Jane Austen

EMMA

MW01031172

Romance CLASSICS

Romance Classics

Published by Trident Press International
801 12th Avenue South
Suite 302
Naples Florida 34102 USA
www.trident-international.com
email: tridentpress@worldnet.att.net

Printed in Australia
ISBN: 1582791945

VOLUME I

Chapter I

Emma Woodhouse, handsome, clever, and rich, with a comfortable home and happy disposition, seemed to unite some of the best blessings of existence; and had lived nearly twenty-one years in the world with very little to distress or vex her.

She was the youngest of the two daughters of a most affectionate, indulgent father; and had, in consequence of her sister's marriage, been mistress of his house from a very early period. Her mother had died too long ago for her to have more than an indistinct remembrance of her caresses; and her place had been supplied by an excellent woman as governess, who had fallen little short of a mother in affection.

Sixteen years had Miss Taylor been in Mr. Woodhouse's family, less as a governess than a friend, very fond of both daughters, but particularly of Emma. Between them it was more the intimacy of sisters. Even before Miss Taylor had ceased to hold the nominal office of governess, the mildness of her temper had hardly allowed her to impose any restraint; and the shadow of authority being now long passed away, they had been living together as friend and friend very mutually attached, and Emma doing just what she liked; highly esteeming Miss Taylor's judgment, but directed chiefly by her own.

The real evils, indeed, of Emma's situation were the power of having rather too much her own way, and a disposition to think a little too well of herself; these were the disadvantages which threatened alloy to her many enjoyments. The danger, however, was at present so unperceived, that they did not by any means rank as misfortunes with her.

Sorrow came—a gentle sorrow—but not at all in the shape of any disagreeable consciousness.—Miss Taylor married. It was Miss Taylor's loss which first brought grief. It was on the wedding-day of this beloved friend that Emma first sat in mournful thought of any continuance. The wedding over, and the bride-people gone, her father and herself were left to dine together, with no prospect of a third to cheer a long evening. Her father composed himself to sleep after dinner, as usual, and she had then only to sit and think of what she had lost.

The event had every promise of happiness for her friend. Mr. Weston was a man of unexceptionable character, easy fortune, suitable age, and pleasant manners; and there was some satisfaction in considering with what self-denying, generous friendship she had always wished and promoted the match; but it was a black morning's work for her. The want of Miss Taylor would be felt every hour of every day. She recalled her past kindness—the kindness, the affection of sixteen years—how she had taught and how she had played with her from five years old—how she had devoted all her powers to attach and amuse her in health—and how nursed her through the various illnesses of childhood. A large debt of gratitude was owing here; but the intercourse of the last seven years, the equal footing and perfect unreserve which had soon followed Isabella's marriage, on their being left to each other, was yet a dearer, tenderer recollection. She had been a friend and companion such as few possessed: intelligent, well-informed, useful, gentle, knowing all the ways of the family, interested in all its concerns, and peculiarly interested in herself, in every pleasure, every scheme of hers—one to whom she could speak every thought as it arose, and who had such an affection for her as could never find fault.

How was she to bear the change?—It was true that her friend was going only half a mile from them; but Emma was aware that great must be the difference between a Mrs. Weston, only half a mile from them, and a Miss Taylor in the house; and with all her advantages, natural and domestic, she was now in great danger of suffering from intellectual solitude. She dearly loved her father, but he was no companion for her. He could not meet her in conversation, rational or playful.

The evil of the actual disparity in their ages (and Mr. Woodhouse had not married early) was much increased by his constitution and habits; for having been a valetudinarian all his life, without activity of mind or body, he was a much older man in ways than in years; and though everywhere beloved for the friendliness of his heart and his amiable temper, his talents could not have recommended him at any time.

Her sister, though comparatively but little removed by matrimony, being settled in London, only sixteen miles off, was much beyond her daily reach; and many a long October and November evening must be struggled through at Hartfield, before Christmas brought the next visit from Isabella and her husband, and their little children, to fill the house, and give her pleasant society again.

Highbury, the large and populous village, almost amounting to a town, to which Hartfield, in spite of its separate lawn, and shrubberies, and name, did really belong, afforded her no equals. The Woodhouses were first in consequence there. All looked up to them. She had many acquaintance in the place, for her father was universally civil, but not one among them who could be accepted in lieu of Miss Taylor for even half a day. It was a melancholy change; and Emma could not but sigh over it, and wish for impossible things, till her father awoke, and made it necessary to be cheerful. His spirits required support. He was a nervous man, easily depressed; fond of every body that he was used to, and hating to part with them; hating change of every kind. Matrimony, as the origin of change, was always disagreeable; and he was by no means yet reconciled to his own daughter's marrying, nor could ever speak of her but with compassion, though it had been entirely a match of affection, when he was now obliged to part with Miss Taylor too; and from his habits of gentle selfishness, and of being never able to suppose that other people could feel differently from himself, he was very much disposed to think Miss Taylor had done as sad a thing for herself as for them, and would have been a great deal happier if she had spent all the rest of her life at Hartfield. Emma smiled and chatted as cheerfully as she could, to keep him from such thoughts; but when tea came, it was impossible for him not to say exactly as he had said at dinner,

"Poor Miss Taylor!—I wish she were here again. What a pity it is that Mr. Weston ever thought of her!"

"I cannot agree with you, papa; you know I cannot. Mr. Weston is such a good-humoured, pleasant, excellent man, that he thoroughly deserves a good wife;—and you would not have had Miss Taylor live with us for ever, and bear all my odd humours, when she might have a house of her own?"

"A house of her own!—But where is the advantage of a house of her own? This is three times as large.—And you have never any odd humours, my dear."

"How often we shall be going to see them, and they coming to see us!—We shall be always meeting! We must begin; we must go and pay wedding visit very soon."

"My dear, how am I to get so far? Randalls is such a distance. I could not walk half so far."

"No, papa, nobody thought of your walking. We must go in the carriage, to be sure."

"The carriage! But James will not like to put the horses to for such a little way;—and where are the poor horses to be while we are paying our visit?"

"They are to be put into Mr. Weston's stable, papa. You know we have settled all that already. We talked it all over with Mr. Weston last night. And as for James, you may be very sure he will always like going to Randalls, because of his daughter's being housemaid there. I only doubt whether he will ever take us anywhere else. That was your doing, papa. You got Hannah that good place. Nobody thought of Hannah till you mentioned her—James is so obliged to you!"

"I am very glad I did think of her. It was very lucky, for I would not have had poor James think himself slighted upon any account; and I am sure she will make a very good servant: she is a civil, pretty-spoken girl; I have a great opinion of her. Whenever I see her, she always curtseys and asks me how I do, in a very pretty manner; and when you have had her here to do needlework, I observe she always turns the lock of the door the right way and never bangs it. I am sure she will be an excellent servant; and it will be a great comfort to poor Miss Taylor to have somebody about her that she is used to see. Whenever James goes over to see his daughter, you know, she will be hearing of us. He will be able to tell her how we all are."

Emma spared no exertions to maintain this happier flow of ideas, and hoped, by the help of backgammon, to get her father tolerably through the evening, and be attacked by no regrets but her own. The backgammon-table was placed; but a visitor immediately afterwards walked in and made it unnecessary.

Mr. Knightley, a sensible man about seven or eight-and-thirty, was not only a very old and intimate friend of the family, but particularly connected with it, as the elder brother of Isabella's husband. He lived about a mile from Highbury, was a frequent visitor, and always welcome, and at this time more welcome than usual, as coming directly from their mutual connexions in London. He had returned to a late dinner, after some days' absence, and now walked up to Hartfield to say that all were well in Brunswick Square. It was a happy circumstance, and animated Mr. Woodhouse for some time. Mr. Knightley had a cheerful manner, which always did him good; and his many inquiries after "poor Isabella" and her children were answered most satisfactorily. When this was over, Mr. Woodhouse gratefully observed, "It is very kind of you, Mr. Knightley, to come out at this late hour to call upon us. I am afraid you must have had a shocking walk."

"Not at all, sir. It is a beautiful moonlight night; and so mild that I must draw back from your great fire."

"But you must have found it very damp and dirty. I wish you may not catch cold."

"Dirty, sir! Look at my shoes. Not a speck on them."

"Well! that is quite surprising, for we have had a vast deal of rain here. It rained dreadfully hard for half an hour while we were at breakfast. I wanted them to put off the wedding."

"By the bye—I have not wished you joy. Being pretty well aware of what sort of joy you must both be feeling, I have been in no hurry with my congratulations; but I hope it all went off tolerably well. How did you all behave? Who cried most?"

"Ah! poor Miss Taylor! 'Tis a sad business."

"Poor Mr. and Miss Woodhouse, if you please; but I cannot possibly say `poor Miss Taylor.' I have a great regard for you and Emma; but when it comes to the question of dependence or independence!—At any rate, it must be better to have only one to please than two."

"Especially when one of those two is such a fanciful, troublesome creature!" said Emma playfully. "That is what you have in your head, I know—and what you would certainly say if my father were not by."

"I believe it is very true, my dear, indeed," said Mr. Woodhouse, with a sigh. "I am afraid I am sometimes very fanciful and troublesome."

"My dearest papa! You do not think I could mean you, or suppose Mr. Knightley to mean you. What a horrible idea! Oh no! I meant only myself. Mr. Knightley loves to find fault with me, you know—in a joke—it is all a joke. We always say what we like to one another."

Mr. Knightley, in fact, was one of the few people who could see faults in Emma Woodhouse, and the only one who ever told her of them: and though this was not particularly agreeable to Emma herself, she knew it would be so much less so to her father, that she would not have him really suspect such a circumstance as her not being thought perfect by every body.

"Emma knows I never flatter her," said Mr. Knightley, "but I meant no reflection on any body. Miss Taylor has been used to have two persons to please; she will now have but one. The chances are that she must be a gainer."

"Well," said Emma, willing to let it pass—"you want to hear about the wedding; and I shall be happy to tell you, for we all behaved charmingly. Every body was punctual, every body in their best looks: not a tear, and hardly a long face to be seen. Oh no; we all felt that we were going to be only half a mile apart, and were sure of meeting every day."

"Dear Emma bears every thing so well," said her father. "But, Mr. Knightley, she is really very sorry to lose poor Miss Taylor, and I am sure she will miss her more than she thinks for."

Emma turned away her head, divided between tears and smiles. "It is impossible that Emma should not miss such a companion," said Mr. Knightley. "We should not like her so well as we do, sir, if we could suppose it; but she knows how much the marriage is to Miss Taylor's advantage; she knows how very acceptable it must be, at Miss Taylor's time of life, to be settled in a home of her own, and how important to her to be secure of a comfortable provision, and therefore cannot allow herself to feel so much pain as pleasure. Every friend of Miss Taylor must be glad to have her so happily married."

"And you have forgotten one matter of joy to me," said Emma, "and a very considerable one—that I made the match myself. I made the match, you know, four years ago; and to have it take place, and be proved in the right, when so many people said Mr. Weston would never marry again, may comfort me for any thing."

Mr. Knightley shook his head at her. Her father fondly replied, "Ah! my dear, I wish you would not make matches and foretell things, for whatever you say always comes to pass. Pray do not make any more matches."

"I promise you to make none for myself, papa; but I must, indeed, for other people. It is the greatest amusement in the world! And after such success, you know!—Every body said that Mr. Weston would never marry again. Oh dear, no! Mr. Weston, who had been a widower so long, and who seemed so perfectly comfortable without a wife, so constantly occupied either in his business in town or among his friends here, always acceptable wherever he went, always cheerful—Mr. Weston need not spend a single evening in the year alone if he did not like it. Oh no! Mr. Weston certainly would never marry again. Some people even talked of a promise to his wife on her deathbed, and others of the son and the uncle not letting him. All manner of solemn nonsense was talked on the subject, but I believed none of it.

"Ever since the day—about four years ago—that Miss Taylor and I met with him in Broadway Lane, when, because it began to drizzle, he darted away with so much gallantry, and borrowed two umbrellas for us from Farmer Mitchell's, I made up my mind on the subject. I planned the match from that hour; and when such success has blessed me in this instance, dear papa, you cannot think that I shall leave off match-making."

"I do not understand what you mean by 'success,'" said Mr. Knightley. "Success supposes endeavour. Your time has been properly and delicately spent, if you have been endeavouring for the last four years to bring about this marriage. A worthy employment for a young lady's mind! But if, which I rather imagine, your making the match, as you call it, means only your planning it, your saying to yourself one idle day, 'I think it would be a very good thing for Miss Taylor if Mr. Weston were to marry her,' and saying it again to yourself every now and then afterwards, why do you talk of success? Where is your merit? What are you proud of? You made a lucky guess; and that is all that can be said."

"And have you never known the pleasure and triumph of a lucky guess?—I pity you.—I thought you cleverer—for, depend upon it a lucky guess is never merely luck. There is always some talent in it. And as to my poor word 'success,' which you quarrel with, I do not know that I am so entirely without any claim to it. You have drawn two pretty pictures; but I think there may be a third—a something between the do-nothing and the do-all. If I had not promoted Mr. Weston's visits here, and given many little encouragements, and smoothed many little matters, it might not have come to any thing after all. I think you must know Hartfield enough to comprehend that."

"A straightforward, open-hearted man like Weston, and a rational, unaffected woman like Miss Taylor, may be safely left to manage their own concerns. You are more likely to have done harm to yourself, than good to them, by interference."

"Emma never thinks of herself, if she can do good to others," rejoined Mr. Woodhouse, understanding but in part. "But, my dear, pray do not make any more matches; they are silly things, and break up one's family circle grievously."

"Only one more, papa; only for Mr. Elton. Poor Mr. Elton! You like Mr. Elton, papa,—I must look about for a wife for him. There is nobody in Highbury who deserves him—and he has been here a whole year, and has fitted up his house so comfortably, that it would be a shame to have him single any longer—and I thought when he was joining their hands to-day, he looked so very much as if he would like to have the same kind office done for him! I think very well of Mr. Elton, and this is the only way I have of doing him a service."

"Mr. Elton is a very pretty young man, to be sure, and a very good young man, and I have a great regard for him. But if you want to shew him any attention, my dear, ask him to come and dine with us some day. That will be a much better thing. I dare say Mr. Knightley will be so kind as to meet him."

"With a great deal of pleasure, sir, at any time," said Mr. Knightley, laughing, "and I agree with you entirely, that it will be a much better thing. Invite him to dinner, Emma, and help him to the best of the fish and the chicken, but leave him to chuse his own wife. Depend upon it, a man of six or seven-and-twenty can take care of himself."

Chapter II

Mr. Weston was a native of Highbury, and born of a respectable family, which for the last two or three generations had been rising into gentility and property. He had received a good education, but, on succeeding early in life to a small independence, had become indisposed for any of the more homely pursuits in which his brothers were engaged, and had satisfied an active, cheerful mind and social temper by entering into the militia of his county, then embodied.

Captain Weston was a general favourite; and when the chances of his military life had introduced him to Miss Churchill, of a great Yorkshire family, and Miss Churchill fell in love with him, nobody was surprized, except her brother and his wife, who had never seen him, and who were full of pride and importance, which the connexion would offend.

Miss Churchill, however, being of age, and with the full command of her fortune—though her fortune bore no proportion to the family-estate—was not to be dissuaded from the marriage, and it took place, to the infinite mortification of Mr. and Mrs. Churchill, who threw her off with due decorum. It was an unsuitable connexion, and did not produce much happiness. Mrs. Weston ought to have found more in it, for she had a husband whose warm heart and sweet temper made him think every thing due to her in return for the great goodness of being in love with him; but though she had one sort of spirit, she had not the best. She had resolution enough to pursue her own will in spite of her brother, but not enough to refrain from unreasonable regrets at that brother's unreasonable anger, nor from missing the luxuries of her former home. They lived beyond their income, but still it was nothing in comparison of Enscombe: she did not cease to love her husband, but she wanted at once to be the wife of Captain Weston, and Miss Churchill of Enscombe.

Captain Weston, who had been considered, especially by the Churchills, as making such an amazing match, was proved to have much the worst of the bargain; for when his wife died, after a three years' marriage, he was rather a poorer man than at first, and with a child to maintain. From the expense of the child, however, he was soon relieved. The boy had, with the additional softening claim of a lingering illness of his mother's, been the means of a sort of reconciliation; and Mr. and Mrs. Churchill, having no children of their own, nor any other young creature of equal kindred to care for, offered to take the whole charge of the little Frank soon after her decease. Some scruples and some reluctance the widower-father may be supposed to have felt; but as they were overcome by other considerations, the child was given up to the care and the wealth of the Churchills, and he had only his own comfort to seek, and his own situation to improve as he could.

A complete change of life became desirable. He quitted the militia and engaged in trade, having brothers already established in a good way in London, which afforded him a favourable opening. It was a concern which brought just employment enough. He had still a small house in Highbury, where most of his leisure days were spent;

and between useful occupation and the pleasures of society, the next eighteen or twenty years of his life passed cheerfully away. He had, by that time, realised an easy competence—enough to secure the purchase of a little estate adjoining Highbury, which he had always longed for—enough to marry a woman as portionless even as Miss Taylor, and to live according to the wishes of his own friendly and social disposition.

It was now some time since Miss Taylor had begun to influence his schemes; but as it was not the tyrannic influence of youth on youth, it had not shaken his determination of never settling till he could purchase Randalls, and the sale of Randalls was long looked forward to; but he had gone steadily on, with these objects in view, till they were accomplished. He had made his fortune, bought his house, and obtained his wife; and was beginning a new period of existence, with every probability of greater happiness than in any yet passed through. He had never been an unhappy man; his own temper had secured him from that, even in his first marriage; but his second must shew him how delightful a well-judging and truly amiable woman could be, and must give him the pleasantest proof of its being a great deal better to choose than to be chosen, to excite gratitude than to feel it.

He had only himself to please in his choice: his fortune was his own; for as to Frank, it was more than being tacitly brought up as his uncle's heir, it had become so avowed an adoption as to have him assume the name of Churchill on coming of age. It was most unlikely, therefore, that he should ever want his father's assistance. His father had no apprehension of it. The aunt was a capricious woman, and governed her husband entirely; but it was not in Mr. Weston's nature to imagine that any caprice could be strong enough to affect one so dear, and, as he believed, so deservedly dear. He saw his son every year in London, and was proud of him; and his fond report of him as a very fine young man had made Highbury feel a sort of pride in him too. He was looked on as sufficiently belonging to the place to make his merits and prospects a kind of common concern.

Mr. Frank Churchill was one of the boasts of Highbury, and a lively curiosity to see him prevailed, though the compliment was so little returned that he had never been there in his life. His coming to visit his father had been often talked of but never achieved.

Now, upon his father's marriage, it was very generally proposed, as a most proper attention, that the visit should take place. There was not a dissentient voice on the subject, either when Mrs. Perry drank tea with Mrs. and Miss Bates, or when Mrs. and Miss Bates returned the visit. Now was the time for Mr. Frank Churchill to come among them; and the hope strengthened when it was understood that he had written to his new mother on the occasion. For a few days, every morning visit in Highbury included some mention of the handsome letter Mrs. Weston had received. "I suppose you have heard of the handsome letter Mr. Frank Churchill has written to Mrs. Weston? I understand it was a very handsome letter, indeed. Mr. Woodhouse told me of it. Mr. Woodhouse saw the letter, and he says he never saw such a handsome letter in his life."

It was, indeed, a highly prized letter. Mrs. Weston had, of course, formed a very favourable idea of the young man; and such a pleasing attention was an irresistible proof of his great good sense, and a most welcome addition to every source and every expression of congratulation which her marriage had already secured. She felt herself a most fortunate woman; and she had lived long enough to know how fortunate she might well be thought, where the only regret was for a partial separation from friends whose friendship for her had never cooled, and who could ill bear to part with her.

She knew that at times she must be missed; and could not think, without pain, of Emma's losing a single pleasure, or suffering an hour's ennui, from the want of her companionableness: but dear Emma was of no feeble character; she was more equal to her situation than most girls would have been, and had sense, and energy, and spirits that might be hoped would bear her well and happily through its little difficulties and privations. And then there was such comfort in the very easy distance of Randalls from Hartfield, so convenient for even solitary female walking, and in Mr. Weston's disposition and circumstances, which would make the approaching season no hindrance to their spending half the evenings in the week together.

Her situation was altogether the subject of hours of gratitude to Mrs. Weston, and of moments only of regret; and her satisfaction—her more than satisfaction—her cheerful enjoyment, was so just and so apparent, that Emma, well as she knew her father, was sometimes taken by surprize at his being still able to pity 'poor Miss Taylor,' when they left her at Randalls in the centre of every domestic comfort, or saw her go away in the evening attended by her pleasant husband to a carriage of her own. But never did she go without Mr. Woodhouse's giving a gentle sigh, and saying, "Ah, poor Miss Taylor! She would be very glad to stay."

There was no recovering Miss Taylor—nor much likelihood of ceasing to pity her; but a few weeks brought some alleviation to Mr. Woodhouse. The compliments of his neighbours were over; he was no longer teased by being wished joy of so sorrowful an event; and the wedding-cake, which had been a great distress to him, was all eat up. His own stomach could bear nothing rich, and he could never believe other people to be different from himself. What was unwholesome to him he regarded as unfit for any body; and he had, therefore, earnestly tried to dissuade them from having any wedding-cake at all, and when that proved vain, as earnestly tried to prevent any body's eating it. He had been at the pains of consulting Mr. Perry, the apothecary, on the subject. Mr. Perry was an intelligent, gentlemanlike man, whose frequent visits were one of the comforts of Mr. Woodhouse's life; and upon being applied to, he could not but acknowledge (though it seemed rather against the bias of inclination) that wedding-cake might certainly disagree with many—perhaps with most people, unless taken moderately. With such an opinion, in confirmation of his own, Mr. Woodhouse hoped to influence every visitor of the newly married pair; but still the cake was eaten; and there was no rest for his benevolent nerves till it was all gone.

There was a strange rumour in Highbury of all the little Perrys being seen with a slice of Mrs. Weston's wedding-cake in their hands: but Mr. Woodhouse would never believe it.

Chapter III

Mr. Woodhouse was fond of society in his own way. He liked very much to have his friends come and see him; and from various united causes, from his long residence at Hartfield, and his good nature, from his fortune, his house, and his daughter, he could command the visits of his own little circle, in a great measure, as he liked. He had not much intercourse with any families beyond that circle; his horror of late hours, and large dinner-parties, made him unfit for any acquaintance but such as would visit him on his own terms. Fortunately for him, Highbury, including Randalls in the same parish, and Donwell Abbey in the parish adjoining, the seat of Mr. Knightley, comprehended many such. Not unfrequently, through Emma's persuasion, he had some of the chosen and the best to dine with him: but evening parties were what he preferred; and, unless he fancied himself at any time unequal to company, there was scarcely an evening in the week in which Emma could not make up a card-table for him.

Real, long-standing regard brought the Westons and Mr. Knightley; and by Mr. Elton, a young man living alone without liking it, the privilege of exchanging any vacant evening of his own blank solitude for the elegancies and society of Mr. Woodhouse's drawing-room, and the smiles of his lovely daughter, was in no danger of being thrown away.

After these came a second set; among the most come-at-able of whom were Mrs. and Miss Bates, and Mrs. Goddard, three ladies almost always at the service of an invitation from Hartfield, and who were fetched and carried home so often, that Mr. Woodhouse thought it no hardship for either James or the horses. Had it taken place only once a year, it would have been a grievance.

Mrs. Bates, the widow of a former vicar of Highbury, was a very old lady, almost past every thing but tea and quadrille. She lived with her single daughter in a very small way, and was considered with all the regard and respect which a harmless old lady, under such untoward circumstances, can excite. Her daughter enjoyed a most uncommon degree of popularity for a woman neither young, handsome, rich, nor married. Miss Bates stood in the very worst predicament in the world for having much of the public favour; and she had no intellectual superiority to make atonement to herself, or frighten those who might hate her into outward respect. She had never boasted either beauty or cleverness. Her youth had passed without distinction, and her middle of life was devoted to the care of a failing mother, and the endeavour to make a small income go as far as possible. And yet she was a happy woman, and a woman whom no one named without good-will. It was her own universal good-will and contented temper which worked such wonders. She loved every body, was interested in every body's happiness, quicksighted to every body's merits; thought herself a most fortunate creature, and surrounded with blessings in such an excellent mother, and so many good neighbours and friends, and a home that wanted for nothing. The simplicity and cheerfulness of her nature, her contented and grateful spirit, were a recommendation to every body, and a mine of felicity to herself. She was a great talker upon little matters, which exactly suited Mr. Woodhouse, full of trivial communications and harmless gossip.

Mrs. Goddard was the mistress of a School—not of a seminary, or an establishment, or any thing which professed, in long sentences of refined nonsense, to combine liberal acquirements with elegant morality, upon new principles and new systems—and where young ladies for enormous pay might be screwed out of health and into vanity—but a real, honest, old-fashioned Boarding-school, where a reasonable quantity of accomplishments were sold at a reasonable price, and where girls might be sent to be out of the way, and scramble themselves into a little education, without any danger of coming back prodigies. Mrs. Goddard's school was in high repute—and very deservedly; for Highbury was reckoned a particularly healthy spot: she had an ample house and garden, gave the children plenty of wholesome food, let them run about a great deal in the summer, and in winter dressed their chilblains with her own hands. It was no wonder that a train of twenty young couple now walked after her to church. She was a plain, motherly kind of woman, who had worked hard in her youth, and now thought herself entitled to the occasional holiday of a tea-visit; and having formerly owed much to Mr. Woodhouse's kindness, felt his particular claim on her to leave her neat parlour, hung round with fancy-work, whenever she could, and win or lose a few sixpences by his fireside.

These were the ladies whom Emma found herself very frequently able to collect; and happy was she, for her father's sake, in the power; though, as far as she was herself concerned, it was no remedy for the absence of Mrs. Weston. She was delighted to see her father look comfortable, and very much pleased with herself for contriving things so well; but the quiet prosings of three such women made her feel that every evening so spent was indeed one of the long evenings she had fearfully anticipated.

As she sat one morning, looking forward to exactly such a close of the present day, a note was brought from Mrs. Goddard, requesting, in most respectful terms, to be allowed to bring Miss Smith with her; a most welcome request: for Miss Smith was a girl of seventeen, whom Emma knew very well by sight, and had long felt an interest in, on account of her beauty. A very gracious invitation was returned, and the evening no longer dreaded by the fair mistress of the mansion.

Harriet Smith was the natural daughter of somebody. Somebody had placed her, several years back, at Mrs. Goddard's school, and somebody had lately raised her from the condition of scholar to that of parlour-boarder. This was all that was generally known of her history. She had no visible friends but what had been acquired at Highbury, and was now just returned from a long visit in the country to some young ladies who had been at school there with her.

She was a very pretty girl, and her beauty happened to be of a sort which Emma particularly admired. She was short, plump, and fair, with a fine bloom, blue eyes, light hair, regular features, and a look of great sweetness, and, before the end of the evening, Emma was as much pleased with her manners as her person, and quite determined to continue the acquaintance.

She was not struck by any thing remarkably clever in Miss Smith's conversation, but she found her altogether very engaging—not inconveniently shy, not unwilling to talk—and yet so far from pushing, shewing so proper and becoming a deference, seeming so pleasantly grateful for being admitted to Hartfield, and so artlessly impressed by the appearance of every thing in so superior a style to what she had been used to, that she must have good sense, and deserve encouragement. Encouragement should be given. Those soft blue eyes, and all those natural graces, should not be wasted on the inferior society of Highbury and its connexions. The acquaintance she had already formed were unworthy of her. The friends from whom she had just parted, though very good sort of people, must be doing her harm. They were a family of the name of Martin, whom Emma well knew by character, as renting a large farm of Mr. Knightley, and residing in the parish of Donwell—very creditably, she believed—she knew Mr. Knightley thought highly of them—but they must be coarse and unpolished, and very unfit to be the intimates of a girl who wanted only a little more knowledge and elegance to be quite perfect. She would notice her; she would improve her;

she would detach her from her bad acquaintance, and introduce her into good society; she would form her opinions and her manners. It would be an interesting, and certainly a very kind undertaking; highly becoming her own situation in life, her leisure, and powers.

She was so busy in admiring those soft blue eyes, in talking and listening, and forming all these schemes in the in-betweens, that the evening flew away at a very unusual rate; and the supper-table, which always closed such parties, and for which she had been used to sit and watch the due time, was all set out and ready, and moved forwards to the fire, before she was aware. With an alacrity beyond the common impulse of a spirit which yet was never indifferent to the credit of doing every thing well and attentively, with the real good-will of a mind delighted with its own ideas, did she then do all the honours of the meal, and help and recommend the minced chicken and scalloped oysters, with an urgency which she knew would be acceptable to the early hours and civil scruples of their guests.

Upon such occasions poor Mr. Woodhouses feelings were in sad warfare. He loved to have the cloth laid, because it had been the fashion of his youth, but his conviction of suppers being very unwholesome made him rather sorry to see any thing put on it; and while his hospitality would have welcomed his visitors to every thing, his care for their health made him grieve that they would eat.

Such another small basin of thin gruel as his own was all that he could, with thorough self-approbation, recommend; though he might constrain himself, while the ladies were comfortably clearing the nicer things, to say:

"Mrs. Bates, let me propose your venturing on one of these eggs. An egg boiled very soft is not unwholesome. Serle understands boiling an egg better than any body. I would not recommend an egg boiled by any body else; but you need not be afraid, they are very small, you see—one of our small eggs will not hurt you. Miss Bates, let Emma help you to a little bit of tart—a very little bit. Ours are all apple-tarts. You need not be afraid of unwholesome preserves here. I do not advise the custard. Mrs. Goddard, what say you to half a glass of wine? A small half-glass, put into a tumbler of water? I do not think it could disagree with you."

Emma allowed her father to talk—but supplied her visitors in a much more satisfactory style, and on the present evening had particular pleasure in sending them away happy. The happiness of Miss Smith was quite equal to her intentions. Miss Woodhouse was so great a personage in Highbury, that the prospect of the introduction had given as much panic as pleasure; but the humble, grateful little girl went off with highly gratified feelings, delighted with the affability with which Miss Woodhouse had treated her all the evening, and actually shaken hands with her at last!

Chapter IV

Harriet Smith's intimacy at Hartfield was soon a settled thing. Quick and decided in her ways, Emma lost no time in inviting, encouraging, and telling her to come very often; and as their acquaintance increased, so did their satisfaction in each other. As a walking companion, Emma had very early foreseen how useful she might find her. In that respect Mrs. Weston's loss had been important. Her father never went beyond the shrubbery, where two divisions of the ground sufficed him for his long walk, or his short, as the year varied; and since Mrs. Weston's marriage her exercise had been too much confined. She had ventured once alone to Randalls, but it was not pleasant; and a Harriet Smith, therefore, one whom she could summon at any time to a walk, would be a valuable addition to her privileges. But in every respect, as she saw more of her, she approved her, and was confirmed in all her kind designs.

Harriet certainly was not clever, but she had a sweet, docile, grateful disposition, was totally free from conceit, and only desiring to be guided by any one she looked up to. Her early attachment to herself was very amiable; and her inclination for good company, and power of appreciating what was elegant and clever, shewed that there was no want of taste, though strength of understanding must not be expected. Altogether she was quite convinced of Harriet Smith's being exactly the young friend she wanted—exactly the something which her home required. Such a friend as Mrs. Weston was out of the question. Two such could never be granted. Two such she did not want. It was quite a different sort of thing, a sentiment distinct and independent. Mrs. Weston was the object of a regard which had its basis in gratitude and esteem. Harriet would be loved as one to whom she could be useful. For Mrs. Weston there was nothing to be done; for Harriet every thing.

Her first attempts at usefulness were in an endeavour to find out who were the parents, but Harriet could not tell. She was ready to tell every thing in her power, but on this subject questions were vain. Emma was obliged to fancy what she liked—but she could never believe that in the same situation she should not have discovered the truth. Harriet had no penetration. She had been satisfied to hear and believe just what Mrs. Goddard chose to tell her; and looked no farther.

Mrs. Goddard, and the teachers, and the girls and the affairs of the school in general, formed naturally a great part of the conversation—and but for her acquaintance with the Martins of Abbey-Mill Farm, it must have been the whole. But the Martins occupied her thoughts a good deal; she had spent two very happy months with them, and now loved to talk of the pleasures of her visit, and describe the many comforts and wonders of the place. Emma encouraged her talkativeness—amused by such a picture of another set of beings, and enjoying the youthful simplicity which could speak with so much exultation of Mrs. Martin's having "two parlours, two very good parlours, indeed; one of them quite as large as Mrs. Goddard's drawing-room; and of her having an upper maid who had lived five-and-twenty years with her; and of their having eight cows, two of them Alderneys, and one a little Welch cow, a very pretty little Welch cow indeed; and of Mrs. Martin's saying as she was so fond of it, it should be called her cow; and of their having a very handsome summer-house in their garden, where some day next year they were all to drink tea:—a very handsome summer-house, large enough to hold a dozen people."

For some time she was amused, without thinking beyond the immediate cause; but as she came to understand the family better, other feelings arose. She had taken up a wrong idea, fancying it was a mother and daughter, a son and son's wife, who all lived together; but when it appeared that the Mr. Martin, who bore a part in the narrative, and was always mentioned with approbation for his great good-nature in doing something or other, was a single man; that there was no young Mrs. Martin, no wife in the case; she did suspect danger to her poor little friend from all this hospitality and kindness, and that, if she were not taken care of, she might be required to sink herself forever.

With this inspiriting notion, her questions increased in number and meaning; and she particularly led Harriet to talk more of Mr. Martin, and there was evidently no dislike to it. Harriet was very ready to speak of the share he had had in their moonlight walks and merry evening games; and dwelt a good deal upon his being so very good-humoured and obliging. He had gone three miles round one day in order to bring her some walnuts, because she had said how fond she was of them, and in every thing else he was so very obliging. He had his shepherd's son into the parlour one night on purpose to sing to her. She was very fond of singing. He could sing a little himself. She believed he was very clever, and understood every thing. He had a very fine flock, and, while she was with them, he had been bid more for his wool than any body in the country. She believed every body spoke well of him. His mother and sisters were very fond of him. Mrs. Martin had told her one day (and there was a blush as she said it,) that it was impossible for any body to be a better son, and therefore she was sure, whenever he married, he would make a good husband. Not that she wanted him to marry. She was in no hurry at all.

"Well done, Mrs. Martin!" thought Emma. "You know what you are about."

"And when she had come away, Mrs. Martin was so very kind as to send Mrs. Goddard a beautiful goose—the finest goose Mrs. Goddard had ever seen. Mrs. Goddard had dressed it on a Sunday, and asked all the three teachers, Miss Nash, and Miss Prince, and Miss Richardson, to sup with her."

"Mr. Martin, I suppose, is not a man of information beyond the line of his own business? He does not read?"

"Oh yes!—that is, no—I do not know—but I believe he has read a good deal—but not what you would think any thing of. He reads the Agricultural Reports, and some other books that lay in one of the window seats—but he reads all them to himself. But sometimes of an evening, before we went to cards, he would read something aloud out of the Elegant Extracts, very entertaining. And I know he has read the Vicar of Wakefield. He never read the Romance of the Forest, nor The Children of the Abbey. He had never heard of such books before I mentioned them, but he is determined to get them now as soon as ever he can."

The next question was—

"What sort of looking man is Mr. Martin?"

"Oh! not handsome—not at all handsome. I thought him very plain at first, but I do not think him so plain now. One does not, you know, after a time. But did you never see him? He is in Highbury every now and then, and he is sure to ride through every week in his way to Kingston. He has passed you very often."

"That may be, and I may have seen him fifty times, but without having any idea of his name. A young farmer, whether on horseback or on foot, is the very last sort of person to raise my curiosity. The yeomanry are precisely the order of people with whom I feel I can have nothing to do. A degree or two lower, and a creditable appearance might interest me; I might hope to be useful to their families in some way or other. But a farmer can need none of my help, and is, therefore, in one sense, as much above my notice as in every other he is below it."

"To be sure. Oh yes! It is not likely you should ever have observed him; but he knows you very well indeed—I mean by sight."

"I have no doubt of his being a very respectable young man. I know, indeed, that he is so, and, as such, wish him well. What do you imagine his age to be?"

"He was four-and-twenty the 8th of last June, and my birthday is the 23rd just a fortnight and a day's difference—which is very odd."

"Only four-and-twenty. That is too young to settle. His mother is perfectly right not to be in a hurry. They seem very comfortable as they are, and if she were to take any pains to marry him, she would probably repent it. Six years hence, if he could meet with a good sort of young woman in the same rank as his own, with a little money, it might be very desirable."

"Six years hence! Dear Miss Woodhouse, he would be thirty years old!"

"Well, and that is as early as most men can afford to marry, who are not born to an independence. Mr. Martin, I imagine, has his fortune entirely to make—cannot be at all beforehand with the world. Whatever money he might come into when his father died, whatever his share of the family property, it is, I dare say, all afloat, all employed in his stock, and so forth; and though, with diligence and good luck, he may be rich in time, it is next to impossible that he should have realised any thing yet."

"To be sure, so it is. But they live very comfortably. They have no indoors man, else they do not want for any thing; and Mrs. Martin talks of taking a boy another year."

"I wish you may not get into a scrape, Harriet, whenever he does marry;—I mean, as to being acquainted with his wife—for though his sisters, from a superior education, are not to be altogether objected to, it does not follow that he might marry any body at all fit for you to notice. The misfortune of your birth ought to make you particularly careful as to your associates. There can be no doubt of your being a gentleman's daughter, and you must support your claim to that station by every thing within your own power, or there will be plenty of people who would take pleasure in degrading you."

"Yes, to be sure, I suppose there are. But while I visit at Hartfield, and you are so kind to me, Miss Woodhouse, I am not afraid of what any body can do."

"You understand the force of influence pretty well, Harriet; but I would have you so firmly established in good society, as to be independent even of Hartfield and Miss Woodhouse. I want to see you permanently well connected, and to that end it will be advisable to have as few odd acquaintance as may be; and, therefore, I say that if you should still be in this country when Mr. Martin marries, I wish you may not be drawn in by your intimacy with the sisters, to be acquainted with the wife, who will probably be some mere farmer's daughter, without education."

"To be sure. Yes. Not that I think Mr. Martin would ever marry any body but what had had some education—and been very well brought up. However, I do not mean to set up my opinion against your's—and I am sure I shall not wish for the acquaintance of his wife. I shall always have a great regard for the Miss Martins, especially Elizabeth, and should be very sorry to give them up, for they are quite as well educated as me. But if he marries a very ignorant, vulgar woman, certainly I had better not visit her, if I can help it."

Emma watched her through the fluctuations of this speech, and saw no alarming symptoms of love. The young man had been the first admirer, but she trusted there was no other hold, and that there would be no serious difficulty, on Harriet's side, to oppose any friendly arrangement of her own.

They met Mr. Martin the very next day, as they were walking on the Donwell road. He was on foot, and after looking very respectfully at her, looked with most unfeigned satisfaction at her companion. Emma was not sorry to have such an opportunity of survey; and walking a few yards forward, while they talked together, soon made her quick eye sufficiently acquainted with Mr. Robert Martin. His appearance was very neat, and he looked like a sensible young man, but his person had no other advantage; and when he came to be contrasted with gentlemen, she thought he must lose all the ground he had gained in Harriet's inclination. Harriet was not insensible of manner; she had voluntarily noticed her father's gentleness with admiration as well as wonder. Mr. Martin looked as if he did not know what manner was.

They remained but a few minutes together, as Miss Woodhouse must not be kept waiting; and Harriet then came running to her with a smiling face, and in a flutter of spirits, which Miss Woodhouse hoped very soon to compose.

"Only think of our happening to meet him!—How very odd! It was quite a chance, he said, that he had not gone round by Randalls. He did not think we ever walked this road. He thought we walked towards Randalls most days. He has not been able to get the Romance of the Forest yet. He was so busy the last time he was at Kingston that he quite forgot it, but he goes again to-morrow. So very odd we should happen to meet! Well, Miss Woodhouse, is he like what you expected? What do you think of him? Do you think him so very plain?"

"He is very plain, undoubtedly—remarkably plain:—but that is nothing compared with his entire want of gentility. I had no right to expect much, and I did not expect much; but I had no idea that he could be so very clownish, so totally without air. I had imagined him, I confess, a degree or two nearer gentility."

"To be sure," said Harriet, in a mortified voice, "he is not so genteel as real gentlemen."

"I think, Harriet, since your acquaintance with us, you have been repeatedly in the company of some such very real gentlemen, that you must yourself be struck with the difference in Mr. Martin. At Hartfield, you have had very good specimens of well educated, well bred men. I should be surprized if, after seeing them, you could be in company with Mr. Martin again without perceiving him to be a very inferior creature—and rather wondering at yourself for having ever thought him at all agreeable before. Do not you begin to feel that now? Were not you struck? I am sure you must have been struck by his awkward look and abrupt manner, and the uncouthness of a voice which I heard to be wholly unmodulated as I stood here."

"Certainly, he is not like Mr. Knightley. He has not such a fine air and way of walking as Mr. Knightley. I see the difference plain enough. But Mr. Knightley is so very fine a man!"

"Mr. Knightley's air is so remarkably good that it is not fair to compare Mr. Martin with him. You might not see one in a hundred with gentleman so plainly written as in Mr. Knightley. But he is not the only gentleman you have been lately used to. What say you to Mr. Weston and Mr. Elton? Compare Mr. Martin with either of them. Compare their manner of carrying themselves; of walking; of speaking; of being silent. You must see the difference."

"Oh yes!—there is a great difference. But Mr. Weston is almost an old man. Mr. Weston must be between forty and fifty."

"Which makes his good manners the more valuable. The older a person grows, Harriet, the more important it is that their manners should not be bad; the more glaring and disgusting any loudness, or coarseness, or awkwardness becomes. What is passable in youth is detestable in later age. Mr. Martin is now awkward and abrupt; what will he be at Mr. Weston's time of life?"

"There is no saying, indeed," replied Harriet rather solemnly.

"But there may be pretty good guessing. He will be a completely gross, vulgar farmer, totally inattentive to appearances, and thinking of nothing but profit and loss."

"Will he, indeed? That will be very bad."

"How much his business engrosses him already is very plain from the circumstance of his forgetting to inquire for the book you recommended. He was a great deal too full of the market to think of any thing else—which is just as it should be, for a thriving man. What has he to do with books? And I have no doubt that he will thrive, and be a very rich man in time—and his being illiterate and coarse need not disturb us."

"I wonder he did not remember the book"—was all Harriet's answer, and spoken with a degree of grave displeasure which Emma thought might be safely left to itself. She, therefore, said no more for some time. Her next beginning was,

"In one respect, perhaps, Mr. Elton's manners are superior to Mr. Knightley's or Mr. Weston's. They have more gentleness. They might be more safely held up as a pattern. There is an openness, a quickness, almost a bluntness in Mr. Weston, which every body likes in him, because there is so much good-humour with it—but that would not do to be copied. Neither would Mr. Knightley's downright, decided, commanding sort of manner, though it suits him very well; his figure, and look, and situation in life seem to allow it; but if any young man were to set about copying him, he would not be sufferable. On the contrary, I think a young man might be very safely recommended to take Mr. Elton as a model. Mr. Elton is good-humoured, cheerful, obliging, and gentle. He seems to me to be grown particularly gentle of late. I do not know whether he has any design of ingratiating himself with either of us, Harriet, by additional softness, but it strikes me that his manners are softer than they used to be. If he means any thing, it must be to please you. Did not I tell you what he said of you the other day?"

She then repeated some warm personal praise which she had drawn from Mr. Elton, and now did full justice to; and Harriet blushed and smiled, and said she had always thought Mr. Elton very agreeable.

Mr. Elton was the very person fixed on by Emma for driving the young farmer out of Harriet's head. She thought it would be an excellent match; and only too palpably desirable, natural, and probable, for her to have much merit in planning it. She feared it was what every body else must think of and predict. It was not likely, however, that any body should have equalled her in the date of the plan, as it had entered her brain during the very first evening of Harriet's coming to Hartfield. The longer she considered it, the greater was her sense of its expediency. Mr. Elton's situation was most suitable, quite the gentleman himself, and without low connexions; at the same time, not of any family that could fairly object to the doubtful birth of Harriet. He had a comfortable home for her, and Emma imagined a very sufficient income; for though the vicarage of Highbury was not large, he was known to have some independent property; and she thought very highly of him as a good-humoured, well-meaning, respectable young man, without any deficiency of useful understanding or knowledge of the world.

She had already satisfied herself that he thought Harriet a beautiful girl, which she trusted, with such frequent meetings at Hartfield, was foundation enough on his side; and on Harriet's there could be little doubt that the idea of being preferred by him would have all the usual weight and efficacy. And he was really a very pleasing young man, a young man whom any woman not fastidious might like. He was reckoned very handsome; his person much admired in general, though not by her, there being a want of elegance of feature which she could not dispense with:—but the girl who could be gratified by a Robert Martin's riding about the country to get walnuts for her might very well be conquered by Mr. Elton's admiration.

Chapter V

"I do not know what your opinion may be, Mrs. Weston," said Mr. Knightley, "of this great intimacy between Emma and Harriet Smith, but I think it a bad thing."

"A bad thing! Do you really think it a bad thing?—why so?"

"I think they will neither of them do the other any good."

"You surprize me! Emma must do Harriet good: and by supplying her with a new object of interest, Harriet may be said to do Emma good. I have been seeing their intimacy with the greatest pleasure. How very differently we feel!—Not think they will do each other any good! This will certainly be the beginning of one of our quarrels about Emma, Mr. Knightley."

"Perhaps you think I am come on purpose to quarrel with you, knowing Weston to be out, and that you must still fight your own battle."

"Mr. Weston would undoubtedly support me, if he were here, for he thinks exactly as I do on the subject. We were speaking of it only yesterday, and agreeing how fortunate it was for Emma, that there should be such a girl in Highbury for her to associate with. Mr. Knightley, I shall not allow you to be a fair judge in this case. You are so much used to live alone, that you do not know the value of a companion; and, perhaps no man can be a good judge of the comfort a woman feels in the society of one of her own sex, after being used to it all her life. I can imagine your objection to Harriet Smith. She is not the superior young woman which Emma's friend ought to be. But on the other hand, as Emma wants to see her better informed, it will be an inducement to her to read more herself. They will read together. She means it, I know."

"Emma has been meaning to read more ever since she was twelve years old. I have seen a great many lists of her drawing-up at various times of books that she meant to read regularly through—and very good lists they were—very well chosen, and very neatly arranged—sometimes alphabetically, and sometimes by some other rule. The list she drew up when only fourteen—I remember thinking it did her judgment so much credit, that I preserved it some time; and I dare say she may have made out a very good list now. But I have done with expecting any course of steady reading from Emma. She will never submit to any thing requiring industry and patience, and a subjection of the fancy to the understanding. Where Miss Taylor failed to stimulate, I may safely affirm that Harriet Smith will do nothing.—You never could persuade her to read half so much as you wished.—You know you could not."

"I dare say," replied Mrs. Weston, smiling, "that I thought so then;—but since we have parted, I can never remember Emma's omitting to do any thing I wished."

"There is hardly any desiring to refresh such a memory as that,"—said Mr. Knightley, feelingly; and for a moment or two he had done. "But I," he soon added, "who have had no such charm thrown over my senses, must still see, hear, and remember. Emma is spoiled by being the cleverest of her family. At ten years old, she had the misfortune of being able to answer questions which puzzled her sister at seventeen. She was always quick and assured: Isabella slow and diffident. And ever since she was twelve, Emma has been mistress of the house and of you all. In her mother she lost the only person able to cope with her. She inherits her mother's talents, and must have been under subjection to her."

"I should have been sorry, Mr. Knightley, to be dependent on your recommendation, had I quitted Mr. Woodhouse's family and wanted another situation; I do not think you would have spoken a good word for me to any body. I am sure you always thought me unfit for the office I held."

"Yes," said he, smiling. "You are better placed here; very fit for a wife, but not at all for a governess. But you were preparing yourself to be an excellent wife all the time you were at Hartfield. You might not give Emma such a complete education as your powers would seem to promise; but you were receiving a very good education from her, on the very material matrimonial point of submitting your own will, and doing as you were bid; and if Weston had asked me to recommend him a wife, I should certainly have named Miss Taylor."

"Thank you. There will be very little merit in making a good wife to such a man as Mr. Weston."

"Why, to own the truth, I am afraid you are rather thrown away, and that with every disposition to bear, there will be nothing to be borne. We will not despair, however. Weston may grow cross from the wantonness of comfort, or his son may plague him."

"I hope not that.—It is not likely. No, Mr. Knightley, do not foretell vexation from that quarter."

"Not I, indeed. I only name possibilities. I do not pretend to Emma's genius for foretelling and guessing. I hope, with all my heart, the young man may be a Weston in merit, and a Churchill in fortune.—But Harriet Smith—I have not half done about Harriet Smith. I think her the very worst sort of companion that Emma could possibly have. She knows nothing herself, and looks upon Emma as knowing every thing. She is a flatterer in all her ways; and so much the worse, because undesigned. Her ignorance is hourly flattery. How can Emma imagine she has any thing to learn herself, while Harriet is presenting such a delightful inferiority? And as for Harriet, I will venture to say that she cannot gain by the acquaintance. Hartfield will only put her out of conceit with all the other places she belongs to. She will grow just refined enough to be uncomfortable with those among whom birth and circumstances have placed her home. I am much mistaken if Emma's doctrines give any strength of mind, or tend at all to make a girl adapt herself rationally to the varieties of her situation in life.—They only give a little polish."

"I either depend more upon Emma's good sense than you do, or am more anxious for her present comfort; for I cannot lament the acquaintance. How well she looked last night!"

"Oh! you would rather talk of her person than her mind, would you? Very well; I shall not attempt to deny Emma's being pretty."

"Pretty! say beautiful rather. Can you imagine any thing nearer perfect beauty than Emma altogether—face and figure?"

"I do not know what I could imagine, but I confess that I have seldom seen a face or figure more pleasing to me than hers. But I am a partial old friend."

"Such an eye!—the true hazle eye—and so brilliant! regular features, open countenance, with a complexion! oh! what a bloom of full health, and such a pretty height and size; such a firm and upright figure! There is health, not merely in her bloom, but in her air, her head, her glance. One hears sometimes of a child being 'the picture of health;' now, Emma always gives me the idea of being the complete picture of grown-up health. She is loveliness itself. Mr. Knightley, is not she?"

"I have not a fault to find with her person," he replied. "I think her all you describe. I love to look at her; and I will add this praise, that I do not think her personally vain. Considering how very handsome she is, she appears to be little occupied with it; her vanity lies another way. Mrs. Weston, I am not to be talked out of my dislike of Harriet Smith, or my dread of its doing them both harm."

"And I, Mr. Knightley, am equally stout in my confidence of its not doing them any harm. With all dear Emma's little faults, she is an excellent creature. Where shall we see a better daughter, or a kinder sister, or a truer friend? No, no; she has qualities which may be trusted; she will never lead any one really wrong; she will make no lasting blunder; where Emma errs once, she is in the right a hundred times."

"Very well; I will not plague you any more. Emma shall be an angel, and I will keep my spleen to myself till Christmas brings John and Isabella. John loves Emma with a reasonable and therefore not a blind affection, and Isabella always thinks as he does; except when he is not quite frightened enough about the children. I am sure of having their opinions with me."

"I know that you all love her really too well to be unjust or unkind; but excuse me, Mr. Knightley, if I take the liberty (I consider myself, you know, as having somewhat of the privilege of speech that Emma's mother might have had) the liberty of hinting that I do not think any possible good can arise from Harriet Smith's intimacy being made a matter of much discussion among you. Pray excuse me;

but supposing any little inconvenience may be apprehended from the intimacy, it cannot be expected that Emma, accountable to nobody but her father, who perfectly approves the acquaintance, should put an end to it, so long as it is a source of pleasure to herself. It has been so many years my province to give advice, that you cannot be surprized, Mr. Knightley, at this little remains of office."

"Not at all," cried he; "I am much obliged to you for it. It is very good advice, and it shall have a better fate than your advice has often found; for it shall be attended to."

"Mrs. John Knightley is easily alarmed, and might be made unhappy about her sister."

"Be satisfied," said he, "I will not raise any outcry. I will keep my ill-humour to myself. I have a very sincere interest in Emma. Isabella does not seem more my sister; has never excited a greater interest; perhaps hardly so great. There is an anxiety, a curiosity in what one feels for Emma. I wonder what will become of her!"

"So do I," said Mrs. Weston gently, "very much."

"She always declares she will never marry, which, of course, means just nothing at all. But I have no idea that she has yet ever seen a man she cared for. It would not be a bad thing for her to be very much in love with a proper object. I should like to see Emma in love, and in some doubt of a return; it would do her good. But there is nobody hereabouts to attach her; and she goes so seldom from home."

"There does, indeed, seem as little to tempt her to break her resolution at present," said Mrs. Weston, "as can well be; and while she is so happy at Hartfield, I cannot wish her to be forming any attachment which would be creating such difficulties on poor Mr. Woodhouse's account. I do not recommend matrimony at present to Emma, though I mean no slight to the state, I assure you."

Part of her meaning was to conceal some favourite thoughts of her own and Mr. Weston's on the subject, as much as possible. There were wishes at Randalls respecting Emma's destiny, but it was not desirable to have them suspected; and the quiet transition which Mr. Knightley soon afterwards made to "What does Weston think of the weather; shall we have rain?" convinced her that he had nothing more to say or surmise about Hartfield.

Chapter VI

Emma could not feel a doubt of having given Harriet's fancy a proper direction and raised the gratitude of her young vanity to a very good purpose, for she found her decidedly more sensible than before of Mr. Elton's being a remarkably handsome man, with most agreeable manners; and as she had no hesitation in following up the assurance of his admiration by agreeable hints, she was soon pretty confident of creating as much liking on Harriet's side, as there could be any occasion for. She was quite convinced of Mr. Elton's being in the fairest way of falling in love, if not in love already. She had no scruple with regard to him. He talked of Harriet, and praised her so warmly, that she could not suppose any thing wanting which a little time would not add. His perception of the striking improvement of Harriet's manner, since her introduction at Hartfield, was not one of the least agreeable proofs of his growing attachment.

"You have given Miss Smith all that she required," said he; "you have made her graceful and easy. She was a beautiful creature when she came to you, but, in my opinion, the attractions you have added are infinitely superior to what she received from nature."

"I am glad you think I have been useful to her; but Harriet only wanted drawing out, and receiving a few, very few hints. She had all the natural grace of sweetness of temper and artlessness in herself. I have done very little."

"If it were admissible to contradict a lady," said the gallant Mr. Elton—

"I have perhaps given her a little more decision of character, have taught her to think on points which had not fallen in her way before."

"Exactly so; that is what principally strikes me. So much superadded decision of character! Skilful has been the hand!"

"Great has been the pleasure, I am sure. I never met with a disposition more truly amiable."

"I have no doubt of it." And it was spoken with a sort of sighing animation, which had a vast deal of the lover. She was not less pleased another day with the manner in which he seconded a sudden wish of hers, to have Harriet's picture.

"Did you ever have your likeness taken, Harriet?" said she: "did you ever sit for your picture?"

Harriet was on the point of leaving the room, and only stopt to say, with a very interesting naivete,

"Oh! dear, no, never."

No sooner was she out of sight, than Emma exclaimed,

"What an exquisite possession a good picture of her would be! I would give any money for it. I almost long to attempt her likeness myself. You do not know it I dare say, but two or three years ago I had a great passion for taking likenesses, and attempted several of my friends, and was thought to have a tolerable eye in general. But from one cause or another, I gave it up in disgust. But really, I could almost venture, if Harriet would sit to me. It would be such a delight to have her picture!"

"Let me entreat you," cried Mr. Elton; "it would indeed be a delight! Let me entreat you, Miss Woodhouse, to exercise so charming a talent in favour of your friend. I know what your drawings are. How could you suppose me ignorant? Is not this room rich in specimens of your landscapes and flowers; and has not Mrs. Weston some inimitable figure-pieces in her drawing-room, at Randalls?"

Yes, good man!—thought Emma—but what has all that to do with taking likenesses? You know nothing of drawing. Don't pretend to be in raptures about mine. Keep your raptures for Harriet's face. "Well, if you give me such kind encouragement, Mr. Elton, I believe I shall try what I can do. Harriet's features are very delicate, which makes a likeness difficult; and yet there is a peculiarity in the shape of the eye and the lines about the mouth which one ought to catch."

"Exactly so—The shape of the eye and the lines about the mouth—I have not a doubt of your success. Pray, pray attempt it. As you will do it, it will indeed, to use your own words, be an exquisite possession."

"But I am afraid, Mr. Elton, Harriet will not like to sit. She thinks so little of her own beauty. Did not you observe her manner of answering me? How completely it meant, 'why should my picture be drawn?'"

"Oh! yes, I observed it, I assure you. It was not lost on me. But still I cannot imagine she would not be persuaded."

Harriet was soon back again, and the proposal almost immediately made; and she had no scruples which could stand many minutes against the earnest pressing of both the others. Emma wished to go to work directly, and therefore produced the portfolio containing her various attempts at portraits, for not one of them had ever been finished, that they might decide together on the best size for Harriet. Her many beginnings were displayed. Miniatures, half-lengths, whole-lengths, pencil, crayon, and water-colours had been all tried in turn. She had always wanted to do every thing, and had made more progress both in drawing and music than many might have done with so little labour as she would ever submit to. She played and sang;—and drew in almost every style; but steadiness had always been wanting; and in nothing had she approached the degree of excellence which she would have been glad to command, and ought not to have failed of. She was not much deceived as to her own skill either as an artist or a musician, but she was not unwilling to have others deceived, or sorry to know her reputation for accomplishment often higher than it deserved.

There was merit in every drawing—in the least finished, perhaps the most; her style was spirited; but had there been much less, or had there been ten times more, the delight and admiration of her two companions would have been the same. They were both in ecstasies. A likeness pleases every body; and Miss Woodhouse's performances must be capital.

"No great variety of faces for you," said Emma. "I had only my own family to study from. There is my father—another of my father—but the idea of sitting for his picture made him so nervous, that I could only take him by stealth; neither of them very like therefore. Mrs. Weston again, and again, and again, you see. Dear Mrs. Weston! always my kindest friend on every occasion. She would sit whenever I asked her. There is my sister; and really quite her own little elegant figure!—and the face not unlike. I should have made a good likeness of her, if she would have sat longer, but she was in such a hurry to have me draw her four children that she would not be quiet. Then, here come all my attempts at three of those four children;—there they are, Henry and John and Bella, from one end of the sheet to the other, and any one of them might do for any one of the rest. She was so eager to have them drawn that I could not refuse;

but there is no making children of three or four years old stand still you know; nor can it be very easy to take any likeness of them, beyond the air and complexion, unless they are coarser featured than any of mama's children ever were. Here is my sketch of the fourth, who was a baby. I took him as he was sleeping on the sofa, and it is as strong a likeness of his cockade as you would wish to see. He had nestled down his head most conveniently. That's very like. I am rather proud of little George. The corner of the sofa is very good. Then here is my last,"—unclosing a pretty sketch of a gentleman in small size, whole-length—"my last and my best—my brother, Mr. John Knightley.—This did not want much of being finished, when I put it away in a pet, and vowed I would never take another likeness. I could not help being provoked; for after all my pains, and when I had really made a very good likeness of it—(Mrs. Weston and I were quite agreed in thinking it very like)—only too handsome—too flattering—but that was a fault on the right side—after all this, came poor dear Isabella's cold approbation of—"Yes, it was a little like—but to be sure it did not do him justice." We had had a great deal of trouble in persuading him to sit at all. It was made a great favour of; and altogether it was more than I could bear; and so I never would finish it, to have it apologised over as an unfavourable likeness, to every morning visitor in Brunswick Square;—and, as I said, I did then forswear ever drawing any body again. But for Harriet's sake, or rather for my own, and as there are no husbands and wives in the case at present, I will break my resolution now."

Mr. Elton seemed very properly struck and delighted by the idea, and was repeating, "No husbands and wives in the case at present indeed, as you observe. Exactly so. No husbands and wives," with so interesting a consciousness, that Emma began to consider whether she had not better leave them together at once. But as she wanted to be drawing, the declaration must wait a little longer.

She had soon fixed on the size and sort of portrait. It was to be a whole-length in water-colours, like Mr. John Knightley's, and was destined, if she could please herself, to hold a very honourable station over the mantelpiece.

The sitting began; and Harriet, smiling and blushing, and afraid of not keeping her attitude and countenance, presented a very sweet mixture of youthful expression to the steady eyes of the artist. But there was no doing any thing, with Mr. Elton fidgeting behind her and watching every touch. She gave him credit for stationing himself where he might gaze and gaze again without offence; but was really obliged to put an end to it, and request him to place himself elsewhere. It then occurred to her to employ him in reading.

"If he would be so good as to read to them, it would be a kindness indeed! It would amuse away the difficulties of her part, and lessen the irksomeness of Miss Smith's."

Mr. Elton was only too happy. Harriet listened, and Emma drew in peace. She must allow him to be still frequently coming to look; any thing less would certainly have been too little in a lover; and he was ready at the smallest intermission of the pencil, to jump up and see the progress, and be charmed.—There was no being displeased with such an encourager, for his admiration made him discern a likeness almost before it was possible. She could not respect his eye, but his love and his complaisance were unexceptionable.

The sitting was altogether very satisfactory; she was quite enough pleased with the first day's sketch to wish to go on. There was no want of likeness, she had been fortunate in the attitude, and as she meant to throw in a little improvement to the figure, to give a little more height, and considerably more elegance, she had great confidence of its being in every way a pretty drawing at last, and of its filling its destined place with credit to them both—a standing memorial of the beauty of one, the skill of the other, and the friendship of both; with as many other agreeable associations as Mr. Elton's very promising attachment was likely to add.

Harriet was to sit again the next day; and Mr. Elton, just as he ought, entreated for the permission of attending and reading to them again.

"By all means. We shall be most happy to consider you as one of the party."

The same civilities and courtesies, the same success and satisfaction, took place on the morrow, and accompanied the whole progress of the picture, which was rapid and happy. Every body who saw it was pleased, but Mr. Elton was in continual raptures, and defended it through every criticism.

"Miss Woodhouse has given her friend the only beauty she wanted,"—observed Mrs. Weston to him—not in the least suspecting that she was addressing a lover.—"The expression of the eye is most correct, but Miss Smith has not those eyebrows and eyelashes. It is the fault of her face that she has them not."

"Do you think so?" replied he. "I cannot agree with you. It appears to me a most perfect resemblance in every feature. I never saw such a likeness in my life. We must allow for the effect of shade, you know."

"You have made her too tall, Emma," said Mr. Knightley.

Emma knew that she had, but would not own it; and Mr. Elton warmly added,

"Oh no! certainly not too tall; not in the least too tall. Consider, she is sitting down—which naturally presents a different—which in short gives exactly the idea—and the proportions must be preserved, you know. Proportions, fore-shortening.—Oh no! it gives one exactly the idea of such a height as Miss Smith's. Exactly so indeed!"

"It is very pretty," said Mr. Woodhouse. "So prettily done! Just as your drawings always are, my dear. I do not know any body who draws so well as you do. The only thing I do not thoroughly like is, that she seems to be sitting out of doors, with only a little shawl over her shoulders—and it makes one think she must catch cold."

"But, my dear papa, it is supposed to be summer; a warm day in summer. Look at the tree."

"But it is never safe to sit out of doors, my dear."

"You, sir, may say any thing," cried Mr. Elton, "but I must confess that I regard it as a most happy thought, the placing of Miss Smith out of doors; and the tree is touched with such inimitable spirit! Any other situation would have been much less in character. The naivete of Miss Smith's manners—and altogether—Oh, it is most admirable! I cannot keep my eyes from it. I never saw such a likeness."

The next thing wanted was to get the picture framed; and here were a few difficulties. It must be done directly; it must be done in London; the order must go through the hands of some intelligent person whose taste could be depended on; and Isabella, the usual doer of all commissions, must not be applied to, because it was December, and Mr. Woodhouse could not bear the idea of her stirring out of her house in the fogs of December. But no sooner was the distress known to Mr. Elton, than it was removed. His gallantry was always on the alert. "Might he be trusted with the commission, what infinite pleasure should he have in executing it! he could ride to London at any time. It was impossible to say how much he should be gratified by being employed on such an errand."

"He was too good!—she could not endure the thought!—she would not give him such a troublesome office for the world,"—brought on the desired repetition of entreaties and assurances,—and a very few minutes settled the business.

Mr. Elton was to take the drawing to London, chuse the frame, and give the directions; and Emma thought she could so pack it as to ensure its safety without much incommoding him, while he seemed mostly fearful of not being incommoded enough.

"What a precious deposit!" said he with a tender sigh, as he received it.

"This man is almost too gallant to be in love," thought Emma. "I should say so, but that I suppose there may be a hundred different ways of being in love. He is an excellent young man, and will suit Harriet exactly; it will be an 'Exactly so,' as he says himself; but he does sigh and languish, and study for compliments rather more than I could endure as a principal. I come in for a pretty good share as a second. But it is his gratitude on Harriet's account."

Chapter VII

The very day of Mr. Elton's going to London produced a fresh occasion for Emma's services towards her friend. Harriet had been at Hartfield, as usual, soon after breakfast; and, after a time, had gone home to return again to dinner: she returned, and sooner than had been talked of, and with an agitated, hurried look, announcing something extraordinary to have happened which she was longing to tell. Half a minute brought it all out. She had heard, as soon as she got back to Mrs. Goddard's, that Mr. Martin had been there an hour before, and finding she was not at home, nor particularly expected, had left a little parcel for her from one of his sisters, and gone away; and on opening this parcel, she had actually found, besides the two songs which she had lent Elizabeth to copy, a letter to herself; and this letter was from him, from Mr. Martin, and contained a direct proposal of marriage. "Who could have thought it? She was so surprized she did not know what to do. Yes, quite a proposal of marriage; and a very good letter, at least she thought so. And he wrote as if he really loved her very much—but she did not know—and so, she was come as fast as she could to ask Miss Woodhouse what she should do.—" Emma was half-ashamed of her friend for seeming so pleased and so doubtful.

"Upon my word," she cried, "the young man is determined not to lose any thing for want of asking. He will connect himself well if he can."

"Will you read the letter?" cried Harriet. "Pray do. I'd rather you would."

Emma was not sorry to be pressed. She read, and was surprized. The style of the letter was much above her expectation. There were not merely no grammatical errors, but as a composition it would not have disgraced a gentleman; the language, though plain, was strong and unaffected, and the sentiments it conveyed very much to the credit of the writer. It was short, but expressed good sense, warm attachment, liberality, propriety, even delicacy of feeling. She paused over it, while Harriet stood anxiously watching for her opinion, with a "Well, well," and was at last forced to add, "Is it a good letter? or is it too short?"

"Yes, indeed, a very good letter," replied Emma rather slowly—"so good a letter, Harriet, that every thing considered, I think one of his sisters must have helped him. I can hardly imagine the young man whom I saw talking with you the other day could express himself so well, if left quite to his own powers, and yet it is not the style of a woman; no, certainly, it is too strong and concise; not diffuse enough for a woman. No doubt he is a sensible man, and I suppose may have a natural talent for—thinks strongly and clearly—and when he takes a pen in hand, his thoughts naturally find proper words. It is so with some men. Yes, I understand the sort of mind. Vigorous, decided, with sentiments to a certain point, not coarse. A better written letter, Harriet (returning it,) than I had expected."

"Well," said the still waiting Harriet;—" well—and—and what shall I do?"

"What shall you do! In what respect? Do you mean with regard to this letter?"

"Yes."

"But what are you in doubt of? You must answer it of course—and speedily."

"Yes. But what shall I say? Dear Miss Woodhouse, do advise me."

"Oh no, no! the letter had much better be all your own. You will express yourself very properly, I am sure. There is no danger of your not being intelligible, which is the first thing. Your meaning must be unequivocal; no doubts or demurs: and such expressions of gratitude and concern for the pain you are inflicting as propriety requires, will present themselves unbidden to your mind, I am persuaded. You need not be prompted to write with the appearance of sorrow for his disappointment."

"You think I ought to refuse him then," said Harriet, looking down.

"Ought to refuse him! My dear Harriet, what do you mean? Are you in any doubt as to that? I thought—but I beg your pardon, perhaps I have been under a mistake. I certainly have been misunderstanding you, if you feel in doubt as to the purport of your answer. I had imagined you were consulting me only as to the wording of it."

Harriet was silent. With a little reserve of manner, Emma continued:

"You mean to return a favourable answer, I collect."

"No, I do not; that is, I do not mean—What shall I do? What would you advise me to do? Pray, dear Miss Woodhouse, tell me what I ought to do."

"I shall not give you any advice, Harriet. I will have nothing to do with it. This is a point which you must settle with your feelings."

"I had no notion that he liked me so very much," said Harriet, contemplating the letter. For a little while Emma persevered in her silence; but beginning to apprehend the bewitching flattery of that letter might be too powerful, she thought it best to say,

"I lay it down as a general rule, Harriet, that if a woman doubts as to whether she should accept a man or not, she certainly ought to refuse him. If she can hesitate as to 'Yes,' she ought to say 'No' directly. It is not a state to be safely entered into with doubtful feelings, with half a heart. I thought it my duty as a friend, and older than yourself, to say thus much to you. But do not imagine that I want to influence you."

"Oh! no, I am sure you are a great deal too kind to—but if you would just advise me what I had best do—No, no, I do not mean that—As you say, one's mind ought to be quite made up—One should not be hesitating—It is a very serious thing.—It will be safer to say 'No,' perhaps.—Do you think I had better say 'No?'"

"Not for the world," said Emma, smiling graciously, "would I advise you either way. You must be the best judge of your own happiness. If you prefer Mr. Martin to every other person; if you think him the most agreeable man you have ever been in company with, why should you hesitate? You blush, Harriet.—Does any body else occur to you at this moment under such a definition? Harriet, Harriet, do not deceive yourself; do not be run away with by gratitude and compassion. At this moment whom are you thinking of?"

The symptoms were favourable.—Instead of answering, Harriet turned away confused, and stood thoughtfully by the fire; and though the letter was still in her hand, it was now mechanically twisted about without regard. Emma waited the result with impatience, but not without strong hopes. At last, with some hesitation, Harriet said—

"Miss Woodhouse, as you will not give me your opinion, I must do as well as I can by myself; and I have now quite determined, and really almost made up my mind—to refuse Mr. Martin. Do you think I am right?"

"Perfectly, perfectly right, my dearest Harriet; you are doing just what you ought. While you were at all in suspense I kept my feelings to myself, but now that you are so completely decided I have no hesitation in approving. Dear Harriet, I give myself joy of this. It would have grieved me to lose your acquaintance, which must have been the consequence of your marrying Mr. Martin. While you were in the smallest degree wavering, I said nothing about it, because I would not influence; but it would have been the loss of a friend to me. I could not have visited Mrs. Robert Martin, of Abbey-Mill Farm. Now I am secure of you for ever."

Harriet had not surmised her own danger, but the idea of it struck her forcibly.

"You could not have visited me!" she cried, looking aghast. "No, to be sure you could not; but I never thought of that before. That would have been too dreadful!—What an escape!—Dear Miss Woodhouse, I would not give up the pleasure and honour of being intimate with you for any thing in the world."

"Indeed, Harriet, it would have been a severe pang to lose you; but it must have been. You would have thrown yourself out of all good society. I must have given you up."

"Dear me!—How should I ever have borne it! It would have killed me never to come to Hartfield any more!"

"Dear affectionate creature!—You banished to Abbey-Mill Farm!—You confined to the society of the illiterate and vulgar all your life! I wonder how the young man could have the assurance to ask it. He must have a pretty good opinion of himself."

"I do not think he is conceited either, in general," said Harriet, her conscience opposing such censure; "at least, he is very good natured, and I shall always feel much obliged to him, and have a great regard for—but that is quite a different thing from—and you know, though he may like me, it does not follow that I should—and certainly I must confess that since my visiting here I have seen people—and if one comes to compare them, person and manners, there is no comparison at all, one is so very handsome and agreeable. However, I do really think Mr. Martin a very amiable young man, and have a great opinion of him; and his being so much attached to me—and his writing such a letter—but as to leaving you, it is what I would not do upon any consideration."

"Thank you, thank you, my own sweet little friend. We will not be parted. A woman is not to marry a man merely because she is asked, or because he is attached to her, and can write a tolerable letter."

"Oh no;—and it is but a short letter too."

Emma felt the bad taste of her friend, but let it pass with a "very true; and it would be a small consolation to her, for the clownish manner which might be offending her every hour of the day, to know that her husband could write a good letter."

"Oh! yes, very. Nobody cares for a letter; the thing is, to be always happy with pleasant companions. I am quite determined to refuse him. But how shall I do? That shall I say?"

Emma assured her there would be no difficulty in the answer, and advised its being written directly, which was agreed to, in the hope of her assistance; and though Emma continued to protest against any assistance being wanted, it was in fact given in the formation of every sentence. The looking over his letter again, in replying to it, had such a softening tendency, that it was particularly necessary to brace her up with a few decisive expressions; and she was so very much concerned at the idea of making him unhappy, and thought so much of what his mother and sisters would think and say, and was so anxious that they should not fancy her ungrateful, that Emma believed if the young man had come in her way at that moment, he would have been accepted after all.

This letter, however, was written, and sealed, and sent. The business was finished, and Harriet safe. She was rather low all the evening, but Emma could allow for her amiable regrets, and sometimes relieved them by speaking of her own affection, sometimes by bringing forward the idea of Mr. Elton.

"I shall never be invited to Abbey-Mill again," was said in rather a sorrowful tone.

"Nor, if you were, could I ever bear to part with you, my Harriet. You are a great deal too necessary at Hartfield to be spared to Abbey-Mill."

"And I am sure I should never want to go there; for I am never happy but at Hartfield."

Some time afterwards it was, "I think Mrs. Goddard would be very much surprized if she knew what had happened. I am sure Miss Nash would—for Miss Nash thinks her own sister very well married, and it is only a linen-draper."

"One should be sorry to see greater pride or refinement in the teacher of a school, Harriet. I dare say Miss Nash would envy you such an opportunity as this of being married. Even this conquest would appear valuable in her eyes. As to any thing superior for you, I suppose she is quite in the dark. The attentions of a certain person can hardly be among the tittle-tattle of Highbury yet. Hitherto I fancy you and I are the only people to whom his looks and manners have explained themselves."

Harriet blushed and smiled, and said something about wondering that people should like her so much. The idea of Mr. Elton was certainly cheering; but still, after a time, she was tender-hearted again towards the rejected Mr. Martin.

"Now he has got my letter," said she softly. "I wonder what they are all doing—whether his sisters know—if he is unhappy, they will be unhappy too. I hope he will not mind it so very much."

"Let us think of those among our absent friends who are more cheerfully employed," cried Emma. "At this moment, perhaps, Mr.

Elton is shewing your picture to his mother and sisters, telling how much more beautiful is the original, and after being asked for it five or six times, allowing them to hear your name, your own dear name."

"My picture!—But he has left my picture in Bond-street."

"Has he so!—Then I know nothing of Mr. Elton. No, my dear little modest Harriet, depend upon it the picture will not be in Bond-street till just before he mounts his horse to-morrow. It is his companion all this evening, his solace, his delight. It opens his designs to his family, it introduces you among them, it diffuses through the party those pleasantest feelings of our nature, eager curiosity and warm prepossession. How cheerful, how animated, how suspicious, how busy their imaginations all are!"

Harriet smiled again, and her smiles grew stronger.

Chapter VIII

Harriet slept at Hartfield that night. For some weeks past she had been spending more than half her time there, and gradually getting to have a bed-room appropriated to herself; and Emma judged it best in every respect, safest and kindest, to keep her with them as much as possible just at present. She was obliged to go the next morning for an hour or two to Mrs. Goddard's, but it was then to be settled that she should return to Hartfield, to make a regular visit of some days.

While she was gone, Mr. Knightley called, and sat some time with Mr. Woodhouse and Emma, till Mr. Woodhouse, who had previously made up his mind to walk out, was persuaded by his daughter not to defer it, and was induced by the entreaties of both, though against the scruples of his own civility, to leave Mr. Knightley for that purpose. Mr. Knightley, who had nothing of ceremony about him, was offering by his short, decided answers, an amusing contrast to the protracted apologies and civil hesitations of the other.

"Well, I believe, if you will excuse me, Mr. Knightley, if you will not consider me as doing a very rude thing, I shall take Emma's advice and go out for a quarter of an hour. As the sun is out, I believe I had better take my three turns while I can. I treat you without ceremony, Mr. Knightley. We invalids think we are privileged people."

"My dear sir, do not make a stranger of me."

"I leave an excellent substitute in my daughter. Emma will be happy to entertain you. And therefore I think I will beg your excuse and take my three turns—my winter walk."

"You cannot do better, sir."

"I would ask for the pleasure of your company, Mr. Knightley, but I am a very slow walker, and my pace would be tedious to you; and, besides, you have another long walk before you, to Donwell Abbey."

"Thank you, sir, thank you; I am going this moment myself; and I think the sooner you go the better. I will fetch your greatcoat and open the garden door for you."

Mr. Woodhouse at last was off; but Mr. Knightley, instead of being immediately off likewise, sat down again, seemingly inclined for more chat. He began speaking of Harriet, and speaking of her with more voluntary praise than Emma had ever heard before.

"I cannot rate her beauty as you do," said he; "but she is a pretty little creature, and I am inclined to think very well of her disposition. Her character depends upon those she is with; but in good hands she will turn out a valuable woman."

"I am glad you think so; and the good hands, I hope, may not be wanting."

"Come," said he, "you are anxious for a compliment, so I will tell you that you have improved her. You have cured her of her school-girl's giggle; she really does you credit."

"Thank you. I should be mortified indeed if I did not believe I had been of some use; but it is not every body who will bestow praise where they may. You do not often overpower me with it."

"You are expecting her again, you say, this morning?"

"Almost every moment. She has been gone longer already than she intended."

"Something has happened to delay her; some visitors perhaps."

"Highbury gossips!—Tiresome wretches!"

"Harriet may not consider every body tiresome that you would."

Emma knew this was too true for contradiction, and therefore said nothing. He presently added, with a smile,

"I do not pretend to fix on times or places, but I must tell you that I have good reason to believe your little friend will soon hear of something to her advantage."

"Indeed! how so? of what sort?"

"A very serious sort, I assure you;" still smiling.

"Very serious! I can think of but one thing—Who is in love with her? Who makes you their confidant?"

Emma was more than half in hopes of Mr. Elton's having dropt a hint. Mr. Knightley was a sort of general friend and adviser, and she knew Mr. Elton looked up to him.

"I have reason to think," he replied, "that Harriet Smith will soon have an offer of marriage, and from a most unexceptionable quarter:—Robert Martin is the man. Her visit to Abbey-Mill, this summer, seems to have done his business. He is desperately in love and means to marry her."

"He is very obliging," said Emma; "but is he sure that Harriet means to marry him?"

"Well, well, means to make her an offer then. Will that do? He came to the Abbey two evenings ago, on purpose to consult me about it. He knows I have a thorough regard for him and all his family, and, I believe, considers me as one of his best friends. He came to ask me whether I thought it would be imprudent in him to settle so early; whether I thought her too young: in short, whether I approved his choice altogether; having some apprehension perhaps of her being considered (especially since your making so much of her) as in a line of society above him. I was very much pleased with all that he said. I never hear better sense from any one than Robert Martin. He always speaks to the purpose; open, straightforward, and very well judging. He told me every thing; his circumstances and plans, and what they all proposed doing in the event of his marriage. He is an excellent young man, both as son and brother. I had no hesitation in advising him to marry. He proved to me that he could afford it; and that being the case, I was convinced he could not do better. I praised the fair lady too, and altogether sent him away very happy. If he had never esteemed my opinion before, he would have thought highly of me then; and, I dare say, left the house thinking me the best friend and counsellor man ever had. This happened the night before last. Now, as we may fairly suppose, he would not allow much time to pass before he spoke to the lady, and as he does not appear to have spoken yesterday, it is not unlikely that he should be at Mrs. Goddard's to-day; and she may be detained by a visitor, without thinking him at all a tiresome wretch."

"Pray, Mr. Knightley," said Emma, who had been smiling to herself through a great part of this speech, "how do you know that Mr. Martin did not speak yesterday?"

"Certainly," replied he, surprized, "I do not absolutely know it; but it may be inferred. Was not she the whole day with you?"

"Come," said she, "I will tell you something, in return for what you have told me. He did speak yesterday—that is, he wrote, and was refused."

This was obliged to be repeated before it could be believed; and Mr. Knightley actually looked red with surprize and displeasure, as he stood up, in tall indignation, and said,

"Then she is a greater simpleton than I ever believed her. What is the foolish girl about?"

"Oh! to be sure," cried Emma, "it is always incomprehensible to a man that a woman should ever refuse an offer of marriage. A man always imagines a woman to be ready for any body who asks her."

"Nonsense! a man does not imagine any such thing. But what is the meaning of this? Harriet Smith refuse Robert Martin? madness, if it is so; but I hope you are mistaken."

"I saw her answer!—nothing could be clearer."

"You saw her answer!—you wrote her answer too. Emma, this is your doing. You persuaded her to refuse him."

"And if I did, (which, however, I am far from allowing) I should not feel that I had done wrong. Mr. Martin is a very respectable young man, but I cannot admit him to be Harriet's equal; and am rather surprized indeed that he should have ventured to address her. By your account, he does seem to have had some scruples. It is a pity that they were ever got over."

"Not Harriet's equal!" exclaimed Mr. Knightley loudly and warmly; and with calmer asperity, added, a few moments afterwards, "No, he is not her equal indeed, for he is as much her superior in sense as in situation. Emma, your infatuation about that girl blinds you. What are Harriet Smith's claims, either of birth, nature or education, to any connexion higher than Robert Martin? She is the natural daughter of nobody knows whom, with probably no settled provision at all, and certainly no respectable relations. She is known only as parlour-boarder at a common school. She is not a sensible girl, nor a girl of any information. She has been taught nothing useful, and is too young and too simple to have acquired any thing herself. At her age she can have no experience, and with her little wit, is not very likely ever to have any that can avail her. She is pretty, and she is good tempered, and that is all. My only scruple in advising the match was on his account, as being beneath his deserts, and a bad connexion for him. I felt that, as to fortune, in all probability he might do much better; and that as to a rational companion or useful helpmate, he could not do worse. But I could not reason so to a man in love, and was willing to trust to there being no harm in her, to her having that sort of disposition, which, in good hands, like his, might be easily led aright and turn out very well. The advantage of the match I felt to be all on her side; and had not the smallest doubt (nor have I now) that there would be a general cry-out upon her extreme good luck. Even your satisfaction I made sure of. It crossed my mind immediately that you would not regret your friend's leaving Highbury, for the sake of her being settled so well. I remember saying to myself, 'Even Emma, with all her partiality for Harriet, will think this a good match.'"

"I cannot help wondering at your knowing so little of Emma as to say any such thing. What! think a farmer, (and with all his sense and all his merit Mr. Martin is nothing more,) a good match for my intimate friend! Not regret her leaving Highbury for the sake of marrying a man whom I could never admit as an acquaintance of my own! I wonder you should think it possible for me to have such feelings. I assure you mine are very different. I must think your statement by no means fair. You are not just to Harriet's claims. They would be estimated very differently by others as well as myself; Mr. Martin may be the richest of the two, but he is undoubtedly her inferior as to rank in society.—The sphere in which she moves is much above his.—It would be a degradation."

"A degradation to illegitimacy and ignorance, to be married to a respectable, intelligent gentleman-farmer!"

"As to the circumstances of her birth, though in a legal sense she may be called Nobody, it will not hold in common sense. She is not to pay for the offence of others, by being held below the level of those with whom she is brought up.—There can scarcely be a doubt that her father is a gentleman—and a gentleman of fortune.—Her allowance is very liberal; nothing has ever been grudged for her improvement or comfort.—That she is a gentleman's daughter, is indubitable to me; that she associates with gentlemen's daughters, no one, I apprehend, will deny.—She is superior to Mr. Robert Martin."

"Whoever might be her parents," said Mr. Knightley, "whoever may have had the charge of her, it does not appear to have been any part of their plan to introduce her into what you would call good society. After receiving a very indifferent education she is left in Mrs. Goddard's hands to shift as she can;—to move, in short, in Mrs. Goddard's line, to have Mrs. Goddard's acquaintance. Her friends evidently thought this good enough for her; and it was good enough. She desired nothing better herself. Till you chose to turn her into a friend, her mind had no distaste for her own set, nor any ambition beyond it. She was as happy as possible with the Martins in the summer. She had no sense of superiority then. If she has it now, you have given it. You have been no friend to Harriet Smith, Emma. Robert Martin would never have proceeded so far, if he had not felt persuaded of her not being disinclined to him. I know him well. He has too much real feeling to address any woman on the haphazard of selfish passion. And as to conceit, he is the farthest from it of any man I know. Depend upon it he had encouragement."

It was most convenient to Emma not to make a direct reply to this assertion; she chose rather to take up her own line of the subject again.

"You are a very warm friend to Mr. Martin; but, as I said before, are unjust to Harriet. Harriet's claims to marry well are not so contemptible as you represent them. She is not a clever girl, but she has better sense than you are aware of, and does not deserve to have her understanding spoken of so slightingly. Waiving that point, however, and supposing her to be, as you describe her, only pretty and good-natured, let me tell you, that in the degree she possesses them, they are not trivial recommendations to the world in general, for she is, in fact, a beautiful girl, and must be thought so by ninety-nine people out of an hundred; and till it appears that men are much more philosophic on the subject of beauty than they are generally supposed; till they do fall in love with well-informed minds instead of handsome faces, a girl, with such loveliness as Harriet, has a certainty of being admired and sought after, of having the power of chusing from among many, consequently a claim to be nice. Her good-nature, too, is not so very slight a claim, comprehending, as it does, real, thorough sweetness of temper and manner, a very humble opinion of herself, and a great readiness to be pleased with other people. I am very much mistaken if your sex in general would not think such beauty, and such temper, the highest claims a woman could possess."

"Upon my word, Emma, to hear you abusing the reason you have, is almost enough to make me think so too. Better be without sense, than misapply it as you do."

"To be sure!" cried she playfully. "I know that is the feeling of you all. I know that such a girl as Harriet is exactly what every man delights in—what at once bewitches his senses and satisfies his judgment. Oh! Harriet may pick and chuse. Were you, yourself, ever to marry, she is the very woman for you. And is she, at seventeen, just entering into life, just beginning to be known, to be wondered at because she does not accept the first offer she receives? No—pray let her have time to look about her."

"I have always thought it a very foolish intimacy," said Mr. Knightley presently, "though I have kept my thoughts to myself; but I now perceive that it will be a very unfortunate one for Harriet. You will puff her up with such ideas of her own beauty, and of what she has a claim to, that, in a little while, nobody within her reach will be good enough for her. Vanity working on a weak head, produces every sort of mischief. Nothing so easy as for a young lady to raise her expectations too high. Miss Harriet Smith may not find offers of marriage flow in so fast, though she is a very pretty girl. Men of sense, whatever you may chuse to say, do not want silly wives. Men of family would not be very fond of connecting themselves with a girl of such obscurity—and most prudent men would be afraid of the inconvenience and disgrace they might be involved in, when the mystery of her parentage came to be revealed. Let her marry Robert Martin, and she is safe, respectable, and happy for ever; but if you encourage her to expect to marry greatly, and teach her to be satisfied with nothing less than a man of consequence and large fortune, she may be a parlour-boarder at Mrs. Goddard's all the rest of her life—or, at least, (for Harriet Smith is a girl who will marry somebody or other,) till she grow desperate, and is glad to catch at the old writing-master's son."

"We think so very differently on this point, Mr. Knightley, that there can be no use in canvassing it. We shall only be making each other more angry. But as to my letting her marry Robert Martin, it is impossible; she has refused him, and so decidedly, I think, as must prevent any second application. She must abide by the evil of having refused him, whatever it may be; and as to the refusal itself, I will not pretend to say that I might not influence her a little; but I assure you there was very little for me or for any body to do. His appearance is so much against him, and his manner so bad, that if she ever were disposed to favour him, she is not now. I can imagine, that before she had seen any body superior, she might tolerate him. He was the brother of her friends, and he took pains to please her; and altogether, having seen nobody better (that must have been his great assistant) she might not, while she was at Abbey-Mill, find him disagreeable. But the case is altered now. She knows now what gentlemen are; and nothing but a gentleman in education and manner has any chance with Harriet."

"Nonsense, errant nonsense, as ever was talked!" cried Mr. Knightley.—"Robert Martin's manners have sense, sincerity, and good-humour to recommend them; and his mind has more true gentility than Harriet Smith could understand."

Emma made no answer, and tried to look cheerfully unconcerned, but was really feeling uncomfortable and wanting him very much to be gone. She did not repent what she had done; she still thought herself a better judge of such a point of female right and refinement than he could be; but yet she had a sort of habitual respect for his judgment in general, which made her dislike having it so loudly against her; and to have him sitting just opposite to her in angry state, was very disagreeable. Some minutes passed in this unpleasant silence, with only one attempt on Emma's side to talk of the weather, but he made no answer. He was thinking. The result of his thoughts appeared at last in these words.

"Robert Martin has no great loss—if he can but think so; and I hope it will not be long before he does. Your views for Harriet are best known to yourself; but as you make no secret of your love of match-making, it is fair to suppose that views, and plans, and projects you have;—and as a friend I shall just hint to you that if Elton is the man, I think it will be all labour in vain."

Emma laughed and disclaimed. He continued,

"Depend upon it, Elton will not do. Elton is a very good sort of man, and a very respectable vicar of Highbury, but not at all likely to make an imprudent match. He knows the value of a good income as well as any body. Elton may talk sentimentally, but he will act rationally. He is as well acquainted with his own claims, as you can be with Harriet's. He knows that he is a very handsome young man, and a great favourite wherever he goes; and from his general way of talking in unreserved moments, when there are only men present, I am convinced that he does not mean to throw himself away. I have heard him speak with great animation of a large family of young ladies that his sisters are intimate with, who have all twenty thousand pounds apiece."

"I am very much obliged to you," said Emma, laughing again. "If I had set my heart on Mr. Elton's marrying Harriet, it would have been very kind to open my eyes; but at present I only want to keep Harriet to myself. I have done with match-making indeed. I could never hope to equal my own doings at Randalls. I shall leave off while I am well."

"Good morning to you,"—said he, rising and walking off abruptly. He was very much vexed. He felt the disappointment of the young man, and was mortified to have been the means of promoting it, by the sanction he had given; and the part which he was persuaded Emma had taken in the affair, was provoking him exceedingly.

Emma remained in a state of vexation too; but there was more indistinctness in the causes of her's, than in his. She did not always feel so absolutely satisfied with herself, so entirely convinced that her opinions were right and her adversary's wrong, as Mr. Knightley. He walked off in more complete self-approbation than he left for her. She was not so materially cast down, however, but that a little time and the return of Harriet were very adequate restoratives. Harriet's staying away so long was beginning to make her uneasy. The possibility of the young man's coming to Mrs. Goddard's that morning, and meeting with Harriet and pleading his own cause, gave alarming ideas. The dread of such a failure after all became the prominent uneasiness; and when Harriet appeared, and in very good spirits, and without having any such reason to give for her long absence, she felt a satisfaction which settled her with her own mind, and convinced her, that let Mr. Knightley think or say what he would, she had done nothing which woman's friendship and woman's feelings would not justify.

He had frightened her a little about Mr. Elton; but when she considered that Mr. Knightley could not have observed him as she had done, neither with the interest, nor (she must be allowed to tell herself, in spite of Mr. Knightley's pretensions) with the skill of such an observer on such a question as herself, that he had spoken it hastily and in anger, she was able to believe, that he had rather said what he wished resentfully to be true, than what he knew any thing about. He certainly might have heard Mr. Elton speak with more unreserve than she had ever done, and Mr. Elton might not be of an imprudent, inconsiderate disposition as to money matters; he might naturally be rather attentive than otherwise to them; but then, Mr. Knightley did not make due allowance for the influence of a strong passion at war with all interested motives. Mr. Knightley saw no such passion, and of course thought nothing of its effects; but she saw too much of it to feel a doubt of its overcoming any hesitations that a reasonable prudence might originally suggest; and more than a reasonable, becoming degree of prudence, she was very sure did not belong to Mr. Elton.

Harriet's cheerful look and manner established hers: she came back, not to think of Mr. Martin, but to talk of Mr. Elton. Miss Nash had been telling her something, which she repeated immediately with great delight. Mr. Perry had been to Mrs. Goddard's to attend a sick child, and Miss Nash had seen him, and he had told Miss Nash, that as he was coming back yesterday from Clayton Park, he had met Mr. Elton, and found to his great surprize, that Mr. Elton was actually on his road to London, and not meaning to return till the morrow, though it was the whist-club night, which he had been never known to miss before; and Mr. Perry had remonstrated with him about it, and told him how shabby it was in him, their best player, to absent himself, and tried very much to persuade him to put off his journey only one day; but it would not do; Mr. Elton had been determined to go on, and had said in a very particular way indeed, that he was going on business which he would not put off for any inducement in the world; and something about a very enviable commission, and being the bearer of something exceedingly precious. Mr. Perry could not quite understand him, but he was very sure there must be a lady in the case, and he told him so; and Mr. Elton only looked very conscious and smiling, and rode off in great spirits. Miss Nash had told her all this, and had talked a great deal more about Mr. Elton; and said, looking so very significantly at her, "that she did not pretend to understand what his business might be, but she only knew that any woman whom Mr. Elton could prefer, she should think the luckiest woman in the world; for, beyond a doubt, Mr. Elton had not his equal for beauty or agreeableness."

Chapter IX

Mr. Knightley might quarrel with her, but Emma could not quarrel with herself. He was so much displeased, that it was longer than usual before he came to Hartfield again; and when they did meet, his grave looks shewed that she was not forgiven. She was sorry, but could not repent. On the contrary, her plans and proceedings were more and more justified and endeared to her by the general appearances of the next few days.

The Picture, elegantly framed, came safely to hand soon after Mr. Elton's return, and being hung over the mantelpiece of the common sitting-room, he got up to look at it, and sighed out his half sentences of admiration just as he ought; and as for Harriet's feelings, they were visibly forming themselves into as strong and steady an attachment as her youth and sort of mind admitted. Emma was soon perfectly satisfied of Mr. Martin's being no otherwise remembered, than as he furnished a contrast with Mr. Elton, of the utmost advantage to the latter.

Her views of improving her little friend's mind, by a great deal of useful reading and conversation, had never yet led to more than a few first chapters, and the intention of going on to-morrow. It was much easier to chat than to study; much pleasanter to let her imagination range and work at Harriet's fortune, than to be labouring to enlarge her comprehension or exercise it on sober facts; and the only literary pursuit which engaged Harriet at present, the only mental provision she was making for the evening of life, was the collecting and transcribing all the riddles of every sort that she could meet with, into a thin quarto of hot-pressed paper, made up by her friend, and ornamented with ciphers and trophies.

In this age of literature, such collections on a very grand scale are not uncommon. Miss Nash, head-teacher at Mrs. Goddard's, had written out at least three hundred; and Harriet, who had taken the first hint of it from her, hoped, with Miss Woodhouse's help, to get a great many more. Emma assisted with her invention, memory and taste; and as Harriet wrote a very pretty hand, it was likely to be an arrangement of the first order, in form as well as quantity.

Mr. Woodhouse was almost as much interested in the business as the girls, and tried very often to recollect something worth their putting in. "So many clever riddles as there used to be when he was young—he wondered he could not remember them! but he hoped he should in time." And it always ended in "Kitty, a fair but frozen maid."

His good friend Perry, too, whom he had spoken to on the subject, did not at present recollect any thing of the riddle kind; but he had desired Perry to be upon the watch, and as he went about so much, something, he thought, might come from that quarter.

It was by no means his daughter's wish that the intellects of Highbury in general should be put under requisition. Mr. Elton was the only one whose assistance she asked. He was invited to contribute any really good enigmas, charades, or conundrums that he might recollect; and she had the pleasure of seeing him most intently at work with his recollections; and at the same time, as she could perceive, most earnestly careful that nothing ungallant, nothing that did not breathe a compliment to the sex should pass his lips. They owed to him their two or three politest puzzles; and the joy and exultation with which at last he recalled, and rather sentimentally recited, that well-known charade,

My first doth affliction denote,
    Which my second is destin'd to feel
And my whole is the best antidote
    That affliction to soften and heal.—

made her quite sorry to acknowledge that they had transcribed it some pages ago already.

"Why will not you write one yourself for us, Mr. Elton?" said she; "that is the only security for its freshness; and nothing could be easier to you."

"Oh no! he had never written, hardly ever, any thing of the kind in his life. The stupidest fellow! He was afraid not even Miss

Woodhouse"—he stopt a moment—"or Miss Smith could inspire him."

The very next day however produced some proof of inspiration. He called for a few moments, just to leave a piece of paper on the table containing, as he said, a charade, which a friend of his had addressed to a young lady, the object of his admiration, but which, from his manner, Emma was immediately convinced must be his own.

"I do not offer it for Miss Smith's collection," said he. "Being my friend's, I have no right to expose it in any degree to the public eye, but perhaps you may not dislike looking at it."

The speech was more to Emma than to Harriet, which Emma could understand. There was deep consciousness about him, and he found it easier to meet her eye than her friend's. He was gone the next moment:—after another moment's pause,

"Take it," said Emma, smiling, and pushing the paper towards Harriet—"it is for you. Take your own."

But Harriet was in a tremor, and could not touch it; and Emma, never loth to be first, was obliged to examine it herself.

To Miss——

CHARADE.

My first displays the wealth and pomp of kings,
Lords of the earth! their luxury and ease.
Another view of man, my second brings,
Behold him there, the monarch of the seas!

But ah! united, what reverse we have!
Man's boasted power and freedom, all are flown;
Lord of the earth and sea, he bends a slave,
And woman, lovely woman, reigns alone.

Thy ready wit the word will soon supply,
May its approval beam in that soft eye!

She cast her eye over it, pondered, caught the meaning, read it through again to be quite certain, and quite mistress of the lines, and then passing it to Harriet, sat happily smiling, and saying to herself, while Harriet was puzzling over the paper in all the confusion of hope and dulness, "Very well, Mr. Elton, very well indeed. I have read worse charades. Courtship—a very good hint. I give you credit for it. This is feeling your way. This is saying very plainly—'Pray, Miss Smith, give me leave to pay my addresses to you. Approve my charade and my intentions in the same glance.'

May its approval beam in that soft eye!

Harriet exactly. Soft is the very word for her eye—of all epithets, the justest that could be given.

Thy ready wit the word will soon supply.

Humph—Harriet's ready wit! All the better. A man must be very much in love, indeed, to describe her so. Ah! Mr. Knightley, I wish you had the benefit of this; I think this would convince you. For once in your life you would be obliged to own yourself mistaken. An excellent charade indeed! and very much to the purpose. Things must come to a crisis soon now."

She was obliged to break off from these very pleasant observations, which were otherwise of a sort to run into great length, by the eagerness of Harriet's wondering questions.

"What can it be, Miss Woodhouse?—what can it be? I have not an idea—I cannot guess it in the least. What can it possibly be? Do try to find it out, Miss Woodhouse. Do help me. I never saw any thing so hard. Is it kingdom? I wonder who the friend was—and who could be the young lady. Do you think it is a good one? Can it be woman?

And woman, lovely woman, reigns alone.

Can it be Neptune?

Behold him there, the monarch of the seas!

Or a trident? or a mermaid? or a shark? Oh, no! shark is only one syllable. It must be very clever, or he would not have brought it. Oh! Miss Woodhouse, do you think we shall ever find it out?"

"Mermaids and sharks! Nonsense! My dear Harriet, what are you thinking of? Where would be the use of his bringing us a charade made by a friend upon a mermaid or a shark? Give me the paper and listen.

For Miss ———, read Miss Smith.

My first displays the wealth and pomp of kings,
Lords of the earth! their luxury and ease.

That is court.

Another view of man, my second brings;
Behold him there, the monarch of the seas!

That is ship;—plain as it can be.—Now for the cream.

But ah! united, (courtship, you know,) what reverse we have!
Man's boasted power and freedom, all are flown.
Lord of the earth and sea, he bends a slave,
And woman, lovely woman, reigns alone.

A very proper compliment!—and then follows the application, which I think, my dear Harriet, you cannot find much difficulty in comprehending. Read it in comfort to yourself. There can be no doubt of its being written for you and to you."

Harriet could not long resist so delightful a persuasion. She read the concluding lines, and was all flutter and happiness. She could not speak. But she was not wanted to speak. It was enough for her to feel. Emma spoke for her.

"There is so pointed, and so particular a meaning in this compliment," said she, "that I cannot have a doubt as to Mr. Elton's intentions. You are his object—and you will soon receive the completest proof of it. I thought it must be so. I thought I could not be so deceived; but now, it is clear; the state of his mind is as clear and decided, as my wishes on the subject have been ever since I knew you. Yes, Harriet, just so long have I been wanting the very circumstance to happen what has happened. I could never tell whether an attachment between you and Mr. Elton were most desirable or most natural. Its probability and its eligibility have really so equalled each other! I am very happy. I congratulate you, my dear Harriet, with all my heart. This is an attachment which a woman may well feel pride in creating. This is a connexion which offers nothing but good. It will give you every thing that you want—consideration, independence, a proper home—it will fix you in the centre of all your real friends, close to Hartfield and to me, and confirm our intimacy for ever. This, Harriet, is an alliance which can never raise a blush in either of us."

"Dear Miss Woodhouse!"—and "Dear Miss Woodhouse," was all that Harriet, with many tender embraces could articulate at first; but when they did arrive at something more like conversation, it was sufficiently clear to her friend that she saw, felt, anticipated, and remembered just as she ought. Mr. Elton's superiority had very ample acknowledgment.

"Whatever you say is always right," cried Harriet, "and therefore I suppose, and believe, and hope it must be so; but otherwise I could not have imagined it. It is so much beyond any thing I deserve. Mr. Elton, who might marry any body! There cannot be two opinions about him. He is so very superior. Only think of those sweet verses—"To Miss ———." Dear me, how clever!—Could it really be meant for me?"

"I cannot make a question, or listen to a question about that. It is a certainty. Receive it on my judgment. It is a sort of prologue to the play, a motto to the chapter; and will be soon followed by matter-of-fact prose."

"It is a sort of thing which nobody could have expected. I am sure, a month ago, I had no more idea myself!—The strangest things do take place!"

"When Miss Smiths and Mr. Eltons get acquainted—they do indeed—and really it is strange; it is out of the common course that what is so evidently, so palpably desirable—what courts the pre-arrangement of other people, should so immediately shape itself into the proper form. You and Mr. Elton are by situation called together; you belong to one another by every circumstance of your respective homes. Your marrying will be equal to the match at Randalls. There does seem to be a something in the air of Hartfield which gives love exactly the right direction, and sends it into the very channel where it ought to flow.

The course of true love never did run smooth—

A Hartfield edition of Shakespeare would have a long note on that passage."

"That Mr. Elton should really be in love with me,—me, of all people, who did not know him, to speak to him, at Michaelmas! And he, the very handsomest man that ever was, and a man that every body looks up to, quite like Mr. Knightley! His company so sought after, that every body says he need not eat a single meal by himself if he does not chuse it; that he has more invitations than there are days in the week. And so excellent in the Church! Miss Nash has put down all the texts he has ever preached from since he came to Highbury. Dear me! When I look back to the first time I saw him! How little did I think!—The two Abbots and I ran into the front room and peeped through the blind when we heard he was going by, and Miss Nash came and scolded us away, and staid to look through herself; however, she called me back presently, and let me look too, which was very good-natured. And how beautiful we thought he looked! He was arm-in-arm with Mr. Cole."

"This is an alliance which, whoever—whatever your friends may be, must be agreeable to them, provided at least they have common sense; and we are not to be addressing our conduct to fools. If they are anxious to see you happily married, here is a man whose amiable character gives every assurance of it;—if they wish to have you settled in the same country and circle which they have chosen to place you in, here it will be accomplished; and if their only object is that you should, in the common phrase, be well married, here is the comfortable fortune, the respectable establishment, the rise in the world which must satisfy them."

"Yes, very true. How nicely you talk; I love to hear you. You understand every thing. You and Mr. Elton are one as clever as the other. This charade!—If I had studied a twelvemonth, I could never have made any thing like it."

"I thought he meant to try his skill, by his manner of declining it yesterday."

"I do think it is, without exception, the best charade I ever read."

"I never read one more to the purpose, certainly."

"It is as long again as almost all we have had before."

"I do not consider its length as particularly in its favour. Such things in general cannot be too short."

Harriet was too intent on the lines to hear. The most satisfactory comparisons were rising in her mind.

"It is one thing," said she, presently—her cheeks in a glow—"to have very good sense in a common way, like every body else, and if there is any thing to say, to sit down and write a letter, and say just what you must, in a short way; and another, to write verses and charades like this."

Emma could not have desired a more spirited rejection of Mr. Martin's prose.

"Such sweet lines!" continued Harriet—"these two last!—But how shall I ever be able to return the paper, or say I have found it out?—Oh! Miss Woodhouse, what can we do about that?"

"Leave it to me. You do nothing. He will be here this evening, I dare say, and then I will give it him back, and some nonsense or other will pass between us, and you shall not be committed.—Your soft eyes shall chuse their own time for beaming. Trust to me."

"Oh! Miss Woodhouse, what a pity that I must not write this beautiful charade into my book! I am sure I have not got one half so good."

"Leave out the two last lines, and there is no reason why you should not write it into your book."

"Oh! but those two lines are"—

—"The best of all. Granted;—for private enjoyment; and for private enjoyment keep them. They are not at all the less written you know, because you divide them. The couplet does not cease to be, nor does its meaning change. But take it away, and all appropriation ceases, and a very pretty gallant charade remains, fit for any collection. Depend upon it, he would not like to have his charade slighted, much better than his passion. A poet in love must be encouraged in both capacities, or neither. Give me the book, I will write it down, and then there can be no possible reflection on you."

Harriet submitted, though her mind could hardly separate the parts, so as to feel quite sure that her friend were not writing down a declaration of love. It seemed too precious an offering for any degree of publicity.

"I shall never let that book go out of my own hands," said she.

"Very well," replied Emma; "a most natural feeling; and the longer it lasts, the better I shall be pleased. But here is my father coming: you will not object to my reading the charade to him. It will be giving him so much pleasure! He loves any thing of the sort, and especially any thing that pays woman a compliment. He has the tenderest spirit of gallantry towards us all!—You must let me read it to him."

Harriet looked grave.

"My dear Harriet, you must not refine too much upon this charade.—You will betray your feelings improperly, if you are too conscious and too quick, and appear to affix more meaning, or even quite all the meaning which may be affixed to it. Do not be overpowered by such a little tribute of admiration. If he had been anxious for secrecy, he would not have left the paper while I was by; but he rather pushed it towards me than towards you. Do not let us be too solemn on the business. He has encouragement enough to proceed, without our sighing out our souls over this charade."

"Oh! no—I hope I shall not be ridiculous about it. Do as you please."

Mr. Woodhouse came in, and very soon led to the subject again, by the recurrence of his very frequent inquiry of "Well, my dears, how does your book go on?—Have you got any thing fresh?"

"Yes, papa; we have something to read you, something quite fresh. A piece of paper was found on the table this morning—(dropt, we suppose, by a fairy)—containing a very pretty charade, and we have just copied it in."

She read it to him, just as he liked to have any thing read, slowly and distinctly, and two or three times over, with explanations of every part as she proceeded—and he was very much pleased, and, as she had foreseen, especially struck with the complimentary conclusion.

"Aye, that's very just, indeed, that's very properly said. Very true. 'Woman, lovely woman.' It is such a pretty charade, my dear, that I can easily guess what fairy brought it.—Nobody could have written so prettily, but you, Emma."

Emma only nodded, and smiled.—After a little thinking, and a very tender sigh, he added,

"Ah! it is no difficulty to see who you take after! Your dear mother was so clever at all those things! If I had but her memory! But I can remember nothing;—not even that particular riddle which you have heard me mention; I can only recollect the first stanza; and there are several.

Kitty, a fair but frozen maid,
    Kindled a flame I yet deplore,
The hood-wink'd boy I called to aid,
Though of his near approach afraid,
    So fatal to my suit before.

And that is all that I can recollect of it—but it is very clever all the way through. But I think, my dear, you said you had got it."

"Yes, papa, it is written out in our second page. We copied it from the Elegant Extracts. It was Garrick's, you know."

"Aye, very true.—I wish I could recollect more of it.

Kitty, a fair but frozen maid.

The name makes me think of poor Isabella; for she was very near being christened Catherine after her grandmama. I hope we shall have her here next week. Have you thought, my dear, where you shall put her—and what room there will be for the children?"

"Oh! yes—she will have her own room, of course; the room she always has;—and there is the nursery for the children,—just as usual, you know. Why should there be any change?"

"I do not know, my dear—but it is so long since she was here!—not since last Easter, and then only for a few days.—Mr. John Knightley's being a lawyer is very inconvenient.—Poor Isabella!—she is sadly taken away from us all!—and how sorry she will be when she comes, not to see Miss Taylor here!"

"She will not be surprized, papa, at least."

"I do not know, my dear. I am sure I was very much surprized when I first heard she was going to be married."

"We must ask Mr. and Mrs. Weston to dine with us, while Isabella is here."

"Yes, my dear, if there is time.—But—(in a very depressed tone)—she is coming for only one week. There will not be time for any thing."

"It is unfortunate that they cannot stay longer—but it seems a case of necessity. Mr. John Knightley must be in town again on the 28th, and we ought to be thankful, papa, that we are to have the whole of the time they can give to the country, that two or three days are not to be taken out for the Abbey. Mr. Knightley promises to give up his claim this Christmas—though you know it is longer since they were with him, than with us."

"It would be very hard, indeed, my dear, if poor Isabella were to be anywhere but at Hartfield."

Mr. Woodhouse could never allow for Mr. Knightley's claims on his brother, or any body's claims on Isabella, except his own. He sat musing a little while, and then said,

"But I do not see why poor Isabella should be obliged to go back so soon, though he does. I think, Emma, I shall try and persuade her to stay longer with us. She and the children might stay very well."

"Ah! papa—that is what you never have been able to accomplish, and I do not think you ever will. Isabella cannot bear to stay behind her husband."

This was too true for contradiction. Unwelcome as it was, Mr. Woodhouse could only give a submissive sigh; and as Emma saw his spirits affected by the idea of his daughter's attachment to her husband, she immediately led to such a branch of the subject as must raise them.

"Harriet must give us as much of her company as she can while my brother and sister are here. I am sure she will be pleased with the children. We are very proud of the children, are not we, papa? I wonder which she will think the handsomest, Henry or John?"

"Aye, I wonder which she will. Poor little dears, how glad they will be to come. They are very fond of being at Hartfield, Harriet."

"I dare say they are, sir. I am sure I do not know who is not."

"Henry is a fine boy, but John is very like his mama. Henry is the eldest, he was named after me, not after his father. John, the second, is named after his father. Some people are surprized, I believe, that the eldest was not, but Isabella would have him called Henry, which I thought very pretty of her. And he is a very clever boy, indeed. They are all remarkably clever; and they have so many pretty ways. They will come and stand by my chair, and say, 'Grandpapa, can you give me a bit of string?' and once Henry asked me for a knife, but I told him knives were only made for grandpapas. I think their father is too rough with them very often."

"He appears rough to you," said Emma, "because you are so very gentle yourself; but if you could compare him with other papas, you would not think him rough. He wishes his boys to be active and hardy; and if they misbehave, can give them a sharp word now and then; but he is an affectionate father—certainly Mr. John Knightley is an affectionate father. The children are all fond of him."

"And then their uncle comes in, and tosses them up to the ceiling in a very frightful way!"

"But they like it, papa; there is nothing they like so much. It is such enjoyment to them, that if their uncle did not lay down the rule of their taking turns, whichever began would never give way to the other."

"Well, I cannot understand it."

"That is the case with us all, papa. One half of the world cannot understand the pleasures of the other."

Later in the morning, and just as the girls were going to separate in preparation for the regular four o'clock dinner, the hero of this inimitable charade walked in again. Harriet turned away; but Emma could receive him with the usual smile, and her quick eye soon discerned in his the consciousness of having made a push—of having thrown a die; and she imagined he was come to see how it might turn up. His ostensible reason, however, was to ask whether Mr. Woodhouse's party could be made up in the evening without him, or whether he should be in the smallest degree necessary at Hartfield. If he were, every thing else must give way; but otherwise his friend Cole had been saying so much about his dining with him—had made such a point of it, that he had promised him conditionally to come.

Emma thanked him, but could not allow of his disappointing his friend on their account; her father was sure of his rubber. He re-urged—she re-declined; and he seemed then about to make his bow, when taking the paper from the table, she returned it—

"Oh! here is the charade you were so obliging as to leave with us; thank you for the sight of it. We admired it so much, that I have ventured to write it into Miss Smith's collection. Your friend will not take it amiss I hope. Of course I have not transcribed beyond the first eight lines."

Mr. Elton certainly did not very well know what to say. He looked rather doubtingly—rather confused; said something about "honour,"—glanced at Emma and at Harriet, and then seeing the book open on the table, took it up, and examined it very attentively. With the view of passing off an awkward moment, Emma smilingly said,

"You must make my apologies to your friend; but so good a charade must not be confined to one or two. He may be sure of every woman's approbation while he writes with such gallantry."

"I have no hesitation in saying," replied Mr. Elton, though hesitating a good deal while he spoke; "I have no hesitation in saying—at least if my friend feels at all as I do—I have not the smallest doubt that, could he see his little effusion honoured as I see it, (looking at the book again, and replacing it on the table), he would consider it as the proudest moment of his life."

After this speech he was gone as soon as possible. Emma could not think it too soon; for with all his good and agreeable qualities, there was a sort of parade in his speeches which was very apt to incline her to laugh. She ran away to indulge the inclination, leaving the tender and the sublime of pleasure to Harriet's share.

Chapter X

Though now the middle of December, there had yet been no weather to prevent the young ladies from tolerably regular exercise; and on the morrow, Emma had a charitable visit to pay to a poor sick family, who lived a little way out of Highbury.

Their road to this detached cottage was down Vicarage Lane, a lane leading at right angles from the broad, though irregular, main street of the place; and, as may be inferred, containing the blessed abode of Mr. Elton. A few inferior dwellings were first to be passed, and then, about a quarter of a mile down the lane rose the Vicarage, an old and not very good house, almost as close to the road as it could be. It had no advantage of situation; but had been very much smartened up by the present proprietor; and, such as it was, there could be no possibility of the two friends passing it without a slackened pace and observing eyes.—Emma's remark was—

"There it is. There go you and your riddle-book one of these days."—Harriet's was—

"Oh, what a sweet house!—How very beautiful!—There are the yellow curtains that Miss Nash admires so much."

"I do not often walk this way now," said Emma, as they proceeded, "but then there will be an inducement, and I shall gradually get intimately acquainted with all the hedges, gates, pools and pollards of this part of Highbury."

Harriet, she found, had never in her life been within side the Vicarage, and her curiosity to see it was so extreme, that, considering exteriors and probabilities, Emma could only class it, as a proof of love, with Mr. Elton's seeing ready wit in her.

"I wish we could contrive it," said she; "but I cannot think of any tolerable pretence for going in;—no servant that I want to inquire about of his housekeeper—no message from my father."

She pondered, but could think of nothing. After a mutual silence of some minutes, Harriet thus began again—

"I do so wonder, Miss Woodhouse, that you should not be married, or going to be married! so charming as you are!"—

Emma laughed, and replied,

"My being charming, Harriet, is not quite enough to induce me to marry; I must find other people charming—one other person at least. And I am not only, not going to be married, at present, but have very little intention of ever marrying at all."

"Ah!—so you say; but I cannot believe it."

"I must see somebody very superior to any one I have seen yet, to be tempted; Mr. Elton, you know, (recollecting herself,) is out of the question: and I do not wish to see any such person. I would rather not be tempted. I cannot really change for the better. If I were to marry, I must expect to repent it."

"Dear me!—it is so odd to hear a woman talk so!"—

"I have none of the usual inducements of women to marry. Were I to fall in love, indeed, it would be a different thing! but I never have been in love; it is not my way, or my nature; and I do not think I ever shall. And, without love, I am sure I should be a fool to change such a situation as mine. Fortune I do not want; employment I do not want; consequence I do not want: I believe few married women are half as much mistress of their husband's house as I am of Hartfield; and never, never could I expect to be so truly beloved and important; so always first and always right in any man's eyes as I am in my father's."

"But then, to be an old maid at last, like Miss Bates!"

"That is as formidable an image as you could present, Harriet; and if I thought I should ever be like Miss Bates! so silly—so satisfied—so smiling—so prosing—so undistinguishing and unfastidious—and so apt to tell every thing relative to every body about me, I would marry to-morrow. But between us, I am convinced there never can be any likeness, except in being unmarried."

"But still, you will be an old maid! and that's so dreadful!"

"Never mind, Harriet, I shall not be a poor old maid; and it is poverty only which makes celibacy contemptible to a generous public! A single woman, with a very narrow income, must be a ridiculous, disagreeable old maid! the proper sport of boys and girls, but a single woman, of good fortune, is always respectable, and may be as sensible and pleasant as any body else. And the distinction is not quite so much against the candour and common sense of the world as appears at first; for a very narrow income has a tendency to contract the mind, and sour the temper. Those who can barely live, and who live perforce in a very small, and generally very inferior, society, may well be illiberal and cross. This does not apply, however, to Miss Bates; she is only too good natured and too silly to suit me; but, in general, she is very much to the taste of every body, though single and though poor. Poverty certainly has not contracted her mind: I really believe, if she had only a shilling in the world, she would be very likely to give away sixpence of it; and nobody is afraid of her: that is a great charm."

"Dear me! but what shall you do? how shall you employ yourself when you grow old?"

"If I know myself, Harriet, mine is an active, busy mind, with a great many independent resources; and I do not perceive why I should be more in want of employment at forty or fifty than one-and-twenty. Woman's usual occupations of hand and mind will be as open to me then as they are now; or with no important variation. If I draw less, I shall read more; if I give up music, I shall take to carpet-work. And as for objects of interest, objects for the affections, which is in truth the great point of inferiority, the want of which is really the great evil to be avoided in not marrying, I shall be very well off, with all the children of a sister I love so much, to care about. There will be enough of them, in all probability, to supply every sort of sensation that declining life can need. There will be enough for every hope and every fear; and though my attachment to none can equal that of a parent, it suits my ideas of comfort better than what is warmer and blinder. My nephews and nieces!—I shall often have a niece with me."

"Do you know Miss Bates's niece? That is, I know you must have seen her a hundred times—but are you acquainted?"

"Oh! yes; we are always forced to be acquainted whenever she comes to Highbury. By the bye, that is almost enough to put one out of conceit with a niece. Heaven forbid! at least, that I should ever bore people half so much about all the Knightleys together, as she does about Jane Fairfax. One is sick of the very name of Jane Fairfax. Every letter from her is read forty times over; her compliments to all friends go round and round again; and if she does but send her aunt the pattern of a stomacher, or knit a pair of garters for her grandmother, one hears of nothing else for a month. I wish Jane Fairfax very well; but she tires me to death."

They were now approaching the cottage, and all idle topics were superseded. Emma was very compassionate; and the distresses of the poor were as sure of relief from her personal attention and kindness, her counsel and her patience, as from her purse. She understood their ways, could allow for their ignorance and their temptations, had no romantic expectations of extraordinary virtue from those for whom education had done so little; entered into their troubles with ready sympathy, and always gave her assistance with as much intelligence as good-will. In the present instance, it was sickness and poverty together which she came to visit; and after remaining there as long as she could give comfort or advice, she quitted the cottage with such an impression of the scene as made her say to Harriet, as they walked away,

"These are the sights, Harriet, to do one good. How trifling they make every thing else appear!—I feel now as if I could think of nothing but these poor creatures all the rest of the day; and yet, who can say how soon it may all vanish from my mind?"

"Very true," said Harriet. "Poor creatures! one can think of nothing else."

"And really, I do not think the impression will soon be over," said Emma, as she crossed the low hedge, and tottering footstep which ended the narrow, slippery path through the cottage garden, and brought them into the lane again. "I do not think it will," stopping to look once more at all the outward wretchedness of the place, and recall the still greater within.

"Oh! dear, no," said her companion.

They walked on. The lane made a slight bend; and when that bend was passed, Mr. Elton was immediately in sight; and so near as to give Emma time only to say farther,

"Ah! Harriet, here comes a very sudden trial of our stability in good thoughts. Well, (smiling,) I hope it may be allowed that if compassion has produced exertion and relief to the sufferers, it has done all that is truly important. If we feel for the wretched, enough to do all we can for them, the rest is empty sympathy, only distressing to ourselves."

Harriet could just answer, "Oh! dear, yes," before the gentleman joined them. The wants and sufferings of the poor family, however, were the first subject on meeting. He had been going to call on them. His visit he would now defer; but they had a very interesting parley about what could be done and should be done. Mr. Elton then turned back to accompany them.

"To fall in with each other on such an errand as this," thought Emma; "to meet in a charitable scheme; this will bring a great increase of love on each side. I should not wonder if it were to bring on the declaration. It must, if I were not here. I wish I were anywhere else."

Anxious to separate herself from them as far as she could, she soon afterwards took possession of a narrow footpath, a little raised on one side of the lane, leaving them together in the main road. But she had not been there two minutes when she found that Harriet's habits of dependence and imitation were bringing her up too, and that, in short, they would both be soon after her. This would not do; she immediately stopped, under pretence of having some alteration to make in the lacing of her half-boot, and stooping down in complete occupation of the footpath, begged them to have the goodness to walk on, and she would follow in half a minute. They did as they were desired; and by the time she judged it reasonable to have done with her boot, she had the comfort of farther delay in her power, being overtaken by a child from the cottage, setting out, according to orders, with her pitcher, to fetch broth from Hartfield. To walk by the side of this child, and talk to and question her, was the most natural thing in the world, or would have been the most natural, had she been acting just then without design; and by this means the others were still able to keep ahead, without any obligation of waiting for her. She gained on them, however, involuntarily: the child's pace was quick, and theirs rather slow; and she was the more concerned at it, from their being evidently in a conversation which interested them. Mr. Elton was speaking with animation, Harriet listening with a very pleased attention; and Emma, having sent the child on, was beginning to think how she might draw back a little more, when they both looked around, and she was obliged to join them.

Mr. Elton was still talking, still engaged in some interesting detail; and Emma experienced some disappointment when she found that he was only giving his fair companion an account of the yesterday's party at his friend Cole's, and that she was come in herself for the Stilton cheese, the north Wiltshire, the butter, the cellery, the beet-root, and all the dessert.

"This would soon have led to something better, of course," was her consoling reflection; "any thing interests between those who love; and any thing will serve as introduction to what is near the heart. If I could but have kept longer away!"

They now walked on together quietly, till within view of the vicarage pales, when a sudden resolution, of at least getting Harriet into the house, made her again find something very much amiss about her boot, and fall behind to arrange it once more. She then broke the lace off short, and dexterously throwing it into a ditch, was presently obliged to entreat them to stop, and acknowledged her inability to put herself to rights so as to be able to walk home in tolerable comfort.

"Part of my lace is gone," said she, "and I do not know how I am to contrive. I really am a most troublesome companion to you both, but I hope I am not often so ill-equipped. Mr. Elton, I must beg leave to stop at your house, and ask your housekeeper for a bit of ribband or string, or any thing just to keep my boot on."

Mr. Elton looked all happiness at this proposition; and nothing could exceed his alertness and attention in conducting them into his house and endeavouring to make every thing appear to advantage. The room they were taken into was the one he chiefly occupied, and looking forwards; behind it was another with which it immediately communicated; the door between them was open, and Emma passed into it with the housekeeper to receive her assistance in the most comfortable manner. She was obliged to leave the door ajar as she found it; but she fully intended that Mr. Elton should close it. It was not closed, however, it still remained ajar; but by engaging the housekeeper in incessant conversation, she hoped to make it practicable for him to chuse his own subject in the adjoining room. For ten minutes she could hear nothing but herself. It could be protracted no longer. She was then obliged to be finished, and make her appearance.

The lovers were standing together at one of the windows. It had a most favourable aspect; and, for half a minute, Emma felt the glory of having schemed successfully. But it would not do; he had not come to the point. He had been most agreeable, most delightful; he had told Harriet that he had seen them go by, and had purposely followed them; other little gallantries and allusions had been dropt, but nothing serious.

"Cautious, very cautious," thought Emma; "he advances inch by inch, and will hazard nothing till he believes himself secure."

Still, however, though every thing had not been accomplished by her ingenious device, she could not but flatter herself that it had been the occasion of much present enjoyment to both, and must be leading them forward to the great event.

Chapter XI

Mr. Elton must now be left to himself. It was no longer in Emma's power to superintend his happiness or quicken his measures. The coming of her sister's family was so very near at hand, that first in anticipation, and then in reality, it became henceforth her prime object of interest; and during the ten days of their stay at Hartfield it was not to be expected—she did not herself expect—that any thing beyond occasional, fortuitous assistance could be afforded by her to the lovers. They might advance rapidly if they would, however; they must advance somehow or other whether they would or no. She hardly wished to have more leisure for them. There are people, who the more you do for them, the less they will do for themselves.

Mr. and Mrs. John Knightley, from having been longer than usual absent from Surry, were exciting of course rather more than the usual interest. Till this year, every long vacation since their marriage had been divided between Hartfield and Donwell Abbey; but all the holidays of this autumn had been given to sea-bathing for the children, and it was therefore many months since they had been seen in a regular way by their Surry connexions, or seen at all by Mr. Woodhouse, who could not be induced to get so far as London, even for poor Isabella's sake; and who consequently was now most nervously and apprehensively happy in forestalling this too short visit.

He thought much of the evils of the journey for her, and not a little of the fatigues of his own horses and coachman who were to bring some of the party the last half of the way; but his alarms were needless; the sixteen miles being happily accomplished, and Mr. and

Mrs. John Knightley, their five children, and a competent number of nursery-maids, all reaching Hartfield in safety. The bustle and joy of such an arrival, the many to be talked to, welcomed, encouraged, and variously dispersed and disposed of, produced a noise and confusion which his nerves could not have borne under any other cause, nor have endured much longer even for this; but the ways of Hartfield and the feelings of her father were so respected by Mrs. John Knightley, that in spite of maternal solicitude for the immediate enjoyment of her little ones, and for their having instantly all the liberty and attendance, all the eating and drinking, and sleeping and playing, which they could possibly wish for, without the smallest delay, the children were never allowed to be long a disturbance to him, either in themselves or in any restless attendance on them.

Mrs. John Knightley was a pretty, elegant little woman, of gentle, quiet manners, and a disposition remarkably amiable and affectionate; wrapt up in her family; a devoted wife, a doating mother, and so tenderly attached to her father and sister that, but for these higher ties, a warmer love might have seemed impossible. She could never see a fault in any of them. She was not a woman of strong understanding or any quickness; and with this resemblance of her father, she inherited also much of his constitution; was delicate in her own health, overcareful of that of her children, had many fears and many nerves, and was as fond of her own Mr. Wingfield in town as her father could be of Mr. Perry. They were alike too, in a general benevolence of temper, and a strong habit of regard for every old acquaintance.

Mr. John Knightley was a tall, gentleman-like, and very clever man; rising in his profession, domestic, and respectable in his private character; but with reserved manners which prevented his being generally pleasing; and capable of being sometimes out of humour. He was not an ill-tempered man, not so often unreasonably cross as to deserve such a reproach; but his temper was not his great perfection; and, indeed, with such a worshipping wife, it was hardly possible that any natural defects in it should not be increased. The extreme sweetness of her temper must hurt his. He had all the clearness and quickness of mind which she wanted, and he could sometimes act an ungracious, or say a severe thing.

He was not a great favourite with his fair sister-in-law. Nothing wrong in him escaped her. She was quick in feeling the little injuries to Isabella, which Isabella never felt herself. Perhaps she might have passed over more had his manners been flattering to Isabella's sister, but they were only those of a calmly kind brother and friend, without praise and without blindness; but hardly any degree of personal compliment could have made her regardless of that greatest fault of all in her eyes which he sometimes fell into, the want of respectful forbearance towards her father. There he had not always the patience that could have been wished. Mr. Woodhouse's peculiarities and fidgetiness were sometimes provoking him to a rational remonstrance or sharp retort equally ill-bestowed. It did not often happen; for Mr. John Knightley had really a great regard for his father-in-law, and generally a strong sense of what was due to him; but it was too often for Emma's charity, especially as there was all the pain of apprehension frequently to be endured, though the offence came not. The beginning, however, of every visit displayed none but the properest feelings, and this being of necessity so short might be hoped to pass away in unsullied cordiality. They had not been long seated and composed when Mr. Woodhouse, with a melancholy shake of the head and a sigh, called his daughter's attention to the sad change at Hartfield since she had been there last.

"Ah, my dear," said he, "poor Miss Taylor—It is a grievous business."

"Oh yes, sir," cried she with ready sympathy, "how you must miss her! And dear Emma, too!—What a dreadful loss to you both!—I have been so grieved for you.—I could not imagine how you could possibly do without her.—It is a sad change indeed.—But I hope she is pretty well, sir."

"Pretty well, my dear—I hope—pretty well.—I do not know but that the place agrees with her tolerably."

Mr. John Knightley here asked Emma quietly whether there were any doubts of the air of Randalls.

"Oh! no—none in the least. I never saw Mrs. Weston better in my life—never looking so well. Papa is only speaking his own regret."

"Very much to the honour of both," was the handsome reply.

"And do you see her, sir, tolerably often?" asked Isabella in the plaintive tone which just suited her father.

Mr. Woodhouse hesitated.—"Not near so often, my dear, as I could wish."

"Oh! papa, we have missed seeing them but one entire day since they married. Either in the morning or evening of every day, excepting one, have we seen either Mr. Weston or Mrs. Weston, and generally both, either at Randalls or here—and as you may suppose, Isabella, most frequently here. They are very, very kind in their visits. Mr. Weston is really as kind as herself. Papa, if you speak in that melancholy way, you will be giving Isabella a false idea of us all. Every body must be aware that Miss Taylor must be missed, but every body ought also to be assured that Mr. and Mrs. Weston do really prevent our missing her by any means to the extent we ourselves anticipated—which is the exact truth."

"Just as it should be," said Mr. John Knightley, "and just as I hoped it was from your letters. Her wish of shewing you attention could not be doubted, and his being a disengaged and social man makes it all easy. I have been always telling you, my love, that I had no idea of the change being so very material to Hartfield as you apprehended; and now you have Emma's account, I hope you will be satisfied."

"Why, to be sure," said Mr. Woodhouse—"yes, certainly—I cannot deny that Mrs. Weston, poor Mrs. Weston, does come and see us pretty often—but then—she is always obliged to go away again."

"It would be very hard upon Mr. Weston if she did not, papa.—You quite forget poor Mr. Weston."

"I think, indeed," said John Knightley pleasantly, "that Mr. Weston has some little claim. You and I, Emma, will venture to take the part of the poor husband. I, being a husband, and you not being a wife, the claims of the man may very likely strike us with equal force. As for Isabella, she has been married long enough to see the convenience of putting all the Mr. Westons aside as much as she can."

"Me, my love," cried his wife, hearing and understanding only in part.—"Are you talking about me?—I am sure nobody ought to be, or can be, a greater advocate for matrimony than I am; and if it had not been for the misery of her leaving Hartfield, I should never have thought of Miss Taylor but as the most fortunate woman in the world; and as to slighting Mr. Weston, that excellent Mr. Weston, I think there is nothing he does not deserve. I believe he is one of the very best-tempered men that ever existed. Excepting yourself and your brother, I do not know his equal for temper. I shall never forget his flying Henry's kite for him that very windy day last Easter—and ever since his particular kindness last September twelvemonth in writing that note, at twelve o'clock at night, on purpose to assure me that there was no scarlet fever at Cobham, I have been convinced there could not be a more feeling heart nor a better man in existence.—If any body can deserve him, it must be Miss Taylor."

"Where is the young man?" said John Knightley. "Has he been here on this occasion—or has he not?"

"He has not been here yet," replied Emma. "There was a strong expectation of his coming soon after the marriage, but it ended in nothing; and I have not heard him mentioned lately."

"But you should tell them of the letter, my dear," said her father. "He wrote a letter to poor Mrs. Weston, to congratulate her, and a very proper, handsome letter it was. She shewed it to me. I thought it very well done of him indeed. Whether it was his own idea you know, one cannot tell. He is but young, and his uncle, perhaps—"

"My dear papa, he is three-and-twenty. You forget how time passes."

"Three-and-twenty!—is he indeed?—Well, I could not have thought it—and he was but two years old when he lost his poor mother! Well, time does fly indeed!—and my memory is very bad. However, it was an exceeding good, pretty letter, and gave Mr. and Mrs. Weston a great deal of pleasure. I remember it was written from Weymouth, and dated Sept. 28th—and began, 'My dear Madam,' but I forget how it went on; and it was signed 'F. C. Weston Churchill.'—I remember that perfectly."

"How very pleasing and proper of him!" cried the good-hearted Mrs. John Knightley. "I have no doubt of his being a most amiable young man. But how sad it is that he should not live at home with his father! There is something so shocking in a child's being taken away from his parents and natural home! I never could comprehend how Mr. Weston could part with him. To give up one's child! I really never could think well of any body who proposed such a thing to any body else."

"Nobody ever did think well of the Churchills, I fancy," observed Mr. John Knightley coolly. "But you need not imagine Mr. Weston to have felt what you would feel in giving up Henry or John. Mr. Weston is rather an easy, cheerful-tempered man, than a man of strong feelings; he takes things as he finds them, and makes enjoyment of them somehow or other, depending, I suspect, much more upon what is called society for his comforts, that is, upon the power of eating and drinking, and playing whist with his neighbours five times a week, than upon family affection, or any thing that home affords."

Emma could not like what bordered on a reflection on Mr. Weston, and had half a mind to take it up; but she struggled, and let it pass. She would keep the peace if possible; and there was something honourable and valuable in the strong domestic habits, the all-sufficiency of home to himself, whence resulted her brother's disposition to look down on the common rate of social intercourse, and those to whom it was important.—It had a high claim to forbearance.

Chapter XII

Mr. Knightley was to dine with them—rather against the inclination of Mr. Woodhouse, who did not like that any one should share with him in Isabella's first day. Emma's sense of right however had decided it; and besides the consideration of what was due to each brother, she had particular pleasure, from the circumstance of the late disagreement between Mr. Knightley and herself, in procuring him the proper invitation.

She hoped they might now become friends again. She thought it was time to make up. Making-up indeed would not do. She certainly had not been in the wrong, and he would never own that he had. Concession must be out of the question; but it was time to appear to forget that they had ever quarrelled; and she hoped it might rather assist the restoration of friendship, that when he came into the room she had one of the children with her—the youngest, a nice little girl about eight months old, who was now making her first visit to Hartfield, and very happy to be danced about in her aunt's arms. It did assist; for though he began with grave looks and short questions, he was soon led on to talk of them all in the usual way, and to take the child out of her arms with all the unceremoniousness of perfect amity. Emma felt they were friends again; and the conviction giving her at first great satisfaction, and then a little sauciness, she could not help saying, as he was admiring the baby,

"What a comfort it is, that we think alike about our nephews and nieces. As to men and women, our opinions are sometimes very different; but with regard to these children, I observe we never disagree."

"If you were as much guided by nature in your estimate of men and women, and as little under the power of fancy and whim in your dealings with them, as you are where these children are concerned, we might always think alike."

"To be sure—our discordancies must always arise from my being in the wrong."

"Yes," said he, smiling—"and reason good. I was sixteen years old when you were born."

"A material difference then," she replied—"and no doubt you were much my superior in judgment at that period of our lives; but does not the lapse of one-and-twenty years bring our understandings a good deal nearer?"

"Yes—a good deal nearer."

"But still, not near enough to give me a chance of being right, if we think differently."

"I have still the advantage of you by sixteen years' experience, and by not being a pretty young woman and a spoiled child. Come, my dear Emma, let us be friends, and say no more about it. Tell your aunt, little Emma, that she ought to set you a better example than to be renewing old grievances, and that if she were not wrong before, she is now."

"That's true," she cried—"very true. Little Emma, grow up a better woman than your aunt. Be infinitely cleverer and not half so conceited. Now, Mr. Knightley, a word or two more, and I have done. As far as good intentions went, we were both right, and I must say that no effects on my side of the argument have yet proved wrong. I only want to know that Mr. Martin is not very, very bitterly disappointed."

"A man cannot be more so," was his short, full answer.

"Ah!—Indeed I am very sorry.—Come, shake hands with me."

This had just taken place and with great cordiality, when John Knightley made his appearance, and "How d'ye do, George?" and "John, how are you?" succeeded in the true English style, burying under a calmness that seemed all but indifference, the real attachment which would have led either of them, if requisite, to do every thing for the good of the other.

The evening was quiet and conversable, as Mr. Woodhouse declined cards entirely for the sake of comfortable talk with his dear Isabella, and the little party made two natural divisions; on one side he and his daughter; on the other the two Mr. Knightleys; their subjects totally distinct, or very rarely mixing—and Emma only occasionally joining in one or the other.

The brothers talked of their own concerns and pursuits, but principally of those of the elder, whose temper was by much the most communicative, and who was always the greater talker. As a magistrate, he had generally some point of law to consult John about, or, at least, some curious anecdote to give; and as a farmer, as keeping in hand the home-farm at Donwell, he had to tell what every field was to bear next year, and to give all such local information as could not fail of being interesting to a brother whose home it had equally been the longest part of his life, and whose attachments were strong. The plan of a drain, the change of a fence, the felling of a tree, and the destination of every acre for wheat, turnips, or spring corn, was entered into with as much equality of interest by John, as his cooler manners rendered possible; and if his willing brother ever left him any thing to inquire about, his inquiries even approached a tone of eagerness.

While they were thus comfortably occupied, Mr. Woodhouse was enjoying a full flow of happy regrets and fearful affection with his daughter.

"My poor dear Isabella," said he, fondly taking her hand, and interrupting, for a few moments, her busy labours for some one of her five children—"How long it is, how terribly long since you were here! And how tired you must be after your journey! You must go to bed early, my dear—and I recommend a little gruel to you before you go.—You and I will have a nice basin of gruel together. My dear Emma, suppose we all have a little gruel."

Emma could not suppose any such thing, knowing as she did, that both the Mr. Knightleys were as unpersuadable on that article as herself;—and two basins only were ordered. After a little more discourse in praise of gruel, with some wondering at its not being taken every evening by every body, he proceeded to say, with an air of grave reflection,

"It was an awkward business, my dear, your spending the autumn at South End instead of coming here. I never had much opinion of the sea air."

"Mr. Wingfield most strenuously recommended it, sir—or we should not have gone. He recommended it for all the children, but particularly for the weakness in little Bella's throat,—both sea air and bathing."

"Ah! my dear, but Perry had many doubts about the sea doing her any good; and as to myself, I have been long perfectly convinced, though perhaps I never told you so before, that the sea is very rarely of use to any body. I am sure it almost killed me once."

"Come, come," cried Emma, feeling this to be an unsafe subject, "I must beg you not to talk of the sea. It makes me envious and miserable;—I who have never seen it! South End is prohibited, if you please. My dear Isabella, I have not heard you make one inquiry about Mr. Perry yet; and he never forgets you."

"Oh! good Mr. Perry—how is he, sir?"

"Why, pretty well; but not quite well. Poor Perry is bilious, and he has not time to take care of himself—he tells me he has not time to take care of himself—which is very sad—but he is always wanted all round the country. I suppose there is not a man in such practice anywhere. But then there is not so clever a man any where."

"And Mrs. Perry and the children, how are they? do the children grow? I have a great regard for Mr. Perry. I hope he will be calling soon. He will be so pleased to see my little ones."

"I hope he will be here to-morrow, for I have a question or two to ask him about myself of some consequence. And, my dear, whenever he comes, you had better let him look at little Bella's throat."

"Oh! my dear sir, her throat is so much better that I have hardly any uneasiness about it. Either bathing has been of the greatest service to her, or else it is to be attributed to an excellent embrocation of Mr. Wingfield's, which we have been applying at times ever since August."

"It is not very likely, my dear, that bathing should have been of use to her—and if I had known you were wanting an embrocation, I would have spoken to—

"You seem to me to have forgotten Mrs. and Miss Bates," said Emma, "I have not heard one inquiry after them."

"Oh! the good Bateses—I am quite ashamed of myself—but you mention them in most of your letters. I hope they are quite well. Good old Mrs. Bates—I will call upon her to-morrow, and take my children.—They are always so pleased to see my children.—And that excellent Miss Bates!—such thorough worthy people!—How are they, sir?"

"Why, pretty well, my dear, upon the whole. But poor Mrs. Bates had a bad cold about a month ago."

"How sorry I am! But colds were never so prevalent as they have been this autumn. Mr. Wingfield told me that he has never known them more general or heavy—except when it has been quite an influenza."

"That has been a good deal the case, my dear; but not to the degree you mention. Perry says that colds have been very general, but not so heavy as he has very often known them in November. Perry does not call it altogether a sickly season."

"No, I do not know that Mr. Wingfield considers it very sickly except—

"Ah! my poor dear child, the truth is, that in London it is always a sickly season. Nobody is healthy in London, nobody can be. It is a dreadful thing to have you forced to live there! so far off!—and the air so bad!"

"No, indeed—we are not at all in a bad air. Our part of London is very superior to most others!—You must not confound us with London in general, my dear sir. The neighbourhood of Brunswick Square is very different from almost all the rest. We are so very airy! I should be unwilling, I own, to live in any other part of the town;—there is hardly any other that I could be satisfied to have my children in: but we are so remarkably airy!—Mr. Wingfield thinks the vicinity of Brunswick Square decidedly the most favourable as to air."

"Ah! my dear, it is not like Hartfield. You make the best of it—but after you have been a week at Hartfield, you are all of you different creatures; you do not look like the same. Now I cannot say, that I think you are any of you looking well at present."

"I am sorry to hear you say so, sir; but I assure you, excepting those little nervous head-aches and palpitations which I am never entirely free from anywhere, I am quite well myself; and if the children were rather pale before they went to bed, it was only because they were a little more tired than usual, from their journey and the happiness of coming. I hope you will think better of their looks to-morrow; for I assure you Mr. Wingfield told me, that he did not believe he had ever sent us off altogether, in such good case. I trust, at least, that you do not think Mr. Knightley looking ill," turning her eyes with affectionate anxiety towards her husband.

"Middling, my dear; I cannot compliment you. I think Mr. John Knightley very far from looking well."

"What is the matter, sir?—Did you speak to me?" cried Mr. John Knightley, hearing his own name.

"I am sorry to find, my love, that my father does not think you looking well—but I hope it is only from being a little fatigued. I could have wished, however, as you know, that you had seen Mr. Wingfield before you left home."

"My dear Isabella,"—exclaimed he hastily—"pray do not concern yourself about my looks. Be satisfied with doctoring and coddling yourself and the children, and let me look as I chuse."

"I did not thoroughly understand what you were telling your brother," cried Emma, "about your friend Mr. Graham's intending to have a bailiff from Scotland, to look after his new estate. What will it answer? Will not the old prejudice be too strong?"

And she talked in this way so long and successfully that, when forced to give her attention again to her father and sister, she had nothing worse to hear than Isabella's kind inquiry after Jane Fairfax; and Jane Fairfax, though no great favourite with her in general, she was at that moment very happy to assist in praising.

"That sweet, amiable Jane Fairfax!" said Mrs. John Knightley.—"It is so long since I have seen her, except now and then for a moment accidentally in town! What happiness it must be to her good old grandmother and excellent aunt, when she comes to visit them! I always regret excessively on dear Emma's account that she cannot be more at Highbury; but now their daughter is married, I suppose Colonel and Mrs. Campbell will not be able to part with her at all. She would be such a delightful companion for Emma."

Mr. Woodhouse agreed to it all, but added,

"Our little friend Harriet Smith, however, is just such another pretty kind of young person. You will like Harriet. Emma could not have a better companion than Harriet."

"I am most happy to hear it—but only Jane Fairfax one knows to be so very accomplished and superior!—and exactly Emma's age."

This topic was discussed very happily, and others succeeded of similar moment, and passed away with similar harmony; but the evening did not close without a little return of agitation. The gruel came and supplied a great deal to be said—much praise and many comments—undoubting decision of its wholesomeness for every constitution, and pretty severe Philippics upon the many houses where it was never met with tolerable;—but, unfortunately, among the failures which the daughter had to instance, the most recent, and therefore most prominent, was in her own cook at South End, a young woman hired for the time, who never had been able to understand what she meant by a basin of nice smooth gruel, thin, but not too thin. Often as she had wished for and ordered it, she had never been able to get any thing tolerable. Here was a dangerous opening.

"Ah!" said Mr. Woodhouse, shaking his head and fixing his eyes on her with tender concern.—The ejaculation in Emma's ear expressed, "Ah! there is no end of the sad consequences of your going to South End. It does not bear talking of." And for a little while she hoped he would not talk of it, and that a silent rumination might suffice to restore him to the relish of his own smooth gruel. After an interval of some minutes, however, he began with,

"I shall always be very sorry that you went to the sea this autumn, instead of coming here."

"But why should you be sorry, sir?—I assure you, it did the children a great deal of good."

"And, moreover, if you must go to the sea, it had better not have been to South End. South End is an unhealthy place. Perry was surprized to hear you had fixed upon South End."

"I know there is such an idea with many people, but indeed it is quite a mistake, sir.—We all had our health perfectly well there, never found the least inconvenience from the mud; and Mr. Wingfield says it is entirely a mistake to suppose the place unhealthy; and I am sure he may be depended on, for he thoroughly understands the nature of the air, and his own brother and family have been there repeatedly."

"You should have gone to Cromer, my dear, if you went anywhere.—Perry was a week at Cromer once, and he holds it to be the best of all the sea-bathing places. A fine open sea, he says, and very pure air. And, by what I understand, you might have had lodgings there quite away from the sea—a quarter of a mile off—very comfortable. You should have consulted Perry."

"But, my dear sir, the difference of the journey;—only consider how great it would have been.—An hundred miles, perhaps, instead of forty."

"Ah! my dear, as Perry says, where health is at stake, nothing else should be considered; and if one is to travel, there is not much to chuse between forty miles and an hundred.—Better not move at all, better stay in London altogether than travel forty miles to get into a worse air. This is just what Perry said. It seemed to him a very ill-judged measure."

Emma's attempts to stop her father had been vain; and when he had reached such a point as this, she could not wonder at her brother-in-law's breaking out.

"Mr. Perry," said he, in a voice of very strong displeasure, "would do as well to keep his opinion till it is asked for. Why does he make it any business of his, to wonder at what I do?—at my taking my family to one part of the coast or another?—I may be allowed, I hope, the use of my judgment as well as Mr. Perry.—I want his directions no more than his drugs." He paused—and growing cooler in a moment, added, with only sarcastic dryness, "If Mr. Perry can tell me how to convey a wife and five children a distance of an hundred and thirty miles with no greater expense or inconvenience than a distance of forty, I should be as willing to prefer Cromer to South End as he could himself."

"True, true," cried Mr. Knightley, with most ready interposition—"very true. That's a consideration indeed.—But John, as to what I was telling you of my idea of moving the path to Langham, of turning it more to the right that it may not cut through the home meadows, I cannot conceive any difficulty. I should not attempt it, if it were to be the means of inconvenience to the Highbury people, but if you call to mind exactly the present line of the path. . . . The only way of proving it, however, will be to turn to our maps. I shall see you at the Abbey to-morrow morning I hope, and then we will look them over, and you shall give me your opinion."

Mr. Woodhouse was rather agitated by such harsh reflections on his friend Perry, to whom he had, in fact, though unconsciously, been attributing many of his own feelings and expressions;—but the soothing attentions of his daughters gradually removed the present evil, and the immediate alertness of one brother, and better recollections of the other, prevented any renewal of it.

Chapter XIII

There could hardly be a happier creature in the world than Mrs. John Knightley, in this short visit to Hartfield, going about every morning among her old acquaintance with her five children, and talking over what she had done every evening with her father and sister. She had nothing to wish otherwise, but that the days did not pass so swiftly. It was a delightful visit;—perfect, in being much too short.

In general their evenings were less engaged with friends than their mornings; but one complete dinner engagement, and out of the house too, there was no avoiding, though at Christmas. Mr. Weston would take no denial; they must all dine at Randalls one day;—even Mr. Woodhouse was persuaded to think it a possible thing in preference to a division of the party.

How they were all to be conveyed, he would have made a difficulty if he could, but as his son and daughter's carriage and horses were actually at Hartfield, he was not able to make more than a simple question on that head; it hardly amounted to a doubt; nor did it occupy Emma long to convince him that they might in one of the carriages find room for Harriet also.

Harriet, Mr. Elton, and Mr. Knightley, their own especial set, were the only persons invited to meet them;—the hours were to be early, as well as the numbers few; Mr. Woodhouse's habits and inclination being consulted in every thing.

The evening before this great event (for it was a very great event that Mr. Woodhouse should dine out, on the 24th of December) had been spent by Harriet at Hartfield, and she had gone home so much indisposed with a cold, that, but for her own earnest wish of being nursed by Mrs. Goddard, Emma could not have allowed her to leave the house. Emma called on her the next day, and found her doom already signed with regard to Randalls. She was very feverish and had a bad sore throat: Mrs. Goddard was full of care and affection, Mr.

Perry was talked of, and Harriet herself was too ill and low to resist the authority which excluded her from this delightful engagement, though she could not speak of her loss without many tears.

Emma sat with her as long as she could, to attend her in Mrs. Goddard's unavoidable absences, and raise her spirits by representing how much Mr. Elton's would be depressed when he knew her state; and left her at last tolerably comfortable, in the sweet dependence of his having a most comfortless visit, and of their all missing her very much. She had not advanced many yards from Mrs. Goddard's door, when she was met by Mr. Elton himself, evidently coming towards it, and as they walked on slowly together in conversation about the invalid—of whom he, on the rumour of considerable illness, had been going to inquire, that he might carry some report of her to Hartfield—they were overtaken by Mr. John Knightley returning from the daily visit to Donwell, with his two eldest boys, whose healthy, glowing faces shewed all the benefit of a country run, and seemed to ensure a quick despatch of the roast mutton and rice pudding they were hastening home for. They joined company and proceeded together. Emma was just describing the nature of her friend's complaint;—"a throat very much inflamed, with a great deal of heat about her, a quick, low pulse, &c. and she was sorry to find from Mrs. Goddard that Harriet was liable to very bad sore-throats, and had often alarmed her with them." Mr. Elton looked all alarm on the occasion, as he exclaimed,

"A sore-throat!—I hope not infectious. I hope not of a putrid infectious sort. Has Perry seen her? Indeed you should take care of yourself as well as of your friend. Let me entreat you to run no risks. Why does not Perry see her?"

Emma, who was not really at all frightened herself, tranquillised this excess of apprehension by assurances of Mrs. Goddard's experience and care; but as there must still remain a degree of uneasiness which she could not wish to reason away, which she would rather feed and assist than not, she added soon afterwards—as if quite another subject,

"It is so cold, so very cold—and looks and feels so very much like snow, that if it were to any other place or with any other party, I should really try not to go out to-day—and dissuade my father from venturing; but as he has made up his mind, and does not seem to feel the cold himself, I do not like to interfere, as I know it would be so great a disappointment to Mr. and Mrs. Weston. But, upon my word, Mr. Elton, in your case, I should certainly excuse myself. You appear to me a little hoarse already, and when you consider what demand of voice and what fatigues to-morrow will bring, I think it would be no more than common prudence to stay at home and take care of yourself to-night."

Mr. Elton looked as if he did not very well know what answer to make; which was exactly the case; for though very much gratified by the kind care of such a fair lady, and not liking to resist any advice of her's, he had not really the least inclination to give up the visit;—but Emma, too eager and busy in her own previous conceptions and views to hear him impartially, or see him with clear vision, was very well satisfied with his muttering acknowledgment of its being "very cold, certainly very cold," and walked on, rejoicing in having extricated him from Randalls, and secured him the power of sending to inquire after Harriet every hour of the evening.

"You do quite right," said she;—"we will make your apologies to Mr. and Mrs. Weston."

But hardly had she so spoken, when she found her brother was civilly offering a seat in his carriage, if the weather were Mr. Elton's only objection, and Mr. Elton actually accepting the offer with much prompt satisfaction. It was a done thing; Mr. Elton was to go, and never had his broad handsome face expressed more pleasure than at this moment; never had his smile been stronger, nor his eyes more exulting than when he next looked at her.

"Well," said she to herself, "this is most strange!—After I had got him off so well, to chuse to go into company, and leave Harriet ill behind!—Most strange indeed!—But there is, I believe, in many men, especially single men, such an inclination—such a passion for dining out—a dinner engagement is so high in the class of their pleasures, their employments, their dignities, almost their duties, that any thing gives way to it—and this must be the case with Mr. Elton; a most valuable, amiable, pleasing young man undoubtedly, and very much in love with Harriet; but still, he cannot refuse an invitation, he must dine out wherever he is asked. What a strange thing love is! he can see ready wit in Harriet, but will not dine alone for her."

Soon afterwards Mr. Elton quitted them, and she could not but do him the justice of feeling that there was a great deal of sentiment in his manner of naming Harriet at parting; in the tone of his voice while assuring her that he should call at Mrs. Goddard's for news of her fair friend, the last thing before he prepared for the happiness of meeting her again, when he hoped to be able to give a better report; and he sighed and smiled himself off in a way that left the balance of approbation much in his favour.

After a few minutes of entire silence between them, John Knightley began with—

"I never in my life saw a man more intent on being agreeable than Mr. Elton. It is downright labour to him where ladies are concerned. With men he can be rational and unaffected, but when he has ladies to please, every feature works."

"Mr. Elton's manners are not perfect," replied Emma; "but where there is a wish to please, one ought to overlook, and one does overlook a great deal. Where a man does his best with only moderate powers, he will have the advantage over negligent superiority. There is such perfect good-temper and good-will in Mr. Elton as one cannot but value."

"Yes," said Mr. John Knightley presently, with some slyness, "he seems to have a great deal of good-will towards you."

"Me!" she replied with a smile of astonishment, "are you imagining me to be Mr. Elton's object?"

"Such an imagination has crossed me, I own, Emma; and if it never occurred to you before, you may as well take it into consideration now."

"Mr. Elton in love with me!—What an idea!"

"I do not say it is so; but you will do well to consider whether it is so or not, and to regulate your behaviour accordingly. I think your manners to him encouraging. I speak as a friend, Emma. You had better look about you, and ascertain what you do, and what you mean to do."

"I thank you; but I assure you you are quite mistaken. Mr. Elton and I are very good friends, and nothing more;" and she walked on, amusing herself in the consideration of the blunders which often arise from a partial knowledge of circumstances, of the mistakes which people of high pretensions to judgment are for ever falling into; and not very well pleased with her brother for imagining her blind and ignorant, and in want of counsel. He said no more.

Mr. Woodhouse had so completely made up his mind to the visit, that in spite of the increasing coldness, he seemed to have no idea of shrinking from it, and set forward at last most punctually with his eldest daughter in his own carriage, with less apparent consciousness of the weather than either of the others; too full of the wonder of his own going, and the pleasure it was to afford at Randalls to see that it was cold, and too well wrapt up to feel it. The cold, however, was severe; and by the time the second carriage was in motion, a few flakes of snow were finding their way down, and the sky had the appearance of being so overcharged as to want only a milder air to produce a very white world in a very short time.

Emma soon saw that her companion was not in the happiest humour. The preparing and the going abroad in such weather, with the sacrifice of his children after dinner, were evils, were disagreeables at least, which Mr. John Knightley did not by any means like; he anticipated nothing in the visit that could be at all worth the purchase; and the whole of their drive to the vicarage was spent by him in expressing his discontent.

"A man," said he, "must have a very good opinion of himself when he asks people to leave their own fireside, and encounter such a day as this, for the sake of coming to see him. He must think himself a most agreeable fellow; I could not do such a thing. It is the greatest absurdity—Actually snowing at this moment!—The folly of not allowing people to be comfortable at home—and the folly of people's not staying comfortably at home when they can! If we were obliged to go out such an evening as this, by any call of duty or business, what a hardship we should deem it;—and here are we, probably with rather thinner clothing than usual, setting forward voluntarily, without excuse, in defiance of the voice of nature, which tells man, in every thing given to his view or his feelings, to stay at home himself, and keep all under shelter that he can;—here are we setting forward to spend five dull hours in another man's house, with nothing to say or to hear that was not said and heard yesterday, and may not be said and heard again to-morrow. Going in dismal weather, to return probably in worse;—four horses and four servants taken out for nothing but to convey five idle, shivering creatures into colder rooms and worse company than they might have had at home."

Emma did not find herself equal to give the pleased assent, which no doubt he was in the habit of receiving, to emulate the "Very true, my love," which must have been usually administered by his travelling companion; but she had resolution enough to refrain from making any answer at all. She could not be complying, she dreaded being quarrelsome; her heroism reached only to silence. She allowed him to talk, and arranged the glasses, and wrapped herself up, without opening her lips.

They arrived, the carriage turned, the step was let down, and Mr. Elton, spruce, black, and smiling, was with them instantly. Emma thought with pleasure of some change of subject. Mr. Elton was all obligation and cheerfulness; he was so very cheerful in his civilities indeed, that she began to think he must have received a different account of Harriet from what had reached her. She had sent while dressing, and the answer had been, "Much the same—not better."

"My report from Mrs. Goddard's," said she presently, "was not so pleasant as I had hoped—'Not better' was my answer."

His face lengthened immediately; and his voice was the voice of sentiment as he answered.

"Oh! no—I am grieved to find—I was on the point of telling you that when I called at Mrs. Goddard's door, which I did the very last thing before I returned to dress, I was told that Miss Smith was not better, by no means better, rather worse. Very much grieved and concerned—I had flattered myself that she must be better after such a cordial as I knew had been given her in the morning."

Emma smiled and answered—"My visit was of use to the nervous part of her complaint, I hope; but not even I can charm away a sore throat; it is a most severe cold indeed. Mr. Perry has been with her, as you probably heard."

"Yes—I imagined—that is—I did not—"

"He has been used to her in these complaints, and I hope to-morrow morning will bring us both a more comfortable report. But it is impossible not to feel uneasiness. Such a sad loss to our party to-day!"

"Dreadful!—Exactly so, indeed.—She will be missed every moment."

This was very proper; the sigh which accompanied it was really estimable; but it should have lasted longer. Emma was rather in dismay when only half a minute afterwards he began to speak of other things, and in a voice of the greatest alacrity and enjoyment.

"What an excellent device," said he, "the use of a sheepskin for carriages. How very comfortable they make it;—impossible to feel cold with such precautions. The contrivances of modern days indeed have rendered a gentleman's carriage perfectly complete. One is so fenced and guarded from the weather, that not a breath of air can find its way unpermitted. Weather becomes absolutely of no consequence. It is a very cold afternoon—but in this carriage we know nothing of the matter.—Ha! snows a little I see."

"Yes," said John Knightley, "and I think we shall have a good deal of it."

"Christmas weather," observed Mr. Elton. "Quite seasonable; and extremely fortunate we may think ourselves that it did not begin yesterday, and prevent this day's party, which it might very possibly have done, for Mr. Woodhouse would hardly have ventured had there been much snow on the ground; but now it is of no consequence. This is quite the season indeed for friendly meetings. At Christmas every body invites their friends about them, and people think little of even the worst weather. I was snowed up at a friend's house once for a week. Nothing could be pleasanter. I went for only one night, and could not get away till that very day se'nnight."

Mr. John Knightley looked as if he did not comprehend the pleasure, but said only, coolly,

"I cannot wish to be snowed up a week at Randalls."

At another time Emma might have been amused, but she was too much astonished now at Mr. Elton's spirits for other feelings. Harriet seemed quite forgotten in the expectation of a pleasant party.

"We are sure of excellent fires," continued he, "and every thing in the greatest comfort. Charming people, Mr. and Mrs. Weston;—Mrs. Weston indeed is much beyond praise, and he is exactly what one values, so hospitable, and so fond of society;—it will be a small party, but where small parties are select, they are perhaps the most agreeable of any. Mr. Weston's dining-room does not accommodate more than ten comfortably; and for my part, I would rather, under such circumstances, fall short by two than exceed by two. I think you will agree with me, (turning with a soft air to Emma,) I think I shall certainly have your approbation, though Mr. Knightley perhaps, from being used to the large parties of London, may not quite enter into our feelings."

"I know nothing of the large parties of London, sir—I never dine with any body."

"Indeed! (in a tone of wonder and pity,) I had no idea that the law had been so great a slavery. Well, sir, the time must come when you will be paid for all this, when you will have little labour and great enjoyment."

"My first enjoyment," replied John Knightley, as they passed through the sweep-gate, "will be to find myself safe at Hartfield again."

Chapter XIV

Some change of countenance was necessary for each gentleman as they walked into Mrs. Weston's drawing-room;—Mr. Elton must compose his joyous looks, and Mr. John Knightley disperse his ill-humour. Mr. Elton must smile less, and Mr. John Knightley more, to fit them for the place.—Emma only might be as nature prompted, and shew herself just as happy as she was. To her it was real enjoyment to be with the Westons. Mr. Weston was a great favourite, and there was not a creature in the world to whom she spoke with such unreserve, as to his wife; not any one, to whom she related with such conviction of being listened to and understood, of being always interesting and always intelligible, the little affairs, arrangements, perplexities, and pleasures of her father and herself. She could tell nothing of Hartfield, in which Mrs. Weston had not a lively concern; and half an hour's uninterrupted communication of all those little matters on which the daily happiness of private life depends, was one of the first gratifications of each.

This was a pleasure which perhaps the whole day's visit might not afford, which certainly did not belong to the present half-hour; but the very sight of Mrs. Weston, her smile, her touch, her voice was grateful to Emma, and she determined to think as little as possible of Mr. Elton's oddities, or of any thing else unpleasant, and enjoy all that was enjoyable to the utmost.

The misfortune of Harriet's cold had been pretty well gone through before her arrival. Mr. Woodhouse had been safely seated long enough to give the history of it, besides all the history of his own and Isabella's coming, and of Emma's being to follow, and had indeed just got to the end of his satisfaction that James should come and see his daughter, when the others appeared, and Mrs. Weston, who had been almost wholly engrossed by her attentions to him, was able to turn away and welcome her dear Emma.

Emma's project of forgetting Mr. Elton for a while made her rather sorry to find, when they had all taken their places, that he was close to her. The difficulty was great of driving his strange insensibility towards Harriet, from her mind, while he not only sat at her elbow, but was continually obtruding his happy countenance on her notice, and solicitously addressing her upon every occasion. Instead of forgetting him, his behaviour was such that she could not avoid the internal suggestion of "Can it really be as my brother imagined? can it be possible for this man to be beginning to transfer his affections from Harriet to me?—Absurd and insufferable!"—Yet he would be so anxious for her being perfectly warm, would be so interested about her father, and so delighted with Mrs. Weston; and at last would begin admiring her drawings with so much zeal and so little knowledge as seemed terribly like a would-be lover, and made it some effort with her to preserve her good manners. For her own sake she could not be rude; and for Harriet's, in the hope that all would yet turn out right, she was even positively civil; but it was an effort; especially as something was going on amongst the others, in the most overpowering period of Mr. Elton's nonsense, which she particularly wished to listen to. She heard enough to know that Mr. Weston was giving some information about his son; she heard the words "my son," and "Frank," and "my son," repeated several times over; and, from a few other half-syllables very much suspected that he was announcing an early visit from his son; but before she could quiet Mr. Elton, the subject was so completely past that any reviving question from her would have been awkward.

Now, it so happened that in spite of Emma's resolution of never marrying, there was something in the name, in the idea of Mr. Frank Churchill, which always interested her. She had frequently thought—especially since his father's marriage with Miss Taylor—that if she were to marry, he was the very person to suit her in age, character and condition. He seemed by this connexion between the families, quite to belong to her. She could not but suppose it to be a match that every body who knew them must think of. That Mr. and Mrs. Weston did think of it, she was very strongly persuaded; and though not meaning to be induced by him, or by any body else, to give up a situation which she believed more replete with good than any she could change it for, she had a great curiosity to see him, a decided intention of finding him pleasant, of being liked by him to a certain degree, and a sort of pleasure in the idea of their being coupled in their friends' imaginations.

With such sensations, Mr. Elton's civilities were dreadfully ill-timed; but she had the comfort of appearing very polite, while feeling very cross—and of thinking that the rest of the visit could not possibly pass without bringing forward the same information again, or the substance of it, from the open-hearted Mr. Weston.—So it proved;—for when happily released from Mr. Elton, and seated by Mr. Weston, at dinner, he made use of the very first interval in the cares of hospitality, the very first leisure from the saddle of mutton, to say to her,

"We want only two more to be just the right number. I should like to see two more here,—your pretty little friend, Miss Smith, and my son—and then I should say we were quite complete. I believe you did not hear me telling the others in the drawing-room that we are expecting Frank. I had a letter from him this morning, and he will be with us within a fortnight."

Emma spoke with a very proper degree of pleasure; and fully assented to his proposition of Mr. Frank Churchill and Miss Smith making their party quite complete.

"He has been wanting to come to us," continued Mr. Weston, "ever since September: every letter has been full of it; but he cannot command his own time. He has those to please who must be pleased, and who (between ourselves) are sometimes to be pleased only by a good many sacrifices. But now I have no doubt of seeing him here about the second week in January."

"What a very great pleasure it will be to you! and Mrs. Weston is so anxious to be acquainted with him, that she must be almost as happy as yourself."

"Yes, she would be, but that she thinks there will be another put-off. She does not depend upon his coming so much as I do: but she does not know the parties so well as I do. The case, you see, is—(but this is quite between ourselves: I did not mention a syllable of it in the other room. There are secrets in all families, you know)—The case is, that a party of friends are invited to pay a visit at Enscombe in January; and that Frank's coming depends upon their being put off. If they are not put off, he cannot stir. But I know they will, because it is a family that a certain lady, of some consequence, at Enscombe, has a particular dislike to: and though it is thought necessary to invite them once in two or three years, they always are put off when it comes to the point. I have not the smallest doubt of the issue. I am as confident of seeing Frank here before the middle of January, as I am of being here myself: but your good friend there (nodding towards the upper end of the table) has so few vagaries herself, and has been so little used to them at Hartfield, that she cannot calculate on their effects, as I have been long in the practice of doing."

"I am sorry there should be any thing like doubt in the case," replied Emma; "but am disposed to side with you, Mr. Weston. If you think he will come, I shall think so too; for you know Enscombe."

"Yes—I have some right to that knowledge; though I have never been at the place in my life.—She is an odd woman!—But I never allow myself to speak ill of her, on Frank's account; for I do believe her to be very fond of him. I used to think she was not capable of being fond of any body, except herself: but she has always been kind to him (in her way—allowing for little whims and caprices, and expecting every thing to be as she likes). And it is no small credit, in my opinion, to him, that he should excite such an affection; for, though I would not say it to any body else, she has no more heart than a stone to people in general; and the devil of a temper."

Emma liked the subject so well, that she began upon it, to Mrs. Weston, very soon after their moving into the drawing-room: wishing her joy—yet observing, that she knew the first meeting must be rather alarming.—Mrs. Weston agreed to it; but added, that she should be very glad to be secure of undergoing the anxiety of a first meeting at the time talked of: "for I cannot depend upon his coming. I cannot be so sanguine as Mr. Weston. I am very much afraid that it will all end in nothing. Mr. Weston, I dare say, has been telling you exactly how the matter stands?"

"Yes—it seems to depend upon nothing but the ill-humour of Mrs. Churchill, which I imagine to be the most certain thing in the world."

"My Emma!" replied Mrs. Weston, smiling, "what is the certainty of caprice?" Then turning to Isabella, who had not been attending before—"You must know, my dear Mrs. Knightley, that we are by no means so sure of seeing Mr. Frank Churchill, in my opinion, as his father thinks. It depends entirely upon his aunt's spirits and pleasure; in short, upon her temper. To you—to my two daughters—I may venture on the truth. Mrs. Churchill rules at Enscombe, and is a very odd-tempered woman; and his coming now, depends upon her being willing to spare him."

"Oh, Mrs. Churchill; every body knows Mrs. Churchill," replied Isabella: "and I am sure I never think of that poor young man without the greatest compassion. To be constantly living with an ill-tempered person, must be dreadful. It is what we happily have never known any thing of; but it must be a life of misery. What a blessing, that she never had any children! Poor little creatures, how unhappy she would have made them!"

Emma wished she had been alone with Mrs. Weston. She should then have heard more: Mrs. Weston would speak to her, with a degree of unreserve which she would not hazard with Isabella; and, she really believed, would scarcely try to conceal any thing relative to the Churchills from her, excepting those views on the young man, of which her own imagination had already given her such instinctive knowledge. But at present there was nothing more to be said. Mr. Woodhouse very soon followed them into the drawing-room. To be sitting long after dinner, was a confinement that he could not endure. Neither wine nor conversation was any thing to him; and gladly did he move to those with whom he was always comfortable.

While he talked to Isabella, however, Emma found an opportunity of saying,

"And so you do not consider this visit from your son as by any means certain. I am sorry for it. The introduction must be unpleasant, whenever it takes place; and the sooner it could be over, the better."

"Yes; and every delay makes one more apprehensive of other delays. Even if this family, the Braithwaites, are put off, I am still afraid that some excuse may be found for disappointing us. I cannot bear to imagine any reluctance on his side; but I am sure there is a great wish on the Churchills' to keep him to themselves. There is jealousy. They are jealous even of his regard for his father. In short, I can feel no dependence on his coming, and I wish Mr. Weston were less sanguine."

"He ought to come," said Emma. "If he could stay only a couple of days, he ought to come; and one can hardly conceive a young man's not having it in his power to do as much as that. A young woman, if she fall into bad hands, may be teazed, and kept at a distance from those she wants to be with; but one cannot comprehend a young man's being under such restraint, as not to be able to spend a week with his father, if he likes it."

"One ought to be at Enscombe, and know the ways of the family, before one decides upon what he can do," replied Mrs. Weston. "One ought to use the same caution, perhaps, in judging of the conduct of any one individual of any one family; but Enscombe, I believe, certainly must not be judged by general rules: she is so very unreasonable; and every thing gives way to her."

"But she is so fond of the nephew: he is so very great a favourite. Now, according to my idea of Mrs. Churchill, it would be most natural, that while she makes no sacrifice for the comfort of the husband, to whom she owes every thing, while she exercises incessant caprice towards him, she should frequently be governed by the nephew, to whom she owes nothing at all."

"My dearest Emma, do not pretend, with your sweet temper, to understand a bad one, or to lay down rules for it: you must let it go its own way. I have no doubt of his having, at times, considerable influence; but it may be perfectly impossible for him to know beforehand when it will be."

Emma listened, and then coolly said, "I shall not be satisfied, unless he comes."

"He may have a great deal of influence on some points," continued Mrs. Weston, "and on others, very little: and among those, on which she is beyond his reach, it is but too likely, may be this very circumstance of his coming away from them to visit us."

Chapter XV

Mr. Woodhouse was soon ready for his tea; and when he had drank his tea he was quite ready to go home; and it was as much as his three companions could do, to entertain away his notice of the lateness of the hour, before the other gentlemen appeared. Mr. Weston was chatty and convivial, and no friend to early separations of any sort; but at last the drawing-room party did receive an augmentation. Mr. Elton, in very good spirits, was one of the first to walk in. Mrs. Weston and Emma were sitting together on a sofa. He joined them immediately, and, with scarcely an invitation, seated himself between them.

Emma, in good spirits too, from the amusement afforded her mind by the expectation of Mr. Frank Churchill, was willing to forget his late improprieties, and be as well satisfied with him as before, and on his making Harriet his very first subject, was ready to listen with most friendly smiles.

He professed himself extremely anxious about her fair friend—her fair, lovely, amiable friend. "Did she know?—had she heard any thing about her, since their being at Randalls?—he felt much anxiety—he must confess that the nature of her complaint alarmed him considerably." And in this style he talked on for some time very properly, not much attending to any answer, but altogether sufficiently awake to the terror of a bad sore throat; and Emma was quite in charity with him.

But at last there seemed a perverse turn; it seemed all at once as if he were more afraid of its being a bad sore throat on her account, than on Harriet's—more anxious that she should escape the infection, than that there should be no infection in the complaint. He began with great earnestness to entreat her to refrain from visiting the sick-chamber again, for the present—to entreat her to promise him not to venture into such hazard till he had seen Mr. Perry and learnt his opinion; and though she tried to laugh it off and bring the subject back into its proper course, there was no putting an end to his extreme solicitude about her. She was vexed. It did appear—there was no concealing it—exactly like the pretence of being in love with her, instead of Harriet; an inconstancy, if real, the most contemptible and abominable! and she had difficulty in behaving with temper. He turned to Mrs. Weston to implore her assistance, "Would not she give him her support?—would not she add her persuasions to his, to induce Miss Woodhouse not to go to Mrs. Goddard's till it were certain that Miss Smith's disorder had no infection? He could not be satisfied without a promise—would not she give him her influence in procuring it?"

"So scrupulous for others," he continued, "and yet so careless for herself! She wanted me to nurse my cold by staying at home to-day, and yet will not promise to avoid the danger of catching an ulcerated sore throat herself. Is this fair, Mrs. Weston?—Judge between us. Have not I some right to complain? I am sure of your kind support and aid."

Emma saw Mrs. Weston's surprize, and felt that it must be great, at an address which, in words and manner, was assuming to himself the right of first interest in her; and as for herself, she was too much provoked and offended to have the power of directly saying any thing to the purpose. She could only give him a look; but it was such a look as she thought must restore him to his senses, and then left the sofa, removing to a seat by her sister, and giving her all her attention.

She had not time to know how Mr. Elton took the reproof, so rapidly did another subject succeed; for Mr. John Knightley now came into the room from examining the weather, and opened on them all with the information of the ground being covered with snow, and of its still snowing fast, with a strong drifting wind; concluding with these words to Mr. Woodhouse:

"This will prove a spirited beginning of your winter engagements, sir. Something new for your coachman and horses to be making their way through a storm of snow."

Poor Mr. Woodhouse was silent from consternation; but every body else had something to say; every body was either surprized or not surprized, and had some question to ask, or some comfort to offer. Mrs. Weston and Emma tried earnestly to cheer him and turn his attention from his son-in-law, who was pursuing his triumph rather unfeelingly.

"I admired your resolution very much, sir," said he, "in venturing out in such weather, for of course you saw there would be snow very soon. Every body must have seen the snow coming on. I admired your spirit; and I dare say we shall get home very well. Another hour or two's snow can hardly make the road impassable;

and we are two carriages; if one is blown over in the bleak part of the common field there will be the other at hand. I dare say we shall be all safe at Hartfield before midnight."

Mr. Weston, with triumph of a different sort, was confessing that he had known it to be snowing some time, but had not said a word, lest it should make Mr. Woodhouse uncomfortable, and be an excuse for his hurrying away. As to there being any quantity of snow fallen or likely to fall to impede their return, that was a mere joke; he was afraid they would find no difficulty. He wished the road might be impassable, that he might be able to keep them all at Randalls; and with the utmost good-will was sure that accommodation might be found for every body, calling on his wife to agree with him, that with a little contrivance, every body might be lodged, which she hardly knew how to do, from the consciousness of there being but two spare rooms in the house.

"What is to be done, my dear Emma?—what is to be done?" was Mr. Woodhouse's first exclamation, and all that he could say for some time. To her he looked for comfort; and her assurances of safety, her representation of the excellence of the horses, and of James, and of their having so many friends about them, revived him a little.

His eldest daughter's alarm was equal to his own. The horror of being blocked up at Randalls, while her children were at Hartfield, was full in her imagination; and fancying the road to be now just passable for adventurous people, but in a state that admitted no delay, she was eager to have it settled, that her father and Emma should remain at Randalls, while she and her husband set forward instantly through all the possible accumulations of drifted snow that might impede them.

"You had better order the carriage directly, my love," said she; "I dare say we shall be able to get along, if we set off directly; and if we do come to any thing very bad, I can get out and walk. I am not at all afraid. I should not mind walking half the way. I could change my shoes, you know, the moment I got home; and it is not the sort of thing that gives me cold."

"Indeed!" replied he. "Then, my dear Isabella, it is the most extraordinary sort of thing in the world, for in general every thing does give you cold. Walk home!—you are prettily shod for walking home, I dare say. It will be bad enough for the horses."

Isabella turned to Mrs. Weston for her approbation of the plan. Mrs. Weston could only approve. Isabella then went to Emma; but Emma could not so entirely give up the hope of their being all able to get away; and they were still discussing the point, when Mr. Knightley, who had left the room immediately after his brother's first report of the snow, came back again, and told them that he had been out of doors to examine, and could answer for there not being the smallest difficulty in their getting home, whenever they liked it, either now or an hour hence. He had gone beyond the sweep—some way along the Highbury road—the snow was nowhere above half an inch deep—in many places hardly enough to whiten the ground; a very few flakes were falling at present, but the clouds were parting, and there was every appearance of its being soon over. He had seen the coachmen, and they both agreed with him in there being nothing to apprehend.

To Isabella, the relief of such tidings was very great, and they were scarcely less acceptable to Emma on her father's account, who was immediately set as much at ease on the subject as his nervous constitution allowed; but the alarm that had been raised could not be appeased so as to admit of any comfort for him while he continued at Randalls. He was satisfied of there being no present danger in returning home, but no assurances could convince him that it was safe to stay; and while the others were variously urging and recommending, Mr. Knightley and Emma settled it in a few brief sentences: thus—

"Your father will not be easy; why do not you go?"

"I am ready, if the others are."

"Shall I ring the bell?"

"Yes, do."

And the bell was rung, and the carriages spoken for. A few minutes more, and Emma hoped to see one troublesome companion deposited in his own house, to get sober and cool, and the other recover his temper and happiness when this visit of hardship were over.

The carriage came: and Mr. Woodhouse, always the first object on such occasions, was carefully attended to his own by Mr. Knightley and Mr. Weston; but not all that either could say could prevent some renewal of alarm at the sight of the snow which had actually fallen, and the discovery of a much darker night than he had been prepared for. "He was afraid they should have a very bad drive.

He was afraid poor Isabella would not like it. And there would be poor Emma in the carriage behind. He did not know what they had best do. They must keep as much together as they could;" and James was talked to, and given a charge to go very slow and wait for the other carriage.

Isabella stept in after her father; John Knightley, forgetting that he did not belong to their party, stept in after his wife very naturally; so that Emma found, on being escorted and followed into the second carriage by Mr. Elton, that the door was to be lawfully shut on them, and that they were to have a tete-a-tete drive. It would not have been the awkwardness of a moment, it would have been rather a pleasure, previous to the suspicions of this very day; she could have talked to him of Harriet, and the three-quarters of a mile would have seemed but one. But now, she would rather it had not happened. She believed he had been drinking too much of Mr. Weston's good wine, and felt sure that he would want to be talking nonsense.

To restrain him as much as might be, by her own manners, she was immediately preparing to speak with exquisite calmness and gravity of the weather and the night; but scarcely had she begun, scarcely had they passed the sweep-gate and joined the other carriage, than she found her subject cut up—her hand seized—her attention demanded, and Mr. Elton actually making violent love to her: availing himself of the precious opportunity, declaring sentiments which must be already well known, hoping—fearing—adoring—ready to die if she refused him; but flattering himself that his ardent attachment and unequalled love and unexampled passion could not fail of having some effect, and in short, very much resolved on being seriously accepted as soon as possible. It really was so. Without scruple—without apology—without much apparent diffidence, Mr. Elton, the lover of Harriet, was professing himself her lover. She tried to stop him; but vainly; he would go on, and say it all. Angry as she was, the thought of the moment made her resolve to restrain herself when she did speak. She felt that half this folly must be drunkenness, and therefore could hope that it might belong only to the passing hour. Accordingly, with a mixture of the serious and the playful, which she hoped would best suit his half and half state, she replied,

"I am very much astonished, Mr. Elton. This to me! you forget yourself—you take me for my friend—any message to Miss Smith I shall be happy to deliver; but no more of this to me, if you please."

"Miss Smith!—message to Miss Smith!—What could she possibly mean!"—And he repeated her words with such assurance of accent, such boastful pretence of amazement, that she could not help replying with quickness,

"Mr. Elton, this is the most extraordinary conduct! and I can account for it only in one way; you are not yourself, or you could not speak either to me, or of Harriet, in such a manner. Command yourself enough to say no more, and I will endeavour to forget it."

But Mr. Elton had only drunk wine enough to elevate his spirits, not at all to confuse his intellects. He perfectly knew his own meaning; and having warmly protested against her suspicion as most injurious, and slightly touched upon his respect for Miss Smith as her friend,—but acknowledging his wonder that Miss Smith should be mentioned at all,—he resumed the subject of his own passion, and was very urgent for a favourable answer.

As she thought less of his inebriety, she thought more of his inconstancy and presumption; and with fewer struggles for politeness, replied,

"It is impossible for me to doubt any longer. You have made yourself too clear. Mr. Elton, my astonishment is much beyond any thing I can express. After such behaviour, as I have witnessed during the last month, to Miss Smith—such attentions as I have been in the daily habit of observing—to be addressing me in this manner—this is an unsteadiness of character, indeed, which I had not supposed possible! Believe me, sir, I am far, very far, from gratified in being the object of such professions."

"Good Heaven!" cried Mr. Elton, "what can be the meaning of this?—Miss Smith!—I never thought of Miss Smith in the whole course of my existence—never paid her any attentions, but as your friend: never cared whether she were dead or alive, but as your friend. If she has fancied otherwise, her own wishes have misled her, and I am very sorry—extremely sorry—But, Miss Smith, indeed!—Oh! Miss Woodhouse! who can think of Miss Smith, when Miss Woodhouse is near! No, upon my honour, there is no unsteadiness of character. I have thought only of you. I protest against having paid the smallest attention to any one else. Every thing that I have said or done, for many weeks past, has been with the sole view of marking my adoration of yourself. You cannot really, seriously, doubt it. No!—(in an accent meant to be insinuating)—I am sure you have seen and understood me."

It would be impossible to say what Emma felt, on hearing this—which of all her unpleasant sensations was uppermost. She was too completely overpowered to be immediately able to reply: and two moments of silence being ample encouragement for Mr. Elton's sanguine state of mind, he tried to take her hand again, as he joyously exclaimed—

"Charming Miss Woodhouse! allow me to interpret this interesting silence. It confesses that you have long understood me."

"No, sir," cried Emma, "it confesses no such thing. So far from having long understood you, I have been in a most complete error with respect to your views, till this moment. As to myself, I am very sorry that you should have been giving way to any feelings—Nothing could be farther from my wishes—your attachment to my friend Harriet—your pursuit of her, (pursuit, it appeared,) gave me great pleasure, and I have been very earnestly wishing you success: but had I supposed that she were not your attraction to Hartfield, I should certainly have thought you judged ill in making your visits so frequent. Am I to believe that you have never sought to recommend yourself particularly to Miss Smith?—that you have never thought seriously of her?"

"Never, madam," cried he, affronted in his turn: "never, I assure you. I think seriously of Miss Smith!—Miss Smith is a very good sort of girl; and I should be happy to see her respectably settled. I wish her extremely well: and, no doubt, there are men who might not object to—Every body has their level: but as for myself, I am not, I think, quite so much at a loss. I need not so totally despair of an equal alliance, as to be addressing myself to Miss Smith!—No, madam, my visits to Hartfield have been for yourself only; and the encouragement I received—"

"Encouragement!—I give you encouragement!—Sir, you have been entirely mistaken in supposing it. I have seen you only as the admirer of my friend. In no other light could you have been more to me than a common acquaintance. I am exceedingly sorry: but it is well that the mistake ends where it does. Had the same behaviour continued, Miss Smith might have been led into a misconception of your views; not being aware, probably, any more than myself, of the very great inequality which you are so sensible of. But, as it is, the disappointment is single, and, I trust, will not be lasting. I have no thoughts of matrimony at present."

He was too angry to say another word; her manner too decided to invite supplication; and in this state of swelling resentment, and mutually deep mortification, they had to continue together a few minutes longer, for the fears of Mr. Woodhouse had confined them to a foot-pace. If there had not been so much anger, there would have been desperate awkwardness; but their straightforward emotions left no room for the little zigzags of embarrassment. Without knowing when the carriage turned into Vicarage Lane, or when it stopped, they found themselves, all at once, at the door of his house; and he was out before another syllable passed.—Emma then felt it indispensable to wish him a good night. The compliment was just returned, coldly and proudly; and, under indescribable irritation of spirits, she was then conveyed to Hartfield.

There she was welcomed, with the utmost delight, by her father, who had been trembling for the dangers of a solitary drive from Vicarage Lane—turning a corner which he could never bear to think of—and in strange hands—a mere common coachman—no James; and there it seemed as if her return only were wanted to make every thing go well: for Mr. John Knightley, ashamed of his ill-humour, was now all kindness and attention; and so particularly solicitous for the comfort of her father, as to seem—if not quite ready to join him in a basin of gruel—perfectly sensible of its being exceedingly wholesome; and the day was concluding in peace and comfort to all their little party, except herself.—But her mind had never been in such perturbation; and it needed a very strong effort to appear attentive and cheerful till the usual hour of separating allowed her the relief of quiet reflection.

Chapter XVI

The hair was curled, and the maid sent away, and Emma sat down to think and be miserable.—It was a wretched business indeed!—Such an overthrow of every thing she had been wishing for!—Such a development of every thing most unwelcome!—Such a blow for Harriet!—that was the worst of all. Every part of it brought pain and humiliation, of some sort or other; but, compared with the evil to Harriet, all was light; and she would gladly have submitted to feel yet more mistaken—more in error—more disgraced by mis-judgment, than she actually was, could the effects of her blunders have been confined to herself.

"If I had not persuaded Harriet into liking the man, I could have borne any thing. He might have doubled his presumption to me—but poor Harriet!"

How she could have been so deceived!—He protested that he had never thought seriously of Harriet—never! She looked back as well as she could; but it was all confusion. She had taken up the idea, she supposed, and made every thing bend to it. His manners, however, must have been unmarked, wavering, dubious, or she could not have been so misled.

The picture!—How eager he had been about the picture!—and the charade!—and an hundred other circumstances;—how clearly they had seemed to point at Harriet. To be sure, the charade, with its "ready wit"—but then the "soft eyes"—in fact it suited neither; it was a jumble without taste or truth. Who could have seen through such thick-headed nonsense?

Certainly she had often, especially of late, thought his manners to herself unnecessarily gallant; but it had passed as his way, as a mere error of judgment, of knowledge, of taste, as one proof among others that he had not always lived in the best society, that with all the gentleness of his address, true elegance was sometimes wanting; but, till this very day, she had never, for an instant, suspected it to mean any thing but grateful respect to her as Harriet's friend.

To Mr. John Knightley was she indebted for her first idea on the subject, for the first start of its possibility. There was no denying that those brothers had penetration. She remembered what Mr. Knightley had once said to her about Mr. Elton, the caution he had given, the conviction he had professed that Mr. Elton would never marry indiscreetly; and blushed to think how much truer a knowledge of his character had been there shewn than any she had reached herself. It was dreadfully mortifying; but Mr. Elton was proving himself, in many respects, the very reverse of what she had meant and believed him; proud, assuming, conceited; very full of his own claims, and little concerned about the feelings of others.

Contrary to the usual course of things, Mr. Elton's wanting to pay his addresses to her had sunk him in her opinion. His professions and his proposals did him no service. She thought nothing of his attachment, and was insulted by his hopes. He wanted to marry well, and having the arrogance to raise his eyes to her, pretended to be in love; but she was perfectly easy as to his not suffering any disappointment that need be cared for. There had been no real affection either in his language or manners. Sighs and fine words had been given in abundance; but she could hardly devise any set of expressions, or fancy any tone of voice, less allied with real love. She need not trouble herself to pity him. He only wanted to aggrandise and enrich himself; and if Miss Woodhouse of Hartfield, the heiress of thirty thousand pounds, were not quite so easily obtained as he had fancied, he would soon try for Miss Somebody else with twenty, or with ten.

But—that he should talk of encouragement, should consider her as aware of his views, accepting his attentions, meaning (in short), to marry him!—should suppose himself her equal in connexion or mind!—look down upon her friend, so well understanding the gradations of rank below him, and be so blind to what rose above, as to fancy himself shewing no presumption in addressing her!—It was most provoking.

Perhaps it was not fair to expect him to feel how very much he was her inferior in talent, and all the elegancies of mind. The very want of such equality might prevent his perception of it; but he must know that in fortune and consequence she was greatly his superior. He must know that the Woodhouses had been settled for several generations at Hartfield, the younger branch of a very ancient family—and that the Eltons were nobody. The landed property of Hartfield certainly was inconsiderable, being but a sort of notch in the Donwell Abbey estate, to which all the rest of Highbury belonged; but their fortune, from other sources, was such as to make them scarcely secondary to Donwell Abbey itself, in every other kind of consequence; and the Woodhouses had long held a high place in the consideration of the neighbourhood which Mr. Elton had first entered not two years ago, to make his way as he could, without any alliances but in trade, or any thing to recommend him to notice but his situation and his civility.—But he had fancied her in love with him; that evidently must have been his dependence; and after raving a little about the seeming incongruity of gentle manners and a conceited head, Emma was obliged in common honesty to stop and admit that her own behaviour to him had been so complaisant and obliging, so full of courtesy and attention, as (supposing her real motive unperceived) might warrant a man of ordinary observation and delicacy, like Mr. Elton, in fancying himself a very decided favourite. If she had so misinterpreted his feelings, she had little right to wonder that he, with self-interest to blind him, should have mistaken hers.

The first error and the worst lay at her door. It was foolish, it was wrong, to take so active a part in bringing any two people together. It was adventuring too far, assuming too much, making light of what ought to be serious, a trick of what ought to be simple. She was quite concerned and ashamed, and resolved to do such things no more.

"Here have I," said she, "actually talked poor Harriet into being very much attached to this man. She might never have thought of him but for me; and certainly never would have thought of him with hope, if I had not assured her of his attachment, for she is as modest and humble as I used to think him. Oh! that I had been satisfied with persuading her not to accept young Martin. There I was quite right. That was well done of me; but there I should have stopped, and left the rest to time and chance. I was introducing her into good company, and giving her the opportunity of pleasing some one worth having; I ought not to have attempted more. But now, poor girl, her peace is cut up for some time. I have been but half a friend to her; and if she were not to feel this disappointment so very much, I am sure I have not an idea of any body else who would be at all desirable for her;—William Coxe—Oh! no, I could not endure William Coxe—a pert young lawyer."

She stopt to blush and laugh at her own relapse, and then resumed a more serious, more dispiriting cogitation upon what had been, and might be, and must be. The distressing explanation she had to make to Harriet, and all that poor Harriet would be suffering, with the awkwardness of future meetings, the difficulties of continuing or discontinuing the acquaintance, of subduing feelings, concealing resentment, and avoiding eclat, were enough to occupy her in most unmirthful reflections some time longer, and she went to bed at last with nothing settled but the conviction of her having blundered most dreadfully.

To youth and natural cheerfulness like Emma's, though under temporary gloom at night, the return of day will hardly fail to bring return of spirits. The youth and cheerfulness of morning are in happy analogy, and of powerful operation; and if the distress be not poignant enough to keep the eyes unclosed, they will be sure to open to sensations of softened pain and brighter hope.

Emma got up on the morrow more disposed for comfort than she had gone to bed, more ready to see alleviations of the evil before her, and to depend on getting tolerably out of it.

It was a great consolation that Mr. Elton should not be really in love with her, or so particularly amiable as to make it shocking to disappoint him—that Harriet's nature should not be of that superior sort in which the feelings are most acute and retentive—and that there could be no necessity for any body's knowing what had passed except the three principals, and especially for her father's being given a moment's uneasiness about it.

These were very cheering thoughts; and the sight of a great deal of snow on the ground did her further service, for any thing was welcome that might justify their all three being quite asunder at present.

The weather was most favourable for her; though Christmas Day, she could not go to church. Mr. Woodhouse would have been miserable had his daughter attempted it, and she was therefore safe from either exciting or receiving unpleasant and most unsuitable ideas. The ground covered with snow, and the atmosphere in that unsettled state between frost and thaw, which is of all others the most unfriendly for exercise, every morning beginning in rain or snow, and every evening setting in to freeze, she was for many days a most honourable prisoner. No intercourse with Harriet possible but by note; no church for her on Sunday any more than on Christmas Day; and no need to find excuses for Mr. Elton's absenting himself.

It was weather which might fairly confine every body at home; and though she hoped and believed him to be really taking comfort in some society or other, it was very pleasant to have her father so well satisfied with his being all alone in his own house, too wise to stir out; and to hear him say to Mr. Knightley, whom no weather could keep entirely from them,—

"Ah! Mr. Knightley, why do not you stay at home like poor Mr. Elton?"

These days of confinement would have been, but for her private perplexities, remarkably comfortable, as such seclusion exactly suited her brother, whose feelings must always be of great importance to his companions; and he had, besides, so thoroughly cleared off his ill-humour at Randalls, that his amiableness never failed him during the rest of his stay at Hartfield. He was always agreeable and obliging, and speaking pleasantly of every body. But with all the hopes of cheerfulness, and all the present comfort of delay, there was still such an evil hanging over her in the hour of explanation with Harriet, as made it impossible for Emma to be ever perfectly at ease.

Chapter XVII

Mr. and Mrs. John Knightley were not detained long at Hartfield. The weather soon improved enough for those to move who must move; and Mr. Woodhouse having, as usual, tried to persuade his daughter to stay behind with all her children, was obliged to see the whole party set off, and return to his lamentations over the destiny of poor Isabella;—which poor Isabella, passing her life with those she doated on, full of their merits, blind to their faults, and always innocently busy, might have been a model of right feminine happiness.

The evening of the very day on which they went brought a note from Mr. Elton to Mr. Woodhouse, a long, civil, ceremonious note, to say, with Mr. Elton's best compliments, "that he was proposing to leave Highbury the following morning in his way to Bath; where, in compliance with the pressing entreaties of some friends, he had engaged to spend a few weeks, and very much regretted the impossibility he was under, from various circumstances of weather and business, of taking a personal leave of Mr. Woodhouse, of whose friendly civilities he should ever retain a grateful sense—and had Mr. Woodhouse any commands, should be happy to attend to them."

Emma was most agreeably surprized.—Mr. Elton's absence just at this time was the very thing to be desired. She admired him for contriving it, though not able to give him much credit for the manner in which it was announced. Resentment could not have been more plainly spoken than in a civility to her father, from which she was so pointedly excluded. She had not even a share in his opening compliments.—Her name was not mentioned;—and there was so striking a change in all this, and such an ill-judged solemnity of leave-taking in his graceful acknowledgments, as she thought, at first, could not escape her father's suspicion.

It did, however.—Her father was quite taken up with the surprize of so sudden a journey, and his fears that Mr. Elton might never get safely to the end of it, and saw nothing extraordinary in his language. It was a very useful note, for it supplied them with fresh matter for thought and conversation during the rest of their lonely evening. Mr. Woodhouse talked over his alarms, and Emma was in spirits to persuade them away with all her usual promptitude.

She now resolved to keep Harriet no longer in the dark. She had reason to believe her nearly recovered from her cold, and it was desirable that she should have as much time as possible for getting the better of her other complaint before the gentleman's return. She went to Mrs. Goddard's accordingly the very next day, to undergo the necessary penance of communication; and a severe one it was.—She had to destroy all the hopes which she had been so industriously feeding—to appear in the ungracious character of the one preferred—and acknowledge herself grossly mistaken and mis-judging in all her ideas on one subject, all her observations, all her convictions, all her prophecies for the last six weeks.

The confession completely renewed her first shame—and the sight of Harriet's tears made her think that she should never be in charity with herself again.

Harriet bore the intelligence very well—blaming nobody—and in every thing testifying such an ingenuousness of disposition and lowly opinion of herself, as must appear with particular advantage at that moment to her friend.

Emma was in the humour to value simplicity and modesty to the utmost; and all that was amiable, all that ought to be attaching, seemed on Harriet's side, not her own. Harriet did not consider herself as having any thing to complain of. The affection of such a man as Mr. Elton would have been too great a distinction.—She never could have deserved him—and nobody but so partial and kind a friend as Miss Woodhouse would have thought it possible.

Her tears fell abundantly—but her grief was so truly artless, that no dignity could have made it more respectable in Emma's eyes—and she listened to her and tried to console her with all her heart and understanding—really for the time convinced that Harriet was the superior creature of the two—and that to resemble her would be more for her own welfare and happiness than all that genius or intelligence could do.

It was rather too late in the day to set about being simple-minded and ignorant; but she left her with every previous resolution confirmed of being humble and discreet, and repressing imagination all the rest of her life. Her second duty now, inferior only to her father's claims, was to promote Harriet's comfort, and endeavour to prove her own affection in some better method than by match-making. She got her to Hartfield, and shewed her the most unvarying kindness, striving to occupy and amuse her, and by books and conversation, to drive Mr. Elton from her thoughts.

Time, she knew, must be allowed for this being thoroughly done; and she could suppose herself but an indifferent judge of such matters in general, and very inadequate to sympathise in an attachment to Mr. Elton in particular; but it seemed to her reasonable that at Harriet's age, and with the entire extinction of all hope, such a progress might be made towards a state of composure by the time of Mr. Elton's return, as to allow them all to meet again in the common routine of acquaintance, without any danger of betraying sentiments or increasing them.

Harriet did think him all perfection, and maintained the non-existence of any body equal to him in person or goodness—and did, in truth, prove herself more resolutely in love than Emma had foreseen; but yet it appeared to her so natural, so inevitable to strive against an inclination of that sort unrequited, that she could not comprehend its continuing very long in equal force.

If Mr. Elton, on his return, made his own indifference as evident and indubitable as she could not doubt he would anxiously do, she could not imagine Harriet's persisting to place her happiness in the sight or the recollection of him.

Their being fixed, so absolutely fixed, in the same place, was bad for each, for all three. Not one of them had the power of removal, or of effecting any material change of society. They must encounter each other, and make the best of it.

Harriet was farther unfortunate in the tone of her companions at Mrs. Goddard's; Mr. Elton being the adoration of all the teachers and great girls in the school; and it must be at Hartfield only that she could have any chance of hearing him spoken of with cooling moderation or repellent truth. Where the wound had been given, there must the cure be found if anywhere; and Emma felt that, till she saw her in the way of cure, there could be no true peace for herself.

Chapter XVIII

Mr. Frank Churchill did not come. When the time proposed drew near, Mrs. Weston's fears were justified in the arrival of a letter of excuse. For the present, he could not be spared, to his "very great mortification and regret; but still he looked forward with the hope of coming to Randalls at no distant period."

Mrs. Weston was exceedingly disappointed—much more disappointed, in fact, than her husband, though her dependence on seeing the young man had been so much more sober: but a sanguine temper, though for ever expecting more good than occurs, does not always pay for its hopes by any proportionate depression. It soon flies over the present failure, and begins to hope again. For half an hour Mr. Weston was surprized and sorry; but then he began to perceive that Frank's coming two or three months later would be a much better plan; better time of year; better weather; and that he would be able, without any doubt, to stay considerably longer with them than if he had come sooner.

These feelings rapidly restored his comfort, while Mrs. Weston, of a more apprehensive disposition, foresaw nothing but a repetition of excuses and delays; and after all her concern for what her husband was to suffer, suffered a great deal more herself.

Emma was not at this time in a state of spirits to care really about Mr. Frank Churchill's not coming, except as a disappointment at Randalls. The acquaintance at present had no charm for her. She wanted, rather, to be quiet, and out of temptation; but still, as it was desirable that she should appear, in general, like her usual self, she took care to express as much interest in the circumstance, and enter as warmly into Mr. and Mrs. Weston's disappointment, as might naturally belong to their friendship.

She was the first to announce it to Mr. Knightley; and exclaimed quite as much as was necessary, (or, being acting a part, perhaps rather more,) at the conduct of the Churchills, in keeping him away. She then proceeded to say a good deal more than she felt, of the advantage of such an addition to their confined society in Surry; the pleasure of looking at somebody new; the gala-day to Highbury entire, which the sight of him would have made; and ending with reflections on the Churchills again, found herself directly involved in a disagreement with Mr. Knightley; and, to her great amusement, perceived that she was taking the other side of the question from her real opinion, and making use of Mrs. Weston's arguments against herself.

"The Churchills are very likely in fault," said Mr. Knightley, coolly; "but I dare say he might come if he would."

"I do not know why you should say so. He wishes exceedingly to come; but his uncle and aunt will not spare him."

"I cannot believe that he has not the power of coming, if he made a point of it. It is too unlikely, for me to believe it without proof."

"How odd you are! What has Mr. Frank Churchill done, to make you suppose him such an unnatural creature?"

"I am not supposing him at all an unnatural creature, in suspecting that he may have learnt to be above his connexions, and to care very little for any thing but his own pleasure, from living with those who have always set him the example of it. It is a great deal more natural than one could wish, that a young man, brought up by those who are proud, luxurious, and selfish, should be proud, luxurious, and selfish too. If Frank Churchill had wanted to see his father, he would have contrived it between September and January. A man at his age—what is he?—three or four-and-twenty—cannot be without the means of doing as much as that. It is impossible."

"That's easily said, and easily felt by you, who have always been your own master. You are the worst judge in the world, Mr. Knightley, of the difficulties of dependence. You do not know what it is to have tempers to manage."

"It is not to be conceived that a man of three or four-and-twenty should not have liberty of mind or limb to that amount. He cannot want money—he cannot want leisure. We know, on the contrary, that he has so much of both, that he is glad to get rid of them at the idlest haunts in the kingdom. We hear of him for ever at some watering-place or other. A little while ago, he was at Weymouth. This proves that he can leave the Churchills."

"Yes, sometimes he can."

"And those times are whenever he thinks it worth his while; whenever there is any temptation of pleasure."

"It is very unfair to judge of any body's conduct, without an intimate knowledge of their situation. Nobody, who has not been in the interior of a family, can say what the difficulties of any individual of that family may be. We ought to be acquainted with Enscombe, and with Mrs. Churchill's temper, before we pretend to decide upon what her nephew can do. He may, at times, be able to do a great deal more than he can at others."

"There is one thing, Emma, which a man can always do, if he chuses, and that is, his duty; not by manoeuvring and finessing, but by vigour and resolution. It is Frank Churchill's duty to pay this attention to his father. He knows it to be so, by his promises and messages; but if he wished to do it, it might be done. A man who felt rightly would say at once, simply and resolutely, to Mrs. Churchill—'Every sacrifice of mere pleasure you will always find me ready to make to your convenience; but I must go and see my father immediately. I know he would be hurt by my failing in such a mark of respect to him on the present occasion, I shall, therefore, set off to-morrow.'—If he would say so to her at once, in the tone of decision becoming a man, there would be no opposition made to his going."

"No," said Emma, laughing; "but perhaps there might be some made to his coming back again. Such language for a young man entirely dependent, to use!—Nobody but you, Mr. Knightley, would imagine it possible. But you have not an idea of what is requisite in situations directly opposite to your own. Mr. Frank Churchill to be making such a speech as that to the uncle and aunt, who have brought him up, and are to provide for him!—Standing up in the middle of the room, I suppose, and speaking as loud as he could!—How can you imagine such conduct practicable?"

"Depend upon it, Emma, a sensible man would find no difficulty in it. He would feel himself in the right; and the declaration—made, of course, as a man of sense would make it, in a proper manner—would do him more good, raise him higher, fix his interest stronger with the people he depended on, than all that a line of shifts and expedients can ever do. Respect would be added to affection. They would feel that they could trust him; that the nephew who had done rightly by his father, would do rightly by them; for they know, as well as he does, as well as all the world must know, that he ought to pay this visit to his father; and while meanly exerting their power to delay it, are in their hearts not thinking the better of him for submitting to their whims. Respect for right conduct is felt by every body. If he would act in this sort of manner, on principle, consistently, regularly, their little minds would bend to his."

"I rather doubt that. You are very fond of bending little minds; but where little minds belong to rich people in authority, I think they have a knack of swelling out, till they are quite as unmanageable as great ones. I can imagine, that if you, as you are, Mr. Knightley, were to be transported and placed all at once in Mr. Frank Churchill's situation, you would be able to say and do just what you have been recommending for him; and it might have a very good effect. The Churchills might not have a word to say in return; but then, you would have no habits of early obedience and long observance to break through. To him who has, it might not be so easy to burst forth at once into perfect independence, and set all their claims on his gratitude and regard at nought. He may have as strong a sense of what would be right, as you can have, without being so equal, under particular circumstances, to act up to it."

"Then it would not be so strong a sense. If it failed to produce equal exertion, it could not be an equal conviction."

"Oh, the difference of situation and habit! I wish you would try to understand what an amiable young man may be likely to feel in directly opposing those, whom as child and boy he has been looking up to all his life."

"Our amiable young man is a very weak young man, if this be the first occasion of his carrying through a resolution to do right against the will of others. It ought to have been a habit with him by this time, of following his duty, instead of consulting expediency. I can allow for the fears of the child, but not of the man. As he became rational, he ought to have roused himself and shaken off all that was unworthy in their authority. He ought to have opposed the first attempt on their side to make him slight his father. Had he begun as he ought, there would have been no difficulty now."

"We shall never agree about him," cried Emma; "but that is nothing extraordinary. I have not the least idea of his being a weak young man: I feel sure that he is not. Mr. Weston would not be blind to folly, though in his own son; but he is very likely to have a more yielding, complying, mild disposition than would suit your notions of man's perfection. I dare say he has; and though it may cut him off from some advantages, it will secure him many others."

"Yes; all the advantages of sitting still when he ought to move, and of leading a life of mere idle pleasure, and fancying himself extremely expert in finding excuses for it. He can sit down and write a fine flourishing letter, full of professions and falsehoods, and persuade himself that he has hit upon the very best method in the world of preserving peace at home and preventing his father's having any right to complain. His letters disgust me."

"Your feelings are singular. They seem to satisfy every body else."

"I suspect they do not satisfy Mrs. Weston. They hardly can satisfy a woman of her good sense and quick feelings: standing in a mother's place, but without a mother's affection to blind her. It is on her account that attention to Randalls is doubly due, and she must doubly feel the omission. Had she been a person of consequence herself, he would have come I dare say; and it would not have signified whether he did or no. Can you think your friend behindhand in these sort of considerations? Do you suppose she does not often say all this to herself? No, Emma, your amiable young man can be amiable only in French, not in English. He may be very 'aimable,' have very good manners, and be very agreeable; but he can have no English delicacy towards the feelings of other people: nothing really amiable about him."

"You seem determined to think ill of him."

"Me!—not at all," replied Mr. Knightley, rather displeased; "I do not want to think ill of him. I should be as ready to acknowledge his merits as any other man; but I hear of none, except what are merely personal; that he is well-grown and good-looking, with smooth, plausible manners."

"Well, if he have nothing else to recommend him, he will be a treasure at Highbury. We do not often look upon fine young men, well-bred and agreeable. We must not be nice and ask for all the virtues into the bargain. Cannot you imagine, Mr. Knightley, what a sensation his coming will produce? There will be but one subject throughout the parishes of Donwell and Highbury; but one interest—one object of curiosity; it will be all Mr. Frank Churchill; we shall think and speak of nobody else."

"You will excuse my being so much over-powered. If I find him conversable, I shall be glad of his acquaintance; but if he is only a chattering coxcomb, he will not occupy much of my time or thoughts."

"My idea of him is, that he can adapt his conversation to the taste of every body, and has the power as well as the wish of being universally agreeable. To you, he will talk of farming; to me, of drawing or music; and so on to every body, having that general information on all subjects which will enable him to follow the lead, or take the lead, just as propriety may require, and to speak extremely well on each; that is my idea of him."

"And mine," said Mr. Knightley warmly, "is, that if he turn out any thing like it, he will be the most insufferable fellow breathing! What! at three-and-twenty to be the king of his company—the great man—the practised politician, who is to read every body's character, and make every body's talents conduce to the display of his own superiority; to be dispensing his flatteries around, that he may make all appear like fools compared with himself! My dear Emma, your own good sense could not endure such a puppy when it came to the point."

"I will say no more about him," cried Emma, "you turn every thing to evil. We are both prejudiced; you against, I for him; and we have no chance of agreeing till he is really here."

"Prejudiced! I am not prejudiced."

"But I am very much, and without being at all ashamed of it. My love for Mr. and Mrs. Weston gives me a decided prejudice in his favour."

"He is a person I never think of from one month's end to another," said Mr. Knightley, with a degree of vexation, which made Emma immediately talk of something else, though she could not comprehend why he should be angry.

To take a dislike to a young man, only because he appeared to be of a different disposition from himself, was unworthy the real liberality of mind which she was always used to acknowledge in him; for with all the high opinion of himself, which she had often laid to his charge, she had never before for a moment supposed it could make him unjust to the merit of another.

VOLUME II

Chapter I

Emma and Harriet had been walking together one morning, and, in Emma's opinion, had been talking enough of Mr. Elton for that day. She could not think that Harriet's solace or her own sins required more; and she was therefore industriously getting rid of the subject as they returned;—but it burst out again when she thought she had succeeded, and after speaking some time of what the poor must suffer in winter, and receiving no other answer than a very plaintive—"Mr. Elton is so good to the poor!" she found something else must be done.

They were just approaching the house where lived Mrs. and Miss Bates. She determined to call upon them and seek safety in numbers. There was always sufficient reason for such an attention; Mrs. and Miss Bates loved to be called on, and she knew she was considered by the very few who presumed ever to see imperfection in her, as rather negligent in that respect, and as not contributing what she ought to the stock of their scanty comforts.

She had had many a hint from Mr. Knightley and some from her own heart, as to her deficiency—but none were equal to counteract the persuasion of its being very disagreeable,—a waste of time—tiresome women—and all the horror of being in danger of falling in with the second-rate and third-rate of Highbury, who were calling on them for ever, and therefore she seldom went near them. But now she made the sudden resolution of not passing their door without going in—observing, as she proposed it to Harriet, that, as well as she could calculate, they were just now quite safe from any letter from Jane Fairfax.

The house belonged to people in business. Mrs. and Miss Bates occupied the drawing-room floor; and there, in the very moderate-sized apartment, which was every thing to them, the visitors were most cordially and even gratefully welcomed; the quiet neat old lady, who with her knitting was seated in the warmest corner, wanting even to give up her place to Miss Woodhouse, and her more active, talking daughter, almost ready to overpower them with care and kindness, thanks for their visit, solicitude for their shoes, anxious inquiries after Mr. Woodhouse's health, cheerful communications about her mother's, and sweet-cake from the beaufet—"Mrs. Cole had just been there, just called in for ten minutes, and had been so good as to sit an hour with them, and she had taken a piece of cake and been so kind as to say she liked it very much; and, therefore, she hoped Miss Woodhouse and Miss Smith would do them the favour to eat a piece too."

The mention of the Coles was sure to be followed by that of Mr. Elton. There was intimacy between them, and Mr. Cole had heard from Mr. Elton since his going away. Emma knew what was coming; they must have the letter over again, and settle how long he had been gone, and how much he was engaged in company, and what a favourite he was wherever he went, and how full the Master of the Ceremonies' ball had been; and she went through it very well, with all the interest and all the commendation that could be requisite, and always putting forward to prevent Harriet's being obliged to say a word.

This she had been prepared for when she entered the house; but meant, having once talked him handsomely over, to be no farther incommoded by any troublesome topic, and to wander at large amongst all the Mistresses and Misses of Highbury, and their card-parties. She had not been prepared to have Jane Fairfax succeed Mr. Elton; but he was actually hurried off by Miss Bates, she jumped away from him at last abruptly to the Coles, to usher in a letter from her niece.

"Oh! yes—Mr. Elton, I understand—certainly as to dancing—Mrs. Cole was telling me that dancing at the rooms at Bath was—Mrs. Cole was so kind as to sit some time with us, talking of Jane; for as soon as she came in, she began inquiring after her, Jane is so very great a favourite there. Whenever she is with us, Mrs. Cole does not know how to shew her kindness enough; and I must say that Jane deserves it as much as any body can. And so she began inquiring after her directly, saying, 'I know you cannot have heard from Jane lately, because it is not her time for writing;' and when I immediately said, 'But indeed we have, we had a letter this very morning,' I do not know that I ever saw any body more surprized. 'Have you, upon your honour?' said she; 'well, that is quite unexpected. Do let me hear what she says.'"

Emma's politeness was at hand directly, to say, with smiling interest—

"Have you heard from Miss Fairfax so lately? I am extremely happy. I hope she is well?"

"Thank you. You are so kind!" replied the happily deceived aunt, while eagerly hunting for the letter.—"Oh! here it is. I was sure it could not be far off; but I had put my huswife upon it, you see, without being aware, and so it was quite hid, but I had it in my hand so very lately that I was almost sure it must be on the table. I was reading it to Mrs. Cole, and since she went away, I was reading it again to my mother, for it is such a pleasure to her—a letter from Jane—that she can never hear it often enough; so I knew it could not be far off, and here it is, only just under my huswife—and since you are so kind as to wish to hear what she says;—but, first of all, I really must, in justice to Jane, apologise for her writing so short a letter—only two pages you see—hardly two—and in general she fills the whole paper and crosses half. My mother often wonders that I can make it out so well. She often says, when the letter is first opened, 'Well, Hetty, now I think you will be put to it to make out all that checker-work'—don't you, ma'am?—And then I tell her, I am sure she would contrive to make it out herself, if she had nobody to do it for her—every word of it—I am sure she would pore over it till she had made out every word. And, indeed, though my mother's eyes are not so good as they were, she can see amazingly well still, thank God! with the help of spectacles. It is such a blessing! My mother's are really very good indeed. Jane often says, when she is here, 'I am sure, grandmama, you must have had very strong eyes to see as you do—and so much fine work as you have done too!—I only wish my eyes may last me as well.'"

All this spoken extremely fast obliged Miss Bates to stop for breath; and Emma said something very civil about the excellence of Miss Fairfax's handwriting.

"You are extremely kind," replied Miss Bates, highly gratified; "you who are such a judge, and write so beautifully yourself. I am sure there is nobody's praise that could give us so much pleasure as Miss Woodhouse's. My mother does not hear; she is a little deaf you know. Ma'am," addressing her, "do you hear what Miss Woodhouse is so obliging to say about Jane's handwriting?"

And Emma had the advantage of hearing her own silly compliment repeated twice over before the good old lady could comprehend it. She was pondering, in the meanwhile, upon the possibility, without seeming very rude, of making her escape from Jane Fairfax's letter, and had almost resolved on hurrying away directly under some slight excuse, when Miss Bates turned to her again and seized her attention.

"My mother's deafness is very trifling you see—just nothing at all. By only raising my voice, and saying any thing two or three times over, she is sure to hear; but then she is used to my voice. But it is very remarkable that she should always hear Jane better than she does me. Jane speaks so distinct! However, she will not find her grandmama at all deafer than she was two years ago; which is saying a great deal at my mother's time of life—and it really is full two years, you know, since she was here. We never were so long without seeing her before, and as I was telling Mrs. Cole, we shall hardly know how to make enough of her now."

"Are you expecting Miss Fairfax here soon?"

"Oh yes; next week."

"Indeed!—that must be a very great pleasure."

"Thank you. You are very kind. Yes, next week. Every body is so surprized; and every body says the same obliging things. I am sure she will be as happy to see her friends at Highbury, as they can be to see her. Yes, Friday or Saturday; she cannot say which, because Colonel Campbell will be wanting the carriage himself one of those days. So very good of them to send her the whole way! But they always do, you know. Oh yes, Friday or Saturday next. That is what she writes about. That is the reason of her writing out of rule, as we call it; for, in the common course, we should not have heard from her before next Tuesday or Wednesday."

"Yes, so I imagined. I was afraid there could be little chance of my hearing any thing of Miss Fairfax to-day."

"So obliging of you! No, we should not have heard, if it had not been for this particular circumstance, of her being to come here so soon. My mother is so delighted!—for she is to be three months with us at least. Three months, she says so, positively, as I am going to have the pleasure of reading to you. The case is, you see, that the Campbells are going to Ireland. Mrs. Dixon has persuaded her father and mother to come over and see her directly. They had not intended to go over till the summer, but she is so impatient to see them again—for till she married, last October, she was never away from them so much as a week, which must make it very strange to be in different kingdoms, I was going to say, but however different countries, and so she wrote a very urgent letter to her mother—or her father, I declare I do not know which it was, but we shall see presently in Jane's letter—wrote in Mr. Dixon's name as well as her own, to press their coming over directly, and they would give them the meeting in Dublin, and take them back to their country seat, Baly-craig, a beautiful place, I fancy. Jane has heard a great deal of its beauty; from Mr. Dixon, I mean—I do not know that she ever heard about it from any body else; but it was very natural, you know, that he should like to speak of his own place while he was paying his addresses—and as Jane used to be very often walking out with them—for Colonel and Mrs. Campbell were very particular about their daughter's not walking out often with only Mr. Dixon, for which I do not at all blame them; of course she heard every thing he might be telling Miss Campbell about his own home in Ireland; and I think she wrote us word that he had shewn them some drawings of the place, views that he had taken himself. He is a most amiable, charming young man, I believe. Jane was quite longing to go to Ireland, from his account of things."

At this moment, an ingenious and animating suspicion entering Emma's brain with regard to Jane Fairfax, this charming Mr. Dixon, and the not going to Ireland, she said, with the insidious design of farther discovery,

"You must feel it very fortunate that Miss Fairfax should be allowed to come to you at such a time. Considering the very particular friendship between her and Mrs. Dixon, you could hardly have expected her to be excused from accompanying Colonel and Mrs. Campbell."

"Very true, very true, indeed. The very thing that we have always been rather afraid of; for we should not have liked to have her at such a distance from us, for months together—not able to come if any thing was to happen. But you see, every thing turns out for the best. They want her (Mr. and Mrs. Dixon) excessively to come over with Colonel and Mrs. Campbell; quite depend upon it; nothing can be more kind or pressing than their joint invitation, Jane says, as you will hear presently; Mr. Dixon does not seem in the least backward in any attention. He is a most charming young man. Ever since the service he rendered Jane at Weymouth, when they were out in that party on the water, and she, by the sudden whirling round of something or other among the sails, would have been dashed into the sea at once, and actually was all but gone, if he had not, with the greatest presence of mind, caught hold of her habit—(I can never think of it without trembling!)—But ever since we had the history of that day, I have been so fond of Mr. Dixon!"

"But, in spite of all her friends' urgency, and her own wish of seeing Ireland, Miss Fairfax prefers devoting the time to you and Mrs. Bates?"

"Yes—entirely her own doing, entirely her own choice; and Colonel and Mrs. Campbell think she does quite right, just what they should recommend; and indeed they particularly wish her to try her native air, as she has not been quite so well as usual lately."

"I am concerned to hear of it. I think they judge wisely. But Mrs. Dixon must be very much disappointed. Mrs. Dixon, I understand, has no remarkable degree of personal beauty; is not, by any means, to be compared with Miss Fairfax."

"Oh! no. You are very obliging to say such things—but certainly not. There is no comparison between them. Miss Campbell always was absolutely plain—but extremely elegant and amiable."

"Yes, that of course."

"Jane caught a bad cold, poor thing! so long ago as the 7th of November, (as I am going to read to you,) and has never been well since. A long time, is not it, for a cold to hang upon her? She never mentioned it before, because she would not alarm us. Just like her! so considerate!—But however, she is so far from well, that her kind friends the Campbells think she had better come home, and try an air that always agrees with her; and they have no doubt that three or four months at Highbury will entirely cure her—and it is certainly a great deal better that she should come here, than go to Ireland, if she is unwell. Nobody could nurse her, as we should do."

"It appears to me the most desirable arrangement in the world."

"And so she is to come to us next Friday or Saturday, and the Campbells leave town in their way to Holyhead the Monday following—as you will find from Jane's letter. So sudden!—You may guess, dear Miss Woodhouse, what a flurry it has thrown me in! If it was not for the drawback of her illness—but I am afraid we must expect to see her grown thin, and looking very poorly. I must tell you what an unlucky thing happened to me, as to that. I always make a point of reading Jane's letters through to myself first, before I read them aloud to my mother, you know, for fear of there being any thing in them to distress her. Jane desired me to do it, so I always do: and so I began to-day with my usual caution; but no sooner did I come to the mention of her being unwell, than I burst out, quite frightened, with 'Bless me! poor Jane is ill!'—which my mother, being on the watch, heard distinctly, and was sadly alarmed at. However, when I read on, I found it was not near so bad as I had fancied at first; and I make so light of it now to her, that she does not think much about it. But I cannot imagine how I could be so off my guard. If Jane does not get well soon, we will call in Mr. Perry. The expense shall not be thought of; and though he is so liberal, and so fond of Jane that I dare say he would not mean to charge any thing for attendance, we could not suffer it to be so, you know. He has a wife and family to maintain, and is not to be giving away his time. Well, now I have just given you a hint of what Jane writes about, we will turn to her letter, and I am sure she tells her own story a great deal better than I can tell it for her."

"I am afraid we must be running away," said Emma, glancing at Harriet, and beginning to rise—"My father will be expecting us. I had no intention, I thought I had no power of staying more than five minutes, when I first entered the house. I merely called, because I would not pass the door without inquiring after Mrs. Bates; but I have been so pleasantly detained! Now, however, we must wish you and Mrs. Bates good morning."

And not all that could be urged to detain her succeeded. She regained the street—happy in this, that though much had been forced on her against her will, though she had in fact heard the whole substance of Jane Fairfax's letter, she had been able to escape the letter itself.

Chapter II

Jane Fairfax was an orphan, the only child of Mrs. Bates's youngest daughter.

The marriage of Lieut. Fairfax of the——regiment of infantry, and Miss Jane Bates, had had its day of fame and pleasure, hope and interest; but nothing now remained of it, save the melancholy remembrance of him dying in action abroad—of his widow sinking under consumption and grief soon afterwards—and this girl.

By birth she belonged to Highbury: and when at three years old, on losing her mother, she became the property, the charge, the consolation, the fondling of her grandmother and aunt, there had seemed every probability of her being permanently fixed there; of her being taught only what very limited means could command, and growing up with no advantages of connexion or improvement, to be engrafted on what nature had given her in a pleasing person, good understanding, and warm-hearted, well-meaning relations.

But the compassionate feelings of a friend of her father gave a change to her destiny. This was Colonel Campbell, who had very highly regarded Fairfax, as an excellent officer and most deserving young man; and farther, had been indebted to him for such attentions, during a severe camp-fever, as he believed had saved his life. These were claims which he did not learn to overlook, though some years passed away from the death of poor Fairfax, before his own return to England put any thing in his power. When he did return, he sought out the child and took notice of her. He was a married man, with only one living child, a girl, about Jane's age: and Jane became their guest, paying them long visits and growing a favourite with all; and before she was nine years old, his daughter's great fondness for her, and his own wish of being a real friend, united to produce an offer from Colonel Campbell of undertaking the whole charge of her education. It was accepted; and from that period Jane had belonged to Colonel Campbell's family, and had lived with them entirely, only visiting her grandmother from time to time.

The plan was that she should be brought up for educating others; the very few hundred pounds which she inherited from her father making independence impossible. To provide for her otherwise was out of Colonel Campbell's power; for though his income, by pay and appointments, was handsome, his fortune was moderate and must be all his daughter's; but, by giving her an education, he hoped to be supplying the means of respectable subsistence hereafter.

Such was Jane Fairfax's history. She had fallen into good hands, known nothing but kindness from the Campbells, and been given an excellent education. Living constantly with right-minded and well-informed people, her heart and understanding had received every advantage of discipline and culture; and Colonel Campbell's residence being in London, every lighter talent had been done full justice to, by the attendance of first-rate masters. Her disposition and abilities were equally worthy of all that friendship could do; and at eighteen or nineteen she was, as far as such an early age can be qualified for the care of children, fully competent to the office of instruction herself; but she was too much beloved to be parted with. Neither father nor mother could promote, and the daughter could not endure it. The evil day was put off. It was easy to decide that she was still too young; and Jane remained with them, sharing, as another daughter, in all the rational pleasures of an elegant society, and a judicious mixture of home and amusement, with only the drawback of the future, the sobering suggestions of her own good understanding to remind her that all this might soon be over.

The affection of the whole family, the warm attachment of Miss Campbell in particular, was the more honourable to each party from the circumstance of Jane's decided superiority both in beauty and acquirements. That nature had given it in feature could not be unseen by the young woman, nor could her higher powers of mind be unfelt by the parents. They continued together with unabated regard however, till the marriage of Miss Campbell, who by that chance, that luck which so often defies anticipation in matrimonial affairs, giving attraction to what is moderate rather than to what is superior, engaged the affections of Mr. Dixon, a young man, rich and agreeable, almost as soon as they were acquainted; and was eligibly and happily settled, while Jane Fairfax had yet her bread to earn.

This event had very lately taken place; too lately for any thing to be yet attempted by her less fortunate friend towards entering on her path of duty; though she had now reached the age which her own judgment had fixed on for beginning. She had long resolved that one-and-twenty should be the period. With the fortitude of a devoted novitiate, she had resolved at one-and-twenty to complete the sacrifice, and retire from all the pleasures of life, of rational intercourse, equal society, peace and hope, to penance and mortification for ever.

The good sense of Colonel and Mrs. Campbell could not oppose such a resolution, though their feelings did. As long as they lived, no exertions would be necessary, their home might be hers for ever; and for their own comfort they would have retained her wholly; but this would be selfishness:—what must be at last, had better be soon. Perhaps they began to feel it might have been kinder and wiser to have resisted the temptation of any delay, and spared her from a taste of such enjoyments of ease and leisure as must now be relinquished. Still, however, affection was glad to catch at any reasonable excuse for not hurrying on the wretched moment. She had never been quite well since the time of their daughter's marriage; and till she should have completely recovered her usual strength, they must forbid her engaging in duties, which, so far from being compatible with a weakened frame and varying spirits, seemed, under the most favourable circumstances, to require something more than human perfection of body and mind to be discharged with tolerable comfort.

With regard to her not accompanying them to Ireland, her account to her aunt contained nothing but truth, though there might be some truths not told. It was her own choice to give the time of their absence to Highbury; to spend, perhaps, her last months of perfect liberty with those kind relations to whom she was so very dear: and the Campbells, whatever might be their motive or motives, whether single, or double, or treble, gave the arrangement their ready sanction, and said, that they depended more on a few months spent in her native air, for the recovery of her health, than on any thing else. Certain it was that she was to come; and that Highbury, instead of welcoming that perfect novelty which had been so long promised it—Mr. Frank Churchill—must put up for the present with Jane Fairfax, who could bring only the freshness of a two years' absence.

Emma was sorry;—to have to pay civilities to a person she did not like through three long months!—to be always doing more than she wished, and less than she ought! Why she did not like Jane Fairfax might be a difficult question to answer; Mr. Knightley had once told her it was because she saw in her the really accomplished young woman, which she wanted to be thought herself; and though the accusation had been eagerly refuted at the time, there were moments of self-examination in which her conscience could not quite acquit her. But "she could never get acquainted with her: she did not know how it was, but there was such coldness and reserve—such apparent indifference whether she pleased or not—and then, her aunt was such an eternal talker!—and she was made such a fuss with by every body!—and it had been always imagined that they were to be so intimate—because their ages were the same, every body had supposed they must be so fond of each other." These were her reasons—she had no better.

It was a dislike so little just—every imputed fault was so magnified by fancy, that she never saw Jane Fairfax the first time after any considerable absence, without feeling that she had injured her; and now, when the due visit was paid, on her arrival, after a two years' interval, she was particularly struck with the very appearance and manners, which for those two whole years she had been depreciating. Jane Fairfax was very elegant, remarkably elegant; and she had herself the highest value for elegance. Her height was pretty, just such as almost every body would think tall, and nobody could think very tall; her figure particularly graceful; her size a most becoming medium, between fat and thin, though a slight appearance of ill-health seemed to point out the likeliest evil of the two. Emma could not but feel all this; and then, her face—her features—there was more beauty in them altogether than she had remembered; it was not regular, but it was very pleasing beauty. Her eyes, a deep grey, with dark eye-lashes and eyebrows, had never been denied their praise; but the skin, which she had been used to cavil at, as wanting colour, had a clearness and delicacy which really needed no fuller bloom. It was a style of beauty, of which elegance was the reigning character, and as such, she must, in honour, by all her principles, admire it:—elegance, which, whether of person or of mind, she saw so little in Highbury. There, not to be vulgar, was distinction, and merit.

In short, she sat, during the first visit, looking at Jane Fairfax with twofold complacency; the sense of pleasure and the sense of rendering justice, and was determining that she would dislike her no longer. When she took in her history, indeed, her situation, as well as her beauty; when she considered what all this elegance was destined to, what she was going to sink from, how she was going to live, it seemed impossible to feel any thing but compassion and respect; especially, if to every well-known particular entitling her to interest, were added the highly probable circumstance of an attachment to Mr. Dixon, which she had so naturally started to herself. In that case, nothing could be more pitiable or more honourable than the sacrifices she had resolved on. Emma was very willing now to acquit her of having seduced Mr. Dixon's actions from his wife, or of any thing mischievous which her imagination had suggested at first. If it were love, it might be simple, single, successless love on her side alone. She might have been unconsciously sucking in the sad poison, while a sharer of his conversation with her friend; and from the best, the purest of motives, might now be denying herself this visit to Ireland, and resolving to divide herself effectually from him and his connexions by soon beginning her career of laborious duty.

Upon the whole, Emma left her with such softened, charitable feelings, as made her look around in walking home, and lament that

Highbury afforded no young man worthy of giving her independence; nobody that she could wish to scheme about for her.

These were charming feelings—but not lasting. Before she had committed herself by any public profession of eternal friendship for Jane Fairfax, or done more towards a recantation of past prejudices and errors, than saying to Mr. Knightley, "She certainly is handsome; she is better than handsome!" Jane had spent an evening at Hartfield with her grandmother and aunt, and every thing was relapsing much into its usual state. Former provocations reappeared. The aunt was as tiresome as ever; more tiresome, because anxiety for her health was now added to admiration of her powers; and they had to listen to the description of exactly how little bread and butter she ate for breakfast, and how small a slice of mutton for dinner, as well as to see exhibitions of new caps and new workbags for her mother and herself; and Jane's offences rose again. They had music; Emma was obliged to play; and the thanks and praise which necessarily followed appeared to her an affectation of candour, an air of greatness, meaning only to shew off in higher style her own very superior performance. She was, besides, which was the worst of all, so cold, so cautious! There was no getting at her real opinion. Wrapt up in a cloak of politeness, she seemed determined to hazard nothing. She was disgustingly, was suspiciously reserved.

If any thing could be more, where all was most, she was more reserved on the subject of Weymouth and the Dixons than any thing. She seemed bent on giving no real insight into Mr. Dixon's character, or her own value for his company, or opinion of the suitableness of the match. It was all general approbation and smoothness; nothing delineated or distinguished. It did her no service however. Her caution was thrown away. Emma saw its artifice, and returned to her first surmises. There probably was something more to conceal than her own preference; Mr. Dixon, perhaps, had been very near changing one friend for the other, or been fixed only to Miss Campbell, for the sake of the future twelve thousand pounds.

The like reserve prevailed on other topics. She and Mr. Frank Churchill had been at Weymouth at the same time. It was known that they were a little acquainted; but not a syllable of real information could Emma procure as to what he truly was. "Was he handsome?"—"She believed he was reckoned a very fine young man." "Was he agreeable?"—"He was generally thought so." "Did he appear a sensible young man; a young man of information?"—"At a watering-place, or in a common London acquaintance, it was difficult to decide on such points. Manners were all that could be safely judged of, under a much longer knowledge than they had yet had of Mr. Churchill. She believed every body found his manners pleasing." Emma could not forgive her.

Chapter III

Emma could not forgive her;—but as neither provocation nor resentment were discerned by Mr. Knightley, who had been of the party, and had seen only proper attention and pleasing behaviour on each side, he was expressing the next morning, being at Hartfield again on business with Mr. Woodhouse, his approbation of the whole; not so openly as he might have done had her father been out of the room, but speaking plain enough to be very intelligible to Emma. He had been used to think her unjust to Jane, and had now great pleasure in marking an improvement.

"A very pleasant evening," he began, as soon as Mr. Woodhouse had been talked into what was necessary, told that he understood, and the papers swept away;—"particularly pleasant. You and Miss Fairfax gave us some very good music. I do not know a more luxurious state, sir, than sitting at one's ease to be entertained a whole evening by two such young women; sometimes with music and sometimes with conversation. I am sure Miss Fairfax must have found the evening pleasant, Emma. You left nothing undone. I was glad you made her play so much, for having no instrument at her grandmother's, it must have been a real indulgence."

"I am happy you approved," said Emma, smiling; "but I hope I am not often deficient in what is due to guests at Hartfield."

"No, my dear," said her father instantly; "that I am sure you are not. There is nobody half so attentive and civil as you are. If any thing, you are too attentive. The muffin last night—if it had been handed round once, I think it would have been enough."

"No," said Mr. Knightley, nearly at the same time; "you are not often deficient; not often deficient either in manner or comprehension. I think you understand me, therefore."

An arch look expressed—"I understand you well enough;" but she said only, "Miss Fairfax is reserved."

"I always told you she was—a little; but you will soon overcome all that part of her reserve which ought to be overcome, all that has its foundation in diffidence. What arises from discretion must be honoured."

"You think her diffident. I do not see it."

"My dear Emma," said he, moving from his chair into one close by her, "you are not going to tell me, I hope, that you had not a pleasant evening."

"Oh! no; I was pleased with my own perseverance in asking questions; and amused to think how little information I obtained."

"I am disappointed," was his only answer.

"I hope every body had a pleasant evening," said Mr. Woodhouse, in his quiet way. "I had. Once, I felt the fire rather too much; but then I moved back my chair a little, a very little, and it did not disturb me. Miss Bates was very chatty and good-humoured, as she always is, though she speaks rather too quick. However, she is very agreeable, and Mrs. Bates too, in a different way. I like old friends; and Miss Jane Fairfax is a very pretty sort of young lady, a very pretty and a very well-behaved young lady indeed. She must have found the evening agreeable, Mr. Knightley, because she had Emma."

"True, sir; and Emma, because she had Miss Fairfax."

Emma saw his anxiety, and wishing to appease it, at least for the present, said, and with a sincerity which no one could question—

"She is a sort of elegant creature that one cannot keep one's eyes from. I am always watching her to admire; and I do pity her from my heart."

Mr. Knightley looked as if he were more gratified than he cared to express; and before he could make any reply, Mr. Woodhouse, whose thoughts were on the Bates's, said—

"It is a great pity that their circumstances should be so confined! a great pity indeed! and I have often wished—but it is so little one can venture to do—small, trifling presents, of any thing uncommon—Now we have killed a porker, and Emma thinks of sending them a loin or a leg; it is very small and delicate—Hartfield pork is not like any other pork—but still it is pork—and, my dear Emma, unless one could be sure of their making it into steaks, nicely fried, as ours are fried, without the smallest grease, and not roast it, for no stomach can bear roast pork—I think we had better send the leg—do not you think so, my dear?"

"My dear papa, I sent the whole hind-quarter. I knew you would wish it. There will be the leg to be salted, you know, which is so very nice, and the loin to be dressed directly in any manner they like."

"That's right, my dear, very right. I had not thought of it before, but that is the best way. They must not over-salt the leg; and then, if it is not over-salted, and if it is very thoroughly boiled, just as Serle boils ours, and eaten very moderately of, with a boiled turnip, and a little carrot or parsnip, I do not consider it unwholesome."

"Emma," said Mr. Knightley presently, "I have a piece of news for you. You like news—and I heard an article in my way hither that I think will interest you."

"News! Oh! yes, I always like news. What is it?—why do you smile so?—where did you hear it?—at Randalls?"

He had time only to say,

"No, not at Randalls; I have not been near Randalls," when the door was thrown open, and Miss Bates and Miss Fairfax walked into the room. Full of thanks, and full of news, Miss Bates knew not which to give quickest. Mr. Knightley soon saw that he had lost his moment, and that not another syllable of communication could rest with him.

"Oh! my dear sir, how are you this morning? My dear Miss Woodhouse—I come quite over-powered. Such a beautiful hind-quarter of pork! You are too bountiful! Have you heard the news? Mr. Elton is going to be married."

Emma had not had time even to think of Mr. Elton, and she was so completely surprized that she could not avoid a little start, and a little blush, at the sound.

"There is my news:—I thought it would interest you," said Mr. Knightley, with a smile which implied a conviction of some part of what had passed between them.

"But where could you hear it?" cried Miss Bates. "Where could you possibly hear it, Mr. Knightley? For it is not five minutes since I received Mrs. Cole's note—no, it cannot be more than five—or at least ten—for I had got my bonnet and spencer on, just ready to come out—I was only gone down to speak to Patty again about the pork—Jane was standing in the passage—were not you, Jane?—for my mother was so afraid that we had not any salting-pan large enough. So I said I would go down and see, and Jane said, 'Shall I go down instead? for I think you have a little cold, and Patty has been washing the kitchen.'—'Oh! my dear,' said I—well, and just then came the note. A Miss Hawkins—that's all I know. A Miss Hawkins of Bath. But, Mr. Knightley, how could you possibly have heard it? for the very moment Mr. Cole told Mrs. Cole of it, she sat down and wrote to me. A Miss Hawkins—"

"I was with Mr. Cole on business an hour and a half ago. He had just read Elton's letter as I was shewn in, and handed it to me directly."

"Well! that is quite—I suppose there never was a piece of news more generally interesting. My dear sir, you really are too bountiful. My mother desires her very best compliments and regards, and a thousand thanks, and says you really quite oppress her."

"We consider our Hartfield pork," replied Mr. Woodhouse—"indeed it certainly is, so very superior to all other pork, that Emma and I cannot have a greater pleasure than—-"

"Oh! my dear sir, as my mother says, our friends are only too good to us. If ever there were people who, without having great wealth themselves, had every thing they could wish for, I am sure it is us. We may well say that 'our lot is cast in a goodly heritage.' Well, Mr. Knightley, and so you actually saw the letter; well—"

"It was short—merely to announce—but cheerful, exulting, of course."—Here was a sly glance at Emma. "He had been so fortunate as to—I forget the precise words—one has no business to remember them. The information was, as you state, that he was going to be married to a Miss Hawkins. By his style, I should imagine it just settled."

"Mr. Elton going to be married!" said Emma, as soon as she could speak. "He will have every body's wishes for his happiness."

"He is very young to settle," was Mr. Woodhouse's observation. "He had better not be in a hurry. He seemed to me very well off as he was. We were always glad to see him at Hartfield."

"A new neighbour for us all, Miss Woodhouse!" said Miss Bates, joyfully; "my mother is so pleased!—she says she cannot bear to have the poor old Vicarage without a mistress. This is great news, indeed. Jane, you have never seen Mr. Elton!—no wonder that you have such a curiosity to see him."

Jane's curiosity did not appear of that absorbing nature as wholly to occupy her.

"No—I have never seen Mr. Elton," she replied, starting on this appeal; "is he—is he a tall man?"

"Who shall answer that question?" cried Emma. "My father would say 'yes,' Mr. Knightley 'no;' and Miss Bates and I that he is just the happy medium. When you have been here a little longer, Miss Fairfax, you will understand that Mr. Elton is the standard of perfection in Highbury, both in person and mind."

"Very true, Miss Woodhouse, so she will. He is the very best young man—But, my dear Jane, if you remember, I told you yesterday he was precisely the height of Mr. Perry. Miss Hawkins,—I dare say, an excellent young woman. His extreme attention to my mother—wanting her to sit in the vicarage pew, that she might hear the better, for my mother is a little deaf, you know—it is not much, but she does not hear quite quick. Jane says that Colonel Campbell is a little deaf. He fancied bathing might be good for it—the warm bath—but she says it did him no lasting benefit. Colonel Campbell, you know, is quite our angel. And Mr. Dixon seems a very charming young man, quite worthy of him. It is such a happiness when good people get together—and they always do. Now, here will be Mr. Elton and Miss Hawkins; and there are the Coles, such very good people; and the Perrys—I suppose there never was a happier or a better couple than Mr. and Mrs. Perry. I say, sir," turning to Mr. Woodhouse, "I think there are few places with such society as Highbury. I always say, we are quite blessed in our neighbours.—My dear sir, if there is one thing my mother loves better than another, it is pork—a roast loin of pork—"

"As to who, or what Miss Hawkins is, or how long he has been acquainted with her," said Emma, "nothing I suppose can be known. One feels that it cannot be a very long acquaintance. He has been gone only four weeks."

Nobody had any information to give; and, after a few more wonderings, Emma said,

"You are silent, Miss Fairfax—but I hope you mean to take an interest in this news. You, who have been hearing and seeing so much of late on these subjects, who must have been so deep in the business on Miss Campbell's account—we shall not excuse your being indifferent about Mr. Elton and Miss Hawkins."

"When I have seen Mr. Elton," replied Jane, " I dare say I shall be interested—but I believe it requires that with me. And as it is some months since Miss Campbell married, the impression may be a little worn off."

"Yes, he has been gone just four weeks, as you observe, Miss Woodhouse," said Miss Bates, "four weeks yesterday.—A Miss Hawkins!—Well, I had always rather fancied it would be some young lady hereabouts; not that I ever—Mrs. Cole once whispered to me—but I immediately said, 'No, Mr. Elton is a most worthy young man—but'—In short, I do not think I am particularly quick at those sort of discoveries. I do not pretend to it. What is before me, I see. At the same time, nobody could wonder if Mr. Elton should have aspired—Miss Woodhouse lets me chatter on, so good-humouredly. She knows I would not offend for the world. How does Miss Smith do? She seems quite recovered now. Have you heard from Mrs. John Knightley lately? Oh! those dear little children. Jane, do you know I always fancy Mr. Dixon like Mr. John Knightley. I mean in person—tall, and with that sort of look—and not very talkative."

"Quite wrong, my dear aunt; there is no likeness at all."

"Very odd! but one never does form a just idea of any body beforehand. One takes up a notion, and runs away with it. Mr. Dixon, you say, is not, strictly speaking, handsome?"

"Handsome! Oh! no—far from it—certainly plain. I told you he was plain."

"My dear, you said that Miss Campbell would not allow him to be plain, and that you yourself—"

"Oh! as for me, my judgment is worth nothing. Where I have a regard, I always think a person well-looking. But I gave what I believed the general opinion, when I called him plain."

"Well, my dear Jane, I believe we must be running away. The weather does not look well, and grandmama will be uneasy. You are too obliging, my dear Miss Woodhouse; but we really must take leave. This has been a most agreeable piece of news indeed. I shall just go round by Mrs. Cole's; but I shall not stop three minutes: and, Jane, you had better go home directly—I would not have you out in a shower!—We think she is the better for Highbury already. Thank you, we do indeed. I shall not attempt calling on Mrs. Goddard, for I really do not think she cares for any thing but boiled pork: when we dress the leg it will be another thing. Good morning to you, my dear sir. Oh! Mr. Knightley is coming too. Well, that is so very!—I am sure if Jane is tired, you will be so kind as to give her your arm.—Mr. Elton, and Miss Hawkins!—Good morning to you."

Emma, alone with her father, had half her attention wanted by him while he lamented that young people would be in such a hurry to marry—and to marry strangers too—and the other half she could give to her own view of the subject. It was to herself an amusing and a very welcome piece of news, as proving that Mr. Elton could not have suffered long; but she was sorry for Harriet: Harriet must feel it—and all that she could hope was, by giving the first information herself, to save her from hearing it abruptly from others. It was now about the time that she was likely to call. If she were to meet Miss Bates in her way!—and upon its beginning to rain, Emma was obliged to expect that the weather would be detaining her at Mrs. Goddard's, and that the intelligence would undoubtedly rush upon her without preparation.

The shower was heavy, but short; and it had not been over five minutes, when in came Harriet, with just the heated, agitated look which hurrying thither with a full heart was likely to give; and the "Oh! Miss Woodhouse, what do you think has happened!" which instantly burst forth, had all the evidence of corresponding perturbation. As the blow was given, Emma felt that she could not now shew greater kindness than in listening; and Harriet, unchecked, ran eagerly through what she had to tell. "She had set out from Mrs. Goddard's half an hour ago—she had been afraid it would rain—she had been afraid it would pour down every moment—but she thought she might get to Hartfield first—she had hurried on as fast as possible; but then, as she was passing by the house where a young woman was making up a gown for her, she thought she would just step in and see how it went on; and though she did not seem to stay half a moment there, soon after she came out it began to rain, and she did not know what to do; so she ran on directly, as fast as she could, and took shelter at Ford's."—Ford's was the principal woollen-draper, linen-draper, and haberdasher's shop united; the shop first in size and fashion in the place.—"And so, there she had set, without an idea of any thing in the world, full ten minutes, perhaps—when, all of a sudden, who should come in—to be sure it was so very odd!—but they always dealt at Ford's—who should come in, but Elizabeth Martin and her brother!—Dear Miss Woodhouse! only think. I thought I should have fainted. I did not know what to do. I was sitting near the door—Elizabeth saw me directly; but he did not; he was busy with the umbrella. I am sure she saw me, but she looked away directly, and took no notice; and they both went to quite the farther end of the shop; and I kept sitting near the door!—Oh! dear; I was so miserable! I am sure I must have been as white as my gown. I could not go away you know, because of the rain; but I did so wish myself anywhere in the world but there.—Oh! dear, Miss Woodhouse—well, at last, I fancy, he looked round and saw me; for instead of going on with her buyings, they began whispering to one another. I am sure they were talking of me; and I could not help thinking that he was persuading her to speak to me—(do you think he was, Miss Woodhouse?)—for presently she came forward—came quite up to me, and asked me how I did, and seemed ready to shake hands, if I would. She did not do any of it in the same way that she used; I could see she was altered; but, however, she seemed to try to be very friendly, and we shook hands, and stood talking some time; but I know no more what I said—I was in such a tremble!—I remember she said she was sorry we never met now; which I thought almost too kind! Dear, Miss Woodhouse, I was absolutely miserable! By that time, it was beginning to hold up, and I was determined that nothing should stop me from getting away—and then—only think!—I found he was coming up towards me too—slowly you know, and as if he did not quite know what to do; and so he came and spoke, and I answered—and I stood for a minute, feeling dreadfully, you know, one can't tell how; and then I took courage, and said it did not rain, and I must go; and so off I set; and I had not got three yards from the door, when he came after me, only to say, if I was going to Hartfield, he thought I had much better go round by Mr. Cole's stables, for I should find the near way quite floated by this rain. Oh! dear, I thought it would have been the death of me! So I said, I was very much obliged to him: you know I could not do less; and then he went back to Elizabeth, and I came round by the stables—I believe I did—but I hardly knew where I was, or any thing about it. Oh! Miss Woodhouse, I would rather done any thing than have it happen: and yet, you know, there was a sort of satisfaction in seeing him behave so pleasantly and so kindly. And Elizabeth, too. Oh! Miss Woodhouse, do talk to me and make me comfortable again."

Very sincerely did Emma wish to do so; but it was not immediately in her power. She was obliged to stop and think. She was not thoroughly comfortable herself. The young man's conduct, and his sister's, seemed the result of real feeling, and she could not but pity them. As Harriet described it, there had been an interesting mixture of wounded affection and genuine delicacy in their behaviour. But she had believed them to be well-meaning, worthy people before; and what difference did this make in the evils of the connexion? It was folly to be disturbed by it. Of course, he must be sorry to lose her—they must be all sorry. Ambition, as well as love, had probably been mortified. They might all have hoped to rise by Harriet's acquaintance: and besides, what was the value of Harriet's description?—So easily pleased—so little discerning;—what signified her praise?

She exerted herself, and did try to make her comfortable, by considering all that had passed as a mere trifle, and quite unworthy of being dwelt on,

"It might be distressing, for the moment," said she; "but you seem to have behaved extremely well; and it is over—and may never—can never, as a first meeting, occur again, and therefore you need not think about it."

Harriet said, "very true," and she "would not think about it;" but still she talked of it—still she could talk of nothing else; and Emma, at last, in order to put the Martins out of her head, was obliged to hurry on the news, which she had meant to give with so much tender caution; hardly knowing herself whether to rejoice or be angry, ashamed or only amused, at such a state of mind in poor Harriet—such a conclusion of Mr. Elton's importance with her!

Mr. Elton's rights, however, gradually revived. Though she did not feel the first intelligence as she might have done the day before, or an hour before, its interest soon increased; and before their first conversation was over, she had talked herself into all the sensations of curiosity, wonder and regret, pain and pleasure, as to this fortunate Miss Hawkins, which could conduce to place the Martins under proper subordination in her fancy.

Emma learned to be rather glad that there had been such a meeting. It had been serviceable in deadening the first shock, without retaining any influence to alarm. As Harriet now lived, the Martins could not get at her, without seeking her, where hitherto they had wanted either the courage or the condescension to seek her; for since her refusal of the brother, the sisters never had been at Mrs. Goddard's; and a twelvemonth might pass without their being thrown together again, with any necessity, or even any power of speech.

Chapter IV

Human nature is so well disposed towards those who are in interesting situations, that a young person, who either marries or dies, is sure of being kindly spoken of.

A week had not passed since Miss Hawkins's name was first mentioned in Highbury, before she was, by some means or other, discovered to have every recommendation of person and mind; to be handsome, elegant, highly accomplished, and perfectly amiable: and when Mr. Elton himself arrived to triumph in his happy prospects, and circulate the fame of her merits, there was very little more for him to do, than to tell her Christian name, and say whose music she principally played.

Mr. Elton returned, a very happy man. He had gone away rejected and mortified—disappointed in a very sanguine hope, after a series of what appeared to him strong encouragement; and not only losing the right lady, but finding himself debased to the level of a very wrong one. He had gone away deeply offended—he came back engaged to another—and to another as superior, of course, to the first, as under such circumstances what is gained always is to what is lost. He came back gay and self-satisfied, eager and busy, caring nothing for Miss Woodhouse, and defying Miss Smith.

The charming Augusta Hawkins, in addition to all the usual advantages of perfect beauty and merit, was in possession of an independent fortune, of so many thousands as would always be called ten; a point of some dignity, as well as some convenience: the story told well; he had not thrown himself away—he had gained a woman of 10,000 l. or thereabouts; and he had gained her with such delightful rapidity—the first hour of introduction had been so very soon followed by distinguishing notice; the history which he had to give Mrs. Cole of the rise and progress of the affair was so glorious—the steps so quick, from the accidental rencontre, to the dinner at Mr. Green's, and the party at Mrs. Brown's—smiles and blushes rising in importance—with consciousness and agitation richly scattered—the lady had been so easily impressed—so sweetly disposed—had in short, to use a most intelligible phrase, been so very ready to have him, that vanity and prudence were equally contented.

He had caught both substance and shadow—both fortune and affection, and was just the happy man he ought to be; talking only of himself and his own concerns—expecting to be congratulated—ready to be laughed at—and, with cordial, fearless smiles, now addressing all the young ladies of the place, to whom, a few weeks ago, he would have been more cautiously gallant.

The wedding was no distant event, as the parties had only themselves to please, and nothing but the necessary preparations to wait for; and when he set out for Bath again, there was a general expectation, which a certain glance of Mrs. Cole's did not seem to contradict, that when he next entered Highbury he would bring his bride.

During his present short stay, Emma had barely seen him; but just enough to feel that the first meeting was over, and to give her the impression of his not being improved by the mixture of pique and pretension, now spread over his air. She was, in fact, beginning very much to wonder that she had ever thought him pleasing at all; and his sight was so inseparably connected with some very disagreeable feelings, that, except in a moral light, as a penance, a lesson, a source of profitable humiliation to her own mind, she would have been thankful to be assured of never seeing him again. She wished him very well; but he gave her pain, and his welfare twenty miles off would administer most satisfaction.

The pain of his continued residence in Highbury, however, must certainly be lessened by his marriage. Many vain solicitudes would be prevented—many awkwardnesses smoothed by it. A Mrs. Elton would be an excuse for any change of intercourse; former intimacy might sink without remark. It would be almost beginning their life of civility again.

Of the lady, individually, Emma thought very little. She was good enough for Mr. Elton, no doubt; accomplished enough for Highbury—handsome enough—to look plain, probably, by Harriet's side. As to connexion, there Emma was perfectly easy; persuaded, that after all his own vaunted claims and disdain of Harriet, he had done nothing. On that article, truth seemed attainable. What she was, must be uncertain; but who she was, might be found out; and setting aside the 10,000 l., it did not appear that she was at all Harriet's superior. She brought no name, no blood, no alliance. Miss Hawkins was the youngest of the two daughters of a Bristol—merchant, of course, he must be called; but, as the whole of the profits of his mercantile life appeared so very moderate, it was not unfair to guess the dignity of his line of trade had been very moderate also. Part of every winter she had been used to spend in Bath; but Bristol was her home, the very heart of Bristol; for though the father and mother had died some years ago, an uncle remained—in the law line—nothing more distinctly honourable was hazarded of him, than that he was in the law line; and with him the daughter had lived. Emma guessed him to be the drudge of some attorney, and too stupid to rise. And all the grandeur of the connexion seemed dependent on the elder sister, who was very well married, to a gentleman in a great way, near Bristol, who kept two carriages! That was the wind-up of the history; that was the glory of Miss Hawkins.

Could she but have given Harriet her feelings about it all! She had talked her into love; but, alas! she was not so easily to be talked out of it. The charm of an object to occupy the many vacancies of Harriet's mind was not to be talked away. He might be superseded by another; he certainly would indeed; nothing could be clearer; even a Robert Martin would have been sufficient; but nothing else, she feared, would cure her. Harriet was one of those, who, having once begun, would be always in love. And now, poor girl! she was considerably worse from this reappearance of Mr. Elton. She was always having a glimpse of him somewhere or other. Emma saw him only once; but two or three times every day Harriet was sure just to meet with him, or just to miss him, just to hear his voice, or see his shoulder, just to have something occur to preserve him in her fancy, in all the favouring warmth of surprize and conjecture. She was, moreover, perpetually hearing about him; for, excepting when at Hartfield, she was always among those who saw no fault in Mr. Elton, and found nothing so interesting as the discussion of his concerns; and every report, therefore, every guess—all that had already occurred, all that might occur in the arrangement of his affairs, comprehending income, servants, and furniture, was continually in agitation around her. Her regard was receiving strength by invariable praise of him, and her regrets kept alive, and feelings irritated by ceaseless repetitions of Miss Hawkins's happiness, and continual observation of, how much he seemed attached!—his air as he walked by the house—the very sitting of his hat, being all in proof of how much he was in love!

Had it been allowable entertainment, had there been no pain to her friend, or reproach to herself, in the waverings of Harriet's mind, Emma would have been amused by its variations. Sometimes Mr. Elton predominated, sometimes the Martins; and each was occasionally useful as a check to the other. Mr. Elton's engagement had been the cure of the agitation of meeting Mr. Martin. The unhappiness produced by the knowledge of that engagement had been a little put aside by Elizabeth Martin's calling at Mrs. Goddard's a few days afterwards. Harriet had not been at home; but a note had been prepared and left for her, written in the very style to touch; a small mixture of reproach, with a great deal of kindness; and till Mr. Elton himself appeared, she had been much occupied by it, continually pondering over what could be done in return, and wishing to do more than she dared to confess. But Mr. Elton, in person, had driven away all such cares. While he staid, the Martins were forgotten; and on the very morning of his setting off for Bath again, Emma, to dissipate some of the distress it occasioned, judged it best for her to return Elizabeth Martin's visit.

How that visit was to be acknowledged—what would be necessary—and what might be safest, had been a point of some doubtful consideration. Absolute neglect of the mother and sisters, when invited to come, would be ingratitude. It must not be: and yet the danger of a renewal of the acquaintance!—

After much thinking, she could determine on nothing better, than Harriet's returning the visit; but in a way that, if they had understanding, should convince them that it was to be only a formal acquaintance. She meant to take her in the carriage, leave her at the Abbey Mill, while she drove a little farther, and call for her again so soon, as to allow no time for insidious applications or dangerous recurrences to the past, and give the most decided proof of what degree of intimacy was chosen for the future.

She could think of nothing better: and though there was something in it which her own heart could not approve—something of ingratitude, merely glossed over—it must be done, or what would become of Harriet?

Chapter V

Small heart had Harriet for visiting. Only half an hour before her friend called for her at Mrs. Goddard's, her evil stars had led her to the very spot where, at that moment, a trunk, directed to The Rev. Philip Elton, White-Hart, Bath, was to be seen under the operation of being lifted into the butcher's cart, which was to convey it to where the coaches past; and every thing in this world, excepting that trunk and the direction, was consequently a blank.

She went, however; and when they reached the farm, and she was to be put down, at the end of the broad, neat gravel walk, which led between espalier apple-trees to the front door, the sight of every thing which had given her so much pleasure the autumn before, was beginning to revive a little local agitation; and when they parted, Emma observed her to be looking around with a sort of fearful curiosity, which determined her not to allow the visit to exceed the proposed quarter of an hour. She went on herself, to give that portion of time to an old servant who was married, and settled in Donwell.

The quarter of an hour brought her punctually to the white gate again; and Miss Smith receiving her summons, was with her without delay, and unattended by any alarming young man. She came solitarily down the gravel walk—a Miss Martin just appearing at the door, and parting with her seemingly with ceremonious civility.

Harriet could not very soon give an intelligible account. She was feeling too much; but at last Emma collected from her enough to understand the sort of meeting, and the sort of pain it was creating. She had seen only Mrs. Martin and the two girls. They had received her doubtingly, if not coolly; and nothing beyond the merest commonplace had been talked almost all the time—till just at last, when Mrs. Martin's saying, all of a sudden, that she thought Miss Smith was grown, had brought on a more interesting subject, and a warmer manner. In that very room she had been measured last September, with her two friends. There were the pencilled marks and memorandums on the wainscot by the window. He had done it. They all seemed to remember the day, the hour, the party, the occasion—to feel the same consciousness, the same regrets—to be ready to return to the same good understanding; and they were just growing again like themselves, (Harriet, as Emma must suspect, as ready as the best of them to be cordial and happy,) when the carriage reappeared, and all was over. The style of the visit, and the shortness of it, were then felt to be decisive. Fourteen minutes to be given to those with whom she had thankfully passed six weeks not six months ago!—Emma could not but picture it all, and feel how justly they might resent, how naturally Harriet must suffer. It was a bad business. She would have given a great deal, or endured a great deal, to have had the Martins in a higher rank of life. They were so deserving, that a little higher should have been enough: but as it was, how could she have done otherwise?—Impossible!—She could not repent. They must be separated; but there was a great deal of pain in the process—so much to herself at this time, that she soon felt the necessity of a little consolation, and resolved on going home by way of Randalls to procure it. Her mind was quite sick of Mr. Elton and the Martins. The refreshment of Randalls was absolutely necessary.

It was a good scheme; but on driving to the door they heard that neither "master nor mistress was at home;" they had both been out some time; the man believed they were gone to Hartfield.

"This is too bad," cried Emma, as they turned away. "And now we shall just miss them; too provoking!—I do not know when I have been so disappointed." And she leaned back in the corner, to indulge her murmurs, or to reason them away; probably a little of both—such being the commonest process of a not ill-disposed mind. Presently the carriage stopt; she looked up; it was stopt by Mr. and Mrs. Weston, who were standing to speak to her. There was instant pleasure in the sight of them, and still greater pleasure was conveyed in sound—for Mr. Weston immediately accosted her with,

"How d'ye do?—how d'ye do?—We have been sitting with your father—glad to see him so well. Frank comes to-morrow—I had a letter this morning—we see him to-morrow by dinner-time to a certainty—he is at Oxford to-day, and he comes for a whole fortnight; I knew it would be so. If he had come at Christmas he could not have staid three days; I was always glad he did not come at Christmas; now we are going to have just the right weather for him, fine, dry, settled weather. We shall enjoy him completely; every thing has turned out exactly as we could wish."

There was no resisting such news, no possibility of avoiding the influence of such a happy face as Mr. Weston's, confirmed as it all was by the words and the countenance of his wife, fewer and quieter, but not less to the purpose. To know that she thought his coming certain was enough to make Emma consider it so, and sincerely did she rejoice in their joy. It was a most delightful reanimation of exhausted spirits. The worn-out past was sunk in the freshness of what was coming; and in the rapidity of half a moment's thought, she hoped Mr. Elton would now be talked of no more.

Mr. Weston gave her the history of the engagements at Enscombe, which allowed his son to answer for having an entire fortnight at his command, as well as the route and the method of his journey; and she listened, and smiled, and congratulated.

"I shall soon bring him over to Hartfield," said he, at the conclusion.

Emma could imagine she saw a touch of the arm at this speech, from his wife.

"We had better move on, Mr. Weston," said she, "we are detaining the girls."

"Well, well, I am ready;"—and turning again to Emma, "but you must not be expecting such a very fine young man; you have only had my account you know; I dare say he is really nothing extraordinary:"—though his own sparkling eyes at the moment were speaking a very different conviction.

Emma could look perfectly unconscious and innocent, and answer in a manner that appropriated nothing.

"Think of me to-morrow, my dear Emma, about four o'clock," was Mrs. Weston's parting injunction; spoken with some anxiety, and meant only for her.

"Four o'clock!—depend upon it he will be here by three," was Mr. Weston's quick amendment; and so ended a most satisfactory meeting. Emma's spirits were mounted quite up to happiness; every thing wore a different air; James and his horses seemed not half so sluggish as before. When she looked at the hedges, she thought the elder at least must soon be coming out; and when she turned round to Harriet, she saw something like a look of spring, a tender smile even there.

"Will Mr. Frank Churchill pass through Bath as well as Oxford?"—was a question, however, which did not augur much.

But neither geography nor tranquillity could come all at once, and Emma was now in a humour to resolve that they should both come in time.

The morning of the interesting day arrived, and Mrs. Weston's faithful pupil did not forget either at ten, or eleven, or twelve o'clock, that she was to think of her at four.

"My dear, dear anxious friend,"—said she, in mental soliloquy, while walking downstairs from her own room, "always overcareful for every body's comfort but your own; I see you now in all your little fidgets, going again and again into his room, to be sure that all is right." The clock struck twelve as she passed through the hall. "'Tis twelve; I shall not forget to think of you four hours hence; and by this time to-morrow, perhaps, or a little later, I may be thinking of the possibility of their all calling here. I am sure they will bring him soon."

She opened the parlour door, and saw two gentlemen sitting with her father—Mr. Weston and his son. They had been arrived only a few minutes, and Mr. Weston had scarcely finished his explanation of Frank's being a day before his time, and her father was yet in the midst of his very civil welcome and congratulations, when she appeared, to have her share of surprize, introduction, and pleasure.

The Frank Churchill so long talked of, so high in interest, was actually before her—he was presented to her, and she did not think too much had been said in his praise; he was a very good looking young man; height, air, address, all were unexceptionable, and his countenance had a great deal of the spirit and liveliness of his father's; he looked quick and sensible. She felt immediately that she should like him; and there was a well-bred ease of manner, and a readiness to talk, which convinced her that he came intending to be acquainted with her, and that acquainted they soon must be.

He had reached Randalls the evening before. She was pleased with the eagerness to arrive which had made him alter his plan, and travel earlier, later, and quicker, that he might gain half a day.

"I told you yesterday," cried Mr. Weston with exultation, "I told you all that he would be here before the time named. I remembered what I used to do myself. One cannot creep upon a journey; one cannot help getting on faster than one has planned; and the pleasure of coming in upon one's friends before the look-out begins, is worth a great deal more than any little exertion it needs."

"It is a great pleasure where one can indulge in it," said the young man, "though there are not many houses that I should presume on so far; but in coming home I felt I might do any thing."

The word home made his father look on him with fresh complacency. Emma was directly sure that he knew how to make himself agreeable; the conviction was strengthened by what followed. He was very much pleased with Randalls, thought it a most admirably arranged house, would hardly allow it even to be very small, admired the situation, the walk to Highbury, Highbury itself, Hartfield still more, and professed himself to have always felt the sort of interest in the country which none but one's own country gives, and the greatest curiosity to visit it. That he should never have been able to indulge so amiable a feeling before, passed suspiciously through Emma's brain; but still, if it were a falsehood, it was a pleasant one, and pleasantly handled. His manner had no air of study or exaggeration. He did really look and speak as if in a state of no common enjoyment.

Their subjects in general were such as belong to an opening acquaintance. On his side were the inquiries,—"Was she a horse-woman?—Pleasant rides?—Pleasant walks?—Had they a large neighbourhood?—Highbury, perhaps, afforded society enough?—There were several very pretty houses in and about it.—Balls—had they balls?—Was it a musical society?"

But when satisfied on all these points, and their acquaintance proportionably advanced, he contrived to find an opportunity, while their two fathers were engaged with each other, of introducing his mother-in-law, and speaking of her with so much handsome praise, so much warm admiration, so much gratitude for the happiness she secured to his father, and her very kind reception of himself, as was an additional proof of his knowing how to please—and of his certainly thinking it worth while to try to please her. He did not advance a word of praise beyond what she knew to be thoroughly deserved by Mrs. Weston; but, undoubtedly he could know very little of the matter. He understood what would be welcome; he could be sure of little else. "His father's marriage," he said, "had been the wisest measure, every friend must rejoice in it; and the family from whom he had received such a blessing must be ever considered as having conferred the highest obligation on him."

He got as near as he could to thanking her for Miss Taylor's merits, without seeming quite to forget that in the common course of things it was to be rather supposed that Miss Taylor had formed Miss Woodhouse's character, than Miss Woodhouse Miss Taylor's. And at last, as if resolved to qualify his opinion completely for travelling round to its object, he wound it all up with astonishment at the youth and beauty of her person.

"Elegant, agreeable manners, I was prepared for," said he; "but I confess that, considering every thing, I had not expected more than a very tolerably well-looking woman of a certain age; I did not know that I was to find a pretty young woman in Mrs. Weston."

"You cannot see too much perfection in Mrs. Weston for my feelings," said Emma; "were you to guess her to be eighteen, I should listen with pleasure; but she would be ready to quarrel with you for using such words. Don't let her imagine that you have spoken of her as a pretty young woman."

"I hope I should know better," he replied; "no, depend upon it, (with a gallant bow,) that in addressing Mrs. Weston I should understand whom I might praise without any danger of being thought extravagant in my terms."

Emma wondered whether the same suspicion of what might be expected from their knowing each other, which had taken strong possession of her mind, had ever crossed his; and whether his compliments were to be considered as marks of acquiescence, or proofs of defiance. She must see more of him to understand his ways; at present she only felt they were agreeable.

She had no doubt of what Mr. Weston was often thinking about. His quick eye she detected again and again glancing towards them with a happy expression; and even, when he might have determined not to look, she was confident that he was often listening.

Her own father's perfect exemption from any thought of the kind, the entire deficiency in him of all such sort of penetration or suspicion, was a most comfortable circumstance. Happily he was not farther from approving matrimony than from foreseeing it.—Though always objecting to every marriage that was arranged, he never suffered beforehand from the apprehension of any; it seemed as if he could not think so ill of any two persons' understanding as to suppose they meant to marry till it were proved against them. She blessed the favouring blindness. He could now, without the drawback of a single unpleasant surmise, without a glance forward at any possible treachery in his guest, give way to all his natural kind-hearted civility in solicitous inquiries after Mr. Frank Churchill's accommodation on his journey, through the sad evils of sleeping two nights on the road, and express very genuine unmixed anxiety to know that he had certainly escaped catching cold—which, however, he could not allow him to feel quite assured of himself till after another night.

A reasonable visit paid, Mr. Weston began to move.—"He must be going. He had business at the Crown about his hay, and a great many errands for Mrs. Weston at Ford's, but he need not hurry any body else." His son, too well bred to hear the hint, rose immediately also, saying,

"As you are going farther on business, sir, I will take the opportunity of paying a visit, which must be paid some day or other, and therefore may as well be paid now. I have the honour of being acquainted with a neighbour of yours, (turning to Emma,) a lady residing in or near Highbury; a family of the name of Fairfax. I shall have no difficulty, I suppose, in finding the house; though Fairfax, I believe, is not the proper name—I should rather say Barnes, or Bates. Do you know any family of that name?"

"To be sure we do," cried his father; "Mrs. Bates—we passed her house—I saw Miss Bates at the window. True, true, you are acquainted with Miss Fairfax; I remember you knew her at Weymouth, and a fine girl she is. Call upon her, by all means."

"There is no necessity for my calling this morning," said the young man; "another day would do as well; but there was that degree of acquaintance at Weymouth which—"

"Oh! go to-day, go to-day. Do not defer it. What is right to be done cannot be done too soon. And, besides, I must give you a hint, Frank; any want of attention to her here should be carefully avoided. You saw her with the Campbells, when she was the equal of every body she mixed with, but here she is with a poor old grandmother, who has barely enough to live on. If you do not call early it will be a slight."

The son looked convinced.

"I have heard her speak of the acquaintance," said Emma; "she is a very elegant young woman."

He agreed to it, but with so quiet a "Yes," as inclined her almost to doubt his real concurrence; and yet there must be a very distinct sort of elegance for the fashionable world, if Jane Fairfax could be thought only ordinarily gifted with it.

"If you were never particularly struck by her manners before," said she, "I think you will to-day. You will see her to advantage; see her and hear her—no, I am afraid you will not hear her at all, for she has an aunt who never holds her tongue."

"You are acquainted with Miss Jane Fairfax, sir, are you?" said Mr. Woodhouse, always the last to make his way in conversation; "then give me leave to assure you that you will find her a very agreeable young lady. She is staying here on a visit to her grandmama and aunt, very worthy people; I have known them all my life. They will be extremely glad to see you, I am sure; and one of my servants shall go with you to shew you the way."

"My dear sir, upon no account in the world; my father can direct me."

"But your father is not going so far; he is only going to the Crown, quite on the other side of the street, and there are a great many houses; you might be very much at a loss, and it is a very dirty walk, unless you keep on the footpath; but my coachman can tell you where you had best cross the street."

Mr. Frank Churchill still declined it, looking as serious as he could, and his father gave his hearty support by calling out, "My good friend, this is quite unnecessary; Frank knows a puddle of water when he sees it, and as to Mrs. Bates's, he may get there from the Crown in a hop, step, and jump."

They were permitted to go alone; and with a cordial nod from one, and a graceful bow from the other, the two gentlemen took leave. Emma remained very well pleased with this beginning of the acquaintance, and could now engage to think of them all at Randalls any hour of the day, with full confidence in their comfort.

Chapter VI

The next morning brought Mr. Frank Churchill again. He came with Mrs. Weston, to whom and to Highbury he seemed to take very cordially. He had been sitting with her, it appeared, most companionably at home, till her usual hour of exercise; and on being desired to chuse their walk, immediately fixed on Highbury.—"He did not doubt there being very pleasant walks in every direction, but if left to him, he should always chuse the same. Highbury, that airy, cheerful, happy-looking Highbury, would be his constant attraction."—Highbury, with Mrs. Weston, stood for Hartfield; and she trusted to its bearing the same construction with him. They walked thither directly.

Emma had hardly expected them: for Mr. Weston, who had called in for half a minute, in order to hear that his son was very handsome, knew nothing of their plans; and it was an agreeable surprize to her, therefore, to perceive them walking up to the house together, arm in arm. She was wanting to see him again, and especially to see him in company with Mrs. Weston, upon his behaviour to whom her opinion of him was to depend. If he were deficient there, nothing should make amends for it. But on seeing them together, she became perfectly satisfied. It was not merely in fine words or hyperbolical compliment that he paid his duty; nothing could be more proper or pleasing than his whole manner to her—nothing could more agreeably denote his wish of considering her as a friend and securing her affection. And there was time enough for Emma to form a reasonable judgment, as their visit included all the rest of the morning. They were all three walking about together for an hour or two—first round the shrubberies of Hartfield, and afterwards in Highbury. He was delighted with every thing; admired Hartfield sufficiently for Mr. Woodhouse's ear; and when their going farther was resolved on, confessed his wish to be made acquainted with the whole village, and found matter of commendation and interest much oftener than Emma could have supposed.

Some of the objects of his curiosity spoke very amiable feelings. He begged to be shewn the house which his father had lived in so long, and which had been the home of his father's father; and on recollecting that an old woman who had nursed him was still living, walked in quest of her cottage from one end of the street to the other; and though in some points of pursuit or observation there was no positive merit, they shewed, altogether, a good-will towards Highbury in general, which must be very like a merit to those he was with.

Emma watched and decided, that with such feelings as were now shewn, it could not be fairly supposed that he had been ever voluntarily absenting himself; that he had not been acting a part, or making a parade of insincere professions; and that Mr. Knightley certainly had not done him justice.

Their first pause was at the Crown Inn, an inconsiderable house, though the principal one of the sort, where a couple of pair of post-horses were kept, more for the convenience of the neighbourhood than from any run on the road; and his companions had not expected to be detained by any interest excited there; but in passing it they gave the history of the large room visibly added; it had been built many years ago for a ball-room, and while the neighbourhood had been in a particularly populous, dancing state, had been occasionally used as such;—but such brilliant days had long passed away, and now the highest purpose for which it was ever wanted was to accommodate a whist club established among the gentlemen and half-gentlemen of the place. He was immediately interested. Its character as a ball-room caught him; and instead of passing on, he stopt for several minutes at the two superior sashed windows which were open, to look in and contemplate its capabilities, and lament that its original purpose should have ceased. He saw no fault in the room, he would acknowledge none which they suggested. No, it was long enough, broad enough, handsome enough. It would hold the very number for comfort. They ought to have balls there at least every fortnight through the winter. Why had not Miss Woodhouse revived the former good old days of the room?—She who could do any thing in Highbury! The want of proper families in the place, and the conviction that none beyond the place and its immediate environs could be tempted to attend, were mentioned; but he was not satisfied. He could not be persuaded that so many good-looking houses as he saw around him, could not furnish numbers enough for such a meeting; and even when particulars were given and families described, he was still unwilling to admit that the inconvenience of such a mixture would be any thing, or that there would be the smallest difficulty in every body's returning into their proper place the next morning. He argued like a young man very much bent on dancing; and Emma was rather surprized to see the constitution of the Weston prevail so decidedly against the habits of the Churchills. He seemed to have all the life and spirit, cheerful feelings, and social inclinations of his father, and nothing of the pride or reserve of Enscombe. Of pride, indeed, there was, perhaps, scarcely enough; his indifference to a confusion of rank, bordered too much on inelegance of mind. He could be no judge, however, of the evil he was holding cheap. It was but an effusion of lively spirits.

At last he was persuaded to move on from the front of the Crown; and being now almost facing the house where the Bateses lodged, Emma recollected his intended visit the day before, and asked him if he had paid it.

"Yes, oh! yes"—he replied; "I was just going to mention it. A very successful visit:—I saw all the three ladies; and felt very much obliged to you for your preparatory hint. If the talking aunt had taken me quite by surprize, it must have been the death of me. As it was, I was only betrayed into paying a most unreasonable visit. Ten minutes would have been all that was necessary, perhaps all that was proper; and I had told my father I should certainly be at home before him—but there was no getting away, no pause; and, to my utter astonishment, I found, when he (finding me nowhere else) joined me there at last, that I had been actually sitting with them very nearly three-quarters of an hour. The good lady had not given me the possibility of escape before."

"And how did you think Miss Fairfax looking?"

"Ill, very ill—that is, if a young lady can ever be allowed to look ill. But the expression is hardly admissible, Mrs. Weston, is it? Ladies can never look ill. And, seriously, Miss Fairfax is naturally so pale, as almost always to give the appearance of ill health.—A most deplorable want of complexion."

Emma would not agree to this, and began a warm defence of Miss Fairfax's complexion. "It was certainly never brilliant, but she would not allow it to have a sickly hue in general; and there was a softness and delicacy in her skin which gave peculiar elegance to the character of her face." He listened with all due deference; acknowledged that he had heard many people say the same—but yet he must confess, that to him nothing could make amends for the want of the fine glow of health. Where features were indifferent, a fine complexion gave beauty to them all; and where they were good, the effect was—fortunately he need not attempt to describe what the effect was.

"Well," said Emma, "there is no disputing about taste.—At least you admire her except her complexion."

He shook his head and laughed.—"I cannot separate Miss Fairfax and her complexion."

"Did you see her often at Weymouth? Were you often in the same society?"

At this moment they were approaching Ford's, and he hastily exclaimed, "Ha! this must be the very shop that every body attends every day of their lives, as my father informs me. He comes to Highbury himself, he says, six days out of the seven, and has always business at Ford's. If it be not inconvenient to you, pray let us go in, that I may prove myself to belong to the place, to be a true citizen of Highbury. I must buy something at Ford's. It will be taking out my freedom.—I dare say they sell gloves."

"Oh! yes, gloves and every thing. I do admire your patriotism. You will be adored in Highbury. You were very popular before you came, because you were Mr. Weston's son—but lay out half a guinea at Ford's, and your popularity will stand upon your own virtues."

They went in; and while the sleek, well-tied parcels of "Men's Beavers" and "York Tan" were bringing down and displaying on the counter, he said—"But I beg your pardon, Miss Woodhouse, you were speaking to me, you were saying something at the very moment of this burst of my amor patriae. Do not let me lose it. I assure you the utmost stretch of public fame would not make me amends for the loss of any happiness in private life."

"I merely asked, whether you had known much of Miss Fairfax and her party at Weymouth."

"And now that I understand your question, I must pronounce it to be a very unfair one. It is always the lady's right to decide on the degree of acquaintance. Miss Fairfax must already have given her account.—I shall not commit myself by claiming more than she may chuse to allow."

"Upon my word! you answer as discreetly as she could do herself. But her account of every thing leaves so much to be guessed, she is so very reserved, so very unwilling to give the least information about any body, that I really think you may say what you like of your acquaintance with her."

"May I, indeed?—Then I will speak the truth, and nothing suits me so well. I met her frequently at Weymouth. I had known the Campbells a little in town; and at Weymouth we were very much in the same set. Colonel Campbell is a very agreeable man, and Mrs. Campbell a friendly, warm-hearted woman. I like them all."

"You know Miss Fairfax's situation in life, I conclude; what she is destined to be?"

"Yes—(rather hesitatingly)—I believe I do."

"You get upon delicate subjects, Emma," said Mrs. Weston smiling; "remember that I am here.—Mr. Frank Churchill hardly knows what to say when you speak of Miss Fairfax's situation in life. I will move a little farther off."

"I certainly do forget to think of her," said Emma, "as having ever been any thing but my friend and my dearest friend."

He looked as if he fully understood and honoured such a sentiment.

When the gloves were bought, and they had quitted the shop again, "Did you ever hear the young lady we were speaking of, play?" said Frank Churchill.

"Ever hear her!" repeated Emma. "You forget how much she belongs to Highbury. I have heard her every year of our lives since we both began. She plays charmingly."

"You think so, do you?—I wanted the opinion of some one who could really judge. She appeared to me to play well, that is, with considerable taste, but I know nothing of the matter myself.—I am excessively fond of music, but without the smallest skill or right of judging of any body's performance.—I have been used to hear her's admired; and I remember one proof of her being thought to play well:—a man, a very musical man, and in love with another woman—engaged to her—on the point of marriage—would yet never ask that other woman to sit down to the instrument, if the lady in question could sit down instead—never seemed to like to hear one if he could hear the other. That, I thought, in a man of known musical talent, was some proof."

"Proof indeed!" said Emma, highly amused.—"Mr. Dixon is very musical, is he? We shall know more about them all, in half an hour, from you, than Miss Fairfax would have vouchsafed in half a year."

"Yes, Mr. Dixon and Miss Campbell were the persons; and I thought it a very strong proof."

"Certainly—very strong it was; to own the truth, a great deal stronger than, if I had been Miss Campbell, would have been at all agreeable to me. I could not excuse a man's having more music than love—more ear than eye—a more acute sensibility to fine sounds than to my feelings. How did Miss Campbell appear to like it?"

"It was her very particular friend, you know."

"Poor comfort!" said Emma, laughing. "One would rather have a stranger preferred than one's very particular friend—with a stranger it might not recur again—but the misery of having a very particular friend always at hand, to do every thing better than one does oneself!—Poor Mrs. Dixon! Well, I am glad she is gone to settle in Ireland."

"You are right. It was not very flattering to Miss Campbell; but she really did not seem to feel it."

"So much the better—or so much the worse:—I do not know which. But be it sweetness or be it stupidity in her—quickness of friendship, or dulness of feeling—there was one person, I think, who must have felt it: Miss Fairfax herself. She must have felt the improper and dangerous distinction."

"As to that—I do not—"

"Oh! do not imagine that I expect an account of Miss Fairfax's sensations from you, or from any body else. They are known to no human being, I guess, but herself. But if she continued to play whenever she was asked by Mr. Dixon, one may guess what one chuses."

"There appeared such a perfectly good understanding among them all—" he began rather quickly, but checking himself, added, "however, it is impossible for me to say on what terms they really were—how it might all be behind the scenes. I can only say that there was smoothness outwardly. But you, who have known Miss Fairfax from a child, must be a better judge of her character, and of how she is likely to conduct herself in critical situations, than I can be."

"I have known her from a child, undoubtedly; we have been children and women together; and it is natural to suppose that we should be intimate,—that we should have taken to each other whenever she visited her friends. But we never did. I hardly know how it has happened; a little, perhaps, from that wickedness on my side which was prone to take disgust towards a girl so idolized and so cried up as she always was, by her aunt and grandmother, and all their set. And then, her reserve—I never could attach myself to any one so completely reserved."

"It is a most repulsive quality, indeed," said he. "Oftentimes very convenient, no doubt, but never pleasing. There is safety in reserve, but no attraction. One cannot love a reserved person."

"Not till the reserve ceases towards oneself; and then the attraction may be the greater. But I must be more in want of a friend, or an agreeable companion, than I have yet been, to take the trouble of conquering any body's reserve to procure one. Intimacy between

Miss Fairfax and me is quite out of the question. I have no reason to think ill of her—not the least—except that such extreme and perpetual cautiousness of word and manner, such a dread of giving a distinct idea about any body, is apt to suggest suspicions of there being something to conceal."

He perfectly agreed with her: and after walking together so long, and thinking so much alike, Emma felt herself so well acquainted with him, that she could hardly believe it to be only their second meeting. He was not exactly what she had expected; less of the man of the world in some of his notions, less of the spoiled child of fortune, therefore better than she had expected. His ideas seemed more moderate—his feelings warmer. She was particularly struck by his manner of considering Mr. Elton's house, which, as well as the church, he would go and look at, and would not join them in finding much fault with. No, he could not believe it a bad house; not such a house as a man was to be pitied for having. If it were to be shared with the woman he loved, he could not think any man to be pitied for having that house. There must be ample room in it for every real comfort. The man must be a blockhead who wanted more.

Mrs. Weston laughed, and said he did not know what he was talking about. Used only to a large house himself, and without ever thinking how many advantages and accommodations were attached to its size, he could be no judge of the privations inevitably belonging to a small one. But Emma, in her own mind, determined that he did know what he was talking about, and that he shewed a very amiable inclination to settle early in life, and to marry, from worthy motives. He might not be aware of the inroads on domestic peace to be occasioned by no housekeeper's room, or a bad butler's pantry, but no doubt he did perfectly feel that Enscombe could not make him happy, and that whenever he were attached, he would willingly give up much of wealth to be allowed an early establishment.

Chapter VII

Emma's very good opinion of Frank Churchill was a little shaken the following day, by hearing that he was gone off to London, merely to have his hair cut. A sudden freak seemed to have seized him at breakfast, and he had sent for a chaise and set off, intending to return to dinner, but with no more important view that appeared than having his hair cut. There was certainly no harm in his travelling sixteen miles twice over on such an errand; but there was an air of foppery and nonsense in it which she could not approve. It did not accord with the rationality of plan, the moderation in expense, or even the unselfish warmth of heart, which she had believed herself to discern in him yesterday. Vanity, extravagance, love of change, restlessness of temper, which must be doing something, good or bad; heedlessness as to the pleasure of his father and Mrs. Weston, indifferent as to how his conduct might appear in general; he became liable to all these charges. His father only called him a coxcomb, and thought it a very good story; but that Mrs. Weston did not like it, was clear enough, by her passing it over as quickly as possible, and making no other comment than that "all young people would have their little whims."

With the exception of this little blot, Emma found that his visit hitherto had given her friend only good ideas of him. Mrs. Weston was very ready to say how attentive and pleasant a companion he made himself—how much she saw to like in his disposition altogether. He appeared to have a very open temper—certainly a very cheerful and lively one; she could observe nothing wrong in his notions, a great deal decidedly right; he spoke of his uncle with warm regard, was fond of talking of him—said he would be the best man in the world if he were left to himself; and though there was no being attached to the aunt, he acknowledged her kindness with gratitude, and seemed to mean always to speak of her with respect. This was all very promising; and, but for such an unfortunate fancy for having his hair cut, there was nothing to denote him unworthy of the distinguished honour which her imagination had given him; the honour, if not of being really in love with her, of being at least very near it, and saved only by her own indifference—(for still her resolution held of never marrying)—the honour, in short, of being marked out for her by all their joint acquaintance.

Mr. Weston, on his side, added a virtue to the account which must have some weight. He gave her to understand that Frank admired her extremely—thought her very beautiful and very charming; and with so much to be said for him altogether, she found she must not judge him harshly. As Mrs. Weston observed, "all young people would have their little whims."

There was one person among his new acquaintance in Surry, not so leniently disposed. In general he was judged, throughout the parishes of Donwell and Highbury, with great candour; liberal allowances were made for the little excesses of such a handsome young man—one who smiled so often and bowed so well; but there was one spirit among them not to be softened, from its power of censure, by bows or smiles—Mr. Knightley. The circumstance was told him at Hartfield; for the moment, he was silent; but Emma heard him almost immediately afterwards say to himself, over a newspaper he held in his hand, "Hum! just the trifling, silly fellow I took him for." She had half a mind to resent; but an instant's observation convinced her that it was really said only to relieve his own feelings, and not meant to provoke; and therefore she let it pass.

Although in one instance the bearers of not good tidings, Mr. and Mrs. Weston's visit this morning was in another respect particularly opportune. Something occurred while they were at Hartfield, to make Emma want their advice; and, which was still more lucky, she wanted exactly the advice they gave.

This was the occurrence:—The Coles had been settled some years in Highbury, and were very good sort of people—friendly, liberal, and unpretending; but, on the other hand, they were of low origin, in trade, and only moderately genteel. On their first coming into the country, they had lived in proportion to their income, quietly, keeping little company, and that little unexpensively; but the last year or two had brought them a considerable increase of means—the house in town had yielded greater profits, and fortune in general had smiled on them. With their wealth, their views increased; their want of a larger house, their inclination for more company. They added to their house, to their number of servants, to their expenses of every sort; and by this time were, in fortune and style of living, second only to the family at Hartfield. Their love of society, and their new dining-room, prepared every body for their keeping dinner-company; and a few parties, chiefly among the single men, had already taken place. The regular and best families Emma could hardly suppose they would presume to invite—neither Donwell, nor Hartfield, nor Randalls. Nothing should tempt her to go, if they did; and she regretted that her father's known habits would be giving her refusal less meaning than she could wish. The Coles were very respectable in their way, but they ought to be taught that it was not for them to arrange the terms on which the superior families would visit them. This lesson, she very much feared, they would receive only from herself; she had little hope of Mr. Knightley, none of Mr. Weston.

But she had made up her mind how to meet this presumption so many weeks before it appeared, that when the insult came at last, it found her very differently affected. Donwell and Randalls had received their invitation, and none had come for her father and herself; and Mrs. Weston's accounting for it with "I suppose they will not take the liberty with you; they know you do not dine out," was not quite sufficient. She felt that she should like to have had the power of refusal; and afterwards, as the idea of the party to be assembled there, consisting precisely of those whose society was dearest to her, occurred again and again, she did not know that she might not have been tempted to accept. Harriet was to be there in the evening, and the Bateses. They had been speaking of it as they walked about Highbury the day before, and Frank Churchill had most earnestly lamented her absence. Might not the evening end in a dance? had been a question of his. The bare possibility of it acted as a farther irritation on her spirits; and her being left in solitary grandeur, even supposing the omission to be intended as a compliment, was but poor comfort.

It was the arrival of this very invitation while the Westons were at Hartfield, which made their presence so acceptable; for though her first remark, on reading it, was that "of course it must be declined," she so very soon proceeded to ask them what they advised her to do, that their advice for her going was most prompt and successful.

She owned that, considering every thing, she was not absolutely without inclination for the party. The Coles expressed themselves so properly—there was so much real attention in the manner of it—so much consideration for her father. "They would have solicited the honour earlier, but had been waiting the arrival of a folding-screen from London, which they hoped might keep Mr. Woodhouse from any draught of air, and therefore induce him the more readily to give them the honour of his company. "Upon the whole, she was very persuadable; and it being briefly settled among themselves how it might be done without neglecting his comfort—how certainly Mrs. Goddard, if not Mrs. Bates, might be depended on for bearing him company—Mr. Woodhouse was to be talked into an acquiescence of his daughter's going out to dinner on a day now near at hand, and spending the whole evening away from him. As for his going, Emma did not wish him to think it possible, the hours would be too late, and the party too numerous. He was soon pretty well resigned.

"I am not fond of dinner-visiting," said he—"I never was. No more is Emma. Late hours do not agree with us. I am sorry Mr. and Mrs. Cole should have done it. I think it would be much better if they would come in one afternoon next summer, and take their tea with us—take us in their afternoon walk; which they might do, as our hours are so reasonable, and yet get home without being out in the damp of the evening. The dews of a summer evening are what I would not expose any body to. However, as they are so very desirous to have dear Emma dine with them, and as you will both be there, and Mr. Knightley too, to take care of her, I cannot wish to prevent it, provided the weather be what it ought, neither damp, nor cold, nor windy." Then turning to Mrs. Weston, with a look of gentle reproach—"Ah! Miss Taylor, if you had not married, you would have staid at home with me."

"Well, sir," cried Mr. Weston, "as I took Miss Taylor away, it is incumbent on me to supply her place, if I can; and I will step to Mrs. Goddard in a moment, if you wish it."

But the idea of any thing to be done in a moment, was increasing, not lessening, Mr. Woodhouse's agitation. The ladies knew better how to allay it. Mr. Weston must be quiet, and every thing deliberately arranged.

With this treatment, Mr. Woodhouse was soon composed enough for talking as usual. "He should be happy to see Mrs. Goddard. He had a great regard for Mrs. Goddard; and Emma should write a line, and invite her. James could take the note. But first of all, there must be an answer written to Mrs. Cole."

"You will make my excuses, my dear, as civilly as possible. You will say that I am quite an invalid, and go no where, and therefore must decline their obliging invitation; beginning with my compliments, of course. But you will do every thing right. I need not tell you what is to be done. We must remember to let James know that the carriage will be wanted on Tuesday. I shall have no fears for you with him. We have never been there above once since the new approach was made; but still I have no doubt that James will take you very safely. And when you get there, you must tell him at what time you would have him come for you again; and you had better name an early hour. You will not like staying late. You will get very tired when tea is over."

"But you would not wish me to come away before I am tired, papa?"

"Oh! no, my love; but you will soon be tired. There will be a great many people talking at once. You will not like the noise."

"But, my dear sir," cried Mr. Weston, "if Emma comes away early, it will be breaking up the party."

"And no great harm if it does," said Mr. Woodhouse. "The sooner every party breaks up, the better."

"But you do not consider how it may appear to the Coles. Emma's going away directly after tea might be giving offence. They are good-natured people, and think little of their own claims; but still they must feel that any body's hurrying away is no great compliment; and Miss Woodhouse's doing it would be more thought of than any other person's in the room. You would not wish to disappoint and mortify the Coles, I am sure, sir; friendly, good sort of people as ever lived, and who have been your neighbours these ten years."

"No, upon no account in the world, Mr. Weston; I am much obliged to you for reminding me. I should be extremely sorry to be giving them any pain. I know what worthy people they are. Perry tells me that Mr. Cole never touches malt liquor. You would not think it to look at him, but he is bilious—Mr. Cole is very bilious. No, I would not be the means of giving them any pain. My dear Emma, we must consider this. I am sure, rather than run the risk of hurting Mr. and Mrs. Cole, you would stay a little longer than you might wish. You will not regard being tired. You will be perfectly safe, you know, among your friends."

"Oh yes, papa. I have no fears at all for myself; and I should have no scruples of staying as late as Mrs. Weston, but on your account. I am only afraid of your sitting up for me. I am not afraid of your not being exceedingly comfortable with Mrs. Goddard. She loves piquet, you know; but when she is gone home, I am afraid you will be sitting up by yourself, instead of going to bed at your usual time—and the idea of that would entirely destroy my comfort. You must promise me not to sit up."

He did, on the condition of some promises on her side: such as that, if she came home cold, she would be sure to warm herself thoroughly; if hungry, that she would take something to eat; that her own maid should sit up for her; and that Serle and the butler should see that every thing were safe in the house, as usual.

Chapter VIII

Frank Churchill came back again; and if he kept his father's dinner waiting, it was not known at Hartfield; for Mrs. Weston was too anxious for his being a favourite with Mr. Woodhouse, to betray any imperfection which could be concealed.

He came back, had had his hair cut, and laughed at himself with a very good grace, but without seeming really at all ashamed of what he had done. He had no reason to wish his hair longer, to conceal any confusion of face; no reason to wish the money unspent, to improve his spirits. He was quite as undaunted and as lively as ever; and, after seeing him, Emma thus moralised to herself:—

"I do not know whether it ought to be so, but certainly silly things do cease to be silly if they are done by sensible people in an impudent way. Wickedness is always wickedness, but folly is not always folly.—It depends upon the character of those who handle it. Mr. Knightley, he is not a trifling, silly young man. If he were, he would have done this differently. He would either have gloried in the achievement, or been ashamed of it. There would have been either the ostentation of a coxcomb, or the evasions of a mind too weak to defend its own vanities.—No, I am perfectly sure that he is not trifling or silly."

With Tuesday came the agreeable prospect of seeing him again, and for a longer time than hitherto; of judging of his general manners, and by inference, of the meaning of his manners towards herself; of guessing how soon it might be necessary for her to throw coldness into her air; and of fancying what the observations of all those might be, who were now seeing them together for the first time.

She meant to be very happy, in spite of the scene being laid at Mr. Cole's; and without being able to forget that among the failings of Mr. Elton, even in the days of his favour, none had disturbed her more than his propensity to dine with Mr. Cole.

Her father's comfort was amply secured, Mrs. Bates as well as Mrs. Goddard being able to come; and her last pleasing duty, before she left the house, was to pay her respects to them as they sat together after dinner; and while her father was fondly noticing the beauty of her dress, to make the two ladies all the amends in her power, by helping them to large slices of cake and full glasses of wine, for whatever unwilling self-denial his care of their constitution might have obliged them to practise during the meal.—She had provided a plentiful dinner for them; she wished she could know that they had been allowed to eat it.

She followed another carriage to Mr. Cole's door; and was pleased to see that it was Mr. Knightley's; for Mr. Knightley keeping no horses, having little spare money and a great deal of health, activity, and independence, was too apt, in Emma's opinion, to get about as he could, and not use his carriage so often as became the owner of Donwell Abbey. She had an opportunity now of speaking her approbation while warm from her heart, for he stopped to hand her out.

"This is coming as you should do," said she; "like a gentleman.—I am quite glad to see you."

He thanked her, observing, "How lucky that we should arrive at the same moment! for, if we had met first in the drawing-room, I doubt whether you would have discerned me to be more of a gentleman than usual.—You might not have distinguished how I came, by my look or manner."

"Yes I should, I am sure I should. There is always a look of consciousness or bustle when people come in a way which they know to be beneath them. You think you carry it off very well, I dare say, but with you it is a sort of bravado, an air of affected unconcern; I always observe it whenever I meet you under those circumstances. Now you have nothing to try for. You are not afraid of being supposed ashamed. You are not striving to look taller than any body else. Now I shall really be very happy to walk into the same room with you."

"Nonsensical girl!" was his reply, but not at all in anger.

Emma had as much reason to be satisfied with the rest of the party as with Mr. Knightley. She was received with a cordial respect which could not but please, and given all the consequence she could wish for. When the Westons arrived, the kindest looks of love, the strongest of admiration were for her, from both husband and wife; the son approached her with a cheerful eagerness which marked her as his peculiar object, and at dinner she found him seated by her—and, as she firmly believed, not without some dexterity on his side.

The party was rather large, as it included one other family, a proper unobjectionable country family, whom the Coles had the advantage of naming among their acquaintance, and the male part of Mr. Cox's family, the lawyer of Highbury. The less worthy females were to come in the evening, with Miss Bates, Miss Fairfax, and Miss Smith; but already, at dinner, they were too numerous for any subject of conversation to be general; and, while politics and Mr. Elton were talked over, Emma could fairly surrender all her attention to the pleasantness of her neighbour. The first remote sound to which she felt herself obliged to attend, was the name of Jane Fairfax. Mrs. Cole seemed to be relating something of her that was expected to be very interesting. She listened, and found it well worth listening to. That very dear part of Emma, her fancy, received an amusing supply. Mrs. Cole was telling that she had been calling on Miss Bates, and as soon as she entered the room had been struck by the sight of a pianoforte—a very elegant looking instrument—not a grand, but a large-sized square pianoforte; and the substance of the story, the end of all the dialogue which ensued of surprize, and inquiry, and congratulations on her side, and explanations on Miss Bates's, was, that this pianoforte had arrived from Broadwood's the day before, to the great astonishment of both aunt and niece—entirely unexpected; that at first, by Miss Bates's account, Jane herself was quite at a loss, quite bewildered to think who could possibly have ordered it—but now, they were both perfectly satisfied that it could be from only one quarter;—of course it must be from Colonel Campbell.

"One can suppose nothing else," added Mrs. Cole, "and I was only surprized that there could ever have been a doubt. But Jane, it seems, had a letter from them very lately, and not a word was said about it. She knows their ways best; but I should not consider their silence as any reason for their not meaning to make the present. They might chuse to surprize her."

Mrs. Cole had many to agree with her; every body who spoke on the subject was equally convinced that it must come from Colonel Campbell, and equally rejoiced that such a present had been made; and there were enough ready to speak to allow Emma to think her own way, and still listen to Mrs. Cole.

"I declare, I do not know when I have heard any thing that has given me more satisfaction!—It always has quite hurt me that Jane Fairfax, who plays so delightfully, should not have an instrument. It seemed quite a shame, especially considering how many houses there are where fine instruments are absolutely thrown away. This is like giving ourselves a slap, to be sure! and it was but yesterday I was telling Mr. Cole, I really was ashamed to look at our new grand pianoforte in the drawing-room, while I do not know one note from another, and our little girls, who are but just beginning, perhaps may never make any thing of it; and there is poor Jane Fairfax, who is mistress of music, has not any thing of the nature of an instrument, not even the pitifullest old spinet in the world, to amuse herself with.—I was saying this to Mr. Cole but yesterday, and he quite agreed with me; only he is so particularly fond of music that he could not help indulging himself in the purchase, hoping that some of our good neighbours might be so obliging occasionally to put it to a better use than we can; and that really is the reason why the instrument was bought—or else I am sure we ought to be ashamed of it.—We are in great hopes that Miss Woodhouse may be prevailed with to try it this evening."

Miss Woodhouse made the proper acquiescence; and finding that nothing more was to be entrapped from any communication of Mrs. Cole's, turned to Frank Churchill.

"Why do you smile?" said she.

"Nay, why do you?"

"Me!—I suppose I smile for pleasure at Colonel Campbell's being so rich and so liberal.—It is a handsome present."

"Very."

"I rather wonder that it was never made before."

"Perhaps Miss Fairfax has never been staying here so long before."

"Or that he did not give her the use of their own instrument—which must now be shut up in London, untouched by any body."

"That is a grand pianoforte, and he might think it too large for Mrs. Bates's house."

"You may say what you chuse—but your countenance testifies that your thoughts on this subject are very much like mine."

"I do not know. I rather believe you are giving me more credit for acuteness than I deserve. I smile because you smile, and shall probably suspect whatever I find you suspect; but at present I do not see what there is to question. If Colonel Campbell is not the person, who can be?"

"What do you say to Mrs. Dixon?"

"Mrs. Dixon! very true indeed. I had not thought of Mrs. Dixon. She must know as well as her father, how acceptable an instrument would be; and perhaps the mode of it, the mystery, the surprize, is more like a young woman's scheme than an elderly man's. It is Mrs. Dixon, I dare say. I told you that your suspicions would guide mine."

"If so, you must extend your suspicions and comprehend Mr. Dixon in them."

"Mr. Dixon.—Very well. Yes, I immediately perceive that it must be the joint present of Mr. and Mrs. Dixon. We were speaking the other day, you know, of his being so warm an admirer of her performance."

"Yes, and what you told me on that head, confirmed an idea which I had entertained before.—I do not mean to reflect upon the good intentions of either Mr. Dixon or Miss Fairfax, but I cannot help suspecting either that, after making his proposals to her friend, he had the misfortune to fall in love with her, or that he became conscious of a little attachment on her side. One might guess twenty things without guessing exactly the right; but I am sure there must be a particular cause for her chusing to come to Highbury instead of going with the Campbells to Ireland. Here, she must be leading a life of privation and penance; there it would have been all enjoyment. As to the pretence of trying her native air, I look upon that as a mere excuse.—In the summer it might have passed; but what can any body's native air do for them in the months of January, February, and March? Good fires and carriages would be much more to the purpose in most cases of delicate health, and I dare say in her's. I do not require you to adopt all my suspicions, though you make so noble a profession of doing it, but I honestly tell you what they are."

"And, upon my word, they have an air of great probability. Mr. Dixon's preference of her music to her friend's, I can answer for being very decided."

"And then, he saved her life. Did you ever hear of that?—A water party; and by some accident she was falling overboard. He caught her."

"He did. I was there—one of the party."

"Were you really?—Well!—But you observed nothing of course, for it seems to be a new idea to you.—If I had been there, I think I should have made some discoveries."

"I dare say you would; but I, simple I, saw nothing but the fact, that Miss Fairfax was nearly dashed from the vessel and that Mr. Dixon caught her.—It was the work of a moment. And though the consequent shock and alarm was very great and much more durable—indeed I believe it was half an hour before any of us were comfortable again—yet that was too general a sensation for any thing of peculiar anxiety to be observable. I do not mean to say, however, that you might not have made discoveries."

The conversation was here interrupted. They were called on to share in the awkwardness of a rather long interval between the courses, and obliged to be as formal and as orderly as the others; but when the table was again safely covered, when every corner dish was placed exactly right, and occupation and ease were generally restored, Emma said,

"The arrival of this pianoforte is decisive with me. I wanted to know a little more, and this tells me quite enough. Depend upon it, we shall soon hear that it is a present from Mr. and Mrs. Dixon."

"And if the Dixons should absolutely deny all knowledge of it we must conclude it to come from the Campbells."

"No, I am sure it is not from the Campbells. Miss Fairfax knows it is not from the Campbells, or they would have been guessed at first. She would not have been puzzled, had she dared fix on them. I may not have convinced you perhaps, but I am perfectly convinced myself that Mr. Dixon is a principal in the business."

"Indeed you injure me if you suppose me unconvinced. Your reasonings carry my judgment along with them entirely. At first, while I supposed you satisfied that Colonel Campbell was the giver, I saw it only as paternal kindness, and thought it the most natural thing in the world. But when you mentioned Mrs. Dixon, I felt how much more probable that it should be the tribute of warm female friendship. And now I can see it in no other light than as an offering of love."

There was no occasion to press the matter farther. The conviction seemed real; he looked as if he felt it. She said no more, other subjects took their turn; and the rest of the dinner passed away; the dessert succeeded, the children came in, and were talked to and admired amid the usual rate of conversation; a few clever things said, a few downright silly, but by much the larger proportion neither the one nor the other—nothing worse than everyday remarks, dull repetitions, old news, and heavy jokes.

The ladies had not been long in the drawing-room, before the other ladies, in their different divisions, arrived. Emma watched the entree of her own particular little friend; and if she could not exult in her dignity and grace, she could not only love the blooming sweetness and the artless manner, but could most heartily rejoice in that light, cheerful, unsentimental disposition which allowed her so many alleviations of pleasure, in the midst of the pangs of disappointed affection. There she sat—and who would have guessed how many tears she had been lately shedding? To be in company, nicely dressed herself and seeing others nicely dressed, to sit and smile and look pretty, and say nothing, was enough for the happiness of the present hour. Jane Fairfax did look and move superior; but Emma suspected she might have been glad to change feelings with Harriet, very glad to have purchased the mortification of having loved—yes, of having loved even Mr. Elton in vain—by the surrender of all the dangerous pleasure of knowing herself beloved by the husband of her friend.

In so large a party it was not necessary that Emma should approach her. She did not wish to speak of the pianoforte, she felt too much in the secret herself, to think the appearance of curiosity or interest fair, and therefore purposely kept at a distance; but by the others, the subject was almost immediately introduced, and she saw the blush of consciousness with which congratulations were received, the blush of guilt which accompanied the name of "my excellent friend Colonel Campbell."

Mrs. Weston, kind-hearted and musical, was particularly interested by the circumstance, and Emma could not help being amused at her perseverance in dwelling on the subject; and having so much to ask and to say as to tone, touch, and pedal, totally unsuspicious of that wish of saying as little about it as possible, which she plainly read in the fair heroine's countenance.

They were soon joined by some of the gentlemen; and the very first of the early was Frank Churchill. In he walked, the first and the handsomest; and after paying his compliments en passant to Miss Bates and her niece, made his way directly to the opposite side of the circle, where sat Miss Woodhouse; and till he could find a seat by her, would not sit at all. Emma divined what every body present must be thinking. She was his object, and every body must perceive it. She introduced him to her friend, Miss Smith, and, at convenient moments afterwards, heard what each thought of the other. "He had never seen so lovely a face, and was delighted with her naivete." And she, "Only to be sure it was paying him too great a compliment, but she did think there were some looks a little like Mr. Elton." Emma restrained her indignation, and only turned from her in silence.

Smiles of intelligence passed between her and the gentleman on first glancing towards Miss Fairfax; but it was most prudent to avoid speech. He told her that he had been impatient to leave the dining-room—hated sitting long—was always the first to move when he could—that his father, Mr. Knightley, Mr. Cox, and Mr. Cole, were left very busy over parish business—that as long as he had staid, however, it had been pleasant enough, as he had found them in general a set of gentlemanlike, sensible men; and spoke so handsomely of Highbury altogether—thought it so abundant in agreeable families—that Emma began to feel she had been used to despise the place rather too much. She questioned him as to the society in Yorkshire—the extent of the neighbourhood about Enscombe, and the sort; and could make out from his answers that, as far as Enscombe was concerned, there was very little going on, that their visitings were among a range of great families, none very near; and that even when days were fixed, and invitations accepted, it was an even chance that Mrs. Churchill were not in health and spirits for going; that they made a point of visiting no fresh person; and that, though he had his separate engagements, it was not without difficulty, without considerable address at times, that he could get away, or introduce an acquaintance for a night.

She saw that Enscombe could not satisfy, and that Highbury, taken at its best, might reasonably please a young man who had more retirement at home than he liked. His importance at Enscombe was very evident. He did not boast, but it naturally betrayed itself, that he had persuaded his aunt where his uncle could do nothing, and on her laughing and noticing it, he owned that he believed (excepting one or two points) he could with time persuade her to any thing. One of those points on which his influence failed, he then mentioned. He had wanted very much to go abroad—had been very eager indeed to be allowed to travel—but she would not hear of it. This had happened the year before. Now, he said, he was beginning to have no longer the same wish.

The unpersuadable point, which he did not mention, Emma guessed to be good behaviour to his father.

"I have made a most wretched discovery," said he, after a short pause.—"I have been here a week to-morrow—half my time. I never knew days fly so fast. A week to-morrow!—And I have hardly begun to enjoy myself. But just got acquainted with Mrs. Weston, and others!—I hate the recollection."

"Perhaps you may now begin to regret that you spent one whole day, out of so few, in having your hair cut."

"No," said he, smiling, "that is no subject of regret at all. I have no pleasure in seeing my friends, unless I can believe myself fit to be seen."

The rest of the gentlemen being now in the room, Emma found herself obliged to turn from him for a few minutes, and listen to Mr. Cole. When Mr. Cole had moved away, and her attention could be restored as before, she saw Frank Churchill looking intently across the room at Miss Fairfax, who was sitting exactly opposite.

"What is the matter?" said she.

He started. "Thank you for rousing me," he replied. "I believe I have been very rude; but really Miss Fairfax has done her hair in so odd a way—so very odd a way—that I cannot keep my eyes from her. I never saw any thing so outree!—Those curls!—This must be a fancy of her own. I see nobody else looking like her!—I must go and ask her whether it is an Irish fashion. Shall I?—Yes, I will—I declare I will—and you shall see how she takes it;—whether she colours."

He was gone immediately; and Emma soon saw him standing before Miss Fairfax, and talking to her; but as to its effect on the young lady, as he had improvidently placed himself exactly between them, exactly in front of Miss Fairfax, she could absolutely distinguish nothing.

Before he could return to his chair, it was taken by Mrs. Weston.

"This is the luxury of a large party," said she:—"one can get near every body, and say every thing. My dear Emma, I am longing to talk to you. I have been making discoveries and forming plans, just like yourself, and I must tell them while the idea is fresh. Do you know how Miss Bates and her niece came here?"

"How?—They were invited, were not they?"

"Oh! yes—but how they were conveyed hither?—the manner of their coming?"

"They walked, I conclude. How else could they come?"

"Very true.—Well, a little while ago it occurred to me how very sad it would be to have Jane Fairfax walking home again, late at night, and cold as the nights are now. And as I looked at her, though I never saw her appear to more advantage, it struck me that she was heated, and would therefore be particularly liable to take cold. Poor girl! I could not bear the idea of it; so, as soon as Mr. Weston came into the room, and I could get at him, I spoke to him about the carriage. You may guess how readily he came into my wishes; and having his approbation, I made my way directly to Miss Bates, to assure her that the carriage would be at her service before it took us home; for I thought it would be making her comfortable at once. Good soul! she was as grateful as possible, you may be sure. 'Nobody was ever so fortunate as herself!'—but with many, many thanks—'there was no occasion to trouble us, for Mr. Knightley's carriage had brought, and was to take them home again.' I was quite surprized;—very glad, I am sure; but really quite surprized. Such a very kind attention—and so thoughtful an attention!—the sort of thing that so few men would think of. And, in short, from knowing his usual ways, I am very much inclined to think that it was for their accommodation the carriage was used at all. I do suspect he would not have had a pair of horses for himself, and that it was only as an excuse for assisting them."

"Very likely," said Emma—"nothing more likely. I know no man more likely than Mr. Knightley to do the sort of thing—to do any thing really good-natured, useful, considerate, or benevolent. He is not a gallant man, but he is a very humane one; and this, considering Jane Fairfax's ill-health, would appear a case of humanity to him;—and for an act of unostentatious kindness, there is nobody whom I would fix on more than on Mr. Knightley. I know he had horses to-day—for we arrived together; and I laughed at him about it, but he said not a word that could betray."

"Well," said Mrs. Weston, smiling, "you give him credit for more simple, disinterested benevolence in this instance than I do; for while Miss Bates was speaking, a suspicion darted into my head, and I have never been able to get it out again. The more I think of it, the more probable it appears. In short, I have made a match between Mr. Knightley and Jane Fairfax. See the consequence of keeping you company!—What do you say to it?"

"Mr. Knightley and Jane Fairfax!" exclaimed Emma. "Dear Mrs. Weston, how could you think of such a thing?—Mr. Knightley!—Mr. Knightley must not marry!—You would not have little Henry cut out from Donwell?—Oh! no, no, Henry must have Donwell. I cannot at all consent to Mr. Knightley's marrying; and I am sure it is not at all likely. I am amazed that you should think of such a thing."

"My dear Emma, I have told you what led me to think of it. I do not want the match—I do not want to injure dear little Henry—but the idea has been given me by circumstances; and if Mr. Knightley really wished to marry, you would not have him refrain on Henry's account, a boy of six years old, who knows nothing of the matter?"

"Yes, I would. I could not bear to have Henry supplanted.—Mr. Knightley marry!—No, I have never had such an idea, and I cannot adopt it now. And Jane Fairfax, too, of all women!"

"Nay, she has always been a first favourite with him, as you very well know."

"But the imprudence of such a match!"

"I am not speaking of its prudence; merely its probability."

"I see no probability in it, unless you have any better foundation than what you mention. His good-nature, his humanity, as I tell you, would be quite enough to account for the horses. He has a great regard for the Bateses, you know, independent of Jane Fairfax—and is always glad to shew them attention. My dear Mrs. Weston, do not take to match-making. You do it very ill. Jane Fairfax mistress of the Abbey!—Oh! no, no;—every feeling revolts. For his own sake, I would not have him do so mad a thing."

"Imprudent, if you please—but not mad. Excepting inequality of fortune, and perhaps a little disparity of age, I can see nothing unsuitable."

"But Mr. Knightley does not want to marry. I am sure he has not the least idea of it. Do not put it into his head. Why should he marry?—He is as happy as possible by himself; with his farm, and his sheep, and his library, and all the parish to manage; and he is extremely fond of his brother's children. He has no occasion to marry, either to fill up his time or his heart."

"My dear Emma, as long as he thinks so, it is so; but if he really loves Jane Fairfax—"

"Nonsense! He does not care about Jane Fairfax. In the way of love, I am sure he does not. He would do any good to her, or her family; but—"

"Well," said Mrs. Weston, laughing, "perhaps the greatest good he could do them, would be to give Jane such a respectable home."

"If it would be good to her, I am sure it would be evil to himself; a very shameful and degrading connexion. How would he bear to have Miss Bates belonging to him?—To have her haunting the Abbey, and thanking him all day long for his great kindness in marrying Jane?—'So very kind and obliging!—But he always had been such a very kind neighbour!' And then fly off, through half a sentence, to her mother's old petticoat. 'Not that it was such a very old petticoat either—for still it would last a great while—and, indeed, she must thankfully say that their petticoats were all very strong.'"

"For shame, Emma! Do not mimic her. You divert me against my conscience. And, upon my word, I do not think Mr. Knightley would be much disturbed by Miss Bates. Little things do not irritate him. She might talk on; and if he wanted to say any thing himself, he would only talk louder, and drown her voice. But the question is not, whether it would be a bad connexion for him, but whether he wishes it; and I think he does. I have heard him speak, and so must you, so very highly of Jane Fairfax! The interest he takes in her—his anxiety about her health—his concern that she should have no happier prospect! I have heard him express himself so warmly on those points!—Such an admirer of her performance on the pianoforte, and of her voice! I have heard him say that he could listen to her for ever. Oh! and I had almost forgotten one idea that occurred to me—this pianoforte that has been sent here by somebody—though we have all been so well satisfied to consider it a present from the Campbells, may it not be from Mr. Knightley? I cannot help suspecting him. I think he is just the person to do it, even without being in love."

"Then it can be no argument to prove that he is in love. But I do not think it is at all a likely thing for him to do. Mr. Knightley does nothing mysteriously."

"I have heard him lamenting her having no instrument repeatedly; oftener than I should suppose such a circumstance would, in the common course of things, occur to him."

"Very well; and if he had intended to give her one, he would have told her so."

"There might be scruples of delicacy, my dear Emma. I have a very strong notion that it comes from him. I am sure he was particularly silent when Mrs. Cole told us of it at dinner."

"You take up an idea, Mrs. Weston, and run away with it; as you have many a time reproached me with doing. I see no sign of attachment—I believe nothing of the pianoforte—and proof only shall convince me that Mr. Knightley has any thought of marrying Jane Fairfax."

They combated the point some time longer in the same way; Emma rather gaining ground over the mind of her friend; for Mrs. Weston was the most used of the two to yield; till a little bustle in the room shewed them that tea was over, and the instrument in preparation;—and at the same moment Mr. Cole approaching to entreat Miss Woodhouse would do them the honour of trying it. Frank Churchill, of whom, in the eagerness of her conversation with Mrs. Weston, she had been seeing nothing, except that he had found a seat by Miss Fairfax, followed Mr. Cole, to add his very pressing entreaties; and as, in every respect, it suited Emma best to lead, she gave a very proper compliance.

She knew the limitations of her own powers too well to attempt more than she could perform with credit; she wanted neither taste nor spirit in the little things which are generally acceptable, and could accompany her own voice well. One accompaniment to her song took her agreeably by surprize—a second, slightly but correctly taken by Frank Churchill. Her pardon was duly begged at the close of the song, and every thing usual followed. He was accused of having a delightful voice, and a perfect knowledge of music; which was properly denied; and that he knew nothing of the matter, and had no voice at all, roundly asserted. They sang together once more; and Emma would then resign her place to Miss Fairfax, whose performance, both vocal and instrumental, she never could attempt to conceal from herself, was infinitely superior to her own.

With mixed feelings, she seated herself at a little distance from the numbers round the instrument, to listen. Frank Churchill sang again. They had sung together once or twice, it appeared, at Weymouth. But the sight of Mr. Knightley among the most attentive, soon drew away half Emma's mind; and she fell into a train of thinking on the subject of Mrs. Weston's suspicions, to which the sweet sounds of the united voices gave only momentary interruptions. Her objections to Mr. Knightley's marrying did not in the least subside. She could see nothing but evil in it. It would be a great disappointment to Mr. John Knightley; consequently to Isabella. A real injury to the children—a most mortifying change, and material loss to them all;—a very great deduction from her father's daily comfort—and, as to herself, she could not at all endure the idea of Jane Fairfax at Donwell Abbey. A Mrs. Knightley for them all to give way to!—No—Mr. Knightley must never marry. Little Henry must remain the heir of Donwell.

Presently Mr. Knightley looked back, and came and sat down by her. They talked at first only of the performance. His admiration was certainly very warm; yet she thought, but for Mrs. Weston, it would not have struck her. As a sort of touchstone, however, she began to speak of his kindness in conveying the aunt and niece; and though his answer was in the spirit of cutting the matter short, she believed it to indicate only his disinclination to dwell on any kindness of his own.

"I often feel concern," said she, "that I dare not make our carriage more useful on such occasions. It is not that I am without the wish; but you know how impossible my father would deem it that James should put-to for such a purpose."

"Quite out of the question, quite out of the question," he replied;—"but you must often wish it, I am sure." And he smiled with such seeming pleasure at the conviction, that she must proceed another step.

"This present from the Campbells," said she—"this pianoforte is very kindly given."

"Yes," he replied, and without the smallest apparent embarrassment.—"But they would have done better had they given her notice of it. Surprizes are foolish things. The pleasure is not enhanced, and the inconvenience is often considerable. I should have expected better judgment in Colonel Campbell."

From that moment, Emma could have taken her oath that Mr. Knightley had had no concern in giving the instrument. But whether he were entirely free from peculiar attachment—whether there were no actual preference—remained a little longer doubtful. Towards the end of Jane's second song, her voice grew thick.

"That will do," said he, when it was finished, thinking aloud—"you have sung quite enough for one evening—now be quiet."

Another song, however, was soon begged for. "One more;—they would not fatigue Miss Fairfax on any account, and would only ask for one more." And Frank Churchill was heard to say, "I think you could manage this without effort; the first part is so very trifling. The strength of the song falls on the second."

Mr. Knightley grew angry.

"That fellow," said he, indignantly, "thinks of nothing but shewing off his own voice. This must not be." And touching Miss Bates, who at that moment passed near—"Miss Bates, are you mad, to let your niece sing herself hoarse in this manner? Go, and interfere. They have no mercy on her."

Miss Bates, in her real anxiety for Jane, could hardly stay even to be grateful, before she stept forward and put an end to all farther singing. Here ceased the concert part of the evening, for Miss Woodhouse and Miss Fairfax were the only young lady performers; but soon (within five minutes) the proposal of dancing—originating nobody exactly knew where—was so effectually promoted by Mr. and Mrs. Cole, that every thing was rapidly clearing away, to give proper space. Mrs. Weston, capital in her country-dances, was seated, and beginning an irresistible waltz; and Frank Churchill, coming up with most becoming gallantry to Emma, had secured her hand, and led her up to the top.

While waiting till the other young people could pair themselves off, Emma found time, in spite of the compliments she was receiving on her voice and her taste, to look about, and see what became of Mr. Knightley. This would be a trial. He was no dancer in general. If he were to be very alert in engaging Jane Fairfax now, it might augur something. There was no immediate appearance. No; he was talking to Mrs. Cole—he was looking on unconcerned; Jane was asked by somebody else, and he was still talking to Mrs. Cole.

Emma had no longer an alarm for Henry; his interest was yet safe; and she led off the dance with genuine spirit and enjoyment. Not more than five couple could be mustered; but the rarity and the suddenness of it made it very delightful, and she found herself well matched in a partner. They were a couple worth looking at.

Two dances, unfortunately, were all that could be allowed. It was growing late, and Miss Bates became anxious to get home, on her mother's account. After some attempts, therefore, to be permitted to begin again, they were obliged to thank Mrs. Weston, look sorrowful, and have done.

"Perhaps it is as well," said Frank Churchill, as he attended Emma to her carriage. "I must have asked Miss Fairfax, and her languid dancing would not have agreed with me, after your's."

Chapter IX

Emma did not repent her condescension in going to the Coles. The visit afforded her many pleasant recollections the next day; and all that she might be supposed to have lost on the side of dignified seclusion, must be amply repaid in the splendour of popularity. She must have delighted the Coles—worthy people, who deserved to be made happy!—And left a name behind her that would not soon die away.

Perfect happiness, even in memory, is not common; and there were two points on which she was not quite easy. She doubted whether she had not transgressed the duty of woman by woman, in betraying her suspicions of Jane Fairfax's feelings to Frank Churchill. It was hardly right; but it had been so strong an idea, that it would escape her, and his submission to all that she told, was a compliment to her penetration, which made it difficult for her to be quite certain that she ought to have held her tongue.

The other circumstance of regret related also to Jane Fairfax; and there she had no doubt. She did unfeignedly and unequivocally regret the inferiority of her own playing and singing. She did most heartily grieve over the idleness of her childhood—and sat down and practised vigorously an hour and a half.

She was then interrupted by Harriet's coming in; and if Harriet's praise could have satisfied her, she might soon have been comforted.

"Oh! if I could but play as well as you and Miss Fairfax!"

"Don't class us together, Harriet. My playing is no more like her's, than a lamp is like sunshine."

"Oh! dear—I think you play the best of the two. I think you play quite as well as she does. I am sure I had much rather hear you. Every body last night said how well you played."

"Those who knew any thing about it, must have felt the difference. The truth is, Harriet, that my playing is just good enough to be praised, but Jane Fairfax's is much beyond it."

"Well, I always shall think that you play quite as well as she does, or that if there is any difference nobody would ever find it out. Mr. Cole said how much taste you had; and Mr. Frank Churchill talked a great deal about your taste, and that he valued taste much more than execution."

"Ah! but Jane Fairfax has them both, Harriet."

"Are you sure? I saw she had execution, but I did not know she had any taste. Nobody talked about it. And I hate Italian singing.—There is no understanding a word of it. Besides, if she does play so very well, you know, it is no more than she is obliged to do, because she will have to teach. The Coxes were wondering last night whether she would get into any great family. How did you think the Coxes looked?"

"Just as they always do—very vulgar."

"They told me something," said Harriet rather hesitatingly;" but it is nothing of any consequence."

Emma was obliged to ask what they had told her, though fearful of its producing Mr. Elton.

"They told me—-that Mr. Martin dined with them last Saturday."

"Oh!"

"He came to their father upon some business, and he asked him to stay to dinner."

"Oh!"

"They talked a great deal about him, especially Anne Cox. I do not know what she meant, but she asked me if I thought I should go and stay there again next summer."

"She meant to be impertinently curious, just as such an Anne Cox should be."

"She said he was very agreeable the day he dined there. He sat by her at dinner. Miss Nash thinks either of the Coxes would be very glad to marry him."

"Very likely.—I think they are, without exception, the most vulgar girls in Highbury."

Harriet had business at Ford's.—Emma thought it most prudent to go with her. Another accidental meeting with the Martins was possible, and in her present state, would be dangerous.

Harriet, tempted by every thing and swayed by half a word, was always very long at a purchase; and while she was still hanging over muslins and changing her mind, Emma went to the door for amusement.—Much could not be hoped from the traffic of even the busiest part of Highbury;—Mr. Perry walking hastily by, Mr. William Cox letting himself in at the office-door, Mr. Cole's carriage-horses returning from exercise, or a stray letter-boy on an obstinate mule, were the liveliest objects she could presume to expect; and when her eyes fell only on the butcher with his tray, a tidy old woman travelling homewards from shop with her full basket, two curs quarrelling over a dirty bone, and a string of dawdling children round the baker's little bow-window eyeing the gingerbread, she knew she had no reason to complain, and was amused enough; quite enough still to stand at the door. A mind lively and at ease, can do with seeing nothing, and can see nothing that does not answer.

She looked down the Randalls road. The scene enlarged; two persons appeared; Mrs. Weston and her son-in-law; they were walking into Highbury;—to Hartfield of course. They were stopping, however, in the first place at Mrs. Bates's; whose house was a little nearer Randalls than Ford's; and had all but knocked, when Emma caught their eye.—Immediately they crossed the road and came forward to her; and the agreeableness of yesterday's engagement seemed to give fresh pleasure to the present meeting. Mrs. Weston informed her that she was going to call on the Bateses, in order to hear the new instrument.

"For my companion tells me," said she, "that I absolutely promised Miss Bates last night, that I would come this morning. I was not aware of it myself. I did not know that I had fixed a day, but as he says I did, I am going now."

"And while Mrs. Weston pays her visit, I may be allowed, I hope," said Frank Churchill, "to join your party and wait for her at Hartfield—if you are going home."

Mrs. Weston was disappointed.

"I thought you meant to go with me. They would be very much pleased."

"Me! I should be quite in the way. But, perhaps—I may be equally in the way here. Miss Woodhouse looks as if she did not want me. My aunt always sends me off when she is shopping. She says I fidget her to death; and Miss Woodhouse looks as if she could almost say the same. What am I to do?"

"I am here on no business of my own," said Emma; "I am only waiting for my friend. She will probably have soon done, and then we shall go home. But you had better go with Mrs. Weston and hear the instrument."

"Well—if you advise it.—But (with a smile) if Colonel Campbell should have employed a careless friend, and if it should prove to have an indifferent tone—what shall I say? I shall be no support to Mrs. Weston. She might do very well by herself. A disagreeable truth would be palatable through her lips, but I am the wretchedest being in the world at a civil falsehood."

"I do not believe any such thing," replied Emma.—"I am persuaded that you can be as insincere as your neighbours, when it is necessary; but there is no reason to suppose the instrument is indifferent. Quite otherwise indeed, if I understood Miss Fairfax's opinion last night."

"Do come with me," said Mrs. Weston, "if it be not very disagreeable to you. It need not detain us long. We will go to Hartfield afterwards. We will follow them to Hartfield. I really wish you to call with me. It will be felt so great an attention! and I always thought you meant it."

He could say no more; and with the hope of Hartfield to reward him, returned with Mrs. Weston to Mrs. Bates's door. Emma watched them in, and then joined Harriet at the interesting counter,—trying, with all the force of her own mind, to convince her that if she wanted plain muslin it was of no use to look at figured; and that a blue ribbon, be it ever so beautiful, would still never match her yellow pattern. At last it was all settled, even to the destination of the parcel.

"Should I send it to Mrs. Goddard's, ma'am?" asked Mrs. Ford.—"Yes—no—yes, to Mrs. Goddard's. Only my pattern gown is at Hartfield. No, you shall send it to Hartfield, if you please. But then, Mrs. Goddard will want to see it.—And I could take the pattern gown home any day. But I shall want the ribbon directly—so it had better go to Hartfield—at least the ribbon. You could make it into two parcels, Mrs. Ford, could not you?"

"It is not worth while, Harriet, to give Mrs. Ford the trouble of two parcels."

"No more it is."

"No trouble in the world, ma'am," said the obliging Mrs. Ford.

"Oh! but indeed I would much rather have it only in one. Then, if you please, you shall send it all to Mrs. Goddard's—I do not know—No, I think, Miss Woodhouse, I may just as well have it sent to Hartfield, and take it home with me at night. What do you advise?"

"That you do not give another half-second to the subject. To Hartfield, if you please, Mrs. Ford."

"Aye, that will be much best," said Harriet, quite satisfied, "I should not at all like to have it sent to Mrs. Goddard's."

Voices approached the shop—or rather one voice and two ladies: Mrs. Weston and Miss Bates met them at the door.

"My dear Miss Woodhouse," said the latter, "I am just run across to entreat the favour of you to come and sit down with us a little while, and give us your opinion of our new instrument; you and Miss Smith. How do you do, Miss Smith?—Very well I thank you.—And I begged Mrs. Weston to come with me, that I might be sure of succeeding."

"I hope Mrs. Bates and Miss Fairfax are—"

"Very well, I am much obliged to you. My mother is delightfully well; and Jane caught no cold last night. How is Mr. Woodhouse?—I am so glad to hear such a good account. Mrs. Weston told me you were here.—Oh! then, said I, I must run across, I am sure Miss Woodhouse will allow me just to run across and entreat her to come in; my mother will be so very happy to see her—and now we are such a nice party, she cannot refuse.—'Aye, pray do,' said Mr. Frank Churchill, 'Miss Woodhouse's opinion of the instrument will be worth having.'—But, said I, I shall be more sure of succeeding if one of you will go with me.—'Oh,' said he, 'wait half a minute, till I have finished my job;'—For, would you believe it, Miss Woodhouse, there he is, in the most obliging manner in the world, fastening in the rivet of my mother's spectacles.—The rivet came out, you know, this morning.—So very obliging!—For my mother had no use of her spectacles—could not put them on. And, by the bye, every body ought to have two pair of spectacles; they should indeed. Jane said so. I meant to take them over to John Saunders the first thing I did, but something or other hindered me all the morning; first one thing, then another, there is no saying what, you know. At one time Patty came to say she thought the kitchen chimney wanted sweeping. Oh, said I, Patty do not come with your bad news to me. Here is the rivet of your mistress's spectacles out. Then the baked apples came home, Mrs. Wallis sent them by her boy; they are extremely civil and obliging to us, the Wallises, always—I have heard some people say that Mrs. Wallis can be uncivil and give a very rude answer, but we have never known any thing but the greatest attention from them. And it cannot be for the value of our custom now, for what is our consumption of bread, you know? Only three of us.—besides dear Jane at present—and she really eats nothing—

makes such a shocking breakfast, you would be quite frightened if you saw it. I dare not let my mother know how little she eats—so I say one thing and then I say another, and it passes off. But about the middle of the day she gets hungry, and there is nothing she likes so well as these baked apples, and they are extremely wholesome, for I took the opportunity the other day of asking Mr. Perry; I happened to meet him in the street. Not that I had any doubt before—I have so often heard Mr. Woodhouse recommend a baked apple. I believe it is the only way that Mr. Woodhouse thinks the fruit thoroughly wholesome. We have apple-dumplings, however, very often. Patty makes an excellent apple-dumpling. Well, Mrs. Weston, you have prevailed, I hope, and these ladies will oblige us."

Emma would be "very happy to wait on Mrs. Bates, &c.," and they did at last move out of the shop, with no farther delay from Miss Bates than,

"How do you do, Mrs. Ford? I beg your pardon. I did not see you before. I hear you have a charming collection of new ribbons from town. Jane came back delighted yesterday. Thank ye, the gloves do very well—only a little too large about the wrist; but Jane is taking them in."

"What was I talking of?" said she, beginning again when they were all in the street.

Emma wondered on what, of all the medley, she would fix.

"I declare I cannot recollect what I was talking of.—Oh! my mother's spectacles. So very obliging of Mr. Frank Churchill! 'Oh!' said he, 'I do think I can fasten the rivet; I like a job of this kind excessively.'—Which you know shewed him to be so very. . . . Indeed I must say that, much as I had heard of him before and much as I had expected, he very far exceeds any thing. . . . I do congratulate you, Mrs. Weston, most warmly. He seems every thing the fondest parent could. . . . 'Oh!' said he, 'I can fasten the rivet. I like a job of that sort excessively.' I never shall forget his manner. And when I brought out the baked apples from the closet, and hoped our friends would be so very obliging as to take some, 'Oh!' said he directly, 'there is nothing in the way of fruit half so good, and these are the finest-looking home-baked apples I ever saw in my life.' That, you know, was so very. . . . And I am sure, by his manner, it was no compliment. Indeed they are very delightful apples, and Mrs. Wallis does them full justice—only we do not have them baked more than twice, and Mr. Woodhouse made us promise to have them done three times—but Miss Woodhouse will be so good as not to mention it. The apples themselves are the very finest sort for baking, beyond a doubt; all from Donwell—some of Mr. Knightley's most liberal supply. He sends us a sack every year; and certainly there never was such a keeping apple anywhere as one of his trees—I believe there is two of them. My mother says the orchard was always famous in her younger days. But I was really quite shocked the other day—for Mr. Knightley called one morning, and Jane was eating these apples, and we talked about them and said how much she enjoyed them, and he asked whether we were not got to the end of our stock. 'I am sure you must be,' said he, 'and I will send you another supply; for I have a great many more than I can ever use. William Larkins let me keep a larger quantity than usual this year. I will send you some more, before they get good for nothing.' So I begged he would not—for really as to ours being gone, I could not absolutely say that we had a great many left—it was but half a dozen indeed; but they should be all kept for Jane; and I could not at all bear that he should be sending us more, so liberal as he had been already; and Jane said the same. And when he was gone, she almost quarrelled with me—No, I should not say quarrelled, for we never had a quarrel in our lives; but she was quite distressed that I had owned the apples were so nearly gone; she wished I had made him believe we had a great many left. Oh, said I, my dear, I did say as much as I could. However, the very same evening William Larkins came over with a large basket of apples, the same sort of apples, a bushel at least, and I was very much obliged, and went down and spoke to William Larkins and said every thing, as you may suppose. William Larkins is such an old acquaintance! I am always glad to see him. But, however, I found afterwards from Patty, that William said it was all the apples of that sort his master had; he had brought them all—and now his master had not one left to bake or boil. William did not seem to mind it himself, he was so pleased to think his master had sold so many; for William, you know, thinks more of his master's profit than any thing; but Mrs. Hodges, he said, was quite displeased at their being all sent away. She could not bear that her master should not be able to have another apple-tart this spring. He told Patty this, but bid her not mind it, and be sure not to say any thing to us about it, for Mrs. Hodges would be cross sometimes, and as long as so many sacks were sold, it did not signify who ate the remainder. And so Patty told me, and I was excessively shocked indeed! I would not have Mr. Knightley know any thing about it for the world! He would be so very. . . . I wanted to keep it from Jane's knowledge; but, unluckily, I had mentioned it before I was aware."

Miss Bates had just done as Patty opened the door; and her visitors walked upstairs without having any regular narration to attend to, pursued only by the sounds of her desultory good-will.

"Pray take care, Mrs. Weston, there is a step at the turning. Pray take care, Miss Woodhouse, ours is rather a dark staircase—rather darker and narrower than one could wish. Miss Smith, pray take care. Miss Woodhouse, I am quite concerned, I am sure you hit your foot. Miss Smith, the step at the turning."

Chapter X

The appearance of the little sitting-room as they entered, was tranquillity itself; Mrs. Bates, deprived of her usual employment, slumbering on one side of the fire, Frank Churchill, at a table near her, most deedily occupied about her spectacles, and Jane Fairfax, standing with her back to them, intent on her pianoforte.

Busy as he was, however, the young man was yet able to shew a most happy countenance on seeing Emma again.

"This is a pleasure," said he, in rather a low voice, "coming at least ten minutes earlier than I had calculated. You find me trying to be useful; tell me if you think I shall succeed."

"What!" said Mrs. Weston, "have not you finished it yet? you would not earn a very good livelihood as a working silversmith at this rate."

"I have not been working uninterruptedly," he replied, "I have been assisting Miss Fairfax in trying to make her instrument stand steadily, it was not quite firm; an unevenness in the floor, I believe. You see we have been wedging one leg with paper. This was very kind of you to be persuaded to come. I was almost afraid you would be hurrying home."

He contrived that she should be seated by him; and was sufficiently employed in looking out the best baked apple for her, and trying to make her help or advise him in his work, till Jane Fairfax was quite ready to sit down to the pianoforte again. That she was not immediately ready, Emma did suspect to arise from the state of her nerves; she had not yet possessed the instrument long enough to touch it without emotion; she must reason herself into the power of performance; and Emma could not but pity such feelings, whatever their origin, and could not but resolve never to expose them to her neighbour again.

At last Jane began, and though the first bars were feebly given, the powers of the instrument were gradually done full justice to. Mrs. Weston had been delighted before, and was delighted again; Emma joined her in all her praise; and the pianoforte, with every proper discrimination, was pronounced to be altogether of the highest promise.

"Whoever Colonel Campbell might employ," said Frank Churchill, with a smile at Emma, "the person has not chosen ill. I heard a good deal of Colonel Campbell's taste at Weymouth; and the softness of the upper notes I am sure is exactly what he and all that party would particularly prize. I dare say, Miss Fairfax, that he either gave his friend very minute directions, or wrote to Broadwood himself. Do not you think so?"

Jane did not look round. She was not obliged to hear. Mrs. Weston had been speaking to her at the same moment.

"It is not fair," said Emma, in a whisper; "mine was a random guess. Do not distress her."

He shook his head with a smile, and looked as if he had very little doubt and very little mercy. Soon afterwards he began again,

"How much your friends in Ireland must be enjoying your pleasure on this occasion, Miss Fairfax. I dare say they often think of you, and wonder which will be the day, the precise day of the instrument's coming to hand. Do you imagine Colonel Campbell knows the business to be going forward just at this time?—Do you imagine it to be the consequence of an immediate commission from him, or that he may have sent only a general direction, an order indefinite as to time, to depend upon contingencies and conveniences?"

He paused. She could not but hear; she could not avoid answering,

"Till I have a letter from Colonel Campbell," said she, in a voice of forced calmness, "I can imagine nothing with any confidence. It must be all conjecture."

"Conjecture—aye, sometimes one conjectures right, and sometimes one conjectures wrong. I wish I could conjecture how soon I shall make this rivet quite firm. What nonsense one talks, Miss Woodhouse, when hard at work, if one talks at all;—your real workmen, I suppose, hold their tongues; but we gentlemen labourers if we get hold of a word—Miss Fairfax said something about conjecturing. There, it is done. I have the pleasure, madam, (to Mrs. Bates,) of restoring your spectacles, healed for the present."

He was very warmly thanked both by mother and daughter; to escape a little from the latter, he went to the pianoforte, and begged Miss Fairfax, who was still sitting at it, to play something more.

"If you are very kind," said he, "it will be one of the waltzes we danced last night;—let me live them over again. You did not enjoy them as I did; you appeared tired the whole time. I believe you were glad we danced no longer; but I would have given worlds—all the worlds one ever has to give—for another half-hour."

She played.

"What felicity it is to hear a tune again which has made one happy!—If I mistake not that was danced at Weymouth."

She looked up at him for a moment, coloured deeply, and played something else. He took some music from a chair near the pianoforte, and turning to Emma, said,

"Here is something quite new to me. Do you know it?—Cramer.—And here are a new set of Irish melodies. That, from such a quarter, one might expect. This was all sent with the instrument. Very thoughtful of Colonel Campbell, was not it?—He knew Miss Fairfax could have no music here. I honour that part of the attention particularly; it shews it to have been so thoroughly from the heart. Nothing hastily done; nothing incomplete. True affection only could have prompted it."

Emma wished he would be less pointed, yet could not help being amused; and when on glancing her eye towards Jane Fairfax she caught the remains of a smile, when she saw that with all the deep blush of consciousness, there had been a smile of secret delight, she had less scruple in the amusement, and much less compunction with respect to her.—This amiable, upright, perfect Jane Fairfax was apparently cherishing very reprehensible feelings.

He brought all the music to her, and they looked it over together.—Emma took the opportunity of whispering,

"You speak too plain. She must understand you."

"I hope she does. I would have her understand me. I am not in the least ashamed of my meaning."

"But really, I am half ashamed, and wish I had never taken up the idea."

"I am very glad you did, and that you communicated it to me. I have now a key to all her odd looks and ways. Leave shame to her. If she does wrong, she ought to feel it."

"She is not entirely without it, I think."

"I do not see much sign of it. She is playing Robin Adair at this moment—his favourite."

Shortly afterwards Miss Bates, passing near the window, descried Mr. Knightley on horse-back not far off.

"Mr. Knightley I declare!—I must speak to him if possible, just to thank him. I will not open the window here; it would give you all cold; but I can go into my mother's room you know. I dare say he will come in when he knows who is here. Quite delightful to have you all meet so!—Our little room so honoured!"

She was in the adjoining chamber while she still spoke, and opening the casement there, immediately called Mr. Knightley's attention, and every syllable of their conversation was as distinctly heard by the others, as if it had passed within the same apartment.

"How d' ye do?—how d'ye do?—Very well, I thank you. So obliged to you for the carriage last night. We were just in time; my mother just ready for us. Pray come in; do come in. You will find some friends here."

So began Miss Bates; and Mr. Knightley seemed determined to be heard in his turn, for most resolutely and commandingly did he say,

"How is your niece, Miss Bates?—I want to inquire after you all, but particularly your niece. How is Miss Fairfax?—I hope she caught no cold last night. How is she to-day? Tell me how Miss Fairfax is."

And Miss Bates was obliged to give a direct answer before he would hear her in any thing else. The listeners were amused; and Mrs. Weston gave Emma a look of particular meaning. But Emma still shook her head in steady scepticism.

"So obliged to you!—so very much obliged to you for the carriage," resumed Miss Bates.

He cut her short with,

"I am going to Kingston. Can I do anything for you?"

"Oh! dear, Kingston—are you?—Mrs. Cole was saying the other day she wanted something from Kingston."

"Mrs. Cole has servants to send. Can I do any thing for you?"

"No, I thank you. But do come in. Who do you think is here?—Miss Woodhouse and Miss Smith; so kind as to call to hear the new pianoforte. Do put up your horse at the Crown, and come in."

"Well," said he, in a deliberating manner, "for five minutes, perhaps."

"And here is Mrs. Weston and Mr. Frank Churchill too!—Quite delightful; so many friends!"

"No, not now, I thank you. I could not stay two minutes. I must get on to Kingston as fast as I can."

"Oh! do come in. They will be so very happy to see you."

"No, no; your room is full enough. I will call another day, and hear the pianoforte."

"Well, I am so sorry!—Oh! Mr. Knightley, what a delightful party last night; how extremely pleasant.—Did you ever see such dancing?—Was not it delightful?—Miss Woodhouse and Mr. Frank Churchill; I never saw any thing equal to it."

"Oh! very delightful indeed; I can say nothing less, for I suppose Miss Woodhouse and Mr. Frank Churchill are hearing every thing that passes. And (raising his voice still more) I do not see why Miss Fairfax should not be mentioned too. I think Miss Fairfax dances very well; and Mrs. Weston is the very best country-dance player, without exception, in England. Now, if your friends have any gratitude, they will say something pretty loud about you and me in return; but I cannot stay to hear it."

"Oh! Mr. Knightley, one moment more; something of consequence—so shocked!—Jane and I are both so shocked about the apples!"

"What is the matter now?"

"To think of your sending us all your store apples. You said you had a great many, and now you have not one left. We really are so shocked! Mrs. Hodges may well be angry. William Larkins mentioned it here. You should not have done it, indeed you should not. Ah! he is off. He never can bear to be thanked. But I thought he would have staid now, and it would have been a pity not to have mentioned. . . . Well, (returning to the room,) I have not been able to succeed. Mr. Knightley cannot stop. He is going to Kingston. He asked me if he could do any thing. . . ."

"Yes," said Jane, "we heard his kind offers, we heard every thing."

"Oh! yes, my dear, I dare say you might, because you know, the door was open, and the window was open, and Mr. Knightley spoke loud. You must have heard every thing to be sure. 'Can I do any thing for you at Kingston?' said he; so I just mentioned. . . . Oh! Miss Woodhouse, must you be going?—You seem but just come—so very obliging of you."

Emma found it really time to be at home; the visit had already lasted long; and on examining watches, so much of the morning was perceived to be gone, that Mrs. Weston and her companion taking leave also, could allow themselves only to walk with the two young ladies to Hartfield gates, before they set off for Randalls.

Chapter XI

It may be possible to do without dancing entirely. Instances have been known of young people passing many, many months successively, without being at any ball of any description, and no material injury accrue either to body or mind;—but when a beginning is made—when the felicities of rapid motion have once been, though slightly, felt—it must be a very heavy set that does not ask for more.

Frank Churchill had danced once at Highbury, and longed to dance again; and the last half-hour of an evening which Mr. Woodhouse was persuaded to spend with his daughter at Randalls, was passed by the two young people in schemes on the subject. Frank's was the first idea; and his the greatest zeal in pursuing it; for the lady was the best judge of the difficulties, and the most solicitous for accommodation and appearance. But still she had inclination enough for shewing people again how delightfully Mr. Frank Churchill and Miss Woodhouse danced—for doing that in which she need not blush to compare herself with Jane Fairfax—and even for simple dancing itself, without any of the wicked aids of vanity—to assist him first in pacing out the room they were in to see what it could be made to hold—and then in taking the dimensions of the other parlour, in the hope of discovering, in spite of all that Mr. Weston could say of their exactly equal size, that it was a little the largest.

His first proposition and request, that the dance begun at Mr. Cole's should be finished there—that the same party should be collected, and the same musician engaged, met with the readiest acquiescence. Mr. Weston entered into the idea with thorough enjoyment, and Mrs. Weston most willingly undertook to play as long as they could wish to dance; and the interesting employment had followed, of reckoning up exactly who there would be, and portioning out the indispensable division of space to every couple.

"You and Miss Smith, and Miss Fairfax, will be three, and the two Miss Coxes five," had been repeated many times over. "And there will be the two Gilberts, young Cox, my father, and myself, besides Mr. Knightley. Yes, that will be quite enough for pleasure. You and Miss Smith, and Miss Fairfax, will be three, and the two Miss Coxes five; and for five couple there will be plenty of room."

But soon it came to be on one side,

"But will there be good room for five couple?—I really do not think there will."

On another,

"And after all, five couple are not enough to make it worth while to stand up. Five couple are nothing, when one thinks seriously about it. It will not do to invite five couple. It can be allowable only as the thought of the moment."

Somebody said that Miss Gilbert was expected at her brother's, and must be invited with the rest. Somebody else believed Mrs. Gilbert would have danced the other evening, if she had been asked. A word was put in for a second young Cox; and at last, Mr. Weston naming one family of cousins who must be included, and another of very old acquaintance who could not be left out, it became a certainty that the five couple would be at least ten, and a very interesting speculation in what possible manner they could be disposed of.

The doors of the two rooms were just opposite each other. "Might not they use both rooms, and dance across the passage?" It seemed the best scheme; and yet it was not so good but that many of them wanted a better. Emma said it would be awkward; Mrs. Weston was in distress about the supper; and Mr. Woodhouse opposed it earnestly, on the score of health. It made him so very unhappy, indeed, that it could not be persevered in.

"Oh! no," said he; "it would be the extreme of imprudence. I could not bear it for Emma!—Emma is not strong. She would catch a dreadful cold. So would poor little Harriet. So you would all. Mrs. Weston, you would be quite laid up; do not let them talk of such a wild thing. Pray do not let them talk of it. That young man (speaking lower) is very thoughtless. Do not tell his father, but that young man is not quite the thing. He has been opening the doors very often this evening, and keeping them open very inconsiderately. He does not think of the draught. I do not mean to set you against him, but indeed he is not quite the thing!"

Mrs. Weston was sorry for such a charge. She knew the importance of it, and said every thing in her power to do it away. Every door was now closed, the passage plan given up, and the first scheme of dancing only in the room they were in resorted to again; and with such good-will on Frank Churchill's part, that the space which a quarter of an hour before had been deemed barely sufficient for five couple, was now endeavoured to be made out quite enough for ten.

"We were too magnificent," said he. "We allowed unnecessary room. Ten couple may stand here very well."

Emma demurred. "It would be a crowd—a sad crowd; and what could be worse than dancing without space to turn in?"

"Very true," he gravely replied; "it was very bad." But still he went on measuring, and still he ended with,

"I think there will be very tolerable room for ten couple."

"No, no," said she, "you are quite unreasonable. It would be dreadful to be standing so close! Nothing can be farther from pleasure than to be dancing in a crowd—and a crowd in a little room!"

"There is no denying it," he replied. "I agree with you exactly. A crowd in a little room—Miss Woodhouse, you have the art of giving pictures in a few words. Exquisite, quite exquisite!—Still, however, having proceeded so far, one is unwilling to give the matter up. It would be a disappointment to my father—and altogether—I do not know that—I am rather of opinion that ten couple might stand here very well."

Emma perceived that the nature of his gallantry was a little self-willed, and that he would rather oppose than lose the pleasure of dancing with her; but she took the compliment, and forgave the rest. Had she intended ever to marry him, it might have been worth while to pause and consider, and try to understand the value of his preference, and the character of his temper; but for all the purposes of their acquaintance, he was quite amiable enough.

Before the middle of the next day, he was at Hartfield; and he entered the room with such an agreeable smile as certified the continuance of the scheme. It soon appeared that he came to announce an improvement.

"Well, Miss Woodhouse," he almost immediately began, "your inclination for dancing has not been quite frightened away, I hope, by the terrors of my father's little rooms. I bring a new proposal on the subject:—a thought of my father's, which waits only your approbation to be acted upon. May I hope for the honour of your hand for the two first dances of this little projected ball, to be given, not at Randalls, but at the Crown Inn?"

"The Crown!"

"Yes; if you and Mr. Woodhouse see no objection, and I trust you cannot, my father hopes his friends will be so kind as to visit him there. Better accommodations, he can promise them, and not a less grateful welcome than at Randalls. It is his own idea. Mrs. Weston sees no objection to it, provided you are satisfied. This is what we all feel. Oh! you were perfectly right! Ten couple, in either of the Randalls rooms, would have been insufferable!—Dreadful!—I felt how right you were the whole time, but was too anxious for securing any thing to like to yield. Is not it a good exchange?—You consent—I hope you consent?"

"It appears to me a plan that nobody can object to, if Mr. and Mrs. Weston do not. I think it admirable; and, as far as I can answer for myself, shall be most happy—It seems the only improvement that could be. Papa, do you not think it an excellent improvement?"

She was obliged to repeat and explain it, before it was fully comprehended; and then, being quite new, farther representations were necessary to make it acceptable.

"No; he thought it very far from an improvement—a very bad plan—much worse than the other. A room at an inn was always damp and dangerous; never properly aired, or fit to be inhabited. If they must dance, they had better dance at Randalls. He had never been in the room at the Crown in his life—did not know the people who kept it by sight.—Oh! no—a very bad plan. They would catch worse colds at the Crown than anywhere."

"I was going to observe, sir," said Frank Churchill, "that one of the great recommendations of this change would be the very little danger of any body's catching cold—so much less danger at the Crown than at Randalls! Mr. Perry might have reason to regret the alteration, but nobody else could."

"Sir," said Mr. Woodhouse, rather warmly, "you are very much mistaken if you suppose Mr. Perry to be that sort of character. Mr. Perry is extremely concerned when any of us are ill. But I do not understand how the room at the Crown can be safer for you than your father's house."

"From the very circumstance of its being larger, sir. We shall have no occasion to open the windows at all—not once the whole evening; and it is that dreadful habit of opening the windows, letting in cold air upon heated bodies, which (as you well know, sir) does the mischief."

"Open the windows!—but surely, Mr. Churchill, nobody would think of opening the windows at Randalls. Nobody could be so imprudent! I never heard of such a thing. Dancing with open windows!—I am sure, neither your father nor Mrs. Weston (poor Miss Taylor that was) would suffer it."

"Ah! sir—but a thoughtless young person will sometimes step behind a window-curtain, and throw up a sash, without its being suspected. I have often known it done myself."

"Have you indeed, sir?—Bless me! I never could have supposed it. But I live out of the world, and am often astonished at what I hear. However, this does make a difference; and, perhaps, when we come to talk it over—but these sort of things require a good deal of consideration. One cannot resolve upon them in a hurry. If Mr. and Mrs. Weston will be so obliging as to call here one morning, we may talk it over, and see what can be done."

"But, unfortunately, sir, my time is so limited—"

"Oh!" interrupted Emma, "there will be plenty of time for talking every thing over. There is no hurry at all. If it can be contrived to be at the Crown, papa, it will be very convenient for the horses. They will be so near their own stable."

"So they will, my dear. That is a great thing. Not that James ever complains; but it is right to spare our horses when we can. If I could be sure of the rooms being thoroughly aired—but is Mrs. Stokes to be trusted? I doubt it. I do not know her, even by sight."

"I can answer for every thing of that nature, sir, because it will be under Mrs. Weston's care. Mrs. Weston undertakes to direct the whole."

"There, papa!—Now you must be satisfied—Our own dear Mrs. Weston, who is carefulness itself. Do not you remember what Mr. Perry said, so many years ago, when I had the measles? 'If Miss Taylor undertakes to wrap Miss Emma up, you need not have any fears, sir.' How often have I heard you speak of it as such a compliment to her!"

"Aye, very true. Mr. Perry did say so. I shall never forget it. Poor little Emma! You were very bad with the measles; that is, you would have been very bad, but for Perry's great attention. He came four times a day for a week. He said, from the first, it was a very good sort—which was our great comfort; but the measles are a dreadful complaint. I hope whenever poor Isabella's little ones have the measles, she will send for Perry."

"My father and Mrs. Weston are at the Crown at this moment," said Frank Churchill, "examining the capabilities of the house. I left them there and came on to Hartfield, impatient for your opinion, and hoping you might be persuaded to join them and give your advice on the spot. I was desired to say so from both. It would be the greatest pleasure to them, if you could allow me to attend you there. They can do nothing satisfactorily without you."

Emma was most happy to be called to such a council; and her father, engaging to think it all over while she was gone, the two young people set off together without delay for the Crown. There were Mr. and Mrs. Weston; delighted to see her and receive her approbation, very busy and very happy in their different way; she, in some little distress; and he, finding every thing perfect.

"Emma," said she, "this paper is worse than I expected. Look! in places you see it is dreadfully dirty; and the wainscot is more yellow and forlorn than any thing I could have imagined."

"My dear, you are too particular," said her husband. "What does all that signify? You will see nothing of it by candlelight. It will be as clean as Randalls by candlelight. We never see any thing of it on our club-nights."

The ladies here probably exchanged looks which meant, "Men never know when things are dirty or not;" and the gentlemen perhaps thought each to himself, "Women will have their little nonsenses and needless cares."

One perplexity, however, arose, which the gentlemen did not disdain. It regarded a supper-room. At the time of the ballroom's being built, suppers had not been in question; and a small card-room adjoining, was the only addition. What was to be done? This card-room would be wanted as a card-room now; or, if cards were conveniently voted unnecessary by their four selves, still was it not too small for any comfortable supper? Another room of much better size might be secured for the purpose; but it was at the other end of the house, and a long awkward passage must be gone through to get at it. This made a difficulty. Mrs. Weston was afraid of draughts for the young people in that passage; and neither Emma nor the gentlemen could tolerate the prospect of being miserably crowded at supper.

Mrs. Weston proposed having no regular supper; merely sandwiches, &c., set out in the little room; but that was scouted as a wretched suggestion. A private dance, without sitting down to supper, was pronounced an infamous fraud upon the rights of men and women; and Mrs. Weston must not speak of it again. She then took another line of expediency, and looking into the doubtful room, observed,

"I do not think it is so very small. We shall not be many, you know."

And Mr. Weston at the same time, walking briskly with long steps through the passage, was calling out,

"You talk a great deal of the length of this passage, my dear. It is a mere nothing after all; and not the least draught from the stairs."

"I wish," said Mrs. Weston, "one could know which arrangement our guests in general would like best. To do what would be most generally pleasing must be our object—if one could but tell what that would be."

"Yes, very true," cried Frank, "very true. You want your neighbours' opinions. I do not wonder at you. If one could ascertain what the chief of them—the Coles, for instance. They are not far off. Shall I call upon them? Or Miss Bates? She is still nearer.—And I do not know whether Miss Bates is not as likely to understand the inclinations of the rest of the people as any body. I think we do want a larger council. Suppose I go and invite Miss Bates to join us?"

"Well—if you please," said Mrs. Weston rather hesitating, "if you think she will be of any use."

"You will get nothing to the purpose from Miss Bates," said Emma. "She will be all delight and gratitude, but she will tell you nothing. She will not even listen to your questions. I see no advantage in consulting Miss Bates."

"But she is so amusing, so extremely amusing! I am very fond of hearing Miss Bates talk. And I need not bring the whole family, you know."

Here Mr. Weston joined them, and on hearing what was proposed, gave it his decided approbation.

"Aye, do, Frank.—Go and fetch Miss Bates, and let us end the matter at once. She will enjoy the scheme, I am sure; and I do not know a properer person for shewing us how to do away difficulties. Fetch Miss Bates. We are growing a little too nice. She is a standing lesson of how to be happy. But fetch them both. Invite them both."

"Both sir! Can the old lady?" . . .

"The old lady! No, the young lady, to be sure. I shall think you a great blockhead, Frank, if you bring the aunt without the niece."

"Oh! I beg your pardon, sir. I did not immediately recollect. Undoubtedly if you wish it, I will endeavour to persuade them both." And away he ran.

Long before he reappeared, attending the short, neat, brisk-moving aunt, and her elegant niece,—Mrs. Weston, like a sweet-tempered woman and a good wife, had examined the passage again, and found the evils of it much less than she had supposed before—indeed very trifling; and here ended the difficulties of decision. All the rest, in speculation at least, was perfectly smooth. All the minor arrangements of table and chair, lights and music, tea and supper, made themselves; or were left as mere trifles to be settled at any time between Mrs. Weston and Mrs. Stokes.—Every body invited, was certainly to come; Frank had already written to Enscombe to propose staying a few days beyond his fortnight, which could not possibly be refused. And a delightful dance it was to be.

Most cordially, when Miss Bates arrived, did she agree that it must. As a counsellor she was not wanted; but as an approver, (a much safer character,) she was truly welcome. Her approbation, at once general and minute, warm and incessant, could not but please; and for another half-hour they were all walking to and fro, between the different rooms, some suggesting, some attending, and all in happy enjoyment of the future. The party did not break up without Emma's being positively secured for the two first dances by the hero of the evening, nor without her overhearing Mr. Weston whisper to his wife, "He has asked her, my dear. That's right. I knew he would!"

Chapter XII

One thing only was wanting to make the prospect of the ball completely satisfactory to Emma—its being fixed for a day within the granted term of Frank Churchill's stay in Surry; for, in spite of Mr. Weston's confidence, she could not think it so very impossible that the Churchills might not allow their nephew to remain a day beyond his fortnight. But this was not judged feasible. The preparations must take their time, nothing could be properly ready till the third week were entered on, and for a few days they must be planning, proceeding and hoping in uncertainty—at the risk—in her opinion, the great risk, of its being all in vain.

Enscombe however was gracious, gracious in fact, if not in word. His wish of staying longer evidently did not please; but it was not opposed. All was safe and prosperous; and as the removal of one solicitude generally makes way for another, Emma, being now certain of her ball, began to adopt as the next vexation Mr. Knightley's provoking indifference about it. Either because he did not dance himself, or because the plan had been formed without his being consulted, he seemed resolved that it should not interest him, determined against its exciting any present curiosity, or affording him any future amusement. To her voluntary communications Emma could get no more approving reply, than,

"Very well. If the Westons think it worth while to be at all this trouble for a few hours of noisy entertainment, I have nothing to say against it, but that they shall not chuse pleasures for me.—Oh! yes, I must be there; I could not refuse; and I will keep as much awake as I can; but I would rather be at home, looking over William Larkins's week's account; much rather, I confess.—Pleasure in seeing dancing!—not I, indeed—I never look at it—I do not know who does.—Fine dancing, I believe, like virtue, must be its own reward. Those who are standing by are usually thinking of something very different."

This Emma felt was aimed at her; and it made her quite angry. It was not in compliment to Jane Fairfax however that he was so indifferent, or so indignant; he was not guided by her feelings in reprobating the ball, for she enjoyed the thought of it to an extraordinary degree. It made her animated—open hearted—she voluntarily said;—

"Oh! Miss Woodhouse, I hope nothing may happen to prevent the ball. What a disappointment it would be! I do look forward to it, I own, with very great pleasure."

It was not to oblige Jane Fairfax therefore that he would have preferred the society of William Larkins. No!—she was more and more convinced that Mrs. Weston was quite mistaken in that surmise. There was a great deal of friendly and of compassionate attachment on his side—but no love.

Alas! there was soon no leisure for quarrelling with Mr. Knightley. Two days of joyful security were immediately followed by the over-throw of every thing. A letter arrived from Mr. Churchill to urge his nephew's instant return. Mrs. Churchill was unwell—far too unwell to do without him; she had been in a very suffering state (so said her husband) when writing to her nephew two days before, though from her usual unwillingness to give pain, and constant habit of never thinking of herself, she had not mentioned it; but now she was too ill to trifle, and must entreat him to set off for Enscombe without delay.

The substance of this letter was forwarded to Emma, in a note from Mrs. Weston, instantly. As to his going, it was inevitable. He must be gone within a few hours, though without feeling any real alarm for his aunt, to lessen his repugnance. He knew her illnesses; they never occurred but for her own convenience.

Mrs. Weston added, "that he could only allow himself time to hurry to Highbury, after breakfast, and take leave of the few friends there whom he could suppose to feel any interest in him; and that he might be expected at Hartfield very soon."

This wretched note was the finale of Emma's breakfast. When once it had been read, there was no doing any thing, but lament and exclaim. The loss of the ball—the loss of the young man—and all that the young man might be feeling!—It was too wretched!—Such a delightful evening as it would have been!—Every body so happy! and she and her partner the happiest!—"I said it would be so," was the only consolation.

Her father's feelings were quite distinct. He thought principally of Mrs. Churchill's illness, and wanted to know how she was treated; and as for the ball, it was shocking to have dear Emma disappointed; but they would all be safer at home.

Emma was ready for her visitor some time before he appeared; but if this reflected at all upon his impatience, his sorrowful look and total want of spirits when he did come might redeem him. He felt the going away almost too much to speak of it. His dejection was most evident. He sat really lost in thought for the first few minutes; and when rousing himself, it was only to say,

"Of all horrid things, leave-taking is the worst."

"But you will come again," said Emma. "This will not be your only visit to Randalls."

"Ah!—(shaking his head)—the uncertainty of when I may be able to return!—I shall try for it with a zeal!—It will be the object of all my thoughts and cares!—and if my uncle and aunt go to town this spring—but I am afraid—they did not stir last spring—I am afraid it is a custom gone for ever."

"Our poor ball must be quite given up."

"Ah! that ball!—why did we wait for any thing?—why not seize the pleasure at once?—How often is happiness destroyed by preparation, foolish preparation!—You told us it would be so.—Oh! Miss Woodhouse, why are you always so right?"

"Indeed, I am very sorry to be right in this instance. I would much rather have been merry than wise."

"If I can come again, we are still to have our ball. My father depends on it. Do not forget your engagement."

Emma looked graciously.

"Such a fortnight as it has been!" he continued; "every day more precious and more delightful than the day before!—every day making me less fit to bear any other place. Happy those, who can remain at Highbury!"

"As you do us such ample justice now," said Emma, laughing, "I will venture to ask, whether you did not come a little doubtfully at first? Do not we rather surpass your expectations? I am sure we do. I am sure you did not much expect to like us. You would not have been so long in coming, if you had had a pleasant idea of Highbury."

He laughed rather consciously; and though denying the sentiment, Emma was convinced that it had been so.

"And you must be off this very morning?"

"Yes; my father is to join me here: we shall walk back together, and I must be off immediately. I am almost afraid that every moment will bring him."

"Not five minutes to spare even for your friends Miss Fairfax and Miss Bates? How unlucky! Miss Bates's powerful, argumentative mind might have strengthened yours."

"Yes—I have called there; passing the door, I thought it better. It was a right thing to do. I went in for three minutes, and was detained by Miss Bates's being absent. She was out; and I felt it impossible not to wait till she came in. She is a woman that one may, that one must laugh at; but that one would not wish to slight. It was better to pay my visit, then"—

He hesitated, got up, walked to a window.

"In short," said he, "perhaps, Miss Woodhouse—I think you can hardly be quite without suspicion"—

He looked at her, as if wanting to read her thoughts. She hardly knew what to say. It seemed like the forerunner of something absolutely serious, which she did not wish. Forcing herself to speak, therefore, in the hope of putting it by, she calmly said,

"You are quite in the right; it was most natural to pay your visit, then"—

He was silent. She believed he was looking at her; probably reflecting on what she had said, and trying to understand the manner. She heard him sigh. It was natural for him to feel that he had cause to sigh. He could not believe her to be encouraging him. A few awkward moments passed, and he sat down again; and in a more determined manner said,

"It was something to feel that all the rest of my time might be given to Hartfield. My regard for Hartfield is most warm"—

He stopt again, rose again, and seemed quite embarrassed.—He was more in love with her than Emma had supposed; and who can say how it might have ended, if his father had not made his appearance? Mr. Woodhouse soon followed; and the necessity of exertion made him composed.

A very few minutes more, however, completed the present trial. Mr. Weston, always alert when business was to be done, and as incapable of procrastinating any evil that was inevitable, as of foreseeing any that was doubtful, said, "It was time to go;" and the young man, though he might and did sigh, could not but agree, to take leave.

"I shall hear about you all," said he; that is my chief consolation. I shall hear of every thing that is going on among you. I have engaged Mrs. Weston to correspond with me. She has been so kind as to promise it. Oh! the blessing of a female correspondent, when one is really interested in the absent!—she will tell me every thing. In her letters I shall be at dear Highbury again."

A very friendly shake of the hand, a very earnest "Good-bye," closed the speech, and the door had soon shut out Frank Churchill. Short had been the notice—short their meeting; he was gone; and Emma felt so sorry to part, and foresaw so great a loss to their little society from his absence as to begin to be afraid of being too sorry, and feeling it too much.

It was a sad change. They had been meeting almost every day since his arrival. Certainly his being at Randalls had given great spirit to the last two weeks—indescribable spirit; the idea, the expectation of seeing him which every morning had brought, the assurance of his attentions, his liveliness, his manners! It had been a very happy fortnight, and forlorn must be the sinking from it into the common course of Hartfield days. To complete every other recommendation, he had almost told her that he loved her. What strength, or what constancy of affection he might be subject to, was another point; but at present she could not doubt his having a decidedly warm admiration, a conscious preference of herself; and this persuasion, joined to all the rest, made her think that she must be a little in love with him, in spite of every previous determination against it.

"I certainly must," said she. "This sensation of listlessness, weariness, stupidity, this disinclination to sit down and employ myself, this feeling of every thing's being dull and insipid about the house!—I must be in love; I should be the oddest creature in the world if I were not—for a few weeks at least. Well! evil to some is always good to others. I shall have many fellow-mourners for the ball, if not for Frank Churchill; but Mr. Knightley will be happy. He may spend the evening with his dear William Larkins now if he likes."

Mr. Knightley, however, shewed no triumphant happiness. He could not say that he was sorry on his own account; his very cheerful look would have contradicted him if he had; but he said, and very steadily, that he was sorry for the disappointment of the others, and with considerable kindness added,

"You, Emma, who have so few opportunities of dancing, you are really out of luck; you are very much out of luck!"

It was some days before she saw Jane Fairfax, to judge of her honest regret in this woeful change; but when they did meet, her composure was odious. She had been particularly unwell, however, suffering from headache to a degree, which made her aunt declare, that had the ball taken place, she did not think Jane could have attended it; and it was charity to impute some of her unbecoming indifference to the languor of ill-health.

Chapter XIII

Emma continued to entertain no doubt of her being in love. Her ideas only varied as to the how much. At first, she thought it was a good deal; and afterwards, but little. She had great pleasure in hearing Frank Churchill talked of; and, for his sake, greater pleasure than ever in seeing Mr. and Mrs. Weston; she was very often thinking of him, and quite impatient for a letter, that she might know how he was, how were his spirits, how was his aunt, and what was the chance of his coming to Randalls again this spring. But, on the other hand, she could not admit herself to be unhappy, nor, after the first morning, to be less disposed for employment than usual; she was still busy and cheerful; and, pleasing as he was, she could yet imagine him to have faults; and farther, though thinking of him so much, and, as she sat drawing or working, forming a thousand amusing schemes for the progress and close of their attachment, fancying interesting dialogues, and inventing elegant letters; the conclusion of every imaginary declaration on his side was that she refused him. Their affection was always to subside into friendship. Every thing tender and charming was to mark their parting; but still they were to part. When she became sensible of this, it struck her that she could not be very much in love; for in spite of her previous and fixed determination never to quit her father, never to marry, a strong attachment certainly must produce more of a struggle than she could foresee in her own feelings.

"I do not find myself making any use of the word sacrifice," said she.—"In not one of all my clever replies, my delicate negatives, is there any allusion to making a sacrifice. I do suspect that he is not really necessary to my happiness. So much the better. I certainly will not persuade myself to feel more than I do. I am quite enough in love. I should be sorry to be more."

Upon the whole, she was equally contented with her view of his feelings.

"He is undoubtedly very much in love—every thing denotes it—very much in love indeed!—and when he comes again, if his affection continue, I must be on my guard not to encourage it.—It would be most inexcusable to do otherwise, as my own mind is quite made up. Not that I imagine he can think I have been encouraging him hitherto. No, if he had believed me at all to share his feelings, he would not have been so wretched. Could he have thought himself encouraged, his looks and language at parting would have been different.—Still, however, I must be on my guard. This is in the supposition of his attachment continuing what it now is; but I do not know that I expect it will; I do not look upon him to be quite the sort of man—I do not altogether build upon his steadiness or constancy.—

His feelings are warm, but I can imagine them rather changeable.—Every consideration of the subject, in short, makes me thankful that my happiness is not more deeply involved.—I shall do very well again after a little while—and then, it will be a good thing over; for they say every body is in love once in their lives, and I shall have been let off easily."

When his letter to Mrs. Weston arrived, Emma had the perusal of it; and she read it with a degree of pleasure and admiration which made her at first shake her head over her own sensations, and think she had undervalued their strength. It was a long, well-written letter, giving the particulars of his journey and of his feelings, expressing all the affection, gratitude, and respect which was natural and honourable, and describing every thing exterior and local that could be supposed attractive, with spirit and precision. No suspicious flourishes now of apology or concern; it was the language of real feeling towards Mrs. Weston; and the transition from Highbury to Enscombe, the contrast between the places in some of the first blessings of social life was just enough touched on to shew how keenly it was felt, and how much more might have been said but for the restraints of propriety.—The charm of her own name was not wanting. Miss Woodhouse appeared more than once, and never without a something of pleasing connexion, either a compliment to her taste, or a remembrance of what she had said; and in the very last time of its meeting her eye, unadorned as it was by any such broad wreath of gallantry, she yet could discern the effect of her influence and acknowledge the greatest compliment perhaps of all conveyed. Compressed into the very lowest vacant corner were these words—"I had not a spare moment on Tuesday, as you know, for Miss Woodhouse's beautiful little friend. Pray make my excuses and adieus to her." This, Emma could not doubt, was all for herself. Harriet was remembered only from being her friend. His information and prospects as to Enscombe were neither worse nor better than had been anticipated; Mrs. Churchill was recovering, and he dared not yet, even in his own imagination, fix a time for coming to Randalls again.

Gratifying, however, and stimulative as was the letter in the material part, its sentiments, she yet found, when it was folded up and returned to Mrs. Weston, that it had not added any lasting warmth, that she could still do without the writer, and that he must learn to do without her. Her intentions were unchanged. Her resolution of refusal only grew more interesting by the addition of a scheme for his subsequent consolation and happiness. His recollection of Harriet, and the words which clothed it, the "beautiful little friend," suggested to her the idea of Harriet's succeeding her in his affections. Was it impossible?—No.—Harriet undoubtedly was greatly his inferior in understanding; but he had been very much struck with the loveliness of her face and the warm simplicity of her manner; and all the probabilities of circumstance and connexion were in her favour.—For Harriet, it would be advantageous and delightful indeed.

"I must not dwell upon it," said she.—"I must not think of it. I know the danger of indulging such speculations. But stranger things have happened; and when we cease to care for each other as we do now, it will be the means of confirming us in that sort of true disinterested friendship which I can already look forward to with pleasure."

It was well to have a comfort in store on Harriet's behalf, though it might be wise to let the fancy touch it seldom; for evil in that quarter was at hand. As Frank Churchill's arrival had succeeded Mr. Elton's engagement in the conversation of Highbury, as the latest interest had entirely borne down the first, so now upon Frank Churchill's disappearance, Mr. Elton's concerns were assuming the most irresistible form.—His wedding-day was named. He would soon be among them again; Mr. Elton and his bride. There was hardly time to talk over the first letter from Enscombe before "Mr. Elton and his bride" was in every body's mouth, and Frank Churchill was forgotten. Emma grew sick at the sound. She had had three weeks of happy exemption from Mr. Elton; and Harriet's mind, she had been willing to hope, had been lately gaining strength. With Mr. Weston's ball in view at least, there had been a great deal of insensibility to other things; but it was now too evident that she had not attained such a state of composure as could stand against the actual approach—new carriage, bell-ringing, and all.

Poor Harriet was in a flutter of spirits which required all the reasonings and soothings and attentions of every kind that Emma could give. Emma felt that she could not do too much for her, that Harriet had a right to all her ingenuity and all her patience; but it was heavy work to be for ever convincing without producing any effect, for ever agreed to, without being able to make their opinions the same. Harriet listened submissively, and said "it was very true—it was just as Miss Woodhouse described—it was not worth while to think about them—and she would not think about them any longer" but no change of subject could avail, and the next half-hour saw her as anxious and restless about the Eltons as before. At last Emma attacked her on another ground.

"Your allowing yourself to be so occupied and so unhappy about Mr. Elton's marrying, Harriet, is the strongest reproach you can make me. You could not give me a greater reproof for the mistake I fell into. It was all my doing, I know. I have not forgotten it, I assure you.—Deceived myself, I did very miserably deceive you—and it will be a painful reflection to me for ever. Do not imagine me in danger of forgetting it."

Harriet felt this too much to utter more than a few words of eager exclamation. Emma continued,

"I have not said, exert yourself Harriet for my sake; think less, talk less of Mr. Elton for my sake; because for your own sake rather, I would wish it to be done, for the sake of what is more important than my comfort, a habit of self-command in you, a consideration of what is your duty, an attention to propriety, an endeavour to avoid the suspicions of others, to save your health and credit, and restore your tranquillity. These are the motives which I have been pressing on you. They are very important—and sorry I am that you cannot feel them sufficiently to act upon them. My being saved from pain is a very secondary consideration. I want you to save yourself from greater pain. Perhaps I may sometimes have felt that Harriet would not forget what was due—or rather what would be kind by me."

This appeal to her affections did more than all the rest. The idea of wanting gratitude and consideration for Miss Woodhouse, whom she really loved extremely, made her wretched for a while, and when the violence of grief was comforted away, still remained powerful enough to prompt to what was right and support her in it very tolerably.

"You, who have been the best friend I ever had in my life—Want gratitude to you!—Nobody is equal to you!—I care for nobody as I do for you!—Oh! Miss Woodhouse, how ungrateful I have been!"

Such expressions, assisted as they were by every thing that look and manner could do, made Emma feel that she had never loved Harriet so well, nor valued her affection so highly before.

"There is no charm equal to tenderness of heart," said she afterwards to herself. "There is nothing to be compared to it. Warmth and tenderness of heart, with an affectionate, open manner, will beat all the clearness of head in the world, for attraction, I am sure it will. It is tenderness of heart which makes my dear father so generally beloved—which gives Isabella all her popularity.—I have it not—but I know how to prize and respect it.—Harriet is my superior in all the charm and all the felicity it gives. Dear Harriet!—I would not change you for the clearest-headed, longest-sighted, best-judging female breathing. Oh! the coldness of a Jane Fairfax!—Harriet is worth a hundred such—And for a wife—a sensible man's wife—it is invaluable. I mention no names; but happy the man who changes Emma for Harriet!"

Chapter XIV

Mrs. Elton was first seen at church: but though devotion might be interrupted, curiosity could not be satisfied by a bride in a pew, and it must be left for the visits in form which were then to be paid, to settle whether she were very pretty indeed, or only rather pretty, or not pretty at all.

Emma had feelings, less of curiosity than of pride or propriety, to make her resolve on not being the last to pay her respects; and she made a point of Harriet's going with her, that the worst of the business might be gone through as soon as possible.

She could not enter the house again, could not be in the same room to which she had with such vain artifice retreated three months ago, to lace up her boot, without recollecting. A thousand vexatious thoughts would recur. Compliments, charades, and horrible blunders; and it was not to be supposed that poor Harriet should not be recollecting too; but she behaved very well, and was only rather pale and silent. The visit was of course short; and there was so much embarrassment and occupation of mind to shorten it, that Emma would not allow herself entirely to form an opinion of the lady, and on no account to give one, beyond the nothing-meaning terms of being "elegantly dressed, and very pleasing."

She did not really like her. She would not be in a hurry to find fault, but she suspected that there was no elegance;—ease, but not elegance.—She was almost sure that for a young woman, a stranger, a bride, there was too much ease. Her person was rather good; her face not unpretty; but neither feature, nor air, nor voice, nor manner, were elegant. Emma thought at least it would turn out so.

As for Mr. Elton, his manners did not appear—but no, she would not permit a hasty or a witty word from herself about his manners. It was an awkward ceremony at any time to be receiving wedding visits, and a man had need be all grace to acquit himself well through it. The woman was better off; she might have the assistance of fine clothes, and the privilege of bashfulness, but the man had only his own good sense to depend on; and when she considered how peculiarly unlucky poor Mr. Elton was in being in the same room at once with the woman he had just married, the woman he had wanted to marry, and the woman whom he had been expected to marry, she must allow him to have the right to look as little wise, and to be as much affectedly, and as little really easy as could be.

"Well, Miss Woodhouse," said Harriet, when they had quitted the house, and after waiting in vain for her friend to begin; "Well, Miss Woodhouse, (with a gentle sigh,) what do you think of her?—Is not she very charming?"

There was a little hesitation in Emma's answer.

"Oh! yes—very—a very pleasing young woman."

"I think her beautiful, quite beautiful."

"Very nicely dressed, indeed; a remarkably elegant gown."

"I am not at all surprized that he should have fallen in love."

"Oh! no—there is nothing to surprize one at all.—A pretty fortune; and she came in his way."

"I dare say," returned Harriet, sighing again, "I dare say she was very much attached to him."

"Perhaps she might; but it is not every man's fate to marry the woman who loves him best. Miss Hawkins perhaps wanted a home, and thought this the best offer she was likely to have."

"Yes," said Harriet earnestly, "and well she might, nobody could ever have a better. Well, I wish them happy with all my heart. And now, Miss Woodhouse, I do not think I shall mind seeing them again. He is just as superior as ever;—but being married, you know, it is quite a different thing. No, indeed, Miss Woodhouse, you need not be afraid; I can sit and admire him now without any great misery. To know that he has not thrown himself away, is such a comfort!—She does seem a charming young woman, just what he deserves. Happy creature! He called her 'Augusta.' How delightful!"

When the visit was returned, Emma made up her mind. She could then see more and judge better. From Harriet's happening not to be at Hartfield, and her father's being present to engage Mr. Elton, she had a quarter of an hour of the lady's conversation to herself, and could composedly attend to her; and the quarter of an hour quite convinced her that Mrs. Elton was a vain woman, extremely well satisfied with herself, and thinking much of her own importance; that she meant to shine and be very superior, but with manners which had been formed in a bad school, pert and familiar; that all her notions were drawn from one set of people, and one style of living; that if not foolish she was ignorant, and that her society would certainly do Mr. Elton no good.

Harriet would have been a better match. If not wise or refined herself, she would have connected him with those who were; but Miss Hawkins, it might be fairly supposed from her easy conceit, had been the best of her own set. The rich brother-in-law near Bristol was the pride of the alliance, and his place and his carriages were the pride of him.

The very first subject after being seated was Maple Grove, "My brother Mr. Suckling's seat;"—a comparison of Hartfield to Maple Grove. The grounds of Hartfield were small, but neat and pretty; and the house was modern and well-built. Mrs. Elton seemed most favourably impressed by the size of the room, the entrance, and all that she could see or imagine. "Very like Maple Grove indeed!—She was quite struck by the likeness!—That room was the very shape and size of the morning-room at Maple Grove; her sister's favourite room."—Mr. Elton was appealed to.—"Was not it astonishingly like?—She could really almost fancy herself at Maple Grove."

"And the staircase—You know, as I came in, I observed how very like the staircase was; placed exactly in the same part of the house. I really could not help exclaiming! I assure you, Miss Woodhouse, it is very delightful to me, to be reminded of a place I am so extremely partial to as Maple Grove. I have spent so many happy months there! (with a little sigh of sentiment). A charming place, undoubtedly. Every body who sees it is struck by its beauty; but to me, it has been quite a home. Whenever you are transplanted, like me, Miss Woodhouse, you will understand how very delightful it is to meet with any thing at all like what one has left behind. I always say this is quite one of the evils of matrimony."

Emma made as slight a reply as she could; but it was fully sufficient for Mrs. Elton, who only wanted to be talking herself.

"So extremely like Maple Grove! And it is not merely the house—the grounds, I assure you, as far as I could observe, are strikingly like. The laurels at Maple Grove are in the same profusion as here, and stand very much in the same way—just across the lawn; and I had a glimpse of a fine large tree, with a bench round it, which put me so exactly in mind! My brother and sister will be enchanted with this place. People who have extensive grounds themselves are always pleased with any thing in the same style."

Emma doubted the truth of this sentiment. She had a great idea that people who had extensive grounds themselves cared very little for the extensive grounds of any body else; but it was not worth while to attack an error so double-dyed, and therefore only said in reply,

"When you have seen more of this country, I am afraid you will think you have overrated Hartfield. Surry is full of beauties."

"Oh! yes, I am quite aware of that. It is the garden of England, you know. Surry is the garden of England."

"Yes; but we must not rest our claims on that distinction. Many counties, I believe, are called the garden of England, as well as Surry."

"No, I fancy not," replied Mrs. Elton, with a most satisfied smile." I never heard any county but Surry called so."

Emma was silenced.

"My brother and sister have promised us a visit in the spring, or summer at farthest," continued Mrs. Elton; "and that will be our time for exploring. While they are with us, we shall explore a great deal, I dare say. They will have their barouche-landau, of course, which holds four perfectly; and therefore, without saying any thing of our carriage, we should be able to explore the different beauties extremely well. They would hardly come in their chaise, I think, at that season of the year. Indeed, when the time draws on, I shall decidedly recommend their bringing the barouche-landau; it will be so very much preferable. When people come into a beautiful country of this sort, you know, Miss Woodhouse, one naturally wishes them to see as much as possible; and Mr. Suckling is extremely fond of exploring. We explored to King's-Weston twice last summer, in that way, most delightfully, just after their first having the barouche-landau. You have many parties of that kind here, I suppose, Miss Woodhouse, every summer?"

"No; not immediately here. We are rather out of distance of the very striking beauties which attract the sort of parties you speak of; and we are a very quiet set of people, I believe; more disposed to stay at home than engage in schemes of pleasure."

"Ah! there is nothing like staying at home for real comfort. Nobody can be more devoted to home than I am. I was quite a proverb for it at Maple Grove. Many a time has Selina said, when she has been going to Bristol, 'I really cannot get this girl to move from the house. I absolutely must go in by myself, though I hate being stuck up in the barouche-landau without a companion; but Augusta, I believe, with her own good-will, would never stir beyond the park paling.' Many a time has she said so; and yet I am no advocate for entire seclusion. I think, on the contrary, when people shut themselves up entirely from society, it is a very bad thing; and that it is much more advisable to mix in the world in a proper degree, without living in it either too much or too little. I perfectly understand your situation, however, Miss Woodhouse—(looking towards Mr. Woodhouse), Your father's state of health must be a great drawback. Why does not he try Bath?—Indeed he should. Let me recommend Bath to you. I assure you I have no doubt of its doing Mr. Woodhouse good."

"My father tried it more than once, formerly; but without receiving any benefit; and Mr. Perry, whose name, I dare say, is not unknown to you, does not conceive it would be at all more likely to be useful now."

"Ah! that's a great pity; for I assure you, Miss Woodhouse, where the waters do agree, it is quite wonderful the relief they give. In my Bath life, I have seen such instances of it! And it is so cheerful a place, that it could not fail of being of use to Mr. Woodhouse's spirits, which, I understand, are sometimes much depressed. And as to its recommendations to you, I fancy I need not take much pains to dwell on them. The advantages of Bath to the young are pretty generally understood. It would be a charming introduction for you, who have lived so secluded a life; and I could immediately secure you some of the best society in the place. A line from me would bring you a little host of acquaintance; and my particular friend, Mrs. Partridge, the lady I have always resided with when in Bath, would be most happy to shew you any attentions, and would be the very person for you to go into public with."

It was as much as Emma could bear, without being impolite. The idea of her being indebted to Mrs. Elton for what was called an introduction—of her going into public under the auspices of a friend of Mrs. Elton's—probably some vulgar, dashing widow, who, with the help of a boarder, just made a shift to live!—The dignity of Miss Woodhouse, of Hartfield, was sunk indeed!

She restrained herself, however, from any of the reproofs she could have given, and only thanked Mrs. Elton coolly; "but their going to Bath was quite out of the question; and she was not perfectly convinced that the place might suit her better than her father." And then, to prevent farther outrage and indignation, changed the subject directly.

"I do not ask whether you are musical, Mrs. Elton. Upon these occasions, a lady's character generally precedes her; and Highbury has long known that you are a superior performer."

"Oh! no, indeed; I must protest against any such idea. A superior performer!—very far from it, I assure you. Consider from how partial a quarter your information came. I am doatingly fond of music—passionately fond;—and my friends say I am not entirely devoid of taste; but as to any thing else, upon my honour my performance is mediocre to the last degree. You, Miss Woodhouse, I well know, play delightfully. I assure you it has been the greatest satisfaction, comfort, and delight to me, to hear what a musical society I am got into. I absolutely cannot do without music. It is a necessary of life to me; and having always been used to a very musical society, both at Maple Grove and in Bath, it would have been a most serious sacrifice. I honestly said as much to Mr. E. when he was speaking of my future home, and expressing his fears lest the retirement of it should be disagreeable; and the inferiority of the house too—knowing what I had been accustomed to—of course he was not wholly without apprehension. When he was speaking of it in that way, I honestly said that the world I could give up—parties, balls, plays—for I had no fear of retirement. Blessed with so many resources within myself, the world was not necessary to me. I could do very well without it. To those who had no resources it was a different thing; but my resources made me quite independent. And as to smaller-sized rooms than I had been used to, I really could not give it a thought. I hoped I was perfectly equal to any sacrifice of that description. Certainly I had been accustomed to every luxury at Maple Grove; but I did assure him that two carriages were not necessary to my happiness, nor were spacious apartments. 'But,' said I, 'to be quite honest, I do not think I can live without something of a musical society. I condition for nothing else; but without music, life would be a blank to me.'"

"We cannot suppose," said Emma, smiling, "that Mr. Elton would hesitate to assure you of there being a very musical society in Highbury; and I hope you will not find he has outstepped the truth more than may be pardoned, in consideration of the motive."

"No, indeed, I have no doubts at all on that head. I am delighted to find myself in such a circle. I hope we shall have many sweet little concerts together. I think, Miss Woodhouse, you and I must establish a musical club, and have regular weekly meetings at your house, or ours. Will not it be a good plan? If we exert ourselves, I think we shall not be long in want of allies. Something of that nature would be particularly desirable for me, as an inducement to keep me in practice; for married women, you know—there is a sad story against them, in general. They are but too apt to give up music."

"But you, who are so extremely fond of it—there can be no danger, surely?"

"I should hope not; but really when I look around among my acquaintance, I tremble. Selina has entirely given up music—never touches the instrument—though she played sweetly. And the same may be said of Mrs. Jeffereys—Clara Partridge, that was—and of the two Milmans, now Mrs. Bird and Mrs. James Cooper; and of more than I can enumerate. Upon my word it is enough to put one in a fright. I used to be quite angry with Selina; but really I begin now to comprehend that a married woman has many things to call her attention. I believe I was half an hour this morning shut up with my housekeeper."

"But every thing of that kind," said Emma, "will soon be in so regular a train—"

"Well," said Mrs. Elton, laughing, "we shall see."

Emma, finding her so determined upon neglecting her music, had nothing more to say; and, after a moment's pause, Mrs. Elton chose another subject.

"We have been calling at Randalls," said she, "and found them both at home; and very pleasant people they seem to be. I like them extremely. Mr. Weston seems an excellent creature—quite a first-rate favourite with me already, I assure you. And she appears so truly good—there is something so motherly and kind-hearted about her, that it wins upon one directly. She was your governess, I think?"

Emma was almost too much astonished to answer; but Mrs. Elton hardly waited for the affirmative before she went on.

"Having understood as much, I was rather astonished to find her so very lady-like! But she is really quite the gentlewoman."

"Mrs. Weston's manners," said Emma, "were always particularly good. Their propriety, simplicity, and elegance, would make them the safest model for any young woman."

"And who do you think came in while we were there?"

Emma was quite at a loss. The tone implied some old acquaintance—and how could she possibly guess?

"Knightley!" continued Mrs. Elton; "Knightley himself!—Was not it lucky?—for, not being within when he called the other day, I had never seen him before; and of course, as so particular a friend of Mr. E.'s, I had a great curiosity. 'My friend Knightley' had been so often mentioned, that I was really impatient to see him; and I must do my caro sposo the justice to say that he need not be ashamed of his friend. Knightley is quite the gentleman. I like him very much. Decidedly, I think, a very gentleman-like man."

Happily, it was now time to be gone. They were off; and Emma could breathe.

"Insufferable woman!" was her immediate exclamation. "Worse than I had supposed. Absolutely insufferable! Knightley!—I could not have believed it. Knightley!—never seen him in her life before, and call him Knightley!—and discover that he is a gentleman! A little upstart, vulgar being, with her Mr. E., and her caro sposo, and her resources, and all her airs of pert pretension and underbred finery. Actually to discover that Mr. Knightley is a gentleman! I doubt whether he will return the compliment, and discover her to be a lady. I could not have believed it! And to propose that she and I should unite to form a musical club! One would fancy we were bosom friends! And Mrs. Weston!—Astonished that the person who had brought me up should be a gentlewoman! Worse and worse. I never met with her equal. Much beyond my hopes. Harriet is disgraced by any comparison. Oh! what would Frank Churchill say to her, if he were here? How angry and how diverted he would be! Ah! there I am—thinking of him directly. Always the first person to be thought of! How I catch myself out! Frank Churchill comes as regularly into my mind!"——

All this ran so glibly through her thoughts, that by the time her father had arranged himself, after the bustle of the Eltons' departure, and was ready to speak, she was very tolerably capable of attending.

"Well, my dear," he deliberately began, "considering we never saw her before, she seems a very pretty sort of young lady; and I dare say she was very much pleased with you. She speaks a little too quick. A little quickness of voice there is which rather hurts the ear. But I believe I am nice; I do not like strange voices; and nobody speaks like you and poor Miss Taylor. However, she seems a very obliging, pretty-behaved young lady, and no doubt will make him a very good wife. Though I think he had better not have married. I made the best excuses I could for not having been able to wait on him and Mrs. Elton on this happy occasion; I said that I hoped I should in the course of the summer. But I ought to have gone before. Not to wait upon a bride is very remiss. Ah! it shews what a sad invalid I am! But I do not like the corner into Vicarage Lane."

"I dare say your apologies were accepted, sir. Mr. Elton knows you."

"Yes: but a young lady—a bride—I ought to have paid my respects to her if possible. It was being very deficient."

"But, my dear papa, you are no friend to matrimony; and therefore why should you be so anxious to pay your respects to a bride? It ought to be no recommendation to you. It is encouraging people to marry if you make so much of them."

"No, my dear, I never encouraged any body to marry, but I would always wish to pay every proper attention to a lady—and a bride, especially, is never to be neglected. More is avowedly due to her. A bride, you know, my dear, is always the first in company, let the others be who they may."

"Well, papa, if this is not encouragement to marry, I do not know what is. And I should never have expected you to be lending your sanction to such vanity-baits for poor young ladies."

"My dear, you do not understand me. This is a matter of mere common politeness and good-breeding, and has nothing to do with any encouragement to people to marry."

Emma had done. Her father was growing nervous, and could not understand her. Her mind returned to Mrs. Elton's offences, and long, very long, did they occupy her.

Chapter XV

Emma was not required, by any subsequent discovery, to retract her ill opinion of Mrs. Elton. Her observation had been pretty correct. Such as Mrs. Elton appeared to her on this second interview, such she appeared whenever they met again,—self-important, presuming, familiar, ignorant, and ill-bred. She had a little beauty and a little accomplishment, but so little judgment that she thought herself coming with superior knowledge of the world, to enliven and improve a country neighbourhood; and conceived Miss Hawkins to have held such a place in society as Mrs. Elton's consequence only could surpass.

There was no reason to suppose Mr. Elton thought at all differently from his wife. He seemed not merely happy with her, but proud. He had the air of congratulating himself on having brought such a woman to Highbury, as not even Miss Woodhouse could equal; and the greater part of her new acquaintance, disposed to commend, or not in the habit of judging, following the lead of Miss

Bates's good-will, or taking it for granted that the bride must be as clever and as agreeable as she professed herself, were very well satisfied; so that Mrs. Elton's praise passed from one mouth to another as it ought to do, unimpeded by Miss Woodhouse, who readily continued her first contribution and talked with a good grace of her being "very pleasant and very elegantly dressed."

In one respect Mrs. Elton grew even worse than she had appeared at first. Her feelings altered towards Emma.—Offended, probably, by the little encouragement which her proposals of intimacy met with, she drew back in her turn and gradually became much more cold and distant; and though the effect was agreeable, the ill-will which produced it was necessarily increasing Emma's dislike. Her manners, too—and Mr. Elton's, were unpleasant towards Harriet. They were sneering and negligent. Emma hoped it must rapidly work Harriet's cure; but the sensations which could prompt such behaviour sunk them both very much.—It was not to be doubted that poor Harriet's attachment had been an offering to conjugal unreserve, and her own share in the story, under a colouring the least favourable to her and the most soothing to him, had in all likelihood been given also. She was, of course, the object of their joint dislike.—When they had nothing else to say, it must be always easy to begin abusing Miss Woodhouse; and the enmity which they dared not shew in open disrespect to her, found a broader vent in contemptuous treatment of Harriet.

Mrs. Elton took a great fancy to Jane Fairfax; and from the first. Not merely when a state of warfare with one young lady might be supposed to recommend the other, but from the very first; and she was not satisfied with expressing a natural and reasonable admiration—but without solicitation, or plea, or privilege, she must be wanting to assist and befriend her.—Before Emma had forfeited her confidence, and about the third time of their meeting, she heard all Mrs. Elton's knight-errantry on the subject.—

"Jane Fairfax is absolutely charming, Miss Woodhouse.—I quite rave about Jane Fairfax.—A sweet, interesting creature. So mild and ladylike—and with such talents!—I assure you I think she has very extraordinary talents. I do not scruple to say that she plays extremely well. I know enough of music to speak decidedly on that point. Oh! she is absolutely charming! You will laugh at my warmth—but, upon my word, I talk of nothing but Jane Fairfax.—And her situation is so calculated to affect one!—Miss Woodhouse, we must exert ourselves and endeavour to do something for her. We must bring her forward. Such talent as hers must not be suffered to remain unknown.—I dare say you have heard those charming lines of the poet,

'Full many a flower is born to blush unseen,
'And waste its fragrance on the desert air.'

We must not allow them to be verified in sweet Jane Fairfax."

"I cannot think there is any danger of it," was Emma's calm answer—"and when you are better acquainted with Miss Fairfax's situation and understand what her home has been, with Colonel and Mrs. Campbell, I have no idea that you will suppose her talents can be unknown."

"Oh! but dear Miss Woodhouse, she is now in such retirement, such obscurity, so thrown away.—Whatever advantages she may have enjoyed with the Campbells are so palpably at an end! And I think she feels it. I am sure she does. She is very timid and silent. One can see that she feels the want of encouragement. I like her the better for it. I must confess it is a recommendation to me. I am a great advocate for timidity—and I am sure one does not often meet with it.—But in those who are at all inferior, it is extremely prepossessing. Oh! I assure you, Jane Fairfax is a very delightful character, and interests me more than I can express."

"You appear to feel a great deal—but I am not aware how you or any of Miss Fairfax's acquaintance here, any of those who have known her longer than yourself, can shew her any other attention than"—

"My dear Miss Woodhouse, a vast deal may be done by those who dare to act. You and I need not be afraid. If we set the example, many will follow it as far as they can; though all have not our situations. We have carriages to fetch and convey her home, and we live in a style which could not make the addition of Jane Fairfax, at any time, the least inconvenient.—I should be extremely displeased if Wright were to send us up such a dinner, as could make me regret having asked more than Jane Fairfax to partake of it. I have no idea of that sort of thing. It is not likely that I should, considering what I have been used to. My greatest danger, perhaps, in housekeeping, may be quite the other way, in doing too much, and being too careless of expense. Maple Grove will probably be my model more than it ought to be—for we do not at all affect to equal my brother, Mr. Suckling, in income.—However, my resolution is taken as to noticing Jane Fairfax.—I shall certainly have her very often at my house, shall introduce her wherever I can, shall have musical parties to draw out her talents, and shall be constantly on the watch for an eligible situation. My acquaintance is so very extensive, that I have little doubt of hearing of something to suit her shortly.—I shall introduce her, of course, very particularly to my brother and sister when they come to us. I am sure they will like her extremely; and when she gets a little acquainted with them, her fears will completely wear off, for there really is nothing in the manners of either but what is highly conciliating.—I shall have her very often indeed while they are with me, and I dare say we shall sometimes find a seat for her in the barouche-landau in some of our exploring parties."

"Poor Jane Fairfax!"—thought Emma.—"You have not deserved this. You may have done wrong with regard to Mr. Dixon, but this is a punishment beyond what you can have merited!—The kindness and protection of Mrs. Elton!—'Jane Fairfax and Jane Fairfax.' Heavens! Let me not suppose that she dares go about, Emma Woodhouse-ing me!—But upon my honour, there seems no limits to the licentiousness of that woman's tongue!"

Emma had not to listen to such paradings again—to any so exclusively addressed to herself—so disgustingly decorated with a "dear Miss Woodhouse." The change on Mrs. Elton's side soon afterwards appeared, and she was left in peace—neither forced to be the very particular friend of Mrs. Elton, nor, under Mrs. Elton's guidance, the very active patroness of Jane Fairfax, and only sharing with others in a general way, in knowing what was felt, what was meditated, what was done.

She looked on with some amusement.—Miss Bates's gratitude for Mrs. Elton's attentions to Jane was in the first style of guileless simplicity and warmth. She was quite one of her worthies—the most amiable, affable, delightful woman—just as accomplished and condescending as Mrs. Elton meant to be considered. Emma's only surprize was that Jane Fairfax should accept those attentions and tolerate Mrs. Elton as she seemed to do. She heard of her walking with the

Eltons, sitting with the Eltons, spending a day with the Eltons! This was astonishing!—She could not have believed it possible that the taste or the pride of Miss Fairfax could endure such society and friendship as the Vicarage had to offer.

"She is a riddle, quite a riddle!" said she.—"To chuse to remain here month after month, under privations of every sort! And now to chuse the mortification of Mrs. Elton's notice and the penury of her conversation, rather than return to the superior companions who have always loved her with such real, generous affection."

Jane had come to Highbury professedly for three months; the Campbells were gone to Ireland for three months; but now the Campbells had promised their daughter to stay at least till Midsummer, and fresh invitations had arrived for her to join them there. According to Miss Bates—it all came from her—Mrs. Dixon had written most pressingly. Would Jane but go, means were to be found, servants sent, friends contrived—no travelling difficulty allowed to exist; but still she had declined it!

"She must have some motive, more powerful than appears, for refusing this invitation," was Emma's conclusion. "She must be under some sort of penance, inflicted either by the Campbells or herself. There is great fear, great caution, great resolution somewhere.—She is not to be with the Dixons. The decree is issued by somebody. But why must she consent to be with the Eltons?—Here is quite a separate puzzle."

Upon her speaking her wonder aloud on that part of the subject, before the few who knew her opinion of Mrs. Elton, Mrs. Weston ventured this apology for Jane.

"We cannot suppose that she has any great enjoyment at the Vicarage, my dear Emma—but it is better than being always at home. Her aunt is a good creature, but, as a constant companion, must be very tiresome. We must consider what Miss Fairfax quits, before we condemn her taste for what she goes to."

"You are right, Mrs. Weston," said Mr. Knightley warmly, "Miss Fairfax is as capable as any of us of forming a just opinion of Mrs. Elton. Could she have chosen with whom to associate, she would not have chosen her. But (with a reproachful smile at Emma) she receives attentions from Mrs. Elton, which nobody else pays her."

Emma felt that Mrs. Weston was giving her a momentary glance; and she was herself struck by his warmth. With a faint blush, she presently replied,

"Such attentions as Mrs. Elton's, I should have imagined, would rather disgust than gratify Miss Fairfax. Mrs. Elton's invitations I should have imagined any thing but inviting."

"I should not wonder," said Mrs. Weston, "if Miss Fairfax were to have been drawn on beyond her own inclination, by her aunt's eagerness in accepting Mrs. Elton's civilities for her. Poor Miss Bates may very likely have committed her niece and hurried her into a greater appearance of intimacy than her own good sense would have dictated, in spite of the very natural wish of a little change."

Both felt rather anxious to hear him speak again; and after a few minutes silence, he said,

"Another thing must be taken into consideration too—Mrs. Elton does not talk to Miss Fairfax as she speaks of her. We all know the difference between the pronouns he or she and thou, the plainest spoken amongst us; we all feel the influence of a something beyond common civility in our personal intercourse with each other—a something more early implanted. We cannot give any body the disagreeable hints that we may have been very full of the hour before. We feel things differently. And besides the operation of this, as a general principle, you may be sure that Miss Fairfax awes Mrs. Elton by her superiority both of mind and manner; and that, face to face, Mrs. Elton treats her with all the respect which she has a claim to. Such a woman as Jane Fairfax probably never fell in Mrs. Elton's way before—and no degree of vanity can prevent her acknowledging her own comparative littleness in action, if not in consciousness."

"I know how highly you think of Jane Fairfax," said Emma. Little Henry was in her thoughts, and a mixture of alarm and delicacy made her irresolute what else to say.

"Yes," he replied, "any body may know how highly I think of her."

"And yet," said Emma, beginning hastily and with an arch look, but soon stopping—it was better, however, to know the worst at once—she hurried on—"And yet, perhaps, you may hardly be aware yourself how highly it is. The extent of your admiration may take you by surprize some day or other."

Mr. Knightley was hard at work upon the lower buttons of his thick leather gaiters, and either the exertion of getting them together, or some other cause, brought the colour into his face, as he answered,

"Oh! are you there?—But you are miserably behindhand. Mr. Cole gave me a hint of it six weeks ago."

He stopped.—Emma felt her foot pressed by Mrs. Weston, and did not herself know what to think. In a moment he went on—

"That will never be, however, I can assure you. Miss Fairfax, I dare say, would not have me if I were to ask her—and I am very sure I shall never ask her."

Emma returned her friend's pressure with interest; and was pleased enough to exclaim,

"You are not vain, Mr. Knightley. I will say that for you."

He seemed hardly to hear her; he was thoughtful—and in a manner which shewed him not pleased, soon afterwards said,

"So you have been settling that I should marry Jane Fairfax?"

"No indeed I have not. You have scolded me too much for match-making, for me to presume to take such a liberty with you. What I said just now, meant nothing. One says those sort of things, of course, without any idea of a serious meaning. Oh! no, upon my word I have not the smallest wish for your marrying Jane Fairfax or Jane any body. You would not come in and sit with us in this comfortable way, if you were married."

Mr. Knightley was thoughtful again. The result of his reverie was, "No, Emma, I do not think the extent of my admiration for her will ever take me by surprize.—I never had a thought of her in that way, I assure you." And soon afterwards, "Jane Fairfax is a very charming young woman—but not even Jane Fairfax is perfect. She has a fault. She has not the open temper which a man would wish for in a wife."

Emma could not but rejoice to hear that she had a fault. "Well," said she, "and you soon silenced Mr. Cole, I suppose?"

"Yes, very soon. He gave me a quiet hint; I told him he was mistaken; he asked my pardon and said no more. Cole does not want to be wiser or wittier than his neighbours."

"In that respect how unlike dear Mrs. Elton, who wants to be wiser and wittier than all the world! I wonder how she speaks of the Coles—what she calls them! How can she find any appellation for them, deep enough in familiar vulgarity? She calls you, Knightley—what can she do for Mr. Cole? And so I am not to be surprized that Jane Fairfax accepts her civilities and consents to be with her. Mrs. Weston, your argument weighs most with me. I can much more readily enter into the temptation of getting away from Miss Bates, than I can believe in the triumph of Miss Fairfax's mind over Mrs. Elton. I have no faith in Mrs. Elton's acknowledging herself the inferior in thought, word, or deed; or in her being under any restraint beyond her own scanty rule of good-breeding. I cannot imagine that she will not be continually insulting her visitor with praise, encouragement, and offers of service; that she will not be continually detailing her magnificent intentions, from the procuring her a permanent situation to the including her in those delightful exploring parties which are to take place in the barouche-landau."

"Jane Fairfax has feeling," said Mr. Knightley—"I do not accuse her of want of feeling. Her sensibilities, I suspect, are strong—and her temper excellent in its power of forbearance, patience, self-controul; but it wants openness. She is reserved, more reserved, I think, than she used to be—And I love an open temper. No—till Cole alluded to my supposed attachment, it had never entered my head. I saw Jane Fairfax and conversed with her, with admiration and pleasure always—but with no thought beyond."

"Well, Mrs. Weston," said Emma triumphantly when he left them, "what do you say now to Mr. Knightley's marrying Jane Fairfax?"

"Why, really, dear Emma, I say that he is so very much occupied by the idea of not being in love with her, that I should not wonder if it were to end in his being so at last. Do not beat me."

Chapter XVI

Every body in and about Highbury who had ever visited Mr. Elton, was disposed to pay him attention on his marriage. Dinner-parties and evening-parties were made for him and his lady; and invitations flowed in so fast that she had soon the pleasure of apprehending they were never to have a disengaged day.

"I see how it is," said she. "I see what a life I am to lead among you. Upon my word we shall be absolutely dissipated. We really seem quite the fashion. If this is living in the country, it is nothing very formidable. From Monday next to Saturday, I assure you we have not a disengaged day!—A woman with fewer resources than I have, need not have been at a loss."

No invitation came amiss to her. Her Bath habits made evening-parties perfectly natural to her, and Maple Grove had given her a taste for dinners. She was a little shocked at the want of two drawing rooms, at the poor attempt at rout-cakes, and there being no ice in the Highbury card-parties. Mrs. Bates, Mrs. Perry, Mrs. Goddard and others, were a good deal behind-hand in knowledge of the world, but she would soon shew them how every thing ought to be arranged. In the course of the spring she must return their civilities by one very superior party—in which her card-tables should be set out with their separate candles and unbroken packs in the true style—and more waiters engaged for the evening than their own establishment could furnish, to carry round the refreshments at exactly the proper hour, and in the proper order.

Emma, in the meanwhile, could not be satisfied without a dinner at Hartfield for the Eltons. They must not do less than others, or she should be exposed to odious suspicions, and imagined capable of pitiful resentment. A dinner there must be. After Emma had talked about it for ten minutes, Mr. Woodhouse felt no unwillingness, and only made the usual stipulation of not sitting at the bottom of the table himself, with the usual regular difficulty of deciding who should do it for him.

The persons to be invited, required little thought. Besides the Eltons, it must be the Westons and Mr. Knightley; so far it was all of course—and it was hardly less inevitable that poor little Harriet must be asked to make the eighth:—but this invitation was not given with equal satisfaction, and on many accounts Emma was particularly pleased by Harriet's begging to be allowed to decline it. "She would rather not be in his company more than she could help. She was not yet quite able to see him and his charming happy wife together, without feeling uncomfortable. If Miss Woodhouse would not be displeased, she would rather stay at home." It was precisely what Emma would have wished, had she deemed it possible enough for wishing. She was delighted with the fortitude of her little friend—for fortitude she knew it was in her to give up being in company and stay at home; and she could now invite the very person whom she really wanted to make the eighth, Jane Fairfax.—Since her last conversation with Mrs. Weston and Mr. Knightley, she was more conscience-stricken about Jane Fairfax than she had often been.—Mr. Knightley's words dwelt with her. He had said that Jane Fairfax received attentions from Mrs. Elton which nobody else paid her.

"This is very true," said she, "at least as far as relates to me, which was all that was meant—and it is very shameful.—Of the same age—and always knowing her—I ought to have been more her friend.—She will never like me now. I have neglected her too long. But I will shew her greater attention than I have done."

Every invitation was successful. They were all disengaged and all happy.—The preparatory interest of this dinner, however, was not yet over. A circumstance rather unlucky occurred. The two eldest little Knightleys were engaged to pay their grandpapa and aunt a visit of some weeks in the spring, and their papa now proposed bringing them, and staying one whole day at Hartfield—which one day would be the very day of this party.—His professional engagements did not allow of his being put off, but both father and daughter were disturbed by its happening so. Mr. Woodhouse considered eight persons at dinner together as the utmost that his nerves could bear—and here would be a ninth—and Emma apprehended that it would be a ninth very much out of humour at not being able to come even to Hartfield for forty-eight hours without falling in with a dinner-party.

She comforted her father better than she could comfort herself, by representing that though he certainly would make them nine, yet he always said so little, that the increase of noise would be very immaterial. She thought it in reality a sad exchange for herself, to have him with his grave looks and reluctant conversation opposed to her instead of his brother.

The event was more favourable to Mr. Woodhouse than to Emma. John Knightley came; but Mr. Weston was unexpectedly summoned to town and must be absent on the very day. He might be able to join them in the evening, but certainly not to dinner. Mr. Woodhouse was quite at ease; and the seeing him so, with the arrival of the little boys and the philosophic composure of her brother on hearing his fate, removed the chief of even Emma's vexation.

The day came, the party were punctually assembled, and Mr. John Knightley seemed early to devote himself to the business of being agreeable. Instead of drawing his brother off to a window while they waited for dinner, he was talking to Miss Fairfax. Mrs. Elton, as elegant as lace and pearls could make her, he looked at in silence—wanting only to observe enough for Isabella's information—but Miss Fairfax was an old acquaintance and a quiet girl, and he could talk to her. He had met her before breakfast as he was returning from a walk with his little boys, when it had been just beginning to rain. It was natural to have some civil hopes on the subject, and he said,

"I hope you did not venture far, Miss Fairfax, this morning, or I am sure you must have been wet.—We scarcely got home in time. I hope you turned directly."

"I went only to the post-office," said she, "and reached home before the rain was much. It is my daily errand. I always fetch the letters when I am here. It saves trouble, and is a something to get me out. A walk before breakfast does me good."

"Not a walk in the rain, I should imagine."

"No, but it did not absolutely rain when I set out."

Mr. John Knightley smiled, and replied,

"That is to say, you chose to have your walk, for you were not six yards from your own door when I had the pleasure of meeting you; and Henry and John had seen more drops than they could count long before. The post-office has a great charm at one period of our lives. When you have lived to my age, you will begin to think letters are never worth going through the rain for."

There was a little blush, and then this answer,

"I must not hope to be ever situated as you are, in the midst of every dearest connexion, and therefore I cannot expect that simply growing older should make me indifferent about letters."

"Indifferent! Oh! no—I never conceived you could become indifferent. Letters are no matter of indifference; they are generally a very positive curse."

"You are speaking of letters of business; mine are letters of friendship."

"I have often thought them the worst of the two," replied he coolly. "Business, you know, may bring money, but friendship hardly ever does."

"Ah! you are not serious now. I know Mr. John Knightley too well—I am very sure he understands the value of friendship as well as any body. I can easily believe that letters are very little to you, much less than to me, but it is not your being ten years older than myself which makes the difference, it is not age, but situation. You have every body dearest to you always at hand, I, probably, never shall again; and therefore till I have outlived all my affections, a post-office, I think, must always have power to draw me out, in worse weather than to-day."

"When I talked of your being altered by time, by the progress of years," said John Knightley, "I meant to imply the change of situation which time usually brings. I consider one as including the other. Time will generally lessen the interest of every attachment not within the daily circle—but that is not the change I had in view for you. As an old friend, you will allow me to hope, Miss Fairfax, that ten years hence you may have as many concentrated objects as I have."

It was kindly said, and very far from giving offence. A pleasant "thank you" seemed meant to laugh it off, but a blush, a quivering lip, a tear in the eye, shewed that it was felt beyond a laugh. Her attention was now claimed by Mr. Woodhouse, who being, according to his custom on such occasions, making the circle of his guests, and paying his particular compliments to the ladies, was ending with her—and with all his mildest urbanity, said,

"I am very sorry to hear, Miss Fairfax, of your being out this morning in the rain. Young ladies should take care of themselves.—Young ladies are delicate plants. They should take care of their health and their complexion. My dear, did you change your stockings?"

"Yes, sir, I did indeed; and I am very much obliged by your kind solicitude about me."

"My dear Miss Fairfax, young ladies are very sure to be cared for.—I hope your good grand-mama and aunt are well. They are some of my very old friends. I wish my health allowed me to be a better neighbour. You do us a great deal of honour to-day, I am sure. My daughter and I are both highly sensible of your goodness, and have the greatest satisfaction in seeing you at Hartfield."

The kind-hearted, polite old man might then sit down and feel that he had done his duty, and made every fair lady welcome and easy.

By this time, the walk in the rain had reached Mrs. Elton, and her remonstrances now opened upon Jane.

"My dear Jane, what is this I hear?—Going to the post-office in the rain!—This must not be, I assure you.—You sad girl, how could you do such a thing?—It is a sign I was not there to take care of you."

Jane very patiently assured her that she had not caught any cold.

"Oh! do not tell me. You really are a very sad girl, and do not know how to take care of yourself.—To the post-office indeed! Mrs. Weston, did you ever hear the like? You and I must positively exert our authority."

"My advice," said Mrs. Weston kindly and persuasively, "I certainly do feel tempted to give. Miss Fairfax, you must not run such risks.—Liable as you have been to severe colds, indeed you ought to be particularly careful, especially at this time of year. The spring I always think requires more than common care. Better wait an hour or two, or even half a day for your letters, than run the risk of bringing on your cough again. Now do not you feel that you had? Yes, I am sure you are much too reasonable. You look as if you would not do such a thing again."

"Oh! she shall not do such a thing again," eagerly rejoined Mrs. Elton. "We will not allow her to do such a thing again:"—and nodding significantly—"there must be some arrangement made, there must indeed. I shall speak to Mr. E. The man who fetches our letters every morning (one of our men, I forget his name) shall inquire for yours too and bring them to you. That will obviate all difficulties you know; and from us I really think, my dear Jane, you can have no scruple to accept such an accommodation."

"You are extremely kind," said Jane; "but I cannot give up my early walk. I am advised to be out of doors as much as I can, I must walk somewhere, and the post-office is an object; and upon my word, I have scarcely ever had a bad morning before."

"My dear Jane, say no more about it. The thing is determined, that is (laughing affectedly) as far as I can presume to determine any thing without the concurrence of my lord and master. You know, Mrs. Weston, you and I must be cautious how we express ourselves. But I do flatter myself, my dear Jane, that my influence is not entirely worn out. If I meet with no insuperable difficulties therefore, consider that point as settled."

"Excuse me," said Jane earnestly, "I cannot by any means consent to such an arrangement, so needlessly troublesome to your servant. If the errand were not a pleasure to me, it could be done, as it always is when I am not here, by my grandmama's."

"Oh! my dear; but so much as Patty has to do!—And it is a kindness to employ our men."

Jane looked as if she did not mean to be conquered; but instead of answering, she began speaking again to Mr. John Knightley.

"The post-office is a wonderful establishment!" said she.—"The regularity and despatch of it! If one thinks of all that it has to do, and all that it does so well, it is really astonishing!"

"It is certainly very well regulated."

"So seldom that any negligence or blunder appears! So seldom that a letter, among the thousands that are constantly passing about the kingdom, is even carried wrong—and not one in a million, I suppose, actually lost! And when one considers the variety of hands, and of bad hands too, that are to be deciphered, it increases the wonder."

"The clerks grow expert from habit.—They must begin with some quickness of sight and hand, and exercise improves them. If you want any farther explanation," continued he, smiling, "they are paid for it. That is the key to a great deal of capacity. The public pays and must be served well."

The varieties of handwriting were farther talked of, and the usual observations made.

"I have heard it asserted," said John Knightley, "that the same sort of handwriting often prevails in a family; and where the same master teaches, it is natural enough. But for that reason, I should imagine the likeness must be chiefly confined to the females, for boys have very little teaching after an early age, and scramble into any hand they can get. Isabella and Emma, I think, do write very much alike. I have not always known their writing apart."

"Yes," said his brother hesitatingly, "there is a likeness. I know what you mean—but Emma's hand is the strongest."

"Isabella and Emma both write beautifully," said Mr. Woodhouse; "and always did. And so does poor Mrs. Weston"—with half a sigh and half a smile at her.

"I never saw any gentleman's handwriting"—Emma began, looking also at Mrs. Weston; but stopped, on perceiving that Mrs.

Weston was attending to some one else—and the pause gave her time to reflect, "Now, how am I going to introduce him?—Am I unequal to speaking his name at once before all these people? Is it necessary for me to use any roundabout phrase?—Your Yorkshire friend—your correspondent in Yorkshire;—that would be the way, I suppose, if I were very bad.—No, I can pronounce his name without the smallest distress. I certainly get better and better.—Now for it."

Mrs. Weston was disengaged and Emma began again—"Mr. Frank Churchill writes one of the best gentleman's hands I ever saw."

"I do not admire it," said Mr. Knightley. "It is too small—wants strength. It is like a woman's writing."

This was not submitted to by either lady. They vindicated him against the base aspersion. "No, it by no means wanted strength—it was not a large hand, but very clear and certainly strong. Had not Mrs. Weston any letter about her to produce?" No, she had heard from him very lately, but having answered the letter, had put it away.

"If we were in the other room," said Emma, "if I had my writing-desk, I am sure I could produce a specimen. I have a note of his.—Do not you remember, Mrs. Weston, employing him to write for you one day?"

"He chose to say he was employed"———

"Well, well, I have that note; and can shew it after dinner to convince Mr. Knightley."

"Oh! when a gallant young man, like Mr. Frank Churchill," said Mr. Knightley dryly, "writes to a fair lady like Miss Woodhouse, he will, of course, put forth his best."

Dinner was on table.—Mrs. Elton, before she could be spoken to, was ready; and before Mr. Woodhouse had reached her with his request to be allowed to hand her into the dining-parlour, was saying—

"Must I go first? I really am ashamed of always leading the way."

Jane's solicitude about fetching her own letters had not escaped Emma. She had heard and seen it all; and felt some curiosity to know whether the wet walk of this morning had produced any. She suspected that it had; that it would not have been so resolutely encountered but in full expectation of hearing from some one very dear, and that it had not been in vain. She thought there was an air of greater happiness than usual—a glow both of complexion and spirits.

She could have made an inquiry or two, as to the expedition and the expense of the Irish mails;—it was at her tongue's end—but she abstained. She was quite determined not to utter a word that should hurt Jane Fairfax's feelings; and they followed the other ladies out of the room, arm in arm, with an appearance of good-will highly becoming to the beauty and grace of each.

Chapter XVII

When the ladies returned to the drawing-room after dinner, Emma found it hardly possible to prevent their making two distinct parties;—with so much perseverance in judging and behaving ill did Mrs. Elton engross Jane Fairfax and slight herself. She and Mrs. Weston were obliged to be almost always either talking together or silent together. Mrs. Elton left them no choice. If Jane repressed her for a little time, she soon began again; and though much that passed between them was in a half-whisper, especially on Mrs. Elton's side, there was no avoiding a knowledge of their principal subjects: The post-office—catching cold—fetching letters—and friendship, were long under discussion; and to them succeeded one, which must be at least equally unpleasant to Jane—inquiries whether she had yet heard of any situation likely to suit her, and professions of Mrs. Elton's meditated activity.

"Here is April come!" said she, "I get quite anxious about you. June will soon be here."

"But I have never fixed on June or any other month—merely looked forward to the summer in general."

"But have you really heard of nothing?"

"I have not even made any inquiry; I do not wish to make any yet."

"Oh! my dear, we cannot begin too early; you are not aware of the difficulty of procuring exactly the desirable thing."

"I not aware!" said Jane, shaking her head; "dear Mrs. Elton, who can have thought of it as I have done?"

"But you have not seen so much of the world as I have. You do not know how many candidates there always are for the first situations. I saw a vast deal of that in the neighbourhood round Maple

Grove. A cousin of Mr. Suckling, Mrs. Bragge, had such an infinity of applications; every body was anxious to be in her family, for she moves in the first circle. Wax-candles in the schoolroom! You may imagine how desirable! Of all houses in the kingdom Mrs. Bragge's is the one I would most wish to see you in."

"Colonel and Mrs. Campbell are to be in town again by midsummer," said Jane. "I must spend some time with them; I am sure they will want it;—afterwards I may probably be glad to dispose of myself. But I would not wish you to take the trouble of making any inquiries at present."

"Trouble! aye, I know your scruples. You are afraid of giving me trouble; but I assure you, my dear Jane, the Campbells can hardly be more interested about you than I am. I shall write to Mrs. Partridge in a day or two, and shall give her a strict charge to be on the look-out for any thing eligible."

"Thank you, but I would rather you did not mention the subject to her; till the time draws nearer, I do not wish to be giving any body trouble."

"But, my dear child, the time is drawing near; here is April, and June, or say even July, is very near, with such business to accomplish before us. Your inexperience really amuses me! A situation such as you deserve, and your friends would require for you, is no everyday occurrence, is not obtained at a moment's notice; indeed, indeed, we must begin inquiring directly."

"Excuse me, ma'am, but this is by no means my intention; I make no inquiry myself, and should be sorry to have any made by my friends. When I am quite determined as to the time, I am not at all afraid of being long unemployed. There are places in town, offices, where inquiry would soon produce something—Offices for the sale—not quite of human flesh—but of human intellect."

"Oh! my dear, human flesh! You quite shock me; if you mean a fling at the slave-trade, I assure you Mr. Suckling was always rather a friend to the abolition."

"I did not mean, I was not thinking of the slave-trade," replied Jane; "governess-trade, I assure you, was all that I had in view; widely different certainly as to the guilt of those who carry it on; but as to the greater misery of the victims, I do not know where it lies. But I only mean to say that there are advertising offices, and that by applying to them I should have no doubt of very soon meeting with something that would do."

"Something that would do!" repeated Mrs. Elton. "Aye, that may suit your humble ideas of yourself;—I know what a modest creature you are; but it will not satisfy your friends to have you taking up with any thing that may offer, any inferior, commonplace situation, in a family not moving in a certain circle, or able to command the elegancies of life."

"You are very obliging; but as to all that, I am very indifferent; it would be no object to me to be with the rich; my mortifications, I think, would only be the greater; I should suffer more from comparison. A gentleman's family is all that I should condition for."

"I know you, I know you; you would take up with any thing; but I shall be a little more nice, and I am sure the good Campbells will be quite on my side; with your superior talents, you have a right to move in the first circle. Your musical knowledge alone would entitle you to name your own terms, have as many rooms as you like, and mix in the family as much as you chose;—that is—I do not know—if you knew the harp, you might do all that, I am very sure; but you sing as well as play;—yes, I really believe you might, even without the harp, stipulate for what you chose;—and you must and shall be delightfully, honourably and comfortably settled before the Campbells or I have any rest."

"You may well class the delight, the honour, and the comfort of such a situation together," said Jane, "they are pretty sure to be equal; however, I am very serious in not wishing any thing to be attempted at present for me. I am exceedingly obliged to you, Mrs. Elton, I am obliged to any body who feels for me, but I am quite serious in wishing nothing to be done till the summer. For two or three months longer I shall remain where I am, and as I am."

"And I am quite serious too, I assure you," replied Mrs. Elton gaily, "in resolving to be always on the watch, and employing my friends to watch also, that nothing really unexceptionable may pass us."

In this style she ran on; never thoroughly stopped by any thing till Mr. Woodhouse came into the room; her vanity had then a change of object, and Emma heard her saying in the same half-whisper to Jane,

"Here comes this dear old beau of mine, I protest!—Only think of his gallantry in coming away before the other men!—what a dear creature he is;—I assure you I like him excessively. I admire all that quaint, old-fashioned politeness; it is much more to my taste than modern ease; modern ease often disgusts me. But this good old Mr. Woodhouse, I wish you had heard his gallant speeches to me at dinner. Oh! I assure you I began to think my caro sposo would be absolutely jealous. I fancy I am rather a favourite; he took notice of my gown. How do you like it?—Selina's choice—handsome, I think, but I do not know whether it is not over-trimmed; I have the greatest dislike to the idea of being over-trimmed—quite a horror of finery. I must put on a few ornaments now, because it is expected of me. A bride, you know, must appear like a bride, but my natural taste is all for simplicity; a simple style of dress is so infinitely preferable to finery. But I am quite in the minority, I believe; few people seem to value simplicity of dress,—show and finery are every thing. I have some notion of putting such a trimming as this to my white and silver poplin. Do you think it will look well?"

The whole party were but just reassembled in the drawing-room when Mr. Weston made his appearance among them. He had returned to a late dinner, and walked to Hartfield as soon as it was over. He had been too much expected by the best judges, for surprize—but there was great joy. Mr. Woodhouse was almost as glad to see him now, as he would have been sorry to see him before. John Knightley only was in mute astonishment.—That a man who might have spent his evening quietly at home after a day of business in London, should set off again, and walk half a mile to another man's house, for the sake of being in mixed company till bed-time, of finishing his day in the efforts of civility and the noise of numbers, was a circumstance to strike him deeply. A man who had been in motion since eight o'clock in the morning, and might now have been still, who had been long talking, and might have been silent, who had been in more than one crowd, and might have been alone!—Such a man, to quit the tranquillity and independence of his own fireside, and on the evening of a cold sleety April day rush out again into the world!—Could he by a touch of his finger have instantly taken back his wife, there would have been a motive; but his coming would probably prolong rather than break up the party. John Knightley looked at him with amazement, then shrugged his shoulders, and said, "I could not have believed it even of him."

Mr. Weston meanwhile, perfectly unsuspicious of the indignation he was exciting, happy and cheerful as usual, and with all the right of being principal talker, which a day spent anywhere from home confers, was making himself agreeable among the rest; and having satisfied the inquiries of his wife as to his dinner, convincing her that none of all her careful directions to the servants had been forgotten, and spread abroad what public news he had heard, was proceeding to a family communication, which, though principally addressed to Mrs. Weston, he had not the smallest doubt of being highly interesting to every body in the room. He gave her a letter, it was from Frank, and to herself; he had met with it in his way, and had taken the liberty of opening it.

"Read it, read it," said he, "it will give you pleasure; only a few lines—will not take you long; read it to Emma."

The two ladies looked over it together; and he sat smiling and talking to them the whole time, in a voice a little subdued, but very audible to every body.

"Well, he is coming, you see; good news, I think. Well, what do you say to it?—I always told you he would be here again soon, did not I?—Anne, my dear, did not I always tell you so, and you would not believe me?—In town next week, you see—at the latest, I dare say; for she is as impatient as the black gentleman when any thing is to be done; most likely they will be there to-morrow or Saturday. As to her illness, all nothing of course. But it is an excellent thing to have Frank among us again, so near as town. They will stay a good while when they do come, and he will be half his time with us. This is precisely what I wanted. Well, pretty good news, is not it? Have you finished it? Has Emma read it all? Put it up, put it up; we will have a good talk about it some other time, but it will not do now. I shall only just mention the circumstance to the others in a common way."

Mrs. Weston was most comfortably pleased on the occasion. Her looks and words had nothing to restrain them. She was happy, she knew she was happy, and knew she ought to be happy. Her congratulations were warm and open; but Emma could not speak so fluently. She was a little occupied in weighing her own feelings, and trying to understand the degree of her agitation, which she rather thought was considerable.

Mr. Weston, however, too eager to be very observant, too communicative to want others to talk, was very well satisfied with what she did say, and soon moved away to make the rest of his friends happy by a partial communication of what the whole room must have overheard already.

It was well that he took every body's joy for granted, or he might not have thought either Mr. Woodhouse or Mr. Knightley particularly delighted. They were the first entitled, after Mrs. Weston and Emma, to be made happy;—from them he would have proceeded to Miss Fairfax, but she was so deep in conversation with John Knightley, that it would have been too positive an interruption; and finding himself close to Mrs. Elton, and her attention disengaged, he necessarily began on the subject with her.

Chapter XVIII

"I hope I shall soon have the pleasure of introducing my son to you," said Mr. Weston.

Mrs. Elton, very willing to suppose a particular compliment intended her by such a hope, smiled most graciously.

"You have heard of a certain Frank Churchill, I presume," he continued—"and know him to be my son, though he does not bear my name."

"Oh! yes, and I shall be very happy in his acquaintance. I am sure Mr. Elton will lose no time in calling on him; and we shall both have great pleasure in seeing him at the Vicarage."

"You are very obliging.—Frank will be extremely happy, I am sure.—He is to be in town next week, if not sooner. We have notice of it in a letter to-day. I met the letters in my way this morning, and seeing my son's hand, presumed to open it—though it was not directed to me—it was to Mrs. Weston. She is his principal correspondent, I assure you. I hardly ever get a letter."

"And so you absolutely opened what was directed to her! Oh! Mr. Weston—(laughing affectedly) I must protest against that.—A most dangerous precedent indeed!—I beg you will not let your neighbours follow your example.—Upon my word, if this is what I am to expect, we married women must begin to exert ourselves!—Oh! Mr. Weston, I could not have believed it of you!"

"Aye, we men are sad fellows. You must take care of yourself, Mrs. Elton.—This letter tells us—it is a short letter—written in a hurry, merely to give us notice—it tells us that they are all coming up to town directly, on Mrs. Churchill's account—she has not been well the whole winter, and thinks Enscombe too cold for her—so they are all to move southward without loss of time."

"Indeed!—from Yorkshire, I think. Enscombe is in Yorkshire?"

"Yes, they are about one hundred and ninety miles from London. A considerable journey."

"Yes, upon my word, very considerable. Sixty-five miles farther than from Maple Grove to London. But what is distance, Mr. Weston, to people of large fortune?—You would be amazed to hear how my brother, Mr. Suckling, sometimes flies about. You will hardly believe me—but twice in one week he and Mr. Bragge went to London and back again with four horses."

"The evil of the distance from Enscombe," said Mr. Weston, "is, that Mrs. Churchill, as we understand, has not been able to leave the sofa for a week together. In Frank's last letter she complained, he said, of being too weak to get into her conservatory without having both his arm and his uncle's! This, you know, speaks a great degree of weakness—but now she is so impatient to be in town, that she means to sleep only two nights on the road.—So Frank writes word. Certainly, delicate ladies have very extraordinary constitutions, Mrs. Elton. You must grant me that."

"No, indeed, I shall grant you nothing. I Always take the part of my own sex. I do indeed. I give you notice—You will find me a formidable antagonist on that point. I always stand up for women—and I assure you, if you knew how Selina feels with respect to sleeping at an inn, you would not wonder at Mrs. Churchill's making incredible exertions to avoid it. Selina says it is quite horror to her—and I believe I have caught a little of her nicety. She always travels with her own sheets; an excellent precaution. Does Mrs. Churchill do the same?"

"Depend upon it, Mrs. Churchill does every thing that any other fine lady ever did. Mrs. Churchill will not be second to any lady in the land for"—

Mrs. Elton eagerly interposed with,

"Oh! Mr. Weston, do not mistake me. Selina is no fine lady, I assure you. Do not run away with such an idea."

"Is not she? Then she is no rule for Mrs. Churchill, who is as thorough a fine lady as any body ever beheld."

Mrs. Elton began to think she had been wrong in disclaiming so warmly. It was by no means her object to have it believed that her sister was not a fine lady; perhaps there was want of spirit in the pretence of it;—and she was considering in what way she had best retract, when Mr. Weston went on.

"Mrs. Churchill is not much in my good graces, as you may suspect—but this is quite between ourselves. She is very fond of Frank, and therefore I would not speak ill of her. Besides, she is out of health now; but that indeed, by her own account, she has always been. I would not say so to every body, Mrs. Elton, but I have not much faith in Mrs. Churchill's illness."

"If she is really ill, why not go to Bath, Mr. Weston?—To Bath, or to Clifton?" "She has taken it into her head that Enscombe is too cold for her. The fact is, I suppose, that she is tired of Enscombe. She has now been a longer time stationary there, than she ever was before, and she begins to want change. It is a retired place. A fine place, but very retired."

"Aye—like Maple Grove, I dare say. Nothing can stand more retired from the road than Maple Grove. Such an immense plantation all round it! You seem shut out from every thing—in the most complete retirement.—And Mrs. Churchill probably has not health or spirits like Selina to enjoy that sort of seclusion. Or, perhaps she may not have resources enough in herself to be qualified for a country life. I always say a woman cannot have too many resources—and I feel very thankful that I have so many myself as to be quite independent of society."

"Frank was here in February for a fortnight."

"So I remember to have heard. He will find an addition to the society of Highbury when he comes again; that is, if I may presume to call myself an addition. But perhaps he may never have heard of there being such a creature in the world."

This was too loud a call for a compliment to be passed by, and Mr. Weston, with a very good grace, immediately exclaimed,

"My dear madam! Nobody but yourself could imagine such a thing possible. Not heard of you!—I believe Mrs. Weston's letters lately have been full of very little else than Mrs. Elton."

He had done his duty and could return to his son.

"When Frank left us," continued he, "it was quite uncertain when we might see him again, which makes this day's news doubly welcome. It has been completely unexpected. That is, I always had a strong persuasion he would be here again soon, I was sure something favourable would turn up—but nobody believed me. He and Mrs. Weston were both dreadfully desponding. 'How could he contrive to come? And how could it be supposed that his uncle and aunt would spare him again?' and so forth—I always felt that something would happen in our favour; and so it has, you see. I have observed, Mrs. Elton, in the course of my life, that if things are going untowardly one month, they are sure to mend the next."

"Very true, Mr. Weston, perfectly true. It is just what I used to say to a certain gentleman in company in the days of courtship, when, because things did not go quite right, did not proceed with all the rapidity which suited his feelings, he was apt to be in despair, and exclaim that he was sure at this rate it would be May before Hymen's saffron robe would be put on for us. Oh! the pains I have been at to dispel those gloomy ideas and give him cheerfuller views! The carriage—we had disappointments about the carriage;—one morning, I remember, he came to me quite in despair."

She was stopped by a slight fit of coughing, and Mr. Weston instantly seized the opportunity of going on.

"You were mentioning May. May is the very month which Mrs. Churchill is ordered, or has ordered herself, to spend in some warmer place than Enscombe—in short, to spend in London; so that we have the agreeable prospect of frequent visits from Frank the whole spring—precisely the season of the year which one should have chosen for it: days almost at the longest; weather genial and pleasant, always inviting one out, and never too hot for exercise. When he was here before, we made the best of it; but there was a good deal of wet, damp, cheerless weather; there always is in February, you know, and we could not do half that we intended. Now will be the time. This will be complete enjoyment; and I do not know, Mrs. Elton, whether the uncertainty of our meetings, the sort of constant expectation there will be of his coming in to-day or to-morrow, and at any hour, may not be more friendly to happiness than having him actually in the house. I think it is so. I think it is the state of mind which gives most spirit and delight. I hope you will be pleased with my son; but you must not expect a prodigy. He is generally thought a fine young man, but do not expect a prodigy. Mrs. Weston's partiality for him is very great, and, as you may suppose, most gratifying to me. She thinks nobody equal to him."

"And I assure you, Mr. Weston, I have very little doubt that my opinion will be decidedly in his favour. I have heard so much in praise of Mr. Frank Churchill.—At the same time it is fair to observe, that I am one of those who always judge for themselves, and are by no means implicitly guided by others. I give you notice that as I find your son, so I shall judge of him.—I am no flatterer."

Mr. Weston was musing.

"I hope," said he presently, "I have not been severe upon poor Mrs. Churchill. If she is ill I should be sorry to do her injustice; but there are some traits in her character which make it difficult for me to speak of her with the forbearance I could wish. You cannot be ignorant, Mrs. Elton, of my connexion with the family, nor of the treatment I have met with; and, between ourselves, the whole blame of it is to be laid to her. She was the instigator. Frank's mother would never have been slighted as she was but for her. Mr. Churchill has pride; but his pride is nothing to his wife's: his is a quiet, indolent, gentlemanlike sort of pride that would harm nobody, and only make himself a little helpless and tiresome; but her pride is arrogance and insolence! And what inclines one less to bear, she has no fair pretence of family or blood. She was nobody when he married her, barely the daughter of a gentleman; but ever since her being turned into a Churchill she has out-Churchill'd them all in high and mighty claims: but in herself, I assure you, she is an upstart."

"Only think! well, that must be infinitely provoking! I have quite a horror of upstarts. Maple Grove has given me a thorough disgust to people of that sort; for there is a family in that neighbourhood who are such an annoyance to my brother and sister from the airs they give themselves! Your description of Mrs. Churchill made me think of them directly. People of the name of Tupman, very lately settled there, and encumbered with many low connexions, but giving themselves immense airs, and expecting to be on a footing with the old established families. A year and a half is the very utmost that they can have lived at West Hall; and how they got their fortune nobody knows. They came from Birmingham, which is not a place to promise much, you know, Mr. Weston. One has not great hopes from Birmingham. I always say there is something direful in the sound: but nothing more is positively known of the Tupmans, though a good many things I assure you are suspected; and yet by their manners they evidently think themselves equal even to my brother, Mr. Suckling, who happens to be one of their nearest neighbours. It is infinitely too bad. Mr. Suckling, who has been eleven years a resident at Maple Grove, and whose father had it before him—I believe, at least—I am almost sure that old Mr. Suckling had completed the purchase before his death."

They were interrupted. Tea was carrying round, and Mr. Weston, having said all that he wanted, soon took the opportunity of walking away.

After tea, Mr. and Mrs. Weston, and Mr. Elton sat down with Mr. Woodhouse to cards. The remaining five were left to their own powers, and Emma doubted their getting on very well; for Mr. Knightley seemed little disposed for conversation; Mrs. Elton was wanting notice, which nobody had inclination to pay, and she was herself in a worry of spirits which would have made her prefer being silent.

Mr. John Knightley proved more talkative than his brother. He was to leave them early the next day; and he soon began with—

"Well, Emma, I do not believe I have any thing more to say about the boys; but you have your sister's letter, and every thing is down at full length there we may be sure. My charge would be much more concise than her's, and probably not much in the same spirit; all that I have to recommend being comprised in, do not spoil them, and do not physic them."

"I rather hope to satisfy you both," said Emma, "for I shall do all in my power to make them happy, which will be enough for Isabella; and happiness must preclude false indulgence and physic."

"And if you find them troublesome, you must send them home again."

"That is very likely. You think so, do not you?"

"I hope I am aware that they may be too noisy for your father—or even may be some encumbrance to you, if your visiting engagements continue to increase as much as they have done lately."

"Increase!"

"Certainly; you must be sensible that the last half-year has made a great difference in your way of life."

"Difference! No indeed I am not."

"There can be no doubt of your being much more engaged with company than you used to be. Witness this very time. Here am I come down for only one day, and you are engaged with a dinner-party!—When did it happen before, or any thing like it? Your neighbourhood is increasing, and you mix more with it. A little while ago, every letter to Isabella brought an account of fresh gaieties; dinners at Mr. Cole's, or balls at the Crown. The difference which Randalls, Randalls alone makes in your goings-on, is very great."

"Yes," said his brother quickly, "it is Randalls that does it all."

"Very well—and as Randalls, I suppose, is not likely to have less influence than heretofore, it strikes me as a possible thing, Emma, that Henry and John may be sometimes in the way. And if they are, I only beg you to send them home."

"No," cried Mr. Knightley, "that need not be the consequence. Let them be sent to Donwell. I shall certainly be at leisure."

"Upon my word," exclaimed Emma, "you amuse me! I should like to know how many of all my numerous engagements take place without your being of the party; and why I am to be supposed in danger of wanting leisure to attend to the little boys. These amazing engagements of mine—what have they been? Dining once with the Coles—and having a ball talked of, which never took place. I can understand you—(nodding at Mr. John Knightley)—your good fortune in meeting with so many of your friends at once here, delights you too much to pass unnoticed. But you, (turning to Mr. Knightley,) who know how very, very seldom I am ever two hours from Hartfield, why you should foresee such a series of dissipation for me, I cannot imagine. And as to my dear little boys, I must say, that if Aunt Emma has not time for them, I do not think they would fare much better with Uncle Knightley, who is absent from home about five hours where she is absent one—and who, when he is at home, is either reading to himself or settling his accounts."

Mr. Knightley seemed to be trying not to smile; and succeeded without difficulty, upon Mrs. Elton's beginning to talk to him.

VOLUME III

Chapter I

A very little quiet reflection was enough to satisfy Emma as to the nature of her agitation on hearing this news of Frank Churchill. She was soon convinced that it was not for herself she was feeling at all apprehensive or embarrassed; it was for him. Her own attachment had really subsided into a mere nothing; it was not worth thinking of;—but if he, who had undoubtedly been always so much the most in love of the two, were to be returning with the same warmth of sentiment which he had taken away, it would be very distressing. If a separation of two months should not have cooled him, there were dangers and evils before her:—caution for him and for herself would be necessary. She did not mean to have her own affections entangled again, and it would be incumbent on her to avoid any encouragement of his.

She wished she might be able to keep him from an absolute declaration. That would be so very painful a conclusion of their present acquaintance! and yet, she could not help rather anticipating something decisive. She felt as if the spring would not pass without bringing a crisis, an event, a something to alter her present composed and tranquil state.

It was not very long, though rather longer than Mr. Weston had foreseen, before she had the power of forming some opinion of Frank Churchill's feelings. The Enscombe family were not in town quite so soon as had been imagined, but he was at Highbury very soon afterwards. He rode down for a couple of hours; he could not yet do more; but as he came from Randalls immediately to Hartfield, she could then exercise all her quick observation, and speedily determine how he was influenced, and how she must act. They met with the utmost friendliness. There could be no doubt of his great pleasure in seeing her. But she had an almost instant doubt of his caring for her as he had done, of his feeling the same tenderness in the same degree. She watched him well. It was a clear thing he was less in love than he had been. Absence, with the conviction probably of her indifference, had produced this very natural and very desirable effect.

He was in high spirits; as ready to talk and laugh as ever, and seemed delighted to speak of his former visit, and recur to old stories: and he was not without agitation. It was not in his calmness that she read his comparative difference. He was not calm; his spirits were evidently fluttered; there was restlessness about him. Lively as he was, it seemed a liveliness that did not satisfy himself; but what decided her belief on the subject, was his staying only a quarter of an hour, and hurrying away to make other calls in Highbury. "He had seen a group of old acquaintance in the street as he passed—he had not stopped, he would not stop for more than a word—but he had the vanity to think they would be disappointed if he did not call, and much as he wished to stay longer at Hartfield, he must hurry off." She had no doubt as to his being less in love—but neither his agitated spirits, nor his hurrying away, seemed like a perfect cure; and she was rather inclined to think it implied a dread of her returning power, and a discreet resolution of not trusting himself with her long.

This was the only visit from Frank Churchill in the course of ten days. He was often hoping, intending to come—but was always prevented. His aunt could not bear to have him leave her. Such was his own account at Randall's. If he were quite sincere, if he really tried to come, it was to be inferred that Mrs. Churchill's removal to London had been of no service to the wilful or nervous part of her disorder. That she was really ill was very certain; he had declared himself convinced of it, at Randalls. Though much might be fancy, he could not doubt, when he looked back, that she was in a weaker state of health than she had been half a year ago. He did not believe it to proceed from any thing that care and medicine might not remove, or at least that she might not have many years of existence before her; but he could not be prevailed on, by all his father's doubts, to say that her complaints were merely imaginary, or that she was as strong as ever.

It soon appeared that London was not the place for her. She could not endure its noise. Her nerves were under continual irritation and suffering; and by the ten days' end, her nephew's letter to

Randalls communicated a change of plan. They were going to remove immediately to Richmond. Mrs. Churchill had been recommended to the medical skill of an eminent person there, and had otherwise a fancy for the place. A ready-furnished house in a favourite spot was engaged, and much benefit expected from the change.

Emma heard that Frank wrote in the highest spirits of this arrangement, and seemed most fully to appreciate the blessing of having two months before him of such near neighbourhood to many dear friends—for the house was taken for May and June. She was told that now he wrote with the greatest confidence of being often with them, almost as often as he could even wish.

Emma saw how Mr. Weston understood these joyous prospects. He was considering her as the source of all the happiness they offered. She hoped it was not so. Two months must bring it to the proof.

Mr. Weston's own happiness was indisputable. He was quite delighted. It was the very circumstance he could have wished for. Now, it would be really having Frank in their neighbourhood. What were nine miles to a young man?—An hour's ride. He would be always coming over. The difference in that respect of Richmond and London was enough to make the whole difference of seeing him always and seeing him never. Sixteen miles—nay, eighteen—it must be full eighteen to Manchester-street—was a serious obstacle. Were he ever able to get away, the day would be spent in coming and returning. There was no comfort in having him in London; he might as well be at Enscombe; but Richmond was the very distance for easy intercourse. Better than nearer!

One good thing was immediately brought to a certainty by this removal,—the ball at the Crown. It had not been forgotten before, but it had been soon acknowledged vain to attempt to fix a day. Now, however, it was absolutely to be; every preparation was resumed, and very soon after the Churchills had removed to Richmond, a few lines from Frank, to say that his aunt felt already much better for the change, and that he had no doubt of being able to join them for twenty-four hours at any given time, induced them to name as early a day as possible.

Mr. Weston's ball was to be a real thing. A very few to-morrows stood between the young people of Highbury and happiness.

Mr. Woodhouse was resigned. The time of year lightened the evil to him. May was better for every thing than February. Mrs. Bates was engaged to spend the evening at Hartfield, James had due notice, and he sanguinely hoped that neither dear little Henry nor dear little John would have any thing the matter with them, while dear Emma were gone.

Chapter II

No misfortune occurred, again to prevent the ball. The day approached, the day arrived; and after a morning of some anxious watching, Frank Churchill, in all the certainty of his own self, reached Randalls before dinner, and every thing was safe.

No second meeting had there yet been between him and Emma. The room at the Crown was to witness it;—but it would be better than a common meeting in a crowd. Mr. Weston had been so very earnest in his entreaties for her arriving there as soon as possible after themselves, for the purpose of taking her opinion as to the propriety and comfort of the rooms before any other persons came, that she could not refuse him, and must therefore spend some quiet interval in the young man's company. She was to convey Harriet, and they drove to the Crown in good time, the Randalls party just sufficiently before them.

Frank Churchill seemed to have been on the watch; and though he did not say much, his eyes declared that he meant to have a delightful evening. They all walked about together, to see that every thing was as it should be; and within a few minutes were joined by the contents of another carriage, which Emma could not hear the sound of at first, without great surprize. "So unreasonably early!" she was going to exclaim; but she presently found that it was a family of old friends, who were coming, like herself, by particular desire, to help Mr. Weston's judgment; and they were so very closely followed by another carriage of cousins, who had been entreated to come early with the same distinguishing earnestness, on the same errand, that it seemed as if half the company might soon be collected together for the purpose of preparatory inspection.

Emma perceived that her taste was not the only taste on which Mr. Weston depended, and felt, that to be the favourite and intimate of a man who had so many intimates and confidantes, was not the very first distinction in the scale of vanity. She liked his open manners, but a little less of open-heartedness would have made him a higher character.—General benevolence, but not general friendship, made a man what he ought to be.—She could fancy such a man. The whole party walked about, and looked, and praised again; and then, having nothing else to do, formed a sort of half-circle round the fire, to observe in their various modes, till other subjects were started, that, though May, a fire in the evening was still very pleasant.

Emma found that it was not Mr. Weston's fault that the number of privy councillors was not yet larger. They had stopped at Mrs. Bates's door to offer the use of their carriage, but the aunt and niece were to be brought by the Eltons.

Frank was standing by her, but not steadily; there was a restlessness, which shewed a mind not at ease. He was looking about, he was going to the door, he was watching for the sound of other carriages,—impatient to begin, or afraid of being always near her.

Mrs. Elton was spoken of. "I think she must be here soon," said he. "I have a great curiosity to see Mrs. Elton, I have heard so much of her. It cannot be long, I think, before she comes."

A carriage was heard. He was on the move immediately; but coming back, said,

"I am forgetting that I am not acquainted with her. I have never seen either Mr. or Mrs. Elton. I have no business to put myself forward."

Mr. and Mrs. Elton appeared; and all the smiles and the proprieties passed.

"But Miss Bates and Miss Fairfax!" said Mr. Weston, looking about. "We thought you were to bring them."

The mistake had been slight. The carriage was sent for them now. Emma longed to know what Frank's first opinion of Mrs. Elton might be; how he was affected by the studied elegance of her dress, and her smiles of graciousness. He was immediately qualifying himself to form an opinion, by giving her very proper attention, after the introduction had passed.

In a few minutes the carriage returned.—Somebody talked of rain.—"I will see that there are umbrellas, sir," said Frank to his father: "Miss Bates must not be forgotten:" and away he went. Mr. Weston was following; but Mrs. Elton detained him, to gratify him by her opinion of his son; and so briskly did she begin, that the young man himself, though by no means moving slowly, could hardly be out of hearing.

"A very fine young man indeed, Mr. Weston. You know I candidly told you I should form my own opinion; and I am happy to say that I am extremely pleased with him.—You may believe me. I never compliment. I think him a very handsome young man, and his manners are precisely what I like and approve—so truly the gentleman, without the least conceit or puppyism. You must know I have a vast dislike to puppies—quite a horror of them. They were never tolerated at Maple Grove. Neither Mr. Suckling nor me had ever any patience with them; and we used sometimes to say very cutting things! Selina, who is mild almost to a fault, bore with them much better."

While she talked of his son, Mr. Weston's attention was chained; but when she got to Maple Grove, he could recollect that there were ladies just arriving to be attended to, and with happy smiles must hurry away.

Mrs. Elton turned to Mrs. Weston. "I have no doubt of its being our carriage with Miss Bates and Jane. Our coachman and horses are so extremely expeditious!—I believe we drive faster than any body.—What a pleasure it is to send one's carriage for a friend!—I understand you were so kind as to offer, but another time it will be quite unnecessary. You may be very sure I shall always take care of them."

Miss Bates and Miss Fairfax, escorted by the two gentlemen, walked into the room; and Mrs. Elton seemed to think it as much her duty as Mrs. Weston's to receive them. Her gestures and movements might be understood by any one who looked on like Emma; but her words, every body's words, were soon lost under the incessant flow of Miss Bates, who came in talking, and had not finished her speech under many minutes after her being admitted into the circle at the fire. As the door opened she was heard,

"So very obliging of you!—No rain at all. Nothing to signify. I do not care for myself. Quite thick shoes. And Jane declares—Well!—

(as soon as she was within the door) Well! This is brilliant indeed!—This is admirable!—Excellently contrived, upon my word. Nothing wanting. Could not have imagined it.—So well lighted up!—Jane, Jane, look!—did you ever see any thing? Oh! Mr. Weston, you must really have had Aladdin's lamp. Good Mrs. Stokes would not know her own room again. I saw her as I came in; she was standing in the entrance. 'Oh! Mrs. Stokes,' said I—but I had not time for more." She was now met by Mrs. Weston.—"Very well, I thank you, ma'am. I hope you are quite well. Very happy to hear it. So afraid you might have a headach!—seeing you pass by so often, and knowing how much trouble you must have. Delighted to hear it indeed. Ah! dear Mrs. Elton, so obliged to you for the carriage!—excellent time. Jane and I quite ready. Did not keep the horses a moment. Most comfortable carriage.—Oh! and I am sure our thanks are due to you, Mrs. Weston, on that score. Mrs. Elton had most kindly sent Jane a note, or we should have been.—But two such offers in one day!—Never were such neighbours. I said to my mother, 'Upon my word, ma'am—.' Thank you, my mother is remarkably well. Gone to Mr. Woodhouse's. I made her take her shawl—for the evenings are not warm—her large new shawl—Mrs. Dixon's wedding-present.—So kind of her to think of my mother! Bought at Weymouth, you know—Mr. Dixon's choice. There were three others, Jane says, which they hesitated about some time. Colonel Campbell rather preferred an olive. My dear Jane, are you sure you did not wet your feet?—It was but a drop or two, but I am so afraid:—but Mr. Frank Churchill was so extremely—and there was a mat to step upon—I shall never forget his extreme politeness.—Oh! Mr. Frank Churchill, I must tell you my mother's spectacles have never been in fault since; the rivet never came out again. My mother often talks of your good-nature. Does not she, Jane?—Do not we often talk of Mr. Frank Churchill?—Ah! here's Miss Woodhouse.—Dear Miss Woodhouse, how do you do?—Very well I thank you, quite well. This is meeting quite in fairy-land!—Such a transformation!—Must not compliment, I know (eyeing Emma most complacently)—that would be rude—but upon my word, Miss Woodhouse, you do look—how do you like Jane's hair?—You are a judge.—She did it all herself. Quite wonderful how she does her hair!—No hairdresser from London I think could.—Ah! Dr. Hughes I declare—and Mrs. Hughes. Must go and speak to Dr. and

Mrs. Hughes for a moment.—How do you do? How do you do?—Very well, I thank you. This is delightful, is not it?—Where's dear Mr. Richard?—Oh! there he is. Don't disturb him. Much better employed talking to the young ladies. How do you do, Mr. Richard?—I saw you the other day as you rode through the town—Mrs. Otway, I protest!—and good Mr. Otway, and Miss Otway and Miss Caroline.—Such a host of friends!—and Mr. George and Mr. Arthur!—How do you do? How do you all do?—Quite well, I am much obliged to you. Never better.—Don't I hear another carriage?—Who can this be?—very likely the worthy Coles.—Upon my word, this is charming to be standing about among such friends! And such a noble fire!—I am quite roasted. No coffee, I thank you, for me—never take coffee.—A little tea if you please, sir, by and bye,—no hurry—Oh! here it comes. Every thing so good!"

Frank Churchill returned to his station by Emma; and as soon as Miss Bates was quiet, she found herself necessarily overhearing the discourse of Mrs. Elton and Miss Fairfax, who were standing a little way behind her.—He was thoughtful. Whether he were overhearing too, she could not determine. After a good many compliments to Jane on her dress and look, compliments very quietly and properly taken, Mrs. Elton was evidently wanting to be complimented herself—and it was, "How do you like my gown?—How do you like my trimming?—How has Wright done my hair?"—with many other relative questions, all answered with patient politeness. Mrs. Elton then said, "Nobody can think less of dress in general than I do—but upon such an occasion as this, when every body's eyes are so much upon me, and in compliment to the Westons—who I have no doubt are giving this ball chiefly to do me honour—I would not wish to be inferior to others. And I see very few pearls in the room except mine.—So Frank Churchill is a capital dancer, I understand.—We shall see if our styles suit.—A fine young man certainly is Frank Churchill. I like him very well."

At this moment Frank began talking so vigorously, that Emma could not but imagine he had overheard his own praises, and did not want to hear more;—and the voices of the ladies were drowned for a while, till another suspension brought Mrs. Elton's tones again distinctly forward.—Mr. Elton had just joined them, and his wife was exclaiming,

"Oh! you have found us out at last, have you, in our seclusion?—I was this moment telling Jane, I thought you would begin to be impatient for tidings of us."

"Jane!"—repeated Frank Churchill, with a look of surprize and displeasure.—"That is easy—but Miss Fairfax does not disapprove it, I suppose."

"How do you like Mrs. Elton?" said Emma in a whisper.

"Not at all."

"You are ungrateful."

"Ungrateful!—What do you mean?" Then changing from a frown to a smile—"No, do not tell me—I do not want to know what you mean.—Where is my father?—When are we to begin dancing?"

Emma could hardly understand him; he seemed in an odd humour. He walked off to find his father, but was quickly back again with both Mr. and Mrs. Weston. He had met with them in a little perplexity, which must be laid before Emma. It had just occurred to Mrs. Weston that Mrs. Elton must be asked to begin the ball; that she would expect it; which interfered with all their wishes of giving Emma that distinction.—Emma heard the sad truth with fortitude.

"And what are we to do for a proper partner for her?" said Mr. Weston. "She will think Frank ought to ask her."

Frank turned instantly to Emma, to claim her former promise; and boasted himself an engaged man, which his father looked his most perfect approbation of—and it then appeared that Mrs. Weston was wanting him to dance with Mrs. Elton himself, and that their business was to help to persuade him into it, which was done pretty soon.—Mr. Weston and Mrs. Elton led the way, Mr. Frank Churchill and Miss Woodhouse followed. Emma must submit to stand second to Mrs. Elton, though she had always considered the ball as peculiarly for her. It was almost enough to make her think of marrying. Mrs. Elton had undoubtedly the advantage, at this time, in vanity completely gratified; for though she had intended to begin with Frank Churchill, she could not lose by the change. Mr. Weston might be his son's superior.—In spite of this little rub, however, Emma was smiling with enjoyment, delighted to see the respectable length of the set as it was forming, and to feel that she had so many hours of unusual festivity before her.—She was more disturbed by Mr. Knightley's not dancing than by any thing else.—There he was, among the standers-by, where he ought not to be; he ought to be dancing,—not classing himself with the husbands, and fathers, and whist-players, who were pretending to feel an interest in the dance till their rubbers were made up,—so young as he looked!—He could not have appeared to greater advantage perhaps anywhere, than where he had placed himself. His tall, firm, upright figure, among the bulky forms and stooping shoulders of the elderly men, was such as Emma felt must draw every body's eyes; and, excepting her own partner, there was not one among the whole row of young men who could be compared with him.—He moved a few steps nearer, and those few steps were enough to prove in how gentlemanlike a manner, with what natural grace, he must have danced, would he but take the trouble.—Whenever she caught his eye, she forced him to smile; but in general he was looking grave. She wished he could love a ballroom better, and could like Frank Churchill better.—He seemed often observing her. She must not flatter herself that he thought of her dancing, but if he were criticising her behaviour, she did not feel afraid. There was nothing like flirtation between her and her partner. They seemed more like cheerful, easy friends, than lovers. That Frank Churchill thought less of her than he had done, was indubitable.

The ball proceeded pleasantly. The anxious cares, the incessant attentions of Mrs. Weston, were not thrown away. Every body seemed happy; and the praise of being a delightful ball, which is seldom bestowed till after a ball has ceased to be, was repeatedly given in the very beginning of the existence of this. Of very important, very recordable events, it was not more productive than such meetings usually are. There was one, however, which Emma thought something of.—The two last dances before supper were begun, and Harriet had no partner;—the only young lady sitting down;—and so equal had been hitherto the number of dancers, that how there could be any one disengaged was the wonder!—But Emma's wonder lessened soon afterwards, on seeing Mr. Elton sauntering about. He would not ask Harriet to dance if it were possible to be avoided: she was sure he would not—and she was expecting him every moment to escape into the card-room.

Escape, however, was not his plan. He came to the part of the room where the sitters-by were collected, spoke to some, and walked about in front of them, as if to shew his liberty, and his resolution of maintaining it. He did not omit being sometimes directly before Miss Smith, or speaking to those who were close to her.—Emma saw it. She was not yet dancing; she was working her way up from the bottom, and had therefore leisure to look around, and by only turning her head a little she saw it all. When she was half-way up the set, the whole group were exactly behind her, and she would no longer allow her eyes to watch; but Mr. Elton was so near, that she heard every syllable of a dialogue which just then took place between him and Mrs. Weston; and she perceived that his wife, who was standing immediately above her, was not only listening also, but even encouraging him by significant glances.—The kind-hearted, gentle Mrs. Weston had left her seat to join him and say, "Do not you dance, Mr. Elton?" to which his prompt reply was, "Most readily, Mrs. Weston, if you will dance with me."

"Me!—oh! no—I would get you a better partner than myself. I am no dancer."

"If Mrs. Gilbert wishes to dance," said he, "I shall have great pleasure, I am sure—for, though beginning to feel myself rather an old married man, and that my dancing days are over, it would give me very great pleasure at any time to stand up with an old friend like Mrs. Gilbert."

"Mrs. Gilbert does not mean to dance, but there is a young lady disengaged whom I should be very glad to see dancing—Miss Smith." "Miss Smith!—oh!—I had not observed.—You are extremely obliging—and if I were not an old married man.—But my dancing days are over, Mrs. Weston. You will excuse me. Any thing else I should be most happy to do, at your command—but my dancing days are over."

Mrs. Weston said no more; and Emma could imagine with what surprize and mortification she must be returning to her seat. This was Mr. Elton! the amiable, obliging, gentle Mr. Elton.—She looked round for a moment; he had joined Mr. Knightley at a little distance, and was arranging himself for settled conversation, while smiles of high glee passed between him and his wife.

She would not look again. Her heart was in a glow, and she feared her face might be as hot.

In another moment a happier sight caught her;—Mr. Knightley leading Harriet to the set!—Never had she been more surprized, seldom more delighted, than at that instant. She was all pleasure and gratitude, both for Harriet and herself, and longed to be thanking him; and though too distant for speech, her countenance said much, as soon as she could catch his eye again.

His dancing proved to be just what she had believed it, extremely good; and Harriet would have seemed almost too lucky, if it had not been for the cruel state of things before, and for the very complete enjoyment and very high sense of the distinction which her happy features announced. It was not thrown away on her, she bounded higher than ever, flew farther down the middle, and was in a continual course of smiles.

Mr. Elton had retreated into the card-room, looking (Emma trusted) very foolish. She did not think he was quite so hardened as his wife, though growing very like her;—she spoke some of her feelings, by observing audibly to her partner,

"Knightley has taken pity on poor little Miss Smith!—Very goodnatured, I declare."

Supper was announced. The move began; and Miss Bates might be heard from that moment, without interruption, till her being seated at table and taking up her spoon.

"Jane, Jane, my dear Jane, where are you?—Here is your tippet. Mrs. Weston begs you to put on your tippet. She says she is afraid there will be draughts in the passage, though every thing has been done—One door nailed up—Quantities of matting—My dear Jane, indeed you must. Mr. Churchill, oh! you are too obliging! How well you put it on!—so gratified! Excellent dancing indeed!—Yes, my dear, I ran home, as I said I should, to help grandmama to bed, and got back again, and nobody missed me.—I set off without saying a word, just as I told you. Grandmama was quite well, had a charming evening with Mr. Woodhouse, a vast deal of chat, and backgammon.—Tea was made downstairs, biscuits and baked apples and wine before she came away: amazing luck in some of her throws: and she inquired a great deal about you, how you were amused, and who were your partners. 'Oh!' said I, 'I shall not forestall Jane; I left her dancing with Mr. George Otway; she will love to tell you all about it herself to-morrow: her first partner was Mr. Elton, I do not know who will ask her next, perhaps Mr. William Cox.' My dear sir, you are too obliging.—Is there nobody you would not rather?—I am not helpless. Sir, you are most kind. Upon my word, Jane on one arm, and me on the other!—Stop, stop, let us stand a little back, Mrs. Elton is going; dear Mrs. Elton, how elegant she looks!—Beautiful lace!—Now we all follow in her train. Quite the queen of the evening!—Well, here we are at the passage. Two steps, Jane, take care of the two steps. Oh! no, there is but one. Well, I was persuaded there were two. How very odd! I was convinced there were two, and there is but one. I never saw any thing equal to the comfort and style—Candles everywhere.—I was telling you of your grandmama, Jane,—There was a little disappointment.—The baked apples and biscuits, excellent in their way, you know; but there was a delicate fricassee of sweetbread and some asparagus brought in at first, and good Mr. Woodhouse, not thinking the asparagus quite boiled enough, sent it all out again. Now there is nothing grandmama loves better than sweetbread and asparagus—so she was rather disappointed, but we agreed we would not speak of it to any body, for fear of its getting round to dear Miss Woodhouse, who would be so very much concerned!—Well, this is brilliant! I am all amazement! could not have supposed any thing!—Such elegance and profusion!—I have seen nothing like it since—Well, where shall we sit? where shall we sit? Anywhere, so that Jane is not in a draught. Where I sit is of no consequence. Oh! do you recommend this side?—Well, I am sure, Mr. Churchill—only it seems too good—but just as you please. What you direct in this house cannot be wrong. Dear Jane, how shall we ever recollect half the dishes for grandmama? Soup too! Bless me! I should not be helped so soon, but it smells most excellent, and I cannot help beginning."

Emma had no opportunity of speaking to Mr. Knightley till after supper; but, when they were all in the ballroom again, her eyes invited him irresistibly to come to her and be thanked. He was warm in his reprobation of Mr. Elton's conduct; it had been unpardonable rudeness; and Mrs. Elton's looks also received the due share of censure.

"They aimed at wounding more than Harriet," said he. "Emma, why is it that they are your enemies?"

He looked with smiling penetration; and, on receiving no answer, added, "She ought not to be angry with you, I suspect, whatever he may be.—To that surmise, you say nothing, of course; but confess, Emma, that you did want him to marry Harriet."

"I did," replied Emma, "and they cannot forgive me."

He shook his head; but there was a smile of indulgence with it, and he only said,

"I shall not scold you. I leave you to your own reflections."

"Can you trust me with such flatterers?—Does my vain spirit ever tell me I am wrong?"

"Not your vain spirit, but your serious spirit.—If one leads you wrong, I am sure the other tells you of it."

"I do own myself to have been completely mistaken in Mr. Elton. There is a littleness about him which you discovered, and which I did not: and I was fully convinced of his being in love with Harriet. It was through a series of strange blunders!"

"And, in return for your acknowledging so much, I will do you the justice to say, that you would have chosen for him better than he has chosen for himself.—Harrict Smith has some first-rate qualities, which Mrs. Elton is totally without. An unpretending, single-minded, artless girl—infinitely to be preferred by any man of sense and taste to such a woman as Mrs. Elton. I found Harriet more conversable than I expected."

Emma was extremely gratified.—They were interrupted by the bustle of Mr. Weston calling on every body to begin dancing again.

"Come Miss Woodhouse, Miss Otway, Miss Fairfax, what are you all doing?—Come Emma, set your companions the example. Every body is lazy! Every body is asleep!"

"I am ready," said Emma, "whenever I am wanted."

"Whom are you going to dance with?" asked Mr. Knightley.

She hesitated a moment, and then replied, "With you, if you will ask me."

"Will you?" said he, offering his hand.

"Indeed I will. You have shewn that you can dance, and you know we are not really so much brother and sister as to make it at all improper."

"Brother and sister! no, indeed."

Chapter III

This little explanation with Mr. Knightley gave Emma considerable pleasure. It was one of the agreeable recollections of the ball, which she walked about the lawn the next morning to enjoy.—She was extremely glad that they had come to so good an understanding respecting the Eltons, and that their opinions of both husband and wife were so much alike; and his praise of Harriet, his concession in her favour, was peculiarly gratifying. The impertinence of the Eltons, which for a few minutes had threatened to ruin the rest of her evening, had been the occasion of some of its highest satisfactions; and she looked forward to another happy result—the cure of Harriet's infatuation.—From Harriet's manner of speaking of the circumstance before they quitted the ballroom, she had strong hopes. It seemed as if her eyes were suddenly opened, and she were enabled to see that Mr. Elton was not the superior creature she had believed him. The fever was over, and Emma could harbour little fear of the pulse being quickened again by injurious courtesy. She depended on the evil feelings of the Eltons for supplying all the discipline of pointed neglect that could be farther requisite.—Harriet rational, Frank Churchill not too much in love, and Mr. Knightley not wanting to quarrel with her, how very happy a summer must be before her!

She was not to see Frank Churchill this morning. He had told her that he could not allow himself the pleasure of stopping at Hartfield, as he was to be at home by the middle of the day. She did not regret it.

Having arranged all these matters, looked them through, and put them all to rights, she was just turning to the house with spirits freshened up for the demands of the two little boys, as well as of their grandpapa, when the great iron sweep-gate opened, and two persons entered whom she had never less expected to see together—Frank Churchill, with Harriet leaning on his arm—actually Harriet!—A moment sufficed to convince her that something extraordinary had happened. Harriet looked white and frightened, and he was trying to cheer her.—The iron gates and the front-door were not twenty yards asunder;—they were all three soon in the hall, and Harriet immediately sinking into a chair fainted away.

A young lady who faints, must be recovered; questions must be answered, and surprizes be explained. Such events are very interesting, but the suspense of them cannot last long. A few minutes made Emma acquainted with the whole.

Miss Smith, and Miss Bickerton, another parlour boarder at Mrs. Goddard's, who had been also at the ball, had walked out together, and taken a road, the Richmond road, which, though apparently public enough for safety, had led them into alarm.—About half a mile beyond Highbury, making a sudden turn, and deeply shaded by elms on each side, it became for a considerable stretch very retired; and when the young ladies had advanced some way into it, they had suddenly perceived at a small distance before them, on a broader patch of greensward by the side, a party of gipsies. A child on the watch, came towards them to beg; and Miss Bickerton, excessively frightened, gave a great scream, and calling on Harriet to follow her, ran up a steep bank, cleared a slight hedge at the top, and made the best of her way by a short cut back to Highbury. But poor Harriet could not follow. She had suffered very much from cramp after dancing, and her first attempt to mount the bank brought on such a return of it as made her absolutely powerless—and in this state, and exceedingly terrified, she had been obliged to remain.

How the trampers might have behaved, had the young ladies been more courageous, must be doubtful; but such an invitation for attack could not be resisted; and Harriet was soon assailed by half a dozen children, headed by a stout woman and a great boy, all clamorous, and impertinent in look, though not absolutely in word.—More and more frightened, she immediately promised them money, and taking out her purse, gave them a shilling, and begged them not to want more, or to use her ill.—She was then able to walk, though but slowly, and was moving away—but her terror and her purse were too tempting, and she was followed, or rather surrounded, by the whole gang, demanding more.

In this state Frank Churchill had found her, she trembling and conditioning, they loud and insolent. By a most fortunate chance his leaving Highbury had been delayed so as to bring him to her assistance at this critical moment. The pleasantness of the morning had induced him to walk forward, and leave his horses to meet him by another road, a mile or two beyond Highbury—and happening to have borrowed a pair of scissors the night before of Miss Bates, and to have forgotten to restore them, he had been obliged to stop at her door, and go in for a few minutes: he was therefore later than he had intended; and being on foot, was unseen by the whole party till almost close to them. The terror which the woman and boy had been creating in Harriet was then their own portion. He had left them completely frightened; and Harriet eagerly clinging to him, and hardly able to speak, had just strength enough to reach Hartfield, before her spirits were quite overcome. It was his idea to bring her to Hartfield: he had thought of no other place.

This was the amount of the whole story,—of his communication and of Harriet's as soon as she had recovered her senses and speech.—He dared not stay longer than to see her well; these several delays left him not another minute to lose; and Emma engaging to give assurance of her safety to Mrs. Goddard, and notice of there being such a set of people in the neighbourhood to Mr. Knightley, he set off, with all the grateful blessings that she could utter for her friend and herself.

Such an adventure as this,—a fine young man and a lovely young woman thrown together in such a way, could hardly fail of suggesting certain ideas to the coldest heart and the steadiest brain. So Emma thought, at least. Could a linguist, could a grammarian, could even a mathematician have seen what she did, have witnessed their appearance together, and heard their history of it, without feeling that circumstances had been at work to make them peculiarly interesting to each other?—How much more must an imaginist, like herself, be on fire with speculation and foresight!—especially with such a groundwork of anticipation as her mind had already made.

It was a very extraordinary thing! Nothing of the sort had ever occurred before to any young ladies in the place, within her memory; no rencontre, no alarm of the kind;—and now it had happened to the very person, and at the very hour, when the other very person was chancing to pass by to rescue her!—It certainly was very extraordinary!—And knowing, as she did, the favourable state of mind of each at this period, it struck her the more. He was wishing to get the better of his attachment to herself, she just recovering from her mania for Mr. Elton. It seemed as if every thing united to promise the most interesting consequences. It was not possible that the occurrence should not be strongly recommending each to the other.

In the few minutes' conversation which she had yet had with him, while Harriet had been partially insensible, he had spoken of her terror, her naivete, her fervour as she seized and clung to his arm, with a sensibility amused and delighted; and just at last, after Harriet's own account had been given, he had expressed his indignation at the abominable folly of Miss Bickerton in the warmest terms. Every thing was to take its natural course, however, neither impelled nor assisted. She would not stir a step, nor drop a hint. No, she had had enough of interference. There could be no harm in a scheme, a mere passive scheme. It was no more than a wish. Beyond it she would on no account proceed.

Emma's first resolution was to keep her father from the knowledge of what had passed,—aware of the anxiety and alarm it would occasion: but she soon felt that concealment must be impossible. Within half an hour it was known all over Highbury. It was the very event to engage those who talk most, the young and the low; and all the youth and servants in the place were soon in the happiness of frightful news. The last night's ball seemed lost in the gipsies. Poor Mr. Woodhouse trembled as he sat, and, as Emma had foreseen, would scarcely be satisfied without their promising never to go beyond the shrubbery again. It was some comfort to him that many inquiries after himself and Miss Woodhouse (for his neighbours knew that he loved to be inquired after), as well as Miss Smith, were coming in during the rest of the day; and he had the pleasure of returning for answer, that they were all very indifferent—which, though not exactly true, for she was perfectly well, and Harriet not much otherwise, Emma would not interfere with. She had an unhappy state of health in general for the child of such a man, for she hardly knew what indisposition was; and if he did not invent illnesses for her, she could make no figure in a message.

The gipsies did not wait for the operations of justice; they took themselves off in a hurry. The young ladies of Highbury might have walked again in safety before their panic began, and the whole history dwindled soon into a matter of little importance but to Emma and her nephews:—in her imagination it maintained its ground, and Henry and John were still asking every day for the story of Harriet and the gipsies, and still tenaciously setting her right if she varied in the slightest particular from the original recital.

Chapter IV

A very few days had passed after this adventure, when Harriet came one morning to Emma with a small parcel in her hand, and after sitting down and hesitating, thus began:

"Miss Woodhouse—if you are at leisure—I have something that I should like to tell you—a sort of confession to make—and then, you know, it will be over."

Emma was a good deal surprized; but begged her to speak. There was a seriousness in Harriet's manner which prepared her, quite as much as her words, for something more than ordinary.

"It is my duty, and I am sure it is my wish," she continued, "to have no reserves with you on this subject. As I am happily quite an altered creature in one respect, it is very fit that you should have the satisfaction of knowing it. I do not want to say more than is necessary—I am too much ashamed of having given way as I have done, and I dare say you understand me."

"Yes," said Emma, "I hope I do."

"How I could so long a time be fancying myself! . . ." cried Harriet, warmly. "It seems like madness! I can see nothing at all extraordinary in him now.—I do not care whether I meet him or not—except that of the two I had rather not see him—and indeed I would go any distance round to avoid him—but I do not envy his wife in the least; I neither admire her nor envy her, as I have done: she is very charming, I dare say, and all that, but I think her very ill-tempered and disagreeable—I shall never forget her look the other night!—However, I assure you, Miss Woodhouse, I wish her no evil.—No, let them be ever so happy together, it will not give me another moment's pang: and to convince you that I have been speaking truth, I am now going to destroy—what I ought to have destroyed long ago—what I ought never to have kept—I know that very well (blushing as she spoke).—However, now I will destroy it all—and it is my particular wish to do it in your presence, that you may see how rational I am grown. Cannot you guess what this parcel holds?" said she, with a conscious look.

"Not the least in the world.—Did he ever give you any thing?"

"No—I cannot call them gifts; but they are things that I have valued very much."

She held the parcel towards her, and Emma read the words Most precious treasures on the top. Her curiosity was greatly excited. Harriet unfolded the parcel, and she looked on with impatience. Within abundance of silver paper was a pretty little Tunbridge-ware box, which Harriet opened: it was well lined with the softest cotton; but, excepting the cotton, Emma saw only a small piece of court-plaister.

"Now," said Harriet, "you must recollect."

"No, indeed I do not."

"Dear me! I should not have thought it possible you could forget what passed in this very room about court-plaister, one of the very last times we ever met in it!—It was but a very few days before I had my sore throat—just before Mr. and Mrs. John Knightley came—I think the very evening.—Do not you remember his cutting his finger with your new penknife, and your recommending court-plaister?—But, as you had none about you, and knew I had, you desired me to supply him; and so I took mine out and cut him a piece; but it was a great deal too large, and he cut it smaller, and kept playing some time with what was left, before he gave it back to me. And so then, in my nonsense, I could not help making a treasure of it—so I put it by never to be used, and looked at it now and then as a great treat."

"My dearest Harriet!" cried Emma, putting her hand before her face, and jumping up, "you make me more ashamed of myself than I can bear. Remember it? Aye, I remember it all now; all, except your saving this relic—I knew nothing of that till this moment—but the cutting the finger, and my recommending court-plaister, and saying I had none about me!—Oh! my sins, my sins!—And I had plenty all the while in my pocket!—One of my senseless tricks!—I deserve to be under a continual blush all the rest of my life.—Well—(sitting down again)—go on—what else?"

"And had you really some at hand yourself? I am sure I never suspected it, you did it so naturally."

"And so you actually put this piece of court-plaister by for his sake!" said Emma, recovering from her state of shame and feeling divided between wonder and amusement. And secretly she added to herself, "Lord bless me! when should I ever have thought of putting by in cotton a piece of court-plaister that Frank Churchill had been pulling about! I never was equal to this."

"Here," resumed Harriet, turning to her box again, "here is something still more valuable, I mean that has been more valuable, because this is what did really once belong to him, which the court-plaister never did."

Emma was quite eager to see this superior treasure. It was the end of an old pencil,—the part without any lead.

"This was really his," said Harriet.—"Do not you remember one morning?—no, I dare say you do not. But one morning—I forget exactly the day—but perhaps it was the Tuesday or Wednesday before that evening, he wanted to make a memorandum in his pocket-book; it was about spruce-beer. Mr. Knightley had been telling him something about brewing spruce-beer, and he wanted to put it down; but when he took out his pencil, there was so little lead that he soon cut it all away, and it would not do, so you lent him another, and this was left upon the table as good for nothing. But I kept my eye on it; and, as soon as I dared, caught it up, and never parted with it again from that moment."

"I do remember it," cried Emma; "I perfectly remember it.—Talking about spruce-beer.—Oh! yes—Mr. Knightley and I both saying we liked it, and Mr. Elton's seeming resolved to learn to like it too. I perfectly remember it.—Stop; Mr. Knightley was standing just here, was not he? I have an idea he was standing just here."

"Ah! I do not know. I cannot recollect.—It is very odd, but I cannot recollect.—Mr. Elton was sitting here, I remember, much about where I am now."—

"Well, go on."

"Oh! that's all. I have nothing more to shew you, or to say—except that I am now going to throw them both behind the fire, and I wish you to see me do it."

"My poor dear Harriet! and have you actually found happiness in treasuring up these things?"

"Yes, simpleton as I was!—but I am quite ashamed of it now, and wish I could forget as easily as I can burn them. It was very wrong of me, you know, to keep any remembrances, after he was married. I knew it was—but had not resolution enough to part with them."

"But, Harriet, is it necessary to burn the court-plaister?—I have not a word to say for the bit of old pencil, but the court-plaister might be useful."

"I shall be happier to burn it," replied Harriet. "It has a disagreeable look to me. I must get rid of every thing.—There it goes, and there is an end, thank Heaven! of Mr. Elton."

"And when," thought Emma, "will there be a beginning of Mr. Churchill?"

She had soon afterwards reason to believe that the beginning was already made, and could not but hope that the gipsy, though she had told no fortune, might be proved to have made Harriet's.—About a fortnight after the alarm, they came to a sufficient explanation, and quite undesignedly. Emma was not thinking of it at the moment, which made the information she received more valuable. She merely said, in the course of some trivial chat, "Well, Harriet, whenever you marry I would advise you to do so and so"—and thought no more of it, till after a minute's silence she heard Harriet say in a very serious tone, "I shall never marry."

Emma then looked up, and immediately saw how it was; and after a moment's debate, as to whether it should pass unnoticed or not, replied,

"Never marry!—This is a new resolution."

"It is one that I shall never change, however."

After another short hesitation, "I hope it does not proceed from—I hope it is not in compliment to Mr. Elton?"

"Mr. Elton indeed!" cried Harriet indignantly.—"Oh! no"—and Emma could just catch the words, "so superior to Mr. Elton!"

She then took a longer time for consideration. Should she proceed no farther?—should she let it pass, and seem to suspect nothing?—Perhaps Harriet might think her cold or angry if she did; or perhaps if she were totally silent, it might only drive Harriet into asking her to hear too much; and against any thing like such an unreserve as had been, such an open and frequent discussion of hopes and chances, she was perfectly resolved.—She believed it would be wiser for her to say and know at once, all that she meant to say and know. Plain dealing was always best. She had previously determined how far she would proceed, on any application of the sort; and it would be safer for both, to have the judicious law of her own brain laid down with speed.—She was decided, and thus spoke—

"Harriet, I will not affect to be in doubt of your meaning. Your resolution, or rather your expectation of never marrying, results from an idea that the person whom you might prefer, would be too greatly your superior in situation to think of you. Is not it so?"

"Oh! Miss Woodhouse, believe me I have not the presumption to suppose—Indeed I am not so mad.—But it is a pleasure to me to admire him at a distance—and to think of his infinite superiority to all the rest of the world, with the gratitude, wonder, and veneration, which are so proper, in me especially."

"I am not at all surprized at you, Harriet. The service he rendered you was enough to warm your heart."

"Service! oh! it was such an inexpressible obligation!—The very recollection of it, and all that I felt at the time—when I saw him coming—his noble look—and my wretchedness before. Such a change! In one moment such a change! From perfect misery to perfect happiness!"

"It is very natural. It is natural, and it is honourable.—Yes, honourable, I think, to chuse so well and so gratefully.—But that it will be a fortunate preference is more that I can promise. I do not advise you to give way to it, Harriet. I do not by any means engage for its being returned. Consider what you are about. Perhaps it will be wisest in you to check your feelings while you can: at any rate do not let them carry you far, unless you are persuaded of his liking you. Be observant of him. Let his behaviour be the guide of your sensations. I give you this caution now, because I shall never speak to you again on the subject. I am determined against all interference. Henceforward I know nothing of the matter. Let no name ever pass our lips. We were very wrong before; we will be cautious now.—He is your superior, no doubt, and there do seem objections and obstacles of a very serious nature; but yet, Harriet, more wonderful things have taken place, there have been matches of greater disparity. But take care of yourself. I would not have you too sanguine; though, however it may end, be assured your raising your thoughts to him, is a mark of good taste which I shall always know how to value."

Harriet kissed her hand in silent and submissive gratitude. Emma was very decided in thinking such an attachment no bad thing for her friend. Its tendency would be to raise and refine her mind—and it must be saving her from the danger of degradation.

Chapter V

In this state of schemes, and hopes, and connivance, June opened upon Hartfield. To Highbury in general it brought no material change. The Eltons were still talking of a visit from the Sucklings, and of the use to be made of their barouche-landau; and Jane Fairfax was still at her grandmother's; and as the return of the Campbells from Ireland was again delayed, and August, instead of Midsummer, fixed for it, she was likely to remain there full two months longer, provided at least she were able to defeat Mrs. Elton's activity in her service, and save herself from being hurried into a delightful situation against her will.

Mr. Knightley, who, for some reason best known to himself, had certainly taken an early dislike to Frank Churchill, was only growing to dislike him more. He began to suspect him of some double dealing in his pursuit of Emma. That Emma was his object appeared indisputable. Every thing declared it; his own attentions, his father's hints, his mother-in-law's guarded silence; it was all in unison; words, conduct, discretion, and indiscretion, told the same story. But while so many were devoting him to Emma, and Emma herself making him over to Harriet, Mr. Knightley began to suspect him of some inclination to trifle with Jane Fairfax. He could not understand it; but there were symptoms of intelligence between them—he thought so at least—symptoms of admiration on his side, which, having once observed, he could not persuade himself to think entirely void of meaning, however he might wish to escape any of Emma's errors of imagination. She was not present when the suspicion first arose. He was dining with the Randalls family, and Jane, at the Eltons'; and he had seen a look, more than a single look, at Miss Fairfax, which, from the admirer of Miss Woodhouse, seemed somewhat out of place. When he was again in their company, he could not help remembering what he had seen; nor could he avoid observations which, unless it were like Cowper and his fire at twilight,

"Myself creating what I saw,"

brought him yet stronger suspicion of there being a something of private liking, of private understanding even, between Frank Churchill and Jane.

He had walked up one day after dinner, as he very often did, to spend his evening at Hartfield. Emma and Harriet were going to walk; he joined them; and, on returning, they fell in with a larger party, who, like themselves, judged it wisest to take their exercise early, as the weather threatened rain; Mr. and Mrs. Weston and their son, Miss Bates and her niece, who had accidentally met. They all united; and, on reaching Hartfield gates, Emma, who knew it was exactly the sort of visiting that would be welcome to her father, pressed them all to go in and drink tea with him. The Randalls party agreed to it immediately; and after a pretty long speech from Miss Bates, which few persons listened to, she also found it possible to accept dear Miss Woodhouse's most obliging invitation.

As they were turning into the grounds, Mr. Perry passed by on horseback. The gentlemen spoke of his horse.

"By the bye," said Frank Churchill to Mrs. Weston presently, "what became of Mr. Perry's plan of setting up his carriage?"

Mrs. Weston looked surprized, and said, "I did not know that he ever had any such plan."

"Nay, I had it from you. You wrote me word of it three months ago."

"Me! impossible!"

"Indeed you did. I remember it perfectly. You mentioned it as what was certainly to be very soon. Mrs. Perry had told somebody, and was extremely happy about it. It was owing to her persuasion, as she thought his being out in bad weather did him a great deal of harm. You must remember it now?"

"Upon my word I never heard of it till this moment."

"Never! really, never!—Bless me! how could it be?—Then I must have dreamt it—but I was completely persuaded—Miss Smith, you walk as if you were tired. You will not be sorry to find yourself at home."

"What is this?—What is this?" cried Mr. Weston, "about Perry and a carriage? Is Perry going to set up his carriage, Frank? I am glad he can afford it. You had it from himself, had you?"

"No, sir," replied his son, laughing, "I seem to have had it from nobody.—Very odd!—I really was persuaded of Mrs. Weston's having mentioned it in one of her letters to Enscombe, many weeks ago, with all these particulars—but as she declares she never heard a syllable of it before, of course it must have been a dream. I am a great dreamer. I dream of every body at Highbury when I am away—and when I have gone through my particular friends, then I begin dreaming of Mr. and Mrs. Perry."

"It is odd though," observed his father, "that you should have had such a regular connected dream about people whom it was not very likely you should be thinking of at Enscombe. Perry's setting up his carriage! and his wife's persuading him to it, out of care for his health—just what will happen, I have no doubt, some time or other; only a little premature. What an air of probability sometimes runs through a dream! And at others, what a heap of absurdities it is! Well, Frank, your dream certainly shews that Highbury is in your thoughts when you are absent. Emma, you are a great dreamer, I think?"

Emma was out of hearing. She had hurried on before her guests to prepare her father for their appearance, and was beyond the reach of Mr. Weston's hint.

"Why, to own the truth," cried Miss Bates, who had been trying in vain to be heard the last two minutes, "if I must speak on this subject, there is no denying that Mr. Frank Churchill might have—I do not mean to say that he did not dream it—I am sure I have sometimes the oddest dreams in the world—but if I am questioned about it, I must acknowledge that there was such an idea last spring; for Mrs. Perry herself mentioned it to my mother, and the Coles knew of it as well as ourselves—but it was quite a secret, known to nobody else, and only thought of about three days. Mrs. Perry was very anxious that he should have a carriage, and came to my mother in great spirits one morning because she thought she had prevailed. Jane, don't you remember grandmama's telling us of it when we got home? I forget where we had been walking to—very likely to Randalls; yes, I think it was to Randalls. Mrs. Perry was always particularly fond of my mother—indeed I do not know who is not—and she had mentioned it to her in confidence; she had no objection to her telling us, of course, but it was not to go beyond: and, from that day to this, I never mentioned it to a soul that I know of. At the same time, I will not positively answer for my having never dropt a hint, because I know I do sometimes pop out a thing before I am aware. I am a talker, you know; I am rather a talker; and now and then I have let a thing escape me which I should not. I am not like Jane; I wish I were.

I will answer for it she never betrayed the least thing in the world. Where is she?—Oh! just behind. Perfectly remember Mrs. Perry's coming.—Extraordinary dream, indeed!"

They were entering the hall. Mr. Knightley's eyes had preceded Miss Bates's in a glance at Jane. From Frank Churchill's face, where he thought he saw confusion suppressed or laughed away, he had involuntarily turned to hers; but she was indeed behind, and too busy with her shawl. Mr. Weston had walked in. The two other gentlemen waited at the door to let her pass. Mr. Knightley suspected in Frank Churchill the determination of catching her eye—he seemed watching her intently—in vain, however, if it were so—Jane passed between them into the hall, and looked at neither.

There was no time for farther remark or explanation. The dream must be borne with, and Mr. Knightley must take his seat with the rest round the large modern circular table which Emma had introduced at Hartfield, and which none but Emma could have had power to place there and persuade her father to use, instead of the small-sized Pembroke, on which two of his daily meals had, for forty years been crowded. Tea passed pleasantly, and nobody seemed in a hurry to move.

"Miss Woodhouse," said Frank Churchill, after examining a table behind him, which he could reach as he sat, "have your nephews taken away their alphabets—their box of letters? It used to stand here. Where is it? This is a sort of dull-looking evening, that ought to be treated rather as winter than summer. We had great amusement with those letters one morning. I want to puzzle you again."

Emma was pleased with the thought; and producing the box, the table was quickly scattered over with alphabets, which no one seemed so much disposed to employ as their two selves. They were rapidly forming words for each other, or for any body else who would be puzzled. The quietness of the game made it particularly eligible for Mr. Woodhouse, who had often been distressed by the more animated sort, which Mr. Weston had occasionally introduced, and who now sat happily occupied in lamenting, with tender melancholy, over the departure of the "poor little boys," or in fondly pointing out, as he took up any stray letter near him, how beautifully Emma had written it.

Frank Churchill placed a word before Miss Fairfax. She gave a slight glance round the table, and applied herself to it. Frank was next to Emma, Jane opposite to them—and Mr. Knightley so placed as to see them all; and it was his object to see as much as he could, with as little apparent observation. The word was discovered, and with a faint smile pushed away. If meant to be immediately mixed with the others, and buried from sight, she should have looked on the table instead of looking just across, for it was not mixed; and Harriet, eager after every fresh word, and finding out none, directly took it up, and fell to work. She was sitting by Mr. Knightley, and turned to him for help. The word was blunder; and as Harriet exultingly proclaimed it, there was a blush on Jane's cheek which gave it a meaning not otherwise ostensible. Mr. Knightley connected it with the dream; but how it could all be, was beyond his comprehension. How the delicacy, the discretion of his favourite could have been so lain asleep! He feared there must be some decided involvement. Disingenuousness and double dealing seemed to meet him at every turn. These letters were but the vehicle for gallantry and trick. It was a child's play, chosen to conceal a deeper game on Frank Churchill's part.

With great indignation did he continue to observe him; with great alarm and distrust, to observe also his two blinded companions. He saw a short word prepared for Emma, and given to her with a look sly and demure. He saw that Emma had soon made it out, and found it highly entertaining, though it was something which she judged it proper to appear to censure; for she said, "Nonsense! for shame!" He heard Frank Churchill next say, with a glance towards Jane, "I will give it to her—shall I?"—and as clearly heard Emma opposing it with eager laughing warmth. "No, no, you must not; you shall not, indeed."

It was done however. This gallant young man, who seemed to love without feeling, and to recommend himself without complaisance, directly handed over the word to Miss Fairfax, and with a particular degree of sedate civility entreated her to study it. Mr. Knightley's excessive curiosity to know what this word might be, made him seize every possible moment for darting his eye towards it, and it was not long before he saw it to be Dixon. Jane Fairfax's perception seemed to accompany his; her comprehension was certainly more equal to the covert meaning, the superior intelligence, of those five letters so arranged. She was evidently displeased; looked up, and seeing herself watched, blushed more deeply than he had ever perceived her, and saying only, "I did not know that proper names were allowed," pushed away the letters with even an angry spirit, and looked resolved to be engaged by no other word that could be offered. Her face was averted from those who had made the attack, and turned towards her aunt.

"Aye, very true, my dear," cried the latter, though Jane had not spoken a word—"I was just going to say the same thing. It is time for us to be going indeed. The evening is closing in, and grandmama will be looking for us. My dear sir, you are too obliging. We really must wish you good night."

Jane's alertness in moving, proved her as ready as her aunt had preconceived. She was immediately up, and wanting to quit the table; but so many were also moving, that she could not get away; and Mr. Knightley thought he saw another collection of letters anxiously pushed towards her, and resolutely swept away by her unexamined. She was afterwards looking for her shawl—Frank Churchill was looking also—it was growing dusk, and the room was in confusion; and how they parted, Mr. Knightley could not tell.

He remained at Hartfield after all the rest, his thoughts full of what he had seen; so full, that when the candles came to assist his observations, he must—yes, he certainly must, as a friend—an anxious friend—give Emma some hint, ask her some question. He could not see her in a situation of such danger, without trying to preserve her. It was his duty.

"Pray, Emma," said he, "may I ask in what lay the great amusement, the poignant sting of the last word given to you and Miss Fairfax? I saw the word, and am curious to know how it could be so very entertaining to the one, and so very distressing to the other."

Emma was extremely confused. She could not endure to give him the true explanation; for though her suspicions were by no means removed, she was really ashamed of having ever imparted them.

"Oh!" she cried in evident embarrassment, "it all meant nothing; a mere joke among ourselves."

"The joke," he replied gravely, "seemed confined to you and Mr. Churchill."

He had hoped she would speak again, but she did not. She would rather busy herself about any thing than speak. He sat a little while in doubt. A variety of evils crossed his mind. Interference—fruitless interference. Emma's confusion, and the acknowledged intimacy, seemed to declare her affection engaged. Yet he would speak. He owed it to her, to risk any thing that might be involved in an unwelcome interference, rather than her welfare; to encounter any thing, rather than the remembrance of neglect in such a cause.

"My dear Emma," said he at last, with earnest kindness, "do you think you perfectly understand the degree of acquaintance between the gentleman and lady we have been speaking of?"

"Between Mr. Frank Churchill and Miss Fairfax? Oh! yes, perfectly.—Why do you make a doubt of it?"

"Have you never at any time had reason to think that he admired her, or that she admired him?"

"Never, never!" she cried with a most open eagerness—"Never, for the twentieth part of a moment, did such an idea occur to me. And how could it possibly come into your head?"

"I have lately imagined that I saw symptoms of attachment between them—certain expressive looks, which I did not believe meant to be public."

"Oh! you amuse me excessively. I am delighted to find that you can vouchsafe to let your imagination wander—but it will not do—very sorry to check you in your first essay—but indeed it will not do. There is no admiration between them, I do assure you; and the appearances which have caught you, have arisen from some peculiar circumstances—feelings rather of a totally different nature—it is impossible exactly to explain:—there is a good deal of nonsense in it—but the part which is capable of being communicated, which is sense, is, that they are as far from any attachment or admiration for one another, as any two beings in the world can be. That is, I presume it to be so on her side, and I can answer for its being so on his. I will answer for the gentleman's indifference."

She spoke with a confidence which staggered, with a satisfaction which silenced, Mr. Knightley. She was in gay spirits, and would have prolonged the conversation, wanting to hear the particulars of his suspicions, every look described, and all the wheres and hows of a circumstance which highly entertained her: but his gaiety did not meet hers. He found he could not be useful, and his feelings were too much irritated for talking. That he might not be irritated into an absolute fever, by the fire which Mr. Woodhouse's tender habits required almost every evening throughout the year, he soon afterwards took a hasty leave, and walked home to the coolness and solitude of Donwell Abbey.

Chapter VI

After being long fed with hopes of a speedy visit from Mr. and Mrs. Suckling, the Highbury world were obliged to endure the mortification of hearing that they could not possibly come till the autumn. No such importation of novelties could enrich their intellectual stores at present. In the daily interchange of news, they must be again restricted to the other topics with which for a while the Sucklings' coming had been united, such as the last accounts of Mrs. Churchill, whose health seemed every day to supply a different report, and the situation of Mrs. Weston, whose happiness it was to be hoped might eventually be as much increased by the arrival of a child, as that of all her neighbours was by the approach of it.

Mrs. Elton was very much disappointed. It was the delay of a great deal of pleasure and parade. Her introductions and recommendations must all wait, and every projected party be still only talked of. So she thought at first;—but a little consideration convinced her that every thing need not be put off. Why should not they explore to Box Hill though the Sucklings did not come? They could go there again with them in the autumn. It was settled that they should go to Box Hill. That there was to be such a party had been long generally known: it had even given the idea of another. Emma had never been to Box Hill; she wished to see what every body found so well worth seeing, and she and Mr. Weston had agreed to chuse some fine morning and drive thither. Two or three more of the chosen only were to be admitted to join them, and it was to be done in a quiet, unpretending, elegant way, infinitely superior to the bustle and preparation, the regular eating and drinking, and picnic parade of the Eltons and the Sucklings.

This was so very well understood between them, that Emma could not but feel some surprise, and a little displeasure, on hearing from Mr. Weston that he had been proposing to Mrs. Elton, as her brother and sister had failed her, that the two parties should unite, and go together; and that as Mrs. Elton had very readily acceded to it, so it was to be, if she had no objection. Now, as her objection was nothing but her very great dislike of Mrs. Elton, of which Mr. Weston must already be perfectly aware, it was not worth bringing forward again:—it could not be done without a reproof to him, which would be giving pain to his wife; and she found herself therefore obliged to consent to an arrangement which she would have done a great deal to avoid; an arrangement which would probably expose her even to the degradation of being said to be of Mrs. Elton's party! Every feeling was offended; and the forbearance of her outward submission left a heavy arrear due of secret severity in her reflections on the unmanageable goodwill of Mr. Weston's temper.

"I am glad you approve of what I have done," said he very comfortably. "But I thought you would. Such schemes as these are nothing without numbers. One cannot have too large a party. A large party secures its own amusement. And she is a good-natured woman after all. One could not leave her out."

Emma denied none of it aloud, and agreed to none of it in private.

It was now the middle of June, and the weather fine; and Mrs. Elton was growing impatient to name the day, and settle with Mr. Weston as to pigeon-pies and cold lamb, when a lame carriage-horse threw every thing into sad uncertainty. It might be weeks, it might be only a few days, before the horse were useable; but no preparations could be ventured on, and it was all melancholy stagnation. Mrs. Elton's resources were inadequate to such an attack.

"Is not this most vexations, Knightley?" she cried.—"And such weather for exploring!—These delays and disappointments are quite odious. What are we to do?—The year will wear away at this rate, and nothing done. Before this time last year I assure you we had had a delightful exploring party from Maple Grove to Kings Weston."

"You had better explore to Donwell," replied Mr. Knightley. "That may be done without horses. Come, and eat my strawberries. They are ripening fast."

If Mr. Knightley did not begin seriously, he was obliged to proceed so, for his proposal was caught at with delight; and the "Oh! I should like it of all things," was not plainer in words than manner. Donwell was famous for its strawberry-beds, which seemed a plea for the invitation: but no plea was necessary; cabbage-beds would have been enough to tempt the lady, who only wanted to be going somewhere. She promised him again and again to come—much oftener than he doubted—and was extremely gratified by such a proof of intimacy, such a distinguishing compliment as she chose to consider it.

"You may depend upon me," said she. "I certainly will come. Name your day, and I will come. You will allow me to bring Jane Fairfax?"

"I cannot name a day," said he, "till I have spoken to some others whom I would wish to meet you."

"Oh! leave all that to me. Only give me a carte-blanche.—I am Lady Patroness, you know. It is my party. I will bring friends with me."

"I hope you will bring Elton," said he: "but I will not trouble you to give any other invitations."

"Oh! now you are looking very sly. But consider—you need not be afraid of delegating power to me. I am no young lady on her preferment. Married women, you know, may be safely authorised. It is my party. Leave it all to me. I will invite your guests."

"No,"—he calmly replied,—"there is but one married woman in the world whom I can ever allow to invite what guests she pleases to Donwell, and that one is—"

"—Mrs. Weston, I suppose," interrupted Mrs. Elton, rather mortified.

"No—Mrs. Knightley;—and till she is in being, I will manage such matters myself."

"Ah! you are an odd creature!" she cried, satisfied to have no one preferred to herself.—"You are a humourist, and may say what you like. Quite a humourist. Well, I shall bring Jane with me—Jane and her aunt.—The rest I leave to you. I have no objections at all to meeting the Hartfield family. Don't scruple. I know you are attached to them."

"You certainly will meet them if I can prevail; and I shall call on Miss Bates in my way home."

"That's quite unnecessary; I see Jane every day:—but as you like. It is to be a morning scheme, you know, Knightley; quite a simple thing. I shall wear a large bonnet, and bring one of my little baskets hanging on my arm. Here,—probably this basket with pink ribbon. Nothing can be more simple, you see. And Jane will have such another. There is to be no form or parade—a sort of gipsy party. We are to walk about your gardens, and gather the strawberries ourselves, and sit under trees;—and whatever else you may like to provide, it is to be all out of doors—a table spread in the shade, you know. Every thing as natural and simple as possible. Is not that your idea?"

"Not quite. My idea of the simple and the natural will be to have the table spread in the dining-room. The nature and the simplicity of gentlemen and ladies, with their servants and furniture, I think is best observed by meals within doors. When you are tired of eating strawberries in the garden, there shall be cold meat in the house."

"Well—as you please; only don't have a great set out. And, by the bye, can I or my housekeeper be of any use to you with our opinion?—Pray be sincere, Knightley. If you wish me to talk to Mrs. Hodges, or to inspect anything—"

"I have not the least wish for it, I thank you."

"Well—but if any difficulties should arise, my housekeeper is extremely clever."

"I will answer for it, that mine thinks herself full as clever, and would spurn any body's assistance."

"I wish we had a donkey. The thing would be for us all to come on donkeys, Jane, Miss Bates, and me—and my caro sposo walking by. I really must talk to him about purchasing a donkey. In a country life I conceive it to be a sort of necessary; for, let a woman have ever so many resources, it is not possible for her to be always shut up at home;—and very long walks, you know—in summer there is dust, and in winter there is dirt."

"You will not find either, between Donwell and Highbury. Donwell Lane is never dusty, and now it is perfectly dry. Come on a donkey, however, if you prefer it. You can borrow Mrs. Cole's. I would wish every thing to be as much to your taste as possible."

"That I am sure you would. Indeed I do you justice, my good friend. Under that peculiar sort of dry, blunt manner, I know you have the warmest heart. As I tell Mr. E., you are a thorough humourist.—Yes, believe me, Knightley, I am fully sensible of your attention to me in the whole of this scheme. You have hit upon the very thing to please me."

Mr. Knightley had another reason for avoiding a table in the shade. He wished to persuade Mr. Woodhouse, as well as Emma, to join the party; and he knew that to have any of them sitting down out of doors to eat would inevitably make him ill. Mr. Woodhouse must not, under the specious pretence of a morning drive, and an hour or two spent at Donwell, be tempted away to his misery.

He was invited on good faith. No lurking horrors were to upbraid him for his easy credulity. He did consent. He had not been at Donwell for two years. "Some very fine morning, he, and Emma, and Harriet, could go very well; and he could sit still with Mrs. Weston, while the dear girls walked about the gardens. He did not suppose they could be damp now, in the middle of the day. He should like to see the old house again exceedingly, and should be very happy to meet Mr. and Mrs. Elton, and any other of his neighbours.—He could not see any objection at all to his, and Emma's, and Harriet's going there some very fine morning. He thought it very well done of Mr. Knightley to invite them—very kind and sensible—much cleverer than dining out.—He was not fond of dining out."

Mr. Knightley was fortunate in every body's most ready concurrence. The invitation was everywhere so well received, that it seemed as if, like Mrs. Elton, they were all taking the scheme as a particular compliment to themselves.—Emma and Harriet professed very high expectations of pleasure from it; and Mr. Weston, unasked, promised to get Frank over to join them, if possible; a proof of approbation and gratitude which could have been dispensed with.—Mr. Knightley was then obliged to say that he should be glad to see him; and Mr. Weston engaged to lose no time in writing, and spare no arguments to induce him to come.

In the meanwhile the lame horse recovered so fast, that the party to Box Hill was again under happy consideration; and at last

Donwell was settled for one day, and Box Hill for the next,—the weather appearing exactly right.

Under a bright mid-day sun, at almost Midsummer, Mr. Woodhouse was safely conveyed in his carriage, with one window down, to partake of this al-fresco party; and in one of the most comfortable rooms in the Abbey, especially prepared for him by a fire all the morning, he was happily placed, quite at his ease, ready to talk with pleasure of what had been achieved, and advise every body to come and sit down, and not to heat themselves.—Mrs. Weston, who seemed to have walked there on purpose to be tired, and sit all the time with him, remained, when all the others were invited or persuaded out, his patient listener and sympathiser.

It was so long since Emma had been at the Abbey, that as soon as she was satisfied of her father's comfort, she was glad to leave him, and look around her; eager to refresh and correct her memory with more particular observation, more exact understanding of a house and grounds which must ever be so interesting to her and all her family.

She felt all the honest pride and complacency which her alliance with the present and future proprietor could fairly warrant, as she viewed the respectable size and style of the building, its suitable, becoming, characteristic situation, low and sheltered—its ample gardens stretching down to meadows washed by a stream, of which the Abbey, with all the old neglect of prospect, had scarcely a sight—and its abundance of timber in rows and avenues, which neither fashion nor extravagance had rooted up.—The house was larger than Hartfield, and totally unlike it, covering a good deal of ground, rambling and irregular, with many comfortable, and one or two handsome rooms.—It was just what it ought to be, and it looked what it was—and Emma felt an increasing respect for it, as the residence of a family of such true gentility, untainted in blood and understanding.—Some faults of temper John Knightley had; but Isabella had connected herself unexceptionably. She had given them neither men, nor names, nor places, that could raise a blush. These were pleasant feelings, and she walked about and indulged them till it was necessary to do as the others did, and collect round the strawberry-beds.—The whole party were assembled, excepting Frank Churchill, who was expected every moment from Richmond; and Mrs. Elton, in all her apparatus of happiness, her large bonnet and her basket, was very ready to lead the way in gathering, accepting, or talking—strawberries, and only strawberries, could now be thought or spoken of.—"The best fruit in England—every body's favourite—always wholesome.—These the finest beds and finest sorts.—Delightful to gather for one's self—the only way of really enjoying them.—Morning decidedly the best time—never tired—every sort good—hautboy infinitely superior—no comparison—the others hardly eatable—hautboys very scarce—Chili preferred—white wood finest flavour of all—price of strawberries in London—abundance about Bristol—Maple Grove—cultivation—beds when to be renewed—gardeners thinking exactly different—no general rule—gardeners never to be put out of their way—delicious fruit—only too rich to be eaten much of—inferior to cherries—currants more refreshing—only objection to gathering strawberries the stooping—glaring sun—tired to death—could bear it no longer—must go and sit in the shade."

Such, for half an hour, was the conversation—interrupted only once by Mrs. Weston, who came out, in her solicitude after her son-in-law, to inquire if he were come—and she was a little uneasy.—She had some fears of his horse.

Seats tolerably in the shade were found; and now Emma was obliged to overhear what Mrs. Elton and Jane Fairfax were talking of.—A situation, a most desirable situation, was in question. Mrs. Elton had received notice of it that morning, and was in raptures. It was not with Mrs. Suckling, it was not with Mrs. Bragge, but in felicity and splendour it fell short only of them: it was with a cousin of Mrs. Bragge, an acquaintance of Mrs. Suckling, a lady known at Maple Grove. Delightful, charming, superior, first circles, spheres, lines, ranks, every thing—and Mrs. Elton was wild to have the offer closed with immediately.—On her side, all was warmth, energy, and triumph—and she positively refused to take her friend's negative, though Miss Fairfax continued to assure her that she would not at present engage in any thing, repeating the same motives which she had been heard to urge before.—Still Mrs. Elton insisted on being authorised to write an acquiescence by the morrow's post.—How Jane could bear it at all, was astonishing to Emma.—She did look vexed, she did speak pointedly—and at last, with a decision of action unusual to her, proposed a removal.—"Should not they walk? Would not Mr. Knightley shew them the gardens—all the gardens?—She wished to see the whole extent."—The pertinacity of her friend seemed more than she could bear.

It was hot; and after walking some time over the gardens in a scattered, dispersed way, scarcely any three together, they insensibly followed one another to the delicious shade of a broad short avenue of limes, which stretching beyond the garden at an equal distance from the river, seemed the finish of the pleasure grounds.—It led to nothing; nothing but a view at the end over a low stone wall with high pillars, which seemed intended, in their erection, to give the appearance of an approach to the house, which never had been there. Disputable, however, as might be the taste of such a termination, it was in itself a charming walk, and the view which closed it extremely pretty.—The considerable slope, at nearly the foot of which the Abbey stood, gradually acquired a steeper form beyond its grounds; and at half a mile distant was a bank of considerable abruptness and grandeur, well clothed with wood;—and at the bottom of this bank, favourably placed and sheltered, rose the Abbey Mill Farm, with meadows in front, and the river making a close and handsome curve around it.

It was a sweet view—sweet to the eye and the mind. English verdure, English culture, English comfort, seen under a sun bright, without being oppressive.

In this walk Emma and Mr. Weston found all the others assembled; and towards this view she immediately perceived Mr. Knightley and Harriet distinct from the rest, quietly leading the way. Mr. Knightley and Harriet!—It was an odd tete-a-tete; but she was glad to see it.—There had been a time when he would have scorned her as a companion, and turned from her with little ceremony. Now they seemed in pleasant conversation. There had been a time also when Emma would have been sorry to see Harriet in a spot so favourable for the Abbey Mill Farm; but now she feared it not. It might be safely viewed with all its appendages of prosperity and beauty, its rich pastures, spreading flocks, orchard in blossom, and light column of smoke ascending.—She joined them at the wall, and found them more engaged in talking than in looking around. He was giving Harriet information as to modes of agriculture, etc. and Emma received a smile which seemed to say, "These are my own concerns. I have a right to talk on such subjects, without being suspected of introducing Robert Martin."—She did not suspect him. It was too old a story.—Robert Martin had probably ceased to think of Harriet.—They took a few turns together along the walk.—The shade was most refreshing, and Emma found it the pleasantest part of the day.

The next remove was to the house; they must all go in and eat;—and they were all seated and busy, and still Frank Churchill did not come. Mrs. Weston looked, and looked in vain. His father would not own himself uneasy, and laughed at her fears; but she could not be cured of wishing that he would part with his black mare. He had expressed himself as to coming, with more than common certainty. "His aunt was so much better, that he had not a doubt of getting over to them."—Mrs. Churchill's state, however, as many were ready to remind her, was liable to such sudden variation as might disappoint her nephew in the most reasonable dependence—and Mrs. Weston was at last persuaded to believe, or to say, that it must be by some attack of Mrs. Churchill that he was prevented coming.—Emma looked at Harriet while the point was under consideration; she behaved very well, and betrayed no emotion.

The cold repast was over, and the party were to go out once more to see what had not yet been seen, the old Abbey fish-ponds; perhaps get as far as the clover, which was to be begun cutting on the morrow, or, at any rate, have the pleasure of being hot, and growing cool again.—Mr. Woodhouse, who had already taken his little round in the highest part of the gardens, where no damps from the river were imagined even by him, stirred no more; and his daughter resolved to remain with him, that Mrs. Weston might be persuaded away by her husband to the exercise and variety which her spirits seemed to need.

Mr. Knightley had done all in his power for Mr. Woodhouse's entertainment. Books of engravings, drawers of medals, cameos, corals, shells, and every other family collection within his cabinets, had been prepared for his old friend, to while away the morning; and the kindness had perfectly answered. Mr. Woodhouse had been exceedingly well amused. Mrs. Weston had been shewing them all to him, and now he would shew them all to Emma;—fortunate in having no other resemblance to a child, than in a total want of taste for what he saw, for he was slow, constant, and methodical.—Before this second looking over was begun, however, Emma walked into the hall for the sake of a few moments' free observation of the entrance and ground-plot of the house—and was hardly there, when Jane Fairfax appeared, coming quickly in from the garden, and with a look of escape.—Little expecting to meet Miss Woodhouse so soon, there was a start at first; but Miss Woodhouse was the very person she was in quest of.

"Will you be so kind," said she, "when I am missed, as to say that I am gone home?—I am going this moment.—My aunt is not aware how late it is, nor how long we have been absent—but I am sure we shall be wanted, and I am determined to go directly.—I have said nothing about it to any body. It would only be giving trouble and distress. Some are gone to the ponds, and some to the lime walk. Till they all come in I shall not be missed; and when they do, will you have the goodness to say that I am gone?"

"Certainly, if you wish it;—but you are not going to walk to Highbury alone?"

"Yes—what should hurt me?—I walk fast. I shall be at home in twenty minutes."

"But it is too far, indeed it is, to be walking quite alone. Let my father's servant go with you.—Let me order the carriage. It can be round in five minutes."

"Thank you, thank you—but on no account.—I would rather walk.—And for me to be afraid of walking alone!—I, who may so soon have to guard others!"

She spoke with great agitation; and Emma very feelingly replied, "That can be no reason for your being exposed to danger now. I must order the carriage. The heat even would be danger.—You are fatigued already."

"I am,"—she answered—"I am fatigued; but it is not the sort of fatigue—quick walking will refresh me.—Miss Woodhouse, we all know at times what it is to be wearied in spirits. Mine, I confess, are exhausted. The greatest kindness you can shew me, will be to let me have my own way, and only say that I am gone when it is necessary."

Emma had not another word to oppose. She saw it all; and entering into her feelings, promoted her quitting the house immediately, and watched her safely off with the zeal of a friend. Her parting look was grateful—and her parting words, "Oh! Miss Woodhouse, the comfort of being sometimes alone!"—seemed to burst from an overcharged heart, and to describe somewhat of the continual endurance to be practised by her, even towards some of those who loved her best.

"Such a home, indeed! such an aunt!" said Emma, as she turned back into the hall again. "I do pity you. And the more sensibility you betray of their just horrors, the more I shall like you."

Jane had not been gone a quarter of an hour, and they had only accomplished some views of St. Mark's Place, Venice, when Frank Churchill entered the room. Emma had not been thinking of him, she had forgotten to think of him—but she was very glad to see him. Mrs. Weston would be at ease. The black mare was blameless; they were right who had named Mrs. Churchill as the cause. He had been detained by a temporary increase of illness in her; a nervous seizure, which had lasted some hours—and he had quite given up every thought of coming, till very late;—and had he known how hot a ride he should have, and how late, with all his hurry, he must be, he believed he should not have come at all. The heat was excessive; he had never suffered any thing like it—almost wished he had staid at home—nothing killed him like heat—he could bear any degree of cold, etc., but heat was intolerable—and he sat down, at the greatest possible distance from the slight remains of Mr. Woodhouse's fire, looking very deplorable.

"You will soon be cooler, if you sit still," said Emma.

"As soon as I am cooler I shall go back again. I could very ill be spared—but such a point had been made of my coming! You will all be going soon I suppose; the whole party breaking up. I met one as I came—Madness in such weather!—absolute madness!"

Emma listened, and looked, and soon perceived that Frank Churchill's state might be best defined by the expressive phrase of being out of humour. Some people were always cross when they were hot. Such might be his constitution; and as she knew that eating and drinking were often the cure of such incidental complaints, she recommended his taking some refreshment; he would find abundance of every thing in the dining-room—and she humanely pointed out the door.

"No—he should not eat. He was not hungry; it would only make him hotter." In two minutes, however, he relented in his own favour; and muttering something about spruce-beer, walked off. Emma returned all her attention to her father, saying in secret—

"I am glad I have done being in love with him. I should not like a man who is so soon discomposed by a hot morning. Harriet's sweet easy temper will not mind it."

He was gone long enough to have had a very comfortable meal, and came back all the better—grown quite cool—and, with good manners, like himself—able to draw a chair close to them, take an interest in their employment; and regret, in a reasonable way, that he should be so late. He was not in his best spirits, but seemed trying to improve them; and, at last, made himself talk nonsense very agreeably. They were looking over views in Swisserland.

"As soon as my aunt gets well, I shall go abroad," said he. "I shall never be easy till I have seen some of these places. You will have my sketches, some time or other, to look at—or my tour to read—or my poem. I shall do something to expose myself."

"That may be—but not by sketches in Swisserland. You will never go to Swisserland. Your uncle and aunt will never allow you to leave England."

"They may be induced to go too. A warm climate may be prescribed for her. I have more than half an expectation of our all going abroad. I assure you I have. I feel a strong persuasion, this morning, that I shall soon be abroad. I ought to travel. I am tired of doing nothing. I want a change. I am serious, Miss Woodhouse, whatever your penetrating eyes may fancy—I am sick of England—and would leave it to-morrow, if I could."

"You are sick of prosperity and indulgence. Cannot you invent a few hardships for yourself, and be contented to stay?"

"I sick of prosperity and indulgence! You are quite mistaken. I do not look upon myself as either prosperous or indulged. I am thwarted in every thing material. I do not consider myself at all a fortunate person."

"You are not quite so miserable, though, as when you first came. Go and eat and drink a little more, and you will do very well. Another slice of cold meat, another draught of Madeira and water, will make you nearly on a par with the rest of us."

"No—I shall not stir. I shall sit by you. You are my best cure."

"We are going to Box Hill to-morrow;—you will join us. It is not Swisserland, but it will be something for a young man so much in want of a change. You will stay, and go with us?"

"No, certainly not; I shall go home in the cool of the evening."

"But you may come again in the cool of to-morrow morning."

"No—It will not be worth while. If I come, I shall be cross."

"Then pray stay at Richmond."

"But if I do, I shall be crosser still. I can never bear to think of you all there without me."

"These are difficulties which you must settle for yourself. Chuse your own degree of crossness. I shall press you no more."

The rest of the party were now returning, and all were soon collected. With some there was great joy at the sight of Frank Churchill; others took it very composedly; but there was a very general distress and disturbance on Miss Fairfax's disappearance being explained. That it was time for every body to go, concluded the subject; and with a short final arrangement for the next day's scheme, they parted. Frank Churchill's little inclination to exclude himself increased so much, that his last words to Emma were,

"Well;—if you wish me to stay and join the party, I will."

She smiled her acceptance; and nothing less than a summons from Richmond was to take him back before the following evening.

Chapter VII

They had a very fine day for Box Hill; and all the other outward circumstances of arrangement, accommodation, and punctuality, were in favour of a pleasant party. Mr. Weston directed the whole, officiating safely between Hartfield and the Vicarage, and every body was in good time. Emma and Harriet went together; Miss Bates and her niece, with the Eltons; the gentlemen on horseback. Mrs. Weston remained with Mr. Woodhouse. Nothing was wanting but to be happy when they got there. Seven miles were travelled in expectation of enjoyment, and every body had a burst of admiration on first arriving; but in the general amount of the day there was deficiency.

There was a languor, a want of spirits, a want of union, which could not be got over. They separated too much into parties. The Eltons walked together; Mr. Knightley took charge of Miss Bates and Jane; and Emma and Harriet belonged to Frank Churchill. And Mr. Weston tried, in vain, to make them harmonise better. It seemed at first an accidental division, but it never materially varied. Mr. and Mrs. Elton, indeed, shewed no unwillingness to mix, and be as agreeable as they could; but during the two whole hours that were spent on the hill, there seemed a principle of separation, between the other parties, too strong for any fine prospects, or any cold collation, or any cheerful Mr. Weston, to remove.

At first it was downright dulness to Emma. She had never seen Frank Churchill so silent and stupid. He said nothing worth hearing—looked without seeing—admired without intelligence—listened without knowing what she said. While he was so dull, it was no wonder that Harriet should be dull likewise; and they were both insufferable.

When they all sat down it was better; to her taste a great deal better, for Frank Churchill grew talkative and gay, making her his first object. Every distinguishing attention that could be paid, was paid to her. To amuse her, and be agreeable in her eyes, seemed all that he cared for—and Emma, glad to be enlivened, not sorry to be flattered, was gay and easy too, and gave him all the friendly encouragement, the admission to be gallant, which she had ever given in the first and most animating period of their acquaintance; but which now, in her own estimation, meant nothing, though in the judgment of most people looking on it must have had such an appearance as no English word but flirtation could very well describe. "Mr. Frank Churchill and Miss Woodhouse flirted together excessively." They were laying themselves open to that very phrase—and to having it sent off in a letter to Maple Grove by one lady, to Ireland by another. Not that Emma was gay and thoughtless from any real felicity; it was rather because she felt less happy than she had expected. She laughed because she was disappointed; and though she liked him for his attentions, and thought them all, whether in friendship, admiration, or playfulness, extremely judicious, they were not winning back her heart. She still intended him for her friend.

"How much I am obliged to you," said he, "for telling me to come to-day!—If it had not been for you, I should certainly have lost all the happiness of this party. I had quite determined to go away again."

"Yes, you were very cross; and I do not know what about, except that you were too late for the best strawberries. I was a kinder friend than you deserved. But you were humble. You begged hard to be commanded to come."

"Don't say I was cross. I was fatigued. The heat overcame me."

"It is hotter to-day."

"Not to my feelings. I am perfectly comfortable to-day."

"You are comfortable because you are under command."

"Your command?—Yes."

"Perhaps I intended you to say so, but I meant self-command. You had, somehow or other, broken bounds yesterday, and run away from your own management; but to-day you are got back again—and as I cannot be always with you, it is best to believe your temper under your own command rather than mine."

"It comes to the same thing. I can have no self-command without a motive. You order me, whether you speak or not. And you can be always with me. You are always with me."

"Dating from three o'clock yesterday. My perpetual influence could not begin earlier, or you would not have been so much out of humour before."

"Three o'clock yesterday! That is your date. I thought I had seen you first in February."

"Your gallantry is really unanswerable. But (lowering her voice)—nobody speaks except ourselves, and it is rather too much to be talking nonsense for the entertainment of seven silent people."

"I say nothing of which I am ashamed," replied he, with lively impudence. "I saw you first in February. Let every body on the Hill hear me if they can. Let my accents swell to Mickleham on one side, and Dorking on the other. I saw you first in February." And then whispering—"Our companions are excessively stupid. What shall we do to rouse them? Any nonsense will serve. They shall talk. Ladies and gentlemen, I am ordered by Miss Woodhouse (who, wherever she is, presides) to say, that she desires to know what you are all thinking of?"

Some laughed, and answered good-humouredly. Miss Bates said a great deal; Mrs. Elton swelled at the idea of Miss Woodhouse's presiding; Mr. Knightley's answer was the most distinct.

"Is Miss Woodhouse sure that she would like to hear what we are all thinking of?"

"Oh! no, no"—cried Emma, laughing as carelessly as she could—"Upon no account in the world. It is the very last thing I would stand the brunt of just now. Let me hear any thing rather than what you are all thinking of. I will not say quite all. There are one or two, perhaps, (glancing at Mr. Weston and Harriet,) whose thoughts I might not be afraid of knowing."

"It is a sort of thing," cried Mrs. Elton emphatically, "which I should not have thought myself privileged to inquire into. Though, perhaps, as the Chaperon of the party—I never was in any circle—exploring parties—young ladies—married women—"

Her mutterings were chiefly to her husband; and he murmured, in reply,

"Very true, my love, very true. Exactly so, indeed—quite unheard of—but some ladies say any thing. Better pass it off as a joke. Every body knows what is due to you."

"It will not do," whispered Frank to Emma; "they are most of them affronted. I will attack them with more address. Ladies and gentlemen—I am ordered by Miss Woodhouse to say, that she waives her right of knowing exactly what you may all be thinking of, and only requires something very entertaining from each of you, in a general way. Here are seven of you, besides myself, (who, she is pleased to say, am very entertaining already,) and she only demands from each of you either one thing very clever, be it prose or verse, original or repeated—or two things moderately clever—or three things very dull indeed, and she engages to laugh heartily at them all."

"Oh! very well," exclaimed Miss Bates, "then I need not be uneasy. 'Three things very dull indeed.' That will just do for me, you know. I shall be sure to say three dull things as soon as ever I open my mouth, shan't I? (looking round with the most good-humoured dependence on every body's assent)—Do not you all think I shall?"

Emma could not resist.

"Ah! ma'am, but there may be a difficulty. Pardon me—but you will be limited as to number—only three at once."

Miss Bates, deceived by the mock ceremony of her manner, did not immediately catch her meaning; but, when it burst on her, it could not anger, though a slight blush shewed that it could pain her.

"Ah!—well—to be sure. Yes, I see what she means, (turning to Mr. Knightley,) and I will try to hold my tongue. I must make myself very disagreeable, or she would not have said such a thing to an old friend."

"I like your plan," cried Mr. Weston. "Agreed, agreed. I will do my best. I am making a conundrum. How will a conundrum reckon?"

"Low, I am afraid, sir, very low," answered his son;—"but we shall be indulgent—especially to any one who leads the way."

"No, no," said Emma, "it will not reckon low. A conundrum of Mr. Weston's shall clear him and his next neighbour. Come, sir, pray let me hear it."

"I doubt its being very clever myself," said Mr. Weston. "It is too much a matter of fact, but here it is.—What two letters of the alphabet are there, that express perfection?"

"What two letters!—express perfection! I am sure I do not know."

"Ah! you will never guess. You, (to Emma), I am certain, will never guess.—I will tell you.—M. and A.—Em-ma.—Do you understand?"

Understanding and gratification came together. It might be a very indifferent piece of wit, but Emma found a great deal to laugh at and enjoy in it—and so did Frank and Harriet.—It did not seem to touch the rest of the party equally; some looked very stupid about it, and Mr. Knightley gravely said,

"This explains the sort of clever thing that is wanted, and Mr. Weston has done very well for himself; but he must have knocked up every body else. Perfection should not have come quite so soon."

"Oh! for myself, I protest I must be excused," said Mrs. Elton; "I really cannot attempt—I am not at all fond of the sort of thing. I had an acrostic once sent to me upon my own name, which I was not at all pleased with. I knew who it came from. An abominable puppy!—You know who I mean (nodding to her husband). These kind of things are very well at Christmas, when one is sitting round the fire; but quite out of place, in my opinion, when one is exploring about the country in summer. Miss Woodhouse must excuse me. I am not one of those who have witty things at every body's service. I do not pretend to be a wit. I have a great deal of vivacity in my own way, but I really must be allowed to judge when to speak and when to hold my tongue. Pass us, if you please, Mr. Churchill. Pass Mr. E., Knightley, Jane, and myself. We have nothing clever to say—not one of us.

"Yes, yes, pray pass me," added her husband, with a sort of sneering consciousness; "I have nothing to say that can entertain Miss Woodhouse, or any other young lady. An old married man—quite good for nothing. Shall we walk, Augusta?"

"With all my heart. I am really tired of exploring so long on one spot. Come, Jane, take my other arm."

Jane declined it, however, and the husband and wife walked off. "Happy couple!" said Frank Churchill, as soon as they were out of hearing:—"How well they suit one another!—Very lucky—marrying as they did, upon an acquaintance formed only in a public place!—They only knew each other, I think, a few weeks in Bath! Peculiarly lucky!—for as to any real knowledge of a person's disposition that Bath, or any public place, can give—it is all nothing; there can be no knowledge. It is only by seeing women in their own homes, among their own set, just as they always are, that you can form any just judgment. Short of that, it is all guess and luck—and will generally be ill-luck. How many a man has committed himself on a short acquaintance, and rued it all the rest of his life!"

Miss Fairfax, who had seldom spoken before, except among her own confederates, spoke now.

"Such things do occur, undoubtedly."—She was stopped by a cough. Frank Churchill turned towards her to listen.

"You were speaking," said he, gravely. She recovered her voice.

"I was only going to observe, that though such unfortunate circumstances do sometimes occur both to men and women, I cannot imagine them to be very frequent. A hasty and imprudent attachment may arise—but there is generally time to recover from it afterwards. I would be understood to mean, that it can be only weak, irresolute characters, (whose happiness must be always at the mercy of chance,) who will suffer an unfortunate acquaintance to be an inconvenience, an oppression for ever."

He made no answer; merely looked, and bowed in submission; and soon afterwards said, in a lively tone,

"Well, I have so little confidence in my own judgment, that whenever I marry, I hope some body will chuse my wife for me. Will you? (turning to Emma.) Will you chuse a wife for me?—I am sure I should like any body fixed on by you. You provide for the family, you know, (with a smile at his father). Find some body for me. I am in no hurry. Adopt her, educate her."

"And make her like myself."

"By all means, if you can."

"Very well. I undertake the commission. You shall have a charming wife."

"She must be very lively, and have hazle eyes. I care for nothing else. I shall go abroad for a couple of years—and when I return, I shall come to you for my wife. Remember."

Emma was in no danger of forgetting. It was a commission to touch every favourite feeling. Would not Harriet be the very creature described? Hazle eyes excepted, two years more might make her all that he wished. He might even have Harriet in his thoughts at the moment; who could say? Referring the education to her seemed to imply it.

"Now, ma'am," said Jane to her aunt, "shall we join Mrs. Elton?"

"If you please, my dear. With all my heart. I am quite ready. I was ready to have gone with her, but this will do just as well. We shall soon overtake her. There she is—no, that's somebody else. That's one of the ladies in the Irish car party, not at all like her.—Well, I declare—"

They walked off, followed in half a minute by Mr. Knightley. Mr. Weston, his son, Emma, and Harriet, only remained; and the young man's spirits now rose to a pitch almost unpleasant. Even Emma grew tired at last of flattery and merriment, and wished herself rather walking quietly about with any of the others, or sitting almost alone, and quite unattended to, in tranquil observation of the beautiful views beneath her. The appearance of the servants looking out for them to give notice of the carriages was a joyful sight; and even the bustle of collecting and preparing to depart, and the solicitude of

Mrs. Elton to have her carriage first, were gladly endured, in the prospect of the quiet drive home which was to close the very questionable enjoyments of this day of pleasure. Such another scheme, composed of so many ill-assorted people, she hoped never to be betrayed into again.

While waiting for the carriage, she found Mr. Knightley by her side. He looked around, as if to see that no one were near, and then said,

"Emma, I must once more speak to you as I have been used to do: a privilege rather endured than allowed, perhaps, but I must still use it. I cannot see you acting wrong, without a remonstrance. How could you be so unfeeling to Miss Bates? How could you be so insolent in your wit to a woman of her character, age, and situation?—Emma, I had not thought it possible."

Emma recollected, blushed, was sorry, but tried to laugh it off.

"Nay, how could I help saying what I did?—Nobody could have helped it. It was not so very bad. I dare say she did not understand me."

"I assure you she did. She felt your full meaning. She has talked of it since. I wish you could have heard how she talked of it—with what candour and generosity. I wish you could have heard her honouring your forbearance, in being able to pay her such attentions, as she was for ever receiving from yourself and your father, when her society must be so irksome."

"Oh!" cried Emma, "I know there is not a better creature in the world: but you must allow, that what is good and what is ridiculous are most unfortunately blended in her."

"They are blended," said he, "I acknowledge; and, were she prosperous, I could allow much for the occasional prevalence of the ridiculous over the good. Were she a woman of fortune, I would leave every harmless absurdity to take its chance, I would not quarrel with you for any liberties of manner. Were she your equal in situation—but, Emma, consider how far this is from being the case. She is poor; she has sunk from the comforts she was born to; and, if she live to old age, must probably sink more. Her situation should secure your compassion. It was badly done, indeed! You, whom she had known from an infant, whom she had seen grow up from a period when her notice was an honour, to have you now, in thoughtless spirits, and the pride of the moment, laugh at her, humble her—and before her niece, too—and before others, many of whom (certainly some,) would be entirely guided by your treatment of her.—This is not pleasant to you, Emma—and it is very far from pleasant to me; but I must, I will,—I will tell you truths while I can; satisfied with proving myself your friend by very faithful counsel, and trusting that you will some time or other do me greater justice than you can do now."

While they talked, they were advancing towards the carriage; it was ready; and, before she could speak again, he had handed her in. He had misinterpreted the feelings which had kept her face averted, and her tongue motionless. They were combined only of anger against herself, mortification, and deep concern. She had not been able to speak; and, on entering the carriage, sunk back for a moment overcome—then reproaching herself for having taken no leave, making no acknowledgment, parting in apparent sullenness, she looked out with voice and hand eager to shew a difference; but it was just too late. He had turned away, and the horses were in motion. She continued to look back, but in vain; and soon, with what appeared unusual speed, they were half way down the hill, and every thing left far behind. She was vexed beyond what could have been expressed—almost beyond what she could conceal. Never had she felt so agitated, mortified, grieved, at any circumstance in her life. She was most forcibly struck. The truth of this representation there was no denying. She felt it at her heart. How could she have been so brutal, so cruel to Miss Bates! How could she have exposed herself to such ill opinion in any one she valued! And how suffer him to leave her without saying one word of gratitude, of concurrence, of common kindness!

Time did not compose her. As she reflected more, she seemed but to feel it more. She never had been so depressed. Happily it was not necessary to speak. There was only Harriet, who seemed not in spirits herself, fagged, and very willing to be silent; and Emma felt the tears running down her cheeks almost all the way home, without being at any trouble to check them, extraordinary as they were.

Chapter VIII

The wretchedness of a scheme to Box Hill was in Emma's thoughts all the evening. How it might be considered by the rest of the party, she could not tell. They, in their different homes, and their different ways, might be looking back on it with pleasure; but in her view it was a morning more completely misspent, more totally bare of rational satisfaction at the time, and more to be abhorred in recollection, than any she had ever passed. A whole evening of back-gammon with her father, was felicity to it. There, indeed, lay real pleasure, for there she was giving up the sweetest hours of the twenty-four to his comfort; and feeling that, unmerited as might be the degree of his fond affection and confiding esteem, she could not, in her general conduct, be open to any severe reproach. As a daughter, she hoped she was not without a heart. She hoped no one could have said to her, "How could you be so unfeeling to your father?—I must, I will tell you truths while I can." Miss Bates should never again—no, never! If attention, in future, could do away the past, she might hope to be forgiven. She had been often remiss, her conscience told her so; remiss, perhaps, more in thought than fact; scornful, ungracious. But it should be so no more. In the warmth of true contrition, she would call upon her the very next morning, and it should be the beginning, on her side, of a regular, equal, kindly intercourse.

She was just as determined when the morrow came, and went early, that nothing might prevent her. It was not unlikely, she thought, that she might see Mr. Knightley in her way; or, perhaps, he might come in while she were paying her visit. She had no objection. She would not be ashamed of the appearance of the penitence, so justly and truly hers. Her eyes were towards Donwell as she walked, but she saw him not.

"The ladies were all at home." She had never rejoiced at the sound before, nor ever before entered the passage, nor walked up the stairs, with any wish of giving pleasure, but in conferring obligation, or of deriving it, except in subsequent ridicule.

There was a bustle on her approach; a good deal of moving and talking. She heard Miss Bates's voice, something was to be done in a hurry; the maid looked frightened and awkward; hoped she would be pleased to wait a moment, and then ushered her in too soon. The aunt and niece seemed both escaping into the adjoining room. Jane she had a distinct glimpse of, looking extremely ill; and, before the door had shut them out, she heard Miss Bates saying, "Well, my dear, I shall say you are laid down upon the bed, and I am sure you are ill enough."

Poor old Mrs. Bates, civil and humble as usual, looked as if she did not quite understand what was going on.

"I am afraid Jane is not very well," said she, "but I do not know; they tell me she is well. I dare say my daughter will be here presently, Miss Woodhouse. I hope you find a chair. I wish Hetty had not gone. I am very little able—Have you a chair, ma'am? Do you sit where you like? I am sure she will be here presently."

Emma seriously hoped she would. She had a moment's fear of Miss Bates keeping away from her. But Miss Bates soon came—"Very happy and obliged"—but Emma's conscience told her that there was not the same cheerful volubility as before—less ease of look and manner. A very friendly inquiry after Miss Fairfax, she hoped, might lead the way to a return of old feelings. The touch seemed immediate.

"Ah! Miss Woodhouse, how kind you are!—I suppose you have heard—and are come to give us joy. This does not seem much like joy, indeed, in me—(twinkling away a tear or two)—but it will be very trying for us to part with her, after having had her so long, and she has a dreadful headach just now, writing all the morning:—such long letters, you know, to be written to Colonel Campbell, and Mrs. Dixon. 'My dear,' said I, 'you will blind yourself'—for tears were in her eyes perpetually. One cannot wonder, one cannot wonder. It is a great change; and though she is amazingly fortunate—such a situation, I suppose, as no young woman before ever met with on first going out—do not think us ungrateful, Miss Woodhouse, for such surprising good fortune—(again dispersing her tears)—but, poor dear soul! if you were to see what a headache she has. When one is in great pain, you know one cannot feel any blessing quite as it may deserve. She is as low as possible. To look at her, nobody would think how delighted and happy she is to have secured such a situation. You will excuse her not coming to you—she is not able—she is gone into her own room—I want her to lie down upon the bed. 'My dear,' said I, 'I shall say you are laid down upon the bed:' but, however, she is not; she is walking about the room. But, now that she has written her letters, she says she shall soon be well. She will be extremely sorry to miss seeing you, Miss Woodhouse, but your kindness will excuse her. You were kept waiting at the door—I was quite ashamed—but somehow there was a little bustle—for it so happened that we had not heard the knock, and till you were on the stairs, we did not know any body was coming. 'It is only Mrs. Cole,' said I, 'depend upon it. Nobody else would come so early.' 'Well,' said she, 'it must be borne some time or other, and it may as well be now.' But then Patty came in, and said it was you. 'Oh!' said I, 'it is Miss Woodhouse: I am sure you will like to see her.'—'I can see nobody,' said she; and up she got, and would go away; and that was what made us keep you waiting—and extremely sorry and ashamed we were. 'If you must go, my dear,' said I, 'you must, and I will say you are laid down upon the bed.'"

Emma was most sincerely interested. Her heart had been long growing kinder towards Jane; and this picture of her present sufferings acted as a cure of every former ungenerous suspicion, and left her nothing but pity; and the remembrance of the less just and less gentle sensations of the past, obliged her to admit that Jane might very naturally resolve on seeing Mrs. Cole or any other steady friend, when she might not bear to see herself. She spoke as she felt, with earnest regret and solicitude—sincerely wishing that the circumstances which she collected from Miss Bates to be now actually determined on, might be as much for Miss Fairfax's advantage and comfort as possible. "It must be a severe trial to them all. She had understood it was to be delayed till Colonel Campbell's return."

"So very kind! " replied Miss Bates. "But you are always kind."

There was no bearing such an "always;" and to break through her dreadful gratitude, Emma made the direct inquiry of—

"Where—may I ask?—is Miss Fairfax going?"

"To a Mrs. Smallridge—charming woman—most superior—to have the charge of her three little girls—delightful children. Impossible that any situation could be more replete with comfort; if we except, perhaps, Mrs. Suckling's own family, and Mrs. Bragge's; but Mrs. Smallridge is intimate with both, and in the very same neighbourhood:—lives only four miles from Maple Grove. Jane will be only four miles from Maple Grove."

"Mrs. Elton, I suppose, has been the person to whom Miss Fairfax owes—"

"Yes, our good Mrs. Elton. The most indefatigable, true friend. She would not take a denial. She would not let Jane say, 'No;' for when Jane first heard of it, (it was the day before yesterday, the very morning we were at Donwell,) when Jane first heard of it, she was quite decided against accepting the offer, and for the reasons you mention; exactly as you say, she had made up her mind to close with nothing till Colonel Campbell's return, and nothing should induce her to enter into any engagement at present—and so she told Mrs. Elton over and over again—and I am sure I had no more idea that she would change her mind!—but that good Mrs. Elton, whose judgment never fails her, saw farther than I did. It is not every body that would have stood out in such a kind way as she did, and refuse to take Jane's answer; but she positively declared she would not write any such denial yesterday, as Jane wished her; she would wait—and, sure enough, yesterday evening it was all settled that Jane should go. Quite a surprize to me! I had not the least idea!—Jane took Mrs. Elton aside, and told her at once, that upon thinking over the advantages of Mrs. Smallridge's situation, she had come to the resolution of accepting it.—I did not know a word of it till it was all settled."

"You spent the evening with Mrs. Elton?"

"Yes, all of us; Mrs. Elton would have us come. It was settled so, upon the hill, while we were walking about with Mr. Knightley. 'You must all spend your evening with us,' said she—'I positively must have you all come.'"

"Mr. Knightley was there too, was he?"

"No, not Mr. Knightley; he declined it from the first; and though I thought he would come, because Mrs. Elton declared she would not let him off, he did not;—but my mother, and Jane, and I, were all there, and a very agreeable evening we had. Such kind friends, you know, Miss Woodhouse, one must always find agreeable, though every body seemed rather fagged after the morning's party. Even pleasure, you know, is fatiguing—and I cannot say that any of them seemed very much to have enjoyed it. However, I shall always think it a very pleasant party, and feel extremely obliged to the kind friends who included me in it."

"Miss Fairfax, I suppose, though you were not aware of it, had been making up her mind the whole day?"

"I dare say she had."

"Whenever the time may come, it must be unwelcome to her and all her friends—but I hope her engagement will have every alleviation that is possible—I mean, as to the character and manners of the family."

"Thank you, dear Miss Woodhouse. Yes, indeed, there is every thing in the world that can make her happy in it. Except the Sucklings and Bragges, there is not such another nursery establishment, so liberal and elegant, in all Mrs. Elton's acquaintance. Mrs. Smallridge, a most delightful woman!—A style of living almost equal to Maple Grove—and as to the children, except the little Sucklings and little Bragges, there are not such elegant sweet children anywhere. Jane will be treated with such regard and kindness!—It will be nothing but pleasure, a life of pleasure.—And her salary!—I really cannot venture to name her salary to you, Miss Woodhouse. Even you, used as you are to great sums, would hardly believe that so much could be given to a young person like Jane."

"Ah! madam," cried Emma, "if other children are at all like what I remember to have been myself, I should think five times the amount of what I have ever yet heard named as a salary on such occasions, dearly earned."

"You are so noble in your ideas!"

"And when is Miss Fairfax to leave you?"

"Very soon, very soon, indeed; that's the worst of it. Within a fortnight. Mrs. Smallridge is in a great hurry. My poor mother does not know how to bear it. So then, I try to put it out of her thoughts, and say, Come ma'am, do not let us think about it any more."

"Her friends must all be sorry to lose her; and will not Colonel and Mrs. Campbell be sorry to find that she has engaged herself before their return?"

"Yes; Jane says she is sure they will; but yet, this is such a situation as she cannot feel herself justified in declining. I was so astonished when she first told me what she had been saying to Mrs. Elton, and when Mrs. Elton at the same moment came congratulating me upon it! It was before tea—stay—no, it could not be before tea, because we were just going to cards—and yet it was before tea, because I remember thinking—Oh! no, now I recollect, now I have it; something happened before tea, but not that. Mr. Elton was called out of the room before tea, old John Abdy's son wanted to speak with him. Poor old John, I have a great regard for him; he was clerk to my poor father twenty-seven years; and now, poor old man, he is bed-ridden, and very poorly with the rheumatic gout in his joints—I must go and see him to-day; and so will Jane, I am sure, if she gets out at all. And poor John's son came to talk to Mr. Elton about relief from the parish; he is very well to do himself, you know, being head man at the Crown, ostler, and every thing of that sort, but still he cannot keep his father without some help; and so, when Mr. Elton came back, he told us what John ostler had been telling him, and then it came out about the chaise having been sent to Randalls to take Mr. Frank Churchill to Richmond. That was what happened before tea. It was after tea that Jane spoke to Mrs. Elton."

Miss Bates would hardly give Emma time to say how perfectly new this circumstance was to her; but as without supposing it possible that she could be ignorant of any of the particulars of Mr. Frank Churchill's going, she proceeded to give them all, it was of no consequence.

What Mr. Elton had learned from the ostler on the subject, being the accumulation of the ostler's own knowledge, and the knowledge of the servants at Randalls, was, that a messenger had come over from Richmond soon after the return of the party from Box Hill—which messenger, however, had been no more than was expected; and that Mr. Churchill had sent his nephew a few lines, containing, upon the whole, a tolerable account of Mrs. Churchill, and only wishing him not to delay coming back beyond the next morning early; but that Mr. Frank Churchill having resolved to go home directly, without waiting at all, and his horse seeming to have got a cold, Tom had been sent off immediately for the Crown chaise, and the ostler had stood out and seen it pass by, the boy going a good pace, and driving very steady.

There was nothing in all this either to astonish or interest, and it caught Emma's attention only as it united with the subject which already engaged her mind. The contrast between Mrs. Churchill's importance in the world, and Jane Fairfax's, struck her; one was every thing, the other nothing—and she sat musing on the difference of woman's destiny, and quite unconscious on what her eyes were fixed, till roused by Miss Bates's saying,

"Aye, I see what you are thinking of, the pianoforte. What is to become of that?—Very true. Poor dear Jane was talking of it just now.—'You must go,' said she. 'You and I must part. You will have no business here.—Let it stay, however,' said she; 'give it houseroom till Colonel Campbell comes back. I shall talk about it to him; he will settle for me; he will help me out of all my difficulties.'—And to this day, I do believe, she knows not whether it was his present or his daughter's."

Now Emma was obliged to think of the pianoforte; and the remembrance of all her former fanciful and unfair conjectures was so little pleasing, that she soon allowed herself to believe her visit had been long enough; and, with a repetition of every thing that she could venture to say of the good wishes which she really felt, took leave.

Chapter IX

Emma's pensive meditations, as she walked home, were not interrupted; but on entering the parlour, she found those who must rouse her. Mr. Knightley and Harriet had arrived during her absence, and were sitting with her father.—Mr. Knightley immediately got up, and in a manner decidedly graver than usual, said,

"I would not go away without seeing you, but I have no time to spare, and therefore must now be gone directly. I am going to London, to spend a few days with John and Isabella. Have you any thing to send or say, besides the 'love,' which nobody carries?"

"Nothing at all. But is not this a sudden scheme?"

"Yes—rather—I have been thinking of it some little time."

Emma was sure he had not forgiven her; he looked unlike himself. Time, however, she thought, would tell him that they ought to be friends again. While he stood, as if meaning to go, but not going—her father began his inquiries.

"Well, my dear, and did you get there safely?—And how did you find my worthy old friend and her daughter?—I dare say they must have been very much obliged to you for coming. Dear Emma has been to call on Mrs. and Miss Bates, Mr. Knightley, as I told you before. She is always so attentive to them!"

Emma's colour was heightened by this unjust praise; and with a smile, and shake of the head, which spoke much, she looked at Mr. Knightley.—It seemed as if there were an instantaneous impression in her favour, as if his eyes received the truth from her's, and all that had passed of good in her feelings were at once caught and honoured.—He looked at her with a glow of regard. She was warmly gratified—and in another moment still more so, by a little movement of more than common friendliness on his part.—He took her hand;—whether she had not herself made the first motion, she could not say—she might, perhaps, have rather offered it—but he took her hand, pressed it, and certainly was on the point of carrying it to his lips—when, from some fancy or other, he suddenly let it go.—Why he should feel such a scruple, why he should change his mind when it was all but done, she could not perceive.—He would have judged better, she thought, if he had not stopped.—The intention, however, was indubitable; and whether it was that his manners had in general so little gallantry, or however else it happened, but she thought nothing became him more.—It was with him, of so simple, yet so dignified a nature.—She could not but recall the attempt with great satisfaction. It spoke such perfect amity.—He left them immediately afterwards—gone in a moment. He always moved with the alertness of a mind which could neither be undecided nor dilatory, but now he seemed more sudden than usual in his disappearance.

Emma could not regret her having gone to Miss Bates, but she wished she had left her ten minutes earlier;—it would have been a great pleasure to talk over Jane Fairfax's situation with Mr. Knightley.—Neither would she regret that he should be going to Brunswick Square, for she knew how much his visit would be enjoyed—but it might have happened at a better time—and to have had longer notice of it, would have been pleasanter.—They parted thorough friends, however; she could not be deceived as to the meaning of his countenance, and his unfinished gallantry;—it was all done to assure her that she had fully recovered his good opinion.—He had been sitting with them half an hour, she found. It was a pity that she had not come back earlier!

In the hope of diverting her father's thoughts from the disagreeableness of Mr. Knightley's going to London; and going so suddenly; and going on horseback, which she knew would be all very bad; Emma communicated her news of Jane Fairfax, and her dependence on the effect was justified; it supplied a very useful check,—interested, without disturbing him. He had long made up his mind to Jane Fairfax's going out as governess, and could talk of it cheerfully, but Mr. Knightley's going to London had been an unexpected blow.

"I am very glad, indeed, my dear, to hear she is to be so comfortably settled. Mrs. Elton is very good-natured and agreeable, and I dare say her acquaintance are just what they ought to be. I hope it is a dry situation, and that her health will be taken good care of. It ought to be a first object, as I am sure poor Miss Taylor's always was with me. You know, my dear, she is going to be to this new lady what Miss Taylor was to us. And I hope she will be better off in one respect, and not be induced to go away after it has been her home so long."

The following day brought news from Richmond to throw every thing else into the background. An express arrived at Randalls to announce the death of Mrs. Churchill! Though her nephew had had no particular reason to hasten back on her account, she had not lived above six-and-thirty hours after his return. A sudden seizure of a different nature from any thing foreboded by her general state, had carried her off after a short struggle. The great Mrs. Churchill was no more.

It was felt as such things must be felt. Every body had a degree of gravity and sorrow; tenderness towards the departed, solicitude for the surviving friends; and, in a reasonable time, curiosity to know where she would be buried. Goldsmith tells us, that when lovely woman stoops to folly, she has nothing to do but to die; and when she stoops to be disagreeable, it is equally to be recommended as a clearer of ill-fame. Mrs. Churchill, after being disliked at least twenty-five years, was now spoken of with compassionate allowances. In one point she was fully justified. She had never been admitted before to be seriously ill. The event acquitted her of all the fancifulness, and all the selfishness of imaginary complaints.

"Poor Mrs. Churchill! no doubt she had been suffering a great deal: more than any body had ever supposed—and continual pain would try the temper. It was a sad event—a great shock—with all her faults, what would Mr. Churchill do without her? Mr. Churchill's loss would be dreadful indeed. Mr. Churchill would never get over it."—Even Mr. Weston shook his head, and looked solemn, and said, "Ah! poor woman, who would have thought it!" and resolved, that his mourning should be as handsome as possible; and his wife sat sighing and moralising over her broad hems with a commiseration and good sense, true and steady. How it would affect Frank was among the earliest thoughts of both. It was also a very early speculation with Emma. The character of Mrs. Churchill, the grief of her husband—her mind glanced over them both with awe and compassion—and then rested with lightened feelings on how Frank might be affected by the event, how benefited, how freed. She saw in a moment all the possible good. Now, an attachment to Harriet Smith would have nothing to encounter. Mr. Churchill, independent of his wife, was feared by nobody; an easy, guidable man, to be persuaded into any thing by his nephew. All that remained to be wished was, that the nephew should form the attachment, as, with all her goodwill in the cause, Emma could feel no certainty of its being already formed.

Harriet behaved extremely well on the occasion, with great self-command. What ever she might feel of brighter hope, she betrayed nothing. Emma was gratified, to observe such a proof in her of strengthened character, and refrained from any allusion that might endanger its maintenance. They spoke, therefore, of Mrs. Churchill's death with mutual forbearance.

Short letters from Frank were received at Randalls, communicating all that was immediately important of their state and plans. Mr. Churchill was better than could be expected; and their first removal, on the departure of the funeral for Yorkshire, was to be to the house of a very old friend in Windsor, to whom Mr. Churchill had been promising a visit the last ten years. At present, there was nothing to be done for Harriet; good wishes for the future were all that could yet be possible on Emma's side.

It was a more pressing concern to shew attention to Jane Fairfax, whose prospects were closing, while Harriet's opened, and whose engagements now allowed of no delay in any one at Highbury, who wished to shew her kindness—and with Emma it was grown into a first wish. She had scarcely a stronger regret than for her past coldness; and the person, whom she had been so many months neglecting, was now the very one on whom she would have lavished every distinction of regard or sympathy. She wanted to be of use to her; wanted to shew a value for her society, and testify respect and consideration. She resolved to prevail on her to spend a day at Hartfield. A note was written to urge it. The invitation was refused, and by a verbal message. "Miss Fairfax was not well enough to write;" and when Mr. Perry called at Hartfield, the same morning, it appeared that she was so much indisposed as to have been visited, though against her own consent, by himself, and that she was suffering under severe headaches, and a nervous fever to a degree, which made him doubt the possibility of her going to Mrs. Smallridge's at the time proposed. Her health seemed for the moment completely deranged—appetite quite gone—and though there were no absolutely alarming symptoms, nothing touching the pulmonary complaint, which was the standing apprehension of the family, Mr. Perry was uneasy about her. He thought she had undertaken more than she was equal to, and that she felt it so herself, though she would not own it. Her spirits seemed overcome. Her present home, he could not but observe, was unfavourable to a nervous disorder:—confined always to one room;—he could have wished it otherwise—and her good aunt, though his very old friend, he must acknowledge to be not the best companion for an invalid of that description. Her care and attention could not be questioned; they were, in fact, only too great. He very much feared that Miss Fairfax derived more evil than good from them. Emma listened with the warmest concern; grieved for her more and more, and looked around eager to discover some way of being useful. To take her—be it only an hour or two—from her aunt, to give her change of air and scene, and quiet rational conversation, even for an hour or two, might do her good; and the following morning she wrote again to say, in the most feeling language she could command, that she would call for her in the carriage at any hour that Jane would name—mentioning that she had Mr. Perry's decided opinion, in favour of such exercise for his patient. The answer was only in this short note:

"Miss Fairfax's compliments and thanks, but is quite unequal to any exercise."

Emma felt that her own note had deserved something better; but it was impossible to quarrel with words, whose tremulous inequality shewed indisposition so plainly, and she thought only of how she might best counteract this unwillingness to be seen or assisted. In spite of the answer, therefore, she ordered the carriage, and drove to Mrs. Bates's, in the hope that Jane would be induced to join her—but it would not do;—Miss Bates came to the carriage door, all gratitude, and agreeing with her most earnestly in thinking an airing might be of the greatest service—and every thing that message could do was tried—but all in vain. Miss Bates was obliged to return without success; Jane was quite unpersuadable; the mere proposal of going out seemed to make her worse.—Emma wished she could have seen her, and tried her own powers; but, almost before she could hint the wish, Miss Bates made it appear that she had promised her niece on no account to let Miss Woodhouse in. "Indeed, the truth was, that poor dear Jane could not bear to see any body—any body at all—Mrs. Elton, indeed, could not be denied—and Mrs. Cole had made such a point—and Mrs. Perry had said so much—but, except them, Jane would really see nobody."

Emma did not want to be classed with the Mrs. Eltons, the Mrs. Perrys, and the Mrs. Coles, who would force themselves anywhere; neither could she feel any right of preference herself—she submitted, therefore, and only questioned Miss Bates farther as to her niece's appetite and diet, which she longed to be able to assist. On that subject poor Miss Bates was very unhappy, and very communicative; Jane would hardly eat any thing:—Mr. Perry recommended nourishing food; but every thing they could command (and never had any body such good neighbours) was distasteful.

Emma, on reaching home, called the housekeeper directly, to an examination of her stores; and some arrowroot of very superior quality was speedily despatched to Miss Bates with a most friendly note. In half an hour the arrowroot was returned, with a thousand thanks from Miss Bates, but "dear Jane would not be satisfied without its being sent back; it was a thing she could not take—and, moreover, she insisted on her saying, that she was not at all in want of any thing."

When Emma afterwards heard that Jane Fairfax had been seen wandering about the meadows, at some distance from Highbury, on the afternoon of the very day on which she had, under the plea of being unequal to any exercise, so peremptorily refused to go out with her in the carriage, she could have no doubt—putting every thing together—that Jane was resolved to receive no kindness from her. She was sorry, very sorry. Her heart was grieved for a state which seemed but the more pitiable from this sort of irritation of spirits, inconsistency of action, and inequality of powers; and it mortified her that she was given so little credit for proper feeling, or esteemed so little worthy as a friend: but she had the consolation of knowing that her intentions were good, and of being able to say to herself, that could Mr. Knightley have been privy to all her attempts of assisting Jane Fairfax, could he even have seen into her heart, he would not, on this occasion, have found any thing to reprove.

Chapter X

One morning, about ten days after Mrs. Churchill's decease, Emma was called downstairs to Mr. Weston, who "could not stay five minutes, and wanted particularly to speak with her."—He met her at the parlour-door, and hardly asking her how she did, in the natural key of his voice, sunk it immediately, to say, unheard by her father,

"Can you come to Randalls at any time this morning?—Do, if it be possible. Mrs. Weston wants to see you. She must see you."

"Is she unwell?"

"No, no, not at all—only a little agitated. She would have ordered the carriage, and come to you, but she must see you alone, and that you know—(nodding towards her father)—Humph!—Can you come?"

"Certainly. This moment, if you please. It is impossible to refuse what you ask in such a way. But what can be the matter?—Is she really not ill?"

"Depend upon me—but ask no more questions. You will know it all in time. The most unaccountable business! But hush, hush!"

To guess what all this meant, was impossible even for Emma. Something really important seemed announced by his looks; but, as her friend was well, she endeavoured not to be uneasy, and settling it with her father, that she would take her walk now, she and Mr.

Weston were soon out of the house together and on their way at a quick pace for Randalls.

"Now,"—said Emma, when they were fairly beyond the sweep gates,—"now Mr. Weston, do let me know what has happened."

"No, no,"—he gravely replied.—"Don't ask me. I promised my wife to leave it all to her. She will break it to you better than I can. Do not be impatient, Emma; it will all come out too soon."

"Break it to me," cried Emma, standing still with terror.—"Good God!—Mr. Weston, tell me at once.—Something has happened in Brunswick Square. I know it has. Tell me, I charge you tell me this moment what it is."

"No, indeed you are mistaken."—

"Mr. Weston do not trifle with me.—Consider how many of my dearest friends are now in Brunswick Square. Which of them is it?—I charge you by all that is sacred, not to attempt concealment."

"Upon my word, Emma."—

"Your word!—why not your honour!—why not say upon your honour, that it has nothing to do with any of them? Good Heavens!—What can be to be broke to me, that does not relate to one of that family?"

"Upon my honour," said he very seriously, "it does not. It is not in the smallest degree connected with any human being of the name of Knightley."

Emma's courage returned, and she walked on.

"I was wrong," he continued, "in talking of its being broke to you. I should not have used the expression. In fact, it does not concern you—it concerns only myself,—that is, we hope.—Humph!—In short, my dear Emma, there is no occasion to be so uneasy about it. I don't say that it is not a disagreeable business—but things might be much worse.—If we walk fast, we shall soon be at Randalls."

Emma found that she must wait; and now it required little effort. She asked no more questions therefore, merely employed her own fancy, and that soon pointed out to her the probability of its being some money concern—something just come to light, of a disagreeable nature in the circumstances of the family,—something which the late event at Richmond had brought forward. Her fancy was very active. Half a dozen natural children, perhaps—and poor

Frank cut off!—This, though very undesirable, would be no matter of agony to her. It inspired little more than an animating curiosity.

"Who is that gentleman on horseback?" said she, as they proceeded—speaking more to assist Mr. Weston in keeping his secret, than with any other view.

"I do not know.—One of the Otways.—Not Frank;—it is not Frank, I assure you. You will not see him. He is half way to Windsor by this time."

"Has your son been with you, then?"

"Oh! yes—did not you know?—Well, well, never mind."

For a moment he was silent; and then added, in a tone much more guarded and demure,

"Yes, Frank came over this morning, just to ask us how we did."

They hurried on, and were speedily at Randalls.—"Well, my dear," said he, as they entered the room—"I have brought her, and now I hope you will soon be better. I shall leave you together. There is no use in delay. I shall not be far off, if you want me."—And Emma distinctly heard him add, in a lower tone, before he quitted the room,—"I have been as good as my word. She has not the least idea."

Mrs. Weston was looking so ill, and had an air of so much perturbation, that Emma's uneasiness increased; and the moment they were alone, she eagerly said,

"What is it my dear friend? Something of a very unpleasant nature, I find, has occurred;—do let me know directly what it is. I have been walking all this way in complete suspense. We both abhor suspense. Do not let mine continue longer. It will do you good to speak of your distress, whatever it may be."

"Have you indeed no idea?" said Mrs. Weston in a trembling voice. "Cannot you, my dear Emma—cannot you form a guess as to what you are to hear?"

"So far as that it relates to Mr. Frank Churchill, I do guess."

"You are right. It does relate to him, and I will tell you directly;" (resuming her work, and seeming resolved against looking up.) "He has been here this very morning, on a most extraordinary errand. It is impossible to express our surprize. He came to speak to his father on a subject,—to announce an attachment—"

She stopped to breathe. Emma thought first of herself, and then of Harriet.

"More than an attachment, indeed," resumed Mrs. Weston; "an engagement—a positive engagement.—What will you say, Emma—what will any body say, when it is known that Frank Churchill and Miss Fairfax are engaged;—nay, that they have been long engaged!"

Emma even jumped with surprize;—and, horror-struck, exclaimed,

"Jane Fairfax!—Good God! You are not serious? You do not mean it?"

"You may well be amazed," returned Mrs. Weston, still averting her eyes, and talking on with eagerness, that Emma might have time to recover—"You may well be amazed. But it is even so. There has been a solemn engagement between them ever since October—formed at Weymouth, and kept a secret from every body. Not a creature knowing it but themselves—neither the Campbells, nor her family, nor his.—It is so wonderful, that though perfectly convinced of the fact, it is yet almost incredible to myself. I can hardly believe it.—I thought I knew him."

Emma scarcely heard what was said.—Her mind was divided between two ideas—her own former conversations with him about Miss Fairfax; and poor Harriet;—and for some time she could only exclaim, and require confirmation, repeated confirmation.

"Well," said she at last, trying to recover herself; "this is a circumstance which I must think of at least half a day, before I can at all comprehend it. What!—engaged to her all the winter—before either of them came to Highbury?"

"Engaged since October,—secretly engaged.—It has hurt me, Emma, very much. It has hurt his father equally. Some part of his conduct we cannot excuse."

Emma pondered a moment, and then replied, "I will not pretend not to understand you; and to give you all the relief in my power, be assured that no such effect has followed his attentions to me, as you are apprehensive of."

Mrs. Weston looked up, afraid to believe; but Emma's countenance was as steady as her words.

"That you may have less difficulty in believing this boast, of my present perfect indifference," she continued, "I will farther tell you, that there was a period in the early part of our acquaintance, when I did like him, when I was very much disposed to be attached to him—nay, was attached—and how it came to cease, is perhaps the wonder. Fortunately, however, it did cease. I have really for some time past, for at least these three months, cared nothing about him. You may believe me, Mrs. Weston. This is the simple truth."

Mrs. Weston kissed her with tears of joy; and when she could find utterance, assured her, that this protestation had done her more good than any thing else in the world could do.

"Mr. Weston will be almost as much relieved as myself," said she. "On this point we have been wretched. It was our darling wish that you might be attached to each other—and we were persuaded that it was so.—Imagine what we have been feeling on your account."

"I have escaped; and that I should escape, may be a matter of grateful wonder to you and myself. But this does not acquit him, Mrs. Weston; and I must say, that I think him greatly to blame. What right had he to come among us with affection and faith engaged, and with manners so very disengaged? What right had he to endeavour to please, as he certainly did—to distinguish any one young woman with persevering attention, as he certainly did—while he really belonged to another?—How could he tell what mischief he might be doing?—How could he tell that he might not be making me in love with him?—very wrong, very wrong indeed."

"From something that he said, my dear Emma, I rather imagine—"

"And how could she bear such behaviour! Composure with a witness! to look on, while repeated attentions were offering to another woman, before her face, and not resent it.—That is a degree of placidity, which I can neither comprehend nor respect."

"There were misunderstandings between them, Emma; he said so expressly. He had not time to enter into much explanation. He was here only a quarter of an hour, and in a state of agitation which did not allow the full use even of the time he could stay—but that there had been misunderstandings he decidedly said. The present crisis, indeed, seemed to be brought on by them; and those misunderstandings might very possibly arise from the impropriety of his conduct."

"Impropriety! Oh! Mrs. Weston—it is too calm a censure. Much, much beyond impropriety!—It has sunk him, I cannot say how it has sunk him in my opinion. So unlike what a man should be!—None of that upright integrity, that strict adherence to truth and principle, that disdain of trick and littleness, which a man should display in every transaction of his life."

"Nay, dear Emma, now I must take his part; for though he has been wrong in this instance, I have known him long enough to answer for his having many, very many, good qualities; and—"

"Good God!" cried Emma, not attending to her.—"Mrs. Smallridge, too! Jane actually on the point of going as governess! What could he mean by such horrible indelicacy? To suffer her to engage herself—to suffer her even to think of such a measure!"

"He knew nothing about it, Emma. On this article I can fully acquit him. It was a private resolution of hers, not communicated to him—or at least not communicated in a way to carry conviction.—Till yesterday, I know he said he was in the dark as to her plans. They burst on him, I do not know how, but by some letter or message—and it was the discovery of what she was doing, of this very project of hers, which determined him to come forward at once, own it all to his uncle, throw himself on his kindness, and, in short, put an end to the miserable state of concealment that had been carrying on so long."

Emma began to listen better.

"I am to hear from him soon," continued Mrs. Weston. "He told me at parting, that he should soon write; and he spoke in a manner which seemed to promise me many particulars that could not be given now. Let us wait, therefore, for this letter. It may bring many extenuations. It may make many things intelligible and excusable which now are not to be understood. Don't let us be severe, don't let us be in a hurry to condemn him. Let us have patience. I must love him; and now that I am satisfied on one point, the one material point, I am sincerely anxious for its all turning out well, and ready to hope that it may. They must both have suffered a great deal under such a system of secresy and concealment."

"His sufferings," replied Emma dryly, "do not appear to have done him much harm. Well, and how did Mr. Churchill take it?"

"Most favourably for his nephew—gave his consent with scarcely a difficulty. Conceive what the events of a week have done in that family! While poor Mrs. Churchill lived, I suppose there could not have been a hope, a chance, a possibility;—but scarcely are her remains at rest in the family vault, than her husband is persuaded to act exactly opposite to what she would have required. What a blessing it is, when undue influence does not survive the grave!—He gave his consent with very little persuasion."

"Ah!" thought Emma, "he would have done as much for Harriet."

"This was settled last night, and Frank was off with the light this morning. He stopped at Highbury, at the Bates's, I fancy, some time—and then came on hither; but was in such a hurry to get back to his uncle, to whom he is just now more necessary than ever, that, as I tell you, he could stay with us but a quarter of an hour.—He was very much agitated—very much, indeed—to a degree that made him appear quite a different creature from any thing I had ever seen him before.—In addition to all the rest, there had been the shock of finding her so very unwell, which he had had no previous suspicion of—and there was every appearance of his having been feeling a great deal."

"And do you really believe the affair to have been carrying on with such perfect secresy?—The Campbells, the Dixons, did none of them know of the engagement?"

Emma could not speak the name of Dixon without a little blush.

"None; not one. He positively said that it had been known to no being in the world but their two selves."

"Well," said Emma, "I suppose we shall gradually grow reconciled to the idea, and I wish them very happy. But I shall always think it a very abominable sort of proceeding. What has it been but a system of hypocrisy and deceit,—espionage, and treachery?—To come among us with professions of openness and simplicity; and such a league in secret to judge us all!—Here have we been, the whole winter and spring, completely duped, fancying ourselves all on an equal footing of truth and honour, with two people in the midst of us who may have been carrying round, comparing and sitting in judgment on sentiments and words that were never meant for both to hear.—They must take the consequence, if they have heard each other spoken of in a way not perfectly agreeable!"

"I am quite easy on that head," replied Mrs. Weston. "I am very sure that I never said any thing of either to the other, which both might not have heard."

"You are in luck.—Your only blunder was confined to my ear, when you imagined a certain friend of ours in love with the lady."

"True. But as I have always had a thoroughly good opinion of Miss Fairfax, I never could, under any blunder, have spoken ill of her; and as to speaking ill of him, there I must have been safe."

At this moment Mr. Weston appeared at a little distance from the window, evidently on the watch. His wife gave him a look which invited him in; and, while he was coming round, added, "Now, dearest Emma, let me intreat you to say and look every thing that may set his heart at ease, and incline him to be satisfied with the match. Let us make the best of it—and, indeed, almost every thing may be fairly said in her favour. It is not a connexion to gratify; but if Mr. Churchill does not feel that, why should we? and it may be a very fortunate circumstance for him, for Frank, I mean, that he should have attached himself to a girl of such steadiness of character and good judgment as I have always given her credit for—and still am disposed to give her credit for, in spite of this one great deviation from the strict rule of right. And how much may be said in her situation for even that error!"

"Much, indeed!" cried Emma feelingly. "If a woman can ever be excused for thinking only of herself, it is in a situation like Jane Fairfax's.—Of such, one may almost say, that 'the world is not their's, nor the world's law.'"

She met Mr. Weston on his entrance, with a smiling countenance, exclaiming,

"A very pretty trick you have been playing me, upon my word! This was a device, I suppose, to sport with my curiosity, and exercise my talent of guessing. But you really frightened me. I thought you had lost half your property, at least. And here, instead of its being a matter of condolence, it turns out to be one of congratulation.—I congratulate you, Mr. Weston, with all my heart, on the prospect of having one of the most lovely and accomplished young women in England for your daughter."

A glance or two between him and his wife, convinced him that all was as right as this speech proclaimed; and its happy effect on his spirits was immediate. His air and voice recovered their usual briskness: he shook her heartily and gratefully by the hand, and entered on the subject in a manner to prove, that he now only wanted time and persuasion to think the engagement no very bad thing. His companions suggested only what could palliate imprudence, or smooth objections; and by the time they had talked it all over together, and he had talked it all over again with Emma, in their walk back to Hartfield, he was become perfectly reconciled, and not far from thinking it the very best thing that Frank could possibly have done.

Chapter XI

"Harriet, poor Harriet!"—Those were the words; in them lay the tormenting ideas which Emma could not get rid of, and which constituted the real misery of the business to her. Frank Churchill had behaved very ill by herself—very ill in many ways,—but it was not so much his behaviour as her own, which made her so angry with him. It was the scrape which he had drawn her into on Harriet's account, that gave the deepest hue to his offence.—Poor Harriet! to be a second time the dupe of her misconceptions and flattery. Mr. Knightley had spoken prophetically, when he once said, "Emma, you have been no friend to Harriet Smith."—She was afraid she had done her nothing but disservice.—It was true that she had not to charge herself, in this instance as in the former, with being the sole and original author of the mischief; with having suggested such feelings as might otherwise never have entered Harriet's imagination; for Harriet had acknowledged her admiration and preference of Frank Churchill before she had ever given her a hint on the subject; but she felt completely guilty of having encouraged what she might have repressed. She might have prevented the indulgence and increase of such sentiments. Her influence would have been enough. And now she was very conscious that she ought to have prevented them.—She felt that she had been risking her friend's happiness on most insufficient grounds. Common sense would have directed her to tell Harriet, that she must not allow herself to think of him, and that there were five hundred chances to one against his ever caring for her.—"But, with common sense," she added, "I am afraid I have had little to do."

She was extremely angry with herself. If she could not have been angry with Frank Churchill too, it would have been dreadful.—As for Jane Fairfax, she might at least relieve her feelings from any present solicitude on her account. Harriet would be anxiety enough; she need no longer be unhappy about Jane, whose troubles and whose ill-health having, of course, the same origin, must be equally under cure.—Her days of insignificance and evil were over.—She would soon be well, and happy, and prosperous.—Emma could now imagine why her own attentions had been slighted. This discovery laid many smaller matters open. No doubt it had been from jealousy.—In Jane's eyes she had been a rival; and well might any thing she could offer of assistance or regard be repulsed. An airing in the Hartfield carriage would have been the rack, and arrowroot from the Hartfield storeroom must have been poison. She understood it all; and as far as her mind could disengage itself from the injustice and selfishness of angry feelings, she acknowledged that Jane Fairfax would have neither elevation nor happiness beyond her desert. But poor Harriet was such an engrossing charge! There was little sympathy to be spared for any body else. Emma was sadly fearful that this second disappointment would be more severe than the first. Considering the very superior claims of the object, it ought; and judging by its apparently stronger effect on Harriet's mind, producing reserve and self-command, it would.—She must communicate the painful truth, however, and as soon as possible. An injunction of secresy had been among Mr. Weston's parting words. "For the present, the whole affair was to be completely a secret. Mr. Churchill had made a point of it, as a token of respect to the wife he had so very recently lost; and every body admitted it to be no more than due decorum."—Emma had promised; but still Harriet must be excepted. It was her superior duty.

In spite of her vexation, she could not help feeling it almost ridiculous, that she should have the very same distressing and delicate office to perform by Harriet, which Mrs. Weston had just gone through by herself. The intelligence, which had been so anxiously announced to her, she was now to be anxiously announcing to another. Her heart beat quick on hearing Harriet's footstep and voice; so, she supposed, had poor Mrs. Weston felt when she was approaching Randalls. Could the event of the disclosure bear an equal resemblance!—But of that, unfortunately, there could be no chance.

"Well, Miss Woodhouse!" cried Harriet, coming eagerly into the room—"is not this the oddest news that ever was?"

"What news do you mean?" replied Emma, unable to guess, by look or voice, whether Harriet could indeed have received any hint.

"About Jane Fairfax. Did you ever hear any thing so strange? Oh!—you need not be afraid of owning it to me, for Mr. Weston has told me himself. I met him just now. He told me it was to be a great secret; and, therefore, I should not think of mentioning it to any body but you, but he said you knew it."

"What did Mr. Weston tell you?"—said Emma, still perplexed.

"Oh! he told me all about it; that Jane Fairfax and Mr. Frank Churchill are to be married, and that they have been privately engaged to one another this long while. How very odd!"

It was, indeed, so odd; Harriet's behaviour was so extremely odd, that Emma did not know how to understand it. Her character appeared absolutely changed. She seemed to propose shewing no agitation, or disappointment, or peculiar concern in the discovery. Emma looked at her, quite unable to speak.

"Had you any idea," cried Harriet, "of his being in love with her?—You, perhaps, might.—You (blushing as she spoke) who can see into every body's heart; but nobody else—"

"Upon my word," said Emma, "I begin to doubt my having any such talent. Can you seriously ask me, Harriet, whether I imagined him attached to another woman at the very time that I was—tacitly, if not openly—encouraging you to give way to your own feelings?—I never had the slightest suspicion, till within the last hour, of Mr. Frank Churchill's having the least regard for Jane Fairfax. You may be very sure that if I had, I should have cautioned you accordingly."

"Me!" cried Harriet, colouring, and astonished. "Why should you caution me?—You do not think I care about Mr. Frank Churchill."

"I am delighted to hear you speak so stoutly on the subject," replied Emma, smiling; "but you do not mean to deny that there was a time—and not very distant either—when you gave me reason to understand that you did care about him?"

"Him!—never, never. Dear Miss Woodhouse, how could you so mistake me?" turning away distressed.

"Harriet!" cried Emma, after a moment's pause—"What do you mean?—Good Heaven! what do you mean?—Mistake you!—Am I to suppose then?—"

She could not speak another word.—Her voice was lost; and she sat down, waiting in great terror till Harriet should answer.

Harriet, who was standing at some distance, and with face turned from her, did not immediately say any thing; and when she did speak, it was in a voice nearly as agitated as Emma's.

"I should not have thought it possible," she began, "that you could have misunderstood me! I know we agreed never to name him—but considering how infinitely superior he is to every body else, I should not have thought it possible that I could be supposed to mean any other person. Mr. Frank Churchill, indeed! I do not know who would ever look at him in the company of the other. I hope I have a better taste than to think of Mr. Frank Churchill, who is like nobody by his side. And that you should have been so mistaken, is amazing!—I am sure, but for believing that you entirely approved and meant to encourage me in my attachment, I should have considered it at first too great a presumption almost, to dare to think of him. At first, if you had not told me that more wonderful things had happened; that there had been matches of greater disparity (those were your very words);—I should not have dared to give way to—I should not have thought it possible—But if you, who had been always acquainted with him——"

"Harriet!" cried Emma, collecting herself resolutely—"Let us understand each other now, without the possibility of farther mistake. Are you speaking of—Mr. Knightley?"

"To be sure I am. I never could have an idea of any body else—and so I thought you knew. When we talked about him, it was as clear as possible."

"Not quite," returned Emma, with forced calmness, "for all that you then said, appeared to me to relate to a different person. I could almost assert that you had named Mr. Frank Churchill. I am sure the service Mr. Frank Churchill had rendered you, in protecting you from the gipsies, was spoken of."

"Oh! Miss Woodhouse, how you do forget!"

"My dear Harriet, I perfectly remember the substance of what I said on the occasion. I told you that I did not wonder at your attachment; that considering the service he had rendered you, it was extremely natural:—and you agreed to it, expressing yourself very warmly as to your sense of that service, and mentioning even what your sensations had been in seeing him come forward to your rescue.—The impression of it is strong on my memory."

"Oh, dear," cried Harriet, "now I recollect what you mean; but I was thinking of something very different at the time. It was not the gipsies—it was not Mr. Frank Churchill that I meant. No! (with some elevation) I was thinking of a much more precious circumstance—of Mr. Knightley's coming and asking me to dance, when Mr. Elton would not stand up with me; and when there was no other partner in the room. That was the kind action; that was the noble benevolence and generosity; that was the service which made me begin to feel how superior he was to every other being upon earth."

"Good God!" cried Emma, "this has been a most unfortunate—most deplorable mistake!—What is to be done?"

"You would not have encouraged me, then, if you had understood me? At least, however, I cannot be worse off than I should have been, if the other had been the person; and now—it is possible——"

She paused a few moments. Emma could not speak.

"I do not wonder, Miss Woodhouse," she resumed, "that you should feel a great difference between the two, as to me or as to any body. You must think one five hundred million times more above me than the other. But I hope, Miss Woodhouse, that supposing—that if—strange as it may appear—. But you know they were your own words, that more wonderful things had happened, matches of greater disparity had taken place than between Mr. Frank Churchill and me; and, therefore, it seems as if such a thing even as this, may have occurred before—and if I should be so fortunate, beyond expression, as to—if Mr. Knightley should really—if he does not mind the disparity, I hope, dear Miss Woodhouse, you will not set yourself against it, and try to put difficulties in the way. But you are too good for that, I am sure."

Harriet was standing at one of the windows. Emma turned round to look at her in consternation, and hastily said,

"Have you any idea of Mr. Knightley's returning your affection?"

"Yes," replied Harriet modestly, but not fearfully—"I must say that I have."

Emma's eyes were instantly withdrawn; and she sat silently meditating, in a fixed attitude, for a few minutes. A few minutes were sufficient for making her acquainted with her own heart. A mind like hers, once opening to suspicion, made rapid progress. She touched—she admitted—she acknowledged the whole truth. Why was it so much worse that Harriet should be in love with Mr. Knightley, than with Frank Churchill? Why was the evil so dreadfully increased by Harriet's having some hope of a return? It darted through her, with the speed of an arrow, that Mr. Knightley must marry no one but herself!

Her own conduct, as well as her own heart, was before her in the same few minutes. She saw it all with a clearness which had never blessed her before. How improperly had she been acting by Harriet! How inconsiderate, how indelicate, how irrational, how unfeeling had been her conduct! What blindness, what madness, had led her on! It struck her with dreadful force, and she was ready to give it every bad name in the world. Some portion of respect for herself, however, in spite of all these demerits—some concern for her own appearance, and a strong sense of justice by Harriet—(there would be no need of compassion to the girl who believed herself loved by Mr. Knightley—but justice required that she should not be made unhappy by any coldness now,) gave Emma the resolution to sit and endure farther with calmness, with even apparent kindness.—For her own advantage indeed, it was fit that the utmost extent of Harriet's hopes should be enquired into; and Harriet had done nothing to forfeit the regard and interest which had been so voluntarily formed and maintained—or to deserve to be slighted by the person, whose counsels had never led her right.—Rousing from reflection, therefore, and subduing her emotion, she turned to Harriet again, and, in a more inviting accent, renewed the conversation; for as to the subject which had first introduced it, the wonderful story of Jane Fairfax, that was quite sunk and lost.—Neither of them thought but of Mr. Knightley and themselves.

Harriet, who had been standing in no unhappy reverie, was yet very glad to be called from it, by the now encouraging manner of such a judge, and such a friend as Miss Woodhouse, and only wanted invitation, to give the history of her hopes with great, though trembling delight.—Emma's tremblings as she asked, and as she listened, were better concealed than Harriet's, but they were not less. Her voice was not unsteady; but her mind was in all the perturbation that such a development of self, such a burst of threatening evil, such a confusion of sudden and perplexing emotions, must create.—She listened with much inward suffering, but with great outward patience, to Harriet's detail.—Methodical, or well arranged, or very well delivered, it could not be expected to be; but it contained, when separated from all the feebleness and tautology of the narration, a substance to sink her spirit—especially with the corroborating circumstances, which her own memory brought in favour of Mr. Knightley's most improved opinion of Harriet.

Harriet had been conscious of a difference in his behaviour ever since those two decisive dances.—Emma knew that he had, on that occasion, found her much superior to his expectation. From that evening, or at least from the time of Miss Woodhouse's encouraging her to think of him, Harriet had begun to be sensible of his talking to her much more than he had been used to do, and of his having indeed quite a different manner towards her; a manner of kindness and sweetness!—Latterly she had been more and more aware of it. When they had been all walking together, he had so often come and walked by her, and talked so very delightfully!—He seemed to want to be acquainted with her. Emma knew it to have been very much the case. She had often observed the change, to almost the same extent.—Harriet repeated expressions of approbation and praise from him—and Emma felt them to be in the closest agreement with what she had known of his opinion of Harriet. He praised her for being without art or affectation, for having simple, honest, generous, feelings.—She knew that he saw such recommendations in Harriet; he had dwelt on them to her more than once.—Much that lived in Harriet's memory, many little particulars of the notice she had received from him, a look, a speech, a removal from one chair to another, a compliment implied, a preference inferred, had been unnoticed, because unsuspected, by Emma. Circumstances that might swell to half an hour's relation, and contained multiplied proofs to her who had seen them, had passed undiscerned by her who now heard them; but the two latest occurrences to be mentioned, the two of strongest promise to Harriet, were not without some degree of witness from Emma herself.—The first, was his walking with her apart from the others, in the lime-walk at Donwell, where they had been walking some time before Emma came, and he had taken pains (as she was convinced) to draw her from the rest to himself—and at first, he had talked to her in a more particular way than he had ever done before, in a very particular way indeed!—(Harriet could not recall it without a blush.) He seemed to be almost asking her, whether her affections were engaged.—But as soon as she (Miss Woodhouse) appeared likely to join them, he changed the subject, and began talking about farming:—The second, was his having sat talking with her nearly half an hour before Emma came back from her visit, the very last morning of his being at Hartfield—though, when he first came in, he had said that he could not stay five minutes—and his having told her, during their conversation, that though he must go to London, it was very much against his inclination that he left home at all, which was much more (as Emma felt) than he had acknowledged to her. The superior degree of confidence towards Harriet, which this one article marked, gave her severe pain.

On the subject of the first of the two circumstances, she did, after a little reflection, venture the following question. "Might he not?—Is not it possible, that when enquiring, as you thought, into the state of your affections, he might be alluding to Mr. Martin—he might have Mr. Martin's interest in view? But Harriet rejected the suspicion with spirit.

"Mr. Martin! No indeed!—There was not a hint of Mr. Martin. I hope I know better now, than to care for Mr. Martin, or to be suspected of it."

When Harriet had closed her evidence, she appealed to her dear Miss Woodhouse, to say whether she had not good ground for hope.

"I never should have presumed to think of it at first," said she, "but for you. You told me to observe him carefully, and let his behaviour be the rule of mine—and so I have. But now I seem to feel that I may deserve him; and that if he does chuse me, it will not be any thing so very wonderful."

The bitter feelings occasioned by this speech, the many bitter feelings, made the utmost exertion necessary on Emma's side, to enable her to say on reply,

"Harriet, I will only venture to declare, that Mr. Knightley is the last man in the world, who would intentionally give any woman the idea of his feeling for her more than he really does."

Harriet seemed ready to worship her friend for a sentence so satisfactory; and Emma was only saved from raptures and fondness, which at that moment would have been dreadful penance, by the sound of her father's footsteps. He was coming through the hall. Harriet was too much agitated to encounter him. "She could not compose herself—Mr. Woodhouse would be alarmed—she had better go;"—with most ready encouragement from her friend, therefore, she passed off through another door—and the moment she was gone, this was the spontaneous burst of Emma's feelings: "Oh God! that I had never seen her!"

The rest of the day, the following night, were hardly enough for her thoughts.—She was bewildered amidst the confusion of all that had rushed on her within the last few hours. Every moment had brought a fresh surprize; and every surprize must be matter of humiliation to her.—How to understand it all! How to understand the deceptions she had been thus practising on herself, and living under!—The blunders, the blindness of her own head and heart!—she sat still, she walked about, she tried her own room, she tried the shrubbery—in every place, every posture, she perceived that she had acted most weakly; that she had been imposed on by others in a most mortifying degree; that she had been imposing on herself in a degree yet more mortifying; that she was wretched, and should probably find this day but the beginning of wretchedness.

To understand, thoroughly understand her own heart, was the first endeavour. To that point went every leisure moment which her father's claims on her allowed, and every moment of involuntary absence of mind.

How long had Mr. Knightley been so dear to her, as every feeling declared him now to be? When had his influence, such influence begun?—When had he succeeded to that place in her affection, which Frank Churchill had once, for a short period, occupied?—She looked back; she compared the two—compared them, as they had always stood in her estimation, from the time of the latter's becoming known to her—and as they must at any time have been compared by her, had it—oh! had it, by any blessed felicity, occurred to her, to institute the comparison.—She saw that there never had been a time when she did not consider Mr. Knightley as infinitely the superior, or when his regard for her had not been infinitely the most dear. She saw, that in persuading herself, in fancying, in acting to the contrary, she had been entirely under a delusion, totally ignorant of her own heart—and, in short, that she had never really cared for Frank Churchill at all!

This was the conclusion of the first series of reflection. This was the knowledge of herself, on the first question of inquiry, which she reached; and without being long in reaching it.—She was most sorrowfully indignant; ashamed of every sensation but the one revealed to her—her affection for Mr. Knightley.—Every other part of her mind was disgusting.

With insufferable vanity had she believed herself in the secret of every body's feelings; with unpardonable arrogance proposed to arrange every body's destiny. She was proved to have been universally mistaken; and she had not quite done nothing—for she had done mischief. She had brought evil on Harriet, on herself, and she too much feared, on Mr. Knightley.—Were this most unequal of all connexions to take place, on her must rest all the reproach of having given it a beginning; for his attachment, she must believe to be produced only by a consciousness of Harriet's;—and even were this not the case, he would never have known Harriet at all but for her folly.

Mr. Knightley and Harriet Smith!—It was a union to distance every wonder of the kind.—The attachment of Frank Churchill and Jane Fairfax became commonplace, threadbare, stale in the comparison, exciting no surprize, presenting no disparity, affording nothing to be said or thought.—Mr. Knightley and Harriet Smith!—Such an elevation on her side! Such a debasement on his! It was horrible to Emma to think how it must sink him in the general opinion, to foresee the smiles, the sneers, the merriment it would prompt at his expense; the mortification and disdain of his brother, the thousand inconveniences to himself.—Could it be?—No; it was impossible.

And yet it was far, very far, from impossible.—Was it a new circumstance for a man of first-rate abilities to be captivated by very inferior powers? Was it new for one, perhaps too busy to seek, to be the prize of a girl who would seek him?—Was it new for any thing in this world to be unequal, inconsistent, incongruous—or for chance and circumstance (as second causes) to direct the human fate?

Oh! had she never brought Harriet forward! Had she left her where she ought, and where he had told her she ought!—Had she not, with a folly which no tongue could express, prevented her marrying the unexceptionable young man who would have made her happy and respectable in the line of life to which she ought to belong—all would have been safe; none of this dreadful sequel would have been.

How Harriet could ever have had the presumption to raise her thoughts to Mr. Knightley!—How she could dare to fancy herself the chosen of such a man till actually assured of it!—But Harriet was less humble, had fewer scruples than formerly.—Her inferiority, whether of mind or situation, seemed little felt.—She had seemed more sensible of Mr. Elton's being to stoop in marrying her, than she now seemed of Mr. Knightley's.—Alas! was not that her own doing too? Who had been at pains to give Harriet notions of self-consequence but herself?—Who but herself had taught her, that she was to elevate herself if possible, and that her claims were great to a high worldly establishment?—If Harriet, from being humble, were grown vain, it was her doing too.

Chapter XII

Till now that she was threatened with its loss, Emma had never known how much of her happiness depended on being first with Mr. Knightley, first in interest and affection.—Satisfied that it was so, and feeling it her due, she had enjoyed it without reflection; and only in the dread of being supplanted, found how inexpressibly important it had been.—Long, very long, she felt she had been first; for, having no female connexions of his own, there had been only Isabella whose claims could be compared with hers, and she had always known exactly how far he loved and esteemed Isabella. She had herself been first with him for many years past. She had not deserved it; she had often been negligent or perverse, slighting his advice, or even wilfully opposing him, insensible of half his merits, and quarrelling with him because he would not acknowledge her false and insolent estimate of her own—but still, from family attachment and habit, and thorough excellence of mind, he had loved her, and watched over her from a girl, with an endeavour to improve her, and an anxiety for her doing right, which no other creature had at all shared. In spite of all her faults, she knew she was dear to him; might she not say, very dear?—When the suggestions of hope, however, which must follow here, presented themselves, she could not presume to indulge them. Harriet Smith might think herself not unworthy of being peculiarly, exclusively, passionately loved by Mr. Knightley. She could not. She could not flatter herself with any idea of blindness in his attachment to her. She had received a very recent proof of its impartiality.—How shocked had he been by her behaviour to Miss Bates! How directly, how strongly had he expressed himself to her on the subject!—Not too strongly for the offence—but far, far too strongly to issue from any feeling softer than upright justice and clear-sighted goodwill.—She had no hope, nothing to deserve the name of hope, that he could have that sort of affection for herself which was now in question; but there was a hope (at times a slight one, at times much stronger,) that Harriet might have deceived herself, and be overrating his regard for her.—Wish it she must, for his sake—be the consequence nothing to herself, but his remaining single all his life. Could she be secure of that, indeed, of his never marrying at all, she believed she should be perfectly satisfied.—Let him but continue the same Mr. Knightley to her and her father, the same Mr. Knightley to all the world; let Donwell and Hartfield lose none of their precious intercourse of friendship and confidence, and her peace would be fully secured.—Marriage, in fact, would not do for her. It would be incompatible with what she owed to her father, and with what she felt for him. Nothing should separate her from her father. She would not marry, even if she were asked by Mr. Knightley.

It must be her ardent wish that Harriet might be disappointed; and she hoped, that when able to see them together again, she might at least be able to ascertain what the chances for it were.—She should see them henceforward with the closest observance; and wretchedly as she had hitherto misunderstood even those she was watching, she did not know how to admit that she could be blinded here.—He was expected back every day. The power of observation would be soon given—frightfully soon it appeared when her thoughts were in one course. In the meanwhile, she resolved against seeing Harriet.—It would do neither of them good, it would do the subject no good, to be talking of it farther.—She was resolved not to be convinced, as long as she could doubt, and yet had no authority for opposing Harriet's confidence. To talk would be only to irritate.—She wrote to her, therefore, kindly, but decisively, to beg that she would not, at present, come to Hartfield; acknowledging it to be her conviction, that all farther confidential discussion of one topic had better be avoided; and hoping, that if a few days were allowed to pass before they met again, except in the company of others—she objected only to a tete-a-tete—they might be able to act as if they had forgotten the conversation of yesterday.—Harriet submitted, and approved, and was grateful.

This point was just arranged, when a visitor arrived to tear Emma's thoughts a little from the one subject which had engrossed them, sleeping or waking, the last twenty-four hours—Mrs. Weston, who had been calling on her daughter-in-law elect, and took Hartfield in her way home, almost as much in duty to Emma as in pleasure to herself, to relate all the particulars of so interesting an interview.

Mr. Weston had accompanied her to Mrs. Bates's, and gone through his share of this essential attention most handsomely; but she having then induced Miss Fairfax to join her in an airing, was now returned with much more to say, and much more to say with satisfaction, than a quarter of an hour spent in Mrs. Bates's parlour, with all the encumbrance of awkward feelings, could have afforded.

A little curiosity Emma had; and she made the most of it while her friend related. Mrs. Weston had set off to pay the visit in a good deal of agitation herself; and in the first place had wished not to go at all at present, to be allowed merely to write to Miss Fairfax instead, and to defer this ceremonious call till a little time had passed, and Mr. Churchill could be reconciled to the engagement's becoming known; as, considering every thing, she thought such a visit could not be paid without leading to reports:—but Mr. Weston had thought differently; he was extremely anxious to shew his approbation to Miss Fairfax and her family, and did not conceive that any suspicion could be excited by it; or if it were, that it would be of any consequence; for "such things," he observed, "always got about." Emma smiled, and felt that Mr. Weston had very good reason for saying so. They had gone, in short—and very great had been the evident distress and confusion of the lady. She had hardly been able to speak a word, and every look and action had shewn how deeply she was suffering from consciousness. The quiet, heart-felt satisfaction of the old lady, and the rapturous delight of her daughter—who proved even too joyous to talk as usual, had been a gratifying, yet almost an affecting, scene. They were both so truly respectable in their happiness, so disinterested in every sensation; thought so much of Jane; so much of every body, and so little of themselves, that every kindly feeling was at work for them. Miss Fairfax's recent illness had offered a fair plea for Mrs. Weston to invite her to an airing; she had drawn back and declined at first, but, on being pressed had yielded; and, in the course of their drive, Mrs. Weston had, by gentle encouragement, overcome so much of her embarrassment, as to bring her to converse on the important subject. Apologies for her seemingly ungracious silence in their first reception, and the warmest expressions of the gratitude she was always feeling towards herself and Mr. Weston, must necessarily open the cause; but when these effusions were put by, they had talked a good deal of the present and of the future state of the engagement. Mrs. Weston was convinced that such conversation must be the greatest relief to her companion, pent up within her own mind as every thing had so long been, and was very much pleased with all that she had said on the subject.

"On the misery of what she had suffered, during the concealment of so many months," continued Mrs. Weston, "she was energetic. This was one of her expressions. 'I will not say, that since I entered into the engagement I have not had some happy moments; but I can say, that I have never known the blessing of one tranquil hour:'—and the quivering lip, Emma, which uttered it, was an attestation that I felt at my heart."

"Poor girl!" said Emma. "She thinks herself wrong, then, for having consented to a private engagement?"

"Wrong! No one, I believe, can blame her more than she is disposed to blame herself. 'The consequence,' said she, 'has been a state of perpetual suffering to me; and so it ought. But after all the punishment that misconduct can bring, it is still not less misconduct. Pain is no expiation. I never can be blameless. I have been acting contrary to all my sense of right; and the fortunate turn that every thing has taken, and the kindness I am now receiving, is what my conscience tells me ought not to be.' 'Do not imagine, madam,' she continued, 'that I was taught wrong. Do not let any reflection fall on the principles or the care of the friends who brought me up. The error has been all my own; and I do assure you that, with all the excuse that present circumstances may appear to give, I shall yet dread making the story known to Colonel Campbell.'"

"Poor girl!" said Emma again. "She loves him then excessively, I suppose. It must have been from attachment only, that she could be led to form the engagement. Her affection must have overpowered her judgment."

"Yes, I have no doubt of her being extremely attached to him."

"I am afraid," returned Emma, sighing, "that I must often have contributed to make her unhappy."

"On your side, my love, it was very innocently done. But she probably had something of that in her thoughts, when alluding to the misunderstandings which he had given us hints of before. One natural consequence of the evil she had involved herself in," she said, "was that of making her unreasonable. The consciousness of having done amiss, had exposed her to a thousand inquietudes, and made her captious and irritable to a degree that must have been—that had been—hard for him to bear. 'I did not make the allowances,' said she, 'which I ought to have done, for his temper and spirits—his delightful spirits, and that gaiety, that playfulness of disposition, which, under any other circumstances, would, I am sure, have been as constantly bewitching to me, as they were at first.' She then began to speak of you, and of the great kindness you had shewn her during her illness; and with a blush which shewed me how it was all connected, desired me, whenever I had an opportunity, to thank you—I could not thank you too much—for every wish and every endeavour to do her good. She was sensible that you had never received any proper acknowledgment from herself."

"If I did not know her to be happy now," said Emma, seriously, "which, in spite of every little drawback from her scrupulous conscience, she must be, I could not bear these thanks;—for, oh! Mrs. Weston, if there were an account drawn up of the evil and the good I have done Miss Fairfax!—Well (checking herself, and trying to be more lively), this is all to be forgotten. You are very kind to bring me these interesting particulars. They shew her to the greatest advantage. I am sure she is very good—I hope she will be very happy. It is fit that the fortune should be on his side, for I think the merit will be all on hers."

Such a conclusion could not pass unanswered by Mrs. Weston. She thought well of Frank in almost every respect; and, what was more, she loved him very much, and her defence was, therefore, earnest. She talked with a great deal of reason, and at least equal affection—but she had too much to urge for Emma's attention; it was soon gone to Brunswick Square or to Donwell; she forgot to attempt to listen; and when Mrs. Weston ended with, "We have not yet had the letter we are so anxious for, you know, but I hope it will soon come," she was obliged to pause before she answered, and at last obliged to answer at random, before she could at all recollect what letter it was which they were so anxious for.

"Are you well, my Emma?" was Mrs. Weston's parting question.

"Oh! perfectly. I am always well, you know. Be sure to give me intelligence of the letter as soon as possible."

Mrs. Weston's communications furnished Emma with more food for unpleasant reflection, by increasing her esteem and compassion, and her sense of past injustice towards Miss Fairfax. She bitterly regretted not having sought a closer acquaintance with her, and blushed for the envious feelings which had certainly been, in some measure, the cause. Had she followed Mr. Knightley's known wishes, in paying that attention to Miss Fairfax, which was every way her due; had she tried to know her better; had she done her part towards intimacy; had she endeavoured to find a friend there instead of in Harriet Smith; she must, in all probability, have been spared from every pain which pressed on her now.—Birth, abilities, and education, had been equally marking one as an associate for her, to be received with gratitude; and the other—what was she?—Supposing even that they had never become intimate friends; that she had never been admitted into Miss Fairfax's confidence on this important matter—which was most probable—still, in knowing her as she ought, and as she might, she must have been preserved from the abominable suspicions of an improper attachment to Mr. Dixon, which she had not only so foolishly fashioned and harboured herself, but had so unpardonably imparted; an idea which she greatly feared had been made a subject of material distress to the delicacy of Jane's feelings, by the levity or carelessness of Frank Churchill's. Of all the sources of evil surrounding the former, since her coming to Highbury, she was persuaded that she must herself have been the worst. She must have been a perpetual enemy. They never could have been all three together, without her having stabbed Jane Fairfax's peace in a thousand instances; and on Box Hill, perhaps, it had been the agony of a mind that would bear no more.

The evening of this day was very long, and melancholy, at Hartfield. The weather added what it could of gloom. A cold stormy rain set in, and nothing of July appeared but in the trees and shrubs, which the wind was despoiling, and the length of the day, which only made such cruel sights the longer visible.

The weather affected Mr. Woodhouse, and he could only be kept tolerably comfortable by almost ceaseless attention on his daughter's side, and by exertions which had never cost her half so much before. It reminded her of their first forlorn tete-a-tete, on the evening of Mrs. Weston's wedding-day; but Mr. Knightley had walked in then, soon after tea, and dissipated every melancholy fancy. Alas! such delightful proofs of Hartfield's attraction, as those sort of visits conveyed, might shortly be over. The picture which she had then drawn of the privations of the approaching winter, had proved erroneous; no friends had deserted them, no pleasures had been lost.—But her present forebodings she feared would experience no similar contradiction. The prospect before her now, was threatening to a degree that could not be entirely dispelled—that might not be even partially brightened. If all took place that might take place among the circle of her friends, Hartfield must be comparatively deserted; and she left to cheer her father with the spirits only of ruined happiness.

The child to be born at Randalls must be a tie there even dearer than herself; and Mrs. Weston's heart and time would be occupied by it. They should lose her; and, probably, in great measure, her husband also.—Frank Churchill would return among them no more; and Miss Fairfax, it was reasonable to suppose, would soon cease to belong to Highbury. They would be married, and settled either at or near Enscombe. All that were good would be withdrawn; and if to these losses, the loss of Donwell were to be added, what would remain of cheerful or of rational society within their reach? Mr. Knightley to be no longer coming there for his evening comfort!—No longer walking in at all hours, as if ever willing to change his own home for their's!—How was it to be endured? And if he were to be lost to them for Harriet's sake; if he were to be thought of hereafter, as finding in Harriet's society all that he wanted; if Harriet were to be the chosen, the first, the dearest, the friend, the wife to whom he looked for all the best blessings of existence; what could be increasing Emma's wretchedness but the reflection never far distant from her mind, that it had been all her own work?

When it came to such a pitch as this, she was not able to refrain from a start, or a heavy sigh, or even from walking about the room for a few seconds—and the only source whence any thing like consolation or composure could be drawn, was in the resolution of her own better conduct, and the hope that, however inferior in spirit and gaiety might be the following and every future winter of her life to the past, it would yet find her more rational, more acquainted with herself, and leave her less to regret when it were gone.

Chapter XIII

The weather continued much the same all the following morning; and the same loneliness, and the same melancholy, seemed to reign at Hartfield—but in the afternoon it cleared; the wind changed into a softer quarter; the clouds were carried off; the sun appeared; it was summer again. With all the eagerness which such a transition gives, Emma resolved to be out of doors as soon as possible. Never had the exquisite sight, smell, sensation of nature, tranquil, warm, and brilliant after a storm, been more attractive to her. She longed for the serenity they might gradually introduce; and on Mr. Perry's coming in soon after dinner, with a disengaged hour to give her father, she lost no time ill hurrying into the shrubbery.—There, with spirits freshened, and thoughts a little relieved, she had taken a few turns, when she saw Mr. Knightley passing through the garden door, and coming towards her.—It was the first intimation of his being returned from London. She had been thinking of him the moment before, as unquestionably sixteen miles distant.—There was time only for the quickest arrangement of mind. She must be collected and calm. In half a minute they were together. The "How d'ye do's" were quiet and constrained on each side. She asked after their mutual friends; they were all well.—When had he left them?—Only that morning. He must have had a wet ride.—Yes.—He meant to walk with her, she found. "He had just looked into the dining-room, and as he was not wanted there, preferred being out of doors."—She thought he neither looked nor spoke cheerfully; and the first possible cause for it, suggested by her fears, was, that he had perhaps been communicating his plans to his brother, and was pained by the manner in which they had been received.

They walked together. He was silent. She thought he was often looking at her, and trying for a fuller view of her face than it suited her to give. And this belief produced another dread. Perhaps he wanted to speak to her, of his attachment to Harriet; he might be watching for encouragement to begin.—She did not, could not, feel equal to lead the way to any such subject. He must do it all himself. Yet she could not bear this silence. With him it was most unnatural. She considered—resolved—and, trying to smile, began—

"You have some news to hear, now you are come back, that will rather surprize you."

"Have I?" said he quietly, and looking at her; "of what nature?"

"Oh! the best nature in the world—a wedding."

After waiting a moment, as if to be sure she intended to say no more, he replied,

"If you mean Miss Fairfax and Frank Churchill, I have heard that already."

"How is it possible?" cried Emma, turning her glowing cheeks towards him; for, while she spoke, it occurred to her that he might have called at Mrs. Goddard's in his way.

"I had a few lines on parish business from Mr. Weston this morning, and at the end of them he gave me a brief account of what had happened."

Emma was quite relieved, and could presently say, with a little more composure,

"You probably have been less surprized than any of us, for you have had your suspicions.—I have not forgotten that you once tried to give me a caution.—I wish I had attended to it—but—(with a sinking voice and a heavy sigh) I seem to have been doomed to blindness."

For a moment or two nothing was said, and she was unsuspicious of having excited any particular interest, till she found her arm drawn within his, and pressed against his heart, and heard him thus saying, in a tone of great sensibility, speaking low,

"Time, my dearest Emma, time will heal the wound.—Your own excellent sense—your exertions for your father's sake—I know you will not allow yourself—." Her arm was pressed again, as he added, in a more broken and subdued accent, "The feelings of the warmest friendship—Indignation—Abominable scoundrel!"—And in a louder, steadier tone, he concluded with, "He will soon be gone. They will soon be in Yorkshire. I am sorry for her. She deserves a better fate."

Emma understood him; and as soon as she could recover from the flutter of pleasure, excited by such tender consideration, replied,

"You are very kind—but you are mistaken—and I must set you right.—I am not in want of that sort of compassion. My blindness to what was going on, led me to act by them in a way that I must always be ashamed of, and I was very foolishly tempted to say and do many things which may well lay me open to unpleasant conjectures, but I have no other reason to regret that I was not in the secret earlier."

"Emma!" cried he, looking eagerly at her, "are you, indeed?"—but checking himself—"No, no, I understand you—forgive me—I am pleased that you can say even so much.—He is no object of regret, indeed! and it will not be very long, I hope, before that becomes the acknowledgment of more than your reason.—Fortunate that your affections were not farther entangled!—I could never, I confess, from your manners, assure myself as to the degree of what you felt—I could only be certain that there was a preference—and a preference which I never believed him to deserve.—He is a disgrace to the name of man.—And is he to be rewarded with that sweet young woman?—Jane, Jane, you will be a miserable creature."

"Mr. Knightley," said Emma, trying to be lively, but really confused—"I am in a very extraordinary situation. I cannot let you continue in your error; and yet, perhaps, since my manners gave such an impression, I have as much reason to be ashamed of confessing that I never have been at all attached to the person we are speaking of, as it might be natural for a woman to feel in confessing exactly the reverse.—But I never have."

He listened in perfect silence. She wished him to speak, but he would not. She supposed she must say more before she were entitled to his clemency; but it was a hard case to be obliged still to lower herself in his opinion. She went on, however.

"I have very little to say for my own conduct.—I was tempted by his attentions, and allowed myself to appear pleased.—An old story, probably—a common case—and no more than has happened to hundreds of my sex before; and yet it may not be the more excusable in one who sets up as I do for Understanding. Many circumstances assisted the temptation. He was the son of Mr. Weston—he was continually here—I always found him very pleasant—and, in short, for (with a sigh) let me swell out the causes ever so ingeniously, they all centre in this at last—my vanity was flattered, and I allowed his attentions. Latterly, however—for some time, indeed—I have had no idea of their meaning any thing.—I thought them a habit, a trick, nothing that called for seriousness on my side. He has imposed on me, but he has not injured me. I have never been attached to him. And now I can tolerably comprehend his behaviour. He never wished to attach me. It was merely a blind to conceal his real situation with another.—It was his object to blind all about him; and no one, I am sure, could be more effectually blinded than myself—except that I was not blinded—that it was my good fortune—that, in short, I was somehow or other safe from him."

She had hoped for an answer here—for a few words to say that her conduct was at least intelligible; but he was silent; and, as far as she could judge, deep in thought. At last, and tolerably in his usual tone, he said,

"I have never had a high opinion of Frank Churchill.—I can suppose, however, that I may have underrated him. My acquaintance with him has been but trifling.—And even if I have not underrated him hitherto, he may yet turn out well.—With such a woman he has a chance.—I have no motive for wishing him ill—and for her sake, whose happiness will be involved in his good character and conduct, I shall certainly wish him well."

"I have no doubt of their being happy together," said Emma; "I believe them to be very mutually and very sincerely attached."

"He is a most fortunate man!" returned Mr. Knightley, with energy. "So early in life—at three-and-twenty—a period when, if a man chuses a wife, he generally chuses ill. At three-and-twenty to have drawn such a prize! What years of felicity that man, in all human calculation, has before him!—Assured of the love of such a woman—the disinterested love, for Jane Fairfax's character vouches for her disinterestedness; every thing in his favour,—equality of situation—I mean, as far as regards society, and all the habits and manners that are important; equality in every point but one—and that one, since the purity of her heart is not to be doubted, such as must increase his felicity, for it will be his to bestow the only advantages she wants.—A man would always wish to give a woman a better home than the one he takes her from; and he who can do it, where there is no doubt of her regard, must, I think, be the happiest of mortals.—Frank Churchill is, indeed, the favourite of fortune. Every thing turns out for his good.—He meets with a young woman at a watering-place, gains her affection, cannot even weary her by negligent treatment—and had he and all his family sought round the world for a perfect wife for him, they could not have found her superior.—His aunt is in the way.—His aunt dies.—He has only to speak.—His friends are eager to promote his happiness.—He had used every body ill—and they are all delighted to forgive him.—He is a fortunate man indeed!"

"You speak as if you envied him."

"And I do envy him, Emma. In one respect he is the object of my envy."

Emma could say no more. They seemed to be within half a sentence of Harriet, and her immediate feeling was to avert the subject, if possible. She made her plan; she would speak of something totally different—the children in Brunswick Square; and she only waited for breath to begin, when Mr. Knightley startled her, by saying,

"You will not ask me what is the point of envy.—You are determined, I see, to have no curiosity.—You are wise—but I cannot be wise. Emma, I must tell you what you will not ask, though I may wish it unsaid the next moment."

"Oh! then, don't speak it, don't speak it," she eagerly cried. "Take a little time, consider, do not commit yourself."

"Thank you," said he, in an accent of deep mortification, and not another syllable followed.

Emma could not bear to give him pain. He was wishing to confide in her—perhaps to consult her;—cost her what it would, she would listen. She might assist his resolution, or reconcile him to it;

she might give just praise to Harriet, or, by representing to him his own independence, relieve him from that state of indecision, which must be more intolerable than any alternative to such a mind as his.—They had reached the house.

"You are going in, I suppose?" said he.

"No,"—replied Emma—quite confirmed by the depressed manner in which he still spoke—"I should like to take another turn. Mr. Perry is not gone." And, after proceeding a few steps, she added—"I stopped you ungraciously, just now, Mr. Knightley, and, I am afraid, gave you pain.—But if you have any wish to speak openly to me as a friend, or to ask my opinion of any thing that you may have in contemplation—as a friend, indeed, you may command me.—I will hear whatever you like. I will tell you exactly what I think."

"As a friend!"—repeated Mr. Knightley.—"Emma, that I fear is a word—No, I have no wish—Stay, yes, why should I hesitate?—I have gone too far already for concealment.—Emma, I accept your offer—Extraordinary as it may seem, I accept it, and refer myself to you as a friend.—Tell me, then, have I no chance of ever succeeding?"

He stopped in his earnestness to look the question, and the expression of his eyes overpowered her.

"My dearest Emma," said he, "for dearest you will always be, whatever the event of this hour's conversation, my dearest, most beloved Emma—tell me at once. Say 'No,' if it is to be said."—She could really say nothing.—"You are silent," he cried, with great animation; "absolutely silent! at present I ask no more."

Emma was almost ready to sink under the agitation of this moment. The dread of being awakened from the happiest dream, was perhaps the most prominent feeling.

"I cannot make speeches, Emma:" he soon resumed; and in a tone of such sincere, decided, intelligible tenderness as was tolerably convincing.—"If I loved you less, I might be able to talk about it more. But you know what I am.—You hear nothing but truth from me.—I have blamed you, and lectured you, and you have borne it as no other woman in England would have borne it.—Bear with the truths I would tell you now, dearest Emma, as well as you have borne with them. The manner, perhaps, may have as little to recommend them. God knows, I have been a very indifferent lover.—But you understand me.—Yes, you see, you understand my feelings—and will return them if you can. At present, I ask only to hear, once to hear your voice."

While he spoke, Emma's mind was most busy, and, with all the wonderful velocity of thought, had been able—and yet without losing a word—to catch and comprehend the exact truth of the whole; to see that Harriet's hopes had been entirely groundless, a mistake, a delusion, as complete a delusion as any of her own—that Harriet was nothing; that she was every thing herself; that what she had been saying relative to Harriet had been all taken as the language of her own feelings; and that her agitation, her doubts, her reluctance, her discouragement, had been all received as discouragement from herself.—And not only was there time for these convictions, with all their glow of attendant happiness; there was time also to rejoice that Harriet's secret had not escaped her, and to resolve that it need not, and should not.—It was all the service she could now render her poor friend; for as to any of that heroism of sentiment which might have prompted her to entreat him to transfer his affection from herself to Harriet, as infinitely the most worthy of the two—or even the more simple sublimity of resolving to refuse him at once and for ever, without vouchsafing any motive, because he could not marry them both, Emma had it not. She felt for Harriet, with pain and with contrition; but no flight of generosity run mad, opposing all that could be probable or reasonable, entered her brain. She had led her friend astray, and it would be a reproach to her for ever; but her judgment was as strong as her feelings, and as strong as it had ever been before, in reprobating any such alliance for him, as most unequal and degrading. Her way was clear, though not quite smooth.—She spoke then, on being so entreated.—What did she say?—Just what she ought, of course. A lady always does.—She said enough to shew there need not be despair—and to invite him to say more himself. He had despaired at one period; he had received such an injunction to caution and silence, as for the time crushed every hope;—she had begun by refusing to hear him.—The change had perhaps been somewhat sudden;—her proposal of taking another turn, her renewing the conversation which she had just put an end to, might be a little extraordinary!—She felt its inconsistency; but Mr. Knightley was so obliging as to put up with it, and seek no farther explanation.

Seldom, very seldom, does complete truth belong to any human disclosure; seldom can it happen that something is not a little disguised, or a little mistaken; but where, as in this case, though the conduct is mistaken, the feelings are not, it may not be very material.—Mr. Knightley could not impute to Emma a more relenting heart than she possessed, or a heart more disposed to accept of his.

He had, in fact, been wholly unsuspicious of his own influence. He had followed her into the shrubbery with no idea of trying it. He had come, in his anxiety to see how she bore Frank Churchill's engagement, with no selfish view, no view at all, but of endeavouring, if she allowed him an opening, to soothe or to counsel her.—The rest had been the work of the moment, the immediate effect of what he heard, on his feelings. The delightful assurance of her total indifference towards Frank Churchill, of her having a heart completely disengaged from him, had given birth to the hope, that, in time, he might gain her affection himself;—but it had been no present hope—he had only, in the momentary conquest of eagerness over judgment, aspired to be told that she did not forbid his attempt to attach her.—The superior hopes which gradually opened were so much the more enchanting.—The affection, which he had been asking to be allowed to create, if he could, was already his!—Within half an hour, he had passed from a thoroughly distressed state of mind, to something so like perfect happiness, that it could bear no other name.

Her change was equal.—This one half-hour had given to each the same precious certainty of being beloved, had cleared from each the same degree of ignorance, jealousy, or distrust.—On his side, there had been a long-standing jealousy, old as the arrival, or even the expectation, of Frank Churchill.—He had been in love with Emma, and jealous of Frank Churchill, from about the same period, one sentiment having probably enlightened him as to the other. It was his jealousy of Frank Churchill that had taken him from the country.—The Box Hill party had decided him on going away. He would save himself from witnessing again such permitted, encouraged attentions.—He had gone to learn to be indifferent.—But he had gone to a wrong place. There was too much domestic happiness in his brother's house; woman wore too amiable a form in it; Isabella was too much like Emma—differing only in those striking inferiorities, which always brought the other in brilliancy before him, for much to have been done, even had his time been longer.—He had stayed on, however, vigorously, day after day—till this very morning's post had conveyed the history of Jane

Fairfax.—Then, with the gladness which must be felt, nay, which he did not scruple to feel, having never believed Frank Churchill to be at all deserving Emma, was there so much fond solicitude, so much keen anxiety for her, that he could stay no longer. He had ridden home through the rain; and had walked up directly after dinner, to see how this sweetest and best of all creatures, faultless in spite of all her faults, bore the discovery.

He had found her agitated and low.—Frank Churchill was a villain.—He heard her declare that she had never loved him. Frank Churchill's character was not desperate.—She was his own Emma, by hand and word, when they returned into the house; and if he could have thought of Frank Churchill then, he might have deemed him a very good sort of fellow.

Chapter XIV

What totally different feelings did Emma take back into the house from what she had brought out!—she had then been only daring to hope for a little respite of suffering;—she was now in an exquisite flutter of happiness, and such happiness moreover as she believed must still be greater when the flutter should have passed away.

They sat down to tea—the same party round the same table—how often it had been collected!—and how often had her eyes fallen on the same shrubs in the lawn, and observed the same beautiful effect of the western sun!—But never in such a state of spirits, never in any thing like it; and it was with difficulty that she could summon enough of her usual self to be the attentive lady of the house, or even the attentive daughter.

Poor Mr. Woodhouse little suspected what was plotting against him in the breast of that man whom he was so cordially welcoming, and so anxiously hoping might not have taken cold from his ride.—Could he have seen the heart, he would have cared very little for the lungs; but without the most distant imagination of the impending evil, without the slightest perception of any thing extraordinary in the looks or ways of either, he repeated to them very comfortably all the articles of news he had received from Mr. Perry, and talked on with much self-contentment, totally unsuspicious of what they could have told him in return.

As long as Mr. Knightley remained with them, Emma's fever continued; but when he was gone, she began to be a little tranquillised and subdued—and in the course of the sleepless night, which was the tax for such an evening, she found one or two such very serious points to consider, as made her feel, that even her happiness must have some alloy. Her father—and Harriet. She could not be alone without feeling the full weight of their separate claims; and how to guard the comfort of both to the utmost, was the question. With respect to her father, it was a question soon answered. She hardly knew yet what Mr. Knightley would ask; but a very short parley with her own heart produced the most solemn resolution of never quitting her father.—She even wept over the idea of it, as a sin of thought. While he lived, it must be only an engagement; but she flattered herself, that if divested of the danger of drawing her away, it might become an increase of comfort to him.—How to do her best by Harriet, was of more difficult decision;—how to spare her from any unnecessary pain; how to make her any possible atonement; how to appear least her enemy?—On these subjects, her perplexity and distress were very great—and her mind had to pass again and again through every bitter reproach and sorrowful regret that had ever surrounded it.—She could only resolve at last, that she would still avoid a meeting with her, and communicate all that need be told by letter; that it would be inexpressibly desirable to have her removed just now for a time from Highbury, and—indulging in one scheme more—nearly resolve, that it might be practicable to get an invitation for her to Brunswick Square.—Isabella had been pleased with Harriet; and a few weeks spent in London must give her some amusement.—She did not think it in Harriet's nature to escape being benefited by novelty and variety, by the streets, the shops, and the children.—At any rate, it would be a proof of attention and kindness in herself, from whom every thing was due; a separation for the present; an averting of the evil day, when they must all be together again.

She rose early, and wrote her letter to Harriet; an employment which left her so very serious, so nearly sad, that Mr. Knightley, in walking up to Hartfield to breakfast, did not arrive at all too soon; and half an hour stolen afterwards to go over the same ground again with him, literally and figuratively, was quite necessary to reinstate her in a proper share of the happiness of the evening before.

He had not left her long, by no means long enough for her to have the slightest inclination for thinking of any body else, when a letter was brought her from Randalls—a very thick letter;—she guessed what it must contain, and deprecated the necessity of reading it.—She was now in perfect charity with Frank Churchill; she wanted no explanations, she wanted only to have her thoughts to herself—and as for understanding any thing he wrote, she was sure she was incapable of it.—It must be waded through, however. She opened the packet; it was too surely so;—a note from Mrs. Weston to herself, ushered in the letter from Frank to Mrs. Weston.

"I have the greatest pleasure, my dear Emma, in forwarding to you the enclosed. I know what thorough justice you will do it, and have scarcely a doubt of its happy effect.—I think we shall never materially disagree about the writer again; but I will not delay you by a long preface.—We are quite well.—This letter has been the cure of all the little nervousness I have been feeling lately.—I did not quite like your looks on Tuesday, but it was an ungenial morning; and though you will never own being affected by weather, I think every body feels a north-east wind.—I felt for your dear father very much in the storm of Tuesday afternoon and yesterday morning, but had the comfort of hearing last night, by Mr. Perry, that it had not made him ill.

"Yours ever,

"A. W."

[To Mrs. Weston.]

WINDSOR–JULY.

MY DEAR MADAM,

"If I made myself intelligible yesterday, this letter will be expected; but expected or not, I know it will be read with candour and indulgence.—You are all goodness, and I believe there will be need of even all your goodness to allow for some parts of my past conduct.—But I have been forgiven by one who had still more to resent. My courage rises while I write. It is very difficult for the prosperous to be humble. I have already met with such success in two applications for pardon, that I may be in danger of thinking myself too sure of yours, and of those among your friends who have had any ground of offence.—You must all endeavour to comprehend the exact nature of my situation when I first arrived at Randalls; you must consider me as having a secret which was to be kept at all hazards. This was the fact. My right to place myself in a situation requiring such concealment, is another question. I shall not discuss it here. For my temptation to think it a right, I refer every caviller to a brick house, sashed windows below, and casements above, in Highbury. I dared not address her openly; my difficulties in the then state of Enscombe must be too well known to require definition; and I was fortunate enough to prevail, before we parted at Weymouth, and to induce the most upright female mind in the creation to stoop in charity to a secret engagement.—Had she refused, I should have gone mad.—But you will be ready to say, what was your hope in doing this?—What did you look forward to?—To any thing, every thing—to time, chance, circumstance, slow effects, sudden bursts, perseverance and weariness, health and sickness. Every possibility of good was before me, and the first of blessings secured, in obtaining her promises of faith and correspondence. If you need farther explanation, I have the honour, my dear madam, of being your husband's son, and the advantage of inheriting a disposition to hope for good, which no inheritance of houses or lands can ever equal the value of.—See me, then, under these circumstances, arriving on my first visit to Randalls;—and here I am conscious of wrong, for that visit might have been sooner paid. You will look back and see that I did not come till Miss Fairfax was in Highbury; and as you were the person slighted, you will forgive me instantly; but I must work on my father's compassion, by reminding him, that so long as I absented myself from his house, so long I lost the blessing of knowing you. My behaviour, during the very happy fortnight which I spent with you, did not, I hope, lay me open to reprehension, excepting on one point. And now I come to the principal, the only important part of my conduct while belonging to you, which excites my own anxiety, or requires very solicitous explanation. With the greatest respect, and the warmest friendship, do I mention Miss Woodhouse; my father perhaps will think I ought to add, with the deepest humiliation.—A few words which dropped from him yesterday spoke his opinion, and some censure I acknowledge myself liable to.—My behaviour to Miss Woodhouse indicated, I believe, more than it ought.—In order to assist a concealment so essential to me, I was led on to make more than an allowable use of the sort of intimacy into which we were immediately thrown.—I cannot deny that Miss Woodhouse was my ostensible object—but I am sure you will believe the declaration, that had I not been convinced of her indifference, I would not have been induced by any selfish views to go on.—Amiable and delightful as Miss Woodhouse is, she never gave me the idea of a young woman likely to be attached; and that she was perfectly free from any tendency to being attached to me, was as much my conviction as my wish.—She received my attentions with an easy, friendly, goodhumoured playfulness, which exactly suited me. We seemed to understand each other. From our relative situation, those attentions were her due, and were felt to be so.—Whether Miss Woodhouse began really to understand me before the expiration of that fortnight, I cannot say;—when I called to take leave of her, I remember that I was within a moment of confessing the truth, and I then fancied she was not without suspicion; but I have no doubt of her having since detected me, at least in some degree.—She may not have surmised the whole, but her quickness must have penetrated a part. I cannot doubt it. You will find, whenever the subject becomes freed from its present restraints, that it did not take her wholly by surprize. She frequently gave me hints of it. I remember her telling me at the ball, that I owed Mrs. Elton gratitude for her attentions to Miss Fairfax.—I hope this history of my conduct towards her will be admitted by you and my father as great extenuation of what you saw amiss. While you considered me as having sinned against Emma Woodhouse, I could deserve nothing from either. Acquit me here, and procure for me, when it is allowable, the acquittal and good wishes of that said Emma Woodhouse, whom I regard with so much brotherly affection, as to long to have her as deeply and as happily in love as myself.—Whatever strange things I said or did during that fortnight, you have now a key to. My heart was in Highbury, and my business was to get my body thither as often as might be, and with the least suspicion. If you remember any queernesses, set them all to the right account.—Of the pianoforte so much talked of, I feel it only necessary to say, that its being ordered was absolutely unknown to Miss F—, who would never have allowed me to send it, had any choice been given her.—The delicacy of her mind throughout the whole engagement, my dear madam, is much beyond my power of doing justice to. You will soon, I earnestly hope, know her thoroughly yourself.—No description can describe her. She must tell you herself what she is—yet not by word, for never was there a human creature who would so designedly suppress her own merit.—Since I began this letter, which will be longer than I foresaw, I have heard from her.—She gives a good account of her own health; but as she never complains, I dare not depend. I want to have your opinion of her looks. I know you will soon call on her; she is living in dread of the visit. Perhaps it is paid already. Let me hear from you without delay; I am impatient for a thousand particulars. Remember how few minutes I was at Randalls, and in how bewildered, how mad a state: and I am not much better yet; still insane either from happiness or misery. When I think of the kindness and favour I have met with, of her excellence and patience, and my uncle's generosity, I am mad with joy: but when I recollect all the uneasiness I occasioned her, and how little I deserve to be forgiven, I am mad with anger. If I could but see her again!—But I must not propose it yet. My uncle has been too good for me to encroach.—I must still add to this long letter. You have not heard all that you ought to hear. I could not give any connected detail yesterday; but the suddenness, and, in one light, the unseasonableness with which the affair burst out, needs explanation; for though the event of the 26th ult., as you will conclude, immediately opened to me the happiest prospects, I should not have presumed on such early measures, but from the very particular circumstances, which left me not an hour to lose. I should myself have shrunk from any thing so hasty, and she would have felt every scruple of mine with multiplied strength and refinement.—But I had no choice. The hasty engagement she had entered into with that woman—Here, my dear madam, I was obliged to leave off abruptly, to recollect and compose myself.—I have been walking over the country, and am now, I hope, rational enough to make the rest of my letter what it ought to be.—It is, in fact, a most mortifying retrospect for me. I behaved shamefully. And here I can admit, that my manners to Miss W., in being unpleasant to Miss F., were highly blameable. She disapproved them, which ought to have been enough.—My plea of concealing the truth she did not think sufficient.—She was displeased; I thought unreasonably so: I thought her, on a thousand occasions, unnecessarily scrupulous and cautious: I thought her even cold. But she was always right. If I had followed her judgment, and subdued my spirits to the level of what she deemed proper, I should have escaped the greatest unhappiness I have ever known.—We quarrelled.—Do you remember the morning spent at Donwell?—There every little dissatisfaction that had occurred before came to a crisis. I was late; I met her walking home by herself, and wanted to walk with her, but she would not suffer it. She absolutely refused to allow me, which I then thought most unreasonable. Now, however, I see nothing in it but a very natural and consistent degree of discretion. While I, to blind the world to our engagement, was behaving one hour with objectionable particularity to another woman, was she to be consenting the next to a proposal which might have made every previous caution useless?—Had we been met walking together between Donwell and Highbury, the truth must have been suspected.—I was mad enough, however, to resent.—I doubted her affection. I doubted it more the next day on Box Hill; when, provoked by such conduct on my side, such shameful, insolent neglect of her, and such apparent devotion to Miss W., as it would have been impossible for any woman of sense to endure, she spoke her resentment in a form of words perfectly intelligible to me.—In short, my dear madam, it was a quarrel blameless on her side, abominable on mine; and I returned the same evening to Richmond, though I might have staid with you till the next morning, merely because I would be as angry with her as possible. Even then, I was not such a fool as not to mean to be reconciled in time; but I was the injured person, injured by her coldness, and I went away determined that she should make the first advances.—I shall always congratulate myself that you were not of the Box Hill party. Had you witnessed my behaviour there, I can hardly suppose you would ever have thought well of me again. Its effect upon her appears in the immediate resolution it produced: as soon as she found I was really gone from Randalls, she closed with the offer of that officious Mrs. Elton; the whole system of whose treatment of her, by the bye, has ever filled me with indignation and hatred. I must not quarrel with a spirit of forbearance which has been so richly extended towards myself; but, otherwise, I should loudly protest against the share of it which that woman has known.—"Jane," indeed!—You will observe that I have not yet indulged myself in calling her by that name, even to you. Think, then, what I must have endured in hearing it bandied between the Eltons with all the vulgarity of needless repetition, and all the insolence of imaginary superiority. Have patience with me, I shall soon have done.—She closed with this offer, resolving to break with me entirely, and wrote the next day to tell me that we never were to meet again.—She felt the engagement to be a source of repentance and misery to each: she dissolved it.—This letter reached me on the very morning of my poor aunt's death. I answered it within an hour; but from the confusion of my mind, and the multiplicity of business falling on me at once, my answer, instead of being sent with all the many other letters of that day, was locked up in my writing-desk; and I, trusting that I had written enough, though but a few lines, to satisfy her, remained without any uneasiness.—I was rather disappointed that I did not hear from her again speedily; but I made excuses for her, and was too busy, and—may I add?—too cheerful in my views to be captious.—We removed to Windsor; and two days afterwards I received a parcel from her, my own letters all returned!—and a few lines at the same time by the post, stating her extreme surprize at not having had the smallest reply to her last; and adding, that as silence on such a point could not be misconstrued, and as it must be equally desirable to both to have every subordinate arrangement concluded as soon as possible, she now sent me, by a safe conveyance, all my letters, and requested, that if I could not directly command hers, so as to send them to Highbury within a week, I would forward them after that period to her at—: in short, the full direction to Mr. Smallridge's, near Bristol, stared me in the face. I knew the name, the place, I knew all about it, and instantly saw what she had been doing. It was perfectly accordant with that resolution of character which I knew her to possess; and the secrecy she had maintained, as to any such design in her former letter, was equally descriptive of its anxious delicacy. For the world would not she have seemed to threaten me.—Imagine the shock; imagine how, till I had actually detected my own blunder, I raved at the blunders of the post.—What was to be done?—One thing only.—I must speak to my uncle. Without his sanction I could not hope to be listened to again.—I spoke; circumstances were in my favour; the late event had softened away his pride, and he was, earlier than I could have anticipated, wholly reconciled and complying; and could say at last, poor man! with a deep sigh, that he wished I might find as much happiness in the marriage state as he had done.—I felt that it would be of a different sort.—Are you disposed to pity me for what I must have suffered in opening the cause to him, for my suspense while all was at stake?—No; do not pity me till I reached Highbury, and saw how ill I had made her. Do not pity me till I saw her wan, sick looks.—I reached Highbury at the time of day when, from my knowledge of their late breakfast hour, I was certain of a good chance of finding her alone.—I was not disappointed; and at last I was not disappointed either in the object of my journey. A great deal of very reasonable, very just displeasure I had to persuade away. But it is done; we are reconciled, dearer, much dearer, than ever, and no moment's uneasiness can ever occur between us again. Now, my dear madam, I will release you; but I could not conclude before. A thousand and a thousand thanks for all the kindness you have ever shewn me, and ten thousand for the attentions your heart will dictate towards her.—If you think me in a way to be happier than I deserve, I am quite of your opinion.—Miss W. calls me the child of good fortune. I hope she is right.—In one respect, my good fortune is undoubted, that of being able to subscribe myself,

Your obliged and affectionate Son,

F. C. WESTON CHURCHILL.

Chapter XV

This letter must make its way to Emma's feelings. She was obliged, in spite of her previous determination to the contrary, to do it all the justice that Mrs. Weston foretold. As soon as she came to her own name, it was irresistible; every line relating to herself was interesting, and almost every line agreeable; and when this charm ceased, the subject could still maintain itself, by the natural return of her former regard for the writer, and the very strong attraction which any picture of love must have for her at that moment. She never stopt till she had gone through the whole; and though it was impossible not to feel that he had been wrong, yet he had been less wrong than she had supposed—and he had suffered, and was very sorry—and he was so grateful to Mrs. Weston, and so much in love with Miss Fairfax, and she was so happy herself, that there was no being severe; and could he have entered the room, she must have shaken hands with him as heartily as ever.

She thought so well of the letter, that when Mr. Knightley came again, she desired him to read it. She was sure of Mrs. Weston's wishing it to be communicated; especially to one, who, like Mr. Knightley, had seen so much to blame in his conduct.

"I shall be very glad to look it over," said he; "but it seems long. I will take it home with me at night."

But that would not do. Mr. Weston was to call in the evening, and she must return it by him.

"I would rather be talking to you," he replied; "but as it seems a matter of justice, it shall be done."

He began—stopping, however, almost directly to say, "Had I been offered the sight of one of this gentleman's letters to his mother-in-law a few months ago, Emma, it would not have been taken with such indifference."

He proceeded a little farther, reading to himself; and then, with a smile, observed, "Humph! a fine complimentary opening: But it is his way. One man's style must not be the rule of another's. We will not be severe."

"It will be natural for me," he added shortly afterwards, "to speak my opinion aloud as I read. By doing it, I shall feel that I am near you. It will not be so great a loss of time: but if you dislike it——"

"Not at all. I should wish it."

Mr. Knightley returned to his reading with greater alacrity.

"He trifles here," said he, "as to the temptation. He knows he is wrong, and has nothing rational to urge.—Bad.—He ought not to have formed the engagement.—'His father's disposition:'—he is unjust, however, to his father. Mr. Weston's sanguine temper was a blessing on all his upright and honourable exertions; but Mr. Weston earned every present comfort before he endeavoured to gain it.—Very true; he did not come till Miss Fairfax was here."

"And I have not forgotten," said Emma, "how sure you were that he might have come sooner if he would. You pass it over very handsomely—but you were perfectly right."

"I was not quite impartial in my judgment, Emma:—but yet, I think—had you not been in the case—I should still have distrusted him."

When he came to Miss Woodhouse, he was obliged to read the whole of it aloud—all that related to her, with a smile; a look; a shake of the head; a word or two of assent, or disapprobation; or merely of love, as the subject required; concluding, however, seriously, and, after steady reflection, thus—

"Very bad—though it might have been worse.—Playing a most dangerous game. Too much indebted to the event for his acquittal.—No judge of his own manners by you.—Always deceived in fact by his own wishes, and regardless of little besides his own convenience.—

Fancying you to have fathomed his secret. Natural enough!—his own mind full of intrigue, that he should suspect it in others.—Mystery; Finesse—how they pervert the understanding! My Emma, does not every thing serve to prove more and more the beauty of truth and sincerity in all our dealings with each other?"

Emma agreed to it, and with a blush of sensibility on Harriet's account, which she could not give any sincere explanation of.

"You had better go on," said she.

He did so, but very soon stopt again to say, "the pianoforte! Ah! That was the act of a very, very young man, one too young to consider whether the inconvenience of it might not very much exceed the pleasure. A boyish scheme, indeed!—I cannot comprehend a man's wishing to give a woman any proof of affection which he knows she would rather dispense with; and he did know that she would have prevented the instrument's coming if she could."

After this, he made some progress without any pause. Frank Churchill's confession of having behaved shamefully was the first thing to call for more than a word in passing.

"I perfectly agree with you, sir,"—was then his remark. "You did behave very shamefully. You never wrote a truer line." And having gone through what immediately followed of the basis of their disagreement, and his persisting to act in direct opposition to Jane Fairfax's sense of right, he made a fuller pause to say, "This is very bad.—He had induced her to place herself, for his sake, in a situation of extreme difficulty and uneasiness, and it should have been his first object to prevent her from suffering unnecessarily.—She must have had much more to contend with, in carrying on the correspondence, than he could. He should have respected even unreasonable scruples, had there been such; but hers were all reasonable. We must look to her one fault, and remember that she had done a wrong thing in consenting to the engagement, to bear that she should have been in such a state of punishment."

Emma knew that he was now getting to the Box Hill party, and grew uncomfortable. Her own behaviour had been so very improper! She was deeply ashamed, and a little afraid of his next look. It was all read, however, steadily, attentively, and without the smallest remark; and, excepting one momentary glance at her, instantly withdrawn, in the fear of giving pain—no remembrance of Box Hill seemed to exist.

"There is no saying much for the delicacy of our good friends, the Eltons," was his next observation.—"His feelings are natural.—

What! actually resolve to break with him entirely!—She felt the engagement to be a source of repentance and misery to each—she dissolved it.—What a view this gives of her sense of his behaviour!—Well, he must be a most extraordinary—"

"Nay, nay, read on.—You will find how very much he suffers."

"I hope he does," replied Mr. Knightley coolly, and resuming the letter. "'Smallridge!'—What does this mean? What is all this?"

"She had engaged to go as governess to Mrs. Smallridge's children—a dear friend of Mrs. Elton's—a neighbour of Maple Grove; and, by the bye, I wonder how Mrs. Elton bears the disappointment?"

"Say nothing, my dear Emma, while you oblige me to read—not even of Mrs. Elton. Only one page more. I shall soon have done. What a letter the man writes!"

"I wish you would read it with a kinder spirit towards him."

"Well, there is feeling here.—He does seem to have suffered in finding her ill.—Certainly, I can have no doubt of his being fond of her. 'Dearer, much dearer than ever.' I hope he may long continue to feel all the value of such a reconciliation.—He is a very liberal thanker, with his thousands and tens of thousands.—'Happier than I deserve.' Come, he knows himself there. 'Miss Woodhouse calls me the child of good fortune.'—Those were Miss Woodhouse's words, were they?—And a fine ending—and there is the letter. The child of good fortune! That was your name for him, was it?"

"You do not appear so well satisfied with his letter as I am; but still you must, at least I hope you must, think the better of him for it. I hope it does him some service with you."

"Yes, certainly it does. He has had great faults, faults of inconsideration and thoughtlessness; and I am very much of his opinion in thinking him likely to be happier than he deserves: but still as he is, beyond a doubt, really attached to Miss Fairfax, and will soon, it may be hoped, have the advantage of being constantly with her, I am very ready to believe his character will improve, and acquire from hers the steadiness and delicacy of principle that it wants. And now, let me talk to you of something else. I have another person's interest at present so much at heart, that I cannot think any longer about Frank Churchill. Ever since I left you this morning, Emma, my mind has been hard at work on one subject."

The subject followed; it was in plain, unaffected, gentlemanlike English, such as Mr. Knightley used even to the woman he was in love with, how to be able to ask her to marry him, without attacking the happiness of her father. Emma's answer was ready at the first word. "While her dear father lived, any change of condition must be impossible for her. She could never quit him." Part only of this answer, however, was admitted. The impossibility of her quitting her father, Mr. Knightley felt as strongly as herself; but the inadmissibility of any other change, he could not agree to. He had been thinking it over most deeply, most intently; he had at first hoped to induce Mr. Woodhouse to remove with her to Donwell; he had wanted to believe it feasible, but his knowledge of Mr. Woodhouse would not suffer him to deceive himself long; and now he confessed his persuasion, that such a transplantation would be a risk of her father's comfort, perhaps even of his life, which must not be hazarded. Mr. Woodhouse taken from Hartfield!—No, he felt that it ought not to be attempted. But the plan which had arisen on the sacrifice of this, he trusted his dearest Emma would not find in any respect objectionable; it was, that he should be received at Hartfield; that so long as her father's happiness in other words his life—required Hartfield to continue her home, it should be his likewise.

Of their all removing to Donwell, Emma had already had her own passing thoughts. Like him, she had tried the scheme and rejected it; but such an alternative as this had not occurred to her. She was sensible of all the affection it evinced. She felt that, in quitting Donwell, he must be sacrificing a great deal of independence of hours and habits; that in living constantly with her father, and in no house of his own, there would be much, very much, to be borne with. She promised to think of it, and advised him to think of it more; but he was fully convinced, that no reflection could alter his wishes or his opinion on the subject. He had given it, he could assure her, very long and calm consideration; he had been walking away from William Larkins the whole morning, to have his thoughts to himself.

"Ah! there is one difficulty unprovided for," cried Emma. "I am sure William Larkins will not like it. You must get his consent before you ask mine."

She promised, however, to think of it; and pretty nearly promised, moreover, to think of it, with the intention of finding it a very good scheme.

It is remarkable, that Emma, in the many, very many, points of view in which she was now beginning to consider Donwell Abbey, was never struck with any sense of injury to her nephew Henry, whose rights as heir-expectant had formerly been so tenaciously regarded. Think she must of the possible difference to the poor little boy; and yet she only gave herself a saucy conscious smile about it, and found amusement in detecting the real cause of that violent dislike of Mr. Knightley's marrying Jane Fairfax, or any body else, which at the time she had wholly imputed to the amiable solicitude of the sister and the aunt.

This proposal of his, this plan of marrying and continuing at Hartfield—the more she contemplated it, the more pleasing it became. His evils seemed to lessen, her own advantages to increase, their mutual good to outweigh every drawback. Such a companion for herself in the periods of anxiety and cheerlessness before her!—Such a partner in all those duties and cares to which time must be giving increase of melancholy!

She would have been too happy but for poor Harriet; but every blessing of her own seemed to involve and advance the sufferings of her friend, who must now be even excluded from Hartfield. The delightful family party which Emma was securing for herself, poor Harriet must, in mere charitable caution, be kept at a distance from. She would be a loser in every way. Emma could not deplore her future absence as any deduction from her own enjoyment. In such a party, Harriet would be rather a dead weight than otherwise; but for the poor girl herself, it seemed a peculiarly cruel necessity that was to be placing her in such a state of unmerited punishment.

In time, of course, Mr. Knightley would be forgotten, that is, supplanted; but this could not be expected to happen very early. Mr. Knightley himself would be doing nothing to assist the cure;—not like Mr. Elton. Mr. Knightley, always so kind, so feeling, so truly considerate for every body, would never deserve to be less worshipped than now; and it really was too much to hope even of Harriet, that she could be in love with more than three men in one year.

Chapter XVI

It was a very great relief to Emma to find Harriet as desirous as herself to avoid a meeting. Their intercourse was painful enough by letter. How much worse, had they been obliged to meet!

Harriet expressed herself very much as might be supposed, without reproaches, or apparent sense of ill-usage; and yet Emma fancied there was a something of resentment, a something bordering on it in her style, which increased the desirableness of their being separate.—It might be only her own consciousness; but it seemed as if an angel only could have been quite without resentment under such a stroke.

She had no difficulty in procuring Isabella's invitation; and she was fortunate in having a sufficient reason for asking it, without resorting to invention.—There was a tooth amiss. Harriet really wished, and had wished some time, to consult a dentist. Mrs. John Knightley was delighted to be of use; any thing of ill health was a recommendation to her—and though not so fond of a dentist as of a Mr. Wingfield, she was quite eager to have Harriet under her care.—When it was thus settled on her sister's side, Emma proposed it to her friend, and found her very persuadable.—Harriet was to go; she was invited for at least a fortnight; she was to be conveyed in Mr. Woodhouse's carriage.—It was all arranged, it was all completed, and Harriet was safe in Brunswick Square.

Now Emma could, indeed, enjoy Mr. Knightley's visits; now she could talk, and she could listen with true happiness, unchecked by that sense of injustice, of guilt, of something most painful, which had haunted her when remembering how disappointed a heart was near her, how much might at that moment, and at a little distance, be enduring by the feelings which she had led astray herself.

The difference of Harriet at Mrs. Goddard's, or in London, made perhaps an unreasonable difference in Emma's sensations; but she could not think of her in London without objects of curiosity and employment, which must be averting the past, and carrying her out of herself.

She would not allow any other anxiety to succeed directly to the place in her mind which Harriet had occupied. There was a communication before her, one which she only could be competent to make—the confession of her engagement to her father; but she would have nothing to do with it at present.—She had resolved to defer the disclosure till Mrs. Weston were safe and well. No additional agitation should be thrown at this period among those she loved—and the evil should not act on herself by anticipation before the appointed time.—A fortnight, at least, of leisure and peace of mind, to crown every warmer, but more agitating, delight, should be hers.

She soon resolved, equally as a duty and a pleasure, to employ half an hour of this holiday of spirits in calling on Miss Fairfax.—She ought to go—and she was longing to see her; the resemblance of their present situations increasing every other motive of goodwill. It would be a secret satisfaction; but the consciousness of a similarity of prospect would certainly add to the interest with which she should attend to any thing Jane might communicate.

She went—she had driven once unsuccessfully to the door, but had not been into the house since the morning after Box Hill, when poor Jane had been in such distress as had filled her with compassion, though all the worst of her sufferings had been unsuspected.—The fear of being still unwelcome, determined her, though assured of their being at home, to wait in the passage, and send up her name.—She heard Patty announcing it; but no such bustle succeeded as poor Miss Bates had before made so happily intelligible.—No; she heard nothing but the instant reply of, "Beg her to walk up;"—and a moment afterwards she was met on the stairs by Jane herself, coming eagerly forward, as if no other reception of her were felt sufficient.—Emma had never seen her look so well, so lovely, so engaging. There was consciousness, animation, and warmth; there was every thing which her countenance or manner could ever have wanted.—She came forward with an offered hand; and said, in a low, but very feeling tone,

"This is most kind, indeed!—Miss Woodhouse, it is impossible for me to express—I hope you will believe——Excuse me for being so entirely without words."

Emma was gratified, and would soon have shewn no want of words, if the sound of Mrs. Elton's voice from the sitting-room had not checked her, and made it expedient to compress all her friendly and all her congratulatory sensations into a very, very earnest shake of the hand.

Mrs. Bates and Mrs. Elton were together. Miss Bates was out, which accounted for the previous tranquillity. Emma could have wished Mrs. Elton elsewhere; but she was in a humour to have patience with every body; and as Mrs. Elton met her with unusual graciousness, she hoped the rencontre would do them no harm.

She soon believed herself to penetrate Mrs. Elton's thoughts, and understand why she was, like herself, in happy spirits; it was being in Miss Fairfax's confidence, and fancying herself acquainted with what was still a secret to other people. Emma saw symptoms of it immediately in the expression of her face; and while paying her own compliments to Mrs. Bates, and appearing to attend to the good old lady's replies, she saw her with a sort of anxious parade of mystery fold up a letter which she had apparently been reading aloud to Miss Fairfax, and return it into the purple and gold reticule by her side, saying, with significant nods,

"We can finish this some other time, you know. You and I shall not want opportunities. And, in fact, you have heard all the essential already. I only wanted to prove to you that Mrs. S. admits our apology, and is not offended. You see how delightfully she writes. Oh! she is a sweet creature! You would have doated on her, had you gone.—But not a word more. Let us be discreet—quite on our good behaviour.—Hush!—You remember those lines—I forget the poem at this moment:

"For when a lady's in the case, "You know all other things give place."

Now I say, my dear, in our case, for lady, read——mum! a word to the wise.—I am in a fine flow of spirits, an't I? But I want to set your heart at ease as to Mrs. S.—My representation, you see, has quite appeased her."

And again, on Emma's merely turning her head to look at Mrs. Bates's knitting, she added, in a half whisper,

"I mentioned no names, you will observe.—Oh! no; cautious as a minister of state. I managed it extremely well."

Emma could not doubt. It was a palpable display, repeated on every possible occasion. When they had all talked a little while in harmony of the weather and Mrs. Weston, she found herself abruptly addressed with,

"Do not you think, Miss Woodhouse, our saucy little friend here is charmingly recovered?—Do not you think her cure does Perry the highest credit?—(here was a side-glance of great meaning at Jane.) Upon my word, Perry has restored her in a wonderful short time!—Oh! if you had seen her, as I did, when she was at the worst!"—And when Mrs. Bates was saying something to Emma, whispered farther, "We do not say a word of any assistance that Perry might have; not a word of a certain young physician from Windsor.—Oh! no; Perry shall have all the credit."

"I have scarce had the pleasure of seeing you, Miss Woodhouse," she shortly afterwards began, "since the party to Box Hill. Very pleasant party. But yet I think there was something wanting. Things did not seem—that is, there seemed a little cloud upon the spirits of some.—So it appeared to me at least, but I might be mistaken. However, I think it answered so far as to tempt one to go again. What say you both to our collecting the same party, and exploring to Box Hill again, while the fine weather lasts?—It must be the same party, you know, quite the same party, not one exception."

Soon after this Miss Bates came in, and Emma could not help being diverted by the perplexity of her first answer to herself, resulting, she supposed, from doubt of what might be said, and impatience to say every thing.

"Thank you, dear Miss Woodhouse, you are all kindness.—It is impossible to say—Yes, indeed, I quite understand—dearest Jane's prospects—that is, I do not mean.—But she is charmingly recovered.—How is Mr. Woodhouse?—I am so glad.—Quite out of my power.—Such a happy little circle as you find us here.—Yes, indeed.—Charming young man!—that is—so very friendly; I mean good Mr. Perry!—such attention to Jane!"—And from her great, her more than commonly thankful delight towards Mrs. Elton for being there, Emma guessed that there had been a little show of resentment towards Jane, from the vicarage quarter, which was now graciously overcome.—After a few whispers, indeed, which placed it beyond a guess, Mrs. Elton, speaking louder, said,

"Yes, here I am, my good friend; and here I have been so long, that anywhere else I should think it necessary to apologise; but, the truth is, that I am waiting for my lord and master. He promised to join me here, and pay his respects to you."

"What! are we to have the pleasure of a call from Mr. Elton?—That will be a favour indeed! for I know gentlemen do not like morning visits, and Mr. Elton's time is so engaged."

"Upon my word it is, Miss Bates.—He really is engaged from morning to night.—There is no end of people's coming to him, on some pretence or other.—The magistrates, and overseers, and churchwardens, are always wanting his opinion. They seem not able to do any thing without him.—'Upon my word, Mr. E.,' I often say, 'rather you than I.—I do not know what would become of my crayons and my instrument, if I had half so many applicants.'—Bad enough as it is, for I absolutely neglect them both to an unpardonable degree.—I believe I have not played a bar this fortnight.—However, he is coming, I assure you: yes, indeed, on purpose to wait on you all." And putting up her hand to screen her words from Emma—"A congratulatory visit, you know.—Oh! yes, quite indispensable."

Miss Bates looked about her, so happily!—

"He promised to come to me as soon as he could disengage himself from Knightley; but he and Knightley are shut up together in deep consultation.—Mr. E. is Knightley's right hand."

Emma would not have smiled for the world, and only said, "Is Mr. Elton gone on foot to Donwell?—He will have a hot walk."

"Oh! no, it is a meeting at the Crown, a regular meeting. Weston and Cole will be there too; but one is apt to speak only of those who lead.—I fancy Mr. E. and Knightley have every thing their own way."

"Have not you mistaken the day?" said Emma. "I am almost certain that the meeting at the Crown is not till to-morrow.—Mr. Knightley was at Hartfield yesterday, and spoke of it as for Saturday."

"Oh! no, the meeting is certainly to-day," was the abrupt answer, which denoted the impossibility of any blunder on Mrs. Elton's side.—"I do believe," she continued, "this is the most troublesome parish that ever was. We never heard of such things at Maple Grove."

"Your parish there was small," said Jane.

"Upon my word, my dear, I do not know, for I never heard the subject talked of."

"But it is proved by the smallness of the school, which I have heard you speak of, as under the patronage of your sister and Mrs. Bragge; the only school, and not more than five-and-twenty children."

"Ah! you clever creature, that's very true. What a thinking brain you have! I say, Jane, what a perfect character you and I should make, if we could be shaken together. My liveliness and your solidity would produce perfection.—Not that I presume to insinuate, however, that some people may not think you perfection already.—But hush!—not a word, if you please."

It seemed an unnecessary caution; Jane was wanting to give her words, not to Mrs. Elton, but to Miss Woodhouse, as the latter plainly saw. The wish of distinguishing her, as far as civility permitted, was very evident, though it could not often proceed beyond a look.

Mr. Elton made his appearance. His lady greeted him with some of her sparkling vivacity.

"Very pretty, sir, upon my word; to send me on here, to be an encumbrance to my friends, so long before you vouchsafe to come!—But you knew what a dutiful creature you had to deal with. You knew I should not stir till my lord and master appeared.—Here have I been sitting this hour, giving these young ladies a sample of true conjugal obedience—for who can say, you know, how soon it may be wanted?"

Mr. Elton was so hot and tired, that all this wit seemed thrown away. His civilities to the other ladies must be paid; but his subsequent object was to lament over himself for the heat he was suffering, and the walk he had had for nothing.

"When I got to Donwell," said he, "Knightley could not be found. Very odd! very unaccountable! after the note I sent him this morning, and the message he returned, that he should certainly be at home till one."

"Donwell!" cried his wife.—"My dear Mr. E., you have not been to Donwell!—You mean the Crown; you come from the meeting at the Crown."

"No, no, that's to-morrow; and I particularly wanted to see Knightley to-day on that very account.—Such a dreadful broiling morning!—I went over the fields too—(speaking in a tone of great ill-usage,) which made it so much the worse. And then not to find him at home! I assure you I am not at all pleased. And no apology left, no message for me. The housekeeper declared she knew nothing of my being expected.—Very extraordinary!—And nobody knew at all which way he was gone. Perhaps to Hartfield, perhaps to the Abbey Mill, perhaps into his woods.—Miss Woodhouse, this is not like our friend Knightley!—Can you explain it?"

Emma amused herself by protesting that it was very extraordinary, indeed, and that she had not a syllable to say for him.

"I cannot imagine," said Mrs. Elton, (feeling the indignity as a wife ought to do,) "I cannot imagine how he could do such a thing by you, of all people in the world! The very last person whom one should expect to be forgotten!—My dear Mr. E., he must have left a message for you, I am sure he must.—Not even Knightley could be so very eccentric;—and his servants forgot it. Depend upon it, that was the case: and very likely to happen with the Donwell servants, who are all, I have often observed, extremely awkward and remiss.—I am sure I would not have such a creature as his Harry stand at our sideboard for any consideration. And as for Mrs. Hodges, Wright holds her very cheap indeed.—She promised Wright a receipt, and never sent it."

"I met William Larkins," continued Mr. Elton, "as I got near the house, and he told me I should not find his master at home, but I did not believe him.—William seemed rather out of humour. He did not know what was come to his master lately, he said, but he could hardly ever get the speech of him. I have nothing to do with William's wants, but it really is of very great importance that I should see Knightley to-day; and it becomes a matter, therefore, of very serious inconvenience that I should have had this hot walk to no purpose."

Emma felt that she could not do better than go home directly. In all probability she was at this very time waited for there; and Mr. Knightley might be preserved from sinking deeper in aggression towards Mr. Elton, if not towards William Larkins.

She was pleased, on taking leave, to find Miss Fairfax determined to attend her out of the room, to go with her even downstairs; it gave her an opportunity which she immediately made use of, to say,

"It is as well, perhaps, that I have not had the possibility. Had you not been surrounded by other friends, I might have been tempted to introduce a subject, to ask questions, to speak more openly than might have been strictly correct.—I feel that I should certainly have been impertinent."

"Oh!" cried Jane, with a blush and an hesitation which Emma thought infinitely more becoming to her than all the elegance of all her usual composure—"there would have been no danger. The danger would have been of my wearying you. You could not have gratified me more than by expressing an interest—. Indeed, Miss Woodhouse, (speaking more collectedly,) with the consciousness which I have of misconduct, very great misconduct, it is particularly consoling to me to know that those of my friends, whose good opinion is most worth preserving, are not disgusted to such a degree as to—I have not time for half that I could wish to say. I long to make apologies, excuses, to urge something for myself. I feel it so very due. But, unfortunately—in short, if your compassion does not stand my friend—"

"Oh! you are too scrupulous, indeed you are," cried Emma warmly, and taking her hand. "You owe me no apologies; and every body to whom you might be supposed to owe them, is so perfectly satisfied, so delighted even—"

"You are very kind, but I know what my manners were to you.—So cold and artificial!—I had always a part to act.—It was a life of deceit!—I know that I must have disgusted you."

"Pray say no more. I feel that all the apologies should be on my side. Let us forgive each other at once. We must do whatever is to be done quickest, and I think our feelings will lose no time there. I hope you have pleasant accounts from Windsor?"

"Very."

"And the next news, I suppose, will be, that we are to lose you—just as I begin to know you."

"Oh! as to all that, of course nothing can be thought of yet. I am here till claimed by Colonel and Mrs. Campbell."

"Nothing can be actually settled yet, perhaps," replied Emma, smiling—"but, excuse me, it must be thought of."

The smile was returned as Jane answered,

"You are very right; it has been thought of. And I will own to you, (I am sure it will be safe), that so far as our living with Mr. Churchill at Enscombe, it is settled. There must be three months, at least, of deep mourning; but when they are over, I imagine there will be nothing more to wait for."

"Thank you, thank you.—This is just what I wanted to be assured of.—Oh! if you knew how much I love every thing that is decided and open!—Good-bye, good-bye."

Chapter XVII

Mrs. Weston's friends were all made happy by her safety; and if the satisfaction of her well-doing could be increased to Emma, it was by knowing her to be the mother of a little girl. She had been decided in wishing for a Miss Weston. She would not acknowledge that it was with any view of making a match for her, hereafter, with either of Isabella's sons; but she was convinced that a daughter would suit both father and mother best. It would be a great comfort to Mr. Weston, as he grew older—and even Mr. Weston might be growing older ten years hence—to have his fireside enlivened by the sports and the nonsense, the freaks and the fancies of a child never banished from home; and Mrs. Weston—no one could doubt that a daughter would be most to her; and it would be quite a pity that any one who so well knew how to teach, should not have their powers in exercise again.

"She has had the advantage, you know, of practising on me," she continued—"like La Baronne d'Almane on La Comtesse d'Ostalis, in Madame de Genlis' Adelaide and Theodore, and we shall now see her own little Adelaide educated on a more perfect plan."

"That is," replied Mr. Knightley, "she will indulge her even more than she did you, and believe that she does not indulge her at all. It will be the only difference."

"Poor child!" cried Emma; "at that rate, what will become of her?"

"Nothing very bad.—The fate of thousands. She will be disagreeable in infancy, and correct herself as she grows older. I am losing all my bitterness against spoilt children, my dearest Emma. I, who am owing all my happiness to you, would not it be horrible ingratitude in me to be severe on them?"

Emma laughed, and replied: "But I had the assistance of all your endeavours to counteract the indulgence of other people. I doubt whether my own sense would have corrected me without it."

"Do you?—I have no doubt. Nature gave you understanding:—Miss Taylor gave you principles. You must have done well. My interference was quite as likely to do harm as good. It was very natural for you to say, what right has he to lecture me?—and I am afraid very natural for you to feel that it was done in a disagreeable manner. I do not believe I did you any good. The good was all to myself, by making you an object of the tenderest affection to me. I could not think about you so much without doating on you, faults and all; and by dint of fancying so many errors, have been in love with you ever since you were thirteen at least."

"I am sure you were of use to me," cried Emma. "I was very often influenced rightly by you—oftener than I would own at the time. I am very sure you did me good. And if poor little Anna Weston is to be spoiled, it will be the greatest humanity in you to do as much for her as you have done for me, except falling in love with her when she is thirteen."

"How often, when you were a girl, have you said to me, with one of your saucy looks—'Mr. Knightley, I am going to do so-and-so; papa says I may, or I have Miss Taylor's leave'—something which, you knew, I did not approve. In such cases my interference was giving you two bad feelings instead of one."

"What an amiable creature I was!—No wonder you should hold my speeches in such affectionate remembrance."

"'Mr. Knightley.'—You always called me, 'Mr. Knightley;' and, from habit, it has not so very formal a sound.—And yet it is formal. I want you to call me something else, but I do not know what."

"I remember once calling you 'George,' in one of my amiable fits, about ten years ago. I did it because I thought it would offend you; but, as you made no objection, I never did it again."

"And cannot you call me 'George' now?"

"Impossible!—I never can call you any thing but 'Mr. Knightley.' I will not promise even to equal the elegant terseness of Mrs. Elton, by calling you Mr. K.—But I will promise," she added presently, laughing and blushing—"I will promise to call you once by your Christian name. I do not say when, but perhaps you may guess where;—in the building in which N. takes M. for better, for worse."

Emma grieved that she could not be more openly just to one important service which his better sense would have rendered her, to the advice which would have saved her from the worst of all her womanly follies—her wilful intimacy with Harriet Smith; but it was too tender a subject.—She could not enter on it.—Harriet was very seldom mentioned between them. This, on his side, might merely proceed from her not being thought of; but Emma was rather inclined to attribute it to delicacy, and a suspicion, from some appearances, that their friendship were declining. She was aware herself, that, parting under any other circumstances, they certainly should have corresponded more, and that her intelligence would not have rested, as it now almost wholly did, on Isabella's letters. He might observe that it was so. The pain of being obliged to practise concealment towards him, was very little inferior to the pain of having made Harriet unhappy.

Isabella sent quite as good an account of her visitor as could be expected; on her first arrival she had thought her out of spirits, which appeared perfectly natural, as there was a dentist to be consulted; but, since that business had been over, she did not appear to find Harriet different from what she had known her before.—Isabella, to be sure, was no very quick observer; yet if Harriet had not been equal to playing with the children, it would not have escaped her. Emma's comforts and hopes were most agreeably carried on, by Harriet's being to stay longer; her fortnight was likely to be a month at least. Mr. and

Mrs. John Knightley were to come down in August, and she was invited to remain till they could bring her back.

"John does not even mention your friend," said Mr. Knightley. "Here is his answer, if you like to see it."

It was the answer to the communication of his intended marriage. Emma accepted it with a very eager hand, with an impatience all alive to know what he would say about it, and not at all checked by hearing that her friend was unmentioned.

"John enters like a brother into my happiness," continued Mr. Knightley, "but he is no complimenter; and though I well know him to have, likewise, a most brotherly affection for you, he is so far from making flourishes, that any other young woman might think him rather cool in her praise. But I am not afraid of your seeing what he writes."

"He writes like a sensible man," replied Emma, when she had read the letter. "I honour his sincerity. It is very plain that he considers the good fortune of the engagement as all on my side, but that he is not without hope of my growing, in time, as worthy of your affection, as you think me already. Had he said any thing to bear a different construction, I should not have believed him."

"My Emma, he means no such thing. He only means—"

"He and I should differ very little in our estimation of the two," interrupted she, with a sort of serious smile—"much less, perhaps, than he is aware of, if we could enter without ceremony or reserve on the subject."

"Emma, my dear Emma—"

"Oh!" she cried with more thorough gaiety, "if you fancy your brother does not do me justice, only wait till my dear father is in the secret, and hear his opinion. Depend upon it, he will be much farther from doing you justice. He will think all the happiness, all the advantage, on your side of the question; all the merit on mine. I wish I may not sink into 'poor Emma' with him at once.—His tender compassion towards oppressed worth can go no farther."

"Ah!" he cried, "I wish your father might be half as easily convinced as John will be, of our having every right that equal worth can give, to be happy together. I am amused by one part of John's letter—did you notice it?—where he says, that my information did not take him wholly by surprize, that he was rather in expectation of hearing something of the kind."

"If I understand your brother, he only means so far as your having some thoughts of marrying. He had no idea of me. He seems perfectly unprepared for that."

"Yes, yes—but I am amused that he should have seen so far into my feelings. What has he been judging by?—I am not conscious of any difference in my spirits or conversation that could prepare him at this time for my marrying any more than at another.—But it was so, I suppose. I dare say there was a difference when I was staying with them the other day. I believe I did not play with the children quite so much as usual. I remember one evening the poor boys saying, 'Uncle seems always tired now.'"

The time was coming when the news must spread farther, and other persons' reception of it tried. As soon as Mrs. Weston was sufficiently recovered to admit Mr. Woodhouse's visits, Emma having it in view that her gentle reasonings should be employed in the cause, resolved first to announce it at home, and then at Randalls.—But how to break it to her father at last!—She had bound herself to do it, in such an hour of Mr. Knightley's absence, or when it came to the point her heart would have failed her, and she must have put it off; but Mr. Knightley was to come at such a time, and follow up the beginning she was to make.—She was forced to speak, and to speak cheerfully too. She must not make it a more decided subject of misery to him, by a melancholy tone herself. She must not appear to think it a misfortune.—With all the spirits she could command, she prepared him first for something strange, and then, in a few words, said, that if his consent and approbation could be obtained—which, she trusted, would be attended with no difficulty, since it was a plan to promote the happiness of all—she and Mr. Knightley meant to marry; by which means Hartfield would receive the constant addition of that person's company whom she knew he loved, next to his daughters and Mrs. Weston, best in the world.

Poor man!—it was at first a considerable shock to him, and he tried earnestly to dissuade her from it. She was reminded, more than once, of having always said she would never marry, and assured that it would be a great deal better for her to remain single; and told of poor Isabella, and poor Miss Taylor.—But it would not do. Emma hung about him affectionately, and smiled, and said it must be so; and that he must not class her with Isabella and Mrs. Weston, whose marriages taking them from Hartfield, had, indeed, made a melancholy change:

but she was not going from Hartfield; she should be always there; she was introducing no change in their numbers or their comforts but for the better; and she was very sure that he would be a great deal the happier for having Mr. Knightley always at hand, when he were once got used to the idea.—Did he not love Mr. Knightley very much?—He would not deny that he did, she was sure.—Whom did he ever want to consult on business but Mr. Knightley?—Who was so useful to him, who so ready to write his letters, who so glad to assist him?—Who so cheerful, so attentive, so attached to him?—Would not he like to have him always on the spot?—Yes. That was all very true. Mr. Knightley could not be there too often; he should be glad to see him every day;—but they did see him every day as it was.—Why could not they go on as they had done?

Mr. Woodhouse could not be soon reconciled; but the worst was overcome, the idea was given; time and continual repetition must do the rest.—To Emma's entreaties and assurances succeeded Mr. Knightley's, whose fond praise of her gave the subject even a kind of welcome; and he was soon used to be talked to by each, on every fair occasion.—They had all the assistance which Isabella could give, by letters of the strongest approbation; and Mrs. Weston was ready, on the first meeting, to consider the subject in the most serviceable light—first, as a settled, and, secondly, as a good one—well aware of the nearly equal importance of the two recommendations to Mr. Woodhouse's mind.—It was agreed upon, as what was to be; and every body by whom he was used to be guided assuring him that it would be for his happiness; and having some feelings himself which almost admitted it, he began to think that some time or other—in another year or two, perhaps—it might not be so very bad if the marriage did take place.

Mrs. Weston was acting no part, feigning no feelings in all that she said to him in favour of the event.—She had been extremely surprized, never more so, than when Emma first opened the affair to her; but she saw in it only increase of happiness to all, and had no scruple in urging him to the utmost.—She had such a regard for Mr. Knightley, as to think he deserved even her dearest Emma; and it was in every respect so proper, suitable, and unexceptionable a connexion, and in one respect, one point of the highest importance, so peculiarly eligible, so singularly fortunate, that now it seemed as if Emma could not safely have attached herself to any other creature, and that she had herself been the stupidest of beings in not having thought of it, and wished it long ago.—How very few of those men in a rank of life to address Emma would have renounced their own home for Hartfield! And who but Mr. Knightley could know and bear with Mr. Woodhouse, so as to make such an arrangement desirable!—The difficulty of disposing of poor Mr. Woodhouse had been always felt in her husband's plans and her own, for a marriage between Frank and Emma. How to settle the claims of Enscombe and Hartfield had been a continual impediment—less acknowledged by Mr. Weston than by herself—but even he had never been able to finish the subject better than by saying—"Those matters will take care of themselves; the young people will find a way." But here there was nothing to be shifted off in a wild speculation on the future. It was all right, all open, all equal. No sacrifice on any side worth the name. It was a union of the highest promise of felicity in itself, and without one real, rational difficulty to oppose or delay it.

Mrs. Weston, with her baby on her knee, indulging in such reflections as these, was one of the happiest women in the world. If any thing could increase her delight, it was perceiving that the baby would soon have outgrown its first set of caps.

The news was universally a surprize wherever it spread; and Mr. Weston had his five minutes share of it; but five minutes were enough to familiarise the idea to his quickness of mind.—He saw the advantages of the match, and rejoiced in them with all the constancy of his wife; but the wonder of it was very soon nothing; and by the end of an hour he was not far from believing that he had always foreseen it.

"It is to be a secret, I conclude," said he. "These matters are always a secret, till it is found out that every body knows them. Only let me be told when I may speak out.—I wonder whether Jane has any suspicion."

He went to Highbury the next morning, and satisfied himself on that point. He told her the news. Was not she like a daughter, his eldest daughter?—he must tell her; and Miss Bates being present, it passed, of course, to Mrs. Cole, Mrs. Perry, and Mrs. Elton, immediately afterwards. It was no more than the principals were prepared for; they had calculated from the time of its being known at Randalls, how soon it would be over Highbury; and were thinking of themselves, as the evening wonder in many a family circle, with great sagacity.

In general, it was a very well approved match. Some might think him, and others might think her, the most in luck. One set might recommend their all removing to Donwell, and leaving Hartfield for the John Knightleys; and another might predict disagreements among their servants; but yet, upon the whole, there was no serious objection raised, except in one habitation, the Vicarage.—There, the surprize was not softened by any satisfaction. Mr. Elton cared little about it, compared with his wife; he only hoped "the young lady's pride would now be contented;" and supposed "she had always meant to catch Knightley if she could;" and, on the point of living at Hartfield, could daringly exclaim, "Rather he than I!"—But Mrs. Elton was very much discomposed indeed.—"Poor Knightley! poor fellow!—sad business for him.—She was extremely concerned; for, though very eccentric, he had a thousand good qualities.—How could he be so taken in?—Did not think him at all in love—not in the least.—Poor Knightley!—There would be an end of all pleasant intercourse with him.—How happy he had been to come and dine with them whenever they asked him! But that would be all over now.—Poor fellow!—No more exploring parties to Donwell made for her. Oh! no; there would be a Mrs. Knightley to throw cold water on every thing.—Extremely disagreeable! But she was not at all sorry that she had abused the housekeeper the other day.—Shocking plan, living together. It would never do. She knew a family near Maple Grove who had tried it, and been obliged to separate before the end of the first quarter.

Chapter XVIII

Time passed on. A few more to-morrows, and the party from London would be arriving. It was an alarming change; and Emma was thinking of it one morning, as what must bring a great deal to agitate and grieve her, when Mr. Knightley came in, and distressing thoughts were put by. After the first chat of pleasure he was silent; and then, in a graver tone, began with,

"I have something to tell you, Emma; some news."

"Good or bad?" said she, quickly, looking up in his face.

"I do not know which it ought to be called."

"Oh! good I am sure.—I see it in your countenance. You are trying not to smile."

"I am afraid," said he, composing his features, "I am very much afraid, my dear Emma, that you will not smile when you hear it."

"Indeed! but why so?—I can hardly imagine that any thing which pleases or amuses you, should not please and amuse me too."

"There is one subject," he replied, "I hope but one, on which we do not think alike." He paused a moment, again smiling, with his eyes fixed on her face. "Does nothing occur to you?—Do not you recollect?—Harriet Smith."

Her cheeks flushed at the name, and she felt afraid of something, though she knew not what.

"Have you heard from her yourself this morning?" cried he. "You have, I believe, and know the whole."

"No, I have not; I know nothing; pray tell me."

"You are prepared for the worst, I see—and very bad it is. Harriet Smith marries Robert Martin."

Emma gave a start, which did not seem like being prepared—and her eyes, in eager gaze, said, "No, this is impossible!" but her lips were closed.

"It is so, indeed," continued Mr. Knightley; "I have it from Robert Martin himself. He left me not half an hour ago."

She was still looking at him with the most speaking amazement.

"You like it, my Emma, as little as I feared.—I wish our opinions were the same. But in time they will. Time, you may be sure, will make one or the other of us think differently; and, in the meanwhile, we need not talk much on the subject."

"You mistake me, you quite mistake me," she replied, exerting herself. "It is not that such a circumstance would now make me unhappy, but I cannot believe it. It seems an impossibility!—You cannot mean to say, that Harriet Smith has accepted Robert Martin. You cannot mean that he has even proposed to her again—yet. You only mean, that he intends it."

"I mean that he has done it," answered Mr. Knightley, with smiling but determined decision, "and been accepted."

"Good God!" she cried.—"Well!"—Then having recourse to her workbasket, in excuse for leaning down her face, and concealing all the exquisite feelings of delight and entertainment which she knew she must be expressing, she added, "Well, now tell me every thing; make this intelligible to me. How, where, when?—Let me know it all. I never was more surprized—but it does not make me unhappy, I assure you.—How—how has it been possible?"

"It is a very simple story. He went to town on business three days ago, and I got him to take charge of some papers which I was wanting to send to John.—He delivered these papers to John, at his chambers, and was asked by him to join their party the same evening to Astley's. They were going to take the two eldest boys to Astley's. The party was to be our brother and sister, Henry, John—and Miss Smith. My friend Robert could not resist. They called for him in their way; were all extremely amused; and my brother asked him to dine with them the next day—which he did—and in the course of that visit (as I understand) he found an opportunity of speaking to Harriet; and certainly did not speak in vain.—She made him, by her acceptance, as happy even as he is deserving. He came down by yesterday's coach, and was with me this morning immediately after breakfast, to report his proceedings, first on my affairs, and then on his own. This is all that I can relate of the how, where, and when. Your friend Harriet will make a much longer history when you see her.—She will give you all the minute particulars, which only woman's language can make interesting.—In our communications we deal only in the great.—However, I must say, that Robert Martin's heart seemed for him, and to me, very overflowing; and that he did mention, without its being much to the purpose, that on quitting their box at Astley's, my brother took charge of Mrs. John Knightley and little John, and he followed with Miss Smith and Henry; and that at one time they were in such a crowd, as to make Miss Smith rather uneasy."

He stopped.—Emma dared not attempt any immediate reply. To speak, she was sure would be to betray a most unreasonable degree of happiness. She must wait a moment, or he would think her mad. Her silence disturbed him; and after observing her a little while, he added,

"Emma, my love, you said that this circumstance would not now make you unhappy; but I am afraid it gives you more pain than you expected. His situation is an evil—but you must consider it as what satisfies your friend; and I will answer for your thinking better and better of him as you know him more. His good sense and good principles would delight you.—As far as the man is concerned, you could not wish your friend in better hands. His rank in society I would alter if I could, which is saying a great deal I assure you, Emma.—You laugh at me about William Larkins; but I could quite as ill spare Robert Martin."

He wanted her to look up and smile; and having now brought herself not to smile too broadly—she did—cheerfully answering,

"You need not be at any pains to reconcile me to the match. I think Harriet is doing extremely well. Her connexions may be worse than his. In respectability of character, there can be no doubt that they are. I have been silent from surprize merely, excessive surprize. You cannot imagine how suddenly it has come on me! how peculiarly unprepared I was!—for I had reason to believe her very lately more determined against him, much more, than she was before."

"You ought to know your friend best," replied Mr. Knightley; "but I should say she was a good-tempered, soft-hearted girl, not likely to be very, very determined against any young man who told her he loved her."

Emma could not help laughing as she answered, "Upon my word, I believe you know her quite as well as I do.—But, Mr. Knightley, are you perfectly sure that she has absolutely and downright accepted him. I could suppose she might in time—but can she already?—Did not you misunderstand him?—You were both talking of other things; of business, shows of cattle, or new drills—and might not you, in the confusion of so many subjects, mistake him?—It was not Harriet's hand that he was certain of—it was the dimensions of some famous ox."

The contrast between the countenance and air of Mr. Knightley and Robert Martin was, at this moment, so strong to Emma's feelings, and so strong was the recollection of all that had so recently passed on Harriet's side, so fresh the sound of those words, spoken with such emphasis, "No, I hope I know better than to think of Robert Martin," that she was really expecting the intelligence to prove, in some measure, premature. It could not be otherwise.

"Do you dare say this?" cried Mr. Knightley. "Do you dare to suppose me so great a blockhead, as not to know what a man is talking of?—What do you deserve?"

"Oh! I always deserve the best treatment, because I never put up with any other; and, therefore, you must give me a plain, direct answer. Are you quite sure that you understand the terms on which Mr. Martin and Harriet now are?"

"I am quite sure," he replied, speaking very distinctly, "that he told me she had accepted him; and that there was no obscurity, nothing doubtful, in the words he used; and I think I can give you a proof that it must be so. He asked my opinion as to what he was now to do. He knew of no one but Mrs. Goddard to whom he could apply for information of her relations or friends. Could I mention any thing more fit to be done, than to go to Mrs. Goddard? I assured him that I could not. Then, he said, he would endeavour to see her in the course of this day."

"I am perfectly satisfied," replied Emma, with the brightest smiles, "and most sincerely wish them happy."

"You are materially changed since we talked on this subject before."

"I hope so—for at that time I was a fool."

"And I am changed also; for I am now very willing to grant you all Harriet's good qualities. I have taken some pains for your sake, and for Robert Martin's sake, (whom I have always had reason to believe as much in love with her as ever,) to get acquainted with her. I have often talked to her a good deal. You must have seen that I did. Sometimes, indeed, I have thought you were half suspecting me of pleading poor Martin's cause, which was never the case; but, from all my observations, I am convinced of her being an artless, amiable girl, with very good notions, very seriously good principles, and placing her happiness in the affections and utility of domestic life.—Much of this, I have no doubt, she may thank you for."

"Me!" cried Emma, shaking her head.—"Ah! poor Harriet!"

She checked herself, however, and submitted quietly to a little more praise than she deserved.

Their conversation was soon afterwards closed by the entrance of her father. She was not sorry. She wanted to be alone. Her mind was in a state of flutter and wonder, which made it impossible for her to be collected. She was in dancing, singing, exclaiming spirits; and till she had moved about, and talked to herself, and laughed and reflected, she could be fit for nothing rational.

Her father's business was to announce James's being gone out to put the horses to, preparatory to their now daily drive to Randalls; and she had, therefore, an immediate excuse for disappearing.

The joy, the gratitude, the exquisite delight of her sensations may be imagined. The sole grievance and alloy thus removed in the prospect of Harriet's welfare, she was really in danger of becoming too happy for security.—What had she to wish for? Nothing, but to grow more worthy of him, whose intentions and judgment had been ever so superior to her own. Nothing, but that the lessons of her past folly might teach her humility and circumspection in future.

Serious she was, very serious in her thankfulness, and in her resolutions; and yet there was no preventing a laugh, sometimes in the very midst of them. She must laugh at such a close! Such an end of the doleful disappointment of five weeks back! Such a heart—such a Harriet!

Now there would be pleasure in her returning—Every thing would be a pleasure. It would be a great pleasure to know Robert Martin.

High in the rank of her most serious and heartfelt felicities, was the reflection that all necessity of concealment from Mr. Knightley would soon be over. The disguise, equivocation, mystery, so hateful to her to practise, might soon be over. She could now look forward to giving him that full and perfect confidence which her disposition was most ready to welcome as a duty.

In the gayest and happiest spirits she set forward with her father; not always listening, but always agreeing to what he said; and, whether in speech or silence, conniving at the comfortable persuasion of his being obliged to go to Randalls every day, or poor Mrs. Weston would be disappointed.

They arrived.—Mrs. Weston was alone in the drawing-room:—but hardly had they been told of the baby, and Mr. Woodhouse received the thanks for coming, which he asked for, when a glimpse was caught through the blind, of two figures passing near the window.

"It is Frank and Miss Fairfax," said Mrs. Weston. "I was just going to tell you of our agreeable surprize in seeing him arrive this morning. He stays till to-morrow, and Miss Fairfax has been persuaded to spend the day with us.—They are coming in, I hope."

In half a minute they were in the room. Emma was extremely glad to see him—but there was a degree of confusion—a number of embarrassing recollections on each side. They met readily and smiling, but with a consciousness which at first allowed little to be said; and having all sat down again, there was for some time such a blank in the circle, that Emma began to doubt whether the wish now indulged, which she had long felt, of seeing Frank Churchill once more, and of seeing him with Jane, would yield its proportion of pleasure. When Mr. Weston joined the party, however, and when the baby was fetched, there was no longer a want of subject or animation—or of courage and opportunity for Frank Churchill to draw near her and say,

"I have to thank you, Miss Woodhouse, for a very kind forgiving message in one of Mrs. Weston's letters. I hope time has not made you less willing to pardon. I hope you do not retract what you then said."

"No, indeed," cried Emma, most happy to begin, "not in the least. I am particularly glad to see and shake hands with you—and to give you joy in person."

He thanked her with all his heart, and continued some time to speak with serious feeling of his gratitude and happiness.

"Is not she looking well?" said he, turning his eyes towards Jane. "Better than she ever used to do?—You see how my father and Mrs. Weston doat upon her."

But his spirits were soon rising again, and with laughing eyes, after mentioning the expected return of the Campbells, he named the name of Dixon.—Emma blushed, and forbade its being pronounced in her hearing.

"I can never think of it," she cried, "without extreme shame."

"The shame," he answered, "is all mine, or ought to be. But is it possible that you had no suspicion?—I mean of late. Early, I know, you had none."

"I never had the smallest, I assure you."

"That appears quite wonderful. I was once very near—and I wish I had—it would have been better. But though I was always doing wrong things, they were very bad wrong things, and such as did me no service.—It would have been a much better transgression had I broken the bond of secrecy and told you every thing."

"It is not now worth a regret," said Emma.

"I have some hope," resumed he, "of my uncle's being persuaded to pay a visit at Randalls; he wants to be introduced to her. When the Campbells are returned, we shall meet them in London, and continue there, I trust, till we may carry her northward.—But now, I am at such a distance from her—is not it hard, Miss Woodhouse?—Till this morning, we have not once met since the day of reconciliation. Do not you pity me?"

Emma spoke her pity so very kindly, that with a sudden accession of gay thought, he cried,

"Ah! by the bye," then sinking his voice, and looking demure for the moment—"I hope Mr. Knightley is well?" He paused.—She coloured and laughed.—"I know you saw my letter, and think you may remember my wish in your favour. Let me return your congratulations.—I assure you that I have heard the news with the warmest interest and satisfaction.—He is a man whom I cannot presume to praise."

Emma was delighted, and only wanted him to go on in the same style; but his mind was the next moment in his own concerns and with his own Jane, and his next words were,

"Did you ever see such a skin?—such smoothness! such delicacy!—and yet without being actually fair.—One cannot call her fair. It is a most uncommon complexion, with her dark eye-lashes and hair—a most distinguishing complexion! So peculiarly the lady in it.—Just colour enough for beauty."

"I have always admired her complexion," replied Emma, archly; "but do not I remember the time when you found fault with her for being so pale?—When we first began to talk of her.—Have you quite forgotten?"

"Oh! no—what an impudent dog I was!—How could I dare—"

But he laughed so heartily at the recollection, that Emma could not help saying,

"I do suspect that in the midst of your perplexities at that time, you had very great amusement in tricking us all.—I am sure you had.—I am sure it was a consolation to you."

"Oh! no, no, no—how can you suspect me of such a thing? I was the most miserable wretch!"

"Not quite so miserable as to be insensible to mirth. I am sure it was a source of high entertainment to you, to feel that you were taking us all in.—Perhaps I am the readier to suspect, because, to tell you the truth, I think it might have been some amusement to myself in the same situation. I think there is a little likeness between us."

He bowed.

"If not in our dispositions," she presently added, with a look of true sensibility, "there is a likeness in our destiny; the destiny which bids fair to connect us with two characters so much superior to our own."

"True, true," he answered, warmly. "No, not true on your side. You can have no superior, but most true on mine.—She is a complete angel. Look at her. Is not she an angel in every gesture? Observe the turn of her throat. Observe her eyes, as she is looking up at my father.—You will be glad to hear (inclining his head, and whispering seriously) that my uncle means to give her all my aunt's jewels. They are to be new set. I am resolved to have some in an ornament for the head. Will not it be beautiful in her dark hair?"

"Very beautiful, indeed," replied Emma; and she spoke so kindly, that he gratefully burst out,

"How delighted I am to see you again! and to see you in such excellent looks!—I would not have missed this meeting for the world. I should certainly have called at Hartfield, had you failed to come."

The others had been talking of the child, Mrs. Weston giving an account of a little alarm she had been under, the evening before, from the infant's appearing not quite well. She believed she had been foolish, but it had alarmed her, and she had been within half a minute of sending for Mr. Perry. Perhaps she ought to be ashamed, but Mr. Weston had been almost as uneasy as herself.—In ten minutes, however, the child had been perfectly well again. This was her history; and particularly interesting it was to Mr. Woodhouse, who commended her very much for thinking of sending for Perry, and only regretted that she had not done it. "She should always send for Perry, if the child appeared in the slightest degree disordered, were it only for a moment. She could not be too soon alarmed, nor send for Perry too often. It was a pity, perhaps, that he had not come last night; for, though the child seemed well now, very well considering, it would probably have been better if Perry had seen it."

Frank Churchill caught the name.

"Perry!" said he to Emma, and trying, as he spoke, to catch Miss Fairfax's eye. "My friend Mr. Perry! What are they saying about Mr. Perry?—Has he been here this morning?—And how does he travel now?—Has he set up his carriage?"

Emma soon recollected, and understood him; and while she joined in the laugh, it was evident from Jane's countenance that she too was really hearing him, though trying to seem deaf.

"Such an extraordinary dream of mine!" he cried. "I can never think of it without laughing.—She hears us, she hears us, Miss Woodhouse. I see it in her cheek, her smile, her vain attempt to frown. Look at her. Do not you see that, at this instant, the very passage of her own letter, which sent me the report, is passing under her eye—that the whole blunder is spread before her—that she can attend to nothing else, though pretending to listen to the others?"

Jane was forced to smile completely, for a moment; and the smile partly remained as she turned towards him, and said in a conscious, low, yet steady voice,

"How you can bear such recollections, is astonishing to me!—They will sometimes obtrude—but how you can court them!"

He had a great deal to say in return, and very entertainingly; but Emma's feelings were chiefly with Jane, in the argument; and on leaving Randalls, and falling naturally into a comparison of the two men, she felt, that pleased as she had been to see Frank Churchill, and really regarding him as she did with friendship, she had never been more sensible of Mr. Knightley's high superiority of character. The happiness of this most happy day, received its completion, in the animated contemplation of his worth which this comparison produced.

Chapter XIX

If Emma had still, at intervals, an anxious feeling for Harriet, a momentary doubt of its being possible for her to be really cured of her attachment to Mr. Knightley, and really able to accept another man from unbiased inclination, it was not long that she had to suffer from the recurrence of any such uncertainty. A very few days brought the party from London, and she had no sooner an opportunity of being one hour alone with Harriet, than she became perfectly satisfied—unaccountable as it was!—that Robert Martin had thoroughly supplanted Mr. Knightley, and was now forming all her views of happiness.

Harriet was a little distressed—did look a little foolish at first: but having once owned that she had been presumptuous and silly, and self-deceived, before, her pain and confusion seemed to die away with the words, and leave her without a care for the past, and with the fullest exultation in the present and future; for, as to her friend's approbation, Emma had instantly removed every fear of that nature, by meeting her with the most unqualified congratulations.—Harriet was most happy to give every particular of the evening at Astley's, and the dinner the next day; she could dwell on it all with the utmost delight. But what did such particulars explain?—The fact was, as Emma could now acknowledge, that Harriet had always liked Robert Martin; and that his continuing to love her had been irresistible.—Beyond this, it must ever be unintelligible to Emma.

The event, however, was most joyful; and every day was giving her fresh reason for thinking so.—Harriet's parentage became known. She proved to be the daughter of a tradesman, rich enough to afford her the comfortable maintenance which had ever been hers, and decent enough to have always wished for concealment.—Such was the blood of gentility which Emma had formerly been so ready to vouch for!—It was likely to be as untainted, perhaps, as the blood of many a gentleman: but what a connexion had she been preparing for Mr. Knightley—or for the Churchills—or even for Mr. Elton!—The stain of illegitimacy, unbleached by nobility or wealth, would have been a stain indeed.

No objection was raised on the father's side; the young man was treated liberally; it was all as it should be: and as Emma became acquainted with Robert Martin, who was now introduced at Hartfield, she fully acknowledged in him all the appearance of sense and worth which could bid fairest for her little friend. She had no doubt of Harriet's happiness with any good-tempered man; but with him, and in the home he offered, there would be the hope of more, of security, stability, and improvement. She would be placed in the midst of those who loved her, and who had better sense than herself; retired enough for safety, and occupied enough for cheerfulness. She would be never led into temptation, nor left for it to find her out. She would be respectable and happy; and Emma admitted her to be the luckiest creature in the world, to have created so steady and persevering an affection in such a man;—or, if not quite the luckiest, to yield only to herself.

Harriet, necessarily drawn away by her engagements with the Martins, was less and less at Hartfield; which was not to be regretted.—The intimacy between her and Emma must sink; their friendship must change into a calmer sort of goodwill; and, fortunately, what ought to be, and must be, seemed already beginning, and in the most gradual, natural manner.

Before the end of September, Emma attended Harriet to church, and saw her hand bestowed on Robert Martin with so complete a satisfaction, as no remembrances, even connected with Mr. Elton as he stood before them, could impair.—Perhaps, indeed, at that time she scarcely saw Mr. Elton, but as the clergyman whose blessing at the altar might next fall on herself.—Robert Martin and Harriet Smith, the latest couple engaged of the three, were the first to be married.

Jane Fairfax had already quitted Highbury, and was restored to the comforts of her beloved home with the Campbells.—The Mr. Churchills were also in town; and they were only waiting for November.

The intermediate month was the one fixed on, as far as they dared, by Emma and Mr. Knightley.—They had determined that their marriage ought to be concluded while John and Isabella were still at Hartfield, to allow them the fortnight's absence in a tour to the seaside, which was the plan.—John and Isabella, and every other friend, were agreed in approving it. But Mr. Woodhouse—how was Mr. Woodhouse to be induced to consent?—he, who had never yet alluded to their marriage but as a distant event.

When first sounded on the subject, he was so miserable, that they were almost hopeless.—A second allusion, indeed, gave less pain.—He began to think it was to be, and that he could not prevent it—a very promising step of the mind on its way to resignation. Still, however, he was not happy. Nay, he appeared so much otherwise, that his daughter's courage failed. She could not bear to see him suffering, to know him fancying himself neglected; and though her understanding almost acquiesced in the assurance of both the Mr. Knightleys, that when once the event were over, his distress would be soon over too, she hesitated—she could not proceed.

In this state of suspense they were befriended, not by any sudden illumination of Mr. Woodhouse's mind, or any wonderful change of his nervous system, but by the operation of the same system in another way.—Mrs. Weston's poultry-house was robbed one night of all her turkeys—evidently by the ingenuity of man. Other poultry-yards in the neighbourhood also suffered.—Pilfering was housebreaking to Mr. Woodhouse's fears.—He was very uneasy; and but for the sense of his son-in-law's protection, would have been under wretched alarm every night of his life. The strength, resolution, and presence of mind of the Mr. Knightleys, commanded his fullest dependence. While either of them protected him and his, Hartfield was safe.—But Mr. John Knightley must be in London again by the end of the first week in November.

The result of this distress was, that, with a much more voluntary, cheerful consent than his daughter had ever presumed to hope for at the moment, she was able to fix her wedding-day—and Mr. Elton was called on, within a month from the marriage of Mr. and

Mrs. Robert Martin, to join the hands of Mr. Knightley and Miss Woodhouse.

The wedding was very much like other weddings, where the parties have no taste for finery or parade; and Mrs. Elton, from the particulars detailed by her husband, thought it all extremely shabby, and very inferior to her own.—"Very little white satin, very few lace veils; a most pitiful business!—Selina would stare when she heard of it."—But, in spite of these deficiencies, the wishes, the hopes, the confidence, the predictions of the small band of true friends who witnessed the ceremony, were fully answered in the perfect happiness of the union.

George Eliot

ADAM BEDE

Romance
CLASSICS

Romance CLASSICS

Published by Trident Press International
801 12th Avenue South
Suite 302
Naples Florida 34102 USA
www.trident-international.com
email: tridentpress@worldnet.att.net

Printed in Australia
ISBN: 158279197X

BOOK ONE

Chapter I   The Workshop

With a single drop of ink for a mirror, the Egyptian sorcerer undertakes to reveal to any chance comer far-reaching visions of the past. This is what I undertake to do for you, reader. With this drop of ink at the end of my pen, I will show you the roomy workshop of Mr. Jonathan Burge, carpenter and builder, in the village of Hayslope, as it appeared on the eighteenth of June, in the year of our Lord 1799.

The afternoon sun was warm on the five workmen there, busy upon doors and window-frames and wainscoting. A scent of pine-wood from a tentlike pile of planks outside the open door mingled itself with the scent of the elder-bushes which were spreading their summer snow close to the open window opposite; the slanting sunbeams shone through the transparent shavings that flew before the steady plane, and lit up the fine grain of the oak panelling which stood propped against the wall. On a heap of those soft shavings a rough, grey shepherd dog had made himself a pleasant bed, and was lying with his nose between his fore-paws, occasionally wrinkling his brows to cast a glance at the tallest of the five workmen, who was carving a shield in the centre of a wooden mantelpiece. It was to this workman that the strong barytone belonged which was heard above the sound of plane and hammer singing—

Awake, my soul, and with the sun
Thy daily stage of duty run;
Shake off dull sloth . . .

Here some measurement was to be taken which required more concentrated attention, and the sonorous voice subsided into a low whistle; but it presently broke out again with renewed vigour—

Let all thy converse be sincere,
Thy conscience as the noonday clear.

Such a voice could only come from a broad chest, and the broad chest belonged to a large-boned, muscular man nearly six feet high, with a back so flat and a head so well poised that when he drew himself up to take a more distant survey of his work, he had the air of a soldier standing at ease. The sleeve rolled up above the elbow showed an arm that was likely to win the prize for feats of strength; yet the long supple hand, with its broad finger-tips, looked ready for works of skill. In his tall stalwartness Adam Bede was a Saxon, and justified his name; but the jet-black hair, made the more noticeable by its contrast with the light paper cap, and the keen glance of the dark eyes that shone from under strongly marked, prominent and mobile eyebrows, indicated a mixture of Celtic blood. The face was large and roughly hewn, and when in repose had no other beauty than such as belongs to an expression of good-humoured honest intelligence.

It is clear at a glance that the next workman is Adam's brother. He is nearly as tall; he has the same type of features, the same hue of hair and complexion; but the strength of the family likeness seems only to render more conspicuous the remarkable difference of expression both in form and face. Seth's broad shoulders have a slight stoop; his eyes are grey; his eyebrows have less prominence and more repose than his brother's; and his glance, instead of being keen, is confiding and benign. He has thrown off his paper cap, and you see that his hair is not thick and straight, like Adam's, but thin and wavy, allowing you to discern the exact contour of a coronal arch that predominates very decidedly over the brow.

The idle tramps always felt sure they could get a copper from Seth; they scarcely ever spoke to Adam.

The concert of the tools and Adam's voice was at last broken by Seth, who, lifting the door at which he had been working intently, placed it against the wall, and said, "There! I've finished my door today, anyhow."

The workmen all looked up; Jim Salt, a burly, red-haired man known as Sandy Jim, paused from his planing, and Adam said to Seth, with a sharp glance of surprise, "What! Dost think thee'st finished the door?"

"Aye, sure," said Seth, with answering surprise; "what's awanting to't?"

A loud roar of laughter from the other three workmen made Seth look round confusedly. Adam did not join in the laughter, but there was a slight smile on his face as he said, in a gentler tone than before, "Why, thee'st forgot the panels."

The laughter burst out afresh as Seth clapped his hands to his head, and coloured over brow and crown.

"Hoorray!" shouted a small lithe fellow called Wiry Ben, running forward and seizing the door. "We'll hang up th' door at fur end o' th' shop an' write on't 'Seth Bede, the Methody, his work.' Here, Jim, lend's hould o' th' red pot."

"Nonsense!" said Adam. "Let it alone, Ben Cranage. You'll mayhap be making such a slip yourself some day; you'll laugh o' th' other side o' your mouth then."

"Catch me at it, Adam. It'll be a good while afore my head's full o' th' Methodies," said Ben.

"Nay, but it's often full o' drink, and that's worse."

Ben, however, had now got the "red pot" in his hand, and was about to begin writing his inscription, making, by way of preliminary, an imaginary S in the air.

"Let it alone, will you?" Adam called out, laying down his tools, striding up to Ben, and seizing his right shoulder. "Let it alone, or I'll shake the soul out o' your body."

Ben shook in Adam's iron grasp, but, like a plucky small man as he was, he didn't mean to give in. With his left hand he snatched the brush from his powerless right, and made a movement as if he would perform the feat of writing with his left. In a moment Adam turned him round, seized his other shoulder, and, pushing him along, pinned him against the wall. But now Seth spoke.

"Let be, Addy, let be. Ben will be joking. Why, he's i' the right to laugh at me—I canna help laughing at myself."

"I shan't loose him till he promises to let the door alone," said Adam.

"Come, Ben, lad," said Seth, in a persuasive tone, "don't let's have a quarrel about it. You know Adam will have his way. You may's well try to turn a waggon in a narrow lane. Say you'll leave the door alone, and make an end on't."

"I binna frighted at Adam," said Ben, "but I donna mind sayin' as I'll let 't alone at your askin', Seth."

"Come, that's wise of you, Ben," said Adam, laughing and relaxing his grasp.

They all returned to their work now; but Wiry Ben, having had the worst in the bodily contest, was bent on retrieving that humiliation by a success in sarcasm.

"Which was ye thinkin' on, Seth," he began—"the pretty parson's face or her sarmunt, when ye forgot the panels?"

"Come and hear her, Ben," said Seth, good-humouredly; "she's going to preach on the Green to-night; happen ye'd get something to think on yourself then, instead o' those wicked songs you're so fond on. Ye might get religion, and that 'ud be the best day's earnings y' ever made."

"All i' good time for that, Seth; I'll think about that when I'm a-goin' to settle i' life; bachelors doesn't want such heavy earnin's. Happen I shall do the coortin' an' the religion both together, as YE do, Seth; but ye wouldna ha' me get converted an' chop in atween ye an' the pretty preacher, an' carry her aff?"

"No fear o' that, Ben; she's neither for you nor for me to win, I doubt. Only you come and hear her, and you won't speak lightly on her again."

"Well, I'm half a mind t' ha' a look at her to-night, if there isn't good company at th' Holly Bush. What'll she take for her text? Happen ye can tell me, Seth, if so be as I shouldna come up i' time for't. Will't be—what come ye out for to see? A prophetess? Yea, I say unto you, and more than a prophetess—a uncommon pretty young woman."

"Come, Ben," said Adam, rather sternly, "you let the words o' the Bible alone; you're going too far now."

"What! Are YE a-turnin' roun', Adam? I thought ye war dead again th' women preachin', a while agoo?"

"Nay, I'm not turnin' noway. I said nought about the women preachin'. I said, You let the Bible alone: you've got a jest-book, han't you, as you're rare and proud on? Keep your dirty fingers to that."

"Why, y' are gettin' as big a saint as Seth. Y' are goin' to th' preachin' to-night, I should think. Ye'll do finely t' lead the singin'. But

I don' know what Parson Irwine 'ull say at his gran' favright Adam Bede a-turnin' Methody."

"Never do you bother yourself about me, Ben. I'm not a-going to turn Methodist any more nor you are—though it's like enough you'll turn to something worse. Mester Irwine's got more sense nor to meddle wi' people's doing as they like in religion. That's between themselves and God, as he's said to me many a time."

"Aye, aye; but he's none so fond o' your dissenters, for all that."

"Maybe; I'm none so fond o' Josh Tod's thick ale, but I don't hinder you from making a fool o' yourself wi't."

There was a laugh at this thrust of Adam's, but Seth said, very seriously. "Nay, nay, Addy, thee mustna say as anybody's religion's like thick ale. Thee dostna believe but what the dissenters and the Methodists have got the root o' the matter as well as the church folks."

"Nay, Seth, lad; I'm not for laughing at no man's religion. Let 'em follow their consciences, that's all. Only I think it 'ud be better if their consciences 'ud let 'em stay quiet i' the church—there's a deal to be learnt there. And there's such a thing as being oversperitial; we must have something beside Gospel i' this world. Look at the canals, an' th' aqueduc's, an' th' coal-pit engines, and Arkwright's mills there at Cromford; a man must learn summat beside Gospel to make them things, I reckon. But t' hear some o' them preachers, you'd think as a man must be doing nothing all's life but shutting's eyes and looking what's agoing on inside him. I know a man must have the love o' God in his soul, and the Bible's God's word. But what does the Bible say? Why, it says as God put his sperrit into the workman as built the tabernacle, to make him do all the carved work and things as wanted a nice hand. And this is my way o' looking at it: there's the sperrit o' God in all things and all times—weekday as well as Sunday—and i' the great works and inventions, and i' the figuring and the mechanics. And God helps us with our headpieces and our hands as well as with our souls; and if a man does bits o' jobs out o' working hours—builds a oven for 's wife to save her from going to the bakehouse, or scrats at his bit o' garden and makes two potatoes grow istead o' one, he's doin' more good, and he's just as near to God, as if he was running after some preacher and a-praying and a-groaning."

"Well done, Adam!" said Sandy Jim, who had paused from his planing to shift his planks while Adam was speaking; "that's the best sarmunt I've heared this long while. By th' same token, my wife's been a-plaguin' on me to build her a oven this twelvemont."

"There's reason in what thee say'st, Adam," observed Seth, gravely. "But thee know'st thyself as it's hearing the preachers thee find'st so much fault with has turned many an idle fellow into an industrious un. It's the preacher as empties th' alehouse; and if a man gets religion, he'll do his work none the worse for that."

"On'y he'll lave the panels out o' th' doors sometimes, eh, Seth?" said Wiry Ben.

"Ah, Ben, you've got a joke again' me as 'll last you your life. But it isna religion as was i' fault there; it was Seth Bede, as was allays a wool-gathering chap, and religion hasna cured him, the more's the pity."

"Ne'er heed me, Seth," said Wiry Ben, "y' are a down-right good-hearted chap, panels or no panels; an' ye donna set up your bristles at every bit o' fun, like some o' your kin, as is mayhap cliverer."

"Seth, lad," said Adam, taking no notice of the sarcasm against himself, "thee mustna take me unkind. I wasna driving at thee in what I said just now. Some 's got one way o' looking at things and some 's got another."

"Nay, nay, Addy, thee mean'st me no unkindness," said Seth, "I know that well enough. Thee't like thy dog Gyp—thee bark'st at me sometimes, but thee allays lick'st my hand after."

All hands worked on in silence for some minutes, until the church clock began to strike six. Before the first stroke had died away, Sandy Jim had loosed his plane and was reaching his jacket; Wiry Ben had left a screw half driven in, and thrown his screwdriver into his tool-basket; Mum Taft, who, true to his name, had kept silence throughout the previous conversation, had flung down his hammer as he was in the act of lifting it; and Seth, too, had straightened his back, and was putting out his hand towards his paper cap. Adam alone had gone on with his work as if nothing had happened. But observing the cessation of the tools, he looked up, and said, in a tone of indignation, "Look there, now! I can't abide to see men throw away their tools i' that way, the minute the clock begins to strike, as if they took no pleasure i' their work and was afraid o' doing a stroke too much."

Seth looked a little conscious, and began to be slower in his preparations for going, but Mum Taft broke silence, and said, "Aye, aye, Adam lad, ye talk like a young un. When y' are six-an'-forty like me, istid o' six-an'-twenty, ye wonna be so flush o' workin' for nought."

"Nonsense," said Adam, still wrathful; "what's age got to do with it, I wonder? Ye arena getting stiff yet, I reckon. I hate to see a man's arms drop down as if he was shot, before the clock's fairly struck, just as if he'd never a bit o' pride and delight in 's work. The very grindstone 'ull go on turning a bit after you loose it."

"Bodderation, Adam!" exclaimed Wiry Ben; "lave a chap aloon, will 'ee? Ye war afinding faut wi' preachers a while agoo—y' are fond enough o' preachin' yoursen. Ye may like work better nor play, but I like play better nor work; that'll 'commodate ye—it laves ye th' more to do."

With this exit speech, which he considered effective, Wiry Ben shouldered his basket and left the workshop, quickly followed by Mum Taft and Sandy Jim. Seth lingered, and looked wistfully at Adam, as if he expected him to say something.

"Shalt go home before thee go'st to the preaching?" Adam asked, looking up.

"Nay; I've got my hat and things at Will Maskery's. I shan't be home before going for ten. I'll happen see Dinah Morris safe home, if she's willing. There's nobody comes with her from Poyser's, thee know'st."

"Then I'll tell mother not to look for thee," said Adam.

"Thee artna going to Poyser's thyself to-night?" said Seth rather timidly, as he turned to leave the workshop.

"Nay, I'm going to th' school."

Hitherto Gyp had kept his comfortable bed, only lifting up his head and watching Adam more closely as he noticed the other workmen departing. But no sooner did Adam put his ruler in his pocket, and begin to twist his apron round his waist, than Gyp ran forward and looked up in his master's face with patient expectation. If Gyp had had a tail he would doubtless have wagged it, but being destitute of that vehicle for his emotions, he was like many other worthy personages, destined to appear more phlegmatic than nature had made him.

"What! Art ready for the basket, eh, Gyp?" said Adam, with the same gentle modulation of voice as when he spoke to Seth.

Gyp jumped and gave a short bark, as much as to say, "Of course." Poor fellow, he had not a great range of expression.

The basket was the one which on workdays held Adam's and Seth's dinner; and no official, walking in procession, could look more resolutely unconscious of all acquaintances than Gyp with his basket, trotting at his master's heels.

On leaving the workshop Adam locked the door, took the key out, and carried it to the house on the other side of the woodyard. It was a low house, with smooth grey thatch and buff walls, looking pleasant and mellow in the evening light. The leaded windows were bright and speckless, and the door-stone was as clean as a white boulder at ebb tide. On the door-stone stood a clean old woman, in a dark-striped linen gown, a red kerchief, and a linen cap, talking to some speckled fowls which appeared to have been drawn towards her by an illusory expectation of cold potatoes or barley. The old woman's sight seemed to be dim, for she did not recognize Adam till he said, "Here's the key, Dolly; lay it down for me in the house, will you?"

"Aye, sure; but wunna ye come in, Adam? Miss Mary's i' th' house, and Mester Burge 'ull be back anon; he'd be glad t' ha' ye to supper wi'm, I'll be's warrand."

"No, Dolly, thank you; I'm off home. Good evening."

Adam hastened with long strides, Gyp close to his heels, out of the workyard, and along the highroad leading away from the village and down to the valley. As he reached the foot of the slope, an elderly horseman, with his portmanteau strapped behind him, stopped his horse when Adam had passed him, and turned round to have another long look at the stalwart workman in paper cap, leather breeches, and dark-blue worsted stockings.

Adam, unconscious of the admiration he was exciting, presently struck across the fields, and now broke out into the tune which had all day long been running in his head:

Let all thy converse be sincere,
Thy conscience as the noonday clear;
For God's all-seeing eye surveys
Thy secret thoughts, thy works and ways.

Chapter II The Preaching

About a quarter to seven there was an unusual appearance of excitement in the village of Hayslope, and through the whole length of its little street, from the Donnithorne Arms to the churchyard gate, the inhabitants had evidently been drawn out of their houses by something more than the pleasure of lounging in the evening sunshine. The Donnithorne Arms stood at the entrance of the village, and a small farmyard and stackyard which flanked it, indicating that there was a pretty take of land attached to the inn, gave the traveller a promise of good feed for himself and his horse, which might well console him for the ignorance in which the weather-beaten sign left him as to the heraldic bearings of that ancient family, the Donnithornes. Mr. Casson, the landlord, had been for some time standing at the door with his hands in his pockets, balancing himself on his heels and toes and looking towards a piece of unenclosed ground, with a maple in the middle of it, which he knew to be the destination of certain grave-looking men and women whom he had observed passing at intervals.

Mr. Casson's person was by no means of that common type which can be allowed to pass without description. On a front view it appeared to consist principally of two spheres, bearing about the same relation to each other as the earth and the moon: that is to say, the lower sphere might be said, at a rough guess, to be thirteen times larger than the upper which naturally performed the function of a mere satellite and tributary. But here the resemblance ceased, for Mr. Casson's head was not at all a melancholy-looking satellite nor was it a "spotty globe," as Milton has irreverently called the moon; on the contrary, no head and face could look more sleek and healthy, and its expression—which was chiefly confined to a pair of round and ruddy cheeks, the slight knot and interruptions forming the nose and eyes being scarcely worth mention—was one of jolly contentment, only tempered by that sense of personal dignity which usually made itself felt in his attitude and bearing. This sense of dignity could hardly be considered excessive in a man who had been butler to "the family" for fifteen years, and who, in his present high position, was necessarily very much in contact with his inferiors. How to reconcile his dignity with the satisfaction of his curiosity by walking towards the Green was the problem that Mr. Casson had been revolving in his mind for the last five minutes; but when he had partly solved it by taking his hands out of his pockets, and thrusting them into the armholes of his waistcoat, by throwing his head on one side, and providing himself with an air of contemptuous indifference to whatever might fall under his notice, his thoughts were diverted by the approach of the horseman whom we lately saw pausing to have another look at our friend Adam, and who now pulled up at the door of the Donnithorne Arms.

"Take off the bridle and give him a drink, ostler," said the traveller to the lad in a smock-frock, who had come out of the yard at the sound of the horse's hoofs.

"Why, what's up in your pretty village, landlord?" he continued, getting down. "There seems to be quite a stir."

"It's a Methodis' preaching, sir; it's been gev hout as a young woman's a-going to preach on the Green," answered Mr. Casson, in a treble and wheezy voice, with a slightly mincing accent. "Will you please to step in, sir, an' tek somethink?"

"No, I must be getting on to Rosseter. I only want a drink for my horse. And what does your parson say, I wonder, to a young woman preaching just under his nose?"

"Parson Irwine, sir, doesn't live here; he lives at Brox'on, over the hill there. The parsonage here's a tumble-down place, sir, not fit for gentry to live in. He comes here to preach of a Sunday afternoon, sir, an' puts up his hoss here. It's a grey cob, sir, an' he sets great store by't. He's allays put up his hoss here, sir, iver since before I hed the Donnithorne Arms. I'm not this countryman, you may tell by my tongue, sir. They're cur'ous talkers i' this country, sir; the gentry's hard work to hunderstand 'em. I was brought hup among the gentry, sir, an' got the turn o' their tongue when I was a bye. Why, what do you think the folks here says for 'hevn't you?'—the gentry, you know, says, 'hevn't you'—well, the people about here says 'hanna yey.' It's what they call the dileck as is spoke hereabout, sir. That's what I've heared Squire Donnithorne say many a time; it's the dileck, says he."

"Aye, aye," said the stranger, smiling. "I know it very well. But you've not got many Methodists about here, surely—in this agricultural spot? I should have thought there would hardly be such a thing as a Methodist to be found about here. You're all farmers, aren't you? The Methodists can seldom lay much hold on THEM."

"Why, sir, there's a pretty lot o' workmen round about, sir. There's Mester Burge as owns the timber-yard over there, he underteks a good bit o' building an' repairs. An' there's the stone-pits not far off. There's plenty of emply i' this countryside, sir. An' there's a fine batch o' Methodisses at Treddles'on—that's the market town about three mile off—you'll maybe ha' come through it, sir. There's pretty nigh a score of 'em on the Green now, as come from there. That's where our people gets it from, though there's only two men of 'em in all Hayslope: that's Will Maskery, the wheelwright, and Seth Bede, a young man as works at the carpenterin'."

"The preacher comes from Treddleston, then, does she?"

"Nay, sir, she comes out o' Stonyshire, pretty nigh thirty mile off. But she's a-visitin' hereabout at Mester Poyser's at the Hall Farm—it's them barns an' big walnut-trees, right away to the left, sir. She's own niece to Poyser's wife, an' they'll be fine an' vexed at her for making a fool of herself i' that way. But I've heared as there's no holding these Methodisses when the maggit's once got i' their head: many of 'em goes stark starin' mad wi' their religion. Though this young woman's quiet enough to look at, by what I can make out; I've not seen her myself."

"Well, I wish I had time to wait and see her, but I must get on. I've been out of my way for the last twenty minutes to have a look at that place in the valley. It's Squire Donnithorne's, I suppose?"

"Yes, sir, that's Donnithorne Chase, that is. Fine hoaks there, isn't there, sir? I should know what it is, sir, for I've lived butler there a-going i' fifteen year. It's Captain Donnithorne as is th' heir, sir—Squire Donnithorne's grandson. He'll be comin' of hage this 'ay-'arvest, sir, an' we shall hev fine doin's. He owns all the land about here, sir, Squire Donnithorne does."

"Well, it's a pretty spot, whoever may own it," said the traveller, mounting his horse; "and one meets some fine strapping fellows about too. I met as fine a young fellow as ever I saw in my life, about half an hour ago, before I came up the hill—a carpenter, a tall, broad-shouldered fellow with black hair and black eyes, marching along like a soldier. We want such fellows as he to lick the French."

"Aye, sir, that's Adam Bede, that is, I'll be bound—Thias Bede's son everybody knows him hereabout. He's an uncommon clever stiddy fellow, an' wonderful strong. Lord bless you, sir—if you'll hex-cuse me for saying so—he can walk forty mile a-day, an' lift a matter o' sixty ston'. He's an uncommon favourite wi' the gentry, sir: Captain Donnithorne and Parson Irwine meks a fine fuss wi' him. But he's a little lifted up an' peppery-like."

"Well, good evening to you, landlord; I must get on."

"Your servant, sir; good evenin'."

The traveller put his horse into a quick walk up the village, but when he approached the Green, the beauty of the view that lay on his right hand, the singular contrast presented by the groups of villagers with the knot of Methodists near the maple, and perhaps yet more, curiosity to see the young female preacher, proved too much for his anxiety to get to the end of his journey, and he paused.

The Green lay at the extremity of the village, and from it the road branched off in two directions, one leading farther up the hill by the church, and the other winding gently down towards the valley. On the side of the Green that led towards the church, the broken line of thatched cottages was continued nearly to the churchyard gate; but on the opposite northwestern side, there was nothing to obstruct the view of gently swelling meadow, and wooded valley, and dark masses of distant hill. That rich undulating district of Loamshire to which Hayslope belonged lies close to a grim outskirt of Stonyshire, over-looked by its barren hills as a pretty blooming sister may sometimes be seen linked in the arm of a rugged, tall, swarthy brother; and in two or three hours' ride the traveller might exchange a bleak treeless region, intersected by lines of cold grey stone, for one where his road wound under the shelter of woods, or up swelling hills, muffled with hedgerows and long meadow-grass and thick corn; and where at every turn he came upon some fine old country-seat nestled in the valley or crowning the slope, some homestead with its long length of barn and its cluster of golden ricks, some grey steeple looking out from a pretty confusion of trees and thatch and dark-red tiles. It was just such a picture as this last that Hayslope Church had made to the traveller as he began to mount the gentle slope leading to its pleasant uplands, and now from his station near the Green he had before him in one view nearly all the other typical features of this pleasant land. High up against the horizon were the huge conical masses of hill, like giant mounds intended to fortify this region of corn and grass against the keen and hungry winds of the north; not distant enough to be clothed in purple mystery, but with sombre greenish sides visibly specked with sheep, whose motion was only revealed by memory, not detected by sight; wooed from day to day by the changing hours, but responding with no change in themselves—left for ever grim and sullen after the flush of morning, the winged gleams of the April noonday, the parting crimson glory of the ripening summer sun. And directly below them the eye rested on a more advanced line of hanging woods, divided by bright patches of pasture or furrowed crops, and not yet deepened into the uniform leafy curtains of high summer, but still showing the warm tints of the young oak and the tender green of the ash and lime. Then came the valley, where the woods grew thicker, as if they had rolled down and hurried together from the patches left smooth on the slope, that they might take the better care of the tall mansion which lifted its parapets and sent its faint blue summer smoke among them. Doubtless there was a large sweep of park and a broad glassy pool in front of that mansion, but the swelling slope of meadow would not let our traveller see them from the village green. He saw instead a foreground which was just as lovely—the level sunlight lying like transparent gold among the gently curving stems of the feathered grass and the tall red sorrel, and the white ambels of the hemlocks lining the bushy hedgerows. It was that moment in summer when the sound of the scythe being whetted makes us cast more lingering looks at the flower-sprinkled tresses of the meadows.

He might have seen other beauties in the landscape if he had turned a little in his saddle and looked eastward, beyond Jonathan Burge's pasture and woodyard towards the green corn-fields and walnut-trees of the Hall Farm; but apparently there was more interest for him in the living groups close at hand. Every generation in the village was there, from old "Feyther Taft" in his brown worsted night-cap, who was bent nearly double, but seemed tough enough to keep on his legs a long while, leaning on his short stick, down to the babies with their little round heads lolling forward in quilted linen caps. Now and then there was a new arrival; perhaps a slouching labourer, who, having eaten his supper, came out to look at the unusual scene with a slow bovine gaze, willing to hear what any one had to say in explanation of it, but by no means excited enough to ask a question. But all took care not to join the Methodists on the Green, and identify themselves in that way with the expectant audience, for there was not one of them that would not have disclaimed the imputation of having come out to hear the "preacher woman"—they had only come out to see "what war a-goin' on, like." The men were chiefly gathered in the neighbourhood of the blacksmith's shop. But do not imagine them gathered in a knot. Villagers never swarm: a whisper is unknown among them, and they seem almost as incapable of an undertone as a cow or a stag. Your true rustic turns his back on his interlocutor, throwing a question over his shoulder as if he meant to run away from the answer, and walking a step or two farther off when the interest of the dialogue culminates. So the group in the vicinity of the blacksmith's door was by no means a close one, and formed no screen in front of Chad Cranage, the blacksmith himself, who stood with his black brawny arms folded, leaning against the door-post, and occasionally sending forth a bellowing laugh at his own jokes, giving them a marked preference over the sarcasms of Wiry Ben, who had renounced the pleasures of the Holly Bush for the sake of seeing life under a new form. But both styles of wit were treated with equal contempt by Mr. Joshua Rann. Mr. Rann's leathern apron and subdued griminess can leave no one in any doubt that he is the village shoemaker; the thrusting out of his chin and stomach and the twirling of his thumbs are more subtle indications, intended to prepare unwary strangers for the discovery that they are in the presence of the parish clerk. "Old Joshway," as he is irreverently called by his neighbours, is in a state of simmering indignation; but he has not yet opened his lips except to say, in a resounding bass undertone, like the tuning of a violoncello, "Sehon, King of the Amorites; for His mercy endureth for ever; and Og the King of Basan: for His mercy endureth for ever"—a quotation which may seem to have slight bearing on the present occasion, but, as with every other anomaly, adequate knowledge will show it to be a natural sequence. Mr. Rann was inwardly maintaining the dignity of the Church in the face of this scandalous irruption of

Methodism, and as that dignity was bound up with his own sonorous utterance of the responses, his argument naturally suggested a quotation from the psalm he had read the last Sunday afternoon.

The stronger curiosity of the women had drawn them quite to the edge of the Green, where they could examine more closely the Quakerlike costume and odd deportment of the female Methodists. Underneath the maple there was a small cart, which had been brought from the wheelwright's to serve as a pulpit, and round this a couple of benches and a few chairs had been placed. Some of the Methodists were resting on these, with their eyes closed, as if wrapt in prayer or meditation. Others chose to continue standing, and had turned their faces towards the villagers with a look of melancholy compassion, which was highly amusing to Bessy Cranage, the blacksmith's buxom daughter, known to her neighbours as Chad's Bess, who wondered "why the folks war amakin' faces a that'ns." Chad's Bess was the object of peculiar compassion, because her hair, being turned back under a cap which was set at the top of her head, exposed to view an ornament of which she was much prouder than of her red cheeks—namely, a pair of large round ear-rings with false garnets in them, ornaments condemned not only by the Methodists, but by her own cousin and namesake Timothy's Bess, who, with much cousinly feeling, often wished "them ear-rings" might come to good.

Timothy's Bess, though retaining her maiden appellation among her familiars, had long been the wife of Sandy Jim, and possessed a handsome set of matronly jewels, of which it is enough to mention the heavy baby she was rocking in her arms, and the sturdy fellow of five in kneebreeches, and red legs, who had a rusty milk-can round his neck by way of drum, and was very carefully avoided by Chad's small terrier. This young olive-branch, notorious under the name of Timothy's Bess's Ben, being of an inquiring disposition, unchecked by any false modesty, had advanced beyond the group of women and children, and was walking round the Methodists, looking up in their faces with his mouth wide open, and beating his stick against the milk-can by way of musical accompaniment. But one of the elderly women bending down to take him by the shoulder, with an air of grave remonstrance, Timothy's Bess's Ben first kicked out vigorously, then took to his heels and sought refuge behind his father's legs.

"Ye gallows young dog," said Sandy Jim, with some paternal pride, "if ye donna keep that stick quiet, I'll tek it from ye. What dy'e mane by kickin' foulks?"

"Here! Gie him here to me, Jim," said Chad Cranage; "I'll tie hirs up an' shoe him as I do th' hosses. Well, Mester Casson," he continued, as that personage sauntered up towards the group of men, "how are ye t' naight? Are ye coom t' help groon? They say folks allays groon when they're hearkenin' to th' Methodys, as if they war bad i' th' inside. I mane to groon as loud as your cow did th' other naight, an' then the praicher 'ull think I'm i' th' raight way."

"I'd advise you not to be up to no nonsense, Chad," said Mr. Casson, with some dignity; "Poyser wouldn't like to hear as his wife's niece was treated any ways disrespectful, for all he mayn't be fond of her taking on herself to preach."

"Aye, an' she's a pleasant-looked un too," said Wiry Ben. "I'll stick up for the pretty women preachin'; I know they'd persuade me over a deal sooner nor th' ugly men. I shouldna wonder if I turn Methody afore the night's out, an' begin to coort the preacher, like Seth Bede."

"Why, Seth's looking rether too high, I should think," said Mr. Casson. "This woman's kin wouldn't like her to demean herself to a common carpenter."

"Tchu!" said Ben, with a long treble intonation, "what's folks's kin got to do wi't? Not a chip. Poyser's wife may turn her nose up an' forget bygones, but this Dinah Morris, they tell me, 's as poor as iver she was—works at a mill, an's much ado to keep hersen. A strappin' young carpenter as is a ready-made Methody, like Seth, wouldna be a bad match for her. Why, Poysers make as big a fuss wi' Adam Bede as if he war a nevvy o' their own."

"Idle talk! idle talk!" said Mr. Joshua Rann. "Adam an' Seth's two men; you wunna fit them two wi' the same last."

"Maybe," said Wiry Ben, contemptuously, "but Seth's the lad for me, though he war a Methody twice o'er. I'm fair beat wi' Seth, for I've been teasin' him iver sin' we've been workin' together, an' he bears me no more malice nor a lamb. An' he's a stout-hearted feller too, for when we saw the old tree all afire a-comin' across the fields one night, an' we thought as it war a boguy, Seth made no more ado, but he up to't as bold as a constable. Why, there he comes out o' Will Maskery's;

an' there's Will hisself, lookin' as meek as if he couldna knock a nail o' the head for fear o' hurtin't. An' there's the pretty preacher woman! My eye, she's got her bonnet off. I mun go a bit nearer."

Several of the men followed Ben's lead, and the traveller pushed his horse on to the Green, as Dinah walked rather quickly and in advance of her companions towards the cart under the maple-tree. While she was near Seth's tall figure, she looked short, but when she had mounted the cart, and was away from all comparison, she seemed above the middle height of woman, though in reality she did not exceed it—an effect which was due to the slimness of her figure and the simple line of her black stuff dress. The stranger was struck with surprise as he saw her approach and mount the cart—surprise, not so much at the feminine delicacy of her appearance, as at the total absence of self-consciousness in her demeanour. He had made up his mind to see her advance with a measured step and a demure solemnity of countenance; he had felt sure that her face would be mantled with the smile of conscious saintship, or else charged with denunciatory bitterness. He knew but two types of Methodist—the ecstatic and the bilious. But Dinah walked as simply as if she were going to market, and seemed as unconscious of her outward appearance as a little boy: there was no blush, no tremulousness, which said, "I know you think me a pretty woman, too young to preach"; no casting up or down of the eyelids, no compression of the lips, no attitude of the arms that said, "But you must think of me as a saint." She held no book in her ungloved hands, but let them hang down lightly crossed before her, as she stood and turned her grey eyes on the people. There was no keenness in the eyes; they seemed rather to be shedding love than making observations; they had the liquid look which tells that the mind is full of what it has to give out, rather than impressed by external objects. She stood with her left hand towards the descending sun, and leafy boughs screened her from its rays; but in this sober light the delicate colouring of her face seemed to gather a calm vividness, like flowers at evening. It was a small oval face, of a uniform transparent whiteness, with an egglike line of cheek and chin, a full but firm mouth, a delicate nostril, and a low perpendicular brow, surmounted by a rising arch of parting between smooth locks of pale reddish hair. The hair was drawn straight back behind the ears, and covered, except for an inch or two above the brow, by a net Quaker cap. The eyebrows, of the same colour as the hair, were perfectly horizontal and firmly pencilled; the eyelashes, though no darker, were long and abundant—nothing was left blurred or unfinished. It was one of those faces that make one think of white flowers with light touches of colour on their pure petals. The eyes had no peculiar beauty, beyond that of expression; they looked so simple, so candid, so gravely loving, that no accusing scowl, no light sneer could help melting away before their glance. Joshua Rann gave a long cough, as if he were clearing his throat in order to come to a new understanding with himself; Chad Cranage lifted up his leather skull-cap and scratched his head; and Wiry Ben wondered how Seth had the pluck to think of courting her.

"A sweet woman," the stranger said to himself, "but surely nature never meant her for a preacher."

Perhaps he was one of those who think that nature has theatrical properties and, with the considerate view of facilitating art and psychology, "makes up," her characters, so that there may be no mistake about them. But Dinah began to speak.

"Dear friends," she said in a clear but not loud voice "let us pray for a blessing."

She closed her eyes, and hanging her head down a little continued in the same moderate tone, as if speaking to some one quite near her: "Saviour of sinners! When a poor woman laden with sins, went out to the well to draw water, she found Thee sitting at the well. She knew Thee not; she had not sought Thee; her mind was dark; her life was unholy. But Thou didst speak to her, Thou didst teach her, Thou didst show her that her life lay open before Thee, and yet Thou wast ready to give her that blessing which she had never sought. Jesus, Thou art in the midst of us, and Thou knowest all men: if there is any here like that poor woman—if their minds are dark, their lives unholy—if they have come out not seeking Thee, not desiring to be taught; deal with them according to the free mercy which Thou didst show to her Speak to them, Lord, open their ears to my message, bring their sins to their minds, and make them thirst for that salvation which Thou art ready to give.

"Lord, Thou art with Thy people still: they see Thee in the night-watches, and their hearts burn within them as Thou talkest with them by the way. And Thou art near to those who have not known Thee: open their eyes that they may see Thee—see Thee weeping over them, and saying 'Ye will not come unto me that ye might have life'—see Thee hanging on the cross and saying, 'Father, forgive them, for they know not what they do'—see Thee as Thou wilt come again in Thy glory to judge them at the last. Amen."

Dinah opened her eyes again and paused, looking at the group of villagers, who were now gathered rather more closely on her right hand.

"Dear friends," she began, raising her voice a little, "you have all of you been to church, and I think you must have heard the clergyman read these words: 'The Spirit of the Lord is upon me, because he hath anointed me to preach the gospel to the poor.' Jesus Christ spoke those words—he said he came TO PREACH THE GOSPEL TO THE POOR. I don't know whether you ever thought about those words much, but I will tell you when I remember first hearing them. It was on just such a sort of evening as this, when I was a little girl, and my aunt as brought me up took me to hear a good man preach out of doors, just as we are here. I remember his face well: he was a very old man, and had very long white hair; his voice was very soft and beautiful, not like any voice I had ever heard before. I was a little girl and scarcely knew anything, and this old man seemed to me such a different sort of a man from anybody I had ever seen before that I thought he had perhaps come down from the sky to preach to us, and I said, 'Aunt, will he go back to the sky to-night, like the picture in the Bible?'

"That man of God was Mr. Wesley, who spent his life in doing what our blessed Lord did—preaching the Gospel to the poor—and he entered into his rest eight years ago. I came to know more about him years after, but I was a foolish thoughtless child then, and I remembered only one thing he told us in his sermon. He told us as 'Gospel' meant 'good news.' The Gospel, you know, is what the Bible tells us about God.

"Think of that now! Jesus Christ did really come down from heaven, as I, like a silly child, thought Mr. Wesley did; and what he came down for was to tell good news about God to the poor. Why, you and me, dear friends, are poor. We have been brought up in poor cottages and have been reared on oat-cake, and lived coarse; and we haven't been to school much, nor read books, and we don't know much about anything but what happens just round us. We are just the sort of people that want to hear good news. For when anybody's well off, they don't much mind about hearing news from distant parts; but if a poor man or woman's in trouble and has hard work to make out a living, they like to have a letter to tell 'em they've got a friend as will help 'em. To be sure, we can't help knowing something about God, even if we've never heard the Gospel, the good news that our Saviour brought us. For we know everything comes from God: don't you say almost every day, 'This and that will happen, please God,' and 'We shall begin to cut the grass soon, please God to send us a little more sunshine'? We know very well we are altogether in the hands of God. We didn't bring ourselves into the world, we can't keep ourselves alive while we're sleeping; the daylight, and the wind, and the corn, and the cows to give us milk—everything we have comes from God. And he gave us our souls and put love between parents and children, and husband and wife. But is that as much as we want to know about God? We see he is great and mighty, and can do what he will: we are lost, as if we was struggling in great waters, when we try to think of him.

"But perhaps doubts come into your mind like this: Can God take much notice of us poor people? Perhaps he only made the world for the great and the wise and the rich. It doesn't cost him much to give us our little handful of victual and bit of clothing; but how do we know he cares for us any more than we care for the worms and things in the garden, so as we rear our carrots and onions? Will God take care of us when we die? And has he any comfort for us when we are lame and sick and helpless? Perhaps, too, he is angry with us; else why does the blight come, and the bad harvests, and the fever, and all sorts of pain and trouble? For our life is full of trouble, and if God sends us good, he seems to send bad too. How is it? How is it?

"Ah, dear friends, we are in sad want of good news about God; and what does other good news signify if we haven't that? For everything else comes to an end, and when we die we leave it all. But God lasts when everything else is gone. What shall we do if he is not our friend?"

Then Dinah told how the good news had been brought, and how the mind of God towards the poor had been made manifest in the life of Jesus, dwelling on its lowliness and its acts of mercy.

"So you see, dear friends," she went on, "Jesus spent his time almost all in doing good to poor people; he preached out of doors to them, and he made friends of poor workmen, and taught them and took pains with them. Not but what he did good to the rich too, for he was full of love to all men, only he saw as the poor were more in want of his help. So he cured the lame and the sick and the blind, and he worked miracles to feed the hungry because, he said, he was sorry for them; and he was very kind to the little children and comforted those who had lost their friends; and he spoke very tenderly to poor sinners that were sorry for their sins.

"Ah, wouldn't you love such a man if you saw him—if he were here in this village? What a kind heart he must have! What a friend he would be to go to in trouble! How pleasant it must be to be taught by him.

"Well, dear friends, who WAS this man? Was he only a good man—a very good man, and no more—like our dear Mr. Wesley, who has been taken from us? . . . He was the Son of God—'in the image of the Father,' the Bible says; that means, just like God, who is the beginning and end of all things—the God we want to know about. So then, all the love that Jesus showed to the poor is the same love that God has for us. We can understand what Jesus felt, because he came in a body like ours and spoke words such as we speak to each other. We were afraid to think what God was before—the God who made the world and the sky and the thunder and lightning. We could never see him; we could only see the things he had made; and some of these things was very terrible, so as we might well tremble when we thought of him. But our blessed Saviour has showed us what God is in a way us poor ignorant people can understand; he has showed us what God's heart is, what are his feelings towards us.

"But let us see a little more about what Jesus came on earth for. Another time he said, 'I came to seek and to save that which was lost';

and another time, 'I came not to call the righteous but sinners to repentance.'

"The LOST! . . . SINNERS! . . . Ah, dear friends, does that mean you and me?"

Hitherto the traveller had been chained to the spot against his will by the charm of Dinah's mellow treble tones, which had a variety of modulation like that of a fine instrument touched with the unconscious skill of musical instinct. The simple things she said seemed like novelties, as a melody strikes us with a new feeling when we hear it sung by the pure voice of a boyish chorister; the quiet depth of conviction with which she spoke seemed in itself an evidence for the truth of her message. He saw that she had thoroughly arrested her hearers. The villagers had pressed nearer to her, and there was no longer anything but grave attention on all faces. She spoke slowly, though quite fluently, often pausing after a question, or before any transition of ideas. There was no change of attitude, no gesture; the effect of her speech was produced entirely by the inflections of her voice, and when she came to the question, "Will God take care of us when we die?" she uttered it in such a tone of plaintive appeal that the tears came into some of the hardest eyes. The stranger had ceased to doubt, as he had done at the first glance, that she could fix the attention of her rougher hearers, but still he wondered whether she could have that power of rousing their more violent emotions, which must surely be a necessary seal of her vocation as a Methodist preacher, until she came to the words, "Lost!—Sinners!" when there was a great change in her voice and manner. She had made a long pause before the exclamation, and the pause seemed to be filled by agitating thoughts that showed themselves in her features. Her pale face became paler; the circles under her eyes deepened, as they did when tears half-gather without falling; and the mild loving eyes took an expression of appalled pity, as if she had suddenly discerned a destroying angel hovering over the heads of the people. Her voice became deep and muffled, but there was still no gesture. Nothing could be less like the ordinary type of the Ranter than Dinah. She was not preaching as she heard others preach, but speaking directly from her own emotions and under the inspiration of her own simple faith.

But now she had entered into a new current of feeling. Her manner became less calm, her utterance more rapid and agitated, as she tried to bring home to the people their guilt their wilful darkness, their state of disobedience to God—as she dwelt on the hatefulness of sin, the Divine holiness, and the sufferings of the Saviour, by which a way had been opened for their salvation. At last it seemed as if, in her yearning desire to reclaim the lost sheep, she could not be satisfied by addressing her hearers as a body. She appealed first to one and then to another, beseeching them with tears to turn to God while there was yet time; painting to them the desolation of their souls, lost in sin, feeding on the husks of this miserable world, far away from God their Father; and then the love of the Saviour, who was waiting and watching for their return.

There was many a responsive sigh and groan from her fellow-Methodists, but the village mind does not easily take fire, and a little smouldering vague anxiety that might easily die out again was the utmost effect Dinah's preaching had wrought in them at present. Yet no one had retired, except the children and "old Feyther Taft," who being too deaf to catch many words, had some time ago gone back to his inglenook. Wiry Ben was feeling very uncomfortable, and almost wishing he had not come to hear Dinah; he thought what she said would haunt him somehow. Yet he couldn't help liking to look at her and listen to her, though he dreaded every moment that she would fix her eyes on him and address him in particular. She had already addressed Sandy Jim, who was now holding the baby to relieve his wife, and the big soft-hearted man had rubbed away some tears with his fist, with a confused intention of being a better fellow, going less to the Holly Bush down by the Stone-pits, and cleaning himself more regularly of a Sunday.

In front of Sandy Jim stood Chad's Bess, who had shown an unwonted quietude and fixity of attention ever since Dinah had begun to speak. Not that the matter of the discourse had arrested her at once, for she was lost in a puzzling speculation as to what pleasure and satisfaction there could be in life to a young woman who wore a cap like Dinah's. Giving up this inquiry in despair, she took to studying Dinah's nose, eyes, mouth, and hair, and wondering whether it was better to have such a sort of pale face as that, or fat red cheeks and round black eyes like her own. But gradually the influence of the general gravity told upon her, and she became conscious of what Dinah was saying. The gentle tones, the loving persuasion, did not touch her, but when the more severe appeals came she began to be frightened. Poor Bessy had always been considered a naughty girl; she was conscious of it; if it was necessary to be very good, it was clear she must be in a bad way. She couldn't find her places at church as Sally Rann could, she had often been tittering when she "curcheyed" to Mr. Irwine; and these religious deficiencies were accompanied by a corresponding slackness in the minor morals, for Bessy belonged unquestionably to that unsoaped lazy class of feminine characters with whom you may venture to "eat an egg, an apple, or a nut." All this she was generally conscious of, and hitherto had not been greatly ashamed of it. But now she began to feel very much as if the constable had come to take her up and carry her before the justice for some undefined offence. She had a terrified sense that God, whom she had always thought of as very far off, was very near to her, and that Jesus was close by looking at her, though she could not see him. For Dinah had that belief in visible manifestations of Jesus, which is common among the Methodists, and she communicated it irresistibly to her hearers: she made them feel that he was among them bodily, and might at any moment show himself to them in some way that would strike anguish and penitence into their hearts.

"See!" she exclaimed, turning to the left, with her eyes fixed on a point above the heads of the people. "See where our blessed Lord stands and weeps and stretches out his arms towards you. Hear what he says: 'How often would I have gathered you as a hen gathereth her chickens under her wings, and ye would not!' . . . and ye would not," she repeated, in a tone of pleading reproach, turning her eyes on the people again. "See the print of the nails on his dear hands and feet. It is your sins that made them! Ah! How pale and worn he looks! He has gone through all that great agony in the garden, when his soul was exceeding sorrowful even unto death, and the great drops of sweat fell like blood to the ground. They spat upon him and buffeted him, they scourged him, they mocked him, they laid the heavy cross on his bruised shoulders. Then they nailed him up. Ah, what pain! His lips are parched with thirst, and they mock him still in this great agony; yet with those parched lips he prays for them, 'Father, forgive them, for they know not what they do.' Then a horror of great darkness fell upon him, and he felt what sinners feel when they are for ever shut out from God. That was the last drop in the cup of bitterness. 'My God, my God!' he cries, 'why hast Thou forsaken me?'

"All this he bore for you! For you—and you never think of him; for you—and you turn your backs on him; you don't care what he has gone through for you. Yet he is not weary of toiling for you: he has risen from the dead, he is praying for you at the right hand of God—'Father, forgive them, for they know not what they do.' And he is upon this earth too; he is among us; he is there close to you now; I see his wounded body and his look of love."

Here Dinah turned to Bessy Cranage, whose bonny youth and evident vanity had touched her with pity.

"Poor child! Poor child! He is beseeching you, and you don't listen to him. You think of ear-rings and fine gowns and caps, and you never think of the Saviour who died to save your precious soul. Your cheeks will be shrivelled one day, your hair will be grey, your poor body will be thin and tottering! Then you will begin to feel that your soul is not saved; then you will have to stand before God dressed in your sins, in your evil tempers and vain thoughts. And Jesus, who stands ready to help you now, won't help you then; because you won't have him to be your Saviour, he will be your judge. Now he looks at you with love and mercy and says, 'Come to me that you may have life'; then he will turn away from you, and say, 'Depart from me into ever-lasting fire!'"

Poor Bessy's wide-open black eyes began to fill with tears, her great red cheeks and lips became quite pale, and her face was distorted like a little child's before a burst of crying.

"Ah, poor blind child!" Dinah went on, "think if it should happen to you as it once happened to a servant of God in the days of her vanity. SHE thought of her lace caps and saved all her money to buy 'em; she thought nothing about how she might get a clean heart and a right spirit—she only wanted to have better lace than other girls. And one day when she put her new cap on and looked in the glass, she saw a bleeding Face crowned with thorns. That face is looking at you now"—here Dinah pointed to a spot close in front of Bessy—"Ah, tear off those follies! Cast them away from you, as if they were stinging adders. They ARE stinging you—they are poisoning your soul—they are dragging you down into a dark bottomless pit, where you will sink for ever, and for ever, and for ever, further away from light and God."

Bessy could bear it no longer: a great terror was upon her, and wrenching her ear-rings from her ears, she threw them down before her, sobbing aloud. Her father, Chad, frightened lest he should be "laid hold on" too, this impression on the rebellious Bess striking him as nothing less than a miracle, walked hastily away and began to work at his anvil by way of reassuring himself. "Folks mun ha' hoss-shoes, praichin' or no praichin': the divil canna lay hould o' me for that," he muttered to himself.

But now Dinah began to tell of the joys that were in store for the penitent, and to describe in her simple way the divine peace and love with which the soul of the believer is filled—how the sense of God's love turns poverty into riches and satisfies the soul so that no uneasy desire vexes it, no fear alarms it: how, at last, the very temptation to sin is extinguished, and heaven is begun upon earth, because no cloud passes between the soul and God, who is its eternal sun.

"Dear friends," she said at last, "brothers and sisters, whom I love as those for whom my Lord has died, believe me, I know what this great blessedness is; and because I know it, I want you to have it too. I am poor, like you: I have to get my living with my hands; but no lord nor lady can be so happy as me, if they haven't got the love of God in their souls. Think what it is—not to hate anything but sin; to be full of love to every creature; to be frightened at nothing; to be sure that all things will turn to good; not to mind pain, because it is our Father's will; to know that nothing—no, not if the earth was to be burnt up, or the waters come and drown us—nothing could part us from God who loves us, and who fills our souls with peace and joy, because we are sure that whatever he wills is holy, just, and good.

"Dear friends, come and take this blessedness; it is offered to you; it is the good news that Jesus came to preach to the poor. It is not like the riches of this world, so that the more one gets the less the rest can have. God is without end; his love is without end—

Its streams the whole creation reach,
So plenteous is the store;
Enough for all, enough for each,
Enough for evermore.

Dinah had been speaking at least an hour, and the reddening light of the parting day seemed to give a solemn emphasis to her closing words. The stranger, who had been interested in the course of her sermon as if it had been the development of a drama—for there is this sort of fascination in all sincere unpremeditated eloquence, which opens to one the inward drama of the speaker's emotions—now turned his horse aside and pursued his way, while Dinah said, "Let us sing a little, dear friends"; and as he was still winding down the slope, the voices of the Methodists reached him, rising and falling in that strange blending of exultation and sadness which belongs to the cadence of a hymn.

Chapter III After the Preaching

IN less than an hour from that time, Seth Bede was walking by Dinah's side along the hedgerow-path that skirted the pastures and green corn-fields which lay between the village and the Hall Farm. Dinah had taken off her little Quaker bonnet again, and was holding it in her hands that she might have a freer enjoyment of the cool evening twilight, and Seth could see the expression of her face quite clearly as he walked by her side, timidly revolving something he wanted to say to her. It was an expression of unconscious placid gravity—of absorption in thoughts that had no connection with the present moment or with her own personality—an expression that is most of all discouraging to a lover. Her very walk was discouraging: it had that quiet elasticity that asks for no support. Seth felt this dimly; he said to himself, "She's too good and holy for any man, let alone me," and the words he had been summoning rushed back again before they had reached his lips. But another thought gave him courage: "There's no man could love her better and leave her freer to follow the Lord's work." They had been silent for many minutes now, since they had done talking about Bessy Cranage; Dinah seemed almost to have forgotten Seth's presence, and her pace was becoming so much quicker that the sense of their being only a few minutes' walk from the yard-gates of the Hall Farm at last gave Seth courage to speak.

"You've quite made up your mind to go back to Snowfield o' Saturday, Dinah?"

"Yes," said Dinah, quietly. "I'm called there. It was borne in upon my mind while I was meditating on Sunday night, as Sister Allen, who's in a decline, is in need of me. I saw her as plain as we see that bit of thin white cloud, lifting up her poor thin hand and beckoning to me. And this morning when I opened the Bible for direction, the first words my eyes fell on were, 'And after we had seen the vision, immediately we endeavoured to go into Macedonia.' If it wasn't for that clear showing of the Lord's will, I should be loath to go, for my heart yearns over my aunt and her little ones, and that poor wandering lamb Hetty Sorrel. I've been much drawn out in prayer for her of late, and I look on it as a token that there may be mercy in store for her."

"God grant it," said Seth. "For I doubt Adam's heart is so set on her, he'll never turn to anybody else; and yet it 'ud go to my heart if he was to marry her, for I canna think as she'd make him happy. It's a deep mystery—the way the heart of man turns to one woman out of all the rest he's seen i' the world, and makes it easier for him to work seven year for HER, like Jacob did for Rachel, sooner than have any other woman for th' asking. I often think of them words, 'And Jacob served seven years for Rachel; and they seemed to him but a few days for the love he had to her.' I know those words 'ud come true with me, Dinah, if so be you'd give me hope as I might win you after seven years was over. I know you think a husband 'ud be taking up too much o' your thoughts, because St. Paul says, 'She that's married careth for the things of the world how she may please her husband'; and may happen you'll think me overbold to speak to you about it again, after what you told me o' your mind last Saturday. But I've been thinking it over again by night and by day, and I've prayed not to be blinded by my own desires, to think what's only good for me must be good for you too. And it seems to me there's more texts for your marrying than ever you can find against it. For St. Paul says as plain as can be in another place, 'I will that the younger women marry, bear children, guide the house, give none occasion to the adversary to speak reproachfully'; and then 'two are better than one'; and that holds good with marriage as well as with other things. For we should be o' one heart and o' one mind, Dinah. We both serve the same Master, and are striving after the same gifts; and I'd never be the husband to make a claim on you as could interfere with your doing the work God has fitted you for. I'd make a shift, and fend indoor and out, to give you more liberty—more than you can have now, for you've got to get your own living now, and I'm strong enough to work for us both."

When Seth had once begun to urge his suit, he went on earnestly and almost hurriedly, lest Dinah should speak some decisive word before he had poured forth all the arguments he had prepared. His cheeks became flushed as he went on his mild grey eyes filled with tears, and his voice trembled as he spoke the last sentence. They had reached one of those very narrow passes between two tall stones, which performed the office of a stile in Loamshire, and Dinah paused as she turned towards Seth and said, in her tender but calm treble notes, "Seth Bede, I thank you for your love towards me, and if I could think of any man as more than a Christian brother, I think it would be you. But my heart is not free to marry. That is good for other women, and it is a great and a blessed thing to be a wife and mother; but 'as God has distributed to every man, as the Lord hath called every man, so let him walk.' God has called me to minister to others, not to have any joys or sorrows of my own, but to rejoice with them that do rejoice, and to weep with those that weep. He has called me to speak his word, and he has greatly owned my work. It could only be on a very clear showing that I could leave the brethren and sisters at Snowfield, who are favoured with very little of this world's good; where the trees are few, so that a child might count them, and there's very hard living for the poor in the winter. It has been given me to help, to comfort, and strengthen the little flock there and to call in many wanderers; and my soul is filled with these things from my rising up till my lying down. My life is too short, and God's work is too great for me to think of making a home for myself in this world. I've not turned a deaf ear to your words, Seth, for when I saw as your love was given to me, I thought it might be a leading of Providence for me to change my way of life, and that we should be fellow-helpers; and I spread the matter before the Lord. But whenever I tried to fix my mind on marriage, and our living together, other thoughts always came in—the times when I've prayed by the sick and dying, and the happy hours I've had preaching, when my heart was filled with love, and the Word was given to me abundantly. And when I've opened the Bible for direction, I've always lighted on some clear word to tell me where my work lay. I believe what you say, Seth, that you would try to be a help and not a hindrance to my work; but I see that our marriage is not God's will—He draws my heart another way. I desire to live and die without husband or children. I seem to have no room in my soul for wants and fears of my own, it has pleased God to fill my heart so full with the wants and sufferings of his poor people."

Seth was unable to reply, and they walked on in silence. At last, as they were nearly at the yard-gate, he said, "Well, Dinah, I must seek for strength to bear it, and to endure as seeing Him who is invisible. But I feel now how weak my faith is. It seems as if, when you are gone, I could never joy in anything any more. I think it's something passing the love of women as I feel for you, for I could be content without your marrying me if I could go and live at Snowfield and be near you. I trusted as the strong love God has given me towards you was a leading for us both; but it seems it was only meant for my trial. Perhaps I feel more for you than I ought to feel for any creature, for I often can't help saying of you what the hymn says—

In darkest shades if she appear,
My dawning is begun;
She is my soul's bright morning-star,
And she my rising sun.

That may be wrong, and I am to be taught better. But you wouldn't be displeased with me if things turned out so as I could leave this country and go to live at Snowfield?"

"No, Seth; but I counsel you to wait patiently, and not lightly to leave your own country and kindred. Do nothing without the Lord's clear bidding. It's a bleak and barren country there, not like this land of Goshen you've been used to. We mustn't be in a hurry to fix and choose our own lot; we must wait to be guided."

"But you'd let me write you a letter, Dinah, if there was anything I wanted to tell you?"

"Yes, sure; let me know if you're in any trouble. You'll be continually in my prayers."

They had now reached the yard-gate, and Seth said, "I won't go in, Dinah, so farewell." He paused and hesitated after she had given him her hand, and then said, "There's no knowing but what you may see things different after a while. There may be a new leading."

"Let us leave that, Seth. It's good to live only a moment at a time, as I've read in one of Mr. Wesley's books. It isn't for you and me to lay plans; we've nothing to do but to obey and to trust. Farewell."

Dinah pressed his hand with rather a sad look in her loving eyes, and then passed through the gate, while Seth turned away to walk lingeringly home. But instead of taking the direct road, he chose to turn back along the fields through which he and Dinah had already passed; and I think his blue linen handkerchief was very wet with tears long before he had made up his mind that it was time for him to set his face steadily homewards. He was but three-and-twenty, and had only just learned what it is to love—to love with that adoration which a young man gives to a woman whom he feels to be greater and better than himself. Love of this sort is hardly distinguishable from religious feeling. What deep and worthy love is so, whether of woman or child, or art or music. Our caresses, our tender words, our still rapture under the influence of autumn sunsets, or pillared vistas, or calm majestic statues, or Beethoven symphonies all bring with them the consciousness that they are mere waves and ripples in an unfathomable ocean of love and beauty; our emotion in its keenest moment passes from expression into silence, our love at its highest flood rushes beyond its object and loses itself in the sense of divine mystery. And this blessed gift of venerating love has been given to too many humble craftsmen since the world began for us to feel any surprise that it should have existed in the soul of a Methodist carpenter half a century ago, while there was yet a lingering after-glow from the time when Wesley and his fellow-labourer fed on the hips and haws of the Cornwall hedges, after exhausting limbs and lungs in carrying a divine message to the poor.

That afterglow has long faded away; and the picture we are apt to make of Methodism in our imagination is not an amphitheatre of green hills, or the deep shade of broad-leaved sycamores, where a crowd of rough men and weary-hearted women drank in a faith which was a rudimentary culture, which linked their thoughts with the past, lifted their imagination above the sordid details of their own narrow lives, and suffused their souls with the sense of a pitying, loving, infinite Presence, sweet as summer to the houseless needy. It is too possible that to some of my readers Methodism may mean nothing more than low-pitched gables up dingy streets, sleek grocers, sponging preachers, and hypocritical jargon—elements which are regarded as an exhaustive analysis of Methodism in many fashionable quarters.

That would be a pity; for I cannot pretend that Seth and Dinah were anything else than Methodists—not indeed of that modern type which reads quarterly reviews and attends in chapels with pillared porticoes, but of a very old-fashioned kind. They believed in present miracles, in instantaneous conversions, in revelations by dreams and visions; they drew lots, and sought for Divine guidance by opening the Bible at hazard; having a literal way of interpreting the Scriptures, which is not at all sanctioned by approved commentators; and it is impossibie for me to represent their diction as correct, or their instruction as liberal. Still—if I have read religious history aright—faith, hope, and charity have not always been found in a direct ratio with a sensibility to the three concords, and it is possible—thank Heaven!—to have very erroneous theories and very sublime feelings. The raw bacon which clumsy Molly spares from her own scanty store that she may carry it to her neighbour's child to "stop the fits," may be a piteously inefficacious remedy; but the generous stirring of neighbourly kindness that prompted the deed has a beneficent radiation that is not lost.

Considering these things, we can hardly think Dinah and Seth beneath our sympathy, accustomed as we may be to weep over the loftier sorrows of heroines in satin boots and crinoline, and of heroes riding fiery horses, themselves ridden by still more fiery passions.

Poor Seth! He was never on horseback in his life except once, when he was a little lad, and Mr. Jonathan Burge took him up behind, telling him to "hold on tight"; and instead of bursting out into wild accusing apostrophes to God and destiny, he is resolving, as he now walks homewards under the solemn starlight, to repress his sadness, to be less bent on having his own will, and to live more for others, as Dinah does.

Chapter IV Home and Its Sorrows

A GREEN valley with a brook running through it, full almost to overflowing with the late rains, overhung by low stooping willows. Across this brook a plank is thrown, and over this plank Adam Bede is passing with his undoubting step, followed close by Gyp with the basket; evidently making his way to the thatched house, with a stack of timber by the side of it, about twenty yards up the opposite slope.

The door of the house is open, and an elderly woman is looking out; but she is not placidly contemplating the evening sunshine; she has been watching with dim eyes the gradually enlarging speck which for the last few minutes she has been quite sure is her darling son Adam. Lisbeth Bede loves her son with the love of a woman to whom her first-born has come late in life. She is an anxious, spare, yet vigorous old woman, clean as a snowdrop. Her grey hair is turned neatly back under a pure linen cap with a black band round it; her broad chest is covered with a buff neckerchief, and below this you see a sort of short bedgown made of blue-checkered linen, tied round the waist and descending to the hips, from whence there is a considerable length of linsey-woolsey petticoat. For Lisbeth is tall, and in other points too there is a strong likeness between her and her son Adam. Her dark eyes are somewhat dim now—perhaps from too much crying—but her broadly marked eyebrows are still black, her teeth are sound, and as she stands knitting rapidly and unconsciously with her work-hardened hands, she has as firmly upright an attitude as when she is carrying a pail of water on her head from the spring. There is the same type of frame and the same keen activity of temperament in mother and son, but it was not from her that Adam got his well-filled brow and his expression of large-hearted intelligence.

Family likeness has often a deep sadness in it. Nature, that great tragic dramatist, knits us together by bone and muscle, and divides us by the subtler web of our brains; blends yearning and repulsion; and ties us by our heart-strings to the beings that jar us at every movement. We hear a voice with the very cadence of our own uttering the thoughts we despise; we see eyes—ah, so like our mother's!—averted from us in cold alienation; and our last darling child startles us with the air and gestures of the sister we parted from in bitterness long years ago. The father to whom we owe our best heritage—the mechanical instinct, the keen sensibility to harmony, the unconscious skill of the modelling hand—galls us and puts us to shame by his daily errors; the long-lost mother, whose face we begin to see in the glass as our own wrinkles come, once fretted our young souls with her anxious humours and irrational persistence.

It is such a fond anxious mother's voice that you hear, as Lisbeth says, "Well, my lad, it's gone seven by th' clock. Thee't allays stay till the last child's born. Thee wants thy supper, I'll warrand. Where's Seth? Gone arter some o's chapellin', I reckon?"

"Aye, aye, Seth's at no harm, mother, thee mayst be sure. But where's father?" said Adam quickly, as he entered the house and glanced into the room on the left hand, which was used as a workshop. "Hasn't he done the coffin for Tholer? There's the stuff standing just as I left it this morning."

"Done the coffin?" said Lisbeth, following him, and knitting uninterruptedly, though she looked at her son very anxiously. "Eh, my lad, he went aff to Treddles'on this forenoon, an's niver come back. I doubt he's got to th' 'Waggin Overthrow' again."

A deep flush of anger passed rapidly over Adam's face. He said nothing, but threw off his jacket and began to roll up his shirt-sleeves again.

"What art goin' to do, Adam?" said the mother, with a tone and look of alarm. "Thee wouldstna go to work again, wi'out ha'in thy bit o' supper?"

Adam, too angry to speak, walked into the workshop. But his mother threw down her knitting, and, hurrying after him, took hold of his arm, and said, in a tone of plaintive remonstrance, "Nay, my lad, my lad, thee munna go wi'out thy supper; there's the taters wi' the gravy in 'em, just as thee lik'st 'em. I saved 'em o' purpose for thee. Come an' ha' thy supper, come."

"Let be!" said Adam impetuously, shaking her off and seizing one of the planks that stood against the wall. "It's fine talking about having supper when here's a coffin promised to be ready at Brox'on by seven o'clock to-morrow morning, and ought to ha' been there now, and not a nail struck yet. My throat's too full to swallow victuals."

"Why, thee canstna get the coffin ready," said Lisbeth. "Thee't work thyself to death. It 'ud take thee all night to do't."

"What signifies how long it takes me? Isn't the coffin promised? Can they bury the man without a coffin? I'd work my right hand off sooner than deceive people with lies i' that way. It makes me mad to think on't. I shall overrun these doings before long. I've stood enough of 'em."

Poor Lisbeth did not hear this threat for the first time, and if she had been wise she would have gone away quietly and said nothing for the next hour. But one of the lessons a woman most rarely learns is never to talk to an angry or a drunken man. Lisbeth sat down on the chopping bench and began to cry, and by the time she had cried enough to make her voice very piteous, she burst out into words.

"Nay, my lad, my lad, thee wouldstna go away an' break thy mother's heart, an' leave thy feyther to ruin. Thee wouldstna ha' 'em carry me to th' churchyard, an' thee not to follow me. I shanna rest i' my grave if I donna see thee at th' last; an' how's they to let thee know as I'm a-dyin', if thee't gone a-workin' i' distant parts, an' Seth belike gone arter thee, and thy feyther not able to hold a pen for's hand shakin', besides not knowin' where thee art? Thee mun forgie thy feyther—thee munna be so bitter again' him. He war a good feyther to thee afore he took to th' drink. He's a clever workman, an' taught thee thy trade, remember, an's niver gen me a blow nor so much as an ill word—no, not even in 's drink. Thee wouldstna ha' 'm go to the workhus—thy own feyther—an' him as was a fine-growed man an' handy at everythin' amost as thee art thysen, five-an'-twenty 'ear ago, when thee wast a baby at the breast."

Lisbeth's voice became louder, and choked with sobs—a sort of wail, the most irritating of all sounds where real sorrows are to be borne and real work to be done. Adam broke in impatiently.

"Now, Mother, don't cry and talk so. Haven't I got enough to vex me without that? What's th' use o' telling me things as I only think too much on every day? If I didna think on 'em, why should I do as I do, for the sake o' keeping things together here? But I hate to be talking where it's no use: I like to keep my breath for doing i'stead o' talking."

"I know thee dost things as nobody else 'ud do, my lad. But thee't allays so hard upo' thy feyther, Adam. Thee think'st nothing too much to do for Seth: thee snapp'st me up if iver I find faut wi' th' lad. But thee't so angered wi' thy feyther, more nor wi' anybody else."

"That's better than speaking soft and letting things go the wrong way, I reckon, isn't it? If I wasn't sharp with him he'd sell every bit o' stuff i' th' yard and spend it on drink. I know there's a duty to be done by my father, but it isn't my duty to encourage him in running headlong to ruin. And what has Seth got to do with it? The lad does no harm as I know of. But leave me alone, Mother, and let me get on with the work."

Lisbeth dared not say any more; but she got up and called Gyp, thinking to console herself somewhat for Adam's refusal of the supper she had spread out in the loving expectation of looking at him while he ate it, by feeding Adam's dog with extra liberality. But Gyp was watching his master with wrinkled brow and ears erect, puzzled at this unusual course of things; and though he glanced at Lisbeth when she called him, and moved his fore-paws uneasily, well knowing that she was inviting him to supper, he was in a divided state of mind, and remained seated on his haunches, again fixing his eyes anxiously on his master. Adam noticed Gyp's mental conflict, and though his anger had made him less tender than usual to his mother, it did not prevent him from caring as much as usual for his dog. We are apt to be kinder to the brutes that love us than to the women that love us. Is it because the brutes are dumb?

"Go, Gyp; go, lad!" Adam said, in a tone of encouraging command; and Gyp, apparently satisfied that duty and pleasure were one, followed Lisbeth into the house-place.

But no sooner had he licked up his supper than he went back to his master, while Lisbeth sat down alone to cry over her knitting. Women who are never bitter and resentful are often the most querulous; and if Solomon was as wise as he is reputed to be, I feel sure that when he compared a contentious woman to a continual dropping on a very rainy day, he had not a vixen in his eye—a fury with long nails, acrid and selfish. Depend upon it, he meant a good creature, who had no joy but in the happiness of the loved ones whom she contributed to make uncomfortable, putting by all the tid-bits for them and spending nothing on herself. Such a woman as Lisbeth, for example—at once patient and complaining, self-renouncing and exacting, brooding the livelong day over what happened yesterday and what is likely to happen to-morrow, and crying very readily both at the good and the evil. But a certain awe mingled itself with her idolatrous love of Adam, and when he said, "Leave me alone," she was always silenced.

So the hours passed, to the loud ticking of the old day-clock and the sound of Adam's tools. At last he called for a light and a draught of water (beer was a thing only to be drunk on holidays), and Lisbeth ventured to say as she took it in, "Thy supper stan's ready for thee, when thee lik'st."

"Donna thee sit up, mother," said Adam, in a gentle tone. He had worked off his anger now, and whenever he wished to be especially kind to his mother, he fell into his strongest native accent and dialect, with which at other times his speech was less deeply tinged. "I'll see to Father when he comes home; maybe he wonna come at all to-night. I shall be easier if thee't i' bed."

"Nay, I'll bide till Seth comes. He wonna be long now, I reckon."

It was then past nine by the clock, which was always in advance of the days, and before it had struck ten the latch was lifted and Seth entered. He had heard the sound of the tools as he was approaching.

"Why, Mother," he said, "how is it as Father's working so late?"

"It's none o' thy feyther as is a-workin'—thee might know that well anoof if thy head warna full o' chapellin'—it's thy brother as does iverything, for there's niver nobody else i' th' way to do nothin'."

Lisbeth was going on, for she was not at all afraid of Seth, and usually poured into his ears all the querulousness which was repressed by her awe of Adam. Seth had never in his life spoken a harsh word to his mother, and timid people always wreak their peevishness on the gentle. But Seth, with an anxious look, had passed into the workshop and said, "Addy, how's this? What! Father's forgot the coffin?"

"Aye, lad, th' old tale; but I shall get it done," said Adam, looking up and casting one of his bright keen glances at his brother. "Why, what's the matter with thee? Thee't in trouble."

Seth's eyes were red, and there was a look of deep depression on his mild face.

"Yes, Addy, but it's what must be borne, and can't be helped. Why, thee'st never been to the school, then?"

"School? No, that screw can wait," said Adam, hammering away again.

"Let me take my turn now, and do thee go to bed," said Seth.

"No, lad, I'd rather go on, now I'm in harness. Thee't help me to carry it to Brox'on when it's done. I'll call thee up at sunrise. Go and eat thy supper, and shut the door so as I mayn't hear Mother's talk."

Seth knew that Adam always meant what he said, and was not to be persuaded into meaning anything else. So he turned, with rather a heavy heart, into the house-place.

"Adam's niver touched a bit o' victual sin' home he's come," said Lisbeth. "I reckon thee'st hed thy supper at some o' thy Methody folks."

"Nay, Mother," said Seth, "I've had no supper yet."

"Come, then," said Lisbeth, "but donna thee ate the taters, for Adam 'ull happen ate 'em if I leave 'em stannin'. He loves a bit o' taters an' gravy. But he's been so sore an' angered, he wouldn't ate 'em, for all I'd putten 'em by o' purpose for him. An' he's been a-threatenin' to go away again," she went on, whimpering, "an' I'm fast sure he'll go some dawnin' afore I'm up, an' niver let me know aforehand, an' he'll niver come back again when once he's gone. An' I'd better niver ha' had a son, as is like no other body's son for the deftness an' th' handiness, an' so looked on by th' grit folks, an' tall an' upright like a poplar-tree, an' me to be parted from him an' niver see 'm no more."

"Come, Mother, donna grieve thyself in vain," said Seth, in a soothing voice. "Thee'st not half so good reason to think as Adam 'ull go away as to think he'll stay with thee. He may say such a thing when he's in wrath—and he's got excuse for being wrathful sometimes—but his heart 'ud never let him go. Think how he's stood by us all when it's been none so easy—paying his savings to free me from going for a soldier, an' turnin' his earnin's into wood for father, when he's got plenty o' uses for his money, and many a young man like him 'ud ha' been married and settled before now. He'll never turn round and knock down his own work, and forsake them as it's been the labour of his life to stand by."

"Donna talk to me about's marr'in'," said Lisbeth, crying afresh. "He's set's heart on that Hetty Sorrel, as 'ull niver save a penny, an' 'ull toss up her head at's old mother. An' to think as he might ha' Mary Burge, an' be took partners, an' be a big man wi' workmen under him, like Mester Burge—Dolly's told me so o'er and o'er again—if it warna as he's set's heart on that bit of a wench, as is o' no more use nor the gillyflower on the wall. An' he so wise at bookin' an' figurin', an' not to know no better nor that!"

"But, Mother, thee know'st we canna love just where other folks 'ud have us. There's nobody but God can control the heart of man. I could ha' wished myself as Adam could ha' made another choice, but I wouldn't reproach him for what he can't help. And I'm not sure but what he tries to o'ercome it. But it's a matter as he doesn't like to be spoke to about, and I can only pray to the Lord to bless and direct him."

"Aye, thee't allays ready enough at prayin', but I donna see as thee gets much wi' thy prayin'. Thee wotna get double earnin's o' this side Yule. Th' Methodies 'll niver make thee half the man thy brother is, for all they're a-makin' a preacher on thee."

"It's partly truth thee speak'st there, Mother," said Seth, mildly; "Adam's far before me, an's done more for me than I can ever do for him. God distributes talents to every man according as He sees good. But thee mustna undervally prayer. Prayer mayna bring money, but it brings us what no money can buy—a power to keep from sin and be content with God's will, whatever He may please to send. If thee wouldst pray to God to help thee, and trust in His goodness, thee wouldstna be so uneasy about things."

"Unaisy? I'm i' th' right on't to be unaisy. It's well seen on THEE what it is niver to be unaisy. Thee't gi' away all thy earnin's, an' niver be unaisy as thee'st nothin' laid up again' a rainy day. If Adam had been as aisy as thee, he'd niver ha' had no money to pay for thee. Take no thought for the morrow—take no thought—that's what thee't allays sayin'; an' what comes on't? Why, as Adam has to take thought for thee."

"Those are the words o' the Bible, Mother," said Seth. "They don't mean as we should be idle. They mean we shouldn't be overanxious and worreting ourselves about what'll happen to-morrow, but do our duty and leave the rest to God's will."

"Aye, aye, that's the way wi' thee: thee allays makes a peck o' thy own words out o' a pint o' the Bible's. I donna see how thee't to know as 'take no thought for the morrow' means all that. An' when the Bible's such a big book, an' thee canst read all thro't, an' ha' the pick o' the texes, I canna think why thee dostna pick better words as donna mean so much more nor they say. Adam doesna pick a that'n; I can understan' the tex as he's allays a-sayin', 'God helps them as helps theirsens.'"

"Nay, Mother," said Seth, "that's no text o' the Bible. It comes out of a book as Adam picked up at the stall at Treddles'on. It was wrote by a knowing man, but overworldly, I doubt. However, that saying's partly true; for the Bible tells us we must be workers together with God."

"Well, how'm I to know? It sounds like a tex. But what's th' matter wi' th' lad? Thee't hardly atin' a bit o' supper. Dostna mean to ha' no more nor that bit o' oat-cake? An' thee lookst as white as a flick o' new bacon. What's th' matter wi' thee?"

"Nothing to mind about, Mother; I'm not hungry. I'll just look in at Adam again, and see if he'll let me go on with the coffin."

"Ha' a drop o' warm broth?" said Lisbeth, whose motherly feeling now got the better of her "nattering" habit. "I'll set two-three sticks a-light in a minute."

"Nay, Mother, thank thee; thee't very good," said Seth, gratefully; and encouraged by this touch of tenderness, he went on: "Let me pray a bit with thee for Father, and Adam, and all of us—it'll comfort thee, happen, more than thee thinkst."

"Well, I've nothin' to say again' it."

Lisbeth, though disposed always to take the negative side in her conversations with Seth, had a vague sense that there was some comfort and safety in the fact of his piety, and that it somehow relieved her from the trouble of any spiritual transactions on her own behalf.

So the mother and son knelt down together, and Seth prayed for the poor wandering father and for those who were sorrowing for him at home. And when he came to the petition that Adam might never be called to set up his tent in a far country, but that his mother might be cheered and comforted by his presence all the days of her pilgrimage, Lisbeth's ready tears flowed again, and she wept aloud.

When they rose from their knees, Seth went to Adam again and said, "Wilt only lie down for an hour or two, and let me go on the while?"

"No, Seth, no. Make Mother go to bed, and go thyself."

Meantime Lisbeth had dried her eyes, and now followed Seth, holding something in her hands. It was the brown-and-yellow platter containing the baked potatoes with the gravy in them and bits of meat which she had cut and mixed among them. Those were dear times, when wheaten bread and fresh meat were delicacies to working people. She set the dish down rather timidly on the bench by Adam's side and said, "Thee canst pick a bit while thee't workin'. I'll bring thee another drop o' water."

"Aye, Mother, do," said Adam, kindly; "I'm getting very thirsty."

In half an hour all was quiet; no sound was to be heard in the house but the loud ticking of the old day-clock and the ringing of Adam's tools. The night was very still: when Adam opened the door to look out at twelve o'clock, the only motion seemed to be in the glowing, twinkling stars; every blade of grass was asleep.

Bodily haste and exertion usually leave our thoughts very much at the mercy of our feelings and imagination; and it was so to-night with Adam. While his muscles were working lustily, his mind seemed as passive as a spectator at a diorama: scenes of the sad past, and probably sad future, floating before him and giving place one to the other in swift sucession.

He saw how it would be to-morrow morning, when he had carried the coffin to Broxton and was at home again, having his breakfast: his father perhaps would come in ashamed to meet his son's glance—would sit down, looking older and more tottering than he had done the morning before, and hang down his head, examining the floor-quarries; while Lisbeth would ask him how he supposed the coffin had been got ready, that he had slinked off and left undone—for Lisbeth was always the first to utter the word of reproach, although she cried at Adam's severity towards his father.

"So it will go on, worsening and worsening," thought Adam; "there's no slipping uphill again, and no standing still when once youve begun to slip down." And then the day came back to him when he was a little fellow and used to run by his father's side, proud to be taken out to work, and prouder still to hear his father boasting to his fellow-workmen how "the little chap had an uncommon notion o' carpentering." What a fine active fellow his father was then! When people asked Adam whose little lad he was, he had a sense of distinction as he answered, "I'm Thias Bede's lad." He was quite sure everybody knew Thias Bede—didn't he make the wonderful pigeon-house at Broxton parsonage? Those were happy days, especially when Seth, who was three years the younger, began to go out working too, and Adam began to be a teacher as well as a learner. But then came the days of sadness, when Adam was someway on in his teens, and Thias began to loiter at the public-houses, and Lisbeth began to cry at home, and to pour forth her plaints in the hearing of her sons. Adam remembered well the night of shame and anguish when he first saw his father quite wild and foolish, shouting a song out fitfully among his drunken companions at the "Waggon Overthrown." He had run away once when he was only eighteen, making his escape in the morning twilight with a little blue bundle over his shoulder, and his "mensuration book" in his pocket, and saying to himself very decidedly that he could bear the vexations of home no longer—he would go and seek his fortune, setting up his stick at the crossways and bending his steps the way it fell. But by the time he got to Stoniton, the thought of his mother and Seth, left behind to endure everything without him, became too importunate, and his resolution failed him. He came back the next day, but the misery and terror his mother had gone through in those two days had haunted her ever since.

"No!" Adam said to himself to-night, "that must never happen again. It 'ud make a poor balance when my doings are cast up at the last, if my poor old mother stood o' the wrong side. My back's broad enough and strong enough; I should be no better than a coward to go away and leave the troubles to be borne by them as aren't half so able. 'They that are strong ought to bear the infirmities of those that are weak, and not to please themselves.' There's a text wants no candle to show't; it shines by its own light. It's plain enough you get into the wrong road i' this life if you run after this and that only for the sake o' making things easy and pleasant to yourself. A pig may poke his nose into the trough and think o' nothing outside it; but if you've got a man's heart and soul in you, you can't be easy a-making your own bed an' leaving the rest to lie on the stones. Nay, nay, I'll never slip my neck out o' the yoke, and leave the load to be drawn by the weak uns. Father's a sore cross to me, an's likely to be for many a long year to come. What then? I've got th' health, and the limbs, and the sperrit to bear it."

At this moment a smart rap, as if with a willow wand, was given at the house door, and Gyp, instead of barking, as might have been expected, gave a loud howl. Adam, very much startled, went at once to the door and opened it. Nothing was there; all was still, as when he opened it an hour before; the leaves were motionless, and the light of the stars showed the placid fields on both sides of the brook quite empty of visible life. Adam walked round the house, and still saw nothing except a rat which darted into the woodshed as he passed. He went in again, wondering; the sound was so peculiar that the moment he heard it it called up the image of the willow wand striking the door. He could not help a little shudder, as he remembered how often his mother had told him of just such a sound coming as a sign when some one was dying. Adam was not a man to be gratuitously superstitious, but he had the blood of the peasant in him as well as of the artisan, and a peasant can no more help believing in a traditional superstition than a horse can help trembling when he sees a camel. Besides, he had that mental combination which is at once humble in the region of mystery and keen in the region of knowledge: it was the depth of his reverence quite as much as his hard common sense which gave him his disinclination to doctrinal religion, and he often checked Seth's argumentative spiritualism by saying, "Eh, it's a big mystery; thee know'st but little about it." And so it happened that Adam was at once penetrating and credulous. If a new building had fallen down and he had been told that this was a divine judgment, he would have said, "May be; but the bearing o' the roof and walls wasn't right, else it wouldn't ha' come down"; yet he believed in dreams and prognostics, and to his dying day he bated his breath a little when he told the story of the stroke with the willow wand. I tell it as he told it, not attempting to reduce it to its natural elements—in our eagerness to explain impressions, we often lose our hold of the sympathy that comprehends them.

But he had the best antidote against imaginative dread in the necessity for getting on with the coffin, and for the next ten minutes his hammer was ringing so uninterruptedly, that other sounds, if there were any, might well be overpowered. A pause came, however, when he had to take up his ruler, and now again came the strange rap, and again Gyp howled. Adam was at the door without the loss of a moment; but again all was still, and the starlight showed there was nothing but the dew-laden grass in front of the cottage.

Adam for a moment thought uncomfortably about his father; but of late years he had never come home at dark hours from Treddleston, and there was every reason for believing that he was then sleeping off his drunkenness at the "Waggon Overthrown." Besides, to Adam, the conception of the future was so inseparable from the painful image of his father that the fear of any fatal accident to him was excluded by the deeply infixed fear of his continual degradation. The next thought that occurred to him was one that made him slip off his shoes and tread lightly upstairs, to listen at the bedroom doors. But both Seth and his mother were breathing regularly.

Adam came down and set to work again, saying to himself, "I won't open the door again. It's no use staring about to catch sight of a sound. Maybe there's a world about us as we can't see, but th' ear's quicker than the eye and catches a sound from't now and then. Some people think they get a sight on't too, but they're mostly folks whose eyes are not much use to 'em at anything else. For my part, I think it's better to see when your perpendicular's true than to see a ghost."

Such thoughts as these are apt to grow stronger and stronger as daylight quenches the candles and the birds begin to sing. By the time the red sunlight shone on the brass nails that formed the initials on the lid of the coffin, any lingering foreboding from the sound of the willow wand was merged in satisfaction that the work was done and the promise redeemed. There was no need to call Seth, for he was already moving overhead, and presently came downstairs.

"Now, lad," said Adam, as Seth made his appearance, "the coffin's done, and we can take it over to Brox'on, and be back again before half after six. I'll take a mouthful o' oat-cake, and then we'll be off."

The coffin was soon propped on the tall shoulders of the two brothers, and they were making their way, followed close by Gyp, out of the little woodyard into the lane at the back of the house. It was but about a mile and a half to Broxton over the opposite slope, and their road wound very pleasantly along lanes and across fields, where the pale woodbines and the dog-roses were scenting the hedgerows, and the birds were twittering and trilling in the tall leafy boughs of oak and elm. It was a strangely mingled picture—the fresh youth of the summer morning, with its Edenlike peace and loveliness, the stalwart strength of the two brothers in their rusty working clothes, and the long coffin on their shoulders. They paused for the last time before a small farmhouse outside the village of Broxton. By six o'clock the task was done, the coffin nailed down, and Adam and Seth were on their way home. They chose a shorter way homewards, which would take them across the fields and the brook in front of the house. Adam had not mentioned to Seth what had happened in the night, but he still retained sufficient impression from it himself to say, "Seth, lad, if Father isn't come home by the time we've had our breakfast, I think it'll be as well for thee to go over to Treddles'on and look after him, and thee canst get me the brass wire I want. Never mind about losing an hour at thy work; we can make that up. What dost say?"

"I'm willing," said Seth. "But see what clouds have gathered since we set out. I'm thinking we shall have more rain. It'll be a sore time for th' haymaking if the meadows are flooded again. The brook's fine and full now: another day's rain 'ud cover the plank, and we should have to go round by the road."

They were coming across the valley now, and had entered the pasture through which the brook ran.

"Why, what's that sticking against the willow?" continued Seth, beginning to walk faster. Adam's heart rose to his mouth: the vague anxiety about his father was changed into a great dread. He made no answer to Seth, but ran forward preceded by Gyp, who began to bark uneasily; and in two moments he was at the bridge.

This was what the omen meant, then! And the grey-haired father, of whom he had thought with a sort of hardness a few hours ago, as certain to live to be a thorn in his side was perhaps even then struggling with that watery death! This was the first thought that flashed through Adam's conscience, before he had time to seize the coat and drag out the tall heavy body. Seth was already by his side, helping him, and when they had it on the bank, the two sons in the first moment knelt and looked with mute awe at the glazed eyes, forgetting that there was need for action—forgetting everything but that their father lay dead before them. Adam was the first to speak.

"I'll run to Mother," he said, in a loud whisper. "I'll be back to thee in a minute."

Poor Lisbeth was busy preparing her sons' breakfast, and their porridge was already steaming on the fire. Her kitchen always looked the pink of cleanliness, but this morning she was more than usually bent on making her hearth and breakfast-table look comfortable and inviting.

"The lads 'ull be fine an' hungry," she said, half-aloud, as she stirred the porridge. "It's a good step to Brox'on, an' it's hungry air o'er the hill—wi' that heavy coffin too. Eh! It's heavier now, wi' poor Bob Tholer in't. Howiver, I've made a drap more porridge nor common this mornin'. The feyther 'ull happen come in arter a bit. Not as he'll ate much porridge. He swallers sixpenn'orth o' ale, an' saves a hap'orth o' por-ridge—that's his way o' layin' by money, as I've told him many a time, an' am likely to tell him again afore the day's out. Eh, poor mon, he takes it quiet enough; there's no denyin' that."

But now Lisbeth heard the heavy "thud" of a running footstep on the turf, and, turning quickly towards the door, she saw Adam enter, looking so pale and overwhelmed that she screamed aloud and rushed towards him before he had time to speak.

"Hush, Mother," Adam said, rather hoarsely, "don't be frightened. Father's tumbled into the water. Belike we may bring him round again. Seth and me are going to carry him in. Get a blanket and make it hot as the fire."

In reality Adam was convinced that his father was dead but he knew there was no other way of repressing his mother's impetuous wailing grief than by occupying her with some active task which had hope in it.

He ran back to Seth, and the two sons lifted the sad burden in heart-stricken silence. The wide-open glazed eyes were grey, like Seth's, and had once looked with mild pride on the boys before whom Thias had lived to hang his head in shame. Seth's chief feeling was awe and distress at this sudden snatching away of his father's soul; but Adam's mind rushed back over the past in a flood of relenting and pity. When death, the great Reconciler, has come, it is never our tenderness that we repent of, but our severity.

Chapter V The Rector

BEFORE twelve o'clock there had been some heavy storms of rain, and the water lay in deep gutters on the sides of the gravel walks in the garden of Broxton Parsonage; the great Provence roses had been cruelly tossed by the wind and beaten by the rain, and all the delicate-stemmed border flowers had been dashed down and stained with the wet soil. A melancholy morning—because it was nearly time hay-harvest should begin, and instead of that the meadows were likely to be flooded.

But people who have pleasant homes get indoor enjoyments that they would never think of but for the rain. If it had not been a wet morning, Mr. Irwine would not have been in the dining-room playing at chess with his mother, and he loves both his mother and chess quite well enough to pass some cloudy hours very easily by their help. Let me take you into that dining-room and show you the Rev. Adolphus Irwine, Rector of Broxton, Vicar of Hayslope, and Vicar of Blythe, a pluralist at whom the severest Church reformer would have found it difficult to look sour. We will enter very softly and stand still in the open doorway, without awaking the glossy-brown setter who is stretched across the hearth, with her two puppies beside her; or the pug, who is dozing, with his black muzzle aloft, like a sleepy president.

The room is a large and lofty one, with an ample mullioned oriel window at one end; the walls, you see, are new, and not yet painted; but the furniture, though originally of an expensive sort, is old and scanty, and there is no drapery about the window. The crimson cloth over the large dining-table is very threadbare, though it contrasts pleasantly enough with the dead hue of the plaster on the walls; but on this cloth there is a massive silver waiter with a decanter of water on it, of the same pattern as two larger ones that are propped up on the sideboard with a coat of arms conspicuous in their centre. You suspect at once that the inhabitants of this room have inherited more blood than wealth, and would not be surprised to find that Mr. Irwine had a finely cut nostril and upper lip; but at present we can only see that he has a broad flat back and an abundance of powdered hair, all thrown backward and tied behind with a black ribbon—a bit of conservatism in costume which tells you that he is not a young man. He will perhaps turn round by and by, and in the meantime we can look at that stately old lady, his mother, a beautiful aged brunette, whose rich-toned complexion is well set off by the complex wrappings of pure white cambric and lace about her head and neck. She is as erect in her comely embonpoint as a statue of Ceres; and her dark face, with its delicate aquiline nose, firm proud mouth, and small, intense, black eye, is so keen and sarcastic in its expression that you instinctively substitute a pack of cards for the chess-men and imagine her telling your fortune. The small brown hand with which she is lifting her queen is laden with pearls, diamonds, and turquoises; and a large black veil is very carefully adjusted over the crown of her cap, and falls in sharp contrast on the white folds about her neck. It must take a long time to dress that old lady in the morning! But it seems a law of nature that she should be dressed so: she is clearly one of those children of royalty who have never doubted their right divine and never met with any one so absurd as to question it.

"There, Dauphin, tell me what that is!" says this magnificent old lady, as she deposits her queen very quietly and folds her arms. "I should be sorry to utter a word disagreeable to your feelings."

"Ah, you witch-mother, you sorceress! How is a Christian man to win a game off you? I should have sprinkled the board with holy water before we began. You've not won that game by fair means, now, so don't pretend it."

"Yes, yes, that's what the beaten have always said of great conquerors. But see, there's the sunshine falling on the board, to show you more clearly what a foolish move you made with that pawn. Come, shall I give you another chance?"

"No, Mother, I shall leave you to your own conscience, now it's clearing up. We must go and plash up the mud a little, mus'n't we, Juno?" This was addressed to the brown setter, who had jumped up at the sound of the voices and laid her nose in an insinuating way on her master's leg. "But I must go upstairs first and see Anne. I was called away to Tholer's funeral just when I was going before."

"It's of no use, child; she can't speak to you. Kate says she has one of her worst headaches this morning."

"Oh, she likes me to go and see her just the same; she's never too ill to care about that."

If you know how much of human speech is mere purposeless impulse or habit, you will not wonder when I tell you that this identical objection had been made, and had received the same kind of answer, many hundred times in the course of the fifteen years that Mr. Irwine's sister Anne had been an invalid. Splendid old ladies, who take a long time to dress in the morning, have often slight sympathy with sickly daughters.

But while Mr. Irwine was still seated, leaning back in his chair and stroking Juno's head, the servant came to the door and said, "If you please, sir, Joshua Rann wishes to speak with you, if you are at liberty."

"Let him be shown in here," said Mrs. Irwine, taking up her knitting. "I always like to hear what Mr. Rann has got to say. His shoes will be dirty, but see that he wipes them Carroll."

In two minutes Mr. Rann appeared at the door with very deferential bows, which, however, were far from conciliating Pug, who gave a sharp bark and ran across the room to reconnoitre the stranger's legs; while the two puppies, regarding Mr. Rann's prominent calf and ribbed worsted stockings from a more sensuous point of view, plunged and growled over them in great enjoyment. Meantime, Mr. Irwine turned round his chair and said, "Well, Joshua, anything the matter at Hayslope, that you've come over this damp morning? Sit down, sit down. Never mind the dogs; give them a friendly kick. Here, Pug, you rascal!"

It is very pleasant to see some men turn round; pleasant as a sudden rush of warm air in winter, or the flash of firelight in the chill dusk. Mr. Irwine was one of those men. He bore the same sort of resemblance to his mother that our loving memory of a friend's face often bears to the face itself: the lines were all more generous, the smile brighter, the expression heartier. If the outline had been less finely cut, his face might have been called jolly; but that was not the right word for its mixture of bonhomie and distinction.

"Thank Your Reverence," answered Mr. Rann, endeavouring to look unconcerned about his legs, but shaking them alternately to keep off the puppies; "I'll stand, if you please, as more becoming. I hope I see you an' Mrs. Irwine well, an' Miss Irwine—an' Miss Anne, I hope's as well as usual."

"Yes, Joshua, thank you. You see how blooming my mother looks. She beats us younger people hollow. But what's the matter?"

"Why, sir, I had to come to Brox'on to deliver some work, and I thought it but right to call and let you know the goins-on as there's been i' the village, such as I hanna seen i' my time, and I've lived in it man and boy sixty year come St. Thomas, and collected th' Easter dues for Mr. Blick before Your Reverence come into the parish, and been at the ringin' o' every bell, and the diggin' o' every grave, and sung i' the choir long afore Bartle Massey come from nobody knows where, wi' his counter-singin' and fine anthems, as puts everybody out but himself—one takin' it up after another like sheep a-bleatin' i' th' fold. I know what belongs to bein' a parish clerk, and I know as I should be wantin' i' respect to Your Reverence, an' church, an' king, if I was t' allow such goins-on wi'out speakin'. I was took by surprise, an' knowed nothin' on it beforehand, an' I was so flustered, I was clean as if I'd lost my tools. I hanna slep' more nor four hour this night as is past an' gone; an' then it was nothin' but nightmare, as tired me worse nor wakin'."

"Why, what in the world is the matter, Joshua? Have the thieves been at the church lead again?"

"Thieves! No, sir—an' yet, as I may say, it is thieves, an' a-thievin' the church, too. It's the Methodisses as is like to get th' upper hand i' th' parish, if Your Reverence an' His Honour, Squire Donnithorne, doesna think well to say the word an' forbid it. Not as I'm a-dictatin' to you, sir; I'm not forgettin' myself so far as to be wise above my betters. Howiver, whether I'm wise or no, that's neither here nor there, but what I've got to say I say—as the young Methodis woman as is at Mester Poyser's was a-preachin' an' a-prayin' on the Green last night, as sure as I'm a-stannin' afore Your Reverence now."

"Preaching on the Green!" said Mr. Irwine, looking surprised but quite serene. "What, that pale pretty young woman I've seen at Poyser's? I saw she was a Methodist, or Quaker, or something of that sort, by her dress, but I didn't know she was a preacher."

"It's a true word as I say, sir," rejoined Mr. Rann, compressing his mouth into a semicircular form and pausing long enough to indicate three notes of exclamation. "She preached on the Green last night; an' she's laid hold of Chad's Bess, as the girl's been i' fits welly iver sin'."

"Well, Bessy Cranage is a hearty-looking lass; I daresay she'll come round again, Joshua. Did anybody else go into fits?"

"No, sir, I canna say as they did. But there's no knowin' what'll come, if we're t' have such preachin's as that a-goin' on ivery week—there'll be no livin' i' th' village. For them Methodisses make folks believe as if they take a mug o' drink extry, an' make theirselves a bit comfortable, they'll have to go to hell for't as sure as they're born. I'm not a tipplin' man nor a drunkard—nobody can say it on me—but I like a extry quart at Easter or Christmas time, as is nat'ral when we're goin' the rounds a-singin', an' folks offer't you for nothin'; or when I'm a-collectin' the dues; an' I like a pint wi' my pipe, an' a neighbourly chat at Mester Casson's now an' then, for I was brought up i' the Church, thank God, an' ha' been a parish clerk this two-an'-thirty year: I should know what the church religion is."

"Well, what's your advice, Joshua? What do you think should be done?"

"Well, Your Reverence, I'm not for takin' any measures again' the young woman. She's well enough if she'd let alone preachin'; an' I hear as she's a-goin' away back to her own country soon. She's Mr. Poyser's own niece, an' I donna wish to say what's anyways disrespectful o' th' family at th' Hall Farm, as I've measured for shoes, little an' big, welly iver sin' I've been a shoemaker. But there's that Will Maskery, sir as is the rampageousest Methodis as can be, an' I make no doubt it was him as stirred up th' young woman to preach last night, an' he'll be a-bringin' other folks to preach from Treddles'on, if his comb isn't cut a bit; an' I think as he should be let know as he isna t' have the makin' an' mendin' o' church carts an' implemen's, let alone stayin' i' that house an' yard as is Squire Donnithorne's."

"Well, but you say yourself, Joshua, that you never knew any one come to preach on the Green before; why should you think they'll come again? The Methodists don't come to preach in little villages like Hayslope, where there's only a handful of labourers, too tired to listen to them. They might almost as well go and preach on the Binton Hills. Will Maskery is no preacher himself, I think."

"Nay, sir, he's no gift at stringin' the words together wi'out book; he'd be stuck fast like a cow i' wet clay. But he's got tongue enough to speak disrespectful about's neebors, for he said as I was a blind

Pharisee—a-usin' the Bible i' that way to find nick-names for folks as are his elders an' betters!—and what's worse, he's been heard to say very unbecomin' words about Your Reverence; for I could bring them as 'ud swear as he called you a 'dumb dog,' an' a 'idle shepherd.' You'll forgi'e me for sayin' such things over again."

"Better not, better not, Joshua. Let evil words die as soon as they're spoken. Will Maskery might be a great deal worse fellow than he is. He used to be a wild drunken rascal, neglecting his work and beating his wife, they told me; now he's thrifty and decent, and he and his wife look comfortable together. If you can bring me any proof that he interferes with his neighbours and creates any disturbance, I shall think it my duty as a clergyman and a magistrate to interfere. But it wouldn't become wise people like you and me to be making a fuss about trifles, as if we thought the Church was in danger because Will Maskery lets his tongue wag rather foolishly, or a young woman talks in a serious way to a handful of people on the Green. We must 'live and let live,' Joshua, in religion as well as in other things. You go on doing your duty, as parish clerk and sexton, as well as you've always done it, and making those capital thick boots for your neighbours, and things won't go far wrong in Hayslope, depend upon it."

"Your Reverence is very good to say so; an' I'm sensable as, you not livin' i' the parish, there's more upo' my shoulders."

"To be sure; and you must mind and not lower the Church in people's eyes by seeming to be frightened about it for a little thing, Joshua. I shall trust to your good sense, now to take no notice at all of what Will Maskery says, either about you or me. You and your neighbours can go on taking your pot of beer soberly, when you've done your day's work, like good churchmen; and if Will Maskery doesn't like to join you, but to go to a prayermeeting at Treddleston instead, let him; that's no business of yours, so long as he doesn't hinder you from doing what you like. And as to people saying a few idle words about us, we must not mind that, any more than the old church-steeple minds the rooks cawing about it. Will Maskery comes to church every Sunday afternoon, and does his wheelwright's business steadily in the week-days, and as long as he does that he must be let alone."

"Ah, sir, but when he comes to church, he sits an' shakes his head, an' looks as sour an' as coxy when we're a-singin' as I should like to fetch him a rap across the jowl—God forgi'e me—an' Mrs. Irwine, an' Your Reverence too, for speakin' so afore you. An' he said as our Christmas singin' was no better nor the cracklin' o' thorns under a pot."

"Well, he's got a bad ear for music, Joshua. When people have wooden heads, you know, it can't be helped. He won't bring the other people in Hayslope round to his opinion, while you go on singing as well as you do."

"Yes, sir, but it turns a man's stomach t' hear the Scripture misused i' that way. I know as much o' the words o' the Bible as he does, an' could say the Psalms right through i' my sleep if you was to pinch me; but I know better nor to take 'em to say my own say wi'. I might as well take the Sacriment-cup home and use it at meals."

"That's a very sensible remark of yours, Joshua; but, as I said before——"

While Mr. Irwine was speaking, the sound of a booted step and the clink of a spur were heard on the stone floor of the entrance-hall, and Joshua Rann moved hastily aside from the doorway to make room for some one who paused there, and said, in a ringing tenor voice,

"Godson Arthur—may he come in?"

"Come in, come in, godson!" Mrs. Irwine answered, in the deep half-masculine tone which belongs to the vigorous old woman, and there entered a young gentleman in a riding-dress, with his right arm in a sling; whereupon followed that pleasant confusion of laughing interjections, and hand-shakings, and "How are you's?" mingled with joyous short barks and wagging of tails on the part of the canine members of the family, which tells that the visitor is on the best terms with the visited. The young gentleman was Arthur Donnithorne, known in Hayslope, variously, as "the young squire," "the heir," and "the captain." He was only a captain in the Loamshire Militia, but to the Hayslope tenants he was more intensely a captain than all the young gentlemen of the same rank in his Majesty's regulars—he outshone them as the planet Jupiter outshines the Milky Way. If you want to know more particularly how he looked, call to your remembrance some tawny-whiskered, brown-locked, clear-complexioned young Englishman whom you have met with in a foreign town, and been proud of as a fellow-countryman—well-washed, high-bred, white-handed, yet looking as if he could deliver well from the left shoulder and floor his man: I will not be so much of a tailor as to trouble your imagination with the difference of costume, and insist on the striped waistcoat, long-tailed coat, and low top-boots.

Turning round to take a chair, Captain Donnithorne said, "But don't let me interrupt Joshua's business—he has something to say."

"Humbly begging Your Honour's pardon," said Joshua, bowing low, "there was one thing I had to say to His Reverence as other things had drove out o' my head."

"Out with it, Joshua, quickly!" said Mr. Irwine.

"Belike, sir, you havena heared as Thias Bede's dead—drownded this morning, or more like overnight, i' the Willow Brook, again' the bridge right i' front o' the house."

"Ah!" exclaimed both the gentlemen at once, as if they were a good deal interested in the information.

"An' Seth Bede's been to me this morning to say he wished me to tell Your Reverence as his brother Adam begged of you particular t' allow his father's grave to be dug by the White Thorn, because his mother's set her heart on it, on account of a dream as she had; an' they'd ha' come theirselves to ask you, but they've so much to see after with the crowner, an' that; an' their mother's took on so, an' wants 'em to make sure o' the spot for fear somebody else should take it. An' if Your Reverence sees well and good, I'll send my boy to tell 'em as soon as I get home; an' that's why I make bold to trouble you wi' it, His Honour being present."

"To be sure, Joshua, to be sure, they shall have it. I'll ride round to Adam myself, and see him. Send your boy, however, to say they shall have the grave, lest anything should happen to detain me. And now, good morning, Joshua; go into the kitchen and have some ale."

"Poor old Thias!" said Mr. Irwine, when Joshua was gone. "I'm afraid the drink helped the brook to drown him. I should have been glad for the load to have been taken off my friend Adam's shoulders in a less painful way. That fine fellow has been propping up his father from ruin for the last five or six years."

"He's a regular trump, is Adam," said Captain Donnithorne. "When I was a little fellow, and Adam was a strapping lad of fifteen, and taught me carpentering, I used to think if ever I was a rich sultan, I would make Adam my grand-vizier. And I believe now he would bear the exaltation as well as any poor wise man in an Eastern story. If ever I live to be a large-acred man instead of a poor devil with a mortgaged allowance of pocket-money, I'll have Adam for my right hand. He shall manage my woods for me, for he seems to have a better notion of those things than any man I ever met with; and I know he would make twice the money of them that my grandfather does, with that miserable old Satchell to manage, who understands no more about timber than an old carp. I've mentioned the subject to my grandfather once or twice, but for some reason or other he has a dislike to Adam, and I can do nothing. But come, Your Reverence, are you for a ride with me? It's splendid out of doors now. We can go to Adam's together, if you like; but I want to call at the Hall Farm on my way, to look at the whelps Poyser is keeping for me."

"You must stay and have lunch first, Arthur," said Mrs. Irwine. "It's nearly two. Carroll will bring it in directly."

"I want to go to the Hall Farm too," said Mr. Irwine, "to have another look at the little Methodist who is staying there. Joshua tells me she was preaching on the Green last night."

"Oh, by Jove!" said Captain Donnithorne, laughing. "Why, she looks as quiet as a mouse. There's something rather striking about her, though. I positively felt quite bashful the first time I saw her—she was sitting stooping over her sewing in the sunshine outside the house, when I rode up and called out, without noticing that she was a stranger, 'Is Martin Poyser at home?' I declare, when she got up and looked at me and just said, 'He's in the house, I believe: I'll go and call him,' I felt quite ashamed of having spoken so abruptly to her. She looked like St. Catherine in a Quaker dress. It's a type of face one rarely sees among our common people."

"I should like to see the young woman, Dauphin," said Mrs. Irwine. "Make her come here on some pretext or other."

"I don't know how I can manage that, Mother; it will hardly do for me to patronize a Methodist preacher, even if she would consent to be patronized by an idle shepherd, as Will Maskery calls me. You should have come in a little sooner, Arthur, to hear Joshua's denunciation of his neighbour Will Maskery. The old fellow wants me to excommunicate the wheelwright, and then deliver him over to the civil arm—that is to say, to your grandfather—to be turned out of house and yard. If I chose to interfere in this business, now, I might get up as pretty a story of hatred and persecution as the Methodists need desire to publish in the next number of their magazine. It wouldn't take me much trouble to persuade Chad Cranage and half a dozen other bull-headed fellows that they would be doing an acceptable service to the Church by hunting Will Maskery out of the village with rope-ends and pitchforks; and then, when I had furnished them with half a sovereign to get gloriously drunk after their exertions, I should have put the climax to as pretty a farce as any of my brother clergy have set going in their parishes for the last thirty years."

"It is really insolent of the man, though, to call you an 'idle shepherd' and a 'dumb dog,'" said Mrs. Irwine. "I should be inclined to check him a little there. You are too easy-tempered, Dauphin."

"Why, Mother, you don't think it would be a good way of sustaining my dignity to set about vindicating myself from the aspersions of Will Maskery? Besides, I'm not so sure that they ARE aspersions. I AM a lazy fellow, and get terribly heavy in my saddle; not to mention that I'm always spending more than I can afford in bricks and mortar, so that I get savage at a lame beggar when he asks me for sixpence. Those poor lean cobblers, who think they can help to regenerate mankind by setting out to preach in the morning twilight before they begin their day's work, may well have a poor opinion of me. But come, let us have our luncheon. Isn't Kate coming to lunch?"

"Miss Irwine told Bridget to take her lunch upstairs," said Carroll; "she can't leave Miss Anne."

"Oh, very well. Tell Bridget to say I'll go up and see Miss Anne presently. You can use your right arm quite well now, Arthur," Mr. Irwine continued, observing that Captain Donnithorne had taken his arm out of the sling.

"Yes, pretty well; but Godwin insists on my keeping it up constantly for some time to come. I hope I shall be able to get away to the regiment, though, in the beginning of August. It's a desperately dull business being shut up at the Chase in the summer months, when one can neither hunt nor shoot, so as to make one's self pleasantly sleepy in the evening. However, we are to astonish the echoes on the 30th of

July. My grandfather has given me carte blanche for once, and I promise you the entertainment shall be worthy of the occasion. The world will not see the grand epoch of my majority twice. I think I shall have a lofty throne for you, Godmamma, or rather two, one on the lawn and another in the ballroom, that you may sit and look down upon us like an Olympian goddess."

"I mean to bring out my best brocade, that I wore at your christening twenty years ago," said Mrs. Irwine. "Ah, I think I shall see your poor mother flitting about in her white dress, which looked to me almost like a shroud that very day; and it WAS her shroud only three months after; and your little cap and christening dress were buried with her too. She had set her heart on that, sweet soul! Thank God you take after your mother's family, Arthur. If you had been a puny, wiry, yellow baby, I wouldn't have stood godmother to you. I should have been sure you would turn out a Donnithorne. But you were such a broad-faced, broad-chested, loud-screaming rascal, I knew you were every inch of you a Tradgett."

"But you might have been a little too hasty there, Mother," said Mr. Irwine, smiling. "Don't you remember how it was with Juno's last pups? One of them was the very image of its mother, but it had two or three of its father's tricks notwithstanding. Nature is clever enough to cheat even you, Mother."

"Nonsense, child! Nature never makes a ferret in the shape of a mastiff. You'll never persuade me that I can't tell what men are by their outsides. If I don't like a man's looks, depend upon it I shall never like HIM. I don't want to know people that look ugly and disagreeable, any more than I want to taste dishes that look disagreeable. If they make me shudder at the first glance, I say, take them away. An ugly, piggish, or fishy eye, now, makes me feel quite ill; it's like a bad smell."

"Talking of eyes," said Captain Donnithorne, "that reminds me that I've got a book I meant to bring you, Godmamma. It came down in a parcel from London the other day. I know you are fond of queer, wizardlike stories. It's a volume of poems, 'Lyrical Ballads.' Most of them seem to be twaddling stuff, but the first is in a different style—'The Ancient Mariner' is the title. I can hardly make head or tail of it as a story, but it's a strange, striking thing. I'll send it over to you; and there are some other books that you may like to see, Irwine—pamphlets about Antinomianism and Evangelicalism, whatever they may be. I can't think what the fellow means by sending such things to me. I've written to him to desire that from henceforth he will send me no book or pamphlet on anything that ends in ISM."

"Well, I don't know that I'm very fond of isms myself; but I may as well look at the pamphlets; they let one see what is going on. I've a little matter to attend to, Arthur," continued Mr. Irwine, rising to leave the room, "and then I shall be ready to set out with you."

The little matter that Mr. Irwine had to attend to took him up the old stone staircase (part of the house was very old) and made him pause before a door at which he knocked gently. "Come in," said a woman's voice, and he entered a room so darkened by blinds and curtains that Miss Kate, the thin middle-aged lady standing by the bedside, would not have had light enough for any other sort of work than the knitting which lay on the little table near her. But at present she was doing what required only the dimmest light—sponging the aching head that lay on the pillow with fresh vinegar. It was a small face, that of the poor sufferer; perhaps it had once been pretty, but now it was worn and sallow. Miss Kate came towards her brother and whispered, "Don't speak to her; she can't bear to be spoken to to-day." Anne's eyes were closed, and her brow contracted as if from intense pain. Mr. Irwine went to the bedside and took up one of the delicate hands and kissed it, a slight pressure from the small fingers told him that it was worth-while to have come upstairs for the sake of doing that. He lingered a moment, looking at her, and then turned away and left the room, treading very gently—he had taken off his boots and put on slippers before he came upstairs. Whoever remembers how many things he has declined to do even for himself, rather than have the trouble of putting on or taking off his boots, will not think this last detail insignificant.

And Mr. Irwine's sisters, as any person of family within ten miles of Broxton could have testified, were such stupid, uninteresting women! It was quite a pity handsome, clever Mrs. Irwine should have had such commonplace daughters. That fine old lady herself was worth driving ten miles to see, any day; her beauty, her well-preserved faculties, and her old-fashioned dignity made her a graceful subject for conversation in turn with the King's health, the sweet new patterns in cotton dresses, the news from Egypt, and Lord Dacey's lawsuit, which was fretting poor Lady Dacey to death. But no one ever thought of mentioning the Miss Irwines, except the poor people in Broxton village, who regarded them as deep in the science of medicine, and spoke of them vaguely as "the gentlefolks." If any one had asked old Job Dummilow who gave him his flannel jacket, he would have answered, "the gentlefolks, last winter"; and widow Steene dwelt much on the virtues of the "stuff" the gentlefolks gave her for her cough. Under this name too, they were used with great effect as a means of taming refractory children, so that at the sight of poor Miss Anne's sallow face, several small urchins had a terrified sense that she was cognizant of all their worst misdemeanours, and knew the precise number of stones with which they had intended to hit Farmer Britton's ducks. But for all who saw them through a less mythical medium, the Miss Irwines were quite superfluous existences—inartistic figures crowding the canvas of life without adequate effect. Miss Anne, indeed, if her chronic headaches could have been accounted for by a pathetic story of disappointed love, might have had some romantic interest attached to her: but no such story had either been known or invented concerning her, and the general impression was quite in accordance with the fact, that both the sisters were old maids for the prosaic reason that they had never received an eligible offer.

Nevertheless, to speak paradoxically, the existence of insignificant people has very important consequences in the world. It can be shown to affect the price of bread and the rate of wages, to call forth many evil tempers from the selfish and many heroisms from the sympathetic, and, in other ways, to play no small part in the tragedy of life. And if that handsome, generous-blooded clergyman, the Rev. Adolphus Irwine, had not had these two hopelessly maiden sisters, his lot would have been shaped quite differently: he would very likely have taken a comely wife in his youth, and now, when his hair was getting grey under the powder, would have had tall sons and blooming daughters—such possessions, in short, as men commonly think will repay them for all the labour they take under the sun. As it was—having with all his three livings no more than seven hundred a-year, and seeing no way of keeping his splendid mother and his sickly sister, not to reckon a second sister, who was usually spoken of without any adjective, in such ladylike ease as became their birth and habits, and at the same time providing for a family of his own—he remained, you see, at the age of eight-and-forty, a bachelor, not making any merit of that renunciation, but saying laughingly, if any one alluded to it, that he made it an excuse for many indulgences which a wife would never have allowed him. And perhaps he was the only person in the world who did not think his sisters uninteresting and superfluous; for his was one of those large-hearted, sweet-blooded natures that never know a narrow or a grudging thought; Epicurean, if you will, with no enthusiasm, no self-scourging sense of duty; but yet, as you have seen, of a sufficiently subtle moral fibre to have an unwearying tenderness for obscure and monotonous suffering. It was his large-hearted indulgence that made him ignore his mother's hardness towards her daughters, which was the more striking from its contrast with her doting fondness towards himself; he held it no virtue to frown at irremediable faults.

See the difference between the impression a man makes on you when you walk by his side in familiar talk, or look at him in his home, and the figure he makes when seen from a lofty historical level, or even in the eyes of a critical neighbour who thinks of him as an embodied system or opinion rather than as a man. Mr. Roe, the "travelling preacher" stationed at Treddleston, had included Mr. Irwine in a general statement concerning the Church clergy in the surrounding district, whom he described as men given up to the lusts of the flesh and the pride of life; hunting and shooting, and adorning their own houses; asking what shall we eat, and what shall we drink, and wherewithal shall we be clothed?—careless of dispensing the bread of life to their flocks, preaching at best but a carnal and soul-benumbing morality, and trafficking in the souls of men by receiving money for discharging the pastoral office in parishes where they did not so much as look on the faces of the people more than once a-year. The ecclesiastical historian, too, looking into parliamentary reports of that period, finds honourable members zealous for the Church, and untainted with any sympathy for the "tribe of canting Methodists," making statements scarcely less melancholy than that of Mr. Roe. And it is impossible for me to say that Mr. Irwine was altogether belied by the generic classification assigned him. He really had no very lofty aims, no theological enthusiasm: if I were closely questioned, I should be obliged to confess that he felt no serious alarms about the souls of his parishioners, and would have thought it a mere loss of time to talk in a doctrinal and awakening manner to old "Feyther Taft," or even to Chad Cranage the blacksmith. If he had been in the habit of speaking theoretically, he would perhaps have said that the only healthy form religion could take in such minds was that of certain dim but strong emotions, suffusing themselves as a hallowing influence over the family affections and neighbourly duties. He thought the custom of baptism more important than its doctrine, and that the religious benefits the peasant drew from the church where his fathers worshipped and the sacred piece of turf where they lay buried were but slightly dependent on a clear understanding of the Liturgy or the sermon. Clearly the rector was not what is called in these days an "earnest" man: he was fonder of church history than of divinity, and had much more insight into men's characters than interest in their opinions; he was neither laborious, nor obviously self-denying, nor very copious in alms-giving, and his theology, you perceive, was lax. His mental palate, indeed, was rather pagan, and found a savouriness in a quotation from Sophocles or Theocritus that was quite absent from any text in Isaiah or Amos. But if you feed your young setter on raw flesh, how can you wonder at its retaining a relish for uncooked partridge in after-life? And Mr. Irwine's recollections of young enthusiasm and ambition were all associated with poetry and ethics that lay aloof from the Bible.

On the other hand, I must plead, for I have an affectionate partiality towards the rector's memory, that he was not vindictive—and some philanthropists have been so; that he was not intolerant—and there is a rumour that some zealous theologians have not been altogether free from that blemish; that although he would probably have declined to give his body to be burned in any public cause, and was far from bestowing all his goods to feed the poor, he had that charity which has sometimes been lacking to very illustrious virtue—he was tender to other men's failings, and unwilling to impute evil. He was one of those men, and they are not the commonest, of whom we can know the best only by following them away from the marketplace, the platform, and the pulpit, entering with them into their own homes, hearing the voice with which they speak to the young and aged about their own hearthstone, and witnessing their thoughtful care for the everyday wants of everyday companions, who take all their kindness as a matter of course, and not as a subject for panegyric.

Such men, happily, have lived in times when great abuses flourished, and have sometimes even been the living representatives of the abuses. That is a thought which might comfort us a little under the opposite fact—that it is better sometimes NOT to follow great reformers of abuses beyond the threshold of their homes.

But whatever you may think of Mr. Irwine now, if you had met him that June afternoon riding on his grey cob, with his dogs running beside him—portly, upright, manly, with a good-natured smile on his finely turned lips as he talked to his dashing young companion on the bay mare, you must have felt that, however ill he harmonized with sound theories of the clerical office, he somehow harmonized extremely well with that peaceful landscape.

See them in the bright sunlight, interrupted every now and then by rolling masses of cloud, ascending the slope from the Broxton side, where the tall gables and elms of the rectory predominate over the tiny whitewashed church. They will soon be in the parish of Hayslope; the grey church-tower and village roofs lie before them to the left, and farther on, to the right, they can just see the chimneys of the Hall Farm.

Chapter VI The Hall Farm

EVIDENTLY that gate is never opened, for the long grass and the great hemlocks grow close against it, and if it were opened, it is so rusty that the force necessary to turn it on its hinges would be likely to pull down the square stone-built pillars, to the detriment of the two stone lionesses which grin with a doubtful carnivorous affability above a coat of arms surmounting each of the pillars. It would be easy enough, by the aid of the nicks in the stone pillars, to climb over the brick wall with its smooth stone coping; but by putting our eyes close to the rusty bars of the gate, we can see the house well enough, and all but the very corners of the grassy enclosure.

It is a very fine old place, of red brick, softened by a pale powdery lichen, which has dispersed itself with happy irregularity, so as to bring the red brick into terms of friendly companionship with the limestone ornaments surrounding the three gables, the windows, and the door-place. But the windows are patched with wooden panes, and the door, I think, is like the gate—it is never opened. How it would groan and grate against the stone fioor if it were! For it is a solid, heavy, handsome door, and must once have been in the habit of shutting with a sonorous bang behind a liveried lackey, who had just seen his master and mistress off the grounds in a carriage and pair.

But at present one might fancy the house in the early stage of a chancery suit, and that the fruit from that grand double row of walnut-trees on the right hand of the enclosure would fall and rot among the grass, if it were not that we heard the booming bark of dogs echoing from great buildings at the back. And now the half-weaned calves that have been sheltering themselves in a gorse-built hovel against the left-hand wall come out and set up a silly answer to that terrible bark, doubtless supposing that it has reference to buckets of milk.

Yes, the house must be inhabited, and we will see by whom; for imagination is a licensed trespasser: it has no fear of dogs, but may climb over walls and peep in at windows with impunity. Put your face to one of the glass panes in the right-hand window: what do you see? A large open fireplace, with rusty dogs in it, and a bare boarded floor; at the far end, fleeces of wool stacked up; in the middle of the floor, some empty corn-bags. That is the furniture of the dining-room. And what through the left-hand window? Several clothes-horses, a pillion, a spinning-wheel, and an old box wide open and stuffed full of coloured rags. At the edge of this box there lies a great wooden doll, which, so far as mutilation is concerned, bears a strong resemblance to the finest Greek sculpture, and especially in the total loss of its nose. Near it there is a little chair, and the butt end of a boy's leather long-lashed whip.

The history of the house is plain now. It was once the residence of a country squire, whose family, probably dwindling down to mere spinsterhood, got merged in the more territorial name of Donnithorne. It was once the Hall; it is now the Hall Farm. Like the life in some coast town that was once a watering-place, and is now a port, where the genteel streets are silent and grass-grown, and the docks and warehouses busy and resonant, the life at the Hall has changed its focus, and no longer radiates from the parlour, but from the kitchen and the farmyard.

Plenty of life there, though this is the drowsiest time of the year, just before hay-harvest; and it is the drowsiest time of the day too, for it is close upon three by the sun, and it is half-past three by Mrs. Poyser's handsome eight-day clock. But there is always a stronger sense of life when the sun is brilliant after rain; and now he is pouring down his beams, and making sparkles among the wet straw, and lighting up every patch of vivid green moss on the red tiles of the cow-shed, and turning even the muddy water that is hurrying along the channel to the drain into a mirror for the yellow-billed ducks, who are seizing the opportunity of getting a drink with as much body in it as possible. There is quite a concert of noises; the great bull-dog, chained against the stables, is thrown into furious exasperation by the unwary approach of a cock too near the mouth of his kennel, and sends forth a thundering bark, which is answered by two fox-hounds shut up in the opposite cow-house; the old top-knotted hens, scratching with their chicks among the straw, set up a sympathetic croaking as the discomfited cock joins them; a sow with her brood, all very muddy as to the legs, and curled as to the tail, throws in some deep staccato notes; our friends the calves are bleating from the home croft; and, under all, a fine ear discerns the continuous hum of human voices.

For the great barn-doors are thrown wide open, and men are busy there mending the harness, under the superintendence of Mr. Goby, the "whittaw," otherwise saddler, who entertains them with the latest Treddleston gossip. It is certainly rather an unfortunate day that Alick, the shepherd, has chosen for having the whittaws, since the morning turned out so wet; and Mrs. Poyser has spoken her mind pretty strongly as to the dirt which the extra nurnber of men's shoes brought into the house at dinnertime. Indeed, she has not yet recovered her equanimity on the subject, though it is now nearly three hours since dinner, and the house-floor is perfectly clean again; as clean as everything else in that wonderful house-place, where the only chance of collecting a few grains of dust would be to climb on the salt-coffer, and put your finger on the high mantel-shelf on which the glittering brass candlesticks are enjoying their summer sinecure; for at this time of year, of course, every one goes to bed while it is yet light, or at least light enough to discern the outline of objects after you have bruised your shins against them. Surely nowhere else could an oak clock-case and an oak table have got to such a polish by the hand: genuine "elbow polish," as Mrs. Poyser called it, for she thanked God she never had any of your varnished rubbish in her house. Hetty Sorrel often took the opportunity, when her aunt's back was turned, of looking at the pleasing reflection of herself in those polished surfaces, for the oak table was usually turned up like a screen, and was more for ornament than for use; and she could see herself sometimes in the great round pewter dishes that were ranged on the shelves above the long deal dinner-table, or in the hobs of the grate, which always shone like jasper.

Everything was looking at its brightest at this moment, for the sun shone right on the pewter dishes, and from their reflecting surfaces pleasant jets of light were thrown on mellow oak and bright brass—and on a still pleasanter object than these, for some of the rays fell on Dinah's finely moulded cheek, and lit up her pale red hair to auburn, as she bent over the heavy household linen which she was mending for her aunt. No scene could have been more peaceful, if Mrs. Poyser, who was ironing a few things that still remained from the Monday's wash, had not been making a frequent clinking with her iron and moving to and fro whenever she wanted it to cool; carrying the keen glance of her blue-grey eye from the kitchen to the dairy, where Hetty was making up the butter, and from the dairy to the back kitchen, where Nancy was taking the pies out of the oven. Do not suppose, however, that Mrs. Poyser was elderly or shrewish in her appearance; she was a good-looking woman, not more than eight-and-thirty, of fair complexion and sandy hair, well-shapen, light-footed. The most conspicuous article in her attire was an ample checkered linen apron, which almost covered her skirt; and nothing could be plainer or less noticeable than her cap and gown, for there was no weakness of which she was less tolerant than feminine vanity, and the preference of ornament to utility. The family likeness between her and her niece Dinah Morris, with the contrast between her keenness and Dinah's seraphic gentleness of expression, might have served a painter as an excellent suggestion for a Martha and Mary. Their eyes were just of the same colour, but a striking test of the difference in their operation was seen in the demeanour of Trip, the black-and-tan terrier, whenever that much-suspected dog unwarily exposed himself to the freezing arctic ray of Mrs. Poyser's glance. Her tongue was not less keen than her eye, and, whenever a damsel came within earshot, seemed to take up an unfinished lecture, as a barrel-organ takes up a tune, precisely at the point where it had left off.

The fact that it was churning day was another reason why it was inconvenient to have the whittaws, and why, consequently, Mrs. Poyser should scold Molly the housemaid with unusual severity. To all appearance Molly had got through her after-dinner work in an exemplary manner, had "cleaned herself" with great dispatch, and now came to ask, submissively, if she should sit down to her spinning till milking time. But this blameless conduct, according to Mrs. Poyser, shrouded a secret indulgence of unbecoming wishes, which she now dragged forth and held up to Molly's view with cutting eloquence.

"Spinning, indeed! It isn't spinning as you'd be at, I'll be bound, and let you have your own way. I never knew your equals for gallowsness. To think of a gell o' your age wanting to go and sit with half-a-dozen men! I'd ha' been ashamed to let the words pass over my lips if I'd been you. And you, as have been here ever since last Michaelmas, and I hired you at Treddles'on stattits, without a bit o' character—as I say, you might be grateful to be hired in that way to a respectable place; and you knew no more o' what belongs to work when you come here than the mawkin i' the field. As poor a two-fisted thing as ever I saw, you know you was. Who taught you to scrub a floor, I should like to know? Why, you'd leave the dirt in heaps i' the corners—anybody 'ud think you'd never been brought up among Christians. And as for spinning, why, you've wasted as much as your wage i' the flax you've spoiled learning to spin. And you've a right to feel that, and not to go about as gaping and as thoughtless as if you was beholding to nobody. Comb the wool for the whittaws, indeed! That's what you'd like to be doing, is it? That's the way with you—that's the road you'd all like to go, headlongs to ruin. You're never easy till you've got some sweetheart as is as big a fool as yourself: you think you'll be finely off when you're married, I daresay, and have got a three-legged stool to sit on, and never a blanket to cover you, and a bit o' oat-cake for your dinner, as three children are a-snatching at."

"I'm sure I donna want t' go wi' the whittaws," said Molly, whimpering, and quite overcome by this Dantean picture of her future, "on'y we allays used to comb the wool for 'n at Mester Ottley's; an' so I just axed ye. I donna want to set eyes on the whittaws again; I wish I may never stir if I do."

"Mr. Ottley's, indeed! It's fine talking o' what you did at Mr. Ottley's. Your missis there might like her floors dirted wi' whittaws for what I know. There's no knowing what people WONNA like—such ways as I've heard of! I never had a gell come into my house as seemed to know what cleaning was; I think people live like pigs, for my part. And as to that Betty as was dairymaid at Trent's before she come to me, she'd ha' left the cheeses without turning from week's end to week's end, and the dairy thralls, I might ha' wrote my name on 'em, when I come downstairs after my illness, as the doctor said it was inflammation—it was a mercy I got well of it. And to think o' your knowing no better, Molly, and been here a-going i' nine months, and not for want o' talking to, neither—and what are you stanning there for, like a jack as is run down, instead o' getting your wheel out? You're a rare un for sitting down to your work a little while after it's time to put by."

"Munny, my iron's twite told; pease put it down to warm."

The small chirruping voice that uttered this request came from a little sunny-haired girl between three and four, who, seated on a high chair at the end of the ironing table, was arduously clutching the handle of a miniature iron with her tiny fat fist, and ironing rags with an assiduity that required her to put her little red tongue out as far as anatomy would allow.

"Cold, is it, my darling? Bless your sweet face!" said Mrs. Poyser, who was remarkable for the facility with which she could relapse from her official objurgatory to one of fondness or of friendly converse. "Never mind! Mother's done her ironing now. She's going to put the ironing things away."

"Munny, I tould 'ike to do into de barn to Tommy, to see de whittawd."

"No, no, no; Totty 'ud get her feet wet," said Mrs. Poyser, carrying away her iron. "Run into the dairy and see cousin Hetty make the butter."

"I tould 'ike a bit o' pum-take," rejoined Totty, who seemed to be provided with several relays of requests; at the same time, taking the opportunity of her momentary leisure to put her fingers into a bowl of starch, and drag it down so as to empty the contents with tolerable completeness on to the ironing sheet.

"Did ever anybody see the like?" screamed Mrs. Poyser, running towards the table when her eye had fallen on the blue stream. "The child's allays i' mischief if your back's turned a minute. What shall I do to you, you naughty, naughty gell?"

Totty, however, had descended from her chair with great swiftness, and was already in retreat towards the dairy with a sort of waddling run, and an amount of fat on the nape of her neck which made her look like the metamorphosis of a white suckling pig.

The starch having been wiped up by Molly's help, and the ironing apparatus put by, Mrs. Poyser took up her knitting which always lay ready at hand, and was the work she liked best, because she could carry it on automatically as she walked to and fro. But now she came and sat down opposite Dinah, whom she looked at in a meditative way, as she knitted her grey worsted stocking.

"You look th' image o' your Aunt Judith, Dinah, when you sit a-sewing. I could almost fancy it was thirty years back, and I was a little gell at home, looking at Judith as she sat at her work, after she'd done the house up; only it was a little cottage, Father's was, and not a big rambling house as gets dirty i' one corner as fast as you clean it in another—but for all that, I could fancy you was your Aunt Judith, only her hair was a deal darker than yours, and she was stouter and broader i' the shoulders. Judith and me allays hung together, though she had such queer ways, but your mother and her never could agree. Ah, your mother little thought as she'd have a daughter just cut out after the very pattern o' Judith, and leave her an orphan, too, for Judith to take care on, and bring up with a spoon when SHE was in the graveyard at Stoniton. I allays said that o' Judith, as she'd bear a pound weight any day to save anybody else carrying a ounce. And she was just the same from the first o' my remembering her; it made no difference in her, as I could see, when she took to the Methodists, only she talked a bit different and wore a different sort o' cap; but she'd never in her life spent a penny on herself more than keeping herself decent."

"She was a blessed woman," said Dinah; "God had given her a loving, self-forgetting nature, and He perfected it by grace. And she was very fond of you too, Aunt Rachel. I often heard her talk of you in the same sort of way. When she had that bad illness, and I was only eleven years old, she used to say, 'You'll have a friend on earth in your Aunt Rachel, if I'm taken from you, for she has a kind heart,' and I'm sure I've found it so."

"I don't know how, child; anybody 'ud be cunning to do anything for you, I think; you're like the birds o' th' air, and live nobody knows how. I'd ha' been glad to behave to you like a mother's sister, if you'd come and live i' this country where there's some shelter and victual for man and beast, and folks don't live on the naked hills, like poultry a-scratching on a gravel bank. And then you might get married to some decent man, and there'd be plenty ready to have you, if you'd only leave off that preaching, as is ten times worse than anything your Aunt Judith ever did. And even if you'd marry Seth Bede, as is a poor wool-gathering Methodist and's never like to have a penny beforehand, I know your uncle 'ud help you with a pig, and very like a cow, for he's allays been good-natur'd to my kin, for all they're poor, and made 'em welcome to the house; and 'ud do for you, I'll be bound, as much as ever he'd do for Hetty, though she's his own niece. And there's linen in the house as I could well spare you, for I've got lots o' sheeting and table-clothing, and towelling, as isn't made up. There's a piece o' sheeting I could give you as that squinting Kitty spun—she was a rare girl to spin, for all she squinted, and the children couldn't abide her; and, you know, the spinning's going on constant, and there's new linen wove twice as fast as the old wears out. But where's the use o' talking, if ye wonna be persuaded, and settle down like any other woman in her senses, i'stead o' wearing yourself out with walking and preaching, and giving away every penny you get, so as you've nothing saved against sickness; and all the things you've got i' the world, I verily believe, 'ud go into a bundle no bigger nor a double cheese. And all because you've got notions i' your head about religion more nor what's i' the Catechism and the Prayer-book."

"But not more than what's in the Bible, Aunt," said Dinah.

"Yes, and the Bible too, for that matter," Mrs. Poyser rejoined, rather sharply; "else why shouldn't them as know best what's in the Bible—the parsons and people as have got nothing to do but learn it—do the same as you do? But, for the matter o' that, if everybody was to do like you, the world must come to a standstill; for if everybody tried to do without house and home, and with poor eating and drinking, and was allays talking as we must despise the things o' the world as you say, I should like to know where the pick o' the stock, and the corn, and the best new-milk cheeeses 'ud have to go. Everybody 'ud be wanting bread made o' tail ends and everybody 'ud be running after everybody else to preach to 'em, istead o' bringing up their families, and laying by against a bad harvest. It stands to sense as that can't be the right religion."

"Nay, dear aunt, you never heard me say that all people are called to forsake their work and their families. It's quite right the land should be ploughed and sowed, and the precious corn stored, and the things of this life cared for, and right that people should rejoice in their families, and provide for them, so that this is done in the fear of the Lord, and that they are not unmindful of the soul's wants while they are caring for the body. We can all be servants of God wherever our lot is cast, but He gives us different sorts of work, according as He fits us for it and calls us to it. I can no more help spending my life in trying to do what I can for the souls of others, than you could help running if you heard little Totty crying at the other end of the house; the voice would go to your heart, you would think the dear child was in trouble or in danger, and you couldn't rest without running to help her and comfort her."

"Ah," said Mrs. Poyser, rising and walking towards the door, "I know it 'ud be just the same if I was to talk to you for hours. You'd make me the same answer, at th' end. I might as well talk to the running brook and tell it to stan' still."

The causeway outside the kitchen door was dry enough now for Mrs. Poyser to stand there quite pleasantly and see what was going on in the yard, the grey worsted stocking making a steady progress in her hands all the while. But she had not been standing there more than five minutes before she came in again, and said to Dinah, in rather a flurried, awe-stricken tone, "If there isn't Captain Donnithorne and Mr. Irwine a-coming into the yard! I'll lay my life they're come to speak about your preaching on the Green, Dinah; it's you must answer 'em, for I'm dumb. I've said enough a'ready about your bringing such disgrace upo' your uncle's family. I wouldn't ha' minded if you'd been Mr. Poyser's own niece—folks must put up wi' their own kin, as they put up wi' their own noses—it's their own flesh and blood. But to think of a niece o' mine being cause o' my husband's being turned out of his farm, and me brought him no fortin but my savin's——"

"Nay, dear Aunt Rachel," said Dinah gently, "you've no cause for such fears. I've strong assurance that no evil will happen to you and my uncle and the children from anything I've done. I didn't preach without direction."

"Direction! I know very well what you mean by direction," said Mrs. Poyser, knitting in a rapid and agitated manner. "When there's a bigger maggot than usial in your head you call it 'direction'; and then nothing can stir you—you look like the statty o' the outside o' Treddles'on church, a-starin' and a-smilin' whether it's fair weather or foul. I hanna common patience with you."

By this time the two gentlemen had reached the palings and had got down from their horses: it was plain they meant to come in. Mrs. Poyser advanced to the door to meet them, curtsying low and trembling between anger with Dinah and anxiety to conduct herself with perfect propriety on the occasion. For in those days the keenest of bucolic minds felt a whispering awe at the sight of the gentry, such as of old men felt when they stood on tiptoe to watch the gods passing by in tall human shape.

"Well, Mrs. Poyser, how are you after this stormy morning?" said Mr. Irwine, with his stately cordiality. "Our feet are quite dry; we shall not soil your beautiful floor."

"Oh, sir, don't mention it," said Mrs. Poyser. "Will you and the captain please to walk into the parlour?"

"No, indeed, thank you, Mrs. Poyser," said the captain, looking eagerly round the kitchen, as if his eye were seeking something it could not find. "I delight in your kitchen. I think it is the most charming room I know. I should like every farmer's wife to come and look at it for a pattern."

"Oh, you're pleased to say so, sir. Pray take a seat," said Mrs. Poyser, relieved a little by this compliment and the captain's evident good-humour, but still glancing anxiously at Mr. Irwine, who, she saw, was looking at Dinah and advancing towards her.

"Poyser is not at home, is he?" said Captain Donnithorne, seating himself where he could see along the short passage to the open dairy-door.

"No, sir, he isn't; he's gone to Rosseter to see Mr. West, the factor, about the wool. But there's Father i' the barn, sir, if he'd be of any use."

"No, thank you; I'll just look at the whelps and leave a message about them with your shepherd. I must come another day and see your husband; I want to have a consultation with him about horses. Do you know when he's likely to be at liberty?"

"Why, sir, you can hardly miss him, except it's o' Treddles'on market-day—that's of a Friday, you know. For if he's anywhere on the farm we can send for him in a minute. If we'd got rid o' the Scantlands, we should have no outlying fields; and I should be glad of it, for if ever anything happens, he's sure to be gone to the Scantlands. Things allays happen so contrairy, if they've a chance; and it's an unnat'ral thing to have one bit o' your farm in one county and all the rest in another."

"Ah, the Scantlands would go much better with Choyce's farm, especially as he wants dairyland and you've got plenty. I think yours is the prettiest farm on the estate, though; and do you know, Mrs. Poyser, if I were going to marry and settle, I should be tempted to turn you out, and do up this fine old house, and turn farmer myself."

"Oh, sir," said Mrs. Poyser, rather alarmed, "you wouldn't like it at all. As for farming, it's putting money into your pocket wi' your right hand and fetching it out wi' your left. As fur as I can see, it's raising victual for other folks and just getting a mouthful for yourself and your children as you go along. Not as you'd be like a poor man as wants to get his bread—you could afford to lose as much money as you liked i' farming—but it's poor fun losing money, I should think, though I understan' it's what the great folks i' London play at more than anything. For my husband heard at market as Lord Dacey's eldest son had lost thousands upo' thousands to the Prince o' Wales, and they said my lady was going to pawn her jewels to pay for him. But you know more about that than I do, sir. But, as for farming, sir, I canna think as you'd like it; and this house—the draughts in it are enough to cut you through, and it's my opinion the floors upstairs are very rotten, and the rats i' the cellar are beyond anything."

"Why, that's a terrible picture, Mrs. Poyser. I think I should be doing you a service to turn you out of such a place. But there's no chance of that. I'm not likely to settle for the next twenty years, till I'm a stout gentleman of forty; and my grandfather would never consent to part with such good tenants as you."

"Well, sir, if he thinks so well o' Mr. Poyser for a tenant I wish you could put in a word for him to allow us some new gates for the Five closes, for my husband's been asking and asking till he's tired, and to think o' what he's done for the farm, and's never had a penny allowed him, be the times bad or good. And as I've said to my husband often and often, I'm sure if the captain had anything to do with it, it wouldn't be so. Not as I wish to speak disrespectful o' them as have got the power i' their hands, but it's more than flesh and blood 'ull bear sometimes, to be toiling and striving, and up early and down late, and hardly sleeping a wink when you lie down for thinking as the cheese may swell, or the cows may slip their calf, or the wheat may grow green again i' the sheaf—and after all, at th' end o' the year, it's like as if you'd been cooking a feast and had got the smell of it for your pains."

Mrs. Poyser, once launched into conversation, always sailed along without any check from her preliminary awe of the gentry. The confidence she felt in her own powers of exposition was a motive force that overcame all resistance.

"I'm afraid I should only do harm instead of good, if I were to speak about the gates, Mrs. Poyser," said the captain, "though I assure you there's no man on the estate I would sooner say a word for than your husband. I know his farm is in better order than any other within ten miles of us; and as for the kitchen," he added, smiling, "I don't believe there's one in the kingdom to beat it. By the by, I've never seen your dairy: I must see your dairy, Mrs. Poyser."

"Indeed, sir, it's not fit for you to go in, for Hetty's in the middle o' making the butter, for the churning was thrown late, and I'm quite ashamed." This Mrs. Poyser said blushing, and believing that the captain was really interested in her milk-pans, and would adjust his opinion of her to the appearance of her dairy.

"Oh, I've no doubt it's in capital order. Take me in," said the captain, himself leading the way, while Mrs. Poyser followed.

Chapter VII The Dairy

THE dairy was certainly worth looking at: it was a scene to sicken for with a sort of calenture in hot and dusty streets—such coolness, such purity, such fresh fragrance of new-pressed cheese, of firm butter, of wooden vessels perpetually bathed in pure water; such soft colouring of red earthenware and creamy surfaces, brown wood and polished tin, grey limestone and rich orange-red rust on the iron weights and hooks and hinges. But one gets only a confused notion of these details when they surround a distractingly pretty girl of seventeen, standing on little pattens and rounding her dimpled arm to lift a pound of butter out of the scale.

Hetty blushed a deep rose-colour when Captain Donnithorne entered the dairy and spoke to her; but it was not at all a distressed blush, for it was inwreathed with smiles and dimples, and with sparkles from under long, curled, dark eyelashes; and while her aunt was discoursing to him about the limited amount of milk that was to be spared for butter and cheese so long as the calves were not all weaned, and a large quantity but inferior quality of milk yielded by the shorthorn, which had been bought on experiment, together with other matters which must be interesting to a young gentleman who would one day be a landlord, Hetty tossed and patted her pound of butter with quite a self-possessed, coquettish air, slyly conscious that no turn of her head was lost.

There are various orders of beauty, causing men to make fools of themselves in various styles, from the desperate to the sheepish; but there is one order of beauty which seems made to turn the heads not only of men, but of all intelligent mammals, even of women. It is a beauty like that of kittens, or very small downy ducks making gentle rippling noises with their soft bills, or babies just beginning to toddle and to engage in conscious mischief—a beauty with which you can never be angry, but that you feel ready to crush for inability to comprehend the state of mind into which it throws you. Hetty Sorrel's was that sort of beauty. Her aunt, Mrs. Poyser, who professed to despise all personal attractions and intended to be the severest of mentors, continually gazed at Hetty's charms by the sly, fascinated in spite of herself; and after administering such a scolding as naturally flowed from her anxiety to do well by her husband's niece—who had no mother of her own to scold her, poor thing!—she would often confess to her husband, when they were safe out of hearing, that she firmly believed, "the naughtier the little huzzy behaved, the prettier she looked."

It is of little use for me to tell you that Hetty's cheek was like a rose-petal, that dimples played about her pouting lips, that her large dark eyes hid a soft roguishness under their long lashes, and that her curly hair, though all pushed back under her round cap while she was at work, stole back in dark delicate rings on her forehead, and about her white shell-like ears; it is of little use for me to say how lovely was the contour of her pink-and-white neckerchief, tucked into her low plum-coloured stuff boddice, or how the linen butter-making apron, with its bib, seemed a thing to be imitated in silk by duchesses, since it fell in such charming lines, or how her brown stockings and thick-soled buckled shoes lost all that clumsiness which they must certainly have had when empty of her foot and ankle—of little use, unless you have seen a woman who affected you as Hetty affected her beholders, for otherwise, though you might conjure up the image of a lovely woman, she would not in the least resemble that distracting kittenlike maiden. I might mention all the divine charms of a bright spring day, but if you had never in your life utterly forgotten yourself in straining your eyes after the mounting lark, or in wandering through the still lanes when the fresh-opened blossoms fill them with a sacred silent beauty like that of fretted aisles, where would be the use of my descriptive catalogue? I could never make you know what I meant by a bright spring day. Hetty's was a spring-tide beauty; it was the beauty of young frisking things, round-limbed, gambolling, circumventing you by a false air of innocence—the innocence of a young star-browed calf, for example, that, being inclined for a promenade out of bounds, leads you a severe steeplechase over hedge and ditch, and only comes to a stand in the middle of a bog.

And they are the prettiest attitudes and movements into which a pretty girl is thrown in making up butter—tossing movements that give a charming curve to the arm, and a sideward inclination of the round white neck; little patting and rolling movements with the palm of the hand, and nice adaptations and finishings which cannot at all be effected without a great play of the pouting mouth and the dark eyes. And then the butter itself seems to communicate a fresh charm—it is so pure, so sweet-scented; it is turned off the mould with such a beautiful firm surface, like marble in a pale yellow light! Moreover, Hetty was particularly clever at making up the butter; it was the one performance of hers that her aunt allowed to pass without severe criticism; so she handled it with all the grace that belongs to mastery.

"I hope you will be ready for a great holiday on the thirtieth of July, Mrs. Poyser," said Captain Donnithorne, when he had sufficiently admired the dairy and given several improvised opinions on Swede turnips and shorthorns. "You know what is to happen then, and I shall expect you to be one of the guests who come earliest and leave latest. Will you promise me your hand for two dances, Miss Hetty? If I don't get your promise now, I know I shall hardly have a chance, for all the smart young farmers will take care to secure you."

Hetty smiled and blushed, but before she could answer, Mrs. Poyser interposed, scandalized at the mere suggestion that the young squire could be excluded by any meaner partners.

"Indeed, sir, you are very kind to take that notice of her. And I'm sure, whenever you're pleased to dance with her, she'll be proud and thankful, if she stood still all the rest o' th' evening."

"Oh no, no, that would be too cruel to all the other young fellows who can dance. But you will promise me two dances, won't you?" the captain continued, determined to make Hetty look at him and speak to him.

Hetty dropped the prettiest little curtsy, and stole a half-shy, half-coquettish glance at him as she said, "Yes, thank you, sir."

"And you must bring all your children, you know, Mrs. Poyser; your little Totty, as well as the boys. I want all the youngest children on the estate to be there—all those who will be fine young men and women when I'm a bald old fellow."

"Oh dear, sir, that 'ull be a long time first," said Mrs. Poyser, quite overcome at the young squire's speaking so lightly of himself, and thinking how her husband would be interested in hearing her recount this remarkable specimen of high-born humour. The captain was thought to be "very full of his jokes," and was a great favourite throughout the estate on account of his free manners. Every tenant was quite sure things would be different when the reins got into his hands—there was to be a millennial abundance of new gates, allowances of lime, and returns of ten per cent.

"But where is Totty to-day?" he said. "I want to see her."

"Where IS the little un, Hetty?" said Mrs. Poyser. "She came in here not long ago."

"I don't know. She went into the brewhouse to Nancy, I think."

The proud mother, unable to resist the temptation to show her Totty, passed at once into the back kitchen, in search of her, not, however, without misgivings lest something should have happened to render her person and attire unfit for presentation.

"And do you carry the butter to market when you've made it?" said the Captain to Hetty, meanwhile.

"Oh no, sir; not when it's so heavy. I'm not strong enough to carry it. Alick takes it on horseback."

"No, I'm sure your pretty arms were never meant for such heavy weights. But you go out a walk sometimes these pleasant evenings, don't you? Why don't you have a walk in the Chase sometimes, now it's so green and pleasant? I hardly ever see you anywhere except at home and at church."

"Aunt doesn't like me to go a-walking only when I'm going somewhere," said Hetty. "But I go through the Chase sometimes."

"And don't you ever go to see Mrs. Best, the housekeeper? I think I saw you once in the housekeeper's room."

"It isn't Mrs. Best, it's Mrs. Pomfret, the lady's maid, as I go to see. She's teaching me tent-stitch and the lace-mending. I'm going to tea with her to-morrow afternoon."

The reason why there had been space for this tete-a-tete can only be known by looking into the back kitchen, where Totty had been discovered rubbing a stray blue-bag against her nose, and in the same moment allowing some liberal indigo drops to fall on her afternoon pinafore. But now she appeared holding her mother's hand—the end of her round nose rather shiny from a recent and hurried application of soap and water.

"Here she is!" said the captain, lifting her up and setting her on the low stone shelf. "Here's Totty! By the by, what's her other name? She wasn't christened Totty."

"Oh, sir, we call her sadly out of her name. Charlotte's her christened name. It's a name i' Mr. Poyser's family: his grandmother was named Charlotte. But we began with calling her Lotty, and now it's got to Totty. To be sure it's more like a name for a dog than a Christian child."

"Totty's a capital name. Why, she looks like a Totty. Has she got a pocket on?" said the captain, feeling in his own waistcoat pockets.

Totty immediately with great gravity lifted up her frock, and showed a tiny pink pocket at present in a state of collapse.

"It dot notin' in it," she said, as she looked down at it very earnestly.

"No! What a pity! Such a pretty pocket. Well, I think I've got some things in mine that will make a pretty jingle in it. Yes! I declare I've got five little round silver things, and hear what a pretty noise they make in Totty's pink pocket." Here he shook the pocket with the five sixpences in it, and Totty showed her teeth and wrinkled her nose in great glee; but, divining that there was nothing more to be got by staying, she jumped off the shelf and ran away to jingle her pocket in the hearing of Nancy, while her mother called after her, "Oh for shame, you naughty gell! Not to thank the captain for what he's given you I'm sure, sir, it's very kind of you; but she's spoiled shameful; her father won't have her said nay in anything, and there's no managing her. It's being the youngest, and th' only gell."

"Oh, she's a funny little fatty; I wouldn't have her different. But I must be going now, for I suppose the rector is waiting for me."

With a "good-bye," a bright glance, and a bow to Hetty Arthur left the dairy. But he was mistaken in imagining himself waited for. The rector had been so much interested in his conversation with Dinah that he would not have chosen to close it earlier; and you shall hear now what they had been saying to each other.

Chapter VIII A Vocation

DINAH, who had risen when the gentlemen came in, but still kept hold of the sheet she was mending, curtsied respectfully when she saw Mr. Irwine looking at her and advancing towards her. He had never yet spoken to her, or stood face to face with her, and her first thought, as her eyes met his, was, "What a well-favoured countenance! Oh that the good seed might fall on that soil, for it would surely flourish." The agreeable impression must have been mutual, for Mr. Irwine bowed to her with a benignant deference, which would have been equally in place if she had been the most dignified lady of his acquaintance.

"You are only a visitor in this neighbourhood, I think?" were his first words, as he seated himself opposite to her.

"No, sir, I come from Snowfield, in Stonyshire. But my aunt was very kind, wanting me to have rest from my work there, because I'd been ill, and she invited me to come and stay with her for a while."

"Ah, I remember Snowfield very well; I once had occasion to go there. It's a dreary bleak place. They were building a cotton-mill there; but that's many years ago now. I suppose the place is a good deal changed by the employment that mill must have brought."

"It IS changed so far as the mill has brought people there, who get a livelihood for themselves by working in it, and make it better for the tradesfolks. I work in it myself, and have reason to be grateful, for thereby I have enough and to spare. But it's still a bleak place, as you say, sir—very different from this country."

"You have relations living there, probably, so that you are attached to the place as your home?"

"I had an aunt there once; she brought me up, for I was an orphan. But she was taken away seven years ago, and I have no other kindred that I know of, besides my Aunt Poyser, who is very good to me, and would have me come and live in this country, which to be sure is a good land, wherein they eat bread without scarceness. But I'm not free to leave Snowfield, where I was first planted, and have grown deep into it, like the small grass on the hill-top."

"Ah, I daresay you have many religious friends and companions there; you are a Methodist—a Wesleyan, I think?"

"Yes, my aunt at Snowfield belonged to the Society, and I have cause to be thankful for the privileges I have had thereby from my earliest childhood."

"And have you been long in the habit of preaching? For I understand you preached at Hayslope last night."

"I first took to the work four years since, when I was twenty-one."

"Your Society sanctions women's preaching, then?"

"It doesn't forbid them, sir, when they've a clear call to the work, and when their ministry is owned by the conversion of sinners and the strengthening of God's people. Mrs. Fletcher, as you may have heard about, was the first woman to preach in the Society, I believe, before she was married, when she was Miss Bosanquet; and Mr. Wesley approved of her undertaking the work. She had a great gift, and there are many others now living who are precious fellow-helpers in the work of the ministry. I understand there's been voices raised against it in the Society of late, but I cannot but think their counsel will come to nought. It isn't for men to make channels for God's Spirit, as they make channels for the watercourses, and say, 'Flow here, but flow not there.'"

"But don't you find some danger among your people—I don't mean to say that it is so with you, far from it—but don't you find sometimes that both men and women fancy themselves channels for God's Spirit, and are quite mistaken, so that they set about a work for which they are unfit and bring holy things into contempt?"

"Doubtless it is so sometimes; for there have been evil-doers among us who have sought to deceive the brethren, and some there are who deceive their own selves. But we are not without discipline and correction to put a check upon these things. There's a very strict order kept among us, and the brethren and sisters watch for each other's souls as they that must give account. They don't go every one his own way and say, 'Am I my brother's keeper?'"

"But tell me—if I may ask, and I am really interested in knowing it—how you first came to think of preaching?"

"Indeed, sir, I didn't think of it at all—I'd been used from the time I was sixteen to talk to the little children, and teach them, and sometimes I had had my heart enlarged to speak in class, and was much drawn out in prayer with the sick. But I had felt no call to preach, for when I'm not greatly wrought upon, I'm too much given to sit still and keep by myself. It seems as if I could sit silent all day long with the thought of God overflowing my soul—as the pebbles lie bathed in the Willow Brook. For thoughts are so great—aren't they, sir? They seem to lie upon us like a deep flood; and it's my besetment to forget where I am and everything about me, and lose myself in thoughts that I could give no account of, for I could neither make a beginning nor ending of them in words. That was my way as long as I can remember; but sometimes it seemed as if speech came to me without any will of my own, and words were given to me that came out as the tears come, because our hearts are full and we can't help it. And those were always times of great blessing, though I had never thought it could be so with me before a congregation of people. But, sir, we are led on, like the little children, by a way that we know not. I was called to preach quite suddenly, and since then I have never been left in doubt about the work that was laid upon me."

"But tell me the circumstances—just how it was, the very day you began to preach."

"It was one Sunday I walked with brother Marlowe, who was an aged man, one of the local preachers, all the way to Hetton-Deeps—that's a village where the people get their living by working in the lead-mines, and where there's no church nor preacher, but they live like sheep without a shepherd. It's better than twelve miles from Snowfield, so we set out early in the morning, for it was summertime; and I had a wonderful sense of the Divine love as we walked over the hills, where there's no trees, you know, sir, as there is here, to make the sky look smaller, but you see the heavens stretched out like a tent, and you feel the everlasting arms around you. But before we got to Hetton, brother Marlowe was seized with a dizziness that made him afraid of falling, for he overworked himself sadly, at his years, in watching and praying, and walking so many miles to speak the Word, as well as carrying on his trade of linen-weaving. And when we got to the village, the people were expecting him, for he'd appointed the time and the place when he was there before, and such of them as cared to hear the Word of Life were assembled on a spot where the cottages was thickest, so as others might be drawn to come. But he felt as he couldn't stand up to preach, and he was forced to lie down in the first of the cottages we came to. So I went to tell the people, thinking we'd go into one of the houses, and I would read and pray with them. But as I passed along by the cottages and saw the aged and trembling women at the doors, and the hard looks of the men, who seemed to have their eyes no more filled with the sight of the Sabbath morning than if they had been dumb oxen that never looked up to the sky, I felt a great movement in my soul, and I trembled as if I was shaken by a strong spirit entering into my weak body. And I went to where the little flock of people was gathered together, and stepped on the low wall that was built against the green hillside, and I spoke the words that were given to me abundantly. And they all came round me out of all the cottages, and many wept over their sins, and have since been joined to the Lord. That was the beginning of my preaching, sir, and I've preached ever since."

Dinah had let her work fall during this narrative, which she uttered in her usual simple way, but with that sincere articulate, thrilling treble by which she always mastered her audience. She stooped now to gather up her sewing, and then went on with it as before. Mr. Irwine was deeply interested. He said to himself, "He must be a miserable prig who would act the pedagogue here: one might as well go and lecture the trees for growing in their own shape."

"And you never feel any embarrassment from the sense of your youth—that you are a lovely young woman on whom men's eyes are fixed?" he said aloud.

"No, I've no room for such feelings, and I don't believe the people ever take notice about that. I think, sir, when God makes His presence felt through us, we are like the burning bush: Moses never took any heed what sort of bush it was—he only saw the brightness of the Lord. I've preached to as rough ignorant people as can be in the villages about Snowfield—men that looked very hard and wild—but they never said an uncivil word to me, and often thanked me kindly as they made way for me to pass through the midst of them."

"THAT I can believe—that I can well believe," said Mr. Irwine, emphatically. "And what did you think of your hearers last night, now? Did you find them quiet and attentive?"

"Very quiet, sir, but I saw no signs of any great work upon them, except in a young girl named Bessy Cranage, towards whom my heart yearned greatly, when my eyes first fell on her blooming youth, given up to folly and vanity. I had some private talk and prayer with her afterwards, and I trust her heart is touched. But I've noticed that in these villages where the people lead a quiet life among the green pastures and the still waters, tilling the ground and tending the cattle, there's a strange deadness to the Word, as different as can be from the great towns, like Leeds, where I once went to visit a holy woman who preaches there. It's wonderful how rich is the harvest of souls up those high-walled streets, where you seemed to walk as in a prison-yard, and the ear is deafened with the sounds of worldly toil. I think maybe it is because the promise is sweeter when this life is so dark and weary, and the soul gets more hungry when the body is ill at ease."

"Why, yes, our farm-labourers are not easily roused. They take life almost as slowly as the sheep and cows. But we have some intelligent workmen about here. I daresay you know the Bedes; Seth Bede, by the by, is a Methodist."

"Yes, I know Seth well, and his brother Adam a little. Seth is a gracious young man—sincere and without offence; and Adam is like the patriarch Joseph, for his great skill and knowledge and the kindness he shows to his brother and his parents."

"Perhaps you don't know the trouble that has just happened to them? Their father, Matthias Bede, was drowned in the Willow Brook last night, not far from his own door. I'm going now to see Adam."

"Ah, their poor aged mother!" said Dinah, dropping her hands and looking before her with pitying eyes, as if she saw the object of her sympathy. "She will mourn heavily, for Seth has told me she's of an anxious, troubled heart. I must go and see if I can give her any help."

As she rose and was beginning to fold up her work, Captain Donnithorne, having exhausted all plausible pretexts for remaining among the milk-pans, came out of the dairy, followed by Mrs. Poyser. Mr. Irwine now rose also, and, advancing towards Dinah, held out his hand, and said, "Good-bye. I hear you are going away soon; but this will not be the last visit you will pay your aunt—so we shall meet again, I hope."

His cordiality towards Dinah set all Mrs. Poyser's anxieties at rest, and her face was brighter than usual, as she said, "I've never asked after Mrs. Irwine and the Miss Irwines, sir; I hope they're as well as usual."

"Yes, thank you, Mrs. Poyser, except that Miss Anne has one of her bad headaches to-day. By the by, we all liked that nice cream-cheese you sent us—my mother especially."

"I'm very glad, indeed, sir. It is but seldom I make one, but I remembered Mrs. Irwine was fond of 'em. Please to give my duty to her, and to Miss Kate and Miss Anne. They've never been to look at my poultry this long while, and I've got some beautiful speckled chickens, black and white, as Miss Kate might like to have some of amongst hers."

"Well, I'll tell her; she must come and see them. Good-bye," said the rector, mounting his horse.

"Just ride slowly on, Irwine," said Captain Donnithorne, mounting also. "I'll overtake you in three minutes. I'm only going to speak to the shepherd about the whelps. Good-bye, Mrs. Poyser; tell your husband I shall come and have a long talk with him soon."

Mrs. Poyser curtsied duly, and watched the two horses until they had disappeared from the yard, amidst great excitement on the part of the pigs and the poultry, and under the furious indignation of the bull-dog, who performed a Pyrrhic dance, that every moment seemed to threaten the breaking of his chain. Mrs. Poyser delighted in this noisy exit; it was a fresh assurance to her that the farm-yard was well guarded, and that no loiterers could enter unobserved; and it was not until the gate had closed behind the captain that she turned into the kitchen again, where Dinah stood with her bonnet in her hand, waiting to speak to her aunt, before she set out for Lisbeth Bede's cottage.

Mrs. Poyser, however, though she noticed the bonnet, deferred remarking on it until she had disburdened herself of her surprise at Mr. Irwine's behaviour.

"Why, Mr. Irwine wasn't angry, then? What did he say to you, Dinah? Didn't he scold you for preaching?"

"No, he was not at all angry; he was very friendly to me. I was quite drawn out to speak to him; I hardly know how, for I had always thought of him as a worldly Sadducee. But his countenance is as pleasant as the morning sunshine."

"Pleasant! And what else did y' expect to find him but pleasant?" said Mrs. Poyser impatiently, resuming her knitting. "I should think his countenance is pleasant indeed! And him a gentleman born, and's got a mother like a picter. You may go the country round and not find such another woman turned sixty-six. It's summat-like to see such a man as that i' the desk of a Sunday! As I say to Poyser, it's like looking at a full crop o' wheat, or a pasture with a fine dairy o' cows in it; it makes you think the world's comfortable-like. But as for such creaturs as you Methodisses run after, I'd as soon go to look at a lot o' bare-ribbed runts on a common. Fine folks they are to tell you what's right, as look as if they'd never tasted nothing better than bacon-sword and sour-cake i' their lives. But what did Mr. Irwine say to you about that fool's trick o' preaching on the Green?"

"He only said he'd heard of it; he didn't seem to feel any displeasure about it. But, dear aunt, don't think any more about that. He told me something that I'm sure will cause you sorrow, as it does me. Thias Bede was drowned last night in the Willow Brook, and I'm thinking that the aged mother will be greatly in need of comfort. Perhaps I can be of use to her, so I have fetched my bonnet and am going to set out."

"Dear heart, dear heart! But you must have a cup o' tea first, child," said Mrs. Poyser, falling at once from the key of B with five sharps to the frank and genial C. "The kettle's boiling—we'll have it ready in a minute; and the young uns 'ull be in and wanting theirs directly. I'm quite willing you should go and see th' old woman, for you're one as is allays welcome in trouble, Methodist or no Methodist; but, for the matter o' that, it's the flesh and blood folks are made on as makes the difference. Some cheeses are made o' skimmed milk and some o' new milk, and it's no matter what you call 'em, you may tell which is which by the look and the smell. But as to Thias Bede, he's better out o' the way nor in—God forgi' me for saying so—for he's done little this ten year but make trouble for them as belonged to him; and I think it 'ud be well for you to take a little bottle o' rum for th' old woman, for I daresay she's got never a drop o' nothing to comfort her inside. Sit down, child, and be easy, for you shan't stir out till you've had a cup o' tea, and so I tell you."

During the latter part of this speech, Mrs. Poyser had been reaching down the tea-things from the shelves, and was on her way towards the pantry for the loaf (followed close by Totty, who had made her appearance on the rattling of the tea-cups), when Hetty came out of the dairy relieving her tired arms by lifting them up, and clasping her hands at the back of her head.

"Molly," she said, rather languidly, "just run out and get me a bunch of dock-leaves: the butter's ready to pack up now."

"D' you hear what's happened, Hetty?" said her aunt.

"No; how should I hear anything?" was the answer, in a pettish tone.

"Not as you'd care much, I daresay, if you did hear; for you're too feather-headed to mind if everybody was dead, so as you could stay upstairs a-dressing yourself for two hours by the clock. But anybody besides yourself 'ud mind about such things happening to them as think a deal more of you than you deserve. But Adam Bede and all his kin might be drownded for what you'd care—you'd be perking at the glass the next minute."

"Adam Bede—drowned?" said Hetty, letting her arms fall and looking rather bewildered, but suspecting that her aunt was as usual exaggerating with a didactic purpose.

"No, my dear, no," said Dinah kindly, for Mrs. Poyser had passed on to the pantry without deigning more precise information. "Not Adam. Adam's father, the old man, is drowned. He was drowned last night in the Willow Brook. Mr. Irwine has just told me about it."

"Oh, how dreadful!" said Hetty, looking serious, but not deeply affected; and as Molly now entered with the dock-leaves, she took them silently and returned to the dairy without asking further questions.

Chapter IX Hetty's World

WHILE she adjusted the broad leaves that set off the pale fragrant butter as the primrose is set off by its nest of green I am afraid Hetty was thinking a great deal more of the looks Captain Donnithorne had cast at her than of Adam and his troubles. Bright, admiring glances from a handsome young gentleman with white hands, a gold chain, occasional regimentals, and wealth and grandeur immeasurable—those were the warm rays that set poor Hetty's heart vibrating and playing its little foolish tunes over and over again. We do not hear that Memnon's statue gave forth its melody at all under the rushing of the mightiest wind, or in response to any other influence divine or human than certain short-lived sunbeams of morning; and we must learn to accommodate ourselves to the discovery that some of those cunningly fashioned instruments called human souls have only a very limited range of music, and will not vibrate in the least under a touch that fills others with tremulous rapture or quivering agony.

Hetty was quite used to the thought that people liked to look at her. She was not blind to the fact that young Luke Britton of Broxton came to Hayslope Church on a Sunday afternoon on purpose that he might see her; and that he would have made much more decided advances if her uncle Poyser, thinking but lightly of a young man whose father's land was so foul as old Luke Britton's, had not forbidden her aunt to encourage him by any civilities. She was aware, too, that Mr. Craig, the gardener at the Chase, was over head and ears in love with her, and had lately made unmistakable avowals in luscious strawberries and hyperbolical peas. She knew still better, that Adam Bede—tall, upright, clever, brave Adam Bede—who carried such authority with all the people round about, and whom her uncle was always delighted to see of an evening, saying that "Adam knew a fine sight more o' the natur o' things than those as thought themselves his betters"—she knew that this Adam, who was often rather stern to other people and not much given to run after the lasses, could be made to turn pale or red any day by a word or a look from her. Hetty's sphere of comparison was not large, but she couldn't help perceiving that Adam was "something like" a man; always knew what to say about things, could tell her uncle how to prop the hovel, and had mended the churn in no time; knew, with only looking at it, the value of the chestnut-tree that was blown down, and why the damp came in the walls, and what they must do to stop the rats; and wrote a beautiful hand that you could read off, and could do figures in his head—a degree of accomplishment totally unknown among the richest farmers of that countryside. Not at all like that slouching Luke Britton, who, when she once walked with him all the way from Broxton to

Hayslope, had only broken silence to remark that the grey goose had begun to lay. And as for Mr. Craig, the gardener, he was a sensible man enough, to be sure, but he was knock-kneed, and had a queer sort of sing-song in his talk; moreover, on the most charitable supposition, he must be far on the way to forty.

Hetty was quite certain her uncle wanted her to encourage Adam, and would be pleased for her to marry him. For those were times when there was no rigid demarcation of rank between the farmer and the respectable artisan, and on the home hearth, as well as in the public house, they might be seen taking their jug of ale together; the farmer having a latent sense of capital, and of weight in parish affairs, which sustained him under his conspicuous inferiority in conversation. Martin Poyser was not a frequenter of public houses, but he liked a friendly chat over his own home-brewed; and though it was pleasant to lay down the law to a stupid neighbour who had no notion how to make the best of his farm, it was also an agreeable variety to learn something from a clever fellow like Adam Bede. Accordingly, for the last three years—ever since he had superintended the building of the new barn—Adam had always been made welcome at the Hall Farm, especially of a winter evening, when the whole family, in patriarchal fashion, master and mistress, children and servants, were assembled in that glorious kitchen, at well-graduated distances from the blazing fire. And for the last two years, at least, Hetty had been in the habit of hearing her uncle say, "Adam Bede may be working for wage now, but he'll be a master-man some day, as sure as I sit in this chair. Mester Burge is in the right on't to want him to go partners and marry his daughter, if it's true what they say; the woman as marries him 'ull have a good take, be't Lady day or Michaelmas," a remark which Mrs. Poyser always followed up with her cordial assent. "Ah," she would say, "it's all very fine having a ready-made rich man, but mayhappen he'll be a ready-made fool; and it's no use filling your pocket full o' money if you've got a hole in the corner. It'll do you no good to sit in a spring-cart o' your own, if you've got a soft to drive you: he'll soon turn you over into the ditch. I allays said I'd never marry a man as had got no brains; for where's the use of a woman having brains of her own if she's tackled to a geck as everybody's a-laughing at? She might as well dress herself fine to sit back'ards on a donkey."

These expressions, though figurative, sufficiently indicated the bent of Mrs. Poyser's mind with regard to Adam; and though she and her husband might have viewed the subject differently if Hetty had been a daughter of their own, it was clear that they would have welcomed the match with Adam for a penniless niece. For what could Hetty have been but a servant elsewhere, if her uncle had not taken her in and brought her up as a domestic help to her aunt, whose health since the birth of Totty had not been equal to more positive labour than the superintendence of servants and children? But Hetty had never given Adam any steady encouragement. Even in the moments when she was most thoroughly conscious of his superiority to her other admirers, she had never brought herself to think of accepting him. She liked to feel that this strong, skilful, keen-eyed man was in her power, and would have been indignant if he had shown the least sign of slipping from under the yoke of her coquettish tyranny and attaching himself to the gentle Mary Burge, who would have been grateful enough for the most trifling notice from him. "Mary Burge, indeed! Such a sallow-faced girl: if she put on a bit of pink ribbon, she looked as yellow as a crow-flower and her hair was as straight as a hank of cotton." And always when Adam stayed away for several weeks from the Hall Farm, and otherwise made some show of resistance to his passion as a foolish one, Hetty took care to entice him back into the net by little airs of meekness and timidity, as if she were in trouble at his neglect. But as to marrying Adam, that was a very different affair! There was nothing in the world to tempt her to do that. Her cheeks never grew a shade deeper when his name was mentioned; she felt no thrill when she saw him passing along the causeway by the window, or advancing towards her unexpectedly in the footpath across the meadow; she felt nothing, when his eyes rested on her, but the cold triumph of knowing that he loved her and would not care to look at Mary Burge. He could no more stir in her the emotions that make the sweet intoxication of young love than the mere picture of a sun can stir the spring sap in the subtle fibres of the plant. She saw him as he was—a poor man with old parents to keep, who would not be able, for a long while to come, to give her even such luxuries as she shared in her uncle's house. And Hetty's dreams were all of luxuries: to sit in a carpeted parlour, and always wear white stockings; to have some large beautiful ear-rings, such as were all the fashion; to have Nottingham lace round the top of her gown, and something to make her handkerchief smell nice, like Miss Lydia Donnithorne's when she drew it out at church; and not to be obliged to get up early or be scolded by anybody. She thought, if Adam had been rich and could have given her these things, she loved him well enough to marry him.

But for the last few weeks a new influence had come over Hetty—vague, atmospheric, shaping itself into no self-confessed hopes or prospects, but producing a pleasant narcotic effect, making her tread the ground and go about her work in a sort of dream, unconscious of weight or effort, and showing her all things through a soft, liquid veil, as if she were living not in this solid world of brick and stone, but in a beatified world, such as the sun lights up for us in the waters. Hetty had become aware that Mr. Arthur Donnithorne would take a good deal of trouble for the chance of seeing her; that he always placed himself at church so as to have the fullest view of her both sitting and standing; that he was constantly finding reason for calling at the Hall Farm, and always would contrive to say something for the sake of making her speak to him and look at him. The poor child no more conceived at present the idea that the young squire could ever be her lover than a baker's pretty daughter in the crowd, whom a young emperor distinguishes by an imperial but admiring smile, conceives that she shall be made empress. But the baker's daughter goes home and dreams of the handsome young emperor, and perhaps weighs the flour amiss while she is thinking what a heavenly lot it must be to have him for a husband. And so, poor Hetty had got a face and a presence haunting her waking and sleeping dreams; bright, soft glances had penetrated her, and suffused her life with a strange, happy languor. The eyes that shed those glances were really not half so fine as Adam's, which sometimes looked at her with a sad, beseeching tenderness, but they had found a ready medium in Hetty's little silly imagination, whereas Adam's could get no entrance through that atmosphere. For three weeks, at least, her inward life had consisted of little else than living through in memory the looks and words Arthur had directed towards her—of little else than recalling the sensations with which she heard his voice outside the house, and saw him enter, and became conscious that his eyes were fixed on her, and then became conscious that a tall figure, looking down on her with eyes that seemed to touch her, was coming nearer in clothes of beautiful texture with an odour like that of a flower-garden borne on the evening breeze. Foolish thoughts! But all this happened, you must remember, nearly sixty years ago, and Hetty was quite uneducated—a simple farmer's girl, to whom a gentleman with a white hand was dazzling as an Olympian god. Until to-day, she had never looked farther into the future than to the next time Captain Donnithorne would come to the Farm, or the next Sunday when she should see him at church; but now she thought, perhaps he would try to meet her when she went to the Chase to-morrow—and if he should speak to her, and walk a little way, when nobody was by! That had never happened yet; and now her imagination, instead of retracing the past, was busy fashioning what would happen to-morrow—whereabout in the Chase she should see him coming towards her, how she should put her new rose-coloured ribbon on, which he had never seen, and what he would say to her to make her return his glance—a glance which she would be living through in her memory, over and over again, all the rest of the day.

In this state of mind, how could Hetty give any feeling to Adam's troubles, or think much about poor old Thias being drowned? Young souls, in such pleasant delirium as hers are as unsympathetic as butterflies sipping nectar; they are isolated from all appeals by a barrier of dreams—by invisible looks and impalpable arms.

While Hetty's hands were busy packing up the butter, and her head filled with these pictures of the morrow, Arthur Donnithorne, riding by Mr. Irwine's side towards the valley of the Willow Brook, had also certain indistinct anticipations, running as an undercurrent in his mind while he was listening to Mr. Irwine's account of Dinah—indistinct, yet strong enough to make him feel rather conscious when Mr. Irwine suddenly said, "What fascinated you so in Mrs. Poyser's dairy, Arthur? Have you become an amateur of damp quarries and skimming dishes?"

Arthur knew the rector too well to suppose that a clever invention would be of any use, so he said, with his accustomed frankness, "No, I went to look at the pretty butter-maker Hetty Sorrel. She's a perfect Hebe; and if I were an artist, I would paint her. It's amazing what pretty girls one sees among the farmers' daughters, when the men are such clowns. That common, round, red face one sees sometimes in the men—all cheek and no features, like Martin Poyser's—comes out in the women of the famuly as the most charming phiz imaginable."

"Well, I have no objection to your contemplating Hetty in an artistic light, but I must not have you feeding her vanity and filling her little noddle with the notion that she's a great beauty, attractive to fine gentlemen, or you will spoil her for a poor man's wife—honest Craig's, for example, whom I have seen bestowing soft glances on her. The little puss seems already to have airs enough to make a husband as miserable as it's a law of nature for a quiet man to be when he marries a beauty. Apropos of marrying, I hope our friend Adam will get settled, now the poor old man's gone. He will only have his mother to keep in future, and I've a notion that there's a kindness between him and that nice modest girl, Mary Burge, from something that fell from old Jonathan one day when I was talking to him. But when I mentioned the subject to Adam he looked uneasy and turned the conversation. I suppose the love-making doesn't run smooth, or perhaps Adam hangs back till he's in a better position. He has independence of spirit enough for two men—rather an excess of pride, if anything."

"That would be a capital match for Adam. He would slip into old Burge's shoes and make a fine thing of that building business, I'll answer for him. I should like to see him well settled in this parish; he would be ready then to act as my grand-vizier when I wanted one. We could plan no end of repairs and improvements together. I've never seen the girl, though, I think—at least I've never looked at her."

"Look at her next Sunday at church—she sits with her father on the left of the reading-desk. You needn't look quite so much at Hetty Sorrel then. When I've made up my mind that I can't afford to buy a tempting dog, I take no notice of him, because if he took a strong fancy to me and looked lovingly at me, the struggle between arithmetic and inclination might become unpleasantly severe. I pique myself on my wisdom there, Arthur, and as an old fellow to whom wisdom had become cheap, I bestow it upon you."

"Thank you. It may stand me in good stead some day though I don't know that I have any present use for it. Bless me! How the brook has overflowed. Suppose we have a canter, now we're at the bottom of the hill."

That is the great advantage of dialogue on horseback; it can be merged any minute into a trot or a canter, and one might have escaped from Socrates himself in the saddle. The two friends were free from the necessity of further conversation till they pulled up in the lane behind Adam's cottage.

Chapter X Dinah Visits Lisbeth

AT five o'clock Lisbeth came downstairs with a large key in her hand: it was the key of the chamber where her husband lay dead. Throughout the day, except in her occasional outbursts of wailing grief, she had been in incessant movement, performing the initial duties to her dead with the awe and exactitude that belong to religious rites. She had brought out her little store of bleached linen, which she had for long years kept in reserve for this supreme use. It seemed but yesterday—that time so many midsummers ago, when she had told Thias where this linen lay, that he might be sure and reach it out for her when SHE died, for she was the elder of the two. Then there had been the work of cleansing to the strictest purity every object in the sacred chamber, and of removing from it every trace of common daily occupation. The small window, which had hitherto freely let in the frosty moonlight or the warm summer sunrise on the working man's slumber, must now be darkened with a fair white sheet, for this was the sleep which is as sacred under the bare rafters as in ceiled houses. Lisbeth had even mended a long-neglected and unnoticeable rent in the checkered bit of bed-curtain; for the moments were few and precious now in which she would be able to do the smallest office of respect or love for the still corpse, to which in all her thoughts she attributed some consciousness. Our dead are never dead to us until we have forgotten them: they can be injured by us, they can be wounded; they know all our penitence, all our aching sense that their place is empty, all the kisses we bestow on the smallest relic of their presence. And the aged peasant woman most of all believes that her dead are conscious. Decent burial was what Lisbeth had been thinking of for herself through years of thrift, with an indistinct expectation that she should know when she was being carried to the churchyard, followed by her husband and her sons; and now she felt as if the greatest work of her life were to be done in seeing that Thias was buried decently before her—under the white thorn, where once, in a dream, she had thought she lay in the coffin, yet all the while saw the sunshine above and smelt the white blossoms that were so thick upon the thorn the Sunday she went to be churched after Adam was born.

But now she had done everything that could be done to-day in the chamber of death—had done it all herself, with some aid from her sons in lifting, for she would let no one be fetched to help her from the village, not being fond of female neighbours generally; and her favourite Dolly, the old housekeeper at Mr. Burge's, who had come to condole with her in the morning as soon as she heard of Thias's death, was too dim-sighted to be of much use. She had locked the door, and now held the key in her hand, as she threw herself wearily into a chair that stood out of its place in the middle of the house floor, where in ordinary times she would never have consented to sit. The kitchen had had none of her attention that day; it was soiled with the tread of muddy shoes and untidy with clothes and other objects out of place. But what at another time would have been intolerable to Lisbeth's habits of order and cleanliness seemed to her now just what should be: it was right that things should look strange and disordered and wretched, now the old man had come to his end in that sad way; the kitchen ought not to look as if nothing had happened. Adam, overcome with the agitations and exertions of the day after his night of hard work, had fallen asleep on a bench in the workshop; and Seth was in the back kitchen making a fire of sticks that he might get the kettle to boil, and persuade his mother to have a cup of tea, an indulgence which she rarely allowed herself.

There was no one in the kitchen when Lisbeth entered and threw herself into the chair. She looked round with blank eyes at the dirt and confusion on which the bright afternoon's sun shone dismally; it was all of a piece with the sad confusion of her mind—that confusion which belongs to the first hours of a sudden sorrow, when the poor human soul is like one who has been deposited sleeping among the ruins of a vast city, and wakes up in dreary amazement, not knowing whether it is the growing or the dying day—not knowing why and whence came this illimitable scene of desolation, or why he too finds himself desolate in the midst of it.

At another time Lisbeth's first thought would have been, "Where is Adam?" but the sudden death of her husband had restored him in these hours to that first place in her affections which he had held six-and-twenty years ago. She had forgotten his faults as we forget the sorrows of our departed childhood, and thought of nothing but the young husband's kindness and the old man's patience. Her eyes continued to wander blankly until Seth came in and began to remove some of the scattered things, and clear the small round deal table that he might set out his mother's tea upon it.

"What art goin' to do?" she said, rather peevishly.

"I want thee to have a cup of tea, Mother," answered Seth, tenderly. "It'll do thee good; and I'll put two or three of these things away, and make the house look more comfortable."

"Comfortable! How canst talk o' ma'in' things comfortable? Let a-be, let a-be. There's no comfort for me no more," she went on, the tears coming when she began to speak, "now thy poor feyther's gone, as I'n washed for and mended, an' got's victual for him for thirty 'ear, an' him allays so pleased wi' iverything I done for him, an' used to be so handy an' do the jobs for me when I war ill an' cumbered wi' th' babby, an' made me the posset an' brought it upstairs as proud as could be, an' carried the lad as war as heavy as two children for five mile an' ne'er grumbled, all the way to Warson Wake, 'cause I wanted to go an' see my sister, as war dead an' gone the very next Christmas as e'er come. An' him to be drownded in the brook as we passed o'er the day we war married an' come home together, an' he'd made them lots o' shelves for me to put my plates an' things on, an' showed 'em me as proud as could be, 'cause he know'd I should be pleased. An' he war to die an' me not to know, but to be a-sleepin' i' my bed, as if I caredna nought about it. Eh! An' me to live to see that! An' us as war young folks once, an' thought we should do rarely when we war married. Let a-be, lad, let a-be! I wonna ha' no tay. I carena if I ne'er ate nor drink no more. When one end o' th' bridge tumbles down, where's th' use o' th' other stannin'? I may's well die, an' foller my old man. There's no knowin' but he'll want me."

Here Lisbeth broke from words into moans, swaying herself backwards and forwards on her chair. Seth, always timid in his behaviour towards his mother, from the sense that he had no influence over her, felt it was useless to attempt to persuade or soothe her till this passion was past; so he contented himself with tending the back kitchen fire and folding up his father's clothes, which had been hanging out to dry since morning—afraid to move about in the room where his mother was, lest he should irritate her further.

But after Lisbeth had been rocking herself and moaning for some minutes, she suddenly paused and said aloud to herself, "I'll go an' see arter Adam, for I canna think where he's gotten; an' I want him to go upstairs wi' me afore it's dark, for the minutes to look at the corpse is like the meltin' snow."

Seth overheard this, and coming into the kitchen again, as his mother rose from her chair, he said, "Adam's asleep in the workshop, mother. Thee'dst better not wake him. He was o'erwrought with work and trouble."

"Wake him? Who's a-goin' to wake him? I shanna wake him wi' lookin' at him. I hanna seen the lad this two hour—I'd welly forgot as he'd e'er growed up from a babby when's feyther carried him."

Adam was seated on a rough bench, his head supported by his arm, which rested from the shoulder to the elbow on the long planing-table in the middle of the workshop. It seemed as if he had sat down for a few minutes' rest and had fallen asleep without slipping from his first attitude of sad, fatigued thought. His face, unwashed since yesterday, looked pallid and clammy; his hair was tossed shaggily about his forehead, and his closed eyes had the sunken look which follows upon watching and sorrow. His brow was knit, and his whole face had an expression of weariness and pain. Gyp was evidently uneasy, for he sat on his haunches, resting his nose on his master's stretched-out leg, and dividing the time between licking the hand that hung listlessly down and glancing with a listening air towards the door. The poor dog was hungry and restless, but would not leave his master, and was waiting impatiently for some change in the scene. It was owing to this feeling on Gyp's part that, when Lisbeth came into the workshop and advanced towards Adam as noiselessly as she could, her intention not to awaken him was immediately defeated; for Gyp's excitement was too great to find vent in anything short of a sharp bark, and in a moment Adam opened his eyes and saw his mother standing before him. It was not very unlike his dream, for his sleep had been little more than living through again, in a fevered delirious way, all that had happened since daybreak, and his mother with her fretful grief was present to him through it all. The chief difference between the reality and the vision was that in his dream Hetty was continually coming before him in bodily presence—strangely mingling herself as an actor in scenes with which she had nothing to do. She was even by the Willow Brook; she made his mother angry by coming into the house; and he met her with her smart clothes quite wet through, as he walked in the rain to Treddleston, to tell the coroner. But wherever Hetty came, his mother was sure to follow soon; and when he opened his eyes, it was not at all startling to see her standing near him.

"Eh, my lad, my lad!" Lisbeth burst out immediately, her wailing impulse returning, for grief in its freshness feels the need of associating its loss and its lament with every change of scene and incident, "thee'st got nobody now but thy old mother to torment thee and be a burden to thee. Thy poor feyther 'ull ne'er anger thee no more; an' thy mother may's well go arter him—the sooner the better—for I'm no good to nobody now. One old coat 'ull do to patch another, but it's good for nought else. Thee'dst like to ha' a wife to mend thy clothes an' get thy victual, better nor thy old mother. An' I shall be nought but cumber, a-sittin' i' th' chimney-corner. (Adam winced and moved uneasily; he dreaded, of all things, to hear his mother speak of Hetty.) But if thy feyther had lived, he'd ne'er ha' wanted me to go to make room for another, for he could no more ha' done wi'out me nor one side o' the scissars can do wi'out th' other. Eh, we should ha' been both flung away together, an' then I shouldna ha' seen this day, an' one buryin' 'ud ha' done for us both."

Here Lisbeth paused, but Adam sat in pained silence—he could not speak otherwise than tenderly to his mother to-day, but he could not help being irritated by this plaint. It was not possible for poor Lisbeth to know how it affected Adam any more than it is possible for a wounded dog to know how his moans affect the nerves of his master. Like all complaining women, she complained in the expectation of being soothed, and when Adam said nothing, she was only prompted to complain more bitterly.

"I know thee couldst do better wi'out me, for thee couldst go where thee likedst an' marry them as thee likedst. But I donna want to say thee nay, let thee bring home who thee wut; I'd ne'er open my lips to find faut, for when folks is old an' o' no use, they may think theirsens well off to get the bit an' the sup, though they'n to swallow ill words wi't. An' if thee'st set thy heart on a lass as'll bring thee nought and waste all, when thee mightst ha' them as 'ud make a man on thee, I'll say nought, now thy feyther's dead an' drownded, for I'm no better nor an old haft when the blade's gone."

Adam, unable to bear this any longer, rose silently from the bench and walked out of the workshop into the kitchen. But Lisbeth followed him.

"Thee wutna go upstairs an' see thy feyther then? I'n done everythin' now, an' he'd like thee to go an' look at him, for he war allays so pleased when thee wast mild to him."

Adam turned round at once and said, "Yes, mother; let us go upstairs. Come, Seth, let us go together."

They went upstairs, and for five minutes all was silence. Then the key was turned again, and there was a sound of footsteps on the stairs. But Adam did not come down again; he was too weary and worn-out to encounter more of his mother's querulous grief, and he went to rest on his bed. Lisbeth no sooner entered the kitchen and sat down than she threw her apron over her head, and began to cry and moan and rock herself as before. Seth thought, "She will be quieter by and by, now we have been upstairs"; and he went into the back kitchen again, to tend his little fire, hoping that he should presently induce her to have some tea.

Lisbeth had been rocking herself in this way for more than five minutes, giving a low moan with every forward movement of her body, when she suddenly felt a hand placed gently on hers, and a sweet treble voice said to her, "Dear sister, the Lord has sent me to see if I can be a comfort to you."

Lisbeth paused, in a listening attitude, without removing her apron from her face. The voice was strange to her. Could it be her sister's spirit come back to her from the dead after all those years? She trembled and dared not look.

Dinah, believing that this pause of wonder was in itself a relief for the sorrowing woman, said no more just yet, but quietly took off her bonnet, and then, motioning silence to Seth, who, on hearing her voice, had come in with a beating heart, laid one hand on the back of Lisbeth's chair and leaned over her, that she might be aware of a friendly presence.

Slowly Lisbeth drew down her apron, and timidly she opened her dim dark eyes. She saw nothing at first but a face—a pure, pale face, with loving grey eyes, and it was quite unknown to her. Her wonder increased; perhaps it WAS an angel. But in the same instant Dinah had laid her hand on Lisbeth's again, and the old woman looked down at it. It was a much smaller hand than her own, but it was not white and delicate, for Dinah had never worn a glove in her life, and her hand bore the traces of labour from her childhood upwards. Lisbeth looked earnestly at the hand for a moment, and then, fixing her eyes again on Dinah's face, said, with something of restored courage, but in a tone of surprise, "Why, ye're a workin' woman!"

"Yes, I am Dinah Morris, and I work in the cotton-mill when I am at home."

"Ah!" said Lisbeth slowly, still wondering; "ye comed in so light, like the shadow on the wall, an' spoke i' my ear, as I thought ye might be a sperrit. Ye've got a'most the face o' one as is a-sittin' on the grave i' Adam's new Bible."

"I come from the Hall Farm now. You know Mrs. Poyser—she's my aunt, and she has heard of your great affliction, and is very sorry; and I'm come to see if I can be any help to you in your trouble; for I know your sons Adam and Seth, and I know you have no daughter; and when the clergyman told me how the hand of God was heavy upon you, my heart went out towards you, and I felt a command to come and be to you in the place of a daughter in this grief, if you will let me."

"Ah! I know who y' are now; y' are a Methody, like Seth; he's tould me on you," said Lisbeth fretfully, her overpowering sense of pain returning, now her wonder was gone. "Ye'll make it out as trouble's a good thing, like HE allays does. But where's the use o' talkin' to me a-that'n? Ye canna make the smart less wi' talkin'. Ye'll ne'er make me believe as it's better for me not to ha' my old man die in's bed, if he must die, an' ha' the parson to pray by him, an' me to sit by him, an' tell him ne'er to mind th' ill words I've gi'en him sometimes when I war angered, an' to gi' him a bit an' a sup, as long as a bit an' a sup he'd swallow. But eh! To die i' the cold water, an' us close to him, an' ne'er to know; an' me a-sleepin', as if I ne'er belonged to him no more nor if he'd been a journeyman tramp from nobody knows where!"

Here Lisbeth began to cry and rock herself again; and Dinah said, "Yes, dear friend, your affliction is great. It would be hardness of heart to say that your trouble was not heavy to bear. God didn't send me to you to make light of your sorrow, but to mourn with you, if you will let me. If you had a table spread for a feast, and was making merry with your friends, you would think it was kind to let me come and sit down and rejoice with you, because you'd think I should like to share those good things; but I should like better to share in your trouble and your labour, and it would seem harder to me if you denied me that. You won't send me away? You're not angry with me for coming?"

"Nay, nay; angered! who said I war angered? It war good on you to come. An' Seth, why donna ye get her some tay? Ye war in a hurry to get some for me, as had no need, but ye donna think o' gettin' 't for them as wants it. Sit ye down; sit ye down. I thank you kindly for comin', for it's little wage ye get by walkin' through the wet fields to see an old woman like me. . . . Nay, I'n got no daughter o' my own—ne'er had one—an' I warna sorry, for they're poor queechy things, gells is; I allays wanted to ha' lads, as could fend for theirsens. An' the lads 'ull be marryin'—I shall ha' daughters eno', an' too many. But now, do ye make the tay as ye like it, for I'n got no taste i' my mouth this day—it's all one what I swaller—it's all got the taste o' sorrow wi't."

Dinah took care not to betray that she had had her tea, and accepted Lisbeth's invitation very readily, for the sake of persuading the old woman herself to take the food and drink she so much needed after a day of hard work and fasting.

Seth was so happy now Dinah was in the house that he could not help thinking her presence was worth purchasing with a life in which grief incessantly followed upon grief; but the next moment he reproached himself—it was almost as if he were rejoicing in his father's sad death. Nevertheless the joy of being with Dinah WOULD triumph—it was like the influence of climate, which no resistance can overcome. And the feeling even suffused itself over his face so as to attract his mother's notice, while she was drinking her tea.

"Thee may'st well talk o' trouble bein' a good thing, Seth, for thee thriv'st on't. Thee look'st as if thee know'dst no more o' care an' cumber nor when thee wast a babby a-lyin' awake i' th' cradle. For thee'dst allays lie still wi' thy eyes open, an' Adam ne'er 'ud lie still a minute when he wakened. Thee wast allays like a bag o' meal as can ne'er be bruised—though, for the matter o' that, thy poor feyther war just such another. But ye've got the same look too" (here Lisbeth turned to Dinah). "I reckon it's wi' bein' a Methody. Not as I'm a-findin' faut wi' ye for't, for ye've no call to be frettin', an' somehow ye looken sorry too. Eh! Well, if the Methodies are fond o' trouble, they're like to thrive: it's a pity they canna ha't all, an' take it away from them as donna like it. I could ha' gi'en 'em plenty; for when I'd gotten my old man I war worreted from morn till night; and now he's gone, I'd be glad for the worst o'er again."

"Yes," said Dinah, careful not to oppose any feeling of Lisbeth's, for her reliance, in her smallest words and deeds, on a divine guidance, always issued in that finest woman's tact which proceeds from acute and ready sympathy; "yes, I remember too, when my dear aunt died, I longed for the sound of her bad cough in the nights, instead of the silence that came when she was gone. But now, dear friend, drink this other cup of tea and eat a little more."

"What!" said Lisbeth, taking the cup and speaking in a less querulous tone, "had ye got no feyther and mother, then, as ye war so sorry about your aunt?"

"No, I never knew a father or mother; my aunt brought me up from a baby. She had no children, for she was never married and she brought me up as tenderly as if I'd been her own child."

"Eh, she'd fine work wi' ye, I'll warrant, bringin' ye up from a babby, an' her a lone woman—it's ill bringin' up a cade lamb. But I daresay ye warna franzy, for ye look as if ye'd ne'er been angered i' your life. But what did ye do when your aunt died, an' why didna ye come to live in this country, bein' as Mrs. Poyser's your aunt too?"

Dinah, seeing that Lisbeth's attention was attracted, told her the story of her early life—how she had been brought up to work hard, and what sort of place Snowfield was, and how many people had a hard life there—all the details that she thought likely to interest Lisbeth. The old woman listened, and forgot to be fretful, unconsciously subject to the soothing influence of Dinah's face and voice. After a while she was persuaded to let the kitchen be made tidy; for Dinah was bent on this, believing that the sense of order and quietude around her would help in disposing Lisbeth to join in the prayer she longed to pour forth at her side. Seth, meanwhile, went out to chop wood, for he surmised that Dinah would like to be left alone with his mother.

Lisbeth sat watching her as she moved about in her still quick way, and said at last, "Ye've got a notion o' cleanin' up. I wouldna mind ha'in ye for a daughter, for ye wouldna spend the lad's wage i' fine clothes an' waste. Ye're not like the lasses o' this countryside. I reckon folks is different at Snowfield from what they are here."

"They have a different sort of life, many of 'em," said Dinah; "they work at different things—some in the mill, and many in the mines, in the villages round about. But the heart of man is the same everywhere, and there are the children of this world and the children of light there as well as elsewhere. But we've many more Methodists there than in this country."

"Well, I didna know as the Methody women war like ye, for there's Will Maskery's wife, as they say's a big Methody, isna pleasant to look at, at all. I'd as lief look at a tooad. An' I'm thinkin' I wouldna mind if ye'd stay an' sleep here, for I should like to see ye i' th' house i' th' mornin'. But mayhappen they'll be lookin for ye at Mester Poyser's."

"No," said Dinah, "they don't expect me, and I should like to stay, if you'll let me."

"Well, there's room; I'n got my bed laid i' th' little room o'er the back kitchen, an' ye can lie beside me. I'd be glad to ha' ye wi' me to speak to i' th' night, for ye've got a nice way o' talkin'. It puts me i' mind o' the swallows as was under the thack last 'ear when they fust begun to sing low an' soft-like i' th' mornin'. Eh, but my old man war fond o' them birds! An' so war Adam, but they'n ne'er comed again this 'ear. Happen THEY'RE dead too."

"There," said Dinah, "now the kitchen looks tidy, and now, dear Mother—for I'm your daughter to-night, you know—I should like you to wash your face and have a clean cap on. Do you remember what David did, when God took away his child from him? While the child was yet alive he fasted and prayed to God to spare it, and he would neither eat nor drink, but lay on the ground all night, beseeching God for the child. But when he knew it was dead, he rose up from the ground and washed and anointed himself, and changed his clothes, and ate and drank; and when they asked him how it was that he seemed to have left off grieving now the child was dead, he said, 'While the child was yet alive, I fasted and wept; for I said, Who can tell whether God will be gracious to me, that the child may live? But now he is dead, wherefore should I fast? Can I bring him back again? I shall go to him, but he shall not return to me.'"

"Eh, that's a true word," said Lisbeth. "Yea, my old man wonna come back to me, but I shall go to him—the sooner the better. Well, ye may do as ye like wi' me: there's a clean cap i' that drawer, an' I'll go i' the back kitchen an' wash my face. An' Seth, thee may'st reach down Adam's new Bible wi' th' picters in, an' she shall read us a chapter. Eh, I like them words—'I shall go to him, but he wonna come back to me.'"

Dinah and Seth were both inwardly offering thanks for the greater quietness of spirit that had come over Lisbeth. This was what Dinah had been trying to bring about, through all her still sympathy and absence from exhortation. From her girlhood upwards she had had experience among the sick and the mourning, among minds hardened and shrivelled through poverty and ignorance, and had gained the subtlest perception of the mode in which they could best be touched and softened into willingness to receive words of spiritual consolation or warning. As Dinah expressed it, "she was never left to herself; but it was always given her when to keep silence and when to speak." And do we not all agree to call rapid thought and noble impulse by the name of inspiration? After our subtlest analysis of the mental process, we must still say, as Dinah did, that our highest thoughts and our best deeds are all given to us.

And so there was earnest prayer—there was faith, love, and hope pouring forth that evening in the littie kitchen. And poor, aged, fretful Lisbeth, without grasping any distinct idea, without going through any course of religious emotions, felt a vague sense of goodness and love, and of something right lying underneath and beyond all this sorrowing life. She couldn't understand the sorrow; but, for these moments, under the subduing influence of Dinah's spirit, she felt that she must be patient and still.

Chapter XI In the Cottage

IT was but half-past four the next morning when Dinah, tired of lying awake listening to the birds and watching the growing light through the little window in the garret roof, rose and began to dress herself very quietly, lest she should disturb Lisbeth. But already some one else was astir in the house, and had gone downstairs, preceded by Gyp. The dog's pattering step was a sure sign that it was Adam who went down; but Dinah was not aware of this, and she thought it was more likely to be Seth, for he had told her how Adam had stayed up working the night before. Seth, however, had only just awakened at the sound of the opening door. The exciting influence of the previous day, heightened at last by Dinah's unexpected presence, had not been counteracted by any bodily weariness, for he had not done his ordinary amount of hard work; and so when he went to bed; it was not till he had tired himself with hours of tossing wakefulness that drowsiness came, and led on a heavier morning sleep than was usual with him.

But Adam had been refreshed by his long rest, and with his habitual impatience of mere passivity, he was eager to begin the new day and subdue sadness by his strong will and strong arm. The white mist lay in the valley; it was going to be a bright warm day, and he would start to work again when he had had his breakfast.

"There's nothing but what's bearable as long as a man can work," he said to himself; "the natur o' things doesn't change, though it seems as if one's own life was nothing but change. The square o' four is sixteen, and you must lengthen your lever in proportion to your weight, is as true when a man's miserable as when he's happy; and the best o' working is, it gives you a grip hold o' things outside your own lot."

As he dashed the cold water over his head and face, he felt completely himself again, and with his black eyes as keen as ever and his thick black hair all glistening with the fresh moisture, he went into the workshop to look out the wood for his father's coffin, intending that he and Seth should carry it with them to Jonathan Burge's and have the coffin made by one of the workmen there, so that his mother might not see and hear the sad task going forward at home.

He had just gone into the workshop when his quick ear detected a light rapid foot on the stairs—certainly not his mother's. He had been in bed and asleep when Dinah had come in, in the evening, and now he wondered whose step this could be. A foolish thought came, and moved him strangely. As if it could be Hetty! She was the last person likely to be in the house. And yet he felt reluctant to go and look and have the clear proof that it was some one else. He stood leaning on a plank he had taken hold of, listening to sounds which his imagination interpreted for him so pleasantly that the keen strong face became suffused with a timid tenderness. The light footstep moved about the kitchen, followed by the sound of the sweeping brush, hardly making so much noise as the lightest breeze that chases the autumn leaves along the dusty path; and Adam's imagination saw a dimpled face, with dark bright eyes and roguish smiles looking backward at this brush, and a rounded figure just leaning a little to clasp the handle. A very foolish thought—it could not be Hetty; but the only way of dismissing such nonsense from his head was to go and see WHO it was, for his fancy only got nearer and nearer to belief while he stood there listening. He loosed the plank and went to the kitchen door.

"How do you do, Adam Bede?" said Dinah, in her calm treble, pausing from her sweeping and fixing her mild grave eyes upon him.

"I trust you feel rested and strengthened again to bear the burden and heat of the day."

It was like dreaming of the sunshine and awaking in the moonlight. Adam had seen Dinah several times, but always at the Hall Farm, where he was not very vividly conscious of any woman's presence except Hetty's, and he had only in the last day or two begun to suspect that Seth was in love with her, so that his attention had not hitherto been drawn towards her for his brother's sake. But now her slim figure, her plain black gown, and her pale serene face impressed him with all the force that belongs to a reality contrasted with a preoccupying fancy. For the first moment or two he made no answer, but looked at her with the concentrated, examining glance which a man gives to an object in which he has suddenly begun to be interested. Dinah, for the first time in her life, felt a painful self-consciousness; there was something in the dark penetrating glance of this strong man so different from the mildness and timidity of his brother Seth. A faint blush came, which deepened as she wondered at it. This blush recalled Adam from his forgetfulness.

"I was quite taken by surprise; it was very good of you to come and see my mother in her trouble," he said, in a gentle grateful tone, for his quick mind told him at once how she came to be there. "I hope my mother was thankful to have you," he added, wondering rather anxiously what had been Dinah's reception.

"Yes," said Dinah, resuming her work, "she seemed greatly comforted after a while, and she's had a good deal of rest in the night, by times. She was fast asleep when I left her."

"Who was it took the news to the Hall Farm?" said Adam, his thoughts reverting to some one there; he wondered whether SHE had felt anything about it.

"It was Mr. Irwine, the clergyman, told me, and my aunt was grieved for your mother when she heard it, and wanted me to come; and so is my uncle, I'm sure, now he's heard it, but he was gone out to Rosseter all yesterday. They'll look for you there as soon as you've got time to go, for there's nobody round that hearth but what's glad to see you."

Dinah, with her sympathetic divination, knew quite well that Adam was longing to hear if Hetty had said anything about their trouble; she was too rigorously truthful for benevolent invention, but she had contrived to say something in which Hetty was tacitly included. Love has a way of cheating itself consciously, like a child who plays at solitary hide-and-seek; it is pleased with assurances that it all the while disbelieves. Adam liked what Dinah had said so much that his mind was directly full of the next visit he should pay to the Hall Farm, when Hetty would perhaps behave more kindly to him than she had ever done before.

"But you won't be there yourself any longer?" he said to Dinah.

"No, I go back to Snowfield on Saturday, and I shall have to set out to Treddleston early, to be in time for the Oakbourne carrier. So I must go back to the farm to-night, that I may have the last day with my aunt and her children. But I can stay here all to-day, if your mother would like me; and her heart seemed inclined towards me last night."

"Ah, then, she's sure to want you to-day. If mother takes to people at the beginning, she's sure to get fond of 'em; but she's a strange way of not liking young women. Though, to be sure," Adam went on, smiling, "her not liking other young women is no reason why she shouldn't like you."

Hitherto Gyp had been assisting at this conversation in motionless silence, seated on his haunches, and alternately looking up in his master's face to watch its expression and observing Dinah's movements about the kitchen. The kind smile with which Adam uttered the last words was apparently decisive with Gyp of the light in which the stranger was to be regarded, and as she turned round after putting aside her sweeping-brush, he trotted towards her and put up his muzzle against her hand in a friendly way.

"You see Gyp bids you welcome," said Adam, "and he's very slow to welcome strangers."

"Poor dog!" said Dinah, patting the rough grey coat, "I've a strange feeling about the dumb things as if they wanted to speak, and it was a trouble to 'em because they couldn't. I can't help being sorry for the dogs always, though perhaps there's no need. But they may well have more in them than they know how to make us understand, for we can't say half what we feel, with all our words."

Seth came down now, and was pleased to find Adam talking with Dinah; he wanted Adam to know how much better she was than all other women. But after a few words of greeting, Adam drew him into the workshop to consult about the coffin, and Dinah went on with her cleaning.

By six o'clock they were all at breakfast with Lisbeth in a kitchen as clean as she could have made it herself. The window and door were open, and the morning air brought with it a mingled scent of southernwood, thyme, and sweet-briar from the patch of garden by the side of the cottage. Dinah did not sit down at first, but moved about, serving the others with the warm porridge and the toasted oat-cake, which she had got ready in the usual way, for she had asked Seth to tell her just what his mother gave them for breakfast. Lisbeth had been unusually silent since she came downstairs, apparently requiring some time to adjust her ideas to a state of things in which she came down like a lady to find all the work done, and sat still to be waited on. Her new sensations seemed to exclude the remembrance of her grief. At last, after tasting the porridge, she broke silence:

"Ye might ha' made the parridge worse," she said to Dinah; "I can ate it wi'out its turnin' my stomach. It might ha' been a trifle thicker an' no harm, an' I allays putten a sprig o' mint in mysen; but how's ye t' know that? The lads arena like to get folks as 'll make their parridge as I'n made it for 'em; it's well if they get onybody as 'll make parridge at all. But ye might do, wi' a bit o' showin'; for ye're a stirrin' body in a mornin', an' ye've a light heel, an' ye've cleaned th' house well enough for a ma'shift."

"Makeshift, mother?" said Adam. "Why, I think the house looks beautiful. I don't know how it could look better."

"Thee dostna know? Nay; how's thee to know? Th' men ne'er know whether the floor's cleaned or cat-licked. But thee'lt know when thee gets thy parridge burnt, as it's like enough to be when I'n gi'en o'er makin' it. Thee'lt think thy mother war good for summat then."

"Dinah," said Seth, "do come and sit down now and have your breakfast. We're all served now."

"Aye, come an' sit ye down—do," said Lisbeth, "an' ate a morsel; ye'd need, arter bein' upo' your legs this hour an' half a'ready. Come, then," she added, in a tone of complaining affection, as Dinah sat down by her side, "I'll be loath for ye t' go, but ye canna stay much longer, I doubt. I could put up wi' ye i' th' house better nor wi' most folks."

"I'll stay till to-night if you're willing," said Dinah. "I'd stay longer, only I'm going back to Snowfield on Saturday, and I must be with my aunt to-morrow."

"Eh, I'd ne'er go back to that country. My old man come from that Stonyshire side, but he left it when he war a young un, an' i' the right on't too; for he said as there war no wood there, an' it 'ud ha' been a bad country for a carpenter."

"Ah," said Adam, "I remember father telling me when I was a little lad that he made up his mind if ever he moved it should be south'ard. But I'm not so sure about it. Bartle Massey says—and he knows the South—as the northern men are a finer breed than the southern, harder-headed and stronger-bodied, and a deal taller. And then he says in some o' those counties it's as flat as the back o' your hand, and you can see nothing of a distance without climbing up the highest trees. I couldn't abide that. I like to go to work by a road that'll take me up a bit of a hill, and see the fields for miles round me, and a bridge, or a town, or a bit of a steeple here and there. It makes you feel the world's a big place, and there's other men working in it with their heads and hands besides yourself."

"I like th' hills best," said Seth, "when the clouds are over your head and you see the sun shining ever so far off, over the Loamford way, as I've often done o' late, on the stormy days. It seems to me as if that was heaven where there's always joy and sunshine, though this life's dark and cloudy."

"Oh, I love the Stonyshire side," said Dinah; "I shouldn't like to set my face towards the countries where they're rich in corn and cattle, and the ground so level and easy to tread; and to turn my back on the hills where the poor people have to live such a hard life and the men spend their days in the mines away from the sunlight. It's very blessed on a bleak cold day, when the sky is hanging dark over the hill, to feel the love of God in one's soul, and carry it to the lonely, bare, stone houses, where there's nothing else to give comfort."

"Eh!" said Lisbeth, "that's very well for ye to talk, as looks welly like the snowdrop-flowers as ha' lived for days an' days when I'n gethered 'em, wi' nothin' but a drop o' water an' a peep o' daylight; but th' hungry foulks had better leave th' hungry country. It makes less mouths for the scant cake. But," she went on, looking at Adam, "donna thee talk o' goin' south'ard or north'ard, an' leavin' thy feyther and mother i' the churchyard, an' goin' to a country as they know nothin' on. I'll ne'er rest i' my grave if I donna see thee i' the churchyard of a Sunday."

"Donna fear, mother," said Adam. "If I hadna made up my mind not to go, I should ha' been gone before now."

He had finished his breakfast now, and rose as he was speaking.

"What art goin' to do?" asked Lisbeth. "Set about thy feyther's coffin?"

"No, mother," said Adam; "we're going to take the wood to the village and have it made there."

"Nay, my lad, nay," Lisbeth burst out in an eager, wailing tone; "thee wotna let nobody make thy feyther's coffin but thysen? Who'd make it so well? An' him as know'd what good work war, an's got a son as is the head o' the village an' all Treddles'on too, for cleverness."

"Very well, mother, if that's thy wish, I'll make the coffin at home; but I thought thee wouldstna like to hear the work going on."

"An' why shouldna I like 't? It's the right thing to be done. An' what's liking got to do wi't? It's choice o' mislikings is all I'n got i' this world. One morsel's as good as another when your mouth's out o' taste. Thee mun set about it now this mornin' fust thing. I wonna ha' nobody to touch the coffin but thee."

Adam's eyes met Seth's, which looked from Dinah to him rather wistfully.

"No, Mother," he said, "I'll not consent but Seth shall have a hand in it too, if it's to be done at home. I'll go to the village this forenoon, because Mr. Burge 'ull want to see me, and Seth shall stay at home and begin the coffin. I can come back at noon, and then he can go."

"Nay, nay," persisted Lisbeth, beginning to cry, "I'n set my heart on't as thee shalt ma' thy feyther's coffin. Thee't so stiff an' masterful, thee't ne'er do as thy mother wants thee. Thee wast often angered wi' thy feyther when he war alive; thee must be the better to him now he's gone. He'd ha' thought nothin' on't for Seth to ma's coffin."

"Say no more, Adam, say no more," said Seth, gently, though his voice told that he spoke with some effort; "Mother's in the right. I'll go to work, and do thee stay at home."

He passed into the workshop immediately, followed by Adam; while Lisbeth, automatically obeying her old habits, began to put away the breakfast things, as if she did not mean Dinah to take her place any longer. Dinah said nothing, but presently used the opportunity of quietly joining the brothers in the workshop.

They had already got on their aprons and paper caps, and Adam was standing with his left hand on Seth's shoulder, while he pointed with the hammer in his right to some boards which they were looking at. Their backs were turned towards the door by which Dinah entered, and she came in so gently that they were not aware of her presence till they heard her voice saying, "Seth Bede!" Seth started, and they both turned round. Dinah looked as if she did not see Adam, and fixed her eyes on Seth's face, saying with calm kindness, "I won't say farewell. I shall see you again when you come from work. So as I'm at the farm before dark, it will be quite soon enough."

"Thank you, Dinah; I should like to walk home with you once more. It'll perhaps be the last time."

There was a little tremor in Seth's voice. Dinah put out her hand and said, "You'll have sweet peace in your mind to-day, Seth, for your tenderness and long-suffering towards your aged mother."

She turned round and left the workshop as quickly and quietly as she had entered it. Adam had been observing her closely all the while, but she had not looked at him. As soon as she was gone, he said, "I don't wonder at thee for loving her, Seth. She's got a face like a lily."

Seth's soul rushed to his eyes and lips: he had never yet confessed his secret to Adam, but now he felt a delicious sense of disburdenment, as he answered, "Aye, Addy, I do love her—too much, I doubt. But she doesna love me, lad, only as one child o' God loves another. She'll never love any man as a husband—that's my belief."

"Nay, lad, there's no telling; thee mustna lose heart. She's made out o' stuff with a finer grain than most o' the women; I can see that clear enough. But if she's better than they are in other things, I canna think she'll fall short of 'em in loving."

No more was said. Seth set out to the village, and Adam began his work on the coffin.

"God help the lad, and me too," he thought, as he lifted the board. "We're like enough to find life a tough job—hard work inside and out. It's a strange thing to think of a man as can lift a chair with his teeth and walk fifty mile on end, trembling and turning hot and cold at only a look from one woman out of all the rest i' the world. It's a mystery we can give no account of; but no more we can of the sprouting o' the seed, for that matter."

Chapter XII In the Wood

THAT same Thursday morning, as Arthur Donnithorne was moving about in his dressing-room seeing his well-looking British person reflected in the old-fashioned mirrors, and stared at, from a dingy olive-green piece of tapestry, by Pharaoh's daughter and her maidens, who ought to have been minding the infant Moses, he was holding a discussion with himself, which, by the time his valet was tying the black silk sling over his shoulder, had issued in a distinct practical resolution.

"I mean to go to Eagledale and fish for a week or so," he said aloud. "I shall take you with me, Pym, and set off this morning; so be ready by half-past eleven."

The low whistle, which had assisted him in arriving at this resolution, here broke out into his loudest ringing tenor, and the corridor, as he hurried along it, echoed to his favourite song from the Beggar's Opera, "When the heart of a man is oppressed with care." Not an heroic strain; nevertheless Arthur felt himself very heroic as he strode towards the stables to give his orders about the horses. His own approbation was necessary to him, and it was not an approbation to be enjoyed quite gratuitously; it must be won by a fair amount of merit. He had never yet forfeited that approbation, and he had considerable reliance on his own virtues. No young man could confess his faults more candidly; candour was one of his favourite virtues; and how can a man's candour be seen in all its lustre unless he has a few failings to talk of? But he had an agreeable confidence that his faults were all of a generous kind—impetuous, warm-blooded, leonine; never crawling, crafty, reptilian. It was not possible for Arthur

Donnithorne to do anything mean, dastardly, or cruel. "No! I'm a devil of a fellow for getting myself into a hobble, but I always take care the load shall fall on my own shoulders." Unhappily, there is no inherent poetical justice in hobbles, and they will sometimes obstinately refuse to inflict their worst consequences on the prime offender, in spite of his loudly expressed wish. It was entirely owing to this deficiency in the scheme of things that Arthur had ever brought any one into trouble besides himself. He was nothing if not good-natured; and all his pictures of the future, when he should come into the estate, were made up of a prosperous, contented tenantry, adoring their landlord, who would be the model of an English gentleman—mansion in first-rate order, all elegance and high taste—jolly housekeeping, finest stud in Loamshire—purse open to all public objects—in short, everything as different as possible from what was now associated with the name of Donnithorne. And one of the first good actions he would perform in that future should be to increase Irwine's income for the vicarage of Hayslope, so that he might keep a carriage for his mother and sisters. His hearty affection for the rector dated from the age of frocks and trousers. It was an affection partly filial, partly fraternal—fraternal enough to make him like Irwine's company better than that of most younger men, and filial enough to make him shrink strongly from incurring Irwine's disapprobation.

You perceive that Arthur Donnithorne was "a good fellow"—all his college friends thought him such. He couldn't bear to see any one uncomfortable; he would have been sorry even in his angriest moods for any harm to happen to his grandfather; and his Aunt Lydia herself had the benefit of that soft-heartedness which he bore towards the whole sex. Whether he would have self-mastery enough to be always as harmless and purely beneficent as his good-nature led him to desire, was a question that no one had yet decided against him; he was but twenty-one, you remember, and we don't inquire too closely into character in the case of a handsome generous young fellow, who will have property enough to support numerous peccadilloes—who, if he should unfortunately break a man's legs in his rash driving, will be able to pension him handsomely; or if he should happen to spoil a woman's existence for her, will make it up to her with expensive bonbons, packed up and directed by his own hand. It would be ridiculous to be prying and analytic in such cases, as if one were inquiring into the character of a confidential clerk. We use round, general, gentlemanly epithets about a young man of birth and fortune; and ladies, with that fine intuition which is the distinguishing attribute of their sex, see at once that he is "nice." The chances are that he will go through life without scandalizing any one; a seaworthy vessel that no one would refuse to insure. Ships, certainly, are liable to casualties, which sometimes make terribly evident some flaw in their construction that would never have been discoverable in smooth water; and many a "good fellow," through a disastrous combination of circumstances, has undergone a like betrayal.

But we have no fair ground for entertaining unfavourable auguries concerning Arthur Donnithorne, who this morning proves himself capable of a prudent resolution founded on conscience. One thing is clear: Nature has taken care that he shall never go far astray with perfect comfort and satisfaction to himself; he will never get beyond that border-land of sin, where he will be perpetually harassed by assaults from the other side of the boundary. He will never be a courtier of Vice, and wear her orders in his button-hole.

It was about ten o'clock, and the sun was shining brilliantly; everything was looking lovelier for the yesterday's rain. It is a pleasant thing on such a morning to walk along the well-rolled gravel on one's way to the stables, meditating an excursion. But the scent of the stables, which, in a natural state of things, ought to be among the soothing influences of a man's life, always brought with it some irritation to Arthur. There was no having his own way in the stables; everything was managed in the stingiest fashion. His grandfather persisted in retaining as head groom an old dolt whom no sort of lever could move out of his old habits, and who was allowed to hire a succession of raw Loamshire lads as his subordinates, one of whom had lately tested a new pair of shears by clipping an oblong patch on Arthur's bay mare. This state of things is naturally embittering; one can put up with annoyances in the house, but to have the stable made a scene of vexation and disgust is a point beyond what human flesh and blood can be expected to endure long together without danger of misanthropy.

Old John's wooden, deep-wrinkled face was the first object that met Arthur's eyes as he entered the stable-yard, and it quite poisoned for him the bark of the two bloodhounds that kept watch there. He could never speak quite patiently to the old blockhead.

"You must have Meg saddled for me and brought to the door at half-past eleven, and I shall want Rattler saddled for Pym at the same time. Do you hear?"

"Yes, I hear, I hear, Cap'n," said old John very deliberately, following the young master into the stable. John considered a young master as the natural enemy of an old servant, and young people in general as a poor contrivance for carrying on the world.

Arthur went in for the sake of patting Meg, declining as far as possible to see anything in the stables, lest he should lose his temper before breakfast. The pretty creature was in one of the inner stables, and turned her mild head as her master came beside her. Little Trot, a tiny spaniel, her inseparable companion in the stable, was comfortably curled up on her back.

"Well, Meg, my pretty girl," said Arthur, patting her neck, "we'll have a glorious canter this morning."

"Nay, your honour, I donna see as that can be," said John.

"Not be? Why not?"

"Why, she's got lamed."

"Lamed, confound you! What do you mean?"

"Why, th' lad took her too close to Dalton's hosses, an' one on 'em flung out at her, an' she's got her shank bruised o' the near foreleg."

The judicious historian abstains from narrating precisely what ensued. You understand that there was a great deal of strong language, mingled with soothing "who-ho's" while the leg was examined; that John stood by with quite as much emotion as if he had been a cunningly carved crab-tree walking-stick, and that Arthur Donnithorne presently repassed the iron gates of the pleasure-ground without singing as he went.

He considered himself thoroughly disappointed and annoyed. There was not another mount in the stable for himself and his servant besides Meg and Rattler. It was vexatious; just when he wanted to get out of the way for a week or two. It seemed culpable in Providence to allow such a combination of circumstances. To be shut up at the Chase with a broken arm when every other fellow in his regiment was enjoying himself at Windsor—shut up with his grandfather, who had the same sort of affection for him as for his parchment deeds! And to be disgusted at every turn with the management of the house and the estate! In such circumstances a man necessarily gets in an ill humour, and works off the irritation by some excess or other. "Salkeld would have drunk a bottle of port every day," he muttered to himself, "but I'm not well seasoned enough for that. Well, since I can't go to Eagledale, I'll have a gallop on Rattler to Norburne this morning, and lunch with Gawaine."

Behind this explicit resolution there lay an implicit one. If he lunched with Gawaine and lingered chatting, he should not reach the Chase again till nearly five, when Hetty would be safe out of his sight in the housekeeper's room; and when she set out to go home, it would be his lazy time after dinner, so he should keep out of her way altogether. There really would have been no harm in being kind to the little thing, and it was worth dancing with a dozen ballroom belles only to look at Hetty for half an hour. But perhaps he had better not take any more notice of her; it might put notions into her head, as Irwine had hinted; though Arthur, for his part, thought girls were not by any means so soft and easily bruised; indeed, he had generally found them twice as cool and cunning as he was himself. As for any real harm in Hetty's case, it was out of the question: Arthur Donnithorne accepted his own bond for himself with perfect confidence.

So the twelve o'clock sun saw him galloping towards Norburne; and by good fortune Halsell Common lay in his road and gave him some fine leaps for Rattler. Nothing like "taking" a few bushes and ditches for exorcising a demon; and it is really astonishing that the Centaurs, with their immense advantages in this way, have left so bad a reputation in history.

After this, you will perhaps be surprised to hear that although Gawaine was at home, the hand of the dial in the courtyard had scarcely cleared the last stroke of three when Arthur returned through the entrance-gates, got down from the panting Rattler, and went into the house to take a hasty luncheon. But I believe there have been men since his day who have ridden a long way to avoid a rencontre, and then galloped hastily back lest they should miss it. It is the favourite stratagem of our passions to sham a retreat, and to turn sharp round upon us at the moment we have made up our minds that the day is our own.

"The cap'n's been ridin' the devil's own pace," said Dalton the coachman, whose person stood out in high relief as he smoked his pipe against the stable wall, when John brought up Rattler.

"An' I wish he'd get the devil to do's grooming for'n," growled John.

"Aye; he'd hev a deal haimabler groom nor what he has now," observed Dalton—and the joke appeared to him so good that, being left alone upon the scene, he continued at intervals to take his pipe from his mouth in order to wink at an imaginary audience and shake luxuriously with a silent, ventral laughter, mentally rehearsing the dialogue from the beginning, that he might recite it with effect in the servants' hall.

When Arthur went up to his dressing-room again after luncheon, it was inevitable that the debate he had had with himself there earlier in the day should flash across his mind; but it was impossible for him now to dwell on the remembrance—impossible to recall the feelings and reflections which had been decisive with him then, any more than to recall the peculiar scent of the air that had freshened him when he first opened his window. The desire to see Hetty had rushed back like an ill-stemmed current; he was amazed himself at the force with which this trivial fancy seemed to grasp him: he was even rather tremulous as he brushed his hair—pooh! it was riding in that break-neck way. It was because he had made a serious affair of an idle matter, by thinking of it as if it were of any consequence. He would amuse himself by seeing Hetty to-day, and get rid of the whole thing from his mind. It was all Irwine's fault. "If Irwine had said nothing, I shouldn't have thought half so much of Hetty as of Meg's lameness." However, it was just the sort of day for lolling in the Hermitage, and he would go and finish Dr. Moore's Zeluco there before dinner. The Hermitage stood in Fir-tree Grove—the way Hetty was sure to come in walking from the Hall Farm. So nothing could be simpler and more natural: meeting Hetty was a mere circumstance of his walk, not its object.

Arthur's shadow flitted rather faster among the sturdy oaks of the Chase than might have been expected from the shadow of a tired man on a warm afternoon, and it was still scarcely four o'clock when he stood before the tall narrow gate leading into the delicious labyrinthine wood which skirted one side of the Chase, and which was called Fir-tree Grove, not because the firs were many, but because they were few. It was a wood of beeches and limes, with here and there a light silver-stemmed birch—just the sort of wood most haunted by the nymphs: you see their white sunlit limbs gleaming athwart the boughs, or peeping from behind the smooth-sweeping outline of a tall lime; you hear their soft liquid laughter—but if you look with a too curious sacrilegious eye, they vanish behind the silvery beeches, they make you believe that their voice was only a running brooklet, perhaps they metamorphose themselves into a tawny squirrel that scampers away and mocks you from the topmost bough. It was not a grove with measured grass or rolled gravel for you to tread upon, but with narrow, hollow-shaped, earthy paths, edged with faint dashes of delicate moss—paths which look as if they were made by the free will of the trees and underwood, moving reverently aside to look at the tall queen of the white-footed nymphs.

It was along the broadest of these paths that Arthur Donnithorne passed, under an avenue of limes and beeches. It was a still afternoon—the golden light was lingering languidly among the upper boughs, only glancing down here and there on the purple pathway and its edge of faintly sprinkled moss: an afternoon in which destiny disguises her cold awful face behind a hazy radiant veil, encloses us in warm downy wings, and poisons us with violet-scented breath. Arthur strolled along carelessly, with a book under his arm, but not looking on the ground as meditative men are apt to do; his eyes WOULD fix themselves on the distant bend in the road round which a little figure must surely appear before long. Ah! There she comes. First a bright patch of colour, like a tropic bird among the boughs; then a tripping figure, with a round hat on, and a small basket under her arm; then a deep-blushing, almost frightened, but bright-smiling girl, making her curtsy with a fluttered yet happy glance, as Arthur came up to her. If Arthur had had time to think at all, he would have thought it strange that he should feel fluttered too, be conscious of blushing too—in fact, look and feel as foolish as if he had been taken by surprise instead of meeting just what he expected. Poor things! It was a pity they were not in that golden age of childhood when they would have stood face to face, eyeing each other with timid liking, then given each other a little butterfly kiss, and toddled off to play together. Arthur would have gone home to his silk-curtained cot, and Hetty to her home-spun pillow, and both would have slept without dreams, and to-morrow would have been a life hardly conscious of a yesterday.

Arthur turned round and walked by Hetty's side without giving a reason. They were alone together for the first time. What an overpowering presence that first privacy is! He actually dared not look at this little butter-maker for the first minute or two. As for Hetty, her feet rested on a cloud, and she was borne along by warm zephyrs; she had forgotten her rose-coloured ribbons; she was no more conscious of her limbs than if her childish soul had passed into a water-lily, resting on a liquid bed and warmed by the midsummer sun-beams. It may seem a contradiction, but Arthur gathered a certain carelessness and confidence from his timidity: it was an entirely different state of mind from what he had expected in such a meeting with Hetty; and full as he was of vague feeling, there was room, in those moments of silence, for the thought that his previous debates and scruples were needless.

"You are quite right to choose this way of coming to the Chase," he said at last, looking down at Hetty; "it is so much prettier as well as shorter than coming by either of the lodges."

"Yes, sir," Hetty answered, with a tremulous, almost whispering voice. She didn't know one bit how to speak to a gentleman like Mr. Arthur, and her very vanity made her more coy of speech.

"Do you come every week to see Mrs. Pomfret?"

"Yes, sir, every Thursday, only when she's got to go out with Miss Donnithorne."

"And she's teaching you something, is she?"

"Yes, sir, the lace-mending as she learnt abroad, and the stocking-mending—it looks just like the stocking, you can't tell it's been mended; and she teaches me cutting-out too."

"What! are YOU going to be a lady's maid?"

"I should like to be one very much indeed." Hetty spoke more audibly now, but still rather tremulously; she thought, perhaps she seemed as stupid to Captain Donnithorne as Luke Britton did to her.

"I suppose Mrs. Pomfret always expects you at this time?"

"She expects me at four o'clock. I'm rather late to-day, because my aunt couldn't spare me; but the regular time is four, because that gives us time before Miss Donnithorne's bell rings."

"Ah, then, I must not keep you now, else I should like to show you the Hermitage. Did you ever see it?"

"No, sir."

"This is the walk where we turn up to it. But we must not go now. I'll show it you some other time, if you'd like to see it."

"Yes, please, sir."

"Do you always come back this way in the evening, or are you afraid to come so lonely a road?"

"Oh no, sir, it's never late; I always set out by eight o'clock, and it's so light now in the evening. My aunt would be angry with me if I didn't get home before nine."

"Perhaps Craig, the gardener, comes to take care of you?"

A deep blush overspread Hetty's face and neck. "I'm sure he doesn't; I'm sure he never did; I wouldn't let him; I don't like him," she said hastily, and the tears of vexation had come so fast that before she had done speaking a bright drop rolled down her hot cheek. Then she felt ashamed to death that she was crying, and for one long instant her happiness was all gone. But in the next she felt an arm steal round her, and a gentle voice said, "Why, Hetty, what makes you cry? I didn't mean to vex you. I wouldn't vex you for the world, you little blossom. Come, don't cry; look at me, else I shall think you won't forgive me."

Arthur had laid his hand on the soft arm that was nearest to him, and was stooping towards Hetty with a look of coaxing entreaty. Hetty lifted her long dewy lashes, and met the eyes that were bent towards her with a sweet, timid, beseeching look. What a space of time those three moments were while their eyes met and his arms touched her! Love is such a simple thing when we have only one-and-twenty summers and a sweet girl of seventeen trembles under our glance, as if she were a bud first opening her heart with wondering rapture to the morning. Such young unfurrowed souls roll to meet each other like two velvet peaches that touch softly and are at rest; they mingle as easily as two brooklets that ask for nothing but to entwine themselves and ripple with ever-interlacing curves in the leafiest hiding-places. While Arthur gazed into Hetty's dark beseeching eyes, it made no difference to him what sort of English she spoke; and even if hoops and powder had been in fashion, he would very likely not have been sensible just then that Hetty wanted those signs of high breeding.

But they started asunder with beating hearts: something had fallen on the ground with a rattling noise; it was Hetty's basket; all her little workwoman's matters were scattered on the path, some of them showing a capability of rolling to great lengths. There was much to be done in picking up, and not a word was spoken; but when Arthur hung the basket over her arm again, the poor child felt a strange difference in his look and manner. He just pressed her hand, and said, with a look and tone that were almost chilling to her, "I have been hindering you; I must not keep you any longer now. You will be expected at the house. Good-bye."

Without waiting for her to speak, he turned away from her and hurried back towards the road that led to the Hermitage, leaving Hetty to pursue her way in a strange dream that seemed to have begun in bewildering delight and was now passing into contrarieties and sadness. Would he meet her again as she came home? Why had he spoken almost as if he were displeased with her? And then run away so suddenly? She cried, hardly knowing why.

Arthur too was very uneasy, but his feelings were lit up for him by a more distinct consciousness. He hurried to the Hermitage, which stood in the heart of the wood, unlocked the door with a hasty wrench, slammed it after him, pitched Zeluco into the most distant corner, and thrusting his right hand into his pocket, first walked four or five times up and down the scanty length of the little room, and then seated himself on the ottoman in an uncomfortable stiff way, as we often do when we wish not to abandon ourselves to feeling.

He was getting in love with Hetty—that was quite plain. He was ready to pitch everything else—no matter where—for the sake of surrendering himself to this delicious feeling which had just disclosed itself. It was no use blinking the fact now—they would get too fond of each other, if he went on taking notice of her—and what would come of it? He should have to go away in a few weeks, and the poor little thing would be miserable. He MUST NOT see her alone again; he must keep out of her way. What a fool he was for coming back from Gawaine's!

He got up and threw open the windows, to let in the soft breath of the afternoon, and the healthy scent of the firs that made a belt round the Hermitage. The soft air did not help his resolution, as he leaned out and looked into the leafy distance. But he considered his resolution sufficiently fixed: there was no need to debate with himself any longer. He had made up his mind not to meet Hetty again; and now he might give himself up to thinking how immensely agreeable it would be if circumstances were different—how pleasant it would have been to meet her this evening as she came back, and put his arm round her again and look into her sweet face. He wondered if the dear little thing were thinking of him too—twenty to one she was. How beautiful her eyes were with the tear on their lashes! He would like to satisfy his soul for a day with looking at them, and he MUST see her again—he must see her, simply to remove any false impression from her mind about his manner to her just now. He would behave in a quiet, kind way to her—just to prevent her from going home with her head full of wrong fancies. Yes, that would be the best thing to do after all.

It was a long while—more than an hour before Arthur had brought his meditations to this point; but once arrived there, he could stay no longer at the Hermitage. The time must be filled up with movement until he should see Hetty again. And it was already late enough to go and dress for dinner, for his grandfather's dinner-hour was six.

Chapter XIII Evening in the Wood

IT happened that Mrs. Pomfret had had a slight quarrel with Mrs. Best, the housekeeper, on this Thursday morning—a fact which had two consequences highly convenient to Hetty. It caused Mrs. Pomfret to have tea sent up to her own room, and it inspired that exemplary lady's maid with so lively a recollection of former passages in Mrs. Best's conduct, and of dialogues in which Mrs. Best had decidedly the inferiority as an interlocutor with Mrs. Pomfret, that Hetty required no more presence of mind than was demanded for using her needle, and throwing in an occasional "yes" or "no." She would have wanted to put on her hat earlier than usual; only she had told Captain Donnithorne that she usually set out about eight o'clock, and if he SHOULD go to the Grove again expecting to see her, and she should be gone! Would he come? Her little butterfly soul fluttered incessantly between memory and dubious expectation. At last the minute-hand of the old-fashioned brazen-faced timepiece was on the last quarter to eight, and there was every reason for its being time to get ready for departure. Even Mrs. Pomfret's preoccupied mind did not prevent her from noticing what looked like a new flush of beauty in the little thing as she tied on her hat before the looking-glass.

"That child gets prettier and prettier every day, I do believe," was her inward comment. "The more's the pity. She'll get neither a place nor a husband any the sooner for it. Sober well-to-do men don't like such pretty wives. When I was a girl, I was more admired than if I had been so very pretty. However, she's reason to be grateful to me for teaching her something to get her bread with, better than farm-house work. They always told me I was good-natured—and that's the truth, and to my hurt too, else there's them in this house that wouldn't be here now to lord it over me in the housekeeper's room."

Hetty walked hastily across the short space of pleasure-ground which she had to traverse, dreading to meet Mr. Craig, to whom she could hardly have spoken civilly. How relieved she was when she had got safely under the oaks and among the fern of the Chase! Even then she was as ready to be startled as the deer that leaped away at her approach. She thought nothing of the evening light that lay gently in the grassy alleys between the fern, and made the beauty of their living green more visible than it had been in the overpowering flood of noon: she thought of nothing that was present. She only saw something that was possible: Mr. Arthur Donnithorne coming to meet her again along the Fir-tree Grove. That was the foreground of Hetty's picture; behind it lay a bright hazy something—days that were not to be as the other days of her life had been. It was as if she had been wooed by a river-god, who might any time take her to his wondrous halls below a watery heaven. There was no knowing what would come, since this strange entrancing delight had come. If a chest full of lace and satin and jewels had been sent her from some unknown source, how could she but have thought that her whole lot was going to change, and that to-morrow some still more bewildering joy would befall her? Hetty had never read a novel; if she had ever seen one, I think the words would have been too hard for her; how then could she find a shape for her expectations? They were as formless as the sweet languid odours of the garden at the Chase, which had floated past her as she walked by the gate.

She is at another gate now—that leading into Fir-tree Grove. She enters the wood, where it is already twilight, and at every step she takes, the fear at her heart becomes colder. If he should not come! Oh, how dreary it was—the thought of going out at the other end of the wood, into the unsheltered road, without having seen him. She reaches the first turning towards the Hermitage, walking slowly—he is not there. She hates the leveret that runs across the path; she hates everything that is not what she longs for. She walks on, happy whenever she is coming to a bend in the road, for perhaps he is behind it. No. She is beginning to cry: her heart has swelled so, the tears stand in her eyes; she gives one great sob, while the corners of her mouth quiver, and the tears roll down.

She doesn't know that there is another turning to the Hermitage, that she is close against it, and that Arthur Donnithorne is only a few yards from her, full of one thought, and a thought of which she only is the object. He is going to see Hetty again: that is the longing which has been growing through the last three hours to a feverish thirst. Not, of course, to speak in the caressing way into which he had unguardedly fallen before dinner, but to set things right with her by a kindness which would have the air of friendly civility, and prevent her from running away with wrong notions about their mutual relation.

If Hetty had known he was there, she would not have cried; and it would have been better, for then Arthur would perhaps have behaved as wisely as he had intended. As it was, she started when he appeared at the end of the side-alley, and looked up at him with two great drops rolling down her cheeks. What else could he do but speak to her in a soft, soothing tone, as if she were a bright-eyed spaniel with a thorn in her foot?

"Has something frightened you, Hetty? Have you seen anything in the wood? Don't be frightened—I'll take care of you now."

Hetty was blushing so, she didn't know whether she was happy or miserable. To be crying again—what did gentlemen think of girls who cried in that way? She felt unable even to say "no," but could only look away from him and wipe the tears from her cheek. Not before a great drop had fallen on her rose-coloured strings—she knew that quite well.

"Come, be cheerful again. Smile at me, and tell me what's the matter. Come, tell me."

Hetty turned her head towards him, whispered, "I thought you wouldn't come," and slowly got courage to lift her eyes to him. That look was too much: he must have had eyes of Egyptian granite not to look too lovingly in return.

"You little frightened bird! Little tearful rose! Silly pet! You won't cry again, now I'm with you, will you?"

Ah, he doesn't know in the least what he is saying. This is not what he meant to say. His arm is stealing round the waist again; it is tightening its clasp; he is bending his face nearer and nearer to the round cheek; his lips are meeting those pouting child-lips, and for a long moment time has vanished. He may be a shepherd in Arcadia for aught he knows, he may be the first youth kissing the first maiden, he may be Eros himself, sipping the lips of Psyche—it is all one.

There was no speaking for minutes after. They walked along with beating hearts till they came within sight of the gate at the end of the wood. Then they looked at each other, not quite as they had looked before, for in their eyes there was the memory of a kiss.

But already something bitter had begun to mingle itself with the fountain of sweets: already Arthur was uncomfortable. He took his arm from Hetty's waist, and said, "Here we are, almost at the end of the Grove. I wonder how late it is," he added, pulling out his watch. "Twenty minutes past eight—but my watch is too fast. However, I'd better not go any further now. Trot along quickly with your little feet, and get home safely. Good-bye."

He took her hand, and looked at her half-sadly, half with a constrained smile. Hetty's eyes seemed to beseech him not to go away yet;

but he patted her cheek and said "Good-bye" again. She was obliged to turn away from him and go on.

As for Arthur, he rushed back through the wood, as if he wanted to put a wide space between himself and Hetty. He would not go to the Hermitage again; he remembered how he had debated with himself there before dinner, and it had all come to nothing—worse than nothing. He walked right on into the Chase, glad to get out of the Grove, which surely was haunted by his evil genius. Those beeches and smooth limes—there was something enervating in the very sight of them; but the strong knotted old oaks had no bending languor in them—the sight of them would give a man some energy. Arthur lost himself among the narrow openings in the fern, winding about without seeking any issue, till the twilight deepened almost to night under the great boughs, and the hare looked black as it darted across his path.

He was feeling much more strongly than he had done in the morning: it was as if his horse had wheeled round from a leap and dared to dispute his mastery. He was dissatisfied with himself, irritated, mortified. He no sooner fixed his mind on the probable consequences of giving way to the emotions which had stolen over him to-day—of continuing to notice Hetty, of allowing himself any opportunity for such slight caresses as he had been betrayed into already—than he refused to believe such a future possible for himself. To flirt with Hetty was a very different affair from flirting with a pretty girl of his own station: that was understood to be an amusement on both sides, or, if it became serious, there was no obstacle to marriage. But this little thing would be spoken ill of directly, if she happened to be seen walking with him; and then those excellent people, the Poysers, to whom a good name was as precious as if they had the best blood in the land in their veins—he should hate himself if he made a scandal of that sort, on the estate that was to be his own some day, and among tenants by whom he liked, above all, to be respected. He could no more believe that he should so fall in his own esteem than that he should break both his legs and go on crutches all the rest of his life. He couldn't imagine himself in that position; it was too odious, too unlike him.

And even if no one knew anything about it, they might get too fond of each other, and then there could be nothing but the misery of parting, after all. No gentleman, out of a ballad, could marry a farmer's niece. There must be an end to the whole thing at once. It was too foolish.

And yet he had been so determined this morning, before he went to Gawaine's; and while he was there something had taken hold of him and made him gallop back. It seemed he couldn't quite depend on his own resolution, as he had thought he could; he almost wished his arm would get painful again, and then he should think of nothing but the comfort it would be to get rid of the pain. There was no knowing what impulse might seize him to-morrow, in this confounded place, where there was nothing to occupy him imperiously through the livelong day. What could he do to secure himself from any more of this folly?

There was but one resource. He would go and tell Irwine—tell him everything. The mere act of telling it would make it seem trivial; the temptation would vanish, as the charm of fond words vanishes when one repeats them to the indifferent. In every way it would help him to tell Irwine. He would ride to Broxton Rectory the first thing after breakfast to-morrow.

Arthur had no sooner come to this determination than he began to think which of the paths would lead him home, and made as short a walk thither as he could. He felt sure he should sleep now: he had had enough to tire him, and there was no more need for him to think.

Chapter XIV The Return Home

WHILE that parting in the wood was happening, there was a parting in the cottage too, and Lisbeth had stood with Adam at the door, straining her aged eyes to get the last glimpse of Seth and Dinah, as they mounted the opposite slope.

"Eh, I'm loath to see the last on her," she said to Adam, as they turned into the house again. "I'd ha' been willin' t' ha' her about me till I died and went to lie by my old man. She'd make it easier dyin'—she spakes so gentle an' moves about so still. I could be fast sure that pictur' was drawed for her i' thy new Bible—th' angel a-sittin' on the big stone by the grave. Eh, I wouldna mind ha'in a daughter like that; but nobody ne'er marries them as is good for aught."

"Well, Mother, I hope thee WILT have her for a daughter; for Seth's got a liking for her, and I hope she'll get a liking for Seth in time."

"Where's th' use o' talkin' a-that'n? She caresna for Seth. She's goin' away twenty mile aff. How's she to get a likin' for him, I'd like to know? No more nor the cake 'ull come wi'out the leaven. Thy figurin' books might ha' tould thee better nor that, I should think, else thee mightst as well read the commin print, as Seth allays does."

"Nay, Mother," said Adam, laughing, "the figures tell us a fine deal, and we couldn't go far without 'em, but they don't tell us about folks's feelings. It's a nicer job to calculate THEM. But Seth's as good-hearted a lad as ever handled a tool, and plenty o' sense, and good-looking too; and he's got the same way o' thinking as Dinah. He deserves to win her, though there's no denying she's a rare bit o' workmanship. You don't see such women turned off the wheel every day."

"Eh, thee't allays stick up for thy brother. Thee'st been just the same, e'er sin' ye war little uns together. Thee wart allays for halving iverything wi' him. But what's Seth got to do with marryin', as is on'y three-an'-twenty? He'd more need to learn an' lay by sixpence. An' as for his desarving her—she's two 'ear older nor Seth: she's pretty near as old as thee. But that's the way; folks mun allays choose by contrairies, as if they must be sorted like the pork—a bit o' good meat wi' a bit o' offal."

To the feminine mind in some of its moods, all things that might be receive a temporary charm from comparison with what is; and since Adam did not want to marry Dinah himself, Lisbeth felt rather peevish on that score—as peevish as she would have been if he HAD wanted to marry her, and so shut himself out from Mary Burge and the partnership as effectually as by marrying Hetty.

It was more than half-past eight when Adam and his mother were talking in this way, so that when, about ten minutes later, Hetty reached the turning of the lane that led to the farmyard gate, she saw Dinah and Seth approaching it from the opposite direction, and waited for them to come up to her. They, too, like Hetty, had lingered a little in their walk, for Dinah was trying to speak words of comfort and strength to Seth in these parting moments. But when they saw

Hetty, they paused and shook hands; Seth turned homewards, and Dinah came on alone.

"Seth Bede would have come and spoken to you, my dear," she said, as she reached Hetty, "but he's very full of trouble to-night."

Hetty answered with a dimpled smile, as if she did not quite know what had been said; and it made a strange contrast to see that sparkling self-engrossed loveliness looked at by Dinah's calm pitying face, with its open glance which told that her heart lived in no cherished secrets of its own, but in feelings which it longed to share with all the world. Hetty liked Dinah as well as she had ever liked any woman; how was it possible to feel otherwise towards one who always put in a kind word for her when her aunt was finding fault, and who was always ready to take Totty off her hands—little tiresome Totty, that was made such a pet of by every one, and that Hetty could see no interest in at all? Dinah had never said anything disapproving or reproachful to Hetty during her whole visit to the Hall Farm; she had talked to her a great deal in a serious way, but Hetty didn't mind that much, for she never listened: whatever Dinah might say, she almost always stroked Hetty's cheek after it, and wanted to do some mending for her. Dinah was a riddle to her; Hetty looked at her much in the same way as one might imagine a little perching bird that could only flutter from bough to bough, to look at the swoop of the swallow or the mounting of the lark; but she did not care to solve such riddles, any more than she cared to know what was meant by the pictures in the Pilgrim's Progress, or in the old folio Bible that Marty and Tommy always plagued her about on a Sunday.

Dinah took her hand now and drew it under her own arm.

"You look very happy to-night, dear child," she said. "I shall think ot you often when I'm at Snowfield, and see your face before me as it is now. It's a strange thing—sometimes when I'm quite alone, sitting in my room with my eyes closed, or walking over the hills, the people I've seen and known, if it's only been for a few days, are brought before me, and I hear their voices and see them look and move almost plainer than I ever did when they were really with me so as I could touch them. And then my heart is drawn out towards them, and I feel their lot as if it was my own, and I take comfort in spreading it before the Lord and resting in His love, on their behalf as well as my own. And so I feel sure you will come before me."

She paused a moment, but Hetty said nothing.

"It has been a very precious time to me," Dinah went on, "last night and to-day—seeing two such good sons as Adam and Seth Bede. They are so tender and thoughtful for their aged mother. And she has been telling me what Adam has done, for these many years, to help his father and his brother; it's wonderful what a spirit of wisdom and knowledge he has, and how he's ready to use it all in behalf of them that are feeble. And I'm sure he has a loving spirit too. I've noticed it often among my own people round Snowfield, that the strong, skilful men are often the gentlest to the women and children; and it's pretty to see 'em carrying the little babies as if they were no heavier than little birds. And the babies always seem to like the strong arm best. I feel sure it would be so with Adam Bede. Don't you think so, Hetty?"

"Yes," said Hetty abstractedly, for her mind had been all the while in the wood, and she would have found it difficult to say what she was assenting to. Dinah saw she was not inclined to talk, but there would not have been time to say much more, for they were now at the yard-gate.

The still twilight, with its dying western red and its few faint struggling stars, rested on the farm-yard, where there was not a sound to be heard but the stamping of the cart-horses in the stable. It was about twenty minutes after sunset. The fowls were all gone to roost, and the bull-dog lay stretched on the straw outside his kennel, with the black-and-tan terrier by his side, when the falling-to of the gate disturbed them and set them barking, like good officials, before they had any distinct knowledge of the reason.

The barking had its effect in the house, for, as Dinah and Hetty approached, the doorway was filled by a portly figure, with a ruddy black-eyed face which bore in it the possibility of looking extremely acute, and occasionally contemptuous, on market-days, but had now a predominant after-supper expression of hearty good-nature. It is well known that great scholars who have shown the most pitiless acerbity in their criticism of other men's scholarship have yet been of a relenting and indulgent temper in private life; and I have heard of a learned man meekly rocking the twins in the cradle with his left hand, while with his right he inflicted the most lacerating sarcasms on an opponent who had betrayed a brutal ignorance of Hebrew. Weaknesses and errors must be forgiven—alas! they are not alien to us—but the man who takes the wrong side on the momentous subject of the Hebrew points must be treated as the enemy of his race. There was the same sort of antithetic mixture in Martin Poyser: he was of so excellent a disposition that he had been kinder and more respectful than ever to his old father since he had made a deed of gift of all his property, and no man judged his neighbours more charitably on all personal matters; but for a farmer, like Luke Britton, for example, whose fallows were not well cleaned, who didn't know the rudiments of hedging and ditching, and showed but a small share of judgment in the purchase of winter stock, Martin Poyser was as hard and implacable as the north-east wind. Luke Britton could not make a remark, even on the weather, but Martin Poyser detected in it a taint of that unsoundness and general ignorance which was palpable in all his farming operations. He hated to see the fellow lift the pewter pint to his mouth in the bar of the Royal George on market-day, and the mere sight of him on the other side of the road brought a severe and critical expression into his black eyes, as different as possible from the fatherly glance he bent on his two nieces as they approached the door. Mr. Poyser had smoked his evening pipe, and now held his hands in his pockets, as the only resource of a man who continues to sit up after the day's business is done.

"Why, lasses, ye're rather late to-night," he said, when they reached the little gate leading into the causeway. "The mother's begun to fidget about you, an' she's got the little un ill. An' how did you leave the old woman Bede, Dinah? Is she much down about the old man? He'd been but a poor bargain to her this five year."

"She's been greatly distressed for the loss of him," said Dinah, "but she's seemed more comforted to-day. Her son Adam's been at home all day, working at his father's coffin, and she loves to have him at home. She's been talking about him to me almost all the day. She has a loving heart, though she's sorely given to fret and be fearful. I wish she had a surer trust to comfort her in her old age."

"Adam's sure enough," said Mr. Poyser, misunderstanding Dinah's wish. "There's no fear but he'll yield well i' the threshing. He's not one o' them as is all straw and no grain. I'll be bond for him any day, as he'll be a good son to the last. Did he say he'd be coming to see us soon? But come in, come in," he added, making way for them; "I hadn't need keep y' out any longer."

The tall buildings round the yard shut out a good deal of the sky, but the large window let in abundant light to show every corner of the house-place.

Mrs. Poyser, seated in the rocking-chair, which had been brought out of the "right-hand parlour," was trying to soothe Totty to sleep. But Totty was not disposed to sleep; and when her cousins entered, she raised herself up and showed a pair of flushed cheeks, which looked fatter than ever now they were defined by the edge of her linen night-cap.

In the large wicker-bottomed arm-chair in the left-hand chimney-nook sat old Martin Poyser, a hale but shrunken and bleached image of his portly black-haired son—his head hanging forward a little, and his elbows pushed backwards so as to allow the whole of his forearm to rest on the arm of the chair. His blue handkerchief was spread over his knees, as was usual indoors, when it was not hanging over his head; and he sat watching what went forward with the quiet OUTWARD glance of healthy old age, which, disengaged from any interest in an inward drama, spies out pins upon the floor, follows one's minutest motions with an unexpectant purposeless tenacity, watches the flickering of the flame or the sun-gleams on the wall, counts the quarries on the floor, watches even the hand of the clock, and pleases itself with detecting a rhythm in the tick.

"What a time o' night this is to come home, Hetty!" said Mrs. Poyser. "Look at the clock, do; why, it's going on for half-past nine, and I've sent the gells to bed this half-hour, and late enough too; when they've got to get up at half after four, and the mowers' bottles to fill, and the baking; and here's this blessed child wi' the fever for what I know, and as wakeful as if it was dinner-time, and nobody to help me to give her the physic but your uncle, and fine work there's been, and half of it spilt on her night-gown—it's well if she's swallowed more nor 'ull make her worse i'stead o' better. But folks as have no mind to be o' use have allays the luck to be out o' the road when there's anything to be done."

"I did set out before eight, aunt," said Hetty, in a pettish tone, with a slight toss of her head. But this clock's so much before the clock at the Chase, there's no telling what time it'll be when I get here."

"What! You'd be wanting the clock set by gentlefolks's time, would you? An' sit up burnin' candle, an' lie a-bed wi' the sun a-bakin' you like a cowcumber i' the frame? The clock hasn't been put forrard for the first time to-day, I reckon."

The fact was, Hetty had really forgotten the difference of the clocks when she told Captain Donnithorne that she set out at eight, and this, with her lingering pace, had made her nearly half an hour later than usual. But here her aunt's attention was diverted from this tender subject by Totty, who, perceiving at length that the arrival of her cousins was not likely to bring anything satisfactory to her in particular, began to cry, "Munny, munny," in an explosive manner.

"Well, then, my pet, Mother's got her, Mother won't leave her; Totty be a good dilling, and go to sleep now," said Mrs. Poyser, leaning back and rocking the chair, while she tried to make Totty nestle against her. But Totty only cried louder, and said, "Don't yock!" So the mother, with that wondrous patience which love gives to the quickest temperament, sat up again, and pressed her cheek against the linen night-cap and kissed it, and forgot to scold Hetty any longer.

"Come, Hetty," said Martin Poyser, in a conciliatory tone, "go and get your supper i' the pantry, as the things are all put away; an' then you can come and take the little un while your aunt undresses herself, for she won't lie down in bed without her mother. An' I reckon YOU could eat a bit, Dinah, for they don't keep much of a house down there."

"No, thank you, Uncle," said Dinah; "I ate a good meal before I came away, for Mrs. Bede would make a kettle-cake for me."

"I don't want any supper," said Hetty, taking off her hat. "I can hold Totty now, if Aunt wants me."

"Why, what nonsense that is to talk!" said Mrs. Poyser. "Do you think you can live wi'out eatin', an' nourish your inside wi' stickin' red ribbons on your head? Go an' get your supper this minute, child; there's a nice bit o' cold pudding i' the safe—just what you're fond of."

Hetty complied silently by going towards the pantry, and Mrs. Poyser went on speaking to Dinah.

"Sit down, my dear, an' look as if you knowed what it was to make yourself a bit comfortable i' the world. I warrant the old woman was glad to see you, since you stayed so long."

"She seemed to like having me there at last; but her sons say she doesn't like young women about her commonly; and I thought just at first she was almost angry with me for going."

"Eh, it's a poor look-out when th' ould folks doesna like the young uns," said old Martin, bending his head down lower, and seeming to trace the pattern of the quarries with his eye.

"Aye, it's ill livin' in a hen-roost for them as doesn't like fleas," said Mrs. Poyser. "We've all had our turn at bein' young, I reckon, be't good luck or ill."

"But she must learn to 'commodate herself to young women," said Mr. Poyser, "for it isn't to be counted on as Adam and Seth 'ull keep bachelors for the next ten year to please their mother. That 'ud be unreasonable. It isn't right for old nor young nayther to make a bargain all o' their own side. What's good for one's good all round i' the long run. I'm no friend to young fellows a-marrying afore they know the difference atween a crab an' a apple; but they may wait o'er long."

"To be sure," said Mrs. Poyser; "if you go past your dinner-time, there'll be little relish o' your meat. You turn it o'er an' o'er wi' your fork, an' don't eat it after all. You find faut wi' your meat, an' the faut's all i' your own stomach."

Hetty now came back from the pantry and said, "I can take Totty now, Aunt, if you like."

"Come, Rachel," said Mr. Poyser, as his wife seemed to hesitate, seeing that Totty was at last nestling quietly, "thee'dst better let Hetty carry her upstairs, while thee tak'st thy things off. Thee't tired. It's time thee wast in bed. Thee't bring on the pain in thy side again."

"Well, she may hold her if the child 'ull go to her," said Mrs. Poyser.

Hetty went close to the rocking-chair, and stood without her usual smile, and without any attempt to entice Totty, simply waiting for her aunt to give the child into her hands.

"Wilt go to Cousin Hetty, my dilling, while mother gets ready to go to bed? Then Totty shall go into Mother's bed, and sleep there all night."

Before her mother had done speaking, Totty had given her answer in an unmistakable manner, by knitting her brow, setting her tiny teeth against her underlip, and leaning forward to slap Hetty on the arm with her utmost force. Then, without speaking, she nestled to her mother again.

"Hey, hey," said Mr. Poyser, while Hetty stood without moving, "not go to Cousin Hetty? That's like a babby. Totty's a little woman, an' not a babby."

"It's no use trying to persuade her," said Mrs. Poyser. "She allays takes against Hetty when she isn't well. Happen she'll go to Dinah."

Dinah, having taken off her bonnet and shawl, had hitherto kept quietly seated in the background, not liking to thrust herself between Hetty and what was considered Hetty's proper work. But now she came forward, and, putting out her arms, said, "Come Totty, come and let Dinah carry her upstairs along with Mother: poor, poor Mother! she's so tired—she wants to go to bed."

Totty turned her face towards Dinah, and looked at her an instant, then lifted herself up, put out her little arms, and let Dinah lift her from her mother's lap. Hetty turned away without any sign of ill humour, and, taking her hat from the table, stood waiting with an air of indifference, to see if she should be told to do anything else.

"You may make the door fast now, Poyser; Alick's been come in this long while," said Mrs. Poyser, rising with an appearance of relief from her low chair. "Get me the matches down, Hetty, for I must have the rushlight burning i' my room. Come, Father."

The heavy wooden bolts began to roll in the house doors, and old Martin prepared to move, by gathering up his blue handkerchief, and reaching his bright knobbed walnut-tree stick from the corner. Mrs. Poyser then led the way out of the kitchen, followed by the gandfather, and Dinah with Totty in her arms—all going to bed by twilight, like the birds. Mrs. Poyser, on her way, peeped into the room where her two boys lay; just to see their ruddy round cheeks on the pillow, and to hear for a moment their light regular breathing.

"Come, Hetty, get to bed," said Mr. Poyser, in a soothing tone, as he himself turned to go upstairs. "You didna mean to be late, I'll be bound, but your aunt's been worrited to-day. Good-night, my wench, good-night."

Chapter XV The Two Bed-Chambers

HETTY and Dinah both slept in the second story, in rooms adjoining each other, meagrely furnished rooms, with no blinds to shut out the light, which was now beginning to gather new strength from the rising of the moon—more than enough strength to enable Hetty to move about and undress with perfect comfort. She could see quite well the pegs in the old painted linen-press on which she hung her hat and gown; she could see the head of every pin on her red cloth pincushion; she could see a reflection of herself in the old-fashioned looking-glass, quite as distinct as was needful, considering that she had only to brush her hair and put on her night-cap. A queer old looking-glass! Hetty got into an ill temper with it almost every time she dressed. It had been considered a handsome glass in its day, and had probably been bought into the Poyser family a quarter of a century before, at a sale of genteel household furniture. Even now an auctioneer could say something for it: it had a great deal of tarnished gilding about it; it had a firm mahogany base, well supplied with drawers, which opened with a decided jerk and sent the contents leaping out from the farthest corners, without giving you the trouble of reaching them; above all, it had a brass candle-socket on each side, which would give it an aristocratic air to the very last. But Hetty objected to it because it had numerous dim blotches sprinkled over the mirror, which no rubbing would remove, and because, instead of swinging backwards and forwards, it was fixed in an upright position, so that she could only get one good view of her head and neck, and that was to be had only by sitting down on a low chair before her dressing-table. And the dressing-table was no dressing-table at all, but a small old chest of drawers, the most awkward thing in the world to sit down before, for the big brass handles quite hurt her knees, and she couldn't get near the glass at all comfortably. But devout worshippers never allow inconveniences to prevent them from performing their religious rites, and Hetty this evening was more bent on her peculiar form of worship than usual.

Having taken off her gown and white kerchief, she drew a key from the large pocket that hung outside her petticoat, and, unlocking one of the lower drawers in the chest, reached from it two short bits of wax candle—secretly bought at Treddleston—and stuck them in the two brass sockets. Then she drew forth a bundle of matches and lighted the candles; and last of all, a small red-framed shilling looking-glass, without blotches. It was into this small glass that she chose to look first after seating herself. She looked into it, smiling and turning her head on one side, for a minute, then laid it down and took out her brush and comb from an upper drawer. She was going to let down her hair, and make herself look like that picture of a lady in Miss Lydia Donnithorne's dressing-room. It was soon done, and the dark hyacinthine curves fell on her neck. It was not heavy, massive, merely rippling hair, but soft and silken, running at every opportunity into delicate rings. But she pushed it all backward to look like the picture, and form a dark curtain, throwing into relief her round white neck. Then she put down her brush and comb and looked at herself, folding her arms before her, still like the picture. Even the old mottled glass couldn't help sending back a lovely image, none the less lovely because Hetty's stays were not of white satin—such as I feel sure heroines must generally wear—but of a dark greenish cotton texture.

Oh yes! She was very pretty. Captain Donnithorne thought so. Prettier than anybody about Hayslope—prettier than any of the ladies she had ever seen visiting at the Chase—indeed it seemed fine ladies were rather old and ugly—and prettier than Miss Bacon, the miller's daughter, who was called the beauty of Treddleston. And Hetty looked at herself to-night with quite a different sensation from what she had ever felt before; there was an invisible spectator whose eye rested on her like morning on the flowers. His soft voice was saying over and over again those pretty things she had heard in the wood; his arm was round her, and the delicate rose-scent of his hair was with her still. The vainest woman is never thoroughly conscious of her own beauty till she is loved by the man who sets her own passion vibrating in return.

But Hetty seemed to have made up her mind that something was wanting, for she got up and reached an old black lace scarf out of the linen-press, and a pair of large ear-rings out of the sacred drawer from which she had taken her candles. It was an old old scarf, full of rents, but it would make a becoming border round her shoulders, and set off the whiteness of her upper arm. And she would take out the little ear-rings she had in her ears—oh, how her aunt had scolded her for having her ears bored!—and put in those large ones. They were but coloured glass and gilding, but if you didn't know what they were made of, they looked just as well as what the ladies wore. And so she sat down again, with the large ear-rings in her ears, and the black lace scarf adjusted round her shoulders. She looked down at her arms: no arms could be prettier down to a little way below the elbow—they were white and plump, and dimpled to match her cheeks; but towards the wrist, she thought with vexation that they were coarsened by butter-making and other work that ladies never did.

Captain Donnithorne couldn't like her to go on doing work: he would like to see her in nice clothes, and thin shoes, and white stockings, perhaps with silk clocks to them; for he must love her very much—no one else had ever put his arm round her and kissed her in that way. He would want to marry her and make a lady of her; she could hardly dare to shape the thought—yet how else could it be? Marry her quite secretly, as Mr. James, the doctor's assistant, married the doctor's niece, and nobody ever found it out for a long while after, and then it was of no use to be angry. The doctor had told her aunt all about it in Hetty's hearing. She didn't know how it would be, but it was quite plain the old Squire could never be told anything about it, for Hetty was ready to faint with awe and fright if she came across him at the Chase. He might have been earth-born, for what she knew. It had never entered her mind that he had been young like other men; he had always been the old Squire at whom everybody was frightened. Oh, it was impossible to think how it would be! But Captain Donnithorne would know; he was a great gentleman, and could have his way in everything, and could buy everything he liked. And nothing could be as it had been again: perhaps some day she should be a grand lady, and ride in her coach, and dress for dinner in a brocaded silk, with feathers in her hair, and her dress sweeping the ground, like Miss Lydia and Lady Dacey, when she saw them going into the dining-room one evening as she peeped through the little round window in the lobby; only she should not be old and ugly like Miss Lydia, or all the same thickness like Lady Dacey, but very pretty, with her hair done in a great many different ways, and sometimes in a pink dress, and sometimes in a white one—she didn't know which she liked best; and Mary Burge and everybody would perhaps see her going out in her carriage—or rather, they would HEAR of it: it was impossible to imagine these things happening at Hayslope in sight of her aunt. At the thought of all this splendour, Hetty got up from her chair, and in doing so caught the little red-framed glass with the edge of her scarf, so that it fell with a bang on the floor; but she was too eagerly occupied with her vision to care about picking it up; and after a momentary start, began to pace with a pigeon-like stateliness backwards and forwards along her room, in her coloured stays and coloured skirt, and the old black lace scarf round her shoulders, and the great glass ear-rings in her ears.

How pretty the little puss looks in that odd dress! It would be the easiest folly in the world to fall in love with her: there is such a sweet babylike roundness about her face and figure; the delicate dark rings of hair lie so charmingly about her ears and neck; her great dark eyes with their long eye-lashes touch one so strangely, as if an imprisoned frisky sprite looked out of them.

Ah, what a prize the man gets who wins a sweet bride like Hetty! How the men envy him who come to the wedding breakfast, and see her hanging on his arm in her white lace and orange blossoms. The dear, young, round, soft, flexible thing! Her heart must be just as soft, her temper just as free from angles, her character just as pliant. If anything ever goes wrong, it must be the husband's fault there: he can make her what he likes—that is plain. And the lover himself thinks so too: the little darling is so fond of him, her little vanities are so bewitching, he wouldn't consent to her being a bit wiser; those kitten-like glances and movements are just what one wants to make one's hearth a paradise. Every man under such circumstances is conscious of being a great physiognomist. Nature, he knows, has a language of her own, which she uses with strict veracity, and he considers himself an adept in the language. Nature has written out his bride's character for him in those exquisite lines of cheek and lip and chin, in those eyelids delicate as petals, in those long lashes curled like the stamen of a flower, in the dark liquid depths of those wonderful eyes. How she will dote on her children! She is almost a child herself, and the little pink round things will hang about her like florets round the central flower; and the husband will look on, smiling benignly, able, whenever he chooses, to withdraw into the sanctuary of his wisdom, towards which his sweet wife will look reverently, and never lift the curtain. It is a marriage such as they made in the golden age, when the men were all wise and majestic and the women all lovely and loving.

It was very much in this way that our friend Adam Bede thought about Hetty; only he put his thoughts into different words. If ever she behaved with cold vanity towards him, he said to himself it is only because she doesn't love me well enough; and he was sure that her love, whenever she gave it, would be the most precious thing a man could possess on earth. Before you despise Adam as deficient in penetration, pray ask yourself if you were ever predisposed to believe evil of any pretty woman—if you ever COULD, without hard head-breaking demonstration, believe evil of the ONE supremely pretty woman who has bewitched you. No: people who love downy peaches are apt not to think of the stone, and sometimes jar their teeth terribly against it.

Arthur Donnithorne, too, had the same sort of notion about Hetty, so far as he had thought of her nature of all. He felt sure she was a dear, affectionate, good little thing. The man who awakes the wondering tremulous passion of a young girl always thinks her affectionate; and if he chances to look forward to future years, probably imagines himself being virtuously tender to her, because the poor thing is so clingingly fond of him. God made these dear women so—and it is a convenient arrangement in case of sickness.

After all, I believe the wisest of us must be beguiled in this way sometimes, and must think both better and worse of people than they deserve. Nature has her language, and she is not unveracious; but we don't know all the intricacies of her syntax just yet, and in a hasty reading we may happen to extract the very opposite of her real meaning. Long dark eyelashes, now—what can be more exquisite? I find it impossible not to expect some depth of soul behind a deep grey eye with a long dark eyelash, in spite of an experience which has shown me that they may go along with deceit, peculation, and stupidity. But if, in the reaction of disgust, I have betaken myself to a fishy eye, there has been a surprising similarity of result. One begins to suspect at length that there is no direct correlation between eyelashes and morals; or else, that the eyelashes express the disposition of the fair one's grandmother, which is on the whole less important to us.

No eyelashes could be more beautiful than Hetty's; and now, while she walks with her pigeonlike stateliness along the room and looks down on her shoulders bordered by the old black lace, the dark fringe shows to perfection on her pink cheek. They are but dim ill-defined pictures that her narrow bit of an imagination can make of the future; but of every picture she is the central figure in fine clothes; Captain Donnithorne is very close to her, putting his arm round her, perhaps kissing her, and everybody else is admiring and envying her—especially Mary Burge, whose new print dress looks very contemptible by the side of Hetty's resplendent toilette. Does any sweet or sad memory mingle with this dream of the future—any loving thought of her second parents—of the children she had helped to tend—of any youthful companion, any pet animal, any relic of her own childhood even? Not one. There are some plants that have hardly any roots: you may tear them from their native nook of rock or wall, and just lay them over your ornamental flower-pot, and they blossom none the worse. Hetty could have cast all her past life behind her and never cared to be reminded of it again. I think she had no feeling at all towards the old house, and did not like the Jacob's Ladder and the long row of hollyhocks in the garden better than other flowers—perhaps not so well. It was wonderful how little she seemed to care about waiting on her uncle, who had been a good father to her—she hardly ever remembered to reach him his pipe at the right time without being told, unless a visitor happened to be there, who would have a better opportunity of seeing her as she walked across the hearth. Hetty did not understand how anybody could be very fond of middle-aged people. And as for those tiresome children, Marty and Tommy and Totty, they had been the very nuisance of her life—as bad as buzzing insects that will come teasing you on a hot day when you want to be quiet. Marty, the eldest, was a baby when she first came to the farm, for the children born before him had died, and so Hetty had had them all three, one after the other, toddling by her side in the meadow, or playing about her on wet days in the half-empty rooms of the large old house. The boys were out of hand now, but Totty was still a day-long plague, worse than either of the others had been, because there was more fuss made about her. And there was no end to the making and mending of clothes. Hetty would have been glad to hear that she should never see a child again; they were worse than the nasty little lambs that the shepherd was always bringing in to be taken special care of in lambing time; for the lambs WERE got rid of sooner or later. As for the young chickens and turkeys, Hetty would have hated the very word "hatching," if her aunt had not bribed her to attend to the young poultry by promising her the proceeds of one out of every brood. The round downy chicks peeping out from under their mother's wing never touched Hetty with any pleasure; that was not the sort of prettiness she cared about, but she did care about the prettiness of the new things she would buy for herself at Treddleston Fair with the money they fetched. And yet she looked so dimpled, so charming, as she stooped down to put the soaked bread under the hen-coop, that you must have been a very acute personage indeed to suspect her of that hardness. Molly, the housemaid, with a turn-up nose and a protuberant jaw, was really a tender-hearted girl, and, as Mrs. Poyser said, a jewel to look after the poultry; but her stolid face showed nothing of this maternal delight, any more than a brown earthenware pitcher will show the light of the lamp within it.

It is generally a feminine eye that first detects the moral deficiencies hidden under the "dear deceit" of beauty, so it is not surprising that Mrs. Poyser, with her keenness and abundant opportunity for observation, should have formed a tolerably fair estimate of what might be expected from Hetty in the way of feeling, and in moments of indignation she had sometimes spoken with great openness on the subject to her husband.

"She's no better than a peacock, as 'ud strut about on the wall and spread its tail when the sun shone if all the folks i' the parish was dying: there's nothing seems to give her a turn i' th' inside, not even when we thought Totty had tumbled into the pit. To think o' that dear cherub! And we found her wi' her little shoes stuck i' the mud an' crying fit to break her heart by the far horse-pit. But Hetty never minded it, I could see, though she's been at the nussin' o' the child ever since it was a babby. It's my belief her heart's as hard as a pebble."

"Nay, nay," said Mr. Poyser, "thee mustn't judge Hetty too hard. Them young gells are like the unripe grain; they'll make good meal by and by, but they're squashy as yet. Thee't see Hetty 'll be all right when she's got a good husband and children of her own."

"I don't want to be hard upo' the gell. She's got cliver fingers of her own, and can be useful enough when she likes and I should miss her wi' the butter, for she's got a cool hand. An' let be what may, I'd strive to do my part by a niece o' yours—an' THAT I've done, for I've taught her everything as belongs to a house, an' I've told her her duty often enough, though, God knows, I've no breath to spare, an' that catchin' pain comes on dreadful by times. Wi' them three gells in the house I'd need have twice the strength to keep 'em up to their work. It's like having roast meat at three fires; as soon as you've basted one, another's burnin'."

Hetty stood sufficiently in awe of her aunt to be anxious to conceal from her so much of her vanity as could be hidden without too great a sacrifice. She could not resist spending her money in bits of finery which Mrs. Poyser disapproved; but she would have been ready to die with shame, vexation, and fright if her aunt had this moment opened the door, and seen her with her bits of candle lighted, and strutting about decked in her scarf and ear-rings. To prevent such a surprise, she always bolted her door, and she had not forgotten to do so to-night. It was well: for there now came a light tap, and Hetty, with a leaping heart, rushed to blow out the candles and throw them into the drawer. She dared not stay to take out her ear-rings, but she threw off her scarf, and let it fall on the floor, before the light tap came again. We shall know how it was that the light tap came, if we leave Hetty for a short time and return to Dinah, at the moment when she had delivered Totty to her mother's arms, and was come upstairs to her bedroom, adjoining Hetty's.

Dinah delighted in her bedroom window. Being on the second story of that tall house, it gave her a wide view over the fields. The thickness of the wall formed a broad step about a yard below the window, where she could place her chair. And now the first thing she did on entering her room was to seat herself in this chair and look out on the peaceful fields beyond which the large moon was rising, just above the hedgerow elms. She liked the pasture best where the milch cows were lying, and next to that the meadow where the grass was half-mown, and lay in silvered sweeping lines. Her heart was very full, for there was to be only one more night on which she would look out on those fields for a long time to come; but she thought little of leaving the mere scene, for, to her, bleak Snowfield had just as many charms. She thought of all the dear people whom she had learned to care for among these peaceful fields, and who would now have a place in her loving remembrance for ever. She thought of the struggles and the weariness that might lie before them in the rest of their life's journey, when she would be away from them, and know nothing of what was befalling them; and the pressure of this thought soon became too strong for her to enjoy the unresponding stillness of the moonlit fields. She closed her eyes, that she might feel more intensely the presence of a Love and Sympathy deeper and more tender than was breathed from the earth and sky. That was often Dinah's mode of praying in solitude. Simply to close her eyes and to feel herself enclosed by the Divine Presence; then gradually her fears, her yearning anxieties for others, melted away like ice-crystals in a warm ocean. She had sat in this way perfectly still, with her hands crossed on her lap and the pale light resting on her calm face, for at least ten minutes when she was startled by a loud sound, apparently of something falling in Hetty's room. But like all sounds that fall on our ears in a state of abstraction, it had no distinct character, but was simply loud and startling, so that she felt uncertain whether she had interpreted it rightly. She rose and listened, but all was quiet afterwards, and she reflected that Hetty might merely have knocked something down in getting into bed. She began slowly to undress; but now, owing to the suggestions of this sound, her thoughts became concentrated on Hetty—that sweet young thing, with life and all its trials before her—the solemn daily duties of the wife and mother—and her mind so unprepared for them all, bent merely on little foolish, selfish pleasures, like a child hugging its toys in the beginning of a long toilsome journey in which it will have to bear hunger and cold and unsheltered darkness. Dinah felt a double care for Hetty, because she shared Seth's anxious interest in his brother's lot, and she had not come to the conclusion that Hetty did not love Adam well enough to marry him. She saw too clearly the absence of any warm, self-devoting love in Hetty's nature to regard the coldness of her behaviour towards Adam as any indication that he was not the man she would like to have for a husband. And this blank in Hetty's nature, instead of exciting Dinah's dislike, only touched her with a deeper pity: the lovely face and form affected her as beauty always affects a pure and tender mind, free from selfish jealousies. It was an excellent divine gift, that gave a deeper pathos to the need, the sin, the sorrow with which it was mingled, as the canker in a lily-white bud is more grievous to behold than in a common pot-herb.

By the time Dinah had undressed and put on her night-gown, this feeling about Hetty had gathered a painful intensity; her imagination had created a thorny thicket of sin and sorrow, in which she saw the poor thing struggling torn and bleeding, looking with tears for rescue and finding none. It was in this way that Dinah's imagination and sympathy acted and reacted habitually, each heightening the other. She felt a deep longing to go now and pour into Hetty's ear all the words of tender warning and appeal that rushed into her mind. But perhaps Hetty was already asleep. Dinah put her ear to the partition and heard still some slight noises, which convinced her that Hetty was not yet in bed. Still she hesitated; she was not quite certain of a divine direction; the voice that told her to go to Hetty seemed no stronger that the other voice which said that Hetty was weary, and that going to her now in an unseasonable moment would only tend to close her heart more obstinately. Dinah was not satisfied without a more unmistakable guidance than those inward voices. There was light enough for her, if she opened her Bible, to discern the text sufficiently to know what it would say to her. She knew the physiognomy of every page, and could tell on what book she opened, sometimes on what chapter, without seeing title or number. It was a small thick Bible, worn quite round at the edges. Dinah laid it sideways on the window ledge, where the light was strongest, and then opened it with her forefinger. The first words she looked at were those at the top of the left-hand page: "And they all wept sore, and fell on Paul's neck and kissed him." That was enough for Dinah; she had opened on that memorable parting at Ephesus, when Paul had felt bound to open his heart in a last exhortation and warning. She hesitated no longer, but, opening her own door gently, went and tapped on Hetty's. We know she had to tap twice, because Hetty had to put out her candles and throw off her black lace scarf; but after the second tap the door was opened immediately. Dinah said, "Will you let me come in, Hetty?" and Hetty, without speaking, for she was confused and vexed, opened the door wider and let her in.

What a strange contrast the two figures made, visible enough in that mingled twilight and moonlight! Hetty, her cheeks flushed and her eyes glistening from her imaginary drama, her beautiful neck and arms bare, her hair hanging in a curly tangle down her back, and the baubles in her ears. Dinah, covered with her long white dress, her pale face full of subdued emotion, almost like a lovely corpse into which the soul has returned charged with sublimer secrets and a sublimer love. They were nearly of the same height; Dinah evidently a little the taller as she put her arm round Hetty's waist and kissed her forehead.

"I knew you were not in bed, my dear," she said, in her sweet clear voice, which was irritating to Hetty, mingling with her own peevish vexation like music with jangling chains, "for I heard you moving; and I longed to speak to you again to-night, for it is the last but one that I shall be here, and we don't know what may happen to-morrow to keep us apart. Shall I sit down with you while you do up your hair?"

"Oh yes," said Hetty, hastily turning round and reaching the second chair in the room, glad that Dinah looked as if she did not notice her ear-rings.

Dinah sat down, and Hetty began to brush together her hair before twisting it up, doing it with that air of excessive indifference which belongs to confused self-consciousness. But the expression of Dinah's eyes gradually relieved her; they seemed unobservant of all details.

"Dear Hetty," she said, "It has been borne in upon my mind to-night that you may some day be in trouble—trouble is appointed for us all here below, and there comes a time when we need more comfort and help than the things of this life can give. I want to tell you that if ever you are in trouble, and need a friend that will always feel for you and love you, you have got that friend in Dinah Morris at Snowfield, and if you come to her, or send for her, she'll never forget this night and the words she is speaking to you now. Will you remember it, Hetty?"

"Yes," said Hetty, rather frightened. "But why should you think I shall be in trouble? Do you know of anything?"

Hetty had seated herself as she tied on her cap, and now Dinah leaned forwards and took her hands as she answered, "Because, dear, trouble comes to us all in this life: we set our hearts on things which it isn't God's will for us to have, and then we go sorrowing; the people we love are taken from us, and we can joy in nothing because they are not with us; sickness comes, and we faint under the burden of our feeble bodies; we go astray and do wrong, and bring ourselves into trouble with our fellow-men. There is no man or woman born into this world to whom some of these trials do not fall, and so I feel that some of them must happen to you; and I desire for you, that while you are young you should seek for strength from your Heavenly Father, that you may have a support which will not fail you in the evil day."

Dinah paused and released Hetty's hands that she might not hinder her. Hetty sat quite still; she felt no response within herself to Dinah's anxious affection; but Dinah's words uttered with solemn pathetic distinctness, affected her with a chill fear. Her flush had died away almost to paleness; she had the timidity of a luxurious pleasure-seeking nature, which shrinks from the hint of pain. Dinah saw the effect, and her tender anxious pleading became the more earnest, till Hetty, full of a vague fear that something evil was some time to befall her, began to cry.

It is our habit to say that while the lower nature can never understand the higher, the higher nature commands a complete view of the lower. But I think the higher nature has to learn this comprehension, as we learn the art of vision, by a good deal of hard experience, often with bruises and gashes incurred in taking things up by the wrong end, and fancying our space wider than it is. Dinah had never seen Hetty affected in this way before, and, with her usual benignant hopefulness, she trusted it was the stirring of a divine impulse. She kissed the sobbing thing, and began to cry with her for grateful joy. But Hetty was simply in that excitable state of mind in which there is no calculating what turn the feelings may take from one moment to another, and for the first time she became irritated under Dinah's caress. She pushed her away impatiently, and said, with a childish sobbing voice, "Don't talk to me so, Dinah. Why do you come to frighten me? I've never done anything to you. Why can't you let me be?"

Poor Dinah felt a pang. She was too wise to persist, and only said mildly, "Yes, my dear, you're tired; I won't hinder you any longer. Make haste and get into bed. Good-night."

She went out of the room almost as quietly and quickly as if she had been a ghost; but once by the side of her own bed, she threw herself on her knees and poured out in deep silence all the passionate pity that filled her heart.

As for Hetty, she was soon in the wood again—her waking dreams being merged in a sleeping life scarcely more fragmentary and confused.

Chapter XVI Links

ARTHUR DONNITHORNE, you remember, is under an engagement with himself to go and see Mr. Irwine this Friday morning, and he is awake and dressing so early that he determines to go before breakfast, instead of after. The rector, he knows, breakfasts alone at half-past nine, the ladies of the family having a different breakfast-hour; Arthur will have an early ride over the hill and breakfast with him. One can say everything best over a meal.

The progress of civilization has made a breakfast or a dinner an easy and cheerful substitute for more troublesome and disagreeable ceremonies. We take a less gloomy view of our errors now our father confessor listens to us over his egg and coffee. We are more distinctly conscious that rude penances are out of the question for gentlemen in an enlightened age, and that mortal sin is not incompatible with an appetite for muffins. An assault on our pockets, which in more barbarous times would have been made in the brusque form of a pistol-shot, is quite a well-bred and smiling procedure now it has become a request for a loan thrown in as an easy parenthesis between the second and third glasses of claret.

Still, there was this advantage in the old rigid forms, that they committed you to the fulfilment of a resolution by some outward deed: when you have put your mouth to one end of a hole in a stone wall and are aware that there is an expectant ear at the other end, you are more likely to say what you came out with the intention of saying than if you were seated with your legs in an easy attitude under the mahogany with a companion who will have no reason to be surprised if you have nothing particular to say.

However, Arthur Donnithorne, as he winds among the pleasant lanes on horseback in the morning sunshine, has a sincere determination to open his heart to the rector, and the swirling sound of the scythe as he passes by the meadow is all the pleasanter to him because of this honest purpose. He is glad to see the promise of settled weather now, for getting in the hay, about which the farmers have been fearful; and there is something so healthful in the sharing of a joy that is general and not merely personal, that this thought about the hay-harvest reacts on his state of mind and makes his resolution seem an easier matter. A man about town might perhaps consider that these influences were not to be felt out of a child's story-book; but when you are among the fields and hedgerows, it is impossible to maintain a consistent superiority to simple natural pleasures.

Arthur had passed the village of Hayslope and was approaching the Broxton side of the hill, when, at a turning in the road, he saw a figure about a hundred yards before him which it was impossible to mistake for any one else than Adam Bede, even if there had been no grey, tailless shepherd-dog at his heels. He was striding along at his usual rapid pace, and Arthur pushed on his horse to overtake him, for he retained too much of his boyish feeling for Adam to miss an opportunity of chatting with him. I will not say that his love for that good fellow did not owe some of its force to the love of patronage: our friend Arthur liked to do everything that was handsome, and to have his handsome deeds recognized.

Adam looked round as he heard the quickening clatter of the horse's heels, and waited for the horseman, lifting his paper cap from his head with a bright smile of recognition. Next to his own brother Seth, Adam would have done more for Arthur Donnithorne than for any other young man in the world. There was hardly anything he would not rather have lost than the two-feet ruler which he always carried in his pocket; it was Arthur's present, bought with his pocket-money when he was a fair-haired lad of eleven, and when he had profited so well by Adam's lessons in carpentering and turning as to embarrass every female in the house with gifts of superfluous thread-reels and round boxes. Adam had quite a pride in the little squire in those early days, and the feeling had only become slightly modified as the fair-haired lad had grown into the whiskered young man. Adam, I confess, was very susceptible to the influence of rank, and quite ready to give an extra amount of respect to every one who had more advantages than himself, not being a philosopher or a proletaire with democratic ideas, but simply a stout-limbed clever carpenter wlth a large fund of reverence in his nature, which inclined him to admit all established claims unless he saw very clear grounds for questioning them. He had no theories about setting the world to rights, but he saw there was a great deal of damage done by building with ill-seasoned timber—by ignorant men in fine clothes making plans for outhouses and workshops and the like without knowing the bearings of things—by slovenly joiners' work, and by hasty contracts that could never be fulfilled without ruining somebody; and he resolved, for his part, to set his face against such doings. On these points he would have maintained his opinion against the largest landed proprietor in Loamshire or Stonyshire either; but he felt that beyond these it would be better for him to defer to people who were more knowing than himself. He saw as plainly as possible how ill the woods on the estate were managed, and the shameful state of the farm-buildings; and if old Squire Donnithorne had asked him the effect of this mismanagement, he would have spoken his opinion without flinching, but the impulse to a respectful demeanour towards a "gentleman" would have been strong within him all the while. The word "gentleman" had a spell for Adam, and, as he often said, he "couldn't abide a fellow who thought he made himself fine by being coxy to's betters." I must remind you again that Adam had the blood of the peasant in his veins, and that since he was in his prime half a century ago, you must expect some of his characteristics to be obsolete.

Towards the young squire this instinctive reverence of Adam's was assisted by boyish memories and personal regard so you may imagine that he thought far more of Arthur's good qualities, and attached far more value to very slight actions of his, than if they had been the qualities and actions of a common workman like himself. He felt sure it would be a fine day for everybody about Hayslope when the young squire came into the estate—such a generous open-hearted disposition as he had, and an "uncommon" notion about improvements and repairs, considering he was only just coming of age. Thus there was both respect and affection in the smile with which he raised his paper cap as Arthur Donnithorne rode up.

"Well, Adam, how are you?" said Arthur, holding out his hand. He never shook hands with any of the farmers, and Adam felt the honour keenly. "I could swear to your back a long way off. It's just the same back, only broader, as when you used to carry me on it. Do you remember?"

"Aye, sir, I remember. It 'ud be a poor look-out if folks didn't remember what they did and said when they were lads. We should think no more about old friends than we do about new uns, then."

"You're going to Broxton, I suppose?" said Arthur, putting his horse on at a slow pace while Adam walked by his side. "Are you going to the rectory?"

"No, sir, I'm going to see about Bradwell's barn. They're afraid of the roof pushing the walls out, and I'm going to see what can be done with it before we send the stuff and the workmen."

"Why, Burge trusts almost everything to you now, Adam, doesn't he? I should think he will make you his partner soon. He will, if he's wise."

"Nay, sir, I don't see as he'd be much the better off for that. A foreman, if he's got a conscience and delights in his work, will do his business as well as if he was a partner. I wouldn't give a penny for a man as 'ud drive a nail in slack because he didn't get extra pay for it."

"I know that, Adam; I know you work for him as well as if you were working for yourself. But you would have more power than you have now, and could turn the business to better account perhaps. The old man must give up his business sometime, and he has no son; I suppose he'll want a son-in-law who can take to it. But he has rather grasping fingers of his own, I fancy. I daresay he wants a man who can put some money into the business. If I were not as poor as a rat, I would gladly invest some money in that way, for the sake of having you settled on the estate. I'm sure I should profit by it in the end. And perhaps I shall be better off in a year or two. I shall have a larger allowance now I'm of age; and when I've paid off a debt or two, I shall be able to look about me."

"You're very good to say so, sir, and I'm not unthankful. But"—Adam continued, in a decided tone—"I shouldn't like to make any offers to Mr. Burge, or t' have any made for me. I see no clear road to a partnership. If he should ever want to dispose of the business, that 'ud be a different matter. I should be glad of some money at a fair interest then, for I feel sure I could pay it off in time."

"Very well, Adam," said Arthur, remembering what Mr. Irwine had said about a probable hitch in the love-making between Adam and Mary Burge, "we'll say no more about it at present. When is your father to be buried?"

"On Sunday, sir; Mr. Irwine's coming earlier on purpose. I shall be glad when it's over, for I think my mother 'ull perhaps get easier then. It cuts one sadly to see the grief of old people; they've no way o' working it off, and the new spring brings no new shoots out on the withered tree."

"Ah, you've had a good deal of trouble and vexation in your life, Adam. I don't think you've ever been hare-brained and light-hearted, like other youngsters. You've always had some care on your mind."

"Why, yes, sir; but that's nothing to make a fuss about. If we're men and have men's feelings, I reckon we must have men's troubles. We can't be like the birds, as fly from their nest as soon as they've got their wings, and never know their kin when they see 'em, and get a fresh lot every year. I've had enough to be thankful for: I've allays had health and strength and brains to give me a delight in my work; and I count it a great thing as I've had Bartle Massey's night-school to go to. He's helped me to knowledge I could never ha' got by myself."

"What a rare fellow you are, Adam!" said Arthur, after a pause, in which he had looked musingly at the big fellow walking by his side. "I could hit out better than most men at Oxford, and yet I believe you would knock me into next week if I were to have a baltle with you."

"God forbid I should ever do that, sir," said Adam, looking round at Arthur and smiling. "I used to fight for fun, but I've never done that since I was the cause o' poor Gil Tranter being laid up for a fortnight. I'll never fight any man again, only when he behaves like a scoundrel. If you get hold of a chap that's got no shame nor conscience to stop him, you must try what you can do by bunging his eyes up."

Arthur did not laugh, for he was preoccupied with some thought that made him say presently, "I should think now, Adam, you never have any struggles within yourself. I fancy you would master a wish that you had made up your mind it was not quite right to indulge, as easily as you would knock down a drunken fellow who was quarrelsome with you. I mean, you are never shilly-shally, first making up your mind that you won't do a thing, and then doing it after all?"

"Well," said Adam, slowly, after a moment's hesitation, "no. I don't remember ever being see-saw in that way, when I'd made my mind up, as you say, that a thing was wrong. It takes the taste out o' my mouth for things, when I know I should have a heavy conscience after 'em. I've seen pretty clear, ever since I could cast up a sum, as you can never do what's wrong without breeding sin and trouble more than you can ever see. It's like a bit o' bad workmanship—you never see th' end o' the mischief it'll do. And it's a poor look-out to come into the world to make your fellow-creatures worse off instead o' better. But there's a difference between the things folks call wrong. I'm not for making a sin of every little fool's trick, or bit o' nonsense anybody may be let into, like some o' them dissenters. And a man may have two minds whether it isn't worthwhile to get a bruise or two for the sake of a bit o' fun. But it isn't my way to be see-saw about anything: I think my fault lies th' other way. When I've said a thing, if it's only to myself, it's hard for me to go back."

"Yes, that's just what I expected of you," said Arthur. "You've got an iron will, as well as an iron arm. But however strong a man's resolution may be, it costs him something to carry it out, now and then. We may determine not to gather any cherries and keep our hands sturdily in our pockets, but we can't prevent our mouths from watering."

"That's true, sir, but there's nothing like settling with ourselves as there's a deal we must do without i' this life. It's no use looking on life as if it was Treddles'on Fair, where folks only go to see shows and get fairings. If we do, we shall find it different. But where's the use o' me talking to you, sir? You know better than I do."

"I'm not so sure of that, Adam. You've had four or five years of experience more than I've had, and I think your life has been a better school to you than college has been to me."

"Why, sir, you seem to think o' college something like what Bartle Massey does. He says college mostly makes people like bladders—just good for nothing but t' hold the stuff as is poured into 'em. But he's got a tongue like a sharp blade, Bartle has—it never touches anything but it cuts. Here's the turning, sir. I must bid you good-morning, as you're going to the rectory."

"Good-bye, Adam, good-bye."

Arthur gave his horse to the groom at the rectory gate, and walked along the gravel towards the door which opened on the garden. He knew that the rector always breakfasted in his study, and the study lay on the left hand of this door, opposite the dining-room. It was a small low room, belonging to the old part of the house—dark with the sombre covers of the books that lined the walls; yet it looked very cheery this morning as Arthur reached the open window. For the morning sun fell aslant on the great glass globe with gold fish in it, which stood on a scagliola pillar in front of the ready-spread bachelor breakfast-table, and by the side of this breakfast-table was a group which would have made any room enticing. In the crimson damask easy-chair sat Mr. Irwine, with that radiant freshness which he always had when he came from his morning toilet; his finely formed plump white hand was playing along Juno's brown curly back; and close to Juno's tail, which was wagging with calm matronly pleasure, the two brown pups were rolling over each other in an ecstatic duet of worrying noises. On a cushion a little removed sat Pug, with the air of a maiden lady, who looked on these familiarities as animal weaknesses, which she made as little show as possible of observing. On the table, at Mr. Irwine~s elbow, lay the first volume of the Foulis AEschylus, which Arthur knew well by sight; and the silver coffee-pot, which Carroll was bringing in, sent forth a fragrant steam which completed the delights of a bachelor breakfast.

"Hallo, Arthur, that's a good fellow! You're just in time," said Mr. Irwine, as Arthur paused and stepped in over the low window-sill. "Carroll, we shall want more coffee and eggs, and haven't you got some cold fowl for us to eat with that ham? Why, this is like old days, Arthur; you haven't been to breakfast with me these five years."

"It was a tempting morning for a ride before breakfast," said Arthur; "and I used to like breakfasting with you so when I was reading with you. My grandfather is always a few degrees colder at breakfast than at any other hour in the day. I think his morning bath doesn't agree with him."

Arthur was anxious not to imply that he came with any special purpose. He had no sooner found himself in Mr. Irwine's presence than the confidence which he had thought quite easy before, suddenly appeared the most difficult thing in the world to him, and at the very moment of shaking hands he saw his purpose in quite a new light. How could he make Irwine understand his position unless he told him those little scenes in the wood; and how could he tell them without looking like a fool? And then his weakness in coming back from Gawaine's, and doing the very opposite of what he intended! Irwine would think him a shilly-shally fellow ever after. However, it must come out in an unpremeditated way; the conversation might lead up to it.

"I like breakfast-time better than any other moment in the day," said Mr. Irwine. "No dust has settled on one's mind then, and it presents a clear mirror to the rays of things. I always have a favourite book by me at breakfast, and I enjoy the bits I pick up then so much, that regularly every morning it seems to me as if I should certainly become studious again. But presently Dent brings up a poor fellow who has killed a hare, and when I've got through my 'justicing,' as Carroll calls it, I'm inclined for a ride round the glebe, and on my way back I meet with the master of the workhouse, who has got a long story of a mutinous pauper to tell me; and so the day goes on, and I'm always the same lazy fellow before evening sets in. Besides, one wants the stimulus of sympathy, and I have never had that since poor D'Oyley left Treddleston. If you had stuck to your books well, you rascal, I should have had a pleasanter prospect before me. But scholarship doesn't run in your family blood."

"No indeed. It's well if I can remember a little inapplicable Latin to adorn my maiden speech in Parliament six or seven years hence. 'Cras ingens iterabimus aequor,' and a few shreds of that sort, will perhaps stick to me, and I shall arrange my opinions so as to introduce them. But I don't think a knowledge of the classics is a pressing want to a country gentleman; as far as I can see, he'd much better have a knowledge of manures. I've been reading your friend Arthur

Young's books lately, and there's nothing I should like better than to carry out some of his ideas in putting the farmers on a better management of their land; and, as he says, making what was a wild country, all of the same dark hue, bright and variegated with corn and cattle. My grandfather will never let me have any power while he lives, but there's nothing I should like better than to undertake the Stonyshire side of the estate—it's in a dismal condition—and set improvements on foot, and gallop about from one place to another and overlook them. I should like to know all the labourers, and see them touching their hats to me with a look of goodwill."

"Bravo, Arthur! A man who has no feeling for the classics couldn't make a better apology for coming into the world than by increasing the quantity of food to maintain scholars—and rectors who appreciate scholars. And whenever you enter on your career of model landlord may I be there to see. You'll want a portly rector to complete the picture, and take his tithe of all the respect and honour you get by your hard work. Only don't set your heart too strongly on the goodwill you are to get in consequence. I'm not sure that men are the fondest of those who try to be useful to them. You know Gawaine has got the curses of the whole neighbourhood upon him about that enclosure. You must make it quite clear to your mind which you are most bent upon, old boy—popularity or usefulness—else you may happen to miss both."

"Oh! Gawaine is harsh in his manners; he doesn't make himself personally agreeable to his tenants. I don't believe there's anything you can't prevail on people to do with kindness. For my part, I couldn't live in a neighbourhood where I was not respected and beloved. And it's very pleasant to go among the tenants here—they seem all so well inclined to me I suppose it seems only the other day to them since I was a little lad, riding on a pony about as big as a sheep. And if fair allowances were made to them, and their buildings attended to, one could persuade them to farm on a better plan, stupid as they are."

"Then mind you fall in love in the right place, and don't get a wife who will drain your purse and make you niggardly in spite of yourself. My mother and I have a little discussion about you sometimes: she says, 'I ll never risk a single prophecy on Arthur until I see the woman he falls in love with.' She thinks your lady-love will rule you as the moon rules the tides. But I feel bound to stand up for you, as my pupil you know, and I maintain that you're not of that watery quality. So mind you don't disgrace my judgment."

Arthur winced under this speech, for keen old Mrs. Irwine's opinion about him had the disagreeable effect of a sinister omen. This, to be sure, was only another reason for persevering in his intention, and getting an additional security against himself. Nevertheless, at this point in the conversation, he was conscious of increased disinclination to tell his story about Hetty. He was of an impressible nature, and lived a great deal in other people's opinions and feelings concerning himself; and the mere fact that he was in the presence of an intimate friend, who had not the slightest notion that he had had any such serious internal struggle as he came to confide, rather shook his own belief in the seriousness of the struggle. It was not, after all, a thing to make a fuss about; and what could Irwine do for him that he could not do for himself? He would go to Eagledale in spite of Meg's lameness—go on Rattler, and let Pym follow as well as he could on the old hack. That was his thought as he sugared his coffee; but the next minute, as he was lifting the cup to his lips, he remembered how thoroughly he had made up his mind last night to tell Irwine. No! He would not be vacillating again—he WOULD do what he had meant to do, this time. So it would be well not to let the personal tone of the conversation altogether drop. If they went to quite indifferent topics, his difficulty would be heightened. It had required no noticeable pause for this rush and rebound of feeling, before he answered, "But I think it is hardly an argument against a man's general strength of character that he should be apt to be mastered by love. A fine constitution doesn't insure one against smallpox or any other of those inevitable diseases. A man may be very firm in other matters and yet be under a sort of witchery from a woman."

"Yes; but there's this difference between love and smallpox, or bewitchment either—that if you detect the disease at an early stage and try change of air, there is every chance of complete escape without any further development of symptoms. And there are certain alternative doses which a man may administer to himself by keeping unpleasant consequences before his mind: this gives you a sort of smoked glass through which you may look at the resplendent fair one and discern her true outline; though I'm afraid, by the by, the smoked glass is apt to be missing just at the moment it is most wanted. I dare-say, now, even a man fortified with a knowledge of the classics might be lured into an imprudent marriage, in spite of the warning given him by the chorus in the Prometheus."

The smile that flitted across Arthur's face was a faint one, and instead of following Mr. Irwine's playful lead, he said, quite seriously—"Yes, that's the worst of it. It's a desperately vexatious thing, that after all one's reflections and quiet determinations, we should be ruled by moods that one can't calculate on beforehand. I don't think a man ought to be blamed so much if he is betrayed into doing things in that way, in spite of his resolutions."

"Ah, but the moods lie in his nature, my boy, just as much as his reflections did, and more. A man can never do anything at variance with his own nature. He carries within him the germ of his most exceptional action; and if we wise people make eminent fools of ourselves on any particular occasion, we must endure the legitimate conclusion that we carry a few grains of folly to our ounce of wisdom."

"Well, but one may be betrayed into doing things by a combination of circumstances, which one might never have done otherwise."

"Why, yes, a man can't very well steal a bank-note unless the bank-note lies within convenient reach; but he won't make us think him an honest man because he begins to howl at the bank-note for falling in his way."

"But surely you don't think a man who struggles against a temptation into which he falls at last as bad as the man who never struggles at all?"

"No, certainly; I pity him in proportion to his struggles, for they foreshadow the inward suffering which is the worst form of Nemesis. Consequences are unpitying. Our deeds carry their terrible consequences, quite apart from any fluctuations that went before—consequences that are hardly ever confined to ourselves. And it is best to fix our minds on that certainty, instead of considering what may be the elements of excuse for us. But I never knew you so inclined for moral discussion, Arthur? Is it some danger of your own that you are considering in this philosophical, general way?"

In asking this question, Mr. Irwine pushed his plate away, threw himself back in his chair, and looked straight at Arthur. He really suspected that Arthur wanted to tell him something, and thought of smoothing the way for him by this direct question. But he was mistaken. Brought suddenly and involuntarily to the brink of confession, Arthur shrank back and felt less disposed towards it than ever. The conversation had taken a more serious tone than he had intended—it would quite mislead Irwine—he would imagine there was a deep passion for Hetty, while there was no such thing. He was conscious of colouring, and was annoyed at his boyishness.

"Oh no, no danger," he said as indifferently as he could. "I don't know that I am more liable to irresolution than other people; only there are little incidents now and then that set one speculating on what might happen in the future."

Was there a motive at work under this strange reluctance of Arthur's which had a sort of backstairs influence, not admitted to himself? Our mental business is carried on much in the same way as the business of the State: a great deal of hard work is done by agents who are not acknowledged. In a piece of machinery, too, I believe there is often a small unnoticeable wheel which has a great deal to do with the motion of the large obvious ones. Possibly there was some such unrecognized agent secretly busy in Arthur's mind at this moment—possibly it was the fear lest he might hereafter find the fact of having made a confession to the rector a serious annoyance, in case he should NOT be able quite to carry out his good resolutions? I dare not assert that it was not so. The human soul is a very complex thing.

The idea of Hetty had just crossed Mr. Irwine's mind as he looked inquiringly at Arthur, but his disclaiming indifferent answer confirmed the thought which had quickly followed—that there could be nothing serious in that direction. There was no probability that Arthur ever saw her except at church, and at her own home under the eye of Mrs. Poyser; and the hint he had given Arthur about her the other day had no more serious meaning than to prevent him from noticing her so as to rouse the little chit's vanity, and in this way perturb the rustic drama of her life. Arthur would soon join his regiment, and be far away: no, there could be no danger in that quarter, even if Arthur's character had not been a strong security against it. His honest, patronizing pride in the good-will and respect of everybody about him was a safeguard even against foolish romance, still more against a lower kind of folly. If there had been anything special on Arthur's mind in the previous conversation, it was clear he was not inclined to enter into details, and Mr. Irwine was too delicate to imply even a friendly curiosity. He perceived a change of subject would be welcome, and said, "By the way, Arthur, at your colonel's birthday fete there were some transparencies that made a great effect in honour of Britannia, and Pitt, and the Loamshire Militia, and, above all, the 'generous youth,' the hero of the day. Don't you think you should get up something of the same sort to astonish our weak minds?"

The opportunity was gone. While Arthur was hesitating, the rope to which he might have clung had drifted away—he must trust now to his own swimming.

In ten minutes from that time, Mr. Irwine was called for on business, and Arthur, bidding him good-bye, mounted his horse again with a sense of dissatisfaction, which he tried to quell by determining to set off for Eagledale without an hour's delay.

BOOK TWO

Chapter XVII In Which the Story Pauses a Little

"THIS Rector of Broxton is little better than a pagan!" I hear one of my readers exclaim. "How much more edifying it would have been if you had made him give Arthur some truly spiritual advice! You might have put into his mouth the most beautiful things—quite as good as reading a sermon."

Certainly I could, if I held it the highest vocation of the novelist to represent things as they never have been and never will be. Then, of course, I might refashion life and character entirely after my own liking; I might select the most unexceptionable type of clergyman and put my own admirable opinions into his mouth on all occasions. But it happens, on the contrary, that my strongest effort is to avoid any such arbitrary picture, and to give a faithful account of men and things as they have mirrored themselves in my mind. The mirror is doubtless defective, the outlines will sometimes be disturbed, the reflection faint or confused; but I feel as much bound to tell you as precisely as I can what that reflection is, as if I were in the witness-box, narrating my experience on oath.

Sixty years ago—it is a long time, so no wonder things have changed—all clergymen were not zealous; indeed, there is reason to believe that the number of zealous clergymen was small, and it is probable that if one among the small minority had owned the livings of Broxton and Hayslope in the year 1799, you would have liked him no better than you like Mr. Irwine. Ten to one, you would have thought him a tasteless, indiscreet, methodistical man. It is so very rarely that facts hit that nice medium required by our own enlightened opinions and refined taste! Perhaps you will say, "Do improve the facts a little, then; make them more accordant with those correct views which it is our privilege to possess. The world is not just what we like; do touch it up with a tasteful pencil, and make believe it is not quite such a mixed entangled affair. Let all people who hold unexceptionable opinions act unexceptionably. Let your most faulty characters always be on the wrong side, and your virtuous ones on the right. Then we shall see at a glance whom we are to condemn and whom we are to approve. Then we shall be able to admire, without the slightest disturbance of our prepossessions: we shall hate and despise with that true ruminant relish which belongs to undoubting confidence."

But, my good friend, what will you do then with your fellow-parishioner who opposes your husband in the vestry? With your newly appointed vicar, whose style of preaching you find painfully below that of his regretted predecessor? With the honest servant who worries your soul with her one failing? With your neighbour, Mrs. Green, who was really kind to you in your last illness, but has said several ill-natured things about you since your convalescence? Nay, with your excellent husband himself, who has other irritating habits besides that of not wiping his shoes? These fellow-mortals, every one, must be accepted as they are: you can neither straighten their noses, nor brighten their wit, nor rectify their dispositions; and it is these people—amongst whom your life is passed—that it is needful you should tolerate, pity, and love: it is these more or less ugly, stupid, inconsistent people whose movements of goodness you should be able to admire—for whom you should cherish all possible hopes, all possible patience. And I would not, even if I had the choice, be the clever novelist who could create a world so much better than this, in which we get up in the morning to do our daily work, that you would be likely to turn a harder, colder eye on the dusty streets and the common green fields—on the real breathing men and women, who can be chilled by your indifference or injured by your prejudice; who can be cheered and helped onward by your fellow-feeling, your forbearance, your outspoken, brave justice.

So I am content to tell my simple story, without trying to make things seem better than they were; dreading nothing, indeed, but falsity, which, in spite of one's best efforts, there is reason to dread. Falsehood is so easy, truth so difficult. The pencil is conscious of a delightful facility in drawing a griffin—the longer the claws, and the larger the wings, the better; but that marvellous facility which we mistook for genius is apt to forsake us when we want to draw a real unexaggerated lion. Examine your words well, and you will find that even when you have no motive to be false, it is a very hard thing to say the exact truth, even about your own immediate feelings—much harder than to say something fine about them which is NOT the exact truth.

It is for this rare, precious quality of truthfulness that I delight in many Dutch paintings, which lofty-minded people despise. I find a source of delicious sympathy in these faithful pictures of a monotonous homely existence, which has been the fate of so many more among my fellow-mortals than a life of pomp or of absolute indigence, of tragic suffering or of world-stirring actions. I turn, without shrinking, from cloud-borne angels, from prophets, sibyls, and heroic warriors, to an old woman bending over her flower-pot, or eating her solitary dinner, while the noonday light, softened perhaps by a screen of leaves, falls on her mob-cap, and just touches the rim of her spinning-wheel, and her stone jug, and all those cheap common things which are the precious necessaries of life to her—or I turn to that village wedding, kept between four brown walls, where an awkward bridegroom opens the dance with a high-shouldered, broad-faced bride, while elderly and middle-aged friends look on, with very irregular noses and lips, and probably with quart-pots in their hands, but with an expression of unmistakable contentment and goodwill. "Foh!" says my idealistic friend, "what vulgar details! What good is there in taking all these pains to give an exact likeness of old women and clowns? What a low phase of life! What clumsy, ugly people!"

But bless us, things may be lovable that are not altogether handsome, I hope? I am not at all sure that the majority of the human race have not been ugly, and even among those "lords of their kind," the British, squat figures, ill-shapen nostrils, and dingy complexions are not startling exceptions. Yet there is a great deal of family love amongst us. I have a friend or two whose class of features is such that the Apollo curl on the summit of their brows would be decidedly trying; yet to my certain knowledge tender hearts have beaten for them, and their miniatures—flattering, but still not lovely—are kissed in secret by motherly lips. I have seen many an excellent matron, who could have never in her best days have been handsome, and yet she had a packet of yellow love-letters in a private drawer, and sweet children showered kisses on her sallow cheeks. And I believe there have been plenty of young heroes, of middle stature and feeble beards, who have felt quite sure they could never love anything more insignificant than a Diana, and yet have found themselves in middle life happily settled with a wife who waddles. Yes! Thank God; human feeling is like the mighty rivers that bless the earth: it does not wait for beauty—it flows with resistless force and brings beauty with it.

All honour and reverence to the divine beauty of form! Let us cultivate it to the utmost in men, women, and children—in our gardens and in our houses. But let us love that other beauty too, which lies in no secret of proportion, but in the secret of deep human sympathy. Paint us an angel, if you can, with a floating violet robe, and a face paled by the celestial light; paint us yet oftener a Madonna, turning her mild face upward and opening her arms to welcome the divine glory; but do not impose on us any aesthetic rules which shall banish from the region of Art those old women scraping carrots with their work-worn hands, those heavy clowns taking holiday in a dingy pot-house, those rounded backs and stupid weather-beaten faces that have bent over the spade and done the rough work of the world—those homes with their tin pans, their brown pitchers, their rough curs, and their clusters of onions. In this world there are so many of these common coarse people, who have no picturesque sentimental wretchedness! It is so needful we should remember their existence, else we may happen to leave them quite out of our religion and philosophy and frame lofty theories which only fit a world of extremes. Therefore, let Art always remind us of them; therefore let us always have men ready to give the loving pains of a life to the faithful representing of commonplace things—men who see beauty in these commonplace things, and delight in showing how kindly the light of heaven falls on them. There are few prophets in the world; few sublimely beautiful women; few heroes. I can't afford to give all my love and reverence to such rarities: I want a great deal of those feelings for my every-day fellow-men, especially for the few in the foreground of the great multitude, whose faces I know, whose hands I touch for whom I have to make way with kindly courtesy. Neither are picturesque lazzaroni or romantic criminals half so frequent as your common labourer, who gets his own bread and eats it vulgarly but creditably with his own pocket-knife. It is more needful that I should have a fibre of sympathy connecting me with that vulgar citizen who weighs out my sugar in a vilely assorted cravat and waistcoat, than with the handsomest rascal in red scarf and green feathers—more needful that my heart should swell with loving admiration at some trait of gentle goodness in the faulty people who sit at the same hearth with me, or in the clergyman of my own parish, who is perhaps rather too corpulent and in other respects is not an Oberlin or a Tillotson, than at the deeds of heroes whom I shall never know except by hearsay, or at the sublimest abstract of all clerical graces that was ever conceived by an able novelist.

And so I come back to Mr. Irwine, with whom I desire you to be in perfect charity, far as he may be from satisfying your demands on the clerical character. Perhaps you think he was not—as he ought to have been—a living demonstration of the benefits attached to a national church? But I am not sure of that; at least I know that the people in Broxton and Hayslope would have been very sorry to part with their clergyman, and that most faces brightened at his approach; and until it can be proved that hatred is a better thing for the soul than love, I must believe that Mr. Irwine's influence in his parish was a more wholesome one than that of the zealous Mr. Ryde, who came there twenty years afterwards, when Mr. Irwine had been gathered to his fathers. It is true, Mr. Ryde insisted strongly on the doctrines of the Reformation, visited his flock a great deal in their own homes, and was severe in rebuking the aberrations of the flesh—put a stop, indeed, to the Christmas rounds of the church singers, as promoting drunkenness and too light a handling of sacred things. But I gathered from Adam Bede, to whom I talked of these matters in his old age, that few clergymen could be less successful in winning the hearts of their parishioners than Mr. Ryde. They learned a great many notions about doctrine from him, so that almost every church-goer under fifty began to distinguish as well between the genuine gospel and what did not come precisely up to that standard, as if he had been born and bred a Dissenter; and for some time after his arrival there seemed to be quite a religious movement in that quiet rural district. "But," said Adam, "I've seen pretty clear, ever since I was a young un, as religion's something else besides notions. It isn't notions sets people doing the right thing—it's feelings. It's the same with the notions in religion as it is with math'matics—a man may be able to work problems straight off in's head as he sits by the fire and smokes his pipe, but if he has to make a machine or a building, he must have a will and a resolution and love something else better than his own ease. Somehow, the congregation began to fall off, and people began to speak light o' Mr. Ryde. I believe he meant right at bottom; but, you see, he was sourish-tempered, and was for beating down prices with the people as worked for him; and his preaching wouldn't go down well with that sauce. And he wanted to be like my lord judge i' the parish, punishing folks for doing wrong; and he scolded 'em from the pulpit as if he'd been a Ranter, and yet he couldn't abide the Dissenters, and was a deal more set against 'em than Mr. Irwine was. And then he didn't keep within his income, for he seemed to think at first go-off that six hundred a-year was to make him as big a man as Mr. Donnithorne. That's a sore mischief I've often seen with the poor curates jumping into a bit of a living all of a sudden. Mr. Ryde was a deal thought on at a distance, I believe, and he wrote books, but as for math'matics and the natur o' things, he was as ignorant as a woman. He was very knowing about doctrines, and used to call 'em the bulwarks of the Reformation; but I've always mistrusted that sort o' learning as leaves folks foolish and unreasonable about business. Now Mester Irwine was as different as could be: as quick!—he understood what you meant in a minute, and he knew all about building, and could see when you'd made a good job. And he behaved as much like a gentleman to the farmers, and th' old women, and the labourers, as he did to the gentry. You never saw HIM interfering and scolding, and trying to play th' emperor. Ah, he was a fine man as ever you set eyes on; and so kind to's mother and sisters. That poor sickly Miss Anne—he seemed to think more of her than of anybody else in the world. There wasn't a soul in the parish had a word to say against him; and his servants stayed with him till they were so old and pottering, he had to hire other folks to do their work."

"Well," I said, "that was an excellent way of preaching in the weekdays; but I daresay, if your old friend Mr. Irwine were to come to life again, and get into the pulpit next Sunday, you would be rather ashamed that he didn't preach better after all your praise of him."

"Nay, nay," said Adam, broadening his chest and throwing himself back in his chair, as if he were ready to meet all inferences, "nobody has ever heard me say Mr. Irwine was much of a preacher. He didn't go into deep speritial experience; and I know there s a deal in a man's inward life as you can't measure by the square, and say, 'Do this and that 'll follow,' and, 'Do that and this 'll follow.' There's things go on in the soul, and times when feelings come into you like a rushing mighty wind, as the Scripture says, and part your life in two a'most, so you look back on yourself as if you was somebody else. Those are things as you can't bottle up in a 'do this' and 'do that'; and I'll go so far with the strongest Methodist ever you'll find. That shows me there's deep speritial things in religion. You can't make much out wi' talking about it, but you feel it. Mr. Irwine didn't go into those things—he preached short moral sermons, and that was all. But then he acted pretty much up to what he said; he didn't set up for being so different from other folks one day, and then be as like 'em as two peas the next. And he made folks love him and respect him, and that was better nor stirring up their gall wi' being overbusy. Mrs. Poyser used to say—you know she would have her word about everything—she said, Mr. Irwine was like a good meal o' victual, you were the better for him without thinking on it, and Mr. Ryde was like a dose o' physic, he gripped you and worreted you, and after all he left you much the same."

"But didn't Mr. Ryde preach a great deal more about that spiritual part of religion that you talk of, Adam? Couldn't you get more out of his sermons than out of Mr. Irwine's?"

"Eh, I knowna. He preached a deal about doctrines. But I've seen pretty clear, ever since I was a young un, as religion's something else besides doctrines and notions. I look at it as if the doctrines was like finding names for your feelings, so as you can talk of 'em when you've never known 'em, just as a man may talk o' tools when he knows their names, though he's never so much as seen 'em, still less handled 'em. I've heard a deal o' doctrine i' my time, for I used to go after the Dissenting preachers along wi' Seth, when I was a lad o' seventeen, and got puzzling myself a deal about th' Arminians and the Calvinists. The Wesleyans, you know, are strong Arminians; and Seth, who could never abide anything harsh and was always for hoping the best, held fast by the Wesleyans from the very first; but I thought I could pick a hole or two in their notions, and I got disputing wi' one o' the class leaders down at Treddles'on, and harassed him so, first o' this side and then o' that, till at last he said, 'Young man, it's the devil making use o' your pride and conceit as a weapon to war against the simplicity o' the truth.' I couldn't help laughing then, but as I was going home, I thought the man wasn't far wrong. I began to see as all this weighing and sifting what this text means and that text means, and whether folks are saved all by God's grace, or whether there goes an ounce o' their own will to't, was no part o' real religion at all. You may talk o' these things for hours on end, and you'll only be all the more coxy and conceited for't. So I took to going nowhere but to church, and hearing nobody but Mr. Irwine, for he said notning but what was good and what you'd be the wiser for remembering. And I found it better for my soul to be humble before the mysteries o' God's dealings, and not be making a clatter about what I could never understand. And they're poor foolish questions after all; for what have we got either inside or outside of us but what comes from God? If we've got a resolution to do right, He gave it us, I reckon, first or last; but I see plain enough we shall never do it without a resolution, and that's enough for me."

Adam, you perceive, was a warm admirer, perhaps a partial judge, of Mr. Irwine, as, happily, some of us still are of the people we have known familiarly. Doubtless it will be despised as a weakness by that lofty order of minds who pant after the ideal, and are oppressed by a general sense that their emotions are of too exquisite a character to find fit objects among their everyday fellowmen. I have often been favoured with the confidence of these select natures, and find them to concur in the experience that great men are overestimated and small men are insupportable; that if you would love a woman without ever looking back on your love as a folly, she must die while you are courting her; and if you would maintain the slightest belief in human heroism, you must never make a pilgrimage to see the hero. I confess I have often meanly shrunk from confessing to these accomplished and acute gentlemen what my own experience has been. I am afraid I have often smiled with hypocritical assent, and gratified them with an epigram on the fleeting nature of our illusions, which any one moderately acquainted with French literature can command at a moment's notice. Human converse, I think some wise man has remarked, is not rigidly sincere. But I herewith discharge my conscience, and declare that I have had quite enthusiastic movements of admiration towards old gentlemen who spoke the worst English, who were occasionally fretful in their temper, and who had never moved in a higher sphere of influence than that of parish overseer; and that the way in which I have come to the conclusion that human nature is lovable—the way I have learnt something of its deep pathos, its sublime mysteries—has been by living a great deal among people more or less commonplace and vulgar, of whom you would perhaps hear nothing very surprising if you were to inquire about them in the neighbourhoods where they dwelt. Ten to one most of the small shopkeepers in their vicinity saw nothing at all in them. For I have observed this remarkable coincidence, that the select natures who pant after the ideal, and find nothing in pantaloons or petticoats great enough to command their reverence and love, are curiously in unison with the narrowest and pettiest. For example, I have often heard Mr. Gedge, the landlord of the Royal Oak, who used to turn a bloodshot eye on his neighbours in the village of Shepperton, sum up his opinion of the people in his own parish—and they were all the people he knew—in these emphatic words: "Aye, sir, I've said it often, and I'll say it again, they're a poor lot i' this parish—a poor lot, sir, big and little." I think he had a dim idea that if he could migrate to a distant parish, he might find neighbours worthy of him; and indeed he did subsequently transfer himself to the Saracen's Head, which was doing a thriving business in the back street of a neighbouring market-town. But, oddly enough, he has found the people up that back street of precisely the same stamp as the inhabitants of Shepperton—"a poor lot, sir, big and little, and them as comes for a go o' gin are no better than them as comes for a pint o' twopenny—a poor lot."

Chapter XVIII Church

"HETTY, Hetty, don't you know church begins at two, and it's gone half after one a'ready? Have you got nothing better to think on this good Sunday as poor old Thias Bede's to be put into the ground, and him drownded i' th' dead o' the night, as it's enough to make one's back run cold, but you must be 'dizening yourself as if there was a wedding i'stid of a funeral?"

"Well, Aunt," said Hetty, "I can't be ready so soon as everybody else, when I've got Totty's things to put on. And I'd ever such work to make her stand still."

Hetty was coming downstairs, and Mrs. Poyser, in her plain bonnet and shawl, was standing below. If ever a girl looked as if she had been made of roses, that girl was Hetty in her Sunday hat and frock. For her hat was trimmed with pink, and her frock had pink spots, sprinkled on a white ground. There was nothing but pink and white about her, except in her dark hair and eyes and her little buckled shoes. Mrs. Poyser was provoked at herself, for she could hardly keep from smiling, as any mortal is inclined to do at the sight of pretty round things. So she turned without speaking, and joined the group outside the house door, followed by Hetty, whose heart was fluttering so at the thought of some one she expected to see at church that she hardly felt the ground she trod on.

And now the little procession set off. Mr. Poyser was in his Sunday suit of drab, with a red-and-green waistcoat and a green watch-ribbon having a large cornelian seal attached, pendant like a plumb-line from that promontory where his watch-pocket was situated; a silk handkerchief of a yellow tone round his neck; and excellent grey ribbed stockings, knitted by Mrs. Poyser's own hand, setting off the proportions of his leg. Mr. Poyser had no reason to be ashamed of his leg, and suspected that the growing abuse of top-boots and other fashions tending to disguise the nether limbs had their origin in a pitiable degeneracy of the human calf. Still less had he reason to be ashamed of his round jolly face, which was good humour itself as he said, "Come, Hetty—come, little uns!" and giving his arm to his wife, led the way through the causeway gate into the yard.

The "little uns" addressed were Marty and Tommy, boys of nine and seven, in little fustian tailed coats and knee-breeches, relieved by rosy cheeks and black eyes, looking as much like their father as a very small elephant is like a very large one. Hetty walked between them, and behind came patient Molly, whose task it was to carry Totty through the yard and over all the wet places on the road; for Totty, having speedily recovered from her threatened fever, had insisted on going to church to-day, and especially on wearing her red-and-black necklace outside her tippet. And there were many wet places for her to be carried over this afternoon, for there had been heavy showers in the morning, though now the clouds had rolled off and lay in towering silvery masses on the horizon.

You might have known it was Sunday if you had only waked up in the farmyard. The cocks and hens seemed to know it, and made only crooning subdued noises; the very bull-dog looked less savage, as if he would have been satisfied with a smaller bite than usual. The sunshine seemed to call all things to rest and not to labour. It was asleep itself on the moss-grown cow-shed; on the group of white ducks nestling together with their bills tucked under their wings; on the old black sow stretched languidly on the straw, while her largest young one found an excellent spring-bed on his mother's fat ribs; on Alick, the shepherd, in his new smock-frock, taking an uneasy siesta, half-sitting, half-standing on the granary steps. Alick was of opinion that church, like other luxuries, was not to be indulged in often by a foreman who had the weather and the ewes on his mind. "Church! Nay—I'n gotten summat else to think on," was an answer which he often uttered in a tone of bitter significance that silenced further question. I feel sure Alick meant no irreverence; indeed, I know that his mind was not of a speculative, negative cast, and he would on no account have missed going to church on Christmas Day, Easter Sunday, and "Whissuntide." But he had a general impression that public worship and religious ceremonies, like other non-productive employments, were intended for people who had leisure.

"There's Father a-standing at the yard-gate," said Martin Poyser. "I reckon he wants to watch us down the field. It's wonderful what sight he has, and him turned seventy-five."

"Ah, I often think it's wi' th' old folks as it is wi' the babbies," said Mrs. Poyser; "they're satisfied wi' looking, no matter what they're looking at. It's God A'mighty's way o' quietening 'em, I reckon, afore they go to sleep."

Old Martin opened the gate as he saw the family procession approaching, and held it wide open, leaning on his stick—pleased to do this bit of work; for, like all old men whose life has been spent in labour, he liked to feel that he was still useful—that there was a better crop of onions in the garden because he was by at the sowing—and that the cows would be milked the better if he stayed at home on a Sunday afternoon to look on. He always went to church on Sacrament Sundays, but not very regularly at other times; on wet Sundays, or whenever he had a touch of rheumatism, he used to read the three first chapters of Genesis instead.

"They'll ha' putten Thias Bede i' the ground afore ye get to the churchyard," he said, as his son came up. "It 'ud ha' been better luck if they'd ha' buried him i' the forenoon when the rain was fallin'; there's no likelihoods of a drop now; an' the moon lies like a boat there, dost see? That's a sure sign o' fair weather—there's a many as is false but that's sure."

"Aye, aye," said the son, "I'm in hopes it'll hold up now."

"Mind what the parson says, mind what the parson says, my lads," said Grandfather to the black-eyed youngsters in knee-breeches, conscious of a marble or two in their pockets which they looked forward to handling, a little, secretly, during the sermon.

"Dood-bye, Dandad," said Totty. "Me doin' to church. Me dot my netlace on. Dive me a peppermint."

Grandad, shaking with laughter at this "deep little wench," slowly transferred his stick to his left hand, which held the gate open, and slowly thrust his finger into the waistcoat pocket on which Totty had fixed her eyes with a confident look of expectation.

And when they were all gone, the old man leaned on the gate again, watching them across the lane along the Home Close, and through the far gate, till they disappeared behind a bend in the hedge. For the hedgerows in those days shut out one's view, even on the better-managed farms; and this afternoon, the dog-roses were tossing out their pink wreaths, the nightshade was in its yellow and purple glory, the pale honeysuckle grew out of reach, peeping high up out of a holly bush, and over all an ash or a sycamore every now and then threw its shadow across the path.

There were acquaintances at other gates who had to move aside and let them pass: at the gate of the Home Close there was half the dairy of cows standing one behind the other, extremely slow to understand that their large bodies might be in the way; at the far gate there was the mare holding her head over the bars, and beside her the liver-coloured foal with its head towards its mother's flank, apparently still much embarrassed by its own straddling existence. The way lay entirely through Mr. Poyser's own fields till they reached the main road leading to the village, and he turned a keen eye on the stock and the crops as they went along, while Mrs. Poyser was ready to supply a running commentary on them all. The woman who manages a dairy has a large share in making the rent, so she may well be allowed to have her opinion on stock and their "keep"—an exercise which strengthens her understanding so much that she finds herself able to give her husband advice on most other subjects.

"There's that shorthorned Sally," she said, as they entered the Home Close, and she caught sight of the meek beast that lay chewing the cud and looking at her with a sleepy eye. "I begin to hate the sight o' the cow; and I say now what I said three weeks ago, the sooner we get rid of her the better, for there's that little yallow cow as doesn't give half the milk, and yet I've twice as much butter from her."

"Why, thee't not like the women in general," said Mr. Poyser; "they like the shorthorns, as give such a lot o' milk. There's Chowne's wife wants him to buy no other sort."

"What's it sinnify what Chowne's wife likes? A poor soft thing, wi' no more head-piece nor a sparrow. She'd take a big cullender to strain her lard wi', and then wonder as the scratchin's run through. I've seen enough of her to know as I'll niver take a servant from her house again—all hugger-mugger—and you'd niver know, when you went in, whether it was Monday or Friday, the wash draggin' on to th' end o' the week; and as for her cheese, I know well enough it rose like a loaf in a tin last year. And then she talks o' the weather bein' i' fault, as there's folks 'ud stand on their heads and then say the fault was i' their boots."

"Well, Chowne's been wanting to buy Sally, so we can get rid of her if thee lik'st," said Mr. Poyser, secretly proud of his wife's superior power of putting two and two together; indeed, on recent market-days he had more than once boasted of her discernment in this very matter of shorthorns. "Aye, them as choose a soft for a wife may's well buy up the shorthorns, for if you get your head stuck in a bog, your legs may's well go after it. Eh! Talk o' legs, there's legs for you," Mrs. Poyser continued, as Totty, who had been set down now the road was dry, toddled on in front of her father and mother. "There's shapes! An' she's got such a long foot, she'll be her father's own child."

"Aye, she'll be welly such a one as Hetty i' ten years' time, on'y she's got THY coloured eyes. I niver remember a blue eye i' my family; my mother had eyes as black as sloes, just like Hetty's."

"The child 'ull be none the worse for having summat as isn't like Hetty. An' I'm none for having her so overpretty. Though for the matter o' that, there's people wi' light hair an' blue eyes as pretty as them wi' black. If Dinah had got a bit o' colour in her cheeks, an' didn't stick that Methodist cap on her head, enough to frighten the cows, folks 'ud think her as pretty as Hetty."

"Nay, nay," said Mr. Poyser, with rather a contemptuous emphasis, "thee dostna know the pints of a woman. The men 'ud niver run after Dinah as they would after Hetty."

"What care I what the men 'ud run after? It's well seen what choice the most of 'em know how to make, by the poor draggle-tails o' wives you see, like bits o' gauze ribbin, good for nothing when the colour's gone."

"Well, well, thee canstna say but what I knowed how to make a choice when I married thee," said Mr. Poyser, who usually settled little conjugal disputes by a compliment of this sort; "and thee wast twice as buxom as Dinah ten year ago."

"I niver said as a woman had need to be ugly to make a good missis of a house. There's Chowne's wife ugly enough to turn the milk an' save the rennet, but she'll niver save nothing any other way. But as for Dinah, poor child, she's niver likely to be buxom as long as she'll make her dinner o' cake and water, for the sake o' giving to them as want. She provoked me past bearing sometimes; and, as I told her, she went clean again' the Scriptur', for that says, 'Love your neighbour as yourself'; 'but,' I said, 'if you loved your neighbour no better nor you do yourself, Dinah, it's little enough you'd do for him. You'd be thinking he might do well enough on a half-empty stomach.' Eh, I wonder where she is this blessed Sunday! Sitting by that sick woman, I daresay, as she'd set her heart on going to all of a sudden."

"Ah, it was a pity she should take such megrims into her head, when she might ha' stayed wi' us all summer, and eaten twice as much as she wanted, and it 'ud niver ha' been missed. She made no odds in th' house at all, for she sat as still at her sewing as a bird on the nest, and was uncommon nimble at running to fetch anything. If Hetty gets married, theed'st like to ha' Dinah wi' thee constant."

"It's no use thinking o' that," said Mrs. Poyser. "You might as well beckon to the flying swallow as ask Dinah to come an' live here comfortable, like other folks. If anything could turn her, I should ha' turned her, for I've talked to her for a hour on end, and scolded her too; for she's my own sister's child, and it behoves me to do what I can for her. But eh, poor thing, as soon as she'd said us 'good-bye' an' got into the cart, an' looked back at me with her pale face, as is welly like her Aunt Judith come back from heaven, I begun to be frightened to think o' the set-downs I'd given her; for it comes over you sometimes as if she'd a way o' knowing the rights o' things more nor other folks have. But I'll niver give in as that's 'cause she's a Methodist, no more nor a white calf's white 'cause it eats out o' the same bucket wi' a black un."

"Nay," said Mr. Poyser, with as near an approach to a snarl as his good-nature would allow; "I'm no opinion o' the Methodists. It's on'y tradesfolks as turn Methodists; you nuver knew a farmer bitten wi' them maggots. There's maybe a workman now an' then, as isn't overclever at's work, takes to preachin' an' that, like Seth Bede. But you see Adam, as has got one o' the best head-pieces hereabout, knows better; he's a good Churchman, else I'd never encourage him for a sweetheart for Hetty."

"Why, goodness me," said Mrs. Poyser, who had looked back while her husband was speaking, "look where Molly is with them lads! They're the field's length behind us. How COULD you let 'em do so, Hetty? Anybody might as well set a pictur' to watch the children as you. Run back and tell 'em to come on."

Mr. and Mrs. Poyser were now at the end of the second field, so they set Totty on the top of one of the large stones forming the true Loamshire stile, and awaited the loiterers Totty observing with complacency, "Dey naughty, naughty boys—me dood."

The fact was that this Sunday walk through the fields was fraught with great excitement to Marty and Tommy, who saw a perpetual drama going on in the hedgerows, and could no more refrain from stopping and peeping than if they had been a couple of spaniels or terriers. Marty was quite sure he saw a yellow-hammer on the boughs of the great ash, and while he was peeping, he missed the sight of a white-throated stoat, which had run across the path and was described with much fervour by the junior Tommy. Then there was a little greenfinch, just fledged, fluttering along the ground, and it seemed quite possible to catch it, till it managed to flutter under the blackberry bush. Hetty could not be got to give any heed to these things, so Molly was called on for her ready sympathy, and peeped with open mouth wherever she was told, and said "Lawks!" whenever she was expected to wonder.

Molly hastened on with some alarm when Hetty had come back and called to them that her aunt was angry; but Marty ran on first, shouting, "We've found the speckled turkey's nest, Mother!" with the instinctive confidence that people who bring good news are never in fault.

"Ah," said Mrs. Poyser, really forgetting all discipline in this pleasant surprise, "that's a good lad; why, where is it?"

"Down in ever such a hole, under the hedge. I saw it first, looking after the greenfinch, and she sat on th' nest."

"You didn't frighten her, I hope," said the mother, "else she'll forsake it."

"No, I went away as still as still, and whispered to Molly—didn't I, Molly?"

"Well, well, now come on," said Mrs. Poyser, "and walk before Father and Mother, and take your little sister by the hand. We must go straight on now. Good boys don't look after the birds of a Sunday."

"But, Mother," said Marty, "you said you'd give half-a-crown to find the speckled turkey's nest. Mayn't I have the half-crown put into my money-box?"

"We'll see about that, my lad, if you walk along now, like a good boy."

The father and mother exchanged a significant glance of amusement at their eldest-born's acuteness; but on Tommy's round face there was a cloud.

"Mother," he said, half-crying, "Marty's got ever so much more money in his box nor I've got in mine."

"Munny, me want half-a-toun in my bots," said Totty.

"Hush, hush, hush," said Mrs. Poyser, "did ever anybody hear such naughty children? Nobody shall ever see their money-boxes any more, if they don't make haste and go on to church."

This dreadful threat had the desired effect, and through the two remaining fields the three pair of small legs trotted on without any serious interruption, notwithstanding a small pond full of tadpoles, alias "bullheads," which the lads looked at wistfully.

The damp hay that must be scattered and turned afresh to-morrow was not a cheering sight to Mr. Poyser, who during hay and corn harvest had often some mental struggles as to the benefits of a day of rest; but no temptation would have induced him to carry on any field-work, however early in the morning, on a Sunday; for had not Michael Holdsworth had a pair of oxen "sweltered" while he was ploughing on Good Friday? That was a demonstration that work on sacred days was a wicked thing; and with wickedness of any sort Martin Poyser was quite clear that he would have nothing to do, since money got by such means would never prosper.

"It a'most makes your fingers itch to be at the hay now the sun shines so," he observed, as they passed through the "Big Meadow." "But it's poor foolishness to think o' saving by going against your conscience. There's that Jim Wakefield, as they used to call 'Gentleman Wakefield,' used to do the same of a Sunday as o' weekdays, and took no heed to right or wrong, as if there was nayther God nor devil. An' what's he come to? Why, I saw him myself last market-day a-carrying a basket wi' oranges in't."

"Ah, to be sure," said Mrs. Poyser, emphatically, "you make but a poor trap to catch luck if you go and bait it wi' wickedness. The money as is got so's like to burn holes i' your pocket. I'd niver wish us to leave our lads a sixpence but what was got i' the rightful way. And as for the weather, there's One above makes it, and we must put up wi't: it's nothing of a plague to what the wenches are."

Notwithstanding the interruption in their walk, the excellent habit which Mrs. Poyser's clock had of taking time by the forelock had secured their arrival at the village while it was still a quarter to two, though almost every one who meant to go to church was already within the churchyard gates. Those who stayed at home were chiefly mothers, like Timothy's Bess, who stood at her own door nursing her baby and feeling as women feel in that position—that nothing else can be expected of them.

It was not entirely to see Thias Bede's funeral that the people were standing about the churchyard so long before service began; that was their common practice. The women, indeed, usually entered the church at once, and the farmers' wives talked in an undertone to each other, over the tall pews, about their illnesses and the total failure of doctor's stuff, recommending dandelion-tea, and other home-made specifics, as far preferable—about the servants, and their growing exorbitance as to wages, whereas the quality of their services declined from year to year, and there was no girl nowadays to be trusted any further than you could see her—about the bad price Mr. Dingall, the Treddleston grocer, was giving for butter, and the reasonable doubts that might be held as to his solvency, notwithstanding that Mrs. Dingall was a sensible woman, and they were all sorry for HER, for she had very good kin. Meantime the men lingered outside, and hardly any of them except the singers, who had a humming and fragmentary rehearsal to go through, entered the church until Mr. Irwine was in the desk. They saw no reason for that premature entrance—what could they do in church if they were there before service began?—and they did not conceive that any power in the universe could take it ill of them if they stayed out and talked a little about "bus'ness."

Chad Cranage looks like quite a new acquaintance to-day, for he has got his clean Sunday face, which always makes his little granddaughter cry at him as a stranger. But an experienced eye would have fixed on him at once as the village blacksmith, after seeing the humble deference with which the big saucy fellow took off his hat and stroked his hair to the farmers; for Chad was accustomed to say that a working-man must hold a candle to a personage understood to be as black as he was himself on weekdays; by which evil-sounding rule of conduct he meant what was, after all, rather virtuous than otherwise, namely, that men who had horses to be shod must be treated with respect. Chad and the rougher sort of workmen kept aloof from the grave under the white thorn, where the burial was going forward; but Sandy Jim, and several of the farm-labourers, made a group round it, and stood with their hats off, as fellow-mourners with the mother and sons. Others held a midway position, sometimes watching the group at the grave, sometimes listening to the conversation of the farmers, who stood in a knot near the church door, and were now joined by Martin Poyser, while his family passed into the church. On the outside of this knot stood Mr. Casson, the landlord of the Donnithorne Arms, in his most striking attitude—that is to say, with the forefinger of his right hand thrust between the buttons of his waistcoat, his left hand in his breeches pocket, and his head very much on one side; looking, on the whole, like an actor who has only a mono-syllabic part entrusted to him, but feels sure that the audience discern his fitness for the leading business; curiously in contrast with old Jonathan Burge, who held his hands behind him and leaned forward, coughing asthmatically, with an inward scorn of all knowingness that could not be turned into cash. The talk was in rather a lower tone than usual to-day, hushed a little by the sound of Mr. Irwine's voice reading the final prayers of the burial-service. They had all had their word of pity for poor Thias, but now they had got upon the nearer subject of their own grievances against Satchell, the Squire's bailiff, who played the part of steward so far as it was not performed by old Mr. Donnithorne himself, for that gentleman had the meanness to receive his own rents and make bargains about his own timber. This subject of conversation was an additional reason for not being loud, since Satchell himself might presently be walking up the paved road to the church door. And soon they became suddenly silent; for Mr. Irwine's voice had ceased, and the group round the white thorn was dispersing itself towards the church.

They all moved aside, and stood with their hats off, while Mr. Irwine passed. Adam and Seth were coming next, with their mother between them; for Joshua Rann officiated as head sexton as well as clerk, and was not yet ready to follow the rector into the vestry. But there was a pause before the three mourners came on: Lisbeth had turned round to look again towards the grave! Ah! There was nothing now but the brown earth under the white thorn. Yet she cried less to-day than she had done any day since her husband's death. Along with all her grief there was mixed an unusual sense of her own importance in having a "burial," and in Mr. Irwine's reading a special service for her husband; and besides, she knew the funeral psalm was going to be sung for him. She felt this counter-excitement to her sorrow still more strongly as she walked with her sons towards the church door, and saw the friendly sympathetic nods of their fellow-parishioners.

The mother and sons passed into the church, and one by one the loiterers followed, though some still lingered without; the sight of Mr. Donnithorne's carriage, which was winding slowly up the hill, perhaps helping to make them feel that there was no need for haste.

But presently the sound of the bassoon and the key-bugles burst forth; the evening hymn, which always opened the service, had begun, and every one must now enter and take his place.

I cannot say that the interior of Hayslope Church was remarkable for anything except for the grey age of its oaken pews—great square pews mostly, ranged on each side of a narrow aisle. It was free, indeed, from the modern blemish of galleries. The choir had two narrow pews to themselves in the middle of the right-hand row, so that it was a short process for Joshua Rann to take his place among them as principal bass, and return to his desk after the singing was over. The pulpit and desk, grey and old as the pews, stood on one side of the arch leading into the chancel, which also had its grey square pews for Mr. Donnithorne's family and servants. Yet I assure you these grey pews, with the buff-washed walls, gave a very pleasing tone to this shabby interior, and agreed extremely well with the ruddy faces and bright waistcoats. And there were liberal touches of crimson toward the chancel, for the pulpit and Mr. Donnithorne's own pew had handsome crimson cloth cushions; and, to close the vista, there was a crimson altar-cloth, embroidered with golden rays by Miss Lydia's own hand.

But even without the crimson cloth, the effect must have been warm and cheering when Mr. Irwine was in the desk, looking benignly round on that simple congregation—on the hardy old men, with bent knees and shoulders, perhaps, but with vigour left for much hedge-clipping and thatching; on the tall stalwart frames and roughly cut bronzed faces of the stone-cutters and carpenters; on the half-dozen well-to-do farmers, with their apple-cheeked families; and on the clean old women, mostly farm-labourers' wives, with their bit of snow-white cap-border under their black bonnets, and with their withered arms, bare from the elbow, folded passively over their chests. For none of the old people held books—why should they? Not one of them could read. But they knew a few "good words" by heart, and their withered lips now and then moved silently, following the service without any very clear comprehension indeed, but with a simple faith in its efflcacy to ward off harm and bring blessing. And now all faces were visible, for all were standing up—the little children on the seats peeping over the edge of the grey pews, while good Bishop Ken's evening hymn was being sung to one of those lively psalm-tunes which died out with the last generation of rectors and choral parish clerks. Melodies die out, like the pipe of Pan, with the ears that love them and listen for them. Adam was not in his usual place among the singers to-day, for he sat with his mother and Seth, and he noticed with surprise that Bartle Massey was absent too—all the more agreeable for Mr. Joshua Rann, who gave out his bass notes with unusual complacency and threw an extra ray of severity into the glances he sent over his spectacles at the recusant Will Maskery.

I beseech you to imagine Mr. Irwine looking round on this scene, in his ample white surplice that became him so well, with his powdered hair thrown back, his rich brown complexion, and his finely cut nostril and upper lip; for there was a certain virtue in that benignant yet keen countenance as there is in all human faces from which a generous soul beams out. And over all streamed the delicious June sunshine through the old windows, with their desultory patches of yellow, red, and blue, that threw pleasant touches of colour on the opposite wall.

I think, as Mr. Irwine looked round to-day, his eyes rested an instant longer than usual on the square pew occupied by Martin Poyser and his family. And there was another pair of dark eyes that found it impossible not to wander thither, and rest on that round pink-and-white figure. But Hetty was at that moment quite careless of any glances—she was absorbed in the thought that Arthur Donnithorne would soon be coming into church, for the carriage must surely be at the church-gate by this time. She had never seen him since she parted with him in the wood on Thursday evening, and oh, how long the time had seemed! Things had gone on just the same as ever since that evening; the wonders that had happened then had brought no changes after them; they were already like a dream. When she heard the church door swinging, her heart beat so, she dared not look up. She felt that her aunt was curtsying; she curtsied herself. That must be old Mr. Donnithorne—he always came first, the wrinkled small old man, peering round with short-sighted glances at the bowing and curtsying congregation; then she knew Miss Lydia was passing, and though Hetty liked so much to look at her fashionable little coal-scuttle bonnet, with the wreath of small roses round it, she didn't mind it to-day. But there were no more curtsies—no, he was not come; she felt sure there was nothing else passing the pew door but the house-keeper's black bonnet and the lady's maid's beautiful straw hat that had once been Miss Lydia's, and then the powdered heads of the butler and footman. No, he was not there; yet she would look now—she might be mistaken—for, after all, she had not looked. So she lifted up her eyelids and glanced timidly at the cushioned pew in the chancel—there was no one but old Mr. Donnithorne rubbing his spectacles with his white handkerchief, and Miss Lydia opening the large gilt-edged prayer-book. The chill disappointment was too hard to bear. She felt herself turning pale, her lips trembling; she was ready to cry. Oh, what SHOULD she do? Everybody would know the reason; they would know she was crying because Arthur was not there. And Mr. Craig, with the wonderful hothouse plant in his button-hole, was staring at her, she knew. It was dreadfully long before the General Confession began, so that she could kneel down. Two great drops WOULD fall then, but no one saw them except good-natured Molly, for her aunt and uncle knelt with their backs towards her. Molly, unable to imagine any cause for tears in church except faintness, of which she had a vague traditional knowledge, drew out of her pocket a queer little flat blue smelling-bottle, and after much labour in pulling the cork out, thrust the narrow neck against Hetty's nostrils. "It donna smell," she whispered, thinking this was a great advantage which old salts had over fresh ones: they did you good without biting your nose. Hetty pushed it away peevishly; but this little flash of temper did what the salts could not have done—it roused her to wipe away the traces of her tears, and try with all her might not to shed any more. Hetty had a certain strength in her vain little nature: she would have borne anything rather than be laughed at, or pointed at with any other feeling than admiration; she would have pressed her own nails into her tender flesh rather than people should know a secret she did not want them to know.

What fluctuations there were in her busy thoughts and feelings, while Mr. Irwine was pronouncing the solemn "Absolution" in her deaf ears, and through all the tones of petition that followed! Anger lay very close to disappointment, and soon won the victory over the conjectures her small ingenuity could devise to account for Arthur's absence on the supposition that he really wanted to come, really wanted to see her again. And by the time she rose from her knees mechanically, because all the rest were rising, the colour had returned to her cheeks even with a heightened glow, for she was framing little indignant speeches to herself, saying she hated Arthur for giving her this pain—she would like him to suffer too. Yet while this selfish tumult was going on in her soul, her eyes were bent down on her prayer-book, and the eyelids with their dark fringe looked as lovely as ever. Adam Bede thought so, as he glanced at her for a moment on rising from his knees.

But Adam's thoughts of Hetty did not deafen him to the service; they rather blended with all the other deep feelings for which the church service was a channel to him this afternoon, as a certain consciousness of our entire past and our imagined future blends itself with all our moments of keen sensibility. And to Adam the church service was the best channel he could have found for his mingled regret, yearning, and resignation; its interchange of beseeching cries for help with outbursts of faith and praise, its recurrent responses and the familiar rhythm of its collects, seemed to speak for him as no other form of worship could have done; as, to those early Christians who had worshipped from their childhood upwards in catacombs, the torch-light and shadows must have seemed nearer the Divine presence than the heathenish daylight of the streets. The secret of our emotions never lies in the bare object, but in its subtle relations to our own past: no wonder the secret escapes the unsympathizing oberver, who might as well put on his spectacles to discern odours.

But there was one reason why even a chance comer would have found the service in Hayslope Church more impressive than in most other village nooks in the kingdom—a reason of which I am sure you have not the slightest suspicion. It was the reading of our friend Joshua Rann. Where that good shoemaker got his notion of reading from remained a mystery even to his most intimate acquaintances. I believe, after all, he got it chiefly from Nature, who had poured some of her music into this honest conceited soul, as she had been known to do into other narrow souls before his. She had given him, at least, a fine bass voice and a musical ear; but I cannot positively say whether these alone had sufficed to inspire him with the rich chant in which he delivered the responses. The way he rolled from a rich deep forte into a melancholy cadence, subsiding, at the end of the last word, into a sort of faint resonance, like the lingering vibrations of a fine violoncello, I can compare to nothing for its strong calm melancholy but the rush and cadence of the wind among the autumn boughs. This may seem a strange mode of speaking about the reading of a parish clerk—a man in rusty spectacles, with stubbly hair, a large occiput, and a prominent crown. But that is Nature's way: she will allow a gentleman of splendid physiognomy and poetic aspirations to sing woefully out of tune, and not give him the slightest hint of it; and takes care that some narrow-browed fellow, trolling a ballad in the corner of a pot-house, shall be as true to his intervals as a bird.

Joshua himself was less proud of his reading than of his singing, and it was always with a sense of heightened importance that he passed from the desk to the choir. Still more to-day: it was a special occasion, for an old man, familiar to all the parish, had died a sad death—not in his bed, a circumstance the most painful to the mind of the peasant—and now the funeral psalm was to be sung in memory of his sudden departure. Moreover, Bartle Massey was not at church, and Joshua's importance in the choir suffered no eclipse. It was a solemn minor strain they sang. The old psalm-tunes have many a wail among them, and the words—

Thou sweep'st us off as with a flood; We vanish hence like dreams—

seemed to have a closer application than usual in the death of poor Thias. The mother and sons listened, each with peculiar feelings. Lisbeth had a vague belief that the psalm was doing her husband good; it was part of that decent burial which she would have thought it a greater wrong to withhold from him than to have caused him many unhappy days while he was living. The more there was said about her husband, the more there was done for him, surely the safer he would be. It was poor Lisbeth's blind way of feeling that human love and pity are a ground of faith in some other love. Seth, who was easily touched, shed tears, and tried to recall, as he had done continually since his father's death, all that he had heard of the possibility that a single moment of consciousness at the last might be a moment of pardon and reconcilement; for was it not written in the very psalm they were singing that the Divine dealings were not measured and circumscribed by time? Adam had never been unable to join in a psalm before. He had known plenty of trouble and vexation since he had been a lad, but this was the first sorrow that had hemmed in his voice, and strangely enough it was sorrow because the chief source of his past trouble and vexation was for ever gone out of his reach. He had not been able to press his father's hand before their parting, and say, "Father, you know it was all right between us; I never forgot what I owed you when I was a lad; you forgive me if I have been too hot and hasty now and then!" Adam thought but little to-day of the hard work and the earnings he had spent on his father: his thoughts ran constantly on what the old man's feelings had been in moments of humiliation, when he had held down his head before the rebukes of his son. When our indignation is borne in submissive silence, we are apt to feel twinges of doubt afterwards as to our own generosity, if not justice; how much more when the object of our anger has gone into everlasting silence, and we have seen his face for the last time in the meekness of death!

"Ah! I was always too hard," Adam said to himself. "It's a sore fault in me as I'm so hot and out o' patience with people when they do wrong, and my heart gets shut up against 'em, so as I can't bring myself to forgive 'em. I see clear enough there's more pride nor love in my soul, for I could sooner make a thousand strokes with th' hammer for my father than bring myself to say a kind word to him. And there went plenty o' pride and temper to the strokes, as the devil WILL be having his finger in what we call our duties as well as our sins. Mayhap the best thing I ever did in my life was only doing what was easiest for myself. It's allays been easier for me to work nor to sit still, but the real tough job for me 'ud be to master my own will and temper and go right against my own pride. It seems to me now, if I was to find Father at home to-night, I should behave different; but there's no knowing—perhaps nothing 'ud be a lesson to us if it didn't come too late. It's well we should feel as life's a reckoning we can't make twice over; there's no real making amends in this world, any more nor you can mend a wrong subtraction by doing your addition right."

This was the key-note to which Adam's thoughts had perpetually returned since his father's death, and the solemn wail of the funeral psalm was only an influence that brought back the old thoughts with stronger emphasis. So was the sermon, which Mr. Irwine had chosen with reference to Thias's funeral. It spoke briefly and simply of the words, "In the midst of life we are in death"—how the present moment is all we can call our own for works of mercy, of righteous dealing, and of family tenderness. All very old truths—but what we thought the oldest truth becomes the most startling to us in the week when we have looked on the dead face of one who has made a part of our own lives. For when men want to impress us with the effect of a new and wonderfully vivid light, do they not let it fall on the most familiar objects, that we may measure its intensity by remembering the former dimness?

Then came the moment of the final blessing, when the forever sublime words, "The peace of God, which passeth all understanding," seemed to blend with the calm afternoon sunshine that fell on the bowed heads of the congregation; and then the quiet rising, the mothers tying on the bonnets of the little maidens who had slept through the sermon, the fathers collecting the prayer-books, until all streamed out through the old archway into the green churchyard and began their neighbourly talk, their simple civilities, and their invitations to tea; for on a Sunday every one was ready to receive a guest—it was the day when all must be in their best clothes and their best humour.

Mr. and Mrs. Poyser paused a minute at the church gate: they were waiting for Adam to Come up, not being contented to go away without saying a kind word to the widow and her sons.

"Well, Mrs. Bede," said Mrs. Poyser, as they walked on together, "you must keep up your heart; husbands and wives must be content when they've lived to rear their children and see one another's hair grey."

"Aye, aye," said Mr. Poyser; "they wonna have long to wait for one another then, anyhow. And ye've got two o' the strapping'st sons i' th' country; and well you may, for I remember poor Thias as fine a broad-shouldered fellow as need to be; and as for you, Mrs. Bede, why you're straighter i' the back nor half the young women now."

"Eh," said Lisbeth, "it's poor luck for the platter to wear well when it's broke i' two. The sooner I'm laid under the thorn the better. I'm no good to nobody now."

Adam never took notice of his mother's little unjust plaints; but Seth said, "Nay, Mother, thee mustna say so. Thy sons 'ull never get another mother."

"That's true, lad, that's true," said Mr. Poyser; "and it's wrong on us to give way to grief, Mrs. Bede; for it's like the children cryin' when the fathers and mothers take things from 'em. There's One above knows better nor us."

"Ah," said Mrs. Poyser, "an' it's poor work allays settin' the dead above the livin'. We shall all on us be dead some time, I reckon—it 'ud be better if folks 'ud make much on us beforehand, i'stid o' beginnin' when we're gone. It's but little good you'll do a-watering the last year's crop."

"Well, Adam," said Mr. Poyser, feeling that his wife's words were, as usual, rather incisive than soothing, and that it would be well to change the subject, "you'll come and see us again now, I hope. I hanna had a talk with you this long while, and the missis here wants you to see what can be done with her best spinning-wheel, for it's got broke, and it'll be a nice job to mend it—there'll want a bit o' turning. You'll come as soon as you can now, will you?"

Mr. Poyser paused and looked round while he was speaking, as if to see where Hetty was; for the children were running on before.

Hetty was not without a companion, and she had, besides, more pink and white about her than ever, for she held in her hand the wonderful pink-and-white hot-house plant, with a very long name—a Scotch name, she supposed, since people said Mr. Craig the gardener was Scotch. Adam took the opportunity of looking round too; and I am sure you will not require of him that he should feel any vexation in observing a pouting expression on Hetty's face as she listened to the gardener's small talk. Yet in her secret heart she was glad to have him by her side, for she would perhaps learn from him how it was Arthur had not come to church. Not that she cared to ask him the question, but she hoped the information would be given spontaneously; for Mr. Craig, like a superior man, was very fond of giving information.

Mr. Craig was never aware that his conversation and advances were received coldly, for to shift one's point of view beyond certain limits is impossible to the most liberal and expansive mind; we are none of us aware of the impression we produce on Brazilian monkeys of feeble understanding—it is possible they see hardly anything in us. Moreover, Mr. Craig was a man of sober passions, and was already in his tenth year of hesitation as to the relative advantages of matrimony and bachelorhood. It is true that, now and then, when he had been a little heated by an extra glass of grog, he had been heard to say of Hetty that the "lass was well enough," and that "a man might do worse"; but on convivial occasions men are apt to express themselves strongly.

Martin Poyser held Mr. Craig in honour, as a man who "knew his business" and who had great lights concerning soils and compost; but he was less of a favourite with Mrs. Poyser, who had more than once said in confidence to her husband, "You're mighty fond o' Craig, but for my part, I think he's welly like a cock as thinks the sun's rose o' purpose to hear him crow." For the rest, Mr. Craig was an estimable gardener, and was not without reasons for having a high opinion of himself. He had also high shoulders and high cheek-bones and hung his head forward a little, as he walked along with his hands in his breeches pockets. I think it was his pedigree only that had the advantage of being Scotch, and not his "bringing up"; for except that he had a stronger burr in his accent, his speech differed little from that of the Loamshire people about him. But a gardener is Scotch, as a French teacher is Parisian.

"Well, Mr. Poyser," he said, before the good slow farmer had time to speak, "ye'll not be carrying your hay to-morrow, I'm thinking. The glass sticks at 'change,' and ye may rely upo' my word as we'll ha' more downfall afore twenty-four hours is past. Ye see that darkish-blue cloud there upo' the 'rizon—ye know what I mean by the 'rizon, where the land and sky seems to meet?"

"Aye, aye, I see the cloud," said Mr. Poyser, "'rizon or no 'rizon. It's right o'er Mike Holdsworth's fallow, and a foul fallow it is."

"Well, you mark my words, as that cloud 'ull spread o'er the sky pretty nigh as quick as you'd spread a tarpaulin over one o' your hay-ricks. It's a great thing to ha' studied the look o' the clouds. Lord bless you! Th' met'orological almanecks can learn me nothing, but there's a pretty sight o' things I could let THEM up to, if they'd just come to me. And how are you, Mrs. Poyser?—thinking o' getherin' the red currants soon, I reckon. You'd a deal better gether 'em afore they're o'er-ripe, wi' such weather as we've got to look forward to. How do ye do, Mistress Bede?" Mr. Craig continued, without a pause, nodding by the way to Adam and Seth. "I hope y' enjoyed them spinach and gooseberries as I sent Chester with th' other day. If ye want vegetables while ye're in trouble, ye know where to come to. It's well known I'm not giving other folks' things away, for when I've supplied the house, the garden s my own spekilation, and it isna every man th' old squire could get as 'ud be equil to the undertaking, let alone asking whether he'd be willing I've got to run my calkilation fine, I can tell you, to make sure o' getting back the money as I pay the squire. I should like to see some o' them fellows as make the almanecks looking as far before their noses as I've got to do every year as comes."

"They look pretty fur, though," said Mr. Poyser, turning his head on one side and speaking in rather a subdued reverential tone. "Why, what could come truer nor that pictur o' the cock wi' the big spurs, as has got its head knocked down wi' th' anchor, an' th' firin', an' the ships behind? Why, that pictur was made afore Christmas, and yit it's come as true as th' Bible. Why, th' cock's France, an' th' anchor's Nelson—an' they told us that beforehand."

"Pee—ee-eh!" said Mr. Craig. "A man doesna want to see fur to know as th' English 'ull beat the French. Why, I know upo' good authority as it's a big Frenchman as reaches five foot high, an' they live upo' spoon-meat mostly. I knew a man as his father had a particular knowledge o' the French. I should like to know what them grasshoppers are to do against such fine fellows as our young Captain Arthur. Why, it 'ud astonish a Frenchman only to look at him; his arm's thicker nor a Frenchman's body, I'll be bound, for they pinch theirsells in wi' stays; and it's easy enough, for they've got nothing i' their insides."

"Where IS the captain, as he wasna at church to-day?" said Adam. "I was talking to him o' Friday, and he said nothing about his going away."

"Oh, he's only gone to Eagledale for a bit o' fishing; I reckon he'll be back again afore many days are o'er, for he's to be at all th' arranging and preparing o' things for the comin' o' age o' the 30th o' July. But he's fond o' getting away for a bit, now and then. Him and th' old squire fit one another like frost and flowers."

Mr. Craig smiled and winked slowly as he made this last observation, but the subject was not developed farther, for now they had reached the turning in the road where Adam and his companions must say "good-bye." The gardener, too, would have had to turn off in the same direction if he had not accepted Mr. Poyser's invitation to tea. Mrs. Poyser duly seconded the invitation, for she would have held it a deep disgrace not to make her neighbours welcome to her house: personal likes and dislikes must not interfere with that sacred custom. Moreover, Mr. Craig had always been full of civilities to the family at the Hall Farm, and Mrs. Poyser was scrupulous in declaring that she had "nothing to say again' him, on'y it was a pity he couldna be hatched o'er again, an' hatched different."

So Adam and Seth, with their mother between them, wound their way down to the valley and up again to the old house, where a saddened memory had taken the place of a long, long anxiety—where Adam would never have to ask again as he entered, "Where's Father?"

And the other family party, with Mr. Craig for company, went back to the pleasant bright house-place at the Hall Farm—all with quiet minds, except Hetty, who knew now where Arthur was gone, but was only the more puzzled and uneasy. For it appeared that his absence was quite voluntary; he need not have gone—he would not have gone if he had wanted to see her. She had a sickening sense that no lot could ever be pleasant to her again if her Thursday night's vision was not to be fulfilled; and in this moment of chill, bare, wintry disappointment and doubt, she looked towards the possibility of being with Arthur again, of meeting his loving glance, and hearing his soft words with that eager yearning which one may call the "growing pain" of passion.

Chapter XIX Adam on a Working Day

NOTWITHSTANDING Mr. Craig's prophecy, the dark-blue cloud dispersed itself without having produced the threatened consequences. "The weather"—as he observed the next morning—"the weather, you see, 's a ticklish thing, an' a fool 'ull hit on't sometimes when a wise man misses; that's why the almanecks get so much credit. It's one o' them chancy things as fools thrive on."

This unreasonable behaviour of the weather, however, could displease no one else in Hayslope besides Mr. Craig. All hands were to be out in the meadows this morning as soon as the dew had risen; the wives and daughters did double work in every farmhouse, that the maids might give their help in tossing the hay; and when Adam was marching along the lanes, with his basket of tools over his shoulder, he caught the sound of jocose talk and ringing laughter from behind the hedges. The jocose talk of hay-makers is best at a distance; like those clumsy bells round the cows' necks, it has rather a coarse sound when it comes close, and may even grate on your ears painfully; but heard from far off, it mingles very prettily with the other joyous sounds of nature. Men's muscles move better when their souls are making merry music, though their merriment is of a poor blundering sort, not at all like the merriment of birds.

And perhaps there is no time in a summer's day more cheering than when the warmth of the sun is just beginning to triumph over the freshness of the morning—when there is just a lingering hint of early coolness to keep off languor under the delicious influence of warmth. The reason Adam was walking along the lanes at this time was because his work for the rest of the day lay at a country-house about three miles off, which was being put in repair for the son of a neighbouring squire; and he had been busy since early morning with the packing of panels, doors, and chimney-pieces, in a waggon which was now gone on before him, while Jonathan Burge himself had ridden to the spot on horseback, to await its arrival and direct the workmen.

This little walk was a rest to Adam, and he was unconsciously under the charm of the moment. It was summer morning in his heart, and he saw Hetty in the sunshine—a sunshine without glare, with slanting rays that tremble between the delicate shadows of the leaves. He thought, yesterday when he put out his hand to her as they came out of church, that there was a touch of melancholy kindness in her face, such as he had not seen before, and he took it as a sign that she had some sympathy with his family trouble. Poor fellow! That touch of melancholy came from quite another source, but how was he to know? We look at the one little woman's face we love as we look at the face of our mother earth, and see all sorts of answers to our own yearnings. It was impossible for Adam not to feel that what had happened in the last week had brought the prospect of marriage nearer to him. Hitherto he had felt keenly the danger that some other man might step in and get possession of Hetty's heart and hand, while he himself was still in a position that made him shrink from asking her to accept him. Even if he had had a strong hope that she was fond of him—and his hope was far from being strong—he had been too heavily burdened with other claims to provide a home for himself and Hetty—a home such as he could expect her to be content with after the comfort and plenty of the Farm. Like all strong natures, Adam had confidence in his ability to achieve something in the future; he felt sure he should some day, if he lived, be able to maintain a family and make a good broad path for himself; but he had too cool a head not to estimate to the full the obstacles that were to be overcome. And the time would be so long! And there was Hetty, like a bright-cheeked apple hanging over the orchard wall, within sight of everybody, and everybody must long for her! To be sure, if she loved him very much, she would be content to wait for him: but DID she love him? His hopes had never risen so high that he had dared to ask her. He was clear-sighted enough to be aware that her uncle and aunt would have looked kindly on his suit, and indeed, without this encouragement he would never have persevered in going to the Farm;

but it was impossible to come to any but fluctuating conclusions about Hetty's feelings. She was like a kitten, and had the same distractingly pretty looks, that meant nothing, for everybody that came near her.

But now he could not help saying to himself that the heaviest part of his burden was removed, and that even before the end of another year his circumstances might be brought into a shape that would allow him to think of marrying. It would always be a hard struggle with his mother, he knew: she would be jealous of any wife he might choose, and she had set her mind especially against Hetty—perhaps for no other reason than that she suspected Hetty to be the woman he HAD chosen. It would never do, he feared, for his mother to live in the same house with him when he was married; and yet how hard she would think it if he asked her to leave him! Yes, there was a great deal of pain to be gone through with his mother, but it was a case in which he must make her feel that his will was strong—it would be better for her in the end. For himself, he would have liked that they should all live together till Seth was married, and they might have built a bit themselves to the old house, and made more room. He did not like "to part wi' th' lad": they had hardly every been separated for more than a day since they were born.

But Adam had no sooner caught his imagination leaping forward in this way—making arrangements for an uncertain future—than he checked himself. "A pretty building I'm making, without either bricks or timber. I'm up i' the garret a'ready, and haven't so much as dug the foundation." Whenever Adam was strongly convinced of any proposition, it took the form of a principle in his mind: it was knowledge to be acted on, as much as the knowledge that damp will cause rust. Perhaps here lay the secret of the hardness he had accused himself of: he had too little fellow-feeling with the weakness that errs in spite of foreseen consequences. Without this fellow-feeling, how are we to get enough patience and charity towards our stumbling, falling companions in the long and changeful journey? And there is but one way in which a strong determined soul can learn it—by getting his heart-strings bound round the weak and erring, so that he must share not only the outward consequence of their error, but their inward suffering. That is a long and hard lesson, and Adam had at present only learned the alphabet of it in his father's sudden death, which, by annihilating in an instant all that had stimulated his indignation, had sent a sudden rush of thought and memory over what had claimed his pity and tenderness.

But it was Adam's strength, not its correlative hardness, that influenced his meditations this morning. He had long made up his mind that it would be wrong as well as foolish for him to marry a blooming young girl, so long as he had no other prospect than that of growing poverty with a growing family. And his savings had been so constantly drawn upon (besides the terrible sweep of paying for Seth's substitute in the militia) that he had not enough money beforehand to furnish even a small cottage, and keep something in reserve against a rainy day. He had good hope that he should be "firmer on his legs" by and by; but he could not be satisfied with a vague confidence in his arm and brain; he must have definite plans, and set about them at once. The partnership with Jonathan Burge was not to be thought of at present—there were things implicitly tacked to it that he could not accept; but Adam thought that he and Seth might carry on a little business for themselves in addition to their journeyman's work, by buying a small stock of superior wood and making articles of household furniture, for which Adam had no end of contrivances. Seth might gain more by working at separate jobs under Adam's direction than by his journeyman's work, and Adam, in his overhours, could do all the "nice" work that required peculiar skill. The money gained in this way, with the good wages he received as foreman, would soon enable them to get beforehand with the world, so sparingly as they would all live now. No sooner had this little plan shaped itself in his mind than he began to be busy with exact calculations about the wood to be bought and the particular article of furniture that should be undertaken first—a kitchen cupboard of his own contrivance, with such an ingenious arrangement of sliding-doors and bolts, such convenient nooks for stowing household provender, and such a symmetrical result to the eye, that every good housewife would be in raptures with it, and fall through all the gradations of melancholy longing till her husband promised to buy it for her. Adam pictured to himself Mrs. Poyser examining it with her keen eye and trying in vain to find out a deficiency; and, of course, close to Mrs. Poyser stood Hetty, and Adam was again beguiled from calculations and contrivances into dreams and hopes. Yes, he would go and see her this evening—it was so long since he had been at the Hall Farm. He would have liked to go to the night-school, to see why Bartle Massey had not been at church yesterday, for he feared his old friend was ill; but, unless he could manage both visits, this last must be put off till to-morrow—the desire to be near Hetty and to speak to her again was too strong.

As he made up his mind to this, he was coming very near to the end of his walk, within the sound of the hammers at work on the refitting of the old house. The sound of tools to a clever workman who loves his work is like the tentative sounds of the orchestra to the violinist who has to bear his part in the overture: the strong fibres begin their accustomed thrill, and what was a moment before joy, vexation, or ambition, begins its change into energy. All passion becomes strength when it has an outlet from the narrow limits of our personal lot in the labour of our right arm, the cunning of our right hand, or the still, creative activity of our thought. Look at Adam through the rest of the day, as he stands on the scaffolding with the two-feet ruler in his hand, whistling low while he considers how a difficulty about a floor-joist or a window-frame is to be overcome; or as he pushes one of the younger workmen aside and takes his place in upheaving a weight of timber, saying, "Let alone, lad! Thee'st got too much gristle i' thy bones yet"; or as he fixes his keen black eyes on the motions of a workman on the other side of the room and warns him that his distances are not right. Look at this broad-shouldered man with the bare muscular arms, and the thick, firm, black hair tossed about like trodden meadow-grass whenever he takes off his paper cap, and with the strong barytone voice bursting every now and then into loud and solemn psalm-tunes, as if seeking an outlet for superfluous strength, yet presently checking himself, apparently crossed by some thought which jars with the singing. Perhaps, if you had not been already in the secret, you might not have guessed what sad memories what warm affection, what tender fluttering hopes, had their home in this athletic body with the broken finger-nails—in this rough man, who knew no better lyrics than he could find in the Old and New Version and an occasional hymn; who knew the smallest possible amount of profane history; and for whom the motion and shape of the earth, the course of the sun, and the changes of the seasons lay in the region of mystery just made visible by fragmentary knowledge. It had cost Adam a great deal of trouble and work in overhours to know what he knew over and above the secrets of his handicraft, and that acquaintance with mechanics and figures, and the nature of the materials he worked with, which was made easy to him by inborn inherited faculty—to get the mastery of his pen, and write a plain hand, to spell without any other mistakes than must in fairness be attributed to the unreasonable character of orthography rather than to any deficiency in the speller, and, moreover, to learn his musical notes and part-singing. Besides all this, he had read his Bible, including the apocryphal books; Poor Richard's Almanac, Taylor's Holy Living and Dying, The Pilgrim's Progress, with Bunyan's Life and Holy War, a great deal of Bailey's Dictionary, Valentine and Orson, and part of a History of Babylon, which Bartle Massey had lent him. He might have had many more books from Bartle Massey, but he had no time for reading "the commin print," as Lisbeth called it, so busy as he was with figures in all the leisure moments which he did not fill up with extra carpentry.

Adam, you perceive, was by no means a marvellous man, nor, properly speaking, a genius, yet I will not pretend that his was an ordinary character among workmen; and it would not be at all a safe conclusion that the next best man you may happen to see with a basket of tools over his shoulder and a paper cap on his head has the strong conscience and the strong sense, the blended susceptibility and self-command, of our friend Adam. He was not an average man. Yet such men as he are reared here and there in every generation of our peasant artisans—with an inheritance of affections nurtured by a simple family life of common need and common industry, and an inheritance of faculties trained in skilful courageous labour: they make their way upwards, rarely as geniuses, most commonly as painstaking honest men, with the skill and conscience to do well the tasks that lie before them. Their lives have no discernible echo beyond the neighbourhood where they dwelt, but you are almost sure to find there some good piece of road, some building, some application of mineral produce, some improvement in farming practice, some reform of parish abuses, with which their names are associated by one or two generations after them. Their employers were the richer for them, the work of their hands has worn well, and the work of their brains has guided well the hands of other men. They went about in their youth in flannel or paper caps, in coats black with coal-dust or streaked with lime and red paint; in old age their white hairs are seen in a place of honour at church and at market, and they tell their well-dressed sons and daughters, seated round the bright hearth on winter evenings, how pleased they were when they first earned their twopence a-day. Others there are who die poor and never put off the workman's coal on weekdays. They have not had the art of getting rich, but they are men of trust, and when they die before the work is all out of them, it is as if some main screw had got loose in a machine; the master who employed them says, "Where shall I find their like?"

Chapter XX Adam Visits the Hall Farm

ADAM came back from his work in the empty waggon—that was why he had changed his clothes—and was ready to set out to the Hall Farm when it still wanted a quarter to seven.

"What's thee got thy Sunday cloose on for?" said Lisbeth complainingly, as he came downstairs. "Thee artna goin' to th' school i' thy best coat?"

"No, Mother," said Adam, quietly. "I'm going to the Hall Farm, but mayhap I may go to the school after, so thee mustna wonder if I'm a bit late. Seth 'ull be at home in half an hour—he's only gone to the village; so thee wutna mind."

"Eh, an' what's thee got thy best cloose on for to go to th' Hall Farm? The Poyser folks see'd thee in 'em yesterday, I warrand. What dost mean by turnin' worki'day into Sunday a-that'n? It's poor keepin' company wi' folks as donna like to see thee i' thy workin' jacket."

"Good-bye, mother, I can't stay," said Adam, putting on his hat and going out.

But he had no sooner gone a few paces beyond the door than Lisbeth became uneasy at the thought that she had vexed him. Of course, the secret of her objection to the best clothes was her suspicion that they were put on for Hetty's sake; but deeper than all her peevishness lay the need that her son should love her. She hurried after him, and laid hold of his arm before he had got half-way down to the brook, and said, "Nay, my lad, thee wutna go away angered wi' thy mother, an' her got nought to do but to sit by hersen an' think on thee?"

"Nay, nay, Mother," said Adam, gravely, and standing still while he put his arm on her shoulder, "I'm not angered. But I wish, for thy own sake, thee'dst be more contented to let me do what I've made up my mind to do. I'll never be no other than a good son to thee as long as we live. But a man has other feelings besides what he owes to's father and mother, and thee oughtna to want to rule over me body and soul. And thee must make up thy mind as I'll not give way to thee where I've a right to do what I like. So let us have no more words about it."

"Eh," said Lisbeth, not willing to show that she felt the real bearing of Adam's words, "and' who likes to see thee i' thy best cloose better nor thy mother? An' when thee'st got thy face washed as clean as the smooth white pibble, an' thy hair combed so nice, and thy eyes a-sparklin'—what else is there as thy old mother should like to look at half so well? An' thee sha't put on thy Sunday cloose when thee lik'st for me—I'll ne'er plague thee no moor about'n."

"Well, well; good-bye, mother," said Adam, kissing her and hurrying away. He saw there was no other means of putting an end to the dialogue. Lisbeth stood still on the spot, shading her eyes and looking after him till he was quite out of sight. She felt to the full all the meaning that had lain in Adam's words, and, as she lost sight of him and turned back slowly into the house, she said aloud to herself—for it was her way to speak her thoughts aloud in the long days when her husband and sons were at their work—"Eh, he'll be tellin' me as he's goin' to bring her home one o' these days; an' she'll be missis o'er me, and I mun look on, belike, while she uses the blue-edged platters, and breaks 'em, mayhap, though there's ne'er been one broke sin' my old man an' me bought 'em at the fair twenty 'ear come next Whis-suntide. Eh!" she went on, still louder, as she caught up her knitting from the table, "but she'll ne'er knit the lad's stockin's, nor foot 'em nayther, while I live; an' when I'm gone, he'll bethink him as nobody 'ull ne'er fit's leg an' foot as his old mother did. She'll know nothin' o' narrowin' an' heelin', I warrand, an' she'll make a long toe as he canna get's boot on. That's what comes o' marr'in' young wenches. I war gone thirty, an' th' feyther too, afore we war married; an' young enough too. She'll be a poor dratchell by then SHE'S thirty, a-marr'in' a-that'n, afore her teeth's all come."

Adam walked so fast that he was at the yard-gate before seven. Martin Poyser and the grandfather were not yet come in from the meadow: every one was in the meadow, even to the black-and-tan terrier—no one kept watch in the yard but the bull-dog; and when Adam reached the house-door, which stood wide open, he saw there was no one in the bright clean house-place. But he guessed where Mrs. Poyser and some one else would be, quite within hearing; so he knocked on the door and said in his strong voice, "Mrs. Poyser within?"

"Come in, Mr. Bede, come in," Mrs. Poyser called out from the dairy. She always gave Adam this title when she received him in her own house. "You may come into the dairy if you will, for I canna justly leave the cheese."

Adam walked into the dairy, where Mrs. Poyser and Nancy were crushing the first evening cheese.

"Why, you might think you war come to a dead-house," said Mrs. Poyser, as he stood in the open doorway; "they're all i' the meadow; but Martin's sure to be in afore long, for they're leaving the hay cocked to-night, ready for carrying first thing to-morrow. I've been forced t' have Nancy in, upo' 'count as Hetty must gether the red currants to-night; the fruit allays ripens so contrairy, just when every hand's wanted. An' there's no trustin' the children to gether it, for they put more into their own mouths nor into the basket; you might as well set the wasps to gether the fruit."

Adam longed to say he would go into the garden till Mr. Poyser came in, but he was not quite courageous enough, so he said, "I could be looking at your spinning-wheel, then, and see what wants doing to it. Perhaps it stands in the house, where I can find it?"

"No, I've put it away in the right-hand parlour; but let it be till I can fetch it and show it you. I'd be glad now if you'd go into the garden and tell Hetty to send Totty in. The child 'ull run in if she's told, an' I know Hetty's lettin' her eat too many currants. I'll be much obliged to you, Mr. Bede, if you'll go and send her in; an' there's the York and Lankester roses beautiful in the garden now—you'll like to see 'em. But you'd like a drink o' whey first, p'r'aps; I know you're fond o' whey, as most folks is when they hanna got to crush it out."

"Thank you, Mrs. Poyser," said Adam; "a drink o' whey's allays a treat to me. I'd rather have it than beer any day."

"Aye, aye," said Mrs. Poyser, reaching a small white basin that stood on the shelf, and dipping it into the whey-tub, "the smell o' bread's sweet t' everybody but the baker. The Miss Irwines allays say, 'Oh, Mrs. Poyser, I envy you your dairy; and I envy you your chickens; and what a beautiful thing a farm-house is, to be sure!' An' I say, 'Yes; a farm-house is a fine thing for them as look on, an' don't know the liftin', an' the stannin', an' the worritin' o' th' inside as belongs to't.'"

"Why, Mrs. Poyser, you wouldn't like to live anywhere else but in a farm-house, so well as you manage it," said Adam, taking the basin; "and there can be nothing to look at pleasanter nor a fine milch cow, standing up to'ts knees in pasture, and the new milk frothing in the pail, and the fresh butter ready for market, and the calves, and the poultry. Here's to your health, and may you allays have strength to look after your own dairy, and set a pattern t' all the farmers' wives in the country."

Mrs. Poyser was not to be caught in the weakness of smiling at a compliment, but a quiet complacency over-spread her face like a stealing sunbeam, and gave a milder glance than usual to her blue-grey eyes, as she looked at Adam drinking the whey. Ah! I think I taste that whey now—with a flavour so delicate that one can hardly distinguish it from an odour, and with that soft gliding warmth that fills one's imagination with a still, happy dreaminess. And the light music of the dropping whey is in my ears, mingling with the twittering of a bird outside the wire network window—the window overlooking the garden, and shaded by tall Guelder roses.

"Have a little more, Mr. Bede?" said Mrs. Poyser, as Adam set down the basin.

"No, thank you; I'll go into the garden now, and send in the little lass."

"Aye, do; and tell her to come to her mother in the dairy."

Adam walked round by the rick-yard, at present empty of ricks, to the little wooden gate leading into the garden—once the well-tended kitchen-garden of a manor-house; now, but for the handsome brick wall with stone coping that ran along one side of it, a true farm-house garden, with hardy perennial flowers, unpruned fruit-trees, and kitchen vegetables growing together in careless, half-neglected abundance. In that leafy, flowery, bushy time, to look for any one in this garden was like playing at "hide-and-seek." There were the tall hollyhocks beginning to flower and dazzle the eye with their pink, white, and yellow; there were the syringas and Guelder roses, all large and disorderly for want of trimming; there were leafy walls of scarlet beans and late peas; there was a row of bushy filberts in one direction, and in another a huge apple-tree making a barren circle under its low-spreading boughs. But what signified a barren patch or two? The garden was so large. There was always a superfluity of broad beans—it took nine or ten of Adam's strides to get to the end of the uncut grass walk that ran by the side of them; and as for other vegetables, there was so much more room than was necessary for them that in the rotation of crops a large flourishing bed of groundsel was of yearly occurrence on one spot or other. The very rose-trees at which Adam stopped to pluck one looked as if they grew wild; they were all huddled together in bushy masses, now flaunting with wide-open petals, almost all of them of the streaked pink-and-white kind, which doubtless dated from the union of the houses of York and Lancaster. Adam was wise enough to choose a compact Provence rose that peeped out half-smothered by its flaunting scentless neighbours, and held it in his hand—he thought he should be more at ease holding something in his hand—as he walked on to the far end of the garden, where he remembered there was the largest row of currant-trees, not far off from the great yew-tree arbour.

But he had not gone many steps beyond the roses, when he heard the shaking of a bough, and a boy's voice saying, "Now, then, Totty, hold out your pinny—there's a duck."

The voice came from the boughs of a tall cherry-tree, where Adam had no difficulty in discerning a small blue-pinafored figure perched in a commodious position where the fruit was thickest. Doubtless Totty was below, behind the screen of peas. Yes—with her bonnet hanging down her back, and her fat face, dreadfully smeared with red juice, turned up towards the cherry-tree, while she held her little round hole of a mouth and her red-stained pinafore to receive the promised downfall. I am sorry to say, more than half the cherries that fell were hard and yellow instead of juicy and red; but Totty spent no time in useless regrets, and she was already sucking the third juiciest when Adam said, "There now, Totty, you've got your cherries. Run into the house with 'em to Mother—she wants you—she's in the dairy. Run in this minute—there's a good little girl."

He lifted her up in his strong arms and kissed her as he spoke, a ceremony which Totty regarded as a tiresome interruption to cherry-eating; and when he set her down she trotted off quite silently towards the house, sucking her cherries as she went along.

"Tommy, my lad, take care you're not shot for a little thieving bird," said Adam, as he walked on towards the currant-trees.

He could see there was a large basket at the end of the row: Hetty would not be far off, and Adam already felt as if she were looking at him. Yet when he turned the corner she was standing with her back towards him, and stooping to gather the low-hanging fruit. Strange that she had not heard him coming! Perhaps it was because she was making the leaves rustle. She started when she became conscious that some one was near—started so violently that she dropped the basin with the currants in it, and then, when she saw it was Adam, she turned from pale to deep red. That blush made his heart beat with a new happiness. Hetty had never blushed at seeing him before.

"I frightened you," he said, with a delicious sense that it didn't signify what he said, since Hetty seemed to feel as much as he did; "let ME pick the currants up."

That was soon done, for they had only fallen in a tangled mass on the grass-plot, and Adam, as he rose and gave her the basin again, looked straight into her eyes with the subdued tenderness that belongs to the first moments of hopeful love.

Hetty did not turn away her eyes; her blush had subsided, and she met his glance with a quiet sadness, which contented Adam because it was so unlike anything he had seen in her before.

"There's not many more currants to get," she said; "I shall soon ha' done now."

"I'll help you," said Adam; and he fetched the large basket, which was nearly full of currants, and set it close to them.

Not a word more was spoken as they gathered the currants. Adam's heart was too full to speak, and he thought Hetty knew all that was in it. She was not indifferent to his presence after all; she had blushed when she saw him, and then there was that touch of sadness about her which must surely mean love, since it was the opposite of her usual manner, which had often impressed him as indifference. And he could glance at her continually as she bent over the fruit, while the level evening sunbeams stole through the thick apple-tree boughs, and rested on her round cheek and neck as if they too were in love with her. It was to Adam the time that a man can least forget in after-life, the time when he believes that the first woman he has ever loved betrays by a slight something—a word, a tone, a glance, the quivering of a lip or an eyelid—that she is at least beginning to love him in return. The sign is so slight, it is scarcely perceptible to the ear or eye—he could describe it to no one—it is a mere feather-touch, yet it seems to have changed his whole being, to have merged an uneasy yearning into a delicious unconsciousness of everything but the present moment. So much of our early gladness vanishes utterly from our memory: we can never recall the joy with which we laid our heads on our mother's bosom or rode on our father's back in childhood. Doubtless that joy is wrought up into our nature, as the sunlight of long-past mornings is wrought up in the soft mellowness of the apricot, but it is gone for ever from our imagination, and we can only BELIEVE in the joy of childhood. But the first glad moment in our first love is a vision which returns to us to the last, and brings with it a thrill of feeling intense and special as the recurrent sensation of a sweet odour breathed in a far-off hour of happiness. It is a memory that gives a more exquisite touch to tenderness, that feeds the madness of jealousy and adds the last keenness to the agony of despair.

Hetty bending over the red bunches, the level rays piercing the screen of apple-tree boughs, the length of bushy garden beyond, his own emotion as he looked at her and believed that she was thinking of him, and that there was no need for them to talk—Adam remembered it all to the last moment of his life.

And Hetty? You know quite well that Adam was mistaken about her. Like many other men, he thought the signs of love for another were signs of love towards himself. When Adam was approaching unseen by her, she was absorbed as usual in thinking and wondering about Arthur's possible return. The sound of any man's footstep would have affected her just in the same way—she would have FELT it might be Arthur before she had time to see, and the blood that forsook her cheek in the agitation of that momentary feeling would have rushed back again at the sight of any one else just as much as at the sight of Adam. He was not wrong in thinking that a change had come over Hetty: the anxieties and fears of a first passion, with which she was trembling, had become stronger than vanity, had given her for the first time that sense of helpless dependence on another's feeling which awakens the clinging deprecating womanhood even in the shallowest girl that can ever experience it, and creates in her a sensibility to kindness which found her quite hard before. For the first time Hetty felt that there was something soothing to her in Adam's timid yet manly tenderness. She wanted to be treated lovingly—oh, it was very hard to bear this blank of absence, silence, apparent indifference, after those moments of glowing love! She was not afraid that Adam would tease her with love-making and flattering speeches like her other admirers; he had always been so reserved to her; she could enjoy without any fear the sense that this strong brave man loved her and was near her. It never entered into her mind that Adam was pitiable too—that Adam too must suffer one day.

Hetty, we know, was not the first woman that had behaved more gently to the man who loved her in vain because she had herself begun to love another. It was a very old story, but Adam knew nothing about it, so he drank in the sweet delusion.

"That'll do," said Hetty, after a little while. "Aunt wants me to leave some on the trees. I'll take 'em in now."

"It's very well I came to carry the basket," said Adam "for it 'ud ha' been too heavy for your little arms."

"No; I could ha' carried it with both hands."

"Oh, I daresay," said Adam, smiling, "and been as long getting into the house as a little ant carrying a caterpillar. Have you ever seen those tiny fellows carrying things four times as big as themselves?"

"No," said Hetty, indifferently, not caring to know the difficulties of ant life.

"Oh, I used to watch 'em often when I was a lad. But now, you see, I can carry the basket with one arm, as if it was an empty nutshell, and give you th' other arm to lean on. Won't you? Such big arms as mine were made for little arms like yours to lean on."

Hetty smiled faintly and put her arm within his. Adam looked down at her, but her eyes were turned dreamily towards another corner of the garden.

"Have you ever been to Eagledale?" she said, as they walked slowly along.

"Yes," said Adam, pleased to have her ask a question about himself. "Ten years ago, when I was a lad, I went with father to see about some work there. It's a wonderful sight—rocks and caves such as you never saw in your life. I never had a right notion o' rocks till I went there."

"How long did it take to get there?"

"Why, it took us the best part o' two days' walking. But it's nothing of a day's journey for anybody as has got a first-rate nag. The captain 'ud get there in nine or ten hours, I'll be bound, he's such a rider. And I shouldn't wonder if he's back again to-morrow; he's too active to rest long in that lonely place, all by himself, for there's nothing but a bit of a inn i' that part where he's gone to fish. I wish he'd got th' estate in his hands; that 'ud be the right thing for him, for it 'ud give him plenty to do, and he'd do't well too, for all he's so young; he's got better notions o' things than many a man twice his age. He spoke very handsome to me th' other day about lending me money to set up i' business; and if things came round that way, I'd rather be beholding to him nor to any man i' the world."

Poor Adam was led on to speak about Arthur because he thought Hetty would be pleased to know that the young squire was so ready to befriend him; the fact entered into his future prospects, which he would like to seem promising in her eyes. And it was true that Hetty listened with an interest which brought a new light into her eyes and a half-smile upon her lips.

"How pretty the roses are now!" Adam continued, pausing to look at them. "See! I stole the prettiest, but I didna mean to keep it myself. I think these as are all pink, and have got a finer sort o' green leaves, are prettier than the striped uns, don't you?"

He set down the basket and took the rose from his button-hole.

"It smells very sweet," he said; "those striped uns have no smell. Stick it in your frock, and then you can put it in water after. It 'ud be a pity to let it fade."

Hetty took the rose, smiling as she did so at the pleasant thought that Arthur could so soon get back if he liked. There was a flash of hope and happiness in her mind, and with a sudden impulse of gaiety she did what she had very often done before—stuck the rose in her hair a little above the left ear. The tender admiration in Adam's face was slightly shadowed by reluctant disapproval. Hetty's love of finery was just the thing that would most provoke his mother, and he himself disliked it as much as it was possible for him to dislike anything that belonged to her.

"Ah," he said, "that's like the ladies in the pictures at the Chase; they've mostly got flowers or feathers or gold things i' their hair, but somehow I don't like to see 'em they allays put me i' mind o' the painted women outside the shows at Treddles'on Fair. What can a woman have to set her off better than her own hair, when it curls so, like yours? If a woman's young and pretty, I think you can see her good looks all the better for her being plain dressed. Why, Dinah Morris looks very nice, for all she wears such a plain cap and gown. It seems to me as a woman's face doesna want flowers; it's almost like a flower itself. I'm sure yours is."

"Oh, very well," said Hetty, with a little playful pout, taking the rose out of her hair. "I'll put one o' Dinah's caps on when we go in, and you'll see if I look better in it. She left one behind, so I can take the pattern."

"Nay, nay, I don't want you to wear a Methodist cap like Dinah's. I daresay it's a very ugly cap, and I used to think when I saw her here as it was nonsense for her to dress different t' other people; but I never rightly noticed her till she came to see mother last week, and then I thought the cap seemed to fit her face somehow as th 'acorn-cup fits th' acorn, and I shouldn't like to see her so well without it. But you've got another sort o' face; I'd have you just as you are now, without anything t' interfere with your own looks. It's like when a man's singing a good tune—you don't want t' hear bells tinkling and interfering wi' the sound."

He took her arm and put it within his again, looking down on her fondly. He was afraid she should think he had lectured her, imagining, as we are apt to do, that she had perceived all the thoughts he had only half-expressed. And the thing he dreaded most was lest any cloud should come over this evening's happiness. For the world he would not have spoken of his love to Hetty yet, till this commencing kindness towards him should have grown into unmistakable love. In his imagination he saw long years of his future life stretching before him, blest with the right to call Hetty his own: he could be content with very little at present. So he took up the basket of currants once more, and they went on towards the house.

The scene had quite changed in the half-hour that Adam had been in the garden. The yard was full of life now: Marty was letting the screaming geese through the gate, and wickedly provoking the gander by hissing at him; the granary-door was groaning on its hinges as Alick shut it, after dealing out the corn; the horses were being led out to watering, amidst much barking of all the three dogs and many "whups" from Tim the ploughman, as if the heavy animals who held down their meek, intelligent heads, and lifted their shaggy feet so deliberately, were likely to rush wildly in every direction but the right. Everybody was come back from the meadow; and when Hetty and Adam entered the house-place, Mr. Poyser was seated in the three-cornered chair, and the grandfather in the large arm-chair opposite, looking on with pleasant expectation while the supper was being laid on the oak table. Mrs. Poyser had laid the cloth herself—a cloth made of homespun linen, with a shining checkered pattern on it, and of an agreeable whitey-brown hue, such as all sensible housewives like to see—none of your bleached "shop-rag" that would wear into holes in no time, but good homespun that would last for two generations. The cold veal, the fresh lettuces, and the stuffed chine might well look tempting to hungry men who had dined at half-past twelve o'clock. On the large deal table against the wall there were bright pewter plates and spoons and cans, ready for Alick and his companions; for the master and servants ate their supper not far off each other; which was all the pleasanter, because if a remark about to-morrow morning's work occurred to Mr. Poyser, Alick was at hand to hear it.

"Well, Adam, I'm glad to see ye," said Mr. Poyser. "What! ye've been helping Hetty to gether the curran's, eh? Come, sit ye down, sit ye down. Why, it's pretty near a three-week since y' had your supper with us; and the missis has got one of her rare stuffed chines. I'm glad ye're come."

"Hetty," said Mrs. Poyser, as she looked into the basket of currants to see if the fruit was fine, "run upstairs and send Molly down. She's putting Totty to bed, and I want her to draw th' ale, for Nancy's busy yet i' the dairy. You can see to the child. But whativer did you let her run away from you along wi' Tommy for, and stuff herself wi' fruit as she can't eat a bit o' good victual?"

This was said in a lower tone than usual, while her husband was talking to Adam; for Mrs. Poyser was strict in adherence to her own rules of propriety, and she considered that a young girl was not to be treated sharply in the presence of a respectable man who was courting her. That would not be fair-play: every woman was young in her turn, and had her chances of matrimony, which it was a point of honour for other women not to spoil—just as one market-woman who has sold her own eggs must not try to balk another of a customer.

Hetty made haste to run away upstairs, not easily finding an answer to her aunt's question, and Mrs. Poyser went out to see after Marty and Tommy and bring them in to supper.

Soon they were all seated—the two rosy lads, one on each side, by the pale mother, a place being left for Hetty between Adam and her uncle. Alick too was come in, and was seated in his far corner, eating cold broad beans out of a large dish with his pocket-knife, and finding a flavour in them which he would not have exchanged for the finest pineapple.

"What a time that gell is drawing th' ale, to be sure!" said Mrs. Poyser, when she was dispensing her slices of stuffed chine. "I think she sets the jug under and forgets to turn the tap, as there's nothing you can't believe o' them wenches: they'll set the empty kettle o' the fire, and then come an hour after to see if the water boils."

"She's drawin' for the men too," said Mr. Poyser. "Thee shouldst ha' told her to bring our jug up first."

"Told her?" said Mrs. Poyser. "Yes, I might spend all the wind i' my body, an' take the bellows too, if I was to tell them gells everything as their own sharpness wonna tell 'em. Mr. Bede, will you take some vinegar with your lettuce? Aye you're i' the right not. It spoils the flavour o' the chine, to my thinking. It's poor eating where the flavour o' the meat lies i' the cruets. There's folks as make bad butter and trusten to the salt t' hide it."

Mrs. Poyser's attention was here diverted by the appearance of Molly, carrying a large jug, two small mugs, and four drinking-cans, all full of ale or small beer—an interesting example of the prehensile power possessed by the human hand. Poor Molly's mouth was rather wider open than usual, as she walked along with her eyes fixed on the double cluster of vessels in her hands, quite innocent of the expression in her mistress's eye.

"Molly, I niver knew your equils—to think o' your poor mother as is a widow, an' I took you wi' as good as no character, an' the times an' times I've told you . . . ."

Molly had not seen the lightning, and the thunder shook her nerves the more for the want of that preparation. With a vague alarmed sense that she must somehow comport herself differently, she hastened her step a little towards the far deal table, where she might set down her cans—caught her foot in her apron, which had become untied, and fell with a crash and a splash into a pool of beer; whereupon a tittering explosion from Marty and Tommy, and a serious "Ello!" from Mr. Poyser, who saw his draught of ale unpleasantly deferred.

"There you go!" resumed Mrs. Poyser, in a cutting tone, as she rose and went towards the cupboard while Molly began dolefully to pick up the fragments of pottery. "It's what I told you 'ud come, over and over again; and there's your month's wage gone, and more, to pay for that jug as I've had i' the house this ten year, and nothing ever happened to't before; but the crockery you've broke sin' here in th' house you've been 'ud make a parson swear—God forgi' me for saying so—an' if it had been boiling wort out o' the copper, it 'ud ha' been the same, and you'd ha' been scalded and very like lamed for life, as there's no knowing but what you will be some day if you go on; for anybody 'ud think you'd got the St. Vitus's Dance, to see the things you've throwed down. It's a pity but what the bits was stacked up for you to see, though it's neither seeing nor hearing as 'ull make much odds to you—anybody 'ud think you war case-hardened."

Poor Molly's tears were dropping fast by this time, and in her desperation at the lively movement of the beer-stream towards Alick's legs, she was converting her apron into a mop, while Mrs. Poyser, opening the cupboard, turned a blighting eye upon her.

"Ah," she went on, "you'll do no good wi' crying an' making more wet to wipe up. It's all your own wilfulness, as I tell you, for there's nobody no call to break anything if they'll only go the right way to work. But wooden folks had need ha' wooden things t' handle. And here must I take the brown-and-white jug, as it's niver been used three times this year, and go down i' the cellar myself, and belike catch my death, and be laid up wi' inflammation . . . ."

Mrs. Poyser had turned round from the cupboard with the brown-and-white jug in her hand, when she caught sight of something at the other end of the kitchen; perhaps it was because she was already trembling and nervous that the apparition had so strong an effect on her; perhaps jug-breaking, like other crimes, has a contagious influence. However it was, she stared and started like a ghost-seer, and the precious brown-and-white jug fell to the ground, parting for ever with its spout and handle.

"Did ever anybody see the like?" she said, with a suddenly lowered tone, after a moment's bewildered glance round the room. "The jugs are bewitched, I think. It's them nasty glazed handles—they slip o'er the finger like a snail."

"Why, thee'st let thy own whip fly i' thy face," said her husband, who had now joined in the laugh of the young ones.

"It's all very fine to look on and grin," rejoined Mrs. Poyser; "but there's times when the crockery seems alive an' flies out o' your hand like a bird. It's like the glass, sometimes, 'ull crack as it stands. What is to be broke WILL be broke, for I never dropped a thing i' my life for want o' holding it, else I should never ha' kept the crockery all these 'ears as I bought at my own wedding. And Hetty, are you mad? Whativer do you mean by coming down i' that way, and making one think as there's a ghost a-walking i' th' house?"

A new outbreak of laughter, while Mrs. Poyser was speaking, was caused, less by her sudden conversion to a fatalistic view of jug-breaking than by that strange appearance of Hetty, which had startled her aunt. The little minx had found a black gown of her aunt's, and pinned it close round her neck to look like Dinah's, had made her hair as flat as she could, and had tied on one of Dinah's high-crowned borderless net caps. The thought of Dinah's pale grave face and mild grey eyes, which the sight of the gown and cap brought with it, made it a laughable surprise enough to see them replaced by Hetty's round rosy cheeks and coquettish dark eyes. The boys got off their chairs and jumped round her, clapping their hands, and even Alick gave a low ventral laugh as he looked up from his beans. Under cover of the noise, Mrs. Poyser went into the back kitchen to send Nancy into the cellar with the great pewter measure, which had some chance of being free from bewitchment.

"Why, Hetty, lass, are ye turned Methodist?" said Mr. Poyser, with that comfortable slow enjoyment of a laugh which one only sees in stout people. "You must pull your face a deal longer before you'll do for one; mustna she, Adam? How come you put them things on, eh?"

"Adam said he liked Dinah's cap and gown better nor my clothes," said Hetty, sitting down demurely. "He says folks looks better in ugly clothes."

"Nay, nay," said Adam, looking at her admiringly; "I only said they seemed to suit Dinah. But if I'd said you'd look pretty in 'em, I should ha' said nothing but what was true."

"Why, thee thought'st Hetty war a ghost, didstna?" said Mr. Poyser to his wife, who now came back and took her seat again. "Thee look'dst as scared as scared."

"It little sinnifies how I looked," said Mrs. Poyser; "looks 'ull mend no jugs, nor laughing neither, as I see. Mr. Bede, I'm sorry you've to wait so long for your ale, but it's coming in a minute. Make yourself at home wi' th' cold potatoes: I know you like 'em. Tommy, I'll send you to bed this minute, if you don't give over laughing. What is there to laugh at, I should like to know? I'd sooner cry nor laugh at the sight o' that poor thing's cap; and there's them as 'ud be better if they could make theirselves like her i' more ways nor putting on her cap. It little becomes anybody i' this house to make fun o' my sister's child, an' her just gone away from us, as it went to my heart to part wi' her. An' I know one thing, as if trouble was to come, an' I was to be laid up i' my bed, an' the children was to die—as there's no knowing but what they will—an' the murrain was to come among the cattle again, an' everything went to rack an' ruin, I say we might be glad to get sight o' Dinah's cap again, wi' her own face under it, border or no border. For she's one o' them things as looks the brightest on a rainy day, and loves you the best when you're most i' need on't."

Mrs. Poyser, you perceive, was aware that nothing would be so likely to expel the comic as the terrible. Tommy, who was of a susceptible disposition, and very fond of his mother, and who had, besides, eaten so many cherries as to have his feelings less under command than usual, was so affected by the dreadful picture she had made of the possible future that he began to cry; and the good-natured father, indulgent to all weaknesses but those of negligent farmers, said to Hetty, "You'd better take the things off again, my lass; it hurts your aunt to see 'em."

Hetty went upstairs again, and the arrival of the ale made an agreeable diversion; for Adam had to give his opinion of the new tap, which could not be otherwise than complimentary to Mrs. Poyser; and then followed a discussion on the secrets of good brewing, the folly of stinginess in "hopping," and the doubtful economy of a farmer's making his own malt. Mrs. Poyser had so many opportunities of expressing herself with weight on these subjects that by the time supper was ended, the ale-jug refilled, and Mr. Poyser's pipe alight she was once more in high good humour, and ready, at Adam's request, to fetch the broken spinning-wheel for his inspection.

"Ah," said Adam, looking at it carefully, "here's a nice bit o' turning wanted. It's a pretty wheel. I must have it up at the turning-shop in the village and do it there, for I've no convenence for turning at home. If you'll send it to Mr. Burge's shop i' the morning, I'll get it done for you by Wednesday. I've been turning it over in my mind," he continued, looking at Mr. Poyser, "to make a bit more convenence at home for nice jobs o' cabinet-making. I've always done a deal at such little things in odd hours, and they're profitable, for there's more workmanship nor material in 'em. I look for me and Seth to get a little business for ourselves i' that way, for I know a man at Rosseter as 'ull take as many things as we should make, besides what we could get orders for round about."

Mr. Poyser entered with interest into a project which seemed a step towards Adam's becoming a "master-man," and Mrs. Poyser gave her approbation to the scheme of the movable kitchen cupboard, which was to be capable of containing grocery, pickles, crockery, and house-linen in the utmost compactness without confusion. Hetty, once more in her own dress, with her neckerchief pushed a little backwards on this warm evening, was seated picking currants near the window, where Adam could see her quite well. And so the time passed pleasantly till Adam got up to go. He was pressed to come again soon, but not to stay longer, for at this busy time sensible people would not run the risk of being sleepy at five o'clock in the morning.

"I shall take a step farther," said Adam, "and go on to see Mester Massey, for he wasn't at church yesterday, and I've not seen him for a week past. I've never hardly known him to miss church before."

"Aye," said Mr. Poyser, "we've heared nothing about him, for it's the boys' hollodays now, so we can give you no account."

"But you'll niver think o' going there at this hour o' the night?" said Mrs. Poyser, folding up her knitting.

"Oh, Mester Massey sits up late," said Adam. "An' the night-school's not over yet. Some o' the men don't come till late—they've got so far to walk. And Bartle himself's never in bed till it's gone eleven."

"I wouldna have him to live wi' me, then," said Mrs. Poyser, "a-dropping candle-grease about, as you're like to tumble down o' the floor the first thing i' the morning."

"Aye, eleven o'clock's late—it's late," said old Martin. "I ne'er sot up so i' MY life, not to say as it warna a marr'in', or a christenin', or a wake, or th' harvest supper. Eleven o'clock's late."

"Why, I sit up till after twelve often," said Adam, laughing, "but it isn't t' eat and drink extry, it's to work extry. Good-night, Mrs. Poyser; good-night, Hetty."

Hetty could only smile and not shake hands, for hers were dyed and damp with currant-juice; but all the rest gave a hearty shake to the large palm that was held out to them, and said, "Come again, come again!"

"Aye, think o' that now," said Mr. Poyser, when Adam was out of on the causeway. "Sitting up till past twelve to do extry work! Ye'll not find many men o' six-an' twenty as 'ull do to put i' the shafts wi' him. If you can catch Adam for a husband, Hetty, you'll ride i' your own spring-cart some day, I'll be your warrant."

Hetty was moving across the kitchen with the currants, so her uncle did not see the little toss of the head with which she answered him. To ride in a spring-cart seemed a very miserable lot indeed to her now.

Chapter XXI The Night-School and the Schoolmaster

Bartle Massey's was one of a few scattered houses on the edge of a common, which was divided by the road to Treddleston. Adam reached it in a quarter of an hour after leaving the Hall Farm; and when he had his hand on the door-latch, he could see, through the curtainless window, that there were eight or nine heads bending over the desks, lighted by thin dips.

When he entered, a reading lesson was going forward and Bartle Massey merely nodded, leaving him to take his place where he pleased. He had not come for the sake of a lesson to-night, and his mind was too full of personal matters, too full of the last two hours he had passed in Hetty's presence, for him to amuse himself with a book till school was over; so he sat down in a corner and looked on with an absent mind. It was a sort of scene which Adam had beheld almost weekly for years; he knew by heart every arabesque flourish in the framed specimen of Bartle Massey's handwriting which hung over the schoolmaster's head, by way of keeping a lofty ideal before the minds of his pupils; he knew the backs of all the books on the shelf running along the whitewashed wall above the pegs for the slates; he knew exactly how many grains were gone out of the ear of Indian corn that hung from one of the rafters; he had long ago exhausted the resources of his imagination in trying to think how the bunch of leathery seaweed had looked and grown in its native element; and from the place where he sat, he could make nothing of the old map of England that hung against the opposite wall, for age had turned it of a fine yellow brown, something like that of a well-seasoned meerschaum. The drama that was going on was almost as familiar as the scene, nevertheless habit had not made him indifferent to it, and even in his present self-absorbed mood, Adam felt a momentary stirring of the old fellow-feeling, as he looked at the rough men painfully holding pen or pencil with their cramped hands, or humbly labouring through their reading lesson.

The reading class now seated on the form in front of the schoolmaster's desk consisted of the three most backward pupils. Adam would have known it only by seeing Bartle Massey's face as he looked over his spectacles, which he had shifted to the ridge of his nose, not requiring them for present purposes. The face wore its mildest expression: the grizzled bushy eyebrows had taken their more acute angle of compassionate kindness, and the mouth, habitually compressed with a pout of the lower lip, was relaxed so as to be ready to speak a helpful word or syllable in a moment. This gentle expression was the more interesting because the schoolmaster's nose, an irregular aquiline twisted a little on one side, had rather a formidable character; and his brow, moreover, had that peculiar tension which always impresses one as a sign of a keen impatient temperament: the blue veins stood out like cords under the transparent yellow skin, and this intimidating brow was softened by no tendency to baldness, for the grey bristly hair, cut down to about an inch in length, stood round it in as close ranks as ever.

"Nay, Bill, nay," Bartle was saying in a kind tone, as he nodded to Adam, "begin that again, and then perhaps, it'll come to you what d-r-y spells. It's the same lesson you read last week, you know."

"Bill" was a sturdy fellow, aged four-and-twenty, an excellent stone-sawyer, who could get as good wages as any man in the trade of his years; but he found a reading lesson in words of one syllable a harder matter to deal with than the hardest stone he had ever had to saw. The letters, he complained, were so "uncommon alike, there was no tellin' 'em one from another," the sawyer's business not being concerned with minute differences such as exist between a letter with its tail turned up and a letter with its tail turned down. But Bill had a firm determination that he would learn to read, founded chiefly on two reasons: first, that Tom Hazelow, his cousin, could read anything "right off," whether it was print or writing, and Tom had sent him a letter from twenty miles off, saying how he was prospering in the world and had got an overlooker's place; secondly, that Sam Phillips, who sawed with him, had learned to read when he was turned twenty, and what could be done by a little fellow like Sam Phillips, Bill considered, could be done by himself, seeing that he could pound Sam into wet clay if circumstances required it. So here he was, pointing his big finger towards three words at once, and turning his head on one side that he might keep better hold with his eye of the one word which was to be discriminated out of the group. The amount of knowledge Bartle Massey must possess was something so dim and vast that Bill's imagination recoiled before it: he would hardly have ventured to deny that the schoolmaster might have something to do in bringing about the regular return of daylight and the changes in the weather.

The man seated next to Bill was of a very different type: he was a Methodist brickmaker who, after spending thirty years of his life in perfect satisfaction with his ignorance, had lately "got religion," and along with it the desire to read the Bible. But with him, too, learning was a heavy business, and on his way out to-night he had offered as usual a special prayer for help, seeing that he had undertaken this hard task with a single eye to the nourishment of his soul—that he might have a greater abundance of texts and hymns wherewith to banish evil memories and the temptations of old habit—or, in brief language, the devil. For the brickmaker had been a notorious poacher, and was suspected, though there was no good evidence against him, of being the man who had shot a neighbouring gamekeeper in the leg. However that might be, it is certain that shortly after the accident referred to, which was coincident with the arrival of an awakening Methodist preacher at Treddleston, a great change had been observed in the brickmaker; and though he was still known in the neighbourhood by his old sobriquet of "Brimstone," there was nothing he held in so much horror as any further transactions with that evil-smelling element. He was a broad-chested fellow. with a fervid temperament, which helped him better in imbibing religious ideas than in the dry process of acquiring the mere human knowledge of the alphabet. Indeed, he had been already a little shaken in his resolution by a brother Methodist, who assured him that the letter was a mere obstruction to the Spirit, and expressed a fear that Brimstone was too eager for the knowledge that puffeth up.

The third beginner was a much more promising pupil. He was a tall but thin and wiry man, nearly as old as Brimstone, with a very pale face and hands stained a deep blue. He was a dyer, who in the course of dipping homespun wool and old women's petticoats had got fired with the ambition to learn a great deal more about the strange secrets of colour. He had already a high reputation in the district for his dyes, and he was bent on discovering some method by which he could reduce the expense of crimsons and scarlets. The druggist at Treddleston had given him a notion that he might save himself a great deal of labour and expense if he could learn to read, and so he had begun to give his spare hours to the night-school, resolving that his "little chap" should lose no time in coming to Mr. Massey's day-school as soon as he was old enough.

It was touching to see these three big men, with the marks of their hard labour about them, anxiously bending over the worn books and painfully making out, "The grass is green," "The sticks are dry," "The corn is ripe"—a very hard lesson to pass to after columns of single words all alike except in the first letter. It was almost as if three rough animals were making humble efforts to learn how they might become human. And it touched the tenderest fibre in Bartle Massey's nature, for such full-grown children as these were the only pupils for whom he had no severe epithets and no impatient tones. He was not gifted with an imperturbable temper, and on music-nights it was apparent that patience could never be an easy virtue to him; but this evening, as he glances over his spectacles at Bill Downes, the sawyer, who is turning his head on one side with a desperate sense of blankness before the letters d-r-y, his eyes shed their mildest and most encouraging light.

After the reading class, two youths between sixteen and nineteen came up with the imaginary bills of parcels, which they had been writing out on their slates and were now required to calculate "off-hand"—a test which they stood with such imperfect success that Bartle Massey, whose eyes had been glaring at them ominously through his spectacles for some minutes, at length burst out in a bitter, high-pitched tone, pausing between every sentence to rap the floor with a knobbed stick which rested between his legs.

"Now, you see, you don't do this thing a bit better than you did a fortnight ago, and I'll tell you what's the reason. You want to learn accounts—that's well and good. But you think all you need do to learn accounts is to come to me and do sums for an hour or so, two or three times a-week; and no sooner do you get your caps on and turn out of doors again than you sweep the whole thing clean out of your mind. You go whistling about, and take no more care what you're thinking of than if your heads were gutters for any rubbish to swill through that happened to be in the way; and if you get a good notion in 'em, it's pretty soon washed out again. You think knowledge is to be got cheap—you'll come and pay Bartle Massey sixpence a-week, and he'll make you clever at figures without your taking any trouble. But knowledge isn't to be got with paying sixpence, let me tell you. If you're to know figures, you must turn 'em over in your heads and keep your thoughts fixed on 'em. There's nothing you can't turn into a sum, for there's nothing but what's got number in it—even a fool. You may say to yourselves, 'I'm one fool, and Jack's another; if my fool's head weighed four pound, and Jack's three pound three ounces and three quarters, how many pennyweights heavier would my head be than Jack's?' A man that had got his heart in learning figures would make sums for himself and work 'em in his head. When he sat at his shoemaking, he'd count his stitches by fives, and then put a price on his stitches, say half a farthing, and then see how much money he could get in an hour; and then ask himself how much money he'd get in a day at that rate; and then how much ten workmen would get working three, or twenty, or a hundred years at that rate—and all the while his needle would be going just as fast as if he left his head empty for the devil to dance in. But the long and the short of it is—I'll have nobody in my night-school that doesn't strive to learn what he comes to learn, as hard as if he was striving to get out of a dark hole into broad daylight. I'll send no man away because he's stupid: if Billy Taft, the idiot, wanted to learn anything, I'd not refuse to teach him. But I'll not throw away good knowledge on people who think they can get it by the sixpenn'orth, and carry it away with 'em as they would an ounce of snuff. So never come to me again, if you can't show that you've been working with your own heads, instead of thinking that you can pay for mine to work for you. That's the last word I've got to say to you."

With this final sentence, Bartle Massey gave a sharper rap than ever with his knobbed stick, and the discomfited lads got up to go with a sulky look. The other pupils had happily only their writing-books to show, in various stages of progress from pot-hooks to round text; and mere pen-strokes, however perverse, were less exasperating to Bartle than false arithmetic. He was a little more severe than usual on Jacob Storey's Z's, of which poor Jacob had written a pageful, all with their tops turned the wrong way, with a puzzled sense that they were not right "somehow." But he observed in apology, that it was a letter you never wanted hardly, and he thought it had only been there "to finish off th' alphabet, like, though ampusand (&) would ha' done as well, for what he could see."

At last the pupils had all taken their hats and said their "Good-nights," and Adam, knowing his old master's habits, rose and said, "Shall I put the candles out, Mr. Massey?"

"Yes, my boy, yes, all but this, which I'll carry into the house; and just lock the outer door, now you're near it," said Bartle, getting his stick in the fitting angle to help him in descending from his stool. He was no sooner on the ground than it became obvious why the stick was necessary—the left leg was much shorter than the right. But the school-master was so active with his lameness that it was hardly thought of as a misfortune; and if you had seen him make his way along the schoolroom floor, and up the step into his kitchen, you would perhaps have understood why the naughty boys sometimes felt that his pace might be indefinitely quickened and that he and his stick might overtake them even in their swiftest run.

The moment he appeared at the kitchen door with the candle in his hand, a faint whimpering began in the chimney-corner, and a brown-and-tan-coloured bitch, of that wise-looking breed with short legs and long body, known to an unmechanical generation as turn-spits, came creeping along the floor, wagging her tail, and hesitating at every other step, as if her affections were painfully divided between the hamper in the chimney-corner and the master, whom she could not leave without a greeting.

"Well, Vixen, well then, how are the babbies?" said the school-master, making haste towards the chimney-corner and holding the candle over the low hamper, where two extremely blind puppies lifted up their heads towards the light from a nest of flannel and wool. Vixen could not even see her master look at them without painful excitement: she got into the hamper and got out again the next moment, and behaved with true feminine folly, though looking all the while as wise as a dwarf with a large old-fashioned head and body on the most abbreviated legs.

"Why, you've got a family, I see, Mr. Massey?" said Adam, smiling, as he came into the kitchen. "How's that? I thought it was against the law here."

"Law? What's the use o' law when a man's once such a fool as to let a woman into his house?" said Bartle, turning away from the hamper with some bitterness. He always called Vixen a woman, and seemed to have lost all consciousness that he was using a figure of speech. "If I'd known Vixen was a woman, I'd never have held the boys from drowning her; but when I'd got her into my hand, I was forced to take to her. And now you see what she's brought me to—the sly, hypocritical wench"—Bartle spoke these last words in a rasping tone of reproach, and looked at Vixen, who poked down her head and turned up her eyes towards him with a keen sense of opprobrium—"and contrived to be brought to bed on a Sunday at church-time. I've wished again and again I'd been a bloody minded man, that I could have strangled the mother and the brats with one cord."

"I'm glad it was no worse a cause kept you from church," said Adam. "I was afraid you must be ill for the first time i' your life. And I was particularly sorry not to have you at church yesterday."

"Ah, my boy, I know why, I know why," said Bartle kindly, going up to Adam and raising his hand up to the shoulder that was almost on a level with his own head. "You've had a rough bit o' road to get over since I saw you—a rough bit o' road. But I'm in hopes there are better times coming for you. I've got some news to tell you. But I must get my supper first, for I'm hungry, I'm hungry. Sit down, sit down."

Bartel went into his little pantry, and brought out an excellent home-baked loaf; for it was his one extravagance in these dear times to eat bread once a-day instead of oat-cake; and he justified it by observing, that what a schoolmaster wanted was brains, and oat-cake ran too much to bone instead of brains. Then came a piece of cheese and a quart jug with a crown of foam upon it. He placed them all on the round deal table which stood against his large arm-chair in the chimney-corner, with Vixen's hamper on one side of it and a window-shelf with a few books piled up in it on the other. The table was as clean as if Vixen had been an excellent housewife in a checkered apron; so was the quarry floor; and the old carved oaken press, table, and chairs, which in these days would be bought at a high price in aristocratic houses, though, in that period of spider-legs and inlaid cupids, Bartle had got them for an old song, where as free from dust as things could be at the end of a summer's day.

"Now, then, my boy, draw up, draw up. We'll not talk about business till we've had our supper. No man can be wise on an empty stomach. But," said Bartle, rising from his chair again, "I must give Vixen her supper too, confound her! Though she'll do nothing with it but nourish those unnecessary babbies. That's the way with these women—they've got no head-pieces to nourish, and so their food all runs either to fat or to brats."

He brought out of the pantry a dish of scraps, which Vixen at once fixed her eyes on, and jumped out of her hamper to lick up with the utmost dispatch.

"I've had my supper, Mr. Massey," said Adam, "so I'll look on while you eat yours. I've been at the Hall Farm, and they always have their supper betimes, you know: they don't keep your late hours."

"I know little about their hours," said Bartle dryly, cutting his bread and not shrinking from the crust. "It's a house I seldom go into, though I'm fond of the boys, and Martin Poyser's a good fellow. There's too many women in the house for me: I hate the sound of women's voices; they're always either a-buzz or a-squeak—always either a-buzz or a-squeak. Mrs. Poyser keeps at the top o' the talk like a fife; and as for the young lasses, I'd as soon look at water-grubs. I know what they'll turn to—stinging gnats, stinging gnats. Here, take some ale, my boy: it's been drawn for you—it's been drawn for you."

"Nay, Mr. Massey," said Adam, who took his old friend's whim more seriously than usual to-night, "don't be so hard on the creaturs God has made to be companions for us. A working-man 'ud be badly off without a wife to see to th' house and the victual, and make things clean and comfortable."

"Nonsense! It's the silliest lie a sensible man like you ever believed, to say a woman makes a house comfortable. It's a story got up because the women are there and something must be found for 'em to do. I tell you there isn't a thing under the sun that needs to be done at all, but what a man can do better than a woman, unless it's bearing children, and they do that in a poor make-shift way; it had better ha' been left to the men—it had better ha' been left to the men. I tell you, a woman 'ull bake you a pie every week of her life and never come to see that the hotter th' oven the shorter the time. I tell you, a woman 'ull make your porridge every day for twenty years and never think of measuring the proportion between the meal and the milk—a little more or less, she'll think, doesn't signify. The porridge WILL be awk'ard now and then: if it's wrong, it's summat in the meal, or it's summat in the milk, or it's summat in the water. Look at me! I make my own bread, and there's no difference between one batch and another from year's end to year's end; but if I'd got any other woman besides Vixen in the house, I must pray to the Lord every baking to give me patience if the bread turned out heavy. And as fŏr cleanliness, my house is cleaner than any other house on the Common, though the half of 'em swarm with women. Will Baker's lad comes to help me in a morning, and we get as much cleaning done in one hour, without any fuss, as a woman 'ud get done in three, and all the while be sending buckets o' water after your ankles, and let the fender and the fire-irons stand in the middle o' the floor half the day for you to break your shins against 'em. Don't tell me about God having made such creatures to be companions for us! I don't say but He might make Eve to be a companion to Adam in Paradise—there was no cooking to be spoilt there, and no other woman to cackle with and make mischief, though you see what mischief she did as soon as she'd an opportunity. But it's an impious, unscriptural opinion to say a woman's a blessing to a man now; you might as well say adders and wasps, and foxes and wild beasts are a blessing, when they're only the evils that belong to this state o' probation, which it's lawful for a man to keep as clear of as he can in this life, hoping to get quit of 'em for ever in another—hoping to get quit of 'em for ever in another."

Bartle had become so excited and angry in the course of his invective that he had forgotten his supper, and only used the knife for the purpose of rapping the table with the haft. But towards the close, the raps became so sharp and frequent, and his voice so quarrelsome, that Vixen felt it incumbent on her to jump out of the hamper and bark vaguely.

"Quiet, Vixen!" snarled Bartle, turning round upon her. "You're like the rest o' the women—always putting in your word before you know why."

Vixen returned to her hamper again in humiliation, and her master continued his supper in a silence which Adam did not choose to interrupt; he knew the old man would be in a better humour when he had had his supper and lighted his pipe. Adam was used to hear him talk in this way, but had never learned so much of Bartle's past life as to know whether his view of married comfort was founded on experience. On that point Bartle was mute, and it was even a secret where he had lived previous to the twenty years in which happily for the peasants and artisans of this neighbourhood he had been settled among them as their only schoolmaster. If anything like a question was ventured on this subject, Bartle always replied, "Oh, I've seen many places—I've been a deal in the south," and the Loamshire men would as soon have thought of asking for a particular town or village in Africa as in "the south."

"Now then, my boy," said Bartle, at last, when he had poured out his second mug of ale and lighted his pipe, "now then, we'll have a little talk. But tell me first, have you heard any particular news to-day?"

"No," said Adam, "not as I remember."

"Ah, they'll keep it close, they'll keep it close, I daresay. But I found it out by chance; and it's news that may concern you, Adam, else I'm a man that don't know a superficial square foot from a solid."

Here Bartle gave a series of fierce and rapid puffs, looking earnestly the while at Adam. Your impatient loquacious man has never any notion of keeping his pipe alight by gentle measured puffs; he is always letting it go nearly out, and then punishing it for that negligence. At last he said, "Satchell's got a paralytic stroke. I found it out from the lad they sent to Treddleston for the doctor, before seven o'clock this morning. He's a good way beyond sixty, you know; it's much if he gets over it."

"Well," said Adam, "I daresay there'd be more rejoicing than sorrow in the parish at his being laid up. He's been a selfish, tale-bearing, mischievous fellow; but, after all, there's nobody he's done so much harm to as to th' old squire. Though it's the squire himself as is to blame—making a stupid fellow like that a sort o' man-of-all-work, just to save th' expense of having a proper steward to look after th' estate. And he's lost more by ill management o' the woods, I'll be bound, than 'ud pay for two stewards. If he's laid on the shelf, it's to be hoped he'll make way for a better man, but I don't see how it's like to make any difference to me."

"But I see it, but I see it," said Bartle, "and others besides me. The captain's coming of age now—you know that as well as I do—and it's to be expected he'll have a little more voice in things. And I know, and you know too, what 'ud be the captain's wish about the woods, if there was a fair opportunity for making a change. He's said in plenty of people's hearing that he'd make you manager of the woods to-morrow, if he'd the power. Why, Carroll, Mr. Irwine's butler, heard him say so to the parson not many days ago. Carroll looked in when we were smoking our pipes o' Saturday night at Casson's, and he told us about it; and whenever anybody says a good word for you, the parson's ready to back it, that I'll answer for. It was pretty well talked over, I can tell you, at Casson's, and one and another had their fling at you; for if donkeys set to work to sing, you're pretty sure what the tune'll be."

"Why, did they talk it over before Mr. Burge?" said Adam; "or wasn't he there o' Saturday?"

"Oh, he went away before Carroll came; and Casson—he's always for setting other folks right, you know—would have it Burge was the man to have the management of the woods. 'A substantial man,' says he, 'with pretty near sixty years' experience o' timber: it 'ud be all very well for Adam Bede to act under him, but it isn't to be supposed the squire 'ud appoint a young fellow like Adam, when there's his elders and betters at hand!' But I said, 'That's a pretty notion o' yours, Casson. Why, Burge is the man to buy timber; would you put the woods into his hands and let him make his own bargains? I think you don't leave your customers to score their own drink, do you? And as for age, what that's worth depends on the quality o' the liquor. It's pretty well known who's the backbone of Jonathan Burge's business.'"

"I thank you for your good word, Mr. Massey," said Adam. "But, for all that, Casson was partly i' the right for once. There's not much likelihood that th' old squire 'ud ever consent t' employ me. I offended him about two years ago, and he's never forgiven me."

"Why, how was that? You never told me about it," said Bartle.

"Oh, it was a bit o' nonsense. I'd made a frame for a screen for Miss Lyddy—she's allays making something with her worsted-work, you know—and she'd given me particular orders about this screen, and there was as much talking and measuring as if we'd been planning a house. However, it was a nice bit o' work, and I liked doing it for her. But, you know, those little friggling things take a deal o' time. I only worked at it in overhours—often late at night—and I had to go to Treddleston over an' over again about little bits o' brass nails and such gear; and I turned the little knobs and the legs, and carved th' open work, after a pattern, as nice as could be. And I was uncommon pleased with it when it was done. And when I took it home, Miss Lyddy sent for me to bring it into her drawing-room, so as she might give me directions about fastening on the work—very fine needle-work, Jacob and Rachel a-kissing one another among the sheep, like a picture—and th' old squire was sitting there, for he mostly sits with her. Well, she was mighty pleased with the screen, and then she wanted to know what pay she was to give me. I didn't speak at random—you know it's not my way; I'd calculated pretty close, though I hadn't made out a bill, and I said, 'One pound thirty.' That was paying for the mater'als and paying me, but none too much, for my work. Th' old squire looked up at this, and peered in his way at the screen, and said, 'One pound thirteen for a gimcrack like that! Lydia, my dear, if you must spend money on these things, why don't you get them at Rosseter, instead of paying double price for clumsy work here? Such things are not work for a carpenter like Adam. Give him a guinea, and no more.' Well, Miss Lyddy, I reckon, believed what he told her, and she's not overfond o' parting with the money herself—she's not a bad woman at bottom, but she's been brought up under his thumb; so she began fidgeting with her purse, and turned as red as her ribbon. But I made a bow, and said, 'No, thank you, madam; I'll make you a present o' the screen, if you please. I've charged the regular price for my work, and I know it's done well; and I know, begging His Honour's pardon, that you couldn't get such a screen at Rosseter under two guineas. I'm willing to give you my work—it's been done in my own time, and nobody's got anything to do with it but me; but if I'm paid, I can't take a smaller price than I asked, because that 'ud be like saying I'd asked more than was just. With your leave, madam, I'll bid you good-morning.' I made my bow and went out before she'd time to say any more, for she stood with the purse in her hand, looking almost foolish. I didn't mean to be disrespectful, and I spoke as polite as I could; but I can give in to no man, if he wants to make it out as I'm trying to overreach him. And in the evening the footman brought me the one pound thirteen wrapped in paper. But since then I've seen pretty clear as th' old squire can't abide me."

"That's likely enough, that's likely enough," said Bartle meditatively. "The only way to bring him round would be to show him what was for his own interest, and that the captain may do—that the captain may do."

"Nay, I don't know," said Adam; "the squire's 'cute enough but it takes something else besides 'cuteness to make folks see what'll be their interest in the long run. It takes some conscience and belief in right and wrong, I see that pretty clear. You'd hardly ever bring round th' old squire to believe he'd gain as much in a straightfor'ard way as by tricks and turns. And, besides, I've not much mind to work under him: I don't want to quarrel with any gentleman, more particular an old gentleman turned eighty, and I know we couldn't agree long. If the captain was master o' th' estate, it 'ud be different: he's got a conscience and a will to do right, and I'd sooner work for him nor for any man living."

"Well, well, my boy, if good luck knocks at your door, don't you put your head out at window and tell it to be gone about its business, that's all. You must learn to deal with odd and even in life, as well as in figures. I tell you now, as I told you ten years ago, when you pommelled young Mike Holdsworth for wanting to pass a bad shilling before you knew whether he was in jest or earnest—you're overhasty and proud, and apt to set your teeth against folks that don't square to your notions. It's no harm for me to be a bit fiery and stiff-backed—I'm an old schoolmaster, and shall never want to get on to a higher perch. But where's the use of all the time I've spent in teaching you writing and mapping and mensuration, if you're not to get for'ard in the world and show folks there's some advantage in having a head on your shoulders, instead of a turnip? Do you mean to go on turning up your nose at every opportunity because it's got a bit of a smell about it that nobody finds out but yourself? It's as foolish as that notion o' yours that a wife is to make a working-man comfortable. Stuff and nonsense! Stuff and nonsense! Leave that to fools that never got beyond a sum in simple addition. Simple addition enough! Add one fool to another fool, and in six years' time six fools more—they're all of the same denomination, big and little's nothing to do with the sum!"

During this rather heated exhortation to coolness and discretion the pipe had gone out, and Bartle gave the climax to his speech by striking a light furiously, after which he puffed with fierce resolution, fixing his eye still on Adam, who was trying not to laugh.

"There's a good deal o' sense in what you say, Mr. Massey," Adam began, as soon as he felt quite serious, "as there always is. But you'll give in that it's no business o' mine to be building on chances that may never happen. What I've got to do is to work as well as I can with the tools and mater'als I've got in my hands. If a good chance comes to me, I'll think o' what you've been saying; but till then, I've got nothing to do but to trust to my own hands and my own head-piece. I'm turning over a little plan for Seth and me to go into the cabinet-making a bit by ourselves, and win a extra pound or two in that way. But it's getting late now—it'll be pretty near eleven before I'm at home, and Mother may happen to lie awake; she's more fidgety nor usual now. So I'll bid you good-night."

"Well, well, we'll go to the gate with you—it's a fine night," said Bartle, taking up his stick. Vixen was at once on her legs, and without further words the three walked out into the starlight, by the side of Bartle's potato-beds, to the little gate.

"Come to the music o' Friday night, if you can, my boy," said the old man, as he closed the gate after Adam and leaned against it.

"Aye, aye," said Adam, striding along towards the streak of pale road. He was the only object moving on the wide common. The two grey donkeys, just visible in front of the gorse bushes, stood as still as limestone images—as still as the grey-thatched roof of the mud cottage a little farther on. Bartle kept his eye on the moving figure till it passed into the darkness, while Vixen, in a state of divided affection, had twice run back to the house to bestow a parenthetic lick on her puppies.

"Aye, aye," muttered the schoolmaster, as Adam disappeared, "there you go, stalking along—stalking along; but you wouldn't have been what you are if you hadn't had a bit of old lame Bartle inside you. The strongest calf must have something to suck at. There's plenty of these big, lumbering fellows 'ud never have known their A B C if it hadn't been for Bartle Massey. Well, well, Vixen, you foolish wench, what is it, what is it? I must go in, must I? Aye, aye, I'm never to have a will o' my own any more. And those pups—what do you think I'm to do with 'em, when they're twice as big as you? For I'm pretty sure the father was that hulking bull-terrier of Will Baker's—wasn't he now, eh, you sly hussy?"

(Here Vixen tucked her tail between her legs and ran forward into the house. Subjects are sometimes broached which a well-bred female will ignore.)

"But where's the use of talking to a woman with babbies?" continued Bartle. "She's got no conscience—no conscience; it's all run to milk."

BOOK THREE

Chapter XXII Going to the Birthday Feast

THE thirtieth of July was come, and it was one of those half-dozen warm days which sometimes occur in the middle of a rainy English summer. No rain had fallen for the last three or four days, and the weather was perfect for that time of the year: there was less dust than usual on the dark-green hedge-rows and on the wild camomile that starred the roadside, yet the grass was dry enough for the little children to roll on it, and there was no cloud but a long dash of light, downy ripple, high, high up in the far-off blue sky. Perfect weather for an outdoor July merry-making, yet surely not the best time of year to be born in. Nature seems to make a hot pause just then: all the loveliest flowers are gone; the sweet time of early growth and vague hopes is past; and yet the time of harvest and ingathering is not come, and we tremble at the possible storms that may ruin the precious fruit in the moment of its ripeness. The woods are all one dark monotonous green; the waggon-loads of hay no longer creep along the lanes, scattering their sweet-smelling fragments on the blackberry branches; the pastures are often a little tanned, yet the corn has not got its last splendour of red and gold; the lambs and calves have lost all traces of their innocent frisky prettiness, and have become stupid young sheep and cows. But it is a time of leisure on the farm—that pause between hay-and corn-harvest, and so the farmers and labourers in Hayslope and Broxton thought the captain did well to come of age just then, when they could give their undivided minds to the flavour of the great cask of ale which had been brewed the autumn after "the heir" was born, and was to be tapped on his twenty-first birthday. The air had been merry with the ringing of church-bells very early this morning, and every one had made haste to get through the needful work before twelve, when it would be time to think of getting ready to go to the Chase.

The midday sun was streaming into Hetty's bedchamber, and there was no blind to temper the heat with which it fell on her head as she looked at herself in the old specked glass. Still, that was the only glass she had in which she could see her neck and arms, for the small hanging glass she had fetched out of the next room—the room that had been Dinah's—would show her nothing below her little chin; and that beautiful bit of neck where the roundness of her cheek melted into another roundness shadowed by dark delicate curls. And to-day she thought more than usual about her neck and arms; for at the dance this evening she was not to wear any neckerchief, and she had been busy yesterday with her spotted pink-and-white frock, that she might make the sleeves either long or short at will. She was dressed now just as she was to be in the evening, with a tucker made of "real" lace, which her aunt had lent her for this unparalleled occasion, but with no ornaments besides; she had even taken out her small round ear-rings which she wore every day. But there was something more to be done, apparently, before she put on her neckerchief and long sleeves, which she was to wear in the day-time, for now she unlocked the drawer that held her private treasures. It is more than a month since we saw her unlock that drawer before, and now it holds new treasures, so much more precious than the old ones that these are thrust into the corner. Hetty would not care to put the large coloured glass ear-rings into her ears now; for see! she has got a beautiful pair of gold and pearls and garnet, lying snugly in a pretty little box lined with white satin. Oh, the delight of taking out that little box and looking at the ear-rings! Do not reason about it, my philosphical reader, and say that Hetty, being very pretty, must have known that it did not signify whether she had on any ornaments or not; and that, moreover, to look at ear-rings which she could not possibly wear out of her bedroom could hardly be a satisfaction, the essence of vanity being a reference to the impressions produced on others; you will never understand women's natures if you are so excessively rational. Try rather to divest yourself of all your rational prejudices, as much as if you were studying the psychology of a canary bird, and only watch the movements of this pretty round creature as she turns her head on one side with an unconscious smile at the ear-rings nestled in the little box. Ah, you think, it is for the sake of the person who has given them to her, and her thoughts are gone back now to the moment when they were put into her hands. No; else why should she have cared to have ear-rings rather than anything else? And I know that she had longed for ear-rings from among all the ornaments she could imagine.

"Little, little ears!" Arthur had said, pretending to pinch them one evening, as Hetty sat beside him on the grass without her hat. "I wish I had some pretty ear-rings!" she said in a moment, almost before she knew what she was saying—the wish lay so close to her lips, it WOULD flutter past them at the slightest breath. And the next day—it was only last week—Arthur had ridden over to Rosseter on purpose to buy them. That little wish so naively uttered seemed to him the prettiest bit of childishness; he had never heard anything like it before; and he had wrapped the box up in a great many covers, that he might see Hetty unwrapping it with growing curiosity, till at last her eyes flashed back their new delight into his.

No, she was not thinking most of the giver when she smiled at the ear-rings, for now she is taking them out of the box, not to press them to her lips, but to fasten them in her ears—only for one moment, to see how pretty they look, as she peeps at them in the glass against the wall, with first one position of the head and then another, like a listening bird. It is impossible to be wise on the subject of ear-rings as one looks at her; what should those delicate pearls and crystals be made for, if not for such ears? One cannot even find fault with the tiny round hole which they leave when they are taken out; perhaps water-nixies, and such lovely things without souls, have these little round holes in their ears by nature, ready to hang jewels in. And Hetty must be one of them: it is too painful to think that she is a woman, with a woman's destiny before her—a woman spinning in young ignorance a light web of folly and vain hopes which may one day close round her and press upon her, a rancorous poisoned garment, changing all at once her fluttering, trivial butterfly sensations into a life of deep human anguish.

But she cannot keep in the ear-rings long, else she may make her uncle and aunt wait. She puts them quickly into the box again and shuts them up. Some day she will be able to wear any ear-rings she likes, and already she lives in an invisible world of brilliant costumes, shimmering gauze, soft satin, and velvet, such as the lady's maid at the Chase has shown her in Miss Lydia's wardrobe. She feels the bracelets on her arms, and treads on a soft carpet in front of a tall mirror. But she has one thing in the drawer which she can venture to wear to-day, because she can hang it on the chain of dark-brown berries which she has been used to wear on grand days, with a tiny flat scent-bottle at the end of it tucked inside her frock; and she must put on her brown berries—her neck would look so unfinished without it. Hetty was not quite as fond of the locket as of the ear-rings, though it was a handsome large locket, with enamelled flowers at the back and a beautiful gold border round the glass, which showed a light-brown slightly waving lock, forming a background for two little dark rings. She must keep it under her clothes, and no one would see it. But Hetty had another passion, only a little less strong than her love of finery, and that other passion made her like to wear the locket even hidden in her bosom. She would always have worn it, if she had dared to encounter her aunt's questions about a ribbon round her neck. So now she slipped it on along her chain of dark-brown berries, and snapped the chain round her neck. It was not a very long chain, only allowing the locket to hang a little way below the edge of her frock. And now she had nothing to do but to put on her long sleeves, her new white gauze neckerchief, and her straw hat trimmed with white to-day instead of the pink, which had become rather faded under the July sun. That hat made the drop of bitterness in Hetty's cup to-day, for it was not quite new—everybody would see that it was a little tanned against the white ribbon—and Mary Burge, she felt sure, would have a new hat or bonnet on. She looked for consolation at her fine white cotton stockings: they really were very nice indeed, and she had given almost all her spare money for them. Hetty's dream of the future could not make her insensible to triumph in the present. To be sure, Captain Donnithorne loved her so that he would never care about looking at other people, but then those other people didn't know how he loved her, and she was not satisfied to appear shabby and insignificant in their eyes even for a short space.

The whole party was assembled in the house-place when Hetty went down, all of course in their Sunday clothes; and the bells had been ringing so this morning in honour of the captain's twenty-first birthday, and the work had all been got done so early, that Marty and Tommy were not quite easy in their minds until their mother had assured them that going to church was not part of the day's festivities. Mr. Poyser had once suggested that the house should be shut up and left to take care of itself; "for," said he, "there's no danger of anybody's breaking in—everybody'll be at the Chase, thieves an' all. If we lock th' house up, all the men can go: it's a day they wonna see twice i' their lives." But Mrs. Poyser answered with great decision: "I never left the house to take care of itself since I was a missis, and I never will. There's been ill-looking tramps enoo' about the place this last week, to carry off every ham an' every spoon we'n got; and they all collogue together, them tramps, as it's a mercy they hanna come and poisoned the dogs and murdered us all in our beds afore we knowed, some Friday night when we'n got the money in th' house to pay the men. And it's like enough the tramps know where we're going as well as we do oursens; for if Old Harry wants any work done, you may be sure he'll find the means."

"Nonsense about murdering us in our beds," said Mr. Poyser; "I've got a gun i' our room, hanna I? and thee'st got ears as 'ud find it out if a mouse was gnawing the bacon. Howiver, if thee wouldstna be easy, Alick can stay at home i' the forepart o' the day, and Tim can come back tow'rds five o'clock, and let Alick have his turn. They may let Growler loose if anybody offers to do mischief, and there's Alick's dog too, ready enough to set his tooth in a tramp if Alick gives him a wink."

Mrs. Poyser accepted this compromise, but thought it advisable to bar and bolt to the utmost; and now, at the last moment before starting, Nancy, the dairy-maid, was closing the shutters of the house-place, although the window, lying under the immediate observation of Alick and the dogs, might have been supposed the least likely to be selected for a burglarious attempt.

The covered cart, without springs, was standing ready to carry the whole family except the men-servants. Mr. Poyser and the grandfather sat on the seat in front, and within there was room for all the women and children; the fuller the cart the better, because then the jolting would not hurt so much, and Nancy's broad person and thick arms were an excellent cushion to be pitched on. But Mr. Poyser drove at no more than a walking pace, that there might be as little risk of jolting as possible on this warm day, and there was time to exchange greetings and remarks with the foot-passengers who were going the same way, specking the paths between the green meadows and the golden cornfields with bits of movable bright colour—a scarlet waistcoat to match the poppies that nodded a little too thickly among the corn, or a dark-blue neckerchief with ends flaunting across a brand-new white smock-frock. All Broxton and all Hayslope were to be at the Chase, and make merry there in honour of "th' heir"; and the old men and women, who had never been so far down this side of the hill for the last twenty years, were being brought from Broxton and Hayslope in one of the farmer's waggons, at Mr. Irwine's suggestion. The church-bells had struck up again now—a last tune, before the ringers came down the hill to have their share in the festival; and before the bells had finished, other music was heard approaching, so that even Old Brown, the sober horse that was drawing Mr. Poyser's cart, began to prick up his ears. It was the band of the Benefit Club, which had mustered in all its glory—that is to say, in bright-blue scarfs and blue favours, and carrying its banner with the motto, "Let brotherly love continue," encircling a picture of a stone-pit.

The carts, of course, were not to enter the Chase. Every one must get down at the lodges, and the vehicles must be sent back.

"Why, the Chase is like a fair a'ready," said Mrs. Poyser, as she got down from the cart, and saw the groups scattered under the great oaks, and the boys running about in the hot sunshine to survey the tall poles surmounted by the fluttering garments that were to be the prize of the successful climbers. "I should ha' thought there wasna so many people i' the two parishes. Mercy on us! How hot it is out o' the shade! Come here, Totty, else your little face 'ull be burnt to a scratchin'! They might ha' cooked the dinners i' that open space an' saved the fires. I shall go to Mrs. Best's room an' sit down."

"Stop a bit, stop a bit," said Mr. Poyser. "There's th' waggin coming wi' th' old folks in't; it'll be such a sight as wonna come o'er again, to see 'em get down an' walk along all together. You remember some on 'em i' their prime, eh, Father?"

"Aye, aye," said old Martin, walking slowly under the shade of the lodge porch, from which he could see the aged party descend. "I remember Jacob Taft walking fifty mile after the Scotch raybels, when they turned back from Stoniton."

He felt himself quite a youngster, with a long life before him, as he saw the Hayslope patriarch, old Feyther Taft, descend from the waggon and walk towards him, in his brown nigbtcap, and leaning on his two sticks.

"Well, Mester Taft," shouted old Martin, at the utmost stretch of his voice—for though he knew the old man was stone deaf, he could not omit the propriety of a greeting—"you're hearty yet. You can enjoy yoursen to-day, for-all you're ninety an' better."

"Your sarvant, mesters, your sarvant," said Feyther Taft in a treble tone, perceiving that he was in company.

The aged group, under care of sons or daughters, themselves worn and grey, passed on along the least-winding carriage-road towards the house, where a special table was prepared for them; while the Poyser party wisely struck across the grass under the shade of the great trees, but not out of view of the house-front, with its sloping lawn and flower-beds, or of the pretty striped marquee at the edge of the lawn, standing at right angles with two larger marquees on each side of the open green space where the games were to be played. The house would have been nothing but a plain square mansion of Queen Anne's time, but for the remnant of an old abbey to which it was united at one end, in much the same way as one may sometimes see a new farmhouse rising high and prim at the end of older and lower farm-offices. The fine old remnant stood a little backward and under the shadow of tall beeches, but the sun was now on the taller and more advanced front, the blinds were all down, and the house seemed asleep in the hot midday. It made Hetty quite sad to look at it: Arthur must be somewhere in the back rooms, with the grand company, where he could not possibly know that she was come, and she should not see him for a long, long while—not till after dinner, when they said he was to come up and make a speech.

But Hetty was wrong in part of her conjecture. No grand company was come except the Irwines, for whom the carriage had been sent early, and Arthur was at that moment not in a back room, but walking with the rector into the broad stone cloisters of the old abbey, where the long tables were laid for all the cottage tenants and the farm-servants. A very handsome young Briton he looked to-day, in high spirits and a bright-blue frock-coat, the highest mode—his arm no longer in a sling. So open-looking and candid, too; but candid people have their secrets, and secrets leave no lines in young faces.

"Upon my word," he said, as they entered the cool cloisters, "I think the cottagers have the best of it: these cloisters make a delightful dining-room on a hot day. That was capital advice of yours, Irwine, about the dinners—to let them be as orderly and comfortable as possible, and only for the tenants: especially as I had only a limited sum after all; for though my grandfather talked of a carte blanche, he couldn't make up his mind to trust me, when it came to the point."

"Never mind, you'll give more pleasure in this quiet way," said Mr. Irwine. "In this sort of thing people are constantly confounding liberality with riot and disorder. It sounds very grand to say that so many sheep and oxen were roasted whole, and everybody ate who liked to come; but in the end it generally happens that no one has had an enjoyable meal. If the people get a good dinner and a moderate quantity of ale in the middle of the day, they'll be able to enjoy the games as the day cools. You can't hinder some of them from getting too much towards evening, but drunkenness and darkness go better together than drunkenness and daylight."

"Well, I hope there won't be much of it. I've kept the Treddleston people away by having a feast for them in the town; and I've got Casson and Adam Bede and some other good fellows to look to the giving out of ale in the booths, and to take care things don't go too far. Come, let us go up above now and see the dinner-tables for the large tenants."

They went up the stone staircase leading simply to the long gallery above the cloisters, a gallery where all the dusty worthless old pictures had been banished for the last three generations—mouldy portraits of Queen Elizabeth and her ladies, General Monk with his eye knocked out, Daniel very much in the dark among the lions, and Julius Caesar on horseback, with a high nose and laurel crown, holding his Commentaries in his hand.

"What a capital thing it is that they saved this piece of the old abbey!" said Arthur. "If I'm ever master here, I shall do up the gallery in first-rate style. We've got no room in the house a third as large as this. That second table is for the farmers' wives and children: Mrs. Best said it would be more comfortable for the mothers and children to be by themselves. I was determined to have the children, and make a regular family thing of it. I shall be 'the old squire' to those little lads and lasses some day, and they'll tell their children what a much finer young fellow I was than my own son. There's a table for the women and children below as well. But you will see them all—you will come up with me after dinner, I hope?"

"Yes, to be sure," said Mr. Irwine. "I wouldn't miss your maiden speech to the tenantry."

"And there will be something else you'll like to hear," said Arthur. "Let us go into the library and I'll tell you all about it while my grandfather is in the drawing-room with the ladies. Something that will surpsise you," he continued, as they sat down. "My grandfather has come round after all."

"What, about Adam?"

"Yes; I should have ridden over to tell you about it, only I was so busy. You know I told you I had quite given up arguing the matter with him—I thought it was hopeless—but yesterday morning he asked me to come in here to him before I went out, and astonished me by saying that he had decided on all the new arrangements he should make in consequence of old Satchell being obliged to lay by work, and that he intended to employ Adam in superintending the woods at a salary of a guinea a-week, and the use of a pony to be kept here. I believe the secret of it is, he saw from the first it would be a profitable plan, but he had some particular dislike of Adam to get over—and besides, the fact that I propose a thing is generally a reason with him for rejecting it. There's the most curious contradiction in my grandfather: I know he means to leave me all the money he has saved, and he is likely enough to have cut off poor Aunt Lydia, who has been a slave to him all her life, with only five hundred a-year, for the sake of giving me all the more; and yet I sometimes think he positively hates me because I'm his heir. I believe if I were to break my neck, he would feel it the greatest misfortune that could befall him, and yet it seems a pleasure to him to make my life a series of petty annoyances."

"Ah, my boy, it is not only woman's love that is [two greek words omitted] as old AEschylus calls it. There's plenty of 'unloving love' in the world of a masculine kind. But tell me about Adam. Has he accepted the post? I don't see that it can be much more profitable than his present work, though, to be sure, it will leave him a good deal of time on his own hands.

"Well, I felt some doubt about it when I spoke to him and he seemed to hesitate at first. His objection was that he thought he should not be able to satisfy my grandfather. But I begged him as a personal favour to me not to let any reason prevent him from accepting the place, if he really liked the employment and would not be giving up anything that was more profitable to him. And he assured me he should like it of all things—it would be a great step forward for him in business, and it would enable him to do what he had long wished to do, to give up working for Burge. He says he shall have plenty of time to superintend a little business of his own, which he and Seth will carry on, and will perhaps be able to enlarge by degrees. So he has agreed at last, and I have arranged that he shall dine with the large tenants to-day; and I mean to announce the appointment to them, and ask them to drink Adam's health. It's a little drama I've got up in honour of my friend Adam. He's a fine fellow, and I like the opportunity of letting people know that I think so."

"A drama in which friend Arthur piques himself on having a pretty part to play," said Mr. Irwine, smiling. But when he saw Arthur colour, he went on relentingly, "My part, you know, is always that of the old fogy who sees nothing to admire in the young folks. I don't like to admit that I'm proud of my pupil when he does graceful things. But I must play the amiable old gentleman for once, and second your toast in honour of Adam. Has your grandfather yielded on the other point too, and agreed to have a respectable man as steward?"

"Oh no," said Arthur, rising from his chair with an air of impatience and walking along the room with his hands in his pockets. "He's got some project or other about letting the Chase Farm and bargaining for a supply of milk and butter for the house. But I ask no questions about it—it makes me too angry. I believe he means to do all the business himself, and have nothing in the shape of a steward. It's amazing what energy he has, though."

"Well, we'll go to the ladies now," said Mr. Irwine, rising too. "I want to tell my mother what a splendid throne you've prepared for her under the marquee."

"Yes, and we must be going to luncheon too," said Arthur. "It must be two o'clock, for there is the gong beginning to sound for the tenants' dinners."

Chapter XXIII Dinner-Time

WHEN Adam heard that he was to dine upstairs with the large tenants, he felt rather uncomfortable at the idea of being exalted in this way above his mother and Seth, who were to dine in the cloisters below. But Mr. Mills, the butler, assured him that Captain Donnithorne had given particular orders about it, and would be very angry if Adam was not there.

Adam nodded and went up to Seth, who was standing a few yards off. "Seth, lad," he said, "the captain has sent to say I'm to dine upstairs—he wishes it particular, Mr. Mills says, so I suppose it 'ud be behaving ill for me not to go. But I don't like sitting up above thee and mother, as if I was better than my own flesh and blood. Thee't not take it unkind, I hope?"

"Nay, nay, lad," said Seth, "thy honour's our honour; and if thee get'st respect, thee'st won it by thy own deserts. The further I see thee above me, the better, so long as thee feel'st like a brother to me. It's because o' thy being appointed over the woods, and it's nothing but what's right. That's a place o' trust, and thee't above a common workman now."

"Aye," said Adam, "but nobody knows a word about it yet. I haven't given notice to Mr. Burge about leaving him, and I don't like to tell anybody else about it before he knows, for he'll be a good bit hurt, I doubt. People 'ull be wondering to see me there, and they'll like enough be guessing the reason and asking questions, for there's been so much talk up and down about my having the place, this last three weeks."

"Well, thee canst say thee wast ordered to come without being told the reason. That's the truth. And mother 'ull be fine and joyful about it. Let's go and tell her."

Adam was not the only guest invited to come upstairs on other grounds than the amount he contributed to the rent-roll. There were other people in the two parishes who derived dignity from their functions rather than from their pocket, and of these Bartle Massey was one. His lame walk was rather slower than usual on this warm day, so Adam lingered behind when the bell rang for dinner, that he might walk up with his old friend; for he was a little too shy to join the Poyser party on this public occasion. Opportunities of getting to Hetty's side would be sure to turn up in the course of the day, and Adam contented himself with that for he disliked any risk of being "joked" about Hetty—the big, outspoken, fearless man was very shy and diffident as to his love-making.

"Well, Mester Massey," said Adam, as Bartle came up "I'm going to dine upstairs with you to-day: the captain's sent me orders."

"Ah!" said Bartle, pausing, with one hand on his back. "Then there's something in the wind—there's something in the wind. Have you heard anything about what the old squire means to do?"

"Why, yes," said Adam; "I'll tell you what I know, because I believe you can keep a still tongue in your head if you like, and I hope you'll not let drop a word till it's common talk, for I've particular reasons against its being known."

"Trust to me, my boy, trust to me. I've got no wife to worm it out of me and then run out and cackle it in everybody's hearing. If you trust a man, let him be a bachelor—let him be a bachelor."

"Well, then, it was so far settled yesterday that I'm to take the management o' the woods. The captain sent for me t' offer it me, when I was seeing to the poles and things here and I've agreed to't. But if anybody asks any questions upstairs, just you take no notice, and turn the talk to something else, and I'll be obliged to you. Now, let us go on, for we're pretty nigh the last, I think."

"I know what to do, never fear," said Bartle, moving on. "The news will be good sauce to my dinner. Aye, aye, my boy, you'll get on.

I'll back you for an eye at measuring and a head-piece for figures, against any man in this county and you've had good teaching—you've had good teaching."

When they got upstairs, the question which Arthur had left unsettled, as to who was to be president, and who vice, was still under discussion, so that Adam's entrance passed without remark.

"It stands to sense," Mr. Casson was saying, "as old Mr. Poyser, as is th' oldest man i' the room, should sit at top o' the table. I wasn't butler fifteen year without learning the rights and the wrongs about dinner."

"Nay, nay," said old Martin, "I'n gi'en up to my son; I'm no tenant now: let my son take my place. Th' ould foulks ha' had their turn: they mun make way for the young uns."

"I should ha' thought the biggest tenant had the best right, more nor th' oldest," said Luke Britton, who was not fond of the critical Mr. Poyser; "there's Mester Holdsworth has more land nor anybody else on th' estate."

"Well," said Mr. Poyser, "suppose we say the man wi' the foulest land shall sit at top; then whoever gets th' honour, there'll be no envying on him."

"Eh, here's Mester Massey," said Mr. Craig, who, being a neutral in the dispute, had no interest but in conciliation; "the schoolmaster ought to be able to tell you what's right. Who's to sit at top o' the table, Mr. Massey?"

"Why, the broadest man," said Bartle; "and then he won't take up other folks' room; and the next broadest must sit at bottom."

This happy mode of settling the dispute produced much laughter—a smaller joke would have sufficed for that Mr. Casson, however, did not feel it compatible with his dignity and superior knowledge to join in the laugh, until it turned out that he was fixed on as the second broadest man. Martin Poyser the younger, as the broadest, was to be president, and Mr. Casson, as next broadest, was to be vice.

Owing to this arrangement, Adam, being, of course, at the bottom of the table, fell under the immediate observation of Mr. Casson, who, too much occupied with the question of precedence, had not hitherto noticed his entrance. Mr. Casson, we have seen, considered Adam "rather lifted up and peppery-like": he thought the gentry made more fuss about this young carpenter than was necessary; they made no fuss about Mr. Casson, although he had been an excellent butler for fifteen years.

"Well, Mr. Bede, you're one o' them as mounts hup'ards apace," he said, when Adam sat down. "You've niver dined here before, as I remember."

"No, Mr. Casson," said Adam, in his strong voice, that could be heard along the table; "I've never dined here before, but I come by Captain Donnithorne's wish, and I hope it's not disagreeable to anybody here."

"Nay, nay," said several voices at once, "we're glad ye're come. Who's got anything to say again' it?"

"And ye'll sing us 'Over the hills and far away,' after dinner, wonna ye?" said Mr. Chowne. "That's a song I'm uncommon fond on."

"Peeh!" said Mr. Craig; "it's not to be named by side o' the Scotch tunes. I've never cared about singing myself; I've had something better to do. A man that's got the names and the natur o' plants in's head isna likely to keep a hollow place t' hold tunes in. But a second cousin o' mine, a drovier, was a rare hand at remembering the Scotch tunes. He'd got nothing else to think on."

"The Scotch tunes!" said Bartle Massey, contemptuously; "I've heard enough o' the Scotch tunes to last me while I live. They're fit for nothing but to frighten the birds with—that's to say, the English birds, for the Scotch birds may sing Scotch for what I know. Give the lads a bagpipe instead of a rattle, and I'll answer for it the corn 'll be safe."

"Yes, there's folks as find a pleasure in undervallying what they know but little about," said Mr. Craig.

"Why, the Scotch tunes are just like a scolding, nagging woman," Bartle went on, without deigning to notice Mr. Craig's remark. "They go on with the same thing over and over again, and never come to a reasonable end. Anybody 'ud think the Scotch tunes had always been asking a question of somebody as deaf as old Taft, and had never got an answer yet."

Adam minded the less about sitting by Mr. Casson, because this position enabled him to see Hetty, who was not far off him at the next table. Hetty, however, had not even noticed his presence yet, for she was giving angry attention to Totty, who insisted on drawing up her feet on to the bench in antique fashion, and thereby threatened to make dusty marks on Hetty's pink-and-white frock. No sooner were the little fat legs pushed down than up they came again, for Totty's eyes were too busy in staring at the large dishes to see where the plum pudding was for her to retain any consciousness of her legs. Hetty got quite out of patience, and at last, with a frown and pout, and gathering tears, she said, "Oh dear, Aunt, I wish you'd speak to Totty; she keeps putting her legs up so, and messing my frock."

"What's the matter wi' the child? She can niver please you," said the mother. "Let her come by the side o' me, then. I can put up wi' her."

Adam was looking at Hetty, and saw the frown, and pout, and the dark eyes seeming to grow larger with pettish half-gathered tears. Quiet Mary Burge, who sat near enough to see that Hetty was cross and that Adam's eyes were fixed on her, thought that so sensible a man as Adam must be reflecting on the small value of beauty in a woman whose temper was bad. Mary was a good girl, not given to indulge in evil feelings, but she said to herself, that, since Hetty had a bad temper, it was better Adam should know it. And it was quite true that if Hetty had been plain, she would have looked very ugly and unamiable at that moment, and no one's moral judgment upon her would have been in the least beguiled. But really there was something quite charming in her pettishness: it looked so much more like innocent distress than ill humour; and the severe Adam felt no movement of disapprobation; he only felt a sort of amused pity, as if he had seen a kitten setting up its back, or a little bird with its feathers ruffled. He could not gather what was vexing her, but it was impossible to him to feel otherwise than that she was the prettiest thing in the world, and that if he could have his way, nothing should ever vex her any more. And presently, when Totty was gone, she caught his eye, and her face broke into one of its brightest smiles, as she nodded to him. It was a bit of flirtation—she knew Mary Burge was looking at them. But the smile was like wine to Adam.

Chapter XXIV The Health-Drinking

WHEN the dinner was over, and the first draughts from the great cask of birthday ale were brought up, room was made for the broad Mr. Poyser at the side of the table, and two chairs were placed at the head.

It had been settled very definitely what Mr. Poyser was to do when the young squire should appear, and for the last five minutes he had been in a state of abstraction, with his eyes fixed on the dark picture opposite, and his hands busy with the loose cash and other articles in his breeches pockets.

When the young squire entered, with Mr. Irwine by his side, every one stood up, and this moment of homage was very agreeable to Arthur. He liked to feel his own importance, and besides that, he cared a great deal for the good-will of these people: he was fond of thinking that they had a hearty, special regard for him. The pleasure he felt was in his face as he said, "My grandfather and I hope all our friends here have enjoyed their dinner, and find my birthday ale good. Mr. Irwine and I are come to taste it with you, and I am sure we shall all like anything the better that the rector shares with us."

All eyes were now turned on Mr. Poyser, who, with his hands still busy in his pockets, began with the deliberateness of a slow-striking clock. "Captain, my neighbours have put it upo' me to speak for 'em to-day, for where folks think pretty much alike, one spokesman's as good as a score. And though we've mayhappen got contrairy ways o' thinking about a many things—one man lays down his land one way an' another another—an' I'll not take it upon me to speak to no man's farming, but my own—this I'll say, as we're all o' one mind about our young squire. We've pretty nigh all on us known you when you war a little un, an' we've niver known anything on you but what was good an' honorable. You speak fair an' y' act fair, an' we're joyful when we look forrard to your being our landlord, for we b'lieve you mean to do right by everybody, an' 'ull make no man's bread bitter to him if you can help it. That's what I mean, an' that's what we all mean; and when a man's said what he means, he'd better stop, for th' ale 'ull be none the better for stannin'. An' I'll not say how we like th' ale yet, for we couldna well taste it till we'd drunk your health in it; but the dinner was good, an' if there's anybody hasna enjoyed it, it must be the fault of his own inside. An' as for the rector's company, it's well known as that's welcome t' all the parish wherever he may be; an' I hope, an' we all hope, as he'll live to see us old folks, an' our children grown to men an' women an' Your Honour a family man. I've no more to say as concerns the present time, an' so we'll drink our young squire's health—three times three."

Hereupon a glorious shouting, a rapping, a jingling, a clattering, and a shouting, with plentiful da capo, pleasanter than a strain of sublimest music in the ears that receive such a tribute for the first time. Arthur had felt a twinge of conscience during Mr. Poyser's speech, but it was too feeble to nullify the pleasure he felt in being praised. Did he not deserve what was said of him on the whole? If there was something in his conduct that Poyser wouldn't have liked if he had known it, why, no man's conduct will bear too close an inspection; and Poyser was not likely to know it; and, after all, what had he done? Gone a little too far, perhaps, in flirtation, but another man in his place would have acted much worse; and no harm would come—no harm should come, for the next time he was alone with Hetty, he would explain to her that she must not think seriously of him or of what had passed. It was necessary to Arthur, you perceive, to be satisfied with himself. Uncomfortable thoughts must be got rid of by good intentions for the future, which can be formed so rapidly that he had time to be uncomfortable and to become easy again before Mr. Poyser's slow speech was finished, and when it was time for him to speak he was quite light-hearted.

"I thank you all, my good friends and neighbours," Arthur said, "for the good opinion of me, and the kind feelings towards me which Mr. Poyser has been expressing on your behalf and on his own, and it will always be my heartiest wish to deserve them. In the course of things we may expect that, if I live, I shall one day or other be your landlord; indeed, it is on the ground of that expectation that my grandfather has wished me to celebrate this day and to come among you now; and I look forward to this position, not merely as one of power and pleasure for myself, but as a means of benefiting my neighbours. It hardly becomes so young a man as I am to talk much about farming to you, who are most of you so much older, and are men of experience; still, I have interested myself a good deal in such matters, and learned as much about them as my opportunities have allowed; and when the course of events shall place the estate in my hands, it will be my first desire to afford my tenants all the encouragement a landlord can give them, in improving their land and trying to bring about a better practice of husbandry. It will be my wish to be looked on by all my deserving tenants as their best friend, and nothing would make me so happy as to be able to respect every man on the estate, and to be respected by him in return. It is not my place at present to enter into particulars; I only meet your good hopes concerning me by telling you that my own hopes correspond to them—that what you expect from me I desire to fulfil; and I am quite of Mr. Poyser's opinion, that when a man has said what he means, he had better stop. But the pleasure I feel in having my own health drunk by you would not be perfect if we did not drink the health of my grandfather, who has filled the place of both parents to me. I will say no more, until you have joined me in drinking his health on a day when he has wished me to appear among you as the future representative of his name and family."

Perhaps there was no one present except Mr. Irwine who thoroughly understood and approved Arthur's graceful mode of proposing his grandfather's health. The farmers thought the young squire knew well enough that they hated the old squire, and Mrs. Poyser said, "he'd better not ha' stirred a kettle o' sour broth." The bucolic mind does not readily apprehend the refinements of good taste. But the toast could not be rejected and when it had been drunk, Arthur said, "I thank you, both for my grandfather and myself; and now there is one more thing I wish to tell you, that you may share my pleasure about it, as I hope and believe you will. I think there can be no man here who has not a respect, and some of you, I am sure, have a very high regard, for my friend Adam Bede. It is well known to every one in this neighbourhood that there is no man whose word can be more depended on than his; that whatever he undertakes to do, he does well, and is as careful for the interests of those who employ him as for his own. I'm proud to say that I was very fond of Adam when I was a little boy, and I have never lost my old feeling for him—I think that shows that I know a good fellow when I find him. It has long been my wish that he should have the management of the woods on the estate, which happen to be very valuable, not only because I think so highly of his character, but because he has the knowledge and the skill which fit him for the place. And I am happy to tell you that it is my grandfather's wish too, and it is now settled that Adam shall manage the woods—a change which I am sure will be very much for the advantage of the estate; and I hope you will by and by join me in drinking his health, and in wishing him all the prosperity in life that he deserves. But there is a still older friend of mine than Adam Bede present, and I need not tell you that it is Mr. Irwine. I'm sure you will agree with me that we must drink no other person's health until we have drunk his. I know you have all reason to love him, but no one of his parishioners has so much reason as I. Come, charge your glasses, and let us drink to our excellent rector—three times three!"

This toast was drunk with all the enthusiasm that was wanting to the last, and it certainly was the most picturesque moment in the scene when Mr. Irwine got up to speak, and all the faces in the room were turned towards him. The superior refinement of his face was much more striking than that of Arthur's when seen in comparison with the people round them. Arthur's was a much commoner British face, and the splendour of his new-fashioned clothes was more akin to the young farmer's taste in costume than Mr. Irwine's powder and the well-brushed but well-worn black, which seemed to be his chosen suit for great occasions; for he had the mysterious secret of never wearing a new-looking coat.

"This is not the first time, by a great many," he said, "that I have had to thank my parishioners for giving me tokens of their goodwill, but neighbourly kindness is among those things that are the more precious the older they get. Indeed, our pleasant meeting to-day is a proof that when what is good comes of age and is likely to live, there is reason for rejoicing, and the relation between us as clergyman and parishioners came of age two years ago, for it is three-and-twenty years since I first came among you, and I see some tall fine-looking young men here, as well as some blooming young women, that were far from looking as pleasantly at me when I christened them as I am happy to see them looking now. But I'm sure you will not wonder when I say that among all those young men, the one in whom I have the strongest interest is my friend Mr. Arthur Donnithorne, for whom you have just expressed your regard. I had the pleasure of being his tutor for several years, and have naturally had opportunities of knowing him intimately which cannot have occurred to any one else who is present; and I have some pride as well as pleasure in assuring you that I share your high hopes concerning him, and your confidence in his possession of those qualities which will make him an excellent landlord when the time shall come for him to take that important position among you. We feel alike on most matters on which a man who is getting towards fifty can feel in common with a young man of one-and-twenty, and he has just been expressing a feeling which I share very heartily, and I would not willingly omit the opportunity of saying so. That feeling is his value and respect for Adam Bede. People in a high station are of course more thought of and talked about and have their virtues more praised, than those whose lives are passed in humble everyday work; but every sensible man knows how necessary that humble everyday work is, and how important it is to us that it should be done well. And I agree with my friend Mr. Arthur Donnithorne in feeling that when a man whose duty lies in that sort of work shows a character which would make him an example in any station, his merit should be acknowledged. He is one of those to whom honour is due, and his friends should delight to honour him. I know Adam Bede well—I know what he is as a workman, and what he has been as a son and brother—and I am saying the simplest truth when I say that I respect him as much as I respect any man living. But I am not speaking to you about a stranger; some of you are his intimate friends, and I believe there is not one here who does not know enough of him to join heartily in drinking his health."

As Mr. Irwine paused, Arthur jumped up and, filling his glass, said, "A bumper to Adam Bede, and may he live to have sons as faithful and clever as himself!"

No hearer, not even Bartle Massey, was so delighted with this toast as Mr. Poyser. "Tough work" as his first speech had been, he would have started up to make another if he had not known the extreme irregularity of such a course. As it was, he found an outlet for his feeling in drinking his ale unusually fast, and setting down his glass with a swing of his arm and a determined rap. If Jonathan Burge and a few others felt less comfortable on the occasion, they tried their best to look contented, and so the toast was drunk with a goodwill apparently unanimous.

Adam was rather paler than usual when he got up to thank his friends. He was a good deal moved by this public tribute—very naturally, for he was in the presence of all his little world, and it was uniting to do him honour. But he felt no shyness about speaking, not being troubled with small vanity or lack of words; he looked neither awkward nor embarrassed, but stood in his usual firm upright attitude, with his head thrown a little backward and his hands perfectly still, in that rough dignity which is peculiar to intelligent, honest, well-built workmen, who are never wondering what is their business in the world.

"I'm quite taken by surprise," he said. "I didn't expect anything o' this sort, for it's a good deal more than my wages. But I've the more reason to be grateful to you, Captain, and to you, Mr. Irwine, and to all my friends here, who've drunk my health and wished me well. It 'ud be nonsense for me to be saying, I don't at all deserve th' opinion you have of me; that 'ud be poor thanks to you, to say that you've known me all these years and yet haven't sense enough to find out a great deal o' the truth about me. You think, if I undertake to do a bit o' work, I'll do it well, be my pay big or little—and that's true. I'd be ashamed to stand before you here if it wasna true. But it seems to me that's a man's plain duty, and nothing to be conceited about, and it's pretty clear to me as I've never done more than my duty; for let us do what we will, it's only making use o' the sperrit and the powers that ha' been given to us. And so this kindness o' yours, I'm sure, is no debt you owe me, but a free gift, and as such I accept it and am thankful. And as to this new employment I've taken in hand, I'll only say that I took it at Captain Donnithorne's desire, and that I'll try to fulfil his expectations. I'd wish for no better lot than to work under him, and to know that while I was getting my own bread I was taking care of his int'rests. For I believe he's one o those gentlemen as wishes to do the right thing, and to leave the world a bit better than he found it, which it's my belief every man may do, whether he's gentle or simple, whether he sets a good bit o' work going and finds the money, or whether he does the work with his own hands. There's no occasion for me to say any more about what I feel towards him: I hope to show it through the rest o' my life in my actions."

There were various opinions about Adam's speech: some of the women whispered that he didn't show himself thankful enough, and seemed to speak as proud as could be; but most of the men were of opinion that nobody could speak more straightfor'ard, and that Adam was as fine a chap as need to be. While such observations were being buzzed about, mingled with wonderings as to what the old squire meant to do for a bailiff, and whether he was going to have a steward, the two gentlemen had risen, and were walking round to the table where the wives and children sat. There was none of the strong ale here, of course, but wine and dessert—sparkling gooseberry for the young ones, and some good sherry for the mothers. Mrs. Poyser was at the head of this table, and Totty was now seated in her lap, bending her small nose deep down into a wine-glass in search of the nuts floating there.

"How do you do, Mrs. Poyser?" said Arthur. "Weren't you pleased to hear your husband make such a good speech to-day?"

"Oh, sir, the men are mostly so tongue-tied—you're forced partly to guess what they mean, as you do wi' the dumb creaturs."

"What! you think you could have made it better for him?" said Mr. Irwine, laughing.

"Well, sir, when I want to say anything, I can mostly find words to say it in, thank God. Not as I'm a-finding faut wi' my husband, for if he's a man o' few words, what he says he'll stand to."

"I'm sure I never saw a prettier party than this," Arthur said, looking round at the apple-cheeked children. "My aunt and the Miss Irwines will come up and see you presently. They were afraid of the noise of the toasts, but it would be a shame for them not to see you at table."

He walked on, speaking to the mothers and patting the children, while Mr. Irwine satisfied himself with standing still and nodding at a distance, that no one's attention might be disturbed from the young squire, the hero of the day. Arthur did not venture to stop near Hetty, but merely bowed to her as he passed along the opposite side. The foolish child felt her heart swelling with discontent; for what woman was ever satisfied with apparent neglect, even when she knows it to be the mask of love? Hetty thought this was going to be the most miserable day she had had for a long while, a moment of chill daylight and reality came across her dream: Arthur, who had seemed so near to her only a few hours before, was separated from her, as the hero of a great procession is separated from a small outsider in the crowd.

Chapter XXV The Games

THE great dance was not to begin until eight o'clock, but for any lads and lasses who liked to dance on the shady grass before then, there was music always at hand—for was not the band of the Benefit Club capable of playing excellent jigs, reels, and hornpipes? And, besides this, there was a grand band hired from Rosseter, who, with their wonderful wind-instruments and puffed-out cheeks, were themselves a delightful show to the small boys and girls. To say nothing of Joshua Rann's fiddle, which, by an act of generous forethought, he had provided himself with, in case any one should be of sufficiently pure taste to prefer dancing to a solo on that instrument.

Meantime, when the sun had moved off the great open space in front of the house, the games began. There were, of course, well-soaped poles to be climbed by the boys and youths, races to be run by the old women, races to be run in sacks, heavy weights to be lifted by the strong men, and a long list of challenges to such ambitious attempts as that of walking as many yards possible on one leg—feats in which it was generally remarked that Wiry Ben, being "the lissom'st, springest fellow i' the country," was sure to be pre-eminent. To crown all, there was to be a donkey-race—that sublimest of all races, conducted on the grand socialistic idea of everybody encouraging everybody else's donkey, and the sorriest donkey winning.

And soon after four o ciock, splendid old Mrs. Irwine, in her damask satin and jewels and black lace, was led out by Arthur, followed by the whole family party, to her raised seat under the striped marquee, where she was to give out the prizes to the victors. Staid, formal Miss Lydia had requested to resign that queenly office to the royal old lady, and Arthur was pleased with this opportunity of gratifying his godmother's taste for stateliness. Old Mr. Donnithorne, the delicately clean, finely scented, withered old man, led out Miss Irwine, with his air of punctilious, acid politeness; Mr. Gawaine brought Miss Lydia, looking neutral and stiff in an elegant peach-blossom silk; and Mr. Irwine came last with his pale sister Anne. No other friend of the family, besides Mr. Gawaine, was invited to-day; there was to be a grand dinner for the neighbouring gentry on the morrow, but to-day all the forces were required for the entertainment of the tenants.

There was a sunk fence in front of the marquee, dividing the lawn from the park, but a temporary bridge had been made for the passage of the victors, and the groups of people standing, or seated here and there on benches, stretched on each side of the open space from the white marquees up to the sunk fence.

"Upon my word it's a pretty sight," said the old lady, in her deep voice, when she was seated, and looked round on the bright scene with its dark-green background; "and it's the last fete-day I'm likely to see, unless you make haste and get married, Arthur. But take care you get a charming bride, else I would rather die without seeing her."

"You're so terribly fastidious, Godmother," said Arthur, "I'm afraid I should never satisfy you with my choice."

"Well, I won't forgive you if she's not handsome. I can't be put off with amiability, which is always the excuse people are making for the existence of plain people. And she must not be silly; that will never do, because you'll want managing, and a silly woman can't manage you. Who is that tall young man, Dauphin, with the mild face? There, standing without his hat, and taking such care of that tall old woman by the side of him—his mother, of course. I like to see that."

"What, don't you know him, Mother?" said Mr. Irwine. "That is Seth Bede, Adam's brother—a Methodist, but a very good fellow. Poor Seth has looked rather down-hearted of late; I thought it was because of his father's dying in that sad way, but Joshua Rann tells me he wanted to marry that sweet little Methodist preacher who was here about a month ago, and I suppose she refused him."

"Ah, I remember hearing about her. But there are no end of people here that I don't know, for they're grown up and altered so since I used to go about."

"What excellent sight you have!" said old Mr. Donnithorne, who was holding a double glass up to his eyes, "to see the expression of that young man's face so far off. His face is nothing but a pale blurred spot to me. But I fancy I have the advantage of you when we come to look close. I can read small print without spectacles."

"Ah, my dear sir, you began with being very near-sighted, and those near-sighted eyes always wear the best. I want very strong spectacles to read with, but then I think my eyes get better and better for things at a distance. I suppose if I could live another fifty years, I should be blind to everything that wasn't out of other people's sight, like a man who stands in a well and sees nothing but the stars."

"See," said Arthur, "the old women are ready to set out on their race now. Which do you bet on, Gawaine?"

"The long-legged one, unless they're going to have several heats, and then the little wiry one may win."

"There are the Poysers, Mother, not far off on the right hand," said Miss Irwine. "Mrs. Poyser is looking at you. Do take notice of her."

"To be sure I will," said the old lady, giving a gracious bow to Mrs. Poyser. "A woman who sends me such excellent cream-cheese is not to be neglected. Bless me! What a fat child that is she is holding on her knee! But who is that pretty girl with dark eyes?"

"That is Hetty Sorrel," said Miss Lydia Donnithorne, "Martin Poyser's niece—a very likely young person, and well-looking too. My maid has taught her fine needlework, and she has mended some lace of mine very respectably indeed—very respectably."

"Why, she has lived with the Poysers six or seven years, Mother; you must have seen her," said Miss Irwine.

"No, I've never seen her, child—at least not as she is now," said Mrs. Irwine, continuing to look at Hetty. "Well-looking, indeed! She's a perfect beauty! I've never seen anything so pretty since my young days. What a pity such beauty as that should be thrown away among the farmers, when it's wanted so terribly among the good families without fortune! I daresay, now, she'll marry a man who would have thought her just as pretty if she had had round eyes and red hair."

Arthur dared not turn his eyes towards Hetty while Mrs. Irwine was speaking of her. He feigned not to hear, and to be occupied with something on the opposite side. But he saw her plainly enough without looking; saw her in heightened beauty, because he heard her beauty praised—for other men's opinion, you know, was like a native climate to Arthur's feelings: it was the air on which they thrived the best, and grew strong. Yes! She was enough to turn any man's head: any man in his place would have done and felt the same. And to give her up after all, as he was determined to do, would be an act that he should always look back upon with pride.

"No, Mother," and Mr. Irwine, replying to her last words; "I can't agree with you there. The common people are not quite so stupid as you imagine. The commonest man, who has his ounce of sense and feeling, is conscious of the difference between a lovely, delicate woman and a coarse one. Even a dog feels a difference in their presence. The man may be no better able than the dog to explain the influence the more refined beauty has on him, but he feels it."

"Bless me, Dauphin, what does an old bachelor like you know about it?"

"Oh, that is one of the matters in which old bachelors are wiser than married men, because they have time for more general contemplation. Your fine critic of woman must never shackle his judgment by calling one woman his own. But, as an example of what I was saying, that pretty Methodist preacher I mentioned just now told me that she had preached to the roughest miners and had never been treated with anything but the utmost respect and kindness by them. The reason is—though she doesn't know it—that there's so much tenderness, refinement, and purity about her. Such a woman as that brings with her 'airs from heaven' that the coarsest fellow is not insensible to."

"Here's a delicate bit of womanhood, or girlhood, coming to receive a prize, I suppose," said Mr. Gawaine. "She must be one of the racers in the sacks, who had set off before we came."

The "bit of womanhood" was our old acquaintance Bessy Cranage, otherwise Chad's Bess, whose large red cheeks and blowsy person had undergone an exaggeration of colour, which, if she had happened to be a heavenly body, would have made her sublime. Bessy, I am sorry to say, had taken to her ear-rings again since Dinah's departure, and was otherwise decked out in such small finery as she could muster. Any one who could have looked into poor Bessy's heart would have seen a striking resemblance between her little hopes and anxieties and Hetty's. The advantage, perhaps, would have been on Bessy's side in the matter of feeling. But then, you see, they were so very different outside! You would have been inclined to box Bessy's ears, and you would have longed to kiss Hetty.

Bessy had been tempted to run the arduous race, partly from mere hedonish gaiety, partly because of the prize. Some one had said there were to be cloaks and other nice clothes for prizes, and she approached the marquee, fanning herself with her handkerchief, but with exultation sparkling in her round eyes.

"Here is the prize for the first sack-race," said Miss Lydia, taking a large parcel from the table where the prizes were laid and giving it to Mrs. Irwine before Bessy came up, "an excellent grogram gown and a piece of flannel."

"You didn't think the winner was to be so young, I suppose, Aunt?" said Arthur. "Couldn't you find something else for this girl, and save that grim-looking gown for one of the older women?"

"I have bought nothing but what is useful and substantial," said Miss Lydia, adjusting her own lace; "I should not think of encouraging a love of finery in young women of that class. I have a scarlet cloak, but that is for the old woman who wins."

This speech of Miss Lydia's produced rather a mocking expression in Mrs. Irwine's face as she looked at Arthur, while Bessy came up and dropped a series of curtsies.

"This is Bessy Cranage, mother," said Mr. Irwine, kindly, "Chad Cranage's daughter. You remember Chad Cranage, the blacksmith?"

"Yes, to be sure," said Mrs. Irwine. "Well, Bessy, here is your prize—excellent warm things for winter. I'm sure you have had hard work to win them this warm day."

Bessy's lip fell as she saw the ugly, heavy gown—which felt so hot and disagreeable too, on this July day, and was such a great ugly thing to carry. She dropped her curtsies again, without looking up, and with a growing tremulousness about the corners of her mouth, and then turned away.

"Poor girl," said Arthur; "I think she's disappointed. I wish it had been something more to her taste."

"She's a bold-looking young person," observed Miss Lydia. "Not at all one I should like to encourage."

Arthur silently resolved that he would make Bessy a present of money before the day was over, that she might buy something more to her mind; but she, not aware of the consolation in store for her, turned out of the open space, where she was visible from the marquee, and throwing down the odious bundle under a tree, began to cry—very much tittered at the while by the small boys. In this situation she was descried by her discreet matronly cousin, who lost no time in coming up, having just given the baby into her husband's charge.

"What's the matter wi' ye?" said Bess the matron, taking up the bundle and examining it. "Ye'n sweltered yoursen, I reckon, running that fool's race. An' here, they'n gi'en you lots o' good grogram and flannel, as should ha' been gi'en by good rights to them as had the sense to keep away from such foolery. Ye might spare me a bit o' this grogram to make clothes for the lad—ye war ne'er ill-natured, Bess; I ne'er said that on ye."

"Ye may take it all, for what I care," said Bess the maiden, with a pettish movement, beginning to wipe away her tears and recover herself.

"Well, I could do wi't, if so be ye want to get rid on't," said the disinterested cousin, walking quickly away with the bundle, lest Chad's Bess should change her mind.

But that bonny-cheeked lass was blessed with an elasticity of spirits that secured her from any rankling grief; and by the time the grand climax of the donkey-race came on, her disappointment was entirely lost in the delightful excitement of attempting to stimulate the last donkey by hisses, while the boys applied the argument of sticks. But the strength of the donkey mind lies in adopting a course inversely as the arguments urged, which, well considered, requires as great a mental force as the direct sequence; and the present donkey proved the first-rate order of his intelligence by coming to a dead standstill just when the blows were thickest. Great was the shouting of the crowd, radiant the grinning of Bill Downes the stone-sawyer and the fortunate rider of this superior beast, which stood calm and stiff-legged in the midst of its triumph.

Arthur himself had provided the prizes for the men, and Bill was made happy with a splendid pocket-knife, supplied with blades and gimlets enough to make a man at home on a desert island. He had hardly returned from the marquee with the prize in his hand, when it began to be understood that Wiry Ben proposed to amuse the company, before the gentry went to dinner, with an impromptu and gratuitous performance—namely, a hornpipe, the main idea of which was doubtless borrowed; but this was to be developed by the dancer in so peculiar and complex a manner that no one could deny him the praise of originality. Wiry Ben's pride in his dancing—an accomplishment productive of great effect at the yearly Wake—had needed only slightly elevating by an extra quantity of good ale to convince him that the gentry would be very much struck with his performance of his hornpipe; and he had been decidedly encouraged in this idea by Joshua Rann, who observed that it was nothing but right to do something to please the young squire, in return for what he had done for them. You will be the less surprised at this opinion in so grave a personage when you learn that Ben had requested Mr. Rann to accompany him on the fiddle, and Joshua felt quite sure that though there might not be much in the dancing, the music would make up for it. Adam Bede, who was present in one of the large marquees, where the plan was being discussed, told Ben he had better not make a fool of himself—a remark which at once fixed Ben's determination: he was not going to let anything alone because Adam Bede turned up his nose at it.

"What's this, what's this?" said old Mr. Donnithorne. "Is it something you've arranged, Arthur? Here's the clerk coming with his fiddle, and a smart fellow with a nosegay in his button-hole."

"No," said Arthur; "I know nothing about it. By Jove, he's going to dance! It's one of the carpenters—I forget his name at this moment."

"It's Ben Cranage—Wiry Ben, they call him," said Mr. Irwine; "rather a loose fish, I think. Anne, my dear, I see that fiddle-scraping is too much for you: you're getting tired. Let me take you in now, that you may rest till dinner."

Miss Anne rose assentingly, and the good brother took her away, while Joshua's preliminary scrapings burst into the "White Cockade," from which he intended to pass to a variety of tunes, by a series of transitions which his good ear really taught him to execute with some skill. It would have been an exasperating fact to him, if he had known it, that the general attention was too thoroughly absorbed by Ben's dancing for any one to give much heed to the music.

Have you ever seen a real English rustic perform a solo dance? Perhaps you have only seen a ballet rustic, smiling like a merry countryman in crockery, with graceful turns of the haunch and insinuating movements of the head. That is as much like the real thing as the "Bird Waltz" is like the song of birds. Wiry Ben never smiled: he looked as serious as a dancing monkey—as serious as if he had been an experimental philosopher ascertaining in his own person the amount of shaking and the varieties of angularity that could be given to the human limbs.

To make amends for the abundant laughter in the striped marquee, Arthur clapped his hands continually and cried "Bravo!" But Ben had one admirer whose eyes followed his movements with a fervid gravity that equalled his own. It was Martin Poyser, who was seated on a bench, with Tommy between his legs.

"What dost think o' that?" he said to his wife. "He goes as pat to the music as if he was made o' clockwork. I used to be a pretty good un at dancing myself when I was lighter, but I could niver ha' hit it just to th' hair like that."

"It's little matter what his limbs are, to my thinking," re-turned Mrs. Poyser. "He's empty enough i' the upper story, or he'd niver come jigging an' stamping i' that way, like a mad grasshopper, for the gentry to look at him. They're fit to die wi' laughing, I can see."

"Well, well, so much the better, it amuses 'em," said Mr. Poyser, who did not easily take an irritable view of things. "But they're going away now, t' have their dinner, I reckon. Well move about a bit, shall we, and see what Adam Bede's doing. He's got to look after the drinking and things: I doubt he hasna had much fun."

Chapter XXVI The Dance

ARTHUR had chosen the entrance-hall for the ballroom: very wisely, for no other room could have heen so airy, or would have had the advantage of the wide doors opening into the garden, as well as a ready entrance into the other rooms. To be sure, a stone floor was not the pleasantest to dance on, but then, most of the dancers had known what it was to enjoy a Christmas dance on kitchen quarries. It was one of those entrance-halls which make the surrounding rooms look like closets—with stucco angels, trumpets, and flower-wreaths on the lofty ceiling, and great medallions of miscellaneous heroes on the walls, alternating with statues in niches. Just the sort of place to be ornamented well with green boughs, and Mr. Craig had been proud to show his taste and his hothouse plants on the occasion. The broad steps of the stone staircase were covered with cushions to serve as seats for the children, who were to stay till half-past nine with the servant-maids to see the dancing, and as this dance was confined to the chief tenants, there was abundant room for every one. The lights were charmingly disposed in coloured-paper lamps, high up among green boughs, and the farmers' wives and daughters, as they peeped in, believed no scene could be more splendid; they knew now quite well in what sort of rooms the king and queen lived, and their thoughts glanced with some pity towards cousins and acquaintances who had not this fine opportunity of knowing how things went on in the great world. The lamps were already lit, though the sun had not long set, and there was that calm light out of doors in which we seem to see all objects more distinctly than in the broad day.

It was a pretty scene outside the house: the farmers and their families were moving about the lawn, among the flowers and shrubs, or along the broad straight road leading from the east front, where a carpet of mossy grass spread on each side, studded here and there with a dark flat-boughed cedar, or a grand pyramidal fir sweeping the ground with its branches, all tipped with a fringe of paler green. The groups of cottagers in the park were gradually diminishing, the young ones being attracted towards the lights that were beginning to gleam from the windows of the gallery in the abbey, which was to be their dancing-room, and some of the sober elder ones thinking it time to go home quietly. One of these was Lisbeth Bede, and Seth went with her—not from filial attention only, for his conscience would not let him join in dancing. It had been rather a melancholy day to Seth: Dinah had never been more constantly present with him than in this scene, where everything was so unlike her. He saw her all the more vividly after looking at the thoughtless faces and gay-coloured dresses of the young women—just as one feels the beauty and the greatness of a pictured Madonna the more when it has been for a moment screened from us by a vulgar head in a bonnet. But this presence of Dinah in his mind only helped him to bear the better with his mother's mood, which had been becoming more and more querulous for the last hour. Poor Lisbeth was suffering from a strange conflict of feelings. Her joy and pride in the honour paid to her darling son Adam was beginning to be worsted in the conflict with the jealousy and fretfulness which had revived when Adam came to tell her that Captain Donnithorne desired him to join the dancers in the hall. Adam was getting more and more out of her reach; she wished all the old troubles back again, for then it mattered more to Adam what his mother said and did.

"Eh, it's fine talkin' o' dancin'," she said, "an' thy father not a five week in's grave. An' I wish I war there too, i'stid o' bein' left to take up merrier folks's room above ground."

"Nay, don't look at it i' that way, Mother," said Adam, who was determined to be gentle to her to-day. "I don't mean to dance—I shall only look on. And since the captain wishes me to be there, it 'ud look as if I thought I knew better than him to say as I'd rather not stay. And thee know'st how he's behaved to me to-day."

"Eh, thee't do as thee lik'st, for thy old mother's got no right t' hinder thee. She's nought but th' old husk, and thee'st slipped away from her, like the ripe nut."

"Well, Mother," said Adam, "I'll go and tell the captain as it hurts thy feelings for me to stay, and I'd rather go home upo' that account: he won't take it ill then, I daresay, and I'm willing." He said this with some effort, for he really longed to be near Hetty this evening.

"Nay, nay, I wonna ha' thee do that—the young squire 'ull be angered. Go an' do what thee't ordered to do, an' me and Seth 'ull go whome. I know it's a grit honour for thee to be so looked on—an' who's to be prouder on it nor thy mother? Hadna she the cumber o' rearin' thee an' doin' for thee all these 'ears?"

"Well, good-bye, then, Mother—good-bye, lad—remember Gyp when you get home," said Adam, turning away towards the gate of the pleasure-grounds, where he hoped he might be able to join the Poysers, for he had been so occupied throughout the afternoon that he had had no time to speak to Hetty. His eye soon detected a distant group, which he knew to be the right one, returning to the house along the broad gravel road, and he hastened on to meet them.

"Why, Adam, I'm glad to get sight on y' again," said Mr. Poyser, who was carrying Totty on his arm. "You're going t' have a bit o' fun, I hope, now your work's all done. And here's Hetty has promised no end o' partners, an' I've just been askin' her if she'd agreed to dance wi' you, an' she says no."

"Well, I didn't think o' dancing to-night," said Adam, already tempted to change his mind, as he looked at Hetty.

"Nonsense!" said Mr. Poyser. "Why, everybody's goin' to dance to-night, all but th' old squire and Mrs. Irwine. Mrs. Best's been tellin' us as Miss Lyddy and Miss Irwine 'ull dance, an' the young squire 'ull pick my wife for his first partner, t' open the ball: so she'll be forced to dance, though she's laid by ever sin' the Christmas afore the little un was born. You canna for shame stand still, Adam, an' you a fine young fellow and can dance as well as anybody."

"Nay, nay," said Mrs. Poyser, "it 'ud be unbecomin'. I know the dancin's nonsense, but if you stick at everything because it's non-sense, you wonna go far i' this life. When your broth's ready-made for you, you mun swallow the thickenin', or else let the broth alone."

"Then if Hetty 'ull d'ance with me," said Adam, yielding either to Mrs. Poyser's argument or to something else, "I'll dance whichever dance she's free."

"I've got no partner for the fourth dance," said Hetty; "I'll dance that with you, if you like."

"Ah," said Mr. Poyser, "but you mun dance the first dance, Adam, else it'll look partic'ler. There's plenty o' nice partners to pick an' choose from, an' it's hard for the gells when the men stan' by and don't ask 'em."

Adam felt the justice of Mr. Poyser's observation: it would not do for him to dance with no one besides Hetty; and remembering that Jonathan Burge had some reason to feel hurt to-day, he resolved to ask Miss Mary to dance with him the first dance, if she had no other partner.

"There's the big clock strikin' eight," said Mr. Poyser; "we must make haste in now, else the squire and the ladies 'ull be in afore us, an' that wouldna look well."

When they had entered the hall, and the three children under Molly's charge had been seated on the stairs, the folding-doors of the drawing-room were thrown open, and Arthur entered in his regimentals, leading Mrs. Irwine to a carpet-covered dais ornamented with hot-house plants, where she and Miss Anne were to be seated with old Mr. Donnithorne, that they might look on at the dancing, like the kings and queens in the plays. Arthur had put on his uniform to please the tenants, he said, who thought as much of his militia dignity as if it had been an elevation to the premiership. He had not the least objection to gratify them in that way: his uniform was very advantageous to his figure.

The old squire, before sitting down, walked round the hall to greet the tenants and make polite speeches to the wives: he was always polite; but the farmers had found out, after long puzzling, that this polish was one of the signs of hardness. It was observed that he gave his most elaborate civility to Mrs. Poyser to-night, inquiring particularly about her health, recommending her to strengthen herself with cold water as he did, and avoid all drugs. Mrs. Poyser curtsied and thanked him with great self-command, but when he had passed on, she whispered to her husband, "I'll lay my life he's brewin' some nasty turn against us. Old Harry doesna wag his tail so for nothin'." Mr. Poyser had no time to answer, for now Arthur came up and said, "Mrs. Poyser, I'm come to request the favour of your hand for the first dance; and, Mr. Poyser, you must let me take you to my aunt, for she claims you as her partner."

The wife's pale cheek flushed with a nervous sense of unwonted honour as Arthur led her to the top of the room; but Mr. Poyser, to whom an extra glass had restored his youthful confidence in his good looks and good dancing, walked along with them quite proudly, secretly flattering himself that Miss Lydia had never had a partner in HER life who could lift her off the ground as he would. In order to balance the honours given to the two parishes, Miss Irwine danced with Luke Britton, the largest Broxton farmer, and Mr. Gawaine led out Mrs. Britton. Mr. Irwine, after seating his sister Anne, had gone to the abbey gallery, as he had agreed with Arthur beforehand, to see how the merriment of the cottagers was prospering. Meanwhile, all the less distinguished couples had taken their places: Hetty was led out by the inevitable Mr. Craig, and Mary Burge by Adam; and now the music struck up, and the glorious country-dance, best of all dances, began.

Pity it was not a boarded floor! Then the rhythmic stamping of the thick shoes would have been better than any drums. That merry stamping, that gracious nodding of the head, that waving bestowal of the hand—where can we see them now? That simple dancing of well-covered matrons, laying aside for an hour the cares of house and dairy, remembering but not affecting youth, not jealous but proud of the young maidens by their side—that holiday sprightliness of portly husbands paying little compliments to their wives, as if their courting days were come again—those lads and lasses a little confused and awkward with their partners, having nothing to say—it would be a pleasant variety to see all that sometimes, instead of low dresses and large skirts, and scanning glances exploring costumes, and languid men in lacquered boots smiling with double meaning.

There was but one thing to mar Martin Poyser's pleasure in this dance: it was that he was always in close contact with Luke Britton, that slovenly farmer. He thought of throwing a little glazed coldness into his eye in the crossing of hands; but then, as Miss Irwine was opposite to him instead of the offensive Luke, he might freeze the wrong person. So he gave his face up to hilarity, unchilled by moral judgments.

How Hetty's heart beat as Arthur approached her! He had hardly looked at her to-day: now he must take her hand. Would he press it? Would he look at her? She thought she would cry if he gave her no sign of feeling. Now he was there—he had taken her hand—yes, he was pressing it. Hetty turned pale as she looked up at him for an instant and met his eyes, before the dance carried him away. That pale look came upon Arthur like the beginning of a dull pain, which clung to him, though he must dance and smile and joke all the same. Hetty would look so, when he told her what he had to tell her; and he should never be able to bear it—he should be a fool and give way again. Hetty's look did not really mean so much as he thought: it was only the sign of a struggle between the desire for him to notice her and the dread lest she should betray the desire to others. But Hetty's face had a language that transcended her feelings. There are faces which nature charges with a meaning and pathos not belonging to the single human soul that flutters beneath them, but speaking the joys and sorrows of foregone generations—eyes that tell of deep love which doubtless has been and is somewhere, but not paired with these eyes—perhaps paired with pale eyes that can say nothing; just as a national language may be instinct with poetry unfelt by the lips that use it. That look of Hetty's oppressed Arthur with a dread which yet had something of a terrible unconfessed delight in it, that she loved him too well. There was a hard task before him, for at that moment he felt he would have given up three years of his youth for the happiness of abandoning himself without remorse to his passion for Hetty.

These were the incongruous thoughts in his mind as he led Mrs. Poyser, who was panting with fatigue, and secretly resolving that neither judge nor jury should force her to dance another dance, to take a quiet rest in the dining-room, where supper was laid out for the guests to come and take it as they chose.

"I've desired Hetty to remember as she's got to dance wi' you, sir," said the good innocent woman; "for she's so thoughtless, she'd be like enough to go an' engage herself for ivery dance. So I told her not to promise too many."

"Thank you, Mrs. Poyser," said Arthur, not without a twinge. "Now, sit down in this comfortable chair, and here is Mills ready to give you what you would like best."

He hurried away to seek another matronly partner, for due honour must be paid to the married women before he asked any of the young ones; and the country-dances, and the stamping, and the gracious nodding, and the waving of the hands, went on joyously.

At last the time had come for the fourth dance—longed for by the strong, grave Adam, as if he had been a delicate-handed youth of eighteen; for we are all very much alike when we are in our first love; and Adam had hardly ever touched Hetty's hand for more than a transient greeting—had never danced with her but once before. His eyes had followed her eagerly to-night in spite of himself, and had taken in deeper draughts of love. He thought she behaved so prettily, so quietly; she did not seem to be flirting at all she smiled less than usual; there was almost a sweet sadness about her. "God bless her!" he said inwardly; "I'd make her life a happy 'un, if a strong arm to work for her, and a heart to love her, could do it."

And then there stole over him delicious thoughts of coming home from work, and drawing Hetty to his side, and feeling her cheek softly pressed against his, till he forgot where he was, and the music and the tread of feet might have been the falling of rain and the roaring of the wind, for what he knew.

But now the third dance was ended, and he might go up to her and claim her hand. She was at the far end of the hall near the staircase, whispering with Molly, who had just given the sleeping Totty into her arms before running to fetch shawls and bonnets from the landing. Mrs. Poyser had taken the two boys away into the dining-room to give them some cake before they went home in the cart with Grandfather and Molly was to follow as fast as possible.

"Let me hold her," said Adam, as Molly turned upstairs; "the children are so heavy when they're asleep."

Hetty was glad of the relief, for to hold Totty in her arms, standing, was not at all a pleasant variety to her. But this second transfer had the unfortunate effect of rousing Totty, who was not behind any child of her age in peevishness at an unseasonable awaking. While Hetty was in the act of placing her in Adam's arms, and had not yet withdrawn her own, Totty opened her eyes, and forthwith fought out with her left fist at Adam's arm, and with her right caught at the string of brown beads round Hetty's neck. The locket leaped out from her frock, and the next moment the string was broken, and Hetty, helpless, saw beads and locket scattered wide on the floor.

"My locket, my locket!" she said, in a loud frightened whisper to Adam; "never mind the beads."

Adam had already seen where the locket fell, for it had attracted his glance as it leaped out of her frock. It had fallen on the raised wooden dais where the band sat, not on the stone floor; and as Adam picked it up, he saw the glass with the dark and light locks of hair under it. It had fallen that side upwards, so the glass was not broken. He turned it over on his hand, and saw the enamelled gold back.

"It isn't hurt," he said, as he held it towards Hetty, who was unable to take it because both her hands were occupied with Totty.

"Oh, it doesn't matter, I don't mind about it," said Hetty, who had been pale and was now red.

"Not matter?" said Adam, gravely. "You seemed very frightened about it. I'll hold it till you're ready to take it," he added, quietly closing his hand over it, that she might not think he wanted to look at it again.

By this time Molly had come with bonnet and shawl, and as soon as she had taken Totty, Adam placed the locket in Hetty's hand. She took it with an air of indifference and put it in her pocket, in her heart vexed and angry with Adam because he had seen it, but determined now that she would show no more signs of agitation.

"See," she said, "they're taking their places to dance; let us go."

Adam assented silently. A puzzled alarm had taken possession of him. Had Hetty a lover he didn't know of? For none of her relations, he was sure, would give her a locket like that; and none of her admirers, with whom he was acquainted, was in the position of an accepted lover, as the giver of that locket must be. Adam was lost in the utter impossibility of finding any person for his fears to alight on. He could only feel with a terrible pang that there was something in Hetty's life unknown to him; that while he had been rocking himself in the hope that she would come to love him, she was already loving another. The pleasure of the dance with Hetty was gone; his eyes, when they rested on her, had an uneasy questioning expression in them; he could think of nothing to say to her; and she too was out of temper and disinclined to speak. They were both glad when the dance was ended.

Adam was determined to stay no longer; no one wanted him, and no one would notice if he slipped away. As soon as he got out of doors, he began to walk at his habitual rapid pace, hurrying along without knowing why, busy with the painful thought that the memory of this day, so full of honour and promise to him, was poisoned for ever. Suddenly, when he was far on through the Chase, he stopped, startled by a flash of reviving hope. After all, he might be a fool, making a great misery out of a trifle. Hetty, fond of finery as she was, might have bought the thing herself. It looked too expensive for that—it looked like the things on white satin in the great jeweller's shop at Rosseter. But Adam had very imperfect notions of the value of such things, and he thought it could certainly not cost more than a guinea. Perhaps Hetty had had as much as that in Christmas boxes, and there was no knowing but she might have been childish enough to spend it in that way; she was such a young thing, and she couldn't help loving finery! But then, why had she been so frightened about it at first, and changed colour so, and afterwards pretended not to care? Oh, that was because she was ashamed of his seeing that she had such a smart thing—she was conscious that it was wrong for her to spend her money on it, and she knew that Adam disapproved of finery. It was a proof she cared about what he liked and disliked. She must have thought from his silence and gravity afterwards that he was very much displeased with her, that he was inclined to be harsh and severe towards her foibles. And as he walked on more quietly, chewing the cud of this new hope, his only uneasiness was that he had behaved in a way which might chill Hetty's feeling towards him. For this last view of the matter must be the true one. How could Hetty have an accepted lover, quite unknown to him? She was never away from her uncle's house for more than a day; she could have no acquaintances that did not come there, and no intimacies unknown to her uncle and aunt. It would be folly to believe that the locket was given to her by a lover. The little ring of dark hair he felt sure was her own; he could form no guess about the light hair under it, for he had not seen it very distinctly. It might be a bit of her father's or mother's, who had died when she was a child, and she would naturally put a bit of her own along with it.

And so Adam went to bed comforted, having woven for himself an ingenious web of probabilities—the surest screen a wise man can place between himself and the truth. His last waking thoughts melted into a dream that he was with Hetty again at the Hall Farm, and that he was asking her to forgive him for being so cold and silent.

And while he was dreaming this, Arthur was leading Hetty to the dance and saying to her in low hurried tones, "I shall be in the wood the day after to-morrow at seven; come as early as you can." And Hetty's foolish joys and hopes, which had flown away for a little space, scared by a mere nothing, now all came fluttering back, unconscious of the real peril. She was happy for the first time this long day, and wished that dance would last for hours. Arthur wished it too; it was the last weakness he meant to indulge in; and a man never lies with more delicious languor under the influence of a passion than when he has persuaded himself that he shall subdue it to-morrow.

But Mrs. Poyser's wishes were quite the reverse of this, for her mind was filled with dreary forebodings as to the retardation of to-morrow morning's cheese in consequence of these late hours. Now that Hetty had done her duty and danced one dance with the young squire, Mr. Poyser must go out and see if the cart was come back to fetch them, for it was half-past ten o'clock, and notwithstanding a mild suggestion on his part that it would be bad manners for them to be the first to go, Mrs. Poyser was resolute on the point, "manners or no manners."

"What! Going already, Mrs. Poyser?" said old Mr. Donnithorne, as she came to curtsy and take leave; "I thought we should not part with any of our guests till eleven. Mrs. Irwine and I, who are elderly people, think of sitting out the dance till then."

"Oh, Your Honour, it's all right and proper for gentlefolks to stay up by candlelight—they've got no cheese on their minds. We're late enough as it is, an' there's no lettin' the cows know as they mustn't want to be milked so early to-morrow mornin'. So, if you'll please t' excuse us, we'll take our leave."

"Eh!" she said to her husband, as they set off in the cart, "I'd sooner ha' brewin' day and washin' day together than one o' these pleasurin' days. There's no work so tirin' as danglin' about an' starin' an' not rightly knowin' what you're goin' to do next; and keepin' your face i' smilin' order like a grocer o' market-day for fear people shouldna think you civil enough. An' you've nothing to show for't when it's done, if it isn't a yallow face wi' eatin' things as disagree."

"Nay, nay," said Mr. Poyser, who was in his merriest mood, and felt that he had had a great day, "a bit o' pleasuring's good for thee sometimes. An' thee danc'st as well as any of 'em, for I'll back thee against all the wives i' the parish for a light foot an' ankle. An' it was a great honour for the young squire to ask thee first—I reckon it was because I sat at th' head o' the table an' made the speech. An' Hetty too—she never had such a partner before—a fine young gentleman in reg'mentals. It'll serve you to talk on, Hetty, when you're an old woman—how you danced wi' th' young squire the day he come o' age."

BOOK FOUR

Chapter XXVII A crisis

IT was beyond the middle of August—nearly three weeks after the birthday feast. The reaping of the wheat had begun in our north midland county of Loamshire, but the harvest was likely still to be retarded by the heavy rains, which were causing inundations and much damage throughout the country. From this last trouble the Broxton and Hayslope farmers, on their pleasant uplands and in their brook-watered valleys, had not suffered, and as I cannot pretend that they were such exceptional farmers as to love the general good better than their own, you will infer that they were not in very low spirits about the rapid rise in the price of bread, so long as there was hope of gathering in their own corn undamaged; and occasional days of sunshine and drying winds flattered this hope.

The eighteenth of August was one of these days when the sunshine looked brighter in all eyes for the gloom that went before. Grand masses of cloud were hurried across the blue, and the great round hills behind the Chase seemed alive with their flying shadows; the sun was hidden for a moment, and then shone out warm again like a recovered joy; the leaves, still green, were tossed off the hedgerow trees by the wind; around the farmhouses there was a sound of clapping doors; the apples fell in the orchards; and the stray horses on the green sides of the lanes and on the common had their manes blown about their faces. And yet the wind seemed only part of the general gladness because the sun was shining. A merry day for the children, who ran and shouted to see if they could top the wind with their voices; and the grown-up people too were in good spirits, inclined to believe in yet finer days, when the wind had fallen. If only the corn were not ripe enough to be blown out of the husk and scattered as untimely seed!

And yet a day on which a blighting sorrow may fall upon a man. For if it be true that Nature at certain moments seems charged with a presentiment of one individual lot must it not also be true that she seems unmindful uncon-scious of another? For there is no hour that has not its births of gladness and despair, no morning brightness that does not bring new sickness to desolation as well as new forces to genius and love. There are so many of us, and our lots are so different, what wonder that Nature's mood is often in harsh contrast with the great crisis of our lives? We are children of a large family, and must learn, as such children do, not to expect that our hurts will be made much of—to be content with little nurture and caressing, and help each other the more.

It was a busy day with Adam, who of late had done almost double work, for he was continuing to act as foreman for Jonathan Burge, until some satisfactory person could be found to supply his place, and Jonathan was slow to find that person. But he had done the extra work cheerfully, for his hopes were buoyant again about Hetty. Every time she had seen him since the birthday, she had seemed to make an effort to behave all the more kindly to him, that she might make him understand she had forgiven his silence and coldness during the dance. He had never mentioned the locket to her again; too happy that she smiled at him—still happier because he observed in her a more subdued air, something that he interpreted as the growth of womanly tenderness and seriousness. "Ah!" he thought, again and again, "she's only seventeen; she'll be thoughtful enough after a while. And her aunt allays says how clever she is at the work. She'll make a wife as Mother'll have no occasion to grumble at, after all." To be sure, he had only seen her at home twice since the birthday; for one Sunday, when he was intending to go from church to the Hall Farm, Hetty had joined the party of upper servants from the Chase and had gone home with them—almost as if she were inclined to encourage Mr. Craig. "She's takin' too much likin' to them folks i' the house keeper's room," Mrs. Poyser remarked. "For my part, I was never overfond o' gentlefolks's servants—they're mostly like the fine ladies' fat dogs, nayther good for barking nor butcher's meat, but on'y for show." And another evening she was gone to Treddleston to buy some things; though, to his great surprise, as he was returning home, he saw her at a distance getting over a stile quite out of the Treddleston road. But, when he hastened to her, she was very kind, and asked him to go in again when he had taken her to the yard gate. She had gone a little farther into the fields after coming from Treddleston because she didn't want to go in, she said: it was so nice to be out of doors, and her aunt always made such a fuss about it if she wanted to go out. "Oh, do come in with me!" she said, as he was going to shake hands with her at the gate, and he could not resist that. So he went in, and Mrs. Poyser was contented with only a slight remark on Hetty's being later than was expected; while Hetty, who had looked out of spirits when he met her, smiled and talked and waited on them all with unusual promptitude.

That was the last time he had seen her; but he meant to make leisure for going to the Farm to-morrow. To-day, he knew, was her day for going to the Chase to sew with the lady's maid, so he would get as much work done as possible this evening, that the next might be clear.

One piece of work that Adam was superintending was some slight repairs at the Chase Farm, which had been hitherto occupied by Satchell, as bailiff, but which it was now rumoured that the old squire was going to let to a smart man in top-boots, who had been seen to ride over it one day. Nothing but the desire to get a tenant could account for the squire's undertaking repairs, though the Saturday-evening party at Mr. Casson's agreed over their pipes that no man in his senses would take the Chase Farm unless there was a bit more ploughland laid to it. However that might be, the repairs were ordered to be executed with all dispatch, and Adam, acting for Mr. Burge, was carrying out the order with his usual energy. But to-day, having been occupied elsewhere, he had not been able to arrive at the Chase Farm till late in the afternoon, and he then discovered that some old roofing, which he had calculated on preserving, had given way. There was clearly no good to be done with this part of the building without pulling it all down, and Adam immediately saw in his mind a plan for building it up again, so as to make the most convenient of cow-sheds and calf-pens, with a hovel for implements; and all without any great expense for materials. So, when the workmen were gone, he sat down, took out his pocket-book, and busied himself with sketching a plan, and making a specification of the expenses that he might show it to Burge the next morning, and set him on persuading the squire to consent. To "make a good job" of anything, however small, was always a pleasure to Adam, and he sat on a block, with his book resting on a planing-table, whistling low every now and then and turning his head on one side with a just perceptible smile of gratification—of pride, too, for if Adam loved a bit of good work, he loved also to think, "I did it!" And I believe the only people who are free from that weakness are those who have no work to call their own. It was nearly seven before he had finished and put on his jacket again; and on giving a last look round, he observed that Seth, who had been working here to-day, had left his basket of tools behind him. "Why, th' lad's forgot his tools," thought Adam, "and he's got to work up at the shop tomorrow. There never was such a chap for wool-gathering; he'd leave his head behind him, if it was loose. However, it's lucky I've seen 'em; I'll carry 'em home."

The buildings of the Chase Farm lay at one extremity of the Chase, at about ten minutes' walking distance from the Abbey. Adam had come thither on his pony, intending to ride to the stables and put up his nag on his way home. At the stables he encountered Mr. Craig, who had come to look at the captain's new horse, on which he was to ride away the day after to-morrow; and Mr. Craig detained him to tell how all the servants were to collect at the gate of the courtyard to wish the young squire luck as he rode out; so that by the time Adam had got into the Chase, and was striding along with the basket of tools over his shoulder, the sun was on the point of setting, and was sending level crimson rays among the great trunks of the old oaks, and touching every bare patch of ground with a transient glory that made it look like a jewel dropt upon the grass. The wind had fallen now, and there was only enough breeze to stir the delicate-stemmed leaves. Any one who had been sitting in the house all day would have been glad to walk now; but Adam had been quite enough in the open air to wish to shorten his way home, and he bethought himself that he might do so by striking across the Chase and going through the Grove, where he had never been for years. He hurried on across the Chase, stalking along the narrow paths between the fern, with Gyp at his heels, not lingering to watch the magnificent changes of the light—hardly once thinking of it—yet feeling its presence in a certain calm happy awe which mingled itself with his busy working-day thoughts. How could he help feeling it? The very deer felt it, and were more timid.

Presently Adam's thoughts recurred to what Mr. Craig had said about Arthur Donnithorne, and pictured his going away, and the changes that might take place before he came back; then they travelled back affectionately over the old scenes of boyish companionship, and dwelt on Arthur's good qualities, which Adam had a pride in, as we all have in the virtues of the superior who honours us. A nature like Adam's, with a great need of love and reverence in it, depends for so much of its happiness on what it can believe and feel about others! And he had no ideal world of dead heroes; he knew little of the life of men in the past; he must find the beings to whom he could cling with loving admiration among those who came within speech of him. These pleasant thoughts about Arthur brought a milder expression than usual into his keen rough face: perhaps they were the reason why, when he opened the old green gate leading into the Grove, he paused to pat Gyp and say a kind word to him.

After that pause, he strode on again along the broad winding path through the Grove. What grand beeches! Adam delighted in a fine tree of all things; as the fisherman's sight is keenest on the sea, so Adam's perceptions were more at home with trees than with other objects. He kept them in his memory, as a painter does, with all the flecks and knots in their bark, all the curves and angles of their boughs, and had often calculated the height and contents of a trunk to a nicety, as he stood looking at it. No wonder that, not-withstanding his desire to get on, he could not help pausing to look at a curious large beech which he had seen standing before him at a turning in the road, and convince himself that it was not two trees wedded together, but only one. For the rest of his life he remembered that moment when he was calmly examining the beech, as a man remembers his last glimpse of the home where his youth was passed, before the road turned, and he saw it no more. The beech stood at the last turning before the Grove ended in an archway of boughs that let in the eastern light; and as Adam stepped away from the tree to continue his walk, his eyes fell on two figures about twenty yards before him.

He remained as motionless as a statue, and turned almost as pale. The two figures were standing opposite to each other, with clasped hands about to part; and while they were bending to kiss, Gyp, who had been running among the brushwood, came out, caught sight of them, and gave a sharp bark. They separated with a start—one hurried through the gate out of the Grove, and the other, turning round, walked slowly, with a sort of saunter, towards Adam who still stood transfixed and pale, clutching tighter the stick with which he held the basket of tools over his shoulder, and looking at the approaching figure with eyes in which amazement was fast turning to fierceness.

Arthur Donnithorne looked flushed and excited; he had tried to make unpleasant feelings more bearable by drinking a little more wine than usual at dinner to-day, and was still enough under its flattering influence to think more lightly of this unwished-for rencontre with Adam than he would otherwise have done. After all, Adam was the best person who could have happened to see him and Hetty together—he was a sensible fellow, and would not babble about it to other people. Arthur felt confident that he could laugh the thing off and explain it away. And so he sauntered forward with elaborate carelessness—his flushed face, his evening dress of fine cloth and fine linen, his hands half-thrust into his waistcoat pockets, all shone upon by the strange evening light which the light clouds had caught up even to the zenith, and were now shedding down between the topmost branches above him.

Adam was still motionless, looking at him as he came up. He understood it all now—the locket and everything else that had been doubtful to him: a terrible scorching light showed him the hidden letters that changed the meaning of the past. If he had moved a muscle, he must inevitably have sprung upon Arthur like a tiger; and in the conflicting emotions that filled those long moments, he had told himself that he would not give loose to passion, he would only speak the right thing. He stood as if petrified by an unseen force, but the force was his own strong will.

"Well, Adam," said Arthur, "you've been looking at the fine old beeches, eh? They're not to be come near by the hatchet, though; this is a sacred grove. I overtook pretty little Hetty Sorrel as I was coming to my den—the Hermitage, there. She ought not to come home this way so late. So I took care of her to the gate, and asked for a kiss for my pains. But I must get back now, for this road is confoundedly damp. Good-night, Adam. I shall see you to-morrow—to say goodbye, you know."

Arthur was too much preoccupied with the part he was playing himself to be thoroughly aware of the expression in Adam's face. He did not look directly at Adam, but glanced carelessly round at the trees and then lifted up one foot to look at the sole of his boot. He cared to say no more—he had thrown quite dust enough into honest Adam's eyes—and as he spoke the last words, he walked on.

"Stop a bit, sir," said Adam, in a hard peremptory voice, without turning round. "I've got a word to say to you."

Arthur paused in surprise. Susceptible persons are more affected by a change of tone than by unexpected words, and Arthur had the susceptibility of a nature at once affectionate and vain. He was still more surprised when he saw that Adam had not moved, but stood with his back to him, as if summoning him to return. What did he mean? He was going to make a serious business of this affair. Arthur felt his temper rising. A patronising disposition always has its meaner side, and in the confusion of his irritation and alarm there entered the feeling that a man to whom he had shown so much favour as to Adam was not in a position to criticize his conduct. And yet he was dominated, as one who feels himself in the wrong always is, by the man whose good opinion he cares for. In spite of pride and temper, there was as much deprecation as anger in his voice when he said, "What do you mean, Adam?"

"I mean, sir"—answered Adam, in the same harsh voice, still without turning round—"I mean, sir, that you don't deceive me by your light words. This is not the first time you've met Hetty Sorrel in this grove, and this is not the first time you've kissed her."

Arthur felt a startled uncertainty how far Adam was speaking from knowledge, and how far from mere inference. And this uncertainty, which prevented him from contriving a prudent answer, heightened his irritation. He said, in a high sharp tone, "Well, sir, what then?"

"Why, then, instead of acting like th' upright, honourable man we've all believed you to be, you've been acting the part of a selfish light-minded scoundrel. You know as well as I do what it's to lead to when a gentleman like you kisses and makes love to a young woman like Hetty, and gives her presents as she's frightened for other folks to see. And I say it again, you're acting the part of a selfish light-minded scoundrel though it cuts me to th' heart to say so, and I'd rather ha' lost my right hand."

"Let me tell you, Adam," said Arthur, bridling his growing anger and trying to recur to his careless tone, "you're not only devilishly impertinent, but you're talking nonsense. Every pretty girl is not such a fool as you, to suppose that when a gentleman admires her beauty and pays her a little attention, he must mean something particular. Every man likes to flirt with a pretty girl, and every pretty girl likes to be flirted with. The wider the distance between them, the less harm there is, for then she's not likely to deceive herself."

"I don't know what you mean by flirting," said Adam, "but if you mean behaving to a woman as if you loved her, and yet not loving her all the while, I say that's not th' action of an honest man, and what isn't honest does come t' harm. I'm not a fool, and you're not a fool, and you know better than what you're saying. You know it couldn't be made public as you've behaved to Hetty as y' have done without her losing her character and bringing shame and trouble on her and her relations. What if you meant nothing by your kissing and your presents? Other folks won't believe as you've meant nothing; and don't tell me about her not deceiving herself. I tell you as you've filled her mind so with the thought of you as it'll mayhap poison her life, and she'll never love another man as 'ud make her a good husband."

Arthur had felt a sudden relief while Adam was speaking; he perceived that Adam had no positive knowledge of the past, and that there was no irrevocable damage done by this evening's unfortunate rencontre. Adam could still be deceived. The candid Arthur had brought himself into a position in which successful lying was his only hope. The hope allayed his anger a little.

"Well, Adam," he said, in a tone of friendly concession, "you're perhaps right. Perhaps I've gone a little too far in taking notice of the pretty little thing and stealing a kiss now and then. You're such a grave, steady fellow, you don't understand the temptation to such trifling. I'm sure I wouldn't bring any trouble or annoyance on her and the good Poysers on any account if I could help it. But I think you look a little too seriously at it. You know I'm going away immediately, so I shan't make any more mistakes of the kind. But let us say good-night"—Arthur here turned round to walk on—"and talk no more about the matter. The whole thing will soon be forgotten."

"No, by God!" Adam burst out with rage that could be controlled no longer, throwing down the basket of tools and striding forward till he was right in front of Arthur. All his jealousy and sense of personal injury, which he had been hitherto trying to keep under, had leaped up and mastered him. What man of us, in the first moments of a sharp agony, could ever feel that the fellow-man who has been the medium of inflicting it did not mean to hurt us? In our instinctive rebellion against pain, we are children again, and demand an active will to wreak our vengeance on. Adam at this moment could only feel that he had been robbed of Hetty—robbed treacherously by the man in whom he had trusted—and he stood close in front of Arthur, with fierce eyes glaring at him, with pale lips and clenched hands, the hard tones in which he had hitherto been constraining himself to express no more than a just indignation giving way to a deep agitated voice that seemed to shake him as he spoke.

"No, it'll not be soon forgot, as you've come in between her and me, when she might ha' loved me—it'll not soon be forgot as you've robbed me o' my happiness, while I thought you was my best friend, and a noble-minded man, as I was proud to work for. And you've been kissing her, and meaning nothing, have you? And I never kissed her i' my life—but I'd ha' worked hard for years for the right to kiss her. And you make light of it. You think little o' doing what may damage other folks, so as you get your bit o' trifling, as means nothing. I throw back your favours, for you're not the man I took you for. I'll never count you my friend any more. I'd rather you'd act as my enemy, and fight me where I stand—it's all th' amends you can make me."

Poor Adam, possessed by rage that could find no other vent, began to throw off his coat and his cap, too blind with passion to notice the change that had taken place in Arthur while he was speaking. Arthur's lips were now as pale as Adam's; his heart was beating violently. The discovery that Adam loved Hetty was a shock which made him for the moment see himself in the light of Adam's indignation, and regard Adam's suffering as not merely a consequence, but an element of his error. The words of hatred and contempt—the first he had ever heard in his life—seemed like scorching missiles that were making ineffaceable scars on him. All screening self-excuse, which rarely falls quite away while others respect us, forsook him for an instant, and he stood face to face with the first great irrevocable evil he had ever committed. He was only twenty-one, and three months ago—nay, much later—he had thought proudly that no man should ever be able to reproach him justly. His first impulse, if there had been time for it, would perhaps have been to utter words of propitiation; but Adam had no sooner thrown off his coat and cap than he became aware that Arthur was standing pale and motionless, with his hands still thrust in his waistcoat pockets.

"What!" he said, "won't you fight me like a man? You know I won't strike you while you stand so."

"Go away, Adam," said Arthur, "I don't want to fight you."

"No," said Adam, bitterly; "you don't want to fight me—you think I'm a common man, as you can injure without answering for it."

"I never meant to injure you," said Arthur, with returning anger. "I didn't know you loved her."

"But you've made her love you," said Adam. "You're a double-faced man—I'll never believe a word you say again."

"Go away, I tell you," said Arthur, angrily, "or we shall both repent."

"No," said Adam, with a convulsed voice, "I swear I won't go away without fighting you. Do you want provoking any more? I tell you you're a coward and a scoundrel, and I despise you."

The colour had all rushed back to Arthur's face; in a moment his right hand was clenched, and dealt a blow like lightning, which sent Adam staggering backward. His blood was as thoroughly up as Adam's now, and the two men, forgetting the emotions that had gone before, fought with the instinctive fierceness of panthers in the deepening twilight darkened by the trees. The delicate-handed gentleman was a match for the workman in everything but strength, and Arthur's skill enabled him to protract the struggle for some long moments. But between unarmed men the battle is to the strong, where the strong is no blunderer, and Arthur must sink under a well-planted blow of Adam's as a steel rod is broken by an iron bar. The blow soon came, and Arthur fell, his head lying concealed in a tuft of fern, so that Adam could only discern his darkly clad body.

He stood still in the dim light waiting for Arthur to rise.

The blow had been given now, towards which he had been straining all the force of nerve and muscle—and what was the good of it? What had he done by fighting? Only satisfied his own passion, only wreaked his own vengeance. He had not rescued Hetty, nor changed the past—there it was, just as it had been, and he sickened at the vanity of his own rage.

But why did not Arthur rise? He was perfectly motionless, and the time seemed long to Adam. Good God! had the blow been too much for him? Adam shuddered at the thought of his own strength, as with the oncoming of this dread he knelt down by Arthur's side and lifted his head from among the fern. There was no sign of life: the eyes and teeth were set. The horror that rushed over Adam completely mastered him, and forced upon him its own belief. He could feel nothing but that death was in Arthur's face, and that he was helpless before it. He made not a single movement, but knelt like an image of despair gazing at an image of death.

Chapter XXVIII A Dilemma

IT was only a few minutes measured by the clock—though Adam always thought it had been a long while—before he perceived a gleam of consciousness in Arthur's face and a slight shiver through his frame. The intense joy that flooded his soul brought back some of the old affection with it.

"Do you feel any pain, sir?" he said, tenderly, loosening Arthur's cravat.

Arthur turned his eyes on Adam with a vague stare which gave way to a slightly startled motion as if from the shock of returning memory. But he only shivered again and said nothing.

"Do you feel any hurt, sir?" Adam said again, with a trembling in his voice.

Arthur put his hand up to his waistcoat buttons, and when Adam had unbuttoned it, he took a longer breath. "Lay my head down," he said, faintly, "and get me some water if you can."

Adam laid the head down gently on the fern again, and emptying the tools out of the flag-basket, hurried through the trees to the edge of the Grove bordering on the Chase, where a brook ran below the bank.

When he returned with his basket leaking, but still half-full, Arthur looked at him with a more thoroughly reawakened consciousness.

"Can you drink a drop out o' your hand, sir?" said Adam, kneeling down again to lift up Arthur's head.

"No," said Arthur, "dip my cravat in and souse it on my head."

The water seemed to do him some good, for he presently raised himself a little higher, resting on Adam's arm.

"Do you feel any hurt inside sir?" Adam asked again

"No—no hurt," said Arthur, still faintly, "but rather done up."

After a while he said, "I suppose I fainted away when you knocked me down."

"Yes, sir, thank God," said Adam. "I thought it was worse."

"What! You thought you'd done for me, eh? Come help me on my legs."

"I feel terribly shaky and dizzy," Arthur said, as he stood leaning on Adam's arm; "that blow of yours must have come against me like a battering-ram. I don't believe I can walk alone."

"Lean on me, sir; I'll get you along," said Adam. "Or, will you sit down a bit longer, on my coat here, and I'll prop y' up. You'll perhaps be better in a minute or two."

"No," said Arthur. "I'll go to the Hermitage—I think I've got some brandy there. There's a short road to it a little farther on, near the gate. If you'll just help me on."

They walked slowly, with frequent pauses, but without speaking again. In both of them, the concentration in the present which had attended the first moments of Arthur's revival had now given way to a vivid recollection of the previous scene. It was nearly dark in the narrow path among the trees, but within the circle of fir-trees round the Hermitage there was room for the growing moonlight to enter in at the windows. Their steps were noiseless on the thick carpet of fir-needles, and the outward stillness seemed to heighten their inward consciousness, as Arthur took the key out of his pocket and placed it in Adam's hand, for him to open the door. Adam had not known before that Arthur had furnished the old Hermitage and made it a retreat for himself, and it was a surprise to him when he opened the door to see a snug room with all the signs of frequent habitation.

Arthur loosed Adam's arm and threw himself on the ottoman. "You'll see my hunting-bottle somewhere," he said. "A leather case with a bottle and glass in."

Adam was not long in finding the case. "There's very little brandy in it, sir," he said, turning it downwards over the glass, as he held it before the window; "hardly this little glassful."

"Well, give me that," said Arthur, with the peevishness of physical depression. When he had taken some sips, Adam said, "Hadn't I better run to th' house, sir, and get some more brandy? I can be there and back pretty soon. It'll be a stiff walk home for you, if you don't have something to revive you."

"Yes—go. But don't say I'm ill. Ask for my man Pym, and tell him to get it from Mills, and not to say I'm at the Hermitage. Get some water too."

Adam was relieved to have an active task—both of them were relieved to be apart from each other for a short time. But Adam's swift pace could not still the eager pain of thinking—of living again with concentrated suffering through the last wretched hour, and looking out from it over all the new sad future.

Arthur lay still for some minutes after Adam was gone, but presently he rose feebly from the ottoman and peered about slowly in the broken moonlight, seeking something. It was a short bit of wax candle that stood amongst a confusion of writing and drawing materials. There was more searching for the means of lighting the candle, and when that was done, he went cautiously round the room, as if wishing to assure himself of the presence or absence of something. At last he had found a slight thing, which he put first in his pocket, and then, on a second thought, took out again and thrust deep down into a waste-paper basket. It was a woman's little, pink, silk neckerchief. He set the candle on the table, and threw himself down on the ottoman again, exhausted with the effort.

When Adam came back with his supplies, his entrance awoke Arthur from a doze.

"That's right," Arthur said; "I'm tremendously in want of some brandy-vigour."

"I'm glad to see you've got a light, sir," said Adam. "I've been thinking I'd better have asked for a lanthorn."

"No, no; the candle will last long enough—I shall soon be up to walking home now."

"I can't go before I've seen you safe home, sir," said Adam, hesitatingly.

"No: it will be better for you to stay—sit down."

Adam sat down, and they remained opposite to each other in uneasy silence, while Arthur slowly drank brandy-and-water, with visibly renovating effect. He began to lie in a more voluntary position, and looked as if he were less overpowered by bodily sensations. Adam was keenly alive to these indications, and as his anxiety about Arthur's condition began to be allayed, he felt more of that impatience which every one knows who has had his just indignation suspended by the physical state of the culprit. Yet there was one thing on his mind to be done before he could recur to remonstrance: it was to confess what had been unjust in his own words. Perhaps he longed all the more to make this confession, that his indignation might be free again; and as he saw the signs of returning ease in Arthur, the words again and again came to his lips and went back, checked by the thought that it would be better to leave everything till to-morrow. As long as they were silent they did not look at each other, and a foreboding came across Adam that if they began to speak as though they remembered the past—if they looked at each other with full recognition—they must take fire again. So they sat in silence till the bit of wax candle flickered low in the socket, the silence all the while becoming more irksome to Adam. Arthur had just poured out some more brandy-and-water, and he threw one arm behind his head and drew up one leg in an attitude of recovered ease, which was an irresistible temptation to Adam to speak what was on his mind.

"You begin to feel more yourself again, sir," he said, as the candle went out and they were half-hidden from each other in the faint moonlight.

"Yes: I don't feel good for much—very lazy, and not inclined to move; but I'll go home when I've taken this dose."

There was a slight pause before Adam said, "My temper got the better of me, and I said things as wasn't true. I'd no right to speak as if you'd known you was doing me an injury: you'd no grounds for knowing it; I've always kept what I felt for her as secret as I could."

He paused again before he went on.

"And perhaps I judged you too harsh—I'm apt to be harsh—and you may have acted out o' thoughtlessness more than I should ha' believed was possible for a man with a heart and a conscience. We're not all put together alike, and we may misjudge one another. God knows, it's all the joy I could have now, to think the best of you."

Arthur wanted to go home without saying any more—he was too painfully embarrassed in mind, as well as too weak in body, to wish for any further explanation to-night. And yet it was a relief to him that Adam reopened the subject in a way the least difficult for him to answer. Arthur was in the wretched position of an open, generous man who has committed an error which makes deception seem a necessity. The native impulse to give truth in return for truth, to meet trust with frank confession, must be suppressed, and duty was becoming a question of tactics. His deed was reacting upon him—was already governing him tyrannously and forcing him into a course that jarred with his habitual feelings. The only aim that seemed admissible to him now was to deceive Adam to the utmost: to make Adam think better of him than he deserved. And when he heard the words of honest retractation—when he heard the sad appeal with which Adam ended—he was obliged to rejoice in the remains of ignorant confidence it implied. He did not answer immediately, for he had to be judicious and not truthful.

"Say no more about our anger, Adam," he said, at last, very languidly, for the labour of speech was unwelcome to him; "I forgive your momentary injustice—it was quite natural, with the exaggerated notions you had in your mind. We shall be none the worse friends in future, I hope, because we've fought. You had the best of it, and that was as it should be, for I believe I've been most in the wrong of the two. Come, let us shake hands."

Arthur held out his hand, but Adam sat still.

"I don't like to say 'No' to that, sir," he said, "but I can't shake hands till it's clear what we mean by't. I was wrong when I spoke as if you'd done me an injury knowingly, but I wasn't wrong in what I said before, about your behaviour t' Hetty, and I can't shake hands with you as if I held you my friend the same as ever till you've cleared that up better."

Arthur swallowed his pride and resentment as he drew back his hand. He was silent for some moments, and then said, as indifferently as he could, "I don't know what you mean by clearing up, Adam. I've told you already that you think too seriously of a little flirtation. But if you are right in supposing there is any danger in it—I'm going away on Saturday, and there will be an end of it. As for the pain it has given you, I'm heartily sorry for it. I can say no more."

Adam said nothing, but rose from his chair and stood with his face towards one of the windows, as if looking at the blackness of the moonlit fir-trees; but he was in reality conscious of nothing but the conflict within him. It was of no use now—his resolution not to speak till to-morrow. He must speak there and then. But it was several minutes before he turned round and stepped nearer to Arthur, standing and looking down on him as he lay.

"It'll be better for me to speak plain," he said, with evident effort, "though it's hard work. You see, sir, this isn't a trifle to me, whatever it may be to you. I'm none o' them men as can go making love first to one woman and then t' another, and don't think it much odds which of 'em I take. What I feel for Hetty's a different sort o' love, such as I believe nobody can know much about but them as feel it and God as has given it to 'em. She's more nor everything else to me, all but my conscience and my good name. And if it's true what you've been saying all along—and if it's only been trifling and flirting as you call it, as 'll be put an end to by your going away—why, then, I'd wait, and hope her heart 'ud turn to me after all. I'm loath to think you'd speak false to me, and I'll believe your word, however things may look."

"You would be wronging Hetty more than me not to believe it," said Arthur, almost violently, starting up from the ottoman and moving away. But he threw himself into a chair again directly, saying, more feebly, "You seem to forget that, in suspecting me, you are casting imputations upon her."

"Nay, sir," Adam said, in a calmer voice, as if he were half-relieved—for he was too straightforward to make a distinction between a direct falsehood and an indirect one—"Nay, sir, things don't lie level between Hetty and you. You're acting with your eyes open, whatever you may do; but how do you know what's been in her mind? She's all but a child—as any man with a conscience in him ought to feel bound to take care on. And whatever you may think, I know you've disturbed her mind. I know she's been fixing her heart on you, for there's a many things clear to me now as I didn't understand before. But you seem to make light o' what she may feel—you don't think o' that."

"Good God, Adam, let me alone!" Arthur burst out impetuously; "I feel it enough without your worrying me."

He was aware of his indiscretion as soon as the words had escaped him.

"Well, then, if you feel it," Adam rejoined, eagerly; "if you feel as you may ha' put false notions into her mind, and made her believe as you loved her, when all the while you meant nothing, I've this demand to make of you—I'm not speaking for myself, but for her. I ask you t' undeceive her before you go away. Y'aren't going away for ever, and if you leave her behind with a notion in her head o' your feeling about her the same as she feels about you, she'll be hankering after you, and the mischief may get worse. It may be a smart to her now, but it'll save her pain i' th' end. I ask you to write a letter—you may trust to my seeing as she gets it. Tell her the truth, and take blame to yourself for behaving as you'd no right to do to a young woman as isn't your equal. I speak plain, sir, but I can't speak any other way. There's nobody can take care o' Hetty in this thing but me."

"I can do what I think needful in the matter," said Arthur, more and more irritated by mingled distress and perplexity, "without giving promises to you. I shall take what measures I think proper."

"No," said Adam, in an abrupt decided tone, "that won't do. I must know what ground I'm treading on. I must be safe as you've put an end to what ought never to ha' been begun. I don't forget what's owing to you as a gentleman, but in this thing we're man and man, and I can't give up."

There was no answer for some moments. Then Arthur said, "I'll see you to-morrow. I can bear no more now; I'm ill." He rose as he spoke, and reached his cap, as if intending to go.

"You won't see her again!" Adam exclaimed, with a flash of recurring anger and suspicion, moving towards the door and placing his back against it. "Either tell me she can never be my wife—tell me you've been lying—or else promise me what I've said."

Adam, uttering this alternative, stood like a terrible fate before Arthur, who had moved forward a step or two, and now stopped, faint, shaken, sick in mind and body. It seemed long to both of them—that inward struggle of Arthur's—before he said, feebly, "I promise; let me go."

Adam moved away from the door and opened it, but when Arthur reached the step, he stopped again and leaned against the door-post.

"You're not well enough to walk alone, sir," said Adam. "Take my arm again."

Arthur made no answer, and presently walked on, Adam following. But, after a few steps, he stood still again, and said, coldly, "I believe I must trouble you. It's getting late now, and there may be an alarm set up about me at home."

Adam gave his arm, and they walked on without uttering a word, till they came where the basket and the tools lay.

"I must pick up the tools, sir," Adam said. "They're my brother's. I doubt they'll be rusted. If you'll please to wait a minute."

Arthur stood still without speaking, and no other word passed between them till they were at the side entrance, where he hoped to get in without being seen by any one. He said then, "Thank you; I needn't trouble you any further."

"What time will it be conven'ent for me to see you to-morrow, sir?" said Adam.

"You may send me word that you're here at five o'clock," said Arthur; "not before."

"Good-night, sir," said Adam. But he heard no reply; Arthur had turned into the house.

Chapter XXIX The Next Morning

ARTHUR did not pass a sleepless night; he slept long and well. For sleep comes to the perplexed—if the perplexed are only weary enough. But at seven he rang his bell and astonished Pym by declaring he was going to get up, and must have breakfast brought to him at eight.

"And see that my mare is saddled at half-past eight, and tell my grandfather when he's down that I'm better this morning and am gone for a ride."

He had been awake an hour, and could rest in bed no longer. In bed our yesterdays are too oppressive: if a man can only get up, though it be but to whistle or to smoke, he has a present which offers some resistance to the past—sensations which assert themselves against tyrannous memories. And if there were such a thing as taking averages of feeling, it would certainly be found that in the hunting and shooting seasons regret, self-reproach, and mortified pride weigh lighter on country gentlemen than in late spring and summer. Arthur felt that he should be more of a man on horseback. Even the presence of Pym, waiting on him with the usual deference, was a reassurance to him after the scenes of yesterday. For, with Arthur's sensitiveness to opinion, the loss of Adam's respect was a shock to his self-contentment which suffused his imagination with the sense that he had sunk in all eyes—as a sudden shock of fear from some real peril makes a nervous woman afraid even to step, because all her perceptions are suffused with a sense of danger.

Arthur's, as you know, was a loving nature. Deeds of kindness were as easy to him as a bad habit: they were the common issue of his weaknesses and good qualities, of his egoism and his sympathy. He didn't like to witness pain, and he liked to have grateful eyes beaming on him as the giver of pleasure. When he was a lad of seven, he one day kicked down an old gardener's pitcher of broth, from no motive but a kicking impulse, not reflecting that it was the old man's dinner; but on learning that sad fact, he took his favourite pencil-case and a silver-hafted knife out of his pocket and offered them as compensation. He had been the same Arthur ever since, trying to make all offences forgotten in benefits. If there were any bitterness in his nature, it could only show itself against the man who refused to be conciliated by him. And perhaps the time was come for some of that bitterness to rise. At the first moment, Arthur had felt pure distress and self-reproach at discovering that Adam's happiness was involved in his relation to Hetty. If there had been a possibility of making Adam tenfold amends—if deeds of gift, or any other deeds, could have restored Adam's contentment and regard for him as a benefactor, Arthur would not only have executed them without hesitation, but would have felt bound all the more closely to Adam, and would never have been weary of making retribution. But Adam could receive no amends; his suffering could not be cancelled; his respect and affection could not be recovered by any prompt deeds of atonement. He stood like an immovable obstacle against which no pressure could avail; an embodiment of what Arthur most shrank from believing in—the irrevocableness of his own wrongdoing. The words of scorn, the refusal to shake hands, the mastery asserted over him in their last conversation in the Hermitage—above all, the sense of having been knocked down, to which a man does not very well reconcile himself, even under the most heroic circumstances—pressed on him with a galling pain which was stronger than compunction. Arthur would so gladly have persuaded himself that he had done no harm! And if no one had told him the contrary, he could have persuaded himself so much better. Nemesis can seldom forge a sword for herself out of our consciences—out of the suffering we feel in the suffering we may have caused: there is rarely metal enough there to make an effective weapon. Our moral sense learns the manners of good society and smiles when others smile, but when some rude person gives rough names to our actions, she is apt to take part against us. And so it was with Arthur: Adam's judgment of him, Adam's grating words, disturbed his self-soothing arguments.

Not that Arthur had been at ease before Adam's discovery. Struggles and resolves had transformed themselves into compunction and anxiety. He was distressed for Hetty's sake, and distressed for his own, that he must leave her behind. He had always, both in making and breaking resolutions, looked beyond his passion and seen that it must speedily end in separation; but his nature was too ardent and tender for him not to suffer at this parting; and on Hetty's account he was filled with uneasiness. He had found out the dream in which she was living—that she was to be a lady in silks and satins—and when he had first talked to her about his going away, she had asked him tremblingly to let her go with him and be married. It was his painful knowledge of this which had given the most exasperating sting to Adam's reproaches. He had said no word with the purpose of deceiving her—her vision was all spun by her own childish fancy—but he was obliged to confess to himself that it was spun half out of his own actions. And to increase the mischief, on this last evening he had not dared to hint the truth to Hetty; he had been obliged to soothe her with tender, hopeful words, lest he should throw her into violent distress. He felt the situation acutely, felt the sorrow of the dear thing in the present, and thought with a darker anxiety of the tenacity which her feelings might have in the future. That was the one sharp point which pressed against him; every other he could evade by hopeful self-persuasion. The whole thing had been secret; the Poysers had not the shadow of a suspicion. No one, except Adam, knew anything of what had passed—no one else was likely to know; for Arthur had impressed on Hetty that it would be fatal to betray, by word or look, that there had been the least intimacy between them; and Adam, who knew half their secret, would rather help them to keep it than betray it. It was an unfortunate business altogether, but there was no use in making it worse than it was by imaginary exaggerations and forebodings of evil that might never come. The temporary sadness for Hetty was the worst consequence; he resolutely turned away his eyes from any bad consequence that was not demonstrably inevitable. But—but

Hetty might have had the trouble in some other way if not in this. And perhaps hereafter he might be able to do a great deal for her and make up to her for all the tears she would shed about him. She would owe the advantage of his care for her in future years to the sorrow she had incurred now. So good comes out of evil. Such is the beautiful arrangement of things!

Are you inclined to ask whether this can be the same Arthur who, two months ago, had that freshness of feeling, that delicate honour which shrinks from wounding even a sentiment, and does not contemplate any more positive offence as possible for it?—who thought that his own self-respect was a higher tribunal than any external opinion? The same, I assure you, only under different conditions. Our deeds determine us, as much as we determine our deeds, and until we know what has been or will be the peculiar combination of outward with inward facts, which constitutes a man's critical actions, it will be better not to think ourselves wise about his character. There is a terrible coercion in our deeds, which may first turn the honest man into a deceiver and then reconcile him to the change, for this reason—that the second wrong presents itself to him in the guise of the only practicable right. The action which before commission has been seen with that blended common sense and fresh untarnished feeling which is the healthy eye of the soul, is looked at afterwards with the lens of apologetic ingenuity, through which all things that men call beautiful and ugly are seen to be made up of textures very much alike. Europe adjusts itself to a fait accompli, and so does an individual character—until the placid adjustment is disturbed by a convulsive retribution.

No man can escape this vitiating effect of an offence against his own sentiment of right, and the effect was the stronger in Arthur because of that very need of self-respect which, while his conscience was still at ease, was one of his best safeguards. Self-accusation was too painful to him—he could not face it. He must persuade himself that he had not been very much to blame; he began even to pity himself for the necessity he was under of deceiving Adam—it was a course so opposed to the honesty of his own nature. But then, it was the only right thing to do.

Well, whatever had been amiss in him, he was miserable enough in consequence: miserable about Hetty; miserable about this letter that he had promised to write, and that seemed at one moment to be a gross barbarity, at another perhaps the greatest kindness he could do to her. And across all this reflection would dart every now and then a sudden impulse of passionate defiance towards all consequences. He would carry Hetty away, and all other considerations might go to . . .

In this state of mind the four walls of his room made an intolerable prison to him; they seemed to hem in and press down upon him all the crowd of contradictory thoughts and conflicting feelings, some of which would fly away in the open air. He had only an hour or two to make up his mind in, and he must get clear and calm. Once on Meg's back, in the fresh air of that fine morning, he should be more master of the situation.

The pretty creature arched her bay neck in the sunshine, and pawed the gravel, and trembled with pleasure when her master stroked her nose, and patted her, and talked to her even in a more caressing tone than usual. He loved her the better because she knew nothing of his secrets. But Meg was quite as well acquainted with her master's mental state as many others of her sex with the mental condition of the nice young gentlemen towards whom their hearts are in a state of fluttering expectation.

Arthur cantered for five miles beyond the Chase, till he was at the foot of a hill where there were no hedges or trees to hem in the road. Then he threw the bridle on Meg's neck and prepared to make up his mind.

Hetty knew that their meeting yesterday must be the last before Arthur went away—there was no possibility of their contriving another without exciting suspicion—and she was like a frightened child, unable to think of anything, only able to cry at the mention of parting, and then put her face up to have the tears kissed away. He could do nothing but comfort her, and lull her into dreaming on. A letter would be a dreadfully abrupt way of awakening her! Yet there was truth in what Adam said—that it would save her from a lengthened delusion, which might be worse than a sharp immediate pain. And it was the only way of satisfying Adam, who must be satisfied, for more reasons than one. If he could have seen her again! But that was impossible; there was such a thorny hedge of hindrances between them, and an imprudence would be fatal. And yet, if he COULD see her again, what good would it do? Only cause him to suffer more from the sight of her distress and the remembrance of it. Away from him she was surrounded by all the motives to self-control.

A sudden dread here fell like a shadow across his imagination—the dread lest she should do something violent in her grief; and close upon that dread came another, which deepened the shadow. But he shook them off with the force of youth and hope. What was the ground for painting the future in that dark way? It was just as likely to be the reverse. Arthur told himself he did not deserve that things should turn out badly. He had never meant beforehand to do anything his conscience disapproved; he had been led on by circumstances. There was a sort of implicit confidence in him that he was really such a good fellow at bottom, Providence would not treat him harshly.

At all events, he couldn't help what would come now: all he could do was to take what seemed the best course at the present moment. And he persuaded himself that that course was to make the way open between Adam and Hetty. Her heart might really turn to Adam, as he said, after a while; and in that case there would have been no great harm done, since it was still Adam's ardent wish to make her his wife. To be sure, Adam was deceived—deceived in a way that Arthur would have resented as a deep wrong if it had been practised on himself. That was a reflection that marred the consoling prospect. Arthur's cheeks even burned in mingled shame and irritation at the thought. But what could a man do in such a dilemma? He was bound in honour to say no word that could injure Hetty: his first duty was to guard her. He would never have told or acted a lie on his own account. Good God! What a miserable fool he was to have brought himself into such a dilemma; and yet, if ever a man had excuses, he had. (Pity that consequences are determined not by excuses but by actions!)

Well, the letter must be written; it was the only means that promised a solution of the difficulty. The tears came into Arthur's eyes as he thought of Hetty reading it; but it would be almost as hard for him to write it; he was not doing anything easy to himself; and this last thought helped him to arrive at a conclusion. He could never deliberately have taken a step which inflicted pain on another and left himself at ease. Even a movement of jealousy at the thought of giving up Hetty to Adam went to convince him that he was making a sacrifice.

When once he had come to this conclusion, he turned Meg round and set off home again in a canter. The letter should be written the first thing, and the rest of the day would be filled up with other business: he should have no time to look behind him. Happily, Irwine and Gawaine were coming to dinner, and by twelve o'clock the next day he should have left the Chase miles behind him. There was some security in this constant occupation against an uncontrollable impulse seizing him to rush to Hetty and thrust into her hand some mad proposition that would undo everything. Faster and faster went the sensitive Meg, at every slight sign from her rider, till the canter had passed into a swift gallop.

"I thought they said th' young mester war took ill last night," said sour old John, the groom, at dinner-time in the servants' hall. "He's been ridin' fit to split the mare i' two this forenoon."

"That's happen one o' the symptims, John," said the facetious coachman.

"Then I wish he war let blood for 't, that's all," said John, grimly.

Adam had been early at the Chase to know how Arthur was, and had been relieved from all anxiety about the effects of his blow by learning that he was gone out for a ride. At five o'clock he was punctually there again, and sent up word of his arrival. In a few minutes Pym came down with a letter in his hand and gave it to Adam, saying that the captain was too busy to see him, and had written everything he had to say. The letter was directed to Adam, but he went out of doors again before opening it. It contained a sealed enclosure directed to Hetty. On the inside of the cover Adam read:

"In the enclosed letter I have written everything you wish. I leave it to you to decide whether you will be doing best to deliver it to Hetty or to return it to me. Ask yourself once more whether you are not taking a measure which may pain her more than mere silence.

"There is no need for our seeing each other again now. We shall meet with better feelings some months hence. A.D."

"Perhaps he's i' th' right on 't not to see me," thought Adam. "It's no use meeting to say more hard words, and it's no use meeting to shake hands and say we're friends again. We're not friends, an' it's better not to pretend it. I know forgiveness is a man's duty, but, to my thinking, that can only mean as you're to give up all thoughts o' taking revenge: it can never mean as you're t' have your old feelings back again, for that's not possible. He's not the same man to me, and I can't feel the same towards him. God help me! I don't know whether I feel the same towards anybody: I seem as if I'd been measuring my work from a false line, and had got it all to measure over again."

But the question about delivering the letter to Hetty soon absorbed Adam's thoughts. Arthur had procured some relief to himself by throwing the decision on Adam with a warning; and Adam, who was not given to hesitation, hesitated here. He determined to feel his way—to ascertain as well as he could what was Hetty's state of mind before he decided on delivering the letter.

Chapter XXX The Delivery of the Letter

THE next Sunday Adam joined the Poysers on their way out of church, hoping for an invitation to go home with them. He had the letter in his pocket, and was anxious to have an opportunity of talking to Hetty alone. He could not see her face at church, for she had changed her seat, and when he came up to her to shake hands, her manner was doubtful and constrained. He expected this, for it was the first time she had met him since she had been aware that he had seen her with Arthur in the Grove.

"Come, you'll go on with us, Adam," Mr. Poyser said when they reached the turning; and as soon as they were in the fields Adam ventured to offer his arm to Hetty. The children soon gave them an opportunity of lingering behind a little, and then Adam said:

"Will you contrive for me to walk out in the garden a bit with you this evening, if it keeps fine, Hetty? I've something partic'lar to talk to you about."

Hetty said, "Very well." She was really as anxious as Adam was that she should have some private talk with him. She wondered what he thought of her and Arthur. He must have seen them kissing, she knew, but she had no conception of the scene that had taken place between Arthur and Adam. Her first feeling had been that Adam would be very angry with her, and perhaps would tell her aunt and uncle, but it never entered her mind that he would dare to say anything to Captain Donnithorne. It was a relief to her that he behaved so kindly to her to-day, and wanted to speak to her alone, for she had trembled when she found he was going home with them lest he should mean "to tell." But, now he wanted to talk to her by herself, she should learn what he thought and what he meant to do. She felt a certain confidence that she could persuade him not to do anything she did not want him to do; she could perhaps even make him believe that she didn't care for Arthur; and as long as Adam thought there was any hope of her having him, he would do just what she liked, she knew. Besides, she MUST go on seeming to encourage Adam, lest her uncle and aunt should be angry and suspect her of having some secret lover.

Hetty's little brain was busy with this combination as she hung on Adam's arm and said "yes" or "no" to some slight observations of his about the many hawthorn-berries there would be for the birds this next winter, and the low-hanging clouds that would hardly hold up till morning. And when they rejoined her aunt and uncle, she could pursue her thoughts without interruption, for Mr. Poyser held that though a young man might like to have the woman he was courting on his arm, he would nevertheless be glad of a little reasonable talk about business the while; and, for his own part, he was curious to heal the most recent news about the Chase Farm. So, through the rest of the walk, he claimed Adam's conversation for himself, and Hetty laid her small plots and imagined her little scenes of cunning blandishment, as she walked along by the hedgerows on honest Adam's arm, quite as well as if she had been an elegantly clad coquette alone in her boudoir. For if a country beauty in clumsy shoes be only shallow-hearted enough, it is astonishing how closely her mental processes may resemble those of a lady in society and crinoline, who applies her refined intellect to the problem of committing indiscretions without compromising herself. Perhaps the resemblance was not much the less because Hetty felt very unhappy all the while. The parting with Arthur was a double pain to her—mingling with the tumult of passion and vanity there was a dim undefined fear that the future might shape itself in some way quite unlike her dream. She clung to the comforting hopeful words Arthur had uttered in their last meeting—"I shall come again at Christmas, and then we will see what can be done." She clung to the belief that he was so fond of her, he would never be happy without her; and she still hugged her secret—that a great gentleman loved her—with gratified pride, as a superiority over all the girls she knew. But the uncertainty of the future, the possibilities to which she could give no shape, began to press upon her like the invisible weight of air; she was alone on her little island of dreams, and all around her was the dark unknown water where Arthur was gone. She could gather no elation of spirits now by looking forward, but only by looking backward to build confidence on past words and caresses. But occasionally, since Thursday evening, her dim anxieties had been almost lost behind the more definite fear that Adam might betray what he knew to her uncle and aunt, and his sudden proposition to talk with her alone had set her thoughts to work in a new way. She was eager not to lose this evening's opportunity; and after tea, when the boys were going into the garden and Totty begged to go with them, Hetty said, with an alacrity that surprised Mrs. Poyser, "I'll go with her, Aunt."

It did not seem at all surprising that Adam said he would go too, and soon he and Hetty were left alone together on the walk by the filbert-trees, while the boys were busy elsewhere gathering the large unripe nuts to play at "cob-nut" with, and Totty was watching them with a puppylike air of contemplation. It was but a short time—hardly two months—since Adam had had his mind filled with delicious hopes as he stood by Hetty's side un this garden. The remembrance of that scene had often been with him since Thursday evening: the sunlight through the apple-tree boughs, the red bunches, Hetty's sweet blush. It came importunately now, on this sad evening, with the low-hanging clouds, but he tried to suppress it, lest some emotion should impel him to say more than was needful for Hetty's sake.

"After what I saw on Thursday night, Hetty," he began, "you won't think me making too free in what I'm going to say. If you was being courted by any man as 'ud make you his wife, and I'd known you was fond of him and meant to have him, I should have no right to speak a word to you about it; but when I see you're being made love to by a gentleman as can never marry you, and doesna think o' marrying you, I feel bound t' interfere for you. I can't speak about it to them as are i' the place o' your parents, for that might bring worse trouble than's needful."

Adam's words relieved one of Hetty's fears, but they also carried a meaning which sickened her with a strengthened foreboding. She was pale and trembling, and yet she would have angrily contradicted Adam, if she had dared to betray her feelings. But she was silent.

"You're so young, you know, Hetty," he went on, almost tenderly, "and y' haven't seen much o' what goes on in the world. It's right for me to do what I can to save you from getting into trouble for want o' your knowing where you're being led to. If anybody besides me knew what I know about your meeting a gentleman and having fine presents from him, they'd speak light on you, and you'd lose your character. And besides that, you'll have to suffer in your feelings, wi' giving your love to a man as can never marry you, so as he might take care of you all your life."

Adam paused and looked at Hetty, who was plucking the leaves from the filbert-trees and tearing them up in her hand. Her little plans and preconcerted speeches had all forsaken her, like an ill-learnt lesson, under the terrible agitation produced by Adam's words. There was a cruel force in their calm certainty which threatened to grapple and crush her flimsy hopes and fancies. She wanted to resist them—she wanted to throw them off with angry contradiction—but the determination to conceal what she felt still governed her. It was nothing more than a blind prompting now, for she was unable to calculate the effect of her words.

"You've no right to say as I love him," she said, faintly, but impetuously, plucking another rough leaf and tearing it up. She was very beautiful in her paleness and agitation, with her dark childish eyes dilated and her breath shorter than usual. Adam's heart yearned over her as he looked at her. Ah, if he could but comfort her, and soothe her, and save her from this pain; if he had but some sort of strength that would enable him to rescue her poor troubled mind, as he would have rescued her body in the face of all danger!

"I doubt it must be so, Hetty," he said, tenderly; "for I canna believe you'd let any man kiss you by yourselves, and give you a gold box with his hair, and go a-walking i' the Grove to meet him, if you didna love him. I'm not blaming you, for I know it 'ud begin by little and little, till at last you'd not be able to throw it off. It's him I blame for stealing your love i' that way, when he knew he could never make you the right amends. He's been trifling with you, and making a plaything of you, and caring nothing about you as a man ought to care."

"Yes, he does care for me; I know better nor you," Hetty burst out. Everything was forgotten but the pain and anger she felt at Adam's words.

"Nay, Hetty," said Adam, "if he'd cared for you rightly, he'd never ha' behaved so. He told me himself he meant nothing by his kissing and presents, and he wanted to make me believe as you thought light of 'em too. But I know better nor that. I can't help thinking as you've been trusting to his loving you well enough to marry you, for all he's a gentleman. And that's why I must speak to you about it, Hetty, for fear you should be deceiving yourself. It's never entered his head the thought o' marrying you."

"How do you know? How durst you say so?" said Hetty, pausing in her walk and trembling. The terrible decision of Adam's tone shook her with fear. She had no presence of mind left for the reflection that Arthur would have his reasons for not telling the truth to Adam. Her words and look were enough to determine Adam: he must give her the letter.

"Perhaps you can't believe me, Hetty, because you think too well of him—because you think he loves you better than he does. But I've got a letter i' my pocket, as he wrote himself for me to give you. I've not read the letter, but he says he's told you the truth in it. But before I give you the letter, consider, Hetty, and don't let it take too much hold on you. It wouldna ha' been good for you if he'd wanted to do such a mad thing as marry you: it 'ud ha' led to no happiness i' th' end."

Hetty said nothing; she felt a revival of hope at the mention of a letter which Adam had not read. There would be something quite different in it from what he thought.

Adam took out the letter, but he held it in his hand still, while he said, in a tone of tender entreaty, "Don't you bear me ill will, Hetty, because I'm the means o' bringing you this pain. God knows I'd ha' borne a good deal worse for the sake o' sparing it you. And think—

there's nobody but me knows about this, and I'll take care of you as if I was your brother. You're the same as ever to me, for I don't believe you've done any wrong knowingly."

Hetty had laid her hand on the letter, but Adam did not loose it till he had done speaking. She took no notice of what he said—she had not listened; but when he loosed the letter, she put it into her pocket, without opening it, and then began to walk more quickly, as if she wanted to go in.

"You're in the right not to read it just yet," said Adam. "Read it when you're by yourself. But stay out a little bit longer, and let us call the children: you look so white and ill, your aunt may take notice of it."

Hetty heard the warning. It recalled to her the necessity of rallying her native powers of concealment, which had half given way under the shock of Adam's words. And she had the letter in her pocket: she was sure there was comfort in that letter in spite of Adam. She ran to find Totty, and soon reappeared with recovered colour, leading Totty, who was making a sour face because she had been obliged to throw away an unripe apple that she had set her small teeth in.

"Hegh, Totty," said Adam, "come and ride on my shoulder—ever so high—you'll touch the tops o' the trees."

What little child ever refused to be comforted by that glorious sense of being seized strongly and swung upward? I don't believe Ganymede cried when the eagle carried him away, and perhaps deposited him on Jove's shoulder at the end. Totty smiled down complacently from her secure height, and pleasant was the sight to the mother's eyes, as she stood at the house door and saw Adam coming with his small burden.

"Bless your sweet face, my pet," she said, the mother's strong love filling her keen eyes with mildness, as Totty leaned forward and put out her arms. She had no eyes for Hetty at that moment, and only said, without looking at her, "You go and draw some ale, Hetty; the gells are both at the cheese."

After the ale had been drawn and her uncle's pipe lighted, there was Totty to be taken to bed, and brought down again in her nightgown because she would cry instead of going to sleep. Then there was supper to be got ready, and Hetty must be continually in the way to give help. Adam stayed till he knew Mrs. Poyser expected him to go, engaging her and her husband in talk as constantly as he could, for the sake of leaving Hetty more at ease. He lingered, because he wanted to see her safely through that evening, and he was delighted to find how much self-command she showed. He knew she had not had time to read the letter, but he did not know she was buoyed up by a secret hope that the letter would contradict everything he had said. It was hard work for him to leave her—hard to think that he should not know for days how she was bearing her trouble. But he must go at last, and all he could do was to press her hand gently as he said "Good-bye," and hope she would take that as a sign that if his love could ever be a refuge for her, it was there the same as ever. How busy his thoughts were, as he walked home, in devising pitying excuses for her folly, in referring all her weakness to the sweet lovingness of her nature, in blaming Arthur, with less and less inclination to admit that his conduct might be extenuated too! His exasperation at Hetty's suffering—and also at the sense that she was possibly thrust for ever out of his own reach—deafened him to any plea for the miscalled friend who had wrought this misery. Adam was a clear-sighted, fair-minded man—a fine fellow, indeed, morally as well as physically. But if Aristides the Just was ever in love and jealous, he was at that moment not perfectly magnanimous. And I cannot pretend that Adam, in these painful days, felt nothing but righteous indignation and loving pity. He was bitterly jealous, and in proportion as his love made him indulgent in his judgment of Hetty, the bitterness found a vent in his feeling towards Arthur.

"Her head was allays likely to be turned," he thought, "when a gentleman, with his fine manners, and fine clothes, and his white hands, and that way o' talking gentlefolks have, came about her, making up to her in a bold way, as a man couldn't do that was only her equal; and it's much if she'll ever like a common man now." He could not help drawing his own hands out of his pocket and looking at them—at the hard palms and the broken finger-nails. "I'm a roughish fellow, altogether; I don't know, now I come to think on't, what there is much for a woman to like about me; and yet I might ha' got another wife easy enough, if I hadn't set my heart on her. But it's little matter what other women think about me, if she can't love me. She might ha' loved me, perhaps, as likely as any other man—there's nobody hereabouts as I'm afraid of, if he hadn't come between us; but now I shall belike be hateful to her because I'm so different to him. And yet there's no telling—she may turn round the other way, when she finds he's made light of her all the while. She may come to feel the vally of a man as 'ud be thankful to be bound to her all his life. But I must put up with it whichever way it is—I've only to be thankful it's been no worse. I am not th' only man that's got to do without much happiness i' this life. There's many a good bit o' work done with a bad heart. It's God's will, and that's enough for us: we shouldn't know better how things ought to be than He does, I reckon, if we was to spend our lives i' puzzling. But it 'ud ha' gone near to spoil my work for me, if I'd seen her brought to sorrow and shame, and through the man as I've always been proud to think on. Since I've been spared that, I've no right to grumble. When a man's got his limbs whole, he can bear a smart cut or two."

As Adam was getting over a stile at this point in his reflections, he perceived a man walking along the field before him. He knew it was Seth, returning from an evening preaching, and made haste to overtake him.

"I thought thee'dst be at home before me," he said, as Seth turned round to wait for him, "for I'm later than usual to-night."

"Well, I'm later too, for I got into talk, after meeting, with John Barnes, who has lately professed himself in a state of perfection, and I'd a question to ask him about his experience. It's one o' them subjects that lead you further than y' expect—they don't lie along the straight road."

They walked along together in silence two or three minutes. Adam was not inclined to enter into the subtleties of religious experience, but he was inclined to interchange a word or two of brotherly affection and confidence with Seth. That was a rare impulse in him, much as the brothers loved each other. They hardly ever spoke of personal matters, or uttered more than an allusion to their family troubles. Adam was by nature reserved in all matters of feeling, and Seth felt a certain timidity towards his more practical brother.

"Seth, lad," Adam said, putting his arm on his brother's shoulder, "hast heard anything from Dinah Morris since she went away?"

"Yes," said Seth. "She told me I might write her word after a while, how we went on, and how mother bore up under her trouble. So I wrote to her a fortnight ago, and told her about thee having a new employment, and how Mother was more contented; and last Wednesday, when I called at the post at Treddles'on, I found a letter from her. I think thee'dst perhaps like to read it, but I didna say anything about it because thee'st seemed so full of other things. It's quite easy t' read—she writes wonderful for a woman."

Seth had drawn the letter from his pocket and held it out to Adam, who said, as he took it, "Aye, lad, I've got a tough load to carry just now—thee mustna take it ill if I'm a bit silenter and crustier nor usual. Trouble doesna make me care the less for thee. I know we shall stick together to the last."

"I take nought ill o' thee, Adam. I know well enough what it means if thee't a bit short wi' me now and then."

"There's Mother opening the door to look out for us," said Adam, as they mounted the slope. "She's been sitting i' the dark as usual. Well, Gyp, well, art glad to see me?"

Lisbeth went in again quickly and lighted a candle, for she had heard the welcome rustling of footsteps on the grass, before Gyp's joyful bark.

"Eh, my lads! Th' hours war ne'er so long sin' I war born as they'n been this blessed Sunday night. What can ye both ha' been doin' till this time?"

"Thee shouldstna sit i' the dark, Mother," said Adam; "that makes the time seem longer."

"Eh, what am I to do wi' burnin' candle of a Sunday, when there's on'y me an' it's sin to do a bit o' knittin'? The daylight's long enough for me to stare i' the booke as I canna read. It 'ud be a fine way o' shortenin' the time, to make it waste the good candle. But which on you's for ha'in' supper? Ye mun ayther be clemmed or full, I should think, seein' what time o' night it is."

"I'm hungry, Mother," said Seth, seating himself at the little table, which had been spread ever since it was light.

"I've had my supper," said Adam. "Here, Gyp," he added, taking some cold potato from the table and rubbing the rough grey head that looked up towards him.

"Thee needstna be gi'in' th' dog," said Lisbeth; "I'n fed him well a'ready. I'm not like to forget him, I reckon, when he's all o' thee I can get sight on."

"Come, then, Gyp," said Adam, "we'll go to bed. Good-night, Mother; I'm very tired."

"What ails him, dost know?" Lisbeth said to Seth, when Adam was gone upstairs. "He's like as if he was struck for death this day or two—he's so cast down. I found him i' the shop this forenoon, arter thee wast gone, a-sittin' an' doin' nothin'—not so much as a booke afore him."

"He's a deal o' work upon him just now, Mother," said Seth, "and I think he's a bit troubled in his mind. Don't you take notice of it, because it hurts him when you do. Be as kind to him as you can, Mother, and don't say anything to vex him."

"Eh, what dost talk o' my vexin' him? An' what am I like to be but kind? I'll ma' him a kettle-cake for breakfast i' the mornin'."

Adam, meanwhile, was reading Dinah's letter by the light of his dip candle.

"DEAR BROTHER SETH—Your letter lay three days beyond my knowing of it at the post, for I had not money enough by me to pay the carriage, this being a time of great need and sickness here, with the rains that have fallen, as if the windows of heaven were opened again; and to lay by money, from day to day, in such a time, when there are so many in present need of all things, would be a want of trust like the laying up of the manna. I speak of this, because I would not have you think me slow to answer, or that I had small joy in your rejoicing at the worldly good that has befallen your brother Adam. The honour and love you bear him is nothing but meet, for God has given him great gifts, and he uses them as the patriarch Joseph did, who, when he was exalted to a place of power and trust, yet yearned with tenderness towards his parent and his younger brother.

"My heart is knit to your aged mother since it was granted me to be near her in the day of trouble. Speak to her of me, and tell her I often bear her in my thoughts at evening time, when I am sitting in the dim light as I did with her, and we held one another's hands, and I spoke the words of comfort that were given to me. Ah, that is a blessed time, isn't it, Seth, when the outward light is fading, and the body is a little wearied with its work and its labour. Then the inward light shines the brighter, and we have a deeper sense of resting on the Divine strength. I sit on my chair in the dark room and close my eyes, and it is as if I was out of the body and could feel no want for evermore. For then, the very hardship, and the sorrow, and the blindness, and the sin I have beheld and been ready to weep over—yea, all the anguish of the children of men, which sometimes wraps me round like sudden darkness—I can bear with a willing pain, as if I was sharing the Redeemer's cross. For I feel it, I feel it—infinite love is suffering too—yea, in the fulness of knowledge it suffers, it yearns, it mourns; and that is a blind self-seeking which wants to be freed from the sorrow wherewith the whole creation groaneth and travaileth. Surely it is not true blessedness to be free from sorrow, while there is sorrow and sin in the world: sorrow is then a part of love, and love does not seek to throw it off. It is not the spirit only that tells me this—I see it in the whole work and word of the Gospel. Is there not pleading in heaven? Is not the Man of Sorrows there in that crucified body wherewith he ascended? And is He not one with the Infinite Love itself—as our love is one with our sorrow?

"These thoughts have been much borne in on me of late, and I have seen with new clearness the meaning of those words, 'If any man love me, let him take up my cross.' I have heard this enlarged on as if it meant the troubles and persecutions we bring on ourselves by confessing Jesus. But surely that is a narrow thought. The true cross of the Redeemer was the sin and sorrow of this world—that was what lay heavy on his heart—and that is the cross we shall share with him, that is the cup we must drink of with him, if we would have any part in that Divine Love which is one with his sorrow.

"In my outward lot, which you ask about, I have all things and abound. I have had constant work in the mill, though some of the other hands have been turned off for a time, and my body is greatly strengthened, so that I feel little weariness after long walking and speaking. What you say about staying in your own country with your mother and brother shows me that you have a true guidance; your lot is appointed there by a clear showing, and to seek a greater blessing elsewhere would be like laying a false offering on the altar and expecting the fire from heaven to kindle it. My work and my joy are here among the hills, and I sometimes think I cling too much to my life among the people here, and should be rebellious if I was called away.

"I was thankful for your tidings about the dear friends at the Hall Farm, for though I sent them a letter, by my aunt's desire, after I came back from my sojourn among them, I have had no word from them. My aunt has not the pen of a ready writer, and the work of the house is sufficient for the day, for she is weak in body. My heart cleaves to her and her children as the nearest of all to me in the flesh—yea, and to all in that house. I am carried away to them continually in my sleep, and often in the midst of work, and even of speech, the thought of them is borne in on me as if they were in need and trouble, which yet is dark to me. There may be some leading here; but I wait to be taught. You say they are all well.

"We shall see each other again in the body, I trust, though, it may be, not for a long while; for the brethren and sisters at Leeds are desirous to have me for a short space among them, when I have a door opened me again to leave Snowfield.

"Farewell, dear brother—and yet not farewell. For those children of God whom it has been granted to see each other face to face, and to hold communion together, and to feel the same spirit working in both can never more be sundered though the hills may lie between. For their souls are enlarged for evermore by that union, and they bear one another about in their thoughts continually as it were a new strength.—Your faithful Sister and fellow-worker in Christ,

DINAH MORRIS."

"I have not skill to write the words so small as you do and my pen moves slow. And so I am straitened, and say but little of what is in my mind. Greet your mother for me with a kiss. She asked me to kiss her twice when we parted."

Adam had refolded the letter, and was sitting meditatively with his head resting on his arm at the head of the bed, when Seth came upstairs.

"Hast read the letter?" said Seth.

"Yes," said Adam. "I don't know what I should ha' thought of her and her letter if I'd never seen her: I daresay I should ha' thought a preaching woman hateful. But she's one as makes everything seem right she says and does, and I seemed to see her and hear her speaking when I read the letter. It's wonderful how I remember her looks and her voice. She'd make thee rare and happy, Seth; she's just the woman for thee."

"It's no use thinking o' that," said Seth, despondingly. "She spoke so firm, and she's not the woman to say one thing and mean another."

"Nay, but her feelings may grow different. A woman may get to love by degrees—the best fire dosna flare up the soonest. I'd have thee go and see her by and by: I'd make it convenient for thee to be away three or four days, and it 'ud be no walk for thee—only between twenty and thirty mile."

"I should like to see her again, whether or no, if she wouldna be displeased with me for going," said Seth.

"She'll be none displeased," said Adam emphatically, getting up and throwing off his coat. "It might be a great happiness to us all if she'd have thee, for mother took to her so wonderful and seemed so contented to be with her."

"Aye," said Seth, rather timidly, "and Dinah's fond o' Hetty too; she thinks a deal about her."

Adam made no reply to that, and no other word but "good-night" passed between them.

Chapter XXXI In Hetty's Bed-Chamber

IT was no longer light enough to go to bed without a candle, even in Mrs. Poyser's early household, and Hetty carried one with her as she went up at last to her bedroom soon after Adam was gone, and bolted the door behind her.

Now she would read her letter. It must—it must have comfort in it. How was Adam to know the truth? It was always likely he should say what he did say.

She set down the candle and took out the letter. It had a faint scent of roses, which made her feel as if Arthur were close to her. She put it to her lips, and a rush of remembered sensations for a moment or two swept away all fear. But her heart began to flutter strangely, and her hands to tremble as she broke the seal. She read slowly; it was not easy for her to read a gentleman's handwriting, though Arthur had taken pains to write plainly.

"DEAREST HETTY—I have spoken truly when I have said that I loved you, and I shall never forget our love. I shall be your true friend as long as life lasts, and I hope to prove this to you in many ways. If I say anything to pain you in this letter, do not believe it is for want of love and tenderness towards you, for there is nothing I would not do for you, if I knew it to be really for your happiness. I cannot bear to think of my little Hetty shedding tears when I am not there to kiss them away; and if I followed only my own inclinations, I should be with her at this moment instead of writing. It is very hard for me to part from her—harder still for me to write words which may seem unkind, though they spring from the truest kindness.

"Dear, dear Hetty, sweet as our love has been to me, sweet as it would be to me for you to love me always, I feel that it would have been better for us both if we had never had that happiness, and that it is my duty to ask you to love me and care for me as little as you can. The fault has all been mine, for though I have been unable to resist the longing to be near you, I have felt all the while that your affection for me might cause you grief. I ought to have resisted my feelings. I should have done so, if I had been a better fellow than I am; but now, since the past cannot be altered, I am bound to save you from any evil that I have power to prevent. And I feel it would be a great evil for you if your affections continued so fixed on me that you could think of no other man who might be able to make you happier by his love than I ever can, and if you continued to look towards something in the future which cannot possibly happen. For, dear Hetty, if I were to do what you one day spoke of, and make you my wife, I should do what you yourself would come to feel was for your misery instead of your welfare. I know you can never be happy except by marrying a man in your own station; and if I were to marry you now, I should only be adding to any wrong I have done, besides offending against my duty in the other relations of life. You know nothing, dear Hetty, of the world in which I must always live, and you would soon begin to dislike me, because there would be so little in which we should be alike.

"And since I cannot marry you, we must part—we must try not to feel like lovers any more. I am miserable while I say this, but nothing else can be. Be angry with me, my sweet one, I deserve it; but do not believe that I shall not always care for you—always be grateful to you—always remember my Hetty; and if any trouble should come that we do not now foresee, trust in me to do everything that lies in my power.

"I have told you where you are to direct a letter to, if you want to write, but I put it down below lest you should have forgotten. Do not write unless there is something I can really do for you; for, dear Hetty, we must try to think of each other as little as we can. Forgive me, and try to forget everything about me, except that I shall be, as long as I live, your affectionate friend,

ARTHUR DONNITHORNE.

Slowly Hetty had read this letter; and when she looked up from it there was the reflection of a blanched face in the old dim glass—a white marble face with rounded childish forms, but with something sadder than a child's pain in it. Hetty did not see the face—she saw nothing—she only felt that she was cold and sick and trembling. The letter shook and rustled in her hand. She laid it down. It was a horrible sensation—this cold and trembling. It swept away the very ideas that produced it, and Hetty got up to reach a warm cloak from her clothes-press, wrapped it round her, and sat as if she were thinking of nothing but getting warm. Presently she took up the letter with a firmer hand, and began to read it through again. The tears came this time—great rushing tears that blinded her and blotched the paper. She felt nothing but that Arthur was cruel—cruel to write so, cruel not to marry her. Reasons why he could not marry her had no existence for her mind; how could she believe in any misery that could come to her from the fulfilment of all she had been longing for and dreaming of? She had not the ideas that could make up the notion of that misery.

As she threw down the letter again, she caught sight of her face in the glass; it was reddened now, and wet with tears; it was almost like a companion that she might complain to—that would pity her. She leaned forward on her elbows, and looked into those dark overflooding eyes and at the quivering mouth, and saw how the tears came thicker and thicker, and how the mouth became convulsed with sobs.

The shattering of all her little dream-world, the crushing blow on her new-born passion, afflicted her pleasure-craving nature with an overpowering pain that annihilated all impulse to resistance, and suspended her anger. She sat sobbing till the candle went out, and then, wearied, aching, stupefied with crying, threw herself on the bed without undressing and went to sleep.

There was a feeble dawn in the room when Hetty awoke, a little after four o'clock, with a sense of dull misery, the cause of which broke upon her gradually as she began to discern the objects round her in the dim light. And then came the frightening thought that she had to conceal her misery as well as to bear it, in this dreary daylight that was coming. She could lie no longer. She got up and went towards the table: there lay the letter. She opened her treasure-drawer: there lay the ear-rings and the locket—the signs of all her short happiness—the signs of the lifelong dreariness that was to follow it. Looking at the little trinkets which she had once eyed and fingered so fondly as the earnest of her future paradise of finery, she lived back in the moments when they had been given to her with such tender caresses, such strangely pretty words, such glowing looks, which filled her with a bewildering delicious surprise—they were so much sweeter than she had thought anything could be. And the Arthur who had spoken to her and looked at her in this way, who was present with her now—whose arm she felt round her, his cheek against hers, his very breath upon her—was the cruel, cruel Arthur who had written that letter, that letter which she snatched and crushed and then opened again, that she might read it once more. The half-benumbed mental condition which was the effect of the last night's violent crying made it necessary to her to look again and see if her wretched thoughts were actually true—if the letter was really so cruel. She had to hold it close to the window, else she could not have read it by the faint light. Yes! It was worse—it was more cruel. She crushed it up again in anger. She hated the writer of that letter—hated him for the very reason that she hung upon him with all her love—all the girlish passion and vanity that made up her love.

She had no tears this morning. She had wept them all away last night, and now she felt that dry-eyed morning misery, which is worse than the first shock because it has the future in it as well as the present. Every morning to come, as far as her imagination could stretch, she would have to get up and feel that the day would have no joy for her. For there is no despair so absolute as that which comes with the first moments of our first great sorrow, when we have not yet known what it is to have suffered and be healed, to have despaired and to have recovered hope. As Hetty began languidly to take off the clothes she had worn all the night, that she might wash herself and brush her hair, she had a sickening sense that her life would go on in this way. She should always be doing things she had no pleasure in, getting up to the old tasks of work, seeing people she cared nothing about, going to church, and to Treddleston, and to tea with Mrs. Best, and carrying no happy thought with her. For her short poisonous delights had spoiled for ever all the little joys that had once made the sweetness of her life—the new frock ready for Treddleston Fair, the party at Mr. Britton's at Broxton wake, the beaux that she would say "No" to for a long while, and the prospect of the wedding that was to come at last when she would have a silk gown and a great many clothes all at once. These things were all flat and dreary to her now; everything would be a weariness, and she would carry about for ever a hopeless thirst and longing.

She paused in the midst of her languid undressing and leaned against the dark old clothes-press. Her neck and arms were bare, her hair hung down in delicate rings—and they were just as beautiful as they were that night two months ago, when she walked up and down this bed-chamber glowing with vanity and hope. She was not thinking of her neck and arms now; even her own beauty was indifferent to her. Her eyes wandered sadly over the dull old chamber, and then looked out vacantly towards the growing dawn. Did a remembrance of Dinah come across her mind? Of her foreboding words, which had made her angry? Of Dinah's affectionate entreaty to think of her as a friend in trouble? No, the impression had been too slight to recur. Any affection or comfort Dinah could have given her would have been as indifferent to Hetty this morning as everything else was except her bruised passion. She was only thinking she could never stay here and go on with the old life—she could better bear something quite new than sinking back into the old everyday round. She would like to run away that very morning, and never see any of the old faces again. But Hetty's was not a nature to face difficulties—to dare to loose her hold on the familiar and rush blindly on some unknown condition. Hers was a luxurious and vain nature—not a passionate one—and if she were ever to take any violent measure, she must be urged to it by the desperation of terror. There was not much room for her thoughts to travel in the narrow circle of her imagination, and she soon fixed on the one thing she would do to get away from her old life: she would ask her uncle to let her go to be a lady's maid. Miss Lydia's maid would help her to get a situation, if she krew Hetty had her uncle's leave.

When she had thought of this, she fastened up her hair and began to wash: it seemed more possible to her to go downstairs and try to behave as usual. She would ask her uncle this very day. On Hetty's blooming health it would take a great deal of such mental suffering as hers to leave any deep impress; and when she was dressed as neatly as usual in her working-dress, with her hair tucked up under her little cap, an indifferent observer would have been more struck with the young roundness of her cheek and neck and the darkness of her eyes and eyelashes than with any signs of sadness about her. But when she took up the crushed letter and put it in her drawer, that she might lock it out of sight, hard smarting tears, having no relief in them as the great drops had that fell last night, forced their way into her eyes. She wiped them away quickly: she must not cry in the daytime. Nobody should find out how miserable she was, nobody should know she was disappointed about anything; and the thought that the eyes of her aunt and uncle would be upon her gave her the self-command which often accompanies a great dread. For Hetty looked out from her secret misery towards the possibility of their ever knowing what had happened, as the sick and weary prisoner might think of the possible pillory. They would think her conduct shameful, and shame was torture. That was poor little Hetty's conscience.

So she locked up her drawer and went away to her early work.

In the evening, when Mr. Poyser was smoking his pipe, and his good-nature was therefore at its superlative moment, Hetty seized the opportunity of her aunt's absence to say, "Uncle, I wish you'd let me go for a lady's maid."

Mr. Poyser took the pipe from his mouth and looked at Hetty in mild surprise for some moments. She was sewing, and went on with her work industriously.

"Why, what's put that into your head, my wench?" he said at last, after he had given one conservative puff.

"I should like it—I should like it better than farm-work."

"Nay, nay; you fancy so because you donna know it, my wench. It wouldn't be half so good for your health, nor for your luck i' life. I'd like you to stay wi' us till you've got a good husband: you're my own niece, and I wouldn't have you go to service, though it was a gentleman's house, as long as I've got a home for you."

Mr. Poyser paused, and puffed away at his pipe.

"I like the needlework," said Hetty, "and I should get good wages."

"Has your aunt been a bit sharp wi' you?" said Mr. Poyser, not noticing Hetty's further argument. "You mustna mind that, my wench—she does it for your good. She wishes you well; an' there isn't many aunts as are no kin to you 'ud ha' done by you as she has."

"No, it isn't my aunt," said Hetty, "but I should like the work better."

"It was all very well for you to learn the work a bit—an' I gev my consent to that fast enough, sin' Mrs. Pomfret was willing to teach you. For if anything was t' happen, it's well to know how to turn your hand to different sorts o' things. But I niver meant you to go to service, my wench; my family's ate their own bread and cheese as fur back as anybody knows, hanna they, Father? You wouldna like your grand-child to take wage?"

"Na-a-y," said old Martin, with an elongation of the word, meant to make it bitter as well as negative, while he leaned forward and looked down on the floor. "But the wench takes arter her mother. I'd hard work t' hould HER in, an' she married i' spite o' me—a feller wi' on'y two head o' stock when there should ha' been ten on's farm—she might well die o' th' inflammation afore she war thirty."

It was seldom the old man made so long a speech, but his son's question had fallen like a bit of dry fuel on the embers of a long unextinguished resentment, which had always made the grandfather more indifferent to Hetty than to his son's children. Her mother's fortune had been spent by that good-for-nought Sorrel, and Hetty had Sorrel's blood in her veins.

"Poor thing, poor thing!" said Martin the younger, who was sorry to have provoked this retrospective harshness. "She'd but bad luck. But Hetty's got as good a chance o' getting a solid, sober husband as any gell i' this country."

After throwing out this pregnant hint, Mr. Poyser recurred to his pipe and his silence, looking at Hetty to see if she did not give some sign of having renounced her ill-advised wish. But instead of that, Hetty, in spite of herself, began to cry, half out of ill temper at the denial, half out of the day's repressed sadness.

"Hegh, hegh!" said Mr. Poyser, meaning to check her playfully, "don't let's have any crying. Crying's for them as ha' got no home, not for them as want to get rid o' one. What dost think?" he continued to his wife, who now came back into the house-place, knitting with fierce rapidity, as if that movement were a necessary function, like the twittering of a crab's antennae.

"Think? Why, I think we shall have the fowl stole before we are much older, wi' that gell forgetting to lock the pens up o' nights. What's the matter now, Hetty? What are you crying at?"

"Why, she's been wanting to go for a lady's maid," said Mr. Poyser. "I tell her we can do better for her nor that."

"I thought she'd got some maggot in her head, she's gone about wi' her mouth buttoned up so all day. It's all wi' going so among them servants at the Chase, as we war fools for letting her. She thinks it 'ud be a finer life than being wi' them as are akin to her and ha' brought her up sin' she war no bigger nor Marty. She thinks there's nothing belongs to being a lady's maid but wearing finer clothes nor she was born to, I'll be bound. It's what rag she can get to stick on her as she's thinking on from morning till night, as I often ask her if she wouldn't like to be the mawkin i' the field, for then she'd be made o' rags inside and out. I'll never gi' my consent to her going for a lady's maid, while she's got good friends to take care on her till she's married to somebody better nor one o' them valets, as is neither a common man nor a gentleman, an' must live on the fat o' the land, an's like enough to stick his hands under his coat-tails and expect his wife to work for him."

"Aye, aye," said Mr. Poyser, "we must have a better husband for her nor that, and there's better at hand. Come, my wench, give over crying and get to bed. I'll do better for you nor letting you go for a lady's maid. Let's hear no more on't."

When Hetty was gone upstairs he said, "I canna make it out as she should want to go away, for I thought she'd got a mind t' Adam Bede. She's looked like it o' late."

"Eh, there's no knowing what she's got a liking to, for things take no more hold on her than if she was a dried pea. I believe that gell,

Molly—as is aggravatin' enough, for the matter o' that—but I believe she'd care more about leaving us and the children, for all she's been here but a year come Michaelmas, nor Hetty would. But she's got this notion o' being a lady's maid wi' going among them servants—we might ha' known what it 'ud lead to when we let her go to learn the fine work. But I'll put a stop to it pretty quick."

"Thee'dst be sorry to part wi' her, if it wasn't for her good," said Mr. Poyser. "She's useful to thee i' the work."

"Sorry? Yes, I'm fonder on her nor she deserves—a little hard-hearted hussy, wanting to leave us i' that way. I can't ha' had her about me these seven year, I reckon, and done for her, and taught her everything wi'out caring about her. An' here I'm having linen spun, an' thinking all the while it'll make sheeting and table-clothing for her when she's married, an' she'll live i' the parish wi' us, and never go out of our sights—like a fool as I am for thinking aught about her, as is no better nor a cherry wi' a hard stone inside it."

"Nay, nay, thee mustna make much of a trifle," said Mr. Poyser, soothingly. "She's fond on us, I'll be bound; but she's young, an' gets things in her head as she can't rightly give account on. Them young fillies 'ull run away often wi'-ou; knowing why."

Her uncle's answers, however, had had another effect on Hetty besides that of disappointing her and making her cry. She knew quite well whom he had in his mind in his allusions to marriage, and to a sober, solid husband; and when she was in her bedroom again, the possibility of her marrying Adam presented itself to her in a new light. In a mind where no strong sympathies are at work, where there is no supreme sense of right to which the agitated nature can cling and steady itself to quiet endurance, one of the first results of sorrow is a desperate vague clutching after any deed that will change the actual condition. Poor Hetty's vision of consequences, at no time more than a narrow fantastic calculation of her own probable pleasures and pains, was now quite shut out by reckless irritation under present suffering, and she was ready for one of those convulsive, motiveless actions by which wretched men and women leap from a temporary sorrow into a lifelong misery.

Why should she not marry Adam? She did not care what she did, so that it made some change in her life. She felt confident that he would still want to marry her, and any further thought about Adam's happiness in the matter had never yet visited her.

"Strange!" perhaps you will say, "this rush of impulse to-wards a course that might have seemed the most repugnant to her present state of mind, and in only the second night of her sadness!"

Yes, the actions of a little trivial soul like Hetty's, struggling amidst the serious sad destinies of a human being, are strange. So are the motions of a little vessel without ballast tossed about on a stormy sea. How pretty it looked with its parti-coloured sail in the sunlight, moored in the quiet bay!

"Let that man bear the loss who loosed it from its moorings."

But that will not save the vessel—the pretty thing that might have been a lasting joy.

Chapter XXXII Mrs. Poyser "Has Her Say Out"

THE next Saturday evening there was much excited discussion at the Donnithorne Arms concerning an incident which had occurred that very day—no less than a second appearance of the smart man in top-boots said by some to be a mere farmer in treaty for the Chase Farm, by others to be the future steward, but by Mr. Casson himself, the personal witness to the stranger's visit, pronounced contemptuously to be nothing better than a bailiff, such as Satchell had been before him. No one had thought of denying Mr. Casson's testimony to the fact that he had seen the stranger; nevertheless, he proffered various corroborating circumstances.

"I see him myself," he said; "I see him coming along by the Crabtree Meadow on a bald-faced hoss. I'd just been t' hev a pint—it was half after ten i' the fore-noon, when I hev my pint as reg'lar as the clock—and I says to Knowles, as druv up with his waggon, 'You'll get a bit o' barley to-day, Knowles,' I says, 'if you look about you'; and then I went round by the rick-yard, and towart the Treddles'on road, and just as I come up by the big ash-tree, I see the man i' top-boots coming along on a bald-faced hoss—I wish I may never stir if I didn't. And I stood still till he come up, and I says, 'Good morning, sir,' I says, for I wanted to hear the turn of his tongue, as I might know whether he was a this-country man; so I says, 'Good morning, sir: it 'll 'old hup for the barley this morning, I think. There'll be a bit got hin, if we've good luck.' And he says, 'Eh, ye may be raight, there's noo tallin',' he says, and I knowed by that"—here Mr. Casson gave a wink—"as he didn't come from a hundred mile off. I daresay he'd think me a hodd talker, as you Loamshire folks allays does hany one as talks the right language."

"The right language!" said Bartle Massey, contemptuously. "You're about as near the right language as a pig's squeaking is like a tune played on a key-bugle."

"Well, I don't know," answered Mr. Casson, with an angry smile. "I should think a man as has lived among the gentry from a by, is likely to know what's the right language pretty nigh as well as a schoolmaster."

"Aye, aye, man," said Bartle, with a tone of sarcastic consolation, "you talk the right language for you. When Mike Holdsworth's goat says ba-a-a, it's all right—it 'ud be unnatural for it to make any other noise."

The rest of the party being Loamsnire men, Mr. Casson had the laugh strongly against him, and wisely fell back on the previous question, which, far from being exhausted in a single evening, was renewed in the churchyard, before service, the next day, with the fresh interest conferred on all news when there is a fresh person to hear it; and that fresh hearer was Martin Poyser, who, as his wife said, "never went boozin' with that set at Casson's, a-sittin' soakin' in drink, and looking as wise as a lot o' cod-fish wi' red faces."

It was probably owing to the conversation she had had with her husband on their way from church concerning this problematic stranger that Mrs. Poyser's thoughts immediately reverted to him when, a day or two afterwards, as she was standing at the house-door with her knitting, in that eager leisure which came to her when the afternoon cleaning was done, she saw the old squire enter the yard on his black pony, followed by John the groom. She always cited it afterwards as a case of prevision, which really had something more in it than her own remarkable penetration, that the moment she set eyes on the squire she said to herself, "I shouldna wonder if he's come about that man as is a-going to take the Chase Farm, wanting Poyser to do something for him without pay. But Poyser's a fool if he does."

Something unwonted must clearly be in the wind, for the old squire's visits to his tenantry were rare; and though Mrs. Poyser had during the last twelvemonth recited many imaginary speeches, meaning even more than met the ear, which she was quite determined to make to him the next time he appeared within the gates of the Hall Farm, the speeches had always remained imaginary.

"Good-day, Mrs. Poyser," said the old squire, peering at her with his short-sighted eyes—a mode of looking at her which, as Mrs. Poyser observed, "allays aggravated me: it was as if you was a insect, and he was going to dab his finger-nail on you."

However, she said, "Your servant, sir," and curtsied with an air of perfect deference as she advanced towards him: she was not the woman to misbehave towards her betters, and fly in the face of the catechism, without severe provocation.

"Is your husband at home, Mrs. Poyser?"

"Yes, sir; he's only i' the rick-yard. I'll send for him in a minute, if you'll please to get down and step in."

"Thank you; I will do so. I want to consult him about a little matter; but you are quite as much concerned in it, if not more. I must have your opinion too."

"Hetty, run and tell your uncle to come in," said Mrs. Poyser, as they entered the house, and the old gentleman bowed low in answer to Hetty's curtsy; while Totty, conscious of a pinafore stained with gooseberry jam, stood hiding her face against the clock and peeping round furtively.

"What a fine old kitchen this is!" said Mr. Donnithorne, looking round admiringly. He always spoke in the same deliberate, well-chiselled, polite way, whether his words were sugary or venomous. "And you keep it so exquisitely clean, Mrs. Poyser. I like these premises, do you know, beyond any on the estate."

"Well, sir, since you're fond of 'em, I should be glad if you'd let a bit o' repairs be done to 'em, for the boarding's i' that state as we're like to be eaten up wi' rats and mice; and the cellar, you may stan' up to your knees i' water in't, if you like to go down; but perhaps you'd rather believe my words. Won't you please to sit down, sir?"

"Not yet; I must see your dairy. I have not seen it for years, and I hear on all hands about your fine cheese and butter," said the squire, looking politely unconscious that there could be any question on which he and Mrs. Poyser might happen to disagree. "I think I see the door open, there. You must not be surprised if I cast a covetous eye on your cream and butter. I don't expect that Mrs. Satchell's cream and butter will bear comparison with yours."

"I can't say, sir, I'm sure. It's seldom I see other folks's butter, though there's some on it as one's no need to see—the smell's enough."

"Ah, now this I like," said Mr. Donnithorne, looking round at the damp temple of cleanliness, but keeping near the door. "I'm sure I should like my breakfast better if I knew the butter and cream came from this dairy. Thank you, that really is a pleasant sight. Unfortunately, my slight tendency to rheumatism makes me afraid of damp: I'll sit down in your comfortable kitchen. Ah, Poyser, how do you do? In the midst of business, I see, as usual. I've been looking at your wife's beautiful dairy—the best manager in the parish, is she not?"

Mr. Poyser had just entered in shirt-sleeves and open waistcoat, with a face a shade redder than usual, from the exertion of "pitching." As he stood, red, rotund, and radiant, before the small, wiry, cool old gentleman, he looked like a prize apple by the side of a withered crab.

"Will you please to take this chair, sir?" he said, lifting his father's arm-chair forward a little: "you'll find it easy."

"No, thank you, I never sit in easy-chairs," said the old gentleman, seating himself on a small chair near the door. "Do you know, Mrs. Poyser—sit down, pray, both of you—I've been far from contented, for some time, with Mrs. Satchell's dairy management. I think she has not a good method, as you have."

"Indeed, sir, I can't speak to that," said Mrs. Poyser in a hard voice, rolling and unrolling her knitting and looking icily out of the window, as she continued to stand opposite the squire. Poyser might sit down if he liked, she thought; she wasn't going to sit down, as if she'd give in to any such smooth-tongued palaver. Mr. Poyser, who looked and felt the reverse of icy, did sit down in his three-cornered chair.

"And now, Poyser, as Satchell is laid up, I am intending to let the Chase Farm to a respectable tenant. I'm tired of having a farm on my own hands—nothing is made the best of in such cases, as you know. A satisfactory bailiff is hard to find; and I think you and I, Poyser, and your excellent wife here, can enter into a little arrangement in consequence, which will be to our mutual advantage."

"Oh," said Mr. Poyser, with a good-natured blankness of imagination as to the nature of the arrangement.

"If I'm called upon to speak, sir," said Mrs. Poyser, after glancing at her husband with pity at his softness, "you know better than me; but I don't see what the Chase Farm is t' us—we've cumber enough wi' our own farm. Not but what I'm glad to hear o' anybody respectable coming into the parish; there's some as ha' been brought in as hasn't been looked on i' that character."

"You're likely to find Mr. Thurle an excellent neighbour, I assure you—such a one as you will feel glad to have accommodated by the little plan I'm going to mention, especially as I hope you will find it as much to your own advantage as his."

"Indeed, sir, if it's anything t' our advantage, it'll be the first offer o' the sort I've heared on. It's them as take advantage that get advantage i' this world, I think. Folks have to wait long enough afore it's brought to 'em."

"The fact is, Poyser," said the squire, ignoring Mrs. Poyser's theory of worldly prosperity, "there is too much dairy land, and too little plough land, on the Chase Farm to suit Thurle's purpose—indeed, he will only take the farm on condition of some change in it: his wife, it appears, is not a clever dairy-woman, like yours. Now, the plan I'm thinking of is to effect a little exchange. If you were to have the Hollow Pastures, you might increase your dairy, which must be so profitable under your wife's management; and I should request you, Mrs. Poyser, to supply my house with milk, cream, and butter at the market prices. On the other hand, Poyser, you might let Thurle have the Lower and Upper Ridges, which really, with our wet seasons, would be a good riddance for you. There is much less risk in dairy land than corn land."

Mr. Poyser was leaning forward, with his elbows on his knees, his head on one side, and his mouth screwed up—apparently absorbed in making the tips of his fingers meet so as to represent with perfect accuracy the ribs of a ship. He was much too acute a man not to see through the whole business, and to foresee perfectly what would be his wife's view of the subject; but he disliked giving unpleasant answers. Unless it was on a point of farming practice, he would rather give up than have a quarrel, any day; and, after all, it mattered more to his wife than to him. So, after a few moments' silence, he looked up at her and said mildly, "What dost say?"

Mrs. Poyser had had her eyes fixed on her husband with cold severity during his silence, but now she turned away her head with a toss, looked icily at the opposite roof of the cow-shed, and spearing her knitting together with the loose pin, held it firmly between her clasped hands.

"Say? Why, I say you may do as you like about giving up any o' your corn-land afore your lease is up, which it won't be for a year come next Michaelmas, but I'll not consent to take more dairy work into my hands, either for love or money; and there's nayther love nor money here, as I can see, on'y other folks's love o' theirselves, and the money as is to go into other folks's pockets. I know there's them as is born t' own the land, and them as is born to sweat on't"—here Mrs. Poyser paused to gasp a little—"and I know it's christened folks's duty to submit to their betters as fur as flesh and blood 'ull bear it; but I'll not make a martyr o' myself, and wear myself to skin and bone, and worret myself as if I was a churn wi' butter a-coming in't, for no landlord in England, not if he was King George himself."

"No, no, my dear Mrs. Poyser, certainly not," said the squire, still confident in his own powers of persuasion, "you must not overwork yourself; but don't you think your work will rather be lessened than increased in this way? There is so much milk required at the Abbey that you will have little increase of cheese and butter making from the addition to your dairy; and I believe selling the milk is the most profitable way of disposing of dairy produce, is it not?"

"Aye, that's true," said Mr. Poyser, unable to repress an opinion on a question of farming profits, and forgetting that it was not in this case a purely abstract question.

"I daresay," said Mrs. Poyser bitterly, turning her head half-way towards her husband and looking at the vacant arm-chair—"I daresay it's true for men as sit i' th' chimney-corner and make believe as everything's cut wi' ins an' outs to fit int' everything else. If you could make a pudding wi' thinking o' the batter, it 'ud be easy getting dinner. How do I know whether the milk 'ull be wanted constant? What's to make me sure as the house won't be put o' board wage afore we're many months older, and then I may have to lie awake o' nights wi' twenty gallons o' milk on my mind—and Dingall 'ull take no more butter, let alone paying for it; and we must fat pigs till we're obliged to beg the butcher on our knees to buy 'em, and lose half of 'em wi' the measles. And there's the fetching and carrying, as 'ud be welly half a day's work for a man an' hoss—that's to be took out o' the profits, I reckon? But there's folks 'ud hold a sieve under the pump and expect to carry away the water."

"That difficulty—about the fetching and carrying—you will not have, Mrs. Poyser," said the squire, who thought that this entrance into particulars indicated a distant inclination to compromise on Mrs. Poyser's part. "Bethell will do that regularly with the cart and pony."

"Oh, sir, begging your pardon, I've never been used t' having gentlefolks's servants coming about my back places, a-making love to both the gells at once and keeping 'em with their hands on their hips listening to all manner o' gossip when they should be down on their knees a-scouring. If we're to go to ruin, it shanna be wi' having our back kitchen turned into a public."

"Well, Poyser," said the squire, shifting his tactics and looking as if he thought Mrs. Poyser had suddenly withdrawn from the proceedings and left the room, "you can turn the Hollows into feeding-land. I can easily make another arrangement about supplying my house. And I shall not forget your readiness to accommodate your landlord as well as a neighbour. I know you will be glad to have your lease renewed for three years, when the present one expires; otherwise, I daresay Thurle, who is a man of some capital, would be glad to take both the farms, as they could be worked so well together. But I don't want to part with an old tenant like you."

To be thrust out of the discussion in this way would have been enough to complete Mrs. Poyser's exasperation, even without the final threat. Her husband, really alarmed at the possibility of their leaving the old place where he had been bred and born—for he believed the old squire had small spite enough for anything—was beginning a mild remonstrance explanatory of the inconvenience he should find in having to buy and sell more stock, with, "Well, sir, I think as it's rether hard . . . " when Mrs. Poyser burst in with the desperate determination to have her say out this once, though it were to rain notices to quit and the only shelter were the work-house.

"Then, sir, if I may speak—as, for all I'm a woman, and there's folks as thinks a woman's fool enough to stan' by an' look on while the men sign her soul away, I've a right to speak, for I make one quarter o' the rent, and save another quarter—I say, if Mr. Thurle's so ready to take farms under you, it's a pity but what he should take this, and see if he likes to live in a house wi' all the plagues o' Egypt in't—wi' the cellar full o' water, and frogs and toads hoppin' up the steps by dozens—and the floors rotten, and the rats and mice gnawing every bit o' cheese, and runnin' over our heads as we lie i' bed till we expect 'em to eat us up alive—as it's a mercy they hanna eat the children long ago. I should like to see if there's another tenant besides Poyser as 'ud put up wi' never having a bit o' repairs done till a place tumbles down—and not then, on'y wi' begging and praying and having to pay half—and being strung up wi' the rent as it's much if he gets enough out o' the land to pay, for all he's put his own money into the ground beforehand. See if you'll get a stranger to lead such a life here as that: a maggot must be born i' the rotten cheese to like it, I reckon. You may run away from my words, sir," continued Mrs. Poyser, following the old squire beyond the door—for after the first moments of stunned surprise he had got up, and, waving his hand towards her with a smile, had walked out towards his pony. But it was impossible for him to get away immediately, for John was walking the pony up and down the yard, and was some distance from the causeway when his master beckoned.

"You may run away from my words, sir, and you may go spinnin' underhand ways o' doing us a mischief, for you've got Old Harry to your friend, though nobody else is, but I tell you for once as we're not dumb creatures to be abused and made money on by them as ha' got the lash i' their hands, for want o' knowing how t' undo the tackle. An' if I'm th' only one as speaks my mind, there's plenty o' the same way o' thinking i' this parish and the next to 't, for your name's no better than a brimstone match in everybody's nose—if it isna two-three old folks as you think o' saving your soul by giving 'em a bit o' flannel and a drop o' porridge. An' you may be right i' thinking it'll take but little to save your soul, for it'll be the smallest savin' y' iver made, wi' all your scrapin.'"

There are occasions on which two servant-girls and a waggoner may be a formidable audience, and as the squire rode away on his black pony, even the gift of short-sightedness did not prevent him from being aware that Molly and Nancy and Tim were grinning not far from him. Perhaps he suspected that sour old John was grinning behind him—which was also the fact. Meanwhile the bull-dog, the black-and-tan terrier, Alick's sheep-dog, and the gander hissing at a safe distance from the pony's heels carried out the idea of Mrs. Poyser's solo in an impressive quartet.

Mrs. Poyser, however, had no sooner seen the pony move off than she turned round, gave the two hilarious damsels a look which drove them into the back kitchen, and unspearing her knitting, began to knit again with her usual rapidity as she re-entered the house.

"Thee'st done it now," said Mr. Poyser, a little alarmed and uneasy, but not without some triumphant amusement at his wife's outbreak.

"Yes, I know I've done it," said Mrs. Poyser; "but I've had my say out, and I shall be th' easier for't all my life. There's no pleasure i' living if you're to be corked up for ever, and only dribble your mind out by the sly, like a leaky barrel. I shan't repent saying what I think, if I live to be as old as th' old squire; and there's little likelihood—for it seems as if them as aren't wanted here are th' only folks as aren't wanted i' th' other world."

"But thee wutna like moving from th' old place, this Michaelmas twelvemonth," said Mr. Poyser, "and going into a strange parish, where thee know'st nobody. It'll be hard upon us both, and upo' Father too."

"Eh, it's no use worreting; there's plenty o' things may happen between this and Michaelmas twelvemonth. The captain may be master afore then, for what we know," said Mrs. Poyser, inclined to take an unusually hopeful view of an embarrassment which had been brought about by her own merit and not by other people's fault.

"I'M none for worreting," said Mr. Poyser, rising from his three-cornered chair and walking slowly towards the door; "but I should be loath to leave th' old place, and the parish where I was bred and born, and Father afore me. We should leave our roots behind us, I doubt, and niver thrive again."

Chapter XXXIII More Links

THE barley was all carried at last, and the harvest suppers went by without waiting for the dismal black crop of beans. The apples and nuts were gathered and stored; the scent of whey departed from the farm-houses, and the scent of brewing came in its stead. The woods behind the Chase, and all the hedgerow trees, took on a solemn splendour under the dark low-hanging skies. Michaelmas was come, with its fragrant basketfuls of purple damsons, and its paler purple daisies, and its lads and lasses leaving or seeking service and winding along between the yellow hedges, with their bundles under their arms. But though Michaelmas was come, Mr. Thurle, that desirable tenant, did not come to the Chase Farm, and the old squire, afler all, had been obliged to put in a new bailiff. It was known throughout the two parishes that the squire's plan had been frustrated because the Poysers had refused to be "put upon," and Mrs. Poyser's outbreak was discussed in all the farm-houses with a zest which was only heightened by frequent repetition. The news that "Bony" was come back from Egypt was comparatively insipid, and the repulse of the French in Italy was nothing to Mrs. Poyser's repulse of the old squire. Mr. Irwine had heard a version of it in every parishioner's house, with the one exception of the Chase. But since he had always, with marvellous skill, avoided any quarrel with Mr. Donnithorne, he could not allow himself the pleasure of laughing at the old gentleman's discomfiture with any one besides his mother, who declared that if she were rich she should like to allow Mrs. Poyser a pension for life, and wanted to invite her to the parsonage that she might hear an account of the scene from Mrs. Poyser's own lips.

"No, no, Mother," said Mr. Irwine; "it was a little bit of irregular justice on Mrs. Poyser's part, but a magistrate like me must not countenance irregular justice. There must be no report spread that I have taken notice of the quarrel, else I shall lose the little good influence I have over the old man."

"Well, I like that woman even better than her cream-cheeses," said Mrs. Irwine. "She has the spirit of three men, with that pale face of hers. And she says such sharp things too."

"Sharp! Yes, her tongue is like a new-set razor. She's quite original in her talk too; one of those untaught wits that help to stock a country with proverbs. I told you that capital thing I heard her say about Craig—that he was like a cock, who thought the sun had risen to hear him crow. Now that's an AEsop's fable in a sentence."

"But it will be a bad business if the old gentleman turns them out of the farm next Michaelmas, eh?" said Mrs. Irwine.

"Oh, that must not be; and Poyser is such a good tenant that Donnithorne is likely to think twice, and digest his spleen rather than turn them out. But if he should give them notice at Lady Day, Arthur and I must move heaven and earth to mollify him. Such old parishioners as they are must not go."

"Ah, there's no knowing what may happen before Lady day," said Mrs. Irwine. "It struck me on Arthur's birthday that the old man was a little shaken: he's eighty-three, you know. It's really an unconscionable age. It's only women who have a right to live as long as that."

"When they've got old-bachelor sons who would be forlorn without them," said Mr. Irwine, laughing, and kissing his mother's hand.

Mrs. Poyser, too, met her husband's occasional forebodings of a notice to quit with "There's no knowing what may happen before Lady day"—one of those undeniable general propositions which are usually intended to convey a particular meaning very far from undeniable. But it is really too hard upon human nature that it should be held a criminal offence to imagine the death even of the king when he is turned eighty-three. It is not to be believed that any but the dullest Britons can be good subjects under that hard condition.

Apart from this foreboding, things went on much as usual in the Poyser household. Mrs. Poyser thought she noticed a surprising improvement in Hetty. To be sure, the girl got "closer tempered, and sometimes she seemed as if there'd be no drawing a word from her with cart-ropes," but she thought much less about her dress, and went after the work quite eagerly, without any telling. And it was wonderful how she never wanted to go out now—indeed, could hardly be persuaded to go; and she bore her aunt's putting a stop to her weekly lesson in fine-work at the Chase without the least grumbling or pouting. It must be, after all, that she had set her heart on Adam at last, and her sudden freak of wanting to be a lady's maid must have been caused by some little pique or misunderstanding between them, which had passed by. For whenever Adam came to the Hall Farm, Hetty seemed to be in better spirits and to talk more than at other times, though she was almost sullen when Mr. Craig or any other admirer happened to pay a visit there.

Adam himself watched her at first with trembling anxiety, which gave way to surprise and delicious hope. Five days after delivering Arthur's letter, he had ventured to go to the Hall Farm again—not without dread lest the sight of him might be painful to her. She was not in the house-place when he entered, and he sat talking to Mr. and Mrs. Poyser for a few minutes with a heavy fear on his heart that they might presently tell him Hetty was ill. But by and by there came a light step that he knew, and when Mrs. Poyser said, "Come, Hetty, where have you been?" Adam was obliged to turn round, though he was afraid to see the changed look there must be in her face. He almost started when he saw her smiling as if she were pleased to see him—looking the same as ever at a first glance, only that she had her cap on, which he had never seen her in before when he came of an evening. Still, when he looked at her again and again as she moved about or sat at her work, there was a change: the cheeks were as pink as ever, and she smiled as much as she had ever done of late, but there was something different in her eyes, in the expression of her face, in all her movements, Adam thought—something harder, older, less child-like. "Poor thing!" he said to himself, "that's allays likely. It's because she's had her first heartache. But she's got a spirit to bear up under it. Thank God for that."

As the weeks went by, and he saw her always looking pleased to see him—turning up her lovely face towards him as if she meant him to understand that she was glad for him to come—and going about her work in the same equable way, making no sign of sorrow, he began to believe that her feeling towards Arthur must have been much slighter than he had imagined in his first indignation and alarm, and that she had been able to think of her girlish fancy that Arthur was in love with her and would marry her as a folly of which she was timely cured. And it perhaps was, as he had sometimes in his more cheerful moments hoped it would be—her heart was really turning with all the more warmth towards the man she knew to have a serious love for her.

Possibly you think that Adam was not at all sagacious in his interpretations, and that it was altogether extremely unbecoming in a sensible man to behave as he did—falling in love with a girl who really had nothing more than her beauty to recommend her, attributing imaginary virtues to her, and even condescending to cleave to her after she had fallen in love with another man, waiting for her kind looks as a patient trembling dog waits for his master's eye to be turned upon him. But in so complex a thing as human nature, we must consider, it is hard to find rules without exceptions. Of course, I know that, as a rule, sensible men fall in love with the most sensible women of their acquaintance, see through all the pretty deceits of coquettish beauty, never imagine themselves loved when they are not loved, cease loving on all proper occasions, and marry the woman most fitted for them in every respect—indeed, so as to compel the approbation of all the maiden ladies in their neighbourhood. But even to this rule an exception will occur now and then in the lapse of centuries, and my friend Adam was one. For my own part, however, I respect him none the less—nay, I think the deep love he had for that sweet, rounded, blossom-like, dark-eyed Hetty, of whose inward self he was really very ignorant, came out of the very strength of his nature and not out of any inconsistent weakness. Is it any weakness, pray, to be wrought on by exquisite music? To feel its wondrous harmonies searching the subtlest windings of your soul, the delicate fibres of life where no memory can penetrate, and binding together your whole being past and present in one unspeakable vibration, melting you in one moment with all the tenderness, all the love that has been scattered through the toilsome years, concentrating in one emotion of heroic courage or resignation all the hard-learnt lessons of self-renouncing sympathy, blending your present joy with past sorrow and your present sorrow with all your past joy? If not, then neither is it a weakness to be so wrought upon by the exquisite curves of a woman's cheek and neck and arms, by the liquid depths of her beseeching eyes, or the sweet childish pout of her lips. For the beauty of a lovely woman is like music: what can one say more? Beauty has an expression beyond and far above the one woman's soul that it clothes, as the words of genius have a wider meaning than the thought that prompted them. It is more than a woman's love that moves us in a woman's eyes—it seems to be a far-off mighty love that has come near to us, and made speech for itself there; the rounded neck, the dimpled arm, move us by something more than their prettiness—by their close kinship with all we have known of tenderness and peace. The noblest nature sees the most of this impersonal expression in beauty (it is needless to say that there are gentlemen with whiskers dyed and undyed who see none of it whatever), and for this reason, the noblest nature is often the most blinded to the character of the one woman's soul that the beauty clothes. Whence, I fear, the tragedy of human life is likely to continue for a long time to come, in spite of mental philosophers who are ready with the best receipts for avoiding all mistakes of the kind.

Our good Adam had no fine words into which he could put his feeling for Hetty: he could not disguise mystery in this way with the appearance of knowledge; he called his love frankly a mystery, as you have heard him. He only knew that the sight and memory of her moved him deeply, touching the spring of all love and tenderness, all faith and courage within him. How could he imagine narrowness, selfishness, hardness in her? He created the mind he believed in out of his own, which was large, unselfish, tender.

The hopes he felt about Hetty softened a little his feeling towards Arthur. Surely his attentions to Hetty must have been of a slight kind; they were altogether wrong, and such as no man in Arthur's position ought to have allowed himself, but they must have had an air of playfulness about them, which had probably blinded him to their danger and had prevented them from laying any strong hold on Hetty's heart. As the new promise of happiness rose for Adam, his indignation and jealousy began to die out. Hetty was not made unhappy; he almost believed that she liked him best; and the thought sometimes crossed his mind that the friendship which had once seemed dead for ever might revive in the days to come, and he would not have to say "good-bye" to the grand old woods, but would like them better because they were Arthur's. For this new promise of happiness following so quickly on the shock of pain had an intoxicating effect on the sober Adam, who had all his life been used to much hardship and moderate hope. Was he really going to have an easy lot after all? It seemed so, for at the beginning of November, Jonathan Burge, finding it impossible to replace Adam, had at last made up his mind to offer him a share in the business, without further condition than that he should continue to give his energies to it and renounce all thought of having a separate business of his own. Son-in-law or no son-in-law, Adam had made himself too necessary to be parted with, and his headwork was so much more important to Burge than his skill in handicraft that his having the management of the woods made little difference in the value of his services; and as to the bargains about the squire's timber, it would be easy to call in a third person. Adam saw here an opening into a broadening path of prosperous work such as he had thought of with ambitious longing ever since he was a lad: he might come to build a bridge, or a town hall, or a factory, for he had always said to himself that Jonathan Burge's building buisness was like an acorn, which might be the mother of a great tree. So he gave his hand to Burge on that bargain, and went home with his mind full of happy visions, in which (my refined reader will perhaps be shocked when I say it) the image of Hetty hovered, and smiled over plans for seasoning timber at a trifling expense, calculations as to the cheapening of bricks per thousand by water-carriage, and a favourite scheme for the strengthening of roofs and walls with a peculiar form of iron girder. What then? Adam's enthusiasm lay in these things; and our love is inwrought in our enthusiasm as electricity is inwrought in the air, exalting its power by a subtle presence.

Adam would be able to take a separate house now, and provide for his mother in the old one; his prospects would justify his marrying very soon, and if Dinah consented to have Seth, their mother would perhaps be more contented to live apart from Adam. But he told himself that he would not be hasty—he would not try Hetty's feeling for him until it had had time to grow strong and firm. However, tomorrow, after church, he would go to the Hall Farm and tell them the news. Mr. Poyser, he knew, would like it better than a five-pound note, and he should see if Hetty's eyes brightened at it. The months would be short with all he had to fill his mind, and this foolish eagerness which had come over him of late must not hurry him into any premature words. Yet when he got home and told his mother the good news, and ate his supper, while she sat by almost crying for joy and wanting him to eat twice as much as usual because of this good-luck, he could not help preparing her gently for the coming change by talking of the old house being too small for them all to go on living in it always.

Chapter XXXIV The Betrothal

IT was a dry Sunday, and really a pleasant day for the 2d of November. There was no sunshine, but the clouds were high, and the wind was so still that the yellow leaves which fluttered down from the hedgerow elms must have fallen from pure decay. Nevertheless, Mrs. Poyser did not go to church, for she had taken a cold too serious to be neglected; only two winters ago she had been laid up for weeks with a cold; and since his wife did not go to church, Mr. Poyser considered that on the whole it would be as well for him to stay away too and "keep her company." He could perhaps have given no precise form to the reasons that determined this conclusion, but it is well known to all experienced minds that our firmest convictions are often dependent on subtle impressions for which words are quite too coarse a medium. However it was, no one from the Poyser family went to church that afternoon except Hetty and the boys; yet Adam was bold enough to join them after church, and say that he would walk home with them, though all the way through the village he appeared to be chiefly occupied with Marty and Tommy, telling them about the squirrels in Binton Coppice, and promising to take them there some day. But when they came to the fields he said to the boys, "Now, then, which is the stoutest walker? Him as gets to th' home-gate first shall be the first to go with me to Binton Coppice on the donkey. But Tommy must have the start up to the next stile, because he's the smallest."

Adam had never behaved so much like a determined lover before. As soon as the boys had both set off, he looked down at Hetty and said,

"Won't you hang on my arm, Hetty?" in a pleading tone, as if he had already asked her and she had refused. Hetty looked up at him smilingly and put her round arm through his in a moment. It was nothing to her, putting her arm through Adam's, but she knew he cared a great deal about having her arm through his, and she wished him to care. Her heart beat no faster, and she looked at the half-bare hedgerows and the ploughed field with the same sense of oppressive dulness as before. But Adam scarcely felt that he was walking. He thought Hetty must know that he was pressing her arm a little—a very little. Words rushed to his lips that he dared not utter—that he had made up his mind not to utter yet—and so he was silent for the length of that field. The calm patience with which he had once waited for Hetty's love, content only with her presence and the thought of the future, had forsaken him since that terrible shock nearly three months ago. The agitations of jealousy had given a new restlessness to his passion—had made fear and uncertainty too hard almost to bear. But though he might not speak to Hetty of his love, he would tell her about his new prospects and see if she would be pleased. So when he was enough master of himself to talk, he said, "I'm going to tell your uncle some news that'll surprise him, Hetty; and I think he'll be glad to hear it too."

"What's that?" Hetty said indifferently.

"Why, Mr. Burge has offered me a share in his business, and I'm going to take it."

There was a change in Hetty's face, certainly not produced by any agreeable impression from this news. In fact she felt a momentary annoyance and alarm, for she had so often heard it hinted by her uncle that Adam might have Mary Burge and a share in the business any day, if he liked, that she associated the two objects now, and the thought immediately occurred that perhaps Adam had given her up because of what had happened lately, and had turned towards Mary Burge. With that thought, and before she had time to remember any reasons why it could not be true, came a new sense of forsakenness and disappointment. The one thing—the one person—her mind had rested on in its dull weariness, had slipped away from her, and peevish misery filled her eyes with tears. She was looking on the ground, but Adam saw her face, saw the tears, and before he had finished saying, "Hetty, dear Hetty, what are you crying for?" his eager rapid thought had flown through all the causes conceivable to him, and had at last alighted on half the true one. Hetty thought he was going to marry Mary Burge—she didn't like him to marry—perhaps she didn't like him to marry any one but herself? All caution was swept away—all reason for it was gone, and Adam could feel nothing but trembling joy. He leaned towards her and took her hand, as he said:

"I could afford to be married now, Hetty—I could make a wife comfortable; but I shall never want to be married if you won't have me."

Hetty looked up at him and smiled through her tears, as she had done to Arthur that first evening in the wood, when she had thought he was not coming, and yet he came. It was a feebler relief, a feebler triumph she felt now, but the great dark eyes and the sweet lips were as beautiful as ever, perhaps more beautiful, for there was a more luxuriant womanliness about Hetty of late. Adam could hardly believe in the happiness of that moment. His right hand held her left, and he pressed her arm close against his heart as he leaned down towards her.

"Do you really love me, Hetty? Will you be my own wife, to love and take care of as long as I live?"

Hetty did not speak, but Adam's face was very close to hers, and she put up her round cheek against his, like a kitten. She wanted to be caressed—she wanted to feel as if Arthur were with her again.

Adam cared for no words after that, and they hardly spoke through the rest of the walk. He only said, "I may tell your uncle and aunt, mayn't I, Hetty?" and she said, "Yes."

The red fire-light on the hearth at the Hall Farm shone on joyful faces that evening, when Hetty was gone upstairs and Adam took the opportunity of telling Mr. and Mrs. Poyser and the grandfather that he saw his way to maintaining a wife now, and that Hetty had consented to have him.

"I hope you have no objections against me for her husband," said Adam; "I'm a poor man as yet, but she shall want nothing as I can work for."

"Objections?" said Mr. Poyser, while the grandfather leaned forward and brought out his long "Nay, nay." "What objections can we ha' to you, lad? Never mind your being poorish as yet; there's money in your head-piece as there's money i' the sown field, but it must ha' time. You'n got enough to begin on, and we can do a deal tow'rt the bit o' furniture you'll want. Thee'st got feathers and linen to spare—plenty, eh?"

This question was of course addressed to Mrs. Poyser, who was wrapped up in a warm shawl and was too hoarse to speak with her usual facility. At first she only nodded emphatically, but she was presently unable to resist the temptation to be more explicit.

"It ud be a poor tale if I hadna feathers and linen," she said, hoarsely, "when I never sell a fowl but what's plucked, and the wheel's a-going every day o' the week."

"Come, my wench," said Mr. Poyser, when Hetty came down, "come and kiss us, and let us wish you luck."

Hetty went very quietly and kissed the big good-natured man.

"There!" he said, patting her on the back, "go and kiss your aunt and your grandfather. I'm as wishful t' have you settled well as if you was my own daughter; and so's your aunt, I'll be bound, for she's done by you this seven 'ear, Hetty, as if you'd been her own. Come, come, now," he went on, becoming jocose, as soon as Hetty had kissed her aunt and the old man, "Adam wants a kiss too, I'll warrant, and he's a right to one now."

Hetty turned away, smiling, towards her empty chair.

"Come, Adam, then, take one," persisted Mr. Poyser, "else y' arena half a man."

Adam got up, blushing like a small maiden—great strong fellow as he was—and, putting his arm round Hetty stooped down and gently kissed her lips.

It was a pretty scene in the red fire-light; for there were no candles—why should there be, when the fire was so bright and was reflected from all the pewter and the polished oak? No one wanted to work on a Sunday evening. Even Hetty felt something like contentment in the midst of all this love. Adam's attachment to her, Adam's caress, stirred no passion in her, were no longer enough to satisfy her vanity, but they were the best her life offered her now—they promised her some change.

There was a great deal of discussion before Adam went away, about the possibility of his finding a house that would do for him to settle in. No house was empty except the one next to Will Maskery's in the village, and that was too small for Adam now. Mr. Poyser insisted that the best plan would be for Seth and his mother to move and leave Adam in the old home, which might be enlarged after a while, for there was plenty of space in the woodyard and garden; but Adam objected to turning his mother out.

"Well, well," said Mr. Poyser at last, "we needna fix everything to-night. We must take time to consider. You canna think o' getting married afore Easter. I'm not for long courtships, but there must be a bit o' time to make things comfortable."

"Aye, to be sure," said Mrs. Poyser, in a hoarse whisper; "Christian folks can't be married like cuckoos, I reckon."

"I'm a bit daunted, though," said Mr. Poyser, "when I think as we may have notice to quit, and belike be forced to take a farm twenty mile off."

"Eh," said the old man, staring at the floor and lifting his hands up and down, while his arms rested on the elbows of his chair, "it's a poor tale if I mun leave th' ould spot an be buried in a strange parish. An' you'll happen ha' double rates to pay," he added, looking up at his son.

"Well, thee mustna fret beforehand, father," said Martin the younger. "Happen the captain 'ull come home and make our peace wi' th' old squire. I build upo' that, for I know the captain 'll see folks righted if he can."

Chapter XXXV The Hidden Dread

IT was a busy time for Adam—the time between the beginning of November and the beginning of February, and he could see little of Hetty, except on Sundays. But a happy time, nevertheless, for it was taking him nearer and nearer to March, when they were to be married, and all the little preparations for their new housekeeping marked the progress towards the longed-for day. Two new rooms had been "run up" to the old house, for his mother and Seth were to live with them after all. Lisbeth had cried so piteously at the thought of leaving Adam that he had gone to Hetty and asked her if, for the love of him, she would put up with his mother's ways and consent to live with her. To his great delight, Hetty said, "Yes; I'd as soon she lived with us as not." Hetty's mind was oppressed at that moment with a worse difficulty than poor Lisbeth's ways; she could not care about them. So Adam was consoled for the disappointment he had felt when Seth had come back from his visit to Snowfield and said "it was no use—Dinah's heart wasna turned towards marrying." For when he told his mother that Hetty was willing they should all live together and there was no more need of them to think of parting, she said, in a more contented tone than he had heard her speak in since it had been settled that he was to be married, "Eh, my lad, I'll be as still as th' ould tabby, an' ne'er want to do aught but th' offal work, as she wonna like t' do. An' then we needna part the platters an' things, as ha' stood on the shelf together sin' afore thee wast born."

There was only one cloud that now and then came across Adam's sunshine: Hetty seemed unhappy sometimes. But to all his anxious, tender questions, she replied with an assurance that she was quite contented and wished nothing different; and the next time he saw her she was more lively than usual. It might be that she was a little overdone with work and anxiety now, for soon after Christmas Mrs. Poyser had taken another cold, which had brought on inflammation, and this illness had confined her to her room all through January. Hetty had to manage everything downstairs, and half-supply Molly's place too, while that good damsel waited on her mistress, and she seemed to throw herself so entirely into her new functions, working with a grave steadiness which was new in her, that Mr. Poyser often told Adam she was wanting to show him what a good housekeeper he would have; but he "doubted the lass was o'erdoing it—she must have a bit o' rest when her aunt could come downstairs."

This desirable event of Mrs. Poyser's coming downstairs happened in the early part of February, when some mild weather thawed the last patch of snow on the Binton Hills. On one of these days, soon after her aunt came down, Hetty went to Treddleston to buy some of the wedding things which were wanting, and which Mrs. Poyser had scolded her for neglecting, observing that she supposed "it was because they were not for th' outside, else she'd ha' bought 'em fast enough."

It was about ten o'clock when Hetty set off, and the slight hoarfrost that had whitened the hedges in the early morning had disappeared as the sun mounted the cloudless sky. Bright February days have a stronger charm of hope about them than any other days in the year. One likes to pause in the mild rays of the sun, and look over the gates at the patient plough-horses turning at the end of the furrow, and think that the beautiful year is all before one. The birds seem to feel just the same: their notes are as clear as the clear air. There are no leaves on the trees and hedgerows, but how green all the grassy fields are! And the dark purplish brown of the ploughed earth and of the bare branches is beautiful too. What a glad world this looks like, as one drives or rides along the valleys and over the hills! I have often thought so when, in foreign countries, where the fields and woods have looked to me like our English Loamshire—the rich land tilled with just as much care, the woods rolling down the gentle slopes to the green meadows—I have come on sormething by the roadside which has reminded me that I am not in Loamshire: an image of a great agony—the agony of the Cross. It has stood perhaps by the clustering apple-blossoms, or in the broad sunshine by the cornfield, or at a turning by the wood where a clear brook was gurgling below; and surely, if there came a traveller to this world who knew nothing of the story of man's life upon it, this image of agony would seem to him strangely out of place in the midst of this joyous nature. He would not know that hidden behind the apple-blossoms, or among the golden corn, or under the shrouding boughs of the wood, there might be a human heart beating heavily with anguish—perhaps a young blooming girl, not knowing where to turn for refuge from swift-advancing shame, understanding no more of this life of ours than a foolish lost lamb wandering farther and farther in the nightfall on the lonely heath, yet tasting the bitterest of life's bitterness.

Such things are sometimes hidden among the sunny fields and behind the blossoming orchards; and the sound of the gurgling brook, if you came close to one spot behind a small bush, would be mingled for your ear with a despairing human sob. No wonder man's religion has much sorrow in it: no wonder he needs a suffering God.

Hetty, in her red cloak and warm bonnet, with her basket in her hand, is turning towards a gate by the side of the Treddleston road, but not that she may have a more lingering enjoyment of the sunshine and think with hope of the long unfolding year. She hardly knows that the sun is shining; and for weeks, now, when she has hoped at all, it has been for something at which she herself trembles and shudders. She only wants to be out of the high-road, that she may walk slowly and not care how her face looks, as she dwells on wretched thoughts; and through this gate she can get into a field-path behind the wide thick hedgerows. Her great dark eyes wander blankly over the fields like the eyes of one who is desolate, homeless, unloved, not the promised bride of a brave tender man. But there are no tears in them: her tears were all wept away in the weary night, before she went to sleep. At the next stile the pathway branches off: there are two roads before her—one along by the hedgerow, which will by and by lead her into the road again, the other across the fields, which will take her much farther out of the way into the Scantlands, low shrouded pastures where she will see nobody. She chooses this and begins to walk a little faster, as if she had suddenly thought of an object towards which it was worth while to hasten. Soon she is in the Scantlands, where the grassy land slopes gradually downwards, and she leaves the level ground to follow the slope. Farther on there is a clump of trees on the low ground, and she is making her way towards it. No, it is not a clump of trees, but a dark shrouded pool, so full with the wintry rains that the under boughs of the elder-bushes lie low beneath the water. She sits down on the grassy bank, against the stooping stem of the great oak that hangs over the dark pool. She has thought of this pool often in the nights of the month that has just gone by, and now at last she is come to see it. She clasps her hands round her knees, and leans forward, and looks earnestly at it, as if trying to guess what sort of bed it would make for her young round limbs.

No, she has not courage to jump into that cold watery bed, and if she had, they might find her—they might find out why she had drowned herself. There is but one thing left to her: she must go away, go where they can't find her.

After the first on-coming of her great dread, some weeks after her betrothal to Adam, she had waited and waited, in the blind vague hope that something would happen to set her free from her terror; but she could wait no longer. All the force of her nature had been concentrated on the one effort of concealment, and she had shrunk with irresistible dread from every course that could tend towards a betrayal of her miserable secret. Whenever the thought of writing to Arthur had occurred to her, she had rejected it. He could do nothing for her that would shelter her from discovery and scorn among the relatives and neighbours who once more made all her world, now her airy dream had vanished. Her imagination no longer saw happiness with Arthur, for he could do nothing that would satisfy or soothe her pride. No, something else would happen—something must happen—to set her free from this dread. In young, childish, ignorant souls there is constantly this blind trust in some unshapen chance: it is as hard to a boy or girl to believe that a great wretchedness will actually befall them as to believe that they will die.

But now necessity was pressing hard upon her—now the time of her marriage was close at hand—she could no longer rest in this blind trust. She must run away; she must hide herself where no familiar eyes could detect her; and then the terror of wandering out into the world, of which she knew nothing, made the possibility of going to Arthur a thought which brought some comfort with it. She felt so helpless now, so unable to fashion the future for herself, that the prospect of throwing herself on him had a relief in it which was stronger than her pride. As she sat by the pool and shuddered at the dark cold water, the hope that he would receive her tenderly—that he would care for her and think for her—was like a sense of lulling warmth, that made her for the moment indifferent to everything else; and she began now to think of nothing but the scheme by which she should get away.

She had had a letter from Dinah lately, full of kind words about the coming marriage, which she had heard of from Seth; and when Hetty had read this letter aloud to her uncle, he had said, "I wish Dinah 'ud come again now, for she'd be a comfort to your aunt when you're gone. What do you think, my wench, o' going to see her as soon as you can be spared and persuading her to come back wi' you? You might happen persuade her wi' telling her as her aunt wants her, for all she writes o' not being able to come." Hetty had not liked the thought of going to Snowfield, and felt no longing to see Dinah, so she only said, "It's so far off, Uncle." But now she thought this proposed visit would serve as a pretext for going away. She would tell her aunt when she got home again that she should like the change of going to Snowfield for a week or ten days. And then, when she got to Stoniton, where nobody knew her, she would ask for the coach that would take her on the way to Windsor. Arthur was at Windsor, and she would go to him.

As soon as Hetty had determined on this scheme, she rose from the grassy bank of the pool, took up her basket, and went on her way to Treddleston, for she must buy the wedding things she had come out for, though she would never want them. She must be careful not to raise any suspicion that she was going to run away.

Mrs. Poyser was quite agreeably surprised that Hetty wished to go and see Dinah and try to bring her back to stay over the wedding. The sooner she went the better, since the weather was pleasant now; and Adam, when he came in the evening, said, if Hetty could set off to-morrow, he would make time to go with her to Treddleston and see her safe into the Stoniton coach.

"I wish I could go with you and take care of you, Hetty," he said, the next morning, leaning in at the coach door; "but you won't stay much beyond a week—the time 'ull seem long."

He was looking at her fondly, and his strong hand beld hers in its grasp. Hetty felt a sense of protection in his presence—she was used to it now: if she could have had the past undone and known no other love than her quiet liking for Adam! The tears rose as she gave him the last look.

"God bless her for loving me," said Adam, as he went on his way to work again, with Gyp at his heels.

But Hetty's tears were not for Adam—not for the anguish that would come upon him when he found she was gone from him for ever. They were for the misery of her own lot, which took her away from this brave tender man who offered up his whole life to her, and threw her, a poor helpless suppliant, on the man who would think it a misfortune that she was obliged to cling to him.

At three o'clock that day, when Hetty was on the coach that was to take her, they said, to Leicester—part of the long, long way to Windsor—she felt dimly that she might be travelling all this weary journey towards the beginning of new misery.

Yet Arthur was at Windsor; he would surely not be angry with her. If he did not mind about her as he used to do, he had promised to be good to her.

BOOK FIVE

Chapter XXXVI The Journey of Hope

A LONG, lonely journey, with sadness in the heart; away from the familiar to the strange: that is a hard and dreary thing even to the rich, the strong, the instructed; a hard thing, even when we are called by duty, not urged by dread.

What was it then to Hetty? With her poor narrow thoughts, no longer melting into vague hopes, but pressed upon by the chill of definite fear, repeating again and again the same small round of memories—shaping again and again the same childish, doubtful images of what was to come—seeing nothing in this wide world but the little history of her own pleasures and pains; with so little money in her pocket, and the way so long and difficult. Unless she could afford always to go in the coaches—and she felt sure she could not, for the journey to Stoniton was more expensive than she had expected—it was plain that she must trust to carriers' carts or slow waggons; and what a time it would be before she could get to the end of her journey! The burly old coachman from Oakbourne, seeing such a pretty young woman among the outside passengers, had invited her to come and sit beside him; and feeling that it became him as a man and a coachman to open the dialogue with a joke, he applied himself as soon as they were off the stones to the elaboration of one suitable in all respects. After many cuts with his whip and glances at Hetty out of the corner of his eye, he lifted his lips above the edge of his wrapper and said, "He's pretty nigh six foot, I'll be bound, isna he, now?"

"Who?" said Hetty, rather startled.

"Why, the sweetheart as you've left behind, or else him as you're goin' arter—which is it?"

Hetty felt her face flushing and then turning pale. She thought this coachman must know something about her. He must know Adam, and might tell him where she was gone, for it is difficult to country people to believe that those who make a figure in their own parish are not known everywhere else, and it was equally difficult to

Hetty to understand that chance words could happen to apply closely to her circumstances. She was too frightened to speak.

"Hegh, hegh!" said the coachman, seeing that his joke was not so gratifying as he had expected, "you munna take it too ser'ous; if he's behaved ill, get another. Such a pretty lass as you can get a sweetheart any day."

Hetty's fear was allayed by and by, when she found that the coachman made no further allusion to her personal concerns; but it still had the effect of preventing her from asking him what were the places on the road to Windsor. She told him she was only going a little way out of Stoniton, and when she got down at the inn where the coach stopped, she hastened away with her basket to another part of the town. When she had formed her plan of going to Windsor, she had not foreseen any difficulties except that of getting away, and after she had overcome this by proposing the visit to Dinah, her thoughts flew to the meeting with Arthur and the question how he would behave to her—not resting on any probable incidents of the journey. She was too entirely ignorant of traveling to imagine any of its details, and with all her store of money—her three guineas—in her pocket, she thought herself amply provided. It was not until she found how much it cost her to get to Stoniton that she began to be alarmed about the journey, and then, for the first time, she felt her ignorance as to the places that must be passed on her way. Oppressed with this new alarm, she walked along the grim Stoniton streets, and at last turned into a shabby little inn, where she hoped to get a cheap lodging for the night. Here she asked the landlord if he could tell her what places she must go to, to get to Windsor.

"Well, I can't rightly say. Windsor must be pretty nigh London, for it's where the king lives," was the answer. "Anyhow, you'd best go t' Ashby next—that's south'ard. But there's as many places from here to London as there's houses in Stoniton, by what I can make out. I've never been no traveller myself. But how comes a lone young woman like you to be thinking o' taking such a journey as that?"

"I'm going to my brother—he's a soldier at Windsor," said Hetty, frightened at the landlord's questioning look. "I can't afford to go by the coach; do you think there's a cart goes toward Ashby in the morning?"

"Yes, there may be carts if anybody knowed where they started from; but you might run over the town before you found out. You'd best set off and walk, and trust to summat overtaking you."

Every word sank like lead on Hetty's spirits; she saw the journey stretch bit by bit before her now. Even to get to Ashby seemed a hard thing: it might take the day, for what she knew, and that was nothing to the rest of the journey. But it must be done—she must get to Arthur. Oh, how she yearned to be again with somebody who would care for her! She who had never got up in the morning without the certainty of seeing familiar faces, people on whom she had an acknowledged claim; whose farthest journey had been to Rosseter on the pillion with her uncle; whose thoughts had always been taking holiday in dreams of pleasure, because all the business of her life was managed for her—this kittenlike Hetty, who till a few months ago had never felt any other grief than that of envying Mary Burge a new ribbon, or being girded at by her aunt for neglecting Totty, must now make her toilsome way in loneliness, her peaceful home left behind for ever, and nothing but a tremulous hope of distant refuge before her. Now for the first time, as she lay down to-night in the strange hard bed, she felt that her home had been a happy one, that her uncle had been very good to her, that her quiet lot at Hayslope among the things and people she knew, with her little pride in her one best gown and bonnet, and nothing to hide from any one, was what she would like to wake up to as a reality, and find that all the feverish life she had known besides was a short nightmare. She thought of all she had left behind with yearning regret for her own sake. Her own misery filled her heart—there was no room in it for other people's sorrow. And yet, before the cruel letter, Arthur had been so tender and loving. The memory of that had still a charm for her, though it was no more than a soothing draught that just made pain bearable. For Hetty could conceive no other existence for herself in future than a hidden one, and a hidden life, even with love, would have had no delights for her; still less a life mingled with shame. She knew no romances, and had only a feeble share in the feelings which are the source of romance, so that well-read ladies may find it difficult to understand her state of mind. She was too ignorant of everything beyond the simple notions and habits in which she had been brought up to have any more definite idea of her probable future than that

Arthur would take care of her somehow, and shelter her from anger and scorn. He would not marry her and make her a lady; and apart from that she could think of nothing he could give towards which she looked with longing and ambition.

The next morning she rose early, and taking only some milk and bread for her breakfast, set out to walk on the road towards Ashby, under a leaden-coloured sky, with a narrowing streak of yellow, like a departing hope, on the edge of the horizon. Now in her faintness of heart at the length and difficulty of her journey, she was most of all afraid of spending her money, and becoming so destitute that she would have to ask people's charity; for Hetty had the pride not only of a proud nature but of a proud class—the class that pays the most poor-rates, and most shudders at the idea of profiting by a poor-rate. It had not yet occurred to her that she might get money for her locket and earrings which she carried with her, and she applied all her small arithmetic and knowledge of prices to calculating how many meals and how many rides were contained in her two guineas, and the odd shillings, which had a melancholy look, as if they were the pale ashes of the other bright-flaming coin.

For the first few miles out of Stoniton, she walked on bravely, always fixing on some tree or gate or projecting bush at the most distant visible point in the road as a goal, and feeling a faint joy when she had reached it. But when she came to the fourth milestone, the first she had happened to notice among the long grass by the roadside, and read that she was still only four miles beyond Stoniton, her courage sank. She had come only this little way, and yet felt tired, and almost hungry again in the keen morning air; for though Hetty was accustomed to much movement and exertion indoors, she was not used to long walks which produced quite a different sort of fatigue from that of household activity. As she was looking at the milestone she felt some drops falling on her face—it was beginning to rain. Here was a new trouble which had not entered into her sad thoughts before, and quite weighed down by this sudden addition to her burden, she sat down on the step of a stile and began to sob hysterically. The beginning of hardship is like the first taste of bitter food—it seems for a moment unbearable; yet, if there is nothing else to satisfy our hunger, we take another bite and find it possible to go on. When Hetty recovered from her burst of weeping, she rallied her fainting courage: it was raining, and she must try to get on to a village where she might find rest and shelter. Presently, as she walked on wearily, she heard the rumbling of heavy wheels behind her; a covered waggon was coming, creeping slowly along with a slouching driver cracking his whip beside the horses. She waited for it, thinking that if the waggoner were not a very sour-looking man, she would ask him to take her up. As the waggon approached her, the driver had fallen behind, but there was something in the front of the big vehicle which encouraged her. At any previous moment in her life she would not have noticed it, but now, the new susceptibility that suffering had awakened in her caused this object to impress her strongly. It was only a small white-and-liver-coloured spaniel which sat on the front ledge of the waggon, with large timid eyes, and an incessant trembling in the body, such as you may have seen in some of these small creatures. Hetty cared little for animals, as you know, but at this moment she felt as if the helpless timid creature had some fellowship with her, and without being quite aware of the reason, she was less doubtful about speaking to the driver, who now came forward—a large ruddy man, with a sack over his shoulders, by way of scarf or mantle.

"Could you take me up in your waggon, if you're going towards Ashby?" said Hetty. "I'll pay you for it."

"Aw," said the big fellow, with that slowly dawning smile which belongs to heavy faces, "I can take y' up fawst enough wi'out bein' paid for't if you dooant mind lyin' a bit closish a-top o' the wool-packs. Where do you coom from? And what do you want at Ashby?"

"I come from Stoniton. I'm going a long way—to Windsor."

"What! Arter some service, or what?"

"Going to my brother—he's a soldier there."

"Well, I'm going no furder nor Leicester—and fur enough too—but I'll take you, if you dooant mind being a bit long on the road. Th' hosses wooant feel YOUR weight no more nor they feel the little doog there, as I puck up on the road a fortni't agoo. He war lost, I b'lieve, an's been all of a tremble iver sin'. Come, gi' us your basket an' come behind and let me put y' in."

To lie on the wool-packs, with a cranny left between the curtains of the awning to let in the air, was luxury to Hetty now, and she half-slept away the hours till the driver came to ask her if she wanted to get down and have "some victual"; he himself was going to eat his dinner at this "public." Late at night they reached Leicester, and so this second day of Hetty's journey was past. She had spent no money except what she had paid for her food, but she felt that this slow journeying would be intolerable for her another day, and in the morning she found her way to a coach-office to ask about the road to Windsor, and see if it would cost her too much to go part of the distance by coach again. Yes! The distance was too great—the coaches were too dear—she must give them up; but the elderly clerk at the office, touched by her pretty anxious face, wrote down for her the names of the chief places she must pass through. This was the only comfort she got in Leicester, for the men stared at her as she went along the street, and for the first time in her life Hetty wished no one would look at her. She set out walking again; but this day she was fortunate, for she was soon overtaken by a carrier's cart which carried her to Hinckley, and by the help of a return chaise, with a drunken postilion—who frightened her by driving like Jehu the son of Nimshi, and shouting hilarious remarks at her, twisting himself backwards on his saddle—she was before night in the heart of woody Warwickshire: but still almost a hundred miles from Windsor, they told her. Oh what a large world it was, and what hard work for her to find her way in it! She went by mistake to Stratford-on-Avon, finding Stratford set down in her list of places, and then she was told she had come a long way out of the right road. It was not till the fifth day that she got to Stony Stratford. That seems but a slight journey as you look at the map, or remember your own pleasant travels to and from the meadowy banks of the Avon. But how wearily long it was to Hetty! It seemed to her as if this country of flat fields, and hedgerows, and dotted houses, and villages, and market-towns—all so much alike to her indifferent eyes—must have no end, and she must go on wandering among them for ever, waiting tired at toll-gates for some cart to come, and then finding the cart went only a little way—a very little way—to the miller's a mile off perhaps; and she hated going into the public houses, where she must go to get food and ask questions, because there were always men lounging there, who stared at her and joked her rudely. Her body was very weary too with these days of new fatigue and anxiety; they had made her look more pale and worn than all the time of hidden dread she had gone through at home. When at last she reached Stony Stratford, her impatience and weariness had become too strong for her economical caution; she determined to take the coach for the rest of the way, though it should cost her all her remaining money. She would need nothing at Windsor but to find Arthur. When she had paid the fare for the last coach, she had only a shilling; and as she got down at the sign of the Green Man in Windsor at twelve o'clock in the middle of the seventh day, hungry and faint, the coachman came up, and begged her to "remember him." She put her hand in her pocket and took out the shilling, but the tears came with the sense of exhaustion and the thought that she was giving away her last means of getting food, which she really required before she could go in search of Arthur. As she held out the shilling, she lifted up her dark tear-filled eyes to the coachman's face and said, "Can you give me back sixpence?"

"No, no," he said, gruffly, "never mind—put the shilling up again."

The landlord of the Green Man had stood near enough to witness this scene, and he was a man whose abundant feeding served to keep his good nature, as well as his person, in high condition. And that lovely tearful face of Hetty's would have found out the sensitive fibre in most men.

"Come, young woman, come in," he said, "and have a drop o' something; you're pretty well knocked up, I can see that."

He took her into the bar and said to his wife, "Here, missis, take this young woman into the parlour; she's a little overcome"—for Hetty's tears were falling fast. They were merely hysterical tears: she thought she had no reason for weeping now, and was vexed that she was too weak and tired to help it. She was at Windsor at last, not far from Arthur.

She looked with eager, hungry eyes at the bread and meat and beer that the landlady brought her, and for some minutes she forgot everything else in the delicious sensations of satisfying hunger and recovering from exhaustion. The landlady sat opposite to her as she ate, and looked at her earnestly. No wonder: Hetty had thrown off her bonnet, and her curls had fallen down. Her face was all the more touching in its youth and beauty because of its weary look, and the good woman's eyes presently wandered to her figure, which in her hurried dressing on her journey she had taken no pains to conceal; moreover, the stranger's eye detects what the familiar unsuspecting eye leaves unnoticed.

"Why, you're not very fit for travelling," she said, glancing while she spoke at Hetty's ringless hand. "Have you come far?"

"Yes," said Hetty, roused by this question to exert more self-command, and feeling the better for the food she had taken. "I've come a good long way, and it's very tiring. But I'm better now. Could you tell me which way to go to this place?" Here Hetty took from her pocket a bit of paper: it was the end of Arthur's letter on which he had written his address.

While she was speaking, the landlord had come in and had begun to look at her as earnestly as his wife had done. He took up the piece of paper which Hetty handed across the table, and read the address.

"Why, what do you want at this house?" he said. It is in the nature of innkeepers and all men who have no pressing business of their own to ask as many questions as possible before giving any information.

"I want to see a gentleman as is there," said Hetty.

"But there's no gentleman there," returned the landlord. "It's shut up—been shut up this fortnight. What gentleman is it you want? Perhaps I can let you know where to find him."

"It's Captain Donnithorne," said Hetty tremulously, her heart beginning to beat painfully at this disappointment of her hope that she should find Arthur at once.

"Captain Donnithorne? Stop a bit," said the landlard, slowly. "Was he in the Loamshire Militia? A tall young officer with a fairish skin and reddish whiskers—and had a servant by the name o' Pym?"

"Oh yes," said Hetty; "you know him—where is he?"

"A fine sight o' miles away from here. The Loamshire Militia's gone to Ireland; it's been gone this fortnight."

"Look there! She's fainting," said the landlady, hastening to support Hetty, who had lost her miserable consciousness and looked like a beautiful corpse. They carried her to the sofa and loosened her dress.

"Here's a bad business, I suspect," said the landlord, as he brought in some water.

"Ah, it's plain enough what sort of business it is," said the wife. "She's not a common flaunting dratchell, I can see that. She looks like a respectable country girl, and she comes from a good way off, to judge by her tongue. She talks something like that ostler we had that come from the north. He was as honest a fellow as we ever had about the house—they're all honest folks in the north."

"I never saw a prettier young woman in my life," said the husband. "She's like a pictur in a shop-winder. It goes to one's 'eart to look at her."

"It 'ud have been a good deal better for her if she'd been uglier and had more conduct," said the landlady, who on any charitable construction must have been supposed to have more "conduct" than beauty. "But she's coming to again. Fetch a drop more water."

Chapter XXXVII The Journey in Despair

HETTY was too ill through the rest of that day for any questions to be addressed to her—too ill even to think with any distinctness of the evils that were to come. She only felt that all her hope was crushed, and that instead of having found a refuge she had only reached the borders of a new wilderness where no goal lay before her. The sensations of bodily sickness, in a comfortable bed, and with the tendance of the good-natured landlady, made a sort of respite for her; such a respite as there is in the faint weariness which obliges a man to throw himself on the sand instead of toiling onward under the scorching sun.

But when sleep and rest had brought back the strength necessary for the keenness of mental suffering—when she lay the next morning looking at the growing light which was like a cruel task-master returning to urge from her a fresh round of hated hopeless labour—she began to think what course she must take, to remember that all her money was gone, to look at the prospect of further wandering among strangers with the new clearness shed on it by the experience of her journey to Windsor. But which way could she turn? It was impossible for her to enter into any service, even if she could obtain it. There was nothing but immediate beggary before her. She thought of a young woman who had been found against the church wall at Hayslope one Sunday, nearly dead with cold and hunger—a tiny infant in her arms. The woman was rescued and taken to the parish. "The parish!" You can perhaps hardly understand the effect of that word on a mind like Hetty's, brought up among people who were somewhat hard in their feelings even towards poverty, who lived among the fields, and had little pity for want and rags as a cruel inevitable fate such as they sometimes seem in cities, but held them a mark of idleness and vice—and it was idleness and vice that brought burdens on the parish. To Hetty the "parish" was next to the prison in obloquy, and to ask anything of strangers—to beg—lay in the same far-off hideous region of intolerable shame that Hetty had all her life thought it impossible she could ever come near. But now the remembrance of that wretched woman whom she had seen herself, on her way from church, being carried into Joshua Rann's, came back upon her with the new terrible sense that there was very little now to divide HER from the same lot. And the dread of bodily hardship mingled with the dread of shame; for Hetty had the luxurious nature of a round soft-coated pet animal.

How she yearned to be back in her safe home again, cherished and cared for as she had always been! Her aunt's scolding about trifles would have been music to her ears now; she longed for it; she used to hear it in a time when she had only trifles to hide. Could she be the same Hetty that used to make up the butter in the dairy with the Guelder roses peeping in at the window—she, a runaway whom her friends would not open their doors to again, lying in this strange bed, with the knowledge that she had no money to pay for what she received, and must offer those strangers some of the clothes in her basket? It was then she thought of her locket and ear-rings, and seeing her pocket lie near, she reached it and spread the contents on the bed before her. There were the locket and ear-rings in the little velvet-lined boxes, and with them there was a beautiful silver thimble which Adam had bought her, the words "Remember me" making the ornament of the border; a steel purse, with her one shilling in it;and a small red-leather case, fastening with a strap. Those beautiful little ear-rings, with their delicate pearls and garnet, that she had tried in her ears with such longing in the bright sunshine on the 30th of July! She had no longing to put them in her ears now: her head with its dark rings of hair lay back languidly on the pillow, and the sadness that rested about her brow and eyes was something too hard for regretful memory. Yet she put her hands up to her ears: it was because there were some thin gold rings in them, which were also worth a little money. Yes, she could surely get some money for her ornaments: those Arthur had given her must have cost a great deal of money. The landlord and landlady had been good to her; perhaps they would help her to get the money for these things.

But this money would not keep her long. What should she do when it was gone? Where should she go? The horrible thought of want and beggary drove her once to think she would go back to her uncle and aunt and ask them to forgive her and have pity on her. But she shrank from that idea again, as she might have shrunk from scorching metal. She could never endure that shame before her uncle and aunt, before Mary Burge, and the servants at the Chase, and the people at Broxton, and everybody who knew her. They should never know what had happened to her. What could she do? She would go away from Windsor—travel again as she had done the last week, and get among the flat green fields with the high hedges round them, where nobody could see her or know her; and there, perhaps, when there was nothing else she could do, she should get courage to drown herself in some pond like that in the Scantlands. Yes, she would get away from Windsor as soon as possible: she didn't like these people at the inn to know about her, to know that she had come to look for Captain Donnithorne. She must think of some reason to tell them why she had asked for him.

With this thought she began to put the things back into her pocket, meaning to get up and dress before the landlady came to her. She had her hand on the red-leather case, when it occurred to her that there might be something in this case which she had forgotten—something worth selling; for without knowing what she should do with her life, she craved the means of living as long as possible; and when we desire eagerly to find something, we are apt to search for it in hopeless places. No, there was nothing but common needles and pins, and dried tulip-petals between the paper leaves where she had written down her little money-accounts. But on one of these leaves there was a name, which, often as she had seen it before, now flashed on Hetty's mind like a newly discovered message. The name was—Dinah Morris, Snowfield. There was a text above it, written, as well as the name, by Dinah's own hand with a little pencil, one evening that they were sitting together and Hetty happened to have the red case lying open before her. Hetty did not read the text now: she was only arrested by the name. Now, for the first time, she remembered without indifference the affectionate kindness Dinah had shown her, and those words of Dinah in the bed-chamber—that Hetty must think of her as a friend in trouble. Suppose she were to go to Dinah, and ask her to help her? Dinah did not think about things as other people did. She was a mystery to Hetty, but Hetty knew she was always kind. She couldn't imagine Dinah's face turning away from her in dark reproof or scorn, Dinah's voice willingly speaking ill of her, or rejoicing in her misery as a punishment. Dinah did not seem to belong to that world of Hetty's, whose glance she dreaded like scorching fire. But even to her Hetty shrank from beseeching and confession. She could not prevail on herself to say, "I will go to Dinah": she only thought of that as a possible alternative, if she had not courage for death.

The good landlady was amazed when she saw Hetty come downstairs soon after herself, neatly dressed, and looking resolutely self-possessed. Hetty told her she was quite well this morning. She had only been very tired and overcome with her journey, for she had come a long way to ask about her brother, who had run away, and they thought he was gone for a soldier, and Captain Donnithorne might know, for he had been very kind to her brother once. It was a lame story, and the landlady looked doubtfully at Hetty as she told it; but there was a resolute air of self-reliance about her this morning, so different from the helpless prostration of yesterday, that the landlady hardly knew how to make a remark that might seem like prying into other people's affairs. She only invited her to sit down to breakfast with them, and in the course of it Hetty brought out her ear-rings and locket, and asked the landlord if he could help her to get money for them. Her journey, she said, had cost her much more than she expected, and now she had no money to get back to her friends, which she wanted to do at once.

It was not the first time the landlady had seen the ornaments, for she had examined the contents of Hetty's pocket yesterday, and she and her husband had discussed the fact of a country girl having these beautiful things, with a stronger conviction than ever that Hetty had been miserably deluded by the fine young officer.

"Well," said the landlord, when Hetty had spread the precious trifles before him, "we might take 'em to the jeweller's shop, for there's one not far off; but Lord bless you, they wouldn't give you a quarter o' what the things are worth. And you wouldn't like to part with 'em?" he added, looking at her inquiringly.

"Oh, I don't mind," said Hetty, hastily, "so as I can get money to go back."

"And they might think the things were stolen, as you wanted to sell 'em," he went on, "for it isn't usual for a young woman like you to have fine jew'llery like that."

The blood rushed to Hetty's face with anger. "I belong to respectable folks," she said; "I'm not a thief."

"No, that you aren't, I'll be bound," said the landlady; "and you'd no call to say that," looking indignantly at her husband. "The things were gev to her: that's plain enough to be seen."

"I didn't mean as I thought so," said the husband, apologetically, "but I said it was what the jeweller might think, and so he wouldn't be offering much money for 'em."

"Well," said the wife, "suppose you were to advance some money on the things yourself, and then if she liked to redeem 'em when she got home, she could. But if we heard nothing from her after two months, we might do as we liked with 'em."

I will not say that in this accommodating proposition the landlady had no regard whatever to the possible reward of her good nature in the ultimate possession of the locket and ear-rings: indeed, the effect they would have in that case on the mind of the grocer's wife had presented itself with remarkable vividness to her rapid imagination. The landlord took up the ornaments and pushed out his lips in a meditative manner. He wished Hetty well, doubtless; but pray, how many of your well-wishers would decline to make a little gain out of you? Your landlady is sincerely affected at parting with you, respects you highly, and will really rejoice if any one else is generous to you; but at the same time she hands you a bill by which she gains as high a percentage as possible.

"How much money do you want to get home with, young woman?" said the well-wisher, at length.

"Three guineas," answered Hetty, fixing on the sum she set out with, for want of any other standard, and afraid of asking too much.

"Well, I've no objections to advance you three guineas," said the landlord; "and if you like to send it me back and get the jewellery again, you can, you know. The Green Man isn't going to run away."

"Oh yes, I'll be very glad if you'll give me that," said Hetty, relieved at the thought that she would not have to go to the jeweller's and be stared at and questioned.

"But if you want the things again, you'll write before long," said the landlady, "because when two months are up, we shall make up our minds as you don't want 'em."

"Yes," said Hetty indifferently.

The husband and wife were equally content with this arrangement. The husband thought, if the ornaments were not redeemed, he could make a good thing of it by taking them to London and selling them. The wife thought she would coax the good man into letting her keep them. And they were accommodating Hetty, poor thing—a pretty, respectable-looking young woman, apparently in a sad case. They declined to take anything for her food and bed: she was quite welcome. And at eleven o'clock Hetty said "Good-bye" to them with the same quiet, resolute air she had worn all the morning, mounting the coach that was to take her twenty miles back along the way she had come.

There is a strength of self-possession which is the sign that the last hope has departed. Despair no more leans on others than perfect contentment, and in despair pride ceases to be counteracted by the sense of dependence.

Hetty felt that no one could deliver her from the evils that would make life hateful to her; and no one, she said to herself, should ever know her misery and humiliation. No; she would not confess even to Dinah. She would wander out of sight, and drown herself where her body would never be found, and no one should know what had become of her.

When she got off this coach, she began to walk again, and take cheap rides in carts, and get cheap meals, going on and on without distinct purpose, yet strangely, by some fascination, taking the way she had come, though she was determined not to go back to her own country. Perhaps it was because she had fixed her mind on the grassy Warwickshire fields, with the bushy tree-studded hedgerows that made a hiding-place even in this leafless season. She went more slowly than she came, often getting over the stiles and sitting for hours under the hedgerows, looking before her with blank, beautiful eyes; fancying herself at the edge of a hidden pool, low down, like that in the Scantlands; wondering if it were very painful to be drowned, and if there would be anything worse after death than what she dreaded in life. Religious doctrines had taken no hold on Hetty's mind. She was one of those numerous people who have had godfathers and god-mothers, learned their catechism, been confirmed, and gone to church every Sunday, and yet, for any practical result of strength in life, or trust in death, have never appropriated a single Christian idea or Christian feeling. You would misunderstand her thoughts during these wretched days, if you imagined that they were influenced either by religious fears or religious hopes.

She chose to go to Stratford-on-Avon again, where she had gone before by mistake, for she remembered some grassy fields on her former way towards it—fields among which she thought she might find just the sort of pool she had in her mind. Yet she took care of her money still; she carried her basket; death seemed still a long way off, and life was so strong in her. She craved food and rest—she hastened towards them at the very moment she was picturing to herself the bank from which she would leap towards death. It was already five days since she had left Windsor, for she had wandered about, always avoiding speech or questioning looks, and recovering her air of proud self-dependence whenever she was under observation, choosing her decent lodging at night, and dressing herself neatly in the morning, and setting off on her way steadily, or remaining under shelter if it rained, as if she had a happy life to cherish.

And yet, even in her most self-conscious moments, the face was sadly different from that which had smiled at itself in the old specked glass, or smiled at others when they glanced at it admiringly. A hard and even fierce look had come in the eyes, though their lashes were as long as ever, and they had all their dark brightness. And the cheek was never dimpled with smiles now. It was the same rounded, pouting, childish prettiness, but with all love and belief in love departed from it—the sadder for its beauty, like that wondrous Medusa-face, with the passionate, passionless lips.

At last she was among the fields she had been dreaming of, on a long narrow pathway leading towards a wood. If there should be a pool in that wood! It would be better hidden than one in the fields. No, it was not a wood, only a wild brake, where there had once been gravel-pits, leaving mounds and hollows studded with brushwood and small trees. She roamed up and down, thinking there was perhaps a pool in every hollow before she came to it, till her limbs were weary, and she sat down to rest. The afternoon was far advanced, and the leaden sky was darkening, as if the sun were setting behind it. After a little while Hetty started up again, feeling that darkness would soon come on; and she must put off finding the pool till to-morrow, and make her way to some shelter for the night. She had quite lost her way in the fields, and might as well go in one direction as another, for aught she knew. She walked through field after field, and no village, no house was in sight; but there, at the corner of this pasture, there was a break in the hedges; the land seemed to dip down a little, and two trees leaned towards each other across the opening. Hetty's heart gave a great heat as she thought there must be a pool there. She walked towards it heavily over the tufted grass, with pale lips and a sense of trembling. It was as if the thing were come in spite of herself, instead of being the object of her search.

There it was, black under the darkening sky: no motion, no sound near. She set down her basket, and then sank down herself on the grass, trembling. The pool had its wintry depth now: by the time it got shallow, as she remembered the pools did at Hayslope, in the summer, no one could find out that it was her body. But then there was her basket—she must hide that too. She must throw it into the water—make it heavy with stones first, and then throw it in. She got up to look about for stones, and soon brought five or six, which she laid down beside her basket, and then sat down again. There was no need to hurry—there was all the night to drown herself in. She sat leaning her elbow on the basket. She was weary, hungry. There were some buns in her basket—three, which she had supplied herself with at the place where she ate her dinner. She took them out now and ate them eagerly, and then sat still again, looking at the pool. The soothed sensation that came over her from the satisfaction of her hunger, and this fixed dreamy attitude, brought on drowsiness, and presently her head sank down on her knees. She was fast asleep.

When she awoke it was deep night, and she felt chill. She was frightened at this darkness—frightened at the long night before her. If she could but throw herself into the water! No, not yet. She began to walk about that she might get warm again, as if she would have more resolution then. Oh how long the time was in that darkness! The bright hearth and the warmth and the voices of home, the secure uprising and lying down, the familiar fields, the familiar people, the Sundays and holidays with their simple joys of dress and feasting—all the sweets of her young life rushed before her now, and she seemed to be stretching her arms towards them across a great gulf. She set her teeth when she thought of Arthur. She cursed him, without knowing what her cursing would do. She wished he too might know desolation, and cold, and a life of shame that he dared not end by death.

The horror of this cold, and darkness, and solitude—out of all human reach—became greater every long minute. It was almost as if she were dead already, and knew that she was dead, and longed to get back to life again. But no: she was alive still; she had not taken the dreadful leap. She felt a strange contradictory wretchedness and exultation: wretchedness, that she did not dare to face death; exultation, that she was still in life—that she might yet know light and warmth again. She walked backwards and forwards to warm herself, beginning to discern something of the objects around her, as her eyes became accustomed to the night—the darker line of the hedge, the rapid motion of some living creature—perhaps a field-mouse—rushing across the grass. She no longer felt as if the darkness hedged her in. She thought she could walk back across the field, and get over the stile; and then, in the very next field, she thought she remembered there was a hovel of furze near a sheepfold. If she could get into that hovel, she would be warmer. She could pass the night there, for that was what Alick did at Hayslope in lambing-time. The thought of this hovel brought the energy of a new hope. She took up her basket and walked across the field, but it was some time before she got in the right direction for the stile. The exercise and the occupation of finding the stile were a stimulus to her, however, and lightened the horror of the darkness and solitude. There were sheep in the next field, and she startled a group as she set down her basket and got over the stile; and the sound of their movement comforted her, for it assured her that her impression was right—this was the field where she had seen the hovel, for it was the field where the sheep were. Right on along the path, and she would get to it. She reached the opposite gate, and felt her way along its rails and the rails of the sheep-fold, till her hand encountered the pricking of the gorsy wall. Delicious sensation! She had found the shelter. She groped her way, touching the prickly gorse, to the door, and pushed it open. It was an ill-smelling close place, but warm, and there was straw on the ground. Hetty sank down on the straw with a sense of escape. Tears came—she had never shed tears before since she left Windsor—tears and sobs of hysterical joy that she had still hold of life, that she was still on the familiar earth, with the sheep near her. The very consciousness of her own limbs was a delight to her: she turned up her sleeves, and kissed her arms with the passionate love of life. Soon warmth and weariness lulled her in the midst of her sobs, and she fell continually into dozing, fancying herself at the brink of the pool again—fancying that she had jumped into the water, and then awaking with a start, and wondering where she was. But at last deep dreamless sleep came; her head, guarded by her bonnet, found a pillow against the gorsy wall, and the poor soul, driven to and fro between two equal terrors, found the one relief that was possible to it—the relief of unconsciousness.

Alas! That relief seems to end the moment it has begun. It seemed to Hetty as if those dozen dreams had only passed into another dream—that she was in the hovel, and her aunt was standing over her with a candle in her hand. She trembled under her aunt's glance, and opened her eyes. There was no candle, but there was light in the hovel—the light of early morning through the open door. And there was a face looking down on her; but it was an unknown face, belonging to an elderly man in a smock-frock.

"Why, what do you do here, young woman?" the man said roughly.

Hetty trembled still worse under this real fear and shame than she had done in her momentary dream under her aunt's glance. She felt that she was like a beggar already—found sleeping in that place. But in spite of her trembling, she was so eager to account to the man for her presence here, that she found words at once.

"I lost my way," she said. "I'm travelling—north'ard, and I got away from the road into the fields, and was overtaken by the dark. Will you tell me the way to the nearest village?"

She got up as she was speaking, and put her hands to her bonnet to adjust it, and then laid hold of her basket.

The man looked at her with a slow bovine gaze, without giving her any answer, for some seconds. Then he turned away and walked towards the door of the hovel, but it was not till he got there that he stood still, and, turning his shoulder half-round towards her, said, "Aw, I can show you the way to Norton, if you like. But what do you do gettin' out o' the highroad?" he added, with a tone of gruff reproof. "Y'ull be gettin' into mischief, if you dooant mind."

"Yes," said Hetty, "I won't do it again. I'll keep in the road, if you'll be so good as show me how to get to it."

"Why dooant you keep where there's a finger-poasses an' folks to ax the way on?" the man said, still more gruffly. "Anybody 'ud think you was a wild woman, an' look at yer."

Hetty was frightened at this gruff old man, and still more at this last suggestion that she looked like a wild woman. As she followed him out of the hovel she thought she would give him a sixpence for telling her the way, and then he would not suppose she was wild. As he stopped to point out the road to her, she put her hand in her pocket to get the six-pence ready, and when he was turning away, without saying good-morning, she held it out to him and said, "Thank you; will you please to take something for your trouble?"

He looked slowly at the sixpence, and then said, "I want none o' your money. You'd better take care on't, else you'll get it stool from yer, if you go trapesin' about the fields like a mad woman a-thatway."

The man left her without further speech, and Hetty held on her way. Another day had risen, and she must wander on. It was no use to think of drowning herself—she could not do it, at least while she had money left to buy food and strength to journey on. But the incident on her waking this morning heightened her dread of that time when her money would be all gone; she would have to sell her basket and clothes then, and she would really look like a beggar or a wild woman, as the man had said. The passionate joy in life she had felt in the night, after escaping from the brink of the black cold death in the pool, was gone now. Life now, by the morning light, with the impression of that man's hard wondering look at her, was as full of dread as death—it was worse; it was a dread to which she felt chained, from which she shrank and shrank as she did from the black pool, and yet could find no refuge from it.

She took out her money from her purse, and looked at it. She had still two-and-twenty shillings; it would serve her for many days more, or it would help her to get on faster to Stonyshire, within reach of Dinah. The thought of Dinah urged itself more strongly now, since the experience of the night had driven her shuddering imagination away from the pool. If it had been only going to Dinah—if nobody besides Dinah would ever know—Hetty could have made up her mind to go to her. The soft voice, the pitying eyes, would have drawn her. But afterwards the other people must know, and she could no more rush on that shame than she could rush on death.

She must wander on and on, and wait for a lower depth of despair to give her courage. Perhaps death would come to her, for she was getting less and less able to bear the day's weariness. And yet—such is the strange action of our souls, drawing us by a lurking desire towards the very ends we dread—Hetty, when she set out again from Norton, asked the straightest road northwards towards Stonyshire, and kept it all that day.

Poor wandering Hetty, with the rounded childish face and the hard, unloving, despairing soul looking out of it—with the narrow heart and narrow thoughts, no room in them for any sorrows but her own, and tasting that sorrow with the more intense bitterness! My heart bleeds for her as I see her toiling along on her weary feet, or seated in a cart, with her eyes fixed vacantly on the road before her, never thinking or caring whither it tends, till hunger comes and makes her desire that a village may be near.

What will be the end, the end of her objectless wandering, apart from all love, caring for human beings only through her pride, clinging to life only as the hunted wounded brute clings to it?

God preserve you and me from being the beginners of such misery!

Chapter XXXVIII The Quest

THE first ten days after Hetty's departure passed as quietly as any other days with the family at the Hall Farm, and with Adam at his daily work. They had expected Hetty to stay away a week or ten days at least, perhaps a little longer if Dinah came back with her, because there might then be somethung to detain them at Snowfield. But when a fortnight had passed they began to feel a little surprise that Hetty did not return; she must surely have found it pleasanter to be with Dinah than any one could have supposed. Adam, for his part, was getting very impatient to see her, and he resolved that, if she did not appear the next day (Saturday), he would set out on Sunday morning to fetch her. There was no coach on a Sunday, but by setting out before it was light, and perhaps getting a lift in a cart by the way, he would arrive pretty early at Snowfield, and bring back Hetty the next day—Dinah too, if she were coming. It was quite time Hetty came home, and he would afford to lose his Monday for the sake of bringing her.

His project was quite approved at the Farm when he went there on Saturday evening. Mrs. Poyser desired him emphatically not to come back without Hetty, for she had been quite too long away, considering the things she had to get ready by the middle of March, and a week was surely enough for any one to go out for their health. As for Dinah, Mrs. Poyser had small hope of their bringing her, unless they could make her believe the folks at Hayslope were twice as miserable as the folks at Snowfield. "Though," said Mrs. Poyser, by way of conclusion, "you might tell her she's got but one aunt left, and SHE'S wasted pretty nigh to a shadder; and we shall p'rhaps all be gone twenty mile farther off her next Michaelmas, and shall die o' broken hearts among strange folks, and leave the children fatherless and motherless."

"Nay, nay," said Mr. Poyser, who certainly had the air of a man perfectly heart-whole, "it isna so bad as that. Thee't looking rarely now, and getting flesh every day. But I'd be glad for Dinah t' come, for she'd help thee wi' the little uns: they took t' her wonderful."

So at daybreak, on Sunday, Adam set off. Seth went with him the first mile or two, for the thought of Snowfield and the possibility that Dinah might come again made him restless, and the walk with Adam in the cold morning air, both in their best clothes, helped to give him a sense of Sunday calm. It was the last morning in February, with a low grey sky, and a slight hoar-frost on the green border of the road and on the black hedges. They heard the gurgling of the full brooklet hurrying down the hill, and the faint twittering of the early birds. For they walked in silence, though with a pleased sense of companionship.

"Good-bye, lad," said Adam, laying his hand on Seth's shoulder and looking at him affectionately as they were about to part. "I wish thee wast going all the way wi' me, and as happy as I am."

"I'm content, Addy, I'm content," said Seth cheerfully. "I'll be an old bachelor, belike, and make a fuss wi' thy children."

The'y turned away from each other, and Seth walked leisurely homeward, mentally repeating one of his favourite hymns—he was very fond of hymns:

Dark and cheerless is the morn
Unaccompanied by thee:
Joyless is the day's return
Till thy mercy's beams I see:
Till thou inward light impart,
Glad my eyes and warm my heart.

Visit, then, this soul of mine,
Pierce the gloom of sin and grief—
Fill me, Radiancy Divine,
Scatter all my unbelief.
More and more thyself display,
Shining to the perfect day.

Adam walked much faster, and any one coming along the Oakbourne road at sunrise that morning must have had a pleasant sight in this tall broad-chested man, striding along with a carriage as upright and firm as any soldier's, glancing with keen glad eyes at the dark-blue hills as they began to show themselves on his way. Seldom in Adam's life had his face been so free from any cloud of anxiety as it was this morning; and this freedom from care, as is usual with constructive practical minds like his, made him all the more observant of the objects round him and all the more ready to gather suggestions from them towards his own favourite plans and ingenious contrivances. His happy love—the knowledge that his steps were carrying him nearer and nearer to Hetty, who was so soon to be his—was to his thoughts what the sweet morning air was to his sensations: it gave him a consciousness of well-being that made activity delightful. Every now and then there was a rush of more intense feeling towards her, which chased away other images than Hetty; and along with that would come a wondering thankfulness that all this happiness was given to him—that this life of ours had such sweetness in it. For Adam had a devout mind, though he was perhaps rather impatient of devout words, and his tenderness lay very close to his reverence, so that the one could hardly be stirred without the other. But after feeling had welled up and poured itself out in this way, busy thought would come back with the greater vigour; and this morning it was intent on schemes by which the roads might be improved that were so imperfect all through the country, and on picturing all the benefits that might come from the exertions of a single country gentleman, if he would set himself to getting the roads made good in his own district.

It seemed a very short walk, the ten miles to Oakbourne, that pretty town within sight of the blue hills, where he break-fasted. After this, the country grew barer and barer: no more rolling woods, no more wide-branching trees near frequent homesteads, no more bushy hedgerows, but greystone walls intersecting the meagre pastures, and dismal wide-scattered greystone houses on broken lands where mines had been and were no longer. "A hungry land," said Adam to himself. "I'd rather go south'ard, where they say it's as flat as a table, than come to live here; though if Dinah likes to live in a country where she can be the most comfort to folks, she's i' the right to live o' this side; for she must look as if she'd come straight from heaven, like th' angels in the desert, to strengthen them as ha' got nothing t' eat." And when at last he came in sight of Snowfield, he thought it looked like a town that was "fellow to the country," though the stream through the valley where the great mill stood gave a pleasant greenness to the lower fields. The town lay, grim, stony, and unsheltered, up the side of a steep hill, and Adam did not go forward to it at present, for Seth had told him where to find Dinah. It was at a thatched cottage outside the town, a little way from the mill—an old cottage, standing sideways towards the road, with a little bit of potato-ground before it. Here Dinah lodged with an elderly couple; and if she and Hetty happened to be out, Adam could learn where they were gone, or when they would be at home again. Dinah might be out on some preaching errand, and perhaps she would have left Hetty at home. Adam could not help hoping this, and as he recognized the cottage by the roadside before him, there shone out in his face that involuntary smile which belongs to the expectation of a near joy.

He hurried his step along the narrow causeway, and rapped at the door. It was opened by a very clean old woman, with a slow palsied shake of the head.

"Is Dinah Morris at home?" said Adam.

"Eh? . . . no," said the old woman, looking up at this tall stranger with a wonder that made her slower of speech than usual. "Will you please to come in?" she added, retiring from the door, as if recollecting herself. "Why, ye're brother to the young man as come afore, arena ye?"

"Yes," said Adam, entering. "That was Seth Bede. I'm his brother Adam. He told me to give his respects to you and your good master."

"Aye, the same t' him. He was a gracious young man. An' ye feature him, on'y ye're darker. Sit ye down i' th' arm-chair. My man isna come home from meeting."

Adam sat down patiently, not liking to hurry the shaking old woman with questions, but looking eagerly towards the narrow twisting stairs in one corner, for he thought it was possible Hetty might have heard his voice and would come down them.

"So you're come to see Dinah Morris?" said the old woman, standing opposite to him. "An' you didn' know she was away from home, then?"

"No," said Adam, "but I thought it likely she might be away, seeing as it's Sunday. But the other young woman—is she at home, or gone along with Dinah?"

The old woman looked at Adam with a bewildered air.

"Gone along wi' her?" she said. "Eh, Dinah's gone to Leeds, a big town ye may ha' heared on, where there's a many o' the Lord's people. She's been gone sin' Friday was a fortnight: they sent her the money for her journey. You may see her room here," she went on, opening a door and not noticing the effect of her words on Adam. He rose and followed her, and darted an eager glance into the little room with its narrow bed, the portrait of Wesley on the wall, and the few books lying on the large Bible. He had had an irrational hope that Hetty might be there. He could not speak in the first moment after seeing that the room was empty; an undefined fear had seized him—something had happened to Hetty on the journey. Still the old woman was so slow of; speech and apprehension, that Hetty might be at Snowfield after all.

"It's a pity ye didna know," she said. "Have ye come from your own country o' purpose to see her?"

"But Hetty—Hetty Sorrel," said Adam, abruptly; "Where is she?"

"I know nobody by that name," said the old woman, wonderingly. "Is it anybody ye've heared on at Snowfield?"

"Did there come no young woman here—very young and pretty—Friday was a fortnight, to see Dinah Morris?"

"Nay; I'n seen no young woman."

"Think; are you quite sure? A girl, eighteen years old, with dark eyes and dark curly hair, and a red cloak on, and a basket on her arm? You couldn't forget her if you saw her."

"Nay; Friday was a fortnight—it was the day as Dinah went away—there come nobody. There's ne'er been nobody asking for her till you come, for the folks about know as she's gone. Eh dear, eh dear, is there summat the matter?"

The old woman had seen the ghastly look of fear in Adam's face. But he was not stunned or confounded: he was thinking eagerly where he could inquire about Hetty.

"Yes; a young woman started from our country to see Dinah, Friday was a fortnight. I came to fetch her back. I'm afraid something has happened to her. I can't stop. Good-bye."

He hastened out of the cottage, and the old woman followed him to the gate, watching him sadly with her shaking head as he almost ran towards the town. He was going to inquire at the place where the Oakbourne coach stopped.

No! No young woman like Hetty had been seen there. Had any accident happened to the coach a fortnight ago? No. And there was no coach to take him back to Oakbourne that day. Well, he would walk: he couldn't stay here, in wretched inaction. But the innkeeper, seeing that Adam was in great anxiety, and entering into this new incident with the eagerness of a man who passes a great deal of time with his hands in his pockets looking into an obstinately monotonous street, offered to take him back to Oakbourne in his own "taxed cart" this very evening. It was not five o'clock; there was plenty of time for Adam to take a meal and yet to get to Oakbourne before ten o'clock. The innkeeper declared that he really wanted to go to Oakbourne, and might as well go to-night; he should have all Monday before him then. Adam, after making an ineffectual attempt to eat, put the food in his pocket, and, drinking a draught of ale, declared himself ready to set off. As they approached the cottage, it occurred to him that he would do well to learn from the old woman where Dinah was to be found in Leeds: if there was trouble at the Hall Farm—he only half-admitted the foreboding that there would be—the Poysers might like to send for Dinah. But Dinah had not left any address, and the old woman, whose memory for names was infirm, could not recall the name of the "blessed woman" who was Dinah's chief friend in the Society at Leeds.

During that long, long journey in the taxed cart, there was time for all the conjectures of importunate fear and struggling hope. In the very first shock of discovering that Hetty had not been to Snowfield, the thought of Arthur had darted through Adam like a sharp pang, but he tried for some time to ward off its return by busying himself with modes of accounting for the alarming fact, quite apart from that intolerable thought. Some accident had happened. Hetty had, by some strange chance, got into a wrong vehicle from Oakbourne: she had been taken ill, and did not want to frighten them by letting them know. But this frail fence of vague improbabilities was soon hurled down by a rush of distinct agonizing fears. Hetty had been deceiving herself in thinking that she could love and marry him: she had been loving Arthur all the while; and now, in her desperation at the nearness of their marriage, she had run away. And she was gone to him. The old indignation and jealousy rose again, and prompted the suspicion that Arthur had been dealing falsely—had written to Hetty—had tempted her to come to him—being unwilling, after all, that she should belong to another man besides himself. Perhaps the whole thing had been contrived by him, and he had given her directions how to follow him to Ireland—for Adam knew that Arthur had been gone thither three weeks ago, having recently learnt it at the Chase. Every sad look of Hetty's, since she had been engaged to Adam, returned upon him now with all the exaggeration of painful retrospect. He had been foolishly sanguine and confident. The poor thing hadn't perhaps known her own mind for a long while; had thought that she could forget Arthur; had been momentarily drawn towards the man who offered her a protecting, faithful love. He couldn't bear to blame her: she never meant to cause him this dreadful pain. The blame lay with that man who had selfishly played with her heart—had perhaps even deliberately lured her away.

At Oakbourne, the ostler at the Royal Oak remembered such a young woman as Adam described getting out of the Treddleston coach more than a fortnight ago—wasn't likely to forget such a pretty lass as that in a hurry—was sure she had not gone on by the Buxton coach that went through Snowfield, but had lost sight of her while he went away with the horses and had never set eyes on her again. Adam then went straight to the house from which the Stonition coach started: Stoniton was the most obvious place for Hetty to go to first, whatever might be her destination, for she would hardly venture on any but the chief coach-roads. She had been noticed here too, and was remembered to have sat on the box by the coachman; but the coachman could not be seen, for another man had been driving on that road in his stead the last three or four days. He could probably be seen at Stoniton, through inquiry at the inn where the coach put up. So the anxious heart-stricken Adam must of necessity wait and try to rest till morning—nay, till eleven o'clock, when the coach started.

At Stoniton another delay occurred, for the old coachman who had driven Hetty would not be in the town again till night. When he did come he remembered Hetty well, and remembered his own joke addressed to her, quoting it many times to Adam, and observing with equal frequency that he thought there was something more than common, because Hetty had not laughed when he joked her. But he declared, as the people had done at the inn, that he had lost sight of Hetty directly she got down. Part of the next morning was consumed in inquiries at every house in the town from which a coach started—(all in vain, for you know Hetty did not start from Stonition by coach, but on foot in the grey morning)—and then in walking out to the first toll-gates on the different lines of road, in the forlorn hope of finding some recollection of her there. No, she was not to be traced any farther; and the next hard task for Adam was to go home and carry the wretched tidings to the Hall Farm. As to what he should do beyond that, he had come to two distinct resolutions amidst the tumult of thought and feeling which was going on within him while he went to and fro. He would not mention what he knew of Arthur Donnithorne's behaviour to Hetty till there was a clear necessity for it: it was still possible Hetty might come back, and the disclosure might be an injury or an offence to her. And as soon as he had been home and done what was necessary there to prepare for his further absence, he would start off to Ireland: if he found no trace of Hetty on the road, he would go straight to Arthur Donnithorne and make himself certain how far he was acquainted with her movements. Several times the thought occurred to him that he would consult Mr. Irwine, but that would be useless unless he told him all, and so betrayed the secret about Arthur. It seems strange that Adam, in the incessant occupation of his mind about Hetty, should never have alighted on the probability that she had gone to Windsor, ignorant that Arthur was no longer there. Perhaps the reason was that he could not conceive Hetty's throwing herself on Arthur uncalled; he imagined no cause that could have driven her to such a step, after that letter written in August. There were but two alternatives in his mind: either Arthur had written to her again and enticed her away, or she had simply fled from her approaching marriage with himself because she found, after all, she could not love him well enough, and yet was afraid of her friends' anger if she retracted.

With this last determination on his mind, of going straight to Arthur, the thought that he had spent two days in inquiries which had proved to be almost useless, was torturing to Adam; and yet, since he would not tell the Poysers his conviction as to where Hetty was gone, or his intention to follow her thither, he must be able to say to them that he had traced her as far as possible.

It was after twelve o'clock on Tuesday night when Adam reached Treddleston; and, unwilling to disturb his mother and Seth, and also to encounter their questions at that hour, he threw himself without undressing on a bed at the "Waggon Overthrown," and slept hard from pure weariness. Not more than four hours, however, for before five o'clock he set out on his way home in the faint morning twilight. He always kept a key of the workshop door in his pocket, so that he could let himself in; and he wished to enter without awaking his mother, for he was anxious to avoid telling her the new trouble himself by seeing Seth first, and asking him to tell her when it should be necessary. He walked gently along the yard, and turned the key gently in the door; but, as he expected, Gyp, who lay in the workshop, gave a sharp bark. It subsided when he saw Adam, holding up his finger at him to impose silence, and in his dumb, tailless joy he must content himself with rubbing his body against his master's legs.

Adam was too heart-sick to take notice of Gyp's fondling. He threw himself on the bench and stared dully at the wood and the signs of work around him, wondering if he should ever come to feel pleasure in them again, while Gyp, dimly aware that there was something wrong with his master, laid his rough grey head on Adam's knee and wrinkled his brows to look up at him. Hitherto, since Sunday afternoon, Adam had been constantly among strange people and in strange places, having no associations with the details of his daily life, and now that by the light of this new morning he was come back to his home and surrounded by the familiar objects that seemed for ever robbed of their charm, the reality—the hard, inevitable reality of his troubles pressed upon him with a new weight. Right before him was an unfinished chest of drawers, which he had been making in spare moments for Hetty's use, when his home should be hers.

Seth had not heard Adam's entrance, but he had been roused by Gyp's bark, and Adam heard him moving about in the room above, dressing himself. Seth's first thoughts were about his brother: he would come home to-day, surely, for the business would be wanting him sadly by to-morrow, but it was pleasant to think he had had a longer holiday than he had expected. And would Dinah come too? Seth felt that that was the greatest happiness he could look forward to for himself, though he had no hope left that she would ever love him well enough to marry him; but he had often said to himself, it was better to be Dinah's friend and brother than any other woman's husband. If he could but be always near her, instead of living so far off!

He came downstairs and opened the inner door leading from the kitchen into the workshop, intending to let out Gyp; but he stood still in the doorway, smitten with a sudden shock at the sight of Adam seated listlessly on the bench, pale, unwashed, with sunken blank eyes, almost like a drunkard in the morning. But Seth felt in an instant what the marks meant—not drunkenness, but some great calamity. Adam looked up at him without speaking, and Seth moved forward towards the bench, himself trembling so that speech did not come readily.

"God have mercy on us, Addy," he said, in a low voice, sitting down on the bench beside Adam, "what is it?"

Adam was unable to speak. The strong man, accustomed to suppress the signs of sorrow, had felt his heart swell like a child's at this first approach of sympathy. He fell on Seth's neck and sobbed.

Seth was prepared for the worst now, for, even in his recollections of their boyhood, Adam had never sobbed before.

"Is it death, Adam? Is she dead?" he asked, in a low tone, when Adam raised his head and was recovering himself.

"No, lad; but she's gone—gone away from us. She's never been to Snowfield. Dinah's been gone to Leeds ever since last Friday was a fortnight, the very day Hetty set out. I can't find out where she went after she got to Stoniton."

Seth was silent from utter astonishment: he knew nothing that could suggest to him a reason for Hetty's going away.

"Hast any notion what she's done it for?" he said, at last.

"She can't ha' loved me. She didn't like our marriage when it came nigh—that must be it," said Adam. He had determined to mention no further reason.

"I hear Mother stirring," said Seth. "Must we tell her?"

"No, not yet," said Adam, rising from the bench and pushing the hair from his face, as if he wanted to rouse himself. "I can't have her told yet; and I must set out on another journey directly, after I've been to the village and th' Hall Farm. I can't tell thee where I'm going, and thee must say to her I'm gone on business as nobody is to know anything about. I'll go and wash myself now." Adam moved towards the door of the workshop, but after a step or two he turned round, and, meeting Seth's eyes with a calm sad glance, he said, "I must take all the money out o' the tin box, lad; but if anything happens to me, all the rest 'll be thine, to take care o' Mother with."

Seth was pale and trembling: he felt there was some terrible secret under all this. "Brother," he said, faintly—he never called Adam "Brother" except in solemn moments—"I don't believe you'll do anything as you can't ask God's blessing on."

"Nay, lad," said Adam, "don't be afraid. I'm for doing nought but what's a man's duty."

The thought that if he betrayed his trouble to his mother, she would only distress him by words, half of blundering affection, half of irrepressible triumph that Hetty proved as unfit to be his wife as she had always foreseen, brought back some of his habitual firmness and self-command. He had felt ill on his journey home—he told her when she came down—had stayed all night at Tredddleston for that reason; and a bad headache, that still hung about him this morning, accounted for his paleness and heavy eyes.

He determined to go to the village, in the first place, attend to his business for an hour, and give notice to Burge of his being obliged to go on a journey, which he must beg him not to mention to any one; for he wished to avoid going to the Hall Farm near breakfast-time, when the children and servants would be in the house-place, and there must be exclamations in their hearing about his having returned without Hetty. He waited until the clock struck nine before he left the work-yard at the village, and set off, through the fields, towards the Farm. It was an immense relief to him, as he came near the Home Close, to see Mr. Poyser advancing towards him, for this would spare him the pain of going to the house. Mr. Poyser was walking briskly this March morning, with a sense of spring business on his mind: he was going to cast the master's eye on the shoeing of a new cart-horse, carrying his spud as a useful companion by the way. His surprise was great when he caught sight of Adam, but he was not a man given to presentiments of evil.

"Why, Adam, lad, is't you? Have ye been all this time away and not brought the lasses back, after all? Where are they?"

"No, I've not brought 'em," said Adam, turning round, to indicate that he wished to walk back with Mr. Poyser.

"Why," said Martin, looking with sharper attention at Adam, "ye look bad. Is there anything happened?"

"Yes," said Adam, heavily. "A sad thing's happened. I didna find Hetty at Snowfield."

Mr. Poyser's good-natured face showed signs of troubled astonishment. "Not find her? What's happened to her?" he said, his thoughts flying at once to bodily accident.

"That I can't tell, whether anything's happened to her. She never went to Snowfield—she took the coach to Stoniton, but I can't learn nothing of her after she got down from the Stoniton coach."

"Why, you donna mean she's run away?" said Martin, standing still, so puzzled and bewildered that the fact did not yet make itself felt as a trouble by him.

"She must ha' done," said Adam. "She didn't like our marriage when it came to the point—that must be it. She'd mistook her feelings."

Martin was silent for a minute or two, looking on the ground and rooting up the grass with his spud, without knowing what he was doing. His usual slowness was always trebled when the subject of speech was painful. At last he looked up, right in Adam's face, saying, "Then she didna deserve t' ha' ye, my lad. An' I feel i' fault myself, for she was my niece, and I was allays hot for her marr'ing ye. There's no amends I can make ye, lad—the more's the pity: it's a sad cut-up for ye, I doubt."

Adam could say nothing; and Mr. Poyser, after pursuing his walk for a little while, went on, "I'll be bound she's gone after trying to get a lady's maid's place, for she'd got that in her head half a year ago, and wanted me to gi' my consent. But I'd thought better on her"—he added, shaking his head slowly and sadly—"I'd thought better on her, nor to look for this, after she'd gi'en y' her word, an' everything been got ready."

Adam had the strongest motives for encouraging this supposition in Mr. Poyser, and he even tried to believe that it might possibly be true. He had no warrant for the certainty that she was gone to Arthur.

"It was better it should be so," he said, as quietly as he could, "if she felt she couldn't like me for a husband. Better run away before than repent after. I hope you won't look harshly on her if she comes back, as she may do if she finds it hard to get on away from home."

"I canna look on her as I've done before," said Martin decisively. "She's acted bad by you, and by all of us. But I'll not turn my back on her: she's but a young un, and it's the first harm I've knowed on her. It'll be a hard job for me to tell her aunt. Why didna Dinah come back wi' ye? She'd ha' helped to pacify her aunt a bit."

"Dinah wasn't at Snowfield. She's been gone to Leeds this fortnight, and I couldn't learn from th' old woman any direction where she is at Leeds, else I should ha' brought it you."

"She'd a deal better be staying wi' her own kin," said Mr. Poyser, indignantly, "than going preaching among strange folks a-that'n."

"I must leave you now, Mr. Poyser," said Adam, "for I've a deal to see to."

"Aye, you'd best be after your business, and I must tell the missis when I go home. It's a hard job."

"But," said Adam, "I beg particular, you'll keep what's happened quiet for a week or two. I've not told my mother yet, and there's no knowing how things may turn out."

"Aye, aye; least said, soonest mended. We'n no need to say why the match is broke off, an' we may hear of her after a bit. Shake hands wi' me, lad: I wish I could make thee amends."

There was something in Martin Poyser's throat at that moment which caused him to bring out those scanty words in rather a broken fashion. Yet Adam knew what they meant all the better, and the two honest men grasped each other's hard hands in mutual understanding.

There was nothing now to hinder Adam from setting off. He had told Seth to go to the Chase and leave a message for the squire, saying that Adam Bede had been obliged to start off suddenly on a journey—and to say as much, and no more, to any one else who made inquiries about him. If the Poysers learned that he was gone away again, Adam knew they would infer that he was gone in search of Hetty.

He had intended to go right on his way from the Hall Farm, but now the impulse which had frequently visited him before—to go to Mr. Irwine, and make a confidant of him—recurred with the new force which belongs to a last opportunity. He was about to start on a long journey—a difficult one—by sea—and no soul would know where he was gone. If anything happened to him? Or, if he absolutely needed help in any matter concerning Hetty? Mr. Irwine was to be trusted; and the feeling which made Adam shrink from telling anything which was her secret must give way before the need there was that she should have some one else besides himself who would be prepared to defend her in the worst extremity. Towards Arthur, even though he might have incurred no new guilt, Adam felt that he was not bound to keep silence when Hetty's interest called on him to speak.

"I must do it," said Adam, when these thoughts, which had spread themselves through hours of his sad journeying, now rushed upon him in an instant, like a wave that had been slowly gathering; "it's the right thing. I can't stand alone in this way any longer."

Chapter XXXIX The Tidings

ADAM turned his face towards Broxton and walked with his swiftest stride, looking at his watch with the fear that Mr. Irwine might be gone out—hunting, perhaps. The fear and haste together produced a state of strong excitement before he reached the rectory gate, and outside it he saw the deep marks of a recent hoof on the gravel.

But the hoofs were turned towards the gate, not away from it, and though there was a horse against the stable door, it was not Mr. Irwine's: it had evidently had a journey this morning, and must belong to some one who had come on business. Mr. Irwine was at home, then; but Adam could hardly find breath and calmness to tell Carroll that he wanted to speak to the rector. The double suffering of certain and uncertain sorrow had begun to shake the strong man. The butler looked at him wonderingly, as he threw himself on a bench in the passage and stared absently at the clock on the opposite wall. The master had somebody with him, he said, but he heard the study door open—the stranger seemed to be coming out, and as Adam was in a hurry, he would let the master know at once.

Adam sat looking at the clock: the minute-hand was hurrying along the last five minutes to ten with a loud, hard, indifferent tick, and Adam watched the movement and listened to the sound as if he had had some reason for doing so. In our times of bitter suffering there are almost always these pauses, when our consciousness is benumbed to everything but some trivial perception or sensation. It is as if semi-idiocy came to give us rest from the memory and the dread which refuse to leave us in our sleep.

Carroll, coming back, recalled Adam to the sense of his burden. He was to go into the study immediately. "I can't think what that strange person's come about," the butler added, from mere incontinence of remark, as he preceded Adam to the door, "he's gone i' the dining-room. And master looks unaccountable—as if he was frightened." Adam took no notice of the words: he could not care about other people's business. But when he entered the study and looked in Mr. Irwine's face, he felt in an instant that there was a new expression in it, strangely different from the warm friendliness it had always worn for him before. A letter lay open on the table, and Mr. Irwine's hand was on it, but the changed glance he cast on Adam could not be owing entirely to preoccupation with some disagreeable business, for he was looking eagerly towards the door, as if Adam's entrance were a matter of poignant anxiety to him.

"You want to speak to me, Adam," he said, in that low constrainedly quiet tone which a man uses when he is determined to suppress agitation. "Sit down here." He pointed to a chair just opposite to him, at no more than a yard's distance from his own, and Adam sat down with a sense that this cold manner of Mr. Irwine's gave an additional unexpected difficulty to his disclosure. But when Adam had made up his mind to a measure, he was not the man to renounce it for any but imperative reasons.

"I come to you, sir," he said, "as the gentleman I look up to most of anybody. I've something very painful to tell you—something as it'll pain you to hear as well as me to tell. But if I speak o' the wrong other people have done, you'll see I didn't speak till I'd good reason."

Mr. Irwine nodded slowly, and Adam went on rather tremulously, "You was t' ha' married me and Hetty Sorrel, you know, sir, o' the fifteenth o' this month. I thought she loved me, and I was th' happiest man i' the parish. But a dreadful blow's come upon me."

Mr. Irwine started up from his chair, as if involuntarily, but then, determined to control himself, walked to the window and looked out.

"She's gone away, sir, and we don't know where. She said she was going to Snowfield o' Friday was a fortnight, and I went last Sunday to fetch her back; but she'd never been there, and she took the coach to Stoniton, and beyond that I can't trace her. But now I'm going a long journey to look for her, and I can't trust t' anybody but you where I'm going."

Mr. Irwine came back from the window and sat down.

"Have you no idea of the reason why she went away?" he said.

"It's plain enough she didn't want to marry me, sir," said Adam. "She didn't like it when it came so near. But that isn't all, I doubt. There's something else I must tell you, sir. There's somebody else concerned besides me."

A gleam of something—it was almost like relief or joy—came across the eager anxiety of Mr. Irwine's face at that moment. Adam was looking on the ground, and paused a little: the next words were hard to speak. But when he went on, he lifted up his head and looked straight at Mr. Irwine. He would do the thing he had resolved to do, without flinching.

"You know who's the man I've reckoned my greatest friend," he said, "and used to be proud to think as I should pass my life i' working for him, and had felt so ever since we were lads . . . ."

Mr. Irwine, as if all self-control had forsaken him, grasped Adam's arm, which lay on the table, and, clutching it tightly like a man in pain, said, with pale lips and a low hurried voice, "No, Adam, no—don't say it, for God's sake!"

Adam, surprised at the violence of Mr. Irwine's feeling, repented of the words that had passed his lips and sat in distressed silence. The grasp on his arm gradually relaxed, and Mr. Irwine threw himself back in his chair, saying, "Go on—I must know it."

"That man played with Hetty's feelings, and behaved to her as he'd no right to do to a girl in her station o' life—made her presents and used to go and meet her out a-walking. I found it out only two days before he went away—found him a-kissing her as they were parting in the Grove. There'd been nothing said between me and Hetty then, though I'd loved her for a long while, and she knew it. But I reproached him with his wrong actions, and words and blows passed between us; and he said solemnly to me, after that, as it had been all nonsense and no more than a bit o' flirting. But I made him write a letter to tell Hetty he'd meant nothing, for I saw clear enough, sir, by several things as I hadn't understood at the time, as he'd got hold of her heart, and I thought she'd belike go on thinking of him and never come to love another man as wanted to marry her. And I gave her the letter, and she seemed to bear it all after a while better than I'd expected . . . and she behaved kinder and kinder to me . . . I daresay she didn't know her own feelings then, poor thing, and they came back upon her when it was too late . . . I don't want to blame her . . . I can't think as she meant to deceive me. But I was encouraged to think she loved me, and—you know the rest, sir. But it's on my mind as he's been false to me, and 'ticed her away, and she's gone to him—and I'm going now to see, for I can never go to work again till I know what's become of her."

During Adam's narrative, Mr. Irwine had had time to recover his self-mastery in spite of the painful thoughts that crowded upon him. It was a bitter remembrance to him now—that morning when Arthur breakfasted with him and seemed as if he were on the verge of a confession. It was plain enough now what he had wanted to confess. And if their words had taken another turn . . . if he himself had been less fastidious about intruding on another man's secrets . . . it was cruel to think how thin a film had shut out rescue from all this guilt and misery. He saw the whole history now by that terrible illumination which the present sheds back upon the past. But every other feeling as it rushed upon his was thrown into abeyance by pity, deep respectful pity, for the man who sat before him—already so bruised, going forth with sad blind resignedness to an unreal sorrow, while a real one was close upon him, too far beyond the range of common trial for him ever to have feared it. His own agitation was quelled by a certain awe that comes over us in the presence of a great anguish, for the anguish he must inflict on Adam was already present to him. Again he put his hand on the arm that lay on the table, but very gently this time, as he said solemnly:

"Adam, my dear friend, you have had some hard trials in your life. You can bear sorrow manfully, as well as act manfully. God requires both tasks at our hands. And there is a heavier sorrow coming upon you than any you have yet known. But you are not guilty—you have not the worst of all sorrows. God help him who has!"

The two pale faces looked at each other; in Adam's there was trembling suspense, in Mr. Irwine's hesitating, shrinking pity. But he went on.

"I have had news of Hetty this morning. She is not gone to him. She is in Stonyshire—at Stoniton."

Adam started up from his chair, as if he thought he could have leaped to her that moment. But Mr. Irwine laid hold of his arm again and said, persuasively, "Wait, Adam, wait." So he sat down.

"She is in a very unhappy position—one which will make it worse for you to find her, my poor friend, than to have lost her for ever."

Adam's lips moved tremulously, but no sound came. They moved again, and he whispered, "Tell me."

"She has been arrested . . . she is in prison."

It was as if an insulting blow had brought back the spirit of resistance into Adam. The blood rushed to his face, and he said, loudly and sharply, "For what?"

"For a great crime—the murder of her child."

"It CAN'T BE!" Adam almost shouted, starting up from his cnair and making a stride towards the door; but he turned round again, setting his back against the bookcase, and looking fiercely at Mr. Irwine. "It isn't possible. She never had a child. She can't be guilty. WHO says it?"

"God grant she may be innocent, Adam. We can still hope she is."

"But who says she is guilty?" said Adam violently. "Tell me everything."

"Here is a letter from the magistrate before whom she was taken, and the constable who arrested her is in the dining-room. She will not confess her name or where she comes from; but I fear, I fear, there can be no doubt it is Hetty. The description of her person corresponds, only that she is said to look very pale and ill. She had a small red-leather pocket-book in her pocket with two names written in it—one at the beginning, 'Hetty Sorrel, Hayslope,' and the other near the end, 'Dinah Morris, Snowfield.' She will not say which is her own name—she denies everything, and will answer no questions, and application has been made to me, as a magistrate, that I may take measures for identifying her, for it was thought probable that the name which stands first is her own name."

"But what proof have they got against her, if it IS Hetty?" said Adam, still violently, with an effort that seemed to shake his whole frame. "I'll not believe it. It couldn't ha' been, and none of us know it."

"Terrible proof that she was under the temptation to commit the crime; but we have room to hope that she did not really commit it. Try and read that letter, Adam."

Adam took the letter between his shaking hands and tried to fix his eyes steadily on it. Mr. Irwine meanwhile went out to give some orders. When he came back, Adam's eyes were still on the first page—he couldn't read—he could not put the words together and make out what they meant. He threw it down at last and clenched his fist.

"It's HIS doing," he said; "if there's been any crime, it's at his door, not at hers. HE taught her to deceive—HE deceived me first. Let 'em put HIM on his trial—let him stand in court beside her, and I'll tell 'em how he got hold of her heart, and 'ticed her t' evil, and then lied to me. Is HE to go free, while they lay all the punishment on her . . . so weak and young?"

The image called up by these last words gave a new direction to poor Adam's maddened feelings. He was silent, looking at the corner of the room as if he saw something there. Then he burst out again, in a tone of appealing anguish, "I can't bear it . . . O God, it's too hard to lay upon me—it's too hard to think she's wicked."

Mr. Irwine had sat down again in silence. He was too wise to utter soothing words at present, and indeed, the sight of Adam before him, with that look of sudden age which sometimes comes over a young face in moments of terrible emotion—the hard bloodless look of the skin, the deep lines about the quivering mouth, the furrows in the brow—the sight of this strong firm man shattered by the invisible stroke of sorrow, moved him so deeply that speech was not easy.

Adam stood motionless, with his eyes vacantly fixed in this way for a minute or two; in that short space he was living through all his love again.

"She can't ha' done it," he said, still without moving his eyes, as if he were only talking to himself: "it was fear made her hide it . . . I forgive her for deceiving me . . . I forgive thee, Hetty . . . thee wast deceived too . . . it's gone hard wi' thee, my poor Hetty . . . but they'll never make me believe it."

He was silent again for a few moments, and then he said, with fierce abruptness, "I'll go to him—I'll bring him back—I'll make him go and look at her in her misery—he shall look at her till he can't forget it—it shall follow him night and day—as long as he lives it shall follow him—he shan't escape wi' lies this time—I'll fetch him, I'll drag him myself."

In the act of going towards the door, Adam paused automatically and looked about for his hat, quite unconscious where he was or who was present with him. Mr. Irwine had followed him, and now took him by the arm, saying, in a quiet but decided tone, "No, Adam, no; I'm sure you will wish to stay and see what good can be done for her, instead of going on a useless errand of vengeance. The punishment will surely fall without your aid. Besides, he is no longer in Ireland. He must be on his way home—or would be, long before you arrived, for his grandfather, I know, wrote for him to come at least ten days ago. I want you now to go with me to Stoniton. I have ordered a horse for you to ride with us, as soon as you can compose yourself."

While Mr. Irwine was speaking, Adam recovered his consciousness of the actual scene. He rubbed his hair off his forehead and listened.

"Remember," Mr. Irwine went on, "there are others to think of, and act for, besides yourself, Adam: there are Hetty's friends, the good Poysers, on whom this stroke will fall more heavily than I can bear to think. I expect it from your strength of mind, Adam—from your sense of duty to God and man—that you will try to act as long as action can be of any use."

In reality, Mr. Irwine proposed this journey to Stoniton for Adam's own sake. Movement, with some object before him, was the best means of counteracting the violence of suffering in these first hours.

"You will go with me to Stoniton, Adam?" he said again, after a moment's pause. "We have to see if it is really Hetty who is there, you know."

"Yes, sir," said Adam, "I'll do what you think right. But the folks at th' Hall Farm?"

"I wish them not to know till I return to tell them myself. I shall have ascertained things then which I am uncertain about now, and I shall return as soon as possible. Come now, the horses are ready."

Chapter XL The Bitter Waters Spread

MR. IRWINE returned from Stoniton in a post-chaise that night, and the first words Carroll said to him, as he entered the house, were, that Squire Donnithorne was dead—found dead in his bed at ten o'clock that morning—and that Mrs. Irwine desired him to say she should be awake when Mr. Irwine came home, and she begged him not to go to bed without seeing her.

"Well, Dauphin," Mrs. Irwine said, as her son entered her room, "you're come at last. So the old gentleman's fidgetiness and low spirits, which made him send for Arthur in that sudden way, really meant something. I suppose Carroll has told you that Donnithorne was found dead in his bed this morning. You will believe my prognostications another time, though I daresay I shan't live to prognosticate anything but my own death."

"What have they done about Arthur?" said Mr. Irwine. "Sent a messenger to await him at Liverpool?"

"Yes, Ralph was gone before the news was brought to us. Dear Arthur, I shall live now to see him master at the Chase, and making good times on the estate, like a generous-hearted fellow as he is. He'll be as happy as a king now."

Mr. Irwine could not help giving a slight groan: he was worn with anxiety and exertion, and his mother's light words were almost intolerable.

"What are you so dismal about, Dauphin? Is there any bad news? Or are you thinking of the danger for Arthur in crossing that frightful Irish Channel at this time of year?"

"No, Mother, I'm not thinking of that; but I'm not prepared to rejoice just now."

"You've been worried by this law business that you've been to Stoniton about. What in the world is it, that you can't tell me?"

"You will know by and by, mother. It would not be right for me to tell you at present. Good-night: you'll sleep now you have no longer anything to listen for."

Mr. Irwine gave up his intention of sending a letter to meet Arthur, since it would not now hasten his return: the news of his grandfather's death would bring him as soon as he could possibly come. He could go to bed now and get some needful rest, before the time came for the morning's heavy duty of carrying his sickening news to the Hall Farm and to Adam's home.

Adam himself was not come back from Stoniton, for though he shrank from seeing Hetty, he could not bear to go to a distance from her again.

"It's no use, sir," he said to the rector, "it's no use for me to go back. I can't go to work again while she's here, and I couldn't bear the sight o' the things and folks round home. I'll take a bit of a room here, where I can see the prison walls, and perhaps I shall get, in time, to bear seeing her."

Adam had not been shaken in his belief that Hetty was innocent of the crime she was charged with, for Mr. Irwine, feeling that the belief in her guilt would be a crushing addition to Adam's load, had kept from him the facts which left no hope in his own mind. There was not any reason for thrusting the whole burden on Adam at once, and Mr. Irwine, at parting, only said, "If the evidence should tell too strongly against her, Adam, we may still hope for a pardon. Her youth and other circumstances will be a plea for her."

"Ah, and it's right people should know how she was tempted into the wrong way," said Adam, with bitter earnestness. "It's right they should know it was a fine gentleman made love to her, and turned her head wi' notions. You'll remember, sir, you've promised to tell my mother, and Seth, and the people at the farm, who it was as led her wrong, else they'll think harder of her than she deserves. You'll be doing her a hurt by sparing him, and I hold him the guiltiest before God, let her ha' done what she may. If you spare him, I'll expose him!"

"I think your demand is just, Adam," said Mr. Irwine, "but when you are calmer, you will judge Arthur more mercifully. I say nothing now, only that his punishment is in other hands than ours."

Mr. Irwine felt it hard upon him that he should have to tell of Arthur's sad part in the story of sin and sorrow—he who cared for Arthur with fatherly affection, who had cared for him with fatherly pride. But he saw clearly that the secret must be known before long, even apart from Adam's determination, since it was scarcely to be supposed that Hetty would persist to the end in her obstinate silence. He made up his mind to withhold nothing from the Poysers, but to tell them the worst at once, for there was no time to rob the tidings of their suddenness. Hetty's trial must come on at the Lent assizes, and they were to be held at Stoniton the next week. It was scarcely to be hoped that Martin Poyser could escape the pain of being called as a witness, and it was better he should know everything as long beforehand as possible.

Before ten o'clock on Thursday morning the home at the Hall Farm was a house of mourning for a misfortune felt to be worse than death. The sense of family dishonour was too keen even in the kind-hearted Martin Poyser the younger to leave room for any compassion towards Hetty. He and his father were simple-minded farmers, proud of their untarnished character, proud that they came of a family which had held up its head and paid its way as far back as its name was in the parish register; and Hetty had brought disgrace on them all—disgrace that could never be wiped out. That was the all-conquering feeling in the mind both of father and son—the scorching sense of disgrace, which neutralised all other sensibility—and Mr. Irwine was struck with surprise to observe that Mrs. Poyser was less severe than her husband. We are often startled by the severity of mild people on exceptional occasions; the reason is, that mild people are most liable to be under the yoke of traditional impressions.

"I'm willing to pay any money as is wanted towards trying to bring her off," said Martin the younger when Mr. Irwine was gone, while the old grandfather was crying in the opposite chair, "but I'll not go nigh her, nor ever see her again, by my own will. She's made our bread bitter to us for all our lives to come, an' we shall ne'er hold up our heads i' this parish nor i' any other. The parson talks o' folks pitying us: it's poor amends pity 'ull make us."

"Pity?" said the grandfather, sharply. "I ne'er wanted folks's pity i' MY life afore . . . an' I mun begin to be looked down on now, an' me turned seventy-two last St. Thomas's, an' all th' underbearers and pall-bearers as I'n picked for my funeral are i' this parish and the next to 't. . . . It's o' no use now . . . I mun be ta'en to the grave by strangers."

"Don't fret so, father," said Mrs. Poyser, who had spoken very little, being almost overawed by her husband's unusual hardness and decision. "You'll have your children wi' you; an' there's the lads and the little un 'ull grow up in a new parish as well as i' th' old un."

"Ah, there's no staying i' this country for us now," said Mr. Poyser, and the hard tears trickled slowly down his round cheeks. "We thought it 'ud be bad luck if the old squire gave us notice this Lady day, but I must gi' notice myself now, an' see if there can anybody be got to come an' take to the crops as I'n put i' the ground; for I wonna stay upo' that man's land a day longer nor I'm forced to't. An' me, as thought him such a good upright young man, as I should be glad when he come to be our landlord. I'll ne'er lift my hat to him again, nor sit i' the same church wi' him . . . a man as has brought shame on respectable folks . . . an' pretended to be such a friend t' everybody . . . .Poor Adam there . . . a fine friend he's been t' Adam, making speeches an' talking so fine, an' all the while poisoning the lad's life, as it's much if he can stay i' this country any more nor we can."

"An' you t' ha' to go into court, and own you're akin t' her," said the old man. "Why, they'll cast it up to the little un, as isn't four 'ear old, some day—they'll cast it up t' her as she'd a cousin tried at the 'sizes for murder."

"It'll be their own wickedness, then," said Mrs. Poyser, with a sob in her voice. "But there's One above 'ull take care o' the innicent child, else it's but little truth they tell us at church. It'll be harder nor ever to die an' leave the little uns, an' nobody to be a mother to 'em."

"We'd better ha' sent for Dinah, if we'd known where she is," said Mr. Poyser; "but Adam said she'd left no direction where she'd be at Leeds."

"Why, she'd be wi' that woman as was a friend t' her Aunt Judith," said Mrs. Poyser, comforted a little by this suggestion of her husbands. "I've often heard Dinah talk of her, but I can't remember what name she called her by. But there's Seth Bede; he's like enough to know, for she's a preaching woman as the Methodists think a deal on."

"I'll send to Seth," said Mr. Poyser. "I'll send Alick to tell him to come, or else to send up word o' the woman's name, an' thee canst write a letter ready to send off to Treddles'on as soon as we can make out a direction."

"It's poor work writing letters when you want folks to come to you i' trouble," said Mrs. Poyser. "Happen it'll be ever so long on the road, an' never reach her at last."

Before Alick arrived with the message, Lisbeth's thoughts too had already flown to Dinah, and she had said to Seth, "Eh, there's no comfort for us i' this world any more, wi'out thee couldst get Dinah Morris to come to us, as she did when my old man died. I'd like her to come in an' take me by th' hand again, an' talk to me. She'd tell me the rights on't, belike—she'd happen know some good i' all this trouble an' heart-break comin' upo' that poor lad, as ne'er done a bit o' wrong in's life, but war better nor anybody else's son, pick the country round. Eh, my lad . . . Adam, my poor lad!"

"Thee wouldstna like me to leave thee, to go and fetch Dinah?" said Seth, as his mother sobbed and rocked herself to and fro.

"Fetch her?" said Lisbeth, looking up and pausing from her grief, like a crying child who hears some promise of consolation. "Why, what place is't she's at, do they say?"

"It's a good way off, mother—Leeds, a big town. But I could be back in three days, if thee couldst spare me."

"Nay, nay, I canna spare thee. Thee must go an' see thy brother, an' bring me word what he's a-doin'. Mester Irwine said he'd come an' tell me, but I canna make out so well what it means when he tells me. Thee must go thysen, sin' Adam wonna let me go to him. Write a letter to Dinah canstna? Thee't fond enough o' writin' when nobody wants thee."

"I'm not sure where she'd be i' that big town," said Seth. "If I'd gone myself, I could ha' found out by asking the members o' the Society. But perhaps if I put Sarah Williamson, Methodist preacher, Leeds, o' th' outside, it might get to her; for most like she'd be wi' Sarah Williamson."

Alick came now with the message, and Seth, finding that Mrs. Poyser was writing to Dinah, gave up the intention of writing himself; but he went to the Hall Farm to tell them all he could suggest about the address of the letter, and warn them that there might be some delay in the delivery, from his not knowing an exact direction.

On leaving Lisbeth, Mr. Irwine had gone to Jonathan Burge, who had also a claim to be acquainted with what was likely to keep Adam away from business for some time; and before six o'clock that evening there were few people in Broxton and Hayslope who had not heard the sad news. Mr. Irwine had not mentioned Arthur's name to Burge, and yet the story of his conduct towards Hetty, with all the dark shadows cast upon it by its terrible consequences, was presently as well known as that his grandfather was dead, and that he was come into the estate. For Martin Poyser felt no motive to keep silence towards the one or two neighbours who ventured to come and shake him sorrowfully by the hand on the first day of his trouble; and Carroll, who kept his ears open to all that passed at the rectory, had framed an inferential version of the story, and found early opportunities of communicating it.

One of those neighbours who came to Martin Poyser and shook him by the hand without speaking for some minutes was Bartle Massey. He had shut up his school, and was on his way to the rectory, where he arrived about half-past seven in the evening, and, sending his duty to Mr. Irwine, begged pardon for troubling him at that hour, but had something particular on his mind. He was shown into the study, where Mr. Irwine soon joined him.

"Well, Bartle?" said Mr. Irwine, putting out his hand. That was not his usual way of saluting the schoolmaster, but trouble makes us treat all who feel with us very much alike. "Sit down."

"You know what I'm come about as well as I do, sir, I daresay," said Bartle.

"You wish to know the truth about the sad news that has reached you . . . about Hetty Sorrel?"

"Nay, sir, what I wish to know is about Adam Bede. I understand you left him at Stoniton, and I beg the favour of you to tell me what's the state of the poor lad's mind, and what he means to do. For as for that bit o' pink-and-white they've taken the trouble to put in jail, I don't value her a rotten nut—not a rotten nut—only for the harm or good that may come out of her to an honest man—a lad I've set such store by—trusted to, that he'd make my bit o' knowledge go a good way in the world . . . . Why, sir, he's the only scholar I've had in this stupid country that ever had the will or the head-piece for mathematics. If he hadn't had so much hard work to do, poor fellow, he might have gone into the higher branches, and then this might never have happened—might never have happened."

Bartle was heated by the exertion of walking fast in an agitated frame of mind, and was not able to check himself on this first occasion of venting his feelings. But he paused now to rub his moist forehead, and probably his moist eyes also.

"You'll excuse me, sir," he said, when this pause had given him time to reflect, "for running on in this way about my own feelings, like that foolish dog of mine howling in a storm, when there's nobody wants to listen to me. I came to hear you speak, not to talk myself—if you'll take the trouble to tell me what the poor lad's doing."

"Don't put yourself under any restraint, Bartle," said Mr. Irwine. "The fact is, I'm very much in the same condition as you just now; I've a great deal that's painful on my mind, and I find it hard work to be quite silent about my own feelings and only attend to others. I share your concern for Adam, though he is not the only one whose sufferings I care for in this affair. He intends to remain at Stoniton till after the trial: it will come on probably a week to-morrow. He has taken a room there, and I encouraged him to do so, because I think it better he should be away from his own home at present; and, poor fellow, he still believes Hetty is innocent—he wants to summon up courage to see her if he can; he is unwilling to leave the spot where she is."

"Do you think the creatur's guilty, then?" said Bartle. "Do you think they'll hang her?"

"I'm afraid it will go hard with her. The evidence is very strong. And one bad symptom is that she denies everything—denies that she has had a child in the face of the most positive evidence. I saw her myself, and she was obstinately silent to me; she shrank up like a frightened animal when she saw me. I was never so shocked in my life as at the change in her. But I trust that, in the worst case, we may obtain a pardon for the sake of the innocent who are involved."

"Stuff and nonsense!" said Bartle, forgetting in his irritation to whom he was speaking. "I beg your pardon, sir, I mean it's stuff and nonsense for the innocent to care about her being hanged. For my own part, I think the sooner such women are put out o' the world the better; and the men that help 'em to do mischief had better go along with 'em for that matter. What good will you do by keeping such vermin alive, eating the victual that 'ud feed rational beings? But if Adam's fool enough to care about it, I don't want him to suffer more than's needful. . . . Is he very much cut up, poor fellow?" Bartle added, taking out his spectacles and putting them on, as if they would assist his imagination.

"Yes, I'm afraid the grief cuts very deep," said Mr. Irwine. "He looks terribly shattered, and a certain violence came over him now and then yesterday, which made me wish I could have remained near him. But I shall go to Stoniton again to-morrow, and I have confidence enough in the strength of Adam's principle to trust that he will be able to endure the worst without being driven to anything rash."

Mr. Irwine, who was involuntarily uttering his own thoughts rather than addressing Bartle Massey in the last sentence, had in his mind the possibility that the spirit of vengeance to-wards Arthur, which was the form Adam's anguish was continually taking, might make him seek an encounter that was likely to end more fatally than the one in the Grove. This possibility heightened the anxiety with which he looked forward to Arthur's arrival. But Bartle thought Mr. Irwine was referring to suicide, and his face wore a new alarm.

"I'll tell you what I have in my head, sir," he said, "and I hope you'll approve of it. I'm going to shut up my school—if the scholars come, they must go back again, that's all—and I shall go to Stoniton and look after Adam till this business is over. I'll pretend I'm come to look on at the assizes; he can't object to that. What do you think about it, sir?"

"Well," said Mr. Irwine, rather hesitatingly, "there would be some real advantages in that . . . and I honour you for your friendship towards him, Bartle. But . . . you must be careful what you say to him, you know. I'm afraid you have too little fellow-feeling in what you consider his weakness about Hetty."

"Trust to me, sir—trust to me. I know what you mean. I've been a fool myself in my time, but that's between you and me. I shan't thrust myself on him only keep my eye on him, and see that he gets some good food, and put in a word here and there."

"Then," said Mr. Irwine, reassured a little as to Bartle's discretion, "I think you'll be doing a good deed; and it will be well for you to let Adam's mother and brother know that you're going."

"Yes, sir, yes," said Bartle, rising, and taking off his spectacles, "I'll do that, I'll do that; though the mother's a whimpering thing—I don't like to come within earshot of her; however, she's a straight-backed, clean woman, none of your slatterns. I wish you good-bye, sir, and thank you for the time you've spared me. You're everybody's friend in this business—everybody's friend. It's a heavy weight you've got on your shoulders."

"Good-bye, Bartle, till we meet at Stoniton, as I daresay we shall."

Bartle hurried away from the rectory, evading Carroll's conversational advances, and saying in an exasperated tone to Vixen, whose short legs pattered beside him on the gravel, "Now, I shall be obliged to take you with me, you good-for-nothing woman. You'd go fretting yourself to death if I left you—you know you would, and perhaps get snapped up by some tramp. And you'll be running into bad company, I expect, putting your nose in every hole and corner where you've no business! But if you do anything disgraceful, I'll disown you—mind that, madam, mind that!"

Chapter XLI The Eve of the Trial

AN upper room in a dull Stoniton street, with two beds in it—one laid on the floor. It is ten o'clock on Thursday night, and the dark wall opposite the window shuts out the moonlight that might have struggled with the light of the one dip candle by which Bartle Massey is pretending to read, while he is really looking over his spectacles at Adam Bede, seated near the dark window.

You would hardly have known it was Adam without being told. His face has got thinner this last week: he has the sunken eyes, the neglected beard of a man just risen from a sick-bed. His heavy black hair hangs over his forehead, and there is no active impulse in him which inclines him to push it off, that he may be more awake to what is around him. He has one arm over the back of the chair, and he seems to be looking down at his clasped hands. He is roused by a knock at the door.

"There he is," said Bartle Massey, rising hastily and unfastening the door. It was Mr. Irwine.

Adam rose from his chair with instinctive respect, as Mr. Irwine approached him and took his hand.

"I'm late, Adam," he said, sitting down on the chair which Bartle placed for him, "but I was later in setting off from Broxton than I intended to be, and I have been incessantly occupied since I arrived. I have done everything now, however—everything that can be done to-night, at least. Let us all sit down."

Adam took his chair again mechanically, and Bartle, for whom there was no chair remaining, sat on the bed in the background.

"Have you seen her, sir?" said Adam tremulously.

"Yes, Adam; I and the chaplain have both been with her this evening."

"Did you ask her, sir . . . did you say anything about me?"

"Yes," said Mr. Irwine, with some hesitation, "I spoke of you. I said you wished to see her before the trial, if she consented."

As Mr. Irwine paused, Adam looked at him with eager, questioning eyes.

"You know she shrinks from seeing any one, Adam. It is not only you—some fatal influence seems to have shut up her heart against her fellow-creatures. She has scarcely said anything more than 'No' either to me or the chaplain. Three or four days ago, before you were mentioned to her, when I asked her if there was any one of her family whom she would like to see—to whom she could open her mind—she said, with a violent shudder, 'Tell them not to come near me—I won't see any of them.'"

Adam's head was hanging down again, and he did not speak. There was silence for a few minutes, and then Mr. Irwine said, "I don't like to advise you against your own feelings, Adam, if they now urge you strongly to go and see her to-morrow morning, even without her consent. It is just possible, notwithstanding appearances to the contrary, that the interview might affect her favourably. But I grieve to say I have scarcely any hope of that. She didn't seem agitated when I mentioned your name; she only said 'No,' in the same cold, obstinate way as usual. And if the meeting had no good effect on her, it would be pure, useless suffering to you—severe suffering, I fear. She is very much changed . . . "

Adam started up from his chair and seized his hat, which lay on the table. But he stood still then, and looked at Mr. Irwine, as if he had a question to ask which it was yet difficult to utter. Bartle Massey rose quietly, turned the key in the door, and put it in his pocket.

"Is he come back?" said Adam at last.

"No, he is not," said Mr. Irwine, quietly. "Lay down your hat, Adam, unless you like to walk out with me for a little fresh air. I fear you have not been out again to-day."

"You needn't deceive me, sir," said Adam, looking hard at Mr. Irwine and speaking in a tone of angry suspicion. "You needn't be afraid of me. I only want justice. I want him to feel what she feels. It's his work . . . she was a child as it 'ud ha' gone t' anybody's heart to look at . . . I don't care what she's done . . . it was him brought her to it. And he shall know it . . . he shall feel it . . . if there's a just God, he shall feel what it is t' ha' brought a child like her to sin and misery."

"I'm not deceiving you, Adam," said Mr. Irwine. "Arthur Donnithorne is not come back—was not come back when I left. I have left a letter for him: he will know all as soon as he arrives."

"But you don't mind about it," said Adam indignantly. "You think it doesn't matter as she lies there in shame and misery, and he knows nothing about it—he suffers nothing."

"Adam, he WILL know—he WILL suffer, long and bitterly. He has a heart and a conscience: I can't be entirely deceived in his character. I am convinced—I am sure he didn't fall under temptation without a struggle. He may be weak, but he is not callous, not coldly selfish. I am persuaded that this will be a shock of which he will feel the effects all his life. Why do you crave vengeance in this way? No amount of torture that you could inflict on him could benefit her."

"No—O God, no," Adam groaned out, sinking on his chair again; "but then, that's the deepest curse of all . . . that's what makes the blackness of it . . . IT CAN NEVER BE UNDONE. My poor Hetty . . . she can never be my sweet Hetty again . . . the prettiest thing God had made—smiling up at me . . . I thought she loved me . . . and was good . . ."

Adam's voice had been gradually sinking into a hoarse undertone, as if he were only talking to himself; but now he said abruptly, looking at Mr. Irwine, "But she isn't as guilty as they say? You don't think she is, sir? She can't ha' done it."

"That perhaps can never be known with certainty, Adam," Mr. Irwine answered gently. "In these cases we sometimes form our judgment on what seems to us strong evidence, and yet, for want of knowing some small fact, our judgment is wrong. But suppose the worst: you have no right to say that the guilt of her crime lies with him, and that he ought to bear the punishment. It is not for us men to apportion the shares of moral guilt and retribution. We find it impossible to avoid mistakes even in determining who has committed a single criminal act, and the problem how far a man is to be held responsible for the unforeseen consequences of his own deed is one that might well make us tremble to look into it. The evil consequences that may lie folded in a single act of selfish indulgence is a thought so awful that it ought surely to awaken some feeling less presumptuous than a rash desire to punish. You have a mind that can understand this fully, Adam, when you are calm. Don't suppose I can't enter into the anguish that drives you into this state of revengeful hatred. But think of this: if you were to obey your passion—for it IS passion, and you deceive yourself in calling it justice—it might be with you precisely as it has been with Arthur; nay, worse; your passion might lead you yourself into a horrible crime."

"No—not worse," said Adam, bitterly; "I don't believe it's worse—I'd sooner do it—I'd sooner do a wickedness as I could suffer for by myself than ha' brought HER to do wickedness and then stand by and see 'em punish her while they let me alone; and all for a bit o' pleasure, as, if he'd had a man's heart in him, he'd ha' cut his hand off sooner than he'd ha' taken it. What if he didn't foresee what's happened? He foresaw enough; he'd no right to expect anything but harm and shame to her. And then he wanted to smooth it off wi' lies. No—there's plenty o' things folks are hanged for not half so hateful as that. Let a man do what he will, if he knows he's to bear the punishment himself, he isn't half so bad as a mean selfish coward as makes things easy t' himself and knows all the while the punishment 'll fall on somebody else."

"There again you partly deceive yourself, Adam. There is no sort of wrong deed of which a man can bear the punishment alone; you can't isolate yourself and say that the evil which is in you shall not spread. Men's lives are as thoroughly blended with each other as the air they breathe: evil spreads as necessarily as disease. I know, I feel the terrible extent of suffering this sin of Arthur's has caused to others; but so does every sin cause suffering to others besides those who commit it. An act of vengeance on your part against Arthur would simply be another evil added to those we are suffering under: you could not bear the punishment alone; you would entail the worst sorrows on every one who loves you. You would have committed an act of blind fury that would leave all the present evils just as they were and add worse evils to them. You may tell me that you meditate no fatal act of vengeance, but the feeling in your mind is what gives birth to such actions, and as long as you indulge it, as long as you do not see that to fix your mind on Arthur's punishment is revenge, and not justice, you are in danger of being led on to the commission of some great wrong. Remember what you told me about your feelings after you had given that blow to Arthur in the Grove."

Adam was silent: the last words had called up a vivid image of the past, and Mr. Irwine left him to his thoughts, while he spoke to

Bartle Massey about old Mr. Donnithorne's funeral and other matters of an indifferent kind. But at length Adam turned round and said, in a more subdued tone, "I've not asked about 'em at th' Hall Farm, sir. Is Mr. Poyser coming?"

"He is come; he is in Stoniton to-night. But I could not advise him to see you, Adam. His own mind is in a very perturbed state, and it is best he should not see you till you are calmer."

"Is Dinah Morris come to 'em, sir? Seth said they'd sent for her."

"No. Mr. Poyser tells me she was not come when he left. They're afraid the letter has not reached her. It seems they had no exact address."

Adam sat ruminating a little while, and then said, "I wonder if Dinah 'ud ha' gone to see her. But perhaps the Poysers would ha' been sorely against it, since they won't come nigh her themselves. But I think she would, for the Methodists are great folks for going into the prisons; and Seth said he thought she would. She'd a very tender way with her, Dinah had; I wonder if she could ha' done any good. You never saw her, sir, did you?"

"Yes, I did. I had a conversation with her—she pleased me a good deal. And now you mention it, I wish she would come, for it is possible that a gentle mild woman like her might move Hetty to open her heart. The jail chaplain is rather harsh in his manner."

"But it's o' no use if she doesn't come," said Adam sadly.

"If I'd thought of it earlier, I would have taken some measures for finding her out," said Mr. Irwine, "but it's too late now, I fear . . . Well, Adam, I must go now. Try to get some rest to-night. God bless you. I'll see you early to-morrow morning."

Chapter XLII The Morning of the Trial

AT one o'clock the next day, Adam was alone in his dull upper room; his watch lay before him on the table, as if he were counting the long minutes. He had no knowledge of what was likely to be said by the witnesses on the trial, for he had shrunk from all the particulars connected with Hetty's arrest and accusation. This brave active man, who would have hastened towards any danger or toil to rescue Hetty from an apprehended wrong or misfortune, felt himself powerless to contemplate irremediable evil and suffering. The susceptibility which would have been an impelling force where there was any possibility of action became helpless anguish when he was obliged to be passive, or else sought an active outlet in the thought of inflicting justice on Arthur. Energetic natures, strong for all strenuous deeds, will often rush away from a hopeless sufferer, as if they were hard-hearted. It is the overmastering sense of pain that drives them. They shrink by an ungovernable instinct, as they would shrink from laceration. Adam had brought himself to think of seeing Hetty, if she would consent to see him, because he thought the meeting might possibly be a good to her—might help to melt away this terrible hardness they told him of. If she saw he bore her no ill will for what she had done to him, she might open her heart to him. But this resolution had been an immense effort—he trembled at the thought of seeing her changed face, as a timid woman trembles at the thought of the surgeon's knife, and he chose now to bear the long hours of suspense rather than encounter what seemed to him the more intolerable agony of witnessing her trial.

Deep unspeakable suffering may well be called a baptism, a regeneration, the initiation into a new state. The yearning memories, the bitter regret, the agonized sympathy, the struggling appeals to the Invisible Right—all the intense emotions which had filled the days and nights of the past week, and were compressing themselves again like an eager crowd into the hours of this single morning, made Adam look back on all the previous years as if they had been a dim sleepy existence, and he had only now awaked to full consciousness. It seemed to him as if he had always before thought it a light thing that men should suffer, as if all that he had himself endured and called sorrow before was only a moment's stroke that had never left a bruise. Doubtless a great anguish may do the work of years, and we may come out from that baptism of fire with a soul full of new awe and new pity.

"O God," Adam groaned, as he leaned on the table and looked blankly at the face of the watch, "and men have suffered like this before . . . and poor helpless young things have suffered like her. . . . Such a little while ago looking so happy and so pretty . . . kissing 'em all, her grandfather and all of 'em, and they wishing her luck. . . . O my poor, poor Hetty . . . dost think on it now?"

Adam started and looked round towards the door. Vixen had begun to whimper, and there was a sound of a stick and a lame walk on the stairs. It was Bartle Massey come back. Could it be all over?

Bartle entered quietly, and, going up to Adam, grasped his hand and said, "I'm just come to look at you, my boy, for the folks are gone out of court for a bit."

Adam's heart beat so violently he was unable to speak—he could only return the pressure of his friend's hand—and Bartle, drawing up the other chair, came and sat in front of him, taking off his hat and his spectacles.

"That's a thing never happened to me before," he observed, "to go out o' the door with my spectacles on. I clean forgot to take 'em off."

The old man made this trivial remark, thinking it better not to respond at all to Adam's agitation: he would gather, in an indirect way, that there was nothing decisive to communicate at present.

"And now," he said, rising again, "I must see to your having a bit of the loaf, and some of that wine Mr. Irwine sent this morning. He'll be angry with me if you don't have it. Come, now," he went on, bringing forward the bottle and the loaf and pouring some wine into a cup, "I must have a bit and a sup myself. Drink a drop with me, my lad—drink with me."

Adam pushed the cup gently away and said, entreatingly, "Tell me about it, Mr. Massey—tell me all about it. Was she there? Have they begun?"

"Yes, my boy, yes—it's taken all the time since I first went; but they're slow, they're slow; and there's the counsel they've got for her puts a spoke in the wheel whenever he can, and makes a deal to do with cross-examining the witnesses and quarrelling with the other lawyers. That's all he can do for the money they give him; and it's a big sum—it's a big sum. But he's a 'cute fellow, with an eye that 'ud pick the needles out of the hay in no time. If a man had got no feelings, it 'ud be as good as a demonstration to listen to what goes on in court; but a tender heart makes one stupid. I'd have given up figures for ever only to have had some good news to bring to you, my poor lad."

"But does it seem to be going against her?" said Adam. "Tell me what they've said. I must know it now—I must know what they have to bring against her."

"Why, the chief evidence yet has been the doctors; all but Martin Poyser—poor Martin. Everybody in court felt for him—it was like one sob, the sound they made when he came down again. The worst was when they told him to look at the prisoner at the bar. It was hard work, poor fellow—it was hard work. Adam, my boy, the blow falls heavily on him as we'l as you; you must help poor Martin; you must show courage. Drink some wine now, and show me you mean to bear it like a man."

Bartle had made the right sort of appeal. Adam, with an air of quiet obedience, took up the cup and drank a little.

"Tell me how SHE looked," he said presently.

"Frightened, very frightened, when they first brought her in; it was the first sight of the crowd and the judge, poor creatur. And there's a lot o' foolish women in fine clothes, with gewgaws all up their arms and feathers on their heads, sitting near the judge: they've dressed themselves out in that way, one 'ud think, to be scarecrows and warnings against any man ever meddling with a woman again. They put up their glasses, and stared and whispered. But after that she stood like a white image, staring down at her hands and seeming neither to hear nor see anything. And she's as white as a sheet. She didn't speak when they asked her if she'd plead 'guilty' or 'not guilty,' and they pleaded 'not guilty' for her. But when she heard her uncle's name, there seemed to go a shiver right through her; and when they told him to look at her, she hung her head down, and cowered, and hid her face in her hands. He'd much ado to speak poor man, his voice trembled so. And the counsellors—who look as hard as nails mostly—I saw, spared him as much as they could. Mr. Irwine put himself near him and went with him out o' court. Ah, it's a great thing in a man's life to be able to stand by a neighbour and uphold him in such trouble as that."

"God bless him, and you too, Mr. Massey," said Adam, in a low voice, laying his hand on Bartle's arm.

"Aye, aye, he's good metal; he gives the right ring when you try him, our parson does. A man o' sense—says no more than's needful. He's not one of those that think they can comfort you with chattering, as if folks who stand by and look on knew a deal better what the trouble was than those who have to bear it. I've had to do with such folks in my time—in the south, when I was in trouble myself. Mr. Irwine is to be a witness himself, by and by, on her side, you know, to speak to her character and bringing up."

"But the other evidence . . . does it go hard against her!" said Adam. "What do you think, Mr. Massey? Tell me the truth."

"Yes, my lad, yes. The truth is the best thing to tell. It must come at last. The doctors' evidence is heavy on her—is heavy. But she's gone on denying she's had a child from first to last. These poor silly women-things—they've not the sense to know it's no use denying what's proved. It'll make against her with the jury, I doubt, her being so obstinate: they may be less for recommending her to mercy, if the verdict's against her. But Mr. Irwine 'ull leave no stone unturned with the judge—you may rely upon that, Adam."

"Is there nobody to stand by her and seem to care for her in the court?" said Adam.

"There's the chaplain o' the jail sits near her, but he's a sharp ferrety-faced man—another sort o' flesh and blood to Mr. Irwine. They say the jail chaplains are mostly the fag-end o' the clergy."

"There's one man as ought to be there," said Adam bitterly. Presently he drew himself up and looked fixedly out of the window, apparently turning over some new idea in his mind.

"Mr. Massey," he said at last, pushing the hair off his forehead, "I'll go back with you. I'll go into court. It's cowardly of me to keep away. I'll stand by her—I'll own her—for all she's been deceitful. They oughtn't to cast her off—her own flesh and blood. We hand folks over to God's mercy, and show none ourselves. I used to be hard sometimes: I'll never be hard again. I'll go, Mr. Massey—I'll go with you."

There was a decision in Adam's manner which would have prevented Bartle from opposing him, even if he had wished to do so. He only said, "Take a bit, then, and another sup, Adam, for the love of me. See, I must stop and eat a morsel. Now, you take some."

Nerved by an active resolution, Adam took a morsel of bread and drank some wine. He was haggard and unshaven, as he had been yesterday, but he stood upright again, and looked more like the Adam Bede of former days.

Chapter XLIII The Verdict

THE place fitted up that day as a court of justice was a grand old hall, now destroyed by fire. The midday light that fell on the close pavement of human heads was shed through a line of high pointed windows, variegated with the mellow tints of old painted glass. Grim dusty armour hung in high relief in front of the dark oaken gallery at the farther end, and under the broad arch of the great mullioned window opposite was spread a curtain of old tapestry, covered with dim melancholy figures, like a dozing indistinct dream of the past. It was a place that through the rest of the year was haunted with the shadowy memories of old kings and queens, unhappy, discrowned, imprisoned; but to-day all those shadows had fled, and not a soul in the vast hall felt the presence of any but a living sorrow, which was quivering in warm hearts.

But that sorrow seemed to have made it itself feebly felt hitherto, now when Adam Bede's tall figure was suddenly seen being ushered to the side of the prisoner's dock. In the broad sunlight of the great hall, among the sleek shaven faces of other men, the marks of suffering in his face were startling even to Mr. Irwine, who had last seen him in the dim light of his small room; and the neighbours from Hayslope who were present, and who told Hetty Sorrel's story by their firesides in their old age, never forgot to say how it moved them when Adam Bede, poor fellow, taller by the head than most of the people round him, came into court and took his place by her side.

But Hetty did not see him. She was standing in the same position Bartle Massey had described, her hands crossed over each other and her eyes fixed on them. Adam had not dared to look at her in the first moments, but at last, when the attention of the court was withdrawn by the proceedings he turned his face towards her with a resolution not to shrink.

Why did they say she was so changed? In the corpse we love, it is the likeness we see—it is the likeness, which makes itself felt the more keenly because something else was and is not. There they were—the sweet face and neck, with the dark tendrils of hair, the long dark lashes, the rounded cheek and the pouting lips—pale and thin, yes, but like Hetty, and only Hetty. Others thought she looked as if some demon had cast a blighting glance upon her, withered up the woman's soul in her, and left only a hard despairing obstinacy. But the mother's yearning, that completest type of the life in another life which is the essence of real human love, feels the presence of the cherished child even in the debased, degraded man; and to Adam, this pale, hard-looking culprit was the Hetty who had smiled at him in the garden under the apple-tree boughs—she was that Hetty's corpse, which he had trembled to look at the first time, and then was unwilling to turn away his eyes from.

But presently he heard something that compelled him to listen, and made the sense of sight less absorbing. A woman was in the witness-box, a middle-aged woman, who spoke in a firm distinct voice. She said, "My name is Sarah Stone. I am a widow, and keep a small shop licensed to sell tobacco, snuff, and tea in Church Lane, Stoniton. The prisoner at the bar is the same young woman who came, looking ill and tired, with a basket on her arm, and asked for a lodging at my house on Saturday evening, the 27th of February. She had taken the house for a public, because there was a figure against the door. And when I said I didn't take in lodgers, the prisoner began to cry, and said she was too tired to go anywhere else, and she only wanted a bed for one night. And her prettiness, and her condition, and something respectable about her clothes and looks, and the trouble she seemed to be in made me as I couldn't find in my heart to send her away at once. I asked her to sit down, and gave her some tea, and asked her where she was going, and where her friends were. She said she was going home to her friends: they were farming folks a good way off, and she'd had a long journey that had cost her more money than she expected, so as she'd hardly any money left in her pocket, and was afraid of going where it would cost her much. She had been obliged to sell most of the things out of her basket, but she'd thankfully give a shilling for a bed. I saw no reason why I shouldn't take the young woman in for the night. I had only one room, but there were two beds in it, and I told her she might stay with me. I thought she'd been led wrong, and got into trouble, but if she was going to her friends, it would be a good work to keep her out of further harm."

The witness then stated that in the night a child was born, and she identified the baby-clothes then shown to her as those in which she had herself dressed the child.

"Those are the clothes. I made them myself, and had kept them by me ever since my last child was born. I took a deal of trouble both for the child and the mother. I couldn't help taking to the little thing and being anxious about it. I didn't send for a doctor, for there seemed no need. I told the mother in the day-time she must tell me the name of her friends, and where they lived, and let me write to them. She said, by and by she would write herself, but not to-day. She would have no nay, but she would get up and be dressed, in spite of everything I could say. She said she felt quite strong enough; and it was wonderful what spirit she showed. But I wasn't quite easy what I should do about her, and towards evening I made up my mind I'd go, after Meeting was over, and speak to our minister about it. I left the house about half-past eight o'clock. I didn't go out at the shop door, but at the back door, which opens into a narrow alley. I've only got the ground-floor of the house, and the kitchen and bedroom both look into the alley. I left the prisoner sitting up by the fire in the kitchen with the baby on her lap. She hadn't cried or seemed low at all, as she did the night before. I thought she had a strange look with her eyes, and she got a bit flushed towards evening. I was afraid of the fever, and I thought I'd call and ask an acquaintance of mine, an experienced woman, to come back with me when I went out. It was a very dark night. I didn't fasten the door behind me; there was no lock; it was a latch with a bolt inside, and when there was nobody in the house I always went out at the shop door. But I thought there was no danger in leaving it unfastened that little while. I was longer than I meant to be, for I had to wait for the woman that came back with me. It was an hour and a half before we got back, and when we went in, the candle was standing burning just as I left it, but the prisoner and the baby were both gone. She'd taken her cloak and bonnet, but she'd left the basket and the things in it. . . . I was dreadful frightened, and angry with her for going. I didn't go to give information, because I'd no thought she meant to do any harm, and I knew she had money in her pocket to buy her food and lodging. I didn't like to set the constable after her, for she'd a right to go from me if she liked."

The effect of this evidence on Adam was electrical; it gave him new force. Hetty could not be guilty of the crime—her heart must have clung to her baby—else why should she have taken it with her? She might have left it behind. The little creature had died naturally, and then she had hidden it. Babies were so liable to death—and there might be the strongest suspicions without any proof of guilt. His mind was so occupied with imaginary arguments against such suspicions, that he could not listen to the cross-examination by Hetty's counsel, who tried, without result, to elicit evidence that the prisoner had shown some movements of maternal affection towards the child. The whole time this witness was being examined, Hetty had stood as motionless as before: no word seemed to arrest her ear. But the sound of the next witness's voice touched a chord that was still sensitive, she gave a start and a frightened look towards him, but immediately turned away her head and looked down at her hands as before. This witness was a man, a rough peasant. He said:

"My name is John Olding. I am a labourer, and live at Tedd's Hole, two miles out of Stoniton. A week last Monday, towards one o'clock in the afternoon, I was going towards Hetton Coppice, and about a quarter of a mile from the coppice I saw the prisoner, in a red cloak, sitting under a bit of a haystack not far off the stile. She got up when she saw me, and seemed as if she'd be walking on the other way. It was a regular road through the fields, and nothing very uncommon to see a young woman there, but I took notice of her because she looked white and scared. I should have thought she was a beggar-woman, only for her good clothes. I thought she looked a bit crazy, but it was no business of mine. I stood and looked back after her, but she went right on while she was in sight. I had to go to the other side of the coppice to look after some stakes. There's a road right through it, and bits of openings here and there, where the trees have been cut down, and some of 'em not carried away. I didn't go straight along the road, but turned off towards the middle, and took a shorter way towards the spot I wanted to get to. I hadn't got far out of the road into one of the open places before I heard a strange cry. I thought it didn't come from any animal I knew, but I wasn't for stopping to look about just then. But it went on, and seemed so strange to me in that place, I couldn't help stopping to look. I began to think I might make some money of it, if it was a new thing. But I had hard work to tell which way it came from, and for a good while I kept looking up at the boughs. And then I thought it came from the ground; and there was a lot of timber-choppings lying about, and loose pieces of turf, and a trunk or two. And I looked about among them, but could find nothing, and at last the cry stopped. So I was for giving it up, and I went on about my business. But when I came back the same way pretty nigh an hour after, I couldn't help laying down my stakes to have another look. And just as I was stooping and laying down the stakes, I saw something odd and round and whitish lying on the ground under a nut-bush by the side of me. And I stooped down on hands and knees to pick it up. And I saw it was a little baby's hand."

At these words a thrill ran through the court. Hetty was visibly trembling; now, for the first time, she seemed to be listening to what a witness said.

"There was a lot of timber-choppings put together just where the ground went hollow, like, under the bush, and the hand came out from among them. But there was a hole left in one place and I could see down it and see the child's head; and I made haste and did away the turf and the choppings, and took out the child. It had got comfortable clothes on, but its body was cold, and I thought it must be dead. I made haste back with it out of the wood, and took it home to my wife. She said it was dead, and I'd better take it to the parish and tell the constable. And I said, 'I'll lay my life it's that young woman's child as I met going to the coppice.' But she seemed to be gone clean out of sight. And I took the child on to Hetton parish and told the constable, and we went on to Justice Hardy. And then we went looking after the young woman till dark at night, and we went and gave information at Stoniton, as they might stop her. And the next morning, another constable came to me, to go with him to the spot where I found the child. And when we got there, there was the prisoner a-sitting against the bush where I found the child; and she cried out when she saw us, but she never offered to move. She'd got a big piece of bread on her lap."

Adam had given a faint groan of despair while this witness was speaking. He had hidden his face on his arm, which rested on the boarding in front of him. It was the supreme moment of his suffering: Hetty was guilty; and he was silently calling to God for help. He heard no more of the evidence, and was unconscious when the case for the prosecution had closed—unconscious that Mr. Irwine was in the witness-box, telling of Hetty's unblemished character in her own parish and of the virtuous habits in which she had been brought up. This testimony could have no influence on the verdict, but it was given as part of that plea for mercy which her own counsel would have made if he had been allowed to speak for her—a favour not granted to criminals in those stern times.

At last Adam lifted up his head, for there was a general movement round him. The judge had addressed the jury, and they were retiring. The decisive moment was not far off Adam felt a shuddering horror that would not let him look at Hetty, but she had long relapsed into her blank hard indifference. All eyes were strained to look at her, but she stood like a statue of dull despair.

There was a mingled rustling, whispering, and low buzzing throughout the court during this interval. The desire to listen was suspended, and every one had some feeling or opinion to express in undertones. Adam sat looking blankly before him, but he did not see the objects that were right in front of his eyes—the counsel and attorneys talking with an air of cool business, and Mr. Irwine in low earnest conversation with the judge—did not see Mr. Irwine sit down again in agitation and shake his head mournfully when somebody whispered to him. The inward action was too intense for Adam to take in outward objects until some strong sensation roused him.

It was not very long, hardly more than a quarter of an hour, before the knock which told that the jury had come to their decision fell as a signal for silence on every ear. It is sublime—that sudden pause of a great multitude which tells that one soul moves in them all. Deeper and deeper the silence seemed to become, like the deepening night, while the jurymen's names were called over, and the prisoner was made to hold up her hand, and the jury were asked for their verdict.

"Guilty."

It was the verdict every one expected, but there was a sigh of disappointment from some hearts that it was followed by no recommendation to mercy. Still the sympathy of the court was not with the prisoner. The unnaturalness of her crime stood out the more harshly by the side of her hard immovability and obstinate silence. Even the verdict, to distant eyes, had not appeared to move her, but those who were near saw her trembling.

The stillness was less intense until the judge put on his black cap, and the chaplain in his canonicals was observed behind him. Then it deepened again, before the crier had had time to command silence. If any sound were heard, it must have been the sound of beating hearts. The judge spoke, "Hester Sorrel . . . ."

The blood rushed to Hetty's face, and then fled back again as she looked up at the judge and kept her wide-open eyes fixed on him, as if fascinated by fear. Adam had not yet turned towards her, there was a deep horror, like a great gulf, between them. But at the words "and then to be hanged by the neck till you be dead," a piercing shriek rang through the hall. It was Hetty's shriek. Adam started to his feet and stretched out his arms towards her. But the arms could not reach her: she had fallen down in a fainting-fit, and was carried out of court.

Chapter XLIV Arthur's Return

WHEN Arthur Donnithorne landed at Liverpool and read the letter from his Aunt Lydia, briefly announcing his grand-father's death, his first feeling was, "Poor Grandfather! I wish I could have got to him to be with him when he died. He might have felt or wished something at the last that I shall never know now. It was a lonely death."

It is impossible to say that his grief was deeper than that. Pity and softened memory took place of the old antagonism, and in his busy thoughts about the future, as the chaise carried him rapidly along towards the home where he was now to be master, there was a continually recurring effort to remember anything by which he could show a regard for his grandfather's wishes, without counteracting his own cherished aims for the good of the tenants and the estate. But it is not in human nature—only in human pretence—for a young man like Arthur, with a fine constitution and fine spirits, thinking well of himself, believing that others think well of him, and having a very ardent intention to give them more and more reason for that good opinion—it is not possible for such a young man, just coming into a splendid estate through the death of a very old man whom he was not fond of, to feel anything very different from exultant joy. Now his real life was beginning; now he would have room and opportunity for action, and he would use them. He would show the Loamshire people what a fine country gentleman was; he would not exchange that career for any other under the sun. He felt himself riding over the hills in the breezy autumn days, looking after favourite plans of drainage and enclosure; then admired on sombre mornings as the best rider on the best horse in the hunt; spoken well of on market-days as a first-rate landlord; by and by making speeches at election dinners, and showing a wonderful knowledge of agriculture; the patron of new ploughs and drills, the severe upbraider of negligent landowners, and withal a jolly fellow that everybody must like—happy faces greeting him everywhere on his own estate, and the neighbouring families on the best terms with him. The Irwines should dine with him every week, and have their own carriage to come in, for in some very delicate way that Arthur would devise, the lay-impropriator of the Hayslope tithes would insist on paying a couple of hundreds more to the vicar; and his aunt should be as comfortable as possible, and go on living at the Chase, if she liked, in spite of her old-maidish ways—at least until he was married, and that event lay in the indistinct background, for Arthur had not yet seen the woman who would play the lady-wife to the first-rate country gentleman.

These were Arthur's chief thoughts, so far as a man's thoughts through hours of travelling can be compressed into a few sentences, which are only like the list of names telling you what are the scenes in a long long panorama full of colour, of detail, and of life. The happy faces Arthur saw greeting him were not pale abstractions, but real ruddy faces, long familiar to him: Martin Poyser was there—the whole Poyser family.

What—Hetty?

Yes; for Arthur was at ease about Hetty—not quite at ease about the past, for a certain burning of the ears would come whenever he thought of the scenes with Adam last August, but at ease about her present lot. Mr. Irwine, who had been a regular correspondent, telling him all the news about the old places and people, had sent him word nearly three months ago that Adam Bede was not to marry Mary Burge, as he had thought, but pretty Hetty Sorrel. Martin Poyser and Adam himself had both told Mr. Irwine all about it—that Adam had been deeply in love with Hetty these two years, and that now it was agreed they were to be married in March. That stalwart rogue Adam was more susceptible than the rector had thought; it was really quite an idyllic love affair; and if it had not been too long to tell in a letter, he would have liked to describe to Arthur the blushing looks and the simple strong words with which the fine honest fellow told his secret. He knew Arthur would like to hear that Adam had this sort of happiness in prospect.

Yes, indeed! Arthur felt there was not air enough in the room to satisfy his renovated life, when he had read that passage in the letter. He threw up the windows, he rushed out of doors into the December air, and greeted every one who spoke to him with an eager gaiety, as if there had been news of a fresh Nelson victory. For the first time that day since he had come to Windsor, he was in true boyish spirits. The load that had been pressing upon him was gone, the haunting fear had vanished. He thought he could conquer his bitterness towards Adam now—could offer him his hand, and ask to be his friend again, in spite of that painful memory which would still make his ears burn. He had been knocked down, and he had been forced to tell a lie: such things make a scar, do what we will. But if Adam were the same again as in the old days, Arthur wished to be the same too, and to have Adam mixed up with his business and his future, as he had always desired before the accursed meeting in August. Nay, he would do a great deal more for Adam than he should otherwise have done, when he came into the estate; Hetty's husband had a special claim on him—Hetty herself should feel that any pain she had suffered through Arthur in the past was compensated to her a hundredfold. For really she could not have felt much, since she had so soon made up her mind to marry Adam.

You perceive clearly what sort of picture Adam and Hetty made in the panorama of Arthur's thoughts on his journey homeward. It was March now; they were soon to be married: perhaps they were already married. And now it was actually in his power to do a great deal for them. Sweet—sweet little Hetty! The little puss hadn't cared for him half as much as he cared for her; for he was a great fool about her still—was almost afraid of seeing her—indeed, had not cared much to look at any other woman since he parted from her. That little figure coming towards him in the Grove, those dark-fringed childish eyes, the lovely lips put up to kiss him—that picture had got no fainter with the lapse of months. And she would look just the same. It was impossible to think how he could meet her: he should certainly tremble. Strange, how long this sort of influence lasts, for he was certainly not in love with Hetty now. He had been earnestly desiring, for months, that she should marry Adam, and there was nothing that contributed more to his happiness in these moments than the thought of their marriage. It was the exaggerating effect of imagination that made his heart still beat a little more quickly at the thought of her. When he saw the little thing again as she really was, as Adam's wife, at work quite prosaically in her new home, he should perhaps wonder at the possibility of his past feelings. Thank heaven it had turned out so well! He should have plenty of affairs and interests to fill his life now, and not be in danger of playing the fool again.

Pleasant the crack of the post-boy's whip! Pleasant the sense of being hurried along in swift ease through English scenes, so like those round his own home, only not quite so charming. Here was a market-town—very much like Treddleston—where the arms of the neighbouring lord of the manor were borne on the sign of the principal inn; then mere fields and hedges, their vicinity to a market-town carrying an agreeable suggestion of high rent, till the land began to assume a trimmer look, the woods were more frequent, and at length a white or red mansion looked down from a moderate eminence, or allowed him to be aware of its parapet and chimneys among the dense-looking masses of oaks and elms—masses reddened now with early buds. And close at hand came the village: the small church, with its red-tiled roof, looking humble even among the faded half-timbered houses; the old green gravestones with nettles round them;

nothing fresh and bright but the children, opening round eyes at the swift post-chaise; nothing noisy and busy but the gaping curs of mysterious pedigree. What a much prettier village Hayslope was! And it should not be neglected like this place: vigorous repairs should go on everywhere among farm-buildings and cottages, and travellers in post-chaises, coming along the Rosseter road, should do nothing but admire as they went. And Adam Bede should superintend all the repairs, for he had a share in Burge's business now, and, if he liked, Arthur would put some money into the concern and buy the old man out in another year or two. That was an ugly fault in Arthur's life, that affair last summer, but the future should make amends. Many men would have retained a feeling of vindictiveness towards Adam, but he would not—he would resolutely overcome all littleness of that kind, for he had certainly been very much in the wrong; and though Adam had been harsh and violent, and had thrust on him a painful dilemma, the poor fellow was in love, and had real provocation. No, Arthur had not an evil feeling in his mind towards any human being: he was happy, and would make every one else happy that came within his reach.

And here was dear old Hayslope at last, sleeping, on the hill, like a quiet old place as it was, in the late afternoon sunlight, and opposite to it the great shoulders of the Binton Hills, below them the purplish blackness of the hanging woods, and at last the pale front of the Abbey, looking out from among the oaks of the Chase, as if anxious for the heir's return. "Poor Grandfather! And he lies dead there. He was a young fellow once, coming into the estate and making his plans. So the world goes round! Aunt Lydia must feel very desolate, poor thing; but she shall be indulged as much as she indulges her fat Fido."

The wheels of Arthur's chaise had been anxiously listened for at the Chase, for to-day was Friday, and the funeral had already been deferred two days. Before it drew up on the gravel of the courtyard, all the servants in the house were assembled to receive him with a grave, decent welcome, befitting a house of death. A month ago, perhaps, it would have been difficult for them to have maintained a suitable sadness in their faces, when Mr. Arthur was come to take possession; but the hearts of the head-servants were heavy that day for another cause than the death of the old squire, and more than one of them was longing to be twenty miles away, as Mr. Craig was, knowing what was to become of Hetty Sorrel—pretty Hetty Sorrel—whom they used to see every week. They had the partisanship of household servants who like their places, and were not inclined to go the full length of the severe indignation felt against him by the farming tenants, but rather to make excuses for him; nevertheless, the upper servants, who had been on terms of neighbourly intercourse with the Poysers for many years, could not help feeling that the longed-for event of the young squire's coming into the estate had been robbed of all its pleasantness.

To Arthur it was nothing surprising that the servants looked grave and sad: he himself was very much touched on seeing them all again, and feeling that he was in a new relation to them. It was that sort of pathetic emotion which has more pleasure than pain in it—which is perhaps one of the most delicious of all states to a good-natured man, conscious of the power to satisfy his good nature. His heart swelled agreeably as he said, "Well, Mills, how is my aunt?"

But now Mr. Bygate, the lawyer, who had been in the house ever since the death, came forward to give deferential greetings and answer all questions, and Arthur walked with him towards the library, where his Aunt Lydia was expecting him. Aunt Lydia was the only person in the house who knew nothing about Hetty. Her sorrow as a maiden daughter was unmixed with any other thoughts than those of anxiety about funeral arrangements and her own future lot; and, after the manner of women, she mourned for the father who had made her life important, all the more because she had a secret sense that there was little mourning for him in other hearts.

But Arthur kissed her tearful face more tenderly than he had ever done in his life before.

"Dear Aunt," he said affectionately, as he held her hand, "YOUR loss is the greatest of all, but you must tell me how to try and make it up to you all the rest of your life."

"It was so sudden and so dreadful, Arthur," poor Miss Lydia began, pouring out her little plaints, and Arthur sat down to listen with impatient patience. When a pause came, he said:

"Now, Aunt, I'll leave you for a quarter of an hour just to go to my own room, and then I shall come and give full attention to everything."

"My room is all ready for me, I suppose, Mills?" he said to the butler, who seemed to be lingering uneasily about the entrance-hall.

"Yes, sir, and there are letters for you; they are all laid on the writing-table in your dressing-room."

On entering the small anteroom which was called a dressing-room, but which Arthur really used only to lounge and write in, he just cast his eyes on the writing-table, and saw that there were several letters and packets lying there; but he was in the uncomfortable dusty condition of a man who has had a long hurried journey, and he must really refresh himself by attending to his toilette a little, before he read his letters. Pym was there, making everything ready for him, and soon, with a delightful freshness about him, as if he were prepared to begin a new day, he went back into his dressing-room to open his letters. The level rays of the low afternoon sun entered directly at the window, and as Arthur seated himself in his velvet chair with their pleasant warmth upon him, he was conscious of that quiet well-being which perhaps you and I have felt on a sunny afternoon when, in our brightest youth and health, life has opened a new vista for us, and long to-morrows of activity have stretched before us like a lovely plain which there was no need for hurrying to look at, because it was all our own.

The top letter was placed with its address upwards: it was in Mr. Irwine's handwriting, Arthur saw at once; and below the address was written, "To be delivered as soon as he arrives." Nothing could have been less surprising to him than a letter from Mr. Irwine at that moment: of course, there was something he wished Arthur to know earlier than it was possible for them to see each other. At such a time as that it was quite natural that Irwine should have something pressing to say. Arthur broke the seal with an agreeable anticipation of soon seeing the writer.

"I send this letter to meet you on your arrival, Arthur, because I may then be at Stoniton, whither I am called by the most painful duty it has ever been given me to perform, and it is right that you should know what I have to tell you without delay.

"I will not attempt to add by one word of reproach to the retribution that is now falling on you: any other words that I could write at this moment must be weak and unmeaning by the side of those in which I must tell you the simple fact.

"Hetty Sorrel is in prison, and will be tried on Friday for the crime of child-murder." . . .

Arthur read no more. He started up from his chair and stood for a single minute with a sense of violent convulsion in his whole frame, as if the life were going out of him with horrible throbs; but the next minute he had rushed out of the room, still clutching the letter—he was hurrying along the corridor, and down the stairs into the hall. Mills was still there, but Arthur did not see him, as he passed like a hunted man across the hall and out along the gravel. The butler hurried out after him as fast as his elderly limbs could run: he guessed, he knew, where the young squire was going.

When Mills got to the stables, a horse was being saddled, and Arthur was forcing himself to read the remaining words of the letter. He thrust it into his pocket as the horse was led up to him, and at that moment caught sight of Mills' anxious face in front of him.

"Tell them I'm gone—gone to Stoniton," he said in a muffled tone of agitation—sprang into the saddle, and set off at a gallop.

Chapter XLV In the Prison

NEAR sunset that evening an elderly gentleman was standing with his back against the smaller entrance-door of Stoniton jail, saying a few last words to the departing chaplain. The chaplain walked away, but the elderly gentleman stood still, looking down on the pavement and stroking his chin with a ruminating air, when he was roused by a sweet clear woman's voice, saying, "Can I get into the prison, if you please?"

He turned his head and looked fixedly at the speaker for a few moments without answering.

"I have seen you before," he said at last. "Do you remember preaching on the village green at Hayslope in Loamshire?"

"Yes, sir, surely. Are you the gentleman that stayed to listen on horseback?"

"Yes. Why do you want to go into the prison?"

"I want to go to Hetty Sorrel, the young woman who has been condemned to death—and to stay with her, if I may be permitted. Have you power in the prison, sir?"

"Yes; I am a magistrate, and can get admittance for you. But did you know this criminal, Hetty Sorrel?"

"Yes, we are kin. My own aunt married her uncle, Martin Poyser. But I was away at Leeds, and didn't know of this great trouble in time to get here before to-day. I entreat you, sir, for the love of our heavenly Father, to let me go to her and stay with her."

"How did you know she was condemned to death, if you are only just come from Leeds?"

"I have seen my uncle since the trial, sir. He is gone back to his home now, and the poor sinner is forsaken of all. I beseech you to get leave for me to be with her."

"What! Have you courage to stay all night in the prison? She is very sullen, and will scarcely make answer when she is spoken to."

"Oh, sir, it may please God to open her heart still. Don't let us delay."

"Come, then," said the elderly gentleman, ringing and gaining admission, "I know you have a key to unlock hearts."

Dinah mechanically took off her bonnet and shawl as soon as they were within the prison court, from the habit she had of throwing them off when she preached or prayed, or visited the sick; and when they entered the jailer's room, she laid them down on a chair unthinkingly. There was no agitation visible in her, but a deep concentrated calmness, as if, even when she was speaking, her soul was in prayer reposing on an unseen support.

After speaking to the jailer, the magistrate turned to her and said, "The turnkey will take you to the prisoner's cell and leave you there for the night, if you desire it, but you can't have a light during the night—it is contrary to rules. My name is Colonel Townley: if I can help you in anything, ask the jailer for my address and come to me. I take some interest in this Hetty Sorrel, for the sake of that fine fellow, Adam Bede. I happened to see him at Hayslope the same evening I heard you preach, and recognized him in court to-day, ill as he looked."

"Ah, sir, can you tell me anything about him? Can you tell me where he lodges? For my poor uncle was too much weighed down with trouble to remember."

"Close by here. I inquired all about him of Mr. Irwine. He lodges over a tinman's shop, in the street on the right hand as you entered the prison. There is an old school-master with him. Now, good-bye: I wish you success."

"Farewell, sir. I am grateful to you."

As Dinah crossed the prison court with the turnkey, the solemn evening light seemed to make the walls higher than they were by day, and the sweet pale face in the cap was more than ever like a white flower on this background of gloom. The turnkey looked askance at her all the while, but never spoke. He somehow felt that the sound of his own rude voice would be grating just then. He struck a light as they entered the dark corridor leading to the condemned cell, and then said in his most civil tone, "It'll be pretty nigh dark in the cell a'ready, but I can stop with my light a bit, if you like."

"Nay, friend, thank you," said Dinah. "I wish to go in alone."

"As you like," said the jailer, turning the harsh key in the lock and opening the door wide enough to admit Dinah. A jet of light from his lantern fell on the opposite corner of the cell, where Hetty was sitting on her straw pallet with her face buried in her knees. It seemed as if she were asleep, and yet the grating of the lock would have been likely to waken her.

The door closed again, and the only light in the cell was that of the evening sky, through the small high grating—enough to discern human faces by. Dinah stood still for a minute, hesitating to speak because Hetty might be asleep, and looking at the motionless heap with a yearning heart. Then she said, softly, "Hetty!"

There was a slight movement perceptible in Hetty's frame—a start such as might have been produced by a feeble electrical shock—but she did not look up. Dinah spoke again, in a tone made stronger by irrepressible emotion, "Hetty . . . it's Dinah."

Again there was a slight startled movement through Hetty's frame, and without uncovering her face, she raised her head a little, as if listening.

"Hetty . . . Dinah is come to you."

After a moment's pause, Hetty lifted her head slowly and timidly from her knees and raised her eyes. The two pale faces were looking at each other: one with a wild hard despair in it, the other full of sad yearning love. Dinah unconsciously opened her arms and stretched them out.

"Don't you know me, Hetty? Don't you remember Dinah? Did you think I wouldn't come to you in trouble?"

Hetty kept her eyes fixed on Dinah's face—at first like an animal that gazes, and gazes, and keeps aloof.

"I'm come to be with you, Hetty—not to leave you—to stay with you—to be your sister to the last."

Slowly, while Dinah was speaking, Hetty rose, took a step forward, and was clasped in Dinah's arms.

They stood so a long while, for neither of them felt the impulse to move apart again. Hetty, without any distinct thought of it, hung on this something that was come to clasp her now, while she was sinking helpless in a dark gulf; and Dinah felt a deep joy in the first sign that her love was welcomed by the wretched lost one. The light got fainter as they stood, and when at last they sat down on the straw pallet together, their faces had become indistinct.

Not a word was spoken. Dinah waited, hoping for a spontaneous word from Hetty, but she sat in the same dull despair, only clutching the hand that held hers and leaning her cheek against Dinah's. It was the human contact she clung to, but she was not the less sinking into the dark gulf.

Dinah began to doubt whether Hetty was conscious who it was that sat beside her. She thought suffering and fear might have driven the poor sinner out of her mind. But it was borne in upon her, as she afterwards said, that she must not hurry God's work: we are overhasty to speak—as if God did not manifest himself by our silent feeling, and make his love felt through ours. She did not know how long they sat in that way, but it got darker and darker, till there was only a pale patch of light on the opposite wall: all the rest was darkness. But she felt the Divine presence more and more—nay, as if she herself were a part of it, and it was the Divine pity that was beating in her heart and was willing the rescue of this helpless one. At last she was prompted to speak and find out how far Hetty was conscious of the present.

"Hetty," she said gently, "do you know who it is that sits by your side?"

"Yes," Hetty answered slowly, "it's Dinah."

"And do you remember the time when we were at the Hall Farm together, and that night when I told you to be sure and think of me as a friend in trouble?"

"Yes," said Hetty. Then, after a pause, she added, "But you can do nothing for me. You can't make 'em do anything. They'll hang me o' Monday—it's Friday now."

As Hetty said the last words, she clung closer to Dinah, shuddering.

"No, Hetty, I can't save you from that death. But isn't the suffering less hard when you have somebody with you, that feels for you—that you can speak to, and say what's in your heart? . . . Yes, Hetty: you lean on me: you are glad to have me with you."

"You won't leave me, Dinah? You'll keep close to me?"

"No, Hetty, I won't leave you. I'll stay with you to the last. . . . But, Hetty, there is some one else in this cell besides me, some one close to you."

Hetty said, in a frightened whisper, "Who?"

"Some one who has been with you through all your hours of sin and trouble—who has known every thought you have had—has seen where you went, where you lay down and rose up again, and all the deeds you have tried to hide in darkness. And on Monday, when I can't follow you—when my arms can't reach you—when death has parted us—He who is with us now, and knows all, will be with you then. It makes no difference—whether we live or die, we are in the presence of God."

"Oh, Dinah, won't nobody do anything for me? Will they hang me for certain? . . . I wouldn't mind if they'd let me live."

"My poor Hetty, death is very dreadful to you. I know it's dreadful. But if you had a friend to take care of you after death—in that other world—some one whose love is greater than mine—who can do everything? . . . If God our Father was your friend, and was willing to save you from sin and suffering, so as you should neither know wicked feelings nor pain again? If you could believe he loved you and would help you, as you believe I love you and will help you, it wouldn't be so hard to die on Monday, would it?"

"But I can't know anything about it," Hetty said, with sullen sadness.

"Because, Hetty, you are shutting up your soul against him, by trying to hide the truth. God's love and mercy can overcome all things—our ignorance, and weakness, and all the burden of our past wickedness—all things but our wilful sin, sin that we cling to, and will not give up. You believe in my love and pity for you, Hetty, but if you had not let me come near you, if you wouldn't have looked at me or spoken to me, you'd have shut me out from helping you. I couldn't have made you feel my love; I couldn't have told you what I felt for you. Don't shut God's love out in that way, by clinging to sin. . . . He can't bless you while you have one falsehood in your soul; his pardoning mercy can't reach you until you open your heart to him, and say, 'I have done this great wickedness; O God, save me, make me pure from sin.' While you cling to one sin and will not part with it, it must drag you down to misery after death, as it has dragged you to misery here in this world, my poor, poor Hetty. It is sin that brings dread, and darkness, and despair: there is light and blessedness for us as soon as we cast it off. God enters our souls then, and teaches us, and brings us strength and peace. Cast it off now, Hetty—now: confess the wickedness you have done—the sin you have been guilty of against your Heavenly Father. Let us kneel down together, for we are in the presence of God."

Hetty obeyed Dinah's movement, and sank on her knees. They still held each other's hands, and there was long silence. Then Dinah said, "Hetty, we are before God. He is waiting for you to tell the truth."

Still there was silence. At last Hetty spoke, in a tone of beseeching—

"Dinah . . . help me . . . I can't feel anything like you . . . my heart is hard."

Dinah held the clinging hand, and all her soul went forth in her voice:

"Jesus, thou present Saviour! Thou hast known the depths of all sorrow: thou hast entered that black darkness where God is not, and hast uttered the cry of the forsaken. Come Lord, and gather of the fruits of thy travail and thy pleading. Stretch forth thy hand, thou who art mighty to save to the uttermost, and rescue this lost one. She is clothed round with thick darkness. The fetters of her sin are upon her, and she cannot stir to come to thee. She can only feel her heart is hard, and she is helpless. She cries to me, thy weak creature. . . . Saviour! It is a blind cry to thee. Hear it! Pierce the darkness! Look upon her with thy face of love and sorrow that thou didst turn on him who denied thee, and melt her hard heart.

"See, Lord, I bring her, as they of old brought the sick and helpless, and thou didst heal them. I bear her on my arms and carry her before thee. Fear and trembling have taken hold on her, but she trembles only at the pain and death of the body. Breathe upon her thy life-giving Spirit, and put a new fear within her—the fear of her sin. Make her dread to keep the accursed thing within her soul. Make her feel the presence of the living God, who beholds all the past, to whom the darkness is as noonday; who is waiting now, at the eleventh hour, for her to turn to him, and confess her sin, and cry for mercy—now, before the night of death comes, and the moment of pardon is for ever fled, like yesterday that returneth not.

"Saviour! It is yet time—time to snatch this poor soul from everlasting darkness. I believe—I believe in thy infinite love. What is my love or my pleading? It is quenched in thine. I can only clasp her in my weak arms and urge her with my weak pity. Thou—thou wilt breathe on the dead soul, and it shall arise from the unanswering sleep of death.

"Yea, Lord, I see thee, coming through the darkness coming, like the morning, with healing on thy wings. The marks of thy agony are upon thee—I see, I see thou art able and willing to save—thou wilt not let her perish for ever. "Come, mighty Saviour! Let the dead hear thy voice. Let the eyes of the blind be opened. Let her see that God encompasses her. Let her tremble at nothing but at the sin that cuts her off from him. Melt the hard heart. Unseal the closed lips: make her cry with her whole soul, 'Father, I have sinned.' . . ."

"Dinah," Hetty sobbed out, throwing her arms round Dinah's neck, "I will speak . . . I will tell . . . I won't hide it any more."

But the tears and sobs were too violent. Dinah raised her gently from her knees and seated her on the pallet again, sitting down by her side. It was a long time before the convulsed throat was quiet, and even then they sat some time in stillness and darkness, holding each other's hands. At last Hetty whispered, "I did do it, Dinah . . . I buried it in the wood . . . the little baby . . . and it cried . . . I heard it cry . . . ever such a way off . . . all night . . . and I went back because it cried."

She paused, and then spoke hurriedly in a louder, pleading tone.

"But I thought perhaps it wouldn't die—there might somebody find it. I didn't kill it—I didn't kill it myself. I put it down there and covered it up, and when I came back it was gone. . . . It was because I was so very miserable, Dinah . . . I didn't know where to go . . . and I tried to kill myself before, and I couldn't. Oh, I tried so to drown myself in the pool, and I couldn't. I went to Windsor—I ran away—did you know? I went to find him, as he might take care of me; and he was gone; and then I didn't know what to do. I daredn't go back home again—I couldn't bear it. I couldn't have bore to look at anybody, for they'd have scorned me. I thought o' you sometimes, and thought I'd come to you, for I didn't think you'd be cross with me, and cry shame on me. I thought I could tell you. But then the other folks 'ud come to know it at last, and I couldn't bear that. It was partly thinking o' you made me come toward Stoniton; and, besides, I was so frightened at going wandering about till I was a beggar-woman, and had nothing; and sometimes it seemed as if I must go back to the farm sooner than that. Oh, it was so dreadful, Dinah . . . I was so miserable . . . I wished I'd never been born into this world. I should never like to go into the green fields again—I hated 'em so in my misery."

Hetty paused again, as if the sense of the past were too strong upon her for words.

"And then I got to Stoniton, and I began to feel frightened that night, because I was so near home. And then the little baby was born, when I didn't expect it; and the thought came into my mind that I might get rid of it and go home again. The thought came all of a sudden, as I was lying in the bed, and it got stronger and stronger . . . I longed so to go back again . . . I couldn't bear being so lonely and coming to beg for want. And it gave me strength and resolution to get up and dress myself. I felt I must do it . . . I didn't know how . . . I thought I'd find a pool, if I could, like that other, in the corner of the field, in the dark. And when the woman went out, I felt as if I was strong enough to do anything . . . I thought I should get rid of all my misery, and go back home, and never let 'em know why I ran away I put on my bonnet and shawl, and went out into the dark street, with the baby under my cloak; and I walked fast till I got into a street a good way off, and there was a public, and I got some warm stuff to drink and some bread. And I walked on and on, and I hardly felt the ground I trod on; and it got lighter, for there came the moon—oh, Dinah, it frightened me when it first looked at me out o' the clouds—it never looked so before; and I turned out of the road into the fields, for I was afraid o' meeting anybody with the moon shining on me. And I came to a haystack, where I thought I could lie down and keep myself warm all night. There was a place cut into it, where I could make me a bed, and I lay comfortable, and the baby was warm against me; and I must have gone to sleep for a good while, for when I woke it was morning, but not very light, and the baby was crying. And I saw a wood a little way off . . . I thought there'd perhaps be a ditch or a pond there . . . and it was so early I thought I could hide the child there, and get a long way off before folks was up. And then I thought I'd go home—I'd get rides in carts and go home and tell 'em I'd been to try and see for a place, and couldn't get one. I longed so for it, Dinah, I longed so to be safe at home. I don't know how I felt about the baby. I seemed to hate it—it was like a heavy weight hanging round my neck; and yet its crying went through me, and I daredn't look at its little hands and face. But I went on to the wood, and I walked about, but there was no water. . . ."

Hetty shuddered. She was silent for some moments, and when she began again, it was in a whisper.

"I came to a place where there was lots of chips and turf, and I sat down on the trunk of a tree to think what I should do. And all of a sudden I saw a hole under the nut-tree, like a little grave. And it darted into me like lightning—I'd lay the baby there and cover it with the grass and the chips. I couldn't kill it any other way. And I'd done it in a minute; and, oh, it cried so, Dinah—I couldn't cover it quite up—I thought perhaps somebody 'ud come and take care of it, and then it wouldn't die. And I made haste out of the wood, but I could hear it crying all the while; and when I got out into the fields, it was as if I was held fast—I couldn't go away, for all I wanted so to go. And I sat against the haystack to watch if anybody 'ud come. I was very hungry, and I'd only a bit of bread left, but I couldn't go away. And after ever such a while—hours and hours—the man came—him in a smock-frock, and he looked at me so, I was frightened, and

I made haste and went on. I thought he was going to the wood and would perhaps find the baby. And I went right on, till I came to a village, a long way off from the wood, and I was very sick, and faint, and hungry. I got something to eat there, and bought a loaf. But I was frightened to stay. I heard the baby crying, and thought the other folks heard it too—and I went on. But I was so tired, and it was getting towards dark. And at last, by the roadside there was a barn—ever such a way off any house—like the barn in Abbot's Close, and I thought I could go in there and hide myself among the hay and straw, and nobody 'ud be likely to come. I went in, and it was half full o' trusses of straw, and there was some hay too. And I made myself a bed, ever so far behind, where nobody could find me; and I was so tired and weak, I went to sleep. . . . But oh, the baby's crying kept waking me, and I thought that man as looked at me so was come and laying hold of me. But I must have slept a long while at last, though I didn't know, for when I got up and went out of the barn, I didn't know whether it was night or morning. But it was morning, for it kept getting lighter, and I turned back the way I'd come. I couldn't help it, Dinah; it was the baby's crying made me go—and yet I was frightened to death. I thought that man in the smock-frock 'ud see me and know I put the baby there. But I went on, for all that. I'd left off thinking about going home—it had gone out o' my mind. I saw nothing but that place in the wood where I'd buried the baby . . . I see it now. Oh Dinah! shall I allays see it?"

Hetty clung round Dinah and shuddered again. The silence seemed long before she went on.

"I met nobody, for it was very early, and I got into the wood . . . .I knew the way to the place . . . the place against the nut-tree; and I could hear it crying at every step. . . . I thought it was alive. . . . I don't know whether I was frightened or glad . . . I don't know what I felt. I only know I was in the wood and heard the cry. I don't know what I felt till I saw the baby was gone. And when I'd put it there, I thought I should like somebody to find it and save it from dying; but when I saw it was gone, I was struck like a stone, with fear. I never thought o' stirring, I felt so weak. I knew I couldn't run away, and everybody as saw me 'ud know about the baby. My heart went like a stone. I couldn't wish or try for anything; it seemed like as if I should stay there for ever, and nothing 'ud ever change. But they came and took me away."

Hetty was silent, but she shuddered again, as if there was still something behind; and Dinah waited, for her heart was so full that tears must come before words. At last Hetty burst out, with a sob, "Dinah, do you think God will take away that crying and the place in the wood, now I've told everything?"

"Let us pray, poor sinner. Let us fall on our knees again, and pray to the God of all mercy."

Chapter XLVI The Hours of Suspense

ON Sunday morning, when the church bells in Stoniton were ringing for morning service, Bartle Massey re-entered Adam's room, after a short absence, and said, "Adam, here's a visitor wants to see you."

Adam was seated with is back towards the door, but he started up and turned round instantly, with a flushed face and an eager look. His face was even thinner and more worn than we have seen it before, but he was washed and shaven this Sunday morning.

"Is it any news?" he said.

"Keep yourself quiet, my lad," said Bartle; "keep quiet. It's not what you're thinking of. It's the young Methodist woman come from the prison. She's at the bottom o' the stairs, and wants to know if you think well to see her, for she has something to say to you about that poor castaway; but she wouldn't come in without your leave, she said. She thought you'd perhaps like to go out and speak to her. These preaching women are not so back'ard commonly," Bartle muttered to himself.

"Ask her to come in," said Adam.

He was standing with his face towards the door, and as Dinah entered, lifting up her mild grey eyes towards him, she saw at once the great change that had come since the day when she had looked up at the tall man in the cottage. There was a trembling in her clear voice as she put her hand into his and said, "Be comforted, Adam Bede, the Lord has not forsaken her."

"Bless you for coming to her," Adam said. "Mr. Massey brought me word yesterday as you was come."

They could neither of them say any more just yet, but stood before each other in silence; and Bartle Massey, too, who had put on his spectacles, seemed transfixed, examining Dinah's face. But he recovered himself first, and said, "Sit down, young woman, sit down," placing the chair for her and retiring to his old seat on the bed.

"Thank you, friend; I won't sit down," said Dinah, "for I must hasten back. She entreated me not to stay long away. What I came for, Adam Bede, was to pray you to go and see the poor sinner and bid her farewell. She desires to ask your forgiveness, and it is meet you should see her to-day, rather than in the early morning, when the time will be short."

Adam stood trembling, and at last sank down on his chair again.

"It won't be," he said, "it'll be put off—there'll perhaps come a pardon. Mr. Irwine said there was hope. He said, I needn't quite give it up."

"That's a blessed thought to me," said Dinah, her eyes filling with tears. "It's a fearful thing hurrying her soul away so fast."

"But let what will be," she added presently. "You will surely come, and let her speak the words that are in her heart. Although her poor soul is very dark and discerns little beyond the things of the flesh, she is no longer hard. She is contrite, she has confessed all to me. The pride of her heart has given way, and she leans on me for help and desires to be taught. This fills me with trust, for I cannot but think that the brethren sometimes err in measuring the Divine love by the sinner's knowledge. She is going to write a letter to the friends at the Hall Farm for me to give them when she is gone, and when I told her you were here, she said, 'I should like to say good-bye to Adam and ask him to forgive me.' You will come, Adam? Perhaps you will even now come back with me."

"I can't," Adam said. "I can't say good-bye while there's any hope. I'm listening, and listening—I can't think o' nothing but that. It can't be as she'll die that shameful death—I can't bring my mind to it."

He got up from his chair again and looked away out of the window, while Dinah stood with compassionate patience. In a minute or two he turned round and said, "I will come, Dinah . . . to-morrow morning . . . if it must be. I may have more strength to bear it, if I know it must be. Tell her, I forgive her; tell her I will come—at the very last."

"I will not urge you against the voice of your own heart," said Dinah. "I must hasten back to her, for it is wonderful how she clings now, and was not willing to let me out of her sight. She used never to make any return to my affection before, but now tribulation has opened her heart. Farewell, Adam. Our heavenly Father comfort you and strengthen you to bear all things." Dinah put out her hand, and Adam pressed it in silence.

Bartle Massey was getting up to lift the stiff latch of the door for her, but before he could reach it, she had said gently, "Farewell, friend," and was gone, with her light step down the stairs.

"Well," said Bartle, taking off his spectacles and putting them into his pocket, "if there must be women to make trouble in the world, it's but fair there should be women to be comforters under it; and she's one—she's one. It's a pity she's a Methodist; but there's no getting a woman without some foolishness or other."

Adam never went to bed that night. The excitement of suspense, heightening with every hour that brought him nearer the fatal moment, was too great, and in spite of his entreaties, in spite of his promises that he would be perfectly quiet, the schoolmaster watched too.

"What does it matter to me, lad?" Bartle said: "a night's sleep more or less? I shall sleep long enough, by and by, underground. Let me keep thee company in trouble while I can."

It was a long and dreary night in that small chamber. Adam would sometimes get up and tread backwards and forwards along the short space from wall to wall; then he would sit down and hide his face, and no sound would be heard but the ticking of the watch on the table, or the falling of a cinder from the fire which the schoolmaster carefully tended. Sometimes he would burst out into vehement speech, "If I could ha' done anything to save her—if my bearing anything would ha' done any good . . . but t' have to sit still, and know it, and do nothing . . . it's hard for a man to bear . . . and to think o' what might ha' been now, if it hadn't been for HIM. . . . O God, it's the very day we should ha' been married."

"Aye, my lad," said Bartle tenderly, "it's heavy—it's heavy. But you must remember this: when you thought of marrying her, you'd a notion she'd got another sort of a nature inside her. You didn't think she could have got hardened in that little while to do what she's done."

"I know—I know that," said Adam. "I thought she was loving and tender-hearted, and wouldn't tell a lie, or act deceitful. How could I think any other way? And if he'd never come near her, and I'd married her, and been loving to her, and took care of her, she might never ha' done anything bad. What would it ha' signified—my having a bit o' trouble with her? It 'ud ha' been nothing to this."

"There's no knowing, my lad—there's no knowing what might have come. The smart's bad for you to bear now: you must have time—you must have time. But I've that opinion of you, that you'll rise above it all and be a man again, and there may good come out of this that we don't see."

"Good come out of it!" said Adam passionately. "That doesn't alter th' evil: HER ruin can't be undone. I hate that talk o' people, as if there was a way o' making amends for everything. They'd more need be brought to see as the wrong they do can never be altered. When a man's spoiled his fellow-creatur's life, he's no right to comfort himself with thinking good may come out of it. Somebody else's good doesn't alter her shame and misery."

"Well, lad, well," said Bartle, in a gentle tone, strangely in contrast with his usual peremptoriness and impatience of contradiction, "it's likely enough I talk foolishness. I'm an old fellow, and it's a good many years since I was in trouble myself. It's easy finding reasons why other folks should be patient."

"Mr. Massey," said Adam penitently, "I'm very hot and hasty. I owe you something different; but you mustn't take it ill of me."

"Not I, lad—not I."

So the night wore on in agitation till the chill dawn and the growing light brought the tremulous quiet that comes on the brink of despair. There would soon be no more suspense.

"Let us go to the prison now, Mr. Massey," said Adam, when he saw the hand of his watch at six. "If there's any news come, we shall hear about it."

The people were astir already, moving rapidly, in one direction, through the streets. Adam tried not to think where they were going, as they hurried past him in that short space between his lodging and the prison gates. He was thankful when the gates shut him in from seeing those eager people.

No; there was no news come—no pardon—no reprieve.

Adam lingered in the court half an hour before he could bring himself to send word to Dinah that he was come. But a voice caught his ear: he could not shut out the words.

"The cart is to set off at half-past seven."

It must be said—the last good-bye: there was no help.

In ten minutes from that time, Adam was at the door of the cell. Dinah had sent him word that she could not come to him; she could not leave Hetty one moment; but Hetty was prepared for the meeting.

He could not see her when he entered, for agitation deadened his senses, and the dim cell was almost dark to him. He stood a moment after the door closed behind him, trembling and stupefied.

But he began to see through the dimness—to see the dark eyes lifted up to him once more, but with no smile in them. O God, how sad they looked! The last time they had met his was when he parted from her with his heart full of joyous hopeful love, and they looked out with a tearful smile from a pink, dimpled, childish face. The face was marble now; the sweet lips were pallid and half-open and quivering; the dimples were all gone—all but one, that never went; and the eyes—O, the worst of all was the likeness they had to Hetty's. They were Hetty's eyes looking at him with that mournful gaze, as if she had come back to him from the dead to tell him of her misery.

She was clinging close to Dinah; her cheek was against Dinah's. It seemed as if her last faint strength and hope lay in that contact, and the pitying love that shone out from Dinah's face looked like a visible pledge of the Invisible Mercy.

When the sad eyes met—when Hetty and Adam looked at each other—she felt the change in him too, and it seemed to strike her with fresh fear. It was the first time she had seen any being whose face seemed to reflect the change in herself: Adam was a new image of the dreadful past and the dreadful present. She trembled more as she looked at him.

"Speak to him, Hetty," Dinah said; "tell him what is in your heart."

Hetty obeyed her, like a little child.

"Adam . . . I'm very sorry . . . I behaved very wrong to you . . . will you forgive me . . . before I die?"

Adam answered with a half-sob, "Yes, I forgive thee Hetty. I forgave thee long ago."

It had seemed to Adam as if his brain would burst with the anguish of meeting Hetty's eyes in the first moments, but the sound of her voice uttering these penitent words touched a chord which had been less strained. There was a sense of relief from what was becoming unbearable, and the rare tears came—they had never come before, since he had hung on Seth's neck in the beginning of his sorrow.

Hetty made an involuntary movement towards him, some of the love that she had once lived in the midst of was come near her again. She kept hold of Dinah's hand, but she went up to Adam and said timidly, "Will you kiss me again, Adam, for all I've been so wicked?"

Adam took the blanched wasted hand she put out to him, and they gave each other the solemn unspeakable kiss of a lifelong parting.

"And tell him," Hetty said, in rather a stronger voice, "tell him . . . for there's nobody else to tell him . . . as I went after him and couldn't find him . . . and I hated him and cursed him once . . . but Dinah says I should forgive him . . . and I try . . . for else God won't forgive me."

There was a noise at the door of the cell now—the key was being turned in the lock, and when the door opened, Adam saw indistinctly that there were several faces there. He was too agitated to see more—even to see that Mr. Irwine's face was one of them. He felt that the last preparations were beginning, and he could stay no longer. Room was silently made for him to depart, and he went to his chamber in loneliness, leaving Bartle Massey to watch and see the end.

Chapter XLVII The Last Moment

IT was a sight that some people remembered better even than their own sorrows—the sight in that grey clear morning, when the fatal cart with the two young women in it was descried by the waiting watching multitude, cleaving its way towards the hideous symbol of a deliberately inflicted sudden death.

All Stoniton had heard of Dinah Morris, the young Methodist woman who had brought the obstinate criminal to confess, and there was as much eagerness to see her as to see the wretched Hetty.

But Dinah was hardly conscious of the multitude. When Hetty had caught sight of the vast crowd in the distance, she had clutched Dinah convulsively.

"Close your eyes, Hetty," Dinah said, "and let us pray without ceasing to God."

And in a low voice, as the cart went slowly along through the midst of the gazing crowd, she poured forth her soul with the wrestling intensity of a last pleading, for the trembling creature that clung to her and clutched her as the only visible sign of love and pity.

Dinah did not know that the crowd was silent, gazing at her with a sort of awe—she did not even know how near they were to the fatal spot, when the cart stopped, and she shrank appalled at a loud shout hideous to her ear, like a vast yell of demons. Hetty's shriek mingled with the sound, and they clasped each other in mutual horror.

But it was not a shout of execration—not a yell of exultant cruelty.

It was a shout of sudden excitement at the appearance of a horseman cleaving the crowd at full gallop. The horse is hot and distressed, but answers to the desperate spurring; the rider looks as if his eyes were glazed by madness, and he saw nothing but what was unseen by others. See, he has something in his hand—he is holding it up as if it were a signal.

The Sheriff knows him: it is Arthur Donnithorne, carrying in his hand a hard-won release from death.

Chapter XLVIII Another Meeting in the Wood

THE next day, at evening, two men were walking from opposite points towards the same scene, drawn thither by a common memory. The scene was the Grove by Donnithorne Chase: you know who the men were.

The old squire's funeral had taken place that morning, the will had been read, and now in the first breathing-space, Arthur

Donnithorne had come out for a lonely walk, that he might look fixedly at the new future before him and confirm himself in a sad resolution. He thought he could do that best in the Grove.

Adam too had come from Stoniton on Monday evening, and today he had not left home, except to go to the family at the Hall Farm and tell them everything that Mr. Irwine had left untold. He had agreed with the Poysers that he would follow them to their new neighbourhood, wherever that might be, for he meant to give up the management of the woods, and, as soon as it was practicable, he would wind up his business with Jonathan Burge and settle with his mother and Seth in a home within reach of the friends to whom he felt bound by a mutual sorrow.

"Seth and me are sure to find work," he said. "A man that's got our trade at his finger-ends is at home everywhere; and we must make a new start. My mother won't stand in the way, for she's told me, since I came home, she'd made up her mind to being buried in another parish, if I wished it, and if I'd be more comfortable elsewhere. It's wonderful how quiet she's been ever since I came back. It seems as if the very greatness o' the trouble had quieted and calmed her. We shall all be better in a new country, though there's some I shall be loath to leave behind. But I won't part from you and yours, if I can help it, Mr. Poyser. Trouble's made us kin."

"Aye, lad," said Martin. "We'll go out o' hearing o' that man's name. But I doubt we shall ne'er go far enough for folks not to find out as we've got them belonging to us as are transported o'er the seas, and were like to be hanged. We shall have that flyin' up in our faces, and our children's after us."

That was a long visit to the Hall Farm, and drew too strongly on Adam's energies for him to think of seeing others, or re-entering on his old occupations till the morrow. "But to-morrow," he said to himself, "I'll go to work again. I shall learn to like it again some time, maybe; and it's right whether I like it or not."

This evening was the last he would allow to be absorbed by sorrow: suspense was gone now, and he must bear the unalterable. He was resolved not to see Arthur Donnithorne again, if it were possible to avoid him. He had no message to deliver from Hetty now, for Hetty had seen Arthur. And Adam distrusted himself—he had learned to dread the violence of his own feeling. That word of Mr. Irwine's—that he must remember what he had felt after giving the last blow to Arthur in the Grove—had remained with him.

These thoughts about Arthur, like all thoughts that are charged with strong feeling, were continually recurring, and they always called up the image of the Grove—of that spot under the overarching boughs where he had caught sight of the two bending figures, and had been possessed by sudden rage.

"I'll go and see it again to-night for the last time," he said; "it'll do me good; it'll make me feel over again what I felt when I'd knocked him down. I felt what poor empty work it was, as soon as I'd done it, before I began to think he might be dead."

In this way it happened that Arthur and Adam were walking towards the same spot at the same time.

Adam had on his working-dress again, now, for he had thrown off the other with a sense of relief as soon as he came home; and if he had had the basket of tools over his shoulder, he might have been taken, with his pale wasted face, for the spectre of the Adam Bede who entered the Grove on that August evening eight months ago. But he had no basket of tools, and he was not walking with the old erectness, looking keenly round him; his hands were thrust in his side pockets, and his eyes rested chiefly on the ground. He had not long entered the Grove, and now he paused before a beech. He knew that tree well; it was the boundary mark of his youth—the sign, to him, of the time when some of his earliest, strongest feelings had left him. He felt sure they would never return. And yet, at this moment, there was a stirring of affection at the remembrance of that Arthur Donnithorne whom he had believed in before he had come up to this beech eight months ago. It was affection for the dead: THAT Arthur existed no longer.

He was disturbed by the sound of approaching footsteps, but the beech stood at a turning in the road, and he could not see who was coming until the tall slim figure in deep mourning suddenly stood before him at only two yards' distance. They both started, and looked at each other in silence. Often, in the last fortnight, Adam had imagined himself as close to Arthur as this, assailing him with words that should be as harrowing as the voice of remorse, forcing upon him a just share in the misery he had caused; and often, too, he had told himself that such a meeting had better not be. But in imagining the meeting he had always seen Arthur, as he had met him on that evening in the Grove, florid, careless, light of speech; and the figure before him touched him with the signs of suffering. Adam knew what suffering was—he could not lay a cruel finger on a bruised man. He felt no impulse that he needed to resist. Silence was more just than reproach. Arthur was the first to speak.

"Adam," he said, quietly, "it may be a good thing that we have met here, for I wished to see you. I should have asked to see you to-morrow."

He paused, but Adam said nothing.

"I know it is painful to you to meet me," Arthur went on, "but it is not likely to happen again for years to come."

"No, sir," said Adam, coldly, "that was what I meant to write to you to-morrow, as it would be better all dealings should be at an end between us, and somebody else put in my place."

Arthur felt the answer keenly, and it was not without an effort that he spoke again.

"It was partly on that subject I wished to speak to you. I don't want to lessen your indignation against me, or ask you to do anything for my sake. I only wish to ask you if you will help me to lessen the evil consequences of the past, which is unchangeable. I don't mean consequences to myself, but to others. It is but little I can do, I know. I know the worst consequences will remain; but something may be done, and you can help me. Will you listen to me patiently?"

"Yes, sir," said Adam, after some hesitation; "I'll hear what it is. If I can help to mend anything, I will. Anger 'ull mend nothing, I know. We've had enough o' that."

"I was going to the Hermitage," said Arthur. "Will you go there with me and sit down? We can talk better there."

The Hermitage had never been entered since they left it together, for Arthur had locked up the key in his desk. And now, when he opened the door, there was the candle burnt out in the socket; there was the chair in the same place where Adam remembered sitting; there was the waste-paper basket full of scraps, and deep down in it, Arthur felt in an instant, there was the little pink silk handkerchief. It would have been painful to enter this place if their previous thoughts had been less painful.

They sat down opposite each other in the old places, and Arthur said, "I'm going away, Adam; I'm going into the army."

Poor Arthur felt that Adam ought to be affected by this announcement—ought to have a movement of sympathy towards him. But Adam's lips remained firmly closed, and the expression of his face unchanged.

"What I want to say to you," Arthur continued, "is this: one of my reasons for going away is that no one else may leave Hayslope—may leave their home on my account. I would do anything, there is no sacrifice I would not make, to prevent any further injury to others through my—through what has happened."

Arthur's words had precisely the opposite effect to that he had anticipated. Adam thought he perceived in them that notion of compensation for irretrievable wrong, that self-soothing attempt to make evil bear the same fruits as good, which most of all roused his indignation. He was as strongly impelled to look painful facts right in the face as Arthur was to turn away his eyes from them. Moreover, he had the wakeful suspicious pride of a poor man in the presence of a rich man. He felt his old severity returning as he said, "The time's past for that, sir. A man should make sacrifices to keep clear of doing a wrong; sacrifices won't undo it when it's done. When people's feelings have got a deadly wound, they can't be cured with favours."

"Favours!" said Arthur, passionately; "no; how can you suppose I meant that? But the Poysers—Mr. Irwine tells me the Poysers mean to leave the place where they have lived so many years—for generations. Don't you see, as Mr. Irwine does, that if they could be persuaded to overcome the feeling that drives them away, it would be much better for them in the end to remain on the old spot, among the friends and neighbours who know them?"

"That's true," said Adam coldly. "But then, sir, folks's feelings are not so easily overcome. It'll be hard for Martin Poyser to go to a strange place, among strange faces, when he's been bred up on the Hall Farm, and his father before him; but then it 'ud be harder for a man with his feelings to stay. I don't see how the thing's to be made any other than hard. There's a sort o' damage, sir, that can't be made up for."

Arthur was silent some moments. In spite of other feelings dominant in him this evening, his pride winced under Adam's mode of treating him. Wasn't he himself suffering? Was not he too obliged to renounce his most cherished hopes? It was now as it had been eight months ago—Adam was forcing Arthur to feel more intensely the irrevocableness of his own wrong-doing. He was presenting the sort of resistance that was the most irritating to Arthur's eager ardent nature. But his anger was subdued by the same influence that had subdued Adam's when they first confronted each other—by the marks of suffering in a long familiar face. The momentary struggle ended in the feeling that he could bear a great deal from Adam, to whom he had been the occasion of bearing so much; but there was a touch of pleading, boyish vexation in his tone as he said, "But people may make injuries worse by unreasonable conduct—by giving way to anger and satisfying that for the moment, instead of thinking what will be the effect in the future.

"If I were going to stay here and act as landlord," he added presently, with still more eagerness—"if I were careless about what I've done—what I've been the cause of, you would have some excuse, Adam, for going away and encouraging others to go. You would have some excuse then for trying to make the evil worse. But when I tell you I'm going away for years—when you know what that means for me, how it cuts off every plan of happiness I've ever formed—it is impossible for a sensible man like you to believe that there is any real ground for the Poysers refusing to remain. I know their feeling about disgrace—Mr. Irwine has told me all; but he is of opinion that they might be persuaded out of this idea that they are disgraced in the eyes of their neighbours, and that they can't remain on my estate, if you would join him in his efforts—if you would stay yourself and go on managing the old woods."

Arthur paused a moment and then added, pleadingly, "You know that's a good work to do for the sake of other people, besides the owner. And you don't know but that they may have a better owner soon, whom you will like to work for. If I die, my cousin Tradgett will have the estate and take my name. He is a good fellow."

Adam could not help being moved: it was impossible for him not to feel that this was the voice of the honest warm-hearted Arthur whom he had loved and been proud of in old days; but nearer memories would not be thrust away. He was silent; yet Arthur saw an answer in his face that induced him to go on, with growing earnestness.

"And then, if you would talk to the Poysers—if you would talk the matter over with Mr. Irwine—he means to see you to-morrow—and then if you would join your arguments to his to prevail on them not to go. . . .I know, of course, that they would not accept any favour from me—I mean nothing of that kind—but I'm sure they would suffer less in the end. Irwine thinks so too. And Mr. Irwine is to have the chief authority on the estate—he has consented to undertake that. They will really be under no man but one whom they respect and like. It would be the same with you, Adam, and it could be nothing but a desire to give me worse pain that could incline you to go."

Arthur was silent again for a little while, and then said, with some agitation in his voice, "I wouldn't act so towards you, I know. If you were in my place and I in yours, I should try to help you to do the best."

Adam made a hasty movement on his chair and looked on the ground. Arthur went on, "Perhaps you've never done anything you've had bitterly to repent of in your life, Adam; if you had, you would be more generous. You would know then that it's worse for me than for you."

Arthur rose from his seat with the last words, and went to one of the windows, looking out and turning his back on Adam, as he continued, passionately, "Haven't I loved her too? Didn't I see her yesterday? Shan't I carry the thought of her about with me as much as you will? And don't you think you would suffer more if you'd been in fault?"

There was silence for several minutes, for the struggle in Adam's mind was not easily decided. Facile natures, whose emotions have little permanence, can hardly understand how much inward resistance he overcame before he rose from his seat and turned towards Arthur. Arthur heard the movement, and turning round, met the sad but softened look with which Adam said, "It's true what you say, sir. I'm hard—it's in my nature. I was too hard with my father, for doing wrong. I've been a bit hard t' everybody but her. I felt as if nobody pitied her enough—her suffering cut into me so; and when I thought the folks at the farm were too hard with her, I said I'd never be hard to anybody myself again. But feeling overmuch about her has perhaps made me unfair to you. I've known what it is in my life to repent and feel it's too late. I felt I'd been too harsh to my father when he was gone from me—I feel it now, when I think of him. I've no right to be hard towards them as have done wrong and repent."

Adam spoke these words with the firm distinctness of a man who is resolved to leave nothing unsaid that he is bound to say; but he went on with more hesitation.

"I wouldn't shake hands with you once, sir, when you asked me—but if you're willing to do it now, for all I refused then . . . "

Arthur's white hand was in Adam's large grasp in an instant, and with that action there was a strong rush, on both sides, of the old, boyish affection.

"Adam," Arthur said, impelled to full confession now, "it would never have happened if I'd known you loved her. That would have helped to save me from it. And I did struggle. I never meant to injure her. I deceived you afterwards—and that led on to worse; but I thought it was forced upon me, I thought it was the best thing I could do. And in that letter I told her to let me know if she were in any trouble: don't think I would not have done everything I could. But I was all wrong from the very first, and horrible wrong has come of it. God knows, I'd give my life if I could undo it."

They sat down again opposite each other, and Adam said, tremulously, "How did she seem when you left her, sir?"

"Don't ask me, Adam," Arthur said; "I feel sometimes as if I should go mad with thinking of her looks and what she said to me, and then, that I couldn't get a full pardon—that I couldn't save her from that wretched fate of being transported—that I can do nothing for her all those years; and she may die under it, and never know comfort any more."

"Ah, sir," said Adam, for the first time feeling his own pain merged in sympathy for Arthur, "you and me'll often be thinking o' the same thing, when we're a long way off one another. I'll pray God to help you, as I pray him to help me."

"But there's that sweet woman—that Dinah Morris," Arthur said, pursuing his own thoughts and not knowing what had been the sense of Adam's words, "she says she shall stay with her to the very last moment—till she goes; and the poor thing clings to her as if she found some comfort in her. I could worship that woman; I don't know what I should do if she were not there. Adam, you will see her when she comes back. I could say nothing to her yesterday—nothing of what I felt towards her. Tell her," Arthur went on hurriedly, as if he wanted to hide the emotion with which he spoke, while he took off his chain and watch, "tell her I asked you to give her this in remembrance of me—of the man to whom she is the one source of comfort, when he thinks of . . . I know she doesn't care about such things—or anything else I can give her for its own sake. But she will use the watch—I shall like to think of her using it."

"I'll give it to her, sir," Adam said, "and tell her your words. She told me she should come back to the people at the Hall Farm."

"And you will persuade the Poysers to stay, Adam?" said Arthur, reminded of the subject which both of them had forgotten in the first interchange of revived friendship. "You will stay yourself, and help Mr. Irwine to carry out the repairs and improvements on the estate?"

"There's one thing, sir, that perhaps you don't take account of," said Adam, with hesitating gentleness, "and that was what made me hang back longer. You see, it's the same with both me and the Poysers: if we stay, it's for our own worldly interest, and it looks as if we'd put up with anything for the sake o' that. I know that's what they'll feel, and I can't help feeling a little of it myself. When folks have got an honourable independent spirit, they don't like to do anything that might make 'em seem base-minded."

"But no one who knows you will think that, Adam. That is not a reason strong enough against a course that is really more generous, more unselfish than the other. And it will be known—it shall be made known, that both you and the Poysers stayed at my entreaty. Adam, don't try to make things worse for me; I'm punished enough without that."

"No, sir, no," Adam said, looking at Arthur with mournful affection. "God forbid I should make things worse for you. I used to wish I could do it, in my passion—but that was when I thought you didn't feel enough. I'll stay, sir, I'll do the best I can. It's all I've got to think of now—to do my work well and make the world a bit better place for them as can enjoy it."

"Then we'll part now, Adam. You will see Mr. Irwine to-morrow, and consult with him about everything."

"Are you going soon, sir?" said Adam.

"As soon as possible—after I've made the necessary arrangements. Good-bye, Adam. I shall think of you going about the old place."

"Good-bye, sir. God bless you."

The hands were clasped once more, and Adam left the Hermitage, feeling that sorrow was more bearable now hatred was gone.

As soon as the door was closed behind him, Arthur went to the waste-paper basket and took out the little pink silk handkerchief.

BOOK SIX

Chapter XLIX At the Hall Farm

THE first autumnal afternoon sunshine of 1801—more than eighteen months after that parting of Adam and Arthur in the Hermitage—was on the yard at the Hall Farm; and the bull-dog was in one of his most excited moments, for it was that hour of the day when the cows were being driven into the yard for their afternoon milking. No wonder the patient beasts ran confusedly into the wrong places, for the alarming din of the bull-dog was mingled with more distant sounds which the timid feminine creatures, with pardonable superstition, imagined also to have some relation to their own movements—with the tremendous crack of the waggoner's whip, the roar of his voice, and the booming thunder of the waggon, as it left the rick-yard empty of its golden load.

The milking of the cows was a sight Mrs. Poyser loved, and at this hour on mild days she was usually standing at the house door, with her knitting in her hands, in quiet contemplation, only heightened to a keener interest when the vicious yellow cow, who had once kicked over a pailful of precious milk, was about to undergo the preventive punishment of having her hinder-legs strapped.

To-day, however, Mrs. Poyser gave but a divided attention to the arrival of the cows, for she was in eager discussion with Dinah, who was stitching Mr. Poyser's shirt-collars, and had borne patiently to have her thread broken three times by Totty pulling at her arm with a sudden insistence that she should look at "Baby," that is, at a large wooden doll with no legs and a long skirt, whose bald head Totty, seated in her small chair at Dinah's side, was caressing and pressing to her fat cheek with much fervour. Totty is larger by more than two years' growth than when you first saw her, and she has on a black frock under her pinafore. Mrs. Poyser too has on a black gown, which seems to heighten the family likeness between her and Dinah. In other respects there is little outward change now discernible in our old friends, or in the pleasant house-place, bright with polished oak and pewter.

"I never saw the like to you, Dinah," Mrs. Poyser was saying, "when you've once took anything into your head: there's no more moving you than the rooted tree. You may say what you like, but I don't believe that's religion; for what's the Sermon on the Mount about, as you're so fond o' reading to the boys, but doing what other folks 'ud have you do? But if it was anything unreasonable they wanted you to do, like taking your cloak off and giving it to 'em, or letting 'em slap you i' the face, I daresay you'd be ready enough. It's only when one 'ud have you do what's plain common sense and good for yourself, as you're obstinate th' other way."

"Nay, dear Aunt," said Dinah, smiling slightly as she went on with her work, "I'm sure your wish 'ud be a reason for me to do anything that I didn't feel it was wrong to do."

"Wrong! You drive me past bearing. What is there wrong, I should like to know, i' staying along wi' your own friends, as are th' happier for having you with 'em an' are willing to provide for you, even if your work didn't more nor pay 'em for the bit o' sparrow's victual y' eat and the bit o' rag you put on? An' who is it, I should like to know, as you're bound t' help and comfort i' the world more nor your own flesh and blood—an' me th' only aunt you've got aboveground, an' am brought to the brink o' the grave welly every winter as comes, an' there's the child as sits beside you 'ull break her little heart when you go, an' the grandfather not been dead a twelvemonth, an' your uncle 'ull miss you so as never was—a-lighting his pipe an' waiting on him, an' now I can trust you wi' the butter, an' have had all the trouble o' teaching you, and there's all the sewing to be done, an' I must have a strange gell out o' Treddles'on to do it—an' all because you must go back to that bare heap o' stones as the very crows fly over an' won't stop at."

"Dear Aunt Rachel," said Dinah, looking up in Mrs. Poyser's face, "it's your kindness makes you say I'm useful to you. You don't really want me now, for Nancy and Molly are clever at their work, and you're in good health now, by the blessing of God, and my uncle is of a cheerful countenance again, and you have neighbours and friends not a few—some of them come to sit with my uncle almost daily. Indeed, you will not miss me; and at Snowfield there are brethren and sisters in great need, who have none of those comforts you have around you. I feel that I am called back to those amongst whom my lot was first cast. I feel drawn again towards the hills where I used to be blessed in carrying the word of life to the sinful and desolate."

"You feel! Yes," said Mrs. Poyser, returning from a parenthetic glance at the cows, "that's allays the reason I'm to sit down wi', when you've a mind to do anything contrairy. What do you want to be preaching for more than you're preaching now? Don't you go off, the Lord knows where, every Sunday a-preaching and praying? An' haven't you got Methodists enow at Treddles'on to go and look at, if church-folks's faces are too handsome to please you? An' isn't there them i' this parish as you've got under hand, and they're like enough to make friends wi' Old Harry again as soon as your back's turned? There's that Bessy Cranage—she'll be flaunting i' new finery three weeks after you're gone, I'll be bound. She'll no more go on in her new ways without you than a dog 'ull stand on its hind-legs when there's nobody looking. But I suppose it doesna matter so much about folks's souls i' this country, else you'd be for staying with your own aunt, for she's none so good but what you might help her to be better."

There was a certain something in Mrs. Poyser's voice just then, which she did not wish to be noticed, so she turned round hastily to look at the clock, and said: "See there! It's tea-time; an' if Martin's i' the rick-yard, he'll like a cup. Here, Totty, my chicken, let mother put your bonnet on, and then you go out into the rick-yard and see if Father's there, and tell him he mustn't go away again without coming t' have a cup o' tea; and tell your brothers to come in too."

Totty trotted off in her flapping bonnet, while Mrs. Poyser set out the bright oak table and reached down the tea-cups.

"You talk o' them gells Nancy and Molly being clever i' their work," she began again; "it's fine talking. They're all the same, clever or stupid—one can't trust 'em out o' one's sight a minute. They want somebody's eye on 'em constant if they're to be kept to their work. An' suppose I'm ill again this winter, as I was the winter before last? Who's to look after 'em then, if you're gone? An' there's that blessed child—something's sure t' happen to her—they'll let her tumble into the fire, or get at the kettle wi' the boiling lard in't, or some mischief as 'ull lame her for life; an' it'll be all your fault, Dinah."

"Aunt," said Dinah, "I promise to come back to you in the winter if you're ill. Don't think I will ever stay away from you if you're in real want of me. But, indeed, it is needful for my own soul that I should go away from this life of ease and luxury in which I have all things too richly to enjoy—at least that I should go away for a short space. No one can know but myself what are my inward needs, and the besetments I am most in danger from. Your wish for me to stay is not a call of duty which I refuse to hearken to because it is against my own desires; it is a temptation that I must resist, lest the love of the creature should become like a mist in my soul shutting out the heavenly light."

"It passes my cunning to know what you mean by ease and luxury," said Mrs. Poyser, as she cut the bread and butter. "It's true there's good victual enough about you, as nobody shall ever say I don't provide enough and to spare, but if there's ever a bit o' odds an' ends as nobody else 'ud eat, you're sure to pick it out . . . but look there! There's Adam Bede a-carrying the little un in. I wonder how it is he's come so early."

Mrs. Poyser hastened to the door for the pleasure of looking at her darling in a new position, with love in her eyes but reproof on her tongue.

"Oh for shame, Totty! Little gells o' five year old should be ashamed to be carried. Why, Adam, she'll break your arm, such a big gell as that; set her down—for shame!"

"Nay, nay," said Adam, "I can lift her with my hand—I've no need to take my arm to it."

Totty, looking as serenely unconscious of remark as a fat white puppy, was set down at the door-place, and the mother enforced her reproof with a shower of kisses.

"You're surprised to see me at this hour o' the day," said Adam.

"Yes, but come in," said Mrs. Poyser, making way for him; "there's no bad news, I hope?"

"No, nothing bad," Adam answered, as he went up to Dinah and put out his hand to her. She had laid down her work and stood up, instinctively, as he approached her. A faint blush died away from her pale cheek as she put her hand in his and looked up at him timidly.

"It's an errand to you brought me, Dinah," said Adam, apparently unconscious that he was holding her hand all the while; "mother's a bit ailing, and she's set her heart on your coming to stay the night with her, if you'll be so kind. I told her I'd call and ask you as I came from the village. She overworks herself, and I can't persuade her to have a little girl t' help her. I don't know what's to be done."

Adam released Dinah's hand as he ceased speaking, and was expecting an answer, but before she had opened her lips Mrs. Poyser said, "Look there now! I told you there was folks enow t' help i' this parish, wi'out going further off. There's Mrs. Bede getting as old and cas'alty as can be, and she won't let anybody but you go a-nigh her hardly. The folks at Snowfield have learnt by this time to do better wi'out you nor she can."

"I'll put my bonnet on and set off directly, if you don't want anything done first, Aunt," said Dinah, folding up her work.

"Yes, I do want something done. I want you t' have your tea, child; it's all ready—and you'll have a cup, Adam, if y' arena in too big a hurry."

"Yes, I'll have a cup, please; and then I'll walk with Dinah. I'm going straight home, for I've got a lot o' timber valuations to write out."

"Why, Adam, lad, are you here?" said Mr. Poyser, entering warm and coatless, with the two black-eyed boys behind him, still looking as much like him as two small elephants are like a large one. "How is it we've got sight o' you so long before foddering-time?"

"I came on an errand for Mother," said Adam. "She's got a touch of her old complaint, and she wants Dinah to go and stay with her a bit."

"Well, we'll spare her for your mother a little while," said Mr. Poyser. "But we wonna spare her for anybody else, on'y her husband."

"Husband!" said Marty, who was at the most prosaic and literal period of the boyish mind. "Why, Dinah hasn't got a husband."

"Spare her?" said Mrs. Poyser, placing a seed-cake on the table and then seating herself to pour out the tea. "But we must spare her, it seems, and not for a husband neither, but for her own megrims. Tommy, what are you doing to your little sister's doll? Making the child naughty, when she'd be good if you'd let her. You shanna have a morsel o' cake if you behave so."

Tommy, with true brotherly sympathy, was amusing himself by turning Dolly's skirt over her bald head and exhibiting her truncated body to the general scorn—an indignity which cut Totty to the heart.

"What do you think Dinah's been a-telling me since dinner-time?" Mrs. Poyser continued, looking at her husband.

"Eh! I'm a poor un at guessing," said Mr. Poyser.

"Why, she means to go back to Snowfield again, and work i' the mill, and starve herself, as she used to do, like a creatur as has got no friends."

Mr. Poyser did not readily find words to express his unpleasant astonishment; he only looked from his wife to Dinah, who had now seated herself beside Totty, as a bulwark against brotherly playfulness, and was busying herself with the children's tea. If he had been given to making general reflections, it would have occurred to him that there was certainly a change come over Dinah, for she never used to change colour; but, as it was, he merely observed that her face was flushed at that moment. Mr. Poyser thought she looked the prettier for it: it was a flush no deeper than the petal of a monthly rose. Perhaps it came because her uncle was looking at her so fixedly; but there is no knowing, for just then Adam was saying, with quiet surprise, "Why, I hoped Dinah was settled among us for life. I thought she'd given up the notion o' going back to her old country."

"Thought! Yes," said Mrs. Poyser, "and so would anybody else ha' thought, as had got their right end up'ards. But I suppose you must be a Methodist to know what a Methodist 'ull do. It's ill guessing what the bats are flying after."

"Why, what have we done to you. Dinah, as you must go away from us?" said Mr. Poyser, still pausing over his tea-cup. "It's like breaking your word, welly, for your aunt never had no thought but you'd make this your home."

"Nay, Uncle," said Dinah, trying to be quite calm. "When I first came, I said it was only for a time, as long as I could be of any comfort to my aunt."

"Well, an' who said you'd ever left off being a comfort to me?" said Mrs. Poyser. "If you didna mean to stay wi' me, you'd better never ha' come. Them as ha' never had a cushion don't miss it."

"Nay, nay," said Mr. Poyser, who objected to exaggerated views. "Thee mustna say so; we should ha' been ill off wi'out her, Lady day was a twelvemont'. We mun be thankful for that, whether she stays or no. But I canna think what she mun leave a good home for, to go back int' a country where the land, most on't, isna worth ten shillings an acre, rent and profits."

"Why, that's just the reason she wants to go, as fur as she can give a reason," said Mrs. Poyser. "She says this country's too comfortable, an' there's too much t' eat, an' folks arena miserable enough. And she's going next week. I canna turn her, say what I will. It's allays the way wi' them meek-faced people; you may's well pelt a bag o' feathers as talk to 'em. But I say it isna religion, to be so obstinate—is it now, Adam?"

Adam saw that Dinah was more disturbed than he had ever seen her by any matter relating to herself, and, anxious to relieve her, if possible, he said, looking at her affectionately, "Nay, I can't find fault with anything Dinah does. I believe her thoughts are better than our guesses, let 'em be what they may. I should ha' been thankful for her to stay among us, but if she thinks well to go, I wouldn't cross her, or make it hard to her by objecting. We owe her something different to that."

As it often happens, the words intended to relieve her were just too much for Dinah's susceptible feelings at this moment. The tears came into the grey eyes too fast to be hidden and she got up hurriedly, meaning it to be understood that she was going to put on her bonnet.

"Mother, what's Dinah crying for?" said Totty. "She isn't a naughty dell."

"Thee'st gone a bit too fur," said Mr. Poyser. "We've no right t' interfere with her doing as she likes. An' thee'dst be as angry as could be wi' me, if I said a word against anything she did."

"Because you'd very like be finding fault wi'out reason," said Mrs. Poyser. "But there's reason i' what I say, else I shouldna say it. It's easy talking for them as can't love her so well as her own aunt does. An' me got so used to her! I shall feel as uneasy as a new sheared sheep when she's gone from me. An' to think of her leaving a parish where she's so looked on. There's Mr. Irwine makes as much of her as if she was a lady, for all her being a Methodist, an' wi' that maggot o' preaching in her head—God forgi'e me if I'm i' the wrong to call it so."

"Aye," said Mr. Poyser, looking jocose; "but thee dostna tell Adam what he said to thee about it one day. The missis was saying, Adam, as the preaching was the only fault to be found wi' Dinah, and Mr. Irwine says, 'But you mustn't find fault with her for that, Mrs. Poyser; you forget she's got no husband to preach to. I'll answer for it, you give Poyser many a good sermon.' The parson had thee there," Mr. Poyser added, laughing unctuously. "I told Bartle Massey on it, an' he laughed too."

"Yes, it's a small joke sets men laughing when they sit a-staring at one another with a pipe i' their mouths," said Mrs. Poyser. "Give Bartle Massey his way and he'd have all the sharpness to himself. If the chaff-cutter had the making of us, we should all be straw, I reckon. Totty, my chicken, go upstairs to cousin Dinah, and see what she's doing, and give her a pretty kiss."

This errand was devised for Totty as a means of checking certain threatening symptoms about the corners of the mouth; for Tommy, no longer expectant of cake, was lifting up his eyelids with his forefingers and turning his eyeballs towards Totty in a way that she felt to be disagreeably personal.

"You're rare and busy now—eh, Adam?" said Mr. Poyser. "Burge's getting so bad wi' his asthmy, it's well if he'll ever do much riding about again."

"Yes, we've got a pretty bit o' building on hand now," said Adam, "what with the repairs on th' estate, and the new houses at Treddles'on."

"I'll bet a penny that new house Burge is building on his own bit o' land is for him and Mary to go to," said Mr. Poyser. "He'll be for laying by business soon, I'll warrant, and be wanting you to take to it all and pay him so much by th' 'ear. We shall see you living on th' hill before another twelvemont's over."

"Well," said Adam, "I should like t' have the business in my own hands. It isn't as I mind much about getting any more money. We've enough and to spare now, with only our two selves and mother; but I should like t' have my own way about things—I could try plans then, as I can't do now."

"You get on pretty well wi' the new steward, I reckon?" said Mr. Poyser.

"Yes, yes; he's a sensible man enough; understands farming—he's carrying on the draining, and all that, capital. You must go some day towards the Stonyshire side and see what alterations they're making. But he's got no notion about buildings. You can so seldom get hold of a man as can turn his brains to more nor one thing; it's just as if they wore blinkers like th' horses and could see nothing o' one side of 'em. Now, there's Mr. Irwine has got notions o' building more nor most architects; for as for th' architects, they set up to be fine fellows, but the most of 'em don't know where to set a chimney so as it shan't be quarrelling with a door. My notion is, a practical builder that's got a bit o' taste makes the best architect for common things; and I've ten times the pleasure i' seeing after the work when I've made the plan myself."

Mr. Poyser listened with an admiring interest to Adam's discourse on building, but perhaps it suggested to him that the building of his corn-rick had been proceeding a little too long without the control of the master's eye, for when Adam had done speaking, he got up and said, "Well, lad, I'll bid you good-bye now, for I'm off to the rick-yard again."

Adam rose too, for he saw Dinah entering, with her bonnet on and a little basket in her hand, preceded by Totty.

"You're ready, I see, Dinah," Adam said; "so we'll set off, for the sooner I'm at home the better."

"Mother," said Totty, with her treble pipe, "Dinah was saying her prayers and crying ever so."

"Hush, hush," said the mother, "little gells mustn't chatter."

Whereupon the father, shaking with silent laughter, set Totty on the white deal table and desired her to kiss him. Mr. and Mrs. Poyser, you perceive, had no correct principles of education.

"Come back to-morrow if Mrs. Bede doesn't want you, Dinah," said Mrs. Poyser: "but you can stay, you know, if she's ill."

So, when the good-byes had been said, Dinah and Adam left the Hall Farm together.

Chapter L In the Cottage

ADAM did not ask Dinah to take his arm when they got out into the lane. He had never yet done so, often as they had walked together, for he had observed that she never walked arm-in-arm with Seth, and he thought, perhaps, that kind of support was not agreeable to her. So they walked apart, though side by side, and the close poke of her little black bonnet hid her face from him.

"You can't be happy, then, to make the Hall Farm your home, Dinah?" Adam said, with the quiet interest of a brother, who has no anxiety for himself in the matter. "It's a pity, seeing they're so fond of you."

"You know, Adam, my heart is as their heart, so far as love for them and care for their welfare goes, but they are in no present need. Their sorrows are healed, and I feel that I am called back to my old work, in which I found a blessing that I have missed of late in the midst of too abundant worldly good. I know it is a vain thought to flee from the work that God appoints us, for the sake of finding a greater blessing to our own souls, as if we could choose for ourselves where we shall find the fulness of the Divine Presence, instead of seeking it where alone it is to be found, in loving obedience. But now, I believe, I have a clear showing that my work lies elsewhere—at least for a time. In the years to come, if my aunt's health should fail, or she should otherwise need me, I shall return."

"You know best, Dinah," said Adam. "I don't believe you'd go against the wishes of them that love you, and are akin to you, without a good and sufficient reason in your own conscience. I've no right to say anything about my being sorry: you know well enough what cause I have to put you above every other friend I've got; and if it had been ordered so that you could ha' been my sister, and lived with us all our lives, I should ha' counted it the greatest blessing as could happen to us now. But Seth tells me there's no hope o' that: your feelings are different, and perhaps I'm taking too much upon me to speak about it."

Dinah made no answer, and they walked on in silence for some yards, till they came to the stone stile, where, as Adam had passed through first and turned round to give her his hand while she mounted the unusually high step, she could not prevent him from seeing her face. It struck him with surprise, for the grey eyes, usually so mild and grave, had the bright uneasy glance which accompanies suppressed agitation, and the slight flush in her cheeks, with which she had come downstairs, was heightened to a deep rose-colour. She looked as if she were only sister to Dinah. Adam was silent with surprise and conjecture for some moments, and then he said, "I hope I've not hurt or displeased you by what I've said, Dinah. Perhaps I was making too free. I've no wish different from what you see to be best, and I'm satisfied for you to live thirty mile off, if you think it right. I shall think of you just as much as I do now, for you're bound up with what I can no more help remembering than I can help my heart beating."

Poor Adam! Thus do men blunder. Dinah made no answer, but she presently said, "Have you heard any news from that poor young man, since we last spoke of him?"

Dinah always called Arthur so; she had never lost the image of him as she had seen him in the prison.

"Yes," said Adam. "Mr. Irwine read me part of a letter from him yesterday. It's pretty certain, they say, that there'll be a peace soon, though nobody believes it'll last long; but he says he doesn't mean to come home. He's no heart for it yet, and it's better for others that he should keep away. Mr. Irwine thinks he's in the right not to come. It's a sorrowful letter. He asks about you and the Poysers, as he always does. There's one thing in the letter cut me a good deal: 'You can't think what an old fellow I feel,' he says; 'I make no schemes now. I'm the best when I've a good day's march or fighting before me.'"

"He's of a rash, warm-hearted nature, like Esau, for whom I have always felt great pity," said Dinah. "That meeting between the brothers, where Esau is so loving and generous, and Jacob so timid and distrustful, notwithstanding his sense of the Divine favour, has always touched me greatly. Truly, I have been tempted sometimes to say that

Jacob was of a mean spirit. But that is our trial: we must learn to see the good in the midst of much that is unlovely."

"Ah," said Adam, "I like to read about Moses best, in th' Old Testament. He carried a hard business well through, and died when other folks were going to reap the fruits. A man must have courage to look at his life so, and think what'll come of it after he's dead and gone. A good solid bit o' work lasts: if it's only laying a floor down, somebody's the better for it being done well, besides the man as does it."

They were both glad to talk of subjects that were not personal, and in this way they went on till they passed the bridge across the Willow Brook, when Adam turned round and said, "Ah, here's Seth. I thought he'd be home soon. Does he know of you're going, Dinah?"

"Yes, I told him last Sabbath."

Adam remembered now that Seth had come home much depressed on Sunday evening, a circumstance which had been very unusual with him of late, for the happiness he had in seeing Dinah every week seemed long to have outweighed the pain of knowing she would never marry him. This evening he had his habitual air of dreamy benignant contentment, until he came quite close to Dinah and saw the traces of tears on her delicate eyelids and eyelashes. He gave one rapid glance at his brother, but Adam was evidently quite outside the current of emotion that had shaken Dinah: he wore his everyday look of unexpectant calm. Seth tried not to let Dinah see that he had noticed her face, and only said, "I'm thankful you're come, Dinah, for Mother's been hungering after the sight of you all day. She began to talk of you the first thing in the morning."

When they entered the cottage, Lisbeth was seated in her armchair, too tired with setting out the evening meal, a task she always performed a long time beforehand, to go and meet them at the door as usual, when she heard the approaching footsteps.

"Coom, child, thee't coom at last," she said, when Dinah went towards her. "What dost mane by lavin' me a week an' ne'er coomin' a-nigh me?"

"Dear friend," said Dinah, taking her hand, "you're not well. If I'd known it sooner, I'd have come."

"An' how's thee t' know if thee dostna coom? Th' lads on'y know what I tell 'em. As long as ye can stir hand and foot the men think ye're hearty. But I'm none so bad, on'y a bit of a cold sets me achin'. An' th' lads tease me so t' ha' somebody wi' me t' do the work—they make me ache worse wi' talkin'. If thee'dst come and stay wi' me, they'd let me alone. The Poysers canna want thee so bad as I do. But take thy bonnet off, an' let me look at thee."

Dinah was moving away, but Lisbeth held her fast, while she was taking off her bonnet, and looked at her face as one looks into a newly gathered snowdrop, to renew the old impressions of purity and gentleness.

"What's the matter wi' thee?" said Lisbeth, in astonishment; "thee'st been a-cryin'."

"It's only a grief that'll pass away," said Dinah, who did not wish just now to call forth Lisbeth's remonstrances by disclosing her intention to leave Hayslope. "You shall know about it shortly—we'll talk of it to-night. I shall stay with you to-night."

Lisbeth was pacified by this prospect. And she had the whole evening to talk with Dinah alone; for there was a new room in the cottage, you remember, built nearly two years ago, in the expectation of a new inmate; and here Adam always sat when he had writing to do or plans to make. Seth sat there too this evening, for he knew his mother would like to have Dinah all to herself.

There were two pretty pictures on the two sides of the wall in the cottage. On one side there was the broad-shouldered, large-featured, hardy old woman, in her blue jacket and buff kerchief, with her dim-eyed anxious looks turned continually on the lily face and the slight form in the black dress that were either moving lightly about in helpful activity, or seated close by the old woman's arm-chair, holding her withered hand, with eyes lifted up towards her to speak a language which Lisbeth understood far better than the Bible or the hymn-book. She would scarcely listen to reading at all to-night. "Nay, nay, shut the book," she said. "We mun talk. I want t' know what thee was cryin' about. Hast got troubles o' thy own, like other folks?"

On the other side of the wall there were the two brothers so like each other in the midst of their unlikeness: Adam with knit brows, shaggy hair, and dark vigorous colour, absorbed in his "figuring"; Seth, with large rugged features, the close copy of his brother's, but with thin, wavy, brown hair and blue dreamy eyes, as often as not looking vaguely out of the window instead of at his book, although it was a newly bought book—Wesley's abridgment of Madame Guyon's life, which was full of wonder and interest for him. Seth had said to Adam, "Can I help thee with anything in here to-night? I don't want to make a noise in the shop."

"No, lad," Adam answered, "there's nothing but what I must do myself. Thee'st got thy new book to read."

And often, when Seth was quite unconscious, Adam, as he paused after drawing a line with his ruler, looked at his brother with a kind smile dawning in his eyes. He knew "th' lad liked to sit full o' thoughts he could give no account of; they'd never come t' anything, but they made him happy," and in the last year or so, Adam had been getting more and more indulgent to Seth. It was part of that growing tenderness which came from the sorrow at work within him.

For Adam, though you see him quite master of himself, working hard and delighting in his work after his inborn inalienable nature, had not outlived his sorrow—had not felt it slip from him as a temporary burden, and leave him the same man again. Do any of us? God forbid. It would be a poor result of all our anguish and our wrestling if we won nothing but our old selves at the end of it—if we could return to the same blind loves, the same self-confident blame, the same light thoughts of human suffering, the same frivolous gossip over blighted human lives, the same feeble sense of that Unknown towards which we have sent forth irrepressible cries in our loneliness. Let us rather be thankful that our sorrow lives in us as an indestructible force, only changing its form, as forces do, and passing from pain into sympathy—the one poor word which includes all our best insight and our best love. Not that this transformation of pain into sympathy had completely taken place in Adam yet. There was still a great remnant of pain, and this he felt would subsist as long as her pain was not a memory, but an existing thing, which he must think of as renewed with the light of every new morning. But we get accustomed to mental as well as bodily pain, without, for all that, losing our sensibility to it. It becomes a habit of our lives, and we cease to imagine a condition of perfect ease as possible for us. Desire is chastened into submission, and we are contented with our day when we have been able to bear our grief in silence and act as if we were not suffering. For it is at such periods that the sense of our lives having visible and invisible relations, beyond any of which either our present or prospective self is the centre, grows like a muscle that we are obliged to lean on and exert.

That was Adam's state of mind in this second autumn of his sorrow. His work, as you know, had always been part of his religion, and from very early days he saw clearly that good carpentry was God's will—was that form of God's will that most immediately concerned him. But now there was no margin of dreams for him beyond this daylight reality, no holiday-time in the working-day world, no moment in the distance when duty would take off her iron glove and breast-plate and clasp him gently into rest. He conceived no picture of the future but one made up of hard-working days such as he lived through, with growing contentment and intensity of interest, every fresh week. Love, he thought, could never be anything to him but a living memory—a limb lopped off, but not gone from consciousness. He did not know that the power of loving was all the while gaining new force within him; that the new sensibilities bought by a deep experience were so many new fibres by which it was possible, nay, necessary to him, that his nature should intertwine with another. Yet he was aware that common affection and friendship were more precious to him than they used to be—that he clung more to his mother and Seth, and had an unspeakable satisfaction in the sight or imagination of any small addition to their happiness. The Poysers, too—hardly three or four days passed but he felt the need of seeing them and interchanging words and looks of friendliness with them. He would have felt this, probably, even if Dinah had not been with them, but he had only said the simplest truth in telling Dinah that he put her above all other friends in the world. Could anything be more natural? For in the darkest moments of memory the thought of her always came as the first ray of returning comfort. The early days of gloom at the Hall Farm had been gradually turned into soft moonlight by her presence; and in the cottage, too, for she had come at every spare moment to soothe and cheer poor Lisbeth, who had been stricken with a fear that subdued even her querulousness at the sight of her darling Adam's grief-worn face. He had become used to watching her light quiet movements, her pretty loving ways to the children, when he went to the Hall Farm; to listen for her voice as for a recurrent music; to think everything she said and did was just right, and could not have been better. In spite of his wisdom, he could not find fault with her for her overindulgence of the children, who had managed to convert Dinah the preacher, before whom a circle of rough men had often trembled a little, into a convenient household slave—though Dinah herself was rather ashamed of this weakness, and had some inward conflict as to her departure from the precepts of Solomon. Yes, there was one thing that might have been better; she might have loved Seth and consented to marry him. He felt a little vexed, for his brother's sake, and he could not help thinking regretfully how Dinah, as Seth's wife, would have made their home as happy as it could be for them all—how she was the one being that would have soothed their mother's last days into peacefulness and rest.

"It's wonderful she doesn't love th' lad," Adam had said sometimes to himself, "for anybody 'ud think he was just cut out for her. But her heart's so taken up with other things. She's one o' those women that feel no drawing towards having a husband and children o' their own. She thinks she should be filled up with her own life then, and she's been used so to living in other folks's cares, she can't bear the thought of her heart being shut up from 'em. I see how it is, well enough. She's cut out o' different stuff from most women: I saw that long ago. She's never easy but when she's helping somebody, and marriage 'ud interfere with her ways—that's true. I've no right to be contriving and thinking it 'ud be better if she'd have Seth, as if I was wiser than she is—or than God either, for He made her what she is, and that's one o' the greatest blessings I've ever had from His hands, and others besides me."

This self-reproof had recurred strongly to Adam's mind when he gathered from Dinah's face that he had wounded her by referring to his wish that she had accepted Seth, and so he had endeavoured to put into the strongest words his confidence in her decision as right—his resignation even to her going away from them and ceasing to make part of their life otherwise than by living in their thoughts, if that separation were chosen by herself. He felt sure she knew quite well enough how much he cared to see her continually—to talk to her with the silent consciousness of a mutual great remembrance. It was not possible she should hear anything but self-renouncing affection and respect in his assurance that he was contented for her to go away; and yet there remained an uneasy feeling in his mind that he had not said quite the right thing—that, somehow, Dinah had not understood him.

Dinah must have risen a little before the sun the next morning, for she was downstairs about five o'clock. So was Seth, for, through Lisbeth's obstinate refusal to have any woman-helper in the house, he had learned to make himself, as Adam said, "very handy in the housework," that he might save his mother from too great weariness; on which ground I hope you will not think him unmanly, any more than you can have thought the gallant Colonel Bath unmanly when he made the gruel for his invalid sister. Adam, who had sat up late at his writing, was still asleep, and was not likely, Seth said, to be down till breakfast-time. Often as Dinah had visited Lisbeth during the last eighteen months, she had never slept in the cottage since that night after Thias's death, when, you remember, Lisbeth praised her deft movements and even gave a modified approval to her porridge. But in that long interval Dinah had made great advances in household cleverness, and this morning, since Seth was there to help, she was bent on bringing everything to a pitch of cleanliness and order that would have satisfied her Aunt Poyser. The cottage was far from that standard at present, for Lisbeth's rheumatism had forced her to give up her old habits of dilettante scouring and polishing. When the kitchen was to her mind, Dinah went into the new room, where Adam had been writing the night before, to see what sweeping and dusting were needed there. She opened the window and let in the fresh morning air, and the smell of the sweet-brier, and the bright low-slanting rays of the early sun, which made a glory about her pale face and pale auburn hair as she held the long brush, and swept, singing to herself in a very low tone—like a sweet summer murmur that you have to listen for very closely—one of Charles Wesley's hymns:

Eternal Beam of Light Divine,
Fountain of unexhausted love,
In whom the Father's glories shine,
Through earth beneath and heaven above;

Jesus! the weary wanderer's rest,
Give me thy easy yoke to bear;

With steadfast patience arm my breast,
With spotless love and holy fear.

Speak to my warring passions, "Peace!"
Say to my trembling heart, "Be still!"
Thy power my strength and fortress is,
For all things serve thy sovereign will.

She laid by the brush and took up the duster; and if you had ever lived in Mrs. Poyser's household, you would know how the duster behaved in Dinah's hand—how it went into every small corner, and on every ledge in and out of sight—how it went again and again round every bar of the chairs, and every leg, and under and over everything that lay on the table, till it came to Adam's papers and rulers and the open desk near them. Dinah dusted up to the very edge of these and then hesitated, looking at them with a longing but timid eye. It was painful to see how much dust there was among them. As she was looking in this way, she heard Seth's step just outside the open door, towards which her back was turned, and said, raising her clear treble, "Seth, is your brother wrathful when his papers are stirred?"

"Yes, very, when they are not put back in the right places," said a deep strong voice, not Seth's.

It was as if Dinah had put her hands unawares on a vibrating chord. She was shaken with an intense thrill, and for the instant felt nothing else; then she knew her cheeks were glowing, and dared not look round, but stood still, distressed because she could not say good-morning in a friendly way. Adam, finding that she did not look round so as to see the smile on his face, was afraid she had thought him serious about his wrathfulness, and went up to her, so that she was obliged to look at him.

"What! You think I'm a cross fellow at home, Dinah?" he said, smilingly.

"Nay," said Dinah, looking up with timid eyes, "not so. But you might be put about by finding things meddled with; and even the man Moses, the meekest of men, was wrathful sometimes."

"Come, then," said Adam, looking at her affectionately, "I'll help you move the things, and put 'em back again, and then they can't get wrong. You're getting to be your aunt's own niece, I see, for particularness."

They began their little task together, but Dinah had not recovered herself sufficiently to think of any remark, and Adam looked at her uneasily. Dinah, he thought, had seemed to disapprove him somehow lately; she had not been so kind and open to him as she used to be. He wanted her to look at him, and be as pleased as he was himself with doing this bit of playful work. But Dinah did not look at him—it was easy for her to avoid looking at the tall man—and when at last there was no more dusting to be done and no further excuse for him to linger near her, he could bear it no longer, and said, in rather a pleading tone, "Dinah, you're not displeased with me for anything, are you? I've not said or done anything to make you think ill of me?"

The question surprised her, and relieved her by giving a new course to her feeling. She looked up at him now, quite earnestly, almost with the tears coming, and said, "Oh, no, Adam! how could you think so?"

"I couldn't bear you not to feel as much a friend to me as I do to you," said Adam. "And you don't know the value I set on the very thought of you, Dinah. That was what I meant yesterday, when I said I'd be content for you to go, if you thought right. I meant, the thought of you was worth so much to me, I should feel I ought to be thankful, and not grumble, if you see right to go away. You know I do mind parting with you, Dinah?"

"Yes, dear friend," said Dinah, trembling, but trying to speak calmly, "I know you have a brother's heart towards me, and we shall often be with one another in spirit; but at this season I am in heaviness through manifold temptations. You must not mark me. I feel called to leave my kindred for a while; but it is a trial—the flesh is weak."

Adam saw that it pained her to be obliged to answer.

"I hurt you by talking about it, Dinah," he said. "I'll say no more. Let's see if Seth's ready with breakfast now."

That is a simple scene, reader. But it is almost certain that you, too, have been in love—perhaps, even, more than once, though you may not choose to say so to all your feminine friends. If so, you will no more think the slight words, the timid looks, the tremulous touches, by which two human souls approach each other gradually, like two little quivering rain-streams, before they mingle into one—you will no more think these things trivial than you will think the first-detected signs of coming spring trivial, though they be but a faint indescribable something in the air and in the song of the birds, and the tiniest perceptible budding on the hedge-row branches. Those slight words and looks and touches are part of the soul's language; and the finest language, I believe, is chiefly made up of unimposing words, such as "light," "sound," "stars," "music"—words really not worth looking at, or hearing, in themselves, any more than "chips" or "sawdust." It is only that they happen to be the signs of something unspeakably great and beautiful. I am of opinion that love is a great and beautiful thing too, and if you agree with me, the smallest signs of it will not be chips and sawdust to you: they will rather be like those little words,"light" and "music," stirring the long-winding fibres of your memory and enriching your present with your most precious past.

Chapter LI Sunday Morning

LISBETH'S touch of rheumatism could not be made to appear serious enough to detain Dinah another night from the Hall Farm, now she had made up her mind to leave her aunt so soon, and at evening the friends must part. "For a long while," Dinah had said, for she had told Lisbeth of her resolve.

"Then it'll be for all my life, an' I shall ne'er see thee again," said Lisbeth. "Long while! I'n got no long while t' live. An' I shall be took bad an' die, an' thee canst ne'er come a-nigh me, an' I shall die a-longing for thee."

That had been the key-note of her wailing talk all day; for Adam was not in the house, and so she put no restraint on her complaining. She had tried poor Dinah by returning again and again to the question, why she must go away; and refusing to accept reasons, which seemed to her nothing but whim and "contrairiness"; and still more, by regretting that she "couldna' ha' one o' the lads" and be her daughter.

"Thee couldstna put up wi' Seth," she said. "He isna cliver enough for thee, happen, but he'd ha' been very good t' thee—he's as handy as can be at doin' things for me when I'm bad, an' he's as fond o' the Bible an' chappellin' as thee art thysen. But happen, thee'dst like a husband better as isna just the cut o' thysen: the runnin' brook isna athirst for th' rain. Adam 'ud ha' done for thee—I know he would—an' he might come t' like thee well enough, if thee'dst stop. But he's as stubborn as th' iron bar—there's no bending him no way but's own. But he'd be a fine husband for anybody, be they who they will, so looked-on an' so cliver as he is. And he'd be rare an' lovin': it does me good on'y a look o' the lad's eye when he means kind tow'rt me."

Dinah tried to escape from Lisbeth's closest looks and questions by finding little tasks of housework that kept her moving about, and as soon as Seth came home in the evening she put on her bonnet to go. It touched Dinah keenly to say the last good-bye, and still more to look round on her way across the fields and see the old woman still standing at the door, gazing after her till she must have been the faintest speck in the dim aged eyes. "The God of love and peace be with them," Dinah prayed, as she looked back from the last stile. "Make them glad according to the days wherein thou hast afflicted them, and the years wherein they have seen evil. It is thy will that I should part from them; let me have no will but thine."

Lisbeth turned into the house at last and sat down in the workshop near Seth, who was busying himself there with fitting some bits of turned wood he had brought from the village into a small workbox, which he meant to give to Dinah before she went away.

"Thee't see her again o' Sunday afore she goes," were her first words. "If thee wast good for anything, thee'dst make her come in again o' Sunday night wi' thee, and see me once more."

"Nay, Mother," said Seth. "Dinah 'ud be sure to come again if she saw right to come. I should have no need to persuade her. She only thinks it 'ud be troubling thee for nought, just to come in to say good-bye over again."

"She'd ne'er go away, I know, if Adam 'ud be fond on her an' marry her, but everything's so contrairy," said Lisbeth, with a burst of vexation.

Seth paused a moment and looked up, with a slight blush, at his mother's face. "What! Has she said anything o' that sort to thee, Mother?" he said, in a lower tone.

"Said? Nay, she'll say nothin'. It's on'y the men as have to wait till folks say things afore they find 'em out."

"Well, but what makes thee think so, Mother? What's put it into thy head?"

"It's no matter what's put it into my head. My head's none so hollow as it must get in, an' nought to put it there. I know she's fond on him, as I know th' wind's comin' in at the door, an' that's anoof. An' he might be willin' to marry her if he know'd she's fond on him, but he'll ne'er think on't if somebody doesna put it into's head."

His mother's suggestion about Dinah's feeling towards Adam was not quite a new thought to Seth, but her last words alarmed him, lest she should herself undertake to open Adam's eyes. He was not sure about Dinah's feeling, and he thought he was sure about Adam's.

"Nay, Mother, nay," he said, earnestly, "thee mustna think o' speaking o' such things to Adam. Thee'st no right to say what Dinah's feelings are if she hasna told thee, and it 'ud do nothing but mischief to say such things to Adam. He feels very grateful and affectionate toward Dinah, but he's no thoughts towards her that 'ud incline him to make her his wife, and I don't believe Dinah 'ud marry him either. I don't think she'll marry at all."

"Eh," said Lisbeth, impatiently. "Thee think'st so 'cause she wouldna ha' thee. She'll ne'er marry thee; thee mightst as well like her t' ha' thy brother."

Seth was hurt. "Mother," he said, in a remonstrating tone, "don't think that of me. I should be as thankful t' have her for a sister as thee wouldst t' have her for a daughter. I've no more thoughts about myself in that thing, and I shall take it hard if ever thee say'st it again."

"Well, well, then thee shouldstna cross me wi' sayin' things arena as I say they are."

"But, Mother," said Seth, "thee'dst be doing Dinah a wrong by telling Adam what thee think'st about her. It 'ud do nothing but mischief, for it 'ud make Adam uneasy if he doesna feel the same to her. And I'm pretty sure he feels nothing o' the sort."

"Eh, donna tell me what thee't sure on; thee know'st nought about it. What's he allays goin' to the Poysers' for, if he didna want t' see her? He goes twice where he used t' go once. Happen he knowsna as he wants t' see her; he knowsna as I put salt in's broth, but he'd miss it pretty quick if it warna there. He'll ne'er think o' marrying if it isna put into's head, an' if thee'dst any love for thy mother, thee'dst put him up to't an' not let her go away out o' my sight, when I might ha' her to make a bit o' comfort for me afore I go to bed to my old man under the white thorn."

"Nay, Mother," said Seth, "thee mustna think me unkind, but I should be going against my conscience if I took upon me to say what Dinah's feelings are. And besides that, I think I should give offence to Adam by speaking to him at all about marrying; and I counsel thee not to do't. Thee may'st be quite deceived about Dinah. Nay, I'm pretty sure, by words she said to me last Sabbath, as she's no mind to marry."

"Eh, thee't as contrairy as the rest on 'em. If it war summat I didna want, it 'ud be done fast enough."

Lisbeth rose from the bench at this, and went out of the workshop, leaving Seth in much anxiety lest she should disturb Adam's mind about Dinah. He consoled himself after a time with reflecting that, since Adam's trouble, Lisbeth had been very timid about speaking to him on matters of feeling, and that she would hardly dare to approach this tenderest of all subjects. Even if she did, he hoped Adam would not take much notice of what she said.

Seth was right in believing that Lisbeth would be held in restraint by timidity, and during the next three days, the intervals in which she had an opportunity of speaking to Adam were too rare and short to cause her any strong temptation. But in her long solitary hours she brooded over her regretful thoughts about Dinah, till they had grown very near that point of unmanageable strength when thoughts are apt to take wing out of their secret nest in a startling manner. And on Sunday morning, when Seth went away to chapel at Treddleston, the dangerous opportunity came.

Sunday morning was the happiest time in all the week to Lisbeth, for as there was no service at Hayslope church till the afternoon, Adam was always at home, doing nothing but reading, an occupation in which she could venture to interrupt him. Moreover, she had always a better dinner than usual to prepare for her sons—very frequently for Adam and herself alone, Seth being often away the entire day—and the smell of the roast meat before the clear fire in the clean kitchen, the clock ticking in a peaceful Sunday manner, her darling Adam seated near her in his best clothes, doing nothing very important, so that she could go and stroke her hand across his hair if she liked, and see him look up at her and smile, while Gyp, rather jealous, poked his muzzle up between them—all these things made poor Lisbeth's earthly paradise.

The book Adam most often read on a Sunday morning was his large pictured Bible, and this morning it lay open before him on the round white deal table in the kitchen; for he sat there in spite of the fire, because he knew his mother liked to have him with her, and it was the only day in the week when he could indulge her in that way. You would have liked to see Adam reading his Bible. He never opened it on a weekday, and so he came to it as a holiday book, serving him for history, biography, and poetry. He held one hand thrust between his waistcoat buttons, and the other ready to turn the pages, and in the course of the morning you would have seen many changes in his face. Sometimes his lips moved in semi-articulation—it was when he came to a speech that he could fancy himself uttering, such as Samuel's dying speech to the people; then his eyebrows would be raised, and the corners of his mouth would quiver a little with sad sympathy—something, perhaps old Isaac's meeting with his son, touched him closely; at other times, over the New Testament, a very solemn look would come upon his face, and he would every now and then shake his head in serious assent, or just lift up his hand and let it fall again. And on some mornings, when he read in the Apocrypha, of which he was very fond, the son of Sirach's keen-edged words would bring a delighted smile, though he also enjoyed the freedom of occasionally differing from an Apocryphal writer. For Adam knew the Articles quite well, as became a good churchman.

Lisbeth, in the pauses of attending to her dinner, always sat opposite to him and watched him, till she could rest no longer without going up to him and giving him a caress, to call his attention to her. This morning he was reading the Gospel according to St. Matthew, and Lisbeth had been standing close by him for some minutes, stroking his hair, which was smoother than usual this morning, and looking down at the large page with silent wonderment at the mystery of letters. She was encouraged to continue this caress, because when she first went up to him, he had thrown himself back in his chair to look at her affectionately and say, "Why, Mother, thee look'st rare and hearty this morning. Eh, Gyp wants me t' look at him. He can't abide to think I love thee the best." Lisbeth said nothing, because she wanted to say so many things. And now there was a new leaf to be turned over, and it was a picture—that of the angel seated on the great stone that has been rolled away from the sepulchre. This picture had one strong association in Lisbeth's memory, for she had been reminded of it when she first saw Dinah, and Adam had no sooner turned the page, and lifted the book sideways that they might look at the angel, than she said, "That's her—that's Dinah."

Adam smiled, and, looking more intently at the angel's face, said, "It is a bit like her; but Dinah's prettier, I think."

"Well, then, if thee think'st her so pretty, why arn't fond on her?"

Adam looked up in surprise. "Why, Mother, dost think I don't set store by Dinah?"

"Nay," said Lisbeth, frightened at her own courage, yet feeling that she had broken the ice, and the waters must flow, whatever mischief they might do. "What's th' use o' settin' store by things as are thirty mile off? If thee wast fond enough on her, thee wouldstna let her go away."

"But I've no right t' hinder her, if she thinks well," said Adam, looking at his book as if he wanted to go on reading. He foresaw a series of complaints tending to nothing. Lisbeth sat down again in the chair opposite to him, as she said:

"But she wouldna think well if thee wastna so contrairy." Lisbeth dared not venture beyond a vague phrase yet.

"Contrairy, mother?" Adam said, looking up again in some anxiety. "What have I done? What dost mean?"

"Why, thee't never look at nothin', nor think o' nothin', but thy figurin, an' thy work," said Lisbeth, half-crying. "An' dost think thee canst go on so all thy life, as if thee wast a man cut out o' timber? An' what wut do when thy mother's gone, an' nobody to take care on thee as thee gett'st a bit o' victual comfortable i' the mornin'?"

"What hast got i' thy mind, Mother?" said Adam, vexed at this whimpering. "I canna see what thee't driving at. Is there anything I could do for thee as I don't do?"

"Aye, an' that there is. Thee might'st do as I should ha' somebody wi' me to comfort me a bit, an' wait on me when I'm bad, an' be good to me."

"Well, Mother, whose fault is it there isna some tidy body i' th' house t' help thee? It isna by my wish as thee hast a stroke o' work to do. We can afford it—I've told thee often enough. It 'ud be a deal better for us."

"Eh, what's the use o' talking o' tidy bodies, when thee mean'st one o' th' wenches out o' th' village, or somebody from Treddles'on as I ne'er set eyes on i' my life? I'd sooner make a shift an' get into my own coffln afore I die, nor ha' them folks to put me in."

Adam was silent, and tried to go on reading. That was the utmost severity he could show towards his mother on a Sunday morning. But Lisbeth had gone too far now to check herself, and after scarcely a minute's quietness she began again.

"Thee mightst know well enough who 'tis I'd like t' ha' wi' me. It isna many folks I send for t' come an' see me. I reckon. An' thee'st had the fetchin' on her times enow."

"Thee mean'st Dinah, Mother, I know," said Adam. "But it's no use setting thy mind on what can't be. If Dinah 'ud be willing to stay at Hayslope, it isn't likely she can come away from her aunt's house, where they hold her like a daughter, and where she's more bound than she is to us. If it had been so that she could ha' married Seth, that 'ud ha' been a great blessing to us, but we can't have things just as we like in this life. Thee must try and make up thy mind to do without her."

"Nay, but I canna ma' up my mind, when she's just cut out for thee; an' nought shall ma' me believe as God didna make her an' send her there o' purpose for thee. What's it sinnify about her bein' a Methody! It 'ud happen wear out on her wi' marryin'."

Adam threw himself back in his chair and looked at his mother. He understood now what she had been aiming at from the beginning of the conversation. It was as unreasonable, impracticable a wish as she had ever urged, but he could not help being moved by so entirely new an idea. The chief point, however, was to chase away the notion from his mother's mind as quickly as possible.

"Mother," he said, gravely, "thee't talking wild. Don't let me hear thee say such things again. It's no good talking o' what can never be. Dinah's not for marrying; she's fixed her heart on a different sort o' life."

"Very like," said Lisbeth, impatiently, "very like she's none for marr'ing, when them as she'd be willin' t' marry wonna ax her. I shouldna ha' been for marr'ing thy feyther if he'd ne'er axed me; an' she's as fond o' thee as e'er I war o' Thias, poor fellow."

The blood rushed to Adam's face, and for a few moments he was not quite conscious where he was. His mother and the kitchen had vanished for him, and he saw nothing but Dinah's face turned up towards his. It seemed as if there were a resurrection of his dead joy. But he woke up very speedily from that dream (the waking was chill and sad), for it would have been very foolish in him to believe his mother's words—she could have no ground for them. He was prompted to express his disbelief very strongly—perhaps that he might call forth the proofs, if there were any to be offered.

"What dost say such things for, Mother, when thee'st got no foundation for 'em? Thee know'st nothing as gives thee a right to say that."

"Then I knowna nought as gi'es me a right to say as the year's turned, for all I feel it fust thing when I get up i' th' morning. She isna fond o' Seth, I reckon, is she? She doesna want to marry HIM? But I can see as she doesna behave tow'rt thee as she daes tow'rt Seth. She makes no more o' Seth's coming a-nigh her nor if he war Gyp, but she's all of a tremble when thee't a-sittin' down by her at breakfast an' a-looking at her. Thee think'st thy mother knows nought, but she war alive afore thee wast born."

"But thee canstna be sure as the trembling means love?" said Adam anxiously.

"Eh, what else should it mane? It isna hate, I reckon. An' what should she do but love thee? Thee't made to be loved—for where's there a straighter cliverer man? An' what's it sinnify her bein' a Methody? It's on'y the marigold i' th' parridge."

Adam had thrust his hands in his pockets, and was looking down at the book on the table, without seeing any of the letters. He was trembling like a gold-seeker who sees the strong promise of gold but sees in the same moment a sickening vision of disappointment. He could not trust his mother's insight; she had seen what she wished to see. And yet—and yet, now the suggestion had been made to him, he remembered so many things, very slight things, like the stirring of the water by an imperceptible breeze, which seemed to him some confirmation of his mother's words.

Lisbeth noticed that he was moved. She went on, "An' thee't find out as thee't poorly aff when she's gone. Thee't fonder on her nor thee know'st. Thy eyes follow her about, welly as Gyp's follow thee."

Adam could sit still no longer. He rose, took down his hat, and went out into the fields.

The sunshine was on them: that early autumn sunshine which we should know was not summer's, even if there were not the touches of yellow on the lime and chestnut; the Sunday sunshine too, which has more than autumnal calmness for the working man; the morning sunshine, which still leaves the dew-crystals on the fine gossamer webs in the shadow of the bushy hedgerows.

Adam needed the calm influence; he was amazed at the way in which this new thought of Dinah's love had taken possession of him, with an overmastering power that made all other feelings give way before the impetuous desire to know that the thought was true. Strange, that till that moment the possibility of their ever being lovers had never crossed his mind, and yet now, all his longing suddenly went out towards that possibility. He had no more doubt or hesitation as to his own wishes than the bird that flies towards the opening through which the daylight gleams and the breath of heaven enters.

The autumnal Sunday sunshine soothed him, but not by preparing him with resignation to the disappointment if his mother—if he himself—proved to be mistaken about Dinah. It soothed him by gentle encouragement of his hopes. Her love was so like that calm sunshine that they seemed to make one presence to him, and he believed in them both alike. And Dinah was so bound up with the sad memories of his first passion that he was not forsaking them, but rather giving them a new sacredness by loving her. Nay, his love for her had grown out of that past: it was the noon of that morning.

But Seth? Would the lad be hurt? Hardly; for he had seemed quite contented of late, and there was no selfish jealousy in him; he had never been jealous of his mother's fondness for Adam. But had he seen anything of what their mother talked about? Adam longed to know this, for he thought he could trust Seth's observation better than his mother's. He must talk to Seth before he went to see Dinah, and, with this intention in his mind, he walked back to the cottage and said to his mother, "Did Seth say anything to thee about when he was coming home? Will he be back to dinner?"

"Aye, lad, he'll be back for a wonder. He isna gone to Treddles'on. He's gone somewhere else a-preachin' and a-prayin'."

"Hast any notion which way he's gone?" said Adam.

"Nay, but he aften goes to th' Common. Thee know'st more o's goings nor I do."

Adam wanted to go and meet Seth, but he must content himself with walking about the near fields and getting sight of him as soon as possible. That would not be for more than an hour to come, for Seth would scarcely be at home much before their dinner-time, which was twelve o'clock. But Adam could not sit down to his reading again, and he sauntered along by the brook and stood leaning against the stiles, with eager intense eyes, which looked as if they saw something very vividly; but it was not the brook or the willows, not the fields or the sky. Again and again his vision was interrupted by wonder at the strength of his own feeling, at the strength and sweetness of this new love—almost like the wonder a man feels at the added power he finds in himself for an art which he had laid aside for a space. How is it that the poets have said so many fine things about our first love, so few about our later love? Are their first poems their best? Or are not those the best which come from their fuller thought, their larger experience, their deeper-rooted affections? The boy's flutelike voice has its own spring charm; but the man should yield a richer deeper music.

At last, there was Seth, visible at the farthest stile, and Adam hastened to meet him. Seth was surprised, and thought something unusual must have happened, but when Adam came up, his face said plainly enough that it was nothing alarming.

"Where hast been?" said Adam, when they were side by side.

"I've been to the Common," said Seth. "Dinah's been speaking the Word to a little company of hearers at Brimstone's, as they call him. They're folks as never go to church hardly—them on the Common—but they'll go and hear Dinah a bit. She's been speaking with power this forenoon from the words, 'I came not to call the righteous, but sinners to repentance.' And there was a little thing happened as was pretty to see. The women mostly bring their children with 'em, but to-day there was one stout curly headed fellow about three or four year old, that I never saw there before. He was as naughty as could be at the beginning while I was praying, and while we was singing, but when we all sat down and Dinah began to speak, th' young un stood stock still all at once, and began to look at her with's mouth open, and presently he ran away from's mother and went to Dinah, and pulled at her, like a little dog, for her to take notice of him. So Dinah lifted him up and held th' lad on her lap, while she went on speaking; and he was as good as could be till he went to sleep—and the mother cried to see him."

"It's a pity she shouldna be a mother herself," said Adam, "so fond as the children are of her. Dost think she's quite fixed against marrying, Seth? Dost think nothing 'ud turn her?"

There was something peculiar in his brother's tone, which made Seth steal a glance at his face before he answered.

"It 'ud be wrong of me to say nothing 'ud turn her," he answered. "But if thee mean'st it about myself, I've given up all thoughts as she can ever be my wife. She calls me her brother, and that's enough."

"But dost think she might ever get fond enough of anybody else to be willing to marry 'em?" said Adam rather shyly.

"Well," said Seth, after some hesitation, "it's crossed my mind sometimes o' late as she might; but Dinah 'ud let no fondness for the creature draw her out o' the path as she believed God had marked out for her. If she thought the leading was not from Him, she's not one to be brought under the power of it. And she's allays seemed clear about that—as her work was to minister t' others, and make no home for herself i' this world."

"But suppose," said Adam, earnestly, "suppose there was a man as 'ud let her do just the same and not interfere with her—she might do a good deal o' what she does now, just as well when she was married as when she was single. Other women of her sort have married—that's to say, not just like her, but women as preached and attended on the sick and needy. There's Mrs. Fletcher as she talks of."

A new light had broken in on Seth. He turned round, and laying his hand on Adam's shoulder, said, "Why, wouldst like her to marry THEE, Brother?"

Adam looked doubtfully at Seth's inquiring eyes and said, "Wouldst be hurt if she was to be fonder o' me than o' thee?"

"Nay," said Seth warmly, "how canst think it? Have I felt thy trouble so little that I shouldna feel thy joy?"

There was silence a few moments as they walked on, and then Seth said, "I'd no notion as thee'dst ever think of her for a wife."

"But is it o' any use to think of her?" said Adam. "What dost say? Mother's made me as I hardly know where I am, with what she's been saying to me this forenoon. She says she's sure Dinah feels for me more than common, and 'ud be willing t' have me. But I'm afraid she speaks without book. I want to know if thee'st seen anything."

"It's a nice point to speak about," said Seth, "and I'm afraid o' being wrong; besides, we've no right t' intermeddle with people's feelings when they wouldn't tell 'em themselves."

Seth paused.

"But thee mightst ask her," he said presently. "She took no offence at me for asking, and thee'st more right than I had, only thee't not in the Society. But Dinah doesn't hold wi' them as are for keeping the Society so strict to themselves. She doesn't mind about making folks enter the Society, so as they're fit t' enter the kingdom o' God. Some o' the brethren at Treddles'on are displeased with her for that."

"Where will she be the rest o' the day?" said Adam.

"She said she shouldn't leave the farm again to-day," said Seth, "because it's her last Sabbath there, and she's going t' read out o' the big Bible wi' the children."

Adam thought—but did not say—"Then I'll go this afternoon; for if I go to church, my thoughts 'ull be with her all the while. They must sing th' anthem without me to-day."

Chapter LII Adam and Dinah

IT was about three o'clock when Adam entered the farmyard and roused Alick and the dogs from their Sunday dozing. Alick said everybody was gone to church "but th' young missis"—so he called Dinah—but this did not disappoint Adam, although the "everybody" was so liberal as to include Nancy the dairymaid, whose works of necessity were not unfrequently incompatible with church-going.

There was perfect stillness about the house. The doors were all closed, and the very stones and tubs seemed quieter than usual. Adam heard the water gently dripping from the pump—that was the only sound—and he knocked at the house door rather softly, as was suitable in that stillness.

The door opened, and Dinah stood before him, colouring deeply with the great surprise of seeing Adam at this hour, when she knew it was his regular practice to be at church. Yesterday he would have said to her without any difficulty, "I came to see you, Dinah: I knew the rest were not at home." But to-day something prevented him from saying that, and he put out his hand to her in silence. Neither of them spoke, and yet both wished they could speak, as Adam entered, and they sat down. Dinah took the chair she had just left; it was at the corner of the table near the window, and there was a book lying on the table, but it was not open. She had been sitting perfectly still, looking at the small bit of clear fire in the bright grate. Adam sat down opposite her, in Mr. Poyser's three-cornered chair.

"Your mother is not ill again, I hope, Adam?" Dinah said, recovering herself. "Seth said she was well this morning."

"No, she's very hearty to-day," said Adam, happy in the signs of Dinah's feeling at the sight of him, but shy.

"There's nobody at home, you see," Dinah said; "but you'll wait. You've been hindered from going to church to-day, doubtless."

"Yes," Adam said, and then paused, before he added, "I was thinking about you: that was the reason."

This confession was very awkward and sudden, Adam felt, for he thought Dinah must understand all he meant. But the frankness of the words caused her immediately to interpret them into a renewal of his brotherly regrets that she was going away, and she answered calmly, "Do not be careful and troubled for me, Adam. I have all things and abound at Snowfield. And my mind is at rest, for I am not seeking my own will in going."

"But if things were different, Dinah," said Adam, hesitatingly. "If you knew things that perhaps you don't know now . . . ."

Dinah looked at him inquiringly, but instead of going on, he reached a chair and brought it near the corner of the table where she was sitting. She wondered, and was afraid—and the next moment her thoughts flew to the past: was it something about those distant unhappy ones that she didn't know?

Adam looked at her. It was so sweet to look at her eyes, which had now a self-forgetful questioning in them—for a moment he forgot that he wanted to say anything, or that it was necessary to tell her what he meant.

"Dinah," he said suddenly, taking both her hands between his, "I love you with my whole heart and soul. I love you next to God who made me."

Dinah's lips became pale, like her cheeks, and she trembled violently under the shock of painful joy. Her hands were cold as death between Adam's. She could not draw them away, because he held them fast.

"Don't tell me you can't love me, Dinah. Don't tell me we must part and pass our lives away from one another."

The tears were trembling in Dinah's eyes, and they fell before she could answer. But she spoke in a quiet low voice.

"Yes, dear Adam, we must submit to another Will. We must part."

"Not if you love me, Dinah—not if you love me," Adam said passionately. "Tell me—tell me if you can love me better than a brother?"

Dinah was too entirely reliant on the Supreme guidance to attempt to achieve any end by a deceptive concealment. She was recovering now from the first shock of emotion, and she looked at Adam with simple sincere eyes as she said, "Yes, Adam, my heart is drawn strongly towards you; and of my own will, if I had no clear showing to the contrary, I could find my happiness in being near you and ministering to you continually. I fear I should forget to rejoice and weep with others; nay, I fear I should forget the Divine presence, and seek no love but yours."

Adam did not speak immediately. They sat looking at each other in delicious silence—for the first sense of mutual love excludes other feelings; it will have the soul all to itself.

"Then, Dinah," Adam said at last, "how can there be anything contrary to what's right in our belonging to one another and spending our lives together? Who put this great love into our hearts? Can anything be holier than that? For we can help one another in everything as is good. I'd never think o' putting myself between you and God, and saying you oughtn't to do this and you oughtn't to do that. You'd follow your conscience as much as you do now."

"Yes, Adam," Dinah said, "I know marriage is a holy state for those who are truly called to it, and have no other drawing; but from my childhood upwards I have been led towards another path; all my peace and my joy have come from having no life of my own, no wants, no wishes for myself, and living only in God and those of his creatures whose sorrows and joys he has given me to know. Those have been very blessed years to me, and I feel that if I was to listen to any voice that would draw me aside from that path, I should be turning my back on the light that has shone upon me, and darkness and doubt would take hold of me. We could not bless each other, Adam, if there were doubts in my soul, and if I yearned, when it was too late, after that better part which had once been given me and I had put away from me."

"But if a new feeling has come into your mind, Dinah, and if you love me so as to be willing to be nearer to me than to other people, isn't that a sign that it's right for you to change your life? Doesn't the love make it right when nothing else would?"

"Adam, my mind is full of questionings about that; for now, since you tell me of your strong love towards me, what was clear to me has become dark again. I felt before that my heart was too strongly drawn towards you, and that your heart was not as mine; and the thought of you had taken hold of me, so that my soul had lost its freedom, and was becoming enslaved to an earthly affection, which made me anxious and careful about what should befall myself. For in all other affection I had been content with any small return, or with none; but my heart was beginning to hunger after an equal love from you. And I had no doubt that I must wrestle against that as a great temptation, and the command was clear that I must go away."

"But now, dear, dear Dinah, now you know I love you better than you love me . . . it's all different now. You won't think o' going. You'll stay, and be my dear wife, and I shall thank God for giving me my life as I never thanked him before."

"Adam, it's hard to me to turn a deaf ear . . . you know it's hard; but a great fear is upon me. It seems to me as if you were stretching out your arms to me, and beckoning me to come and take my ease and live for my own delight, and Jesus, the Man of Sorrows, was standing looking towards me, and pointing to the sinful, and suffering, and afflicted. I have seen that again and again when I have been sitting in stillness and darkness, and a great terror has come upon me lest I should become hard, and a lover of self, and no more bear willingly the Redeemer's cross."

Dinah had closed her eyes, and a faint shudder went through her. "Adam," she went on, "you wouldn't desire that we should seek a good through any unfaithfulness to the light that is in us; you wouldn't believe that could be a good. We are of one mind in that."

"Yes, Dinah," said Adam sadly, "I'll never be the man t' urge you against your conscience. But I can't give up the hope that you may come to see different. I don't believe your loving me could shut up your heart—it's only adding to what you've been before, not taking away from it. For it seems to me it's the same with love and happiness as with sorrow—the more we know of it the better we can feel what other people's lives are or might be, and so we shall only be more tender to 'em, and wishful to help 'em. The more knowledge a man has, the better he'll do's work; and feeling's a sort o' knowledge."

Dinah was silent; her eyes were fixed in contemplation of something visible only to herself. Adam went on presently with his pleading, "And you can do almost as much as you do now. I won't ask you to go to church with me of a Sunday. You shall go where you like among the people, and teach 'em; for though I like church best, I don't put my soul above yours, as if my words was better for you to follow than your own conscience. And you can help the sick just as much, and you'll have more means o' making 'em a bit comfortable; and you'll be among all your own friends as love you, and can help 'em and be a blessing to 'em till their dying day. Surely, Dinah, you'd be as near to God as if you was living lonely and away from me."

Dinah made no answer for some time. Adam was still holding her hands and looking at her with almost trembling anxiety, when she turned her grave loving eyes on his and said, in rather a sad voice, "Adam there is truth in what you say, and there's many of the brethren and sisters who have greater strength than I have, and find their hearts enlarged by the cares of husband and kindred. But I have not faith that it would be so with me, for since my affections have been set above measure on you, I have had less peace and joy in God. I have felt as it were a division in my heart. And think how it is with me, Adam. That life I have led is like a land I have trodden in blessedness since my childhood; and if I long for a moment to follow the voice which calls me to another land that I know not, I cannot but fear that my soul might hereafter yearn for that early blessedness which I had forsaken; and where doubt enters there is not perfect love. I must wait for clearer guidance. I must go from you, and we must submit ourselves entirely to the Divine Will. We are sometimes required to lay our natural lawful affections on the altar."

Adam dared not plead again, for Dinah's was not the voice of caprice or insincerity. But it was very hard for him; his eyes got dim as he looked at her.

"But you may come to feel satisfied . . . to feel that you may come to me again, and we may never part, Dinah?"

"We must submit ourselves, Adam. With time, our duty will be made clear. It may be when I have entered on my former life, I shall find all these new thoughts and wishes vanish, and become as things that were not. Then I shall know that my calling is not towards marriage. But we must wait."

"Dinah," said Adam mournfully, "you can't love me so well as I love you, else you'd have no doubts. But it's natural you shouldn't, for I'm not so good as you. I can't doubt it's right for me to love the best thing God's ever given me to know."

"Nay, Adam. It seems to me that my love for you is not weak, for my heart waits on your words and looks, almost as a little child waits on the help and tenderness of the strong on whom it depends. If the thought of you took slight hold of me, I should not fear that it would be an idol in the temple. But you will strengthen me—you will not hinder me in seeking to obey to the uttermost."

"Let us go out into the sunshine, Dinah, and walk together. I'll speak no word to disturb you."

They went out and walked towards the fields, where they would meet the family coming from church. Adam said, "Take my arm, Dinah," and she took it. That was the only change in their manner to each other since they were last walking together. But no sadness in the prospect of her going away—in the uncertainty of the issue—could rob the sweetness from Adam's sense that Dinah loved him. He thought he would stay at the Hall Farm all that evening. He would be near her as long as he could.

"Hey-day! There's Adam along wi' Dinah," said Mr. Poyser, as he opened the far gate into the Home Close, "I couldna think how he happened away from church. Why," added good Martin, after a moment's pause, "what dost think has just jumped into my head?"

"Summat as hadna far to jump, for it's just under our nose. You mean as Adam's fond o' Dinah."

"Aye! hast ever had any notion of it before?"

"To be sure I have," said Mrs. Poyser, who always declined, if possible, to be taken by surprise. "I'm not one o' those as can see the cat i' the dairy an' wonder what she's come after."

"Thee never saidst a word to me about it."

"Well, I aren't like a bird-clapper, forced to make a rattle when the wind blows on me. I can keep my own counsel when there's no good i' speaking."

"But Dinah 'll ha' none o' him. Dost think she will?"

"Nay," said Mrs. Poyser, not sufficiently on her guard against a possible surprise, "she'll never marry anybody, if he isn't a Methodist and a cripple."

"It 'ud ha' been a pretty thing though for 'em t' marry," said Martin, turning his head on one side, as if in pleased contemplation of his new idea. "Thee'dst ha' liked it too, wouldstna?"

"Ah! I should. I should ha' been sure of her then, as she wouldn't go away from me to Snowfield, welly thirty mile off, and me not got a creatur to look to, only neighbours, as are no kin to me, an' most of 'em women as I'd be ashamed to show my face, if my dairy things war like their'n. There may well be streaky butter i' the market. An' I should be glad to see the poor thing settled like a Christian woman, with a house of her own over her head; and we'd stock her well wi' linen and feathers, for I love her next to my own children. An' she makes one feel safer when she's i' the house, for she's like the driven snow: anybody might sin for two as had her at their elbow."

"Dinah," said Tommy, running forward to meet her, "mother says you'll never marry anybody but a Methodist cripple. What a silly you must be!" a comment which Tommy followed up by seizing Dinah with both arms, and dancing along by her side with incommodious fondness.

"Why, Adam, we missed you i' the singing to-day," said Mr. Poyser. "How was it?"

"I wanted to see Dinah—she's going away so soon," said Adam.

"Ah, lad! Can you persuade her to stop somehow? Find her a good husband somewhere i' the parish. If you'll do that, we'll forgive you for missing church. But, anyway, she isna going before the harvest supper o' Wednesday, and you must come then. There's Bartle Massey comin', an' happen Craig. You'll be sure an' come, now, at seven? The missis wunna have it a bit later."

"Aye," said Adam, "I'll come if I can. But I can't often say what I'll do beforehand, for the work often holds me longer than I expect. You'll stay till the end o' the week, Dinah?"

"Yes, yes!" said Mr. Poyser. "We'll have no nay."

"She's no call to be in a hurry," observed Mrs. Poyser. "Scarceness o' victual 'ull keep: there's no need to be hasty wi' the cooking. An' scarceness is what there's the biggest stock of i' that country."

Dinah smiled, but gave no promise to stay, and they talked of other things through the rest of the walk, lingering in the sunshine to look at the great flock of geese grazing, at the new corn-ricks, and at the surprising abundance of fruit on the old pear-tree; Nancy and Molly having already hastened home, side by side, each holding, carefully wrapped in her pocket-handkerchief, a prayer-book, in which she could read little beyond the large letters and the Amens.

Surely all other leisure is hurry compared with a sunny walk through the fields from "afternoon church"—as such walks used to be in those old leisurely times, when the boat, gliding sleepily along the canal, was the newest locomotive wonder; when Sunday books had most of them old brown-leather covers, and opened with remarkable precision always in one place. Leisure is gone—gone where the spinning-wheels are gone, and the pack-horses, and the slow waggons, and the pedlars, who brought bargains to the door on sunny afternoons. Ingenious philosophers tell you, perhaps, that the great work of the steam-engine is to create leisure for mankind. Do not believe them: it only creates a vacuum for eager thought to rush in. Even idleness is eager now—eager for amusement; prone to excursion-trains, art museums, periodical literature, and exciting novels; prone even to scientific theorizing and cursory peeps through microscopes. Old Leisure was quite a different personage. He only read one newspaper, innocent of leaders, and was free from that periodicity of sensations which we call post-time. He was a contemplative, rather stout gentleman, of excellent digestion; of quiet perceptions, undiseased by hypothesis; happy in his inability to know the causes of things, preferring the things themselves. He lived chiefly in the country, among pleasant seats and homesteads, and was fond of sauntering by the fruit-tree wall and scenting the apricots when they were warmed by the morning sunshine, or of sheltering himself under the orchard boughs at noon, when the summer pears were falling. He knew nothing of weekday services, and thought none the worse of the Sunday sermon if it allowed him to sleep from the text to the blessing; liking the afternoon service best, because the prayers were the shortest, and not ashamed to say so; for he had an easy, jolly conscience, broad-backed like himself, and able to carry a great deal of beer or port-wine, not being made squeamish by doubts and qualms and lofty aspirations. Life was not a task to him, but a sinecure. He fingered the guineas in his pocket, and ate his dinners, and slept the sleep of the irresponsible, for had he not kept up his character by going to church on the Sunday afternoons?

Fine old Leisure! Do not be severe upon him, and judge him by our modern standard. He never went to Exeter Hall, or heard a popular preacher, or read Tracts for the Times or Sartor Resartus.

Chapter LIII The Harvest Supper

AS Adam was going homeward, on Wednesday evening, in the six o'clock sunlight, he saw in the distance the last load of barley winding its way towards the yard-gate of the Hall Farm, and heard the chant of "Harvest Home!" rising and sinking like a wave. Fainter and fainter, and more musical through the growing distance, the falling dying sound still reached him, as he neared the Willow Brook. The low westering sun shone right on the shoulders of the old Binton Hills, turning the unconscious sheep into bright spots of light; shone on the windows of the cottage too, and made them a-flame with a glory beyond that of amber or amethyst. It was enough to make Adam feel that he was in a great temple, and that the distant chant was a sacred song.

"It's wonderful," he thought, "how that sound goes to one's heart almost like a funeral bell, for all it tells one o' the joyfullest time o' the year, and the time when men are mostly the thankfullest. I suppose it's a bit hard to us to think anything's over and gone in our lives; and there's a parting at the root of all our joys. It's like what I feel about Dinah. I should never ha' come to know that her love 'ud be the greatest o' blessings to me, if what I counted a blessing hadn't been wrenched and torn away from me, and left me with a greater need, so as I could crave and hunger for a greater and a better comfort."

He expected to see Dinah again this evening, and get leave to accompany her as far as Oakbourne; and then he would ask her to fix some time when he might go to Snowfield, and learn whether the last best hope that had been born to him must be resigned like the rest. The work he had to do at home, besides putting on his best clothes, made it seven before he was on his way again to the Hall Farm, and it was questionable whether, with his longest and quickest strides, he should be there in time even for the roast beef, which came after the plum pudding, for Mrs. Poyser's supper would be punctual.

Great was the clatter of knives and pewter plates and tin cans when Adam entered the house, but there was no hum of voices to this accompaniment: the eating of excellent roast beef, provided free of expense, was too serious a business to those good farm-labourers to be performed with a divided attention, even if they had had anything to say to each other—which they had not. And Mr. Poyser, at the head of the table, was too busy with his carving to listen to Bartle Massey's or Mr. Craig's ready talk.

"Here, Adam," said Mrs. Poyser, who was standing and looking on to see that Molly and Nancy did their duty as waiters, "here's a place kept for you between Mr. Massey and the boys. It's a poor tale you couldn't come to see the pudding when it was whole."

Adam looked anxiously round for a fourth woman's figure, but Dinah was not there. He was almost afraid of asking about her; besides, his attention was claimed by greetings, and there remained the hope that Dinah was in the house, though perhaps disinclined to festivities on the eve of her departure.

It was a goodly sight—that table, with Martin Poyser's round good-humoured face and large person at the head of it helping his servants to the fragrant roast beef and pleased when the empty plates came again. Martin, though usually blest with a good appetite, really forgot to finish his own beef to-night—it was so pleasant to him to look on in the intervals of carving and see how the others enjoyed their supper; for were they not men who, on all the days of the year except Christmas Day and Sundays, ate their cold dinner, in a makeshift manner, under the hedgerows, and drank their beer out of wooden bottles—with relish certainly, but with their mouths towards the zenith, after a fashion more endurable to ducks than to human bipeds. Martin Poyser had some faint conception of the flavour such men must find in hot roast beef and fresh-drawn ale. He held his head on one side and screwed up his mouth, as he nudged Bartle Massey, and watched half-witted Tom Tholer, otherwise known as "Tom Saft," receiving his second plateful of beef. A grin of delight broke over Tom's face as the plate was set down before him, between his knife and fork, which he held erect, as if they had been sacred tapers. But the delight was too strong to continue smouldering in a grin—it burst out the next instant in a long-drawn "haw, haw!" followed by a sudden collapse into utter gravity, as the knife and fork darted down on the prey. Martin Poyser's large person shook with his silent unctuous laugh. He turned towards Mrs. Poyser to see if she too had been observant of Tom, and the eyes of husband and wife met in a glance of good-natured amusement.

"Tom Saft" was a great favourite on the farm, where he played the part of the old jester, and made up for his practical deficiencies by his success in repartee. His hits, I imagine, were those of the flail, which falls quite at random, but nevertheless smashes an insect now and then. They were much quoted at sheep-shearing and haymaking times, but I refrain from recording them here, lest Tom's wit should prove to be like that of many other bygone jesters eminent in their day—rather of a temporary nature, not dealing with the deeper and more lasting relations of things.

Tom excepted, Martin Poyser had some pride in his servants and labourers, thinking with satisfaction that they were the best worth their pay of any set on the estate. There was Kester Bale, for example (Beale, probably, if the truth were known, but he was called Bale, and was not conscious of any claim to a fifth letter), the old man with the close leather cap and the network of wrinkles on his sun-browned face. Was there any man in Loamshire who knew better the "natur" of all farming work? He was one of those invaluable labourers who can not only turn their hand to everything, but excel in everything they turn their hand to. It is true Kester's knees were much bent outward by this time, and he walked with a perpetual curtsy, as if he were among the, most reverent of men. And so he was; but I am obliged to admit that the object of his reverence was his own skill, towards which he performed some rather affecting acts of worship. He always thatched the ricks—for if anything were his forte more than another, it was thatching—and when the last touch had been put to the last beehive rick, Kester, whose home lay at some distance from the farm, would take a walk to the rick-yard in his best clothes on a Sunday morning and stand in the lane, at a due distance, to contemplate his own thatching walking about to get each rick from the proper point of view. As he curtsied along, with his eyes upturned to the straw knobs imitative of golden globes at the summits of the beehive ricks, which indeed were gold of the best sort, you might have imagined him to be engaged in some pagan act of adoration. Kester was an old bachelor and reputed to have stockings full of coin, concerning which his master cracked a joke with him every pay-night: not a new unseasoned joke, but a good old one, that had been tried many times before and had worn well. "Th' young measter's a merry mon," Kester frequently remarked; for having begun his career by frightening away the crows under the last Martin Poyser but one, he could never cease to account the reigning Martin a young master. I am not ashamed of commemorating old Kester. You and I are indebted to the hard hands of such men—hands that have long ago mingled with the soil they tilled so faithfully, thriftily making the best they could of the earth's fruits, and receiving the smallest share as their own wages.

Then, at the end of the table, opposite his master, there was Alick, the shepherd and head-man, with the ruddy face and broad shoulders, not on the best terms with old Kester; indeed, their intercourse was confined to an occasional snarl, for though they probably differed little concerning hedging and ditching and the treatment of ewes, there was a profound difference of opinion between them as to their own respective merits. When Tityrus and Meliboeus happen to be on the same farm, they are not sentimentally polite to each other. Alick, indeed, was not by any means a honeyed man. His speech had usually something of a snarl in it, and his broad-shouldered aspect something of the bull-dog expression—"Don't you meddle with me, and I won't meddle with you." But he was honest even to the splitting of an oat-grain rather than he would take beyond his acknowledged share, and as "close-fisted" with his master's property as if it had been his own—throwing very small handfuls of damaged barley to the chickens, because a large handful affected his imagination painfully with a sense of profusion. Good-tempered Tim, the waggoner, who loved his horses, had his grudge against Alick in the matter of corn. They rarely spoke to each other, and never looked at each other, even over their dish of cold potatoes; but then, as this was their usual mode of behaviour towards all mankind, it would be an unsafe conclusion that they had more than transient fits of unfriendliness. The bucolic character at Hayslope, you perceive, was not of that entirely genial, merry, broad-grinning sort, apparently observed in most districts visited by artists. The mild radiance of a smile was a rare sight on a field-labourer's face, and there was seldom any gradation between bovine gravity and a laugh. Nor was every labourer so honest as our friend Alick. At this very table, among Mr. Poyser's men, there is that big Ben Tholoway, a very powerful thresher, but detected more than once in carrying away his master's corn in his pockets—an action which, as Ben was not a philosopher, could hardly be ascribed to absence of mind. However, his master had forgiven him, and continued to employ him, for the Tholoways had lived on the Common time out of mind, and had always worked for the Poysers. And on the whole, I daresay, society was not much the worse because Ben had not six months of it at the treadmill, for his views of depredation were narrow, and the House of Correction might have enlarged them. As it was, Ben ate his roast beef to-night with a serene sense of having stolen nothing more than a few peas and beans as seed for his garden since the last harvest supper, and felt warranted in thinking that Alick's suspicious eye, for ever upon him, was an injury to his innocence.

But NOW the roast beef was finished and the cloth was drawn, leaving a fair large deal table for the bright drinking-cans, and the foaming brown jugs, and the bright brass candlesticks, pleasant to behold. NOW, the great ceremony of the evening was to begin—the harvest-song, in which every man must join. He might be in tune, if he liked to be singular, but he must not sit with closed lips. The movement was obliged to be in triple time; the rest was ad libitum.

As to the origin of this song—whether it came in its actual state from the brain of a single rhapsodist, or was gradually perfected by a school or succession of rhapsodists, I am ignorant. There is a stamp of unity, of individual genius upon it, which inclines me to the former hypothesis, though I am not blind to the consideration that this unity may rather have arisen from that consensus of many minds which was a condition of primitive thought, foreign to our modern consciousness. Some will perhaps think that they detect in the first quatrain an indication of a lost line, which later rhapsodists, failing in imaginative vigour, have supplied by the feeble device of iteration. Others, however, may rather maintain that this very iteration is an original felicity, to which none but the most prosaic minds can be insensible.

The ceremony connected with the song was a drinking ceremony. (That is perhaps a painful fact, but then, you know, we cannot reform our forefathers.) During the first and second quatrain, sung decidedly forte, no can was filled.

Here's a health unto our master,
The founder of the feast;
Here's a health unto our master
And to our mistress!

And may his doings prosper,
Whate'er he takes in hand,

For we are all his servants,
And are at his command.

But now, immediately before the third quatrain or chorus, sung fortissimo, with emphatic raps of the table, which gave the effect of cymbals and drum together, Alick's can was filled, and he was bound to empty it before the chorus ceased.

Then drink, boys, drink!
And see ye do not spill,
For if ye do, ye shall drink two,
For 'tis our master's will.

When Alick had gone successfully through this test of steady-handed manliness, it was the turn of old Kester, at his right hand—and so on, till every man had drunk his initiatory pint under the stimulus of the chorus. Tom Saft—the rogue—took care to spill a little by accident; but Mrs. Poyser (too officiously, Tom thought) interfered to prevent the exaction of the penalty.

To any listener outside the door it would have been the reverse of obvious why the "Drink, boys, drink!" should have such an immediate and often-repeated encore; but once entered, he would have seen that all faces were at present sober, and most of them serious—it was the regular and respectable thing for those excellent farm-labourers to do, as much as for elegant ladies and gentlemen to smirk and bow over their wine-glasses. Bartle Massey, whose ears were rather sensitive, had gone out to see what sort of evening it was at an early stage in the ceremony, and had not finished his contemplation until a silence of five minutes declared that "Drink, boys, drink!" was not likely to begin again for the next twelvemonth. Much to the regret of the boys and Totty: on them the stillness fell rather flat, after that glorious thumping of the table, towards which Totty, seated on her father's knee, contributed with her small might and small fist.

When Bartle re-entered, however, there appeared to be a general desire for solo music after the choral. Nancy declared that Tim the waggoner knew a song and was "allays singing like a lark i' the stable," whereupon Mr. Poyser said encouragingly, "Come, Tim, lad, let's hear it." Tim looked sheepish, tucked down his head, and said he couldn't sing, but this encouraging invitation of the master's was echoed all round the table. It was a conversational opportunity: everybody could say, "Come, Tim," except Alick, who never relaxed into the frivolity of unnecessary speech. At last, Tim's next neighbour, Ben Tholoway, began to give emphasis to his speech by nudges, at which Tim, growing rather savage, said, "Let me alooan, will ye? Else I'll ma' ye sing a toon ye wonna like." A good-tempered waggoner's patience has limits, and Tim was not to be urged further.

"Well, then, David, ye're the lad to sing," said Ben, willing to show that he was not discomfited by this check. "Sing 'My loove's a roos wi'out a thorn.'"

The amatory David was a young man of an unconscious abstracted expression, which was due probably to a squint of superior intensity rather than to any mental characteristic; for he was not indifferent to Ben's invitation, but blushed and laughed and rubbed his sleeve over his mouth in a way that was regarded as a symptom of yielding. And for some time the company appeared to be much in earnest about the desire to hear David's song. But in vain. The lyricism of the evening was in the cellar at present, and was not to be drawn from that retreat just yet.

Meanwhile the conversation at the head of the table had taken a political turn. Mr. Craig was not above talking politics occasionally, though he piqued himself rather on a wise insight than on specific information. He saw so far beyond the mere facts of a case that really it was superfluous to know them.

"I'm no reader o' the paper myself," he observed to-night, as he filled his pipe, "though I might read it fast enough if I liked, for there's Miss Lyddy has 'em and 's done with 'em i' no time. But there's Mills, now, sits i' the chimney-corner and reads the paper pretty nigh from morning to night, and when he's got to th' end on't he's more addle-headed than he was at the beginning. He's full o' this peace now, as they talk on; he's been reading and reading, and thinks he's got to the bottom on't. 'Why, Lor' bless you, Mills,' says I, 'you see no more into this thing nor you can see into the middle of a potato. I'll tell you what it is: you think it'll be a fine thing for the country. And I'm not again' it—mark my words—I'm not again' it. But it's my opinion as there's them at the head o' this country as are worse enemies to us nor Bony and all the mounseers he's got at 's back; for as for the mounseers, you may skewer half-a-dozen of 'em at once as if they war frogs.'"

"Aye, aye," said Martin Poyser, listening with an air of much intelligence and edification, "they ne'er ate a bit o' beef i' their lives. Mostly sallet, I reckon."

"And says I to Mills," continued Mr. Craig, "'Will you try to make me believe as furriners like them can do us half th' harm them ministers do with their bad government? If King George 'ud turn 'em all away and govern by himself, he'd see everything righted. He might take on Billy Pitt again if he liked; but I don't see myself what we want wi' anybody besides King and Parliament. It's that nest o' ministers does the mischief, I tell you.'"

"Ah, it's fine talking," observed Mrs. Poyser, who was now seated near her husband, with Totty on her lap—"it's fine talking. It's hard work to tell which is Old Harry when everybody's got boots on."

"As for this peace," said Mr. Poyser, turning his head on one side in a dubitative manner and giving a precautionary puff to his pipe between each sentence, "I don't know. Th' war's a fine thing for the country, an' how'll you keep up prices wi'out it? An' them French are a wicked sort o' folks, by what I can make out. What can you do better nor fight 'em?"

"Ye're partly right there, Poyser," said Mr. Craig, "but I'm not again' the peace—to make a holiday for a bit. We can break it when we like, an' I'm in no fear o' Bony, for all they talk so much o' his cliverness. That's what I says to Mills this morning. Lor' bless you, he sees no more through Bony! . . . why, I put him up to more in three minutes than he gets from's paper all the year round. Says I, 'Am I a gardener as knows his business, or arn't I, Mills? Answer me that.' 'To be sure y' are, Craig,' says he—he's not a bad fellow, Mills isn't, for a butler, but weak i' the head. 'Well,' says I, 'you talk o' Bony's cliverness; would it be any use my being a first-rate gardener if I'd got nought but a quagmire to work on?' 'No,' says he. 'Well,' I says, 'that's just what it is wi' Bony. I'll not deny but he may be a bit cliver—he's no Frenchman born, as I understand—but what's he got at's back but mounseers?'"

Mr. Craig paused a moment with an emphatic stare after this triumphant specimen of Socratic argument, and then added, thumping the table rather fiercely, "Why, it's a sure thing—and there's them 'ull bear witness to't—as i' one regiment where there was one man a-missing, they put the regimentals on a big monkey, and they fit him as the shell fits the walnut, and you couldn't tell the monkey from the mounseers!"

"Ah! Think o' that, now!" said Mr. Poyser, impressed at once with the political bearings of the fact and with its striking interest as an anecdote in natural history.

"Come, Craig," said Adam, "that's a little too strong. You don't believe that. It's all nonsense about the French being such poor sticks. Mr. Irwine's seen 'em in their own country, and he says they've plenty o' fine fellows among 'em. And as for knowledge, and contrivances, and manufactures, there's a many things as we're a fine sight behind 'em in. It's poor foolishness to run down your enemies. Why, Nelson and the rest of 'em 'ud have no merit i' beating 'em, if they were such offal as folks pretend."

Mr. Poyser looked doubtfully at Mr. Craig, puzzled by this opposition of authorities. Mr. Irwine's testimony was not to be disputed; but, on the other hand, Craig was a knowing fellow, and his view was less startling. Martin had never "heard tell" of the French being good for much. Mr. Craig had found no answer but such as was implied in taking a long draught of ale and then looking down fixedly at the proportions of his own leg, which he turned a little outward for that purpose, when Bartle Massey returned from the fireplace, where he had been smoking his first pipe in quiet, and broke the silence by saying, as he thrust his forefinger into the canister, "Why, Adam, how happened you not to be at church on Sunday? Answer me that, you rascal. The anthem went limping without you. Are you going to disgrace your schoolmaster in his old age?"

"No, Mr. Massey," said Adam. "Mr. and Mrs. Poyser can tell you where I was. I was in no bad company."

"She's gone, Adam—gone to Snowfield," said Mr. Poyser, reminded of Dinah for the first time this evening. "I thought you'd ha' persuaded her better. Nought 'ud hold her, but she must go yesterday forenoon. The missis has hardly got over it. I thought she'd ha' no sperrit for th' harvest supper."

Mrs. Poyser had thought of Dinah several times since Adam had come in, but she had had "no heart" to mention the bad news.

"What!" said Bartle, with an air of disgust. "Was there a woman concerned? Then I give you up, Adam."

"But it's a woman you'n spoke well on, Bartle," said Mr. Poyser. "Come now, you canna draw back; you said once as women wouldna ha' been a bad invention if they'd all been like Dinah."

"I meant her voice, man—I meant her voice, that was all," said Bartle. "I can bear to hear her speak without wanting to put wool in my ears. As for other things, I daresay she's like the rest o' the women—thinks two and two 'll come to make five, if she cries and bothers enough about it."

"Aye, aye!" said Mrs. Poyser; "one 'ud think, an' hear some folks talk, as the men war 'cute enough to count the corns in a bag o' wheat wi' only smelling at it. They can see through a barn-door, they can. Perhaps that's the reason THEY can see so little o' this side on't."

Martin Poyser shook with delighted laughter and winked at Adam, as much as to say the schoolmaster was in for it now.

"Ah!" said Bartle sneeringly, "the women are quick enough—they're quick enough. They know the rights of a story before they hear it, and can tell a man what his thoughts are before he knows 'em himself."

"Like enough," said Mrs. Poyser, "for the men are mostly so slow, their thoughts overrun 'em, an' they can only catch 'em by the tail. I can count a stocking-top while a man's getting's tongue ready an' when he outs wi' his speech at last, there's little broth to be made on't. It's your dead chicks take the longest hatchin'. Howiver, I'm not denyin' the women are foolish: God Almighty made 'em to match the men."

"Match!" said Bartle. "Aye, as vinegar matches one's teeth. If a man says a word, his wife 'll match it with a contradiction; if he's a mind for hot meat, his wife 'll match it with cold bacon; if he laughs, she'll match him with whimpering. She's such a match as the horse-fly is to th' horse: she's got the right venom to sting him with—the right venom to sting him with."

"Yes," said Mrs. Poyser, "I know what the men like—a poor soft, as 'ud simper at 'em like the picture o' the sun, whether they did right or wrong, an' say thank you for a kick, an' pretend she didna know which end she stood uppermost, till her husband told her. That's what a man wants in a wife, mostly; he wants to make sure o' one fool as 'ull tell him he's wise. But there's some men can do wi'out that—they think so much o' themselves a'ready. An' that's how it is there's old bachelors."

"Come, Craig," said Mr. Poyser jocosely, "you mun get married pretty quick, else you'll be set down for an old bachelor; an' you see what the women 'ull think on you."

"Well," said Mr. Craig, willing to conciliate Mrs. Poyser and setting a high value on his own compliments, "I like a cleverish woman—a woman o' sperrit—a managing woman."

"You're out there, Craig," said Bartle, dryly; "you're out there. You judge o' your garden-stuff on a better plan than that. You pick the things for what they can excel in—for what they can excel in. You don't value your peas for their roots, or your carrots for their flowers. Now, that's the way you should choose women. Their cleverness 'll never come to much—never come to much—but they make excellent simpletons, ripe and strong-flavoured."

"What dost say to that?" said Mr. Poyser, throwing himself back and looking merrily at his wife.

"Say!" answered Mrs. Poyser, with dangerous fire kindling in her eye. "Why, I say as some folks' tongues are like the clocks as run on strikin', not to tell you the time o' the day, but because there's summat wrong i' their own inside . . . "

Mrs. Poyser would probably have brought her rejoinder to a further climax, if every one's attention had not at this moment been called to the other end of the table, where the lyricism, which had at first only manifested itself by David's sotto voce performance of "My love's a rose without a thorn," had gradually assumed a rather deafening and complex character. Tim, thinking slightly of David's vocalization, was impelled to supersede that feeble buzz by a spirited commencement of "Three Merry Mowers," but David was not to be put down so easily, and showed himself capable of a copious crescendo, which was rendering it doubtful whether the rose would not predominate over the mowers, when old Kester, with an entirely unmoved and immovable aspect, suddenly set up a quavering treble—as if he had been an alarum, and the time was come for him to go off.

The company at Alick's end of the table took this form of vocal entertainment very much as a matter of course, being free from musical prejudices; but Bartle Massey laid down his pipe and put his fingers in his ears; and Adam, who had been longing to go ever since he had heard Dinah was not in the house, rose and said he must bid good-night.

"I'll go with you, lad," said Bartle; "I'll go with you before my ears are split."

"I'll go round by the Common and see you home, if you like, Mr. Massey," said Adam.

"Aye, aye!" said Bartle; "then we can have a bit o' talk together. I never get hold of you now."

"Eh! It's a pity but you'd sit it out," said Martin Poyser. "They'll all go soon, for th' missis niver lets 'em stay past ten."

But Adam was resolute, so the good-nights were said, and the two friends turned out on their starlight walk together.

"There's that poor fool, Vixen, whimpering for me at home," said Bartle. "I can never bring her here with me for fear she should be struck with Mrs. Poyser's eye, and the poor bitch might go limping for ever after."

"I've never any need to drive Gyp back," said Adam, laughing. "He always turns back of his own head when he finds out I'm coming here."

"Aye, aye," said Bartle. "A terrible woman!—made of needles, made of needles. But I stick to Martin—I shall always stick to Martin. And he likes the needles, God help him! He's a cushion made on purpose for 'em."

"But she's a downright good-natur'd woman, for all that," said Adam, "and as true as the daylight. She's a bit cross wi' the dogs when they offer to come in th' house, but if they depended on her, she'd take care and have 'em well fed. If her tongue's keen, her heart's tender: I've seen that in times o' trouble. She's one o' those women as are better than their word."

"Well, well," said Bartle, "I don't say th' apple isn't sound at the core; but it sets my teeth on edge—it sets my teeth on edge."

Chapter LIV The Meeting on the Hill

ADAM understood Dinah's haste to go away, and drew hope rather than discouragement from it. She was fearful lest the strength of her feeling towards him should hinder her from waiting and listening faithfully for the ultimate guiding voice from within.

"I wish I'd asked her to write to me, though," he thought. "And yet even that might disturb her a bit, perhaps. She wants to be quite quiet in her old way for a while. And I've no right to be impatient and interrupting her with my wishes. She's told me what her mind is, and she's not a woman to say one thing and mean another. I'll wait patiently."

That was Adam's wise resolution, and it throve excellently for the first two or three weeks on the nourishment it got from the remembrance of Dinah's confession that Sunday afternoon. There is a wonderful amount of sustenance in the first few words of love. But towards the middle of October the resolution began to dwindle perceptibly, and showed dangerous symptoms of exhaustion. The weeks were unusually long: Dinah must surely have had more than enough time to make up her mind. Let a woman say what she will after she has once told a man that she loves him, he is a little too flushed and exalted with that first draught she offers him to care much about the taste of the second. He treads the earth with a very elastic step as he walks away from her, and makes light of all difficulties. But that sort of glow dies out: memory gets sadly diluted with time, and is not strong enough to revive us. Adam was no longer so confident as he had been. He began to fear that perhaps Dinah's old life would have too strong a grasp upon her for any new feeling to triumph. If she had not felt this, she would surely have written to him to give him some comfort; but it appeared that she held it right to discourage him. As Adam's confidence waned, his patience waned with it, and he thought he must write himself. He must ask Dinah not to leave him in painful doubt longer than was needful. He sat up late one night to write her a letter, but the next morning he burnt it, afraid of its effect. It would be worse to have a discouraging answer by letter than from her own lips, for her presence reconciled him to her will.

You perceive how it was: Adam was hungering for the sight of Dinah, and when that sort of hunger reaches a certain stage, a lover is likely to still it though he may have to put his future in pawn.

But what harm could he do by going to Snowfield? Dinah could not be displeased with him for it. She had not forbidden him to go. She must surely expect that he would go before long. By the second Sunday in October this view of the case had become so clear to Adam that he was already on his way to Snowfield, on horseback this time, for his hours were precious now, and he had borrowed Jonathan Burge's good nag for the journey.

What keen memories went along the road with him! He had often been to Oakbourne and back since that first journey to Snowfield, but beyond Oakbourne the greystone walls, the broken country, the meagre trees, seemed to be telling him afresh the story of that painful past which he knew so well by heart. But no story is the same to us after a lapse of time—or rather, we who read it are no longer the same interpreters—and Adam this morning brought with him new thoughts through that grey country, thoughts which gave an altered significance to its story of the past.

That is a base and selfish, even a blasphemous, spirit which rejoices and is thankful over the past evil that has blighted or crushed another, because it has been made a source of unforeseen good to ourselves. Adam could never cease to mourn over that mystery of human sorrow which had been brought so close to him; he could never thank God for another's misery. And if I were capable of that narrow-sighted joy in Adam's behalf, I should still know he was not the man to feel it for himself. He would have shaken his head at such a sentiment and said, "Evil's evil, and sorrow's sorrow, and you can't alter it's natur by wrapping it up in other words. Other folks were not created for my sake, that I should think all square when things turn out well for me."

But it is not ignoble to feel that the fuller life which a sad experience has brought us is worth our own personal share of pain. Surely it is not possible to feel otherwise, any more than it would be possible for a man with cataract to regret the painful process by which his dim blurred sight of men as trees walking had been exchanged for clear outline and effulgent day. The growth of higher feeling within us is like the growth of faculty, bringing with it a sense of added strength. We can no more wish to return to a narrower sympathy than a painter or a musician can wish to return to his cruder manner, or a philosopher to his less complete formula.

Something like this sense of enlarged being was in Adam's mind this Sunday morning, as he rode along in vivid recollection of the past. His feeling towards Dinah, the hope of passing his life with her, had been the distant unseen point towards which that hard journey from Snowfield eighteen months ago had been leading him. Tender and deep as his love for Hetty had been—so deep that the roots of it would never be torn away—his love for Dinah was better and more precious to him, for it was the outgrowth of that fuller life which had come to him from his acquaintance with deep sorrow. "It's like as if it was a new strength to me," he said to himself, "to love her and know as she loves me. I shall look t' her to help me to see things right. For she's better than I am—there's less o' self in her, and pride. And it's a feeling as gives you a sort o' liberty, as if you could walk more fearless, when you've more trust in another than y' have in yourself. I've always been thinking I knew better than them as belonged to me, and that's a poor sort o' life, when you can't look to them nearest to you t' help you with a bit better thought than what you've got inside you a'ready."

It was more than two o'clock in the afternoon when Adam came in sight of the grey town on the hill-side and looked searchingly towards the green valley below, for the first glimpse of the old thatched roof near the ugly red mill. The scene looked less harsh in the soft October sunshine than it had in the eager time of early spring, and the one grand charm it possessed in common with all wide-stretching woodless regions—that it filled you with a new consciousness of the overarching sky—had a milder, more soothing influence than usual, on this almost cloudless day. Adam's doubts and fears melted under this influence as the delicate weblike clouds had gradually melted away into the clear blue above him. He seemed to see Dinah's gentle face assuring him, with its looks alone, of all he longed to know.

He did not expect Dinah to be at home at this hour, but he got down from his horse and tied it at the little gate, that he might ask where she was gone to-day. He had set his mind on following her and bringing her home. She was gone to Sloman's End, a hamlet about three miles off, over the hill, the old woman told him—had set off directly after morning chapel, to preach in a cottage there, as her habit was. Anybody at the town would tell him the way to Sloman's End. So Adam got on his horse again and rode to the town, putting up at the old inn and taking a hasty dinner there in the company of the too chatty landlord, from whose friendly questions and reminiscences he was glad to escape as soon as possible and set out towards Sloman's End. With all his haste it was nearly four o'clock before he could set off, and he thought that as Dinah had gone so early, she would perhaps already be near returning. The little, grey, desolate-looking hamlet, unscreened by sheltering trees, lay in sight long before he reached it, and as he came near he could hear the sound of voices singing a hymn. "Perhaps that's the last hymn before they come away," Adam thought. "I'll walk back a bit and turn again to meet her, farther off the village." He walked back till he got nearly to the top of the hill again, and seated himself on a loose stone, against the low wall, to watch till he should see the little black figure leaving the hamlet and winding up the hill. He chose this spot, almost at the top of the hill, because it was away from all eyes—no house, no cattle, not even a nibbling sheep near—no presence but the still lights and shadows and the great embracing sky.

She was much longer coming than he expected. He waited an hour at least watching for her and thinking of her, while the afternoon shadows lengthened and the light grew softer. At last he saw the little black figure coming from between the grey houses and gradually approaching the foot of the hill. Slowly, Adam thought, but Dinah was really walking at her usual pace, with a light quiet step. Now she was beginning to wind along the path up the hill, but Adam would not move yet; he would not meet her too soon; he had set his heart on meeting her in this assured loneliness. And now he began to fear lest he should startle her too much. "Yet," he thought, "she's not one to be overstartled; she's always so calm and quiet, as if she was prepared for anything."

What was she thinking of as she wound up the hill? Perhaps she had found complete repose without him, and had ceased to feel any need of his love. On the verge of a decision we all tremble: hope pauses with fluttering wings.

But now at last she was very near, and Adam rose from the stone wall. It happened that just as he walked forward, Dinah had paused and turned round to look back at the village—who does not pause and look back in mounting a hill? Adam was glad, for, with the fine instinct of a lover, he felt that it would be best for her to hear his voice before she saw him. He came within three paces of her and then said, "Dinah!" She started without looking round, as if she connected the sound with no place. "Dinah!" Adam said again. He knew quite well what was in her mind. She was so accustomed to think of impressions as purely spiritual monitions that she looked for no material visible accompaniment of the voice.

But this second time she looked round. What a look of yearning love it was that the mild grey eyes turned on the strong dark-eyed man! She did not start again at the sight of him; she said nothing, but moved towards him so that his arm could clasp her round.

And they walked on so in silence, while the warm tears fell. Adam was content, and said nothing. It was Dinah who spoke first.

"Adam," she said, "it is the Divine Will. My soul is so knit to yours that it is but a divided life I live without you. And this moment, now you are with me, and I feel that our hearts are filled with the same love. I have a fulness of strength to bear and do our heavenly Father's Will that I had lost before."

Adam paused and looked into her sincere eyes.

"Then we'll never part any more, Dinah, till death parts us."

And they kissed each other with a deep joy.

What greater thing is there for two human souls than to feel that they are joined for life—to strengthen each other in all labour, to rest on each other in all sorrow, to minister to each other in all pain, to be one with each other in silent unspeakable memories at the moment of the last parting?

Chapter LV Marriage Bells

IN little more than a month after that meeting on the hill—on a rimy morning in departing November—Adam and Dinah were married.

It was an event much thought of in the village. All Mr. Burge's men had a holiday, and all Mr. Poyser's, and most of those who had a holiday appeared in their best clothes at the wedding. I think there was hardly an inhabitant of Hayslope specially mentioned in this history and still resident in the parish on this November morning who was not either in church to see Adam and Dinah married, or near the church door to greet them as they came forth. Mrs. Irwine and her daughters were waiting at the churchyard gates in their carriage (for they had a carriage now) to shake hands with the bride and bridegroom and wish them well; and in the absence of Miss Lydia Donnithorne at Bath, Mrs. Best, Mr. Mills, and Mr. Craig had felt it incumbent on them to represent "the family" at the Chase on the occasion. The churchyard walk was quite lined with familiar faces, many of them faces that had first looked at Dinah when she preached on the Green. And no wonder they showed this eager interest on her marriage morning, for nothing like Dinah and the history which had brought her and Adam Bede together had been known at Hayslope within the memory of man.

Bessy Cranage, in her neatest cap and frock, was crying, though she did not exactly know why; for, as her cousin Wiry Ben, who stood near her, judiciously suggested, Dinah was not going away, and if Bessy was in low spirits, the best thing for her to do was to follow Dinah's example and marry an honest fellow who was ready to have her. Next to Bessy, just within the church door, there were the Poyser children, peeping round the corner of the pews to get a sight of the mysterious ceremony; Totty's face wearing an unusual air of anxiety at the idea of seeing cousin Dinah come back looking rather old, for in Totty's experience no married people were young.

I envy them all the sight they had when the marriage was fairly ended and Adam led Dinah out of church. She was not in black this morning, for her Aunt Poyser would by no means allow such a risk of incurring bad luck, and had herself made a present of the wedding dress, made all of grey, though in the usual Quaker form, for on this point Dinah could not give way. So the lily face looked out with sweet gravity from under a grey Quaker bonnet, neither smiling nor blushing, but with lips trembling a little under the weight of solemn feelings. Adam, as he pressed her arm to his side, walked with his old erectness and his head thrown rather backward as if to face all the world better. But it was not because he was particularly proud this morning, as is the wont of bridegrooms, for his happiness was of a kind that had little reference to men's opinion of it. There was a tinge of sadness in his deep joy; Dinah knew it, and did not feel aggrieved.

There were three other couples, following the bride and bridegroom: first, Martin Poyser, looking as cheery as a bright fire on this rimy morning, led quiet Mary Burge, the bridesmaid; then came Seth serenely happy, with Mrs. Poyser on his arm; and last of all Bartle Massey, with Lisbeth—Lisbeth in a new gown and bonnet, too busy with her pride in her son and her delight in possessing the one daughter she had desired to devise a single pretext for complaint.

Bartle Massey had consented to attend the wedding at Adam's earnest request, under protest against marriage in general and the marriage of a sensible man in particular. Nevertheless, Mr. Poyser had a joke against him after the wedding dinner, to the effect that in the vestry he had given the bride one more kiss than was necessary.

Behind this last couple came Mr. Irwine, glad at heart over this good morning's work of joining Adam and Dinah. For he had seen Adam in the worst moments of his sorrow; and what better harvest from that painful seed-time could there be than this? The love that had brought hope and comfort in the hour of despair, the love that had found its way to the dark prison cell and to poor Hetty's darker soul—this strong gentle love was to be Adam's companion and helper till death.

There was much shaking of hands mingled with "God bless you's" and other good wishes to the four couples, at the churchyard gate, Mr. Poyser answering for the rest with unwonted vivacity of tongue, for he had all the appropriate wedding-day jokes at his command. And the women, he observed, could never do anything but put finger in eye at a wedding. Even Mrs. Poyser could not trust herself to speak as the neighbours shook hands with her, and Lisbeth began to cry in the face of the very first person who told her she was getting young again.

Mr. Joshua Rann, having a slight touch of rheumatism, did not join in the ringing of the bells this morning, and, looking on with some contempt at these informal greetings which required no official co-operation from the clerk, began to hum in his musical bass, "Oh what a joyful thing it is," by way of preluding a little to the effect he intended to produce in the wedding psalm next Sunday.

"That's a bit of good news to cheer Arthur," said Mr. Irwine to his mother, as they drove off. "I shall write to him the first thing when we get home."

Epilogue

IT is near the end of June, in 1807. The workshops have been shut up half an hour or more in Adam Bede's timber-yard, which used to be Jonathan Burge's, and the mellow evening light is falling on the pleasant house with the buff walls and the soft grey thatch, very much as it did when we saw Adam bringing in the keys on that June evening nine years ago.

There is a figure we know well, just come out of the house, and shading her eyes with her hands as she looks for something in the distance, for the rays that fall on her white borderless cap and her pale auburn hair are very dazzling. But now she turns away from the sunlight and looks towards the door.

We can see the sweet pale face quite well now: it is scarcely at all altered—only a little fuller, to correspond to her more matronly figure, which still seems light and active enough in the plain black dress.

"I see him, Seth," Dinah said, as she looked into the house. "Let us go and meet him. Come, Lisbeth, come with Mother."

The last call was answered immediately by a small fair creature with pale auburn hair and grey eyes, little more than four years old, who ran out silently and put her hand into her mother's.

"Come, Uncle Seth," said Dinah.

"Aye, aye, we're coming," Seth answered from within, and presently appeared stooping under the doorway, being taller than usual by the black head of a sturdy two-year-old nephew, who had caused some delay by demanding to be carried on uncle's shoulder.

"Better take him on thy arm, Seth," said Dinah, looking fondly at the stout black-eyed fellow. "He's troublesome to thee so."

"Nay, nay: Addy likes a ride on my shoulder. I can carry him so for a bit." A kindness which young Addy acknowledged by drumming his heels with promising force against Uncle Seth's chest. But to walk by Dinah's side, and be tyrannized over by Dinah's and Adam's children, was Uncle Seth's earthly happiness.

"Where didst see him?" asked Seth, as they walked on into the adjoining field. "I can't catch sight of him anywhere."

"Between the hedges by the roadside," said Dinah. "I saw his hat and his shoulder. There he is again."

"Trust thee for catching sight of him if he's anywhere to be seen," said Seth, smiling. "Thee't like poor mother used to be. She was always on the look out for Adam, and could see him sooner than other folks, for all her eyes got dim."

"He's been longer than he expected," said Dinah, taking Arthur's watch from a small side pocket and looking at it; "it's nigh upon seven now."

"Aye, they'd have a deal to say to one another," said Seth, "and the meeting 'ud touch 'em both pretty closish. Why, it's getting on towards eight years since they parted."

"Yes," said Dinah, "Adam was greatly moved this morning at the thought of the change he should see in the poor young man, from the sickness he has undergone, as well as the years which have changed us all. And the death of the poor wanderer, when she was coming back to us, has been sorrow upon sorrow."

"See, Addy," said Seth, lowering the young one to his arm now and pointing, "there's Father coming—at the far stile."

Dinah hastened her steps, and little Lisbeth ran on at her utmost speed till she clasped her father's leg. Adam patted her head and lifted her up to kiss her, but Dinah could see the marks of agitation on his face as she approached him, and he put her arm within his in silence.

"Well, youngster, must I take you?" he said, trying to smile, when Addy stretched out his arms—ready, with the usual baseness of infancy, to give up his Uncle Seth at once, now there was some rarer patronage at hand.

"It's cut me a good deal, Dinah," Adam said at last, when they were walking on.

"Didst find him greatly altered?" said Dinah.

"Why, he's altered and yet not altered. I should ha' known him anywhere. But his colour's changed, and he looks sadly. However, the doctors say he'll soon be set right in his own country air. He's all sound in th' inside; it's only the fever shattered him so. But he speaks just the same, and smiles at me just as he did when he was a lad. It's wonderful how he's always had just the same sort o' look when he smiles."

"I've never seen him smile, poor young man," said Dinah.

"But thee wilt see him smile, to-morrow," said Adam. "He asked after thee the first thing when he began to come round, and we could talk to one another. 'I hope she isn't altered,' he said, 'I remember her face so well.' I told him 'no,'" Adam continued, looking fondly at the eyes that were turned towards his, "only a bit plumper, as thee'dst a right to be after seven year. 'I may come and see her to-morrow, mayn't I?' he said; 'I long to tell her how I've thought of her all these years.'"

"Didst tell him I'd always used the watch?" said Dinah.

"Aye; and we talked a deal about thee, for he says he never saw a woman a bit like thee. 'I shall turn Methodist some day,' he said, 'when she preaches out of doors, and go to hear her.' And I said, 'Nay, sir, you can't do that, for Conference has forbid the women preaching, and she's given it up, all but talking to the people a bit in their houses.'"

"Ah," said Seth, who could not repress a comment on this point, "and a sore pity it was o' Conference; and if Dinah had seen as I did, we'd ha' left the Wesleyans and joined a body that 'ud put no bonds on Christian liberty."

"Nay, lad, nay," said Adam, "she was right and thee wast wrong. There's no rules so wise but what it's a pity for somebody or other. Most o' the women do more harm nor good with their preaching—they've not got Dinah's gift nor her sperrit—and she's seen that, and she thought it right to set th' example o' submitting, for she's not held from other sorts o' teaching. And I agree with her, and approve o' what she did."

Seth was silent. This was a standing subject of difference rarely alluded to, and Dinah, wishing to quit it at once, said, "Didst remember, Adam, to speak to Colonel Donnithorne the words my uncle and aunt entrusted to thee?"

"Yes, and he's going to the Hall Farm with Mr. Irwine the day after to-morrow. Mr. Irwine came in while we were talking about it, and he would have it as the Colonel must see nobody but thee to-morrow. He said—and he's in the right of it—as it'll be bad for him t' have his feelings stirred with seeing many people one after another. 'We must get you strong and hearty,' he said, 'that's the first thing to be done, Arthur, and then you shall have your own way. But I shall keep you under your old tutor's thumb till then.' Mr. Irwine's fine and joyful at having him home again."

Adam was silent a little while, and then said, "It was very cutting when we first saw one another. He'd never heard about poor Hetty till Mr. Irwine met him in London, for the letters missed him on his journey. The first thing he said to me, when we'd got hold o' one another's hands was, 'I could never do anything for her, Adam—she lived long enough for all the suffering—and I'd thought so of the time when I might do something for her. But you told me the truth when you said to me once, "There's a sort of wrong that can never be made up for."'"

"Why, there's Mr. and Mrs. Poyser coming in at the yard gate," said Seth.

"So there is," said Dinah. "Run, Lisbeth, run to meet Aunt Poyser. Come in, Adam, and rest; it has been a hard day for thee."

Jane Austen

PRIDE AND PREJUDICE

Romance CLASSICS

Romance CLASSICS

Published by Trident Press International
801 12th Avenue South
Suite 302
Naples Florida 34102 USA
www.trident-international.com
email: tridentpress@worldnet.att.net

Printed in Australia
ISBN: 1582791937

Chapter 1

It is a truth universally acknowledged, that a single man in possession of a large fortune must be in want of a wife.

However little known the feelings or views of such a man may be on his first entering a neighbourhood, this truth is so well fixed in the minds of the surrounding families, that he is considered the rightful property of someone or other of their daughters.

"My dear Mr. Bennet," said his lady to him one day, "have you heard that Netherfield Park is let at last?"

Mr. Bennet replied that he had not.

"But it is, returned she; "for Mrs. Long has just been here, and she told me all about it.

Mr. Bennet made no answer.

"Do you not want to know who has taken it?" cried his wife impatiently.

"YOU want to tell me, and I have no objection to hearing it."

This was invitation enough.

"Why, my dear, you must know, Mrs. Long says that Netherfield is taken by a young man of large fortune from the north of England; that he came down on Monday in a chaise and four to see the place, and was so much delighted with it, that he agreed with Mr. Morris immediately; that he is to take possession before Michaelmas, and some of his servants are to be in the house by the end of next week."

"What is his name?"

"Bingley."

"Is he married or single?"

"Oh! Single, my dear, to be sure! A single man of large fortune; four or five thousand a year. What a fine thing for our girls!"

"How so? How can it affect them?"

"My dear Mr. Bennet," replied his wife, "how can you be so tiresome! You must know that I am thinking of his marrying one of them."

"Is that his design in settling here?"

"Design! Nonsense, how can you talk so! But it is very likely that he MAY fall in love with one of them, and therefore you must visit him as soon as he comes."

"I see no occasion for that. You and the girls may go, or you may send them by themselves, which perhaps will be still better, for as you are as handsome as any of them, Mr. Bingley may like you the best of the party."

"My dear, you flatter me. I certainly HAVE had my share of beauty, but I do not pretend to be anything extraordinary now. When a woman has five grown-up daughters, she ought to give over thinking of her own beauty."

"In such cases, a woman has not often much beauty to think of."

"But, my dear, you must indeed go and see Mr. Bingley when he comes into the neighbourhood."

"It is more than I engage for, I assure you."

"But consider your daughters. Only think what an establishment it would be for one of them. Sir William and Lady Lucas are determined to go, merely on that account, for in general, you know, they visit no newcomers. Indeed you must go, for it will be impossible for US to visit him if you do not."

"You are over-scrupulous, surely. I dare say Mr. Bingley will be very glad to see you; and I will send a few lines by you to assure him of my hearty consent to his marrying whichever he chooses of the girls; though I must throw in a good word for my little Lizzy."

"I desire you will do no such thing. Lizzy is not a bit better than the others; and I am sure she is not half so handsome as Jane, nor half so good-humoured as Lydia. But you are always giving HER the preference."

"They have none of them much to recommend them," replied he; "they are all silly and ignorant like other girls; but Lizzy has something more of quickness than her sisters."

"Mr. Bennet, how CAN you abuse your own children in such a way? You take delight in vexing me. You have no compassion for my poor nerves."

"You mistake me, my dear. I have a high respect for your nerves. They are my old friends. I have heard you mention them with consideration these last twenty years at least."

Mr. Bennet was so odd a mixture of quick parts, sarcastic humour, reserve, and caprice, that the experience of three-and-twenty years had been insufficient to make his wife understand his character. HER mind was less difficult to develop. She was a woman of mean understanding, little information, and uncertain temper. When she was discontented, she fancied herself nervous. The business of her life was to get her daughters married; its solace was visiting and news.

Chapter 2

Mr. Bennet was among the earliest of those who waited on Mr. Bingley. He had always intended to visit him, though to the last always assuring his wife that he should not go; and till the evening after the visit was paid she had no knowledge of it. It was then disclosed in the following manner:—Observing his second daughter employed in trimming a hat, he suddenly addressed her with:

"I hope Mr. Bingley will like it, Lizzy."

"We are not in a way to know WHAT Mr. Bingley likes," said her mother resentfully, "since we are not to visit."

"But you forget, mamma," said Elizabeth, "that we shall meet him at the assemblies, and that Mrs. Long promised to introduce him."

"I do not believe Mrs. Long will do any such thing. She has two nieces of her own. She is a selfish, hypocritical woman, and I have no opinion of her."

"No more have I," said Mr. Bennet; "and I am glad to find that you do not depend on her serving you."

Mrs. Bennet deigned not to make any reply, but, unable to contain herself, began scolding one of her daughters.

"Don't keep coughing so, Kitty, for Heaven's sake! Have a little compassion on my nerves. You tear them to pieces."

"Kitty has no discretion in her coughs," said her father; "she times them ill."

"I do not cough for my own amusement," replied Kitty fretfully. "When is your next ball to be, Lizzy?"

"To-morrow fortnight."

"Aye, so it is," cried her mother, "and Mrs. Long does not come back till the day before; so it will be impossible for her to introduce him, for she will not know him herself."

"Then, my dear, you may have the advantage of your friend, and introduce Mr. Bingley to HER."

"Impossible, Mr. Bennet, impossible, when I am not acquainted with him myself; how can you be so teasing?"

"I honour your circumspection. A fortnight's acquaintance is certainly very little. One cannot know what a man really is by the end of a fortnight. But if WE do not venture somebody else will; and after all, Mrs. Long and her daughters must stand their chance; and, therefore, as she will think it an act of kindness, if you decline the office, I will take it on myself."

The girls stared at their father. Mrs. Bennet said only, "Nonsense, nonsense!"

"What can be the meaning of that emphatic exclamation?" cried he. "Do you consider the forms of introduction, and the stress that is laid on them, as nonsense? I cannot quite agree with you THERE. What say you, Mary? For you are a young lady of deep reflection, I know, and read great books and make extracts."

Mary wished to say something sensible, but knew not how.

"While Mary is adjusting her ideas," he continued, "let us return to Mr. Bingley."

"I am sick of Mr. Bingley," cried his wife.

"I am sorry to hear THAT; but why did not you tell me that before? If I had known as much this morning I certainly would not have called on him. It is very unlucky; but as I have actually paid the visit; we cannot escape the acquaintance now."

The astonishment of the ladies was just what he wished; that of Mrs. Bennet perhaps surpassing the rest; though, when the first tumult of joy was over, she began to declare that it was what she had expected all the while.

"How good it was in you, my dear Mr. Bennet! But I knew I should persuade you at last. I was sure you loved your girls too well to neglect such an acquaintance. Well, how pleased I am! and it is such a good joke, too, that you should have gone this morning and never said a word about it till now."

"Now, Kitty, you may cough as much as you choose," said Mr. Bennet; and, as he spoke, he left the room, fatigued with the raptures of his wife.

What an excellent father you have, girls!" said she, when the door was shut. "I do not know how you will ever make him amends for his kindness; or me, either, for that matter. At our time of life it is not so pleasant, I can tell you, to be making new acquaintances every day; but for your sakes, we would do anything. Lydia, my love, though you ARE the youngest, I dare say Mr. Bingley will dance with you at the next ball."

"Oh!" said Lydia stoutly, "I am not afraid; for though I AM the youngest, I'm the tallest."

The rest of the evening was spent in conjecturing how soon he would return Mr. Bennet's visit, and determining when they should ask him to dinner.

Chapter 3

Not all that Mrs. Bennet, however, with the assistance of her five daughters, could ask on the subject, was sufficient to draw from her husband any satisfactory description of Mr. Bingley. They attacked him in various way—with barefaced questions, ingenious suppositions, and distant surmises; but he eluded the skill of them all, and they were at last obliged to accept the second-hand intelligence of their neighbour, Lady Lucas. Her report was highly favourable. Sir William had been delighted with him. He was quite young, wonderfully handsome, extremely agreeable, and, to crown the whole, he meant to be at the next assembly with a large party. Nothing could be more delightful! To be fond of dancing was a certain step towards falling in love; and very lively hopes of Mr. Bingley's heart were entertained.

"If I can but see one of my daughters happily settled at Netherfield," said Mrs. Bennet to her husband, "and all the others equally well married, I shall have nothing to wish for."

In a few days Mr. Bingley returned Mr. Bennet's visit, and sat about ten minutes with him in his library. He had entertained hopes of being admitted to a sight of the young ladies, of whose beauty he had heard much; but he saw only the father. The ladies were somewhat more fortunate, for they had the advantage of ascertaining from an upper window that he wore a blue coat, and rode a black horse.

An invitation to dinner was soon afterwards dispatched; and already had Mrs. Bennet planned the courses that were to do credit to her housekeeping, when an answer arrived which deferred it all. Mr. Bingley was obliged to be in town the following day, and, consequently, unable to accept the honour of their invitation, etc. Mrs. Bennet was quite disconcerted. She could not imagine what business he could have in town so soon after his arrival in Hertfordshire; and she began to fear that he might be always flying about from one place to another, and never settled at Netherfield as he ought to be. Lady Lucas quieted her fears a little by starting the idea of his being gone to London only to get a large party for the ball; and a report soon followed, that Mr. Bingley was to bring twelve ladies and seven gentlemen with him to the assembly. The girls grieved over such a number of ladies, but were comforted the day before the ball by hearing, that instead of twelve he brought only six with him from London—his five sisters and a cousin. And when the party entered the assembly room it consisted of only five altogether—Mr. Bingley, his two sisters, the husband of the eldest, and another young man.

Mr. Bingley was good-looking and gentlemanlike; he had a pleasant countenance, and easy, unaffected manners. His sisters were fine women, with an air of decided fashion. His brother-in-law, Mr. Hurst, merely looked the gentleman; but his friend Mr. Darcy soon drew the attention of the room by his fine, tall person, handsome features, noble mien, and the report which was in general circulation within five minutes after his entrance, of his having ten thousand a year. The gentlemen pronounced him to be a fine figure of a man, the ladies declared he was much handsomer than Mr. Bingley, and he was looked at with great admiration for about half the evening, till his manners gave a disgust which turned the tide of his popularity; for he was discovered to be proud; to be above his company, and above being pleased; and not all his large estate in Derbyshire could then save him from having a most forbidding, disagreeable countenance, and being unworthy to be compared with his friend.

Mr. Bingley had soon made himself acquainted with all the principal people in the room; he was lively and unreserved, danced every dance, was angry that the ball closed so early, and talked of giving one himself at Netherfield. Such amiable qualities must speak for themselves. What a contrast between him and his friend! Mr. Darcy danced only once with Mrs. Hurst and once with Miss Bingley, declined being introduced to any other lady, and spent the rest of the evening in walking about the room, speaking occasionally to one of his own party. His character was decided. He was the proudest, most disagreeable man in the world, and everybody hoped that he would never come there again. Amongst the most violent against him was Mrs. Bennet, whose dislike of his general behaviour was sharpened into particular resentment by his having slighted one of her daughters.

Elizabeth Bennet had been obliged, by the scarcity of gentlemen, to sit down for two dances; and during part of that time, Mr. Darcy had been standing near enough for her to hear a conversation between him and Mr. Bingley, who came from the dance for a few minutes, to press his friend to join it.

"Come, Darcy," said he, "I must have you dance. I hate to see you standing about by yourself in this stupid manner. You had much better dance."

"I certainly shall not. You know how I detest it, unless I am particularly acquainted with my partner. At such an assembly as this it would be insupportable. Your sisters are engaged, and there is not another woman in the room whom it would not be a punishment to me to stand up with."

"I would not be so fastidious as you are," cried Mr. Bingley, "for a kingdom! Upon my honour, I never met with so many pleasant girls in my life as I have this evening; and there are several of them you see uncommonly pretty."

"YOU are dancing with the only handsome girl in the room," said Mr. Darcy, looking at the eldest Miss Bennet.

"Oh! She is the most beautiful creature I ever beheld! But there is one of her sisters sitting down just behind you, who is very pretty, and I dare say very agreeable. Do let me ask my partner to introduce you."

"Which do you mean?" and turning round he looked for a moment at Elizabeth, till catching her eye, he withdrew his own and coldly said: "She is tolerable, but not handsome enough to tempt ME; I am in no humour at present to give consequence to young ladies who are slighted by other men. You had better return to your partner and enjoy her smiles, for you are wasting your time with me."

Mr. Bingley followed his advice. Mr. Darcy walked off; and Elizabeth remained with no very cordial feelings toward him. She told the story, however, with great spirit among her friends; for she had a lively, playful disposition, which delighted in anything ridiculous.

The evening altogether passed off pleasantly to the whole family. Mrs. Bennet had seen her eldest daughter much admired by the Netherfield party. Mr. Bingley had danced with her twice, and she had been distinguished by his sisters. Jane was as much gratified by this as her mother could be, though in a quieter way. Elizabeth felt Jane's pleasure. Mary had heard herself mentioned to Miss Bingley as the most accomplished girl in the neighbourhood; and Catherine and Lydia had been fortunate enough never to be without partners, which was all that they had yet learnt to care for at a ball. They returned, therefore, in good spirits to Longbourn, the village where they lived, and of which they were the principal inhabitants. They found Mr. Bennet still up. With a book he was regardless of time; and on the present occasion he had a good deal of curiosity as to the events of an evening which had raised such splendid expectations. He had rather hoped that his wife's views on the stranger would be disappointed; but he soon found out that he had a different story to hear.

"Oh! my dear Mr. Bennet," as she entered the room, "we have had a most delightful evening, a most excellent ball. I wish you had been there. Jane was so admired, nothing could be like it. Everybody said how well she looked; and Mr. Bingley thought her quite beautiful, and danced with her twice! Only think of THAT, my dear; he actually danced with her twice! and she was the only creature in the room that he asked a second time. First of all, he asked Miss Lucas. I was so vexed to see him stand up with her! But, however, he did not admire her at all; indeed, nobody can, you know; and he seemed quite struck with Jane as she was going down the dance. So he inquired who she was, and got introduced, and asked her for the two next. Then the two third he danced with Miss King, and the two fourth with Maria Lucas, and the two fifth with Jane again, and the two sixth with Lizzy, and the BOULANGER—"

"If he had had any compassion for ME," cried her husband impatiently, "he would not have danced half so much! For God's sake, say no more of his partners. O that he had sprained his ankle in the first place!"

"Oh! my dear, I am quite delighted with him. He is so excessively handsome! And his sisters are charming women. I never in my life saw anything more elegant than their dresses. I dare say the lace upon Mrs. Hurst's gown—"

Here she was interrupted again. Mr. Bennet protested against any description of finery. She was therefore obliged to seek another branch of the subject, and related, with much bitterness of spirit and some exaggeration, the shocking rudeness of Mr. Darcy.

"But I can assure you," she added, "that Lizzy does not lose much by not suiting HIS fancy; for he is a most disagreeable, horrid man, not at all worth pleasing. So high and so conceited that there was no enduring him! He walked here, and he walked there, fancying himself so very great! Not handsome enough to dance with! I wish you had been there, my dear, to have given him one of your set-downs. I quite detest the man."

Chapter 4

When Jane and Elizabeth were alone, the former, who had been cautious in her praise of Mr. Bingley before, expressed to her sister just how very much she admired him.

"He is just what a young man ought to be," said she, "sensible, good-humoured, lively; and I never saw such happy manners!—so much ease, with such perfect good breeding!"

"He is also handsome," replied Elizabeth, "which a young man ought likewise to be, if he possibly can. His character is thereby complete."

"I was very much flattered by his asking me to dance a second time. I did not expect such a compliment."

"Did not you? I did for you. But that is one great difference between us. Compliments always take YOU by surprise, and ME never. What could be more natural than his asking you again? He could not help seeing that you were about five times as pretty as every other woman in the room. No thanks to his gallantry for that. Well, he certainly is very agreeable, and I give you leave to like him. You have liked many a stupider person."

"Dear Lizzy!"

"Oh! you are a great deal too apt, you know, to like people in general. You never see a fault in anybody. All the world are good and agreeable in your eyes. I never heard you speak ill of a human being in your life."

"I would not wish to be hasty in censuring anyone; but I always speak what I think."

"I know you do; and it is THAT which makes the wonder. With YOUR good sense, to be so honestly blind to the follies and nonsense of others! Affectation of candour is common enough—one meets with it everywhere. But to be candid without ostentation or design—to take the good of everybody's character and make it still better, and say nothing of the bad—belongs to you alone. And so you like this man's sisters, too, do you? Their manners are not equal to his."

"Certainly not—at first. But they are very pleasing women when you converse with them. Miss Bingley is to live with her brother, and keep his house; and I am much mistaken if we shall not find a very charming neighbour in her."

Elizabeth listened in silence, but was not convinced; their behaviour at the assembly had not been calculated to please in general; and with more quickness of observation and less pliancy of temper than her sister, and with a judgement too unassailed by any attention to herself, she was very little disposed to approve them. They were in fact very fine ladies; not deficient in good humour when they were pleased, nor in the power of making themselves agreeable when they chose it, but proud and conceited. They were rather handsome, had been educated in one of the first private seminaries in town, had a fortune of twenty thousand pounds, were in the habit of spending more than they ought, and of associating with people of rank, and were therefore in every respect entitled to think well of themselves, and meanly of others. They were of a respectable family in the north of England; a circumstance more deeply impressed on their memories than that their brother's fortune and their own had been acquired by trade.

Mr. Bingley inherited property to the amount of nearly a hundred thousand pounds from his father, who had intended to purchase an estate, but did not live to do it. Mr. Bingley intended it likewise, and sometimes made choice of his county; but as he was now provided with a good house and the liberty of a manor, it was doubtful to many of those who best knew the easiness of his temper, whether he might not spend the remainder of his days at Netherfield, and leave the next generation to purchase.

His sisters were anxious for his having an estate of his own; but, though he was now only established as a tenant, Miss Bingley was by no means unwilling to preside at his table—nor was Mrs. Hurst, who had married a man of more fashion than fortune, less disposed to consider his house as her home when it suited her. Mr. Bingley had not been or age two years, when he was tempted by an accidental recommendation to look at Netherfield House. He did look at it, and into it for half-an-hour—was pleased with the situation and the principal rooms, satisfied with what the owner said in its praise, and took it immediately.

Between him and Darcy there was a very steady friendship, in spite of great opposition of character. Bingley was endeared to Darcy by the easiness, openness, and ductility of his temper, though no disposition could offer a greater contrast to his own, and though with his own he never appeared dissatisfied. On the strength of Darcy's regard, Bingley had the firmest reliance, and of his judgement the highest opinion. In understanding, Darcy was the superior. Bingley was by no means deficient, but Darcy was clever. He was at the same time haughty, reserved, and fastidious, and his manners, though well-bred, were not inviting. In that respect his friend had greatly the advantage. Bingley was sure of being liked wherever he appeared, Darcy was continually giving offense.

The manner in which they spoke of the Meryton assembly was sufficiently characteristic. Bingley had never met with more pleasant people or prettier girls in his life; everybody had been most kind and attentive to him; there had been no formality, no stiffness; he had soon felt acquainted with all the room; and, as to Miss Bennet, he could not conceive an angel more beautiful. Darcy, on the contrary, had seen a collection of people in whom there was little beauty and no fashion, for none of whom he had felt the smallest interest, and from none received either attention or pleasure. Miss Bennet he acknowledged to be pretty, but she smiled too much.

Mrs. Hurst and her sister allowed it to be so—but still they admired her and liked her, and pronounced her to be a sweet girl, and one whom they would not object to know more of. Miss Bennet was therefore established as a sweet girl, and their brother felt authorized by such commendation to think of her as he chose.

Chapter 5

Within a short walk of Longbourn lived a family with whom the Bennets were particularly intimate. Sir William Lucas had been formerly in trade in Meryton, where he had made a tolerable fortune, and risen to the honour of knighthood by an address to the king during his mayoralty. The distinction had perhaps been felt too strongly. It had given him a disgust to his business, and to his residence in a small market town; and, in quitting them both, he had removed with his family to a house about a mile from Meryton, denominated from that period Lucas Lodge, where he could think with pleasure of his own importance, and, unshackled by business, occupy himself solely in being civil to all the world. For, though elated by his rank, it did not render him supercilious; on the contrary, he was all attention to everybody. By nature inoffensive, friendly, and obliging, his presentation at St. James's had made him courteous.

Lady Lucas was a very good kind of woman, not too clever to be a valuable neighbour to Mrs. Bennet. They had several children. The eldest of them, a sensible, intelligent young woman, about twenty-seven, was Elizabeth's intimate friend.

That the Miss Lucases and the Miss Bennets should meet to talk over a ball was absolutely necessary; and the morning after the assembly brought the former to Longbourn to hear and to communicate. "YOU began the evening well, Charlotte," said Mrs. Bennet with civil self-command to Miss Lucas. "YOU were Mr. Bingley's first choice."

"Yes; but he seemed to like his second better."

"Oh! you mean Jane, I suppose, because he danced with her twice. To be sure that DID seem as if he admired her—indeed I rather believe he DID—I heard something about it—but I hardly know what—something about Mr. Robinson."

"Perhaps you mean what I overheard between him and Mr. Robinson; did not I mention it to you? Mr. Robinson's asking him how he liked our Meryton assemblies, and whether he did not think there were a great many pretty women in the room, and WHICH he thought the prettiest? and his answering immediately to the last question: Oh! the eldest Miss Bennet, beyond a doubt; there cannot be two opinions on that point.'"

"Upon my word! Well, that is very decided indeed—that does seem as if—but, however, it may all come to nothing, you know."

"MY overhearings were more to the purpose than YOURS, Eliza," said Charlotte. "Mr. Darcy is not so well worth listening to as his friend, is he?—poor Eliza!—to be only just TOLERABLE."

"I beg you would not put it into Lizzy's head to be vexed by his ill-treatment, for he is such a disagreeable man, that it would be quite a misfortune to be liked by him. Mrs. Long told me last night that he sat close to her for half-an-hour without once opening his lips."

"Are you quite sure, ma'am?—is not there a little mistake?" said Jane. "I certainly saw Mr. Darcy speaking to her."

"Aye—because she asked him at last how he liked Netherfield, and he could not help answering her; but she said he seemed quite angry at being spoke to."

"Miss Bingley told me," said Jane, "that he never speaks much, unless among his intimate acquaintances. With THEM he is remarkably agreeable."

"I do not believe a word of it, my dear. If he had been so very agreeable, he would have talked to Mrs. Long. But I can guess how it was; everybody says that he is eat up with pride, and I dare say he had heard somehow that Mrs. Long does not keep a carriage, and had come to the ball in a hack chaise."

"I do not mind his not talking to Mrs. Long," said Miss Lucas, "but I wish he had danced with Eliza."

"Another time, Lizzy," said her mother, "I would not dance with HIM, if I were you."

"I believe, ma'am, I may safely promise you NEVER to dance with him."

"His pride," said Miss Lucas, "does not offend ME so much as pride often does, because there is an excuse for it. One cannot wonder that so very fine a young man, with family, fortune, everything in his favour, should think highly of himself. If I may so express it, he has a RIGHT to be proud."

"That is very true," replied Elizabeth, "and I could easily forgive HIS pride, if he had not mortified MINE."

"Pride," observed Mary, who piqued herself upon the solidity of her reflections, "is a very common failing, I believe. By all that I have ever read, I am convinced that it is very common indeed; that human nature is particularly prone to it, and that there are very few of us who do not cherish a feeling of self-complacency on the score of some quality or other, real or imaginary. Vanity a pride are different things, though the words are often used synonymously. A person may be proud without being vain. Pride relates more to our opinion of ourselves, vanity to what we would have others think of us."

"If I were as rich as Mr. Darcy," cried a young Lucas, who came with his sisters, "I should not care how proud I was. I would keep a pack of foxhounds, and drink a bottle of wine a day."

"Then you would drink a great deal more than you ought," said Mrs. Bennet; "and if I were to see you at it, I should take away your bottle directly."

The boy protested that she should not; she continued to declare that she would, and the argument ended only with the visit.

Chapter 6

The ladies of Longbourn soon waited on those of Netherfield. The visit was soon returned in due form. Miss Bennet's pleasing manners grew on the goodwill of Mrs. Hurst and Miss Bingley; and though the mother was found to be intolerable, and the younger sisters not worth speaking to, a wish of being better acquainted with THEM was expressed towards the two eldest. By Jane, this attention was received with the greatest pleasure, but Elizabeth still saw superciliousness in their treatment of everybody, hardly excepting even her sister, and could not like them; though their kindness to Jane, such as it was, had a value as arising in all probability from the influence of their brother's admiration. It was generally evident whenever they met, that he DID admire her and to HER it was equally evident that Jane was yielding to the preference which she had begun to entertain for him from the first, and was in a way to be very much in love; but she considered with pleasure that it was not likely to be discovered by the world in general, since Jane united, with great strength of feeling, a composure of temper and a uniform cheerfulness of manner which would guard her from the suspicions of the impertinent. She mentioned this to her friend Miss Lucas.

"It may perhaps be pleasant," replied Charlotte, "to be able to impose on the public in such a case; but it is sometimes a disadvantage to be so very guarded. If a woman conceals her affection with the same skill from the object of it, she may lose the opportunity of fixing him; and it will then be but poor consolation to believe the world equally in the dark. There is so much of gratitude or vanity in almost every attachment, that it is not safe to leave any to itself. We can all BEGIN freely—a slight preference is natural enough; but there are very few of us who have heart enough to be really in love without encouragement. In nine cases out of ten a women had better show MORE affection than she feels. Bingley, likes your sister, undoubtedly; but he may never do more than like her, if she does not help him on."

"But she does help him on, as much as her nature will allow. If I can perceive her regard for him, he must be a simpleton, indeed, not to discover it too."

"Remember, Eliza, that he does not know Jane's disposition as you do."

"But if a woman is partial to a man, and does not endeavour to conceal it, he must find it out."

"Perhaps he must, if he sees enough of her. But, though Bingley and Jane meet tolerably often, it is never for many hours together; and, as they always see each other in large mixed parties, it is impossible that every moment should be employed in conversing together. Jane should therefore make the most of every half-hour in which she can command his attention. When she is secure of him, there will be more leisure for falling in love as much as she chooses."

"Your plan is a good one," replied Elizabeth, "where nothing is in question but the desire of being well married, and if I were determined to get a rich husband, or any husband, I dare say I should adopt it. But these are not Jane's feelings; she is not acting by design. As yet, she cannot even be certain of the degree of her own regard nor of its reasonableness. She has known him only a fortnight. She danced four dances with him at Meryton; she saw him one morning at his own house, and has since dined with him in company four times. This is not quite enough to make her understand his character."

"Not as you represent it. Had she merely DINED with him, she might only have discovered whether he had a good appetite; but you must remember that four evenings have also been spent together—and four evenings may do a great deal."

"Yes; these four evenings have enabled them to ascertain that they both like Vingt-un better than Commerce; but with respect to any other leading characteristic, I do not imagine that much has been unfolded."

"Well," said Charlotte, "I wish Jane success with all my heart; and if she were married to him to-morrow, I should think she had as good a chance of happiness as if she were to be studying his character for a twelvemonth. Happiness in marriage is entirely a matter of chance. If the dispositions of the parties are ever so well known to each other or ever so similar beforehand, it does not advance their felicity in the least. They always continue to grow sufficiently unlike afterwards to have their share of vexation; and it is better to know as little as possible of the defects of the person with whom you are to pass your life."

"You make me laugh, Charlotte; but it is not sound. You know it is not sound, and that you would never act in this way yourself."

Occupied in observing Mr. Bingley's attentions to her sister, Elizabeth was far from suspecting that she was herself becoming an object of some interest in the eyes of his friend. Mr. Darcy had at first scarcely allowed her to be pretty; he had looked at her without admiration at the ball; and when they next met, he looked at her only to criticise. But no sooner had he made it clear to himself and his friends that she hardly had a good feature in her face, than he began to find it was rendered uncommonly intelligent by the beautiful expression of her dark eyes. To this discovery succeeded some others equally mortifying. Though he had detected with a critical eye more than one failure of perfect symmetry in her form, he was forced to acknowledge her figure to be light and pleasing; and in spite of his asserting that her manners were not those of the fashionable world, he was caught by their easy playfulness. Of this she was perfectly unaware; to her he was only the man who made himself agreeable nowhere, and who had not thought her handsome enough to dance with.

He began to wish to know more of her, and as a step towards conversing with her himself, attended to her conversation with others. His doing so drew her notice. It was at Sir William Lucas's, where a large party were assembled.

"What does Mr. Darcy mean," said she to Charlotte, "by listening to my conversation with Colonel Forster?"

"That is a question which Mr. Darcy only can answer."

"But if he does it any more I shall certainly let him know that I see what he is about. He has a very satirical eye, and if I do not begin by being impertinent myself, I shall soon grow afraid of him."

On his approaching them soon afterwards, though without seeming to have any intention of speaking, Miss Lucas defied her friend to mention such a subject to him; which immediately provoking Elizabeth to do it, she turned to him and said:

"Did you not think, Mr. Darcy, that I expressed myself uncommonly well just now, when I was teasing Colonel Forster to give us a ball at Meryton?"

"With great energy; but it is always a subject which makes a lady energetic."

"You are severe on us."

"It will be HER turn soon to be teased," said Miss Lucas. "I am going to open the instrument, Eliza, and you know what follows."

"You are a very strange creature by way of a friend!—always wanting me to play and sing before anybody and everybody! If my vanity had taken a musical turn, you would have been invaluable; but as it is, I would really rather not sit down before those who must be in the habit of hearing the very best performers." On Miss Lucas's persevering, however, she added, "Very well, if it must be so, it must." And gravely glancing at Mr. Darcy, "There is a fine old saying, which everybody here is of course familiar with: 'Keep your breath to cool your porridge'; and I shall keep mine to swell my song."

Her performance was pleasing, though by no means capital. After a song or two, and before she could reply to the entreaties of several that she would sing again, she was eagerly succeeded at the instrument by her sister Mary, who having, in consequence of being the only plain one in the family, worked hard for knowledge and accomplishments, was always impatient for display.

Mary had neither genius nor taste; and though vanity had given her application, it had given her likewise a pedantic air and conceited manner, which would have injured a higher degree of excellence than she had reached. Elizabeth, easy and unaffected, had been listened to with much more pleasure, though not playing half so well; and Mary, at the end of a long concerto, was glad to purchase praise and gratitude by Scotch and Irish airs, at the request of her younger sisters, who, with some of the Lucases, and two or three officers, joined eagerly in dancing at one end of the room.

Mr. Darcy stood near them in silent indignation at such a mode of passing the evening, to the exclusion of all conversation, and was too much engrossed by his thoughts to perceive that Sir William Lucas was his neighbour, till Sir William thus began:

"What a charming amusement for young people this is, Mr. Darcy! There is nothing like dancing after all. I consider it as one of the first refinements of polished society."

"Certainly, sir; and it has the advantage also of being in vogue amongst the less polished societies of the world. Every savage can dance."

Sir William only smiled. "Your friend performs delightfully," he continued after a pause, on seeing Bingley join the group; "and I doubt not that you are an adept in the science yourself, Mr. Darcy."

"You saw me dance at Meryton, I believe, sir."

"Yes, indeed, and received no inconsiderable pleasure from the sight. Do you often dance at St. James's?"

"Never, sir."

"Do you not think it would be a proper compliment to the place?"

"It is a compliment which I never play to any place if I can avoid it."

"You have a house in town, I conclude?"

Mr. Darcy bowed.

"I had once had some thought of fixing in town myself—for I am fond of superior society; but I did not feel quite certain that the air of London would agree with Lady Lucas."

He paused in hopes of an answer; but his companion was not disposed to make any; and Elizabeth at that instant moving towards them, he was struck with the action of doing a very gallant thing, and called out to her:

"My dear Miss Eliza, why are you not dancing? Mr. Darcy, you must allow me to present this young lady to you as a very desirable partner. You cannot refuse to dance, I am sure when so much beauty is before you." And, taking her hand, he would have given it to Mr. Darcy who, though extremely surprised, was not unwilling to receive it, when she instantly drew back, and said with some discomposure to Sir William:

"Indeed, sir, I have not the least intention of dancing. I entreat you not to suppose that I moved this way in order to beg for a partner."

Mr. Darcy, with grave propriety, requested to be allowed the honour of her hand, but in vain. Elizabeth was determined; nor did Sir William at all shake her purpose by his attempt at persuasion.

"You excel so much in the dance, Miss Eliza, that it is cruel to deny me the happiness of seeing you; and though this gentleman dislikes the amusement in general, he can have no objection, I am sure, to oblige us for one half-hour."

"Mr. Darcy is all politeness," said Elizabeth, smiling.

"He is, indeed; but, considering the inducement, my dear Miss Eliza, we cannot wonder at his complaisance—for who would object to such a partner?"

Elizabeth looked archly, and turned away. Her resistance had not injured her with the gentleman, and he was thinking of her with some complacency, when thus accosted by Miss Bingley:

"I can guess the subject of your reverie."

"I should imagine not."

"You are considering how insupportable it would be to pass many evenings in this manner—in such society; and indeed I am quite of you opinion. I was never more annoyed! The insipidity, and yet the noise—the nothingness, and yet the self-importance of all those people! What would I give to hear your strictures on them!"

"You conjecture is totally wrong, I assure you. My mind was more agreeably engaged. I have been meditating on the very great pleasure which a pair of fine eyes in the face of a pretty woman can bestow."

Miss Bingley immediately fixed her eyes on his face, a desired he would tell her what lady had the credit of inspiring such reflections. Mr. Darcy replied with great intrepidity:

"Miss Elizabeth Bennet."

"Miss Elizabeth Bennet!" repeated Miss Bingley. "I am all astonishment. How long has she been such a favourite?—and pray, when am I to wish you joy?"

"That is exactly the question which I expected you to ask. A lady's imagination is very rapid; it jumps from admiration to love, from love to matrimony, in a moment. I knew you would be wishing me joy."

"Nay, if you are serious about it, I shall consider the matter is absolutely settled. You will be having a charming mother-in-law, indeed; and, of course, she will always be at Pemberley with you."

He listened to her with perfect indifference while she chose to entertain herself in this manner; and as his composure convinced her that all was safe, her wit flowed long.

Chapter 7

Mr. Bennet's property consisted almost entirely in an estate of two thousand a year, which, unfortunately for his daughters, was entailed, in default of heirs male, on a distant relation; and their mother's fortune, though ample for her situation in life, could but ill supply the deficiency of his. Her father had been an attorney in Meryton, and had left her four thousand pounds.

She had a sister married to a Mr. Phillips, who had been a clerk to their father and succeeded him in the business, and a brother settled in London in a respectable line of trade.

The village of Longbourn was only one mile from Meryton; a most convenient distance for the young ladies, who were usually tempted thither three or four times a week, to pay their duty to their aunt and to a milliner's shop just over the way. The two youngest of the family, Catherine and Lydia, were particularly frequent in these attentions; their minds were more vacant than their sisters', and when nothing better offered, a walk to Meryton was necessary to amuse their morning hours and furnish conversation for the evening; and however bare of news the country in general might be, they always contrived to learn some from their aunt. At present, indeed, they were well supplied both with news and happiness by the recent arrival of a militia regiment in the neighbourhood; it was to remain the whole winter, and Meryton was the headquarters.

Their visits to Mrs. Phillips were now productive of the most interesting intelligence. Every day added something to their knowledge of the officers' names and connections. Their lodgings were not long a secret, and at length they began to know the officers themselves. Mr.

Phillips visited them all, and this opened to his nieces a store of felicity unknown before. They could talk of nothing but officers; and Mr. Bingley's large fortune, the mention of which gave animation to their mother, was worthless in their eyes when opposed to the regimentals of an ensign.

After listening one morning to their effusions on this subject, Mr. Bennet coolly observed:

"From all that I can collect by your manner of talking, you must be two of the silliest girls in the country. I have suspected it some time, but I am now convinced."

Catherine was disconcerted, and made no answer; but Lydia, with perfect indifference, continued to express her admiration of Captain Carter, and her hope of seeing him in the course of the day, as he was going the next morning to London.

"I am astonished, my dear," said Mrs. Bennet, "that you should be so ready to think your own children silly. If I wished to think slightingly of anybody's children, it should not be of my own, however."

"If my children are silly, I must hope to be always sensible of it."

"Yes—but as it happens, they are all of them very clever."

"This is the only point, I flatter myself, on which we do not agree. I had hoped that our sentiments coincided in every particular, but I must so far differ from you as to think our two youngest daughters uncommonly foolish."

"My dear Mr. Bennet, you must not expect such girls to have the sense of their father and mother. When they get to our age, I dare say they will not think about officers any more than we do. I remember the time when I liked a red coat myself very well—and, indeed, so I do still at my heart; and if a smart young colonel, with five or six thousand a year, should want one of my girls I shall not say nay to him; and I thought Colonel Forster looked very becoming the other night at Sir William's in his regimentals."

"Mamma," cried Lydia, "my aunt says that Colonel Forster and Captain Carter do not go so often to Miss Watson's as they did when they first came; she sees them now very often standing in Clarke's library."

Mrs. Bennet was prevented replying by the entrance of the footman with a note for Miss Bennet; it came from Netherfield, and the servant waited for an answer. Mrs. Bennet's eyes sparkled with pleasure, and she was eagerly calling out, while her daughter read:

"Well, Jane, who is it from? What is it about? What does he say? Well, Jane, make haste and tell us; make haste, my love."

"It is from Miss Bingley," said Jane, and then read it aloud.

> "MY DEAR FRIEND,—
>
> "If you are not so compassionate as to dine to-day with Louisa and me, we shall be in danger of hating each other for the rest of our lives, for a whole day's tete-a-tete between two women can never end without a quarrel. Come as soon as you can on receipt of this. My brother and the gentlemen are to dine with the officers.—Yours ever,
>
> "CAROLINE BINGLEY"

"With the officers!" cried Lydia. "I wonder my aunt did not tell us of THAT."

"Dining out," said Mrs. Bennet, "that is very unlucky."

"Can I have the carriage?" said Jane.

"No, my dear, you had better go on horseback, because it seems likely to rain; and then you must stay all night."

"That would be a good scheme," said Elizabeth, "if you were sure that they would not offer to send her home."

"Oh! but the gentlemen will have Mr. Bingley's chaise to go to Meryton, and the Hursts have no horses to theirs."

"I had much rather go in the coach."

"But, my dear, your father cannot spare the horses, I am sure. They are wanted in the farm, Mr. Bennet, are they not?

"They are wanted in the farm much oftener than I can get them."

"But if you have got them to-day," said Elizabeth, "my mother's purpose will be answered."

She did at last extort from her father an acknowledgment that the horses were engaged; Jane was therefore obliged to go on horseback, and her mother attended her to the door with many cheerful prognostics of a bad day. Her hopes were answered; Jane had not been gone long before it rained hard. Her sisters were uneasy for her, but her mother was delighted. The rain continued the whole evening without intermission; Jane certainly could not some back.

"This was a lucky idea of mine, indeed!" said Mrs. Bennet more than once, as if the credit of making it rain were all her own. Till the next morning, however, she was not aware of all the felicity of her contrivance. Breakfast was scarcely over when a servant from Netherfield brought the following note for Elizabeth:

"MY DEAREST LIZZY,

"I find myself very unwell this morning, which, I suppose, is to be imputed to my getting wet through yesterday. My kind friends will not hear of my returning till I am better. They insist also on my seeing Mr. Jones—therefore do not be alarmed if you should hear of his having been to me—and, excepting a sore throat and headache, there is not much the matter with me.—Yours, etc."

"Well, my dear," said Mr. Bennet, when Elizabeth had read the note aloud, "if your daughter should have a dangerous fit of illness—if she should die, it would be a comfort to know that it was all in pursuit of Mr. Bingley, and under your orders."

"Oh! I am not afraid of her dying. People do not die of little trifling colds. She will be taken good care of. As long as she stays there, it is all very well. I would go an see her if I could have the carriage."

Elizabeth, feeling really anxious, was determined to go to her, though the carriage was not to be had; and as she was no horsewoman, walking was her only alternative. She declared her resolution.

"How can you be so silly," cried her mother, "as to think of such a thing, in all this dirt! You will not be fit to be seen when you get there."

"I shall be very fit to see Jane—which is all I want."

"Is this a hint to me, Lizzy," said her father, "to send for the horses?"

""No, indeed, I do not wish to avoid the walk. The distance is nothing when one has a motive; only three miles. I shall be back by dinner."

"I admire the activity of your benevolence," observed Mary, "but every impulse of feeling should be guided by reason; and, in my opinion, exertion should always be in proportion to what is required."

"We will go as far as Meryton with you," said Catherine and Lydia. Elizabeth accepted their company, and the three young ladies set off together.

"If we make haste," said Lydia, as they walked along, "perhaps we may see something of Captain Carter before he goes."

"In Meryton they parted; the two youngest repaired to the lodgings of one of the officers' wives, and Elizabeth continued her walk alone, crossing field after field at a quick pace, jumping over stiles and springing over puddles with impatient activity, and finding herself at last within view of the house, with weary ankles, dirty stockings, and a face glowing with the warmth of exercise.

She was shown into the breakfast-parlour, where all but Jane were assembled, and where her appearance created a great deal of surprise. That she should have walked three miles so early in the day, in such dirty weather, and by herself, was almost incredible to Mrs. Hurst and Miss Bingley; and Elizabeth was convinced that they held her in contempt for it. She was received, however, very politely by them; and in their brother's manners there was something better than politeness; there was good humour and kindness. Mr. Darcy said very little, and Mr. Hurst nothing at all. The former was divided between admiration of the brilliancy which exercise had given to her complexion, and doubt as to the occasion's justifying her coming so far alone. The latter was thinking only of his breakfast.

Her inquiries after her sister were not very favourably answered. Miss Bennet had slept ill, and though up, was very feverish, and not well enough to leave her room. Elizabeth was glad to be taken to her immediately; and Jane, who had only been withheld by the fear of giving alarm or inconvenience from expressing in her note how much she longed for such a visit, was delighted at her entrance. She was not equal, however, to much conversation, and when Miss Bingley left them together, could attempt little besides expressions of gratitude for the extraordinary kindness she was treated with. Elizabeth silently attended her.

When breakfast was over they were joined by the sisters; and Elizabeth began to like them herself, when she saw how much affection and solicitude they showed for Jane. The apothecary came, and having examined his patient, said, as might be supposed, that she had caught a violent cold, and that they must endeavour to get the better of it; advised her to return to bed, and promised her some draughts. The advice was followed readily, for the feverish symptoms increased, and her head ached acutely. Elizabeth did not quit her room for a moment; nor were the other ladies often absent; the gentlemen being out, they had, in fact, nothing to do elsewhere.

When the clock struck three, Elizabeth felt that she must go, and very unwillingly said so. Miss Bingley offered her the carriage, and she only wanted a little pressing to accept it, when Jane testified such concern in parting with her, that Miss Bingley was obliged to convert the offer of the chaise to an invitation to remain at Netherfield for the present. Elizabeth most thankfully consented, and a servant was dispatched to Longbourn to acquaint the family with her stay and bring back a supply of clothes.

Chapter 8

At five o'clock the two ladies retired to dress, and at half-past six Elizabeth was summoned to dinner. To the civil inquiries which then poured in, and amongst which she had the pleasure of distinguishing the much superior solicitude of Mr. Bingley's, she could not make a very favourable answer. Jane was by no means better. The sisters, on hearing this, repeated three or four times how much they were grieved, how shocking it was to have a bad cold, and how excessively they disliked being ill themselves; and then thought no more of the matter: and their indifference towards Jane when not immediately before them restored Elizabeth to the enjoyment of all her former dislike.

Their brother, indeed, was the only one of the party whom she could regard with any complacency. His anxiety for Jane was evident, and his attentions to herself most pleasing, and they prevented her feeling herself so much an intruder as she believed she was considered by the others. She had very little notice from any but him. Miss Bingley was engrossed by Mr. Darcy, her sister scarcely less so; and as for Mr. Hurst, by whom Elizabeth sat, he was an indolent man, who lived only to eat, drink, and play at cards; who, when he found her to prefer a plain dish to a ragout, had nothing to say to her.

When dinner was over, she returned directly to Jane, and Miss Bingley began abusing her as soon as she was out of the room. Her manners were pronounced to be very bad indeed, a mixture of pride and impertinence; she had no conversation, no style, no beauty. Mrs. Hurst thought the same, and added:

"She has nothing, in short, to recommend her, but being an excellent walker. I shall never forget her appearance this morning. She really looked almost wild."

"She did, indeed, Louisa. I could hardly keep my countenance. Very nonsensical to come at all! Why must SHE be scampering about the country, because her sister had a cold? Her hair, so untidy, so blowsy!"

"Yes, and her petticoat; I hope you saw her petticoat, six inches deep in mud, I am absolutely certain; and the gown which had been let down to hide it not doing its office."

"Your picture may be very exact, Louisa," said Bingley; "but this was all lost upon me. I thought Miss Elizabeth Bennet looked remarkably well when she came into the room this morning. Her dirty petticoat quite escaped my notice."

"YOU observed it, Mr. Darcy, I am sure," said Miss Bingley; "and I am inclined to think that you would not wish to see YOUR sister make such an exhibition."

"Certainly not."

"To walk three miles, or four miles, or five miles, or whatever it is, above her ankles in dirt, and alone, quite alone! What could she mean by it? It seems to me to show an abominable sort of conceited independence, a most country-town indifference to decorum."

"It shows an affection for her sister that is very pleasing," said Bingley.

"I am afraid, Mr. Darcy," observed Miss Bingley in a half whisper, "that this adventure has rather affected your admiration of her fine eyes."

"Not at all," he replied; "they were brightened by the exercise." A short pause followed this speech, and Mrs. Hurst began again:

"I have a excessive regard for Miss Jane Bennet, she is really a very sweet girl, and I wish with all my heart she were well settled. But with such a father and mother, and such low connections, I am afraid there is no chance of it."

"I think I have heard you say that their uncle is an attorney on Meryton."

"Yes; and they have another, who lives somewhere near Cheapside."

"That is capital," added her sister, and they both laughed heartily.

"If they had uncles enough to fill ALL Cheapside," cried Bingley, "it would not make them one jot less agreeable."

"But it must very materially lessen their chance of marrying men of any consideration in the world," replied Darcy.

To this speech Bingley made no answer; but his sisters gave it their hearty assent, and indulged their mirth for some time at the expense of their dear friend's vulgar relations.

With a renewal of tenderness, however, they returned to her room on leaving the dining-parlour, and sat with her till summoned to coffee. She was still very poorly, and Elizabeth would not quit her at all, till late in the evening, when she had the comfort of seeing her sleep, and when it seemed to her rather right than pleasant that she should go downstairs herself. On entering the drawing-room she found the whole party at loo, and was immediately invited to join them; but suspecting them to be playing high, she declined it, for the short time she could stay below, with a book. Mr. Hurst looked at her with astonishment.

"Do you prefer reading to cards?" said he; "that is rather singular."

"Miss Eliza Bennet," said Miss Bingley, "despises cards. She is a great reader, and has no pleasure in anything else."

"I deserve neither such praise nor such censure," cried Elizabeth; "I am NOT a great reader, and I have pleasure in many things."

"In nursing your sister I am sure you have pleasure,"said Bingley; "and I hope it will be soon increased by seeing her quite well."

Elizabeth thanked him from her heart, and then walked towards the table where a few books were lying. He immediately offered to fetch her others—all that his library afforded.

"And I wish my collection were larger for your benefit and my own credit; but I am an idle fellow, and though I have not many, I have more than I ever looked into."

Elizabeth assured him that she could suit herself perfectly with those in the room.

"I am astonished," said Miss Bingley, "that my father should have left so small a collection of books. What a delightful library you have at Pemberley, Mr. Darcy!"

"It ought to be good," he replied, "it has been the work of many generations."

"And then you have added so much to it yourself, you are always buying books."

"I cannot comprehend the neglect of a family library in such days as these."

"Neglect! I am sure you neglect nothing that can add to the beauties of that noble place. Charles, when you build YOUR house, I wish it may be half as delightful as Pemberley."

"I wish it may."

"But I would really advise you to make your purchase in that neighbourhood, and take Pemberley for a kind of model. There is not a finer county in England than Derbyshire."

"With all my heart; I will buy Pemberley itself if Darcy will sell it."

"I am talking of possibilities, Charles."

"Upon my word, Caroline, I should think it more possible to get Pemberley by purchase than by imitation."

Elizabeth was so much caught with what passed, as to leave her very little attention for her book; and soon laying it wholly aside, she drew near the card-table, and stationed herself between Mr. Bingley and his eldest sister, to observe the game."

"Is Miss Darcy much grown since the spring?" said Miss Bingley; "will she be as tall as I am?"

"I think she will. She is now about Miss Elizabeth Bennet's height, or rather taller."

"How I long to see her again! I never met with anybody who delighted me so much. Such a countenance, such manners! And so extremely accomplished for her age! Her performance on the pianoforte is exquisite."

"It is amazing to me," said Bingley, "how young ladies can have patience to be so very accomplished as they all are."

"All young ladies accomplished! My dear Charles, what do you mean?"

"Yes, all of them, I think. They all paint tables, cover screens, and net purses. I scarcely know anyone who cannot do all this, and I am sure I never heard a young lady spoken of for the first time, without being informed that she was very accomplished."

"Your list of the common extent of accomplishments," said Darcy, "has too much truth. The word is applied to many a woman who deserves it no otherwise than by netting a purse or covering a screen. But I am very far from agreeing with you in your estimation of ladies in general. I cannot boast of knowing more than half-a-dozen, in the whole range of my acquaintance, that are really accomplished."

"Nor I, I am sure," said Miss Bingley.

"Then," observed Elizabeth, "you must comprehend a great deal in your idea of an accomplished woman."

"Yes, I do comprehend a great deal in it."

"Oh! certainly," cried his faithful assistant, "no one can be really esteemed accomplished who does not greatly surpass what is usually met with. A woman must have a thorough knowledge of music, singing, drawing, dancing, and the modern languages, to deserve the word; and besides all this, she must possess a certain something in her air and manner of walking, the tone of her voice, her address and expressions, or the word will be but half-deserved."

"All this she must possess," added Darcy, "and to all this she must yet add something more substantial, in the improvement of her mind by extensive reading."

"I am no longer surprised at your knowing ONLY six accomplished women. I rather wonder now at your knowing ANY."

"Are you so severe upon your own sex as to doubt the possibility of all this?

"I never saw such a woman. I never saw such capacity, and taste, and application, and elegance, as you describe united."

Mrs. Hurst and Miss Bingley both cried out against the injustice of her implied doubt, and were both protesting that they knew many women who answered this description, when Mr. Hurst called them to order, with bitter complaints of their inattention to what was going forward. As all conversation was thereby at an end, Elizabeth soon afterwards left the room.

"Elizabeth Bennet," said Miss Bingley, when the door was closed on her, "is one of those young ladies who seek to recommend themselves to the other sex by undervaluing their own; and with many men, I dare say, it succeeds. But, in my opinion, it is a paltry device, a very mean art."

"Undoubtedly," replied Darcy, to whom this remark was chiefly addressed, "there is a meanness in ALL the arts which ladies sometimes condescend to employ for captivation. Whatever bears affinity to cunning is despicable."

Miss Bingley was not so entirely satisfied with this reply as to continue the subject.

Elizabeth joined them again only to say that her sister was worse, and that she could not leave her. Bingley urged Mr. Jones being sent for immediately; while his sisters, convinced that no country advice could be of any service, recommended an express to town for one of the most eminent physicians. This she would not hear of; but she was not so unwilling to comply with their brother's proposal; and it was settled that Mr. Jones should be sent for early in the morning, if Miss Bennet were not decidedly better. Bingley was quite uncomfortable; his sisters declared that they were miserable: They solaced their wretchedness, however, by duets after supper, while he could find no better relief to his feelings than by giving his housekeeper directions that every attention might be paid to the sick lady and her sister.

Chapter 9

Elizabeth passed the chief of the night in her sister's room, and in the morning had the pleasure of being able to send a tolerable answer to the inquiries which she very early received from Mr. Bingley by a housemaid, and some time afterwards from the two elegant ladies who waited on his sisters. In spite of this amendment, however, she requested to have a note sent to Longbourn, desiring her mother to visit Jane, and form her own judgement of her situation. The note was immediately dispatched, and its contents as quickly complied with. Mrs. Bennet, accompanied by her two youngest girls, reached Netherfield soon after the family breakfast.

Had she found Jane in any apparent danger, Mrs. Bennet would have been very miserable; but being satisfied on seeing her that her illness was not alarming, she had no wish of her recovering immediately, as her restoration to health would probably remove her from Netherfield. She would not listen, therefore, to her daughter's proposal of being carried home; neither did the apothecary, who arrived about the same time, think it at all advisable. After sitting a little while with Jane, on Miss Bingley's appearance and invitation, the mother and three daughter all attended her into the breakfast parlour. Bingley met them with hopes that Mrs. Bennet had not found Miss Bennet worse than she expected.

"Indeed I have, sir," was her answer. "She is a great deal too ill to be moved. Mr. Jones says we must not think of moving her. We must trespass a little longer on your kindness."

"Removed!" cried Bingley. "It must not be thought of. My sister, I am sure, will not hear of her removal."

"You may depend upon it, madam," said Miss Bingley, with cold civility, "that Miss Bennet will receive every possible attention while she remains with us."

Mrs. Bennet was profuse in hr acknowledgements.

"I am sure," she added, "if it was not for such good friends I do not know what would become of her, for she is very ill indeed, and suffers a vast deal, though with the greatest patience in the world, which is always the way with her, for she has, without exception, the sweetest temper I have ever met with. I often tell my other girls they are nothing to HER. You have a sweet room here, Mr. Bingley, and a charming prospect over the gravel walk. I do not know a place in the country that is equal to Netherfield. You will not think of quitting it in a hurry, I hope, though you have but a short lease."

"Whatever I do is done in a hurry," replied he; "and therefore if I should resolve to quit Netherfield, I should probably be off in five minutes. At present, however, I consider myself as quite fixed here."

"That is exactly what I should have supposed of you," said Elizabeth.

"You begin to comprehend me, do you?" cried he, turning towards her.

"Oh! yes—I understand you perfectly."

"I wish I might take this for a compliment; but to be so easily seen through I am afraid is pitiful."

"That is as it happens. It does not follow that a deep, intricate character is more or less estimable than such a one as yours."

"Lizzy," cried her mother, "remember where you are, and do not run on in the wild manner that you are suffered to do at home."

"I did not know before," continued Bingley immediately, "that your were a studier of character. It must be an amusing study."

""Yes, but intricate characters are the MOST amusing. They have at least that advantage."

"The country," said Darcy, "can in general supply but a few subjects for such a study. In a country neighbourhood you move in a very confined and unvarying society."

"But people themselves alter so much, that there is something new to be observed in them for ever."

"Yes, indeed," cried Mrs. Bennet, offended by his manner of mentioning a country neighbourhood. "I assure you there is quite as much of THAT going on in the country as in town."

Everybody was surprised, and Darcy, after looking at her for a moment, turned silently away. Mrs. Bennet, who fancied she had gained a complete victory over him, continued her triumph.

"I cannot see that London has any great advantage over the country, for my part, except the shops and public places. The country is a vast deal pleasanter, is it not, Mr. Bingley?"

"When I am in the country," he replied, "I never wish to leave it; and when I am in town it is pretty much the same. They have each their advantages, and I can be equally happy in either."

"Aye—that is because you have the right disposition. But that gentleman," looking at Darcy, "seemed to think the country was nothing at all."

"Indeed, mamma, you are mistaken," said Elizabeth, blushing for her mother. "You quite mistook Mr. Darcy. He only meant that there was not such a variety of people to be met with in the country as in the town, which you must acknowledge to be true."

"Certainly, my dear, nobody said there were; but as to not meeting with many people in this neighbourhood, I believe there are few neighbourhoods larger. I know we dine with four-and-twenty families."

Nothing but concern for Elizabeth could enable Bingley to keep his countenance. His sister was less delicate, and directed her eyes towards Mr. Darcy with a very expressive smile. Elizabeth, for the sake of saying something that might turn her mother's thoughts, now asked her if Charlotte Lucas had been at Longbourn since HER coming away.

"Yes, she called yesterday with her father. What an agreeable man Sir William is, Mr. Bingley, is not he? So much the man of fashion! So genteel and easy! He had always something to say to everybody. THAT is my idea of good breeding; and those persons who fancy themselves very important, and never open their mouths, quite mistake the matter."

"Did Charlotte dine with you?"

"No, she would go home. I fancy she was wanted about mince-pies. For my part, Mr. Bingley, I always keep servants that can do their own work; MY daughters are brought up very differently. But everybody is to judge for themselves, and the Lucases are a very good sort of girls, I assure you. It is a pity they are not handsome! Not that I think Charlotte so VERY plain—but then she is our particular friend."

"She seems a very pleasant young woman."

"Oh! dear, yes; but you must own she is very plain. Lady Lucas herself has often said so, and envied me Jane's beauty. I do not like to boast of my own child, but to be sure, Jane—one does not often see anybody better looking. It is what everybody says. I do not trust my own partiality. When she was only fifteen, there was a man at my brother Gardiner's in town so much in love with her that my sister-in-law was sure he would make her an offer before we came away. But, however, he did not. Perhaps he thought her too young. However, he wrote some verses on her, and very pretty they were."

"And so ended his affection," said Elizabeth impatiently. "There has been many a one, I fancy, overcome in the same way. I wonder who first discovered the efficacy of poetry in driving away love!"

"I have been used to consider poetry as the FOOD of love," said Darcy.

"Of a fine, stout, healthy love it may. Everything nourishes what is strong already. But if it be only a slight, thin sort of inclination, I am convinced that one good sonnet will starve it entirely away."

Darcy only smiled; and the general pause which ensued made Elizabeth tremble lest her mother should be exposing herself again. She longed to speak, but could think of nothing to say; and after a short silence Mrs. Bennet began repeating her thanks to Mr. Bingley for his kindness to Jane, with an apology for troubling him also with Lizzy. Mr. Bingley was unaffectedly civil in his answer, and forced his younger sister to be civil also, and say what the occasion required. She performed her part indeed without much graciousness, but Mrs. Bennet was satisfied, and soon afterwards ordered her carriage. Upon this signal, the youngest of her daughters put herself forward. The two girls had been whispering to each other during the whole visit, and the result of it was, that the youngest should tax Mr. Bingley with having promised on his first coming into the country to give a ball at Netherfield.

Lydia was a stout, well-grown girl of fifteen, with a fine complexion and good-humoured countenance; a favourite with her mother, whose affection had brought her into public at an early age. She had high animal spirits, and a sort of natural self-consequence, which the attention of the officers, to whom her uncle's good dinners, and her own easy manners recommended her, had increased into assurance. She was very equal, therefore, to address Mr. Bingley on the subject of the ball, and abruptly reminded him that it would be the most shameful thing in the world if he did not keep it. His answer to this sudden attack was delightful to her mother's ear:

"I am perfectly ready, I assure you, to keep my engagement; and when your sister is recovered, you shall, if you please, name the very day of the ball. But you would not wish to be dancing when she is ill."

Lydia declared herself satisfied. "Oh! yes—it would be much better to wait till Jane was well, and by that time most likely Captain Carter would be at Meryton again. And when you have given YOUR ball," she added, "I shall insist on their giving one also. I shall tell Colonel Forster it will be quite a shame if he does not."

Mrs. Bennet and her daughter then departed, and Elizabeth returned instantly to Jane, leaving her own and her relations' behaviour to the remarks of the two ladies and Mr. Darcy; the latter of whom, however, could not be prevailed on to join in their censure of HER, in spite of all Miss Bingley's witticisms on FINE EYES.

Chapter 10

The day passed much as the day before had done. Mrs. Hurst and Miss Bingley had spent some hours of the morning with the invalid, who continued, though slowly, to mend; and in the evening Elizabeth joined their party in the drawing-room. The loo-table, however, did not appear. Mr. Darcy was writing, and Miss Bingley, seated near him, was watching the progress of his letter and repeatedly calling his attention by messages to his sister. Mr. Hurst and Mr. Bingley were at piquet, and Mrs. Hurst was observing their game.

Elizabeth took up some needlework, and was sufficiently amused in attending to what passed between Darcy and his companion. The perpetual commendations of the lady, either on his handwriting, or on the evenness of his lines, or on the length of his letter, with the perfect unconcern with which her praises were received, formed a curious dialogue, and was exactly in union with her opinion of each.

"How delighted Miss Darcy will be to receive such a letter!"

He made no answer.

"You write uncommonly fast."

"You are mistaken. I write rather slowly."

"How many letters you must have occasion to write in the course of a year! Letters of business, too! How odious I should think them!"

"It is fortunate, then, that they fall to my lot instead of yours."

"Pray tell your sister that I long to see her."

"I have already told her so once, by your desire."

"I am afraid you do not like your pen. Let me mend it for you. I mend pens remarkably well."

"Thank you—but I always mend my own."

"How can you contrive to write so even?"

He was silent.

"Tell your sister I am delighted to hear of her improvement on the harp; and pray let her know that I am quite in raptures with her beautiful little design for a table, and I think it infinitely superior to Miss Grantley's."

"Will you give me leave to defer your raptures till I write again? At present I have not room to do them justice."

"Oh! It is of no consequence. I shall see her in January. But do you always write such charming long letters to her, Mr. Darcy?"

"They are generally long; but whether always charming it is not for me to determine."

"It is a rule with me, that a person who can write a long letter with ease, cannot write ill."

"That will not do for a compliment to Darcy, Caroline," cried her brother, "because he does not write with ease. He studies too much for words of four syllables. Do not you, Darcy?"

"My style of writing is very different from yours."

"Oh!" cried Miss Bingley, "Charles writes in the most careless way imaginable. He leaves out half his words, and blots the rest."

"My ideas flow so rapidly that I have not time to express them—by which means my letters sometimes convey no ideas at all to my correspondents."

"Your humility, Mr. Bingley," said Elizabeth, "must disarm reproof."

"Nothing is more deceitful," said Darcy, "than the appearance of humility. It is often only carelessness of opinion, and sometimes an indirect boast."

"And which of the two do you call MY little recent piece of modesty?"

"The indirect boast; for you are really proud of your defects in writing, because you consider them as proceeding from a rapidity of thought and carelessness of execution, which, if not estimable, you think at least highly interesting. The power of doing anything with quickness is always prized much by the possessor, and often without any attention to the imperfection of the performance. When you told Mrs. Bennet this morning, that if you ever resolved upon quitting Netherfield you should be gone in five minutes, you meant it to be a sort of panegyric, of compliment to yourself—and yet what is there so very laudable in a precipitance which must leave very necessary business undone, and can be of no real advantage to yourself or anyone else?"

"Nay," cried Bingley, "this is too much, to remember at night all the foolish things that were said in the morning. And, yet, upon my honour, I believe what I said of myself to be true, and I believe it at this moment. At least, therefore, I did not assume the character of needless precipitance merely to show off before the ladies."

"I dare say you believed it; but I am by no means convinced that you would be gone with such celerity. Your conduct would be quite as dependent on chance as that of any man I know; and if, as you were mounting your horse, a friend were to say, Bingley, you had better stay till next week,' you would probably do it, you would probably not go—and at another word, might stay a month."

"You have only proved by this," cried Elizabeth, "that Mr. Bingley did not do justice to his own disposition. You have shown him off now much more than he did himself."

"I am exceedingly gratified," said Bingley, "by your converting what my friend says into a compliment on the sweetness of my temper. But I am afraid you are giving it a turn which that gentleman did by no means intend; for he would certainly think better of me, if under such a circumstance I were to give a flat denial, and ride off as fast as I could."

"Would Mr. Darcy then consider the rashness of your original intentions as atoned for by your obstinacy in adhering to it?"

"Upon my word, I cannot exactly explain the matter; Darcy must speak for himself."

"You expect me to account for opinions which you choose to call mine, but which I have never acknowledged. Allowing the case, however, to stand according to your representation, you must remember, Miss Bennet, that the friend who is supposed to desire his return to the house, and the delay of his plan, has merely desired it, asked it without offering one argument in favour of its propriety."

"To yield readily—easily—to the PERSUASION of a friend is no merit with you."

"To yield without conviction is no compliment to the understanding of either."

"You appear to me, Mr. Darcy, to allow nothing for the influence of friendship and affection. A regard for the requester would often make one readily yield to a request, without waiting for arguments to reason one into it. I am not particularly speaking of such a case as you have supposed about Mr. Bingley. We may as well wait, perhaps, till the circumstance occurs before we discuss the discretion of his behaviour thereupon. But in general and ordinary cases between friend and friend, where one of them is desired by the other to change a resolution of no very great moment, should you think ill of that person for complying with the desire, without waiting to be argued into it?"

"Will it not be advisable, before we proceed on this subject, to arrange with rather more precision the degree of importance which is to appertain to this request, as well as the degree of intimacy subsisting between the parties?"

"By all means," cried Bingley; "let us hear all the particulars, not forgetting their comparative height and size; for that will have more weight in the argument, Miss Bennet, than you may be aware of. I assure you, that if Darcy were not such a great tall fellow, in comparison with myself, that I should not pay him half so much deference. I declare I do not know a more awful object than Darcy, on particular occasions, and in particular places; at his own house especially, and of a Sunday evening, when he has nothing to do."

Mr. Darcy smiled; but Elizabeth thought she could perceive that he was rather offended, and therefore checked her laugh. Miss Bingley warmly resented the indignity he had received, in an expostulation with her brother for talking such nonsense.

"I see your design, Bingley," said his friend. "You dislike an argument, and want to silence this."

"Perhaps I do. Arguments are too much like disputes. If you and Miss Bennet will defer yours till I am out of the room, I shall be very thankful; and then you may say whatever you like of me."

"What you ask," said Elizabeth, "is no sacrifice on my side; and Mr. Darcy had much better finish his letter."

Mr. Darcy took her advice, and did finish his letter.

When that business was over, he applied to Miss Bingley and Elizabeth for an indulgence of some music. Miss Bingley moved with some alacrity to the pianoforte; and, after a polite request that Elizabeth would lead the way which the other as politely and more earnestly negatived, she seated herself.

Mrs. Hurst sang with her sister, and while they were thus employed, Elizabeth could not help observing, as she turned over some music-books that lay on the instrument, how frequently Mr. Darcy's eyes were fixed on her. She hardly knew how to suppose that she could be an object of admiration to so great a man; and yet that he should look at her because he disliked her, was still more strange. She could only imagine, however, at last that she drew his notice because there was something more wrong and reprehensible, according to his ideas of right, than in any other person present. The supposition did not pain her. She liked him too little to care for his approbation.

After playing some Italian songs, Miss Bingley varied the charm by a lively Scotch air; and soon afterwards Mr. Darcy, drawing near Elizabeth, said to her:

"Do not you feel a great inclination, Miss Bennet, to seize such an opportunity of dancing a reel?"

She smiled, but made no answer. He repeated the question, with some surprise at her silence.

"Oh!" said she, "I heard you before, but I could not immediately determine what to say in reply. You wanted me, I know, to say Yes,' that you might have the pleasure of despising my taste; but I always delight in overthrowing those kind of schemes, and cheating a person of their meditated contempt. I have, therefore, made up my mind to tell you, that I do not want to dance a reel at all—and now despise me if you dare."

""Indeed I do not dare."

Elizabeth, having rather expected to affront him, was amazed at his gallantry; but there was a mixture of sweetness and archness in her manner which made it difficult for her to affront anybody; and Darcy had never been so bewitched by any woman as he was by her. He really believed, that were it not for the inferiority of her connections, he should be in some danger.

Miss Bingley saw, or suspected enough to be jealous; and her great anxiety for the recovery of her dear friend Jane received some assistance from her desire of getting rid of Elizabeth.

She often tried to provoke Darcy into disliking her guest, by talking of their supposed marriage, and planning his happiness in such an alliance.

"I hope," said she, as they were walking together in the shrubbery the next day, "you will give your mother-in-law a few hints, when this desirable event takes place, as to the advantage of holding her tongue; and if you can compass it, do sure the younger girls of running after officers. And, if I may mention so delicate a subject, endeavour to check that little something, bordering on conceit and impertinence, which your lady possesses."

"Have you anything else to propose for my domestic felicity?"

"Oh! yes. Do let the portraits of your uncle and aunt Phillips get placed in the gallery at Pemberley. Put them next to your great-uncle the judge. They are in the same profession, you know, only in different lines. As for your Elizabeth's picture, you must not have it taken, for what painter could do justice to those beautiful eyes?"

"It would not be easy, indeed, to catch their expression, but their colour and shape, and the eyelashes, so remarkably fine, might be copied."

At that moment they were met from another walk by Mrs. Hurst and Elizabeth herself.

"I did not know that you intended to walk," said Miss Bingley, in some confusion, lest they had been overheard.

"You used us abominably ill, "answered Mrs. Hurst, "running away without telling us that you were coming out."

Then taking the disengaged arm of Mr. Darcy, she left Elizabeth to walk by herself. The path just admitted three. Mr. Darcy felt their rudeness, and immediately said:

"This walk is not wide enough for our party. We had better go into the avenue."

But Elizabeth, who had not the least inclination to remain with them, laughingly answered:

"No, no; stay where you are. You are charmingly grouped, and appear to uncommon advantage. The picturesque would be spoilt by admitting a fourth. Good-bye."

She then ran gaily off, rejoicing, as she rambled about, in the hope of being at home again in a day or two. Jane was already so much recovered as to intend leaving her room for a couple of hours that evening.

Chapter 11

When the ladies removed after dinner, Elizabeth ran up to her sister, and seeing her well guarded from cold, attended her into the drawing-room, where she was welcomed by her two friends with many professions of pleasure; and Elizabeth had never seen them so agreeable as they were during the hour which passed before the gentlemen appeared. Their powers of conversation were considerable. They could describe an entertainment with accuracy, relate an anecdote with humour, and laugh at their acquaintance with spirit.

But when the gentlemen entered, Jane was no longer the first object; Miss Bingley's eyes were instantly turned toward Darcy, and she had something to say to him before he had advanced many steps. He addressed himself to Miss Bennet, with a polite congratulation; Mr. Hurst also made her a slight bow, and said he was "very glad"; but diffuseness and warmth remained for Bingley's salutation. He was full of joy and attention. The first half-hour was spent in piling up the fire, lest she should suffer from the change of room; and she removed at his desire to the other side of the fireplace, that she might be further from the door. He then sat down by her, and talked scarcely to anyone else. Elizabeth, at work in the opposite corner, saw it all with great delight.

When tea was over, Mr. Hurst reminded his sister-in-law of the card-table—but in vain. She had obtained private intelligence that Mr. Darcy did not wish for cards; and Mr. Hurst soon found even his open petition rejected. She assured him that no one intended to play, and the silence of the whole party on the subject seemed to justify her. Mr. Hurst had therefore nothing to do, but to stretch himself on one of the sofas and go to sleep. Darcy took up a book; Miss Bingley did the same; and Mrs. Hurst, principally occupied in playing with her bracelets and rings, joined now and then in her brother's conversation with Miss Bennet.

Miss Bingley's attention was quite as much engaged in watching Mr. Darcy's progress through HIS book, as in reading her own; and she was perpetually either making some inquiry, or looking at his page. She could not win him, however, to any conversation; he merely answered her question, and read on. At length, quite exhausted by the attempt to be amused with her own book, which she had only chosen because it was the second volume of his, she gave a great yawn and said, "How pleasant it is to spend an evening in this way! I declare after all there is no enjoyment like reading! How much sooner one tires of anything than of a book! When I have a house of my own, I shall be miserable if I have not an excellent library."

No one made any reply. She then yawned again, threw aside her book, and cast her eyes round the room in quest for some amusement; when hearing her brother mentioning a ball to Miss Bennet, she turned suddenly towards him and said:

"By the bye, Charles, are you really serious in meditating a dance at Netherfield? I would advise you, before you determine on it, to consult the wishes of the present party; I am much mistaken if there are not some among us to whom a ball would be rather a punishment than a pleasure."

"If you mean Darcy," cried her brother, "he may go to bed, if he chooses, before it begins—but as for the ball, it is quite a settled thing; and as soon as Nicholls has made white soup enough, I shall send round my cards."

"I should like balls infinitely better," she replied, "if they were carried on in a different manner; but there is something insufferably tedious in the usual process of such a meeting. It would surely be much more rational if conversation instead of dancing were made the order of the day."

"Much more rational, my dear Caroline, I dare say, but it would not be near so much like a ball."

Miss Bingley made no answer, and soon afterwards she got up and walked about the room. Her figure was elegant, and she walked well; but Darcy, at whom it was all aimed, was still inflexibly studious. In the desperation of her feelings, she resolved on one effort more, and, turning to Elizabeth, said:

"Miss Eliza Bennet, let me persuade you to follow my example, and take a turn about the room. I assure you it is very refreshing after sitting so long in one attitude."

Elizabeth was surprised, but agreed to it immediately. Miss Bingley succeeded no less in the real object of her civility; Mr. Darcy looked up. He was as much awake to the novelty of attention in that quarter as Elizabeth herself could be, and unconsciously closed his book. He was directly invited to join their party, but he declined it, observing that he could imagine but two motives for their choosing to walk up and down the room together, with either of which motives his joining them would interfere. "What could he mean? She was dying to know what could be his meaning?"—and asked Elizabeth whether she could at all understand him?

"Not at all," was her answer; "but depend upon it, he means to be severe on us, and our surest way of disappointing him will be to ask nothing about it."

Miss Bingley, however, was incapable of disappointing Mr. Darcy in anything, and persevered therefore in requiring an explanation of his two motives.

"I have not the smallest objection to explaining them," said he, as soon as she allowed him to speak. "You either choose this method of passing the evening because you are in each other's confidence, and have secret affairs to discuss, or because you are conscious that your figures appear to the greatest advantage in walking; if the first, I would be completely in your way, and if the second, I can admire you much better as I sit by the fire."

"Oh! shocking!" cried Miss Bingley. "I never heard anything so abominable. How shall we punish him for such a speech?"

"Nothing so easy, if you have but the inclination," said Elizabeth. "We can all plague and punish one another. Tease him—laugh at him. Intimate as you are, you must know how it is to be done."

"But upon my honour, I do NOT. I do assure you that my intimacy has not yet taught me THAT. Tease calmness of manner and presence of mind! No, no—feel he may defy us there. And as to laughter, we will not expose ourselves, if you please, by attempting to laugh without a subject. Mr. Darcy may hug himself."

"Mr. Darcy is not to be laughed at!" cried Elizabeth. "That is an uncommon advantage, and uncommon I hope it will continue, for it would be a great loss to ME to have many such acquaintances. I dearly love a laugh."

"Miss Bingley," said he, "has given me more credit than can be. The wisest and the best of men—nay, the wisest and best of their actions—may be rendered ridiculous by a person whose first object in life is a joke."

"Certainly," replied Elizabeth—"there are such people, but I hope I am not one of THEM. I hope I never ridicule what is wise and good. Follies and nonsense, whims and inconsistencies, DO divert me, I own, and I laugh at them whenever I can. But these, I suppose, are precisely what you are without."

"Perhaps that is not possible for anyone. But it has been the study of my life to avoid those weaknesses which often expose a strong understanding to ridicule."

"Such as vanity and pride."

"Yes, vanity is a weakness indeed. But pride—where there is a real superiority of mind, pride will be always under good regulation."

Elizabeth turned away to hide a smile.

"Your examination of Mr. Darcy is over, I presume," said Miss Bingley; "and pray what is the result?"

"I am perfectly convinced by it that Mr. Darcy has no defect. He owns it himself without disguise."

"No," said Darcy, "I have made no such pretension. I have faults enough, but they are not, I hope, of understanding. My temper I dare not vouch for. It is, I believe, too little yielding—certainly too little for the convenience of the world. I cannot forget the follies and vices of other so soon as I ought, nor their offenses against myself. My feelings are not puffed about with every attempt to move them. My temper would perhaps be called resentful. My good opinion once lost, is lost forever."

"THAT is a failing indeed!" cried Elizabeth. "Implacable resentment IS a shade in a character. But you have chosen your fault well. I really cannot LAUGH at it. You are safe from me."

"There is, I believe, in every disposition a tendency to some particular evil—a natural defect, which not even the best education can overcome."

"And YOUR defect is to hate everybody."

"And yours," he replied with a smile, "is willfully to misunderstand them."

"Do let us have a little music," cried Miss Bingley, tired of a conversation in which she had no share. "Louisa, you will not mind my waking Mr. Hurst?"

Her sister had not the smallest objection, and the pianoforte was opened; and Darcy, after a few moments' recollection, was not sorry for it. He began to feel the danger of paying Elizabeth too much attention.

Chapter 12

In consequence of an agreement between the sisters, Elizabeth wrote the next morning to their mother, to beg that the carriage might be sent for them in the course of the day. But Mrs. Bennet, who had calculated on her daughters remaining at Netherfield till the following Tuesday, which would exactly finish Jane's week, could not bring herself to receive them with pleasure before. Her answer, therefore, was not propitious, at least not to Elizabeth's wishes, for she was impatient to get home. Mrs. Bennet sent them word that they could not possibly have the carriage before Tuesday; and in her postscript it was added, that if Mr. Bingley and his sister pressed them to stay longer, she could spare them very well. Against staying longer, however, Elizabeth was positively resolved—nor did she much expect it would be asked; and fearful, on the contrary, as being considered as intruding themselves needlessly long, she urged Jane to borrow Mr. Bingley's carriage immediately, and at length it was settled that their original design of leaving Netherfield that morning should be mentioned, and the request made.

The communication excited many professions of concern; and enough was said of wishing them to stay at least till the following day to work on Jane; and till the morrow their going was deferred. Miss Bingley was then sorry that she had proposed the delay, for her jealousy and dislike of one sister much exceeded her affection for the other.

The master of the house heard with real sorrow that they were to go so soon, and repeatedly tried to persuade Miss Bennet that it would not be safe for her—that she was not enough recovered; but Jane was firm where she felt herself to be right.

To Mr. Darcy it was welcome intelligence—Elizabeth had been at Netherfield long enough. She attracted him more than he liked—and Miss Bingley was uncivil to HER, and more teasing than usual to himself. He wisely resolved to be particularly careful that no sign of admiration should NOW escape him, nothing that could elevate her with the hope of influencing his felicity; sensible that if such an idea had been suggested, his behaviour during the last day must have material weight in confirming or crushing it. Steady to his purpose, he scarcely spoke ten words to her through the whole of Saturday, and though they were at one time left by themselves for half-an-hour, he adhered most conscientiously to his book, and would not even look at her.

On Sunday, after morning service, the separation, so agreeable to almost all, took place. Miss Bingley's civility to Elizabeth increased at last very rapidly, as well as her affection for Jane; and when they parted, after assuring the latter of the pleasure it would always give her to see her either at Longbourn or Netherfield, and embracing her most tenderly, she even shook hands with the former. Elizabeth took leave of the whole party in the liveliest of spirits.

They were not welcomed home very cordially by their mother. Mrs. Bennet wondered at their coming, and thought them very wrong to give so much trouble, and was sure Jane would have caught cold again. But their father, though very laconic in his expressions of pleasure, was really glad to see them; he had felt their importance in the family circle. The evening conversation, when they were all assembled, had lost much of its animation, and almost all its sense by the absence of Jane and Elizabeth.

They found Mary, as usual, deep in the study of thorough-bass and human nature; and had some extracts to admire, and some new observations of threadbare morality to listen to. Catherine and Lydia had information for them of a different sort. Much had been done and much had been said in the regiment since the preceding Wednesday; several of the officers had dined lately with their uncle, a private had been flogged, and it had actually been hinted that colonel Foster was going to be married.

Chapter 13

"I hope, my dear," said Mr. Bennet to his wife, as they were at breakfast the next morning, "that you have ordered a good dinner to-day, because I have reason to expect an addition to our family party."

"Who do you mean, my dear? I know of nobody that is coming, I am sure, unless Charlotte Lucas should happen to call in—And I hope MY dinners are good enough for her. I do not believe she often sees such at home."

"The person of whom I speak is a gentleman, and a stranger."

Mrs. Bennet's eyes sparkled. "A gentleman and a stranger! It is Mr. Bingley, I am sure! Well, I am sure I shall be extremely glad to see Mr. Bingley. But—good Lord! how unlucky! There is not a bit of fish to be got to-day. Lydia, my love, ring the bell—I must speak to Hill this moment."

"It is NOT Mr. Bingley," said her husband; "it is a person whom I never saw in the whole course of my life."

This roused a general astonishment; and he had the pleasure of being eagerly questioned by his wife and his five daughters at once.

After amusing himself some time with their curiosity, he thus explained:

"About a month ago I received this letter; and about a fortnight ago I answered it, for I thought it a case of some delicacy, and requiring early attention. It is from my cousin, Mr. Collins, who, when I am dead, may turn you all out of this house as soon as he pleases."

"Oh! my dear," cried his wife, "I cannot bear to hear that mentioned. Pray do not talk of that odious man. I do think it is the hardest thing in the world, that your estate should be entailed away from your own children; and I am sure, if I had been you, I should have tried long ago to do something or other about it."

Jane and Elizabeth tried to explain to her the nature of an entail. They had often attempted to do it before, but it was a subject on which Mrs. Bennet was beyond the reach of reason, and she continued to rail bitterly against the cruelty of settling and estate away from a family of five daughters, in favour of a man whom nobody cared anything about.

"It certainly is a most iniquitous affair," said Mr. Bennet, "and nothing can clear Mr. collins from the guilt of inheriting Longbourn. But if you will listen to his letter, you may perhaps be a little softened by his manner of expressing himself."

"No, that I am sure I shall not; and I think it is very impertinent of him to write to you at all, and very hypocritical. I hate such false friends. Why could he not keep on quarreling with you, as his father did before him?"

"Why, indeed; he does seem to have had some filial scruples on that head, as you will hear."

"Hunsford, near Westerham, Kent,
"15th October.

"Dear Sir,—

"The disagreement subsisting between yourself and my late honoured father always gave me much uneasiness, and since I have had the misfortune to lose him, I have frequently wished to heal the breach; but for some time I was kept back by my own doubts, fearing lest it might seem disrespectful to his memory for me to be on good terms with anyone with whom it had always pleased him to be at variance,—There, Mrs. Bennet.'—My mind, however, is now made up on the subject, for having received ordination at Easter, I have been so fortunate as to be distinguished by the patronage of the Right Honourable Lady Catherine de Bourgh, widow of Sir Lewis de Bourgh, whose bounty and beneficence has preferred me to the valuable rectory of this parish, where it shall be my earnest endeavour to demean myself with grateful respect towards her Ladyship, and be ever ready to perform those rites and ceremonies which are instituted by the Church of England. As a clergyman, moreover, I feel it my duty to promote and establish the blessing of peace in all families within in the reach of my influence; and on these grounds I flatter myself that my present overtures are highly commendable, and that the circumstance of my being next in the entail of Longbourn estate will be kindly overlooked on your side, and not lead you to reject the offered olive-branch. I cannot otherwise than be concerned at being the means of injuring your amiable daughters, and beg leave to apologise for it, as well as to assure you of my readiness to make them every possible amends—but of this hereafter. If you should have no objection to receive me into your house, I propose myself the satisfaction of waiting on you and your family, Monday, November 18th, by four o'clock, and shall probably trespass on your hospitality till the Saturday se'ennight following, which I can do without any inconvenience, as Lady Catherine is far from objecting to my occasional absence on a Sunday, provided that some other clergyman is engaged to do the duty of the day.—I remain, dear sir, with respectful compliments to your lady and daughters, your well-wisher and friend,

"WILLIAM COLLINS"

"At four o'clock, therefore, we may expect this peace-making gentleman," said Mr. Bennet, as he folded up the letter. "He seems to be a most conscientious and polite young man, upon my word, and I doubt not will prove a valuable acquaintance, especially if Lady Catherine should be so indulgent as to let him come to us again."

"There is some sense in what he says about the girls, however, and if he is disposed to make them any amends, I shall not be the person to discourage him."

"Though it is difficult," said Jane, "to guess in what way he can mean to make us the atonement he thinks our due, the wish is certainly to his credit."

Elizabeth was chiefly struck by his extraordinary deference for Lady Catherine, and his kind intention of christening, marrying, and burying his parishioners whenever it were required.

"He must be an oddity, I think," said she. "I cannot make him out. There is something very pompous in his style. And what can he mean by apologising for being next in the entail? We cannot suppose he would help it if he could. Could he be a sensible man, sir?"

"No, my dear, I think not. I have great hopes of finding him quite the reverse. Thee is a mixture of servility and self-importance in his letter, which promises well. I am impatient to see him."

"In point of composition," said Mary, "the letter does not seem defective. The idea of the olive-branch perhaps is not wholly new, yet I think it is well expressed."

To Catherine and Lydia, neither the letter nor its writer were in any degree interesting. It was next to impossible that their cousin should come in a scarlet coat, and it was now some weeks since they had received pleasure from the society of a man in any other colour. As for their mother, Mr. Collins's letter had done away much of her ill-will, and she was preparing to see him with a degree of composure which astonished her husband and daughters.

Mr. Collins was punctual to his time, and was received with great politeness by the whole family. Mr. Bennet indeed said little; but the ladies were ready enough to talk, and Mr. Collins seemed neither in need of encouragement, nor inclined to be silent himself. He was a tall, heavy-looking young man of five-and-twenty. His air was grave and stately, and his manners were very formal. He had not been long seated before he complimented Mrs. Bennet on having so fine a family of daughters; said he had heard much of their beauty, but that in this instance fame had fallen short of the truth; and added, that he did not doubt her seeing them all in due time disposed of in marriage. This gallantry was not much to the taste of some of his hearers; but Mrs. Bennet, who quarreled with no compliments, answered most readily.

"You are very kind, I am sure; and I wish with all my heart it may prove so, for else they will be destitute enough. Things are settled so oddly."

"You allude, perhaps, to the entail of this estate."

"Ah! sir, I do indeed. It is a grievous affair to my poor girls, you must confess. Not that I mean to find fault with YOU, for such things I know are all chance in this world. There is no knowing how estates will go when once they come to be entailed."

"I am very sensible, madam, of the hardship to my fair cousins, and could say much on the subject, but that I am cautious of appearing forward and precipitate. But I can assure the young ladies that I come prepared to admire them. At present I will not say more; but, perhaps, when we are better acquainted—"

He was interrupted by a summons to dinner; and the girls smiled on each other. They were not the only objects of Mr. Collin's admiration. The hall, the dining-room, and all its furniture, were examined and praised; and his commendation of everything would have touched Mrs. Bennet's heart, but for the mortifying supposition of his viewing it all as his own future property. The dinner too in its turn was highly admired; and he begged to know to which of his fair cousins the excellency of its cooking was owing. But he was set right there by Mrs. Bennet, who assured him with some asperity that they were very well able to keep a good cook, and that her daughters had nothing to do in the kitchen. He begged pardon for having displeased her. In a softened tone she declared herself not at all offended; but he continued to apologise for about a quarter of an hour.

Chapter 14

During dinner, Mr. Bennet scarcely spoke at all; but when the servants were withdrawn, he thought it time to have some conversation with his guest, and therefore started a subject in which he expected him to shine, by observing that he seemed very fortunate in his patroness. Lady Catherine de Bourgh's attention to his wishes, and consideration for his comfort, appeared very remarkable. Mr. Bennet could not have chosen better. Mr. Collins was eloquent in her praise. The subject elevated him to more than usual solemnity of manner, and with a most important aspect he protested that "he had never in his life witnessed such behaviour in a person of rank—such affability and condescension, as he had himself experienced from Lady Catherine. She had been graciously pleased to approve of both of the discourses which he had already had the honour of preaching before her. She had also asked him twice to dine at Rosings, and had sent for him only the Saturday before, to make up her pool of quadrille in the evening. Lady Catherine was reckoned proud by many people he knew, but HE had never seen anything but affability in her. She had always spoken to him as she would to any other gentleman; she made not the smallest objection to his joining in the society of the neighbourhood nor to his leaving the parish occasionally for a week or two, to visit his relations. She had even condescended to advise him to marry as soon as he could, provided he chose with discretion; and had once paid him a visit in his humble parsonage, where she had perfectly approved all the alterations he had been making, and had even vouchsafed to suggest some herself—some shelves in the closet upstairs."

"That is all very proper and civil, I am sure," said Mrs. Bennet, "and I dare say she is a very agreeable woman. It is a pity that great ladies in general are not more like her. Does she live near you, sir?"

"The garden in which stands my humble abode is separated only by a lane from Rosings Park, her ladyship's residence."

"I think you said she was a widow, sir? Has she any family?"

"She has only one daughter, the heiress of Rosings, and of very extensive property."

"Ah!" said Mrs. Bennet, shaking her head, "then she is better off than many girls. And what sort of young lady is she? Is she handsome?"

"She is a most charming young lady indeed. Lady Catherine herself says that, in point of true beauty, Miss de Bourgh is far superior to the handsomest of her sex, because there is that in her features which marks the young lady of distinguished birth. She is unfortunately of a sickly constitution, which has prevented her from making that progress in many accomplishments which she could not have otherwise failed of, as I am informed by the lady who superintended her education, and who still resides with them. But she is perfectly amiable, and often condescends to drive by my humble abode in her little phaeton and ponies."

"Has she been presented? I do not remember her name among the ladies at court."

"Her indifferent state of health unhappily prevents her being in town; and by that means, as I told Lady Catherine one day, has deprived the British court of its brightest ornaments. Her ladyship seemed pleased with the idea; and you may imagine that I am happy on every occasion to offer those little delicate compliments which are always acceptable to ladies. I have more than once observed to Lady Catherine, that her charming daughter seemed born to be a duchess, and that the most elevated rank, instead of giving her consequence, would be adorned by her. These are the kind of little things which please her ladyship, and it is a sort of attention which I conceive myself peculiarly bound to pay."

"You judge very properly," said Mr. Bennet, "and it is happy for you that you possess the talent of flattering with delicacy. May I ask whether these pleasing attentions proceed from the impulse of the moment, or are the result of previous study?"

"They arise chiefly from what is passing at the time, and though I sometimes amuse myself with suggesting and arranging such little elegant compliments as may be adapted to ordinary occasions, I always wish to give them as unstudied an air as possible."

Mr. Bennet's expectations were fully answered. His cousin was as absurd as he had hoped, and he listened to him with the keenest enjoyment, maintaining at the same time the most resolute composure of countenance, and, except in an occasional glance at Elizabeth, requiring no partner in his pleasure.

By tea-time, however, the dose had been enough, and Mr. Bennet was glad to take his guest into the drawing-room again, and, when tea was over, glad to invite him to read aloud to the ladies. Mr. Collins readily assented, and a book was produced; but, on beholding it (for everything announced it to be from a circulating library), he started back, and begging pardon, protested that he never read novels. Kitty stared at him, and Lydia exclaimed. Other books were produced, and after some deliberation he chose Fordyce's Sermons. Lydia gaped as he opened the volume, and before he had, with very monotonous solemnity, read three pages, she interrupted him with:

"Do you know, mamma, that my uncle Phillips talks of turning away Richard; and if he does, Colonel Forster will hire him. My aunt told me so herself on Saturday. I shall walk to Meryton to-morrow to hear more about it, and to ask when Mr. Denny comes back from town."

Lydia was bid by her two eldest sisters to hold her tongue; but Mr. Collins, much offended, laid aside his book, and said:

"I have often observed how little young ladies are interested by books of a serious stamp, though written solely for their benefit. It amazes me, I confess; for, certainly, there can be nothing so advantageous to them as instruction. But I will no longer importune my young cousin."

Then turning to Mr. Bennet, he offered himself as his antagonist at backgammon. Mr. Bennet accepted the challenge, observing that he acted very wisely in leaving the girls to their own trifling amusements. Mrs. Bennet and her daughters apologised most civilly for Lydia's interruption, and promised that it should not occur again, if he would resume his book; but Mr. Collins, after assuring them that he bore his young cousin no ill-will, and should never resent her behaviour as any affront, seated himself at another table with Mr. Bennet, and prepared for backgammon.

Chapter 15

Mr. Collins was not a sensible man, and the deficiency of nature had been but littleassisted by education or society; the greatest part of his life having been spent under the guidance of an illiterate and miserly father; and though he belonged to one of the universities, he had merely kept the necessary terms, without forming at it any useful acquaintance. The subjection in which his father had brought him up had given him originally great humility of manner; but it was now a good deal counteracted by the self-conceit of a weak head, living in retirement, and the consequential feelings of early and unexpected prosperity. A fortunate chance had recommended him to Lady Catherine de Bourgh when the living of Hunsford was vacant; and the respect which he felt for her high rank, and his veneration for her as his patroness, mingling with a very good opinion of himself, of his authority as a clergyman, and his right as a rector, made him altogether a mixture of pride and obsequiousness, self-importance and humility.

Having now a good house and a very sufficient income, he intended to marry; and in seeking a reconciliation with the Longbourn family he had a wife in view, as he meant to choose one of the daughters, if he found them as handsome and amiable as they were represented by common report. This was his plan off amends—of atonement—for inheriting their father's estate; and he thought it an excellent one, full of eligibility and suitableness, and excessively generous and disinterested on his own part.

His plan did not vary on seeing them. Miss Bennet's lovely face confirmed his views, and established all his strictest notions of what was due to seniority; and for the first evening SHE was his settled choice. The next morning, however, made an alteration; for in a quarter of an hour's tete-a-tete with Mrs. Bennet before breakfast, a conversation beginning with his parsonage-house, and leading naturally to the avowal of his hopes, that a mistress might be found for it at Longbourn, produced from her, amid very complaisant smiles and general encouragement, a caution against the very Jane he had fixed on. "As to her YOUNGER daughters, she could not take upon her to say—she could not positively answer—but she did not KNOW of any prepossession; her ELDEST daughter, she must just mention—she felt it incumbent on her to hint, was likely to be very soon engaged."

Mr. Collins had only to change from Jane to Elizabeth—and it was soon done—done while Mrs. Bennet was stirring the fire. Elizabeth, equally next to Jane in birth and beauty, succeeded her of course.

Mrs. Bennet treasured up the hint, and trusted that she might soon have two daughters married; and the man whom she could not bear to speak of the day before was now high in her good graces.

Lydia's intention of walking to Meryton was not forgotten; every sister except Mary agreed to go with her; and Mr. Collins was to attend them, at the request of Mr. Bennet, who was most anxious to get rid of him, and have his library to himself; for thither Mr. Collins had followed him after breakfast; and there he would continue, nominally engaged with one of the largest folios in the collection, but really talking to Mr. Bennet, with little cessation, of his house and garden at Hunsford. Such doings discomposed Mr. Bennet exceedingly. In his library he had been always sure of leisure and tranquillity; and though prepared, as he told Elizabeth, to meet with folly and conceit in every other room of the house, he was used to be free from them there; his civility, therefore, was most prompt in inviting Mr. Collins to join his daughters in their walk; and Mr. Collins, being in fact much better fitted for a walker than a reader, was extremely pleased to close his large book, and go.

In pompous nothings on his side, and civil assents on that of his cousins, their time passed till they entered Meryton. The attention of the younger ones was then no longer to be gained by him. Their eyes were immediately wandering up in the street in quest of the officers, and nothing less than a very smart bonnet indeed, or a really new muslin in a shop window, could recall them.

But the attention of every lady was soon caught by a young man, whom they had never seen before, of most gentlemanlike appearance, walking with another officer on the other side of the way. The officer was the very Mr. Denny concerning whose return from London Lydia came to inquire, and he bowed as they passed. All were struck with the stranger's air, all wondered who he could be; and Kitty and Lydia, determined if possible to find out, led the way across the street, under pretense of wanting something in an opposite shop, and fortunately had just gained the pavement when the two gentlemen, turning back, had reached the same spot. Mr. Denny addressed them directly, and entreated permission to introduce his friend, Mr. Wickham, who had returned with him the day before from town, and he was happy to say had accepted a commission in their corps. This was exactly as it should be; for the young man wanted only regimentals to make him completely charming. His appearance was greatly in his favour; he had all the best part of beauty, a fine countenance, a good figure, and very pleasing address. The introduction was followed up on his side by a happy readiness of conversation—a readiness at the same time perfectly correct and unassuming; and the whole party were still standing and talking together very agreeably, when the sound of horses drew their notice, and Darcy and Bingley were seen riding down the street. On distinguishing the ladies of the group, the two gentlemen came directly towards them, and began the usual civilities. Bingley was the principal spokesman, and Miss Bennet the principal object. He was then, he said, on his way to Longbourn on purpose to inquire after her. Mr. Darcy corroborated it with a bow, an was beginning to determine not to fix his eyes on Elizabeth, when they were suddenly arrested by the sight of the stranger, and Elizabeth happening to see the countenance of both as they looked at each other, was all astonishment at the effect of the meeting. Both changed colour, one looked white, the other red. Mr. Wickham, after a few moments, touched his hat—a salutation which Mr. Darcy just deigned to return. What could be the meaning of it? It was impossible to imagine; it was impossible not to long to know.

In another minute, Mr. Bingley, but without seeming to have noticed what passed, took leave and rode on with his friend.

Mr. Denny and Mr. Wickham walked with the young ladies to the door of Mr. Phillip's house, and then made their bows, in spite of Miss Lydia's pressing entreaties that they should come in, and even in spite of Mrs. Phillips throwing up the parlour window and loudly seconding the invitation.

Mrs. Phillips was always glad to see her nieces; and the two eldest, from their recent absence, were particularly welcome, and she was eagerly expressing her surprise at their sudden return home, which, as their own carriage had not fetched them, she should have known nothing about, if she had not happened to see Mr. Jones's shop-boy in the street, who had told her that they were not to send any more draughts to Netherfield because the Miss Bennets were come away, when her civility was claimed towards Mr. Collins by Jane's introduction of him. She received him with her very best politeness, which he returned with as much more, apologising for his intrusion, without any previous acquaintance with her, which he could not help flattering himself, however, might be justified by his relationship to the young ladies who introduced him to her notice. Mrs. Phillips was quite awed by such an excess of good breeding; but her contemplation of one stranger was soon put to an end by exclamations and inquiries about the other; of whom, however, she could only tell her nieces what they already knew, that Mr. Denny had brought him from London, and that he was to have a lieutenant's commission in the ______shire. She had been watching him the last hour, she said, as he walked up and down the street, and had Mr. Wickham appeared, Kitty and Lydia would certainly have continued the occupation, but unluckily no one passed windows now except a few of the officers, who, in comparison with the stranger, were become "stupid, disagreeable fellows." Some of them were to dine with the Phillipses the next day, and their aunt promised to make her husband call on Mr. Wickham, and give him an invitation also, if the family from Longbourn would come in the evening. This was agreed to, and Mrs. Phillips protested that they would have a nice comfortable noisy game of lottery tickets, and a little bit of hot supper afterwards. The prospect of such delights was very cheering, and they parted in mutual good spirits. Mr. Collins repeated his apologies in quitting the room, and was assured with unwearying civility that they were perfectly needless.

As they walked home, Elizabeth related to Jane what she had seen pass between the two gentlemen; but though Jane would have defended either or both, had they appeared to be in the wrong, she could no more explain such behaviour than her sister.

Mr. Collins on his return highly gratified Mrs. Bennet by admiring Mrs' Phillips's manners and politeness. He protested that, except Lady Catherine and her daughter, he had never seen a more elegant woman; for she had not only received him with the utmost civility, but even pointedly included him in her invitation for the next evening, although utterly unknown to her before. Something, he supposed, might be attributed to his connection with them, but yet he had never met with so much attention in the whole course of his life.

Chapter 16

As no objection was made to the young people's engagement with their aunt, and all Mr. Collins's scruples of leaving Mr. and Mrs. Bennet for a single evening during his visit were most steadily resisted, the coach conveyed him and his five cousins at a suitable hour to Meryton; and the girls had the pleasure of hearing, as they entered the drawing-room, that Mr. Wickham had accepted their uncle's invitation, and was then in the house.

When this information was given, and they had all taken their seats, Mr. collins was at leisure to look around him and admire, and he was so much struck with the size and furniture of the apartment, that he declared he might almost have supposed himself in the small summer breakfast parlour at Rosings; a comparison that did not at first convey much gratification; but when Mrs. Phillips understood from him what Rosings was, and who was its proprietor—when she had listened to the description of only one of Lady Catherine's drawing-rooms, and found that the chimney-piece alone had cost eight hundred pounds, she felt all the force of the compliment, and would hardly have resented a comparison with the housekeeper's room.

In describing to her all the grandeur of Lady Catherine and her mansion, with occasional digressions in praise of his own humble abode, and the improvements it was receiving, he was happily employed until the gentlemen joined them; and he found in Mrs. Phillips a very attentive listener, whose opinion of his consequence increased with what she heard, and who was resolving to retail it all among her neighbours as soon as she could. To the girls, who could not listen to their cousin, and who had nothing to do but to wish for an instrument, and examine their own indifferent imitations of china on the mantelpiece, the interval of waiting appeared very long. It was over at last, however. The gentlemen did approach, and when Mr. Wickham walked into the room, Elizabeth felt that she had neither been seeing him before, nor thinking of him since, with the smallest degree of unreasonable admiration. The officers of the ______shire were in general a very creditable, gentlemanlike set, and the best of them were of the present party; but Mr. Wickham was as far beyond them all in person, countenance, air, and walk, as THEY were superior to the broad-faced, stuffy uncle Phillips, breathing port wine, who followed them into the room.

Mr. Wickham was the happy man towards whom almost every female eye was turned, and Elizabeth was the happy woman by whom he finally seated himself; and the agreeable manner in which he immediately fell into conversation, though it was only on its being a wet night, made her feel that the commonest, dullest, most threadbare topic might be rendered interesting by the skill of the speaker.

With such rivals for the notice of the fair as Mr. Wickham and the officers, Mr. Collins seemed to sink into insignificance; to the young ladies he certainly was nothing; but he had still at intervals a kind listener in Mrs. Phillips, and was by her watchfulness, most abundantly supplied with coffee and muffin. When the card-tables were placed, he had the opportunity of obliging her in turn, by sitting down to whist.

"I know little of the game at present," said he, "but I shall be glad to improve myself, for in my situation in life—"Mrs. Phillips was very glad for his compliance, but could not wait for his reason.

Mr. Wickham did not play at whist, and with ready delight was he received at the other table between Elizabeth and Lydia. At first there seemed danger of Lydia's engrossing him entirely, for she was a most determined talked; but being likewise extremely fond of lottery tickets, she soon grew too much interested in the game, too eager in making bets and exclaiming after prizes to have attention for anyone in particular. Allowing for the common demands of the game, Mr. Wickham was therefore at leisure to talk to Elizabeth, and she was very willing to hear him, though what she chiefly wished to hear she could not hope to be told—the history of his acquaintance with Mr. Darcy. She dared not even mention that gentleman. Her curiosity, however, was unexpectedly relieved. Mr. Wickham began the subject himself. He inquired how far Netherfield was from Meryton; and, after receiving her answer, asked in a hesitating manner how long Mr. Darcy had been staying there.

"About a month," said Elizabeth; and then, unwilling to let the subject drop, added, "he is a man of very large property in Derbyshire, I understand."

"Yes," replied Mr. Wickham; "his estate there is a noble one. A clear ten thousand per annum. You could not have met with a person more capable of giving you certain information on that head than myself, for I have been connected with his family in a particular manner from my infancy."

Elizabeth could not but look surprised.

"You may well be surprised, Miss Bennet, at such an assertion, after seeing, as you probably might, the very cold manner of our meeting yesterday. Are you much acquainted with Mr. Darcy?"

"As much as I ever wish to be," cried Elizabeth very warmly. "I have spent four days in the same house with him, and I think him very disagreeable."

"I have no right to give MY opinion," said Wickham, "as to his being agreeable or otherwise. I am not qualified to form one. I have known him too long and too well to be a fair judge. It is impossible for ME to be impartial. But I believe your opinion of him would in general astonish—and perhaps you would not express it quite so strongly anywhere else. Here you are in your own family."

"Upon my word, I say no more HERE than I might say in any house in the neighbourhood, except Netherfield. He is not at all liked in Hertfordshire. Everybody is disgusted with his pride. You will not find him more favourably spoken of by any one."

"I cannot pretend to be sorry," said Wickham, after a short interruption, "that he or that any man should not be estimated beyond their deserts; but with HIM I believe it does not often happen. The world is blinded by his fortune and consequence, or frightened by his high and imposing manners, and sees him only as he chooses to be seen."

I should take him, even on MY slight acquaintance, to be an ill-tempered man." Wickham shook his head.

"I wonder," said he, at the next opportunity of speaking, "whether he is likely to be in this country much longer."

"I do not at all know; but I HEARD nothing of his going away when I was at Netherfield. I hope your plans in favour of the ______shire will not be affected by his being in the neighbourhood."

"Oh! no—it is not for ME to be driven away by Mr. Darcy. If HE wishes to avoid seeing ME, he must go. We are not on friendly terms, and it always gives me pain to meet him, but I have no reason for avoiding HIM but what I might proclaim before all the world, a sense of very great ill-usage, and most painful regrets at his being what he is. His father, Miss Bennet, the late Mr. Darcy, was one of the best men that ever breathed, and the truest friend I ever had; and I can never be in company with this Mr. Darcy without being grieved to the soul by a thousand tender recollections. His behaviour to myself has been scandalous; but I verily believe I could forgive him anything and everything, rather than his disappointing the hopes and disgracing the memory of his father."

Elizabeth found the interest of the subject increase, and listened with all her heart; but the delicacy of it prevented further inquiry.

Mr. Wickham began to speak on more general topics, Meryton, the neighbourhood, the society, appearing highly pleased with all that he had yet seen, and speaking of the latter with gentle but very intelligible gallantry.

"It was the prospect of constant society, and good society," he added, "which was my chief inducement to enter the ______shire. I knew it to be a most respectable, agreeable corps, and my friend Denny tempted me further by his account of their present quarters, and the very great attentions and excellent acquaintances Meryton had procured them. Society, I own, is necessary to me. I have been a disappointed man, and my spirits will not bear solitude. I MUST have employment and society. A military life is not what I was intended for, but circumstances have now made it eligible. The church OUGHT to have been my profession—I was brought up for the church, and I should at this time have been in possession of a most valuable living, had it pleased the gentleman we were speaking of just now."

"Indeed!"

"Yes—the late Mr. Darcy bequeathed me the next presentation of the best living in his gift. He was my godfather, and excessively attached to me. I cannot do justice to his kindness. He meant to provide for me amply, and thought he had done it; but when the living fell, it was given elsewhere."

"Good heavens!" cried Elizabeth; "but how could THAT be? How could his will be disregarded? Why did you not seek legal redress?"

"There was just such an informality in the terms of the bequest as to give me no hope from law. A man of honour could not have doubted the intention, but Mr. Darcy chose to doubt it—or to treat it as a merely conditional recommendation, and to assert that I had forfeited all claim to it by extravagance, imprudence—in short anything or nothing. Certain it is, that the living became vacant two years ago, exactly as I was of an age to hold it, and that it was given to another man; and no less certain is it, that I cannot accuse myself of having really done anything to deserve to lose it. I have a warm, unguarded temper, and I may have spoken my opinion OF him, and TO him, too freely. I can recall nothing worse. But the fact is, that we are very different sort of men, and that he hates me."

"This is quite shocking! He deserves to be publicly disgraced."

"Some time or other he WILL be—but it shall not be by ME. Till I can forget his father, I can never defy or expose HIM."

Elizabeth honoured him for such feelings, and thought him handsomer than ever as he expressed them.

"But what," said she, after a pause, "can have been his motive? What can have induced him to behave so cruelly?"

"A thorough, determined dislike of me—a dislike which I cannot but attribute in some measure to jealousy. Had the late Mr. Darcy liked me less, his son might have borne with me better; but his father's uncommon attachment to me irritated him, I believe, very early in life. He had not a temper to bear the sort of competition in which we stood—the sort of preference which was often given me."

"I had not thought Mr. Darcy so bad as this—though I have never liked him. I had not thought so very ill of him. I had supposed him to be despising his fellow-creatures in general, but did not suspect him of descending to such malicious revenge, such injustice, such inhumanity as this."

After a few minutes' reflection, however, she continued, "I DO remember his boasting one day, at Netherfield, of the implacability of his resentments, of his having an unforgiving temper. His disposition must be dreadful."

"I will not trust myself on the subject," replied Wickham; "I can hardly be just to him."

Elizabeth was again deep in thought, and after a time exclaimed, "to treat in such a manner the godson, the friend, the favorite of his father!" She could have added, "a young man, too, like YOU, whose very countenance may vouch for your being amiable"—but she contented herself with, "and one, too, who had probably been his companion from childhood, connected together, as I think you said, in the closest manner!"

"We were born in the same parish, within the same park; the greatest part of our youth was passed together; inmates of the same house, sharing the same amusements, objects of the same parental care. MY father began life in the profession which your uncle, Mr. Phillips, appears to do so much credit to—but he gave up everything to be of use to the late Mr. Darcy and devoted all his time to the care of the Pemberley property. He was most highly esteemed by Mr. Darcy, a most intimate, confidential friend. Mr. Darcy often acknowledged himself to be under the greatest obligations to my father's active superintendence, and when, immediately before my father's death, Mr. Darcy gave him a voluntary promise of providing for me, I am convinced that he felt it to be as much a debt of gratitude to HIM, as of his affection to myself."

"How strange!" cried Elizabeth. "How abominable! I wonder that the very pride of this Mr. Darcy has not made him just to you! If from no better motive, that he should not have been too proud to be dishonest—for dishonesty I must call it."

"It IS wonderful," replied Wickham, "for almost all his actions may be traced to pride; and pride had often been his best friend. It has connected him nearer with virtue than with any other feeling. But we are none of us consistent, and in his behaviour to me there were stronger impulses even than pride."

"Can such abominable pride as his have ever done him good?"

"Yes. It has often led him to be liberal and generous, to give his money freely, to display hospitality, to assist his tenants, and relieve the poor. Family pride, and FILIAL pride—for he is very proud of what his father was—have done this. Not to appear to disgrace his family, to degenerate from the popular qualities, or lose the influence of the Pemberley House, is a powerful motive. He has also BROTHERLY pride, which, with SOME brotherly affection, makes him a very kind and careful guardian of his sister, and you will hear him generally cried up as the most attentive and best of brothers."

"What sort of girl is Miss Darcy?"

He shook his head. "I wish I could call her amiable. It gives me pain to speak ill of a Darcy. But she is too much like her brother—very, very proud. As a child, she was affectionate and pleasing, and extremely fond of me; and I have devoted hours and hours to her amusement. But she is nothing to me now. She is a handsome girl, about fifteen or sixteen, and, I understand, highly accomplished. Since her father's death, her home has been London, where a lady lives with her, and superintends her education."

After many pauses and many trials of other subjects, Elizabeth could not help reverting once more to the first, and saying:

"I am astonished at his intimacy with Mr. Bingley! How can Mr. Bingley, who seems good humour itself, and is, I really believe, truly amiable, be in friendship with such a man? How can they suit each other? Do you know Mr. Bingley?"

"Not at all."

"He is a sweet-tempered, amiable, charming man. He cannot know what Mr. Darcy is."

"Probably not; but Mr. Darcy can please where he chooses. He does not want abilities. He can be a conversible companion if he thinks it worth his while. Among those who are at all his equals in consequence, he is a very different man from what he is to the less prosperous. His pride never deserts him; but with the rich he is liberal-minded, just, sincere, rational, honourable, and perhaps agreeable—allowing something for fortune and figure."

The whist party soon afterwards breaking up, the players gathered round the other table and Mr. Collins took his station between his cousin Elizabeth and Mrs. Phillips. The usual inquiries as to his success was made by the latter. It had not been very great; he had lost every point; but when Mrs. Phillips began to express her concern thereupon, he assured her with much earnest gravity that it was not of the least importance, that he considered the money as a mere trifle, and begged that she would not make herself uneasy.

I know very well, madam," said he, "that when persons sit down to a card table, they must take their chances of these things, and happily I am not in such circumstances as to make five shillings any object. There are undoubtedly many who could not say the same, but thanks to Lady Catherine de Bourgh, I am removed far beyond the necessity of regarding little matters."

Mr. Wickham's attention was caught; and after observing Mr,. Collins for a few moments, he asked Elizabeth in a low voice whether her relation was very intimately acquainted with the family of de Bourgh.

"Lady Catherine de Bourgh," she replied, "has very lately given him a living. I hardly know how Mr. Collins was first introduced to her notice, but he certainly has not known her long."

"You know of course that Lady Catherine de Bourgh and Lady Anne Darcy were sisters; consequently that she is aunt to the present Mr. Darcy."

"No, indeed, I did not. I knew nothing at all of Lady Catherine's connections. I never heard of her existence till the day before yesterday."

"Her daughter, Miss de Bourgh, will have a very large fortune, and it is believed that she and her cousin will unite the two estates."

This information made Elizabeth smile, as she thought of poor Miss Bingley. Vain indęed must be all her attentions, vain and useless her affection for his sister and her praise of himself, if he were already self-destined for another.

"Mr. Collins," siad she, "speaks highly both of Lady Catherine and her daughter; but from some particulars that he has related of her ladyship, I suspect his gratitude misleads him, and that in spite of her being his patroness, she is an arrogant, conceited woman."

"I believe her to be both in a great degree," replied Wickham; "I have not seen her for many years, but I very well remember that I never liked her, and that her manners were dictatorial and insolent. She has the reputation of being remarkably sensible and clever; but I rather believe she derives part of her abilities from her rank and fortune, part from her authoritative manner, and the rest from the pride for her nephew, who chooses that every one connected with him should have an understanding of the first class."

Elizabeth allowed that he had given a very rational account of it, and they continued talking together, with mutual satisfaction till supper put an end to cards, and gave the rest of the ladies their share of Mr. Wickham's attentions. There could be no conversation in the noise of

Mrs. Phillips' supper party, but his manners recommended him to everybody. Whatever he said, was said well; and whatever he did, done gracefully. Elizabeth went away with her head full of him. She could think of nothing but of Mr. Wickham, and of what he had told her, all the way home; but there was not time for her even to mention his name as they went, for neither Lydia nor Mr. Collins were once silent. Lydia talked incessantly of lottery tickets, of the fish she had lost and the fish she had won; and Mr. Collins in describing the civility of Mr. and Mrs. Phillips, protesting that he did not in the least regard his losses at whist, enumerating all the dishes at supper, and repeatedly fearing that he crowded his cousins, had more to say than he could well manage before the carriage stopped at Longbourn House.

Chapter 17

Elizabeth related to Jane the next day what had passed between Mr. Wickham and herself. Jane listened with astonishment and concern; she knew not how to believe that Mr. Darcy could be so unworthy of Mr. Bingley's regard; and yet, it was not in her nature to question the veracity of a young man of such amiable appearance as Wickham. The possibility of his having endured such unkindness, was enough to interest all her tender feelings; and nothing remained therefore to be done, but to think well of them both, to defend the conduct of each, and throw into the account of accident or mistake whatever could not be otherwise explained.

"They have both," said she, "been deceived, I dare say, in some way or other, pf which we can form no idea. Interested people have perhaps misrepresented each to the other. It is, in short, impossible for us to conjecture the causes or circumstances which may have alienated them, without actual blame on either side."

"Very true, indeed; and now, my dear Jane, what have you got to say on behalf of the interested people who have probably been concerned in the business? Do clear THEM too, or we shall be obliged to think ill of somebody?"

"Laugh as much as you choose, but you will not laugh me out of my opinion. My dearest Lizzy, do but consider in what a disgraceful light it places Mr. Darcy, to be treating his father's favourite in such a manner, one whom his father had promised to provide for. It is impossible. No man of common humanity, no man who had any value for his character, could be capable of it. Can his most intimate friends be so excessively deceived in him? Oh! no."

"I can much more easily believe Mr. Bingley's being imposed on, than that Mr. Wickham should invent such a history of himself as he gave me last night; names, facts, everything mentioned without ceremony. If it be not so, let Mr. Darcy contradict it. Besides, there was truth in his looks."

"It is difficult indeed—it is distressing. One does not know what to think."

"I beg your pardon; one knows exactly what to think."

But Jane could think with certainty on only one point—that Mr. Bingley, if he HAD been imposed on, would have much to suffer when the affair became public.

The two young ladies were summoned from the shrubbery, where this conversation passed, by the arrival of the very persons of whom they had been speaking; Mr. Bingley and his sisters came to give their personal invitation for the long-expected ball at Netherfield, which was fixed for the following Tuesday. The two ladies were delighted to see their dear friend again, called it an age since they had met, and repeatedly asked what she had been doing with herself since their separation. To the rest of the family they paid little attention; avoiding Mrs. Bennet as much as possible, saying not much to Elizabeth, and nothing at all to the others. They were soon gone again, rising from their seats with an activity which took their brother by surprise, and hurrying off as if eager to escape from Mrs. Bennet's civilities.

The prospect of the Netherfield ball was extremely agreeable to every female of the family. Mrs. Bennet chose to consider it as given in compliment to her eldest daughter, and was particularly flattered by receiving the invitation from Mr. Bingley himself, instead of a ceremonious card. Jane pictured to herself a happy evening in the society of her two friends, and the attentions of her brother; and Elizabeth thought with pleasure of dancing a great deal with Mr. Wickham, and of seeing a confirmation of everything in Mr. Darcy's look and behavior. The happiness anticipated by Catherine and Lydia depended less on any single event, or any particular person, for though they each, like Elizabeth, meant to dance half the evening with Mr. Wickham, he was be no means the only partner who could satisfy them, and a ball was, at any rate, a ball. And even Mary could assure her family that she had no disinclination for it.

"While I can have my mornings to myself," said she, "it is enough—I think it is no sacrifice to join occasionally in evening engagements. Society has claims on us all; and I profess myself one of hose who consider intervals of recreation and amusement as desirable for everybody."

Elizabeth's spirits were so high on this occasion, that though she did not often speak unnecessarily to Mr. Collins, she could not help asking him whether he intended to accept Mr. Bingley's invitation, and if he did, whether he would think it proper to join in the evening's amusement; and she was rather surprised to find that he entertained no scruple whatever on that head, and was very far from dreading a rebuke either from the Archbishop, or Lady Catherine de Bourgh, by venturing to dance.

"I am by no means of the opinion, I assure you," said he, "that a ball of this kind, given by a young man of character, to respectable people, can have any evil tendency; and I am so far from objecting to dancing myself, that I shall hope to be honoured with the hands of all my fair cousins in the course of the evening; and I take this opportunity of soliciting yours, Miss Elizabeth, for the two first dances especially, a preference which I trust my cousin Jane will attribute to the right cause, and not to any disrespect for her."

Elizabeth felt herself completely taken in. She had fully proposed being engaged by Mr. Wickham for those very dances; and to have Mr. Collins instead! her liveliness had never been worse times. There was no help for it, however. Mr. Wickham's happiness and her own were perforce delayed a little longer, and Mr. Collins' proposal accepted with as good a grace as she could. She was not better the pleased with his gallantry from the idea it suggested of something more. It now first struck her, that SHE was selected from among her sisters as worthy of being mistress of Hunsford Parsonage, and of assisting to form a quadrille table at Rosings, in the absence of more eligible visitors. The idea soon reached to conviction, as she observed his increasing civilities toward herself, and heard his frequent attempt at a compliment on her wit and vivacity; and though more astonished than gratified herself by this effect of her charms, it was not long before her mother gave her to understand that the probability of their marriage was extremely agreeable to HER. Elizabeth, however, did not choose to take the hint, being well aware that a serious dispute must be the consequence of any reply. Mr. Collins might never make the offer, and, till he did, it was useless to quarrel about him.

If there had not been a Netherfield ball to prepare for and talk of, the younger Miss Bennets would have been in a very pitiable state at this time, for form the day of the invitation, to the day of the ball, there was such a succession of rain as prevented their walking to Meryton once. No aunt, no officers, no news could be sought after—the very shoe-roses for Netherfield were got by proxy. Even Elizabeth might have found some trial of her patience in weather which totally suspended the improvement of her acquaintance with Mr. Wickham; and nothing less than a dance on Tuesday, could have made such a Friday, Saturday, Sunday, and Monday endurable to Kitty and Lydia.

Chapter 18

Till Elizabeth entered the drawing-room at Netherfield, and looked in vain for Mr. Wickham among the cluster of red coats there assembled, a doubt of his being present had never occurred to her. The certainty of meeting him had not been checked by any of those recollections that might not unreasonably have alarmed her. She had dressed with more than usual care, and prepared in the highest spirits for the conquest of all that remained unsubdued of his heart, trusting that it was not more than might be won in the course of the evening. But in an instant arose the dreadful suspicion of his being purposely omitted for Mr. Darcy's pleasure in the Bingleys' invitation to the officers; and though this was not exactly the case, the absolute fact of his absence was pronounced by his friend Denny, to whom Lydia eagerly applied, and who told them that Wickham had been obliged to go to town on business the day before, and was not yet returned; adding, with a significant smile, "I do not imagine his business would have called him away just now, if he had not wanted to avoid a certain gentleman here."

This part of his intelligence, though unheard by Lydia, was caught by Elizabeth, and, as it assured her that Darcy was not less answerable for Wickham's absence than if her first surmise had been just, every feeling of displeasure against the former was so sharpened by immediate disappointment, that she could hardly reply with tolerable civility to the polite inquiries which he directly afterwards approached to make. Attendance, forbearance, patience with Darcy, was injury to Wickham. She was resolved against any sort of conversation with him, and turned away with a degree of ill-humour which she could not wholly surmount even in speaking to Mr. Bingley, whose blind partiality provoked her.

But Elizabeth was not formed for ill-humour; and though every prospect of her own was destroyed for the evening, it could not dwell long on her spirits; and having told all her griefs to Charlotte Lucas, whom she had not seen for a week, she was soon able to make a voluntary transition to the oddities of her cousin, and to point him out to her particular notice. The first two dances, however, brought a return of distress; they were dances of mortification. Mr. Collins, awkward and solemn, apologising instead of attending, and often moving wrong without being aware of it, gave her all the shame and misery which disagreeable partner for a couple of dances can give. The moment of her release from him was ecstasy.

She danced next with an officer, and had the refreshment of talking of Wickham, and of hearing that he was universally liked. When those dances were over, she returned to Charlotte Lucas, and was in conversation with her, when she found herself suddenly addressed by Mr. Darcy who took her so much by surprise in his application for her hand, that, without knowing what she did, she accepted him. He walked away again immediately, and she was left to fret over her own want of presence of mind; Charlotte tried to console her:

"I dare say you will find him very agreeable."

"Heaven forbid! THAT would be the greatest misfortune of all! To find a man agreeable whom on is determined to hate! Do not wish me such an evil."

When the dancing recommenced, however, and Darcy approached to claim her hand, Charlotte could not help cautioning her in a whisper, not to be a simpleton, and allow her fancy for Wickham to make her appear unpleasant in the eyes of a man ten times his consequence. Elizabeth made no answer, and took her place in the set, amazed at the dignity to which she was arrived in being allowed to stand opposite to Mr. Darcy, and reading in her neighbours' looks, their equal amazement in beholding it. They stood for some time without speaking a word; and she began to imagine that their silence was to last through the two dances, and at first was resolved not to break it; till suddenly fancying that it would be the greater punishment to her partner to oblige him to talk, she made some slight observation on the dance. He replied, and was again silent. After a pause of some minutes, she addressed him a second time with:—"It is YOUR turn to say something now, Mr. Darcy.

I talked about the dance, and YOU ought to make some sort of remark on the size of the room, or the number of couples."

He smiled, and assured her that whatever she wished him to say should be said.

"Very well. That reply will do for the present. Perhaps by and by I may observe that private balls are much pleasanter than public ones. But NOW we may be silent."

"Do you talk by rule, then, while you are dancing?"

"Sometimes. One must speak a little, you know. It would look odd to be entirely silent for half an hour together; and yet for the advantage of SOME, conversation ought to be so arranged, as that they may have the trouble of saying as little as possible."

"Are you consulting your own feelings in the present case, or do you imagine that you are gratifying mine?"

"Both," replied Elizabeth archly; "for I have always seen a great similarity in the turn of our minds. We are each of an unsocial, taciturn disposition, unwilling to speak, unless we expect to say something that will amaze the whole room, and be handed down to posterity with all the eclat of a proverb."

"This is no very striking resemblance of your own character, I am sure," said he. "How near it may be to MINE, I cannot pretend to say. YOU think it a faithful portrait undoubtedly."

"I must not decide on my own performance."

He made no answer, and they were again silent till they had gone down the dance, when he asked her if she and her sisters did not very often walk to Meryton? She answered in the affirmative, and, unable to resist the temptation, added, "When you met us there the other day, we had just been forming a new acquaintance."

The effect was immediate. A deeper shade of hauteur overspread his features, but he said not a word, and Elizabeth, though blaming herself for her own weakness, could not go on. At length Darcy spoke, and in a constrained manner said, "Mr. Wickham is blessed with such happy manners as may ensure his MAKING friends—whether he may be equally capable of RETAINING them, is less certain."

"He has been so unlucky as to lose YOUR friendship," replied Elizabeth with emphasis, "and in a manner which he is likely to suffer from all his life."

Darcy made no answer, and seemed desirous of changing the subject. At that moment, Sir William Lucas appeared close to them, meaning to pass through the set to the other side of the room; but on perceiving Mr. Darcy, he stopped with a bow of superior courtesy to compliment him on his dancing and his partner.

"I have been most highly gratified indeed, my dear sir. Such very superior dancing is not often seen. It is evident that you belong to the first circles. Allow me to say, however, that your fair partner does not disgrace you, and that I must hope to have this pleasure often repeated, especially when a certain desirable event, my dear Eliza (glancing at her sister and Bingley) shall take place. What congratulations will then flow in! I appeal to Mr. Darcy:—but let me not interrupt you, sir. You will not thank me for detaining you from the bewitching converse of that young lady, whose bright eyes are also upbraiding me."

The latter part of this address was scarcely heard by Darcy; but Sir William's allusion to his friend seemed to strike him forcibly, and his eyes were directed with a very serious expression towards Bingley and Jane, who were dancing together. Recovering himself, however, shortly, he turned to his partner, and said, "Sir William's interruption has made me forget what we were talking of."

"I do not think we were speaking at all. Sir William could not have interrupted two people in the room who had less to say for themselves. We have tried two or three subjects already without success, and what we are to talk of next I cannot imagine."

"What think you of books?" said he, smiling.

"Books—oh! no. I am sure we never read the same, or not with the same feelings."

"I am sorry you think so; but if that be the case, there can at least be no want of subject. We may compare our different opinions."

"No—I cannot talk of books in a ball-room; my head is always full of something else."

"The PRESENT always occupies you in such scenes—does it?" said he, with a look of doubt.

"Yes, always," she replied, without knowing what she said, for her thoughts had wandered far from the subject, as soon afterwards appeared by her suddenly exclaiming, "I remember hearing you once say, Mr. Darcy, that you hardly ever forgave, that you resentment once created was unappeasable. You are very cautious, I suppose, as to its BEING CREATED."

"I am," said he, with a firm voice.

"And never allow yourself to be blinded by prejudice?"

"I hope not."

"It is particularly incumbent on those who never change their opinion, to be secure of judging properly at first.

"May I ask to what these questions tend?"

"Merely to the illustration of YOUR character," said she, endeavouring to shake off her gravity. "I am trying to make it out."

"And what is your success?"

She shook her head. "I do not get on at all. I hear such different accounts of you as puzzle me exceedingly."

"I can readily believe," answered he gravely, "that reports may vary greatly with respect to me; and I could wish, Miss Bennet, that you were not to sketch my character at the present moment, as there is reason to fear that the performance would reflect no credit on either."

"But if I do not take your likeness now, I may never have another opportunity."

"I would by no means suspend any pleasure of yours," he coldly replied. She said no more, and they went down the other dance and parted in silence; and on each side dissatisfied, though not to an equal degree, for in Darcy's breast there was a tolerable powerful feeling towards her, which soon procured her pardon, and directed all his anger against another.

They had not long separated, when Miss Bingley came towards her, and with an expression of civil disdain accosted her:—"So, Miss Eliza, I hear you are quite delighted with George Wickham! Your sister has been talking to me about him, and asking me a thousand questions; and I find that the young man quite forgot to tell you, among his other communication, that he was the son of old Wickham, the late Mr. Darcy's steward. Let me recommend you, however, as a friend, not to give implicit confidence to all his assertions; for as to Mr. Darcy's using him ill, it is perfectly false; for, on the contrary, he has always been remarkably kind to him, though George Wickham has treated Mr. Darcy in a most infamous manner. I do not know the particulars, but I know very well that Mr. Darcy is not in the least to blame, that he cannot bear to hear George Wickham mentioned, and that though my brother thought that he could not well avoid including him in his invitation to the officers, he was excessively glad to find that he had taken himself out of the way. His coming into the country at all is a most insolent thing, indeed, and I wonder how he could presume to do it. I pity you, Miss Eliza, for this discovery of your favourite's guilt; but really, considering his descent, one could not expect much better."

"His guilt and his descent appear by your account to be the same," said Elizabeth angrily; "for I have heard you accuse him of nothing worse than of being the son of Mr. Darcy's steward, and of THAT, I can assure you, he informed me himself."

"I beg your pardon," replied Miss Bingley, turning away with a sneer. "Excuse my interference: it was kindly meant."

"Insolent girl!" said Elizabeth to herself. "You are much mistaken if you expect to influence me by such a paltry attack as this. I see nothing in it but your own wilful ignorance and the malice of Mr. Darcy." She then sought her eldest sister, who has undertaken to make inquiries on the same subject of Bingley. Jane met her with a smile of such sweet complacency, a glow of such happy expression, as sufficiently marked how well she was satisfied with the occurrences of the evening. Elizabeth instantly read her feelings, and at that moment solicitude for Wickham, resentment against his enemies, and everything else, gave way before the hope of Jane's being in the fairest way for happiness.

"I want to know," said she, with a countenance no less smiling than her sister's, "what you have learnt about Mr. Wickham. But perhaps you have been too pleasantly engaged to think of any third person; in which case you may be sure of my pardon."

"No," replied Jane, "I have not forgotten him; but I have nothing satisfactory to tell you. Mr. Bingley does not know the whole of his history, and is quite ignorant of the circumstances which have principally offended Mr. Darcy; but he will vouch for the good conduct, the probity, and honour of his friend, and is perfectly convinced that Mr. Wickham has deserved much less attention from Mr. Darcy than he has received; and I am sorry to say by his account as well as his sister's, Mr. Wickham is by no means a respectable young man. I am afraid he has been very imprudent, and has deserved to lose Mr. Darcy's regard."

"Mr. Bingley does not know Mr. Wickham himself?"

"No; he never saw him till the other morning at Meryton."

"This account then is what he has received from Mr. Darcy. I am satisfied. But what does he say of the living?"

"He does not exactly recollect the circumstances, though he has heard them from Mr. Darcy more than once, but he believes that it was left to him CONDITIONALLY only."

"I have not a doubt of Mr. Bingley's sincerity," said Elizabeth warmly; "but you must excuse my not being convinced by assurances only. Mr. Bingley's defense of his friend was a very able one, I dare say; but since he is unacquainted with several parts of the story, and has learnt the rest from that friend himself, I shall venture to still think of both gentlemen as I did before."

She then changed the discourse to one more gratifying to each, and on which there could be no difference of sentiment. Elizabeth listened with delight to the happy, though modest hopes which Jane entertained of Mr. Bingley's regard, and said all in her power to heighten her confidence in it. On their being joined by Mr. Bingley himself, Elizabeth withdrew to Miss Lucas; to whose inquiry after the pleasantness of her last partner she had scarcely replied, before Mr. Collins came up to them, and told her with great exultation that he had just been so fortunate as to make a most important discovery.

"I have found out," said he, "by a singular accident, that there is now in the room a near relation of my patroness. I happened to overhear the gentleman himself mentioning to the young lady who does the honours of the house the names of his cousin Miss de Bourgh, and of her mother Lady Catherine. How wonderfully these sort of things occur! Who would have thought of my meeting with, perhaps, a nephew of Lady Catherine de Bourgh in his assembly! I am most thankful that the discovery is made in time for me to pay my respects to him, which I am now going to do, and trust he will excuse my not having done it before. My total ignorance of the connection must plead my apology."

"You are not going to introduce yourself to Mr. Darcy!"

"Indeed I am. I shall entreat his pardon for not having done it earlier. I believe him to be Lady Catherine's NEPHEW. It will be in my power to assure him that her ladyship was quite well yesterday se'nnight."

Elizabeth tried hard to dissuade him from such a scheme, assuring him that Mr. Darcy would consider his addressing him without introduction as an impertinent freedom, rather than a compliment to his aunt; that it was not in the least necessary there should be any notice on either side; and that if it were, it must belong to Mr. Darcy, the superior in consequence, to begin the acquaintance. Mr. Collins listened to her with the determined air of following his own inclination, and, when she ceased speaking, replied thus:—"My dear Miss Elizabeth, I have the highest opinion in the world in your excellent judgement in all matters within the scope of your understanding; but permit me to say, that there must be a wide difference between the established forms of ceremony amongst the laity, and those which regulate the clergy; for, give me leave to observe that I consider the clerical office as equal in point of dignity with the highest rank in the kingdom—provided that a proper humility of behaviour is at the same time maintained. You must therefore allow me to follow the dictates of my conscience on this occasion, which leads me to perform what I look on as a point of duty. Pardon me for neglecting to profit by your advice, which on every other subject shall be my constant guide, though in the case before us I consider myself more fitted by education and habitual study to decide on what is right than a young lady like yourself." And with a low bow he left her to attack Mr. Darcy, whose reception of his advances she eagerly watched, and whose astonishment at being so addressed was very evident. Her cousin prefaced his speech with a solemn bow and though she could not hear a word of it, she felt as if hearing it all, and saw in the motion of his lips the words "apology," "Hunsford," and "Lady Catherine de Bourgh." It vexed her to see him expose himself to such a man. Mr. Darcy was eyeing him with unrestrained wonder, and when at last Mr. Collins allowed him time to speak, replied with an air of distant civility. Mr. Collins, however, was not discouraged from speaking again, and Mr. Darcy's contempt seemed abundantly increasing with the length of his second speech, and at the end of it he only made him a slight bow, and moved another way. Mr. Collins then returned to Elizabeth.

"I have no reason, I assure you," said he, "to be dissatisfied with my reception. Mr. Darcy seemed much pleased with the attention. He answered me with the utmost civility, and even paid me the compliment of saying that he was so well convinced of Lady Catherine's discernment as to be certain she could never bestow a favour unworthily. It was really a very handsome thought. Upon the whole, I am much pleased with him."

As Elizabeth had no longer any interest of her own to pursue, she turned her attention almost entirely on her sister and Mr. Bingley; and the train of agreeable reflections which her observations gave birth to, made her perhaps almost as happy as Jane. She saw her in idea settled in that very house, in all the felicity which a marriage of true affection could bestow; and she felt capable, under such circumstances, of endeavouring even to like Bingley's two sisters. Her mother's thoughts she plainly saw were bent the same way, and she determined not to venture near her, lest she might hear too much. When they sat down to supper, therefore, she considered it a most unlucky perverseness which placed them within one of each other; and deeply was she vexed to find that her mother was talking to that one person (Lady Lucas) freely, openly, and of nothing else but her expectation that Jane would soon be married to Mr. Bingley. It was an animating subject, and Mrs. Bennet seemed incapable of fatigue while enumerating the advantages of the match. His being such a charming young man, and so rich, and living but three miles from them, were the first points of self-gratulation; and then it was such a comfort to think how fond the two sisters were of Jane, and to be certain that they must desire the connection as much as she could do. It was, moreover, such a promising thing for her younger daughters, as Jane's marrying so greatly must throw them in the way of other rich men; and lastly, it was so pleasant at her time of life to be able to consign her single daughters to the care of their sister, that she might not be obliged to go into company more than she liked. It was necessary to make this circumstance a matter of pleasure, because on such occasions it is the etiquette; but no one was less likely than Mrs. Bennet to find comfort in staying home at any period of her life. She concluded with many good wishes that Lady Lucas might soon be equally fortunate, though evidently and triumphantly believing there was no chance of it.

In vain did Elizabeth endeavour to check the rapidity of her mother's words, or persuade her to describe her felicity in a less audible whisper; for, to her inexpressible vexation, she could perceive that the chief of it was overheard by Mr. Darcy, who sat opposite to them. Her mother only scolded her for being nonsensical.

"What is Mr. Darcy to me, pray, that I should be afraid of him? I am sure we owe him no such particular civility as to be obliged to say nothing HE may not like to hear."

"For heaven's sake, madam, speak lower. What advantage can it be for you to offend Mr. Darcy? You will never recommend yourself to his friend by so doing!"

Nothing that she could say, however, had any influence. Her mother would talk of her views in the same intelligible tone. Elizabeth blushed and blushed again with shame and vexation. She could not help frequently glancing her eye at Mr. Darcy, though every glance convinced her of what she dreaded; for though he was not always looking at her mother, she was convinced that his attention was invariably fixed by her. The expression of his face changed gradually from indignant contempt to a composed and steady gravity.

At length, however, Mrs. Bennet had no more to say; and Lady Lucas, who had been long yawning at the repetition of delights which she saw no likelihood of sharing, was left to the comforts of cold ham and chicken. Elizabeth now began to revive. But not long was the interval of tranquillity; for, when supper was over, singing was talked of, and she had the mortification of seeing Mary, after very little entreaty, preparing to oblige the company. By many significant looks and silent entreaties, did she endeavour to prevent such a proof of complaisance, but in vain; Mary would not understand them; such an opportunity of exhibiting was delightful to her, and she began her song. Elizabeth's eyes were fixed on her with most painful sensations, and she watched her progress through the several stanzas with an impatience which was very ill rewarded at their close; for Mary, on receiving, amongst the thanks of the table, the hint of a hope that she might be prevailed on to favour them again, after the pause of half a minute began another. Mary's powers were by no means fitted for such a display; her voice was weak, and her manner affected. Elizabeth was in agonies. She looked at Jane, to see how she bore it; but Jane was very composedly talking to Bingley. She looked at his two sisters, and saw them making signs of derision at each other, and at Darcy, who continued, however, imperturbably grave. She looked at her father to entreat his interference, lest Mary should be singing all night. He took the hint, and when Mary had finished her second song, said aloud, "That will do extremely well, child. You have delighted us long enough. Let the other young ladies have time to exhibit."

Mary, though pretending not to hear, was somewhat disconcerted; and Elizabeth, sorry for her, and sorry for her father's speech, was afraid her anxiety had done no good. Others of the party were now applied to.

"If I," said Mr. Collins, "were so fortunate as to be able to sing, I should have great pleasure, I am sure, in obliging the company with an air; for I consider music as a very innocent diversion, and perfectly compatible with the profession of a clergyman. I do not mean, however, to assert that we can be justified in devoting too much of our time to music, for there are certainly other things to be attended to. The rector of a parish has much to do. In the first place, he must make such an agreement for tithes as a may be beneficial to himself and not offensive to his patron. He must write his own sermons; and the time that remains will not be too much for his parish duties, and the care and improvement of his dwelling, which he cannot be excused from making as a comfortable as a possible. And I do not think it of light importance that he should have attentive and conciliatory manner towards everybody, especially towards those to whom he owes his preferment. I cannot acquit him of that duty; nor could I think well of the man who should omit an occasion of testifying his respect towards anybody connected with the family." And with a bow to Mr. Darcy, he concluded his speech, which had been spoken so loud as a to be heard by half the room. Many stared—many smiled; but no one looked more amused than Mr. Bennet himself, while his wife seriously commended Mr. Collins for having spoken so sensibly, and observed in a half-whisper to Lady Lucas, that he was a remarkably clever, good kind of young man.

To Elizabeth it appeared that, had her family made an agreement to expose themselves as a much as a they could during the evening, it would have been impossible for them to play their parts with more spirit or finer success; and happy did she think it for Bingley and her sister that some of the exhibition had escaped his notice, and that his feelings were not of a sort to be much distressed by the folly which he must have witnessed. That his two sisters and Mr. Darcy, however, should have such an opportunity of ridiculing her relations, was bad enough, and she could not determine whether the silent contempt of the gentleman, or the insolent smiles of the ladies, were more intolerable.

The rest of the evening brought her little amusement. She was teased by Mr. Collins, who continued most perseveringly by her side, and though he could not prevail on her to dance with him again, put it out of her power to dance with others. In vain did she entreat him to stand up with somebody else, and offer to introduce him to any young lady in the room. He assured her, that as to dancing, he was perfectly indifferent to it; that his chief object was by delicate attentions to recommend himself to her and that he should therefore make a point of remaining close to her the whole evening. There was no arguing upon such a project. She owed her greatest relief to her friend Miss Lucas, who often joined them, and good-naturedly engaged Mr. Collins's conversation to herself.

She was at least free from the offense of Mr. Darcy's further notice; though often standing within a very short distance of her, quite disengaged, he never came near enough to speak. She felt it to be the probable consequence of her allusions to Mr. Wickham, and rejoiced in it.

The Longbourn party were the last of all the company to depart, and, by a manoeuvre of Mrs. Bennet, had to wait for their carriage a quarter of an hour after everybody else was gone, which gave them time to see how heartily they were wished away by some of the family. Mrs. Hurst and her sister scarcely opened their mouths, except to complain of fatigue, and were evidently impatient to have the house to themselves. They repulsed every attempt of Mrs. Bennet at conversation, and by so doing threw a languor over the whole party, which was very little relieved by the long speeches of Mr. Collins, who was complimenting Mr. Bingley and his sisters on the elegance of their entertainment, and the hospitality and politeness which had marked their behaviour to their guests. Darcy said nothing at all. Mr. Bennet, in equal silence, was enjoying the scene. Mr. Bingley and Jane were standing together, a little detached from the rest, and talked only to each other. Elizabeth preserved as steady a silence as either Mrs. Hurst or Miss Bingley; and even Lydia was too much fatigued to utter more than the occasional exclamation of "Lord, how tired I am!" accompanied by a violent yawn.

When at length they arose to take leave, Mrs. Bennet was most pressingly civil in her hope of seeing the whole family soon at Longbourn, and addressed herself especially to Mr. Bingley, to assure him how happy he would make them by eating a family dinner with them at any time, without the ceremony of a formal invitation. Bingley was all grateful pleasure, and he readily engaged for taking the earliest opportunity of waiting on her, after his return from London, whither he was obliged to go the next day for a short time.

Mrs. Bennet was perfectly satisfied, and quitted the house under the delightful persuasion that, allowing for the necessary preparations of settlements, new carriages, and wedding clothes, she should undoubtedly see her daughter settled at Netherfield in the course of three or four months. Of having another daughter married to Mr. Collins, she thought with equal certainty, and with considerable, though not equal, pleasure. Elizabeth was the least dear to her of all her children; and though the man and the match were quite good enough for HER, the worth of each was eclipsed by Mr. Bingley and Netherfield.

Chapter 19

The next day opened a new scene at Longbourn. Mr. Collins made his declaration in form. Having resolved to do it without loss of time, as his leave of absence extended only to the following Saturday, and having no feelings of diffidence to make it distressing to himself even at the moment, he set about it in a very orderly manner, with all the observances, which he supposed a regular part of the business. On finding Mrs. Bennet, Elizabeth, and one of the younger girls together, soon after breakfast, he addressed the mother in these words: "May I hope, madam, for your interest with your fair daughter Elizabeth, when I solicit for the honour of a private audience with her in the course of this morning?"

Before Elizabeth had time for anything but a blush of surprise, Mrs. Bennet answered instantly, "Oh dear!—yes—certainly. I am sure Lizzy will be very happy—I am sure she can have no objection, Come, Kitty, I want you upstairs." And, gathering her work together, she was hastening away, when Elizabeth called out:

"Dear madam, do not go. I beg you will not go. Mr. Collins must excuse me. He can have nothing to say to me that anybody need not hear. I am going away myself."

"No, no, nonsense, Lizzy. I desire you to stay where you are." And upon Elizabeth's seeming really, with vexed and embarrassed looks, about to escape, she added: "Lizzy, I INSIST upon your staying and hearing Mr. Collins."

Elizabeth would not oppose such and injunction—and a moment's consideration making her also sensible that it would be wisest to get it over as soon and as quietly as possible, she sat down again and tried to conceal, by incessant employment the feelings which were divided between distress and diversion. Mrs. Bennet and Kitty walked off, and as soon as they were gone, Mr. Collins began.

"Believe me, my dear Miss Elizabeth, that your modesty, so far from doing you any disservice, rather adds to your other perfections. You would have been less amiable in my eyes had there NOT been this little unwillingness; but allow me to assure you, that I have your respected mother's permission for this address. You can hardly doubt the purport of my discourse, however your natural delicacy may lead you to dissemble; my attentions have been too marked to be mistaken. Almost as soon as I entered the house, I singled you out as the companion of my future life. But before I am run away with by my feelings on this subject, perhaps it would be advisable for me to state my reasons for marrying—and, moreover, for coming into Hertfordshire with the design of selecting a wife, as I certainly did."

The idea of Mr. Collins, with all his solemn composure, being run away with by his feelings, made Elizabeth so near laughing, that she could not use the short pause he allowed in any attempt to stop him further, and he continued:

"My reasons for marrying are, first, that I think it a right thing for every clergyman in easy circumstances (like myself) to set the example of matrimony in his parish; secondly, that I am convinced that it will add very greatly to my happiness; and thirdly—which perhaps I ought to have mentioned earlier, that it is the particular advice and recommendation of the very noble lady whom I have the honour of calling patroness. Twice has she condescended to give me her opinion (unasked too!) on this subject; and it was but the very Saturday night before I left Hunsford—between our pools at quadrille, while Mrs. Jenkins was arranging Miss de Bourgh's footstool, that she said, Mr. Collins, you must marry. A clergyman like you must marry. Choose properly, choose a gentlewoman for MY sake; and for your OWN, let her be an active, useful sort of person, not brought up high, but able to make a small income go a good way. This is my advice. Find such a woman as soon as you can, bring her to Hunsford, and I will visit her.' Allow me, by the way, to observe, my fair cousin, that I do not reckon the notice and kindness of Lady Catherine de Bourgh as among the least of the advantages in my power to offer. You will find her manners beyond anything I can describe; and your wit and vivacity, I think, must be acceptable to her, especially when tempered with the silence and respect which her rank will inevitably excite. Thus much for my general intention in favour of matrimony; it remains to be told why my views were directed towards Longbourn instead of my own neighbourhood, where I can assure you there are many amiable young women. But the fact is, that being, as I am, to inherit this estate after the death of your honoured father (who, however, may live many years longer), I could not satisfy myself without resolving to choose a wife from among his daughters, that the loss to them might be as little as possible, when the melancholy event takes place—which, however, as I have already said, may not be for several years. This has been my motive, my fair cousin, and I flatter myself it will not sink me in your esteem. And now nothing remains but for me but to assure you in the most animated language of the violence of my affection. To fortune I am perfectly indifferent, and shall make no demand of that nature on your father, since I am well aware that it could not be complied with; and that one thousand pounds in the four per cents, which will not be yours till after your mother's decease, is all that you may ever be entitled to. On that head, therefore, I shall be uniformly silent; and you may assure yourself that no ungenerous reproach shall ever pass my lips when we are married."

It was absolutely necessary to interrupt him now.

"You are too hasty, sir," she cried. "You forget that I have made no answer. Let me do it without further loss of time. Accept my thanks for the compliment you are paying me. I am very sensible of the honour of your proposals, but it is impossible for me to do otherwise than to decline them."

"I am not now to learn," replied Mr. Collins, with a formal wave of the hand, "that it is usual with young ladies to reject the addresses of the man whom they secretly mean to accept, when he first applies for their favour; and that sometimes the refusal is repeated a second, or even a third time. I am therefore by no means discouraged by what you have just said, and shall hope to lead you to the altar ere long."

"Upon my word, sir," cried Elizabeth, "your hope is a rather extraordinary one after my declaration. I do assure you that I am not one of those young ladies (if such young ladies there are) who are so daring as to risk their happiness on the chance of being asked a second time. I am perfectly serious in my refusal. You could not make ME happy, and I am convinced that I am the last woman in the world who could make you so. Nay, were your friend Lady Catherine to know me, I am persuaded she would find me in every respect ill qualified for the situation."

"Were it certain that Lady Catherine would think so," said Mr. Collins very gravely—"but I cannot imagine that her ladyship would at all disapprove of you. And you may be certain when I have the honour of seeing her again, I shall speak in the very highest terms of your modesty, economy, and other amiable qualification."

"Indeed, Mr. Collins, all praise of me will be unnecessary. You must give me leave to judge for myself, and pay me the compliment of believing what I say. I wish you very happy and very rich, and by refusing you hand, do all in my power to prevent your being otherwise. In making me the offer, you must have satisfied the delicacy of your feelings with regard to my family, and may take possession of Longbourn estate whenever it falls, without any self-reproach. This matter may be considered, therefore, as finally settled." And rising as she thus spoke, she would have quitted the room, had Mr. Collins not thus addressed her:

"When I do myself the honour of speaking to you next on the subject, I shall hope to receive a more favourable answer than you have now given me; though I am far from accusing you of cruelty at present, because I know it to be the established custom of your sex to reject a man on the first application, and perhaps you have even now said as much to encourage my suit as would be consistent with the true delicacy of the female character."

"Really, Mr. Collins," cried Elizabeth with some warmth, "you puzzle me exceedingly. If what I have hitherto said can appear to you in the form of encouragement, I know not how to express my refusal in such a way as to convince you of its being one."

"You must give me leave to flatter myself, my dear cousin, that your refusal of my addresses is merely words of course. My reasons for believing it are briefly these: It does not appear to me that my hand is unworthy your acceptance, or that the establishment I can offer would be any other than highly desirable. My situation in life, my connections with the family of de Bourgh, and my relationship to your own, are circumstances highly in my favour; and you should take it into further consideration, that in spite of your manifold attractions, it is by no means certain that another offer of marriage may ever be made you. Your portion is unhappily so small that it will in all likelihood undo the effects of your loveliness and amiable qualifications. As I must therefore conclude that you are not serious in your rejection of me, I shall choose to attribute it to your wish of increasing my love by suspense, according to the usual practice of elegant females."

"I do assure you, sir, that I have no pretensions whatever to that kind of elegance which consists in tormenting a respectable man. I would rather be paid the compliment of being believed sincere. I thank you again and again for the honour you have done me in your proposals, but to accept them is absolutely impossible. My feelings in every respect forbid it. Can I speak plainer? Do not consider me now as an elegant female, intending to plague you, but as a rational creature, speaking the truth from her heart."

"You are uniformly charming!" cried he, with an air of awkward gallantry; "and I am persuaded that when sanctioned by the express authority of both your excellent parents, my proposals will not fail of being acceptable."

To such perseverance in wilful self-deception Elizabeth would make no reply, and immediately and in silence withdrew, determined, that if he persisted in considering her repeated refusals as flattering encouragement, to apply to her father, whose negative might be uttered in such a manner as to be decisive, and whose behavior at least could not be mistaken for the affectation and coquetry of an elegant female.

Chapter 20

Mr. Collins was not left long to the silent contemplation of his successful love; for Mrs. Bennet, having dawdled about in the vestibule to watch for the end of the conference, no sooner saw Elizabeth open the door and with quick step pass her towards the staircase, than she entered the breakfast-room, and congratulated both him and herself in warm terms on the happy prospect or their nearer connection. Mr. Collins received and returned these felicitations with equal pleasure, and then proceeded to relate the particulars of their interview, with the result of which he trusted he had every reason to be satisfied, since the refusal which his cousin had steadfastly given him would naturally flow from her bashful modesty and the genuine delicacy of her character.

This information, however, startled Mrs. Bennet; she would have been glad to be equally satisfied that her daughter had meant to encourage him by protesting against his proposals, but she dared not believe it, and could not help saying so.

"But, depend upon it, Mr. Collins," she added, "that Lizzy shall be brought to reason. I will speak to her about it directly. She is a very headstrong, foolish girl, and does not know her own interest but I will MAKE her know it."

"Pardon me for interrupting you, madam," cried Mr. Collins; "but if she is really headstrong and foolish, I know not whether she would altogether be a very desirable wife to a man in my situation, who naturally looks for happiness in the marriage state. If therefore she actually persists in rejecting my suit, perhaps it were better not to force her into accepting me, because if liable to such defects of temper, she could not contribute much to my felicity."

"Sir, you quite misunderstand me," said Mrs. Bennet, alarmed. "Lizzy is only headstrong in such matters as these. In everything else she is as good-natured a girl as ever lived. I will go directly to Mr. Bennet, and we shall very soon settle it with her, I am sure."

She would not give him time to reply, but hurrying instantly to her husband, called out as she entered the library, "Oh! Mr. Bennet, you are wanted immediately; we are all in an uproar. You must come and make

Lizzy marry Mr. Collins, for she vows she will not have him, and if you do not make haste he will change his mind and not have HER."

Mr. Bennet raised his eyes from his book as she entered, and fixed them on her face with a calm unconcern which was not in the least altered by her communication.

"I have not the pleasure of understanding you," said he, when she had finished her speech. "Of what are you talking?"

"Of Mr. Collins and Lizzy. Lizzy declares she will not have Mr. Collins, and Mr. Collins begins to say that he will not have Lizzy."

"And what am I to do on the occasion? It seems an hopeless business."

"Speak to Lizzy about it yourself. Tell her that you insist upon her marrying him."

"Let her be called down. She shall hear my opinion."

Mrs. Bennet rang the bell, and Miss Elizabeth was summoned to the library.

"Come here, child," cried her father as she appeared. "I have sent for you on an affair of importance. I understand that Mr. Collins has made you an offer of marriage. Is it true?" Elizabeth replied that it was. "Very well—and this offer of marriage you have refused?"

"I have, sir."

"Very well. We now come to the point. Your mother insists upon your accepting it. Is it not so, Mrs. Bennet?"

"Yes, or I will never see her again."

"An unhappy alternative is before you, Elizabeth. From this day you must be a stranger to one of your parents. Your mother will never see you again if you do NOT marry Mr. Collins, and I will never see you again if you DO."

Elizabeth could not but smile at such a conclusion of such a beginning, but Mrs. Bennet, who had persuaded herself that her husband regarded the affair as she wished, was excessively disappointed.

"What do you mean, Mr. Bennet, in talking this way? You promised me to INSIST upon her marrying him."

"My dear," replied her husband, "I have two small favours to request. First, that you will allow me the free use of my understanding on the present occasion; and secondly, of my room. I shall be glad to have the library to myself as soon as may be."

Not yet, however, in spite of her disappointment in her husband, did Mrs. Bennet give up the point. She talked to Elizabeth again and again; coaxed and threatened her by turns. She endeavoured to secure Jane in her interest; but Jane, with all possible mildness, declined interfering; and Elizabeth, sometimes with real earnestness, and sometimes with playful gaiety, replied to her attacks. Though her manner varied, however, her determination never did.

Mr. Collins, meanwhile, was meditating in solitude on what had passed. He thought too well of himself to comprehend on what motives his cousin could refuse him; and though his pride was hurt, he suffered in no other way. His regard for her was quite imaginary; and the possibility of her deserving her mother's reproach prevented his feeling any regret.

While the family were in this confusion, Charlotte Lucas came to spend the day with them. She was met in the vestibule by Lydia, who, flying to her, cried in a half whisper, "I am glad you are come, for there is such fun here! What do you think has happened this morning? Mr. Collins has made an offer to Lizzy, and she will not have him."

Charlotte hardly had time to answer, before they were joined by Kitty, who came to tell the same news; and no sooner had they entered the breakfast-room, where Mrs. Bennet was alone, than she likewise began on the subject, calling on Miss Lucas for her compassion, and entreating her to persuade her friend Lizzy to comply with the wishes of all her family. "Pray do, my dear Miss Lucas," she added in a melancholy tone, "for nobody is on my side, nobody takes part with me. I am cruelly used, nobody feels for my poor nerves."

Charlotte's reply was spared by the entrance of Jane and Elizabeth.

"Aye, there she comes," continued Mrs. Bennet, "looking as unconcerned as may be, and caring no more for us than if we were at York, provided she can have her own way. But I tell you, Miss Lizzy—if you take it into your head to go on refusing every offer of marriage in this way, you will never get a husband at all—and I am sure I do not know who is to maintain you when your father is dead. I shall not be able to keep you—and so I warn you. I have done with you from this very day. I told you in the library, you know, that I should never speak to you again, and you will find me as good as my word. I have no pleasure in talking to undutiful children. Not that I have much pleasure, indeed, in talking to anybody. People who suffer as I do from nervous complaints can have no great inclination for talking. Nobody can tell what I suffer! But it is always so. Those who do not complain are never pitied."

Her daughters listened in silence to this effusion, sensible that any attempt to reason with her or soothe her would only increase the irritation. She talked on, therefore, without interruption from any of them, till they were joined by Mr. Collins, who entered the room with an air more stately than usual, and on perceiving whom, she said to the girls, "Now, I do insist upon it, that you, all of you, hold your tongues, and let me and Mr. Collins have a little conversation together."

Elizabeth passed quietly out of the room, Jane and Kitty followed, but Lydia stood her ground, determined to hear all she could; and Charlotte, detained first by the civility of Mr. Collins, whose inquiries after herself and all her family were very minute, and then by a little curiosity, satisfied herself with walking to the window and pretending not to hear. In a doleful voice Mrs. Bennet began the projected conversation: "Oh! Mr. Collins!"

"My dear madam, " replied he, "let us be for ever silent on this point. Far be it from me," he presently continued, in a voice that marked his displeasure, "to resent the behaviour of your daughter. Resignation to inevitable evils is the evil duty of us all; the peculiar duty of a young man who has been so fortunate as I have been in early preferment; and I trust I am resigned. Perhaps not the less so from feeling a doubt of my positive happiness had my fair cousin honoured me with her hand; for I have often observed that resignation is never so perfect as when the blessing denied begins to lose somewhat of its value in our estimation. You will not, I hope, consider me as showing any disrespect to your family, my dear madam, by thus withdrawing my pretensions to your daughter's favour, without having paid yourself and Mr. Bennet to compliment of requesting you to interpose your authority in my behalf. My conduct may, I fear, be objectionable in having accepted my dismission from your daughter's lips instead of your own. But we are all liable to error. I have certainly meant well through the whole affair. My object has been to secure an amiable companion for myself, with due consideration for the advantage of all your family, and if my MANNER has been at all reprehensible, I here beg leave to apologise."

Chapter 21

The discussion of Mr. Collins's offer was now nearly at an end, and Elizabeth had only to suffer from the uncomfortable feelings necessarily attending it, and occasionally from some peevish allusions of her mother. As for the gentleman himself, HIS feelings were chiefly expressed, not by embarrassment or dejection, or by trying to avoid her, but by stiffness of manner and resentful silence. He scarcely ever spoke to her, and the assiduous attentions which he had been so sensible of himself were transferred for the rest of the day to Miss Lucas, whose civility in listening to him was a seasonable relief to them all, and especially to her friend.

The morrow produced no abatement of Mrs. Bennet's ill-humour or ill health. Mr. Collins was also in the same state of angry pride. Elizabeth had hoped that his resentment might shorten his visit, but his plan did not appear in the least affected by it. He was always to have gone on Saturday, and to Saturday he meant to stay.

After breakfast, the girls walked to Meryton to inquire if Mr. Wickham were returned, and to lament over his absence from the Netherfield ball. He joined them on their entering the town, and attended them to their aunt's where his regret and vexation, and the concern of everybody, was well talked over. To Elizabeth, however, he voluntarily acknowledged that the necessity of his absence HAD been self-imposed.

"I found," said he, "as the time drew near that I had better not meet Mr. Darcy; that to be in the same room, the same party with him for so many hours together, might be more than I could bear, and that scenes might arise unpleasant to more than myself."

She highly approved his forbearance, and they had leisure for a full discussion of it, and for all the commendation which they civilly bestowed on each other, as Wickham and another officer walked back with them to Longbourn, and during the walk he particularly attended to her. His accompanying them was a double advantage; she felt all the compliment it offered to herself, and it was most acceptable as an occasion of introducing him to her father and mother.

Soon after their return, a letter was delivered to Miss Bennet; it came from Netherfield. The envelope contained a sheet of elegant, little, hot-pressed paper, well covered with a lady's fair, flowing hand; and Elizabeth saw her sister's countenance change as she read it, and saw her dwelling intently on some particular passages. Jane recollected herself soon, and putting the letter away, tried to join with her usual cheerfulness in the general conversation; but Elizabeth felt an anxiety on the subject which drew off her attention even from Wickham; and no sooner had he and he companion taken leave, than a glance from Jane invited her to follow her upstairs. When they had gained their own room, Jane, taking out her letter, said, "This is from Caroline Bingley;

what it contains has surprised me a good deal. The whole party have left Netherfield by this time, and are on their way to town—and without any intention of coming back again. You shall hear what she says."

She then read the first sentence aloud, which comprised the information of their having just resolved to follow their brother to town directly, and of their meaning to dine in Grosvenor Street, where Mr. Hurst had a house. The next was in these words: "I do not pretend to regret anything I shall leave in Hertfordshire, except your society, my dearest friend; but we will hope, at some future period, to enjoy many returns of that delightful intercourse we have known, and in the meanwhile may lessen the pain of separation by a very frequent and most unreserved correspondence. I depend on you for that." To these high-flown expressions Elizabeth listened with all the insensibility of distrust; and though the suddenness of their removal surprised her, she saw nothing in it really to lament; it was not to be supposed that their absence from Netherfield would prevent Mr. Bingley's being there; and as to the loss of their society, she was persuaded that Jane must cease to regard it, in the enjoyment of his.

"It is unlucky," said she, after a short pause, "that you should not be able to see your friends before they leave the country. But may we not hope that the period of future happiness to which Miss Bingley looks forward may arrive earlier than she is aware, and that the delightful intercourse you have known as friends will be renewed with yet greater satisfaction as sisters? Mr. Bingley will not be detained in London by them."

"Caroline decidedly says that none of the party will return into Hertfordshire this winter. I will read it to you:

"'When my brother left us yesterday, he imagined that the business which took him to London might be concluded in three or four days; but as we are certain it cannot be so, and at the same time convinced that when Charles gets to town he will be in no hurry to leave it again, we have determined on following him thither, that he may not be obliged to spend his vacant hours in a comfortless hotel. Many of my acquaintances are already there for the winter; I wish that I could hear that you, my dearest friend, had any intention of making one of the crowd—but of that I despair. I sincerely hope your Christmas in Hertfordshire may abound in the gaieties which that season generally brings, and that your beaux will be so numerous as to prevent your feeling the loss of the three of whom we shall deprive you.'"

"It is evident by this," added Jane, "that he comes back no more this winter."

"It is only evident that Miss Bingley does not mean that he SHOULD."

"Why will you think so? It must be his own doing. He is his own master. But you do not know ALL. I WILL read you the passage which particularly hurts me. I will have no reserves from YOU."

"'Mr. Darcy is impatient to see his sister; and, to confess the truth, WE are scarcely less eager to meet her again. I really do not think Georgiana Darcy has her equal for beauty, elegance, and accomplishments; and the affection she inspires in Louisa and myself is heightened into something still more interesting, from the hope we dare entertain of her being hereafter our sister. I do not know whether I ever before mentioned to you my feelings on this subject; but I will not leave the country without confiding them, and I trust you will not esteem them unreasonable. My brother admires her greatly already; he will have frequent opportunity now of seeing her on the most intimate footing; her relations all wish the connection as much as his own; and a sister's partiality is not misleading me, I think, when I call Charles most capable of engaging any woman's heart. With all these circumstances to favour an attachment, and nothing to prevent it, am I wrong, my dearest Jane, in indulging the hope of an event which will secure the happiness of so many?'"

"What do you think of THIS sentence, my dear Lizzy?" said Jane as she finished it. "Is it not clear enough? Does it not expressly declare that Caroline neither expects nor wishes me to be her sister; that she is perfectly convinced of her brother's indifference; and that if she suspects the nature of my feelings for him, she means (most kindly!) to put me on my guard? Can there be any other opinion on the subject?"

"Yes, there can; for mine is totally different. Will you hear it?"

"Most willingly."

You shall have it in a few words. Miss Bingley sees that her brother is in love with you, and wants him to marry Miss Darcy. She follows him to town in hope of keeping him there, and tries to persuade you that he does not care about you."

Jane shook her head.

""Indeed, Jane, you ought to believe me. No one who has ever seen you together can doubt his affection. Miss Bingley, I am sure, cannot. She is not such a simpleton. Could she have seen half as much love in

Mr. Darcy for herself, she would have ordered her wedding clothes. But the case is this: We are not rich enough or grand enough for them; and she is the more anxious to get Miss Darcy for her brother, from the notion that when there has been ONE intermarriage, she may have less trouble in achieving a second: in which there is certainly some ingenuity, and I dare say it would succeed, if Miss de Bourgh were out of the way. But, my dearest Jane, you cannot seriously imagine that because Miss Bingley tells you her brother greatly admires Miss Darcy, he is in the smallest degree less sensible of YOUR merit than when he took leave of you on Tuesday, or that it will be in her power to persuade him that, instead of being in love with you, he is very much in love with her friend."

"If we thought alike of Miss Bingley," replied Jane, "your representation of all this might make me quite easy. But I know the foundation is unjust. Caroline is incapable of wilfully deceiving anyone; and all that I can hope in this case is that she is deceiving herself."

"That is right. You could not have started a more happy idea, since you will not take comfort in mine. Believe her to be deceived, by all means. You have now done your duty by her, and must fret no longer."

"But, my dear sister, can I be happy, even supposing the best, in accepting a man whose sisters and friends are all wishing him to marry elsewhere?"

"You must decide for yourself," said Elizabeth; "and if, upon mature deliberation, you find that the misery of disobliging his two sisters is more than equivalent to the happiness of being his wife, I advise you by all means to refuse him."

"How can you talk so?" said Jane, faintly smiling. "You must know that though I should be exceedingly grieved at their disapprobation, I could not hesitate."

"I did not think you would; and that being the case, I cannot consider your situation with much compassion."

"But if he returns no more this winter, my choice will never be required. A thousand things may arise in six months!"

The idea of his returning no more Elizabeth treated with the utmost contempt. It appeared to her merely the suggestion of Caroline's interested wishes, and she could not for a moment suppose that those wishes, however openly or artfully spoken, could influence a young man so totally independent of everyone.

She represented to her sister as forcibly as possible what she felt on the subject, and had soon the pleasure of seeing its happy effect. Jane's temper was not desponding, and she was gradually led to hope, though the diffidence of affection sometimes overcame the hope, that Bingley would return to Netherfield and answer every wish of her heart.

They agreed that Mrs. Bennet should only hear of the departure of the family, without being alarmed on the score of the gentleman's conduct; but even this partial communication gave her a great deal of concern, and she bewailed it as exceedingly unlucky that the ladies should happen to go away just as they were all getting so intimate together. After lamenting it, however, at some length, she had the consolation that Mr. Bingley would be soon down again and soon dining at Longbourn, and the conclusion of all was the comfortable declaration, that though he had been invited only to a family dinner, she would take care to have two full courses.

Chapter 22

The Bennets were engaged to dine with the Lucases and again during the chief of the day was Miss Lucas so kind as to listen to Mr. Collins. Elizabeth took an opportunity of thanking her. "It keeps him in good humour," said she, "and I am more obliged to you than I can express." Charlotte assured her friend of her satisfaction in being useful, and that it amply repaid her for the little sacrifice of her time. This was very amiable, but Charlotte's kindness extended farther than Elizabeth had any conception of; its object was nothing else than to secure her from any return of Mr. Collins's addresses, by engaging them towards herself. Such was Miss Lucas's scheme; and appearances were so favourable, that when they parted at night, she would have felt almost secure of success if he had not been to leave Hertfordshire so very soon. But here she did injustice to the fire and independence of his character, for it led him to escape out of Longbourn House the next morning with admirable slyness, and hasten to Lucas Lodge to throw himself at her feet. He was anxious to avoid the notice of his cousins, from a conviction that if they saw him depart, they could not fail to conjecture his design, and he was not willing to have the attempt known till its success might be known likewise; for though feeling almost secure, and with reason, for Charlotte had been tolerably encouraging, he was comparatively diffident since the adventure of Wednesday. His reception, however, was of the most flattering kind. Miss Lucas perceived him from an upper window as he walked towards the house, and instantly set out to meet him accidentally in the lane. But little had she dared to hope that so much love and eloquence awaited her there.

In as short a time as Mr. Collins's long speeches would allow, everything was settled between them to the satisfaction of both; and as they entered the house he earnestly entreated her to name the day that was to make him the happiest of men; and though such a solicitation must be waived for the present, the lady felt no inclination to trifle with his happiness. The stupidity with which he was favoured by nature must guard his courtship from any charm that could make a woman wish for its continuance; and Miss Lucas, who accepted him solely from the pure and disinterested desire of an establishment, cared not how soon that establishment were gained.

Sir William and Lady Lucas were speedily applied to for their consent; and it was bestowed with a most joyful alacrity. Mr. Collins's present circumstances made it a most eligible match for their daughter, to whom they could give little fortune; and his prospects of future wealth were exceedingly fair. Lady Lucas began directly to calculate, with more interest than the matter had ever excited before, how many years longer Mr. Bennet was likely to live; and Sir William gave it as his decided opinion, that whenever Mr. Collins should be in possession of the Longbourn estate, it would be highly expedient that both he and his wife should make their appearance at St. James's. The whole family, in short, were properly overjoyed on the occasion. The younger girls formed hopes of COMING OUT a year or two sooner than they might otherwise have done; and the boys were relieved from their apprehension of Charlotte's dying an old maid. Charlotte herself was tolerably composed. She had gained her point, and had time to consider of it. Her reflections were in general satisfactory. Mr. Collins, to be sure, was neither sensible nor agreeable; his society was irksome, and his attachment to her must be imaginary. But still he would be her husband. Without thinking highly either of men or matrimony, marriage had always been her object; it was the only provision for well-educated young women of small fortune, and however uncertain of giving happiness, must be their pleasantest preservative from want. This preservative she had now obtained; and at the age of twenty-seven, without having ever been handsome, she felt all the good luck of it. The least agreeable circumstance in the business was the surprise it must occasion to Elizabeth Bennet, whose friendship she valued beyond that of any other person. Elizabeth would wonder, and probably would blame her; and though her resolution was not to be shaken, her feelings must be hurt by such a disapprobation. She resolved to give her the information herself, and therefore charged Mr. Collins, when he returned to Longbourn to dinner, to drop no hint of what had passed before any of the family. A promise of secrecy was of course very dutifully given, but it could not be kept without difficulty; for the curiosity excited by his long absence burst forth in such very direct questions on his return as required some ingenuity to evade, and he was at the same time exercising great self-denial, for he was longing to publish his prosperous love.

As he was to begin his journey too early on the morrow to see any of the family, the ceremony of leave-taking was performed when the ladies moved for the night; and Mrs. Bennet, with great politeness and cordiality, said how happy they should be to see him at Longbourn again, whenever his engagements might allow him to visit them.

"My dear madam," he replied, "this invitation is particularly gratifying, because it is what I have been hoping to receive; and you may be very certain that I shall avail myself of it as soon as possible."

They were all astonished; and Mr. Bennet, who could by no means wish for so speedy a return, immediately said:

"But is there not danger of Lady Catherine's disapprobation here, my good sir? You had better neglect your relations than run the risk of offending your patroness."

"My dear sir," replied Mr. Collins," I am particularly obliged to you for this friendly caution, and you may depend upon my not taking so material a step without her ladyship's concurrence."

"You cannot be too much upon your guard. Risk anything rather than her displeasure; and if you find it likely to be raised by your coming to us again, which I should think exceedingly probable, stay quietly at home, and be satisfied that WE shall take no offence."

"Believe me, my dear sir, my gratitude is warmly excited, by such affectionate attention; and depend upon it, you will speedily receive from me a letter of thanks for this, and for every other mark of your regard during my stay in Hertfordshire. As for my fair cousins, though my absence may not be long enough to render it necessary, I shall now take the liberty of wishing them health and happiness, not excepting my cousin Elizabeth."

With proper civilities the ladies then withdrew; all of them equally surprised that he meditated a quick return. Mrs. Bennet wished to understand by it that he thought of paying his addresses to one of her younger girls, and Mary might have been prevailed on to accept him. She rated his abilities much higher than any of the others; there was a solidity in his reflections which often struck her, and though by no means so clever as herself, she thought that if encouraged to read and improve himself by such an example as hers, he might become a very agreeable companion. But on the following morning, every hope of this kind was done away. Miss Lucas called soon after breakfast, and in a private conference with Elizabeth related the event of the day before.

The possibility of Mr. Collins's fancying herself in love with her friend had once occurred to Elizabeth within the last day or two; but that Charlotte could encourage him seemed almost as far from possibility as she could encourage him herself, and her astonishment was consequently so great as to overcome at first the bounds of decorum, and she could not help crying out:

"Engaged to Mr. Collins! My dear Charlotte—impossible!"

The steady countenance which Miss Lucas had commanded in telling her story, gave way to a momentary confusion here on receiving so direct a reproach; though, as it was no more than she expected, she soon regained her composure, and calmly replied:

"Why should you be surprised, my dear Eliza? Do you think it incredible that Mr. Collins should be able to procure any woman's good opinion, because he was not so happy as to succeed with you?"

But Elizabeth had now recollected herself, and making a strong effort for it, was able to assure with tolerable firmness that the prospect of their relationship was highly grateful to her, and that she wished her all imaginable happiness.

"I see what you are feeling," replied Charlotte. "You must be surprised, very much surprised—so lately as Mr. Collins was wishing to marry you. But when you have had time to think it over, I hope you will be satisfied with what I have done. I amd not romantic, you know; I never was. I ask only a comfortable home; and considering Mr. Collins's character, connection, and situation in life, I am convinced that my chance of happiness with him is as fair as most people can boast on entering the marriage state."

Elizabeth quietly answered "Undoubtedly"; and after an awkward pause, they returned to the rest of the family. Charlotte did not stay much longer, and Elizabeth was then left to reflect on what she had heard. It was a long time before she became at all reconciled to the idea of so unsuitable a match. The strangeness of Mr. Collins's making two offers of marriage within three days was nothing in comparison of his being now accepted. She had always felt that Charlotte's opinion of matrimony was not exactly like her own, but she had not supposed it to be possible that, when called into action, she would have sacrificed every better feeling to worldly advantage. Charlotte the wife of Mr. Collins was a most humiliating picture! And to the pang of a friend disgracing herself and sunk in her esteem, was added the distressing conviction that it was impossible for that friend to be tolerably happy in the lot she had chosen.

Chapter 23

Elizabeth was sitting with her mother and sisters, reflecting on what she had heard, and doubting whether she was authorised to mention it, when Sir William Lucas himself appeared, sent by his daughter, to announce her engagement to the family. With many compliments to them, and much self-gratulation on the prospect of a connection between the houses, he unfolded the matter—to an audience not merely wondering, but incredulous; for Mrs. Bennet, with more perseverance than politeness, protested he must be entirely mistaken; and Lydia, always unguarded and often uncivil, boisterously exclaimed:

"Good Lord! Sir William, how can you tell such a story? Do not you know that Mr. Collins wants to marry Lizzy?"

Nothing less than the complaisance of a courtier could have borne without anger such treatment; but Sir William's good breeding carried him through it all; and though he begged leave to be positive as to the truth of his information, he listened to all their impertinence with the most forbearing courtesy.

Elizabeth, feeling it incumbent on her to relieve him from so unpleasant a situation, now put herself forward to confirm his account, by mentioning her prior knowledge of it from Charlotte herself; and endeavoured to put a stop to the exclamations of her mother and sisters by the earnestness of her congratulations to Sir William, in which she was readily joined by Jane, and by making a variety of remarks on the happiness that might be expected from the match, the excellent character of Mr. Collins, and the convenient distance of Hunsford from London.

Mrs. Bennet was in fact too much overpowered to say a great deal while Sir William remained; but no sooner had he left them than her feelings found a rapid vent. In the first place, she persisted in disbelieving the whole of the matter; secondly, she was very sure that Mr. Collins had been taken in; thirdly, she trusted that they would never be happy together; and fourthly, that the match might be broken off. Two inferences, however, were plainly deduced from the whole: one, that Elizabeth was the real cause of the mischief; and the other that she herself had been barbarously misused by them all; and on these two points she principally dwelt during the rest of the day. Nothing could console and nothing could appease her. Nor did that day wear out her resentment. A week elapsed before she could see Elizabeth without scolding her, a month passed away before she could speak to Sir William or Lady Lucas without being rude, and many months were gone before she could at all forgive her daughter.

Mr. Bennet's emotions were much more tranquil on the occasion, and such as he did experience he pronounced to be of a most agreeable sort; for it gratified him, he said, to discover that Charlotte Lucas, whom he had been used to think tolerably sensible, was as foolish as his wife, and more foolish than his daughter!

Jane confessed herself a little surprised at the match; but she said less of her astonishment than of her earnest desire for their happiness; nor could Elizabeth persuade her to consider it as improbable. Kitty and Lydia were far from envying Miss Lucas, for Mr. Collins was only a clergyman; and it affected them in no other way than as a piece of news to spread at Meryton.

Lady Lucas could not be insensible of triumph on being able to retort on Mrs. Bennet the comfort of having a daughter well married; and she called at Longbourn rather oftener than usual to say how happy she was, though Mrs. Bennet's sour looks and ill-natured remarks might have been enough to drive happiness away.

Between Elizabeth and Charlotte there was a restraint which kept them mutually silent on the subject; and Elizabeth felt persuaded that no real confidence could ever subsist between them again. Her disappointment in Charlotte made her turn with fonder regard to her sister, of whose rectitude and delicacy she was sure her opinion could never be shaken, and for whose happiness she grew daily more anxious, as Bingley had now been gone a week and nothing more was heard of his return.

Jane had sent Caroline an early answer to her letter, and was counting the days till she might reasonably hope to hear again. The promised letter of thanks from Mr. Collins arrived on Tuesday, addressed to their father, and written with all the solemnity of gratitude which a twelvemonth's abode in the family might have prompted. After discharging his conscience on that head, he proceeded to inform them, with many rapturous expressions, of his happiness in having obtained the affection of their amiable neighbour, Miss Lucas, and then explained that it was merely with the view of enjoying her society that he had been so ready to close with their kind wish of seeing him again at Longbourn, whither he hoped to be able to return on Monday fortnight; for Lady Catherine, he added, so heartily approved his marriage, that she wished it to take place as soon as possible, which he trusted would be an unanswerable argument with his amiable Charlotte to name an early day for making him the happiest of men.

Mr. Collins's return into Hertfordshire was no longer a matter of pleasure to Mrs. Bennet. On the contrary, she was as much disposed to complain of it as her husband. It was very strange that he should come to Longbourn instead of to Lucas Lodge; it was also very inconvenient and exceedingly troublesome. She hated having visitors in the house while her health was so indifferent, and lovers were of all people the most disagreeable. Such were the gentle murmurs of Mrs. Bennet, and they gave way only to the greater distress of Mr. Bingley's continued absence.

Neither Jane nor Elizabeth were comfortable on this subject. Day after day passed away without bringing any other tidings of him than the report which shortly prevailed in Meryton of his coming no more to Netherfield the whole winter; a report which highly incensed Mrs. Bennet, and which she never failed to contradict as a most scandalous falsehood.

Even Elizabeth began to fear—not that Bingley was indifferent—but that his sisters would be successful in keeping him away. Unwilling as she was to admit an idea so destructive of Jane's happiness, and so dishonorable to the stability of her lover, she could not prevent its frequently occurring. The united efforts of his two unfeeling sisters and of his overpowering friend, assisted by the attractions of Miss Darcy and the amusements of London might be too much, she feared, for the strength of his attachment.

As for Jane, HER anxiety under this suspense was, of course, more painful than Elizabeth's, but whatever she felt she was desirous of concealing, and between herself and Elizabeth, therefore, the subject was never alluded to. But as no such delicacy restrained her mother, an hour seldom passed in which she did not talk of Bingley, express her impatience for his arrival, or even require Jane to confess that if he did not come back she would think herself very ill used. It needed all Jane's steady mildness to bear these attacks with tolerable tranquillity.

Mr. Collins returned most punctually on Monday fortnight, but his reception at Longbourn was not quite so gracious as it had been on his first introduction. He was too happy, however, to need much attention; and luckily for the others, the business of love-making relieved them from a great deal of his company. The chief of every day was spent by him at Lucas Lodge, and he sometimes returned to Longbourn only in time to make an apology for his absence before the family went to bed.

Mrs. Bennet was really in a most pitiable state. The very mention of anything concerning the match threw her into an agony of ill-humour, and wherever she went she was sure of hearing it talked of. The sight of Miss Lucas was odious to her. As her successor in that house, she regarded her with jealous abhorrence. Whenever Charlotte came to see them, she concluded her to be anticipating the hour of possession; and whenever she spoke in a low voice to Mr. Collins, was convinced that they were talking of the Longbourn estate, and resolving to turn herself and her daughters out of the house, as soon as Mr. Bennet were dead. She complained bitterly of all this to her husband.

"Indeed, Mr. Bennet," said she, "it is very hard to think that Charlotte Lucas should ever be mistress of this house, that I should be forced to make way for HER, and live to see her take her place in it!"

"My dear, do not give way to such gloomy thoughts. Let us hope for better things. Let us flatter ourselves that I may be the survivor."

This is not very consoling to Mrs. Bennet, and therefore, instead of making any answer, she went on as before.

"I cannot bear to think that they should have all this estate. If it was not for the entail, I should not mind it."

"What should not you mind?"

"I should not mind anything at all."

"Let us be thankful that you are preserved from a state of such insensibility."

"I never can be thankful, Mr. Bennet, for anything about the entail. How anyone could have the conscience to entail away an estate from one's own daughters, I cannot understand; and all for the sake of Mr. Collins too! Why should HE have it more than anybody else?"

"I leave it to yourself to determine," said Mr. Bennet.

Chapter 24

Miss Bingley's letter arrived, and put an end to doubt. The very first sentence conveyed the assurance of their being all settled in London for the winter, and concluded with her brother's regret at not having had time to pay his respects to his friends in Hertfordshire before he left the country.

Hope was over, entirely over; and when Jane could attend to the rest of the letter, she found little, except the professed affection of the writer, that could give her any comfort. Miss Darcy's praise occupied the chief of it. Her many attractions were again dwelt on, and Caroline boasted joyfully of their increasing intimacy, and ventured to predict the accomplishment of the wishes which had been unfolded in her former letter. She wrote also with great pleasure of her brother's being an inmate of Mr. Darcy's house, and mentioned with raptures some plans of the latter with regard to new furniture.

Elizabeth, to whom Jane very soon communicated the chief of all this, heard it in silent indignation. Her heart was divided between concern for her sister, and resentment against all others. To Caroline's assertion of her brother's being partial to Miss Darcy she paid no credit. That he was really fond of Jane, she doubted no more than she had ever done; and much as she had always been disposed to like him, she could not think without anger, hardly without contempt, on that easiness of temper, that want of proper resolution, which now made him the slave of his designing friends, and led him to sacrifice of his own happiness to the caprice of their inclination. Had his own happiness, however, been the only sacrifice, he might have been allowed to sport with it in whatever manner he thought best, but her sister's was involved in it, as she thought he must be sensible himself. It was a subject, in short, on which reflection would be long indulged, and must be unavailing. She could think of nothing else; and yet whether Bingley's regard had really died away, or were suppressed by his friends' interference; whether he had been aware of Jane's attachment, or whether it had escaped his observation; whatever were the case, though her opinion of him must be materially affected by the difference, her sister's situation remained the same, her peace equally wounded.

A day or two passed before Jane had courage to speak of her feelings to Elizabeth; but at last, on Mrs. Bennet's leaving them together, after a longer irritation than usual about Netherfield and its master, she could not help saying:

"Oh, that my dear mother had more command over herself! She can have no idea of the pain she gives me by her continual reflections on him. But I will not repine. It cannot last long. He will be forgot, and we shall all be as we were before."

Elizabeth looked at her sister with incredulous solicitude, but said nothing.

"You doubt me," cried Jane, slightly colouring; "indeed, you have no reason. He may live in my memory as the most amiable man of my acquaintance, but that is all. I have nothing either to hope or fear, and nothing to reproach him with. Thank God! I have not THAT pain. A little time, therefore—I shall certainly try to get the better."

With a stronger voice she soon added, "I have this comfort immediately, that it has not been more than an error of fancy on my side, and that it has done no harm to anyone but myself."

"My dear Jane!" exclaimed Elizabeth, "you are too good. Your sweetness and disinterestedness are really angelic; I do not know what to say to you. I feel as if I had never done you justice, or loved you as you deserve."

Miss Bennet eagerly disclaimed all extraordinary merit, and threw back the praise on her sister's warm affection.

"Nay," said Elizabeth, "this is not fair. YOU wish to think all the world respectable, and are hurt if I speak ill of anybody. I only want to think YOU perfect, and you set yourself against it. Do not be afraid of my running into any excess, of my encroaching on your privilege of universal good-will. You need not. There are few people whom I really love, and still fewer of whom I think well. The more I see of the world, the more am I dissatisfied with it; and every day confirms my belief of the inconsistency of all human characters, and of the little dependence that can be placed on the appearance of merit or sense. I have met with two instances lately, one I will not mention; the other is Charlotte's marriage. It is unaccountable! In every view it is unaccountable!"

"My dear Lizzy, do not give way to such feelings as these. They will ruin your happiness. You do not make allowance enough for difference of situation and temper. Consider Mr. Collins's respectability, and Charlotte's steady, prudent character. Remember that she is one of a large family; that as to fortune, it is a most eligible match; and be ready to believe, for everybody's sake, that she may feel something like regard and esteem for our cousin."

"To oblige you, I would try to believe almost anything, but no one else could be benefited by such a belief as this; for were I persuaded that Charlotte had any regard for him, I should only think worse of her understanding than I now do of her heart. My dear Jane, Mr. Collins is a conceited, pompous, narrow-minded, silly man; you know he is, as well as I do; and you must feel, as well as I do, that the woman who married him cannot have a proper way of thinking. You shall not defend her, though it is Charlotte Lucas. You shall not, for the sake of one individual, change the meaning of principle and integrity, nor endeavour to persuade yourself or me, that selfishness is prudence, and insensibility of danger security for happiness."

"I must think your language too strong in speaking of both," replied Jane; "and I hope you will be convinced of it by seeing them happy together. But enough of this. You alluded to something else. You mentioned TWO instances. I cannot misunderstand you, but I entreat you, dear Lizzy, not to pain me by thinking THAT PERSON to blame, and saying your opinion of him is sunk. We must not be so ready to fancy ourselves intentionally injured. We must not expect a lively young man to be always so guarded and circumspect. It is very often nothing but our own vanity that deceives us. Women fancy admiration means more than it does."

"And men take care that they should."

"If it is designedly done, they cannot be justified; but I have no idea of there being so much design in the world as some persons imagine.

"I am far from attributing any part of Mr. Bingley's conduct to design," said Elizabeth; "but without scheming to do wrong, or to make others unhappy, there may be error, and there may be misery. Thoughtlessness, want of attention to other people's feelings, and want of resolution, will do the business."

"And do you impute it to either of those?"

"Yes; to the last. But if I go on, I shall displease you by saying what I think of persons you esteem Stop me whilst you can."

"You persist, then, in supposing his sisters influence him?"

Yes, in conjunction with his friend."

"I cannot believe it. Why should they try to influence him? They can only wish his happiness; and if he is attached to me, no other woman can secure it."

"Your first position is false. They may wish many things besides his happiness; they may wish his increase of wealth and consequence; they may wish him to marry a girl who has all the importance of money, great connections, and pride."

"Beyond a doubt, they do wish him to choose Miss Darcy," replied Jane; "but this may be from better feelings than you are supposing. They have known her much longer than they have known me; no wonder if they love her better. But, whatever may be their own wishes, it is very unlikely they should have opposed their brother's. What sister would think herself at liberty to do it, unless there were something very objectionable? If they believed him attached to me, they would not try to part us; if he were so, they could not succeed. By supposing such an affection, you make everybody acting unnaturally and wrong, and me most unhappy. Do not distress me by the idea. I am not ashamed of having been mistaken—or, at least, it is light, it is nothing in comparison of what I should feel in thinking ill of him or his sisters. Let me take it in the best light, in the light in which it may be understood."

Elizabeth could not oppose such a wish; and from this time Mr. Bingley's name was scarcely ever mentioned between them."

Mrs. Bennet still continued to wonder and repine at his returning no more, and though a day seldom passed in which Elizabeth did not account for it clearly, there was little chance of her ever considering it with less perplexity. Her daughter endeavoured to convince her of what she did not believe herself, that his attentions to Jane had been merely the effect of a common and transient liking, which ceased when he saw her no more; but though the probability of the statement was admitted at the time, she had the same story to repeat every day. Mrs. Bennet's best comfort was that Mr. Bingley must be down again in the summer.

Mr. Bennet treated the matter differently. "So, Lizzy," said he one day, "your sister is crossed in love, I find. I congratulate her. Next to being married, a girl likes to be crossed a little in love now and then. It is something to think of, and it gives her a sort of distinction among her companions. When is your turn to come? You will hardly bear to be long outdone by Jane. Now is your time. Here are officers enough in Meryton to disappoint all the young ladies in the country. Let Wickham be your man. He is a pleasant fellow, and would jilt you creditably."

"Thank you, sir, but a less agreeable man would satisfy me. We must not all expect Jane's good fortune."

"True," said Mr. Bennet, "but it is a comfort to think that whatever of that kind may befall you, you have an affectionate mother who will make the most of it."

Mr. Wickham's society was of material service in dispelling the gloom which the late perverse occurrences had thrown on many of the Longbourn family. They saw him often, and to his other recommendations was now added that of general unreserve. The whole of what Elizabeth had already heard, his claims on Mr. Darcy, and all that he had suffered from him, was now openly acknowledged and publicly canvassed; and everybody was pleased to know how much they had always disliked Mr. Darcy before they had known anything of the matter.

Miss Bennet was the only creature who could suppose there might be any extenuating circumstances in the case, unknown to the society of Hertfordshire; her mild and steady candour always pleaded for allowances, and urged the possibility of mistakes—but by everybody else Mr. Darcy was condemned as the worst of men.

Chapter 25

After a week spent in professions of love and schemes of felicity, Mr. Collins was called from his amiable Charlotte by the arrival of Saturday. The pain of separation, however, might be alleviated on his side, by preparations for the reception of his bride; as he had reason to hope, that shortly after his return into Hertfordshire, the day would be fixed that was to make him the happiest of men. He took leave of his relations at Longbourn with as much solemnity as before; wished his fair cousins health and happiness again, and promised their father another letter of thanks.

On the following Monday, Mrs. Bennet had the pleasure of receiving her brother and his wife, who came as usual to spend the Christmas at Longbourn. Mr. Gardiner was a sensible, gentlemanlike man, greatly superior to his sister, as well by nature as education. The Netherfield ladies would have had difficulty in believing that a man who lived by trade, and within view of his own warehouses, could have been so well-bred and agreeable. Mrs. Gardiner, who was several years younger than Mrs. Bennet and Mrs. Phillips, was an amiable, intelligent, elegant woman, and a great favourite with all her Longbourn nieces. Between the two eldest and herself especially, there subsisted a particular regard. They had frequently been staying with her in town.

The first part of Mrs. Gardiner's business on her arrival was to distribute her presents and describe the newest fashions. When this was done she had a less active part to play. It became her turn to listen. Mrs. Bennet had many grievances to relate, and much to complain of. They had all been very ill-used since she last saw her sister. Two of her girls had been upon the point of marriage, and after all there was nothing in it.

"I do not blame Jane," she continued, "for Jane would have got Mr. Bingley if she could. But Lizzy! Oh, sister! It is very hard to think that she might have been Mr. Collins's wife by this time, had it not been for her own perverseness. He made her an offer in this very room, and she refused him. The consequence of it is, that Lady Lucas will have a daughter married before I have, and that the Longbourn estate is just as much entailed as ever. The Lucases are very artful people indeed, sister. They are all for what they can get. I am sorry to say it of them, but so it is. It makes me very nervous and poorly, to be thwarted so in my own family, and to have neighbours who think of themselves before anybody else. However, your coming just at this time is the greatest of comforts, and I am very glad to hear what you tell us, of long sleeves."

Mrs. Gardiner, to whom the chief of this news had been given before, in the course of Jane and Elizabeth's correspondence with her, made her sister a slight answer, and, in compassion to her nieces, turned the conversation.

When alone with Elizabeth afterwards, she spoke more on the subject.

"It seems likely to have been a desirable match for Jane," said she. "I am sorry it went off. But these things happen so often! A young man, such as you describe Mr. Bingley, so easily falls in love with a pretty girl for a few weeks, and when accident separates them, so easily forgets her, that these sort of inconsistencies are very frequent."

"An excellent consolation in its way," said Elizabeth, "but it will not do for US. We do not suffer by accident. It does not often happen that the interference of friends will persuade a young man of independent fortune to think no more of a girl whom he was violently in love with only a few days before."

"But that expression of violently in love' is so hackneyed, so doubtful, so indefinite, that it gives me very little idea. It is as often applied to feelings which arise from a half-hour's acquaintance, as to a real, strong attachment. Pray, how VIOLENT WAS Mr. Bingley's love?"

"I never saw a more promising inclination; he was growing quite inattentive to other people, and wholly engrossed by her. Every time they met, it was more decided and remarkable. At his own ball he offended two or three young ladies, by not asking them to dance; and I spoke to him twice myself, without receiving an answer. Could there be finer symptoms? Is not general incivility the very essence of love?"

"Oh, yes! of that kind of love which I suppose him to have felt. Poor Jane! I am sorry for her, because, with her disposition, she may not get over it immediately. It had better have happened to YOU, Lizzy; you would have laughed yourself out of it sooner. But do you think she would be prevailed upon to go back with us? Change of scene might be of service—and perhaps a little relief from home may be as useful as anything."

Elizabeth was exceedingly pleased with this proposal, and felt persuaded of her sister's ready acquiescence.

"I hope," added Mrs. Gardiner, "that no consideration with regard to this young man will influence her. We live in so different a part of town, all our connections are so different, and, as you well know, we go out so little, that it is very improbable that they should meet at all, unless he really comes to see her."

"And THAT is quite impossible; for he is now in the custody of his friend, and Mr. Darcy would no more suffer him to call on Jane in such a part of London! My dear aunt, how could you think of it? Mr. Darcy may perhaps have HEARD of such a place as Gracechurch Street, but he would hardly think a month's ablution enough to cleanse him from its impurities, were he once to enter it; and depend upon it, Mr. Bingley never stirs without him."

"So much the better. I hope they will not meet at all. But does not Jane correspond with his sister? SHE will not be able to help calling."

"She will drop the acquaintance entirely."

But in spite of the certainty in which Elizabeth affected to place this point, as well as the still more interesting one of Bingley's being withheld from seeing Jane, she felt a solicitude on the subject which convinced her, on examination, that she did not consider it entirely hopeless. It was possible, and sometimes she thought it probable, that his affection might be reanimated, and the influence of his friends successfully combated by the more natural influence of Jane's attractions.

Miss Bennet accepted her aunt's invitation with pleasure; and the Bingleys were no otherwise in her thoughts at the same time, than as she hoped by Caroline's not living in the same house with her brother, she might occasionally spend a morning with her, without any danger of seeing him.

The Gardiners stayed a week at Longbourn; and what with the Plillipses, the Lucases, and the officers, there was not a day without its engagement. Mrs. Bennet had so carefully provided for the entertainment of her brother and sister, that they did not once sit down to a family dinner. When the engagement was for home, some of the officers always made part of it—of which officers Mr. Wickham was sure to be one; and on these occasion, Mrs. Gardiner, rendered suspicious by Elizabeth's warm commendation, narrowly observed them both. Without supposing them, from what she saw, to be very seriously in love, their preference of each other was plain enough to make her a little uneasy; and she resolved to speak to Elizabeth on the subject before she left Hertfordshire, and represent to her the imprudence of encouraging such an attachment.

To Mrs. Gardiner, Wickham had one means of affording pleasure, unconnected with his general powers. About ten or a dozen years ago, before her marriage, she had spent a considerable time in that very part of Derbyshire to which he belonged. They had, therefore, many acquaintances in common; and though Wickham had been little there since the death of Darcy's father, it was yet in his power to give her fresher intelligence of her former friends than she had been in the way of procuring.

Mrs. Gardiner had seen Pemberly, and known the late Mr. Darcy by character perfectly well. Here consequently was an inexhaustible subject of discourse. In comparing her recollection of Pemberly with the minute description which Wickham could give, and in bestowing her tribute of praise on the character of its late possessor, she was delighting both him and herself. On being made acquainted with the present Mr. Darcy's treatment of him, she tried to remember some of that gentleman's reputed disposition when quite a lad which might agree with it, and was confident at last that she recollected having heard Mr. Fitzwilliam Darcy formerly spoken of as a very proud, ill-natured boy.

Chapter 26

Mrs. Gardiner's caution to Elizabeth was punctually and kindly given on the first favourable opportunity of speaking to her alone; after honestly telling her what she thought, she thus went on:

"You are too sensible a girl, Lizzy, to fall in love merely because you are warned against it; and, therefore, I am not afraid of speaking openly. Seriously, I would have you be on your guard. Do not involve yourself or endeavour to involve him in an affection which the want of fortune would make so very imprudent. I have nothing to say against HIM; he is a most interesting young man; and if he had the fortune he ought to have, I should think you could not do better. But as it is, you must not let your fancy run away with you. You have sense, and we all expect you to use it. Your father would depend on YOUR resolution and good conduct, I am sure. You must not disappoint your father."

"My dear aunt, this is being serious indeed."

"Yes, and I hope to engage you to be serious likewise."

"Well, then, you need not be under any alarm. I will take care of myself, and of Mr. Wickham too. He shall not be in love with me, if I can prevent it."

"Elizabeth, you are not serious now."

"I beg your pardon, I will try again. At present I am not in love with Mr. Wickham; no, I certainly am not. But he is, beyond all comparison, the most agreeable man I ever saw—and if he becomes really attached to me—I believe it will be better that he should not. I see the imprudence of it. Oh! THAT abominable Mr. Darcy! My father's opinion of me does me the greatest honour, and I should be miserable to forfeit it. My father, however, is partial to Mr. Wickham. In short, my dear aunt, I should be very sorry to be the means of making any of you unhappy; but since we see every day that where there is affection, young people are seldom withheld by immediate want of fortune from entering into engagements with each other, how can I promise to be wiser than so many of my fellow-creatures if I am tempted, or how am I even to know that it would be wisdom to resist? All that I can promise you, therefore, is not to be in a hurry. I will not be in a hurry to believe myself his first object. When I am in company with him, I will not be wishing. In short, I will do my best."

"Perhaps it will be as well if you discourage his coming here so very often. At least, you should not REMIND you mother of inviting him."

"As I did the other day," said Elizabeth with a conscious smile: "very true, it will be wise in me to refrain from THAT. But do not imagine that he is always here so often. It is on your account that he has been so frequently invited this week. You know my mother's ideas as to the necessity of constant company for her friends. But really, and upon my honour, I will try to do what I think to be the wisest; and now I hope you are satisfied."

Her aunt assured her that she was, and Elizabeth having thanked her for the kindness of her hints, they parted; a wonderful instance of advice being given on such a point, without being resented.

Mr. Collins returned into Hertfordshire soon after it had been quitted by the Gardiners and Jane; but as he took up his abode with the Lucases, his arrival was no great inconvenience to Mrs. Bennet. His marriage was now fast approaching, and she was at length so far resigned as to think it inevitable, and even repeatedly to say, in an ill-natured tone, that she "WISHED they might be happy." Thursday was to be the wedding day, and on Wednesday Miss Lucas paid her farewell visit; and when she rose to take leave, Elizabeth, ashamed of her mother's ungracious and reluctant good wishes, and sincerely affected herself, accompanied her out of the room. As they went downstairs together, Charlotte said:

"I shall depend on hearing from you very often, Eliza."

"THAT you certainly shall."

"And I have another favour to ask you. Will you come and see me?"

"We shall often meet, I hope, in Hertfordshire."

"I am not likely to leave Kent for some time. Promise me, therefore, to come to Hunsford."

Elizabeth could not refuse, though she foresaw little pleasure in the visit.

"My father and Maria are coming to me in March," added Charlotte, "and I hope you will consent to be of the party. Indeed, Eliza, you will be as welcome as either of them."

The wedding took place: the bride and bridegroom set off for Kent from the church door, and everybody had as much to say, or to hear, on the subject as usual. Elizabeth soon heard from her friend; and their correspondence was as regular and frequent as it had ever been; that it should be equally unreserved was impossible. Elizabeth could never address her without feeling that all the comfort of intimacy was over, and though determined not to slacken as a correspondent, it was for the sake of what had been, rather than what was. Charlotte's first letters were received with a good deal of eagerness; there could not but be curiosity to know how she would speak of her new home, how she would like Lady Catherine, and how happy she would dare pronounce herself to be; though, when the letters were read, Elizabeth felt that Charlotte expressed herself on every point exactly as she might have foreseen. She wrote cheerfully, seemed surrounded with comforts, and mentioned nothing which she could not praise. The house, furniture, neighbourhood, and roads, were all to her taste, and Lady Catherine's behaviour was most friendly and obliging. It was Mr. Collins's picture of Hunsford and Rosings rationally softened; and Elizabeth perceived that she must wait for her own visit there to know the rest.

Jane had already written a few lines to her sister to announce their safe arrival in London; and when she wrote again, Elizabeth hoped it would be in her power to say something of the Bingleys.

Her impatience for this second letter was as well rewarded as impatience generally is. Jane had been a week in town without either seeing or hearing from Caroline. She accounted for it, however, by supposing that her last letter to her friend from Longbourn had by some accident been lost.

"My aunt," she continued, "is going to-morrow into that part of the town, and I shall take the opportunity of calling in Grosvenor Street."

She wrote again when the visit was paid, and she had seen Miss Bingley. "I did not think Caroline in spirits," were her words, "but she was very glad to see me, and reproached me for giving her no notice of my coming to London. I was right, therefore, my last letter had never reached her. I inquired after their brother, of course. He was well, but so much engaged with Mr. Darcy that they scarcely ever saw him. I found that Miss Darcy was expected to dinner. I wish I could see her. My visit was not long, as Caroline and Mrs. Hurst were going out. I dare say I shall see them soon here."

Elizabeth shook her head over this letter. It convinced her that accident only could discover to Mr. Bingley her sister's being in town.

Four weeks passed away, and Jane saw nothing of him. She endeavoured to persuade herself that she did not regret it; but she could no longer be blind to Miss Bingley's inattention. After waiting at home every morning for a fortnight, and inventing every evening a fresh excuse for her, the visitor did at last appear; but the shortness of her stay, and yet more, the alteration of her manner would allow Jane to deceive herself no longer. The letter which she wrote on this occasion to her sister will prove what she felt.

"My dearest Lizzy will, I am sure, be incapable of triumphing in her better judgement, at my expense, when I confess myself to have been entirely deceived in Miss Bingley's regard for me. But, my dear sister, though the event has proved you right, do not think me obstinate if I still assert that, considering what her behaviour was, my confidence was as natural as your suspicion. I do not at all comprehend her reason for wishing to be intimate with me; but if the same circumstances were to happen again, I am sure I should be deceived again. Caroline did not return my visit till yesterday; and not a note, not a line, did I receive in the meantime. When she did come, it was very evident that she had no pleasure in it; she made a slight, formal apology, for not calling before, said not a word of wishing to see me again, and was in every respect so altered a creature, that when she went away I was perfectly resolved to continue the acquaintance no longer. I pity, though I cannot help blaming her. She was very wrong in singling me out as she did; I can safely say that every advance to intimacy began on her side. But I pity her, because she must feel that she has been acting wrong, and because I am very sure that anxiety for her brother is the cause of it. I need not explain myself farther; and though WE know this anxiety to be quite needless, yet if she feels it, it will easily account for her behaviour to me; and so deservedly dear as he is to his sister, whatever anxiety she must feel on his behalf is natural and amiable. I cannot but wonder, however, at her having any such fears now, because, if he had at all cared about me, we must have met, long ago. He knows of my being in town, I am certain, from something she said herself; and yet it would seem, by her manner of talking, as if she wanted to persuade herself that he is really partial to Miss Darcy. I cannot understand it. If I were not afraid of judging harshly, I should be almost tempted to say that there is a strong appearance of duplicity in all this. But I will endeavour to banish every painful thought, and think only of what will make me happy—your affection, and the invariable kindness of my dear uncle and aunt. Let me hear from you very soon. Miss Bingley said something of his never returning to Netherfield again, of giving up the house, but not with any certainty. We had better not mention it. I am extremely glad that you have such pleasant accounts from our friends at Hunsford. Pray go to see them, with Sir William and Maria. I am sure you will be very comfortable there.—Yours, etc."

* * *

This letter gave Elizabeth some pain; but her spirits returned as she considered that Jane wold no longer be duped, by the sister at least. All expectation from the brother was now absolutely over. She would not even wish for a renewal of his attentions. His character sunk on every review of it; and as a punishment for him, as well as a possible advantage to Jane, she seriously hoped he might really soon marry Mr. Darcy's sister, as by Wickham's account, she would make him abundantly regret what he had thrown away.

Mrs. Gardiner about this time reminded Elizabeth of her promise concerning that gentleman, and required information; and Elizabeth had such to send as might rather give contentment to her aunt than to herself. His apparent partiality had subsided, his attentions were over, he was the admirer of some one else. Elizabeth was watchful enough to see it all, but she could see it and write of it without material pain. Her heart had been but slightly touched, and her vanity was satisfied with believing that SHE would have been his only choice, had fortune permitted it. The sudden acquisition of ten thousand pounds was the most remarkable charm of the young lady to whom he was now rendering himself agreeable; but Elizabeth, less clear-sighted perhaps in this case than in Charlotte's, did not quarrel with him for his wish of independence. Nothing, on the contrary, could be more natural; and while able to suppose that it cost him a few struggle to relinquish her, she was ready to allow it a wise and desirable measure for both, and could very sincerely wish him happy.

All this was acknowledged to Mrs. Gardiner; and after relating the circumstances, she thus went on:—"I am now convinced, my dear aunt, that I have never been much in love; for had I really experiences that pure and elevating passion, I should at present detest his very name, and wish him all manner of evil. But my feelings are not only cordial towards HIM; they are even impartial towards Miss King. I cannot find out that I hate her at all, or that I am in the least unwilling to think her a very good sort of girl. There can be no love in all this. My watchfulness has been effectual; and though I certainly should be a more interesting object to all my acquaintances were I distractedly in love with him, I cannot say that I regret my comparative insignificance. Importance may sometimes be purchased too dearly. Kitty and Lydia take his defection much more to heart than I do. They are young in the ways of the world, and not yet open to the mortifying conviction that handsome young men must have something to live on as well as the plain."

Chapter 27

With no greater events than these in the Longbourn family, and otherwise diversified by little beyond the walks to Meryton, sometimes dirty and sometimes cold, did January and February pass away. March was to take Elizabeth to Hunsford. She had not at first thought very seriously of going thither; but Charlotte, she soon found, was depending on the plan and she gradually learned to consider it herself with greater pleasure as well as greater certainty. Absence had increased her desire of seeing Charlotte again, and weakened her disgust of Mr. Collins. There was novelty in the scheme, and as, with such a mother and such uncompanionable sisters, home could not be faultless, a little change was not unwelcome for its own sake. The journey would moreover give her a peep at Jane; and, in short, as the time drew near, she would have been very sorry for any delay. Everything, however, went on smoothly, and was finally settled according to Charlotte's first sketch. She was to accompany Sir William and his second daughter. The improvement of spending a night in London was added in time, and the plan became perfect as plan could be.

The only pain was in leaving her father, who would certainly miss her, and who, when it came to the point, so little liked her going, that he told her to write to him, and almost promised to answer her letter.

The farewell between herself and Mr. Wickham was perfectly friendly; on his side even more. His present pursuit could not make him forget that Elizabeth had been the first to excite and to deserve his attention, the first to listen and to pity, the first to be admired; and in his manner of bidding her adieu, wishing her every enjoyment, reminding her of what she was to expect in Lady Catherine de Bourgh, and trusting their opinion of her—their opinion of everybody—would always coincide, there was a solicitude, an interest which she felt must ever attach her to him with a most sincere regard; and she parted from him convinced that, whether married or single, he must always be her model of the amiable and pleasing.

Her fellow-travellers the next day were not of a kind to make her think him less agreeable. Sir William Lucas, and his daughter Maria, a good-humoured girl, but as empty-headed as himself, had nothing to say that could be worth hearing, and were listened to with about as much delight as the rattle of the chaise. Elizabeth loved absurdities, but she had known Sir William's too long. He could tell her nothing new of the wonders of his presentation and knighthood; and his civilities were worn out, like his information.

It was a journey of only twenty-four miles, and they began it so early as to be in Gracechurch Street by noon. As they drove to Mr. Gardiner's door, Jane was at a drawing-room window watching their arrival; when they entered the passage she was there to welcome them, and Elizabeth, looking earnestly in her face, was pleased to see it healthful and lovely as ever. On the stairs were a troop of little boys and girls, whose eagerness for their cousin's appearance would not allow them to wait in the drawing-room, and whose shyness, as they had not seen her for a twelvemonth, prevented their coming lower. All was joy and kindness. The day passed most pleasantly away; the morning in bustle and shopping, and the evening at one of the theatres.

Elizabeth then contrived to sit by her aunt. Their first object was her sister; and she was more grieved than astonished to hear, in reply to her minute inquiries, that though Jane always struggled to support her spirits, there were periods of dejection. It was reasonable, however, to hope that they would not continue long. Mrs. Gardiner gave her the particulars also of Miss Bingley's visit in Gracechurch Street, and repeated conversations occurring at different times between Jane and herself, which proved that the former had, from her heart, given up the acquaintance.

Mrs. Gardiner then rallied her niece on Wickham's desertion, and complimented her on bearing it so well.

"But my dear Elizabeth," she added, "what sort of girl is Miss King? I should be sorry to think our friend mercenary."

"Pray, my dear aunt, what is the difference in matrimonial affairs, between the mercenary and the prudent motive? Where does discretion end, and avarice begin? Last Christmas you were afraid of his marrying me, because it would be imprudent; and now, because he is trying to get a girl with only ten thousand pounds, you want to find out that he is mercenary."

"If you will only tell me what sort of girl Miss King is, I shall know what to think."

"She is a very good kind of girl, I believe. I know no harm of her."

"But he paid her not the smallest attention till her grandfather's death made her mistress of this fortune."

"No—what should he? If it were not allowable for him to gain MY affections because I had no money, what occasion could there be for making love to a girl whom he did not care about, and who was equally poor?"

"But there seems an indelicacy in directing his attentions towards her so soon after this event."

"A man in distressed circumstances has not time for all those elegant decorums which other people may observe. If SHE does not object to it, why should WE?"

"HER not objecting does not justify HIM. It only shows her being deficient in something herself—sense or feeling."

"Well," cried Elizabeth, "have it as you choose. HE shall be mercenary, and SHE shall be foolish."

"No, Lizzy, that is what I do NOT choose. I should be sorry, you know, to think ill of a young man who has lived so long in Derbyshire."

"Oh! if that is all, I have a very poor opinion of young men who live in Derbyshire; and their intimate friends who live in Hertfordshire are not much better. I am sick of them all. Thank Heaven! I am going tomorrow where I shall find a man who has not one agreeable quality, who has neither manner nor sense to recommend him. Stupid men are the only ones worth knowing, after all."

"Take care, Lizzy; that speech savours strongly of disappointment."

Before they were separated by the conclusion of the play, she had the unexpected happiness of an invitation to accompany her uncle and aunt in a tour of pleasure which they proposed taking in the summer.

"We have not determined how far it shall carry us," said Mrs. Gardiner, "but, perhaps, to the Lakes."

No scheme could have been more agreeable to Elizabeth, and her acceptance of the invitation was most ready and grateful. "Oh, my dear, dear aunt," she rapturously cried, "what delight! what felicity! You give me fresh life and vigour. Adieu to disappointment and spleen. What are young men to rocks and mountains? Oh! what hours of transport we shall spend! And when we DO return, it shall not be like other travellers, without being able to give one accurate idea of anything. We WILL know where we have gone—we WILL recollect what we have seen. Lakes, mountains, and rivers shall not be jumbled together in our imaginations; nor when we attempt to describe any particular scene, will we begin quarreling about its relative situation. Let OUR first effusions be less insupportable than those of the generality of travellers."

Chapter 28

Every object in the next day's journey was new and interesting to Elizabeth; and her spirits were in a state of enjoyment; for she had seen her sister looking so well as to banish all fear for her health, and the prospect of her northern tour was a constant source of delight.

When they left the high road for the lane to Hunsford, every eye was in search of the Parsonage, and every turning expected to bring it in view. The palings of Rosings Park was their boundary on one side. Elizabeth smiled at the recollection of all that she had heard of its inhabitants.

At length the Parsonage was discernible. The garden sloping to the road, the house standing in it, the green pales, and the laurel hedge, everything declared they were arriving. Mr. Collins and Charlotte appeared at the door, and the carriage stopped at the small gate which led by a short gravel walk to the house, amidst the nods and smiles of the whole party. In a moment they were all out of the chaise, rejoicing at the sight of each other. Mrs. Collins welcomed her friend with the liveliest pleasure, and Elizabeth was more and more satisfied with coming when she found herself so affectionately received. She saw instantly that her cousin's manner were not altered by his marriage; his formal civility was just what it had been, and he detained her some minutes at the gate to hear and satisfy his inquiries after all her family. They were then, with no other delay than his pointing out the neatness of the entrance taken into the house; and as soon as they were in the parlour, he welcomed them a second time, with ostentatious formality to his humble abode, and punctually repeated all his wife's offers of refreshment.

Elizabeth was prepared to see him in his glory; and she could not help in fancying that in displaying the good proportion of the room, its aspect and its furniture, he addressed himself particularly to her, as if wishing to make her feel what she had lost in refusing him. But though everything seemed neat and comfortable, she was not able to gratify him by any sigh of repentance, and rather looked with wonder at her friend that she could have so cheerful an air with such a companion. When Mr. Collins said anything of which his wife might reasonably be ashamed, which certainly was not unseldom, she involuntarily turned her eye on Charlotte. Once of twice she could discern a faint blush; but in general Charlotte wisely did not hear. After sitting long enough to admire every article of furniture in the room, from the sideboard to the fender, to give an account of their journey, and of all that had happened in London, Mr. Collins invited them to take a stroll in the garden, which was large and well laid out, and to the cultivation of which he attended himself. To work in this garden was one of his most respectable pleasures; and Elizabeth admired the command of countenance with which Charlotte talked of the healthfulness of the exercise, and owned she encouraged it as much as possible. Here, leading the way through every walk and cross walk, and scarcely allowing them an interval to utter the praises he asked for, every view was pointed out with a minuteness which left beauty entirely behind. He could number the fields in every direction, and could tell how many tress there were in the most distant clump. But of all the views which his garden, or which the country or kingdom could boast, none were to be compared with the prospect of Rosings, afforded by an opening in the trees that bordered the park nearly opposite the front of his house. It was a handsome modern building, well situated on rising ground.

From his garden, Mr. Collins would have led them round his two meadows; but the ladies, not having shoes to encounter the remains of a white frost, turned back; and while Sir William accompanied him, Charlotte took her sister and friend over the house, extremely well pleased, probably, to have the opportunity of showing it without her husband's help. It was rather small, but well built and convenient; and everything was fitted up and arranged with a neatness and consistency of which Elizabeth gave Charlotte all the credit. When Mr. Collins could be forgotten, there was really an air of great comfort throughout, and by

Charlotte's evident enjoyment of it, Elizabeth supposed he must be often forgotten.

She had already learnt that Lady Catherine was still in the country. It was spoken of again while they were at dinner, when Mr. Collins joining in, observed:

"Yes, Miss Elizabeth, you will have the honour of seeing Lady Catherine de Bourgh on the ensuing Sunday at church, and I need not say you will be delighted with her. She is all affability and condescension, and I doubt not but you will be honoured with some portion of her notice when service is over. I have scarcely any hesitation in saying she will include you and my sister Maria in every invitation with which she honours us during your stay here. Her behaviour to my dear Charlotte is charming. We dine at Rosings twice every week, and are never allowed to walk home. Her ladyship's carriage is regularly ordered for us. I SHOULD say, one of her ladyship's carriages, for she has several."

"Lady Catherine is a very respectable, sensible woman indeed, added Charlotte, "and a most attentive neighbour."

"Very true, my dear, that is exactly what I say. She is the sort of woman whom one cannot regard with too much deference."

The evening was spent chiefly in talking over Hertfordshire news, and telling again what had already been written; and when it closed, Elizabeth, in the solitude of her chamber, had to meditate upon Charlotte's degree of contentment, to understand her address in guiding, and composure in bearing with, her husband, and to acknowledge that it was all done very well. She had also to anticipate how her visit would pass, the quiet tenor of their usual employments, the vexatious interruptions of Mr. Collins, and the gaieties of their intercourse with Rosings. A lively imagination soon settled it all.

About the middle of the next day, as she was in her room getting ready for a walk, a sudden noise below seemed to speak the whole house in confusion; and, after listening a moment, she heard somebody running upstairs in a violent hurry, and calling loudly after her. She opened the door and met Maria in the landing place, who, breathless with agitation, cried out—

"Oh, my dear Eliza! pray make haste and come into the dining-room, for there is such a sight to be seen! I will not tell you what it is. Make haste, and come down this moment."

Elizabeth asked questions in vain; Maria would tell her nothing more, and down they ran into the dining-room, which fronted the lane, in quest of this wonder! It was two ladies stopping in a low phaeton at the garden gate.

"And is this all?" cried Elizabeth. "I expected at least that the pigs were got into the garden, and here is nothing but Lady Catherine and her daughter."

"La! my dear," said Maria, quite shocked at the mistake, "it is not Lady Catherine. The old lady is Mrs. Jenkins, who lives with them; the other is Miss de Bourgh. Only look at her. She is quite a little creature. Who would have thought that she could be so thin and small?"

"She is abominably rude to keep Charlotte out of doors in all this wind. Why does she not come in?"

"Oh, Charlotte says she hardly ever does. It is the greatest of favours when Miss de Bourgh comes in."

"I like her appearance," said Elizabeth, struck with other ideas. "She looks sickly and cross. Yes, she will do for him very well. She will make him a very proper wife."

Mr. Collins and Charlotte were both standing at the gate in conversation with the ladies; and Sir William, to Elizabeth's high diversion, was stationed in the doorway, in earnest contemplation of the greatness before him, and constantly bowing whenever Miss de Bourgh looked that way.

At length there was nothing more to be said; the ladies drove on, and the others returned into the house. Mr. Collins no sooner saw the two girls than he began to congratulate them on their good fortune, which Charlotte explained by letting them know that the whole party was asked to dine at Rosings the next day.

Chapter 29

Mr. Collins's triumph, in consequence of this invitation, was complete. The power of displaying the grandeur of his patroness to his wondering visitors, and of letting them see her civility towards himself and his wife, was exactly what he had wished for; and that an opportunity of doing it should be given so soon, was such an instance of Lady Catherine's condescension, as he knew not how to admire enough.

"I confess," said he, "that I should not have been at all surprised by her ladyship's asking us on Sunday to drink tea and spend the evening at Rosings. I rather expected, from my knowledge of her affability, that it would happen. But who could have foreseen such an attention as this? Who could have imagined that we should receive an invitation to dine there (an invitation, moreover, including the whole party) so immediately after your arrival!"

"I am the less surprised at what has happened," replied Sir William, "from that knowledge of what the manners of the great really are, which my situation in life has allowed me to acquire. About the court, such instances of elegant breeding are not uncommon."

Scarcely anything was talked of the whole day or next morning but their visit to Rosings. Mr. Collins was carefully instructing them in what they were to expect, that the sight of such rooms, so many servants, and so splendid a dinner, might not wholly overpower them.

When the ladies were separating for the toilette. Her said to Elizabeth—

"Do not make yourself uneasy, my dear cousin, about your apparel. Lady Catherine is far from requiring that elegance of dress in us which becomes herself and her daughter. I would advise you merely to put on whatever of your clothes is superior to the rest—there is no occasion for anything more. Lady Catherine will not think the worse of you for being simply dressed. She likes to have the distinction of rank preserved."

While they were dressing, he came two or three times to their different doors, to recommend their being quick, as Lady Catherine very much objected to be kept waiting for her dinner. Such formidable accounts of her ladyship, and her manner of living, quite frightened Maria Lucas who had been little used to company, and she looked forward to her introduction at Rosings with as much apprehension as her father had done to his presentation at St. James's.

As the weather was fine, they had a pleasant walk of about half a mile across the park. Every park has its beauty and its prospects; and Elizabeth saw much to be pleased with, though she could not be in such raptures as Mr. Collins expected the scene to inspire, and was but slightly affected by his enumeration of the windows in front of the house, and his relation of what the glazing altogether had originally cost Sir Lewis de Bourgh.

When they ascended the steps to the hall, Maria's alarm was every moment increasing, and even Sir William did not look perfectly calm. Elizabeth's courage did not fail her. She had heard nothing of Lady Catherine that spoke her awful from any extraordinary talents or miraculous virtue, and the mere stateliness of money or rank she thought she could witness without trepidation.

From the entrance-hall, of which Mr. Collins pointed out, with a rapturous air, the fine proportion and the finished ornaments, they followed the servants through an ante-chamber, to the room where Lady Catherine, her daughter, and Mrs. Jenkinson were sitting. Her ladyship, with great condescension, arose to receive them; and as Mrs. Collins had settled it with her husband that the office of introduction should be hers, it was performed in a proper manner, without any of those apologies and thanks which he would have thought necessary.

In spite of having been at St. James's Sir William was so completely awed by the grandeur surrounding him, that he had but just courage enough to make a very low bow, and take his seat without saying a word; and his daughter, frightened almost out of her senses, sat on the edge of her chair, not knowing which way to look. Elizabeth found herself quite equal to the scene, and could observe the three ladies before her composedly. Lady Catherine was a tall, large woman, with strongly-marked features, which might once have been handsome. Her air was not conciliating, nor was her manner of receiving them such as to make her visitors forget their inferior rank. She was not rendered formidable by silence; but whatever she said was spoken in so authoritative a tone, as marked her self-importance, and brought Mr. Wickham immediately to Elizabeth's mind; and from the observation of the day altogether, she believed Lady Catherine to be exactly what he represented.

When, after examining the mother, in whose countenance and deportment she soon found some resemblance of Mr. Darcy, she turned her eyes on the daughter, she could almost have joined in Maria's astonishment at her being so thin and so small. There was neither in figure nor face any likeness between the ladies. Miss de Bourgh was pale and sickly; her features, though not plain, were insignificant; and she spoke very little, except in a low voice, to Mrs. Jenkinson, in whose appearance there was nothing remarkable, and who was entirely engaged in listening to what she said, and placing a screen in the proper direction before her eyes.

After sitting a few minutes, they were all sent to one of the windows to admire the view, Mr. Collins attending them to point out its beauties, and Lady Catherine kindly informing them that it was much better worth looking at in the summer.

The dinner was exceedingly handsome, and there were all the servants and all the articles of plate which Mr. Collins had promised; and, as he had likewise foretold, he took his seat at the bottom of the table, by her ladyship's desire, and looked as if he felt that life could furnish nothing greater. He carved, and ate, and praised with delighted alacrity; and every dish was commended, first by him and then by Sir William, who was now enough recovered to echo whatever his son-in-law said, in a manner which Elizabeth wondered Lady Catherine could bear. But Lady Catherine seemed gratified by their excessive admiration, and gave most gracious smiles, especially when any dish on the table proved a novelty to them. The party did not supply much conversation. Elizabeth was ready to speak whenever there was an opening, but she was seated between Charlotte and Miss de Bourgh—the former of whom was engaged in listening to Lady Catherine, and the latter said not a word to her all dinner-time. Miss Jenkinson was chiefly employed in watching how little Miss de Bourgh ate, pressing her to try some other dish, and fearing she was indisposed. Maria thought speaking out of the question, and the gentlemen did nothing but eat and admire.

When the ladies returned to the drawing-room, there was little to be done but to hear Lady Catherine talk, which she did without any intermission till coffee came in, delivering her opinion on every subject in so decisive a manner, as proved that she was not used to have her judgement controverted. She inquired into Charlotte's domestic concerns familiarly and minutely, gave her a great deal of advice as to the management of them all; told her how everything ought to be regulated in so small a family as hers, and instructed her as to the care of her cows and her poultry. Elizabeth found that nothing was beneath this great lady's attention, which could furnish her with an occasion of dictating to others. In the intervals of her discourse with Mrs. Collins, she addressed a variety of questions to Maria and Elizabeth, but especially to the latter, of whose connections she knew the least, and who she observed to Mrs. Collins was a very genteel, pretty kind of girl. She asked her, at different times, how many sisters she had, whether they were older or younger than herself, whether any of them were likely to be married, whether they were handsome, where they had been educated, what carriage her father kept, and what had been her mother's maiden name? Elizabeth felt all the impertinence of her questions but answered them very composedly. Lady Catherine then observed,

"Your father's estate is entailed on Mr. Collins, I think. For your sake," turning to Charlotte, "I am glad of it; but otherwise I see no occasion for entailing estates from the female line. It was not thought necessary in Sir Lewis de Bourgh's family. Do you play and sing, Miss Bennet?"

"A little."

"Oh! then—some time or other we shall be happy to hear you. Our instrument is a capital one, probably superior to______ You shall try it some day. Do your sisters play and sing?"

"One of them does."

"Why did not you all learn? You ought all to have learned. The Miss Webbs all play, and their father has not so good an income as yours. Do you draw?"

"No, not at all."

"What, none of you?"

"Not one."

"That is very strange. But I suppose you had no opportunity. Your mother should have taken you to town every spring for the benefit of masters."

"My mother would have had no objection, but my father hates London."

"Has your governess left you?"

"We never had any governess."

"No governess! How was that possible? Five daughters brought up at home without a governess! I never heard of such a thing. Your mother must have been quite a slave to your education."

Elizabeth could hardly help smiling as she assured her that had not been the case.

"Then, who taught you? who attended to you? Without a governess, you must have been neglected."

"Compared with some families, I believe we were; but such of us as wished to learn never wanted the means. We were always encouraged to read, and had all the masters that were necessary. Those who chose to be idle, certainly might."

"Aye, no doubt; but that is what a governess will prevent, and if I had known your mother, I should have advised her most strenuously to engage one. I always say that nothing is to be done in education without steady and regular instruction, and nobody but a governess can give it. It is wonderful how many families I have been the means of supplying in that way. I am always glad to get a young person well placed out. Four nieces of Mrs. Jenkinson are most delightfully situated through my means; and it was but the other day that I recommended another young person, who was merely accidentally mentioned to me, and the family are quite delighted with her. Mrs. Collins, did I tell you of Lady Metcalf's calling yesterday to thank me? She finds Miss Pope a treasure. 'Lady Catherine,' said she, 'you have given me a treasure.' Are any of your younger sisters out, Miss Bennet?"

"Yes, ma'am, all."

"All! What, all five out at once? Very odd! And you only the second. The younger ones out before the elder ones are married! Your younger sisters must be very young?"

"Yes, my youngest is not sixteen. Perhaps SHE is full young to be much in company. But really, ma'am, I think it would be very hard upon younger sisters, that they should not have their share of society and amusement, because the elder may not have the means or inclination to marry early. The last-born has as good a right to the pleasures of youth at the first. And to be kept back on SUCH a motive! I think it would not be very likely to promote sisterly affection or delicacy of mind."

"Upon my word," said her ladyship, "you give your opinion very decidedly for so young a person. Pray, what is your age?"

"With three younger sisters grown up," replied Elizabeth, smiling, "your ladyship can hardly expect me to own it."

Lady Catherine seemed quite astonished at not receiving a direct answer; and Elizabeth suspected herself to be the first creature who had ever dared to trifle with so much dignified impertinence.

"You cannot be more than twenty, I am sure, therefore you need not conceal your age."

"I am not one-and-twenty."

When the gentlemen had joined them, and tea was over, the card-tables were placed. Lady Catherine, Sir William, and Mr. and Mrs. Collins sat down to quadrille; and as Miss de Bourgh chose to play at cassino, the two girls had the honour of assisting Mrs. Jenkinson to make up her party. Their table was superlatively stupid. Scarcely a syllable was uttered that did not relate to the game, except when Mrs. Jenkinson expressed her fears of Mis de Bourgh's being too hot or too cold, or having too much or too little light. A great deal more passed at the other table. Lady Catherine was generally speaking—stating the mistakes of the three others, or relating some anecdote of herself. Mr.

Collins was employed in agreeing to everything her ladyship said, thanking her for every fish he won, and apologising if he thought he won too many. Sir William did not say much. He was storing his memory with anecdotes and noble names.

When Lady Catherine and her daughter had played as long as they chose, the tables were broken up, the carriage was offered to Mrs. Collins, gratefully accepted and immediately ordered. The party then gathered round the fire to hear Lady Catherine determine what weather they were to have on the morrow. From these instructions they were summoned by the arrival of the coach; and with many speeches of thankfulness on Mr. Collins's side and as many bows on Sir William's they departed. As soon as they had driven from the door, Elizabeth was called on by her cousin to give her opinion of all that she had seen at Rosings, which, for Charlotte's sake, she made more favourable than it really was. But her commendation, though costing her some trouble, could by no means satisfy Mr. Collins, and he was very soon obliged to take her ladyship's praise into his own hands.

Chapter 30

Sir William stayed only a week at Hunsford, but his visit was long enough to convince him of his daughter's being most comfortably settled, and of her possessing such a husband and such a neighbour as were not often met with. While Sir William was with them, Mr. Collins devoted his morning to driving him out in his gig, and showing him the country; but when he went away, the whole family returned to their usual employments, and Elizabeth was thankful to find that they did not see more of her cousin by the alteration, for the chief of the time between breakfast and dinner was now passed by him either at work in the garden or in reading and writing, and looking out of the window in his own book-room, which fronted the road. The room in which the ladies sat was backwards. Elizabeth had at first rather wondered that Charlotte should not prefer the dining-parlour for common use; it was a better sized room, and had a more pleasant aspect; but she soon saw that her friend had an excellent reason for what she did, for Mr. Collins would undoubtedly have been much less in his own apartment had they sat in one equally lively; and she gave Charlotte credit for the arrangement.

From the drawing-room they could distinguish nothing in the lane, and were indebted to Mr. Collins for the knowledge of what carriages went along, and how often especially Miss de Bourgh drove by in her phaeton, which he never failed coming to inform them of, though it happened almost every day. She not unfrequently stopped at the Parsonage, and had a few minutes' conversation with Charlotte, but was scarcely ever prevailed upon to get out.

Very few days passed in which Mr. Collins did not walk to Rosings, and not many in which his wife did not think it necessary to go likewise; and till Elizabeth recollected that there might be other family livings to be disposed of, she could not understand the sacrifice of so many hours. Now and then they were honoured with a call from her ladyship, and nothing escaped her observation that was passing in the room during these visits. She examined into their employments, looked at their work, and advised them to do it differently; found fault with the arrangement of the furniture; or detected the housemaid in negligence; and if she accepted any refreshment, seemed to do it only for the sake of finding out that Mrs. Collins's joints of eat were too large for her family.

Elizabeth soon perceived, that though this great lady was not in commission of the peace of the county, she was a most active magistrate in her own parish, the minutest concerns of which were carried to her by Mr. Collins; and whenever any of the cottagers were disposed to be quarrelsome, discontented, or too poor, she sallied forth into the village to settle their differences, silence their complaints, and scold them into harmony and plenty.

The entertainment of dining at Rosings was repeated about twice a week; and, allowing for the loss of Sir William, and there being only one card-table in the evening, every such entertainment was the counterpart of the first. Their other engagements were few, as the style of living in the neighbourhood in general was beyond Mr. Collins's reach. This, however, was no evil to Elizabeth, and upon the whole she spent her time comfortably enough; there were half-hours of pleasant conversation with Charlotte, and the weather was so fine for the time of year that she had often great enjoyment out of doors. Her favourite walk, and where she frequently went while the others were calling on Lady Catherine, was along the open grove which edged that side of the park, where there was a nice sheltered path, which no one seemed to value but herself, and where she felt beyond the reach of Lady Catherine's curiosity.

In this quiet way, the first fortnight of her visit soon passed away. Easter was approaching, and the week preceding it was to bring an addition to the family at Rosings, which in so small a circle must be important. Elizabeth had heard soon after her arrival that Mr. Darcy was expected there in the course of a few weeks, and though there were not many of her acquaintances whom she did not prefer, his coming would furnish one comparatively new to look at in their Rosings parties, and she might be amused in seeing how hopeless Miss Bingley's designs on him were, by his behaviour to his cousin, for whom he was evidently destined by Lady Catherine, who talked of his coming with the greatest satisfaction, spoke of him in terms of the highest admiration, and seemed almost angry to find that he had already been frequently seen by Miss Lucas and herself.

His arrival was soon known at the Parsonage; for Mr. Collins was walking the whole morning within view of the lodges opening into Hunsford Lane, in order to have the earliest

assurance of it, and after making his bow as the carriage turned into the Park, hurried home with the great intelligence. On the following morning he hastened to Rosings to pay his respects. There were two nephews of Lady Catherine to require them, for Mr. Darcy had brought with him a Colonel Fitzwilliam, the younger son of his uncle Lord ______, and, to the great surprise of all the party, when Mr. Collins returned, the gentleman accompanied him. Charlotte had seen them from her husband's room, crossing the road, and immediately running into the other, told the girls what an honour they might expect, adding:

"I may thank you, Eliza, for this piece of civility. Mr. Darcy would never have come so soon to wait upon me."

Elizabeth had scarcely time to disclaim all right to the compliment, before their approach was announced by the door-bell, and shortly afterwards the three gentlemen entered the room. Colonel Fitzwilliam, who led the way, was about thirty, not handsome, but in person and address most truly the gentleman. Mr. Darcy looked just as he had been used to look in Hertfordshire—paid his compliments, with his usual reserve, to Mrs. Collins, and whatever might be his feelings toward her friend, met her with every appearance of composure. Elizabeth merely curtseyed to him without saying a word.

Colonel Fitzwilliam entered into conversation directly with the readiness and ease of a well-bred man, and talked very pleasantly; but his cousin, after having addressed a slight observation on the house and garden to Mrs. Collins, sat for some time without speaking to anybody. At length, however, his civility was so far awakened as to inquire of Elizabeth after the health of her family. She answered him in the usual way, and after a moment's pause, added:

"My eldest sister has been in town these three months. Have you never happened to see her there?"

She was perfectly sensible that he never had; but she wished to see whether he would betray any consciousness of what had passed between the Bingleys and Jane, and she thought he looked a little confused as he answered that he had never been so fortunate as to meet Miss Bennet. The subject was pursued no farther, and the gentlemen soon afterwards went away.

Chapter 31

Colonel Fitzwilliam's manners were very much admired at the Parsonage, and the ladies all felt that he must add considerably to the pleasures of their engagements at Rosings. It was some days, however, before they received any invitation thither—for while there were visitors in the house, they could not be necessary; and it was not till Easter-day, almost a week after the gentlemen's arrival, that they were honoured by such an attention, and then they were merely asked on leaving church to come there in the evening. For the last week they had seen very little of Lady Catherine or her daughter. Colonel Fitzwilliam had called at the Parsonage more than once during the time, but Mr. Darcy they had seen only at church.

The invitation was accepted of course, and at a proper hour they joined the party in Lady Catherine's drawing-room. Her ladyship received them civilly, but it was plain that their company was by no means so acceptable as when she could get nobody else; and she was, in fact, almost engrossed by her nephews, speaking to them, especially to Darcy, much more than to any other person in the room.

Colonel Fitzwilliam seemed really glad to see them; anything was a welcome relief to him at Rosings; and Mrs. Collins's pretty friend had moreover caught his fancy very much. He now seated himself by her, and talked so agreeably of Kent and Hertfordshire, of travelling and staying at home, of new books and music, that Elizabeth had never been half so well entertained in that room before; and they conversed with so much spirit and flow, as to draw the attention of Lady Catherine herself, as well as of Mr. Darcy. HIS eyes had been soon and repeatedly turned towards them with a look of curiosity; and that her ladyship, after a while, shared the feeling, was more openly acknowledged, for she did not scruple to call out:

"What is that you are saying, Fitzwilliam? What is it you are talking of? What are you telling Miss Bennet? Let me hear what it is."

"We are speaking of music, madam," said he, when no longer able to avoid a reply.

"Of music! Then pray speak aloud. It is of all subjects my delight. I must have my share in the conversation if you are speaking of music. There are few people in England, I suppose, who have more true enjoyment of music than myself, or a better natural taste. If I had ever learnt, I should have been a great proficient. And so would Anne, if her health had allowed her to apply. I am confident that she would have performed delightfully. How does Georgiana get on, Darcy?"

Mr. Darcy spoke with affectionate praise of his sister's proficiency.

"I am very glad to hear such a good account of her," said Lady Catherine; "and pray tell her from me, that she cannot expect to excel if she does not practice a good deal."

"I assure you, madam," he replied, "that she does not need such advice. She practises very constantly."

"So much the better. It cannot be done too much; and when I next write to her, I shall charge her not to neglect it on any account. I often tell young ladies that no excellence in music is to be acquired without constant practice. I have told Miss Bennet several times, that she will never play really well unless she practises more; and though Mrs. Collins has no instrument, she is very welcome, as I have often told her, to come to Rosings every day, and play on the pianoforte in Mrs. Jenkinson's room. She would be in nobody's way, you know, in that part of the house."

Mr. Darcy looked a little ashamed of his aunt's ill-breeding, and made no answer.

When coffee was over, Colonel Fitzwilliam reminded Elizabeth of having promised to play to him; and she sat down directly to the instrument. He drew a chair near her. Lady Catherine listened to half a song, and then talked, as before, to her other nephew; till the latter walked away from her, and making with his usual deliberation towards the pianoforte stationed himself so as to command a full view of the fair performer's countenance. Elizabeth saw what he was doing, and at the first convenient pause, turned to him with an arch smile, and said:

"You mean to frighten me, Mr. Darcy, by coming in all this state to hear me? I will not be alarmed though your sister DOES play so well. There is a stubbornness about me that never can bear to be frightened at the will of others. My courage always rises at every attempt to intimidate me."

"I shall not say you are mistaken," he replied, "because you could not really believe me to entertain any design of alarming you; and I have had the pleasure of your acquaintance long enough to know that you find great enjoyment in occasionally professing opinions which in fact are not your own."

Elizabeth laughed heartily at this picture of herself, and said to Colonel Fitzwilliam, "Your cousin will give you a very pretty notion of me, and teach you not to believe a word I say. I am particularly unlucky in meeting with a person so able to expose my real character, in a part of the world where I had hoped to pass myself off with some degree of credit. Indeed, Mr. Darcy, it is very ungenerous in you to mention all that you knew to my disadvantage in Hertfordshire—and, give me leave to say, very impolitic too—for it is provoking me to retaliate, and such things may come out as will shock your relations to hear."

"I am not afraid of you," said he, smilingly.

"Pray let me hear what you have to accuse him of," cried Colonel Fitzwilliam. "I should like to know how he behaves among strangers."

"You shall hear then—but prepare yourself for something very dreadful. The first time of my ever seeing him in Hertfordshire, you must know, was at a ball—and at this ball, what do you think he did? He danced only four dances, though gentlemen were scarce; and, to my certain knowledge, more than one young lady was sitting down in want of a partner. Mr. Darcy, you cannot deny the fact."

"I had not at that time the honour of knowing any lady in the assembly beyond my own party."

"True; and nobody can ever be introduced in a ball-room. Well, Colonel Fitzwilliam, what do I play next? My fingers wait your orders."

"Perhaps," said Darcy, "I should have judged better, had I sought an introduction; but I am ill-qualified to recommend myself to strangers."

Shall we ask your cousin the reason of this?" said Elizabeth, still addressing Colonel Fitzwilliam. "Shall we ask him why a man of sense and education, and who has lived in the world, is ill qualified to recommend himself to strangers?"

"I can answer your question," said Fitzwilliam, "without applying to him. It is because he will not give himself the trouble."

"I certainly have not the talent which some people possess," said Darcy, "of conversing easily with those I have never seen before. I cannot catch their tone of conversation, or appear interested in their concerns, as I often see done."

"My fingers," said Elizabeth, "do not move over this instrument in the masterly manner which I see so many women's do. They have not the same force or rapidity, and do not produce the same expression. But then I have always supposed it to be my own fault—because I will not take the trouble of practising. It is not that I do not believe MY fingers as capable as any other woman's of superior execution."

Darcy smiled and said, "You are perfectly right. You have employed your time much better. No one admitted to the privilege of hearing you can think anything wanting. We neither of us perform to strangers."

Here they were interrupted by Lady Catherine, who called out to know what they were talking of. Elizabeth immediately began playing again. Lady Catherine approached, and, after listening for a few minutes, said to Darcy:

"Miss Bennet would not play at all amiss if she practised more, and could have the advantage of a London master. She has a very good notion of fingering, though her taste is not equal to Anne's. Anne would have been a delightful performer, had her health allowed her to learn."

Elizabeth looked at Darcy to see how cordially he assented to his cousin's praise; but neither at that moment nor at any other could she discern any symptom of love; and from the whole of his behaviour to Miss de Bourgh she derived this comfort for Miss Bingley, that he might have been just as likely to marry HER, had she been his relation.

Lady Catherine continued her remarks on Elizabeth's performance, mixing with them many instructions on execution and taste. Elizabeth received them with all the forbearance of civility, and, at the request of the gentlemen, remained at the instrument till her ladyship's carriage was ready to take them all home.

Chapter 32

Elizabeth was sitting by herself the next morning, and writing to Jane while Mrs. Collins and Maria were gone on business into the village, when she was startled by a ring at the door, the certain signal of a visitor. As she had heard no carriage, she thought it not unlikely to be Lady Catherine, and under that apprehension was putting away her half-finished letter that she might escape all impertinent questions, when the door opened, and, to her very great surprise, Mr. Darcy, and Mr. Darcy only, entered the room.

He seemed astonished too on finding her alone, and apologised for his intrusion by letting her know that he had understood all the ladies were to be within.

They then sat down, and when her inquiries after Rosings were made, seemed in danger of sinking into total silence. It was absolutely necessary, therefore, to think of something, and in this emergence recollecting WHEN she had seen him last in Hertfordshire, and feeling curious to know what he would say on the subject of their hasty departure, she observed:

"How very suddenly you all quitted Netherfield last November, Mr. Darcy! It must have been a most agreeable surprise to Mr. Bingley to see you all after him so soon; for, if I recollect right, he went but the day before. He and his sisters were well, I hope, when you left London?"

"Perfectly so, I thank you."

She found that she was to receive no other answer, and, after a short pause added:

"I think I have understood that Mr. Bingley has not much idea of ever returning to Netherfield again?"

"I have never heard him say so; but it is probable that he may spend very little of his time there in the future. He has many friends, and is at a time of life when friends and engagements are continually increasing."

"If he means to be but little at Netherfield, it would be better for the neighbourhood that he should give up the place entirely, for then we might possibly get a settled family there. But, perhaps, Mr. Bingley did not take the house so much for the convenience of the neighbourhood as for his own, and we must expect him to keep it or quit it on the same principle."

"I should not be surprised," said Darcy, "if he were to give it up as soon as any eligible purchase offers."

Elizabeth made no answer. She was afraid of talking longer of his friend; and, having nothing else to say, was now determined to leave the trouble of finding a subject to him.

He took the hint, and soon began with, "This seems a very comfortable house. Lady Catherine, I believe, did a great deal to it when Mr. Collins first came to Hunsford."

"I believe she did—and I am sure she could not have bestowed her kindness on a more grateful object."

"Mr. Collins appears to be very fortunate in his choice of a wife."

"Yes, indeed, his friends may well rejoice in his having met with one of the very few sensible women who would have accepted him, or have made him happy if they had. My friend has an excellent understanding—though I am not certain that I consider her marrying Mr. Collins as the wisest thing she ever did. She seems perfectly happy, however, and in a prudential light it is certainly a very good match for her."

"It must be very agreeable for her to be settled within so easy a distance of her own family and friends."

"An easy distance, do you call it? It is nearly fifty miles."

"And what is fifty miles of good road? Little more than half a day's journey. Yes, I call it a very easy distance."

I should never have considered the distance as one of the ADVANTAGES of the match," cried Elizabeth. "I should never have said Mrs. Collins was settled NEAR her family."

"It is a proof of your own attachment to Hertfordshire. Anything beyond the very neighbourhood of Longbourn, I suppose, would appear far."

As he spoke there was a sort of smile which Elizabeth fancied she understood; he must be supposing her to be thinking of Jane and Netherfield, and she blushed as she answered:

"I do not mean to say that a woman may not be settled too near her family. The far and the near must be relative, and depend on many varying circumstances. Where there is fortune to make the expenses of travelling unimportant, distance becomes no evil. But that is not the case HERE. Mr. and Mrs. Collins have a comfortable income, but not such a one as will allow of frequent journeys—and I am persuaded my friend would not call herself NEAR her family under less than HALF the present distance."

Mr. Darcy drew his chair a little towards her, and said, "YOU cannot have a right to such very strong local attachment. YOU cannot have been always at Longbourn."

Elizabeth looked surprised. The gentleman experienced some change of feeling; he drew back his chair, took a newspaper from the table, and glancing over it, said, in a colder voice:

"Are you pleased with Kent?"

A short dialogue on the subject of the county ensued, on either side calm and concise—and soon put an end to by the entrance of Charlotte and her sister, just returned from her walk. The tete-a-tete surprised them. Mr. Darcy related the mistake which had occasioned his intruding on Miss Bennet, and after sitting a few minutes longer without saying much to anybody, went away.

"What can be the meaning of this?" said Charlotte, as soon as he was gone. "My dear, Eliza, he must be in love with you, or he would never have called us in this familiar way."

But when Elizabeth told of his silence; it did not seem very likely, even to Charlotte's wishes, to be the case; and after various conjectures, they could at last only suppose his visit to proceed from the difficulty of finding anything to do, which was the more probable from the time of year. All field sports were over. Within doors there was Lady Catherine, books, and a billiard-table, but gentlemen cannot always be within doors; and in the nearness of the Parsonage, or the pleasantness of the walk to it, or of the people who lived in it, the two cousins found a temptation from this period of walking thither almost every day. They called at various times of the morning, sometimes separately, sometimes together, and now and then accompanied by their aunt. It was plain to them all that Colonel Fitzwilliam came because he had pleasure in their society, a persuasion which of course recommended him still more; and Elizabeth was reminded by her own satisfaction in being with him, as well as by his evident admiration of her, of her former favourite George Wickham; and though, in comparing them, she saw there was less captivating softness in Colonel Fitzwilliam's manners, she believed he might have the best informed mind. But why Mr. Darcy came so often to the Parsonage, it was more difficult to understand. It could not be for society, as he frequently sat there ten minutes together without opening his lips; and when he did speak, it seemed the effect of necessity rather than of choice—a sacrifice to propriety, not a pleasure to himself. He seldom appeared really animated. Mrs. Collins knew not what to make of him. Colonel Fitzwilliam's occasionally laughing at his stupidity, proved that he was generally different, which her own knowledge of him could not have told her; and as she would liked to have believed this change the effect of love, and the object of that love her friend Eliza, she set herself seriously to work to find it out. She watched him whenever they were at Rosings, and whenever he came to Hunsford; but without much success. He certainly looked at her friend a great deal, but the expression of that look was disputable. It was an earnest, steadfast gaze, but she often doubted whether there were much admiration in it, and sometimes it seemed nothing but absence of mind.

She had once or twice suggested to Elizabeth the possibility of his being partial to her, but Elizabeth always laughed at the idea; and Mrs. Collins did not think it right to press the subject, from the danger of raising expectations which might only end in disappointment; for in her opinion it admitted not of a doubt, that all her friend's dislike would vanish, if she could suppose him to be in her power.

In her kind schemes for Elizabeth, she sometimes planned her marrying colonel Fitzwilliam. He was beyond comparison the most pleasant man; he certainly admired her, and his situation in life was most eligible; but, to counterbalance these advantages, Mr. Darcy had considerable patronage in the church, and his cousin could have none at all.

Chapter 33

More than once did Elizabeth, in her ramble within the park, unexpectedly meet Mr. Darcy. She felt all the perverseness of the mischance that should bring him where no one else was brought, and, to prevent its ever happening again, took care to inform him at first that it was a favourite haunt of hers. How it could occur a second time, therefore, was very odd! Yet it did, and even a third. It seemed like wilful ill-nature, or a voluntary penance, for on these occasions it was not merely a few formal inquiries and an awkward pause and then away, but he actually thought it necessary to turn back and walk with her. He never said a great deal, nor did she give herself the trouble of talking or of listening much; but it struck her in the course of their third rencontre that he was asking some odd unconnected questions—about her pleasure in being at Hunsford, her love of solitary walks, and her opinion of Mr. and Mrs. Collins's happiness; and that in speaking of Rosings and her not perfectly understanding the house, he seemed to expect that whenever she came into Kent again she would be staying THERE too. His words seemed to imply it. Could he have Colonel Fitzwilliam in his thoughts? She supposed, if he meant anything, he must mean and allusion to what might arise in that quarter. It distressed her a little, and she was quite glad to find herself at the gate in the pales opposite the Parsonage.

She was engaged one day as she walked in perusing Jane's last letter, and dwelling on some passages which proved that Jane had not written in spirits, when, instead of being again surprised by Mr. Darcy, she saw on looking up that Colonel Fitzwilliam was meeting her. Putting away the letter immediately and forcing a smile, she said:

"I did not know before that you ever walked this way."

"I have been making the tour of the park," he replied, "as I generally do every year, and intend to close it with a call at the Parsonage. Are you going much farther?"

"No, I should have turned in a moment."

And accordingly she did turn, and they walked towards the Parsonage together.

"Do you certainly leave Kent on Saturday?" said she.

"Yes—if Darcy does not put it off again. But I am at his disposal. He arranges the business just as he pleases."

"And if not able to please himself in the arrangement, he has at least pleasure in the great power of choice. I do not know anybody who seems more to enjoy the power of doing what he likes than Mr. Darcy."

"He likes to have his own way very well," replied Colonel Fitzwilliam. "But so we all do. It is only that he has better means of having it than many others, because he is rich, and many others are poor. I speak feelingly. A younger son, you know, must be inured to self-denial and dependence."

"In my opinion, the younger son of an earl can know very little of either. Now seriously, what have you ever known of self-denial and dependence? When have you been prevented by want of money from going wherever you chose, or procuring anything you had a fancy for?"

"These are home questions—and perhaps I cannot say that I have experienced many hardships of that nature. But in matters of greater weight, I may suffer from want of money. Younger sons cannot marry where they like."

"Unless where they like women of fortune, which I think they very often do."

Our habits of expense make us too dependent, and there are too many in my rank of life who can afford to marry without some attention to money."

"Is this," thought Elizabeth, "meant for me?" and she coloured at the idea; but, recovering herself, said in a lively tone, "And pray, what is the usual price of an earl's younger son? Unless the elder brother is very sickly, I suppose you would not ask above fifty thousand pounds."

He answered her in the same style, and the subject dropped. To interrupt a silence which might make him fancy her affected with what had passed, she soon afterwards said:

"I imagine your cousin brought you down with him chiefly for the sake of having someone at his disposal. I wonder he does not marry, to secure a lasting convenience of that kind. But, perhaps, his sister does as well for the present, and, as she is under his sole care, he may do what he likes with her."

"No," said Colonel Fitzwilliam, "that is an advantage which he must divide with me. I am joined with him in the guardianship of Miss Darcy."

"Are you indeed? And pray what sort of guardians do you make? Does your charge give you much trouble? Young ladies of her age are sometimes a little difficult to manage, and if she has the true Darcy spirit, she may like to have her own way."

As she spoke she observed him looking at her earnestly; and the manner in which he immediately asked her why she supposed Miss Darcy likely to give them any uneasiness, convinced her that she had somehow or other got pretty near the truth. She directly replied:

"You need not be frightened. I never heard any harm of her; and I dare say she is one of the most tractable creatures in the world. She is a very great favourite with some ladies of my acquaintance, Mrs. Hurst and Miss Bingley. I think I have heard you say that you know them."

"I know them a little. Their brother is a pleasant gentlemanlike man—he is a great friend of Darcy's."

"Oh! yes," said Elizabeth drily; "Mr. Darcy is uncommonly kind to Mr. Bingley, and takes a prodigious deal of care of him."

"Care of him! Yes, I really believe Darcy DOES take care of him in those points where he most wants care. From something that he told me in our journey hither, I have reason to think Bingley very much indebted to him. But I ought to beg his pardon, for I have no right to suppose that Bingley was the person meant. It was all conjecture."

"What is it you mean?"

"It is a circumstance which Darcy could not wish to be generally known, because if it were to get round to the lady's family, it would be an unpleasant thing."

"You may depend upon my not mentioning it."

"And remember that I have not much reason for supposing it to be Bingley. What he told me was merely this: that he congratulated himself on having lately saved a friend from the inconveniences of a most imprudent marriage, but without mentioning names or any other particulars, and I only suspected it to be Bingley from believing him the kind of young man to get into a scrape of that sort, and from knowing them to have been together the whole of last summer."

"Did Mr. Darcy give you reasons for this interference?"

"I understood that there were some very strong objections against the lady."

"And what arts did he use to separate them?"

"He did not talk to me of his own arts," said Fitzwilliam, smiling. "He only told me what I have now told you."

Elizabeth made no answer, and walked on, her heart swelling with indignation. After watching her a little, Fitzwilliam asked her why she was so thoughtful.

"I am thinking of what you have been telling me," said she. "Your cousin's conduct does not suit my feelings. Why was he to be the judge?"

"You are rather disposed to call his interference officious?"

"I do not see what right Mr. Darcy had to decide on the propriety of his friend's inclination, or why, upon his own judgement alone, he was to determine and direct in what manner his friend was to be happy. But," she continued, recollecting herself, "as we know none of the particulars, it is not fair to condemn him. It is not to be supposed that there was much affection in the case."

"That is not an unnatural surmise," said Fitzwilliam, "but it is a lessening of the honour of my cousin's triumph very sadly."

This was spoken jestingly; but it appeared to her so just a picture of Mr. Darcy, that she would not trust herself with an answer, and therefore, abruptly changing the conversation talked on indifferent matters until they reached the Parsonage. There, shut into her own room, as soon as their visitor left them, she could think without interruption of all that she had heard. It was not to be supposed that any other people could be meant than those with whom she was connected. There could not exist in the world TWO men over whom Mr. Darcy could have such boundless influence. That he had been concerned in the measures taken to separate Bingley and Jane she had never doubted; but she had always attributed to Miss Bingley the principal design and arrangement of them. If his own vanity, however, did not mislead him, HE was the cause, his pride and caprice were the cause, of all that Jane had suffered, and still continued to suffer. He had ruined for a while every hope of happiness for the most affectionate, generous heart in the world; and no one could say how lasting an evil he might have inflicted.

"There were some very strong objections against the lady," were Colonel Fitzwilliam's words; and those strong objections probably were, her having one uncle who was a country attorney, and another who was in business in London.

"To Jane herself," she exclaimed, "there could be no possibility of objection; all loveliness and goodness as she is!—her understanding excellent, her mind improved, and her manners captivating. Neither could anything be urged against my father, who, though with some peculiarities, has abilities Mr. Darcy himself need not disdain, and respectability which he will probably never each." When she thought of her mother, her confidence gave way a little; but she would not allow that any objections THERE had material weight with Mr. Darcy, whose pride, she was convinced, would receive a deeper wound from the want of importance in his friend's connections, than from their want of sense; and she was quite decided, at last, that he had been partly governed by this worst kind of pride, and partly by the wish of retaining Mr. Bingley for his sister.

The agitation and tears which the subject occasioned, brought on a headache; and it grew so much worse towards the evening, that, added to her unwillingness to see Mr. Darcy, it determined her not to attend her cousins to Rosings, where they were engaged to drink tea. Mrs. Collins, seeing that she was really unwell, did not press her to go and as much as possible prevented her husband from pressing her; but Mr. Collins could not conceal his apprehension of Lady Catherine's being rather displeased by her staying at home.

Chapter 34

When they were gone, Elizabeth, as if intending to exasperate herself as much as possible against Mr. Darcy, chose for her employment the examination of all the letters which Jane had written to her since her being in Kent. They contained no actual complaint, nor was there any revival of past occurrences, or any communication of present suffering. But in all, and in almost every line of each, there was a want of that cheerfulness which had been used to characterise her style, and which, proceeding from the serenity of a mind at ease with itself and kindly disposed towards everyone, had been scarcely ever clouded. Elizabeth noticed every sentence conveying the idea of uneasiness, with an attention which it had hardly received on the first perusal. Mr. Darcy's shameful boast of what misery he had been able to inflict gave her a keener sense of her sister's sufferings. It was some consolation to think that his visit to Rosings was to end on the day after the next—and, a still greater, that in less than a fortnight she should herself be with Jane again, and enabled to contribute to the recovery of her spirits, by all that affection could do.

She could not think of Darcy's leaving Kent without remembering that his cousin was to go with him; but Colonel Fitzwilliam had made it clear that he had no intentions at all, and agreeable as he was, she did not mean to be unhappy about him.

While settling this point, she was suddenly roused by the sound of the door-bell, and her spirits were a little fluttered by the idea of its being Colonel Fitzwilliam himself, who had once before called late in the evening, and might now come to inquire particularly after her. But this idea was soon banished, and her spirits were very differently affected, when, to her utter amazement, she saw Mr. Darcy walk into the room. In an hurried manner he immediately began an inquiry after her health, imputing his visit to a wish of hearing that she were better. She answered him with cold civility. He sat down for a few moments, and then getting up, walked about the room. Elizabeth was surprised, but said not a word.

After a silence of several minutes, he came towards her in an agitated manner, and thus began:

"In vain I have struggled. It will not do. My feelings will not be repressed. You must allow me to tell you how ardently I admire and love you."

Elizabeth's astonishment was beyond expression. She stared, coloured, doubted, and was silent. This he considered sufficient encouragement; and the avowal of all that he felt, and had long felt for her, immediately followed. He spoke well; but there were feelings besides those of the heart to be detailed; and he was not more eloquent on the subject of tenderness than of pride. His sense of her inferiority—of its being a degradation—of the family obstacles which had always opposed to inclination, were dwelt on with a warmth which seemed due to the consequence he was wounding, but was very unlikely to recommend his suit.

In spite of her deeply-rooted dislike, she could not be insensible to the compliment of such a man's affection, and though her intentions did not vary for an instant, she was at first sorry for the pain he was to receive; till, roused to resentment by his subsequent language, she lost all compassion in anger. She tried, however, to compose herself to answer him with patience, when he should have done. He concluded with representing to her the strength of that attachment which, in spite of all his endeavours, he had found impossible to conquer; and with expressing his hope that it would now be rewarded by her acceptance of his hand. As he said this, she could easily see that he had no doubt of a favourable answer. He SPOKE of apprehension and anxiety, but his countenance expressed real security. Such a circumstance could only exasperate farther, and, when he ceased, the colour rose into her cheeks, and she said:

"In such cases as this, it is, I believe, the established mode to express a sense of obligation for the sentiments avowed, however unequally they may be returned. It is natural that obligation should be felt, and if I could FEEL gratitude, I would now thank you. But I cannot—I have never desired your good opinion, and you have certainly bestowed it most unwillingly. I am sorry to have occasioned pain to anyone. It has been most unconsciously done, however, and I hope will be of short duration. The feelings which, you tell me, have long prevented the acknowledgment of your regard, can have little difficulty in overcoming it after this explanation."

Mr. Darcy, who was leaning against the mantelpiece with his eyes fixed on her face, seemed to catch her words with no less resentment than surprise. His complexion became pale with anger, and the disturbance of his mind was visible in every feature. He was struggling for the appearance of composure, and would not open his lips till he believed himself to have attained it. The pause was to Elizabeth's feelings dreadful. At length, with a voice of forced calmness, he said:

"And this is the reply which I am to have the honour of expecting: I might, perhaps, wish to be informed why, with so little ENDEAVOUR at civility, I am thus rejected. But it is of small importance."

"I might as well inquire," replied she, " why with so evident a desire of offending and insulting me, you chose to tell me that you liked me against your will, against your reason, and even against your character? Was not this some excuse for incivility, if I WAS uncivil? But I have other provocations. You know I have. Had not my feelings decided against you—had they been indifferent, or had they even been favourable, do you think that any consideration would tempt me to accept the man who has been the means of ruining, perhaps for ever, the happiness of a most beloved sister?"

As she pronounced these words, Mr. Darcy changed colour; but the emotion was short, and he listened without attempting to interrupt her while she continued:

"I have every reason in the world to think ill of you. No motive can excuse the unjust and ungenerous part you acted THERE. You dare not, you cannot deny, that you have been the principal, if not the only means of dividing them from each other—of exposing one to the censure of the world for caprice and instability, and the other to its derision for disappointed hopes, and involving them both in misery of the acutest kind."

She paused, and saw with no slight indignation that he was listening with an air which proved him wholly unmoved by any feeling of remorse. He even looked at her with a smile of affected incredulity.

"Can you deny that you have done it?" she repeated.

With assumed tranquillity he then replied: "I have no wish of denying that I did everything in my power to separate my friend from your sister, or that I rejoice in my success. Towards HIM I have been kinder than towards myself."

Elizabeth disdained the appearance of noticing this civil reflection, but its meaning did not escape, nor was it likely to conciliate her.

"But it is not merely this affair," she continued, "on which my dislike is founded. Long before it had taken place my opinion of you was decided. Your character was unfolded in the recital which I received many months ago from Mr. Wickham. On this subject, what can you have to say? In what imaginary act of friendship can you here defend yourself? or under what misrepresentation can you here impose upon others?"

"You take an eager interest in that gentleman's concerns," said Darcy, in a less tranquil tone, and with a heightened colour.

"Who that knows what his misfortunes have been, can help feeling an interest in him?"

"His misfortunes!" repeated Darcy contemptuously; "yes, his misfortunes have been great indeed."

"And of your infliction," cried Elizabeth with energy. "You have reduced him to his present state of poverty—comparative poverty. You have withheld the advantages which you must know to have been designed for him. You have deprived the best years of his life of that independence which was no less his due than his desert. You have done all this! and yet you can treat the mention of his misfortune with contempt and ridicule."

"And this," cried Darcy, as he walked with quick steps across the room, "Is your opinion of me! This is the estimation in which you hold me! I thank you for explaining it so fully. My faults, according to this calculation, are heavy indeed! But perhaps," added he, stopping in his walk, and turning towards her, "these offenses might have been overlooked, had not your pride been hurt by my honest confession of the scruples that had long prevented my forming any serious design. These bitter accusations might have been suppressed, had I, with greater policy, concealed my struggles, and flattered you into the belief of my being impelled by unqualified, unalloyed inclination; by reason, by reflection, by everything. But disguise of every sort is my abhorrence. Nor am I ashamed of the feelings I related. They were natural and just. Could you expect me to rejoice in the inferiority of your connections?—to congratulate myself on the hope of relations, whose condition in life is so decidedly beneath my own?"

Elizabeth felt herself growing more angry every moment; yet she tried to the utmost to speak with composure when she said:

"You are mistaken, Mr. Darcy, if you suppose that the mode of your declaration affected me in any other way, than as it spared the concern which I might have felt in refusing you, had you behaved in a more gentlemanlike manner."

She saw him start at this, but he said nothing, and she continued:

"You could not have made the offer of your hand in any possible way that would have tempted me to accept it."

Again his astonishment was obvious; and he looked at her with an expression of mingled incredulity and mortification. She went on:

"From the very beginning—from the first moment, I may almost say—of my acquaintance with you, your manners, impressing me with the fullest belief of your arrogance, your conceit, and your selfish disdain of the feelings of others, were such as to form the groundwork of disapprobation on which succeeding events have built so immovable a dislike; and I had not known you a month before I felt that you were the last man in the world whom I could ever be prevailed on to marry."

"You have said quite enough, madam. I perfectly comprehend your feelings, and have now only to be ashamed of what my own have been. Forgive me for having taken up so much of your time, and accept my best wishes for your health and happiness."

And with these words he hastily left the room, and Elizabeth heard him the next moment open the front door and quit the house.

The tumult of her mind, was now painfully great. She knew not how to support herself, and from actual weakness sat down and cried for half-an-hour. Her astonishment, as she reflected on what had passed, was increased by every review of it. That she should receive an offer of marriage from Mr. Darcy! That he should have been in love with her for so many months! So much in love as to wish to marry her in spite of all the objections which had made him prevent his friend's marrying her sister, and which must appear at least with equal force in his own case—was almost incredible! It was gratifying to have inspired unconsciously so strong an affection. But his pride, his abominable pride—his shameless avowal of what he had done with respect to Jane—his unpardonable assurance in acknowledging, though he could not justify it, and the unfeeling manner in which he had mentioned Mr. Wickham, his cruelty towards whom he had not attempted to deny, soon overcame the pity which the consideration of his attachment had for a moment excited. She continued in very agitated reflections till the sound of Lady Catherine's carriage made her feel how unequal she was to encounter Charlotte's observation, and hurried her away to her room.

Chapter 35

Elizabeth awoke the next morning to the same thoughts and meditations which had at length closed her eyes. She could not yet recover from the surprise of what had happened; it was impossible to think of anything else; and, totally indisposed for employment, she resolved, soon after breakfast, to indulge herself in air and exercise. She was proceeding directly to her favourite walk, when the recollection of Mr. Darcy's sometimes coming there stopped her, and instead of entering the park, she turned up the lane, which led farther from the turnpike-road. The park paling was still the boundary on one side, and she soon passed one of the gates into the ground.

After walking two or three times along that part of the lane, she was tempted, by the pleasantness of the morning, to stop at the gates and look into the park. The five weeks which she had now passed in Kent had made a great difference in the country, and every day was adding to the verdure of the early trees. She was on the point of continuing her walk, when she caught a glimpse of a gentleman within the sort of grove which edged the park; he was moving that way; and, fearful of its being Mr. Darcy, she was directly retreating. But the person who advanced was now near enough to see her, and stepping forward with eagerness, pronounced her name. She had turned away; but on hearing herself called, though in a voice which proved it to be Mr. Darcy, she moved again towards the gate. He had by that time reached it also, and, holding out a letter, which she instinctively took, said, with a look of haughty composure, "I have been walking in the grove some time in the hope of meeting you. Will you do me the honour of reading that letter?" And then, with a slight bow, turned again into the plantation, and was soon out of sight.

With no expectation of pleasure, but with the strongest curiosity, Elizabeth opened the letter, and, to her still increasing wonder, perceived an envelope containing two sheets of letter-paper, written quite through, in a very close hand. The envelope itself was likewise full. Pursuing her way along the lane, she then began it. It was dated from Rosings, at eight o'clock in the morning, and was as follows:—

"Be not alarmed, madam, on receiving this letter, by the apprehension of its containing any repetition of those sentiments or renewal of those offers which were last night so disgusting to you. I write without any intention of paining you, or humbling myself, by dwelling on wishes which, for the happiness of both, cannot be too soon forgotten; and the effort which the formation and the perusal of this letter must occasion, should have been spared had not my character required it to be written and read. You must, therefore, pardon the freedom with which I demand your attention; your feelings, I know, will bestow it unwillingly, but I demand it of your justice.

"Two offenses of a very different nature, and by no means of equal magnitude, you last night laid to my charge. The first mentioned was, that, regardless of the sentiments of either, I had detached Mr. Bingley from your sister, and the other, that I had, in defiance of various claims, in defiance of honour and humanity, ruined the immediate prosperity and blasted the prospects of Mr. Wickham. Wilfully and wantonly to have thrown off the companion of my youth, the acknowledged favourite of my father, a young man who had scarcely any other dependence than on our patronage, and who had been brought up to expect its exertion, would be a depravity, to which the separation of two young persons, whose affection could be the growth of only a few weeks, could bear no comparison. But from the severity of that blame which was last night so liberally bestowed, respecting each circumstance, I shall hope to be in the future secured, when the following account of my actions and their motives has been read. If, in the explanation of them, which is due to myself, I am under the necessity of relating feelings which may be offensive to yours, I can only say that I am sorry. The necessity must be obeyed, and further apology would be absurd.

"I had not been long in Hertfordshire, before I saw, in common with others, that Bingley preferred your elder sister to any other young woman in the country. But it was not till the evening of the dance at Netherfield that I had any apprehension of his feeling a serious attachment. I had often seen him in love before. At that ball, while I had the honour of dancing with you, I was first made acquainted, by Sir William Lucas's accidental information, that Bingley's attentions to your sister had given rise to a general expectation of their marriage. He spoke of it as a certain event, of which the time alone could be undecided. From that moment I observed my friend's behaviour attentively; and I could then perceive that his partiality for Miss Bennet was beyond what I had ever witnessed in him. Your sister I also watched. Her look and manners were open, cheerful, and engaging as ever, but without any symptom of peculiar regard, and I remained convinced from the evening's scrutiny, that though she received his attentions with pleasure, she did not invite them by any participation of sentiment. If YOU have not been mistaken here, I must have been in error. Your superior knowledge of your sister must make the latter probable. If it be so, if I have been misled by such error to inflict pain on her, your resentment has not been unreasonable. But I shall not scruple to assert, that the serenity of your sister's countenance and air was such as might have given the most acute observer a conviction that, however amiable her temper, her heart was not likely to be easily touched. That I was desirous of believing her indifferent is certain—but I will venture to say that my investigation and decisions are not usually influenced by my hopes or fears. I did not believe her to be indifferent because I wished it; I believed it on impartial conviction, as truly as I wished it in reason. My objections to the marriage were not merely those which I last night acknowledged to have the utmost force of passion to put aside, in my own case; the want of connection could not be so great an evil to my friend as to me. But there were other causes of repugnance; causes which, though still existing, and existing to an equal degree in both instances, I had myself endeavoured to forget, because they were not immediately before me. These causes must be stated, though briefly. The situation of your mother's family, though objectionable, was nothing in comparison to that total want of propriety so frequently, so almost uniformly betrayed by herself, by your three younger sisters, and occasionally even by your father. Pardon me. It pains me to offend you. But amidst your concern for the defects of your nearest relations, and your displeasure at this representation of them, let it give you consolation to consider that, to have conducted yourselves so as to avoid any share of the like censure, is praise no less generally bestowed on you and your elder sister, than it is honourable to the sense and disposition of both. I will only say farther that from what passed that evening my opinion of all parties was confirmed, and every inducement heightened which could have led me before to preserve my friend from what I esteemed a most unhappy connection. He left Netherfield for London, on the day following, as you, I am certain, remember, with the design of soon returning.

"The part which I acted is now to be explained. His sisters' uneasiness had been equally excited with my own; our coincidence of feeling was soon discovered, and, alike sensible that no time was to be lost in detaching their brother, we shortly resolved on joining him directly in London. We accordingly went—and there I readily engaged in the office of pointing out to my friend the certain evils of such a choice. I described, and enforced them earnestly. But, however this remonstrance might have staggered or delayed his determination, I do not suppose that it would ultimately have prevented the marriage, had it not been seconded by the assurance that I hesitated not in giving, of your sister's indifference. He had before believed her to return his affection with sincere, if not with equal regard. But Bingley has great natural modesty, with a stronger dependence on my judgement than on his own. To convince him, therefore, that he had deceived himself, was no very difficult point. To persuade him against returning into Hertfordshire, when that conviction had been given, was scarcely the work of a moment. I cannot blame myself for having done thus much. There is but one part of my conduct in the whole affair on which I do not reflect with satisfaction; it is, that I condescended to adopt the measures of art so far as to conceal from him your sister's being in town. I knew it myself, as it was known to Miss Bingley; but her brother is even yet ignorant of it. That they might have met without ill consequence is perhaps probable; but his regard did not appear to me enough extinguished for him to see her without some danger. Perhaps this concealment, this disguise was beneath me; it is done, however, and it was done for the best. On this subject I have nothing more to say, no other apology to offer. If I have wounded your sister's feelings, it was unknowingly done and though the motives which governed me may to you very naturally appear insufficient, I have not yet learnt to condemn them.

"With respect to that other, more weighty accusation, of having injured Mr. Wickham, I can only refute it by laying before you the whole of his connection with my family. Of what he has PARTICULARLY accused me I am ignorant; but of the truth of what I shall relate, I can summon more than one witness of undoubted veracity.

"Mr. Wickham is the son of a very respectable man, who had for many years the management of all the Pemberley estates, and whose good conduct in the discharge of his trust naturally inclined my father to be of service to him; and on George Wickham, who was his godson, his kindness was therefore liberally bestowed. My father supported him at school, and afterwards at Cambridge—most important assistance, as his own father, always poor from the extravagance of his wife, would have been unable to give him a gentleman's education. My father was not only fond of this young man's society, whose manner were always engaging; he had also the highest opinion of him, and hoping the church would be his profession, intended to provide for him in it. As for myself, it is many, many years since I first began to think of him in a very different manner. The vicious propensities—the want of principle, which he was careful to guard from the knowledge of his best friend, could not escape the observation of a young man of nearly the same age with himself, and who had opportunities of seeing him in unguarded moments, which Mr. Darcy could not have. Here again shall give you pain—to what degree you only can tell. But whatever may be the sentiments which Mr. Wickham has created, a suspicion of their nature shall not prevent me from unfolding his real character—it adds even another motive.

"My excellent father died about five years ago; and his attachment to Mr. Wickham was to the last so steady, that in his will he particularly recommended it to me, to promote his advancement in the best manner that his profession might allow—and if he took orders, desired that a valuable family living might be his as soon as it became vacant. There was also a legacy of one thousand pounds. His own father did not long survive mine, and within half a year from these events, Mr. Wickham wrote to inform me that, having finally resolved against taking orders, he hoped I should not think it unreasonable for him to expect some more immediate pecuniary advantage, in lieu of the preferment, by which he could not be benefited. He had some intention, he added, of studying law, and I must be aware that the interest of one thousand pounds would be a very insufficient support therein. I rather wished, than believed him to be sincere—but, at any rate, was perfectly ready to accede to his proposal. I knew that Mr. Wickham ought not to be a clergyman; the business was therefore soon settled—he resigned all claim to assistance in the church, were it possible that he could ever be in a situation to receive it, and accepted in return three thousand pounds. All connection between us seemed now dissolved. I thought too ill of him to invite him to Pemberley, or admit his society in town. In town I believe he chiefly lived, but his studying the law was a mere pretence, and being now free from all restraint, his life was a life of idleness and dissipation. For about three years I heard little of him; but on the decease of the incumbent of the living which had been designed for him, he applied to me again by letter for the presentation. His circumstances, he assured me, and I had no difficulty in believing it, were exceedingly bad. He had found the law a most unprofitable study, and was now absolutely resolved on being ordained, if I would present him to the living in question—of which he trusted there could be little doubt, as he was well assured that I had no other person to provide for, and I could not have forgotten my revered father's intentions. You will hardly blame me for refusing to comply with this entreaty, or for resisting every repetition to it. His resentment was in proportion to the distress of his circumstances—and he was doubtless as violent in his abuse of me to others as in his reproaches to myself. After this period every appearance of acquaintance was dropped. How he lived I know not. But last summer he was again most painfully obtruded on my notice.

"I must now mention a circumstance which I would wish to forget myself, and which no obligation less than the present should induce me to unfold to any human being. Having said thus much, I feel no doubt of your secrecy. My sister, who is more than ten years my junior, was left to the guardianship of my mother's nephew, Colonel Fitzwilliam, and myself. About a year ago, she was taken from school, and an establishment formed for her in London; and last summer she went with the lady who presided over it, to Ramsgate; and thither also went Mr. Wickham, undoubtedly by design; for there proved to have been a prior acquaintance between him and Mrs. Younge, in whose character we were most unhappily deceived; and by her connivance and aid, he so far recommended himself to Georgiana, whose affectionate heart retained a strong impression of his kindness to her as a child, that she was persuaded to believe herself in love, and to consent to an elopement. She was then but fifteen, which must be her excuse; and after stating her imprudence, I am happy to add, that I owed the knowledge of it to herself. I joined them unexpectedly a day or two before the intended elopement, and then Georgiana, unable to support the idea of grieving and offending a brother whom she almost looked up to as a father, acknowledged the whole to me. You may imagine what I felt and how I acted. Regard for my sister's credit and feelings prevented any public exposure; but I wrote to Mr. Wickham, who left the place immediately, and Mrs. Younge was of course removed from her charge. Mr. Wickham's object was unquestionably my sister's fortune, which is thirty thousand pounds; but I cannot help supposing that the hope of revenging himself on me was a strong inducement. His revenge would have been complete indeed.

"This, madam, is a faithful narrative of every event in which we have been concerned together; and if you do not absolutely reject it as false, you will, I hope, acquit me henceforth of cruelty towards Mr. Wickham. I know not in what manner, under what form of falsehood he had imposed on you; but his success is not perhaps to be wondered at, ignorant as you previously were of everything concerning either. Detection could not be in your power, and suspicion certainly not in your inclination.

"You may possibly wonder why all this was not told you last night; but I was not then master enough of myself to know what could or ought to be revealed. For the truth of everything here related, I can appeal more particularly to the testimony of Colonel Fitzwilliam, who, from our near relationship and constant intimacy, and, still more, as one of the executors of my father's will, has been unavoidably acquainted with every particular of these transactions. If your abhorrence of ME should make MY assertions valueless, you cannot be prevented by the same cause from confiding in my cousin; and that there may be the possibility of consulting him, I shall endeavour to find some opportunity of putting this letter in your hands in the course of the morning. I will only add, God bless you,

"FITZWILLIAM DARCY"

Chapter 36

If Elizabeth, when Mr. Darcy gave her the letter, did not expect it to contain a renewal of his offers, she had formed no expectation at all of its contents. But such as they were, it may well be supposed how eagerly she went through them, and what a contrariety of emotion they excited. Her feelings as she read were scarcely to be defined. With amazement did she first understand that he believed any apology to be in his power; and steadfastly was she persuaded, that he could have no explanation to give, which a just sense of shame would not conceal. With a strong prejudice against everything he might say, she began his account of what had happened at Netherfield. She read with an eagerness which hardly left her power of comprehension, and from impatience of knowing what the next sentence might bring, was incapable of attending to the sense of the one before her eyes. His belief of her sister's insensibility she instantly resolved to be false; and his account of the real, the worst objections to the match, made her too angry to have any wish of doing him justice. He expressed no regret for what he had done which satisfied her; his style was not penitent, but haughty. It was all pride and insolence.

But when this subject was succeeded by his account of Mr. Wickham—when she read with somewhat clearer attention a relation of events which, if true, must overthrow every cherished opinion of his worth, and which bore so alarming an affinity to his own history of himself—her feelings were yet more acutely painful and more difficult of definition. Astonishment, apprehension, and even horror, oppressed her. She wished to discredit it entirely, repeatedly exclaiming, "This must be false! This cannot be! This must be the grossest falsehood!"—and when she had gone through the whole letter, though scarcely knowing anything of the last page or two, put it hastily away, protesting that she would not regard it, that she would never look in it again.

In this perturbed state of mind, with thoughts that could rest on nothing, she walked on; but it would not do; in half a minute the letter was unfolded again, and collecting herself as well as she could, she again began the mortifying perusal of all that related to Wickham, and commanded herself so far as to examine the meaning of every sentence. The account of his connection with the Pemberley family was exactly what he had related himself; and the kindness of the late Mr. Darcy, though she had not before known its extent, agreed equally well with his own words. So far each recital confirmed the other; but when she came to the will, the difference was great. What Wickham had said of the living was fresh in her memory, and as she recalled his very words, it was impossible not to feel that there was gross duplicity on one side or the other; and, for a few moments, she flattered herself that her wishes did not err. But when she read and re-read with the closest attention, the particulars immediately following of Wickham's resigning all pretensions to the living, of his receiving in lieu so considerable a sum as three thousand pounds, again was she forced to hesitate. She put down the letter, weighed every circumstance with what she meant to be impartiality—deliberated on the probability of each statement—but with little success. On both sides it was only assertion. Again she read on; but every line proved more clearly that the affair, which she had believed it impossible that any contrivance could so represent as to render Mr. Darcy's conduct in it less than infamous, was capable of a turn which must make him entirely blameless throughout the whole.

The extravagance and general profligacy which he scrupled not to lay at Mr. Wickham's charge, exceedingly shocked her; the more so, as she could bring no proof of its injustice. She had never heard of him before his entrance into the ______shire Militia, in which he had engaged at the persuasion of the young man who, on meeting him accidentally in town, had there renewed a slight acquaintance. Of his former way of life nothing had been known in Hertfordshire but what he told himself. As to his real character, had information been in her power, she had never felt a wish of inquiring. His countenance, voice, and manner had established him at once in the possession of every virtue. She tried to recollect some instance of goodness, some distinguished trait of integrity or benevolence, that might rescue him from the attacks of Mr. Darcy; or at least, by the predominance of virtue, atone for those casual errors under which she would endeavour to class what Mr. Darcy had described as the idleness and vice of many years' continuance. But no such recollection befriended her. She could see him instantly before her, in every charm of air and address; but she could remember no more substantial good than the general approbation of the neighbourhood, and the regard which his social powers had gained him in the mess. After pausing on this point a considerable while, she once more continued to read. But, alas! the story which followed, of his designs on Miss Darcy, received some confirmation from what had passed between Colonel Fitzwilliam and herself only the morning before; and at last she was referred for the truth of every particular to Colonel Fitzwilliam himself—from whom she had previously received the information of his near concern in all his cousin's affairs, and whose character she had no reason to question. At one time she had almost resolved on applying to him, but the idea was checked by the awkwardness of the application, and at length wholly banished by the conviction that Mr. Darcy would never have hazarded such a proposal, if he had not been well assured of his cousin's corroboration.

She perfectly remembered everything that had passed in conversation between Wickham and herself, in their first evening at Mr. Phillips's. Many of his expressions were still fresh in her memory. She was NOW struck with the impropriety of such communications to a stranger, and wondered it had escaped her before. She saw the indelicacy of putting himself forward as he had done, and the inconsistency of his professions with his conduct. She remembered that he had boasted of having no fear of seeing Mr. Darcy—that Mr. Darcy might leave the country, but that HE should stand his ground; yet he had avoided the Netherfield ball the very next week. She remembered also that, till the Netherfield family had quitted the country, he had told his story to no one but herself; but that after their removal it had been everywhere discussed; that he had then no reserves, no scruples in sinking Mr. Darcy's character, though he had assured her that respect for the father would always prevent his exposing the son.

How differently did everything now appear in which he was concerned! His attentions to Miss King were now the consequence of views solely and hatefully mercenary; and the mediocrity of her fortune proved no longer the moderation of his wishes, but his eagerness to grasp at anything. His behaviour to herself could now have had no tolerable motive; he had either been deceived with regard to her fortune, or had been gratifying his vanity by encouraging the preference which she believed she had most incautiously shown. Every lingering struggle in his favour grew fainter and fainter; and in farther justification of Mr. Darcy, she could not but allow Mr. Bingley, when questioned by Jane, had long ago asserted his blamelessness in the affair; that proud and repulsive as were his manners, she had never, in the whole course of their acquaintance—an acquaintance which had latterly brought them much together, and given her a sort of intimacy with his ways—seen anything that betrayed him to be unprincipled or unjust—anything that spoke him of irreligious or immoral habits; that among his own connections he was esteemed and valued—that even Wickham had allowed him merit as a brother, and that she had often heard him speak so affectionately of his sister as to prove him capable of some amiable feeling; that had his actions been what Mr. Wickham represented them, so gross a violation of everything right could hardly have been concealed from the world; and that friendship between a person capable of it, and such an amiable man as Bingley, was incomprehensible.

She grew absolutely ashamed of herself. Of neither Darcy nor Wickham could she think without feeling she had been blind, partial, prejudiced, absurd.

"How despicably I have acted!" she cried; "I, who have prided myself on my discernment! I, who have valued myself on my abilities! who have often disdained the generous candour of my sister, and gratified my vanity in useless or blameable mistrust! How humiliating is this discovery! yet, how just a humiliation! Had I been in love, I could not have been more wretchedly blind! But vanity, not love, has been my folly. Pleased with the preference of one, and offended by the neglect of the other, on the very beginning of our acquaintance, I have courted prepossession and ignorance, and driven reason away, where either were concerned. Till this moment I never knew myself."

From herself to Jane—from Jane to Bingley, her thoughts were in a line which soon brought to her recollection that Mr. Darcy's explanation THERE had appeared very insufficient, and she read it again. Widely different was the effect of a second perusal. How could she deny that credit to his assertions in one instance, which she had been obliged to give in the other? He declared himself to be totally unsuspicious of her sister's attachment; and she could not help remembering what Charlotte's opinion had always been. Neither could she deny the justice of his description of Jane. She felt that Jane's feelings, though fervent, were little displayed, and that there was a constant complacency in her air and manner not often united with great sensibility.

When she came to that part of the letter in which her family were mentioned in terms of such mortifying, yet merited reproach, her sense of shame was severe. The justice of the charge struck her too forcibly for denial, and the circumstances to which he particularly alluded as having passed at the Netherfield ball, and as confirming all his first disapprobation, could not have made a stronger impression on his mind than on hers. The compliment to herself and her sister was not unfelt. It soothed, but it could not console her for the contempt which had thus been self-attracted by the rest of her family; and as she considered that Jane's disappointment had in fact been the work of her nearest relations, and reflected how materially the credit of both must be hurt by such impropriety of conduct, she felt depressed beyond anything she had ever known before.

After wandering along the lane for two hours, giving way to every variety of thought—re-considering events, determining probabilities, and reconciling herself, as well as she could, to a change so sudden and so important, fatigue, and a recollection of her long absence, made her at length return home; and she entered the house with the wish of appearing cheerful as usual, and the resolution of repressing such reflections as must make her unfit for conversation.

She was immediately told that the two gentlemen from Rosings had each called during her absence; Mr. Darcy, only for a few minutes, to take leave—but that Colonel Fitzwilliam had been sitting with them at least an hour, hoping for her return, and almost resolving to walk after her till she could be found. Elizabeth could but just AFFECT concern in missing him; she really rejoiced at it. Colonel Fitzwilliam was no longer an object; she could think only of her letter.

Chapter 37

The two gentlemen left Rosings the next morning, and Mr. Collins having been in waiting near the lodges, to make them his parting obeisance, was able to bring home the pleasing intelligence, of their appearing in very good health, and in as tolerable spirits as could be expected, after the melancholy scene so lately gone through at Rosings. To Rosings he then hastened, to console Lady Catherine and her daughter; and on his return brought back, with great satisfaction, a message from her ladyship, importing that she felt herself so dull as to make her very desirous of having them all to dine with her.

Elizabeth could not see Lady Catherine without recollecting that, had she chosen it, she might by this time have been presented to her as her future niece; nor could she think, without a smile, of what her ladyship's indignation would have been. "What would she have said? how would she have behaved?" were questions with which she amused herself.

Their first subject was the diminution of the Rosings party. "I assure you, I feel it exceedingly," said Lady Catherine; "I believe no one feels the loss of friends so much as I do. But I am particularly attached to these young men, and know them to be so much attached to me! They were excessively sorry to go! But so they always are. The dear Colonel rallied his spirits tolerably till just at last; but Darcy seemed to feel it most acutely, more, I think, than last year. His attachment to Rosings certainly increases."

Mr. Collins had a compliment, and an allusion to throw in here, which were kindly smiled on by the mother and daughter.

Lady Catherine observed, after dinner, that Miss Bennet seemed out of spirits. And immediately accounting for it by herself, by supposing that she did not like to go home again so soon, she added:

"But if that is the case, you must write to your mother and beg that you may stay a little longer. Mrs. Collins will be very glad of your company, I am sure."

"I am much obliged to your ladyship for your kind invitation," replied Elizabeth, "but it is not in my power to accept it. I must be in town next Saturday."

"Why, at that rate, you will have been here only six weeks. I expected you to stay two months. I told Mrs. Collins so before you came. There can be no occasion for your going so soon. Mrs. Bennet could certainly spare you for another fortnight."

"But my father cannot. He wrote last week to hurry my return."

"Oh! your father of course may spare you, if your mother can. Daughters are never of so much consequence to a father. And if you will stay another MONTH complete, it will be in my power to take one of you as far as London, for I am going there early in June, for a week; and as Dawson does not object to the barouche-box, there will be very good room for one of you—and indeed, if the weather should happen to be cool, I should not object to taking you both, as you are neither of you large."

"You are all kindness, madam; but I believe we must abide by our original plan."

Lady Catherine seemed resigned. "Mrs. Collins, you must send a servant with them. You know I always speak my mind, and I cannot bear the idea of two young women travelling post by themselves. It is highly improper. You must contrive to send somebody. I have the greatest dislike in the world to that sort of thing. Young women should always be properly guarded and attended, according to their situation in life. When my niece Georgiana went to Ramsgate last summer, I made a point of her having two men-servants go with her. Miss Darcy, the daughter of Mr. Darcy, of Pemberley, and Lady Anne, could not have appeared with propriety in a different manner. I am excessively attentive to all those things. You must send John with the young ladies, Mrs. Collins. I am glad it occurred to me to mention it; for it would really be discreditable to YOU to let them go alone."

"My uncle is to send a servant for us."

"Oh! Your uncle! He keeps a man-servant, does he? I am very glad you have somebody who thinks of these things. Where shall you change horses? Oh! Bromley, of course. If you mention my name at the Bell, you will be attended to."

Lady Catherine had many other questions to ask respecting their journey, and as she did not answer them all herself, attention was necessary, which Elizabeth believed to be lucky for her; or, with a mind so occupied, she might have forgotten where she was. Reflection must be reserved for solitary hours; whenever she was alone, she gave way to it as the greatest relief; and not a day went by without a solitary walk, in which she might indulge in all the delight of unpleasant recollections.

Mr. Darcy's letter she was in a fair way of soon knowing by heart. She studied every sentence; and her feelings towards its writer were at times widely different. When she remembered the style of his address, she was still full of indignation; but when she considered how unjustly she had condemned and upbraided him, her anger was turned against herself; and his disappointed feelings became the object of compassion. His attachment excited gratitude, his general character respect; but she could not approve him; nor could she for a moment repent her refusal, or feel the slightest inclination ever to see him again. In her own past behaviour, there was a constant source of vexation and regret; and in the unhappy defects of her family, a constant source of vexation and regret; and in the unhappy defects of her family, a subject of yet heavier chagrin. They were hopeless of remedy. Her father, contented with laughing at them, would never exert himself to restrain the wild giddiness of his youngest daughters; and her mother, with manners so far from right herself, was entirely insensible of the evil. Elizabeth had frequently united with Jane in an endeavour to check the imprudence of Catherine and Lydia; but while they were supported by their mother's indulgence, what chance could there be of improvement? Catherine, weak-spirited, irritable, and completely under Lydia's guidance, had been always affronted by their advice; and Lydia, self-willed and careless, would scarcely give them a hearing. They were ignorant, idle, and vain. While there was an officer in Meryton, they would flirt with him; and while Meryton was within a walk of Longbourn, they would be going there forever.

Anxiety on Jane's behalf was another prevailing concern; and Mr. Darcy's explanation, by restoring Bingley to all her former good opinion, heightened the sense of what Jane had lost. His affection was proved to have been sincere, and his conduct cleared of all blame, unless any could attach to the implicitness of his confidence in his friend. How grievous then was the thought that, of a situation so desirable in every respect, so replete with advantage, so promising for happiness, Jane had been deprived, by the folly and indecorum of her own family!

Their engagements at Rosings were as frequent during the last week of her stay as they had been at first. The very last evening was spent there; and her ladyship again inquired minutely into the particulars of their journey, gave them directions as to the best method of packing, and was so urgent on the necessity of placing gowns in the only right way, that Maria thought herself obliged, on her return, to undo all the work of the morning, and pack her trunk afresh.

When they parted, Lady Catherine, with great condescension, wished them a good journey, and invited them to come to Hunsford again next year; and Miss de Bourgh exerted herself so far as to curtsey and hold out her hand to both.

Chapter 38

On Saturday morning Elizabeth and Mr. Collins met for breakfast a few minutes before the others appeared; and he took the opportunity of paying the parting civilities which he deemed indispensably necessary.

"I know not, Miss Elizabeth," said he, "whether Mrs. Collins has yet expressed her sense of your kindness in coming to us; but I am very certain you will not leave the house without receiving her thanks for it. The favor of your company has been much felt, I assure you. We know how little there is to tempt any one to our humble abode. Our plain manner of living, our small rooms and few domestics, and the little we see of the world, must make Hunsford extremely dull to a young lady like yourself; but I hope you will believe us grateful for the condescension, and that we have done everything in our power to prevent your spending your time unpleasantly."

Elizabeth was eager with her thanks and assurances of happiness. She had spent six weeks with great enjoyment; and the pleasure of being with Charlotte, and the kind attentions she had received, must make HER feel the obliged. Mr. Collins was gratified, and with a more smiling solemnity replied:

"It gives me great pleasure to hear that you have passed your time not disagreeably. We have certainly done our best; and most fortunately having it in our power to introduce you to very superior society, and, from our connection with Rosings, the frequent means of varying the humble home scene, I think we may flatter ourselves that your Hunsford visit cannot have been entirely irksome. Our situation with regard to Lady Catherine's family is indeed the sort of extraordinary advantage and blessing which few can boast. You see on what a footing we are. You see how continually we are engaged there. In truth I must acknowledge that, with all the disadvantages of this humble parsonage, I should not think anyone abiding in it an object of compassion, while they are sharers of our intimacy at Rosings."

Words were insufficient for the elevation of his feelings; and he was obliged to walk about the room, while Elizabeth tried to unite civility and truth in a few short sentences.

"You may, in fact, carry a very favourable report of us into Hertfordshire, my dear cousin. I flatter myself at least that you will be able to do so. Lady Catherine's great attentions to Mrs. Collins you have been a daily witness of; and altogether I trust it does not appear that your friend has drawn an unfortunate______ But on this point it will be as well to be silent. Only let me assure you, my dear Miss Elizabeth, that I can from my heart most cordially wish you equal felicity in marriage. My dear Charlotte and I have but one mind and one way of thinking. There is in everything a most remarkable resemblance of character and ideas between us. We seem to have been designed for each other."

Elizabeth could safely say that it was a great happiness where that was the case, and with equal sincerity could add, that she firmly believed and rejoiced in his domestic comforts. She was not sorry, however, to have the recital of them interrupted by the lady from whom they sprang. Poor Charlotte! it was melancholy to leave her to such society! But she had chosen it with her eyes open; and though evidently regretting that her visitors were to go, she did not seem to ask for compassion. Her home and her housekeeping, her parish and her poultry, and all their dependent concerns, had not yet lost their charms.

At length the chaise arrived, the trunks were fastened on, the parcels placed within, and it was pronounced to be ready. After an affectionate parting between the friends, Elizabeth was attended to the carriage by Mr. Collins, and as they walked down the garden he was commissioning her with his best respects to all her family, not forgetting his thanks for the kindness he had received at Longbourn in the winter, and his compliments to Mr. and Mrs. Gardiner, though unknown. He then handed her in, Maria followed, and the door was on the point of being closed, when he suddenly reminded them, with some consternation, that they had hitherto forgotten to leave any message for the ladies at Rosings.

"But," he added, "you will of course wish to have your humble respects delivered to them, with your grateful thanks for their kindness to you while you have been here."

Elizabeth made no objection; the door was then allowed to be shut, and the carriage drove off.

"Good gracious!" cried Maria, after a few minutes' silence, "it seems but a day or two since we first came! and yet how many things have happened!"

"A great many indeed," said her companion with a sigh.

"We have dined nine times at Rosings, besides drinking tea there twice! How much I shall have to tell!"

Elizabeth added privately, "And how much I shall have to conceal!"

Their journey was performed without much conversation, or any alarm; and within four hours of their leaving Hunsford they reached Mr. Gardiner's house, where they were to remain a few days.

Jane looked well, and Elizabeth had little opportunity of studying her spirits, amidst the various engagements which the kindness of her aunt had reserved for them. But Jane was to go home with her, and at Longbourn there would be leisure enough for observation.

It was not without an effort, meanwhile, that she could wait even for Longbourn, before she told her sister of Mr. Darcy's proposals. To know that she had the power of revealing what would so exceedingly astonish Jane, and must, at the same time, so highly gratify whatever of her own vanity she had not yet been able to reason away, was such a temptation to openness as nothing could have conquered but the state of indecision in which she remained as to the extent of what she should communicate; and her fear, if she once entered on the subject, of being hurried into repeating something of Bingley which might only grieve her sister further.

Chapter 39

It was the second week in May, in which the three young ladies set out together from Gracechurch Street for the town of ______, in Hertfordshire; and, as they drew near the appointed inn where Mr. Bennet's carriage was to meet them, they quickly perceived, in token of the coachman's punctuality, both Kitty and Lydia looking out of a dining-room upstairs. These two girls had been above an hour in the place, happily employed in visiting an opposite milliner, watching the sentinel on guard, and dressing a salad and cucumber.

After welcoming their sisters, they triumphantly displayed a table set out with such cold meat as an inn larder usually affords, exclaiming, "Is not this nice? Is not this an agreeable surprise?"

"And we mean to treat you all," added Lydia, "but you must lend us the money, for we have just spent ours at the shop out there." Then, showing her purchases—"Look here, I have bought this bonnet. I do not think it is very pretty; but I thought I might as well buy it as not. I shall pull it to pieces as soon as I get home, and see if I can not make it up any better."

And when her sisters abused it as ugly, she added, with perfect unconcern, "Oh! but there were two or three much uglier in the shop; and when I have bought some prettier-coloured satin to trim it with fresh, I think it will be very tolerable. Besides, it will not much signify what one wears this summer, after the ______shire have left Meryton, and they are going in a fortnight."

"Are they indeed!" cried Elizabeth, with the greatest satisfaction.

"They are going to be encamped near Brighton; and I do so want papa to take us all there for the summer! It would be such a delicious scheme; and I dare say would hardly cost anything at all. Mamma would like to go too of all things! Only think what a miserable summer else we shall have!"

"Yes," thought Elizabeth, "THAT would be a delightful scheme indeed, and completely do for us at once. Good Heaven! Brighton, and a whole campful of soldiers, to us, who have been overset already by one poor regiment of militia, and the monthly balls of Meryton!"

"Now I have got some news for you," said Lydia, as they sat down at table. "What do you think? It is excellent news—capital news—and about a certain person we all like!"

Jane and Elizabeth looked at each other, and the waiter was told he need not stay. Lydia laughed, and said:

"Aye, that is just like your formality and discretion. You thought the waiter must not hear, as if he cared! I dare say he often hears worse things said than I am going to say. But he is an ugly fellow! I am glad he is gone. I never saw such a long chin in my life. Well, but now for my news; it is about dear Wickham; too good for the waiter, is it not? There is no danger of Wickham's marrying Mary King. There's for you! She is gone down to her uncle at Liverpool: gone to stay. Wickham is safe."

"And Mary King is safe!" added Elizabeth; "safe from a connection imprudent as to fortune."

"She is a great fool for going away, if she liked him."

"But I hope there is no strong attachment on either side," said Jane.

"I am sure there is not on HIS. I will answer for it, he never cared three straws about her—who could about such a nasty little freckled thing?"

Elizabeth was shocked to think that, however incapable of such coarseness of EXPRESSION herself, the coarseness of the SENTIMENT was little other than her own breast had harboured and fancied liberal!

As soon as all had ate, and the elder ones paid, the carriage was ordered; and after some contrivance, the whole party, with all their boxes, work-bags, and parcels, and the unwelcome addition of Kitty's and Lydia's purchases, were seated in it.

"How nicely we are all crammed in," cried Lydia. "I am glad I bought my bonnet, if it is only for the fun of having another bandbox! Well, now let us be quite comfortable and snug, and talk and laugh all the way home. And in the first place, let us hear what has happened to you all since you went away. Have you seen any pleasant men? Have you had any flirting? I was in great hopes that one of you would have got a husband before you came back. Jane will be quite an old maid soon, I declare. She is almost three-and-twenty! My aunt Phillips wants you so to get husbands, you can't think. She says Lizzy had better have taken Mr. Collins; but I do not think there would have been any fun in it. Lord! how I should like to be married before any of you! and then I would chaperon you about to all the balls. Dear me! we had such a good piece of fun the other day at Colonel Forster's. Kitty and me were to spend the day there, and Mrs. Forster promised to have a little dance in the evening; (by the bye, Mrs. Forster and me are SUCH friends!) and so she asked the two Harringtons to come, but Harriet was ill, and so Pen was forced to come by herself; and then, what do you think we did? We dressed up Chamberlayne in woman's clothes on purpose to pass for a lady, only think what fun! Not a soul knew of it, but Colonel and Mrs. Forster, and Kitty and me, except my aunt, for we were forced to borrow one of her gowns; and you cannot imagine how well he looked! When Denny, and Wickham, and Pratt, and two or three more of the men came in, they did not know him in the least. Lord! how I laughed! and so did Mrs. Forster. I thought I should have died. And THAT made the men suspect something, and then they soon found out what was the matter."

With such kinds of histories of their parties and good jokes, did Lydia, assisted by Kitty's hints and additions, endeavour to amuse her companions all the way to Longbourn. Elizabeth listened as little as she could, but there was no escaping the frequent mention of Wickham's name.

Their reception at home was most kind. Mrs. Bennet rejoiced to see Jane in undiminished beauty; and more than once during dinner did Mr. Bennet say voluntarily to Elizabeth:

"I am glad you are come back, Lizzy."

Their party in the dining-room was large, for almost all the Lucases came to meet Maria and hear the news; and various were the subjects that occupied them: Lady Lucas was inquiring of Maria, after the welfare and poultry of her eldest daughter; Mrs. Bennet was doubly engaged, on one hand collecting an account of the present fashions from Jane, who sat some way below her, and, on the other, retailing them all to the younger Lucases; and Lydia, in a voice rather louder than any other person's, was enumerating the various pleasures of the morning to anybody who would hear her.

"Oh! Mary," said she, "I wish you had gone with us, for we had such fun! As we went along, Kitty and I drew up the blinds, and pretended there was nobody in the coach; and I should have gone so all the way, if Kitty had not been sick; and when we got to the George, I do think we behaved very handsomely, for we treated the other three with the nicest cold luncheon in the world, and if you would have gone, we would have treated you too. And then when we came away it was such fun! I thought we never should have got into the coach. I was ready to die of laughter. And then we were so merry all the way home! we talked and laughed so loud, that anybody might have heard us ten miles off!"

To this Mary very gravely replied, "Far be it from me, my dear sister, to depreciate such pleasures! They would doubtless be congenial with the generality of female minds. But I confess they would have no charms for ME—I should infinitely prefer a book."

But of this answer Lydia heard not a word. She seldom listened to anybody for more than half a minute, and never attended to Mary at all.

In the afternoon Lydia was urgent with the rest of the girls to walk to Meryton, and to see how everybody went on; but Elizabeth steadily opposed the scheme. It should not be said that the Miss Bennets could not be at home half a day before they were in pursuit of the officers. There was another reason too for her opposition. She dreaded seeing Mr. Wickham again, and was resolved to avoid it as long as possible. The comfort to HER of the regiment's approaching removal was indeed beyond expression. In a fortnight they were to go—and once gone, she hoped there could be nothing more to plague her on his account.

She had not been many hours at home before she found that the Brighton scheme, of which Lydia had given them a hint at the inn, was under frequent discussion between her parents. Elizabeth saw directly that her father had not the smallest intention of yielding; but his answers were at the same time so vague and equivocal, that her mother, though often disheartened, had never yet despaired of succeeding at last.

Chapter 40

Elizabeth's impatience to acquaint Jane with what had happened could no longer be overcome; and at length, resolving to suppress every particular in which her sister was concerned, and preparing her to be surprised, she related to her the next morning the chief of the scene between Mr. Darcy and herself.

Miss Bennet's astonishment was soon lessened by the strong sisterly partiality which made any admiration of Elizabeth appear perfectly natural; and all surprise was shortly lost in other feelings. She was sorry that Mr. Darcy should have delivered his sentiments in a manner so little suited to recommend them; but still more was she grieved for the unhappiness which her sister's refusal must have given him.

"His being so sure of succeeding was wrong," said she, "and certainly ought not to have appeared; but consider how much it must increase his disappointment!"

"Indeed," replied Elizabeth, "I am heartily sorry for him; but he has other feelings, which will probably soon drive away his regard for me. You do not blame me, however, for refusing him?"

"Blame you! Oh, no."

"But you blame me for having spoken so warmly of Wickham?"

"No—I do not know that you were wrong in saying what you did."

"But you WILL know it, when I tell you what happened the very next day."

She then spoke of the letter, repeating the whole of its contents as far as they concerned George Wickham. What a stroke was this for poor Jane! who would willingly have gone through the world without believing that so much wickedness existed in the whole race of mankind, as was here collected in one individual. Nor was Darcy's vindication, though grateful to her feelings, capable of consoling her for such discovery. Most earnestly did she labour to prove the probability of error, and seek to clear the one without involving the other.

"This will not do," said Elizabeth; "you never will be able to make both of them good for anything. Take your choice, but you must be satisfied with only one. There is but such a quantity of merit between them; just enough to make one good sort of man; and of late it has been shifting about pretty much. For my part, I am inclined to believe it all Darcy's; but you shall do as you choose."

It was some time, however, before a smile could be extorted from Jane.

"I do not know when I have been more shocked," said she. "Wickham so very bad! It is almost past belief. And poor Mr. Darcy! Dear Lizzy, only consider what he must have suffered. Such a disappointment! and with the knowledge of your ill opinion, too! and having to relate such a thing of his sister! It is really too distressing. I am sure you must feel it so."

"Oh! no, my regret and compassion are all done away by seeing you so full of both. I know you will do him such ample justice, that I am growing every moment more unconcerned and indifferent. Your profusion makes me saving; and if you lament over him much longer, my heart will be as light as a feather."

"Poor Wickham! there is such an expression of goodness in his countenance! such an openness and gentleness in his manner!"

"There certainly was some great mismanagement in the education of those two young men. One has got all the goodness, and the other all the appearance of it."

"I never thought Mr. Darcy so deficient in the APPEARANCE of it as you used to do."

"And yet I meant to be uncommonly clever in taking so decided a dislike to him, without any reason. It is such a spur to one's genius, such an opening for wit, to have a dislike of that kind. One may be continually abusive without saying anything just; but one cannot always be laughing at a man without now and then stumbling on something witty."

"Lizzy, when you first read that letter, I am sure you could not treat the matter as you do now."

"Indeed, I could not. I was uncomfortable enough, I may say unhappy. And with no one to speak to about what I felt, no Jane to comfort me and say that I had not been so very weak and vain and nonsensical as I knew I had! Oh! how I wanted you!"

"How unfortunate that you should have used such very strong expressions in speaking of Wickham to Mr. Darcy, for now they DO appear wholly undeserved."

"Certainly. But the misfortune of speaking with bitterness is a most natural consequence of the prejudices I had been encouraging. There is one point on which I want your advice. I want to be told whether I ought, or ought not, to make our acquaintances in general understand Wickham's character."

Miss Bennet paused a little, and then replied, "Surely there can be no occasion for exposing him so dreadfully. What is your opinion?"

"That it ought not to be attempted. Mr. Darcy has not authorised me to make his communication public. On the contrary, every particular relative to his sister was meant to be kept as much as possible to myself; and if I endeavour to undeceive people as to the rest of his conduct, who will believe me? The general prejudice against Mr. Darcy is so violent, that it would be the death of half the good people in Meryton to attempt to place him in an amiable light. I am not equal to it. Wickham will soon be gone; and therefore it will not signify to anyone here what he really is. Some time hence it will be all found out, and then we may laugh at their stupidity in not knowing it before. At present I will say nothing about it."

"You are quite right. To have his errors made public might ruin him for ever. He is now, perhaps, sorry for what he has done, and anxious to re-establish a character. We must not make him desperate."

The tumult of Elizabeth's mind was allayed by this conversation. She had got rid of two of the secrets which had weighed on her for a fortnight, and was certain of a willing listener in Jane, whenever she might wish to talk again of either. But there was still something lurking behind, of which prudence forbade the disclosure. She dared not relate the other half of Mr. Darcy's letter, nor explain to her sister how sincerely she had been valued by her friend. Here was knowledge in which no one could partake; and she was sensible that nothing less than a perfect understanding between the parties could justify her in throwing off this last encumbrance of mystery. "And then," said she, "if that very improbable event should ever take place, I shall merely be able to tell what Bingley may tell in a much more agreeable manner himself. The liberty of communication cannot be mine till it has lost all its value!"

She was now, on being settled at home, at leisure to observe the real state of her sister's spirits. Jane was not happy. She still cherished a very tender affection for Bingley. Having never even fancied herself in love before, her regard had all the warmth of first attachment, and, from her age and disposition, greater steadiness than most first attachments often boast; and so fervently did she value his remembrance, and prefer him to every other man, that all her good sense, and all her attention to the feelings of her friends, were requisite to check the indulgence of those regrets which must have been injurious to her own health and their tranquillity.

"Well, Lizzy," said Mrs. Bennet one day, "what is your opinion NOW of this sad business of Jane's? For my part, I am determined never to speak of it again to anybody. I told my sister Phillips so the other day. But I cannot find out that Jane saw anything of him in London. Well, he is a very undeserving young man—and I do not suppose there's the least chance in the world of her ever getting him now. There is no talk of his coming to Netherfield again in the summer; and I have inquired of everybody, too, who is likely to know."

"I do not believe he will ever live at Netherfield any more."

"Oh well! it is just as he chooses. Nobody wants him to come. Though I shall always say he used my daughter extremely ill; and if I was her, I would not have put up with it. Well, my comfort is, I am sure Jane will die of a broken heart; and then he will be sorry for what he has done."

But as Elizabeth could not receive comfort from any such expectation, she made no answer.

"Well, Lizzy," continued her mother, soon afterwards, "and so the Collinses live very comfortable, do they? Well, well, I only hope it will last. And what sort of table do they keep? Charlotte is an excellent manager, I dare say. If she is half as sharp as her mother, she is saving enough. There is nothing extravagant in THEIR housekeeping, I dare say."

"No, nothing at all."

"A great deal of good management, depend upon it. Yes, yes. THEY will take care not to outrun their income. THEY will never be distressed for money. Well, much good may it do them! And so, I suppose, they often talk of having Longbourn when your father is dead. They look upon it as quite their own, I dare say, whenever that happens."

"It was a subject which they could not mention before me."

"No; it would have been strange if they had; but I make no doubt they often talk of it between themselves. Well, if they can be easy with an estate that is not lawfully their own, so much the better. I should be ashamed of having one that was only entailed on me."

Chapter 41

The first week of their return was soon gone. The second began. It was the last of the regiment's stay in Meryton, and all the young ladies in the neighbourhood were drooping apace. The dejection was almost universal. The elder Miss Bennets alone were still able to eat, drink, and sleep, and pursue the usual course of their employments. Very frequently were they reproached for this insensibility by Kitty and Lydia, whose own misery was extreme, and who could not comprehend such hard-heartedness in any of the family.

"Good Heaven! what is to become of us? What are we to do?" would they often exclaiming the bitterness of woe. "How can you be smiling so, Lizzy?"

Their affectionate mother shared all their grief; she remembered what she had herself endured on a similar occasion, five-and twenty years ago.

"I am sure," said she, "I cried for two days together when Colonel Miller's regiment went away. I thought I should have broken my heart."

"I am sure I shall break MINE," said Lydia.

"If one could but go to Brighton!" observed Mrs. Bennet.

"Oh, yes!—if one could but go to Brighton! But papa is so disagreeable."

"A little sea-bathing would set me up forever."

"And my aunt Phillips is sure it would do ME a great deal of good," added Kitty.

Such were the kind of lamentations resounding perpetually through Longbourn House. Elizabeth tried to be diverted by them; but all sense of pleasure was lost in shame. She felt anew the justice of Mr. Darcy's objections; and never had she been so much disposed to pardon his interference in the views of his friend.

But the gloom of Lydia's prospect was shortly cleared away; for she received an invitation from Mrs. Forster, the wife of the colonel of the regiment, to accompany her to Brighton. This invaluable friend was a very young woman, and very lately married. A resemblance in good humour and good spirits had recommended her and Lydia to each other, and out of their THREE months' acquaintance they had been intimate TWO.

The rapture of Lydia on this occasion, her adoration of Mrs. Forster, the delight of Mrs. Bennet, and the mortification of Kitty, are scarcely to be described. Wholly inattentive to her sister's feelings, Lydia flew about the house in restless ecstasy, calling for every one's congratulations, and laughing and talking with more violence than ever; whilst the luckless Kitty continued in the parlour repined at her fate in terms as unreasonable as her accent was peevish.

"I cannot see why Mrs. Forster should not ask ME as well as Lydia," said she, "Though I am NOT her particular friend. I have just as much right to be asked as she has, and more too, for I am two years older."

In vain did Elizabeth attempt to make her reasonable, and Jane to make her resigned. As for Elizabeth herself, this invitation was so far from exciting in her the same feelings as in her mother and Lydia, that she considered it as the death warrant of all possibility of common sense for the latter; and detestable as such a step must make her were it known, she could not help secretly advising her father not to let her go. She represented to him all the improprieties of Lydia's general behaviour, the little advantage she could derive from the friendship of such a woman as Mrs. Forster, and the probability of her being yet more imprudent with such a companion at Brighton, where the temptations must be greater than at home. He heard her attentively, and then said:

"Lydia will never be easy until she has exposed herself in some public place or other, and we can never expect her to do it with so little expense or inconvenience to her family as under the present circumstances."

"If you were aware," said Elizabeth, "of the very great disadvantage to us all which must arise from the public notice of Lydia's unguarded and imprudent manner—nay, which has already arisen from it, I am sure you would judge differently in the affair."

"Already arisen?" repeated Mr. Bennet. "What, has she frightened away some of your lovers? Poor little Lizzy! But do not be cast down. Such squeamish youths as cannot bear to be connected with a little absurdity are not worth a regret. Come, let me see the list of pitiful fellows who have been kept aloof by Lydia's folly."

"Indeed you are mistaken. I have no such injuries to resent. It is not of particular, but of general evils, which I am now complaining. Our importance, our respectability in the world must be affected by the wild volatility, the assurance and disdain of all restraint which mark Lydia's character. Excuse me, for I must speak plainly. If you, my dear father, will not take the trouble of checking her exuberant spirits, and of teaching her that her present pursuits are not to be the business of her life, she will soon be beyond the reach of amendment. Her character will be fixed, and she will, at sixteen, be the most determined flirt that ever made herself or her family ridiculous; a flirt, too, in the worst and meanest degree of flirtation; without any attraction beyond youth and a tolerable person; and, from the ignorance and emptiness of her mind, wholly unable to ward off any portion of that universal contempt which her rage for admiration will excite. In this danger Kitty also is comprehended. She will follow wherever Lydia leads. Vain, ignorant, idle, and absolutely uncontrolled! Oh! my dear father, can you suppose it possible that they will not be censured and despised wherever they are known, and that their sisters will not be often involved in the disgrace?"

Mr. Bennet saw that her whole heart was in the subject, and affectionately taking her hand said in reply:

"Do not make yourself uneasy, my love. Wherever you and Jane are known you must be respected and valued; and you will not appear to less advantage for having a couple of—or I may say, three—very silly sisters. We shall have no peace at Longbourn if Lydia does not go to Brighton. Let her go, then. Colonel Forster is a sensible man, and will keep her out of any real mischief; and she is luckily too poor to be an object of prey to anybody. At Brighton she will be of less importance even as a common flirt than she has been here. The officers will find women better worth their notice. Let us hope, therefore, that her being there may teach her her own insignificance. At any rate, she cannot grow many degrees worse, without authorising us to lock her up for the rest of her life."

With this answer Elizabeth was forced to be content; but her own opinion continued the same, and she left him disappointed and sorry. It was not in her nature, however, to increase her vexations by dwelling on them. She was confident of having performed her duty, and to fret over unavoidable evils, or augment them by anxiety, was no part of her disposition.

Had Lydia and her mother known the substance of her conference with her father, their indignation would hardly have found expression in their united volubility. In Lydia's imagination, a visit to Brighton comprised ever possibility of earthly happiness. She saw, with the creative eye of fancy, the streets of that gay bathing-place covered with officers. She saw herself the object to tens and to scores of them at present unknown. She saw all the glories of the camp—its tents stretched forth in beauteous uniformity of lines, crowded with the young and the gay, and dazzling with scarlet; and, to complete the view, she saw herself seated beneath a tent, tenderly flirting with at least six officers at once.

Had she known her sister sought to tear her from such prospects and such realities as these, what would have been her sensations? They could have been understood only by her mother, who might have felt nearly the same. Lydia's going to Brighton was all that consoled her for her melancholy conviction of her husband's never intending to go there himself.

But they were entirely ignorant of what had passed; and their raptures continued, with little intermission, to the very day of Lydia's leaving home.

Elizabeth was now to see Mr. Wickham for the last time. Having been frequently in company with him since her return, agitation was pretty well over; the agitations of formal partiality entirely so. She had even learnt to detect, in the very gentleness which had first delighted her, an affectation and a sameness to disgust and weary. In his present behaviour to herself, moreover, she had a fresh source of displeasure, for the inclination he soon testified of renewing those intentions which had marked the early part of their acquaintance could only serve, after what had since passed, to provoke her. She lost all concern for him in finding herself thus selected as the object of such idle and frivolous gallantry; and while she steadily repressed it, could not but feel the reproof contained in his believing, that however long, and for whatever cause, his attentions had been withdrawn, her vanity would be gratified, and her preference secured at any time by their renewal.

On the very last day of the regiment's remaining at Meryton, he dined, with other of the officers, at Longbourn; and so little was

Elizabeth disposed to part from him in good humour, that on his making some inquiry as to the manner in which her time had passed at Hunsford, she mentioned Colonel Fitzwilliam's and Mr. Darcy's having both spent three weeks at Rosings, and asked him, if he was acquainted with the former.

He looked surprised displeased, alarmed; but with a moment's recollection and a returning smile, replied, that he had formerly seen him often; and, after observing that he was a very gentlemanlike man, asked her how she had liked him. Her answer was warmly in his favour. With an air of indifference he soon afterwards added:

"How long did you say he was at Rosings?"

"Nearly three weeks."

"And you saw him frequently?"

"Yes, almost every day."

"His manners are very different from his cousin's."

"Yes, very different. But I think Mr. Darcy improves upon acquaintance."

"Indeed!" cried Mr. Wickham with a look which did not escape her. "And pray, may I ask?—" But checking himself, he added, in a gayer tone, "Is it in address that he improves? Has he deigned to add aught of civility to his ordinary style?—for I dare not hope," he continued in a lower and more serious tone, "that he is improved in essentials."

"Oh, no!" said Elizabeth. "In essentials, I believe, he is very much what he ever was."

While she spoke, Wickham looked as if scarcely knowing whether to rejoice over her words, or to distrust their meaning. There was a something in her countenance which made him listen with an apprehensive and anxious attention, while she added:

"When I said that he improved on acquaintance, I did not mean that his mind or his manners were in a state of improvement, but that, from knowing him better, his disposition was better understood."

Wickham's alarm now appeared in a heightened complexion and agitated look; for a few minuted he was silent, till, shaking off his embarrassment, he turned to her again, and said in the gentlest of accents:

"You, who so well know my feeling towards Mr. Darcy, will readily comprehend how sincerely I must rejoice that he is wise enough to assume even the APPEARANCE of what is right. His pride, in that direction, may be of service, if not to himself, to many others, for it must only deter him from such foul misconduct as I have suffered by. I only fear that the sort of cautiousness to which you, I imagine, have been alluding, is merely adopted on his visits to his aunt, of whose good opinion and judgement he stands much in awe. His fear of her has always operated, I know, when they were together; and a good deal is to be imputed to his wish of forwarding the match with Miss de Bourgh, which I am certain he has very much at heart."

Elizabeth could not repress a smile at this, but she answered only by a slight inclination of the head. She saw that he wanted to engage her on the old subject of his grievances, and she was in no humour to indulge him. The rest of the evening passed with the APPEARANCE, on his side, of usual cheerfulness, but with no further attempt to distinguish Elizabeth; and they parted at last with mutual civility, and possibly a mutual desire of never meeting again.

When the party broke up, Lydia returned with Mrs. Forster to Meryton, from whence they were to set out early the next morning. The separation between her and her family was rather noisy than pathetic. Kitty was the only one who shed tears; but she did weep from vexation and envy. Mrs. Bennet was diffuse in her good wishes for the felicity of her daughter, and impressive in her injunctions that she should not miss the opportunity of enjoying herself as much as possible—advice which there was every reason to believe would be well attended to; and in the clamorous happiness of Lydia herself in bidding farewell, the more gentle adieux of her sisters were uttered without being heard.

Chapter 42

Had Elizabeth's opinion been all drawn from her own family, she could not have formed a very pleasing opinion of conjugal felicity or domestic comfort. Her father, captivated by youth and beauty, and that appearance of good humour which youth and beauty generally give, had married a woman whose weak understanding and illiberal mind had very early in their marriage put and end to all real affection for her. Respect, esteem, and confidence had vanished for ever; and all his views of domestic happiness were overthrown. But Mr. Bennet was not of a disposition to seek comfort for the disappointment which his own imprudence had brought on, in any of those pleasures which too often console the unfortunate for their folly of their vice. He was fond of the country and of books; and from these tastes had arisen his principal enjoyments. To his wife he was very little otherwise indebted, than as her ignorance and folly had contributed to his amusement. This is not the sort of happiness which a man would in general wish to owe to his wife; but where other powers of entertainment are wanting, the true philosopher will derive benefit from such as are given.

Elizabeth, however, had never been blind to the impropriety of her father's behaviour as a husband. She had always seen it with pain; but respecting his abilities, and grateful for his affectionate treatment of herself, she endeavoured to forget what she could not overlook, and to banish from her thoughts that continual breach of conjugal obligation and decorum which, in exposing his wife to the contempt of her own children, was so highly reprehensible. But she had never felt so strongly as now the disadvantages which must attend the children of so unsuitable a marriage, nor ever been so fully aware of the evils arising from so ill-judged a direction of talents; talents, which, rightly used, might at least have preserved the respectability of his daughters, even if incapable of enlarging the mind of his wife.

When Elizabeth had rejoiced over Wickham's departure she found little other cause for satisfaction in the loss of the regiment. Their parties abroad were less varied than before, and at home she had a mother and sister whose constant repinings at the dullness of everything around them threw a real gloom over their domestic circle; and, though Kitty might in time regain her natural degree of sense, since the disturbers of her brain were removed, her other sister, from whose disposition greater evil might be apprehended, was likely to be hardened in all her folly and assurance by a situation of such double danger as a watering-place and a camp. Upon the whole, therefore, she found, what has been sometimes been found before, that an event to which she had been looking with impatient desire did not, in taking place, bring all the satisfaction she had promised herself. It was consequently necessary to name some other period for the commencement of actual felicity—to have some other point on which her wishes and hopes might be fixed, and by again enjoying the pleasure of anticipation, console herself for the present, and prepare for another disappointment. Her tour to the Lakes was now the object of her happiest thoughts; it was her best consolation for all the uncomfortable hours which the discontentedness of her mother and Kitty made inevitable; and could she have included Jane in the scheme, every part of it would have been perfect.

"But it is fortunate," thought she, "that I have something to wish for. Were the whole arrangement complete, my disappointment would be certain. But here, by carrying with me one ceaseless source of regret in my sister's absence, I may reasonably hope to have all my expectations of pleasure realised. A scheme of which every part promises delight can never be successful; and general disappointment is only warded off by the defence of some little peculiar vexation."

When Lydia went away she promised to write very often and very minutely to her mother and Kitty; but her letters were always long expected, and always very short. Those to her mother contained little else than that they were just returned from the library, where such and such officers had attended them, and where she had seen such beautiful ornaments as made her quite wild; that she had a new gown, or a new parasol, which she would have described more fully, but was obliged to leave off in a violent hurry, as Mrs. Forster called her, and they were going off to the camp; and from her correspondence with her sister, there was still less to be learnt—for her letters to Kitty, though rather longer, were much too full of lines under the words to be made public.

After the first fortnight or three weeks of her absence, health, good humour, and cheerfulness began to reappear at Longbourn. Everything wore a happier aspect. The families who had been in town for the winter came back again, and summer finery and summer engagements arose. Mrs. Bennet was restored to her usual querulous serenity; and, by the middle of June, Kitty was so much recovered as to be able to enter Meryton without tears; an event of such happy promise as to make Elizabeth hope that by the following Christmas she might be so tolerably reasonable as not to mention an officer above once a day, unless, by some cruel and malicious arrangement at the War Office, another regiment should be quartered in Meryton.

The time fixed for the beginning of their northern tour was now fast approaching, and a fortnight only was wanting of it, when a letter arrived from Mrs. Gardiner, which at once delayed its commencement and curtailed its extent. Mr. Gardiner would be prevented by business from setting out till a fortnight later in July, and must be in London again within a month, and as that left too short a period for them to go so far, and see so much as they had proposed, or at least to see it with the leisure and comfort they had built on, they were obliged to give up the Lakes, and substitute a more contracted tour, and, according to the present plan, were to go no farther northwards than Derbyshire. In that county there was enough to be seen to occupy the chief of their three weeks; and to Mrs. Gardiner it had a peculiarly strong attraction. The town where she had formerly passed some years of her life, and where they were now to spend a few days, was probably as great an object of her curiosity as all the celebrated beauties of Matlock, Chatsworth, Dovedale, or the Peak.

Elizabeth was excessively disappointed; she had set her heart on seeing the Lakes, and still thought there might have been time enough. But it was her business to be satisfied—and certainly her temper to be happy; and all was soon right again.

With the mention of Derbyshire there were many ideas connected. It was impossible for her to see the word without thinking of Pemberley and its owner. "But surely," said she, "I may enter his county without impunity, and rob it of a few petrified spars without his perceiving me."

The period of expectation was now doubled. Four weeks were to pass away before her uncle and aunt's arrival. But they did pass away, and Mr. and Mrs. Gardiner, with their four children, did at length appear at Longbourn. The children, two girls of six and eight years old, and two younger boys, were to be left under the particular care of their cousin Jane, who was the general favourite, and whose steady sense and sweetness of temper exactly adapted her for attending to them in every way—teaching them, playing with them, and loving them.

The Gardiners stayed only one night at Longbourn, and set off the next morning with Elizabeth in pursuit of novelty and amusement. One enjoyment was certain—that of suitableness of companions; a suitableness which comprehended health and temper to bear inconveniences—cheerfulness to enhance every pleasure—and affection and intelligence, which might supply it among themselves if there were disappointments abroad.

It is not the object of this work to give a description of Derbyshire, nor of any of the remarkable places through which their route thither lay; Oxford, Blenheim, Warwick, Kenilworth, Birmingham, &c., are sufficiently known. A small part of Derbyshire is all the present concern. To the little town of Lambton, the scene of Mrs. Gardiner's former residence, and where she had lately learned some acquaintance still remained, they bent their steps, after having seen all the principal wonders of the country; and within five miles of Lambton, Elizabeth found from her aunt that Pemberley was situated. It was not in their direct road, nor more than a mile or two out of it. In talking over their route the evening before, Mrs. Gardiner expressed an inclination to see the place again. Mr. Gardiner declared his willingness, and Elizabeth was applied to for her approbation.

"My love, should not you like to see a place of which you have heard so much?" said her aunt; "a place, too, with which so many of your acquaintances are connected. Wickham passed all his youth there, you know."

Elizabeth was distressed. She felt that she had no business at Pemberley, and was obliged to assume a disinclination for seeing it. She must own that she was tired of seeing great houses; after going over so many, she really had no pleasure in fine carpets or satin curtains.

Mrs. Gardiner abused her stupidity. If it were merely a fine house richly furnished," said she, "I should not care about it myself; but the grounds are delightful. They have some of the finest woods in the country."

Elizabeth said no more—but her mind could not acquiesce. The possibility of meeting Mr. Darcy, while viewing the place, instantly occurred. It would be dreadful! She blushed at the very idea, and thought it would be better to speak openly to her aunt than to run such a risk. But against this there were objections; and she finally resolved that it could be the last resource, if her private inquiries to the absence of the family were unfavourably answered.

Accordingly, when she retired at night, she asked the chambermaid whether Pemberley were not a very fine place? what was the name of its proprietor? and, with no little alarm, whether the family were down for the summer? A most welcome negative followed the last question—and her alarms now being removed, she was at leisure to feel a great deal of curiosity to see the house herself; and when the subject was revived the next morning, and she was again applied to, could readily answer, and with a proper air of indifference, that she had not really any dislike to the scheme. To Pemberley, therefore, they were to go.

Chapter 43

Elizabeth, as they drove along, watched for the first appearance of Pemberley Woods with some perturbation; and when at length they turned in at the lodge, her spirits were in a high flutter.

The park was very large, and contained great variety of ground. They entered it in one of its lowest points, and drove for some time through a beautiful wood stretching over a wide extent.

Elizabeth's mind was too full for conversation, but she saw and admired every remarkable spot and point of view. They gradually ascended for half-a-mile, and then found themselves at the top of a considerable eminence, where the wood ceased, and the eye was instantly caught by Pemberley House, situated on the opposite side of a valley, into which the road with some abruptness wound. It was a large, handsome stone building, standing well on rising ground, and backed by a ridge of high woody hills; and in front, a stream of some natural importance was swelled into greater, but without any artificial appearance. Its banks were neither formal nor falsely adorned. Elizabeth was delighted. She had never seen a place for which nature had done more, or where natural beauty had been so little counteracted by an awkward taste. They were all of them warm in their admiration; and at that moment she felt that to be mistress of Pemberley might be something!

They descended the hill, crossed the bridge, and drove to the door; and, while examining the nearer aspect of the house, all her apprehension of meeting its owner returned. She dreaded lest the chambermaid had been mistaken. On applying to see the place, they were admitted into the hall; and Elizabeth, as they waited for the housekeeper, had leisure to wonder at her being where she was.

The housekeeper came; a respectable-looking elderly woman, much less fine, and more civil, than she had any notion of finding her. They followed her into the dining-parlour. It was a large, well proportioned room, handsomely fitted up. Elizabeth, after slightly surveying it, went to a window to enjoy its prospect. The hill, crowned with wood, which they had descended, receiving increased abruptness from the distance, was a beautiful object. Every disposition of the ground was good; and she looked on the whole scene, the river, the trees scattered on its banks and the winding of the valley, as far as she could trace it, with delight. As they passed into other rooms these objects were taking different positions; but from every window there were beauties to be seen. The rooms were lofty and handsome, and their furniture suitable to the fortune of its proprietor; but Elizabeth saw, with admiration of his taste, that it was neither gaudy nor uselessly fine; with less of splendour, and more real elegance, than the furniture of Rosings.

"And of this place," thought she, "I might have been mistress! With these rooms I might now have been familiarly acquainted! Instead of viewing them as a stranger, I might have rejoiced in them as my own, and welcomed to them as visitors my uncle and aunt. But no," recollecting herself—"that could never be; my uncle and aunt would have been lost to me; I should not have been allowed to invite them."

This was a lucky recollection—it saved her from something very like regret.

She longed to inquire of the housekeeper whether her master was really absent, but had not the courage for it. At length however, the question was asked by her uncle; and she turned away with alarm, while Mrs. Reynolds replied that he was, adding, "But we expect him to-morrow, with a large party of friends." How rejoiced was Elizabeth that their own journey had not by any circumstance been delayed a day!

Her aunt now called her to look at a picture. She approached and saw the likeness of Mr. Wickham, suspended, amongst several other miniatures, over the mantelpiece. Her aunt asked her, smilingly, how she liked it. The housekeeper came forward, and told them it was a picture of a young gentleman, the son of her late master's steward, who had been brought up by him at his own expense. "He is now gone into the army," she added; "but I am afraid he has turned out very wild."

Mrs. Gardiner looked at her niece with a smile, but Elizabeth could not return it.

"And that," said Mrs Reynolds, pointing to another of the miniatures, "is my master—and very like him. It was drawn at the same time as the other—about eight years ago."

"I have heard much of your master's fine person," said Mrs. Gardiner, looking at the picture; "it is a handsome face. But, Lizzy, you can tell us whether it is like or not."

Mrs. Reynolds respect for Elizabeth seemed to increase on this intimation of her knowing her master.

"Does that young lady know Mr. Darcy?"

Elizabeth coloured, and said: "A little."

"And do not you think him a very handsome gentleman, ma'am?"

"Yes, very handsome."

"I am sure I know none so handsome; but in the gallery upstairs you will see a finer, larger picture of him than this. This room was my late master's favourite room, and these miniatures are just as they used to be then. He was very fond of them."

This accounted to Elizabeth for Mr. Wickham's being among them.

Mrs. Reynolds then directed their attention to one of Miss Darcy, drawn when she was only eight years old.

"And is Miss Darcy as handsome as her brother?" said Mrs. Gardiner.

"Oh! yes—the handsomest young lady that ever was seen; and so accomplished!—She plays and sings all day long. In the next room is a new instrument just come down for her—a present from my master; she comes here to-morrow with him."

Mr. Gardiner, whose manners were very easy and pleasant, encouraged her communicativeness by his questions and remarks: Mrs. Reynolds, either by pride or attachment, had evidently great pleasure in talking of her master and his sister.

"Is your master much at Pemberley in the course of the year?"

"Not so much as I could wish, sir; but I dare say he may spend half his time here; and Miss Darcy is always down for the summer months."

"Except," thought Elizabeth, "when she goes to Ramsgate."

"If your master would marry, you might see more of him."

"Yes, sir; but I do not know when THAT will be. I do not know who is good enough for him."

Mr. and Mrs. Gardiner smiled. Elizabeth could not help saying, "It is very much to his credit, I am sure, that you should think so."

"I say no more than the truth, and everybody will say that knows him," replied the other. Elizabeth thought this was going pretty far; and she listened with increasing astonishment as the housekeeper added, "I have never known a cross word from him in my life, and I have known him ever since he was four years old."

This was praise, of all others most extraordinary, most opposite to her ideas. That he was not a good-tempered man had been her firmest opinion. Her keenest attention was awakened; she longed to hear more, and was grateful to her uncle for saying:

"There are very few people of whom so much can be said. You are lucky in having such a master."

"Yes, sir, I know I am. If I were to go through the world, I could not meet with a better. But I have always observed, that they who are good-natured when children, are good-natured when they grow up; and he was always the sweetest-tempered, most generous-hearted boy in the world."

Elizabeth almost stared at her. "Can this be Mr. Darcy?" thought she.

"His father was an excellent man," said Mrs. Gardiner.

"Yes, ma'am, that he was indeed; and his son will be just like him—just as affable to the poor."

Elizabeth listened, wondered, doubted, and was impatient for more. Mrs. Reynolds could interest her on no other point. She related the subjects of the pictures, the dimensions of the rooms, and the price of the furniture, in vain, Mr. Gardiner, highly amused by the kind of family prejudice to which he attributed her excessive commendation of her master, soon led again to the subject; and she dwelt with energy on his many merits as they proceeded together up the great staircase.

"He is the best landlord, and the best master," said she, "that ever lived; not like the wild young men nowadays, who think of nothing but themselves. There is not one of his tenants or servants but will give him a good name. Some people call him proud; but I am sure I never saw anything of it. To my fancy, it is only because he does not rattle away like other young men."

"In what an amiable light does this place him!" thought Elizabeth.

"This fine account of him," whispered her aunt as they walked, "is not quite consistent with his behaviour to our poor friend."

"Perhaps we might be deceived."

"That is not very likely; our authority was too good."

On reaching the spacious lobby above they were shown into a very pretty sitting-room, lately fitted up with greater elegance and lightness than the apartments below; and were informed that it was but just done to give pleasure to Miss Darcy, who had taken a liking to the room when last at Pemberley.

"He is certainly a good brother," said Elizabeth, as she walked towards one of the windows.

Mrs. Reynolds anticipated Miss Darcy's delight, when she should enter the room. "And this is always the way with him," she added. "Whatever can give his sister any pleasure is sure to be done in a moment. There is nothing he would not do for her."

The picture-gallery, and two or three of the principal bedrooms, were all that remained to be shown. In the former were many good paintings; but Elizabeth knew nothing of the art; and from such as had been already visible below, she had willingly turned to look at some drawings of Miss Darcy's, in crayons, whose subjects were usually more interesting, and also more intelligible.

In the gallery there were many family portraits, but they could have little to fix the attention of a stranger. Elizabeth walked in quest of the only face whose features would be known to her. At last it arrested her—and she beheld a striking resemblance to Mr. Darcy, with such a smile over the face as she remembered to have sometimes seen when he looked at her. She stood several minutes before the picture, in earnest contemplation, and returned to it again before they quitted the gallery. Mrs. Reynolds informed them that it had been taken in his father's lifetime.

There was certainly at this moment, in Elizabeth's mind, a more gentle sensation towards the original than she had ever felt at the height of their acquaintance. The commendation bestowed on him by Mrs. Reynolds was of no trifling nature. What praise is more valuable than the praise of an intelligent servant? As a brother, a landlord, a master, she considered how many people's happiness were in his guardianship!—how much of pleasure or pain was it in his power to bestow!—how much of good or evil must be done by him! Every idea that had been brought forward by the housekeeper was favourable to his character, and as she stood before the canvas on which he was represented, and fixed his eyes upon herself, she thought of his regard with a deeper sentiment of gratitude than it had ever raised before; she remembered its warmth, and softened its impropriety of expression.

When all of the house that was open to general inspection had been seen, they returned downstairs, and, taking leave of the housekeeper, were consigned over to the gardener, who met them at the hall-door.

As they walked across the hall towards the river, Elizabeth turned back to look again; her uncle and aunt stopped also, and while the former was conjecturing as to the date of the building, the owner of it himself suddenly came forward from the road, which led behind it to the stables.

They were within twenty yards of each other, and so abrupt was his appearance, that it was impossible to avoid his sight. Their eyes instantly met, and the cheeks of both were overspread with the deepest blush. He absolutely started, and for a moment seemed immovable from surprise; but shortly recovering himself, advanced towards the party, and spoke to Elizabeth, if not in terms of perfect composure, at least of perfect civility.

She had instinctively turned away; but stopping on his approach, received his compliments with an embarrassment impossible to be overcome. Had his first appearance, or his resemblance to the picture they had just been examining, been insufficient to assure the other two that they now saw Mr. Darcy, the gardener's expression of surprise, on beholding his master, must immediately have told it. They stood a little aloof while he was talking to their niece, who, astonished and confused, scarcely dared lift her eyes to his face, and knew not what answer she returned to his civil inquiries after her family. Amazed at the alteration of his manner since they last parted, every sentence that he uttered was increasing her embarrassment; and every idea of the impropriety of her being found there recurring to her mind, the few minutes in which they continued were some of the most uncomfortable in her life. Nor did he seem much more at ease; when he spoke, his accent had none of its usual sedateness; and he repeated his inquiries as to the time of her having left Longbourn, and of her having stayed in Derbyshire, so often, and in so hurried a way, as plainly spoke the distraction of his thoughts.

At length every idea seemed to fail him; and, after standing a few moments without saying a word, he suddenly recollected himself, and took leave.

The others then joined her, and expressed admiration of his figure; but Elizabeth heard not a word, and wholly engrossed by her own feelings, followed them in silence. She was overpowered by shame and vexation. Her coming there was the most unfortunate, the most ill-judged thing in the world! How strange it must appear to him! In what a disgraceful light might it not strike so vain a man! It might seem as if she had purposely thrown herself in his way again! Oh! why did she come? Or, why did he thus come a day before he was expected? Had they been only ten minutes sooner, they should have been beyond the reach of his discrimination; for it was plain that he was that moment arrived—that moment alighted from his horse or his carriage. She blushed again and again over the perverseness of the meeting. And his behaviour, so strikingly altered—what could it mean? That he should even speak to her was amazing!—but to speak with such civility, to inquire after her family! Never in her life had she seen his manners so little dignified, never had he spoken with such gentleness as on this unexpected meeting. What a contrast did it offer to his last address in Rosings Park, when he put his letter into her hand! She knew not what to think, or how to account for it.

They had now entered a beautiful walk by the side of the water, and every step was bringing forward a nobler fall of ground, or a finer reach of the woods to which they were approaching; but it was some time before Elizabeth was sensible of any of it; and, though she answered mechanically to the repeated appeals of her uncle and aunt, and seemed to direct her eyes to such objects as they pointed out, she distinguished no part of the scene. Her thoughts were all fixed on that one spot of Pemberley House, whichever it might be, where Mr. Darcy then was. She longed to know what at the moment was passing in his mind—in what manner he thought of her, and whether, in defiance of everything, she was still dear to him. Perhaps he had been civil only because he felt himself at ease; yet there had been THAT in his voice which was not like ease. Whether he had felt more of pain or of pleasure in seeing her she could not tell, but he certainly had not seen her with composure.

At length, however, the remarks of her companions on her absence of mind aroused her, and she felt the necessity of appearing more like herself.

They entered the woods, and bidding adieu to the river for a while, ascended some of the higher grounds; when, in spots where the opening of the trees gave the eye power to wander, were many charming views of the valley, the opposite hills, with the long range of woods overspreading many, and occasionally part of the stream. Mr. Gardiner expressed a wish of going round the whole park, but feared it might be beyond a walk. With a triumphant smile they were told that it was ten miles round. It settled the matter; and they pursued the accustomed circuit; which brought them again, after some time, in a descent among hanging woods, to the edge of the water, and one of its narrowest parts. They crossed it by a simple bridge, in character with the general air of the scene; it was a spot less adorned than any they had yet visited; and the valley, here contracted into a glen, allowed room only for the stream, and a narrow walk amidst the rough coppice-wood which bordered it. Elizabeth longed to explore its windings; but when they had crossed the bridge, and perceived their distance from the house, Mrs. Gardiner, who was not a great walker, could go no farther, and thought only of returning to the carriage as quickly as possible. Her niece was, therefore, obliged to submit, and they took their way towards the house on the opposite side of the river, in the nearest direction; but their progress was slow, for Mr. Gardiner, though seldom able to indulge the taste, was very fond of fishing, and was so much engaged in watching the occasional appearance of some trout in the water, and talking to the man about them, that he advanced but little. Whilst wandering on in this slow manner, they were again surprised, and Elizabeth's astonishment was quite equal to what it had been at first, by the sight of Mr. Darcy approaching them, and at no great distance. The walk here being here less sheltered than on the other side, allowed them to see him before they met. Elizabeth, however astonished, was at least more prepared for an interview than before, and resolved to appear and to speak with calmness, if we really intended to meet them. For a few moments, indeed, she felt that he would probably strike into some other path. The idea lasted while a turning in the walk concealed him from their view; the turning past, he was immediately before them. With a glance, she saw that he had lost none of his recent civility; and, to imitate his politeness, she began as they to admire the beauty of the place; but she had not got beyond the words "delightful," and "charming," when some unlucky recollections obtruded, and she fancied that praise of Pemberley from her might be mischievously construed. Her colour changed, and she said no more.

Mrs. Gardiner was standing a little behind; and on her pausing, he asked her if she would do him the honour of introducing him to her friends. This was a stroke of civility for which she was quite unprepared; and she could hardly suppress a smile at his being now seeking the acquaintance of some of those very people against whom his pride had revolted in his offer to herself. "What will be his surprise," thought she, "when he knows who they are? He takes them now for people of fashion."

The introduction, however, was immediately made; and as she named their relationship to herself, she stole a sly look at him, to see how he bore it, and was not without the expectation of his decamping as fast as he could from such disgraceful companions. That he was SURPRISED by the connection was evident; he sustained it, however, with fortitude, and so far from going away, turned his back with them, and entered into conversation with Mr. Gardiner. Elizabeth could not but be pleased, could not but triumph. It was consoling that he should know she had some relations for whom there was no need to blush. She listened most attentively to all that passed between them, and gloried in every expression, every sentence of her uncle, which marked his intelligence, his taste, or his good manners.

The conversation soon turned upon fishing; and she heard Mr. Darcy invite him, with the greatest civility, to fish there as often as he chose while he continued in the neighbourhood, offering at the same time to supply him with fishing tackle, and pointing out those parts of the stream where there was usually most sport. Mrs. Gardiner, who was walking arm-in-arm with Elizabeth, gave her a look expressive of wonder. Elizabeth said nothing, but it gratified her exceedingly; the compliment must be all for herself. Her astonishment, however, was extreme, and continually was she repeating, "Why is he so altered? From what can it proceed? It cannot be for ME—it cannot be for MY sake that his manners are thus softened. My reproofs at Hunsford could not work such a change as this. It is impossible that he should still love me."

After walking some time in this way, the two ladies in front, the two gentlemen behind, on resuming their places, after descending to the brink of the river for the better inspection of some curious water-plant, there chanced to be a little alteration. It originated in Mrs. Gardiner, who, fatigued by the exercise of the morning, found Elizabeth's arm inadequate to her support, and consequently preferred her husband's. Mr. Darcy took her place by her niece, and they walked on together. After a short silence, the lady first spoke. She wished him to know that she had been assured of his absence before she came to the place, and accordingly began by observing, that his arrival had been very unexpected—"for your housekeeper," she added, "informed us that you would certainly not be here till to-morrow; and indeed, before we left Bakewell, we understood that you were not immediately expected in the country." He acknowledged the truth of it all, and said that business with his steward had occasioned his coming forward a few hours before the rest of the party with whom he had been travelling. "They will join me early to-morrow ," he continued, "and among them are some who will claim an acquaintance with you—Mr. Bingley and his sisters."

Elizabeth answered only by a slight bow. Her thoughts were instantly driven back to the time when Mr. Bingley's name had been the last mentioned between them; and, if she might judge by his complexion, HIS mind was not very differently engaged.

"There is also one other person in the party," he continued after a pause, "who more particularly wishes to be known to you. Will you allow me, or do I ask too much, to introduce my sister to your acquaintance during your stay at Lambton?"

The surprise of such an application was great indeed; it was too great for her to know in what manner she acceded to it. She immediately felt that whatever desire Miss Darcy might have of being acquainted with her must be the work of her brother, and, without looking farther, it was satisfactory; it was gratifying to know that is resentment had not made him think really ill of her.

They now walked on in silence, each of them deep in thought. Elizabeth was not comfortable; that was impossible; but she was flattered and pleased. His wish of introducing his sister to her was a compliment of the highest kind. They soon outstripped the others, and when they had reached the carriage, Mr. and Mrs. Gardiner were half a quarter of a mile behind.

He then asked her to walk into the house—but she declared herself not tired, and they stood together on the lawn. At such a time much might have been said, and silence was very awkward. She wanted to talk, but there seemed to be an embargo on every subject. At last she recollected that she had been travelling, and they talked of Matlock and Dovedale with great perseverance. Yet time and her aunt moved slowly—and her patience and her ideas were nearly worn our before the tete-a-tete was over. On Mr. and Mrs' Gardiner's coming up they were all pressed to go into the house and take some refreshment; but this was declined, and they parted on each side with utmost politeness. Mr. Darcy handed the ladies into the carriage; and when it drove off, Elizabeth saw him walking slowly towards the house.

The observations of her uncle and aunt now began; and each of them pronounced him to be infinitely superior to anything they had expected. "He is perfectly well behaved, polite, and unassuming," said her uncle.

"There IS something a little stately in him, to be sure," replied her aunt, "but it is confined to his air, and is not unbecoming. I can now say with the housekeeper, that though some people may call him proud, I have seen nothing of it."

"I was never more surprised than by his behaviour to us. It was more than civil; it was really attentive; and there was no necessity for such attention. His acquaintance with Elizabeth was very trifling."

"To be sure, Lizzy," said her aunt, "he is not so handsome as Wickham; or, rather, he has not Wickham's countenance, for his features are perfectly good. But how came you to tell me that he was so disagreeable?"

Elizabeth excused herself as well as she could; said that she had liked him better when they had met in Kent than before, and that she had never seen him so pleasant as this morning.

"But perhaps he may be a little whimsical in his civilities," replied her uncle. "Your great men often are; and therefore I shall not take him at his word, as he might change his mind another day, and warn me off his grounds."

Elizabeth felt that they had entirely misunderstood his character, but said nothing.

"From what we have seen of him," continued Mrs. Gardiner, "I really should not have thought that he could have behaved in so cruel a way by anybody as he has done by poor Wickham. He has not an ill-natured look. On the contrary, there is something pleasing about his mouth when he speaks. And there is something of dignity in his countenance that would not give one an unfavourable idea of his heart. But, to be sure, the good lady who showed us his house did give him a most flaming character! I could hardly help laughing aloud sometimes. But he is a liberal master, I suppose, and THAT in the eye of a servant comprehends every virtue."

Elizabeth here felt herself called on to say something in vindication of his behaviour to Wickham; and therefore gave them to understand, in as guarded a manner as she could, that by what she had heard from his relations in Kent, his actions were capable of a very different construction; and that his character was by no means so faulty, nor Wickham's so amiable, as they had been considered in Hertfordshire. In confirmation of this, she related the particulars of all the pecuniary transactions in which they had been connected, without actually naming her authority, but stating as such as might be relied on.

Mrs. Gardiner was surprised and concerned; but as they were now approaching the scene of her former pleasures, every idea gave way to the charm of recollection; and she was too much engaged in pointing out to her husband all the interesting spots in its environs to think of anything else. Fatigued as she had been by the morning's walk they had no sooner dined than she set off again in quest of her former acquaintance, and the evening was spent in the satisfactions of a intercourse renewed after many years' discontinuance.

The occurrences of the day were too full of interest to leave Elizabeth much attention for any of these new friends; and she could do nothing but think, and think with wonder, of Mr. Darcy's civility, and, above all, of his wishing her to be acquainted with his sister.

Chapter 44

Elizabeth had settled it that Mr. Darcy would bring his sister to visit her the very day after her reaching Pemberley; and was consequently resolved not to be out of sight of the inn the whole of that morning. But her conclusion was false; for on the very morning after their arrival at Lambton, these visitors came. They had been walking about the place with some of their new friends, and were just returning to the inn to dress themselves for dining with the same family, when the sound of a carriage drew them to a window, and they saw a gentleman and a lady in a curricle driving up the street. Elizabeth immediately recognizing the livery, guessed what it meant, and imparted no small degree of her surprise to her relations by acquainting them with the honour which she expected. Her uncle and aunt were all amazement; and the embarrassment of her manner as she spoke, joined to the circumstance itself, and many of the circumstances of the preceding day, opened to them a new idea on the business. Nothing had ever suggested it before, but they felt that there was no other way of accounting for such attentions from such a quarter than by supposing a partiality for their niece. While these newly-born notions were passing in their heads, the perturbation of Elizabeth's feelings was at every moment increasing. She was quite amazed at her own discomposure; but amongst other causes of disquiet, she dreaded lest the partiality of the brother should have said too much in her favour; and, more than commonly anxious to please, she naturally suspected that every power of pleasing would fail her.

She retreated from the window, fearful of being seen; and as she walked up and down the room, endeavouring to compose herself, saw such looks of inquiring surprise in her uncle and aunt as made everything worse.

Miss Darcy and her brother appeared, and this formidable introduction took place. With astonishment did Elizabeth see that her new acquaintance was at least as much embarrassed as herself. Since her being at Lambton, she had heard that Miss Darcy was exceedingly proud; but the observation of a very few minutes convinced her that she was only exceedingly shy. She found it difficult to obtain even a word from her beyond a monosyllable.

Miss Darcy was tall, and on a larger scale than Elizabeth; and, though little more than sixteen, her figure was formed, and her appearance womanly and graceful. She was less handsome than her brother; but there was sense and good humour in her face, and her manners were perfectly unassuming and gentle. Elizabeth, who had expected to find in her as acute and unembarrassed an observer as ever Mr. Darcy had been, was much relieved by discerning such different feelings.

They had not long been together before Mr. Darcy told her that Bingley was also coming to wait on her; and she had barely time to express her satisfaction, and prepare for such a visitor, when Bingley's quick step was heard on the stairs, and in a moment he entered the room. All Elizabeth's anger against him had been long done away; but had she still felt any, it could hardly have stood its ground against the unaffected cordiality with which he expressed himself on seeing her again. He inquired in a friendly, though general way, after her family, and looked and spoke with the same good-humoured ease that he had ever done.

To Mr. and Mrs. Gardiner he was scarcely a less interesting personage than to herself. They had long wished to see him. The whole party before them, indeed, excited a lively attention. The suspicions which had just arisen of Mr. Darcy and their niece directed their observation towards each with an earnest though guarded inquiry; and they soon drew from those inquiries the full conviction that one of them at least knew what it was to love. Of the lady's sensations they remained a little in doubt; but that the gentleman was overflowing with admiration was evident enough.

Elizabeth, on her side, had much to do. She wanted to ascertain the feelings of each of her visitors; she wanted to compose her own, and to make herself agreeable to all; and in the latter object, where she feared most to fail, she was most sure of success, for those to whom she endeavoured to give pleasure were prepossessed in her favour. Bingley was ready, Georgiana was eager, and Darcy determined, to be pleased.

In seeing Bingley, her thoughts naturally flew to her sister; and, oh! how ardently did she long to know whether any of his were directed in a like manner. Sometimes she could fancy that he talked less than on former occasions, and once or twice pleased herself with the notion that, as he looked at her, he was trying to trace a resemblance . But, though this might be imaginary, she could not be deceived as to his behaviour to Miss Darcy, who had been set up as a rival to Jane. No look appeared on either side that spoke particular regard. Nothing occurred between them that could justify the hopes of his sister. On this point she was soon satisfied; and two or three little circumstances occurred ere they parted, which, in her anxious interpretation, denoted a recollection of Jane not untinctured by tenderness, and a wish of saying more that might lead to the mention of her, had he dared. He observed to her, at a moment when the others were talking together, and in a tone which had something of real regret, that it "was a very long time since he had had the pleasure of seeing her"; and, before she could reply, he added, "It is above eight months. We have not met since the 26th of November, when we were all dancing together at Netherfield."

Elizabeth was pleased to find his memory so exact; and he afterwards took occasion to ask her, when unattended to by any of the rest, whether ALL her sisters were at Longbourn. There was not much in the question, nor in the preceding remark; but there was a look and a manner which gave them meaning.

It was not often that she could turn her eyes on Mr. Darcy himself; but, whenever she did catch a glimpse, she saw an expression of general complaisance, and in all that he said she heard an accent so removed from hauteur or disdain of his companions, as convinced her that the improvement of manners which she had yesterday witnessed however temporary its existence might prove, had at least outlived one day. When she saw him thus seeking the acquaintance and courting the good opinion of people with whom any intercourse a few months ago would have been a disgrace—when she saw him thus civil, not only to herself, but to the very relations whom he had openly disdained, and recollected their last lively scene in Hunsford Parsonage—the difference, the change was so great, and struck so forcibly on her mind, that she could hardly restrain her astonishment from being visible. Never, even in the company of his dear friends at Netherfield, or his dignified relations at Rosings, had she seen him so desirous to please, so free from self-consequence or unbending reserve, as now, when no importance could result from the success of his endeavours, and when even the acquaintance of those to whom his attentions were addressed would draw down the ridicule and censure of the ladies both of Netherfield as Rosings.

Their visitors stayed with them above half-an-hour; and when they arose to depart, Mr. Darcy called on his sister to join him in expressing their wish of seeing Mr. and Mrs. Gardiner, and Miss Bennet, to dinner at Pemberley, before they left the country. Miss Darcy, though with a diffidence which marked her little in the habit of giving invitations, readily obeyed. Mrs. Gardiner looked at her niece, desirous of knowing how SHE, whom the invitation most concerned, felt disposed as to its acceptance, but Elizabeth had turned away her head. Presuming however, that this studied avoidance spoke rather a momentary embarrassment than any dislike of the proposal, and seeing in her husband, who was fond or society, a perfect willingness to accept it, she ventured to engage for her attendance, and the day after the next was fixed on.

Bingley expressed great pleasure in the certainty of seeing Elizabeth again, having still a great deal to say to her, and many inquiries to make after all their Hertfordshire friends. Elizabeth, construing all this into a wish of hearing her speak of her sister, was pleased, and on this account, as well as some others, found herself, when their visitors left them, capable of considering the last half-hour with some satisfaction, though while it was passing, the enjoyment of it had been little. Eager to be alone, and fearful of inquiries or hints from her uncle and aunt, she stayed with them only long enough to hear their favourable opinion of Bingley, and then hurried away to dress.

But she had no reason to fear Mr. and Mrs. Gardiner's curiosity; it was not their wish to force her communication. It was evident that she was much better acquainted with Mr. Darcy than they had before any idea of; it was evident that he was very much in love with her. They saw much to interest, but nothing to justify inquiry.

Of Mr. Darcy it was now a matter of anxiety to think well; and, as far as their acquaintance reached, there was no fault to find. They could not be untouched by his politeness; and had they drawn his character from their own feelings and his servant's report, without any reference to any other account, the circle in Hertfordshire to which he was known would not have recognized it for Mr. Darcy. There was now an interest, however, in believing the housekeeper; and they soon became sensible that the authority of a servant who had known him since he was four years old, and whose own manners indicated respectability, was not to be hastily rejected. Neither had anything occurred in the intelligence of their Lambton friends that could materially lessen its weight. They had nothing to accuse him of but pride; pride he probably had, and if not, it would certainly be imputed by the inhabitants of a small market-town where the family did not visit. It was acknowledged, however, that he was a liberal man, and did much good among the poor.

With respect to Wickham, the travellers soon found that he was not held there in much estimation; for though the chief of his concerns with the son of his patron were imperfectly understood, it was yet a well-known fact that, on his quitting Derbyshire, he had left many debts behind him, which Mr. Darcy afterwards discharged.

As for Elizabeth, her thoughts were at Pemberley this evening more than the last; and the evening, though as it passed it seemed long, was not long enough to determine her feelings towards ONE in that mansion; and she lay awake two whole hours endeavouring to make them out. She certainly did not hate him. No; hatred had vanished long ago, and she had almost as long been ashamed of ever feeling a dislike against him, that could be so called. The respect created by the conviction of his valuable qualities, though at first unwillingly admitted, had for some time ceased to be repugnant to her feeling; and it was now heightened into somewhat of a friendlier nature, by the testimony so highly in his favour, and bringing forward his disposition in so amiable a light, which yesterday had produced. But above all, above respect and esteem, there was a motive within her of goodwill which could not be overlooked. It was gratitude; gratitude, not merely for having once loved her, but for loving her still well enough to forgive all the petulance and acrimony of her manner in rejecting him, and all the unjust accusations accompanying her rejection. He who, she had been persuaded, would avoid her as his greatest enemy, seemed, on this accidental meeting, most eager to preserve the acquaintance, and without any indelicate display of regard, or any peculiarity of manner, where their two selves only were concerned, was soliciting the good opinion of her friends, and bent on making her known to his sister. Such a change in a man of so much pride exciting not only astonishment but gratitude—for to love, ardent love, it must be attributed; and as such its impression on her was of a sort to be encouraged, as by no means unpleasing, though it could not be exactly defined. She respected, she esteemed, he was grateful to him, she felt a real interest in his welfare; and she only wanted to know how far she wished that welfare to depend upon herself, and how far it would be for the happiness of both that she should employ the power, which her fancy told her she still possessed, of bringing on her the renewal of his addresses.

It had been settled in the evening between the aunt and the niece, that such a striking civility as Miss Darcy's in coming to see them on the very day of her arrival at Pemberley, for she had reached it only to a late breakfast, ought to be imitated, though it could not be equalled, by some exertion of politeness on their side; and, consequently, that it would be highly expedient to wait on her at Pemberley the following morning. They were, therefore, to go. Elizabeth was pleased; though when she asked herself the reason, she had very little to say in reply.

Mr. Gardiner left them soon after breakfast. The fishing scheme had been renewed the day before, and a positive engagement made of his meeting some of the gentlemen at Pemberley before noon.

Chapter 45

Convinced as Elizabeth now was that Miss Bingley's dislike of her had originated in jealousy, she could not help feeling how unwelcome her appearance at Pemberley must be to her, and was curious to know with how much civility on that lady's side the acquaintance would now be renewed.

On reaching the house, they were shown through the hall into the saloon, whose northern aspect rendered it delightful for summer. Its windows opening to the ground, admitted a most refreshing view of the high woody hills behind the house, and of the beautiful oaks and Spanish chestnuts which were scattered over the intermediate lawn.

In this house they were received by Miss Darcy, who was sitting there with Mrs. Hurst and Miss Bingley, and the lady with whom she lived in London. Georgiana's reception of them was very civil, but attended with all the embarrassment which, though proceeding from shyness and the fear of doing wrong, would easily give to those who felt themselves inferior the belief of her being proud and reserved. Mrs. Gardiner and her niece, however, did her justice, and pitied her.

By Mrs. Hurst and Miss Bingley they were noticed only by a curtsey; and, on their being seated, a pause, awkward as such pauses must always be, succeeded for a few moments. It was first broken by Mrs. Annesley, a genteel, agreeable-looking woman, whose endeavour to introduce some kind of discourse proved her to be more truly well-bred than either of the others; and between her and Mrs. Gardiner, with occasional help from Elizabeth, the conversation was carried on. Miss Darcy looked as if she wished for courage enough to join in it; and sometimes did venture a short sentence when there was least danger of its being heard.

Elizabeth soon saw that she was herself closely watched by Miss Bingley, and that she could not speak a word, especially to Miss Darcy, without calling her attention. This observation would not have prevented her from trying to talk to the latter, had they not been seated at an inconvenient distance; but she was not sorry to be spared the necessity of saying much. Her own thoughts were employing her. She expected every moment that some of the gentlemen would enter the room. She wished, she feared that the master of the house might be amongst them; and whether she wished or feared it most, she could scarcely determine. After sitting in this manner a quarter of an hour without hearing Miss Bingley's voice, Elizabeth was roused by receiving from her a cold inquiry after the health of her family. She answered with equal indifference and brevity, and the others said no more.

The next variation which their visit afforded was produced by the entrance of the servants with cold meat, cake, and a variety of all the entrance of servants with cold meat, cake, and a variety of all the finest fruits in season; but this did not take place till after many a significant look and smile from Mrs. Annesley to Miss Darcy had been given, to remind her of her post. There was now employment for the whole party—for though they could not all talk, they could all eat; and the beautiful pyramids of grapes, nectarines, and peaches soon collected them round the table.

While thus engaged, Elizabeth had a fair opportunity of deciding whether she most feared or wished for the appearance of Mr. Darcy, by the feelings which prevailed on his entering the room; and then, though but a moment before she had believed her wishes to predominate, she began to regret that he came.

He had been some time with Mr. Gardiner, who, with two or three other gentlemen from the house, was engaged by the river, and had left him only on learning that the ladies of the family intended a visit to Georgiana that morning. No sooner did he appear than Elizabeth wisely resolved to be perfectly easy and unembarrassed; a resolution the more necessary to be made, but perhaps not the more easily kept, because she saw that the suspicions of the whole party were awakened against them, and that there was scarcely an eye which did not watch his behaviour when he first came into the room. In no countenance was attentive curiosity so strongly marked as in Miss Bingley's, in spite of the smiles which overspread her face whenever she spoke to one of its objects; for jealousy had not yet made her desperate, and her attentions to Mr. Darcy were by no means over. Miss Darcy, on her brother's entrance, exerted herself much more to talk, and Elizabeth saw that she was anxious for his sister and herself to get acquainted, and forwarded as much as possible, every attempt at conversation on either side. Miss Bingley saw all this likewise; and, in the imprudence of anger, took the first opportunity of saying, with sneering civility:

"Pray, Miss Eliza, are not the ______shire Militia removed from Meryton? They must be a great loss to YOUR family."

In Darcy's presence she dared not mention Wickham's name; but Elizabeth instantly comprehended that he was uppermost in her thoughts; and the various recollections connected with him gave her a moment's distress; but exerting herself vigorously to repel the ill-natured attack, she presently answered the question in a tolerably detached tone. While she spoke, an involuntary glance showed her Darcy, with a heightened complexion, earnestly looking at her, and his sister overcome with confusion, and unable to lift up her eyes. Had Miss Bingley know what pain she was then giving her beloved friend, she undoubtedly would have refrained from the hint; but she had merely intended to discompose Elizabeth by bringing forward the idea of a man to whom she believed her partial, to make her betray a sensibility which might injure her in Darcy's opinion, and, perhaps, to remind the latter of all the follies and absurdities by which some part of her family were connected with that corps. Not a syllable had ever reached her of Miss Darcy's meditated elopement. To no creature had it been revealed, where secrecy was possible, except to Elizabeth; and from all Bingley's connections her brother was particularly anxious to conceal it, from the very wish which Elizabeth had long ago attributed to him, of their becoming hereafter her own. He had certainly formed such a plan, and without meaning that it should effect his endeavour to separate him from Miss Bennet, it is probable that it might add something to his lively concern for the welfare of his friend.

Elizabeth's collected behaviour, however, soon quieted his emotion; and as Miss Bingley, vexed and disappointed, dared not approach nearer to Wickham, Georgiana also recovered in time, though not enough to be able to speak any more. Her brother, whose eye she feared to meet, scarcely recollected her interest in the affair, and the very circumstance which had been designed to turn his thoughts from Elizabeth seemed to have fixed them on her more and more cheerfully.

Their visit did not continue long after the question and answer above mentioned; and while Mr. Darcy was attending them to their carriage Miss Bingley was venting her feelings in criticisms on Elizabeth's person, behaviour, and dress. But Georgiana would not join her. Her brother's recommendation was enough to ensure her favour; his judgement could not err. And he had spoken in such terms of Elizabeth as to leave Georgiana without the power of finding her otherwise than lovely and amiable. When Darcy returned to the saloon, Miss Bingley could not help repeating to him some part of what she had been saying to his sister.

"How very ill Miss Eliza Bennet looks this morning, Mr. Darcy," she cried; "I never in my life saw anyone so much altered as she is since the winter. She is grown so brown and coarse! Louisa and I were agreeing that we should not have known her again."

However little Mr. Darcy might have liked such an address, he contented himself with coolly replying that he perceived no other alteration than her being rather tanned, no miraculous consequence of travelling in the summer.

"For my own part," she rejoined, "I must confess that I never could see any beauty in her. Her face is too thin; her complexion has no brilliancy; and her features are not at all handsome. Her nose wants character—there is nothing marked in its lines. Her teeth are tolerable, but not out of the common way; and as for her eyes, which have sometimes been called so fine, I could never see anything extraordinary in them. They have a sharp, shrewish look, which I do not like at all; and in her air altogether there is a self-sufficiency without fashion, which is intolerable."

Persuaded as Miss Bingley was that Darcy admired Elizabeth, this was not the best method of recommending herself; but angry people are not always wise; and in seeing him at last look somewhat nettled, she had all the success she expected. He was resolutely silent, however, and, from a determination of making him speak, she continued:

"I remember, when we first knew her in Hertfordshire, how amazed we all were to find that she was a reputed beauty; and I particularly recollect your saying one night, after they had been dining at Netherfield, SHE a beauty! I should as soon call her mother a wit.' But afterwards she seemed to improve on you, and I believe you thought her rather pretty at one time."

"Yes," replied Darcy, who could contain himself no longer, "but THAT was only when I first saw her, for it is many months since I have considered her as one of the handsomest women of my acquaintances."

He then went away, and Miss Bingley was left to all the satisfaction of having forced him to say what gave no one any pain but herself.

Mrs. Gardiner and Elizabeth talked of all that had occurred during their visit, as they returned, except what had particularly interested them both. The look and behaviour of everybody they had seen were discussed, except of the person who had mostly engaged their attention. They talked of his sister, his friends, his house, his fruit—of everything but himself; yet Elizabeth was longing to know what Mrs. Gardiner thought of him, and Mrs. Gardiner would have been highly gratified by her niece's beginning the subject.

Chapter 46

Elizabeth had been a good deal disappointed in not finding a letter from Jane on their first arrival at Lambton; and this disappointment had been renewed on each of the mornings that had now been spent there; but on the third her repining was over, and her sister justified, by the receipt of two letters from her at once, on one of which was marked that it had been missent elsewhere. Elizabeth was not surprised at it, as Jane had written the direction remarkably ill.

They had just been preparing to walk as the letters came in; and her uncle and aunt, leaving her to enjoy them in quiet, set off by themselves. The one missent must first be attended to; it had been written five days ago. The beginning contained an account of all their little parties and engagements, with such news as the country afforded; but the latter half, which was dated a day later, and written in evident agitation, gave more important intelligence. It was to this effect:

"Since writing the above, dearest Lizzy, something has occurred of a most unexpected and serious nature; but I am afraid of alarming you—be assured that we are all well. What I have to say relates to poor Lydia. An express came at twelve last night, just as we were all gone to bed, from Colonel Forster, to inform us that she was gone off to Scotland with one of his officers; to own the truth, with Wickham! Imagine our surprise. To Kitty, however, it does not seem so wholly unexpected. I am very, very sorry. So imprudent a match on both sides! But I am willing to hope the best, and that his character has been misunderstood. Thoughtless and indiscreet I can easily believe him, but this step (and let us rejoice over it) marks nothing bad at heart. His choice is disinterested at least, for he must know my father can give her nothing. Our poor mother is sadly grieved. My father bears it better. How thankful am I that we never let them know what has been said against him! we must forget it ourselves. They were off Saturday night about twelve, as is conjectured, but were not missed till yesterday morning at eight. The express was sent off directly. My dear Lizzy, they must have passed within ten miles of us. Colonel Forster gives us reason to expect him here soon. Lydia left a few lines for his wife, informing her of their intention. I must conclude, for I cannot be long from my poor mother. I am afraid you will not be able to `make it out, but I hardly know what I have written."

Without allowing herself time for consideration, and scarcely knowing what she felt, Elizabeth on finishing this letter instantly seized the other, and opening it with the utmost impatience, read as follows: it had been written a day later than the conclusion of the first.

"By this time, my dearest sister, you have received my hurried letter; I wish this may be more intelligible, but though not confined for time, my head is so bewildered that I cannot answer for being coherent. Dearest Lizzy, I hardly know what I would write, but I have bad news for you, and it cannot be delayed. Imprudent as the marriage between Mr. Wickham and our poor Lydia would be, we are now anxious to be assured it has taken place, for there is but too much reason to fear they are not gone to Scotland. Colonel Forster came yesterday, having left

Brighton the day before, not many hours after the express. Though Lydia's short letter to Mrs. F. gave them to understand that they were going to Gretna Green, something was dropped by Denny expressing his belief that W. never intended to go there, or to marry Lydia at all, which was repeated to Colonel F., who, instantly taking the alarm, set off from B., intending to trace their route. He did trace them easily to Clapham, but no further; for on entering that place, they removed into a hackney coach, and dismissed the chaise that brought them from Epsom. All that is known after this is, that they were seen to continue the London road. I know not what to think. After making every possible inquiry on that side London, Colonel F. came on into Hertfordshire, anxiously renewing them at all the turnpikes, and at the inns in Barnet and Hatfield, but without any success—no such people had been seen to pass through. With the kindest concern he came on to Longbourn, and broke his apprehensions to us in a manner most creditable to his heart. I am sincerely grieved for him and Mrs. F., but no one can throw any blame on them. Our distress, my dear Lizzy, is very great. My father and mother believe the worst, but I cannot think so ill of him. Many circumstances might make it more eligible for them to be married privately in town than to pursue their first plan; and even if HE could form such a design against a young woman of Lydia's connections, which is not likely, can I suppose her so lost to everything? Impossible! I grieve to find, however, that Colonel F. is not disposed to depend upon their marriage; he shook his head when I expressed my hopes, and said he fear W. was not a man to be trusted. My poor mother is really ill, and keeps her room. Could she exert herself, it would be better; but this is not to be expected. And as to my father, I never in my life saw him so affected. Poor Kitty has anger for having concealed their attachment; but as it was a matter of confidence, one cannot wonder. I am truly glad, dearest Lizzy, that you have been spared something of these distressing scenes; but now, as the first shock is over, shall I own that I long for your return? I am not so selfish, however, as to press for it, if inconvenient. Adieu! I take up my pen again to do what I have just told you I would not; but circumstances are such that I cannot help earnestly begging you all to come here as soon as possible. I know my dear uncle and aunt so well, that I am not afraid of requesting it, though I have still something more to ask of the former. My father is going to London with Colonel Forster instantly, to try to discover her. What he means to do I am sure I know not; but his excessive distress will not allow him to pursue any measure in the best and safest way, and Colonel Forster is obliged to be at Brighton again to-morrow evening. In such and exigence, my uncle's advice and assistance would be everything in the world; he will immediately comprehend what I must feel, and I rely upon his goodness."

"Oh! where, where is my uncle?" cried Elizabeth, darting from her seat as she finished the letter, in eagerness to follow him, without losing a moment of the time so precious; but as she reached the door it was opened by a servant, and Mr. Darcy appeared. Her pale face and impetuous manner made him start, and before he could recover himself to speak, she, in whose mind every idea was superseded by Lydia's situation, hastily exclaimed, "I beg your pardon, but I must leave you. I must find Mr. Gardiner this moment, on business that cannot be delayed; I have not an instant to loose."

"Good God! what is the matter?" cried he, with more feeling than politeness; then recollecting himself, "I will not detain you a minute; but let me, or let the servant go after Mr. and Mrs. Gardiner. You are not well enough; you cannot go yourself."

Elizabeth hesitated, but her knees trembled under her and she felt how little would be gained by her attempting to pursue them. Calling back the servant, therefore, she commissioned him, though in so breathless an accent as made her almost unintelligible, to fetch his master and mistress home instantly.

On his quitting the room she sat down, unable to support herself, and looking so miserably ill, that it was impossible for Darcy to leave her, or to refrain from saying, in a tone of gentleness and commiseration, "Let me call your maid. Is there nothing you could take to give you present relief? A glass of wine; shall I get you one? You are very ill."

"No, I thank you," she replied, endeavouring to recover herself. "There is nothing the matter with me. I am quite well; I am only distressed by some dreadful news which I have just received from Longbourn."

She burst into tears as she alluded to it, and for a few minutes could not speak another word. Darcy, in wretched suspense, could only say something indistinctly of his concern, and observe her in compassionate silence. At length she spoke again. "I have just had a letter from Jane, with such dreadful news. It cannot be concealed from any one. My younger sister has left all her friends—has eloped; has thrown herself into the power of—of Mr. Wickham. They are gone off together from Brighton. YOU know him too well to doubt the rest. She has no money, no connections, nothing that can tempt him to—she is lost for ever."

Darcy was fixed in astonishment. "When I consider," she added in a yet more agitated voice, "that I might have prevented it! I, who knew what he was. Had I but explained some part of it only—some part of what I learnt, to my own family! Had his character been known, this could not have happened. But it is all—all too late now."

"I am grieved indeed," cried Darcy; "grieved—shocked. But is it certain—absolutely certain?"

"Oh, yes! They left Brighton together on Sunday night, and were traced almost to London, but not beyond; they are certainly not gone to Scotland."

"And what has been done, what has been attempted, to recover her?"

"My father is gone to London, and Jane has written to beg my uncle's immediate assistance; and we shall be off, I hope, in half-an-hour. But nothing can be done—I know very well that nothing can be done. How is such a man to be worked on? How are they even to be discovered? I have not the smallest hope. It is every way horrible!"

Darcy shook his head in silent acquiescence.

"When MY eyes were opened to his real character—Oh! had I known what I ought, what I dared to do! But I knew not—I was afraid of doing too much. Wretched, wretched mistake!"

Darcy made no answer. He seemed scarcely to hear her, and was walking up and down the room in earnest meditation, his brow contracted, his air gloomy. Elizabeth soon observed, and instantly understood it. Her power was sinking; everything MUST sink under such a proof of family weakness, such an assurance of the deepest disgrace. She could neither wonder nor condemn, but the belief of his self-conquest brought nothing to her consolatory to her bosom, afforded no palliation of her distress. It was, on the contrary, exactly calculated to make her understand her own wishes; and never had she so honestly felt that she could have loved him, as now, when all love must be vain.

But self, though it would intrude, could not engross her. Lydia—the humiliation, the misery she was bringing on them all, soon swallowed up every private care; and covering her face with her handkerchief, Elizabeth was soon lost to everything else; and, after a pause of several minutes, was only recalled to a sense of her situation by the voice of her companion, who, in a manner which, though it spoke compassion, spoke likewise restraint, said, "I am afraid you have been long desiring my absence, nor have I anything to plead in excuse of my stay, but real, though unavailing concern. Would to Heaven that anything could be either said or done on my part that might offer consolation to such distress! But I will not torment you with vain wishes, which may seem purposely to ask for your thanks. This unfortunate affair will, I fear, prevent my sister's having the pleasure of seeing you at Pemberley to-day."

"Oh, yes. Be so kind as to apologise for us to Miss Darcy. Say that urgent business calls us home immediately. Conceal the unhappy truth as long as it is possible, I know it cannot be long."

He readily assured her of his secrecy; again expressed his sorrow for her distress, wished it a happier conclusion than there was at present reason to hope, and leaving his compliments for her relations, with only one serious, parting look went away.

As he quitted the room, Elizabeth felt how improbable it was that they should ever see each other again on such terms of cordiality as had marked their several meetings in Derbyshire; and as she threw a retrospective glance over the whole of their acquaintance, so full of contradictions and varieties, sighed at the perverseness of those feelings which would now have promoted its continuance, and would formerly have rejoiced in its termination.

If gratitude and esteem are good foundations of affection, Elizabeth's change of sentiment will be neither improbable nor faulty. But if otherwise—if regard springing from such sources is unreasonable or unnatural, in comparison of what is so often described as arising on a first interview with its object, and even before two words have been exchanged, nothing can be said in her defence, except that she had given somewhat of a trial to the latter method in her partiality for Wickham, and that its ill success might, perhaps, authorise her to seek the other less interesting mode of attachment. Be that as it may, she saw him go with regret; and in this early example of what Lydia's infamy must produce, found additional anguish as she reflected on that wretched business. Never, since reading Jane's second letter, had she entertained a hope of Wickham's meaning to marry her. No one but

Jane, she thought, could flatter herself with such an expectation. Surprise was the least of her feelings on this development. While the contents of the first letter remained in her mind, she was all surprise—all astonishment that Wickham should marry a girl whom it was impossible he could marry for money; and how Lydia could ever have attached him had appeared incomprehensible. But no it was all too natural. For such an attachment as this she might have sufficient charm; and though she did not suppose Lydia to be deliberately engaging in an elopement without the intention of marriage, she had no difficulty in believing that neither her virtue nor her understanding would preserve her from falling an easy prey.

She had never perceived, while the regiment was in Hertfordshire, that Lydia had any partiality for him; but she was convinced that Lydia wanted only encouragement to attach herself to anybody. Sometimes one officer, sometimes another, had been her favourite, as their attentions raised them in her opinion. Her affections had continually been fluctuating but never without an object. The mischief of neglect and mistaken indulgence towards such a girl—oh! how acutely did she now feel it!

She was wild to be at home—to hear, to see, to be upon the spot to share with Jane in the cares that must now fall wholly upon her, in a family so deranged, a father absent, a mother incapable of exertion, and requiring constant attendance; and though almost persuaded that nothing could be done for Lydia, her uncle's interference seemed of the utmost importance, and till he entered the room her impatience was severe. Mr. and Mrs. Gardiner had hurried back in alarm, supposing by the servant's account that their niece was taken suddenly ill; but satisfying them instantly on that head, she eagerly communicated the cause of their summons, reading the two letters aloud, and dwelling on the postscript of the last with trembling energy, though Lydia had never been a favourite with them, Mr. and Mrs. Gardiner could not but be deeply afflicted. Not Lydia only, but all were concerned in it; and after the first exclamations of surprise and horror, Mr. Gardiner promised every assistance in his power. Elizabeth, though expecting no less, thanked him with tears of gratitude; and all three being actuated by one spirit, everything relating to their journey was speedily settled. They were to be off as soon as possible. "But what is to be done about Pemberley?" cried Mrs. Gardiner. "John told us Mr. Darcy was here when you sent for us; was it so?"

"Yes; and I told him we should not be able to keep our engagement. THAT is all settled."

"What is all settled?" repeated the other, as she ran into her room to prepare. "And are they upon such terms as for her to disclose the real truth? Oh, that I knew how it was!"

But wishes were vain, or at least could only serve to amuse her in the hurry and confusion of the following hour. Had Elizabeth been at leisure to be idle, she would have remained certain that all employment was impossible to one so wretched as herself; but she had her share of business as well as her aunt, and amongst the rest there were notes to be written to all their friends at Lambton, with false excuses for their sudden departure. An hour, however, saw the whole completed; and Mr. Gardiner meanwhile having settled his account at the inn, nothing remained to be done but to go; and Elizabeth, after all the misery of the morning, found herself, in a shorter space of time than she could have supposed, seated in the carriage, and on the road to Longbourn.

Chapter 47

"I have been thinking it over again, Elizabeth," said her uncle, as they drove from the town; "and really, upon serious consideration, I am much more inclined than I was to judge as your eldest sister does on the matter. It appears to me so very unlikely that any young man should form such a design against a girl who is by no means unprotected or friendless, and who was actually staying in his colonel's family, that I am strongly inclined to hope the best. Could he expect that her friends would not step forward? Could he expect to be noticed again by the regiment, after such an affront to Colonel Forster? His temptation is not adequate to the risk!"

"Do you really think so?" cried Elizabeth, brightening up for a moment.

"Upon my word," said Mrs. Gardiner, "I begin to be of your uncle's opinion. It is really too great a violation of decency, honour, and interest, for him to be guilty of. I cannot think so very ill of Wickham. Can you yourself, Lizzy, so wholly give him up, as to believe him capable of it?"

"Not, perhaps, of neglecting his own interest; but of every other neglect I can believe him capable. If, indeed, it should be so! But I dare not hope it. Why should they not go on to Scotland if that had been the case?"

"In the first place," replied Mr. Gardiner, "there is no absolute proof that they are not gone to Scotland."

"Oh! but their removing from the chaise into a hackney coach is such a presumption! And, besides, no traces of them were to be found on the Barnet road."

"Well, then—supposing them to be in London. They may be there, though for the purpose of concealment, for no more exceptional purpose. It is not likely that money should be very abundant on either side; and it might strike them that they could be more economically, though less expeditiously, married in London than in Scotland."

But why all this secrecy? Why any fear of detection? Why must their marriage be private? Oh, no, no—this is not likely. His most particular friend, you see by Jane's account, was persuaded of his never intending to marry her. Wickham will never marry a woman without some money. He cannot afford it. And what claims has Lydia—what attraction has she beyond youth, health, and good humour that could make him, for her sake, forego every chance of benefiting himself by marrying well? As to what restraint the apprehensions of disgrace in the corps might throw on a dishonourable elopement with her, I am not able to judge; for I know nothing of the effects that such a step might produce. But as to your other objection, I am afraid it will hardly hold good. Lydia has no brothers to step forward; and he might imagine, from my father's behaviour, from his indolence and the little attention he has ever seemed to give to what was going forward in his family, that HE would do as little, and think as little about it, as any father could do, in such a matter."

"But can you think that Lydia is so lost to everything but love of him as to consent to live with him on any terms other than marriage?"

"It does seem, and it is most shocking indeed," replied Elizabeth, with tears in her eyes, "that a sister's sense of decency and virtue in such a point should admit of doubt. But, really, I know not what to say. Perhaps I am not doing her justice. But she is very young; she has never been taught to think on serious subjects; and for the last half-year, nay, for a twelvemonth—she has been given up to nothing but amusement and vanity. She has been allowed to dispose of her time in the most idle and frivolous manner, and to adopt any opinions that came in her way. Since the ______shire were first quartered in Meryton, nothing but love, flirtation, and officers have been in her head. She has been doing everything in her power by thinking and talking on the subject, to give greater—what shall I call it? susceptibility to her feelings; which are naturally lively enough. And we all know that Wickham has every charm of person and address that can captivate a woman."

"But you see that Jane," said her aunt, "does not think so very ill of Wickham as to believe him capable of the attempt."

"Of whom does Jane ever think ill? And who is there, whatever might be their former conduct, that she would think capable of such an attempt, till it were proved against them? But Jane knows, as well as I do, what Wickham really is. We both know that he has been profligate in every sense of the word; that he has neither integrity nor honour; that he is as false and deceitful as he is insinuating."

"And do you really know all this?" cried Mrs. Gardiner, whose curiosity as to the mode of her intelligence was all alive.

"I do indeed," replied Elizabeth, colouring. "I told you, the other day, of his infamous behaviour to Mr. Darcy; and you yourself, when last at Longbourn, heard in what manner he spoke of the man who had behaved with such forbearance and liberality towards him. And there are other circumstances which I am not at liberty—which it is not worth while to relate; but his lies about the whole Pemberley family are endless. From what he said of Miss Darcy I was thoroughly prepared to see a proud, reserved, disagreeable girl. Yet he knew to the contrary himself. He must know that she was as amiable and unpretending as we have found her."

"But does Lydia know nothing of this? can she be ignorant of what you and Jane seem so well to understand?"

"Oh, yes! that, that is the worst of all. Till I was in Kent, and saw so much both of Mr. Darcy and his relation Colonel Fitzwilliam, I was ignorant of the truth myself. And when I returned home, the ______shire was to leave Meryton in a week or fortnight's time. As that was the case, neither Jane, to whom I related the whole, nor I, thought it necessary to make our knowledge public; for of what use could it apparently be to any one, that the good opinion which all the neighbourhood had of him should then be overthrown? And even when it was settled that Lydia should go with Mrs. Forster, the necessity of opening her eyes to his character never occurred to me. That SHE could be in any danger from the deception never entered my head. That such a consequence as THIS could ensue, you may easily believe, was far enough from my thoughts."

"When they all removed to Brighton, therefore, you had no reason, I suppose, to believe them fond of each other?"

"Not the slightest. I can remember no symptom of affection on either side; and had anything of the kind been perceptible, you must be aware that ours is not a family on which it could be thrown away. When first he entered the corps, she was ready enough to admire him; but so we all were. Every girl in or near Meryton was out of her senses about him for the first two months; but he never distinguished HER by any particular attention; and, consequently, after a moderate period of extravagant and wild admiration, her fancy for him gave way, and others of the regiment, who treated her with more distinction, again became her favourites."

It may be easily believed, that however little of novelty could be added to their fears, hopes, and conjectures, on this interesting subject, by its repeated discussion, no other could detain them from it long, during the whole of the journey. From Elizabeth's thoughts it was never absent. Fixed there by the keenest of all anguish, self-reproach, she could find no interval of ease or forgetfulness.

They travelled as expeditiously as possible, and, sleeping one night on the road, reached Longbourn by dinner time the next day. It was a comfort to Elizabeth to consider that Jane could not have been wearied by long expectations.

The little Gardiners, attracted by the sight of a chaise, were standing on the steps of the house as they entered the paddock; and, when the carriage drove up to the door, the joyful surprise that lighted up their faces, and displayed itself over their whole bodies, in a variety of capers and frisks, was the first pleasing earnest of their welcome.

Elizabeth jumped out; and, after giving each of them a hasty kiss, hurried into the vestibule, where Jane, who came running down from her mother's apartment, immediately met her.

Elizabeth, as she affectionately embraced her, whilst tears filled the eyes of both, lost not a moment in asking whether anything had been heard of the fugitives.

"Not yet," replied Jane. "But now that my dear uncle is come, I hope everything will be well."

"Is my father in town?"

"Yes, he went on Tuesday, as I wrote you word."

"And have you heard from him often?"

"We have heard only twice. He wrote me a few lines on Wednesday to say that he had arrived in safety, and to give me his directions, which I particularly begged him to do. He merely added that he should not write again till he had something of importance to mention."

"And my mother—how is she? How are you all?"

"My mother is tolerably well, I trust; though her spirits are greatly shaken. She is upstairs and will have great satisfaction in seeing you all. She does not yet leave her dressing-room. Mary and Kitty are, thank Heaven, are quite well."

"But you—how are you?" cried Elizabeth. "You look pale. How much you must have gone through!"

Her sister, however, assured her of her being perfectly well; and their conversation, which had been passing while Mr. and Mrs. Gardiner were engaged with their children,. Was now put an end to by the approach of the whole party. Jane ran to her uncle and aunt, and welcomed and thanked them both, with alternate smiles and tears.

When they were all in the drawing-room, the questions which Elizabeth had already asked were of course repeated by the others, and they soon found that Jane had no intelligence to give. The sanguine hope of good, however, which the benevolence of her heart suggested had not yet deserted her; she still expected that it would all end well, and that every morning would bring some letter, either from Lydia or her father, to explain their proceedings, and, perhaps, announce their marriage.

Mrs. Bennet, to whose apartment they all repaired, after a few minutes' conversation together, received them exactly as might be expected; with tears and lamentations of regret, invectives against the villainous conduct of Wickham, and complaints of her own sufferings and ill-usage; blaming everybody but the person to whose ill-judging indulgence the errors of her daughter must principally be owing.

"If I had been able," said she, "to carry my point in going to Brighton, with all my family, THIS would not have happened; but poor dear Lydia had nobody to take care of her. Why did the Forsters ever let her go out of their sight? I am sure there was some great neglect or other on their side, for she is not the kind of girl to do such a thing if she had been well looked after. I always thought they were very unfit to have the charge of her; but I was overruled, as I always am. Poor dear child! And now here's Mr. Bennet gone away, and I know he will fight Wickham, wherever he meets him and then he will be killed, and what is to become of us all? The Collinses will turn us out before he is cold in his grave, and if you are not kind to us, brother, I do not know what we shall do."

They all exclaimed against such terrific ideas; and Mr. Gardiner, after general assurances of his affection for her and all her family, told her that he meant to be in London the very next day, and would assist Mr. Bennet in every endeavour for recovering Lydia.

"Do not give way to useless alarm," added he; "though it is right to be prepared for the worst, there is no occasion to look on it a certain. It is not quite a week since they left Brighton. In a few days more we may gain some news of them; and till we know that they are not married, and have no design of marrying, do not let us give the matter over as lost. As soon as I get to town I shall go to my brother, and make him come home with me to Gracechurch Street; and then we may consult together as to what is to be done."

"Oh! my dear brother," replied Mrs. Bennet, "that is exactly what I could most wish for. And now do, when you get to town, find them out, wherever they may be; and if they are not married already, MAKE them marry. And as for wedding clothes, do not let them wait for that, but tell Lydia she shall have as much money as she chooses to buy them, after they are married. And, above all, keep Mr. Bennet from fighting. Tell him what a dreadful state I am in, that I am frighted out of my wits—and have such tremblings, such flutterings, all over me—such spasms in my side and pains in my head, and such beatings at heart, that I can get no rest by night nor by day. And tell my dear Lydia not to give any directions about her clothes till she has seen me, for she does not know which are the best warehouses. Oh, brother, how kind you are! I know you will contrive it all."

But Mr. Gardiner, though he assured her again of his earnest endeavours in the cause, could not avoid recommending moderation to her, as well in her hopes as her fear; and after talking with her in this manner till dinner was on the table, they all left her to vent all her feelings on the housekeeper, who attended in the absence of her daughters.

Though her brother and sister were persuaded that there was no real occasion for such a seclusion from the family, they did not attempt to oppose it, for they knew that she had not prudence enough to hold her tongue before the servants, while they waited at table, and judged it better that ONE only of the household, and the one whom they could most trust should comprehend all her fears and solicitude on the subject.

In the dining-room they were soon joined by Mary and Kitty, who had been too busily engaged in their separate apartments to make their appearance before. One came from her books, and the other from her toilette. The faces of both, however, were tolerably calm; and no change was visible in either, except that the loss of her favourite sister, or the anger which she had herself incurred in this business, had given more of fretfulness than usual to the accents of Kitty. As for Mary, she was mistress enough of herself to whisper to Elizabeth, with a countenance of grave reflection, soon after they were seated at table:

"This is a most unfortunate affair, and will probably be much talked of. But we must stem the tide of malice, and pour into the wounded bosoms of each other the balm of sisterly consolation."

Then, perceiving in Elizabeth no inclination of replying, she added, "Unhappy as the event must be for Lydia, we may draw from it this useful lesson: that loss of virtue in a female is irretrievable; that one false step involves her in endless ruin; that her reputation is no less brittle than it is beautiful; and that she cannot be too much guarded in her behaviour towards the undeserving of the other sex."

Elizabeth lifted up her eyes in amazement, but was too much oppressed to make any reply. Mary, however, continued to console herself with such kind of moral extractions from the evil before them.

In the afternoon, the two elder Miss Bennets were able to be for half-an-hour by themselves; and Elizabeth instantly availed herself of the opportunity of making any inquiries, which Jane was equally eager to satisfy. After joining in general lamentations over the dreadful sequel of this event, which Elizabeth considered as all but certain, and Miss Bennet could not assert to be wholly impossible, the former continued the subject, by saying, "But tell me all and everything about it which I have not already heard. Give me further particulars. What did Colonel Forster say? Had they no apprehension of anything before the elopement took place? They must have seen them together for ever."

"Colonel Forster did own that he had often suspected some partiality, especially on Lydia's side, but nothing to give him any alarm. I am so grieved for him! His behaviour was attentive and kind to the utmost. He WAS coming to us, in order to assure us of his concern, before he had any idea of their not being gone to Scotland: when that apprehension first got abroad, it hastened his journey."

"And was Denny convinced that Wickham would not marry? Did he know of their intending to go off? Had Colonel Forster seen Denny himself?"

"Yes; but, when questioned by HIM, Denny denied knowing anything of their plans, and would not give his real opinion about it. He did not repeat his persuasion of their not marrying—and from THAT, I am inclined to hope, he might have been misunderstood before."

"And till Colonel Forster came himself, not one of you entertained a doubt, I suppose, of their being really married?"

"How was it possible that such an idea should enter our brains? I felt a little uneasy—a little fearful of my sister's happiness with him in marriage, because I knew that his conduct had not been always quite right. My father and mother knew nothing of that; they only felt how imprudent a match it must be. Kitty then owned, with a very natural triumph on knowing more than the rest of us, that in Lydia's last letter she had prepared her for such a step. She had known, it seems, of their being in love with each other, many weeks."

"But not before they went to Brighton?"

"No, I believe not."

"And did Colonel Forster appear to think well of Wickham himself? Does he know he real character?"

"I must confess that he did not speak so well of Wickham as he formerly did. He believed him to be imprudent and extravagant. And since this sad affair has taken place, it is said that he left Meryton greatly in debt; but I hope this may be false."

"Oh, Jane, had we been less secret, had we told what we knew of him, this could not have happened!"

"Perhaps it would have been better," replied her sister. "But to expose the former faults of any person without knowing what their present feelings were, seemed unjustifiable. We acted with the best intentions."

"Could Colonel Forster repeat the particulars of Lydia's note to his wife?"

"He brought it with him for us to see."

Jane then took it from her pocket-book, and gave it to Elizabeth. These were the contents:

"MY DEAR HARRIET,—

"You will laugh when you know where I am gone, and I cannot help laughing myself at your surprise to-morrow morning, as soon as I am missed. I am going to Gretna Green, and if you cannot guess with who, I shall think you a simpleton, for there is but one man in the world I love, and he is an angel. I should never be happy without him, so think it no harm to be off. You need not send them word at Longbourn of my going, if you do not like it, for it will make the surprise the greater, when I write to them and sign my name Lydia Wickham.' What a good joke it will be! I can hardly write for laughing. Pray make my excuses to Pratt for not keeping my engagement, and dancing with him to-night. Tell him I hope he will excuse me when he knows all; and tell him I will dance with him at the next ball we meet, with great pleasure. I shall send for my clothes when I get to Longbourn; but I wish you would tell Sally to mend a great slit in my worked muslin gown before they are packed up. Good-bye. Give my love to Colonel Forster. I hope you will drink to our good journey. Your affectionate friend,

"Lydia Bennet."

"Oh! thoughtless, thoughtless Lydia!" cried Elizabeth when she had finished it. What a letter is this, to be written at such a moment! But at least it shows that SHE was serious on the subject of their journey. Whatever he might afterwards persuade her to, it was not on her side a SCHEME of infamy. My poor father! how he must have felt it!"

I never saw any one so shocked. He could not speak a word for full ten minutes. My mother was taken ill immediately, and the whole house in such confusion!"

"Oh! Jane," cried Elizabeth, "was there a servant belonging to it who did not know the whole story before the end of the day?"

"I do not know. I hope there was. But to be guarded at such a time is very difficult. My mother was in hysterics, and though I endeavoured to give her every assistance in my power, I am afraid I did not do so much as I might have done! But the horror of what might possibly happen almost took from me my faculties."

"Your attendance upon her has been too much for you. You do not look well. Oh that I had been with you! you have had every care and anxiety upon yourself alone."

"Mary and Kitty have been very kind, and would have shared in every fatigue, I am sure; but I did not think it right for either of them. Kitty is slight and delicate; and Mary studies so much, that her hours of repose should not be broken in on. My aunt Phillips came to Longbourn on Tuesday, after my father went away; and was so good as to stay till Thursday with me. She was of great use and comfort to us all. And Lady Lucas has been very kind; she walked here on Wednesday morning to condole with us, and offered her services, or any of her daughters', if they should be of use to us."

"She had better have stayed at home," cried Elizabeth; "perhaps she MEANT well, but, under such a misfortune as this, one cannot see too little of one's neighbours. Assistance is impossible; condolence insufferable. Let them triumph over us at a distance, and be satisfied."

She then proceeded to inquire into the measures which her father had intended to pursue, while in town, for the recovery of his daughter.

"He meant I believe," replied Jane, "to go to Epsom, the place where they last changed horses, see the postilions and try if anything could be made out from them. His principal object must be to discover the number of the hackney coach which took them from Clapham. It had come with a fare from London; and as he thought that the circumstance of a gentleman and lady's removing from one carriage into another might be remarked he meant to make inquiries at Clapham. If he could anyhow discover at what house the coachman had before set down his fare, he determined to make inquiries there, and hoped it might not be impossible to find out the stand and number of the coach. I do not know of any other designs that he had formed; but he was in such a hurry to be gone, and his spirits so greatly discomposed, that I had difficulty in finding out even so much as this."

Chapter 48

The whole party were in hopes of a letter from Mr. Bennet the next morning, but the post came in without bringing a single line from him. His family knew him to be, on all common occasions, a most negligent and dilatory correspondent; but at such a time they had hoped for exertion. They were forced to conclude that he had no pleasing intelligence to send; but even of THAT they would have been glad to be certain. Mr. Gardiner had waited only for the letters before he set off.

When he was gone, they were certain at least of receiving constant information of what was going on, and their uncle promised, at parting, to prevail on Mr. Bennet to return to Longbourn, as soon as he could, to the great consolation of his sister, who considered it as the only security for her husband's not being killed in a duel.

Mrs. Gardiner and the children were to remain in Hertfordshire a few days longer, as the former thought her presence might be serviceable to her nieces. She shared in their attendance on Mrs. Bennet, and was a great comfort to them in their hours of freedom. Their other aunt also visited them frequently, and always, as she said, with the design of cheering and heartening them up—though, as she never came without reporting some fresh instance of Wickham's extravagance or irregularity, she seldom went away without leaving them more dispirited than she found them.

All Meryton seemed striving to blacken the man who, but three months before, had been almost an angel of light. He was declared to be in debt to every tradesman in the place, and his intrigues all honoured with the title of seduction, had been extended into every tradesman's family. Everybody declared that he was the wickedest young man in the world; and everybody began to find out that they had always distrusted the appearance of his goodness. Elizabeth, though she did not credit above half of what was said, believed enough to make her former assurance of her sister's ruin more certain; and even Jane, who believed still less of it, became almost hopeless, more especially as the time was now come when, if they had gone to Scotland, which she had never before entirely despaired of, they must in all probability have gained some news of them.

Mr. Gardiner left Longbourn on Sunday; on Tuesday his wife received a letter from him; it told them that, on his arrival, he had immediately found out his brother, and persuaded him to come to Gracechurch Street; that Mr. Bennet had been to Epsom and Clapham, before his arrival, but without gaining any satisfactory information; and that he was now determined to inquire at all the principal hotels in town, as Mr. Bennet thought it possible they might have gone to one of them, on their first coming to London, before they procured lodgings. Mr. Gardiner himself did not expect any success from this measure, but as his brother was eager in it, he meant to assist him in pursuing it. He added that Mr. Bennet seemed wholly disinclined at present to leave London and promised to write again very soon. There was also a postscript to this effect:

"I have written to Colonel Forster to desire him to find out, if possible, from some of the young man's intimates in the regiment, whether Wickham has any relations or connections who would be likely to know in what part of town he has now concealed himself. If there were any one that one could apply to with a probability of gaining such a clue as that, it might be of essential consequence. At present we have nothing to guide us. Colonel Forster will, I dare say, do everything in his power to satisfy us on this head. But, on second thoughts, perhaps, Lizzy could tell us what relations he has now living, better than any other person."

Elizabeth was at no loss to understand from whence this deference to her authority proceeded; but it was not in her power to give any information of so satisfactory a nature as the compliment deserved. She had never heard of his having had any relations, except a father and mother, both of whom had been dead many years. It was possible, however, that some of his companions in the ______shire might be able to give more information; and though she was not very sanguine in expecting it, the application was a something to look forward to.

Every day at Longbourn was now a day of anxiety; but the most anxious part of each was when the post was expected. The arrival of letters was the grand object of every morning's impatience. Through letters, whatever of good or bad was to be told would be communicated, and every succeeding day was expected to bring some news of importance.

But before they heard again from Mr. Gardiner, a letter arrived for their father, from a different quarter, from Mr. Collins; which, as Jane had received directions to open all that came for him in his absence, she accordingly read; and Elizabeth, who knew what curiosities his letters always were, looked over her, and read it likewise. It was as follows:

> "MY DEAR SIR,
>
> "I feel myself called upon, by our relationship, and my situation in life, to condole with you on the grievous affliction you are now suffering under, of which we were yesterday informed by a letter from Hertfordshire. Be assured, my dear sir, that Mrs. Collins and myself sincerely sympathise with you and all your respectable family, in your present distress, which must be of the bitterest kind, because proceeding from a cause which no time can remove. No arguments shall be wanting on my part that can alleviate so severe a misfortune—or that may comfort you, under a circumstance that must be of all others the most afflicting to a parent's mind. The death of your daughter

would have been a blessing in comparison of this. And it is the more to be lamented, because there is reason to suppose as my dear Charlotte informs me, that this licentiousness of behaviour in your daughter has proceeded from a faulty degree of indulgence; though, at the same time, for the consolation of yourself and Mrs. Bennet, I am inclined to think that her own disposition must be naturally bad, or she could not be guilty of such an enormity, at so early an age. Howsoever that may be, you are grievously to be pitied; in which opinion I am not only joined by Mrs. Collins, but likewise by Lady Catherine and her daughter, to whom I have related the affair. They agree with me in apprehending that this false step in one daughter will be injurious to the fortunes of all the others; for who, as Lady Catherine herself condescendingly says, will connect themselves with such a family? And this consideration leads me moreover to reflect, with augmented satisfaction, on a certain event of last November; for had it been otherwise, I must have been involved in all your sorrow and disgrace. Let me then advise you, dear sir, to console yourself as much as possible, to throw off your unworthy child from your affection for ever, and leave her to reap the fruits of her own heinous offense.—I am, dear sir, etc., etc."

Mr. Gardiner did not write again till he had received an answer from Colonel Forster; and then he had nothing of a pleasant nature to send. It was not known that Wickham had a single relationship with whom he kept up any connection, and it was certain that he had no near one living. His former acquaintances had been numerous; but since he had been in the militia, it did not appear that he was on terms of particular friendship with any of them. There was no one, therefore, who could be pointed out as likely to give any news of him. And in the wretched state of his own finances, there was a very powerful motive for secrecy, in addition to his fear of discovery by Lydia's relations, for it had just transpired that he had left gaming debts behind him to a very considerable amount. Colonel Forster believed that more than a thousand pounds would be necessary to clear his expenses at Brighton. He owed a good deal in town, but his debts of honour were still more formidable. Mr. Gardiner did not attempt to conceal these particulars from the Longbourn family. Jane heard them with horror. "A gamester!" she cried. "This is wholly unexpected. I had not an idea of it."

Mr. Gardiner added in his letter, that they might expect to see their father at home on the following day, which was Saturday. Rendered spiritless by the ill-success of all their endeavours, he had yielded to his brother-in-law's entreaty that he would return to his family, and leave it to him to do whatever occasion might suggest to be advisable for continuing their pursuit. When Mrs. Bennet was told of this, she did not express so much satisfaction as her children expected, considering what her anxiety for his life had been before.

"What, is he coming home, and without poor Lydia?" she cried. "Sure he will not leave London before he has found them. Who is to fight Wickham, and make him marry her, if he comes away?"

As Mrs. Gardiner began to wish to be at home, it was settled that she and the children should go to London, at the same time that Mr. Bennet came from it. The coach, therefore, took them the first stage of their journey, and brought its master back to Longbourn.

Mrs. Gardiner went away in all the perplexity about Elizabeth and her Derbyshire friend that had attended her from that part of the world. His name had never been voluntarily mentioned before them by her niece; and the kind of half-expectation which Mrs. Gardiner had formed, of their being followed by a letter from him, had ended in nothing. Elizabeth had received none since her return that could come from Pemberley.

The present unhappy state of the family rendered any other excuse for the lowness of her spirits unnecessary; nothing, therefore, could be fairly conjectured from THAT, though Elizabeth, who was by this time tolerably well acquainted with her own feelings, was perfectly aware that, had she known nothing of Darcy, she could have borne the dread of Lydia's infamy somewhat better. It would have spared her, she thought, one sleepless night out of two.

When Mr. Bennet arrived, he had all the appearance of his usual philosophic composure. He said as little as he had ever been in the habit of saying; made no mention of the business that had taken him away, and it was some time before his daughters had courage to speak of it.

It was not till the afternoon, when he had joined them at tea, that Elizabeth ventured to introduce the subject; and then, on her briefly expressing her sorrow for what he must have endured, he replied, "Say nothing of that. Who should suffer but myself? It has been my own doing, and I ought to feel it."

"You must not be too severe upon yourself," replied Elizabeth.

"You may well warn me against such an evil. Human nature is so prone to fall into it! No, Lizzy, let me once in my life feel how much I have been to blame. I am not afraid of being overpowered by the impression. It will pass away soon enough."

"Do you suppose them to be in London?"

"Yes; where else can they be so well concealed?"

"And Lydia used to want to go to London," added Kitty.

"She is happy then," said her father drily; "and her residence there will probably be of some duration."

Then after a short silence he continued:

"Lizzy, I bear you no ill-will for being justified in your advice to me last May, which, considering the event, shows some greatness of mind."

They were interrupted by Miss Bennet, who came to fetch her mother's tea.

"This is a parade," he cried, "which does one good; it gives such an elegance to misfortune! Another day I will do the same; I will sit in my library, in my nightcap and powdering gown, and give as much trouble as I can; or, perhaps, I may defer it till Kitty runs away."

"I am not going to run away, papa," said Kitty fretfully. "If I should ever go to Brighton, I would behave better than Lydia."

"YOU go to Brighton. I would not trust you so near it as Eastbourne for fifty pounds! No, Kitty, I have at last learnt to be cautious, and you will feel the effects of it. No officer is ever to enter into my house again, nor even to pass through the village. Balls will be absolutely prohibited, unless you stand up with one of your sisters. And you are never to stir out of doors till you can prove that you have spent ten minutes of every day in a rational manner."

Kitty, who took all these threats in a serious light, began to cry.

"Well, well," said he, "do not make yourself unhappy. If you are a good girl for the next ten years, I will take you to a review at the end of them."

Chapter 49

Two days after Mr. Bennet's return, as Jane and Elizabeth were walking together in the shrubbery behind the house, they saw the housekeeper coming towards them, and, concluding that she came to call them to their mother, went forward to meet her; but, instead of the expected summons, when they approached her, she said to Miss Bennet, "I beg your pardon, madam, for interrupting you, but I was in hopes you might have got some good news from town, so I took the liberty of coming to ask."

"What do you mean, Hill? We have heard nothing from town."

"Dear madam," cried Mrs. Hill, in great astonishment, "don't you know there is an express come for master from Mr. Gardiner? He has been here this half-hour, and master has had a letter."

Away ran the girls, too eager to get in to have time for speech. They ran through the vestibule into the breakfast-room; from thence to the library; their father was in neither; and they were on the point of seeking him upstairs with their mother, when they were met by the butler, who said:

"If you are looking for my master, ma'am, he is walking towards the little copse."

Upon this information, they instantly passed through the hall once more, and ran across the lawn after their father, who was deliberately pursuing his way towards a small wood on one side of the paddock.

Jane, who was not so light nor so much in the habit of running as Elizabeth, soon lagged behind, while her sister, panting for breath, came up with him, and eagerly cried out:

"Oh, papa, what news—what news? Have you heard from my uncle?"

"Yes I have had a letter from him by express."

"Well, and what news does it bring—good or bad?"

"What is there of good to be expected?" said he, taking the letter from his pocket. "But perhaps you would like to read it."

Elizabeth impatiently caught it from his hand. Jane now came up.

"Read it aloud," said their father, "for I hardly know myself what it is about."

* * *

"Gracechurch Street, Monday,"

"August 2.

"MY DEAR BROTHER,—"At last I am able to send you some tidings of my niece, and such as, upon the whole, I hope it will give you satisfaction. Soon after you left me on Saturday, I was fortunate enough to find out in what part of London they were. The particulars I reserve till we meet; it is enough to know they are discovered. I have seen them both—"

"Then it is as I always hoped," cried Jane; "they are married!"
Elizabeth read on:

"I have seen them both. They are not married, nor can I find there was any intention of being so; but if you are willing to perform the engagements which I have ventured to make on your side, I hope it will not be long before they are. All that is required of you is, to assure to your daughter, by settlement, her equal share of the five thousand pounds secured among your children after the decease of yourself and my sister; and, moreover, to enter into an engagement of allowing her, during your life, one hundred pounds per annum. These are conditions which, considering everything, I had no hesitation in complying with, as far as I thought myself privileged, for you. I shall send this by express, that no time may be lost in bringing me your answer. You will easily comprehend, from these particulars, that Mr. Wickham's circumstances are not so hopeless as they are generally believed to be. The world has been deceived in that respect; and I am happy to say there will be some little money, even when all his debts are discharged, to settle on my niece, in addition to her own fortune. If, as I conclude will be the case, you send me full powers to act in your name throughout the whole of this business, I will immediately give directions to Haggerston for preparing a proper settlement. There will not be the smallest occasion for your coming to town again; therefore stay quiet at Longbourn, and depend on my diligence and care. Send back your answer as fast as you can, and be careful to write explicitly. We have judged it best that my niece should be married from this house, of which I hope you will approve. She comes to us to-day. I shall write again as soon as anything more is determined on. Yours, etc.,

"EDW. GARDINER."

"Is it possible?" cried Elizabeth, when she had finished. "Can it be possible that he will marry her?"

"Wickham is not so undeserving, then, as we thought him," said her sister. "My dear father, I congratulate you."

"And have you answered the letter?" cried Elizabeth.

"No; but it must be done soon."

Most earnestly did she then entreaty him to lose no more time before he wrote.

"Oh! my dear father," she cried, "come back and write immediately. Consider how important every moment is in such a case."

"Let me write for you," said Jane, "if you dislike the trouble yourself."

"I dislike it very much," he replied; "but it must be done."

And so saying, he turned back with them, and walked towards the house.

"And may I ask—" said Elizabeth; "but the terms, I suppose, must be complied with."

"Complied with! I am only ashamed of his asking so little."

"And they MUST marry! Yet he is SUCH a man!"

"Yes, yes, they must marry. There is nothing else to be done. But there are two things that I want very much to know; one is, how much money your uncle has laid down to bring it about; and the other, how am I ever to pay him."

"Money! My uncle!" cried Jane, "what do you mean, sir?"

"I mean, that no man in his senses would marry Lydia on so slight a temptation as one hundred a year during my life, and fifty after I am gone."

"That is very true," said Elizabeth; "though it had not occurred to me before. His debts to be discharged, and something still to remain! Oh! it must be my uncle's doings! Generous, good man, I am afraid he has distressed himself. A small sum could not do all this."

"No," said her father; "Wickham's a fool if he takes her with a farthing less than ten thousand pounds. I should be sorry to think so ill of him, in the very beginning of our relationship."

"Ten thousand pounds! Heaven forbid! How is half such a sum to be repaid?"

Mr. Bennet made no answer, and each of them, deep in thought, continued silent till they reached the house. Their father then went on to the library to write, and the girls walked into the breakfast-room.

"And they are really to be married!" cried Elizabeth, as soon as they were by themselves. "How strange this is! And for THIS we are to be thankful. That they should marry, small as is their chance of happiness, and wretched as is his character, we are forced to rejoice. Oh, Lydia!"

"I comfort myself with thinking," replied Jane, "that he certainly would not marry Lydia if he had not a real regard for her. Though our kind uncle has done something towards clearing him, I cannot believe that ten thousand pounds, or anything like it, has been advanced. He has children of his own, and may have more. How could he spare half ten thousand pounds?"

"If he were ever able to learn what Wickham's debts have been," said Elizabeth, "and how much is settled on his side on our sister, we shall exactly know what Mr. Gardiner has done for them, because Wickham has not sixpence of his own. The kindness of my uncle and aunt can never be requited. Their taking her home, and affording her their personal protection and countenance, is such a sacrifice to her advantage as years of gratitude cannot enough acknowledge. By this time she is actually with them! If such goodness does not make her miserable now, she will never deserve to be happy! What a meeting for her, when she first sees my aunt!"

"We must endeavour to forget all that has passed on either side," said Jane: "I hope and trust they will yet be happy. His consenting to marry her is a proof, I will believe, that he is come to a right way of thinking. Their mutual affection will steady them; and I flatter myself they will settle so quietly, and live in so rational a manner, as may in time make their past imprudence forgotten."

"Their conduct has been such," replied Elizabeth, "as neither you, nor I, nor anybody can ever forget. It is useless to talk of it."

It now occurred to the girls that their mother was in all likelihood perfectly ignorant of what had happened. They went to the library, therefore, and asked their father whether he would not wish them to make it known to her. He was writing and, without raising his head, coolly replied:

"Just as you please."

"May we take my uncle's letter to read to her?"

"Take whatever you like, and get away."

Elizabeth took the letter from his writing-table, and they went upstairs together. Mary and Kitty were both with Mrs. Bennet: one communication would, therefore, do for all. After a slight preparation for good news, the letter was read aloud. Mrs. Bennet could hardly contain herself. As soon as Jane had read Mr. Gardiner's hope of Lydia's being soon married, her joy burst forth, and every following sentence added to its exuberance. She was now in an irritation as violent from delight, as she had ever been fidgety from alarm and vexation. To know that her daughter would be married was enough. She was disturbed by no fear for her felicity, nor humbled by any remembrance of her misconduct.

"My dear, dear Lydia!" she cried. "This is delightful indeed! She will be married! I shall see her again! She will be married at sixteen! My good, kind brother! I knew how it would be. I knew he would manage everything! How I long to see her! and to see dear Wickham too! But the clothes, the wedding clothes! I will write to my sister Gardiner about them directly. Lizzy, my dear, run down to your father, and ask him how much he will give her. Stay, stay, I will go myself. Ring the bell, Kitty, for Hill. I will put on my things in a moment. My dear, dear Lydia! How merry we shall be together when we meet!"

Her eldest daughter endeavoured to give some relief to the violence of these transports, by leading her thoughts to the obligations which Mr. Gardiner's behaviour laid them all under.

"For we must attribute this happy conclusion," she added, "in a great measure to his kindness. We are persuaded that he has pledged himself to assist Mr. Wickham with money."

"Well," cried her mother, "it is all very right; who should do it but her own uncle? If he had not had a family of his own, I and my children must have had all his money, you know; and it is the first time we have ever had anything from him, except a few presents. Well! I am so happy! In a short time I shall have a daughter married. Mrs. Wickham! How well it sounds! And she was only sixteen last June. My dear Jane, I am in such a flutter, that I am sure I can't write; so I will dictate, and you write for me. We will settle with your father about the money afterwards; but the things should be ordered immediately."

She was then proceeding to all the particulars of calico, muslin, and cambric, and would shortly have dictated some very plentiful orders, had not Jane, though with some difficulty, persuaded her to wait till her father was at leisure to be consulted. One day's delay, she observed, would be of small importance; and her mother was too happy to be quite so obstinate as usual. Other schemes, too, came into her head.

"I will go to Meryton," said she, "as soon as I am dressed, and tell the good, good news to my sister Philips. And as I come back, I can call on Lady Lucas and Mrs. Long. Kitty, run down and order the carriage. An airing would do me a great deal of good, I am sure. Girls, can I do anything for you in Meryton? Oh! Here comes Hill! My dear Hill, have you heard the good news? Miss Lydia is going to be married; and you shall all have a bowl of punch to make merry at her wedding."

Mrs. Hill began instantly to express her joy. Elizabeth received her congratulations amongst the rest, and then, sick of this folly, took refuge in her own room, that she might think with freedom.

Poor Lydia's situation must, at best, be bad enough; but that it was no worse, she had need to be thankful. She felt it so; and though, in looking forward, neither rational happiness nor worldly prosperity could be justly expected for her sister, in looking back to what they had feared, only two hours ago, she felt all the advantages of what they had gained.

Chapter 50

Mr. Bennet had very often wished before this period of his life that, instead of spending his whole income, he had laid by an annual sum for the better provision of his children, and of his wife, if she survived him. He now wished it more than ever. Had he done his duty in that respect, Lydia need not have been indebted to her uncle for whatever of honour or credit could now be purchased for her. The satisfaction of prevailing on one of the most worthless young men in Great Britain to be her husband might then have rested in its proper place.

He was seriously concerned that a cause of so little advantage to anyone should be forwarded at the sole expense of his brother-in-law, and he was determined, if possible, to find out the extent of his assistance, and to discharge the obligation as soon as he could.

When first Mr. Bennet had married, economy was held to be perfectly useless, for, of course, they were to have a son. The son was to join in cutting off the entail, as soon as he should be of age, and the widow and younger children would by that means be provided for. Five daughters successively entered the world, but yet the son was to come; and Mrs. Bennet, for many years after Lydia's birth, had been certain that he would. This event had at last been despaired of, but it was then too late to be saving. Mrs. Bennet had no turn for economy, and her husband's love of independence had alone prevented their exceeding their income.

Five thousand pounds was settled by marriage articles on Mrs. Bennet and the children. But in what proportions it should be divided amongst the latter depended on the will of the parents. This was one point, with regard to Lydia, at least, which was now to be settled, and Mr. Bennet could have no hesitation in acceding to the proposal before him. In terms of grateful acknowledgment for the kindness of his brother, though expressed most concisely, he then delivered on paper his perfect approbation of all that was done, and his willingness to fulfil the engagements that had been made for him. He had never before supposed that, could Wickham be prevailed on to marry his daughter, it would be done with so little inconvenience to himself as by the present arrangement. He would scarcely be ten pounds a year the loser by the hundred that was to be paid them; for, what with her board and pocket allowance, and the continual presents in money which passed to her through her mother's hands, Lydia's expenses had been very little within that sum.

That it would be done with such trifling exertion on his side, too, was another very welcome surprise; for his wish at present was to have as little trouble in the business as possible. When the first transports of rage which had produced his activity in seeking her were over, he naturally returned to all his former indolence. His letter was soon dispatched; for, though dilatory in undertaking business, he was quick in its execution. He begged to know further particulars of what he was indebted to his brother, but was too angry with Lydia to send any message to her.

The good news spread quickly through the house, and with proportionate speed through the neighbourhood. It was borne in the latter with decent philosophy. To be sure, it would have been more for the advantage of conversation had Miss Lydia Bennet come upon the town; or, as the happiest alternative, been secluded from the world, in some distant farmhouse. But there was much to be talked of in marrying her; and the good-natured wishes for her well-doing which had proceeded before from all the spiteful old ladies in Meryton lost but a little of their spirit in this change of circumstances, because with such an husband her misery was considered certain.

It was a fortnight since Mrs. Bennet had been downstairs; but on this happy day she again took her seat at the head of her table, and in spirits oppressively high. No sentiment of shame gave a damp to her triumph. The marriage of a daughter, which had been the first object of her wishes since Jane was sixteen, was now on the point of accomplishment, and her thoughts and her words ran wholly on those attendants of elegant nuptials, fine muslins, new carriages, and servants. She was busily searching through the neighbourhood for a proper situation for her daughter, and, without knowing of considering what their income might be, rejected many as deficient in size and importance.

"Haye Park might do," said she, "if the Gouldings could quit it—or the great house at Stoke, if the drawing-room were larger; but Ashworth is too far off! I could not bear to have her ten miles from me; and as for Pulvis Lodge, the attics are dreadful."

Her husband allowed her to talk on without interruption while the servants remained. But when they had withdrawn, he said to her: "Mrs. Bennet, before you take any or all of these houses for your son and daugher, let us come to a right understanding. Into ONE house in this neighbourhood they shall never have admittance. I will not encourage the impudence of either, by receiving them at Longbourn."

A long dispute followed this declaration; but Mr. Bennet was firm. It soon led to another; and Mrs. Bennet found, with amazement and horror, that her husband would not advance a guinea to buy clothes for his daughter. He protested that she should receive from him no mark of affection whatever on the occasion. Mrs. Bennet could hardly comprehend it. That his anger could be carried to such a point of inconceivable resentment as to refuse his daughter a privilege without which her marriage would scarcely seem valid, exceeded all she could believe possible. She was more alive to the disgrace which her want of new clothes must reflect on her daugher's nuptials, than to any sense of shame at her eloping and living with Wickham a fortnight before they took place.

Elizabeth was now most heartily sorry that she had, from the distress of the moment, been led to make Mr. Darcy acquainted with with their fears for her sister; for since her marriage would so shortly give the proper termination to the elopement, they might hope to conceal its unfavourable beginning from all those who were not immediately on the spot.

She had no fear of its spreading farther through his means. There were few people on whose secrecy she would have more confidently depended; but, at the same time, there was no one whose knowledge of a sister's frailty would have mortified her so much—not, however, from any fear of disadvantage from it individually to herself, for, at any rate, there seemed a gulf impassable between them. Had Lydia's marriage been concluded on the most honourable terms, it was not to be supposed that Mr. Darcy would connect himself with a family where, to every other objection, would now be added an alliance and relationship of the nearest kind with a man whom he so justly scorned.

From such a connection she could not wonder that he would shrink. The wish of procuring her regard, which she had assured herself of his feeling in Derbyshire, could not in rational expectation survive such a blow as this. She was humbled, she was grieved; she repented, though she hardly knew of what. She became jealous of his esteem, when she could no longer hope to be benefited by it. She wanted to hear of him, when there seemed the least chance of gaining intelligence. She was convinced that she could have been happy with him, when it was no longer likely they should meet.

What a triumph for him, as she often thought, could he know that the proposals which she had proudly spurned only four months ago, would now have been most gladly and gratefully received! He was as generous, she doubted not, as the most generous of his sex; but while he was mortal, there must be a triumph.

She began now to comprehend that he was exactly the man who, in disposition and talents, would most suit her. His understanding and temper, though unlike her own, would have answered all her wishes. It was an union that must have been to the advantage of both: by her ease and liveliness, his mind might have been softened, his manners improved; and from his judgement, information, and knowledge of the world, she must have received benefit of greater importance.

But no such happy marriage could now teach the admiring multitude what connubial felicity really was. An union of a different tendency , and precluding the possiblity of the other, was soon to be formed in their family.

How Wickham and Lydia were to be supported in tolerable independence, she could not imagine. But how little of permanent happiness could belong to a couple who were only brought together because their passions were stronger than their virtue, she could easily conjecture.

Mr. Gardiner soon wrote again to his brother. To Mr. Bennet's acknowledgments he briefly replied, with assurance of his eagerness to promote the welfare of any of his family; and concluded with entreaties that the subject might never be mentioned to him again. The principal purport of his letter was to inform them that Mr. Wickham had resolved on quitting the militia.

"It was greatly my wish that he should do so," he added, "as soon as his marriage was fixed on. And I think you will agree with me, in considering the removal from that corps as highly advisable, both on his account and my niece's. It is Mr. Wickham's intention to go into the regulars; and among his former friends, there are still some who are able and willing to assist him in the army. He has the promise of an ensigncy in General ______'s regiment, now quartered in the North. It is an advantage to have it so far from this part of the kingdom. He promises fairly; and I hope among different people, where they may each have a character to preserve, they will both be more prudent. I have written to Colonel Forster, to inform him of our present arrangements, and to request that he will satisfy the various creditors of Mr. Wickham in and near Brighton, with assurances of speedy payment, for which I have pledged myself. And will you give yourself the trouble of carrying similar assurances to his creditors in Meryton, of whom I shall subjoin a list according to his information? He has given in all his debts; I hope at least he has not deceived us. Haggerston has our directions, and all will be completed in a week. They will then join his regiment, unless they are first invited to Longbourn; and I understand from Mrs. Gardiner, that my niece is very desirous of seeing you all before she leaves the South. She is well, and begs to be dutifully remembered to you and your mother.—Yours, etc.,

"E. GARDINER."

Mr. Bennet and his daughters saw all the advantages of Wickham's removal from the ______shire as clearly as Mr. Gardiner could do. But Mrs. Bennet was not so well pleased with it. Lydia's being settled in the North, just when she had expected most pleasure and pride in her company, for she had by no means given up her plan of their residing in Hertfordshire, was a severe disappointment; and, besides, it was such a pity that Lydia should be taken from a regiment where she was acquainted with everybody, and had so many favourites.

"She is so fond of Mrs. Forster, "said she, "it will be quite shocking to send her away! And there are several of the young men, too, that she likes very much. The officers may not be so pleasant in General ______'s regiment."

His daughter's request, for such it might be considered, of being admitted into her family again before she set off for the North, received at first an absolute negative. But Jane and Elizabeth, who agreed in wishing, for the sake of their sister's feelings and consequence, that she should be noticed on her marriage by her parents, urged him so earnestly yet so rationally and so mildly, to receive her and her husband at Longbourn, as soon as they were married, that he was prevailed on to think as they thought, and act as they wished. And their mother had the satisfaction of knowing that she would be able to show her married daughter in the neighbourhood before she was banished to the North. When Mr. Bennet wrote again to his brother, therefore, he sent his permission for them to come; and it was settled, that as soon as the ceremony was over, they should proceed to Longbourn. Elizabeth was surprised, however, that Wickham should consent to such a scheme, and had she consulted only her own inclination, any meeting with him would have been the last object of her wishes.

Chapter 51

THEIR sister's wedding day arrived; and Jane and Elizabeth felt for her probably more than she felt for herself. The carriage was sent to meet them at ______, and they were to return in it by dinner-time. Their arrival was dreaded by the elder Miss Bennets, and Jane more especially, who gave Lydia the feelings which would have attended herself, had she been the culprit, and was wretched in the thought of what her sister must endure.

They came. The family were assembled in the breakfast room to receive them. Smiles decked the face of Mrs. Bennet as the carriage drove up to the door; her husband looked impenetrably grave; her daughters, alarmed, anxious, uneasy.

Lydia's voice was heard in the vestibule; the door was thrown open, and she ran into the room. Her mother stepped forwards, embraced her, and welcomed her with rapture; gave her hand, with an affectionate smile, to Wickham, who followed his lady; and wished them both joy with an alacrity which shewed no doubt of their happiness.

Their reception from Mr. Bennet, to whom they then turned, was not quite so cordial. His countenance rather gained in austerity; and he scarcely opened his lips. The easy assurance of the young couple, indeed, was enough to provoke him. Elizabeth was disgusted, and even Miss Bennet was shocked. Lydia was Lydia still; untamed, unabashed, wild, noisy, and fearless. She turned from sister to sister, demanding their congratulations; and when at length they all sat down, looked eagerly round the room, took notice of some little alteration in it, and observed, with a laugh, that it was a great while since she had been there.

Wickham was not at all more distressed than herself, but his manners were always so pleasing, that had his character and his marriage been exactly what they ought, his smiles and his easy address, while he claimed their relationship, would have delighted them all. Elizabeth had not before believed him quite equal to such assurance; but she sat down, resolving within herself to draw no limits in future to the impudence of an impudent man. She blushed, and Jane blushed; but the cheeks of the two who caused their confusion suffered no variation of colour.

There was no want of discourse. The bride and her mother could neither of them talk fast enough; and Wickham, who happened to sit near Elizabeth, began enquiring after his acquaintance in that neighbourhood, with a good humoured ease which she felt very unable to equal in her replies. They seemed each of them to have the happiest memories in the world. Nothing of the past was recollected with pain; and Lydia led voluntarily to subjects which her sisters would not have alluded to for the world.

"Only think of its being three months," she cried, "since I went away; it seems but a fortnight I declare; and yet there have been things enough happened in the time. Good gracious! when I went away, I am sure I had no more idea of being married till I came back again! though I thought it would be very good fun if I was."

Her father lifted up his eyes. Jane was distressed. Elizabeth looked expressively at Lydia; but she, who never heard nor saw any thing of which she chose to be insensible, gaily continued, "Oh! mamma, do the people here abouts know I am married to-day? I was afraid they might not; and we overtook William Goulding in his curricle, so I was determined he should know it, and so I let down the side-glass next to him, and took off my glove, and let my hand just rest upon the window frame, so that he might see the ring, and then I bowed and smiled like any thing."

Elizabeth could bear it no longer. She got up, and ran out of the room; and returned no more, till she heard them passing through the hall to the dining parlour. She then joined them soon enough to see Lydia, with anxious parade, walk up to her mother's right hand, and hear her say to her eldest sister, "Ah! Jane, I take your place now, and you must go lower, because I am a married woman."

It was not to be supposed that time would give Lydia that embarrassment from which she had been so wholly free at first. Her ease and good spirits increased. She longed to see Mrs. Phillips, the Lucases, and all their other neighbours, and to hear herself called "Mrs. Wickham" by each of them; and in the mean time, she went after dinner to shew her ring, and boast of being married, to Mrs. Hill and the two housemaids.

"Well, mamma," said she, when they were all returned to the breakfast room, "and what do you think of my husband? Is not he a charming man? I am sure my sisters must all envy me. I only hope they may have half my good luck. They must all go to Brighton. That is the place to get husbands. What a pity it is, mamma, we did not all go."

"Very true; and if I had my will, we should. But my dear Lydia, I don't at all like your going such a way off. Must it be so?"

"Oh, lord! yes;—there is nothing in that. I shall like it of all things. You and papa, and my sisters, must come down and see us. We shall be at Newcastle all the winter, and I dare say there will be some balls, and I will take care to get good partners for them all."

"I should like it beyond any thing!" said her mother.

"And then when you go away, you may leave one or two of my sisters behind you; and I dare say I shall get husbands for them before the winter is over."

"I thank you for my share of the favour," said Elizabeth; "but I do not particularly like your way of getting husbands."

Their visitors were not to remain above ten days with them. Mr. Wickham had received his commission before he left London, and he was to join his regiment at the end of a fortnight.

No one but Mrs. Bennet regretted that their stay would be so short; and she made the most of the time by visiting about with her daughter, and having very frequent parties at home. These parties were acceptable to all; to avoid a family circle was even more desirable to such as did think, than such as did not.

Wickham's affection for Lydia was just what Elizabeth had expected to find it; not equal to Lydia's for him. She had scarcely needed her present observation to be satisfied, from the reason of things, that their elopement had been brought on by the strength of her love, rather than by his; and she would have wondered why, without violently caring for her, he chose to elope with her at all, had she not felt certain that his flight was rendered necessary by distress of circumstances; and if that were the case, he was not the young man to resist an opportunity of having a companion.

Lydia was exceedingly fond of him. He was her dear Wickham on every occasion; no one was to be put in competition with him. He did every thing best in the world; and she was sure he would kill more birds on the first of September, than any body else in the country.

One morning, soon after their arrival, as she was sitting with her two elder sisters, she said to Elizabeth,

"Lizzy, I never gave you an account of my wedding, I believe. You were not by, when I told mamma and the others all about it. Are not you curious to hear how it was managed?"

"No really," replied Elizabeth; "I think there cannot be too little said on the subject."

"La! You are so strange! But I must tell you how it went off. We were married, you know, at St. Clement's, because Wickham's lodgings were in that parish. And it was settled that we should all be there by eleven o'clock. My uncle and aunt and I were to go together; and the others were to meet us at the church. Well, Monday morning came, and I was in such a fuss! I was so afraid, you know, that something would happen to put it off, and then I should have gone quite distracted. And there was my aunt, all the time I was dressing, preaching and talking away just as if she was reading a sermon. However, I did not hear above one word in ten, for I was thinking, you may suppose, of my dear Wickham. I longed to know whether he would be married in his blue coat."

"Well, and so we breakfasted at ten as usual; I thought it would never be over; for, by the bye, you are to understand, that my uncle and aunt were horrid unpleasant all the time I was with them. If you'll believe me, I did not once put my foot out of doors, though I was there a fortnight. Not one party, or scheme, or any thing. To be sure London was rather thin, but, however, the Little Theatre was open. Well, and so just as the carriage came to the door, my uncle was called away upon business to that horrid man Mr. Stone. And then, you know, when once they get together, there is no end of it. Well, I was so frightened I did not know what to do, for my uncle was to give me away; and if we were beyond the hour, we could not be married all day. But, luckily, he came back again in ten minutes' time, and then we all set out. However, I recollected afterwards that if he had been prevented going, the wedding need not be put off, for Mr. Darcy might have done as well."

"Mr. Darcy!" repeated Elizabeth, in utter amazement.

"Oh, yes!—he was to come there with Wickham, you know, But gracious me! I quite forgot! I ought not to have said a word about it. I promised them so faithfully! What will Wickham say? It was to be such a secret!"

"If it was to be secret," said Jane, "say not another word on the subject. You may depend upon my seeking no further."

"Oh! certainly," said Elizabeth, though burning with curiosity; "we will ask you no questions."

"Thank you," said Lydia, "for if you did, I should certainly tell you all, and then Wickham would be angry."

On such encouragement to ask, Elizabeth was forced to put it out of her power, by running away.

But to live in ignorance on such a point was impossible; or at least it was impossible not to try for information. Mr. Darcy had been at her sister's wedding. It was exactly a scene, and exactly among people, where he had apparently least to do, and least temptation to go. Conjectures as to the meaning of it, rapid and wild, hurried into her brain; but she was satisfied with none. Those that best pleased her, as placing his conduct in the noblest light, seemed most improbable. She could not bear such suspense; and hastily seizing a sheet of paper, wrote a short letter to her aunt, to request an explanation of what Lydia had dropt, if it were compatible with the secrecy which had been intended.

"You may readily comprehend," she added, "what my curiosity must be to know how a person unconnected with any of us, and (comparatively speaking) a stranger to our family, should have been amongst you at such a time. Pray write instantly, and let me understand it—unless it is, for very cogent reasons, to remain in the secrecy which Lydia seems to think necessary; and then I must endeavour to be satisfied with ignorance."

"Not that I shall, though," she added to herself, as she finished the letter; "and my dear aunt, if you do not tell me in an honourable manner, I shall certainly be reduced to tricks and stratagems to find it out."

Jane's delicate sense of honour would not allow her to speak to Elizabeth privately of what Lydia had let fall; Elizabeth was glad of it;—till it appeared whether her inquiries would receive any satisfaction, she had rather be without a confidante.

Chapter 52

ELIZABETH had the satisfaction of receiving an answer to her letter as soon as she possibly could. She was no sooner in possession of it than, hurrying into the little copse, where she was least likely to be interrupted, she sat down on one of the benches and prepared to be happy; for the length of the letter convinced her that it did not contain a denial.

> "Gracechurch-street, Sept. 6.
>
> "MY DEAR NIECE,
>
> "I have just received your letter, and shall devote this whole morning to answering it, as I foresee that a little writing will not comprise what I have to tell you. I must confess myself surprised by your application; I did not expect it from you. Don't think me angry, however, for I only mean to let you know that I had not imagined such enquiries to be necessary on your side. If you do not choose to understand me, forgive my impertinence. Your uncle is as much surprised as I am—and nothing but the belief of your being a party concerned would have allowed him to act as he has done. But if you are really innocent and ignorant, I must be more explicit.
>
> "On the very day of my coming home from Longbourn, your uncle had a most unexpected visitor. Mr. Darcy called, and was shut up with him several hours. It was all over before I arrived; so my curiosity was not so dreadfully racked as your's seems to have been. He came to tell Mr. Gardiner that he had found out where your sister and Mr. Wickham were, and that he had seen and talked with them both; Wickham repeatedly, Lydia once. From what I can collect, he left Derbyshire only one day after ourselves, and came to town with the resolution of hunting for them. The motive professed was his conviction of its being owing to himself that Wickham's worthlessness had not been so well known as to make it impossible for any

young woman of character to love or confide in him. He generously imputed the whole to his mistaken pride, and confessed that he had before thought it beneath him to lay his private actions open to the world. His character was to speak for itself. He called it, therefore, his duty to step forward, and endeavour to remedy an evil which had been brought on by himself. If he had another motive, I am sure it would never disgrace him. He had been some days in town, before he was able to discover them; but he had something to direct his search, which was more than we had; and the consciousness of this was another reason for his resolving to follow us.

" There is a lady, it seems, a Mrs. Younge, who was some time ago governess to Miss Darcy, and was dismissed from her charge on some cause of disapprobation, though he did not say what. She then took a large house in Edward-street, and has since maintained herself by letting lodgings. This Mrs. Younge was, he knew, intimately acquainted with Wickham; and he went to her for intelligence of him as soon as he got to town. But it was two or three days before he could get from her what he wanted. She would not betray her trust, I suppose, without bribery and corruption, for she really did know where her friend was to be found. Wickham indeed had gone to her on their first arrival in London, and had she been able to receive them into her house, they would have taken up their abode with her. At length, however, our kind friend procured the wished-for direction. They were in ______ street. He saw Wickham, and afterwards insisted on seeing Lydia. His first object with her, he acknowledged, had been to persuade her to quit her present disgraceful situation, and return to her friends as soon as they could be prevailed on to receive her, offering his assistance, as far as it would go. But he found Lydia absolutely resolved on remaining where she was. She cared for none of her friends; she wanted no help of his; she would not hear of leaving Wickham. She was sure they should be married some time or other, and it did not much signify when. Since such were her feelings, it only remained, he thought, to secure and expedite a marriage, which, in his very first conversation with Wickham, he easily learnt had never been his design. He confessed himself obliged to leave the regiment, on account of some debts of honour, which were very pressing; and scrupled not to lay all the ill-consequences of Lydia's flight on her own folly alone. He meant to resign his commission immediately; and as to his future situation, he could conjecture very little about it. He must go somewhere, but he did not know where, and he knew he should have nothing to live on.

"Mr. Darcy asked him why he had not married your sister at once. Though Mr. Bennet was not imagined to be very rich, he would have been able to do something for him, and his situation must have been benefited by marriage. But he found, in reply to this question, that Wickham still cherished the hope of more effectually making his fortune by marriage in some other country. Under such circumstances, however, he was not likely to be proof against the temptation of immediate relief.

"They met several times, for there was much to be discussed. Wickham of course wanted more than he could get; but at length was reduced to be reasonable.

"Every thing being settled between them, Mr. Darcy's next step was to make your uncle acquainted with it, and he first called in Gracechurch-street the evening before I came home. But Mr. Gardiner could not be seen, and Mr. Darcy found, on further enquiry, that your father was still with him, but would quit town the next morning. He did not judge your father to be a person whom he could so properly consult as your uncle, and therefore readily postponed seeing him till after the departure of the former. He did not leave his name, and till the next day it was only known that a gentleman had called on business.

"On Saturday he came again. Your father was gone, your uncle at home, and, as I said before, they had a great deal of talk together.

"They met again on Sunday, and then I saw him too. It was not all settled before Monday: as soon as it was, the express was sent off to Longbourn. But our visitor was very obstinate. I fancy, Lizzy, that obstinacy is the real defect of his character, after all. He has been accused of many faults at different times, but this is the true one. Nothing was to be done that he did not do himself; though I am sure (and I do not speak it to be thanked, therefore say nothing about it), your uncle would most readily have settled the whole.

"They battled it together for a long time, which was more than either the gentleman or lady concerned in it deserved. But at last your uncle was forced to yield, and instead of being allowed to be of use to his niece, was forced to put up with only having the probable credit of it, which went sorely against the grain; and I really believe your letter this morning gave him great pleasure, because it required an explanation that would rob him of his borrowed feathers, and give the praise where it was due. But, Lizzy, this must go no farther than yourself, or Jane at most.

"You know pretty well, I suppose, what has been done for the young people. His debts are to be paid, amounting, I believe, to considerably more than a thousand pounds, another thousand in addition to her own settled upon her, and his commission purchased. The reason why all this was to be done by him alone, was such as I have given above. It was owing to him, to his reserve and want of proper consideration, that Wickham's character had been so misunderstood, and consequently that he had been received and noticed as he was. Perhaps there was some truth in this; though I doubt whether his reserve, or anybody's reserve, can be answerable for the event. But in spite of all this fine talking, my dear Lizzy, you may rest perfectly assured that your uncle would never have yielded, if we had not given him credit for another interest in the affair.

"When all this was resolved on, he returned again to his friends, who were still staying at Pemberley; but it was agreed that he should be in London once more when the wedding took place, and all money matters were then to receive the last finish.

"I believe I have now told you every thing. It is a relation which you tell me is to give you great surprise; I hope at least it will not afford you any displeasure. Lydia came to us; and Wickham had constant admission to the house. He was exactly what he had been when I knew him in Hertfordshire; but I would not tell you how little I was satisfied with her behaviour while she staid with us, if I had not perceived, by Jane's letter last Wednesday, that her conduct on coming home was exactly of a piece with it, and therefore what I now tell you can give you no fresh pain. I talked to her repeatedly in the most serious manner, representing to her all the wickedness of what she had done, and all the unhappiness she had brought on her family. If she heard me, it was by good luck, for I am sure she did not listen. I was sometimes quite provoked, but then I recollected my dear Elizabeth and Jane, and for their sakes had patience with her.

"Mr. Darcy was punctual in his return, and as Lydia informed you, attended the wedding. He dined with us the next day, and was to leave town again on Wednesday or Thursday. Will you be very angry with me, my dear Lizzy, if I take this opportunity of saying (what I was never bold enough to say before) how much I like him. His behaviour to us has, in every respect, been as pleasing as when we were in Derbyshire. His understanding and opinions all please me; he wants nothing but a little more liveliness, and that, if he marry prudently, his wife may teach him. I thought him very sly;—he hardly ever mentioned your name. But slyness seems the fashion.

"Pray forgive me if I have been very presuming, or at least do not punish me so far as to exclude me from P. I shall never be quite happy till I have been all round the park. A low phaeton, with a nice little pair of ponies, would be the very thing.

"But I must write no more. The children have been wanting me this half hour. Your's, very sincerely,

M. GARDINER."

The contents of this letter threw Elizabeth into a flutter of spirits, in which it was difficult to determine whether pleasure or pain bore the greatest share. The vague and unsettled suspicions which uncertainty had produced of what Mr. Darcy might have been doing to forward her sister's match, which she had feared to encourage as an exertion of goodness too great to be probable, and at the same time dreaded to be just, from the pain of obligation, were proved beyond their greatest extent to be true! He had followed them purposely to town, he had taken on himself all the trouble and mortification attendant on such a research; in which supplication had been necessary to a woman whom he must abominate and despise, and where he was reduced to meet, frequently meet, reason with, persuade, and finally bribe, the man whom he always most wished to avoid, and whose very name it was punishment to him to pronounce. He had done all this for a girl whom he could neither regard nor esteem. Her heart did whisper that he had done it for her. But it was a hope shortly checked by other considerations, and she soon felt that even her vanity was insufficient, when required to depend on his affection for her—for a woman who had already refused him—as able to overcome a sentiment so natural as abhorrence against relationship with Wickham. Brother-in-law of Wickham! Every kind of pride must revolt from the connection. He had, to be sure, done much. She was ashamed to think how much. But he had given a reason for his interference, which asked no extraordinary stretch of belief. It was reasonable that he should feel he had been wrong; he had liberality, and he had the means of exercising it; and though she would not place herself as his principal inducement, she could, perhaps, believe that remaining partiality for her might assist his endeavours in a cause where her peace of mind must be materially concerned. It was painful, exceedingly painful, to know that they were under obligations to a person who could never receive a return. They owed the restoration of Lydia, her character, every thing, to him. Oh! how heartily did she grieve over every ungracious sensation she had ever encouraged, every saucy speech she had ever directed towards him. For herself she was humbled; but she was proud of him. Proud that in a cause of compassion and honour, he had been able to get the better of himself. She read over her aunt's commendation of him again and again. It was hardly enough; but it pleased her. She was even sensible of some pleasure, though mixed with regret, on finding how steadfastly both she and her uncle had been persuaded that affection and confidence subsisted between Mr. Darcy and herself.

She was roused from her seat, and her reflections, by some one's approach; and before she could strike into another path, she was overtaken by Wickham.

"I am afraid I interrupt your solitary ramble, my dear sister?" said he, as he joined her.

"You certainly do," she replied with a smile; "but it does not follow that the interruption must be unwelcome."

"I should be sorry indeed, if it were. We were always good friends; and now we are better."

"True. Are the others coming out?"

"I do not know. Mrs. Bennet and Lydia are going in the carriage to Meryton. And so, my dear sister, I find, from our uncle and aunt, that you have actually seen Pemberley."

She replied in the affirmative.

"I almost envy you the pleasure, and yet I believe it would be too much for me, or else I could take it in my way to Newcastle. And you saw the old housekeeper, I suppose? Poor Reynolds, she was always very fond of me. But of course she did not mention my name to you."

"Yes, she did."

"And what did she say?"

"That you were gone into the army, and she was afraid had—not turned out well. At such a distance as that, you know, things are strangely misrepresented."

"Certainly," he replied, biting his lips. Elizabeth hoped she had silenced him; but he soon afterwards said,

"I was surprised to see Darcy in town last month. We passed each other several times. I wonder what he can be doing there."

"Perhaps preparing for his marriage with Miss de Bourgh," said Elizabeth. "It must be something particular, to take him there at this time of year."

"Undoubtedly. Did you see him while you were at Lambton? I thought I understood from the Gardiners that you had."

"Yes; he introduced us to his sister."

"And do you like her?"

"Very much."

"I have heard, indeed, that she is uncommonly improved within this year or two. When I last saw her, she was not very promising. I am very glad you liked her. I hope she will turn out well."

"I dare say she will; she has got over the most trying age."

"Did you go by the village of Kympton?"

"I do not recollect that we did."

"I mention it, because it is the living which I ought to have had. A most delightful place!—Excellent Parsonage House! It would have suited me in every respect."

"How should you have liked making sermons?"

"Exceedingly well. I should have considered it as part of my duty, and the exertion would soon have been nothing. One ought not to repine;—but, to be sure, it would have been such a thing for me! The quiet, the retirement of such a life would have answered all my ideas of happiness! But it was not to be. Did you ever hear Darcy mention the circumstance, when you were in Kent?"

"I have heard from authority, which I thought as good, that it was left you conditionally only, and at the will of the present patron."

"You have. Yes, there was something in that; I told you so from the first, you may remember."

"I did hear, too, that there was a time, when sermon-making was not so palatable to you as it seems to be at present; that you actually declared your resolution of never taking orders, and that the business had been compromised accordingly."

"You did! and it was not wholly without foundation. You may remember what I told you on that point, when first we talked of it."

They were now almost at the door of the house, for she had walked fast to get rid of him; and unwilling, for her sister's sake, to provoke him, she only said in reply, with a good-humoured smile,

"Come, Mr. Wickham, we are brother and sister, you know. Do not let us quarrel about the past. In future, I hope we shall be always of one mind."

She held out her hand; he kissed it with affectionate gallantry, though he hardly knew how to look, and they entered the house.

Chapter 53

MR. Wickham was so perfectly satisfied with this conversation that he never again distressed himself, or provoked his dear sister Elizabeth, by introducing the subject of it; and she was pleased to find that she had said enough to keep him quiet.

The day of his and Lydia's departure soon came, and Mrs. Bennet was forced to submit to a separation, which, as her husband by no means entered into her scheme of their all going to Newcastle, was likely to continue at least a twelvemonth.

"Oh! my dear Lydia," she cried, "when shall we meet again?"

"Oh, lord! I don't know. Not these two or three years, perhaps."

"Write to me very often, my dear."

"As often as I can. But you know married women have never much time for writing. My sisters may write to me. They will have nothing else to do."

Mr. Wickham's adieus were much more affectionate than his wife's. He smiled, looked handsome, and said many pretty things.

"He is as fine a fellow," said Mr. Bennet, as soon as they were out of the house, "as ever I saw. He simpers, and smirks, and makes love to us all. I am prodigiously proud of him. I defy even Sir William Lucas himself to produce a more valuable son-in-law."

The loss of her daughter made Mrs. Bennet very dull for several days.

"I often think," said she, "that there is nothing so bad as parting with one's friends. One seems so forlorn without them."

"This is the consequence, you see, Madam, of marrying a daughter," said Elizabeth. "It must make you better satisfied that your other four are single."

"It is no such thing. Lydia does not leave me because she is married, but only because her husband's regiment happens to be so far off. If that had been nearer, she would not have gone so soon."

But the spiritless condition which this event threw her into was shortly relieved, and her mind opened again to the agitation of hope, by an article of news which then began to be in circulation. The housekeeper at Netherfield had received orders to prepare for the arrival of her master, who was coming down in a day or two, to shoot there for several weeks. Mrs. Bennet was quite in the fidgets. She looked at Jane, and smiled and shook her head by turns.

"Well, well, and so Mr. Bingley is coming down, sister," (for Mrs. Phillips first brought her the news). "Well, so much the better. Not that I care about it, though. He is nothing to us, you know, and I am sure I never want to see him again. But, however, he is very welcome to come to Netherfield, if he likes it. And who knows what may happen? But that is nothing to us. You know, sister, we agreed long ago never to mention a word about it. And so, is it quite certain he is coming?"

"You may depend on it," replied the other, "for Mrs. Nicholls was in Meryton last night; I saw her passing by, and went out myself on purpose to know the truth of it; and she told me that it was certain true. He comes down on Thursday at the latest, very likely on Wednesday. She was going to the butcher's, she told me, on purpose to order in some meat on Wednesday, and she has got three couple of ducks just fit to be killed."

Miss Bennet had not been able to hear of his coming without changing colour. It was many months since she had mentioned his name to Elizabeth; but now, as soon as they were alone together, she said,

"I saw you look at me to-day, Lizzy, when my aunt told us of the present report; and I know I appeared distressed. But don't imagine it was from any silly cause. I was only confused for the moment, because I felt that I should be looked at. I do assure you that the news does not affect me either with pleasure or pain. I am glad of one thing, that he comes alone; because we shall see the less of him. Not that I am afraid of myself, but I dread other people's remarks."

Elizabeth did not know what to make of it. Had she not seen him in Derbyshire, she might have supposed him capable of coming there with no other view than what was acknowledged; but she still thought him partial to Jane, and she wavered as to the greater probability of his coming there with his friend's permission, or being bold enough to come without it.

"Yet it is hard," she sometimes thought, "that this poor man cannot come to a house which he has legally hired, without raising all this speculation! I will leave him to himself."

In spite of what her sister declared, and really believed to be her feelings in the expectation of his arrival, Elizabeth could easily perceive that her spirits were affected by it. They were more disturbed, more unequal, than she had often seen them.

The subject which had been so warmly canvassed between their parents, about a twelvemonth ago, was now brought forward again.

"As soon as ever Mr. Bingley comes, my dear," said Mrs. Bennet, "you will wait on him of course."

"No, no. You forced me into visiting him last year, and promised, if I went to see him, he should marry one of my daughters. But it ended in nothing, and I will not be sent on a fool's errand again."

His wife represented to him how absolutely necessary such an attention would be from all the neighbouring gentlemen, on his returning to Netherfield.

"'Tis an etiquette I despise," said he. "If he wants our society, let him seek it. He knows where we live. I will not spend my hours in running after my neighbours every time they go away and come back again."

"Well, all I know is, that it will be abominably rude if you do not wait on him. But, however, that shan't prevent my asking him to dine here, I am determined. We must have Mrs. Long and the Gouldings soon. That will make thirteen with ourselves, so there will be just room at table for him."

Consoled by this resolution, she was the better able to bear her husband's incivility; though it was very mortifying to know that her neighbours might all see Mr. Bingley, in consequence of it, before they did. As the day of his arrival drew near:

"I begin to be sorry that he comes at all," said Jane to her sister. "It would be nothing; I could see him with perfect indifference, but I can hardly bear to hear it thus perpetually talked of. My mother means well; but she does not know, no one can know, how much I suffer from what she says. Happy shall I be, when his stay at Netherfield is over!"

"I wish I could say any thing to comfort you," replied Elizabeth; "but it is wholly out of my power. You must feel it; and the usual satisfaction of preaching patience to a sufferer is denied me, because you have always so much."

Mr. Bingley arrived. Mrs. Bennet, through the assistance of servants, contrived to have the earliest tidings of it, that the period of anxiety and fretfulness on her side might be as long as it could. She counted the days that must intervene before their invitation could be sent; hopeless of seeing him before. But on the third morning after his arrival in Hertfordshire, she saw him, from her dressing-room window, enter the paddock and ride towards the house.

Her daughters were eagerly called to partake of her joy. Jane resolutely kept her place at the table; but Elizabeth, to satisfy her mother, went to the window—she looked,—she saw Mr. Darcy with him, and sat down again by her sister.

"There is a gentleman with him, mamma," said Kitty; "who can it be?"

"Some acquaintance or other, my dear, I suppose; I am sure I do not know."

"La!" replied Kitty, "it looks just like that man that used to be with him before. Mr. what's-his-name. That tall, proud man."

"Good gracious! Mr. Darcy!—and so it does, I vow. Well, any friend of Mr. Bingley's will always be welcome here, to be sure; but else I must say that I hate the very sight of him."

Jane looked at Elizabeth with surprise and concern. She knew but little of their meeting in Derbyshire, and therefore felt for the awkwardness which must attend her sister, in seeing him almost for the first time after receiving his explanatory letter. Both sisters were uncomfortable enough. Each felt for the other, and of course for themselves; and their mother talked on, of her dislike of Mr. Darcy, and her resolution to be civil to him only as Mr. Bingley's friend, without being heard by either of them. But Elizabeth had sources of uneasiness which could not be suspected by Jane, to whom she had never yet had courage to shew Mrs. Gardiner's letter, or to relate her own change of sentiment towards him. To Jane, he could be only a man whose proposals she had refused, and whose merit she had undervalued; but to her own more extensive information, he was the person to whom the whole family were indebted for the first of benefits, and whom she regarded herself with an interest, if not quite so tender, at least as reasonable and just as what Jane felt for Bingley. Her astonishment at his coming—at his coming to Netherfield, to Longbourn, and voluntarily seeking her again, was almost equal to what she had known on first witnessing his altered behaviour in Derbyshire.

The colour which had been driven from her face, returned for half a minute with an additional glow, and a smile of delight added lustre to her eyes, as she thought for that space of time that his affection and wishes must still be unshaken. But she would not be secure.

"Let me first see how he behaves," said she; "it will then be early enough for expectation."

She sat intently at work, striving to be composed, and without daring to lift up her eyes, till anxious curiosity carried them to the face of her sister as the servant was approaching the door. Jane looked a little paler than usual, but more sedate than Elizabeth had expected. On the gentlemen's appearing, her colour increased; yet she received them with tolerable ease, and with a propriety of behaviour equally free from any symptom of resentment or any unnecessary complaisance.

Elizabeth said as little to either as civility would allow, and sat down again to her work, with an eagerness which it did not often command. She had ventured only one glance at Darcy. He looked serious, as usual; and, she thought, more as he had been used to look in Hertfordshire, than as she had seen him at Pemberley. But, perhaps he could not in her mother's presence be what he was before her uncle and aunt. It was a painful, but not an improbable, conjecture.

Bingley, she had likewise seen for an instant, and in that short period saw him looking both pleased and embarrassed. He was received by Mrs. Bennet with a degree of civility which made her two daughters ashamed, especially when contrasted with the cold and ceremonious politeness of her curtsey and address to his friend.

Elizabeth, particularly, who knew that her mother owed to the latter the preservation of her favourite daughter from irremediable infamy, was hurt and distressed to a most painful degree by a distinction so ill applied.

Darcy, after enquiring of her how Mr. and Mrs. Gardiner did, a question which she could not answer without confusion, said scarcely any thing. He was not seated by her; perhaps that was the reason of his silence; but it had not been so in Derbyshire. There he had talked to her friends, when he could not to herself. But now several minutes elapsed without bringing the sound of his voice; and when occasionally, unable to resist the impulse of curiosity, she raised he eyes to his face, she as often found him looking at Jane as at herself, and frequently on no object but the ground. More thoughtfulness and less anxiety to please, than when they last met, were plainly expressed. She was disappointed, and angry with herself for being so.

"Could I expect it to be otherwise!" said she. "Yet why did he come?"

She was in no humour for conversation with any one but himself; and to him she had hardly courage to speak.

She enquired after his sister, but could do no more.

"It is a long time, Mr. Bingley, since you went away," said Mrs. Bennet.

He readily agreed to it. "I began to be afraid you would never come back again. People did say you meant to quit the place entirely at

Michaelmas; but, however, I hope it is not true. A great many changes have happened in the neighbourhood, since you went away. Miss Lucas is married and settled. And one of my own daughters. I suppose you have heard of it; indeed, you must have seen it in the papers. It was in the Times and the Courier, I know; though it was not put in as it ought to be. It was only said, "Lately, George Wickham, Esq. to Miss Lydia Bennet," without there being a syllable said of her father, or the place where she lived, or any thing. It was my brother Gardiner's drawing up too, and I wonder how he came to make such an awkward business of it. Did you see it?"

Bingley replied that he did, and made his congratulations. Elizabeth dared not lift up her eyes. How Mr. Darcy looked, therefore, she could not tell.

"It is a delightful thing, to be sure, to have a daughter well married," continued her mother, "but at the same time, Mr. Bingley, it is very hard to have her taken such a way from me. They are gone down to Newcastle, a place quite northward, it seems, and there they are to stay I do not know how long. His regiment is there; for I suppose you have heard of his leaving the ______shire, and of his being gone into the regulars. Thank Heaven! he has some friends, though perhaps not so many as he deserves."

Elizabeth, who knew this to be levelled at Mr. Darcy, was in such misery of shame, that she could hardly keep her seat. It drew from her, however, the exertion of speaking, which nothing else had so effectually done before; and she asked Bingley whether he meant to make any stay in the country at present. A few weeks, he believed.

"When you have killed all your own birds, Mr. Bingley," said her mother, "I beg you will come here, and shoot as many as you please on Mr. Bennet's manor. I am sure he will be vastly happy to oblige you, and will save all the best of the covies for you."

Elizabeth's misery increased, at such unnecessary, such officious attention! Were the same fair prospect to arise at present as had flattered them a year ago, every thing, she was persuaded, would be hastening to the same vexatious conclusion. At that instant, she felt that years of happiness could not make Jane or herself amends for moments of such painful confusion.

"The first wish of my heart," said she to herself, "is never more to be in company with either of them. Their society can afford no pleasure that will atone for such wretchedness as this! Let me never see either one or the other again!"

Yet the misery, for which years of happiness were to offer no compensation, received soon afterwards material relief, from observing how much the beauty of her sister re-kindled the admiration of her former lover. When first he came in, he had spoken to her but little; but every five minutes seemed to be giving her more of his attention. He found her as handsome as she had been last year; as good natured, and as unaffected, though not quite so chatty. Jane was anxious that no difference should be perceived in her at all, and was really persuaded that she talked as much as ever. But her mind was so busily engaged, that she did not always know when she was silent.

When the gentlemen rose to go away, Mrs. Bennet was mindful of her intended civility, and they were invited and engaged to dine at Longbourn in a few days time.

"You are quite a visit in my debt, Mr. Bingley," she added, "for when you went to town last winter, you promised to take a family dinner with us, as soon as you returned. I have not forgot, you see; and I assure you, I was very much disappointed that you did not come back and keep your engagement."

Bingley looked a little silly at this reflection, and said something of his concern at having been prevented by business. They then went away.

Mrs. Bennet had been strongly inclined to ask them to stay and dine there that day; but, though she always kept a very good table, she did not think any thing less than two courses could be good enough for a man on whom she had such anxious designs, or satisfy the appetite and pride of one who had ten thousand a year.

Chapter 54

As soon as they were gone, Elizabeth walked out to recover her spirits; or in other words, to dwell without interruption on those subjects that must deaden them more. Mr. Darcy's behaviour astonished and vexed her.

"Why, if he came only to be silent, grave, and indifferent," said she, "did he come at all?"

She could settle it in no way that gave her pleasure.

"He could be still amiable, still pleasing, to my uncle and aunt, when he was in town; and why not to me? If he fears me, why come hither? If he no longer cares for me, why silent? Teazing, teazing, man! I will think no more about him."

Her resolution was for a short time involuntarily kept by the approach of her sister, who joined her with a cheerful look, which shewed her better satisfied with their visitors, than Elizabeth.

"Now," said she, "that this first meeting is over, I feel perfectly easy. I know my own strength, and I shall never be embarrassed again by his coming. I am glad he dines here on Tuesday. It will then be publicly seen that, on both sides, we meet only as common and indifferent acquaintance."

"Yes, very indifferent indeed," said Elizabeth, laughingly. "Oh, Jane, take care."

"My dear Lizzy, you cannot think me so weak, as to be in danger now?"

"I think you are in very great danger of making him as much in love with you as ever."

They did not see the gentlemen again till Tuesday; and Mrs. Bennet, in the meanwhile, was giving way to all the happy schemes, which the good humour and common politeness of Bingley, in half an hour's visit, had revived.

On Tuesday there was a large party assembled at Longbourn; and the two who were most anxiously expected, to the credit of their punctuality as sportsmen, were in very good time. When they repaired to the dining-room, Elizabeth eagerly watched to see whether Bingley would take the place, which, in all their former parties, had belonged to him, by her sister. Her prudent mother, occupied by the same ideas, forbore to invite him to sit by herself. On entering the room, he seemed to hesitate; but Jane happened to look round, and happened to smile: it was decided. He placed himself by her.

Elizabeth, with a triumphant sensation, looked towards his friend. He bore it with noble indifference, and she would have imagined that Bingley had received his sanction to be happy, had she not seen his eyes likewise turned towards Mr. Darcy, with an expression of half-laughing alarm.

His behaviour to her sister was such, during dinner time, as shewed an admiration of her, which, though more guarded than formerly, persuaded Elizabeth, that if left wholly to himself, Jane's happiness, and his own, would be speedily secured. Though she dared not depend upon the consequence, she yet received pleasure from observing his behaviour. It gave her all the animation that her spirits could boast; for she was in no cheerful humour. Mr. Darcy was almost as far from her as the table could divide them. He was on one side of her mother. She knew how little such a situation would give pleasure to either, or make either appear to advantage. She was not near enough to hear any of their discourse, but she could see how seldom they spoke to each other, and how formal and cold was their manner whenever they did. Her mother's ungraciousness, made the sense of what they owed him more painful to Elizabeth's mind; and she would, at times, have given any thing to be privileged to tell him that his kindness was neither unknown nor unfelt by the whole of the family.

She was in hopes that the evening would afford some opportunity of bringing them together; that the whole of the visit would not pass away without enabling them to enter into something more of conversation than the mere ceremonious salutation attending his entrance. Anxious and uneasy, the period which passed in the drawing-room, before the gentlemen came, was wearisome and dull to a degree that almost made her uncivil. She looked forward to their entrance as the point on which all her chance of pleasure for the evening must depend.

"If he does not come to me, then," said she, "I shall give him up for ever."

The gentlemen came; and she thought he looked as if he would have answered her hopes; but, alas! the ladies had crowded round the table, where Miss Bennet was making tea, and Elizabeth pouring out the coffee, in so close a confederacy that there was not a single vacancy near her which would admit of a chair. And on the gentlemen's approaching, one of the girls moved closer to her than ever, and said, in a whisper,

"The men shan't come and part us, I am determined. We want none of them; do we?"

Darcy had walked away to another part of the room. She followed him with her eyes, envied every one to whom he spoke, had scarcely patience enough to help anybody to coffee; and then was enraged against herself for being so silly!

"A man who has once been refused! How could I ever be foolish enough to expect a renewal of his love? Is there one among the sex, who would not protest against such a weakness as a second proposal to the same woman? There is no indignity so abhorrent to their feelings!"

She was a little revived, however, by his bringing back his coffee cup himself; and she seized the opportunity of saying,

"Is your sister at Pemberley still?"

"Yes, she will remain there till Christmas."

"And quite alone? Have all her friends left her?"

"Mrs. Annesley is with her. The others have been gone on to Scarborough, these three weeks."

She could think of nothing more to say; but if he wished to converse with her, he might have better success. He stood by her, however, for some minutes, in silence; and, at last, on the young lady's whispering to Elizabeth again, he walked away.

When the tea-things were removed, and the card tables placed, the ladies all rose, and Elizabeth was then hoping to be soon joined by him, when all her views were overthrown by seeing him fall a victim to her mother's rapacity for whist players, and in a few moments after seated with the rest of the party. She now lost every expectation of pleasure. They were confined for the evening at different tables, and she had nothing to hope, but that his eyes were so often turned towards her side of the room, as to make him play as unsuccessfully as herself.

Mrs. Bennet had designed to keep the two Netherfield gentlemen to supper; but their carriage was unluckily ordered before any of the others, and she had no opportunity of detaining them.

"Well girls," said she, as soon as they were left to themselves, "What say you to the day? I think every thing has passed off uncommonly well, I assure you. The dinner was as well dressed as any I ever saw. The venison was roasted to a turn—and everybody said they never saw so fat a haunch. The soup was fifty times better than what we had at the Lucases' last week; and even Mr. Darcy acknowledged, that the partridges were remarkably well done; and I suppose he has two or three French cooks at least. And, my dear Jane, I never saw you look in greater beauty. Mrs. Long said so too, for I asked her whether you did not. And what do you think she said besides? "Ah! Mrs. Bennet, we shall have her at Netherfield at last." She did indeed. I do think Mrs. Long is as good a creature as ever lived—and her nieces are very pretty behaved girls, and not at all handsome: I like them prodigiously."

Mrs. Bennet, in short, was in very great spirits; she had seen enough of Bingley's behaviour to Jane, to be convinced that she would get him at last; and her expectations of advantage to her family, when in a happy humour, were so far beyond reason, that she was quite disappointed at not seeing him there again the next day, to make his proposals.

"It has been a very agreeable day," said Miss Bennet to Elizabeth. "The party seemed so well selected, so suitable one with the other. I hope we may often meet again."

Elizabeth smiled.

"Lizzy, you must not do so. You must not suspect me. It mortifies me. I assure you that I have now learnt to enjoy his conversation as an agreeable and sensible young man, without having a wish beyond it. I am perfectly satisfied, from what his manners now are, that he never had any design of engaging my affection. It is only that he is blessed with greater sweetness of address, and a stronger desire of generally pleasing, than any other man."

"You are very cruel," said her sister, "you will not let me smile, and are provoking me to it every moment."

"How hard it is in some cases to be believed!"

"And how impossible in others!"

"But why should you wish to persuade me that I feel more than I acknowledge?"

"That is a question which I hardly know how to answer. We all love to instruct, though we can teach only what is not worth knowing. Forgive me; and if you persist in indifference, do not make me your confidante."

Chapter 55

A few days after this visit, Mr. Bingley called again, and alone. His friend had left him that morning for London, but was to return home in ten days time. He sat with them above an hour, and was in remarkably good spirits. Mrs. Bennet invited him to dine with them; but, with many expressions of concern, he confessed himself engaged elsewhere.

"Next time you call," said she, "I hope we shall be more lucky."

He should be particularly happy at any time, etc. etc.; and if she would give him leave, would take an early opportunity of waiting on them.

"Can you come to-morrow?"

Yes, he had no engagement at all for to-morrow; and her invitation was accepted with alacrity.

He came, and in such very good time that the ladies were none of them dressed. In ran Mrs. Bennet to her daughter's room, in her dressing gown, and with her hair half finished, crying out, "My dear Jane, make haste and hurry down. He is come—Mr. Bingley is come.—He is, indeed. Make haste, make haste. Here, Sarah, come to Miss Bennet this moment, and help her on with her gown. Never mind Miss Lizzy's hair."

"We will be down as soon as we can," said Jane; "but I dare say Kitty is forwarder than either of us, for she went up stairs half an hour ago."

"Oh! hang Kitty! what has she to do with it? Come be quick, be quick! Where is your sash, my dear?"

But when her mother was gone, Jane would not be prevailed on to go down without one of her sisters.

The same anxiety to get them by themselves was visible again in the evening. After tea, Mr. Bennet retired to the library, as was his custom, and Mary went up stairs to her instrument. Two obstacles of the five being thus removed, Mrs. Bennet sat looking and winking at Elizabeth and Catherine for a considerable time, without making any impression on them. Elizabeth would not observe her; and when at last Kitty did, she very innocently said, "What is the matter mamma? What do you keep winking at me for? What am I to do?"

"Nothing child, nothing. I did not wink at you."

She then sat still five minutes longer; but unable to waste such a precious occasion, she suddenly got up, and saying to Kitty, "Come here, my love, I want to speak to you," took her out of the room. Jane instantly gave a look at Elizabeth which spoke her distress at such premeditation, and her intreaty that she would not give in to it.

In a few minutes, Mrs. Bennet half-opened the door and called out, "Lizzy, my dear, I want to speak with you."

Elizabeth was forced to go. "We may as well leave them by themselves you know;" said her mother, as soon as she was in the hall. "Kitty and I are going up stairs to sit in my dressing room."

Elizabeth made no attempt to reason with her mother, but remained quietly in the hall, till she and Kitty were out of sight, then returned into the drawing room.

Mrs. Bennet's schemes for this day were ineffectual. Bingley was every thing that was charming, except the professed lover of her daughter. His ease and cheerfulness rendered him a most agreeable addition to their evening party; and he bore with the ill-judged officiousness of the mother, and heard all her silly remarks with a forbearance and command of countenance particularly grateful to the daughter.

He scarcely needed an invitation to stay supper; and before he went away, an engagement was formed, chiefly through his own and Mrs. Bennet's means, for his coming next morning to shoot with her husband.

After this day, Jane said no more of her indifference. Not a word passed between the sisters concerning Bingley; but Elizabeth went to bed in the happy belief that all must speedily be concluded, unless Mr. Darcy returned within the stated time. Seriously, however, she felt tolerably persuaded that all this must have taken place with that gentleman's concurrence.

Bingley was punctual to his appointment; and he and Mr. Bennet spent the morning together, as had been agreed on. The latter was much more agreeable than his companion expected. There was nothing of presumption or folly in Bingley that could provoke his ridicule, or disgust him into silence; and he was more communicative, and less eccentric, than the other had ever seen him. Bingley of course returned with him to dinner; and in the evening Mrs. Bennet's invention was again at work to get every body away from him and her daughter. Elizabeth, who had a letter to write, went into the breakfast room for that purpose soon after tea; for as the others were all going to sit down to cards, she could not be wanted to counteract her mother's schemes.

But on returning to the drawing room, when her letter was finished, she saw, to her infinite surprise, there was reason to fear that her mother had been too ingenious for her. On opening the door, she perceived her sister and Bingley standing together over the hearth, as if engaged in earnest conversation; and had this led to no suspicion, the faces of both, as they hastily turned round and moved away from each other, would have told it all. Their situation was awkward enough; but her's she thought was still worse. Not a syllable was uttered by either;

and Elizabeth was on the point of going away again, when Bingley, who as well as the other had sat down, suddenly rose, and whispering a few words to her sister, ran out of the room.

Jane could have no reserves from Elizabeth, where confidence would give pleasure; and instantly embracing her, acknowledged, with the liveliest emotion, that she was the happiest creature in the world.

"'Tis too much!" she added, "by far too much. I do not deserve it. Oh! why is not every body as happy?"

Elizabeth's congratulations were given with a sincerity, a warmth, a delight, which words could but poorly express. Every sentence of kindness was a fresh source of happiness to Jane. But she would not allow herself to stay with her sister, or say half that remained to be said for the present.

"I must go instantly to my mother;" she cried. "I would not on any account trifle with her affectionate solicitude; or allow her to hear it from any one but myself. He is gone to my father already. Oh! Lizzy, to know that what I have to relate will give such pleasure to all my dear family! how shall I bear so much happiness!"

She then hastened away to her mother, who had purposely broken up the card party, and was sitting up stairs with Kitty.

Elizabeth, who was left by herself, now smiled at the rapidity and ease with which an affair was finally settled, that had given them so many previous months of suspense and vexation.

"And this," said she, "is the end of all his friend's anxious circumspection! of all his sister's falsehood and contrivance! the happiest, wisest, most reasonable end!"

In a few minutes she was joined by Bingley, whose conference with her father had been short and to the purpose.

"Where is your sister?" said he hastily, as he opened the door.

"With my mother up stairs. She will be down in a moment, I dare say."

He then shut the door, and, coming up to her, claimed the good wishes and affection of a sister. Elizabeth honestly and heartily expressed her delight in the prospect of their relationship. They shook hands with great cordiality; and then, till her sister came down, she had to listen to all he had to say of his own happiness, and of Jane's perfections; and in spite of his being a lover, Elizabeth really believed all his expectations of felicity to be rationally founded, because they had for basis the excellent understanding, and super-excellent disposition of Jane, and a general similarity of feeling and taste between her and himself.

It was an evening of no common delight to them all; the satisfaction of Miss Bennet's mind gave a glow of such sweet animation to her face, as made her look handsomer than ever. Kitty simpered and smiled, and hoped her turn was coming soon. Mrs. Bennet could not give her consent or speak her approbation in terms warm enough to satisfy her feelings, though she talked to Bingley of nothing else for half an hour; and when Mr. Bennet joined them at supper, his voice and manner plainly shewed how really happy he was.

Not a word, however, passed his lips in allusion to it, till their visitor took his leave for the night; but as soon as he was gone, he turned to his daughter, and said,

"Jane, I congratulate you. You will be a very happy woman."

Jane went to him instantly, kissed him, and thanked him for his goodness.

"You are a good girl;" he replied, "and I have great pleasure in thinking you will be so happily settled. I have not a doubt of your doing very well together. Your tempers are by no means unlike. You are each of you so complying, that nothing will ever be resolved on; so easy, that every servant will cheat you; and so generous, that you will always exceed your income."

"I hope not so. Imprudence or thoughtlessness in money matters would be unpardonable in me."

"Exceed their income! My dear Mr. Bennet," cried his wife, "what are you talking of? Why, he has four or five thousand a year, and very likely more." Then addressing her daughter, "Oh! my dear, dear Jane, I am so happy! I am sure I shan't get a wink of sleep all night. I knew how it would be. I always said it must be so, at last. I was sure you could not be so beautiful for nothing! I remember, as soon as ever I saw him, when he first came into Hertfordshire last year, I thought how likely it was that you should come together. Oh! he is the handsomest young man that ever was seen!"

Wickham, Lydia, were all forgotten. Jane was beyond competition her favourite child. At that moment, she cared for no other. Her younger sisters soon began to make interest with her for objects of happiness which she might in future be able to dispense.

Mary petitioned for the use of the library at Netherfield; and Kitty begged very hard for a few balls there every winter.

Bingley, from this time, was of course a daily visitor at Longbourn; coming frequently before breakfast, and always remaining till after supper; unless when some barbarous neighbour, who could not be enough detested, had given him an invitation to dinner which he thought himself obliged to accept.

Elizabeth had now but little time for conversation with her sister; for while he was present, Jane had no attention to bestow on any one else; but she found herself considerably useful to both of them in those hours of separation that must sometimes occur. In the absence of Jane, he always attached himself to Elizabeth, for the pleasure of talking of her; and when Bingley was gone, Jane constantly sought the same means of relief.

"He has made me so happy," said she, one evening, "by telling me that he was totally ignorant of my being in town last spring! I had not believed it possible."

"I suspected as much," replied Elizabeth. "But how did he account for it?"

"It must have been his sister's doing. They were certainly no friends to his acquaintance with me, which I cannot wonder at, since he might have chosen so much more advantageously in many respects. But when they see, as I trust they will, that their brother is happy with me, they will learn to be contented, and we shall be on good terms again; though we can never be what we once were to each other."

"That is the most unforgiving speech," said Elizabeth, "that I ever heard you utter. Good girl! It would vex me, indeed, to see you again the dupe of Miss Bingley's pretended regard."

"Would you believe it, Lizzy, that when he went to town last November, he really loved me, and nothing but a persuasion of my being indifferent would have prevented his coming down again!"

"He made a little mistake to be sure; but it is to the credit of his modesty."

This naturally introduced a panegyric from Jane on his diffidence, and the little value he put on his own good qualities.

Elizabeth was pleased to find that he had not betrayed the interference of his friend; for, though Jane had the most generous and forgiving heart in the world, she knew it was a circumstance which must prejudice her against him.

"I am certainly the most fortunate creature that ever existed!" cried Jane. "Oh! Lizzy, why am I thus singled from my family, and blessed above them all! If I could but see you as happy! If there were but such another man for you!"

"If you were to give me forty such men, I never could be so happy as you. Till I have your disposition, your goodness, I never can have your happiness. No, no, let me shift for myself; and, perhaps, if I have very good luck, I may meet with another Mr. Collins in time."

The situation of affairs in the Longbourn family could not be long a secret. Mrs. Bennet was privileged to whisper it to Mrs. Philips, and she ventured, without any permission, to do the same by all her neighbours in Meryton.

The Bennets were speedily pronounced to be the luckiest family in the world, though only a few weeks before, when Lydia had first run away, they had been generally proved to be marked out for misfortune.

Chapter 56

ONE morning, about a week after Bingley's engagement with Jane had been formed, as he and the females of the family were sitting together in the dining room, their attention was suddenly drawn to the window, by the sound of a carriage; and they perceived a chaise and four driving up the lawn. It was too early in the morning for visitors, and besides, the equipage did not answer to that of any of their neighbours. The horses were post; and neither the carriage, nor the livery of the servant who preceded it, were familiar to them. As it was certain, however, that somebody was coming, Bingley instantly prevailed on Miss Bennet to avoid the confinement of such an intrusion, and walk away with him into the shrubbery. They both set off, and the conjectures of the remaining three continued, though with little satisfaction, till the door was thrown open and their visitor entered. It was Lady Catherine de Bourgh.

They were of course all intending to be surprised; but their astonishment was beyond their expectation; and on the part of Mrs. Bennet and Kitty, though she was perfectly unknown to them, even inferior to what Elizabeth felt.

She entered the room with an air more than usually ungracious, made no other reply to Elizabeth's salutation than a slight inclination of the head, and sat down without saying a word. Elizabeth had mentioned her name to her mother on her ladyship's entrance, though no request of introduction had been made.

Mrs. Bennet, all amazement, though flattered by having a guest of such high importance, received her with the utmost politeness. After sitting for a moment in silence, she said very stiffly to Elizabeth,

"I hope you are well, Miss Bennet. That lady, I suppose, is your mother."

Elizabeth replied very concisely that she was.

"And that I suppose is one of your sisters."

"Yes, madam," said Mrs. Bennet, delighted to speak to a Lady Catherine. "She is my youngest girl but one. My youngest of all is lately married, and my eldest is somewhere about the grounds, walking with a young man who, I believe, will soon become a part of the family."

"You have a very small park here," returned Lady Catherine after a short silence.

"It is nothing in comparison of Rosings, my lady, I dare say; but I assure you it is much larger than Sir William Lucas's."

"This must be a most inconvenient sitting room for the evening, in summer; the windows are full west."

Mrs. Bennet assured her that they never sat there after dinner, and then added,

"May I take the liberty of asking your ladyship whether you left Mr. and Mrs. Collins well."

"Yes, very well. I saw them the night before last."

Elizabeth now expected that she would produce a letter for her from Charlotte, as it seemed the only probable motive for her calling. But no letter appeared, and she was completely puzzled.

Mrs. Bennet, with great civility, begged her ladyship to take some refreshment; but Lady Catherine very resolutely, and not very politely, declined eating any thing; and then, rising up, said to Elizabeth,

"Miss Bennet, there seemed to be a prettyish kind of a little wilderness on one side of your lawn. I should be glad to take a turn in it, if you will favour me with your company."

"Go, my dear," cried her mother, "and shew her ladyship about the different walks. I think she will be pleased with the hermitage."

Elizabeth obeyed, and running into her own room for her parasol, attended her noble guest down stairs. As they passed through the hall, Lady Catherine opened the doors into the dining-parlour and drawing-room, and pronouncing them, after a short survey, to be decent looking rooms, walked on.

Her carriage remained at the door, and Elizabeth saw that her waiting-woman was in it. They proceeded in silence along the gravel walk that led to the copse; Elizabeth was determined to make no effort for conversation with a woman who was now more than usually insolent and disagreeable.

"How could I ever think her like her nephew?" said she, as she looked in her face.

As soon as they entered the copse, Lady Catherine began in the following manner:—

"You can be at no loss, Miss Bennet, to understand the reason of my journey hither. Your own heart, your own conscience, must tell you why I come."

Elizabeth looked with unaffected astonishment.

"Indeed, you are mistaken, Madam. I have not been at all able to account for the honour of seeing you here."

"Miss Bennet," replied her ladyship, in an angry tone, "you ought to know, that I am not to be trifled with. But however insincere you may choose to be, you shall not find me so. My character has ever been celebrated for its sincerity and frankness, and in a cause of such moment as this, I shall certainly not depart from it. A report of a most alarming nature reached me two days ago. I was told that not only your sister was on the point of being most advantageously married, but that you, that Miss Elizabeth Bennet, would, in all likelihood, be soon afterwards united to my nephew, my own nephew, Mr. Darcy. Though I know it must be a scandalous falsehood, though I would not injure him so much as to suppose the truth of it possible, I instantly resolved on setting off for this place, that I might make my sentiments known to you."

"If you believed it impossible to be true," said Elizabeth, colouring with astonishment and disdain, "I wonder you took the trouble of coming so far. What could your ladyship propose by it?"

"At once to insist upon having such a report universally contradicted."

"Your coming to Longbourn, to see me and my family," said Elizabeth coolly, "will be rather a confirmation of it; if, indeed, such a report is in existence."

"If! Do you then pretend to be ignorant of it? Has it not been industriously circulated by yourselves? Do you not know that such a report is spread abroad?"

"I never heard that it was."

"And can you likewise declare, that there is no foundation for it?"

"I do not pretend to possess equal frankness with your ladyship. You may ask questions which I shall not choose to answer."

"This is not to be borne. Miss Bennet, I insist on being satisfied. Has he, has my nephew, made you an offer of marriage?"

"Your ladyship has declared it to be impossible."

"It ought to be so; it must be so, while he retains the use of his reason. But your arts and allurements may, in a moment of infatuation, have made him forget what he owes to himself and to all his family. You may have drawn him in."

"If I have, I shall be the last person to confess it."

"Miss Bennet, do you know who I am? I have not been accustomed to such language as this. I am almost the nearest relation he has in the world, and am entitled to know all his dearest concerns."

"But you are not entitled to know mine; nor will such behaviour as this, ever induce me to be explicit."

"Let me be rightly understood. This match, to which you have the presumption to aspire, can never take place. No, never. Mr. Darcy is engaged to my daughter. Now what have you to say?"

"Only this; that if he is so, you can have no reason to suppose he will make an offer to me."

Lady Catherine hesitated for a moment, and then replied,

"The engagement between them is of a peculiar kind. From their infancy, they have been intended for each other. It was the favourite wish of his mother, as well as of her's. While in their cradles, we planned the union: and now, at the moment when the wishes of both sisters would be accomplished in their marriage, to be prevented by a young woman of inferior birth, of no importance in the world, and wholly unallied to the family! Do you pay no regard to the wishes of his friends? To his tacit engagement with Miss De Bourgh? Are you lost to every feeling of propriety and delicacy? Have you not heard me say that from his earliest hours he was destined for his cousin?"

"Yes, and I had heard it before. But what is that to me? If there is no other objection to my marrying your nephew, I shall certainly not be kept from it by knowing that his mother and aunt wished him to marry Miss De Bourgh. You both did as much as you could in planning the marriage. Its completion depended on others. If Mr. Darcy is neither by honour nor inclination confined to his cousin, why is not he to make another choice? And if I am that choice, why may not I accept him?"

"Because honour, decorum, prudence, nay, interest, forbid it. Yes, Miss Bennet, interest; for do not expect to be noticed by his family or friends, if you wilfully act against the inclinations of all. You will be censured, slighted, and despised, by every one connected with him. Your alliance will be a disgrace; your name will never even be mentioned by any of us."

"These are heavy misfortunes," replied Elizabeth. "But the wife of Mr. Darcy must have such extraordinary sources of happiness necessarily attached to her situation, that she could, upon the whole, have no cause to repine."

"Obstinate, headstrong girl! I am ashamed of you! Is this your gratitude for my attentions to you last spring? Is nothing due to me on that score? Let us sit down. You are to understand, Miss Bennet, that I came here with the determined resolution of carrying my purpose; nor will I be dissuaded from it. I have not been used to submit to any person's whims. I have not been in the habit of brooking disappointment."

"That will make your ladyship's situation at present more pitiable; but it will have no effect on me."

"I will not be interrupted. Hear me in silence. My daughter and my nephew are formed for each other. They are descended, on the maternal side, from the same noble line; and, on the father's, from respectable, honourable, and ancient—though untitled—families. Their fortune on both sides is splendid. They are destined for each other by the voice of every member of their respective houses; and what is to divide them? The upstart pretensions of a young woman without family, connections, or fortune. Is this to be endured! But it must not, shall not be. If you were sensible of your own good, you would not wish to quit the sphere in which you have been brought up."

"In marrying your nephew, I should not consider myself as quitting that sphere. He is a gentleman; I am a gentleman's daughter; so far we are equal."

"True. You are a gentleman's daughter. But who was your mother? Who are your uncles and aunts? Do not imagine me ignorant of their condition."

"Whatever my connections may be," said Elizabeth, "if your nephew does not object to them, they can be nothing to you."

"Tell me once for all, are you engaged to him?"

Though Elizabeth would not, for the mere purpose of obliging Lady Catherine, have answered this question, she could not but say, after a moment's deliberation, "I am not."

Lady Catherine seemed pleased.

"And will you promise me, never to enter into such an engagement?"

"I will make no promise of the kind."

"Miss Bennet I am shocked and astonished. I expected to find a more reasonable young woman. But do not deceive yourself into a belief that I will ever recede. I shall not go away till you have given me the assurance I require."

"And I certainly never shall give it. I am not to be intimidated into anything so wholly unreasonable. Your ladyship wants Mr. Darcy to marry your daughter; but would my giving you the wished-for promise make their marriage at all more probable? Supposing him to be attached to me, would my refusing to accept his hand make him wish to bestow it on his cousin? Allow me to say, Lady Catherine, that the arguments with which you have supported this extraordinary application have been as frivolous as the application was ill-judged. You have widely mistaken my character, if you think I can be worked on by such persuasions as these. How far your nephew might approve of your interference in his affairs, I cannot tell; but you have certainly no right to concern yourself in mine. I must beg, therefore, to be importuned no farther on the subject."

"Not so hasty, if you please. I have by no means done. To all the objections I have already urged, I have still another to add. I am no stranger to the particulars of your youngest sister's infamous elopement. I know it all; that the young man's marrying her was a patched-up business, at the expence of your father and uncles. And is such a girl to be my nephew's sister? Is her husband, is the son of his late father's steward, to be his brother? Heaven and earth!—of what are you thinking? Are the shades of Pemberley to be thus polluted?"

"You can now have nothing farther to say," she resentfully answered. "You have insulted me in every possible method. I must beg to return to the house."

And she rose as she spoke. Lady Catherine rose also, and they turned back. Her ladyship was highly incensed.

"You have no regard, then, for the honour and credit of my nephew! Unfeeling, selfish girl! Do you not consider that a connection with you must disgrace him in the eyes of everybody?"

"Lady Catherine, I have nothing farther to say. You know my sentiments."

"You are then resolved to have him?"

"I have said no such thing. I am only resolved to act in that manner, which will, in my own opinion, constitute my happiness, without reference to you, or to any person so wholly unconnected with me."

"It is well. You refuse, then, to oblige me. You refuse to obey the claims of duty, honour, and gratitude. You are determined to ruin him in the opinion of all his friends, and make him the contempt of the world."

"Neither duty, nor honour, nor gratitude," replied Elizabeth, "have any possible claim on me, in the present instance. No principle of either would be violated by my marriage with Mr. Darcy. And with regard to the resentment of his family, or the indignation of the world, if the former were excited by his marrying me, it would not give me one moment's concern—and the world in general would have too much sense to join in the scorn."

"And this is your real opinion! This is your final resolve! Very well. I shall now know how to act. Do not imagine, Miss Bennet, that your ambition will ever be gratified. I came to try you. I hoped to find you reasonable; but, depend upon it, I will carry my point."

In this manner Lady Catherine talked on, till they were at the door of the carriage, when, turning hastily round, she added, "I take no leave of you, Miss Bennet. I send no compliments to your mother. You deserve no such attention. I am most seriously displeased."

Elizabeth made no answer; and without attempting to persuade her ladyship to return into the house, walked quietly into it herself. She heard the carriage drive away as she proceeded up stairs. Her mother impatiently met her at the door of the dressing-room, to ask why Lady Catherine would not come in again and rest herself.

"She did not choose it," said her daughter, "she would go."

"She is a very fine-looking woman! and her calling here was prodigiously civil! for she only came, I suppose, to tell us the Collinses were well. She is on her road somewhere, I dare say, and so, passing through Meryton, thought she might as well call on you. I suppose she had nothing particular to say to you, Lizzy?"

Elizabeth was forced to give into a little falsehood here; for to acknowledge the substance of their conversation was impossible.

CHAPTER 57

The discomposure of spirits which this extraordinary visit threw Elizabeth into, could not be easily overcome; nor could she, for many hours, learn to think of it less than incessantly. Lady Catherine, it appeared, had actually taken the trouble of this journey from Rosings, for the sole purpose of breaking off her supposed engagement with Mr. Darcy. It was a rational scheme, to be sure! but from what the report of their engagement could originate, Elizabeth was at a loss to imagine; till she recollected that his being the intimate friend of Bingley, and her being the sister of Jane, was enough, at a time when the expectation of one wedding made every body eager for another, to supply the idea. She had not herself forgotten to feel that the marriage of her sister must bring them more frequently together. And her neighbours at Lucas lodge, therefore (for through their communication with the Collinses, the report, she concluded, had reached lady Catherine), had only set that down as almost certain and immediate, which she had looked forward to as possible at some future time.

In revolving Lady Catherine's expressions, however, she could not help feeling some uneasiness as to the possible consequence of her persisting in this interference. From what she had said of her resolution to prevent their marriage, it occurred to Elizabeth that she must meditate an application to her nephew; and how he might take a similar representation of the evils attached to a connection with her, she dared not pronounce. She knew not the exact degree of his affection for his aunt, or his dependence on her judgment, but it was natural to suppose that he thought much higher of her ladyship than she could do; and it was certain that, in enumerating the miseries of a marriage with one whose immediate connections were so unequal to his own, his aunt would address him on his weakest side. With his notions of dignity, he would probably feel that the arguments, which to Elizabeth had appeared weak and ridiculous, contained much good sense and solid reasoning.

If he had been wavering before as to what he should do, which had often seemed likely, the advice and intreaty of so near a relation might settle every doubt, and determine him at once to be as happy as dignity unblemished could make him. In that case he would return no more. Lady Catherine might see him in her way through town; and his engagement to Bingley of coming again to Netherfield must give way.

"If, therefore, an excuse for not keeping his promise should come to his friend within a few days," she added, "I shall know how to understand it. I shall then give over every expectation, every wish of his constancy. If he is satisfied with only regretting me, when he might have obtained my affections and hand, I shall soon cease to regret him at all."

The surprise of the rest of the family, on hearing who their visitor had been, was very great; but they obligingly satisfied it, with the same kind of supposition which had appeased Mrs. Bennet's curiosity; and Elizabeth was spared from much teazing on the subject.

The next morning, as she was going down stairs, she was met by her father, who came out of his library with a letter in his hand.

"Lizzy," said he, "I was going to look for you; come into my room."

She followed him thither; and her curiosity to know what he had to tell her was heightened by the supposition of its being in some manner connected with the letter he held. It suddenly struck her that it might be from Lady Catherine; and she anticipated with dismay all the consequent explanations.

She followed her father to the fire place, and they both sat down. He then said,

"I have received a letter this morning that has astonished me exceedingly. As it principally concerns yourself, you ought to know its contents. I did not know before, that I had two daughters on the brink of matrimony. Let me congratulate you on a very important conquest."

The colour now rushed into Elizabeth's cheeks in the instantaneous conviction of its being a letter from the nephew, instead of the aunt; and she was undetermined whether most to be pleased that he explained himself at all, or offended that his letter was not rather addressed to herself; when her father continued,

"You look conscious. Young ladies have great penetration in such matters as these; but I think I may defy even your sagacity, to discover the name of your admirer. This letter is from Mr. Collins."

"From Mr. Collins! and what can he have to say?"

"Something very much to the purpose of course. He begins with congratulations on the approaching nuptials of my eldest daughter, of which, it seems, he has been told by some of the good-natured, gossiping Lucases. I shall not sport with your impatience, by reading what he says on that point. What relates to yourself, is as follows." "Having thus offered you the sincere congratulations of Mrs. Collins and myself on this happy event, let me now add a short hint on the subject of another; of which we have been advertised by the same authority. Your daughter Elizabeth, it is presumed, will not long bear the name of Bennet, after her elder sister has resigned it, and the chosen partner of her fate may be reasonably looked up to as one of the most illustrious personages in this land."

"Can you possibly guess, Lizzy, who is meant by this?" "This young gentleman is blessed, in a peculiar way, with every thing the heart of mortal can most desire,—splendid property, noble kindred, and extensive patronage. Yet in spite of all these temptations, let me warn my cousin Elizabeth, and yourself, of what evils you may incur by a precipitate closure with this gentleman's proposals, which, of course, you will be inclined to take immediate advantage of."

"Have you any idea, Lizzy, who this gentleman is? But now it comes out."

"My motive for cautioning you is as follows. We have reason to imagine that his aunt, Lady Catherine de Bourgh, does not look on the match with a friendly eye."

"Mr. Darcy, you see, is the man! Now, Lizzy, I think I have surprised you. Could he, or the Lucases, have pitched on any man within the circle of our acquaintance, whose name would have given the lie more effectually to what they related? Mr. Darcy, who never looks at any woman but to see a blemish, and who probably never looked at you in his life! It is admirable!"

Elizabeth tried to join in her father's pleasantry, but could only force one most reluctant smile. Never had his wit been directed in a manner so little agreeable to her.

"Are you not diverted?"

"Oh! yes. Pray read on."

"After mentioning the likelihood of this marriage to her ladyship last night, she immediately, with her usual condescension, expressed what she felt on the occasion; when it become apparent, that on the score of some family objections on the part of my cousin, she would never give her consent to what she termed so disgraceful a match. I thought it my duty to give the speediest intelligence of this to my cousin, that she and her noble admirer may be aware of what they are about, and not run hastily into a marriage which has not been properly sanctioned." "Mr. Collins moreover adds," "I am truly rejoiced that my cousin Lydia's sad business has been so well hushed up, and am only concerned that their living together before the marriage took place should be so generally known. I must not, however, neglect the duties of my station, or refrain from declaring my amazement at hearing that you received the young couple into your house as soon as they were married. It was an encouragement of vice; and had I been the rector of Longbourn, I should very strenuously have opposed it. You ought certainly to forgive them as a Christian, but never to admit them in your sight, or allow their names to be mentioned in your hearing." "That is his notion of Christian forgiveness! The rest of his letter is only about his dear Charlotte's situation, and his expectation of a young olive-branch. But, Lizzy, you look as if you did not enjoy it. You are not going to be Missish, I hope, and pretend to be affronted at an idle report. For what do we live, but to make sport for our neighbours, and laugh at them in our turn?"

"Oh!" cried Elizabeth, "I am excessively diverted. But it is so strange!"

"Yes—that is what makes it amusing. Had they fixed on any other man it would have been nothing; but his perfect indifference, and your pointed dislike, make it so delightfully absurd! Much as I abominate writing, I would not give up Mr. Collins's correspondence for any consideration. Nay, when I read a letter of his, I cannot help giving him the preference even over Wickham, much as I value the impudence and hypocrisy of my son-in-law. And pray, Lizzy, what said Lady Catherine about this report? Did she call to refuse her consent?"

To this question his daughter replied only with a laugh; and as it had been asked without the least suspicion, she was not distressed by his repeating it. Elizabeth had never been more at a loss to make her feelings appear what they were not. It was necessary to laugh, when she would rather have cried. Her father had most cruelly mortified her, by what he said of Mr. Darcy's indifference, and she could do nothing but wonder at such a want of penetration, or fear that perhaps, instead of his seeing too little, she might have fancied too much.

Chapter 58

Instead of receiving any such letter of excuse from his friend, as Elizabeth half expected Mr. Bingley to do, he was able to bring Darcy with him to Longbourn before many days had passed after Lady Catherine's visit. The gentlemen arrived early; and, before Mrs. Bennet had time to tell him of their having seen his aunt, of which her daughter sat in momentary dread, Bingley, who wanted to be alone with Jane, proposed their all walking out. It was agreed to. Mrs. Bennet was not in the habit of walking; Mary could never spare time; but the remaining five set off together. Bingley and Jane, however, soon allowed the others to outstrip them. They lagged behind, while Elizabeth, Kitty, and Darcy were to entertain each other. Very little was said by either; Kitty was too much afraid of him to talk; Elizabeth was secretly forming a desperate resolution; and perhaps he might be doing the same.

They walked towards the Lucases, because Kitty wished to call upon Maria; and as Elizabeth saw no occasion for making it a general concern, when Kitty left them she went boldly on with him alone. Now was the moment for her resolution to be executed, and, while her courage was high, she immediately said,

"Mr. Darcy, I am a very selfish creature; and, for the sake of giving relief to my own feelings, care not how much I may be wounding your's. I can no longer help thanking you for your unexampled kindness to my poor sister. Ever since I have known it, I have been most anxious to acknowledge to you how gratefully I feel it. Were it known to the rest of my family, I should not have merely my own gratitude to express."

"I am sorry, exceedingly sorry," replied Darcy, in a tone of surprise and emotion, "that you have ever been informed of what may, in a mistaken light, have given you uneasiness. I did not think Mrs. Gardiner was so little to be trusted."

"You must not blame my aunt. Lydia's thoughtlessness first betrayed to me that you had been concerned in the matter; and, of course, I could not rest till I knew the particulars. Let me thank you again and again, in the name of all my family, for that generous compassion which induced you to take so much trouble, and bear so many mortifications, for the sake of discovering them."

"If you will thank me," he replied, "let it be for yourself alone. That the wish of giving happiness to you might add force to the other inducements which led me on, I shall not attempt to deny. But your family owe me nothing. Much as I respect them, I believe I thought only of you."

Elizabeth was too much embarrassed to say a word. After a short pause, her companion added, "You are too generous to trifle with me. If your feelings are still what they were last April, tell me so at once. My affections and wishes are unchanged, but one word from you will silence me on this subject for ever."

Elizabeth, feeling all the more than common awkwardness and anxiety of his situation, now forced herself to speak; and immediately, though not very fluently, gave him to understand that her sentiments had undergone so material a change, since the period to which he alluded, as to make her receive with gratitude and pleasure his present assurances. The happiness which this reply produced, was such as he had probably never felt before; and he expressed himself on the occasion as sensibly and as warmly as a man violently in love can be supposed to do. Had Elizabeth been able to encounter his eye, she might have seen how well the expression of heartfelt delight, diffused over his face, became him; but, though she could not look, she could listen, and he told her of feelings, which, in proving of what importance she was to him, made his affection every moment more valuable.

They walked on, without knowing in what direction. There was too much to be thought, and felt, and said, for attention to any other objects. She soon learnt that they were indebted for their present good understanding to the efforts of his aunt, who did call on him in her return through London, and there relate her journey to Longbourn, its motive, and the substance of her conversation with Elizabeth; dwelling emphatically on every expression of the latter which, in her ladyship's apprehension, peculiarly denoted her perverseness and assurance; in the belief that such a relation must assist her endeavours to obtain that promise from her nephew which she had refused to give. But, unluckily for her ladyship, its effect had been exactly contrariwise.

"It taught me to hope," said he, "as I had scarcely ever allowed myself to hope before. I knew enough of your disposition to be certain that, had you been absolutely, irrevocably decided against me, you would have acknowledged it to Lady Catherine, frankly and openly."

Elizabeth coloured and laughed as she replied, "Yes, you know enough of my frankness to believe me capable of that. After abusing you so abominably to your face, I could have no scruple in abusing you to all your relations."

"What did you say of me, that I did not deserve? For, though your accusations were ill-founded, formed on mistaken premises, my behaviour to you at the time had merited the severest reproof. It was unpardonable. I cannot think of it without abhorrence."

"We will not quarrel for the greater share of blame annexed to that evening," said Elizabeth. "The conduct of neither, if strictly examined, will be irreproachable; but since then, we have both, I hope, improved in civility."

"I cannot be so easily reconciled to myself. The recollection of what I then said, of my conduct, my manners, my expressions during the whole of it, is now, and has been many months, inexpressibly painful to me. Your reproof, so well applied, I shall never forget: ``had you behaved in a more gentleman-like manner." Those were your words. You know not, you can scarcely conceive, how they have tortured me;—though it was some time, I confess, before I was reasonable enough to allow their justice."

"I was certainly very far from expecting them to make so strong an impression. I had not the smallest idea of their being ever felt in such a way."

"I can easily believe it. You thought me then devoid of every proper feeling, I am sure you did. The turn of your countenance I shall never forget, as you said that I could not have addressed you in any possible way that would induce you to accept me."

"Oh! do not repeat what I then said. These recollections will not do at all. I assure you that I have long been most heartily ashamed of it."

Darcy mentioned his letter. "Did it," said he, "did it soon make you think better of me? Did you, on reading it, give any credit to its contents?"

She explained what its effect on her had been, and how gradually all her former prejudices had been removed.

"I knew," said he, "that what I wrote must give you pain, but it was necessary. I hope you have destroyed the letter. There was one part especially, the opening of it, which I should dread your having the power of reading again. I can remember some expressions which might justly make you hate me."

"The letter shall certainly be burnt, if you believe it essential to the preservation of my regard; but, though we have both reason to think my opinions not entirely unalterable, they are not, I hope, quite so easily changed as that implies."

"When I wrote that letter," replied Darcy, "I believed myself perfectly calm and cool, but I am since convinced that it was written in a dreadful bitterness of spirit."

"The letter, perhaps, began in bitterness, but it did not end so. The adieu is charity itself. But think no more of the letter. The feelings of the person who wrote, and the person who received it, are now so widely different from what they were then, that every unpleasant circumstance attending it ought to be forgotten. You must learn some of my philosophy. Think only of the past as its remembrance gives you pleasure."

"I cannot give you credit for any philosophy of the kind. Your retrospections must be so totally void of reproach, that the contentment arising from them is not of philosophy, but, what is much better, of innocence. But with me, it is not so. Painful recollections will intrude which cannot, which ought not, to be repelled. I have been a selfish being all my life, in practice, though not in principle. As a child I was taught what was right, but I was not taught to correct my temper. I was given good principles, but left to follow them in pride and conceit. Unfortunately an only son (for many years an only child), I was spoilt by my parents, who, though good themselves (my father, particularly, all that was benevolent and amiable), allowed, encouraged, almost taught me to be selfish and overbearing; to care for none beyond my own family circle; to think meanly of all the rest of the world; to wish at least to think meanly of their sense and worth compared with my own. Such I was, from eight to eight and twenty; and such I might still have been but for you, dearest, loveliest Elizabeth! What do I not owe you! You taught me a lesson, hard indeed at first, but most advantageous. By you, I was properly humbled. I came to you without a doubt of my reception. You shewed me how insufficient were all my pretensions to please a woman worthy of being pleased."

"Had you then persuaded yourself that I should?"

"Indeed I had. What will you think of my vanity? I believed you to be wishing, expecting my addresses."

"My manners must have been in fault, but not intentionally, I assure you. I never meant to deceive you, but my spirits might often lead me wrong. How you must have hated me after that evening?"

"Hate you! I was angry perhaps at first, but my anger soon began to take a proper direction."

"I am almost afraid of asking what you thought of me, when we met at Pemberley. You blamed me for coming?"

"No indeed; I felt nothing but surprise."

"Your surprise could not be greater than mine in being noticed by you. My conscience told me that I deserved no extraordinary politeness, and I confess that I did not expect to receive more than my due."

"My object then," replied Darcy, "was to shew you, by every civility in my power, that I was not so mean as to resent the past; and I hoped to obtain your forgiveness, to lessen your ill opinion, by letting you see that your reproofs had been attended to. How soon any other wishes introduced themselves I can hardly tell, but I believe in about half an hour after I had seen you."

He then told her of Georgiana's delight in her acquaintance, and of her disappointment at its sudden interruption; which naturally leading to the cause of that interruption, she soon learnt that his resolution of following her from Derbyshire in quest of her sister had been formed before he quitted the inn, and that his gravity and thoughtfulness there had arisen from no other struggles than what such a purpose must comprehend.

She expressed her gratitude again, but it was too painful a subject to each, to be dwelt on farther.

After walking several miles in a leisurely manner, and too busy to know any thing about it, they found at last, on examining their watches, that it was time to be at home.

"What could become of Mr. Bingley and Jane!" was a wonder which introduced the discussion of their affairs. Darcy was delighted with their engagement; his friend had given him the earliest information of it.

"I must ask whether you were surprised?" said Elizabeth.

"Not at all. When I went away, I felt that it would soon happen."

"That is to say, you had given your permission. I guessed as much." And though he exclaimed at the term, she found that it had been pretty much the case.

"On the evening before my going to London," said he, "I made a confession to him, which I believe I ought to have made long ago. I told him of all that had occurred to make my former interference in his affairs absurd and impertinent. His surprise was great. He had never had the slightest suspicion. I told him, moreover, that I believed myself mistaken in supposing, as I had done, that your sister was indifferent to him; and as I could easily perceive that his attachment to her was unabated, I felt no doubt of their happiness together."

Elizabeth could not help smiling at his easy manner of directing his friend.

"Did you speak from your own observation," said she, "when you told him that my sister loved him, or merely from my information last spring?"

"From the former. I had narrowly observed her during the two visits which I had lately made here; and I was convinced of her affection."

"And your assurance of it, I suppose, carried immediate conviction to him."

"It did. Bingley is most unaffectedly modest. His diffidence had prevented his depending on his own judgment in so anxious a case, but his reliance on mine made every thing easy. I was obliged to confess one thing, which for a time, and not unjustly, offended him. I could not allow myself to conceal that your sister had been in town three months last winter, that I had known it, and purposely kept it from him. He was angry. But his anger, I am persuaded, lasted no longer than he remained in any doubt of your sister's sentiments. He has heartily forgiven me now."

Elizabeth longed to observe that Mr. Bingley had been a most delightful friend; so easily guided that his worth was invaluable; but she checked herself. She remembered that he had yet to learn to be laughed at, and it was rather too early to begin. In anticipating the happiness of Bingley, which of course was to be inferior only to his own, he continued the conversation till they reached the house. In the hall they parted.

Chapter 59

"My dear Lizzy, where can you have been walking to?" was a question which Elizabeth received from Jane as soon as she entered their room, and from all the others when they sat down to table. She had only to say in reply, that they had wandered about, till she was beyond her own knowledge. She coloured as she spoke; but neither that, nor any thing else, awakened a suspicion of the truth.

The evening passed quietly, unmarked by any thing extraordinary. The acknowledged lovers talked and laughed, the unacknowledged were silent. Darcy was not of a disposition in which happiness overflows in mirth; and Elizabeth, agitated and confused, rather knew that she was happy than felt herself to be so; for, besides the immediate embarrassment, there were other evils before her. She anticipated what would be felt in the family when her situation became known; she was aware that no one liked him but Jane; and even feared that with the others it was a dislike which not all his fortune and consequence might do away.

At night she opened her heart to Jane. Though suspicion was very far from Miss Bennet's general habits, she was absolutely incredulous here.

"You are joking, Lizzy. This cannot be!—engaged to Mr. Darcy! No, no, you shall not deceive me. I know it to be impossible."

"This is a wretched beginning indeed! My sole dependence was on you; and I am sure nobody else will believe me, if you do not. Yet, indeed, I am in earnest. I speak nothing but the truth. He still loves me, and we are engaged."

Jane looked at her doubtingly. "Oh, Lizzy! it cannot be. I know how much you dislike him."

"You know nothing of the matter. That is all to be forgot. Perhaps I did not always love him so well as I do now. But in such cases as these, a good memory is unpardonable. This is the last time I shall ever remember it myself."

Miss Bennet still looked all amazement. Elizabeth again, and more seriously assured her of its truth.

"Good Heaven! can it be really so! Yet now I must believe you," cried Jane. "My dear, dear Lizzy, I would—I do congratulate you—but are you certain? forgive the question—are you quite certain that you can be happy with him?"

"There can be no doubt of that. It is settled between us already, that we are to be the happiest couple in the world. But are you pleased, Jane? Shall you like to have such a brother?"

"Very, very much. Nothing could give either Bingley or myself more delight. But we considered it, we talked of it as impossible. And do you really love him quite well enough? Oh, Lizzy! do any thing rather than marry without affection. Are you quite sure that you feel what you ought to do?"

"Oh, yes! You will only think I feel more than I ought to do, when I tell you all."

"What do you mean?"

"Why, I must confess that I love him better than I do Bingley. I am afraid you will be angry."

"My dearest sister, now be serious. I want to talk very seriously. Let me know every thing that I am to know, without delay. Will you tell me how long you have loved him?"

"It has been coming on so gradually, that I hardly know when it began. But I believe I must date it from my first seeing his beautiful grounds at Pemberley."

Another intreaty that she would be serious, however, produced the desired effect; and she soon satisfied Jane by her solemn assurances of attachment. When convinced on that article, Miss Bennet had nothing farther to wish.

"Now I am quite happy," said she, "for you will be as happy as myself. I always had a value for him. Were it for nothing but his love of you, I must always have esteemed him; but now, as Bingley's friend and your husband, there can be only Bingley and yourself more dear to me. But Lizzy, you have been very sly, very reserved with me. How little did you tell me of what passed at Pemberley and Lambton! I owe all that I know of it to another, not to you."

Elizabeth told her the motives of her secrecy. She had been unwilling to mention Bingley; and the unsettled state of her own feelings had made her equally avoid the name of his friend. But now she would no longer conceal from her his share in Lydia's marriage. All was acknowledged, and half the night spent in conversation.

"Good gracious!" cried Mrs. Bennet, as she stood at a window the next morning, "if that disagreeable Mr. Darcy is not coming here again with our dear Bingley! What can he mean by being so tiresome as to be always coming here? I had no notion but he would go a-shooting, or something or other, and not disturb us with his company. What shall we do with him? Lizzy, you must walk out with him again, that he may not be in Bingley's way."

Elizabeth could hardly help laughing at so convenient a proposal; yet was really vexed that her mother should be always giving him such an epithet.

As soon as they entered, Bingley looked at her so expressively, and shook hands with such warmth, as left no doubt of his good information; and he soon afterwards said aloud, "Mrs. Bennet, have you no more lanes hereabouts in which Lizzy may lose her way again to-day?"

"I advise Mr. Darcy, and Lizzy, and Kitty," said Mrs. Bennet, "to walk to Oakham Mount this morning. It is a nice long walk, and Mr. Darcy has never seen the view."

"It may do very well for the others," replied Mr. Bingley; "but I am sure it will be too much for Kitty. Won't it, Kitty?" Kitty owned that she had rather stay at home. Darcy professed a great curiosity to see the view from the Mount, and Elizabeth silently consented. As she went up stairs to get ready, Mrs. Bennet followed her, saying,

"I am quite sorry, Lizzy, that you should be forced to have that disagreeable man all to yourself. But I hope you will not mind it: it is all for Jane's sake, you know; and there is no occasion for talking to him, except just now and then. So, do not put yourself to inconvenience."

During their walk, it was resolved that Mr. Bennet's consent should be asked in the course of the evening. Elizabeth reserved to herself the application for her mother's. She could not determine how her mother would take it; sometimes doubting whether all his wealth and grandeur would be enough to overcome her abhorrence of the man. But whether she were violently set against the match, or violently delighted with it, it was certain that her manner would be equally ill adapted to do credit to her sense; and she could no more bear that Mr. Darcy should hear the first raptures of her joy, than the first vehemence of her disapprobation.

In the evening, soon after Mr. Bennet withdrew to the library, she saw Mr. Darcy rise also and follow him, and her agitation on seeing it was extreme. She did not fear her father's opposition, but he was going to be made unhappy; and that it should be through her means—that she, his favourite child, should be distressing him by her choice, should be filling him with fears and regrets in disposing of her—was a wretched reflection, and she sat in misery till Mr. Darcy appeared again, when, looking at him, she was a little relieved by his smile. In a few minutes he approached the table where she was sitting with Kitty; and, while pretending to admire her work said in a whisper, "Go to your father, he wants you in the library." She was gone directly.

Her father was walking about the room, looking grave and anxious. "Lizzy," said he, "what are you doing? Are you out of your senses, to be accepting this man? Have not you always hated him?"

How earnestly did she then wish that her former opinions had been more reasonable, her expressions more moderate! It would have spared her from explanations and professions which it was exceedingly awkward to give; but they were now necessary, and she assured him, with some confusion, of her attachment to Mr. Darcy.

"Or, in other words, you are determined to have him. He is rich, to be sure, and you may have more fine clothes and fine carriages than Jane. But will they make you happy?"

"Have you any other objection," said Elizabeth, "than your belief of my indifference?"

"None at all. We all know him to be a proud, unpleasant sort of man; but this would be nothing if you really liked him."

"I do, I do like him," she replied, with tears in her eyes, "I love him. Indeed he has no improper pride. He is perfectly amiable. You do not know what he really is; then pray do not pain me by speaking of him in such terms."

"Lizzy," said her father, "I have given him my consent. He is the kind of man, indeed, to whom I should never dare refuse any thing, which he condescended to ask. I now give it to you, if you are resolved on having him. But let me advise you to think better of it. I know your disposition, Lizzy. I know that you could be neither happy nor respectable, unless you truly esteemed your husband; unless you looked up to him as a superior. Your lively talents would place you in the greatest danger in an unequal marriage. You could scarcely escape discredit and misery. My child, let me not have the grief of seeing you unable to respect your partner in life. You know not what you are about."

Elizabeth, still more affected, was earnest and solemn in her reply; and at length, by repeated assurances that Mr. Darcy was really the object of her choice, by explaining the gradual change which her estimation of him had undergone, relating her absolute certainty that his affection was not the work of a day, but had stood the test of many months suspense, and enumerating with energy all his good qualities, she did conquer her father's incredulity, and reconcile him to the match.

"Well, my dear," said he, when she ceased speaking, "I have no more to say. If this be the case, he deserves you. I could not have parted with you, my Lizzy, to any one less worthy." To complete the favourable impression, she then told him what Mr. Darcy had voluntarily done for Lydia. He heard her with astonishment.

"This is an evening of wonders, indeed! And so, Darcy did every thing: made up the match, gave the money, paid the fellow's debts, and got him his commission! So much the better. It will save me a world of trouble and economy. Had it been your uncle's doing, I must and would have paid him; but these violent young lovers carry every thing their own way. I shall offer to pay him to-morrow; he will rant and storm about his love for you, and there will be an end of the matter." He then recollected her embarrassment a few days before, on his reading Mr. Collins's letter; and after laughing at her some time, allowed her at last to go—saying, as she quitted the room, "If any young men come for Mary or Kitty, send them in, for I am quite at leisure."

Elizabeth's mind was now relieved from a very heavy weight; and, after half an hour's quiet reflection in her own room, she was able to join the others with tolerable composure. Every thing was too recent for gaiety, but the evening passed tranquilly away; there was no longer any thing material to be dreaded, and the comfort of ease and familiarity would come in time.

When her mother went up to her dressing-room at night, she followed her, and made the important communication. Its effect was most extraordinary; for on first hearing it, Mrs. Bennet sat quite still, and unable to utter a syllable. Nor was it under many, many minutes that she could comprehend what she heard; though not in general backward to credit what was for the advantage of her family, or that came in the shape of a lover to any of them. She began at length to recover, to fidget about in her chair, get up, sit down again, wonder, and bless herself.

"Good gracious! Lord bless me! only think! dear me! Mr. Darcy! Who would have thought it! And is it really true? Oh! my sweetest Lizzy! how rich and how great you will be! What pin-money, what jewels, what carriages you will have! Jane's is nothing to it—nothing at all. I am so pleased—so happy. Such a charming man!—so handsome! so tall!—Oh, my dear Lizzy! pray apologise for my having disliked him so much before. I hope he will overlook it. Dear, dear Lizzy. A house in town! Every thing that is charming! Three daughters married! Ten thousand a year! Oh, Lord! What will become of me. I shall go distracted."

This was enough to prove that her approbation need not be doubted: and Elizabeth, rejoicing that such an effusion was heard only by herself, soon went away. But before she had been three minutes in her own room, her mother followed her.

"My dearest child," she cried, "I can think of nothing else! Ten thousand a year, and very likely more! 'Tis as good as a Lord! And a special licence. You must and shall be married by a special licence. But my dearest love, tell me what dish Mr. Darcy is particularly fond of, that I may have it tomorrow."

This was a sad omen of what her mother's behaviour to the gentleman himself might be; and Elizabeth found that, though in the certain possession of his warmest affection, and secure of her relations' consent, there was still something to be wished for. But the morrow passed off much better than she expected; for Mrs. Bennet luckily stood in such awe of her intended son-in-law that she ventured not to speak to him, unless it was in her power to offer him any attention, or mark her deference for his opinion.

Elizabeth had the satisfaction of seeing her father taking pains to get acquainted with him; and Mr. Bennet soon assured her that he was rising every hour in his esteem.

"I admire all my three sons-in-law highly," said he. "Wickham, perhaps, is my favourite; but I think I shall like your husband quite as well as Jane's."

Chapter 60

Elizabeth's spirits soon rising to playfulness again, she wanted Mr. Darcy to account for his having ever fallen in love with her. "How could you begin?" said she. "I can comprehend your going on charmingly, when you had once made a beginning; but what could set you off in the first place?"

"I cannot fix on the hour, or the spot, or the look, or the words, which laid the foundation. It is too long ago. I was in the middle before I knew that I had begun."

"My beauty you had early withstood, and as for my manners—my behaviour to you was at least always bordering on the uncivil, and I never spoke to you without rather wishing to give you pain than not. Now be sincere; did you admire me for my impertinence?"

"For the liveliness of your mind, I did."

"You may as well call it impertinence at once. It was very little less. The fact is, that you were sick of civility, of deference, of officious attention. You were disgusted with the women who were always speaking, and looking, and thinking for your approbation alone. I roused, and interested you, because I was so unlike them. Had you not been really amiable, you would have hated me for it; but in spite of the pains you took to disguise yourself, your feelings were always noble and just; and in your heart, you thoroughly despised the persons who so assiduously courted you. There—I have saved you the trouble of accounting for it; and really, all things considered, I begin to think it perfectly reasonable. To be sure, you knew no actual good of me—but nobody thinks of that when they fall in love."

"Was there no good in your affectionate behaviour to Jane while she was ill at Netherfield?"

"Dearest Jane! who could have done less for her? But make a virtue of it by all means. My good qualities are under your protection, and you are to exaggerate them as much as possible; and, in return, it belongs to me to find occasions for teazing and quarrelling with you as often as may be; and I shall begin directly by asking you what made you so unwilling to come to the point at last. What made you so shy of me, when you first called, and afterwards dined here? Why, especially, when you called, did you look as if you did not care about me?"

"Because you were grave and silent, and gave me no encouragement."

"But I was embarrassed."

"And so was I."

"You might have talked to me more when you came to dinner."

"A man who had felt less, might."

"How unlucky that you should have a reasonable answer to give, and that I should be so reasonable as to admit it! But I wonder how long you would have gone on, if you had been left to yourself. I wonder when you would have spoken, if I had not asked you! My resolution of thanking you for your kindness to Lydia had certainly great effect. Too much, I am afraid; for what becomes of the moral, if our comfort springs from a breach of promise? for I ought not to have mentioned the subject. This will never do."

"You need not distress yourself. The moral will be perfectly fair. Lady Catherine's unjustifiable endeavours to separate us were the means of removing all my doubts. I am not indebted for my present happiness to your eager desire of expressing your gratitude. I was not in a humour to wait for any opening of your's. My aunt's intelligence had given me hope, and I was determined at once to know every thing."

"Lady Catherine has been of infinite use, which ought to make her happy, for she loves to be of use. But tell me, what did you come down to Netherfield for? Was it merely to ride to Longbourn and be embarrassed? or had you intended any more serious consequence?"

"My real purpose was to see you, and to judge, if I could, whether I might ever hope to make you love me. My avowed one, or what I avowed to myself, was to see whether your sister were still partial to Bingley, and if she were, to make the confession to him which I have since made."

"Shall you ever have courage to announce to Lady Catherine what is to befall her?"

"I am more likely to want more time than courage, Elizabeth. But it ought to done, and if you will give me a sheet of paper, it shall be done directly."

"And if I had not a letter to write myself, I might sit by you and admire the eveness of your writing, as another young lady once did. But I have an aunt, too, who must not be longer neglected."

From an unwillingness to confess how much her intimacy with Mr. Darcy had been over-rated, Elizabeth had never yet answered Mrs. Gardiner's long letter; but now, having that to communicate which she knew would be most welcome, she was almost ashamed to find that her uncle and aunt had already lost three days of happiness, and immediately wrote as follows:

> "I would have thanked you before, my dear aunt, as I ought to have done, for your long, kind, satisfactory, detail of particulars; but to say the truth, I was too cross to write. You supposed more than really existed. But now suppose as much as you chuse; give a loose to your fancy, indulge your imagination in every possible flight which the subject will afford, and unless you believe me actually married, you cannot greatly err. You must write again very soon, and praise him a great deal more than you did in your last. I thank you, again and again, for not going to the Lakes. How could I be so silly as to wish it! Your idea of the ponies is delightful. We will go round the Park every day. I am the happiest creature in the world. Perhaps other people have said so before, but not one with such justice. I am happier even

than Jane; she only smiles, I laugh. Mr. Darcy sends you all the love in the world that he can spare from me. You are all to come to Pemberley at Christmas.—Yours, etc."

Mr. Darcy's letter to Lady Catherine was in a different style; and still different from either was what Mr. Bennet sent to Mr. Collins, in reply to his last.

"DEAR SIR,

"I must trouble you once more for congratulations. Elizabeth will soon be the wife of Mr. Darcy. Console Lady Catherine as well as you can. But, if I were you, I would stand by the nephew. He has more to give. —Yours sincerely, etc."

Miss Bingley's congratulations to her brother, on his approaching marriage, were all that was affectionate and insincere. She wrote even to Jane on the occasion, to express her delight, and repeat all her former professions of regard. Jane was not deceived, but she was affected; and though feeling no reliance on her, could not help writing her a much kinder answer than she knew was deserved.

The joy which Miss Darcy expressed on receiving similar information, was as sincere as her brother's in sending it. Four sides of paper were insufficient to contain all her delight, and all her earnest desire of being loved by her sister.

Before any answer could arrive from Mr. Collins, or any congratulations to Elizabeth from his wife, the Longbourn family heard that the Collinses were come themselves to Lucas lodge. The reason of this sudden removal was soon evident. Lady Catherine had been rendered so exceedingly angry by the contents of her nephew's letter, that Charlotte, really rejoicing in the match, was anxious to get away till the storm was blown over. At such a moment, the arrival of her friend was a sincere pleasure to Elizabeth, though in the course of their meetings she must sometimes think the pleasure dearly bought, when she saw Mr. Darcy exposed to all the parading and obsequious civility of her husband. He bore it, however, with admirable calmness. He could even listen to Sir William Lucas, when he complimented him on carrying away the brightest jewel of the country, and expressed his hopes of their all meeting frequently at St. James's, with very decent composure. If he did shrug his shoulders, it was not till Sir William was out of sight.

Mrs. Philips's vulgarity was another, and perhaps a greater, tax on his forbearance; and though Mrs. Philips, as well as her sister, stood in too much awe of him to speak with the familiarity which Bingley's good humour encouraged, yet, whenever she did speak, she must be vulgar. Nor was her respect for him, though it made her more quiet, at all likely to make her more elegant. Elizabeth did all she could to shield him from the frequent notice of either, and was ever anxious to keep him to herself, and to those of her family with whom he might converse without mortification; and though the uncomfortable feelings arising from all this took from the season of courtship much of its pleasure, it added to the hope of the future; and she looked forward with delight to the time when they should be removed from society so little pleasing to either, to all the comfort and elegance of their family party at Pemberley.

Chapter 61

Happy for all her maternal feelings was the day on which Mrs. Bennet got rid of her two most deserving daughters. With what delighted pride she afterwards visited Mrs. Bingley, and talked of Mrs. Darcy, may be guessed. I wish I could say, for the sake of her family, that the accomplishment of her earnest desire in the establishment of so many of her children produced so happy an effect as to make her a sensible, amiable, well-informed woman for the rest of her life; though perhaps it was lucky for her husband, who might not have relished domestic felicity in so unusual a form, that she still was occasionally nervous and invariably silly.

Mr. Bennet missed his second daughter exceedingly; his affection for her drew him oftener from home than any thing else could do. He delighted in going to Pemberley, especially when he was least expected.

Mr. Bingley and Jane remained at Netherfield only a twelvemonth. So near a vicinity to her mother and Meryton relations was not desirable even to his easy temper, or her affectionate heart. The darling wish of his sisters was then gratified; he bought an estate in a neighbouring county to Derbyshire, and Jane and Elizabeth, in addition to every other source of happiness, were within thirty miles of each other.

Kitty, to her very material advantage, spent the chief of her time with her two elder sisters. In society so superior to what she had generally known, her improvement was great. She was not of so ungovernable a temper as Lydia; and, removed from the influence of Lydia's example, she became, by proper attention and management, less irritable, less ignorant, and less insipid. From the farther disadvantage of Lydia's society she was of course carefully kept, and though Mrs. Wickham frequently invited her to come and stay with her, with the promise of balls and young men, her father would never consent to her going.

Mary was the only daughter who remained at home; and she was necessarily drawn from the pursuit of accomplishments by Mrs. Bennet's being quite unable to sit alone. Mary was obliged to mix more with the world, but she could still moralize over every morning visit; and as she was no longer mortified by comparisons between her sisters' beauty and her own, it was suspected by her father that she submitted to the change without much reluctance.

As for Wickham and Lydia, their characters suffered no revolution from the marriage of her sisters. He bore with philosophy the conviction that Elizabeth must now become acquainted with whatever of his ingratitude and falsehood had before been unknown to her; and in spite of every thing, was not wholly without hope that Darcy might yet be prevailed on to make his fortune. The congratulatory letter which Elizabeth received from Lydia on her marriage, explained to her that, by his wife at least, if not by himself, such a hope was cherished. The letter was to this effect:

> "MY DEAR LIZZY,
> I wish you joy. If you love Mr. Darcy half as well as I do my dear Wickham, you must be very happy. It is a great comfort to have you so rich, and when you have nothing else to do, I hope you will think of us. I am sure Wickham would like a place at court very much, and I do not think we shall have quite money enough to live upon without some help. Any place would do, of about three or four hundred a year; but however, do not speak to Mr. Darcy about it, if you had rather not.—Yours, etc."

As it happened that Elizabeth had much rather not, she endeavoured in her answer to put an end to every intreaty and expectation of the kind. Such relief, however, as it was in her power to afford, by the practice of what might be called economy in her own private expences, she frequently sent them. It had always been evident to her that such an income as theirs, under the direction of two persons so extravagant in their wants, and heedless of the future, must be very insufficient to their support; and whenever they changed their quarters, either Jane or herself were sure of being applied to for some little assistance towards discharging their bills. Their manner of living, even when the restoration of peace dismissed them to a home, was unsettled in the extreme. They were always moving from place to place in quest of a cheap situation, and always spending more than they ought. His affection for her soon sunk into indifference; her's lasted a little longer; and in spite of her youth and her manners, she retained all the claims to reputation which her marriage had given her.

Though Darcy could never receive him at Pemberley, yet, for Elizabeth's sake, he assisted him farther in his profession. Lydia was occasionally a visitor there, when her husband was gone to enjoy himself in London or Bath; and with the Bingleys they both of them frequently staid so long, that even Bingley's good humour was overcome, and he proceeded so far as to talk of giving them a hint to be gone.

Miss Bingley was very deeply mortified by Darcy's marriage; but as she thought it advisable to retain the right of visiting at Pemberley, she dropt all her resentment; was fonder than ever of Georgiana, almost as attentive to Darcy as heretofore, and paid off every arrear of civility to Elizabeth.

Pemberley was now Georgiana's home; and the attachment of the sisters was exactly what Darcy had hoped to see. They were able to love each other even as well as they intended. Georgiana had the highest opinion in the world of Elizabeth; though at first she often listened with an astonishment bordering on alarm at her lively, sportive, manner of talking to her brother. He, who had always inspired in herself a respect which almost overcame her affection, she now saw the object of open pleasantry. Her mind received knowledge which had never before fallen in her way. By Elizabeth's instructions, she began to comprehend that a woman may take liberties with her husband which a brother will not always allow in a sister more than ten years younger than himself.

Lady Catherine was extremely indignant on the marriage of her nephew; and as she gave way to all the genuine frankness of her character in her reply to the letter which announced its arrangement, she sent him language so very abusive, especially of Elizabeth, that for some time all intercourse was at an end. But at length, by Elizabeth's persuasion, he was prevailed on to overlook the offence, and seek a reconciliation; and, after a little farther resistance on the part of his aunt, her resentment gave way, either to her affection for him, or her curiosity to see how his wife conducted herself; and she condescended to wait on them at Pemberley, in spite of that pollution which its woods had received, not merely from the presence of such a mistress, but the visits of her uncle and aunt from the city.

With the Gardiners, they were always on the most intimate terms. Darcy, as well as Elizabeth, really loved them; and they were both ever sensible of the warmest gratitude towards the persons who, by bringing her into Derbyshire, had been the means of uniting them.

Louisa May Alcott

LITTLE WOMEN

Romance
CLASSICS

Romance CLASSICS

Published by Trident Press International
801 12th Avenue South
Suite 302
Naples Florida 34102 USA
www.trident-international.com
email: tridentpress@worldnet.att.net

Printed in Australia
ISBN: 1582791961

LITTLE WOMEN PART I

Chapter One

"Christmas won't be Christmas without any presents," grumbled Jo, lying on the rug.

"It's so dreadful to be poor!" sighed Meg, looking down at her old dress.

"I don't think it's fair for some girls to have plenty of pretty things, and other girls nothing at all," added little Amy, with an injured sniff.

"We've got Father and Mother, and each other," said Beth contentedly from her corner.

The four young faces on which the firelight shone brightened at the cheerful words, but darkened again as Jo said sadly, "We haven't got Father, and shall not have him for a long time." She didn't say "perhaps never," but each silently added it, thinking of Father far away, where the fighting was.

Nobody spoke for a minute; then Meg said in an altered tone, "You know the reason Mother proposed not having any presents this Christmas was because it is going to be a hard winter for everyone; and she thinks we ought not to spend money for pleasure, when our men are suffering so in the army. We can't do much, but we can make our little sacrifices, and ought to do it gladly. But I am afraid I don't." And Meg shook her head, as she thought regretfully of all the pretty things she wanted.

"But I don't think the little we should spend would do any good. We've each got a dollar, and the army wouldn't be much helped by our giving that. I agree not to expect anything from Mother or you, but I do want to buy UNDINE AND SINTRAM for myself. I've wanted it so long," said Jo, who was a bookworm.

"I planned to spend mine in new music," said Beth, with a little sigh, which no one heard but the hearth brush and kettle holder.

"I shall get a nice box of Faber's drawing pencils. I really need them," said Amy decidedly.

"Mother didn't say anything about our money, and she won't wish us to give up everything. Let's each buy what we want, and have a little fun. I'm sure we work hard enough to earn it," cried Jo, examining the heels of her shoes in a gentlemanly manner.

"I know I do—teaching those tiresome children nearly all day, when I'm longing to enjoy myself at home," began Meg, in the complaining tone again.

"You don't have half such a hard time as I do," said Jo. "How would you like to be shut up for hours with a nervous, fussy old lady, who keeps you trotting, is never satisfied, and worries you till you you're ready to fly out the window or cry?"

"It's naughty to fret, but I do think washing dishes and keeping things tidy is the worst work in the world. It makes me cross, and my hands get so stiff, I can't practice well at all." And Beth looked at her rough hands with a sigh that any one could hear that time.

"I don't believe any of you suffer as I do," cried Amy, "for you don't have to go to school with impertinent girls, who plague you if you don't know your lessons, and laugh at your dresses, and label your father if he isn't rich, and insult you when your nose isn't nice."

"If you mean libel, I'd say so, and not talk about labels, as if Papa was a pickle bottle," advised Jo, laughing.

"I know what I mean, and you needn't be statirical about it. It's proper to use good words, and improve your vocabilary," returned Amy, with dignity.

"Don't peck at one another, children. Don't you wish we had the money Papa lost when we were little, Jo? Dear me! How happy and good we'd be, if we had no worries!" said Meg, who could remember better times.

"You said the other day you thought we were a deal happier than the King children, for they were fighting and fretting all the time, in spite of their money."

"So I did, Beth. Well, I think we are. For though we do have to work, we make fun of ourselves, and are a pretty jolly set, as Jo would say."

"Jo does use such slang words!" observed Amy, with a reproving look at the long figure stretched on the rug.

Jo immediately sat up, put her hands in her pockets, and began to whistle.

"Don't, Jo. It's so boyish!"

"That's why I do it."

"I detest rude, unladylike girls!"

"I hate affected, niminy-piminy chits!"

"Birds in their little nests agree," sang Beth, the peacemaker, with such a funny face that both sharp voices softened to a laugh, and the "pecking" ended for that time.

"Really, girls, you are both to be blamed," said Meg, beginning to lecture in her elder-sisterly fashion."You are old enough to leave off boyish tricks, and to behave better, Josephine. It didn't matter so much when you were a little girl, but now you are so tall, and turn up your hair, you should remember that you are a young lady."

"I'm not! And if turning up my hair makes me one, I'll wear it in two tails till I'm twenty," cried Jo, pulling off her net, and shaking down a chestnut mane. "I hate to think I've got to grow up, and be Miss March, and wear long gowns, and look as prim as a China Aster! It's bad enough to be a girl, anyway, when I like boy's games and work and manners! I can't get over my disappointment in not being a boy. And it's worse than ever now, for I'm dying to go and fight with Papa. And I can only stay home and knit, like a poky old woman!"

And Jo shook the blue army sock till the needles rattled like castanets, and her ball bounded across the room.

"Poor Jo! It's too bad, but it can't be helped. So you must try to be contented with making your name boyish, and playing brother to us girls," said Beth, stroking the rough head with a hand that all the dish washing and dusting in the world could not make ungentle in its touch.

"As for you, Amy," continued Meg, "you are altogether to particular and prim. Your airs are funny now, but you'll grow up an affected little goose, if you don't take care. I I like your nice manners and refined ways of speaking, when you don't try to be elegant. But your absurd words are as bad as Jo's slang."

"If Jo is a tomboy and Amy a goose, what am I, please?" asked Beth, ready to share the lecture.

"You're a dear, and nothing else," answered Meg warmly, and no one contradicted her, for the 'Mouse' was the pet of the family.

As young readers like to know 'how people look', we will take this moment to give them a little sketch of the four sisters, who sat knitting away in the twilight, while the December snow fell quietly without, and the fire crackled cheerfully within. It was a comfortable room, though the carpet was faded and the furniture very plain, for a good picture or two hung on the walls, books filled the recesses, chrysanthemums and Christmas roses bloomed in the windows, and a pleasant atmosphere of home peace pervaded it.

Margaret, the eldest of the four, was sixteen, and very pretty, being plump and fair, with large eyes, plenty of soft brown hair, a sweet mouth, and white hands, of which she was rather vain. Fifteen-year-old Jo was very tall, thin, and brown, and reminded one of a colt, for she never seemed to know what to do with her long limbs, which were very much in her way. She had a decided mouth, a comical nose, and sharp, gray eyes, which appeared to see everything, and were by turns fierce, funny, or thoughtful. Her long, thick hair was her one beauty, but it was usually bundled into a net, to be out of her way. Round shoulders had Jo, big hands and feet, a flyaway look to her clothes, and the uncomfortable appearance of a girl who was rapidly shooting up into a woman and didn't like it. Elizabeth, or Beth, as everyone called her, was a rosy, smooth-haired, bright-eyed girl of thirteen, with a shy manner, a timid voice, and a ;peaceful expression which was seldom disturbed. Her father called her 'Little Miss Tranquility', and the name suited her excellently, for she seemed to live in a happy world of her own, only venturing out to meet the few whom she trusted and loved. Amy, though the youngest, was a most important person, in her own opinion at least. A regular snow maiden, with blue eyes, and yellow hair curling on her shoulders, pale and slender, and always carrying herself like a young lady mindful of her manners. What the characters of the four sisters were we will leave to be found out.

The clock struck six and, having swept up the hearth, Beth put a pair of slippers down to warm. Somehow the sight of the old shoes had a good effect upon the girls, for Mother was coming, and everyone brightened to welcome her. Meg stopped lecturing, and lighted the lamp, Amy got out of the easy chair without being asked, and Jo forgot how tired she was as she sat up to hold the slippers nearer to the blaze.

"They are quite worn out. Marmee must have a new pair."

"I thought I'd get her some with my dollar," said Beth.

"No, I shall!" cried Amy.

"I'm the oldest," began Meg, but Jo cut in with a decided, "I'm the man of the family now Papa is away, and I shall provide the slippers, for he told me to take special care of Mother while he was gone."

"I'll tell you what we'll do," said Beth, "let's each get her something for Christmas, land not get anything for ourselves."

"That's like you, dear! What will we get?" exclaimed Jo.

Everyone thought soberly for a minute, then Meg announced, as if the idea was suggested by the sight of her own pretty hands, "I shall give her a nice pair of gloves."

"Army shoes, best to be had," cried Jo.

"Some handkerchiefs, all hemmed," said Beth.

"I'll get a little bottle of cologne. She likes it, and it won't cost much, so I'll have some left to buy my pencils," added Amy.

"How will we give the things?" asked Meg.

"Put them on the table, and bring her in and see her open the bundles. Don't you remember how we used to do on our birthdays?" answered Jo.

"I used to be so frightened when it was my turn to sit in the chair with the crown on, and see you all come marching round to give the presents, with a kiss. I liked the things and the kisses, but it was dreadful to have you sit looking at me while I opened the bundles," said Beth, who was toasting her face and the bread for tea at the same time.

"Let Marmee think we are getting things for ourselves, and then surprise her. We must go shopping tomorrow afternoon, Meg. There is so much to do about the play for Christmas night," said Jo, marching up and down, with her hands behind her back, and her nose in the air.

"I don't mean to act any more after this time. I'm getting too old for such things," observed Meg, who was as much a child as ever about 'dressing-up' frolics.

"You won't stop, I know, as long as you can trail round in a white gown with your hair down, and wear gold-paper jewelry. You are the best actress we've got, and there'll be an end of everything if you quit the boards," said Jo. "We ought to rehearse tonight. Come here, Amy, and do the fainting scene, for you are as stiff as a poker in that."

"I can't help it. I never saw anyone faint, and I don't choose to make myself all black and blue, tumbling flat as you do. If I can go down easily, I'll drop. If I can't, I shall fall into a chair and be graceful. I don't care if Hugo does come at me with a pistol," returned Amy, who was not gifted with dramatic power, but was chosen because she was small enough to be borne out shrieking by the villain of the piece.

"Do it this way. Clasp your hands so, and stagger across the room, crying frantically, 'Roderigo Save me! Save me!' and away went Jo, with a melodramatic scream which was truly thrilling.

Amy followed, but she poked her hands out stiffly before her, and jerked herself along as if she went by machinery, and her "Ow!" was more suggestive of pins being run into her than of fear and anguish. Jo gave a despairing groan, and Meg laughed outright, while Beth let her bread burn as she watched the fun with interest. "It's no use! Do the best you can when the time comes, and if the audience laughs, don't blame me. Come on, Meg."

"Then things went smoothly, for Don Pedro defied the world in a speech of two pages without a single break. Hagar, the witch, chanted an awful incantation over her kettleful of simmering toads, with weird effect. Roderigo rent his chains asunder manfully, and Hugo died in agonies of remorse and arsenic, with a wild, "Ha! Ha!"

"It's the best we've had yet," said Meg, as the dead villain sat up and rubbed his elbows.

"I don't see how you can write and act such splendid things, Jo. You're a regular Shakespeare!" exclaimed Beth, who firmly believed that her sisters were gifted with wonderful genius in all things.

"Not quite," replied Jo modestly. "I do think THE WITCHES CURSE, an Operatic Tragedy is rather a nice thing, but I'd like to try McBETH, if we only had a trapdoor for Banquo. I always wanted to do the killing part. 'Is that a dagger that I see before me?" muttered Jo, rolling her eyes and clutching at the air, as she had seen a famous tragedian do.

"No, it's the toasting fork, with Mother's shoe on it instead of the bread. Beth's stage-struck!" cried Meg, and the rehearsal ended in a general burst of laughter.

"Glad to find you so merry, my girls," said a cheery voice at the door, and actors and audience turned to welcome a tall, motherly lady with a 'can I help you' look about her which was truly delightful. She was not elegantly dressed, but a noble-looking woman, and the girls thought the gray cloak and unfashionable bonnet covered the most splendid mother in the world.

"Well, dearies, how have you got on today? There was so much to do, getting the boxes ready to go tomorrow, that I didn't come home to dinner. Has anyone called, Beth? How is your cold, Meg? Jo, you look tired to death. Come and kiss me, baby."

While making these maternal inquiries Mrs. March got her wet things off, her warm slippers on, and sitting down in the easy chair, drew Amy to her lap, preparing to enjoy the happiest hour of her busy day. The girls flew about, trying to make things comfortable, each in her own way. Meg arranged the tea table, Jo brought wood and set chairs, dropping, over-turning, and clattering everything she touched. Beth trotted to and fro between parlor kitchen, quiet and busy, while Amy gave directions to everyone, as she sat with her hands folded.

As they gathered about the table, Mrs. March said, with a particularly happy face, "I've got a treat for you after supper."

A quick, bright smile went round like a streak of sunshine. Beth clapped her hands, regardless of the biscuit she held, and Jo tossed up her napkin, crying, "A letter! A letter! Three cheers for Father!"

"Yes, a nice long letter. He is well, and thinks he shall get through the cold season better than we feared. He sends all sorts of loving wishes for Christmas, and an especial message to you girls," said Mrs. March, patting her pocket as if she had got a treasure there.

"Hurry and get done! Don't stop to quirk your little finger and simper over your plate, Amy," cried Jo, choking on her tea and dropping her bread, butter side down, on the carpet in her haste to get at the treat.

Beth ate no more, but crept away to sit in her shadowy corner and brood over the delight to come, till the others were ready.

"I think it was so splendid in Father to go as chaplain when he was too old to be drafted, and not strong enough for a soldier," said Meg warmly.

"Don't I wish I could go as a drummer, a vivan—what's its name? Or a nurse, so I could be near him and help him," exclaimed Jo, with a groan.

"It must be very disagreeable to sleep in a tent, and eat all sorts of bad-tasting things, and drink out of a tin mug," sighed Amy.

"When will he come home, Marmee? asked Beth, with a little quiver in her voice.

"Not for many months, dear, unless he is sick. He will stay and do his work faithfully as long as he can, and we won't ask for him back a minute sooner than he can be spared. Now come and hear the letter."

They all drew to the fire, Mother in the big chair with Beth at her feet, Meg and Amy perched on either arm of the chair, and Jo leaning on the back, where no one would see any sign of emotion if the letter should happen to be touching. Very few letters were written in those hard times that were not touching, especially those which fathers sent home. In this one little was said of the hardships endured, the dangers faced, or the homesickness conquered. It was a cheerful, hopeful letter, full of lively descriptions of camp life, marches, and military news, and only at the end did the writer's heart over-flow with fatherly love and longing for the little girls at home.

"Give them all of my dear love and a kiss. Tell them I think of them by day, pray for them by night, and find my best comfort in their affection at all times. A year seems very long to wait before I see them, but remind them that while we wait we may all work, so that these hard days need not be wasted. I know they will remember all I said to them, that they will be loving children to you, will do their duty faithfully, fight their bosom enemies bravely, and conquer themselves so beautifully that when I come back to them I may be fonder and prouder than ever of my little women." Everybody sniffed when they came to that part. Jo wasn't ashamed of the great tear that dropped off the end of her nose, and Amy never minded the rumpling of her curls as she hid her face on her mother's shoulder and sobbed out, "I am a selfish girl! But I'll truly try to be better, so he mayn't be disappointed in me by-and-by."

We all will," cried Meg. "I think too much of my looks and hate to work, but won't any more, if I can help it."

"I'll try and be what he loves to call me, 'a little woman' and not be rough and wild, but do my duty here instead of wanting to be somewhere else," said Jo, thinking that keeping her temper at home was a much harder task than facing a rebel or two down South.

Beth said nothing, but wiped away her tears with the blue army sock and began to knit with all her might, losing no time in doing the duty that lay nearest her, while she resolved in her quiet little soul to be all that Father hoped to find her when the year brought round the happy coming home.

Mrs. March broke the silence that followed Jo's words, by saying in her cheery voice, "Do you remember how you used to play Pilgrims Progress when you were little things? Nothing delighted you more than to have me tie my piece bags on your backs for burdens, give you hats and sticks and rolls of paper, and let you travel through the house from the cellar, which was the City of Destruction, up, up, to the housetop, where you had all the lovely things you could collect to make a Celestial City."

"What fun it was, especially going by the lions, fighting Apollyon, and passing through the valley where the hob-goblins were," said Jo.

"I liked the place where the bundles fell off and tumbled downstairs," said Meg.

"I don't remember much about it, except that I was afraid of the cellar and the dark entry, and always liked the cake and milk we had up at the top. If I wasn't too old for such things, I'd rather like to play it over again," said Amy, who began to talk of renouncing childish things at the mature age of twelve.

"We never are too old for this, my dear, because it is a play we are playing all the time in one way or another. Out burdens are here, our road is before us, and the longing for goodness and happiness is the guide that leads us through many troubles and mistakes to the peace which is a true Celestial City. Now, my little pilgrims, suppose you begin again, not in play, but in earnest, and see how far on you can get before Father comes home."

"Really, Mother? Where are our bundles?" asked Amy, who was a very literal young lady.

"Each of you told what your burden was just now, except Beth. I rather think she hasn't got any," said her mother.

"Yes, I have. Mine is dishes and dusters, and envying girls with nice pianos, and being afraid of people."

Beth's bundle was such a funny one that everybody wanted to laugh, but nobody did, for it would have hurt her feelings very much.

"Let us do it," said Meg thoughtfully. "It is only another name for trying to be good, and the story may help us, for though we do want to be good, it's hard work and we forget, and don't do our best."

"We were in the Slough of Despond tonight, and Mother came and pulled us out as Help did in the book. We ought to have our roll of directions, like Christian. What shall we do about that?" asked Jo, delighted with the fancy which lent a little romance to the very dull task of doing her duty.

"Look under your pillows christmas morning, and you will find your guidebook," replied Mrs. March.

They talked over the new plan while old Hannah cleared the table, then out came the four little work baskets, and the needles flew as the girls made sheets for Aunt March. It was uninteresting sewing, but tonight no one grumbled. They adopted Jo's plan of dividing the long seams into four parts, and calling the quarters Europe, Asia, Africa, and America, and in that way got on capitally, especially when they talked about the different countries as they stitched their way through them.

At nine they stopped work, and sang, as usual, before they went to bed. No one but Beth could get much music out of the old piano, but she had a way of softly touching the yellow keys and making a pleasant accompaniment to the simple songs they sang. Meg had a voice like a flute, and she and herr mother led the little choir. Amy chirped like a cricket, and Jo wandered through the airs at her own sweet will, always coming out at the wrong place with a croak or a quaver that spoiled the most pensive tune. They had always done this from the time they could lisp . . .

Crinkle, crinkle, 'ittle 'tar,

and it had become a household custom, for the mother was a born singer. The first sound in the morning was her voice as she went about the house singing like a lark, and the last sound at night was the same cheery sound, for the girls never grew too old for that familiar lullaby.

Chapter Two

Jo was the first to wake in the gray dawn of Christmas morning. No stockings hung at the fireplace, and for a moment she felt as much disappointed as she did long ago, when her little sock fell down because it was crammed so full of goodies. Then she remembered her mother's promise and, slipping her hand under her pillow, drew out a little crimson-covered book. She knew it very well, for it was that beautiful old story of the best life ever lived, and Jo felt that it was a true guidebook for any pilgrim going on a long journey. She woke Meg with a "Merry Christmas," and bade her see what was under her pillow. A green-covered book appeared, with the same picture inside, and a few words written by their mother, which made their one present very precious in their eyes. Presently Beth and Amy woke to rummage and find their little books also, one dove-colored, the other blue, and all sat looking at and talking about them, while the east grew rosy with the coming day.

In spite of her small vanities, Margaret had a sweet and pious nature, which unconsciously influenced her sisters, especially Jo, who loved her very tenderly, and obeyed her because her advice was so gently given.

"Girls," said Meg seriously, looking from the tumbled head beside her to the two little night-capped ones in the room beyond, "Mother wants us to read and love and mind these books, and we must begin at once. We used to be faithful about it, but since Father went away and all this war trouble unsettled us, we have neglected many things. You can do as you please, but I shall keep my book on the table here and read a little every morning as soon as I wake, for I know it will do me good and help me through the day."

Then she opened her new book and began to read. Jo put her arm round her and, leaning cheek to cheek, read also, with the quiet expression so seldom seen on her restless face.

"How good Meg is! Come, Amy, let's do as they do. I'll help you with the hard words, and they" explain things if we don't understand," whispered Beth, very much impressed by the pretty books and her sisters, example.

"I'm glad mine is blue," said Amy. and then the rooms were very still while the pages were softly turned, and the winter sunshine crept in to touch the bright heads and serious faces with a Christmas greeting.

"Where is Mother?" asked Meg, as she and Jo ran down to thank her for their gifts, half an hour later.

"Goodness only knows. some poor creeter came a-beggin', and your ma went straight off to see what was needed. There never was such a woman for givin' away vittles and drink, clothes and firin'," replied Hannah, who had lived with the family since Meg was born, and was considered by them all more as a friend than a servant.

"She will be back soon, I think, so fry your cakes, and have everything ready," said Meg, looking over the presents which were collected in a basket and kept under the sofa, ready to be produced at the proper time. "why, where is Amy's bottle of cologne?" she added, as the little flask did not appear.

"She took it out a minute ago, and went off with it to put a ribbon on it, or some such notion," replied Jo, dancing about the room to take the first stiffness off the new army slippers.

"How nice my handkerchiefs look, don't they? Hannah washed and ironed them for me, and I marked them all myself," said Beth, looking proudly at the somewhat uneven letters which had cost her such labor.

"Bless the child! She's gone and put 'Mother' on them instead of 'M. March'. How funny!" cried Jo, taking one up.

"Isn't that right? I thought it was better to do it so, because Meg's initials are M.M., and I don't want anyone to use these but Marmee," said Beth;, looking troubled.

"It's all right, dear, and a very pretty idea, quite sensible too, for no one can ever mistake now. It will please her very much, I know," said Meg, with a frown for Jo and a smile for Beth.

"There's Mother. Hide the basket, quick!" cried Jo, as a door slammed and steps sounded in the hall.

Amy came in hastily, and looked rather abashed when she saw her sisters all waiting for her.

"Where have you been, and what are you hiding behind you?" asked Meg, surprised to see, by her hood and cloak, that lazy Amy had been out so early.

"Don't laugh at me, Jo! I didn't mean anyone should know till the time came. I only meant to change the little bottle for a big one, and I gave all my money to get it, and I'm truly trying not to be selfish any more."

As she spoke, Amy showed the handsome flask which replaced the cheap one, and looked so earnest and humble in her little effort to forget herself that Meg hugged her on the spot, and Jo pronounced her 'a trump', while Beth ran to the window, and picked her finest rose to ornament the stately bottle.

"You see I felt ashamed of my present, after reading and talking about being good this morning, so I ran round the corner and changed it the minute I was up, and I'm so glad, for mine is the handsomest now."

Another bang of the street door sent the basket under the sofa, and the girls to the table, eager for breakfast.

"Merry Christmas, Marmee! Many of them! Thank you for our books. We read some, and mean to every day," they all cried in chorus. "Merry Christmas, little daughters! I'm glad you began at once, and hope you will keep on. But I want to say one word before we sit down. Not far away from here lies a poor woman with a little newborn baby. Six children are huddled into one bed to keep from freezing, for they have no fire. There is nothing to eat over there, and the oldest boy came to tell me they were suffering hunger and cold. My girls, will you give them your breakfast as a Christmas present?"

They were all unusually hungry, having waited nearly an hour, and for a minute no one spoke, only a minute, for Jo exclaimed impetuously, "I'm so glad you came before we began!"

"May I go and help carry the things to the poor little children?" asked Beth eagerly.

"I shall take the cream and the muffings," added Amy, heroically giving up the article she most liked.

Meg was already covering the buckwheats, and piling the bread into one big plate.

"I thought you'd do it," said Mrs. March, smiling as if satisfied. "You shall all go and help me, and when we come back we will have bread and milk for breakfast, and make it up at dinnertime."

They were soon ready, and the procession set out. Fortunately it was early, and they went through back streets, so few people saw them, and no one laughed at the queer party.

A poor, bare, miserable room it was, with broken windows, no fire, ragged bedclothes, a sick mother, wailing baby, and a group of pale, hungry children cuddled under one old quilt, trying to keep warm.

How the big eyes stared and the blue lips smiled as the girls went in.

"Ach, mein Gott! It is good angels come to us!" said the poor woman, crying for joy.

"Funny angels in hoods and mittens," said Jo, and set them to laughing.

In a few minutes it really did seem as if kind spirits had been at work there. Hannah, who had carried wood, made a fire, and stopped up the broken panes with old hats and her own cloak. Mrs. March gave the mother tea and gruel, and comforted her with promises of help, while she dressed the little baby as tenderly as if it had been her own. The girls meantime spread the table, set the children round the fire, and fed them like so many hungry birds, laughing, talking, and trying to understand the funny broken English.

"Das ist gut!" "Die Engel-kinder!" cried the poor things as they ate and warmed their purple hands at the comfortable blaze. The girls had never been called angel children before, and thought it very agreeable, especially Jo, who had been considered a 'Sancho' ever since she was born. That was a very happy breakfast, though they didn't get any of it. And when they went away, leaving comfort behind, I think there were not in all the city four merrier people than the hungry little girls who gave away their breakfasts and contented themselves with bread and milk on Christmas morning.

"That's loving our neighbor better than ourselves, and I like it," said Meg, as they set out their presents while their mother was upstairs collecting clothes for the poor Hummels.

Not a very splendid show, but there was a great deal of love done up in the few little bundles, and the tall vase of red roses, white chrysanthemums, and trailing vines, which stood in the middle, gave quite an elegant air to the table.

"She's coming! Strike up, Beth! Open the door, Amy! Three cheers for Marmee!" cried Jo, prancing about while Meg went to conduct Mother to the seat of honor.

Beth played her gayest march, amy threw open the door, and Meg enacted escort with great dignity. Mrs. March was both surprised and touched, and smiled with her eyes full as she examined her presents and read the little notes which accompanied them. The slippers went on at once, a new handkerchief was slipped into her pocket, well scented with Amy's cologne, the rose was fastened in her bosom, and the nice gloves were pronounced a perfect fit.

There was a good deal of laughing and kissing and explaining, in the simple, loving fashion which makes these home festivals so pleasant at the time, so sweet to remember long afterward, and then all fell to work.

The morning charities and ceremonies took so much time that the rest of the day was devoted to preparations for the evening festivities. Being still too young to go often to the theater, and not rich enough to afford any great outlay for private performances, the girls put their wits to work, and necessity being the mother of invention, made whatever they needed. Very clever were some of their productions, pasteboard guitars, antique lamps made of old-fashioned butter boats covered with silver paper, gorgeous robes of old cotton, glittering with tin spangles from a pickle factory, and armor covered with the same useful diamond shaped bits left inn sheets when the lids of preserve pots were cut out. The big chamber was the scene of many innocent revels.

No gentleman were admitted, so Jo played male parts to her heart's content and took immense satisfaction in a pair of russet leather boots given her by a friend, who knew a lady who knew an actor. These boots, an old foil, and a slashed doublet once used by an artist for some picture, were Jo's chief treasures and appeared on all occasions. The smallness of the company made it necessary for the two principal actors to take several parts apiece, and they certainly deserved some credit for the hard work they did in learning three or four different parts, whisking in and out of various costumes, and managing the stage besides. It was excellent drill for their memories, a harmless amusement, and employed many hours which otherwise would have been idle, lonely, or spent in less profitable society.

On christmas night, a dozen girls piled onto the bed which was the dress circle, and sat before the blue and yellow chintz curtains in a most flattering state of expectancy. There was a good deal of rustling and whispering behind the curtain, a trifle of lamp smoke, and an occasional giggle from Amy, who was apt to get hysterical in the excitement of the moment. Presently a bell sounded, the curtains flew apart, and the OPERATIC TRAGEDY began.

"A gloomy wood," according to the one playbill, was represented by a few shrubs in pots, green baize on the floor, and a cave in the distance. This cave was made with a clothes horse for a roof, bureaus for walls, and in it was a small furnace in full blast, with a black pot on it and an old witch bending over it.

The stage was dark and the glow of the furnace had a fine effect, especially as real steam issued from the kettle when the witch took off the cover. A moment was allowed for the first thrill to subside, then Hugo, the villain, stalked in with a clanking sword at his side, a slouching hat, black beard, mysterious cloak, and the boots. After pacing to and fro in much agitation, he struck his forehead, and burst out in a wild strain, singing of his hatred to Roderigo, his love for Zara, and his pleasing resolution to kill the one and win the other. The gruff tones of Hugo's voice, with an occasional shout when his feelings overcame him, were very impressive, and the audience applauded the moment he paused for breath. bowing with the air of one accustomed to public praise, he stole to the cavern and ordered Hagar to come forth with a commanding, "What ho, minion! I need thee!"

Out came Meg, with gray horsehair hanging about her face, a red and black robe, a staff, and cabalistic signs upon her cloak. Hugo demanded a potion to make Zara adore him, and one destroy Roderigo. Hagar, in a fine dramatic melody, promised both, and proceeded to call up the spirit who would bring the love philter.

> Hither, hither, from thy home, Airy sprite, I bid thee come! Born of roses, fed on dew, Charms and potions canst thou brew? Bring me here, with elfin speed, The fragrant philter which I need. Make it sweet and swift and strong, Spirit, answer now my song!

A soft strain of music sounded, and then at the back of the cave appeared a little figure in cloudy white, with glittering wings, golden hair, and a garland of roses on its head. Waving a wand, it sang . . .

> Hither I come, From my airy home, Afar in the silver moon. Take the magic spell, And use it well, Or its power will vanish soon!

And dropping a small, gilded bottle at the witch's feet, the spirit vanished. Another chant from Hagar produced another apparition, not a lovely one, for with a bang an ugly black imp appeared and, having croaked a reply, tossed a dark bottle at Hugo and disappeared with a mocking laugh. Having warbled his thanks and put the potions in his boots, Hugo departed, and Hagar informed the audience that as he had killed a few of her friends in times past, she had cursed him, and intends to thwart his plans, and be revenged on him. Then the curtain fell, and the audience reposed and ate candy while discussing the merits of the play.

A good deal of hammering went on before the curtain rose again, but when it became evident what a masterpiece of stage carpentery had been got up, no one murmured at the delay. It was truly superb. A tower rose to the ceiling, halfway up appeared a window with a lamp burning in it, and behind the white curtain appeared Zara in a lovely blue and silver dress, waiting for Roderigo. He came in gorgeous array, with plumed cap, red cloak, chestnut lovelocks, a guitar, and the boots, of course. Kneeling at the foot of the tower, he sang a serenade in melting tones. Zara replied and, after a musical dialogue, consented to fly. Then came the grand effect of the play. Roderigo produced a rope ladder, with five steps to it, threw up one end, and invited Zara to descend. Timidly she crept from her lattice, put her hand on Roderigo's shoulder, and was about to leap gracfully down when "Alas! Alas for Zara!" she forgot her train. It caught in the window, the tower tottered, leaned forward, fell with a crash, and buried the unhappy lovers in the ruins.

A universal shriek arose as the russet boots waved wildly from the wreck and a golden head emerged, exclaiming, "I told you so! I told you so!" With wonderful presence of mind, Don Pedro, the cruel sire, rushed in, dragged out his daughter, with a hasty aside . . .

"Don't laugh! Act as if it was all right!" and, ordering Roderigo up, banished him form the kingdom with wrath and scorn. Though decidedly shaken by the fall from the tower upon him, Roderigo defied the old gentleman and refused to stir. This dauntless example fired Zara. She also defied her sire, and he ordered them both to the deepest dungeons of the castle. A stout little retainer came in with chains and led them away, looking very much frightened and evidently forgetting the speech he ought to have made.

Act third was the castle hall, and here Hagar appeared, having come to free the lovers and finish Hugo. She hears him coming and hides, sees him put the potions into two cups of wine and bid the the timid little servant, "Bear them to the captives in their cells, and tell them I shall come anon." The servant takes Hugo aside to tell him something, and Hagar changes the cups for two others which are harmless. Ferdinando, the 'minion', carries them away, and Hagar puts back the cup which holds the poison meant for Roderigo. Hugo, getting thirsty after a long warble, drinks it, loses his wits, and after a good deal of clutching and stamping, falls flat and dies, while Hagar informs him what she has done in a song of exquisite power and melody.

This was a truly thrilling scene, though some persons might have thought that the sudden tumbling down of a quantity of long red hair rather marred the effect of the villain's death. He was called before the curtain, and with great propriety appeared, leading Hagar, whose singing was considered more wonderful than all the rest of the performance put together.

Act fourth displayed the despairing Roderigo on the point of stabbing himself because he has been told that Zara has deserted him. Just as the dagger is at his heart, a lovely song is sung under his window, informing him that Zara is true but in danger, and he can save her if he will. A key is thrown in, which unlocks the door, and in a spasm of rapture he tears off his chains and rushes away to find and rescue his lady love.

Act fifth opened with a stormy scene between Zara and Don Pedro. He wishes her to go into a convent, but she won't hear of it, and after a touching appeal, is about to faint when Roderigo dashes in and demands her hand. Don Pedro refuses, because he is not rich. They shout and gesticulate tremendously but cannot agree, and Rodrigo is about to bear away the exhausted Zara, when the timid servant enters with a letter and a bag from Hagar, who has mysteriously disappeared. The latter informs the party that she bequeths untold wealth to the young pair and an awful doom to Don Pedro, if he doesn't make them happy. The bag is opened, and several quarts of tin money shower down upon the stage till it is quite glorified with the glitter. This entirely softens the stern sire. He consents without a murmur, all join in a joyful chorus, and the curtain falls upon the lovers kneeling to receive Don Pedro's blessing in attitudes of the most romantic grace.

Tumultuous applause followed but received an unexpected check, for the cot bed, on which the dress circle was built, suddenly shut up and extinguished the enthusiastic audience. Roderigo and Don Pedro flew to the rescue, and all were taken out unhurt, though many were speechless with laughter. the excitement had hardly subsided when Hannah appeared, with "Mrs. March's compliments, and would the ladies walk down to supper."

This was a surprise even to the actors, and when they saw the table, they looked at one another in rapturous amazement. It was like Marmee to get up a little treat for them, but anything so fine as this was unheard of since the departed days of plenty. There was ice cream, actually two dishes of it, pink and white, and cake and fruit and distracting french bonbons and, in the middle of the table, four great bouquets of hot house flowers.

It quite took their breath away, and they stared first at the table and then at their mother, who looked as if she enjoyed it immensely. "Is it fairies?" asked Amy.

"Santa Claus," said Beth.

"Mother did it." And Meg smiled her sweetest, in spite of her gray beard and white eyebrows.

"Aunt March had a good fit and sent the supper," cried Jo, with a sudden inspiration.

"All wrong. Old Mr. Laurence sent it," replied Mrs. March.

"The Laurence boy's grandfather! What in the world put such a thing into his head? We don't know him!' exclaimed Meg.

"Hannah told one of his servants about your breakfast party. He is an odd old gentleman, but that pleased him. He knew my father years ago, and he sent me a polite note this afternoon, saying he hoped I would allow him to express his friendly feeling toward my children by sending them a few trifles in honor of the day. I could not refuse, and so you have a little feast at night to make up for the bread-and-milk breakfast."

"That boy; put it into his head, I know he did! He's a capital fellow, and I wish we could get acquainted. He looks as if he'd like to know us but he's bashful, and Meg is so prim she won't let me speak to him when we pass," said Jo, as the plates went round, and the ice began to melt out of sight, with ohs and ahs of satisfaction.

"You mean the people who live in the big house next door, don't you?" asked one of the girls. "My mother knows old Mr. Laurence, but says he's very proud and doesn't like to mix with his neighbors. He keeps his grandson shut up, when he isn't riding or walking with his tutor, and makes him study very hard. We invited him to our party, but he didn't come. Mother says he's very nice, though he never speaks to us girls."

"Our cat ran away once, and he brought her back, and we talked over the fence, and were getting on capitally, all about cricket, and so on, when he saw Meg coming, and walked off. I mean to know him some day, for he needs fun, I'm sure he does," said Jo decidedly.

"I like his manners, and he looks like a little gentleman, so I've no objection to your knowing him, if a proper opportunity comes. He brought the flowers himself, and I should have asked him in, if I had been sure what was going on upstairs. He looked so wistful as he went away, hearing the frolic and evidently having none of his own."

"It's a mercy you didn't, Mother!" laughed Jo, looking at her boots. "But we'll have another play sometime that he can see. Perhaps he'll help act. Wouldn't that be jolly?"

"I never had such a fine bouquet before! How pretty it is!" And Meg examined her flowers with great interest.

"They are lovely. But Beth's roses are sweeter to me," said Mrs. March, smelling the half-dead posy in her belt.

Beth nestled up to her, and whispered softly, "I wish I could send my bunch to Father. I'm afraid he isn't having such a merry Christmas as we are."

Chapter Three

"Jo! Jo! Where are you?" cried Meg at the foot of the garret stairs.

"Here!" answered a husky voice from above, and, running up, Meg found her sister eating apples and crying over the Heir of Redclyffe, wrapped up in a comforter on an old three-legged sofa by the sunny window. This was Jo's favorite refuge, and here she loved to retire with half a dozen russets and a nice book, to enjoy the quiet and the society of a pet rat who lived near by and didn't mind her a particle. As Meg appeared, Scrabble whisked into his hole. Jo shook the tears off her cheeks and waited to hear the news.

"Such fun! Only see! A regular note of invitation from Mrs. Gardiner for tomorrow night!" cried Meg, waving the precious paper and then proceeding to read it with girlish delight.

"'Mrs. Gardiner would be happy to see Miss March and Miss Josephine at a little dance on New Year's Eve.' Marmee is willing we should go, now what shall we wear?"

"What's the use of asking that, when you know we shall wear our poplins, because we haven't got anything else?" answered Jo with her mouth full.

"If I only had a silk!" sighed Meg. "Mother says I may when I'm eighteen perhaps, but two years is an everlasting time to wait."

"I'm sure our pops look like silk, and they are nice enough for us. Yours is as good as new, but I forgot the burn and the tear in mine. Whatever shall I do? The burn shows badly, and I can't take any out."

"You must sit still all you can and keep your back out of sight. The front is all right. I shall have a new ribbon for my hair, and Marmee will lend me her little pearl pin, and my new slippers are lovely, and my gloves will do, though they aren't as nice as I'd like."

"Mine are spoiled with lemonade, and I can't get any new ones, so I shall have to go without," said Jo, who never troubled herself much about dress.

"You must have gloves, or I won't go," cried Meg decidedly. "Gloves are more important than anything else. You can't dance without them, and if you don't I should be so mortified." "Then I'll stay still. I don't care much for company dancing. It's no fun to go sailing round. I like to fly about and cut capers."

"You can't ask Mother for new ones, they are so expensive, and you are so careless. She said when you spoiled the others that she shouldn't get you any more this winter. Can't you make them do?"

"I can hold them crumpled up in my hand, so no one will know how stained they are. That's all I can do. No! I'll tell you how we can manage, each wear one good one and carry a bad one. Don't you see?"

"Your hands are bigger than mine, and you will stretch my glove dreadfully," began Meg, whose gloves were a tender point with her.

"Then I'll go without. I don't care what people say!" cried Jo, taking up her book.

"You may have it, you may! Only don't stain it, and do behave nicely. Don't put your hands behind you, or stare, or say 'Christopher Columbus!' will you?"

"Don't worry about me. I'll be as prim ad I can and not get into any scrapes, if I can help it. Now go and answer your note, and let me finish this splendid story."

So Meg went away to 'accept with thanks', look over her dress, and sing blithely as she did up her one real lace frill, while Jo finished her story, her four apples, and had a game of romps with Scrabble.

On New Year's Eve the parlor was deserted, for the two younger girls played dressing maids and the two elder were absorbed in the all-important business of 'getting ready for the party'. Simple as the toilets were, there was a great deal of running up and down, laughing and talking, and at one time a strong smell of burned hair pervaded the house. Meg wanted a few curls about her face, and Jo undertook to pinch the papered locks with a pair of hot tongs.

"Ought they to smoke like that?" asked Beth from her perch on the bed.

"It's the dampness drying," replied Jo.

"What a queer smell! It's like burned feathers," observed Amy, smoothing her own pretty curls with a superior air.

"There, now I'll take off the papers and you'll see a cloud of little ringlets," said Jo, putting down the tongs.

She did take off the papers, but no cloud of ringlets appeared, for the hair came with the papers, and the horrified hairdresser laid a row of little scorched bundles on the bureau before her victim.

"Oh, oh, oh! What have you done? I'm spoiled! I can't go! My hair, oh, my hair!" wailed Meg, looking with despair at the uneven frizzle on her forehead.

"Just my luck! You shouldn't have asked me to do it. I always spoil everything. I'm so sorry, but the tongs were too hot, and so I've made a mess," groaned poor Jo, regarding the little black pancakes with tears of regret.

"It isn't spoiled. Just frizzle it, and tie your ribbon so the ends come on your forehead a bit, and it will look like the last fashion. I've seen many girls do it so," said Amy consolingly.

"Serves me right for trying to be fine. I wish I'd let my hair alone," cried Meg petulantly.

"So do I, it was so smooth and pretty. But it will soon grow out again," said Beth, coming to kiss and comfort the shorn sheep.

After various lesser mishaps, Meg was finished at last, and by the united exertions of the entire family Jo's hair was got up and her dress on. They looked very well in their simple suits, Meg's in silvery drab, with a blue velvet snood, lace frills, and the pearl pin. Jo in maroon, with a stiff, gentlemanly linen collar, and a white chrysanthemum or two for her only ornament. Each put on one nice light glove, and carried one soiled one, and all pronounced the effect "quite easy and fine". Meg's high-heeled slippers were very tight and hurt her, though she would not own it, and Jo's nineteen hairpins all seemed stuck straight into her head, which was not exactly comfortable, but, dear me, let us be elegant or die.

"Have a good time, dearies!" said Mrs. March, as the sisters went daintily down the walk. "Don't eat much supper, and come away at eleven when I send Hannah for you." As the gate clashed behind them, a voice cried from a window . . .

"Girls, girls! Have you you both got nice pocket handkerchiefs?"

"Yes, yes, spandy nice, and Meg has cologne on hers," cried Jo, adding with a laugh as they went on, "I do believe Marmee would ask that if we were all running away from an earthquake.

"It is one of her aristocratic tastes, and quite proper, for a real lady is always known by neat boots, gloves, and handkerchief," replied Meg, who had a good many little 'aristocratic tastes' of her own.

"Now don't forget to keep the bad breadth out of sight, Jo. Is my sash right? And does my hair look very bad?" said Meg, as she turned from the glass in Mrs. Gardiner's dressing room after a prolonged prink. "I know I shall forget. If you see me doing anything wrong, just remind me by a wink, will you?" returned Jo, giving her collar a twitch and her head a hasty brush.

"No, winking isn't ladylike. I'll lift my eyebrows if any thing is wrong, and nod if you are all right. Now hold your shoulder straight, and take short steps, and don't shake hands if you are introduced to anyone. It isn't the thing."

"How do you learn all the proper ways? I never can. Isn't that music gay?"

Down they went, feeling a trifle timid, for they seldom went to parties, and informal as this little gathering was, it was an event to them. Mrs. Gardiner, a stately old lady, greeted them kindly and handed them over to the eldest of her six daughters. Meg knew Sallie and was at her ease very soon, but Jo, who didn't care much for girls or girlish gossip, stood about, with her back carefully against the wall, and felt as much out of place as a colt in a flower garden. Half a dozen jovial lads were talking about skates in another part of the room, and she longed to go and join them, for skating was one of the joys of her life. She telegraphed her wish to Meg, but the eyebrows went up so alarmingly that she dared not stir. No one came to talk to her, and one by one the group dwindled away till she was left alone. She could not roam about and amuse herself, for the burned breadth would show, so she stared at people rather forlornly till the dancing began. Meg was asked at once, and the tight slippers tripped about so briskly that none would have guessed the pain their wearer suffered smilingly. Jo saw a big red headed youth approaching her corner, and fearing he meant to engage her, she slipped into a curtained recess, intending to peep and enjoy herself in peace. Unfortunately, another bashful person had chosen the same refuge, for, as the curtain fell behind her, she found herself face to face with the 'Laurence boy'.

"Dear me, I didn't know anyone was here!" stammered Jo, preparing to back out as speedily as she had bounced in.

But the boy laughed and said pleasantly, though he looked a little startled, "Don't mind me, stay if you like."

"Shan't I disturb you?"

"Not a bit. I only came here because I don't know many people and felt rather strange at first, you know."

"So did I. Don't go away, please, unless you'd rather."

The boy sat down again and looked at his pumps, till Jo said, trying to be polite and easy, "I think I've had the pleasure of seeing you before. You live near us, don't you?"

"Next door." And he looked up and laughed outright, for Jo's prim manner was rather funny when he remembered how they had chatted about cricket when he brought the cat home.

That put Jo at her ease and she laughed too, as she said, in her heartiest way, "We did have such a good time over your nice Christmas present."

"Grandpa sent it."

"But you put it into his head, didn't you, now?"

"How is your cat, Miss March?" asked the boy, trying to look sober while his black eyes shone with fun.

"Nicely, thank you, Mr. Laurence. But I am not Miss March, I'm only Jo," returned the young lady.

"I'm not Mr. Laurence, I'm only Laurie."

"Laurie Laurence, what an odd name."

"My first name is theodore, but I don't like it, for the fellows called me Dora, so I made the say Laurie instead."

"I hate my name, too, so sentimental! I wish every one would say Jo instead of Josephine. How did you make the boys stop calling you Dora?"

"I thrashed 'em."

"I can't thrash Aunt March, so I suppose I shall have to bear it." And Jo resigned herself with a sigh.

"Don't you like to dance, Miss Jo?" asked Laurie, looking as if he thought the name suited her.

"I like it well enough if there is plenty of room, and everyone is lively. In a place like this I'm sure to upset something, tread on people's toes, or do something dreadful, so I keep out of mischief and let Meg sail about. Don't you dance?"

"Sometimes. You see I've been abroad a good many years, and haven't been into company enough yet to know how you do things here."

"Abroad!." cried Jo. "Oh, tell me about it! I love dearly to hear people describe their travels."

Laurie didn't seem to know where to begin, but Jo's eager questions soon set him going, and he told her how he had been at school in Vevay, where the boys never wore hats and had a fleet of boats on the lake, and for holiday fun went on walking trips about Switzerland with their teachers.

"Don't I wish I'd been there!" cried Jo. "Did you go to Paris?"

"We spent last winter there."

"Can you talk French?"

"We were not allowed to speak anything else at Vevay."

"Do say some! I can read it, but can't pronounce."

"Quel nom a cetter jeune demoiselle en les pantoulles jolis?"

"How nicely you do it! Let me see . . .you said, 'Who is the young lady in the pretty slippers', didn't you?"

"Oui, mademoiselle."

"It's my sister Margaret, and you knew it was! Do you think she is pretty?"

"Yes, she makes me think of the German girls, she looks so fresh and quiet, and dances like a lady."

Jo quite glowed with pleasure at this boyish praise of her sister, and stored it up to repeat to Meg. Both peeped and critisized and chatted till they felt like old acquaintances. Laurie's bashfulness soon wore off, for Jo's gentlemanly demeanor amused and set him at his ease, and Jo was her merry self again, because her dress was forgotten and nobody lifted their eyebrows at her. She liked the 'Laurence boy' better than ever and took several good looks at him, so that she might describe him to the girls, for they had no brothers, very few male cousins, and boys were almost unknown creatures to them.

"Curly black hair, brown skin, big black eyes, handsome nose, fine teeth, small hands and feet, taller than I am, very polite, for a boy, and altogether jolly. Wonder how old he is?"

It was on the tip of Jo's tongue to ask, but she checked herself in time and, with unusual tact, tried to find out in a roundabout way.

"I suppose you are going to college soon? I see you pegging away at your books, no, I mean studying hard." And Jo blushed at the dreadful 'pegging' which had escaped her.

Laurie smiled but didn't seem shocked, and answered with a shrug. "Not for a year or two. I won't go before seventeen, anyway."

"Aren't you but fifteen?" asked Jo, looking at the tall lad, whom she had imagined seventeen already.

"Sixteen, next month."

"How I wish I was going to college! You don't look as if you liked it."

"I hate it! Nothing but grinding or skylarking. And I don't like the way fellows do either, in this country." "What do you like?"

"To live in Italy, and to enjoy myself in my own way."

Jo wanted very much to ask what his own way was, but his black brows looked rather threatening as he knit them, so she changed the subject by saying, as her foot kept time, "That's a splendid polka! Why don't you go and try it?"

"If you will come too," he answered, with a gallant little bow.

"I can't, for I told meg I wouldn't, because . . ." There Jo stopped, and looked undecided whether to tell or to laugh.

"Because, what?"

"You won't tell?"

"Never!"

"Well, I have a bad trick of standing before the fire, and so I burn my frocks, and I scorched this one, and though it's nicely mended, it shows, and Meg told me to keep still so no one would see it. You may laugh, if you want to. It is funny, I know."

But Laurie didn't laugh. He only looked dawn a minute, and the expression of his face puzzled Jo when he said very gently, "Never mind that. I'll tell you how we can manage. There's a long hall out there, and we can dance grandly, and no one will see us. Please come."

Jo thanked him and gladly went, wishing she had two neat gloves when she saw the nice, pearl-colored ones her partner wore. The hall was empty, and they had a grand polka, for Laurie danced well, and taught her the German step, which delighted Jo, being full of swing and spring. When the music stopped, they sat down on the stairs to get their breath, and Laurie was in the midst of an account of a students' festival at Heidelberg when Meg appeared in search of her sister. She beckoned, and Jo reluctantly followed her into a side room, where she found her on a sofa, holding her foot, and looking pale.

"I've sprained my ankle. That stupid high heel turned and gave me a sad wrench. It aches so, I can hardly stand, and I don't know how I'm ever going to get home," she said, rocking to and fro in pain.

"I knew you'd hurt your feet with those silly shoes. I'm sorry. But I don't see what you can do, except get a carriage, or stay here all night," answered Jo, softly rubbing the poor ankle as she spoke.

"I can't have a carriage without its costing ever so much. I dare say I can't get one at all, for most people come in their own, and it's a long way to the stable, and no one to send." "I'll go."

"No, indeed! It's past nine, and dark as Egypt. I can't stop here, for the house is full. Sallie has some girls staying with her. I'll rest till Hannah comes, and then do the best I can."

"I'll ask Laurie. He will go," said Jo," looking relieved as the idea occurred to her.

"Mercy, no! Don't ask or tell anyone. Get me my rubbers, and put these slippers with our things. I can't dance anymore, but as soon as supper is over, watch for Hannah and tell me the minute she comes."

"They are going out to supper now. I'll stay with you. I'd rather."

"No, dear, run along, and bring me some coffee. I'm so tired I can't stir."

So Meg reclined, with rubbers well hidden, and Jo went blundering away to the dining room, which she found after going into a china closet, and opening the door of a room where old Mr. Gardiner was taking a little private refreshment. Making a dart at the table, she secured the coffee, which she immediately spilled, thereby making the front of her dress as bad as the back.

"Oh, dear, what a blunderbuss I am!" exclaimed Jo, finishing Meg's glove by scrubbing her gown with it.

"Can I help you?" said a friendly voice. And there was Laurie, with a full cup in one hand and a plate of ice in the other.

"I was trying to get something for Meg, who is very tired, and someone shook me, and here I am in a nice state," answered Jo, glancing dismally from the stained skirt to the coffee-colored glove.

"Too bad! I was looking for someone to give this to. May I take it to your sister?"

"Oh, thank you! I'll show you where she is. I don't offer to take it myself, for I should only get into another scrape if I did."

Jo led the way, and as if used to waiting on ladies, Laurie drew up a little table, brought a second installment of coffee and ice for Jo, and was so obliging that even particular Meg pronounced him a 'nice boy'. They had a merry time over the bonbons and mottoes, and were in the midst of a quiet game of BUZZ, with two or three other young people who had strayed in, when Hannah appeared. Meg forgot her foot and rose so quickly that she was forced to catch hold of Jo, with an exclamation of pain.

"Hush! Don't say anything," she whispered, adding aloud, "It's nothing. I turned my foot a little, that's all," and limped upstairs to put her things on. Hannah scolded, Meg cried, and Jo was at her wits' end, till se decided to take things into her own hands. Slipping out, she ran down and, finding a servant, asked if he could get her a carriage. It happened to be a hired waiter who knew nothing about the neighborhood and Jo was looking round for help when Laurie, who had heard what she said, came up and offered his grandfather's carriage, which had just come for him, he said.

"It's so early! You can't mean to go yet?" began Jo. looking relieved but hesitating to accept the offer.

"I always go early, I do, truly! Please let me take you home. It's all on my way, you know, and it rains, they say."

That settled it, and telling him of Meg's mishap, Jo gratefully accepted and rushed up to bring down the rest of the party. Hannah hated rain as much as a cat does so she made no trouble, and they rolled away in the luxurious close carriage, feeling very festive and elegant. Laurie went on the box so Meg could keep her foot up, and the girls talked over their party in freedom.

"I had a capital time. Did you?' asked Jo, rumpling up her hair, and making herself comfortable.

"Yes, till I hurt myself. Sallie's friend, Annie Moffat, took a fancy to me, and asked me to come and spend a week with her when Sallie does. She is going in the spring when the opera comes, and it will be perfectly splendid, if Mother only lets me go," answered Meg, cheering up at the thought.

"I saw you dancing with the red headed man I ran away from. Was he nice?"

"Oh. very! His hair is auburn, not red, and he was very polite, and I had a delicious redowa with him."

"He looked like a grasshopper in a fit when he did the new step. Laurie and I couldn't help laughing. Did you hear us?"

"No, but it was very rude. What were you about all that time, hidden away there?"

Jo told her adventures, and by the time she had finished they were at home. With many thanks, they said good night and crept in, hoping to disturb no one, but the instant their door creaked, two little nightcaps bobbed up, and two sleepy but eager voices cried out . . .

"Tell about the party! Tell about the party!"

With what Meg called 'a great want of manners' Jo had saved some bonbons for the little girls, and they soon subsided, after hearing the most thrilling events of the evening.

"I declare, it really seems like being a fine young lady, to come home from the party in a carriage and sit in my dressing gown wit a maid to wait on me," said Meg, as Jo bound up her foot with arnica and brushed her hair.

"I don't believe fine young ladies enjoy themselves a bit more than we do, in spite of our burned hair, old gowns, one glove apiece and tight slippers that sprain our ankles when we are silly enough to wear them," And I think Jo was quite right.

Chapter Four

"Oh, dear, how hard it does seem to take up our packs and go on," sighed Meg the morning after the party, for now the holidays were over, the week of merrymaking did not fit her for going on easily with the task she never liked.

"I wish it was Christmas or New Year's all the time. Wouldn't it be fun?" answered Jo, yawning dismally.

"We shouldn't enjoy ourselves half so much as we do now. But it does seem so nice to have little suppers and bouquets, and go to parties, and drive home, and read and rest, and not work. It's like other people, you know, and I always envy girls who do such things, I'm so fond of luxury," said Meg, trying to decide which of two shabby gowns was the least shabby.

"Well, we can't have it, so don't let us grumble but shoulder our bundles and trudge along as cheerfully as Marmee does. I'm sure Aunt March is a regular Old Man of the Sea to me, but I suppose when I've learned to carry her without complaining, she will tumble off, or get so light that I shan't mind her."

This idea tickled Jo's fancy and put her in good spirits, but Meg didn't brighten, for her burden, consisting of four spoiled children, seemed heavier than ever. She had not heart enough even to make herself pretty as usual by putting on a blue neck ribbon and dressing her hair in the most becoming way.

"Where's the use of looking nice, when no one sees me but those cross midgets, and no one cares whether I'm pretty or not?" she muttered, shutting her drawer with a jerk. "I shall have to toil and moil all my days, with only little bits of fun now and then, and get old and ugly and sour, because I'm poor and can't enjoy my life as other girls do. It's a shame!"

So Meg went down, wearing an injured look, and wasn't at all agreeable at breakfast time. Everyone seemed rather out of sorts and inclined to croak.

Beth had a headache and lay on the sofa, trying to comfort herself with the cat and three kittens. Amy was fretting because her lessons were not learned, and she couldn't find her rubbers. Jo would whistle and make a great racket getting ready.

Mrs. March was very busy trying to finish a letter, which must go at once, and Hannah had the grumps, for being up late didn't suit her.

"There never was such a cross family!" cried Jo, losing her temper when she had upset an inkstand, broken both boot lacings, and sat down upon her hat.

"You're the crossest person in it!" returned Amy, washing out the sum that was all wrong with the tears that had fallen on her slate.

"Beth, if you don't keep these horrid cats down cellar I'll have them drowned," exclaimed Meg angrily as she tried to get rid of the kitten which had scrambled up her back and stuck like a burr just out of reach.

Jo laughed, Meg scolded, Beth implored, and Amy wailed because she couldn't remember how much nine times twelve was.

"Girls, girls, do be quiet one minute! I must get this off by the early mail, and you drive me distracted with your worry," cried Mrs. March, crossing out the third spoiled sentence in her letter.

There was a momentary lull, broken by Hannah, who stalked in, laid two hot turnovers on the table, and stalked out again. These turnovers were an institution, and the girls called them 'muffs', for they had no others and found the hot pies very comforting to their hands on cold mornings.

Hannah never forgot to make them, no matter how busy or grumpy she might be, for the walk was long and bleak. The poor things got no other lunch and were seldom home before two.

"Cuddle your cats and get over your headache, Bethy. Goodbye, Marmee. We are a set of rascals this morning, but we'll come home regular angels. Now then, Meg!" And Jo tramped away, feeling that the pilgrims were not setting out as they ought to do.

They always looked back before turning the corner, for their mother was always at the window to nod and smile, and wave her hand to them. Somehow it seemed as if they couldn't have got through the day without that, for whatever their mood might be, the last glimpse of that motherly face was sure to affect them like sunshine.

"If Marmee shook her fist instead of kissing her hand to us, it would serve us right, for more ungrateful wretches than we are were never seen," cried Jo, taking a remorseful satisfaction in the snowy walk and bitter wind. "Don't use such dreadful expressions," replied Meg from the depths of the veil in which she had shrouded herself like a nun sick of the world.

"I like good strong words that mean something," replied Jo, catching her hat as it took a leap off her head preparatory to flying away altogether.

"Call yourself any names you like, but I am neither a rascal nor a wretch and I don't choose to be called so."

"You're a blighted being, and decidedly cross today because you can't sit in the lap of luxury all the time. Poor dear, just wait till I make my fortune, and you shall revel in carriages and ice cream and high-heeled slippers, and posies, and red-headed boys to dance with."

"How ridiculous you are, Jo!" But Meg laughed at the nonsense and felt better in spite of herself.

"Lucky for you I am, for if I put on crushed airs and tried to be dismal, as you do, we should be in a nice state. Thank goodness, I can always find something funny to keep me up. Don't croak any more, but come home jolly, there's a dear."

Jo gave her sister an encouraging pat on the shoulder as they parted for the day, each going a different way, each hugging her little warm turnover, and each trying to be cheerful in spite of wintry weather, hard work, and the unsatisfied desires of pleasure-loving youth.

When Mr. March lost his property in trying to help an unfortunate friend, the two oldest girls begged to be allowed to do something toward their own support, at least. Believing that they could not begin too early to cultivate energy, industry, and independence, their parents consented, and both fell to work with the hearty good will which in spite of all obstacles is sure to succeed at last.

Margaret found a place as nursery governess and felt rich with her small salary. As she said, she was 'fond of luxury', and her chief trouble was poverty. She found it harder to bear than the others because she could remember a time when home was beautiful, life full of ease and pleasure, and want of any kind unknown. She tried not to be envious or discontented, but it was very natural that the young girl should long for pretty things, gay friends, accomplishments, and a happy life. At the Kings' she daily saw all she wanted, for the children's older sisters were just out, and Meg caught frequent glimpses of dainty ball dresses and bouquets, heard lively gossip about theaters, concerts, sleighing parties, and merrymakings of all kinds, and saw money lavished on trifles which would have been so precious to her. Poor Meg seldom complained, but a sense of injustice made her feel bitter toward everyone sometimes, for she had not yet learned to know how rich she was in the blessings which alone can make life happy.

Jo happened to suit Aunt March, who was lame and needed an active person to wait upon her. The childless old lady had offered to adopt one of the girls when the troubles came, and was much offended because her offer was declined. Other friends told the Marches that they had lost all chance of being remembered in the rich old lady's will, but the unworldly Marches only said . . .

"We can't give up our girls for a dozen fortunes. Rich or poor, we will keep together and be happy in one another."

The old lady wouldn't speak to them for a time, but happening to meet Jo at at a friend's, something in her comical face and blunt manners struck the old lady's fancy, and she proposed to take her for a companion. This did not suit Jo at all, but she accepted the place since nothing better appeared and, to every one's surprise, got on remarkably well with her irascible relative. There was an occasional tempest, and once Jo marched home, declaring she couldn't bear it longer, but Aunt March always cleared up quickly, and sent for her to come back again with such urgency that she could not refuse, for in her heart she rather liked the peppery old lady.

I suspect that the real attraction was a large library of fine books, which was left to dust and spiders since Uncle March died. Jo remembered the kind old gentleman, who used to let her build railroads and bridges with his big dictionaries, tell her stories about queer pictures in his Latin books, and buy her cards of gingerbread whenever he met her in the street. The dim, dusty room, with the busts staring down from the tall bookcases, the cozy chairs, the globes, and best of all, the wilderness of books in which she could wander where she liked, made the library a region of bliss to her.

The moment Aunt March took her nap, or was busy with company, Jo hurried to this quiet place, and curling herself up in the easy chair, devoured poetry, romance, history, travels, and pictures like a regular bookworm. But, like all happiness, it did not last long, for as sure as she had just reached the heart of the story, the sweetest verse of a song, or the most perilous adventure of her traveler, a shrill voice called, "Josy-phine! Josy-phine! and she had to leave her paradise to wind yarn, wash the poodle, or read Belsham's Essays by the hour together.

Jo's ambition was to do something very splendid. What it was, she had no idea as yet, but left it for time to tell her, and meanwhile, found her greatest affliction in the fact that she couldn't read, run, and ride as much as she liked. A quick temper, sharp tongue, and restless spirit were always getting her into scrapes, and her life was a series of ups and downs, which were both comic and pathetic. But the training she received at Aunt March's was just what she needed, and the thought that she was doing something to support herself made her happy in spite of the perpetual "Josy-phine!"

Beth was too bashful to go to school.It had been tried, but she suffered so much that it was given up, and she did her lessons at home with her father. Even when he went away, and her mother was called to devote her skill and energy to Soldiers' Aid Societies, Beth went faithfully on by herself and did the best she could. She was a housewifely little creature, and helped Hannah keep home neat and comfortable for the workers, never thinking of any reward but to be loved. Long, quiet days she spent, not lonely nor idle, for her little world was peopled with imaginary friends, and she was by nature a busy bee. There were six dolls to be taken up and dressed every morning, for Beth was a child still and and loved her pets as well as ever. Not one whole or handsome one among them, all were outcasts till Beth took them in, for when her sisters outgrew these idols, they passed to her because Amy would have nothing old or ugly. Beth cherished them all the more tenderly for that very reason, and set up a hospital for infirm dolls. No pins were ever stuck into their cotton vitals, no harsh words or blows were ever given them, no neglect ever saddened the heart or the most repulsive, but all were fed and clothed, nursed and caressed with an affection which never failed. One forlorn fragment of dollanity had belonged to Jo and, having led a tempestuous life, was left a wreck in the rag bag, from which dreary poorhouse it was rescued by Beth and taken to her refuge. Having no top to its head, she tied on a neat little cap, and as both arms and legs were gone, she hid these deficiencies by folding it in a blanket and devoting her best bed to this chronic invalid. If anyone had known the care lavished on that dolly, I think it would have touched their hearts, even while they laughed. She brought it bits of bouquets, she read to it, took it out to breathe fresh air, hidden under her coat, she sang it lullabies and never went to be without kissing its dirty face and whispering tenderly, "I hope you'll have a good night, my poor dear."

Beth had her troubles as well as the others, and not being an angel but a very human little girl, she often 'wept a little weep' as Jo said, because she couldn't take music lessons and have a fine piano. She loved music so dearly, tried so hard to learn, and practiced away so patiently at the jingling old instrument, that it did seem as if someone (not to hint Aunt March) ought to help her. Nobody did, however, and nobody saw Beth wipe the tears off the yellow keys, that wouldn't keep in tune, when she was all alone. She sang like a little lark about her work, never was too tired for Marmee and the girls, and day after day said hopefully to herself," I know I'll get my music some time, if I'm good."

There are many Beths in the world, shy and quiet, sitting in corners till needed, and living for others so cheerfully that no one sees the sacrifices till the little cricket on the hearth stops chirping, and the sweet, sunshiny presence vanishes, leaving silence and shadow behind.

If anybody had asked Amy what the greatest trial of her life was, she would have answered at once, "My nose." When she was a baby, Jo had accidently dropped her into the coal hod, and Amy insisted that the fall had ruined her nose forever. It was not big nor red, like poor 'Petrea's', it was only rather flat, and all the pinching in the world could not give it an aristocratic point. No one minded it but herself, and it was doing its best to grow, but Amy felt deeply the want of a Grecian nose, and drew whole sheets of handsome ones to console herself.

"Little Raphael," as her sisters called her, had a decided talent for drawing, and was never so happy as when copying flowers, designing fairies, or illustrating stories with queer specimens of art. Her teachers complained that instead of doing her sums she covered her slate with animals, the blank pages of her atlas were used to copy maps on, and caricatures of the most ludicrous description came fluttering out of all her books at unlucky moments. She got through her lessons as well as she could, and managed to escape reprimands by being a model of deportment. She was a great favorite with her mates, being good-tempered and possessing the happy art of pleasing without effort. Her little airs and graces were much admired, so were her accomplishments, for besides her drawing, she could play twelve tunes, crochet, and read French without mispronouncing more than two-thirds of the words. She had a plaintive way of saying, "When Papa was rich we did so-and-so," which was very touching, and her long words were considered 'perfectly elegant' by the girls.

Amy was in a fair way to be spoiled, for everyone petted her, and her small vanities and selfishnesses were growing nicely. One thing, however, rather quenched the vanities. She had to wear her cousin's clothes. Now Florence's mama hadn't a particle of taste, and Amy suffered deeply at having to wear a red instead of a blue bonnet, unbecoming gowns, and fussy aprons that did not fit. Everything was good, well made, and little worn, but Amy's artistic eyes were much afflicted, especially this winter, when her school dress was a dull purple with yellow dots and no trimming.

"My only comfort," she said to Meg, with tears in her eyes, "is that Mother doesn't take tucks in my dresses whenever I'm naughty, as Maria Parks's mother does. My dear, it's really dreadful, for sometimes she is so bad her frock is up to her knees, and she can't come to school. When I think of this deggerredation, I fell that I can bear even my flat nose and purple gown with yellow skyrockets on it."

Meg was Amy's confidante and monitor, and by some strange attraction of opposites Jo was gentle Beth's. To Jo alone did the shy child tell her thoughts, and over her big harum-scarum sister Beth unconsciously exercised more influence than anyone in the family. The two older girls were a great deal to one another, but each took one of the younger sisters into her keeping and watched over her in her own way, 'playing mother' they called it, and put their sisters in the places of discarded dolls with the maternal instinct of litte women.

"Has anybody got anything to tell? It's been such a dismal day I'm really dying for some amusement," said Meg, as they sat sewing together that evening.

"I had a queer time with Aunt today, and, as I got the best of it, I'll tell you about it," began Jo, who dearly loved to tell stories. "I was reading that everlasting Belsham, and droning away as I always do, for Aunt soon drops off, and then I take out some nice book, and read like fury till she wakes up. I actually made myself sleepy, and before she began to nod, I gave such a gape that she asked me what I meant by opening my mouth wide enough to take the whole book in at once.

"I wish I could, and be done with it," said I, trying not to be saucy.

"Then she gave me a long lecture on my sins, and told me to sit and think them over while she just 'lost' herself for a moment. She never finds herself very soon, so the minute her cap began to bob like a top-heavy dahlia, I whipped the VICAR OF WAKEFIELD out of my pocket, and read away, with one eye on him and one on Aunt. I'd just got to where they all tumbled into the water when I forgot and laughed out loud. Aunt woke up and, being more good-natured after her nap, told me to read a bit and show what frivolous work I preferred to the worthy and instructive Belsham. I did my very best, and she liked it, though she only said . . .

"I don't understand what it's all about. Go back and begin it, child."

"Back I went, and made the Primroses as interesting as ever I could. Once I was wicked enough to stop in a thrilling place, and say meekly, "I'm afraid it tires you, ma'am. Shan't I stop now?"

"She caught up her knitting, which had dropped out of her hands, gave me a sharp look through her specs, and said, in her short way, 'Finish the chapter, and don't be impertinent, miss.'"

"Did she own she liked it?" asked Meg.

"Oh, bless you, no! But she let old Belsham rest, and when I ran back after my gloves this afternoon, there she was, so hard at the Vicar that she didn't hear me laugh as I danced a jig in the hall because of the good time coming. What a pleasant life she might have if only she chose! I don't envy her much, in spite of her money, for after all rich people have about as many worries as poor ones, I think," added Jo.

"That reminds me," said Meg, "that I've got something to tell. It isn't funny, like Jo's story, but I thought about it a good deal as I came home. At the Kings' today I found everybody in a flurry, and one of the children said that her oldest brother had done something dreadful, and Papa had sent him away. I heard Mrs. King crying and Mr. King talking very loud, and Grace and Ellen turned away their faces when they passed me, so I shouldn't see how red and swollen their eyes were. I didn't ask any questions, of course, but I felt so sorry for them and was rather glad I hadn't any wild brothers to do wicked things and disgrace the family."

"I think being disgraced in school is a great deal tryinger than anything bad boys can do," said Amy, shaking her head, as if her experience of life had been a deep one. "Susie Perkins came to school today with a lovely red carnelian ring. I wanted it dreadfully, and wished I was her with all my might. Well, she drew a picture of Mr. Davis, with a monstrous nose and a hump, and the words, 'Young ladies, my eye is upon you!' coming out of his mouth in a balloon thing. We were laughing over it when all of a sudden his eye was on us, and he ordered Susie to bring up her slate. She was parrylized with fright, but she went, and oh, what do you think he did? He took her by the ear—the ear! Just fancy how horrid!—and led her to the recitation platform, and made her stand there half and hour, holding the slate so everyone could see."

"Didn't the girls laugh at the picture?" asked Jo, who relished the scrape.

"Laugh? Not one! They sat still as mice, and Susie cried quarts, I know she did. I didn't envy her then, for I felt that millions of carnelian rings wouldn't have made me happy after that. I never, never should have got over such a agonizing mortification." And Amy went on with her work, in the proud consciousness of virtue and the successful utterance of two long words in a breath.

"I saw something I liked this morning, and I meant to tell it at dinner, but I forgot," said Beth, putting Jo's topsy-turvy basket in order as she talked. "When I went to get some oysters for Hannah, Mr. Laurence was in the fish shop, but he didn't see me, for I kept behind the fish barrel, and he was busy with Mr. Cutter the fishman. A poor woman came in with a pail a mop, and asked Mr. Cutter if he would let her do some scrubbing for a bit of fish, because she hadn't any dinner for her children, and had been disappointed of a day's work. Mr. Cutter was in a hurry and said 'No', rather crossly, so she was going away, looking hungry and sorry, when Mr. Laurence hooked up a big fish with the crooked end of his cane and held it out to her. She was so glad and surprised she took it right into her arms, and thanked him over and over. He told her to 'go along and cook it', and she hurried off, so happy! Wasn't it good of him? Oh, she did look so funny, hugging the big, slippery fish, and hoping Mr. Laurence's bed in heaven would be 'aisy'."

When they had laughed at Beth's story, they asked their mother for one, and after a moments thought, she said soberly, "As I sat cutting out blue flannel jackets today at the rooms, I felt very anxious about Father, and thought how lonely and helpless we should be, if anything happened to him. It was not a wise thing to do, but I kept on worrying till an old man came in with an order for some clothes. He sat down near me, and I began to talk to him, for he looked poor and tired and anxious.

"'Have you sons in the army?' I asked, for the note he brought was not to me. "Yes, ma'am. I had four, but two were killed, one is a prisoner, and I'm going to the other, who is very sick in a Washington hospital.' he answered quietly.

"'You have done a great deal for your country, sir, ' I said, feeling respect now, instead of pity.

"'Not a mite more than I ought, ma'am. I'd go myself, if I was any use. As I ain't, I give my boys, and give 'em free.'

"He spoke so cheerfully, looked so sincere, and seemed so glad to give his all, that I was ashamed of myself. I'd given one man and thought it too much, while he gave four without grudging them. I had all my girls to comfort me at home, and his last son was waiting, miles away, to say good-by to him, perhaps! I felt so rich, so happy thinking of my blessings, that I made him a nice bundle, gave him some money, and thanked him heartily for the lesson he had taught me."

"Tell another story, Mother, one with a moral to it, like this. I like to think about them afterward, if they are real and not too preachy," said Jo, after a minute's silence.

Mrs. March smiled and began at once, for she had told stories to this little audience for many years, and knew how to please them.

"Once upon a time, there were four girls, who had enough to eat and drink and wear, a good many comforts and pleasures, kind friends and parents who loved them dearly, and yet they were not contented." (Here the listeners stole sly looks at one another, and began to sew diligently.) "These girls were anxious to be good and made many excellent resolutions, but they did not keep them very well, and were constantly saying, 'If only we had this, ' or 'If we could only do that, ' quite forgetting how much they already had, and how many things they actually could do. So they asked an old woman what spell they could use to make them happy, and she said, 'When you feel discontented, think over your blessings, and be grateful.'" (Here Jo looked up quickly, as if about to speak, but changed her mind, seeing that the story was not done yet.)

"Being sensible girls, they decided to try her advice, and soon were surprised to see how well off they were. One discovered that money couldn't keep shame and sorrow out of rich people's houses, another that, though she was poor, she was a great deal happier, with her youth, health, and good spirits, than a certain fretful, feeble old lady who couldn't enjoy her comforts, a third that, disagreeable as it was to help get dinner, it was harder still to go begging for it and the fourth, that even carnelian rings were not so valuable as good behavior. So they agreed to stop complaining, to enjoy the blessings already possessed, and try to deserve them, lest they should be taken away entirely, instead of increased, and I believe they were never disappointed or sorry that they took the old woman's advice."

"Now, Marmee, that is very cunning of you to turn our own stories against us, and give us a sermon instead of a romance!" cried Meg. "I like that kind of sermon. It's the sort Father used to tell us," said Beth thoughtfully, putting the needles straight on Jo's cushion.

"I don't complain near as much as the others do, and I shall be more careful than ever now, for I've had warning from Susies's downfall," said Amy morally.

"We needed that lesson, and we won't forget it. If we do so, you just say to us, as old Chloe did in UNCLE TOM, 'Tink ob yer marcies, chillen! 'Tink ob yer marcies!'" added Jo, who could not, for the life of her, help getting a morsel of fun out of the little sermon, though she took it to heart as much as any of them.

Chapter Five

"What in the world are you going to do now, Jo." asked Meg one snowy afternoon, as her sister came tramping through the hall, in rubber boots, old sack, and hood, with a broom in one hand and a shovel in the other.

"Going out for exercise," answered Jo with a mischievous twinkle in her eyes.

"I should think two long walks this morning would have been enough! It's cold and dull out, and I advise you to stay warm and dry by the fire, as I do," said Meg with a shiver.

"Never take advice! Can't keep still all day, and not being a pussycat, I don't like to doze by the fire. I like adventures, and I'm going to find some."

Meg went back to toast her feet and read IVANHOE, and Jo began to dig paths with great energy. The snow was light, and with her broom she soon swept a path all round the garden, for Beth to walk in when the sun came out and the invalid dolls needed air. Now, the garden separated the Marches' house from that of Mr. Laurence. Both stood in a suburb of the city, which was still countrylike, with groves and lawns, large gardens, and quiet streets. A low hedge parted the two estates. On one side was an old, brown house, looking rather bare and shabby, robbed of the vines that in summer covered its walls and the flowers, which then surrounded it. On the other side was a stately stone mansion, plainly betokening every sort of comfort and luxury, from the big coach house and well-kept grounds to the conservatory and the glimpses of lovely things one caught between the rich curtains.

Yet it seemed a lonely, lifeless sort of house, for no children frolicked on the lawn, no motherly face ever smiled at the windows, and few people went in and out, except the old gentleman and his grandson.

To Jo's lively fancy, this fine house seemed a kind of enchanted palace, full of splendors and delights which no one enjoyed. She had long wanted to behold these hidden glories, and to know the Laurence boy, who looked as if he would like to be known, if he only knew how to begin. Since the party, she had been more eager than ever, and had planned many ways of making friends with him, but he had not been seen lately, and Jo began to think he had gone away, when she one day spied a brown face at an upper window, looking wistfully down into their garden, where Beth and Amy were snow-balling one another.

"That boy is suffering for society and fun," she said to herself. "His grandpa does not know what's good for him, and keeps him shut up all alone. He needs a party of jolly boys to play with, or somebody young and lively. I've a great mind to go over and tell the old gentleman so!"

The idea amused Jo. who liked to do daring things and was always scandalizing Meg by her queer performances. The plan of 'going over' was not forgotten. And when the snowy afternoon came, Jo resolved to try what could be done. She saw Mr. Lawrence drive off, and then sallied out to dig her way down to the hedge, where she paused and took a survey. All quiet, curtains down at the lower windows, servants out of sight, and nothing human visible but a curly black head leaning on a thin hand at the upper window.

"There he is," thought Jo, "Poor boy! All alone and sick this dismal day. It's a shame! I'll toss up a snowball and make him look out, and then say a kind word to him."

Up went a handful of soft snow, and the head turned at once, showing a face which lost its listless look in a minute, as the big eyes brightened and the mouth began to smile. Jo nodded and laughed, and flourished her broom as she called out . . .

"How do you do? Are you sick?"

Laurie opened the window, and croaked out as hoarsely as a raven . . .

"Better, thank you. I've had a bad cold, and been shut up a week."

"I'm sorry. What do you amuse yourself with?"

"Nothing. It's dull as tombs up here."

"Don't you read?"

"Not much. They won't let me."

"Can't somebody read to you?"

"Grandpa does sometimes, but my books don't interest him, and I hate to ask Brooke all the time."

"Have someone come and see you then."

"There isn't anyone I'd like to see. Boys make such a row, and my head is weak."

"Isn't there some nice girl who'd read and amuse you? Girls are quiet and like to play nurse."

"Don't know any."

"You know us," began Jo, then laughed and stopped.

"So I do! Will you come, please?" cried Laurie.

"I'm not quiet and nice, but I'll come, if Mother will let me. I'll go ask her. Shut the window, like a good boy, and wait till I come."

With that, Jo shouldered her broom and marched into the house, wondering what they would all say to her. Laurie was in a flutter of excitement at the idea of having company, and flew about to get ready, for as Mrs. March said, he was 'a little gentleman'. and did honor to the coming guest by brushing his curly pate, putting on a fresh color, and trying tidy up the room, which in spite of half a dozen servants, was anything but neat. Presently there came a loud ring, than a decided voice, asking for 'Mr. laurie', and a surprised-looking servant came running up to announce a young lady.

"All right, show her up, it's Miss Jo, "said Laurie, going to the door of his little parlor to meet Jo, who appeared, looking rosy and quite at her ease, with a covered dish in one hand and Beth's three kittens in the other.

"Here I am, bag and baggage," she said briskly. "Mother sent her love, and was glad if I could do anything for you. Meg wanted me to bring some of her blancmange, she makes it very nicely, and Beth thought her cats would be comforting. I knew you'd laugh at them, but I couldn't refuse, she was so anxious to do something."

It so happened that Beth's funny loan was just the thing, for in laughing over the kits, Laurie forgot his bashfulness, and grew sociable at once.

"That looks too pretty to eat," he said, smiling with pleasure, as Jo uncovered the dish, and showed the blancmange, surrounded by a garland of green leaves, and the scarlet flowers of Amy's pet geranium.

"It isn't anything, only they all felt kindly and wanted to show it. Tell the girl to put it away for your tea. It's so simple you can eat it, and being soft, it will slip down without hurting your sore throat. What a cozy room this is!"

"It might be it it was kept nice, but the maids are lazy, and I don't know how to make them mind. It worries me though."

"I'll right it up in two minutes, for it only needs to have the hearth brushed, so—and the things made straight on the mantelpiece, so—and the books put here, and the bottles there, and your sofa turned from the light, and the pillows plumped up a bit. Now then, you're fixed."

And so he was, for, as she laughed and talked, Jo had whisked things into place and given quite a different air to the room. Laurie watched her in respectful silence, and when she beckoned him to his sofa, he sat down with a sigh of satisfaction, saying gratefully . . .

"How kind you are! Yes, that's what it wanted. Now please take the big chair and let me do something to amuse my company."

"No, I came to amuse you. Shall I read aloud?" and Jo looked affectionately toward some inviting books near by.

"Thank you! I've read all those, and if you don't mind, I'd rather talk," answered Laurie.

"Not a bit. I'll talk all day if you'll only set me going. Beth says I never know when to stop."

"Is Beth the rosy one, who stays at home good deal and sometimes goes out with a little basket?" asked Laurie with interest.

"Yes, that's Beth. She's my girl, and a regular good one she is, too."

"The pretty one is Meg, and the curly-haired one is Amy, I believe?"

Laurie colored up, but answered frankly, "Why, you see I often hear you calling to one another, and when I'm alone up here, I can't help looking over at your house, you always seem to be having such good times. I beg your pardon for being so rude, but sometimes you forget to put down the curtain at the window where the flowers are. And when the lamps are lighted, it's like looking at a picture to see the fire, and you all around the table with your mother. Her face is right opposite, and it looks so sweet behind the flowers, I can't help watching it. I haven't got any mother, you know." And Laurie poked the fire to hide a little twitching of the lips that he could not control.

The solitary, hungry look in his eyes went straight to Jo's warm heart. she had been so simply taught that there was no nonsense in her head, and at fifteen she was as innocent and frank as any child. Laurie was sick and lonely, and feeling how rich she was in home and happiness, she gladly tried to share it with him. Her face was very friendly and her sharp voice unusually gentle as she said . . .

"We'll never draw that curtain any more, and I give you leave to look as much as you like. I just wish, though, instead of peeping, you'd come over and see us. Mother is so splendid, she'd do you heaps of good, and Beth would sing to you if I begged her to, and Amy would dance. Meg and I would make you laugh over our funny stage properties, and we'd have jolly times. Wouldn't your grandpa let you?"

"I think he would, if your mother asked him. He's very kind, though he does not look so, and he lets me do what I like, pretty much, only he's afraid I might be a bother to strangers," began Laurie, brightening more and more.

"We are not strangers, we are neighbors, and you needn't think you'd be a bother. We want to know you, and I've been trying to do it this ever so long. We haven't been here a great while, you know, but we have got acquainted with all our neighbors but you."

"You see, Grandpa lives among his books, and doesn't mind much what happens outside. Mr. Brooke, my tutor, doesn't stay here, you know, and I have no one to go about with me, so I just stop at home and get on as I can."

"That's bad. You ought to make an effort and go visiting everywhere you are asked, then you'll have plenty of friends, and pleasant places to go to. Never mind being bashful. It won't last long if you keep going."

Laurie turned red again, but wasn't offended at being accused of bashfulness, for there was so much good will in Jo it was impossible not to take her blunt speeches as kindly as they were meant.

"Do you like your school?" asked the boy, changing the subject, after a little pause, during which he stared at the fire and Jo looked about her, well pleased.

"Don't go to school, I'm a businessman—girl, I mean. I go to wait on my great-aunt, and a dear, cross old soul she is, too," answered Jo.

Laurie opened his mouth to ask another question, but remembering just in time that it wasn't manners to make too many inquiries into people's affairs, he shut it again, and looked uncomfortable.

Jo liked his good breeding, and didn't mind having a laugh at Aunt March, so she gave him a lively description of the fidgety old lady, her fat poodle, the parrot that talked Spanish, and the library where she reveled.

Laurie enjoyed that immensely, and when she told about the prim old gentleman who came once to woo Aunt March, and in the middle of a fine speech, how Poll had tweaked his wig off to his great dismay, the boy lay back and laughed till the tears ran down his cheeks, and a maid popped her head in to see what was the matter.

"Oh! That does me no end of good. Tell on, please," he said, taking his face out of the sofa cushion, red and shining with merriment.

Much elated with her success, Jo did 'tell on', all about their plays and plans, their hopes and fears for Father, and the most interesting events of the little world in which the sisters lived. Then they got to talking about books, and to Jo's delight, she found that Laurie loved them as well as she did, and had read even more than herself.

"If you like them so much, come down and see ours. Grandfather is out, so you needn't be afraid," said Laurie, getting up.

"I'm not afraid of anything," returned Jo, with a toss of the head.

"I don't believe you are!" exclaimed the boy, looking at her with much admiration, though he privately thought she would have good reason to be a trifle afraid of the old gentleman, if she met hem in some of his moods.

The atmosphere of the whole house being summerlike, Laurie led the way from room to room, letting Jo stop to examine whatever struck her fancy. And so, at last they came to the library, where she clapped her hands and pranced, as she always did when especially delighted. It was lined with books, and there were pictures and statues, and distracting little cabinets full of coins and curiosities, and Sleepy Hollow chairs, and queer tables, and bronzes, and best of all, a great open fireplace with quaint tiles all round it.

"What richness!" sighed Jo, sinking into the depth of a velour chair and gazing about her with an air of intense satisfaction. "Theodore Laurence, you ought to be the happiest boy in the world," she added impressively.

"A fellow can't live on books," said Laurie, shaking his head as he perched on a table opposite.

Before he could more, a bell rang, and Jo flew up, exclaiming with alarm, "Mercy me! It's your grandpa!"

"Well, what if it is? You are not afraid of anything, you know," returned the boy, looking wicked.

"I think I am a little bit afraid of him, but I don't know why I should be. Marmee said I might come, and I don't think you're any the worse for it," said Jo, composing herself, though she kept her eyes on the door.

"I'm a great deal better for it, and ever so much obliged. I'm only afraid you are very tired of talking to me. It was so pleasant, I couldn't bear to stop," said Laurie gratefully.

"The doctor to see you, sir," and the maid beckoned as she spoke.

"Would you mind if I left you for a minute? I suppose I must see him," said Laurie.

"Don't mind me. I'm happy as a cricket here," answered Jo.

Laurie went away, and his guest amused herself in her own way. She was standing before a fine portrait of the old gentleman when the door opened again, and without turning, she said decidedly, "I'm sure now that I shouldn't be afraid of him, for he's got kind eyes, though his mouth is grim, and he looks as if he had a tremendous will of his own. He isn't as handsome as my grandfather, but I like him."

"Thank you, ma'am," said a gruff voice behind her, and there, to her great dismay, stood old Mr. Laurence.

Poor Jo blushed till she couldn't blush any redder, and her heart began to beat uncomfortably fast as she thought what she had said. For a minute a wild desire to run away possessed her, but that was cowardly, and the girls would laugh at her, so she resolved to stay and get out of the scrape as she could. A second look showed her that the living eyes, under the bushy eyebrows, were kinder even than the painted ones, and there was a sly twinkle in them, which lessened her fear a good deal. The gruff voice was gruffer than ever, as the old gentleman said abruptly, after the dreadful pause, "So you're not afraid of me, hey?"

"Not much, sir."

"And you don't think me as handsome as your grandfather?"

"Not quite, sir."

"And I've got a tremendous will, have I?"

"I only said I thought so."

"But you like me in spite of it?"

"Yes, I do, sir."

That answer pleased the old gentleman. He gave a short laugh, shook hands with her, and, putting his finger under her chin, turned up her face, examined it gravely, and let it go, saying with a nod, "You've got your grandfather's spirit, if you haven't his face. He was a fine man, my dear, but what is better, he was a brave and an honest one, and I was proud to be his friend."

"Thank you, sir," And Jo was quite comfortable after that, for it suited her exactly.

"What have you been doing to this boy of mine, hey?" was the next question, sharply put.

"Only trying to be neighborly, sir." And Jo to how her visit came about.

"You think he needs cheering up a bit, do you?"

"Yes, sir, he seems a little lonely, and young folks would do him good perhaps. We are only girls, but we should be glad to help if we could, for we don't forget the splendid Christmas present you sent us," said Jo eagerly.

"Tut, tut, tut! That was the boy's affair. How is the poor woman?"

"Doing nicely, sir." And off went Jo, talking very fast, as she told all about the Hummels, in whom her mother had interested richer friends than they were.

"Just her father's way of doing good. I shall come and see your mother some fine day. Tell her so. There's the tea bell, we have it early on the boy's account. Come down and go on being neighborly."

"If you'd like to have me, sir."

"Shouldn't ask you, if I didn't." And Mr. Laurence offered her his arm with old-fashioned courtesy.

"What would Meg say to this?" thought Jo, as she was marched away, while her eyes danced with fun as she imagined herself telling the story at home.

"Hey! Why, what the dickens has come to the fellow?" said the old gentleman, as Laurie came running downstairs and brought up with a start of surprise at the astounding sight of Jo arm in arm with his redoubtable grandfather.

"I didn't know you'd come, sir," he began, as Jo gave him a triumphant little glance.

"That's evident, by the way you racket downstairs. Come to your tea, sir, and behave like a gentleman." And having pulled the boy's hair by way of a caress, Mr. Laurence walked on, while Laurie went through a series of comic evolutions behind their backs, which nearly produced an explosion of laughter from Jo.

The old gentleman did not say much as he drank his four cups of tea, but he watched the young people, who soon chatted away like old friends, and the change in his grandson did not escape him. There was color, light, and life in the boy's face now, vivacity in his manner, and genuine merriment in his laugh.

"She's right, the lad is lonely. I'll see what these little girls can do for him," thought Mr. Laurence, as he looked and listened. He liked Jo, for her odd, blunt ways suited him, and she seemed to understand the boy almost as well as if she had been one herself.

If the Laurences had been what Jo called 'prim and poky', she would not have got on at all, for such people always made her shy and awkward. But finding them free and easy, she was so herself, and made a good impression. When they rose she proposed to go, but Laurie said he had something more to show her, and took her away to the conservatory, which had been lighted for her benefit. It seemed quite fairylike to Jo, as she went up and down the walks, enjoying the blooming walls on either side, the soft light, the damp sweet air, and the wonderful vines and trees that hung about her, while her new friend cut the finest flowers till his hands were full. Then he tied them up, saying, with the happy look Jo liked to see, "Please give these to your mother, and tell her I like the medicine she sent me very much."

They found Mr. Laurence standing before the fire in the great drawing room, by Jo's attention was entirely absorbed by a grand piano, which stood open.

"Do you play?" she asked, turning to Laurie with a respectful expression.

"Sometimes," he answered modestly.

"Please do now. I want to hear it, so I can tell Beth."

"Won't you first?"

"Don't know how. Too stupid to learn, but I love music dearly."

So Laurie played and Jo listened, with her nose luxuriously buried in heliotrope and tea roses. Her respect and regard for the 'Laurence' boy increased very much, for he played remarkably well and didn't put on any airs. She wished Beth could hear him, but she did not say so, only praised him till he was quite abashed, and his grandfather came to his rescue.

"That will do, that will do, young lady. too many sugarplums are not good for him. His music isn't bad, but I hope he will do as well in more important things. Going? well, I'm much obliged to you, and I hope you'll come again. My respects to your mother. Good night, Doctor Jo."

He shook hands kindly, but looked as if something did not please him. When they got into the hall, Jo asked Laurie if she had said something amiss. He shook his head.

"No, it was me. He doesn't like to hear me play."

"Why not?"

"I'll tell you some day. John is going home with you, as I can't." "No need of that. I am not a young lady, and it's only a step. Take care of yourself, won't you?"

"Yes, but you will come again, I hope?"

"If you promise to come and see us after you are well."

"I will."

"Good night, Laurie!" "Good night, Jo, good night!"

When all the afternoon's adventures had been told, the family felt inclined to go visiting in a body, for each found something very attractive in the big house on the other side of the hedge. Mrs. March wanted to talk of her father with the old man who had not forgotten him, Meg longed to walk in the conservatory, Beth sighed for the grand piano. and Amy was eager to see the fine pictures and statues.

"Mother, why didn't Mr. Laurence like to have Laurie play?" asked Jo, who was of an inquiring disposition.

"I am not sure, but I think it was because his son, Laurie's father, married an Italian lady, a musician, which displeased the old man, who is very proud. The lady was good and lovely and accomplished, but he did not like her, and never saw his son after he married. They both died when Laurie was a little child, and then his grandfather took him home. I fancy the boy, who was born in Italy, is not very strong, and the old man is afraid of losing him, which makes him so careful. Laurie comes naturally by his love of music, for he is like his mother, and I dare say his grandfather fears that he may want to be a musician. At any rate, his skill reminds him of the woman he did not like, and so he 'glowered' as Jo said."

"Dear me, how romantic!" exclaimed Meg.

"How silly!" said Jo. "Let him be a musician if he wants to, and not plague his life out sending him to college, when he hates to go."

"That's why he has such handsome black eyes and pretty manners, I suppose. Italians are always nice," said Meg, who was a little sentimental.

"What do you know about his eyes and his manners? You never spoke to him, hardly," cried Jo, who was not sentimental.

"I saw him at the party, and what you tell shows that he knows how to behave. That was a nice little speech about the medicine Mother sent him."

"He meant the blanc mange, I suppose." "How stupid you are, child! He meant you, of course."

"Did he?" And Jo opened her eyes as if it had never occurred to her before.

"I never saw such a girl! You don't know a compliment when you get it," said Meg, with the air of a young lady who knew all about the matter.

"I think they are great nonsense, and I'll thank you not to be silly and spoil my fun. Laurie's a nice boy and I like him, and I won't have any sentimental stuff about compliments and such rubbish. We'll all be good to him because he hasn't got any mother, and he may come over and see us, mayn't he, Marmee?"

"Yes, Jo, your little friend is very welcome, and I hope Meg will remember that children should be children as long as they can."

"I don't call myself a child, and I'm not in my teens yet," observed Amy. "What do you say, Beth?"

"I was thinking about our 'PILGRIM'S PROGRESS,'" answered Beth, who had not heard a word. "How we got out of the Slough and through the Wicket Gate by resolving to be good, and up the steep hill by trying, and that maybe the house over there, full of splendid things, is going to be our Palace Beautiful."

"We have got to get by the lions first," said Jo, as if she rather liked the prospect.

Chapter Six

The big house did prove a Palace Beautiful, though it took some time for all to get in, and Beth found it very hard to pass the lions. Old Mr. Laurence was the biggest one, but after he had called, said something funny or kind to each one of the girls, and talked over old times with their mother, nobody felt much afraid of him, except timid Beth. The other lion was the fact that they were poor and Laurie rich, for this made them shy of accepting favors which they could not return. But, after a while, they found that he considered them the benefactors, and could not do enough to show how grateful he was for Mrs. March's motherly welcome, their cheerful society, and the comfort he took in that humble home of theirs. So they soon forgot their pride and interchanged kindnesses without stopping to think which was the greater.

All sorts of pleasant things happened about that time, for the new friendship flourished like grass in spring. Every one liked Laurie, and he privately informed his tutor that "the Marches were regularly splendid girls." With the delightful enthusiasm of youth, they took the solitary boy into their midst and made much of him, and he found something very charming in the innocent companionship of these simple-hearted girls. Never having known mother or sisters, he was quick to feel the influences they brought about him, and their busy, lively ways made him ashamed of the indolent life he led. He was tired of books, and found people so interesting now that Mr. Brooke was obliged to make very unsatisfactory reports, for Laurie was always playing truant and running over to the Marches'.

"Never mind, let him take a holiday, and make it up afterward," said the old gentleman. "The good lady next door says he is studying too hard and needs young society, amusement, and exercise. I suspect she is right, and that I've been coddling the fellow as if I'd been his grandmother. Let him do what he likes, as long as he is happy. He can't get into mischief in that little nunnery over there, and Mrs. March is doing more for him than we can."

What good times they had, to be sure. Such plays and tableaux, such sleigh rides and skating frolics, such pleasant evenings in the old parlor, and now and then such gay little parties at the great house. Meg could walk in the conservatory whenever she liked and revel in bouquets, Jo browsed over the new library voraciously, and convulsed the old gentleman with her criticisms, Amy copied pictures and enjoyed beauty to her heart's content, and Laurie played 'lord of the manor' in the most delightful style.

But Beth, though yearning for the grand piano, could not pluck up courage to go to the 'Mansion of Bliss', as Meg called it. She went once with Jo, but the old gentleman, not being aware of her infirmity, stared at her so hard from under his heavy eyebrows, and said "Hey!" so loud, that he frightened her so much her 'feet chattered on the floor', she never told her mother, and she ran away, declaring she would never go there any more, not even for the dear piano. No persuasions or enticements could overcome her fear, till, the fact coming to Mr. Laurence's ear in some mysterious way, he set about mending matters. During one of the brief calls he made, he artfully led the conversation to music, and talked away about great singers whom he had seen, fine organs he had heard, and told such charming anecdotes that Beth found it impossible to stay in her distant corner, but crept nearer and nearer, as if fascinated. At the back of his chair she stopped and stood listening, with her great eyes wide open and her cheeks red with excitement of this unusual performance. Taking no more notice of her than if she had been a fly, Mr. Laurence talked on about Laurie's lessons and teachers. And presently, as if the idea had just occurred to him, he said to Mrs. March . . .

"The boy neglects his music now, and I'm glad of it, for he was getting too fond of it. But the piano suffers for want of use. Wouldn't some of your girls like to run over, and practice on it now and then, just to keep it in tune, you know, ma'am?"

Beth took a step forward, and pressed her hands tightly together to keep from clapping them, for this was an irresistible temptation, and the thought of practicing on that splendid instrument quite took her breath away. Before Mrs. March could reply, Mr. Laurence went on with an odd little nod and smile . . .

"They needn't see or speak to anyone, but run in at any time. For I'm shut up in my study at the other end of the house, Laurie is out a great deal, and the servants are never near the drawing room after nine o'clock."

Here he rose, as if going, and Beth made up her mind to speak, for that last arrangement left nothing to be desired. "Please, tell the young ladies what I say, and if they don't care to come, why, never mind." Here a little hand slipped into his, and Beth looked up at him with a face full of gratitude, as she said, in her earnest yet timid way . . .

"Oh sir, they do care, very very much!" "Are you the musical girl?" he asked, without any startling "Hey!" as he looked down at her very kindly.

"I'm Beth. I love it dearly, and I'll come, if you are quite sure nobody will hear me, and be disturbed," she added, fearing to be rude, and trembling at her own boldness as she spoke.

"Not a soul, my dear. The house is empty half the day, so come and drum away as much as you like, and I shall be obliged to you."

"How kind you are, sir!"

Beth blushed like a rose under the friendly look he wore, but she was not frightened now, and gave the hand a grateful squeeze because she had no words to thank him for the precious gift he had given her. The old gentleman softly stroked the hair off her forehead, and, stooping down, he kissed herr, saying, in a tone few people ever heard . . .

"I had a little girl once, with eyes like these. God bless you, my dear! Good day. madam." And away he went, in a great hurry.

Beth had a rapture with her mother, and then rushed up to impart the glorious news to her family of invalids, as the girls were not home. How blithely she sang that evening, and how they all laughed at her because she woke Amy in the night by playing the piano on her face in her sleep. Next day, having seen both the old and young gentleman out of the house, Beth, after two or three retreats, fairly got in at the side door, and made her way as noiselessly as any mouse to the drawing room where her idol stood. Quite by accident, of course, some pretty, easy music lay on the piano, and with trembling fingers and frequent stops to listen and look about, Beth at last touched the great instrument, and straightway forgot her fear, herself, and everything else but the unspeakable delight which the music gave her, for it was like the voice of a beloved friend.

She stayed till Hannah came to take her home to dinner, but she had no appetite, and could only sit and smile upon everyone in a general state of beatitude.

After that, the little brown hood slipped through the hedge nearly every day, and the great drawing room was haunted by a tuneful spirit that came and went unseen. She never knew that

Mr. Laurence opened his study door to hear the old-fashioned airs he liked. She never saw Laurie mount guard in the hall to warn the servants away. She never suspected that the exercise books and new songs which she found in the rack were put there for her especial benefit, and when he talked to her about music at home, she only thought how kind he was to tell things that helped her so much. So she enjoyed herself heartily, and found, what isn't always the case, that her granted wish was all she had hoped. Perhaps it was because she was so grateful for this blessing that a greater was given her. At any rate she deserved both. "Mother, I'm going to work Mr. Laurence a pair of slippers. He is so kind to me, I must thank him, and I don't know any other way. Can I do it?" asked Beth, a few weeks after that eventful call of his.

"Yes, dear. It will please him very much, and be a nice way of thanking him. The girls will help you about them, and I will pay for the making up," replied Mrs. March, who took peculiar pleasure in granting Beth's requests because she so seldom asked anything for herself.

After many serious discussions with Meg and Jo, the pattern was chosen, the materials bought, and the slippers begun. A cluster of grave yet cheerful pansies on a deeper purple ground was pronounced very appropriate and pretty, and beth worked away early and late, with occasional lifts over hard parts. She was a nimble little needlewoman, and they were finished before anyone got tired of them. Then she wrote a short, simple note, and with Laurie's help, got them smuggled onto the study table one morning before the old gentleman was up.

When this excitement was over, Beth waited to see what would happen. All day passed a a part of the next before any acknowledgement arrived, and she was beginning to fear she had offended her crochety friend. On the afternoon of the second day, she went out to do an errand, and give poor Joanna, the invalid doll, her daily exercise. As she came up the street, on her return, she saw three, yes, four heads popping in and out of the parlor windows, and the moment they saw her, several hands were waved, and several joyful voices screamed . . .

"Here's a letter from the old gentleman! Come quick, and read it!"

"Oh, Beth, he's sent you . . ." began Amy, gesticulating with unseemly energy, but she got no further, for Jo quenched her by slamming down the window.

Beth hurried on in a flutter of suspense. At the door her sisters seized and bore her to the parlor in a triumphal procession, all pointing and all saying at once, "Look there! Look there!" Beth did look, and turned pale with delight and surprise, for there stood a little cabinet piano, with a letter lying on the glossy lid, directed like a sign board to "Miss Elizabeth March."

"For me?" gasped Beth, holding onto Jo and feeling as if she should tumble down, it was such an overwhelming thing altogether.

"Yes, all for you, my precious! Isn't it splendid of him? Don't you think he's the dearest old man in the world? Here's the key in the letter. We didn't open it, but we are dying to know what he says," cried Jo, hugging her sister and offering the note.

"You read it! I can't, I feel so queer! Oh, it is too lovely!" and Beth hid her face in Jo's apron, quite upset by her present.

Jo opened the paper and began to laugh, for the first worked she saw were . . .

"Miss March: "Dear Madam—" "How nice it sounds! I wish someone would write to me so!" said Amy, who thought the old-fashioned address very elegant.

"'I have had many pairs of slippers in my life, but I never had any that suited me so well as yours, '" continues Jo. "'Heartsease is my favorite flower, and these will always remind me of the gentle giver. I like to pay my debts, so I know you will allow 'the old gentleman' to send you something which once belonged to the little grand daughter he lost. With hearty thanks and best wishes, I remain "'Your grateful friend and humble servant, "'JAMES LAURENCE'

"There, Beth, that's an honor to be proud of, I'm sure! Laurie told me how fond Mr.Laurence used to be of the child who died, and how he kept all her little things carefully. Just think, he's given you her piano. That comes of having big blue eyes and loving music," said Jo, trying to soothe Beth, who trembled and looked more excited than she had ever been before.

"See the cunning brackets to hold candles, and the nice green sild, puckered up, with a gold rose in the middle, and the pretty rack and stool, all complete," added Meg, opening the instrument and displaying its beauties.

"'Your humble servant, James Laurence'. Only think of his writing that to you. I'll tell the girls. They'll think it's splendid," said Amy, much impressed by the note.

"Try it, honey. Let's hear the sound of the baby pianny," said Hannah, who always took a share in the family joys and sorrows.

So Beth tried it, and everyone pronounced it the most remarkable piano ever heard. It had evidently been newly tuned and put in apple-pie order, but, perfect as it was, I think the real charm lay in the happiest of all happy faces which leaned over it, as Beth lovingly touched the beautiful black and white keys and pressed the bright pedals.

"You'll have to go and thank him," said Jo, by way of a joke, for the idea of the child's really going never entered her head.

"Yes, I mean to. I guess I'll go no, before I get frightened thinking about it." And, to the utter amazement of the assembled family, Beth walked deliberately down the garden, through the hedge, and in at the Laurences' door.

"Well, I wish I may die if it ain't the queerest thing I ever see! The pianny has turned her head! She'd never have gone in her right mind," cried Hannah, staring after her, while the girls were rendered quite speechless by the miracle.

They would have been still more amazed if they had seen what Beth did afterward. If you will believe me, she went and knocked at the study door before she gave herself time to think, and when a gruff voice called out, "come in!" she did go in, right up to Mr. Laurence, who looked quite taken aback, and held out her hand, saying, with only a small quaver in her voice, "I came to thank you, sir, for . . ." But she didn't finish, for he looked so friendly that she forgot her speech and, only remembering that he had lost the little girl he loved, she put both arms round his neck and kissed him.

If the roof of the house had suddenly flown off, the old gentleman wouldn't have been more astonished. But he liked it. Oh, dear, yes, he liked it amazingly! And was so touched and pleased by that confiding little kiss that all his crustiness vanished, and he just set her on his knee, and laid his wrinkled cheek against her rosy one, feeling as if he had got his own little grand daughter back again. Beth ceased to fear him from that moment, and sat there talking to him as cozily as if she had known him all her life, for love casts out fear, and gratitude can conquer pride. When she went home, he walked with her to her own gate, shook hands cordially, and touched his hat as he marched back again, looking very stately and erect, like a handsome, soldierly old gentleman, as he was.

When the girls saw that performance, Jo began to dance a jig, by way of expressing her satisfaction, Amy nearly fell out of the window in her surprise, and Meg exclaimed, with up-lifted hands, "Well, I do believe the world is coming to an end.

Chapter Seven

"That boy is a perfect cyclops, isn't he?" said Amy one day, as Laurie clattered by on horseback, with a flourish of his whip as he passed.

"How dare you say so, when he's got both his eyes? And very handsome ones they are, too," cried Jo, who resented any slighting remarks about her friend.

"I didn't day anything about his eyes, and I don't see why you need fire up when I admire his riding."

"Oh, my goodness! That little goose means a centaur, and she called him a Cyclops," exclaimed Jo, with a burst of laughter. "You needn't be so rude, it's only a 'lapse of lingy', as Mr. Davis says," retorted Amy, finishing Jo with her Latin. "I just wish I had a little of the money Laurie spends on that horse," she added, as if to herself, yet hoping her sisters would hear.

"Why?" asked Meg kindly, for Jo had gone off in another laugh at Amy's second blunder.

"I need it so much. I'm dreadfully in debt, and it won't be my turn to have the rag money for a month."

"In debt, Amy? What do you mean?" And Meg looked sober.

"Why, I owe at least a dozen pickled limes, and I can't pay them, you know, till I have money, for Marmee forbade my having anything charged at the shop."

"Tell me all about it. Are limes the fashion now? It used to be pricking bits of rubber to make balls." And Meg tried to keep her countenance, Amy looked so grave and important.

"Why, you see, the girls are always buying them, and unless you want to be thought mean, you must do it too. It's nothing but limes now, for everyone is sucking them in their desks in schooltime, and trading them off for pencils, bead rings, paper dolls, or something else, at recess. If one girl likes another, she gives her a lime. If she's mad with her, she eats one before her face, and doesn't offer even a suck. They treat by turns, and I've had ever so many but haven't returned them, and I ought for they are debts of honor, you know."

"How much will pay them off and restore your credit?" asked Meg, taking out her purse."

"A quarter would more than do it, and leave a few cents over for a treat for you. Don't you like limes?"

"Not much. You may have my share. Here's the money. Make it last as long as you can, for it isn't very plenty, you know."

"Oh, thank you! It must be so nice to have pocket money! I'll have a grand feast, for I haven't tasted a lime this week. I felt delicate about taking any, as I couldn't return them, and I'm actually suffering for one."

Next day Amy was rather late at school, but could not resist the temptation of displaying, with pardonable pride, a moist brown-paper parcel, before she consigned it to the inmost recesses of her desk. During the next few minutes the rumor that Amy March had got twenty-four delicious limes (she ate one on the way) and was going to treat circulated through her 'set', and the attentions of her friends became quite overwhelming. Katy Brown invited her to her next party on the spot. Mary Kinglsey insisted on lending her her watch till recess, and Jenny Snow, a satirical young lady, who had basely twitted Amy upon her limeless state, promptly buried the hatchet and offered to furnish answers to certain appalling sums. But Amy had not forgotten Miss Snow's cutting remarks about 'some persons whose noses were not too flat to smell other people's limes, and stuck-up people who were not too proud to ask for them', and she instantly crushed 'that Snow girl's' hopes by the withering telegram, "You needn't be so polite all of a sudden, for you won't get any."

A distinguished personage happened to visit the school that morning, and Amy's beautifully drawn maps received praise, which honor to her foe rankled in the soul of Miss Snow, and caused Miss March to assume the airs of a studious young peacock. But, alas, alas! Pride goes before a fall, and the revengeful Snow turned the tables with disastrous success. No sooner had the guest paid the usual stale compliments and bowed himself out, than Jenny, under pretense of asking an important question, informed Mr. Davis, the teacher, that Amy March had pickled limes in her desk.

Now Mr. Davis had declared limes a contraband article, and solemnly vowed to publicly ferrule the first person who was found breaking the law. This much-enduring man had succeeded in banishing chewing gum after a long and stormy war, had made a bonfire of the confiscated novels and newspapers, had suppressed a private post office, had forbidden distortions of the face, nicknames, and caricatures, and done all that one man could do to keep half a hundred rebellious girls in order. Boys are trying enough to human patience, goodness knows, but girls are infinitely more so, especially to nervous gentlemen with tyrannical tempers and no more talent for teaching than Dr. Blimber. Mr. Davis knew any quantity of Greek, Latin, algebra, and ologies of all sorts so he was called a fine teacher, and manners, morals, feelings, and examples were not considered of any particular importance. It was a most unfortunate moment for denouncing Amy, and Jenny knew it. Mr. Davis had evidently taken his coffee too strong that morning, there was an east wind, which always affected his neuralgia, and his pupils had not done him the credit which he felt he deserved. Therefore, to use the expressive, if not elegant, language of a schoolgirl, "He was as nervous as a witch and as cross as a bear". The word 'limes' was like fire to powder, his yellow face flushed, and he rapped on his desk with an energy which made Jenny skip to her seat with unusual rapidity.

"Young ladies, attention, if you please!"

At the stern order the buzz ceased, and fifty pairs of blue, black, gray, and brown eyes were obediently fixed upon his awful countenance.

"Miss March, come to the desk."

Amy rose to comply with outward composure, but a secret fear oppressed her, for the limes weighed upon her conscience.

"Bring with you the limes you have in your desk," was the unexpected command which arrested her before she got out of her seat.

"Don't take all." whispered her neighbor, a young lady of great presence of mind.

Amy hastily shook out half a dozen and laid the rest down before Mr. Davis, feeling that any man possessing a human heart would relent when that delicious perfume met his nose. Unfortunately, Mr. Davis particularly detested the odor of the fashionable pickle, and disgust added to his wrath.

"Is that all?"

"Not quite," stammered Amy.

"Bring the rest immediately."

With a despairing glance at her set, she obeyed.

"You are sure there are no more?'

"I never lie, sir."

"So I see. Now take these disgusting things two by two, and throw them out of the window."

There was a simultaneous sigh, which created quite a little gust, as the last hope fled, and the treat was ravished from their longing lips. Scarlet with shame and anger, Amy went to and fro six dreadful times, and as each doomed couple, looking oh, so plump and juicy, fell from her reluctant hands, a shout from the street completed the anguish of the girls, for it told them that their feast was being exulted over by the little Irish children, who were their sworn foes. This—this was too much. All flashed indignant or appealing glances at the inexorable Davis, and one passionate lime lover burst into tears.

As Amy returned from her last trip, Mr. Davis gave a portentous "Hem!" and said, in his most impressive manner . . .

"Young ladies, you remember what I said to you a week ago. I am sorry this has happened, but I never allow my rules to be infringed, and I never break my word. Miss March, hold out your hand."

Amy started, and put both hands behind her, turning on him an imploring look which pleaded for her better than the words she could not utter. She was rather a favorite with 'old Davis', as, of course, he was called, and it's my private belief that he would have broken his word if the indignation of one irrepressible young lady had not found vent in a hiss. That hiss, faint as it was, irritated the irascible gentleman, and sealed the culprit's fate.

"Your hand, Miss March!" was the only answer her mute appeal received, and too proud to cry or beseech, Amy set her teeth, threw bach her head defiantly, and bore without flinching several tingling blows on her little palm. They were neither many nor heavy, but that made no difference to her. For the first time in her life she had been struck, and the disgrace, in her eyes, was as deep as if he had knocked her down.

"You will now stand on the platform till recess," said Mr. Davis, resolved to do the thing thoroughly, since he had begun.

That was dreadful. It would have been bad enough to go to her seat, and see the pitying faces of her friends, or the satisfied ones of her few enemies, but to face the whole school, with that shame fresh upon her, seemed impossible, and for a second she felt as if she could only drop down where she stood, and break her heart with crying. A bitter sense of wrong and the thought of Jenny Snow helped her to bear it, and, taking the ignominious place, she fixed her eyes on the stove funnel above what now seemed a sea of faces, and stood there, so motionless and white that the girls found it hard to study with that pathetic figure before them.

During the fifteen minutes that followed, the proud and sensitive little girl suffered a shame and pain which she never forgot. To others it might seem a ludicrous or trivial affair, but to her it was a hard experience, for during the twelve years of her life she had been governed by love alone, and a blow of that sort had never touched her before. The smart of her hand and the ache of her heart were forgotten in the sting of the thought, "I shall have to tell at home, and they will be so disappointed in me!"

The fifteen minutes seemed an hour, but they came to an end at last, and the word 'Recess!' had never seemed so welcome to her before.

"You can go, Miss March," said Mr. Davis, looking, as he felt, uncomfortable.

He did not soon forget the reproachful glance Amy gave him, as she went, without a word to anyone, straight into the anteroom, snatched her things, and left the place "forever," as she passionately declared to herself. She was in a sad state when she got home, and when the older girls arrived, some time later, an indignation meeting was held at once. Mrs. March did not say much but looked disturbed, and comforted her afflicted little daughter in her tenderest manner. Meg bathed the insulted hand with glycerine and tears, Beth felt that even her beloved kittens would fail as a balm for griefs like this, Jo wrathfully proposed that Mr. Davis be arrested without delay, and Hannah shook her fist at the 'villain' and pounded potatoes for dinner as if she had him under her pestle.

No notice was taken of Amy's flight, except by her mates, but the sharp-eyed demoiselles discovered that Mr. Davis was quite benignant in the afternoon, also unusually nervous. Just before school closed, Jo appeared, wearing a grim expression as she stalked up to the desk, and delivered a letter from her mother, then collected Amy's property, and departed, carefully scraping the mud from her boots on the door mat, as if she shook that dust of the place off her feet.

"Yes, you can have a vacation from school, but I want you to study a little every day with Beth," said Mrs. March that evening. "I don't approve of corporal punishment, especially for girls. I dislike Mr. Davis's manner of teaching and don't think the girls you associate with are doing you any good, so I shall ask your father's advice before I send you anywhere else."

"That's good! I wish all the girls would leave, and spoil his old school. It's perfectly maddening to think of those lovely limes," sighed Amy, with the air of a martyr.

"I am not sorry you lost them, for you broke the rules, and deserved some punishment for disobedience," was the severe reply, which rather disappointed the young lady, who expected nothing but sympathy.

"Do you mean you are glad I was disgraced before the whole school?" cried Amy.

"I should not have chosen that way of mending a fault," replied her mother, "but I'm not sure that it won't do you more good than a molder method. You are getting to be rather conceited, my dear, and it is quite time you set about correcting it. You have a good many little gifts and virtues, but there is no need of parading them, for conceit spoils the finest genius. There is not much danger that real talent or goodness will be overlooked long, even if it is, the consciousness of possessing and using it well should satisfy one, and the great charm of all power is modesty."

"So it is!" cried Laurie, who was playing chess in a corner with Jo. "I knew a girl once, who had a really remarkable talent for music, and she didn't know it, never guessed what sweet little things she composed when she was alone, and wouldn't have believed it if anyone had told her."

"I wish I'd known that nice girl. Maybe she would have helped me, I'm so stupid," said Beth, who stood beside him, listening eagerly.

"You do know her, and she helps you better than anyone else could," answered Laurie, looking at her with such mischievous meaning in his merry black eyes that Beth suddenly turned very red, and hid her face in the sofa cushion, quite overcome by such an unexpected discovery.

Jo let Laurie win the game to pay for that praise of her Beth, who could not be prevailed upon to play for them after her compliment. So Laurie did his best, and sang delightfully, being in a particularly lively humor, for to the Marches he seldom showed the moody side of his character. When he was gone, amy, who had been pensive all evening, said suddenly, as if busy over some new idea, "Is Laurie an accomplished boy?"

"Yes, he has had an excellent education, and has much talent. He will make a fine man, if not spoiled by petting," replied her mother.

"And he isn't conceited, is he?" asked Amy.

"Not in the least. That is why he is so charming and we all like him so much." "I see. It's nice to have accomplishments and be elegant, but not to show off or get perked up," said Amy thoughtfully.

"These things are always seen and felt in a person's manner and conversations, if modestly used, but it is not necessary to display them," said Mrs. March.

"Any more than it's proper to wear all your bonnets and gowns and ribbons at once, that folks may know you've got them," added Jo, and the lecture ended in a laugh.

Chapter Eight

"Girls, where are you going?" asked Amy, coming into their room one Saturday afternoon, and finding them getting ready to go out with an air of secrecy which excited her curiosity.

"Never mind. Little girls shouldn't ask questions," returned Jo sharply.

Now if there is anything mortifying to out feelings when we are young, it is to be told that, and to be bidden to "run away, dear" is still more trying to us. Amy bridled up at this insult, and determined to find out the secret, if she teased for an hour. Turning to Meg, who never refused her anything very long, she said coaxingly, "Do tell me! I should think you might let me go, too, for Beth is fussing over her piano, and I haven't got anything to do, and am so lonely."

"I can't, dear, because you aren't invited," began Meg, but Jo broke in impatiently, "Now, Meg, be quiet or you will spoil it all. You can't go, Amy, so don't be a baby and whine about it."

"You are going somewhere with Laurie, I know you are. You were whispering and laughing together on the sofa last night, and you stopped when I came in. Aren't you going with him?"

"Yes, we are. Now do be still, and stop bothering."

Amy held her tongue, but used her eyes, and saw Meg slip a fan into her pocket.

"I know! I know! You're going to the theater to see the SEVEN CASTLES!" she cried, adding resolutely, "and I shall go, for Mother said I might see it, and I've got my rag money, and it was mean not to tell me in time."

"Just listen to me a minute, and be a good child," said Meg soothingly. "Mother doesn't wish you to go this week, because your eyes are not well enough yet to bear the light of this fairy piece. Next week you can go with Beth and Hannah, and have a nice time."

"I don't like that half as well as going with you and Laurie. Please let me. I've been sick with this cold so long, and shut up, I'm dying for some fun. Do, Meg! I'll be ever so good," pleaded Amy, looking as pathetic as she could.

"Suppose we take her. I don't believe Mother would mind, if we bundle her up well," began Meg.

"If she goes I shan't, and if I don't, Laurie won't like it, and it will be very rude, after he invited only us, to go and drag in Amy. I should think she'd hate to poke herself where she isn't wanted," said Jo crossly, for she disliked the trouble of overseeing a fidgety child when she wanted to enjoy herself.

Her tone and manner angered Amy, who began to put her boots on, saying, in her most aggravating way, "I shall go. Meg says I may, and if I pay for myself, Laurie hasn't anything to do with it."

"You can't sit with us, for our seats are reserved, and you mustn't sit alone, so Laurie will give you his place, and that will spoil our pleasure. Or he'll get another seat for you, and that isn't proper when you weren't asked. You shan't stir a step, so you may just stay where you are," scolded Jo, crosser than ever, having just pricked her finger in her hurry.

Sitting on the floor with one boot on, Amy began to cry and Meg to reason with her, when Laurie called from below, and the two girls hurried down, leaving their sister wailing. For now and then she forgot her grown-up ways and acted like a spoiled child. Just as the party was setting out, Amy called over the banisters in a threatening tone, "You'll be sorry for this, Jo March, see if you ain't."

"Fiddlesticks!" returned Jo, slamming the door.

They had a charming time, for THE SEVEN CASTLES OF THE DIAMOND LAKE was as brilliant and wonderful as heart could wish. But in spite of the comical red imps, sparkling elves, and the gorgeous princes and princesses, Jo's pleasure had a drop of bitterness in it. The fairy queen's yellow curls reminded her of Amy, and between the acts she amused herself with wondering what her sister would do to make her 'sorry for it'. She and Amy had had many lively skirmishes in the course of their lives, for both had quick tempers and were apt to be violent when fairly roused. Amy teased Jo, and Jo irritated Amy, and semioccasional explosions occurred, of which both were much ashamed afterward.

Although the oldest, Jo had the least self-control, and had hard times trying to curb the fiery spirit which was continually getting her into trouble. Her anger never lasted long, and having humbly confessed her fault, she sincerely repented and tried to do better. Her sisters used to say that they rather liked to get Jo into a fury because she was such an angel afterward. Poor Jo tried desperately to be good, but her bosom enemy was always ready to flame up and defeat her, and it took years of patient effort to subdue it.

When they got home, they found amy reading in the parlor. She assumed an injured air as they came in, never lifted her eyes from her book, or asked a single question. Perhaps curiosity might have conquered resentment, if Beth had not been there to inquire and receive a glowing description of the play. On going up to put away her best hat, Jo's first look was toward the bureau, for in their last quarrel Amy had soothed her feelings by turning Jo's top drawer upside down on the floor. Everything was in its place, however, and after a hasty glance into her various closets, bags, and boxes, Jo decided that Amy had forgiven and forgotten her wrongs.

There Jo was mistaken, for next day she made a discovery which produced a tempest. Meg, Beth, and Amy were sitting together, late in the afternoon, when Jo burst into the room, looking excited and demanding breathlessly, "Has anyone taken my book?"

Meg and Beth said, "No." at once, and looked surprised. Amy poked the fire and said nothing. Jo saw her color rise and was down upon her in a minute.

"Amy, you've got it!"

"No, I haven't."

"You know where it is, then!"

"No, I don't."

"That's a fib!" cried Jo, taking her by the shoulders, and looking fierce enough to frighten a much braver child than Amy.

"It isn't. I haven't got it, don't know where it is now, and don't care."

"You know something about it, and you'd better tell at once, or I'll make you." And Jo gave her a slight shake.

"Scold as much as you like, you'll never see your silly old book again," cried Amy, getting excited in her turn.

"why not?"

"I burned it up."

"What! My little book I was so fond of, and worked over, and meant to finish before Father got home? Have you really burned it?" said Jo, turning very pale, while her eyes kindled and her hands clutched Amy nervously.

"Yes, I did! I told you I'd make you pay for being so cross yesterday, and I have, so . . ."

Amy got no farther, for Jo's hot temper mastered her, and she shook Amy till her teeth chattered in her head, crying in a passion of grief and anger . . .

"You wicked, wicked girl! I never can write it again, and I'll never forgive you as long as I live."

Meg flew to rescue Amy, and Beth to pacify Jo, but Jo was quite beside herself, and with a parting box on her sister's ear, she rushed out of the room up to the old sofa in the garret, and finished her fight alone.

The storm cleared up below, for Mrs. March came home, and, having heard the story, soon brought Amy to a sense of the wrong she had done her sister. Jo's book was the pride of her heart, and was regarded by her family as a literary sprout of great promise. It was only half a dozen little fairy tales, but Jo had worked over them patiently, putting her whole heart into her work, hoping to make something good enough to print. She had just copied them with great care, and had destroyed the old manuscript, so that Amy's bonfire had consumed the loving work of several years. It seemed a small loss to others, but to Jo it was a dreadful calamity, and she felt that it never could be made up to her. Beth mourned as for a departed kitten, and Meg refused to defend her pet. Mrs. March looked grave and grieved, and Amy felt that no one would love her till she had asked pardon for the act which she now regretted more than any of them.

When the tea bell rang, Jo appeared, looking so grim and unapproachable that it took all Amy's courage to say meekly . . .

"Please forgive me, Jo. I'm very, very sorry."

"I never shall forgive you," was Jo's stern answer, and from that moment she ignored Amy entirely.

No one spoke of the great trouble, not even Mrs. March, for all had learned by experience that when Jo was in that mood words were wasted, and the wisest course was to wait till some little accident, or her own generous nature, softened Jo's resentment and healed the breach. It was not a happy evening, for though they sewed as usual, while their mother read aloud from Bremer, Scott, or Edgeworth, something was wanting, and the sweet home peace was disturbed. They felt this most when singing time came, for Beth could only play, Jo stood dumb as a stone, and Amy broke down, so Meg and Mother sang alone. But in spite of their efforts to be as cheery as larks, the flutelike voices did not seem to chord as well as usual, and all felt out of tune.

As Jo received her good-night kiss, Mrs. March whispered gently, "My dear, don't let the sun go down upon your anger. Forgive each other, help each other, and begin again tomorrow."

Jo wanted to lay her head down on that motherly bosom, and cry her grief and anger all away, but tears were an unmanly weakness, and she felt so deeply injured that she really couldn't quite forgive yet. So she winked hard, shook her head, and said gruffly because Amy was listening, "It was an abominable thing, and she doesn't deserve to be forgiven."

With that she marched off to bed, and there was no merry or confidential gossip that night.

Amy was much offended that her overtures of peace had been repulsed, and began to wish she had not humbled herself, to feel more injured than ever, and to plume herself on her superior virtue in a way which was particularly exasperating. Jo still looked like a thunder cloud, and nothing went well all day. It was bitter cold in the morning, she dropped her precious turnover in the gutter, Aunt March had an attack of the fidgets, Meg was sensitive, Beth would look grieved and wistful when she got home, and Amy kept making remarks about people who were always talking about being good and yet wouldn't even try when other people set them a virtuous example. "Everybody is so hateful, I'll ask Laurie to go skating. He is always kind and jolly, and will put me to rights, I know," said Jo to herself, and off she went.

Amy heard the clash of skates, and looked out with an impatient exclamation.

"There! She promised I should go next time, for this is the last ice we shall have. But it's no use to ask such a crosspatch to take me."

"Don't say that. You were very naughty, and it is hard to forgive the loss of her precious little book, but I think she might do it now, and I guess she will, if you try her at the right minute," said Meg. "Go after them. Don't say anything till Jo has got good-natured with Laurie, than take a quiet minute and just kiss her, or do some kind thing, and I'm sure she'll be friends again with all her heart."

"I'll try," said Amy, for the advice suited her, and after a flurry to get ready, she ran after the friends, who were just disappearing over the hill.

It was not far to the river, but both were ready before Amy reached them. Jo saw her coming, and turned her back. Laurie did not see, for he was carefully skating along the shore, sounding the ice, for a warm spell had preceded the cold snap.

"I'll go on to the first bend, and see if it's all right before we begin to race," Amy heard him say, as he shot away, looking like a young Russian in his fur-trimmed coat and cap.

Jo heard Amy panting after her run, stamping her feet and blowing on her fingers as she tried to put her skates on, but Jo never turned and went slowly zigzagging down the river, taking a bitter, unhappy sort of satisfaction in her sister's troubles. She had cherished her anger till it grew strong and took possession of her, as evil thoughts and feelings always do unless cast out at once. As Laurie turned the bend, he shouted back . . .

"Keep near the shore. It isn't safe in the middle." Jo heard, but Amy was struggling to her feet and did not catch a word. Jo glanced over her shoulder, and the little demon she was harboring said in her ear . . .

"No matter whether she heard or not, let her take care of herself."

Laurie had vanished round the bend, Jo was just at the turn, and Amy, far behind, striking out toward the the smoother ice in the middle of the river. For a minute Jo stood still with a strange feeling in her heart, then she resolved to go on, but something held and turned her round, just in time to see Amy throw up her hands and go down, with a sudden crash of rotten ice, the splash of water, and a cry that made Jo's heart stand still with fear. She tried to call Laurie, but her voice was gone. She tried to rush forward, but her feet seemed to have no strength in them, and for a second, she could only stand motionless, staring with a terror-stricken face at the little blue hood above the black water. Something rushed swiftly by her, and Laurie's voice cried out . . .

"Bring a rail. Quick, quick!"

How she did it, she never knew, but for the next few minutes she worked as if possessed, blindly obeying Laurie, who was quite self-possessed, and lying flat, held Amy up by his arm and hockey stick till Jo dragged a rail from the fence, and together they got the child out, more frightened than hurt.

"Now then, we must walk her home as fast as we can. Pile our things on her, while I get off these confounded skates," cried Laurie, wrapping his coat round Amy, and tugging away at the straps which never seemed so intricate before.

Shivering, dripping, and crying, they got Amy home, and after an exciting time of it, she fell asleep, rolled in blankets before a hot fire. During the bustle Jo had scarcely spoken but flown about, looking pale and wild, with her things half off, her dress torn, and her hands cut and bruised by ice and rails and refractory buckles. When Amy was comfortably asleep, the house quiet, and Mrs. March sitting by the bed, she called Jo to her and began to bind up the hurt hands.

"Are you sure she is safe?" whispered Jo, looking remorsefully at the golden head, which might have been swept away from her sight forever under the treacherous ice.

"Quite safe, dear. she is not hurt, and won't even take cold, I think, you were so sensible in covering and getting her home quickly," replied her mother cheerfully.

"Laurie did it all. I only let her go. Mother, if she should die, it would be my fault." And Jo dropped down beside the bed in a passion of penitent tears, telling all that had happened, bitterly condemning her hardness of heart, and sobbing out her gratitude for being spared the heavy punishment which might have come upon her. "It's my dreadful temper! I try to cure it, I think I have, and then it breaks out worse than ever. OH, Mother, what shall I do? What shall I do?" cried poor Jo, in despair.

"Watch and pray, dear, never get tired of trying, and never think it is impossible to conquer your fault," said Mrs. March, drawing the blowzy head to her shoulder and kissing the wet cheek so tenderly that Jo cried even harder.

"You don't know, you can't guess how bad it is! It seems as if I could do anything when I'm in a passion. I get so savage, I could hurt anyone and enjoy it. I'm afraid I shall do something dreadful some day, and spoil my life, and make everybody hate me. Oh, Mother, help me, do help me!"

"I will, my child, I will. Don't cry so bitterly, but remember this day, and resolve with all your soul that you will never know another like it. Jo, dear, we all have our temptations, some far greater than yours, and it often takes us all our lives to conquer them. You think your temper is the worst in the world, but mine used to be just like it."

"Yours, Mother? Why, you are never angry!" And for the moment Jo forgot remorse in surprise.

"I've been trying to cure it for forty years, and have only succeeded in controlling it. I am angry nearly every day of my life, Jo, but I have learned not to show it, and I still hope to learn not to feel it, though it may take me another forty years to do so."

The patience and the humility of the face she loved so well was a better lesson to Jo than the wisest lecture, the sharpest reproof. She felt comforted at once by the sympathy and confidence given her. The knowledge that her mother had a fault like hers, and tried to mend it, made her own easier to bear and strengthened her resolution to cure it, though forty years seemed rather a long time to watch and pray to a girl of fifteen.

"Mother, are you angry when you fold your lips tight together and go out of the room sometimes, when Aunt March scolds or people worry you?" asked Jo, feeling nearer and dearer to her mother than ever before.

"Yes, I've learned to check the hasty words that rise to my lips, and when I feel that they mean to break out against my will,

I just go away for a minute, and give myself a little shake for being so weak and wicked," answered Mrs. March with a sigh and a smile, as she smoothed and fastened up Jo's disheveled hair.

"How did you learn to keep still? That is what troubles me, for the sharp words fly out before I know what I'm about, and the more I say the worse I get, till it's a pleasure to hurt people's feelings and say dreadful things. Tell me how you do it, Marmee dear." "My good mother used to help me . . ."

"As you do us . . ." interrupted Jo, with a grateful kiss.

"But I lost her when I was a little older than you are, and for years had to struggle on alone, for I was too proud to confess my weakness to anyone else. I had a hard time, Jo, and shed a good many bitter tears over my failures, for in spite of my efforts I never seemed to get on. Then your father came, and I was so happy that i found it easy to be good. But by-and-by, when I had four little daughters round me and we were poor, then the old trouble began again, for I am not patient by nature, and it tried me very much to see my children wanting anything."

"Poor Mother! What helped you then?"

"Your father, Jo. He never loses patience, never doubts or complains, but always hopes, and works and waits so cheerfully that one is ashamed to do otherwise before him. He helped and comforted me, and showed me that I must try to practice all the virtues I would have my little girls possess, for I was their example. It was easier to try for your sakes than for my own. A startled or surprised look from one of you when I spoke sharply rebuked me more than any words could have done, and the love, respect, and confidence of my children was the sweetest reward I could receive for my efforts to be the woman I would have them copy."

"Oh, Mother, if I'm ever half as good as you, I shall be satisfied," cried Jo, much touched.

"I hope you will be a great deal better, dear, but you must keep watch over your 'bosom enemy', as father calls it, or it may sadden, if not spoil your life. You have had a warning. Remember it, and try with heart and soul to master this quick temper, before it brings you greater sorrow and regret than you have known today."

"I will try, Mother, I truly will. But you must help me, remind me, and keep me from flying out. I used to see Father sometimes put his finger on his lips, and look at you with a very kind but sober face, and you always folded your lips tight and went away. Was he reminding you then?" asked Jo softly.

"Yes. I asked him to help me so, and he never forgot it, but saved me from many a sharp word by that little gesture and kind look."

Jo saw that her mother's eyes filled and her lips trembled as she spoke, and fearing that she had said too much, she whispered anxiously, "Was it wrong to watch you and to speak of it? I didn't mean to be rude, but it's so comfortable to say all I think to you, and feel so safe and happy here."

"Mu Jo, you may say anything to your mother, for it is my greatest happiness and pride to feel that my girls confide in me and know how much I love them."

"I thought I'd grieved you."

"No, dear, but speaking of Father reminded me how much I miss him, how much I owe him, and how faithfully I should watch and work to keep his little daughters safe and good for him."

"Yet you told him to go, Mother, and didn't cry when he went, and never complain now, or seem as if you needed any help," said Jo, wondering.

"I gave my best to the country I love, and kept my tears till he was gone. Why should I complain, when we both have merely done our duty and will surely be the happier for it in the end? If I don't seem to need help, it is because I have a better friend, even than Father, to comfort and sustain me. My child, the troubles and temptations of your life are beginning and may be many, but you can overcome and outlive them all if you learn to feel the strength and tenderness of your Heavenly Father as you do that of your earthly one. The more you love and trust Him, and the less you will depend on human power and wisdom. His love and care never tire or change, can never be taken from you, but my become the source of lifelong peace, happiness, and strength. Believe this heartily, and go to God with all your little cares, and hopes, and sins, and sorrows, as freely and confidingly as you come to your mother."

Jo's only answer was to hold her mother close, and in the silence which followed the sincerest prayer she had ever prayed left her heart without words. For in that sad yet happy hour, she had learned not only the bitterness of remorse and despair, but the sweetness of self-denial and self-control, and led by her mother's hand, she had drawn nearer to the Friend who always welcomes every child with a love stronger than that of any father, tenderer than that of any mother.

Amy stirred and sighed in her sleep, and as if eager to begin at once to mend her fault, l Jo looked up with an expression on her face which it had never worn before.

"I let the sun go down on my anger. I wouldn't forgive her, and today, if it hadn't been for Laurie, it might have been too late! How could I be so wicked?" said Jo, half aloud, as she leaned over her sister softly stroking the wet hair scattered on the pillow.

As if she heard, Amy opened her eyes, and held out her arms, with a smile that went straight to Jo's heart. Neither said a word, but they hugged one another close, in spite of the blankets, and everything was forgiven and forgotten in one hearty kiss.

Chapter Nine

"I do think it was the most fortunate thing in the world that those children should have the measles just now," said Meg, one April day, as she stood packing the 'go abroady' trunk in her room, surrounded by her sisters.

"And so nice of Annie Moffat not to forget her promise. A whole fortnight of fun will be regularly splendid," replied Jo, looking like a windmill as she folded skirts with her long arms.

"And such lovely weather, I'm so glad of that," added Beth, tidily sorting neck and hair ribbons in her best box, lent for the great occasion.

"I wish I was going to have a fine time and wear all these nice things," said Amy with her mouth full of pins, as she artistically replenished her sister's cushion.

"I wish you were all going, but as you can't, I shall keep my adventures to tell you when I come back. I'm sure it's the least I can do when you have been so kind, lending me things and helping me get ready," said Meg, glancing round the room at the very simple outfit, which seemed nearly perfect in their eyes.

"What did Mother give you out of the treasure box?" asked Amy, who had not been present at the opening of a certain cedar chest in which Mrs. March kept a few relics of past splendor, as gifts for her girls when the proper time came.

"A pair of silk stockings, that pretty carved fan, and a lovely blue sash. I wanted the violet silk, but there isn't time to make it over, so I must be contented with my old tarlatan."

"It will look nice over my new muslin skirt, and the sash will set it off beautifully. I wish I hadn't smashed my coral bracelet, for you might have had it," said Jo, who loved to give and lend, but whose possessions were usually too dilapidated to be of much use.

"There is a lovely old-fashioned pearl set in the treasure chest, but Mother said real flowers were the prettiest ornament for a young girl, and Laurie promised to send me all I want," replied Meg. "Now, let me see, there's my new gray walking suit, just curl up the feather in my hat, Beth, then my poplin for Sunday and the small party, it looks heavy for spring, doesn't it? The violet silk would be so nice. Oh, dear!"

"Never mind, you've got the tarlatan for the big party, and you always look like an angel in white," said Amy, brooding over the little store of finery in which her soul delighted.

"It isn't low-necked, and it doesn't sweep enough, but it will have to do. My blue housedress looks so well, turned and freshly trimmed, that I feel as if I'd got a new one. My silk sacque isn't a bit the fashion, and my bonnet doesn't look like Sallie's. I didn't like to say anything, but I was sadly disappointed in my umbrella. I told Mother black with a white handle, but she forgot and bought a green one with a yellowish handle. It's strong and neat, so I ought not to complain, but I know I shall feel ashamed of it beside Annie's silk one with a gold top," sighed Meg, surveying the little umbrella with great disfavor.

"Change it," advised Jo.

"I won't be so silly, or hurt Marmee's feelings, when she took so much pains to get my things. It's a nonsensical notion of mine, and I'm not going to give up to it. My silk stockings and two pairs of new gloves are my comfort. You are a dear to lend me yours, Jo. I feel so rich and sort of elegant, with two new pairs, and the old ones cleaned up for common." And Meg took a refreshing peep at her glove box. "Annie Moffat has blue and pink bows on her nightcaps. Would you put some on mine?" she asked, as Beth brought up a pile of snowy muslins, fresh from Hannah's hands.

"No, I wouldn't, for the smart caps won't match the plain gowns without any trimming on them. Poor folks shouldn't rig," said Jo decidedly.

"I wonder if I shall ever be happy enough to have real lace on my clothes and bows on my caps?" said Meg impatiently.

"You said the other day that you'd be perfectly happy if you could only go to Annie Moffat's," observed Beth in her quiet way.

"So I did! Well, I am happy, and I won't fret, but it does seem as if the more one gets the more one wants, doesn't it? There now, the trays are ready, and everything in but my ball dress, which I shall leave for Mother to pack," said Meg, cheering up, as she glanced from the half-filled trunk to the many times pressed and mended white tarlatan, which she called her 'ball dress' with an important air.

The next day was fine, and Meg departed in style for a fortnight of novelty and pleasure. Mrs. March had consented to the visit rather reluctantly, fearing that Margaret would come back more discontented than she went. But she begged so hard, and Sallie had promised to take good care of her, and a little pleasure seemed so delightful after a winter of irksome work that the mother yielded, and the daughter went to take her first taste of fashionable life.

The Moffats were very fashionable, and simple Meg was rather daunted, at first, by the splendor of the house and the elegance of its occupants. But they were kindly people, in spite of the frivolous life they led, and soon put their guest at her ease. Perhaps Meg felt, without understanding why, that they were not particularly cultivated or intelligent people, and that all their gilding could not quite conceal the ordinary material of which they were made. It certainly was agreeable to fare sumptuously, drive in a fine carriage, wear her best frock every day, and do nothing but enjoy herself. It suited her exactly, and soon she began to imitate the manners and conversation of those about her, to put on little airs and graces, use French phrases, crimp her hair, take in her dresses, and talk about the fashions as well as she could. The more she saw of Annie Moffat's pretty things, the more she envied her and sighed to be rich. Home now looked bare and dismal as she thought of it, work grew harder than ever, and she felt that she was a very destitute and much-injured girl, in spite of the new gloves and silk stockings.

She had not much time for repining, however, for the three young girls were busily employed in 'having a good time'. They shopped, walked, rode, and called all day, went to theaters and operas or frolicked at home in the evening, for Annie had many friends and knew how to entertain them. Her older sisters were very fine young ladies, and one was engaged, which was extremely interesting and romantic, Meg thought. Mr. Moffat was a fat, jolly old gentleman, who knew her father, and Mrs. Moffat, a fat, jolly old lady, who took as great a fancy to Meg as her daughter had done. Everyone petted her, and 'Daisey', as they called her, was in a fair way to have her head turned.

When the evening for the small party came, she found that the poplin wouldn't do at all, for the other girls were putting on thin dresses and making themselves very fine indeed. So out came the tarlatan, looking older, limper, and shabbier than ever beside Sallie's crisp new one. Meg saw the girls glance at it and then at one another, and her cheeks began to burn, for with all her gentleness she was very proud. No one said a word about it, but Sallie offered to dress her hair, and Annie to tie her sash, and Belle, the engaged sister, praised her white arms. But in their kindness Meg saw only pity for her poverty, and her heart felt very heavy as she stood by herself, while the others laughed, chattered, and flew about like gauzy butterflies. The hard, bitter feeling was getting pretty bad, when the maid brought in a box of flowers. Before she could speak, Annie had the cover off, and all were exclaiming at the lovely roses, heath, and fern within.

"It's for Belle, of course, George always sends her some, but these are altogether ravishing," cried Annie, with a great sniff.

"They are for Miss March, the man said. And here's a note," put in the maid, holding it to Meg.

"What fun! Who are they from? Didn't know you had a lover," cried the girls, fluttering about Meg in a high state of curiosity and surprise.

"The note is from Mother, and the flowers from Laurie," said Meg simply, yet much gratified that he had not forgotten her.

"Oh, indeed!" said Annie with a funny look, as Meg slipped the note into her pocket as a sort of talisman against envy, vanity, and false pride, for the few loving words had done her good, and the flowers cheered her up by their beauty.

Feeling almost happy again, she laid by a few ferns and roses for herself, and quickly made up the rest in dainty bouquets for the breasts, hair, or skirts of her friends, offering them so prettily that Clara, the elder sister, told her she was 'the sweetest little thing she ever saw', and they looked quite charmed with her small attention. Somehow the kind act finished her despondency, and when all the rest went to show themselves to Mrs. Moffat, she saw a happy, bright-eyed face in the mirror, as she laid her ferns against her rippling hair and fastened the roses in the dress that didn't strike her as so very shabby now.

She enjoyed herself very much that evening, for she danced to her heart's content. Everyone was very kind, and she had three compliments. Annie made her sing, and some one said she had a remarkably fine voice. Major Lincoln asked who 'the fresh little girl with the beautiful eyes' was, and Mr. Moffat insisted on dancing with her because she 'didn't dawdle, but had some spring in her', as he gracefully expressed it. So altogether she had a very nice time, till she overheard a bit of conversation, which disturbed her extremely. She was sitting just inside the conservatory, waiting for her partner to bring her an ice, when she heard a voice ask on the other side of the flowery wall . . .

"How old is he?"

"Sixteen or seventeen, I should say," replied another voice.

"It would be a grand thing for one of those girls, wouldn't it? Sallie says they are very intimate now, and the old man quite dotes on them."

"Mrs. M. has made her plans, I dare say, and will play her cards well, early as it is. The girl evidently doesn't think of it yet," said Mrs. Moffat.

"She told that fib about her momma, as if she did know, and colored up when the flowers came quite prettily. Poor thing! She'd be so nice if she was only got up in style. Do you think she'd be offended if we offered to lend her a dress for Thursday?" asked another voice.

"She's proud, but I don't believe she'd mind, for that dowdy tarlatan is all she has got. She may tear it tonight, and that will be a good excuse for offering a decent one."

Here Meg's partner appeared, to find her looking much flushed and rather agitated. She was proud, and her pride was useful just then, for it helped her hide her mortification, anger, and disgust at what she had just heard. For, innocent and unsuspicious as she was, she could not help understanding the gossip of her friends. She tried to forget it, but could not, and kept repeating to herself, "Mrs. M. has made her plans," "that fib about her mamma," and 'dowdy tarlatan," till she was ready to cry and rush home to tell her troubles and ask for advice. As that was impossible, she did her best to seem gay, and being rather excited, she succeeded so well that no one dreamed what an effort she was making. She was very glad when it was all over and she was quiet in her bed, where she could think and wonder and fume till her head ached and her hot cheeks were cooled by a few natural tears. Those foolish, yet well meant words, had opened a new world to Meg, and much disturbed the peace of the old one in which till now she had lived as happily as a child.

Her innocent friendship with Laurie was spoiled by the silly speeches she had overheard. Her faith in her mother was a little shaken by the worldly plans attributed to her by Mrs. Moffat, who judged others by herself, and the sensible resolution to be contented with the simple wardrobe which suited a poor man's daughter was weakened by the unnecessary pity of girls who thought a shabby dress one of the greatest calamities under heaven.

Poor Meg had a restless night, and got up heavy-eyed, unhappy, half resentful toward her friends, and half ashamed of herself for not speaking out frankly and setting everything right. Everybody dawdled that morning, and it was noon before the girls found energy enough even to take up their worsted work. Something in the manner of her friends struck Meg at once. They treated her with more respect, she thought, took quite a tender interest in what she said, and looked at her with eyes that plainly betrayed curiosity. All this surprised and flattered her, though she did not understand it till Miss Belle looked up from her writing, and said, with a sentimental air . . .

"Daisy, dear, I've sent an invitation to your friend, Mr. Laurence, for Thursday. We should like to know him, and it's only a proper compliment to you."

Meg colored, but a mischievous fancy to tease the girls made her reply demurely, "You are very kind, but I'm afraid he won't come."

"Why not, Cherie?" asked Miss Belle.

"He's too old."

"My child, what do you mean? What is his age, I beg to know!" cried Miss Clara.

"Nearly seventy, I believe," answered Meg, counting stitches to hide the merriment in her eyes.

"You sly creature! Of course we meant the young man," exclaimed Miss Belle, laughing.

"There isn't any, Laurie is only a little boy." And Meg laughed also at the queer look which the sisters exchanged as she thus described her supposed lover. "About you age," Nan said.

"Nearer my sister Jo's, I am seventeen in August," returned Meg, tossing her head.

"It's very nice of him to send you flowers, isn't it?" said Annie, looking wise about nothing.

"Yes, he often does, to all of us, for their house is full, and we are so fond of them. My mother and old Mr. Laurence are friends, you know, so it is quite natural that we children should play together." And Meg hoped they would say no more.

"It's evident Daisy isn't out yet," said Miss Clara to Belle with a nod.

"Quite a pastoral state of innocence all round," returned Miss Belle with a shrug.

"I'm going out to get some little matters for my girls. Can I do anything for you, young ladies?" asked Mrs. Moffat, lumbering in like an elephant in silk and lace.

"No, thank you, ma'am," replied Sallie. "I've got my new pink silk for Thursday and don't want a thing."

"Nor I . . ." began Meg, but stopped because it occurred to her that she did want several things and could not have them.

"What shall you wear?" asked Sallie.

"My old white one again, if I can mend it fit to be seen, it got sadly torn last night," said Meg, trying to speak quite easily, but feeling very uncomfortable.

"Why don't you send home for another?" said Sallie, who was not an observing young lady.

"I haven't got any other." It cost Meg an effort to say that, but Sallie did not see it and exclaimed in amiable surprise, "Only that?" How funny . . ." She did not finish her speech, for Belle shook her head at her and broke in, saying kindly . . .

"Not at all. Where is the use of having a lot of dresses when she isn't out yet? There's no need of sending home, Daisy, even if you had a dozen, for I've got a sweet blue silk laid away, which I've outgrown, and you shall wear it to please me, won't you, dear?"

"You are very kind, but I don't mind my old dress if you don't, it does well enough for a little girl like me," said Meg.

"Now do let me please myself by dressing you up in style. I admire to do it, and you'd be a regular little beauty with a touch here and there. I shan't let anyone see you till you are done, and then we'll burst upon them like Cinderella and her godmother going to the ball," said Belle in her persuasive tone.

Meg couldn't refuse the offer so kindly made, for a desire to see if she would be 'a little beauty' after touching up caused her to accept and forget all her former uncomfortable feelings toward the Moffats.

On the Thursday evening, Belle shut herself up with her maid, and between them they turned Meg into a fine lady. They crimped and curled her hair, they polished her neck and arms with some fragrant powder, touched her lips with coralline salve to make them redder, and Hortense would have added 'a soupcon of rouge', if Meg had not rebelled. They laced her into a sky-blue dress, which was so tight she could hardly breathe and so low in the neck that modest Meg blushed at herself in the mirror. A set of silver filagree was added, bracelets, necklace, brooch, and even earrings, for Hortense tied them on with a bit of pink silk which did not show. A cluster of tea-rose buds at the bosom and a ruche, reconciled Meg to the display of her pretty, white shoulders, and a pair of high-heeled silk boots satisfied the last wish of her heart. A lace handkerchief, a plumy fan, and a bouquet in a shoulder holder finished her off, and Miss Belle surveyed her with the satisfaction of a little girl with a newly dressed doll.

"Mademoiselle is chatmante, tres jolie, is she not?" cried Hortense, clasping her hands in an affected rapture.

"Come and show yourself," said Miss Belle, leading the way to the room where the others were waiting.

As Meg went rustling after, with her long skirts trailing, her earrings tinkling, her curls waving, and her heart beating, she felt as if her fun had really begun at last, for the mirror had plainly told her that she was 'a little beauty'. Her friends repeated the pleasing phrase enthusiastically, and for several minutes she stood, like a jackdaw in the fable, enjoying her borrowed plumes, while the rest chattered like a party of magpies.

"While I dress, do you drill her, Nan, in the management of her skirt and those French heels, or she will trip herself up. Take your silver butterfly, and catch up that long curl on the left side of her head, Clara, and don't any of you disturb the charming work of my hands," said Belle, as she hurried away, looking well pleased with her success.

"You don't look a bit like yourself, but you are very nice. I'm nowhere beside you, for Belle has heaps of taste, and you're quite French, I assure you. Let your flowers hang, don't be so careful of them, and be sure you don't trip," returned Sallie, trying not to care that Meg was prettier than herself.

Keeping that warning carefully in mind, Margaret got safely downstairs and sailed into the drawing rooms where the Moffats and a few early guests were assembled. She very soon discovered that there is a charm about fine clothes which attracts a certain class of people and secures their respect. Several young ladies, who had taken no notice of her before, were very affectionate all of a sudden. Several young gentlemen, who had only stared at her at the other party, now not only stared, but asked to be introduced, and said all manner of foolish but agreeable things to her, and several old ladies, who sat on the sofas, and criticized the rest of the party, inquired who she was with an air of interest. She heard Mrs. Moffat reply to one of them . . .

"Daisy March—father a colonel in the army—one of our first families, but reverses of fortune, you know; intimate friends of the Laurences; sweet creature, I assure you; my Ned is quite wild about her."

"Dear me!" said the old lady, putting up her glass for another observation of Meg, who tried to look as if she had not heard and been rather shocked at Mrs. Moffat's fibs. The 'queer feeling' did not pass away, but she imagined herself acting the new part of fine lady and so got on pretty well, though the tight dress gave her a side-ache, the train kept getting under her feet, and she was in constant fear lest her earrings should fly off and get lost or broken. She was flirting her fan and laughing at the feeble jokes of a young gentleman who tried to be witty, when she suddenly stopped laughing and looked confused, for just opposite, she saw Laurie. He was staring at her with undisguised surprise, and disapproval also, she thought, for though he bowed and smiled, yet something in his honest eyes made her blush and wish she had her old dress on. To complete her confusion, she saw Belle nudge Annie, and both glance from her to Laurie, who, she was happy to see, looked unusually boyish and shy.

"Silly creatures, to put such thoughts into my head. I won't care for it, or let it change me a bit," thought Meg, and rustled across the room to shake hands with her friend.

"I'm glad you came, I was afraid you wouldn't." she said, with her most grown-up air.

"Jo wanted me to come, and tell her how you looked, so I did," answered Laurie, without turning his eyes upon her, though he half smiled at her maternal tone.

"What shall you tell her?" asked Meg, full of curiosity to know his opinion of her, yet feeling ill at ease with him for the first time.

"I shall say I didn't know you, for you look so grown-up and unlike yourself, I'm quite afraid of you," he said, fumbling at his glove button.

"How absurd of you! The girls dressed me up for fun, and I rather like it. Wouldn't Jo stare if she saw me?" said Meg, bent on making him say whether he thought her improved or not. "Yes, I think she would," returned Laurie gravely.

"Don't you like me so?' asked Meg.

"No, I don't," was the blunt reply.

"Why not?" in an anxious tone.

He glanced at her frizzled head, bare shoulders, and fantastically trimmed dress with an expression that abashed her more than his answer, which had not particle of his usual politeness in it.

"I don't like fuss and feathers."

That was altogether too much from a lad younger than herself, and Meg walked away, saying petulantly, "You are the rudest boy I ever saw."

Feeling very much ruffled, she went and stood at a quiet window to cool her cheeks, for the tight dress gave her an uncomfortably brilliant color. As she stood there, Major Lincoln passed by, and a minute after she heard him saying to his mother . . .

"They are making a fool of that little girl. I wanted you to see her, but they have spoiled her entirely. She's nothing but a doll tonight."

"Oh, dear!" sighed Meg. "I wish I'd been sensible and worn my own things, then I should not have disgusted other people, or felt so uncomfortable and ashamed of myself."

She leaned her forehead on the cool pane, and stood half hidden by the curtains, never minding that her favorite waltz had begun, till some one touched her, and turning, she saw Laurie, looking penitent, as he said, with his very best bow and his hand out . . .

"Please forgive my rudeness, and come and dance with me."

"I'm afraid it will be to disagreeable to you," said Meg, trying to look offended and failing entirely.

"Not a bit of it, I'm dying to do it. Come, I'll be good. I don't like your gown, but I do think you are just splendid." And he waved his hands, as if words failed to express his admiration.

Meg smiled and relented, and whispered as they stood waiting to catch the time, "Take care my skirt doesn't trip you up. It's the plague of my life and I was a goose to wear it."

"Pin it round your neck, and then it will be useful," said Laurie, looking down at the little blue boots, which he evidently approved of. Away they went fleetly and gracefully, for having practiced at home, they were well matched, and the blithe young couple were a pleasant sight to see, as they twirled merrily round and round, feeling more friendly than ever after their small tiff.

"Laurie, I want you to do me a favor, will you?' said Meg, as he stood fanning her when her breath gave out, which it did very soon though she would not own why.

"Won't I!" said Laurie, with alacrity.

"Please don't tell them at home about my dress tonight. They won't understand the joke, and it will worry Mother.'

"Then why did you do it?" said Laurie's eyes, so plainly that Meg hastily added . . .

"I shall tell them myself all about it, and 'fess' to Mother how silly I've been. But I'd rather do it myself. So you'll not tell, will you?"

"I give you my word I won't, only what shall I say when they ask me?"

"Just say I looked pretty well and was having a good time."

"I'll say the first with all my heart, but how about the other? You don't look as if you were having a good time. Are you?' And Laurie looked at her with an expression which made her answer in a whisper . . .

"No, not just now. Don't think I'm horrid. I only wanted a little fun, but this sort doesn't pay, I find, and I'm getting tired of it."

"Here comes Ned Moffat. What does he want?" said Laurie, knitting his black brows as if he did not regard his young host in the light of a pleasant addition to the party.

"He put his name down for three dances, and I suppose he's coming for them. What a bore!" said Meg, assuming a languid air which amused Laurie immensely.

He did not speak to her again till suppertime, when he saw her drinking champagne with Ned and his friend Fisher, who were behaving 'like a pair of fools', as Laurie said to himself, for he felt a brotherly sort of right to watch over the Marches and fight their battles whenever a defender was needed.

"You'll have a splitting headache tomorrow, if you drink much of that. I wouldn't, Meg, your mother doesn't like it, you know," he whispered, leaning over her chair, as Ned turned to refill her glass and Fisher stooped to pick up her fan.

"I'm not Meg tonight, I'm 'a doll' who does all sorts of crazy things. Tomorrow I shall put away my 'fuss and feathers' and be desperately good again," se answered with an affected little laugh.

"Wish tomorrow was here, then," muttered Laurie, walking off, ill-pleased at the change he saw in her.

Meg danced and flirted, chattered and giggled, as the other girls did. After supper she undertook the German, and blundered through it, nearly upsetting her partner with her long skirt, and romping in a way that scandalized Laurie, who looked on and meditated a lecture. But he got no chance to deliver it, for Meg kept away from him till he came to say good night.

"Remember!" she said, trying to smile, for the splitting headache had already begun.

"Silence a' la mort," replied Laurie, with a melodramatic flourish, as he went away.

This little bit of byplay excited Annie's curiosity, but Meg was too tired for gossip and went to bed, feeling as if she had been to a masquerade and hadn't enjoyed herself as much as she expected. She was sick all the next day, and on Saturday went home, quite used up with her fortnight's fun and feeling that she had 'sat in the lap of luxury' long enough.

"It does seem pleasant to be quiet, and not have company manners on all the time. Home is a nice place, though it isn't splendid," said Meg, looking about her with a restful expression, as she sat with her mother and Jo on the Sunday evening.

"I'm glad to hear you say so, dear, for I was afraid home would seem dull and poor to you after your fine quarters," replied her mother, who had given her many anxious looks that day. For motherly eyes are quick to see any change in children's faces.

Meg had told her adventures gayly and said over and over what a charming time she had had, but something still seemed to weigh upon her spirits, and when the younger girls were gone to bed, she sat thoughtfully staring at the fire, saying little and looking worried. As the clock struck nine and Jo proposed bed, Meg suddenly left her chair and, taking Beth's stool, leaned her elbows on her mother's knee, saying bravely . . .

"Marmee, I want to 'fess.'"

"I thought so. What is it, dear?"

"Shall I go away?" asked Jo discreetly.

"Of course not. Don't I always tell you everything? I was ashamed to speak of it before the younger children, but I want you to know all the dreadful things I did at the Moffats.'"

"We are prepared," said Mrs. March, smiling but looking a little anxious.

"I told you they dressed me up, but I didn't tell you that they powdered and squeezed and frizzled, and made me look like a fashion plate. Laurie thought I wasn't proper. I know he did, though he didn't say so, and one man called me 'a doll'. I knew it was silly, but they flattered me and said I was a beauty, and quantities of nonsense, so I let them make a fool of me."

"Is that all?" asked Jo, as Mrs. March looked silently at the downcast face of her pretty daughter, and could not find it in her heart to blame her little follies.

"No, I drank champagne and romped and tried to flirt, and was altogether abominable," said Meg self-reproachfully.

"There is something more, I think." And Mrs. March smoothed the soft cheek, which suddenly grew rosy as Meg answered slowly . . .

"Yes. It's very silly, but I want to tell it, because I hate to have people say and think such things about us and Laurie."

Then she told the various bits of gossip she had heard at the Moffats', and as she spoke, Jo saw her mother fold her lips tightly, as if ill pleased that such ideas should be put into Meg's innocent mind.

"Well, if that isn't the greatest rubbish I ever heard," cried Jo indignantly. "Why didn't you pop out and tell them so on the spot?'

"I couldn't, it was so embarrassing for me. I couldn't help hearing at first, and then I was so angry and ashamed, I didn't remember that I ought to go away."

"Just wait till I see Annie Moffat, and I'll show you how to settle such ridiculous stuff. The idea of having 'plans' and being kind to Laurie because he's rich and may marry us by-and-by! Won't he shout when I tell him what those silly things say about us poor children?" And Jo laughed, as if on second thoughts the thing struck her as a good joke.

"If you tell Laurie, I'll never forgive you! She mustn't, must she, Mother?" said Meg, looking distressed.

"No, never repeat that foolish gossip, and forget it as soon as you can," said Mrs. March gravely. "I was very unwise to let you go among people of whom I know so little, kind, I dare say, but worldly, ill-bred, and full of these vulgar ideas about young people. I am more sorry than I can express for the mischief this visit may have done you, Meg."

"Don't be sorry, I won't let it hurt me. I'll forget all the bad and remember only the good, for I did enjoy a great deal, and thank you very much for letting me go. I'll not be sentimental or dissatisfied, Mother. I know I'm a silly little girl, and I'll stay with you till I'm fit to take care of myself. But it is nice to be praised and admired, and I can't help saying I like it," said Meg, looking half ashamed of the confession.

"That is perfectly natural, and quite harmless, if the liking does not become a passion and lead one to do foolish or unmaidenly things. Learn to know and value the praise which is worth having, and to excite the admiration of excellent people by being modest as well as pretty, Meg."

Margaret sat thinking a moment, while Jo stood with her hands behind her, looking both interested and a little perplexed, for it was a new thing to see Meg blushing and talking about admiration, lovers, and things of that sort. And Jo felt as if during that fortnight her sister had grown up amazingly, and was drifting away from her into a world where she could not follow.

"Mother, do you have 'plans', as Mrs. Moffat said?" asked Meg bashfully.

"Yes, my dear, I have a great many, all mothers do, but mine differ somewhat from Mrs. Moffat's, I suspect. I will tell you some of them, for the time has come when a word may set this romantic little head and heart of yours right, on a very serious subject. You are young, Meg, but not too young to understand me, and mothers' lips are the fittest to speak of such things to girls like you. Jo, your turn will come in time, perhaps, so listen to my 'plans' and help me carry them out, if they are good."

Jo went and sat on one arm of the chair, looking as if she thought they were about to join in some very solemn affair. Holding a hand of each, and watching the two young faces wistfully, Mrs. March said, in her serious yet cheery way . . .

"I want my daughters to be beautiful, accomplished, and good. To be admired, loved, and respected. To have a happy youth, to be well and wisely married, and to lead useful, pleasant lives, with as little care and sorrow to try them as God sees fit to send. To be loved and chosen by a good man is the best and sweetest thing which can happen to a woman, and I sincerely hope my girls may know this beautiful experience. It is natural to think of it, Meg, right to hope and wait for it, and wise to prepare for it, so that when the happy time comes, you may feel ready for the duties and worthy of the joy. My dear girls, I am ambitious for you, but not to have you make a dash in the world, marry rich men merely because they are rich, or have splendid houses, which are not homes because love is wanting. Money is a needful and precious thing, and when well used, a noble thing, but I never want you to think it is the first or only prize to strive for. I'd rather see you poor men's wives, if you were happy, beloved, contented, than queens on thrones, without self-respect and peace."

"Poor girls don't stand any chance, Belle says, unless they put themselves forward," sighed Meg.

"Then we'll be old maids," said Jo stoutly. "right, Jo. Better be happy old maids than unhappy wives, or unmaidenly girls, running about to find husbands," said Mrs. March decidedly. "Don't be troubled, Meg, poverty seldom daunts a sincere lover. Some of the best and most honored women I know were poor girls, but so love-worthy that they were not allowed to be old maids. Leave these things to time. Make this home happy, so that you may be fit for homes of your own, if they are offered you, and contented here if they are not. One thing remember, my girls. Mother is always ready to be your confidante, Father to be your friend, and both of hope and trust that our daughters, whether married or single, will be the pride and comfort of out lives."

"We will, Marmee, we will!" cried both, with all their hearts, as she bade them good night.

Chapter Ten

As spring came on, a new set of amusements became the fashion, and the lengthening days gave long afternoons for work and play of all sorts. The garden had to be put in order, and each sister had a quarter of the little plot to do what she liked with. Hannah used to say, "I'd know which each of them gardings belonged to, ef I see 'em in Chiny," and so she might, for the girls' tastes differed as much as their characters. Meg's had roses and heliotrope, myrtle, and a little orange tree in it. Jo's bed was never alike two seasons, for she was always trying experiments. This year it was to be a plantation of sun flowers, the seeds of which cheerful land aspiring plant were to feed Aunt Cockle-top and her family of chicks. Beth had old-fashioned fragrant flowers in her garden, sweet peas and mignonette, larkspur, pinks, pansies, and southernwood, with chickweed for the birds and catnip for the pussies. Amy had a bower in hers, rather small and earwiggy, but very pretty to look at, with honeysuckle and morning-glories hanging their colored horns and bells in graceful wreaths all over it, tall white lilies, delicate ferns, and as many brilliant, picturesque plants as would consent to blossom there.

Gardening, walks, rows on the river, and flower hunts employed the fine days, and for rainy ones, they had house diversions, some old, some new, all more or less original. One of these was the 'P.C.', for as secret societies were the fashion, it was thought proper to have one, and as all of the girls admired Dickens, they called themselves the Pickwick Club. With a few interruptions, they had kept this up for a year, and met every

Saturday evening in the big garret, on which occasions the ceremonies were as follows: Three chairs were arranged in a row before a table on which was a lamp, also four white badges, with a big 'P.C.' in different colors on each, and the weekly newspaper called, The Pickwick Portfolio, to which all contributed something, while Jo, who reveled in pens and ink, was the editor. At seven o'clock, the four members ascended to the clubroom, tied their badges round their heads, and took their seats with great solemnity. Meg, as the eldest, was Samuel Pickwick, Jo, being of a literary turn, Augustus Snodgrass, Beth, because she was round and rosy, Tracy Tupman, and Amy, who was always trying to do what she couldn't, was Nathaniel Winkle. Pickwick, the president, read the paper, which was filled with original tales, poetry, local news, funny advertisements, and hints, in which they good-naturedly reminded each other of their faults and short comings. On one occasion, Mr. Pickwick put on a pair of spectacles without any glass, rapped upon the table, hemmed, and having stared hard at Mr. Snodgrass, who was tilting back in his chair, till he arranged himself properly, began to read:

"THE PICKWICK PORTFOLIO"

MAY 20, 18—
POET'S CORNER
ANNIVERSARY ODE

Again we meet to celebrate With badge and solemn rite, Our fifty-second anniversary, In Pickwick Hall, tonight.

We all are here in perfect health, None gone from our small band: Again we see each well-known face, And press each friendly hand.

Our Pickwick, always at his post, With reverence we greet, As, spectacles on nose, he reads Our well-filled weekly sheet.

Although he suffers from a cold, We joy to hear him speak, For words of wisdom from him fall, In spite of croak or squeak.

Old six-foot Snodgrass looms on high, With elephantine grace, And beams upon the company, With brown and jovial face.

Poetic fire lights up his eye, He struggles 'gainst his lot. Behold ambition on his brow, And on his nose, a blot.

Next our peaceful Tupman comes, So rosy, plump, and sweet, Who chokes with laughter at the puns, And tumbles off his seat.

Prim little Winkle too is here, With every hair in place, A model of propriety, Though he hates to wash his face.

The year is gone, we still unite To joke and laugh and read, And tread the path of literature That doth to glory lead.

Long may our paper prosper well, Our club unbroken be, And coming years their blessings pour On the useful, gay 'P. C.'. A. SNODGRASS

THE MASKED MARRIAGE (A Tale Of Venice)

Gondola after gondola swept up to the marble steps, and left its lovely load to swell the brilliant throng that filled the stately halls of Count Adelon. Knights and ladies, elves and pages, monks and flower girls, all mingled gaily in the dance. Sweet voices and rich melody filled the air, and so with mirth and music the masquerade went on. "Has your Highness seen the Lady viola tonight?" asked a gallant troubadour of the fairy queen who floated down the hall upon his arm. "Yes, is she not lovely, though so sad! Her dress is well chosen, too, for in a week she weds Count Antonio, whom she passionately hates."

"By my faith, I envy him. Yonder he comes, arrayed like a bridegroom, except the black mask. When that is off we shall see how he regards the fair maid whose heart he cannot win, though her stern father bestows her hand," returned the troubadour.

"Tis whispered that she loves the young English artist who haunts her steps, and is spurned by the old Count," said the lady, as they joined the dance. The revel was at its height when a priest appeared, and withdrawing the young pair to an alcove, hung with purple velvet, he motioned them to kneel. Instant silence fell on the gay throng, and not a sound, but he dash of fountains or the rustle of orange groves sleeping in the moonlight, broke the hush, as Count de Adelon spoke thus:

"My lords and ladies, pardon the ruse by which I have gathered you here to witness the marriage of my daughter. Father, we wait your services." All eyes turned toward the bridal party, and a murmur of amazement went through the throng, for neither bride nor groom removed their masks. Curiosity and wonder possessed all hearts, but respect restrained all tongues till the holy rite was over. Then the eager spectators gathered round the count, demanding an explanation.

"Gladly would I give it if I could, but I only know that it was the whim of my timid Viola, and I yielded to it. Now, my children, let the play end. Unmask and receive my blessing."

But neither bent the knee, for the young bridegroom replied in a tone that startled all listeners as the mask fell, disclosing the noble face of Ferdinand Devereux, the artist lover, and leaning on the breast where now flashed the star of an English earl was the lovely Viola, radiant with joy and beauty.

"My lord, you scornfully bade me claim your daughter when I could boast as high a name and vast a fortune as the Count antonio. I can do more, for even your ambitious soul cannot refuse the Earl of Devereux and De Vere, when he gives his ancient name and boundless wealth in return for the beloved hand of this fair lady, now my wife.

The count stood like one changed to stone, and turning to the bewildered crowd, Ferdinand added, with a gay smile of triumph, "To you, my gallant friends, I can only wish that your wooing may prosper as mine has done, and that you may all win as fair a bride as I have by this masked marriage." S. PICKWICK

Why is the P. C. like the Tower of Babel? It is full of unruly members.

THE HISTORY OF A SQUASH

Once upon a time a farmer planted a little seed. in his garden, and after a while it sprouted and became a vine and bore many squashes. One day in October, when they were ripe, he picked one and took it to market. A gorcerman bought and put it in his shop. That same morning, a little girl in a brown hat and blue dress, with a round face and snub nose, went and bought it for her mother. She lugged it home, cut it up, and boiled it in the big pot, mashed some of it salt and butter, for dinner. And to the rest she added a pint of milk, two eggs, four spoons of sugar, nutmeg, and some crackers, put it in a deep dish, and baked it till it was brown and nice, and next day it was eaten by a family named March. T. TUPMAN

Mr. Pickwick, Sir:-I address you upon the subject of sin the sinner I mean is a man named Winkle who makes trouble in his club by laughing and sometimes won't write his piece in this fine paper I hope you will pardon his badness and let him send a French fable because he can't write out of his head as he has so many lessons to do and no brains in future I will try to take time by the fetlock and prepare some work which will be all commy la fo that means all right I am in haste as it is nearly school time Yours respectably, N. WINKLE

[The above is a manly and handsome aknowledgment of past misdemeanors. If our young friend studied punctuation, it would be well.]

A SAD ACCIDENT

On Friday last, we were startled by a violent shock in our basement, followed by cries of distress. On rushing in a body to the cellar, we discovered our beloved President prostrate upon the floor, having tripped and fallen while getting wood for domestic purposes. A perfect scene of ruin met our eyes, for in his fall Mr. Pickwick had plunged his head and shoulders into a tub of water, upset a keg of soft soap upon his manly form, and torn his garments badly. On being removed from this perilous situation, it was discovered that he had suffered no injury but several bruises, and we are happy to add, is now doing well. ED.

THE PUBLIC BEREAVEMENT

It is our painful duty to record the sudden and mysterious disappearance of our cherished friend, Mrs. Snowball Pat Paw. This lovely and beloved cat was the pet of a large circle of warm and admiring friends; for her beauty attracted all eyes, her graces and virtues endeared her to all hearts, and her loss is deeply felt by the whole community.

When last seen, she was sitting at the gate, watching the butcher's cart, and it is feared that some villain, tempted by her charms, basely stole her. Weeks have passed, but no trace of her has been discovered, and we relinquish all hope, tie a black ribbon to her basket, set aside her dish, and weep for her as one lost to us forever.

A sympathizing friend sends the following gem:

A LAMENT (FOR S. B. PAT PAW)

We mourn the loss of our little pet, And sigh o'er her hapless fate, For never more by the fire she'll sit, Nor play by the old green gate.

The little grave where her infant sleeps Is 'neath the chestnut tree. But o'er her grave we may not weep, We know not where it may be.

Her empty bed, her idle ball, Will never see her more; No gentle tap, no loving purr Is heard at the parlor door.

Another cat comes after her mice, A cat with a dirty face, But she does not hunt as our darling did, Nor play with her airy grace.

Her stealthy paws tread the very hall Where Snowball used to play, But she only spits at the dogs our pet So gallantly drove away.

She is useful and mild, and does her best, But she is not fair to see, And we cannot give her your place dear, Nor worship her as we worship thee. A.S.

ADVERTISEMENTS

Miss Oranthy Bluggage, the accomplished strong-minded lecturer, will deliver her famous lecture on "WOMAN AND

HER POSITION" at Pickwick Hall, next Saturday Evening, after the usual performances.

A weekly meeting will be held at Kitchen place, to teach young ladies how to cook. Hannah Brown will preside, and all are invited to attend.

The DUSTPAN SOCIETY will meet on Wednesday next, and parade in the upper story of the Club House. All members to appear in uniform and shoulder their brooms at nine precisely.

Mrs. Beth Bouncer will open her new assortment of Doll's Millinery next week. The latest Paris fashions have arrived, and orders are respectfully solicited.

A new play will appear at the Barnville Theatre, in the course of a few weeks, which will surpass anything ever seen on the American stage. The Greek Slave, or Constantine the Avenger, is the name of this thrilling drama.!!!

HINTS

If S.P. didn't use so much soap on his hands, he wouldn't always be late at breakfast. A.S. is requested not to whistle in the street. T.T please don't forget Amy's napkin. N.W. must not fret because his dress has not nine tucks.

WEEKLY REPORT

Meg—Good. Jo—Bad. Beth—Very Good. Amy—Middling.

As the President finished reading the paper (which I beg leave to assure my readers is a bona fide copy of one written by bona fide girls once upon a time), a round of applause followed, and then Mr. Snodgrass rose to make a proposition.

"Mr. President and gentlemen," he began, assuming a parliamentary attitude and tone, "I wish to propose the admission of a new member—one who highly deserves the honor, would be deeply grateful for it, and would add immensely to the spirit of the club, the literary value of the paper, and be no end jolly and nice. I propose Mr. Theodore Laurence as an honorary member of the P. C. Come now, do have him."

Jo's sudden change of tone made the girls laugh, but all looked rather anxious, and no one said a word as Snodgrass took his seat.

"We'll put it to a vote," said the President. "All in favor of this motion please to manifest it by saying, 'Aye.'"

"Contrary-minded say, 'No.'"

Meg and Amy were contrary-minded, and Mr. Winkle rose to say with great elegance, "We don't wish any boys, they only joke and bounce about. This is a ladies' club, and we wish to be private and proper."

"I'm afraid he'll laugh at our paper, and make fun of us afterward," observed Pickwick, pulling the little curl on her forehead, as she always did when doubtful.

Up rose Snodgrass, very much in earnest. "Sir, I give you my word as a gentleman, Laurie won't do anything of the sort. He likes to write, and he'll give a tone to our contributions and keep us from being sentimental, don't you see? We can do so little for him, and he does so much for us, I think the least we can do is to offer him a place here, and make him welcome if he comes."

This artful allusion to benefits conferred brought Tupman to his feet, looking as if he had quite made up his mind.

"Yes, we ought to do it, even if we are afraid. I say he may come, and his grandpa, too, if he likes."

This spirited burst from Beth electrified the club, and Jo left her seat to shake hands approvingly. "Now then, vote again. Everybody remember it's our Laurie, and say, 'Aye!'" cried Snodgrass excitedly.

"Aye! Aye! Aye!" replied three voices at once.

"Good! Bless you! Now, as there's nothing like 'taking time by the fetlock', as Winkle characteristically observes, allow me to present the new member." And, to the dismay of the rest of the club, Jo threw open the door of the closet, and displayed Laurie sitting on a rag bag, flushed and twinkling with suppressed laughter.

"You rogue! You traitor! Jo, how could you?" cried the three girls, as Snodgrass led her friend triumphantly forth, and producing both a chair and a badge, installed him in a jiffy.

"The coolness of you two rascals is amazing," began Mr. Pickwick, trying to get up an awful frown and only succeeding in producing an amiable smile. But the new member was equal to the occasion, and rising, with a grateful salutation to the Chair, said in the most engaging manner, "Mr. President and ladies—I beg pardon, gentlemen—allow me to introduce myself as Sam Weller, the very humble servant of the club."

"Good! Good!" cried Jo, pounding with the handle of the old warming pan on which she leaned.

"My faithful friend and noble patron," continued Laurie with a wave of the hand, "who has so flatteringly presented me, is not to be blamed for the base stratagem of tonight. I planned it, and she only gave in after lots of teasing."

"Come now, don't lay it all on yourself. You know I proposed the cupboard," broke in Snodgrass, who was enjoying the joke amazingly.

"Never mind what she says. I'm the wretch that did it, sir," said the new member, with a Welleresque nod to Mr. Pickwick. "But on my honor, I never will do so again, and henceforth devote myself to the interest of this immortal club."

"Hear! Hear!" cried Jo, clashing the lid of the warming pan like a cymbal.

"Go on, go on!" added Winkle and Tupman, while the President bowed benignly.

"I merely wish to say, that as a slight token of my gratitude for the honor done me, and as a means of promoting friendly relations between adjoining nations, I have set up a post office in the hedge in the lower corner of the garden, a fine, spacious building with padlocks on the doors and every convenience for the mails, also the females, if I may be allowed the expression. It's the old martin house, but I've stopped up the door and made the roof open, so it will hold all sorts of things, and save our valuable time. Letters, manuscripts, books, and bundles can be passed in there, and as each nation has a key, it will be uncommonly nice, I fancy. Allow me to present the club key, and with many thanks for your favor, take my seat."

Great applause as Mr. Weller deposited a little key on the table and subsided, the warming pan clashed and waved wildly, and it was some time before order could be restored. A long discussion followed, and everyone came out surprising, for everyone did her best. So it was an unusually lively meeting, and did not adjourn till a late hour, when it broke up with three shrill cheers for the new member. No one ever regretted the admittance of Sam Weller, for a more devoted, well-behaved, and jovial member no club could have. He certainly did add 'spirit' to the meetings, and 'a tone' to the paper, for his orations convulsed his hearers and his contributions were excellent, being patriotic, classical, comical, or dramatic, but never sentimental. Jo regarded them as worthy of Bacon, Milton, or Shakespeare, and remodeled her own works with good effect, she thought.

The P. O. was a capital little institution, and flourished wonderfully, for nearly as many queer things passed through it as through the real post office. Tragedies and cravats, poetry and pickles, garden seeds and long letters, music and gingerbread, rubbers, invitations, scoldings, and puppies. The old gentleman liked the fun, and amused himself by sending odd bundles, mysterious messages, and funny telegrams, and his gardener, who was smitten with Hannah's charms, actually sent a love letter to Jo's care. How they laughed when the secret came out, never dreaming how many love letters that little post office would hold in the years to come.

Chapter Eleven

"The first of June! The Kings are off to the seashore tomorrow, and I'm free. Three months' vacation—how I shall enjoy it!" exclaimed Meg, coming home one warm day to find Jo laid upon the sofa in an unusual state of exhaustion, while Beth took off her dusty boots, and Amy made lemonade for the refreshment of the whole party.

"Aunt March went today, for which, oh, be joyful!" said Jo. "I was mortally afraid she'd ask me to go with her. If she had, I should have felt as if I ought to do it, but Plumfield is about as gay as a churchyard, you know, and I'd rather be excused. We had a flurry getting the old lady off, and I had a fright every time she spoke to me, for I was in such a hurry to be through that I was uncommonly helpful and sweet, and feared she'd find it impossible to part from me. I quaked till she was fairly in the carriage, and had a final fright, for as it drove of, she popped out her head, saying, 'Josyphine, won't you—?' I didn't hear any more, for I basely turned and fled. I did actually run, and whisked round the corner whee I felt safe."

"Poor old Jo! She came in looking as if bears were after her," said Beth, as she cuddled her sister's feet with a motherly air.

"Aunt March is a regular samphire, is she not?" observed Amy, tasting her mixture critically.

"She means vampire, not seaweed, but it doesn't matter. It's too warm to be particular about one's parts of speech," murmured Jo.

"What shall you do all your vacation?" asked Amy, changing the subject with tact.

"I shall lie abed late, and do nothing," replied Meg, from the depths of the rocking chair. "I've been routed up early all winter and had to spend my days working for other people, so now I'm going to rest and revel to my heart's content."

"No," said Jo, "that dozy way wouldn't suit me. I've laid in a heap of books, and I'm going to improve my shining hours reading on my perch in the old apple tree, when I'm not having l..."

"Don't say 'larks!'" implored Amy, as a return snub for the samphire' correction.

"I'll say 'nightingales' then, with Laurie. That's proper and appropriate, since he's a warbler."

"Don't let us do any lessons, Beth, for a while, but play all the time and rest, as the girls mean to," proposed Amy.

"Well, I will, if Mother doesn't mind. I want to learn some new songs, and my children need fitting up for the summer. They are dreadfully out of order and really suffering for clothes."

"May we, Mother?" asked Meg, turning to Mrs. March, who sat sewing in what they called 'Marmee's corner'. "You may try your experiment for a week and see how you like it. I think by Saturday night you will find that all play and no work is as bad as all work and no play."

"Oh, dear, no! It will be delicious, I'm sure," said Meg complacently.

"I now propose a toast, as my 'friend and pardner, Sairy Gamp', says. Fun forever, and no grubbing!" cried Jo, rising, glass in hand, as the lemonade went round.

They all drank it merrily, and began the experiment by lounging for the rest of the day. Next morning, Meg did not appear till ten o'clock. Her solitary breakfast did not taste nice, and the room seemed lonely and untidy, for Jo had not filled the vases, Beth had not dusted, and Amy's books lay scattered about. Nothing was neat and pleasant but 'Marmee's corner', which looked as usual. And there Meg sat, to 'rest and read', which meant to yawn and imagine what pretty summer dresses she would get with her salary. Jo spent the morning on the river with Laurie and the afternoon reading and crying over The Wide, Wide World, up in the apple tree. Beth began by rummaging everything out of the big closet where her family resided, but getting tired before half done, she left her establishment topsy-turvy and went to her music, rejoicing that she had no dishes to wash. Amy arranged her bower, put on her best white frock, smoothed her curls, and sat down to draw under the honeysuckle, hoping someone would see and inquire who the young artist was. As no one appeared but an inquisitive daddy-longlegs, who examined her work with interest, she went to walk, got caught in a shower, and came home dripping.

At teatime they compared notes, and all agreed that it had been a delightful, though unusually long day. Meg, who went shopping in the afternoon and got a 'sweet blue muslin, had discovered, after she had cut the breadths off, that it wouldn't wash, which mishap made her slightly cross. Jo had burned the skin off her nose boating, and got a raging headache by reading too long. Beth was worried by the confusion of her closet and the difficulty of learning three or four songs at once, and Amy deeply regretted the damage done her frock, for Katy Brown's party was to be the next day and now like Flora McFlimsey, she had 'nothing to wear'. But these were mere trifles, and they assured their mother that the experiment was working finely. She smiled, said nothing, and with Hannah's help did their neglected work, keeping home pleasant and the domestic machinery running smoothly. It was astonishing what a peculiar and uncomfortable state of things was produced by the 'resting and reveling' process. The days kept getting longer and longer, the weather was unusually variable and so were tempers, and unsettled feeling possessed everyone, and Satan found plenty of mischief for the idle hands to do. As the height of luxury, Meg put out some of her sewing, and then found time hang so heavily that she fell to snipping and spoiling her clothes in her attempts to furbish them up a'la Moffat. Jo read till her eyes gave out and she was sick of books, got so fidgety that even good-natured Laurie had a quarrel with her, and so reduced in spirits that she desperately wished she had gone with Aunt March. Beth got on pretty well, for she was constantly forgetting that it was to be all play and no work, and fell back into her old ways now and then. But something in the air affected her, and more than once her tranquility was much disturbed, so much so that on one occasion she actually shook poor dear Joanna and told her she was a fright'. Amy fared worst of all, for her resources were small, and when her sisters left her to amuse herself, she soon found that accomplished and important little self a great burden. She didn't like dolls, fairy tales were childish, and one couldn't draw all the time. Tea parties didn't amount to much neither did picnics unless very well conducted. "If one could have a fine house, full of nice girls, or go traveling, the summer would be delightful, but to stay at home with three selfish sisters and a grown-up boy was enough to try the patience of a Boaz," complained Miss Malaprop, after several days devoted to pleasure, fretting, and ennui.

No one would own that they were tired of the experiment, but by Friday night each acknowledged to herself that she was glad the week was nearly done. Hoping to impress the lesson more deeply, Mrs. March, who had a good deal of humor, resolved to finish off the trial in an appropriate manner, so she gave Hannah a holiday and let the girls enjoy the full effect of the play system.

When they got up on Saturday morning, there was no fire in the kitchen, no breakfast in the dining room, and no mother anywhere to be seen.

"Mercy on us! What has happened?" cried Jo, staring about her in dismay.

Meg ran upstairs and soon came back again, looking relieved but rather bewildered, and a little ashamed.

"Mother isn't sick, only very tired, and she says she is going to stay quietly in her room all day and let us do the best we can. It's a very queer thing for her to do, she doesn't act a bit like herself. But she says it has been a hard week for her, so we mustn't grumble but take care of ourselves."

"That's easy enough, and I like the idea, I'm aching for something to do, that is, some new amusement, you know," added Jo quickly.

In fact it was an immense relief to them all to have a little work, and they took hold with a will, but soon realized the truth of Hannah's saying, "Housekeeping ain't no joke." There was plenty of food in the larder, and while Beth and Amy set the table, Meg and Jo got breakfast, wondering as they did why servants ever talked about hard work.

"I shall take some up to Mother, though she said we were not to think of her, for she'd take care of herself," said Meg, who presided and felt quite matronly behind the teapot.

So a tray was fitted out before anyone began, and taken up with the cook's compliments. The boiled tea was very bitter, the omelet scorched, and the biscuits speckled with saleratus, but Mrs. March received her repast with thanks and laughed heartily over it after Jo was gone.

"Poor little souls, they will have a hard time, I'm afraid, but they won't suffer, and it will do them good," she said, producing the more palatable viands with which she had provided herself, and disposing of the bad breakfast, so that their feelings might not be hurt, a motherly little deception for which they were grateful.

Many were the complaints below, and great the chagrin of the head cook at her failures. "Never mind, I'll get the dinner and be servant, you be mistress, keep your hands nice, see company, and give orders," said Jo, who knew still less than Meg, about culinary affairs.

This obliging offer was gladly accepted, and Margaret retired to the parlor, which she hastily put in order by whisking the litter under the sofa and shutting the blinds to save the trouble of dusting. Jo, with perfect faith in her own powers and a friendly desire to make up the quarrel, immediately put a note in the office, inviting Laurie to dinner.

"You'd better see what you have got before you think of having company," said Meg, when informed of the hospitable but rash act.

"Oh, there's corned beef and plenty of poatoes, and I shall get some asparagus and a lobster, 'for a relish', as Hannah says. We'll have lettuce and make a salad. I don't know how, but the book tells. I'll have blancmange and strawberries for dessert, and coffee too, if you want to be elegant."

"Don't try too many messes, Jo, for you can't make anything but gingerbread and molasses candy fit to eat. I wash my hands of the dinner party, and since you have asked Laurie on your own responsibility, you may just take care of him."

"I don't want you to do anything but be civil to him and help to the pudding. You'll give me your advice if I get in a muddle, won't you?" asked Jo, rather hurt.

"Yes, but I don't know much, except about bread and a few trifles. You had better ask Mother's leave before you order anything," returned Meg prudently.

"Of course I shall. I'm not a fool." And Jo went off in a huff at the doubts expressed of her powers.

"Get what you like, and don't disturb me. I'm going out to dinner and can't worry about things at home," said Mrs. March, when Jo spoke to her. "I never enjoyed housekeeping, and I'm going to take a vacation today, and read, write, go visiting, and amuse myself."

The unusual spectacle of her busy mother rocking comfortably and reading early in the morning made Jo feel as if some unnatural phenomenon had occurred, for an eclipse, an earthquake, or a volcanic eruption would hardly have seemed stranger.

"Everything is out of sorts, somehow," she said to herself, going downstairs. "There's Beth crying, that's a sure sign that something is wrong in this family. If Amy is bothering, I'll shake her."

Feeling very much out of sorts herself, Jo hurried into the parlor to find Beth sobbing over Pip, the canary, who lay dead in the cage with his little claws pathetically extended, as if imploring the food for want of which he had died.

"It's all my fault, I forgot him, there isn't a seed or a drop left. Oh, Pip! Oh, Pip! How could I be so cruel to you?" cried Beth, taking the poor thing in her hands and trying to restore him.

Jo peeped into his half-open eye, felt his little heart, and finding him stiff and cold, shook her head, and offered her domino box for a coffin.

"Put him in the oven, and maybe his will get warm and revive," said Amy hopefully.

"He's been starved, and he shan't be baked now he's dead. I'll make him a shroud, and he shall be buried in the garden, and I'll never have another bird, never, my Pip! For I am too bad to own one," murmured Beth, sitting on the floor with her pet folded in her hands. "The funeral shall be this afternoon, and we will all go. Now, don't cry, Bethy. It's a pity, but nothing goes right this week, and Pip has had the worst of the experiment.

Make the shroud, and lay him in my box, and after the dinner party, we'll have a nice little funeral," said Jo, beginning to feel as if she had undertaken a good deal.

Leaving the others to console Beth, she departed to the kitchen, which was in a most discouraging state of confusion. Putting on a big apron, she fell to work and got the dishes piled up ready for washing, when she discovered that the fire was out.

"Here's a sweet prospect!" muttered Jo, slamming the stove door open, and poking vigorously among the cinders.

Having rekindled the fire, she thought she would go to market while the water heated. The walk revived her spirits, and flattering herself that she had made good bargins, she trudged home again, after buying a very young lobster, some very old asparagus, and two boxes of acid strawberries. By the time she got cleared up, the dinner arrived and the stove was red-hot. Hannah had left a pan of bread to rise, Meg had worked it up early, set it on the hearth for a second rising, and forgotten it. Meg was entertaining Sallie Gardiner in the parlor, when the door flew open and a floury, crocky, flushed, and disheveled figure appeared, demanding tartly . . .

"I say, isn't bread 'riz' enough when it runs over the pans?"

Sallie began to laugh, but Meg nodded and lifted her eyebrows as high as they would go, which caused the apparition to vanish and put the sour bread into the oven without further delay. Mrs. March went out, after peeping here and there to see how matters went, also saying a word of comfort to Beth, who sat making a winding sheet, while the dear departed lay in state in the domino box. A strange sense of helplessness fell upon the girls as the gray bonnet vanished round the corner, and despair seized them when a few minutes later Miss Crocker appeared, and said she'd come to dinner. Now this lady was a thin, yellow spinster, with a sharp nose and inquisitive eyes, who saw everything and gossiped about all she saw. They disliked her, but had been taught to be kind to her, simply because she was old and poor and had few friends. So Meg gave her the easy chair and tried to entertain her, while she asked questions, critsized everything, and told stories of the people whom she knew.

Language cannot describe the anxieties, experiences, and exertions which Jo underwent that morning, and the dinner she served up became a standing joke. Fearing to ask any more advice, she did her best alone, and discovered that something more than energy and good will is necessary to make a cook. She boiled the asparagus for an hour and was grieved to find the heads cooked off and the stalks harder than ever. The bread burned black, for the salad dressing so aggravated her that she could not make it fit to ear. The lobster was a scarlet mystery to her, but she hammered and poked till it was unshelled and its meager proportions concealed in a grove of lettuce leaves. The potatoes had to be hurried, not to keep the asparagus waiting, and were not done at the last. The blancmange was lumpy, and the strawberries not as ripe as they looked, having been skilfully 'deaconed'.

"Well, they can eat beef and bread and butter, if they are hungry, only it's mortifying to have to spend your whole morning for nothing," thought Jo, as she rang the bell half an hour later than usual, and stood, hot, tired, and dispirited, surveying the feast spread before Laurie, accustomed to all sorts of elegance, and Miss Crocker, whose tattling tongue would report them far and wide.

Poor Jo would gladly have gone under the table, as one thing after another was tasted and left, while Amy giggled, Meg looked distressed, Miss Crocker pursed her lips, and Laurie talked and laughed with all his might to give a cheerful tone to the festive scene. Jo's one strong point was the fruit, for she had sugared it well, and had a pitcher of rich cream to eat with it. Her hot cheeks cooled a trifle, and she drew a long breath as the pretty glass plates went round, and everyone looked graciously at the little rosy islands floating in a sea of cream. Miss

Crocker tasted first, made a wry face, and drank some water hastily. Jo, who refused, thinking there might not be enough, for they dwindled sadly after the picking over, glanced at Laurie, but he was eating away manfully, though there was a slight pucker about his mouth and he kept his eye fixed on his plate. Amy, who was fond of delicate fare, took a heaping spoonful, choked, hid her face in her napkin, and left the table precipitately.

"Oh, what is it?" exclaimed Jo, trembling.

"Salt instead of sugar, and the cream is sour," replied Meg with a tragic gesture.

Jo uttered a groan and fell back in her chair, remembering that she had given a last hasty powdering to the berries out of one of the two boxes on the kitchen table, and had neglected to put the milk in the refrigerator. She turned scarlet and was on the verge of crying, when she met Laurie's eyes, which would look merry in spite of his heroic efforts. The comical side of the affair suddenly struck her, and she laughed till the tears ran down her cheeks. So did everyone else, even 'Croaker' as the girls called the old lady, and the unfortunate dinner ended gaily, with bread and butter, olives and fun.

"I haven't strength of mind enough to clear up now, so we will sober ourselves with a funeral," said Jo, as they rose, and Miss Crocker made ready to go, being eager to tell the new story at another friend's dinner table.

They did sober themselves for Beth's sake. Laurie dug a grave under the ferns in the grove, little Pip was laid in, with many tears by his tender-hearted mistress, and covered with moss, while a wreath of violets and chickweed was hung on the stone which bore his epitaph, composed by Jo while she struggled with the dinner.

> Here lies Pip March, Who died the 7th of June; Loved and lamented sore, And not forgotten soon.

At the conclusion of the ceremonies, Beth retired to her room, overcome with emotion and lobster, but there was no place of repose, for the beds were not made, and she found her grief much assuaged by beating up the pillows and putting things in order. Meg helped Jo clear away the remains of the feast, which took half the afternoon and left them so tired that they agreed to be contented with tea and toast for supper.

Laurie took Amy to drive, which was a deed of charity, for the sour cream seemed to have had a bad effect upon her temper. Mrs. March came home to find the three older girls hard at work in the middle of the afternoon, and a glance at the closet gave her an idea of the success of one part of the experiment.

Before the housewives could rest, several people called, and there was a scramble to get ready to see them. Then tea must be got, errands done, and one or two necessary bits of sewing neglected until the last minute. As twilight fell, dewy and still, one by one they gathered on the porch where the June roses were budding beautifully, and each groaned or sighed as she sat down, as if tired or troubled.

"What a dreadful day this has been!" began Jo, usually the first to speak.

"It has seemed shorter than usual, but so uncomfortable," said Meg.

"Not a bit like home," added Amy.

"It can't seem so without Marmee and little Pip," sighed Beth, glancing with full eyes at the empty cage above her head.

"Here's Mother, dear, and you shall have another bird tomorrow, if you want it."

As she spoke, Mrs. March came and took her place among them, looking as if her holiday had not been much pleasanter than theirs.

"Are you satisfied with your experiment, girls, or do you want another week of it?" she asked, as Beth nestled up to her and the rest turned toward her with brightening faces, as flowers turn toward the sun.

"I don't!" cried Jo decidedly.

"Nor I," echoed the others.

"You think then, that it is better to have a few duties and live a little for others, do you?"

"Lounging and larking doesn't pay," observed Jo, shaking her head. "I'm tired of it and mean to go to work at something right off."

"Suppose you learn plain cooking. That's a useful accomplishment, which no woman should be without," said Mrs. March, laughing inaudibly at the recollection of Jo's dinner party, for she had met Miss Crocker and heard her account of it.

"Mother, did you go away and let everything be, just to see how we'd get on?" cried Meg, who had had suspicions all day.

"Yes, I wanted you to see how the comfort of all depends on each doing her share faithfully. While Hannah and I did your work, you got on pretty well, though I don't think you were very happy or amiable. So I thought, as a little lesson, I would show you what happens when everyone thinks only of herself. Don't you feel that it is pleasanter to help one another, to have daily duties which make leisure sweet when it comes, and to bear and forbear, that home may be comfortable and lovely to us all?"

"We do, Mother we do!" cried the girls.

"Then let me advise you to take up your little burdens again, for though they seem heavy sometimes, they are good for us, and lighten as we learn to carry them. Work is wholesome, and there is plenty for everyone. It keeps us from ennui and mischief, is good for health and spirits, and gives us a sense of power and independence better than money or fashion."

"We'll work like bees, and love it too, see if we don't," said Jo. "I'll learn plain cooking for my holiday task, and the dinner party I have shall be a success."

"I'll make the set of shirts for father, instead of letting you do it, Marmee. I can and I will, though I'm not fond of sewing. That will be better than fussing over my own things, which are plenty nice enough as they are." said Meg.

"I'll do my lessons every day, and not spend so much time with my music and dolls. I am a stupid thing, and ought to be studying, not playing," was Beth's resolution, while Amy followed their example by heroically declaring, "I shall learn to make buttonholes, and attend to my parts of speech."

"Very good! Then I am quite satisfied with the experiment, and fancy that we shall not have to repeat it, only don't go to the other extreme and delve like slaves. Have regular hours for work and play, make each day both useful and pleasant, and prove that you understand the worth of time by employing it well. Then youth will be delightful, old age will bring few regrets, and life become a beautiful success, in spite of poverty."

"We'll remember, Mother!" And they did.

Chapter Tweleve

Beth was postmistress, for, being most at home, she could attend to it regularly, and dearly liked the daily task of unlocking the little door and distributing the mail. One July day she came in with her hands full, and went about the house leaving letters and parcels like the penny post.

"Here's your posy, Mother! Laurie never forgets that," she said, putting the fresh nosegay in the vase that stood in 'Marmee's corner', and was kept supplied by the affectionate boy.

"Miss Meg March, one letter and a glove," continued Beth, delivering the articles to her sister, who sat near her mother, stitching wristbands.

"Why, I left a pair over there, and here is only one," said Meg, looking at the gray cotton glove. "Didn't you drop the other in the garden?"

"No, I'm sure I didn't, for there was only one in the office."

"I hate to have odd gloves! Never mind, the other may be found. My letter is only a translation of the German song I wanted. I think Mr. Brooke did it, for this isn't Laurie's writing."

Mrs. March glanced at Meg, who was looking very pretty in her gingham morning gown, with the little curls blowing about her forehead, and very womanly, as she sat sewing at her little worktable, full of tidy white rolls, so unconscious of the thought in her mother's mind as she sewed and sang, while her fingers flew and her thoughts were busied with girlish fancies as innocent and fresh as the pansies in her belt, that Mrs. March smiled and was satisfied.

"Two letters for Doctor Jo, a book, and a funny old hat, which covered the whole post office and stuck outside," said Beth, laughing as she went into the study where Jo sat writing.

"What a sly fellow Laurie is! I said I wished bigger hats were the fashion, because I burn my face every hot day. He said, 'Why mind the fashion? Wear a big hat, and be comfortable!' I said I would if I had one, and he has sent me this to try me. I'll wear it for fun, and show him I don't care for the fashion." And hanging the antique broadbrim on a bust of Plato, Jo read her letters.

One from her mother made her cheeks glow and her eyes fill, for it said to her . . .

My Dear:

I write a little word to tell you with how much satisfaction I watch your efforts to control your temper. You say nothing about your trials, failures, or successes, and think, perhaps, that no one sees them but the Friend whose help you daily ask, if I may trust the well-worn cover of your guidebook. I, too, have seen them all, and heartily believe in the sincerity of your resolution, since it begins to bear fruit. Go on, dear, patiently and bravely, and always believe that no one sympathizes more tenderly with you than your loving . . .

Mother

"That does me good! That's worth millions of money and pecks of praise. Oh, Marmee, I do try! I will keep on trying, and not get tired, since I have you to help me."

Laying her head on her arms, Jo wet her little romance with a few happy tears. for she had thought that no one saw and appreciated her efforts to be good, and this assurance was doubly precious, doubly encouraging, because unexpected and from the person whose commendation she most valued. Feeling stronger than ever to meet and subdue her Apollyon, she pinned the note inside her frock, as a shield and a reminder, lest she be taken unaware, and proceeded to open her other letter, quite ready for either good or bad news. In a big, dashing hand, Laurie wrote . . .

Dear Jo, What ho!

Some english girls and boys are coming to see me tomorrow and I want to have a jolly time. If it's fine, I'm going to pitch my tent in Longmeadow, and row up the whole crew to lunch and croquet—have a fire, make messes, gypsy fashion, and all sorts of larks. They are nice people, and like such things. Brooke will go to keep us boys steady, and Kate Vaughn will play propriety for the girls. I want you all to come, can't let Beth off at any price, and nobody shall worry her. Don't bother about rations, I'll see to that and everything else, only do come, there's a good fellow!

In a tearing hurry, Yours ever, Laurie.

"Here's richness!" cried Jo, flying in to tell the news to Meg.

"Of course we can go, Mother? It will be such a help to Laurie, for I can row, and Meg see to the lunch, and the children be useful in some way."

"I hope the Vaughns are not fine grown-up people. Do you know anything about them, Jo?" asked Meg.

"Only that there are four of them. Kate is older than you, Fred and Frank (twins) about my age, and a little girl (Grace), who is nine or ten. Laurie knew them abroad, and liked the boys. I fancied, from the way he primmed up his mouth in speaking of her, that he didn't admire Kate much."

"I'm so glad my French print is clean, it's just the thing and so becoming!" observed Meg complacently. "Have you anything decent, Jo?"

"Scarlet and gray boating suit, good enough for me. I shall row and tramp about, so I don't want any starch to think of. You'll come, Betty?"

"If you won't let any boys talk to me."

"Not a boy!"

"I like to please Laurie, and I'm not afraid of Mr. Brooke, he is so kind. But I don't want to play, or sing, or say anything. I'll work hard and not trouble anyone, and you'll take care of me, Jo, so I'll go."

"That's my good girl. You do try to fight off your shyness, and I love you for it. Fighting faults isn't easy, as I know, and a cheery word kind of gives a lift. Thank you, Mother," And Jo gave the thin cheek a grateful kiss, more precious to Mrs. March than if it had given back the rosy roundness of her youth.

"I had a box of chocolate drops, and the picture I wanted to copy," said Amy, showing her mail.

"And I got a note from Mr. Laurence, asking me to come over and play to him tonight, before the lamps are lighted, and I shall go," added Beth, whose friendship with the old gentleman prospered finely. "Now let's fly round, and do double duty today, so that we can play tomorrow with free minds," said Jo, preparing to replace her pen with a broom.

When the sun peeped into the girls' room early next morning to promise them a fine day, he saw a comical sight. Each had made such preparation for the fete as seemed necessary and proper. Meg had an extra row of little curlpapers across her forehead, Jo had copiously anointed her afflicted face with cold cream, Beth had taken Joanna to bed with her to atone for the approaching separation, and Amy had capped the climax by putting a colthespin on her nose to uplift the offending feature. It was one of the kind artists use to hold the paper on their drawing boards, therefore quite appropriate and effective for the purpose it was now being put. This funny spectacle appeared to amuse the sun, for he burst out with such radiance that Jo woke up and roused her sisters by a hearty laugh at Amy's ornament.

Sunshine and laughter were good omens for a pleasure party, and soon a lively bustle began in both houses. Beth, who was ready first, kept reporting what went on next door, and enlivened her sisters' toilets by frequent telegrams from the window.

"There goes the man with the tent! I see Mrs. Barker doing up the lunch in a hamper and a great basket. Now Mr. Laurence is looking up at the sky and the weathercock. I wish he would go too. There's Laurie, looking like a sailor, nice boy! Oh, mercy me! Here's a carriage full of people, a tall lady, a little girl, and two dreadful boys. One is lame, poor thing, he's got a crutch. Laurie didn't tell us that. Be quick, girls! It's getting late. Why, there is Ned Moffat, I do declare. Meg, isn't that the man who bowed to you one day when we were shopping?"

"So it is. How queer that he should come. I thought he was at the mountains. There is Sallie. I'm glad she got back in time. Am I all right, Jo?" cried Meg in a flutter.

"A regular daisy. Hold up your dress and put your hat on straight, it looks sentimental tipped that way and will fly off at the first puff. Now then, come on!"

"Oh, Jo, you are not going to wear that awful hat? It's too absurd! You shall not make a guy of yourself," remonstrated Meg, as Jo tied down with a red ribbon the broad-brimmed, old-fashioned leghorn Laurie had sent for a joke.

"I just will, though, for it's capital, so shady, light, and big. It will make fun, and I don't mind being a guy if I'm comfortable." With that Jo marched straight away and the rest followed, a bright little band of sisters, all looking their best in summer suits, with happy faces under the jaunty hatbrims.

Laurie ran to meet and present them to his friends in the most cordial manner. The lawn was the reception room, and for several minutes a lively scene was enacted there. Meg was grateful to see that Miss Kate, though twenty, was dressed with a simplicity which American girls would do well to imitate, and who was much flattered by Mr. Ned's assurances that he came especially to see her. Jo understood why Laurie 'primmed up his mouth' when speaking of Kate, for that young lady had a stand-off-don't-touch-me air, which contrasted strongly with the free and easy demeanor of the other girls. Beth took an observation of the new boys and decided that the lame one was not 'dreadful', but gentle and feeble, and she would be kind to him on that account. Amy found Grace a well-mannered, merry, little person, and after staring dumbly at one another for a few minutes, they suddenly became very good friends.

Tents, lunch, and croquet utensils having been sent on beforehand, the party was soon embarked, and the two boats pushed off together, leaving Mr. Laurence waving his hat on the shore. Laurie and Jo rowed one boat, Mr. Brooke and Ned the other, while Fred Vaughn, the riotous twin, did his best to upset both by paddling about in a wherry like a disturbed water bug. Jo's funny hat deserved a vote of thanks, for it was of general utility. It broke the ice in the beginning by producing a laugh, it created quite a refreshing breeze, flapping to and fro as she rowed, and would make an excellent umbrella for the whole party, if a shower came up, she said. Miss Kate decided that she was 'odd', but rather clever, and smiled upon her from afar.

Meg, in the other boat, was delightfully situated, face to face with the rowers, who both admired the prospect and feathered their oars with uncommon 'skill and dexterity'. Mr. Brooke was a grave, silent young man, with handsome brown eyes and a pleasant voice. Meg liked his quiet manners and considered him a walking encyclopedia of useful knowledge. He never talked to her much, but he looked at her a good deal, and she felt sure that he did not regard her with aversion. Ned, being in college, of course put on all the airs which freshmen think it their bounden duty to assume. He was not very wise, but very good-natured, and altogether an excellent person to carry on a picnic. Sallie Gardiner was absorbed in keeping her white pique dress clean and chattering with the ubiquitous Fred, who kept Beth in constant terror by his pranks.

It was not far to Longmeadow, but the tent was pitched and the wickets down by the time they arrived. A pleasant green field, with three wide-spreading oaks in the middle and a smooth strip of turf for croquet.

"Welcome to Camp Laurence!" said the young host, as they landed with exclamations of delight.

"Brooke is commander in chief, I am commissary general, the other fellows are staff officers, and you, ladies, are company. The tent is for your especial benefit and that oak is your drawing room, this is the messroom and the third is the camp kitchen. Now, let's have a game before it gets hot, and then we'll see about dinner."

Frank, Beth, Amy, and Grace sat down to watch the game played by the other eight. Mr. Brooke chose Meg, Kate, and Fred. Laurie took Sallie, Jo, and Ned. The English played well, but the Americans played better, and contested every inch of the ground as strongly as if the spirit of '76 inspired them. Jo and Fred had several skirmishes and once narrowly escaped high words. Jo was through the last wicket and had missed the stroke, which failure ruffled her a good deal. Fred was close behind her and his turn came before hers. He gave a stroke, his ball hit the wicket, and stopped an inch on the wrong side. No one was very near, and running up to examine, he gave it a sly nudge with his toe, which put it just an inch on the right side.

"I'm through! Now, Miss Jo, I'll settle you, and get in first," cried the young gentleman, swinging his mallet for another blow.

"You pushed it. I saw you. It's my turn now," said Jo sharply.

"Upon my word, I didn't move it. It rolled a bit, perhaps, but that is allowed. So, stand off please, and let me have a go at the stake."

"We don't cheat in America, but you can, if you choose," said Jo angrily.

"Yankees are a deal the most tricky, everybody knows. There you go!" returned Fred, croqueting her ball far away.

Jo opened her lips to say something rude, but checked herself in time, colored up to her forehead and stood a minute, hammering down a wicket with all her might, while Fred hit the stake and declared himself out with much exultation. She went off to get her ball, and was a long time finding it among the bushes, but she came back, looking cool and quiet, and waited her turn patiently. It took several strokes to regain the place she had lost, and when she got there, the other side had nearly won, for Kate's ball was the last but one and lay near the stake.

"By George, it's all up with us! Goodbye, Kate. Miss Jo owes me one, so you are finished," cried Fred excitedly, as they all drew near to see the finish.

"Yankees have a trick of being generous to their enemies," said Jo, with a look that made the lad redden, "especially when they beat them," she added, as, leaving Kate's ball untouched, she won the game by a clever stroke.

Laurie threw up his hat, then remembered that it wouldn't do to exult over the defeat of his guests, and stopped in the middle of the cheer to whisper to his friend, "Good for you, Jo! He did cheat, I saw him. We can't tell him so, but he won't do it again, take my word for it."

Meg drew her aside, under pretense of pinning up a loose braid, and said approvingly, "It was dreadfully provoking, but you kept your temper, and I'm so glad, Jo."

"Don't praise me, Meg, for I could box his ears this minute. I should certainly have boiled over if I hadn't stayed among the nettles till I got my rage under control enough to hold my tongue.. It's simmering now, so I hope he'll keep out of my way," returned Jo, biting her lips as she glowered at Fred from under her big hat.

"Time for lunch," said Mr. Brooke, looking at his watch. "Commissary general, will you make the fire and get water, while Miss March, Miss Sallie, and I spread the table? Who can make good coffee?"

"Jo can," said Meg, glad to recommend her sister. So Jo, feeling that her late lessons in cookery were to do her honor, went to preside over the coffeepot, while the children collected dry sticks, and the boys made a fire and got water from a spring near by. Miss Kate sketched and Frank talked to Beth, who was making little mats of braided rushes to serve as plates.

The commander in chief and his aides soon spread the tablecloth with an inviting array of eatables and drinkables, prettily decorated with green leaves. Jo announced that the coffee was ready, and everyone settled themselves to a hearty meal, for youth is seldom dyspeptic, and exercise develops wholesome appetites. A very merry lunch it was, for everything seemed fresh and funny, and frequent peals of laughter startled a venerable horse who fed near by. There was a pleasing inequality in the table, which produced many mishaps to cups and plates, acorns dropped in the milk, little black ants partook of the refreshments without being invited, and fuzzy caterpillars swung down from the tree to see what was going on. Three white-headed children peeped over the fence, and an objectionable dog barked at them from the other side of the river with all his might and main.

"There's salt here," said Laurie, as he handed Jo a saucer of berries.

"Thank you, I prefer spiders," she replied, fishing up two unwary little ones who had gone to a creamy death. "How dare you remind me of that horrid dinner party, when your's is so nice in every way?' added Jo, as they both laughed and ate out of one plate, the china having run short.

"I had an uncommonly good time that day, and haven't got over it yet. This is no credit to me, you know, I don't do anything. It's you and Meg and Brooke who make it all go, and I'm no end obliged to you. what shall we do when we can't eat anymore?" asked Laurie, feeling that his trump card had been played when lunch was over.

"Have games till it's cooler. I brought Authors, and I dare say Miss Kate knows something new and nice. Go and ask her. She's company, and you ought to stay with her more."

"Aren't you company too? I thought she'd suit Brooke, but he keeps talking to Meg, and Kate just stares at them through that ridiculous glass of hers'. I'm going, so you needn't try to preach propriety, for you can't do it, Jo."

Miss Kate did know several new games, and as the girls would not, and the boys could not, eat any more, they all adjourned to the drawing room to play Rig-marole.

"One person begins a story, any nonsense you like, and tells as long as he pleases, only taking care to stop short at some exciting point, when the next takes it up and does the same. It's very funny when well done, and makes a perfect jumble of tragical comical stuff to laugh over. Please start it, Mr. Brooke," said Kate, with a commanding air, which surprised Meg, who treated the tutor with as much respect as any other gentleman.

Lying on the grass at the feet of the two young ladies, Mr. Brooke obediently began the story, with the handsome brown eyes steadily fixed upon the sunshiny river.

"Once on a time, a knight went out into the world to seek his fortune, for he had nothing but his sword and his shield. He traveled a long while, nearly eight-and-twenty years, and had a hard time of it, till he came to the palace of a good old king, who had offered a reward to anyone who could tame and train a fine but unbroken colt, of which he was very fond. The knight agreed to try, and got on slowly but surely, for the colt was a gallant fellow, and soon learned to love his new master, though he was freakish and wild. Every day, when he gave his lessons to this pet of the king's, the knight rode him through the city, and as he rode, he looked everywhere for a certain beautiful face, which he had seen many times in his dreams, but never found. One day, as he went prancing down a quiet street, he saw at the window of a ruinous castle the lovely face. He was delighted, inquired who lived in this old castle, and was told that several captive princesses were kept there by a spell, and spun all day to lay up money to buy their liberty. The knight wished intensely that he could free them, but he was poor and could only go by each day, watching for the sweet face and longing to see it out in the sunshine. At last he resolved to get into the castle and ask how he could help them. He went and knocked. The great door flew open, and he beheld . . ."

"A ravishingly lovely lady, who exclaimed, with a cry of rapture, 'At last! At last!'" continued Kate, who had read French novels, and admired the style. "'Tis she!' cried Count Gustave, and fell at her feet in an ecstasy of joy. 'Oh, rise!' she said, extending a hand of marble fairness. 'Never! Till you tell me how I may rescue you, ' swore the knight, still kneeling. 'Alas, my cruel fate condemns me to remain here till my tyrant is destroyed.' 'Where is the villain?' 'In the mauve salon. Go, brave heart, and save me from despair.' 'I obey, and return victorious or dead!' With these thrilling words he rushed away, and flinging open the door of the mauve salon, was about to enter, when he received . . ." "A stunning blow from the big Greek lexicon, which an old fellow in a black gown fired at him," said Ned. "Instantly, Sir What's-his-name recovered himself, pitched the tyrant out of the window, and turned to join the lady, victorious, but with a bump on his brow, found the door locked, tore up the curtains, made a rope ladder, got halfway down when the ladder broke, and he went headfirst into the moat, sixty feet below. Could swim like a duck, paddled round the castle till he came to a little door guarded by two stout fellows, knocked their heads together till they cracked like a couple of nuts, then, by a trifling exertion of his prodigious strength, he smashed in the door, went up a pair of stone steps covered with dust a foot thick, toads as big as your fist, and spiders that would frighten you into hysterics, MIss March. At the top of these steps he came plump upon a sight that took his breath away and chilled his blood . . ."

"A tall figure, all in white with a veil over its face and a lamp in its wasted hand," went on Meg. "It beckoned, gliding noiselessly before him down a corridor as dark and cold as any tomb. Shadowy effigies in armor stood on either side, a dead silence reigned, the lamp burned blue, and the ghostly figure ever and anon turned its face toward him, showing the glitter of awful eyes through its white veil. They reached a curtained door, behind which sounded lovely music. He sprang forward to enter, but the specter plucked him back, and waved threateningly before him a . . ."

"Snuffbox," said Jo, in a sepulchral tone, which convulsed the audience. "'Thankee, ' said the knight politely, as he took a pinch and sneezed seven times so violently that his head fell off. 'Ha! Ha!' laughed the ghost, and having peeped through the keyhole at the princesses spinning away for dear life, the evil spirit picked up her victim and put him in a large tin box, where there were eleven other knights packed together without their heads, like sardines, who all rose and began to . . ."

"Dance a hornpipe," cut in Fred, as Jo paused for breath, "and, as they danced, the rubbishy old castle turned to a man-of-war in full sail. 'Up with the jib, reef the tops'l halliards, helm hard alee, and man the guns!' roared the captain, as a Portuguese pirate hove in sight, with a flag black as ink flying from her foremast. 'Go in and win, my hearties!' says the captain, and a tremendous fight began. Of course the British beat, they always do."

"No, they don't!" cried Jo, aside.

"Having taken the pirate captain prisoner, sailed slap over the schooner, whose decks were piled high with dead and whose lee scuppers ran blood, for the order had been 'Cutlasses, and die hard!' 'Bosun's mate, take a bight of the flying-jib sheet, and start this villain if he doesn't confess his sins double quick, ' said the British captain. The Portuguese held his tongue like a brick, and walked the plank, while the jolly tars cheered like mad. But the sly dog dived, came up under the man-of-war, scuttled her, and down she went, with all sail set, 'To the bottom of the sea, sea, sea' where . . ." "Oh, gracious! What shall I say?" cried Sallie, as Fred ended his rigmarole, in which he had jumbled together pell-mell nautical phrases and facts out of one of his favorite books. "Well, they went to the bottom, and a nice mermaid welcomed them, but was much grieved on finding the box of headless knights, and kindly pickled them in brine, hoping to discover the mystery about them, for being a woman, she was curious. By-and-by a diver came down, and the mermaid said, 'I'll give you a box of pearls if you can take it up, ' for she wanted to restore the poor things to life, and couldn't raise the heavy load herself. So the diver hoisted it up, and was much disappointed on opening it to find no pearls. He left it in a great lonely field, where it was found by a . . ."

"Little goose girl, who kept a hundred fat geese in the field," said Amy, when Sallie's invention gave out. "The little girl was sorry for them, and asked an old woman what she should do to help them. 'Your geese will tell you, they know everything.' said the old woman. So she asked what she should use for new heads, since the old ones were lost, and all the geese opened their hundred mouths and screamed . . ."

"'Cabbages!'" continued Laurie promptly. "'Just the thing, ' said the girl, and ran to get twelve fine ones from her garden. She put them on, the knights revived at once, thanked her, and went on their way rejoicing, never knowing the difference, for there were so many other heads like them in the world that no one thought anything of it. The knight in whom I'm interest went back to find the pretty face, and learned that the princesses had spun themselves free and all gone and married, but one. He was in a great state of mind at that, and mounting the colt, who stood by him through thick and thin, rushed to the castle to see which was left. Peeping over the hedge, he saw the queen of his affections picking flowers in her garden. 'Will you give me a rose?' said he. 'You must come and get it. I can't come to you, it isn't proper, ' said she, as sweet as honey. He tried to climb over the hedge, but it seemed to grow higher and higher. Then he tried to push through, but it grew thicker and thicker, and he was in despair. So he patiently broke twig after twig till he had made a little hole through which he peeped, saying imploringly, 'Let me in! Let me in!' But the pretty princess did not seem to understand, for she picked her roses quietly, and left him to fight his way in. Whether he did or not, Frank will tell you."

"I can't. I'm not playing, I never do," said Frank, dismayed at the sentimental predicament out of which he was to rescue the absurd couple. Beth had disappeared behind Jo, and Grace was asleep.

"So the poor knight is to be left sticking in the hedge, is he?" asked Mr. Brooke, still watching the river, and playing with the wild rose in his buttonhole.

"I guess the princess gave him a posy, and opened the gate after a while," said Laurie, smiling to himself, as he threw acorns at his tutor.

"What a piece of nonsense we have made! With practice we might do something quite clever. Do you know Truth?"

"I hope so," said Meg soberly.

"The game, I mean?"

"what is it?" said Fred.

"Why, you pile up your hands, choose a number, and draw out in turn, and the person who draws at the number has to answer truly any question put by the rest. It's great fun."

"Let's try it," said Jo, who liked new experiments.

Miss Kate and Mr. Booke, Meg, and Ned declined, but Fred, Sallie, Jo, and Laurie piled and drew, and the lot fell to Laurie.

"Who are your heroes?" asked Jo.

"Grandfather and Napoleon."

"Which lady here do you think prettiest?" said Sallie.

"Margaret."

"Which do you like best?" from Fred.

"Jo, of course." "What silly questions you ask!" And Jo gave a disdainful shrug as the rest laughed at Laurie's matter-of-fact tone.

"Try again. Truth isn't a bad game," said Fred.

"It's a very good one for you," retorted Jo in a low voice. Her turn came next.

"What is your greatest fault?' asked Fred, by way of testing in her the virtue he lacked himself.

"A quick temper."

"What do you most wish for?" said Laurie.

"A pair of boot lacings," returned Jo, guessing and defeating his purpose.

"Not a true answer. You must say what you really do want most."

"Genius. Don't you wish you could give it to me, Laurie?" And she slyly smiled in his disappointed face.

"What virtues do you most admire in a man?" asked Sallie.

"Courage and honesty."

"Now my turn," said Fred, as his hand came last.

"Let's give it to him," whispered Laurie to Jo, who nodded and asked at once . . .

"Didn't you cheat at croquet?'

"Well, yes, a little bit."

"Good! Didn't you take your story out of THE SEA LION?" said Laurie.

"Rather."

"Don't you think the English nation perfect in every respect?" asked Sallie.

"I should be ashamed of myself if I didn't."

"He's a true John Bull. Now, Miss Sallie, you shall have a chance without waiting to draw. I'll harrow up your feelings first by asking if you don't think you are something of a flirt," said Laurie, as Jo nodded to Fred as a sign that peace was declared.

"You impertinent boy! Of course I'm not," exclaimed Sallie, with an air that proved the contrary.

"What do you hate most?" asked Fred.

"Spiders and rice pudding."

"What do you like best?" asked Jo.

"Dancing and French gloves."

"Well, I think Truth is a very silly play. Let's have a sensible game of Authors to refresh our minds," proposed Jo.

Ned, frank, and the little girls joined in this, and while it went on, the three elders sat apart, talking. Miss Kate took out her sketch again, and Margaret watched her, while Mr. Brooke lay on the grass with a book, which he did not read.

"How beautifully you do it! I wish I could draw," said Meg, with mingled admiration and regret in her voice.

"Why don't you learn? I should think you had taste and talent for it," replied Miss Kate graciously.

"I haven't time."

"Your mamma prefers other accomplishments, I fancy. So did mine, but I proved to her that I had talent by taking a few lessons privately, and then she was quite willing I should go on. Can't you do the same with your governess?"

"I have none."

"I forgot young ladies in America go to school more than with us. Very fine schools they are, too, Papa says. You go to a private one, I suppose?"

"I don't go at all. I am a governess myself."

"Oh. indeed!" said Miss Kate, but she might as well have said, "Dear me, how dreadful!" for her tone implied it, and something in her face made Meg color, and wish she had not been so frank.

Mr. Brooke looked up and said quickly, Young ladies in America love independence as much as their ancestors did, and are admired and respected for supporting themselves."

"Oh, yes, of course it's very nice and proper in them to do so. We have many most respectable and worthy young women who do the same and are employed by the nobility, because, being the daughters of gentlemen, they are both well bred and accomplished, you know," said Miss Kate in a patronizing tone that hurt Meg's pride, and made her work seem not only more distasteful, but degrading.

"Did the German song suit, Miss March?" inquired Mr. Brooke, breaking an awkward pause.

"Oh, yes! It was very sweet, and I'm much obliged to whoever translated it for me." And Meg's downcast face brightened as she spoke.

"Don't you read German?" asked Miss Kate with a look of surprise.

"Not very well. My father, who taught me, is away, and I don't get on very fast alone, for I've no one to correct my pronunciation."

"Try a little now. Here is Schiller's Mary Stuart and a tutor who loves to teach." And Mr. Brooke laid his book on her lap with an inviting smile.

"It's so hard I'm afraid to try," said Meg, grateful, but bashful in the presence of the accomplished young lady beside her.

"I'll read a bit to encourage you." And Miss Kate read one of the most beautiful passages in a perfectly correct but perfectly expressionless manner.

Mr. Brooke made no comment as she returned the book to Meg, who said innocently, "I thought it was poetry." "Some of it is. Try this passage."

There was a queer smile about Mr. Brooke's mouth as he opened at poor Mary's lament.

Meg obediently following the long grass-blade which her new tutor used to point with, read slowly and timidly, unconsciously making poetry of the hard words by the soft intonation of her musical voice. Down the page went the green guide, and presently, forgetting her listener in the beauty of the sad scene, Meg read as if alone, giving a little touch of tragedy to the words of the unhappy queen. If she had seen the brown eyes then, she would have stopped short, but she never looked up, and the lesson was not spoiled for her.

"Very well indeed!" said Mr. Brooke, as she paused, quite ignoring her many mistakes, and looking as if he did indeed love to teach.

Miss Kate put up her glass, and, having taken a survey of the little tableau before her, shut her sketch book, saying with condescension, "You've a nice accent and in time will be a clever reader. I advise you to learn, for German is a valuable accomplishment to teachers. I must look after Grace, she is romping." And Miss Kate strolled away, adding to herself with a shrug, "I didn't come to chaperone a governess, though she is young and pretty. What odd people these Yankees are. I'm afraid Laurie will be quite spoiled among them."

"I forgot that English people rather turn up their noses at governesses and don't treat them as we do," said Meg, looking after the retreating figure with an annoyed expression.

"Tutors also have rather a hard time of it there, as I know to my sorrow. There's no place like America for us workers, Miss Margaret." And Mr. Brooke looked so contented and cheerful that Meg was ashamed to lament her hard lot.

"I'm glad I live in it then. I don't like my work, but I get a good deal of satisfaction out of it after all, so I won't complain. I only wished I liked teaching as you do."

"I think you would if you had Laurie for a pupil. I shall be very sorry to lose him next year," said Mr. Brooke, busily punching holes in the turf.

"Going to college, I suppose?" Meg's lips asked the question, but her eyes added, "And what becomes of you?"

"Yes, it's high time he went, for he is ready, and as soon as he is off, I shall turn soldier. I am needed."

"I am glad of that!" exclaimed Meg. "I should think every young man would want to go, though it is hard for the mothers and sisters who stay at home," she added sorrowfully. "I have neither, and very few friends to care whether I live or die," said Mr. Brooke rather bitterly as he absently put the dead rose in the hole he had made and covered it up, like a little grave.

"Laurie and his grandfather would care a great deal, and we should all be very sorry to have any harm happen to you," said Meg heartily.

"Thank you, that sounds pleasant," began Mr. Brooke, looking cheerful again, but before he could finish his speech, Ned, mounted on the old horse, came lumbering up to display his equestrian skill before the young ladies, and there was no more quiet that day.

"Don't you love to ride?" asked Grace of Amy, as they stood resting after a race round the field with the others, led by Ned.

"I dote upon it. My sister, Meg, used to ride when Papa was rich, but we don't keep any horses now, except Ellen Tree," added Amy, laughing.

"Tell me about Ellen Tree. Is it a donkey?" asked Grace curiously.

"Why, you see, Jo is crazy about horses and so am I, but we've only got an old sidesaddle and no horse. Out in our garden is an apple tree that has a nice low branch, so Jo put the saddle on it, fixed some reins on the part that turns up, and we bounce away on Ellen Tree whenever we like."

"How funny!" laughed Grace. "I have a pony at home, and ride nearly every day in the park with Fred and Kate. It's very nice, for my friends go too, and the Row is full of ladies and gentlemen."

"Dear, how charming! I hope I shall go abroad some day, but I'd rather go to Rome than the row," said Amy, who had not the remotest idea what the Row was and wouldn't have asked for the world.

Frank, sitting just behind the little girls, heard what they were saying, and pushed his crutch away from him with an impatient gesture as he watched the active lads going through all sorts of comical gymnastics. Beth, who was collecting the scattered Author cards, looked up and said, in her shy yet friendly way, "I'm afraid you are tired. Can I do anything for you?"

"Talk to me, please. It's dull, sitting by myself," answered Frank, who had evidently been used to being made much of at home.

If he asked her to deliver a Latin oration, it would not have seemed a more impossible task to bashful Beth, but there was no place to run to, no Jo to hide behind now, and the poor boy looked so wistfully at her that she bravely resolved to try.

"What do you like to talk about?" she asked, fumbling over the cards and dropping half as she tried to tie them up.

"Well, I like to hear about cricket and boating and hunting," said Frank, who had not yet learned to suit his amusements to his strength.

My heart! What shall I do? I don't know anything about them, thought Beth, and forgetting the boy's misfortune in her flurry, she said, hoping to make him talk, "I never saw any hunting, but I suppose you know all about it."

"I did once, but I can never hunt again, for I got hurt leaping a confounded five-barred gate, so there are no more horses and hounds for me," said Frank with a sigh that made Beth hate herself for her innocent blunder.

"Your deer are much prettier than our ugly buffaloes," she said, turning to the prairies for help and feeling glad that she had read one of the boys' books in which Jo delighted.

Buffaloes proved soothing and satisfactory, and in her eagerness to amuse another, Beth forgot herself, and was quite unconscious of her sisters' surprise and delight at the unusual spectacle of Beth talking away to one of the dreadful boys, against whom she had begged protection.

"Bless her heart! She pities him, so she is good to him," aid Jo, beaming at her from the croquet ground.

"I always said she was a little saint," added Meg, as if there could be no further doubt of it.

"I haven't heard Frank laugh so much for ever so long," said Grace to Amy, as they sat discussing dolls and making tea sets out of the acorn cups.

"My sister Beth is a very fastidious girl, when she likes to be," said Amy, well pleased at Beth's success. She meant 'facinating', but as Grace didn't know the exact meaning of either word, fastidious sounded well and made a good impression.

An impromptu circus, fox and geese, and an amicable game of croquet finished the afternoon. At sunset the tent was struck, hampers packed, wickets pulled up, boats loaded, and the whole party floated down the river, singing at the tops of their voices. Ned, getting sentimental, warbled a serenade with the pensive refrain . . .

Alone, alone, ah! Woe, alone,
and at the lines . . .

We each are young, we each have a heart, Oh, why should we stand thus coldly apart?

he looked at Meg with such a lackadiasical expression that she laughed outright and spoiled his song.

"How can you be so cruel to me?" he whispered, under cover of a lively chorus. "You've kept close to that starched-up Englishwoman all day, and now you snub me."

"I didn't mean to, but you looked so funny I really couldn't help it," replied Meg, passing over the first part of his reproach, for it was quite true that she had shunned him, remembering the Moffat party and the talk after it.

Ned was offended and turned to Sallie for consolation, saying to her rather pettishly, "There isn't a bit of flirt in that girl, is there?"

"Not a particle, but she's a dear," returned Sallie, defending her friend even while confessing her shortcomings.

"She's not a stricken deer anyway," said Ned, trying to be witty, and succeeding as well as very young gentlemen usually do.

On the lawn where it had gathered, the little party separated with cordial good nights and good-bys, for the Vaughns were going to Canada. As the four sisters went home through the garden, Miss Kate looked after them, saying, without the patronizing tone in her voice, "In spite of their demonstrative manners, American girls are very nice when one knows them."

"I quite agree with you," said Mr. Brooke.

Chapter Thirteen

Laurie lay luxuriously swinging to and fro in his hammock one warm September afternoon, wondering what his neighbors were about, but too lazy to go and find out. He was in one of his moods, for the day had been both unprofitable and unsatisfactory, and he was wishing he could live it over again. The hot weather made him indolent, and he had shirked his studies, tried Mr. Brooke's patience to the utmost, displeased his grandfather by practicing half the afternoon, frightened the maidservants half out of their wits by mischievously hinting that one of his dogs was going mad, and, after high words with the stableman about some fancied neglect of his horse, he had flung himself into his hammock to fume over the stupidity of the world in general, till the peace of the lovely day quieted him in spite of himself. Staring up into the green gloom of the horse-chestnut trees above him, he dreamed dreams of all sorts, and was just imagining himself tossing on the ocean in a voyage round the world, when the sound of voices brought him ashore in a flash. Peeping through the meshes of the hammock, he saw the Marches coming out, as if bound on some expedition.

"What in the world are those girls about now?" thought Laurie, opening his sleepy eyes to take a good look, for there was something rather peculiar in the appearance of his neighbors. Each wore a large, flapping hat, a brown linen pouch slung over one shoulder, and carried a long staff. Meg had a cushion, Jo a book, Beth a basket, and Amy a portfolio. All walked quietly through the garden, out at the little back gate, and began to climb the hill that lay between the house and river.

"Well, that's cool," said Laurie to himself, "to have a picnic and never ask me! They can't be going in the boat, for they haven't got the key. Perhaps they forgot it. I'll take it to them, and see what's going on."

Though possessed of half a dozen hats, it took him some time to find one, then there was a hunt for the key, which was at last discovered in his pocket, so that the girls were quite out of sight when leaped the fence and ran after them. Taking the shortest way to the boathouse, he waited for them to appear, but no one came, and he went up the hill to take an observation. A grove of pines covered one part of it, and from the heart of this green spot came a clearer sound than the soft sigh of the pines or the drowsy chirp of the crickets.

"Here's a landscape!" thought Laurie, peeping through the bushes, and looking wide-awake and good-natured already.

It was a rather pretty little picture, for the sisters sat together in the shady nook, with sun and shadow flickering over them, the aromatic wind lifting their hair and cooling their hot cheeks, and all the little wood people going on with their affairs as if these were no strangers but old friends. Meg sat upon her cushion, sewing daintily with her white hands, and looking as fresh and sweet as a rose in her pink dress among the green. Beth was sorting the cones that lay thick under the hemlock near by, for she made pretty things with them. Amy was sketching a group of ferns, and Jo was knitting as she read aloud. A shadow passed over the boy's face as he watched them, feeling that he ought to go away because uninvited, yet lingering because home seemed very lonely and this quiet party in the woods most attractive to his restless spirit. He stood so still that a squirrel, busy with it's harvesting, ran dawn a pine close beside him, saw him suddenly and skipped back, scolding so shrilly that Beth looked up, espied the wistful face behind the birches, and beckoned with a reassuring smile.

"May I come in, please? Or shall I be a bother?" he asked, advancing slowly.

Meg lifted her eyebrows, but Jo scowled at her defiantly and said at once, "Of course you may. We should have asked you before, only we thought you wouldn't care for such a girl's game as this."

"I always like your games, but if Meg doesn't want me, I'll go away."

"I've no objection, if you do something. It's against the rules to be idle here," replied Meg gravely but graciously.

"Much obliged. I'll do anything if you'll let me stop a bit, for it's as dull as the Desert of Sahara down there. Shall I sew, read, cone, draw, or do all at once? Bring on your bears. I'm ready." And Laurie sat down with a submissive expression delightful to behold.

"Finish this story while I set my heel," said Jo, handing him the book.

"Yes'm." was the meek answer, as he began, doing his best to prove his gratitude for the favor of admission into the 'Busy Bee Society'.

The story was not a long one, and when it was finished, he ventured to ask a few questions as a reward of merit.

"Please, ma'am, could I inquire if this highly instructive and charming institution is a new one?"

"Would you tell him?" asked Meg of her sisters.

"He'll laugh," said Amy warningly.

"Who cares?" said Jo.

"I guess he'll like it," added Beth.

"Of course I shall! I give you my word I won't laugh. Tell away, Jo, and don't be afraid."

"The idea of being afraid of you! Well, you see we used to play Pilgrim's Progress, and we have been going on with it in earnest, all winter and summer."

"Yes, I know," said Laurie, nodding wisely.

"Who told you?" demanded Jo.

"Spirits."

"No, I did. I wanted to amuse him one night when you were all away, and he was rather dismal. He did like it, so don't scold, Jo," said Beth meekly.

"You can't keep a secret. Never mind, it saves trouble now."

"Go on, please," said Laurie, as Jo became absorbed in her work, looking a trifle displeased.

"Oh, didn't she tell you about this new plan of ours? Well, we have tried not to waste our holiday, but each has had a task and worked at it with a will. The vacation is nearly over, the stints are all done, and we are ever so glad that we didn't dawdle."

"Yes, I should think so," and Laurie thought regretfully of his own idle days. "Mother likes to have us out-of-doors as much as possible, so we bring our work here and have nice times. For the fun of it we bring our things in these bags, wear the old hats, use poles to climb the hill, and play pilgrims, as we used to do years ago. We call this hill the Delectable Mountain, for we can look far away and see the country where we hope to live some time."

Jo pointed, and Laurie sat up to examine, for through an opening in the wood one could look cross the wide, blue river, the meadows on the other side, far over the outskirts of the great city, to the green hills that rose to meet the sky. The sun was low, and the heavens glowed with the splendor of an autumn sunset. Gold and purple clouds lay on the hilltops, and rising high into the ruddy light were silvery white peaks that shone like the airy spires of some Celestial City.

"How beautiful that is!" said Laurie softly, for he was quick to see and feel beauty of any kind.

"It's often so, and we like to watch it, for it is never the same, but always splendid," replied Amy, wishing she could paint it.

"Jo talks about the country where we hope to live sometime—the real country, she means, with pigs and chickens and haymaking. It would be nice, but I wish the beautiful country up there was real, and we could ever go to it," said Beth musingly.

"There is a lovelier country even than that, where we shall go, by-and-by, when we are good enough," answered Meg with her sweetest voice.

"It seems so long to wait, so hard to do. I want to fly away at once, as those swallows fly, and go in at that splendid gate."

"You'll get there, Beth, sooner or later, no fear of that," said Jo. "I'm the one that will have to fight and work, and climb and wait, and maybe never get in after all."

"you'll have me for company, if that's any comfort. I shall have to do a deal of traveling before I come in sight of your Celestial City. If I arrive late, you'll say a good word for me, won't you, Beth?"

Something in the boy's face troubled his little friend, but she said cheerfully, with her quiet eyes on the changing clouds, "If people really want to go, and really try all their lives, I think they will get in, for I don't believe there are any locks on that door or any guards at the gate. I always imagine it is as it is in the picture, where the shining ones stretch out their hands to welcome poor Christian as he comes up from the river.

"Wouldn't it be fun if all the castles in the air which we make could come true, and we could live in them?" said Jo, after a little pause.

"I've made such quantities it would be hard to choose which I'd have," said Laurie, lying flat and throwing cones at the squirrel who had betrayed him.

"You'd have to take your favorite one. What is it?" asked Meg.

"If I tell mine, will you tell yours?"

"Yes, if the girls will too."

"We will. Now, Laurie."

"After I'd seen as much of the world as I want to, I'd like to settle in Germany and have just as much music as I choose. I'm to be a famous musician myself, and all creation is to rush to hear me. And I'm never to be bothered about money or business, but just enjoy myself and live for what I like. That's my favorite castle. What's yours, Meg?"

Margaret seemed to find it a little hard to tell hers, and waved a brake before her face, as if to disperse imaginary gnats, while she said slowly, "I should like a lovely house, full of all sorts of luxurious things—nice food, pretty clothes, handsome furniture, pleasant people, and heaps of money. I am to be mistress of it, and manage it as I like, with plenty of servants, so I never need work a bit. How I should enjoy it! For I wouldn't be idle, but do good, and make everyone love me dearly."

"Wouldn't you have a master for your castle in the air?" asked Laurie slyly.

"I said 'pleasant people', you know," And Meg carefully tied up her shoe as she spoke, so that no one saw her face.

"Why don't you say you'd have a splendid, wise, good husband and some angelic little children? You know your castle wouldn't be perfect without," said blunt Jo, who had no tender fancies yet, and rather scorned romance, except in books.

"You'd have nothing but horses, inkstands, and novels in yours," answered Meg petulantly.

"Wouldn't I though? I'd have a stable full of Arabian steeds, rooms piled high with books, and I'd write out of a magic inkstand, so that my works should be as famous as Laurie's music. I want to do something splendid before I go into my castle, something heroic or wonderful that won't be forgotten after I'm dead. I don't know what, but I'm on the watch for it, and mean to astonish you all some day. I think I shall write books, and get rich and famous, that would suit me, so that is my favorite dream."

"Mine is to stay at home safe with Father and Mother, and help take care of the family," said Beth contentedly.

"Don't you wish for anything else?" asked Laurie. "Since I had my little piano, I am perfectly satisfied. I only wish we may all keep well and be together, nothing else."

"I have ever so many wishes, but the pet one is to be an artist, and go to Rome, and do fine pictures, and be the best artist in the whole world," was Amy's modest desire.

"We're an ambitious set, aren't we? Every one of us, but Beth, wants to be rich and famous, and gorgeous in every respect. I do wonder if any of us will ever get our wishes," said Laurie, chewing grass like a meditative calf.

"I've got the key to my castle in the air, but whether I can unlock the door remains to be seen," observed Jo mysteriously.

"I've got the key to mine, but I'm not allowed to try it. Hang college!" muttered Laurie with an impatient sigh.

"Here's mine!" and Amy waved her pencil.

"I haven't got any," said Meg forlornly.

"Yes, you have," said Laurie at once.

"Where?"

"In your face."

"Nonsense, that's of no use." "Wait and see if it doesn't bring you something worth having," replied the boy, laughing at the thought of a charming little secret which he fancied he knew.

Meg colored behind the brake, but asked no questions and looked across the river with the same expectant expression which Mr. Brooke had worn when he told the story of the knight.

"If we are all alive ten years hence, let's meet, and see how many of us have got our wishes, or how much nearer we are then than now," said Jo, always ready with a plan.

"Bless me! How old I shall be, twenty-seven!" exclaimed Meg, who felt grown up already, having just reached seventeen.

"You and I will be twenty-six, Teddy, Beth twenty-four, and Amy twenty-two. What a venerable party!" said Jo.

"I hope I shall have done something to be proud of by that time, but I'm such a lazy dog, I'm afraid I shall dawdle, Jo."

"You need a motive, Mother says, and when you get it, she is sure you'll work splendidly."

"Is she? By Jupiter, I will, if I only get the chance!" cried Laurie, sitting up with sudden energy. "I ought to be satisfied to please Grandfather, and I do try, but it's working against the grain, you see, and comes hard. He wants me to be an India merchant, as he was, and I'd rather be shot. I hate tea and sild and spices, and every sort of rubbish his old ships bring, and I don't care how soon they go to the bottom when I own them. Going to college ought to satisfy him, for if I give him four years he ought to let me off from the business. But he's set, and I've got to do just as he did, unless I break away and please myself, as my father did. If there was anyone left to stay with the old gentleman, I'd do it tomorrow."

Laurie spoke excitedly, and looked ready to carry his threat into execution on the slightest provocation, for he was growing up very fast and, in spite of his indolent ways, had a young man's hatred of subjection, a young man's restless longing to try the world for himself.

"I advise you to sail away in one of your ships, and never come home again till you have tried your own way," said Jo, whose imagination was fired by the thought of such a daring exploit, and whose sympathy was excited by what she called 'Teddy's Wrongs'.

"That's not right, Jo. You mustn't talk in that way, and Laurie mustn't take your bad advice. You should do just what your grandfather wishes, my dear boy," said Meg in her most maternal tone. "Do your best at college, and when he sees that you try to please him, I'm sure he won't be hard on you or unjust to you. As you say, there is no one else to stay with and love him, and you'd never forgive yourself if you left him without his permission. Don't be dismal or fret, but do your duty and you'll get your reward, as good Mr. Brooke has, by being respected and loved."

"What do you know about him?" asked Laurie, grateful for the good advice, but objecting to the lecture, and glad to turn the conversation from himself after his unusual outbreak.

"Only what your grandpa told us about him, how he took good care of his own mother till she died, and wouldn't go abroad as tutor to some nice person because he wouldn't leave her. And how he provides now for an old woman who nursed his mother, and never tells anyone, but is just as generous and patient and good as he can be."

"So he is, dear old fellow!" said Laurie heartily, as Meg paused, looking flushed and earnest with her story. "It's like Grandpa to find out all about him without letting him know, and to tell all his goodness to others, so that they might like him. Brooke couldn't understand why your mother was so kind to him, asking him over with me and treating him in her beautiful friendly way. He thought she was just perfect, and talked about it for days and days, and went on about you all in flaming style. If ever I do get my wish, you see what I'll do for Booke."

"Begin to do something now by not plaguing his life out," said Meg sharply.

"How do you know I do, Miss?" "I can always tell by his face when he goes away. If you have been good, he looks satisfied and walks briskly. If you have plagued him, he's sober and walks slowly, as if he wanted to go back and do his work better."

"Well, I like that? So you keep an account of my good and bad marks in Brooke's face, do you? I see him bow and smile as he passes your window, but I didn't know you'd got up a telegraph."

"We haven't. Don't be angry, and oh, don't tell him I said anything! It was only to show that I cared how you get on, and what is said here is said in confidence, you know," cried Meg, much alarmed at the thought of what might follow from her careless speech.

"I don't tell tales," replied Laurie, with his 'high and mighty' air, as Jo called a certain expression which he occasionally wore. "Only if Brooke is going to be a thermometer, I must mind and have fair weather for him to report."

"Please don't be offended. I didn't meant to preach or tell tales or be silly. I only thought Jo was encouraging you in a feeling which you'd be sorry for by-and-by. You are so kind to us, we feel as if you were our brother and say just what we think. Forgive me, I meant it kindly." And Meg offered her hand with a gesture both affectionate and timid.

Ashamed of his momentary pique, Laurie squeezed the kind little hand, and said frankly, "I'm the one to be forgiven. I'm cross and have been out of sorts all day. I like to have you tell me my faults and be sisterly, so don't mind if I am grumpy sometimes. I thank you all the same."

Bent on showing that he was not offended, he made himself as agreeable as possible, wound cotton for Meg, recited poetry to please Jo, shook down cones for Beth, and helped Amy with her ferns, proving himself a fit person to belong to the 'Busy Bee Society'. In the midst of an animated discussion on the domestic habits of turtles (one of those amiable creatures having strolled up from the river), the faint sound of a bell warned them that Hannah had put the tea 'to draw', and they would just have time to get home to supper.

"May I come again?" asked Laurie.

"Yes, if your are good, and love your book, as the boys in the primer are told to do," said Meg, smiling.

"I'll try."

"Then you may come, and I'll teach you to knit as the Scotchmen do. There's a demand for socks just now," added Jo, waving hers like a big blue worsted banner as they parted at the gate.

That night, when Beth played to Mr. Laurence in the twilight, Laurie, standing in the shadow of the curtain, listened to the little David, whose simple music always quieted his moody spirit, and watched the old man, who sat with his gray head on his hand, thinking tender thoughts of the dead child he had loved so much. Remembering the conversation of the afternoon, the boy said to himself, with the resolve to make the sacrifice cheerfully, "I'll let my castle go, and stay with the dear old gentleman while he needs me, for I am all he has."

Chapter Fourteen

Jo was very busy in the garret, for the October days began to grow chilly, and the afternoons were short. For two or three hours the sun lay warmly in the high window, showing Jo seated on the old sofa, writing busily, with her papers spread out upon a trunk before her, while Scrabble, the pet rat, promenaded the beams overhead, accompanied by his oldest son, a fine young fellow, who was evidently very proud of his whiskers. Quite absorbed in her work, Jo scribbled away till the last page was filled, when she signed her name with a flourish and threw down her pen, exclaiming . . .

"There, I've done my best! If this won't suit I shall have to wait till I can do better."

Lying back on the sofa, she read the manuscript carefully through, making dashes here and there, and putting in many exclamation points, which looked like little balloons. Then she tied it up with a smart red ribbon, and sat a minute looking at it with a sober, wistful expression, which plainly showed how ernest her work had been. Jo's desk up here was an old tin kitchen which hung against the wall. It it she kept her papers, and a few books, safely shut away from Scrabble, who, being likewise of a literary turn, was fond of making a circulating library of such books as were left in his way by eating the leaves. From this tin receptacle Jo produced another manuscript, and putting both in her pocket, crept quietly downstairs, leaving her friends to nibble on her pens and taste her ink.

She put on her hat and jacket as noiselessly as possible, and going to the back entry window, got out upon the roof of a low porch, swung herself down to the grassy bank, and took a roundabout way to the road. Once there, she composed herself, hailed a passing omnibus, and rolled away to town, looking very merry and mysterious.

If anyone had been watching her, he would have thought her movements decidedly peculiar, for on alighting, she went off at a great pace till she reached a certain number in a certain busy street. Having found the place with some difficulty, she went into the doorway, looked up the dirty stairs, and after standing stock still a minute, suddenly dived into the street and walked away as rapidly as she came. This maneuver she repeated several times, to the great amusement of a black-eyed young gentleman lounging in the window of a building opposite. On returning for the third time, Jo gave herself a shake, pulled her hat over her eyes, and walked up the stairs, looking as if she were going to have all her teeth out.

There was a dentist's sign, among others, which adorned the entrance, and after staring a moment at the pair of artificial jaws which slowly opened and shut to draw attention to a fine set of teeth, the young gentleman put on his coat, took his hat, and went down to post himself in the opposite doorway, saying with a smile and a shiver, "It's like her to come alone, but if she has a bad time she'll need someone to help her home."

In ten minutes Jo came running downstairs with a very red face and the general appearance of a person who had just passed through a trying ordeal of some sort. When she saw the young gentleman she looked anything but pleased, and passed him with a nod. But he followed, asking with an air of sympathy, "Did you have a bad time?"

"Not very."

"You got through quickly."

"Yes, thank goodness!"

"Why did you go alone?"

"Didn't want anyone to know."

"You're the oddest fellow I ever saw. How many did you have out?"

Jo looked at her friend as if she did not understand him, then began to laugh as if mightily amused at something.

"There are two which I want to have come out, but I must wait a week."

"What are you laughing at? You are up to some mischief, Jo," said Laurie, looking mystified.

"So are you. What were you doing, sir, up in that billiard saloon?"

"Begging your pardon, ma'am, it wasn't a billiard saloon, but a gymnasium, and I was taking a lesson in fencing."

"I'm glad of that."

"why?"

"You can teach me, and then when we play HAMLET, you can be Laertes, and we'll make a fine thing of the fencing scene."

"Laurie burst out with a hearty boy's laugh, which made several passers-by smile in spite of themselves.

"I'll teach you whether we play HAMLET or not. It's grand fun and will straighten you up capitally. But I don't believe that was your only reason for saying 'I'm glad' in that decided way, was it now?"

"No, I was glad that you were not in the saloon, because I hope you never go to such places. Do you?"

"Not often."

"I wish you wouldn't."

"It's no harm, Jo. I have billiards at home, but it's no fun unless you have good players, so, as I'm fond of it, I come sometimes and have a game with Ned Moffat or some of the other fellows."

"Oh, dear, I'm so sorry, for you'll get to liking it better and better, and will waste time and money, and grow like those dreadful boys. I did hope you'd stay respectable and be a satisfaction to your friends," said Jo, shaking her head.

"Can't a fellow take a little innocent amusement now and then without losing his respectability?" asked Laurie, looking nettled.

"That depends upon how and where he takes it. I don't like Ned and his set, and wish you'd keep out of it. Mother won't let us have him at our house, though he wants to come. And if you grow like him she won't be willing to have us frolic together as we do now." "Won't she?" asked Laurie anxiously.

"No, she can't bear fashionable young men, and she'd shut us all up in bandboxes rather than have us associate with them."

"Well, she needn't get out her bandboxes yet. I'm not a fashionable party and don't mean to be, but I do like harmless larks now and then, don't you?"

"Yes, nobody minds them, so lark away, but don't get wild, will you? Or there will be an end of all our good times."

"I'll be a double distilled saint."

"I can't bear saints. Just be a simple, honest, respectable boy, and we'll never desert you. I don't know what I should do if you acted like Mr. King's son. He had plenty of money, but didn't know how to spend it, and got tipsy and gambled, and ran away, and forged his father's name, I believe, and was altogether horrid."

"You think I'm likely to do the same? Much obliged."

"No, I don't—oh, dear, no!—but I hear people talking about money being such a temptation, and I sometimes wish you were poor. I shouldn't worry then."

"Do you worry about me, Jo?"

"A little, when you look moody and discontented, as you sometimes do, for you've got such a strong will, if you once get started wrong, I'm afraid it would be hard to stop you."

Laurie walked in silence a few minutes, and Jo watched him, wishing she had held her tongue, for his eyes looked angry, though his lips smiled as if at her warnings.

"Are you going to deliver lectures all the way home?" he asked presently.

"Of course not. Why?"

"Because if you are, I'll take a bus. If you're not, I'd like to walk with you and tell you something very interesting."

"I won't preach any more, and I'd like to hear the news immensely."

"Very well, then, come on. It's a secret, and if I tell you, you must tell me yours."

"I haven't got any," began Jo, but stopped suddenly, remembering that she had.

"You know you have—you can't hide anything, so up and fess, or I won't tell," cried Laurie.

"Is your secret a nice one?"

"Oh, isn't it! All about people you know, and such fun! You ought to hear it, and I've been aching to tell it this long time. Come, you begin."

"You'll not say anything about it at home, will you?"

"Not a word."

"And you won't tease me in private?"

"I never tease."

"Yes, you do. You get everything you want out of people. I don't know how you do it, but you are a born wheedler."

"Thank you. Fire away."

"Well, I've left two stories with a newspaperman, and he's to give his answer next week," whispered Jo, in her confidant's ear.

"Hurrah for Miss March, the celebrated American authoress!" cried Laurie, throwing up his hat and catching it again, to the great delight of two ducks, four cats, five hens, and half a dozen Irish children, for they were out of the city now.
"Hush! It won't come to anything, I dare say, but I couldn't rest till I had tried, and I said nothing about it because I didn't want anyone else to be disappointed."

"It won't fail. Why, Jo, your stories are works of Shakespeare compared to half the rubbish that is published every day. Won't it be fun to see them in print, and shan't we feel proud of our authoress?"

Jo's eyes sparkled, for it is always pleasant to be believed in, and a friend's praise is always sweeter than a dozen newspaper puffs.

"Where's your secret? Play fair, Teddy, or I'll never believe you again," she said, trying to extinguish the brilliant hopes that blazed up at a word of encouragement.

"I may get into a scrape for telling, but I didn't promise not to, so I will, for I never feel easy in my mind till I've told you any plummy bit of news I get. I know where Meg's glove is."

"Is that all? said Jo, looking disappointed, as Laurie nodded and twinkled with a face full of mysterious intelligence.

"It's quite enough for the present, as you'll agree when I tell you where it is."

"Tell, then."

Laurie bent, and whispered three words in Jo's ear, which produced a comical change. She stood and stared at him for a minute, looking both surprised and displeased, then walked on, saying sharply, "How do you know?"

"Saw it."

"Where?'

"Pocket."

"All this time?"

"Yes, isn't that romantic?"

"No, it's horrid."

"Don't you like it?"

"Of course I don't. It's ridiculous, it won't be allowed. My patience! What would Meg say?"

"You are not to tell anyone. Mind that."

"I didn't promise."

"That was understood, and I trusted you."

"Well, I won't for the present, anyway, but I'm disgusted, and wish you hadn't told me."

"I thought you'd be pleased."

"At the idea of anybody coming to take Meg away? No, thank you."

"You'll feel better about it when somebody comes to take you away."

"I'd like to see anyone try it," cried Jo fiercely.

"So should I!" And Laurie chuckled at the idea.

"I don't think secrets agree with me, I feel rumpled up in my mind since you told me that," said Jo rather ungratefully.

"Race down this hill with me, and you'll be all right," suggested Laurie.

No one was in sight, the smooth road sloped invitingly before her, and finding the temptation irresistible, Jo darted away, soon leaving hat and comb behind her and scattering hairpins as she ran. Laurie reached the goal first and was quite satisfied with the success of his treatment, for his Atalanta came panting up with flying hair, bright eyes, ruddy cheeks, and no signs of dissatisfaction in her face.

"I wish I was a horse, then I could run for miles in this splendid air, and not lose my breath. It was capital, but see what a guy it's made me. Go, pick up my things, like a cherub, as you are," said Jo, dropping down under a maple tree, which was carpeting the bank with crimson leaves.

Laurie leisurely departed to recover the lost property, and Jo bundled up her braids, hoping no one would pass by till she was tidy again. But someone did pass, and who should it be but Meg, looking particularly ladylike in her state and festival suit, for she had been making calls.

"What in the world are you doing here?" she asked, regarding her disheveled sister with well-bred surprise.

"Getting leaves," meekly answered Jo, sorting the rosy handful she had just swept up.

"And hairpins," added Laurie, throwing half a dozen into Jo's lap. "They grow on this road, Meg, so do combs and brown straw hats."

"You have been running, Jo. How could you? When will you stop such romping ways?" said Meg reprovingly, as she settled her cuffs and smoothed her hair, with which the wind had taken liberties.

"Never till I'm stiff and old and have to use a crutch. Don't try to make me grow up before my time, Meg. It's hard enough to have you change all of a sudden. Let me be a little girl as long as I can."

As she spoke, Jo bent over the leaves to hide the trembling of her lips, for lately she had felt that Margaret was fast getting to be a woman, and Laurie's secret made her dread the separation which must surely come some time and now seemed very near.

He saw the trouble in her face and drew Meg's attention from it by asking quickly, "Where have you been calling, all so fine?"

"At the Gardiners', and Sallie has been telling me all about Belle Moffat's wedding. It was very splendid, and they have gone to spend the winter in Paris. Just think how delightful that must be!"

"Do you envy her, Meg?" said Laurie.

"I'm afraid I do."

"I'm glad of it!" muttered Jo, tying on her hat with a jerk.

"Why?" asked Meg, looking surprised.

"Because if you care much about riches, you will never go and marry a poor man," said Jo, frowning at Laurie, who was mutely warning her to mind what she said.

"I shall never 'go and marry' anyone," observed Meg, walking on with great dignity while the others followed, laughing, whispering, skipping stones, and 'behaving like children', as Meg said to herself, though she might have been tempted to join them if she had not had her best dress on.

For a week or two, Jo behaved so queerly that her sisters were quite bewildered. She rushed to the door when the postman rang, was rude to Mr. Brooke whenever they met, would sit looking at Meg with a woe-begone face, occasionally jumping up to shake and then kiss her in a very mysterious manner. Laurie and she were always making signs to one another, and talking about 'Spread Eagles' till the girls declared they had both lost their wits. On the second Saturday after Jo got out of the window, Meg, as she sat sewing at her window, was scandalized by the sight of Laurie chasing Jo all over the garden and finally capturing her in Amy's bower. What went on there, Meg could not see, but shrieks of laughter were heard, followed by the murmur of voices and a great flapping of newspapers.

"What shall we do with that girl? She never will behave like a young lady," sighed Meg, as she watched the race with a disapproving face.

"I hope she won't. She is so funny and dear as she is," said Beth, who had never betrayed that she was a little hurt at Jo's having secrets with anyone but her.

"It's very trying, but we never can make her commy la fo," added Amy, who sat making some new frills for herself, with her curls tied up in a very becoming way., two agreeable things that made her feel unusually elegant and ladylike.

In a few minutes Jo bounced in, laid herself on the sofa, and affected to read.

"Have you anything interesting there?" asked Meg, with condescension.

"Nothing but a story, won't amount to much, I guess," returned Jo, carefully keeping the name of the paper out of sight.

"You'd better read it aloud. That will amuse us and keep you out of mischief," said Amy in her most grown-up tone.

"What's the name?" asked Beth, wondering why Jo kept her face behind the sheet.

"The Rival Painters."

"That sounds well. Read it," said Meg.

With a loud "Hem!" and a long breath, Jo began to read very fast. The girls listened with interest, for the tale was romantic, and somewhat pathetic, as most of the characters died in the end. "I like that about the splendid picture," was Amy's approving remark, as Jo paused.

"I prefer the lovering part. Viola and Angelo are two of our favorite names, isn't that queer?" said Meg, wiping her eyes, for the lovering part was tragical.

"Who wrote it?" asked Beth, who had caught a glimpse of Jo's face.

The reader suddenly sat up, cast away the paper, displaying a flushed countenance, and with a funny mixture of solemnity and excitement replied in a loud voice, "Your sister."

"You?" cried Meg, dropping her work.

"It's very good," said Amy critically.

"I knew it! I knew it! Oh, my Jo, I am so proud!" And Beth ran to hug her sister and exult over this splendid success.

Dear me, how delighted they all were, to be sure! How Meg wouldn't believe it till she saw the words. "Miss Josephine March," actually printed in the paper. How graciously Amy critisized the artistic parts of the story, and offered hints for a sequel, which unfortunately couldn't be carried out, as the hero and heroine were dead. How Beth got excited, and skipped and sang with joy. How Hannah came in to exclaim, "Sakes alive, well I never!" in great astonishment at 'that Jo's doin's'. How proud Mrs. March was when she knew it. How Jo laughed, with tears in her eyes, as she declared she might as well be a peacock and done with it. and how th 'Spread Eagle' might be said to flap his wings triumphantly over the House of March, as the paper passed from hand to hand.

"Tell us about it." "When did it come?" "How much did you get for it?" "What will Father say?" "Won't Laurie laugh?" cried the family, all in one breath as they clustered about Jo, for these foolish, affectionate people mad a jubilee of every little household joy.

"Stop jabbering, girls, and I'll tell you everything," said Jo, wondering if Miss Burney felt any grander over her Evilina than she did over her 'Rival Painters'. Having told how she disposed of her tales, Jo added, "And when I went to get my answer, the man said he liked them both, but didn't pay beginners, only let them print in his paper, and noticed the stories. It was good practice, he said, and when the beginners improved, anyone would pay. So I let him have the two stories, and today this was sent to me, and Laurie caught me with it and insisted on seeing it, so I let him. And he said it was good, and I shall write more, and he's going to get the next paid for, and I am so happy, for in time I may be able to support myself and help the girls."

Jo's breath gave out here, and wrapping her head in the paper, she bedewed her little story with a few natural tears, for to be independent and earn the praise of those she loved were the dearest wishes of her heart, and this seemed to be the first step toward that happy end.

Chapter Fifteen

"November is the most disagreeable month in the whole year," said Margaret, standing at the window one dull afternoon, looking out at the frostbitten garden.

"That's the reason I was born in it," observed Jo pensively, quite unconscious of the blot on her nose.

"If something very pleasant should happen now, we should think it a delightful month," said Beth, who took a hopeful view of everything, even November.

"I dare say, but nothing pleasant ever does happen in this family," said Meg, who was out of sorts. "We go grubbing along day after day, without a bit of change, and very little fun. We might as well be in a treadmill."

"My patience, how blue we are!" cried Jo. "I don't much wonder, poor dear, for you see other girls having splendid times, while you grind, grind, year in and year out. Oh, don't I wish I could manage things for you as I do for my heroines! You're pretty enough and good enough already, so I'd have some rich relation leave you a fortune unexpectedly. Then you'd dash out as an heiress, scorn everyone who has slighted you, go abroad, and come home my Lady Something in a blaze of splendor and elegance."

"People don't have fortunes left them in that style nowadays, men have to work and women marry for money. It's a dreadfully unjust world," said Meg bitterly.

"Jo and I are going to make fortunes for you all. Just wait ten years, and see if we don't," said Amy, who sat in a corner making mud pies, as Hannah called her little clay models of birds, fruit, and faces.

"Can't wait, and I'm afraid I haven't much faith in ink and dirt, though I'm grateful for your good intentions.

Meg sighed, and turned to the frostbitten garden again. Jo groaned and leaned both elbows on the table in a despondent attitude, but Amy spatted away energetically, and Beth, who sat at the other window, said, smiling, "Two pleasant things are going to happen right away. Marmee is coming down the street, and Laurie is tramping through the garden as if he had something nice to tell."

In they both came, Mrs. March with her usual question, "Any letter from Father, girls?" and Laurie to say in his persuasive way, "Won't some of you come for a drive? I've been working away at mathematics till my head is in a muddle, and I'm going to freshen my wits by a brisk turn. It's a dull day, but the air isn't bad, and I'm going to take Brooke home, so it will be gay inside, if it isn't out. Come, Jo, you and Beth will go, won't you?"

"Of course we will."

"Much obliged, but I'm busy." And Meg whisked out her workbasket, for she had agreed with her mother that it was best, for her at least, not to drive too often with the young gentleman.

"We three will be ready in a minute," cried Amy, running away to wash her hands.

"Can I do anything for you, Madam Mother?" asked Laurie, leaning over Mrs. March's chair with the affectionate look and tone he always gave her.

"No, thank you, except call at the office, if you'll be so kind, dear. It's our day for a letter, and the postman hasn't been. Father is as regular as the sun, but there's some delay on the way, perhaps."

A sharp ring interrupted her, and a minute after Hannah came in with a letter.

"It's one of them horrid telegraph things, mum," she said, handling it as if she was afraid it would explode and do some damage.

At the word 'telegraph', Mrs. March snatched it, read the two lines it contained, and dropped back into her chair as white as if the little paper had sent a bullet to her heart. Laurie dashed downstairs for water, while Meg and Hannah supported her, and Jo read aloud, in a frightened voice . . .

Mrs. March: Your husband is very ill. Come at once. S. HALE Blank Hospital, Washington.

How still the room was as they listened breathlessly, how strangely the day darkened outside, and how suddenly the whole world seemed to change, as the girls gathered about their mother, feeling as if all the happiness and support of their lives was about to be taken from them.

Mrs. March was herself again directly, read the message over, and stretched out her arms to her daughters, saying, in a tone they never forgot, "I shall go at once, but it may be too late. Oh, children, children, help me to bear it!"

For several minutes there was nothing but the sound of sobbing in the room, mingled with broken words of comfort, tender assurances of help, and hopeful whispers that died away in tears. Poor Hannah was the first to recover, and with unconscious wisdom she set all the rest a good example, for with her, work was panacea for most afflictions.

"The Lord keep the dear man! I won't waste no time a-cryin', but git your things ready right away, mum," she said heartily, as she wiped her face on her apron, gave her mistress a warm shake of the hand with her own hard one, and went away to work like three women in one.

"She's right, there's no time for tears now. Be calm, girls, and let me think."

They tried to be calm, poor things, as their mother sat up, looking pale but steady, and put away her grief to think and plan for them.

"Where's Laurie?' she asked presently, when she had collected her thoughts and decided on the first duties to be done.

"Here, ma'am. Oh, let me do something!" cried the boy, hurrying from the next room whither he had withdrawn, feeling that their first sorrow was too sacred for even his friendly eyes to see.

"Send a telegram saying I will come at once. The next train goes early in the morning. I'll take that."

"What else? The horses are ready. I can go anywhere, do anything," he said, looking ready to fly to the ends of the earth.

"Leave a note at Aunt March's. Jo, give me that pen and paper."

Tearing off the blank side of one of her newly copied pages, Jo drew the table before her mother, well knowing that money for the long, sad journey must be borrowed, and feeling as if she could do anything to add to a little to the sum for her father.

"Now go, dear, but don't kill yourself driving at a desperate pace. There is no need of that."

Mrs. March's warning was evidently thrown away, for five minutes later Laurie tore by the window on his own fleet horse, riding as if for his life.

"Jo, run to the rooms, and tell Mrs. King that I can't come. On the way get these things. I'll put them down, they'll be needed and I must go prepared for nursing. Hospital stores are not always good. Beth, go and ask Mr. Laurence for a couple of bottles of old wine. I'm not too proud to beg for Father. He shall have the best of everything. Amy, tell Hannah to get down the black trunk, and Meg, come and help me find my things, for I'm half bewildered."

Writing, thinking, and directing all at once might well bewilder the poor lady, and Meg begged her to sit quietly in her room for a little while, and let them work. Everyone scattered like leaves before a gust of wind, and the quiet, happy household was broken up as suddenly as if the paper had been an evil spell.

Mr. Laurence came hurrying back with Beth, bringing every comfort the kind old gentleman could think of for the invalid, and friendliest promises of protection for the girls during the mother's absence, which comforted her very much. There was nothing he didn't offer, from his own dressing gown to himself as escort. But the last was impossible. Mrs. March would not hear of the old gentleman's undertaking the long journey, yet an expression of relief was visible when he spoke of it, for anxiety ill fits one for traveling. He saw the look, knit his heavy eyebrows, rubbed his hands, and marched abruptly away, saying he'd be back directly. No one had time to think of him again till, as Meg ran through the entry, with a pair of rubbers in one hand and a cup of tea in the other, she came suddenly upon Mr. Brooke.

"I'm very sorry to hear of this, Miss March," he said, in the kind, quiet tone which sounded very pleasantly to her perturbed spirit. "I came to offer myself as escort to your mother. Mr. Laurence has commissions for me in Washington, and it will give me real satisfaction to be of service to her there."

Down dropped the rubbers, and the tea was very near following, as Meg put out her hand, with a face so full of gratitude that Mr. Brooke would have felt repaid for a much greater sacrifice than the trifling one of time and comfort which he was about to take.

"How kind you all are! Mother will accept, I'm sure, and it will be such a relief to know that she has someone to take care of her. Thank you very, very much!"

Meg spoke earnestly, and forgot herself entirely till something in the brown eyes looking down at her made her remember the cooling tea, and lead the way into the parlor, saying she would call her mother.

Everything was arranged by the time Laurie returned with a note from Aunt March, enclosing the desired sum, and a few lines repeating what she had often said before, that she had always told them it was absurd for March to go into the army, always predicted that no good would come of it, and she hoped they would take her advice the next time. Mrs. March put the note in the fire, the money in her purse, and went on with her preparations, with her lips folded tightly in a way which Jo would have understood if she had been there.

The short afternoon wore away. All other errands were done, and Meg and her mother busy at some necessary needlework, while Beth and Amy goth tea, and Hannah finished her ironing with what she called a 'slap and a bang', but still Jo did not come. They began to get anxious, and Laurie went off to find her, for no one knew what freak Jo might take into her head. He missed her, however, and she came walking in with a very queer expression of countenance, for there was a mixture of fun and fear, satisfaction and regret in it, which puzzled the family as much as did the roll of bills she laid before her mother, saying with a little choke in her voice, "That's my contribution toward making Father comfortable and bringing him home!"
"My dear, where did you get it? Twenty-five dollars! Jo, I hope you haven't done anything rash?"

"No, it's mine honestly. I didn't beg, borrow, or steal it. I earned it, and I don't think you'll blame me, for I only sold what was my own."

As she spoke, Jo took off her bonnet, and a general outcry arose, for all her abundant hair was cut short.

"Your hair! Your beautiful hair!" "Oh, Jo, how could you? Your one beauty." "My dear girl, there was no need of this." "She doesn't look like my Jo any more, but I love her dearly for it!"

As everyone exclaimed, and Beth hugged the cropped head tenderly, Jo assumed an indifferent air, which did not deceive anyone a particle, and said, rumpling up the brown bush and trying to look as if she liked it, "It doesn't affect the fate of the nation, so don't wail, Beth. It will be good for my vanity, I getting too proud of my wig. It will do my brains good to have that mop taken off. My head feels deliciously light and cool, and the barber said I could soon have a curly crop, which will be boyish, becoming, and easy to keep in order. I'm satisfied, so please take the money and let's have supper."

"Tell me all about it, Jo. I am not quite satisfied, but I can't blame you, for I know how willingly you sacrificed your vanity, as you call it, to your love. But, my dear, it was not necessary, and I'm afraid you will regret it one of these days," said Mrs. March.

"No, I won't!" returned Jo stoutly, feeling much relieved that her prank was not entirely condemned.

"What made you do it?" asked Amy, who would as soon have thought of cutting off her head as her pretty hair.

"Well, I was wild to to something for Father," replied Jo, as they gathered about the table, for healthy young people can eat even in the midst of trouble. "I hate to borrow as much as Mother does, and I knew Aunt March would croak, she always does, if you ask for a ninepence. Meg gave all her quarterly salary toward the rent, and I only got some clothes with mine, so I felt wicked, and was bound to have some money, if I sold the nose off my face to get it."

"You needn't feel wicked, my child! You had no winter things and got the simplest with your own hard earnings," said Mrs. March with a look that warmed Jo's heart.

"I hadn't the least idea of selling my hair at first, but as I went along I kept thinking what I could do, and feeling as if I'd like to dive into some of the rich stores and help myself. In a barber's window I saw tails of hair with the prices marked, and one black tail, not so thick as mine, was forty dollars. It came to me all of a sudden that I had one thing to make money out of, and without stopping to think, I walked in, asked if they bought hair, and what they would give for mine."

"I don't see how you dared to do it," said Beth in a tone of awe.

"Oh, he was a little man who looked as if he merely lived to oil his hair. He rather stared at first, as if he wasn't used to having girls bounce into his shop and ask him to buy their hair. He said he didn't care about mine, it wasn't the fashionable color, and he never paid much for it in the first place. The work he put it into it made it dear, and so on. It was getting late, and I was afraid if it wasn't done right away that I shouldn't have it done at all, and you know when I start to do a thing, I hate to give it up. So I begged him to take it, and told him why I was in such a hurry. It was silly, I dare say, but it changed his mind, for I got rather excited, and told the story in my topsy-turvy way, and his wife heard, and said so kindly, 'Take it, Thomas, and oblige the young lady. I'd do as much for our Jimmy any day if I had a spire of hair worth selling.'"

"Who was Jimmy?" asked Amy, who liked to have things explained as they went along.

"Her son, she said, who was in the army. How friendly such things make strangers feel, don't they? She talked away all the time the man clipped, and diverted my mind nicely."

"Didn't you feel dreadfully when the first cut came?" asked Meg, with a shiver.

"I took a last look at my hair while the man got his things, and that was the end of it. I never snivel over trifles like that. I will confess, though, I felt queer when I saw the dear old hair laid out on the table, and felt only the short rough ends of my head. It almost seemed as if I'd an arm or leg off. The woman saw me look at it, and picked out a long lock for me to keep. I'll give it to you, Marmee, just to remember past glories by, for a crop is so comfortable I don't think I shall ever have a mane again."

Mrs. March folded the wavy chestnut lock, and laid it away with a short gray one in her desk. She only said, "Thank you, deary," but something in her face made the girls change the subject, and talk as cheerfully as they could about Mr. Brooke's kindness, the prospect of a fine day tomorrow, and the happy times they would have when Father came home to be nursed.

No one wanted to go to bed when at ten o'clock Mrs. March put by the last finished job, and said, "Come girls." Beth went to the piano and played the father's favorite hymn. All began bravely, but broke down one by one till Beth was left alone, singing with all her heart, for to her music was always a sweet consoler.

"Go to bed and don't talk, for we must be up early and shall need all the sleep we can get. Good night, my darlings," said Mrs. March, as the hymn ended, for no one cared to try another.

They kissed her quietly, and went to bed as silently as if the dear invalid lay in the next room. Beth and Amy soon fell asleep in spite of the great trouble, but Meg lay awake, thinking the most serious thoughts she had ever known in her short life. Jo lay motionless, and her sister fancied that she was asleep, till a stifled sob made her exclaim, as she touched a wet cheek . . .

"Jo, dear, what is it? Are you crying about father?"

"No, not now."

"What then?"

"My . . .My hair!" burst out poor Jo, trying vainly to smother her emotion in the pillow.

It did not seem at all comical to Meg, who kissed and caressed the afflicted heroine in the tenderest manner.

"I'm not sorry," protested Jo, with a choke. "I'd do it again tomorrow, if I could. It's only the vain part of me that goes and cries in this silly way. Don't tell anyone, it's all over now. I thought you were asleep, so I just made a little private moan for my one beauty. How came you to be awake?"

"I can't sleep, I'm so anxious," said Meg.

"Think about something pleasant, and you'll soon drop off."

"I tried it, but felt wider awake than ever."

"What did you think of?"

"Handsome faces—eyes particularly," answered Meg, smiling to herself in the dark. "What color do you like best?"

"Brown, that is, sometimes. Blue are lovely."

Jo, laughed, and Meg sharply ordered her not to talk, then amiably promised to make her hair curl, and fell asleep to dream of living in her castle in the air.

The clocks were striking midnight and the rooms were very still as a figure glided quietly from bed to bed, smoothing a coverlet here, settling a pillow there, and pausing to look long and tenderly at each unconscious face, to kiss each with lips that mutely blessed, and to pray the fervent prayers which only mothers utter. As she lifted the curtain to look out into the dreary night, the moon broke suddenly from behind the clouds and shone upon her like a bright, benignant face, which seemed to whisper in the silence," Be comforted, dear soul! There is always light behind the clouds."

Chapter Sixteen

In the cold gray dawn the sisters lit their lamp and read their chapter with an earnestness never felt before. For now the shadow of a real trouble had come, the little books were full of help and comfort, and as they dressed, they agreed to say goodbye cheerfully and hopefully, and send their mother on her anxious journey unsaddened by tears or complaints from them. Everything seemed very strange when they went down, so dim and still outside, so full of light and bustle within. Breakfast at that early hour seemed odd, and even Hannah's familiar face looked unnatural as she flew about her kitchen with her nightcap on. The big trunk stood ready in the hall, Mother's cloak and bonnet lay on the sofa, and Mother herself sat trying to eat, but looking so pale and worn with sleeplessness and anxiety that the girls found it very hard to keep their resolution. Meg's eyes kept filling in spite of herself, Jo was obliged to hide her face in the kitchen roller more than once, ant the little girls wore a grave, troubled expression, as if sorrow was a new experience to them.

Nobody talked much, but as the time drew very near and they sat waiting for the carriage, Mrs. March said to the girls, who were all busied about her, one folding her shawl, another smoothing out the strings of her bonnet, a third putting on her overshoes, and a forth fastening up her travelling bag . . .

"Children, I leave you to Hannah's care and Mr. Laurence's protection. Hannah is faithfulness itself, and our good neighbor will guard you as if you were his own. I have no fears for you, yet I am anxious that you should take this trouble rightly. Don't grieve and fret when I am gone, or think that you can be idle and comfort yourselves by being idle and trying to forget. Go on with your work as usual, for work is a blessed solace. Hope and keep busy, and whatever happens, remember that you never can be fatherless."

"Yes, Mother."

"Meg, dear, be prudent, watch over your sisters, consult Hannah, and in any perplexity, go to Mr. Laurence. Be patient, Jo, don't get despondent or do rash things, write to me often, and be my brave girl, ready to help and cheer all. Beth, comfort yourself with your music, and be faithful to the little home duties, and You Amy, help all you can, be obedient, and keep happy safe at home."

"We will, Mother! We will!"

The rattle of an approaching carriage made them all start and listen. That was the hard minute, but the girls stood it well. No one cried, no one ran away or uttered a lamentation, though their hearts were very heavy as they sent loving messages to Father, remembering, as they spoke that it might be too late to deliver them. They kissed their mother quietly, clung about her tenderly, and tried to wave their hands cheerfully when she drove away.

Laurie and his grandfather came over to see her off, and Mr. Brooke looked so strong and sensible and kind that the girls christened him 'Mr. Greatheart' on the spot.

"Goodby, my darlings! God bless and keep us all!" whispered Mrs. March, as she kissed one dear little face after the other, and hurried into the carriage.

As she rolled away, the sun came out, and looking back, she saw it shining on the group at the gate like a good omen. They saw it also, and smiled and waved their hands, and the last thing she beheld as she turned the corner was the four bright faces, and behind them like a bodyguard, old Mr. Laurence, faithful Hannah, and devoted Laurie.

"How kind everyone is to us!" she said, turning to find fresh proof of it in the respectful sympathy of the young man's face.

"I don't see how they can help it," returned Mr. Brooke, laughing so infectiously that Mrs. March could not help smiling. And so the journey began with the good omens of sunshine, smiles, and cheerful words.

"I feel as if there had been an earthquake," said Jo, as their neighbors went home to breakfast, leaving them to rest and refresh themselves.

"It seems as if half the house was gone," added Meg forlornly.

Beth opened her lips to say something, but could only point to the pile of nicely mended hose which lay on Mother's table, showing that even in her last hurried moments she had thought and worked for them. It was a little thing, but it went straight to their hearts, and in spite of their brave resolutions, they all broke down and cried bitterly.

Hannah wisely allowed them to relieve their feelings, and when the shower showed signs of clearing up, she came to the rescue, armed with a coffeepot.

"Now, ny dear young ladies, remember what your ma said, and don't fret. Come and have a cup of coffee all round, and then let's fall to work and be a credit to the family."

Coffee was a treat, and Hannah showed great tact in making it that morning. No one could resist her persuasive nods, or the fragrant invitation issuing from the nose of the coffee pot. They drew up to the table, exchanged their handkerchiefs for napkins, and in ten minutes were all right again.

"'Hope and keep busy', that's the motto for us, so let's see who will remember it best. I shall go to Aunt March, as usual. Oh, won't she lecture though!" said Jo, as she sipped with returning spirit.

"I shall go to my Kings, though I'd much rather stay at home and attend to things here," said Meg, wishing she hadn't made her eyes so red.

"No need of that. Beth and I can keep house perfectly well," put in Amy, with an important air. "Hannah will tell us what to do, and we'll have everything nice when you come home," added Beth, getting out her mop and dish tub without delay.

"I think anxiety is very interesting," observed Amy, eating sugar pensively.

The girls couldn't help laughing, and felt better for it, though Meg shook her head at the young lady who could find consolation in a sugar bowl.

The sight of the turnovers made Jo sober again, and when the two went out to their daily tasks, they looked sorrowfully back at the window where they were accustomed to see their mother's face. It was gone, but Beth had remembered the little household ceremony, and there she was, nodding away at them like a rosyfaced mandarin.

"That's so like my Beth!" said Jo, waving her hat, with a grateful face. "Goodbye, Meggy, I hope the Kings won't strain today. Don't fret about Father, dear," she added, as they parted.

"And I hope Aunt March won't croak. Your hair is becoming, and it looks very boyish and nice," returned Meg, trying not to smile at the curly head, which looked comically small on her tall sister's shoulders.

"That's my only comfort." And, touching her hat a' la Laurie, away went Jo, feeling like a shorn sheep on a wintry day.

News from their father comforted the girls very much, for though dangerously ill, the presence of the best and tenderest of nurses had already done him good. Mr. Brooke sent a bulletin every day, and as the head of the family, Meg insisted on reading the dispatches, which grew more cheerful as the week passed. At first, everyone was eager to write, and plump envelopes were carefully poked into the letter box by one or other of the sisters, who felt rather important with their Washington correspondence. As one of these packets contained characteristic notes from the party, we will rob an imaginary mail, and read them.

My dearest Mother:

It is impossible to tell you how happy your last letter made us, for the news was so good we couldn't help laughing and crying over it. How very kind Mr. Brooke is, and how fortunate that Mr. Laurence's business detains him near you so long, since he is so useful to you and Father. The girls are all as good as gold. Jo helps me with the sewing, and insists on doing all sorts of hard jobs. I should be afraid she might overdo, if I didn't know her 'moral fit' wouldn't last long. Beth is as regular about her tasks as a clock, and never forgets what you told her. She grieves about Father, and looks sober except when she is at her little piano. Amy minds me nicely, and I take great care of her. She does her own hair, and I am teaching her to make buttonholes and mend her stockings. She tries very hard, and I know you will be pleased with her improvement when you come. Mr. Laurence watches over us like a motherly old hen, as Jo says, and Laurie is very kind and neighborly. He and Jo keep us merry, for we get pretty blue sometimes, and feel like orphans, with you so far away. Hannah is a perfect saint. She does not scold at all, and always calls me Miss Margaret, which is quite proper, you know, and treats me with respect. We are all well and busy, but we long, day and night, to have you back. Give my dearest love to Father, and believe me, ever your own . . .

MEG

This note, prettily written on scented paper, was a great contrast to the next, which was scribbled on a big sheet of thin foreign paper, ornamented with blots and all manner of flourishes and curly-tailed letters.

My precious Marmee:

Three cheers for dear Father! Brooke was a trump to telegraph right off, and let us know the minute he was better. I rushed up garret when the letter came, and tried to thank god for being so good to us, but I could only cry, and say, "I'm glad! I'm glad!" Didn't that do as well as a regular prayer? For I felt a great many in my heart. We have such funny times, and now I can enjoy them, for everyone is so desperately good, it's like living in a nest of turtledoves. You'd laugh to see Meg head the table and try to be motherish. She gets prettier every day, and I'm in love with her sometimes. The children are regular archangels, and I—well, I'm Jo, and never shall be anything else. Oh, I must tell you that I came near having a quarrel with Laurie. I freed my mind about a silly little thing, and he was offended. I was right, but didn't speak as I ought, and he marched home, saying he wouldn't come again till I begged pardon. I declared I wouldn't and got mad. It lasted all day. I felt bad and wanted you very much. Laurie and I are both so proud, it's hard to beg pardon. But I thought he'd come to it, for I was in the right. He didn't come, and just at night I remembered what you said when Amy fell into the river. I read my little book, felt better, resolved not to let the sun set on my anger, and ran over to tell Laurie I was sorry. I met him at the gate, coming for the same thing. We both laughed, begged each other's pardon, and felt all good and comfortable again.

I made a 'pome' yesterday, when I was helping Hannah wash, and as Father likes my silly little things, I put it in to amuse him. Give him my lovingest hug that ever was, and kiss yourself a dozen times for your . . .

TOPSY-TURVY JO

A SONG FROM THE SUDS

Queen of my tub, I merrily sing, While the white foam rises high, And sturdily wash and rinse and wring, And fasten the clothes to dry. Then out in the free fresh air they swing, Under the sunny sky.

I wish we could wash from out hearts and souls The stains of the week away, And let water and air by their magic make Ourselves as pure as they. Then on the earth there would be indeed, A glorious washing day!

Along the path of a useful life, Will heartsease ever bloom. The busy mind has no time to think Of sorrow or care or gloom. And anxious thoughts may be swept away, As we bravely wield a broom.

I am glad a task to me is given, To labor at day by day, For it brings me health and strength and hope, And I cheerfully learn to say, "Head, you may think, Heart, you may feel, But, Hand, you shall work alway!"

Dear Mother,

There is only room for me to send my love, and some pressed pansies from the root I have been keeping safe in the house for Father to see. I read every morning, try to be good all day, and sing myself to sleep with Father's tune. I can't sing 'LAND OF THE LEAL' now, it makes me cry. Everyone is very kind, and we are as happy as we can be without you. Amy wants the rest of the page, so I must stop. I didn't forget to cover the holders, and I wind the clock and air the rooms every day.

Kiss dear Father on the cheek he calls mine. Oh, do come soon to your loving . . .

LITTLE BETH

Ma Chere Mamma,

We are all well I do my lessons always and never corroberate the girls—Meg says I mean contradick so I put in both words and you can take the properest. Meg is a great comfort to me and lets me have jelly every night at tea its so good for me Jo says because it keeps me sweet tempered. Laurie is not as respeckful as he ought to be now I am almost in my teens, he calls me Chick and hurts my feelings by talking French to me very fast when I say Merci or Bon jour as Hattie King does. The sleeves of my blue dress were all worn out, and Meg put in new ones, but the full front came wrong and they are more blue than the dress. I felt bad but did not fret I bear my troubles well but I do wish Hannah would put more starch in my aprons and have buckwheats every day. Can't she? Didn't I make that interrigation point nice? Meg says my punchtuation and spelling are disgraceful and I am mortyfied but dear me I have so many things to do, I can't stop. Adieu, I send heaps of love to Papa. Your affectionate daughter . . .

AMY CURTIS MARCH

Dear Mis March,

I jes drop a line to say we git on fust rate. The girls is clever and fly round right smart. Miss Meg is going to make a proper good housekeeper. She hes the liking for it, and gits the hang of things surprisin quick. Jo doos beat all for goin ahead, but she don't stop to cal'k'late fust, and you never know where she's like to bring up. She done out a tub of clothes on Monday, but she starched 'em afore they was wrenched, and blued a pink calico dress till I thought I should a died a laughin. Beth is the best of little creeters, and a sight of help to me, bein so forehanded and dependable. She tries to learn everything, and really goes to market beyond her years, likewise keeps accounts, with my help, quite wonderful. We have got on very economical so fur. I don't let the girls hev coffee only once a week, accordin to your wish, and keep em on plain wholesome vittles. Amy does well without frettin, wearin her best clothes and eatin sweet stuff. Mr. Laurie is as full of didoes as usual, and turns the house upside down frequent, but he heartens the girls, so I let em hev full swing. The old gentleman send heaps of things, and is rather wearin, but means wal, and it aint my place to say nothin. My bread is riz, so no more at this time. I send my duty to Mr. March, and hope he's seen the last of his Pewmonia.

Yours respectful,
Hannah Mullet

Head Nurse of Ward No. 2,

All serene on the Rappahannock, troops in fine condition, commisary department well conducted, the Home Guard under Colonel Teddy always on duty, Commander in Chief General Laurence reviews the army daily, Quartermaster

Mullet keeps order in camp, and Major Lion does picket duty at night. A salute of twenty-four guns was fired on reciept of good news from Washington, and a dress parade took place at headquarters. Commander in chief sends best wishes, in which he is heartily joined by . . .

COLONEL TEDDY

Dear Madam:

The little girls are all well. Beth and my boy report daily. Hannah is a model servant, and guards pretty Meg like a dragon. Glad the fine weather holds. Pray make Brooke useful, and draw on me for funds if expenses exceed your estimate. Don't let your husband want anything. Thank God he is mending.

Your sincere friend and servant, JAMES LAURENCE

Chapter Seventeen

For a week the amount of virtue in the old house would have supplied the neighborhood. It was really amazing, for everyone seemed in a heavenly frame of mind, and self-denial was all the fashion. Relieved of their first anxiety about their father, girls insensibly relaxed their praiseworthy efforts a little, and began to fall back into old ways. They did not forget their motto, but hoping and keeping busy seemed to grow easier, and after such tremendous exertions, they felt that Endeavor deserved a holiday, and gave it a good many.

Jo caught a bad cold through neglect to cover the shorn head enough, and was ordered to stay at home till she was better, for Aunt March didn't like to hear people read with colds in their heads. Jo liked this, and after an energetic rummage from garret to cellar, subsided on the sofa to nurse her cold with arsenicum and books. Amy found that housework and art did not go well together, and returned to her mud pies. Meg went daily to her pupils, and sewed, or thought she did, at home, but much time was spent in writing long letters to her mother, or reading the Washington dispatches over and over. Beth kept on, with only slight relapses into idleness or grieving.

All the little duties were faithfully done each day, and many of her sisters' also, for they were forgetful, and the house seemed like a clock whose pendulum was gone a-visiting. When her heart got heavy with longings for Mother or fears for Father, she went away into a certain closet, hid her face in the folds of a dear old gown, and made her little moan and prayed her little prayer quietly by herself. Nobody knew what cheered her up after a sober fit, but everyone felt how sweet and helpful Beth was, and fell into a way of going to her for comfort or advice in their small affairs.

All were unconscious that this experience was a test of character, and when the first excitement was over, felt that they had done well and deserved praise. So they did, but their mistake was in ceasing to do well, and they learned this lesson through much anxiety and regret.

"Meg, I wish you'd go and see the Hummels. You know Mother told us not to forget them." said Beth, ten days after Mrs. March's departure.

"I'm too tired to go this afternoon," re;lied Meg, rocking comfortably as she sewed.

"Can't you, Jo?' asked Beth.

"Too stormy for me with my cold."

"I thought it was almost well."

"It's well enough for me to go out with Laurie, but not well enough to go to the Hummels,'" said Jo, laughing, but looking a little ashamed of her inconsistency.

"Why don't you go yourself?" asked Meg.

"I have been every day, but the baby is sick, and I don't know what to do for it. Mrs. Hummel goes away to work, and Lottchen takes care of it. But it gets sicker and sicker, and I think you or Hannah ought to go."

Beth spoke earnestly, and Meg promised she would go tomorrow.

"Ask Hannah for some nice little mess, and take it round, Beth, the air will do you good," said Jo, adding apologetically, "I'd go but I want to finish my writing."

"My head aches and I'm tired, so I thought maybe some of you would go," said Beth.

"Amy will be in presently, and she will run down for us, suggested Meg.

So Beth lay down on the sofa, the others returned to their work, and the Hummels were forgotten. An hour passed. Amy did not come, Meg went to her room to try on a new dress, Jo was absorbed in her story, and Hannah was sound asleep before the kitchen fire, when Beth quietly put on her hood, filled her basket with odds and ends for the poor children, and went out into the chilly air with a heavy head and a grieved look in her patient eyes. It was late when she came back, and no one saw her creep upstairs and shut herself into her mother's room. Half an hour after, Jo went to 'Mother's closet' for something, and there found little Beth sitting on the medicine chest, looking very grave, with red eyes and a camphor bottle in her hand.

"Christopher Columbus! What's the matter?" cried Jo, as Beth put out her hand as if to warn her off, and asked quickly, "You've had the scarlet fever, havent't you?"

"Years ago, when Meg did. Why?'

"Then I'll tell you. Oh, Jo, the baby's dead!"

"What baby?"

"Mrs. Hummel's. It died in my lap before she got home," cried Beth with a sob.

"My poor dear, how dreadful for you! I ought to have gone," said Jo, taking her sister in her arms as she sat down in her mother's bit chair, with a remorseful face.

"It wasn't dreadful, Jo, only so sad! I saw in a minute it was sicker, but Lottchen said her mother had gone for a doctor, so I took Baby and let Lotty rest. It seemed asleep, but all of a sudden if gave a little cry and trembled, and then lay very still. I tried to warm its feet, and Lotty gave it some milk, but it didn't stir, and I knew it was dead."

"Don't cry, dear! What did you do?"

"I just sat and held it softly till Mrs. Hummel came with the doctor. He said it was dead, and looked at Heinrich and Minna, who have sore throats. 'Scarlet fever, ma'am. Ought to have called me before, ' he said crossly. Mrs. Hummel told him she was poor, and had tried to cure baby herself, but now it was too late, and she could only ask him to help the others and trust to charity for his pay. He smiled then, and was kinder, but it was very sad, and I cried with them till he turned round all of a sudden, and told me to go home and take belladonna right away, or I'd have the fever."

"No, you won't!" cried Jo, hugging her close, with a frightened look. "Oh, Beth, if you should be sick I never could forgive myself! What shall we do?"

"Don't be frightened, I guess I shan't have it badly. I looked in Mother's book, and saw that it begins with headache, sore throat, and queer feelings like mine, so I did take some belladonna, and I feel better," said Beth, laying her cold hands on her hot forehead and trying to look well.

"If Mother was only at home!" exclaimed Jo, seizing the book, and feeling that Washington was an immense way off. She read a page, looked at Beth, felt her head, peeped into her throat, and then said gravely, "You've been over the baby every day for more than a week, and among the others who are going to have it, so I'm afraid you are going to have it, Beth. I'll call Hannah, she knows all about sickness." "Don't let Amy come. She never had it, and I should hate to give it to her. Can't you and Meg have it over again?" asked Beth, anxiously.

"I guess not. Don't care if I do. Serve me right, selfish pig, to let you go, and stay writing rubbish myself!" muttered Jo, as she went to consult Hannah.

The good soul was wide awake in a minute, and took the lead at once, assuring that there was no need to worry; every one had scarlet fever, and if rightly treated, nobody died, all of which Jo believed, and felt much relieved as they went up to call Meg.

"Now I'll tell you what we'll do," said Hannah, when she had examined and questioned Beth, "we will have Dr. Bangs, just to take a look at you, dear, and see that we start right. Then we'll send Amy off to Aunt March's for a spell, to keep her out of harm's way, and one of you girls can stay at home and amuse Beth for a day or two."

"I shall stay, of course, I'm oldest," began Meg, looking anxious and self-reproachful.

"I shall, because it's my fault she is sick. I told Mother I'd do the errands, and I haven't," said Jo decidedly.

"Which will you have, Beth? There ain't no need of but one," aid Hannah.

"Jo, please." And Beth leaned her head against her sister with a contented look, which effectually settled that point.

"I'll go and tell Amy," said Meg, feeling a little hurt, yet rather relieved on the whole, for she did not like nursing, and Jo did.

Amy rebelled outright, and passionately declared that she had rather have the fever than go to Aunt March. Meg reasoned, pleaded, and commanded, all in vain. Amy protested that she would not go, and Meg left her in despair to ask Hannah what should be done. Before she came back, Laurie walked into the parlor to find Amy sobbing, with her head in the sofa cushions. She told her story, expecting to be consoled, but Laurie only put his hands in his pockets and walked about the room, whistling softly, as he knit his brows in deep thought. Presently he sat down beside her, and said, in his most wheedlesome tone, "Now be a sensible little woman, and do as they say. No, don't cry, but hear what a jolly plan I've got. You go to Aunt March's, and I'll come and take you out every day, driving or walking, and we'll have capital times. Won't that be better than moping here?"

"I don't wish to be sent off as if I was in the way," began Amy, in an injured voice.

"Bless your heart, child, it's to keep you well. You don't want to be sick, do you?"

"No, I'm sure I don't, but I dare say I shall be, for I've been with Beth all the time."

"That's the very reason you ought to go away at once, so that you may escape it. Change of air and care will keep you well, I dare say, or if it does not entirely, you will have the fever more lightly. I advise you to be off as soon as you can, for scarlet fever is no joke, miss."

"But it's dull at Aunt March's, and she is so cross," said Amy, looking rather frightened.

"It won't be dull with me popping; in every day to tell you how Beth is, and take you out gallivanting. The old lady likes me, and I'll be as sweet as possible to her, so she won't peck at us, whatever we do."

"Will you take me out in the trotting wagon with Puck?"

"On my honor as a gentleman."

"And come every single day?"

"See if I don't/"

"And bring me back the minute Beth is well?"

"The identical minute."

"And go to the theater, truly?"

"A dozen theaters, if we may."

"Well—I guess I will," said Amy slowly.

"Good girl! Call Meg, and tell her you'll give in," said Laurie, with an approving pat, which annoyed Amy more than the 'giving in'.

Meg and Jo came running down to behold the miracle which had been wrought, and Amy, feeling very precious and self-sacrificing, promised to go, if the doctor said Beth was going to be ill.

"How is the little dear?" asked Laurie, for Beth was his especial pet, and he felt more anxious about her than he liked to show.

"She is lying down on Mother's bed, and feels better. The baby's death troubled her, but I dare say she has only got cold. Hannah says she thinks so, but she looks worried, and that makes me fidgety," answered Meg.

"What a trying world it is!" said Jo, rumpling up her hair in a fretful way. "No sooner do we get out of one trouble than down comes another. There doesn't seem to be anything to hold on to when Mother's gone, so I'm all at sea."

"Well, don't make a porcupine of yourself, it isn't becoming. Settle your wig, Jo, and tell me if I shall telegraph to your mother, or do anything?" asked Laurie, who never had been reconciled to the loss of his friend's one beauty.

"That is what troubles me," said Meg. "I think we ought to tell her if Beth is really ill, but Hannah says we mustn't, for Mother can't leave Father, and it will only make them anxious. Beth won't be sick long, and Hannah knows just what to do, and Mother said we were to mind her, so I suppose we must, but it doesn't seem quite right to me."

"Hum, well, I can't say. Suppose you ask Grandfather after the doctor has been."

"We will. Jo, go and get Dr. Bangs at once," commanded Meg. "We can't decide anything till he has been."

"Stay where you are, Jo. I'm errand boy to this establishment," said Laurie, taking up his cap.

"I'm afraid you are busy," began Meg.

"No, I've done my lessons for the day."

"Do you study in vacation time?" asked Jo.

"I follow the good example my neighbors set me," was Laurie's answer, as he swung himself out of the room.

"I have great hopes for my boy," observed Jo, watching him fly over the fence with an approving smile.

"He does very well, for a boy," was Meg's somewhat ungracious answer, for the subject did not interest her.

Dr. Bangs came, said Beth had symptoms of the fever, but he thought she would have it lightly, though he looked sober over the Hummel story. Amy was ordered off at once, and provided with something to ward off danger, she departed in great state, with Jo and Laurie as escort.

Aunt March received them with her usual hospitality.

"What do you want now?" she asked, looking sharply over her spectacles, while the parrot, sitting on the back of her chair, called out . . .

"Go away. No boys allowed here."

Laurie retired to the window, and Jo told her story.

"No more than I expected, if you are allowed to go poking about among poor folks. Amy can stay and make herself useful if she isn't sick, which I've no doubt she will be, looks like it now. Don't cry, child, it worries me to hear people sniff." Amy was on the point of crying, but Laurie slyly pulled the parrot's tail, which caused Polly to utter an astonished croak and call out, "Bless my boots!" in such a funny way, that she laughed instead.

"What do you hear from your mother?" asked the old lady gruffly.

"Father is much better," replied Jo, trying to keep sober.

"Oh, is her? Well, that won't last long, I fancy. March never had any stamina," was the cheerful reply.

"Ha, ha! Never say die, take a pinch of snuff, goodbye, goodbye!" squalled Polly, dancing on her perch, and clawing at the old lady's cap as Laurie tweaked him in the rear.

"Hold your tongue, you disrespectful old bird! And, Jo, you'd better go at once. It isn't proper to be gadding about so late with a rattlepated boy like . . ."

"Hold your tongue, you disrespectful old bird!" cried Polly, tumbling off the chair with a bounce, and running to peck the 'rattlepated' boy, who was shaking with laughter at the last speech.

"I don't think I can bear it, but I'll try," thought Amy, as she was left alone with Aunt March.

"Get along, you fright!" screamed Polly, and at that rude speech Amy could not restrain a sniff.

Chapter Eighteen

Beth did have the fever, and was much sicker than anyone but Hannah and the doctor suspected. The girls knew nothing about illness, and Mr. Laurence was not allowed to see her, so Hannah had everything her own way, and busy Dr. Bangs did his best, but left a good deal to the excellent nurse. Meg stayed at home, lest she should infect the Kings, and kept house, feeling very anxious and a little guilty when she wrote letters in which no mention was made of Beth's illness. She could not think it right to deceive her mother, but she had been bidden to mind Hannah, and Hannah wouldn't hear of 'Mrs. March bein' told, and worried just for sech a trifle.'

Jo devoted herself to Beth day and night, not a hard task, for Beth was very patient, and bore her pain uncomplainingly as long as she could control herself. But there came a time when during the fever fits she began to talk in a hoarse, broken voice, to play on the coverlet as if on her beloved little piano, and try to sing with a throat so swollen that there was no music left, a time when she did not know the familiar faces around her, but addressed them by wrong names, and called imploringly for her mother. Then Jo grew frightened, Meg begged to be allowed to write the truth, and even Hannah said she 'would think of it, though there was no danger yet'. A letter from Washington added to their trouble, for Mr. March had had a relapse, and could not think of coming home for a long while.

How dark the days seemed now, how sad and lonely the house, and how heavy were the hearts of the sisters as they worked and waited, while the shadow of death hovered over the once happy home. Then it was that Margaret, sitting alone with tears dropping often on her work, felt how rich she had been in things more precious than any luxuries money could buy—in love, protection, peace, and health, the real blessings of life. Then it was that Jo, living in the darkened room, with that suffering little sister always before her eyes and that pathetic voice sounding in her ears, learned to see the beauty and to sweetness of Beth's nature, to feel how deep and tender a place she filled in all hearts, and to acknowledge the worth of Beth's unselfish ambition to live for others, and make home happy by that exercise of those simple virtues which all may possess, and which all should love and value more than talent, wealth, or beauty. And Amy, in her exile, longed eagerly to be at home, that she might work for Beth, feeling now that no service would be hard or irksome, and remembering, with regretful grief, how many neglected tasks those willing hands had done for her. Laurie haunted the house like a restless ghost, and Mr. Laurence locke the grand piano, because he could not bear to be reminded of the young neighbor who used to make the twilight pleasant for him. Everyone missed Beth. The milkman, baker, grocer, and butcher inquired how she did, poor Mrs. Hummel came to beg pardon for her thoughtlessness and to get a shroud for Minna, the neighbors sent all sorts of comforts and good wishes, and even those who knew her best were surprised to find how many friends shy little Beth had made.

Meanwhile she lay on her bed with old Joanna at her side, for even in her wanderings she did not forget her forlorn protege. She longed for her cats, but would not have them brought, lest they should get sick, and in her quiet hours she was full of anxiety about Jo. She sent loving messages to Amy, bade them tell her mother that she would write soon, and often begged for pencil and paper to try to say a word, that Father might not think she had neglected him. But soon even these intervals of consciousness ended, and she lay hour after hour, tossing to and fro, with incoherent words on her lips, or sank into a heavy sleep which brought her no refreshment. Dr. Bangs came twice a day, Hannah sat up at night, Meg kept a telegram in her desk all ready to send off at any minute, and Jo never stirred from Beth's side.

The first of December was a wintry day indeed to them, for a bitter wind blew, snow fell fast, and the year seemed getting ready for its death. When Dr. Bangs came that morning, he looked long at Beth, held the hot hand in both his own for a minute, and laid it gently down, saying, in a low voice to Hannah, "If Mrs. March can leave her husband she'd better be sent for."

Hannah nodded without speaking, for her lips twitched nervously, Meg dropped down into a chair as the strength seemed to go out of her limbs at the sound of those words, and Jo, standing with a pale face for a minute, ran to the parlor, snatched up the telegram, and throwing on her things, rushed out into the storm. She was soon back, and while noiselessly taking off her cloak, Laurie came in with a letter, saying that Mr. March was mending again. Jo read it thankfully, but the heavy weight did not seem lifted off her heart, and her face was so full of misery that Laurie asked quickly, "What is it? Is Beth worse?"

"I've sent for Mother," said Jo, tugging at her rubber boots with a tragic expression.

"Good for you, Jo! Did you do it on your own responsibility?" asked Laurie, as he seated her in the hall chair and took off the rebellious boots, seeing how her hands shook.

"No. The doctor told us to."

"Oh, Jo, it's not so bad as that?" cried Laurie, with a startled face.

"Yes, it is. She doesn't know us, she doesn't even talk about the flocks of green doves, as she calls the vine leaves on the wall. She doesn't look like my Beth, and there's nobody to help us bear it. Mother and father both gone, and God seems so far away I can't find Him."

As the tears streamed fast down poor Jo's cheeks, she stretched out her hand in a helpless sort of way, as if groping in the dark, and Laurie took it in his, whispering as well as he could with a lump in his throat, "I'm here. Hold on tome, Jo, dear!"

She could not speak, but she did 'hold on', and the warm grasp of the friendly human hand comforted her sore heart, and seemed to lead her nearer to the Divine arm which alone could uphold her in her trouble.

Laurie longed to say something tender and comfortable, but no fitting words came to him, so he stood silent, gently stroking her bent head as her mother used to do. It was the best thing he could have done, far more soothing than the most eloquent words, for Jo felt the unspoken sympathy, and in the silence learned the sweet solace which affection administers to sorrow. Soon she dried the tears which had relieved her, and looked up with a grateful face.

"Thank you, Teddy, I'm better now. I don't feel so forlorn, and will try to bear it if it comes."

"Keep hoping for the best, that will help you, Jo. Soon your mother will be here, and then everything will be all right."

"I'm so glad Father is better. Now she won't feel so bad about leaving him. Oh, me! It does seem as if all the troubles came in a heap, and I got the heaviest part on my shoulders," sighed Jo, spreading her wet handkerchief over her knees to dry.

"Doesn't Meg pull fair?" asked Laurie, looking indignant.

"Oh, yes, she tries to, but she can't love Bethy as I do, and she won't miss her as I shall. Beth is my conscience, and I can't give her up. I can't! I can't!"

Down went Jo's face into the wet handkerchief, and she cried despairingly, for she had kept up bravely till now and never shed a tear. Laurie drew his hand across his eyes, but could not speak till he had subdued the choky feeling in his throat and steadied his lips. It might be unmanly, but he couldn't help it, and I am glad of it. Presently, as Jo's sobs quieted, he said hopefully, "I don't think she will die. She's so good, and we all love her so much, I don't believe God will take her away yet."

"The good and dear people always do die," groaned Jo, but she stopped crying, for her friend's words cheered her up in spite of her own doubts and fears.

"Poor girl, you're worn out. It isn't like you to be forlorn. Stop a bit. I'll hearten you up in a jiffy."

Laurie went off two stairs at a time, and Jo laid her wearied head down on Beth's little brown hood, which no one had thought of moving from the table where she left it. It must have possessed some magic, for the submissive spirit of its gentle owner seemed to enter into Jo, and when Laurie came running down with a glass of wine, she took it with a smile, and said bravely, "I drink—Health to my Beth! You are a good doctor, Teddy, and such a comfortable friend. How can I ever pay you?" she added, as the wine refreshed her body, as the kind words had done her troubled mind.

"I'll send my bill, by-and-by, and tonight I'll give you something that will warm the cockles of your heart better than quarts of wine," said Laurie, beaming at her with a face of suppressed satisfaction at something.

"What is it?" cried Jo, forgetting her woes for a minute in her wonder.

"I telegraphed to your mother yesterday, and Brooke answered she'd come at once, and she'll be here tonight, and everything will be all right. Aren't you glad I did it?"

Laurie spoke very fast, and turned red and excited all in a minute, for he had kept his plot a secret, for fear of disappointing the girls or harming Beth. Jo grew quite white, flew out of her chair, and the moment he stopped speaking she electrified him by throwing her arms round his neck, and crying out, with a joyful cry, "Oh, Laurie! Oh, Mother! I am so glad!" She did not weep again, but laughed hysterically, and trembled and clung to her friend as if she was a little bewildered by the sudden news.

Laurie, though decidedly amazed, behaved with great presence of mind. He patted her back soothingly, and finding that she was recovering, followed it up by a bashful kiss or two, which brought Jo round at once. Holding on to the banisters, she put him gently away, saying breathlessly, "Oh, don't! I didn't mean to, it was dreadful of me, but you were such a dear to go and do it in spite of Hannah that I couldn't help flying at you. Tell me all about it, and don't give me wine again, it makes me act so."

"I don't mind," laughed Laurie, as he settled his tie. "Why, you see I got fidgety, and so did Grandpa. We thought Hannah was overdoing the authority business, and your mother ought to know. She'd never forgive us if Beth . . . Well, if anything happened, you know. So I got grandpa to say it was high time we did something, and off I pelted to the office yesterday, for the doctor looked sober, and Hannah most took my head off when I proposed a telegram. I never can bear to be 'lorded over', so that settled my mind, and I did it. Your mother will come, I know, and the late train is in at two A.M. I shall go for her, and you've only got to bottle up your rapture, and keep Beth quiet till that blessed lady gets here."

"Laurie, you're an angel! How shall I ever thank you?"

"Fly at me again. I rather liked it," said Laurie, looking mischievous, a thing he had not done for a fortnight.

"No, thank you. I'll do it by proxy, when your grandpa comes. Don't tease, but go home and rest, for you'll be up half the night. Bless you, Teddy, bless you!"

Jo had backed into a corner, and as she finished her speech, she vanished precipitately into the kitchen, where she sat down upon a dresser and told the assembled cats that she was "happy, oh, so happy!" while Laurie departed, feeling that he had made a rather neat thing of it.

"That's the interferingest chap I ever see, but I forgive him and do hope Mrs. March is coming right away," said Hannah, with an air of relief, when Jo told the good news.

Meg had a quiet rapture, and then brooded over the letter, while Jo set the sickroom in order, and Hannah 'knocked up a couple of pies in case of company unexpected". A breath of fresh air seemed to blow through the house, and something better than sunshine brightened the quiet rooms. Everything appeared to feel the hopeful change. Beth's bird began to chirp again, and a half-blown rose was discovered on Amy's bush in the window. The fires seemed to burn with unusual cheeriness, and every time the girls met, their pale faces broke into smiles as they hugged one another, whispering encouragingly, "Mother's coming, dear! Mother's coming!" Every one rejoiced but Beth. She lay in that heavy stupor, alike unconscious of hope and joy, doubt and danger. It was a piteous sight, the once rosy face so changed and vacant, the once busy hands so weak and wasted, the once smiling lips quite dumb, and the once pretty, well-kept hair scattered rough and tangled on the pillow. All day she say so, only rousing now and then to mutter, "Water!" with lips so parched they could hardly shape the word. All day Jo and Meg hovered over her, watching, waiting, hoping, and trusting in God and Mother, and all day the snow fell, the bitter wind raged, and the hours dragged slowly by. But night came at last, and every time the clock struck, the sisters, still sitting on either side of the bed, looked at each other with brightening eyes, for each hour brought help nearer. The doctor had been in to say that some change, for better or worse, would probably take place about midnight, at which time he would return.

Hannah, quite worn out, lay down on the sofa at the bed's foot and fell fast asleep, Mr. Laurence marched to and fro in the parlor, feeling that he would rather face a rebel battery than Mrs. March's countenance as she entered. Laurie lay on the rug, pretending to rest, but staring into the fire with the thoughtful look which made his black eyes beautifully soft and clear.

The girls never forgot that night, for no sleep came to them as they kept their watch, with that dreadful sense of powerlessness which comes to us in hours like those.

"If God spares Beth, I never will complain again," whispered Meg earnestly.

"If god spares Beth, I'll try to love and serve Him all my life," answered Jo, with equal fervor.

"I wish I had no heart, it aches so," sighed Meg, after a pause.

"If life is often as hard as this, I don't see how we ever shall get through it," added her sister despondently.

Here the clock struck twelve, and both forgot themselves in watching Beth, for they fancied a change passed over her wan face. The house was still as death, and nothing but the wailing of the wind broke the deep hush. Weary Hannah slept on, and no one but the sisters saw the pale shadow which seemed to fall upon the little bed. An hour went by, and nothing happened except Laurie's quiet departure for the station. Another hour, still no one came, and anxious fears of delay in the storm, or accidents by the way, or, worst of all, a great grief at Washington, haunted the girls.

It was past two, when Jo, who stood at the window thinking how dreary the world looked in its winding sheet of snow, heard a movement by the bed, and turning quickly, saw Meg kneeling before their mother's easy chair with her face hidden. A dreadful fear passed coldly over Jo, as she thought, "Beth is dead, and Meg is afraid to tell me."

She was back at her post in an instant, and to her excited eyes a great change seemed to have taken place. The fever flush and the look of pain were gone, and the beloved little face looked so pale and peaceful in its utter repose that Jo felt no desire to weep or to lament. Leaning low over this dearest of her sisters, she kissed the damp forehead with her heart on her lips, and softly whispered, "Goodby, my Beth. Goodby!"

As if awaked by the stir, Hannah started out of her sleep, hurried to the bed, looked at Beth, felt her hands, listened at her lips, and then, throwing her apron over her head, sat down to rock to and fro, exclaiming, under her breath, "The fever's turned, she's sleepin' nat'ral, her skin's damp, and she breathes easy. Praise be given! Oh, my goodness me!"

Before the girls could believe the happy truth, the doctor came to confirm it. He was a homely man, but they thought his face quite heavenly when he smiled and said, with a fatherly look at them, "Yes, my dears, I think the little girl will pull through this time. Keep the house quiet, let her sleep, and when she wakes, give her . . ."

What they were to give, neither heard, for both crept into the dark hall, and, sitting on the stairs, held each other close, rejoicing with hearts too full for words. When they went back to be kissed and cuddled by faithful Hannah, they found Beth lying, as she used to do, with her cheek pillowed on her hand, the dreadful pallor gone, and breathing quietly, as if just fallen asleep.

"If Mother would only come now!" said Jo, as the winter night began to wane.

"See," said Meg, coming up with a white, half-opened rose, "I thought this would hardly be ready to lay in Beth's hand tomorrow if she—went away from us. But it has blossomed in the night, and now I mean to put it in my vase here, so that when the darling wakes, the first thing she sees will be the little rose, and Mother's face."

Never had the sun risen so beautifully, and never had the world seemed so lovely as it did to the heavy eyes of Meg and Jo, as they looked out in the early morning, when their long, sad vigil was done.

"It looks like a fairy world," said Meg, smiling to herself, as she stood behind the curtain, watching the dazzling sight.

"Hark!" cried Jo, starting to her feet.

Yes, there was a sound of bells at the door below, a cry from Hannah, and then Laurie's voice saying in a joyful whisper, "Girls, she's come! She's come!"

Chapter Nineteen

While these things were happening at home, Amy was having hard times at Aunt March's. She felt her exile deeply, and for the first time in her life, realized how much she was beloved and petted at home. Aunt March never petted any one. She did not approve of it, but she meant to be kind, for the well-behaved little girl pleased her very much, and Aunt March had a soft place in her old heart for her nephew's children, though she didn't think it proper to confess it. She really did her best to make Amy happy, but, dear me, what mistakes she made. Some old people keep young at heart in spite of wrinkles and gray hairs, can sympathize with children's little cares and joys, make them feel at home, and can hide wise lessons under pleasant plays, giving and receiving friendship in the sweetest way. But Aunt March had not this gift, and she worried Amy very much with her rules and orders, her prim ways, and long, prosy talks. Finding the child more docile and amiable than her sister, the old lady felt it her duty to try and counteract, as far as possible, the bad effects of home freedom and indulgence. So she took Amy by the hand, and taught her as she herself had been taught sixty years ago, a process which carried dismay to Amy's soul, and made her feel like a fly in the web of a very strict spider.

She had to wash the cups every morning, and polish up the old-fashioned spoons, the fat silver teapot, and the glasses till they shone. Then she must dust the room, and what a trying job that was. Not a speck escaped Aunt March's eye, and all the furniture had claw legs and much carving, which was never dusted to suit. Then Polly had to be fed, the lap dog combed, and a dozen trips upstairs and down to get things or deliver orders, for the old lady was very lame and seldom left her big chair. After these tiresome labors, she must do her lessons, which was a daily trial of every virtue she possessed. Then she was allowed one hour for exercise or play, and didn't she enjoy it?

Laurie came every day, and wheedled Aunt March till Amy was allowed to go out with him, when they walked and rode and had capital times. After dinner, she had to read aloud, and sit still while the old lady slept, which she usually did for an hour, as she dropped off over the first page. Then patchwork or towels appeared, and Amy sewed with outward meekness and inward rebellion till dusk, when she was allowed to amuse herself as she liked till teatime. The evenings were the worst of all, for Aunt March fell to telling long stories about her youth, which were so unutterably dull that Amy was always ready to go to be, intending to cry over her hard fate, but usually going to sleep before she had squeezed out more than a tear or two.

If it had not been for Laurie, and old Esther, the maid, she felt that she never could have got through that dreadful time. The parrot alone was enough to drive her distracted, for he soon felt that she did not admire him, and revenged himself by being as mischievous as possible. He pulled her hair whenever she came near him, upset his bread and milk to plague her when she had newly cleaned his cage, made Mop bark by pecking at him while Madam dozed, called her names before company, and behaved in all respects like an reprehensible old bird. Then she could not endure the dog, a fat, cross beast who snarled and yelped at her when she made his toilet, and who lay on his back with all his legs in the air and a most idiotic expression of countenance when he wanted something to eat, which was about a dozen times a day. The cook was bad-tempered, the old coachman was deaf, and Esther the only one who ever took any notice of the young lady.

Esther was a Frenchwoman, who had lived with'Madame', as she called her mistress, for many years, and who rather tyrannized over the old lady, who could not get along without her. Her real name was Estelle, but Aunt March ordered her to change it, and she obeyed, on condition that she was never asked to change her religion. She took a fancy to Mademoiselle, and amused her very much with odd stories of her life in France, when Amy sat with her while she got up Madam's laces. She also allowed her to roam about the great house, and examine the curious and pretty things stored away in the big wardrobes and the ancient chests, for Aunt March hoarded like a magpie. Amy's chief delight was an Indian cabinet, full of queer drawers, little pigeonholes, and secret places, in which were kept all sorts of ornaments, some precious, some merely curious, all more or less antique. To examine and arrange these things gave Amy great satisfaction, especially the jewel cases, in which on velvet cushions reposed the ornaments which had adorned a belle forty years ago. There was the garnet set which Aunt March wore when she came out, the pearls her father gave her on her wedding day, her lover's diamonds, the jet mourning rings and pins, the queer lockets, with portraits of dead friends and weeping willows made of hair inside, the baby bracelets her one little daughter had worn, Uncle March's big watch, with the red seal so many childish hands had played with, and in a box all by itself lay Aunt March's wedding ring, too small now for her fat finger, but put carefully away like the most precious jewel of them all.

"Which would Mademoiselle choose if she had her will?" asked Esther, wo always sat near to watch over and lock up the valuables.

"I like the diamonds best, but there is no necklace among them, and I'm fond of necklaces, they are so becoming. I should choose this if I might," replied Amy, looking with great admiration at a string of gold and ebony beads from which hung a heavy cross of the same.

"I, too, covet that, but not as a necklace. Ah, no! To me it is a rosary, and as such I should use it like a good catholic," said Esther, eyeing the handsome thing wistfully.

"Is it meant to use as you use the string of good-smelling wooden beads hanging over your glass?" asked Amy.

"Truly, yes, to pray with. It would be pleasing to the saints if one used so fine a rosary as this, instead of wearing it as a vain bijou."

"You seem to take a great deal of comfort in your prayers, Esther, and always come down looking quiet and satisfied. I wish I could."

"If Mademoiselle was a Catholic, she would find true comfort, but as that is not to be, it would be well if you went apart each day to meditate and pray, as did the good mistress whom I served before Madame. She had a little chapel, and in it found solacement for much trouble."

"Would it be right for me to do so too?" asked Amy, who in her loneliness felt the need of help of some sort, and found that she was apt to forget her little book, now that Beth was not there to remind her of it.

"It would be excellent and charming, and I shall gladly arrange the little dressing room for you if you like it. Say nothing to Madame, but when she sleeps go you and sit alone a while to think good thoughts, and pray the dear God preserve your sister."

Esther was truly pious, and quite sincere in her advice, for she had an affectionate heart, and felt much for the sisters in their anxiety. Amy liked the idea, and gave her leave to arrange the light closet next her room, hoping it would do her good.

"I wish I knew where all these pretty things would go when Aunt March dies," she said, as she slowly replaced the shining rosary and shut the jewel cases one by one.

"To you and your sisters. I know it, Madame confides in me. I witnessed her will, and it is to be so," whispered Esther smiling.

"How nice! But I wish she'd let us have them now. Procrastination is not agreeable," observed Amy, taking a last look at the diamonds.

"It is too soon yet for the young ladies to wear these things. The first one who is affianced will have the pearls, Madame has said it, and I have a fancy that the little turquoise ring will be given to you when you go, for Madame approves your good behavior and charming manners."

"Do you think so? Oh, I'll be a lamb, if I can only have that lovely ring! It's ever so much prettier than Kitty Bryant's. I do like Aunt March after all." And Amy tried on the blue ring with a delighted face and a firm resolve to earn it.

From that day she was a model of obedience, and the old lady complacently admired the success of her training. Esther fitted up the closet with a little table, placed a footstool before it, and over it a picture taken from one of the shut-up rooms. She thought it was of no great value, but, being appropriate, she borrowed it, well knowing that Madame would never know it, nor care if she did. It was, however, a very valuable copy of one of the famous pictures of the world, and Amy's beauty-loving eyes were never tired of looking up at the sweet face of the Divine Mother, while her tender thoughts of her own were busy at her heart. On the table she laid her little testament and hymnbook, kept a vase always full of the best flowers Laurie brought her, and came every day to 'sit alone' thinking good thoughts, and praying the dear God to preserve her sister. Esther had given her a rosary of black beads with a silver cross, but Amy hung it up and did not use it, feeling doubtful as to its fitness for Protestant prayers.

The little girl was very sincere in all this, for being left alone outside the safe home nest, she felt the need of some kind hand to hold by so sorely that she instinctively turned to the strong and tender Friend, whose fatherly love most closely surrounds His little children. She missed her mother's help to understand and rule herself, but having been taught where to look, she did her best to find the way and walk in it confidingly. But Amy was a young pilgrim, and just now her burden seemed very heavy. She tried to forget herself, to keep cheerful, and be satisfied with doing right, though no one saw or praised her for it. In her first effort at being very, very good, she decided to make her will, as Aunt March had done, so that if she did fall ill and die, her possessions might be justly and generously divided. It cost her a pang even to think of giving up the little treasures which in her eyes were as precious as the old lady's jewels.

During one of her play hours she wrote out the important document as well as she could, with some help from Esther as to certain legal terms, and when the good-natured Frenchwoman had signed her name, Amy felt relieved and laid it by to show Laurie, whom she wanted as a second witness. As it was a rainy day, she went upstairs to amuse herself in one of the large chambers, and took Polly with her for company. In this room there was a wardrobe full of old-fashioned costumes with which Esther allowed her to play, and it was her favorite amusement to array herself in the faded brocades, and parade up and down before the long mirror, making stately curtsies, and sweeping her train about with a rustle which delighted her ears. So busy was she on this day that she did not hear Laurie's ring nor see his face peeping in at her as she gravely promenaded to and fro, flirting her fan and tossing her head, on which she wore a great pink turban, contrasting oddly with her blue brocade dress and yellow quilted petticoat. She was obliged to walk carefully, for she had on highheeled shoes, and, as Laurie told Jo afterward, it was a comical sight to see her mince along in her gay suit, with Polly sidilng and bridling just behind her, imitating her as well as he could, and occasionally stopping to laugh or exclaim, "Ain't we fine? Get along, you fright! Hold your tongue! Kiss me, dear! Ha! Ha!"

Having with difficulty restrained an explosion of merriment, lest it should offend her majesty, Laurie tapped and was graciously received.

"Sit down and rest while I put these things away, then I want to consult you about a very serious matter," said Amy, when she had shown her splendor and driven Polly into a cor ner. "That bird is the trial of my life," she continued, removing the pink mountain from her head, while Laurie seated himself astride a chair. "Yesterday, when Aunt was asleep and I was trying to be as still as a mouse, Polly began to squall and flap about in his cage, so I went to let him out, and found a big spider there. I poked it out, and it ran under the bookcase. Polly marched straight after it, stooped down and peeped under the bookcase, saying, in his funny way, with a cock of his eye, 'Come out and take a walk, my dear.' I couldn't help laughing, which made Poll swear, and Aunt woke up and scolded us both."

"Did the spider accept the old fellow's invitation?" asked Laurie, yawning.

"Yes, out it came, and away ran Polly, frightened to death, and scrambled up on Aunt's chair, calling out, 'Catch her! Catch her! Catch her!' as I chased the spider."

"That's a lie! Oh, lor!" cried the parrot, pecking at Laurie's toes.

"I'd wring your neck if you were mine, you old torment," cried Laurie, shaking his fist at the bird, who put his head on one side and gravely croaked, "Allyluyer! Bless your buttons, dear!"

"Now I'm ready," said Amy, shutting the wardrobe and taking a piece of paper out of her pocket. "I want you to read that, please, and tell me if it is legal and right. I felt I ought to do it, for life is uncertain and I don't want any ill feeling over my tomb."

Laurie bit his lips, and turning a little from the pensive speaker, read the following document, with praiseworthy gravity, considering the spelling:

MY LAST WILL AND TESTIMENT

I, Amy Curtis March, being in my sane mind, go give and bequeethe all my earthly property—viz.to wit:—namely

To my father, my best pictures, sketches, maps, and works of art, including frames. Also my $100, to do what he likes with.

To my mother, all my clothes, except the blue apron with pockets—also my likeness, and my medal, with much love.

To my dear sister Margaret, I give my turkquoise ring (if I get it), also my green box with the doves on it, also my; piece of real lace for her neck, and my sketch of her as a memorial of her 'little girl'.

To Jo I leave my breastpin, the one mended with sealing wax, also my bronze inkstand—she lost the cover—and my most precious plaster rabbit, because I am sorry I burned up her story.

To Beth (if she lives after me) I give my dolls and the little bureau, my fan, my linen collars and my new slippers if she can wear them being thin when she gets well. And I herewith also leave her my regret that I ever made fun of old Joanna.

To my friend and neighbor Theodore Laurence I bequeethe my paper mashay portfolio, my clay model of a horse though he did say it hadn't any neck. Also in return for his great kindness in the hour of affliction any one of my artistic works he likes, Noter Dame is the best.

To our venerable benefactor Mr. Laurence I leave my purple box with a looking glass in the cover which will be nice for his pens and remind him of the departed girl who thanks him for his favors to her family, especially Beth.

I wish my favorite playmate Kitty Bryant to have the blue silk apron and my gold-bead ring with a kiss.

To Hannah I give the bandbox she wanted and all the patchwork I leave hoping she 'will remember me, when it you see'.

And now having disposed of my most valuable property I hope all will be satisfied and not blame the dead. I forgive everyone, and trust we may all meet when the trump shall sound. Amen.

To this will and testiment I set my hand and seal on this 20th day of Nov. Anni Domino 1861.

Amy Curtis March

Witnesses:

Estelle Valnor, Theodore Laurence.

The last name was written in pencil, and Amy explained that he was to rewrite it in ink and seal it up for her properly.

"What put it into your head? Did anyone tell you about Beth's giving away her things?" asked Laurie soberly, as Amy laid a bit of red tape, with sealing wax, a taper, and a standish before him.

She explained and then asked anxiously, "What about Beth?"

"I'm sorry I spoke, but as I did, I'll tell you. She felt so ill one day that she told Jo she wanted to give her piano to Meg, her cats to you, and the poor old doll to Jo, who would love it for her sake. She was sorry she had so little to give, and left locks of hair to the rest of us, and her best love to Grandpa. She never thought of a will."

Laurie was signing and sealing as he spoke, and did not look up till a great tear dropped on the paper. Amy's face was full of trouble, but she only said, "Don't people put sort of postscripts to their wills, sometimes?"

"Yes, 'codicils', they call them."

"Put one in mine then, that I wish all my curls cut off, and given round to my friends. I forgot it, but I want it done though it will spoil my looks."

Laurie added it, smiling at Amy's last and greatest sacrifice. Then he amused her for an hour, and was much interested in all her trials. But when he came to go, Amy held him back to whisper with trembling lips, "Is there really any danger about Beth?"

"I'm afraid there is, but we must hope for the best, so don't cry, dear." And Laurie put his arm about her with a brotherly gesture which was very comforting.

When he had gone, she went to her little chapel, and sitting in the twilight, prayed for Beth, with streaming tears and an aching heart, feeling that a million turquoise rings would not console her for the loss of her gentle little sister.

Chapter Twenty

I don't think I have any words in which to tell the meeting of the mother and daughters. Such hours are beautiful to live, but very hard to describe, so I will leave it to the imagination of my readers, merely saying that the house was full of genuine happiness, and that Meg's tender hope was realized, for when Beth woke from that long, healing sleep, the first objects on which her eyes fell were the little rose and Mother's face. Too weak to wonder at anything, she only smiled and nestled close in the loving arms about her, feeling that the hungry longing was satisfied at last. Then she slept again, and the girls waited upon their mother, for she would not unclasp the thin hand which clung to hers even in sleep.

Hannah had 'dished up' and astonishing breakfast for the traveler, finding it impossible to vent her excitement in any other way, and Meg and Jo fed their mother like dutiful young storks, while they listened to her whispered account of Father's state, Mr. Brooke's promise to stay and nurse him, the delays which the storm occasioned on the homeward journey, and the unspeakable comfort Laurie's hopeful face had given her when she arrived, worn out with fatigue, anxiety, and cold.

What a strange yet pleasant day that was. So brilliant and gay without, for all the world seemed abroad to welcome the first snow. So quiet and reposeful within, for everyone slept, spent with watching, and a Sabbath stillness reigned through the house, while nodding Hannah mounted guard at the door. With a blissful sense of burdens lifted off, Meg and Jo closed their weary eyes, and lay at rest, like storm-beaten boats safe at anchor in a quiet harbor. Mrs. March would not leave Beth's side, but rested in the big chair, waking often to look at, touch, and brood over her child, like a miser over some recovered treasure.

Laurie meanwhile posted off to comfort Amy, and told his story so well that Aunt March actually 'sniffed' herself, and never once said "I told you so". Amy came out so strong on this occasion that I think the good thoughts in the little chapel really began to bear fruit. She dried her tears quickly, restrained her impatience to see her mother, and never even thought of the turquoise ring, when the old lady heartily agreed in Laurie's opinion, that she behaved 'like a capital little woman'. Even Polly seemed impressed, for he called her a good girl, blessed her buttons, and begged her to "come and take a walk, dear", in his most affable tone. She would very gladly have gone out to enjoy the bright wintry weather, but discovering that Laurie was dropping with sleep in spite of manful efforts to conceal the fact, she persuaded him to rest on the sofa, while she wrote a note to her mother. She was a long time about it, and when she returned, he was stretched out with both arms under his head, sound asleep, while Aunt March had pulled down the curtains and sat doing nothing in an unusual fit of benignity.

After a while, they began to think he was not going to wake up till night, and I'm not sure that he would, had he not been effectually roused by Amy's cry of joy at sight of her mother. There probably were a good many happy little girls in and about the city that day, but it is my private opinion that Amy was the happiest of all, when she sat in her mother's lap and told her trials, receiving consolation and compensation in the shape of approving smiles and fond caresses. They were alone together in the chapel, to which her mother did not object when its purpose was explained to her.

"On the contrary, I like it very much, dear," looking from the dusty rosary to the well-worn little book, and the lovely picture with its garland of evergreen. "It is an excellent plan to have some place where we can go to be quiet, when things vex or grieve us. There are a good many hard times in this life of ours, but we can always bear them if we ask help in the right way. I think my little girl is learning this."

"Yes, Mother, and when I go home I mean to have a corner in the big closet to put my books and the copy of that picture which I've tried to make. The woman's face is not good, it's too beautiful for me to draw, but the baby is done better, and I love it very much. I like to think He was a little child once, for then I don't seem so far away, and that helps me."

As Amy pointed to the smiling Christ child on his Mother's knee, Mrs. March saw something on the lifted hand that made her smile. She said nothing, but Amy understood the look, and after a minute's pause, she added gravely, "I wanted to speak to you about this, but I forgot it. Aunt gave me the ring today. She called me to her and kissed me, and put it on my finger, and said I was a credit to her, and she'd like to keep me always. She gave that funny guard to keep the turquoise on, as it's too big. I'd like to wear them Mother, can I?"

"They are very pretty, but I think you're rather too young for such ornaments, Amy," said Mrs. March, looking at the plump little hand, with the band of sky-blue stones on the forefinger, and the quaint guard formed of two tiny golden hands clasped together.

"I'll try not to be vain," said Amy. "I don't think I like it only because it's so pretty, but I want to wear it as the girl in the story wore her bracelet, to remind me of something."

"Do you mean Aunt March?" asked her mother, laughing.

"No, to remind me not to be selfish." Amy looked so earnest and sincere about it that her mother stopped laughing, and listened respectfully to the little plan.

"I've thought a great deal lately about my 'bundle of naughties', and being selfish is the largest one in it, so I'm going to try hard to cure it, if I can. Beth isn't selfish, and that's the reason everyone loves her and feels so bad at the thoughts of losing her. People wouldn't feel so bat about me if I was sick, and I don't deserve to have them, but I'd like to be loved and missed by a great many friends, so I'm going to try and be like Beth all I can. I'm apt to forget my resolutions, but if I had something always about me to remind me, I guess I should do better. May we try this way?"

"Yes, but I have more faith in the corner of the big closet. Wear your ring, dear, and do your best. I think you will prosper, for the sincere wish to be good is half the battle. Now I must go back to Beth. Keep up your heart, little daughter, and we will soon have you home again."

That evening while Meg was writing to her father to report the traveler's safe arrival, Jo slipped upstairs into Beth's room, and finding her mother in her usual place, stood a minute twisting her fingers in her hair, with a worried gesture and an undecided look.

"What is it, deary?' asked Mrs. March, holding out her hand, with a face which invited confidence.

"I want to tell you something, Mother."

"About Meg?"

"How quickly you guessed! Yes, it's about her, and though it's a little thing, it fidgets me."

"Beth is asleep. Speak low, and tell me all about it. That Moffat hasn't been here, I hope?" asked Mrs. March rather sharply.

"No. I should have shut the door in his face if he had," said Jo, settling herself on the floor at her mother's feet. "Last summer Meg left a pair of gloves over at the Laurences' and only one was returned. We forgot about it, till Teddy told me that Mr. Brooke owned that he liked Meg but didn't dare say so, she was so young and he so poor. Now, isn't it a dreadful state of things?"

"Do you think Meg cares for him?" asked Mrs. March, with an anxious look.

"Mercy me! I don't know anything about love and such nonsense!" cried Jo, with a funny mixture of interest and contempt. "In novels, the girls show it by starting and blushing, fainting away, growing thin, and acting like fools. Now Meg does not do anything of the sort. She eats and drinks and sleeps like a sensible creature, she looks straight in my face when I talk about that man, and only blushes a little bit when Teddy jokes about lovers. I forbid him to do it, but he doesn't mind me as he ought."

"Then you fancy that Meg is not interested in John?'

"Who?" cried Jo, staring.

"Mr. Brooke. I call him 'John' now. We fell into the way of doing so at the hospital, and he likes it."

"Oh, dear! I know you'll take his part. He's been good to Father, and you won't send him away, but let Meg marry him, if she wants to. Mean thing! To go petting Papa and helping you, just to wheedle you into liking him." And Jo pulled her hair again with a wrathful tweak.

"My dear, don't get angry about it, and I will tell you how it happened. John went with me at Mr. Laurence's request, and was so devoted to poor Father that we couldn't help getting fond of him. He was perfectly open and honorable about Meg, for he told us he loved her, but would earn a comfortable home before he asked her to marry him. He only wanted our leave to love her and work for her, and the right to make her love him if he could. He is a truly excellent young man, and we could not refuse to listen to him, but I will not consent to Meg's engaging herself so young."

"Of course not. It would be idiotic! I knew there was mischief brewing. I felt it, and now it's worse than I imagined. I just wish I could marry Meg myself, and keep her safe in the family."

This odd arrangement made Mrs. March smile, but she said gravely, "Jo, I confide in you and don't wish you to say anything to Meg yet. When John comes back, and I see them together, I can judge better of her feelings toward him."

"She'll see those handsome eyes that she talks about, and then it will be all up with her. She's got such a soft heart, it will melt like butter in the sun if anyone looks sentimentlly at her. She read the short reports he sent more than she did your letters, and pinched me when I spoke of it, and likes brown eyes, and doesn't think John an ugly name, and she'll go and fall in love, and there's an end of peace and fun, and cozy times together. I see it all! They'll go lovering around the house, and we shall have to dodge. Meg will be absorbed and no good to me any more. Brooke will scratch up a fortune somehow, carry her off, and make a hole in the family, and I shall break my heart, and everything will be abominably uncomfortable. Oh, dear me! Why weren't we all boys, then there wouldn't be any bother."

Jo leaned her chin on her knees in a disconsolate attitude and shook her fist at the reprehensible John. Mrs. March sighed, and Jo looked up with an air of relief.

"You don't like it, Mother? I'm glad of it. Let's send him about his business, and not tell Meg a word of it, but all be happy together as we always have been."

"I did wrong to sigh, Jo. It is natural and right you should all go to homes of your own in time, but I do want to keep my girls as long as I can, and I am sorry that this happened so soon, for Meg is only seventeen and it will be some years before John can make a home for her. Your father and I have agreed that she shall not bind herself in any way, nor be married, before twenty. If she and John love one another, they can wait, and test the love by doing so. She is conscientious, and I have no fear of her treating him unkindly. My pretty, tender hearted girl! I hope things will go happily with her."

"Hadn't you rather have her marry a rich man?" asked Jo, as her mother's voice faltered a little over the last words.

"Money is a good and useful thing, Jo, and I hope my girls will never feel the need of it too bitterly not be tempted by too much. I should like to know that John was firmly established in some good business, which gave him an income large enough to keep free from debt and make Meg comfortable. I'm not ambitious for a splendid fortune, a fashionable position, or a great name for my girls. If rank and money come with love and virtue, also, I should accept them gratefully, and enjoy your good fortune, but I know, by experience, how much genuine happiness can be had in a plain little house, where the daily bread is earned, and some privations give sweetness to the few pleasures. I am content to see Meg begin humbly, for if I am not mistaken, she will be rich in the possession of a good man's heart, and that is better than a fortune."

"I understand, Mother, and quite agree, but I'm disappointed about Meg, for I'd planned to have her marry Teddy by-and-by and sit in the lap of luxury all her days. Wouldn't it be nice?" asked Jo, looking up with a brighter face.

"He is younger than she, you know," began Mrs. March, but Jo broke in . . .

"Only a little, he's old for his age, and tall, and can be quite grown-up in his manners if he likes. Then he's rich and generous and good, and loves us all, and I say it's a pity my plan is spoiled."

"I'm afraid Laurie is hardly grown-up enough for Meg, and altogether too much of a weathercock just now for anyone to depend on. Don't make plans, Jo, but let time and their own hearts mate your friends. We can't meddle safely in such matters, and had better not get 'romantic rubbish' as you call it, into our heads, lest it spoil our friendship."

"Well, I won't, but I hate to see things going all crisscross and getting snarled up, when a pull her and a snip there would straighten it out. I wish wearing flatirons on our heads would keep us from growing up. But buds will be roses, and kittens cats, more's the pity!"

"What's that about flatirons and cats?" asked Meg, as she crept into the room with the finished letter in her hand.

"Only one of my stupid speeches. I'm going to bed. Come, Peggy," said Jo, unfolding herself like an animated puzzle.

"Quite right, and beautifully written. Please add that I send my love to John," said Mrs. March, as she glanced over the letter and gave it back.

"Do you call him 'John'?" asked Meg, smiling, with her innocent eyes looking down into her mother's.

"Yes, he has been like a son to us, and we are very fond of him," replied Mrs. March, returning the look with a keen one.

"I'm glad of that, he is so lonely. Good night, Mother, dear. It is so inexpressibly comfortable to have you here," was Meg's answer.

The kiss her mother gave her was a very tender one, and as she went away, Mrs. March said, with a mixture of satisfaction and regret, "She does not love John yet, but will soon learn to.

Chapter Twenty-One

Jo's face was a study next day, for the secret rather weighed upon her, and she found it hard not to look mysterious and important. Meg observed it, but did not trouble herself to make inquiries, for she had learned that the best way to manage Jo was by the law of contraries, so she felt sure of being told everything if she did not ask. She was rather surprised, therefore, when the silence remained unbroken, and Jo assumed a patronizing air, which decidedly aggravated Meg, who in turn assumed an air of dignified reserve and devoted herself to her mother. This left Jo to her own devices, for Mrs. March had taken her place as nurse, and bade her rest, exercise, and amuse herself after her long confinement. Amy being gone, Laurie was her only refuge, and much as she enjoyed his society, she rather dreaded him just then, for he was an incorrigible tease, and she feared he would coax the secret from her.

She was quite right, for the mischief-loving lad no sooner suspected a mystery than he set himself to find it out, and led Jo a trying life of it. He wheedled, bribed, ridiculed, threatened, and scolded; affected indifference, that he might surprise the truth from her; declared her knew, then that he didn't care; and at last, by dint of perseverance, he satisfied himself that it concerned Meg and Mr. Brooke. Feeling indignant that he was not taken into his tutor's confidence, he set his wits to work to devise some proper retaliation for the slight.

Meg meanwhile had apparently forgotten the matter and was absorbed in preparations for her father's return, but all of a sudden a change seemed to come over her, and, for a day or two, she was quite unlike herself. She started when spoken to, blushed when looked at, was very quiet, and sat over her sewing, with a timid, troubled look on her face. To her mother's inquiries she answered that she was quite well, and Jo's she silenced by begging to be let alone.

"She feels it in the air—love, I mean—and she's going very fast. She's got most of the symptoms—is twittery and cross, doesn't eat, lies awake, and mopes in corners. I caught her singing that song he gave her, and once she said 'John', as you do, and then turned as red as a poppy. whatever shall we do?" said Jo, looking ready for any measures, however violent.

"Nothing but wait. Let her alone, be kind and patient, and Father's coming will settle everything," replied her mother.

"Here's a note to you, Meg, all sealed up. How odd! Teddy never seals mine," said Jo next day, as she distributed the contents of the little post office.

Mrs. March and Jo were deep in their own affairs, when a sound from Meg made them look up to see her staring at her note with a frightened face.

"My child, what is it?" cried her mother, running to her, while Jo tried to take the paper which had done the mischief.

"It's all a mistake, he didn't send it. Oh, Jo, how could you do it?" and Meg hid her face in her hands, crying as if her heart were quite broken.

"Me! I've done nothing! What's she talking about?" cried Jo, bewildered.

Meg's mild eyes kindled with anger as she pulled a crumpled note from her pocket and threw it at Jo, saying reproachfully, "You wrote it, and that bad boy helped you. How could you be so rude, so mean, and cruel to us both?"

Jo hardly heard her, for she and her mother were reading the note, which was written in a peculiar hand.

> "My Dearest Margaret,
>
> "I can no longer restrain my passion, and must know my fate before I return. I dare not tell your parents yet, but I think they would consent if they knew that we adored one another. Mr. Laurence will help me to some good place, and then, my sweet girl, you will make me happy. I implore you to say nothing to your family yet, but to send one word of hope through Laurie to,
>
> "Your devoted John."

"Oh, the little villain! That's the way he meant to pay me for keeping my word to Mother. I'll give him a hearty scolding and bring him over to beg pardon," cried Jo, burning to execute immediate justice. But her mother held her back, saying, with a look she seldom wore . . .

"Stop, Jo, you must clear yourself first. You have played so many pranks that I am afraid you have had a hand in this."

"On my word, Mother, I haven't! I never saw that note before, and don't know anything about it, as true as I live!" said

Jo, so earnestly that they believed her. "If I had taken part in it I'd have done it better than this, and have written a sensible note. I should think you'd have known Mr. Brooke wouldn't write such stuff as that," she added, scornfully tossing down the paper.

"It's like his writing," faltered Meg, comparing it with the note in her hand. "Oh, Meg, you didn't answer it?" cried Mrs. March quickly.

"Yes, I did!" and Meg hid her face again, overcome with shame.

"Here's a scrape! Do let me bring that wicked boy over to explain and be lectured. I can't rest till I get hold of him." And Jo made for the door again.

"Hush! Let me handle this, for it is worse than I thought. Margaret, tell me the whole story," commanded Mrs. March, sitting down by Meg, yet keeping hold of Jo, lest she should fly off.

"I received the first letter from Laurie, who didn't look as if he knew anything about it," began Meg, without looking up. "I was worried at first and meant to tell you, then I remembered how you liked Mr. Brooke, so I thought you wouldn't mind if I kept my little secret for a few days. I'm so silly that I liked to think no one knew, and while I was deciding what to say, I felt like the girls in books, who have such things to do. Forgive me, Mother, I'm paid for my silliness now. I never can look him in the face again."

"What did you say to him?' asked Mrs. March.

"I only said I was too young to do anything about it yet, that I didn't wish to have secrets from you, and he must speak to father. I was very grateful for his kindness, and would be his friend, but nothing more, for a long while."

Mrs. March smiled, as if well pleased, and Jo clapped her hands, exclaiming, with a laugh, "You are almost equal to Caroline Percy, who was a pattern of prudence! Tell on, Meg. What did he say to that?"

"He writes in a different way entirely, telling me that he never sent any love letter at all, and is very sorry that my roguish sister, Jo, should take liberties with our names. It's very kind and respectful, but think how dreadful for me!"

Meg leaned against her mother, looking the image of despair, and Jo tramped about the room, calling Laurie names. All of a sudden she stopped, caught up the two notes, and after looking at them closely, said decidedly, "I don't believe Brooke ever saw either of these letters. Teddy wrote both, and keeps yours to crow over me with because I wouldn't tell him my secret."

"Don't have any secrets, Jo. Tell it to Mother and keep out of trouble, as I should have done," said Meg warningly.

"Bless you, child! Mother told me."

"That will do, Jo. I'll comfort Meg while you go and get Laurie. I shall sift the matter to the bottom, and put a stop to such pranks at once." Away ran Jo, and Mrs. March gently told Meg Mr. Brooke's real feelings. "Now, dear, what are your own? Do you love him enough to wait till her can make a home for you, or will you keep yourself quite free for the present?"

"I've been so scared and worried, I don't want to have anything to do with lovers for a long while, perhaps never,"

answered Meg petulantly. "If John doesn't know anything about this nonsense, don't tell him, and make Jo and Laurie hold their tongues. I won't be deceived and plagued and made a fool of. It's a shame!"

Seeing Meg's usually gentle temper was roused and her pride hurt by this mischievous joke, Mrs. March soothed her by promises of entire silence and great discretion for the future. The instant Laurie's step was heard in the hall, Meg fled into the study, and Mrs. March received the culprit alone. Jo had not told him why he was wanted, fearing he wouldn't come, but he knew the minute he saw Mrs. March's face, and stood twirling his hat with a guilty air which convicted him at once. Jo was dismissed, but chose to march up and down the hall like a sentinel, having some fear that the prisoner might bolt. The sound of voices in the parlor rose and fell for half an hour, but what happened during that interview the girls never knew.

When they were called in, Laurie was standing by their mother with such a penitent face that Jo forgave him on the spot, but did not think it wise to betray the fact. Meg received his humble apology, and was much comforted by the assurance that Brooke knew nothing of the joke.

"I'll never tell him to my dying day, wild horses shan't drag it out of me, so you'll forgive me, Meg, and I'll do anything to show how out-and-out sorry I am," he added, looking very much ashamed of himself.

"I'll try, but it was a very ungentlemanly thing to do, I didn't think you could be so sly and malicious, Laurie," replied Meg, trying to hid her maidenly confusion under a gravely reproachful air.

"It was altogether abominable, and I don't deserve to be spoken to for a month, but you will, though, won't you?" And Laurie folded his hands together with such and imploring gesture, as he spoke in his irresistibly persuasive tone, that it was impossible to frown upon him in spite of his scandalous behavior.

Meg pardoned him, and Mrs. March's grave face relaxed, in spite of her efforts to keep sober, when she heard him declare that he would atone for his sins by all sorts of penances, and abase himself like a worm before the injured damsel.

Jo stood aloof, meanwhile, trying to harden her heart against him, and succeeding only in primming up her face into an expression of entire disapprobation. Laurie looked at her once or twice, but as she showed no sign of relenting, he felt injured, and turned his back on her till the others were done with him, when he made her a low bow and walked off without a word.

As soon as he had gone, she wished she had been more forgiving, and when Meg and her mother went upstairs, she felt lonely and longed for Teddy. After resisting for some time, she yielded to the impulse, and armed with a book to return, went over to the big house.

"Is Mr. Laurence in?" asked Jo, of a housemaid, who was coming downstairs.

"Yes, Miss, but I don't believe he's seeable just yet."

"Why not? Is he ill?"

"La, no Miss, but he's had a scene with Mr. Laurie, who is in one of his tantrums about something, which vexes the old gentleman, so I dursn't go nigh him."

"Where is Laurie?'

"Shut up in his room, and he won't answer, though I've been a-tapping. I don't know what's to become of the dinner, for it's ready, and there's no one to eat it."

"I'll go and see what the matter is. I'm not afraid of either of them."

Up went Jo, and knocked smartly on the door of Laurie's little study.

"Stop that, or I'll open the door and make you!" called out the young gentleman in a threatening tone.

Jo immediately knocked again. The door flew open, and in she bounced before Laurie could recover from his surprise. Seeing that he really was out of temper, Jo, who knew how to manage him, assumed a contrite expression, and going artistically down upon her knees, said meekly, "Please forgive me for being so cross. I came to make it up, and can't go away till I have."

"It's all right. Get up, and don't be a goose, Jo," was the cavalier reply to her petition.

"Thank you, I will. Could I ask what's the matter? You don't look exactly easy in your mind."

"I've been shaken, and I won't bear it!" growled Laurie indignantly.

"Who did it?" demanded Jo.

"Grandfather. If it had been anyone else I'd have . . ." And the injured youth finished his sentence by an energetic gesture of the right arm.

"That's nothing. I often shake you, and you don't mind," said Jo soothingly.

"Pooh! You're a girl, and it's fun, but I'll allow no man to shake me!"

"I don't think anyone would care to try it, if you looked as much like a thundercloud as you do now. Why were you treated so?"

"Just because I wouldn't say what your mother wanted me for. I'd promised not to tell, and of course I wasn't going to break my word."

"Couldn't you satisfy your grandpa in any other way?"

"No, he would have the truth, the whole truth, and nothing but the truth. I'd have told my part of the scrape, if I could without bringing Meg in. As I couldn't, I held my tongue, and bore the scolding till the old gentleman collared me. Then I bolted, for fear I should forget myself."

"It wasn't nice, but he's sorry, I know, so go down and make up. I'll help you."

"Hanged if I do! I'm not going to be lectured and pummelled by everyone, just for a bit of a frolic. I was sorry about Meg, and begged pardon like a man, but I won't do it again, when I wasn't in the wrong."

"He didn't know that."

"He ought to trust me, and not act as if I was a baby. It's no use, Jo, he's got to learn that I'm able to take care of myself, and don't need anyone's apron string to hold on by." "What pepper pots you are! " sighed Jo. "How do you mean to settle this affair?"

"Well, he ought to beg pardon, and believe me when I say I can't tell him what the fuss's about."

"Bless you! He won't do that."

"I won't go down till he does."

"Now, Teddy, be sensible. Let it pass, and I'll explain what I can. You can't stay here, so what's the use of being melodramatic?"

"I don't intend to stay here long, anyway. I'll slip off and take a journey somewhere, and when Grandpa misses me he'll come round fast enough." "I dare say, but you ought not to go and worry him."

"Don't preach. I'll go to Washington and see Brooke. It's gay there, and I'll enjoy myself after the troubles."

"What fun you'd have! I wish I could run off too," said Jo, forgetting her part of mentor in lively visions of martial life at the capital.

"Come on, then! Why not? You go and surprise your father, and I'll stir up old Brooke. It would be a glorious joke. Let's do it, Jo. We'll leave a letter saying we are all right, and trot off at once. I've got money enough. It will do you good, and no harm, as you go to your father."

For a moment Jo looked as if she would agree, for wild as the plan was, it just suited her. She was tired of care and confinement, longed for change, and thoughts of her father blended temptingly with the novel charms of camps and hospitals, liberty and fun. Her eyes kindled as they turned wistfully toward the window, but they fell on the old house opposite, and she shook her head with sorrowful decision.

"If I was a boy, we'd run away together, and have a capital time, but as I'm a miserable girl, I must be proper and stop at home. Don't tempt me, Teddy, it's a crazy plan."

"That's the fun of it," began Laurie, who had got a willful fit on him and was possessed to break out of bounds in some way.

"Hold your tongue!" cried Jo, covering her ears. "'Prunes and prisms' are my doom, and I may as well make up my mind to it. I came here to moralize, not to hear things that make me skip to think of."

"I know Meg would wet-blanket such a proposal, but I thought you had more spirit," began Laurie insinuatingly.

"Bad boy, be quiet! Sit down and think of your own sins, don't go making me add to mine. If I get your grandpa to apologize for the shaking, will you give up running away?" asked Jo seriously.

"Yes, but you won't do it," answered Laurie, who wished to make up, but felt that his outraged dignity must be appeased first.

"If I can manage the young one, I can the old one," muttered Jo, as she walked away, leaving Laurie bent over a railroad map with his head propped up on both hands.

"Come in!" And Mr. Laurence's gruff voice sounded gruffer than ever, as Jo tapped at his door.

"It's only me, Sir, come to return a book," she said blandly, as she entered.

"Want any more?" asked the old gentleman, looking grim and vexed, but trying not to show it.

"Yes, please. I like old Sam so well, I think I'll try the second volume," returned Jo, hoping to propitiate him by accepting a second dose of Boswell's Johnson, as he had recommended that lively work.

The shaggy eyebrows unbent a little as he rolled the steps toward the shelf where the Johnsonian literature was placed. Jo skipped up, and sitting on the top step, affected to be searching for her book, but was really wondering how best to introduce the dangerous object of her visit. Mr. Laurence seemed to suspect that something was brewing in her mind, for after taking several brisk turns about the room, he faced round on her, speaking so abruptly that Rasselas tumbled face downward on the floor.

"What has that boy been about? Don't try to shield him. I know he has been in mischief by the way he acted when he came home. I can't get a word from him, and when I threatened to shake the truth out of him he bolted upstairs and locked himself into his room."

"He did wrong, but we forgave him, and all promised not to say a word to anyone," began Jo reluctantly.

"That won't do. He shall not shelter himself behind a promise from you softhearted girls. If he's done anything amiss, he shall confess, beg pardon, and be punished. Out with it, Jo. I won't be kept in the dark."

Mr. Laurence looked so alarming and spoke so sharply that Jo would have gladly run away, if she could, but she was perched aloft on the steps, and he stood at the foot, a lion in the path, so she had to stay and brave it out.

"Indeed, Sir, I cannot tell. Mother forbade it. Laurie has confessed, asked pardon, and been punished quite enough. We don't keep silence to shield him, but someone else, and it will make more trouble if you interfere. Please don't. It was partly my fault, but it's all right now. So let's forget it, and talk about the RAMBLER or something pleasant."

"Hang the RAMBLER! Come down and give me your word that this harum-scarum boy of mine hasn't done anything ungrateful or impertinent. If he has, after all your kindness to him, I'll thrash him with my own hands."

The threat sounded awful, but did not alarm Jo, for she knew the irascible old gentleman would never lift a finger against his grandson, whatever he might say to the contrary. She obediently descended, and made as light of the prank as she could without betraying Meg or forgetting the truth.

"Hum . . . ha . . . well, if the boy held his tongue because he promised, and not from obstinacy, I'll forgive him. He's a stubborn fellow and hard to manage," said Mr. Laurence, rubbing up his hair till it looked as if he had been out in a gale, and smoothing the frown from his brow with an air of relief.

"So am I, but a kind word will govern me when all the king's horses and all the king's men couldn't," said Jo, trying to say a kind word for her friend, who seemed to get out of one scrape only to fall into another.

"You think I'm not kind to him, hey?" was the sharp answer.

"Oh, dear no, Sir. You are rather too kind sometimes, and then just a trifle hasty when he tries your patience. Don't you think you are?"

Jo was determined to have it out now, and tried to look quite placid, though she quaked a little after her bold speech. To her great relief and surprise, the old gentleman only threw his spectacles onto the table with a rattle and exclaimed frankly, "You're right, girl, I am! I love the boy, but he tries my patience past bearing, and I know how it will end, if we go on so."

"I'll tell you, he'll run away." Jo was sorry for that speech the minute it was made. She meant to warn him that Laurie would not bear much restraint, and hoped he would be more forebearing with the lad.

Mr. Laurence's ruddy face changed suddenly, and he sat down, with a troubled glance at the picture of a handsome man, which hung over his table. It was Laurie's father, who had run away in his youth, and married against the imperious old man's will. Jo fancied her remembered and regretted the past, and she wished she had held her tongue.

"He won't do it unless he is very much worried, and only threatens it sometimes, when he gets tired of studying. I often think I should like to, especially since my hair was cut, so if you ever miss us, you may advertise for two boys and look among the ships bound for India."

She laughed as she spoke, and Mr. Laurence looked relieved, evidently taking the whole as a joke.

"You hussy, how dare you talk in that way? Where's your respect for me, and your proper bringing up? Bless the boys and girls! What torments they are, yet we can't do without them," he said, pinching her cheeks good-humoredly. "Go and bring that boy down to his dinner, tell him it's all right, and advise him not to put on tragedy airs with his grandfather. I won't bear it."

"He won't come, Sir. He feels badly because you didn't believe him when he said he couldn't tell. I think the shaking hurt his feelings very much."

Jo tried to look pathetic but must have failed, for Mr. Laurence began to laugh, and she knew the day was won.

"I'm sorry for that, and ought to thank him for not shaking me, I suppose. What the dickens does the fellow expect?" And the old gentleman looked a trifle ashamed of his own testiness.

"If I were you, I'd write him an apology, Sir. He says he won't come down till he has one, and talks about Washington, and goes on in an absurd way. A formal apology will make him see how foolish he is, and bring him down quite amiable. Try it. He likes fun, and this was is better than talking. I'll carry it up, and teach him his duty."

Mr. Laurence gave her a sharp look, and put on his spectacles, saying slowly, "You're a sly puss, but I don't mind being managed by you and Beth. Here, give me a bit of paper, and let us have done with this nonsense."

The note was written in the terms which one gentleman would use to another after offering some deep insult. Jo dropped a kiss on the top of Mr. Laurence's bald head, and ran up to slip the apology under Laurie's door, advising him through the keyhole to be submissive, decorous, and a few other agreeable impossibilities. Finding the door locked again, she left the note to do its work, and was going quietly away, when the young gentleman slid down the banisters, and waited for her at the bottom, saying, with his most virtuous expression of countenance, "What a good fellow you are, Jo! Did you get blown up?" he added, laughing.

"No, he was pretty mild, on the whole."

"AH! I got it all round. Even you cast me off over there, and I felt just ready to go to the deuce," he began apologetically.

"Don't talk that way, turn over a new leaf and begin again, Teddy, my son."

"I keep turning over new leaves, and spoiling them, as I used to spoil my copybooks, and I make so many beginnings there never will be an end," he said dolefully.

"Go and eat your dinner, you'll feel better after it. Men always croak when they are hungry," and Jo whisked out at the front door after that.

"That's a 'label' on my 'sect'," answered Laurie, quoting Amy, as he went to partake of humble pie dutifully with his grandfather, who was quite saintly in temper and overwhelmingly respectful in manner all the rest of the day.

Everyone thought the matter ended and the little cloud blown over, but the mischief was done, for though others forgot it, Meg remembered. She never alluded to a certain person, but she thought of him a good deal, dreamed dreams more than ever, and once Jo, rummaging her sister's desk for stamps, found a bit of paper scribbled over with the words, 'Mrs. John Brooke', whereat she groaned tragically and cast it into the fire, feeling that Laurie's prank had hastened the evil day for her.

Chapter Twenty-Two

Like sunshine after a storm were the peaceful weeks which followed. The invalids improved rapidly, and Mr. March began to talk or returning early in the new year. Beth was soon able to lie on the study sofa all day, amusing herself with the well-beloved cats at first, and in time with doll's sewing, which had fallen sadly behindhand. Her once active limbs were so stiff and feeble that Jo took her for a daily airing about the house in her strong arms. Meg cheerfully blackened and burned her white hands cooking delicate messes for 'the dear', while Amy, a loyal slave of the ring, celebrated her return by giving away as many of her treasures as she could prevail on her sisters to accept.

As Christmas approached, the usual mysteries began to haunt the house, and Jo frequently convulsed the family by proposing utterly impossible or magnificently absurd ceremonies, in honor of this unusually merry Christmas. Laurie was equally impracticable, and would have had bonfires, skyrockets, and triumphal arches, if he had had his own way. After many skirmishes and snubbings, the ambitious pair were considered effectually quenched and went about with forlorn faces, which were rather belied by explosions of laughter when the two got together.

Several days of unusually mild weather fitly ushered in a splendid Christmas Day. Hannah 'felt in her bones' that it was going to be an unusually fine day, and she proved herself a true prophetess, for everybody and everything seemed bound to produce a grand success. To begin with, Mr. March wrote that he should soon be with them, then Beth felt uncommonly well that morning, and, being dressed in her mother's gift, a soft crimson merino wrapper, was borne in high triumph to the window to behold the offering of Jo and Laurie. The Unquenchables had done their best to be worthy of the name, for like elves they had worked by night and conjured up a comical surprise. Out in the garden stood a stately snow maiden, crowned with holly, bearing a basket of fruit and flowers in one hand, a great roll of music in the other, a perfect rainbow of an Afghan round her chilly shoulders, and a Christmas carol issuing from her lips on a pink paper streamer.

THE JUNGFRAU TO BETH

God bless you, dear Queen Bess! May nothing you dismay, But health and peace and happiness Be yours, this Christmas day. Here's fruit to feed our busy bee, And flowers for her nose. Here's music for her pianee, An afghan for her toes,

A portrait of Joanna, see, By Raphael No. 2, Who laboured with great industry To make it fair and true.

Accept a ribbon red, I beg, For Madam Purrer's tail, And ice cream made by lovely Peg, A Mont Blanc in a pail.

Their dearest love my makers laid Within my breast of snow. Accept it, and the Alpine maid, From Laurie and from Jo.

How Beth laughed when she saw it, how Laurie ran up and down to bring in the gifts, and what ridiculous speeches Jo made as she presented them.

"I'm so full of happiness, that if Father was only here, I couldn't hold one drop more," said Beth, quite sighing with contentment as Jo carried her off to the study to rest after the excitement, and to refresh herself with some of the delicious grapes the 'Jungfrau' had sent her.

"So am I," added Jo, slapping the pocket wherein reposed the long-desired UNDINE AND SINTRAM.

"I'm sure I am," echoed Amy, poring over the engraved copy of the Madonna and Child, which her mother had given her in a pretty frame.

"Of course I am!" cried Meg, smoothing the silvery folds of her first sild dress, for Mr. Laurence had insisted on giving it. "How can I be otherwise?" said Mrs. March gratefully, as her eyes went from her husband's letter to Beth's smiling face, and her hand carressed the brooch made of gray and golden, chestnut and dark brown hair, which the girls had just fastened on her breast.

Now and then, in this workaday world, things do happen in the delightful storybook fashion, and what a comfort it is. Half an hour after everyone had said they were so happy they could only hold one drop more, the drop came. Laurie opened the parlor door and popped his head in very quietly. He might just as well have turned a somersault and uttered an Indian war whoop, for his face was so full of suppressed excitement and his voice so treacherously joyful that everyone jumped up, though he only said, in a queer, breathless voice, "Here's another Christmas present for the March family."

Before the words were well out of his mouth, he was whisked away somehow, and in his place appeared a tall man, muffled up to the eyes, leaning on the arm of another tall man, who tried to say something and couldn't. Of course there was a general stampede, and for several minutes everybody seemed to lose their wits, for the strangest things were done, and no one said a word.

Mr. March became invisible in the embrace of four pairs of loving arms. Jo disgraced herself by nearly fainting away, and had to be doctored by Laurie in the china closet. Mr. Brooke kissed Meg entirely by mistake, as he somewhat incoherently explained. And Amy, the dignified, tumbled over a stool, and never stopping to get up, hugged and cried over her father's boots in the most touching manner. Mrs. March was the first to recover herself, and held up her hand with a warning, "Hush! Remember Beth."

But it was too late. The study door flew open, the little red wrapper appeared on the threshold, joy put strength into the feeble limbs, and Beth ran straight into her father's arms. Never mind what happened just after that, for the full hearts overflowed, washing away the bitterness of the past and leaving only the sweetness of the present.

It was not at all romantic, but a hearty laugh set everybody straight again, for Hannah was discovered behind the door, sobbing over the fat turkey, which she had forgotten to put down when she rushed up from the kitchen. As the laugh subsided, Mrs. March began to thank Mr. Brooke for his faithful care of her husband, at which Mr. Brooke suddenly remembered that Mr. March needed rest, and seizing Laurie, he precipitately retired. Then the two invalids were ordered to repose, which they did, by both sitting in one big chair and talking hard.

Mr. March told how he had longed to surprise them, and how, when the fine weather came, he had been allowed by his doctor, to take advantage of it, how devoted Brooke had been, and how he was altogether a most estimable and upright young man. Why Mr. March paused a minute just there, and after a glance at Meg, who was violently poking the fire, looked at his wife with an inquiring lift of the eyebrows, I leave you to imagine. Also why Mrs. March gently nodded her head and asked, rather abruptly, if he wouldn't like to have something to eat. Jo saw and understood the look, and she stalked grimly away to get wine and beef tea, muttering to herself as she slammed the door, "I hate estimable young men with brown eyes!"

There never was such a Christmas dinner as they had that day. The fat turkey was a sight to behold, when Hannah sent him up, stuffed, browned, and decorated. So was the plum pudding, which melted in one's mouth, likewise the jellies, in which

Amy reveled like a fly in a honeypot. Everything turned out well, which was a mercy, Hannah said, "For my mind was that flustered, Mum, that it's a merrycle I didn't roast the pudding, and stuff the turkey with raisins, let alone bilin' of it in a cloth."

Mr. Laurence and his grandson dined with them, also Mr. Brooke, at whom Jo glowered darkly, to Laurie's infinite amusement. Two easy chairs stood side by side at the head of the table, in which sat Beth and her father, feasting modestly on chicken and a little fruit. They drank healths, told stories, sang songs, 'reminisced', as the old folks say, and had a thoroughly good time. A sleigh ride had been planned, but the girls would not leave their father, so the guests departed early, and as twilight gathered, the happy family sat together round the fire.

"Just a year ago we were groaning over the dismal Christmas we expected to have. Do you remember?" asked Jo, breaking a short pause which had followed a long conversation about many things.

"Rather a pleasant year on the whole!" said Meg, smiling at the fire, and congratulating herself on having treated Mr. Brooke with dignity.

"I think it's been a pretty hard one," observed Amy, watching the light shine on her ring with thoughtful eyes.

"i'm glad it's over, because we've got you back," whispered Beth, who sat on her father's knee.

"Rather a rough road for you to travel, my little pilgrims, especially the latter part of it. But you have got on bravely, and I think the burdens are in a fair way to tumble off very soon," said Mr. March, looking with fatherly satisfaction at the four young faces gathered round him.

"How do you know? Did Mother tell you?' asked Jo.

"Not much. Straws show which way the wind blows, and I've made several discoveries today."

"Oh, tell us what they are!" cried Meg, who sat beside him.

"Here is one." And taking up the hand which lay on the arm of his chair, he pointed to the roughened forefinger, a burn on the back, and two or three little hard spots on the palm. "I remember a time when this hand was white and smooth, and your first care was to keep it so. It was very pretty then, but to me it is much prettier now, for in this seeming blemishes I read a little history. A burnt offering has been made to vanity, this hardened palm has earned something better than blisters, and I'm sure the sewing done by these pricked fingers will last a long time, so much good will went into the stitches. Meg, my dear, I value the womanly skill which keeps home happy more than white hands or fashionable accomplishments. I'm proud to shake this good, industrious little hand, and hope I shall not soon be asked to give it away."

If Meg had wanted a reward for hours of patient labor, she received it in the hearty pressure of her father's hand and the approving smile he gave her.

"What about Jo? Please say something nice, for she has tried so hard and been so very, very good to me," said Beth in her father's ear.

He laughed and looked across at the tall girl who sat opposite, with and unusually mild expression in her face.

"In spite of the curly crop, I don't see the 'son Jo' whom I left a year ago," said Mr. March. "I see a young lady who pins her collar straight, laces her boots neatly, and neither whistles, talks slang, nor lies on the rug as she used to do. Her face is rather thin and pale just now, with watching and anxiety, but I like to look at it, for it has grown gentler, and her voice is lower. She doesn't bounce, but moves quietly, and takes care of a certain little person in a motherly way which delights me. I rather miss my wild girl, but if I get a strong, helpful, tenderhearted woman in her place, I shall feel quite satisfied. I don't know whether the shearing sobered our black sheep, but I do know that in all

Washington I couldn't find anything beautiful enough to be bought with the five-and-twenty dollars my good girl sent me."

Jo's keen eyes were rather dim for a minute, and her thin face grew rosy in the firelight as she received her father's praise, feeling that she did deserve a portion of it.

"Now, Beth," said Amy, longing for her turn, but ready to wait.

"There's so little of her, I'm afraid to say much, for fear she will slip away altogether, though she is not so shy as she used to be," began their father cheerfully. But recollecting how nearly he had lost her, he held her close, saying tenderly, with her cheek against his own, "I've got you safe, my Beth, and I'll keep you so, please God."

After a minute's silence, he looked down at Amy, who sat on the cricket at his feet, and said, with a caress of the shining hair . . .

"I observed that Amy took drumsticks at dinner, ran errands for her mother all the afternoon, gave Meg her place tonight, and has waited on every on with patience and good humor. I also observe that she does not fret much nor look in the glass, and has not even mentioned a very pretty ring which she wears, so I conclude that she has learned to think of other people more and of herself less, and has decided to try and mold her character as carefully as she molds her little clay figures. I am glad of this, for though I should be very proud of a graceful statue made by her, I shall be infinitely prouder of a lovable daughter with a talent for making life beautiful to herself and others."

"What are you thinking of, Beth?" asked Jo, when Amy had thanked her father and told about her ring.

"I read in PILGRIM'S PROGRESS today how, after many troubles, christian and Hopeful came to a pleasant green meadow where lilies bloomed all year round, and there they rested happily, as we do now, before they went on to their journey's end," answered Beth, adding, as she slipped out of her father's arms and went to the instrument, "It's singing time now, and I want to be in my old place. I'll try to sing the song of the shepherd boy which the Pilgrims heard. I made the music for Father, because he likes the verses."

So, sitting at the dear little piano, Beth softly touched the keys, and in the sweet voice they had never thought to hear again, sang to her own accompaniment the quaint hymn, which was a singularly fitting song for her.

> He that is down need fear no fall, He that is low no pride.
> He that is humble ever shall Have God to be his guide.
>
> I am content with what I have, Little be it, or much. And, Lord! Contentment still I crave, Because Thou savest such.
>
> Fulness to them a burden is, That go on pilgrimage. Here little, and hereafter bliss, Is best from age to age!

Chapter Twenty-Three

Like bees swarming after their queen, mother and daughters hovered about Mr. March the next day, neglecting everything to look at, wait upon, and listen to the new invalid, who was in a fair way to be killed by kindness. As he sat propped up in a big chair by Beth's sofa, with the other three close by, and Hannah popping in her head now and then 'to peek at the dear man', nothing seemed needed to complete their happiness. But something was needed, and the elder ones felt it, though none confessed the fact. Mr. and Mrs. March looked at one another with an anxious expression, as their eyes followed Meg. Jo had sudden fits of sobriety, and was seen to shake her fist at Mr.

Brooke's umbrella, which had been left in the hall. Meg was absent-minded, shy, and silent, started when the bell rang, and colored when John's name was mentioned. Amy said, "Everyone seemed waiting for something, and couldn't settle down, which was queer, since Father was safe at home," and Beth innocently wondered why their neighbors didn't run over as usual.

Laurie went by in the afternoon, and seeing Meg at the window, seemed suddenly possessed with a melodramatic fit, for he fell down on one knee in the snow, beat his breast, tore his hair, and clasped his hands imploringly, as if begging some boon. And when Meg told him to behave himself and go away, he wrung imaginary tears out of his handkerchief, and staggered round the corner as if in utter despair.

"What does the goose mean?" said Meg, laughing and trying to look unconscious.

"He's showing you how your John will go on by-and-by. Touchin, isn't it?" answered Jo scornfully.

"Don't say my John, it isn't proper or true," but Meg's voice lingered over the words as if they sounded pleasant to her. "Please don't plague me, Jo, I've told you I don't care much about him, and there isn't to be anything said, but we are all to be friendly, and go on as before."

"We can't, for something has been said, and Laurie's mischief has spoiled you for me. I see it, and so does Mother. You are not like your old self a bit, and seem ever so far away from me. I don't mean to plague you and will bear it like a man, but I do wish it was all settled. I hate to wait, so if you mean ever to do it, make haste and have it over quickly," said Jo pettishly.

"I can't say anything till he speaks, and he won't, because Father said I was too young," began Meg, bending over her work with a queer little smile, which suggested that she did not quite agree with her father on that point.

"If he did speak, you wouldn't know what to say, but would cry or blush, or let him have his own way, instead of giving a good, decided no."

"I'm not so silly and weak as you think. I know just what I should say, for I've planned it all, so I needn't be taken unawares. There's no knowing what may happen, and I wished to be prepared."

Jo couldn't help smiling at the important air which Meg had unconsciously assumed and which was as becoming as the pretty color varying in her cheeks.

"Would you mind telling me what you'd say?" asked Jo more respectfully.

"Not at all. You are sixteen now, quite old enough to be my confidente, and my experience will be useful to you by-and-by, perhaps, in your own affairs of this sort."

"Don't mean to have any. It's fun to watch other people philander, but I should feel like a fool doing it myself," said Jo, looking alarmed at the thought.

"I think not, if you liked anyone very much, and he liked you." Meg spoke as if to herself, and glanced out at the lane where she had often seen lovers walking together in the summer twilight.

"I thought you were going to tell your speech to that man," said Jo, rudely shortening her sister's little reverie.

"Oh, I should merely say, quite calmly and decidedly, 'Thank you, Mr. Brooke, you are very kind, but I agree with Father that I am too young to enter into any engagement at present, so please say no more, but let us be friends as we were.'"

"Hum, that's stiff and cool enough! I don't believe you'll ever say it, and I know he won't be satisfied if you do. If he goes on like the rejected lovers in books, you'll give in, rather than hurt his feelings."

"No, I won't. I shall tell him I've made up my mind, and shall walk out of the room with dignity."

Meg rose as she spoke, and was just going to rehearse the dignified exit, when a step in the hall made her fly into her seat and begin to sew as fast as if her life depended on finishing that particular seam in a given time. Jo smothered a laugh at the sudden change, and when someone gave a modest tap, opened the door with a grim aspect which was anything but hospitable.

"Good afternoon. I came to get my umbrella, that is, to see how your father finds himself today," said Mr. Brooke, getting a trifle confused as his eyes went from one telltale face to the other.

"It's very well, he's in the rack. I'll get him, and tell it you are here." And having jumbled her father and the umbrella well together in her reply, Jo slipped out of the room to give Meg a chance to make her speech and air her dignity. But the instant she vanished, Meg began to sidle toward the door, murmuring . . .

"Mother will like to see you. Pray sit down, I'll call her."

"Don't go. Are you afraid of me, Margaret?" And Mr. Brooke looked so hurt that Meg thought she must have done something very rude. She blushed up to the little curls on her forehead, for he had never called her Margaret before, and she was surprised to find how natural and sweet it seemed to hear him say it. Anxious to appear friendly and at her ease, she put out her hand with a confiding gesture, and said gratefully . . .

"How can I be afraid when you have been so kind to Father? I only wish I could thank you for it."

"Shall I tell you how?" asked Mr. Brooke, holding the small hand fast in both his own, and looking down at Meg with so much love in the brown eyes that her heart began to flutter, and she both longed to run away and to stop and listen.

"Oh no, please don't, I'd rather not," she said, trying to withdraw her hand, and looking frightened in spite of her denial.

"I won't trouble you. I only want to know if you care for me a little, Meg. I love you so much, dear," added Mr. Brooke tenderly.

This was the moment for the calm, proper speech, but Meg didn't make it. She forgot every word of it, hung her head, and answered, "I don't know," so softly that John had to stoop down to catch the foolish little reply.

He seemed to think it was worth the trouble, for he smiled to himself as if quite satisfied, pressed the plump hand gratefully, and said in his most persuasive tone, "Will you try and find out? I want to know so much, for I can't go to work with any heart until I learn whether I am to have my reward in the end or not."

"I'm too young," faltered Meg, wondering was she was so fluttered, yet rather enjoying it.

"I'll wait, and in the meantime, you could be learning to like me. Would it be a very hard lesson, dear?"

"Not if I chose to learn it, but . . ."

"Please choose to learn, Meg. I love you to teach, and this is easier than German," broke in John, getting possession of the other hand, so that she had no way of hiding her face as he bent to look into it.

His tone was properly beseeching, but stealing a shy look at him, Meg saw that his eyes were merry as well as tender, and that he wore the satisfied smile of one who had no doubt of his success. This nettled her. Annie Moffat's foolish lessons in coquetry came into her mind, and the love of power, which sleeps in the bosoms of the best of little women, woke up all of a sudden and took possession of her. She felt excited and strange, and not knowing what else to do, followed a capricious impulse, and, withdrawing her hands, said petulantly, "I don't choose. Please go away and let me be!"

Poor Mr. Brooke looked as if his lovely castle in the air was tumbling about his ears, for he had never seen Meg in such a mood before, and it rather bewildered him.

"Do you really mean that?" he asked anxiously, following her as she walked away.

"Yes, I do. I don't want to be worried about such things. Father says I needn't, it's too soon and I'd rather not."

"Mayn't I hope you'll change your mind by-and-by? I'll wait and say nothing till you have had more time. Don't play with me, Meg. I didn't think that of you."

"Don't think of me at all. I'd rather you wouldn't," said Meg, taking a naughty satisfaction in trying her lover's patience and her own power. He was grave and pale now, and looked decidedly more like the novel heroes whom she admired, but he neither slapped his forehead nor tramped about the room as they did. He just stood looking at her so wistfully, so tenderly, that she found her heart relenting in spite of herself. What would have happened next I cannot say, if Aunt March had not come hobbling in at this interesting minute.

The old lady couldn't resist her longing to see her nephew, for she had met Laurie as she took her airing, and hearing of Mr. March's arrival, drove straight out to see him. The family were all busy in the back part of the house, and she had made her way quietly in, hoping to surprise them. She did surprise two of them so much that Meg started as if she had seen a ghost, and Mr. Brooke vanished into the study.

"Bless me, what's all this?" cried the old lady with a rap of her cane as she glanced from the pale young gentleman to the scarlet young lady.

"It's Father's friend. I'm so surprised to see you!" stammered Meg, feeling that she was in for a lecture now.

"That's evident," returned Aunt March, sitting down. "But what is Father's friend saying to make you look like a peony? There's mischief going on, and I insist upon knowing what it is," with another rap.

"We were only talking. Mr. Brooke came for his umbrella," began Meg, wishing that Mr. Brooke and the umbrella were safely out of the house.

"Brooke? That boy's tutor? Ah! I understand now. I know all about it. Jo blundered into a wrong message in one of your Father's letters, and I made her tell me. You haven't gone and accepted him, child?" cried Aunt March, looking scandalized.

"Hush! He'll hear. Shan't I call Mother?" said Meg, much troubled.

"Not yet. I've something to say to you, and I must free my mind at once. Tell me, do you mean to marry this Cook? If you do, not one penny of my money ever goes to you. Remember that, and be a sensible girl," said the old lady impressively.

Now Aunt March possessed in perfection the art of rousing the spirit of opposition in the gentlest people, and enjoyed doing it. The best of us have a spice of perversity in us, especially when we are young and in love. If Aunt March had begged Meg to accept John Brooke, she would probably have declared she couldn't think of it, but as she was preemptorily ordered not to like him, she immediately made up her mind that she would. Inclination as well as perversity made the decision easy, and being already much excited, Meg opposed the old lady with unusual spirit. "I shall marry whom I please, Aunt March, and you can leave your money to anyone you like," she said, nodding her head with a resolute air.

"Highty-tighty! Is that the way you take my advice, Miss? You'll be sorry for it by-and-by, when you've tried love in a cottage and found it a failure."

"It can't be a worse one than some people find in big houses," retorted Meg.

Aunt March put on her glasses and took a look at the girl, for she did not know her in this new mood. Meg hardly knew herself, she felt so brave and independent, so glad to defend John and assert her right to love him, if she liked. Aunt March saw that she had begun wrong, and after a little pause, made a fresh start, saying as mildly as she could, "Now, Meg, my dear, be reasonable and take my advice. I mean it kindly, and don't want you to spoil your whole life by making a mistake at the beginning. You ought to marry well and help your family. It's your duty to make a rich match and it ought to be impressed upon you."

"Father and Mother don't think so. They like John though he is poor."

"Your parents, my dear, have no more worldly wisdom than a pair of babies."

"I'm glad of it," cried Meg stoutly.

Aunt March took no notice, but went on with her lecture. "This Rook is poor and hasn't got any rich relations, has he?"

"No, but he has many warm friends."

"You can't live on friends, try it and see how cool they'll grow. He hasn't any business, has he?"

"Not yet. Mr. Laurence is going to help him."

"That won't last long. James Laurence is a crotchety old fellow and not to be depended on. So you intend to marry a man without money, position, or business, and go on working harder than you do now, when you might be comfortable all your days by minding me and doing better? I thought you had more sense, Meg."

"I couldn't do better if I waited half my life! John is good and wise, he's got heaps of talent, he's willing to work and sure to get on, he's so energetic and brave. Everyone likes and respects him, and I'm proud to think he cares for me, though I'm so poor and young and silly," said Meg, looking prettier than ever in her earnestness.

"He knows you have got rich relations, child. That's the secret of his liking, I suspect."

"Aunt March, how dare you say such a thing? John is above such meanness, and I won't listen to you a minute if you talk so," cried Meg indignantly, forgetting everything but the injustice of the old lady's suspicions. "My John wouldn't marry for money, any more than I would. We are willing to work and we mean to wait. I'm not afraid of being poor, for I've been happy so far, and I know I shall be with him because he loves me, and I . . ."

Meg stopped there, remembering all of a sudden that she hadn't made up her mind, that she had told 'her John' to go away, and that he might be overhearing her inconsistent remarks.

Aunt March was very angry, for she had set her heart on having her pretty niece make a fine match, and something in the girl's happy young face made the lonely old woman feel both sad and sour.

"Well, I wash my hands of the whole affair! You are a willful child, and you've lost more than you know by this piece of folly. No, I won't stop. I'm disappointed in you, and haven't spirits to see your father now. Don't expect anything from me when you are married. Your Mr. Book's friends must take care of you. I'm done with you forever."

And slamming the door in Meg's face, Aunt March drove off in high dudgeon. She seemed to take all the girl's courage with her, for when left alone, Meg stood for a moment, undecided whether to laugh or cry. Before she could make up her mind, she was taken possession of by Mr. Brooke, who said all in one breath, "I couldn't help hearing, Meg. Thank you for defending me, and Aunt March for proving that you do care for me a little bit."

"I didn't know how much till she abused you," began Meg.

"And I needn't go away, but my stay and be happy, may I, dear?"

Here was another fine chance to make the crushing speech and the stately exit, but Meg never thought of doing either, and disgraced herself forever in Jo's eyes by meekly whispering, "Yes, John," and hiding her face on Mr. Brooke's waistcoat.

Fifteen minutes after Aunt March's departure, Jo came softly downstairs, paused an instant at the parlor door, and hearing no sound within, nodded and smiled with a satisfied expression, saying to herself, "She has seen him away as we planned, and that affair is settled. I'll go and hear the fun, and have a good laugh over it."

But poor Jo never got her laugh, for she was transfixed upon the threshold by a spectacle which held her there, staring with her mouth nearly as wide open as her eyes. Going in to exult over a fallen enemy and to praise a strong-minded sister for the banishment of an objectionable lover, it certainly was a shock to behold the aforesaid enemy serenely sitting on the sofa, with the strongminded sister enthroned upon his knee and wearing an expression of the most abject submission. Jo gave a sort of gasp, as if a cold shower bath had suddenly fallen upon her, for such an unexpected turning of the tables actually took her breath away. At the odd sound the lovers turned and saw her. Meg jumped up, looking both proud and shy, but 'that man', as Jo called him, actually laughed and said coolly, as he kissed the astonished newcomer, "Sister Jo, congratulate us!"

That was adding insult to injury, it was altogether too much, and making some wild demonstration with her hands, Jo vanished without a word. Rushing upstairs, she startled the invalids by exclaiming tragically as she burst into the room, "Oh, do somebody go down quick! John Brooke is acting dreadfully, and Meg likes it!"

Mr. and Mrs. March left the room with speed, and casting herself upon the be, Jo cried and scolded tempestuously as she told the awful news to Beth and Amy. The little girls, however, considered it a most agreeable and interesting event, and Jo got little comfort from them, so she went up to her refuge in the garret, and confided her troubles to the rats.

Nobody ever knew what went on in the parlor that afternoon, but a great deal of talking was done, and quiet Mr. Brooke astonished his friends by the eloquence and spirit with which he pleaded his suit, told his plans, and persuaded them to arrange everything just as he wanted it.

The tea bell rang before he had finished describing the paradise which he meant to earn for Meg, and he proudly took her in to supper, both looking so happy that Jo hadn't the heart to be jealous or dismal. Amy was very much impressed by John's devotion and Meg's dignity, Beth beamed at them from a distance, while Mr. and Mrs. March surveyed the young couple with such tender satisfaction that it was perfectly evident Aunt March was right in calling them as 'unworldly as a pair of babies'. No one ate much, but everyone looked very happy, and the old room seemed to brighten up amazingly when the first romance of the family began there.

"You can't say nothing pleasant ever happens now, can you, Meg?" said Amy, trying to decide how she would group the lovers in a sketch she was planning to make. "No, I'm sure I can't. How much has happened since I said that! It seems a year ago," answered Meg, who was in a blissful dream lifted far above such common things as bread and butter.

"The joys come close upon the sorrows this time, and I rather think the changes have begun," said Mrs. March. "In most families there comes, now and then, a year full of events. This has been such a one, but it ends well, after all."

"Hope the next will end better," muttered Jo, who found it very hard to see Meg absorbed in a stranger before her face, for Jo loved a few persons very dearly and dreaded to have their affection lost or lessened in any way. "I hope the third year from this will end better. I mean it shall, if I live to work out my plans," said Mr. Brooke, smiling at Meg, as if everything had become possible to him now.

"Doesn't it seem very long to wait?" asked Amy, who was in a hurry for the wedding.

"I've got so much to learn before I shall be ready, it seems a short time to me," answered Meg, with a sweet gravity in her face never seen there before.

"You have only to wait, I am to do the work," said John beginning his labors by picking up Meg's napkin, with an expression which caused Jo to shake her head, and then say to herself with an air of relief as the front door banged, "Here comes Laurie. Now we shall have some sensible conversation."

But Jo was mistaken, for Laurie came prancing in, overflowing with good spirits, bearing a great bridal-looking bouquet for 'Mrs. John Brooke', and evidently laboring under the delusion that the whole affair had been brought about by his excellent management.

"I knew Brooke would have it all his own way, he always does, for when he makes up his mind to accomplish anything, it's done though the sky falls," said Laurie, when he had presented his offering and his congratulations.

"Much obliged for that recommendation. I take it as a good omen for the future and invite you to my wedding on the spot," answered Mr. Brooke, who felt at peace with all mankind, even his mischievous pupil.

"I'll come if I'm at the ens of the earth, for the sight of Jo's face alone on that occasion would be worth a long journey. You don't look festive, ma'am, what's the matter?" asked Laurie, following her into a corner of the parlor, whither all had adjourned to greet Mr. Laurence.

"I don't approve of the match, but I've made up my mind to bear it, and shall not say a word against it," said Jo solemnly. "You can't know how hard it is for me to give up Meg," she continued with a little quiver in her voice. "You don't give her up. You only go halves," said Laurie consolingly.

"It can never be the same again. I've lost my dearest friend," sighed Jo.

"You've got me, anyhow. I'm not good for much, I know, but I'll stand by you, Jo, all the days of my life. Upon my word I will!" And Laurie meant what he said.

"I know you will, and I'm ever so much obliged. You are always a great comfort to me, Teddy," returned Jo, gratefully shaking hands. "Well, now, don't be dismal, there's a good fellow. It's all right you see. Meg is happy, Brooke will fly round and get settled immediately, Grandpa will attend to him, and it will be very jolly to see Meg in her own little house. We'll have capital times after she is gone, for I shall be through college before long, and then we'll go abroad on some nice trip or other. Wouldn't that console you?"

"I rather think it would, but there's no knowing what may happen in three years," said Jo thoughtfully.

"That's true. Don't you wish you could take a look forward and wee where we shall all be then? I do," returned Laurie.

"I think not, for I might see something sad, and everyone looks so happy now, I don't believe they could be much improved." And Jo's eyes went slowly round the room, brightening as they looked, for the prospect was a pleasant one.

Father and Mother sat together, quietly reliving the first chapter of the romance which for them began some twenty years ago. Amy was drawing the lovers, who sat apart in a beautiful world of their own, the light of which touched their faces with a grace the little artist could not copy. Beth lay on her sofa, talking cheerily with her old friend, who held her little hand as if he felt that it possessed the power to lead him along the peaceful way she walked. Jo lounged in her favorite low seat, with the grave quiet look which best became her, and Laurie, leaning on the back of her chair, his chin on a level with her curly head, smiled with his friendliest aspect, and nodded at her in the long glass which reflected them both.

So the curtain falls upon Meg, Jo, Beth, and Amy. Whether it ever rises again, depends upon the reception giveN the first act of the domestic drama called LITTLE WOMEN.

LITTLE WOMEN PART 2

Chapter Twenty-Four

In order that we may start afresh and go to Meg's wedding with free minds, it will be well to begin with a little gossip about the Marches. And here let me premise that if any of the elders think there is too much 'lovering' in the story, as I fear they may (I'm not afraid the young folks will make that objection), I can only say with Mrs. March, "What can you expect when I have four gay girls in the house, and a dashing young neighbor over the way?"

The three years that have passed have brought but few changes to the quiet family. The war is over, and Mr. March safely at home, busy with his books and the small parish which found in him a minister by nature as by grace, a quiet, studious man, rich in the wisdom that is better than learning, the charity which calls all mankind 'brother', the piety that blossoms into character, making it august and lovely.

These attributes, in spite of poverty and the strict integrity which shut him out from the more worldly successes, attracted to him many admirable persons, as naturally as sweet herbs draw bees, and as naturally he gave them the honey into which fifty years of hard experience had distilled no bitter drop. Earnest young men found the gray-headed scholar as young at heart as they, thoughtful or troubled women instinctively brought their doubts to him, sure of finding the gentlest sympathy, the wisest counsel. Sinners told their sins to the pure-hearted old man and were both rebuked and saved. Gifted men found a companion in him. Ambitious men caught glimpses of nobler ambitions than their own, and even worldlings confessed that his beliefs were beautiful and true, although 'they wouldn't pay'.

To outsiders the five energetic women seemed to rule the house, and so they did in many things, but the quiet scholar, sitting among his books, was still the head of the family, the household conscience, anchor, and comforter, for to him the busy, anxious women always turned in troublous times, finding him, in the truest sense of those sacred words, husband and father.

The girls gave their hearts into their mother's keeping, their souls into their father's, and to both parents, who lived and labored so faithfully for them, they gave a love that grew with their growth and bound them tenderly together by the sweetest tie which blesses life and outlives death.

Mrs. March is as brisk and cheery, though rather grayer, than when we saw her last, and just now so absorbed in Meg's affairs that the hospitals and homes still full of wounded 'boys' and soldiers' widows, decidedly miss the motherly missionary's visits.

John Brooke did his duty manfully for a year, got wounded, was sent home, and not allowed to return. He received no stars or bars, but he deserved them, for he cheerfully risked all he had, and life and love are very precious when both are in full bloom. Perfectly resigned to his discharge, he devoted himself to getting well, preparing for business, and earning a home for Meg. With the good sense and sturdy independence that characterized him, he refused Mr. Laurence's more generous offers, and accepted the place of bookkeeper, feeling better satisfied to begin with an honestly earned salary than by running any risks with borrowed money.

Meg had spent the time in working as well as waiting, growing womanly in character, wise in housewifely arts, and prettier than ever, for love is a great beautifier. She had her girlish ambitions and hopes, and felt some disappointment at the humble way in which the new life must begin. Ned Moffat had just married Sallie Gardiner, and Meg couldn't help contrasting their fine house and carriage, many gifts, and splendid outfit with her own, and secretly wishing she could have the same. But somehow envy and discontent soon vanished when she thought of all the patient love and labor John had put into the little home awaiting her, and when they sat together in the twilight, talking over their small plans, the future always grew so beautiful and bright that she forgot Sallie's splendor and felt herself the richest, happiest girl in Christendom.

Jo never went back to Aunt March, for the old lady took such a fancy to AMy that she bribed her with the offer of drawing lessons from one of the best teachers going, and for the sake of this advantage, Amy would have served a far harder mistress. So she gave her mornings to duty, her afternoons to pleasure, and prospered finely. Jo meantime devoted herself to literature and Beth, who remained delicate long after the fever was a thing of the past. Not an invalid exactly, but never again the rosy, healthy creature she had been, yet always hopeful, happy, and serene, and busy with the quiet duties she loved, everyone's friend, and an angel in the house, long before those who loved her most had learned to know it.

As long as THE SPREAD EAGLE paid her a dollar a column for her 'rubbish', as she called it, Jo felt herself a woman of means, and spun her little romances diligently. But great plans fermented in her busy brain and ambitious mind, and the old tin kitchen in the garret held a slowly increasing pile of blotted manuscript, which was one day to place the name of March upon the roll of fame.

Laurie, having dutifully gone to college to please his grandfather, was now getting through it in the easiest possible manner to please himself. A universal favorite, thanks to money, manners, much talent, and the kindest heart that ever got its owner into scrapes by trying to get other people out of them, he stood in great danger of being spoiled, and probably would have been, like many another promising boy, if he had not possessed a talisman against evil in the memory of the kind old man who was bound up in his success, the motherly friend who watched over him as if he were her son, and last, but not least by any means, the knowledge that four innocent girls loved, admired, and believed in him with all their hearts.

Being only 'a glorious human boy', of course he frolicked and flirted, grew dandified, aquatic, sentimental, or gymnastic, as college fashions ordained, hazed and was hazed, talked slang, and more than once came perilously near suspension and expulsion. But as high spirits and the love of fun were the causes of these pranks, he always managed to save himself by frank confession, honorable atonement, or the irresistible power of persuasion which he possessed in perfection. In fact, he rather prided himself on his narrow escapes, and liked to thrill the girls with graphic accounts of his triumphs over wrathful tutors, dignified professors, and vanquished enemies. The 'men of my class', were heroes in the eyes of the girls, who never wearied of the exploits of 'our fellows', and were frequently allowed to bask in the smiles of these great creatures, when Laurie brought them home with him.

Amy especially enjoyed this high honor, and became quite a belle among them, for her ladyship early felt and learned to use the gift of fascination with which she was endowed. Meg was too much absorbed in her private and particular John to care for any other lords of creation, and Beth too shy to do more than peep at them and wonder how Amy dared to order them about so, but Jo felt quite in her own element, and found it very difficult to refrain from imitating the gentlemanly attitudes, phrases, and feats, which seemed more natural to her than the decorums prescribed for young ladies. They all liked Jo immensely, but never fell in love with her, though very few escaped without paying the tribute of a sentimental sigh or two at Amy's shrine. And speaking of sentiment brings us very naturally to the 'Dovecote'.

That was the name of the little brown house Mr. Brooke had prepared for Meg's first home. Laurie had christened it, saying it was highly appropriate to the gentle lovers who 'went on together like a pair of turtledoves, with first a bill and then a coo'. It was a tiny house, with a little garden behind and a lawn about as big as a pocket handkerchief in the front. Here Meg meant to have a fountain, shrubbery, and a profusion of lovely flowers, though just at present the fountain was represented by a weather-beaten urn, very like a dilapidated slopbowl, the shrubbery consisted of several young larches, undecided whether to live or die, and the profusion of flowers was merely hinted by regiments of sticks to show where seeds were planted. But inside, it was altogether charming, and the happy bride saw no fault from garret to cellar. To be sure, the hall was so narrow it was fortunate that they had no piano, for one never could have been got in whole, the dining room was so small that six people were a tight fit, and the kitchen stairs seemed built for the express purpose of precipitating both servants and china pell-mell into the coalbin. But once get used to these slight blemishes and nothing could be more complete, for good sense and good taste had presided over the furnishing, and the result was highly satisfactory. There were no marble-topped tables, long mirrors, or lace curtains in the little parlor, but simple furniture, plenty of books, a fine picture or two, a stand of flowers in the bay window, and, scattered all about, the pretty gifts which came from friendly hands and were the fairer for the loving messages they brought.

I don't think the Parian Psyche Laurie gave lost any of its beauty because John put up the bracket it stood upon, that any upholsterer could have draped the plain muslin curtains more gracefully than Amy's artistic hand, or that any store-room was ever better provided with good wishes, merry words, and happy hopes than that in which Jo and her mother put away Meg's few boxes, barrels, and bundles, and I am morally certain that the spandy new kitchen never could have looked so cozy and neat if Hannah had not arranged every pot and pan a dozen times over, and laid the fire all ready for lighting the minute 'Mis. Brooke came home'. I also doubt if any young matron ever began life with so rich a supply of dusters, holders, and piece bags, for Beth made enough to last till the silver wedding came round, and invented three different kinds of dishcloths for the express service of the bridal china.

People who hire all these things done for them never know what they lose, for the homeliest tasks get beautified if loving hands do them, and Meg found so many proofs of this that everything in her small nest, from the kitchen roller to the silver vase on her parlor table, was eloquent of home love and tender forethought.

What happy times they had planning together, what solemn shopping excursions, what funny mistakes they made, and what shouts of laughter arose over Laurie's ridiculous bargains. In his love of jokes, this young gentleman, though nearly through college, was a much of a boy as ever. His last whim had been to bring with him on his weekly visits some new, useful, and ingenious article for the young housekeeper. Now a bag of remarkable clothespins, next, a wonderful nutmeg grater which fell to pieces at the first trial, a knife cleaner that spoiled all the knives, or a sweeper that picked the nap neatly off the carpet and left the dirt, labor-saving soap that took the skin off one's hands, infallible cements which stuck firmly to nothing but the fingers of the deluded buyer, and every kind of tinware, from a toy savings bank for odd pennies, to a wonderful boiler which would wash articles in its own steam with every prospect of exploding in the process.

In vain Meg begged him to stop. John laughed at him, and Jo called him 'Mr. Toodles'. He was possessed with a mania for patronizing Yankee ingenuity, and seeing his friends fitly furnished forth. So each week beheld some fresh absurdity.

Everything was done at last, even to Amy's arranging different colored soaps to match the different colored rooms, and Beth's setting the table for the first meal.

"Are you satisfied? Does it seem like home, and do you feel as if you should be happy here?" asked Mrs. March, as she and her daughter went through the new kingdom arm in arm, for just then they seemed to cling together more tenderly than ever.

"Yes, Mother, perfectly satisfied, thanks to you all, and so happy that I can't talk about it," with a look that was far better than words.

"If she only had a servant or two it would be all right," said Amy, coming out of the parlor, where she had been trying to decide whether the bronze Mercury looked best on the whatnot or the mantlepiece.

"Mother and I have talked that over, and I have made up my mind to try her way first. There will be so little to do that with Lotty to run my errands and help me here and there, I shall only have enough work to keep me from getting lazy or homesick," answered Meg tranquilly.

"Sallie Moffat has four," began Amy.

"If Meg had four, the house wouldn't hold them, and master and missis would have to camp in the garden," broke in Jo, who, enveloped in a big blue pinafore, was giving the last polish to the door handles.

"Sallie isn't a poor man's wife, and many maids are in keeping with her fine establishment. Meg and John begin humbly, but I have a feeling that there will be quite as much happiness in the little house as in the big one. It's a great mistake for young girls like Meg to leave themselves nothing to do but dress, give orders, and gossip. When I was first married, I used to long for my new clothes to wear out or get torn, so that i might have the pleasure of mending them, for I got heartily sick of doing fancywork and tending my pocket handkerchief."

"Why didn't you go into the kitchen and make messes, as Sallie says she does to amuse herself, though they never turn out well and the servants laugh at her," said Meg.

"I did after a while, not to 'mess' but to learn of Hannah how things should be done, that my servants need not laugh at me. It was play then, but there came a time when I was truly grateful that I not only possessed the will but the power to cook wholesome food for my little girls, and help myself when I could no longer afford to hire help. You begin at the other end, Meg, dear, but the lessons you learn now will be of use to you by-and-by when John is a richer man, for the mistress of a house, however splendid, should know how work ought to be done, if she wishes to be well and honestly served."

"Yes, Mother, I'm sure of that," said Meg, listening respectfully to the little lecture, for the best of women will hold forth upon the all absorbing subject of house keeping. "Do you know I like this room most of all in my baby house," added Meg, a minute after, as they went upstairs and she looked into her well-stored linen closet.

Beth was there, laying the snowy piles smoothly on the shelves and exulting over the goodly array. All three laughed as Meg spoke, for that linen closet was a joke. You see, having said that if Meg married 'that Brooke' she shouldn't have a cent of her money, Aunt March was rather in a quandary when time had appeased her wrath and made her repent her vow. She never broke her word, and was much exercised in her mind how to get round it, and at last devised a plan whereby she could satisfy herself. Mrs. Carrol, Florence's mamma, was ordered to buy, have made, and marked a generous supply of house and table linen, and send it as her present, all of which was faithfully done, but the secret leaked out, and was greatly enjoyed by the family, for Aunt March tried to look utterly unconscious, and insisted that she could give nothing but the old-fashioned pearls long promised to the first bride.

"That's a housewifely taste which I am glad to see. I had a young friend who set up housekeeping with six sheets, but she had finger bowls for company and that satisfied her," said Mrs. March, patting the damask tablecloths, with a truly feminine appreciation of their fineness.

"I haven't a single finger bowl, but this is a setout that will last me all my days, Hannah says." And Meg looked quite contented, as well she might.

A tall, broad-shouldered young fellow, with a cropped head, a felt basin of a hat, and a flyaway coat, came tramping down the road at a great pace, walked over the low fence without stopping to open the gate, straight up to Mrs. March, with both hands out and a hearty . . .

"Here I am, Mother! Yes, it's all right."

The last words were in answer to the look the elder lady gave him, a kindly questioning look which the handsome eyes met so frankly that the little ceremony closed, as usual, with a motherly kiss.

"For Mrs. John Brooke, with the maker's congratulations and compliments. Bless you, Beth! What a refreshing spectacle you are, Jo. Amy, you are getting altogether too handsome for a single lady."

As Laurie spoke, he delivered a brown paper parcel to Meg, pilled Beth's hair ribbon, stared at Jo's bib pinafore, and fell into an attitude of mock rapture before Amy, then shook hands all round, and everyone began to talk.

"Where is John?" asked Meg anxiously.

"Stopped to get the license for tomorrow, ma'am."

"Which side won the last match, Teddy?" inquired Jo, who persisted in feeling an interest in manly sports despite her nineteen years.

"Ours, of course. Wish you'd been there to see."

"How is the lovely Miss Randal?" asked Amy with a significant smile.

"More cruel than ever. Don't you see how I'm pining away?" And Laurie gave his broad chest a sounding slap and heaved a melodramatic sigh.

"What's the last joke? Undo the bundle and see, Meg," said Beth, eying the knobby parcel with curiosity.

"It's a useful thing to have in the house in case of fire or thieves," observed Laurie, as a watchman's rattle appeared, amid the laughter of the girls.

"Any time when John is away and you get frightened, Mrs. Meg, just swing that out of the front window, and it will rouse the neighborhood in a jiffy. Nice thing, isn't it?" And Laurie gave them a sample of its powers that made them cover up their ears.

"There's gratitude for you! And speaking of gratitude reminds me to mention that you may thank Hannah for saving your wedding cake from destruction. I saw it going into your house as I came by, and if she hadn't defended it manfully I'd have had a pick at it, for it looked like a remarkably plummy one."

"I wonder if you will ever grow up, Laurie," said Meg in a matronly tone.

"I'm doing my best, ma'am, but can't get much higher, I'm afraid, as six feet is about all men can do in these degenerate days," responded the young gentleman, whose head was about level with the little chandelier.

"I suppose it would be profanation to eat anything in this spick-and-span bower, so as I'm tremendously hungry, I propose an adjournment," he added presently.

"Mother and I are going to wait for John. There are some last things to settle," said Meg, bustling away.

"Beth and I are going over to Kitty Bryant's to get more flowers for tomorrow," added Amy, tying a picturesque hat over her picturesque curls, and enjoying the effect as much as anybody.

"Come, Jo, don't desert a fellow. I'm in such a state of exhaustion I can't get home without help. Don't take off your apron, whatever you do, it's peculiarly becoming," said Laurie, as Jo bestowed his especial aversion in her capacious pocket and offered her arm to support his feeble steps.

"Now, Teddy, I want to talk seriously to you about tomorrow," began Jo, as they strolled away together. "You must promise to behave well, and not cut up any pranks, and spoil our plans."

"Not a prank."

"And don't say funny things when we ought to be sober."

"I never do. You are the one for that."

"And I implore you not to look at me during the ceremony. I shall certainly laugh if you do."

"You won't see me, you'll be crying so hard that the thick fog round you will obscure the prospect."

"I never cry unless for some great affliction."

"Such as fellows going to college, hey?" cut in Laurie, with suggestive laugh.

"Don't be a peacock. I only moaned a trifle to keep the girls company." "Exactly. I say, Jo, how is Grandpa this week? Pretty amiable?"

"Very. Why, have you got into a scrape and want to know how he'll take it?" asked Jo rather sharply.

"Now, Jo, do you think I'd look your mother in the face and say 'All right', if it wasn't?" And Laurie stopped short, with an injured air.

"No, I don't."

"Then don't go and be suspicious. I only want some money," said Laurie, walking on again, appeased by her hearty tone.

"You spend a great deal, Teddy."

"Bless you, I don't spend it, it spends itself somehow, and is gone before I know it."

"You are so generous and kind-hearted that you let people borrow, and can't say 'No' to anyone. We heard about Henshaw and all you did for him. If you always spent money in that way, no one would blame you," said Jo warmly.

"Oh, he made a mountain out of a molehill. You wouldn't have me let that fine fellow work himself to death just for want of a little help, when he is worth a dozen of us lazy chaps, would you?"

"Of course not, but I don't see the use of your having seventeen waistcoats, endless neckties, and a new hat every time you come home. I thought you'd got over the dandy period, but every now and then it breaks out in a new spot. Just now it's the fashion to be hideous, to make your head look like a scrubbing brush, wear a strait jacket, orange gloves, and clumping square-toed boots. If it was cheap ugliness, I'd say nothing, but it costs as much as the other, and I don't get any satisfaction out of it."

Laurie threw back his head, and laughed so heartily at this attack, that the felt hat fell off, and Jo walked on it, which insult only afforded him an opportunity for expatiating on the advantages of a rough-and-ready costume, as he folded up the maltreated hat, and stuffed it into his pocket.

"Don't lecture any more, there's a good soul! I have enough all through the week, and like to enjoy myself when I come home. I'll get myself up regardless of expense tomorrow and be a satisfaction to my friends."

"I'll leave you in peace if you'll only let your hair grow. I'm not aristocratic, but I do object to being seen with a person who looks like a young prize fighter," observed Jo severely.

"This unassuming style promotes study, that's why we adopt it," returned Laurie, who certainly could not be accused of vanity, having voluntarily sacrificed a handsome curly crop to the demand for quarterinch-long stubble.

"By the way, Jo, I think that little Parker is really getting desperate about Amy. He talks of her constantly, writes poetry, and moons about in a most suspicious manner. He'd better nip his little passion in the bud, hadn't he?" added Laurie, in a confidential, elder brotherly tone, after a minute's silence.

"Of course he had. We don't want any more marrying in this family for years to come. Mercy on us, what are the children thinking of?" And Jo looked as much scandalized as if Amy and little Parker were not yet in their teens.

"It's a fast age, and I don't know what we are coming to, ma'am. You are a mere infant, but you'll go next, Jo, and we'll be left lamenting," said Laurie, shaking his head over the degeneracy of the times.

"Don't be alarmed. I'm not one of the agreeable sort. Nobody will want me, and it's a mercy, for there should always be one old maid in a family."

"You won't give anyone a chance," said Laurie, with a sidelong glance and a little more color than before in his sunburned face. "You won't show the soft side of your character, and if a fellow gets a peep at it by accident and can't help showing that he likes it, you treat him as Mrs. Gummidge did her sweetheart, throw cold water over him, and get so thorny no one dares touch or look at you."

"I don't like that sort of thing. I'm too busy to be worried with nonsense, and I think it's dreadful to break up families so. Now don't say any more about it. Meg's wedding has turned all our heads, and we talk of nothing but lovers and such absurdities. I don't wish to get cross, so let's change the subject." And Jo looked quite ready to fling cold water on the slightest provocation.

Whatever his feelings might have been, Laurie found a vent for them in a long low whistle and the fearful prediction as they parted at the gate, "Mark my words, Jo, you'll go next."

Chapter Twenty-Five

The June roses over the porch were awake bright and early on that morning, rejoicing with all their hearts in the cloudless sunshine, like friendly little neighbors, as they were. Quite flushed with excitement were their ruddy faces, as they swung in the wind, whispering to one another what they had seen, for some peeped in at the dining room windows where the feast was spread, some climbed up to nod and smile at the sisters as they dressed the bride, others waved a welcome to those who came and went on various errands in garden, porch, and hall, and all, from the rosiest full-blown flower to the palest baby bud, offered their tribute of beauty and fragrance to the gentle mistress who had loved and tended them so long.

Meg looked very like a rose herself, for all that was best and sweetest in heart and soul seemed to bloom into her face that day, making it fair and tender, with a charm more beautiful than beauty. Neither silk, lace, nor orange flowers would she have. "I don't want a fashionable wedding, but only those about me whom I love, and to them I wish to look and be my familiar self."

So she made her wedding gown herself, sewing into it the tender hopes and innocent romances of a girlish heart. her sisters braided up her pretty hair, and the only ornaments she wore were the lilies of the valley, which 'her John' liked best of all the flowers that grew.

"You do look just like our own dear Meg, only so very sweet and lovely that I should hug you if it wouldn't crumple your dress," cried Amy, surveying her with delight when all was done.

"Then I am satisfied. But please hug and kiss me, everyone, and don't mind my dress. I want a great many crumples of this sort put into it today." And Meg opened her arms to her sisters, who clung about her with April faces for a minute, feeling that the new love had not changed the old.

"Now I'm going to tie John's cravat for him, and then to stay a few minutes with Father quietly in the study." And Meg ran down to perform these little ceremonies, and then to follow her mother wherever she went, conscious that in spite of the smiles on the motherly face, there was a secret sorrow hid in the motherly heart at the flight of the first bird from the nest.

As the younger girls stand together, giving the last touches to their simple toilet, it may be a good time to tell of a few changes which three years have wrought in their appearance, for all are looking their best just now.

Jo's angles are much softened, she has learned to carry herself with ease, if not grace. The curly crop has lengthened into a thick coil, more becoming to the small head atop of the tall figure. There is a fresh color in her brown cheeks, a soft shine in her eyes, and only gentle words fall from her sharp tongue today.

Beth has grown slender, pale, and more quiet than ever. The beautiful, kind eyes are larger, and in them lies an expression that saddens one, although it is not sad itself. It is the shadow of pain which touches the young face with such pathetic patience, but Beth seldom complains and always speaks hopefully of 'being better soon'.

Amy is with truth considered 'the flower of the family', for at sixteen she has the air and bearing of a full-grown woman, not beautiful, but possessed of that indescribable charm called grace. One saw it in the lines of her figure, the make and motion of her hands, the flow of her dress, the droop of her hair, unconscious yet harmonious, and as attractive to many as beauty itself. Amy's nose still afflicted her, for it never would grow Grecian, so did her mouth, being too wide, and having a decided chin. These offending features gave character to her whole face, but she never could see it, and consoled herself with her wonderfully fair complexion, keen blue eyes, and curls more golden and abundant than ever.

All three wore suits of thin silver gray (their best gowns for the summer), with blush roses in hair and bosom, and all three looked just what they were, fresh-faced, happy-hearted girls, pausing a moment in their busy lives to read with wistful eyes the sweetest chapter in the romance of womanhood.

There were to be no ceremonious performances, everything was to be as natural and homelike as possible, so when Aunt March arrived, she was scandalized to see the bride come running to welcome and lead her in, to find the bridegroom fastening up a garland that had fallen down, and to catch a glimpse of the paternal minister marching upstairs with a grave countenance and a wine bottle under each arm.

"Upon my word, here's a state of things!" cried the old lady, taking the seat of honor prepared for her, and settling the folds of her lavender moire with a great rustle. "You oughtn't to be seen till the last minute, child."

"I'm not a show, Aunty, and no one is coming to stare at me, to criticize my dress, or count the cost of my luncheon. I'm too happy to care what anyone says or thinks, and I'm going to have my little wedding just as I like it. John, dear, here's your hammer." And away went Meg to help 'that man' in his highly improper employment.

Mr. Brooke didn't even say, "Thank you," but as he stooped for the unromantic tool, he kissed his little bride behind the folding door, with a look that made Aunt March whisk out her pocket handkerchief with a sudden dew in her sharp old eyes.

A crash, a cry, and a laugh from Laurie, accompanied by the indecorous exclamation, "Jupiter Ammon! Jo's upset the cake again!" caused a momentary flurry, which was hardly over when a flock of cousins arrived, and 'the party came in', as Beth used to say when a child.

"Don't let that young giant come near me, he worries me worse than mosquitoes," whispered the old lady to Amy, as the rooms filled and Laurie's black head towered above the rest.

"He has promised to be very good today, and he can be perfectly elegant if he likes," returned Amy, and gliding away to warn Hercules to beware of the dragon, which warning caused him to haunt the old lady with a devotion that nearly distracted her.

There was no bridal procession, but a sudden silence fell upon the room as Mr. March and the young couple took their places under the green arch. Mother and sisters gathered close, as if loath to give Meg up. The fatherly voice broke more than once, which only seemed to make the service more beautiful and solemn. The bridegroom's hand trembled visibly, and no one heard his replies. But Meg looked straight up in her husband's eyes, and said, "I will!" with such tender trust in her own face and voice that her mother's heart rejoiced and Aunt March sniffed audibly.

Jo did not cry, though she was very near it once, and was only saved from a demonstration by the consciousness that Laurie was staring fixedly at her, with a comical mixture of merriment and emotion in his wicked black eyes. Beth kept her face hidden on her mother's shoulder, but Amy stood like a graceful statue, with a most becoming ray of sunshine touching her white forehead and the flower in her hair.

It wasn't at all the thing, I'm afraid, but the minute she was fairly married, Meg cried, "The first kiss for Marmee!" and turning, gave it with her heart on her lips. During the next fifteen minutes she looked more like a rose than ever, for everyone availed themselves of their privileges to the fullest extent, from Mr. Laurence to old Hannah, who, adorned with a headdress fearfully and wonderfully made, fell upon her in the hall, crying with a sob and a chuckle, "Bless you, deary, a hundred times! The cake ain't hurt a mite, and everything looks lovely."

Everybody cleared up after that, and said something brilliant, or tried to, which did just as well, for laughter is ready when hearts are light. There was no display of gifts, for they were already in the little house, nor was there an elaborate breakfast, but a plentiful lunch of cake and fruit, dressed with flowers. Mr. Laurence and Aunt March shrugged and smiled at one another when water, lemonade, and coffee were found to be to only sorts of nectar which the three Hebes carried around. No one said anything, till Laurie, who insisted on serving the bride, appeared before her, with a loaded salver in his hand and a puzzled expression on his face.

"Has Jo smashed all the bottles by accident?" he whispered, "or am I merely laboring under a delusion that I saw some lying about loose this morning?"

"No, your grandfather kindly offered us his best, and Aunt March actually sent some, but Father put away a little for Beth, and dispatched the rest to the Soldier's Home. You know he thinks that wine should be used only in illness, and Mother says that neither she nor her daughters will ever offer it to any young man under her roof."

Meg spoke seriously and expected to see Laurie frown or laugh, but he did neither, for after a quick look at her, he said, in his impetuous way, "I like that! For I've seen enough harm done to wish other women would think as you do."

"You are not made wise by experience, I hope?" And there was an anxious accent in Meg's voice.

"No. I give you my word for it. Don't think too well of me, either, this is not one of my temptations. Being brought up where wine is as common as water and almost as harmless, I don't care for it, but when a pretty girl offers it, one doesn't like to refuse, you see."

"But you will, for the sake of others, if not for your own. Come, Laurie, promise, and give me one more reason to call this the happiest day of my life."

A demand so sudden and so serious made the young man hesitate a moment, for ridicule is often harder to bear than self-denial. Meg knew that if he gave the promise he would keep it at all costs, and feeling her power, used it as a woman may for her friend's good. She did not speak, but she looked up at him with a face made very eloquent by happiness, and a smile which said, "No one can refuse me anything today."

Laurie certainly could not, and with an answering smile, he gave her his hand, saying heartily, "I promise, Mrs. Brooke!"

"I thank you, very, very much."

"And I drink 'long life to your resolution', Teddy," cried Jo, baptizing him with a splash of lemonade, as she waved her glass and beamed approvingly upon him.

So the toast was drunk, the pledge made and loyally kept in spite of many temptations, for with instinctive wisdom, the girls seized a happy moment to do their friend a service, for which he thanked them all his life.

After lunch, people strolled about, by twos and threes, through the house and garden, enjoying the sunshine without and within. Meg and John happened to be standing together in the middle of the grass plot, when Laurie was seized with an inspiration which put the finishing touch to this unfashionable wedding.

"All the married people take hands and dance round the new-made husband and wife, as the Germans do, while we bachelors and spinsters prance in couples outside!" cried Laurie, promenading down the path with Amy, with such infectious spirit and skill that everyone else followed their example without a murmur. Mr. and Mrs. March, Aunt and Uncle Carrol began it, others rapidly joined in, even Sallie Moffat, after a moment's hesitation, threw her train over her arm and whisked Ned into the ring. But the crowning joke was Mr. Laurence and Aunt March, for when the stately old gentleman chass'ed solemnly up to the old lady, she just tucked her cane under arm, and hopped briskly away to join hands with the rest and dance about the bridal pair, while the young folks pervaded the garden like butterflies on a midsummer day.

Want of breath brought the impromptu ball to a close, and then people began to go.

"I wish you well, my dear, I heartily wish you well, but I think you'll be sorry for it," said Aunt March to Meg, adding to the bridegroom, as he led her to the carriage, "You've got a treasure, young man, see that you deserve it."

"That is the prettiest wedding I've been to for an age, Ned, and I don't see why, for there wasn't a bit of style about it," observed Mrs. Moffat to her husband, as they drove away.

"Laurie, my lad, if you ever want to indulge in this sort of thing, get one of those little girls to help you, and I shall be perfectly satisfied," said Mr. Laurence, settling himself in his easy chair to rest after the excitement of the morning.

"I'll do my best to gratify you, Sir," was Laurie's unusually dutiful reply, as he carefully unpinned the posy Jo had put in his buttonhole.

The little house was not far away, and the only bridal journey Meg had was the quiet walk with John from the old home to the new. When she came down, looking like a pretty Quakeress in her dovecolored suit and straw bonnet tied with white, they all gathered about her to say goodby, as tenderly as if she had been going to make the grand tour.

"Don't feel that I am separated from you, Marmee dear, or that I love you any the less for loving John so much," she said, clinging to her mother, with full eyes for a moment. "I shall come every day, Father, and expect to keep my old place in all your hearts, though I am married. Beth is going to be with me a great deal, and the other girls will drop in now and then to laugh at my housekeeping struggles. Thank you all for my happy wedding day. Goodby, goodby!"

They stood watching her, with faces full of love and hope and tender pride as she walked away, leaning on her husband's arm, with her hands full of flowers and the June sunshine brightening her happy face—and so Meg's married life began.

Chapter Twenty-Six

It takes people a long time to learn the difference between talent and genius, especially ambitious young men and women. Amy was learning this distinction through much tribulation, for mistaking enthusiasm for inspiration, she attempted every branch of art with youthful audacity. For a long time there was a lull in the 'mud-pie' business, and she devoted herself to the finest pen-and-ink drawing, in which she showed such taste and skill that her graceful handiwork proved both pleasant and profitable. But over-strained eyes caused pen and ink to be laid aside for a bold attempt at poker sketching.

While this attack lasted, the family lived in constant fear of a conflagration, for the odor of burning wood pervaded the house at all hours, smoke issued from attic and shed with alarming frequency, red-hot pokers lay about promiscuously, and Hannah never went to bed without a pail of water and the dinner bell at her door in case of fire. Raphael's face was found boldly executed on the underside of the moulding board, and Bacchus on the head of a beer barrel. A chanting cherub adorned the cover of the sugar bucket, and attempts to portray Romeo and Juliet supplied kindling for some time.

From fire to oil was a natural transition for burned fingers, and Amy fell to painting with undiminished ardor. An artist friend fitted her out with his castoff palettes, brushes, and colors, and she daubed away, producing pastoral and marine views such as were never seen on land or sea. Her monstrosities in the way of cattle would have taken prizes at an agricultural fair, and the perilous pitching of her vessels would have produced seasickness in the most nautical observer, if the utter disregard to all known rules of shipbuilding and rigging had not convulsed him with laughter at the first glance. Swarthy boys and dark-eyed Madonnas, staring at you from one corner of the studio, suggested Murillo. Oily brown shadows of faces with a lurid streak in the wrong place, meant Rembrandt. Buxom ladies and dropiscal infants, Rubens, and Turner appeared in tempests of blue thunder, orange lightning, brown rain, and purple clouds, with a tomato-colored splash in the middle, which might be the sun or a bouy, a sailor's shirt or a king's robe, as the spectator pleased.

Charcoal portraits came next, and the entire family hung in a row, looking as wild and crocky as if just evoked from a coal-bin. Softened into crayon sketches, they did better, for the likenesses were good, and Amy's hair, Jo's nose, Meg's mouth, and Laurie's eyes were pronounced 'wonderfully fine'. A return to clay and plaster followed, and ghostly casts of her acquaintances haunted corners of the house, or tumbled off closet shelves onto people's heads. Children were enticed in as models, till their incoherent accounts of her mysterious doings caused Miss Amy to be regarded in the light of a young ogress. Her efforts in this line, however, were brought to an abrupt close by an untoward accident, which quenched her ardor. Other models failing her for a time, she undertook to cast her own pretty foot, and the family were one day alarmed by an unearthly bumping and screaming and running to the rescue, found the young enthusiast hopping wildly about the shed with her foot held fast in a pan full of plaster, which had hardened with unexpected rapidity. With much difficulty and some danger she was dug out, for Jo was so overcome with laughter while she excavated that her knife went too far, cut the poor foot, and left a lasting memorial of one artistic attempt, at least.

After this Amy subsided, till a mania for sketching from nature set her to haunting river, field, and wood, for picturesque studies, and sighing for ruins to copy. She caught endless colds sitting on damp grass to book 'delicious bit', composed of a stone, a stump, one mushroom, and a broken mullein stalk, or 'a heavenly mass of clouds', that looked like a choice display of featherbeds when done. She sacrificed her complexion floating on the river in the midsummer sun to study light and shade, and got a wrinkle over her nose trying after 'points of sight', or whatever the squint-and-string performance is called.

If 'genius is eternal patience', as Michelangelo affirms, Amy had some claim to the divine attribute, for she persevered in spite of all obstacles, failures, and discouragements, firmly believing that in time she should do something worthy to be called 'high art'.

She was learning, doing, and enjoying other things, meanwhile, for she had resolved to be an attractive and accomplished woman, even if she never became a great artist. Here she succeeded better, for she was one of those happily created beings who please without effort, make friends everywhere, and take life so gracefully and easily that less fortunate souls are tempted to believe that such are born under a lucky star. Everybody liked her, for among her good gifts was tact. She had an instinctive sense of what was pleasing and proper, always said the right thing to the right person, did just what suited the time and place, and was so self-possessed that her sisters used to say, "If Amy went to court without any rehearsal beforehand, she'd know exactly what to do."

One of her weaknesses was a desire to move in 'our best society', without being quite sure what the best really was. Money, position, fashionable accomplishments, and elegant manners were most desirable things in her eyes, and she liked to associate with those who possessed them, often mistaking the false for the true, and admiring what was not admirable. Never forgetting that by birth she was a gentlewoman, she cultivated her aristocratic tastes and feelings, so that when the opportunity came she might be ready to take the place from which poverty now excluded her.

"My lady," as her friends called her, sincerely desired to be a genuine lady, and was so at heart, but had yet to learn that money cannot buy refinement of nature, that rank does not always confer nobility, and that true breeding makes itself felt in spite of external drawbacks.

"I want to ask a favor of you, Mamma," Amy said, coming in with an important air one day.

"Well, little girl, what is it?" replied her mother, in whose eyes the stately young lady still remained 'the baby'.

"Our drawing class breaks up next week, and before the girls separate for the summer, I want to ask them out here for a day. They are wild to see the river, sketch the broken bridge, and copy some of the things they admire in my book. They have been very kind to me in many ways, and I am grateful, for they are all rich and I know I am poor, yet they never made any difference."

"Why should they?" And Mrs. March put the question with what the girls called her 'Maria Theresa air'.

"You know as well as I that it does make a difference with nearly everyone, so don't ruffle up like a dear, motherly hen, when your chickens get pecked by smarter birds. The ugly duckling turned out a swan, you know." And Amy smiled without bitterness, for she possessed a happy temper and hopeful spirit.

Mrs. March laughed, and smoothed down her maternal pride as she asked, "Well, my swan, what is your plan?"

"I should like to ask the girls out to lunch next week, to take them for a drive to the places they want to see, a row on the river, perhaps, and make a little artistic fete for them."

"That looks feasible. What do you want for lunch? Cake, sandwiches, fruit, and coffee will be all that is necessary, I suppose?"

"Oh, dear, no! We must have cold tongue and chicken, French chocolate and ice cream, besides. The girls are used to such things, and I want my lunch to be proper and elegant, though I do work for my living."

"How many young ladies are there?" asked her mother, beginning to look sober.

"Twelve or fourteen in the class, but I dare say they won't all come."

"Bless me, child, you will have to charter an omnibus to carry them about."

"Why, Mother, how can you think of such a thing? Not more than six or eight will probably come, so I shall hire a beach wagon and borrow Mr. Laurence's cherry-bounce." (Hannah's pronunciation of charabanc.)

"All of this will be expensive, Amy."

"Not very. I've calculated the cost, and I'll pay for it myself."

"Don't you think, dear, that as these girls are used to such things, and the best we can do will be nothing new, that some simpler plan would be pleasanter to them, as a change if nothing more, and much better for us than buying or borrowing what we don't need, and attempting a style not in keeping with our circumstances?"

"If I can't have it as I like, I don't care to have it at all. I know that I can carry it out perfectly well, if you and the girls will help a little, and I don't see why I can't if I'm willing to pay for it," said Amy, with the decision which opposition was apt to change into obstinacy.

Mrs. March knew that experience was an excellent teacher, and when it was possible she left her children to learn alone the lessons which she would gladly have made easier, if they had not objected to taking advice as much as they did salts and senna.

"Very well, Amy, if your heart is set upon it, and you see your way through without too great an outlay of money, time, and temper, I'll say no more. Talk it over with the girls, and whichever way you decide, I'll do my best to help you."

"Thanks, Mother, you are always so kind." And away went Amy to lay her plan before her sisters. Meg agreed at once, and promised to her aid, gladly offering anything she possessed, from her little house itself to her very best saltspoons. But Jo frowned upon the whole project and would have nothing to do with it at first.

"Why in the world should you spend your money, worry your family, and turn the house upside down for a parcel of girls who don't care a sixpence for you? I thought you had too much pride and sense to truckle to any mortal woman just because she wears French boots and rides in a coupe," said Jo, who, being called from the tragic climax of her novel, was not in the best mood for social enterprises.

"I don't truckle, and I hate being patronized as much as you do!" returned Amy indignantly, for the two still jangled when such questions arose. "The girls do care for me, and I for them, and there's a great deal of kindness and sense and talent among them, in spite of what you call fashionable nonsense. You don't care to make people like you, to go into good society, and cultivate your manners and tastes. I do, and I mean to make the most of every chance that comes. You can go through the world with your elbows out and your nose in the air, and call it independence, if you like. That's not my way."

When Amy had whetted her tongue and freed her mind she usually got the best of it, for she seldom failed to have common sense on her side, while Jo carried her love of liberty and hate of conventionalities to such an unlimited extent that she naturally found herself worsted in an argument. Amy's definition of Jo's idea of independence was such a good hit that both burst out laughing, and the discussion took a more amiable turn. Much against her will, Jo at length consented to sacrifice a day to Mrs. Grundy, and help her sister through what she regarded as 'a nonsensical business'.

The invitations were sent, nearly all accepted, and the following Monday was set apart for the grand event. Hannah was out of humor because her week's work was deranged, and prophesied that "ef the washin' and ironin' warn't done reg'lar, nothin' would go well anywheres". This hitch in the mainspring of the domestic machinery had a bad effect upon the whole concern, but Amy's motto was 'Nil desperandum', and having made up her mind what to do, she proceeded to do it in spite of all obstacles. To begin with, Hannah's cooking didn't turn out well. The chicken was tough, the tongue too salt, and the chocolate wouldn't froth properly. Then the cake and ice cost more than Amy expected, so did the wagon, and various other expenses, which seemed trifling at the outset, counted up rather alarmingly afterward. Beth got a cold and took to her bed. Meg had an unusual number of callers to keep her at home, and Jo was in such a divided state of mind that her breakages, accidents, and mistakes were uncommonly numerous, serious, and trying.

It it was not fair on Monday, the young ladies were to come on Tuesday, and arrangement which aggravated Jo and Hannah to the last degree. On Monday morning the weather was in that undecided state which is more exasperating than a steady pour. It drizzled a little, shone a little, blew a little, and didn't make up its mind till it was too late for anyone else to make up theirs. Amy was up at dawn, hustling people out of their beds and through their breakfasts, that the house might be got in order. The parlor struck her as looking uncommonly shabby, but without stopping to sigh for what she had not, she skillfully made the best of what she had, arranging chairs over the worn places in the carpet, covering stains on the walls with homemade statuary, which gave an artistic air to the room, as did the lovely vases of flowers Jo scattered about.

The lunch looked charming, and as she surveyed it, she sincerely hoped it would taste well, and that the borrowed glass, china, and silver would get safely home again. The carriages were promised, Meg and Mother were all ready to do the honors, Beth was able to help Hannah behind the scenes, Jo had engaged to be as lively and amiable as an absent mind, and aching head, and a very decided disapproval of everybody and everything would allow, and as she wearily dressed, Amy cheered herself with anticipations of the happy moment when, lunch safely over, she should drive away with her friends for an afternoon of artistic delights, for the 'cherry bounce' and the broken bridge were her strong points.

Then came the hours of suspense, during which she vibrated from parlor to porch, while public opinion varied like the weathercock. A smart shower at eleven had evidently quenched the enthusiasm of the young ladies who were to arrive at twelve, for nobody came, and at two the exhausted family sat down in a blaze of sunshine to consume the perishable portions of the feast, that nothing might be lost.

"No doubt about the weather today, they will certainly come, so we must fly round and be ready for them," said Amy, as the sun woke her next morning. She spoke briskly, but in her secret soul she wished she had said nothing about Tuesday, for her interest like her cake was getting a little stale.

"I can't get any lobsters, so you will have to do without salad today," said Mr. March, coming in half an hour later, with an expression of placid despair.

"Use the chicken then, the toughness won't matter in a salad," advised his wife.

"Hannah left it on the kitchen table a minute, and the kittens got at it. I'm very sorry, amy," added Beth, who was still a patroness of cats.

"Then I must have a lobster, for tongue alone won't do," said Amy decidedly.

"Shall I rush into town and demand one?" asked Jo, with the magnanimity of a martyr.

"You'd come bringing it home under your arm without any paper, just to try me. I'll go myself," answered Amy, whose temper was beginning to fail.

Shrouded in a thick veil and armed with a genteel traveling basket, she departed, feeling that a cool drive would soothe her ruffled spirit and fit her for the labors of the day. After some delay, the object of her desire was procured, likewise a bottle of dressing to prevent further loss of time at home, and off she drove again, well pleased with her own forethought.

As the omnibus contained only one other passenger, a sleepy old lady, Amy pocketed her veil and beguiled the tedium of the way by trying to find out where all her money had gone to. So busy was she with her card full of refractory figures that she did not observe a newcomer, who entered without stopping the vehicle, till a masculine voice said, "Good morning, Miss March," and, looking up, she beheld one of Laurie's most elegant college friends. Fervently hoping that he would get out before she did, Amy utterly ignored the basket at her feet, and congratulating herself that she had on her new traveling dress, returned the young man's greeting with her usual suavity and spirit.

They got on excellently, for Amy's chief care was soon set at rest by learning that the gentleman would leave first, and she was chatting away in a peculiarly lofty strain, when the old lady got out. In stumbling to the door, she upset the basket, and—oh horror!—the lobster, in all its vulgar size and brilliancy, was revealed to the highborn eyes of a Tudor.

"By Jove, she's forgotten her dinner!" cried the unconscious youth, poking the scarlet monster into its place with his cane, and preparing to hand out the basket after the old lady.

"Please don't—it's—it's mine," murmured Amy, with a face nearly as red as her fish.

"Oh, really, I beg pardon. It's an uncommonly fine one, isn't it?" said Tudor, with great presence of mind, and an air of sober interest that did credit to his breeding.

Amy recovered herself in a breath, set her basket boldly on the seat, and said, laughing, "Don't you wish you were to have some of the salad he's going to make, and to see the charming young ladies who are to eat it?"

Now that was tact, for two of the ruling foibles of the masculine mind were touched. The lobster was instantly surrounded by a halo of pleasing reminiscences, and curiosity about 'the charming young ladies' diverted his mind from the comical mishap.

"I suppose he'll laugh and joke over it with Laurie, but I shan't see them, that's a comfort," thought Amy, as Tudor bowed and departed.

She did not mention this meeting at home (though she discovered that, thanks to the upset, her new dress was much damaged by the rivulets of dressing that meandered down the skirt), but went through with the preparations which now seemed more irksome than before, and at twelve o'clock all was ready again. feeling that the neighbors were interested in her movements, she wished to efface the memory of yesterday's failure by a grand success today, so she ordered the 'cherry bounce', and drove away in state to meet and escort her guests to the banquet.

"There's the rumble, they're coming! I'll go onto the porch and meet them. It looks hospitable, and I want the poor child to have a good time after all her trouble," said Mrs. March, suiting the action to the word. But after one glance, she retired, with an indescribable expression, for looking quite lost in the big carriage, sat Amy and one young lady.

"Run, Beth, and help Hannah clear half the things off the table. It will be too absurd to put a luncheon for twelve before a single girl," cried Jo, hurrying away to the lower regions, too excited to stop even for a laugh.

In came Amy, quite calm and delightfully cordial to the one guest who had kept her promise. The rest of the family, being of a dramatic turn, played their parts equally well, and Miss Eliott found them a most hilarious set, for it was impossible to control entirely the merriment which possessed them. The remodeled lunch being gaily partaken of, the studio and garden visited, and art discussed with enthusiasm, Amy ordered a buggy (alas for the elegant cherry-bounce), and drove her friend quietly about the neighborhood till sunset, when 'the party went out'.

As she came walking in, looking very tired but as composed as ever, she observed that every vestige of the unfortunate fete had disappeared, except a suspicious pucker about the corners of Jo's mouth.

"You've had a loverly afternoon for your drive, dear," said her mother, as respectfully as if the whole twelve had come.

"Miss Eliott is a very sweet girl, and seemed to enjoy herself, I thought," observed Beth, with unusual warmth.

"Could you spare me some of your cake? I really need some, I have so much company, and I can't make such delicious stuff as yours," asked Meg soberly.

"Take it all. I'm the only one here who likes sweet things, and it will mold before I can dispose of it," answered Amy, thinking with a sigh of the generous store she had laid in for such an end as this.

"It's a pity Laurie isn't here to help us," began Jo, as they sat down to ice cream and salad for the second time in two days.

A warning look from her mother checked any further remarks, and the whole family ate in heroic silence, till Mr. March mildly observed, "salad was one of the favorite dishes of the ancients, and Evelyn . . ." Here a general explosion of laughter cut short the 'history of salads', to the great surprise of the learned gentleman.

"Bundle everything into a basket and send it to the Hummels. Germans like messes. I'm sick of the sight of this, and there's no reason you should all die of a surfeit because I've been a fool," cried Amy, wiping her eyes. "I thought I should have died when I saw you two girls rattling about in the what-you-call-it, like two little kernels in a very big nutshell, and Mother waiting in state to receive the throng," sighed Jo, quite spent with laughter.

"I'm very sorry you were disappointed, dear, but we all did our best to satisfy you," said Mrs. March, in a tone full of motherly regret.

"I am satisfied. I've done what I undertook, and it's not my fault that it failed. I comfort myself with that," said Amy with a little quiver in her voice. "I thank you all very much for helping me, and I'll thank you still more if you won't allude to it for a month, at least."

No one did for several months, but the word 'fete' always produced a general smile, and Laurie's birthday gift to Amy was a tiny coral lobster in the shape of a charm for her watch guard.

Chapter Twenty-Seven

Fortune suddenly smiled upon Jo, and dropped a good luck penny in her path. Not a golden penny, exactly, but I doubt if half a million would have given more real happiness then did the little sum that came to her in this wise.

Every few weeks she would shut herself up in her room, put on her scribbling suit, and 'fall into a vortex', as she expressed it, writing away at her novel with all her heart and soul, for till that was finished she could find no peace. Her 'scribbling suit' consisted of a black woolen pinafore on which she could wipe her pen at will, and a cap of the same material, adorned with a cheerful red bow, into which she bundled her hair when the decks were cleared for action. This cap was a beacon to the inquiring eyes of her family, who during these periods kept their distance, merely popping in their heads semi-occasionally to ask, with interest, "Does genius burn, Jo?" They did not always venture even to ask this question, but took an observation of the cap, and judged accordingly. If this expressive article of dress was drawn low upon the forehead, it was a sign that hard work was going on, in exciting moments it was pushed rakishly askew, and when despair seized the author it was plucked wholly off, and cast upon the floor, and cast upon the floor. At such times the intruder silently withdrew, and not until the red bow was seen gaily erect upon the gifted brow, did anyone dare address Jo.

She did not think herself a genius by any means, but when the writing fit came on, she gave herself up to it with entire abandon, and led a blissful life, unconscious of want, care, or bad weather, while she sat safe and happy in an imaginary world, full of friends almost as real and dear to her as any in the flesh. Sleep forsook her eyes, meals stood untasted, day and night were all too short to enjoy the happiness which blessed her only at such times, and made these hours worth living, even if they bore no other fruit. The devine afflatus usually lasted a week or two, and then she emerged from her 'vortex', hungry, sleepy, cross, or despondent.

She was just recovering from one of these attacks when she was prevailed upon to escort Miss Crocker to a lecture, and in return for her virtue was rewarded with a new idea. It was a People's Course, the lecture on the Pyramids, and Jo rather wondered at the choice of such a subject for such an audience, but took it for granted that some great social evil would be remedied or some great want supplied by unfolding the glories of the Pharaohs to an audience whose thoughts were busy with the price of coal and flour, and whose lives were spent in trying to solve harder riddles than that of the Sphinx.

They were early, and while Miss Crocker set the heel of her stocking, Jo amused herself by examining the faces of the people who occupied the seat with them. On her left were two matrons, with massive foreheads and bonnets to match, discussing Women's Rights and making tatting. Beyond sat a pair of humble lovers, artlessly holding each other by the hand, a somber spinster eating peppermints out of a paper bag, and an old gentleman taking his preparatory nap behind a yellow bandanna. On her right, her only neighbor was a studious looking lad absorbed in a newspaper.

It was a pictorial sheet, and Jo examined the work of art nearest her, idly wondering what fortuitous concatenation of circumstances needed the melodramatic illustration of an Indian in full war costume, tumbling over a precipice with a wolf at his throat, while two infuriated young gentlemen, with unnaturally small feet and big eyes, were stabbing each other close by, and a disheveled female was flying away in the background with her mouth wide open. Pausing to turn a page, the lad saw her looking and, with boyish good nature offered half his paper, saying bluntly, "want to read it? That's a first-rate story."

Jo accepted it with a smile, for she had never outgrown her liking for lads, and soon found herself involved in the usual labyrinth of love, mystery, and murder, for the story belonged to that class of light literature in which the passions have a holiday, and when the author's invention fails, a grand catastrophe clears the stage of one half the dramatis personae, leaving the other half to exult over their downfall.

"Prime, isn't it?" asked the boy, as her eye went down the last paragraph of her portion.

"I think you and I could do as well as that if we tried," returned Jo, amused at his admiration of the trash.

"I should think I was a pretty lucky chap if I could. She makes a good living out of such stories, they say." And he pointed to the name of Mrs. S.L.A.N.G. Northbury, under the title of the tale.

"Do you know her?" asked Jo, with sudden interest.

"No, but I read all her pieces, and I know a fellow who works in the office where this paper is printed." "Do you say she makes a good living out of stories like this?" And Jo looked more respectfully at the agitated group and thickly sprinkled exclamation points that adorned the page.

"Guess she does! She knows just what folks like, and gets paid well for writing it."

Here the lecture began, but Jo heard very little of it, for while Professor Sands was prosing away about Belzoni, Cheops, scarabei, and hieroglyphics, she was covertly taking down the address of the paper, and boldly resolving to try for the hundred-dollar prize offered in its columns for a sensational story.

By the time the lecture ended and the audience awoke, she had built up a splendid fortune for herself (not the first founded on paper), and was already deep in the concoction of her story, being unable to decide whether the duel should come before the elopement or after the murder.

she said nothing of her plan at home, but fell to work next day, much to the disquiet of her mother, who always looked a little anxious when 'genius took to burning'. Jo had never tried this style before, contenting herself with very mild romances for THE SPREAD EAGLE. Her experience and miscellaneous reading were of service now, for they gave her some idea of dramatic effect, and supplied plot, language, and costumes. Her story was as full of desperation and despair as her limited acquaintance with those uncomfortable emotions enabled her to make it, and having located it in Lisbon, she wound up with an earthquake, as a striking and appropriate denouement. The manuscript was privately dispatched, accompanied by a note, modestly saying that if the tale didn't get the prize, which the writer hardly dared expect, she would be very glad to receive any sum it might be considered worth.

Six weeks is a long time to wait, and a still longer time for a girl to keep a secret, but Jo did both, and was just beginning to give up all hope of ever seeing her manuscript again, when a letter arrived which almost took her breath away, for on opening it, a check for a hundred dollars fell into her lap. For a minute she stared at it as if it had been a snake, then she read her letter and began to cry. If the amiable gentleman who wrote that kindly note could have known what intense happiness he was giving a fellow creature, I think he would devote his leisure hours, if he has any, to that amusement, for Jo valued the letter more than the money, because it was encouraging, and after years of effort it was so pleasant to find that she had learned to do something, though it was only to write a sensation story.

A prouder young woman was seldom seen than she, when, having composed herself, she electrified the family by appearing before them with the letter in one hand, the check in the other, announcing that she had won the prize. Of course there was a great jubilee, and when the story came everyone read and praised it, though after her father had told her that the language was good, the romance fresh and hearty, and the tragedy quite thrilling, he shook his head, and said in his unworldly way . . .

"You can do better than this, Jo. Aim at the highest, and never mind the money."

"I think the money is the best part of it. What will you do with such a fortune?" asked Amy, regarding the magic slip of paper with a reverential eye.

"Send Beth and Mother to the seaside for a month or two," answered Jo promptly.

To the seaside they went, after much discussion, and though Beth didn't come home as plump and rosy as could be desired, she was much better, while Mrs. March declared she felt ten years younger. So Jo was satisfied with the investment of her prize money, and fell to work with a cheery spirit, bent on earning more of those delightful checks. She did earn several that year, and began to feel herself a power in the house, for by the magic of a pen, her 'rubbish' turned into comforts for them all. The Duke's Daughter paid the butcher's bill, A Phantom Hand put down a new carpet, and the Curse of the Coventrys proved the blessing of the Marches in the way of groceries and gowns.

Wealth is certainly a most desirable thing, but poverty has its sunny side, and one of the sweet uses of adversity is the genuine satisfaction which comes from hearty work of head or hand, and to the inspiration of necessity, we owe half the wise, beautiful, and useful blessings of the world. Jo enjoyed a taste of this satisfaction, and ceased to envy richer girls, taking great comfort in the knowledge that she could supply her own wants, and need ask no one for a penny.

Little notice was taken of her stories, but they found a market, and encouraged by this fact, she resolved to make a bold stroke for fame and fortune. Having copied her novel for the fourth time, read it to all her confidential friends, and submitted it with fear and trembling to three publishers, she at last disposed of it, on condition that she would cut it down one third, and omit all the parts which she particularly admired.

"Now I must either bundle it back in to my tin kitchen to mold, pay for printing it myself, or chop it up to suit purchasers and get what I can for it. Fame is a very good thing to have in the house, but cash is more convenient, so I wish to take the sense of the meeting on this important subject," said Jo, calling a family council.

"Don't spoil your book, my girl, for there is more in it than you know, and the idea is well worked out. Let it wait and ripen," was her father's advice, and he practiced what he preached, having waited patiently thirty years for fruit of his own to ripen, and being in no haste to gather it even now when it was sweet and mellow.

"It seems to me that Jo will profit more by taking the trial than by waiting," said Mrs. March. "Criticism is the best test of such work, for it will show her both unsuspected merits and faults, and help her to do better next time. We are too partial, but the praise and blame of outsiders will prove useful, even if she gets but little money."

"Yes," said Jo, knitting her brows, "that's just it. I've been fussing over the thing so long, I really don't know whether it's good, bad, or indifferent. It will be a great help to have cool, impartial persons take a look at it, and tell me what they think of it."

"I wouldn't leave a word out of it. You'll spoil it if you do, for the interest of the story is more in the minds than in the actions of the people, and it will be all a muddle if you don't explain as you go on," said Meg, who firmly believed that this book was the most remarkable novel ever written.

"But Mr. Allen says, 'Leave out the explanations, make it brief and dramatic, and let the characters tell the story,'" interrupted Jo, turning to the publisher's note.

"Do as he tells you. He knows what will sale, and we don't. Make a good, popular book, and get as much money as you can. By-and-by, when you've got a name, you can afford to digress, and have philosophical and metaphysical people in your novels," said Amy, who took a strictly practical view of the subject.

"Well," said Jo, laughing, "if my people are 'philosophical and metaphysical', it isn't my fault, for I know nothing about such things, except what I hear father say;, sometimes. If I've got some of his wise ideas jumbled up with my romance, so much the better for me. Now, Beth, what do you say?"

"I should so like to see it printed soon," was all Beth said, and smiled in saying it. But there was an unconscious emphasis on the last word, and a wistful look in the eyes that never lost their childlike candor, which chilled Jo's heart for a minute with a forboding fear, and decided her to make her little venture 'soon'.

So, with Spartan firmness, the young authoress laid her first-born on her table, and chopped it up as ruthlessly as any ogre. In the hope of pleasing everyone, she took everyone's advice, and like the old man and his donkey in the fable suited nobody.

Her father liked the metaphysical streak which had unconsciously got into it, so that was allowed to remain though she had her doubts about it. Her mother thought that there was a trifle too much description. Out, therefore it came, and with it many necessary links in the story. Meg admired the tragedy, so Jo piled up the agony to suit her, while Amy objected to the fun, and, with the best intentions in life, Jo quenched the spritly scenes which relieved the somber character of the story. Then, to complicate the ruin, she cut it down one third, and confidingly sent the poor little romance, like a picked robin, out into the big, busy world to try its fate.

Well, it was printed, and she got three hundred dollars for it, likewise plenty of praise and blame, both so much greater than she expected that she was thrown into a state of bewilderment from which it took her some time to recover.

"You said, Mother, that criticism would help me. But how can it, when it's so contradictory that I don't know whether I've written a promising book or broken all the ten commandments?" cried poor Jo, turning over a heap of notices, the perusal of which filled her with pride and joy one minute, wrath and dismay the next. "This man says, 'An exquisite book, full of truth, beauty, and earnestness.

All is sweet, pure, and healthy.'" continued the perplexed authoress. "The next, 'The theory of the book is bad, full of morbid fancies, spiritualistic ideas, and unnatural characters.' Now, as I had no theory of any kind, don't believe in Spiritualism, and copied my characters from life, I don't see how this critic can be right. Another says, 'It's one of the best American novels which has appeared for years.' (I know better than that), and the next asserts that 'Though it is original, and written with great force and feeling, it is a dangerous book.' 'Tisn't! Some make fun of it, some overpraise, and nearly all insist that I had a deep theory to expound, when I only wrote it for the pleasure and the money. I wish I'd printed the whole or not at all, for I do hate to be so misjudged."

Her family and friends administered comfort and commendation liberally. Yet it was a hard time for sensitive, high-spirited Jo, who meant so well and had apparently done so ill. But it did her good, for those whose opinion had real value gave her the critism which is an author's best education, and when the first soreness was over, she could laugh at her poor little book, yet believe in it still, and feel herself the wiser and stronger for the buffeting she had received.

"Not being a genius, like Keats, it won't kill me," she said stoutly, "and I've got the joke on my side, after all, for the parts that were taken straight out of real life are denounced as impossible and absurd, and the scenes that I made up out of my own silly head are pronounced 'charmingly natural, tender, and true'. So I'll comfort myself with that, and when I'm ready, I'll up again and take another."

Chapter Twenty-Eight

Like most other young matrons, Meg began her married life with the determination to be a model housekeeper. John should find home a paradise, he should always see a smiling face, should fare sumptuously every day, and never know the loss of a button. She brought so much love, energy, and cheerfulness to the work that she could not but succeed, in spite of some obstacles. Her paradise was not a tranquil one, for the little woman fussed, was over-anxious to please, and bustled about like a true Martha, cumbered with many cares. She was too tired, sometimes, even to smile, John grew dyspeptic after a course of dainty dishes and ungratefully demanded plain fare. As for buttons, she soon learned to wonder where they went, to shake her head over the carelessness of men, and to threaten to make him sew them on himself, and see if his work would stand impatient and clumsy fingers any better than hers.

They were very happy, even after they discovered that they couldn't live on love alone. John did not find Meg's beauty diminished, though she beamed at him from behind the familiar coffee pot. Nor did Meg miss any of the romance from the daily parting, when her husband followed up his kiss with the tender inquiry, "Shall I send some veal or mutton for dinner, darling?" The little house ceased to be a glorified bower, but it became a home, and the young couple soon felt that it was a change for the better. At first they played keep-house, and frolicked over it like children. Then John took steadily to business, feeling the cares of the head of a family upon his shoulders, and Meg laid by her cambric wrappers, put on a big apron, and fell to work, as before said, with more energy than discretion.

While the cooking mania lasted she went through Mrs. Cornelius's Receipt Book as if it were a mathematical exercise, working out the problems with patience and care. Sometimes her family were invited in to help eat up a too bounteous feast of successes, or Lotty would be privately dispatched with a batch of failures, which were to be concealed from all eyes in the convenient stomachs of the little Hummels. An evening with John over the account books usually produced a temporary lull in the culinary enthusiasm, and a frugal fit would ensue, during which the poor man was put through a course of bread pudding, hash, and warmed-over coffee, which tried his soul, although he bore it with praiseworthy fortitude. Before the golden mean was found, however, Meg added to her domestic possessions what young couples seldom get on long without, a family jar.

Fired a with housewifely wish to see her storeroom stocked with homemade preserves, she undertook to put up her own currant jelly. John was requested to order home a dozen or so of little pots and an extra quantity of sugar, for their own currants were ripe and were to be attended to at once. As John firmly believed that 'my wife' was equal to anything, and took a natural pride in her skill, he resolved that she should be gratified, and their only crop of fruit laid by in a most pleasing form for winter use. Home came four dozen delightful little pots, half a barrel of sugar, and a small boy to pick the currants for her. With her pretty hair tucked into a little cap, arms bared to the elbow, and a checked apron which had a coquettish look in spite of the bib, the young housewife fell to work, feeling no doubts about her success, for hadn't she seen Hannah do it hundreds of times? The array of pots rather amazed her at first, but John was so fond of jelly, and the nice little jars would look so well on the top shelf, that Meg resolved to fill them all, and spend a long day picking, boiling, straining, and fussing over her jelly. She did her best, she asked advice of Mrs. Cornelius, she racked her brain to remember what Hannah did that she left undone, she reboiled, resugared, and restrained, but that dreadful stuff wouldn't 'jell'.

She longed to run home, bib and all, and ask Mother to lend her a hand, but John and she had agreed that they would never annoy anyone with their private worries, experiments, or quarrels. They had laughed over that last word as if the idea it suggested was a most preposterous one, but they had held to their resolve, and whenever they could get on without help they did so, and no one interfered, for Mrs. March had advised the plan. So Meg wrestled alone with the refractory sweetmeats all that hot summer day, and at five o'clock sat down in her topsy-turvey kitchen, wrung her bedaubed hands, lifted up her voice and wept.

Now, in the first flush of the new life, she had often said, "My husband shall always feel free to bring a friend home whenever he likes. I shall always be prepared. There shall be no flurry, no scolding, no discomfort, but a neat house, a cheerful wife, and a good dinner. John, dear, never stop to ask my leave, invite whom you please, and be sure of a welcome from me."

How charming that was, to be sure! John quite glowed with pride to hear her say it, and felt what a blessed thing it was to have a superior wife. But, although they had had company from time to time, it never happened to be unexpected, and Meg had never had an opportunity to distinguish herself till now. It always happens so in this vale of tears, there is an inevitability about such things which we can only wonder at, deplore, and bear as we best can.

If John had not forgotten all about the jelly, it really would have been unpardonable in him to choose that day, of all the days in the year, to bring a friend home to dinner unexpectedly. Congratulating himself that a handsome repast had been ordered that morning, feeling sure that it would be ready to the minute, and indulging in pleasant anticipations of the charming effect it would produce, when his pretty wife came running out to meet him, he escorted his friend to his mansion, with the irrepressible satisfaction of a young host and husband.

It is a world of disappointments, as John discovered when he reached the Dovecote. the front door usually stood hospitably open. Now it was not only shut, but locked, and yesterday's mud still adorned the steps. The parlor windows were closed and curtained, no picture of the pretty wife sewing on the piazza, in white, with a distracting little bow in her hair, or a bright-eyed hostess, smiling a shy welcome as she greeted her guest. Nothing of the sort, for not a soul appeared but a sanginary-looking boy asleep under the current bushes.

"I'm afraid something has happened. Step into the garden, Scott, while I look up Mrs. Brooke," said John, alarmed at the silence and solitude.

Round the house he hurried, led by a pungent smell of burned sugar, and Mr. Scott strolled after him, with a queer look on his face. He paused discreetly at a distance when Brooke disappeared, but he could both see and hear, and being a bachelor, enjoyed the prospect mightily.

In the kitchen reigned confusion and despair. One edition of jelly was trickled from pot to pot, another lay upon the floor, and a third was burning gaily on the stove. Lotty, with Teutonic phlegm, was calmly eating bread and currant wine, for the jelly was still in a hopelessly liquid state, while Mrs. Brooke, with her apron over her head, sat sobbing dismally.

"My dearest girl, what is the matter?" cried John, rushing in, with awful visions of scalded hands, sudden news of affliction, and secret consternation at the thought of the guest in the garden.

"Oh, John, I am so tired and hot and cross and worried! I've been at it till I'm all worn out. Do come and help me or I shall die!" And the exhausted housewife cast herself upon his breast, giving him a sweet welcome in every sense of the word, for her pinafore had been baptized at the same time as the floor.

"What worries you dear? Has anything dreadful happened?" asked the anxious John, tenderly kissing the crown of the little cap, which was all askew.

"Yes," sobbed Meg despairingly.

"Tell me quick, then. Don't cry. I can bear anything better than that. Out with it, love."

"The . . .The jelly won't jell and I don't know what to do!"

John Brooke laughed then as he never dared to laugh afterward, and the derisive Scott smiled involuntarily as he heard the hearty peal, which put the finishing stroke to poor Meg's woe.

"Is that all? Fling it out of the window, and don't bother any more about it. I'll buy you quarts if you want it, but for heaven's sake don't have hysterics, for I've brought Jack Scott home to dinner, and . . ."

John got no further, for Meg cast him off, and clasped her hands with a tragic gesture as she fell into a chair, exclaiming in a tone of mingled indignation, reproach, and dismay . . .

"A man to dinner, and everything in a mess! John Brooke, how could you do such a thing?"

"Hush, he's in the garden! I forgot the confounded jelly, but it can't be helped now," said John, surveying the prospect with an anxious eye.

"You ought to have sent word, or told me this morning, and you ought to have remembered how busy I was," continued Meg petulantly, for even turtledoves will peck when ruffled.

"I didn't know it this morning, and there was no time to send word, for I met him on the way out. I never thought of asking leave, when you have always told me to do as I liked. I never tried it before, and hang me if I ever do again!" added John, with an aggrieved air.

"I should hope not! Take him away at once. I can't see him, and there isn't any dinner."

"Well, I like that! Where's the beef and vegetables I sent home, and the pudding you promised?" cried John, rushing to the larder. "I hadn't time to cook anything. I meant to dine at Mother's. I'm sorry, but I was so busy," and Meg's tears began again.

John was a mild man, but he was human, and after a long day's work to come home tired, hungry, and hopeful, to find a chaotic house, an empty table, and a cross wife was not exactly conductive to repose of mind or manner. He restrained himself however, and the little squall would have blown over, but for one unlucky word.

"It's a scrape, I acknowledge, but if you will lend a hand, we'll pull through and have a good time yet. Don't cry, dear, but just exert yourself a bit, and fix us up something to eat. We're both as hungry as hunters, so we shan't mind what it is. Give us the cold meat, and bread and cheese. We won't ask for jelly."

He meant it to be a good-natured joke, but that one word sealed his fate. Meg thought it was too cruel to hint about her sad failure, and the last atom of patience vanished as he spoke.

"You must get yourself out of the scrape as you can. I'm too used up to 'exert' myself for anyone. It's like a man to propose a bone and vulgar bread and cheese for company. I won't have anything of the sort in my house. Take that Scott up to Mother's, and tell him I'm away, sick, dead, anything. I won't see him, and you two can laugh at me and my jelly as much as you like. You won't have anything else here." And having delivered her defiance all on one breath, Meg cast away her pinafore and precipitately left the field to bemoan herself in her own room.

What those two creatures did in her absence, she never knew, but Mr. scott was not taken 'up to Mother's', and when Meg descended, after they had strolled away together, she found traces of a promiscuous lunch which filled her with horror. Lotty reported that they had eaten "a much, and greatly laughed, and the master bid her throw away all the sweet stuff, and hide the pots."

Meg longed to go and tell Mother, but a sense of shame at her own short comings, of loyalty to John, "who might be cruel, but nobody should know it," restrained her, and after a summary cleaning up, she dressed herself prettily, and sat down to wait for John to come and be forgiven.

Unfortunately, John didn't come, not seeing the matter in that light. He had carried it off as a good joke with Scott, excused his little wife as well as he could, and played the host so hospitably that his friend enjoyed the impromptu dinner, and promised to come again, but John was angry, though he did not show it, he felt that Meg had deserted him in his hour of need. "It wasn't fair to tell a man to bring folks home any time, with perfect freedom, and when he took you at your word, to flame up and blame him, and leave him in the lurch, to be laughed at or pitied. No, by George, it wasn't! And Meg must know it."

He had fumed inwardly during the feast, but when the flurry was over and he strolled home after seeing Scott off, a milder mood came over him. "Poor little thing! It was hard upon her when she tried so heartily to please me. She was wrong, of course, but then she was young. I must be patient and teach her." He hoped she had not gone home—he hated gossip and interference. For a minute he was ruffled again at the mere thought of it, and then the fear that Meg would cry herself sick softened his heart, and sent him on at a quicker pace, resolving to be calm and kind, but firm, quite firm, and show her where she had failed in her duty to her spouse.

Meg likewise resolved to be 'calm and kind, but firm', and show him his duty. She longed to run to meet him, and beg pardon, and be kissed and comforted, as she was sure of being, but, of course, she did nothing of the sort, and when she saw John coming, began to hum quite naturally, as she rocked and sewed, like a lady of leisure in her best parlor.

John was a little disappointed not to find a tender Niobe, but feeling that his dignity demanded the first apology, he made none, only came leisurely in and laid himself upon the sofa with the singularly relevant remark, "We are going to have a new moon, my dear."

"I've no objection," was Meg's equally soothing remark. A few other topics of general interest were introduced by Mr. Brooke and wet-blanketed by Mrs. Brooke, and conversation languished. John went to one window, unfolded his paper, and wrapped himself in it, figuratively speaking. Meg went to the other window, and sewed as if new rosettes for slippers were among the necessaries of life. Neither spoke. Both looked quite 'calm and firm', and both felt desperately uncomfortable.

"Oh, dear," thought Meg, "married life is very trying, and does need infinite patience as well as love, as Mother says." The word 'Mother' suggested other maternal counsels given long ago, and received with unbelieving protests.

"John is a good man, but he has his faults, and you must learn to see and bear with them, remembering your own. He is very decided, but never will be obstinate, if you reason kindly, not oppose impatiently. He is very accurate, and particular about the truth—a good trait, though you call him 'fussy'. Never deceive him by look or word, Meg, and he will give you the confidence you deserve, the support you need. He has a temper, not like ours—one flash and then all over—but the white, still anger that is seldom stirred, but once kindled is hard to quench. Be careful, be very careful, not to wake his anger against yourself, for peace and happiness depend on keeping his respect. Watch yourself, be the first to ask pardon if you both err, and guard against the little piques, misunderstandings, and hasty words that often pave the way for bitter sorrow and regret."

These words came back to Meg, as she sat sewing in the sunset, especially the last. This was the first serious disagreement, her own hasty speeches sounded both silly and unkind, as she recalled them, her own anger looked childish now, and thoughts of poor John coming home to such a scene quite melted her heart. She glanced at him with tears in her eyes, but he did not see them. She put down her work and got up, thinking, "I will be the first to say, 'Forgive me', but he did not seem to hear her. She went very slowly across the room, for pride was hard to swallow, and stood by him, but he did not turn his head. For a minute she felt as if she really couldn't do it, then came the thought, This is the beginning. I'll do my part, and have nothing to reproach myself with," and stooping sown, she softly kissed her husband on the forehead. Of course that settled it. The penitent kiss was better than a world of words, and John had her on his knee in a minute, saying tenderly . . .

"It was too bad to laugh at the poor little jelly pots. Forgive me, dear. I never will again!"

But he did, oh bless you, yes, hundreds of times, and so did Meg, both declaring that it was the sweetest jelly they ever made, for family peace was preserved in that little family jar.

After this, Meg had Mr. Scott to dinner by special invitation, and served him up a pleasant feast without a cooked wife for the first course, on which occasion she was so gay and gracious, and made everything go off so charmingly, that Mr. Scott told John he was a lucky fellow, and shook his head over the hardships of bachelorhood all the way home.

In the autumn, new trials and experiences came to Meg. Sallie Moffat renewed her friendship, was always running out for a dish of gossip at the little house, or inviting 'that poor dear' to come in and spend the day at the big house. It was pleasant, for in dull weather Meg often felt lonely. All were busy at home, John absent till night, and nothing to do but sew, or read, or potter about. So it naturally fell out that Meg got into the way of gadding and gossiping with her friend. Seeing Sallie's pretty things made her long for such, and pity herself because she had not got them. Sallie was very kind, and often offered her the coveted trifles, but Meg declined them, knowing that John wouldn't like it, and then this foolish little woman went and did what John disliked even worse.

She knew her husband's income, and she loved to feel that he trusted her, not only with his happiness, but what some men seem to value more—his money. She knew where it was, was free to take what she liked, and all he asked was that she should keep account of every penny, pay bills once a month, and remember that she was a poor man's wife. Till now she had done well, been prudent and exact, kept her little account books neatly, and showed them to him monthly without fear. But that autumn the serpent got into Meg's paradise, and tempted her like many a modern Eve, not with apples, but with dress. Meg didn't like to be pitied and made to feel poor. It irritated her, but she was ashamed to confess it, and now and then she tried to console herself by buying something pretty, so that Sallie needn't think she had to economize. She always felt wicked after it, for the pretty things were seldom necessaries, but then they cost so little, it wasn't worth worrying about, so the trifles increased unconsciously, and in the shopping excursions she was no longer a passive looker-on.

But the trifles cost more than one would imagine, and when she cast up her accounts at the end of the month the sum total rather scared her. John was busy that month and left the bills to her, the next month he was absent, but the third he had a grand quarterly settling up, and Meg never forgot it. A few days before she had done a dreadful thing, and it weighed upon her conscience. Sallie had been buying silks, and Meg longed for a new one, just a handsome light one for parties, her black silk was so common, and thin things for evening wear were only proper for girls. Aunt March usually gave the sisters a present of twenty-five dollars apiece at New Year's. That was only a month to wait, and here was a lovely violet silk going at a bargain, and she had the money, if she only dared to take it. John always said what was his was hers, but would he think it right to spend not only the prospective five-and-twenty, but another five-and-twenty out of the household fund? That was the question. Sallie had urged her to do it, had offered to lend the money, and with the best intentions in life had tempted Meg beyond her strength. In an evil moment the shopman held up the lovely, shimmering folds, and said, "A bargain, I assure, you, ma'am." She answered, "I'll take it," and it was cut off and paid for, and Sallie had exulted, and she had laughed as if it were a thing of no consequence, and driven away, feeling as if she had stolen something, and the police were after her.

When she got home, she tried to assuage the pangs of remorse by spreading forth the lovely silk, but it looked less silvery now, didn't become her, after all, and the words 'fifty dollars' seemed stamped like a pattern down each breadth. She put it away, but it haunted her, not delightfully as a new dress should, but dreadfully like the ghost of a folly that was not easily laid. When John got out his books that night, Meg's heart sank, and for the first time in her married life, she was afraid of her husband. The kind, brown eyes looked as if they could be stern, and though he was unusually merry, she fancied he had found her out, but didn't mean to let her know it. The house bills were all paid, the books all in order. John had praised her, and was undoing the old pocketbook which they called the 'bank', when Meg, knowing that it was quite empty, stopped his hand, saying nervously . . .

"You haven't seen my private expense book yet."

John never asked to see it, but she always insisted on his doing so, and used to enjoy his masculine amazement at the queer things women wanted, and made him guess what piping was, demand fiercely the meaning of a hug-me-tight, or wonder how a little thing composed of three rosebuds, a bit of velvet, and a pair of strings, could possibly be a bonnet, and cost six dollars. That night he looked as if he would like the fun of quizzing her figures and pretending to be horrified at her extravagance, as he often did, being particularly proud of his prudent wife.

The little book was brought slowly out and laid down before him. Meg got behind his chair under pretense of smoothing the wrinkles out of his tired forehead, and standing there, she said, with her panic increasing with every word . . .

"John, dear, I'm ashamed to show you my book, for I've really been dreadfully extravagant lately. I go about so much I must have things, you know, and Sallie advised my getting it, so I did, and my New Year's money will partly pay for it, but I was sorry after I had done it, for I knew you'd think it wrong in me."

John laughed, and drew her round beside him, saying goodhumoredly, "Don't go and hide. I won't beat you if you have got a pair of killing boots. I'm rather proud of my wife's feet, and don't mind if she does pay eight or nine dollars for her boots, if they are good ones."

That had been one of her last 'trifles', and John's eye had fallen on it as he spoke. "Oh, what will he say when he comes to that awful fifty dollars!" thought Meg, with a shiver.

"It's worse than boots, it's a silk dress," she said, with the calmness of desperation, for she wanted the worst over.

"Well, dear, what is the 'dem'd total', as Mr. Mantalini says?"

That didn't sound like John, and she knew he was looking up at her with the straightforward look that she had always been ready to meet and answer with one as frank till now. She turned the page and her head at the same time, pointing to the sum which would have been bad enough without the fifty, but which was appalling to her with that added. For a minute the room was very still, then John said slowly—but she could feel it cost him an effort to express no displeasure— . . .

"Well, I don't know that fifty is much for a dress, with all the furbelows and notions you have to have to finish it off these days."

"It isn't made or trimmed," sighed Meg, faintly, for a sudden recollection of the cost still to be incurred quite overwhelmed her.

"Twenty-five yards of silk seems a good deal to cover one small woman, but I've no doubt my wife will look as fine as Ned Moffat's when she gets it on," said John dryly.

"I know you are angry, John, but I can't help it. I don't mean to waste your money, and I didn't think those little things would count up so. I can't resist them when I see Sallie buying all she wants, and pitying me because I don't. I try to be contented, but it is hard, and I'm tired of being poor."

The last words were spoken so low she thought he did not hear them, but he did, and they wounded him deeply, for he had denied himself many pleasures for Meg's sake. She could have bitten her tongue out the minute she had said it, for John pushed the books away and got up, saying with a little quiver in his voice, "I was afraid of this. I do my best, Meg." If he had scolded her, or even shaken her, it would not have broken her heart like those few words. She ran to him and held him close, crying, with repentant tears, "Oh, John, my dear, kind, hard-working boy. I didn't mean it! It was so wicked, so untrue and ungrateful, how could I say it! Oh, how could I say it!" He was very kind, forgave her readily, and did not utter one reproach, but Meg knew that she had done and said a thing which would not be forgotten soon, although he might never allude to it again. She had promised to love him for better or worse, and then she, his wife, had reproached him with his poverty, after spending his earnings recklessly. It was dreadful, and the worst of it was John went on so quietly afterward, just as if nothing had happened, except that he stayed in town later, and worked at night when she had gone to cry herself to sleep. A week or remorse nearly made Meg sick, and the discovery that John had countermanded the order for his new greatcoat reduced her to a state of despair which was pathetic to behold. He had simply said, in answer to her surprised inquiries as to the change, "I can't afford it, my dear."

Meg said no more, but a few minutes after he found her in the hall with her face buried in the old greatcoat, crying as if her heart would break.

They had a long talk that night, and Meg learned to love her husband better for his poverty, because it seemed to have made a man of him, given him the strength and courage to fight his own way, and taught him a tender patience with which to bear and comfort the natural longings and failures of those he loved.

Next day she put her pride in her pocket, went to Sallie, told the truth, and asked her to buy the silk as a favor. The good-natured Mrs. Moffat willingly did so, and had the delicacy not to make her a present of it immediately afterward. Then Meg ordered home the greatcoat, and when John arrived, she put it on, and asked him how he liked her new silk gown. One can imagine what answer he made, how he received his present, and what a blissful state of things ensued. John came home early, Meg gadded no more, and that greatcoat was put on in the morning by a very happy husband, and taken off at night by a most devoted little wife. So the year rolled round, and at mid-summer there came to Meg a new experience, the deepest and tenderest of a woman's life.

Laurie came sneaking into the kitchen of the Dovecote one Saturday, with an excited face, and was received with the clash of cymbals, for Hannah clapped her hands with a saucepan in one and the cover in the other.

"How's the little mamma? Where is everybody? Why didn't you tell me before I came home?" began Laurie in a loud whisper.

"Happy as a queen, the dear! Every soul of 'em is upstairs a worshipin'. We didn't want no hurrycanes round. Now you go into the parlor, and I'll send 'em down to you," with which somewhat involved reply Hannah vanished, chuckling ecstatically.

Presently Jo appeared, proudly bearing a flannel bundle laid forth upon a large pillow. Jo's face was very sober, but her eyes twinkled, and there was an odd sound in her voice of repressed emotion of some sort.

"Shut your eyes and hold out your arms," she said invitingly.

Laurie backed precipitately into a corner, and put his hands behind him with an imploring gesture. "No, thank you. I'd rather not. I shall drop it or smash it, as sure as fate."

"Then you shan't see your nevvy," said Jo decidedly, turning as if to go.

"I will, I will! Only you must be responsible for damages." And obeying orders, Laurie heroically shut his eyes while something was put into his arms. A peal of laughter from Jo, Amy, Mrs. March, Hannah, and John caused him to open them the next minute, to find himself invested with two babies instead of one.

No wonder they laughed, for the expression of his face was droll enough to convulse a Quaker, as he stood and stared wildly from the unconscious innocents to the hilarious spectators with such dismay that Jo sat down on the floor and screamed.

"Twins, by Jupiter!" was all he said for a minute, then turning to the women with an appealing look that was comically piteous, he added, "Take 'em quick, somebody! I'm going to laugh, and I shall drop 'em."

Jo rescued his babies, and marched up and down, with one on each are, as if already initiated into the mysteries of baby-tending, while Laurie laughed till the tears ran down his cheeks.

"It's the best joke of the season, isn't it? I wouldn't have told you, for I set my heart on surprising you, and I flatter myself I've done it," said Jo, when she got her breath.

"I never was more staggered in my life. Isn't it fun? Are they boys? What are you going to name them? Let's have another look. Hold me up, Jo, for upon my life it's one too many for me," returned Laurie, regarding the infants with the air of a big, benevolent Newfoundland looking at a pair of infantile kittens.

"Boy and girl. Aren't they beauties?" said the proud papa, beaming upon the little red squirmers as if they were unfledged angels.

"Most remarkable children I ever saw. Which is which?" and Laurie bent like a well-sweep to examine the prodigies.

"Amy put a blue ribbon on the boy and a pink on the girl, French fashion, so you can always tell. Besides, one has blue eyes and one brown. Kiss them, Uncle Teddy," said wicked Jo.

"I'm afraid they mightn't like it," began Laurie, with unusual timidity in such matters.

"Of course they will, they are used to it now. Do it this minute, sir!" commanded Jo, fearing he might propose a proxy.

Laurie screwed up his face and obeyed with a gingerly peck at each little cheek that produced another laugh, and made the babies squeal.

"There, I knew they didn't like it! That's the boy, see him kick, he hits out with his fists like a good one. Now then, young Brooke, pitch into a man of your own size, will you?" cried Laurie, delighted with a poke in the face from a tiny fist, flapping aimlessly about.

"He's to be named John Laurence, and the girl Margaret, after mother and grandmother. We shall call her Daisey, so as not to have two Megs, and I suppose the mannie will be Jack, unless we find a better name," said Amy, with aunt-like interest.

"Name him Demijohn, and call him Demi for short," said Laurie

"Daisy and Demi, just the thing! I knew Teddy would do it," cried Jo clapping her hands.

Teddy certainly had done it that time, for the babies were 'Daisy' and 'Demi' to the end of the chapter.

Chapter Twenty-Nine

"Come, Jo, it's time."

"For what?"

"You don't mean to say you have forgotten that you promised to make half a dozen calls with me today?"

"I've done a good many rash and foolish things in my life, but I don't think I ever was mad enough to say I'd make six calls in one day, when a single one upsets me for a week."

"Yes, you did, it was a bargain between us. I was to finish the crayon of Beth for you, and you were to go properly with me, and return our neighbors' visits."

"If it was fair, that was in the bond, and I stand to the letter of my bond, Shylock. There is a pile of clouds in the east, it's not fair, and I don't go."

"Now, that's shirking. It's a lovely day, no prospect of rain, and you pride yourself on keeping; promises, so be honorable, come and do your duty, and then be at peace for another six months."

At that minute Jo was particularly absorbed in dressmaking, for she was mantua-maker general to the family, and took especial credit to herself because she could use a needle as well as a pen. It was very provoking to be arrested in the act of a first tryingon, and ordered out to make calls in her best array on a warm July day. She hated calls of the formal sort, and never made any till Amy compelled her with a bargain, bribe, or promise. In the present instance there was no escape, and having clashed her scissors rebelliously, while protesting that she smelled thunder, she gave in, put away her work, and taking up her hat and gloves with an air of resignation, told Amy the victim was ready.

"Jo March, you are perverse enough to provoke a saint! You don't intend to make calls in that state, I hope," cried Amy, surveying her with amazement.

"Why not? I'm neat and cool and comfortable, quite proper for a dusty walk on a warm day. If people care more for my clothes than they do for me, I don't wish to see them. You can dress for both, and be as elegant as you please. It pays for you to be fine. It doesn't for me, and furbelows only worry me."

"Oh, dear!" sighed Amy, "now she's in a contrary fit, and will drive me distracted before I can get her properly ready. I'm sure it's no pleasure to me to go today, but it's a debt we owe society, and there's no one to pay it but you and me. I'll do anything for you, Jo, if you'll only dress yourself nicely, and come and help me do the civil. You can talk so well, look so aristocratic in your best things, and behave so beautifully, if you try, that I'm proud of you. I'm afraid to go alone, do come and take care of me."

"You're an artful little puss to flatter and wheedle your cross old sister in that way. The idea of my being aristocratic and well-bred, and your being afraid to go anywhere alone! I don't know which is the most absurd. Well, I'll go if I must, and do my best. You shall be commander of the expedition, and I'll obey blindly, will that satisfy you?" said Jo, with a sudden change from perversity to lamblike submission.

"You're a perfect cherub! Now put on all your best things, and I'll tell you how to behave at each place, so that you will make a good impression. I want people to like you, and they would if you'd only try to be a little more agreeable. Do your hair the pretty way, and put the pink rose in your bonnet. It's becoming, and you look too sober in your plain suit. Take your light gloves and the embroidered handkerchief. We'll stop at Meg's, and borrow her white sunshade, and then you can have my dove-colored one."

While Amy dressed, she issued her orders, and Jo obeyed them, not without entering her protest, however, for she sighed as she rustled into her new organdie, frowned darkly at herself as she tied her bonnet strings in an irreproachable bow, wrestled viciously with pins as she put on her collar, wrinkled up her features generally as she shook out the handkerchief, whose embroidery was as irritating to her nose as the present mission was to her feelings, and when she had squeezed her hands into tight gloves with three buttons and a tassel, as the last touch of elegance, she turned to Amy with an imbecile expression of countenance, saying meekly . . .

"I'm perfectly miserable, but if you consider me presentable, I die happy."

"You're highly satisfactory. turn slowly round, and let me get a careful view." Jo revolved, and Amy gave a touch here and there, then fell back, with her head on one side, observing graciously, "Yes, you'll do. Your head is all I could ask, for that white bonnet with the rose is quite ravishing. Hold back your shoulders, and carry your hands easily, no matter if your gloves do pinch. There's one thing you can do well, Jo, that is, wear a shawl. I can't, but it's very nice to see you, and I'm so glad Aunt March gave you that lovely one. It's simple, but handsome, and those folds over the arm are really artistic. Is the point of my mantle in the middle, and have I looped my dress evenly? I like to show my boots, for my feet are pretty, though my nose isn't."

"You are a thing of beauty and a joy forever," said Jo, looking through her hand with the air of a connoisseur at the blue feather against the golden hair. “Am I to drag my best dress through the dust, or loop it up, please, ma’am?”

“Hold it yup when you walk, but drop it in the house. The sweeping style suits you best, and you must learn to trail your skirts gracefully. You haven’t half buttoned one cuff, do it at once. You’ll never look finished if you are not careful about the little details, for they make yup the pleasing whole.”

Jo sighed, and proceeded to burst the buttons off her glove, in doing up her cuff, but at last both were ready, and sailed away, looking as ‘pretty as picters’, Hannah said, as she hung out of the upper window to watch them.

“Now, Jo dear, the Chesters consider themselves very elegant people, so I want you to put on your best deportment. Don’t make any of your abrupt remarks, or do anything odd, will you? Just be calm, cool, and quiet, that’s safe and ladylike, and you can easily do it for fifteen minutes,” said Amy, as they approached the first place, having borrowed the white parasol and been inspected by Meg, with a baby on each arm.

“Let me see. ‘Calm, cool, and quiet’, yes, I think I can promise that. I’ve played the part of a prim young lady on the stage, and I’ll try it off. My powers are great, as you shall see, so be easy in your mind, my child.”

Amy looked relieved, but naughty Jo took her at her word, for during the first call she sat with every limb gracefully composed, every fold correctly draped, calm as a summer sea, cool as a snowbank, and as silent as the sphinx. In vain Mrs. Chester alluded to her ‘charming novel’, and the Misses Chester introduced parties, picnics, the opera, and the fashions. Each and all were answered by a smile, a bow, and a demure “Yes” or “No” with the chill on. In vain Amy telegraphed the word ‘talk’, tried to draw her out, and administered covert pokes with her foot. Jo sat as if blandly unconcious of it all, with deportment like Maud’s face, ‘icily regular, splendidly null’.

"What a haughty, uninteresting creature that oldest Miss March is!" was the unfortunately audible remark of one of the ladies, as the door closed upon their guests. Jo laughed noiselessly all through the hall, but Amy looked disgusted at the failure of her instructions, and very naturally laid the blame upon Jo.

"How could you mistake me so? I merely meant you to be properly dignified and composed, and you made yourself a perfect stock and stone. Try to be sociable at the Lamb's'. Gossip as other girls do, and be interested in dress and flirtations and whatever nonsense comes up. They move in the best society, are valuable persons for us to know, and I wouldn't fail to make a good impression there for anything."

"I'll be agreeable. I'll gossip and giggle, and have horrors and raptures over any trifle you like. I rather enjoy this, and now I'll imitate what is called 'a charming girl'. I can do it, for I have May Chester as a model, and I'll improve upon her. See if the Lambs don't say, 'What a lively, nice creature that Jo March is!"

Amy felt anxious, as well she might, for when Jo turned freakish there was no knowing where she would stop. Amy's face was a study when she saw her sister skim into the next drawing room, kiss all the young ladies with effusion, beam graciously upon the young gentlemen, and join in the chat with a spirit which amazed the beholder. Amy was taken possession of by Mrs. Lamb, with whom she was a favorite, and forced to hear a long account of Lucretia's last attack, while three delightful young gentlemen hovered near, waiting for a pause when they might rush in and rescue her. So situated, she was powerless to check Jo, who seemed possessed by a spirit of mischief, and talked away as volubly as the lady. A knot of heads gathered about her, and Amy strained her ears to hear what was going on, for broken sentences filled her with curiosity, and frequent peals of laughter made her wild to share the fun. One may imagine her suffering on overhearing fragments of this sort of conversation.

"She rides splendidly. who taught her?"

"No one. She used to practice mounting, holding the reins, and sitting straight on an old saddle in a tree. Now she rides anything, for she doesn't know what fear is, and the stableman lets her have horses cheap because she trains them to carry ladies so well. She has such a passion for it, I often tell her if everything else fails, she can be a horsebreaker, and get her living so."

At this awful speech Amy contained herself with difficulty, for the impression was being given that she was rather a fast young lady, which was her especial aversion. But what could she do? For the old lady was in the middle of her story, and long before it was done, Jo was off again, make more droll revelations and committing still more fearful blunders.

"Yes, Amy was in despair that day, for all the good beasts were gone, and of three left, one was lame, one blind, and the other so balky that you had to put dirt in his mouth before he would start. Nice animal for a pleasure party, wasn't it?"

"Which did she choose?" asked one of the laughing gentlemen, who enjoyed the subject.

"None of them. She heard of a young horse at the farm house over the river, and though a lady had never ridden him, she resolved to try, because he was handsome and spirited. Her struggles were really pathetic. There was no one to bring the horse to the saddle, so she took the saddle to the horse. My dear creature, she actually rowed it over the river, put it on her head, and marched up to the barn to the utter amazement of the old man!"

"Did she ride the horse?'

"Of course she did, and had a capital time. I expected to see her brought home in fragments, but she managed him perfectly, and was the life of the party."

"Well, I call that plucky!" And young Mr. Lamb turned an approving glance upon Amy, wondering what his mother could be saying to make the girl look so red and uncomfortable.

She was still redder and more uncomfortable a moment after, when a sudden turn in the conversation introduced the subject of dress. One of the young ladies asked Jo where she got the pretty drab hat she wore to the picnic and stupid Jo, instead of mentioning the place where it was bought two years ago, must needs answer with unnecessary frankness, "Oh, Amy painted it. You can't buy those soft shades, so we paint ours any color we like. It's a great comfort to have an artistic sister."

"Isn't that an original idea?" cried Miss Lamb, who found Jo great fun.

"That's nothing compared to some of her brilliant performances. There's nothing the child can't do. Why, she wanted a pair of blue boots for Sallie's party, so she just painted her soiled white ones the loveliest shade of sky blue you ever saw, and they looked exactly like satin," added Jo, with an air of pride in her sister's accomplishments that exasperated Amy till she felt that it would be a relief to throw her cardcase at her.

"We read a story of yours the other day, and enjoyed it very much," observed the elder Miss Lamb, wishing to compliment the literary lady, who did not look the character just then, it must be confessed.

Any mention of her 'works' always had a bad effect upon Jo, who either grew rigid and looked offended, or changed the subject with a brusque remark, as now. "Sorry you could find nothing better to read. I write that rubbish because it sells, and ordinary people like it. Are you going to New York this winter?'

As Miss Lamb had 'enjoyed' the story, this speech was not exactly grateful or complimentary. The minute it was made Jo saw her mistake, but fearing to make the matter worse, suddenly remembered that it was for her to make the first move toward departure, and did so with an abruptness that left three people with half-finished sentences in their mouths.

"Amy, we must go. Good-by, dear, do come and see us. We are pining for a visit. I don't dare to ask you, Mr. Lamb, but if you should come, I don't think I shall have the heart to send you away."

Jo said this with such a droll imitation of May Chester's gushing style that Amy got out of the room as rapidly as possible, feeling a strong desire to laugh and cry at the same time.

"Didn't I do well?" asked Jo, with a satisfied air as they walked away.

"Nothing could have been worse," was Amy's crushing reply. "What possessed you to tell those stories about my saddle, and the hats and boots, and all the rest of it?"

"Why, it's funny, and amuses people. They know we are poor, so it's no use pretending that we have grooms, buy three or four hats a season, and have things as easy and fine as they do."

"You needn't go and tell them all our little shifts, and expose our; poverty in that perfectly unnecessary way. You haven't a bit of proper pride, and never will learn when to hold your tongue and when to speak," said Amy despairingly.

Poor Jo looked abashed, and silently chafed the end of her nose with the stiff handkerchief, as if performing a penance for her misdemeanors.

"How shall I behave here?" she asked, as they approached the third mansion.

"Just as you please. I wash my hands of you," was Amy's short answer.

"Then I'll enjoy myself. The boys are at home, and we'll have a comfortable time. Goodness knows I need a little change, for elegance has a bad effect upon my constitution," returned Jo gruffly, being disturbed by her failure to suit.

An enthusiastic welcome from three big boys and several pretty children speedily soothed her ruffled feelings, and leaving

Amy to entertain the hostess and Mr. Tudor, who happened to be calling likewise, Jo devoted herself to the young folks and found the change refreshing. She listened to college stories with deep interest, caressed pointers and poodles without a murmur, agreed heartily that "Tom Brown was a brick," regardless of the improper form of praise, and when one lad proposed a visit to his turtle tank, she went with an alacrity which caused Mamma to smile upon her, as that motherly lady settled the cap which was left in a ruinous condition by filial hugs, bearlike but affectionate, and dearer to her than the most faultless coiffure from the hands of an inspired Frenchwoman.

Leaving her sister to her own devices, Amy proceeded to enjoy herself to her heart's content. Mr. Tudor's uncle had married an English lady who was third cousin to a living lord, and Amy regarded the whole family with great respect, for in spite of her American birth and breeding, she possessed that reverence for titles which haunts the best of us—that unacknowledged loyalty to the early faith in kings which set the most democratic nation under the sun in ferment at the coming of a royal yellow-haired laddie, some years ago, and which still has something to do with the love the young country bears the old, like that of a big son for an imperious little mother, who held him while she could, and let him go with a farewell scolding when he rebelled. But even the satisfaction of talking with a distant connection of the British nobility did not render Amy forgetful of time, and when the proper number of minutes had passed, she reluctantly tore herself from this aristocratic society, and looked about for Jo, fervently hoping that her incorrigible sister would not be found in any position which should bring disgrace upon the name of March.

It might have been worse, but Amy considered it bad. For Jo sat on the grass, with an encampment of boys about her, and a dirty-footed dog reposing on the skirt of her state and festival dress, as she related one of Laurie's pranks to her admiring audience. One small child was poking turtles with Amy's cherished parasol, a second was eating gingerbread over Jo's best bonnet, and a third playing ball with her gloves. but all were enjoying themselves, and when Jo collected her damaged property to go, her escort accompanied her, begging her to come again, "It was such fun to hear about Laurie's larks."

"Capital boys, aren't they? I feel quite young and brisk again after that." said Jo, strolling along with her hands behind her, partly from habit, partly to conceal the bespattered parasol.

"Why do you always avoid Mr. Tudor?" asked Amy, wisely refraining from any comment upon Jo's dilapidated appearance.

"Don't like him, he puts on airs, snubs his sisters, worries his father, a nd doesn't speak respectfully of his mother. Laurie says he is fast, and I don't consider him a desirable acquaintance, so I let him alone."

"You might treat him civilly, at least. You gave him a cool nod, and just now you bowed and smiled in the politest way to Tommy Chamberlain, whose father keeps a grocery store. If you had just reversed the nod and the bow, it would have been right," said Amy reprovingly.

"No, it wouldn't," returned Jo, "I neither like, respect, nor admire Tudor, though his grandfather's uncle's nephew's niece was a third cousin to a lord. Tommy is poor and bashful and good and very clever. I think well of him, and like to show that I do, for he is a gentleman in spite of the brown paper parcels."

"It's no use trying to argue with you," began Amy.

"Not the least, my dear," interrupted Jo, "so let us look amiable, and drop a card here, as the Kings are evidently out, for which I'm deeply grateful."

The family cardcase having done its duty the girls walked on, and Jo uttered another thanksgiving on reaching the fifth house, and being told that the young ladies were engaged.

"Now let us go home, and never mind Aunt March today. We can run down there any time, and it's really a pity to trail through the dust in our best bibs and tuckers, when we are tired and cross."

"Speak for yourself, if you please. Aunt March likes to have us pay her the compliment of coming in style, and making a formal call. It's a little thing to do, but it gives her pleasure, and I don't believe it will hurt your things half so much as letting dirty dogs and clumping boys spoil them. Stoop down, and let me take the crumbs off of your bonnet."

"What a good girl you are, Amy!" said Jo, with a repentant glance from her own damaged costume to that of her sister, which was fresh and spotless still. "I wish it was as easy for me to do little things to please people as it is for you. I think of them, but it takes too much time to do them, so I wait for a chance to confer a great favor, and let the small ones slip, but they tell best in the end, I fancy."

Amy smiled and was mollified at once, saying with a maternal air, "Women should learn to be agreeable, particularly poor ones, for they have no other way of repaying the kindnesses they receive. If you'd remember that, and practice it, you'd be better liked than I am, because there is more of you."

"I'm a crotchety old thing, and always shall be, but I'm willing to own that you are right, only it's easier for me to risk my life for a person than to be pleasant to him when I don't feel like it. It's a great misfortune to have such strong likes and dislikes, isn't it?"

"It's a greater not to be able to hide them. I don't mind saying that I don't approve of Tudor any more than you do, but I'm not called upon to tell him so. Neither are you, and there is no use in making yourself disagreeable because he is."

"But I think girls ought to show when they disapprove of young men, and how can they do it except by their manners?

Preaching does not do any good, as I know to my sorrow, since I've had Teddie to manage. But there are many little ways in which I can influence him without a word, and I say we ought to do it to others if we can."

"Teddy is a remarkable boy, and can't be taken as a sample of other boys," said Amy, in a tone of solemn conviction, which would have convulsed the 'remarkable boy' if he had heard it. "If we were belles, or women of wealth and position, we might do something, perhaps, but for us to frown at one set of young gentlemen because we don't approve of them, and smile upon another set because we do, wouldn't have a particle of effect, and we should only be considered odd and puritanical."

"So we are to countenance things and people which we detest, merely because we are not belles and millionaires, are we? That's a nice sort of morality."

"I can't argue about it, I only know that it's the way of the world, and people who set themselves against it only get laughed at for their pains. I don't like reformers, and I hope you never try to be one."

"I do like them, and I shall be one if I can, for in spite of the laughing the world would never get on without them. We can't agree about that. for you belong to the old set, and I to the new. You will get on the best, but I shall have the liveliest time of it. I should rather enjoy the brickbats and hooting, I think."

"Well, compose yourself now, and don't worry Aunt with your new ideas."

"I'll try not to, but I'm always possessed to burst out with some particularly blunt speech or revolutionary sentiment before her. It's my doom, and I can't help it."

They found Aunt Carrol with the old lady, both absorbed in some very interesting subject, but they dropped it as the girls came in, with a conscious look which betrayed that they had been talking about their nieces. Jo was not in a good humor, and the perverse fit returned, but Amy, who had virtuously done her duty, kept her temper and pleased everybody, was in a most angelic frame of mind. This amiable spirit was felt at once, and both aunts 'my deared' her affectionately, looking what they afterward said emphatically, "That child improves every day."

"Are you going to help about the fair, dear?" asked Mrs. Carrol, as Amy sat down beside her with the confiding air elderly people like so well in the young.

"Yes, Aunt. Mrs. Chester asked me if I would, and I offered to tend a table, as I have nothing but my time to give."

"I'm not," put in Jo decidedly. "I hate to be patronized, and the Chesters think it's a great favor to allow us to help with their highly connected fair. I wonder you consented, Amy, they only want you to work."

"I am willing to work. It's for the freedmen as well as the Chesters, and I think it very kind of them to let me share the labor and the fun. Patronage does not trouble me when it is well meant."

"Quite right and proper. I like your grateful spirit, my dear. It's a pleasure to help people who appreciate our efforts. Some do not, and that is trying," observed Aunt March, looking over her spectacles at Jo, who sat apart, rocking herself, with a somewhat morose expression.

If Jo had only known what a great happiness was wavering in the balance for one of them, she would have turned dove-like in a minute, but unfortunately, we don't have windows in our breasts, and cannot see what goes on in the minds of our friends. Better for us that we cannot as a general thing, but now and then it would be such a comfort, such a saving of time and temper. By her next speech, Jo deprived herself of several years of pleasure, and received a timely lesson in the art of holding her tongue.

"I don't like favors, they oppress and make me feel like a slave. I'd rather do everything for myself, and be perfectly independent."

"Ahem!" coughed Aunt Carrol softly, with a look at Aunt March.

"I told you so," said Aunt March, with a decided nod to Aunt Carrol.

Mercifully unconscious of what she had done, Jo sat with her nose in the air, and a revolutionary aspect which was anything but inviting.

"Do you speak French, dear?" asked Mrs. Carrol, laying a hand on Amy's.

"Pretty well, thanks to Aunt March, who lets Esther talk to me as often as I like," replied amy, with a grateful look, which caused the old lady to smile affably.

"How are you about languages?" asked Mrs. Carrol of JO.

"Don't know a word. I'm very stupid about studying anything, can't bear French, it's such a slippery, silly sort of language," was the brusque reply.

Another look passed between the ladies, and Aunt March said to Amy, 'You are quite strong and well no, dear, I believe? Eyes don't trouble you any more, do they?"

"Not at all, thank you, ma'am. I'm very well, and mean to do great things next winter, so that I may be ready for Rome, whenever that joyful time arrives."

"Good girl! You deserve to go, and I'm sure you will some day," said Aunt March, with an approving; pat on the head, as Amy picked up her ball for her.

Crosspatch, draw the latch, Sit by the fire and spin,

squalled Polly, bending down from his perch on the back of her chair to peep into Jo's face, with such a comical air of impertinent inquiry that it was impossible to help laughing.

"Most observing bird," said the old lady.

"Come and take a walk, my dear?" cried Polly, hopping toward the china closet, with a look suggestive of a lump of sugar.

"Thank you, I will. Come Amy." And Jo brought the visit to an end, feeling more strongly than ever that calls did have a bad effect upon her constitution. She shook hands in a gentlemanly manner, but Amy kissed both the aunts, and the girls departed, leaving behind them the impression of shadow and sunshine, which impression caused Aunt March to say, as they vanished . . .

"You'd better do it, Mary. I'll supply the money. And Aunt Carrol to reply decidedly, "I certainly will, if her father and mother consent."

Chapter Thirty

Mrs. Chester's fair was so very elegant and select that it was considered a great honor by the young ladies of the neighborhood to be invited to take a table, and everyone was much interest in the matter. Amy was asked, but Jo was not, which was fortunate for all parties, as her elbows were decidedly akimbo at this period of her life, and it took a good many hard knocks to teach her how to get on easily. The 'haughty, uninteresting creature' was let severely alone, but Amy's talent and taste were duly complimented by the offer of the art table, and she exerted herself to prepare and secure appropriate and valuable contributions to it.

Everything went on smoothly till the day before the fair opened, then there occurred one of the little skirmishes which it is almost impossible to avoid, when some five-and-twenty women, old and young, with all their private piques and prejudices, try to work together.

May Chester was rather jealous of Amy because the latter was a greater favorite than herself, and just at this time several trifling circumstances occurred to increase the feeling. Amy's dainty pen-and-ink work entirely eclipsed May's painted vases—that was one thorn. Then the all conquering Tudor had danced four times with Amy at a late party and only once with May—that was thorn number two. But the chief grievance that rankled in her soul, and gave an excuse for her unfriendly conduct, was a rumor which some obliging gossip had whispered to her, that the March girls had made fun of her at the Lambs'. All the blame of this should have fallen upon Jo, for her naughty imitation had been too lifelike to escape detection, and the frolicsome Lambs had permitted the joke to escape. No hint of this had reached the culprits, however, and Amy's dismay can be imagined, when, the very evening before the fair, as she was putting the last touches to her pretty table, Mrs. Chester, who, of course, resented the supposed ridicule of her daughter, said, in a bland tone, but with a cold look . . .

"I find, dear, that there is some feeling among the young ladies about my giving this table to anyone but my girls. As this is the most prominent, and some say the most attractive table of all, and they are the chief getters-up of the fair, it is thought best for them to take this place. I'm sorry, but I know you are too sincerely interested in the cause to mind a little personal disappointment, and you shall have another table if you like."

Mrs. Chester fancied beforehand that it would be easy to deliver this little speech, but when the time came, she found it rather difficult to utter it naturally, with Amy's unsuspicious eyes looking straight at her full of surprise and trouble.

"Amy felt that there was something behind this, but would not guess what, and said quietly, feeling hurt, and showing that she did, "Perhaps you had rather I took no table at all?"

"Now, my dear, don't have any ill feeling, I beg. It's merely a matter of expediency, you see, my girls will naturally take the lead, and this table is considered their proper place. I think it very appropriate to you, and feel very grateful for your efforts to make it so pretty, but we must give up our private wishes, of course, and I will see that you have a good place elsewhere.

Wouldn't you like the flower table? The little girls undertook it, but they are discouraged. You could make a charming thing of it, and the flower table is always attractive you know."

"Especially to gentlemen," added May, with a look which enlightened Amy as to one cause of her sudden fall from favor. She colored angrily, but took no other notice of that girlish sarcasm, and answered with unexpected amiability . . .

"It shall be as you please, Mrs. Chester. I'll give up my place here at once, and attend to the flowers, if you like."

"You can put your own things on your own table, if you prefer," began May, feeling a little conscience-stricken, as she looked at the pretty racks, the painted shells, and quaint illuminations Amy had so carefully made and so gracefully arranged. She meant it kindly, but Amy mistook her meaning, and said quickly . . .

"Oh, certainly, if they are in your way," and sweeping her contributions into her apron, pell-mell, she walked off, feeling that herself and her works of art had been insulted past forgiveness.

"Now she's mad. Oh, dear, I wish I hadn't asked you to speak, Mama," said May, looking disconsolately at the empty spaces on her table.

"Girls' quarrels are soon over," returned her mother, feeling a trifle ashamed of her own part in this one, as well she might.

The little girls hailed Amy and her treasures with delight, which cordial reception somewhat soothed her perturbed spirit, and she fell to work, determined to succeed florally, if she could not artistically. But everything seemed against her. It was late, and she was tired. Everyone was too busy with their own affairs to help her, and the little girls were only hindrances, for the dears fussed and chattered like so many magpies, making a great deal of confusion in their artless efforts to preserve the most perfect order. The evergreen arch wouldn't stay firm after she got it up, but wiggled and threatened to tumble down on her head when the hanging baskets were filled. Her best tile got a splash of water, which left a sephia tear on the Cupid's cheek. She bruised her hands with hammering, and got cold working in a draft, which last affliction filled her with apprehensions for the morrow. Any girl reader who has suffered like afflictions will sympathize with poor Amy and wish her well through her task.

There was great indignation at home when she told her story that evening. Her mother said it was a shame, but told her she had done right. Beth declared she wouldn't go to the fair at all, and Jo demanded why she didn't take all her pretty things and leave those mean people to get on without her.

"Because they are mean is no reason why i should be. I hate such things, and though I think I've a right to be hurt, I don't intend to show it. They will feel that more than angry speeches or huffy actions, won't they, Marmee?"

"That's the right spirit, my dear. A kiss for a blow is always best, though it's not very easy to give it sometimes," said her mother, with the air of one who had learned the difference between preaching and practicing.

In spite of various very natural temptations to resent and retaliate, Amy adhered to her resolution all the next day, bent on conquering her enemy by kindness. She began well, thanks to a silent reminder that came to her unexpectedly, but most opportunely. As she arranged her table that morning, while the little girls were in the anteroom filling the baskets, she took up her pet production, a little book, the antique cover of which her father had found among his treasures, and in which on leaves of vellum she had beautifully illuminated different texts. As she turned the pages rich in dainty devices with very pardonable pride, her eye fell upon one verse that made her stop and think. Framed in a brilliant scrollwork of scarlet, blue and gold, with little spirits of good will helping one another up and down among the thorns and flowers, were the words, "Thou shalt love thy neighbor as thyself."

"I ought, but I don't," thought Amy, as her eye went from the bright page to May's discontented face behind the big vases, that could not hide the vacancies her pretty work had once filled. Amy stood a minute, turning the leaves in her hand, reading on each some sweet rebuke for all heartburnings and uncharitableness of spirit. Many wise and true sermons are preached us every day by unconscious ministers in street, school, office, or home. Even a fair table may become a pulpit, if it can offer the good and helpful words which are never out of season. Amy's conscience preached her a little sermon from that text, then and there, and she did what many of us do not always do, took the sermon to heart, and straightway put it in practice. A group of girls were standing about May's table, admiring the pretty things, and talking over the change of saleswomen. They dropped their voices, but Amy knew they were speaking of her, hearing one side of the story and judging accordingly. It was not pleasant, but a better spirit had come over her, and presently a chance offered for proving it. She heard May say sorrowfully . . .

"It's too bad, for there is no time to make other things, and I don't want to fill up with odds and ends. The table was just complete then. Now it's spoiled."

"I dare say she'd put them back if you asked her," suggested someone.

"How could I after all the fuss?" began May, but she did not finish, for Amy's voice came across the hall, saying pleasantly . . .

"You may have them, and welcome, without asking, if you want them. I was just thinking I'd offer to put them back, for they belong to your table rather than mine. Here they are, please take them, and forgive me if I was hasty in carrying them away last night."

As she spoke, Amy returned her contribution, with a nod and a smile, and hurried away again, feeling that it was easier to do a friendly thing than it was to stay and be thanked for it.

"Now, I call that lovely of her, don't you?" cried one girl.

May's answer was inaudible, but another young lady, whose temper was evidently a little soured by making lemonade, added, with a disagreeable laugh, "Very lovely, for she knew she wouldn't sell them at her own table."

Now, that was hard. When we make little sacrifices we like to have them appreciated, at least, and for a minute Amy was sorry she had done it, feeling that virtue was not always its won reward. But it is, as she presently discovered, for her spirits began to rise, and her table to blossom under her skillful hands, the girls were very kind, and that one little act seemed to have cleared the atmosphere amazingly.

It was a very long day and a hard one for Amy, as she sat behind her table, often quite alone, for the little girls deserted very soon. Few cared to buy flowers in summer, and her bouquets began to droop long before night.

The art table was the most attractive in the room. There was a crowd about it all day long, and the tenders were constantly flying to and fro with important faces and rattling money boxes. Amy often looked wistfully across, longing to be there, where she felt at home and happy, instead of in a corner with nothing to do. It might seem no hardship to some of us, but to a pretty, blithe young girl, it was not only tedious, but very trying, and the thought of Laurie and his friends made it a real martyrdom.

She did not go home till night, and then she looked so pale and quiet that they knew the day had been a hard one, though she made no complaint, and did not even tell what she had done. Her mother gave her an extra cordial cup of tea. Beth helped her dress, and made a charming little wreath for her hair, while Jo astonished her family by getting herself up with unusual care, and hinting darkly that the tables were about to be turned.

"Don't do anything rude, pray Jo. I won't have any fuss made, so let it all pass and behave yourself," begged Amy, as she departed early, hoping to find a reinforcement of flowers to refresh her poor little table.

"I merely intend to make myself entrancingly agreeable to ever one I know, and to keep them in your corner as long as possible. Teddy and his boys will lend a hand, and we'll have a good time yet." returned Jo, leaning over the gate to watch for Laurie. Presently the familiar tramp was heard in the dusk, and she ran out to meet him.

"Is that my boy?"

"As sure as this is my girl!" And Laurie tucked her hand under his arm with the air of a man whose every wish was gratified.

"Oh, teddy, such doings!" And Jo told Amy's wrongs with sisterly zeal.

"A flock of our fellows are going to drive over by-and-by, and I'll be hanged if I don't make them buy every flower she's got, and camp down before her table afterward," said Laurie, espousing her cause with warmth.

"The flowers are not at all nice, Amy says, and the fresh ones may not arrive in time. I don't wish to be unjust or suspicious, but I shouldn't wonder if they never came at all. When people do one mean thing they are very likely to do another," observed Jo in a disgusted tone.

"Didn't Hayes give you the best out of our gardens? I told him to."

"I didn't know that, he forgot, I suppose, and, as your grandpa was poorly, I didn't like to worry him by asking, though I did want some."

"Now, Jo, how could you think there was any need of asking? They are just as much yours as mine. Don't we always go halves in everything?" began Laurie, in the tone that always made Jo turn thorny.

"Gracious, I hope not! Half of some of your things wouldn't suit me at all. But we mustn't stand philandering here. I've got to help Amy, so you go and make yourself splendid, and if you'll be so very kind as to let Hayes take a few nice flowers up to the Hall, I'll bless you forever."

"Couldn't you do it now?" asked Laurie, so suggestively that Jo shut the gate in his face with inhospitable haste, and called through the bars, "Go away, Teddy, I'm busy."

Thanks to the conspirators, the tables were turned that night, for Hayes sent up a wilderness of flowers, with a loverly basket arranged in his best manner for a centerpiece. Then the March family turned out en masse, and Jo exerted herself to some purpose, for people not only came, but stayed, laughing at her nonsense, admiring Amy's taste, and apparently enjoying themselves very much. Laurie and his friends gallantly threw themselves into the breach, bought up the bouquets, encamped before the table, and made that corner the liveliest spot in the room. Amy was in her element now, and out of gratitude, if nothing more, was as spritely and gracious as possible, coming to the conclusion, about that time, that virtue was it's own reward, after all.

Jo behaved herself with exemplary propriety, and when Amy was happily surrounded by her guard of honor, Jo circulated about the hall, picking up various bits of gossip, which enlightened her upon the subject of the Chester change of base. She reproached herself for her share of the ill feeling and resolved to exonerate Amy as soon as possible. She also discovered what Amy had done about the things in the morning, and considered her a model of magnanimity. As she passed the art table, she glanced over it for her sister's things, but saw no sign of them. "Tucked away out of sight, I dare say," thought Jo, who could forgiver her own wrongs, but hotly resented any insult offered her family.

"Good evening, Miss Jo. How does Amy get on?" asked May with a conciliatory air, for she wanted to show that she also could be generous.

"She has sold everything she had that was worth selling, and now she is enjoying herself. The flower table is always attractive, you know, 'especially to gentlemen.'"

Jo couldn't resist giving that little slap, but May took it so meekly she regretted it a minute after, and fell to praising the great vases, which still remained unsold.

"Is Amy's illumination anywhere about? I took a fancy to buy that for Father," said Jo, very anxious to learn the fate of her sister's work.

"Everything of Amy's sold long ago. I took care that the right people saw them, and they made a nice little sum of money for us," returned May, who had overcome sundry small temptations, as well as Amy had, that day.

Much gratified, Jo rushed back to tell the good news, and Amy looked both touched and surprised by the report of May's word and manner.

"Now, gentlemen, I want you to go and do your duty by the other tables as generously as you have by mine, especially the art table," she said, ordering out 'Teddy's own', as the girls called the college friends.

"'Charge, Chester, charge!' is the motto for that table, but do your duty like men, and you'll get your money's worth of art in every sense of the word," said the irrepressible Jo, as the devoted phalanx prepared to take the field.

"To hear is to obey, but March is fairer far than May," said little Parker, making a frantic effort to be both witty and tender, and getting promptly quenched by Laurie, who said . . .

"Very well, my son, for a small boy!" and walked him off, with a paternal pat on the head.

"Buy the vases," whispered Amy to Laurie, as a final heaping of coals of fire on her enemy's head.

To May's great delight, Mr. Laurence not only bought the vases, but pervaded the hall with one under each arm. The other gentlemen speculated with equal rashness in all sorts of frail trifles, and wandered helplessly about afterward, burdened with wax flowers, painted fans, filigree portfolios, and other useful and appropriate purchases.

Aunt Carrol was there, heard the story, looked pleased, and said something to Mrs. March in a corner, which made the latter lady beam with satisfaction, and watch Amy with a face full of mingled pride and anxiety, though she did not betray the cause of her pleasure till several days later.

The fair was pronounced a success, and when May bade Amy goodnight, she did not gush as usual, but gave her an affectionate kiss, and a look which said 'forgive and forget'. That satisfied Amy, and when she got home she found the vases paraded on the parlor chimney piece with a great bouquet in each. "The reward of merit for a magnanimous March," as Laurie announced with a flourish.

"You've a deal more principle and generosity and nobleness of character than I ever gave you credit for, Amy. You've behaved sweetly, and I respect you with all my heart," said Jo warmly, as they brushed their hair together late that night.

"Yes, we all do, and love her for being so ready to forgive. It must have been dreadfully hard, after working so long and setting your heart on selling your own pretty things. I don't believe I could have done it as kindly as you did," added Beth from her pillow.

"Why, girls, you needn't praise me so. I only did as I'd be done by. You laugh at me when I say I want to be a lady, but I mean a true gentlewoman in mind and manners, and I try to do it as far as I know how. I can't explain exactly, but I want to be above the little meannesses and follies and faults that spoil so many women. I'm far from it now, but I do my best, and hope in time to be what Mother is."

Amy spoke earnestly, and Jo said, with a cordial hug, "I understand now what you mean, and I'll never laugh at you again. You are getting on faster than you think, and I'll take lessons of you in true politeness, for you've learned the secret, I believe. Try away, deary, you'll get your reward some day, and no one will be more delighted than I shall."

A week later Amy did get her reward, and poor Jo found it hard to be delighted. A letter came from Aunt Carrol, and Mrs. March's face was illuminated to such a degree when she read it that Jo and Beth, who were with her, demanded what the glad tiding were.

"Aunt Carrol is going abroad next month, and wants . . ."

"Me to go with her!" burst in Jo, flying out of her chair in an uncontrollable rapture.

"No, dear, not you. It's Amy."

"Oh, Mother! She's too young, it's my turn first. I've wanted it so long. It would do me so much good, and be so altogether splendid. I must go!"

"I'm afraid it's impossible, Jo. Aunt says Amy, decidedly, and it is not for us to dictate when she offers such a favor."

"It's always so. Amy has all the fun and I have all the work. It isn't fair, oh, it isn't fair!" cried Jo passionately.

"I'm afraid it's partly your own fault, dear. When Aunt spoke to me the other day, she regretted your blunt manners and too independent spirit, and here she writes, as if quoting something you had said—'I planned at first to ask Jo, but as 'favors burden her', and she 'hates French', I think I won't venture to invite her. Amy is more docile, will make a good companion for Flo, and receive gratefully any help the trip may give her."

"Oh, my tongue, my abominable tongue! Why can't I learn to keep it quiet?' groaned Jo, remembering words which had been her undoing. When she had heard the explanation of the quoted phrases, Mrs. March said sorrowfully . . .

"I wish you could have gone, but there is no hope of it this time, so try to bear it cheerfully, and don't sadden Amy's pleasure by reproaches or regrets."

"I'll try," said Jo, winking hard as she knelt down to pick up the basket she had joyfully upset. "I'll take a leaf out of her book, and try not only to seem glad, but to be so, and not grudge her one minute of happiness. But it won't be easy, for it is a dreadful disappointment." And poor Jo bedewed the little fat pincushion she held with several very bitter tears. "Jo, dear, I'm very selfish, but I couldn't spare you, and I'm glad you are not going quite yet," whispered Beth, embracing her, basket and all, with such a clinging touch and loving face that Jo felt comforted in spite of the sharp regret that made her want to box her own ears, and humbly beg Aunt Carrol to burden her with this favor, and see how gratefully she would bear it.

By the time Amy came in, Jo was able to take her part in the family jubilation, not quite as heartily as usual, perhaps, but without repinings at Amy's good fortune. The young lady herself received the news as tidings of great joy, went about in a solemn sort of rapture, and began to sort her colors and pack her pencils that evening, leaving such trifles as clothes, money, and passports to those less absorbed in visions of art than herself.

"It isn't a mere pleasure trip to me, girls," she said impressively, as she scraped her best palette. "It will decide my career, for if I have any genius, I shall find it out in Rome, and will do something to prove it."

"Suppose you haven't?" said Jo, sewing away, with red eyes, at the new collars which were to be handed over to Amy.

"Then I shall come home and teach drawing for my living," replied the aspirant for fame, with philosophic composure. But she made a wry face at the prospect, and scratched away at her palette as if bent on vigorous measures before she gave up her hopes.

"No, you won't. You hate hard work, and you'll marry some rich man, and come home to sit in the lap of luxury all your days," said Jo.

"Your predictions sometimes come to pass, but I don't believe that one will. I'm sure I wish it would, for if I can't be an artist myself, I should like to be able to help those who are," said Amy, smiling, as if the part of Lady Bountiful would suit her better than that of a poor drawing teacher.

"Hum!" said Jo, with a sigh. "If you wish it you'll have it, for your wishes are always granted—mine never."

"Would you like to go?" asked Amy, thoughtfully patting her nose with her knife.

"Rather!"

"Well, in a year or two I'll send for you, and we'll dig in the Forum for relics, and carry out all the plans we've made so many times."

"Thank you. I'll remind you of your promise when that joyful day comes, if it ever does," returned Jo, accepting the vague but magnificent offer as gratefully as she could. "There was not much time for preparation, and the house was in a ferment till Amy was off. Jo bore up very well till the last flutter of blue ribbon vanished, when she retired to her refuge, the garret, and cried till she couldn't cry any more. Amy likewise bore up stoutly till the steamer sailed. Then just as the gangway was about to be withdrawn, it suddenly came over her that a whole ocean was soon to roll between her and those who loved her best, and she clung to Laurie, the last lingerer, saying with a sob . . .

"Oh, take care of them for me, and if anything should happen . . . "

"I will, dear, I will, and if anything happens, I'll come and comfort you," whispered Laurie, little dreaming that he would be called upon to keep his word.

So Amy sailed away to find the Old World, which is always new and beautiful to young eyes, while her father and friend watched her from the shore, fervently hoping that none but gentle fortunes would befall the happy-hearted girl, who waved her hand to them till they could see nothing but the summer sunshine dazzling on the sea.

Chapter Thirty-One

London

Dearest People, Here I really sit at a front window of the Bath Hotel, Piccadilly. It's not a fashionable place, but Uncle stopped here years ago, and won't go anywhere else. However, we don't mean to stay long, so it's no great matter. Oh, I can't begin to tell you how I enjoy it all! I never can, so I'll only give you bits out of my notebook, for I've done nothing but sketch and scribble since I started.

I sent a line from Halifax, when I felt pretty miserable, but after that I got on delightfully, seldom ill, on deck all day, with plenty of pleasant people to amuse me. Everyone was very kind to me, especially the officers. Don't laugh, Jo, gentlemen really are very necessary aboard ship, to hold on to, or to wait upon one, and as they have nothing to do, it's a mercy to make them useful, otherwise they would smoke themselves to death, I'm afraid.

Aunt and Flo were poorly all the way, and liked to be let alone, so when I had done what I could for them, I went and enjoyed myself. Such walks on deck, such sunsets, such splendid air and waves! It was almost as exciting as riding a fast horse, when we went rushing on so grandly. I wish Beth could have come, it would have done her so much good. As for Jo, she would have gone up and sat on the maintop jib, or whatever the high thing is called, made friends with the engineers, and tooted on the captain's speaking trumpet, she'd have been in such a state of rapture.

It was all heavenly, but I was glad to see the Irish coast, and found it very lovely, so green and sunny, with brown cabins here and there, ruins on some of the hills, and gentlemen's countryseats in the valleys, with deer feeding in the parks. It was early in the morning, but I didn't regret getting up to see it, for the bay was full of little boats, the shore so picturesque, and a rosy sky overhead. I never shall forget it.

At Queenstown on of my new acquaintances left us, Mr. Lennox, and when I said something about the Lakes of Killarney, he sighed and and, with a look at me . . .

"Oh, have you e'er heard of Kate Kearney? She lives on the banks of Killarney; From the glance of her eye, Shun danger and fly, For fatal's the glance of Kate Kearney."

Wasn't that nonsensical?

We only stopped at Liverpool a few hours. It's a dirty, noisy place, and I was glad to leave it. Uncle rushed out and bought a pair of dogskin gloves, some ugly, thick shoes, and an umbrella, and got shaved 'a la mutton chop, the first thing. Then he flattered himself that he looked like a true Briton, but the first time he had the mud cleaned off his shoes, the little bootblack knew that an American stood in them, and said, with a grin, "There yer har, sir. I've given 'em the latest Yankee shine." It amused Uncle immensely. Oh, I must tell you what that absurd Lennox did! He got his friend Ward, who came on with us, to order a bouquet for me, and the first thing I saw in my room was a lovely one, with "Robert Lennox's compliments," on the card. Wasn't that fun, girls? I like traveling.

I never shall get to London if I don't hurry. The trip was like riding through a long picture gallery, full of lovely landscapes. The farmhouses were my delight, with thatched roofs, ivy up to the eaves, latticed windows, and stout women with rosy children at the doors. The very cattle looked more tranquil than ours, as they stood knee-deep in clover, and the hens had a contented cluck, as if they never got nervous like Yankee biddies. Such perfect color I never saw, the grass so green, sky so blue, grain so yellow, woods so dark, I was in a rapture all the way. So was Flo, and we kept bouncing from one side to the other, trying to see everything while we were whisking along at the rate of sixty miles an hour. Aunt was tired and went to sleep, but Uncle read his guidebook, and wouldn't be astonished at anything. This is the way we went on. Amy, flying up—"Oh, that must be Kenilworth, that gray place among the trees!" Flo, darting to my window—"How sweet! We must go there sometime, won't we Papa?" Uncle, calmly admiring his boots—"No, my dear, not unless you want beer, that's a brewery."

A pause—then Flo cried out, "Bless me, there's a gallows and a man going up." "Where, where?" shrieks Amy, staring out at two tall posts with a crossbeam and some dangling chains. "A colliery," remarks Uncle, with a twinkle of the eye. "Here's a lovely flock of lambs all lying down," says Amy. "See, Papa, aren't they pretty?" added Flo sentimentally. "Geese, young ladies," returns Uncle, in a tone that keeps us quiet till Flo settles down to enjoy the FLIRTATIONS OF CAPTAIN CAVENDISH, and I have the scenery all to myself.

Of course it rained when we got to London, and there was nothing to be seen but fog and umbrellas. We rested, unpacked, and shopped a little between the showers. Aunt Mary got me some new things, for I came off in such a hurry I wasn't half ready. A white hat and blue feather, a muslin dress to match, and the loveliest mantle you ever saw. Shopping in Regent Street is perfectly splendid. Things seem so cheap, nice ribbons only sixpence a yard. I laid in a stock, but shall get my gloves in Paris. Doesn't that sound sort of elegant and rich?

Flo and I, for the fun of it, ordered a hansom cab, while Aunt and Uncle were out, and went for a drive, though we learned afterward that it wasn't the thing for young ladies to ride in them alone. It was so droll! For when we were shut in by the wooden apron, the man drove so fast that Flo was frightened, and told me to stop him. but he was up outside behind somewhere, and I couldn't get at him. He didn't hear me call, nor see me flap my parasol in front, and there we were, quite helpless, rattling away, and whirling around corners at a breakneck pace. At last, in my despair, I saw a little door in the roof, and on poking it open, a red eye appeared, and a beery voice said . . .

"Now, then, mum?"

I gave my order as soberly as I could, and slamming down the door, with an "Aye, aye, mum," the man made his horse walk, as if going to a funeral. I poked again and said, "A little faster," then off he went, helter-skelter as before, and we resigned ourselves to our fate.

Today was fair, and we went to Hyde Park, close by, for we are more aristocratic than we look. The Duke of Devonshire lives near. I often see his footmen lounging at the back gate, and the Duke of Wellington's house is not far off. Such sights as I saw, my dear! It was as good as Punch, for there were fat dowagers rolling about in their red and yellow coaches, with gorgeous Jeameses in silk stockings and velvet coats, up behind, and powdered coachmen in front. Smart maids, with the rosiest children I ever saw, handsome girls, looking half asleep, dandies in queer English hats and lavender kids lounging about, and tall soldiers, in short red jackets and muffin caps stuck on one side, looking so funny I longed to sketch them.

Rotten Row means 'Route de Roi', or the king's way, but now it's more like a riding school than anything else. The horses are splendid, and the men, especially the grooms, ride well, but the women are stiff, and bounce, which isn't according to our rules. I longed to show them a tearing American gallop, for they trotted solemnly up and down, in their scant habits and high hats, looking like the women in a toy Noah's Ark. Everyone rides—old men, stout ladies, little children—and the young folks do a deal of flirting here, I say a pair exchange rose buds, for it's the thing to wear one in the button-hole, and I thought it rather a nice little idea.

In the P.M. to Westminster Abbey, but don't expect me to describe it, that's impossible, so I'll only say it was sublime! This evening we are going to see Fechter, which will be an appropriate end to the happiest day of my life.

It's very late, but I can't let my letter go in the morning without telling you what happened last evening. Who do you think came in, as we were at tea? Laurie's English friends, Fred and Frank Vaughn! I was so surprised, for I shouldn't have known them but for the cards. both are tall fellows with whiskers, Fred handsome in the English style, and Frank much better, for he only limps slightly, and uses no crutches. They had heard from Laurie where we were to be, and came to ask us to their house, but Uncle won't go, so we shall return the call, and see them as we can. They went to the theater with us, and we did have such a good time, for Frank devoted himself to Flo, and Fred and I talked over past, present, and future fun as if we had know each other all our days. Tell Beth Frank asked for her, and was sorry to hear of her ill health. Fred laughed when I spoke of Jo, and sent his 'respectful compliments to the big hat'. Neither of them had forgotten Camp Laurence, or the fun we had there. What ages ago it seems, doesn't it?

Aunt is tapping on the wall for the third time, so I must stop. I really feel like a dissipated London fine lady, writing here so late, with my room full of pretty things, and my head a jumble of parks, theaters, new gowns, and gallant creatures who say "Ah!" and twirl their blond mustaches with the true English lordliness. I long to see you all, and in spite of my nonsense am, as ever, your loving . . .
AMY

PARIS

Dear girls,

In my last I told you about our London visit, how kind the Vaughns were, and what pleasant parties they made for us. I enjoyed the trips to Hampton Court and the Kensington Museum more than anything else, for at Hampton I saw Raphael's cartoons, and at the Museum, rooms full of pictures by Turner, Lawrence, Reynolds, Hogarth, and the other great creatures. The day in Richmond Park was charming, for we had a regular English picnic, and I had more splendid oaks and groups of deer than I could copy, also heard a nightingale, and saw larks go up. We 'did' London to our heart's content, thanks to Fred and Frank, and were sorry to go away, for though English people are slow to take you in, when they once make up their minds to do it they cannot be outdone in hospitality, I think. The Vaughns hope to meet us in Rome next winter, and I shall be dreadfully disappointed if they don't, for Grace and I are great friends, and the boys very nice fellows, especially Fred.

Well, we were hardly settled here, when he turned up again, saying he had come for a holiday, and was going to Switzerland. Aunt looked sober at first, but he was so cool about it she couldn't say a word. And now we get on nicely, and are very glad he came, for he speaks French like a native, and I don't know what we should do without him. Uncle doesn't know ten words, and insists on talking English very loud, as if it would make people understand him. Aunt's pronunciation is old-fashioned, and Flo and I, though we flattered ourselves that we knew a good deal, find we don't, and are very grateful to have Fred do the 'parley vooing', as Uncle calls it.

Such delightful times as we are having! Sight-seeing from morning till night, stopping for nice lunches in the gay cafes, and meeting with all sorts of droll adventures.

Rainy days I spend in the Louvre, revelling in pictures. Jo would turn up her naughty nose at some of the finest, because she has no soul for art, but I have, and I'm cultivation eye and taste as fast as I can. She would like the relics of great people better, for I've seen her Napoleon's cocked hat and gray coat, his baby's cradle and his old toothbrush, also Marie Antoinette's little shoe, the ring of Saint Denis, Charlemagne's sword, and many other interesting things. I'll talk for hours about them when I come, but haven't time to write.

The Palais Royale is a heavenly place, so full of bijouterie and lovely things that I'm nearly distracted because I can't buy them. Fred wanted to get me some, but of course I didn't allow it. Then the Bois and Champs Elysees are tres magnifique. I've seen the imperial family several times, the emperor an ugly, hard-looking man, the empress pale and pretty, but dressed in bad taste, I thought—purple dress, green hat, and yellow gloves. Little Nap is a handsome boy, who sits chatting to his tutor, and kissed his hand to the people as he passes in his four-horse barouche, with postilions in red satin jackets and a mounted guard before and behind.

We often walk in the Tuileries Gardens, for they are lovely, though the antique Luxembourg Gardens suit me better. Pere la Chaise is very curious, for many of the tombs are like small rooms, and looking in, one sees a table, with images or pictures of the dead, and chairs for the mourners to sit in when they come to lament. That is so Frenchy.

Our rooms are on the Rue de Rivoli, and sitting on the balcony, we look up and down the long, brilliant street. It is so pleasant that we spend our evenings talking there when too tired with our day's work to go out. Fred is very entertaining, and is altogether the most agreeable young man I ever knew—except Laurie, whose manners are more charming. I wish Fred was dark, for I don't fancy light men, however, the Vaughns are very rich and come of an excellent family, so I won't find fault with their yellow hair, as my own is yellower.

Next week we are off to Germany and Switzerland, and as we shall travel fast, I shall only be able to give you hasty letters. I keep my diary, and try to 'remember correctly and describe clearly all that I see and admire', as Father advised. It is good practice for me, and with my sketchbook will give you a better idea of my tour than these scribbles.

Adieu, I embrace you tenderly. VOTRE AMIE

HEIDELBERG

My dear Mamma,

Having a quiet hour before we leave for Berne, I'll try to tell you what has happened, for some of it is very important, as you will see.

The sail up the Rhine was perfect, and I just sat and enjoyed it with all my might. Get Father's old guidebooks and read about it. I haven't words beautiful enough to describe it. At Coblenz we had a lovely time, for some students from Bonn, with whom Fred got acquainted on the boat, gave us a serenade. It was a moonlight night, and about one o'clock Flo and I were waked by the most delicious music under our windows. We flew up, and hid behind the curtains, but sly peeps showed us Fred and the students singing away down below. It was the most romantic thing I ever saw—the river, the bridge of boats, the great fortress opposite, moonlight everywhere, and music fit to melt a heart of stone.

When they were done we threw down some flowers, and saw them scramble for them, kiss their hands to the invisible ladies, and go laughing away, to smoke and drink beer, I suppose. Next morning Fred showed me one of the crumpled flowers in his vest pocket, and looked very sentimental. I laughed at him, and said I didn't throw it, but Flo, which seemed to disgust him, for he tossed it out of the window, and turned sensible again. I'm afraid I'm going to have trouble with that boy, it begins to look like it.

The baths at Nassau were very gay, so was Baden-Baden, where Fred lost some money, and I scolded him. He needs someone to look after him when Frank is not with him. Kate said once she hoped he'd marry soon, and I quite agree with her that it would be well for him. Frankfurt was delightful. I saw Goeth's house, Schiller's statue, and Dannecker's famous Ariadne. It was very lovely, but I should have enjoyed it more if I had known the story better. I didn't like to ask, as everyone knew it or pretended they did. I wish Jo would tell me all about it. I ought to have read more, for I find I don't know anything, and it mortifies me.

Now comes the serious part, for it happened here, and Fred has just gone. He has been so kind and jolly that we all got quite fond of him. I never thought of anything but a traveling friendship till the serenade night. Since then I've begun to feel that the moonlight walks, balcony talks, and daily adventures were something more to him than fun. I haven't flirted, Mother, truly, but remembered what you said to me, and have done my very best. I can't help it if people like me. I don't try to make them, and it worries me if I don't care for them, though Jo says I haven't got any heart. Now I know Mother will shake her head, and the girls say, "Oh, the mercenary little wretch!", but I've made up my mind, and if Fred asks me, I shall accept him, though I'm not madly in love. I like him, and we get on comfortably together. He is handsome, young, clever enough, and very rich—ever so much richer than the Laurences. I don't think his family would object, and I should be very happy, for they are all kind, well-bred, generous people, and they like me. Fred, as the eldest twin, will have the estate, I suppose, and such a splendid one it is! A city house in a fashionable street, not so showy as our big houses, but twice as comfortable and full of solid luxury, such as English people believe in. I like it, for it's genuine. I've seen the plate, the family jewels, the old servants, and pictures of the country place, with its park, great house, lovely grounds, and fine horses. Oh, it would be all I should ask! And I'd rather have it than any title such as girls snap up so readily, and find nothing behind. I may be mercenary, but I hate poverty, and don't mean to bear it a minute longer than I can help. One of us must marry well. Meg didn't, Jo won't, Beth can't yet, so I shall, and make everything okay all round. I wouldn't marry a man I hated or despised. You may be sure of that, and though Fred is not my model hero, he does very well, and in time I should get fond enough of him if he was very fond of me, and let me do just as I liked. So I've been turning the matter over in my mind the last week, for it was impossible to help seeing that Fred liked me. He said nothing, but little things showed it. He never goes with Flo, always gets on my side of the carriage, table, or promenade, looks sentimental when we are alone, and frowns at anyone else who ventures to speak tome. Yesterday at dinner, when an Austrian officer stared at us and then said something to his friend, a rakish-looking baron, about 'ein wonderschones Blondchen', Fred looked as fierce as a lion, and cut his meat so savagely it nearly flew off his plate. He isn't one of the cool, stiff Englishmen, but is rather peppery, for he has Scotch blood in him, as one might guess from his bonnie blue eyes.

Well, last evening we went up to the castle about sunset, at least all of us but Fred, who was to meet us there after going to the Post Restante for letters. We had a charming time poking about the ruins, the vaults where the monster tun is, and the beautiful gardens made by the elector long ago for his English wife. I liked the great terrace best, for the view was divine, so while the rest went to see the rooms inside, I sat there trying to sketch the gray stone lion's head on the wall, with scarlet woodbine sprays hanging round it. I felt as if I'd got into a romance, sitting there, watching the Meckar rolling through the valley, listening to the music of the Austrian band below, and waiting for my lover, like a real storybook girl. I had a feeling that something was going to happen and I was ready for it. I didn't feel blushy or quakey, but quite cool and only a little excited.

By-and-by I heard Fred's voice, and then he came hurrying through the great arch to find me. He looked so troubled that I forgot all about myself, and asked what the matter was. He said he'd just got a letter begging him to come home, for Frank was very ill. So he was going at once on the night train and only had time to say good-by. I was very sorry for him, and disappointed for myself, but only for a minute because he said, as he shook hands, and said it in a way that I could not mistake, "I shall soon come back, you won't forget me, Amy?"

I didn't promise, but I looked at him, and he seemed satisfied, and there was no time for anything but messages and good-byes, for he was off in an hour, and we all miss him very much. I know he wanted to speak, but I think, from something he once hinted, that he had promised his father not to do anything of the sort yet a while, for is is a rash boy, and the old gentleman dreads a foreign daughter-in-law. We shall soon meet in Rome, and then, if I don't change my mind, I'll say "Yes, thank you," when he says "Will you, please?"

Of course this is all very private, but I wished you to know what was going on. Don't be anxious about me, remember I am your 'prudent Amy', and be sure I will do nothing rashly. Send me as much advice as you like. I'll use it if I can. I wish I could see you for a good talk, Marmee. Love and trust me.

Ever your AMY

Chapter Thirty-Two

"Jo, I'm anxious about Beth."

"Why, Mother, she has seemed unusually well since the babies came."

"It's not her health that troubles me now, it's her spirits. I'm sure there is something on her mind, and I want you to discover what it is."

"What makes you think so, Mother?"

"She sits alone a good deal, and doesn't talk to her father as much as she used. I found her crying over the babies the other day. When she sings, the songs are always sad ones, and now and then I see a look in her face that I don't understand. This isn't like Beth, and it worries me."

"Have you asked her about it?'

"I have tried once or twice, but she either evaded my questions or looked so distressed that I stopped. I never force my children's confidence, and I seldom have to wait for long."

Mrs. March glanced at Jo as she spoke, but the face opposite seemed quite unconscious of any secret disquietude but Beth's, and after sewing thoughtfully for a minute, Jo said, "I think she is growing up, and so begins to dream dreams, and have hopes and fears and fidgets, without knowing why or being able to explain them. Why, Mother, Beth's eighteen, but we don't realize it, and treat her like a child, forgetting she's a woman."

"So she is. Dear heart, how fast you do grow up," returned her mother with a sigh and a smile.

"Can't be helped, Marmee, so you must resign yourself to all sorts of worries, and let your birds hop out of the nest, one by one. I promise never to hop very far, if that is any comfort to you."

"It's a great comfort, Jo. I always feel strong when you are at home, now Meg is gone. Beth is too feeble and Amy too young to depend upon, but when the tug comes, you are always ready."

"Why, you know I don't mind hard jobs much, and there must always be one scrub in a family. Amy is splendid in fine works and I'm not, but I feel in my element when all the carpets are to be taken up, or half the family fall sick at once. Amy is distinguishing herself abroad, but if anything is amiss at home, I'm your man."

"I leave Beth to your hands, then, for she will open her tender little heart to her Jo sooner than to anyone else. Be very kind, and don't let her think anyone watches or talks about; her. If she only would get quite strong and cheerful again, I shouldn't have a wish in the world."

"Happy woman! I've got heaps."

"My dear, what are they?"

"I'll settle Bethy's troubles, and then I'll tell you mine. They are not very wearing, so they'll keep." And Jo stitched away, with a wise nod which set her mother's heart at rest about her for the present at least.

While apparently absorbed in her own affairs, Jo watched Beth, and after many conflicting conjectures, finally settled upon one which seemed to explain the change in her. A slight incident gave Jo the clue to the mystery, she thought, and lively fancy, loving heart did the rest. She was affecting to write busily one Saturday afternoon, when she and Beth were alone together. Yet as she scribbled, she kept her eye on her sister, who seemed unusually quiet. Sitting at the window, Beth's work often dropped into her lap, and she leaned her head upon her hand, in a dejected attitude, while her eyes rested on the dull, autumnal landscape. Suddenly some one passed below, whistling like an operatic blackbird, and a voice called out, "All serene! Coming in tonight."

Beth started, leaned forward, smiled and nodded, watched the passer-by till his quick tramp died away, then said softly as if to herself, "How strong and well and happy that dear boy looks."

"Hum!" said Jo, still intent upon her sister's face, for the bright color faded as quickly as it came, the smile vanished, and presently a tear lay shining on the window ledge. Beth whisked it off, and in her half-averted face read a tender sorrow that made her own eyes fill. Fearing to betray herself, she slipped away, murmuring something about needing more paper.

"Mercy on me, Beth loves Laurie!" she said, sitting down in her own room, pale with the shock of the discovery which she believed she had just made. "I never dreamed of such a thing. What will Mother say? I wonder if her . . ." there Jo stopped and turned scarlet with a sudden thought. "If he shouldn't love back again, how dreadful it would be. He must. I'll make him!" And she shook her head threateningly at the picture of the mischievous-looking boy laughing at her from the wall. "Oh dear, we are growing up with a vengeance. Here's Meg married and a mamma, Amy flourishing away at Paris, and Beth in love. I'm the only one that has sense enough to keep out of mischief." Jo thought intently for a minute with her eyes fixed on the picture, then she smoothed out her wrinkled forehead and said, with a decided nod at the face opposite, "No thank you, sir, you're very charming, but you've no more stability than a weathercock. So you needn't write touching notes and smile in that insinuating way, for it won't do a bit of good, and I won't have it."

Then she sighed, and fell into a reverie from which she did not wake till the early twilight sent her down to take new observations, which only confirmed her suspicion. Though Laurie flirted with Amy and joked with Jo, his manner to Beth had always been peculiarly kind and gentle, but so was everybody's. Therefore, no one thought of imagining that he cared more for her than for the others. Indeed, a general impression had prevailed in the family of late that 'our boy' was getting fonder than ever of Jo, who, however, wouldn't hear a word upon the subject and scolded violently if anyone dared to suggest it. If they had known the various tender passages which had been nipped in the bud, they would have had the immense satisfaction of saying, "I told you so." But Jo hated 'philandering', and wouldn't allow it, always having a joke or a smile ready at the least sign of impending danger. When Laurie first went to college, he fell in love about once a month, but these small flames were as brief as ardent, did no damage, and much amused Jo, who took great interest in the alternations of hop, despair, and resignation, which were confided to her in their weekly conferences. But there came a time when Laurie ceased to worship at many shrines, hinted darkly at one all-absorbing passion, and indulged occasionally in Byronic fits of gloom. Then he avoided the tender subject altogether, wrote philosophical notes to Jo, turned studious, and gave out that he was going to 'dig', intending to graduate in a blaze of glory. This suited the young lady better than twilight confidences, tender pressures of the hand, and eloquent glances of the eye, for with Jo, brain developed earlier than heart, and she preferred imaginary heroes to real ones, because when tired of them, the former could be shut up in the tin kitchen till called for, and the latter were less manageable.

Things were in this state when the grand discovery was made, and Jo watched Laurie that night as she had never done before. If she had not got the new idea into her head, she would have seen nothing unusual in the fact that Beth was very quiet, and Laurie very kind to her. But having given the rein to her lively fancy, it galloped away with her at a great pace, and common sense, being rather weakened by a long course or romance writing, did not come to the rescue. As usual Beth lay on the sofa and Laurie sat in a low chair close by, amusing her with all sorts of gossip, for she depended on her weekly 'spin', and he never disappointed her. But that evening Jo fancied that Beth's eyes rested on the lively, dark face beside her with peculiar pleasure, and that she listened with intense interest to an account of some exciting cricket match, though the phrases, 'caught off a tice', 'stumped off his ground", and 'the leg hit for three', were as intelligible to her as Sanskrit. She also fancied, having set her heart upon seeing it, that she saw a certain increase of gentleness in Laurie's manner, that he dropped his voice now and then, laughed less than usual, was a little absent—minded, and settled the afghan over Beth's feet with an assiduity that was really almost tender.

"Who knows? Stranger things have happened," thought Jo, as she fussed about the room. "She will make quite an angel of him, and he will make life delightfully easy and pleasant for the dear, if they only love each other. I don't see how he can help it, and I do believe he would if the rest of us were out of the way."

As everyone was out of the way but herself, Jo began to feel that she ought to dispose of herself with all speed. But where should she go? And burning to lay herself upon the shrine of sisterly devotion, she sat down to settle that point.

Now, the old sofa was a regular patriarch of a sofa—long, broad, well-cushioned, and low, a trifle shabby, as well it might be, for the girls had slept and sprawled on it as babies, fished over the back, rode on the arms, and had menageries under it as children, and rested tired heads, dreamed dreams, and listened to tender talk on it as young women. They all loved it, for it was a family refuge, and one corner had always been Jo's favorite lounging place. Among the many pillows that adorned the venerable couch was one, hard, round, covered with prickly horsehair, and furnished with a knobby button at each end. This repulsive pillow was her especial property, being used as a weapon of defense, a barricade, or a stern preventive of too much slumber.

Laurie knew this pillow well, and had cause to regard it with deep aversion, having been unmercifully pummeled with it in former days when romping was allowed, and now frequently debarred by it from the seat he most coveted next ot Jo in the sofa corner. If 'the sausage' as the called it, stood on end, it was a sign that he might approach and repose, but if it lay flat across the sofa, woe to man, woman, or child who dared disturb it! That evening Jo forgot to barricade her corner, and had not been in her seat five minutes, before a massive form appeared beside her, and with both arms spread over the sofa back, both long legs stretched out before him, Laurie exclaimed, with a sigh of satisfaction . . .

"Now, this is filling at the price."

"No slang," snapped Jo, slamming down the pillow. But it was too late, there was no room for it, and coasting onto the floor, it disappeared in a most mysterious manner.

"Come, Jo, don't be thorny. After studying himself to a skeleton all the week, a fellow deserves petting and ought to get it."

"Beth will pet you. I'm busy."

"No, she's not to be bothered with me, but you like that sort of thing, unless you've suddenly lost your taste for it. Have you? Do you hate your boy, and want to fire pillows at him?"

Anything more wheedlesome than that touching appeal was seldom heard, but Jo quenched 'her boy' by turning on him with a stern query, "How many bouquets have you sent Miss Randal this week?"

"Not one, upon my word. She's engaged. Now then."

"I'm glad of it, that's one of your foolish extravagances, sending flowers and things to girls for whom you don't care two pins," continued Jo reprovingly.

"Sensible girls for whom I do care whole papers of pins won't let me send them 'flowers and things', so what can I do? My feelings need a' vent'."

"Mother doesn't approve of flirting even in fun, and you do flirt desperately, Teddy."

"I'd give anything if I could answer, 'So do you'. As I can't, I'll merely say that I don't see any harm in that pleasant little game, if all parties understand that it's only play."

"Well, it does look pleasant, but I can't learn how it's done. I've tried, because one feels awkward in company not to do as everybody else id doing, but I don't seem to get on", said Jo, forgetting to play mentor.

"Take lessons of Amy, she has a regular talent for it."

"Yes, she does it very prettily, and never seems to go too far. I suppose it's natural to some people to please without trying, and others to always say and do the wrong thing in the wrong place."

"I'm glad you can't flirt. It's really refreshing to see a sensible, straightforward girl, who can be jolly and kind without making a fool of herself. Between ourselves, Jo, some of the girls I know really do go on at such a rate I'm ashamed of them. They don't mean any harm, I'm sure, but if they knew how we fellows talked about them afterward, they'd mend their ways, I fancy."

"They do the same, and as their tongues are the sharpest, you fellows get the worst of it, for you are as silly as they, every bit. If you behaved properly, they would, but knowing you like their nonsense, they keep it up, and then you blame them."

"Much you know about it, ma'am," said Laurie in a superior tone. "We don't like romps and flirts, though we may act as if we did sometimes. The pretty, modest girls are never talked about, except respectfully, among gentleman. Bless your innocent soul! If you could be in my place for a month you'd see things that would astonish you a trifle. Upon my word, when I see one of those harum-scarum girls, I always want to say with our friend Cock Robin . . .

"Out upon you, fie upon you, Bold-faced jig!"

It was impossible to help laughing at the funny conflict between Laurie's chivalrous reluctance to speak ill of womankind, and his very natural dislike of the unfeminine folly of which fashionable society showed him many samples. Jo knew that 'young Laurence' was regarded as a most eligible parti by worldly mamas, was much smiled upon by their daughters, and flattered enough by ladies of all ages to make a coxcomb of him, so she watched him rather jealously, fearing he would be spoiled, and rejoiced more than she confessed to find that he still believed in modest girls. Returning suddenly to her admonitory tone, she said, dropping her voice, "If you must have a 'went', Teddy, go and devote yourself to one of the 'pretty, modest girls' whom you do respect, and not waste your time with the silly ones."

"You really advise it?" And Laurie looked at her with an odd mixture of anxiety and merriment in his face.

"Yes, I do, but you'd better wait till you are through college, on the whole, and be fitting yourself for the place meantime. You're not half good enough for—well, whoever the modest girl may be." And Jo looked a little queer likewise, for a name had almost escaped her.

"That I'm not!" acquiesced Laurie, with an expression of humility quite new to him, as he dropped his eyes and absently wound Jo's apron tassel round his finger.

"Mercy on us, this will never do," thought Jo, adding aloud, "Go and sing to me. I'm dying for some music, and always like yours."

"I'd rather stay here, thank you."

"Well, you can't, there isn't room. Go and make yourself useful, since you are too big to be ornamental. I thought you hated to be tied to a woman's apron string?" retorted Jo, quoting certain rebellious words of his own.

"Ah, that depends on who wears the apron!" and Laurie gave an audacious tweak at the tassel.

"Are you going?" demanded Jo, diving for the pillow.

He fled at once, and the minute it was well, "Up with the bonnets of bonnie Dundee," she slipped away to return no more till the young gentleman departed in high dudgeon.

Jo lay long awake that night, and was just dropping off when the sound of a stifled sob made her fly to Beth's bedside, with the anxious inquiry, "What is it, dear?"

"I thought you were asleep," sobbed Beth.

"Is it the old pain, my precious?'

"No, it's a new one, but I can bear it." And Beth tried to check her tears.

"Tell me all about it, and let me cure it as I often did the other."

"You can't, there is no cure." There Beth's voice gave way, and clinging to her sister, she cried so despairingly that Jo was frightened.

"Where is it? Shall I call Mother?"

"No, no, don't call her, don't tell her. I shall be better soon. Lie down here and 'poor' my head. I'll be quiet and go to sleep, indeed I will." Jo obeyed, but as her hand went softly to and fro across Beth's hot forehead and wet eyelids, her heart was very full and she longed to speak. But young as she was, Jo had learned that hearts, like flowers, cannot be rudely handled, but must open naturally, so though she believed she knew the cause of Beth's new pain, she only said, in her tenderest tone, "Does anything trouble you, deary?"

"Yes, Jo," after a long pause.

"Wouldn't it comfort you to tell me what it is?"

"not now, not yet."

"Then I won't ask, but remember, Bethy, that Mother and Jo are always glad to hear and help you, if they can."

"I know it. I'll tell you by-and-by."

"Is the pain better now?"

"Oh, yes, much better, you are so comfortable, Jo."

"Go to sleep, dear. I'll stay with you."

So cheek to cheek they fell asleep, and on the morrow Beth seemed quite herself again, for at eighteen neither heads nor hearts ache long, and a loving word can medicine most ills.

But Jo had made up her mind, and after pondering over a project for some days, she confided it to her mother.

"You asked me the other day what my wishes were. I'll tell you one of them, Marmee," she began, as they sat along together. "I want to go away somewhere this winter for a change."

"Why, Jo?" And her mother looked up quickly, as if the words suggested a double meaning.

With her eyes on her work Jo answered soberly, "I want something new. I feel restless and anxious to be seeing, doing, and learning more than I am. I brood too much over my own small affairs, and need stirring up, so as I can be spared this winter, I'd like to hop a little way and try my wings."

"Where will you hop?"

"To New York. I had a bright idea yesterday, and this is it. You know Mrs. Kirke wrote to you for some respectable young person to teach her children and sew. It's rather hard to find just the thing, but I think I should suit if I tried."

"My dear, go out to service in that great boarding house!" And Mrs. March looked surprised, but not displeased.

"It's not exactly going out to service, for Mrs. Kirke is your friend—the kindest soul that ever lived—and would make things pleasant for me, I know. Her family is separate from the rest, and no one knows me there. Don't care if they do. It's honest work, and I'm not ashamed of it."

"Nor I. But your writing?"

"All the better for the change. I shall see and hear new things, get new ideas, and even if I haven't much time there, I shall bring home quantities of material for my rubbish."

"I have no doubt of it, but are these your only reasons for this sudden fancy?'

"No, Mother."

"May I know the others?"

Jo looked up and Jo looked down, then said slowly, with sudden color in her cheeks. "It may be vain and wrong to say it, but—I'm afraid—Laurie is getting too fond of me."

"Then you don't care for him in the way it is evident he begins to care for you?' And Mrs. March looked anxious as she put the question.

"Mercy, no! I love the dear boy, as I always have, and am immensely proud of him, but as for anything more, it's out of the question."

"I'm glad of that, Jo."

"Why, please?'

"Because, dear, I don't think you suited to one another. As friends you are very happy, and your frequent quarrels soon blow over, but I fear you would both rebel if you were mated for life. You are too much alike and too fond of freedom, not to mention hot tempers and strong wills, to get on happily together, in a relation which needs infinite patience and forbearance, as well as love."

"That's just the feeling I had, though I couldn't express it. I'm glad you think he is only beginning to care for me. It would trouble me sadly to make him unhappy, for I couldn't fall in love with the dear old fellow merely out of gratitude, could I?"

"You are sure of his feeling for you?"

The color deepened in Jo's cheeks as she answered, with the look of mingled pleasure, pride, and pain which young girls wear when speaking of first lovers, "I'm afraid it is so, Mother. He hasn't said anything, but he looks a great deal. I think I had better go away before it comes to anything."

"I agree with you, and if it can be managed you shall go."

Jo looked relieved, and after a pause, said, smiling, "How Mrs. Moffat would wonder at your want of management, if she knew, and how she will rejoice that Annie may still hope."

"AH, Jo, mothers may differ in their management, but the hope is the same in all—the desire to see their children happy. Meg is so, and I am content with her success. You I leave to enjoy your liberty till you tire of it, for only then will you find that there is something sweeter. Amy is my chief care now, but her good sense will help ;her. For Beth, I indulge no hopes except that she may be well. By the way, she seems brighter this last day or two. Have you spoken to her?'

"Yes, she owned she had a trouble, and promised to tell me by-and-by. I said no more, for I think I know it," And Jo told her little story.

Mrs. March shook her head, and did not take so romantic a view of the case, but looked grave, and repeated her opinion that for Laurie's sake Jo should go away for a time.

"Let us say nothing about it to him till the plan is settled, then I'll run away before he can collect his wits and be tragic. Beth must think I'm going to please myself, as I am, for I can't talk about Laurie to her. But she can pet and comfort him after I'm gone, and so cure him of this romantic notion. He's been through so many little trials of the sort, he's used to it, and will soon get over his lovelornity."

Jo spoke hopefully, but could not rid herself of the foreboding fear that this 'little trial' would be harder than the others, and that Laurie would not get over his 'lovelornity' as easily as heretofore.

The plan was talked over in a family council and agreed upon, for Mrs. Kirke gladly accepted Jo, and promised to make a pleasant home for her. The teaching would render her independent, and such leisure as she got might be made profitable by writing, while the new scenes and society would be both useful and agreeable. Jo liked the prospect and was eager to be gone, for the home nest was growing too narrow for her restless nature and adventurous spirit. When all was settled, with fear and trembling she told Laurie, but to her surprise he took it very quietly. He had been graver than usual of late, but very pleasant, and when jokingly accused of turning over a new leaf, he answered soberly, "So I am, and I mean this one shall stay turned."

Jo was very much relieved that one of his virtuous fits should come on just then, and made her preparations with a lightened heart, for Beth seemed more cheerful, and hoped she was doing the best for all.

"One thing I leave in your especial care," she said, the night before she left.

"You mean your papers?" asked Beth. "No, my boy. Be very good to him, won't you?"

"Of course I will, but I can't fill your place, and he'll miss you sadly."

"It won't hurt him, so remember, I leave him in your charge, to plague, pet, and keep in order."

"I'll do my best, for your sake," promised Beth, wondering why Jo looked at her so queerly.

When Laurie said good-by, he whispered significantly, "It won't do a bit of good, Jo. My eye is on you, so mind what you do, or I'll come and bring you home."

Chapter Thirty-Three

New York, November

Dear Marmee and Beth,

I'm going to write you a regular volume, for I've got heaps to tell, though I'm not a fine young lady traveling on the continent. When I lost sight of Father's dear old face, I felt a trifle blue, and might have shed a briny drop or two, if an Irish lady with four small children, all crying more or less, hadn't diverted my mind, for I amused myself by dropping gingerbread nuts over the seat every time they opened their mouths to roar.

Soon the sun came out, and taking it as a good omen, I cleared up likewise and enjoyed my journey with all my heart.

Mrs. Kirke welcomed me so kindly I felt at home at once, even in that big house full of strangers. She gave me a funny little sky parlor—all she had, but there is a stove in it, and a nice table in a sunny window, so I can sit here and write whenever I like. A fine view and a church tower opposite atone for the many stairs, and I took a fancy to my den on the spot. The nursery, where I am to teach and sew, is a pleasant room next Mrs. Kirke's private parlor, and thc two little girls are pretty children, rather spoiled, I fancy, but they took to me after telling them The Seven Bad Pigs, and I've no doubt I shall make a model governess.

I am to have my meals with the children, if I prefer it to the great table, and for the present I do, for I am bashful, though no one will believe it.

"Now, my dear, make yourself at home," said Mrs. K. in her motherly way, "I'm on the drive from morning to night, as you may suppose with such a family, but a great anxiety will be off my mind if I know the children are safe with you. My rooms are always open to you, and your own shall be as comfortable as I can make it. There are some pleasant people in the house if you feel sociable, and your evenings are always free. Come to me if anything goes wrong, and be as happy as you can. There's the tea bell, I must run and change my cap." And off she bustled, leaving me to settle myself in my new nest.

As I went downstairs soon after, I saw something I liked. The flights are very long in this tall house, and as I stood waiting at the head of the third one for a little servant girl to lumber up, I saw a gentleman come along behind her, take the heavy hod of coal out of her hand, carry it all the way up, put it down at a door near by, and walk away, saying, with a kind nod and a foreign accent, "It goes better so. The little back is too young to haf such heaviness."

Wasn't it good of him? I like such things, for as Father says, trifles show character. When I mentioned it to Mrs. K., that evening, she laughed, and said, "That must have been Professor Bhaer, he's always doing things of that sort."

Mrs. K. told me he was from Berlin, very learned and good, but poor as a church mouse, and gives lessons to support himself and two little orphan nephews whom he is educating here, according to the wishes of his sister, who married an American. Not a very romantic story, but it interested me, and I was glad to hear that Mrs. K. lends him her parlor for some of his scholars. There is a glass door between it and the nursery, and I mean to peep at him, and then I'll tell you how he looks. He's almost forty, so it's no harm, Marmee.

After tea and a go-to-bed romp with the little girls, I attacked the big workbasket, and had a quiet evening chatting with my new friend. I shall keep a journal-letter, and send it once a week, so goodnight, and more tomorrow.

Tuesday Eve

Had a lively time in my seminary this morning, for the children acted like Sancho, and at one time I really thought I should shake them all round. Some good angel inspired me to try gymnastics, and I kept it up till they were glad to sit down and keep still. After luncheon, the girl took them out for a walk, and I went to my needlework like little Mabel 'with a willing mind'. I was thanking my stars that I'd learned to make nice buttonholes, when the parlor door opened and shut, and someone began to hum, Kennst Du Das Land, like a big bumblebee. It was dreadfully improper, I know, but I couldn't resist the temptation, and lifting one end of the curtain before the glass door, I peeped in.

Professor Bhaer was there, and while he arranged his books, I took a good look at him. A regular German—rather stout, with brown hair tumbled all over his head, a bushy beard, good nose, the kindest eyes I ever saw, and a splendid big voice that does one's ears good, after our sharp or slipshod American gabble. His clothes were rusty, his hands were large, and he hadn't a really handsome feature in his face, except his beautiful teeth, yet I liked him, for he had a fine head, his linen was very nice, and he looked like a gentleman, though two buttons were off his coat and there was a patch on one shoe. He looked sober in spite of his humming, till he went to the window to turn the hyacinth bulbs toward thc sun, and strokc thc cat, who received him like an old friend. Then he smiled, and when a tap came at the door, called out in a loud, brisk tone, "Herein!"

I was just going to run, when I caught sight of a morsel of a child carrying a big book, and stopped, to see what was going on.

"Me wants me Bhaer," said the mite, slamming down her book and running to meet him.

"Thou shalt haf thy Bhaer. Come, then, and take a goot hug from him, my Tina," said the Professor, catching her up with a laugh, and holding her so high over his head that she had to stoop her little face to kiss him.

"Now me mus tuddy my lessin," went on the funny little thing. So he put her up at the table, opened the great dictionary she had brought, and gave her a paper and pencil, and she scribbled away, turning a leaf now and then, and passing her little fat finger down the page, as if finding a word, so soberly that I nearly betrayed myself by a laugh, while Mr. Bhaer stood stroking her pretty hair with a fatherly look that made me think she must be his own, though she looked more French than German.

Another knock and the appearance of two young ladies sent me back to my work, and there I virtuously remained through all the noise and gabbling that went on next door. One of the girls kept laughing affectedly, and saying, "Now Professor," in a coquettish tone, and the other pronounced her German with an accent that must have made it hard for him to keep sober.

Both seemed to try his patience sorely, for more than once I heard him say emphatically, "No, no, it is not so, you haf not attend to what I say," and once there was a loud rap, as if he struck the table with his book, followed by the despairing exclamation, "Prut! It all goes bad this day."

Poor man, I pitied him, and when the girls were gone, took just one more peep to see if he survived it. He seemed to have thrown himself back in his chair, tired out, and sat there with his eyes shut till the clock struck two, when he jumped up, put his books in his pocket, as if ready for another lesson, and taking little Tina who had fallen asleep on the sofa in his arms, he carried her quietly away. I fancy he has a hard life of it. Mrs. Kirke asked me if I wouldn't go down to the five o'clock dinner, and feeling a little bit homesick, I thought I would, just to see what sort of people are under the same roof with me. So I made myself respectable and tried to slip in behind Mrs. Kirke, but as she is short and I'm tall, my efforts at concealment were rather a failure. She gave me a seat by her, and after my face cooled off, I plucked up courage and looked about me. The long table was full, and every—one intent on getting their dinner, the gentlemen especially, who seemed to be eating on time, for they bolted in every sense of the word, vanishing as soon as they were done. There was the usual assortment of young men absorbed in themselves, young couples absorbed in each other, married ladies in their babies, and old gentlemen in politics. I don't think I shall care to have much to do with any of them, except one sweetfaced maiden lady, who looks as if she had something in her.

Cast away at the very bottom of the table was the Professor, shouting answers to the questions of a very inquisitive, deaf old gentleman on one side, and talking philosophy with a Frenchman on the other. If Amy had been here, she'd have turned her back on him forever because, sad to relate, he had a great appetite, and shoveled in his dinner in a manner which would have horrified 'her ladyship'. I didn't mind, for I like 'to see folks eat with a relish', as Hannah says, and the poor man must have needed a deal of food after teaching idiots all day.

As I went upstairs after dinner, two of the young men were settling their hats before the hall mirror, and I heard one say low to the other, "Who's the new party?"

"Governess, or something of that sort."

"What the deuce is she at our table for?"

"Friend of the old lady's."

"Handsome head, but no style."

"Not a bit of it. Give us a light and come on."

I felt angry at first, and then I didn't care, for a governess is as good as a clerk, and I've got sense, if I haven't style, which is more than some people have, judging from the remarks of the elegant beings who clattered away, smoking like bad chimneys. I hate ordinary people!

Thursday

Yesterday was a quiet day spent in teaching, sewing, and writing in my little room, which is very cozy, with a light and fire. I picked up a few bits of news and was introduced to the Professor. It seems that Tina is the child of the Frenchwoman who does the fine ironing in the laundry here. The little thing has lost her heart to Mr. Bhaer, and follows him about the house like a dog whenever he is at home, which delights him, as he is very fond of children, though a 'bacheldore'. Kitty and Minnie Kirk likewise regard him with affection, and tell all sorts of stories about the plays he invents, the presents he brings, and the splendid tales he tells. The younger men quiz him, it seems, call him Old Fritz, Lager Beer, Ursa Major, and make all manner of jokes on his name. But he enjoys it like a boy, Mrs. Kirke says, and takes it so good-naturedly that they all like him in spite of his foreign ways.

The maiden lady is a Miss Norton, rich, cultivated, and kind. She spoke to me at dinner today (for I went to table again, it's such fun to watch people), and asked me to come and see her at her room. She has fine books and pictures, knows interesting persons, and seems friendly, so I shall make myself agreeable, for I do want to get into good society, only it isn't the same sort that Amy likes.

I was in our parlor last evening when Mr. Bhaer came in with some newspapers for Mrs. Kirke. She wasn't there, but Minnie, who is a little old woman, introduced me very prettily. "This is Mamma's friend, Miss March."

"Yes, and she's jolly and we like her lots," added Kitty, who is and 'enfant terrible'.

We both bowed, and then we laughed, for the prim introduction and the blunt addition were rather a comical contrast.

"Ah, yes, I hear these naughty ones go to vex you, Mees Marsch. If so again, call at me and I come," he said, with a threatening frown that delighted the little wretches.

I promised I would, and he departed, but it seems as if I was doomed to see a good deal of him, for today as I passed his door on my way out, by accident I knocked against it with my umbrella. It flew open, and there he stood in his dressing gown, with a big blue sock on one hand and a darning needle in the other. He didn't seem at all ashamed of it, for when I explained and hurried on, he waved his hand, sock and all, saying in his loud, cheerful way . . .

"You haf a fine day to make your walk. Bon voyage, Mademoiselle."

I laughed all the way downstairs, but it was a little pathetic, also to think of the poor man having to mend his own clothes. The German gentlemen embroider, I know, but darning hose is another thing and not so pretty.

Saturday

Nothing has happened to write about, except a call on Miss Norton, who has a room full of pretty things, and who was very charming, for she showed me all her treasures, and asked me if I would sometimes go with her to lectures and concerts, as her escort, if I enjoyed them. She put it as a favor, but I'm sure Mrs. Kirke has told her about us, and she does it out of kindness to me. I'm as proud as Lucifer, but such favors from such people don't burden me, and I accepted gratefully. When I got back to the nursery there was such an uproar in the parlor that I looked in, and there was Mr. Bhaer down on his hands and knees, with Tina on his back, Kitty leading him with a jump rope, and Minnie feeding two small boys with seedcakes, as they roared and ramped in cages built of chairs.

"We are playing nargerie," explained Kitty.

"Dis is mine effalunt!" added Tina, holding on by the Professor's hair.

"Mamma always allows us to do what we like Saturday afternoon, when Franz and Emil come, doesn't she, Mr. Bhaer?" said Minnie.

The 'effalunt' sat up, looking as much in earnest as any of them, and said soberly to me, "I gif you my wort it is so, if we make too large a noise you shall say Hush! to us, and we go more softly."

I promised to do so, but left the door open and enjoyed the fun as much as they did, for a more glorious frolic I never witnessed. They played tag and soldiers, danced and sang, and when it began to grow dark they all piled onto the sofa about the Professor, while he told charming fairy stories of the storks on the chimney tops, and the little 'koblods', who ride the snowflakes as they fall. I wish Americans were as simple and natural as Germans, don't you?

I'm so fond of writing, I should go spinning on forever if motives of economy didn't stop me, for though I've used thin paper and written fine, I tremble to think of the stamps this long letter will need. Pray forward Amy's as soon as you can spare them. My small news will sound very flat after her splendors, but you will like them, I know. Is Teddy studying so hard that he can't find time to write to his friends? Take good care of him for me, Beth, and tell me all about the babies, and give heaps of love to everyone. From your faithful Jo.

P.S. On reading over my letter, it strikes me as rather Bhaery, but I am always interested in odd people, and I really had nothing else to write about. Bless you!

DECEMBER

My Precious Betsey,

As this is to be a scribble-scrabble letter, I direct it to you, for it may amuse you, and give you some idea of my goings on, for though quiet, they are rather amusing, for which, oh, be joyful! After what Amy would call Herculaneum efforts, in the way of mental and moral agriculture, my young ideas begin to shoot and my little twigs to bend as I could wish. They are not so interesting tome as Tina and the boys, but I do my duty by them, and they are fond of me. Franz and Emil are jolly little lads, quite after my own heart, for the mixture of German and American spirit in the produces a constant state of effervescence. Saturday afternoons are riotous times, whether spent in the house or out, for on pleasant days they all go to walk, like a seminary, with the Professor and myself to keep order, and then such fun!

We are very good friends now, and I've begun to take lessons. I really couldn't help it, and it all came about in such a droll way that I must tell you. To begin at the beginning, Mrs. Kirke called to me one day as I passed Mr. Bhaer's room where she was rummaging.

"Did you ever see such a den, my dear? Just come and help me put these books to rights, for I've turned everything upside down, trying to discover what he has done with the six new handkerchiefs I gave him not long ago."

I went in, and while we worked I looked about me, for it was 'a den' to be sure. Books and papers everywhere, a broken meerschaum, and an old flute over the mantlepiece as if done with, a ragged bird without any tail chirped on one window seat, and a box of white mice adorned the other. Half-finished boats and bits of string lay among the manuscripts. Dirty little boots stood drying before the fire, and traces of the dearly beloved boys, for whom he makes a slave of himself, were to be seen all over the room. After a grand rummage three of the missing articles were found, one over the bird cage, one covered with ink, and a third burned brown, having been used as a holder.

"Such a man!" laughed good-natured Mrs. K., as she put the relics in the rag bay. "I suppose the others are torn up to rig ships, bandage cut fingers, or make kite tails. It's dreadful, but I can't scold him. He's so absent-minded and goodnatured, he lets those boys ride over him roughshod. I agreed to do his washing and mending, but he forgets to give out his things and I forget to look them over, so he comes to a sad pass sometimes."

"Let me mend them," said I. "I don't mind it, and he needn't know. I'd like to, he's so kind to me about bringing my letters and lending books."

So I have got his things in order, and knit heels into two pairs of the socks, for they were boggled out of shape with his queer darns. Nothing was said, and I hoped he wouldn't find it out, but one day last week he caught me at it. Hearing the lessons he gives to others has interested and amused me so much that I took a fancy to lear, for Tina runs in and out, leaving the door open, and I can hear. I had been sitting near this door, finishing off the last sock, and trying to understand what he said to a new scholar, who is as stupid as I am. The girl had gone, and I thought he had also, it was so still, and I was busily gabbling over a verb, and rocking to and fro in a most absurd way, when a little crow made me look up, and there was Mr. Bhaer looking and laughing quietly, while he made signs to Tina not to betray him.

"So!" he said, as I stopped and stared like a goose, "you peep at me, I peep at you, and this is not bad, but see, I am not pleasanting when I say, haf you a wish for German?"

"Yes, but you are too busy. I am too stupid to learn," I blundered out, as red as a peony.

"Prut! We will make the time, and we fail not to find the sense. At efening I shall gif a little lesson with much gladness, for look you, Mees Marsch, I haf this debt to pay." And he pointed to my work 'Yes, ' they say to one another, these so kind ladies, 'he is a stupid old fellow, he will see not what we do, he will never observe that his sock heels go not in holes any more, he will think his buttons grow out new when they fall, and believe that strings make theirselves.' "Ah! But I haf an eye, and I see much. I haf a heart, and I feel thanks for this. Come, a little lesson then and now, or no more good fairy works for me and mine."

Of course I couldn't say anything after that, and as it really is a splendid opportunity, I made the bargain, and we began. I took four lessons, and then I stuck fast in a grammatical bog. The Professor was very patient with me, but it must have been torment to him, and now and then he'd look at me with such an expression of mild despair that it was a toss-up with me whether to laugh or cry. I tried both ways, and when it came to a sniff or utter mortification and woe, he just threw the grammar on to the floor and marched out of the room. I felt myself disgraced and deserted forever, but didn't blame him a particle, and was scrambling my papers together, meaning to rush upstairs and shake myself hard, when in he came, as brisk and beaming as if I'd covered myself in glory.

"Now we shall try a new way. You and I will read these pleasant little MARCHEN together, and dig no more in that dry book, that goes in the corner for making us trouble."

He spoke so kindly, and opened Hans Andersons's fairy tales so invitingly before me, that I was more ashamed than ever, and went at my lesson in a neck-or-nothing style that seemed to amuse him immensely. I forgot my bashfulness, and pegged away (no other word will express it) with all my might, tumbling over long words, pronouncing according to inspiration of the minute, and doing my very best. When I finished reading my first page, and stopped for breath, he clapped his hands and cried out in his hearty way, "Das ist gut!' Now we go well! My turn. I do him in German, gif me your ear." And away he went, rumbling out the words with his strong voice and a relish which was good to see as well as hear. Fortunately the story was the CONSTANT TIN SOLDIER, which is droll, you know, so I could laugh, and I did, though I didn't understand half he read, for I couldn't help it, he was so earnest, I so excited, and the whole thing so comical. After that we got on better, and now I read my lessons pretty well, for this way of studying suits me, and I can see that the grammar gets tucked into the tales and poetry as one gives pills in jelly. I like it very much, and he doesn't seem tired of it yet, which is very good of him, isn't it? I mean to give him something on

Christmas, for I dare not offer money. Tell me something nice, Marmee.

I'm glad Laurie seems so happy and busy, that he has given up smoking and lets his hair grow. You see Beth manages him better than I did. I'm not jealous, dear, do your best, only don't make a saint of him. I'm afraid I couldn't like him without a spice of human naughtiness. Read him bits of my letters. I haven't time to write much, and that will do just as well. Thank Heaven Beth continues so comfortable.

JANUARY

A Happy New Year to you all, my dearest family, which of course includes Mr. L. and a young man by the name of Teddy. I can't tell you how much I enjoyed your Christmas bundle, for i didn't get it till night and had given up hoping. Your letter came in the morning, but you said nothing about a parcel, meaning it for a surprise, so I was disappointed, for I'd had a 'kind of feeling' that you wouldn't forget me. I felt a little low in my mind as I sat up in my room after tea, and when the big, muddy, battered-looking bundle was brought to me, I just hugged it and pranced. It was so homey and refreshing that I sat down on the floor and read and looked and ate and laughed and cried, in my usual absurd way. The things were just what I wanted, and all the better for being made instead of bought. Beth's new 'ink bib' was capital, and Hannah's box of hard gingerbread will be a treasure. I'll be sure and wear the nice flannels you sent, Marmee, and read carefully the books Father has marked. Thank you all, heaps and heaps!

Speaking of books reminds me that I'm getting rich in that line, for on New Year's Day Mr. Bhaer gave me a fine Shakespeare. It is one he values much, and I've often admired it, set up in the place of honor with his German Bible, Plato, Homer, and Milton, so you may imagine how I felt when he brought it down, without its cover, and showed me my own name in it, "from my friend Friedrich Bhaer".

"You say often you wish a library. Here I gif you one, for between these lids (he meant covers) is many books in one. Read him well, and he will help you much, for the study of character in this book will help you to read it in the world and paint it with your pen."

I thanked him as well as I could, and talk now about 'my library', as if I had a hundred books. I never knew how much there was in Shakespeare before, but then I never had a Bhaer to explain it to me. Now don't laugh at his horrid name. It isn't pronounced either Bear or Beer, as people will say it, but something between the two, as only Germans can give it. I'm glad you both like what I tell you about him, and hope you will know him some day. Mother would admire his warm heart, Father his wise head. I admire both, and feel rich in my new 'friend Friedrich Bhaer'.

Not having much money, or knowing what he'd like, I got several little things, and put them about the room, where he would find them unexpectedly. They were useful, pretty, or funny, a new standish on his table, a little vase for his flower, he always has one, or a bit of green in a glass, to keep him fresh, he says, and a holder for his blower, so that he needn't burn up what Amy calls 'mouchoirs'. I made it like those Beth invented, a big butterfly with a fat body, and black and yellow wings, worsted feelers, and bead eyes. It took his fancy immensely, and he put it on his mantlepiece as an article of virtue, so it was rather a failure after all. Poor as he is, he didn't forget a servant or a child in the house, and not a soul here, from the French laundrywoman to Miss Norton forgot him. I was so glad of that.

They got up a masquerade, and had a gay time New Year's Eve. I didn't mean to go down, having no dress. But at the last minute, Mrs. Kirke remembered some old brocades, and Miss Norton lent me lace and feathers. So I dressed up as Mrs. Malaprop, and sailed in with a mask on. No one knew me, for I disguised my voice, and no one dreamed of the silent, haughty Miss March (for they think I am very stiff and cool, most of them, and so I am to whippersnappers) could dance and dress, and burst out into a 'nice derangement of epitaphs, like an allegory on the banks of the Nile'. I enjoyed it very much, and when we unmasked it was fun to see them stare at me. I heard one of the young men tell another that he knew I'd been an actress, in fact, he thought he remembered seeing me at one of the minor theaters. Meg will relish that joke. Mr. Bhaer was Nick Bottom, and Tina was Titania, a perfect little fairy in his arms. To see them dance was 'quite a landscape', to use a Teddyism.

I had a very happy New Year, after all, and when I thought it over in my room, I felt as if I was getting on a little in spite of my many failures, for I'm cheerful all the time now, work with a will, and take more interest in other people than I used to, which is satisfactory. Bless you all! Ever your loving . . . Jo

Chapter Thirty-Four

Though very happy in the social atmosphere about her, and very busy with the daily work that earned her bread and made it sweeter for the effort, Jo still found time for literary labors. The purpose which now took possession of her was a natural one to a poor and ambitious girl, but the means she took to gain her end were not the best. She saw that money conferred power, therefore, she resolved to have, not to be used for herself alone, but for those whom she loved more than life.

The dream of filling home with comforts, giving Beth everything she wanted, from strawberries in winter to an organ in her bedroom, going abroad herself, and always having more than enough, so that she might indulge in the luxury of charity, had been for years Jo's most cherished castle in the air.

The prize-story experience had seemed to open a way which might, after long traveling and much uphill work, lead to this delightful chateau en Espagne. But the novel disaster quenched her courage for a time, for public opinion is a giant which has frightened stouter-hearted Jacks on bigger beanstalks than hers. Like that immortal hero, she reposed awhile after the first attempt, which resulted in a tumble and the least lovely of the giant's treasures, if I remember rightly. But the 'up again and take another' spirit was as strong in Jo as in Jack, so she scrambled up on the shady side this time and got more booty, but nearly left behind her what was far more precious than the moneybags.

She took to writing sensation stories, for in those dark ages, even all-perfect America read rubbish. She told no one, but concocted a 'thrilling tale', and boldly carried it herself to Mr. Dashwood, editor of the Weekly Volcano. She had never read Sartor Resartus, but she had a womanly instinct that clothes possess an influence more powerful over many than the worth of character or the magic of manners. So she dressed herself in her best, and trying to persuade herself that she was neither excited nor nervous, bravely climbed two pairs of dark and dirty stairs to find herself in a disorderly room, a cloud of cigar smoke, and the presence of three gentlemen, sitting with their heels rather higher than their hats, which articles of dress none of them took the trouble to remove on her appearance. somewhat daunted by this reception, Jo hesitated on the threshold, murmuring in much embarrassment . . .

"Excuse me, I was looking for the Weekly Volcano office. I wished to see Mr. Dashwood."

Down went the highest pair of heels, up rose the smokiest gentleman, and carefully cherishing his cigar between his fingers, he advanced with a nod and a countenance expressive of nothing but sleep. Feeling that she must get through the matter somehow, Jo produced her manuscript and, blushing redder and redder with each sentence, blundered out fragments of the little speech carefully prepared for the occasion.

"A friend of mine desired me to offer—a story—just as an experiment—would like your opinion—be glad to write more if this suits."

While she blushed and blundered, Mr. Dashwood had taken the manuscript, and was turning over the leaves with a pair of rather dirty fingers, and casting critical glances up and down the neat pages.

"Not a first attempt, I take it?" observing that the pages were numbered, covered only on one side, and not tied up with a ribbon—sure sign of a novice.

"No, sir. She has had some experience, and got a prize for a tale in the BLARNEYSTONE BANNER."

"Oh, did she?" And Mr. Dashwood gave JO a quick look, which seemed to take note of everything she had on, from the bow in her bonnet to the buttons on her boots. "Well, you can leave it, if you like. We've more of this sort of thing on hand than we know what to do with at present, but I'll run my eye over it, and give you an answer next week."

Now, Jo did not like to leave it, for Mr. Dashwood didn't suit her at all, but, under the circumstances, there was nothing for her to do but bow and walk away, looking particularly tall and dignified, as she was apt to do when nettled or abashed. Just then she was both, for it was perfectly evident from the knowing glances exchanged among the gentlemen that her little fiction of 'my friend' was considered a good joke, and a laugh, produced by some inaudible remark of the editor, as he closed the door, completed her discomfiture. Half resolving never to return, she went home, and worked off her irritation by stitching pinafores vigorously, and in an hour or two was cool enough to laugh over the scene and long for next week.

When she went again, Mr. Dashwood was alone, whereat she rejoiced. Mr. Dashwood was much wider awake than before, which was agreeable and Mr. Dashwood was not too deeply absorbed in a cigar to remember his manners, so the second interview was much more comfortable than the first.

"We'll take this (editors never say I), if you don't object to a few alterations. It's too long, but omitting the passages I've marked will make it just the right length," he said, in a businesslike tone.

Jo hardly knew her own MS again, so crumpled and underscored were its pages and paragraphs, but feeling as a tender patent might on being asked to cut off her baby's legs in order that it might fit into a new cradle, she looked at the marked passages and was surprised to find that all the moral reflections—which she had carefully put in as ballast for much romance—had been stricken out.

"But, Sir, I thought every story should have some sort of a moral, so I took care to have a few of my sinners repent."

Mr. Dashwoods's editorial gravity relaxed into a smile, for Jo had forgotten her 'friend', and spoken as only an author could.

"People want to be amused, not preached at, you know. Morals don't sell nowadays." Which was not quite a correct statement, by the way.

"You think it would do with these alterations, then?"

"Yes, it's a new plot, and pretty well worked up—language good, and so on," was Mr. Dashwood's affable reply.

"What do you—that is, what compensation—" began Jo, not exactly knowing how to express herself.

"Oh, yes, well, we give from twenty-five to thirty for things of this sort. Pay when it comes out," returned Mr. Dashwood, as if that point had escaped him. Such trifles do escape the editorial mind, it is said.

"Very well, you can have it," said Jo, handing back the story with a satisfied air, for after the dollar-a-column work, even twenty-five seemed good pay.

"Shall I tell my friend you will take another if she has one better than this?" asked Jo, unconscious of her little slip of the tongue, and emboldened by her success.

"Well, we'll look at it. Can't promise to take it. Tell her to make it short and spicy, and never mind the moral. What name would your friend like to put on it?" in a careless tone.

"None at all, if you please, she doesn't wish her name to appear and has no nom de plume," said Jo, blushing in spite of herself.

"Just as she likes, of course. The tale will be out next week. Will you call for the money, or shall I send it?" asked Mr. Dashwood, who felt a natural desire to know who his new contributor might be.

"I'll call. Good morning, Sir."

As she departed, Mr. Dashwood put up his feet, with the graceful remark, "Poor and proud, as usual, but she'll do."

Following Mr. Dashwood's directions, and making Mrs. Northbury her model, Jo rashly took a plunge into the frothy sea of sensational literature, but thanks to the life preserver thrown her by a friend, she came up again not much the worse for her ducking.

Like most young scribblers, she went abroad for her characters and scenery, and banditti, counts, gypsies, nuns, and duchesses appeared upon her stage, and played their parts with as much accuracy and spirit as could be expected. Her readers were not particular about such trifles as grammar, punctuation, and probability, and Mr. Dashwood graciously permitted her to fill his columns at the lowest prices, not thinking it necessary to tell her that the real cause of his hospitality was the fact that one of his hacks, on being offered higher wages, had basely left him in the lurch.

She soon became interested in her work, for her emaciated purse grew stout, and the little hoard she was making to take Beth to the mountains next summer grew slowly but surely as the weeks passed. One thing disturbed her satisfaction, and that was that she did not tell them at home. She had a feeling that Father and Mother would not approve, and preferred to have her own way first, and beg pardon afterward. It was easy to keep her secret, for no name appeared with her stories. Mr. Dashwood had of course found it out very soon, but promised to be dumb, and for a wonder kept his word.

She thought it would do her no harm, for she sincerely meant to write nothing of which she would be ashamed, and quieted all pricks of conscience by anticipations of the happy minute when she should show her earnings and laugh over her well-kept secret.

But Mr. Dashwood rejected any but thrilling tales, and as thrills could not be produced except by harrowing up the souls of the readers, history and romance, land and sea, science and art, police records and lunatic asylums, had to be ransacked for the purpose. Jo soon found that her innocent experience had given her but few glimpses of the tragic world which underlies society, so regarding it in a business light, she set about supplying her deficiencies with characteristic energy. Eager to find material for stories, and bent on making them original in plot, if not masterly in execution, she searched newspapers for accidents, incidents, and crimes. She excited the suspicions of public librarians by asking for works on poisons. She studied faces in the street, and characters, good, bad, and indifferent, all about her. She delved in the dust of ancient times for facts or fictions so old that they were as good as new, and introduced herself to folly, sin, and misery, as well as her limited opportunities allowed. She thought she was prospering finely, but unconsciously she was beginning to desecrate some of the womanliest attributes of a woman's character. She was living in bad society, and imaginary though it was, its influence affected her, for she was feeding heart and fancy on dangerous and unsubstantial food, and was fast brushing the innocent bloom from her nature by a premature acquaintance with the darker side of life, which comes soon enough to all of us.

She was beginning to feel rather than see this, for much describing of other people's passions and feelings set her to studying and speculating about her own. a morbid amusement in which healthy young minds do not voluntarily indulge. Wrongdoing always brings its own punishment, and when Jo most needed hers, she got it.

I don't know whether the study of Shakespeare helped her to read character, or the natural instinct of a woman for what was honest, brave, and strong, but while endowing her imaginary heroes with every perfection under the sun, Jo was discovering a live hero, who interested her in spite of many human imperfections. Mr. Bhaer, in one of their conversations, had advised her to study simple, true, and lovely characters, wherever she found them, as good training for a writer. Jo took him at his word, for she coolly turned round and studied him—a proceeding which would have much surprised him, had he know it, for the worthy Professor was very humble in his own conceit.

Why everybody liked him was what puzzled Jo, at first. He was neither rich nor great, young nor handsome, in no respect what is called fascinating, imposing, or brilliant, and yet he was as attractive as a genial fire, and people seemed to gather about him as naturally as about a warm hearth. He was poor, yet always appeared to be giving something away; a stranger, yet everyone was his friend; no longer young, but as happy-hearted as a boy; plain and peculiar, yet his face looked beautiful to many, and his oddities were freely forgiven for his sake. Jo often watched him, trying to discover the charm, and at last decided that it was benevolence which worked the miracle. If he had any sorrow, 'it sat with its head under its wing', and he turned only his sunny side to the world. There were lines upon his forehead, but Time seemed to have touched him gently, remembering how kind he was to others. The pleasant curves about his mouth were the memorials of many friendly words and cheery laughs, his eyes were never cold or hard, and his big hand had a warm, strong grasp that was more expressive than words.

His very clothes seemed to partake of the hospitable nature of the wearer. They looked as if they were at ease, and liked to make him comfortable. His capacious waistcoat was sugges-tive of a large heart underneath. His rusty coat had a social air, and the baggy pockets plainly proved that little hands often went in empty and came out full. His very boots were benevolent, and his collars never stiff and raspy like other people's.

"That's it!" said Jo to herself, when she at length discovered that genuine good will toward one's fellow men could beautify and dignify even a stout German teacher, who shoveled in his dinner, darned his own socks, and was burdened with the name of Bhaer.

Jo valued goodness highly, but she also possessed a most feminine respect for intellect, and a little discovery which she made about the Professor added much to her regard for him. He never spoke of himself, and no one ever knew that in his native city he had been a man much honored and esteemed for learning and integrity, till a countryman came to see him. He never spoke of himself, and in a conversation with Miss Norton divulged the pleasing fact. From her Jo learned it, and liked it all the better because Mr. Bhaer had never told it. She felt proud to know that he was an honored Professor in Berlin, though only a poor language-master in America, and his homely, hard-working life was much beautified by the spice of romance which this discovery gave it. Another and a better gift than intellect was shown her in a most unexpected manner. Miss Norton had the entree into most society, which Jo would have had no chance of seeing but for her. The solitary woman felt an interest in the ambitious girl, and kindly conferred many favors of this sort both on Jo and the Professor. She took them with her one night to a select symposium, held in honor of several celebrities.

Jo went prepared to bow down and adore the mighty ones whom she had worshiped with youthful enthusiasm afar off. But her reverence for genius received a severe shock that night, and it took her some time to recover from the discovery that the great creatures were only men and women after all. Imagine her dismay, on stealing a glance of timid admiration at the poet whose lines suggested an ethereal being fed on 'spirit, fire, and dew', to behold him devouring his supper with an ardor which flushed his intellectual countenance. Turning as from a fallen idol, she made other discoveries which rapidly dispelled her romantic illusions. The great novelist vibrated between two decanters with the regularity of a pendulum; the famous divine flirted openly with one of the Madame de Staels of the age, who looked daggers at another Corinne, who was amiably satirizing her, after outmaneuvering her in efforts to absorb the profound philosopher, who imbibed tea Johnsonianly and appeared to slumber, the loquacity of the lady rendering speech impossible. The scientific celebrities, forgetting their mollusks and glacial periods, gossiped about art, while devoting themselves to oysters and ices with characteristic energy; the young musician, who was charming the city like a second Orpheus, talked horses; and the specimen of the British nobility present happened to be the most ordinary man of the party.

Before the evening was half over, Jo felt so completely disillusioned, that she sat down in a corner to recover herself. Mr. Bhaer soon joined her, looking rather out of his element, and presently several of the philosophers, each mounted on his hobby, came ambling up to hold an intellectual tournament in the recess. The conversations were miles beyond Jo's comprehension, but she enjoyed it, though Kant and Hegel were unknown gods, the Subjective and Objective unintelligible terms, and the only thing 'evolved from her inner consciousness' was a bad headache after it was all over. It dawned upon her gradually that the world was being picked to pieces, and put together on new and, according to the talkers, on infinitely better principles than before, that religion was in a fair way to be reasoned into nothingness, and intellect was to be the only God. Jo knew nothing about philosophy or metaphysics of any sort, but a curious excitement, half pleasurable, half painful, came over her as she listened with a sense of being turned adrift into time and space, like a young balloon out on a holiday.

She looked round to see how the Professor liked it, and found him looking at her with the grimest expression she had ever seen him wear. He shook his head and beckoned her to come away, but she was fascinated just then by the freedom of Speculative Philosophy, and kept her seat, trying to find out what the wise gentlemen intended to rely upon after they had annihilated all the old beliefs.

Now, Mr. Bhaer was a diffident man and slow to offer his own opinions, not because they were unsettled, but too sincere and earnest to be lightly spoken. As he glanced from Jo to several other young people, attracted by the brilliancy of the philosophic pyrotechnics, he knit his brows and longed to speak, fearing that some inflammable young soul would be led astray by the rockets, to find when the display was over that they had only an empty stick or a scorched hand.

He bore it as long as he could, but when he was appealed to for an opinion, he blazed up with honest indignation and defended religion with all the eloquence of truth—an eloquence which made his broken English musical and his plain face beautiful. He had a hard fight, for the wise men argued well, but he didn't know when he was beaten and stood to his colors like a man. Somehow, as he talked, the world got right again to Jo. The old beliefs, that had lasted so long, seemed better than the new. God was not a blind force, and immortality was not a pretty fable, but a blessed fact. She felt as if she had solid ground under her feet again, and when Mr. Bhaer paused, outtalked but not one whit convinced, Jo wanted to clap her hands and thank him.

She did neither, but she remembered the scene, and gave the Professor her heartiest respect, for she knew it cost him an effort to speak out then and there, because his conscience would not let him be silent. She began to see that character is a better possession than money, rank, intellect, or beauty, and to feel that if greatness is what a wise man has defined it to be, 'truth, reverence, and good will', then her friend friedrich Bhaer was not only good, but great.

This belief strengthened daily. She valued his esteem, she coveted his respect, she wanted to be worthy of his friendship, and just when the wish was sincerest, she came near to losing everything. It all grew out of a cocked hat, for one evening the Professor came in to give Jo her lesson with a paper soldier cap on his head, which Tina had put there and he had forgotten to take off.

"It's evident he doesn't look in his glass before coming down," thought Jo, with a smile, as he said "Goot efening," and sat soberly down, quite unconscious of the ludicrous contrast between his subject and his headgear, for he was going to read her the Death of Wallenstein.

She said nothing at first, for she liked to hear him laugh out his big, hearty laugh when anything funny happened, so she left him to discover it for himself, and presently forgot all about it, for to hear a German read Schiller is rather an absorbing occupation. After the reading came the lesson, which was a lively one, for Jo was in a gay mood that night, and the cocked hat kept her eyes dancing with merriment. The Professor didn't know what to make of her, and stopped at last to ask with an air of mild surprise that was irresistible . . .

"Mees Marsch, for what do you laugh in your master's face? Haf you no respect for me, that you go on so bad?"

"How can I be respectful, Sir, when you forget to take your hat off?" said Jo.

Lifting his hand to his head, the absent-minded Professor gravely felt and removed the little cocked hat, looked at it a minute, and then threw back his head and laughed like a merry bass viol.

"Ah! I see him now, it is that imp Tina who makes me a fool with my cap. Well, it is nothing, but see you, if this lesson goes not well, you too shall wear him."

But the lesson did not go at all for a few minutes because Mr. Bhaer caught sight of a picture on the hat, and unfolding it, said with great disgust, "I wish these papers did not come in the house. They are not for children to see, nor young people to read. It is not well, and I haf no patience with those who make this harm."

Jo glanced at the sheet and saw a pleasing illustration composed of a lunatic, a corpse, a villian, and a viper. She did not like it, but the impulse that made her turn it over was not one of displeasure but fear, because for a minute she fancied the paper was the Volcano. It was not, however, and her panic subsided as she remembered that even if it had been and one of her own tales in it, there would have been no name to betray her. She had betrayed herself, however, by a look and a blush, for though an absent man, the Professor saw a good deal more than people fancied. He knew that Jo wrote, and had met her down among the newspaper offices more than once, but as she never spoke of it, he asked no questions in spite of a strong desire to see her work. Now it occurred to him that she was doing what she was ashamed to own, and it troubled him. He did not say to himself, "It is none of my business. I've no right to say anything," as many people would have done. He only remembered that she was young and poor, a girl far away from mother's love and father's care, and he was moved to help her with an impulse as quick and natural as that which would prompt him to put out his hand to save a baby from a puddle. All this flashed through his mind in a minute, but not a trace of it appeared in his face, and by the time the paper was turned, and Jo's needle threaded, he was ready to say quite naturally, but very gravely . . .

"Yes, you are right to put it from you. I do not think that good young girls should see such things. They are made pleasant to some, but I would more rather give my boys gunpowder to play with than this bad trash."

"All may not be bad, only silly, you know, and if there is a demand for it, I don't see any harm in supplying it. Many very respectable people make an honest living out of what are called sensation stories," said Jo, scratching gathers so energetically that a row of little slits followed her pin.

"There is a demand for whisky, but I think you and I do not care to sell it. If the respectable people knew what harm they did, they would not feel that the living was honest. They haf no right to put poison in the sugarplum, and let the small ones eat it. No, they should think a little, and sweep mud in the street before they do this thing."

Mr. Bhaer spoke warmly, and walked to the fire, crumpling the paper in his hands. Jo sat still, looking as if the fire had come to her, for her cheeks burned long after the cocked hat had turned to smoke and gone harmlessly up the chimney.

"I should like much to send all the rest after him," muttered the Professor, coming back with a relieved air.

Jo thought what a blaze her pile of papers upstairs would make, and her hard-earned money lay rather heavily on her conscience at that minute. Then she thought consolingly to herself, "Mine are not like that, they are only silly, never bad, so I won't be worried," and taking up her book, she said, with a studious face, "Shall we go on, Sir? I'll be very good and proper now."

"I shall hope so," was all he said, but he meant more than she imagined, and the grave, kind look he gave her made her feel as if the words Weekly Volcano were printed in large type on her forehead.

As soon as she went to her room, she got out her papers, and carefully reread every one of her stories. Being a little shortsighted, Mr. Bhaer sometimes used eye glasses, and Jo had tried them once, smiling to see how they magnified the fine print of her book. Now she seemed to have on the Professor's mental or moral spectacles also, for the faults of these poor stories glared at her dreadfully and filled her with dismay.

"They are trash, and will soon be worse trash if I go on, for each is more sensational than the last. I've gone blindly on, hurting myself and other people, for the sake of money. I know it's so, for I can't read this stuff in sober earnest without being horribly ashamed of it, and what should I do if they were seen at home or Mr. Bhaer got hold of them?"

Jo turned hot at the bare idea, and stuffed the whole bundle into her stove, nearly setting the chimney afire with the blaze.

"Yes, that's the best place for such inflammable nonsense. I'd better burn the house down, I suppose, than let other people blow themselves up with my gunpowder," she thought as she watched the Demon of the Jura whisk away, a little black cinder with fiery eyes.

But when nothing remained of all her three month's work except a heap of ashes and the money in her lap, Jo looked sober, as she sat on the floor, wondering what she ought to do about her wages.

"I think I haven't done much harm yet, and may keep this to pay for my time," she said, after a long meditation, adding impatiently, "I almost wish I hadn't any conscience, it's so inconvenient. If I didn't care about doing right, and didn't feel uncomfortable when doing wrong, I should get on capitally. I can't help wishing sometimes, that Mother and Father hadn't been so particular about such things."

Ah, Jo, instead of wishing that, thank God that 'Father and Mother were particular'. and pity from your heart those who have no such guardians to hedge them round with principles which may seem like prison walls to impatient youth, but which will prove sure foundations to build character upon in womanhood.

Jo wrote no more sensational stories, deciding that the money did not pay for her share of the sensation, but going to the other extreme, as is the way with people of her stamp, she took a course of Mrs. Sherwood, Miss Edgeworth, and Hannah More, and then produced a tale which might have been more properly called an essay or a sermon, so intensely moral was it. She had her doubts about it from the beginning, for her lively fancy and girlish romance felt as ill at ease in the new style as she would have done masquerading in the stiff and cumbrous costume of the last century. She sent this didactic gem to several markets, but it found no purchaser, and she was inclined to agree with Mr. Dashwood that morals didn't sell.

Then she tried a child's story, which she could easily have disposed of if she had not been mercenary enough to demand filthy lucre for it. The only person who offered enough to make it worth her while to try juvenile literature was a worthy gentleman who felt it his mission to convert all the world to his particular belief. But much as she liked to write for children, Jo could not consent to depict all her naughty boys as being eaten by bears or tossed by mad bulls because they did not go to a particular Sabbath school, nor all the good infants who did go as rewarded by every kind of bliss, from gilded gingerbread to escorts of angels when they departed this life with psalms or sermons on their lisping tongues. So nothing came of these trials, and Jo corked up her inkstand, and said in a fit of very wholesome humility . . .

"I don't know anything. I'll wait until I do before I try again, and meantime, 'sweep mud in the street' if I can't do better, that's honest, at least." Which decision proved that her second tumble down the beanstalk had done her some good.

While these internal revolutions were going on, her external life had been as busy and uneventful as usual, and if she sometimes looked serious or a little sad no one observed it but Professor Bhaer. He did it so quietly that Jo never knew he was watching to see if she would accept and profit by his reproof, but she stood the test, and he was satisfied, for though no words passed between them, he knew that she had given up writing. Not only did he guess it by the fact that the second finger of her right hand was no longer inky, but she spent her evenings downstairs now, was met no more among newspaper offices, and studied with a dogged patience, which assured him that she was bent on occupying her mind with something useful, if not pleasant.

He helped her in many ways, proving himself a true friend, and Jo was happy, for while her pen lay idle, she was learning other lessons besides German, and laying a foundation for the sensation story of her own life.

It was a pleasant winter and a long one, for she did not leave Mrs. Kirke till June. Everyone seemed sorry when the time came. The children were inconsolable, and Mr. Bhaer's hair stuck straight up all over his head, for he always rumpled it wildly when disturbed in mind.

"Going home? Ah, you are happy that you haf a home to go in," he said, when she told him, and sat silently pulling his beard in the corner, while she held a little levee on that last evening.

She was going early, so she bade them all goodbye overnight, and when his turn came, she said warmly, "Now, Sir, you won't forget to come and see us, if you ever travel our way, will you? I'll never forgive you if you do, for I want them all to know my friend."

"Do you? Shall I come?" he asked, looking down at her with an eager expression which she did not see.

"Yes, come next month. Laurie graduates then, and you'd enjoy commencement as something new."

"That is your best friend, of whom you speak?" he said in an altered tone.

"Yes, my boy Teddy. I'm very proud of him and should like you to see him."

Jo looked up then, quite unconscious of anything but her own pleasure in the prospect of showing them to one another. Something in Mr. Bhaer's face suddenly recalled the fact that she might find Laurie more than a 'best friend', and simply because she particularly wished not to look as if anything was the matter, she involuntarily began to blush, and the more she tried not to, the redder she grew. If it had not been for Tina on her knee. She didn't know what would have become of her. Fortunately the child was moved to hug her, so she managed to hide her face an instant, hoping the Professor did not see it. But he did, and his own changed again from that momentary anxiety to its usual expression, as he said cordially . . .

"I fear I shall not make the time for that, but I wish the friend much success, and you all happiness. Gott bless you!" And with that, he shook hands warmly, shouldered Tina, and went away.

But after the boys were abed, he sat long before his fire with the tired look on his face and the 'heimweh', or homesickness, lying heavy at his heart. Once, when he remembered Jo as she sat with the little child in her lap and that new softness in her face, he leaned his head on his hands a minute, and then roamed about the room, as if in search of something that he could not find.

"It is not for me, I must not hope it now," he said to himself, with a sigh that was almost a groan. Then, as if reproaching himself for the longing that he could not repress, he went and kissed the two tousled heads upon the pillow, took down his seldom-used meerschaum, and opened his Plato.

He did his best and did it manfully, but I don't think he found that a pair of rampant boys, a pipe, or even the divine Plato, were very satisfactory substitutes for wife and child at home.

Early as it was, he was at the station next morning to see Jo off, and thanks to him, she began her solitary journey with the pleasant memory of a familiar face smiling its farewell, a bunch of violets to keep her company, and best of all, the happy thought, "Well, the winter's gone, and I've written no books, earned no fortune, but I've made a friend worth having and I'll try to keep him all my life."

Chapter Thirty-Five

Whatever his motive might have been, Laurie studied to some purpose that year, for he graduated with honor, and gave the Latin oration with the grace of a Phillips and the eloquence of a Demosthenes, so his friends said. They were all there, his grandfather—oh, so proud—Mr. and Mrs. March, John and Meg, Jo and Beth, and all exulted over him with the sincere admiration which boys make light of at the time, but fail to win from the world by any after-triumphs.

"I've got to stay for this confounded supper, but I shall be home early tomorrow. You'll come and meet me as usual, girls?" Laurie said, as he put the sisters into the carriage after the joys of the day were over. He said 'girls', but he meant Jo, for she was the only one who kept up the old custom. She had not the heart to refuse her splendid, successful boy anything, and answered warmly . . .

"I'll come, Teddy, rain or shine, and march before you, playing 'Hail the conquering hero comes' on a jew's-harp."

Laurie thanked her with a look that made her think in a sudden panic, "Oh, deary me! I know he'll say something, and then what shall I do?"

Evening meditation and morning work somewhat allayed her fears, and having decided that she wouldn't be vain enough to think people were going to propose when she had given them every reason to know what her answer would be, she set forth at the appointed time, hoping Teddy wouldn't do anything to make her hurt his poor feelings. A call at Meg's, and a refreshing sniff and sip at the Daisy and Demijohn, still further fortified her for the tete-a-tete, but when she saw a stalwart figure looming in the distance, she had a strong desire to turn about and run away.

"Where's the jew's-harp, Jo?" cried Laurie, as soon as he was within speaking distance.

"I forgot it." And Jo took heart again, for that salutation could not be called loverlike.

She always used to take his arm on these occasions, now she did not, and he made no complaint, which was a bad sign, but talked on rapidly about all sorts of faraway subjects, till they turned from the road into the little path that led homeward through the grove. Then he walked more slowly, suddenly lost his fine flow of language, and now and then a dreadful pause occurred. To rescue the conversation from one of the wells of silence into which it kept falling, Jo said hastily, "Now you must have a good long holiday!"

"I intend to."

Something in his resolute tone made Jo look up quickly to find him looking down at her with an expression that assured her the dreaded moment had come, and made her put out her hand with an imploring, "No, Teddy. Please don't!"

"I will, and you must hear me. It's no use, Jo, we've got to have it out, and the sooner the better for both of us," he answered, getting flushed and excited all at once.

"Say what you like then. I'll listen," said Jo, with a desperate sort of patience.

Laurie was a young lover, but he was in earnest, and meant to 'have it out', if he died in the attempt, so he plunged into the subject with characteristic impetuousity, saying in a voice that would get choky now and then, in spite of manful efforts to keep it steady . . . "I've loved you ever since I've known you, Jo, couldn't help it, you've been so good to me. I've tried to show it, but you wouldn't let me. Now I'm going to make you hear, and give me an answer, for I can't go on so any longer."

"I wanted to save you this. I thought you'd understand . . ." began Jo, finding it a great deal harder than she expected.

"I know you did, but the girls are so queer you never know what they mean. They say no when they mean yes, and drive a man out of his wits just for the fun of it," returned Laurie, entrenching himself behind an undeniable fact.

"I don't. I never wanted to make you care for me so, and I went away to keep you from it if I could."

"I thought so. It was like you, but it was no use. I only loved you all the more, and I worked hard to please you, and I gave up billiards and everything you didn't like, and waited and never complained, for I hoped you'd love me, though I'm not half good enough . . ." Here there was a choke that couldn't be controlled, so he decapitated buttercups while he cleared his 'confounded throat'.

"You, you are, you're a great deal too good for me, and I'm so grateful to you, and so proud and fond of you, I don't know why I can't love you as you want me to. I've tried, but I can't change the feeling, and it would be a lie to say I do when I don't."

"Really, truly, Jo?"

He stopped short, and caught both her hands as he put his question with a look that she did not soon forget.

"Really, truly, dear."

They were in the grove now, close by the stile, and when the last words fell reluctantly from Jo's lips, Laurie dropped her hands and turned as if to go on, but for once in his life the fence was too much for him. So he just laid his head down on the mossy post, and stood so still that Jo was frightened.

"Oh, Teddy, I'm sorry, so desperately sorry, I could kill myself if it would do any good! I wish you wouldn't take it so hard, I can't help it. You know it's impossible for people to make themselves love other people if they don't," cried Jo inelegantly but remorsefully, as she softly patted his shoulder, remembering the time when he had comforted her so long ago.

"They do sometimes," said a muffled voice from the post. "I don't believe it's the right sort of love, and I'd rather not try it," was the decided answer.

There was a long pause, while a blackbird sung blithely on the willow by the river, and the tall grass rustled in the wind. Presently Jo said very soberly, as she sat down on the step of the stile, "Laurie, I want to tell you something."

He started as if he had been shot, threw up his head, and cried out in a fierce tone, "Don't tell me that, Jo, I can't bear it now!"

"Tell what?" she asked, wondering at his violence.

"That you love that old man."

"What old man?" demanded Jo, thinking he must mean his grandfather.

"That devilish Professor you were always writing about. If you say you love him, I know I shall do something desperate." And he looked as if he would keep his word, as he clenched his hands with a wrathful spark in his eyes.

Jo wanted to laugh, but restrained herself and said warmly, for she too, was getting excited with all this, "Don't swear, Teddy! He isn't old, nor anything bad, but good and kind, and the best friend I've got, next to you. Pray, don't fly into a passion. I want to be kind, but I know I shall get angry if you abuse my Professor. I haven't the least idea of loving him or anybody else."

"But you will after a while, and then what will become of me?"

"You'll love someone else too, like a sensible boy, and forget all this trouble."

"I can't love anyone else, and I'll never forget you, Jo, Never! Never!" with a stamp to emphasize his passionate words.

"What shall I do with him?" sighed Jo, finding that emotions were more unmanagable than she expected. "You haven't heard what I wanted to tell you. Sit down and listen, for indeed I want to do right and make you happy," she said, hoping to soothe him with a little reason, which proved that she knew nothing about love.

Seeing a ray of hope in that last speech, Laurie threw himself down on the grass at her feet, leaned his arm on the lower step of the stile, and looked up at her with an expectant face. Now that arrangement was not conducive to calm speech or clear thought on Jo's part, for how could she say hard things to her boy while he watched her with eyes full of love and longing, and lashes still wet with the bitter drop or two her hardness of heart had wrung from him? She gently turned his head away, saying, as she stroked the wavy hair which had been allowed to grow for her sake—how touching that was, to be sure! "I agree with Mother that you and I are not suited to each other, because our quick tempers and strong wills would probably make us very miserable, if we were so foolish as to . . ." Jo paused a little over the last word, but Laurie uttered it with a rapturous expression.

"Marry—no we shouldn't! If you loved me, Jo, I should be a perfect saint, for you could make me anything you like."

"No, I can't. I've tried and failed, and I won't risk our happiness by such a serious experiment. We don't agree and we never shall, so we'll be good friends all our lives, but we won't go and do anything rash."

"Yes, we will if we get the chance," muttered Laurie rebelliously.

"Now do be reasonable, and take a sensible view of the case," implored Jo, almost at her wit's end.

"I won't be reasonable. I don't want to take what you call 'a sensible view'. It won't help me, and it only makes it harder. I don't believe you've got any heart."

"I wish I hadn't."

There was a little quiver in Jo's voice, and thinking it a good omen, Laurie turned round, bringing all his persuasive powers to bear as he said, in the wheedlesome tone that had never been so dangerously wheedlesome before, "Don't disappoint us, dear! Everyone expects it. Grandpa has set his heart upon it, your people like it, and I can't get on without you. Say you will, and let's be happy. Do, do!"

Not until months afterward did Jo understand how she had the strength of mind to hold fast to the resolution she had made when she decided that she did not love her boy, and never could.

It was very hard to do, but she did it, knowing that delay was both useless and cruel.

"I can't say 'yes' truly, so I won't say it at all. You'll see that I'm right, by-and-by, and thank me for it . . ." she began solemnly.

"I'll be hanged if I do!" And Laurie bounced up off the grass, burning with indignation at the very idea.

"Yes, you will!" persisted Jo. "You'll get over this after a while, and find some lovely accomplished girl, who will adore you, and make a fine mistress for your fine house. I shouldn't. I'm homely and awkward and odd and old, and you'd be ashamed of me, and we should quarrel—we can't help it even now, you see-and I shouldn't like elegant society and you would, and you'd hate my scribbling, and I couldn't get on without it, and we should be unhappy, and wish we hadn't done it, and everything would be horrid!"

"Anything more?" asked asked Laurie, finding it hard to listen patiently to this prophetic burst.

"Nothing more, except that I don't believe I shall ever marry. I'm happy as I am, and love my liberty too well to be in a hurry to give it up for any mortal man."

"I know better!" broke in Laurie. "You think so now, but there'll come a time when you will care for somebody, and you'll love him tremendously, and live and die for him. I know you will, it's your way, and I shall have to stand by and see it." And the despairing lover cast his hat upon the ground with a gesture that would have seemed comical, if his face had not been so tragic.

"Yes, I will live and die for him, if her ever comes and makes me love him in spite of myself, and you must do the best you can!" cried Jo, losing patience with poor Teddy. "I've done my best, but you won't be reasonable, and it's selfish of you to keep teasing for what I can't give. I shall always be fond of you, very fond indeed, as a friend, but I'll never marry you, and the sooner you believe it the better for both of us—so now!"

That speech was like gunpowder. Laurie looked at her a minute as if he did not quite know what to do with himself, then turned sharply away, saying in a desperate sort of tone, "You'll be sorry some day, Jo."

"Oh, where are you going?" she cried, for his face frightened her.

"To the devil!" was the consoling answer.

For a minute Jo's heart stood still, as he swung himself down the bank toward the river, but it takes much folly, sin or misery to send a young man to a violent death, and Laurie was not one of the weak sort who are conquered by a single failure. He had no thought of a melodramatic plunge, but some blind instinct led him to fling hat and coat into his boat, and row away with all his might, making better time up the river than he had done in any race. Jo drew a long breath and unclasped her hands as she watched the poor fellow trying to outstrip the trouble which he carried in his heart.

"That will do him good, and he'll come home in such a tender, penitent state of mind, that I shan't dare to see him." she said, adding, as she went slowly home, feeling as if she had murdered some innocent thing, and buried it under the leaves. "Now I must go and prepare Mr. Laurence to be very kind to my poor boy. I wish he'd love Beth, perhaps he may in time, but I begin to think I was mistaken about her. Oh dear! How can girls like to have lovers and refuse them? I think it's dreadful." Being sure that no one could do it so well as herself, she went straight to Mr. Laurence, told the hard story bravely through, and then broke down, crying so dismally over her own insensibility that the kind old gentleman, though sorely disappointed, did not utter a reproach. He found it difficult to understand how any girl could help loving Laurie, and hoped she would change her mind, but he knew even better than Jo that love cannot be forced, so he shook his head sadly and resolved to carry his boy out of harm's way, for Young

Impetuosity's parting words to Jo disturbed him more than he would confess.

When Laurie came home, dead tired but quite composed, his grandfather met him as if he knew nothing, and kept up the delusion very successfully for an hour or two. But when they sat together in the twilight, the time they used to enjoy so much, it was hard work for the old man to ramble on as usual, and harder still for the young one to listen to praises of the last year's success, which to him now seemed like love's labor lost. He bore it as long as he could, then went to his piano and began to play. The window's were open, and Jo, walking in the garden with Beth, for once understood music better than her sister, for he played the 'SONATA PATHETIQUE', and played it as he never did before.

"That's very fine, I dare say, but it's sad enough to make one cry. Give us something gayer, lad," said Mr. Laurence, whose kind old heart was full of sympathy, which he longed to show but knew not how.

Laurie dashed into a livelier strain, played stormily for several minutes, and would have got through bravely, if in a momentary lull Mrs. March's voice had not been heard calling, "Jo, dear, come in. I want you."

Just what Laurie longed to say, with a different meaning! As he listened, he lost his place, the music ended with a broken chord, and the musician sat silent in the dark.

"I can't stand this," muttered the old gentleman. Up he got, groped his way to the piano, laid a kind hand on either of the broad shoulders, and said, as gently as a woman, "I know, my boy, I know."

No answer for an instant, then Laurie asked sharply, "Who told you?"

"Jo herself."

"Then there's an end of it!" And he shook off his grandfather's hands with an impatient motion, for though grateful for the sympathy, his man's pride could not bear a man's pity.

"Not quite. I want to say one thing, and then there shall be an end of it," returned Mr. Laurence with unusual mildness. "You won't care to stay at home now, perhaps?"

"I don't intend to run away from a girl. Jo can't prevent my seeing her, and I shall stay and do it as long as I like," interrupted Laurie in a defiant tone.

"Not if you are the gentleman I think you. I'm disappointed, but the girl can't help it, and the only thing left for you to do is to go away for a time. Where will you go?"

"Anywhere. I don't care what becomes of me." And Laurie got up with a reckless laugh that grated on his grandfather's ear.

"Take it like a man, and don't do anything rash, for God's sake. Why not go abroad, as you planned, and forget it?"

"I can't."

"But you've been wild to go, and I promised you should when you got through college."

"Ah, but I didn't mean to go alone!" And Laurie walked fast through the room with an expression which it was well his grandfather did not see.

"I don't ask you to go alone. There's someone ready and glad to go with you, anywhere in the world."

"Who, Sir?' stopping to listen.

"Myself."

Laurie came back as quickly as he went, and put out his hand, saying huskily, "I'm a selfish brute, but—you know—Grandfather—"

"Lord help me, yes, I do know, for I've been through it all before, once in my own young days, and then with your father. Now, my dear boy, just sit quietly down and hear my plan. It's all settled, and can be carried out at once," said Mr. Laurence, keeping hold of the young man, as if fearful that he would break away as his father had done before him.

"Well, sir, what is it?" And Laurie sat down, without a sign of interest in face or voice.

"There is business in London that needs looking after. I meant you should attend to it, but I can do it better myself, and things here will get on very well with Brooke to manage them. My partners do almost everything, I'm merely holding on until you take my place, and can be off at any time."

"But you hate traveling, Sir. I can't ask it of you at your age," began Laurie, who was grateful for the sacrifice, but much preferred to go alone, if he went at all. The old gentleman knew that perfectly well, and particularly desired to prevent it, for the mood in which he found his grandson assured him that it would not be wise to leave him to his own devices. So, stifling a natural regret at the thought of the home comforts he would leave behind him, he said stoutly, Bless your soul, I'm not superannuated yet. I quite enjoy the idea. It will do me good, and my old bones won't suffer, for traveling nowadays is almost as easy as sitting in a chair."

A restless movement from Laurie suggested that his chair was not easy, or that he did not like the plan, and made the old man add hastily, "I don't mean to be a marplot or a burden. I go because I think you'd feel happier than if I was left behind. I don't intend to gad about with you, but leave you free to go where you like, while I amuse myself in my own way. I've friends in London and Paris, and should like to visit them. Meantime you can go to Italy, Germany, Switzerland, where you will, and enjoy pictures, music, scenery, and adventures to your heart's content."

Now, Laurie felt just then that his heart was entirely broken and the world a howling wilderness, but at the sound of certain words which the old gentleman artfully introduced into his closing sentence, the broken heart gave an unexpected leap, and a green oasis or two suddenly appeared in the howling wilderness. He sighed, and then said, in a spiritless tone, "Just as you like, Sir. It doesn't matter where I go or what I do."

"It does to me, remember that, my lad. I give you entire liberty, but I trust you to make an honest use of it. Promise me that, Laurie."

"Anything you like, Sir."

"Good," thought the old gentleman. "You don't care now, but there'll come a time when that promise will keep you out of mischief, or I'm much mistaken."

Being an energetic individual, Mr. Laurence struck while the iron was hot, and before the blighted being recovered spirit enough to rebel, they were off. During the time necessary for preparation, Laurie bore himself as young gentleman usually do in such cases. He was moody, irritable, and pensive by turns, lost his appetite, neglected his dress and devoted much time to playing tempestuously on his piano, avoided Jo, but consoled himself by staring at her from his window, with a tragic face that haunted her dreams by night and oppressed her with a heavy sense of guilt by day. Unlike some sufferers, he never spoke of his unrequited passion, and would allow no one, not even Mrs. March, to attempt consolation or offer sympathy. On some accounts, this was a relief to his friends, but the weeks before his departure were very uncomfortable, and everyone rejoiced that the 'poor, dear fellow was going away to forget his trouble, and come home happy'. Of course, he smiled darkly at their delusion, but passed it by with the sad superiority of one who knew that his fidelity like his love was unalterable.

When the parting came he affected high spirits, to conceal certain inconvenient emotions which seemed inclined to assert themselves. This gaiety did not impose upon anybody, but they tried to look as if it did for his sake, and he got on very well till Mrs. March kissed him, whit a whisper full of motherly solicitude. Then feeling that he was going very fast, he hastily embraced them all round, not forgetting the afflicted Hannah, and ran downstairs as if for his life. Jo followed a minute after to wave her hand to him if he looked round. He did look round, came back, put his arms about her as she stood on the step above him, and looked up at her with a face that made his short appeal eloquent and pathetic.

"Oh, Jo, can't you?"

"Teddy, dear, I wish I could!"

That was all, except a little pause. Then Laurie straightened himself up, said, "It's all right, never mind," and went away without another word. Ah, but it wasn't all right, and Jo did mind, for while the curly head lay on her arm a minute after her hard answer, she felt as if she had stabbed her dearest friend, and when he left her without a look behind him, she knew that the boy Laurie never would come again.

Chapter Thirty-Six

When Jo came home that spring, she had been struck with the change in Beth. No one spoke of it or seemed aware of it, for it had come too gradually to startle those who saw her daily, but to eyes sharpened by absence, it was very plain and a heavy weight fell on Jo's heart as she saw her sister's face. It was no paler and but littler thinner than in the autumn, yet there was a strange, transparent look about it, as if the mortal was being slowly refined away, and the immortal shining through the frail flesh with an indescribably pathetic beauty. Jo saw and felt it, but said nothing at the time, and soon the first impression lost much of its power, for Beth seemed happy, no one appeared to doubt that she was better, and presently in other cares Jo fora time forgot her fear.

But when Laurie was gone, and peace prevailed again, the vague anxiety returned and haunted her. She had confessed her sins and been forgiven, but when she showed her savings and proposed a mountain trip, Beth had thanked her heartily, but begged not to go so far away from home. Another little visit to the seashore would suit her better, and as Grandma could not be prevailed upon to leave the babies, Jo took Beth down to the quiet place, where she could live much in the open air, and let the fresh sea breezes blow a little color into her pale cheeks.

It was not a fashionable place, but even among the pleasant people there, the girls made few friends, preferring to live for one another. Beth was too shy to enjoy society, and Jo too wrapped up in her to care for anyone else. So they were all in all to each other, and came and went, quite unconscious of the interest they exited in those about them, who watched with sympathetic eyes the strong sister and the feeble one, always together, as if they felt instinctively that a long separation was not far away.

They did feel it, yet neither spoke of it, for often between ourselves and those nearest and dearest to us there exists a reserve which it is very hard to overcome. Jo felt as if a veil had fallen between her heart and Beth's, but when she put out her hand to lift it up, there seemed something sacred in the silence, and she waited for Beth to speak. She wondered, and was thankful also, that her parents did not seem to see what she saw, and during the quiet weeks when the shadows grew so plain to her, she said nothing of it to those at home, believing that it would tell itself when Beth came back no better. She wondered still more if her sister really guessed the hard truth, and what thoughts were passing through her mind during the long hours when she lay on the warm rocks with her head in Jo's lap, while the winds blew healthfully over her and the sea made music at her feet.

One day Beth told her. Jo thought she was asleep, she lay so still, and putting down her book, sat looking at her with wistful eyes, trying to see signs of hope in the faint color on Beth's cheeks. But she could not find enough to satisfy her, for the cheeks were very thin, and the hands seemed too feeble to hold even the rosy little shells they had been collecting. It came to her then more bitterly than ever that Beth was slowly drifting away form her, and her arms instinctively tightened their hold upon the dearest treasure she possessed. For a minute her eyes were too dim for seeing, and when they cleared, Beth was looking up at her so tenderly that there was hardly any need for her to say, "Jo, dear, I'm glad you know it. I've tried to tell you, but I couldn't."

There was no answer except her sister's cheek against her own, not even tears, for when most deeply moved, Jo did not cry. She was the weaker then, land Beth tried to comfort and sustain her, with her arms about her and the soothing words she whispered in her ear.

"I've known it for a good while, dear, and now I'm used to it, it isn't hard to think of or to bear. Try to see it so and don't be troubled about me, because it's best, indeed it is."

"Is this what made you so unhappy in the autumn, Beth? You did not feel it then, land keep it to yourself so long, did you?" asked Jo, refusing to see or say that it was best, but glad to know that Laurie had no part in Beth's trouble.

"Yes, I gave up hoping then, but I didn't like to own it. I tried to think it was a sick fancy, and would not let it trouble anyone. But when I saw you all so well and strong and full of happy plans, it was hard to feel that I could never be like you, and then I was miserable, Jo."

"Oh, Beth, and you didn't tell me, didn't let me comfort and help you? How could you shut me out, bear it all alone?"

Jo's voice was full of tender reproach, and her heart ached to think of the solitary struggle that must have gone on while Beth learned to say goodbye to health, love, and live, and take up her cross so cheerfully.

"Perhaps it was wrong, but I tried to do right. I wasn't sure, no one said anything, and I hoped I was mistaken. It would have been selfish to frighten you all when Marmee was so anxious about Meg, and Amy away, and you so happy with Laurie—at least I thought so then."

"And I thought you loved him, Beth, and I went away because I couldn't," cried Jo, glad to say all the truth.

Beth looked so amazed at the idea that Jo smiled in spite of her pain, and added softly, "Then you didn't, dearie? I was afraid it was so, and imagined your poor little heart full of lovelornity all that while."

"Why, Jo, how could I, when he was so fond of you?" asked Beth, as innocently as a child. "I do love him dearly. He is so good to me, how can I help It? But he could never be anything to me but my brother. I hope he truly will be, sometime."

"Not through me," said Jo decidedly. "Amy is left for him, and they would suit excellently, but I have no heart for such things, now. I don't care what becomes of anybody but you, Beth. You must get well."

"I want to, oh, so much! I try, but every day I lose a little, and feel more sure that I shall never gain it back. It's like the tide, Jo, when it turns, it goes slowly, but it can't be stopped.."

"It shall be stopped, your tide must not turn so soon, nineteen is too young, Beth. I can't let you go. I'll work and pray and fight against it. I'll keep you in spite of everything. There must be ways, it can't be too late. God won't be so cruel as to take you from me," cried poor Jo rebelliously, for her spirit was far less piously submissive than Beth's.

Simple, sincere people seldom speak much of their piety. It shows itself in acts rather than in words, and has more influence than homilies or protestations. Beth could not reason upon or explain the faith that gave her courage and patience to give up life, and cheerfully wait for death. Like a confiding child, she asked no questions, but left everything to God and nature, Father and Mother of us all, feeling sure that they, and they only, could teach and strengthen heart and spirit for this life and the life to come. She did not rebuke Jo with saintly speeches, only loved her better for her passionate affection, and clung more closely to the dear human love, from which our Father never means us to be weaned, but through which He draws us closer to Himself. She could not say, "I'm glad to go," for life was very sweet for her. She could only sob out, "I try to be willing," while she held fast to Jo, as the first bitter wave of this great sorrow broke over them together.

By and by Beth said, with recovered serenity, "You'll tell them this when we go home?"

"I think they will see it without words," sighed Jo, for now it seemed to her that Beth changed every day.

"Perhaps not. I've heard that the people who love best are often blindest to such things. If they don't see it, you will tell them for me. I don't want any secrets, and it's kinder to prepare them. Meg has John and the babies to comfort her, but you must stand by Father and Mother, won't you Jo?"

"If I can. But, Beth, I don't give up yet. I'm going to believe that it is a sick fancy, and not let you think it's true." said Jo, trying to speak cheerfully.

Beth lay a minute thinking, and then said in her quiet way, "I don't know how to express myself, and shouldn't try to anyone but you, because I can't speak out except to my Jo. I only mean to say that I have a feeling that it never was intended I should live long. I'm not like the rest of you. I never made any plans about what I'd do when I grew up. I never thought of being married, as you all did. I couldn't seem to imagine myself anything but stupid little Beth, trotting about at home, of no use anywhere but there. I never wanted to go away, and the hard part now is the leaving you all. I'm not afraid, but it seems as if I should be homesick for you even in heaven."

Jo could not speak, and for several minutes there was no sound but the sigh of the wind and the lapping of the tide. A white-winged gull flew by, with the flash of sunshine on its silvery breast. Beth watched it till it vanished, and her eyes were full of sadness. A little gray-coated sand bird came tripping over the beach 'peeping' softly to itself, as if enjoying the sun and sea. It came quite close to Beth, and looked at her with a friendly eye and sat upon a warm stone, dressing its wet feathers, quite at home. Beth smiled and felt comforted, for the tiny thing seemed to offer its small friendship and remind her that a pleasant world was still to be enjoyed.

"Dear little bird! See, Jo, how tame it is. I like peeps better than the gulls. They are not so wild and handsome, but they seem happy, confiding little things. I used to call them my birds last summer, and Mother said they reminded her of me—busy, quaker-colored creatures, always near the shore, and always chirping that contented little song of theirs. You are the gull, Jo, strong and wild, fond of the storm and the wind, flying far out to sea, and happy all alone. Meg is the turtledove, and Amy is like the lark she write about, trying to get up among the clouds, but always dropping down into its nest again. Dear little girl! She's so ambitious, but her heart is good and tender, and no matter how high she flies, she never will forget home. I hope I shall see her again, but she seems so far away."

"She is coming in the spring, and I mean that you shall be all ready to see and enjoy her. I'm going to have you well and rosy by that time." began Jo, feeling that of all the changes in Beth, the talking change was the greatest, for it seemed to cost no effort now, and she thought aloud in a way quite unlike bashful Beth.

"Jo, dear, don't hope any more. It won't do any good. I'm sure of that. We won't be miserable, but enjoy being together while we wait. We'll have happy times, for I don't suffer much, and I think the tide will go out easily, if you help me."

Jo leaned down to kiss the tranquil face, and with that silent kiss, she dedicated herself soul and body to Beth.

She was right. There was no need of any words when they got home, for Father and Mother saw plainly now what they had prayed to be saved from seeing. Tired with her short journey, Beth went at once to bed, saying how glad she was to be home, and when Jo went down, she found that she would be spared the hard task of telling Beth's secret. Her father stood leaning his head on the mantelpiece and did not turn as she came in, but her mother stretched out her arms as if for help, and Jo went to comfort her without a word.

Chapter Thirty-Seven

At three o'clock in the afternoon, all the fashionable world at Nice may be seen on the Promenade des Anglais—a charming place, for the wide walk, bordered with palms, flowers, and tropical shrubs, is bounded on one side by the sea, on the other by the grand drive, lined with hotels and villas, while beyond lie orange orchards and the hills. Many nations are represented, many languages spoken, many costumes worn, and on a sunny day the spectacle is as gay and brilliant as a carnival. Haughty English, lively French, sober Germans, handsome Spaniards, ugly Russians, meek Jews, free-and-easy Americans, all drive, sit, or saunter here, chatting over the news, and criticzing the latest celebrity who has arrived—Ristori or Dickens, Victor Emmanuel or the Queen of the Sandwich Islands. The equipages are as varied as the company and attract as much attention, especially the low basket barouches in which ladies drive themselves, with a pair of dashing ponies, gay nets to keep their voluminous flounces from overflowing the diminutive vehicles, and little grooms on the perch behind.

Along this walk, on Christmas Day, a tall young man walked slowly, with his hands behind him, and a somewhat absent expression of countenance. He looked like an Italian, was dressed like an Englishman, and had the independent air of an American—a combination which caused sundry pairs of feminine eyes to look approvingly after him, and sundry dandies in black velvet suits, with rose-colored neckties, buff gloves, and orange flowers in their buttonholes, to shrug their shoulders, and then envy him his inches. There were plenty of pretty faces to admire, but the young man took little notice of them, except to glance now and then at some blonde girl in blue. Presently he strolled out of the promenade and stood a moment at the crossing, as if undecided whether to go and listen to the band in the Jardin Publique, or to wander along the beach toward Castle Hill. The quick trot of ponies feet made him look up, as one of the little carriages, containing a single young lady, came rapidly down the street. The lady was young, blonde, and dressed in blue. He stared a minute, then his whole face woke up, and, waving his hat like a boy, he hurried forward to meet her.

"Oh, Laurie, is it really you? I thought you'd never come!" cried Amy, dropping the reins and holding out both hands, to the great scandalization of a French mamma, who hastened her daughter's steps, lest she should be demoralized by beholding the free manners of these 'mad English'.

"I was detained by the way, but I promised to spend Christmas with you, and here I am."

"How is your grandfather? When did you come? Where are you staying?"

"Very well—last night—at the Chauvain. I called at your hotel, but you were out."

"I have so much to say, I don't know where to begin! Get in and we can talk at our ease. I was going for a drive and longing for company. Flo's saving up for tonight."

"What happens then, a ball?"

"A Christmas party at out hotel. There are many Americans there, and they give it in honor of the day. You'll go with us, of course? Aunt will be charmed."

"Thank you. Where now?" asked Laurie, leaning back and folding his arms, a proceeding which suited Amy, who preferred to drive, for her parasol whip and blue reins over the white ponies backs afforded her infinite satisfaction.

"I'm going to the bankers first for letters, and then to Castle Hill. The view is so lovely, and I like to feed the peacocks. Have you ever been there?"

"Often, years ago, but I don't mind having a look at it."

"Now tell me all about yourself. The last I heard of you, your grandfather wrote that he expected you from Berlin." "Yes, I spent a month there and then joined him in Paris, where he has settled for the winter. He has friends there and finds plenty to amuse him, so I go and come, and we got on capitally."

"That's a sociable arrangement," said Amy, missing something in Laurie's manner, though she couldn't tell what.

"Why, you see, he hates to travel, and I hate to keep still, so we each suit ourselves, and there is no trouble. I am often with him, and he enjoys my adventures, while I like to feel that someone is glad to see me when I get back from my wanderings. Dirty old hole, isn't it?" he added, with a look of disgust as they drove along the boulevard to the Place Napoleon in the old city.

"The dirt is picturesque, so I don't mind. The river and the hills are delicious, and these glimpses of the narrow cross streets are my delight. Now we shall have to wait for that procession to pass. It's going to the Church of St. John."

While Laurie listlessly watched the procession of priests under their canopies, white-veiled nuns bearing lighted tapers, and some brotherhood in blue chanting as they walked, Amy watched him, and felt a new sort of shyness steal over her, for he was changed, and she could not find the merry-faced boy she left in the moody-looking man beside her. He was handsomer than ever and greatly improved, she thought, but now that the flush of pleasure at meeting her was over, he looked tired and spiritless—not sick, nor exactly unhappy, but older and graver than a year or two of prosperous life should have made him. She couldn't understand it and did not venture to ask questions, so she shook her head and touched up her ponies, as the procession wound away across the arches of the Paglioni bridge and vanished in the church.

"Que pensez-vous?" she said, airing her French, which had improved in quantity, if not in quality, since she came abroad.

"That mademoiselle has made good use of her time, and the result is charming," replied Laurie, bowing with his hand on his heart and an admiring look.

She blushed with pleasure, but somehow the compliment did not satisfy her like the blunt praises he used to give her at home, when he promenaded round her on festival occasions, and tole her she was 'altogether jolly', with a hearty smile and an approving pat on the head. She didn't like the new tone, for though not blase, it sounded indifferent in spite of the look.

"If that's the way he's going to grow up, I wish he's stay a boy," she thought, with a curious sense of disappointment and discomfort, trying meantime to seem quite easy and gay.

At Avigdor's she found the precious home letters and, giving the reins to Laurie, read them luxuriously as they wound up the shady road between green hedges, where tea roses bloomed as freshly as in June.

"Beth is very poorly, Mother says. I often think I ought to go home, but they all say 'stay'. So I do, for I shall never have another chance like this," said Amy, looking sober over one page.

"I think you are right, there. You could do nothing at home, and it is a great comfort to them to know that you are well and happy, and enjoying so much, my dear."

He drew a little nearer, and looked more like his old self as he said that, and the fear that sometimes weighed on Amy's heart was lightened, for the look, the act, the brotherly 'my dear', seemed to assure her that if any trouble did come, she would not be alone in a strange land. Presently she laughed and showed him a small sketch of Jo in her scribbling suit, with the bow rampantly erect upon her cap, and issuing from her mouth the words, 'Genius burns!'.

Laurie smiled, took it, put it in his vest pocket 'to keep it from blowing away', and listened with interest to the lively letter Amy read him.

"This will be a regularly merry Christmas to me, with presents in the morning, you and letters in the afternoon, and a party at night," said Amy, as they alighted among the ruins of the old fort, and a flock of splendid peacocks came trooping about them, tamely waiting to be fed. While Amy stood laughing on the bank above him as she scattered crumbs to the brilliant birds, Laurie looked at her as she had looked at him, with a natural curiosity to see what changes time and absence had wrought. He found nothing to perplex or disappoint, much to admire and approve, for overlooking a few little affectations of speech and manner, she was as sprightly and graceful as ever, with the addition of that indescribable something in dress and bearing which we call elegance. Always mature for her age, she had gained a certain aplomb in both carriage and conversation, which made her seem more of a woman of the world than she was, but her old petulance now and then showed itself, her strong will still held its own, and her native frankness was unspoiled by foreign polish.

Laurie did not read all this while he watched her feed the peacocks, but he saw enough to satisfy and interest him, and carried away a pretty little picture of a bright-faced girl standing in the sunshine, which brought out the soft hue of her dress, the fresh color of her cheeks, the golden gloss of her hair, and made her a prominent figure in the pleasant scene.

As they came up onto the stone plateau that crowns the hill, Amy waved her hand as if welcoming him to her favorite haunt, and said, pointing here and there, "Do you remember the Cathedral and the Corso, the fishermen dragging their nets in the bay, and the lovely road to Villa Franca, Schubert's Tower, just below, and best of all, that speck far out to sea which they say ils Corsica?"

"I remember. It's not much changed," he answered without enthusiasm.

"What Jo would give for a sight of that famous speck!" said Amy, feeling in good spirits and anxious to see him so also.

"Yes," was all he said, but he turned and strained his eyes to see the island which a greater usurper than even Napoleon now made interesting in his sight.

"Take a good look at it for her sake, and then come and tell me what you have been doing with yourself all this while," said Amy, seating herself, ready for a good talk.

But she did not get it, for though he joined her and answered all her questions freely, she could only learn that he had roved about the Continent and been to Greece. So after idling away an hour, they drove home again, and having paid his respects to Mrs. Carrol, Laurie left them, promising to return in the evening.

It must be recorded of Amy that she deliberately prinked that night. Time and absence had done its work on both the young people. She had seen her old friend in a new light, not as 'our boy', but as a handsome and agreeable man, and she was conscious of a very natural desire to find favor in his sight. Amy knew her good points, and made the most of them with the taste and skill which is a fortune to a poor and pretty woman.

Tarlatan and tulle were cheap at Nice, so she enveloped herself in them on such occasions, and following the sensible English fashion of simple dress for young girls, got up charming little toilettes with fresh flowers, a few trinkets, and all manner of dainty devices, which were both inexpensive and effective. It must be confessed that the artist sometimes got possession of the woman, and indulged in antique coiffures, statuesque attitudes, and classic draperies. But, dear heart, we all have out little weaknesses, and find it easy to pardon such in the young, who satisfy our eyes with their comeliness, and keep our hearts merry with their artless vanities.

"I do want him to think I look well, and tell them so at home," said Amy to herself, as she put on Flo's old white silk ball dress, and covered it with a cloud of fresh illusion, out of which her white shoulders and golden head emerged with a most artistic effect. Her hair she had the sense to let alone, after gathering up the thick waves and curls into a Hebe-like knot at the back of her head.

"It's not the fashion, but it's becoming, and I can't afford to make a fright of myself," she used to say, when advised to frizzle, puff, or braid, as the latest style commanded.

Having no ornaments fine enough for this important occasion, Amy looped her fleecy skirts with rosy clusters of azalea, and framed the white shoulders in delicate green vines. Remembering the painted boots, she surveyed her white satin slippers with girlish satisfaction, and chassed down the room, admiring her aristocratic feet all by herself.

"My new fan just matches my flowers, my gloves fit to a charm, and the real lace on Aunt's mouchoir gives an air to my whole dress. If I only had a classical nose and mouth I should be perfectly happy," she said, surveying herself with a critical eye and a candle in each hand.

In spite of this affliction, she looked unusually gay and graceful as she glided away. She seldom ran—it did not suit her style, she thought, for being tall, the stately and Junoesque was more appropriate than the sportive or piquante. She walked up and down the long saloon while waiting for Laurie, and once arranged herself under the chandelier, which had a good effect upon her hair, then she thought better of it, and went away to the other end of the room, as if ashamed of the girlish desire to have the first view a propitious one. It so happened that she could not have done a better thing, for Laurie came in so quietly she did not hear him, and as she stood at the distant window, with her head half turned and one hand gathering up her dress, the slender, white figure against the red curtains was as effective as a well-placed statue.

"Good evening, Diana!" said Laurie, with the look of satisfaction she liked to see in his eyes when they rested on her.

"Good evening, Apollo!" she answered, smiling back at him, for he too looked unusually debonair, and the thought of entering the ballroom on the arm of such a personable man caused Amy to pity the four plain Misses Davis from the bottom of her heart.

"Here are your flowers. I arranged them myself, remembering that you didn't like what Hannah calls a 'sot-bookay', said Laurie, handing her a delicate nosegay, in a holder that she had long coveted as she daily passed it in Cardiglia's window.

"How kind you are!" she exclaimed gratefully. "If I'd known you were coming I'd have had something ready for you today, though not as pretty as this, I'm afraid."

"Thank you. It isn't what it should be, but you have improved it," he added, as she snapped the silver bracelet on her wrist.

"Please don't."

"I thought you liked that sort of thing."

"Not from you, it doesn't sound natural, and I like your old bluntness better."

"I'm glad of it," he answered, with a look of relief, then buttoned her gloves for her, and asked if his tie was straight, just as he used to do when they went to parties together at home.

The company assembled in the long salle a manger that evening was such as one sees nowhere but on the Continent. The hospitable Americans had invited every acquaintance they had in Nice, and having no prejudice against titles, secured a few to add luster to their Christmas ball.

A Russian prince condescended to sit in a corner for an hour and talk with a massive lady, dressed like Hamlet's mother in black velvet with a pearl bridle under her chin. A Polish count, aged eighteen, devoted himself to the ladies, who pronounced him, 'a fascinating dear', and a German Serene Something, having come to supper alone, roamed vaguely about, seeking what he might devour. Baron Rothschild's private secretary, a largenosed Jew in tight boots, affably beamed upon the world, as if his master's name crowned him with a golden halo. A stout Frenchman, who knew the Emperor, came to indulge his mania for dancing, and Lady de Jones, a British matron, adorned the scene with her little family of eight. Of course, there were many light-footed, shrill-voiced American girls, handsome, lifeless-looking English ditto, and a few plain but piquante French demoiselles, likewise the usual set of traveling young gentlemen who disported themselves gaily, while mammas of all nations lined the walls and smiled upon them benignly when they danced with their daughters.

Any young girl can imagine Amy's state of mind when she 'took the stage' that night, leaning on Laurie's arm. She knew she looked well, she loved to dance, she felt that her foot was on her native heath in a ballroom, and enjoyed the delightful sense of power which comes when young girls first discover the new and lovely kingdom they are born to rule by virtue of beauty, youth, and womanhood. She did pity the Davis girls, who were awkward, plain, and destitute of escort, except a grim papa and three grimmer maiden aunts, and she bowed to them in her friendliest manner as she passed, which was good of her, as it permitted them to see her dress, and burn with curiosity to know who her distinguished-looking friend might be. With the first burst of the band, Amy's color rose, her eyes began to sparkle, and her feet to tap the floor impatiently, for she danced well and wanted Laurie to know it. Therefore the shock she received can better be imagined than described, when he said in a perfectly tranquil tone, "Do you care to dance?"

"One usually does at a ball."

Her amazed look and quick answer caused Laurie to repair his error as fast as possible.

"I meant the first dance. May I have the honor?"

"I can give you one if I put off the Count. He dances devinely, but he will excuse me, as you are an old friend," said Amy, hoping that the name would have a good effect, and show Laurie that she was not to be trifled with.

"Nice little boy, but rather a short Pole to support

'. . . A daughter of the gods,
Devinely tall, and most devinely fair,'"

was all the satisfaction she got, however.

The set in which they found themselves was composed of English, and Amy was compelled to walk decorously through a cotillion, feeling all the while as if she could dance the tarantella with relish. Laurie resigned her to the 'nice little boy', and went to do his duty to Flo, without securing Amy for the joys to come, which reprehensible want of forethought was properly punished, for she immediately engaged herself till supper, meaning to relent if he then gave any signs penitence. She showed him her ball book with demure satisfaction when he strolled instead of rushed up to claim her for the next, a glorious polka redowa. But his polite regrets didn't impose upon her, and when she galloped away with the Count, she saw Laurie sit down by her aunt with an actual expression of relief.

That was unpardonable, and Amy took no more notice of him for a long while, except a word now and then when she came to her chaperon between the dances for a necessary pin or a moment's rest. Her anger had a good effect, however, for she hid it under a smiling face, and seemed unusually blithe and brilliant. Laurie's eyes followed her with pleasure, for she neither romped nor sauntered, but danced with spirit and grace, making the delightsome pastime what it should be. He very naturally fell to studying her from this new point of view, and before the evening was half over, had decided that 'little Amy was going to make a very charming woman'.

It was a lively scene, for soon the spirit of the social season took possession of everyone, and Christmas merriment made all faces shine, hearts happy, and heels light. The musicians fiddled, tooted, and banged as if they enjoyed it, everybody danced who could, and those who couldn't admired their neighbors with uncommon warmth. The air was dark with Davises, and many Jones gamboled like a flock of young giraffes. The golden secretary darted through the room like a meteor with a dashing frenchwoman who carped the floor with her pink satin train. The serene Teuton found the supper table and was happy, eating steadily through the bill of fare, and dismayed the garcons by the ravages he committed. But the Emperor's friend covered himself with glory, for he danced everything, whether he knew it or not, and introduced impromptu pirouettes when the figures bewildered him. The boyish abandon of that stout man was charming to behold, for though he 'carried weight', he danced like an India-rubber ball. He ran, he flew, he pranced, his face glowed, his bald head shown, his coattails waved wildly, his pumps actually twinkled in the air, and when the music stopped, he wiped the drops from his brow, and beamed upon his fellow men like a French Pickwick without glasses.

Amy and her Pole distinguished themselves by equal enthusiasm but more graceful agility, and Laurie found himself involuntarily keeping time to the rhythmic rise and fall of the white slippers as they flew by as indefatigably as if winged. When little Vladimir finally relinquished her, with assurances that he was 'desolated to leave so early', she was ready to rest, and see how her recreant knight had borne his punishment.

It had been successful, for at three-and-twenty, blighted affections find a balm in friendly society, and young nerves will thrill, young blood dance, and healthy young spirits rise, when subjected to the enchantment of beauty, light, music, and motion. Laurie had a waked-up look as he rose to give her his seat, and when he hurried away to bring her some supper, she said to herself, with a satisfied smile, "Ah, I thought that would do him good!"

"You look like Balzac's 'FEMME PEINTE PAR ELLE-NENE,'" he said, as he fanned her with one hand and held her coffee cup in the other.

"My rouge won't come off." And Amy rubbed her brilliant cheek, and showed him her white glove with a sober simplicity that made him laugh outright.

"What do you call this stuff?" he asked, touching a fold of her dress that had blown over his knee.

"Illusion."

"Good name for it. It's very pretty—new thing, isn't it?"

"It's as old as the hills. You have seen it on dozens of girls, and you never found out that it was pretty till now? Stupide!"

"I never saw it on you before, which accounts for the mistake, you see."

"None of that, it is forbidden. I'd rather take coffee than compliments just now. No, don't lounge, it makes me nervous."

Laurie sat bold upright, and meekly took her empty plate feeling an odd sort of pleasure in having 'little Amy' order him about, for she had lost her shyness now, and felt an irrestible desire to trample on him, as girls have a delightful way of doing when lords of creation show any signs of subjection.

"Where did you learn all this sort of thing?" he asked with a quizzical look.

"As 'this sort of thing' is rather a vague expression, would you kindly explain?" returned Amy, knowing perfectly well what he meant, but wickedly leaving him to describe what is indescribable.

"Well—the general air, the style, the self-possession, the—the—illusion—you know", laughed Laurie, breaking down and helping himself out of his quandary with the new word.

Amy was gratified, but of course didn't show it, and demurely answered, "Foreign life polishes one in spite of one's self. I study as well as play, and as for this"—with a little gesture toward her dress—"why, tulle is cheap, posies to be had for nothing, and I am used to making the most of my poor little things."

Amy rather regretted that last sentence, fearing it wasn't in good taste, but Laurie liked her better for it, and found himself both admiring and respecting the brave patience that made the most of opportunity, and the cheerful spirit that covered poverty with flowers. Amy did not know why he looked at her so kindly, now why he filled up her book with his own name, and devoted himself to her for the rest of the evening in the most delightful manner, but the impulse that wrought this agreeable change was the result of one of the new impressions which both of them were unconsciously giving and receiving.

Chapter Thirty-Eight

In France the young girls have a dull time of it till they are married, when 'Vive la liberte!' becomes their motto. In America, as everyone knows, girls early sign the declaration of independence, and enjoy their freedom with republican zest, but the young matrons usually abdicate with the first heir to the throne and go into a seclusion almost as close as a French nunnery, though by no means as quiet. Whether they like it or not, they are virtually put upon the shelf as soon as the wedding excitement is over, and most of them might exclaim, as did a very pretty woman the other day, "I'm as handsome as ever, but no one takes any notice of me because I'm married."

Not being a belle or even a fashionable lady, Meg did not experience this affliction till her babies were a year old, for in her little world primitive customs prevailed, and she found herself more admired and beloved than ever.

As she was a womanly little woman, the maternal instinct was very strong, and she was entirely absorbed in her children, to the utter exclusion of everything and everybody else. Day and night she brooded over them with tireless devotion and anxiety, leaving John to the tender mercies of the help, for an Irish lady now presided over the kitchen department. Being a domestic man, John decidedly missed the wifely attentions he had been accustomed to receive, but as he adored his babies, he cheerfully relinquished his comfort for a time, supposing with masculine ignorance that peace would soon be restored. But three months passed, and there was no return of repose. Meg looked worn and nervous, the babies absorbed every minute of her time, the house was neglected, and Kitty, the cook, who took life 'aisy', kept him on short commons. When he went out in the morning he was bewildered by small commissions for the captive mamma, if he came gaily in at night, eager to embrace his family, he was quenched by a "Hush! They are just asleep after worrying all day." If he proposed a little amusement at home, "No, it would disturb the babies." If he hinted at a lecture or a concert, he was answered with a reproachful look, and a decided "Leave my children for pleasure, never!" His sleep was broken by infant wails and visions of a phantom figure pacing noiselessly to and fro in the watches of the night. His meals were interrupted by the frequent flight of the presiding genius, who deserted him, half-helped, if a muffled chirp sounded from the nest above. And when he read his paper of an evening, Demi's colic got into the shipping list and Daisy's fall affected the price of stocks, for Mrs. Brooke was only interested in domestic news.

The poor man was very uncomfortable, for the children had bereft him of his wife, home was merely a nursery and the perpetual 'hushing' made him feel like a brutal intruder whenever he entered the sacred precincts of Babyland. He bore it very patiently for six months, and when no signs of amendment appeared, he did what other paternal exiles do—tried to get a little comfort elsewhere. Scott had married and gone to housekeeping not far off, and John fell into the way of running over for an hour or two of an evening, when his own parlor was empty, and his own wife singing lullabies that seemed to have no end. Mrs. Scott was a lively, pretty girl, with nothing to do but be agreeable, and she performed her mission most successfully. The parlor was always bright and attractive, the chessboard ready, the piano in tune, plenty of gay gossip, and a nice little supper set forth in tempting style.

John would have preferred his own fireside if it had not been so lonely, but as it was he gratefully took the next best thing and enjoyed his neighbor's society.

Meg rather approved of the new arrangement at first, and found it a relief to know that John was having a good time instead of dozing in the parlor, or tramping about the house and waking the children. But by-and-by, when the teething worry was over and the idols went to sleep at proper hours, leaving Mamma time to rest, she began to miss John, and find her work-basket dull company, when he was not sitting opposite in his old dressing gown, comfortably scorching his slippers on the fender. She would not ask him to stay at home, but felt injured because he did not know that she wanted him without being told, entirely forgetting the many evenings he had waited for her in vain. She was nervous and worn out with watching and worry, and in that unreasonable frame of mind which the best of mothers occasionally experience when domestic cares oppress them. Want of exercise robs them of cheerfulness, and too much devotion to that idol of American women, the teapot, makes them feel as if they were all nerve and no muscle.

"Yes," she would say, looking in the glass, "I'm getting old and ugly. John doesn't find me interesting any longer, so he leaves his faded wife and goes to see his pretty neighbor, who has no incumbrances. Well, the babies love me, they don't care if I am thin and pale and haven't time to crimp my hair, they are my comfort, and some day John will see what I've gladly sacrificed for them, won't he, my precious?"

To which pathetic appeal daisy would answer with a coo, or Demi with a crow, and Meg would put by her lamentations for a maternal revel, which soothed her solitude for the time being. But the pain increased as politics absorbed John, who was always running over to discuss interesting points with Scott, quite unconscious that Meg missed him. Not a word did she say, however, till her mother found her in tears one day, and insisted on knowing what the matter was, for Meg's drooping spirits had not escaped her observation.

"I wouldn't tell anyone except you, Mother, but I really do need advice, for if John goes on much longer I might as well be widowed," replied Mrs. Brooke, drying her tears on Daisy's bib with an injured air.

"Goes on how, my dear?" asked her mother anxiously.

"He's away all day, and at night when I want to see him, he is continually going over to the Scotts'. It isn't fair that I should have the hardest work, and never any amusement. Men are very selfish, even the best of them."

"So are women. Don't blame John till you see where you are wrong yourself."

"But it can't be right for him to neglect me."

"Don't you neglect him?"

"Why, Mother, I thought you'd take my part!"

"So I do, as far as sympathizing goes, but I think the fault is yours, Meg."

"I don't see how."

"Let me show you. Did John ever neglect you, as you call it, while you made it a point to give him your society of an evening, his only leisure time?"

"No, but I can't do it now, with two babies to tend."

"I think you could, dear, and I think you ought. May I speak quite freely, and will you remember that it's Mother who blames as well as Mother who sympathizes?"

"Indeed I will! Speak to me as if I were little Meg again. I often feel as if I needed teaching more than ever since these babies look to me for everything."

Meg drew her low chair beside her mother's, and with a little interruption in either lap, the two women rocked and talked lovingly together, feeling that the tie of motherhood made them more one than ever.

"You have only made the mistake that most young wives make-forgotten your duty to your husband in your love for your children. A very natural and forgivable mistake, Meg, but one that had better be remedied before you take to different ways, for children should draw you nearer than ever, not separate you, as if they were all yours, and John had nothing to do but support them. I've seen it for some weeks, but have not spoken, feeling sure it would come right in time."

"I'm afraid it won't. If I ask him to stay, he'll think I'm jealous, and I wouldn't insult him by such an idea. He doesn't see that I want him, and I don't know how to tell him without words."

"Make it so pleasant he won't want to go away. My dear, he's longing for his little home, but it isn't home without you, and you are always in the nursery."

"Oughtn't I to be there?"

"Not all the time, too much confinement makes you nervous, and then you are unfitted for everything. Besides, you owe something to John as well as to the babies. Don't neglect husband for children, don't shut him out of the nursery, but teach him how to help in it. His place is there as well as yours, and the children need him. Let him feel that he has a part to do, and he will do it gladly and faithfully, and it will be better for you all."

"You really think so, Mother?"

"I know it, Meg, for I've tried it, and I seldom give advice unless I've proved its practicability. When you and Jo were little, I went on just as you are, feeling as if I didn't do my duty unless I devoted myself wholly to you. Poor Father took to his books, after I had refused all offers of help, and left me to try my experiment alone. I struggled along as well as I could, but Jo was too much for me. I nearly spoiled her by indulgence. You were poorly, and I worried about you till I fell sick myself. Then Father came to the rescue, quietly managed everything, and made himself so helpful that I saw my mistake, and never have been able to got on without him since. That is the secret of our home happiness. He does not let business wean him from the little cares and duties that affect us all, and I try not to let domestic worries destroy my interest in his pursuits. Each do our part alone in many things, but at home we work together, always."

"It is so, Mother, and my great wish is to be to my husband and children what you have been to yours. Show me how, I'll do anything you say."

"You were always my docile daughter. Well, dear, if I were you, I'd let John have more to do with the management of Demi, for the boy needs training, and it's none too soon to begin. Then I'd do what I have often proposed, let Hannah come and help you. She is a capital nurse, and you may trust the precious babies to her while you do more housework. You need the exercise, Hannah would enjoy the rest, and John would find his wife again. Go out more, keep cheerful as well as busy, for you are the sunshine-maker of the family, and if you get dismal there is no fair weather. Then I'd try to take an interest in whatever

John likes—talk with him, let him read to you, exchange ideas, and help each other in that way. Don't shut yourself up in a bandbox because you are a woman, but understand what is going on, and educate yourself to take your part in the world's work, for it all affects you and yours."

"John is so sensible, I'm afraid he will think I'm stupid if I ask questions about politics and things."

"I don't believe he would. Love covers a multitude of sins, and of whom could you ask more freely than of him? Try it, and see if he doesn't find your society far more agreeable than Mrs. Scott's suppers."

"I will. Poor John! I'm afraid I have neglected him sadly, but I thought I was right, and he never said anything."

"He tried not to be selfish, but he has felt rather forlorn, I fancy. This is just the time, Meg, when young married people are apt to grow apart, and the very time when they ought to be most together, for the first tenderness soon wears off, unless care is taken to preserve it. And no time is so beautiful and precious to parents as the first years of the little lives given to them to train. Don't let John be a stranger to the babies, for they will do more to keep him safe and happy in this world of trial and temptation than anything else, and through them you will learn to know and love one another as you should. Now, dear, good-by. Think over Mother's preachment, act upon it if it seems good, and God bless you all."

Meg did think it over, found it good, and acted upon it, though the first attempt was not made exactly as she planned to have it. Of course the children tyrannized over her, and ruled the house as soon as they found out that kicking and squalling brought them whatever they wanted. Mamma was an abject slave to their caprices, but Papa was not so easily subjugated, and occasionally afflicted his tender spouse by an attempt at paternal discipline with his obstreperous son. For Demi inherited a trifle of his sire's firmness of character, we won't call it obstinacy, and when he made up his little to have or to do anything, all the king's horses and all the king's men could not change that pertinacious little mind. Mamma thought the dear too young to be taught to conquer his prejudices, but Papa believed that it never was too soon to learn obedience. So Master Demi early discovered that when he undertook to 'wrastle' with 'Parpar', he always got the worst of it, yet like the Englishman, baby respected the man who conquered him, and loved the father whose grave "No, no," was more impressive than all Mamma's love pats. A few days after the talk with her mother, Meg resolved to try a social evening with John, so she ordered a nice supper, set the parlor in order, dressed herself prettily, and put the children to bed early, that nothing should interfere with her experiment. But unfortunately Demi's most unconquerable prejudice was against going to bed, and that night he decided to go on a rampage. So poor Meg sang and rocked, told stories and tried every sleep-prevoking wile she could devise, but all in vain, the big eyes wouldn't shut, and long after Daisy had gone to byelow, like the chubby little bunch of good nature she was, naughty Demi lay staring at the light, with the most discouragingly wide-awake expression of countenance.

"Will Demi lie still like a good boy, while Mamma runs down and gives poor Papa his tea?" asked Meg, as the hall door softly closed, and the well-known step went tip-toeing into the dining room.

"Me has tea!" said Demi, preparing to join in the revel.

"No, but I'll save you some little cakies for breakfast, if you'll go bye-by like Daisy. Will you, lovey?"

"Iss!" and Demi shut his eyes tight, as if to catch sleep and hurry the desired day.

Taking advantage of the propitious moment, Meg slipped away and ran down to greet her husband with a smiling face and the little blue bow in her hair which was his especial admiration. He saw it at once and said with pleased surprise, "Why, little mother, how gay we are tonight. Do you expect company?"

"Only you, dear."

"No, I'm tired of being dowdy, so I dressed up as a change. You always make yourself nice for table, no matter how tired you are, so why shouldn't I when I have the time?'

"I do it out of respect for you, my dear," said old-fashioned John.

"Ditto, ditto, Mr. Brooke," laughed Meg, looking young and pretty again, as she nodded to him over the teapot.

"Well, it's altogether delightful, and like old times. This tastes right. I drink your health, dear." And John sipped his tea with an air of reposeful rapture, which was of very short duration however, for as he put down his cup, the door handle rattled mysteriously, and a little voice was heard, saying impatiently . . .

"Opy doy. Me's tummin!"

"It's that naughty boy. I told him to go to sleep alone, and here he is, downstairs, getting his death a-cold pattering over that canvas," said Meg, answering the call.

"Mornin' now," announced Demi in joyful tone as he entered, with his long nightgown gracefully festooned over his arm and every curl bobbing gayly as he pranced about the table, eyeing the 'cakies' with loving glances.

"No, it isn't morning yet. You must go to bed, and not trouble poor Mamma. Then you can have the little cake with sugar on it."

"Me loves Parpar," said the artful one, preparing to climb the paternal knee and revel in forbidden joys. But John shook his head, and said to Meg . . .

"If you told him to stay up there, and go to sleep alone, make him do it, or he will never learn to mind you."

"Yes, of course. Come, Demi." And Meg led her son away, feeling a strong desire to spank the little marplot who hopped beside her, laboring under the delusion that the bribe was to be administered as soon as they reached the nursery.

Nor was he disappointed, for that shortsighted woman actually gave him a lump of sugar, tucked him into his bed, and forbade any more promenades till morning.

"Iss!" said Demi the perjured, blissfully sucking his sugar, and regarding his first attempt as eminently successful.

Meg returned to her place, and supper was progressing pleasantly, when the little ghost walked again and exposed the maternal delinquencies by boldly demanding, "More sudar, Marmar."

"Now this won't do," said John, hardening his heart against the engaging little sinner. "We shall never know any peace till that child learns togo to bed properly. You have made a slave of yourself long enough. Give him one lesson, and then there will be an end of it. Put him in his bed and leave him, Meg."

"He won't stay there, he never does unless I sit by him."

"I'll manage him. Demi, go upstairs, and get into your bed, as Mamma bids you."

"S'ant!" replied the young rebel, helping himself to the coveted 'cakie', and beginning to eat the same with calm audacity.

"You must never say that to Papa. I shall carry you if you don't go yourself."

"Go 'way, me don't love Parpar." And Demi retired to his mother's skirts for protection.

But even that refuge proved unavailing, for he was delivered over to the enemy, with a "Be gentle with him, John," which struck the culprit with dismay, for when Mamma deserted him, then the judgment day was at hand. Bereft of his cake, defrauded of his frolic, and borne away by a strong hand to that detested bed, poor Demi could not restrain his wrath, but openly defied Papa, and kicked and screamed lustily all the way upstairs. The minute he was put into bed on one side, he rolled out on the other, and made for the door, only to be ignominiously caught up by the tail of his little toga and put back again, which lively performance was kept up till the young man's strength gave out, when he devoted himself to roaring at the top of his voice. This vocal exercise usually conquered Meg, but John sat as unmoved as the post which is popularly believed to be deaf. No coaxing, no sugar, no lullaby, no story, even the light was put out and only the red glow of the fire enlivened the 'big dark' which Demi regarded with curiosity rather than fear. This new order of things disgusted him, and he howled dismally for 'Marmar', as his angry passions subsided, and recollections of his tender bondwoman returned to the captive autocrat. The plaintive wail which succeeded the passionate roar went to Meg's heart, and she ran up to say beseechingly . . .

"Let me stay with him, he'll be good now, John."

"No, my dear. I've told him he must go to sleep, as you bid him, and he must, if I stay here all night."

"But he'll cry himself sick," pleaded Meg, reproaching herself for deserting her boy.

"No, he won't, he's so tired he will soon drop off and then the matter is settled, for he will understand that he has got to mind. Don't interfere, I'll manage him."

"He's my child, and I can't have his spirit broken by harshness."

"He's my child, and I won't have his temper spoiled by indulgence. Go down, my dear, and leave the boy to me."

When John spoke in that masterful tone, Meg always obeyed, and never regretted her docility.

"Please let me kiss him once, John?"

"Certainly. Demi, say good night to Mamma, and let her go and rest, for she is very tired with taking care of you all day."

Meg always insisted upon it that the kiss won the victory, for after it was given, Demi sobbed more quietly, and lay quite still at the bottom of the bed, whither he had wriggled in his anguish of mind.

"Poor little man, he's worn out with sleep and crying. I'll cover him up, and then go and set Meg's heart at rest." thought

John, creeping to the bedside, hoping to find his rebellious heir asleep.

But he wasn't, for the moment his father peeped at him, Demi's eyes opened, his little chin began to quiver, and he put up his arms, saying with a penitent hiccough, "Me's dood, now."

Sitting on the stairs outside Meg wondered at the long silence which followed the uproar, and after imagining all sorts of impossible accidents, she slipped into the room to set her fears at rest. Demi lay fast asleep, not in his usual spreadeagle attitude, but in a subdued bunch, cuddled close in the circle of his father's arm and holding his father's finger, as if he felt that justice was tempered with mercy, and had gone to sleep a sadder and wiser baby. So held, John had waited with a womanly patience till the little hand relaxed its hold, and while waiting had fallen asleep, more tired by that tussle with his son than with his whole day's work.

As Meg stood watching the two faces on the pillow, she smiled to herself, and then slipped away again, saying in a satisfied tone, "I never need fear that John will be too harsh with my babies. He does know how to manage them, and will be a great help, for Demi is getting too much for me."

When John came down at last, expecting to find a pensive or reproachful wife, he was agreeably surprised to find Meg placidly trimming a bonnet, and to be greeted with the request to read something about the election, if he was not too tired. John saw in a minute that a revolution of some kind was going on, but wisely asked no questions, knowing that Meg was such a transparent little person, she couldn't keep a secret to save her life, and therefore the clue would soon appear. He read a long debate with the most amiable readiness and then explained it in his most lucid manner, while Meg tried to look deeply interested, to ask intelligent questions, and keep her thoughts from wandering from the state of the nation to the state of her bonnet. In her secret soul, however, she decided that politics were as bad as mathematics, and the the mission of politicians seemed to be calling each other names, but she kept these feminine ideas to herself, and when John paused, shook her head and said with what she thought diplomatic ambiguity, "Well, I really don't see what we are coming to."

John laughed, and watched her for a minute, as she poised a pretty little preparation of lace and flowers on her hand, and regarded it with the genuine interest which his harangue had failed to waken.

"She is trying to like politics for my sake, so I'll try and like millinery for hers, that's only fair," thought John the Just, adding aloud, "That's very pretty. Is it what you call a breakfast cap?"

"My dear man, it's a bonnet! My very best go-to-concert-and-theater bonnet."

"I beg your pardon, it was so small, I naturally mistook it for one of the flyaway things you sometimes wear. How do you keep it on?"

"These bits of lace are fastened under the chin with a rosebud, so." And Meg illustrated by putting on the bonnet and regarding him with an air of calm satisfaction that was irresistible.

"It's a love of a bonnet, but I prefer the face inside, for it looks young and happy again." And John kissed the smiling face, to the great detriment of the rosebud under the chin.

"I'm glad you like it, for I want you to take me to one of the new concerts some night. I really need some music to put me in tune. Will you, please?"

"Of course I will, with all my heart, or anywhere else you like. You have been shut up so long, it will do you no end of good, and I shall enjoy it, of all things. What put it into your head, little mother?"

"Well, I had a talk with Marmee the other day, and told her how nervous and cross and out of sorts I felt, and she said I needed change and less care, so Hannah is to help me with the children, and I'm to see to things about the house more, and now and then have a little fun, just to keep me from getting to be a fidgety, broken-down old woman before my time. It's only an experiment, John, and I want to try it for your sake as much as for mine, because I've neglected you shamefully lately, and I'm going to make home what it used to be, if I can. You don't object, I hope?"

Never mind what John said, or what a very narrow escape the little bonnet had from utter ruin. All that we have any business to know is that John did not appear to object, judging from the changes which gradually took place in the house and its inmates. It was not all Paradise by any means, but everyone was better for the division of labor system. The children throve under the paternal rule, for accurate, stedfast John brought order and obedience into Babydom, while Meg recovered her spirits and composed her nerves by plenty of wholesome exercise, a little pleasure, and much confidential conversation with her sensible husband. Home grew homelike again, and John had no wish to leave it, unless he took Meg with him. The Scotts came to the Brookes' now, and everyone found the little house a cheerful place, full of happiness, content, and family love. Even Sallie Moffatt liked to go there. "It is always so quiet and pleasant here, it does me good, Meg," she used to say, looking about her with wistful eyes, as if trying to discover the charm, that she might use it in her great house, full of splendid lonliness, for there were no riotous, sunny-faced babies there, and Ned lived in a world of lis own, where there was no place for her.

This household happiness did not come all at once, but John and Meg had found the key to it, and each year of Married life taught them how to use it, unlocking the treasuries of real home love and mutual helpfulness, which the poorest may possess, and the richest cannot buy. This is the sort of shelf on which young wives and mothers may consent to be laid, safe from the restless fret and fever of the world, finding loyal lovers in the little sons and daughters who cling to them, undaunted by sorrow, poverty, or age, walking side by side, through fair and stormy weather, with a faithful friend, who is, in the true sense of the good old Saxon word, the 'house-band', and learning, as Meg learned, that a woman's happiest kingdom is home, her highest honor the art of ruling it not as a queen, but as a wise wife and mother.

Chapter Thirty-Nine

Laurie went to Nice intending to stay a week, and remained a month. He was tired of wandering about alone, and Amy's familiar presence seemed to give a homelike charm to the foreign scenes in which she bore a part. He rather missed the 'petting' he used to receive, and enjoyed a taste of it again, for no attentions, however flattering, from strangers, were half so pleasant as the sisterly adoration of the girls at home. Amy never would pet him like the others, but she was very glad to see him now, and quite clung to him, feeling that he was the representative of the dear family for whom she longed more than she would confess. They naturally took comfort in each other's society and were much together, riding, walking, dancing, or dawdling, for at Nice no one can be very industrious during the gay season. But, while apparently amusing themselves in the most careless fashion, they were half-consciously making discoveries and forming opinions about each other. Amy rose daily in the estimation of her friend, but he sank in hers, and each felt the truth before a word was spoken. Amy tried to please, and succeeded, for she was grateful for the many pleasures he gave her, and repaid him with the little services to which womanly women know how to lend an indescribable charm. Laurie made no effort of any kind, but just let himself drift along as comfortably as possible, trying to forget, and feeling that all women owed him a kind word because one had been cold to him. It cost him no effort to be generous, and he would have given Amy all the trinkets in Nice if she would have taken them, but at the same time he felt that he could not change the opinion she was forming of him, and he rather dreaded the keen blue eyes that seemed to watch him with such half-sorrowful, half-scornful surprise.

"All the rest have gone to Monaco for the day. I preferred to stay at home and write letters. They are done now, and I am going to Valrosa to sketch, will you come?' said Amy, as she joined Laurie one lovely day when he lounged in as usual about noon.

"Well, yes, but isn't it rather warm for such a long walk?" he answered slowly, for the shaded salon looked inviting after the glare without.

"I'm going to have the little carriage, and Baptiste can drive, so you'll have nothing to do but hold your umbrella, and keep your gloves nice," returned Amy, with a sarcastic glance at the immaculate kids, which were a weak point with Laurie.

"Then I'll go with pleasure." And he put out his hand for her sketchbook. But she tucked it under her arm with a sharp . . .

"Don't trouble yourself. It's no exertion to me, but you don't look equal to it."

Laurie lifted his eyebrows and followed at a leisurely pace as she ran downstairs, but when they got into the carriage he took the reins himself, and left little Baptiste nothing to do but fold his arms and fall asleep on his perch.

The two never quarreled. Amy was too well-bred, and just now Laurie was too lazy, so in a minute he peeped under her hatbrim with an inquiring air. She answered him with a smile, and they went on together in the most amicable manner.

It was a lovely drive, along winding roads rich in the picturesque scenes that delight beauty-loving eyes. Here an ancient monastery, whence the solemn chanting of the monks came down to them. There a bare-legged shepherd, in wooden shoes, pointed hat, and rough jacket over one shoulder, sat piping on a stone while his goats skipped among the rocks or lay at his feet. Meek, mouse-colored donkeys, laden with panniers of freshly cut grass passed by, with a pretty girl in a capaline sitting between the green piles, or an old woman spinning with a distaff as she went. Brown, soft-eyed children ran out from the quaint stone hovels to offer nosegays, or bunches of oranges still on the bough. Gnarled olive trees covered the hills with their dusky foliage, fruit hung golden in the orchard, and great scarlet anemones fringed the roadside, while beyond green slopes and craggy heights, the Maritime Alps rose sharp and white against the blue Italian sky.

Valrosa well deserved its name, for in that climate of perpetual summer roses blossomed everywhere. They overhung the archway, thrust themselves between the bars of the great gate with a sweet welcome to passers-by, and lined the avenue, winding through lemon trees and feathery palms up to the villa on the hill. Every shadowy nook, where seats invited one to stop and rest, was a mass of bloom, every cool grotto had its marble nymph smiling from a veil of flowers and every fountain reflected crimson, white, or pale pink roses, leaning down to smile at their own beauty. Roses covered the walls of the house, draped the cornices, climbed the pillars, and ran riot over the balustrade of the wide terrace, whence one looked down on the sunny Mediterranean, and the white-walled city on its shore.

"This is a regular honeymoon paradise, isn't it? Did you ever see such roses?" asked Amy, pausing on the terrace to enjoy the view, and a luxurious whiff of perfume that came wandering by.

"No, nor felt such thorns," returned Laurie, with his thumb in his mouth, after a vain attempt to capture a solitary scarlet flower that grew just beyond his reach.

"Try lower down, and pick those that have no thorns," said Amy, gathering three of the tiny cream-colored ones that starred the wall behind her. She put them in his buttonhole as a peace offering, and he stood a minute looking down at them with a curious expression, for in the Italian part of his nature there was a touch of superstition, and he was just then in that state of half-sweet, half-bitter melancholy, when imaginative young men find significance in trifles and food for romance everywhere. He had thought of Jo in reaching after the thorny red rose, for vivid flowers became her, and she had often worn ones like that from the greenhouse at home. The pale roses Amy gave him were the sort that the Italians lay in dead hands, never in bridal wreaths, and for a moment he wondered if the omen was for Jo or for himself, but the next instant his American common sense got the better of sentimentality, and he laughed a heartier laugh than Amy had heard since he came.

"It's good advice, you'd better take it and save your fingers," she said, thinking her speech amused him.

"Thank you, I will," he answered in jest, and a few months later he did it in earnest.

"Laurie, when are you going to your grandfather?" she asked presently, as she settled herself on a rustic seat.

"Very soon."

"You have said that a dozen times within the last three weeks."

"I dare say, short answers save trouble."

"He expects you, and you really ought to go."

"Hospitable creature! I know it."

"Then why don't you do it?"

"Natural depravity, I suppose."

"Natural indolence, you mean. It's really dreadful!" And Amy looked severe.

"Not so bad as it seems, for I should only plague him if I went, so I might as well stay and plague you a little longer, you can bear it better, in fact I think it agrees with you excellently." And Laurie composed himself for a lounge on the broad ledge of the balustrade.

Amy shook her head and opened her sketchbook with an air of resignation, but she had made up her mind to lecture 'that boy' and in a minute she began again.

"What are you doing just now?"

"Watching lizards."

"No, no. I mean what do you intend and wish to do?"

"Smoke a cigarette, if you'll allow me."

"How provoking you are! I don't approve of cigars and I will only allow it on condition that you let me put you into my sketch. I need a figure."

"With all the pleasure in life. How will you have me, full length or three-quarters, on my head or my heels? I should respectfully suggest a recumbent posture, then put yourself in also and call it 'Dolce far niente.'"

"Stay as you are, and go to sleep if you like. I intend to work hard," said Amy in her most energetic tone.

"What delightful enthusiasm!" And he leaned against a tall urn with an ir of entire satisfaction.

"What would Jo say if she saw you now?" asked Amy impatiently, hoping to stir him up by the mention of her still more energetic sister's name.

"As usual, 'Go away, Teddy. I'm busy!'" He laughed as he spoke, but the laugh was not natural, and a shade passed over his face, for the utterance of the familiar name touched the wound that was not healed yet. Both tone and shadow struck Amy, for she had seen and heard them before, and now she looked up in time to catch a new expression on Laurie's face—a hard bitter look, full of pain, dissatisfaction, and regret. It was gone before she could study it and the listless expression back again. She watched him for a moment with artistic pleasure, thinking how like an Italian he looked, as he lay basking in the sun with uncovered head and eyes full of southern dreaminess, for he seemed to have forgotten her and fallen into a reverie.

"You look like the effigy of a young knight asleep on his tomb," she said, carefully tracing the well-cut profile defined against the dark stone.

"Wish I was!"

"That's a foolish wish, unless you have spoiled your life. You are so changed, I sometimes think—" There Amy stopped, with a half-timid, half-wistful look, more significant than her unfinished speech.

Laurie saw and understood the affectionate anxiety which she hesitated to express, and looking straight into her eyes, said, just as he used to say it to her mother, "It's all right, ma'am."

That satisfied her and set at rest the doubts that had begun to worry her lately. It also touched her, and she showed that it did, by the cordial tone in which she said . . .

"I'm glad of that! I didn't think you'd been a very bad boy, but I fancied you might have wasted money at that wicked Baden-Baden, lost your heart to some charming Frenchwoman with a husband, or got into some of the scrapes that young men seem to consider a necessary part of a foreign tour. Don't stay out there in the sun, come and lie on the grass here and 'let us be friendly', as Jo used to say when we got in the sofa corner and told secrets."

Laurie obediently threw himself down on the turf, and began to amuse himself by sticking daisies into the ribbons of Amy's hat, that lay there.

"I'm all ready for the secrets." And he glanced up with a decided expression of interest in his eyes.

"I've none to tell. You may begin."

"Haven't one to bless myself with. I thought perhaps you'd had some news from home.."

"You have heard all that has come lately. Don't you hear often? I fancied Jo would send you volumes."

"She's very busy. I'm roving about so, it's impossible to be regular, you know. When do you begin your great work of art, Raphaella?' he asked. changing the subject abruptly after another pause, in which he had been wondering if Amy knew his secret and wanted to talk about it.

"Never," she answered, with a despondent but decided air. "Rome took all the vanity out of me, for after seeing the wonders there, I felt too insignificant to live and gave up all my foolish hopes in despair."

"Why should you, with so much energy and talent?"

"That's just why, because talent isn't genius, and no amount of energy can make it so. I want to be great, or nothing. I won't be a common-place dauber, so I don't intend to try any more."

"And what are you going to do with yourself now, if I may ask?"

"Polish up my other talents, and be an ornament to society, if I get the chance."

It was a characteristic speech, and sounded daring, but audacity becomes young people, and Amy's ambition had a good foundation. Laurie smiled, but he liked the spirit with which she took up a new purpose when a long-cherished one died, and spent no time lamenting.

"Good! And here is where Fred Vaughn comes in, I fancy."

Amy preserved a discreet silence, but there was a conscious look in her downcast face that made Laurie sit up and say gravely, "Now I'm going to play brother, and ask questions. May I?"

"I don't promise to answer."

"Your face will, if your tongue won't. You aren't woman of the world enough yet to hide your feelings, my dear. I heard rumors about Fred and you last year, and it's my private opinion that if he had not been called home so suddenly and detained so long, something would have come of it, hey?"

"That's not for me to say," was Amy's grim reply, but her lips would smile, and there was a traitorous sparkle of the eye which betrayed that she knew her power and enjoyed the knowledge.

"You are not engaged, I hope?" And Laurie looked very elder-brotherly and grave all of a sudden.

"No."

"But you will be, if he comes back and goes properly down on his knees, won't you?"

"Very likely."

"Then you are fond of old Fred?"

"I could be, if I tried."

"But you don't intend to try till the proper moment? Bless my soul, what unearthly prudence! He's a good fellow, Amy, but not the man I fancied you'd like."

"He is rich, a gentleman, and has delightful manners," began Amy, trying to be quite cool and dignified, but feeling a little ashamed of herself, in spite of the sincerity of her intentions.

"I understand. Queens of society can't get on without money, so you mean to make a good match, and start in that way? Quite right and proper, as the world goes, but it sounds odd from the lips of one of your mother's girls."

"True, nevertheless."

A short speech, but the quiet decision with which it was uttered contrasted curiously with the young speaker. Laurie felt this instinctively and laid himself down again, with a sense of disappointment which he could not explain. His look and silence, as well as a certain inward self-disapproval, ruffled Amy, and made her resolve to deliver her lecture without delay.

"I wish you'd do me the favor to rouse yourself a little," she said sharply.

"Do it for me, there's a dear girl."

"I could, if I tried." And she looked as if she would like doing it in the most summary style.

"Try, then. I give you leave," returned Laurie, who enjoyed having someone to tease, after his long abstinence from his favorite pastime.

"You'd be angry in five minutes."

"I'm never angry with you. It takes two flints to make a fire. You are as cool and soft as snow."

"You don't know what I can do. Snow produces a glow and a tingle, if applied rightly. Your indifference is half affectation, and a good stirring up would prove it."

"Stir away, it won't hurt me and it may amuse you, as the big man said when his little wife beat him. Regard me in the light of a husband or a carpet, and beat till you are tired, if that sort of exercise agrees with you."

Being decidedly nettled herself, and longing to see him shake off the apathy that so altered him, Amy sharpened both tongue and pencil, and began.

"Flo and I have got a new name for you. It's Lazy Laurence. How do you like it?"

She thought it would annoy him, but he only folded his arms under his head, with an imperturbable, "That's not bad. Thank you, ladies."

"Do you want to know what I honestly think of you?"

"Pining to be told."

"Well, I despise you." If she had even said 'I hate you' in a petulant or coquettish tone, he would have laughed and rather liked it, but the grave, almost sad, accent in her voice made him open his eyes, and ask quickly . . .

"Why, if you please?"

"Because, with every chance for being good, useful, and happy, you are faulty, lazy, and miserable."

"Strong language, mademoiselle."

"If you like it, I'll go on."

"Pray do, it's quite interesting."

"I thought you'd find it so. Selfish people always like to talk about themselves."

"Am I selfish?" The question slipped out involuntarily and in a tone of surprise, for the one virtue on which he prided himself was generosity.

"Yes, very selfish," continued Amy, in a calm, cool voice, twice as effective just then as an angry one. "I'll show you how, for I've studied you while we were frolicking, and I'm not at all satisfied with you. Here you have been abroad nearly six months, and done nothing but waste time and money and disappoint your friends."

"Isn't a fellow to have any pleasure after a four-year grind?"

"You don't look as if you'd had much. At any rate, you are none the better for it, as far as I can see. I said when we first met that you had improved. Now I take it all back, for I don't think you half so nice as when I left you at home. You have grown abominably lazy, you like gossip, and waste time on frivolous things, you are contented to be petted and admired by silly people, instead of being loved and respected by wise ones. With money, talent, position, health, and beauty, ah you like that old Vanity! But it's the truth, so I can't help saying it, with all these splendid things to use and enjoy, you can find nothing to do but dawdle, and instead of being the man you ought to be, you are only . . ." There she stopped, with a look that had both pain and pity in it.

"Saint Laurence on a gridiron," added Laurie, blandly finishing the sentence. But the lecture began to take effect, for there was a wide-awake sparkle in his eyes now and a half-angry, half-injured expression replaced the former indifference.

"I supposed you'd take it so. You men tell us we are angels, and say we can make you what we will, but the instant we honestly try to do you good, you laugh at us and won't listen, which proves how much your flattery is worth." Amy spoke bitterly, and turned her back on the exasperating martyr at her feet.

In a minute a hand came down over the page, so that she could not draw, and Laurie's voice said, with a droll imitation of a penitent child, "I will be good, oh, I will be good!"

But Amy did not laugh, for she was in earnest, and tapping on the outspread hand with her pencil, said soberly, "Aren't you ashamed of a hand like that? It's as soft and white as a woman's, and looks as if it never did anything but wear Jouvin's best gloves and pick flowers for ladies. You are not a dandy, thank Heaven, so I'm glad to see there are no diamonds or big seal rings on it, only the little old one Jo gave you so long ago. Dear soul, I wish she was here to help me!"

"So do I!"

The hand vanished as suddenly as it came, and there was energy enough in the echo of her wish to suit even Amy. She glanced down at him with a new thought in her mind, but he was lying with his hat half over his face, as if for shade, and his mustache hid his mouth. She only saw his chest rise and fall, with a long breath that might have been a sigh, and the hand that wore the ring nestled down into the grass, as if to hide something too precious or too tender to be spoken of. All in a minute various hints and trifles assumed shape and significance in Amy's mind, and told her what her sister never had confided to her. She remembered that Laurie never spoke voluntarily of Jo, she recalled the shadow on his face just now, the change in his character, and the wearing of the little old ring which was no ornament to a handsome hand. Girls are quick to read such signs and feel their eloquence. Amy had fancied that perhaps a love trouble was at the bottom of the alteration, and now she was sure of it. Her keen eyes filled, and when she spoke again, it was in a voice that could be beautifully soft and kind when she chose to make it so.

"I know I have no right to talk so to you, Laurie, and if you weren't the sweetest-tempered fellow in the world, you'd be very angry with me. But we are all so fond and proud of you, I couldn't bear to think they should be disappointed in you at home as I have been, though, perhaps they would understand the change better than I do."

"I think they would," came from under the hat, in a grim tone, quite as touching as a broken one.

"They ought to have told me, and not let me go blundering and scolding, when I should have been more kind and patient than ever. I never did like that Miss Randal and now I hate her!" said artful Amy, wishing to be sure of her facts this time.

"Hang Miss Randal!" And Laurie knocked the hat off his face with a look that left no doubt of his sentiments toward that young lady.

"I beg pardon, I thought . . ." And there she paused diplomatically.

"No, you didn't, you knew perfectly well I never cared for anyone but Jo," Laurie said that in his old, impetuous tone, and turned his face away as he spoke.

"I did think so, but as they never said anything about it, and you came away, I supposed I was mistaken. And Jo wouldn't be kind to you? Why, I was sure she loved you dearly."

"She was kind, but not in the right way, and it's lucky for her she didn't love me, if I'm the good-for-nothing fellow you think me. It's her fault though, and you may tell her so."

The hard, bitter look came back again as he said that, and it troubled Amy, for she did not know what balm to apply.

"I was wrong, I didn't know. I'm very sorry I was so cross, but I can't help wishing you'd bear it better, Teddy, dear."

"Don't, that's her name for me!" And Laurie put up his hand with a quick gesture to stop the words spoken in Jo's half-kind, half-reproachful tone. "Wait till you've tried it yourself," he added in a low voice, as he pulled up the grass by the handful.

"I'd take it manfully, and be respected if i couldn't be loved," said Amy, with the decision of one who knew nothing about it.

Now, Laurie flattered himself that he had borne it remarkably well, making no moan, asking no sympathy, and taking his trouble away to live it down alone. Amy's lecture put the Matter in a new light, and for the first time it did look weak and selfish to lose heart at the first failure, and shut himself up in moody indifference. He felt as if suddenly shaken out of a pensive dream and found it impossible to go to sleep again. Presently he sat up and asked slowly, "Do you think Jo would despise me as you do?"

"Yes, if she saw you now. She hates lazy people. Why don't you do something splendid, and make her love you?"

"I did my best, but it was no use."

"Graduating well, you mean? That was no more than you ought to have done, for your grandfather's sake. It would have been shameful to fail after spending so much time and money, when everyone knew that you could do well."

"I did fail, say what you will, for Jo wouldn't love me,"

began Laurie, leaning his head on his hand in a despondent attitude.

"No, you didn't, and you'll say so in the end, for it did you good, and proved that you could do something if you tried. If you'd only set about another task of some sort, you'd soon be your hearty, happy self again, and forget your trouble."

"That's impossible."

"Try it and see. You needn't shrug your shoulders, and think, 'Much she knows about such things'. I don't pretend to be wise, but I am observing, and I see a great deal more than you'd imagine. I'm interested in other people's experiences and inconsistencies, and though I can't explain, I remember and use them for my own benefit. Love Jo all your days, if you choose, but don't let it spoil you, for it's wicked to throw away so many good gifts because you can't have the one you want. There, I won't lecture any more, for I know you'll wake up and be a man in spite of that hardhearted girl."

Neither spoke for several minutes. Laurie sat turning the little ring on his finger, and Amy put the last touches to the hasty sketch she had been working at while she talked. Presently she put it on his knee, merely saying, "How do you like that?"

He looked and then he smiled, as he could not well help doing, for it was capitally done, the long, lazy figure on the grass, with listless face, half-shut eyes, and one hand holding a cigar, from which came the little wreath of smoke that encircled the dreamer's head.

"How well you draw!" he said, with a genuine surprise and pleasure at her skill, adding, with a half-laugh, "Yes, that's me."

"As you are. This is as you were." And Amy laid another sketch beside the one he held.

It was not nearly so well done, but there was a life and spirit in it which atoned for many faults, and it recalled the past so vividly that a sudden change swept over the young man's face as he looked. Only a rough sketch of Laurie taming a horse. Hat and coat were off, and every line of the active figure, resolute face, and commanding attitude was full of energy and meaning. The handsome brute, just subdued, stood arching his neck under the tightly drawn rein, with one foot impatiently pawing the ground, and ears pricked up as if listening for the voice that had mastered him. In the ruffled mane. The rider's breezy hair and erect attitude, there was a suggestion of suddenly arrested motion, of strength, courage, and youthful buoyancy that contrasted sharply with the supine grace of the 'DOLCE FAR NIENTE' sketch. Laurie said nothing but as his eye went from one to the other, Amy say him flush up and fold his lips together as if he read and accepted the little lesson she had given him. That satisfied her, and without waiting for him to speak, she said, in her sprightly way . . .

"Don't you remember the day you played Rarey with Puck, and we all looked on? Meg and Beth were frightened, but Jo clapped and pranced, and I sat on the fence and drew you. I found that sketch in my portfolio the other day, touched it up, and kept it to show you."

"Much obliged. You've improved immensely since then, and I congratulate you. May I venture to suggest in 'a honeymoon paradise' that five o'clock is the dinner hour at your hotel?"

Laurie rose as he spoke, returned the pictures with a smile and a bow and looked at his watch, as if to remind her that even moral lectures should have an end. He tried to resume his former easy, indifferent air, but it was an affectation now, for the rousing had been more effacious than he would confess. Amy felt the shade of coldness in his manner, and said to herself...

"Now, I've offended him. Well, if it does him good, I'm glad, if it makes him hate me, I'm sorry, but it's true, and I can't take back a word of it."

They laughed and chatted all the way home, and little Baptist, up behind, thought that monsieur and madamoiselle were in charming spirits. But both felt ill at ease. The friendly frankness was disturbed, the sunshine had a shadow over it, and despite their apparent gaiety, there was a secret discontent in the heart of each.

"Shall we see you this evening, mon frere?" asked Amy, as they parted at her aunt's door.

"Unfortunately I have an engagement. Au revoir, madamoiselle." And Laurie bent as if to kiss her hand, in the foreign fashion, which became him better than many men. Something in his face made Amy say quickly and warmly...

"No, be yourself with me, Laurie, and part in the good old way. I'd rather have a hearty English handshake than all the sentimental salutations in France."

"Goodbye, dear." And with these words, uttered in the tone she liked, Laurie left her, after a handshake almost painful in its heartiness.

Next morning, instead of the usual call, Amy received a note which made her smile at the beginning and sigh at the end.

> My Dear Mentor,
>
> Please make my adieux to your aunt, and exult within yourself, for 'Lazy Laurence' has gone to his grandpa, like the best of boys. A pleasant winter to you, and may the gods grant you a blissful honeymoon at Valrosa! I think Fred would be benefited by a rouser. Tell him so, with my congratulations.
>
> Yours gratefully, Telemachus

"Good boy! I'm glad he's gone," said Amy, with an approving smile. The next minute her face fell as she glanced about the empty room, adding, with an involuntary sigh, "Yes, I am glad, but how I shall miss him."

Chapter Forty

When the first bitterness was over, the family accepted the inevitable, and tried to bear it cheerfully, helping one another by the increased affection which comes to bind households tenderly together in times of trouble. They put away their grief, and each did his or her part toward making that last year a happy one.

The pleasantest room in the house was set apart for Beth, and in it was gathered everything that she most loved, flowers, pictures, her piano, the little worktable, and the beloved pussies. Father's best books found their way there, Mother's easy chair, Jo's desk, Amy's finest sketches, and every day Meg brought her babies on a loving pilgrimage, to make sunshine for Aunty Beth. John quietly set apart a little sum, that he might enjoy the pleasure of keeping the invalid supplied with the fruit she loved and longed for. Old Hannah never wearied of concocting dainty dishes to tempt a capricious appetite, dropping tears as she worked, and from across the sea came little gifts and cheerful letters, seeming to bring breaths of warmth and fragrance from lands that know no winter.

Here, cherished like a household saint in its shrine, sat Beth, tranquil and busy as ever, for nothing could change the sweet, unselfish nature, and even while preparing to leave life, she tried to make it happier for those who should remain behind. The feeble fingers were never idle, and one of her pleasures was to make little things for the school children daily passing to and fro, to drop a pair of mittens from her window for a pair of purple hands, a needlebook for some small mother of many dolls, penwipers for young penmen toiling through forests of pothooks, scrapbooks for picture-loving eyes, and all manner of pleasant devices, till the reluctant climbers of the ladder of learning found their way strewn with flowers, as it were, and came to regard the gentle giver as a sort of fairy godmother, who sat above there, and showered down gifts miraculously suited to their tastes and needs. If Beth had wanted any reward, she found it in the bright little faces always turned up to her window, with nods and smiles, and the droll little letters which came to her, full of blots and gratitude.

The first few months were very happy ones, and Beth often used to look round, and say "How beautiful this is!" as they all sat together in her sunny room, the babies kicking and crowing on the floor, mother and sisters working near, and father reading, in his pleasant voice, from the wise old books which seemed rich in good and comfortable words, as applicable now as when written centuries ago, a little chapel, where a paternal priest taught his flock the hard lessons all must learn, trying to show them that hope can comfort love, and faith make resignation possible. Simple sermons, that went straight to the souls of those who listened, for the father's heart was in the minister's religion, and the frequent falter in the voice gave a double eloquence to the words he spoke or read.

It was well for all that this peaceful time was given them as preparation for the sad hours to come, for by-and-by, Beth said the needle was 'so heavy', and put it down forever. Talking wearied her, faces troubled her, pain claimed her for its own, and her tranquil spirit was sorrowfully perturbed by the ills that vexed her feeble flesh. Ah me! Such heavy days, such long, long nights, such aching hearts and imploring prayers, when those who loved her best were forced to see the thin hands stretched out to them beseechingly, to hear the bitter cry, "Help me, help me!" and to feel that there was no help. A sad eclipse of the serene soul, a sharp struggle of the young life with death, but both were mercifully brief, and then the natural rebellion over, the old peace returned more beautiful than ever. With the wreck of her frail body, Beth's soul grew strong, and though she said little, those about her felt that she was ready, saw that the first pilgrim called was likewise the fittest, and waited with her on the shore, trying to see the Shining Ones coming to receive her when she crossed the river.

Jo never left her for an hour since Beth had said "I feel stronger when you are here." She slept on a couch in the room, waking often to renew the fire, to feed, lift, or wait upon the patient creature who seldom asked for anything, and 'tried not to be a trouble'. All day she haunted the room, jealous of any other nurse, and prouder of being chosen then than of any honor her life ever brought her. Precious and helpful hours to Jo, for now her heart received the teaching that it needed. Lessons in patience were so sweetly taught her that she could not fail to learn them, charity for all, the lovely spirit that can forgive and truly forget unkindness, the loyalty to duty that makes the hardest easy, and the sincere faith that fears nothing, but trusts undoubtingly.

Often when she woke Jo found Beth reading in her well-worn little book, heard her singing softly, to beguile the sleepless night, or saw her lean her face upon her hands, while slow tears dropped through the transparent fingers, and Jo would lie watching her with thoughts too deep for tears, feeling that Beth, in her simple, unselfish way, was trying to wean herself from the dear old life, and fit herself for the life to come, by sacred words of comfort, quiet prayers, and the music she loved so well.

Seeing this did more for Jo than the wisest sermons, the saintliest hymns, the most fervent prayers that any voice could utter. For with eyes made clear by many tears, and a heart softened by the tenderest sorrow, she recognized the beauty of her sister's life—uneventful, unambitious, yet full of the genuine virtues which 'smell sweet, and blossom in the dust', the self-forgetfulness that makes the humblest on earth remembered soonest in heaven, the true success which is possible to all.

One night when Beth looked among the books upon her table, to find something to make her forget the mortal weariness that was almost as hard to bear as pain, as she turned the leaves of her old favorite, Pilgrims's Progress, she found a little paper, scribbled over in Jo's hand. The name caught her eye and the blurred look of the lines made her sure that tears had fallen on it.

"Poor Jo! She's fast asleep, so I won't wake her to ask leave. She shows me all her things, and I don't think she'll mind if I look at this", thought Beth, with a glance at her sister, who lay on the rug, with the tongs beside her, ready to wake up the minute the log fell apart.

MY BETH

Sitting patient in the shadow Till the blessed light shall come, A serene and saintly presence Sanctifies our troubled home. Earthly joys and hopes and sorrows Break like ripples on the strand Of the deep and solemn river Where her willing feet now stand.

O my sister, passing from me, Out of human care and strife, Leave me, as a gift, those virtues Which have beautified your life. Dear, bequeath me that great patience Which has power to sustain A cheerful, uncomplaining spirit In its prison-house of pain.

Give me, for I need it sorely, Of that courage, wise and sweet, Which has made the path of duty Green beneath your willing feet. Give me that unselfish nature, That with charity devine Can pardon wrong for love's dear sake—Meek heart, forgive me mine!

Thus our parting daily loseth Something of its bitter pain, And while learning this hard lesson, My great loss becomes my gain. For the touch of grief will render My wild nature more serene, Give to life new aspirations, A new trust in the unseen.

Henceforth, safe across the river, I shall see forever more A beloved, household spirit Waiting for me on the shore. Hope and faith, born of my sorrow, Guardian angels shall become, And the sister gone before me By their hands shall lead me home.

Blurred and blotted, faulty and feeble as the lines were, they brought a look of inexpressible comfort to Beth's face, for her one regret had been that she had done so little, and this seemed to assure her that her life had not been useless, that her death would not bring the despair she feared. As she sat with the paper folded between her hands, the charred log fell asunder. Jo started up, revived the blaze, and crept to the bedside, hoping Beth slept.

"Not asleep, but so happy, dear. See, I found this and read it. I knew you wouldn't care. Have I been all that to you, Jo?" she asked, with wistful, humble earnestness.

"OH, Beth, so much, so much!" And Jo's head went down upon the pillow beside her sister's.

"Then I don't feel as if I'd wasted my life. I'm not so good as you make me, but I have tried to do right. And now, when it's too late to begin even to do better, it's such a comfort to know that someone loves me so much, and feels as if I'd helped them."

"More than any one in the world, Beth. I used to think I couldn't let you go, but I'm learning to feel that I don't lose you, that you'll be more to me than ever, and death can't part us, though it seems to."

"I know it cannot, and I don't fear it any longer, for I'm sure I shall be your Beth still, to love and help you more than ever. You must take my place, Jo, and be everything to Father and Mother when I'm gone. They will turn to you, don't fail them, and if it's hard to work alone, remember that I don't forget you, and that you'll be happier in doing that than writing splendid books or seeing all the world, for love is the only thing that we can carry with us when we go, and it makes the go easy."

"I'll try, Beth." And then and there Jo renounced her old ambition, pledged herself to a new and better one, acknowledging the poverty of other desires, and feeling the blessed solace of a belief in the immortality of love.

So the spring days came and went, the sky grew clearer, the earth greener, the flowers were up fairly early, and the birds came back in time to say goodbye to Beth, who, like a tired but trustful child, clung to the hands that had led her all her life, as Father and Mother guided her tenderly through the Valley of the Shadow, and gave her up to God.

Seldom except in books do the dying utter memorable words, see visions, or depart with beatified countenances, and those who have sped many parting souls know that to most the end comes as naturally and simply as sleep. As Beth had hoped, the 'tide went out easily', and in the dark hour before dawn, on the bosom where she had drawn her first breath, she quietly drew her last, with no farewell but one loving look, one little sigh.

With tears and prayers and tender hands, Mother and sisters made her ready for the long sleep that pain would never mar again, seeing with grateful eyes the beautiful serenity that soon replaced the pathetic patience that had wrung their hearts so long, and feeling with reverent joy that to their darling death was a benignant angel, not a phantom full of dread.

When morning came, for the first time in many months the fire was out, Jo's place was empty, and the room was very still. But a bird sang blithely on a budding bough, close by, the snowdrops blossomed freshly at the window, and the spring sunshine streamed in like a benediction over the placid face upon the pillow, a face so full of painless peace that those who loved it best smiled through their tears, and thanked God that Beth was well at last.

Chapter Forty-One

Amy's lecture did Laurie good, though, of course, he did not own it till long afterward. Men seldom do, for when women are the advisers, the lords of creation don't take the advice till they have persuaded themselves that it is just what they intended to do. Then they act upon it, and, if it succeeds, they give the weaker vessel half the credit of it. If it fails, they generously give her the whole. Laurie went back to his grandfather, and was so dutifully devoted for several weeks that the old gentleman declared the climate of Nice had improved him wonderfully, and he had better try it again. There was nothing the young gentleman would have liked better, but elephants could not have dragged him back after the scolding he had received. Pride forbid, and whenever the longing grew very strong, he fortified his resolution by repeating the words that had made the deepest impression, "I despise you." "Go and do something splendid that will make her love you."

Laurie turned the matter over in his mind so often that he soon brought himself to confess that he had been selfish and lazy, but then when a man has a great sorrow, he should be indulged in all sorts of vagaries till he has lived it down. He felt that his blighted affections were quite dead now, and though he should never cease to be a faithful mourner, there was no occasion to wear his weeds ostentatiously. Jo wouldn't love him, but he might make her respect and admire him by doing something which should prove that a girl's no had not spoiled his life. He had always meant to do something, and Amy's advice was quite unnecessary. He had only been waiting till the aforesaid blighted affections were decently interred. That being done, he felt that he was ready to 'hide his stricken heart, and still toil on'.

As Goethe, when he had a joy or a grief, put it into a song, so Laurie resolved to embalm his love sorrow in music, and to compose a Requiem which should harrow up Jo's soul and melt the heart of every hearer. Therefore the next time the old gentleman found him getting restless and moody and ordered him off, he went to Vienna, where he had musical friends, and fell to work with the firm determination to distinguish himself. But whether the sorrow was too vast to be embodied in music, or music too ethereal to uplift a mortal woe, he soon discovered that the Requiem was beyond him just at present. It was evident that his mind was not in working order yet, and his ideas needed clarifying, for often in the middle of a plaintive strain, he would find himself humming a dancing tune that vividly recalled the Christmas ball at Nice, especially the stout Frenchman, and put an effectual stop to tragic composition for the time being.

Then he tried an opera, for nothing seemed impossible in the beginning, but here again unforeseen difficulties beset him. He wanted Jo for his heroine, and called upon his memory to supply him with tender recollections and romantic visions of his love. But memory turned traitor, and as if possessed by the perverse spirit of the girl, would only recall Jo's oddities, faults, and freaks, would only show her in the most unsentimental aspects—beating mats with her head tied up in a bandana, barricading herself with the sofa pillow, or throwing cold water over his passion a la Gummidge—and an irresistable laugh spoiled the pensive picture he was endeavoring to paint. Jo wouldn't be put into the opera at any price, and he had to give her up with a "Bless that girl, what a torment she is!" and a clutch at his hair, as became a distracted composer.

When he looked about him for another and a less intractable damsel to immortalize in melody, memory produced one with the most obliging readiness. This phantom wore many faces, but it always had golden hair, was enveloped in a diaphanous cloud, and floated airily before his mind's eye in a pleasing chaos of roses, peacocks, white ponies, and blue ribbons. He did not give the complacent wraith any name, but he took her for his heroine and grew quite fond of her, as well he might, for he gifted her with every gift and grace under the sun, and escorted her, unscathed, through trials which would have annihilated any mortal woman.

Thanks to this inspiration, he got on swimmingly for a time, but gradually the work lost its charm, and he forgot to compose, while he sat musing, pen in hand, or roamed about the gay city to get some new ideas and refresh his mind, which seemed to be in a somewhat unsettled state that winter. He did not do much, but he thought a great deal and was conscious of a change of some sort going on in spite of himself. "It's genius simmering, perhaps. I'll let it simmer, and see what comes of it," he said, with a secret suspicion all the while that it wasn't genius, but something far more common. Whatever it was, it simmered to some purpose, for he grew more and more discontented with his desultory life, began to long for some real and earnest work to go at, soul and body, and finally came to the wise conclusion that everyone who loved music was not a composer. Returning from one of Mozart's grand operas, splendidly performed at the Royal Theatre, he looked over his own, played a few of the best parts, sat staring at the busts of Mendelssohn, Beethoven, and bach, who stared benignly back again. Then suddenly he tore up his music sheets, one by one, and as the last fluttered out of his hand, he said soberly to himself . . .

"She is right! Talent isn't genius, and you can't make it so. That music has taken the vanity out of my as Rome took it out of her, and I won't be a humbug any longer. Now what shall I do?"

That seemed a hard question to answer, and Laurie began to wish he had to work for his daily bread. Now if ever, occurred an eligible opportunity for 'going to the devil', as he once forcibly expressed it, for he had plenty of money and nothing to do, and Satan is proverbially fond of providing employment for full and idle hands. The poor fellow had temptations enough from without and from within, but he withstood them pretty well, for much as he valued liberty, he valued good faith and confidence more, so his promise to his grandfather, and his desire to be able to look honestly into the eyes of the women who loved him, and say "All's well," kept him safe and steady.

Very likely some Mrs. Grundy will observe, "I don't believe it, boys will be boys, young men must sow their wild oats, and women must not expect miracles." I dare say you don't, Mrs. Grundy, but it's true nevertheless. Women work a good many miracles, and I have a persuasion that they may perform even that of raising the standard of manhood by refusing to echo such sayings. Let the boys be boys, the longer the better, and let the young men sow their wild oats if they must. But mothers, sisters, and friends may help to make the crop a small one, and keep many tares from spoiling the harvest, by believing, and showing that they believe, in the possibility of loyalty to the virtues which make men manliest in good women's eyes. If it is a feminine delusion, leave us to enjoy it while we may, for without it half the beauty and the romance of life is lost, and sorrowful forebodings would embitter all our hopes of the brave, tenderhearted little lads, who still love their mothers better than themselves and are not ashamed to own it.

Laurie thought that the task of forgetting his love for Jo would absorb all his powers for years, but to his great surprise he discovered it grew easier every day. He refused to believe it at first, got angry with himself, and couldn't understand it, but these hearts of ours are curious and contrary things, and time and nature work their will in spite of us. Laurie's heart wouldn't ache. The wound persisted in healing with a rapidity that astonished him, and instead of trying to forget, he found himself trying to remember. He had not foreseen this turn of affairs, and was not prepared for it. He was disgusted with himself, surprised at his own fickleness, and full of a queer mixture of disappointment and relief that he could recover from such a tremendous blow so soon. He carefully stirred up the embers of his lost love, but they refused to burst into a blaze. There was only a comfortable glow that warmed and did him good without putting him into a fever, and he was reluctantly obliged to confess that the boyish passion was slowly subbsiding into a more tranquil sentiment, very tender, a little sad and resentful still, but that was sure to pass away in time, leaving a brotherly affection which would last unbroken to the end.

As the word 'brotherly' passed through his mind in one of his reveries, he smiled, and glanced up at the picture of Mozart that was before him . . .

"Well, he was a great man, and when he couldn't have one sister he took the other, and was happy."

Laurie did not utter the words, but he thought them, and the next instant kissed the little old ring, saying to himself, "No, I won't! I haven't forgotten, I never can. I'll try again, and if that fails, why then . . .

Leaving his sentence unfinished, he seized pen and paper and wrote to Jo, telling her that he could not settle to anything while there was the least hope of her changing her mind. Couldn't she, wouldn't she, and let him come home and be happy? While waiting for an answer he did nothing, but he did it energetically, for he was in a fever of impatience. It came at last, and settled his mind effectually on one point, for Jo decidedly couldn't and wouldn't. She was wrapped up in Beth, and never wished to hear the word love again. Then she begged him to be happy with somebody else, but always keep a little corner of his ghart for his loving sister Jo. In a postscript she desired him not to tell Amy that Beth was worse, she was coming home in the spring and there was no need of saddening the remainder of her stay. That would be time enough, please God, but Laurie must write to her often, and not let her feel lonely, homesick or anxious.

"So I will, at once. Poor little girl, it will be a sad going home for her, I'm afraid." And Laurie opened his desk, as if writing to Amy had been the proper conclusion of the sentence left unfinished some weeks before.

But he did not write the letter that day, for as he rummaged out his best paper, he came across something which changed his purpose. Tumbling about in one part of the desk among bills, passports, and business documents of various kinds were several of Jo's letters, and in another compartment were three notes from Amy, carefully tied up with one of her blue ribbons and sweetly suggestive of the little dead roses put away inside. with a half-repentant, half-amused expression, Laurie gathered up all

Jo's letters, smoothed, folded, and put them neatly into a small drawer of the desk, stood a minute turning the ring thoughtfully on his finger, then slowly drew it off, laid it with the letters, locked the drawer, and went out to hear High Mass at Saint Stefan's, feeling as if there had been a funeral, and though not overwhelmed with affliction, this seemed a more proper way to spend the rest of the day than in writing letters to charming young ladies.

The letter went very soon, however, and was promptly answered, for Amy was homesick, and confessed it in the most delightfully confiding manner. The correspondence flourished famously, and letters flew to and fro with unfailing regularity all through the early spring. Laurie sold his busts, made allumettes of his opera, and went back to Paris, hoping somebody would arrive before long. He wanted desperately to go to Nice, but would not till he was asked, and Amy would not ask him, for just then she was having little experiences of her own, which made her rather wish to avoid the quizzical eyes of 'out boy'.

Fred Vaughn had returned, and put the question to which she had once decided to answer, "Yes, thank you," but now she said, "No, thank you," kindly but steadily, for when the time came, her courage failed her, and she found that something more than money and position was needed to satisfy the new longing that filled her heart so full of tender hopes and fears. The words, "Fred is a good fellow, but not at all the man I fancied you would ever like," and Laurie's face when he uttered them, kept returning to her as pertinaciously as her own did when she said in look, if not in words, "I shall marry for money." It troubled her to remember that now, she wished she could take it back, it sounded so unwomanly. She didn't want Laurie to think her a heartless, worldly creature. She didn't care to be a queen of society now half so much as she did to be a lovable woman. She was so glad he didn't hate her for the dreadful things she said, but took them so beautifully and was kinder than ever. His letters were such a comfort, for the home letters were very irregular and not half so satisfactory as his when they did come. It was not only a pleasure, but a duty to answer them, for the poor fellow was forlorn, and needed petting, since Jo persisted in being stonyhearted. She ought to have made an effort and tried to love him. It couldn't be very hard, many people would be proud and glad to have such a dear boy care for them. But Jo never would act like other girls, so there was nothing to do but be very kind and treat him like a brother.

If all brothers were treated as well as Laurie was at this period, they would be a much happier race of beings than they are. Amy never lectured now. She asked his opinion on all subjects, she was interested in everything he did, made charming little presents for him, and sent him two letters a week, full of lively gossip, sisterly confidences, and captivating sketches of the lovely scenes about her. As few brothers are complimented by having their letters carried about in their sister's pockets, read and reread diligently, cried over when short, kissed when long, and treasured carefully, we will not hint that Amy did any of these fond and foolish things. But she certainly did grow a little pale and pensive that spring, lost much of her relish for society, and went out sketching alone a good deal. She never had much to show when she came home, but was studying nature, I dare say, while she sat for hours, with her hands folded, on the terrace at Valrosa, or absently sketched any fancy that occurred to her, a stalwart knight carved on a tomb, a young man asleep in the grass, with his hat over his eyes, or a curly haired girl in gorgeous array, promenading down a ballroom on the arm of a tall gentleman, both faces being left a blur according to the last fashion in art, which was safe but not altogether satisfactory.

Her aunt thought that she regretted her answer to Fred, and finding denials useless and explanations impossible, Amy left her to think what she liked, taking care that Laurie should know that Fred had gone to Egypt. That was all, but he understood it, and looked relieved, as he said to himself, with a venerable air . . .

"I was sure she would think better of it. Poor old fellow! I've been through it all, and I can sympathize."

With that he heaved a great sigh, and then, as if he had discharged his duty to the past, put his feet up on the sofa and enjoyed Amy's letter luxuriously.

While these changes were going on abroad, trouble had come at home. But the letter telling that Beth was failing never reached Amy, and when the next found her at Vevay, for the heat had driven them from Nice in May, and they had travelled slowly to Switzerland, by way of Genoa and the Italian lakes. She bore it very well, and quietly submitted to the family decree that she should nôt shorten her visit, for since it was too late to say goodbye to Beth, she had better stay, and let absence soften her sorrow. But her heart was very heavy, she longed to be at home, and every day looked wistfully across the lake, waiting for Laurie to come and comfort her.

He did come very soon, for the same mail brought letters to them both, but he was in Germany, and it took some days to reach him. The moment he read it, he packed his knapsack, bade adieu to his fellow pedestrians, and was off to keep his promise, with a heart full of joy and sorrow, hope and suspense.

He knew Vevay well, and as soon as the boat touched the little quay, he hurried along the shore to La Tour, where the Carrols were living en pension. The garcon was in despair that the whole family had gone to take a promenade on the lake, but no, the blonde mademoiselle might be in the chateau garden. If monsier would give himself the pain of sitting down, a flash of time should present her. But monsieur could not wait even a 'flash of time', and in the middle of the speech departed to find mademoiselle himself.

A pleasant old garden on the borders of the lovely lake, with chestnuts rustling overhead, ivy climbing everywhere, and the black shadow of the tower falling far across the sunny water. At one corner of the wide, low wall was a seat, and here Amy often came to read or work, or console herself with the beauty all about her. She was sitting here that day, leaning her head on her hand, with a homesick heart and heavy eyes, thinking of Beth and wondering why Laurie did not come. She did not hear him cross the courtyard beyond, nor see him pause in the archway that led from the subterranean path into the garden. He stood a minute looking at her with new eyes, seeing what no one had ever seen before, the tender side of Amy's character. Everything about her mutely suggested love and sorrow, the blotted letters in her lap, the black ribbon that tied up her hair, the womanly pain and patience in her face, even the little ebony cross at her throat seemed pathetic to Laurie, for he had given it to her, and she wore it as her only ornament. If he had any doubts about the reception she would give him, they were set at rest the minute she looked up and saw him, for dropping everything, she ran to him, exclaiming in a tone of unmistakable love and longing . . .

"Oh, Laurie, Laurie, I knew you'd come to me!"

I think everything was said and settled then, for as they stood together quite silent for a moment, with the dark head bent down protectingly over the light one, Amy felt that no one could comfort and sustain her so well as Laurie, and Laurie decided that Amy was the only woman in the world who could fill Jo's place and make him happy. He did not tell her so, but she was not disappointed, for both felt the truth, were satisfied, and gladly left the rest to silence.

In a minute Amy went back to her place, and while she dried her tears, Laurie gathered up the scattered papers, finding in the sight of sundry well-worn letters and suggestive sketches good omens for the future. As he sat down beside her, amy felt shy again, and turned rosy red at the recollection of her impulsive greeting.

"I couldn't help it, I felt so lonely and sad, and was so very glad to see you. It was such a surprise to look up and find you, just as I was beginning to fear you wouldn't come," she said, trying in vain to speak quite naturally.

"I came the minute I heard. I wish I could say something to comfort you for the loss of dear little Beth, but I can only feel, and . . ." He could not get any further, for her too turned bashful all of a sudden, and did not quite know what to say. He longed to lay Amy's head down on his shoulder, and tell her to have a good cry, but he did not dare, so took her hand instead, and gave it a sympathetic squeeze that was better than words.

"You needn't say anything, this comforts me," she said softly. "Beth is well and happy, and I mustn't wish her back, but I dread the going home, much as I long to see them all. We won't talk about it now, for it makes me cry, and I want to enjoy you while you stay. You needn't go right back, need you?"

"Not if you want me, dear."

"I do, so much. Aunt and Flo are very kind, but you seem like one of the family, and it would be so comfortable to have you for a little while."

Amy spoke and looked so like a homesick child whose heart was full that Laurie forgot his bashfulness all at once, and gave her just what she wanted—the petting she was used to and the cheerful conversation she needed.

"Poor little soul, you look as if you'd grieved yourself half sick! I'm going to take care of you, so don't cry any more, but come and walk about with me, the wind is too chilly for you to sit still," he said, in the half-caressing, half-commanding way that Amy liked, as he tied on her hat, drew her arm through his, and began to pace up and down the sunny walk under the new-leaved chestnuts. He felt more at ease upon his legs, and Amy found it pleasant to have a strong arm to lean upon, a familiar face to smile at her, and a kind voice to talk delightfully for her alone.

The quaint old garden had sheltered many pairs of lovers, and seemed expressly made for them, so sunny and secluded was it, with nothing but the tower to overlook them, and the wide lake to carry away the echo of their words, as it rippled by below. For an hour this new pair walked and talked, or rested on the wall, enjoying the sweet influences which gave such a charm to time and place, and when an unromantic dinner bell warned them away, Amy felt as if she left her burden of lonliness and sorrow behind her in the chateau garden.

The moment Mrs. Carrol saw the girl's altered face, she was illuminated with a new idea, and exclaimed to herself, "Now I understand it all—the child has been pining for young Laurence. Bless my heart, I never thought of such a thing!"

With praiseworthy discretion, the good lady said nothing, and betrayed no sign of enlightenment, but cordially urged Laurie to stay and begged Amy to enjoy his society, for it would do her more good than so much solitude. Amy was a model of docility, and as her aunt was a good deal occupied with Flo, she was left to entertain her friend, and did it with more than her usual success.

At Nice, Laurie had lounged and Amy had scolded. At Vevay, Laurie was never idle, but always walking, riding, boating, or studying in the most energetic manner, while Amy admired everything he did and followed his example as far and as fast as she could. He said the change was owing to the climate, and she did not contradict him, being glad of a like excuse for her own recovered health and spirits.

The invigorating air did them both good, and much exercise worked wholesome changes in minds as well as bodies. They seemed to get clearer views of life and duty up there among the everlasting hills. The fresh winds blew away desponding doubts, delusive fancies, and moody mists. The warm spring sunshine brought out all sorts of aspiring ideas, tender hopes, and happy thoughts. The lake seemed to wash away the troubles of the past, and the grand old mountains to look benignly down upon them saying, "Little children, love one another."

In spite of the new sorrow, it was a very happy time, so happy that Laurie could not bear to disturb it by a word. It took him a little while to recover from his surprise at the cure of his first, and as he had firmly believed, his last and only love. He consoled himself for the seeming disloyalty by the thought that Jo's sister was almost the same as Jo's self, and the conviction that it would have been impossible to love any other woman but Amy so soon and so well. His first wooing had been of the tempestuous order, and he looked back upon ;it as if through a long vista of years with a feeling of compassion blended with regret. He was not ashamed of it, but put it away as one of the bittersweet experiences of his life, for which he could be grateful when the pain was over. His second wooing, he resolved, should be as calm and simple as possible. There was no need of having a scene, hardly any need of telling Amy that he loved her, she knew it without words and had given him his answer long ago. It all came about so naturally that no one could complain, and he knew that everybody would be pleased, even Jo. But when our first little passion has been crushed, we are apt to be wary and slow in making a second trial, so Laurie let the days pass, enjoying every hour, and leaving to chance the utterance of the word that would put an end to the first and sweetest part of his new romance.

He had rather imagined that the denoument would take place in the chateau garden by moonlight, and in the most graceful and decorus manner, but it turned out exactly the reverse, for the matter was settled on the lake at noonday in a few blunt words. They had been floating about all the morning, from gloomy St. Gingolf to sunny Montreux, with the Alps of

Savoy on one side, Mont St. Bernard and the Dent du Midi on the other, pretty Vevay in the valley, and Lausanne upon the hill beyond, a cloudless blue sky overhead, and the bluer lake below, dotted with the picturesque boats that look like white-winged gulls.

They had been talking of Bonnivard, as they glided past Chillon, and of Rousseau, as they looked up at Clarens, where he wrote his Heloise. Neither had read it, but they knew it was a love story, and each privately wondered if it was half as interesting as their own. Amy had been dabbling her hand in the water during the little pause that fell between them, and when she looked up, Laurie was leaning on his oars with an expression in his eyes that made her say hastily, merely for the sake of saying something.

"You must be tired. Rest a little, and let me row. It will do me good, for since you came I have been altogether lazy and luxurious."

"I'm not tired, but you may take an oar, if you like. There's room enough, though I have to sit nearly in the middle, else the boat won't trim," returned Laurie, as if he rather liked the arrangment.

Feeling that she had not mended matters much, Amy took the offered third of a seat, shook her hair over her face, and accepted an oar. She rowed as well as she did many other things, and though she used both hands, and Laurie but one, the oars kept time, and the boat went smoothly through the water.

"How well we pull together, don't we?" said Amy, who objected to silence just then.

"So well that I wish we might always pull in the same boat. Will you, Amy?" very tenderly.

"Yes, Laurie," very low.

Then they both stopped rowing, and unconsciously added a pretty little tableau of human love and happiness to the dissolving views reflected in the lake.

Chapter Forty-Two

It was easy to promise self-abnegation when self was wrapped up in another, and heart and soul were purified by a sweet example. But when the helpful voice was silent, the daily lesson over, the beloved presence gone, and nothing remained but lonliness and grief, then Jo found her promise very hard to keep. How could she 'comfort Father and Mother' when her own heart ached with a ceaseless longing for her sister, how could she 'make the house cheerful' when all its light and warmth and beauty seemed to have deserted it when Beth left the old home for the new, and where in all the world could she 'find some useful, happy work to do', that would take the place of the loving service which had been its own reward? She tried in a blind, hopeless way to do her duty, secretly rebelling against it all the while, for it seemed unjust that her few joys should be lessened, her burdens made heavier, and life get harder and harder as she toiled along. Some people seemed to get all sunshine, and some all shadow. It was not fair, for she tried more than Amy to be good, but never got any reward, only disappointment, trouble and hard work.

Poor Jo, these were dark days to her, for something like despair came over her when she thought of spending all her life in that quiet house, devoted to humdrum cares, a few small pleasures, and the duty that never seemed to grow any easier. "I can't do it. I wasn't meant for a life like this, and I know I shall break away and do something desperate if somebody doesn't come and help me," she said to herself, when her first efforts failed and she fell into the moody, miserable state of mind which often comes when strong wills have to yield to the inevitable.

But someone did come and help her, though Jo did not recognize her good angels at once because they wore familiar shapes and used the simple spells best fitted to poor humanity. Often she started up at night, thinking Beth called her, and when the sight of the little empty bed made her cry with the bitter cry of unsubmissive sorrow, "Oh, Beth, come back! Come back!" she did not stretch out her yearning arms in vain. For, as quick to hear her sobbing as she had been to hear her sister's faintest whisper, her mother came to comfort her, not with words only, but the patient tenderness that soothes by a touch, tears that were mute reminders of a greater grief than Jo's, and broken whispers, more eloquent than prayers, because hopeful resignation went hand-in-hand with natural sorrow. Sacred moments, when heart talked to heart in the silence of the night, turning affliction to a blessing, which chastened grief and strengthned love. Feeling this, Jo's burden seemed easier to bear, duty grew sweeter, and life looked more endurable, seen from the safe shelter of her mother's arms.

When aching heart was a little comforted, troubled mind likewise found help, for one day she went to the study, and leaning over the good gray head lifted to welcome her with a tranquil smile, she said very humbly, "Father, talk to me as you did to Beth. I need it more than she did, for I'm all wrong."

"My dear, nothing can comfort me like this," he answered, with a falter in his voice, and both arms round her, as if he too, needed help, and did not fear to ask for it.

Then, sitting in Beth's little chair close beside him, Jo told her troubles, the resentful sorrow for her loss, the fruitless efforts that discouraged her, the want of faith that made life look so dark, and all the sad bewilderment which we call despair. She gave him entire confidence, he gave her the help she needed, and both found consolation in the act. For the time had come when they could talk together not only as father and daughter, but as man and woman, able and glad to serve each other with mutual sympathy as well as mutual love. Happy, thoughtful times there in the old study which Jo called 'the church of one member', and from which she came with fresh courage, recovered cheerfulness, and a more submissive spirit. For the parents who had taught one child to meet death without fear, were trying now to teach another to accept life without despondency or distrust, and to use its beautiful opportunities with gratitude and power.

Other helps had Jo—humble, wholesome duties and delights that would not be denied their part in serving her, and which she slowly learned to see and value. Brooms and dishcloths never could be as distasteful as they once had been, for Beth had presided over both, and something of her housewifely spirit seemed to linger around the little mop and the old brush, never thrown away. As she used them, Jo found herself humming the songs Beth used to hum, imitating Beth's orderly ways, and giving the little touches here and there that kept everything fresh and cozy, which was the first step toward making home happy, though she didn't know it till Hannah said with an approving squeeze of the hand . . .

"You thoughtful creeter, you're determined we shan't miss that dear lamb ef you can help it. We don't say much, but we see it, and the Lord will bless you for't, see ef He don't."

As they sat sewing together, Jo discovered how much improved her sister Meg was, how well she could talk, how much she knew about good, womanly impulses, thoughts, and feelings, how happy she was in husband and children, and how much they were all doing for each other.

"Marriage is an excellent thing, after all. I wonder if I should blossom out half as well as you have, if I tried it?" said Jo, as she constructed a kite for Demi in the topsy-turvy nursery.

"It's just what you need to bring out the tender womanly half of your nature, Jo. You are like a chestnut burr, prickly outside, but silky-soft within, and a sweet kernal, if one can only get at it. Love will make you show your heart one day, and then the rough burr will fall off."

"Frost opens chestnut burrs, ma'am, and it takes a good shake to bring them down. Boys go nutting, and I don't care to be bagged by them," returned Jo, pasting away at the kite which no wind that blows would ever carry up, for Daisy had tied herself on as a bob.

Meg laughed, for she was glad to see a glimmer of Jo's old spirit, but she felt it her duty to enforce her opinion by every argument in her power, and the sisterly chats were not wasted, especially as two of Meg's most effective arguments were the babies, whom Jo loved tenderly. Grief is the best opener of some hearts, and Jo's was nearly ready for the bag. A little more sunshine to ripen the nut, then, not a boy's impatient shake, but a man's hand reached up to pick it gently from the burr, and find the kernal sound and sweet. If she suspected this, she would have shut up tight, and been more prickly than ever, fortunately she wasn't thinking about herself, so when the time came, down she dropped.

Now, if she had been the heroine of a moral storybook, she ought at this period of her life to have become quite saintly, renounced the world, and gone about doing good in a mortified bonnet, with tracts in her pocket. But, you see, Jo wasn't a heroine, she was only a struggling human girl like hundreds of others, and she just acted out her nature, being sad, cross, listless, or energetic, as the mood suggested. It's highly virtuous to say we'll be good, but we can't do it all at once, and it takes a long pull, a strong pull, and a pull all together before some of us even get our feet set in the right way. Jo had got so far, she was learning to do her duty, and to feel unhappy if she did not, but to do it cheerfully, ah, that was another thing! She had often said she wanted to do something splendid, no matter how hard, and now she had her wish, for what could be more beautiful than to devote her life to Father and Mother, trying to make home as happy to them as they had to her? And if difficulties were necessary to increase the splendor of the effort, what could be harder for a restless, ambitious girl than to give up her own hopes, plans, and desires, and cheerfully live for others?

Providence had taken her at her word. Here was the task, not what she had expected, but better because self had no part in it. Now, could she do it? She decided that she would try, and in her first attempt she found the helps I have suggested. Still another was given her, and she took it, not as a reward, but as a comfort, as Christian took the refreshment afforded by the little arbor where he rested, as he climbed the hill called Difficulty.

"Why don't you write? That always used to make you happy," said her mother once, when the desponding fit overshadowed Jo.

"I've no heart to write, and if I had, nobody cares for my things."

"We do. Write something for us, and never mind the rest of the world. Try it, dear. I'm sure it would do you good, and please us very much."

"Don't believe I can." But Jo got out her desk and began to overhaul her half-finished manuscripts.

An hour afterward her mother peeped in and there she was, scratching away, with her black pinafore on, and an absorbed expression, which caused Mrs. March to smile and slip away, well pleased with the success of her suggestion. Jo never knew how it happened, but something got into that story that went straight to the hearts of those who read it, for when her family had laughed and cried over it, her father sent it, much against her will, to one of the popular magazines, and to her utter surprise, it was not only paid for, but others requested. Letters from several persons, whose praise was honor, followed the appearance of the little story, newspapers copied it, and strangers as well as friends, admired it. For a small thing it was a great success, and Jo was more astonished than when her novel was commended and condemned all at once.

"I don't understand it. What can there be in a simple little story like that to make people praise it so?" she said, quite bewildered.

"There is truth in it, Jo, that's the secret. Humor and pathos make it alive, and you have found your style at last. You wrote with not thoughts of fame and money, and put your heart into it, my daughter. You have had the bitter, now comes the sweet. Do your best, and grow as happy as we are in your success."

"If there is anything good or true in what I write, it isn't mine. I owe it all to you and Mother and Beth," said Jo, more touched by her father's words than by any amount of praise from the world.

So taught by love and sorrow, Jo wrote her little stories, and sent them away to make friends for themselves and her, finding it a very charitable world to such humble wanderers, for they were kindly welcomed, and sent home comfortable tokens to their mother, like dutiful children whom good fortune overtakes.

When Amy and Laurie wrote of their engagement, Mrs. March feared that Jo would find it difficult to rejoice over it, but her fears were soon set at rest, for thought Jo looked grave at first, she took it very quietly, and was full of hopes and plans for 'the children' before she read the letter twice. It was a sort of written duet, wherein each glorified the other in loverlike fashion, very pleasant to read and satisfactory to think of, for no one had any objection to make.

"You like it, Mother?" said Jo, as they laid down the closely written sheets and looked at one another.

"Yes, I hoped it would be so, ever since Amy wrote that she had refused Fred. I felt sure then that something better than what you call the 'mercenary spirit' had come over her, and a hint here and there in her letters made me suspect that love and Laurie would win the day."

"How sharp you are, Marmee, and how silent! You never said a worked to me."

"Mothers have need of sharp eyes and discreet tongues when they have girls to manage. I was half afraid to put the idea into your head, lest you should write and congratulate them before the thing was settled."

"I'm not the scatterbrain I was. You may trust me. I'm sober and sensible enough for anyone's confidante now."

"So you are, my dear, and I should have made you mine, only I fancied it might pain you to learn that your Teddy loved someone else."

"Now, Mother, did you really think I could be so silly and selfish, after I'd refused his love, when it was freshest, if not best?"

"I knew you were sincere then, Jo, but lately I have thought that if he came back, and asked again, you might perhaps, feel like giving another answer. Forgive me, dear, I can't help seeing that you are very lonely, and sometimes there is a hungry look in your eyes that goes to my heart. So I fancied that your boy might fill the empty place if he tried now."

"No, Mother, it is better as it ia, and I'm glad Amy has learned to love him. But you are right in one thing. I am lonely, and perhaps if Teddy had tried again, I might have said 'Yes', not because I love him any more, but because I care more to be loved than when he went away."

"I'm glad of that, Jo, for it shows that you are getting on. There are plenty to love you, so try to be satisfied with Father and Mother, sisters and brothers, friends and babies, till the best lover of all comes to give you your reward."

"Mothers are the best lovers in the world, but I don't mind whispering to Marmee that I'd like to try all kinds. It's very curious, but the more I try to satisfy myself with all sorts of natural affections, the more I seem to want. I'd no idea hearts could take in so many. Mine is so elastic, it never seems full now, and I used to be quite contented with my family. I don't understand it."

"I do." And Mrs. March smiled her wise smile, as Jo turned back the leaves to read what Amy said of Laurie.

"It is so beautiful to be loved as Laurie loves me. He isn't sentimental, doesn't say much about it, but I see and feel it in all he says and does, and it makes me so happy and so humble that I don't seem to be the same girl I was. I never knew how good and generous and tender he was till now, for he lets me read his heart, and I find it full of noble impulses and hopes and purposes, and am so proud to know it's mine. He says he feels as if he 'could make a prosperous voyage now with me aboard as mate, and lots of love for ballast'. I pray he may, and try to be all he believes me, for I love my gallant captain with all my heart and soul and might, and never will desert him, while God lets us be together. Oh, Mother, I never knew how much like heaven this world could be, when two people love and live for one another!"

"And that's our cool, reserved, and worldly Amy! Truly, love does work miracles. How very, very happy they must be!" And Jo laid the rustling sheets together with a careful hand, as one might shut the covers of a lovely romance, which holds the reader fast till the end comes, and he finds himself alone in the workaday world again.

By-and-by Jo roamed away upstairs, for it was rainy, and she could not walk. A restless spirit possessed her, and the old feeling came again, not bitter as it once was, but a sorrowfully patient wonder why one sister should have all she asked, the other nothing. It was not true, she knew that and tried to put it away, but the natural craving for affection was strong, and Amy's happiness woke the hungry longing for someone to 'love with heart and soul, and cling to while God let them be together'. Up in the garret, where Jo's unquiet wanderings ended stood four little wooden chests in a row, each marked with its owners name, and each filled with relics of the childhood and girlhood ended now for all. Jo glanced into them, and when she came to her own, leaned her chin on the edge, and stared absently at the chaotic collection, till a bundle of old exercise books caught her eye. She drew them out, turned them over, and relived that pleasant winter at kind Mrs. Kirke's. She had smiled at first, then she looked thoughtful, next sad, and when she came to a little message written in the Professor's hand, her lips began to tremble, the books slid out of her lap, and she sat looking at the friendly words, as they took a new meaning, and touched a tender spot in her heart.

"Wait for me, my friend. I may be a little late, but I shall surely come."

"Oh, if he only would! So kine, so good, so patient with me always, my dear old Fritz. I didn't value him half enough when I had him, but now how I should love to see him, for everyone seems going away from me, and I'm all alone."

And holding the little paper fast, as if it were a promise yet to be fulfilled, Jo laid her head down on a comfortable rag bag, and cried, as if in opposition to the rain pattering on the roof.

Was it all self-pity, loneliness, or low spirits? Or was it the waking up of a sentiment which had bided its time as patiently as its inspirer? Who shall say?

Chapter Forty-Three

Jo was alone in the twilight, lying on the old sofa, looking at the fire, and thinking. It was her favorite way of spending the hour of dusk. No one disturbed her, and she used to lie there on Beth's little red pillow, planning stories, dreaming dreams, or thinking tender thoughts of the sister who never seemed far away. Her face looked tired, grave, and rather sad, for tomorrow was her birthday, and she was thinking how fast the years went by, how old she was getting, and how little she seemed to have accomplished. Almost twenty-five, and nothing to show for it. Jo was mistaken in that. There was a good deal to show, and by-and-by she saw, and was grateful for it.

"An old maid, that's what I'm to be. A literary spinster, with a pen for a spouse, a family of stories for children, and twenty years hence a morsel of fame, perhaps, when, like poor Johnson, I'm old and can't enjoy it, solitary, and can't share it, independent, and don't need it. Well, I needn't be a sour saint nor a selfish sinner, and, I dare say, old maids are very comfortable when they get used to it, but . . ." And there Jo sighed, as if the prospect was not inviting.

It seldom is, at first, and thirty seems the end of all things to five-and-twenty. But it's not as bad as it looks, and one can get on quite happily if one has something in one's self to fall back upon. At twenty-five, girls begin to talk about being old maids, but secretly resolve that they never will be. At thirty they say nothing about it, but quietly accept the fact, and if sensible, console themselves by remembering that they have twenty more useful, happy years, in which they may be learning to grow old gracefully. Don't laugh at the spinsters, dear girls, for often very tender, tragic romances are hidden away in the hearts that beat so quietly under the sober gowns, and many silent sacrifices of youth, health, ambition, love itself, make the faded faces beautiful in God's sight. Even the sad, sour sisters should be kindly dealt with, because they have missed the sweetest part of life, if for no other reason. And looking at them with compassion, not contempt, girls in their bloom should remember that they too may miss the blossom time. That rosy cheeks don't last forever, that silver threads will come in the bonnie brown hair, and that, by-and-by, kindness and respect will be as sweet as love and admiration now.

Gentlemen, which means boys, be courteous to the old maids, no matter how poor and plain and prim, for the only chivalry worth having is that which is the readiest to pay deference to the old, protect the feeble, and serve womankind, regardless of rank, age, or color. Just recollect the good aunts who have not only lectured and fussed, but nursed and petted, too often without thanks, the scrapes they have helped you out of, the tips they have given you from their small store, the stitches the patient old fingers have set for you, the steps the willing old feet have taken, and gratefully pay the dear old ladies the little attentions that women love to receive as long as they live. The bright-eyed girls are quick to see such traits, and will like you all the better for them, and if death, almost the only power that can part mother and son, should rob you of yours, you will be sure to find a tender welcome and maternal cherishing from some Aunt Priscilla, who has kept the warmest corner of her lonely old heart for 'the best nevvy in the world'.

Jo must have fallen asleep (as I dare say my reader has during this little homily), for suddenly Laurie's ghost seemed to stand before her, a substantial, lifelike ghost, leaning over her with the very look he used to wear when he felt a good deal and didn't like to show it. But, like Jenny in the ballad . . .

She could not think it he,

and lay staring up at him in startled silence, till he stooped and kissed her. Then she knew him, and flew up, crying joyfully . . .

"Oh my Teddy! Oh my Teddy!"

"Dear Jo, you are glad to see me, then?"

"Glad! My blessed boy, words can't express my gladness. Where's Amy?" "Your mother has got her down at Meg's. We stopped there by the way, and there was no getting my wife out of their clutches."

"Your what?" cried Jo, for Laurie uttered those two words with an unconscious pride and satisfaction which betrayed him.

"Oh, the dickens! Now I've done it." And he looked so guilty that Jo was down on him like a flash.

"You've gone and got married!"

"Yes, please, but I never will again." And he went down upon his knees, with a penitent clasping of hands, and a face full of mischief, mirth, and triumph.

"Actually married?"

"Very much so, thank you."

"Mercy on us. What dreadful thing will you do next?" And Jo fell into her seat with a gasp.

"A characteristic, but not exactly complimentary, congratulation," returned Laurie, still in an abject attitude, but beaming with satisfaction.

"What can you expect, when you take one's breath away, creeping in like a burglar, and letting cats out of bags like that? Get up, you ridiculous boy, and tell me all about it."

"Not a word, unless you let me come in my old place, and promise not to barricade."

Jo laughed at that as she had not done for many a long day, and patted the sofa invitingly, as she said in a cordial tone, "The old pillow is up garret, and we don't need it now. So, come and fess, Teddy."

"How good it sounds to hear you say 'Teddy'! No one ever calls me that but you." And Laurie sat down with an air of great content.

"What does Amy call you?"

"My lord."

"That's like her. Well, you look it." And Jo's eye plainly betrayed that she found her boy comelier than ever.

The pillow was gone, but there was a barricade, nevertheless, a natural one, raised by time absence, and change of heart. Both felt it, and for a minute looked at one another as if that invisible barrier cast a little shadow over them. It was gone directly however, for Laurie said, with a vain attempt at dignity . . .

"Don't I look like a married man and the head of a family?"
"Not a bit, and you never will. You've grown bigger and bonnier, but you are the same scapegrace as ever."

"Now really, Jo, you ought to treat me with more respect," began Laurie, who enjoyed it all immensely.

"How can I, when the mere idea of you, married and settled, is so irresistibly funny that I can't keep sober!" answered Jo, smiling all over her face, so infectiously that they had another laugh, and then settled down for a good talk, quite in the pleasant old fashion.

"It's no use your going out in the cold to get Amy, for they are all coming up presently. I couldn't wait. I wanted to be the one to tell you the grand surprise, and have 'first skim' as we used to say when we squabbled about the cream."

"Of course you did, and spoiled your story by beginning at the wrong end. Now, start right, and tell me how it all happened. I'm pining to know."

"Well, I did it to please Amy," began Laurie, with a twinkle that made Jo exclaim . . .

"Fib number one. Amy did it to please you. Go on, and tell the truth, if you can, sir."

"Now she's beginning to marm it. Isn't it jolly to hear her?" said Laurie to the fire, and the fire glowed and sparkled as if it quite agreed. "It's all the same, you know, she and I being one. We planned to come home with the Carrols, a month or more ago, but they suddenly changed their minds, and decided to pass another winter in Paris. But Grandpa wanted to come home. He went to please me, and I couldn't let him go along, neither could I leave Amy, and Mrs. Carrol had got English notions about chaperons and such nonsense, and wouldn't let Amy come with us. So I just settled the difficulty by saying, 'Let's be married, and then we can do as we like.'"

"Of course you did. You always have things to suit you."

"Not always." And something in Laurie's voice made Jo say hastily . . .

"How did you ever get Aunt to agree?"

"It was hard work, but between us, we talked her over, for we had heaps of good reasons on our side. There wasn't time to write and ask leave, but you all liked it, had consented to it by-and-by, and it was only 'taking time by the fetlock', as my wife says."

"Aren't we proud of those two word, and don't we like to say them?" interrupted Jo, addressing the fire in her turn, and watching with delight the happy light it seemed to kindle in the eyes that had been so tragically gloomy when she saw them last. "A trifle, perhaps, she's such a captivating little woman I can't help being proud of her. Well, then Uncle and Aunt were there to play propriety. We were so absorbed in one another we were of no mortal use apart, and that charming arrangement would make everything easy all round, so we did it."

"When, where, how?" asked Jo, in a fever of feminine interest and curiosity, for she could not realize it a particle.

"Six weeks ago, at the American consul's, in Paris, a very quiet wedding of course, for even in our happiness we didn't forget dear little Beth."

Jo put her hand in his as he said that, and Laurie gently smoothed the little red pillow, which he remembered well.

"Why didn't you let us know afterward?" asked Jo, in a quieter tone, when they had sat quite still a minute.

"We wanted to surprise you. We thought we were coming directly home, at first, but the dear old gentleman, as soon as we were married, found he couldn't be ready under a month, at least, and sent us off to spend our honeymoon wherever we liked. Amy had once called Valrosa a regular honeymoon home, so we went there, and were as happy as people are but once in their lives. My faith! Wasn't it love among the roses!"

Laurie seemed to forget Jo for a minute, and Jo was glad of it, for the fact that he told her these things so freely and so naturally assured her that he had quite forgiven and forgotten. She tried to draw away her hand, but as if he guessed the thought that prompted the half-involuntary impulse, Laurie held it fast, and said, with a manly gravity she had never seen in him before . . .

"Jo, dear, I want to say one thing, and then we'll put it by forever. As I told you in my letter when I wrote that Amy had been so kind to me, I never shall stop loving you, but the love is altered, and I have learned to see that it is better as it is. Amy and you changed places in my heart, that's all. I think it was meant to be so, and would have come about naturally, if I had waited, as you tried to make me, but I never could be patient, and so I got a heartache. I was a boy then, headstrong and violent, and it took a hard lesson to show me my mistake. For it was one, Jo, as you said, and I found it out, after making a fool of myself. Upon my word, I was so tumbled up in my mind, at one time, that I didn't know which I loved best, you or Amy, and tried to love you both alike. But I couldn't, and when I saw her in Switzerland, everything seemed to clear up all at once. You both got into your right places, and I felt sure that it was well off with the old love before it was on with the new, that I could honestly share my heart between sister Jo and wife Amy, and love them dearly. Will you believe it, and go back to the happy old times when we first knew one another?"

"I'll believe it, with all my heart, but, Teddy, we never can be boy and girl again. The happy old times can't come back, and we mustn't expect it. We are man and woman now, with sober work to do, for playtime is over, and we must give up frolicking. I'm sure you feel this. I see the change in you, and you'll find it in me. I shall miss my boy, but I shall love the man as much, and admire him more, because he means to be what I hoped he would. We can't be little playmates any longer, but we will be brother and sister, to love and help one another all our lives, won't we, Laurie?"

He did not say a word, but took the hand she offered him, and laid his face down on it for a minute, feeling that out of the grave of a boyish passion, there had risen a beautiful, strong friendship to bless them both. Presently Jo said cheerfully, for she didn't the coming home to be a sad one, "I can't make it true that you children are really married and going to set up housekeeping. Why, it seems only yesterday that I was buttoning Amy's pinafore, and pulling your hair when you teased. Mercy me, how time does fly!"

"As one of the children is older than yourself, you needn't talk so like a grandma. I flatter myself I'm a 'gentleman growed' as Peggotty said of David, and when you see Amy, you'll find her rather a precocious infant," said Laurie, looking amused at her maternal air.

"You may be a little older in years, but I'm ever so much older in feeling, Teddy. Women always are, and this last year has been such a hard one that I feel forty."

"Poor Jo! We left you to bear it alone, while we went pleasuring. You are older. Here's a line, and there's another. Unless you smile, your eyes look sad, and when I touched the cushion, just now, I found a tear on it. You've had a great deal to bear, and had to bear it all alone. What a selfish beast I've been!" And Laurie pulled his own hair, with a remorseful look.

But Jo only turned over the traitorous pillow, and answered, in a tone which she tried to make more cheerful, "No, I had Father and Mother to help me, and the dear babies to comfort me, and the thought that you and Amy were safe and happy, to make the troubles here easier to bear. I am lonely, sometimes, but I dare say it's good for me, and . . ."

"You never shall be again," broke in Laurie, putting his arm about her, as if to fence out every human ill. "Amy and I can't get on without you, so you must come and teach 'the children' to keep house, and go halves in everything, just as we used to do, and let us pet you, and all be blissfully happy and friendly together."

"If I shouldn't be in the way, it would be very pleasant. I begin to feel quite young already, for somehow all my troubles seemed to fly away when you came. You always were a comfort,

Teddy." And Jo leaned her head on his shoulder, just as she did years ago, when Beth lay ill and Laurie told her to hold on to him.

He looked down at her, wondering if she remembered the time, but Jo was smiling to herself, as if in truth her troubles had all vanished at his coming.

"You are the same Jo still, dropping tears about one minute, and laughing the next. You look a little wicked now. What is it, Grandma?"

"I was wondering how you and Amy get on together."

"Like angels!"

"Yes, of course, but which rules?"

"I don't mind telling you that she does now, at least I let her think so, it pleases her, you know. By-and-by we shall take turns, for marriage, they say, halves one's rights and doubles one's duties."

"You'll go on as you begin, and Amy will rule you all the days of your life."

"Well, she does it so imperceptibly that I don't think I shall mind much. She is the sort of woman who knows how to rule well. In fact, I rather like it, for she winds one round her finger as softly and prettily as a skein of silk, and makes you feel as if she was doing you a favor all the while."

"That ever I should live to see you a henpecked husband and enjoying it!" cried Jo, with uplifted hands.

It was good to see Laurie square his shoulders, and smile with masculine scorn at that insinuation, as he replied, with his "high and mighty" air, "Amy is too well-bred for that, and I am not the sort of man to submit to it. My wife and I respect ourselves and one another too much ever to tyrannize or quarrel."

Jo like that, and thought the new dignity very becoming, but the boy seemed changing very fast into the man, and regret mingled with her pleasure.

"I am sure of that. Amy and you never did quarrel as we used to. She is the sun and I the wind, in the fable, and the sun managed the man best, you remember."

"She can blow him up as well as shine on him," laughed Laurie. "such a lecture as I got at Nice! I give you my word it was a deal worse than any or your scoldings, a regular rouser. I'll tell you all about it sometime, she never will, because after telling me that she despised and was ashamed of me, she lost her heart to the despicable party and married the good-for-nothing."

"What baseness! Well, if she abuses you, come to me, and I'll defend you."

"I look as if I needed it, don't I?" said Laurie, getting up and striking an attitude which suddenly changed from the imposing to the rapturous, as Amy's voice was heard calling, "Where is she? Where's my dear old Jo?"

In trooped the whole family, and everyone was hugged and kissed all over again, and after several vain attempts, the three wanderers were set down to be looked at and exulted over. Mr. Laurence, hale and hearty as ever, was quite as much improved as the others by his foreign tour, for the crustiness seemed to be nearly gone, and the old-fashioned courtliness had received a polish which made it kindlier than ever. It was good to see him beam at 'my children', as he called the young pair. It was better still to see Amy pay him the daughterly duty and affection which completely won his old heart, and best of all, to watch Laurie revolve about the two, as if never tired of enjoying the pretty picture they made.

The minute she put her eyes upon Amy, Meg became conscious that her own dress hadn't a Parisian air, that young Mrs. Mofffat would be entirely eclipsed by young Mrs. Laurence, and that 'her ladyship' was altogether a most elegant and graceful woman. Jo thought, as she watched the pair, "How well they look together! I was right, and Laurie has found the beautiful, accomplished girl who will become his home better than clumsy old Jo, and be a pride, not a torment to him." Mrs. March and her husband smiled and nodded at each other with happy faces, for they saw that their youngest had done well, not only in worldly things, but the better wealth of love, confidence, and happiness.

For Amy's face was full of the soft brightness which betokens a peaceful heart, her voice had a new tenderness in it, and the cool, prim carriage was changed to a gentle dignity, both womanly and winning. No little affectations marred it, and the cordial sweetness of her manner was more charming than the new beauty or the old grace, for it stamped her at once with the unmistakable sign of the true gentlewoman she had hoped to become.

"Love has done much for our little girl," said her mother softly.

"She has had a good example before her all her life, my dear," Mr. March whispered back, with a loving look at the worn face and gray head beside him.

Daisy found it impossible to keep her eyes off her 'pitty aunty', but attached herself like a lap dog to the wonderful chatelaine full of delightful charms. Demi paused to consider the new relationship before he compromised himself by the rash acceptance of a bribe, which took the tempting form of a family of wooden bears from Berne. A flank movement produced an unconditional surrender, however, for Laurie knew where to have him.

"Young man, when I first had the honor of making your acquaintance you hit me in the face. Now I demand the satisfaction of a gentleman," and with that the tall uncle proceeded to toss and tousle the small nephew in a way that damaged his philosophical dignity as much as it delighted his boyish soul.

"Blest if she ain't in silk from head to foot? Ain't it a relishin' sight to see her settin' there as fine as a fiddle, anch a happy procession as filed away into the little dining room! Mr. March proudly escorted Mrs. Laurence. Mrs. March as proudly leaned on the arm of 'my son'. The old gentleman took Jo, with a whispered, "You must be my girl now," and a glance at the empty corner by the fire, that made Jo whisper back, "I'll try to fill her place, sir.

The twins pranced behind, feeling that the millennium was at hand, for everyone was so busy with the newcomers that they were left to revel at their own sweet will, and you may be sure they made the most of the opportunity. Didn't they steal sips of tea, stuff gingerbread ad libitum, get a hot biscuit apiece, and as a crowning trespass, didn't they each whisk a captivating little tart into their tiny pockets, there to stick and crumble treacherously, teaching them that both human nature and a pastry are frail? Burdened with the guilty consciousness of the sequestered tarts, and fearing that Dodo's sharp eyes would pierce the thin disguise of cambric and merino which hid their booty, the little sinners attached themselves to 'Dranpa', who hadn't his spectacles on. Amy, who was handed about like refreshments, returned to the parlor on Father Laurence's arm. The others paired off as before, and this arrangement left Jo companionless. She did not mind it at the minute, for she lingered to answer Hannah's eager inquiry.

"Will Miss Amy ride in her coop (coupe), and use all them lovely silver dishes that's stored away over yander?"

"Shouldn't wonder if she drove six white horses, ate off gold plate, and wore diamonds and point lace every day. Teddy thinks nothing too good for her," returned Jo with infinite satisfaction.

"No more there is! Will you have hash or fishballs for breakfast?" asked Hannah, who wisely mingled poetry and prose.

"I don't care." And Jo shut the door, feeling that food was an uncongenial topic just then. She stood a minute looking at the party vanishing above, and as Demi's short plaid legs toiled up the last stair, a sudden sense of lonliness came over her so strongly that she looked about her with dim eyes, as if to find something to lean upon, for even Teddy had deserted her. If she had known what birthday gift was coming every minute nearer and nearer, she would not have said to herself, "I'll weep a little weep when I go to bed. It won't do to be dismal now." Then she drew her hand over her eyes, for one of her boyish habits was never to know where her handkerchief was, and had just managed to call up a smile when there came a knock at the porch door.

She opened with hospitable haste, and started as if another ghost had come to surprise her, for there stood a tall bearded gentleman, beaming on her from the darkness like a midnight sun.

"Oh, Mr. Bhaer, I am so glad to see you!" cried Jo, with a clutch, as if she feared the night would swallow him up before she could get him in.

"And I to see Miss Marsch, but no, you haf a party," and the Professor paused as the sound of voices and the tap of dancing feet came down to them.

"No, we haven't, only the family. My sister and friends have just come home, and we are all very happy. Come in, and make one of us."

Though a very social man, I think Mr. Bhaer would have gone decorously away, and come again another day, but how could he, when Jo shut the door behind him, and bereft him of his hat? Perhaps her face had something to do with it, for she forgot to hide her joy at seeing him, and showed it with a frankness that proved irresistible to the solitary man, whose welcome far exceeded his boldest hopes.

"If I shall not be Monsieur de Trop, I will so gladly see them all. You haf been ill, my friend?"

He put the question abruptly, for, as Jo hung up his coat, the light fell on her face, and he saw a change in it.

"Not ill, but tired and sorrowful. We have had trouble since I saw you last."

"Ah, yes, I know. My heart was sore for you when I heard that." And he shook hands again, with such a sympathetic face that Jo felt as if no comfort could equal the look of the kind eyes, the grasp of the big, warm hand.

"Father, Mother, this is my friend, Professor Bhaer," she said, with a face and tone of such irrepressible pride and pleasure that she might as well have blown a trumpet and opened the door with a flourish.

If the stranger had any doubts about his reception, they were set at rest in a minute by the cordial welcome he received. Everyone greeted him kindly, for Jo's sake at first, but very soon they liked him for his own. They could not help it, for he carried the talisman that opens all hearts, and these simple people warmed to him at once, feeling even the more friendly because he was poor. For poverty enriches those who live above it, and is a sure passport to truly hospitable spirits. Mr. Bhaer sat looking about him with the air of a traveler who knocks at a strange door, and when it opens, finds himself at home. The children went to him like bees to a honeypot, and establishing themselves on each knee, proceeded to captivate him by rifling his pockets, pulling his beard, and investigating his watch, with juvenile audacity. The women telegraphed their approval to one another, and Mr. March, feeling that he had got a kindred spirit, opened his choicest stores for his guest's benefit, while silent John listened and enjoyed the talk, but said not a word, and Mr. Laurence found it impossible to go to sleep.

If Jo had not been otherwise engaged, Laurie's behavior would have amused her, for a faint twinge, not of jealousy, but something like suspicion, caused that gentleman to stand aloof at first, and observe the newcomer with brotherly circumspection. But it did not last long. He got interested in spite of himself, and before he knew it, was drawn into the circle. For Mr.

Bhaer talked well in this genial atmosphere, and did himself justice. He seldom spoke to Laurie, but he looked at him often, and a shadow would pass across his face, as if regretting his own lost youth, as he watched the young man in his prime. Then his eyes would turn to Jo so wistfully that she would have surely answered the mute inquiry if she had seen it. But Jo had her own eyes to take care of, and feeling that they could not be trusted, she prudently kept them on the little sock she was knitting, like a model maiden aunt.

A stealthy glance now and then refreshed her like sips of fresh water after a dusty walk, for the sidelong peeps showed her several propitious omens. Mr. Bhaer's face had lost the absent-minded expression, and looked all alive with interest in the present moment, actually young and handsome, she thought, forgetting to compare him with Laurie, as she usually did strange men, to their great detriment. Then he seemed quite inspired, though the burial customs of the ancients, to which the conversation had strayed, might not be considered an exhilarating topic. Jo quite glowed with triumph when Teddy got quenched in an argument, and thought to herself, as she watched her father's absorbed face, "How he would enjoy having such a man as my Professor to talk with every day!" Lastly, Mr. Bhaer was dressed in a new suit of black, which made him look more like a gentleman than ever. His bushy hair had been cut and smoothly brushed, but didn't stay in order long, for in exciting moments, he rumpled it up in the droll way he used to do, and Jo liked it rampantly erect better than flat, because she thought it gave his fine forehead a Jove-like aspect. Poor Jo, how she did glorify that plain man, as she sat knitting away so quietly, yet letting nothing escape her, not even the fact that Mr. Bhaer actually had gold sleeve-buttons in his immaculate wristbands.

"Dear old fellow! He couldn't have got himself up with more care if he'd been going a-wooing," said Jo to herself, and then a sudden thought born of the words made her blush so dreadfully that she had to drop her ball, and go down after it to hide her face.

The maneuver did not succeed as well as she expected, however, for though just in the act of setting fire to a funeral pyre, the Professor dropped his torch, metaphorically speaking, and made a dive after the little blue ball. Of course they bumped their heads smartly together, saw stars, and both came up flushed and laughing, without the ball, to resume their seats, wishing they had not left them.

Nobody knew where the evening went to, for Hannah skillfully abstracted the babies at an early hour, nodding like two rosy poppies, and Mr. Laurence went home to rest. The others sat round the fire, talking away, utterly regardless of the lapse of time, till Meg, whose maternal was impressed with a firm conviction that Daisy had tumbled out of be, and Demi set his nightgown afire studying the structure of matches, made a move to go.

"We must have our sing, in the good old way, for we are all together again once more," said Jo, feeling that a good shout would be a safe and pleasant vent for the jubilant emotions of her soul.

They were not all there. But no one found the words thougtless or untrue, for Beth still seemed among them, a peaceful presence, invisible, but dearer than ever, since death could not break the household league that love made disoluble. The little chair stood in its old place. The tidy basket, with the bit of work she left unfinished when the needle grew 'so heavy', was still on its accustomed shelf. The beloved instrument, seldom touched now had not been moved, and above it Beth's face, serene and smiling, as in the early days, looked down upon them, seeming to say, "Be happy. I am here."

"Play something, Amy. Let them hear how much you have improved," said Laurie, with pardonable pride in his promising pupil.

But Amy whispered, with full eyes, as she twirled the faded stool, "Not tonight, dear. I can't show off tonight."

But she did show something better than brilliancy or skill, for she sang Beth's songs with a tender music in her voice which the best master could not have taught, and touched the listener's hearts with a sweeter power than any other inspiration could have given her. The room was very still, when the clear voice failed suddenly at the last line of Beth's favorite hymn. It was hard to say . . .

Earth hath no sorrow that heaven cannot heal;

and Amy leaned against her husband, who stood behind her, feeling that her welcome home was not quite perfect without Beth's kiss.

"Now, we must finish with Mignon's song, for Mr. Bhaer sings that," said Jo, before the pause grew painful. And Mr. Bhaer cleared his throat with a gratified "Hem!" as he stepped into the corner where Jo stood, saying . . .

"You will sing with me? We go excellently well together."

A pleasing fiction, by the way, for Jo had no more idea of music than a grasshopper. But she would have consented if he had proposed to sing a whole opera, and warbled away, blissfully regardless of time and tune. It didn't much matter, for Mr. Bhaer sang like a true German, heartily and well, and Jo soon subsided into a subdued hum, that she might listen to the mellow voice that seemed to sing for her alone.

Know'st thou the land where the citron blooms,

used to be the Professor's favorite line, for 'das land' meant Germany to him, but now he seemed to dwell, with peculiar warmth and melody, upon the words . . .

There, oh there, might I with thee, O, my beloved, go

and one listener was so thrilled by the tender invitation that she longed to say she did know the land, and would joyfully depart thither whenever he liked The song was considered a great success, and the singer retired covered with laurels. But a few minutes afterward, he forgot his manners entirely, and stared at Amy putting on her bonnet, for she had been introduced simply as 'my sister', and on one had called her by her new name since her came. He forgot himself still further when Laurie said, in his most gracious manner, at parting . . .

"My wife and I are very glad to meet you, sir. Please remember that there is always a welcome waiting for you over the way."

Then the Professor thanked him so heartily, and looked so suddenly illuminated with satisfaction, that Laurie thought him the most delightfully demonstrative old fellow he ever met.

"I too shall go, but I shall gladly come again, if you will gif me leave, dear madame, for a little business in the city will keep me here some days."

He spoke to Mrs. March, but he looked at Jo, and the mother's voice gave as cordial an assent as did the daughter's eyes, for Mrs. March was not so blind to her children's interest as Mrs. Moffat supposed.

"I suspect that is a wise man," remarked Mr. March, with placid satisfaction, from the hearthrug, after the last guest had gone.

"I know he is a good one," added Mrs. March, with decided approval, as she wound up the clock.

"I thought you'd like him," was all Jo said, as she slipped away to her bed.

She wondered what the business was that brought Mr. Bhaer to the city, and finally decided that he had been appointed to some great honor, somewhere, but had been too modest to mention the fact. If she had seen his face when, safe in his own room, he looked at the picture of a severe and rigid young lady, with a good deal of hair, who appeared to be gazing darkly into futurity, it might have thrown some light upon the subject, especially when he turned off the gas, and kissed the picture in the dark.

Chapter Forty-Four

"Please, Madam Mother, could you lend me my wife for half an hour? The luggage has come, and I've been making hay of Amy's Paris finery, trying to find some things I want," said Laurie, coming in the next day to find Mrs. Laurence sitting in her mother's lap, as if being made 'the baby' again.

"Certainly. Go, dear, I forgot that you have any home but this." And Mrs. March pressed the white hand that wore the wedding ring, as if asking pardon for her maternal covetousness.

"I shouldn't have come over if I could have helped it, but I can't get on without my little woman any more than a . . ."

"Weathercock can without the wind," suggested Jo, as he paused for a simile. Jo had grown quite her own saucy self again since Teddy came home.

"Exactly, for Amy keeps me pointing due west most of the time, with only an occasional whiffle round to the south, and I haven't had an easterly spell since I was married. Don't know anything about the north, but am altogether salubrious and balmy, hey, my lady?"

"Lovely weather so far. I don't know how long it will last, but I'm not afraid of storms, for I'm learning how to sail my ship. Come home, dear, and I'll find your bootjack. I suppose that's what you are rummaging after among my things. Men are so helpless, Mother," said Amy, with a matronly air, which delighted her husband.

"What are you going to do with yourselves after you get settled?" asked Jo, buttoning Amy's cloak as she used to button her pinafores.

"We have our plans. We don't mean to say much about them yet, because we are such very new brooms, but we don't intend to be idle. I'm going into business with a devotion that shall delight Grandfather, and prove to him that I'm not spoiled. I need something of the sort to keep me steady. I'm tired of dawdling, and mean to work like a man."

"And Amy, what is she going to do?" asked Mrs. March, well pleased at Laurie's decision and the energy with which he spoke.

"After doing the civil all round, and airing our best bonnet, we shall astonish you by the elegant hospitalities of our mansion, the brilliant society we shall draw about us, and the beneficial influence we shall exert over the world at large. That's about it, isn't it, Madame Recamier?" asked Laurie with a quizzical look at Amy.

"Time will show. Come away, Impertinence, and don't shock my family by calling me names before their faces," answered Amy, resolving that there should be a home with a good wife in it before she set up a salon as a queen of society.

"How happy those children seem together!" observed Mr. March, finding it difficult to become absorbed in his Aristotle after the young couple had gone.

"Yes, and I think it will last," added Mrs. March, with the restful expression of a pilot who has brought a ship safely into port.

"I know it will. Happy Amy!" And Jo sighed, then smiled brightly as Professor Bhaer opened the gate with an impatient push.

Later in the evening, when his mind had been set at rest about the bootjack, Laurie said suddenly to his wife, "Mrs. Laurence."

"My Lord!"

"That man intends to marry our Jo!"

"I hope so, don't you, dear?"

"Well, my love, I consider him a trump, in the fullest sense of that expressive word, but I do wish he was a little younger and a good deal richer."

"Now, Laurie, don't be too fastidious and worldly-minded. If they love one another it doesn't matter a particle how old they are nor how poor. Women never should marry for money . . ." Amy caught herself up short as the words escaped her, and looked at her husband, who replied, with malicious gravity . . .

"Certainly not, though you do hear charming girls say that they intend to do it sometimes. If my memory serves me, you once thought it your duty to make a rich match. That accounts, perhaps, for your marrying a good-for-nothing like me."

"Oh, my dearest boy, don't, don't say that! I forgot you were rich when I said 'Yes'. I'd have married you if you hadn't a penny, and I sometimes wish you were poor that I might show how much I love you." And Amy, who was very dignified in public and very fond in private, gave convincing proofs of the truth of her words.

"You don't really think I am such a mercenary creature as I tried to be once, do you? It would break my heart if you didn't believe that I'd gladly pull in the same boat with you, even if you had to get your living by rowing on the lake."2

"Am I an idiot and a brute? How could I think so, when you refused a richer man for me, and won't let me give you half I want to now, when I have the right? Girls do it every day, poor things, and are taught to think it is their only salvation, but you had better lessons, and though I trembled for you at one time, I was not disappointed, for the daughter was true to the mother's teaching. I told Mamma so yesterday, and she looked as glad and grateful as if I'd given her a check for a million, to be spent in charity. You are not listening to my moral remarks, Mrs. Laurence." And Laurie paused, for Amy's eyes had an absent look, though fixed upon his face.

"Yes, I am, and admiring the mple in your chin at the same time. I don't wish to make you vain, but I must confess that I'm prouder of my handsome husband than of all his money. Don't laugh, but your nose is such a comfort to me." And Amy softly caressed the well-cut feature with artistic satisfaction.

Laurie had received many compliments in his life, but never one that suited him better, as he plainly showed though he did laugh at his wife's peculiar taste, while she said slowly, "May I ask you a question, dear?"

"Of course, you may."

"Shall you care if Jo does marry Mr. Bhaer?"

"Oh, that's the trouble is it? I thought there was something in the dimple that didn't quite suit you. Not being a dog in the manger, but the happiest fellow alive, I assure you I can dance at Jo's wedding with a heart as light as my heels. Do you doubt it, my darling?"

Amy looked up at him, and was satisfied. Her little jealous fear vanished forever, and she thanked him, with a face full of love and confidence.

"I wish we could do something for that capital old Professor. Couldn't we invent a rich relation, who shall obligingly die out there in Germany, and leave him a tidy little fortune?" said Laurie, when they began to pace up and down the long drawing room, arm in arm, as they were fond of doing, in memory of the chateau garden.

"Jo would find us out, and spoil it all. She is very proud of him, just as he is, and said yesterday that she thought poverty was a beautiful thing."

"Bless her dear heart! She won't think so when she has a literary husband, and a dozen little professors and professorins to support. We won't interfere now, but watch our chance, and do them a good turn in spite of themselves. I owe Jo for a part of my education, and she believes in people's paying their honest debts, so I'll get round her in that way."

"How delightful it is to be able to help others, isn't it? That was always one of my dreams, to have the power of giving freely, and thanks to you, the dream has come true."

"Ah, we'll do quantities of good, won't we? There's one sort of poverty that I particularly like to help. Out-and-out beggars get taken care of, but poor gentle folks fare badly, because they won't ask, and people don't dare to offer charity. Yet there are a thousand ways of helping them, if one only knows how to do it so delicately that it does not offend. I must say, I like to serve a decayed gentleman better than a blarneying beggar. I suppose it's wrong, but I do, though it is harder."

"Because it takes a gentleman to do it," added the other member of the domestic admiration society.

"Thank you, I'm afraid I don't deserve that pretty compliment. But I was going to say that while I was dawdling about abroad, I saw a good many talented young fellows making all sorts of sacrifices, and enduring real hardships, that they might realize their dreams. Splendid fellows, some of them, working like heros, poor and friendless, but so full of courage, patience, and ambition that I was ashamed of myself, and longed to give them a right good lift. Those are people whom it's a satisfaction to help, for if they've got genius, it's an honor to be allowed to serve them, and not let it be lost or delayed for want of fuel to keep the pot boiling. If they haven't, it's a pleasure to comfort the poor souls, and keep them from despair when they find it out."

"Yes, indeed, and there's another class who can't ask, and who suffer in silence. I know something of it, for I belonged to it before you made a princess of me, as the king does the beggar-maid in the old story. Ambitious girls have a hard time, Laurie, and often have to see youth, health, and precious opportunities go by, just for want of a little help at the right minute. People have been very kind to me, and whenever I see girls struggling along, as we used to do, I want to put out my hand and help them, as I was helped."

"And so you shall, like an angel as you are!" cried Laurie, resolving, with a glow of philanthropic zeal, to found and endow an institution for the express benefit of young women with artistic tendencies. "Rich people have no right to sit down and enjoy themselves, or let their money accumulate for others to waste. It's not half so sensible to leave legacies when one dies as it is to use the money wisely while alive, and enjoy making one's fellow creatures happy with it. We'll have a good time ourselves, and add an extra relish to our own pleasure by giving other people a generous taste. Will you be a little Dorcal, going about emptying a big basket of comforts, and filling it up with good deeds?"

"With all my heart, if you will be a brave St. Martin, stopping as you ride gallantly through the world to share your cloak with the beggar."

"It's a bargain, and we shall get the best of it!"

So the young pair shook hands upon it, and then paced happily on again, feeling that their pleasant home was more homelike because they hoped to brighten other homes, believing that their own feet would walk more uprightly along the flowery path before them, if they smoothed rough ways for other feet, and feeling that their hearts were more closely knit together by a love which could tenderly remember those less blest than they.

Chapter Forty-Five

I cannot feel that I have done my duty as humble historian of the March family, without devoting at least one chapter to the two most precious and important members of it. Daisy and Demi had now arrived at years of discretion, for in this fast age babies of three or four assert their rights, and get them, too, which is more than many of their elders do. If there ever were a pair of twins in danger of being utterly spoiled by adoration, it was these prattling Brookes. Of course they were the most remarkable children ever born, as will be shown when I mention that they walked at eight months, talked fluently at twelve months, and at two years they took their places at table, and behaved with a propriety which charmed all beholders. At three, Daisy demanded a 'needler', and actually made a bag with four stitches in it. She likewise set up housekeeping in the sideboard, and managed a microscopic cooking stove with a skill that brought tears of pride to Hannah's eyes, while Demi learned his letters with his grandfather, who invented a new mode of teaching the alphabet by forming letters with his arms and legs, thus uniting gymnastics for head and heels. The boy early developed a mechanical genius which delighted his father and distracted his mother, for he tried to imitate every machine he saw, and kept the nursery in a chaotic condition, with his 'sewinsheen', a mysterious structure of string, chairs, clothespins, and spools, for wheels to go 'wound and wound'. Also a basket hung over the back of a chair, in which he vainly tried to hoist his too confiding sister, who, with feminine devotion, allowed her little head to be bumped till rescued, when the young inventor indignantly remarked, "Why, Marmar, dat's my lellywaiter, and me's trying to pull her up."

Though utterly unlike in character, the twins got on remarkably well together, and seldom quarreled more than thrice a day. Of course, Demi tyrannized over Daisy, and gallantly defended her from every other aggressor, while Daisy made a galley slave of herself, and adored her brother as the one perfect being in the world. A rosy, chubby, sunshiny little soul was Daisy, who found her way to everybody's heart, and nestled there. One of the captivating children, who seem made to be kissed and cuddled, adorned and adored like little goddesses, and produced for general approval on all festive occasions. Her small virtues were so sweet that she would have been quite angelic if a few small naughtinesses had not kept her delightfully human. It was all fair weather in her world, and every morning she scrambled up to the window in her little nightgown to look our, and say, no matter whether it rained or shone, "Oh, pitty day, oh, pitty day!" Everyone was a friend, and she offered kisses to a stranger so confidingly that the most inveterate bachelor relented, and baby-lovers became faithful worshipers.

"Me loves evvybody," she once said, opening her arms, with her spoon in one hand, and her mug in the other, as if eager to embrace and nourish the whole world.

As she grew, her mother began to feel that the Dovecote would be blessed by the presence of an inmate as serene and loving as that which had helped to make the old house home, and to pray that she might be spared a loss like that which had lately taught them how long they had entertained an angel unawares. Her grandfather often called her 'Beth', and her grandmother watched over her with untiring devotion, as if trying to atone for some past mistake, which no eye but her own could see.

Demi, like a true Yankee, was of an inquiring turn, wanting to know everything, and often getting much disturbed because he could not get satisfactory answers to his perpetual "What for?"

He also possessed a philosophic bent, to the great delight of his grandfather, who used to hold Socratic conversations with him, in which the precocious pupil occasionally posed his teacher, to the undisguised satisfaction of the womenfolk.

"What makes my legs go, Dranpa?" asked the young philosopher, surveying those active portions of his frame with a meditative air, while resting after a go-to-bed frolic one night.

"It's your little mind, Demi," replied the sage, stroking the yellow head respectfully.

"What is a little mine?"

"It is something which makes your body move, as the spring made the wheels go in my watch when I showed it to you."

"Open me. I want to see it go wound."

"I can't do that any more than you could open the watch. God winds you up, and you go till He stops you."

"Does I?" And Demi's brown eyes grew big and bright as he took in the new thought. "Is I wounded up like the watch?"

"Yes, but I can't show you how, for it is done when we don't see."

Demi felt his back, as if expecting to find it like that of the watch, and then gravely remarked, "I dess Dod does it when I's asleep."

A careful explanation followed, to which he listened so attentively that his anxious grandmother said, "My dear, do you think it wise to talk about such things to that baby? He's getting great bumps over his eyes, and learning to ask the most unanswerable questions."

"If he is old enough to ask the question he is old enough to receive true answers. I am not putting the thoughts into his head, but helping him unfold those already there. These children are wiser than we are, and I have no doubt the boy understands every word I have said to him. Now, Demi, tell me where you keep your mind."

If the boy had replied like Alcibiades, "By the gods, Socrates, I cannot tell," his grandfather would not have been surprised, but when, after standing a moment on one leg, like a meditative young stork, he answered, in a tone of calm conviction, "In my little belly," the old gentleman could only join in Grandma's laugh, and dismiss the class in metaphysics.

There might have been cause for maternal anxiety, if Demi had not given convincing proofs that he was a true boy, as well as a budding philosopher, for often, after a discussion which caused Hannah to prophesy, with ominous nods, "That child ain't long for this world," he would turn about and set her fears at rest by some of the pranks with which dear, dirty, naughty little rascals distract and delight their parent's souls.

Meg made many moral rules, and tried to keep them, but what mother was ever proof against the winning wiles, the ingenious evasions, or the tranquil audacity of the miniature men and women who so early show themselves accomplished Artful Dodgers?

"No more raisins, Demi. They'll make you sick," says Mamma to the young person who offers his services in the kitchen with unfailing regularity on plum-pudding day.

"Me likes to be sick."

"I don't want to have you, so run away and help Daisy make patty cakes."

He reluctantly departs, but his wrongs weigh upon his spirit, and by-and-by when an opportunity comes to redress them, he outwits Mamma by a shrewd bargain.

"Now you have been good children, and I'll play anything you like," says Meg, as she leads her assistant cooks upstairs, when the pudding is safely bouncing in the pot.

"Truly, Marmar?" asks Demi, with a brilliant idea in his well-powdered head.

"Yes, truly. Anything you say," replies the shortsighted parent, preparing herself to sing, "The Three Little Kittens" half a dozen times over, or to take her family to "Buy a penny bun," regardless of wind or limb. But Demi corners her by the cool reply . . .

"Then we'll go and eat up all the raisins."

Aunt Dodo was chief playmate and confidante of both children, and the trio turned the little house topsy-turvy. Aunt Amy was as yet only a name to them, Aunt Beth soon faded into a pleasantly vague memory, but Aunt Dodo was a living reality, and they made the most of her, for which compliment she was deeply grateful. But when Mr. Bhaer came, Jo neglected her playfellows, and dismay and desolation fell upon their little souls. Daisy, who was fond of going about peddling kisses, lost her best customer and became bankrupt. Demi, with infantile penetration, soon discovered that Dodo like to play with 'the bear-man' better than she did him, but though hurt, he concealed his anguish, for he hadn't the heart to insult a rival who kept a mine of chocolate drops in his waistcoat pocket, and a watch that could be taken out of its case and freely shaken by ardent admirers.

Some persons might have considered these pleasing liberties as bribes, but Demi didn't see it in that light, and continued to patronize the 'the bear-man' with pensive affability, while Daisy bestowed her small affections upon him at the third call, and considered his shoulder her throne, his arm her refuge, his gifts treasures surpassing worth.

Gentlemen are sometimes seized with sudden fits of admiration for the young relatives of ladies whom they honor with their regard, but this counterfeit philoprogenitiveness sits uneasily upon them, and does not deceive anybody a particle. Mr. Bhaer's devotion was sincere, however likewise effective—for honesty is the best policy in love as in law. He was one of the men who are at home with children, and looked particularly well when little faces made a pleasant contrast with his manly one. His business, whatever it was, detained him from day to day, but evening seldom failed to bring him out to see—well, he always asked for Mr. March, so I suppose he was the attraction. The excellent papa labored under the delusion that he was, and reveled in long discussions with the kindred spirit, till a chance remark of his more observing grandson suddenly enlightened him.

Mr. Bhaer came in one evening to pause on the threshold of the study, astonished by the spectacle that met his eye. Prone upon the floor lay Mr. March, with his respectable legs in the air, and beside him, likewise prone, was Demi, trying to imitate the attitude with his own short, scarlet-stockinged legs, both grovelers so seriously absorbed that they were unconscious of spectators, till Mr. Bhaer laughed his sonorous laugh, and Jo cried out, with a scandalized face . . .

"Father, Father, here's the Professor!"

Down went the black legs and up came the gray head, as the preceptor said, with undisturbed dignity, "Good evening, Mr. Bhaer. Excuse me for a moment. We are just finishing our lesson. Now, Demi, make the letter and tell its name."

"I knows him!" And, after a few convulsive efforts, the red legs tok the shape of a pair of compasses, and the intelligent pupil triumphantly shouted, "It's a We, Dranpa, it's a We!"

"He's a born Weller," laughed Jo, as her parent gathered himself up, and her nephew tried to stand on his head, as the only mode of expressing his satisfaction that school was over.

"What have you been at today, bubchen?" asked Mr. Bhaer, picking up the gymnast.

"Me went to see little Mary."

"And what did you there?"

"I kissed her," began Demi, with artless frankness. "Prut! Thou beginnest early. What did the little Mary say to that?" asked Mr. Bhaer, continuing to confess the young sinner, who stood upon the knee, exploring the waistcoat pocket.

"Oh, she liked it, and she kissed me, and I liked it. Don't little boys like little girls?" asked Demi, with his mouth full, and an air of bland satisfaction.

"You precious chick! Who put that into your head?" said Jo, enjoying the innocent revelation as much as the Professor.

"'Tisn't in mine head, it's in mine mouf," answered literal Demi, putting out his tongue, with a chocolate drop on it, thinking she alluded to confectionery, not ideas.

"Thou shouldst save some for the little friend. Sweets to the sweet, mannling." And Mr. Bhaer offered Jo some, with a look that made her wonder if chocolate was not the nectar drunk by the gods. Demi also saw the smile, was impressed by it, and artlessy inquired . . .

"Do great boys like great girls, to, 'Fessor?"

Like young Washington, Mr. Bhaer 'couldn't tell a lie', so he gave the somewhat vague reply that he believed they did sometimes, in a tone that made Mr. March put down his clothes-brush, glance at Jo's retiring face, and then sink into his chair, looking as if the 'precocious chick' had put an idea into his head that was both sweet and sour.

Why Dodo, when she caught him in the china closet half an hour afterward, nearly squeezed the breath out of his little body with a tender embrace, instead of shaking him for being there, and why she followed up this novel performance by the unexpected gift of a big slice of bread and jelly, remained one of the problems over which Demi puzzled his small wits, and was forced to leave unsolved forever.

Chapter Forty-Six

While Laurie and Amy were taking conjugal strolls over velvet carpets, as they set their house in order, and planned a blissful future, Mr. Bhaer and Jo were enjoying promenades of a different sort, along muddy roads and sodden fields.

"I always do take a walk toward evening, and I don't know why I should give it up, just because I happen to meet the Professor on his way out," said Jo to herself, after two or three encounters, for though there were two paths to Meg's whichever one she took she was sure to meet him., either going or returning. He was always walking rapidly, and never seemed to see her until quite close, when he would look as if his short-sighted eyes had failed to recognize the approaching lady till that moment. Then, if she was going to Meg's he always had something for the babies. If her face was turned homeward, he had merely strolled down to see the river, and was just returning, unless they were tired of his frequent calls.

Under the circumstances, what could Jo do but greet him civilly, and invite him in? If she was tired of his visits, she concealed her weariness with perfect skill, and took care that there should be coffee for supper, "as Friedrich—I mean Mr. Bhaer—doesn't like tea."

By the second week, everyone knew perfectly well what was going on, yet everyone tried to look as if they were stone-blind to the changes in Jo's face. They never asked why she sang about her work, did up her hair three times a day, and got so blooming with her evening exercise. And no one seemed to have the slightest suspicion that Professor Bhaer, while talking philosophy with the father, was giving the daughter lessons in love.

Jo couldn't even lose her heart in a decorous manner, but sternly tried to quench her feelings, and failing to do so, led a somewhat agitated life. She was mortally afraid of being laughed at for surrendering, after her many and vehement declarations of independence. Laurie was her especial dread, but thanks to the new manager, he behaved with praiseworthy propriety, never called Mr. Bhaer 'a capital old fellow' in public, never alluded, in the remotest manner, to Jo's improved appearance, or expressed the least surprise at seeing the Professor's hat on the Marches' table nearly every evening. But he exulted in private and longed for the time to come when he could give Jo a piece of plate, with a bear and a ragged staff on it as an appropriate coat of arms.

For a fortnight, the Professor came and went with lover-like regularity. Then he stayed away for three whole days, and made no sign, a proceeding which caused everybody to look sober, and Jo to become pensive, at first, and then—alas for romance—very cross.

"Disgusted, I dare say, and gone home as suddenly as he came. It's nothing tome, of course, but I should think he would have come and bid us goodbye like a gentleman," she said to herself, with a despairing look at the gate, as she put on her things for the customary walk one dull afternoon.

"You'd better take the little umbrella, dear. It looks like rain," said her mother, observing that she had on her new bonnet, but not alluding to the fact. "Yes, Marmee, do you want anything in town? I've got to run in and get some paper," returned Jo, pulling out the bow under her chin before the glass as an excuse for not looking at her mother.

"Yes, I want some twilled silesia, a paper of number nine needles, and two yards of narrow lavender ribbon. Have you got your thick boots on, and something warm under your cloak?"

"I believe so," answered Jo absently.

"If you happen to meet Mr. Bhaer, bring him home to tea. I quite long to see the dear man," added Mrs. March.

Jo heard that, but made no answer, except to kiss her mother, and walk rapidly away, thinking with a glow of gratitude, in spite of her heartache, "How good she is to me! What do girls do who haven't any mothers to help them through their troubles?"

The dry-goods stores were not down among the counting-houses, banks, and wholesale warerooms, where gentlemen most do congregate, but Jo found herself in that part of the city before she did a single errand, loitering along as if waiting for someone, examining engineering instruments in one window and samples of wool in another, with most unfeminine interest, tumbling over barrels, being half-smothered by descending bales, and hustled unceremoniously by busy men who looked as if they wondered 'how the deuce she got there'. A drop of rain on her cheek recalled her thoughts from baffled hopes to ruined ribbons. For the drops continued to fall, and being a woman as well as a lover, she felt that, though it was too late to save her heart, she might her bonnet. Now she remembered the little umbrella, which she had forgotten to take in her hurry to be off, but regret was unavailing, and nothing could be done but borrow one or submit to to a drenching. She looked up at the lowering sky, down at the crimson bow already flecked with black, forward along the muddy street, then one long, lingering look behind, at a certain grimy warehouse, with 'Hoffmann, Swartz, & Co.' over the door, and said to herself, with a sternly reproachful air . . .

"It serves me right! what business had I to put on all my best things and come philandering down here, hoping to see the Professor? Jo, I'm ashamed of you! No, you shall not go there to borrow an umbrella, or find out where he is, from his friends. You shall trudge away, and do your errands in the rain, and if you catch your death and ruin your bonnet, it's no more than you deserve. Now then!"

With that she rushed across the street so impetuously that she narrowly escaped annihilation from a passing truck, and precipitated herself into the arms of a stately old gentleman, who said, "I beg pardon, ma'am," and looked mortally offended. Somewhat daunted, Jo righted herself, spread her handkerchief over the devoted ribbons, and putting temptation behind her, hurried on, with increasing dampness about the ankles, and much clashing of umbrellas overhead. The fact that a somewhat dilapidated blue one remained stationary above the unprotected bonnet attracted her attention, and looking up, she saw Mr. Bhaer looking down.

"I feel to know the strong-minded lady who goes so bravely under many horse noses, and so fast through much mus. What do you down here, my friend?"

"I'm shopping."

Mr. Bhaer smiled, as he glanced from the pickle factory on one side to the wholesale hide and leather concern on the other, but her only said politely, "You haf no umbrella. May I go also, and take for you the bundles?"

"Yes, thank you."

Jo's cheeks were as red as her ribbon, and she wondered what he thought of her, but she didn't care, for in a minute she found herself walking away arm in arm with her Professor, feeling as if the sun had suddenly burst out with uncommon brilliancy, that the world was all right again, and that one thoroughly happy woman was paddling through the wet that day.

"We thought you had gone," said Jo hastily, for she knew he was looking at her. Her bonnet wasn't big enough to hide her face, and she feared he might think the joy it betrayed unmaidenly.

"Did you believe that I should go with no farewell to those who haf been so heavenly kind tome?" he asked so reproachfully that she felt as if she had insulted him by the suggestion, and answered heartily . . .

"No, I didn't. I knew you were busy about your own affairs, but we rather missed you, Father and Mother especially."

"And you?"

"I'm always glad to see you, sir."

In her anxiety to keep her voice quite calm, Jo made it rather cool, and the frosty little monosyllable at the end seemed to chill the Professor, for his smile vanished, as he said gravely . . .

"I thank you, and come one more time before I go."

"You are going, then?"

"I haf no longer any business here, it is done."

"Successfully, I hope?" said Jo, for the bitterness of disappointment was in that short reply of his.

"I ought to think so, for I haf a way opened to me by which I can make my bread and gif my Junglings much help."

"Tell me, please! I like to know all about the—the boys," said Jo eagerly.

"That is so kind, I gladly tell you. My friends find for me a place in a college, where I teach as at home, and earn enough to make the way smooth for Franz and Emil. For this I should be grateful, should I not?"

"Indeed you should. How splendid it will be to have you doing what you like, and be able to see you often, and the boys!" cried Jo, clinging to the lads as an excuse for the satisfaction she could not help betraying.

"Ah! But we shall not meet often, I fear, this place is at the West."

"So far away!" And Jo left her skirts to their fate, as if it didn't matter now what became of her clothes or herself.

Mr. Bhaer could read several languages, but he had not learned to read women yet. He flattered himself that he knew Jo pretty well, and was, therefore, much amazed by the contradictions of voice, face, and manner, which she showed him in rapid succession that day, for she was in half a dozen different moods in the course of half an hour. When she met him she looked surprised, though it was impossible to help suspecting that she had come for that express purpose. When he offered her his arm, she took it with a look that filled him with delight, but when he asked if she missed him, she gave such a chilly, formal reply that despair fell upon him. On learning his good fortune she almost clapped her hands. Was the joy all for the boys? Then on hearing his destination, she said, "So far away!" in a tone of despair that lifted him on to a pinnacle of hope, but the next minute she tumbled him down again by observing, like one entirely absorbed in the matter . . .

"Here's the place for my errands. Will you come in? It won't take long."

Jo rather prided herself upon her shopping capabilities, and particularly wished to impress her escort with the neatness and dispatch with which she would accomplish the business. But owing to the flutter she was in, everything went amiss. She upset the tray of needles, forgot the silesia was to be 'twilled' till it was cut off, gave the wrong change, and covered herself with confusion by asking for lavender ribbon at the calico counter. Mr. Bhaer stood by, watching her blush and blunder, and as he watched, his own bewilderment seemed to subside, for he was beginning to see that on some occasions, women, like dreams, go by contraries.

When they came out, he put the parcel under his arm with a more cheerful aspect, and splashed through the puddles as if he rather enjoyed it on the whole.

"Should we no do a little what you call shopping for the babies, and haf a farewell feast tonight if I go for my last call at your so pleasant home?" he asked, stopping before a window full of fruit and flowers.

"What will we buy?" asked Jo, ignoring the latter part of his speech, and sniffing the mingled odors with an affectation of delight as they went in.

"May they haf oranges and figs?" asked Mr. Bhaer, with a paternal air.

"They eat them when they can get them." "Do you care for nuts?"

"Like a squirrel."

"Hamburg grapes. Yes, we shall drink to the Fatherland in those?"

Jo frowned upon that piece of extravagance, and asked why he didn't buy a frail of dated, a cask of raisins, and a bag of almonds, and be done with it? Whereat Mr. Bhaer confiscated her purse, produced his own, and finished the marketing by buying several pounds of grapes, a pot of rosy daisies, and a pretty jar of honey, to be regarded in the light of a demijohn. Then distorting his pockets with knobby bundles, and giving her the flowers to hold, he put up the old umbrella, and they traveled on again.

"Miss Marsch, I haf a great favor to ask of you," began the Professor, after a moist promenade of half a block.

"Yes, sir." And Jo's heart began to beat so hard she was afraid he would hear it.

"I am bold to say it in spite of the rain, because so short a time remains to me."

"Yes, sir." And Jo nearly crushed the small flowerpot with the sudden squeeze she gave it.

"I wish to get a little dress for my Tina, and I am too stupid to go alone. Will you kindly gif me a word of taste and help?"

"Yes, sir." And JO felt as calm and cool all of a sudden as if she had stepped into a refrigerator.

"Perhaps also a shawl for Tina's mother, she is so poor and sick, and the husband is such a care. Yes, yes, a thick, warm shawl would be a friendly thing to take the little mother."

"I'll do it with pleasure, Mr. Bhaer. I'm going very fast, and he's getting dearer every minute," added Jo to herself, then with a mental shake she entered into the business with an energy that was pleasant to behold. Mr. Bhaer left it all to her, so she chose a pretty gown for Tina, and then ordered out the shawls. The clerk, being a married man, condescended to take an interest in the couple, who appeared to be shopping for their family.

"Your lady may prefer this. It's a superior article, a most desirable color, quite chaste and genteel," he said, shaking out a comfortable gray shawl, and throwing it over Jo's shoulders.

"Does this suit you, Mr. Bhaer?" she asked, turning her back to him, and feeling deeply grateful for the chance of hiding her face. "Excellently well, we will haf it," answered the Professor, smiling to himself as he paid for it, while Jo continued to rummage the counters like a confirmed bargain-hunter.

"Now shall we go home?" he asked, as if the words were very pleasant to him.

"Yes, it's late, and I'm so tired." Jo's voice was more pathetic than she knew. For now the sun seemed to have gone in as suddenly as it came out, and the world grew muddy and miserable again, and for the first time she discovered that her feet were cold, her head ached, and that her heart was colder than the former, fuller of pain than the latter. Mr. Bhaer was going away, he only cared for her as a friend, it was all a mistake, and the sooner it was over the better. With this idea in her head, she hailed an approaching omnibus with such a hasty gesture that the daisies flew out of the pot and were badly damaged.

"This is not our omniboos," said the Professor, waving the loaded vehicle away, and stopping to pick up the poor little flowers.

"I beg your pardon. I didn't see the name distinctly. Never mind, I can walk. I'm used to plodding in the mud," returned Jo, winking hard, because she would have died rather than openly wipe her eyes. Mr. Bhaer saw the drops on her cheeks, though she turned her head away. The sight seemed to touch him very much, for suddenly stooping down, he asked in a tone that meant a great deal, "Heart's dearest, why do you cry?"

Now, if Jo had not been new to this sort of thing she would have said she wasn't crying, had a cold in her head, or told any other feminine fib proper to the occasion. Instead of which, that undignified creature answered, with an irrepressible sob, "Because you are going away."

"Ach, mein Gott, that is so good!" cried Mr. Bhaer, managing to clasp his hands in spite of the umbrella and the bundles, "Jo, I haf nothing but much love to gif you. I came to see if you could care for it, and I waited to be sure that I was something more than a friend. Am I? Can you make a little place in your heart for old Fritz?" he added, all in one breath.

"Oh, yes!" said Jo, and he was quite satisfied, for she folded both hands over his are, and looked up at him with an expression that plainly showed how happy she would be to walk through life beside him, even though she had no better shelter than the old umbrella, if he carried it.

It was certainly proposing under difficulties, for even if he had desired to do so, Mr. Bhaer could not go down upon his knees, on account of the mud. Neither could he offer Jo his hand, except figuratively, for both were full. Much less could he indulge in tender remonstrations in the open street, though he was near it. So the only way in which he could express his rapture was to look at her, with an expression which glorified his face to such a degree that there actually seemed to be little rainbows in the drops that sparkled on his beard. If he had not loved Jo very much, I don't think he could have done it then, for she looked far from lovely, with her skirts in a deplorable state, her rubber boots splashed to the ankle, and her bonnet a ruin. Fortunately, Mr. Bhaer considered her the most beautiful woman living, and she found him more 'Jove-like" than ever, though his hatbrim was quite limp with the little rills trickling thence upon his shoulders (for he held the umbrella all over Jo), and every finger of his gloves needed mending.

Passers-by probably thought them a pair of harmless lunatics, for they entirely forgot to hail a bus, and strolled leisurely along, oblivious of deepening dusk and fog. Little they cared what anybody thought, for they were enjoying the happy hour that seldom comes but once in any life, the magical moment which bestows youth on the old, beauty on the plain, wealth on the poor, and gives human hearts a foretaste of heaven. The Professor looked as if he had conquered a kingdom, and the world had nothing more to offer him in the way of bliss. While Jo trudged beside him, feeling as if her place had always been there, and wondering how she ever could have chosen any other lot. Of course, she was the first to speak—intelligibly, I mean, for the emotional remarks which followed her impetuous "Oh, yes!" were not of a coherent or reportable character.

"Friedrich, why didn't you . . ."

"Ah, heaven, she gifs me the name that no one speaks since Minna died!" cried the Professor, pausing in a puddle to regard her with grateful delight.

"I always call you so to myself—I forgot, but I won't unless you like it."

"Like it? It is more sweet to me than I can tell. Say 'thou', also, and I shall say your language is almost as beautiful as mine."

"Isn't 'thou' a little sentimental?" asked Jo, privately thinking it a lovely monosyllable.

"Sentimental? Yes. Thank Gott, we Germans believe in sentiment, and keep ourselves young mit it. Your English 'you' is so cold, say 'thou', heart's dearest, it means so much to me," pleaded Mr. Bhaer, more like a romantic student than a grave professor.

"Well, then, why didn't thou tell me all this sooner?" asked Jo bashfully.

"Now I shall haf to show thee all my heart, and I so gladly will, because thou must take care of it hereafter. See, then, my Jo—ah, the dear, funny little name—I had a wish to tell something the day I said goodbye in New York, but I thought the handsome friend was betrothed to thee, and so I spoke not. Wouldst thou have said 'Yes', then, if I had spoken?"

"I don't know. I'm afraid not, for I didn't have any heart just then."

"Prut! That I do not believe. It was asleep till the fairy prince came through the wood, and waked it up. Ah, well, 'Die erste Liebe ist die beste', but that I should not expect."

"Yes, the first love is the best, but be so contented, for I never had another. Teddy was only a boy, and soon got over his little fancy," said Jo, anxious to correct the Professor's mistake.

"Good! Then I shall rest happy, and be sure that thou givest me all. I haf waited so long, I am grown selfish, as thou wilt find, Professorin."

"I like that," cried Jo, delighted with her new name. "Now tell me what brought you, at last, just when I wanted you?"

"This." And Mr. Bhaer took a little worn paper out of his waistcoat pocket.

Jo unfolded it, and looked much abashed, for it was one of her own contributions to a paper that paid for poetry, which accounted for her sending it an occasional attempt.

"How could that bring you?" she asked, wondering what he meant.

"I found it by chance. I knew it by the names and the initials, and in it there was one little verse that seemed to call me. Read and find him. I will see that you go not in the wet."

IN THE GARRET

Four little chests all in a row, Dim with dust, and worn by time, All fashioned and filled, long ago, By children now in their prime. Four little keys hung side by side, With faded ribbons, brave and gay When fastened there, with childish pride, Long ago, on a rainy day. Four little names, one on each lid, Carved out by a boyish hand, And underneath there lieth hid Histories of the happpy band Once playing here, and pausing oft To hear the sweet refrain, That came and went on the roof aloft, In the falling summer rain.

"Meg" on the first lid, smooth and fair. I look in with loving eyes, For folded here, with well-known care, A goodly gathering lies, The record of a peaceful life—Gifts to gentle child and girl, A bridal gown, lines to a wife, A tiny shoe, a baby curl. No toys in this first chest remain, For all are carried away, In their old age, to join again In another small Meg's play. Ah, happy mother! Well I know You hear, like a sweet refrain, Lullabies ever soft and low In the falling summer rain.

"Jo" on the next lid, scratched and worn, And within a motley store Of headless, dolls, of schoolbooks torn, Birds and beasts that speak no more, Spoils brought home from the fairy ground Only trod by youthful feet, Dreams of a future never found, Memories of a past still sweet, Half-writ poems, stories wild, April letters, warm and cold, Diaries of a wilful child, Hints of a woman early old, A woman in a lonely home, Hearing, like a sad refrain—"Be worthy, love, and love will come," In the falling summer rain.

My Beth! the dust is always swept From the lid that bears your name, As if by loving eyes that wept, By careful hands that often came. Death cannonized for us one saint, Ever less human than divine, And still we lay, with tender plaint, Relics in this household shrine—The silver bell, so seldom rung, The little cap which last she wore, The fair, dead Catherine that hung By angels borne above her door. The songs she sang, without lament, In her prison-house of pain, Forever are they sweetly blent With the falling summer rain.

Upon the last lid's polished field—Legend now both fair and true A gallant knight bears on his shield, "Amy" in letters gold and blue. Within lie snoods that bound her hair, Slippers that have danced their last, Faded flowers laid by with care, Fans whose airy toils are past, Gay valentines, all ardent flames, Trifles that have borne their part In girlish hopes and fears and shames, The record of a maiden heart Now learning fairer, truer spells, Hearing, like a blithe refrain, The silver sound of bridal bells In the falling summer rain.

Four little chests all in a row, Dim with dust, and worn by time, Four women, taught by weal and woe To love and labor in their prime. Four sisters, parted for an hour, None lost, one only gone before, Made by love's immortal power, Nearest and dearest evermore. Oh, when these hidden stores of ours Lie open to the Father's sight, May they be rich in golden hours, Deeds that show fairer for the light, Lives whose brave music long shall ring, Like a spirit-stirring strain, Souls that shall gladly soar and sing In the long sunshine after rain.

"It's very bad poetry, but I felt it when I wrote it, one day when I was very lonely, and had a good cry on a rag bag. I never thought it would go where it could tell tales," said Jo, tearing up the verses the Professor had treasured so long.

"Let it go, it has done it's duty, and I will haf a fresh one when I read all the brown book in which she keeps her little secrets," said Mr. Bhaer with a smile as he watched the fragments fly away on the wind. "Yes," he added earnestly, "I read that, and I think to myself, She has a sorrow, she is lonely, she would find comfort in true love. I haf a heart full, full for her. Shall I not go and say, "If this is not too poor a thing to gif for what I shall hope to receive, take it in Gott's name?"

"And so you came to find that it was not too poor, but the one precious thing I needed," whispered Jo.

"I had no courage to think that at first, heavenly kind as was your welcome to me. But soon I began to hope, and then I said, 'I will haf her if I die for it,' and so I will!" cried Mr. Bhaer, with a defiant nod, as if the walls of mist closing round them were barriers which he was to surmount or valiantly knock down.

Jo thought that was splendid, and resolved to be worthy of her knight, though he did not come prancing on a charger in gorgeous array.

"What made you stay away so long?" she asked presently, finding it so pleasant to ask confidential questions and get delightful answers that she could not keep silent.

"It was not easy, but I could not find the heart to take you from that so happy home until I could haf a prospect of one to gif you, after much time, perhaps, and hard work. How could I ask you to gif up so much for a poor old fellow, who has no fortune but a little learning?"

"I'm glad you are poor. I couldn't bear a rich husband," said Jo decidedly, adding in a softer tone, "Don't fear poverty. I've known it long enough to lose my dread and be happy working for those I love, and don't call yourself old—

forty is the prime of life. I couldn't help loving you if you were seventy!"

The Professor found that so touching that he would have been glad of his handkerchief, if he could have got at it. As her couldn't, Jo wiped his eyes for him, and said, laughing, as she took away a bundle or two . . .

"I may be strong-minded, but no one can say I'm out of my sphere now, for woman's special mission is supposed to be drying tears and bearing burdens. I'm to carry my share, Friedrich, and help to earn the home. Make up your mind to that, or I'll never go," she added resolutely, as he tried to reclaim his load.

"We shall see. Haf you patience to wait a long time, Jo? I must go away and do my work alone. I must help my boys first, because, even for you, I may not break my word to Minna. Can you forgif that, and be happy while we hope and wait?"

"Yes, I know I can, for we love one another, and that makes all the rest easy to bear. I have my duty, also, and my work. I couldn't enjoy myself if I neglected them even for you, so there's no need of hurry or impatience. You can do your part out West, I can do mine here, and both be happy hoping for the best, and leaving the future to be as God wills."

"Ah! Thou gifest me such hope and courage, and I haf nothing to gif back but a full heart and these empty hands," cried the Professor, quite overcome.

Jo never, never would learn to be proper, for when he said that as they stood upon the steps, she just put both hands into his, whispering tenderly, "Not empty now," and stooping down, kissed her Friedrich under the umbrella. It was dreadful, but she would have done it if the flock of draggle-tailed sparrows on the hedge had been human beings, for she was very far gone indeed, and quite regardless of everything but her own happiness. Though it came in such a very simple guise, that was the crowning moment of both their lives, when, turning from the night and storm and loneliness to the household light and warmth and peace waiting to receive them, with a glad "Welcome home!" Jo led her lover in, and shut the door.

Chapter Forty-Seven

For a year Jo and her Professor worked and waited, hoped and loved, met occasionally, and wrote such voluminous letters that the rise in the price of paper was accounted for, Laurie said. The second year began rather soberly, for their prospects did not brighten, and Aunt March died suddenly. But when their first sorrow was over—for they loved the old lady in spite of her sharp tongue—they found they had cause for rejoicing, for she had left Plumfield to Jo, which made all sorts of joyful things possible.

"It's a fine old place, and will bring a handsome sum, for of course you intend to sell it," said Laurie, as they were all talking the matter over some weeks later.

"No, I don't," was Jo's decided answer, as she petted the fat poodle, whom she had adopted, out of respect to his former mistress.

"You don't mean to live there?"

"Yes, I do."

"But, my dear girl, it's an immense house, and will take a power of money to keep it in order. The garden and orchard alone need two or three men, and farming isn't in Bhaer's line, I take it."

"He'll try his hand at it there, if I propose it."

"And you expect to live on the produce of the place? Well, that sounds paradisiacal, but you'll find it desperate hard work."

"The crop we are going to raise is a profitable one," And Jo laughed.

"Of what is this fine crop to consist, ma'am?"

"Boys. I want to open a school for little lads—a good, happy, homelike school, with me to take care of them and Fritz to teach them." "That's a truly Joian plan for you! Isn't that just like her?" cried Laurie, appealing to the family, who looked as much surprised as he.

"I like it," said Mrs. March decidedly.

"So do I," added her husband, who welcomed the thought of a chance for trying the Socratic method of education on modern youth.

"It will be an immense care for Jo," said Meg, stroking the head or her one all-absorbing son.

"Jo can do it, and be happy in it. It's a splendid idea. Tell us all about it," cried Mr. Laurence, who had been longing to lend the lovers a hand, but knew that they would refuse his help.

"I knew you'd stand by me, sir. Amy does too—I see it in her eyes, though she prudently waits to turn it over in her mind before she speaks. Now, my dear people," continued Jo earnestly, "just understand that this isn't a new idea of mine, but a long cherished plan. Before my Fritz came, I used to think how, when I'd made my fortune, and no one needed me at home, I'd hire a big house, and pick up some poor, forlorn little lads who hadn't any mothers, and take care of them, and make life jolly for them before it was too late. I see so many going to ruin for want of help at the right minute, I love so to do anything for them, I seem to feel their wants, and sympathize with their troubles, and oh, I should so like to be a mother to them!"

Mrs. March held out her hand to Jo, who took it, smiling, with tears in her eyes, and went on in the old enthusiastic way, which they had not seen for a long while.

"I told my plan to Fritz once, and he said it was just what he would like, and agreed to try it when we got rich. Bless his dear heart, he's been doing it all his life—helping poor boys, I mean, not getting rich, that he'll never be. Money doesn't stay in his pocket long enough to lay up any. But now, thanks to my good old aunt, who loved me better than I ever deserved, I'm rich, at least I feel so, and we can live at Plumfield perfectly well, if we have a flourishing school. It's just the place for boys, the house is big, and the furniture strong and plain. There's plenty of room for dozens inside, and splendid grounds outside. They could help in the garden and orchard. Such work is healthy, isn't it, sir? Then Fritz could train and teach in his own way, and Father will help him. I can feed and nurse and pet and scold them, and Mother will be my stand-by. I've always longed for lots of boys, and never had enough, now I can fill the house full and revel in the little dears to my heart's content. Think what luxury—Plumfield my own, and a wilderness of boys to enjoy it with me."

As Jo waved her hands and gave a sigh of rapture, the family went off into a gale of merriment, and Mr. Laurence laughed till they thought he'd have an apoplectic fit.

"I don't see anything funny," she said gravely, when she could be heard. "Nothing could be more natural and proper than for my Professor to open a school, and for me to prefer to reside in my own estate."

"She is putting on airs already," said Laurie, who regarded the idea in the light of a capital joke. "But may I inquire how you intend to support the establishment? If all the pupils are little ragamuffins, I'm afraid your crop won't be profitable in a worldly sense, Mr. Bhaer."

"Now don't be a wet-blanket, Teddy. Of course I shall have rich pupils, also—perhaps begin with such altogether. Then, when I've got a start, I can take in a ragamuffin or two, just for a relish. Rich people's children often need care and comfort, as well as poor. I've seen unfortunate little creatures left to servants, or backward ones pushed forward, when it's real cruelty. Some are naughty through mismanagment or neglect, and some lose their mothers. Besides, the best have to get through the hobbledehoy age, and that's the very time they need most patience and kindness. People laugh at them, and hustle them about, try to keep them out of sight, and expect them to turn all at once from pretty children into fine young men. They don't complain much—plucky little souls—but they feel it. I've been through some-thing of it, and I know all about it. I've a special interest in such young bears, and like to show them that I see the warm, honest, well-meaning boys' hearts, in spite of the clumsy arms and legs and the topsy-turvy heads. I've had experience, too, for haven't I brought up one boy to be a pride and honor to his family?"

"I'll testify that you tried to do it," said Laurie with a grateful look.

"And I've succeeded beyond my hopes, for here you are, a steady, sensible businessman, doing heaps of good with your money, and laying up the blessings of the poor, instead of dollars. But you are not merely a businessman, you love good and beautiful things, enjoy them yourself, and let others go halves, as you always did in the old times. I am proud of you, Teddy, for you get better every year, and everyone feels it, though you won't let them say so. Yes, and when I have my flock, I'll just point to you, and say 'There's your model, my lads.'"

Poor Laurie didn't know where to look, for, man though he was, something of the old bashfulness came over him as this burst of praise made all faces turn approvingly upon him.

"I say, Jo, that's rather too much," he began, just in his old boyish way. "You have all done more for me than I can ever thank you for, except by doing my best not to disapoint you. You have rather cast me off lately, Jo, but I've had the best of help, nevertheless. So, if I've got on at all, you may thank these two for it." And he laid one hand gently on his grandfather's head, and the other on Amy's golden one, for the three were never far apart.

"I do think that families are the most beautiful things in all the world!" burst out Jo, who was in an unusually up-lifted frame of mind just then. "When I have one of my own, I hope it will be as happy as the three I know and love the best. If John and my Fritz were only here, it would be quite a little heaven on earth," she added more quietly. And that night when she went to her room after a blissful evening of family counsels, hopes, and plans, her heart was so full of happiness that she could only calm it by kneeling beside the empty bed always near her own, and thinking tender thoughts of Beth. It was a very astonishing year altogether, for things seemed to happen in an unusually rapid and delightful manner. Almost before she knew where she was, Jo found herself married and settled at Plumfield. Then a family of six or seven boys sprung up like mushrooms, and flourished surprisingly, poor boys as well as rich, for Mr. Laurence was continually finding some touching case of destitution, and begging the Bhaers to take pity on the child, and he would gladly pay a trifle for its support. In this way, the sly old gentleman got round proud Jo, and furnished her with the style of boy in which she most delighted.

Of course it was uphill work at first, and Jo made queer mistakes, but the wise Professor steered her safely into calmer waters, and the most rampant ragamuffin was conquered in the end. How Jo did enjoy her 'wilderness of boys', and how poor, dear Aunt March would have lamented had she been there to see the sacred precincts of prim, well-ordered Plumfield overrun with Toms, Dicks, and Harrys! There was a sort of poetic justice about it, after all, for the old lady had been the terror of the boys for miles around, and now the exiles feasted freely on forbidden plums, kicked up the gravel with profane boots unreproved, and played cricket in the big field where the irritable 'cow with a crumpled horn' used to invite rash youths to come and be tossed. It became a sort of boys' paradise, and Laurie suggested that it should be called the 'Bhaer-garten', as a compliment to its master and appropriate to its inhabitants.

It never was a fashionable school, and the Professor did not lay up a fortune, but it was just what Jo intended it to be—'a happy, homelike place for boys, who needed teaching, care, and kindness'. Every room in the big house was soon full. Every little plot in the garden soon had its owner. A regular menagerie appeared in barn and shed, for pet animals were allowed. And three times a day, Jo smiled at her Fritz from the head of a long table lined on either side with rows of happy young faces, which all turned to her with affectionate eyes, confiding words, and grateful hearts, full of love for 'Mother Bhaer'. She had boys enough now, and did not tire of them, though they were not angels, by any means, and some of them caused both Professor and Professorin much trouble and anxiety. But her faith in the good spot which exists in the heart of the naughtiest, sauciest, most tantalizing little ragamuffin gave her patience, skill, and in time success, for no mortal boy could hold out long with Father Bhaer shining on him as benevolently as the sun, and Mother Bhaer forgiving him seventy times seven. Very precious to Jo was the friendship of the lads, their penitent sniffs and whispers after wrongdoing, their droll or touching little confidences, their pleasant enthusiasms, hopes, and plans, even their misfortunes, for they only endeared them to her all the more. There were slow boys and bashful boys, feeble boys and riotous boys, boys that lisped and boys that stuttered, one or two lame ones, and a merry little quadroon, who could not be taken in elsewhere, but who was welcome to the 'Bhaer-garten', though some people predicted that his admission would ruin the school.

Yes, Jo was a very happy woman there, in spite of hard work, much anxiety, and a perpetual racket. She enjoyed it heartily and found the applause of her boys more satisfying than any praise of the world, for now she told no stories except to her flock of enthusiastic believers and admirers. As the years went on, two little lads of her own came to increase her happiness—Rob, named for Grandpa, and Teddy, a happy-go-lucky baby, who seemed to have inherited his papa's sunshiny temper as well as his mother's lively spirit. How they ever grew up alive in that whirlpool of boys was a mystery to their grandma and aunts, but they flourished like dandelions in spring, and their rough nurses loved and served them well.

There were a great many holidays at Plumfield, and one of the most delightful was the yearly apple-picking. For then the Marches, Laurences, Brookes. And Bhaers turned out in full force and made a day of it. Five years after Jo's wedding, one of these fruitful festivals occurred, a mellow October day, when the air was full of an exhilarating freshness which made the spirits rise and the blood dance healthily in the veins. The old orchard wore its holiday attire. Goldenrod and asters fringed the mossy walls. Grasshoppers skipped briskly in the sere grass, and crickets chirped like fairy pipers at a feast. Squirrels were busy with their small harvesting. Birds twittered their adieux from the alders in the lane, and every tree stood ready to send down its shower of red or yellow apples at the first shake. Everybody was there. Everybody laughed and sang, climbed up and tumbled down. Everybody declared that there never had been such a perfect day or such a jolly set to enjoy it, and everyone gave themselves up to the simple pleasures of the hour as freely as if there were no such things as care or sorrow in the world.

Mr. March strolled placidly about, quoting Tusser, Cowley, and Columella to Mr. Laurence, while enjoying . . .

The gentle apple's winey juice.

The Professor charged up and down the green aisles like a stout Teutonic knight, with a pole for a lance, leading on the boys, who made a hook and ladder company of themselves, and performed wonders in the way of ground and lofty tumbling. Laurie devoted himself to the little ones, rode his small daughter in a bushel-basket, took Daisy up among the bird's nests, and kept adventurous Rob from breaking his neck. Mrs. March and

Meg sat among the apple piles like a pair of Pomonas, sorting the contributions that kept pouring in, while Amy with a beautiful motherly expression in her face sketched the various groups, and watched over one pale lad, who sat adoring her with his little crutch beside him.

Jo was in her element that day, and rushed about, with her gown pinned up, and her hat anywhere but on her head, and her baby tucked under her arm, ready for any lively adventure which might turn up. Little Teddy bore a charmed life, for nothing ever happened to him, and Jo never felt any anxiety when he was whisked up into a tree by one lad, galloped off on the back of another, or supplied with sour russets by his indulgent papa, who labored under the Germanic delusion that babies could digest anything, from pickled cabbage to buttons, nails, and their own small shoes. She knew that little Ted would turn up again in time, safe and rosy, dirty and serene, and she always received him back with a hearty welcome, for Jo loved her babies tenderly.

At four o'clock a lull took place, and baskets remained empty, while the apple pickers rested and compared rents and bruises. Then Jo and Meg, with a detachment of the bigger boys, set forth the supper on the grass, for an out-of-door tea was always the crowning joy of the day. The land literally flowed with milk and honey on such occasions, for the lads were not required to sit at table, but allowed to partake of refreshment as they liked—freedom being the sauce best beloved by the boyish soul. They availed themselves of the rare privilege to the fullest extent, for some tried the pleasing experiment of drinking mild while standing on their heads, others lent a charm to leapfrog by eating pie in the pauses of the game, cookies were sown broadcast over the field, and apple turnovers roosted in the trees like a new style of bird. The little girls had a private tea party, and Ted roved among the edibles at his own sweet will.

When no one could eat any more, the Professor proposed the first regular toast, which was always drunk at such times—"Aunt March, God bless her!" A toast heartily given by the good man, who never forgot how much he owed her, and quietly drunk by the boys, who had been taught to keep her memory green.

"Now, Grandma's sixtieth birthday! Long life to her, with three times three!"

That was given with a will, as you may well believe, and the cheering once begun, it was hard to stop it. Everybody's health was proposed, form Mr. Laurence, who was considered their special patron, to the astonished guinea pig, who had strayed from its proper sphere in search of its young master. Demi, as the oldest grandchild, then presented the queen of the day with various gifts, so numerous that they were transported to the festive scene in a wheelbarrow. Funny presents, some of them, but what would have been defects to other eyes were ornaments to Grandma's—for the children's gifts were all their own. Every stitch Daisy's patient little fingers had put into the handkerchiefs she hemmed was better than embroidery to Mrs. March. Demi's miracle of mechanical skill, though the cover wouldn't shut, Rob's footstool had a wiggle in its uneven legs that she declared was soothing, and no page of the costly book Amy's child gave her was so fair as that on which appeared in tipsy capitals, the words—"To dear Grandma, from her little Beth."

During the ceremony the boys had mysteriously disappeared, and when Mrs. March had tried to thank her children, and broken down, while Teddy wiped her eyes on his pinafore, the Professor suddenly began to sing. Then, from above him, voice after voice took up the words, and from tree to tree echoed the music of the unseen choir, as the boys sang with all their hearts the little song that Jo had written, Laurie set to music, and the Professor trained his lads to give with the best effect. This was something altogether new, and it proved a grand success, for Mrs. March couldn't get over her surprise, and insisted on shaking hands with every one of the featherless birds, from tall Franz and Emil to the little quadroon, who had the sweetest voice of all.

After this, the boys dispersed for a final lark, leaving Mrs. March and her daughters under the festival tree.

"I don't think I ever ought to call myself 'unlucky Jo' again, when my greatest wish has been so beautifully gratified," said Mrs. Bhaer, taking Teddy's little fist out of the milk pitcher, in which he was rapturously churning.

"And yet your life is very different from the one you pictured so long ago. Do you remember our castles in the air?" asked Amy, smiling as she watched Laurie and John playing cricket with the boys.

"Dear fellows! It does my heart good to see them forget business and frolic for a day," answered Jo, who now spoke in a maternal way of all mankind. "Yes, I remember, but the life I wanted then seems selfish, lonely, and cold to me now. I haven't given up the hope that I may write a good book yet, but I can wait, and I'm sure it will be all the better for such experiences and illustrations as these." And Jo pointed from the lively lads in the distance to her father, leaning on the Professor's arm, as they walked to and fro in the sunshine, deep in one of the conversations which both enjoyed so much, and then to her mother, sitting enthroned among her daughters, with their children in her lap and at her feet, as if all found help and happiness in the face which never could grow old to them.

"My castle was the most nearly realized of all. I asked for splendid things, to be sure, but in my heart I knew I should be satisfied, if I had a little home, and John, and some dear children like these. I've got them all, thank God, and am the happiest woman in the world." And Meg laid her hand on her tall boy's head, with a face full of tender and devout content.

"My castle is very different from what I planned, but I would not alter it, though, like Jo, I don't relinquish all my artistic hopes, or confine myself to helping others fulfill their dreams of beauty. I've begun to model a figure of baby, and Laurie says it is the best thing I've ever done. I think so, myself, and mean to do it in marble, so that, whatever happens, I may at least keep the image of my little angel."

As Amy spoke, a great tear dropped on the golden hair of the sleeping child in her arms, for her one well-beloved daughter was a frail little creature and the dread of losing her was the shadow over Amy's sunshine. This cross was doing much for both father and mother, for one love and sorrow bound them closely together. Amy's nature was growing sweeter, deeper, and more tender. Laurie was growing more serious, strong, and firm, and both were learning that beauty, youth, good fortune, even love itself, cannot keep care and pain, loss and sorrow, from the most blessed for . . .

> Into each life some rain must fall, Some days must be dark and sad and dreary.

"She is growing better, I am sure of it, my dear. Don't despond, but hope and keep happy," said Mrs. March, as tenderhearted Daisy stooped from her knee to lay her rosy cheek against her little cousin's pale one.

"I never ought to, while I have you to cheer me up, Marmee, and Laurie to take more than half of every burden," replied Amy warmly. "He never lets me see his anxiety, but is so sweet and patient with me, so devoted to Beth, and such a stay and comfort to me always that I can't love him enough. So, in spite of my one cross, I can say with Meg, 'Thank God, I'm a happy woman.'"

"There's no need for me to say it, for everyone can see that I'm far happier than I deserve," added Jo, glancing from her good husband to her chubby children, tumbling on the grass beside her. "Fritz is getting gray and stout. I'm growing as thin as a shadow, and am thirty. We never shall be rich, and Plumfield may burn up any night, for that incorrigible Tommy Bangs will smoke sweet-fern cigars under the bed-clothes, though he's set himself afire three times already. But in spite of these unromantic facts, I have nothing to complain of, and never was so jolly in my life. Excuse the remark, but living among boys, I can't help using their expressions now and then."

"Yes, Jo, I think your harvest will be a good one," began Mrs. March, frightening away a big black cricket that was staring Teddy out of countenance.

"Not half so good as yours, Mother. Here it is, and we never can thank you enough for the patient sowing and reaping you have done," cried Jo, with the loving impetuosity which she never would outgrow.

"I hope there will be more wheat and fewer tares every year," said Amy softly.

"A large sheaf, but I know there's room in your heart for it, Marmee dear," added Meg's tender voice.

Touched to the heart, Mrs. March could only stretch out her arms, as if to gather children and grandchildren to herself, and say, with face and voice full of motherly love, gratitude, and humility . . .

"Oh, my girls, however long you may live, I never can wish you a greater happiness than this!"

Emily Brontë

WUTHERING HEIGHTS

Romance CLASSICS

Romance CLASSICS

Published by Trident Press International
801 12th Avenue South
Suite 302
Naples Florida 34102 USA
www.trident-international.com
email: tridentpress@worldnet.att.net

Printed in Australia
ISBN: 1582791953

Chapter I

1801.—I have just returned from a visit to my landlord—the solitary neighbour that I shall be troubled with. This is certainly a beautiful country! In all England, I do not believe that I could have fixed on a situation so completely removed from the stir of society. A perfect misanthropist's heaven: and Mr. Heathcliff and I are such a suitable pair to divide the desolation between us. A capital fellow! He little imagined how my heart warmed towards him when I beheld his black eyes withdraw so suspiciously under their brows, as I rode up, and when his fingers sheltered themselves, with a jealous resolution, still further in his waistcoat, as I announced my name.

'Mr. Heathcliff?' I said.

A nod was the answer.

'Mr. Lockwood, your new tenant, sir. I do myself the honour of calling as soon as possible after my arrival, to express the hope that I have not inconvenienced you by my perseverance in soliciting the occupation of Thrushcross Grange: I heard yesterday you had had some thoughts—'

'Thrushcross Grange is my own, sir,' he interrupted, wincing. 'I should not allow any one to inconvenience me, if I could hinder it—walk in!'

The 'walk in' was uttered with closed teeth, and expressed the sentiment, 'Go to the Deuce:' even the gate over which he leant manifested no sympathising movement to the words; and I think that circumstance determined me to accept the invitation: I felt interested in a man who seemed more exaggeratedly reserved than myself.

When he saw my horse's breast fairly pushing the barrier, he did put out his hand to unchain it, and then sullenly preceded me up the causeway, calling, as we entered the court,—'Joseph, take Mr. Lockwood's horse; and bring up some wine.'

'Here we have the whole establishment of domestics, I suppose,' was the reflection suggested by this compound order. 'No wonder the grass grows up between the flags, and cattle are the only hedge-cutters.'

Joseph was an elderly, nay, an old man: very old, perhaps, though hale and sinewy. 'The Lord help us!' he soliloquised in an undertone of peevish displeasure, while relieving me of my horse: looking, meantime, in my face so sourly that I charitably conjectured he must have need of divine aid to digest his dinner, and his pious ejaculation had no reference to my unexpected advent.

Wuthering Heights is the name of Mr. Heathcliff's dwelling. 'Wuthering' being a significant provincial adjective, descriptive of the atmospheric tumult to which its station is exposed in stormy weather. Pure, bracing ventilation they must have up there at all times, indeed: one may guess the power of the north wind blowing over the edge, by the excessive slant of a few stunted firs at the end of the house; and by a range of gaunt thorns all stretching their limbs one way, as if craving alms of the sun. Happily, the architect had foresight to build it strong: the narrow windows are deeply set in the wall, and the corners defended with large jutting stones.

Before passing the threshold, I paused to admire a quantity of grotesque carving lavished over the front, and especially about the principal door; above which, among a wilderness of crumbling griffins and shameless little boys, I detected the date '1500,' and the name 'Hareton Earnshaw.' I would have made a few comments, and requested a short history of the place from the surly owner; but his attitude at the door appeared to demand my speedy entrance, or complete departure, and I had no desire to aggravate his impatience previous to inspecting the penetralium.

One stop brought us into the family sitting-room, without any introductory lobby or passage: they call it here 'the house' pre-eminently. It includes kitchen and parlour, generally; but I believe at Wuthering Heights the kitchen is forced to retreat altogether into another quarter: at least I distinguished a chatter of tongues, and a clatter of culinary utensils, deep within; and I observed no signs of roasting, boiling, or baking, about the huge fireplace; nor any glitter of copper saucepans and tin cullenders on the walls. One end, indeed, reflected splendidly both light and heat from ranks of immense pewter dishes, interspersed with silver jugs and tankards, towering row after row, on a vast oak dresser, to the very roof. The latter had never been under-drawn: its entire anatomy lay bare to an inquiring eye, except where a frame of wood laden with oatcakes and clusters of legs of beef, mutton, and ham, concealed it. Above the chimney were sundry villainous old guns, and a couple of horse-pistols: and, by way of ornament, three gaudily-painted canisters disposed along its ledge. The floor was of smooth, white stone; the chairs, high-backed, primitive structures, painted green: one or two heavy black ones lurking in the shade. In an arch under the dresser reposed a huge, liver-coloured bitch pointer, surrounded by a swarm of squealing puppies; and other dogs haunted other recesses.

The apartment and furniture would have been nothing extraordinary as belonging to a homely, northern farmer, with a stubborn countenance, and stalwart limbs set out to advantage in knee-breeches and gaiters. Such an individual seated in his arm-chair, his mug of ale frothing on the round table before him, is to be seen in any circuit of five or six miles among these hills, if you go at the right time after dinner. But Mr. Heathcliff forms a singular contrast to his abode and style of living. He is a dark-skinned gipsy in aspect, in dress and manners a gentleman: that is, as much a gentleman as many a country squire: rather slovenly, perhaps, yet not looking amiss with his negligence, because he has an erect and handsome figure; and rather morose. Possibly, some people might suspect him of a degree of under-bred pride; I have a sympathetic chord within that tells me it is nothing of the sort: I know, by instinct, his reserve springs from an aversion to showy displays of feeling—to manifestations of mutual kindliness. He'll love and hate equally under cover, and esteem it a species of impertinence to be loved or hated again. No, I'm running on too fast: I bestow my own attributes over-liberally on him. Mr. Heathcliff may have entirely dissimilar reasons for keeping his hand out of the way when he meets a would-be acquaintance, to those which actuate me. Let me hope my constitution is almost peculiar: my dear mother used to say I should never have a comfortable home; and only last summer I proved myself perfectly unworthy of one.

While enjoying a month of fine weather at the sea-coast, I was thrown into the company of a most fascinating creature: a real goddess in my eyes, as long as she took no notice of me. I 'never told my love' vocally; still, if looks have language, the merest idiot might have guessed I was over head and ears: she understood me at last, and looked a return—the sweetest of all imaginable looks. And what did I do? I confess it with shame—shrunk icily into myself, like a snail; at every glance retired colder and farther; till finally the poor innocent was led to doubt her own senses, and, overwhelmed with confusion at her supposed mistake, persuaded her mamma to decamp. By this curious turn of disposition I have gained the reputation of deliberate heartlessness; how undeserved, I alone can appreciate.

I took a seat at the end of the hearthstone opposite that towards which my landlord advanced, and filled up an interval of silence by attempting to caress the canine mother, who had left her nursery, and was sneaking wolfishly to the back of my legs, her lip curled up, and her white teeth watering for a snatch. My caress provoked a long, guttural gnarl.

'You'd better let the dog alone,' growled Mr. Heathcliff in unison, checking fiercer demonstrations with a punch of his foot. 'She's not accustomed to be spoiled—not kept for a pet.' Then, striding to a side door, he shouted again, 'Joseph!'

Joseph mumbled indistinctly in the depths of the cellar, but gave no intimation of ascending; so his master dived down to him, leaving me VIS-A-VIS the ruffianly bitch and a pair of grim shaggy sheep-dogs, who shared with her a jealous guardianship over all my movements. Not anxious to come in contact with their fangs, I sat still; but, imagining they would scarcely understand tacit insults, I unfortunately indulged in winking and making faces at the trio, and some turn of my physiognomy so irritated madam, that she suddenly broke into a fury and leapt on my knees. I flung her back, and hastened to interpose the table between us. This proceeding aroused the whole hive: half-a-dozen four-footed fiends, of various sizes and ages, issued from hidden dens to the common centre. I felt my heels and coat-laps peculiar subjects of assault; and parrying off the larger combatants as effectually as I could with the poker, I was constrained to demand, aloud, assistance from some of the household in re-establishing peace.

Mr. Heathcliff and his man climbed the cellar steps with vexatious phlegm: I don't think they moved one second faster than usual, though the hearth was an absolute tempest of worrying and yelping. Happily, an inhabitant of the kitchen made more despatch: a lusty dame, with tucked-up gown, bare arms, and fire-flushed cheeks, rushed into the midst of us flourishing a frying-pan: and used that weapon, and her tongue, to such purpose, that the storm subsided magically, and she only remained, heaving like a sea after a high wind, when her master entered on the scene.

'What the devil is the matter?' he asked, eyeing me in a manner that I could ill endure, after this inhospitable treatment.

'What the devil, indeed!' I muttered. 'The herd of possessed swine could have had no worse spirits in them than those animals of yours, sir. You might as well leave a stranger with a brood of tigers!'

'They won't meddle with persons who touch nothing,' he remarked, putting the bottle before me, and restoring the displaced table. 'The dogs do right to be vigilant. Take a glass of wine?'

'No, thank you.'

'Not bitten, are you?'

'If I had been, I would have set my signet on the biter.' Heathcliff's countenance relaxed into a grin.

'Come, come,' he said, 'you are flurried, Mr. Lockwood. Here, take a little wine. Guests are so exceedingly rare in this house that I and my dogs, I am willing to own, hardly know how to receive them. Your health, sir?'

I bowed and returned the pledge; beginning to perceive that it would be foolish to sit sulking for the misbehaviour of a pack of curs; besides, I felt loth to yield the fellow further amusement at my expense; since his humour took that turn. He—probably swayed by prudential consideration of the folly of offending a good tenant-relaxed a little in the laconic style of chipping off his pronouns and auxiliary verbs, and introduced what he supposed would be a subject of interest to me,—a discourse on the advantages and disadvantages of my present place of retirement. I found him very intelligent on the topics we touched; and before I went home, I was encouraged so far as to volunteer another visit to-morrow. He evidently wished no repetition of my intrusion. I shall go, notwithstanding. It is astonishing how sociable I feel myself compared with him.

Chapter II

YESTERDAY afternoon set in misty and cold. I had half a mind to spend it by my study fire, instead of wading through heath and mud to Wuthering Heights. On coming up from dinner, however, (N.B.—I dine between twelve and one o'clock; the housekeeper, a matronly lady, taken as a fixture along with the house, could not, or would not, comprehend my request that I might be served at five)—on mounting the stairs with this lazy intention, and stepping into the room, I saw a servant-girl on her knees surrounded by brushes and coal-scuttles, and raising an infernal dust as she extinguished the flames with heaps of cinders. This spectacle drove me back immediately; I took my hat, and, after a four-miles' walk, arrived at Heathcliff's garden-gate just in time to escape the first feathery flakes of a snow-shower.

On that bleak hill-top the earth was hard with a black frost, and the air made me shiver through every limb. Being unable to remove the chain, I jumped over, and, running up the flagged causeway bordered with straggling gooseberry-bushes, knocked vainly for admittance, till my knuckles tingled and the dogs howled.

'Wretched inmates!' I ejaculated, mentally, 'you deserve perpetual isolation from your species for your churlish inhospitality. At least, I would not keep my doors barred in the day-time. I don't care—I will get in!' So resolved, I grasped the latch and shook it vehemently. Vinegar-faced Joseph projected his head from a round window of the barn.

'What are ye for?' he shouted. 'T' maister's down i' t' fowld. Go round by th' end o' t' laith, if ye went to spake to him.'

'Is there nobody inside to open the door?' I hallooed, responsively.

'There's nobbut t' missis; and shoo'll not oppen 't an ye mak' yer flaysome dins till neeght.'

'Why? Cannot you tell her whom I am, eh, Joseph?'

'Nor-ne me! I'll hae no hend wi't,' muttered the head, vanishing.

The snow began to drive thickly. I seized the handle to essay another trial; when a young man without coat, and shouldering a pitchfork, appeared in the yard behind. He hailed me to follow him, and, after marching through a wash-house, and a paved area containing a coal-shed, pump, and pigeon-cot, we at length arrived in the huge, warm, cheerful apartment where I was formerly received. It glowed delightfully in the radiance of an immense fire, compounded of coal, peat, and wood; and near the table, laid for a plentiful evening meal, I was pleased to observe the 'missis,' an individual whose existence I had never previously suspected. I bowed and waited, thinking she would bid me take a seat. She looked at me, leaning back in her chair, and remained motionless and mute.

'Rough weather!' I remarked. 'I'm afraid, Mrs. Heathcliff, the door must bear the consequence of your servants' leisure attendance: I had hard work to make them hear me.'

She never opened her mouth. I stared—she stared also: at any rate, she kept her eyes on me in a cool, regardless manner, exceedingly embarrassing and disagreeable.

'Sit down,' said the young man, gruffly. 'He'll be in soon.'

I obeyed; and hemmed, and called the villain Juno, who deigned, at this second interview, to move the extreme tip of her tail, in token of owning my acquaintance.

'A beautiful animal!' I commenced again. 'Do you intend parting with the little ones, madam?'

'They are not mine,' said the amiable hostess, more repellingly than Heathcliff himself could have replied.

'Ah, your favourites are among these?' I continued, turning to an obscure cushion full of something like cats.

'A strange choice of favourites!' she observed scornfully.

Unluckily, it was a heap of dead rabbits. I hemmed once more, and drew closer to the hearth, repeating my comment on the wildness of the evening.

'You should not have come out,' she said, rising and reaching from the chimney-piece two of the painted canisters.

Her position before was sheltered from the light; now, I had a distinct view of her whole figure and countenance. She was slender, and apparently scarcely past girlhood: an admirable form, and the most exquisite little face that I have ever had the pleasure of beholding; small features, very fair; flaxen ringlets, or rather golden, hanging loose on her delicate neck; and eyes, had they been agreeable in expression, that would have been irresistible: fortunately for my susceptible heart, the only sentiment they evinced hovered between scorn and a kind of desperation, singularly unnatural to be detected there. The canisters were almost out of her reach; I made a motion to aid her; she turned upon me as a miser might turn if any one attempted to assist him in counting his gold.

'I don't want your help,' she snapped; 'I can get them for myself.'

'I beg your pardon!' I hastened to reply.

'Were you asked to tea?' she demanded, tying an apron over her neat black frock, and standing with a spoonful of the leaf poised over the pot.

'I shall be glad to have a cup,' I answered.

'Were you asked?' she repeated.

'No,' I said, half smiling. 'You are the proper person to ask me.'

She flung the tea back, spoon and all, and resumed her chair in a pet; her forehead corrugated, and her red under-lip pushed out, like a child's ready to cry.

Meanwhile, the young man had slung on to his person a decidedly shabby upper garment, and, erecting himself before the blaze, looked down on me from the corner of his eyes, for all the world as if there were some mortal feud unavenged between us. I began to doubt whether he were a servant or not: his dress and speech were both rude, entirely devoid of the superiority observable in Mr. and Mrs. Heathcliff; his thick brown curls were rough and uncultivated, his whiskers encroached bearishly over his cheeks, and his hands were embrowned like those of a common labourer: still his bearing was free, almost haughty, and he showed none of a domestic's assiduity in attending on the lady of the house. In the absence of clear proofs of his condition, I deemed it best to abstain from noticing his curious conduct; and, five minutes afterwards, the entrance of Heathcliff relieved me, in some measure, from my uncomfortable state.

'You see, sir, I am come, according to promise!' I exclaimed, assuming the cheerful; 'and I fear I shall be weather-bound for half an hour, if you can afford me shelter during that space.'

'Half an hour?' he said, shaking the white flakes from his clothes; 'I wonder you should select the thick of a snow-storm to ramble about in. Do you know that you run a risk of being lost in the marshes? People familiar with these moors often miss their road on such evenings; and I can tell you there is no chance of a change at present.'

'Perhaps I can get a guide among your lads, and he might stay at the Grange till morning—could you spare me one?'

'No, I could not.'

'Oh, indeed! Well, then, I must trust to my own sagacity.'

'Umph!'

'Are you going to mak' the tea?' demanded he of the shabby coat, shifting his ferocious gaze from me to the young lady.

'Is HE to have any?' she asked, appealing to Heathcliff.

'Get it ready, will you?' was the answer, uttered so savagely that I started. The tone in which the words were said revealed a genuine bad nature. I no longer felt inclined to call Heathcliff a capital fellow. When the preparations were finished, he invited me with—'Now, sir, bring forward your chair.' And we all, including the rustic youth, drew round the table: an austere silence prevailing while we discussed our meal.

I thought, if I had caused the cloud, it was my duty to make an effort to dispel it. They could not every day sit so grim and taciturn;

and it was impossible, however ill-tempered they might be, that the universal scowl they wore was their every-day countenance.

'It is strange,' I began, in the interval of swallowing one cup of tea and receiving another—'it is strange how custom can mould our tastes and ideas: many could not imagine the existence of happiness in a life of such complete exile from the world as you spend, Mr. Heathcliff; yet, I'll venture to say, that, surrounded by your family, and with your amiable lady as the presiding genius over your home and heart—'

'My amiable lady!' he interrupted, with an almost diabolical sneer on his face. 'Where is she—my amiable lady?'

'Mrs. Heathcliff, your wife, I mean.'

'Well, yes—oh, you would intimate that her spirit has taken the post of ministering angel, and guards the fortunes of Wuthering Heights, even when her body is gone. Is that it?'

Perceiving myself in a blunder, I attempted to correct it. I might have seen there was too great a disparity between the ages of the parties to make it likely that they were man and wife. One was about forty: a period of mental vigour at which men seldom cherish the delusion of being married for love by girls: that dream is reserved for the solace of our declining years. The other did not look seventeen.

Then it flashed on me—'The clown at my elbow, who is drinking his tea out of a basin and eating his broad with unwashed hands, may be her husband: Heathcliff junior, of course. Here is the consequence of being buried alive: she has thrown herself away upon that boor from sheer ignorance that better individuals existed! A sad pity—I must beware how I cause her to regret her choice.' The last reflection may seem conceited; it was not. My neighbour struck me as bordering on repulsive; I knew, through experience, that I was tolerably attractive.

'Mrs. Heathcliff is my daughter-in-law,' said Heathcliff, corroborating my surmise. He turned, as he spoke, a peculiar look in her direction: a look of hatred; unless he has a most perverse set of facial muscles that will not, like those of other people, interpret the language of his soul.

'Ah, certainly—I see now: you are the favoured possessor of the beneficent fairy,' I remarked, turning to my neighbour.

This was worse than before: the youth grew crimson, and clenched his fist, with every appearance of a meditated assault. But he seemed to recollect himself presently, and smothered the storm in a brutal curse, muttered on my behalf: which, however, I took care not to notice.

'Unhappy in your conjectures, sir,' observed my host; 'we neither of us have the privilege of owning your good fairy; her mate is dead. I said she was my daughter-in-law: therefore, she must have married my son.'

'And this young man is—'

'Not my son, assuredly.'

Heathcliff smiled again, as if it were rather too bold a jest to attribute the paternity of that bear to him.

'My name is Hareton Earnshaw,' growled the other; 'and I'd counsel you to respect it!'

'I've shown no disrespect,' was my reply, laughing internally at the dignity with which he announced himself.

He fixed his eye on me longer than I cared to return the stare, for fear I might be tempted either to box his ears or render my hilarity audible. I began to feel unmistakably out of place in that pleasant family circle. The dismal spiritual atmosphere overcame, and more than neutralised, the glowing physical comforts round me; and I resolved to be cautious how I ventured under those rafters a third time.

The business of eating being concluded, and no one uttering a word of sociable conversation, I approached a window to examine the weather. A sorrowful sight I saw: dark night coming down prematurely, and sky and hills mingled in one bitter whirl of wind and suffocating snow.

'I don't think it possible for me to get home now without a guide,' I could not help exclaiming. 'The roads will be buried already; and, if they were bare, I could scarcely distinguish a foot in advance.'

'Hareton, drive those dozen sheep into the barn porch. They'll be covered if left in the fold all night: and put a plank before them,' said Heathcliff.

'How must I do?' I continued, with rising irritation.

There was no reply to my question; and on looking round I saw only Joseph bringing in a pail of porridge for the dogs, and Mrs. Heathcliff leaning over the fire, diverting herself with burning a bundle of matches which had fallen from the chimney-piece as she restored the tea-canister to its place. The former, when he had deposited his burden, took a critical survey of the room, and in cracked tones grated out—'Aw wonder how yah can faishion to stand thear i' idleness un war, when all on 'ems goan out! Bud yah're a nowt, and it's no use talking—yah'll niver mend o'yer ill ways, but goa raight to t' divil, like yer mother afore ye!'

I imagined, for a moment, that this piece of eloquence was addressed to me; and, sufficiently enraged, stepped towards the aged rascal with an intention of kicking him out of the door. Mrs. Heathcliff, however, checked me by her answer.

'You scandalous old hypocrite!' she replied. 'Are you not afraid of being carried away bodily, whenever you mention the devil's name? I warn you to refrain from provoking me, or I'll ask your abduction as a special favour! Stop! look here, Joseph,' she continued, taking a long, dark book from a shelf; 'I'll show you how far I've progressed in the Black Art: I shall soon be competent to make a clear house of it. The red cow didn't die by chance; and your rheumatism can hardly be reckoned among providential visitations!'

'Oh, wicked, wicked!' gasped the elder; 'may the Lord deliver us from evil!'

'No, reprobate! you are a castaway—be off, or I'll hurt you seriously! I'll have you all modelled in wax and clay! and the first who passes the limits I fix shall—I'll not say what he shall be done to—but, you'll see! Go, I'm looking at you!'

The little witch put a mock malignity into her beautiful eyes, and Joseph, trembling with sincere horror, hurried out, praying, and ejaculating 'wicked' as he went. I thought her conduct must be prompted by a species of dreary fun; and, now that we were alone, I endeavoured to interest her in my distress.

'Mrs. Heathcliff,' I said earnestly, 'you must excuse me for troubling you. I presume, because, with that face, I'm sure you cannot help being good-hearted. Do point out some landmarks by which I may know my way home: I have no more idea how to get there than you would have how to get to London!'

'Take the road you came,' she answered, ensconcing herself in a chair, with a candle, and the long book open before her. 'It is brief advice, but as sound as I can give.'

'Then, if you hear of me being discovered dead in a bog or a pit full of snow, your conscience won't whisper that it is partly your fault?'

'How so? I cannot escort you. They wouldn't let me go to the end of the garden wall.'

'YOU! I should be sorry to ask you to cross the threshold, for my convenience, on such a night,' I cried. 'I want you to tell me my way, not to SHOW it: or else to persuade Mr. Heathcliff to give me a guide.'

'Who? There is himself, Earnshaw, Zillah, Joseph and I. Which would you have?'

'Are there no boys at the farm?'

'No; those are all.'

'Then, it follows that I am compelled to stay.'

'That you may settle with your host. I have nothing to do with it.'

'I hope it will be a lesson to you to make no more rash journeys on these hills,' cried Heathcliff's stern voice from the kitchen entrance. 'As to staying here, I don't keep accommodations for visitors: you must share a bed with Hareton or Joseph, if you do.'

'I can sleep on a chair in this room,' I replied.

'No, no! A stranger is a stranger, be he rich or poor: it will not suit me to permit any one the range of the place while I am off guard!' said the unmannerly wretch.

With this insult my patience was at an end. I uttered an expression of disgust, and pushed past him into the yard, running against Earnshaw in my haste. It was so dark that I could not see the means of exit; and, as I wandered round, I heard another specimen of their civil behaviour amongst each other. At first the young man appeared about to befriend me.

'I'll go with him as far as the park,' he said.

'You'll go with him to hell!' exclaimed his master, or whatever relation he bore. 'And who is to look after the horses, eh?'

'A man's life is of more consequence than one evening's neglect of the horses: somebody must go,' murmured Mrs. Heathcliff, more kindly than I expected.

'Not at your command!' retorted Hareton. 'If you set store on him, you'd better be quiet.'

'Then I hope his ghost will haunt you; and I hope Mr. Heathcliff will never get another tenant till the Grange is a ruin,' she answered, sharply.

'Hearken, hearken, shoo's cursing on 'em!' muttered Joseph, towards whom I had been steering.

He sat within earshot, milking the cows by the light of a lantern, which I seized unceremoniously, and, calling out that I would send it back on the morrow, rushed to the nearest postern.

'Maister, maister, he's staling t' lanthern!' shouted the ancient, pursuing my retreat. 'Hey, Gnasher! Hey, dog! Hey Wolf, holld him, holld him!'

On opening the little door, two hairy monsters flew at my throat, bearing me down, and extinguishing the light; while a mingled guffaw from Heathcliff and Hareton put the copestone on my rage and humiliation. Fortunately, the beasts seemed more bent on stretching their paws, and yawning, and flourishing their tails, than devouring me alive; but they would suffer no resurrection, and I was forced to lie till their malignant masters pleased to deliver me: then, hatless and trembling with wrath, I ordered the miscreants to let me out—on their peril to keep me one minute longer—with several incoherent threats of retaliation that, in their indefinite depth of virulency, smacked of King Lear.

The vehemence of my agitation brought on a copious bleeding at the nose, and still Heathcliff laughed, and still I scolded. I don't know what would have concluded the scene, had there not been one person at hand rather more rational than myself, and more benevolent than my entertainer. This was Zillah, the stout housewife; who at length issued forth to inquire into the nature of the uproar. She thought that some of them had been laying violent hands on me; and, not daring to attack her master, she turned her vocal artillery against the younger scoundrel.

'Well, Mr. Earnshaw,' she cried, 'I wonder what you'll have agait next? Are we going to murder folk on our very door-stones? I see this house will never do for me—look at t' poor lad, he's fair choking! Wisht, wisht; you mun'n't go on so. Come in, and I'll cure that: there now, hold ye still.'

With these words she suddenly splashed a pint of icy water down my neck, and pulled me into the kitchen. Mr. Heathcliff followed, his accidental merriment expiring quickly in his habitual moroseness.

I was sick exceedingly, and dizzy, and faint; and thus compelled perforce to accept lodgings under his roof. He told Zillah to give me a glass of brandy, and then passed on to the inner room; while she condoled with me on my sorry predicament, and having obeyed his orders, whereby I was somewhat revived, ushered me to bed.

Chapter III

WHILE leading the way upstairs, she recommended that I should hide the candle, and not make a noise; for her master had an odd notion about the chamber she would put me in, and never let anybody lodge there willingly. I asked the reason. She did not know, she answered: she had only lived there a year or two; and they had so many queer goings on, she could not begin to be curious.

Too stupefied to be curious myself, I fastened my door and glanced round for the bed. The whole furniture consisted of a chair, a clothes-press, and a large oak case, with squares cut out near the top resembling coach windows. Having approached this structure, I looked inside, and perceived it to be a singular sort of old-fashioned couch, very conveniently designed to obviate the necessity for every member of the family having a room to himself. In fact, it formed a little closet, and the ledge of a window, which it enclosed, served as a table. I slid back the panelled sides, got in with my light, pulled them together again, and felt secure against the vigilance of Heathcliff, and every one else.

The ledge, where I placed my candle, had a few mildewed books piled up in one corner; and it was covered with writing scratched on the paint. This writing, however, was nothing but a name repeated in all kinds of characters, large and small—CATHERINE EARNSHAW, here and there varied to CATHERINE HEATHCLIFF, and then again to CATHERINE LINTON.

In vapid listlessness I leant my head against the window, and continued spelling over Catherine Earnshaw—Heathcliff—Linton, till my eyes closed; but they had not rested five minutes when a glare of white letters started from the dark, as vivid as spectres-the air swarmed with Catherines; and rousing myself to dispel the obtrusive name, I discovered my candle-wick reclining on one of the antique volumes, and perfuming the place with an odour of roasted calf-skin. I snuffed it off, and, very ill at ease under the influence of cold and lingering nausea, sat up and spread open the injured tome on my knee. It was a Testament, in lean type, and smelling dreadfully musty: a fly-leaf bore the inscription-'Catherine Earnshaw, her book,' and a date some quarter of a century back. I shut it, and took up another and another, till I had examined all. Catherine's library was select, and its state of dilapidation proved it to have been well used, though not altogether for a legitimate purpose: scarcely one chapter had escaped, a pen-and-ink commentary—at least the appearance of one-covering every morsel of blank that the printer had left. Some were detached sentences; other parts took the form of a regular diary, scrawled in an unformed, childish hand. At the top of an extra page (quite a treasure, probably, when first lighted on) I was greatly amused to behold an excellent caricature of my friend Joseph,—rudely, yet powerfully sketched. An immediate interest kindled within me for the unknown Catherine, and I began forthwith to decipher her faded hieroglyphics.

'An awful Sunday,' commenced the paragraph beneath. 'I wish my father were back again. Hindley is a detestable substitute—his conduct to Heathcliff is atrocious—H. and I are going to rebel—we took our initiatory step this evening.

'All day had been flooding with rain; we could not go to church, so Joseph must needs get up a congregation in the garret; and, while Hindley and his wife basked downstairs before a comfortable fire-doing anything but reading their Bibles, I'll answer for it—Heathcliff, myself, and the unhappy ploughboy were commanded to take our prayer-books, and mount: we were ranged in a row, on a sack of corn, groaning and shivering, and hoping that Joseph would shiver too, so that he might give us a short homily for his own sake. A vain idea! The service lasted precisely three hours; and yet my brother had the face to exclaim, when he saw us descending, "What, done already?" On Sunday evenings we used to be permitted to play, if we did not make much noise; now a mere titter is sufficient to send us into corners.

'"You forget you have a master here," says the tyrant. "I'll demolish the first who puts me out of temper! I insist on perfect sobriety and silence. Oh, boy! was that you? Frances darling, pull his hair as you go by: I heard him snap his fingers." Frances pulled his hair heartily, and then went and seated herself on her husband's knee, and there they were, like two babies, kissing and talking nonsense by the hour—foolish palaver that we should be ashamed of. We made ourselves as snug as our means allowed in the arch of the dresser. I had just fastened our pinafores together, and hung them up for a curtain, when in comes Joseph, on an errand from the stables. He tears down my handiwork, boxes my ears, and croaks:

'"T' maister nobbut just buried, and Sabbath not o'ered, und t' sound o' t' gospel still i' yer lugs, and ye darr be laiking! Shame on ye!

sit ye down, ill childer! there's good books eneugh if ye'll read 'em: sit ye down, and think o' yer sowls!"

'Saying this, he compelled us so to square our positions that we might receive from the far-off fire a dull ray to show us the text of the lumber he thrust upon us. I could not bear the employment. I took my dingy volume by the scroop, and hurled it into the dog-kennel, vowing I hated a good book. Heathcliff kicked his to the same place. Then there was a hubbub!

'"Maister Hindley!" shouted our chaplain. "Maister, coom hither! Miss Cathy's riven th' back off 'Th' Helmet o' Salvation,' un' Heathcliff's pawsed his fit into t' first part o' 'T' Brooad Way to Destruction!' It's fair flaysome that ye let 'em go on this gait. Ech! th' owd man wad ha' laced 'em properly—but he's goan!"

'Hindley hurried up from his paradise on the hearth, and seizing one of us by the collar, and the other by the arm, hurled both into the back-kitchen; where, Joseph asseverated, "owd Nick would fetch us as sure as we were living: and, so comforted, we each sought a separate nook to await his advent. I reached this book, and a pot of ink from a shelf, and pushed the house-door ajar to give me light, and I have got the time on with writing for twenty minutes; but my companion is impatient, and proposes that we should appropriate the dairy-woman's cloak, and have a scamper on the moors, under its shelter. A pleasant suggestion—and then, if the surly old man come in, he may believe his prophecy verified—we cannot be damper, or colder, in the rain than we are here.'

* * * * * *

I suppose Catherine fulfilled her project, for the next sentence took up another subject: she waxed lachrymose.

'How little did I dream that Hindley would ever make me cry so!' she wrote. 'My head aches, till I cannot keep it on the pillow; and still I can't give over. Poor Heathcliff! Hindley calls him a vagabond, and won't let him sit with us, nor eat with us any more; and, he says, he and I must not play together, and threatens to turn him out of the house if we break his orders. He has been blaming our father (how dared he?) for treating H. too liberally; and swears he will reduce him to his right place—'

* * * * * *

I began to nod drowsily over the dim page: my eye wandered from manuscript to print. I saw a red ornamented title—'Seventy

Times Seven, and the First of the Seventy-First.' A Pious Discourse delivered by the Reverend Jabez Branderham, in the Chapel of Gimmerden Sough.' And while I was, half-consciously, worrying my brain to guess what Jabez Branderham would make of his subject, I sank back in bed, and fell asleep. Alas, for the effects of bad tea and bad temper! What else could it be that made me pass such a terrible night? I don't remember another that I can at all compare with it since I was capable of suffering.

I began to dream, almost before I ceased to be sensible of my locality. I thought it was morning; and I had set out on my way home, with Joseph for a guide. The snow lay yards deep in our road; and, as we floundered on, my companion wearied me with constant reproaches that I had not brought a pilgrim's staff: telling me that I could never get into the house without one, and boastfully flourishing a heavy-headed cudgel, which I understood to be so denominated. For a moment I considered it absurd that I should need such a weapon to gain admittance into my own residence. Then a new idea flashed across me. I was not going there: we were journeying to hear the famous Jabez Branderham preach, from the text—'Seventy Times Seven;' and either Joseph, the preacher, or I had committed the 'First of the Seventy-First,' and were to be publicly exposed and excommunicated.

We came to the chapel. I have passed it really in my walks, twice or thrice; it lies in a hollow, between two hills: an elevated hollow, near a swamp, whose peaty moisture is said to answer all the purposes of embalming on the few corpses deposited there. The roof has been kept whole hitherto; but as the clergyman's stipend is only twenty pounds per annum, and a house with two rooms, threatening speedily to determine into one, no clergyman will undertake the duties of pastor: especially as it is currently reported that his flock would rather let him starve than increase the living by one penny from their own pockets. However, in my dream, Jabez had a full and attentive congregation; and he preached—good God! what a sermon; divided into FOUR HUNDRED AND NINETY parts, each fully equal to an ordinary address from the pulpit, and each discussing a separate sin! Where he searched for them, I cannot tell. He had his private manner of interpreting the phrase, and it seemed necessary the brother should sin different sins on every occasion. They were of the most curious character: odd transgressions that I never imagined previously.

Oh, how weary I grow. How I writhed, and yawned, and nodded, and revived! How I pinched and pricked myself, and rubbed my eyes, and stood up, and sat down again, and nudged Joseph to inform me if he would EVER have done. I was condemned to hear all out: finally, he reached the 'FIRST OF THE SEVENTY-FIRST.' At that crisis, a sudden inspiration descended on me; I was moved to rise and denounce Jabez Branderham as the sinner of the sin that no Christian need pardon.

'Sir,' I exclaimed, 'sitting here within these four walls, at one stretch, I have endured and forgiven the four hundred and ninety heads of your discourse. Seventy times seven times have I plucked up my hat and been about to depart—Seventy times seven times have you preposterously forced me to resume my seat. The four hundred and ninety-first is too much. Fellow-martyrs, have at him! Drag him down, and crush him to atoms, that the place which knows him may know him no more!'

'THOU ART THE MAN!' cried Jabez, after a solemn pause, leaning over his cushion. 'Seventy times seven times didst thou gapingly contort thy visage—seventy times seven did I take counsel with my soul—Lo, this is human weakness: this also may be absolved! The First of the Seventy-First is come. Brethren, execute upon him the judgment written. Such honour have all His saints!'

With that concluding word, the whole assembly, exalting their pilgrim's staves, rushed round me in a body; and I, having no weapon to raise in self-defence, commenced grappling with Joseph, my nearest and most ferocious assailant, for his. In the confluence of the multitude, several clubs crossed; blows, aimed at me, fell on other sconces. Presently the whole chapel resounded with rappings and counter rappings: every man's hand was against his neighbour; and Branderham, unwilling to remain idle, poured forth his zeal in a shower of loud taps on the boards of the pulpit, which responded so smartly that, at last, to my unspeakable relief, they woke me. And what was it that had suggested the tremendous tumult? What had played Jabez's part in the row? Merely the branch of a fir-tree that touched my lattice as the blast wailed by, and rattled its dry cones against the panes! I listened doubtingly an instant; detected the disturber, then turned and dozed, and dreamt again: if possible, still more disagreeably than before.

This time, I remembered I was lying in the oak closet, and I heard distinctly the gusty wind, and the driving of the snow; I heard, also, the fir bough repeat its teasing sound, and ascribed it to the right cause: but it annoyed me so much, that I resolved to silence it, if possible; and, I thought, I rose and endeavoured to unhasp the casement. The hook was soldered into the staple: a circumstance observed by me when awake, but forgotten. 'I must stop it, nevertheless!' I muttered, knocking my knuckles through the glass, and stretching an arm out to seize the importunate branch; instead of which, my fingers closed on the fingers of a little, ice-cold hand! The intense horror of nightmare came over me: I tried to draw back my arm, but the hand clung to it, and a most melancholy voice sobbed, 'Let me in—let me in!' 'Who are you?' I asked, struggling, meanwhile, to disengage myself. 'Catherine Linton,' it replied, shiveringly (why did I think of LINTON? I had read EARNSHAW twenty times for Linton)—'I'm come home: I'd lost my way on the moor!' As it spoke, I discerned, obscurely, a child's face looking through the window. Terror made me cruel; and, finding it useless to attempt shaking the creature off, I pulled its wrist on to the broken pane, and rubbed it to and fro till the blood ran down and soaked the bedclothes: still it wailed, 'Let me in!' and maintained its tenacious gripe, almost maddening me with fear. 'How can I!' I said at length. 'Let ME go, if you want me to let you in!' The fingers relaxed, I snatched mine through the hole, hurriedly piled the books up in a pyramid against it, and stopped my ears to exclude the lamentable prayer. I seemed to keep them closed above a quarter of an hour; yet, the instant I listened again, there was the doleful cry moaning on! 'Begone!' I shouted. 'I'll never let you in, not if you beg for twenty years.' 'It is twenty years,' mourned the voice: 'twenty years. I've been a waif for twenty years!' Thereat began a feeble scratching outside, and the pile of books moved as if thrust forward. I tried to jump up; but could not stir a limb; and so yelled aloud, in a frenzy of fright. To my confusion, I discovered the yell was not ideal: hasty footsteps approached my chamber door; somebody pushed it open, with a vigorous hand, and a light glimmered through the squares at the top of the bed. I sat shuddering yet, and wiping the perspiration from my forehead: the intruder appeared to hesitate, and muttered to himself. At last, he said, in a half-whisper, plainly not expecting an answer, 'Is any one here?' I considered it best to confess my presence; for I knew

Heathcliff's accents, and feared he might search further, if I kept quiet. With this intention, I turned and opened the panels. I shall not soon forget the effect my action produced.

Heathcliff stood near the entrance, in his shirt and trousers; with a candle dripping over his fingers, and his face as white as the wall behind him. The first creak of the oak startled him like an electric shock: the light leaped from his hold to a distance of some feet, and his agitation was so extreme, that he could hardly pick it up.

'It is only your guest, sir,' I called out, desirous to spare him the humiliation of exposing his cowardice further. 'I had the misfortune to scream in my sleep, owing to a frightful nightmare. I'm sorry I disturbed you.'

'Oh, God confound you, Mr. Lockwood! I wish you were at the—' commenced my host, setting the candle on a chair, because he found it impossible to hold it steady. 'And who showed you up into this room?' he continued, crushing his nails into his palms, and grinding his teeth to subdue the maxillary convulsions. 'Who was it? I've a good mind to turn them out of the house this moment?'

'It was your servant Zillah,' I replied, flinging myself on to the floor, and rapidly resuming my garments. 'I should not care if you did, Mr. Heathcliff; she richly deserves it. I suppose that she wanted to get another proof that the place was haunted, at my expense. Well, it is—swarming with ghosts and goblins! You have reason in shutting it up, I assure you. No one will thank you for a doze in such a den!'

'What do you mean?' asked Heathcliff, 'and what are you doing? Lie down and finish out the night, since you ARE here; but, for heaven's sake! don't repeat that horrid noise: nothing could excuse it, unless you were having your throat cut!'

'If the little fiend had got in at the window, she probably would have strangled me!' I returned. 'I'm not going to endure the persecutions of your hospitable ancestors again. Was not the Reverend Jabez Branderham akin to you on the mother's side? And that minx, Catherine Linton, or Earnshaw, or however she was called-she must have been a changeling—wicked little soul! She told me she had been walking the earth these twenty years: a just punishment for her mortal transgressions, I've no doubt!'

Scarcely were these words uttered when I recollected the association of Heathcliff's with Catherine's name in the book, which had completely slipped from my memory, till thus awakened. I blushed at my inconsideration: but, without showing further consciousness of the offence, I hastened to add—'The truth is, sir, I passed the first part of the night in—' Here I stopped afresh—I was about to say 'perusing those old volumes,' then it would have revealed my knowledge of their written, as well as their printed, contents; so, correcting myself, I went on—'in spelling over the name scratched on that window-ledge. A monotonous occupation, calculated to set me asleep, like counting, or—'

'What CAN you mean by talking in this way to ME!' thundered Heathcliff with savage vehemence. 'How—how DARE you, under my roof?—God! he's mad to speak so!' And he struck his forehead with rage.

I did not know whether to resent this language or pursue my explanation; but he seemed so powerfully affected that I took pity and proceeded with my dreams; affirming I had never heard the appellation of 'Catherine Linton' before, but reading it often over produced an impression which personified itself when I had no longer my imagination under control. Heathcliff gradually fell back into the shelter of the bed, as I spoke; finally sitting down almost concealed behind it. I guessed, however, by his irregular and intercepted breathing, that he struggled to vanquish an excess of violent emotion. Not liking to show him that I had heard the conflict, I continued my toilette rather noisily, looked at my watch, and soliloquised on the length of the night: 'Not three o'clock yet! I could have taken oath it had been six. Time stagnates here: we must surely have retired to rest at eight!'

'Always at nine in winter, and rise at four,' said my host, suppressing a groan: and, as I fancied, by the motion of his arm's shadow, dashing a tear from his eyes. 'Mr. Lockwood,' he added, 'you may go into my room: you'll only be in the way, coming down-stairs so early: and your childish outcry has sent sleep to the devil for me.'

'And for me, too,' I replied. 'I'll walk in the yard till daylight, and then I'll be off; and you need not dread a repetition of my intrusion. I'm now quite cured of seeking pleasure in society, be it country or town. A sensible man ought to find sufficient company in himself.'

'Delightful company!' muttered Heathcliff. 'Take the candle, and go where you please. I shall join you directly. Keep out of the yard, though, the dogs are unchained; and the house—Juno mounts sentinel there, and—nay, you can only ramble about the steps and passages. But, away with you! I'll come in two minutes!'

I obeyed, so far as to quit the chamber; when, ignorant where the narrow lobbies led, I stood still, and was witness, involuntarily, to a piece of superstition on the part of my landlord which belied, oddly, his apparent sense. He got on to the bed, and wrenched open the lattice, bursting, as he pulled at it, into an uncontrollable passion of tears. 'Come in! come in!' he sobbed. 'Cathy, do come. Oh, do—ONCE more! Oh! my heart's darling! hear me THIS time, Catherine, at last!' The spectre showed a spectre's ordinary caprice: it gave no sign of being; but the snow and wind whirled wildly through, even reaching my station, and blowing out the light.

There was such anguish in the gush of grief that accompanied this raving, that my compassion made me overlook its folly, and I drew off, half angry to have listened at all, and vexed at having related my ridiculous nightmare, since it produced that agony; though WHY was beyond my comprehension. I descended cautiously to the lower regions, and landed in the back-kitchen, where a gleam of fire, raked compactly together, enabled me to rekindle my candle. Nothing was stirring except a brindled, grey cat, which crept from the ashes, and saluted me with a querulous mew.

Two benches, shaped in sections of a circle, nearly enclosed the hearth; on one of these I stretched myself, and Grimalkin mounted the other. We were both of us nodding ere any one invaded our retreat, and then it was Joseph, shuffling down a wooden ladder that vanished in the roof, through a trap: the ascent to his garret, I suppose. He cast a sinister look at the little flame which I had enticed to play between the ribs, swept the cat from its elevation, and bestowing himself in the vacancy, commenced the operation of stuffing a three-inch pipe with tobacco. My presence in his sanctum was evidently esteemed a piece of impudence too shameful for remark: he silently applied the tube to his lips, folded his arms, and puffed away. I let him enjoy the luxury unannoyed; and after sucking out his last wreath, and heaving a profound sigh, he got up, and departed as solemnly as he came.

A more elastic footstep entered next; and now I opened my mouth for a 'good-morning,' but closed it again, the salutation unachieved; for Hareton Earnshaw was performing his orison SOTTO VOCE, in a series of curses directed against every object he touched, while he rummaged a corner for a spade or shovel to dig through the drifts. He glanced over the back of the bench, dilating his nostrils, and thought as little of exchanging civilities with me as with my companion the cat. I guessed, by his preparations, that egress was allowed, and, leaving my hard couch, made a movement to follow him. He noticed this, and thrust at an inner door with the end of his spade, intimating by an inarticulate sound that there was the place where I must go, if I changed my locality.

It opened into the house, where the females were already astir; Zillah urging flakes of flame up the chimney with a colossal bellows; and Mrs. Heathcliff, kneeling on the hearth, reading a book by the aid of the blaze. She held her hand interposed between the furnace-heat and her eyes, and seemed absorbed in her occupation; desisting from it only to chide the servant for covering her with sparks, or to push away a dog, now and then, that snoozled its nose overforwardly into her face. I was surprised to see Heathcliff there also. He stood by the fire, his back towards me, just finishing a stormy scene with poor Zillah; who ever and anon interrupted her labour to pluck up the corner of her apron, and heave an indignant groan.

'And you, you worthless—' he broke out as I entered, turning to his daughter-in-law, and employing an epithet as harmless as duck, or sheep, but generally represented by a dash—. 'There you are, at your idle tricks again! The rest of them do earn their bread—you live on my charity! Put your trash away, and find something to do. You shall pay me for the plague of having you eternally in my sight—do you hear, damnable jade?'

'I'll put my trash away, because you can make me if I refuse,' answered the young lady, closing her book, and throwing it on a chair. 'But I'll not do anything, though you should swear your tongue out, except what I please!'

Heathcliff lifted his hand, and the speaker sprang to a safer distance, obviously acquainted with its weight. Having no desire to be entertained by a cat-and-dog combat, I stepped forward briskly, as if eager to partake the warmth of the hearth, and innocent of any knowledge of the interrupted dispute. Each had enough decorum to suspend further hostilities: Heathcliff placed his fists, out of temptation, in his pockets; Mrs. Heathcliff curled her lip, and walked to a seat far off, where she kept her word by playing the part of a statue during the remainder of my stay. That was not long.

I declined joining their breakfast, and, at the first gleam of dawn, took an opportunity of escaping into the free air, now clear, and still, and cold as impalpable ice.

My landlord halloed for me to stop ere I reached the bottom of the garden, and offered to accompany me across the moor. It was well he did, for the whole hill-back was one billowy, white ocean; the swells and falls not indicating corresponding rises and depressions in the ground: many pits, at least, were filled to a level; and entire ranges of mounds, the refuse of the quarries, blotted from the chart which my yesterday's walk left pictured in my mind. I had remarked on one side of the road, at intervals of six or seven yards, a line of upright stones, continued through the whole length of the barren: these were erected and daubed with lime on purpose to serve as guides in the dark, and also when a fall, like the present, confounded the deep swamps on either hand with the firmer path: but, excepting a dirty dot pointing up here and there, all traces of their existence had vanished: and my companion found it necessary to warn me frequently to steer to the right or left, when I imagined I was following, correctly, the windings of the road.

We exchanged little conversation, and he halted at the entrance of Thrushcross Park, saying, I could make no error there. Our adieux were limited to a hasty bow, and then I pushed forward, trusting to my own resources; for the porter's lodge is untenanted as yet. The distance from the gate to the grange is two miles; I believe I managed to make it four, what with losing myself among the trees, and sinking up to the neck in snow: a predicament which only those who have experienced it can appreciate. At any rate, whatever were my wanderings, the clock chimed twelve as I entered the house; and that gave exactly an hour for every mile of the usual way from Wuthering Heights.

My human fixture and her satellites rushed to welcome me; exclaiming, tumultuously, they had completely given me up: everybody conjectured that I perished last night; and they were wondering how they must set about the search for my remains. I bid them be quiet, now that they saw me returned, and, benumbed to my very heart, I dragged up-stairs; whence, after putting on dry clothes, and pacing to and fro thirty or forty minutes, to restore the animal heat, I adjourned to my study, feeble as a kitten: almost too much so to enjoy the cheerful fire and smoking coffee which the servant had prepared for my refreshment.

Chapter IV

WHAT vain weathercocks we are! I, who had determined to hold myself independent of all social intercourse, and thanked my stars that, at length, I had lighted on a spot where it was next to impracticable—I, weak wretch, after maintaining till dusk a struggle with low spirits and solitude, was finally compelled to strike my colours; and under pretence of gaining information concerning the necessities of my establishment, I desired Mrs. Dean, when she brought in supper, to sit down while I ate it; hoping sincerely she would prove a regular gossip, and either rouse me to animation or lull me to sleep by her talk.

'You have lived here a considerable time,' I commenced; 'did you not say sixteen years?'

'Eighteen, sir: I came when the mistress was married, to wait on her; after she died, the master retained me for his housekeeper.'

'Indeed.'

There ensued a pause. She was not a gossip, I feared; unless about her own affairs, and those could hardly interest me. However, having studied for an interval, with a fist on either knee, and a cloud of meditation over her ruddy countenance, she ejaculated—'Ah, times are greatly changed since then!'

'Yes,' I remarked, 'you've seen a good many alterations, I suppose?'

'I have: and troubles too,' she said.

'Oh, I'll turn the talk on my landlord's family!' I thought to myself. 'A good subject to start! And that pretty girl-widow, I should like to know her history: whether she be a native of the country, or, as is more probable, an exotic that the surly INDIGENAE will not recognise for kin.' With this intention I asked Mrs. Dean why Heathcliff let Thrushcross Grange, and preferred living in a situation and residence so much inferior. 'Is he not rich enough to keep the estate in good order?' I inquired.

'Rich, sir!' she returned. 'He has nobody knows what money, and every year it increases. Yes, yes, he's rich enough to live in a finer house than this: but he's very near—close-handed; and, if he had meant to flit to Thrushcross Grange, as soon as he heard of a good tenant he could not have borne to miss the chance of getting a few hundreds more. It is strange people should be so greedy, when they are alone in the world!'

'He had a son, it seems?'

'Yes, he had one—he is dead.'

'And that young lady, Mrs. Heathcliff, is his widow?'

'Yes.'

'Where did she come from originally?'

'Why, sir, she is my late master's daughter: Catherine Linton was her maiden name. I nursed her, poor thing! I did wish Mr. Heathcliff would remove here, and then we might have been together again.'

'What! Catherine Linton?' I exclaimed, astonished. But a minute's reflection convinced me it was not my ghostly Catherine. Then,' I continued, 'my predecessor's name was Linton?'

'It was.'

'And who is that Earnshaw: Hareton Earnshaw, who lives with Mr. Heathcliff? Are they relations?'

'No; he is the late Mrs. Linton's nephew.'

'The young lady's cousin, then?'

'Yes; and her husband was her cousin also: one on the mother's, the other on the father's side: Heathcliff married Mr. Linton's sister.'

'I see the house at Wuthering Heights has "Earnshaw" carved over the front door. Are they an old family?'

'Very old, sir; and Hareton is the last of them, as our Miss Cathy is of us—I mean, of the Lintons. Have you been to Wuthering Heights? I beg pardon for asking; but I should like to hear how she is!'

'Mrs. Heathcliff? she looked very well, and very handsome; yet, I think, not very happy.'

'Oh dear, I don't wonder! And how did you like the master?'

'A rough fellow, rather, Mrs. Dean. Is not that his character?

'Rough as a saw-edge, and hard as whinstone! The less you meddle with him the better.'

'He must have had some ups and downs in life to make him such a churl. Do you know anything of his history?'

'It's a cuckoo's, sir—I know all about it: except where he was born, and who were his parents, and how he got his money at first. And Hareton has been cast out like an unfledged dunnock! The unfortunate lad is the only one in all this parish that does not guess how he has been cheated.'

'Well, Mrs. Dean, it will be a charitable deed to tell me something of my neighbours: I feel I shall not rest if I go to bed; so be good enough to sit and chat an hour.'

'Oh, certainly, sir! I'll just fetch a little sewing, and then I'll sit as long as you please. But you've caught cold: I saw you shivering, and you must have some gruel to drive it out.'

The worthy woman bustled off, and I crouched nearer the fire; my head felt hot, and the rest of me chill: moreover, I was excited, almost to a pitch of foolishness, through my nerves and brain. This caused me to feel, not uncomfortable, but rather fearful (as I am still) of serious effects from the incidents of to-day and yesterday. She returned presently, bringing a smoking basin and a basket of work; and, having placed the former on the hob, drew in her seat, evidently pleased to find me so companionable.

Before I came to live here, she commenced—waiting no farther invitation to her story—I was almost always at Wuthering Heights; because my mother had nursed Mr. Hindley Earnshaw, that was Hareton's father, and I got used to playing with the children: I ran errands too, and helped to make hay, and hung about the farm ready for anything that anybody would set me to. One fine summer morning—it was the beginning of harvest, I remember—Mr. Earnshaw, the old master, came down-stairs, dressed for a journey; and, after he had told Joseph what was to be done during the day, he turned to Hindley, and Cathy, and me—for I sat eating my porridge with them—and he said, speaking to his son, 'Now, my bonny man, I'm going to Liverpool to-day, what shall I bring you? You may choose what you like: only let it be little, for I shall walk there and back: sixty miles each way, that is a long spell!' Hindley named a fiddle, and then he asked Miss Cathy; she was hardly six years old, but she could ride any horse in the stable, and she chose a whip. He did not forget me; for he had a kind heart, though he was rather severe sometimes. He promised to bring me a pocketful of apples and pears, and then he kissed his children, said good-bye, and set off.

It seemed a long while to us all—the three days of his absence—and often did little Cathy ask when he would be home. Mrs. Earnshaw expected him by supper-time on the third evening, and she put the meal off hour after hour; there were no signs of his coming, however, and at last the children got tired of running down to the gate to look. Then it grew dark; she would have had them to bed, but they begged sadly to be allowed to stay up; and, just about eleven o'clock, the door-latch was raised quietly, and in stepped the master. He threw himself into a chair, laughing and groaning, and bid them all stand off, for he was nearly killed—he would not have such another walk for the three kingdoms.

'And at the end of it to be flighted to death!' he said, opening his great-coat, which he held bundled up in his arms. 'See here, wife! I was never so beaten with anything in my life: but you must e'en take it as a gift of God; though it's as dark almost as if it came from the devil.'

We crowded round, and over Miss Cathy's head I had a peep at a dirty, ragged, black-haired child; big enough both to walk and talk: indeed, its face looked older than Catherine's; yet when it was set on its feet, it only stared round, and repeated over and over again some gibberish that nobody could understand. I was frightened, and Mrs. Earnshaw was ready to fling it out of doors: she did fly up, asking how he could fashion to bring that gipsy brat into the house, when they had their own bairns to feed and fend for? What he meant to do with it, and whether he were mad? The master tried to explain the matter; but he was really half dead with fatigue, and all that I could make out, amongst her scolding, was a tale of his seeing it starving, and houseless, and as good as dumb, in the streets of Liverpool, where he picked it up and inquired for its owner. Not a soul knew to whom it belonged, he said; and his money and time being both limited, he thought it better to take it home with him at once, than run into vain expenses there: because he was determined he would not leave it as he found it. Well, the conclusion was, that my mistress grumbled herself calm; and Mr. Earnshaw told me to wash it, and give it clean things, and let it sleep with the children.

Hindley and Cathy contented themselves with looking and listening till peace was restored: then, both began searching their father's pockets for the presents he had promised them. The former was a boy of fourteen, but when he drew out what had been a fiddle, crushed to morsels in the great-coat, he blubbered aloud; and Cathy, when she learned the master had lost her whip in attending on the stranger, showed her humour by grinning and spitting at the stupid little thing; earning for her pains a sound blow from her father, to teach her cleaner manners. They entirely refused to have it in bed with them, or even in their room; and I had no more sense, so I put it on the landing of the stairs, hoping it might he gone on the morrow. By chance, or else attracted by hearing his voice, it crept to Mr. Earnshaw's door, and there he found it on quitting his chamber.

Inquiries were made as to how it got there; I was obliged to confess, and in recompense for my cowardice and inhumanity was sent out of the house.

This was Heathcliff's first introduction to the family. On coming back a few days afterwards (for I did not consider my banishment perpetual), I found they had christened him 'Heathcliff': it was the name of a son who died in childhood, and it has served him ever since, both for Christian and surname. Miss Cathy and he were now very thick; but Hindley hated him: and to say the truth I did the same; and we plagued and went on with him shamefully: for I wasn't reasonable enough to feel my injustice, and the mistress never put in a word on his behalf when she saw him wronged.

He seemed a sullen, patient child; hardened, perhaps, to ill-treatment: he would stand Hindley's blows without winking or shedding a tear, and my pinches moved him only to draw in a breath and open his eyes, as if he had hurt himself by accident, and nobody was to blame. This endurance made old Earnshaw furious, when he discovered his son persecuting the poor fatherless child, as he called him. He took to Heathcliff strangely, believing all he said (for that matter, he said precious little, and generally the truth), and petting him up far above Cathy, who was too mischievous and wayward for a favourite.

So, from the very beginning, he bred bad feeling in the house; and at Mrs. Earnshaw's death, which happened in less than two years after, the young master had learned to regard his father as an oppressor rather than a friend, and Heathcliff as a usurper of his parent's affections and his privileges; and he grew bitter with brooding over these injuries. I sympathised a while; but when the children fell ill of the measles, and I had to tend them, and take on me the cares of a woman at once, I changed my idea. Heathcliff was dangerously sick; and while he lay at the worst he would have me constantly by his pillow: I suppose he felt I did a good deal for him, and he hadn't wit to guess that I was compelled to do it. However, I will say this, he was the quietest child that ever nurse watched over. The difference between him and the others forced me to be less partial. Cathy and her brother harassed me terribly: he was as uncomplaining as a lamb; though hardness, not gentleness, made him give little trouble.

He got through, and the doctor affirmed it was in a great measure owing to me, and praised me for my care. I was vain of his commendations, and softened towards the being by whose means I earned them, and thus Hindley lost his last ally: still I couldn't dote on Heathcliff, and I wondered often what my master saw to admire so much in the sullen boy; who never, to my recollection, repaid his indulgence by any sign of gratitude. He was not insolent to his benefactor, he was simply insensible; though knowing perfectly the hold he had on his heart, and conscious he had only to speak and all the house would be obliged to bend to his wishes. As an instance, I remember Mr. Earnshaw once bought a couple of colts at the parish fair, and gave the lads each one. Heathcliff took the handsomest, but it soon fell lame, and when he discovered it, he said to Hindley—

'You must exchange horses with me: I don't like mine; and if you won't I shall tell your father of the three thrashings you've given me this week, and show him my arm, which is black to the shoulder.' Hindley put out his tongue, and cuffed him over the ears. 'You'd better do it at once,' he persisted, escaping to the porch (they were in the stable): 'you will have to: and if I speak of these blows, you'll get them again with interest.' 'Off, dog!' cried Hindley, threatening him with an iron weight used for weighing potatoes and hay. 'Throw it,' he replied, standing still, 'and then I'll tell how you boasted that you would turn me out of doors as soon as he died, and see whether he will not turn you out directly.' Hindley threw it, hitting him on the breast, and down he fell, but staggered up immediately, breathless and white; and, had not I prevented it, he would have gone just so to the master, and got full revenge by letting his condition plead for him, intimating who had caused it. 'Take my colt, Gipsy, then!' said young Earnshaw. 'And I pray that he may break your neck: take him, and he damned, you beggarly interloper! and wheedle my father out of all he has: only afterwards show him what you are, imp of Satan.—And take that, I hope he'll kick out your brains!'

Heathcliff had gone to loose the beast, and shift it to his own stall; he was passing behind it, when Hindley finished his speech by knocking him under its feet, and without stopping to examine whether his hopes were fulfilled, ran away as fast as he could. I was surprised to witness how coolly the child gathered himself up, and went on with his intention; exchanging saddles and all, and then sitting down on a bundle of hay to overcome the qualm which the violent blow occasioned, before he entered the house. I persuaded him easily to let me lay the blame of his bruises on the horse: he minded little what tale was told since he had what he wanted. He complained so seldom, indeed, of such stirs as these, that I really thought him not vindictive: I was deceived completely, as you will hear.

Chapter V

IN the course of time Mr. Earnshaw began to fail. He had been active and healthy, yet his strength left him suddenly; and when he was confined to the chimney-corner he grew grievously irritable. A nothing vexed him; and suspected slights of his authority nearly threw him into fits. This was especially to be remarked if any one attempted to impose upon, or domineer over, his favourite: he was painfully jealous lest a word should be spoken amiss to him; seeming to have got into his head the notion that, because he liked Heathcliff, all hated, and longed to do him an ill-turn. It was a disadvantage to the lad; for the kinder among us did not wish to fret the master, so we humoured his partiality; and that humouring was rich nourishment to the child's pride and black tempers. Still it became in a manner necessary; twice, or thrice, Hindley's manifestation of scorn, while his father was near, roused the old man to a fury: he seized his stick to strike him, and shook with rage that he could not do it.

At last, our curate (we had a curate then who made the living answer by teaching the little Lintons and Earnshaws, and farming his bit of land himself) advised that the young man should be sent to college; and Mr. Earnshaw agreed, though with a heavy spirit, for he said—'Hindley was nought, and would never thrive as where he wandered.'

I hoped heartily we should have peace now. It hurt me to think the master should be made uncomfortable by his own good deed. I fancied the discontent of age and disease arose from his family disagreements; as he would have it that it did: really, you know, sir, it was in his sinking frame. We might have got on tolerably, notwithstanding, but for two people—Miss Cathy, and Joseph, the servant: you saw him, I daresay, up yonder. He was, and is yet most likely, the wearisomest self-righteous Pharisee that ever ransacked a Bible to rake the promises to himself and fling the curses to his neighbours. By his knack of sermonising and pious discoursing, he contrived to make a great impression on Mr. Earnshaw; and the more feeble the master became, the more influence he gained. He was relentless in worrying him about his soul's concerns, and about ruling his children rigidly. He encouraged him to regard Hindley as a reprobate; and, night after night, he regularly grumbled out a long string of tales against Heathcliff and Catherine: always minding to flatter Earnshaw's weakness by heaping the heaviest blame on the latter.

Certainly she had ways with her such as I never saw a child take up before; and she put all of us past our patience fifty times and oftener in a day: from the hour she came down-stairs till the hour she went to bed, we had not a minute's security that she wouldn't be in mischief. Her spirits were always at high-water mark, her tongue always going—singing, laughing, and plaguing everybody who would not do the same. A wild, wicked slip she was—but she had the bonniest eye, the sweetest smile, and lightest foot in the parish: and, after all, I believe she meant no harm; for when once she made you cry in good earnest, it seldom happened that she would not keep you company, and oblige you to be quiet that you might comfort her. She was much too fond of Heathcliff. The greatest punishment we could invent for her was to keep her separate from him: yet she got chided more than any of us on his account. In play, she liked exceedingly to act the little mistress; using her hands freely, and commanding her companions: she did so to me, but I would not bear slapping and ordering; and so I let her know.

Now, Mr. Earnshaw did not understand jokes from his children: he had always been strict and grave with them; and Catherine, on her part, had no idea why her father should be crosser and less patient in his ailing condition than he was in his prime. His peevish reproofs wakened in her a naughty delight to provoke him: she was never so happy as when we were all scolding her at once, and she defying us with her bold, saucy look, and her ready words; turning Joseph's religious curses into ridicule, baiting me, and doing just what her father hated most—showing how her pretended insolence, which he thought real, had more power over Heathcliff than his kindness: how the boy would do HER bidding in anything, and HIS only when it suited his own inclination. After behaving as badly as possible all day, she sometimes came fondling to make it up at night. 'Nay, Cathy,' the old man would say, 'I cannot love thee, thou'rt worse than thy brother. Go, say thy prayers, child, and ask God's pardon. I doubt thy mother and I must rue that we ever reared thee!' That made her cry, at first;

and then being repulsed continually hardened her, and she laughed if I told her to say she was sorry for her faults, and beg to be forgiven.

But the hour came, at last, that ended Mr. Earnshaw's troubles on earth. He died quietly in his chair one October evening, seated by the fire-side. A high wind blustered round the house, and roared in the chimney: it sounded wild and stormy, yet it was not cold, and we were all together—I, a little removed from the hearth, busy at my knitting, and Joseph reading his Bible near the table (for the servants generally sat in the house then, after their work was done). Miss Cathy had been sick, and that made her still; she leant against her father's knee, and Heathcliff was lying on the floor with his head in her lap. I remember the master, before he fell into a doze, stroking her bonny hair—it pleased him rarely to see her gentle—and saying, 'Why canst thou not always be a good lass, Cathy?' And she turned her face up to his, and laughed, and answered, 'Why cannot you always be a good man, father?' But as soon as she saw him vexed again, she kissed his hand, and said she would sing him to sleep. She began singing very low, till his fingers dropped from hers, and his head sank on his breast. Then I told her to hush, and not stir, for fear she should wake him. We all kept as mute as mice a full half-hour, and should have done so longer, only Joseph, having finished his chapter, got up and said that he must rouse the master for prayers and bed. He stepped forward, and called him by name, and touched his shoulder; but he would not move: so he took the candle and looked at him. I thought there was something wrong as he set down the light; and seizing the children each by an arm, whispered them to 'frame up-stairs, and make little din—they might pray alone that evening-he had summut to do.'

'I shall bid father good-night first,' said Catherine, putting her arms round his neck, before we could hinder her. The poor thing discovered her loss directly—she screamed out—'Oh, he's dead, Heathcliff! he's dead!' And they both set up a heart-breaking cry.

I joined my wail to theirs, loud and bitter; but Joseph asked what we could be thinking of to roar in that way over a saint in heaven. He told me to put on my cloak and run to Gimmerton for the doctor and the parson. I could not guess the use that either would be of, then. However, I went, through wind and rain, and brought one, the doctor, back with me; the other said he would come in the morning.

Leaving Joseph to explain matters, I ran to the children's room: their door was ajar, I saw they had never lain down, though it was past midnight; but they were calmer, and did not need me to console them. The little souls were comforting each other with better thoughts than I could have hit on: no parson in the world ever pictured heaven so beautifully as they did, in their innocent talk; and, while I sobbed and listened, I could not help wishing we were all there safe together.

Chapter VI

MR. HINDLEY came home to the funeral; and—a thing that amazed us, and set the neighbours gossiping right and left—he brought a wife with him. What she was, and where she was born, he never informed us: probably, she had neither money nor name to recommend her, or he would scarcely have kept the union from his father.

She was not one that would have disturbed the house much on her own account. Every object she saw, the moment she crossed the threshold, appeared to delight her; and every circumstance that took place about her: except the preparing for the burial, and the presence of the mourners. I thought she was half silly, from her behaviour while that went on: she ran into her chamber, and made me come with her, though I should have been dressing the children: and there she sat shivering and clasping her hands, and asking repeatedly—'Are they gone yet?' Then she began describing with hysterical emotion the effect it produced on her to see black; and started, and trembled, and, at last, fell a-weeping—and when I asked what was the matter, answered, she didn't know; but she felt so afraid of dying! I imagined her as little likely to die as myself. She was rather thin, but young, and fresh-complexioned, and her eyes sparkled as bright as diamonds. I did remark, to be sure, that mounting the stairs made her breathe very quick; that the least sudden noise set her all in a quiver, and that she coughed troublesomely sometimes: but I knew nothing of what these symptoms portended, and had no impulse to sympathise with her. We don't in general take to foreigners here, Mr. Lockwood, unless they take to us first.

Young Earnshaw was altered considerably in the three years of his absence. He had grown sparer, and lost his colour, and spoke and dressed quite differently; and, on the very day of his return, he told

Joseph and me we must thenceforth quarter ourselves in the back-kitchen, and leave the house for him. Indeed, he would have carpeted and papered a small spare room for a parlour; but his wife expressed such pleasure at the white floor and huge glowing fireplace, at the pewter dishes and delf-case, and dog-kennel, and the wide space there was to move about in where they usually sat, that he thought it unnecessary to her comfort, and so dropped the intention.

She expressed pleasure, too, at finding a sister among her new acquaintance; and she prattled to Catherine, and kissed her, and ran about with her, and gave her quantities of presents, at the beginning. Her affection tired very soon, however, and when she grew peevish, Hindley became tyrannical. A few words from her, evincing a dislike to Heathcliff, were enough to rouse in him all his old hatred of the boy. He drove him from their company to the servants, deprived him of the instructions of the curate, and insisted that he should labour out of doors instead; compelling him to do so as hard as any other lad on the farm.

Heathcliff bore his degradation pretty well at first, because Cathy taught him what she learnt, and worked or played with him in the fields. They both promised fair to grow up as rude as savages; the young master being entirely negligent how they behaved, and what they did, so they kept clear of him. He would not even have seen after their going to church on Sundays, only Joseph and the curate reprimanded his carelessness when they absented themselves; and that reminded him to order Heathcliff a flogging, and Catherine a fast from dinner or supper. But it was one of their chief amusements to run away to the moors in the morning and remain there all day, and the after punishment grew a mere thing to laugh at. The curate might set as many chapters as he pleased for Catherine to get by heart, and Joseph might thrash Heathcliff till his arm ached; they forgot everything the minute they were together again: at least the minute they had contrived some naughty plan of revenge; and many a time I've cried to myself to watch them growing more reckless daily, and I not daring to speak a syllable, for fear of losing the small power I still retained over the unfriended creatures. One Sunday evening, it chanced that they were banished from the sitting-room, for making a noise, or a light offence of the kind; and when I went to call them to supper, I could discover them nowhere. We searched the house, above and below, and the yard and stables; they were invisible: and, at last,

Hindley in a passion told us to bolt the doors, and swore nobody should let them in that night. The household went to bed; and I, too, anxious to lie down, opened my lattice and put my head out to hearken, though it rained: determined to admit them in spite of the prohibition, should they return. In a while, I distinguished steps coming up the road, and the light of a lantern glimmered through the gate. I threw a shawl over my head and ran to prevent them from waking Mr. Earnshaw by knocking. There was Heathcliff, by himself: it gave me a start to see him alone.

'Where is Miss Catherine?' I cried hurriedly. 'No accident, I hope?' 'At Thrushcross Grange,' he answered; 'and I would have been there too, but they had not the manners to ask me to stay.' 'Well, you will catch it!' I said: 'you'll never be content till you're sent about your business. What in the world led you wandering to Thrushcross Grange?' 'Let me get off my wet clothes, and I'll tell you all about it, Nelly,' he replied. I bid him beware of rousing the master, and while he undressed and I waited to put out the candle, he continued—'Cathy and I escaped from the wash-house to have a ramble at liberty, and getting a glimpse of the Grange lights, we thought we would just go and see whether the Lintons passed their Sunday evenings standing shivering in corners, while their father and mother sat eating and drinking, and singing and laughing, and burning their eyes out before the fire. Do you think they do? Or reading sermons, and being catechised by their manservant, and set to learn a column of Scripture names, if they don't answer properly?' 'Probably not,' I responded. 'They are good children, no doubt, and don't deserve the treatment you receive, for your bad conduct.' 'Don't cant, Nelly,' he said: 'nonsense! We ran from the top of the Heights to the park, without stopping—Catherine completely beaten in the race, because she was barefoot. You'll have to seek for her shoes in the bog to-morrow. We crept through a broken hedge, groped our way up the path, and planted ourselves on a flower-plot under the drawing-room window. The light came from thence; they had not put up the shutters, and the curtains were only half closed. Both of us were able to look in by standing on the basement, and clinging to the ledge, and we saw—ah! it was beautiful—a splendid place carpeted with crimson, and crimson-covered chairs and tables, and a pure white ceiling bordered by gold, a shower of glass-drops hanging in silver chains from the centre, and shimmering with little soft tapers. Old Mr. and Mrs. Linton were not there; Edgar and his sisters had it entirely to themselves. Shouldn't they have been happy? We should have thought ourselves in heaven! And now, guess what your good children were doing? Isabella—I believe she is eleven, a year younger than Cathy—lay screaming at the farther end of the room, shrieking as if witches were running red-hot needles into her. Edgar stood on the hearth weeping silently, and in the middle of the table sat a little dog, shaking its paw and yelping; which, from their mutual accusations, we understood they had nearly pulled in two between them. The idiots! That was their pleasure! to quarrel who should hold a heap of warm hair, and each begin to cry because both, after struggling to get it, refused to take it. We laughed outright at the petted things; we did despise them! When would you catch me wishing to have what Catherine wanted? or find us by ourselves, seeking entertainment in yelling, and sobbing, and rolling on the ground, divided by the whole room? I'd not exchange, for a thousand lives, my condition here, for Edgar Linton's at Thrushcross Grange—not if I might have the privilege of flinging Joseph off the highest gable, and painting the house-front with Hindley's blood!'

'Hush, hush!' I interrupted. 'Still you have not told me, Heathcliff, how Catherine is left behind?'

'I told you we laughed,' he answered. 'The Lintons heard us, and with one accord they shot like arrows to the door; there was silence, and then a cry, "Oh, mamma, mamma! Oh, papa! Oh, mamma, come here. Oh, papa, oh!" They really did howl out something in that way. We made frightful noises to terrify them still more, and then we dropped off the ledge, because somebody was drawing the bars, and we felt we had better flee. I had Cathy by the hand, and was urging her on, when all at once she fell down. "Run, Heathcliff, run!" she whispered. "They have let the bull-dog loose, and he holds me!" The devil had seized her ankle, Nelly: I heard his abominable snorting. She did not yell out—no! she would have scorned to do it, if she had been spitted on the horns of a mad cow. I did, though: I vociferated curses enough to annihilate any fiend in Christendom; and I got a stone and thrust it between his jaws, and tried with all my might to cram it down his throat. A beast of a servant came up with a lantern, at last, shouting—"Keep fast, Skulker, keep fast!" He changed his note, however, when he saw Skulker's game. The dog was throttled off; his huge, purple tongue hanging half a foot out of his mouth, and his pendent lips streaming with bloody slaver. The man took Cathy up; she was sick: not from fear, I'm certain, but from pain. He carried her in; I followed, grumbling execrations and vengeance. "What prey, Robert?" hallooed Linton from the entrance. "Skulker has caught a little girl, sir," he replied; "and there's a lad here," he added, making a clutch at me, "who looks an out-and-outer! Very like the robbers were for putting them through the window to open the doors to the gang after all were asleep, that they might murder us at their ease. Hold your tongue, you foul-mouthed thief, you! you shall go to the gallows for this. Mr. Linton, sir, don't lay by your gun." "No, no, Robert," said the old fool. "The rascals knew that yesterday was my rent-day: they thought to have me cleverly. Come in; I'll furnish them a reception. There, John, fasten the chain. Give Skulker some water, Jenny. To beard a magistrate in his stronghold, and on the Sabbath, too! Where will their insolence stop? Oh, my dear Mary, look here! Don't be afraid, it is but a boy—yet the villain scowls so plainly in his face; would it not be a kindness to the country to hang him at once, before he shows his nature in acts as well as features?" He pulled me under the chandelier, and Mrs. Linton placed her spectacles on her nose and raised her hands in horror. The cowardly children crept nearer also, Isabella lisping—"Frightful thing! Put him in the cellar, papa. He's exactly like the son of the fortune-teller that stole my tame pheasant. Isn't he, Edgar?"

'While they examined me, Cathy came round; she heard the last speech, and laughed. Edgar Linton, after an inquisitive stare, collected sufficient wit to recognise her. They see us at church, you know, though we seldom meet them elsewhere. "That's Miss Earnshaw?" he whispered to his mother, "and look how Skulker has bitten her—how her foot bleeds!"

'"Miss Earnshaw? Nonsense!" cried the dame; "Miss Earnshaw scouring the country with a gipsy! And yet, my dear, the child is in mourning—surely it is—and she may be lamed for life!"

'"What culpable carelessness in her brother!" exclaimed Mr. Linton, turning from me to Catherine. "I've understood from Shielders"' (that was the curate, sir) '"that he lets her grow up in absolute heathenism. But who is this? Where did she pick up this companion? Oho! I declare he is that strange acquisition my late neighbour made, in his journey to Liverpool—a little Lascar, or an American or Spanish castaway."

'"A wicked boy, at all events," remarked the old lady, "and quite unfit for a decent house! Did you notice his language, Linton? I'm shocked that my children should have heard it."

'I recommenced cursing—don't be angry, Nelly—and so Robert was ordered to take me off. I refused to go without Cathy; he dragged me into the garden, pushed the lantern into my hand, assured me that Mr. Earnshaw should be informed of my behaviour, and, bidding me march directly, secured the door again. The curtains were still looped up at one corner, and I resumed my station as spy; because, if Catherine had wished to return, I intended shattering their great glass panes to a million of fragments, unless they let her out. She sat on the sofa quietly. Mrs. Linton took off the grey cloak of the dairy-maid which we had borrowed for our excursion, shaking her head and expostulating with her, I suppose: she was a young lady, and they made a distinction between her treatment and mine. Then the woman-servant brought a basin of warm water, and washed her feet; and Mr. Linton mixed a tumbler of negus, and Isabella emptied a plateful of cakes into her lap, and Edgar stood gaping at a distance. Afterwards, they dried and combed her beautiful hair, and gave her a pair of enormous slippers, and wheeled her to the fire; and I left her, as merry as she could be, dividing her food between the little dog and Skulker, whose nose she pinched as he ate; and kindling a spark of spirit in the vacant blue eyes of the Lintons—a dim reflection from her own enchanting face. I saw they were full of stupid admiration; she is so immeasurably superior to them—to everybody on earth, is she not, Nelly?'

'There will more come of this business than you reckon on,' I answered, covering him up and extinguishing the light. 'You are incurable, Heathcliff; and Mr. Hindley will have to proceed to extremities, see if he won't.' My words came truer than I desired. The luckless adventure made Earnshaw furious. And then Mr. Linton, to mend matters, paid us a visit himself on the morrow, and read the young master such a lecture on the road he guided his family, that he was stirred to look about him, in earnest. Heathcliff received no flogging, but he was told that the first word he spoke to Miss Catherine should ensure a dismissal; and Mrs. Earnshaw undertook to keep her sister-in-law in due restraint when she returned home; employing art, not force: with force she would have found it impossible.

Chapter VII

CATHY stayed at Thrushcross Grange five weeks: till Christmas. By that time her ankle was thoroughly cured, and her manners much improved. The mistress visited her often in the interval, and commenced her plan of reform by trying to raise her self-respect with fine clothes and flattery, which she took readily; so that, instead of a wild, hatless little savage jumping into the house, and rushing to squeeze us all breathless, there 'lighted from a handsome black pony a very dignified person, with brown ringlets falling from the cover of a feathered beaver, and a long cloth habit, which she was obliged to hold up with both hands that she might sail in. Hindley lifted her from her horse, exclaiming delightedly, 'Why, Cathy, you are quite a beauty! I should scarcely have known you: you look like a lady now. Isabella Linton is not to be compared with her, is she, Frances?' 'Isabella has not her natural advantages,' replied his wife: 'but she must mind and not grow wild again here. Ellen, help Miss Catherine off with her things—Stay, dear, you will disarrange your curls—let me untie your hat.'

I removed the habit, and there shone forth beneath a grand plaid silk frock, white trousers, and burnished shoes; and, while her eyes sparkled joyfully when the dogs came bounding up to welcome her, she dared hardly touch them lest they should fawn upon her splendid garments. She kissed me gently: I was all flour making the Christmas cake, and it would not have done to give me a hug; and then she looked round for Heathcliff. Mr. and Mrs. Earnshaw watched anxiously their meeting; thinking it would enable them to judge, in some measure, what grounds they had for hoping to succeed in separating the two friends.

Heathcliff was hard to discover, at first. If he were careless, and uncared for, before Catherine's absence, he had been ten times more so since. Nobody but I even did him the kindness to call him a dirty boy, and bid him wash himself, once a week; and children of his age seldom have a natural pleasure in soap and water. Therefore, not to mention his clothes, which had seen three months' service in mire and dust, and his thick uncombed hair, the surface of his face and hands was dismally beclouded. He might well skulk behind the settle, on beholding such a bright, graceful damsel enter the house, instead of a rough-headed counterpart of himself, as he expected. 'Is Heathcliff not here?' she demanded, pulling off her gloves, and displaying fingers wonderfully whitened with doing nothing and staying indoors.

'Heathcliff, you may come forward,' cried Mr. Hindley, enjoying his discomfiture, and gratified to see what a forbidding young blackguard he would be compelled to present himself. 'You may come and wish Miss Catherine welcome, like the other servants.'

Cathy, catching a glimpse of her friend in his concealment, flew to embrace him; she bestowed seven or eight kisses on his cheek within the second, and then stopped, and drawing back, burst into a laugh, exclaiming, 'Why, how very black and cross you look! and how—how funny and grim! But that's because I'm used to Edgar and Isabella Linton. Well, Heathcliff, have you forgotten me?'

She had some reason to put the question, for shame and pride threw double gloom over his countenance, and kept him immovable.

'Shake hands, Heathcliff,' said Mr. Earnshaw, condescendingly; 'once in a way, that is permitted.'

'I shall not,' replied the boy, finding his tongue at last; 'I shall not stand to be laughed at. I shall not bear it!' And he would have broken from the circle, but Miss Cathy seized him again.

'I did not mean to laugh at you,' she said; 'I could not hinder myself: Heathcliff, shake hands at least! What are you sulky for? It was only that you looked odd. If you wash your face and brush your hair, it will be all right: but you are so dirty!'

She gazed concernedly at the dusky fingers she held in her own, and also at her dress; which she feared had gained no embellishment from its contact with his.

'You needn't have touched me!' he answered, following her eye and snatching away his hand. 'I shall be as dirty as I please: and I like to be dirty, and I will be dirty.'

With that he dashed headforemost out of the room, amid the merriment of the master and mistress, and to the serious disturbance of Catherine; who could not comprehend how her remarks should have produced such an exhibition of bad temper.

After playing lady's-maid to the new-comer, and putting my cakes in the oven, and making the house and kitchen cheerful with great fires, befitting Christmas-eve, I prepared to sit down and amuse myself by singing carols, all alone; regardless of Joseph's affirmations that he considered the merry tunes I chose as next door to songs. He had retired to private prayer in his chamber, and Mr. and Mrs.

Earnshaw were engaging Missy's attention by sundry gay trifles bought for her to present to the little Lintons, as an acknowledgment of their kindness. They had invited them to spend the morrow at Wuthering Heights, and the invitation had been accepted, on one condition: Mrs. Linton begged that her darlings might be kept carefully apart from that 'naughty swearing boy.'

Under these circumstances I remained solitary. I smelt the rich scent of the heating spices; and admired the shining kitchen utensils, the polished clock, decked in holly, the silver mugs ranged on a tray ready to be filled with mulled ale for supper; and above all, the speckless purity of my particular care—the scoured and well-swept floor. I gave due inward applause to every object, and then I remembered how old Earnshaw used to come in when all was tidied, and call me a cant lass, and slip a shilling into my hand as a Christmas-box; and from that I went on to think of his fondness for Heathcliff, and his dread lest he should suffer neglect after death had removed him: and that naturally led me to consider the poor lad's situation now, and from singing I changed my mind to crying. It struck me soon, however, there would be more sense in endeavouring to repair some of his wrongs than shedding tears over them: I got up and walked into the court to seek him. He was not far; I found him smoothing the glossy coat of the new pony in the stable, and feeding the other beasts, according to custom.

'Make haste, Heathcliff!' I said, 'the kitchen is so comfortable; and Joseph is up-stairs: make haste, and let me dress you smart before Miss Cathy comes out, and then you can sit together, with the whole hearth to yourselves, and have a long chatter till bedtime.'

He proceeded with his task, and never turned his head towards me.

'Come—are you coming?' I continued. 'There's a little cake for each of you, nearly enough; and you'll need half-an-hour's donning.'

I waited five minutes, but getting no answer left him. Catherine supped with her brother and sister-in-law: Joseph and I joined at an unsociable meal, seasoned with reproofs on one side and sauciness on the other. His cake and cheese remained on the table all night for the fairies. He managed to continue work till nine o'clock, and then marched dumb and dour to his chamber. Cathy sat up late, having a world of things to order for the reception of her new friends: she came into the kitchen once to speak to her old one; but he was gone, and she only stayed to ask what was the matter with him, and then went back. In the morning he rose early; and, as it was a holiday, carried his ill-humour on to the moors; not re-appearing till the family were departed for church. Fasting and reflection seemed to have brought him to a better spirit. He hung about me for a while, and having screwed up his courage, exclaimed abruptly—'Nelly, make me decent, I'm going to be good.'

'High time, Heathcliff,' I said; 'you HAVE grieved Catherine: she's sorry she ever came home, I daresay! It looks as if you envied her, because she is more thought of than you.'

The notion of ENVYING Catherine was incomprehensible to him, but the notion of grieving her he understood clearly enough.

'Did she say she was grieved?' he inquired, looking very serious.

'She cried when I told her you were off again this morning.'

'Well, I cried last night,' he returned, 'and I had more reason to cry than she.'

'Yes: you had the reason of going to bed with a proud heart and an empty stomach,' said I. 'Proud people breed sad sorrows for themselves. But, if you be ashamed of your touchiness, you must ask pardon, mind, when she comes in. You must go up and offer to kiss her, and say—you know best what to say; only do it heartily, and not as if you thought her converted into a stranger by her grand dress. And now, though I have dinner to get ready, I'll steal time to arrange you so that Edgar Linton shall look quite a doll beside you: and that he does. You are younger, and yet, I'll be bound, you are taller and twice as broad across the shoulders; you could knock him down in a twinkling; don't you feel that you could?'

Heathcliff's face brightened a moment; then it was overcast afresh, and he sighed.

'But, Nelly, if I knocked him down twenty times, that wouldn't make him less handsome or me more so. I wish I had light hair and a fair skin, and was dressed and behaved as well, and had a chance of being as rich as he will be!'

'And cried for mamma at every turn,' I added, 'and trembled if a country lad heaved his fist against you, and sat at home all day for a shower of rain. Oh, Heathcliff, you are showing a poor spirit! Come to the glass, and I'll let you see what you should wish. Do you mark those two lines between your eyes; and those thick brows, that, instead of rising arched, sink in the middle; and that couple of black fiends, so deeply buried, who never open their windows boldly, but lurk glinting under them, like devil's spies? Wish and learn to smooth away the surly wrinkles, to raise your lids frankly, and change the fiends to confident, innocent angels, suspecting and doubting nothing, and always seeing friends where they are not sure of foes. Don't get the expression of a vicious cur that appears to know the kicks it gets are its desert, and yet hates all the world, as well as the kicker, for what it suffers.'

'In other words, I must wish for Edgar Linton's great blue eyes and even forehead,' he replied. 'I do—and that won't help me to them.'

'A good heart will help you to a bonny face, my lad,' I continued, 'if you were a regular black; and a bad one will turn the bonniest into something worse than ugly. And now that we've done washing, and combing, and sulking—tell me whether you don't think yourself rather handsome? I'll tell you, I do. You're fit for a prince in disguise. Who knows but your father was Emperor of China, and your mother an Indian queen, each of them able to buy up, with one week's income, Wuthering Heights and Thrushcross Grange together? And you were kidnapped by wicked sailors and brought to England. Were I in your place, I would frame high notions of my birth; and the thoughts of what I was should give me courage and dignity to support the oppressions of a little farmer!'

So I chattered on; and Heathcliff gradually lost his frown and began to look quite pleasant, when all at once our conversation was interrupted by a rumbling sound moving up the road and entering the court. He ran to the window and I to the door, just in time to behold the two Lintons descend from the family carriage, smothered in cloaks and furs, and the Earnshaws dismount from their horses: they often rode to church in winter. Catherine took a hand of each of the children, and brought them into the house and set them before the fire, which quickly put colour into their white faces.

I urged my companion to hasten now and show his amiable humour, and he willingly obeyed; but ill luck would have it that, as he opened the door leading from the kitchen on one side, Hindley opened it on the other. They met, and the master, irritated at seeing him clean and cheerful, or, perhaps, eager to keep his promise to Mrs. Linton, shoved him back with a sudden thrust, and angrily bade Joseph 'keep the fellow out of the room—send him into the garret till dinner is over. He'll be cramming his fingers in the tarts and stealing the fruit, if left alone with them a minute.'

'Nay, sir,' I could not avoid answering, 'he'll touch nothing, not he: and I suppose he must have his share of the dainties as well as we.'

'He shall have his share of my hand, if I catch him downstairs till dark,' cried Hindley. 'Begone, you vagabond! What! you are attempting the coxcomb, are you? Wait till I get hold of those elegant locks—see if I won't pull them a bit longer!'

'They are long enough already,' observed Master Linton, peeping from the doorway; 'I wonder they don't make his head ache. It's like a colt's mane over his eyes!'

He ventured this remark without any intention to insult; but Heathcliff's violent nature was not prepared to endure the appearance of impertinence from one whom he seemed to hate, even then, as a rival. He seized a tureen of hot apple sauce (the first thing that came under his gripe) and dashed it full against the speaker's face and neck; who instantly commenced a lament that brought Isabella and Catherine hurrying to the place. Mr. Earnshaw snatched up the culprit directly and conveyed him to his chamber; where, doubtless, he administered a rough remedy to cool the fit of passion, for he appeared red and breathless. I got the dishcloth, and rather spitefully scrubbed Edgar's nose and mouth, affirming it served him right for meddling. His sister began weeping to go home, and Cathy stood by confounded, blushing for all.

'You should not have spoken to him!' she expostulated with Master Linton. 'He was in a bad temper, and now you've spoilt your visit; and he'll be flogged: I hate him to be flogged! I can't eat my dinner. Why did you speak to him, Edgar?'

'I didn't,' sobbed the youth, escaping from my hands, and finishing the remainder of the purification with his cambric pocket-handkerchief. 'I promised mamma that I wouldn't say one word to him, and I didn't.'

'Well, don't cry,' replied Catherine, contemptuously; 'you're not killed. Don't make more mischief; my brother is coming: be quiet! Hush, Isabella! Has anybody hurt you?'

'There, there, children—to your seats!' cried Hindley, bustling in. 'That brute of a lad has warmed me nicely. Next time, Master Edgar, take the law into your own fists—it will give you an appetite!'

The little party recovered its equanimity at sight of the fragrant feast. They were hungry after their ride, and easily consoled, since no real harm had befallen them. Mr. Earnshaw carved bountiful plate-fuls, and the mistress made them merry with lively talk. I waited behind her chair, and was pained to behold Catherine, with dry eyes and an indifferent air, commence cutting up the wing of a goose before her. 'An unfeeling child,' I thought to myself; 'how lightly she dismisses her old playmate's troubles. I could not have imagined her to be so selfish.' She lifted a mouthful to her lips: then she set it down again: her cheeks flushed, and the tears gushed over them. She slipped her fork to the floor, and hastily dived under the cloth to conceal her emotion. I did not call her unfeeling long; for I perceived she was in purgatory throughout the day, and wearying to find an opportunity of getting by herself, or paying a visit to Heathcliff, who had been locked up by the master: as I discovered, on endeavouring to introduce to him a private mess of victuals.

In the evening we had a dance. Cathy begged that he might be liberated then, as Isabella Linton had no partner: her entreaties were vain, and I was appointed to supply the deficiency. We got rid of all gloom in the excitement of the exercise, and our pleasure was increased by the arrival of the Gimmerton band, mustering fifteen strong: a trumpet, a trombone, clarionets, bassoons, French horns, and a bass viol, besides singers. They go the rounds of all the respectable houses, and receive contributions every Christmas, and we esteemed it a first-rate treat to hear them. After the usual carols had been sung, we set them to songs and glees. Mrs. Earnshaw loved the music, and so they gave us plenty.

Catherine loved it too: but she said it sounded sweetest at the top of the steps, and she went up in the dark: I followed. They shut the house door below, never noting our absence, it was so full of people. She made no stay at the stairs'-head, but mounted farther, to the garret where Heathcliff was confined, and called him. He stubbornly declined answering for a while: she persevered, and finally persuaded him to hold communion with her through the boards. I let the poor things converse unmolested, till I supposed the songs were going to cease, and the singers to get some refreshment: then I clambered up the ladder to warn her. Instead of finding her outside, I heard her voice within. The little monkey had crept by the skylight of one garret, along the roof, into the skylight of the other, and it was with the utmost difficulty I could coax her out again. When she did come, Heathcliff came with her, and she insisted that I should take him into the kitchen, as my fellow-servant had gone to a neighbour's, to be removed from the sound of our 'devil's psalmody,' as it pleased him to call it. I told them I intended by no means to encourage their tricks: but as the prisoner had never broken his fast since yesterday's dinner, I would wink at his cheating Mr. Hindley that once. He went down: I set him a stool by the fire, and offered him a quantity of good things: but he was sick and could eat little, and my attempts to entertain him were thrown away. He leant his two elbows on his knees, and his chin on his hands and remained rapt in dumb meditation. On my inquiring the subject of his thoughts, he answered gravely—'I'm trying to settle how I shall pay Hindley back. I don't care how long I wait, if I can only do it at last. I hope he will not die before I do!'

'For shame, Heathcliff!' said I. 'It is for God to punish wicked people; we should learn to forgive.'

'No, God won't have the satisfaction that I shall,' he returned. 'I only wish I knew the best way! Let me alone, and I'll plan it out: while I'm thinking of that I don't feel pain.'

'But, Mr. Lockwood, I forget these tales cannot divert you. I'm annoyed how I should dream of chattering on at such a rate; and your gruel cold, and you nodding for bed! I could have told Heathcliff's history, all that you need hear, in half a dozen words.'

Thus interrupting herself, the housekeeper rose, and proceeded to lay aside her sewing; but I felt incapable of moving from the hearth, and I was very far from nodding. 'Sit still, Mrs. Dean,' I cried; 'do sit still another half-hour. You've done just right to tell the story leisurely. That is the method I like; and you must finish it in the same style. I am interested in every character you have mentioned, more or less.'

'The clock is on the stroke of eleven, sir.'

'No matter—I'm not accustomed to go to bed in the long hours. One or two is early enough for a person who lies till ten.'

'You shouldn't lie till ten. There's the very prime of the morning gone long before that time. A person who has not done one-half his day's work by ten o'clock, runs a chance of leaving the other half undone.'

'Nevertheless, Mrs. Dean, resume your chair; because to-morrow I intend lengthening the night till afternoon. I prognosticate for myself an obstinate cold, at least.'

'I hope not, sir. Well, you must allow me to leap over some three years; during that space Mrs. Earnshaw—'

'No, no, I'll allow nothing of the sort! Are you acquainted with the mood of mind in which, if you were seated alone, and the cat licking its kitten on the rug before you, you would watch the operation so intently that puss's neglect of one ear would put you seriously out of temper?'

'A terribly lazy mood, I should say.'

'On the contrary, a tiresomely active one. It is mine, at present; and, therefore, continue minutely. I perceive that people in these regions acquire over people in towns the value that a spider in a dungeon does over a spider in a cottage, to their various occupants; and yet the deepened attraction is not entirely owing to the situation of the looker-on. They DO live more in earnest, more in themselves, and less in surface, change, and frivolous external things. I could fancy a love for life here almost possible; and I was a fixed unbeliever in any love of a year's standing. One state resembles setting a hungry man down to a single dish, on which he may concentrate his entire appetite and do it justice; the other, introducing him to a table laid out by French cooks: he can perhaps extract as much enjoyment from the whole; but each part is a mere atom in his regard and remembrance.'

'Oh! here we are the same as anywhere else, when you get to know us,' observed Mrs. Dean, somewhat puzzled at my speech.

'Excuse me,' I responded; 'you, my good friend, are a striking evidence against that assertion. Excepting a few provincialisms of slight consequence, you have no marks of the manners which I am habituated to consider as peculiar to your class. I am sure you have thought a great deal more than the generality of servants think. You have been compelled to cultivate your reflective faculties for want of occasions for frittering your life away in silly trifles.'

Mrs. Dean laughed.

'I certainly esteem myself a steady, reasonable kind of body,' she said; 'not exactly from living among the hills and seeing one set of faces, and one series of actions, from year's end to year's end; but I have undergone sharp discipline, which has taught me wisdom; and then, I have read more than you would fancy, Mr. Lockwood. You could not open a book in this library that I have not looked into, and got something out of also: unless it be that range of Greek and Latin, and that of French; and those I know one from another: it is as much as you can expect of a poor man's daughter. However, if I am to follow my story in true gossip's fashion, I had better go on; and instead of leaping three years, I will be content to pass to the next summer—the summer of 1778, that is nearly twenty-three years ago.'

Chapter VIII

ON the morning of a fine June day my first bonny little nursling, and the last of the ancient Earnshaw stock, was born. We were busy with the hay in a far-away field, when the girl that usually brought our breakfasts came running an hour too soon across the meadow and up the lane, calling me as she ran.

'Oh, such a grand bairn!' she panted out. 'The finest lad that ever breathed! But the doctor says missis must go: he says she's been in a consumption these many months. I heard him tell Mr. Hindley: and now she has nothing to keep her, and she'll be dead before winter. You must come home directly. You're to nurse it, Nelly: to feed it with sugar and milk, and take care of it day and night. I wish I were you, because it will be all yours when there is no missis!'

'But is she very ill?' I asked, flinging down my rake and tying my bonnet.

'I guess she is; yet she looks bravely,' replied the girl, 'and she talks as if she thought of living to see it grow a man. She's out of her head for joy, it's such a beauty! If I were her I'm certain I should not die: I should get better at the bare sight of it, in spite of Kenneth. I was fairly mad at him. Dame Archer brought the cherub down to master, in the house, and his face just began to light up, when the old croaker steps forward, and says he-"Earnshaw, it's a blessing your wife has been spared to leave you this son. When she came, I felt convinced we shouldn't keep her long; and now, I must tell you, the winter will probably finish her. Don't take on, and fret about it too much: it can't be helped. And besides, you should have known better than to choose such a rush of a lass!"'

'And what did the master answer?' I inquired.

'I think he swore: but I didn't mind him, I was straining to see the bairn,' and she began again to describe it rapturously. I, as zealous as herself, hurried eagerly home to admire, on my part; though I was very sad for Hindley's sake. He had room in his heart only for two idols—his wife and himself: he doted on both, and adored one, and I couldn't conceive how he would bear the loss.

When we got to Wuthering Heights, there he stood at the front door; and, as I passed in, I asked, 'how was the baby?'

'Nearly ready to run about, Nell!' he replied, putting on a cheerful smile.

'And the mistress?' I ventured to inquire; 'the doctor says she's—'

'Damn the doctor!' he interrupted, reddening. 'Frances is quite right: she'll be perfectly well by this time next week. Are you going upstairs? will you tell her that I'll come, if she'll promise not to talk. I left her because she would not hold her tongue; and she must—tell her Mr. Kenneth says she must be quiet.'

I delivered this message to Mrs. Earnshaw; she seemed in flighty spirits, and replied merrily, 'I hardly spoke a word, Ellen, and there he has gone out twice, crying. Well, say I promise I won't speak: but that does not bind me not to laugh at him!'

Poor soul! Till within a week of her death that gay heart never failed her; and her husband persisted doggedly, nay, furiously, in affirming her health improved every day. When Kenneth warned him that his medicines were useless at that stage of the malady, and he needn't put him to further expense by attending her, he retorted, 'I know you need not—she's well—she does not want any more attendance from you! She never was in a consumption. It was a fever; and it is gone: her pulse is as slow as mine now, and her cheek as cool.'

He told his wife the same story, and she seemed to believe him; but one night, while leaning on his shoulder, in the act of saying she thought she should be able to get up to-morrow, a fit of coughing took her—a very slight one—he raised her in his arms; she put her two hands about his neck, her face changed, and she was dead.

As the girl had anticipated, the child Hareton fell wholly into my hands. Mr. Earnshaw, provided he saw him healthy and never heard him cry, was contented, as far as regarded him. For himself, he grew desperate: his sorrow was of that kind that will not lament. He neither wept nor prayed; he cursed and defied: execrated God and man, and gave himself up to reckless dissipation. The servants could not bear his tyrannical and evil conduct long: Joseph and I were the only two that would stay. I had not the heart to leave my charge; and besides, you know, I had been his foster-sister, and excused his behaviour more readily than a stranger would. Joseph remained to hector over tenants and labourers; and because it was his vocation to be where he had plenty of wickedness to reprove.

The master's bad ways and bad companions formed a pretty example for Catherine and Heathcliff. His treatment of the latter was enough to make a fiend of a saint. And, truly, it appeared as if the lad WERE possessed of something diabolical at that period. He delighted to witness Hindley degrading himself past redemption; and became daily more notable for savage sullenness and ferocity. I could not half tell what an infernal house we had. The curate dropped calling, and nobody decent came near us, at last; unless Edgar Linton's visits to Miss Cathy might be an exception. At fifteen she was the queen of the country-side; she had no peer; and she did turn out a haughty, head-strong creature! I own I did not like her, after infancy was past; and I vexed her frequently by trying to bring down her arrogance: she never took an aversion to me, though. She had a wondrous constancy to old attachments: even Heathcliff kept his hold on her affections unalterably; and young Linton, with all his superiority, found it difficult to make an equally deep impression. He was my late master: that is his portrait over the fireplace. It used to hang on one side, and his wife's on the other; but hers has been removed, or else you might see something of what she was. Can you make that out?

Mrs. Dean raised the candle, and I discerned a soft-featured face, exceedingly resembling the young lady at the Heights, but more pensive and amiable in expression. It formed a sweet picture. The long light hair curled slightly on the temples; the eyes were large and serious; the figure almost too graceful. I did not marvel how Catherine Earnshaw could forget her first friend for such an individual. I marvelled much how he, with a mind to correspond with his person, could fancy my idea of Catherine Earnshaw.

'A very agreeable portrait,' I observed to the house-keeper. 'Is it like?'

'Yes,' she answered; 'but he looked better when he was animated; that is his everyday countenance: he wanted spirit in general.'

Catherine had kept up her acquaintance with the Lintons since her five-weeks' residence among them; and as she had no temptation to show her rough side in their company, and had the sense to be ashamed of being rude where she experienced such invariable courtesy, she imposed unwittingly on the old lady and gentleman by her ingenious cordiality; gained the admiration of Isabella, and the heart and soul of her brother: acquisitions that flattered her from the first—for she was full of ambition—and led her to adopt a double character without exactly intending to deceive any one. In the place where she heard Heathcliff termed a 'vulgar young ruffian,' and 'worse than a brute,' she took care not to act like him; but at home she had small inclination to practise politeness that would only be laughed at, and restrain an unruly nature when it would bring her neither credit nor praise.

Mr. Edgar seldom mustered courage to visit Wuthering Heights openly. He had a terror of Earnshaw's reputation, and shrunk from encountering him; and yet he was always received with our best attempts at civility: the master himself avoided offending him, knowing why he came; and if he could not be gracious, kept out of the way. I rather think his appearance there was distasteful to Catherine; she was not artful, never played the coquette, and had evidently an objection to her two friends meeting at all; for when Heathcliff expressed contempt of Linton in his presence, she could not half coincide, as she did in his absence; and when Linton evinced disgust and antipathy to Heathcliff, she dared not treat his sentiments with indifference, as if depreciation of her playmate were of scarcely any consequence to her. I've had many a laugh at her perplexities and untold troubles, which she vainly strove to hide from my mockery. That sounds ill-natured: but she was so proud it became really impossible to pity her distresses, till she should be chastened into more humility. She did bring herself, finally, to confess, and to confide in me: there was not a soul else that she might fashion into an adviser.

Mr. Hindley had gone from home one afternoon, and Heathcliff presumed to give himself a holiday on the strength of it. He had reached the age of sixteen then, I think, and without having bad features, or being deficient in intellect, he contrived to convey an impression of inward and outward repulsiveness that his present aspect retains no traces of. In the first place, he had by that time lost the benefit of his early education: continual hard work, begun soon and concluded late, had extinguished any curiosity he once possessed in pursuit of knowledge, and any love for books or learning. His childhood's sense of superiority, instilled into him by the favours of old Mr. Earnshaw, was faded away. He struggled long to keep up an equality with Catherine in her studies, and yielded with poignant though silent regret: but he yielded completely; and there was no prevailing on him to take a step in the way of moving upward, when he found he must, necessarily, sink beneath his former level. Then personal appearance sympathised with mental deterioration: he acquired a slouching gait and ignoble look; his naturally reserved disposition was exaggerated into an almost idiotic excess of unsociable moroseness; and he took a grim pleasure, apparently, in exciting the aversion rather than the esteem of his few acquaintance.

Catherine and he were constant companions still at his seasons of respite from labour; but he had ceased to express his fondness for her in words, and recoiled with angry suspicion from her girlish caresses, as if conscious there could be no gratification in lavishing such marks of affection on him. On the before-named occasion he came into the house to announce his intention of doing nothing, while I was assisting Miss Cathy to arrange her dress: she had not reckoned on his taking it into his head to be idle; and imagining she would have the whole place to herself, she managed, by some means, to inform Mr. Edgar of her brother's absence, and was then preparing to receive him.

'Cathy, are you busy this afternoon?' asked Heathcliff. 'Are you going anywhere?'

'No, it is raining,' she answered.

'Why have you that silk frock on, then?' he said. 'Nobody coming here, I hope?'

'Not that I know of,' stammered Miss: 'but you should be in the field now, Heathcliff. It is an hour past dinnertime: I thought you were gone.'

'Hindley does not often free us from his accursed presence,' observed the boy. 'I'll not work any more to-day: I'll stay with you.'

'Oh, but Joseph will tell,' she suggested; 'you'd better go!'

'Joseph is loading lime on the further side of Penistone Crags; it will take him till dark, and he'll never know.'

So, saying, he lounged to the fire, and sat down. Catherine reflected an instant, with knitted brows—she found it needful to smooth the way for an intrusion. 'Isabella and Edgar Linton talked of calling this afternoon,' she said, at the conclusion of a minute's silence. 'As it rains, I hardly expect them; but they may come, and if they do, you run the risk of being scolded for no good.'

'Order Ellen to say you are engaged, Cathy,' he persisted; 'don't turn me out for those pitiful, silly friends of yours! I'm on the point, sometimes, of complaining that they—but I'll not—'

'That they what?' cried Catherine, gazing at him with a troubled countenance. 'Oh, Nelly!' she added petulantly, jerking her head away from my hands, 'you've combed my hair quite out of curl! That's enough; let me alone. What are you on the point of complaining about, Heathcliff?'

'Nothing—only look at the almanack on that wall;' he pointed to a framed sheet hanging near the window, and continued, 'The crosses are for the evenings you have spent with the Lintons, the dots for those spent with me. Do you see? I've marked every day.'

'Yes—very foolish: as if I took notice!' replied Catherine, in a peevish tone. 'And where is the sense of that?'

'To show that I DO take notice,' said Heathcliff.

'And should I always be sitting with you?' she demanded, growing more irritated. 'What good do I get? What do you talk about? You might be dumb, or a baby, for anything you say to amuse me, or for anything you do, either!'

'You never told me before that I talked too little, or that you disliked my company, Cathy!' exclaimed Heathcliff, in much agitation.

'It's no company at all, when people know nothing and say nothing,' she muttered.

Her companion rose up, but he hadn't time to express his feelings further, for a horse's feet were heard on the flags, and having knocked gently, young Linton entered, his face brilliant with delight at the unexpected summon she had received. Doubtless Catherine marked the difference between her friends, as one came in and the other went out. The contrast resembled what you see in exchanging a bleak, hilly, coal country for a beautiful fertile valley; and his voice and greeting were as opposite as his aspect. He had a sweet, low manner of speaking, and pronounced his words as you do: that's less gruff than we talk here, and softer.

'I'm not come too soon, am I?' he said, casting a look at me: I had begun to wipe the plate, and tidy some drawers at the far end in the dresser.

'No,' answered Catherine. 'What are you doing there, Nelly?'

'My work, Miss,' I replied. (Mr. Hindley had given me directions to make a third party in any private visits Linton chose to pay.)

She stepped behind me and whispered crossly, 'Take yourself and your dusters off; when company are in the house, servants don't commence scouring and cleaning in the room where they are!'

'It's a good opportunity, now that master is away,' I answered aloud: 'he hates me to be fidgeting over these things in his presence. I'm sure Mr. Edgar will excuse me.'

'I hate you to be fidgeting in MY presence,' exclaimed the young lady imperiously, not allowing her guest time to speak: she had failed to recover her equanimity since the little dispute with Heathcliff.

'I'm sorry for it, Miss Catherine,' was my response; and I proceeded assiduously with my occupation.

She, supposing Edgar could not see her, snatched the cloth from my hand, and pinched me, with a prolonged wrench, very spitefully on the arm. I've said I did not love her, and rather relished mortifying her vanity now and then: besides, she hurt me extremely; so I started up from my knees, and screamed out, 'Oh, Miss, that's a nasty trick! You have no right to nip me, and I'm not going to bear it.'

'I didn't touch you, you lying creature!' cried she, her fingers tingling to repeat the act, and her ears red with rage. She never had power to conceal her passion, it always set her whole complexion in a blaze.

'What's that, then?' I retorted, showing a decided purple witness to refute her.

She stamped her foot, wavered a moment, and then, irresistibly impelled by the naughty spirit within her, slapped me on the cheek: a stinging blow that filled both eyes with water.

'Catherine, love! Catherine!' interposed Linton, greatly shocked at the double fault of falsehood and violence which his idol had committed.

'Leave the room, Ellen!' she repeated, trembling all over.

Little Hareton, who followed me everywhere, and was sitting near me on the floor, at seeing my tears commenced crying himself, and sobbed out complaints against 'wicked aunt Cathy,' which drew her fury on to his unlucky head: she seized his shoulders, and shook him till the poor child waxed livid, and Edgar thoughtlessly laid hold of her hands to deliver him. In an instant one was wrung free, and the astonished young man felt it applied over his own ear in a way that could not be mistaken for jest. He drew back in consternation. I lifted Hareton in my arms, and walked off to the kitchen with him, leaving the door of communication open, for I was curious to watch how they would settle their disagreement. The insulted visitor moved to the spot where he had laid his hat, pale and with a quivering lip.

'That's right!' I said to myself. 'Take warning and begone! It's a kindness to let you have a glimpse of her genuine disposition.'

'Where are you going?' demanded Catherine, advancing to the door.

He swerved aside, and attempted to pass.

'You must not go!' she exclaimed, energetically.

'I must and shall!' he replied in a subdued voice.

'No,' she persisted, grasping the handle; 'not yet, Edgar Linton: sit down; you shall not leave me in that temper. I should be miserable all night, and I won't be miserable for you!'

'Can I stay after you have struck me?' asked Linton.

Catherine was mute.

'You've made me afraid and ashamed of you,' he continued; 'I'll not come here again!'

Her eyes began to glisten and her lids to twinkle.

'And you told a deliberate untruth!' he said.

'I didn't!' she cried, recovering her speech; 'I did nothing deliberately. Well, go, if you please—get away! And now I'll cry—I'll cry myself sick!'

She dropped down on her knees by a chair, and set to weeping in serious earnest. Edgar persevered in his resolution as far as the court; there he lingered. I resolved to encourage him.

'Miss is dreadfully wayward, sir,' I called out. 'As bad as any marred child: you'd better be riding home, or else she will be sick, only to grieve us.'

The soft thing looked askance through the window: he possessed the power to depart as much as a cat possesses the power to leave a mouse half killed, or a bird half eaten. Ah, I thought, there will be no saving him: he's doomed, and flies to his fate! And so it was: he turned abruptly, hastened into the house again, shut the door behind him; and when I went in a while after to inform them that Earnshaw had come home rabid drunk, ready to pull the whole place about our ears (his ordinary frame of mind in that condition), I saw the quarrel had merely effected a closer intimacy—had broken the outworks of youthful timidity, and enabled them to forsake the disguise of friendship, and confess themselves lovers.

Intelligence of Mr. Hindley's arrival drove Linton speedily to his horse, and Catherine to her chamber. I went to hide little Hareton, and to take the shot out of the master's fowling-piece, which he was fond of playing with in his insane excitement, to the hazard of the lives of any who provoked, or even attracted his notice too much; and I had hit upon the plan of removing it, that he might do less mischief if he did go the length of firing the gun.

Chapter IX

HE entered, vociferating oaths dreadful to hear; and caught me in the act of stowing his son sway in the kitchen cupboard. Hareton was impressed with a wholesome terror of encountering either his wild beast's fondness or his madman's rage; for in one he ran a chance of being squeezed and kissed to death, and in the other of being flung into the fire, or dashed against the wall; and the poor thing remained perfectly quiet wherever I chose to put him.

'There, I've found it out at last!' cried Hindley, pulling me back by the skin of my neck, like a dog. 'By heaven and hell, you've sworn between you to murder that child! I know how it is, now, that he is always out of my way. But, with the help of Satan, I shall make you swallow the carving-knife, Nelly! You needn't laugh; for I've just crammed Kenneth, head-downmost, in the Black-horse marsh; and two is the same as one—and I want to kill some of you: I shall have no rest till I do!'

'But I don't like the carving-knife, Mr. Hindley,' I answered; 'it has been cutting red herrings. I'd rather be shot, if you please.'

'You'd rather be damned!' he said; 'and so you shall. No law in England can hinder a man from keeping his house decent, and mine's abominable! Open your mouth.' He held the knife in his hand, and pushed its point between my teeth: but, for my part, I was never much afraid of his vagaries. I spat out, and affirmed it tasted detestably—I would not take it on any account.

'Oh!' said he, releasing me, 'I see that hideous little villain is not Hareton: I beg your pardon, Nell. If it be, he deserves flaying alive for not running to welcome me, and for screaming as if I were a goblin. Unnatural cub, come hither! I'll teach thee to impose on a good-hearted, deluded father. Now, don't you think the lad would be handsomer cropped? It makes a dog fiercer, and I love something fierce—get me a scissors—something fierce and trim! Besides, it's infernal affectation—devilish conceit it is, to cherish our ears—we're asses enough without them. Hush, child, hush! Well then, it is my darling! wisht, dry thy eyes—there's a joy; kiss me. What! it won't? Kiss me, Hareton! Damn thee, kiss me! By God, as if I would rear such a monster! As sure as I'm living, I'll break the brat's neck.'

Poor Hareton was squalling and kicking in his father's arms with all his might, and redoubled his yells when he carried him up-stairs and lifted him over the banister. I cried out that he would frighten the child into fits, and ran to rescue him. As I reached them, Hindley leant forward on the rails to listen to a noise below; almost forgetting what he had in his hands. 'Who is that?' he asked, hearing some one approaching the stairs'-foot. I leant forward also, for the purpose of signing to Heathcliff, whose step I recognised, not to come further; and, at the instant when my eye quitted Hareton, he gave a sudden spring, delivered himself from the careless grasp that held him, and fell.

There was scarcely time to experience a thrill of horror before we saw that the little wretch was safe. Heathcliff arrived underneath just at the critical moment; by a natural impulse he arrested his descent, and setting him on his feet, looked up to discover the author of the accident. A miser who has parted with a lucky lottery ticket for five shillings, and finds next day he has lost in the bargain five thousand pounds, could not show a blanker countenance than he did on beholding the figure of Mr. Earnshaw above. It expressed, plainer than words could do, the intensest anguish at having made himself the instrument of thwarting his own revenge. Had it been dark, I daresay he would have tried to remedy the mistake by smashing Hareton's skull on the steps; but, we witnessed his salvation; and I was presently below with my precious charge pressed to my heart. Hindley descended more leisurely, sobered and abashed.

'It is your fault, Ellen,' he said; 'you should have kept him out of sight: you should have taken him from me! Is he injured anywhere?'

'Injured!' I cried angrily; 'if he is not killed, he'll be an idiot! Oh! I wonder his mother does not rise from her grave to see how you use him. You're worse than a heathen—treating your own flesh and blood in that manner!' He attempted to touch the child, who, on finding himself with me, sobbed off his terror directly. At the first finger his father laid on him, however, he shrieked again louder than before, and struggled as if he would go into convulsions.

'You shall not meddle with him!' I continued. 'He hates you—they all hate you—that's the truth! A happy family you have; and a pretty state you're come to!'

'I shall come to a prettier, yet, Nelly,' laughed the misguided man, recovering his hardness. 'At present, convey yourself and him away. And hark you, Heathcliff! clear you too quite from my reach and hearing. I wouldn't murder you to-night; unless, perhaps, I set the house on fire: but that's as my fancy goes.'

While saying this he took a pint bottle of brandy from the dresser, and poured some into a tumbler.

'Nay, don't!' I entreated. 'Mr. Hindley, do take warning. Have mercy on this unfortunate boy, if you care nothing for yourself!'

'Any one will do better for him than I shall,' he answered.

'Have mercy on your own soul!' I said, endeavouring to snatch the glass from his hand.

'Not I! On the contrary, I shall have great pleasure in sending it to perdition to punish its Maker,' exclaimed the blasphemer. 'Here's to its hearty damnation!'

He drank the spirits and impatiently bade us go; terminating his command with a sequel of horrid imprecations too bad to repeat or remember.

'It's a pity he cannot kill himself with drink,' observed Heathcliff, muttering an echo of curses back when the door was shut. 'He's doing his very utmost; but his constitution defies him. Mr. Kenneth says he would wager his mare that he'll outlive any man on this side Gimmerton, and go to the grave a hoary sinner; unless some happy chance out of the common course befall him.'

I went into the kitchen, and sat down to lull my little lamb to sleep. Heathcliff, as I thought, walked through to the barn. It turned out afterwards that he only got as far as the other side the settle, when he flung himself on a bench by the wall, removed from the fire and remained silent.

I was rocking Hareton on my knee, and humming a song that began,—

It was far in the night, and the bairnies grat,
The mither beneath the mools heard that,

when Miss Cathy, who had listened to the hubbub from her room, put her head in, and whispered,—'Are you alone, Nelly?'

'Yes, Miss,' I replied.

She entered and approached the hearth. I, supposing she was going to say something, looked up. The expression of her face seemed disturbed and anxious. Her lips were half asunder, as if she meant to speak, and she drew a breath; but it escaped in a sigh instead of a sentence. I resumed my song; not having forgotten her recent behaviour.

'Where's Heathcliff?' she said, interrupting me.

'About his work in the stable,' was my answer.

He did not contradict me; perhaps he had fallen into a doze. There followed another long pause, during which I perceived a drop or two trickle from Catherine's cheek to the flags. Is she sorry for her shameful conduct?—I asked myself. That will be a novelty: but she may come to the point—as she will—I sha'n't help her! No, she felt small trouble regarding any subject, save her own concerns.

'Oh, dear!' she cried at last. 'I'm very unhappy!'

'A pity,' observed I. 'You're hard to please; so many friends and so few cares, and can't make yourself content!'

'Nelly, will you keep a secret for me?' she pursued, kneeling down by me, and lifting her winsome eyes to my face with that sort of look which turns off bad temper, even when one has all the right in the world to indulge it.

'Is it worth keeping?' I inquired, less sulkily.

'Yes, and it worries me, and I must let it out! I want to know what I should do. To-day, Edgar Linton has asked me to marry him, and I've given him an answer. Now, before I tell you whether it was a consent or denial, you tell me which it ought to have been.'

'Really, Miss Catherine, how can I know?' I replied. 'To be sure, considering the exhibition you performed in his presence this afternoon, I might say it would be wise to refuse him: since he asked you after that, he must either be hopelessly stupid or a venturesome fool.'

'If you talk so, I won't tell you any more,' she returned, peevishly rising to her feet. 'I accepted him, Nelly. Be quick, and say whether I was wrong!'

'You accepted him! Then what good is it discussing the matter? You have pledged your word, and cannot retract.'

'But say whether I should have done so—do!' she exclaimed in an irritated tone; chafing her hands together, and frowning.

'There are many things to be considered before that question can be answered properly,' I said, sententiously. 'First and foremost, do you love Mr. Edgar?'

'Who can help it? Of course I do,' she answered.

Then I put her through the following catechism: for a girl of twenty-two it was not injudicious.

'Why do you love him, Miss Cathy?'

'Nonsense, I do—that's sufficient.'

'By no means; you must say why?'

'Well, because he is handsome, and pleasant to be with.'

'Bad!' was my commentary.

'And because he is young and cheerful.'

'Bad, still.'

'And because he loves me.'

'Indifferent, coming there.'

'And he will be rich, and I shall like to be the greatest woman of the neighbourhood, and I shall be proud of having such a husband.'

'Worst of all. And now, say how you love him?'

'As everybody loves—You're silly, Nelly.'

'Not at all—Answer.'

'I love the ground under his feet, and the air over his head, and everything he touches, and every word he says. I love all his looks, and all his actions, and him entirely and altogether. There now!'

'And why?'

'Nay; you are making a jest of it: it is exceedingly ill-natured! It's no jest to me!' said the young lady, scowling, and turning her face to the fire.

'I'm very far from jesting, Miss Catherine,' I replied. 'You love Mr. Edgar because he is handsome, and young, and cheerful, and rich, and loves you. The last, however, goes for nothing: you would love him without that, probably; and with it you wouldn't, unless he possessed the four former attractions.'

'No, to be sure not: I should only pity him—hate him, perhaps, if he were ugly, and a clown.'

'But there are several other handsome, rich young men in the world: handsomer, possibly, and richer than he is. What should hinder you from loving them?'

'If there be any, they are out of my way: I've seen none like Edgar.'

'You may see some; and he won't always be handsome, and young, and may not always be rich.'

'He is now; and I have only to do with the present. I wish you would speak rationally.'

'Well, that settles it: if you have only to do with the present, marry Mr. Linton.'

'I don't want your permission for that—I SHALL marry him: and yet you have not told me whether I'm right.'

'Perfectly right; if people be right to marry only for the present. And now, let us hear what you are unhappy about. Your brother will be pleased; the old lady and gentleman will not object, I think; you will escape from a disorderly, comfortless home into a wealthy, respectable one; and you love Edgar, and Edgar loves you. All seems smooth and easy: where is the obstacle?'

'HERE! and HERE!' replied Catherine, striking one hand on her forehead, and the other on her breast: 'in whichever place the soul lives. In my soul and in my heart, I'm convinced I'm wrong!'

'That's very strange! I cannot make it out.'

'It's my secret. But if you will not mock at me, I'll explain it: I can't do it distinctly; but I'll give you a feeling of how I feel.'

She seated herself by me again: her countenance grew sadder and graver, and her clasped hands trembled.

'Nelly, do you never dream queer dreams?' she said, suddenly, after some minutes' reflection.

'Yes, now and then,' I answered.

'And so do I. I've dreamt in my life dreams that have stayed with me ever after, and changed my ideas: they've gone through and through me, like wine through water, and altered the colour of my mind. And this is one: I'm going to tell it—but take care not to smile at any part of it.'

'Oh! don't, Miss Catherine!' I cried. 'We're dismal enough without conjuring up ghosts and visions to perplex us. Come, come, be merry and like yourself! Look at little Hareton! HE'S dreaming nothing dreary. How sweetly he smiles in his sleep!'

'Yes; and how sweetly his father curses in his solitude! You remember him, I daresay, when he was just such another as that chubby thing: nearly as young and innocent. However, Nelly, I shall oblige you to listen: it's not long; and I've no power to be merry to-night.'

'I won't hear it, I won't hear it!' I repeated, hastily.

I was superstitious about dreams then, and am still; and Catherine had an unusual gloom in her aspect, that made me dread something from which I might shape a prophecy, and foresee a fearful catastrophe. She was vexed, but she did not proceed. Apparently taking up another subject, she recommenced in a short time.

'If I were in heaven, Nelly, I should be extremely miserable.'

'Because you are not fit to go there,' I answered. 'All sinners would be miserable in heaven.'

'But it is not for that. I dreamt once that I was there.'

'I tell you I won't hearken to your dreams, Miss Catherine! I'll go to bed,' I interrupted again.

She laughed, and held me down; for I made a motion to leave my chair.

'This is nothing,' cried she: 'I was only going to say that heaven did not seem to be my home; and I broke my heart with weeping to come back to earth; and the angels were so angry that they flung me out into the middle of the heath on the top of Wuthering Heights; where I woke sobbing for joy. That will do to explain my secret, as well as the other. I've no more business to marry Edgar Linton than I have to be in heaven; and if the wicked man in there had not brought Heathcliff so low, I shouldn't have thought of it. It would degrade me to marry Heathcliff now; so he shall never know how I love him: and that, not because he's handsome, Nelly, but because he's more myself than I am. Whatever our souls are made of, his and mine are the same; and Linton's is as different as a moonbeam from lightning, or frost from fire.'

Ere this speech ended I became sensible of Heathcliff's presence. Having noticed a slight movement, I turned my head, and saw him rise from the bench, and steal out noiselessly. He had listened till he heard Catherine say it would degrade her to marry him, and then he stayed to hear no further. My companion, sitting on the ground, was prevented by the back of the settle from remarking his presence or departure; but I started, and bade her hush!

'Why?' she asked, gazing nervously round.

'Joseph is here,' I answered, catching opportunely the roll of his cartwheels up the road; 'and Heathcliff will come in with him. I'm not sure whether he were not at the door this moment.'

'Oh, he couldn't overhear me at the door!' said she. 'Give me Hareton, while you get the supper, and when it is ready ask me to sup with you. I want to cheat my uncomfortable conscience, and be convinced that Heathcliff has no notion of these things. He has not, has he? He does not know what being in love is!'

'I see no reason that he should not know, as well as you,' I returned; 'and if you are his choice, he'll be the most unfortunate creature that ever was born! As soon as you become Mrs. Linton, he loses friend, and love, and all! Have you considered how you'll bear the separation, and how he'll bear to be quite deserted in the world? Because, Miss Catherine—'

'He quite deserted! we separated!' she exclaimed, with an accent of indignation. 'Who is to separate us, pray? They'll meet the fate of Milo! Not as long as I live, Ellen: for no mortal creature. Every Linton on the face of the earth might melt into nothing before I could consent to forsake Heathcliff. Oh, that's not what I intend—that's not what I mean! I shouldn't be Mrs. Linton were such a price demanded! He'll be as much to me as he has been all his lifetime. Edgar must shake off his antipathy, and tolerate him, at least. He will, when he learns my true feelings towards him. Nelly, I see now you think me a selfish wretch; but did it never strike you that if Heathcliff and I married, we should be beggars? whereas, if I marry Linton I can aid Heathcliff to rise, and place him out of my brother's power.'

'With your husband's money, Miss Catherine?' I asked. 'You'll find him not so pliable as you calculate upon: and, though I'm hardly a judge, I think that's the worst motive you've given yet for being the wife of young Linton.'

'It is not,' retorted she; 'it is the best! The others were the satisfaction of my whims: and for Edgar's sake, too, to satisfy him. This is for the sake of one who comprehends in his person my feelings to Edgar and myself. I cannot express it; but surely you and everybody have a notion that there is or should be an existence of yours beyond you. What were the use of my creation, if I were entirely contained here? My great miseries in this world have been Heathcliff's miseries, and I watched and felt each from the beginning: my great thought in living is himself. If all else perished, and HE remained, I should still continue to be; and if all else remained, and he were annihilated, the universe would turn to a mighty stranger: I should not seem a part of it.—My love for Linton is like the foliage in the woods: time will change it, I'm well aware, as winter changes the trees. My love for Heathcliff resembles the eternal rocks beneath: a source of little visible delight, but necessary. Nelly, I AM Heathcliff! He's always, always in my mind: not as a pleasure, any more than I am always a pleasure to myself, but as my own being. So don't talk of our separation again: it is impracticable; and—'

She paused, and hid her face in the folds of my gown; but I jerked it forcibly away. I was out of patience with her folly!

'If I can make any sense of your nonsense, Miss,' I said, 'it only goes to convince me that you are ignorant of the duties you undertake in marrying; or else that you are a wicked, unprincipled girl. But trouble me with no more secrets: I'll not promise to keep them.'

'You'll keep that?' she asked, eagerly.

'No, I'll not promise,' I repeated.

She was about to insist, when the entrance of Joseph finished our conversation; and Catherine removed her seat to a corner, and nursed Hareton, while I made the supper. After it was cooked, my fellow-servant and I began to quarrel who should carry some to Mr. Hindley; and we didn't settle it till all was nearly cold. Then we came to the agreement that we would let him ask, if he wanted any; for we feared particularly to go into his presence when he had been some time alone.

'And how isn't that nowt comed in fro' th' field, be this time? What is he about? girt idle seeght!' demanded the old man, looking round for Heathcliff.

'I'll call him,' I replied. 'He's in the barn, I've no doubt.'

I went and called, but got no answer. On returning, I whispered to Catherine that he had heard a good part of what she said, I was sure; and told how I saw him quit the kitchen just as she complained of her brother's conduct regarding him. She jumped up in a fine fright, flung Hareton on to the settle, and ran to seek for her friend herself; not taking leisure to consider why she was so flurried, or how her talk would have affected him. She was absent such a while that Joseph proposed we should wait no longer. He cunningly conjectured they were staying away in order to avoid hearing his protracted blessing. They were 'ill eneugh for ony fahl manners,' he affirmed. And on their behalf he added that night a special prayer to the usual quarter-of-an-hour's supplication before meat, and would have tacked another to the end of the grace, had not his young mistress broken in upon him with a hurried command that he must run down the road, and, wherever Heathcliff had rambled, find and make him re-enter directly!

'I want to speak to him, and I MUST, before I go upstairs,' she said. 'And the gate is open: he is somewhere out of hearing; for he would not reply, though I shouted at the top of the fold as loud as I could.'

Joseph objected at first; she was too much in earnest, however, to suffer contradiction; and at last he placed his hat on his head, and walked grumbling forth. Meantime, Catherine paced up and down the floor, exclaiming—'I wonder where he is—I wonder where he can be! What did I say, Nelly? I've forgotten. Was he vexed at my bad humour this afternoon? Dear! tell me what I've said to grieve him? I do wish he'd come. I do wish he would!'

'What a noise for nothing!' I cried, though rather uneasy myself. 'What a trifle scares you! It's surely no great cause of alarm that Heathcliff should take a moonlight saunter on the moors, or even lie too sulky to speak to us in the hay-loft. I'll engage he's lurking there. See if I don't ferret him out!'

I departed to renew my search; its result was disappointment, and Joseph's quest ended in the same.

'Yon lad gets war und war!' observed he on re-entering. 'He's left th' gate at t' full swing, and Miss's pony has trodden dahn two rigs o' corn, and plottered through, raight o'er into t' meadow! Hahsomdiver, t' maister 'ull play t' devil to-morn, and he'll do weel. He's patience itsseln wi' sich careless, offald craters—patience itsseln he is! Bud he'll not be soa allus—yah's see, all on ye! Yah mun'n't drive him out of his heead for nowt!'

'Have you found Heathcliff, you ass?' interrupted Catherine. 'Have you been looking for him, as I ordered?'

'I sud more likker look for th' horse,' he replied. 'It 'ud be to more sense. Bud I can look for norther horse nur man of a neeght loike this—as black as t' chimbley! und Heathcliff's noan t' chap to coom at MY whistle—happen he'll be less hard o' hearing wi' YE!'

It WAS a very dark evening for summer: the clouds appeared inclined to thunder, and I said we had better all sit down; the approaching rain would be certain to bring him home without further trouble. However, Catherine would hot be persuaded into tranquillity. She kept wandering to and fro, from the gate to the door, in a state of agitation which permitted no repose; and at length took up a permanent situation on one side of the wall, near the road: where, heedless of my expostulations and the growling thunder, and the great drops that began to plash around her, she remained, calling at intervals, and then listening, and then crying outright. She beat Hareton, or any child, at a good passionate fit of crying.

About midnight, while we still sat up, the storm came rattling over the Heights in full fury. There was a violent wind, as well as thunder, and either one or the other split a tree off at the corner of the building: a huge bough fell across the roof, and knocked down a portion of the east chimney-stack, sending a clatter of stones and soot into the kitchen-fire. We thought a bolt had fallen in the middle of us; and Joseph swung on to his knees, beseeching the Lord to remember the patriarchs Noah and Lot, and, as in former times, spare the righteous, though he smote the ungodly. I felt some sentiment that it must be a judgment on us also. The Jonah, in my mind, was Mr. Earnshaw; and I shook the handle of his den that I might ascertain if he were yet living. He replied audibly enough, in a fashion which made my companion vociferate, more clamorously than before, that a wide distinction might be drawn between saints like himself and sinners like his master. But the uproar passed away in twenty minutes, leaving us all unharmed; excepting Cathy, who got thoroughly drenched for her obstinacy in refusing to take shelter, and standing bonnetless and shawl-less to catch as much water as she could with her hair and clothes. She came in and lay down on the settle, all soaked as she was, turning her face to the back, and putting her hands before it.

'Well, Miss!' I exclaimed, touching her shoulder; 'you are not bent on getting your death, are you? Do you know what o'clock it is? Half-past twelve. Come, come to bed! there's no use waiting any longer on that foolish boy: he'll be gone to Gimmerton, and he'll stay there now. He guesses we shouldn't wait for him till this late hour: at least, he guesses that only Mr. Hindley would be up; and he'd rather avoid having the door opened by the master.'

'Nay, nay, he's noan at Gimmerton,' said Joseph. 'I's niver wonder but he's at t' bothom of a bog-hoile. This visitation worn't for nowt, and I wod hev' ye to look out, Miss—yah muh be t' next. Thank Hivin for all! All warks togither for gooid to them as is chozzen, and piked out fro' th' rubbidge! Yah knaw whet t' Scripture ses.' And he began quoting several texts, referring us to chapters and verses where we might find them.

I, having vainly begged the wilful girl to rise and remove her wet things, left him preaching and her shivering, and betook myself to bed with little Hareton, who slept as fast as if everyone had been sleeping round him. I heard Joseph read on a while afterwards; then I distinguished his slow step on the ladder, and then I dropped asleep.

Coming down somewhat later than usual, I saw, by the sunbeams piercing the chinks of the shutters, Miss Catherine still seated near the fireplace. The house-door was ajar, too; light entered from its unclosed windows; Hindley had come out, and stood on the kitchen hearth, haggard and drowsy.

'What ails you, Cathy?' he was saying when I entered: 'you look as dismal as a drowned whelp. Why are you so damp and pale, child?'

'I've been wet,' she answered reluctantly, 'and I'm cold, that's all.'

'Oh, she is naughty!' I cried, perceiving the master to be tolerably sober. 'She got steeped in the shower of yesterday evening, and there she has sat the night through, and I couldn't prevail on her to stir.'

Mr. Earnshaw stared at us in surprise. 'The night through,' he repeated. 'What kept her up? not fear of the thunder, surely? That was over hours since.'

Neither of us wished to mention Heathcliff's absence, as long as we could conceal it; so I replied, I didn't know how she took it into her head to sit up; and she said nothing. The morning was fresh and cool; I threw back the lattice, and presently the room filled with sweet scents from the garden; but Catherine called peevishly to me, 'Ellen, shut the window. I'm starving!' And her teeth chattered as she shrank closer to the almost extinguished embers.

'She's ill,' said Hindley, taking her wrist; 'I suppose that's the reason she would not go to bed. Damn it! I don't want to be troubled with more sickness here. What took you into the rain?'

'Running after t' lads, as usuald!' croaked Joseph, catching an opportunity from our hesitation to thrust in his evil tongue. 'If I war yah, maister, I'd just slam t' boards i' their faces all on 'em, gentle and simple! Never a day ut yah're off, but yon cat o' Linton comes sneaking hither; and Miss Nelly, shoo's a fine lass! shoo sits watching for ye i' t' kitchen; and as yah're in at one door, he's out at t'other; and, then, wer grand lady goes a-courting of her side! It's bonny behaviour, lurking amang t' fields, after twelve o' t' night, wi' that fahl, flaysome divil of a gipsy, Heathcliff! They think I'M blind; but I'm noan: nowt ut t' soart!—I seed young Linton boath coming and going, and I seed YAH' (directing his discourse to me), 'yah gooid fur nowt, slattenly witch! nip up and bolt into th' house, t' minute yah heard t' maister's horse-fit clatter up t' road.'

'Silence, eavesdropper!' cried Catherine; 'none of your insolence before me! Edgar Linton came yesterday by chance, Hindley; and it was I who told him to be off: because I knew you would not like to have met him as you were.'

'You lie, Cathy, no doubt,' answered her brother, 'and you are a confounded simpleton! But never mind Linton at present: tell me, were you not with Heathcliff last night? Speak the truth, now. You need not he afraid of harming him: though I hate him as much as ever, he did me a good turn a short time since that will make my conscience tender of breaking his neck. To prevent it, I shall send him about his business this very morning; and after he's gone, I'd advise you all to look sharp: I shall only have the more humour for you.'

'I never saw Heathcliff last night,' answered Catherine, beginning to sob bitterly: 'and if you do turn him out of doors, I'll go with him. But, perhaps, you'll never have an opportunity: perhaps, he's gone.' Here she burst into uncontrollable grief, and the remainder of her words were inarticulate.

Hindley lavished on her a torrent of scornful abuse, and bade her get to her room immediately, or she shouldn't cry for nothing! I obliged her to obey; and I shall never forget what a scene she acted when we reached her chamber: it terrified me. I thought she was going mad, and I begged Joseph to run for the doctor. It proved the commencement of delirium: Mr. Kenneth, as soon as he saw her, pronounced her dangerously ill; she had a fever. He bled her, and he told me to let her live on whey and water-gruel, and take care she did not throw herself downstairs or out of the window; and then he left: for he had enough to do in the parish, where two or three miles was the ordinary distance between cottage and cottage.

Though I cannot say I made a gentle nurse, and Joseph and the master were no better, and though our patient was as wearisome and headstrong as a patient could be, she weathered it through. Old Mrs. Linton paid us several visits, to be sure, and set things to rights, and scolded and ordered us all; and when Catherine was convalescent, she insisted on conveying her to Thrushcross Grange: for which deliverance we were very grateful. But the poor dame had reason to repent of her kindness: she and her husband both took the fever, and died within a few days of each other.

Our young lady returned to us saucier and more passionate, and haughtier than ever. Heathcliff had never been heard of since the evening of the thunder-storm; and, one day, I had the misfortune, when she had provoked me exceedingly, to lay the blame of his disappearance on her: where indeed it belonged, as she well knew. From that period, for several months, she ceased to hold any communication with me, save in the relation of a mere servant. Joseph fell under a ban also: he would speak his mind, and lecture her all the same as if she were a little girl; and she esteemed herself a woman, and our mistress, and thought that her recent illness gave her a claim to be treated with consideration. Then the doctor had said that she would not bear crossing much; she ought to have her own way; and it was nothing less than murder in her eyes for any one to presume to stand up and contradict her. From Mr. Earnshaw and his companions she kept aloof; and tutored by Kenneth, and serious threats of a fit that often attended her rages, her brother allowed her whatever she pleased to demand, and generally avoided aggravating her fiery temper. He was rather too indulgent in humouring her caprices; not from affection, but from pride: he wished earnestly to see her bring honour to the family by an alliance with the Lintons, and as long as she let him alone she might trample on us like slaves, for aught he cared! Edgar Linton, as multitudes have been before and will be after him, was infatuated: and believed himself the happiest man alive on the day he led her to Gimmerton Chapel, three years subsequent to his father's death.

Much against my inclination, I was persuaded to leave Wuthering Heights and accompany her here, Little Hareton was nearly five years old, and I had just begun to teach him his letters. We made a sad parting; but Catherine's tears were more powerful than ours. When I refused to go, and when she found her entreaties did not move me, she went lamenting to her husband and brother. The former offered me munificent wages; the latter ordered me to pack up: he wanted no women in the house, he said, now that there was no mistress; and as to Hareton, the curate should take him in hand, by-and-by. And so I had but one choice left: to do as I was ordered. I told the master he got rid of all decent people only to run to ruin a little faster; I kissed Hareton, said good-by; and since then he has been a stranger: and it's very queer to think it, but I've no doubt he has completely forgotten all about Ellen Dean, and that he was ever more than all the world to her and she to him!

At this point of the housekeeper's story she chanced to glance towards the time-piece over the chimney; and was in amazement on seeing the minute-hand measure half-past one. She would not hear of staying a second longer: in truth, I felt rather disposed to defer the sequel of her narrative myself. And now that she is vanished to her rest, and I have meditated for another hour or two, I shall summon courage to go also, in spite of aching laziness of head and limbs.

Chapter X

A CHARMING introduction to a hermit's life! Four weeks' torture, tossing, and sickness! Oh, these bleak winds and bitter northern skies, and impassable roads, and dilatory country surgeons! And oh, this dearth of the human physiognomy! and, worse than all, the terrible intimation of Kenneth that I need not expect to be out of doors till spring!

Mr. Heathcliff has just honoured me with a call. About seven days ago he sent me a brace of grouse—the last of the season. Scoundrel! He is not altogether guiltless in this illness of mine; and that I had a great mind to tell him. But, alas! how could I offend a man who was charitable enough to sit at my bedside a good hour, and talk on some other subject than pills and draughts, blisters and leeches? This is quite an easy interval. I am too weak to read; yet I feel as if I could enjoy something interesting. Why not have up Mrs. Dean to finish her tale? I can recollect its chief incidents, as far as she had gone. Yes: I remember her hero had run off, and never been heard of for three years; and the heroine was married. I'll ring: she'll be delighted to find me capable of talking cheerfully. Mrs. Dean came.

'It wants twenty minutes, sir, to taking the medicine,' she commenced.

'Away, away with it!' I replied; 'I desire to have—'

'The doctor says you must drop the powders.'

'With all my heart! Don't interrupt me. Come and take your seat here. Keep your fingers from that bitter phalanx of vials. Draw your knitting out of your pocket—that will do—now continue the history of Mr. Heathcliff, from where you left off, to the present day. Did he finish his education on the Continent, and come back a gentleman? or did he get a sizar's place at college, or escape to America, and earn honours by drawing blood from his foster-country? or make a fortune more promptly on the English highways?'

'He may have done a little in all these vocations, Mr. Lockwood; but I couldn't give my word for any. I stated before that I didn't know how he gained his money; neither am I aware of the means he took to raise his mind from the savage ignorance into which it was sunk: but, with your leave, I'll proceed in my own fashion, if you think it will amuse and not weary you. Are you feeling better this morning?'

'Much.'

'That's good news.'

I got Miss Catherine and myself to Thrushcross Grange; and, to my agreeable disappointment, she behaved infinitely better than I dared to expect. She seemed almost over-fond of Mr. Linton; and even to his sister she showed plenty of affection. They were both very attentive to her comfort, certainly. It was not the thorn bending to the honeysuckles, but the honeysuckles embracing the thorn. There were no mutual concessions: one stood erect, and the others yielded: and who can be ill-natured and bad-tempered when they encounter neither opposition nor indifference? I observed that Mr. Edgar had a deep-rooted fear of ruffling her humour. He concealed it from her; but if ever he heard me answer sharply, or saw any other servant grow cloudy at some imperious order of hers, he would show his trouble by a frown of displeasure that never darkened on his own account. He many a time spoke sternly to me about my pertness; and averred that the stab of a knife could not inflict a worse pang than he suffered at seeing his lady vexed. Not to grieve a kind master, I learned to be less touchy; and, for the space of half a year, the gunpowder lay as harmless as sand, because no fire came near to explode it. Catherine had seasons of gloom and silence now and then: they were respected with sympathising silence by her husband, who ascribed them to an alteration in her constitution, produced by her perilous illness; as she was never subject to depression of spirits before. The return of sunshine was welcomed by answering sunshine from him. I believe I may assert that they were really in possession of deep and growing happiness.

It ended. Well, we MUST be for ourselves in the long run; the mild and generous are only more justly selfish than the domineering; and it ended when circumstances caused each to feel that the one's interest was not the chief consideration in the other's thoughts. On a mellow evening in September, I was coming from the garden with a heavy basket of apples which I had been gathering. It had got dusk, and the moon looked over the high wall of the court, causing undefined shadows to lurk in the corners of the numerous projecting portions of the building. I set my burden on the house-steps by the kitchen-door, and lingered to rest, and drew in a few more breaths of the soft, sweet air; my eyes were on the moon, and my back to the entrance, when I heard a voice behind me say,—'Nelly, is that you?'

It was a deep voice, and foreign in tone; yet there was something in the manner of pronouncing my name which made it sound familiar. I turned about to discover who spoke, fearfully; for the doors were shut, and I had seen nobody on approaching the steps. Something stirred in the porch; and, moving nearer, I distinguished a tall man dressed in dark clothes, with dark face and hair. He leant against the side, and held his fingers on the latch as if intending to open for himself. 'Who can it be?' I thought. 'Mr. Earnshaw? Oh, no! The voice has no resemblance to his.'

'I have waited here an hour,' he resumed, while I continued staring; 'and the whole of that time all round has been as still as death. I dared not enter. You do not know me? Look, I'm not a stranger!'

A ray fell on his features; the cheeks were sallow, and half covered with black whiskers; the brows lowering, the eyes deep-set and singular. I remembered the eyes.

'What!' I cried, uncertain whether to regard him as a worldly visitor, and I raised my hands in amazement. 'What! you come back? Is it really you? Is it?'

'Yes, Heathcliff,' he replied, glancing from me up to the windows, which reflected a score of glittering moons, but showed no lights from within. 'Are they at home? where is she? Nelly, you are not glad! you needn't be so disturbed. Is she here? Speak! I want to have one word with her—your mistress. Go, and say some person from Gimmerton desires to see her.'

'How will she take it?' I exclaimed. 'What will she do? The surprise bewilders me—it will put her out of her head! And you ARE Heathcliff! But altered! Nay, there's no comprehending it. Have you been for a soldier?'

'Go and carry my message,' he interrupted, impatiently. 'I'm in hell till you do!'

He lifted the latch, and I entered; but when I got to the parlour where Mr. and Mrs. Linton were, I could not persuade myself to proceed. At length I resolved on making an excuse to ask if they would have the candles lighted, and I opened the door.

They sat together in a window whose lattice lay back against the wall, and displayed, beyond the garden trees, and the wild green park, the valley of Gimmerton, with a long line of mist winding nearly to its top (for very soon after you pass the chapel, as you may have noticed, the sough that runs from the marshes joins a beck which follows the bend of the glen). Wuthering Heights rose above this silvery vapour; but our old house was invisible; it rather dips down on the other side. Both the room and its occupants, and the scene they gazed on, looked wondrously peaceful. I shrank reluctantly from performing my errand; and was actually going away leaving it unsaid, after having put my question about the candles, when a sense of my folly compelled me to return, and mutter, 'A person from Gimmerton wishes to see you ma'am.'

'What does he want?' asked Mrs. Linton.

'I did not question him,' I answered.

'Well, close the curtains, Nelly,' she said; 'and bring up tea. I'll be back again directly.'

She quitted the apartment; Mr. Edgar inquired, carelessly, who it was.

'Some one mistress does not expect,' I replied. 'That Heathcliff—you recollect him, sir—who used to live at Mr. Earnshaw's.'

'What! the gipsy—the ploughboy?' he cried. 'Why did you not say so to Catherine?'

'Hush! you must not call him by those names, master,' I said. 'She'd be sadly grieved to hear you. She was nearly heartbroken when he ran off. I guess his return will make a jubilee to her.'

Mr. Linton walked to a window on the other side of the room that overlooked the court. He unfastened it, and leant out. I suppose they were below, for he exclaimed quickly: 'Don't stand there, love! Bring the person in, if it be anyone particular.' Ere long, I heard the click of the latch, and Catherine flew up-stairs, breathless and wild; too excited to show gladness: indeed, by her face, you would rather have surmised an awful calamity.

'Oh, Edgar, Edgar!' she panted, flinging her arms round his neck. 'Oh, Edgar darling! Heathcliff's come back—he is!' And she tightened her embrace to a squeeze.

'Well, well,' cried her husband, crossly, 'don't strangle me for that! He never struck me as such a marvellous treasure. There is no need to be frantic!'

'I know you didn't like him,' she answered, repressing a little the intensity of her delight. 'Yet, for my sake, you must be friends now. Shall I tell him to come up?'

'Here,' he said, 'into the parlour?'

'Where else?' she asked.

He looked vexed, and suggested the kitchen as a more suitable place for him. Mrs. Linton eyed him with a droll expression—half angry, half laughing at his fastidiousness.

'No,' she added, after a while; 'I cannot sit in the kitchen. Set two tables here, Ellen: one for your master and Miss Isabella, being gentry; the other for Heathcliff and myself, being of the lower orders. Will that please you, dear? Or must I have a fire lighted elsewhere? If so, give directions. I'll run down and secure my guest. I'm afraid the joy is too great to be real!'

She was about to dart off again; but Edgar arrested her.

'YOU bid him step up,' he said, addressing me; 'and, Catherine, try to be glad, without being absurd. The whole household need not witness the sight of your welcoming a runaway servant as a brother.'

I descended, and found Heathcliff waiting under the porch, evidently anticipating an invitation to enter. He followed my guidance without waste of words, and I ushered him into the presence of the master and mistress, whose flushed cheeks betrayed signs of warm talking. But the lady's glowed with another feeling when her friend appeared at the door: she sprang forward, took both his hands, and led him to Linton; and then she seized Linton's reluctant fingers and crushed them into his. Now, fully revealed by the fire and candlelight, I was amazed, more than ever, to behold the transformation of Heathcliff. He had grown a tall, athletic, well-formed man; beside whom my master seemed quite slender and youth-like. His upright carriage suggested the idea of his having been in the army. His countenance was much older in expression and decision of feature than Mr. Linton's; it looked intelligent, and retained no marks of former degradation. A half-civilised ferocity lurked yet in the depressed brows and eyes full of black fire, but it was subdued; and his manner was even dignified: quite divested of roughness, though stern for grace. My master's surprise equalled or exceeded mine: he remained for a minute at a loss how to address the ploughboy, as he had called him. Heathcliff dropped his slight hand, and stood looking at him coolly till he chose to speak.

'Sit down, sir,' he said, at length. 'Mrs. Linton, recalling old times, would have me give you a cordial reception; and, of course, I am gratified when anything occurs to please her.'

'And I also,' answered Heathcliff, 'especially if it be anything in which I have a part. I shall stay an hour or two willingly.'

He took a seat opposite Catherine, who kept her gaze fixed on him as if she feared he would vanish were she to remove it. He did not raise his to her often: a quick glance now and then sufficed; but it flashed back, each time more confidently, the undisguised delight he drank from hers. They were too much absorbed in their mutual joy to suffer embarrassment. Not so Mr. Edgar: he grew pale with pure annoyance: a feeling that reached its climax when his lady rose, and stepping across the rug, seized Heathcliff's hands again, and laughed like one beside herself.

'I shall think it a dream to-morrow!' she cried. 'I shall not be able to believe that I have seen, and touched, and spoken to you once more. And yet, cruel Heathcliff! you don't deserve this welcome. To be absent and silent for three years, and never to think of me!'

'A little more than you have thought of me,' he murmured. 'I heard of your marriage, Cathy, not long since; and, while waiting in the yard below, I meditated this plan—just to have one glimpse of your face, a stare of surprise, perhaps, and pretended pleasure; afterwards settle my score with Hindley; and then prevent the law by doing execution on myself. Your welcome has put these ideas out of my mind; but beware of meeting me with another aspect next time! Nay, you'll not drive me off again. You were really sorry for me, were you? Well, there was cause. I've fought through a bitter life since I last heard your voice; and you must forgive me, for I struggled only for you!'

'Catherine, unless we are to have cold tea, please to come to the table,' interrupted Linton, striving to preserve his ordinary tone, and a due measure of politeness. 'Mr. Heathcliff will have a long walk, wherever he may lodge to-night; and I'm thirsty.'

She took her post before the urn; and Miss Isabella came, summoned by the bell; then, having handed their chairs forward, I left the room. The meal hardly endured ten minutes. Catherine's cup was never filled: she could neither eat nor drink. Edgar had made a slop in his saucer, and scarcely swallowed a mouthful. Their guest did not protract his stay that evening above an hour longer. I asked, as he departed, if he went to Gimmerton?

'No, to Wuthering Heights,' he answered: 'Mr. Earnshaw invited me, when I called this morning.'

Mr. Earnshaw invited HIM! and HE called on Mr. Earnshaw! I pondered this sentence painfully, after he was gone. Is he turning out a bit of a hypocrite, and coming into the country to work mischief under a cloak? I mused: I had a presentiment in the bottom of my heart that he had better have remained away.

About the middle of the night, I was wakened from my first nap by Mrs. Linton gliding into my chamber, taking a seat on my bedside, and pulling me by the hair to rouse me.

'I cannot rest, Ellen,' she said, by way of apology. 'And I want some living creature to keep me company in my happiness! Edgar is sulky, because I'm glad of a thing that does not interest him: he refuses to open his mouth, except to utter pettish, silly speeches; and he affirmed I was cruel and selfish for wishing to talk when he was so sick and sleepy. He always contrives to be sick at the least cross! I gave a few sentences of commendation to Heathcliff, and he, either for a headache or a pang of envy, began to cry: so I got up and left him.'

'What use is it praising Heathcliff to him?' I answered. 'As lads they had an aversion to each other, and Heathcliff would hate just as much to hear him praised: it's human nature. Let Mr. Linton alone about him, unless you would like an open quarrel between them.'

'But does it not show great weakness?' pursued she. 'I'm not envious: I never feel hurt at the brightness of Isabella's yellow hair and the whiteness of her skin, at her dainty elegance, and the fondness all the family exhibit for her. Even you, Nelly, if we have a dispute sometimes, you back Isabella at once; and I yield like a foolish mother: I call her a darling, and flatter her into a good temper. It pleases her brother to see us cordial, and that pleases me. But they are very much alike: they are spoiled children, and fancy the world was made for their accommodation; and though I humour both, I think a smart chastisement might improve them all the same.'

'You're mistaken, Mrs. Linton,' said I. 'They humour you: I know what there would be to do if they did not. You can well afford to indulge their passing whims as long as their business is to anticipate all your desires. You may, however, fall out, at last, over something of equal consequence to both sides; and then those you term weak are very capable of being as obstinate as you.'

'And then we shall fight to the death, sha'n't we, Nelly?' she returned, laughing. 'No! I tell you, I have such faith in Linton's love, that I believe I might kill him, and he wouldn't wish to retaliate.'

I advised her to value him the more for his affection.

'I do,' she answered, 'but he needn't resort to whining for trifles. It is childish and, instead of melting into tears because I said that Heathcliff was now worthy of anyone's regard, and it would honour the first gentleman in the country to be his friend, he ought to have said it for me, and been delighted from sympathy. He must get accustomed to him, and he may as well like him: considering how Heathcliff has reason to object to him, I'm sure he behaved excellently!'

'What do you think of his going to Wuthering Heights?' I inquired. 'He is reformed in every respect, apparently: quite a Christian: offering the right hand of fellowship to his enemies all around!'

'He explained it,' she replied. 'I wonder as much as you. He said he called to gather information concerning me from you, supposing you resided there still; and Joseph told Hindley, who came out and fell to questioning him of what he had been doing, and how he had been living; and finally, desired him to walk in. There were some persons sitting at cards; Heathcliff joined them; my brother lost some money to him, and, finding him plentifully supplied, he requested that he would come again in the evening: to which he consented. Hindley is too reckless to select his acquaintance prudently: he doesn't trouble himself to reflect on the causes he might have for mistrusting one whom he has basely injured. But Heathcliff affirms his principal reason for resuming a connection with his ancient persecutor is a wish to instal himself in quarters at walking distance from the Grange, and an attachment to the house where we lived together; and likewise a hope that I shall have more opportunities of seeing him there than I could have if he settled in Gimmerton. He means to offer liberal payment for permission to lodge at the Heights; and doubtless my brother's covetousness will prompt him to accept the terms: he was always greedy; though what he grasps with one hand he flings away with the other.'

'It's a nice place for a young man to fix his dwelling in!' said I. 'Have you no fear of the consequences, Mrs. Linton?'

'None for my friend,' she replied: 'his strong head will keep him from danger; a little for Hindley: but he can't be made morally worse than he is; and I stand between him and bodily harm. The event of this evening has reconciled me to God and humanity! I had risen in angry rebellion against Providence. Oh, I've endured very, very bitter misery, Nelly! If that creature knew how bitter, he'd be ashamed to cloud its removal with idle petulance. It was kindness for him which induced me to bear it alone: had I expressed the agony I frequently felt, he would have been taught to long for its alleviation as ardently as I. However, it's over, and I'll take no revenge on his folly; I can afford to suffer anything hereafter! Should the meanest thing alive slap me on the cheek, I'd not only turn the other, but I'd ask pardon for provoking it; and, as a proof, I'll go make my peace with Edgar instantly. Good-night! I'm an angel!'

In this self-complacent conviction she departed; and the success of her fulfilled resolution was obvious on the morrow: Mr. Linton had not only abjured his peevishness (though his spirits seemed still subdued by Catherine's exuberance of vivacity), but he ventured no objection to her taking Isabella with her to Wuthering Heights in the afternoon; and she rewarded him with such a summer of sweetness and affection in return as made the house a paradise for several days; both master and servants profiting from the perpetual sunshine.

Heathcliff—Mr. Heathcliff I should say in future—used the liberty of visiting at Thrushcross Grange cautiously, at first: he seemed estimating how far its owner would bear his intrusion. Catherine, also, deemed it judicious to moderate her expressions of pleasure in receiving him; and he gradually established his right to be expected. He retained a great deal of the reserve for which his boyhood was remarkable; and that served to repress all startling demonstrations of feeling. My master's uneasiness experienced a lull, and further circumstances diverted it into another channel for a space.

His new source of trouble sprang from the not anticipated misfortune of Isabella Linton evincing a sudden and irresistible attraction towards the tolerated guest. She was at that time a charming young lady of eighteen; infantile in manners, though possessed of keen wit, keen feelings, and a keen temper, too, if irritated. Her brother, who loved her tenderly, was appalled at this fantastic preference. Leaving aside the degradation of an alliance with a nameless man, and the possible fact that his property, in default of heirs male, might pass into such a one's power, he had sense to comprehend Heathcliff's disposition: to know that, though his exterior was altered, his mind was unchangeable and unchanged. And he dreaded that mind: it revolted him: he shrank forebodingly from the idea of committing Isabella to its keeping. He would have recoiled still more had he been aware that her attachment rose unsolicited, and was bestowed where it awakened no reciprocation of sentiment; for the minute he discovered its existence he laid the blame on Heathcliff's deliberate designing.

We had all remarked, during some time, that Miss Linton fretted and pined over something. She grew cross and wearisome; snapping at and teasing Catherine continually, at the imminent risk of exhausting her limited patience. We excused her, to a certain extent, on the plea of ill-health: she was dwindling and fading before our eyes. But one day, when she had been peculiarly wayward, rejecting her breakfast, complaining that the servants did not do what she told them; that the mistress would allow her to be nothing in the house, and Edgar neglected her; that she had caught a cold with the doors being left open, and we let the parlour fire go out on purpose to vex her, with a hundred yet more frivolous accusations, Mrs. Linton peremptorily insisted that she should get to bed; and, having scolded her heartily, threatened to send for the doctor. Mention of Kenneth caused her to exclaim, instantly, that her health was perfect, and it was only Catherine's harshness which made her unhappy.

'How can you say I am harsh, you naughty fondling?' cried the mistress, amazed at the unreasonable assertion. 'You are surely losing your reason. When have I been hash, tell me?'

'Yesterday,' sobbed Isabella, 'and now!'

'Yesterday!' said her sister-in-law. 'On what occasion?'

'In our walk along the moor: you told me to ramble where I pleased, while you sauntered on with Mr. Heathcliff?'

'And that's your notion of harshness?' said Catherine, laughing. 'It was no hint that your company was superfluous? We didn't care whether you kept with us or not; I merely thought Heathcliff's talk would have nothing entertaining for your ears.'

'Oh, no,' wept the young lady; 'you wished me away, because you knew I liked to be there!'

'Is she sane?' asked Mrs. Linton, appealing to me. 'I'll repeat our conversation, word for word, Isabella; and you point out any charm it could have had for you.'

'I don't mind the conversation,' she answered: 'I wanted to be with—'

"Well?' said Catherine, perceiving her hesitate to complete the sentence.

'With him: and I won't be always sent off!' she continued, kindling up. 'You are a dog in the manger, Cathy, and desire no one to be loved but yourself!'

'You are an impertinent little monkey!' exclaimed Mrs. Linton, in surprise. 'But I'll not believe this idiotcy! It is impossible that you can covet the admiration of Heathcliff—that you consider him an agreeable person! I hope I have misunderstood you, Isabella?'

'No, you have not,' said the infatuated girl. 'I love him more than ever you loved Edgar, and he might love me, if you would let him!'

'I wouldn't be you for a kingdom, then!' Catherine declared, emphatically: and she seemed to speak sincerely. 'Nelly, help me to convince her of her madness. Tell her what Heathcliff is: an unreclaimed creature, without refinement, without cultivation; an arid wilderness of furze and whinstone. I'd as soon put that little canary into the park on a winter's day, as recommend you to bestow your heart on him! It is deplorable ignorance of his character, child, and nothing else, which makes that dream enter your head. Pray, don't imagine that he conceals depths of benevolence and affection beneath a stern exterior! He's not a rough diamond—a pearl-containing oyster of a rustic: he's a fierce, pitiless, wolfish man. I never say to him, "Let this or that enemy alone, because it would be ungenerous or cruel to harm them;" I say, "Let them alone, because I should hate them to be wronged:" and he'd crush you like a sparrow's egg, Isabella, if he found you a troublesome charge. I know he couldn't love a Linton; and yet he'd be quite capable of marrying your fortune and expectations: avarice is growing with him a besetting sin. There's my picture: and I'm his friend—so much so, that had he thought seriously to catch you, I should, perhaps, have held my tongue, and let you fall into his trap.'

Miss Linton regarded her sister-in-law with indignation.

'For shame! for shame!' she repeated, angrily. 'You are worse than twenty foes, you poisonous friend!'

'Ah! you won't believe me, then?' said Catherine. 'You think I speak from wicked selfishness?'

'I'm certain you do,' retorted Isabella; 'and I shudder at you!'

'Good!' cried the other. 'Try for yourself, if that be your spirit: I have done, and yield the argument to your saucy insolence.'—

'And I must suffer for her egotism!' she sobbed, as Mrs. Linton left the room. 'All, all is against me: she has blighted my single consolation. But she uttered falsehoods, didn't she? Mr. Heathcliff is not a fiend: he has an honourable soul, and a true one, or how could he remember her?'

'Banish him from your thoughts, Miss,' I said. 'He's a bird of bad omen: no mate for you. Mrs. Linton spoke strongly, and yet I can't contradict her. She is better acquainted with his heart than I, or any one besides; and she never would represent him as worse than he is. Honest people don't hide their deeds. How has he been living? how has he got rich? why is he staying at Wuthering Heights, the house of a man whom he abhors? They say Mr. Earnshaw is worse and worse since he came. They sit up all night together continually, and Hindley has been borrowing money on his land, and does nothing but play and drink: I heard only a week ago—it was Joseph who told me—I met him at Gimmerton: "Nelly," he said, "we's hae a crowner's 'quest enow, at ahr folks'. One on 'em 's a'most getten his finger cut off wi' hauding t' other fro' stickin' hisseln loike a cawlf. That's maister, yeah knaw, 'at 's soa up o' going tuh t' grand 'sizes. He's noan feared o' t' bench o' judges, norther Paul, nur Peter, nur John, nur Matthew, nor noan on 'em, not he! He fair likes—he langs to set his brazened face agean 'em! And yon bonny lad Heathcliff, yah mind, he's a rare 'un. He can girn a laugh as well 's onybody at a raight divil's jest. Does he niver say nowt of his fine living amang us, when he goes to t' Grange? This is t' way on 't:—up at sun-down: dice, brandy, cloised shutters, und can'le-light till next day at noon: then, t'fooil gangs banning und raving to his cham'er, makking dacent fowks dig thur fingers i' thur lugs fur varry shame; un' the knave, why he can caint his brass, un' ate, un' sleep, un' off to his neighbour's to gossip wi' t' wife. I' course, he tells Dame Catherine how her fathur's goold runs into his pocket, and her fathur's son gallops down t' broad road, while he flees afore to oppen t' pikes!" Now, Miss Linton, Joseph is an old rascal, but no liar; and, if his account of Heathcliff's conduct be true, you would never think of desiring such a husband, would you?'

'You are leagued with the rest, Ellen!' she replied. 'I'll not listen to your slanders. What malevolence you must have to wish to convince me that there is no happiness in the world!'

Whether she would have got over this fancy if left to herself, or persevered in nursing it perpetually, I cannot say: she had little time to reflect. The day after, there was a justice-meeting at the next town; my master was obliged to attend; and Mr. Heathcliff, aware of his absence, called rather earlier than usual. Catherine and Isabella were sitting in the library, on hostile terms, but silent: the latter alarmed at her recent indiscretion, and the disclosure she had made of her secret feelings in a transient fit of passion; the former, on mature consideration, really offended with her companion; and, if she laughed again at her pertness, inclined to make it no laughing matter to her. She did laugh as she saw Heathcliff pass the window. I was sweeping the hearth, and I noticed a mischievous smile on her lips. Isabella, absorbed in her meditations, or a book, remained till the door opened; and it was too late to attempt an escape, which she would gladly have done had it been practicable.

'Come in, that's right!' exclaimed the mistress, gaily, pulling a chair to the fire. 'Here are two people sadly in need of a third to thaw the ice between them; and you are the very one we should both of us choose. Heathcliff, I'm proud to show you, at last, somebody that dotes on you more than myself. I expect you to feel flattered. Nay, it's not Nelly; don't look at her! My poor little sister-in-law is breaking her heart by mere contemplation of your physical and moral beauty. It lies in your own power to be Edgar's brother! No, no, Isabella, you sha'n't run off,' she continued, arresting, with feigned playfulness, the confounded girl, who had risen indignantly. 'We were quarrelling like cats about you, Heathcliff; and I was fairly beaten in protestations of devotion and admiration: and, moreover, I was informed that if I would but have the manners to stand aside, my rival, as she will have herself to be, would shoot a shaft into your soul that would fix you for ever, and send my image into eternal oblivion!'

'Catherine!' said Isabella, calling up her dignity, and disdaining to struggle from the tight grasp that held her, 'I'd thank you to adhere to the truth and not slander me, even in joke! Mr. Heathcliff, be kind enough to bid this friend of yours release me: she forgets that you and I are not intimate acquaintances; and what amuses her is painful to me beyond expression.'

As the guest answered nothing, but took his seat, and looked thoroughly indifferent what sentiments she cherished concerning him, she turned and whispered an earnest appeal for liberty to her tormentor.

'By no means!' cried Mrs. Linton in answer. 'I won't be named a dog in the manger again. You SHALL stay: now then! Heathcliff, why don't you evince satisfaction at my pleasant news? Isabella swears that the love Edgar has for me is nothing to that she entertains for you. I'm sure she made some speech of the kind; did she not, Ellen? And she has fasted ever since the day before yesterday's walk, from sorrow and rage that I despatched her out of your society under the idea of its being unacceptable.'

'I think you belie her,' said Heathcliff, twisting his chair to face them. 'She wishes to be out of my society now, at any rate!'

And he stared hard at the object of discourse, as one might do at a strange repulsive animal: a centipede from the Indies, for instance, which curiosity leads one to examine in spite of the aversion it raises. The poor thing couldn't bear that; she grew white and red in rapid succession, and, while tears beaded her lashes, bent the strength of her small fingers to loosen the firm clutch of Catherine; and perceiving that as fast as she raised one finger off her arm another closed down, and she could not remove the whole together, she began to make use of her nails; and their sharpness presently ornamented the detainer's with crescents of red.

'There's a tigress!' exclaimed Mrs. Linton, setting her free, and shaking her hand with pain. 'Begone, for God's sake, and hide your vixen face! How foolish to reveal those talons to him. Can't you fancy the conclusions he'll draw? Look, Heathcliff! they are instruments that will do execution—you must beware of your eyes.'

'I'd wrench them off her fingers, if they ever menaced me,' he answered, brutally, when the door had closed after her. 'But what did you mean by teasing the creature in that manner, Cathy? You were not speaking the truth, were you?'

'I assure you I was,' she returned. 'She has been dying for your sake several weeks, and raving about you this morning, and pouring forth a deluge of abuse, because I represented your failings in a plain light, for the purpose of mitigating her adoration. But don't notice it further: I wished to punish her sauciness, that's all. I like her too well, my dear Heathcliff, to let you absolutely seize and devour her up.'

'And I like her too ill to attempt it,' said he, 'except in a very ghoulish fashion. You'd hear of odd things if I lived alone with that mawkish, waxen face: the most ordinary would be painting on its white the colours of the rainbow, and turning the blue eyes black, every day or two: they detestably resemble Linton's.'

'Delectably!' observed Catherine. 'They are dove's eyes—angel's!'

'She's her brother's heir, is she not?' he asked, after a brief silence.

'I should be sorry to think so,' returned his companion. 'Half a dozen nephews shall erase her title, please heaven! Abstract your mind from the subject at present: you are too prone to covet your neighbour's goods; remember THIS neighbour's goods are mine.'

'If they were MINE, they would be none the less that,' said Heathcliff; 'but though Isabella Linton may be silly, she is scarcely mad; and, in short, we'll dismiss the matter, as you advise.'

From their tongues they did dismiss it; and Catherine, probably, from her thoughts. The other, I felt certain, recalled it often in the course of the evening. I saw him smile to himself—grin rather—and lapse into ominous musing whenever Mrs. Linton had occasion to be absent from the apartment.

I determined to watch his movements. My heart invariably cleaved to the master's, in preference to Catherine's side: with reason I imagined, for he was kind, and trustful, and honourable; and she-she could not be called OPPOSITE, yet she seemed to allow herself such wide latitude, that I had little faith in her principles, and still less sympathy for her feelings. I wanted something to happen which might have the effect of freeing both Wuthering Heights and the Grange of Mr. Heathcliff quietly; leaving us as we had been prior to his advent. His visits were a continual nightmare to me; and, I suspected, to my master also. His abode at the Heights was an oppression past explaining. I felt that God had forsaken the stray sheep there to its own wicked wanderings, and an evil beast prowled between it and the fold, waiting his time to spring and destroy.

Chapter XI

SOMETIMES, while meditating on these things in solitude, I've got up in a sudden terror, and put on my bonnet to go see how all was at the farm. I've persuaded my conscience that it was a duty to warn him how people talked regarding his ways; and then I've recollected his confirmed bad habits, and, hopeless of benefiting him, have flinched from re-entering the dismal house, doubting if I could bear to be taken at my word.

One time I passed the old gate, going out of my way, on a journey to Gimmerton. It was about the period that my narrative has reached: a bright frosty afternoon; the ground bare, and the road hard and dry. I came to a stone where the highway branches off on to the moor at your left hand; a rough sand-pillar, with the letters W. H. cut on its north side, on the east, G., and on the south-west, T. G. It serves as a guide-post to the Grange, the Heights, and village. The sun shone yellow on its grey head, reminding me of summer; and I cannot say why, but all at once a gush of child's sensations flowed into my heart. Hindley and I held it a favourite spot twenty years before. I gazed long at the weather-worn block; and, stooping down, perceived a hole near the bottom still full of snail-shells and pebbles, which we were fond of storing there with more perishable things; and, as fresh as reality, it appeared that I beheld my early playmate seated on the withered turf: his dark, square head bent forward, and his little hand scooping out the earth with a piece of slate. 'Poor Hindley!' I exclaimed, involuntarily. I started: my bodily eye was cheated into a momentary belief that the child lifted its face and stared straight into mine! It vanished in a twinkling; but immediately I felt an irresistible yearning to be at the Heights. Superstition urged me to comply with this impulse: supposing he should be dead! I thought—or should die soon!—supposing it were a sign of death! The nearer I got to the house the more agitated I grew; and on catching sight of it I trembled in every limb. The apparition had outstripped me: it stood looking through the gate. That was my first idea on observing an elf-locked, brown-eyed boy setting his ruddy countenance against the bars. Further reflection suggested this must be Hareton, MY Hareton, not altered greatly since I left him, ten months since.

'God bless thee, darling!' I cried, forgetting instantaneously my foolish fears. 'Hareton, it's Nelly! Nelly, thy nurse.'

He retreated out of arm's length, and picked up a large flint.

'I am come to see thy father, Hareton,' I added, guessing from the action that Nelly, if she lived in his memory at all, was not recognised as one with me.

He raised his missile to hurl it; I commenced a soothing speech, but could not stay his hand: the stone struck my bonnet; and then ensued, from the stammering lips of the little fellow, a string of curses, which, whether he comprehended them or not, were delivered with practised emphasis, and distorted his baby features into a shocking expression of malignity. You may be certain this grieved more than angered me. Fit to cry, I took an orange from my pocket, and offered it to propitiate him. He hesitated, and then snatched it from my hold; as if he fancied I only intended to tempt and disappoint him. I showed another, keeping it out of his reach.

'Who has taught you those fine words, my bairn?' I inquired. 'The curate?'

'Damn the curate, and thee! Gie me that,' he replied.

'Tell us where you got your lessons, and you shall have it,' said I. 'Who's your master?'

'Devil daddy,' was his answer.

'And what do you learn from daddy?' I continued.

He jumped at the fruit; I raised it higher. 'What does he teach you?' I asked.

'Naught,' said he, 'but to keep out of his gait. Daddy cannot bide me, because I swear at him.'

'Ah! and the devil teaches you to swear at daddy?' I observed.

'Ay—nay,' he drawled.

'Who, then?'

'Heathcliff.'

'I asked if he liked Mr. Heathcliff.'

'Ay!' he answered again.

Desiring to have his reasons for liking him, I could only gather the sentences—'I known't: he pays dad back what he gies to me—he curses daddy for cursing me. He says I mun do as I will.'

'And the curate does not teach you to read and write, then?' I pursued.

'No, I was told the curate should have his—teeth dashed down his—throat, if he stepped over the threshold—Heathcliff had promised that!'

I put the orange in his hand, and bade him tell his father that a woman called Nelly Dean was waiting to speak with him, by the garden gate. He went up the walk, and entered the house; but, instead of Hindley, Heathcliff appeared on the door-stones; and I turned directly and ran down the road as hard as ever I could race, making no halt till I gained the guide-post, and feeling as scared as if I had raised a goblin. This is not much connected with Miss Isabella's affair: except that it urged me to resolve further on mounting vigilant guard, and doing my utmost to cheek the spread of such bad influence at the Grange: even though I should wake a domestic storm, by thwarting Mrs. Linton's pleasure.

The next time Heathcliff came my young lady chanced to be feeding some pigeons in the court. She had never spoken a word to her sister-in-law for three days; but she had likewise dropped her fretful complaining, and we found it a great comfort. Heathcliff had not the habit of bestowing a single unnecessary civility on Miss Linton, I knew. Now, as soon as he beheld her, his first precaution was to take a sweeping survey of the house-front. I was standing by the kitchen-window, but I drew out of sight. He then stepped across the pavement to her, and said something: she seemed embarrassed, and desirous of getting away; to prevent it, he laid his hand on her arm. She averted her face: he apparently put some question which she had no mind to answer. There was another rapid glance at the house, and supposing himself unseen, the scoundrel had the impudence to embrace her.

'Judas! Traitor!' I ejaculated. 'You are a hypocrite, too, are you? A deliberate deceiver.'

'Who is, Nelly?' said Catherine's voice at my elbow: I had been over-intent on watching the pair outside to mark her entrance.

'Your worthless friend!' I answered, warmly: 'the sneaking rascal yonder. Ah, he has caught a glimpse of us—he is coming in! I wonder will he have the heart to find a plausible excuse for making love to Miss, when he told you he hated her?'

Mrs. Linton saw Isabella tear herself free, and run into the garden; and a minute after, Heathcliff opened the door. I couldn't withhold giving some loose to my indignation; but Catherine angrily insisted on silence, and threatened to order me out of the kitchen, if I dared to be so presumptuous as to put in my insolent tongue.

'To hear you, people might think you were the mistress!' she cried. 'You want setting down in your right place! Heathcliff, what are you about, raising this stir? I said you must let Isabella alone!—I beg you will, unless you are tired of being received here, and wish Linton to draw the bolts against you!'

'God forbid that he should try!' answered the black villain. I detested him just then. 'God keep him meek and patient! Every day I grow madder after sending him to heaven!'

'Hush!' said Catherine, shutting the inner door! 'Don't vex me. Why have you disregarded my request? Did she come across you on purpose?'

'What is it to you?' he growled. 'I have a right to kiss her, if she chooses; and you have no right to object. I am not YOUR husband: YOU needn't be jealous of me!'

'I'm not jealous of you,' replied the mistress; 'I'm jealous for you. Clear your face: you sha'n't scowl at me! If you like Isabella, you shall marry her. But do you like her? Tell the truth, Heathcliff! There, you won't answer. I'm certain you don't.'

'And would Mr. Linton approve of his sister marrying that man?' I inquired.

'Mr. Linton should approve,' returned my lady, decisively.

'He might spare himself the trouble,' said Heathcliff: 'I could do as well without his approbation. And as to you, Catherine, I have a mind to speak a few words now, while we are at it. I want you to be aware that I KNOW you have treated me infernally—infernally! Do you hear? And if you flatter yourself that I don't perceive it, you are a fool; and if you think I can be consoled by sweet words, you are an idiot: and if you fancy I'll suffer unrevenged, I'll convince you of the contrary, in a very little while! Meantime, thank you for telling me your sister-in-law's secret: I swear I'll make the most of it. And stand you aside!'

'What new phase of his character is this?' exclaimed Mrs. Linton, in amazement. 'I've treated you infernally—and you'll take your revenge! How will you take it, ungrateful brute? How have I treated you infernally?'

'I seek no revenge on you,' replied Heathcliff, less vehemently. 'That's not the plan. The tyrant grinds down his slaves and they don't turn against him; they crush those beneath them. You are welcome to torture me to death for your amusement, only allow me to amuse myself a little in the same style, and refrain from insult as much as you are able. Having levelled my palace, don't erect a hovel and complacently admire your own charity in giving me that for a home. If I imagined you really wished me to marry Isabel, I'd cut my throat!'

'Oh, the evil is that I am NOT jealous, is it?' cried Catherine. 'Well, I won't repeat my offer of a wife: it is as bad as offering Satan a lost soul. Your bliss lies, like his, in inflicting misery. You prove it. Edgar is restored from the ill-temper he gave way to at your coming; I begin to be secure and tranquil; and you, restless to know us at peace, appear resolved on exciting a quarrel. Quarrel with Edgar, if you please, Heathcliff, and deceive his sister: you'll hit on exactly the most efficient method of revenging yourself on me.'

The conversation ceased. Mrs. Linton sat down by the fire, flushed and gloomy. The spirit which served her was growing intractable: she could neither lay nor control it. He stood on the hearth with folded arms, brooding on his evil thoughts; and in this position I left them to seek the master, who was wondering what kept Catherine below so long.

'Ellen,' said he, when I entered, 'have you seen your mistress?'

'Yes; she's in the kitchen, sir,' I answered. 'She's sadly put out by Mr. Heathcliff's behaviour: and, indeed, I do think it's time to arrange his visits on another footing. There's harm in being too soft, and now it's come to this—.' And I related the scene in the court, and, as near as I dared, the whole subsequent dispute. I fancied it could not be very prejudicial to Mrs. Linton; unless she made it so afterwards, by assuming the defensive for her guest. Edgar Linton had difficulty in hearing me to the close. His first words revealed that he did not clear his wife of blame.

'This is insufferable!' he exclaimed. 'It is disgraceful that she should own him for a friend, and force his company on me! Call me two men out of the hall, Ellen. Catherine shall linger no longer to argue with the low ruffian—I have humoured her enough.'

He descended, and bidding the servants wait in the passage, went, followed by me, to the kitchen. Its occupants had recommenced their angry discussion: Mrs. Linton, at least, was scolding with renewed vigour; Heathcliff had moved to the window, and hung his head, somewhat cowed by her violent rating apparently. He saw the master first, and made a hasty motion that she should be silent; which she obeyed, abruptly, on discovering the reason of his intimation.

'How is this?' said Linton, addressing her; 'what notion of propriety must you have to remain here, after the language which has been held to you by that blackguard? I suppose, because it is his ordinary talk you think nothing of it: you are habituated to his baseness, and, perhaps, imagine I can get used to it too!'

'Have you been listening at the door, Edgar?' asked the mistress, in a tone particularly calculated to provoke her husband, implying both carelessness and contempt of his irritation. Heathcliff, who had raised his eyes at the former speech, gave a sneering laugh at the latter; on purpose, it seemed, to draw Mr. Linton's attention to him. He succeeded; but Edgar did not mean to entertain him with any high flights of passion.

'I've been so far forbearing with you, sir,' he said quietly; 'not that I was ignorant of your miserable, degraded character, but I felt you were only partly responsible for that; and Catherine wishing to keep up your acquaintance, I acquiesced—foolishly. Your presence is a moral poison that would contaminate the most virtuous: for that cause, and to prevent worse consequences, I shall deny you hereafter admission into this house, and give notice now that I require your instant departure. Three minutes' delay will render it involuntary and ignominious.

Heathcliff measured the height and breadth of the speaker with an eye full of derision.

'Cathy, this lamb of yours threatens like a bull!' he said. 'It is in danger of splitting its skull against my knuckles. By God! Mr. Linton, I'm mortally sorry that you are not worth knocking down!'

My master glanced towards the passage, and signed me to fetch the men: he had no intention of hazarding a personal encounter. I obeyed the hint; but Mrs. Linton, suspecting something, followed; and when I attempted to call them, she pulled me back, slammed the door to, and locked it.

'Fair means!' she said, in answer to her husband's look of angry surprise. 'If you have not courage to attack him, make an apology, or allow yourself to be beaten. It will correct you of feigning more valour than you possess. No, I'll swallow the key before you shall get it! I'm delightfully rewarded for my kindness to each! After constant indulgence of one's weak nature, and the other's bad one, I earn for thanks two samples of blind ingratitude, stupid to absurdity! Edgar, I was defending you and yours; and I wish Heathcliff may flog you sick, for daring to think an evil thought of me!'

It did not need the medium of a flogging to produce that effect on the master. He tried to wrest the key from Catherine's grasp, and for safety she flung it into the hottest part of the fire; whereupon Mr. Edgar was taken with a nervous trembling, and his countenance grew deadly pale. For his life he could not avert that excess of emotion: mingled anguish and humiliation overcame him completely. He leant on the back of a chair, and covered his face.

'Oh, heavens! In old days this would win you knighthood!' exclaimed Mrs. Linton. 'We are vanquished! we are vanquished! Heathcliff would as soon lift a finger at you as the king would march his army against a colony of mice. Cheer up! you sha'n't be hurt! Your type is not a lamb, it's a sucking leveret.'

'I wish you joy of the milk-blooded coward, Cathy!' said her friend. 'I compliment you on your taste. And that is the slavering, shivering thing you preferred to me! I would not strike him with my fist, but I'd kick him with my foot, and experience considerable satisfaction. Is he weeping, or is he going to faint for fear?'

The fellow approached and gave the chair on which Linton rested a push. He'd better have kept his distance: my master quickly sprang erect, and struck him full on the throat a blow that would have levelled a slighter man. It took his breath for a minute; and while he choked, Mr. Linton walked out by the back door into the yard, and from thence to the front entrance.

'There! you've done with coming here,' cried Catherine. 'Get away, now; he'll return with a brace of pistols and half-a-dozen assistants. If he did overhear us, of course he'd never forgive you. You've played me an ill turn, Heathcliff! But go—make haste! I'd rather see Edgar at bay than you.'

'Do you suppose I'm going with that blow burning in my gullet?' he thundered. 'By hell, no! I'll crush his ribs in like a rotten hazel-nut before I cross the threshold! If I don't floor him now, I shall murder him some time; so, as you value his existence, let me get at him!'

'He is not coming,' I interposed, framing a bit of a lie. 'There's the coachman and the two gardeners; you'll surely not wait to be thrust into the road by them! Each has a bludgeon; and master will, very likely, be watching from the parlour-windows to see that they fulfil his orders.'

The gardeners and coachman were there: but Linton was with them. They had already entered the court. Heathcliff, on the second thoughts, resolved to avoid a struggle against three underlings: he seized the poker, smashed the lock from the inner door, and made his escape as they tramped in.

Mrs. Linton, who was very much excited, bade me accompany her up-stairs. She did not know my share in contributing to the disturbance, and I was anxious to keep her in ignorance.

'I'm nearly distracted, Nelly!' she exclaimed, throwing herself on the sofa. 'A thousand smiths' hammers are beating in my head! Tell Isabella to shun me; this uproar is owing to her; and should she or any one else aggravate my anger at present, I shall get wild. And, Nelly, say to Edgar, if you see him again to-night, that I'm in danger of being seriously ill. I wish it may prove true. He has startled and distressed me shockingly! I want to frighten him. Besides, he might come and begin a string of abuse or complainings; I'm certain I should recriminate, and God knows where we should end! Will you do so, my good Nelly? You are aware that I am no way blamable in this matter. What possessed him to turn listener? Heathcliff's talk was outrageous, after you left us; but I could soon have diverted him from Isabella, and the rest meant nothing. Now all is dashed wrong; by the fool's craving to hear evil of self, that haunts some people like a demon! Had Edgar never gathered our conversation, he would never have been the worse for it. Really, when he opened on me in that unreasonable tone of displeasure after I had scolded Heathcliff till I was hoarse for him, I did not care hardly what they did to each other; especially as I felt that, however the scene closed, we should all be driven asunder for nobody knows how long! Well, if I cannot keep Heathcliff for my friend—if Edgar will be mean and jealous, I'll try to break their hearts by breaking my own. That will be a prompt way of finishing all, when I am pushed to extremity! But it's a deed to be reserved for a forlorn hope; I'd not take Linton by surprise with it. To this point he has been discreet in dreading to provoke me; you must represent the peril of quitting that policy, and remind him of my passionate temper, verging, when kindled, on frenzy. I wish you could dismiss that apathy out of that countenance, and look rather more anxious about me.'

The stolidity with which I received these instructions was, no doubt, rather exasperating: for they were delivered in perfect sincerity; but I believed a person who could plan the turning of her fits of passion to account, beforehand, might, by exerting her will, manage to control herself tolerably, even while under their influence; and I did not wish to 'frighten' her husband, as she said, and multiply his annoyances for the purpose of serving her selfishness. Therefore I said nothing when I met the master coming towards the parlour; but I took the liberty of turning back to listen whether they would resume their quarrel together. He began to speak first.

'Remain where you are, Catherine,' he said; without any anger in his voice, but with much sorrowful despondency. 'I shall not stay. I am neither come to wrangle nor be reconciled; but I wish just to learn whether, after this evening's events, you intend to continue your intimacy with—'

'Oh, for mercy's sake,' interrupted the mistress, stamping her foot, 'for mercy's sake, let us hear no more of it now! Your cold blood cannot be worked into a fever: your veins are full of ice-water; but mine are boiling, and the sight of such chillness makes them dance.'

'To get rid of me, answer my question,' persevered Mr. Linton. 'You must answer it; and that violence does not alarm me. I have found that you can be as stoical as anyone, when you please. Will you give up Heathcliff hereafter, or will you give up me? It is impossible for you to be MY friend and HIS at the same time; and I absolutely REQUIRE to know which you choose.'

'I require to be let alone?' exclaimed Catherine, furiously. 'I demand it! Don't you see I can scarcely stand? Edgar, you—you leave me!'

She rang the bell till it broke with a twang; I entered leisurely. It was enough to try the temper of a saint, such senseless, wicked rages! There she lay dashing her head against the arm of the sofa, and grinding her teeth, so that you might fancy she would crash them to splinters! Mr. Linton stood looking at her in sudden compunction and fear. He told me to fetch some water. She had no breath for speaking. I brought a glass full; and as she would not drink, I sprinkled it on her face. In a few seconds she stretched herself out stiff, and turned up her eyes, while her cheeks, at once blanched and livid, assumed the aspect of death. Linton looked terrified.

'There is nothing in the world the matter,' I whispered. I did not want him to yield, though I could not help being afraid in my heart.

'She has blood on her lips!' he said, shuddering.

'Never mind!' I answered, tartly. And I told him how she had resolved, previous to his coming, on exhibiting a fit of frenzy. I incautiously gave the account aloud, and she heard me; for she started up—her hair flying over her shoulders, her eyes flashing, the muscles of her neck and arms standing out preternaturally. I made up my mind for broken bones, at least; but she only glared about her for an instant, and then rushed from the room. The master directed me to follow; I did, to her chamber-door: she hindered me from going further by securing it against me.

As she never offered to descend to breakfast next morning, I went to ask whether she would have some carried up. 'No!' she replied, peremptorily. The same question was repeated at dinner and tea; and again on the morrow after, and received the same answer. Mr. Linton, on his part, spent his time in the library, and did not inquire concerning his wife's occupations. Isabella and he had had an hour's interview, during which he tried to elicit from her some sentiment of proper horror for Heathcliff's advances: but he could make nothing of her evasive replies, and was obliged to close the examination unsatisfactorily; adding, however, a solemn warning, that if she were so insane as to encourage that worthless suitor, it would dissolve all bonds of relationship between herself and him.

Chapter XII

WHILE Miss Linton moped about the park and garden, always silent, and almost always in tears; and her brother shut himself up among books that he never opened—wearying, I guessed, with a continual vague expectation that Catherine, repenting her conduct, would come of her own accord to ask pardon, and seek a reconciliation—and SHE fasted pertinaciously, under the idea, probably, that at every meal Edgar was ready to choke for her absence, and pride alone held him from running to cast himself at her feet; I went about my household duties, convinced that the Grange had but one sensible soul in its walls, and that lodged in my body. I wasted no condolences on Miss, nor any expostulations on my mistress; nor did I pay much attention to the sighs of my master, who yearned to hear his lady's name, since he might not hear her voice. I determined they should come about as they pleased for me; and though it was a tiresomely slow process, I began to rejoice at length in a faint dawn of its progress: as I thought at first.

Mrs. Linton, on the third day, unbarred her door, and having finished the water in her pitcher and decanter, desired a renewed supply, and a basin of gruel, for she believed she was dying. That I set down as a speech meant for Edgar's ears; I believed no such thing, so I kept it to myself and brought her some tea and dry toast. She ate and drank eagerly, and sank back on her pillow again, clenching her hands and groaning. 'Oh, I will die,' she exclaimed, 'since no one cares anything about me. I wish I had not taken that.' Then a good while after I heard her murmur, 'No, I'll not die—he'd be glad—he does not love me at all—he would never miss me!'

'Did you want anything, ma'am?' I inquired, still preserving my external composure, in spite of her ghastly countenance and strange, exaggerated manner.

'What is that apathetic being doing?' she demanded, pushing the thick entangled locks from her wasted face. 'Has he fallen into a lethargy, or is he dead?'

'Neither,' replied I; 'if you mean Mr. Linton. He's tolerably well, I think, though his studies occupy him rather more than they ought: he is continually among his books, since he has no other society.'

I should not have spoken so if I had known her true condition, but I could not get rid of the notion that she acted a part of her disorder.

'Among his books!' she cried, confounded. 'And I dying! I on the brink of the grave! My God! does he know how I'm altered?' continued she, staring at her reflection in a mirror hanging against the opposite wall. 'Is that Catherine Linton? He imagines me in a pet—in play, perhaps. Cannot you inform him that it is frightful earnest? Nelly, if it be not too late, as soon as I learn how he feels, I'll choose between these two: either to starve at once—that would be no punishment unless he had a heart—or to recover, and leave the country. Are you speaking the truth about him now? Take care. Is he actually so utterly indifferent for my life?'

'Why, ma'am,' I answered, 'the master has no idea of your being deranged; and of course he does not fear that you will let yourself die of hunger.'

'You think not? Cannot you tell him I will?' she returned. 'Persuade him! speak of your own mind: say you are certain I will!'

'No, you forget, Mrs. Linton,' I suggested, 'that you have eaten some food with a relish this evening, and to-morrow you will perceive its good effects.'

'If I were only sure it would kill him,' she interrupted, 'I'd kill myself directly! These three awful nights I've never closed my lids—and oh, I've been tormented! I've been haunted, Nelly! But I begin to fancy you don't like me. How strange! I thought, though everybody hated and despised each other, they could not avoid loving me. And they have all turned to enemies in a few hours: they have, I'm positive; the people here. How dreary to meet death, surrounded by their cold faces! Isabella, terrified and repelled, afraid to enter the room, it would be so dreadful to watch Catherine go. And Edgar standing solemnly by to see it over; then offering prayers of thanks to God for restoring peace to his house, and going back to his BOOKS! What in the name of all that feels has he to do with BOOKS, when I am dying?'

She could not bear the notion which I had put into her head of Mr. Linton's philosophical resignation. Tossing about, she increased her feverish bewilderment to madness, and tore the pillow with her teeth; then raising herself up all burning, desired that I would open the window. We were in the middle of winter, the wind blew strong from the north-east, and I objected. Both the expressions flitting over her face, and the changes of her moods, began to alarm me terribly; and brought to my recollection her former illness, and the doctor's injunction that she should not be crossed. A minute previously she was violent; now, supported on one arm, and not noticing my refusal to obey her, she seemed to find childish diversion in pulling the feathers from the rents she had just made, and ranging them on the sheet according to their different species: her mind had strayed to other associations.

'That's a turkey's,' she murmured to herself; 'and this is a wild duck's; and this is a pigeon's. Ah, they put pigeons' feathers in the pillows—no wonder I couldn't die! Let me take care to throw it on the floor when I lie down. And here is a moor-cock's; and this—I should know it among a thousand—it's a lapwing's. Bonny bird; wheeling over our heads in the middle of the moor. It wanted to get to its nest, for the clouds had touched the swells, and it felt rain coming. This feather was picked up from the heath, the bird was not shot: we saw its nest in the winter, full of little skeletons. Heathcliff set a trap over it, and the old ones dared not come. I made him promise he'd never shoot a lapwing after that, and he didn't. Yes, here are more! Did he shoot my lapwings, Nelly? Are they red, any of them? Let me look.'

'Give over with that baby-work!' I interrupted, dragging the pillow away, and turning the holes towards the mattress, for she was removing its contents by handfuls. 'Lie down and shut your eyes: you're wandering. There's a mess! The down is flying about like snow.'

I went here and there collecting it.

'I see in you, Nelly,' she continued dreamily, 'an aged woman: you have grey hair and bent shoulders. This bed is the fairy cave under Penistone crags, and you are gathering elf-bolts to hurt our heifers; pretending, while I am near, that they are only locks of wool. That's what you'll come to fifty years hence: I know you are not so now. I'm not wandering: you're mistaken, or else I should believe you really WERE that withered hag, and I should think I WAS under Penistone Crags; and I'm conscious it's night, and there are two candles on the table making the black press shine like jet.'

'The black press? where is that?' I asked. 'You are talking in your sleep!'

'It's against the wall, as it always is,' she replied. 'It DOES appear odd—I see a face in it!'

'There's no press in the room, and never was,' said I, resuming my seat, and looping up the curtain that I might watch her.

'Don't YOU see that face?' she inquired, gazing earnestly at the mirror.

And say what I could, I was incapable of making her comprehend it to be her own; so I rose and covered it with a shawl.

'It's behind there still!' she pursued, anxiously. 'And it stirred. Who is it? I hope it will not come out when you are gone! Oh! Nelly, the room is haunted! I'm afraid of being alone!'

I took her hand in mine, and bid her be composed; for a succession of shudders convulsed her frame, and she would keep straining her gaze towards the glass.

'There's nobody here!' I insisted. 'It was YOURSELF, Mrs. Linton: you knew it a while since.'

'Myself!' she gasped, 'and the clock is striking twelve! It's true, then! that's dreadful!'

Her fingers clutched the clothes, and gathered them over her eyes. I attempted to steal to the door with an intention of calling her husband; but I was summoned back by a piercing shriek—the shawl had dropped from the frame.

'Why, what is the matter?' cried I. 'Who is coward now? Wake up! That is the glass—the mirror, Mrs. Linton; and you see yourself in it, and there am I too by your side.'

Trembling and bewildered, she held me fast, but the horror gradually passed from her countenance; its paleness gave place to a glow of shame.

'Oh, dear! I thought I was at home,' she sighed. 'I thought I was lying in my chamber at Wuthering Heights. Because I'm weak, my brain got confused, and I screamed unconsciously. Don't say anything; but stay with me. I dread sleeping: my dreams appal me.'

'A sound sleep would do you good, ma'am,' I answered: 'and I hope this suffering will prevent your trying starving again.'

'Oh, if I were but in my own bed in the old house!' she went on bitterly, wringing her hands. 'And that wind sounding in the firs by the lattice. Do let me feel it—it comes straight down the moor—do let me have one breath!' To pacify her I held the casement ajar a few seconds. A cold blast rushed through; I closed it, and returned to my post. She lay still now, her face bathed in tears. Exhaustion of body had entirely subdued her spirit: our fiery Catherine was no better than a wailing child.

'How long is it since I shut myself in here?' she asked, suddenly reviving.

'It was Monday evening,' I replied, 'and this is Thursday night, or rather Friday morning, at present.'

'What! of the same week?' she exclaimed. 'Only that brief time?'

'Long enough to live on nothing but cold water and ill-temper,' observed I.

'Well, it seems a weary number of hours,' she muttered doubtfully: 'it must be more. I remember being in the parlour after they had quarrelled, and Edgar being cruelly provoking, and me running into this room desperate. As soon as ever I had barred the door, utter blackness overwhelmed me, and I fell on the floor. I couldn't explain to Edgar how certain I felt of having a fit, or going raging mad, if he persisted in teasing me! I had no command of tongue, or brain, and he did not guess my agony, perhaps: it barely left me sense to try to escape from him and his voice. Before I recovered sufficiently to see and hear, it began to be dawn, and, Nelly, I'll tell you what I thought, and what has kept recurring and recurring till I feared for my reason. I thought as I lay there, with my head against that table leg, and my eyes dimly discerning the grey square of the window, that I was enclosed in the oak-panelled bed at home; and my heart ached with some great grief which, just waking, I could not recollect. I pondered, and worried myself to discover what it could be, and, most strangely, the whole last seven years of my life grew a blank! I did not recall that they had been at all. I was a child; my father was just buried, and my misery arose from the separation that Hindley had ordered between me and Heathcliff. I was laid alone, for the first time; and, rousing from a dismal doze after a night of weeping, I lifted my hand to push the panels aside: it struck the table-top! I swept it along the carpet, and then memory burst in: my late anguish was swallowed in a paroxysm of despair. I cannot say why I felt so wildly wretched: it must have been temporary derangement; for there is scarcely cause. But, supposing at twelve years old I had been wrenched from the Heights, and every early association, and my all in all, as Heathcliff was at that time, and been converted at a stroke into Mrs. Linton, the lady of Thrushcross Grange, and the wife of a stranger: an exile, and outcast, thenceforth, from what had been my world. You may fancy a glimpse of the abyss where I grovelled! Shake your head as you will, Nelly, you have helped to unsettle me! You should have spoken to Edgar, indeed you should, and compelled him to leave me quiet! Oh, I'm burning! I wish I were out of doors! I wish I were a girl again, half savage and hardy, and free; and laughing at injuries, not maddening under them! Why am I so changed? why does my blood rush into a hell of tumult at a few words? I'm sure I should be myself were I once among the heather on those hills. Open the window again wide: fasten it open! Quick, why don't you move?'

'Because I won't give you your death of cold,' I answered.

'You won't give me a chance of life, you mean,' she said, sullenly. 'However, I'm not helpless yet; I'll open it myself.'

And sliding from the bed before I could hinder her, she crossed the room, walking very uncertainly, threw it back, and bent out, careless of the frosty air that cut about her shoulders as keen as a knife. I entreated, and finally attempted to force her to retire. But I soon found her delirious strength much surpassed mine (she was delirious, I became convinced by her subsequent actions and ravings). There was no moon, and everything beneath lay in misty darkness: not a light gleamed from any house, far or near all had been extinguished long ago: and those at Wuthering Heights were never visible—still she asserted she caught their shining.

'Look!' she cried eagerly, 'that's my room with the candle in it, and the trees swaying before it; and the other candle is in Joseph's garret. Joseph sits up late, doesn't he? He's waiting till I come home that he may lock the gate. Well, he'll wait a while yet. It's a rough journey, and a sad heart to travel it; and we must pass by Gimmerton Kirk to go that journey! We've braved its ghosts often together, and dared each other to stand among the graves and ask them to come. But, Heathcliff, if I dare you now, will you venture? If you do, I'll keep you. I'll not lie there by myself: they may bury me twelve feet deep, and throw the church down over me, but I won't rest till you are with me. I never will!'

She paused, and resumed with a strange smile. 'He's considering-he'd rather I'd come to him! Find a way, then! not through that kirkyard. You are slow! Be content, you always followed me!'

Perceiving it vain to argue against her insanity, I was planning how I could reach something to wrap about her, without quitting my hold of herself (for I could not trust her alone by the gaping lattice), when, to my consternation, I heard the rattle of the door-handle, and Mr. Linton entered. He had only then come from the library; and, in passing through the lobby, had noticed our talking and been attracted by curiosity, or fear, to examine what it signified, at that late hour.

'Oh, sir!' I cried, checking the exclamation risen to his lips at the sight which met him, and the bleak atmosphere of the chamber. 'My poor mistress is ill, and she quite masters me: I cannot manage her at all; pray, come and persuade her to go to bed. Forget your anger, for she's hard to guide any way but her own.'

'Catherine ill?' he said, hastening to us. 'Shut the window, Ellen! Catherine! why—'

He was silent. The haggardness of Mrs. Linton's appearance smote him speechless, and he could only glance from her to me in horrified astonishment.

'She's been fretting here,' I continued, 'and eating scarcely anything, and never complaining: she would admit none of us till this evening, and so we couldn't inform you of her state, as we were not aware of it ourselves; but it is nothing.'

I felt I uttered my explanations awkwardly; the master frowned. 'It is nothing, is it, Ellen Dean?' he said sternly. 'You shall account more clearly for keeping me ignorant of this!' And he took his wife in his arms, and looked at her with anguish.

At first she gave him no glance of recognition: he was invisible to her abstracted gaze. The delirium was not fixed, however; having weaned her eyes from contemplating the outer darkness, by degrees she centred her attention on him, and discovered who it was that held her.

'Ah! you are come, are you, Edgar Linton?' she said, with angry animation. 'You are one of those things that are ever found when least wanted, and when you are wanted, never! I suppose we shall have plenty of lamentations now—I see we shall—but they can't keep me from my narrow home out yonder: my resting-place, where I'm bound before spring is over! There it is: not among the Lintons, mind, under the chapel-roof, but in the open air, with a head-stone; and you may please yourself whether you go to them or come to me!'

'Catherine, what have you done?' commenced the master. 'Am I nothing to you any more? Do you love that wretch Heath—'

'Hush!' cried Mrs. Linton. 'Hush, this moment! You mention that name and I end the matter instantly by a spring from the window! What you touch at present you may have; but my soul will be on that hill-top before you lay hands on me again. I don't want you, Edgar: I'm past wanting you. Return to your books. I'm glad you possess a consolation, for all you had in me is gone.'

'Her mind wanders, sir,' I interposed. 'She has been talking nonsense the whole evening; but let her have quiet, and proper attendance, and she'll rally. Hereafter, we must be cautious how we vex her.'

'I desire no further advice from you,' answered Mr. Linton. 'You knew your mistress's nature, and you encouraged me to harass her. And not to give me one hint of how she has been these three days! It was heartless! Months of sickness could not cause such a change!'

I began to defend myself, thinking it too bad to be blamed for another's wicked waywardness. 'I knew Mrs. Linton's nature to be headstrong and domineering,' cried I: 'but I didn't know that you wished to foster her fierce temper! I didn't know that, to humour her, I should wink at Mr. Heathcliff. I performed the duty of a faithful servant in telling you, and I have got a faithful servant's wages! Well, it will teach me to be careful next time. Next time you may gather intelligence for yourself!'

'The next time you bring a tale to me you shall quit my service, Ellen Dean,' he replied.

'You'd rather hear nothing about it, I suppose, then, Mr. Linton?' said I. 'Heathcliff has your permission to come a-courting to Miss, and to drop in at every opportunity your absence offers, on purpose to poison the mistress against you?'

Confused as Catherine was, her wits were alert at applying our conversation.

'Ah! Nelly has played traitor,' she exclaimed, passionately. 'Nelly is my hidden enemy. You witch! So you do seek elf-bolts to hurt us! Let me go, and I'll make her rue! I'll make her howl a recantation!'

A maniac's fury kindled under her brows; she struggled desperately to disengage herself from Linton's arms. I felt no inclination to tarry the event; and, resolving to seek medical aid on my own responsibility, I quitted the chamber.

In passing the garden to reach the road, at a place where a bridle hook is driven into the wall, I saw something white moved irregularly, evidently by another agent than the wind. Notwithstanding my hurry, I stayed to examine it, lest ever after I should have the conviction impressed on my imagination that it was a creature of the other world. My surprise and perplexity were great on discovering, by touch more than vision, Miss Isabella's springer, Fanny, suspended by a handkerchief, and nearly at its last gasp. I quickly released the animal, and lifted it into the garden. I had seen it follow its mistress up-stairs when she went to bed; and wondered much how it could have got out there, and what mischievous person had treated it so. While untying the knot round the hook, it seemed to me that I repeatedly caught the beat of horses' feet galloping at some distance; but there were such a number of things to occupy my reflections that I hardly gave the circumstance a thought: though it was a strange sound, in that place, at two o'clock in the morning.

Mr. Kenneth was fortunately just issuing from his house to see a patient in the village as I came up the street; and my account of Catherine Linton's malady induced him to accompany me back immediately. He was a plain rough man; and he made no scruple to speak his doubts of her surviving this second attack; unless she were more submissive to his directions than she had shown herself before.

'Nelly Dean,' said he, 'I can't help fancying there's an extra cause for this. What has there been to do at the Grange? We've odd reports up here. A stout, hearty lass like Catherine does not fall ill for a trifle; and that sort of people should not either. It's hard work bringing them through fevers, and such things. How did it begin?'

'The master will inform you,' I answered; 'but you are acquainted with the Earnshaws' violent dispositions, and Mrs. Linton caps them all. I may say this; it commenced in a quarrel. She was struck during a tempest of passion with a kind of fit. That's her account, at least: for she flew off in the height of it, and locked herself up. Afterwards, she refused to eat, and now she alternately raves and remains in a half dream; knowing those about her, but having her mind filled with all sorts of strange ideas and illusions.'

'Mr. Linton will be sorry?' observed Kenneth, interrogatively.

' Sorry? he'll break his heart should anything happen!' I replied. 'Don't alarm him more than necessary.'

'Well, I told him to beware,' said my companion; 'and he must bide the consequences of neglecting my warning! Hasn't he been intimate with Mr. Heathcliff lately?'

'Heathcliff frequently visits at the Grange,' answered I, 'though more on the strength of the mistress having known him when a boy, than because the master likes his company. At present he's discharged from the trouble of calling; owing to some presumptuous aspirations after Miss Linton which he manifested. I hardly think he'll be taken in again.'

'And does Miss Linton turn a cold shoulder on him?' was the doctor's next question.

'I'm not in her confidence,' returned I, reluctant to continue the subject.

'No, she's a sly one,' he remarked, shaking his head. 'She keeps her own counsel! But she's a real little fool. I have it from good authority that last night (and a pretty night it was!) she and Heathcliff were walking in the plantation at the back of your house above two hours; and he pressed her not to go in again, but just mount his horse and away with him! My informant said she could only put him off by pledging her word of honour to be prepared on their first meeting after that: when it was to be he didn't hear; but you urge Mr. Linton to look sharp!'

This news filled me with fresh fears; I outstripped Kenneth, and ran most of the way back. The little dog was yelping in the garden yet. I spared a minute to open the gate for it, but instead of going to the house door, it coursed up and down snuffing the grass, and would have escaped to the road, had I not seized it and conveyed it in with me. On ascending to Isabella's room, my suspicions were confirmed: it was empty. Had I been a few hours sooner Mrs. Linton's illness might have arrested her rash step. But what could be done now? There was a bare possibility of overtaking them if pursued instantly. I could not pursue them, however; and I dared not rouse the family, and fill the place with confusion; still less unfold the business to my master, absorbed as he was in his present calamity, and having no heart to spare for a second grief! I saw nothing for it but to hold my tongue, and suffer matters to take their course; and Kenneth being arrived, I went with a badly composed countenance to announce him. Catherine lay in a troubled sleep: her husband had succeeded in soothing the excess of frenzy; he now hung over her pillow, watching every shade and every change of her painfully expressive features.

The doctor, on examining the case for himself, spoke hopefully to him of its having a favourable termination, if we could only preserve around her perfect and constant tranquillity. To me, he signified the threatening danger was not so much death, as permanent alienation of intellect.

I did not close my eyes that night, nor did Mr. Linton: indeed, we never went to bed; and the servants were all up long before the usual hour, moving through the house with stealthy tread, and exchanging whispers as they encountered each other in their vocations. Every one was active but Miss Isabella; and they began to remark how sound she slept: her brother, too, asked if she had risen, and seemed impatient for her presence, and hurt that she showed so little anxiety for her sister-in-law. I trembled lest he should send me to call her; but I was spared the pain of being the first proclaimant of her flight. One of the maids, a thoughtless girl, who had been on an early errand to Gimmerton, came panting up-stairs, open-mouthed, and dashed into the chamber, crying: 'Oh, dear, dear! What mun we have next? Master, master, our young lady—'

'Hold your noise!' cried, I hastily, enraged at her clamorous manner.

'Speak lower, Mary—What is the matter?' said Mr. Linton. 'What ails your young lady?'

'She's gone, she's gone! Yon' Heathcliff's run off wi' her!' gasped the girl.

'That is not true!' exclaimed Linton, rising in agitation. 'It cannot be: how has the idea entered your head? Ellen Dean, go and seek her. It is incredible: it cannot be.'

As he spoke he took the servant to the door, and then repeated his demand to know her reasons for such an assertion.

'Why, I met on the road a lad that fetches milk here,' she stammered, 'and he asked whether we weren't in trouble at the Grange. I thought he meant for missis's sickness, so I answered, yes. Then says he, "There's somebody gone after 'em, I guess?" I stared. He saw I knew nought about it, and he told how a gentleman and lady had stopped to have a horse's shoe fastened at a blacksmith's shop, two miles out of Gimmerton, not very long after midnight! and how the blacksmith's lass had got up to spy who they were: she knew them both directly. And she noticed the man—Heathcliff it was, she felt certain: nob'dy could mistake him, besides—put a sovereign in her father's hand for payment. The lady had a cloak about her face; but having desired a sup of water, while she drank it fell back, and she saw her very plain. Heathcliff held both bridles as they rode on, and they set their faces from the village, and went as fast as the rough roads would let them. The lass said nothing to her father, but she told it all over Gimmerton this morning.'

I ran and peeped, for form's sake, into Isabella's room; confirming, when I returned, the servant's statement. Mr. Linton had resumed his seat by the bed; on my re-entrance, he raised his eyes, read the meaning of my blank aspect, and dropped them without giving an order, or uttering a word.

'Are we to try any measures for overtaking and bringing her back,' I inquired. 'How should we do?'

'She went of her own accord,' answered the master; 'she had a right to go if she pleased. Trouble me no more about her. Hereafter she is only my sister in name: not because I disown her, but because she has disowned me.'

And that was all he said on the subject: he did not make single inquiry further, or mention her in any way, except directing me to send what property she had in the house to her fresh home, wherever it was, when I knew it.

Chapter XIII

FOR two months the fugitives remained absent; in those two months, Mrs. Linton encountered and conquered the worst shock of what was denominated a brain fever. No mother could have nursed an only child more devotedly than Edgar tended her. Day and night he was watching, and patiently enduring all the annoyances that irritable nerves and a shaken reason could inflict; and, though Kenneth remarked that what he saved from the grave would only recompense his care by forming the source of constant future anxiety—in fact, that his health and strength were being sacrificed to preserve a mere ruin of humanity—he knew no limits in gratitude and joy when Catherine's life was declared out of danger; and hour after hour he would sit beside her, tracing the gradual return to bodily health, and flattering his too sanguine hopes with the illusion that her mind would settle back to its right balance also, and she would soon be entirely her former self.

The first time she left her chamber was at the commencement of the following March. Mr. Linton had put on her pillow, in the morning, a handful of golden crocuses; her eye, long stranger to any gleam of pleasure, caught them in waking, and shone delighted as she gathered them eagerly together.

'These are the earliest flowers at the Heights,' she exclaimed. 'They remind me of soft thaw winds, and warm sunshine, and nearly melted snow. Edgar, is there not a south wind, and is not the snow almost gone?'

'The snow is quite gone down here, darling,' replied her husband; 'and I only see two white spots on the whole range of moors: the sky is blue, and the larks are singing, and the becks and brooks are all brim full. Catherine, last spring at this time, I was longing to have you under this roof; now, I wish you were a mile or two up those hills: the air blows so sweetly, I feel that it would cure you.'

'I shall never be there but once more,' said the invalid; 'and then you'll leave me, and I shall remain for ever. Next spring you'll long again to have me under this roof, and you'll look back and think you were happy to-day.'

Linton lavished on her the kindest caresses, and tried to cheer her by the fondest words; but, vaguely regarding the flowers, she let the tears collect on her lashes and stream down her cheeks unheeding. We knew she was really better, and, therefore, decided that long confinement to a single place produced much of this despondency, and it might be partially removed by a change of scene. The master told me to light a fire in the many-weeks' deserted parlour, and to set an easy-chair in the sunshine by the window; and then he brought her down, and she sat a long while enjoying the genial heat, and, as we expected, revived by the objects round her: which, though familiar, were free from the dreary associations investing her hated sick chamber. By evening she seemed greatly exhausted; yet no arguments could persuade her to return to that apartment, and I had to arrange the parlour sofa for her bed, till another room could be prepared. To obviate the fatigue of mounting and descending the stairs, we fitted up this, where you lie at present—on the same floor with the parlour; and she was soon strong enough to move from one to the other, leaning on Edgar's arm. Ah, I thought myself, she might recover, so waited on as she was. And there was double cause to desire it, for on her existence depended that of another: we cherished the hope that in a little while Mr. Linton's heart would be gladdened, and his lands secured from a stranger's gripe, by the birth of an heir.

I should mention that Isabella sent to her brother, some six weeks from her departure, a short note, announcing her marriage with Heathcliff. It appeared dry and cold; but at the bottom was dotted in with pencil an obscure apology, and an entreaty for kind remembrance and reconciliation, if her proceeding had offended him: asserting that she could not help it then, and being done, she had now no power to repeal it. Linton did not reply to this, I believe; and, in a fortnight more, I got a long letter, which I considered odd, coming from the pen of a bride just out of the honeymoon. I'll read it: for I keep it yet. Any relic of the dead is precious, if they were valued living.

DEAR ELLEN, it begins,—I came last night to Wuthering Heights, and heard, for the first time, that Catherine has been, and is yet, very ill. I must not write to her, I suppose, and my brother is either too angry or too distressed to answer what I sent him. Still, I must write to somebody, and the only choice left me is you.

Inform Edgar that I'd give the world to see his face again—that my heart returned to Thrushcross Grange in twenty-four hours after I left it, and is there at this moment, full of warm feelings for him, and Catherine! I CAN'T FOLLOW IT THOUGH—(these words are underlined)—they need not expect me, and they may draw what conclusions they please; taking care, however, to lay nothing at the door of my weak will or deficient affection.

The remainder of the letter is for yourself alone. I want to ask you two questions: the first is,—How did you contrive to preserve the common sympathies of human nature when you resided here? I cannot recognise any sentiment which those around share with me.

The second question I have great interest in; it is this—Is Mr. Heathcliff a man? If so, is he mad? And if not, is he a devil? I sha'n't tell my reasons for making this inquiry; but I beseech you to explain, if you can, what I have married: that is, when you call to see me; and you must call, Ellen, very soon. Don't write, but come, and bring me something from Edgar.

Now, you shall hear how I have been received in my new home, as I am led to imagine the Heights will be. It is to amuse myself that I dwell on such subjects as the lack of external comforts: they never occupy my thoughts, except at the moment when I miss them. I should laugh and dance for joy, if I found their absence was the total of my miseries, and the rest was an unnatural dream!

The sun set behind the Grange as we turned on to the moors; by that, I judged it to be six o'clock; and my companion halted half an hour, to inspect the park, and the gardens, and, probably, the place itself, as well as he could; so it was dark when we dismounted in the paved yard of the farm-house, and your old fellow-servant, Joseph, issued out to receive us by the light of a dip candle. He did it with a courtesy that redounded to his credit. His first act was to elevate his torch to a level with my face, squint malignantly, project his under-lip, and turn away. Then he took the two horses, and led them into the stables; reappearing for the purpose of locking the outer gate, as if we lived in an ancient castle.

Heathcliff stayed to speak to him, and I entered the kitchen—a dingy, untidy hole; I daresay you would not know it, it is so changed since it was in your charge. By the fire stood a ruffianly child, strong in limb and dirty in garb, with a look of Catherine in his eyes and about his mouth.

'This is Edgar's legal nephew,' I reflected—'mine in a manner; I must shake hands, and—yes—I must kiss him. It is right to establish a good understanding at the beginning.'

I approached, and, attempting to take his chubby fist, said—'How do you do, my dear?'

He replied in a jargon I did not comprehend.

'Shall you and I be friends, Hareton?' was my next essay at conversation.

An oath, and a threat to set Throttler on me if I did not 'frame off' rewarded my perseverance.

'Hey, Throttler, lad!' whispered the little wretch, rousing a half-bred bull-dog from its lair in a corner. 'Now, wilt thou be ganging?' he asked authoritatively.

Love for my life urged a compliance; I stepped over the threshold to wait till the others should enter. Mr. Heathcliff was nowhere visible; and Joseph, whom I followed to the stables, and requested to accompany me in, after staring and muttering to himself, screwed up his nose and replied—'Mim! mim! mim! Did iver Christian body hear aught like it? Minching un' munching! How can I tell whet ye say?'

'I say, I wish you to come with me into the house!' I cried, thinking him deaf, yet highly disgusted at his rudeness.

'None o' me! I getten summut else to do,' he answered, and continued his work; moving his lantern jaws meanwhile, and surveying my dress and countenance (the former a great deal too fine, but the latter, I'm sure, as sad as he could desire) with sovereign contempt.

I walked round the yard, and through a wicket, to another door, at which I took the liberty of knocking, in hopes some more civil servant might show himself. After a short suspense, it was opened by a tall, gaunt man, without neckerchief, and otherwise extremely slovenly; his features were lost in masses of shaggy hair that hung on his shoulders; and HIS eyes, too, were like a ghostly Catherine's with all their beauty annihilated.

'What's your business here?' he demanded, grimly. 'Who are you?'

'My name was Isabella Linton,' I replied. 'You've seen me before, sir. I'm lately married to Mr. Heathcliff, and he has brought me here—I suppose, by your permission.'

'Is he come back, then?' asked the hermit, glaring like a hungry wolf.

'Yes—we came just now,' I said; 'but he left me by the kitchen door; and when I would have gone in, your little boy played sentinel over the place, and frightened me off by the help of a bull-dog.'

'It's well the hellish villain has kept his word!' growled my future host, searching the darkness beyond me in expectation of discovering Heathcliff; and then he indulged in a soliloquy of execrations, and threats of what he would have done had the 'fiend' deceived him.

I repented having tried this second entrance, and was almost inclined to slip away before he finished cursing, but ere I could execute that intention, he ordered me in, and shut and re-fastened the door. There was a great fire, and that was all the light in the huge apartment, whose floor had grown a uniform grey; and the once brilliant pewter-dishes, which used to attract my gaze when I was a girl, partook of a similar obscurity, created by tarnish and dust. I inquired whether I might call the maid, and be conducted to a bedroom! Mr. Earnshaw vouchsafed no answer. He walked up and down, with his hands in his pockets, apparently quite forgetting my presence; and his abstraction was evidently so deep, and his whole aspect so misanthropical, that I shrank from disturbing him again.

You'll not be surprised, Ellen, at my feeling particularly cheerless, seated in worse than solitude on that inhospitable hearth, and remembering that four miles distant lay my delightful home, containing the only people I loved on earth; and there might as well be the Atlantic to part us, instead of those four miles: I could not overpass them! I questioned with myself—where must I turn for comfort? and—mind you don't tell Edgar, or Catherine-above every sorrow beside, this rose pre-eminent: despair at finding nobody who could or would be my ally against Heathcliff! I had sought shelter at Wuthering Heights, almost gladly, because I was secured by that arrangement from living alone with him; but he knew the people we were coming amongst, and he did not fear their intermeddling.

I sat and thought a doleful time: the clock struck eight, and nine, and still my companion paced to and fro, his head bent on his breast, and perfectly silent, unless a groan or a bitter ejaculation forced itself out at intervals. I listened to detect a woman's voice in the house, and filled the interim with wild regrets and dismal anticipations, which, at last, spoke audibly in irrepressible sighing and weeping. I was not aware how openly I grieved, till Earnshaw halted opposite, in his measured walk, and gave me a stare of newly-awakened surprise. Taking advantage of his recovered attention, I exclaimed—'I'm tired with my journey, and I want to go to bed! Where is the maid-servant? Direct me to her, as she won't come to me!'

'We have none,' he answered; 'you must wait on yourself!'

'Where must I sleep, then?' I sobbed; I was beyond regarding self-respect, weighed down by fatigue and wretchedness.

'Joseph will show you Heathcliff's chamber,' said he; 'open that door—he's in there.'

I was going to obey, but he suddenly arrested me, and added in the strangest tone—'Be so good as to turn your lock, and draw your bolt—don't omit it!'

'Well!' I said. 'But why, Mr. Earnshaw?' I did not relish the notion of deliberately fastening myself in with Heathcliff.

'Look here!' he replied, pulling from his waistcoat a curiously-constructed pistol, having a double-edged spring knife attached to the barrel. 'That's a great tempter to a desperate man, is it not? I cannot resist going up with this every night, and trying his door. If once I find it open he's done for; I do it invariably, even though the minute before I have been recalling a hundred reasons that should make me refrain: it is some devil that urges me to thwart my own schemes by killing him. You fight against that devil for love as long as you may; when the time comes, not all the angels in heaven shall save him!'

I surveyed the weapon inquisitively. A hideous notion struck me: how powerful I should be possessing such an instrument! I took it from his hand, and touched the blade. He looked astonished at the expression my face assumed during a brief second: it was not horror, it was covetousness. He snatched the pistol back, jealously; shut the knife, and returned it to its concealment.

'I don't care if you tell him,' said he. 'Put him on his guard, and watch for him. You know the terms we are on, I see: his danger does not shock you.'

'What has Heathcliff done to you?' I asked. 'In what has he wronged you, to warrant this appalling hatred? Wouldn't it be wiser to bid him quit the house?'

'No!' thundered Earnshaw; 'should he offer to leave me, he's a dead man: persuade him to attempt it, and you are a murderess! Am I to lose ALL, without a chance of retrieval? Is Hareton to be a beggar? Oh, damnation! I WILL have it back; and I'll have HIS gold too; and then his blood; and hell shall have his soul! It will be ten times blacker with that guest than ever it was before!'

You've acquainted me, Ellen, with your old master's habits. He is clearly on the verge of madness: he was so last night at least. I shuddered to be near him, and thought on the servant's ill-bred moroseness as comparatively agreeable. He now recommenced his moody walk, and I raised the latch, and escaped into the kitchen. Joseph was bending over the fire, peering into a large pan that swung above it; and a wooden bowl of oatmeal stood on the settle close by. The contents of the pan began to boil, and he turned to plunge his hand into the bowl; I conjectured that this preparation was probably for our supper, and, being hungry, I resolved it should be eatable; so, crying out sharply, 'I'LL make the porridge!' I removed the vessel out of his reach, and proceeded to take off my hat and riding-habit. 'Mr. Earnshaw,' I continued, 'directs me to wait on myself: I will. I'm not going to act the lady among you, for fear I should starve.'

'Gooid Lord!' he muttered, sitting down, and stroking his ribbed stockings from the knee to the ankle. 'If there's to be fresh ortherings—just when I getten used to two maisters, if I mun hev' a MISTRESS set o'er my heead, it's like time to be flitting. I niver DID think to see t' day that I mud lave th' owld place—but I doubt it's nigh at hand!'

This lamentation drew no notice from me: I went briskly to work, sighing to remember a period when it would have been all merry fun; but compelled speedily to drive off the remembrance. It racked me to recall past happiness and the greater peril there was of conjuring up its apparition, the quicker the thible ran round, and the faster the handfuls of meal fell into the water. Joseph beheld my style of cookery with growing indignation.

'Thear!' he ejaculated. 'Hareton, thou willn't sup thy porridge toneeght; they'll be naught but lumps as big as my neive. Thear, agean! I'd fling in bowl un' all, if I wer ye! There, pale t' guilp off, un' then ye'll hae done wi' 't. Bang, bang. It's a mercy t' bothom isn't deaved out!'

It WAS rather a rough mess, I own, when poured into the basins; four had been provided, and a gallon pitcher of new milk was brought from the dairy, which Hareton seized and commenced drinking and spilling from the expansive lip. I expostulated, and desired that he should have his in a mug; affirming that I could not taste the liquid treated so dirtily. The old cynic chose to be vastly offended at this nicety; assuring me, repeatedly, that 'the barn was every bit as good' as I, 'and every bit as wollsome,' and wondering how I could fashion to be so conceited. Meanwhile, the infant ruffian continued sucking; and glowered up at me defyingly, as he slavered into the jug.

'I shall have my supper in another room,' I said. 'Have you no place you call a parlour?'

'PARLOUR!' he echoed, sneeringly, 'PARLOUR! Nay, we've noa PARLOURS. If yah dunnut loike wer company, there's maister's; un' if yah dunnut loike maister, there's us.'

'Then I shall go up-stairs,' I answered; 'show me a chamber.'

I put my basin on a tray, and went myself to fetch some more milk. With great grumblings, the fellow rose, and preceded me in my ascent: we mounted to the garrets; he opened a door, now and then, to look into the apartments we passed.

'Here's a rahm,' he said, at last, flinging back a cranky board on hinges. 'It's weel eneugh to ate a few porridge in. There's a pack o' corn i' t' corner, thear, meeterly clane; if ye're feared o' muckying yer grand silk cloes, spread yer hankerchir o' t' top on't.'

The 'rahm' was a kind of lumber-hole smelling strong of malt and grain; various sacks of which articles were piled around, leaving a wide, bare space in the middle.

'Why, man,' I exclaimed, facing him angrily, 'this is not a place to sleep in. I wish to see my bed-room.'

'BED-RUME!' he repeated, in a tone of mockery. 'Yah's see all t' BED-RUMES thear is—yon's mine.'

He pointed into the second garret, only differing from the first in being more naked about the walls, and having a large, low, curtainless bed, with an indigo-coloured quilt, at one end.

'What do I want with yours?' I retorted. 'I suppose Mr. Heathcliff does not lodge at the top of the house, does he?'

'Oh! it's Maister HATHECLIFF'S ye're wanting?' cried he, as if making a new discovery. 'Couldn't ye ha' said soa, at onst? un' then, I mud ha' telled ye, baht all this wark, that that's just one ye cannut see—he allas keeps it locked, un' nob'dy iver mells on't but hisseln.'

'You've a nice house, Joseph,' I could not refrain from observing, 'and pleasant inmates; and I think the concentrated essence of all the madness in the world took up its abode in my brain the day I linked my fate with theirs! However, that is not to the present purpose—there are other rooms. For heaven's sake be quick, and let me settle somewhere!'

He made no reply to this adjuration; only plodding doggedly down the wooden steps, and halting, before an apartment which, from that halt and the superior quality of its furniture, I conjectured to be the best one. There was a carpet—a good one, but the pattern was obliterated by dust; a fireplace hung with cut-paper, dropping to pieces; a handsome oak-bedstead with ample crimson curtains of rather expensive material and modern make; but they had evidently experienced rough usage: the vallances hung in festoons, wrenched from their rings, and the iron rod supporting them was bent in an arc on one side, causing the drapery to trail upon the floor. The chairs were also damaged, many of them severely; and deep indentations deformed the panels of the walls. I was endeavouring to gather resolution for entering and taking possession, when my fool of a guide announced,—'This here is t' maister's.' My supper by this time was cold, my appetite gone, and my patience exhausted. I insisted on being provided instantly with a place of refuge, and means of repose.

'Whear the divil?' began the religious elder. 'The Lord bless us! The Lord forgie us! Whear the HELL wdd ye gang? ye marred, wearisome nowt! Ye've seen all but Hareton's bit of a cham'er. There's not another hoile to lig down in i' th' hahse!'

I was so vexed, I flung my tray and its contents on the ground; and then seated myself at the stairs'-head, hid my face in my hands, and cried.

'Ech! ech!' exclaimed Joseph. 'Weel done, Miss Cathy! weel done, Miss Cathy! Howsiver, t' maister sall just tum'le o'er them brooken pots; un' then we's hear summut; we's hear how it's to be. Gooid-for-naught madling! ye desarve pining fro' this to Churstmas, flinging t' precious gifts o'God under fooit i' yer flaysome rages! But I'm mista'en if ye shew yer sperrit lang. Will Hathecliff bide sich bonny ways, think ye? I nobbut wish he may catch ye i' that plisky. I nobbut wish he may.'

And so he went on scolding to his den beneath, taking the candle with him; and I remained in the dark. The period of reflection succeeding this silly action compelled me to admit the necessity of smothering my pride and choking my wrath, and bestirring myself to remove its effects. An unexpected aid presently appeared in the shape of Throttler, whom I now recognised as a son of our old Skulker: it had spent its whelphood at the Grange, and was given by my father to Mr. Hindley. I fancy it knew me: it pushed its nose against mine by way of salute, and then hastened to devour the porridge; while I groped from step to step, collecting the shattered earthenware, and drying the spatters of milk from the banister with my pocket-handkerchief. Our labours were scarcely over when I heard Earnshaw's tread in the passage; my assistant tucked in his tail, and pressed to the wall; I stole into the nearest doorway. The dog's endeavour to avoid him was unsuccessful; as I guessed by a scutter down-stairs, and a prolonged, piteous yelping. I had better luck: he passed on, entered his chamber, and shut the door. Directly after Joseph came up with Hareton, to put him to bed. I had found shelter in Hareton's room, and the old man, on seeing me, said,—'They's rahm for boath ye un' yer pride, now, I sud think i' the hahse. It's empty; ye may hev' it all to yerseln, un' Him as allus maks a third, i' sich ill company!'

Gladly did I take advantage of this intimation; and the minute I flung myself into a chair, by the fire, I nodded, and slept. My slumber was deep and sweet, though over far too soon. Mr. Heathcliff awoke me; he had just come in, and demanded, in his loving manner, what I was doing there? I told him the cause of my staying up so late—that he had the key of our room in his pocket. The adjective OUR gave mortal offence. He swore it was not, nor ever should be, mine; and he'd—but I'll not repeat his language, nor describe his habitual conduct: he is ingenious and unresting in seeking to gain my abhorrence! I sometimes wonder at him with an intensity that deadens my fear: yet, I assure you, a tiger or a venomous serpent could not rouse terror in me equal to that which he wakens. He told me of Catherine's illness, and accused my brother of causing it promising that I should be Edgar's proxy in suffering, till he could get hold of him.

I do hate him—I am wretched—I have been a fool! Beware of uttering one breath of this to any one at the Grange. I shall expect you every day—don't disappoint me!—ISABELLA.

Chapter XIV

AS soon as I had perused this epistle I went to the master, and informed him that his sister had arrived at the Heights, and sent me a letter expressing her sorrow for Mrs. Linton's situation, and her ardent desire to see him; with a wish that he would transmit to her, as early as possible, some token of forgiveness by me.

'Forgiveness!' said Linton. 'I have nothing to forgive her, Ellen. You may call at Wuthering Heights this afternoon, if you like, and say that I am not angry, but I'm sorry to have lost her; especially as I can never think she'll be happy. It is out of the question my going to see her, however: we are eternally divided; and should she really wish to oblige me, let her persuade the villain she has married to leave the country.'

'And you won't write her a little note, sir?' I asked, imploringly.

'No,' he answered. 'It is needless. My communication with Heathcliff's family shall be as sparing as his with mine. It shall not exist!'

Mr. Edgar's coldness depressed me exceedingly; and all the way from the Grange I puzzled my brains how to put more heart into what he said, when I repeated it; and how to soften his refusal of even a few lines to console Isabella. I daresay she had been on the watch for me since morning: I saw her looking through the lattice as I came up the garden causeway, and I nodded to her; but she drew back, as if afraid of being observed. I entered without knocking. There never was such a dreary, dismal scene as the formerly cheerful house presented! I must confess, that if I had been in the young lady's place, I would, at least, have swept the hearth, and wiped the tables with a duster. But she already partook of the pervading spirit of neglect which encompassed her. Her pretty face was wan and listless; her hair uncurled: some locks hanging lankly down, and some carelessly twisted round her head. Probably she had not touched her dress since yester evening. Hindley was not there. Mr. Heathcliff sat at a table, turning over some papers in his pocket-book; but he rose when I appeared, asked me how I did, quite friendly, and offered me a chair. He was the only thing there that seemed decent; and I thought he never looked better. So much had circumstances altered their positions, that he would certainly have struck a stranger as a born and bred gentleman; and his wife as a thorough little slattern! She came forward eagerly to greet me, and held out one hand to take the expected letter. I shook my head. She wouldn't understand the hint, but followed me to a sideboard, where I went to lay my bonnet, and importuned me in a whisper to give her directly what I had brought. Heathcliff guessed the meaning of her manoeuvres, and said—'If you have got anything for Isabella (as no doubt you have, Nelly), give it to her. You needn't make a secret of it: we have no secrets between us.'

'Oh, I have nothing,' I replied, thinking it best to speak the truth at once. 'My master bid me tell his sister that she must not expect either a letter or a visit from him at present. He sends his love, ma'am, and his wishes for your happiness, and his pardon for the grief you have occasioned; but he thinks that after this time his household and the household here should drop intercommunication, as nothing could come of keeping it up.'

Mrs. Heathcliff's lip quivered slightly, and she returned to her seat in the window. Her husband took his stand on the hearthstone, near me, and began to put questions concerning Catherine. I told him as much as I thought proper of her illness, and he extorted from me, by cross-examination, most of the facts connected with its origin. I blamed her, as she deserved, for bringing it all on herself; and ended by hoping that he would follow Mr. Linton's example and avoid future interference with his family, for good or evil.

'Mrs. Linton is now just recovering,' I said; 'she'll never be like she was, but her life is spared; and if you really have a regard for her, you'll shun crossing her way again: nay, you'll move out of this country entirely; and that you may not regret it, I'll inform you Catherine Linton is as different now from your old friend Catherine Earnshaw, as that young lady is different from me. Her appearance is changed greatly, her character much more so; and the person who is compelled, of necessity, to be her companion, will only sustain his affection hereafter by the remembrance of what she once was, by common humanity, and a sense of duty!'

'That is quite possible,' remarked Heathcliff, forcing himself to seem calm: 'quite possible that your master should have nothing but common humanity and a sense of duty to fall back upon. But do you imagine that I shall leave Catherine to his DUTY and HUMANITY? and can you compare my feelings respecting Catherine to his? Before you leave this house, I must exact a promise from you that you'll get me an interview with her: consent, or refuse, I WILL see her! What do you say?'

'I say, Mr. Heathcliff,' I replied, 'you must not: you never shall, through my means. Another encounter between you and the master would kill her altogether.'

'With your aid that may be avoided,' he continued; 'and should there be danger of such an event—should he be the cause of adding a single trouble more to her existence—why, I think I shall be justified in going to extremes! I wish you had sincerity enough to tell me whether Catherine would suffer greatly from his loss: the fear that she would restrains me. And there you see the distinction between our feelings: had he been in my place, and I in his, though I hated him with a hatred that turned my life to gall, I never would have raised a hand against him. You may look incredulous, if you please! I never would have banished him from her society as long as she desired his. The moment her regard ceased, I would have torn his heart out, and drunk his blood! But, till then—if you don't believe me, you don't know me—till then, I would have died by inches before I touched a single hair of his head!'

'And yet,' I interrupted, 'you have no scruples in completely ruining all hopes of her perfect restoration, by thrusting yourself into her remembrance now, when she has nearly forgotten you, and involving her in a new tumult of discord and distress.'

'You suppose she has nearly forgotten me?' he said. 'Oh, Nelly! you know she has not! You know as well as I do, that for every thought she spends on Linton she spends a thousand on me! At a most miserable period of my life, I had a notion of the kind: it haunted me on my return to the neighbourhood last summer; but only her own assurance could make me admit the horrible idea again. And then, Linton would be nothing, nor Hindley, nor all the dreams that ever I dreamt. Two words would comprehend my future—DEATH and HELL: existence, after losing her, would be hell. Yet I was a fool to fancy for a moment that she valued Edgar Linton's attachment more than mine. If he loved with all the powers of his puny being, he couldn't love as much in eighty years as I could in a day. And Catherine has a heart as deep as I have: the sea could be as readily contained in that horse-trough as her whole affection be monopolised by him. Tush! He is scarcely a degree dearer to her than her dog, or her horse. It is not in him to be loved like me: how can she love in him what he has not?'

'Catherine and Edgar are as fond of each other as any two people can be,' cried Isabella, with sudden vivacity. 'No one has a right to talk in that manner, and I won't hear my brother depreciated in silence!'

'Your brother is wondrous fond of you too, isn't he?' observed Heathcliff, scornfully. 'He turns you adrift on the world with surprising alacrity.'

'He is not aware of what I suffer,' she replied. 'I didn't tell him that.'

'You have been telling him something, then: you have written, have you?'

'To say that I was married, I did write—you saw the note.'

'And nothing since?'

'No.'

'My young lady is looking sadly the worse for her change of condition,' I remarked. 'Somebody's love comes short in her case, obviously; whose, I may guess; but, perhaps, I shouldn't say.'

'I should guess it was her own,' said Heathcliff. 'She degenerates into a mere slut! She is tired of trying to please me uncommonly early. You'd hardly credit it, but the very morrow of our wedding she was weeping to go home. However, she'll suit this house so much the better for not being over nice, and I'll take care she does not disgrace me by rambling abroad.'

'Well, sir,' returned I, 'I hope you'll consider that Mrs. Heathcliff is accustomed to be looked after and waited on; and that she has been brought up like an only daughter, whom every one was ready to serve. You must let her have a maid to keep things tidy about her, and you must treat her kindly. Whatever be your notion of Mr. Edgar, you cannot doubt that she has a capacity for strong attachments, or she wouldn't have abandoned the elegancies, and comforts, and friends of her former home, to fix contentedly, in such a wilderness as this, with you.'

'She abandoned them under a delusion,' he answered; 'picturing in me a hero of romance, and expecting unlimited indulgences from my chivalrous devotion. I can hardly regard her in the light of a rational creature, so obstinately has she persisted in forming a fabulous notion of my character and acting on the false impressions she cherished. But, at last, I think she begins to know me: I don't perceive the silly smiles and grimaces that provoked me at first; and the senseless incapability of discerning that I was in earnest when I gave her my opinion of her infatuation and herself. It was a marvellous effort of perspicacity to discover that I did not love her. I believed, at one time, no lessons could teach her that! And yet it is poorly learnt; for this morning she announced, as a piece of appalling intelligence, that I had actually succeeded in making her hate me! A positive labour of Hercules, I assure you! If it be achieved, I have cause to return thanks. Can I trust your assertion, Isabella? Are you sure you hate me? If I let you alone for half a day, won't you come sighing and wheedling to me again? I daresay she would rather I had seemed all tenderness before you: it wounds her vanity to have the truth exposed. But I don't care who knows that the passion was wholly on one side: and I never told her a lie about it. She cannot accuse me of showing one bit of deceitful softness. The first thing she saw me do, on coming out of the Grange, was to hang up her little dog; and when she pleaded for it, the first words I uttered were a wish that I had the hanging of every being belonging to her, except one: possibly she took that exception for herself. But no brutality disgusted her: I suppose she has an innate admiration of it, if only her precious person were secure from injury! Now, was it not the depth of absurdity—of genuine idiotcy, for that pitiful, slavish, mean-minded brach to dream that I could love her? Tell your master, Nelly, that I never, in all my life, met with such an abject thing as she is. She even disgraces the name of Linton; and I've sometimes relented, from pure lack of invention, in my experiments on what she could endure, and still creep shamefully cringing back! But tell him, also, to set his fraternal and magisterial heart at ease: that I keep strictly within the limits of the law. I have avoided, up to this period, giving her the slightest right to claim a separation; and, what's more, she'd thank nobody for dividing us. If she desired to go, she might: the nuisance of her presence outweighs the gratification to be derived from tormenting her!'

'Mr. Heathcliff,' said I, 'this is the talk of a madman; your wife, most likely, is convinced you are mad; and, for that reason, she has borne with you hitherto: but now that you say she may go, she'll doubtless avail herself of the permission. You are not so bewitched, ma'am, are you, as to remain with him of your own accord?'

'Take care, Ellen!' answered Isabella, her eyes sparkling irefully; there was no misdoubting by their expression the full success of her partner's endeavours to make himself detested. 'Don't put faith in a single word he speaks. He's a lying fiend! a monster, and not a human being! I've been told I might leave him before; and I've made the attempt, but I dare not repeat it! Only, Ellen, promise you'll not mention a syllable of his infamous conversation to my brother or Catherine. Whatever he may pretend, he wishes to provoke Edgar to desperation: he says he has married me on purpose to obtain power over him; and he sha'n't obtain it—I'll die first! I just hope, I pray, that he may forget his diabolical prudence and kill me! The single pleasure I can imagine is to die, or to see him dead!'

'There—that will do for the present!' said Heathcliff. 'If you are called upon in a court of law, you'll remember her language, Nelly! And take a good look at that countenance: she's near the point which would suit me. No; you're not fit to be your own guardian, Isabella, now; and I, being your legal protector, must retain you in my custody, however distasteful the obligation may be. Go up-stairs; I have something to say to Ellen Dean in private. That's not the way: up-stairs, I tell you! Why, this is the road upstairs, child!'

He seized, and thrust her from the room; and returned muttering—'I have no pity! I have no pity! The more the worms writhe, the more I yearn to crush out their entrails! It is a moral teething; and I grind with greater energy in proportion to the increase of pain.'

'Do you understand what the word pity means?' I said, hastening to resume my bonnet. 'Did you ever feel a touch of it in your life?'

'Put that down!' he interrupted, perceiving my intention to depart. 'You are not going yet. Come here now, Nelly: I must either persuade or compel you to aid me in fulfilling my determination to see Catherine, and that without delay. I swear that I meditate no harm: I don't desire to cause any disturbance, or to exasperate or insult Mr. Linton; I only wish to hear from herself how she is, and why she has been ill; and to ask if anything that I could do would be of use to her. Last night I was in the Grange garden six hours, and I'll return there to-night; and every night I'll haunt the place, and every day, till I find an opportunity of entering. If Edgar Linton meets me, I shall not hesitate to knock him down, and give him enough to insure his quiescence while I stay. If his servants oppose me, I shall threaten them off with these pistols. But wouldn't it be better to prevent my coming in contact with them, or their master? And you could do it so easily. I'd warn you when I came, and then you might let me in unobserved, as soon as she was alone, and watch till I departed, your conscience quite calm: you would be hindering mischief.'

I protested against playing that treacherous part in my employer's house: and, besides, I urged the cruelty and selfishness of his destroying Mrs. Linton's tranquillity for his satisfaction. 'The commonest occurrence startles her painfully,' I said. 'She's all nerves, and she couldn't bear the surprise, I'm positive. Don't persist, sir! or else I shall be obliged to inform my master of your designs; and he'll take measures to secure his house and its inmates from any such unwarrantable intrusions!'

'In that case I'll take measures to secure you, woman!' exclaimed Heathcliff; 'you shall not leave Wuthering Heights till to-morrow morning. It is a foolish story to assert that Catherine could not bear to see me; and as to surprising her, I don't desire it: you must prepare her—ask her if I may come. You say she never mentions my name, and that I am never mentioned to her. To whom should she mention me if I am a forbidden topic in the house? She thinks you are all spies for her husband. Oh, I've no doubt she's in hell among you! I guess by her silence, as much as anything, what she feels. You say she is often restless, and anxious-looking: is that a proof of tranquillity? You talk of her mind being unsettled. How the devil could it be otherwise in her frightful isolation? And that insipid, paltry creature attending her from DUTY and HUMANITY! From PITY and CHARITY! He might as well plant an oak in a flower-pot, and expect it to thrive, as imagine he can restore her to vigour in the soil of his shallow cares? Let us settle it at once: will you stay here, and am I to fight my way to Catherine over Linton and his footman? Or will you be my friend, as you have been hitherto, and do what I request? Decide! because there is no reason for my lingering another minute, if you persist in your stubborn ill-nature!'

Well, Mr. Lockwood, I argued and complained, and flatly refused him fifty times; but in the long run he forced me to an agreement. I engaged to carry a letter from him to my mistress; and should she consent, I promised to let him have intelligence of Linton's next absence from home, when he might come, and get in as he was able: I wouldn't be there, and my fellow-servants should be equally out of the way. Was it right or wrong? I fear it was wrong, though expedient. I thought I prevented another explosion by my compliance; and I thought, too, it might create a favourable crisis in Catherine's mental illness: and then I remembered Mr. Edgar's stern rebuke of my carrying tales; and I tried to smooth away all disquietude on the subject, by affirming, with frequent iteration, that that betrayal of trust, if it merited so harsh an appellation, should be the last. Notwithstanding, my journey homeward was sadder than my journey thither; and many misgivings I had, ere I could prevail on myself to put the missive into Mrs. Linton's hand.

But here is Kenneth; I'll go down, and tell him how much better you are. My history is DREE, as we say, and will serve to while away another morning.

Dree, and dreary! I reflected as the good woman descended to receive the doctor: and not exactly of the kind which I should have chosen to amuse me. But never mind! I'll extract wholesome medicines from Mrs. Dean's bitter herbs; and firstly, let me beware of the fascination that lurks in Catherine Heathcliff's brilliant eyes. I should be in a curious taking if I surrendered my heart to that young person, and the daughter turned out a second edition of the mother.

Chapter XV

ANOTHER week over—and I am so many days nearer health, and spring! I have now heard all my neighbour's history, at different sittings, as the housekeeper could spare time from more important occupations. I'll continue it in her own words, only a little condensed. She is, on the whole, a very fair narrator, and I don't think I could improve her style.

In the evening, she said, the evening of my visit to the Heights, I knew, as well as if I saw him, that Mr. Heathcliff was about the place; and I shunned going out, because I still carried his letter in my pocket, and didn't want to be threatened or teased any more. I had made up my mind not to give it till my master went somewhere, as I could not guess how its receipt would affect Catherine. The consequence was, that it did not reach her before the lapse of three days. The fourth was Sunday, and I brought it into her room after the family were gone to church. There was a manservant left to keep the house with me, and we generally made a practice of locking the doors during the hours of service; but on that occasion the weather was so warm and pleasant that I set them wide open, and, to fulfil my engagement, as I knew who would be coming, I told my companion that the mistress wished very much for some oranges, and he must run over to the village and get a few, to be paid for on the morrow. He departed, and I went up-stairs.

Mrs. Linton sat in a loose white dress, with a light shawl over her shoulders, in the recess of the open window, as usual. Her thick, long hair had been partly removed at the beginning of her illness, and now she wore it simply combed in its natural tresses over her temples and neck. Her appearance was altered, as I had told Heathcliff; but when she was calm, there seemed unearthly beauty in the change. The flash of her eyes had been succeeded by a dreamy and melancholy softness; they no longer gave the impression of looking at the objects around her: they appeared always to gaze beyond, and far beyond—you would have said out of this world. Then, the paleness of her face—its haggard aspect having vanished as she recovered flesh—and the peculiar expression arising from her mental state, though painfully suggestive of their causes, added to the touching interest which she awakened; and—invariably to me, I know, and to any person who saw her, I should think-refuted more tangible proofs of convalescence, and stamped her as one doomed to decay.

A book lay spread on the sill before her, and the scarcely perceptible wind fluttered its leaves at intervals. I believe Linton had laid it there: for she never endeavoured to divert herself with reading, or occupation of any kind, and he would spend many an hour in trying to entice her attention to some subject which had formerly been her amusement. She was conscious of his aim, and in her better moods endured his efforts placidly, only showing their uselessness by now and then suppressing a wearied sigh, and checking him at last with the saddest of smiles and kisses. At other times, she would turn petulantly away, and hide her face in her hands, or even push him off angrily; and then he took care to let her alone, for he was certain of doing no good.

Gimmerton chapel bells were still ringing; and the full, mellow flow of the beck in the valley came soothingly on the ear. It was a sweet substitute for the yet absent murmur of the summer foliage, which drowned that music about the Grange when the trees were in leaf. At Wuthering Heights it always sounded on quiet days following a great thaw or a season of steady rain. And of Wuthering Heights Catherine was thinking as she listened: that is, if she thought or listened at all; but she had the vague, distant look I mentioned before, which expressed no recognition of material things either by ear or eye.

'There's a letter for you, Mrs. Linton,' I said, gently inserting it in one hand that rested on her knee. 'You must read it immediately, because it wants an answer. Shall I break the seal?' 'Yes,' she answered, without altering the direction of her eyes. I opened it—it was very short. 'Now,' I continued, 'read it.' She drew away her hand, and let it fall. I replaced it in her lap, and stood waiting till it should please her to glance down; but that movement was so long delayed that at last I resumed—'Must I read it, ma'am? It is from Mr. Heathcliff.'

There was a start and a troubled gleam of recollection, and a struggle to arrange her ideas. She lifted the letter, and seemed to peruse it; and when she came to the signature she sighed: yet still I found she had not gathered its import, for, upon my desiring to hear her reply, she merely pointed to the name, and gazed at me with mournful and questioning eagerness.

'Well, he wishes to see you,' said I, guessing her need of an interpreter. 'He's in the garden by this time, and impatient to know what answer I shall bring.'

As I spoke, I observed a large dog lying on the sunny grass beneath raise its ears as if about to bark, and then smoothing them back, announce, by a wag of the tail, that some one approached whom it did not consider a stranger. Mrs. Linton bent forward, and listened breathlessly. The minute after a step traversed the hall; the open house was too tempting for Heathcliff to resist walking in: most likely he supposed that I was inclined to shirk my promise, and so resolved to trust to his own audacity. With straining eagerness Catherine gazed towards the entrance of her chamber. He did not hit the right room directly: she motioned me to admit him, but he found it out ere I could reach the door, and in a stride or two was at her side, and had her grasped in his arms.

He neither spoke nor loosed his hold for some five minutes, during which period he bestowed more kisses than ever he gave in his life before, I daresay: but then my mistress had kissed him first, and I plainly saw that he could hardly bear, for downright agony, to look into her face! The same conviction had stricken him as me, from the instant he beheld her, that there was no prospect of ultimate recovery there—she was fated, sure to die.

'Oh, Cathy! Oh, my life! how can I bear it?' was the first sentence he uttered, in a tone that did not seek to disguise his despair. And now he stared at her so earnestly that I thought the very intensity of his gaze would bring tears into his eyes; but they burned with anguish: they did not melt.

'What now?' said Catherine, leaning back, and returning his look with a suddenly clouded brow: her humour was a mere vane for constantly varying caprices. 'You and Edgar have broken my heart, Heathcliff! And you both come to bewail the deed to me, as if you were the people to be pitied! I shall not pity you, not I. You have killed me—and thriven on it, I think. How strong you are! How many years do you mean to live after I am gone?'

Heathcliff had knelt on one knee to embrace her; he attempted to rise, but she seized his hair, and kept him down.

'I wish I could hold you,' she continued, bitterly, 'till we were both dead! I shouldn't care what you suffered. I care nothing for your sufferings. Why shouldn't you suffer? I do! Will you forget me? Will you be happy when I am in the earth? Will you say twenty years hence, "That's the grave of Catherine Earnshaw? I loved her long ago, and was wretched to lose her; but it is past. I've loved many others since: my children are dearer to me than she was; and, at death, I shall not rejoice that I are going to her: I shall be sorry that I must leave them!" Will you say so, Heathcliff?'

'Don't torture me till I'm as mad as yourself,' cried he, wrenching his head free, and grinding his teeth.

The two, to a cool spectator, made a strange and fearful picture. Well might Catherine deem that heaven would be a land of exile to her, unless with her mortal body she cast away her moral character also. Her present countenance had a wild vindictiveness in its white cheek, and a bloodless lip and scintillating eye; and she retained in her closed fingers a portion of the locks she had been grasping. As to her companion, while raising himself with one hand, he had taken her arm with the other; and so inadequate was his stock of gentleness to the requirements of her condition, that on his letting go I saw four distinct impressions left blue in the colourless skin.

'Are you possessed with a devil,' he pursued, savagely, 'to talk in that manner to me when you are dying? Do you reflect that all those words will be branded in my memory, and eating deeper eternally after you have left me? You know you lie to say I have killed you: and, Catherine, you know that I could as soon forget you as my existence! Is it not sufficient for your infernal selfishness, that while you are at peace I shall writhe in the torments of hell?'

'I shall not be at peace,' moaned Catherine, recalled to a sense of physical weakness by the violent, unequal throbbing of her heart, which beat visibly and audibly under this excess of agitation. She said nothing further till the paroxysm was over; then she continued, more kindly—

'I'm not wishing you greater torment than I have, Heathcliff. I only wish us never to be parted: and should a word of mine distress you hereafter, think I feel the same distress underground, and for my own sake, forgive me! Come here and kneel down again! You never harmed me in your life. Nay, if you nurse anger, that will be worse to remember than my harsh words! Won't you come here again? Do!'

Heathcliff went to the back of her chair, and leant over, but not so far as to let her see his face, which was livid with emotion. She bent round to look at him; he would not permit it: turning abruptly, he walked to the fireplace, where he stood, silent, with his back towards us. Mrs. Linton's glance followed him suspiciously: every movement woke a new sentiment in her. After a pause and a prolonged gaze, she resumed; addressing me in accents of indignant disappointment:—

'Oh, you see, Nelly, he would not relent a moment to keep me out of the grave. THAT is how I'm loved! Well, never mind. That is not MY Heathcliff. I shall love mine yet; and take him with me: he's in my soul. And,' added she musingly, 'the thing that irks me most is this shattered prison, after all. I'm tired of being enclosed here. I'm wearying to escape into that glorious world, and to be always there: not seeing it dimly through tears, and yearning for it through the walls of an aching heart: but really with it, and in it. Nelly, you think you are better and more fortunate than I; in full health and strength: you are sorry for me—very soon that will be altered. I shall be sorry for YOU. I shall be incomparably beyond and above you all. I WONDER he won't be near me!' She went on to herself. 'I thought he wished it. Heathcliff, dear! you should not be sullen now. Do come to me, Heathcliff.'

In her eagerness she rose and supported herself on the arm of the chair. At that earnest appeal he turned to her, looking absolutely desperate. His eyes, wide and wet, at last flashed fiercely on her; his breast heaved convulsively. An instant they held asunder, and then how they met I hardly saw, but Catherine made a spring, and he caught her, and they were locked in an embrace from which I thought my mistress would never be released alive: in fact, to my eyes, she seemed directly insensible. He flung himself into the nearest seat, and on my approaching hurriedly to ascertain if she had fainted, he gnashed at me, and foamed like a mad dog, and gathered her to him with greedy jealousy. I did not feel as if I were in the company of a creature of my own species: it appeared that he would not understand, though I spoke to him; so I stood off, and held my tongue, in great perplexity.

A movement of Catherine's relieved me a little presently: she put up her hand to clasp his neck, and bring her cheek to his as he held her; while he, in return, covering her with frantic caresses, said wildly—

'You teach me now how cruel you've been—cruel and false. WHY did you despise me? WHY did you betray your own heart, Cathy? I have not one word of comfort. You deserve this. You have killed yourself. Yes, you may kiss me, and cry; and wring out my kisses and tears: they'll blight you—they'll damn you. You loved me—then what RIGHT had you to leave me? What right—answer me—for the poor fancy you felt for Linton? Because misery and degradation, and death, and nothing that God or Satan could inflict would have parted us, YOU, of your own will, did it. I have not broken your heart—YOU have broken it; and in breaking it, you have broken mine. So much the worse for me that I am strong. Do I want to live? What kind of living will it be when you—oh, God! would YOU like to live with your soul in the grave?'

'Let me alone. Let me alone,' sobbed Catherine. 'If I've done wrong, I'm dying for it. It is enough! You left me too: but I won't upbraid you! I forgive you. Forgive me!'

'It is hard to forgive, and to look at those eyes, and feel those wasted hands,' he answered. 'Kiss me again; and don't let me see your eyes! I forgive what you have done to me. I love MY murderer—but YOURS! How can I?'

They were silent—their faces hid against each other, and washed by each other's tears. At least, I suppose the weeping was on both sides; as it seemed Heathcliff could weep on a great occasion like this.

I grew very uncomfortable, meanwhile; for the afternoon wore fast away, the man whom I had sent off returned from his errand, and

I could distinguish, by the shine of the western sun up the valley, a concourse thickening outside Gimmerton chapel porch.

'Service is over,' I announced. 'My master will be here in half an hour.'

Heathcliff groaned a curse, and strained Catherine closer: she never moved.

Ere long I perceived a group of the servants passing up the road towards the kitchen wing. Mr. Linton was not far behind; he opened the gate himself and sauntered slowly up, probably enjoying the lovely afternoon that breathed as soft as summer.

'Now he is here,' I exclaimed. 'For heaven's sake, hurry down! You'll not meet any one on the front stairs. Do be quick; and stay among the trees till he is fairly in.'

'I must go, Cathy,' said Heathcliff, seeking to extricate himself from his companion's arms. 'But if I live, I'll see you again before you are asleep. I won't stray five yards from your window.'

'You must not go!' she answered, holding him as firmly as her strength allowed. 'You SHALL not, I tell you.'

'For one hour,' he pleaded earnestly.

'Not for one minute,' she replied.

'I MUST—Linton will be up immediately,' persisted the alarmed intruder.

He would have risen, and unfixed her fingers by the act—she clung fast, gasping: there was mad resolution in her face.

'No!' she shrieked. 'Oh, don't, don't go. It is the last time! Edgar will not hurt us. Heathcliff, I shall die! I shall die!'

'Damn the fool! There he is,' cried Heathcliff, sinking back into his seat. 'Hush, my darling! Hush, hush, Catherine! I'll stay. If he shot me so, I'd expire with a blessing on my lips.'

And there they were fast again. I heard my master mounting the stairs—the cold sweat ran from my forehead: I was horrified.

'Are you going to listen to her ravings?' I said, passionately. 'She does not know what she says. Will you ruin her, because she has not wit to help herself? Get up! You could be free instantly. That is the most diabolical deed that ever you did. We are all done for—master, mistress, and servant.'

I wrung my hands, and cried out; and Mr. Linton hastened his step at the noise. In the midst of my agitation, I was sincerely glad to observe that Catherine's arms had fallen relaxed, and her head hung down.

'She's fainted, or dead,' I thought: 'so much the better. Far better that she should be dead, than lingering a burden and a misery-maker to all about her.'

Edgar sprang to his unbidden guest, blanched with astonishment and rage. What he meant to do I cannot tell; however, the other stopped all demonstrations, at once, by placing the lifeless-looking form in his arms.

'Look there!' he said. 'Unless you be a fiend, help her first—then you shall speak to me!'

He walked into the parlour, and sat down. Mr. Linton summoned me, and with great difficulty, and after resorting to many means, we managed to restore her to sensation; but she was all bewildered; she sighed, and moaned, and knew nobody. Edgar, in his anxiety for her, forgot her hated friend. I did not. I went, at the earliest opportunity, and besought him to depart; affirming that Catherine was better, and he should hear from me in the morning how she passed the night.

'I shall not refuse to go out of doors,' he answered; 'but I shall stay in the garden: and, Nelly, mind you keep your word to-morrow. I shall be under those larch-trees. Mind! or I pay another visit, whether Linton be in or not.'

He sent a rapid glance through the half-open door of the chamber, and, ascertaining that what I stated was apparently true, delivered the house of his luckless presence.

Chapter XVI

ABOUT twelve o'clock that night was born the Catherine you saw at Wuthering Heights: a puny, seven-months' child; and two hours after the mother died, having never recovered sufficient consciousness to miss Heathcliff, or know Edgar. The latter's distraction at his bereavement is a subject too painful to be dwelt on; its after-effects showed how deep the sorrow sunk. A great addition, in my eyes, was his being left without an heir. I bemoaned that, as I gazed on the feeble orphan; and I mentally abused old Linton for (what was only natural partiality) the securing his estate to his own daughter, instead of his son's. An unwelcomed infant it was, poor thing! It might have wailed out of life, and nobody cared a morsel, during those first hours of existence. We redeemed the neglect afterwards; but its beginning was as friendless as its end is likely to be.

Next morning—bright and cheerful out of doors—stole softened in through the blinds of the silent room, and suffused the couch and its occupant with a mellow, tender glow. Edgar Linton had his head laid on the pillow, and his eyes shut. His young and fair features were almost as deathlike as those of the form beside him, and almost as fixed: but HIS was the hush of exhausted anguish, and HERS of perfect peace. Her brow smooth, her lids closed, her lips wearing the expression of a smile; no angel in heaven could be more beautiful than she appeared. And I partook of the infinite calm in which she lay: my mind was never in a holier frame than while I gazed on that untroubled image of Divine rest. I instinctively echoed the words she had uttered a few hours before: 'Incomparably beyond and above us all! Whether still on earth or now in heaven, her spirit is at home with God!'

I don't know if it be a peculiarity in me, but I am seldom otherwise than happy while watching in the chamber of death, should no frenzied or despairing mourner share the duty with me. I see a repose that neither earth nor hell can break, and I feel an assurance of the endless and shadowless hereafter—the Eternity they have entered—where life is boundless in its duration, and love in its sympathy, and joy in its fulness. I noticed on that occasion how much selfishness there is even in a love like Mr. Linton's, when he so regretted Catherine's blessed release! To be sure, one might have doubted, after the wayward and impatient existence she had led, whether she merited a haven of peace at last. One might doubt in seasons of cold reflection; but not then, in the presence of her corpse. It asserted its own tranquillity, which seemed a pledge of equal quiet to its former inhabitant.

Do you believe such people are happy in the other world, sir? I'd give a great deal to know.

I declined answering Mrs. Dean's question, which struck me as something heterodox. She proceeded:

Retracing the course of Catherine Linton, I fear we have no right to think she is; but we'll leave her with her Maker.

The master looked asleep, and I ventured soon after sunrise to quit the room and steal out to the pure refreshing air. The servants thought me gone to shake off the drowsiness of my protracted watch; in reality, my chief motive was seeing Mr. Heathcliff. If he had remained among the larches all night, he would have heard nothing of the stir at the Grange; unless, perhaps, he might catch the gallop of the messenger going to Gimmerton. If he had come nearer, he would probably be aware, from the lights flitting to and fro, and the opening and shutting of the outer doors, that all was not right within. I wished, yet feared, to find him. I felt the terrible news must be told, and I longed to get it over; but how to do it I did not know. He was there—at least, a few yards further in the park; leant against an old ash-tree, his hat off, and his hair soaked with the dew that had gathered on the budded branches, and fell pattering round him. He had been standing a long time in that position, for I saw a pair of ousels passing and repassing scarcely three feet from him, busy in building their nest, and regarding his proximity no more than that of a piece of timber. They flew off at my approach, and he raised his eyes and spoke:—'She's dead!' he said; 'I've not waited for you to learn that. Put your handkerchief away—don't snivel before me. Damn you all! she wants none of your tears!'

I was weeping as much for him as her: we do sometimes pity creatures that have none of the feeling either for themselves or others. When I first looked into his face, I perceived that he had got intelligence of the catastrophe; and a foolish notion struck me that his heart was quelled and he prayed, because his lips moved and his gaze was bent on the ground.

'Yes, she's dead!' I answered, checking my sobs and drying my cheeks. 'Gone to heaven, I hope; where we may, every one, join her, if we take due warning and leave our evil ways to follow good!'

'Did SHE take due warning, then?' asked Heathcliff, attempting a sneer. 'Did she die like a saint? Come, give me a true history of the event. How did—?'

He endeavoured to pronounce the name, but could not manage it; and compressing his mouth he held a silent combat with his inward agony, defying, meanwhile, my sympathy with an unflinching, ferocious stare. 'How did she die?' he resumed, at last—fain, notwithstanding his hardihood, to have a support behind him; for, after the struggle, he trembled, in spite of himself, to his very finger-ends.

'Poor wretch!' I thought; 'you have a heart and nerves the same as your brother men! Why should you be anxious to conceal them? Your pride cannot blind God! You tempt him to wring them, till he forces a cry of humiliation.'

'Quietly as a lamb!' I answered, aloud. 'She drew a sigh, and stretched herself, like a child reviving, and sinking again to sleep; and five minutes after I felt one little pulse at her heart, and nothing more!'

'And—did she ever mention me?' he asked, hesitating, as if he dreaded the answer to his question would introduce details that he could not bear to hear.

'Her senses never returned: she recognised nobody from the time you left her,' I said. 'She lies with a sweet smile on her face; and her latest ideas wandered back to pleasant early days. Her life closed in a gentle dream—may she wake as kindly in the other world!'

'May she wake in torment!' he cried, with frightful vehemence, stamping his foot, and groaning in a sudden paroxysm of ungovernable passion. 'Why, she's a liar to the end! Where is she? Not THERE—not in heaven—not perished—where? Oh! you said you cared nothing for my sufferings! And I pray one prayer-I repeat it till my tongue stiffens—Catherine Earnshaw, may you not rest as long as I am living; you said I killed you—haunt me, then! The murdered DO haunt their murderers, I believe. I know that ghosts HAVE wandered on earth. Be with me always—take any form—drive me mad! only DO not leave me in this abyss, where I cannot find you! Oh, God! it is unutterable! I CANNOT live without my life! I CANNOT live without my soul!'

He dashed his head against the knotted trunk; and, lifting up his eyes, howled, not like a man, but like a savage beast being goaded to death with knives and spears. I observed several splashes of blood about the bark of the tree, and his hand and forehead were both stained; probably the scene I witnessed was a repetition of others acted during the night. It hardly moved my compassion—it appalled me: still, I felt reluctant to quit him so. But the moment he recollected himself enough to notice me watching, he thundered a command for me to go, and I obeyed. He was beyond my skill to quiet or console!

Mrs. Linton's funeral was appointed to take place on the Friday following her decease; and till then her coffin remained uncovered, and strewn with flowers and scented leaves, in the great drawing-room. Linton spent his days and nights there, a sleepless guardian; and—a circumstance concealed from all but me—Heathcliff spent his nights, at least, outside, equally a stranger to repose. I held no communication with him: still, I was conscious of his design to enter, if he could; and on the Tuesday, a little after dark, when my master, from sheer fatigue, had been compelled to retire a couple of hours, I went and opened one of the windows; moved by his perseverance to give him a chance of bestowing on the faded image of his idol one final adieu. He did not omit to avail himself of the opportunity, cautiously and briefly; too cautiously to betray his presence by the slightest noise. Indeed, I shouldn't have discovered that he had been there, except for the disarrangement of the drapery about the corpse's face, and for observing on the floor a curl of light hair, fastened with a silver thread; which, on examination, I ascertained to have been taken from a locket hung round Catherine's neck. Heathcliff had opened the trinket and cast out its contents, replacing them by a black lock of his own. I twisted the two, and enclosed them together.

Mr. Earnshaw was, of course, invited to attend the remains of his sister to the grave; he sent no excuse, but he never came; so that, besides her husband, the mourners were wholly composed of tenants and servants. Isabella was not asked.

The place of Catherine's interment, to the surprise of the villagers, was neither in the chapel under the carved monument of the Lintons, nor yet by the tombs of her own relations, outside. It was dug on a green slope in a corner of the kirk-yard, where the wall is so low that heath and bilberry-plants have climbed over it from the moor; and peat-mould almost buries it. Her husband lies in the same spot now; and they have each a simple headstone above, and a plain grey block at their feet, to mark the graves.

Chapter XVII

THAT Friday made the last of our fine days for a month. In the evening the weather broke: the wind shifted from south to north-east, and brought rain first, and then sleet and snow. On the morrow one could hardly imagine that there had been three weeks of summer: the primroses and crocuses were hidden under wintry drifts; the larks were silent, the young leaves of the early trees smitten and blackened. And dreary, and chill, and dismal, that morrow did creep over! My master kept his room; I took possession of the lonely parlour, converting it into a nursery: and there I was, sitting with the moaning doll of a child laid on my knee; rocking it to and fro, and watching, meanwhile, the still driving flakes build up the uncurtained window, when the door opened, and some person entered, out of breath and laughing! My anger was greater than my astonishment for a minute. I supposed it one of the maids, and I cried—'Have done! How dare you show your giddiness here; What would Mr. Linton say if he heard you?'

'Excuse me!' answered a familiar voice; 'but I know Edgar is in bed, and I cannot stop myself.'

With that the speaker came forward to the fire, panting and holding her hand to her side.

'I have run the whole way from Wuthering Heights!' she continued, after a pause; 'except where I've flown. I couldn't count the number of falls I've had. Oh, I'm aching all over! Don't be alarmed! There shall be an explanation as soon as I can give it; only just have the goodness to step out and order the carriage to take me on to Gimmerton, and tell a servant to seek up a few clothes in my wardrobe.'

The intruder was Mrs. Heathcliff. She certainly seemed in no laughing predicament: her hair streamed on her shoulders, dripping with snow and water; she was dressed in the girlish dress she commonly wore, befitting her age more than her position: a low frock with short sleeves, and nothing on either head or neck. The frock was of light silk, and clung to her with wet, and her feet were protected merely by thin slippers; add to this a deep cut under one ear, which only the cold prevented from bleeding profusely, a white face scratched and bruised, and a frame hardly able to support itself through fatigue; and you may fancy my first fright was not much allayed when I had had leisure to examine her.

'My dear young lady,' I exclaimed, 'I'll stir nowhere, and hear nothing, till you have removed every article of your clothes, and put on dry things; and certainly you shall not go to Gimmerton to-night, so it is needless to order the carriage.'

'Certainly I shall,' she said; 'walking or riding: yet I've no objection to dress myself decently. And—ah, see how it flows down my neck now! The fire does make it smart.'

She insisted on my fulfilling her directions, before she would let me touch her; and not till after the coachman had been instructed to get ready, and a maid set to pack up some necessary attire, did I obtain her consent for binding the wound and helping to change her garments.

'Now, Ellen,' she said, when my task was finished and she was seated in an easy-chair on the hearth, with a cup of tea before her, 'you sit down opposite me, and put poor Catherine's baby away: I don't like to see it! You mustn't think I care little for Catherine, because I behaved so foolishly on entering: I've cried, too, bitterly—yes, more than any one else has reason to cry. We parted unreconciled, you remember, and I sha'n't forgive myself. But, for all that, I was not going to sympathise with him—the brute beast! Oh, give me the poker! This is the last thing of his I have about me:' she slipped the gold ring from her third finger, and threw it on the floor. 'I'll smash it!' she continued, striking it with childish spite, 'and then I'll burn it!' and she took and dropped the misused article among the coals. 'There! he shall buy another, if he gets me back again. He'd be capable of coming to seek me, to tease Edgar. I dare not stay, lest that notion should possess his wicked head! And besides, Edgar has not been kind, has he? And I won't come suing for his assistance; nor will I bring him into more trouble. Necessity compelled me to seek shelter here; though, if I had not learned he was out of the way, I'd have halted at the kitchen, washed my face, warmed myself, got you to bring what I wanted, and departed again to anywhere out of the reach of my accursed—of that incarnate goblin! Ah, he was in such a fury! If he had caught me! It's a pity Earnshaw is not his match in strength: I wouldn't have run till I'd seen him all but demolished, had Hindley been able to do it!'

'Well, don't talk so fast, Miss!' I interrupted; 'you'll disorder the handkerchief I have tied round your face, and make the cut bleed again. Drink your tea, and take breath, and give over laughing: laughter is sadly out of place under this roof, and in your condition!'

'An undeniable truth,' she replied. 'Listen to that child! It maintains a constant wail—send it out of my hearing for an hour; I sha'n't stay any longer.'

I rang the bell, and committed it to a servant's care; and then I inquired what had urged her to escape from Wuthering Heights in such an unlikely plight, and where she meant to go, as she refused remaining with us.

'I ought, and I wished to remain,' answered she, 'to cheer Edgar and take care of the baby, for two things, and because the Grange is my right home. But I tell you he wouldn't let me! Do you think he could bear to see me grow fat and merry—could bear to think that we were tranquil, and not resolve on poisoning our comfort? Now, I have the satisfaction of being sure that he detests me, to the point of its annoying him seriously to have me within ear-shot or eyesight: I notice, when I enter his presence, the muscles of his countenance are involuntarily distorted into an expression of hatred; partly arising from his knowledge of the good causes I have to feel that sentiment for him, and partly from original aversion. It is strong enough to make me feel pretty certain that he would not chase me over England, supposing I contrived a clear escape; and therefore I must get quite away. I've recovered from my first desire to be killed by him: I'd rather he'd kill himself! He has extinguished my love effectually, and so I'm at my ease. I can recollect yet how I loved him; and can dimly imagine that I could still be loving him, if—no, no! Even if he had doted on me, the devilish nature would have revealed its existence somehow. Catherine had an awfully perverted taste to esteem him so dearly, knowing him so well. Monster! would that he could be blotted out of creation, and out of my memory!'

'Hush, hush! He's a human being,' I said. 'Be more charitable: there are worse men than he is yet!'

'He's not a human being,' she retorted; 'and he has no claim on my charity. I gave him my heart, and he took and pinched it to death, and flung it back to me. People feel with their hearts, Ellen: and since he has destroyed mine, I have not power to feel for him: and I would not, though he groaned from this to his dying day, and wept tears of blood for Catherine! No, indeed, indeed, I wouldn't!' And here Isabella began to cry; but, immediately dashing the water from her lashes, she recommenced. 'You asked, what has driven me to flight at last? I was compelled to attempt it, because I had succeeded in rousing his rage a pitch above his malignity. Pulling out the nerves with red hot pincers requires more coolness than knocking on the head. He was worked up to forget the fiendish prudence he boasted of, and proceeded to murderous violence. I experienced pleasure in being able to exasperate him: the sense of pleasure woke my instinct of self-preservation, so I fairly broke free; and if ever I come into his hands again he is welcome to a signal revenge.

'Yesterday, you know, Mr. Earnshaw should have been at the funeral. He kept himself sober for the purpose—tolerably sober: not going to bed mad at six o'clock and getting up drunk at twelve. Consequently, he rose, in suicidal low spirits, as fit for the church as for a dance; and instead, he sat down by the fire and swallowed gin or brandy by tumblerfuls.

'Heathcliff—I shudder to name him! has been a stranger in the house from last Sunday till to-day. Whether the angels have fed him, or his kin beneath, I cannot tell; but he has not eaten a meal with us for nearly a week. He has just come home at dawn, and gone up-stairs to his chamber; looking himself in—as if anybody dreamt of coveting his company! There he has continued, praying like a Methodist: only the deity he implored is senseless dust and ashes; and God, when addressed, was curiously confounded with his own black father! After concluding these precious orisons—and they lasted generally till he grew hoarse and his voice was strangled in his throat—he would be off again; always straight down to the Grange! I wonder Edgar did not send for a constable, and give him into custody! For me, grieved as I was about Catherine, it was impossible to avoid regarding this season of deliverance from degrading oppression as a holiday.

'I recovered spirits sufficient to bear Joseph's eternal lectures without weeping, and to move up and down the house less with the foot of a frightened thief than formerly. You wouldn't think that I should cry at anything Joseph could say; but he and Hareton are detestable companions. I'd rather sit with Hindley, and hear his awful talk, than with "t' little maister" and his staunch supporter, that odious old man! When Heathcliff is in, I'm often obliged to seek the kitchen and their society, or starve among the damp uninhabited chambers; when he is not, as was the case this week, I establish a table and chair at one corner of the house fire, and never mind how Mr. Earnshaw may occupy himself; and he does not interfere with my arrangements. He is quieter now than he used to be, if no one provokes him: more sullen and depressed, and less furious. Joseph affirms he's sure he's an altered man: that the Lord has touched his heart, and he is saved "so as by fire." I'm puzzled to detect signs of the favourable change: but it is not my business.

'Yester-evening I sat in my nook reading some old books till late on towards twelve. It seemed so dismal to go up-stairs, with the wild snow blowing outside, and my thoughts continually reverting to the kirk-yard and the new-made grave! I dared hardly lift my eyes from the page before me, that melancholy scene so instantly usurped its place. Hindley sat opposite, his head leant on his hand; perhaps meditating on the same subject. He had ceased drinking at a point below irrationality, and had neither stirred nor spoken during two or three hours. There was no sound through the house but the moaning wind, which shook the windows every now and then, the faint crackling of the coals, and the click of my snuffers as I removed at intervals the long wick of the candle. Hareton and Joseph were probably fast asleep in bed. It was very, very sad: and while I read I sighed, for it seemed as if all joy had vanished from the world, never to be restored.

'The doleful silence was broken at length by the sound of the kitchen latch: Heathcliff had returned from his watch earlier than usual; owing, I suppose, to the sudden storm. That entrance was fastened, and we heard him coming round to get in by the other. I rose with an irrepressible expression of what I felt on my lips, which induced my companion, who had been staring towards the door, to turn and look at me.

'"I'll keep him out five minutes," he exclaimed. "You won't object?"

'"No, you may keep him out the whole night for me," I answered. "Do! put the key in the look, and draw the bolts."

'Earnshaw accomplished this ere his guest reached the front; he then came and brought his chair to the other side of my table, leaning over it, and searching in my eyes for a sympathy with the burning hate that gleamed from his: as he both looked and felt like an assassin, he couldn't exactly find that; but he discovered enough to encourage him to speak.

'"You, and I," he said, "have each a great debt to settle with the man out yonder! If we were neither of us cowards, we might combine to discharge it. Are you as soft as your brother? Are you willing to endure to the last, and not once attempt a repayment?"

'"I'm weary of enduring now," I replied; "and I'd be glad of a retaliation that wouldn't recoil on myself; but treachery and violence are spears pointed at both ends; they wound those who resort to them worse than their enemies."

'"Treachery and violence are a just return for treachery and violence!" cried Hindley. "Mrs. Heathcliff, I'll ask you to do nothing; but sit still and be dumb. Tell me now, can you? I'm sure you would have as much pleasure as I in witnessing the conclusion of the fiend's existence; he'll be YOUR death unless you overreach him; and he'll be MY ruin. Damn the hellish villain! He knocks at the door as if he were master here already! Promise to hold your tongue, and before that clock strikes—it wants three minutes of one—you're a free woman!"

'He took the implements which I described to you in my letter from his breast, and would have turned down the candle. I snatched it away, however, and seized his arm.

'"I'll not hold my tongue!" I said; "you mustn't touch him. Let the door remain shut, and be quiet!"

'"No! I've formed my resolution, and by God I'll execute it!" cried the desperate being. "I'll do you a kindness in spite of yourself, and Hareton justice! And you needn't trouble your head to screen me; Catherine is gone. Nobody alive would regret me, or be ashamed, though I cut my throat this minute—and it's time to make an end!"

'I might as well have struggled with a bear, or reasoned with a lunatic. The only resource left me was to run to a lattice and warn his intended victim of the fate which awaited him.

'"You'd better seek shelter somewhere else to-night!" I exclaimed, in rather a triumphant tone. "Mr. Earnshaw has a mind to shoot you, if you persist in endeavouring to enter."

'"You'd better open the door, you—" he answered, addressing me by some elegant term that I don't care to repeat.

'"I shall not meddle in the matter," I retorted again. "Come in and get shot, if you please. I've done my duty."

'With that I shut the window and returned to my place by the fire; having too small a stock of hypocrisy at my command to pretend any anxiety for the danger that menaced him. Earnshaw swore passionately at me: affirming that I loved the villain yet; and calling me all sorts of names for the base spirit I evinced. And I, in my secret heart (and conscience never reproached me), thought what a blessing it would be for HIM should Heathcliff put him out of misery; and what a blessing for ME should he send Heathcliff to his right abode! As I sat nursing these reflections, the casement behind me was banged on to the floor by a blow from the latter individual, and his black countenance looked blightingly through. The stanchions stood too close to suffer his shoulders to follow, and I smiled, exulting in my fancied security. His hair and clothes were whitened with snow, and his sharp cannibal teeth, revealed by cold and wrath, gleamed through the dark.

'"Isabella, let me in, or I'll make you repent!" he "girned," as Joseph calls it.

'"I cannot commit murder," I replied. "Mr. Hindley stands sentinel with a knife and loaded pistol."

'"Let me in by the kitchen door," he said.

'"Hindley will be there before me," I answered: "and that's a poor love of yours that cannot bear a shower of snow! We were left at peace in our beds as long as the summer moon shone, but the moment a blast of winter returns, you must run for shelter! Heathcliff, if I were you, I'd go stretch myself over her grave and die like a faithful dog. The world is surely not worth living in now, is it? You had distinctly impressed on me the idea that Catherine was the whole joy of your life: I can't imagine how you think of surviving her loss."

'"He's there, is he?" exclaimed my companion, rushing to the gap: "If I can get my arm out I can hit him!"

'I'm afraid, Ellen, you'll set me down as really wicked; but you don't know all, so don't judge. I wouldn't have aided or abetted an attempt on even HIS life for anything. Wish that he were dead, I must; and therefore I was fearfully disappointed, and unnerved by terror for the consequences of my taunting speech, when he flung himself on Earnshaw's weapon and wrenched it from his grasp.

'The charge exploded, and the knife, in springing back, closed into its owner's wrist. Heathcliff pulled it away by main force, slitting up the flesh as it passed on, and thrust it dripping into his pocket. He then took a stone, struck down the division between two windows, and sprang in. His adversary had fallen senseless with excessive pain and the flow of blood, that gushed from an artery or a large vein. The ruffian kicked and trampled on him, and dashed his head repeatedly against the flags, holding me with one hand, meantime, to prevent me summoning Joseph. He exerted preterhuman self-denial in abstaining from finishing him completely; but getting out of breath, he finally desisted, and dragged the apparently inanimate body on to the settle. There he tore off the sleeve of Earnshaw's coat, and bound up the wound with brutal roughness; spitting and cursing during the operation as energetically as he had kicked before. Being at liberty, I lost no time in seeking the old servant; who, having gathered by degrees the purport of my hasty tale, hurried below, gasping, as he descended the steps two at once.

'"What is ther to do, now? what is ther to do, now?"

'"There's this to do," thundered Heathcliff, "that your master's mad; and should he last another month, I'll have him to an asylum. And how the devil did you come to fasten me out, you toothless hound? Don't stand muttering and mumbling there. Come, I'm not going to nurse him. Wash that stuff away; and mind the sparks of your candle—it is more than half brandy!"

'"And so ye've been murthering on him?" exclaimed Joseph, lifting his hands and eyes in horror. "If iver I seed a seeght loike this! May the Lord—"

'Heathcliff gave him a push on to his knees in the middle of the blood, and flung a towel to him; but instead of proceeding to dry it up, he joined his hands and began a prayer, which excited my laughter from its odd phraseology. I was in the condition of mind to be shocked at nothing: in fact, I was as reckless as some malefactors show themselves at the foot of the gallows.

'"Oh, I forgot you," said the tyrant. "You shall do that. Down with you. And you conspire with him against me, do you, viper? There, that is work fit for you!"

'He shook me till my teeth rattled, and pitched me beside Joseph, who steadily concluded his supplications, and then rose, vowing he would set off for the Grange directly. Mr. Linton was a magistrate, and though he had fifty wives dead, he should inquire into this. He was so obstinate in his resolution, that Heathcliff deemed it expedient to compel from my lips a recapitulation of what had taken place; standing over me, heaving with malevolence, as I reluctantly delivered the account in answer to his questions. It required a great deal of labour to satisfy the old man that Heathcliff was not the aggressor; especially with my hardly-wrung replies. However, Mr. Earnshaw soon convinced him that he was alive still; Joseph hastened to administer a dose of spirits, and by their succour his master presently regained motion and consciousness. Heathcliff, aware that his opponent was ignorant of the treatment received while insensible, called him deliriously intoxicated; and said he should not notice his atrocious conduct further, but advised him to get to bed. To my joy, he left us, after giving this judicious counsel, and Hindley stretched himself on the hearthstone. I departed to my own room, marvelling that I had escaped so easily.

'This morning, when I came down, about half an hour before noon, Mr. Earnshaw was sitting by the fire, deadly sick; his evil genius, almost as gaunt and ghastly, leant against the chimney. Neither appeared inclined to dine, and, having waited till all was cold on the table, I commenced alone. Nothing hindered me from eating heartily, and I experienced a certain sense of satisfaction and superiority, as, at intervals, I cast a look towards my silent companions, and felt the comfort of a quiet conscience within me. After I had done, I ventured on the unusual liberty of drawing near the fire, going round Earnshaw's seat, and kneeling in the corner beside him.

'Heathcliff did not glance my way, and I gazed up, and contemplated his features almost as confidently as if they had been turned to stone. His forehead, that I once thought so manly, and that I now think so diabolical, was shaded with a heavy cloud; his basilisk eyes were nearly quenched by sleeplessness, and weeping, perhaps, for the lashes were wet then: his lips devoid of their ferocious sneer, and sealed in an expression of unspeakable sadness. Had it been another, I would have covered my face in the presence of such grief. In HIS case, I was gratified; and, ignoble as it seems to insult a fallen enemy, I couldn't miss this chance of sticking in a dart: his weakness was the only time when I could taste the delight of paying wrong for wrong.'

'Fie, fie, Miss!' I interrupted. 'One might suppose you had never opened a Bible in your life. If God afflict your enemies, surely that ought to suffice you. It is both mean and presumptuous to add your torture to his!'

'In general I'll allow that it would be, Ellen,' she continued; 'but what misery laid on Heathcliff could content me, unless I have a hand in it? I'd rather he suffered less, if I might cause his sufferings and he might KNOW that I was the cause. Oh, I owe him so much. On only one condition can I hope to forgive him. It is, if I may take an eye for an eye, a tooth for a tooth; for every wrench of agony return a wrench: reduce him to my level. As he was the first to injure, make him the first to implore pardon; and then—why then, Ellen, I might show you some generosity. But it is utterly impossible I can ever be revenged, and therefore I cannot forgive him. Hindley wanted some water, and I handed him a glass, and asked him how he was.

'"Not as ill as I wish," he replied. "But leaving out my arm, every inch of me is as sore as if I had been fighting with a legion of imps!"

'"Yes, no wonder," was my next remark. "Catherine used to boast that she stood between you and bodily harm: she meant that certain persons would not hurt you for fear of offending her. It's well people don't REALLY rise from their grave, or, last night, she might have witnessed a repulsive scene! Are not you bruised, and cut over your chest and shoulders?"

'"I can't say," he answered, "but what do you mean? Did he dare to strike me when I was down?"

'"He trampled on and kicked you, and dashed you on the ground," I whispered. "And his mouth watered to tear you with his teeth; because he's only half man: not so much, and the rest fiend."

'Mr. Earnshaw looked up, like me, to the countenance of our mutual foe; who, absorbed in his anguish, seemed insensible to anything around him: the longer he stood, the plainer his reflections revealed their blackness through his features.

'"Oh, if God would but give me strength to strangle him in my last agony, I'd go to hell with joy," groaned the impatient man, writhing to rise, and sinking back in despair, convinced of his inadequacy for the struggle.

'"Nay, it's enough that he has murdered one of you," I observed aloud. "At the Grange, every one knows your sister would have been living now had it not been for Mr. Heathcliff. After all, it is preferable to be hated than loved by him. When I recollect how happy we were—how happy Catherine was before he came—I'm fit to curse the day."

'Most likely, Heathcliff noticed more the truth of what was said, than the spirit of the person who said it. His attention was roused, I saw, for his eyes rained down tears among the ashes, and he drew his breath in suffocating sighs. I stared full at him, and laughed scornfully. The clouded windows of hell flashed a moment towards me; the fiend which usually looked out, however, was so dimmed and drowned that I did not fear to hazard another sound of derision.

'"Get up, and begone out of my sight," said the mourner.

'I guessed he uttered those words, at least, though his voice was hardly intelligible.

'"I beg your pardon," I replied. "But I loved Catherine too; and her brother requires attendance, which, for her sake, I shall supply. Now, that she's dead, I see her in Hindley: Hindley has exactly her eyes, if you had not tried to gouge them out, and made them black and red; and her—"

'"Get up, wretched idiot, before I stamp you to death!" he cried, making a movement that caused me to make one also.

'"But then," I continued, holding myself ready to flee, "if poor Catherine had trusted you, and assumed the ridiculous, contemptible, degrading title of Mrs. Heathcliff, she would soon have presented a similar picture! SHE wouldn't have borne your abominable behaviour quietly: her detestation and disgust must have found voice."

'The back of the settle and Earnshaw's person interposed between me and him; so instead of endeavouring to reach me, he snatched a dinner-knife from the table and flung it at my head. It struck beneath my ear, and stopped the sentence I was uttering; but, pulling it out, I sprang to the door and delivered another; which I hope went a little deeper than his missile. The last glimpse I caught of him was a furious rush on his part, checked by the embrace of his host; and both fell locked together on the hearth. In my flight through the kitchen I bid Joseph speed to his master; I knocked over Hareton, who was hanging a litter of puppies from a chair-back in the doorway; and, blessed as a soul escaped from purgatory, I bounded, leaped, and flew down the steep road; then, quitting its windings, shot direct across the moor, rolling over banks, and wading through marshes: precipitating myself, in fact, towards the beacon-light of the Grange. And far rather would I be condemned to a perpetual dwelling in the infernal regions than, even for one night, abide beneath the roof of Wuthering Heights again.'

Isabella ceased speaking, and took a drink of tea; then she rose, and bidding me put on her bonnet, and a great shawl I had brought, and turning a deaf ear to my entreaties for her to remain another hour, she stepped on to a chair, kissed Edgar's and Catherine's portraits, bestowed a similar salute on me, and descended to the carriage, accompanied by Fanny, who yelped wild with joy at recovering her mistress. She was driven away, never to revisit this neighbourhood: but a regular correspondence was established between her and my master when things were more settled. I believe her new abode was in the south, near London; there she had a son born a few months subsequent to her escape. He was christened Linton, and, from the first, she reported him to be an ailing, peevish creature.

Mr. Heathcliff, meeting me one day in the village, inquired where she lived. I refused to tell. He remarked that it was not of any moment, only she must beware of coming to her brother: she should not be with him, if he had to keep her himself. Though I would give no information, he discovered, through some of the other servants, both her place of residence and the existence of the child. Still, he didn't molest her: for which forbearance she might thank his aversion, I suppose. He often asked about the infant, when he saw me; and on hearing its name, smiled grimly, and observed: 'They wish me to hate it too, do they?'

'I don't think they wish you to know anything about it,' I answered.

'But I'll have it,' he said, 'when I want it. They may reckon on that!'

Fortunately its mother died before the time arrived; some thirteen years after the decease of Catherine, when Linton was twelve, or a little more.

On the day succeeding Isabella's unexpected visit I had no opportunity of speaking to my master: he shunned conversation, and was fit for discussing nothing. When I could get him to listen, I saw it pleased him that his sister had left her husband; whom he abhorred with an intensity which the mildness of his nature would scarcely seem to allow. So deep and sensitive was his aversion, that he refrained from going anywhere where he was likely to see or hear of Heathcliff. Grief, and that together, transformed him into a complete hermit: he threw up his office of magistrate, ceased even to attend church, avoided the village on all occasions, and spent a life of entire seclusion within the limits of his park and grounds; only varied by solitary rambles on the moors, and visits to the grave of his wife, mostly at evening, or early morning before other wanderers were abroad. But he was too good to be thoroughly unhappy long. HE didn't pray for Catherine's soul to haunt him. Time brought resignation, and a melancholy sweeter than common joy. He recalled her memory with ardent, tender love, and hopeful aspiring to the better world; where he doubted not she was gone.

And he had earthly consolation and affections also. For a few days, I said, he seemed regardless of the puny successor to the departed: that coldness melted as fast as snow in April, and ere the tiny thing could stammer a word or totter a step it wielded a despot's sceptre in his heart. It was named Catherine; but he never called it the name in full, as he had never called the first Catherine short: probably because Heathcliff had a habit of doing so. The little one was always Cathy: it formed to him a distinction from the mother, and yet a connection with her; and his attachment sprang from its relation to her, far more than from its being his own.

I used to draw a comparison between him and Hindley Earnshaw, and perplex myself to explain satisfactorily why their conduct was so opposite in similar circumstances. They had both been fond husbands, and were both attached to their children; and I could not see how they shouldn't both have taken the same road, for good or evil. But, I thought in my mind, Hindley, with apparently the stronger head, has shown himself sadly the worse and the weaker man. When his ship struck, the captain abandoned his post; and the crew, instead of trying to save her, rushed into riot and confusion, leaving no hope for their luckless vessel. Linton, on the contrary, displayed the true courage of a loyal and faithful soul: he trusted God; and God comforted him. One hoped, and the other despaired: they chose their own lots, and were righteously doomed to endure them. But you'll not want to hear my moralising, Mr. Lockwood; you'll judge, as well as I can, all these things: at least, you'll think you will, and that's the same. The end of Earnshaw was what might have been expected; it followed fast on his sister's: there were scarcely six months between them. We, at the Grange, never got a very succinct account of his state preceding it; all that I did learn was on occasion of going to aid in the preparations for the funeral. Mr. Kenneth came to announce the event to my master.

'Well, Nelly,' said he, riding into the yard one morning, too early not to alarm me with an instant presentiment of bad news, 'it's yours and my turn to go into mourning at present. Who's given us the slip now, do you think?'

'Who?' I asked in a flurry.

'Why, guess!' he returned, dismounting, and slinging his bridle on a hook by the door. 'And nip up the corner of your apron: I'm certain you'll need it.'

'Not Mr. Heathcliff, surely?' I exclaimed.

'What! would you have tears for him?' said the doctor. 'No, Heathcliff's a tough young fellow: he looks blooming to-day. I've just seen him. He's rapidly regaining flesh since he lost his better half.'

'Who is it, then, Mr. Kenneth?' I repeated impatiently.

'Hindley Earnshaw! Your old friend Hindley,' he replied, 'and my wicked gossip: though he's been too wild for me this long while. There! I said we should draw water. But cheer up! He died true to his character: drunk as a lord. Poor lad! I'm sorry, too. One can't help missing an old companion: though he had the worst tricks with him that ever man imagined, and has done me many a rascally turn. He's barely twenty-seven, it seems; that's your own age: who would have thought you were born in one year?'

I confess this blow was greater to me than the shock of Mrs. Linton's death: ancient associations lingered round my heart; I sat down in the porch and wept as for a blood relation, desiring Mr. Kenneth to get another servant to introduce him to the master. I could not hinder myself from pondering on the question—'Had he had fair play?' Whatever I did, that idea would bother me: it was so tiresomely pertinacious that I resolved on requesting leave to go to Wuthering Heights, and assist in the last duties to the dead. Mr. Linton was extremely reluctant to consent, but I pleaded eloquently for the friendless condition in which he lay; and I said my old master and foster-brother had a claim on my services as strong as his own. Besides, I reminded him that the child Hareton was his wife's nephew, and, in the absence of nearer kin, he ought to act as its guardian; and he ought to and must inquire how the property was left, and look over the concerns of his brother-in-law. He was unfit for attending to such matters then, but he bid me speak to his lawyer; and at length permitted me to go. His lawyer had been Earnshaw's also: I called at the village, and asked him to accompany me. He shook his head, and advised that Heathcliff should be let alone; affirming, if the truth were known, Hareton would be found little else than a beggar.

'His father died in debt,' he said; 'the whole property is mortgaged, and the sole chance for the natural heir is to allow him an opportunity of creating some interest in the creditor's heart, that he may be inclined to deal leniently towards him.'

When I reached the Heights, I explained that I had come to see everything carried on decently; and Joseph, who appeared in sufficient distress, expressed satisfaction at my presence. Mr. Heathcliff said he did not perceive that I was wanted; but I might stay and order the arrangements for the funeral, if I chose.

'Correctly,' he remarked, 'that fool's body should he buried at the cross-roads, without ceremony of any kind. I happened to leave him ten minutes yesterday afternoon, and in that interval he fastened the two doors of the house against me, and he has spent the night in drinking himself to death deliberately! We broke in this morning, for we heard him sporting like a horse; and there he was, laid over the settle: flaying and scalping would not have wakened him. I sent for Kenneth, and he came; but not till the beast had changed into carrion: he was both dead and cold, and stark; and so you'll allow it was useless making more stir about him!'

The old servant confirmed this statement, but muttered:

'I'd rayther he'd goan hisseln for t' doctor! I sud ha,' taen tent o' t' maister better nor him—and he warn't deead when I left, naught o' t' soart!'

I insisted on the funeral being respectable. Mr. Heathcliff said I might have my own way there too: only, he desired me to remember that the money for the whole affair came out of his pocket. He maintained a hard, careless deportment, indicative of neither joy nor sorrow: if anything, it expressed a flinty gratification at a piece of difficult work successfully executed. I observed once, indeed, something like exultation in his aspect: it was just when the people were bearing the coffin from the house. He had the hypocrisy to represent a mourner: and previous to following with Hareton, he lifted the unfortunate child on to the table and muttered, with peculiar gusto, 'Now, my bonny lad, you are MINE! And we'll see if one tree won't grow as crooked as another, with the same wind to twist it!' The unsuspecting thing was pleased at this speech: he played with Heathcliff's whiskers, and stroked his cheek; but I divined its meaning, and observed tartly, 'That boy must go back with me to Thrushcross Grange, sir. There is nothing in the world less yours than he is!'

'Does Linton say so?' he demanded.

'Of course—he has ordered me to take him,' I replied.

'Well,' said the scoundrel, 'we'll not argue the subject now: but I have a fancy to try my hand at rearing a young one; so intimate to your master that I must supply the place of this with my own, if he attempt to remove it. I don't engage to let Hareton go undisputed; but I'll be pretty sure to make the other come! Remember to tell him.'

This hint was enough to bind our hands. I repeated its substance on my return; and Edgar Linton, little interested at the commencement, spoke no more of interfering. I'm not aware that he could have done it to any purpose, had he been ever so willing.

The guest was now the master of Wuthering Heights: he held firm possession, and proved to the attorney—who, in his turn, proved it to Mr. Linton—that Earnshaw had mortgaged every yard of land he owned for cash to supply his mania for gaming; and he, Heathcliff, was the mortgagee. In that manner Hareton, who should now be the first gentleman in the neighbourhood, was reduced to a state of complete dependence on his father's inveterate enemy; and lives in his own house as a servant, deprived of the advantage of wages: quite unable to right himself, because of his friendlessness, and his ignorance that he has been wronged.

Chapter XVIII

THE twelve years, continued Mrs. Dean, following that dismal period were the happiest of my life: my greatest troubles in their passage rose from our little lady's trifling illnesses, which she had to experience in common with all children, rich and poor. For the rest, after the first six months, she grew like a larch, and could walk and talk too, in her own way, before the heath blossomed a second time over Mrs. Linton's dust. She was the most winning thing that ever brought sunshine into a desolate house: a real beauty in face, with the Earnshaws' handsome dark eyes, but the Lintons' fair skin and small features, and yellow curling hair. Her spirit was high, though not rough, and qualified by a heart sensitive and lively to excess in its affections. That capacity for intense attachments reminded me of her mother: still she did not resemble her: for she could be soft and mild as a dove, and she had a gentle voice and pensive expression: her anger was never furious; her love never fierce: it was deep and tender. However, it must be acknowledged, she had faults to foil her gifts. A propensity to be saucy was one; and a perverse will, that indulged children invariably acquire, whether they be good tempered or cross. If a servant chanced to vex her, it was always—'I shall tell papa!' And if he reproved her, even by a look, you would have thought it a heart-breaking business: I don't believe he ever did speak a harsh word to her. He took her education entirely on himself, and made it an amusement. Fortunately, curiosity and a quick intellect made her an apt scholar: she learned rapidly and eagerly, and did honour to his teaching.

Till she reached the age of thirteen she had not once been beyond the range of the park by herself. Mr. Linton would take her with him a mile or so outside, on rare occasions; but he trusted her to no one else. Gimmerton was an unsubstantial name in her ears; the chapel, the only building she had approached or entered, except her own home. Wuthering Heights and Mr. Heathcliff did not exist for her: she was a perfect recluse; and, apparently, perfectly contented. Sometimes, indeed, while surveying the country from her nursery window, she would observe—

'Ellen, how long will it be before I can walk to the top of those hills? I wonder what lies on the other side—is it the sea?'

'No, Miss Cathy,' I would answer; 'it is hills again, just like these.'

'And what are those golden rocks like when you stand under them?' she once asked.

The abrupt descent of Penistone Crags particularly attracted her notice; especially when the setting sun shone on it and the topmost heights, and the whole extent of landscape besides lay in shadow. I explained that they were bare masses of stone, with hardly enough earth in their clefts to nourish a stunted tree.

'And why are they bright so long after it is evening here?' she pursued.

'Because they are a great deal higher up than we are,' replied I; 'you could not climb them, they are too high and steep. In winter the frost is always there before it comes to us; and deep into summer I have found snow under that black hollow on the north-east side!'

'Oh, you have been on them!' she cried gleefully. 'Then I can go, too, when I am a woman. Has papa been, Ellen?'

'Papa would tell you, Miss,' I answered, hastily, 'that they are not worth the trouble of visiting. The moors, where you ramble with him, are much nicer; and Thrushcross Park is the finest place in the world.'

'But I know the park, and I don't know those,' she murmured to herself. 'And I should delight to look round me from the brow of that tallest point: my little pony Minny shall take me some time.'

One of the maids mentioning the Fairy Cave, quite turned her head with a desire to fulfil this project: she teased Mr. Linton about it; and he promised she should have the journey when she got older. But Miss Catherine measured her age by months, and, 'Now, am I old enough to go to Penistone Crags?' was the constant question in her mouth. The road thither wound close by Wuthering Heights. Edgar had not the heart to pass it; so she received as constantly the answer, 'Not yet, love: not yet.'

I said Mrs. Heathcliff lived above a dozen years after quitting her husband. Her family were of a delicate constitution: she and Edgar both lacked the ruddy health that you will generally meet in these parts. What her last illness was, I am not certain: I conjecture, they died of the same thing, a kind of fever, slow at its commencement, but incurable, and rapidly consuming life towards the close. She wrote to inform her brother of the probable conclusion of a four-months' indisposition under which she had suffered, and entreated him to come to her, if possible; for she had much to settle, and she wished to bid him adieu, and deliver Linton safely into his hands. Her hope was that Linton might be left with him, as he had been with her: his father, she would fain convince herself, had no desire to assume the burden of his maintenance or education. My master hesitated not a moment in complying with her request: reluctant as he was to leave home at ordinary calls, he flew to answer this; commanding Catherine to my peculiar vigilance, in his absence, with reiterated orders that she must not wander out of the park, even under my escort he did not calculate on her going unaccompanied.

He was away three weeks. The first day or two my charge sat in a corner of the library, too sad for either reading or playing: in that quiet state she caused me little trouble; but it was succeeded by an interval of impatient, fretful weariness; and being too busy, and too old then, to run up and down amusing her, I hit on a method by which she might entertain herself. I used to send her on her travels round the grounds—now on foot, and now on a pony; indulging her with a patient audience of all her real and imaginary adventures when she returned.

The summer shone in full prime; and she took such a taste for this solitary rambling that she often contrived to remain out from breakfast till tea; and then the evenings were spent in recounting her fanciful tales. I did not fear her breaking bounds; because the gates were generally looked, and I thought she would scarcely venture forth alone, if they had stood wide open. Unluckily, my confidence proved misplaced. Catherine came to me, one morning, at eight o'clock, and said she was that day an Arabian merchant, going to cross the Desert with his caravan; and I must give her plenty of provision for herself and beasts: a horse, and three camels, personated by a large hound and a couple of pointers. I got together good store of dainties, and slung them in a basket on one side of the saddle; and she sprang up as gay as a fairy, sheltered by her wide-brimmed hat and gauze veil from the July sun, and trotted off with a merry laugh, mocking my cautious counsel to avoid galloping, and come back early. The naughty thing never made her appearance at tea. One traveller, the hound, being an old dog and fond of its ease, returned; but neither Cathy, nor the pony, nor the two pointers were visible in any direction: I despatched emissaries down this path, and that path, and at last went wandering in search of her myself. There was a labourer working at a fence round a plantation, on the borders of the grounds. I inquired of him if he had seen our young lady.

'I saw her at morn,' he replied: 'she would have me to cut her a hazel switch, and then she leapt her Galloway over the hedge yonder, where it is lowest, and galloped out of sight.'

You may guess how I felt at hearing this news. It struck me directly she must have started for Penistone Crags. 'What will become of her?' I ejaculated, pushing through a gap which the man was repairing, and making straight to the high-road. I walked as if for a wager, mile after mile, till a turn brought me in view of the Heights; but no Catherine could I detect, far or near. The Crags lie about a mile and a half beyond Mr. Heathcliff's place, and that is four from the Grange, so I began to fear night would fall ere I could reach them. 'And what if she should have slipped in clambering among them,' I reflected, 'and been killed, or broken some of her bones?' My suspense was truly painful; and, at first, it gave me delightful relief to observe, in hurrying by the farmhouse, Charlie, the fiercest of the pointers, lying under a window, with swelled head and bleeding ear. I opened the wicket and ran to the door, knocking vehemently for admittance. A woman whom I knew, and who formerly lived at Gimmerton, answered: she had been servant there since the death of Mr. Earnshaw.

'Ah,' said she, 'you are come a-seeking your little mistress! Don't be frightened. She's here safe: but I'm glad it isn't the master.'

'He is not at home then, is he?' I panted, quite breathless with quick walking and alarm.

'No, no,' she replied: 'both he and Joseph are off, and I think they won't return this hour or more. Step in and rest you a bit.'

I entered, and beheld my stray lamb seated on the hearth, rocking herself in a little chair that had been her mother's when a child.

Her hat was hung against the wall, and she seemed perfectly at home, laughing and chattering, in the best spirits imaginable, to Hareton—now a great, strong lad of eighteen—who stared at her with considerable curiosity and astonishment: comprehending precious little of the fluent succession of remarks and questions which her tongue never ceased pouring forth.

'Very well, Miss!' I exclaimed, concealing my joy under an angry countenance. 'This is your last ride, till papa comes back. I'll not trust you over the threshold again, you naughty, naughty girl!'

'Aha, Ellen!' she cried, gaily, jumping up and running to my side. 'I shall have a pretty story to tell to-night; and so you've found me out. Have you ever been here in your life before?'

'Put that hat on, and home at once,' said I. 'I'm dreadfully grieved at you, Miss Cathy: you've done extremely wrong! It's no use pouting and crying: that won't repay the trouble I've had, scouring the country after you. To think how Mr. Linton charged me to keep you in; and you stealing off so! It shows you are a cunning little fox, and nobody will put faith in you any more.'

'What have I done?' sobbed she, instantly checked. 'Papa charged me nothing: he'll not scold me, Ellen—he's never cross, like you!'

'Come, come!' I repeated. 'I'll tie the riband. Now, let us have no petulance. Oh, for shame! You thirteen years old, and such a baby!'

This exclamation was caused by her pushing the hat from her head, and retreating to the chimney out of my reach.

'Nay,' said the servant, 'don't be hard on the bonny lass, Mrs. Dean. We made her stop: she'd fain have ridden forwards, afeard you should be uneasy. Hareton offered to go with her, and I thought he should: it's a wild road over the hills.'

Hareton, during the discussion, stood with his hands in his pockets, too awkward to speak; though he looked as if he did not relish my intrusion.

'How long am I to wait?' I continued, disregarding the woman's interference. 'It will be dark in ten minutes. Where is the pony, Miss Cathy? And where is Phoenix? I shall leave you, unless you be quick; so please yourself.'

'The pony is in the yard,' she replied, 'and Phoenix is shut in there. He's bitten—and so is Charlie. I was going to tell you all about it; but you are in a bad temper, and don't deserve to hear.'

I picked up her hat, and approached to reinstate it; but perceiving that the people of the house took her part, she commenced capering round the room; and on my giving chase, ran like a mouse over and under and behind the furniture, rendering it ridiculous for me to pursue. Hareton and the woman laughed, and she joined them, and waxed more impertinent still; till I cried, in great irritation,—'Well, Miss Cathy, if you were aware whose house this is you'd be glad enough to get out.'

'It's YOUR father's, isn't it?' said she, turning to Hareton.

'Nay,' he replied, looking down, and blushing bashfully.

He could not stand a steady gaze from her eyes, though they were just his own.

'Whose then—your master's?' she asked.

He coloured deeper, with a different feeling, muttered an oath, and turned away.

'Who is his master?' continued the tiresome girl, appealing to me. 'He talked about "our house," and "our folk." I thought he had been the owner's son. And he never said Miss: he should have done, shouldn't he, if he's a servant?'

Hareton grew black as a thunder-cloud at this childish speech. I silently shook my questioner, and at last succeeded in equipping her for departure.

'Now, get my horse,' she said, addressing her unknown kinsman as she would one of the stable-boys at the Grange. 'And you may come with me. I want to see where the goblin-hunter rises in the marsh, and to hear about the FAIRISHES, as you call them: but make haste! What's the matter? Get my horse, I say.'

'I'll see thee damned before I be THY servant!' growled the lad.

"You'll see me WHAT!' asked Catherine in surprise.

'Damned—thou saucy witch!' he replied.

'There, Miss Cathy! you see you have got into pretty company,' I interposed. 'Nice words to be used to a young lady! Pray don't begin to dispute with him. Come, let us seek for Minny ourselves, and begone.'

'But, Ellen,' cried she, staring fixed in astonishment, 'how dare he speak so to me? Mustn't he be made to do as I ask him? You wicked creature, I shall tell papa what you said.—Now, then!'

Hareton did not appear to feel this threat; so the tears sprang into her eyes with indignation. 'You bring the pony,' she exclaimed, turning to the woman, 'and let my dog free this moment!'

'Softly, Miss,' answered she addressed: 'you'll lose nothing by being civil. Though Mr. Hareton, there, be not the master's son, he's your cousin: and I was never hired to serve you.'

'HE my cousin!' cried Cathy, with a scornful laugh.

'Yes, indeed,' responded her reprover.

'Oh, Ellen! don't let them say such things,' she pursued in great trouble. 'Papa is gone to fetch my cousin from London: my cousin is a gentleman's son. That my—' she stopped, and wept outright; upset at the bare notion of relationship with such a clown.

'Hush, hush!' I whispered; 'people can have many cousins and of all sorts, Miss Cathy, without being any the worse for it; only they needn't keep their company, if they be disagreeable and bad.'

'He's not—he's not my cousin, Ellen!' she went on, gathering fresh grief from reflection, and flinging herself into my arms for refuge from the idea.

I was much vexed at her and the servant for their mutual revelations; having no doubt of Linton's approaching arrival, communicated by the former, being reported to Mr. Heathcliff; and feeling as confident that Catherine's first thought on her father's return would be to seek an explanation of the latter's assertion concerning her rude-bred kindred. Hareton, recovering from his disgust at being taken for a servant, seemed moved by her distress; and, having fetched the pony round to the door, he took, to propitiate her, a fine crooked-legged terrier whelp from the kennel, and putting it into her hand, bid her whist! for he meant nought. Pausing in her lamentations, she surveyed him with a glance of awe and horror, then burst forth anew.

I could scarcely refrain from smiling at this antipathy to the poor fellow; who was a well-made, athletic youth, good-looking in features, and stout and healthy, but attired in garments befitting his daily occupations of working on the farm and lounging among the moors after rabbits and game. Still, I thought I could detect in his physiognomy a mind owning better qualities than his father ever possessed. Good things lost amid a wilderness of weeds, to be sure, whose rankness far over-topped their neglected growth; yet, notwithstanding, evidence of a wealthy soil, that might yield luxuriant crops under other and favourable circumstances. Mr. Heathcliff, I believe, had not treated him physically ill; thanks to his fearless nature, which offered no temptation to that course of oppression: he had none of the timid susceptibility that would have given zest to ill-treatment, in Heathcliff s judgment. He appeared to have bent his malevolence on making him a brute: he was never taught to read or write; never rebuked for any bad habit which did not annoy his keeper; never led a single step towards virtue, or guarded by a single precept against vice. And from what I heard, Joseph contributed much to his deterioration, by a narrow-minded partiality which prompted him to flatter and pet him, as a boy, because he was the head of the old family. And as he had been in the habit of accusing Catherine Earnshaw and Heathcliff, when children, of putting the master past his patience, and compelling him to seek solace in drink by what he termed their 'offald ways,' so at present he laid the whole burden of Hareton's faults on the shoulders of the usurper of his property. If the lad swore, he wouldn't correct him: nor however culpably he behaved. It gave Joseph satisfaction, apparently, to watch him go the worst lengths: he allowed that the lad was ruined: that his soul was abandoned to perdition; but then he reflected that Heathcliff must answer for it. Hareton's blood would be required at his hands; and there lay immense consolation in that thought. Joseph had instilled into him a pride of name, and of his lineage; he would, had he dared, have fostered hate between him and the present owner of the Heights: but his dread of that owner amounted to superstition; and he confined his feelings regarding him to muttered innuendoes and private comminations. I don't pretend to be intimately acquainted with the mode of living customary in those days at Wuthering Heights: I only speak from hearsay; for I saw little. The villagers affirmed Mr. Heathcliff was NEAR, and a cruel hard landlord to his tenants; but the house, inside, had regained its ancient aspect of comfort under female management, and the scenes of riot common in Hindley's time were not now enacted within its walls. The master was too gloomy to seek companionship with any people, good or bad; and he is yet.

This, however, is not making progress with my story. Miss Cathy rejected the peace-offering of the terrier, and demanded her own dogs, Charlie and Phoenix. They came limping and hanging their heads; and we set out for home, sadly out of sorts, every one of us. I could not wring from my little lady how she had spent the day; except that, as I supposed, the goal of her pilgrimage was Penistone Crags; and she arrived without adventure to the gate of the farm-house, when Hareton happened to issue forth, attended by some canine followers, who attacked her train. They had a smart battle, before their owners could separate them: that formed an introduction. Catherine told Hareton who she was, and where she was going; and asked him to show her the way: finally, beguiling him to accompany her. He opened the mysteries of the Fairy Cave, and twenty other queer places. But, being in disgrace, I was not favoured with a description of the interesting objects she saw. I could gather, however, that her guide had been a favourite till she hurt his feelings by addressing him as a servant; and Heathcliff's housekeeper hurt hers by calling him her cousin. Then the language he had held to her rankled in her heart; she who was always 'love,' and 'darling,' and 'queen,' and 'angel,' with everybody at the Grange, to be insulted so shockingly by a stranger! She did not comprehend it; and hard work I had to obtain a promise that she would not lay the grievance before her father. I explained how he objected to the whole household at the Heights, and how sorry he would be to find she had been there; but I insisted most on the fact, that if she revealed my negligence of his orders, he would perhaps be so angry that I should have to leave; and Cathy couldn't bear that prospect: she pledged her word, and kept it for my sake. After all, she was a sweet little girl.

Chapter XIX

A LETTER, edged with black, announced the day of my master's return, Isabella was dead; and he wrote to bid me get mourning for his daughter, and arrange a room, and other accommodations, for his youthful nephew. Catherine ran wild with joy at the idea of welcoming her father back; and indulged most sanguine anticipations of the innumerable excellencies of her 'real' cousin. The evening of their expected arrival came. Since early morning she had been busy ordering her own small affairs; and now attired in her new black frock—poor thing! her aunt's death impressed her with no definite sorrow—she obliged me, by constant worrying, to walk with her down through the grounds to meet them.

'Linton is just six months younger than I am,' she chattered, as we strolled leisurely over the swells and hollows of mossy turf, under shadow of the trees. 'How delightful it will be to have him for a playfellow! Aunt Isabella sent papa a beautiful lock of his hair; it was lighter than mine—more flaxen, and quite as fine. I have it carefully preserved in a little glass box; and I've often thought what a pleasure it would be to see its owner. Oh! I am happy—and papa, dear, dear papa! Come, Ellen, let us run! come, run.'

She ran, and returned and ran again, many times before my sober footsteps reached the gate, and then she seated herself on the grassy bank beside the path, and tried to wait patiently; but that was impossible: she couldn't be still a minute.

'How long they are!' she exclaimed. 'Ah, I see, some dust on the road—they are coming! No! When will they be here? May we not go a little way—half a mile, Ellen, only just half a mile? Do say Yes: to that clump of birches at the turn!'

I refused staunchly. At length her suspense was ended: the travelling carriage rolled in sight. Miss Cathy shrieked and stretched out her arms as soon as she caught her father's face looking from the window. He descended, nearly as eager as herself; and a considerable interval elapsed ere they had a thought to spare for any but themselves. While they exchanged caresses I took a peep in to see after Linton. He was asleep in a corner, wrapped in a warm, fur-lined cloak, as if it had been winter. A pale, delicate, effeminate boy, who might have been taken for my master's younger brother, so strong was the resemblance: but there was a sickly peevishness in his aspect that Edgar Linton never had. The latter saw me looking; and having shaken hands, advised me to close the door, and leave him undisturbed; for the journey had fatigued him. Cathy would fain have taken one glance, but her father told her to come, and they walked together up the park, while I hastened before to prepare the servants.

'Now, darling,' said Mr. Linton, addressing his daughter, as they halted at the bottom of the front steps: 'your cousin is not so strong or so merry as you are, and he has lost his mother, remember, a very short time since; therefore, don't expect him to play and run about with you directly. And don't harass him much by talking: let him be quiet this evening, at least, will you?'

'Yes, yes, papa,' answered Catherine: 'but I do want to see him; and he hasn't once looked out.'

The carriage stopped; and the sleeper being roused, was lifted to the ground by his uncle.

'This is your cousin Cathy, Linton,' he said, putting their little hands together. 'She's fond of you already; and mind you don't grieve her by crying to-night. Try to be cheerful now; the travelling is at an end, and you have nothing to do but rest and amuse yourself as you please.'

'Let me go to bed, then,' answered the boy, shrinking from Catherine's salute; and he put his fingers to remove incipient tears.

'Come, come, there's a good child,' I whispered, leading him in. 'You'll make her weep too—see how sorry she is for you!'

I do not know whether it was sorrow for him, but his cousin put on as sad a countenance as himself, and returned to her father. All three entered, and mounted to the library, where tea was laid ready. I proceeded to remove Linton's cap and mantle, and placed him on a chair by the table; but he was no sooner seated than he began to cry afresh. My master inquired what was the matter.

'I can't sit on a chair,' sobbed the boy.

'Go to the sofa, then, and Ellen shall bring you some tea,' answered his uncle patiently.

He had been greatly tried, during the journey, I felt convinced, by his fretful ailing charge. Linton slowly trailed himself off, and lay down. Cathy carried a footstool and her cup to his side. At first she sat silent; but that could not last: she had resolved to make a pet of her little cousin, as she would have him to be; and she commenced stroking his curls, and kissing his cheek, and offering him tea in her saucer, like a baby. This pleased him, for he was not much better: he dried his eyes, and lightened into a faint smile.

'Oh, he'll do very well,' said the master to me, after watching them a minute. 'Very well, if we can keep him, Ellen. The company of a child of his own age will instil new spirit into him soon, and by wishing for strength he'll gain it.'

'Ay, if we can keep him!' I mused to myself; and sore misgivings came over me that there was slight hope of that. And then, I thought, how ever will that weakling live at Wuthering Heights? Between his father and Hareton, what playmates and instructors they'll be. Our doubts were presently decided—even earlier than I expected. I had just taken the children up-stairs, after tea was finished, and seen Linton asleep—he would not suffer me to leave him till that was the case—I had come down, and was standing by the table in the hall, lighting a bedroom candle for Mr. Edgar, when a maid stepped out of the kitchen and informed me that Mr. Heathcliff's servant Joseph was at the door, and wished to speak with the master.

'I shall ask him what he wants first,' I said, in considerable trepidation. 'A very unlikely hour to be troubling people, and the instant they have returned from a long journey. I don't think the master can see him.'

Joseph had advanced through the kitchen as I uttered these words, and now presented himself in the hall. He was donned in his Sunday garments, with his most sanctimonious and sourest face, and, holding his hat in one hand, and his stick in the other, he proceeded to clean his shoes on the mat.

'Good-evening, Joseph,' I said, coldly. 'What business brings you here to-night?'

'It's Maister Linton I mun spake to,' he answered, waving me disdainfully aside.

'Mr. Linton is going to bed; unless you have something particular to say, I'm sure he won't hear it now,' I continued. 'You had better sit down in there, and entrust your message to me.'

'Which is his rahm?' pursued the fellow, surveying the range of closed doors.

I perceived he was bent on refusing my mediation, so very reluctantly I went up to the library, and announced the unseasonable visitor, advising that he should be dismissed till next day. Mr. Linton had no time to empower me to do so, for Joseph mounted close at my heels, and, pushing into the apartment, planted himself at the far side of the table, with his two fists clapped on the head of his stick, and began in an elevated tone, as if anticipating opposition—

'Hathecliff has sent me for his lad, and I munn't goa back 'bout him.'

Edgar Linton was silent a minute; an expression of exceeding sorrow overcast his features: he would have pitied the child on his own account; but, recalling Isabella's hopes and fears, and anxious wishes for her son, and her commendations of him to his care, he grieved bitterly at the prospect of yielding him up, and searched in his heart how it might be avoided. No plan offered itself: the very exhibition of any desire to keep him would have rendered the claimant more peremptory: there was nothing left but to resign him. However, he was not going to rouse him from his sleep.

'Tell Mr. Heathcliff,' he answered calmly, 'that his son shall come to Wuthering Heights to-morrow. He is in bed, and too tired to go the distance now. You may also tell him that the mother of Linton desired him to remain under my guardianship; and, at present, his health is very precarious.'

'Noa!' said Joseph, giving a thud with his prop on the floor, and assuming an authoritative air. 'Noa! that means naught. Hathecliff maks noa 'count o' t' mother, nor ye norther; but he'll heu' his lad; und I mun tak' him—soa now ye knaw!'

'You shall not to-night!' answered Linton decisively. 'Walk down stairs at once, and repeat to your master what I have said. Ellen, show him down. Go—'

And, aiding the indignant elder with a lift by the arm, he rid the room of him and closed the door.

'Varrah weell!' shouted Joseph, as he slowly drew off. 'To-morn, he's come hisseln, and thrust HIM out, if ye darr!'

Chapter XX

TO obviate the danger of this threat being fulfilled, Mr. Linton commissioned me to take the boy home early, on Catherine's pony; and, said he—'As we shall now have no influence over his destiny, good or bad, you must say nothing of where he is gone to my daughter: she cannot associate with him hereafter, and it is better for her to remain in ignorance of his proximity; lest she should be restless, and anxious to visit the Heights. Merely tell her his father sent for him suddenly, and he has been obliged to leave us.'

Linton was very reluctant to be roused from his bed at five o'clock, and astonished to be informed that he must prepare for further travelling; but I softened off the matter by stating that he was going to spend some time with his father, Mr. Heathcliff, who wished to see him so much, he did not like to defer the pleasure till he should recover from his late journey.

'My father!' he cried, in strange perplexity. 'Mamma never told me I had a father. Where does he live? I'd rather stay with uncle.'

'He lives a little distance from the Grange,' I replied; 'just beyond those hills: not so far, but you may walk over here when you get hearty. And you should be glad to go home, and to see him. You must try to love him, as you did your mother, and then he will love you.'

'But why have I not heard of him before?' asked Linton. 'Why didn't mamma and he live together, as other people do?'

'He had business to keep him in the north,' I answered, 'and your mother's health required her to reside in the south.'

'And why didn't mamma speak to me about him?' persevered the child. 'She often talked of uncle, and I learnt to love him long ago. How am I to love papa? I don't know him.'

'Oh, all children love their parents,' I said. 'Your mother, perhaps, thought you would want to be with him if she mentioned him often to you. Let us make haste. An early ride on such a beautiful morning is much preferable to an hour's more sleep.'

'Is SHE to go with us,' he demanded, 'the little girl I saw yesterday?'

'Not now,' replied I.

'Is uncle?' he continued.

'No, I shall be your companion there,' I said.

Linton sank back on his pillow and fell into a brown study.

'I won't go without uncle,' he cried at length: 'I can't tell where you mean to take me.'

I attempted to persuade him of the naughtiness of showing reluctance to meet his father; still he obstinately resisted any progress towards dressing, and I had to call for my master's assistance in coaxing him out of bed. The poor thing was finally got off, with several delusive assurances that his absence should be short: that Mr. Edgar and Cathy would visit him, and other promises, equally ill-founded, which I invented and reiterated at intervals throughout the way. The pure heather-scented air, the bright sunshine, and the gentle canter of Minny, relieved his despondency after a while. He began to put questions concerning his new home, and its inhabitants, with greater interest and liveliness.

'Is Wuthering Heights as pleasant a place as Thrushcross Grange?' he inquired, turning to take a last glance into the valley, whence a light mist mounted and formed a fleecy cloud on the skirts of the blue.

'It is not so buried in trees,' I replied, 'and it is not quite so large, but you can see the country beautifully all round; and the air is healthier for you—fresher and drier. You will, perhaps, think the building old and dark at first; though it is a respectable house: the next best in the neighbourhood. And you will have such nice rambles on the moors. Hareton Earnshaw—that is, Miss Cathy's other cousin, and so yours in a manner—will show you all the sweetest spots; and you can bring a book in fine weather, and make a green hollow your study; and, now and then, your uncle may join you in a walk: he does, frequently, walk out on the hills.'

'And what is my father like?' he asked. 'Is he as young and handsome as uncle?'

'He's as young,' said I; 'but he has black hair and eyes, and looks sterner; and he is taller and bigger altogether. He'll not seem to you so gentle and kind at first, perhaps, because it is not his way: still, mind you, be frank and cordial with him; and naturally he'll be fonder of you than any uncle, for you are his own.'

'Black hair and eyes!' mused Linton. 'I can't fancy him. Then I am not like him, am I?'

'Not much,' I answered: not a morsel, I thought, surveying with regret the white complexion and slim frame of my companion, and his large languid eyes—his mother's eyes, save that, unless a morbid touchiness kindled them a moment, they had not a vestige of her sparkling spirit.

'How strange that he should never come to see mamma and me!' he murmured. 'Has he ever seen me? If he has, I must have been a baby. I remember not a single thing about him!'

'Why, Master Linton,' said I, 'three hundred miles is a great distance; and ten years seem very different in length to a grown-up person compared with what they do to you. It is probable Mr. Heathcliff proposed going from summer to summer, but never found a convenient opportunity; and now it is too late. Don't trouble him with questions on the subject: it will disturb him, for no good.'

The boy was fully occupied with his own cogitations for the remainder of the ride, till we halted before the farmhouse garden-gate. I watched to catch his impressions in his countenance. He surveyed the carved front and low-browed lattices, the straggling gooseberry-bushes and crooked firs, with solemn intentness, and then shook his head: his private feelings entirely disapproved of the exterior of his new abode. But he had sense to postpone complaining: there might be compensation within. Before he dismounted, I went and opened the door. It was half-past six; the family had just finished breakfast: the servant was clearing and wiping down the table. Joseph stood by his master's chair telling some tale concerning a lame horse; and Hareton was preparing for the hayfield.

'Hallo, Nelly!' said Mr. Heathcliff, when he saw me. 'I feared I should have to come down and fetch my property myself. You've brought it, have you? Let us see what we can make of it.'

He got up and strode to the door: Hareton and Joseph followed in gaping curiosity. Poor Linton ran a frightened eye over the faces of the three.

'Sure-ly,' said Joseph after a grave inspection, 'he's swopped wi' ye, Maister, an' yon's his lass!'

Heathcliff, having stared his son into an ague of confusion, uttered a scornful laugh.

'God! what a beauty! what a lovely, charming thing!' he exclaimed. 'Hav'n't they reared it on snails and sour milk, Nelly? Oh, damn my soul! but that's worse than I expected—and the devil knows I was not sanguine!'

I bid the trembling and bewildered child get down, and enter. He did not thoroughly comprehend the meaning of his father's speech, or whether it were intended for him: indeed, he was not yet certain that the grim, sneering stranger was his father. But he clung to me with growing trepidation; and on Mr. Heathcliff's taking a seat and bidding him 'come hither' he hid his face on my shoulder and wept.

'Tut, tut!' said Heathcliff, stretching out a hand and dragging him roughly between his knees, and then holding up his head by the chin. 'None of that nonsense! We're not going to hurt thee, Linton—isn't that thy name? Thou art thy mother's child, entirely! Where is my share in thee, puling chicken?'

He took off the boy's cap and pushed back his thick flaxen curls, felt his slender arms and his small fingers; during which examination Linton ceased crying, and lifted his great blue eyes to inspect the inspector.

'Do you know me?' asked Heathcliff, having satisfied himself that the limbs were all equally frail and feeble.

'No,' said Linton, with a gaze of vacant fear.

'You've heard of me, I daresay?'

'No,' he replied again.

'No! What a shame of your mother, never to waken your filial regard for me! You are my son, then, I'll tell you; and your mother was a wicked slut to leave you in ignorance of the sort of father you possessed. Now, don't wince, and colour up! Though it is something to see you have not white blood. Be a good lad; and I'll do for you. Nelly, if you be tired you may sit down; if not, get home again. I guess you'll report what you hear and see to the cipher at the Grange; and this thing won't be settled while you linger about it.'

'Well,' replied I, 'I hope you'll be kind to the boy, Mr. Heathcliff, or you'll not keep him long; and he's all you have akin in the wide world, that you will ever know—remember.'

'I'll be very kind to him, you needn't fear,' he said, laughing. 'Only nobody else must be kind to him: I'm jealous of monopolising his affection. And, to begin my kindness, Joseph, bring the lad some breakfast. Hareton, you infernal calf, begone to your work. Yes, Nell,' he added, when they had departed, 'my son is prospective owner of your place, and I should not wish him to die till I was certain of being his successor. Besides, he's MINE, and I want the triumph of seeing MY descendant fairly lord of their estates; my child hiring their children to till their fathers' lands for wages. That is the sole consideration which can make me endure the whelp: I despise him for himself, and hate him for the memories he revives! But that consideration is sufficient: he's as safe with me, and shall be tended as carefully as your master tends his own. I have a room up-stairs, furnished for him in handsome style; I've engaged a tutor, also, to come three times a week, from twenty miles' distance, to teach him what he pleases to learn. I've ordered Hareton to obey him: and in fact I've arranged everything with a view to preserve the superior and the gentleman in him, above his associates. I do regret, however, that he so little deserves the trouble: if I wished any blessing in the world, it was to find him a worthy object of pride; and I'm bitterly disappointed with the whey-faced, whining wretch!'

While he was speaking, Joseph returned bearing a basin of milk-porridge, and placed it before Linton: who stirred round the homely mess with a look of aversion, and affirmed he could not eat it. I saw the old man-servant shared largely in his master's scorn of the child; though he was compelled to retain the sentiment in his heart, because Heathcliff plainly meant his underlings to hold him in honour.

'Cannot ate it?' repeated he, peering in Linton's face, and subduing his voice to a whisper, for fear of being overheard. 'But Maister Hareton nivir ate naught else, when he wer a little 'un; and what wer gooid enough for him's gooid enough for ye, I's rayther think!'

'I SHA'N'T eat it!' answered Linton, snappishly. 'Take it away.'

Joseph snatched up the food indignantly, and brought it to us.

'Is there aught ails th' victuals?' he asked, thrusting the tray under Heathcliff's nose.

'What should ail them?' he said.

'Wah!' answered Joseph, 'yon dainty chap says he cannut ate 'em. But I guess it's raight! His mother wer just soa—we wer a'most too mucky to sow t' corn for makking her breead.'

'Don't mention his mother to me,' said the master, angrily. 'Get him something that he can eat, that's all. What is his usual food, Nelly?'

I suggested boiled milk or tea; and the housekeeper received instructions to prepare some. Come, I reflected, his father's selfishness may contribute to his comfort. He perceives his delicate constitution, and the necessity of treating him tolerably. I'll console Mr. Edgar by acquainting him with the turn Heathcliff's humour has taken. Having no excuse for lingering longer, I slipped out, while Linton was engaged in timidly rebuffing the advances of a friendly sheep-dog. But he was too much on the alert to be cheated: as I closed the door, I heard a cry, and a frantic repetition of the words—

'Don't leave me! I'll not stay here! I'll not stay here!'

Then the latch was raised and fell: they did not suffer him to come forth. I mounted Minny, and urged her to a trot; and so my brief guardianship ended.

Chapter XXI

WE had sad work with little Cathy that day: she rose in high glee, eager to join her cousin, and such passionate tears and lamentations followed the news of his departure that Edgar himself was obliged to soothe her, by affirming he should come back soon: he added, however, 'if I can get him'; and there were no hopes of that. This promise poorly pacified her; but time was more potent; and though still at intervals she inquired of her father when Linton would return, before she did see him again his features had waxed so dim in her memory that she did not recognise him.

When I chanced to encounter the housekeeper of Wuthering Heights, in paying business visits to Gimmerton, I used to ask how the young master got on; for he lived almost as secluded as Catherine herself, and was never to be seen. I could gather from her that he continued in weak health, and was a tiresome inmate. She said Mr. Heathcliff seemed to dislike him ever longer and worse, though he took some trouble to conceal it: he had an antipathy to the sound of his voice, and could not do at all with his sitting in the same room with him many minutes together. There seldom passed much talk between them: Linton learnt his lessons and spent his evenings in a small apartment they called the parlour: or else lay in bed all day: for he was constantly getting coughs, and colds, and aches, and pains of some sort.

'And I never know such a fainthearted creature,' added the woman; 'nor one so careful of hisseln. He WILL go on, if I leave the window open a bit late in the evening. Oh! it's killing, a breath of night air! And he must have a fire in the middle of summer; and Joseph's bacca-pipe is poison; and he must always have sweets and dainties, and always milk, milk for ever—heeding naught how the rest of us are pinched in winter; and there he'll sit, wrapped in his furred cloak in his chair by the fire, with some toast and water or other slop on the hob to sip at; and if Hareton, for pity, comes to amuse him—Hareton is not bad-natured, though he's rough-they're sure to part, one swearing and the other crying. I believe the master would relish Earnshaw's thrashing him to a mummy, if he were not his son; and I'm certain he would be fit to turn him out of doors, if he knew half the nursing he gives hisseln. But then he won't go into danger of temptation: he never enters the parlour, and should Linton show those ways in the house where he is, he sends him up-stairs directly.'

I divined, from this account, that utter lack of sympathy had rendered young Heathcliff selfish and disagreeable, if he were not so originally; and my interest in him, consequently, decayed: though still I was moved with a sense of grief at his lot, and a wish that he had been left with us. Mr. Edgar encouraged me to gain information: he thought a great deal about him, I fancy, and would have run some risk to see him; and he told me once to ask the housekeeper whether he ever came into the village? She said he had only been twice, on horseback, accompanying his father; and both times he pretended to be quite knocked up for three or four days afterwards. That housekeeper left, if I recollect rightly, two years after he came; and another, whom I did not know, was her successor; she lives there still.

Time wore on at the Grange in its former pleasant way till Miss Cathy reached sixteen. On the anniversary of her birth we never manifested any signs of rejoicing, because it was also the anniversary of my late mistress's death. Her father invariably spent that day alone in the library; and walked, at dusk, as far as Gimmerton kirkyard, where he would frequently prolong his stay beyond midnight. Therefore Catherine was thrown on her own resources for amusement. This twentieth of March was a beautiful spring day, and when her father had retired, my young lady came down dressed for going out, and said she asked to have a ramble on the edge of the moor with me: Mr. Linton had given her leave, if we went only a short distance and were back within the hour.

'So make haste, Ellen!' she cried. 'I know where I wish to go; where a colony of moor-game are settled: I want to see whether they have made their nests yet.'

'That must be a good distance up,' I answered; 'they don't breed on the edge of the moor.'

'No, it's not,' she said. 'I've gone very near with papa.'

I put on my bonnet and sallied out, thinking nothing more of the matter. She bounded before me, and returned to my side, and was off again like a young greyhound; and, at first, I found plenty of entertainment in listening to the larks singing far and near, and enjoying the sweet, warm sunshine; and watching her, my pet and my delight, with her golden ringlets flying loose behind, and her bright cheek, as soft and pure in its bloom as a wild rose, and her eyes radiant with cloudless pleasure. She was a happy creature, and an angel, in those days. It's a pity she could not be content.

'Well,' said I, 'where are your moor-game, Miss Cathy? We should be at them: the Grange park-fence is a great way off now.'

'Oh, a little further—only a little further, Ellen,' was her answer, continually. 'Climb to that hillock, pass that bank, and by the time you reach the other side I shall have raised the birds.'

But there were so many hillocks and banks to climb and pass, that, at length, I began to be weary, and told her we must halt, and retrace our steps. I shouted to her, as she had outstripped me a long way; she either did not hear or did not regard, for she still sprang on, and I was compelled to follow. Finally, she dived into a hollow; and before I came in sight of her again, she was two miles nearer Wuthering Heights than her own home; and I beheld a couple of persons arrest her, one of whom I felt convinced was Mr. Heathcliff himself.

Cathy had been caught in the fact of plundering, or, at least, hunting out the nests of the grouse. The Heights were Heathcliff's land, and he was reproving the poacher.

'I've neither taken any nor found any,' she said, as I toiled to them, expanding her hands in corroboration of the statement. 'I didn't mean to take them; but papa told me there were quantities up here, and I wished to see the eggs.'

Heathcliff glanced at me with an ill-meaning smile, expressing his acquaintance with the party, and, consequently, his malevolence towards it, and demanded who 'papa' was?

'Mr. Linton of Thrushcross Grange,' she replied. 'I thought you did not know me, or you wouldn't have spoken in that way.'

'You suppose papa is highly esteemed and respected, then?' he said, sarcastically.

'And what are you?' inquired Catherine, gazing curiously on the speaker. 'That man I've seen before. Is he your son?'

She pointed to Hareton, the other individual, who had gained nothing but increased bulk and strength by the addition of two years to his age: he seemed as awkward and rough as ever.

'Miss Cathy,' I interrupted, 'it will be three hours instead of one that we are out, presently. We really must go back.'

'No, that man is not my son,' answered Heathcliff, pushing me aside. 'But I have one, and you have seen him before too; and, though your nurse is in a hurry, I think both you and she would be the better for a little rest. Will you just turn this nab of heath, and walk into my house? You'll get home earlier for the ease; and you shall receive a kind welcome.'

I whispered Catherine that she mustn't, on any account, accede to the proposal: it was entirely out of the question.

'Why?' she asked, aloud. 'I'm tired of running, and the ground is dewy: I can't sit here. Let us go, Ellen. Besides, he says I have seen his son. He's mistaken, I think; but I guess where he lives: at the farm-house I visited in coming from Penistone' Crags. Don't you?'

'I do. Come, Nelly, hold your tongue—it will he a treat for her to look in on us. Hareton, get forwards with the lass. You shall walk with me, Nelly.'

'No, she's not going to any such place,' I cried, struggling to release my arm, which he had seized: but she was almost at the door-stones already, scampering round the brow at full speed. Her appointed companion did not pretend to escort her: he shied off by the road-side, and vanished.

'Mr. Heathcliff, it's very wrong,' I continued: 'you know you mean no good. And there she'll see Linton, and all will be told as soon as ever we return; and I shall have the blame.'

'I want her to see Linton,' he answered; 'he's looking better these few days; it's not often he's fit to be seen. And we'll soon persuade her to keep the visit secret: where is the harm of it?'

'The harm of it is, that her father would hate me if he found I suffered her to enter your house; and I am convinced you have a bad design in encouraging her to do so,' I replied.

'My design is as honest as possible. I'll inform you of its whole scope,' he said. 'That the two cousins may fall in love, and get married. I'm acting generously to your master: his young chit has no expectations, and should she second my wishes she'll be provided for at once as joint successor with Linton.'

'If Linton died,' I answered, 'and his life is quite uncertain, Catherine would be the heir.'

'No, she would not,' he said. 'There is no clause in the will to secure it so: his property would go to me; but, to prevent disputes, I desire their union, and am resolved to bring it about.'

'And I'm resolved she shall never approach your house with me again,' I returned, as we reached the gate, where Miss Cathy waited our coming.

Heathcliff bade me be quiet; and, preceding us up the path, hastened to open the door. My young lady gave him several looks, as if she could not exactly make up her mind what to think of him; but now he smiled when he met her eye, and softened his voice in addressing her; and I was foolish enough to imagine the memory of her mother might disarm him from desiring her injury. Linton stood on the hearth. He had been out walking in the fields, for his cap was on, and he was calling to Joseph to bring him dry shoes. He had grown tall of his age, still wanting some months of sixteen. His features were pretty yet, and his eye and complexion brighter than I remembered them, though with merely temporary lustre borrowed from the salubrious air and genial sun.

'Now, who is that?' asked Mr. Heathcliff, turning to Cathy. 'Can you tell?'

'Your son?' she said, having doubtfully surveyed, first one and then the other.

'Yes, yes,' answered he: 'but is this the only time you have beheld him? Think! Ah! you have a short memory. Linton, don't you recall your cousin, that you used to tease us so with wishing to see?'

'What, Linton!' cried Cathy, kindling into joyful surprise at the name. 'Is that little Linton? He's taller than I am! Are you Linton?'

The youth stepped forward, and acknowledged himself: she kissed him fervently, and they gazed with wonder at the change time had wrought in the appearance of each. Catherine had reached her full height; her figure was both plump and slender, elastic as steel, and her whole aspect sparkling with health and spirits. Linton's looks and movements were very languid, and his form extremely slight; but there was a grace in his manner that mitigated these defects, and rendered him not unpleasing. After exchanging numerous marks of fondness with him, his cousin went to Mr. Heathcliff, who lingered by the door, dividing his attention between the objects inside and those that lay without: pretending, that is, to observe the latter, and really noting the former alone.

'And you are my uncle, then!' she cried, reaching up to salute him. 'I thought I liked you, though you were cross at first. Why don't you visit at the Grange with Linton? To live all these years such close neighbours, and never see us, is odd: what have you done so for?'

'I visited it once or twice too often before you were born,' he answered. 'There—damn it! If you have any kisses to spare, give them to Linton: they are thrown away on me.'

'Naughty Ellen!' exclaimed Catherine, flying to attack me next with her lavish caresses. 'Wicked Ellen! to try to hinder me from entering. But I'll take this walk every morning in future: may I, uncle? and sometimes bring papa. Won't you be glad to see us?'

'Of course,' replied the uncle, with a hardly suppressed grimace, resulting from his deep aversion to both the proposed visitors. 'But stay,' he continued, turning towards the young lady. 'Now I think of it, I'd better tell you. Mr. Linton has a prejudice against me:

we quarrelled at one time of our lives, with unchristian ferocity; and, if you mention coming here to him, he'll put a veto on your visits altogether. Therefore, you must not mention it, unless you be careless of seeing your cousin hereafter: you may come, if you will, but you must not mention it.'

'Why did you quarrel?' asked Catherine, considerably crestfallen.

'He thought me too poor to wed his sister,' answered Heathcliff, 'and was grieved that I got her: his pride was hurt, and he'll never forgive it.'

'That's wrong!' said the young lady: 'some time I'll tell him so. But Linton and I have no share in your quarrel. I'll not come here, then; he shall come to the Grange.'

'It will be too far for me,' murmured her cousin: 'to walk four miles would kill me. No, come here, Miss Catherine, now and then: not every morning, but once or twice a week.'

The father launched towards his son a glance of bitter contempt.

'I am afraid, Nelly, I shall lose my labour,' he muttered to me. 'Miss Catherine, as the ninny calls her, will discover his value, and send him to the devil. Now, if it had been Hareton!—Do you know that, twenty times a day, I covet Hareton, with all his degradation? I'd have loved the lad had he been some one else. But I think he's safe from HER love. I'll pit him against that paltry creature, unless it bestir itself briskly. We calculate it will scarcely last till it is eighteen. Oh, confound the vapid thing! He's absorbed in drying his feet, and never looks at her.-Linton!'

'Yes, father,' answered the boy.

'Have you nothing to show your cousin anywhere about, not even a rabbit or a weasel's nest? Take her into the garden, before you change your shoes; and into the stable to see your horse.'

'Wouldn't you rather sit here?' asked Linton, addressing Cathy in a tone which expressed reluctance to move again.

'I don't know,' she replied, casting a longing look to the door, and evidently eager to be active.

He kept his seat, and shrank closer to the fire. Heathcliff rose, and went into the kitchen, and from thence to the yard, calling out for Hareton. Hareton responded, and presently the two re-entered. The young man had been washing himself, as was visible by the glow on his cheeks and his wetted hair.

'Oh, I'll ask YOU, uncle,' cried Miss Cathy, recollecting the housekeeper's assertion. 'That is not my cousin, is he?'

'Yes,' he, replied, 'your mother's nephew. Don't you like him!'

Catherine looked queer.

'Is he not a handsome lad?' he continued.

The uncivil little thing stood on tiptoe, and whispered a sentence in Heathcliff's ear. He laughed; Hareton darkened: I perceived he was very sensitive to suspected slights, and had obviously a dim notion of his inferiority. But his master or guardian chased the frown by exclaiming—

'You'll be the favourite among us, Hareton! She says you are a—What was it? Well, something very flattering. Here! you go with her round the farm. And behave like a gentleman, mind! Don't use any bad words; and don't stare when the young lady is not looking at you, and be ready to hide your face when she is; and, when you speak, say your words slowly, and keep your hands out of your pockets. Be off, and entertain her as nicely as you can.'

He watched the couple walking past the window. Earnshaw had his countenance completely averted from his companion. He seemed studying the familiar landscape with a stranger's and an artist's interest. Catherine took a sly look at him, expressing small admiration. She then turned her attention to seeking out objects of amusement for herself, and tripped merrily on, lilting a tune to supply the lack of conversation.

'I've tied his tongue,' observed Heathcliff. 'He'll not venture a single syllable all the time! Nelly, you recollect meat his age—nay, some years younger. Did I ever look so stupid: so "gaumless," as Joseph calls it?'

'Worse,' I replied, 'because more sullen with it.'

'I've a pleasure in him,' he continued, reflecting aloud. 'He has satisfied my expectations. If he were a born fool I should not enjoy it half so much. But he's no fool; and I can sympathise with all his feelings, having felt them myself. I know what he suffers now, for instance, exactly: it is merely a beginning of what he shall suffer, though. And he'll never be able to emerge from his bathos of coarseness and ignorance. I've got him faster than his scoundrel of a father secured me, and lower; for he takes a pride in his brutishness. I've taught him to scorn everything extra-animal as silly and weak. Don't you think Hindley would be proud of his son, if he could see him?

almost as proud as I am of mine. But there's this difference; one is gold put to the use of paving-stones, and the other is tin polished to ape a service of silver. MINE has nothing valuable about it; yet I shall have the merit of making it go as far as such poor stuff can go. HIS had first-rate qualities, and they are lost: rendered worse than unavailing. I have nothing to regret; he would have more than any but I are aware of. And the best of it is, Hareton is damnably fond of me! You'll own that I've outmatched Hindley there. If the dead villain could rise from his grave to abuse me for his offspring's wrongs, I should have the fun of seeing the said offspring fight him back again, indignant that he should dare to rail at the one friend he has in the world!'

Heathcliff chuckled a fiendish laugh at the idea. I made no reply, because I saw that he expected none. Meantime, our young companion, who sat too removed from us to hear what was said, began to evince symptoms of uneasiness, probably repenting that he had denied himself the treat of Catherine's society for fear of a little fatigue. His father remarked the restless glances wandering to the window, and the hand irresolutely extended towards his cap.

'Get up, you idle boy!' he exclaimed, with assumed heartiness.

'Away after them! they are just at the corner, by the stand of hives.'

Linton gathered his energies, and left the hearth. The lattice was open, and, as he stepped out, I heard Cathy inquiring of her unsociable attendant what was that inscription over the door? Hareton stared up, and scratched his head like a true clown.

'It's some damnable writing,' he answered. 'I cannot read it.'

'Can't read it?' cried Catherine; 'I can read it: it's English. But I want to know why it is there.'

Linton giggled: the first appearance of mirth he had exhibited.

'He does not know his letters,' he said to his cousin. 'Could you believe in the existence of such a colossal dunce?'

'Is he all as he should be?' asked Miss Cathy, seriously; 'or is he simple: not right? I've questioned him twice now, and each time he looked so stupid I think he does not understand me. I can hardly understand him, I'm sure!'

Linton repeated his laugh, and glanced at Hareton tauntingly; who certainly did not seem quite clear of comprehension at that moment.

'There's nothing the matter but laziness; is there, Earnshaw?' he said. 'My cousin fancies you are an idiot. There you experience the consequence of scorning "book-larning," as you would say. Have you noticed, Catherine, his frightful Yorkshire pronunciation?'

'Why, where the devil is the use on't?' growled Hareton, more ready in answering his daily companion. He was about to enlarge further, but the two youngsters broke into a noisy fit of merriment: my giddy miss being delighted to discover that she might turn his strange talk to matter of amusement.

'Where is the use of the devil in that sentence?' tittered Linton. 'Papa told you not to say any bad words, and you can't open your mouth without one. Do try to behave like a gentleman, now do!'

'If thou weren't more a lass than a lad, I'd fell thee this minute, I would; pitiful lath of a crater!' retorted the angry boor, retreating, while his face burnt with mingled rage and mortification! for he was conscious of being insulted, and embarrassed how to resent it.

Mr. Heathcliff having overheard the conversation, as well as I, smiled when he saw him go; but immediately afterwards cast a look of singular aversion on the flippant pair, who remained chattering in the door-way: the boy finding animation enough while discussing Hareton's faults and deficiencies, and relating anecdotes of his goings on; and the girl relishing his pert and spiteful sayings, without considering the ill-nature they evinced. I began to dislike, more than to compassionate Linton, and to excuse his father in some measure for holding him cheap.

We stayed till afternoon: I could not tear Miss Cathy away sooner; but happily my master had not quitted his apartment, and remained ignorant of our prolonged absence. As we walked home, I would fain have enlightened my charge on the characters of the people we had quitted: but she got it into her head that I was prejudiced against them.

'Aha!' she cried, 'you take papa's side, Ellen: you are partial I know; or else you wouldn't have cheated me so many years into the notion that Linton lived a long way from here. I'm really extremely angry; only I'm so pleased I can't show it! But you must hold your tongue about MY uncle; he's my uncle, remember; and I'll scold papa for quarrelling with him.'

And so she ran on, till I relinquished the endeavour to convince her of her mistake. She did not mention the visit that night, because she did not see Mr. Linton. Next day it all came out, sadly to my chagrin; and still I was not altogether sorry: I thought the burden of directing and warning would be more efficiently borne by him than me. But he was too timid in giving satisfactory reasons for his wish that she should shun connection with the household of the Heights, and Catherine liked good reasons for every restraint that harassed her petted will.

'Papa!' she exclaimed, after the morning's salutations, 'guess whom I saw yesterday, in my walk on the moors. Ah, papa, you started! you've not done right, have you, now? I saw—but listen, and you shall hear how I found you out; and Ellen, who is in league with you, and yet pretended to pity me so, when I kept hoping, and was always disappointed about Linton's coming back!'

She gave a faithful account of her excursion and its consequences; and my master, though he cast more than one reproachful look at me, said nothing till she had concluded. Then he drew her to him, and asked if she knew why he had concealed Linton's near neighbourhood from her? Could she think it was to deny her a pleasure that she might harmlessly enjoy?

'It was because you disliked Mr. Heathcliff,' she answered.

'Then you believe I care more for my own feelings than yours, Cathy?' he said. 'No, it was not because I disliked Mr. Heathcliff, but because Mr. Heathcliff dislikes me; and is a most diabolical man, delighting to wrong and ruin those he hates, if they give him the slightest opportunity. I knew that you could not keep up an acquaintance with your cousin without being brought into contact with him; and I knew he would detest you on my account; so for your own good, and nothing else, I took precautions that you should not see Linton again. I meant to explain this some time as you grew older, and I'm sorry I delayed it.'

'But Mr. Heathcliff was quite cordial, papa,' observed Catherine, not at all convinced; 'and he didn't object to our seeing each other: he said I might come to his house when I pleased; only I must not tell you, because you had quarrelled with him, and would not forgive him for marrying aunt Isabella. And you won't. YOU are the one to be blamed: he is willing to let us be friends, at least; Linton and I; and you are not.'

My master, perceiving that she would not take his word for her uncle-in-law's evil disposition, gave a hasty sketch of his conduct to

Isabella, and the manner in which Wuthering Heights became his property. He could not bear to discourse long upon the topic; for though he spoke little of it, he still felt the same horror and detestation of his ancient enemy that had occupied his heart ever since Mrs. Linton's death. 'She might have been living yet, if it had not been for him!' was his constant bitter reflection; and, in his eyes, Heathcliff seemed a murderer. Miss Cathy—conversant with no bad deeds except her own slight acts of disobedience, injustice, and passion, arising from hot temper and thoughtlessness, and repented of on the day they were committed—was amazed at the blackness of spirit that could brood on and cover revenge for years, and deliberately prosecute its plans without a visitation of remorse. She appeared so deeply impressed and shocked at this new view of human nature—excluded from all her studies and all her ideas till now—that Mr. Edgar deemed it unnecessary to pursue the subject. He merely added: 'You will know hereafter, darling, why I wish you to avoid his house and family; now return to your old employments and amusements, and think no more about them.'

Catherine kissed her father, and sat down quietly to her lessons for a couple of hours, according to custom; then she accompanied him into the grounds, and the whole day passed as usual: but in the evening, when she had retired to her room, and I went to help her to undress, I found her crying, on her knees by the bedside.

'Oh, fie, silly child!' I exclaimed. 'If you had any real griefs you'd be ashamed to waste a tear on this little contrariety. You never had one shadow of substantial sorrow, Miss Catherine. Suppose, for a minute, that master and I were dead, and you were by yourself in the world: how would you feel, then? Compare the present occasion with such an affliction as that, and be thankful for the friends you have, instead of coveting more.'

'I'm not crying for myself, Ellen,' she answered, 'it's for him. He expected to see me again to-morrow, and there he'll be so disappointed: and he'll wait for me, and I sha'n't come!'

'Nonsense!' said I, 'do you imagine he has thought as much of you as you have of him? Hasn't he Hareton for a companion? Not one in a hundred would weep at losing a relation they had just seen twice, for two afternoons. Linton will conjecture how it is, and trouble himself no further about you.'

'But may I not write a note to tell him why I cannot come?' she asked, rising to her feet. 'And just send those books I promised to lend him? His books are not as nice as mine, and he wanted to have them extremely, when I told him how interesting they were. May I not, Ellen?'

'No, indeed! no, indeed!' replied I with decision. 'Then he would write to you, and there'd never be an end of it. No, Miss Catherine, the acquaintance must be dropped entirely: so papa expects, and I shall see that it is done.'

'But how can one little note—?' she recommenced, putting on an imploring countenance.

'Silence!' I interrupted. 'We'll not begin with your little notes. Get into bed.'

She threw at me a very naughty look, so naughty that I would not kiss her good-night at first: I covered her up, and shut her door, in great displeasure; but, repenting half-way, I returned softly, and lo! there was Miss standing at the table with a bit of blank paper before her and a pencil in her hand, which she guiltily slipped out of sight on my entrance.

'You'll get nobody to take that, Catherine,' I said, 'if you write it; and at present I shall put out your candle.'

I set the extinguisher on the flame, receiving as I did so a slap on my hand and a petulant 'cross thing!' I then quitted her again, and she drew the bolt in one of her worst, most peevish humours. The letter was finished and forwarded to its destination by a milk-fetcher who came from the village; but that I didn't learn till some time afterwards. Weeks passed on, and Cathy recovered her temper; though she grew wondrous fond of stealing off to corners by herself and often, if I came near her suddenly while reading, she would start and bend over the book, evidently desirous to hide it; and I detected edges of loose paper sticking out beyond the leaves. She also got a trick of coming down early in the morning and lingering about the kitchen, as if she were expecting the arrival of something; and she had a small drawer in a cabinet in the library, which she would trifle over for hours, and whose key she took special care to remove when she left it.

One day, as she inspected this drawer, I observed that the playthings and trinkets which recently formed its contents were transmuted into bits of folded paper. My curiosity and suspicions were roused; I determined to take a peep at her mysterious treasures; so, at night, as soon as she and my master were safe upstairs, I searched, and readily found among my house keys one that would fit the lock.

Having opened, I emptied the whole contents into my apron, and took them with me to examine at leisure in my own chamber. Though I could not but suspect, I was still surprised to discover that they were a mass of correspondence-daily almost, it must have been—from Linton Heathcliff: answers to documents forwarded by her. The earlier dated were embarrassed and short; gradually, however, they expanded into copious love-letters, foolish, as the age of the writer rendered natural, yet with touches here and there which I thought were borrowed from a more experienced source. Some of them struck me as singularly odd compounds of ardour and flatness; commencing in strong feeling, and concluding in the affected, wordy style that a schoolboy might use to a fancied, incorporeal sweetheart. Whether they satisfied Cathy I don't know; but they appeared very worthless trash to me. After turning over as many as I thought proper, I tied them in a handkerchief and set them aside, relocking the vacant drawer.

Following her habit, my young lady descended early, and visited the kitchen: I watched her go to the door, on the arrival of a certain little boy; and, while the dairymaid filled his can, she tucked something into his jacket pocket, and plucked something out. I went round by the garden, and laid wait for the messenger; who fought valorously to defend his trust, and we spilt the milk between us; but I succeeded in abstracting the epistle; and, threatening serious consequences if he did not look sharp home, I remained under the wall and perused Miss Cathy's affectionate composition. It was more simple and more eloquent than her cousin's: very pretty and very silly. I shook my head, and went meditating into the house. The day being wet, she could not divert herself with rambling about the park; so, at the conclusion of her morning studies, she resorted to the solace of the drawer. Her father sat reading at the table; and I, on purpose, had sought a bit of work in some unripped fringes of the window-curtain, keeping my eye steadily fixed on her proceedings. Never did any bird flying back to a plundered nest, which it had left brimful of chirping young ones, express more complete despair, in its anguished cries and flutterings, than she by her single 'Oh!' and the change that transfigured her late happy countenance. Mr. Linton looked up.

'What is the matter, love? Have you hurt yourself?' he said.

His tone and look assured her HE had not been the discoverer of the hoard.

'No, papa!' she gasped. 'Ellen! Ellen! come up-stairs—I'm sick!'

I obeyed her summons, and accompanied her out.

'Oh, Ellen! you have got them,' she commenced immediately, dropping on her knees, when we were enclosed alone. 'Oh, give them to me, and I'll never, never do so again! Don't tell papa. You have not told papa, Ellen? say you have not? I've been exceedingly naughty, but I won't do it any more!'

With a grave severity in my manner I bade her stand up.

'So,' I exclaimed, 'Miss Catherine, you are tolerably far on, it seems: you may well be ashamed of them! A fine bundle of trash you study in your leisure hours, to be sure: why, it's good enough to be printed! And what do you suppose the master will think when I display it before him? I hav'n't shown it yet, but you needn't imagine I shall keep your ridiculous secrets. For shame! and you must have led the way in writing such absurdities: he would not have thought of beginning, I'm certain.'

'I didn't! I didn't!' sobbed Cathy, fit to break her heart. 'I didn't once think of loving him till—'

'LOVING!' cried I, as scornfully as I could utter the word. 'LOVING! Did anybody ever hear the like! I might just as well talk of loving the miller who comes once a year to buy our corn. Pretty loving, indeed! and both times together you have seen Linton hardly four hours in your life! Now here is the babyish trash. I'm going with it to the library; and we'll see what your father says to such LOVING.'

She sprang at her precious epistles, but I hold them above my head; and then she poured out further frantic entreaties that I would burn them—do anything rather than show them. And being really fully as much inclined to laugh as scold—for I esteemed it all girlish vanity—I at length relented in a measure, and asked,—'If I consent to burn them, will you promise faithfully neither to send nor receive a letter again, nor a book (for I perceive you have sent him books), nor locks of hair, nor rings, nor playthings?'

'We don't send playthings,' cried Catherine, her pride overcoming her shame.

'Nor anything at all, then, my lady?' I said. 'Unless you will, here I go.'

'I promise, Ellen!' she cried, catching my dress. 'Oh, put them in the fire, do, do!'

But when I proceeded to open a place with the poker the sacrifice was too painful to be borne. She earnestly supplicated that I would spare her one or two.

'One or two, Ellen, to keep for Linton's sake!'

I unknotted the handkerchief, and commenced dropping them in from an angle, and the flame curled up the chimney.

'I will have one, you cruel wretch!' she screamed, darting her hand into the fire, and drawing forth some half-consumed fragments, at the expense of her fingers.

'Very well—and I will have some to exhibit to papa!' I answered, shaking back the rest into the bundle, and turning anew to the door.

She emptied her blackened pieces into the flames, and motioned me to finish the immolation. It was done; I stirred up the ashes, and interred them under a shovelful of coals; and she mutely, and with a sense of intense injury, retired to her private apartment. I descended to tell my master that the young lady's qualm of sickness was almost gone, but I judged it best for her to lie down a while. She wouldn't dine; but she reappeared at tea, pale, and red about the eyes, and marvellously subdued in outward aspect. Next morning I answered the letter by a slip of paper, inscribed, 'Master Heathcliff is requested to send no more notes to Miss Linton, as she will not receive them.' And, henceforth, the little boy came with vacant pockets.

Chapter XXII

SUMMER drew to an end, and early autumn: it was past Michaelmas, but the harvest was late that year, and a few of our fields were still uncleared. Mr. Linton and his daughter would frequently walk out among the reapers; at the carrying of the last sheaves they stayed till dusk, and the evening happening to be chill and damp, my master caught a bad cold, that settled obstinately on his lungs, and confined him indoors throughout the whole of the winter, nearly without intermission.

Poor Cathy, frightened from her little romance, had been considerably sadder and duller since its abandonment; and her father insisted on her reading less, and taking more exercise. She had his companionship no longer; I esteemed it a duty to supply its lack, as much as possible, with mine: an inefficient substitute; for I could only spare two or three hours, from my numerous diurnal occupations, to follow her footsteps, and then my society was obviously less desirable than his.

On an afternoon in October, or the beginning of November—a fresh watery afternoon, when the turf and paths were rustling with moist, withered leaves, and the cold blue sky was half hidden by clouds—dark grey streamers, rapidly mounting from the west, and boding abundant rain—I requested my young lady to forego her ramble, because I was certain of showers. She refused; and I unwillingly donned a cloak, and took my umbrella to accompany her on a stroll to the bottom of the park: a formal walk which she generally affected if low-spirited—and that she invariably was when Mr. Edgar had been worse than ordinary, a thing never known from his confession, but guessed both by her and me from his increased silence and the melancholy of his countenance. She went sadly on: there was no running or bounding now, though the chill wind might well have tempted her to race. And often, from the side of my eye, I could detect her raising a hand, and brushing something off her cheek. I gazed round for a means of diverting her thoughts. On one side of the road rose a high, rough bank, where hazels and stunted oaks, with their roots half exposed, held uncertain tenure: the soil was too loose for the latter; and strong winds had blown some nearly horizontal. In summer Miss Catherine delighted to climb along these trunks, and sit in the branches, swinging twenty feet above the ground; and I, pleased with her agility and her light, childish heart, still considered it proper to scold every time I caught her at such an elevation, but so that she knew there was no necessity for descending. From dinner to tea she would lie in her breeze-rocked cradle, doing nothing except singing old songs-my nursery lore—to herself, or watching the birds, joint tenants, feed and entice their young ones to fly: or nestling with closed lids, half thinking, half dreaming, happier than words can express.

'Look, Miss!' I exclaimed, pointing to a nook under the roots of one twisted tree. 'Winter is not here yet. There's a little flower up yonder, the last bud from the multitude of bluebells that clouded those turf steps in July with a lilac mist. Will you clamber up, and pluck it to show to papa?' Cathy stared a long time at the lonely blossom trembling in its earthy shelter, and replied, at length—'No, I'll not touch it: but it looks melancholy, does it not, Ellen?'

'Yes,' I observed, 'about as starved and suckless as you your cheeks are bloodless; let us take hold of hands and run. You're so low, I daresay I shall keep up with you.'

'No,' she repeated, and continued sauntering on, pausing at intervals to muse over a bit of moss, or a tuft of blanched grass, or a fungus spreading its bright orange among the heaps of brown foliage; and, ever and anon, her hand was lifted to her averted face.

'Catherine, why are you crying, love?' I asked, approaching and putting my arm over her shoulder. 'You mustn't cry because papa has a cold; be thankful it is nothing worse.'

She now put no further restraint on her tears; her breath was stifled by sobs.

'Oh, it will be something worse,' she said. 'And what shall I do when papa and you leave me, and I am by myself? I can't forget your words, Ellen; they are always in my ear. How life will be changed, how dreary the world will be, when papa and you are dead.'

'None can tell whether you won't die before us,' I replied. 'It's wrong to anticipate evil. We'll hope there are years and years to come before any of us go: master is young, and I am strong, and hardly forty-five. My mother lived till eighty, a canty dame to the last. And suppose Mr. Linton I were spared till he saw sixty, that would be more years than you have counted, Miss. And would it not be foolish to mourn a calamity above twenty years beforehand?'

'But Aunt Isabella was younger than papa,' she remarked, gazing up with timid hope to seek further consolation.

'Aunt Isabella had not you and me to nurse her,' I replied. 'She wasn't as happy as Master: she hadn't as much to live for. All you need do, is to wait well on your father, and cheer him by letting him see you cheerful; and avoid giving him anxiety on any subject: mind that, Cathy! I'll not disguise but you might kill him if you were wild and reckless, and cherished a foolish, fanciful affection for the son of a person who would be glad to have him in his grave; and allowed him to discover that you fretted over the separation he has judged it expedient to make.'

'I fret about nothing on earth except papa's illness,' answered my companion. 'I care for nothing in comparison with papa. And I'll never—never—oh, never, while I have my senses, do an act or say a word to vex him. I love him better than myself, Ellen; and I know it by this: I pray every night that I may live after him; because I would rather be miserable than that he should be: that proves I love him better than myself.'

'Good words,' I replied. 'But deeds must prove it also; and after he is well, remember you don't forget resolutions formed in the hour of fear.'

As we talked, we neared a door that opened on the road; and my young lady, lightening into sunshine again, climbed up and seated herself on the top of the wall, reaching over to gather some hips that bloomed scarlet on the summit branches of the wild-rose trees shadowing the highway side: the lower fruit had disappeared, but only birds could touch the upper, except from Cathy's present station. In stretching to pull them, her hat fell off; and as the door was locked, she proposed scrambling down to recover it. I bid her be cautious lest she got a fall, and she nimbly disappeared. But the return was no such easy matter: the stones were smooth and neatly cemented, and the rose-bushes and black-berry stragglers could yield no assistance in re-ascending. I, like a fool, didn't recollect that, till I heard her laughing and exclaiming—'Ellen! you'll have to fetch the key, or else I must run round to the porter's lodge. I can't scale the ramparts on this side!'

'Stay where you are,' I answered; 'I have my bundle of keys in my pocket: perhaps I may manage to open it; if not, I'll go.'

Catherine amused herself with dancing to and fro before the door, while I tried all the large keys in succession. I had applied the last, and found that none would do; so, repeating my desire that she would remain there, I was about to hurry home as fast as I could, when an approaching sound arrested me. It was the trot of a horse; Cathy's dance stopped also.

'Who is that?' I whispered.

'Ellen, I wish you could open the door,' whispered back my companion, anxiously.

'Ho, Miss Linton!' cried a deep voice (the rider's), 'I'm glad to meet you. Don't be in haste to enter, for I have an explanation to ask and obtain.'

'I sha'n't speak to you, Mr. Heathcliff,' answered Catherine. 'Papa says you are a wicked man, and you hate both him and me; and Ellen says the same.'

'That is nothing to the purpose,' said Heathcliff. (He it was.) 'I don't hate my son, I suppose; and it is concerning him that I demand your attention. Yes; you have cause to blush. Two or three months since, were you not in the habit of writing to Linton? making love in play, eh? You deserved, both of you, flogging for that! You especially, the elder; and less sensitive, as it turns out. I've got your letters, and if you give me any pertness I'll send them to your father. I presume you grew weary of the amusement and dropped it, didn't you? Well, you dropped Linton with it into a Slough of Despond. He was in earnest: in love, really. As true as I live, he's dying for you; breaking his heart at your fickleness: not figuratively, but actually. Though Hareton has made him a standing jest for six weeks, and I have used more serious measures, and attempted to frighten him out of his idiotcy, he gets worse daily; and he'll be under the sod before summer, unless you restore him!'

'How can you lie so glaringly to the poor child?' I called from the inside. 'Pray ride on! How can you deliberately get up such paltry falsehoods? Miss Cathy, I'll knock the lock off with a stone: you won't believe that vile nonsense. You can feel in yourself it is impossible that a person should die for love of a stranger.'

'I was not aware there were eavesdroppers,' muttered the detected villain. 'Worthy Mrs. Dean, I like you, but I don't like your double-dealing,' he added aloud. 'How could YOU lie so glaringly as to affirm I hated the "poor child"? and invent bugbear stories to terrify her from my door-stones? Catherine Linton (the very name warms me), my bonny lass, I shall be from home all this week; go and see if have not spoken truth: do, there's a darling! Just imagine your father in my place, and Linton in yours; then think how you would value your careless lover if he refused to stir a step to comfort you, when your father himself entreated him; and don't, from pure stupidity, fall into the same error. I swear, on my salvation, he's going to his grave, and none but you can save him!'

The lock gave way and I issued out.

'I swear Linton is dying,' repeated Heathcliff, looking hard at me. 'And grief and disappointment are hastening his death. Nelly, if you won't let her go, you can walk over yourself. But I shall not return till this time next week; and I think your master himself would scarcely object to her visiting her cousin.'

'Come in,' said I, taking Cathy by the arm and half forcing her to re-enter; for she lingered, viewing with troubled eyes the features of the speaker, too stern to express his inward deceit.

He pushed his horse close, and, bending down, observed—'Miss Catherine, I'll own to you that I have little patience with Linton; and Hareton and Joseph have less. I'll own that he's with a harsh set. He pines for kindness, as well as love; and a kind word from you would be his best medicine. Don't mind Mrs. Dean's cruel cautions; but be generous, and contrive to see him. He dreams of you day and night, and cannot be persuaded that you don't hate him, since you neither write nor call.'

I closed the door, and rolled a stone to assist the loosened lock in holding it; and spreading my umbrella, I drew my charge underneath: for the rain began to drive through the moaning branches of the trees, and warned us to avoid delay. Our hurry prevented any comment on the encounter with Heathcliff, as we stretched towards home; but I divined instinctively that Catherine's heart was clouded now in double darkness. Her features were so sad, they did not seem hers: she evidently regarded what she had heard as every syllable true.

The master had retired to rest before we came in. Cathy stole to his room to inquire how he was; he had fallen asleep. She returned, and asked me to sit with her in the library. We took our tea together; and afterwards she lay down on the rug, and told me not to talk, for she was weary. I got a book, and pretended to read. As soon as she supposed me absorbed in my occupation, she recommenced her silent weeping: it appeared, at present, her favourite diversion. I suffered her to enjoy it a while; then I expostulated: deriding and ridiculing all Mr. Heathcliff's assertions about his son, as if I were certain she would coincide. Alas! I hadn't skill to counteract the effect his account had produced: it was just what he intended.

'You may be right, Ellen,' she answered; 'but I shall never feel at ease till I know. And I must tell Linton it is not my fault that I don't write, and convince him that I shall not change.'

What use were anger and protestations against her silly credulity? We parted that night—hostile; but next day beheld me on the road to Wuthering Heights, by the side of my wilful young mistress's pony. I couldn't bear to witness her sorrow: to see her pale, dejected countenance, and heavy eyes: and I yielded, in the faint hope that Linton himself might prove, by his reception of us, how little of the tale was founded on fact.

Chapter XXIII

THE rainy night had ushered in a misty morning—half frost, half drizzle—and temporary brooks crossed our path—gurgling from the uplands. My feet were thoroughly wetted; I was cross and low; exactly the humour suited for making the most of these disagreeable things. We entered the farm-house by the kitchen way, to ascertain whether Mr. Heathcliff were really absent: because I put slight faith in his own affirmation.

Joseph seemed sitting in a sort of elysium alone, beside a roaring fire; a quart of ale on the table near him, bristling with large pieces of toasted oat-cake; and his black, short pipe in his mouth. Catherine ran to the hearth to warm herself. I asked if the master was in? My question remained so long unanswered, that I thought the old man had grown deaf, and repeated it louder.

'Na—ay!' he snarled, or rather screamed through his nose. 'Na—ay! yah muh goa back whear yah coom frough.'

'Joseph!' cried a peevish voice, simultaneously with me, from the inner room. 'How often am I to call you? There are only a few red ashes now. Joseph! come this moment.'

Vigorous puffs, and a resolute stare into the grate, declared he had no ear for this appeal. The housekeeper and Hareton were invisible; one gone on an errand, and the other at his work, probably. We knew Linton's tones, and entered.

'Oh, I hope you'll die in a garret, starved to death!' said the boy, mistaking our approach for that of his negligent attendant.

He stopped on observing his error: his cousin flew to him.

'Is that you, Miss Linton?' he said, raising his head from the arm of the great chair, in which he reclined. 'No—don't kiss me: it takes my breath. Dear me! Papa said you would call,' continued he, after recovering a little from Catherine's embrace; while she stood by looking very contrite. 'Will you shut the door, if you please? you left it open; and those—those DETESTABLE creatures won't bring coals to the fire. It's so cold!'

I stirred up the cinders, and fetched a scuttleful myself. The invalid complained of being covered with ashes; but he had a tiresome cough, and looked feverish and ill, so I did not rebuke his temper.

'Well, Linton,' murmured Catherine, when his corrugated brow relaxed, 'are you glad to see me? Can I do you any good?'

'Why didn't you come before?' he asked. 'You should have come, instead of writing. It tired me dreadfully writing those long letters. I'd far rather have talked to you. Now, I can neither bear to talk, nor anything else. I wonder where Zillah is! Will you' (looking at me) 'step into the kitchen and see?'

I had received no thanks for my other service; and being unwilling to run to and fro at his behest, I replied—'Nobody is out there but Joseph.'

'I want to drink,' he exclaimed fretfully, turning away. 'Zillah is constantly gadding off to Gimmerton since papa went: it's miserable! And I'm obliged to come down here—they resolved never to hear me up-stairs.'

'Is your father attentive to you, Master Heathcliff?' I asked, perceiving Catherine to be checked in her friendly advances.

'Attentive? He makes them a little more attentive at least,' he cried. 'The wretches! Do you know, Miss Linton, that brute Hareton laughs at me! I hate him! indeed, I hate them all: they are odious beings.'

Cathy began searching for some water; she lighted on a pitcher in the dresser, filled a tumbler, and brought it. He bid her add a spoonful of wine from a bottle on the table; and having swallowed a small portion, appeared more tranquil, and said she was very kind.

'And are you glad to see me?' asked she, reiterating her former question and pleased to detect the faint dawn of a smile.

'Yes, I am. It's something new to hear a voice like yours!' he replied. 'But I have been vexed, because you wouldn't come. And papa swore it was owing to me: he called me a pitiful, shuffling, worthless thing; and said you despised me; and if he had been in my place, he would be more the master of the Grange than your father by this time. But you don't despise me, do you, Miss—?'

'I wish you would say Catherine, or Cathy,' interrupted my young lady. 'Despise you? No! Next to papa and Ellen, I love you better than anybody living. I don't love Mr. Heathcliff, though; and I dare not come when he returns: will he stay away many days?'

'Not many,' answered Linton; 'but he goes on to the moors frequently, since the shooting season commenced; and you might spend an hour or two with me in his absence. Do say you will. I think I should not be peevish with you: you'd not provoke me, and you'd always be ready to help me, wouldn't you?'

'Yes" said Catherine, stroking his long soft hair: 'if I could only get papa's consent, I'd spend half my time with you. Pretty Linton! I wish you were my brother.'

'And then you would like me as well as your father?' observed he, more cheerfully. 'But papa says you would love me better than him and all the world, if you were my wife; so I'd rather you were that.'

'No, I should never love anybody better than papa,' she returned gravely. 'And people hate their wives, sometimes; but not their sisters and brothers: and if you were the latter, you would live with us, and papa would be as fond of you as he is of me.'

Linton denied that people ever hated their wives; but Cathy affirmed they did, and, in her wisdom, instanced his own father's aversion to her aunt. I endeavoured to stop her thoughtless tongue. I couldn't succeed till everything she knew was out. Master Heathcliff, much irritated, asserted her relation was false.

'Papa told me; and papa does not tell falsehoods,' she answered pertly.

'MY papa scorns yours!' cried Linton. 'He calls him a sneaking fool.'

'Yours is a wicked man,' retorted Catherine; 'and you are very naughty to dare to repeat what he says. He must be wicked to have made Aunt Isabella leave him as she did.'

'She didn't leave him,' said the boy; 'you sha'n't contradict me.'

'She did,' cried my young lady.

'Well, I'll tell you something!' said Linton. 'Your mother hated your father: now then.'

'Oh!' exclaimed Catherine, too enraged to continue.

'And she loved mine,' added he.

'You little liar! I hate you now!' she panted, and her face grew red with passion.

'She did! she did!' sang Linton, sinking into the recess of his chair, and leaning back his head to enjoy the agitation of the other disputant, who stood behind.

'Hush, Master Heathcliff!' I said; 'that's your father's tale, too, I suppose.'

'It isn't: you hold your tongue!' he answered. 'She did, she did, Catherine! she did, she did!'

Cathy, beside herself, gave the chair a violent push, and caused him to fall against one arm. He was immediately seized by a suffocating cough that soon ended his triumph. It lasted so long that it frightened even me. As to his cousin, she wept with all her might, aghast at the mischief she had done: though she said nothing. I held him till the fit exhausted itself. Then he thrust me away, and leant his head down silently. Catherine quelled her lamentations also, took a seat opposite, and looked solemnly into the fire.

'How do you feel now, Master Heathcliff?' I inquired, after waiting ten minutes.

'I wish SHE felt as I do,' he replied: 'spiteful, cruel thing! Hareton never touches me: he never struck me in his life. And I was better today: and there—' his voice died in a whimper.

'I didn't strike you!' muttered Cathy, chewing her lip to prevent another burst of emotion.

He sighed and moaned like one under great suffering, and kept it up for a quarter of an hour; on purpose to distress his cousin apparently, for whenever he caught a stifled sob from her he put renewed pain and pathos into the inflexions of his voice.

'I'm sorry I hurt you, Linton,' she said at length, racked beyond endurance. 'But I couldn't have been hurt by that little push, and I had no idea that you could, either: you're not much, are you, Linton? Don't let me go home thinking I've done you harm. Answer! speak to me.'

'I can't speak to you,' he murmured; 'you've hurt me so that I shall lie awake all night choking with this cough. If you had it you'd know what it was; but YOU'LL be comfortably asleep while I'm in agony, and nobody near me. I wonder how you would like to pass those fearful nights!' And he began to wail aloud, for very pity of himself.

'Since you are in the habit of passing dreadful nights,' I said, 'it won't be Miss who spoils your ease: you'd be the same had she never come. However, she shall not disturb you again; and perhaps you'll get quieter when we leave you.'

'Must I go?' asked Catherine dolefully, bending over him. 'Do you want me to go, Linton?'

'You can't alter what you've done,' he replied pettishly, shrinking from her; 'unless you alter it for the worse by teasing me into a fever.'

'Well, then, I must go?' she repeated.

'Let me alone, at least,' said he; 'I can't bear your talking.'

She lingered, and resisted my persuasions to departure a tiresome while; but as he neither looked up nor spoke, she finally made a movement to the door, and I followed. We were recalled by a scream. Linton had slid from his seat on to the hearthstone, and lay writhing in the mere perverseness of an indulged plague of a child, determined to be as grievous and harassing as it can. I thoroughly gauged his disposition from his behaviour, and saw at once it would be folly to attempt humouring him. Not so my companion: she ran back in terror, knelt down, and cried, and soothed, and entreated, till he grew quiet from lack of breath: by no means from compunction at distressing her.

'I shall lift him on to the settle,' I said, 'and he may roll about as he pleases: we can't stop to watch him. I hope you are satisfied, Miss Cathy, that you are not the person to benefit him; and that his condition of health is not occasioned by attachment to you. Now, then, there he is! Come away: as soon as he knows there is nobody by to care for his nonsense, he'll be glad to lie still.'

She placed a cushion under his head, and offered him some water; he rejected the latter, and tossed uneasily on the former, as if it were a stone or a block of wood. She tried to put it more comfortably.

'I can't do with that,' he said; 'it's not high enough.'

Catherine brought another to lay above it.

'That's too high,' murmured the provoking thing.

'How must I arrange it, then?' she asked despairingly.

He twined himself up to her, as she half knelt by the settle, and converted her shoulder into a support.

'No, that won't do,' I said. 'You'll be content with the cushion, Master Heathcliff. Miss has wasted too much time on you already: we cannot remain five minutes longer.'

'Yes, yes, we can!' replied Cathy. 'He's good and patient now. He's beginning to think I shall have far greater misery than he will tonight, if I believe he is the worse for my visit: and then I dare not come again. Tell the truth about it, Linton; for I musn't come, if I have hurt you.'

'You must come, to cure me,' he answered. 'You ought to come, because you have hurt me: you know you have extremely! I was not as ill when you entered as I am at present—was I?'

'But you've made yourself ill by crying and being in a passion.—I didn't do it all,' said his cousin. 'However, we'll be friends now. And you want me: you would wish to see me sometimes, really?'

'I told you I did,' he replied impatiently. 'Sit on the settle and let me lean on your knee. That's as mamma used to do, whole afternoons together. Sit quite still and don't talk: but you may sing a song, if you can sing; or you may say a nice long interesting ballad—one of those you promised to teach me; or a story. I'd rather have a ballad, though: begin.'

Catherine repeated the longest she could remember. The employment pleased both mightily. Linton would have another, and after that another, notwithstanding my strenuous objections; and so they went on until the clock struck twelve, and we heard Hareton in the court, returning for his dinner.

'And to-morrow, Catherine, will you be here to-morrow?' asked young Heathcliff, holding her frock as she rose reluctantly.

'No,' I answered, 'nor next day neither.' She, however, gave a different response evidently, for his forehead cleared as she stooped and whispered in his ear.

'You won't go to-morrow, recollect, Miss!' I commenced, when we were out of the house. 'You are not dreaming of it, are you?'

She smiled.

'Oh, I'll take good care,' I continued: 'I'll have that lock mended, and you can escape by no way else.'

'I can get over the wall,' she said laughing. 'The Grange is not a prison, Ellen, and you are not my gaoler. And besides, I'm almost seventeen: I'm a woman. And I'm certain Linton would recover quickly if he had me to look after him. I'm older than he is, you know, and wiser: less childish, am I not? And he'll soon do as I direct him, with some slight coaxing. He's a pretty little darling when he's good. I'd make such a pet of him, if he were mine. We should, never quarrel, should we after we were used to each other? Don't you like him, Ellen?'

'Like him!' I exclaimed. 'The worst-tempered bit of a sickly slip that ever struggled into its teens. Happily, as Mr. Heathcliff conjectured, he'll not win twenty. I doubt whether he'll see spring, indeed. And small loss to his family whenever he drops off. And lucky it is for us that his father took him: the kinder he was treated, the more tedious and selfish he'd be. I'm glad you have no chance of having him for a husband, Miss Catherine.'

My companion waxed serious at hearing this speech. To speak of his death so regardlessly wounded her feelings.

'He's younger than I,' she answered, after a protracted pause of meditation, 'and he ought to live the longest: he will—he must live as long as I do. He's as strong now as when he first came into the north; I'm positive of that. It's only a cold that ails him, the same as papa has. You say papa will get better, and why shouldn't he?'

'Well, well,' I cried, 'after all, we needn't trouble ourselves; for listen, Miss,—and mind, I'll keep my word,—if you attempt going to Wuthering Heights again, with or without me, I shall inform Mr. Linton, and, unless he allow it, the intimacy with your cousin must not be revived.'

'It has been revived,' muttered Cathy, sulkily.

'Must not be continued, then,' I said.

'We'll see,' was her reply, and she set off at a gallop, leaving me to toil in the rear.

We both reached home before our dinner-time; my master supposed we had been wandering through the park, and therefore he demanded no explanation of our absence. As soon as I entered I hastened to change my soaked shoes and stockings; but sitting such awhile at the Heights had done the mischief. On the succeeding morning I was laid up, and during three weeks I remained incapacitated for attending to my duties: a calamity never experienced prior to that period, and never, I am thankful to say, since.

My little mistress behaved like an angel in coming to wait on me, and cheer my solitude; the confinement brought me exceedingly low. It is wearisome, to a stirring active body: but few have slighter reasons for complaint than I had. The moment Catherine left Mr. Linton's room she appeared at my bedside. Her day was divided between us; no amusement usurped a minute: she neglected her meals, her studies, and her play; and she was the fondest nurse that ever watched. She must have had a warm heart, when she loved her father so, to give so much to me. I said her days were divided between us; but the master retired early, and I generally needed nothing after six o'clock, thus the evening was her own. Poor thing! I never considered what she did with herself after tea. And though frequently, when she looked in to bid me good-night, I remarked a fresh colour in her cheeks and a pinkness over her slender fingers, instead of fancying the line borrowed from a cold ride across the moors, I laid it to the charge of a hot fire in the library.

Chapter XXIV

AT the close of three weeks I was able to quit my chamber and move about the house. And on the first occasion of my sitting up in the evening I asked Catherine to read to me, because my eyes were weak. We were in the library, the master having gone to bed: she consented, rather unwillingly, I fancied; and imagining my sort of books did not suit her, I bid her please herself in the choice of what she perused. She selected one of her own favourites, and got forward steadily about an hour; then came frequent questions.

'Ellen, are not you tired? Hadn't you better lie down now? You'll be sick, keeping up so long, Ellen.'

'No, no, dear, I'm not tired,' I returned, continually.

Perceiving me immovable, she essayed another method of showing her disrelish for her occupation. It changed to yawning, and stretching, and—

'Ellen, I'm tired.'

'Give over then and talk,' I answered.

That was worse: she fretted and sighed, and looked at her watch till eight, and finally went to her room, completely overdone with sleep; judging by her peevish, heavy look, and the constant rubbing she inflicted on her eyes. The following night she seemed more impatient still; and on the third from recovering my company she complained of a headache, and left me. I thought her conduct odd; and having remained alone a long while, I resolved on going and inquiring whether she were better, and asking her to come and lie on the sofa, instead of up-stairs in the dark. No Catherine could I discover up-stairs, and none below. The servants affirmed they had not seen her. I listened at Mr. Edgar's door; all was silence. I returned to her apartment, extinguished my candle, and seated myself in the window.

The moon shone bright; a sprinkling of snow covered the ground, and I reflected that she might, possibly, have taken it into her head to walk about the garden, for refreshment. I did detect a figure creeping along the inner fence of the park; but it was not my young mistress: on its emerging into the light, I recognised one of the grooms. He stood a considerable period, viewing the carriage-road through the grounds; then started off at a brisk pace, as if he had detected something, and reappeared presently, leading Miss's pony;

and there she was, just dismounted, and walking by its side. The man took his charge stealthily across the grass towards the stable. Cathy entered by the casement-window of the drawing-room, and glided noiselessly up to where I awaited her. She put the door gently too, slipped off her snowy shoes, untied her hat, and was proceeding, unconscious of my espionage, to lay aside her mantle, when I suddenly rose and revealed myself. The surprise petrified her an instant: she uttered an inarticulate exclamation, and stood fixed.

'My dear Miss Catherine,' I began, too vividly impressed by her recent kindness to break into a scold, 'where have you been riding out at this hour? And why should you try to deceive me by telling a tale? Where have you been? Speak!'

'To the bottom of the park,' she stammered. 'I didn't tell a tale.'

'And nowhere else?' I demanded.

'No,' was the muttered reply.

'Oh, Catherine!' I cried, sorrowfully. 'You know you have been doing wrong, or you wouldn't be driven to uttering an untruth to me. That does grieve me. I'd rather be three months ill, than hear you frame a deliberate lie.'

She sprang forward, and bursting into tears, threw her arms round my neck.

'Well, Ellen, I'm so afraid of you being angry,' she said. 'Promise not to be angry, and you shall know the very truth: I hate to hide it.'

We sat down in the window-seat; I assured her I would not scold, whatever her secret might be, and I guessed it, of course; so she commenced—

'I've been to Wuthering Heights, Ellen, and I've never missed going a day since you fell ill; except thrice before, and twice after you left your room. I gave Michael books and pictures to prepare Minny every evening, and to put her back in the stable: you mustn't scold him either, mind. I was at the Heights by half-past six, and generally stayed till half-past eight, and then galloped home. It was not to amuse myself that I went: I was often wretched all the time. Now and then I was happy: once in a week perhaps. At first, I expected there would be sad work persuading you to let me keep my word to Linton: for I had engaged to call again next day, when we quitted him; but, as you stayed up-stairs on the morrow, I escaped that trouble. While Michael was refastening the lock of the park door in the afternoon, I got possession of the key, and told him how my cousin wished me to visit him, because he was sick, and couldn't come to the Grange; and how papa would object to my going: and then I negotiated with him about the pony. He is fond of reading, and he thinks of leaving soon to get married; so he offered, if I would lend him books out of the library, to do what I wished: but I preferred giving him my own, and that satisfied him better.

'On my second visit Linton seemed in lively spirits; and Zillah (that is their housekeeper) made us a clean room and a good fire, and told us that, as Joseph was out at a prayer-meeting and Hareton Earnshaw was off with his dogs—robbing our woods of pheasants, as I heard afterwards—we might do what we liked. She brought me some warm wine and gingerbread, and appeared exceedingly good-natured, and Linton sat in the arm-chair, and I in the little rocking chair on the hearth-stone, and we laughed and talked so merrily, and found so much to say: we planned where we would go, and what we would do in summer. I needn't repeat that, because you would call it silly.

'One time, however, we were near quarrelling. He said the pleasantest manner of spending a hot July day was lying from morning till evening on a bank of heath in the middle of the moors, with the bees humming dreamily about among the bloom, and the larks singing high up overhead, and the blue sky and bright sun shining steadily and cloudlessly. That was his most perfect idea of heaven's happiness: mine was rocking in a rustling green tree, with a west wind blowing, and bright white clouds flitting rapidly above; and not only larks, but throstles, and blackbirds, and linnets, and cuckoos pouring out music on every side, and the moors seen at a distance, broken into cool dusky dells; but close by great swells of long grass undulating in waves to the breeze; and woods and sounding water, and the whole world awake and wild with joy. He wanted all to lie in an ecstasy of peace; I wanted all to sparkle and dance in a glorious jubilee. I said his heaven would be only half alive; and he said mine would be drunk: I said I should fall asleep in his; and he said he could not breathe in mine, and began to grow very snappish. At last, we agreed to try both, as soon as the right weather came; and then we kissed each other and were friends.

'After sitting still an hour, I looked at the great room with its smooth uncarpeted floor, and thought how nice it would be to play in, if we removed the table; and I asked Linton to call Zillah in to help us, and we'd have a game at blindman's-buff; she should try to catch us: you used to, you know, Ellen. He wouldn't: there was no pleasure in it, he said; but he consented to play at ball with me. We found two in a cupboard, among a heap of old toys, tops, and hoops, and battledores and shuttlecocks. One was marked C., and the other H.; I wished to have the C., because that stood for Catherine, and the H. might be for Heathcliff, his name; but the bran came out of H., and Linton didn't like it. I beat him constantly: and he got cross again, and coughed, and returned to his chair. That night, though, he easily recovered his good humour: he was charmed with two or three pretty songs—YOUR songs, Ellen; and when I was obliged to go, he begged and entreated me to come the following evening; and I promised. Minny and I went flying home as light as air; and I dreamt of Wuthering Heights and my sweet, darling cousin, till morning.

'On the morrow I was sad; partly because you were poorly, and partly that I wished my father knew, and approved of my excursions: but it was beautiful moonlight after tea; and, as I rode on, the gloom cleared. I shall have another happy evening, I thought to myself; and what delights me more, my pretty Linton will. I trotted up their garden, and was turning round to the back, when that fellow Earnshaw met me, took my bridle, and bid me go in by the front entrance. He patted Minny's neck, and said she was a bonny beast, and appeared as if he wanted me to speak to him. I only told him to leave my horse alone, or else it would kick him. He answered in his vulgar accent, "It wouldn't do mitch hurt if it did;" and surveyed its legs with a smile. I was half inclined to make it try; however, he moved off to open the door, and, as he raised the latch, he looked up to the inscription above, and said, with a stupid mixture of awkwardness and elation: "Miss Catherine! I can read yon, now."

'"Wonderful," I exclaimed. "Pray let us hear you—you ARE grown clever!"

'He spelt, and drawled over by syllables, the name—"Hareton Earnshaw."

'"And the figures?" I cried, encouragingly, perceiving that he came to a dead halt.

'"I cannot tell them yet," he answered.

'"Oh, you dunce!" I said, laughing heartily at his failure.

'The fool stared, with a grin hovering about his lips, and a scowl gathering over his eyes, as if uncertain whether he might not join in my mirth: whether it were not pleasant familiarity, or what it really was, contempt. I settled his doubts, by suddenly retrieving my gravity and desiring him to walk away, for I came to see Linton, not him. He reddened—I saw that by the moonlight—dropped his hand from the latch, and skulked off, a picture of mortified vanity. He imagined himself to be as accomplished as Linton, I suppose, because he could spell his own name; and was marvellously discomfited that I didn't think the same.'

'Stop, Miss Catherine, dear!'—I interrupted. 'I shall not scold, but I don't like your conduct there. If you had remembered that Hareton was your cousin as much as Master Heathcliff, you would have felt how improper it was to behave in that way. At least, it was praiseworthy ambition for him to desire to be as accomplished as Linton; and probably he did not learn merely to show off: you had made him ashamed of his ignorance before, I have no doubt; and he wished to remedy it and please you. To sneer at his imperfect attempt was very bad breeding. Had you been brought up in his circumstances, would you be less rude? He was as quick and as intelligent a child as ever you were; and I'm hurt that he should be despised now, because that base Heathcliff has treated him so unjustly.'

'Well, Ellen, you won't cry about it, will you?' she exclaimed, surprised at my earnestness. 'But wait, and you shall hear if he conned his A B C to please me; and if it were worth while being civil to the brute. I entered; Linton was lying on the settle, and half got up to welcome me.

'"I'm ill to-night, Catherine, love," he said; "and you must have all the talk, and let me listen. Come, and sit by me. I was sure you wouldn't break your word, and I'll make you promise again, before you go."

'I knew now that I mustn't tease him, as he was ill; and I spoke softly and put no questions, and avoided irritating him in any way. I had brought some of my nicest books for him: he asked me to read a little of one, and I was about to comply, when Earnshaw burst the door open: having gathered venom with reflection. He advanced direct to us, seized Linton by the arm, and swung him off the seat.

'"Get to thy own room!" he said, in a voice almost inarticulate with passion; and his face looked swelled and furious. "Take her there if she comes to see thee: thou shalln't keep me out of this. Begone wi' ye both!"

'He swore at us, and left Linton no time to answer, nearly throwing him into the kitchen; and he clenched his fist as I followed, seemingly longing to knock me down. I was afraid for a moment, and I let one volume fall; he kicked it after me, and shut us out. I heard a malignant, crackly laugh by the fire, and turning, beheld that odious Joseph standing rubbing his bony hands, and quivering.

'"I wer sure he'd sarve ye out! He's a grand lad! He's getten t' raight sperrit in him! HE knaws—ay, he knaws, as weel as I do, who sud be t' maister yonder—Ech, ech, ech! He made ye skift properly! Ech, ech, ech!"

'"Where must we go?" I asked of my cousin, disregarding the old wretch's mockery.

'Linton was white and trembling. He was not pretty then, Ellen: oh, no! he looked frightful; for his thin face and large eyes were wrought into an expression of frantic, powerless fury. He grasped the handle of the door, and shook it: it was fastened inside.

'"If you don't let me in, I'll kill you!—If you don't let me in, I'll kill you!" he rather shrieked than said. "Devil! devil!—I'll kill you—I'll kill you!"

Joseph uttered his croaking laugh again.

'"Thear, that's t' father!" he cried. "That's father! We've allas summut o' either side in us. Niver heed, Hareton, lad—dunnut be 'feard—he cannot get at thee!"

'I took hold of Linton's hands, and tried to pull him away; but he shrieked so shockingly that I dared not proceed. At last his cries were choked by a dreadful fit of coughing; blood gushed from his mouth, and he fell on the ground. I ran into the yard, sick with terror; and called for Zillah, as loud as I could. She soon heard me: she was milking the cows in a shed behind the barn, and hurrying from her work, she inquired what there was to do? I hadn't breath to explain; dragging her in, I looked about for Linton. Earnshaw had come out to examine the mischief he had caused, and he was then conveying the poor thing up-stairs. Zillah and I ascended after him; but he stopped me at the top of the steps, and said I shouldn't go in: I must go home. I exclaimed that he had killed Linton, and I WOULD enter. Joseph locked the door, and declared I should do "no sich stuff," and asked me whether I were "bahn to be as mad as him." I stood crying till the housekeeper reappeared. She affirmed he would be better in a bit, but he couldn't do with that shrieking and din;-and she took me, and nearly carried me into the house.

'Ellen, I was ready to tear my hair off my head! I sobbed and wept so that my eyes were almost blind; and the ruffian you have such sympathy with stood opposite: presuming every now and then to bid me "wisht," and denying that it was his fault; and, finally, frightened by my assertions that I would tell papa, and that he should be put in prison and hanged, he commenced blubbering himself, and hurried out to hide his cowardly agitation. Still, I was not rid of him: when at length they compelled me to depart, and I had got some hundred yards off the premises, he suddenly issued from the shadow of the road-side, and checked Minny and took hold of me.

'"Miss Catherine, I'm ill grieved," he began, "but it's rayther too bad—"

'I gave him a cut with my whip, thinking perhaps he would murder me. He let go, thundering one of his horrid curses, and I galloped home more than half out of my senses.

'I didn't bid you good-night that evening, and I didn't go to Wuthering Heights the next: I wished to go exceedingly; but I was strangely excited, and dreaded to hear that Linton was dead, sometimes; and sometimes shuddered at the thought of encountering Hareton. On the third day I took courage: at least, I couldn't bear longer suspense, and stole off once more. I went at five o'clock, and walked; fancying I might manage to creep into the house, and up to Linton's room, unobserved. However, the dogs gave notice of my approach. Zillah received me, and saying "the lad was mending nicely," showed me into a small, tidy, carpeted apartment, where, to my inexpressible joy, I beheld Linton laid on a little sofa, reading one of my books. But he would neither speak to me nor look at me, through a whole hour, Ellen: he has such an unhappy temper. And what quite confounded me, when he did open his mouth, it was to utter the falsehood that I had occasioned the uproar, and Hareton was not to blame! Unable to reply, except passionately, I got up and walked from the room. He sent after me a faint "Catherine!" He did not reckon on being answered so: but I wouldn't turn back; and the morrow was the second day on which I stayed at home, nearly determined to visit him no more. But it was so miserable going to bed and getting up, and never hearing anything about him, that my resolution melted into air before it was properly formed. It had appeared wrong to take the journey once; now it seemed wrong to refrain. Michael came to ask if he must saddle Minny; I said "Yes," and considered myself doing a duty as she bore me over the hills. I was forced to pass the front windows to get to the court: it was no use trying to conceal my presence.

'"Young master is in the house," said Zillah, as she saw me making for the parlour. I went in; Earnshaw was there also, but he quitted the room directly. Linton sat in the great arm-chair half asleep; walking up to the fire, I began in a serious tone, partly meaning it to be true—

'"As you don't like me, Linton, and as you think I come on purpose to hurt you, and pretend that I do so every time, this is our last meeting: let us say good-bye; and tell Mr. Heathcliff that you have no wish to see me, and that he mustn't invent any more falsehoods on the subject."

'"Sit down and take your hat off, Catherine," he answered. "You are so much happier than I am, you ought to be better. Papa talks enough of my defects, and shows enough scorn of me, to make it natural I should doubt myself. I doubt whether I am not altogether as worthless as he calls me, frequently; and then I feel so cross and bitter, I hate everybody! I am worthless, and bad in temper, and bad in spirit, almost always; and, if you choose, you may say good-bye: you'll get rid of an annoyance. Only, Catherine, do me this justice: believe that if I might be as sweet, and as kind, and as good as you are, I would be; as willingly, and more so, than as happy and as healthy. And believe that your kindness has made me love you deeper than if I deserved your love: and though I couldn't, and cannot help showing my nature to you, I regret it and repent it; and shall regret and repent it till I die!"

'I felt he spoke the truth; and I felt I must forgive him: and, though we should quarrel the next moment, I must forgive him again. We were reconciled; but we cried, both of us, the whole time I stayed: not entirely for sorrow; yet I WAS sorry Linton had that distorted nature. He'll never let his friends be at ease, and he'll never be at ease himself! I have always gone to his little parlour, since that night; because his father returned the day after.

'About three times, I think, we have been merry and hopeful, as we were the first evening; the rest of my visits were dreary and troubled: now with his selfishness and spite, and now with his sufferings: but I've learned to endure the former with nearly as little resentment as the latter. Mr. Heathcliff purposely avoids me: I have hardly seen him at all. Last Sunday, indeed, coming earlier than usual, I heard him abusing poor Linton cruelly for his conduct of the night before. I can't tell how he knew of it, unless he listened. Linton had certainly behaved provokingly: however, it was the business of nobody but me, and I interrupted Mr. Heathcliff's lecture by entering and telling him so. He burst into a laugh, and went away, saying he was glad I took that view of the matter. Since then, I've told Linton he must whisper his bitter things. Now, Ellen, you have heard all. I can't be prevented from going to Wuthering Heights, except by inflicting misery on two people; whereas, if you'll only not tell papa, my going need disturb the tranquillity of none. You'll not tell, will you? It will be very heartless, if you do.'

'I'll make up my mind on that point by to-morrow, Miss Catherine,' I replied. 'It requires some study; and so I'll leave you to your rest, and go think it over.'

I thought it over aloud, in my master's presence; walking straight from her room to his, and relating the whole story: with the exception of her conversations with her cousin, and any mention of Hareton. Mr. Linton was alarmed and distressed, more than he would acknowledge to me. In the morning, Catherine learnt my betrayal of her confidence, and she learnt also that her secret visits were to end. In vain she wept and writhed against the interdict, and implored her father to have pity on Linton: all she got to comfort her was a promise that he would write and give him leave to come to the Grange when he pleased; but explaining that he must no longer expect to see Catherine at Wuthering Heights. Perhaps, had he been aware of his nephew's disposition and state of health, he would have seen fit to withhold even that slight consolation.

Chapter XXV

'THESE things happened last winter, sir,' said Mrs. Dean; 'hardly more than a year ago. Last winter, I did not think, at another twelve months' end, I should be amusing a stranger to the family with relating them! Yet, who knows how long you'll be a stranger? You're too young to rest always contented, living by yourself; and I some way fancy no one could see Catherine Linton and not love her. You smile; but why do you look so lively and interested when I talk about her? and why have you asked me to hang her picture over your fireplace? and why—?'

'Stop, my good friend!' I cried. 'It may be very possible that I should love her; but would she love me? I doubt it too much to venture my tranquillity by running into temptation: and then my home is not here. I'm of the busy world, and to its arms I must return. Go on. Was Catherine obedient to her father's commands?'

'She was,' continued the housekeeper. 'Her affection for him was still the chief sentiment in her heart; and he spoke without anger: he spoke in the deep tenderness of one about to leave his treasure amid perils and foes, where his remembered words would be the only aid that he could bequeath to guide her. He said to me, a few days afterwards, "I wish my nephew would write, Ellen, or call. Tell me, sincerely, what you think of him: is he changed for the better, or is there a prospect of improvement, as he grows a man?"

'"He's very delicate, sir," I replied; "and scarcely likely to reach manhood: but this I can say, he does not resemble his father; and if Miss Catherine had the misfortune to marry him, he would not be beyond her control: unless she were extremely and foolishly indulgent. However, master, you'll have plenty of time to get acquainted with him and see whether he would suit her: it wants four years and more to his being of age."'

Edgar sighed; and, walking to the window, looked out towards Gimmerton Kirk. It was a misty afternoon, but the February sun shone dimly, and we could just distinguish the two fir-trees in the yard, and the sparely-scattered gravestones.

'I've prayed often,' he half soliloquised, 'for the approach of what is coming; and now I begin to shrink, and fear it. I thought the memory of the hour I came down that glen a bridegroom would be less sweet than the anticipation that I was soon, in a few months, or, possibly, weeks, to be carried up, and laid in its lonely hollow! Ellen, I've been very happy with my little Cathy: through winter nights and summer days she was a living hope at my side. But I've been as happy musing by myself among those stones, under that old church: lying, through the long June evenings, on the green mound of her mother's grave, and wishing—yearning for the time when I might lie beneath it. What can I do for Cathy? How must I quit her? I'd not care one moment for Linton being Heathcliff's son; nor for his taking her from me, if he could console her for my loss. I'd not care that Heathcliff gained his ends, and triumphed in robbing me of my last blessing! But should Linton be unworthy—only a feeble tool to his father—I cannot abandon her to him! And, hard though it be to crush her buoyant spirit, I must persevere in making her sad while I live, and leaving her solitary when I die. Darling! I'd rather resign her to God, and lay her in the earth before me.'

'Resign her to God as it is, sir,' I answered, 'and if we should lose you—which may He forbid—under His providence, I'll stand her friend and counsellor to the last. Miss Catherine is a good girl: I don't fear that she will go wilfully wrong; and people who do their duty are always finally rewarded.'

Spring advanced; yet my master gathered no real strength, though he resumed his walks in the grounds with his daughter. To her inexperienced notions, this itself was a sign of convalescence; and then his cheek was often flushed, and his eyes were bright; she felt sure of his recovering. On her seventeenth birthday, he did not visit the churchyard: it was raining, and I observed—'You'll surely not go out to-night, sir?'

He answered,—'No, I'll defer it this year a little longer.' He wrote again to Linton, expressing his great desire to see him; and, had the invalid been presentable, I've no doubt his father would have permitted him to come. As it was, being instructed, he returned an answer, intimating that Mr. Heathcliff objected to his calling at the Grange; but his uncle's kind remembrance delighted him, and he hoped to meet him sometimes in his rambles, and personally to petition that his cousin and he might not remain long so utterly divided.

That part of his letter was simple, and probably his own. Heathcliff knew he could plead eloquently for Catherine's company, then.

'I do not ask,' he said, 'that she may visit here; but am I never to see her, because my father forbids me to go to her home, and you forbid her to come to mine? Do, now and then, ride with her towards the Heights; and let us exchange a few words, in your presence! We have done nothing to deserve this separation; and you are not angry with me: you have no reason to dislike me, you allow, yourself. Dear uncle! send me a kind note to-morrow, and leave to join you anywhere you please, except at Thrushcross Grange. I believe an interview would convince you that my father's character is not mine: he affirms I am more your nephew than his son; and though I have faults which render me unworthy of Catherine, she has excused them, and for her sake, you should also. You inquire after my health—it is better; but while I remain cut off from all hope, and doomed to solitude, or the society of those who never did and never will like me, how can I be cheerful and well?'

Edgar, though he felt for the boy, could not consent to grant his request; because he could not accompany Catherine. He said, in summer, perhaps, they might meet: meantime, he wished him to continue writing at intervals, and engaged to give him what advice and comfort he was able by letter; being well aware of his hard position in his family. Linton complied; and had he been unrestrained, would probably have spoiled all by filling his epistles with complaints and lamentations. but his father kept a sharp watch over him; and, of course, insisted on every line that my master sent being shown; so, instead of penning his peculiar personal sufferings and distresses, the themes constantly uppermost in his thoughts, he harped on the cruel obligation of being held asunder from his friend and love; and gently intimated that Mr. Linton must allow an interview soon, or he should fear he was purposely deceiving him with empty promises.

Cathy was a powerful ally at home; and between them they at length persuaded my master to acquiesce in their having a ride or a walk together about once a week, under my guardianship, and on the moors nearest the Grange: for June found him still declining. Though he had set aside yearly a portion of his income for my young lady's fortune, he had a natural desire that she might retain—or at least return in a short time to—the house of her ancestors; and he considered her only prospect of doing that was by a union with his heir; he had no idea that the latter was failing almost as fast as himself; nor had any one, I believe: no doctor visited the Heights, and no one saw Master Heathcliff to make report of his condition among us. I, for my part, began to fancy my forebodings were false, and that he must be actually rallying, when he mentioned riding and walking on the moors, and seemed so earnest in pursuing his object. I could not picture a father treating a dying child as tyrannically and wickedly as I afterwards learned Heathcliff had treated him, to compel this apparent eagerness: his efforts redoubling the more imminently his avaricious and unfeeling plans were threatened with defeat by death.

Chapter XXVI

SUMMER was already past its prime, when Edgar reluctantly yielded his assent to their entreaties, and Catherine and I set out on our first ride to join her cousin. It was a close, sultry day: devoid of sunshine, but with a sky too dappled and hazy to threaten rain: and our place of meeting had been fixed at the guide-stone, by the cross-roads. On arriving there, however, a little herd-boy, despatched as a messenger, told us that,—'Maister Linton wer just o' this side th' Heights: and he'd be mitch obleeged to us to gang on a bit further.'

'Then Master Linton has forgot the first injunction of his uncle,' I observed: 'he bid us keep on the Grange land, and here we are off at once.'

'Well, we'll turn our horses' heads round when we reach him,' answered my companion; 'our excursion shall lie towards home.'

But when we reached him, and that was scarcely a quarter of a mile from his own door, we found he had no horse; and we were forced to dismount, and leave ours to graze. He lay on the heath, awaiting our approach, and did not rise till we came within a few yards. Then he walked so feebly, and looked so pale, that I immediately exclaimed,—'Why, Master Heathcliff, you are not fit for enjoying a ramble this morning. How ill you do look!'

Catherine surveyed him with grief and astonishment: she changed the ejaculation of joy on her lips to one of alarm; and the congratulation on their long-postponed meeting to an anxious inquiry, whether he were worse than usual?

'No—better—better!' he panted, trembling, and retaining her hand as if he needed its support, while his large blue eyes wandered timidly over her; the hollowness round them transforming to haggard wildness the languid expression they once possessed.

'But you have been worse,' persisted his cousin; 'worse than when I saw you last; you are thinner, and—'

'I'm tired,' he interrupted, hurriedly. 'It is too hot for walking, let us rest here. And, in the morning, I often feel sick-papa says I grow so fast.'

Badly satisfied, Cathy sat down, and he reclined beside her.

'This is something like your paradise,' said she, making an effort at cheerfulness. 'You recollect the two days we agreed to spend in the place and way each thought pleasantest? This is nearly yours, only there are clouds; but then they are so soft and mellow: it is nicer than sunshine. Next week, if you can, we'll ride down to the Grange Park, and try mine.'

Linton did not appear to remember what she talked of and he had evidently great difficulty in sustaining any kind of conversation. His lack of interest in the subjects she started, and his equal incapacity to contribute to her entertainment, were so obvious that she could not conceal her disappointment. An indefinite alteration had come over his whole person and manner. The pettishness that might be caressed into fondness, had yielded to a listless apathy; there was less of the peevish temper of a child which frets and teases on purpose to be soothed, and more of the self-absorbed moroseness of a confirmed invalid, repelling consolation, and ready to regard the good-humoured mirth of others as an insult. Catherine perceived, as well as I did, that he held it rather a punishment, than a gratification, to endure our company; and she made no scruple of proposing, presently, to depart. That proposal, unexpectedly, roused Linton from his lethargy, and threw him into a strange state of agitation. He glanced fearfully towards the Heights, begging she would remain another half-hour, at least.

'But I think,' said Cathy, 'you'd be more comfortable at home than sitting here; and I cannot amuse you to-day, I see, by my tales, and songs, and chatter: you have grown wiser than I, in these six months; you have little taste for my diversions now: or else, if I could amuse you, I'd willingly stay.'

'Stay to rest yourself,' he replied. 'And, Catherine, don't think or say that I'm VERY unwell: it is the heavy weather and heat that make me dull; and I walked about, before you came, a great deal for me. Tell uncle I'm in tolerable health, will you?'

'I'll tell him that YOU say so, Linton. I couldn't affirm that you are,' observed my young lady, wondering at his pertinacious assertion of what was evidently an untruth.

'And be here again next Thursday,' continued he, shunning her puzzled gaze. 'And give him my thanks for permitting you to come—my best thanks, Catherine. And—and, if you DID meet my father, and he asked you about me, don't lead him to suppose that I've been extremely silent and stupid: don't look sad and downcast, as you are doing—he'll be angry.'

'I care nothing for his anger,' exclaimed Cathy, imagining she would be its object.

'But I do,' said her cousin, shuddering. 'DON'T provoke him against me, Catherine, for he is very hard.'

'Is he severe to you, Master Heathcliff?' I inquired. 'Has he grown weary of indulgence, and passed from passive to active hatred?'

Linton looked at me, but did not answer; and, after keeping her seat by his side another ten minutes, during which his head fell drowsily on his breast, and he uttered nothing except suppressed moans of exhaustion or pain, Cathy began to seek solace in looking for bilberries, and sharing the produce of her researches with me: she did not offer them to him, for she saw further notice would only weary and annoy.

'Is it half-an-hour now, Ellen?' she whispered in my ear, at last. 'I can't tell why we should stay. He's asleep, and papa will be wanting us back.'

'Well, we must not leave him asleep,' I answered; 'wait till lie wakes, and be patient. You were mighty eager to set off, but your longing to see poor Linton has soon evaporated!'

'Why did HE wish to see me?' returned Catherine. 'In his crossest humours, formerly, I liked him better than I do in his present curious mood. It's just as if it were a task he was compelled to perform—

this interview—for fear his father should scold him. But I'm hardly going to come to give Mr. Heathcliff pleasure; whatever reason he may have for ordering Linton to undergo this penance. And, though I'm glad he's better in health, I'm sorry he's so much less pleasant, and so much less affectionate to me.'

'You think HE IS better in health, then?' I said.

'Yes,' she answered; 'because he always made such a great deal of his sufferings, you know. He is not tolerably well, as he told me to tell papa; but he's better, very likely.'

'There you differ with me, Miss Cathy,' I remarked; 'I should conjecture him to be far worse.'

Linton here started from his slumber in bewildered terror, and asked if any one had called his name.

'No,' said Catherine; 'unless in dreams. I cannot conceive how you manage to doze out of doors, in the morning.'

'I thought I heard my father,' he gasped, glancing up to the frowning nab above us. 'You are sure nobody spoke?'

'Quite sure,' replied his cousin. 'Only Ellen and I were disputing concerning your health. Are you truly stronger, Linton, than when we separated in winter? If you be, I'm certain one thing is not stronger—your regard for me: speak,—are you?'

The tears gushed from Linton's eyes as he answered, 'Yes, yes, I am!' And, still under the spell of the imaginary voice, his gaze wandered up and down to detect its owner.

Cathy rose. 'For to-day we must part,' she said. 'And I won't conceal that I have been sadly disappointed with our meeting; though I'll mention it to nobody but you: not that I stand in awe of Mr. Heathcliff.'

'Hush,' murmured Linton; 'for God's sake, hush! He's coming.' And he clung to Catherine's arm, striving to detain her; but at that announcement she hastily disengaged herself, and whistled to Minny, who obeyed her like a dog.

'I'll be here next Thursday,' she cried, springing to the saddle. 'Good-bye. Quick, Ellen!'

And so we left him, scarcely conscious of our departure, so absorbed was he in anticipating his father's approach.

Before we reached home, Catherine's displeasure softened into a perplexed sensation of pity and regret, largely blended with vague, uneasy doubts about Linton's actual circumstances, physical and social: in which I partook, though I counselled her not to say much; for a second journey would make us better judges. My master requested an account of our ongoings. His nephew's offering of thanks was duly delivered, Miss Cathy gently touching on the rest: I also threw little light on his inquiries, for I hardly knew what to hide and what to reveal.

Chapter XXVII

SEVEN days glided away, every one marking its course by the henceforth rapid alteration of Edgar Linton's state. The havoc that months had previously wrought was now emulated by the inroads of hours. Catherine we would fain have deluded yet; but her own quick spirit refused to delude her: it divined in secret, and brooded on the dreadful probability, gradually ripening into certainty. She had not the heart to mention her ride, when Thursday came round; I mentioned it for her, and obtained permission to order her out of doors: for the library, where her father stopped a short time daily—the brief period he could bear to sit up—and his chamber, had become her whole world. She grudged each moment that did not find her bending over his pillow, or seated by his side. Her countenance grew wan with watching and sorrow, and my master gladly dismissed her to what he flattered himself would be a happy change of scene and society; drawing comfort from the hope that she would not now be left entirely alone after his death.

He had a fixed idea, I guessed by several observations he let fall, that, as his nephew resembled him in person, he would resemble him in mind; for Linton's letters bore few or no indications of his defective character. And I, through pardonable weakness, refrained from correcting the error; asking myself what good there would be in disturbing his last moments with information that he had neither power nor opportunity to turn to account.

We deferred our excursion till the afternoon; a golden afternoon of August: every breath from the hills so full of life, that it seemed whoever respired it, though dying, might revive. Catherine's face was just like the landscape—shadows and sunshine flitting over it in rapid succession; but the shadows rested longer, and the sunshine was more transient; and her poor little heart reproached itself for even that passing forgetfulness of its cares.

We discerned Linton watching at the same spot he had selected before. My young mistress alighted, and told me that, as she was resolved to stay a very little while, I had better hold the pony and remain on horseback; but I dissented: I wouldn't risk losing sight of the charge committed to me a minute; so we climbed the slope of heath together. Master Heathcliff received us with greater animation on this occasion: not the animation of high spirits though, nor yet of joy; it looked more like fear.

'It is late!' he said, speaking short and with difficulty. 'Is not your father very ill? I thought you wouldn't come.'

'WHY won't you be candid?' cried Catherine, swallowing her greeting. 'Why cannot you say at once you don't want me? It is strange, Linton, that for the second time you have brought me here on purpose, apparently to distress us both, and for no reason besides!'

Linton shivered, and glanced at her, half supplicating, half ashamed; but his cousin's patience was not sufficient to endure this enigmatical behaviour.

'My father IS very ill,' she said; 'and why am I called from his bedside? Why didn't you send to absolve me from my promise, when you wished I wouldn't keep it? Come! I desire an explanation: playing and trifling are completely banished out of my mind; and I can't dance attendance on your affectations now!'

'My affectations!' he murmured; 'what are they? For heaven's sake, Catherine, don't look so angry! Despise me as much as you please; I am a worthless, cowardly wretch: I can't be scorned enough; but I'm too mean for your anger. Hate my father, and spare me for contempt.'

'Nonsense!' cried Catherine in a passion. 'Foolish, silly boy! And there! he trembles: as if I were really going to touch him! You needn't bespeak contempt, Linton: anybody will have it spontaneously at your service. Get off! I shall return home: it is folly dragging you from the hearth-stone, and pretending—what do we pretend? Let go my frock! If I pitied you for crying and looking so very frightened, you should spurn such pity. Ellen, tell him how disgraceful this conduct is. Rise, and don't degrade yourself into an abject reptile—DON'T!'

With streaming face and an expression of agony, Linton had thrown his nerveless frame along the ground: he seemed convulsed with exquisite terror.

'Oh!' he sobbed, 'I cannot bear it! Catherine, Catherine, I'm a traitor, too, and I dare not tell you! But leave me, and I shall be killed! DEAR Catherine, my life is in your hands: and you have said you loved me, and if you did, it wouldn't harm you. You'll not go, then? kind, sweet, good Catherine! And perhaps you WILL consent—and he'll let me die with you!'

My young lady, on witnessing his intense anguish, stooped to raise him. The old feeling of indulgent tenderness overcame her vexation, and she grew thoroughly moved and alarmed.

'Consent to what?' she asked. 'To stay! tell me the meaning of this strange talk, and I will. You contradict your own words, and distract me! Be calm and frank, and confess at once all that weighs on your heart. You wouldn't injure me, Linton, would you? You wouldn't let any enemy hurt me, if you could prevent it? I'll believe you are a coward, for yourself, but not a cowardly betrayer of your best friend.'

'But my father threatened me,' gasped the boy, clasping his attenuated fingers, 'and I dread him—I dread him! I DARE not tell!'

'Oh, well!' said Catherine, with scornful compassion, 'keep your secret: I'M no coward. Save yourself: I'm not afraid!'

Her magnanimity provoked his tears: he wept wildly, kissing her supporting hands, and yet could not summon courage to speak out. I was cogitating what the mystery might be, and determined Catherine should never suffer to benefit him or any one else, by my good will; when, hearing a rustle among the ling, I looked up and saw Mr. Heathcliff almost close upon us, descending the Heights. He didn't cast a glance towards my companions, though they were sufficiently near for Linton's sobs to be audible; but hailing me in the almost hearty tone he assumed to none besides, and the sincerity of which I couldn't avoid doubting, he said—

'It is something to see you so near to my house, Nelly. How are you at the Grange? Let us hear. The rumour goes,' he added, in a lower tone, 'that Edgar Linton is on his death-bed: perhaps they exaggerate his illness?'

'No; my master is dying,' I replied: 'it is true enough. A sad thing it will be for us all, but a blessing for him!'

'How long will he last, do you think?' he asked.

'I don't know,' I said.

'Because,' he continued, looking at the two young people, who were fixed under his eye—Linton appeared as if he could not venture to stir or raise his head, and Catherine could not move, on his account—'because that lad yonder seems determined to beat me; and I'd thank his uncle to be quick, and go before him! Hallo! has the whelp been playing that game long? I DID give him some lessons about snivelling. Is he pretty lively with Miss Linton generally?'

'Lively? no—he has shown the greatest distress,' I answered. 'To see him, I should say, that instead of rambling with his sweetheart on the hills, he ought to be in bed, under the hands of a doctor.'

'He shall be, in a day or two,' muttered Heathcliff. 'But first—get up, Linton! Get up!' he shouted. 'Don't grovel on the ground there up, this moment!'

Linton had sunk prostrate again in another paroxysm of helpless fear, caused by his father's glance towards him, I suppose: there was nothing else to produce such humiliation. He made several efforts to obey, but his little strength was annihilated for the time, and he fell back again with a moan. Mr. Heathcliff advanced, and lifted him to lean against a ridge of turf.

'Now,' said he, with curbed ferocity, 'I'm getting angry and if you don't command that paltry spirit of yours—DAMN you! get up directly!'

'I will, father,' he panted. 'Only, let me alone, or I shall faint. I've done as you wished, I'm sure. Catherine will tell you that I—that I—have been cheerful. Ah! keep by me, Catherine; give me your hand.'

'Take mine,' said his father; 'stand on your feet. There now—she'll lend you her arm: that's right, look at her. You would imagine I was the devil himself, Miss Linton, to excite such horror. Be so kind as to walk home with him, will you? He shudders if I touch him.'

'Linton dear!' whispered Catherine, 'I can't go to Wuthering Heights: papa has forbidden me. He'll not harm you: why are you so afraid?'

'I can never re-enter that house,' he answered. 'I'm NOT to re-enter it without you!'

'Stop!' cried his father. 'We'll respect Catherine's filial scruples. Nelly, take him in, and I'll follow your advice concerning the doctor, without delay.'

'You'll do well,' replied I. 'But I must remain with my mistress: to mind your son is not my business.'

'You are very stiff,' said Heathcliff, 'I know that: but you'll force me to pinch the baby and make it scream before it moves your charity. Come, then, my hero. Are you willing to return, escorted by me?'

He approached once more, and made as if he would seize the fragile being; but, shrinking back, Linton clung to his cousin, and implored her to accompany him, with a frantic importunity that admitted no denial. However I disapproved, I couldn't hinder her: indeed, how could she have refused him herself? What was filling him with dread we had no means of discerning; but there he was, powerless under its gripe, and any addition seemed capable of shocking him into idiotcy. We reached the threshold; Catherine walked in, and I stood waiting till she had conducted the invalid to a chair, expecting her out immediately; when Mr. Heathcliff, pushing me forward, exclaimed—'My house is not stricken with the plague, Nelly; and I have a mind to be hospitable to-day: sit down, and allow me to shut the door.'

He shut and locked it also. I started.

'You shall have tea before you go home,' he added. 'I am by myself. Hareton is gone with some cattle to the Lees, and Zillah and Joseph are off on a journey of pleasure; and, though I'm used to being alone, I'd rather have some interesting company, if I can get it. Miss Linton, take your seat by HIM. I give you what I have: the present is hardly worth accepting; but I have nothing else to offer. It is Linton, I mean. How she does stare! It's odd what a savage feeling I have to anything that seems afraid of me! Had I been born where laws are less strict and tastes less dainty, I should treat myself to a slow vivisection of those two, as an evening's amusement.'

He drew in his breath, struck the table, and swore to himself, 'By hell! I hate them.'

'I am not afraid of you!' exclaimed Catherine, who could not hear the latter part of his speech. She stepped close up; her black eyes flashing with passion and resolution. 'Give me that key: I will have it!' she said. 'I wouldn't eat or drink here, if I were starving.'

Heathcliff had the key in his hand that remained on the table. He looked up, seized with a sort of surprise at her boldness; or, possibly, reminded, by her voice and glance, of the person from whom she inherited it. She snatched at the instrument, and half succeeded in getting it out of his loosened fingers: but her action recalled him to the present; he recovered it speedily.

'Now, Catherine Linton,' he said, 'stand off, or I shall knock you down; and, that will make Mrs. Dean mad.'

Regardless of this warning, she captured his closed hand and its contents again. 'We will go!' she repeated, exerting her utmost efforts to cause the iron muscles to relax; and finding that her nails made no impression, she applied her teeth pretty sharply. Heathcliff glanced at me a glance that kept me from interfering a moment. Catherine was too intent on his fingers to notice his face. He opened them suddenly, and resigned the object of dispute; but, ere she had well secured it, he seized her with the liberated hand, and, pulling her on his knee, administered with the other a shower of terrific slaps on both sides of the head, each sufficient to have fulfilled his threat, had she been able to fall.'

At this diabolical violence I rushed on him furiously. 'You villain!' I began to cry, 'you villain!' A touch on the chest silenced me: I am stout, and soon put out of breath; and, what with that and the rage, I staggered dizzily back and felt ready to suffocate, or to burst a blood-vessel. The scene was over in two minutes; Catherine, released, put her two hands to her temples, and looked just as if she were not sure whether her ears were off or on. She trembled like a reed, poor thing, and leant against the table perfectly bewildered.

'I know how to chastise children, you see,' said the scoundrel, grimly, as he stooped to repossess himself of the key, which had dropped to the floor. 'Go to Linton now, as I told you; and cry at your ease! I shall be your father, to-morrow—all the father you'll have in a few days—and you shall have plenty of that. You can bear plenty; you're no weakling: you shall have a daily taste, if I catch such a devil of a temper in your eyes again!'

Cathy ran to me instead of Linton, and knelt down and put her burning cheek on my lap, weeping aloud. Her cousin had shrunk into a corner of the settle, as quiet as a mouse, congratulating himself, I dare say, that the correction had alighted on another than him. Mr. Heathcliff, perceiving us all confounded, rose, and expeditiously made the tea himself. The cups and saucers were laid ready. He poured it out, and handed me a cup.

'Wash away your spleen,' he said. 'And help your own naughty pet and mine. It is not poisoned, though I prepared it. I'm going out to seek your horses.'

Our first thought, on his departure, was to force an exit somewhere. We tried the kitchen door, but that was fastened outside: we looked at the windows—they were too narrow for even Cathy's little figure.

'Master Linton,' I cried, seeing we were regularly imprisoned, 'you know what your diabolical father is after, and you shall tell us, or I'll box your ears, as he has done your cousin's.'

'Yes, Linton, you must tell,' said Catherine. 'It was for your sake I came; and it will be wickedly ungrateful if you refuse.'

'Give me some tea, I'm thirsty, and then I'll tell you,' he answered. 'Mrs. Dean, go away. I don't like you standing over me. Now, Catherine, you are letting your tears fall into my cup. I won't drink that. Give me another.' Catherine pushed another to him, and wiped her face. I felt disgusted at the little wretch's composure, since he was no longer in terror for himself. The anguish he had exhibited on the moor subsided as soon as ever he entered Wuthering Heights; so I guessed he had been menaced with an awful visitation of wrath if he failed in decoying us there; and, that accomplished, he had no further immediate fears.

'Papa wants us to be married,' he continued, after sipping some of the liquid. 'And he knows your papa wouldn't let us marry now; and he's afraid of my dying if we wait; so we are to be married in the morning, and you are to stay here all night; and, if you do as he wishes, you shall return home next day, and take me with you.'

'Take you with her, pitiful changeling!' I exclaimed. 'YOU marry? Why, the man is mad! or he thinks us fools, every one. And do you imagine that beautiful young lady, that healthy, hearty girl, will tie herself to a little perishing monkey like you? Are you cherishing the notion that anybody, let alone Miss Catherine Linton, would have you for a husband? You want whipping for bringing us in here at all, with your dastardly puling tricks: and-don't look so silly, now! I've a very good mind to shake you severely, for your contemptible treachery, and your imbecile conceit.'

I did give him a slight shaking; but it brought on the cough, and he took to his ordinary resource of moaning and weeping, and Catherine rebuked me.

'Stay all night? No,' she said, looking slowly round. 'Ellen, I'll burn that door down but I'll get out.'

And she would have commenced the execution of her threat directly, but Linton was up in alarm for his dear self again. He clasped her in his two feeble arms sobbing:—'Won't you have me, and save me? not let me come to the Grange? Oh, darling Catherine! you mustn't go and leave, after all. You MUST obey my father—you MUST!'

'I must obey my own,' she replied, 'and relieve him from this cruel suspense. The whole night! What would he think? He'll be distressed already. I'll either break or burn a way out of the house. Be quiet! You're in no danger; but if you hinder me-Linton, I love papa better than you!' The mortal terror he felt of Mr. Heathcliff's anger restored to the boy his coward's eloquence. Catherine was near distraught: still, she persisted that she must go home, and tried entreaty in her turn, persuading him to subdue his selfish agony. While they were thus occupied, our jailor re-entered.

'Your beasts have trotted off,' he said, 'and—now Linton! snivelling again? What has she been doing to you? Come, come—have done, and get to bed. In a month or two, my lad, you'll be able to pay her back her present tyrannies with a vigorous hand. You're pining for pure love, are you not? nothing else in the world: and she shall have you! There, to bed! Zillah won't be here to-night; you must undress yourself. Hush! hold your noise! Once in your own room, I'll not come near you: you needn't fear. By chance, you've managed tolerably. I'll look to the rest.'

He spoke these words, holding the door open for his son to pass, and the latter achieved his exit exactly as a spaniel might which suspected the person who attended on it of designing a spiteful squeeze. The lock was re-secured. Heathcliff approached the fire, where my mistress and I stood silent. Catherine looked up, and instinctively raised her hand to her cheek: his neighbourhood revived a painful sensation. Anybody else would have been incapable of regarding the childish act with sternness, but he scowled on her and muttered—'Oh! you are not afraid of me? Your courage is well disguised: you seem damnably afraid!'

'I AM afraid now,' she replied, 'because, if I stay, papa will be miserable: and how can I endure making him miserable—when he—when he—Mr. Heathcliff, let ME go home! I promise to marry Linton: papa would like me to: and I love him. Why should you wish to force me to do what I'll willingly do of myself?'

'Let him dare to force you,' I cried. 'There's law in the land, thank God! there is; though we be in an out-of-the-way place. I'd inform if he were my own son: and it's felony without benefit of clergy!'

'Silence!' said the ruffian. 'To the devil with your clamour! I don't want YOU to speak. Miss Linton, I shall enjoy myself remarkably in thinking your father will be miserable: I shall not sleep for satisfaction. You could have hit on no surer way of fixing your residence under my roof for the next twenty-four hours than informing me that such an event would follow. As to your promise to marry Linton, I'll take care you shall keep it; for you shall not quit this place till it is fulfilled.'

'Send Ellen, then, to let papa know I'm safe!' exclaimed Catherine, weeping bitterly. 'Or marry me now. Poor papa! Ellen, he'll think we're lost. What shall we do?'

'Not he! He'll think you are tired of waiting on him, and run off for a little amusement,' answered Heathcliff. 'You cannot deny that you entered my house of your own accord, in contempt of his injunctions to the contrary. And it is quite natural that you should desire amusement at your age; and that you would weary of nursing a sick man, and that man ONLY your father. Catherine, his happiest days were over when your days began. He cursed you, I dare say, for coming into the world (I did, at least); and it would just do if he cursed you as HE went out of it. I'd join him. I don't love you! How should I? Weep away. As far as I can see, it will be your chief diversion hereafter; unless Linton make amends for other losses: and your provident parent appears to fancy he may. His letters of advice and consolation entertained me vastly. In his last he recommended my jewel to be careful of his; and kind to her when he got her. Careful and kind—that's paternal. But Linton requires his whole stock of care and kindness for himself. Linton can play the little tyrant well. He'll undertake to torture any number of cats, if their teeth be drawn and their claws pared. You'll be able to tell his uncle fine tales of his KINDNESS, when you get home again, I assure you.'

'You're right there!' I said; 'explain your son's character. Show his resemblance to yourself: and then, I hope, Miss Cathy will think twice before she takes the cockatrice!'

'I don't much mind speaking of his amiable qualities now,' he answered; 'because she must either accept him or remain a prisoner, and you along with her, till your master dies. I can detain you both, quite concealed, here. If you doubt, encourage her to retract her word, and you'll have an opportunity of judging!'

'I'll not retract my word,' said Catherine. 'I'll marry him within this hour, if I may go to Thrushcross Grange afterwards. Mr. Heathcliff, you're a cruel man, but you're not a fiend; and you won't, from MERE malice, destroy irrevocably all my happiness. If papa thought I had left him on purpose, and if he died before I returned, could I bear to live? I've given over crying: but I'm going to kneel here, at your knee; and I'll not get up, and I'll not take my eyes from your face till you look back at me! No, don't turn away! DO LOOK! you'll see nothing to provoke you. I don't hate you. I'm not angry that you struck me. Have you never loved ANYBODY in all your life, uncle? NEVER? Ah! you must look once. I'm so wretched, you can't help being sorry and pitying me.'

'Keep your eft's fingers off; and move, or I'll kick you!' cried Heathcliff, brutally repulsing her. 'I'd rather be hugged by a snake. How the devil can you dream of fawning on me? I DETEST you!'

He shrugged his shoulders: shook himself, indeed, as if his flesh crept with aversion; and thrust back his chair; while I got up, and opened my mouth, to commence a downright torrent of abuse. But I was rendered dumb in the middle of the first sentence, by a threat that I should be shown into a room by myself the very next syllable I uttered. It was growing dark—we heard a sound of voices at the garden-gate. Our host hurried out instantly: HE had his wits about him; WE had not. There was a talk of two or three minutes, and he returned alone.

'I thought it had been your cousin Hareton,' I observed to Catherine. 'I wish he would arrive! Who knows but he might take our part?'

'It was three servants sent to seek you from the Grange,' said Heathcliff, overhearing me. 'You should have opened a lattice and called out: but I could swear that chit is glad you didn't. She's glad to be obliged to stay, I'm certain.'

At learning the chance we had missed, we both gave vent to our grief without control; and he allowed us to wail on till nine o'clock. Then he bid us go upstairs, through the kitchen, to Zillah's chamber; and I whispered my companion to obey: perhaps we might contrive to get through the window there, or into a garret, and out by its skylight. The window, however, was narrow, like those below, and the garret trap was safe from our attempts; for we were fastened in as before. We neither of us lay down: Catherine took her station by the lattice, and watched anxiously for morning; a deep sigh being the only answer I could obtain to my frequent entreaties that she would try to rest. I seated myself in a chair, and rocked to and fro, passing harsh judgment on my many derelictions of duty; from which, it struck me then, all the misfortunes of my employers sprang. It was not the case, in reality, I am aware; but it was, in my imagination, that dismal night; and I thought Heathcliff himself less guilty than I.

At seven o'clock he came, and inquired if Miss Linton had risen. She ran to the door immediately, and answered, 'Yes.' 'Here, then,' he said, opening it, and pulling her out. I rose to follow, but he turned the lock again. I demanded my release.

'Be patient,' he replied; 'I'll send up your breakfast in a while.'

I thumped on the panels, and rattled the latch angrily and Catherine asked why I was still shut up? He answered, I must try to endure it another hour, and they went away. I endured it two or three hours; at length, I heard a footstep: not Heathcliff's.

'I've brought you something to eat,' said a voice; 'oppen t' door!'

Complying eagerly, I beheld Hareton, laden with food enough to last me all day.

'Tak' it,' he added, thrusting the tray into my hand.

'Stay one minute,' I began.

'Nay,' cried he, and retired, regardless of any prayers I could pour forth to detain him.

And there I remained enclosed the whole day, and the whole of the next night; and another, and another. Five nights and four days I remained, altogether, seeing nobody but Hareton once every morning; and he was a model of a jailor: surly, and dumb, and deaf to every attempt at moving his sense of justice or compassion.

Chapter XXVIII

ON the fifth morning, or rather afternoon, a different step approached—lighter and shorter; and, this time, the person entered the room. It was Zillah; donned in her scarlet shawl, with a black silk bonnet on her head, and a willow-basket swung to her arm.

'Eh, dear! Mrs. Dean!' she exclaimed. 'Well! there is a talk about you at Gimmerton. I never thought but you were sunk in the Blackhorse marsh, and missy with you, till master told me you'd been found, and he'd lodged you here! What! and you must have got on an island, sure? And how long were you in the hole? Did master save you, Mrs. Dean? But you're not so thin—you've not been so poorly, have you?'

'Your master is a true scoundrel!' I replied. 'But he shall answer for it. He needn't have raised that tale: it shall all be laid bare!'

'What do you mean?' asked Zillah. 'It's not his tale: they tell that in the village—about your being lost in the marsh; and I calls to Earnshaw, when I come in—"Eh, they's queer things, Mr. Hareton, happened since I went off. It's a sad pity of that likely young lass, and cant Nelly Dean." He stared. I thought he had not heard aught, so I told him the rumour. The master listened, and he just smiled to himself, and said, "If they have been in the marsh, they are out now, Zillah. Nelly Dean is lodged, at this minute, in your room. You can tell her to flit, when you go up; here is the key. The bog-water got into her head, and she would have run home quite flighty; but I fixed her till she came round to her senses. You can bid her go to the Grange at once, if she be able, and carry a message from me, that her young lady will follow in time to attend the squire's funeral."'

'Mr. Edgar is not dead?' I gasped. 'Oh! Zillah, Zillah!'

'No, no; sit you down, my good mistress,' she replied; 'you're right sickly yet. He's not dead; Doctor Kenneth thinks he may last another day. I met him on the road and asked.'

Instead of sitting down, I snatched my outdoor things, and hastened below, for the way was free. On entering the house, I looked about for some one to give information of Catherine. The place was filled with sunshine, and the door stood wide open; but nobody seemed at hand. As I hesitated whether to go off at once, or return and seek my mistress, a slight cough drew my attention to the hearth. Linton lay on the settle, sole tenant, sucking a stick of sugar-candy, and pursuing my movements with apathetic eyes. 'Where is Miss Catherine?' I demanded sternly, supposing I could frighten him into giving intelligence, by catching him thus, alone. He sucked on like an innocent.

'Is she gone?' I said.

'No,' he replied; 'she's upstairs: she's not to go; we won't let her.'

'You won't let her, little idiot!' I exclaimed. 'Direct me to her room immediately, or I'll make you sing out sharply.'

'Papa would make you sing out, if you attempted to get there,' he answered. 'He says I'm not to be soft with Catherine: she's my wife, and it's shameful that she should wish to leave me. He says she hates me and wants me to die, that she may have my money; but she shan't have it: and she shan't go home! She never shall!-she may cry, and be sick as much as she pleases!'

He resumed his former occupation, closing his lids, as if he meant to drop asleep.

'Master Heathcliff,' I resumed, 'have you forgotten all Catherine's kindness to you last winter, when you affirmed you loved her, and when she brought you books and sung you songs, and came many a time through wind and snow to see you? She wept to miss one evening, because you would be disappointed; and you felt then that she was a hundred times too good to you: and now you believe the lies your father tells, though you know he detests you both. And you join him against her. That's fine gratitude, is it not?'

The corner of Linton's mouth fell, and he took the sugar-candy from his lips.

'Did she come to Wuthering Heights because she hated you?' I continued. 'Think for yourself! As to your money, she does not even know that you will have any. And you say she's sick; and yet you leave her alone, up there in a strange house! You who have felt what it is to be so neglected! You could pity your own sufferings; and she pitied them, too; but you won't pity hers! I shed tears, Master Heathcliff, you see—an elderly woman, and a servant merely—and you, after pretending such affection, and having reason to worship her almost, store every tear you have for yourself, and lie there quite at ease. Ah! you're a heartless, selfish boy!'

'I can't stay with her,' he answered crossly. 'I'll not stay by myself. She cries so I can't bear it. And she won't give over, though I say I'll call my father. I did call him once, and he threatened to strangle her if she was not quiet; but she began again the instant he left the room, moaning and grieving all night long, though I screamed for vexation that I couldn't sleep.'

'Is Mr. Heathcliff out?' I inquired, perceiving that the wretched creature had no power to sympathize with his cousin's mental tortures.

'He's in the court,' he replied, 'talking to Doctor Kenneth; who says uncle is dying, truly, at last. I'm glad, for I shall be master of the Grange after him. Catherine always spoke of it as her house. It isn't hers! It's mine: papa says everything she has is mine. All her nice books are mine; she offered to give me them, and her pretty birds, and her pony Minny, if I would get the key of our room, and let her out; but I told her she had nothing to give, they ware all, all mine. And then she cried, and took a little picture from her neck, and said I should have that; two pictures in a gold case, on one side her mother, and on the other uncle, when they were young. That was yesterday—I said they were mine, too; and tried to get them from her. The spiteful thing wouldn't let me: she pushed me off, and hurt me. I shrieked out-that frightens her—she heard papa coming, and she broke the hinges and divided the case, and gave me her mother's portrait; the other she attempted to hide: but papa asked what was the matter, and I explained it. He took the one I had away, and ordered her to resign hers to me; she refused, and he—he struck her down, and wrenched it off the chain, and crushed it with his foot.'

'And were you pleased to see her struck?' I asked: having my designs in encouraging his talk.

'I winked,' he answered: 'I wink to see my father strike a dog or a horse, he does it so hard. Yet I was glad at first—she deserved punishing for pushing me: but when papa was gone, she made me come to the window and showed me her cheek cut on the inside, against her teeth, and her mouth filling with blood; and then she gathered up the bits of the picture, and went and sat down with her face to the wall, and she has never spoken to me since: and I sometimes think she can't speak for pain. I don't like to think so; but she's a naughty thing for crying continually; and she looks so pale and wild, I'm afraid of her.'

'And you can get the key if you choose?' I said.

'Yes, when I am up-stairs,' he answered; 'but I can't walk up-stairs now.'

'In what apartment is it?' I asked.

'Oh,' he cried, 'I shan't tell YOU where it is. It is our secret. Nobody, neither Hareton nor Zillah, is to know. There! you've tired me—go away, go away!' And he turned his face on to his arm, and shut his eyes again.

I considered it best to depart without seeing Mr. Heathcliff, and bring a rescue for my young lady from the Grange. On reaching it, the astonishment of my fellow-servants to see me, and their joy also, was intense; and when they heard that their little mistress was safe, two or three were about to hurry up and shout the news at Mr. Edgar's door:

but I bespoke the announcement of it myself. How changed I found him, even in those few days! He lay an image of sadness and resignation awaiting his death. Very young he looked: though his actual age was thirty-nine, one would have called him ten years younger, at least. He thought of Catherine; for he murmured her name. I touched his hand, and spoke.

'Catherine is coming, dear master!' I whispered; 'she is alive and well; and will be here, I hope, to-night.'

I trembled at the first effects of this intelligence: he half rose up, looked eagerly round the apartment, and then sank back in a swoon. As soon as he recovered, I related our compulsory visit, and detention at the Heights. I said Heathcliff forced me to go in: which was not quite true. I uttered as little as possible against Linton; nor did I describe all his father's brutal conduct—my intentions being to add no bitterness, if I could help it, to his already over-flowing cup.

He divined that one of his enemy's purposes was to secure the personal property, as well as the estate, to his son: or rather himself; yet why he did not wait till his decease was a puzzle to my master, because ignorant how nearly he and his nephew would quit the world together. However, he felt that his will had better be altered: instead of leaving Catherine's fortune at her own disposal, he determined to put it in the hands of trustees for her use during life, and for her children, if she had any, after her. By that means, it could not fall to Mr. Heathcliff should Linton die.

Having received his orders, I despatched a man to fetch the attorney, and four more, provided with serviceable weapons, to demand my young lady of her jailor. Both parties were delayed very late. The single servant returned first. He said Mr. Green, the lawyer, was out when he arrived at his house, and he had to wait two hours for his re-entrance; and then Mr. Green told him he had a little business in the village that must be done; but he would be at Thrushcross Grange before morning. The four men came back unaccompanied also. They brought word that Catherine was ill: too ill to quit her room; and Heathcliff would not suffer them to see her. I scolded the stupid fellows well for listening to that tale, which I would not carry to my master; resolving to take a whole bevy up to the Heights, at daylight, and storm it literally, unless the prisoner were quietly surrendered to us. Her father SHALL see her, I vowed, and vowed again, if that devil be killed on his own doorstones in trying to prevent it!

Happily, I was spared the journey and the trouble. I had gone down-stairs at three o'clock to fetch a jug of water; and was passing through the hall with it in my hand, when a sharp knock at the front door made me jump. 'Oh! it is Green,' I said, recollecting myself—'only Green,' and I went on, intending to send somebody else to open it; but the knock was repeated: not loud, and still importunately. I put the jug on the banister and hastened to admit him myself. The harvest moon shone clear outside. It was not the attorney. My own sweet little mistress sprang on my neck sobbing, 'Ellen, Ellen! Is papa alive?'

'Yes,' I cried: 'yes, my angel, he is, God be thanked, you are safe with us again!'

She wanted to run, breathless as she was, up-stairs to Mr. Linton's room; but I compelled her to sit down on a chair, and made her drink, and washed her pale face, chafing it into a faint colour with my apron. Then I said I must go first, and tell of her arrival; imploring her to say, she should be happy with young Heathcliff. She stared, but soon comprehending why I counselled her to utter the falsehood, she assured me she would not complain.

I couldn't abide to be present at their meeting. I stood outside the chamber-door a quarter of an hour, and hardly ventured near the bed, then. All was composed, however: Catherine's despair was as silent as her father's joy. She supported him calmly, in appearance; and he fixed on her features his raised eyes that seemed dilating with ecstasy.

He died blissfully, Mr. Lockwood: he died so. Kissing her cheek, he murmured,—'I am going to her; and you, darling child, shall come to us!' and never stirred or spoke again; but continued that rapt, radiant gaze, till his pulse imperceptibly stopped and his soul departed. None could have noticed the exact minute of his death, it was so entirely without a struggle.

Whether Catherine had spent her tears, or whether the grief were too weighty to let them flow, she sat there dry-eyed till the sun rose: she sat till noon, and would still have remained brooding over that deathbed, but I insisted on her coming away and taking some repose. It was well I succeeded in removing her, for at dinner-time appeared the lawyer, having called at Wuthering Heights to get his instructions how to behave. He had sold himself to Mr. Heathcliff: that was the cause of his delay in obeying my master's summons. Fortunately, no thought of worldly affairs crossed the latter's mind, to disturb him, after his daughter's arrival.

Mr. Green took upon himself to order everything and everybody about the place. He gave all the servants but me, notice to quit. He would have carried his delegated authority to the point of insisting that Edgar Linton should not be buried beside his wife, but in the chapel, with his family. There was the will, however, to hinder that, and my loud protestations against any infringement of its directions. The funeral was hurried over; Catherine, Mrs. Linton Heathcliff now, was suffered to stay at the Grange till her father's corpse had quitted it.

She told me that her anguish had at last spurred Linton to incur the risk of liberating her. She heard the men I sent disputing at the door, and she gathered the sense of Heathcliff's answer. It drove her desperate. Linton who had been conveyed up to the little parlour soon after I left, was terrified into fetching the key before his father re-ascended. He had the cunning to unlock and re-lock the door, without shutting it; and when he should have gone to bed, he begged to sleep with Hareton, and his petition was granted for once. Catherine stole out before break of day. She dared not try the doors lest the dogs should raise an alarm; she visited the empty chambers and examined their windows; and, luckily, lighting on her mother's, she got easily out of its lattice, and on to the ground, by means of the fir-tree close by. Her accomplice suffered for his share in the escape, notwithstanding his timid contrivances.

Chapter XXIX

THE evening after the funeral, my young lady and I were seated in the library; now musing mournfully—one of us despairingly—on our loss, now venturing conjectures as to the gloomy future.

We had just agreed the best destiny which could await Catherine would be a permission to continue resident at the Grange; at least during Linton's life: he being allowed to join her there, and I to remain as housekeeper. That seemed rather too favourable an arrangement to be hoped for; and yet I did hope, and began to cheer up under the prospect of retaining my home and my employment, and, above all, my beloved young mistress; when a servant—one of the discarded ones, not yet departed—rushed hastily in, and said 'that devil Heathcliff' was coming through the court: should he fasten the door in his face?

If we had been mad enough to order that proceeding, we had not time. He made no ceremony of knocking or announcing his name: he was master, and availed himself of the master's privilege to walk straight in, without saying a word. The sound of our informant's voice directed him to the library; he entered and motioning him out, shut the door.

It was the same room into which he had been ushered, as a guest, eighteen years before: the same moon shone through the window; and the same autumn landscape lay outside. We had not yet lighted a candle, but all the apartment was visible, even to the portraits on the wall: the splendid head of Mrs. Linton, and the graceful one of her husband. Heathcliff advanced to the hearth. Time had little altered his person either. There was the same man: his dark face rather sallower and more composed, his frame a stone or two heavier, perhaps, and no other difference. Catherine had risen with an impulse to dash out, when she saw him.

'Stop!' he said, arresting her by the arm. 'No more runnings away! Where would you go? I'm come to fetch you home; and I hope you'll be a dutiful daughter and not encourage my son to further disobedience. I was embarrassed how to punish him when I discovered his part in the business: he's such a cobweb, a pinch would annihilate him; but you'll see by his look that he has received his due! I brought him down one evening, the day before yesterday, and just set him in a chair, and never touched him afterwards. I sent Hareton out, and we had the room to ourselves. In two hours, I called Joseph to carry him up again; and since then my presence is as potent on his nerves as a ghost; and I fancy he sees me often, though I am not near. Hareton says he wakes and shrieks in the night by the hour together, and calls you to protect him from me; and, whether you like your precious mate, or not, you must come: he's your concern now; I yield all my interest in him to you.'

'Why not let Catherine continue here,' I pleaded, 'and send Master Linton to her? As you hate them both, you'd not miss them: they can only be a daily plague to your unnatural heart.'

'I'm seeking a tenant for the Grange,' he answered; 'and I want my children about me, to be sure. Besides, that lass owes me her services for her bread. I'm not going to nurture her in luxury and idleness after Linton is gone. Make haste and get ready, now; and don't oblige me to compel you.'

'I shall,' said Catherine. 'Linton is all I have to love in the world, and though you have done what you could to make him hateful to me, and me to him, you cannot make us hate each other. And I defy you to hurt him when I am by, and I defy you to frighten me!'

'You are a boastful champion,' replied Heathcliff; 'but I don't like you well enough to hurt him: you shall get the full benefit of the torment, as long as it lasts. It is not I who will make him hateful to you—it is his own sweet spirit. He's as bitter as gall at your desertion and its consequences: don't expect thanks for this noble devotion. I heard him draw a pleasant picture to Zillah of what he would do if he were as strong as I: the inclination is there, and his very weakness will sharpen his wits to find a substitute for strength.'

'I know he has a bad nature,' said Catherine: 'he's your son. But I'm glad I've a better, to forgive it; and I know he loves me, and for that reason I love him. Mr. Heathcliff YOU have NOBODY to love you; and, however miserable you make us, we shall still have the revenge of thinking that your cruelty arises from your greater misery. You ARE miserable, are you not? Lonely, like the devil, and envious like him? NOBODY loves you—NOBODY will cry for you when you die! I wouldn't be you!'

Catherine spoke with a kind of dreary triumph: she seemed to have made up her mind to enter into the spirit of her future family, and draw pleasure from the griefs of her enemies.

'You shall be sorry to be yourself presently,' said her father-in-law, 'if you stand there another minute. Begone, witch, and get your things!'

She scornfully withdrew. In her absence I began to beg for Zillah's place at the Heights, offering to resign mine to her; but he would suffer it on no account. He bid me be silent; and then, for the first time, allowed himself a glance round the room and a look at the pictures. Having studied Mrs. Linton's, he said—'I shall have that home. Not because I need it, but—' He turned abruptly to the fire, and continued, with what, for lack of a better word, I must call a smile—'I'll tell you what I did yesterday! I got the sexton, who was digging Linton's grave, to remove the earth off her coffin lid, and I opened it. I thought, once, I would have stayed there: when I saw her face again—it is hers yet!—he had hard work to stir me; but he said it would change if the air blew on it, and so I struck one side of the coffin loose, and covered it up: not Linton's side, damn him! I wish he'd been soldered in lead. And I bribed the sexton to pull it away when I'm laid there, and slide mine out too; I'll have it made so: and then by the time Linton gets to us he'll not know which is which!'

'You were very wicked, Mr. Heathcliff!' I exclaimed; 'were you not ashamed to disturb the dead?'

'I disturbed nobody, Nelly,' he replied; 'and I gave some ease to myself. I shall be a great deal more comfortable now; and you'll have a better chance of keeping me underground, when I get there. Disturbed her? No! she has disturbed me, night and day, through eighteen years—incessantly—remorselessly—till yesternight; and yesternight I was tranquil. I dreamt I was sleeping the last sleep by that sleeper, with my heart stopped and my cheek frozen against hers.'

'And if she had been dissolved into earth, or worse, what would you have dreamt of then?' I said.

'Of dissolving with her, and being more happy still!' he answered. 'Do you suppose I dread any change of that sort? I expected such a transformation on raising the lid—but I'm better pleased that it should not commence till I share it. Besides, unless I had received a distinct impression of her passionless features, that strange feeling would hardly have been removed. It began oddly. You know I was wild after she died; and eternally, from dawn to dawn, praying her to return to me her spirit! I have a strong faith in ghosts: I have a conviction that they can, and do, exist among us! The day she was buried, there came a fall of snow. In the evening I went to the churchyard. It blew bleak as winter—all round was solitary. I didn't fear that her fool of a husband would wander up the glen so late; and no one else had business to bring them there. Being alone, and conscious two yards of loose earth was the sole barrier between us, I said to myself—'I'll have her in my arms again! If she be cold, I'll think it is this north wind that chills ME; and if she be motionless, it is sleep." I got a spade from the tool-house, and began to delve with all my might—it scraped the coffin; I fell to work with my hands; the wood commenced cracking about the screws; I was on the point of attaining my object, when it seemed that I heard a sigh from some one above, close at the edge of the grave, and bending down. "If I can only get this off," I muttered, "I wish they may shovel in the earth over us both!" and I wrenched at it more desperately still. There was another sigh, close at my ear. I appeared to feel the warm breath of it displacing the sleet-laden wind. I knew no living thing in flesh and blood was by; but, as certainly as you perceive the approach to some substantial body in the dark, though it cannot be discerned, so certainly I felt that Cathy was there: not under me, but on the earth. A sudden sense of relief flowed from my heart through every limb. I relinquished my labour of agony, and turned consoled at once: unspeakably consoled. Her presence was with me: it remained while I re-filled the grave, and led me home. You may laugh, if you will; but I was sure I should see her there. I was sure she was with me, and I could not help talking to her. Having reached the Heights, I rushed eagerly to the door. It was fastened; and, I remember, that accursed Earnshaw and my wife opposed my entrance. I remember stopping to kick the breath out of him, and then hurrying up-stairs, to my room and hers. I looked round impatiently—I felt her by me—I could ALMOST see her, and yet I COULD NOT! I ought to have sweat blood then, from the anguish of my yearning—from the fervour of my supplications to have but one glimpse! I had not one. She showed herself, as she often was in life, a devil to me! And, since then, sometimes more and sometimes less, I've been the sport of that intolerable torture! Infernal! keeping my nerves at such a stretch that, if they had not resembled catgut, they would long ago have relaxed to the feebleness of Linton's. When I sat in the house with Hareton, it seemed that on going out I should meet her; when I walked on the moors I should meet her coming in. When I went from home I hastened to return; she MUST be somewhere at the Heights, I was certain! And when I slept in her chamber—I was beaten out of that. I couldn't lie there; for the moment I closed my eyes, she was either outside the window, or sliding back the panels, or entering the room, or even resting her darling head on the same pillow as she did when a child; and I must open my lids to see. And so I opened and closed them a hundred times a night—to be always disappointed! It racked me! I've often groaned aloud, till that old rascal Joseph no doubt believed that my conscience was playing the fiend inside of me. Now, since I've seen her, I'm pacified—a little. It was a strange way of killing: not by inches, but by fractions of hairbreadths, to beguile me with the spectre of a hope through eighteen years!'

Mr. Heathcliff paused and wiped his forehead; his hair clung to it, wet with perspiration; his eyes were fixed on the red embers of the fire, the brows not contracted, but raised next the temples; diminishing the grim aspect of his countenance, but imparting a peculiar look of trouble, and a painful appearance of mental tension towards one absorbing subject. He only half addressed me, and I maintained silence. I didn't like to hear him talk! After a short period he resumed his meditation on the picture, took it down and leant it against the sofa to contemplate it at better advantage; and while so occupied Catherine entered, announcing that she was ready, when her pony should be saddled.

'Send that over to-morrow,' said Heathcliff to me; then turning to her, he added: 'You may do without your pony: it is a fine evening, and you'll need no ponies at Wuthering Heights; for what journeys you take, your own feet will serve you. Come along.'

'Good-bye, Ellen!' whispered my dear little mistress.

As she kissed me, her lips felt like ice. 'Come and see me, Ellen; don't forget.'

'Take care you do no such thing, Mrs. Dean!' said her new father. 'When I wish to speak to you I'll come here. I want none of your prying at my house!'

He signed her to precede him; and casting back a look that cut my heart, she obeyed. I watched them, from the window, walk down the garden. Heathcliff fixed Catherine's arm under his: though she disputed the act at first evidently; and with rapid strides he hurried her into the alley, whose trees concealed them.

Chapter XXX

I HAVE paid a visit to the Heights, but I have not seen her since she left: Joseph held the door in his hand when I called to ask after her, and wouldn't let me pass. He said Mrs. Linton was 'thrang,' and the master was not in. Zillah has told me something of the way they go on, otherwise I should hardly know who was dead and who living. She thinks Catherine haughty, and does not like her, I can guess by her talk. My young lady asked some aid of her when she first came; but Mr. Heathcliff told her to follow her own business, and let his daughter-in-law look after herself; and Zillah willingly acquiesced, being a narrow-minded, selfish woman. Catherine evinced a child's annoyance at this neglect; repaid it with contempt, and thus enlisted my informant among her enemies, as securely as if she had done her some great wrong. I had a long talk with Zillah about six weeks ago, a little before you came, one day when we foregathered on the moor; and this is what she told me.

'The first thing Mrs. Linton did,' she said, 'on her arrival at the Heights, was to run up-stairs, without even wishing good-evening to me and Joseph; she shut herself into Linton's room, and remained till morning. Then, while the master and Earnshaw were at breakfast, she entered the house, and asked all in a quiver if the doctor might be sent for? her cousin was very ill.

'"We know that!" answered Heathcliff; "but his life is not worth a farthing, and I won't spend a farthing on him."

'"But I cannot tell how to do," she said; "and if nobody will help me, he'll die!"

'"Walk out of the room," cried the master, "and let me never hear a word more about him! None here care what becomes of him; if you do, act the nurse; if you do not, lock him up and leave him."

'Then she began to bother me, and I said I'd had enough plague with the tiresome thing; we each had our tasks, and hers was to wait on Linton: Mr. Heathcliff bid me leave that labour to her.

'How they managed together, I can't tell. I fancy he fretted a great deal, and moaned hisseln night and day; and she had precious little rest: one could guess by her white face and heavy eyes. She sometimes came into the kitchen all wildered like, and looked as if she would fain beg assistance; but I was not going to disobey the master: I never dare disobey him, Mrs. Dean; and, though I thought it wrong that Kenneth should not be sent for, it was no concern of mine either to advise or complain, and I always refused to meddle. Once or twice, after we had gone to bed, I've happened to open my door again and seen her sitting crying on the stairs'-top; and then I've shut myself in quick, for fear of being moved to interfere. I did pity her then, I'm sure: still I didn't wish to lose my place, you know.

'At last, one night she came boldly into my chamber, and frightened me out of my wits, by saying, "Tell Mr. Heathcliff that his son is dying—I'm sure he is, this time. Get up, instantly, and tell him."

'Having uttered this speech, she vanished again. I lay a quarter of an hour listening and trembling. Nothing stirred—the house was quiet.

'She's mistaken, I said to myself. He's got over it. I needn't disturb them; and I began to doze. But my sleep was marred a second time by a sharp ringing of the bell—the only bell we have, put up on purpose for Linton; and the master called to me to see what was the matter, and inform them that he wouldn't have that noise repeated.

'I delivered Catherine's message. He cursed to himself, and in a few minutes came out with a lighted candle, and proceeded to their room. I followed. Mrs. Heathcliff was seated by the bedside, with her hands folded on her knees. Her father-in-law went up, held the light to Linton's face, looked at him, and touched him; afterwards he turned to her.

'"Now—Catherine," he said, "how do you feel?"

'She was dumb.

'"How do you feel, Catherine?" he repeated.

'"He's safe, and I'm free," she answered: "I should feel well—but," she continued, with a bitterness she couldn't conceal, "you have left me so long to struggle against death alone, that I feel and see only death! I feel like death!"

'And she looked like it, too! I gave her a little wine. Hareton and Joseph, who had been wakened by the ringing and the sound of feet, and heard our talk from outside, now entered. Joseph was fain, I believe, of the lad's removal; Hareton seemed a thought bothered: though he was more taken up with staring at Catherine than thinking of Linton. But the master bid him get off to bed again: we didn't want his help. He afterwards made Joseph remove the body to his chamber, and told me to return to mine, and Mrs. Heathcliff remained by herself.

'In the morning, he sent me to tell her she must come down to breakfast: she had undressed, and appeared going to sleep, and said she was ill; at which I hardly wondered. I informed Mr. Heathcliff, and he replied,—"Well, let her be till after the funeral; and go up now and then to get her what is needful; and, as soon as she seems better, tell me."'

Cathy stayed upstairs a fortnight, according to Zillah; who visited her twice a day, and would have been rather more friendly, but her attempts at increasing kindness were proudly and promptly repelled.

Heathcliff went up once, to show her Linton's will. He had bequeathed the whole of his, and what had been her, moveable property, to his father: the poor creature was threatened, or coaxed, into that act during her week's absence, when his uncle died. The lands, being a minor, he could not meddle with. However, Mr. Heathcliff has claimed and kept them in his wife's right and his also: I suppose legally; at any rate, Catherine, destitute of cash and friends, cannot disturb his possession.

'Nobody,' said Zillah, 'ever approached her door, except that once, but I; and nobody asked anything about her. The first occasion of her coming down into the house was on a Sunday afternoon. She had cried out, when I carried up her dinner, that she couldn't bear any longer being in the cold; and I told her the master was going to Thrushcross Grange, and Earnshaw and I needn't hinder her from descending; so, as soon as she heard Heathcliff's horse trot off, she made her appearance, donned in black, and her yellow curls combed back behind her ears as plain as a Quaker: she couldn't comb them out.

'Joseph and I generally go to chapel on Sundays:' the kirk, you know, has no minister now, explained Mrs. Dean; and they call the Methodists' or Baptists' place (I can't say which it is) at Gimmerton, a chapel. 'Joseph had gone,' she continued, 'but I thought proper to bide at home. Young folks are always the better for an elder's over-looking; and Hareton, with all his bashfulness, isn't a model of nice behaviour. I let him know that his cousin would very likely sit with us, and she had been always used to see the Sabbath respected; so he had as good leave his guns and bits of indoor work alone, while she stayed. He coloured up at the news, and cast his eyes over his hands and clothes. The train-oil and gunpowder were shoved out of sight in a minute. I saw he meant to give her his company; and I guessed, by his way, he wanted to be presentable; so, laughing, as I durst not laugh when the master is by, I offered to help him, if he would, and joked at his confusion. He grew sullen, and began to swear.

'Now, Mrs. Dean,' Zillah went on, seeing me not pleased by her manner, 'you happen think your young lady too fine for Mr. Hareton; and happen you're right: but I own I should love well to bring her pride a peg lower. And what will all her learning and her daintiness do for her, now? She's as poor as you or I: poorer, I'll be bound: you're saying, and I'm doing my little all that road.'

Hareton allowed Zillah to give him her aid; and she flattered him into a good humour; so, when Catherine came, half forgetting her former insults, he tried to make himself agreeable, by the housekeeper's account.

'Missis walked in,' she said, 'as chill as an icicle, and as high as a princess. I got up and offered her my seat in the arm-chair. No, she turned up her nose at my civility. Earnshaw rose, too, and bid her come to the settle, and sit close by the fire: he was sure she was starved.

'"I've been starved a month and more," she answered, resting on the word as scornful as she could.

'And she got a chair for herself, and placed it at a distance from both of us. Having sat till she was warm, she began to look round, and discovered a number of books on the dresser; she was instantly upon her feet again, stretching to reach them: but they were too high up. Her cousin, after watching her endeavours a while, at last summoned courage to help her; she held her frock, and he filled it with the first that came to hand.

'That was a great advance for the lad. She didn't thank him; still, he felt gratified that she had accepted his assistance, and ventured to stand behind as she examined them, and even to stoop and point out what struck his fancy in certain old pictures which they contained; nor was he daunted by the saucy style in which she jerked the page from his finger: he contented himself with going a bit farther back and looking at her instead of the book. She continued reading, or seeking for something to read. His attention became, by degrees, quite centred in the study of her thick silky curls: her face he couldn't see, and she couldn't see him. And, perhaps, not quite awake to what he did, but attracted like a child to a candle, at last he proceeded from staring to touching; he put out his hand and stroked one curl, as gently as if it were a bird. He might have stuck a knife into her neck, she started round in such a taking.

'"Get away this moment! How dare you touch me? Why are you stopping there?" she cried, in a tone of disgust. "I can't endure you! I'll go upstairs again, if you come near me."

'Mr. Hareton recoiled, looking as foolish as he could do: he sat down in the settle very quiet, and she continued turning over her volumes another half hour; finally, Earnshaw crossed over, and whispered to me.

'Will you ask her to read to us, Zillah? I'm stalled of doing naught; and I do like—I could like to hear her! Dunnot say I wanted it, but ask of yourseln."

'"Mr. Hareton wishes you would read to us, ma'am," I said, immediately. "He'd take it very kind—he'd be much obliged."

'She frowned; and looking up, answered—

'"Mr. Hareton, and the whole set of you, will be good enough to understand that I reject any pretence at kindness you have the hypocrisy to offer! I despise you, and will have nothing to say to any of you! When I would have given my life for one kind word, even to see one of your faces, you all kept off. But I won't complain to you! I'm driven down here by the cold; not either to amuse you or enjoy your society."

'"What could I ha' done?" began Earnshaw. "How was I to blame?"

'"Oh! you are an exception," answered Mrs. Heathcliff. "I never missed such a concern as you."

'"But I offered more than once, and asked," he said, kindling up at her pertness, "I asked Mr. Heathcliff to let me wake for you—"

'"Be silent! I'll go out of doors, or anywhere, rather than have your disagreeable voice in my ear!" said my lady.

'Hareton muttered she might go to hell, for him! and unslinging his gun, restrained himself from his Sunday occupations no longer. He talked now, freely enough; and she presently saw fit to retreat to her solitude: but the frost had set in, and, in spite of her pride, she was forced to condescend to our company, more and more. However, I took care there should be no further scorning at my good nature: ever since, I've been as stiff as herself; and she has no lover or liker among us: and she does not deserve one; for, let them say the least word to her, and she'll curl back without respect of any one. She'll snap at the master himself, and as good as dares him to thrash her; and the more hurt she gets, the more venomous she grows.'

At first, on hearing this account from Zillah, I determined to leave my situation, take a cottage, and get Catherine to come and live with me: but Mr. Heathcliff would as soon permit that as he would set up Hareton in an independent house; and I can see no remedy, at present, unless she could marry again; and that scheme it does not come within my province to arrange.

Thus ended Mrs. Dean's story. Notwithstanding the doctor's prophecy, I am rapidly recovering strength; and though it be only the second week in January, I propose getting out on horseback in a day or two, and riding over to Wuthering Heights, to inform my landlord that I shall spend the next six months in London; and, if he likes, he may look out for another tenant to take the place after October. I would not pass another winter here for much.

Chapter XXXI

YESTERDAY was bright, calm, and frosty. I went to the Heights as I proposed: my housekeeper entreated me to bear a little note from her to her young lady, and I did not refuse, for the worthy woman was not conscious of anything odd in her request. The front door stood open, but the jealous gate was fastened, as at my last visit; I knocked and invoked Earnshaw from among the garden-beds; he unchained it, and I entered. The fellow is as handsome a rustic as need be seen. I took particular notice of him this time; but then he does his best apparently to make the least of his advantages.

I asked if Mr. Heathcliff were at home? He answered, No; but he would be in at dinner-time. It was eleven o'clock, and I announced my intention of going in and waiting for him; at which he immediately flung down his tools and accompanied me, in the office of watchdog, not as a substitute for the host.

We entered together; Catherine was there, making herself useful in preparing some vegetables for the approaching meal; she looked more sulky and less spirited than when I had seen her first. She hardly raised her eyes to notice me, and continued her employment with the same disregard to common forms of politeness as before; never returning my bow and good-morning by the slightest acknowledgment.

'She does not seem so amiable,' I thought, 'as Mrs. Dean would persuade me to believe. She's a beauty, it is true; but not an angel.'

Earnshaw surlily bid her remove her things to the kitchen. 'Remove them yourself,' she said, pushing them from her as soon as she had done; and retiring to a stool by the window, where she began to carve figures of birds and beasts out of the turnip-parings in her lap. I approached her, pretending to desire a view of the garden; and, as I fancied, adroitly dropped Mrs. Dean's note on to her knee, unnoticed by Hareton—but she asked aloud, 'What is that?' And chucked it off.

'A letter from your old acquaintance, the housekeeper at the Grange,' I answered; annoyed at her exposing my kind deed, and fearful lest it should be imagined a missive of my own. She would gladly have gathered it up at this information, but Hareton beat her; he seized and put it in his waistcoat, saying Mr. Heathcliff should look at it first. Thereat, Catherine silently turned her face from us, and, very stealthily, drew out her pocket-handkerchief and applied it to her eyes; and her cousin, after struggling awhile to keep down his softer feelings, pulled out the letter and flung it on the floor beside her, as ungraciously as he could. Catherine caught and perused it eagerly; then she put a few questions to me concerning the inmates, rational and irrational, of her former home; and gazing towards the hills, murmured in soliloquy:

'I should like to be riding Minny down there! I should like to be climbing up there! Oh! I'm tired—I'm STALLED, Hareton!' And she leant her pretty head back against the sill, with half a yawn and half a sigh, and lapsed into an aspect of abstracted sadness: neither caring nor knowing whether we remarked her.

'Mrs. Heathcliff,' I said, after sitting some time mute, 'you are not aware that I am an acquaintance of yours? so intimate that I think it strange you won't come and speak to me. My housekeeper never wearies of talking about and praising you; and she'll be greatly disappointed if I return with no news of or from you, except that you received her letter and said nothing!'

She appeared to wonder at this speech, and asked,—

'Does Ellen like you?'

'Yes, very well,' I replied, hesitatingly.

'You must tell her,' she continued, 'that I would answer her letter, but I have no materials for writing: not even a book from which I might tear a leaf.'

'No books!' I exclaimed. 'How do you contrive to live here without them? if I may take the liberty to inquire. Though provided with a large library, I'm frequently very dull at the Grange; take my books away, and I should be desperate!'

'I was always reading, when I had them,' said Catherine; 'and Mr. Heathcliff never reads; so he took it into his head to destroy my books. I have not had a glimpse of one for weeks. Only once, I searched through Joseph's store of theology, to his great irritation; and once, Hareton, I came upon a secret stock in your room—some Latin and Greek, and some tales and poetry: all old friends. I brought the last here—and you gathered them, as a magpie gathers silver spoons, for the mere love of stealing! They are of no use to you; or else you concealed them in the bad spirit that, as you cannot enjoy them, nobody else shall. Perhaps YOUR envy counselled Mr. Heathcliff to rob me of my treasures? But I've most of them written on my brain and printed in my heart, and you cannot deprive me of those!'

Earnshaw blushed crimson when his cousin made this revelation of his private literary accumulations, and stammered an indignant denial of her accusations.

'Mr. Hareton is desirous of increasing his amount of knowledge,' I said, coming to his rescue. 'He is not ENVIOUS, but EMULOUS of your attainments. He'll be a clever scholar in a few years.'

'And he wants me to sink into a dunce, meantime,' answered Catherine. 'Yes, I hear him trying to spell and read to himself, and pretty blunders he makes! I wish you would repeat Chevy Chase as you did yesterday: it was extremely funny. I heard you; and I heard you turning over the dictionary to seek out the hard words, and then cursing because you couldn't read their explanations!'

The young man evidently thought it too bad that he should be laughed at for his ignorance, and then laughed at for trying to remove it. I had a similar notion; and, remembering Mrs. Dean's anecdote of his first attempt at enlightening the darkness in which he had been reared, I observed,—'But, Mrs. Heathcliff, we have each had a commencement, and each stumbled and tottered on the threshold; had our teachers scorned instead of aiding us, we should stumble and totter yet.'

'Oh!' she replied, 'I don't wish to limit his acquirements: still, he has no right to appropriate what is mine, and make it ridiculous to me with his vile mistakes and mispronunciations! Those books, both prose and verse, are consecrated to me by other associations; and I hate to have them debased and profaned in his mouth! Besides, of all, he has selected my favourite pieces that I love the most to repeat, as if out of deliberate malice.'

Hareton's chest heaved in silence a minute: he laboured under a severe sense of mortification and wrath, which it was no easy task to suppress. I rose, and, from a gentlemanly idea of relieving his embarrassment, took up my station in the doorway, surveying the external prospect as I stood. He followed my example, and left the room; but presently reappeared, bearing half a dozen volumes in his hands, which he threw into Catherine's lap, exclaiming,—'Take them! I never want to hear, or read, or think of them again!'

'I won't have them now,' she answered. 'I shall connect them with you, and hate them.'

She opened one that had obviously been often turned over, and read a portion in the drawling tone of a beginner; then laughed, and threw it from her. 'And listen,' she continued, provokingly, commencing a verse of an old ballad in the same fashion.

But his self-love would endure no further torment: I heard, and not altogether disapprovingly, a manual cheek given to her saucy tongue. The little wretch had done her utmost to hurt her cousin's sensitive though uncultivated feelings, and a physical argument was the only mode he had of balancing the account, and repaying its effects on the inflictor. He afterwards gathered the books and hurled them on the fire. I read in his countenance what anguish it was to offer that sacrifice to spleen. I fancied that as they consumed, he recalled the pleasure they had already imparted, and the triumph and ever-increasing pleasure he had anticipated from them; and I fancied I guessed the incitement to his secret studies also. He had been content with daily labour and rough animal enjoyments, till Catherine crossed his path. Shame at her scorn, and hope of her approval, were his first prompters to higher pursuits; and instead of guarding him from one and winning him to the other, his endeavours to raise himself had produced just the contrary result.

'Yes that's all the good that such a brute as you can get from them!' cried Catherine, sucking her damaged lip, and watching the conflagration with indignant eyes.

'You'd BETTER hold your tongue, now,' he answered fiercely.

And his agitation precluded further speech; he advanced hastily to the entrance, where I made way for him to pass. But ere he had crossed the door-stones, Mr. Heathcliff, coming up the causeway, encountered him, and laying hold of his shoulder asked,—'What's to do now, my lad?'

'Naught, naught,' he said, and broke away to enjoy his grief and anger in solitude.

Heathcliff gazed after him, and sighed.

'It will be odd if I thwart myself,' he muttered, unconscious that I was behind him. 'But when I look for his father in his face, I find HER every day more! How the devil is he so like? I can hardly bear to see him.'

He bent his eyes to the ground, and walked moodily in. There was a restless, anxious expression in his countenance. I had never remarked there before; and he looked sparer in person. His daughter-in-law, on perceiving him through the window, immediately escaped to the kitchen, so that I remained alone.

'I'm glad to see you out of doors again, Mr. Lockwood,' he said, in reply to my greeting; 'from selfish motives partly: I don't think I could readily supply your loss in this desolation. I've wondered more than once what brought you here.'

'An idle whim, I fear, sir,' was my answer; 'or else an idle whim is going to spirit me away. I shall set out for London next week; and I must give you warning that I feel no disposition to retain Thrushcross Grange beyond the twelve months I agreed to rent it. I believe I shall not live there any more.'

'Oh, indeed; you're tired of being banished from the world, are you?' he said. 'But if you be coming to plead off paying for a place you won't occupy, your journey is useless: I never relent in exacting my due from any one.'

'I'm coming to plead off nothing about it,' I exclaimed, considerably irritated. 'Should you wish it, I'll settle with you now,' and I drew my note-book from my pocket.

'No, no,' he replied, coolly; 'you'll leave sufficient behind to cover your debts, if you fail to return: I'm not in such a hurry. Sit down and take your dinner with us; a guest that is safe from repeating his visit can generally be made welcome. Catherine bring the things in: where are you?'

Catherine reappeared, bearing a tray of knives and forks.

'You may get your dinner with Joseph,' muttered Heathcliff, aside, 'and remain in the kitchen till he is gone.'

She obeyed his directions very punctually: perhaps she had no temptation to transgress. Living among clowns and misanthropists, she probably cannot appreciate a better class of people when she meets them.

With Mr. Heathcliff, grim and saturnine, on the one hand, and Hareton, absolutely dumb, on the other, I made a somewhat cheerless meal, and bade adieu early. I would have departed by the back way, to get a last glimpse of Catherine and annoy old Joseph; but Hareton received orders to lead up my horse, and my host himself escorted me to the door, so I could not fulfil my wish.

'How dreary life gets over in that house!' I reflected, while riding down the road. 'What a realisation of something more romantic than a fairy tale it would have been for Mrs. Linton Heathcliff, had she and I struck up an attachment, as her good nurse desired, and migrated together into the stirring atmosphere of the town!'

Chapter XXXII

1802.—This September I was invited to devastate the moors of a friend in the north, and on my journey to his abode, I unexpectedly came within fifteen miles of Gimmerton. The ostler at a roadside public-house was holding a pail of water to refresh my horses, when a cart of very green oats, newly reaped, passed by, and he remarked,—'Yon's frough Gimmerton, nah! They're allas three wick' after other folk wi' ther harvest.'

'Gimmerton?' I repeated—my residence in that locality had already grown dim and dreamy. 'Ah! I know. How far is it from this?'

'Happen fourteen mile o'er th' hills; and a rough road,' he answered.

A sudden impulse seized me to visit Thrushcross Grange. It was scarcely noon, and I conceived that I might as well pass the night under my own roof as in an inn. Besides, I could spare a day easily to arrange matters with my landlord, and thus save myself the trouble of invading the neighbourhood again. Having rested awhile, I directed my servant to inquire the way to the village; and, with great fatigue to our beasts, we managed the distance in some three hours.

I left him there, and proceeded down the valley alone. The grey church looked greyer, and the lonely churchyard lonelier. I distinguished a moor-sheep cropping the short turf on the graves. It was sweet, warm weather—too warm for travelling; but the heat did not hinder me from enjoying the delightful scenery above and below: had I seen it nearer August, I'm sure it would have tempted me to waste a month among its solitudes. In winter nothing more dreary, in summer nothing more divine, than those glens shut in by hills, and those bluff, bold swells of heath.

I reached the Grange before sunset, and knocked for admittance; but the family had retreated into the back premises, I judged, by one thin, blue wreath, curling from the kitchen chimney, and they did not hear. I rode into the court. Under the porch, a girl of nine or ten sat knitting, and an old woman reclined on the housesteps, smoking a meditative pipe.

'Is Mrs. Dean within?' I demanded of the dame.

'Mistress Dean? Nay!' she answered, 'she doesn't bide here: shoo's up at th' Heights.'

'Are you the housekeeper, then?' I continued.

'Eea, aw keep th' hause,' she replied.

'Well, I'm Mr. Lockwood, the master. Are there any rooms to lodge me in, I wonder? I wish to stay all night.'

'T' maister!' she cried in astonishment. 'Whet, whoiver knew yah wur coming? Yah sud ha' send word. They's nowt norther dry nor mensful abaht t' place: nowt there isn't!'

She threw down her pipe and bustled in, the girl followed, and I entered too; soon perceiving that her report was true, and, moreover, that I had almost upset her wits by my unwelcome apparition, I bade her be composed. I would go out for a walk; and, meantime she must try to prepare a corner of a sitting-room for me to sup in, and a bed-room to sleep in. No sweeping and dusting, only good fire and dry sheets were necessary. She seemed willing to do her best; though she thrust the hearth-brush into the grates in mistake for the poker, and malappropriated several other articles of her craft: but I retired, confiding in her energy for a resting-place against my return. Wuthering Heights was the goal of my proposed excursion. An afterthought brought me back, when I had quitted the court.

'All well at the Heights?' I inquired of the woman.

'Eea, f'r owt ee knaw!' she answered, skurrying away with a pan of hot cinders.

I would have asked why Mrs. Dean had deserted the Grange, but it was impossible to delay her at such a crisis, so I turned away and made my exit, rambling leisurely along, with the glow of a sinking sun behind, and the mild glory of a rising moon in front—one fading, and the other brightening—as I quitted the park, and climbed the stony by-road branching off to Mr. Heathcliff's dwelling. Before I arrived in sight of it, all that remained of day was a beamless amber light along the west: but I could see every pebble on the path, and every blade of grass, by that splendid moon. I had neither to climb the gate nor to knock—it yielded to my hand. That is an improvement, I thought. And I noticed another, by the aid of my nostrils; a fragrance of stocks and wallflowers wafted on the air from amongst the homely fruit-trees.

Both doors and lattices were open; and yet, as is usually the case in a coal-district, a fine red fire illumined the chimney: the comfort which the eye derives from it renders the extra heat endurable. But the house of Wuthering Heights is so large that the inmates have plenty of space for withdrawing out of its influence; and accordingly what inmates there were had stationed themselves not far from one of the windows. I could both see them and hear them talk before I entered, and looked and listened in consequence; being moved thereto by a mingled sense of curiosity and envy, that grew as I lingered.

'Con-TRARY!' said a voice as sweet as a silver bell. 'That for the third time, you dunce! I'm not going to tell you again. Recollect, or I'll pull your hair!'

'Contrary, then,' answered another, in deep but softened tones. 'And now, kiss me, for minding so well.'

'No, read it over first correctly, without a single mistake.'

The male speaker began to read: he was a young man, respectably dressed and seated at a table, having a book before him. His handsome features glowed with pleasure, and his eyes kept impatiently wandering from the page to a small white hand over his shoulder, which recalled him by a smart slap on the cheek, whenever its owner detected such signs of inattention. Its owner stood behind; her light, shining ringlets blending, at intervals, with his brown looks, as she bent to superintend his studies; and her face—it was lucky he could not see her face, or he would never have been so steady. I could; and I bit my lip in spite, at having thrown away the chance I might have had of doing something besides staring at its smiting beauty.

The task was done, not free from further blunders; but the pupil claimed a reward, and received at least five kisses; which, however, he generously returned. Then they came to the door, and from their conversation I judged they were about to issue out and have a walk on the moors. I supposed I should be condemned in Hareton Earnshaw's heart, if not by his mouth, to the lowest pit in the infernal regions if I showed my unfortunate person in his neighbourhood then; and feeling very mean and malignant, I skulked round to seek refuge in the kitchen. There was unobstructed admittance on that side also; and at the door sat my old friend Nelly Dean, sewing and singing a song; which was often interrupted from within by harsh words of scorn and intolerance, uttered in far from musical accents.

'I'd rayther, by th' haulf, hev' 'em swearing i' my lugs fro'h morn to neeght, nor hearken ye hahsiver!' said the tenant of the kitchen, in answer to an unheard speech of Nelly's. 'It's a blazing shame, that I cannot oppen t' blessed Book, but yah set up them glories to sattan, and all t' flaysome wickednesses that iver were born into th' warld! Oh! ye're a raight nowt; and shoo's another; and that poor lad 'll be lost atween ye. Poor lad!' he added, with a groan; 'he's witched: I'm sartin on't. Oh, Lord, judge 'em, for there's norther law nor justice among wer rullers!'

'No! or we should be sitting in flaming fagots, I suppose,' retorted the singer. 'But wisht, old man, and read your Bible like a Christian, and never mind me. This is "Fairy Annie's Wedding"—a bonny tune—it goes to a dance.'

Mrs. Dean was about to recommence, when I advanced; and recognising me directly, she jumped to her feet, crying—'Why, bless you, Mr. Lockwood! How could you think of returning in this way? All's shut up at Thrushcross Grange. You should have given us notice!'

'I've arranged to be accommodated there, for as long as I shall stay,' I answered. 'I depart again to-morrow. And how are you transplanted here, Mrs. Dean? tell me that.'

'Zillah left, and Mr. Heathcliff wished me to come, soon after you went to London, and stay till you returned. But, step in, pray! Have you walked from Gimmerton this evening?'

'From the Grange,' I replied; 'and while they make me lodging room there, I want to finish my business with your master; because I don't think of having another opportunity in a hurry.'

'What business, sir?' said Nelly, conducting me into the house. 'He's gone out at present, and won't return soon.'

'About the rent,' I answered.

'Oh! then it is with Mrs. Heathcliff you must settle,' she observed; 'or rather with me. She has not learnt to manage her affairs yet, and I act for her: there's nobody else.'

I looked surprised.

'Ah! you have not heard of Heathcliff's death, I see,' she continued.

'Heathcliff dead!' I exclaimed, astonished. 'How long ago?'

'Three months since: but sit down, and let me take your hat, and I'll tell you all about it. Stop, you have had nothing to eat, have you?'

'I want nothing: I have ordered supper at home. You sit down too. I never dreamt of his dying! Let me hear how it came to pass. You say you don't expect them back for some time—the young people?'

'No—I have to scold them every evening for their late rambles: but they don't care for me. At least, have a drink of our old ale; it will do you good: you seem weary.'

She hastened to fetch it before I could refuse, and I heard Joseph asking whether 'it warn't a crying scandal that she should have followers at her time of life? And then, to get them jocks out o' t' maister's cellar! He fair shaamed to 'bide still and see it.'

She did not stay to retaliate, but re-entered in a minute, bearing a reaming silver pint, whose contents I lauded with becoming earnestness. And afterwards she furnished me with the sequel of Heathcliff's history. He had a 'queer' end, as she expressed it.

I was summoned to Wuthering Heights, within a fortnight of your leaving us, she said; and I obeyed joyfully, for Catherine's sake. My first interview with her grieved and shocked me: she had altered so much since our separation. Mr. Heathcliff did not explain his reasons for taking a new mind about my coming here; he only told me he wanted me, and he was tired of seeing Catherine: I must make the little parlour my sitting-room, and keep her with me. It was enough if he were obliged to see her once or twice a day. She seemed pleased at this arrangement; and, by degrees, I smuggled over a great number of books, and other articles, that had formed her amusement at the Grange; and flattered myself we should get on in tolerable comfort. The delusion did not last long. Catherine, contented at first, in a brief space grew irritable and restless. For one thing, she was forbidden to move out of the garden, and it fretted her sadly to be confined to its narrow bounds as spring drew on; for another, in following the house, I was forced to quit her frequently, and she complained of loneliness: she preferred quarrelling with Joseph in the kitchen to sitting at peace in her solitude. I did not mind their skirmishes: but Hareton was often obliged to seek the kitchen also, when the master wanted to have the house to himself! and though in the beginning she either left it at his approach, or quietly joined in my occupations, and shunned remarking or addressing him—and though he was always as sullen and silent as possible—after a while, she changed her behaviour, and became incapable of letting him alone: talking at him; commenting on his stupidity and idleness; expressing her wonder how he could endure the life he lived—how he could sit a whole evening staring into the fire, and dozing.

'He's just like a dog, is he not, Ellen?' she once observed, 'or a cart-horse? He does his work, eats his food, and sleeps eternally! What a blank, dreary mind he must have! Do you ever dream, Hareton? And, if you do, what is it about? But you can't speak to me!'

Then she looked at him; but he would neither open his mouth nor look again.

'He's, perhaps, dreaming now,' she continued. 'He twitched his shoulder as Juno twitches hers. Ask him, Ellen.'

'Mr. Hareton will ask the master to send you up-stairs, if you don't behave!' I said. He had not only twitched his shoulder but clenched his fist, as if tempted to use it.

'I know why Hareton never speaks, when I am in the kitchen,' she exclaimed, on another occasion. 'He is afraid I shall laugh at him. Ellen, what do you think? He began to teach himself to read once; and, because I laughed, he burned his books, and dropped it: was he not a fool?'

'Were not you naughty?' I said; 'answer me that.'

'Perhaps I was,' she went on; 'but I did not expect him to be so silly. Hareton, if I gave you a book, would you take it now? I'll try!'

She placed one she had been perusing on his hand; he flung it off, and muttered, if she did not give over, he would break her neck.

'Well, I shall put it here,' she said, 'in the table-drawer; and I'm going to bed.'

Then she whispered me to watch whether he touched it, and departed. But he would not come near it; and so I informed her in the morning, to her great disappointment. I saw she was sorry for his persevering sulkiness and indolence: her conscience reproved her for frightening him off improving himself: she had done it effectually. But her ingenuity was at work to remedy the injury: while I ironed, or pursued other such stationary employments as I could not well do in the parlour, she would bring some pleasant volume and read it aloud to me. When Hareton was there, she generally paused in an interesting part, and left the book lying about: that she did repeatedly; but he was as obstinate as a mule, and, instead of snatching at her bait, in wet weather he took to smoking with Joseph; and they sat like automatons, one on each side of the fire, the elder happily too deaf to understand her wicked nonsense, as he would have called it, the younger doing his best to seem to disregard it. On fine evenings the latter followed his shooting expeditions, and Catherine yawned and sighed, and teased me to talk to her, and ran off into the court or garden the moment I began; and, as a last resource, cried, and said she was tired of living: her life was useless.

Mr. Heathcliff, who grew more and more disinclined to society, had almost banished Earnshaw from his apartment. Owing to an accident at the commencement of March, he became for some days a fixture in the kitchen. His gun burst while out on the hills by himself; a splinter cut his arm, and he lost a good deal of blood before he could reach home. The consequence was that, perforce, he was condemned to the fireside and tranquillity, till he made it up again. It suited Catherine to have him there: at any rate, it made her hate her room up-stairs more than ever: and she would compel me to find out business below, that she might accompany me.

On Easter Monday, Joseph went to Gimmerton fair with some cattle; and, in the afternoon, I was busy getting up linen in the kitchen. Earnshaw sat, morose as usual, at the chimney corner, and my little mistress was beguiling an idle hour with drawing pictures on the window-panes, varying her amusement by smothered bursts of songs, and whispered ejaculations, and quick glances of annoyance and impatience in the direction of her cousin, who steadfastly smoked, and looked into the grate. At a notice that I could do with her no longer intercepting my light, she removed to the hearthstone. I bestowed little attention on her proceedings, but, presently, I heard her begin—'I've found out, Hareton, that I want—that I'm glad—that I should like you to be my cousin now, if you had not grown so cross to me, and so rough.'

Hareton returned no answer.

'Hareton, Hareton, Hareton! do you hear?' she continued.

'Get off wi' ye!' he growled, with uncompromising gruffness.

'Let me take that pipe,' she said, cautiously advancing her hand and abstracting it from his mouth.

Before he could attempt to recover it, it was broken, and behind the fire. He swore at her and seized another.

'Stop,' she cried, 'you must listen to me first; and I can't speak while those clouds are floating in my face.'

'Will you go to the devil!' he exclaimed, ferociously, 'and let me be!'

'No,' she persisted, 'I won't: I can't tell what to do to make you talk to me; and you are determined not to understand. When I call you stupid, I don't mean anything: I don't mean that I despise you. Come, you shall take notice of me, Hareton: you are my cousin, and you shall own me.'

'I shall have naught to do wi' you and your mucky pride, and your damned mocking tricks!' he answered. 'I'll go to hell, body and soul, before I look sideways after you again. Side out o' t' gate, now, this minute!'

Catherine frowned, and retreated to the window-seat chewing her lip, and endeavouring, by humming an eccentric tune, to conceal a growing tendency to sob.

'You should be friends with your cousin, Mr. Hareton,' I interrupted, 'since she repents of her sauciness. It would do you a great deal of good: it would make you another man to have her for a companion.'

'A companion!' he cried; 'when she hates me, and does not think me fit to wipe her shoon! Nay, if it made me a king, I'd not be scorned for seeking her good-will any more.'

'It is not I who hate you, it is you who hate me!' wept Cathy, no longer disguising her trouble. 'You hate me as much as Mr. Heathcliff does, and more.'

'You're a damned liar,' began Earnshaw: 'why have I made him angry, by taking your part, then, a hundred times? and that when you sneered at and despised me, and—Go on plaguing me, and I'll step in yonder, and say you worried me out of the kitchen!'

'I didn't know you took my part,' she answered, drying her eyes; 'and I was miserable and bitter at everybody; but now I thank you, and beg you to forgive me: what can I do besides?'

She returned to the hearth, and frankly extended her hand. He blackened and scowled like a thunder-cloud, and kept his fists resolutely clenched, and his gaze fixed on the ground. Catherine, by instinct, must have divined it was obdurate perversity, and not dislike, that prompted this dogged conduct; for, after remaining an instant undecided, she stooped and impressed on his cheek a gentle kiss. The little rogue thought I had not seen her, and, drawing back, she took her former station by the window, quite demurely. I shook my head reprovingly, and then she blushed and whispered—'Well! what should I have done, Ellen? He wouldn't shake hands, and he wouldn't look: I must show him some way that I like him-that I want to be friends.'

Whether the kiss convinced Hareton, I cannot tell: he was very careful, for some minutes, that his face should not be seen, and when he did raise it, he was sadly puzzled where to turn his eyes.

Catherine employed herself in wrapping a handsome book neatly in white paper, and having tied it with a bit of ribbon, and addressed it to 'Mr. Hareton Earnshaw,' she desired me to be her ambassadress, and convey the present to its destined recipient.

'And tell him, if he'll take it, I'll come and teach him to read it right,' she said; 'and, if he refuse it, I'll go upstairs, and never tease him again.'

I carried it, and repeated the message; anxiously watched by my employer. Hareton would not open his fingers, so I laid it on his knee. He did not strike it off, either. I returned to my work. Catherine leaned her head and arms on the table, till she heard the slight rustle of the covering being removed; then she stole away, and quietly seated herself beside her cousin. He trembled, and his face glowed: all his rudeness and all his surly harshness had deserted him: he could not summon courage, at first, to utter a syllable in reply to her questioning look, and her murmured petition.

'Say you forgive me, Hareton, do. You can make me so happy by speaking that little word.'

He muttered something inaudible.

'And you'll be my friend?' added Catherine, interrogatively.

'Nay, you'll be ashamed of me every day of your life,' he answered; 'and the more ashamed, the more you know me; and I cannot bide it.'

'So you won't be my friend?' she said, smiling as sweet as honey, and creeping close up.

I overheard no further distinguishable talk, but, on looking round again, I perceived two such radiant countenances bent over the page of the accepted book, that I did not doubt the treaty had been ratified on both sides; and the enemies were, thenceforth, sworn allies.

The work they studied was full of costly pictures; and those and their position had charm enough to keep them unmoved till Joseph came home. He, poor man, was perfectly aghast at the spectacle of Catherine seated on the same bench with Hareton Earnshaw, leaning her hand on his shoulder; and confounded at his favourite's endurance of her proximity: it affected him too deeply to allow an observation on the subject that night. His emotion was only revealed by the immense sighs he drew, as he solemnly spread his large Bible on the table, and overlaid it with dirty bank-notes from his pocket-book, the produce of the day's transactions. At length he summoned Hareton from his seat.

'Tak' these in to t' maister, lad,' he said, 'and bide there. I's gang up to my own rahm. This hoile's neither mensful nor seemly for us: we mun side out and seearch another.'

'Come, Catherine,' I said, 'we must "side out" too: I've done my ironing. Are you ready to go?'

'It is not eight o'clock!' she answered, rising unwillingly.

'Hareton, I'll leave this book upon the chimney-piece, and I'll bring some more to-morrow.'

'Ony books that yah leave, I shall tak' into th' hahse,' said Joseph, 'and it'll be mitch if yah find 'em agean; soa, yah may plase yerseln!'

Cathy threatened that his library should pay for hers; and, smiling as she passed Hareton, went singing up-stairs: lighter of heart, I venture to say, than ever she had been under that roof before; except, perhaps, during her earliest visits to Linton.

The intimacy thus commenced grew rapidly; though it encountered temporary interruptions. Earnshaw was not to be civilized with a wish, and my young lady was no philosopher, and no paragon of patience; but both their minds tending to the same point—one loving and desiring to esteem, and the other loving and desiring to be esteemed—they contrived in the end to reach it.

You see, Mr. Lockwood, it was easy enough to win Mrs. Heathcliff's heart. But now, I'm glad you did not try. The crown of all my wishes will be the union of those two. I shall envy no one on their wedding day: there won't be a happier woman than myself in England!

Chapter XXXIII

ON the morrow of that Monday, Earnshaw being still unable to follow his ordinary employments, and therefore remaining about the house, I speedily found it would be impracticable to retain my charge beside me, as heretofore. She got downstairs before me, and out into the garden, where she had seen her cousin performing some easy work; and when I went to bid them come to breakfast, I saw she had persuaded him to clear a large space of ground from currant and gooseberry bushes, and they were busy planning together an importation of plants from the Grange.

I was terrified at the devastation which had been accomplished in a brief half-hour; the black-currant trees were the apple of Joseph's eye, and she had just fixed her choice of a flower-bed in the midst of them.

'There! That will be all shown to the master,' I exclaimed, 'the minute it is discovered. And what excuse have you to offer for taking such liberties with the garden? We shall have a fine explosion on the head of it: see if we don't! Mr. Hareton, I wonder you should have no more wit than to go and make that mess at her bidding!'

'I'd forgotten they were Joseph's,' answered Earnshaw, rather puzzled; 'but I'll tell him I did it.'

We always ate our meals with Mr. Heathcliff. I held the mistress's post in making tea and carving; so I was indispensable at table. Catherine usually sat by me, but to-day she stole nearer to Hareton; and I presently saw she would have no more discretion in her friendship than she had in her hostility.

'Now, mind you don't talk with and notice your cousin too much,' were my whispered instructions as we entered the room. 'It will certainly annoy Mr. Heathcliff, and he'll be mad at you both.'

'I'm not going to,' she answered.

The minute after, she had sidled to him, and was sticking primroses in his plate of porridge.

He dared not speak to her there: he dared hardly look; and yet she went on teasing, till he was twice on the point of being provoked to laugh. I frowned, and then she glanced towards the master: whose mind was occupied on other subjects than his company, as his countenance evinced; and she grew serious for an instant, scrutinizing him with deep gravity. Afterwards she turned, and recommenced her nonsense; at last, Hareton uttered a smothered laugh. Mr. Heathcliff started; his eye rapidly surveyed our faces, Catherine met it with her accustomed look of nervousness and yet defiance, which he abhorred.

'It is well you are out of my reach,' he exclaimed. 'What fiend possesses you to stare back at me, continually, with those infernal eyes? Down with them! and don't remind me of your existence again. I thought I had cured you of laughing.'

'It was me,' muttered Hareton.

'What do you say?' demanded the master.

Hareton looked at his plate, and did not repeat the confession. Mr. Heathcliff looked at him a bit, and then silently resumed his breakfast and his interrupted musing. We had nearly finished, and the two young people prudently shifted wider asunder, so I anticipated no further disturbance during that sitting: when Joseph appeared at the door, revealing by his quivering lip and furious eyes that the outrage committed on his precious shrubs was detected. He must have seen Cathy and her cousin about the spot before he examined it, for while his jaws worked like those of a cow chewing its cud, and rendered his speech difficult to understand, he began:—

'I mun hev' my wage, and I mun goa! I HED aimed to dee wheare I'd sarved fur sixty year; and I thowt I'd lug my books up into t' garret, and all my bits o' stuff, and they sud hev' t' kitchen to theirseln; for t' sake o' quietness. It wur hard to gie up my awn hearth-stun, but I thowt I COULD do that! But nah, shoo's taan my garden fro' me, and by th' heart, maister, I cannot stand it! Yah may bend to th' yoak an ye will—I noan used to 't, and an old man doesn't sooin get used to new barthens. I'd rayther arn my bite an' my sup wi' a hammer in th' road!'

'Now, now, idiot!' interrupted Heathcliff, 'cut it short! What's your grievance? I'll interfere in no quarrels between you and Nelly. She may thrust you into the coal-hole for anything I care.'

'It's noan Nelly!' answered Joseph. 'I sudn't shift for Nelly-nasty ill nowt as shoo is. Thank God! SHOO cannot stale t' sowl o' nob'dy! Shoo wer niver soa handsome, but what a body mud look at her 'bout winking. It's yon flaysome, graceless quean, that's witched our lad, wi' her bold een and her forrard ways—till—Nay! it fair bursts my heart! He's forgotten all I've done for him, and made on him, and goan and riven up a whole row o' t' grandest currant-trees i' t' garden!' and here he lamented outright; unmanned by a sense of his bitter injuries, and Earnshaw's ingratitude and dangerous condition.

'Is the fool drunk?' asked Mr. Heathcliff. 'Hareton, is it you he's finding fault with?'

'I've pulled up two or three bushes,' replied the young man; 'but I'm going to set 'em again.'

'And why have you pulled them up?' said the master.

Catherine wisely put in her tongue.

'We wanted to plant some flowers there,' she cried. 'I'm the only person to blame, for I wished him to do it.'

'And who the devil gave YOU leave to touch a stick about the place?' demanded her father-in-law, much surprised. 'And who ordered YOU to obey her?' he added, turning to Hareton.

The latter was speechless; his cousin replied—'You shouldn't grudge a few yards of earth for me to ornament, when you have taken all my land!'

'Your land, insolent slut! You never had any,' said Heathcliff.

'And my money,' she continued; returning his angry glare, and meantime biting a piece of crust, the remnant of her breakfast.

'Silence!' he exclaimed. 'Get done, and begone!'

'And Hareton's land, and his money,' pursued the reckless thing. 'Hareton and I are friends now; and I shall tell him all about you!'

The master seemed confounded a moment: he grew pale, and rose up, eyeing her all the while, with an expression of mortal hate.

'If you strike me, Hareton will strike you,' she said; 'so you may as well sit down.'

'If Hareton does not turn you out of the room, I'll strike him to hell,' thundered Heathcliff. 'Damnable witch! dare you pretend to rouse him against me? Off with her! Do you hear? Fling her into the kitchen! I'll kill her, Ellen Dean, if you let her come into my sight again!'

Hareton tried, under his breath, to persuade her to go.

'Drag her away!' he cried, savagely. 'Are you staying to talk?' And he approached to execute his own command.

'He'll not obey you, wicked man, any more,' said Catherine; 'and he'll soon detest you as much as I do.'

'Wisht! wisht!' muttered the young man, reproachfully; 'I will not hear you speak so to him. Have done.'

'But you won't let him strike me?' she cried.

'Come, then,' he whispered earnestly.

It was too late: Heathcliff had caught hold of her.

'Now, YOU go!' he said to Earnshaw. 'Accursed witch! this time she has provoked me when I could not bear it; and I'll make her repent it for ever!'

He had his hand in her hair; Hareton attempted to release her looks, entreating him not to hurt her that once. Heathcliff's black eyes flashed; he seemed ready to tear Catherine in pieces, and I was just worked up to risk coming to the rescue, when of a sudden his fingers relaxed; he shifted his grasp from her head to her arm, and gazed intently in her face. Then he drew his hand over his eyes, stood a moment to collect himself apparently, and turning anew to Catherine, said, with assumed calmness—'You must learn to avoid putting me in a passion, or I shall really murder you some time! Go with Mrs. Dean, and keep with her; and confine your insolence to her ears. As to Hareton Earnshaw, if I see him listen to you, I'll send him seeking his bread where he can get it! Your love will make him an outcast and a beggar. Nelly, take her; and leave me, all of you! Leave me!'

I led my young lady out: she was too glad of her escape to resist; the other followed, and Mr. Heathcliff had the room to himself till dinner. I had counselled Catherine to dine up-stairs; but, as soon as he perceived her vacant seat, he sent me to call her. He spoke to none of us, ate very little, and went out directly afterwards, intimating that he should not return before evening.

The two new friends established themselves in the house during his absence; where I heard Hareton sternly cheek his cousin, on her offering a revelation of her father-in-law's conduct to his father. He said he wouldn't suffer a word to be uttered in his disparagement: if he were the devil, it didn't signify; he would stand by him; and he'd rather she would abuse himself, as she used to, than begin on Mr. Heathcliff. Catherine was waxing cross at this; but he found means to make her hold her tongue, by asking how she would like HIM to speak ill of her father? Then she comprehended that Earnshaw took the master's reputation home to himself; and was attached by ties stronger than reason could break-chains, forged by habit, which it would be cruel to attempt to loosen. She showed a good heart, thenceforth, in avoiding both complaints and expressions of antipathy concerning Heathcliff; and confessed to me her sorrow that she had endeavoured to raise a bad spirit between him and Hareton: indeed, I don't believe she has ever breathed a syllable, in the latter's hearing, against her oppressor since.

When this slight disagreement was over, they were friends again, and as busy as possible in their several occupations of pupil and teacher. I came in to sit with them, after I had done my work; and I felt so soothed and comforted to watch them, that I did not notice how time got on. You know, they both appeared in a measure my children: I had long been proud of one; and now, I was sure, the other would be a source of equal satisfaction. His honest, warm, and intelligent nature shook off rapidly the clouds of ignorance and degradation in which it had been bred; and Catherine's sincere commendations acted as a spur to his industry. His brightening mind brightened his features, and added spirit and nobility to their aspect: I could hardly fancy it the same individual I had beheld on the day I discovered my little lady at Wuthering Heights, after her expedition to the Crags. While I admired and they laboured, dusk drew on, and with it returned the master. He came upon us quite unexpectedly, entering by the front way, and had a full view of the whole three, ere we could raise our heads to glance at him. Well, I reflected, there was never a pleasanter, or more harmless sight; and it will be a burning shame to scold them. The red fire-light glowed on their two bonny heads, and revealed their faces animated with the eager interest of children; for, though he was twenty-three and she eighteen, each had so much of novelty to feel and learn, that neither experienced nor evinced the sentiments of sober disenchanted maturity.

They lifted their eyes together, to encounter Mr. Heathcliff: perhaps you have never remarked that their eyes are precisely similar, and they are those of Catherine Earnshaw. The present Catherine has no other likeness to her, except a breadth of forehead, and a certain arch of the nostril that makes her appear rather haughty, whether she will or not. With Hareton the resemblance is carried farther: it is singular at all times, THEN it was particularly striking; because his senses were alert, and his mental faculties wakened to unwonted activity. I suppose this resemblance disarmed Mr. Heathcliff: he walked to the hearth in evident agitation; but it quickly subsided as he looked at the young man: or, I should say, altered its character; for it was there yet. He took the book from his hand, and glanced at the open page, then returned it without any observation; merely signing Catherine away: her companion lingered very little behind her, and I was about to depart also, but he bid me sit still.

'It is a poor conclusion, is it not?' he observed, having brooded awhile on the scene he had just witnessed: 'an absurd termination to my violent exertions? I get levers and mattocks to demolish the two houses, and train myself to be capable of working like Hercules, and when everything is ready and in my power, I find the will to lift a slate off either roof has vanished! My old enemies have not beaten me; now would be the precise time to revenge myself on their representatives: I could do it; and none could hinder me. But where is the use? I don't care for striking: I can't take the trouble to raise my hand! That sounds as if I had been labouring the whole time only to exhibit a fine trait of magnanimity. It is far from being the case: I have lost the faculty of enjoying their destruction, and I am too idle to destroy for nothing.

'Nelly, there is a strange change approaching; I'm in its shadow at present. I take so little interest in my daily life that I hardly remember to eat and drink. Those two who have left the room are the only objects which retain a distinct material appearance to me; and that appearance causes me pain, amounting to agony. About HER I won't speak; and I don't desire to think; but I earnestly wish she were invisible: her presence invokes only maddening sensations. HE moves me differently: and yet if I could do it without seeming insane, I'd never see him again! You'll perhaps think me rather inclined to become so,' he added, making an effort to smile, 'if I try to describe the thousand forms of past associations and ideas he awakens or embodies. But you'll not talk of what I tell you; and my mind is so eternally secluded in itself, it is tempting at last to turn it out to another.

'Five minutes ago Hareton seemed a personification of my youth, not a human being; I felt to him in such a variety of ways, that it would have been impossible to have accosted him rationally. In the first place, his startling likeness to Catherine connected him fearfully with her. That, however, which you may suppose the most potent to arrest my imagination, is actually the least: for what is not connected with her to me? and what does not recall her? I cannot look down to this floor, but her features are shaped in the flags! In every cloud, in every tree—filling the air at night, and caught by glimpses in every object by day—I am surrounded with her image! The most ordinary faces of men and women—my own features—mock me with a resemblance. The entire world is a dreadful collection of memoranda that she did exist, and that I have lost her! Well, Hareton's aspect was the ghost of my immortal love; of my wild endeavours to hold my right; my degradation, my pride, my happiness, and my anguish—

'But it is frenzy to repeat these thoughts to you: only it will let you know why, with a reluctance to be always alone, his society is no benefit; rather an aggravation of the constant torment I suffer: and it partly contributes to render me regardless how he and his cousin go on together. I can give them no attention any more.'

'But what do you mean by a CHANGE, Mr. Heathcliff?' I said, alarmed at his manner: though he was neither in danger of losing his senses, nor dying, according to my judgment: he was quite strong and healthy; and, as to his reason, from childhood he had a delight in dwelling on dark things, and entertaining odd fancies. He might have had a monomania on the subject of his departed idol; but on every other point his wits were as sound as mine.

'I shall not know that till it comes,' he said; 'I'm only half conscious of it now.'

'You have no feeling of illness, have you?' I asked.

'No, Nelly, I have not,' he answered.

'Then you are not afraid of death?' I pursued.

'Afraid? No!' he replied. 'I have neither a fear, nor a presentiment, nor a hope of death. Why should I? With my hard constitution and temperate mode of living, and unperilous occupations, I ought to, and probably SHALL, remain above ground till there is scarcely a black hair on my head. And yet I cannot continue in this condition! I have to remind myself to breathe-almost to remind my heart to beat! And it is like bending back a stiff spring: it is by compulsion that I do the slightest act not prompted by one thought; and by compulsion that I notice anything alive or dead, which is not associated with one universal idea. I have a single wish, and my whole being and faculties are yearning to attain it. They have yearned towards it so long, and so unwaveringly, that I'm convinced it will be reached—and soon—because it has devoured my existence: I am swallowed up in the anticipation of its fulfilment. My confessions have not relieved me; but they may account for some otherwise unaccountable phases of humour which I show. O God! It is a long fight; I wish it were over!'

He began to pace the room, muttering terrible things to himself, till I was inclined to believe, as he said Joseph did, that conscience had turned his heart to an earthly hell. I wondered greatly how it would end. Though he seldom before had revealed this state of mind, even by looks, it was his habitual mood, I had no doubt: he asserted it himself; but not a soul, from his general bearing, would have conjectured the fact. You did not when you saw him, Mr. Lockwood: and at the period of which I speak, he was just the same as then; only fonder of continued solitude, and perhaps still more laconic in company.

Chapter XXXIV

FOR some days after that evening Mr. Heathcliff shunned meeting us at meals; yet he would not consent formally to exclude Hareton and Cathy. He had an aversion to yielding so completely to his feelings, choosing rather to absent himself; and eating once in twenty-four hours seemed sufficient sustenance for him.

One night, after the family were in bed, I heard him go downstairs, and out at the front door. I did not hear him re-enter, and in the morning I found he was still away. We were in April then: the weather was sweet and warm, the grass as green as showers and sun could make it, and the two dwarf apple-trees near the southern wall in full bloom. After breakfast, Catherine insisted on my bringing a chair and sitting with my work under the fir-trees at the end of the house; and she beguiled Hareton, who had perfectly recovered from his accident, to dig and arrange her little garden, which was shifted to that corner by the influence of Joseph's complaints. I was comfortably revelling in the spring fragrance around, and the beautiful soft blue overhead, when my young lady, who had run down near the gate to procure some primrose roots for a border, returned only half laden, and informed us that Mr. Heathcliff was coming in. 'And he spoke to me,' she added, with a perplexed countenance.

'What did he say?' asked Hareton.

'He told me to begone as fast as I could,' she answered. 'But he looked so different from his usual look that I stopped a moment to stare at him.'

'How?' he inquired.

'Why, almost bright and cheerful. No, ALMOST nothing—VERY MUCH excited, and wild, and glad!' she replied.

'Night-walking amuses him, then,' I remarked, affecting a careless manner: in reality as surprised as she was, and anxious to ascertain the truth of her statement; for to see the master looking glad would not be an every-day spectacle. I framed an excuse to go in. Heathcliff stood at the open door; he was pale, and he trembled: yet, certainly, he had a strange joyful glitter in his eyes, that altered the aspect of his whole face.

'Will you have some breakfast?' I said. 'You must be hungry, rambling about all night!' I wanted to discover where he had been, but I did not like to ask directly.

'No, I'm not hungry,' he answered, averting his head, and speaking rather contemptuously, as if he guessed I was trying to divine the occasion of his good humour.

I felt perplexed: I didn't know whether it were not a proper opportunity to offer a bit of admonition.

'I don't think it right to wander out of doors,' I observed, 'instead of being in bed: it is not wise, at any rate this moist season. I daresay you'll catch a bad cold or a fever: you have something the matter with you now!'

'Nothing but what I can bear,' he replied; 'and with the greatest pleasure, provided you'll leave me alone: get in, and don't annoy me.'

I obeyed: and, in passing, I noticed he breathed as fast as a cat.

'Yes!' I reflected to myself, 'we shall have a fit of illness. I cannot conceive what he has been doing.'

That noon he sat down to dinner with us, and received a heaped-up plate from my hands, as if he intended to make amends for previous fasting.

'I've neither cold nor fever, Nelly,' he remarked, in allusion to my morning's speech; 'and I'm ready to do justice to the food you give me.'

He took his knife and fork, and was going to commence eating, when the inclination appeared to become suddenly extinct. He laid them on the table, looked eagerly towards the window, then rose and went out. We saw him walking to and fro in the garden while we concluded our meal, and Earnshaw said he'd go and ask why he would not dine: he thought we had grieved him some way.

'Well, is he coming?' cried Catherine, when her cousin returned.

'Nay,' he answered; 'but he's not angry: he seemed rarely pleased indeed; only I made him impatient by speaking to him twice; and then he bid me be off to you: he wondered how I could want the company of anybody else.'

I set his plate to keep warm on the fender; and after an hour or two he re-entered, when the room was clear, in no degree calmer: the same unnatural—it was unnatural—appearance of joy under his black brows; the same bloodless hue, and his teeth visible, now and then, in a kind of smile; his frame shivering, not as one shivers with chill or weakness, but as a tight-stretched cord vibrates—a strong thrilling, rather than trembling.

I will ask what is the matter, I thought; or who should? And I exclaimed—'Have you heard any good news, Mr. Heathcliff? You look uncommonly animated.'

'Where should good news come from to me?' he said. 'I'm animated with hunger; and, seemingly, I must not eat.'

'Your dinner is here,' I returned; 'why won't you get it?'

'I don't want it now,' he muttered, hastily: 'I'll wait till supper. And, Nelly, once for all, let me beg you to warn Hareton and the other away from me. I wish to be troubled by nobody: I wish to have this place to myself.'

'Is there some new reason for this banishment?' I inquired. 'Tell me why you are so queer, Mr. Heathcliff? Where were you last night? I'm not putting the question through idle curiosity, but—'

'You are putting the question through very idle curiosity,' he interrupted, with a laugh. 'Yet I'll answer it. Last night I was on the threshold of hell. To-day, I am within sight of my heaven. I have my eyes on it: hardly three feet to sever me! And now you'd better go! You'll neither see nor hear anything to frighten you, if you refrain from prying.'

Having swept the hearth and wiped the table, I departed; more perplexed than ever.

He did not quit the house again that afternoon, and no one intruded on his solitude; till, at eight o'clock, I deemed it proper, though unsummoned, to carry a candle and his supper to him. He was leaning against the ledge of an open lattice, but not looking out: his face was turned to the interior gloom. The fire had smouldered to ashes; the room was filled with the damp, mild air of the cloudy evening; and so still, that not only the murmur of the beck down Gimmerton was distinguishable, but its ripples and its gurgling over the pebbles, or through the large stones which it could not cover. I uttered an ejaculation of discontent at seeing the dismal grate, and commenced shutting the casements, one after another, till I came to his.

'Must I close this?' I asked, in order to rouse him; for he would not stir.

The light flashed on his features as I spoke. Oh, Mr. Lockwood, I cannot express what a terrible start I got by the momentary view! Those deep black eyes! That smile, and ghastly paleness! It appeared to me, not Mr. Heathcliff, but a goblin; and, in my terror, I let the candle bend towards the wall, and it left me in darkness.

'Yes, close it,' he replied, in his familiar voice. 'There, that is pure awkwardness! Why did you hold the candle horizontally? Be quick, and bring another.'

I hurried out in a foolish state of dread, and said to Joseph—'The master wishes you to take him a light and rekindle the fire.' For I dared not go in myself again just then.

Joseph rattled some fire into the shovel, and went: but he brought it back immediately, with the supper-tray in his other hand, explaining that Mr. Heathcliff was going to bed, and he wanted nothing to eat till morning. We heard him mount the stairs directly; he did not proceed to his ordinary chamber, but turned into that with the panelled bed: its window, as I mentioned before, is wide enough for anybody to get through; and it struck me that he plotted another midnight excursion, of which he had rather we had no suspicion.

'Is he a ghoul or a vampire?' I mused. I had read of such hideous incarnate demons. And then I set myself to reflect how I had tended him in infancy, and watched him grow to youth, and followed him almost through his whole course; and what absurd nonsense it was to yield to that sense of horror. 'But where did he come from, the little dark thing, harboured by a good man to his bane?' muttered Superstition, as I dozed into unconsciousness. And I began, half dreaming, to weary myself with imagining some fit parentage for him; and, repeating my waking meditations, I tracked his existence over again, with grim variations; at last, picturing his death and funeral: of which, all I can remember is, being exceedingly vexed at having the task of dictating an inscription for his monument, and consulting the sexton about it; and, as he had no surname, and we could not tell his age, we were obliged to content ourselves with the single word, 'Heathcliff.' That came true: we were. If you enter the kirkyard, you'll read, on his headstone, only that, and the date of his death.

Dawn restored me to common sense. I rose, and went into the garden, as soon as I could see, to ascertain if there were any footmarks under his window. There were none. 'He has stayed at home,' I thought, 'and he'll be all right to-day.' I prepared breakfast for the household, as was my usual custom, but told Hareton and Catherine to get theirs ere the master came down, for he lay late. They preferred taking it out of doors, under the trees, and I set a little table to accommodate them.

On my re-entrance, I found Mr. Heathcliff below. He and Joseph were conversing about some farming business; he gave clear, minute directions concerning the matter discussed, but he spoke rapidly, and turned his head continually aside, and had the same excited expression, even more exaggerated. When Joseph quitted the room he took his seat in the place he generally chose, and I put a basin of coffee before him. He drew it nearer, and then rested his arms on the table, and looked at the opposite wall, as I supposed, surveying one particular portion, up and down, with glittering, restless eyes, and with such eager interest that he stopped breathing during half a minute together.

'Come now,' I exclaimed, pushing some bread against his hand, 'eat and drink that, while it is hot: it has been waiting near an hour.'

He didn't notice me, and yet he smiled. I'd rather have seen him gnash his teeth than smile so.

'Mr. Heathcliff! master!' I cried, 'don't, for God's sake, stare as if you saw an unearthly vision.'

'Don't, for God's sake, shout so loud,' he replied. 'Turn round, and tell me, are we by ourselves?'

'Of course,' was my answer; 'of course we are.'

Still, I involuntarily obeyed him, as if I was not quite sure. With a sweep of his hand he cleared a vacant space in front among the breakfast things, and leant forward to gaze more at his ease.

Now, I perceived he was not looking at the wall; for when I regarded him alone, it seemed exactly that he gazed at something within two yards' distance. And whatever it was, it communicated, apparently, both pleasure and pain in exquisite extremes: at least the anguished, yet raptured, expression of his countenance suggested that idea. The fancied object was not fixed, either: his eyes pursued it with unwearied diligence, and, even in speaking to me, were never weaned away. I vainly reminded him of his protracted abstinence from food: if he stirred to touch anything in compliance with my entreaties, if he stretched his hand out to get a piece of bread, his fingers clenched before they reached it, and remained on the table, forgetful of their aim.

I sat, a model of patience, trying to attract his absorbed attention from its engrossing speculation; till he grew irritable, and got up, asking why I would not allow him to have his own time in taking his meals? and saying that on the next occasion I needn't wait: I might set the things down and go. Having uttered these words he left the house, slowly sauntered down the garden path, and disappeared through the gate.

The hours crept anxiously by: another evening came. I did not retire to rest till late, and when I did, I could not sleep. He returned after midnight, and, instead of going to bed, shut himself into the room beneath. I listened, and tossed about, and, finally, dressed and descended. It was too irksome to lie there, harassing my brain with a hundred idle misgivings.

I distinguished Mr. Heathcliff's step, restlessly measuring the floor, and he frequently broke the silence by a deep inspiration, resembling a groan. He muttered detached words also; the only one I could catch was the name of Catherine, coupled with some wild term of endearment or suffering; and spoken as one would speak to a person present; low and earnest, and wrung from the depth of his soul. I had not courage to walk straight into the apartment; but I desired to divert him from his reverie, and therefore fell foul of the kitchen fire, stirred it, and began to scrape the cinders. It drew him forth sooner than I expected. He opened the door immediately, and said—'Nelly, come here—is it morning? Come in with your light.'

'It is striking four,' I answered. 'You want a candle to take up-stairs: you might have lit one at this fire.'

'No, I don't wish to go up-stairs,' he said. 'Come in, and kindle ME a fire, and do anything there is to do about the room.'

'I must blow the coals red first, before I can carry any,' I replied, getting a chair and the bellows

He roamed to and fro, meantime, in a state approaching distraction; his heavy sighs succeeding each other so thick as to leave no space for common breathing between.

'When day breaks I'll send for Green,' he said; 'I wish to make some legal inquiries of him while I can bestow a thought on those matters, and while I can act calmly. I have not written my will yet; and how to leave my property I cannot determine. I wish I could annihilate it from the face of the earth.'

'I would not talk so, Mr. Heathcliff,' I interposed. 'Let your will be a while: you'll be spared to repent of your many injustices yet! I never expected that your nerves would be disordered: they are, at present, marvellously so, however; and almost entirely through your own fault. The way you've passed these three last days might knock up a Titan. Do take some food, and some repose. You need only look at yourself in a glass to see how you require both. Your cheeks are hollow, and your eyes blood-shot, like a person starving with hunger and going blind with loss of sleep.'

'It is not my fault that I cannot eat or rest,' he replied. 'I assure you it is through no settled designs. I'll do both, as soon as I possibly can. But you might as well bid a man struggling in the water rest within arms' length of the shore! I must reach it first, and then I'll rest. Well, never mind Mr. Green: as to repenting of my injustices, I've done no injustice, and I repent of nothing. I'm too happy; and yet I'm not happy enough. My soul's bliss kills my body, but does not satisfy itself.'

'Happy, master?' I cried. 'Strange happiness! If you would hear me without being angry, I might offer some advice that would make you happier.'

'What is that?' he asked. 'Give it.'

'You are aware, Mr. Heathcliff,' I said, 'that from the time you were thirteen years old you have lived a selfish, unchristian life; and probably hardly had a Bible in your hands during all that period. You must have forgotten the contents of the book, and you may not have space to search it now. Could it be hurtful to send for some one—some minister of any denomination, it does not matter which—to explain it, and show you how very far you have erred from its precepts; and how unfit you will be for its heaven, unless a change takes place before you die?'

'I'm rather obliged than angry, Nelly,' he said, 'for you remind me of the manner in which I desire to be buried. It is to be carried to the churchyard in the evening. You and Hareton may, if you please, accompany me: and mind, particularly, to notice that the sexton obeys my directions concerning the two coffins! No minister need come; nor need anything be said over me.—I tell you I have nearly attained MY heaven; and that of others is altogether unvalued and uncovered by me.'

'And supposing you persevered in your obstinate fast, and died by that means, and they refused to bury you in the precincts of the kirk?' I said, shocked at his godless indifference. 'How would you like it?'

'They won't do that,' he replied: 'if they did, you must have me removed secretly; and if you neglect it you shall prove, practically, that the dead are not annihilated!'

As soon as he heard the other members of the family stirring he retired to his den, and I breathed freer. But in the afternoon, while Joseph and Hareton were at their work, he came into the kitchen again, and, with a wild look, bid me come and sit in the house: he wanted somebody with him. I declined; telling him plainly that his strange talk and manner frightened me, and I had neither the nerve nor the will to be his companion alone.

'I believe you think me a fiend,' he said, with his dismal laugh: 'something too horrible to live under a decent roof.' Then turning to Catherine, who was there, and who drew behind me at his approach, he added, half sneeringly,—'Will YOU come, chuck? I'll not hurt you. No! to you I've made myself worse than the devil. Well, there is ONE who won't shrink from my company! By God! she's relentless. Oh, damn it! It's unutterably too much for flesh and blood to bear—even mine.'

He solicited the society of no one more. At dusk he went into his chamber. Through the whole night, and far into the morning, we heard him groaning and murmuring to himself. Hareton was anxious to enter; but I bid him fetch Mr. Kenneth, and he should go in and see him. When he came, and I requested admittance and tried to open the door, I found it locked; and Heathcliff bid us be damned. He was better, and would be left alone; so the doctor went away.

The following evening was very wet: indeed, it poured down till day-dawn; and, as I took my morning walk round the house, I observed the master's window swinging open, and the rain driving straight in. He cannot be in bed, I thought: those showers would drench him through. He must either be up or out. But I'll make no more ado, I'll go boldly and look.'

Having succeeded in obtaining entrance with another key, I ran to unclose the panels, for the chamber was vacant; quickly pushing them aside, I peeped in. Mr. Heathcliff was there—laid on his back. His eyes met mine so keen and fierce, I started; and then he seemed to smile. I could not think him dead: but his face and throat were washed with rain; the bed-clothes dripped, and he was perfectly still. The lattice, flapping to and fro, had grazed one hand that rested on the sill; no blood trickled from the broken skin, and when I put my fingers to it, I could doubt no more: he was dead and stark!

I hasped the window; I combed his black long hair from his forehead; I tried to close his eyes: to extinguish, if possible, that frightful, life-like gaze of exultation before any one else beheld it. They would not shut: they seemed to sneer at my attempts; and his parted lips and sharp white teeth sneered too! Taken with another fit of cowardice, I cried out for Joseph. Joseph shuffled up and made a noise, but resolutely refused to meddle with him.

'Th' divil's harried off his soul,' he cried, 'and he may hev' his carcass into t' bargin, for aught I care! Ech! what a wicked 'un he looks, girning at death!' and the old sinner grinned in mockery. I thought he intended to cut a caper round the bed; but suddenly composing himself, he fell on his knees, and raised his hands, and returned thanks that the lawful master and the ancient stock were restored to their rights.

I felt stunned by the awful event; and my memory unavoidably recurred to former times with a sort of oppressive sadness. But poor Hareton, the most wronged, was the only one who really suffered much. He sat by the corpse all night, weeping in bitter earnest. He pressed its hand, and kissed the sarcastic, savage face that every one else shrank from contemplating; and bemoaned him with that strong grief which springs naturally from a generous heart, though it be tough as tempered steel.

Mr. Kenneth was perplexed to pronounce of what disorder the master died. I concealed the fact of his having swallowed nothing for four days, fearing it might lead to trouble, and then, I am persuaded, he did not abstain on purpose: it was the consequence of his strange illness, not the cause.

We buried him, to the scandal of the whole neighbourhood, as he wished. Earnshaw and I, the sexton, and six men to carry the coffin, comprehended the whole attendance. The six men departed when they had let it down into the grave: we stayed to see it covered. Hareton, with a streaming face, dug green sods, and laid them over the brown mould himself: at present it is as smooth and verdant as its companion mounds—and I hope its tenant sleeps as soundly. But the country folks, if you ask them, would swear on the Bible that he WALKS: there are those who speak to having met him near the church, and on the moor, and even within this house. Idle tales, you'll say, and so say I. Yet that old man by the kitchen fire affirms he has seen two on 'em looking out of his chamber window on every rainy night since his death:-and an odd thing happened to me about a month ago. I was going to the Grange one evening—a dark evening, threatening thunder—and, just at the turn of the Heights, I encountered a little boy with a sheep and two lambs before him; he was crying terribly; and I supposed the lambs were skittish, and would not be guided.

'What is the matter, my little man?' I asked.

'There's Heathcliff and a woman yonder, under t' nab,' he blubbered, 'un' I darnut pass 'em.'

I saw nothing; but neither the sheep nor he would go on so I bid him take the road lower down. He probably raised the phantoms from thinking, as he traversed the moors alone, on the nonsense he had heard his parents and companions repeat. Yet, still, I don't like being out in the dark now; and I don't like being left by myself in this grim house: I cannot help it; I shall be glad when they leave it, and shift to the Grange.

'They are going to the Grange, then?' I said.

'Yes,' answered Mrs. Dean, 'as soon as they are married, and that will be on New Year's Day.'

'And who will live here then?'

'Why, Joseph will take care of the house, and, perhaps, a lad to keep him company. They will live in the kitchen, and the rest will be shut up.'

'For the use of such ghosts as choose to inhabit it?' I observed.

'No, Mr. Lockwood,' said Nelly, shaking her head. 'I believe the dead are at peace: but it is not right to speak of them with levity.'

At that moment the garden gate swung to; the ramblers were returning.

'THEY are afraid of nothing,' I grumbled, watching their approach through the window. 'Together, they would brave Satan and all his legions.'

As they stepped on to the door-stones, and halted to take a last look at the moon—or, more correctly, at each other by her light—I felt irresistibly impelled to escape them again; and, pressing a remembrance into the hand of Mrs. Dean, and disregarding her expostulations at my rudeness, I vanished through the kitchen as they opened the house-door; and so should have confirmed Joseph in his opinion of his fellow-servant's gay indiscretions, had he not fortunately recognised me for a respectable character by the sweet ring of a sovereign at his feet.

My walk home was lengthened by a diversion in the direction of the kirk. When beneath its walls, I perceived decay had made progress, even in seven months: many a window showed black gaps deprived of glass; and slates jutted off here and there, beyond the right line of the roof, to be gradually worked off in coming autumn storms.

I sought, and soon discovered, the three headstones on the slope next the moor: on middle one grey, and half buried in the heath; Edgar Linton's only harmonized by the turf and moss creeping up its foot; Heathcliff's still bare.

I lingered round them, under that benign sky: watched the moths fluttering among the heath and harebells, listened to the soft wind breathing through the grass, and wondered how any one could ever imagine unquiet slumbers for the sleepers in that quiet earth.

Charlotte Brontë

JANE EYRE

Romance CLASSICS

Romance CLASSICS

Published by Trident Press International
801 12th Avenue South
Suite 302
Naples Florida 34102 USA
www.trident-international.com
email: tridentpress@worldnet.att.net

Printed in Australia
ISBN: 1582791783

PREFACE

A preface to the first edition of "Jane Eyre" being unnecessary, I gave none: this second edition demands a few words both of acknowledgment and miscellaneous remark.

My thanks are due in three quarters.

To the Public, for the indulgent ear it has inclined to a plain tale with few pretensions.

To the Press, for the fair field its honest suffrage has opened to an obscure aspirant.

To my Publishers, for the aid their tact, their energy, their practical sense and frank liberality have afforded an unknown and unrecommended Author.

The Press and the Public are but vague personifications for me, and I must thank them in vague terms; but my Publishers are definite: so are certain generous critics who have encouraged me as only large-hearted and high-minded men know how to encourage a struggling stranger; to them, i.e., to my Publishers and the select Reviewers, I say cordially, Gentlemen, I thank you from my heart.

Having thus acknowledged what I owe those who have aided and approved me, I turn to another class; a small one, so far as I know, but not, therefore, to be overlooked. I mean the timorous or carping few who doubt the tendency of such books as "Jane Eyre:" in whose eyes whatever is unusual is wrong; whose ears detect in each protest against bigotry—that parent of crime—an insult to piety, that regent of God on earth. I would suggest to such doubters certain obvious distinctions; I would remind them of certain simple truths.

Conventionality is not morality. Self-righteousness is not religion. To attack the first is not to assail the last. To pluck the mask from the face of the Pharisee, is not to lift an impious hand to the Crown of Thorns.

These things and deeds are diametrically opposed: they are as distinct as is vice from virtue. Men too often confound them: they should not be confounded: appearance should not be mistaken for truth; narrow human doctrines, that only tend to elate and magnify a few, should not be substituted for the world-redeeming creed of Christ. There is—I repeat it—a difference; and it is a good, and not a bad action to mark broadly and clearly the line of separation between them.

The world may not like to see these ideas dissevered, for it has been accustomed to blend them; finding it convenient to make external show pass for sterling worth—to let white-washed walls vouch for clean shrines. It may hate him who dares to scrutinise and expose—to rase the gilding, and show base metal under it—to penetrate the sepulchre, and reveal charnel relics: but hate as it will, it is indebted to him.

Ahab did not like Micaiah, because he never prophesied good concerning him, but evil; probably he liked the sycophant son of Chenaannah better; yet might Ahab have escaped a bloody death, had he but stopped his ears to flattery, and opened them to faithful counsel.

There is a man in our own days whose words are not framed to tickle delicate ears: who, to my thinking, comes before the great ones of society, much as the son of Imlah came before the throned Kings of Judah and Israel; and who speaks truth as deep, with a power as prophet-like and as vital—a mien as dauntless and as daring. Is the satirist of "Vanity Fair" admired in high places? I cannot tell; but I think if some of those amongst whom he hurls the Greek fire of his sarcasm, and over whom he flashes the levin-brand of his denunciation, were to take his warnings in time—they or their seed might yet escape a fatal Rimoth-Gilead.

Why have I alluded to this man? I have alluded to him, Reader, because I think I see in him an intellect profounder and more unique than his contemporaries have yet recognised; because I regard him as the first social regenerator of the day—as the very master of that working corps who would restore to rectitude the warped system of things; because I think no commentator on his writings has yet found the comparison that suits him, the terms which rightly characterise his talent. They say he is like Fielding: they talk of his wit, humour, comic powers. He resembles Fielding as an eagle does a vulture: Fielding could stoop on carrion, but Thackeray never does. His wit is bright, his humour attractive, but both bear the same relation to his serious genius that the mere lambent sheet-lightning playing under the edge of the summer-cloud does to the electric death-spark hid in its womb. Finally, I have alluded to Mr. Thackeray, because to him—if he will accept the tribute of a total stranger—I have dedicated this second edition of "JANE EYRE."

CURRER BELL.

December 21st, 1847.

NOTE TO THE THIRD EDITION

I avail myself of the opportunity which a third edition of "Jane Eyre" affords me, of again addressing a word to the Public, to explain that my claim to the title of novelist rests on this one work alone. If, therefore, the authorship of other works of fiction has been attributed to me, an honour is awarded where it is not merited; and consequently, denied where it is justly due.

This explanation will serve to rectify mistakes which may already have been made, and to prevent future errors.

CURRER BELL.

April 13th, 1848.

Chapter I

There was no possibility of taking a walk that day. We had been wandering, indeed, in the leafless shrubbery an hour in the morning; but since dinner (Mrs. Reed, when there was no company, dined early) the cold winter wind had brought with it clouds so sombre, and a rain so penetrating, that further out-door exercise was now out of the question.

I was glad of it: I never liked long walks, especially on chilly afternoons: dreadful to me was the coming home in the raw twilight, with nipped fingers and toes, and a heart saddened by the chidings of Bessie, the nurse, and humbled by the consciousness of my physical inferiority to Eliza, John, and Georgiana Reed.

The said Eliza, John, and Georgiana were now clustered round their mama in the drawing-room: she lay reclined on a sofa by the fireside, and with her darlings about her (for the time neither quarrelling nor crying) looked perfectly happy. Me, she had dispensed from joining the group; saying, "She regretted to be under the necessity of keeping me at a distance; but that until she heard from Bessie, and could discover by her own observation, that I was endeavouring in good earnest to acquire a more sociable and child-like disposition, a more attractive and sprightly manner—something lighter, franker, more natural, as it were—she really must exclude me from privileges intended only for contented, happy, little children."

"What does Bessie say I have done?" I asked.

"Jane, I don't like cavillers or questioners; besides, there is something truly forbidding in a child taking up her elders in that manner. Be seated somewhere; and until you can speak pleasantly, remain silent."

A breakfast-room adjoined the drawing-room, I slipped in there. It contained a bookcase: I soon possessed myself of a volume, taking care that it should be one stored with pictures. I mounted into the window-seat: gathering up my feet, I sat cross-legged, like a Turk; and, having drawn the red moreen curtain nearly close, I was shrined in double retirement.

Folds of scarlet drapery shut in my view to the right hand; to the left were the clear panes of glass, protecting, but not separating me from the drear November day. At intervals, while turning over the leaves of my book, I studied the aspect of that winter afternoon. Afar, it offered a pale blank of mist and cloud; near a scene of wet lawn and storm-beat shrub, with ceaseless rain sweeping away wildly before a long and lamentable blast.

I returned to my book—Bewick's History of British Birds: the letterpress thereof I cared little for, generally speaking; and yet there were certain introductory pages that, child as I was, I could not pass quite as a blank. They were those which treat of the haunts of sea-fowl; of "the solitary rocks and promontories" by them only inhabited; of the coast of Norway, studded with isles from its southern extremity, the Lindeness, or Naze, to the North Cape—

"Where the Northern Ocean, in vast whirls,
Boils round the naked, melancholy isles
Of farthest Thule; and the Atlantic surge
Pours in among the stormy Hebrides."

Nor could I pass unnoticed the suggestion of the bleak shores of Lapland, Siberia, Spitzbergen, Nova Zembla, Iceland, Greenland, with "the vast sweep of the Arctic Zone, and those forlorn regions of dreary space,—that reservoir of frost and snow, where firm fields of ice, the accumulation of centuries of winters, glazed in Alpine heights above heights, surround the pole, and concentre the multiplied rigours of extreme cold." Of these death-white realms I formed an idea of my own: shadowy, like all the half-comprehended notions that float dim through children's brains, but strangely impressive. The words in these introductory pages connected themselves with the succeeding vignettes, and gave significance to the rock standing up alone in a sea of billow and spray; to the broken boat stranded on a desolate coast; to the cold and ghastly moon glancing through bars of cloud at a wreck just sinking.

I cannot tell what sentiment haunted the quite solitary churchyard, with its inscribed headstone; its gate, its two trees, its low horizon, girdled by a broken wall, and its newly-risen crescent, attesting the hour of eventide.

The two ships becalmed on a torpid sea, I believed to be marine phantoms.

The fiend pinning down the thief's pack behind him, I passed over quickly: it was an object of terror.

So was the black horned thing seated aloof on a rock, surveying a distant crowd surrounding a gallows.

Each picture told a story; mysterious often to my undeveloped understanding and imperfect feelings, yet ever profoundly interesting: as interesting as the tales Bessie sometimes narrated on winter evenings, when she chanced to be in good humour; and when, having brought her ironing-table to the nursery hearth, she allowed us to sit about it, and while she got up Mrs. Reed's lace frills, and crimped her nightcap borders, fed our eager attention with passages of love and adventure taken from old fairy tales and other ballads; or (as at a later period I discovered) from the pages of Pamela, and Henry, Earl of Moreland.

With Bewick on my knee, I was then happy: happy at least in my way. I feared nothing but interruption, and that came too soon. The breakfast-room door opened.

"Boh! Madam Mope!" cried the voice of John Reed; then he paused: he found the room apparently empty.

"Where the dickens is she!" he continued. "Lizzy! Georgy! (calling to his sisters) Joan is not here: tell mama she is run out into the rain—bad animal!"

"It is well I drew the curtain," thought I; and I wished fervently he might not discover my hiding-place: nor would John Reed have found it out himself; he was not quick either of vision or conception; but Eliza just put her head in at the door, and said at once—

"She is in the window-seat, to be sure, Jack."

And I came out immediately, for I trembled at the idea of being dragged forth by the said Jack.

"What do you want?" I asked, with awkward diffidence.

"Say, 'What do you want, Master Reed?'" was the answer. "I want you to come here;" and seating himself in an arm-chair, he intimated by a gesture that I was to approach and stand before him.

John Reed was a schoolboy of fourteen years old; four years older than I, for I was but ten: large and stout for his age, with a dingy and unwholesome skin; thick lineaments in a spacious visage, heavy limbs and large extremities. He gorged himself habitually at table, which made him bilious, and gave him a dim and bleared eye and flabby cheeks. He ought now to have been at school; but his mama had taken him home for a month or two, "on account of his delicate health." Mr. Miles, the master, affirmed that he would do very well if he had fewer cakes and sweetmeats sent him from home; but the mother's heart turned from an opinion so harsh, and inclined rather to the more refined idea that John's sallowness was owing to over-application and, perhaps, to pining after home.

John had not much affection for his mother and sisters, and an antipathy to me. He bullied and punished me; not two or three times in the week, nor once or twice in the day, but continually: every nerve I had feared him, and every morsel of flesh in my bones shrank when he came near. There were moments when I was bewildered by the terror he inspired, because I had no appeal whatever against either his menaces or his inflictions; the servants did not like to offend their young master by taking my part against him, and Mrs. Reed was blind and deaf on the subject: she never saw him strike or heard him abuse me, though he did both now and then in her very presence, more frequently, however, behind her back.

Habitually obedient to John, I came up to his chair: he spent some three minutes in thrusting out his tongue at me as far as he could without damaging the roots: I knew he would soon strike, and while dreading the blow, I mused on the disgusting and ugly appearance of him who would presently deal it. I wonder if he read that notion in my face; for, all at once, without speaking, he struck suddenly and strongly. I tottered, and on regaining my equilibrium retired back a step or two from his chair.

"That is for your impudence in answering mama awhile since," said he, "and for your sneaking way of getting behind curtains, and for the look you had in your eyes two minutes since, you rat!"

Accustomed to John Reed's abuse, I never had an idea of replying to it; my care was how to endure the blow which would certainly follow the insult.

"What were you doing behind the curtain?" he asked.

"I was reading."

"Show the book."

I returned to the window and fetched it thence.

"You have no business to take our books; you are a dependent, mama says; you have no money; your father left you none; you ought to beg, and not to live here with gentlemen's children like us, and eat the same meals we do, and wear clothes at our mama's expense. Now, I'll teach you to rummage my bookshelves: for they ARE mine; all the house belongs to me, or will do in a few years. Go and stand by the door, out of the way of the mirror and the windows."

I did so, not at first aware what was his intention; but when I saw him lift and poise the book and stand in act to hurl it, I instinctively started aside with a cry of alarm: not soon enough, however; the volume was flung, it hit me, and I fell, striking my head against the door and cutting it. The cut bled, the pain was sharp: my terror had passed its climax; other feelings succeeded.

"Wicked and cruel boy!" I said. "You are like a murderer—you are like a slave-driver—you are like the Roman emperors!"

I had read Goldsmith's History of Rome, and had formed my opinion of Nero, Caligula, &c. Also I had drawn parallels in silence, which I never thought thus to have declared aloud.

"What! what!" he cried. "Did she say that to me? Did you hear her, Eliza and Georgiana? Won't I tell mama? but first—"

He ran headlong at me: I felt him grasp my hair and my shoulder: he had closed with a desperate thing. I really saw in him a tyrant, a murderer. I felt a drop or two of blood from my head trickle down my neck, and was sensible of somewhat pungent suffering: these sensations for the time predominated over fear, and I received him in frantic sort. I don't very well know what I did with my hands, but he called me "Rat! Rat!" and bellowed out aloud. Aid was near him: Eliza and Georgiana had run for Mrs. Reed, who was gone upstairs: she now came upon the scene, followed by Bessie and her maid Abbot. We were parted: I heard the words—

"Dear! dear! What a fury to fly at Master John!"

"Did ever anybody see such a picture of passion!"

Then Mrs. Reed subjoined—

"Take her away to the red-room, and lock her in there." Four hands were immediately laid upon me, and I was borne upstairs.

Chapter II

I resisted all the way: a new thing for me, and a circumstance which greatly strengthened the bad opinion Bessie and Miss Abbot were disposed to entertain of me. The fact is, I was a trifle beside myself; or rather OUT of myself, as the French would say: I was conscious that a moment's mutiny had already rendered me liable to strange penalties, and, like any other rebel slave, I felt resolved, in my desperation, to go all lengths.

"Hold her arms, Miss Abbot: she's like a mad cat."

"For shame! for shame!" cried the lady's-maid. "What shocking conduct, Miss Eyre, to strike a young gentleman, your benefactress's son! Your young master."

"Master! How is he my master? Am I a servant?"

"No; you are less than a servant, for you do nothing for your keep. There, sit down, and think over your wickedness."

They had got me by this time into the apartment indicated by Mrs. Reed, and had thrust me upon a stool: my impulse was to rise from it like a spring; their two pair of hands arrested me instantly.

"If you don't sit still, you must be tied down," said Bessie. "Miss Abbot, lend me your garters; she would break mine directly."

Miss Abbot turned to divest a stout leg of the necessary ligature. This preparation for bonds, and the additional ignominy it inferred, took a little of the excitement out of me.

"Don't take them off," I cried; "I will not stir."

In guarantee whereof, I attached myself to my seat by my hands.

"Mind you don't," said Bessie; and when she had ascertained that I was really subsiding, she loosened her hold of me; then she and Miss

Abbot stood with folded arms, looking darkly and doubtfully on my face, as incredulous of my sanity.

"She never did so before," at last said Bessie, turning to the Abigail.

"But it was always in her," was the reply. "I've told Missis often my opinion about the child, and Missis agreed with me. She's an underhand little thing: I never saw a girl of her age with so much cover."

Bessie answered not; but ere long, addressing me, she said—"You ought to be aware, Miss, that you are under obligations to Mrs. Reed: she keeps you: if she were to turn you off, you would have to go to the poorhouse."

I had nothing to say to these words: they were not new to me: my very first recollections of existence included hints of the same kind. This reproach of my dependence had become a vague sing-song in my ear: very painful and crushing, but only half intelligible. Miss Abbot joined in—

"And you ought not to think yourself on an equality with the Misses Reed and Master Reed, because Missis kindly allows you to be brought up with them. They will have a great deal of money, and you will have none: it is your place to be humble, and to try to make yourself agreeable to them."

"What we tell you is for your good," added Bessie, in no harsh voice, "you should try to be useful and pleasant, then, perhaps, you would have a home here; but if you become passionate and rude, Missis will send you away, I am sure."

"Besides," said Miss Abbot, "God will punish her: He might strike her dead in the midst of her tantrums, and then where would she go? Come, Bessie, we will leave her: I wouldn't have her heart for anything. Say your prayers, Miss Eyre, when you are by yourself; for if you don't repent, something bad might be permitted to come down the chimney and fetch you away."

They went, shutting the door, and locking it behind them.

The red-room was a square chamber, very seldom slept in, I might say never, indeed, unless when a chance influx of visitors at Gateshead Hall rendered it necessary to turn to account all the accommodation it contained: yet it was one of the largest and stateliest chambers in the mansion. A bed supported on massive pillars of mahogany, hung with curtains of deep red damask, stood out like a tabernacle in the centre; the two large windows, with their blinds always drawn down, were half shrouded in festoons and falls of similar drapery; the carpet was red; the table at the foot of the bed was covered with a crimson cloth; the walls were a soft fawn colour with a blush of pink in it; the wardrobe, the toilet-table, the chairs were of darkly polished old mahogany. Out of these deep surrounding shades rose high, and glared white, the piled-up mattresses and pillows of the bed, spread with a snowy Marseilles counterpane. Scarcely less prominent was an ample cushioned easy-chair near the head of the bed, also white, with a footstool before it; and looking, as I thought, like a pale throne.

This room was chill, because it seldom had a fire; it was silent, because remote from the nursery and kitchen; solemn, because it was known to be so seldom entered. The house-maid alone came here on Saturdays, to wipe from the mirrors and the furniture a week's quiet dust: and Mrs. Reed herself, at far intervals, visited it to review the contents of a certain secret drawer in the wardrobe, where were stored divers parchments, her jewel-casket, and a miniature of her deceased husband; and in those last words lies the secret of the red-room—the spell which kept it so lonely in spite of its grandeur.

Mr. Reed had been dead nine years: it was in this chamber he breathed his last; here he lay in state; hence his coffin was borne by the undertaker's men; and, since that day, a sense of dreary consecration had guarded it from frequent intrusion.

My seat, to which Bessie and the bitter Miss Abbot had left me riveted, was a low ottoman near the marble chimney-piece; the bed rose before me; to my right hand there was the high, dark wardrobe, with subdued, broken reflections varying the gloss of its panels; to my left were the muffled windows; a great looking-glass between them repeated the vacant majesty of the bed and room. I was not quite sure whether they had locked the door; and when I dared move, I got up and went to see. Alas! yes: no jail was ever more secure. Returning, I had to cross before the looking-glass; my fascinated glance involuntarily explored the depth it revealed. All looked colder and darker in that visionary hollow than in reality: and the strange little figure there gazing at me, with a white face and arms specking the gloom, and glittering eyes of fear moving where all else was still, had the effect of a real spirit: I thought it like one of the tiny phantoms, half fairy, half imp, Bessie's evening stories represented as coming out of lone, ferny dells in moors, and appearing before the eyes of belated travellers. I returned to my stool.

Superstition was with me at that moment; but it was not yet her hour for complete victory: my blood was still warm; the mood of the revolted slave was still bracing me with its bitter vigour; I had to stem a rapid rush of retrospective thought before I quailed to the dismal present.

All John Reed's violent tyrannies, all his sisters' proud indifference, all his mother's aversion, all the servants' partiality, turned up in my disturbed mind like a dark deposit in a turbid well. Why was I always suffering, always browbeaten, always accused, for ever condemned? Why could I never please? Why was it useless to try to win any one's favour? Eliza, who was headstrong and selfish, was respected. Georgiana, who had a spoiled temper, a very acrid spite, a captious and insolent carriage, was universally indulged. Her beauty, her pink cheeks and golden curls, seemed to give delight to all who looked at her, and to purchase indemnity for every fault. John no one thwarted, much less punished; though he twisted the necks of the pigeons, killed the little pea-chicks, set the dogs at the sheep, stripped the hothouse vines of their fruit, and broke the buds off the choicest plants in the conservatory: he called his mother "old girl," too; sometimes reviled her for her dark skin, similar to his own; bluntly disregarded her wishes; not unfrequently tore and spoiled her silk attire; and he was still "her own darling." I dared commit no fault: I strove to fulfil every duty; and I was termed naughty and tiresome, sullen and sneaking, from morning to noon, and from noon to night.

My head still ached and bled with the blow and fall I had received: no one had reproved John for wantonly striking me; and because I had turned against him to avert farther irrational violence, I was loaded with general opprobrium.

"Unjust!—unjust!" said my reason, forced by the agonising stimulus into precocious though transitory power: and Resolve, equally wrought up, instigated some strange expedient to achieve escape from insupportable oppression—as running away, or, if that could not be effected, never eating or drinking more, and letting myself die.

What a consternation of soul was mine that dreary afternoon! How all my brain was in tumult, and all my heart in insurrection! Yet in what darkness, what dense ignorance, was the mental battle fought! I could not answer the ceaseless inward question—WHY I thus suffered; now, at the distance of—I will not say how many years, I see it clearly.

I was a discord in Gateshead Hall: I was like nobody there; I had nothing in harmony with Mrs. Reed or her children, or her chosen vassalage. If they did not love me, in fact, as little did I love them. They were not bound to regard with affection a thing that could not sympathise with one amongst them; a heterogeneous thing, opposed to them in temperament, in capacity, in propensities; a useless thing, incapable of serving their interest, or adding to their pleasure; a noxious thing, cherishing the germs of indignation at their treatment, of contempt of their judgment. I know that had I been a sanguine, brilliant, careless, exacting, handsome, romping child—though equally dependent and friendless—Mrs. Reed would have endured my presence more complacently; her children would have entertained for me more of the cordiality of fellow-feeling; the servants would have been less prone to make me the scapegoat of the nursery.

Daylight began to forsake the red-room; it was past four o'clock, and the beclouded afternoon was tending to drear twilight. I heard the rain still beating continuously on the staircase window, and the wind howling in the grove behind the hall; I grew by degrees cold as a stone, and then my courage sank. My habitual mood of humiliation, self-doubt, forlorn depression, fell damp on the embers of my decaying ire. All said I was wicked, and perhaps I might be so; what thought had I been but just conceiving of starving myself to death? That certainly was a crime: and was I fit to die? Or was the vault under the chancel of Gateshead Church an inviting bourne? In such vault I had been told did Mr. Reed lie buried; and led by this thought to recall his idea, I dwelt on it with gathering dread. I could not remember him; but I knew that he was my own uncle—my mother's brother—that he had taken me when a parentless infant to his house; and that in his last moments he had required a promise of Mrs. Reed that she would rear and maintain me as one of her own children. Mrs. Reed probably considered she had kept this promise; and so she had, I dare say, as well as her nature would permit her; but how could she really like an interloper not of her race, and unconnected with her, after her husband's death, by any tie? It must have been most irksome to find herself bound by a hard-wrung pledge to stand in the stead of a parent to a strange child she could not love, and to see an uncongenial alien permanently intruded on her own family group.

A singular notion dawned upon me. I doubted not—never doubted—that if Mr. Reed had been alive he would have treated me kindly; and now, as I sat looking at the white bed and overshadowed walls—occasionally also turning a fascinated eye towards the dimly gleaning mirror—I began to recall what I had heard of dead men, troubled in their graves by the violation of their last wishes, revisiting the earth to punish the perjured and avenge the oppressed; and I thought Mr. Reed's spirit, harassed by the wrongs of his sister's child, might quit its abode—whether in the church vault or in the unknown world of the departed—and rise before me in this chamber. I wiped my tears and hushed my sobs, fearful lest any sign of violent grief might waken a preternatural voice to comfort me, or elicit from the gloom some haloed face, bending over me with strange pity. This idea, consolatory in theory, I felt would be terrible if realised: with all my might I endeavoured to stifle it—I endeavoured to be firm. Shaking my hair from my eyes, I lifted my head and tried to look boldly round the dark room; at this moment a light gleamed on the wall. Was it, I asked myself, a ray from the moon penetrating some aperture in the blind? No; moonlight was still, and this stirred; while I gazed, it glided up to the ceiling and quivered over my head. I can now conjecture readily that this streak of light was, in all likelihood, a gleam from a lantern carried by some one across the lawn: but then, prepared as my mind was for horror, shaken as my nerves were by agitation, I thought the swift darting beam was a herald of some coming vision from another world. My heart beat thick, my head grew hot; a sound filled my ears, which I deemed the rushing of wings; something seemed near me; I was oppressed, suffocated: endurance broke down; I rushed to the door and shook the lock in desperate effort. Steps came running along the outer passage; the key turned, Bessie and Abbot entered.

"Miss Eyre, are you ill?" said Bessie.

"What a dreadful noise! it went quite through me!" exclaimed Abbot.

"Take me out! Let me go into the nursery!" was my cry.

"What for? Are you hurt? Have you seen something?" again demanded Bessie.

"Oh! I saw a light, and I thought a ghost would come." I had now got hold of Bessie's hand, and she did not snatch it from me.

"She has screamed out on purpose," declared Abbot, in some disgust. "And what a scream! If she had been in great pain one would have excused it, but she only wanted to bring us all here: I know her naughty tricks."

"What is all this?" demanded another voice peremptorily; and Mrs. Reed came along the corridor, her cap flying wide, her gown rustling stormily. "Abbot and Bessie, I believe I gave orders that Jane Eyre should be left in the red-room till I came to her myself."

"Miss Jane screamed so loud, ma'am," pleaded Bessie.

"Let her go," was the only answer. "Loose Bessie's hand, child: you cannot succeed in getting out by these means, be assured. I abhor artifice, particularly in children; it is my duty to show you that tricks will not answer: you will now stay here an hour longer, and it is only on condition of perfect submission and stillness that I shall liberate you then."

"O aunt! have pity! Forgive me! I cannot endure it—let me be punished some other way! I shall be killed if—"

"Silence! This violence is all most repulsive:" and so, no doubt, she felt it. I was a precocious actress in her eyes; she sincerely looked on me as a compound of virulent passions, mean spirit, and dangerous duplicity.

Bessie and Abbot having retreated, Mrs. Reed, impatient of my now frantic anguish and wild sobs, abruptly thrust me back and locked me in, without farther parley. I heard her sweeping away; and soon after she was gone, I suppose I had a species of fit: unconsciousness closed the scene.

Chapter III

The next thing I remember is, waking up with a feeling as if I had had a frightful nightmare, and seeing before me a terrible red glare, crossed with thick black bars. I heard voices, too, speaking with a hollow sound, and as if muffled by a rush of wind or water: agitation, uncertainty, and an all-predominating sense of terror confused my faculties. Ere long, I became aware that some one was handling me; lifting me up and supporting me in a sitting posture, and that more tenderly than I had ever been raised or upheld before. I rested my head against a pillow or an arm, and felt easy.

In five minutes more the cloud of bewilderment dissolved: I knew quite well that I was in my own bed, and that the red glare was the nursery fire. It was night: a candle burnt on the table; Bessie stood at the bed-foot with a basin in her hand, and a gentleman sat in a chair near my pillow, leaning over me.

I felt an inexpressible relief, a soothing conviction of protection and security, when I knew that there was a stranger in the room, an individual not belonging to Gateshead., and not related to Mrs. Reed. Turning from Bessie (though her presence was far less obnoxious to me than that of Abbot, for instance, would have been), I scrutinised the face of the gentleman: I knew him; it was Mr. Lloyd, an apothecary, sometimes called in by Mrs. Reed when the servants were ailing: for herself and the children she employed a physician.

"Well, who am I?" he asked.

I pronounced his name, offering him at the same time my hand: he took it, smiling and saying, "We shall do very well by-and-by." Then he laid me down, and addressing Bessie, charged her to be very careful that I was not disturbed during the night. Having given some further directions, and intimates that he should call again the next day, he departed; to my grief: I felt so sheltered and befriended while he sat in the chair near my pillow; and as he closed the door after him, all the room darkened and my heart again sank: inexpressible sadness weighed it down.

"Do you feel as if you should sleep, Miss?" asked Bessie, rather softly.

Scarcely dared I answer her; for I feared the next sentence might be rough. "I will try."

"Would you like to drink, or could you eat anything?"

"No, thank you, Bessie."

"Then I think I shall go to bed, for it is past twelve o'clock; but you may call me if you want anything in the night."

Wonderful civility this! It emboldened me to ask a question.

"Bessie, what is the matter with me? Am I ill?"

"You fell sick, I suppose, in the red-room with crying; you'll be better soon, no doubt."

Bessie went into the housemaid's apartment, which was near. I heard her say—

"Sarah, come and sleep with me in the nursery; I daren't for my life be alone with that poor child to-night: she might die; it's such a strange thing she should have that fit: I wonder if she saw anything. Missis was rather too hard."

Sarah came back with her; they both went to bed; they were whispering together for half-an-hour before they fell asleep. I caught scraps of their conversation, from which I was able only too distinctly to infer the main subject discussed.

"Something passed her, all dressed in white, and vanished"—"A great black dog behind him"—"Three loud raps on the chamber door"—"A light in the churchyard just over his grave," &c. &c.

At last both slept: the fire and the candle went out. For me, the watches of that long night passed in ghastly wakefulness; strained by dread: such dread as children only can feel.

No severe or prolonged bodily illness followed this incident of the red-room; it only gave my nerves a shock of which I feel the reverberation to this day. Yes, Mrs. Reed, to you I owe some fearful pangs of mental suffering, but I ought to forgive you, for you knew not what you did: while rending my heart-strings, you thought you were only uprooting my bad propensities.

Next day, by noon, I was up and dressed, and sat wrapped in a shawl by the nursery hearth. I felt physically weak and broken down: but my worse ailment was an unutterable wretchedness of mind: a wretchedness which kept drawing from me silent tears; no sooner had I wiped one salt drop from my cheek than another followed. Yet, I thought, I ought to have been happy, for none of the Reeds were there, they were all gone out in the carriage with their mama. Abbot, too, was sewing in another room, and Bessie, as she moved hither and thither, putting away toys and arranging drawers, addressed to me every now and then a word of unwonted kindness. This state of things should have been to me a paradise of peace, accustomed as I was to a life of ceaseless reprimand and thankless fagging; but, in fact, my racked nerves were now in such a state that no calm could soothe, and no pleasure excite them agreeably.

Bessie had been down into the kitchen, and she brought up with her a tart on a certain brightly painted china plate, whose bird of paradise, nestling in a wreath of convolvuli and rosebuds, had been wont to stir in me a most enthusiastic sense of admiration; and which plate I had often petitioned to be allowed to take in my hand in order to examine it more closely, but had always hitherto been deemed unworthy of such a privilege. This precious vessel was now placed on my knee, and I was cordially invited to eat the circlet of delicate pastry upon it. Vain favour! coming, like most other favours long deferred and often wished for, too late! I could not eat the tart; and the plumage of the bird, the tints of the flowers, seemed strangely faded: I put both plate and tart away. Bessie asked if I would have a book: the word BOOK acted as a transient stimulus, and I begged her to fetch Gulliver's Travels from the library. This book I had again and again perused with delight. I considered it a narrative of facts, and discovered in it a vein of interest deeper than what I found in fairy tales: for as to the elves, having sought them in vain among foxglove leaves and bells, under mushrooms and beneath the ground-ivy mantling old wall-nooks, I had at length made up my mind to the sad truth, that they were all gone out of England to some savage country where the woods were wilder and thicker, and the population more scant; whereas, Lilliput and Brobdignag being, in my creed, solid parts of the earth's surface, I doubted not that I might one day, by taking a long voyage, see with my own eyes the little fields, houses, and trees, the diminutive people, the tiny cows, sheep, and birds of the one realm; and the corn-fields forest-high, the mighty mastiffs, the monster cats, the tower-like men and women, of the other. Yet, when this cherished volume was now placed in my hand—when I turned over its leaves, and sought in its marvellous pictures the charm I had, till now, never failed to find—all was eerie and dreary; the giants were gaunt goblins, the pigmies malevolent and fearful imps, Gulliver a most desolate wanderer in most dread and dangerous regions. I closed the book, which I dared no longer peruse, and put it on the table, beside the untasted tart.

Bessie had now finished dusting and tidying the room, and having washed her hands, she opened a certain little drawer, full of splendid shreds of silk and satin, and began making a new bonnet for Georgiana's doll. Meantime she sang: her song was—

> "In the days when we went gipsying,
> A long time ago."

I had often heard the song before, and always with lively delight; for Bessie had a sweet voice,—at least, I thought so. But now, though her voice was still sweet, I found in its melody an indescribable sadness. Sometimes, preoccupied with her work, she sang the refrain very low, very lingeringly; "A long time ago" came out like the saddest cadence of a funeral hymn. She passed into another ballad, this time a really doleful one.

"My feet they are sore, and my limbs they are weary;
Long is the way, and the mountains are wild;
Soon will the twilight close moonless and dreary
Over the path of the poor orphan child.

Why did they send me so far and so lonely,
Up where the moors spread and grey rocks are piled?
Men are hard-hearted, and kind angels only
Watch o'er the steps of a poor orphan child.

Yet distant and soft the night breeze is blowing,
Clouds there are none, and clear stars beam mild,
God, in His mercy, protection is showing,
Comfort and hope to the poor orphan child.

Ev'n should I fall o'er the broken bridge passing,
Or stray in the marshes, by false lights beguiled,
Still will my Father, with promise and blessing,
Take to His bosom the poor orphan child.

There is a thought that for strength should avail me,
Though both of shelter and kindred despoiled;
Heaven is a home, and a rest will not fail me;
God is a friend to the poor orphan child."

"Come, Miss Jane, don't cry," said Bessie as she finished. She might as well have said to the fire, "don't burn!" but how could she divine the morbid suffering to which I was a prey? In the course of the morning Mr. Lloyd came again.

"What, already up!" said he, as he entered the nursery. "Well, nurse, how is she?"

Bessie answered that I was doing very well.

"Then she ought to look more cheerful. Come here, Miss Jane: your name is Jane, is it not?"

"Yes, sir, Jane Eyre."

"Well, you have been crying, Miss Jane Eyre; can you tell me what about? Have you any pain?"

"No, sir."

"Oh! I daresay she is crying because she could not go out with Missis in the carriage," interposed Bessie.

"Surely not! why, she is too old for such pettishness."

I thought so too; and my self-esteem being wounded by the false charge, I answered promptly, "I never cried for such a thing in my life: I hate going out in the carriage. I cry because I am miserable."

"Oh fie, Miss!" said Bessie.

The good apothecary appeared a little puzzled. I was standing before him; he fixed his eyes on me very steadily: his eyes were small and grey; not very bright, but I dare say I should think them shrewd now: he had a hard-featured yet good-natured looking face. Having considered me at leisure, he said—

"What made you ill yesterday?"

"She had a fall," said Bessie, again putting in her word.

"Fall! why, that is like a baby again! Can't she manage to walk at her age? She must be eight or nine years old."

"I was knocked down," was the blunt explanation, jerked out of me by another pang of mortified pride; "but that did not make me ill," I added; while Mr. Lloyd helped himself to a pinch of snuff.

As he was returning the box to his waistcoat pocket, a loud bell rang for the servants' dinner; he knew what it was. "That's for you, nurse," said he; "you can go down; I'll give Miss Jane a lecture till you come back."

Bessie would rather have stayed, but she was obliged to go, because punctuality at meals was rigidly enforced at Gateshead Hall.

"The fall did not make you ill; what did, then?" pursued Mr. Lloyd when Bessie was gone.

"I was shut up in a room where there is a ghost till after dark."

I saw Mr. Lloyd smile and frown at the same time.

"Ghost! What, you are a baby after all! You are afraid of ghosts?"

"Of Mr. Reed's ghost I am: he died in that room, and was laid out there. Neither Bessie nor any one else will go into it at night, if they can help it; and it was cruel to shut me up alone without a candle,—so cruel that I think I shall never forget it."

"Nonsense! And is it that makes you so miserable? Are you afraid now in daylight?"

"No: but night will come again before long: and besides,—I am unhappy,—very unhappy, for other things."

"What other things? Can you tell me some of them?"

How much I wished to reply fully to this question! How difficult it was to frame any answer! Children can feel, but they cannot analyse their feelings; and if the analysis is partially effected in thought, they know not how to express the result of the process in words. Fearful, however, of losing this first and only opportunity of relieving my grief by imparting it, I, after a disturbed pause, contrived to frame a meagre, though, as far as it went, true response.

"For one thing, I have no father or mother, brothers or sisters."

"You have a kind aunt and cousins."

Again I paused; then bunglingly enounced—

"But John Reed knocked me down, and my aunt shut me up in the red-room."

Mr. Lloyd a second time produced his snuff-box.

"Don't you think Gateshead Hall a very beautiful house?" asked he. "Are you not very thankful to have such a fine place to live at?"

"It is not my house, sir; and Abbot says I have less right to be here than a servant."

"Pooh! you can't be silly enough to wish to leave such a splendid place?"

"If I had anywhere else to go, I should be glad to leave it; but I can never get away from Gateshead till I am a woman."

"Perhaps you may—who knows? Have you any relations besides Mrs. Reed?"

"I think not, sir."

"None belonging to your father?"

"I don't know. I asked Aunt Reed once, and she said possibly I might have some poor, low relations called Eyre, but she knew nothing about them."

"If you had such, would you like to go to them?"

I reflected. Poverty looks grim to grown people; still more so to children: they have not much idea of industrious, working, respectable poverty; they think of the word only as connected with ragged clothes, scanty food, fireless grates, rude manners, and debasing vices: poverty for me was synonymous with degradation.

"No; I should not like to belong to poor people," was my reply.

"Not even if they were kind to you?"

I shook my head: I could not see how poor people had the means of being kind; and then to learn to speak like them, to adopt their manners, to be uneducated, to grow up like one of the poor women I saw sometimes nursing their children or washing their clothes at the cottage doors of the village of Gateshead: no, I was not heroic enough to purchase liberty at the price of caste.

"But are your relatives so very poor? Are they working people?"

"I cannot tell; Aunt. Reed says if I have any, they must be a beggarly set: I should not like to go a begging."

"Would you like to go to school?"

Again I reflected: I scarcely knew what school was: Bessie sometimes spoke of it as a place where young ladies sat in the stocks, wore backboards, and were expected to be exceedingly genteel and precise: John Reed hated his school, and abused his master; but John Reed's tastes were no rule for mine, and if Bessie's accounts of school-discipline (gathered from the young ladies of a family where she had lived before coming to Gateshead) were somewhat appalling, her details of certain accomplishments attained by these same young ladies were, I thought, equally attractive. She boasted of beautiful paintings of landscapes and flowers by them executed; of songs they could sing and pieces they could play, of purses they could net, of French books they could translate; till my spirit was moved to emulation as I listened. Besides, school would be a complete change: it implied a long journey, an entire separation from Gateshead, an entrance into a new life.

"I should indeed like to go to school," was the audible conclusion of my musings.

"Well, well! who knows what may happen?" said Mr. Lloyd, as he got up. "The child ought to have change of air and scene," he added, speaking to himself; "nerves not in a good state."

Bessie now returned; at the same moment the carriage was heard rolling up the gravel-walk.

"Is that your mistress, nurse?" asked Mr. Lloyd. "I should like to speak to her before I go."

Bessie invited him to walk into the breakfast-room, and led the way out. In the interview which followed between him and Mrs. Reed, I presume, from after-occurrences, that the apothecary ventured to recommend my being sent to school; and the recommendation was no doubt readily enough adopted; for as Abbot said, in discussing the subject with Bessie when both sat sewing in the nursery one night, after I was in bed, and, as they thought, asleep, "Missis was, she dared say, glad enough to get rid of such a tiresome, ill-conditioned child, who always looked as if she were watching everybody, and scheming plots underhand." Abbot, I think, gave me credit for being a sort of infantine Guy Fawkes.

On that same occasion I learned, for the first time, from Miss Abbot's communications to Bessie, that my father had been a poor clergyman; that my mother had married him against the wishes of her friends, who considered the match beneath her; that my grandfather Reed was so irritated at her disobedience, he cut her off without a shilling; that after my mother and father had been married a year, the latter caught the typhus fever while visiting among the poor of a large manufacturing town where his curacy was situated, and where that disease was then prevalent: that my mother took the infection from him, and both died within a month of each other.

Bessie, when she heard this narrative, sighed and said, "Poor Miss Jane is to be pitied, too, Abbot."

"Yes," responded Abbot; "if she were a nice, pretty child, one might compassionate her forlornness; but one really cannot care for such a little toad as that."

"Not a great deal, to be sure," agreed Bessie: "at any rate, a beauty like Miss Georgiana would be more moving in the same condition."

"Yes, I doat on Miss Georgiana!" cried the fervent Abbot. "Little darling!—with her long curls and her blue eyes, and such a sweet colour as she has; just as if she were painted!—Bessie, I could fancy a Welsh rabbit for supper."

"So could I—with a roast onion. Come, we'll go down." They went.

Chapter IV

From my discourse with Mr. Lloyd, and from the above reported conference between Bessie and Abbot, I gathered enough of hope to suffice as a motive for wishing to get well: a change seemed near,—I desired and waited it in silence. It tarried, however: days and weeks passed: I had regained my normal state of health, but no new allusion was made to the subject over which I brooded. Mrs. Reed surveyed me at times with a severe eye, but seldom addressed me: since my illness, she had drawn a more marked line of separation than ever between me and her own children; appointing me a small closet to sleep in by myself, condemning me to take my meals alone, and pass all my time in the nursery, while my cousins were constantly in the drawing-room. Not a hint, however, did she drop about sending me to school: still I felt an instinctive certainty that she would not long endure me under the same roof with her; for her glance, now more than ever, when turned on me, expressed an insuperable and rooted aversion.

Eliza and Georgiana, evidently acting according to orders, spoke to me as little as possible: John thrust his tongue in his cheek whenever he saw me, and once attempted chastisement; but as I instantly turned against him, roused by the same sentiment of deep ire and desperate revolt which had stirred my corruption before, he thought it better to desist, and ran from me tittering execrations, and vowing I had burst his nose. I had indeed levelled at that prominent feature as hard a blow as my knuckles could inflict; and when I saw that either that or my look daunted him, I had the greatest inclination to follow up my advantage to purpose; but he was already with his mama. I heard him in a blubbering tone commence the tale of how "that nasty Jane Eyre" had flown at him like a mad cat: he was stopped rather harshly—

"Don't talk to me about her, John: I told you not to go near her; she is not worthy of notice; I do not choose that either you or your sisters should associate with her."

Here, leaning over the banister, I cried out suddenly, and without at all deliberating on my words—

"They are not fit to associate with me."

Mrs. Reed was rather a stout woman; but, on hearing this strange and audacious declaration, she ran nimbly up the stair, swept me like a whirlwind into the nursery, and crushing me down on the edge of my crib, dared me in an emphatic voice to rise from that place, or utter one syllable during the remainder of the day.

"What would Uncle Reed say to you, if he were alive?" was my scarcely voluntary demand. I say scarcely voluntary, for it seemed as if my tongue pronounced words without my will consenting to their utterance: something spoke out of me over which I had no control.

"What?" said Mrs. Reed under her breath: her usually cold composed grey eye became troubled with a look like fear; she took her hand from my arm, and gazed at me as if she really did not know whether I were child or fiend. I was now in for it.

"My Uncle Reed is in heaven, and can see all you do and think; and so can papa and mama: they know how you shut me up all day long, and how you wish me dead."

Mrs. Reed soon rallied her spirits: she shook me most soundly, she boxed both my ears, and then left me without a word. Bessie supplied the hiatus by a homily of an hour's length, in which she proved beyond a doubt that I was the most wicked and abandoned child ever reared under a roof. I half believed her; for I felt indeed only bad feelings surging in my breast.

November, December, and half of January passed away. Christmas and the New Year had been celebrated at Gateshead with the usual festive cheer; presents had been interchanged, dinners and evening parties given. From every enjoyment I was, of course, excluded: my share of the gaiety consisted in witnessing the daily apparelling of Eliza and Georgiana, and seeing them descend to the drawing-room, dressed out in thin muslin frocks and scarlet sashes, with hair elaborately ringletted; and afterwards, in listening to the sound of the piano or the harp played below, to the passing to and fro of the butler and footman, to the jingling of glass and china as refreshments were handed, to the broken hum of conversation as the drawing-room door opened and closed. When tired of this occupation, I would retire from the stairhead to the solitary and silent nursery: there, though somewhat sad, I was not miserable. To speak truth, I had not the least wish to go into company, for in company I was very rarely noticed; and if Bessie had but been kind and companionable, I should have deemed it a treat to spend the evenings quietly with her, instead of passing them under the formidable eye of Mrs. Reed, in a room full of ladies and gentlemen. But Bessie, as soon as she had dressed her young ladies, used to take herself off to the lively regions of the kitchen and housekeeper's room, generally bearing the candle along with her. I then sat with my doll on my knee till the fire got low, glancing round occasionally to make sure that nothing worse than myself haunted the shadowy room; and when the embers sank to a dull red, I undressed hastily, tugging at knots and strings as I best might, and sought shelter from cold and darkness in my crib. To this crib I always took my doll; human beings must love something, and, in the dearth of worthier objects of affection, I contrived to find a pleasure in loving and cherishing a faded graven image, shabby as a miniature scarecrow. It puzzles me now to remember with what absurd sincerity I doated on this little toy, half fancying it alive and capable of sensation. I could not sleep unless it was folded in my night-gown; and when it lay there safe and warm, I was comparatively happy, believing it to be happy likewise.

Long did the hours seem while I waited the departure of the company, and listened for the sound of Bessie's step on the stairs: sometimes she would come up in the interval to seek her thimble or her scissors, or perhaps to bring me something by way of supper—a bun or a cheese-cake—then she would sit on the bed while I ate it, and when I had finished, she would tuck the clothes round me, and twice she kissed me, and said, "Good night, Miss Jane." When thus gentle, Bessie seemed to me the best, prettiest, kindest being in the world; and I wished most intensely that she would always be so pleasant and amiable, and never push me about, or scold, or task me unreasonably, as she was too often wont to do. Bessie Lee must, I think, have been a girl of good natural capacity, for she was smart in all she did, and had a remarkable knack of narrative; so, at least, I judge from the impression made on me by her nursery tales. She was pretty too, if my recollections of her face and person are correct. I remember her as a slim young woman, with black hair, dark eyes, very nice features, and good, clear complexion; but she had a capricious and hasty temper, and indifferent ideas of principle or justice: still, such as she was, I preferred her to any one else at Gateshead Hall.

It was the fifteenth of January, about nine o'clock in the morning: Bessie was gone down to breakfast; my cousins had not yet been summoned to their mama; Eliza was putting on her bonnet and warm garden-coat to go and feed her poultry, an occupation of which she was fond: and not less so of selling the eggs to the housekeeper and hoarding up the money she thus obtained. She had a turn for traffic, and a marked propensity for saving; shown not only in the vending of eggs and chickens, but also in driving hard bargains with the gardener about flower-roots, seeds, and slips of plants; that functionary having orders from Mrs. Reed to buy of his young lady all the products of her parterre she wished to sell: and Eliza would have sold the hair off her head if she could have made a handsome profit thereby. As to her money, she first secreted it in odd corners, wrapped in a rag or an old curl-paper; but some of these hoards having been discovered by the housemaid, Eliza, fearful of one day losing her valued treasure, consented to intrust it to her mother, at a usurious rate of interest—fifty or sixty per cent.; which interest she exacted every quarter, keeping her accounts in a little book with anxious accuracy.

Georgiana sat on a high stool, dressing her hair at the glass, and interweaving her curls with artificial flowers and faded feathers, of which she had found a store in a drawer in the attic. I was making my bed, having received strict orders from Bessie to get it arranged before she returned (for Bessie now frequently employed me as a sort of under-nurserymaid, to tidy the room, dust the chairs, &c.). Having spread the quilt and folded my night-dress, I went to the window-seat to put in order some picture-books and doll's house furniture scattered there; an abrupt command from Georgiana to let her playthings alone (for the tiny chairs and mirrors, the fairy plates and cups, were her property) stopped my proceedings; and then, for lack of other occupation, I fell to breathing on the frost-flowers with which the window was fretted, and thus clearing a space in the glass through which I might look out on the grounds, where all was still and petrified under the influence of a hard frost.

From this window were visible the porter's lodge and the carriage-road, and just as I had dissolved so much of the silver-white foliage veiling the panes as left room to look out, I saw the gates thrown open and a carriage roll through. I watched it ascending the drive with indifference; carriages often came to Gateshead, but none ever brought visitors in whom I was interested; it stopped in front of the house, the door-bell rang loudly, the new-comer was admitted. All this being nothing to me, my vacant attention soon found livelier attraction in the spectacle of a little hungry robin, which came and chirruped on the twigs of the leafless cherry-tree nailed against the wall near the casement. The remains of my breakfast of bread and milk stood on the table, and having crumbled a morsel of roll, I was tugging at the sash to put out the crumbs on the window-sill, when Bessie came running upstairs into the nursery.

"Miss Jane, take off your pinafore; what are you doing there? Have you washed your hands and face this morning?" I gave another tug before I answered, for I wanted the bird to be secure of its bread: the sash yielded; I scattered the crumbs, some on the stone sill, some on the cherry-tree bough, then, closing the window, I replied—

"No, Bessie; I have only just finished dusting."

"Troublesome, careless child! and what are you doing now? You look quite red, as if you had been about some mischief: what were you opening the window for?"

I was spared the trouble of answering, for Bessie seemed in too great a hurry to listen to explanations; she hauled me to the wash-stand, inflicted a merciless, but happily brief scrub on my face and hands with soap, water, and a coarse towel; disciplined my head with a bristly brush, denuded me of my pinafore, and then hurrying me to the top of the stairs, bid me go down directly, as I was wanted in the breakfast-room.

I would have asked who wanted me: I would have demanded if Mrs. Reed was there; but Bessie was already gone, and had closed the nursery-door upon me. I slowly descended. For nearly three months, I had never been called to Mrs. Reed's presence; restricted so long to the nursery, the breakfast, dining, and drawing-rooms were become for me awful regions, on which it dismayed me to intrude.

I now stood in the empty hall; before me was the breakfast-room door, and I stopped, intimidated and trembling. What a miserable little poltroon had fear, engendered of unjust punishment, made of me in those days! I feared to return to the nursery, and feared to go forward to the parlour; ten minutes I stood in agitated hesitation; the vehement ringing of the breakfast-room bell decided me; I MUST enter.

"Who could want me?" I asked inwardly, as with both hands I turned the stiff door-handle, which, for a second or two, resisted my efforts. "What should I see besides Aunt Reed in the apartment?—a man or a woman?" The handle turned, the door unclosed, and passing through and curtseying low, I looked up at—a black pillar!—such, at least, appeared to me, at first sight, the straight, narrow, sable-clad shape standing erect on the rug: the grim face at the top was like a carved mask, placed above the shaft by way of capital.

Mrs. Reed occupied her usual seat by the fireside; she made a signal to me to approach; I did so, and she introduced me to the stony stranger with the words: "This is the little girl respecting whom I applied to you."

HE, for it was a man, turned his head slowly towards where I stood, and having examined me with the two inquisitive-looking grey eyes which twinkled under a pair of bushy brows, said solemnly, and in a bass voice, "Her size is small: what is her age?"

"Ten years."

"So much?" was the doubtful answer; and he prolonged his scrutiny for some minutes. Presently he addressed me—"Your name, little girl?"

"Jane Eyre, sir."

In uttering these words I looked up: he seemed to me a tall gentleman; but then I was very little; his features were large, and they and all the lines of his frame were equally harsh and prim.

"Well, Jane Eyre, and are you a good child?"

Impossible to reply to this in the affirmative: my little world held a contrary opinion: I was silent. Mrs. Reed answered for me by an expressive shake of the head, adding soon, "Perhaps the less said on that subject the better, Mr. Brocklehurst."

"Sorry indeed to hear it! she and I must have some talk;" and bending from the perpendicular, he installed his person in the armchair opposite Mrs. Reed's. "Come here," he said.

I stepped across the rug; he placed me square and straight before him. What a face he had, now that it was almost on a level with mine! what a great nose! and what a mouth! and what large prominent teeth!

"No sight so sad as that of a naughty child," he began, "especially a naughty little girl. Do you know where the wicked go after death?"

"They go to hell," was my ready and orthodox answer.

"And what is hell? Can you tell me that?"

"A pit full of fire."

"And should you like to fall into that pit, and to be burning there for ever?"

"No, sir."

"What must you do to avoid it?"

I deliberated a moment; my answer, when it did come, was objectionable: "I must keep in good health, and not die."

"How can you keep in good health? Children younger than you die daily. I buried a little child of five years old only a day or two since,—a good little child, whose soul is now in heaven. It is to be feared the same could not be said of you were you to be called hence."

Not being in a condition to remove his doubt, I only cast my eyes down on the two large feet planted on the rug, and sighed, wishing myself far enough away.

"I hope that sigh is from the heart, and that you repent of ever having been the occasion of discomfort to your excellent benefactress."

"Benefactress! benefactress!" said I inwardly: "they all call Mrs. Reed my benefactress; if so, a benefactress is a disagreeable thing."

"Do you say your prayers night and morning?" continued my interrogator.

"Yes, sir."

"Do you read your Bible?"

"Sometimes."

"With pleasure? Are you fond of it?"

"I like Revelations, and the book of Daniel, and Genesis and Samuel, and a little bit of Exodus, and some parts of Kings and Chronicles, and Job and Jonah."

"And the Psalms? I hope you like them?"

"No, sir."

"No? oh, shocking! I have a little boy, younger than you, who knows six Psalms by heart: and when you ask him which he would rather have, a gingerbread-nut to eat or a verse of a Psalm to learn, he says: 'Oh! the verse of a Psalm! angels sing Psalms;' says he, 'I wish to be a little angel here below;' he then gets two nuts in recompense for his infant piety."

"Psalms are not interesting," I remarked.

"That proves you have a wicked heart; and you must pray to God to change it: to give you a new and clean one: to take away your heart of stone and give you a heart of flesh."

I was about to propound a question, touching the manner in which that operation of changing my heart was to be performed, when Mrs. Reed interposed, telling me to sit down; she then proceeded to carry on the conversation herself.

"Mr. Brocklehurst, I believe I intimated in the letter which I wrote to you three weeks ago, that this little girl has not quite the character and disposition I could wish: should you admit her into Lowood school, I should be glad if the superintendent and teachers were requested to keep a strict eye on her, and, above all, to guard against her worst fault, a tendency to deceit. I mention this in your hearing, Jane, that you may not attempt to impose on Mr. Brocklehurst."

Well might I dread, well might I dislike Mrs. Reed; for it was her nature to wound me cruelly; never was I happy in her presence; however carefully I obeyed, however strenuously I strove to please her, my efforts were still repulsed and repaid by such sentences as the above. Now, uttered before a stranger, the accusation cut me to the heart; I dimly perceived that she was already obliterating hope from the new phase of existence which she destined me to enter; I felt, though I could not have expressed the feeling, that she was sowing aversion and unkindness along my future path; I saw myself transformed under Mr. Brocklehurst's eye into an artful, noxious child, and what could I do to remedy the injury?

"Nothing, indeed," thought I, as I struggled to repress a sob, and hastily wiped away some tears, the impotent evidences of my anguish.

"Deceit is, indeed, a sad fault in a child," said Mr. Brocklehurst; "it is akin to falsehood, and all liars will have their portion in the lake burning with fire and brimstone; she shall, however, be watched, Mrs. Reed. I will speak to Miss Temple and the teachers."

"I should wish her to be brought up in a manner suiting her prospects," continued my benefactress; "to be made useful, to be kept humble: as for the vacations, she will, with your permission, spend them always at Lowood."

"Your decisions are perfectly judicious, madam," returned Mr. Brocklehurst. "Humility is a Christian grace, and one peculiarly appropriate to the pupils of Lowood; I, therefore, direct that especial care shall be bestowed on its cultivation amongst them. I have studied how best to mortify in them the worldly sentiment of pride; and, only the other day, I had a pleasing proof of my success. My second daughter, Augusta, went with her mama to visit the school, and on her return she exclaimed: 'Oh, dear papa, how quiet and plain all the girls at Lowood look, with their hair combed behind their ears, and their long pinafores, and those little holland pockets outside their frocks—they are almost like poor people's children! and,' said she, 'they looked at my dress and mama's, as if they had never seen a silk gown before.'"

"This is the state of things I quite approve," returned Mrs. Reed; "had I sought all England over, I could scarcely have found a system more exactly fitting a child like Jane Eyre. Consistency, my dear Mr. Brocklehurst; I advocate consistency in all things."

"Consistency, madam, is the first of Christian duties; and it has been observed in every arrangement connected with the establishment of Lowood: plain fare, simple attire, unsophisticated accommodations, hardy and active habits; such is the order of the day in the house and its inhabitants."

"Quite right, sir. I may then depend upon this child being received as a pupil at Lowood, and there being trained in conformity to her position and prospects?"

"Madam, you may: she shall be placed in that nursery of chosen plants, and I trust she will show herself grateful for the inestimable privilege of her election."

"I will send her, then, as soon as possible, Mr. Brocklehurst; for, I assure you, I feel anxious to be relieved of a responsibility that was becoming too irksome."

"No doubt, no doubt, madam; and now I wish you good morning. I shall return to Brocklehurst Hall in the course of a week or two: my good friend, the Archdeacon, will not permit me to leave him sooner. I shall send Miss Temple notice that she is to expect a new girl, so that there will he no difficulty about receiving her. Good-bye."

"Good-bye, Mr. Brocklehurst; remember me to Mrs. and Miss Brocklehurst, and to Augusta and Theodore, and Master Broughton Brocklehurst."

"I will, madam. Little girl, here is a book entitled the 'Child's Guide,' read it with prayer, especially that part containing 'An account of the awfully sudden death of Martha G-, a naughty child addicted to falsehood and deceit.'"

With these words Mr. Brocklehurst put into my hand a thin pamphlet sewn in a cover, and having rung for his carriage, he departed.

Mrs. Reed and I were left alone: some minutes passed in silence; she was sewing, I was watching her. Mrs. Reed might be at that time some six or seven and thirty; she was a woman of robust frame, square-shouldered and strong-limbed, not tall, and, though stout, not obese: she had a somewhat large face, the under jaw being much developed and very solid; her brow was low, her chin large and prominent, mouth and nose sufficiently regular; under her light eyebrows glimmered an eye devoid of ruth; her skin was dark and opaque, her hair nearly flaxen; her constitution was sound as a bell—illness never came near her; she was an exact, clever manager; her household and tenantry were thoroughly under her control; her children only at times defied her authority and laughed it to scorn; she dressed well, and had a presence and port calculated to set off handsome attire.

Sitting on a low stool, a few yards from her arm-chair, I examined her figure; I perused her features. In my hand I held the tract containing the sudden death of the Liar, to which narrative my attention had been pointed as to an appropriate warning. What had just passed; what Mrs. Reed had said concerning me to Mr. Brocklehurst; the whole tenor of their conversation, was recent, raw, and stinging in my mind; I had felt every word as acutely as I had heard it plainly, and a passion of resentment fomented now within me.

Mrs. Reed looked up from her work; her eye settled on mine, her fingers at the same time suspended their nimble movements.

"Go out of the room; return to the nursery," was her mandate. My look or something else must have struck her as offensive, for she spoke with extreme though suppressed irritation. I got up, I went to the door; I came back again; I walked to the window, across the room, then close up to her.

SPEAK I must: I had been trodden on severely, and MUST turn: but how? What strength had I to dart retaliation at my antagonist? I gathered my energies and launched them in this blunt sentence—

"I am not deceitful: if I were, I should say I loved you; but I declare I do not love you: I dislike you the worst of anybody in the world except John Reed; and this book about the liar, you may give to your girl, Georgiana, for it is she who tells lies, and not I."

Mrs. Reed's hands still lay on her work inactive: her eye of ice continued to dwell freezingly on mine.

"What more have you to say?" she asked, rather in the tone in which a person might address an opponent of adult age than such as is ordinarily used to a child.

That eye of hers, that voice stirred every antipathy I had. Shaking from head to foot, thrilled with ungovernable excitement, I continued—

"I am glad you are no relation of mine: I will never call you aunt again as long as I live. I will never come to see you when I am grown up; and if any one asks me how I liked you, and how you treated me, I will say the very thought of you makes me sick, and that you treated me with miserable cruelty."

"How dare you affirm that, Jane Eyre?"

"How dare I, Mrs. Reed? How dare I? Because it is the TRUTH. You think I have no feelings, and that I can do without one bit of love or kindness; but I cannot live so: and you have no pity. I shall remember how you thrust me back—roughly and violently thrust me back—into the red-room, and locked me up there, to my dying day; though I was in agony; though I cried out, while suffocating with distress, 'Have mercy! Have mercy, Aunt Reed!' And that punishment you made me suffer because your wicked boy struck me—knocked me down for nothing. I will tell anybody who asks me questions, this exact tale. People think you a good woman, but you are bad, hard-hearted. YOU are deceitful!"

Ere I had finished this reply, my soul began to expand, to exult, with the strangest sense of freedom, of triumph, I ever felt. It seemed as if an invisible bond had burst, and that I had struggled out into unhoped-for liberty. Not without cause was this sentiment: Mrs. Reed looked frightened; her work had slipped from her knee; she was lifting up her hands, rocking herself to and fro, and even twisting her face as if she would cry.

"Jane, you are under a mistake: what is the matter with you? Why do you tremble so violently? Would you like to drink some water?"

"No, Mrs. Reed."

"Is there anything else you wish for, Jane? I assure you, I desire to be your friend."

"Not you. You told Mr. Brocklehurst I had a bad character, a deceitful disposition; and I'll let everybody at Lowood know what you are, and what you have done."

"Jane, you don't understand these things: children must be corrected for their faults."

"Deceit is not my fault!" I cried out in a savage, high voice.

"But you are passionate, Jane, that you must allow: and now return to the nursery—there's a dear—and lie down a little."

"I am not your dear; I cannot lie down: send me to school soon, Mrs. Reed, for I hate to live here."

"I will indeed send her to school soon," murmured Mrs. Reed sotto voce; and gathering up her work, she abruptly quitted the apartment.

I was left there alone—winner of the field. It was the hardest battle I had fought, and the first victory I had gained: I stood awhile on the rug, where Mr. Brocklehurst had stood, and I enjoyed my conqueror's solitude. First, I smiled to myself and felt elate; but this fierce pleasure subsided in me as fast as did the accelerated throb of my pulses. A child cannot quarrel with its elders, as I had done; cannot give its furious feelings uncontrolled play, as I had given mine, without experiencing afterwards the pang of remorse and the chill of reaction. A ridge of lighted heath, alive, glancing, devouring, would have been a meet emblem of my mind when I accused and menaced Mrs. Reed: the same ridge, black and blasted after the flames are dead, would have represented as meetly my subsequent condition, when half-an-hour's silence and reflection had shown me the madness of my conduct, and the dreariness of my hated and hating position.

Something of vengeance I had tasted for the first time; as aromatic wine it seemed, on swallowing, warm and racy: its after-flavour, metallic and corroding, gave me a sensation as if I had been poisoned. Willingly would I now have gone and asked Mrs. Reed's pardon; but I knew, partly from experience and partly from instinct, that was the way to make her repulse me with double scorn, thereby re-exciting every turbulent impulse of my nature.

I would fain exercise some better faculty than that of fierce speaking; fain find nourishment for some less fiendish feeling than that of sombre indignation. I took a book—some Arabian tales; I sat down and endeavoured to read. I could make no sense of the subject; my own thoughts swam always between me and the page I had usually found fascinating. I opened the glass-door in the breakfast-room: the shrubbery was quite still: the black frost reigned, unbroken by sun or breeze, through the grounds. I covered my head and arms with the skirt of my frock, and went out to walk in a part of the plantation which was quite sequestrated; but I found no pleasure in the silent trees, the falling fir-cones, the congealed relics of autumn, russet leaves, swept by past winds in heaps, and now stiffened together. I leaned against a gate, and looked into an empty field where no sheep were feeding, where the short grass was nipped and blanched. It was a very grey day; a most opaque sky, "onding on snaw," canopied all; thence flakes felt it intervals, which settled on the hard path and on the hoary lea without melting. I stood, a wretched child enough, whispering to myself over and over again, "What shall I do?—what shall I do?"

All at once I heard a clear voice call, "Miss Jane! where are you? Come to lunch!"

It was Bessie, I knew well enough; but I did not stir; her light step came tripping down the path.

"You naughty little thing!" she said. "Why don't you come when you are called?"

Bessie's presence, compared with the thoughts over which I had been brooding, seemed cheerful; even though, as usual, she was somewhat cross. The fact is, after my conflict with and victory over Mrs. Reed, I was not disposed to care much for the nursemaid's transitory anger; and I WAS disposed to bask in her youthful lightness of heart. I just put my two arms round her and said, "Come, Bessie! don't scold."

The action was more frank and fearless than any I was habituated to indulge in: somehow it pleased her.

"You are a strange child, Miss Jane," she said, as she looked down at me; "a little roving, solitary thing: and you are going to school, I suppose?"

I nodded.

"And won't you be sorry to leave poor Bessie?"

"What does Bessie care for me? She is always scolding me."

"Because you're such a queer, frightened, shy little thing. You should be bolder."

"What! to get more knocks?"

"Nonsense! But you are rather put upon, that's certain. My mother said, when she came to see me last week, that she would not like a little one of her own to be in your place.—Now, come in, and I've some good news for you."

"I don't think you have, Bessie."

"Child! what do you mean? What sorrowful eyes you fix on me! Well, but Missis and the young ladies and Master John are going out to tea this afternoon, and you shall have tea with me. I'll ask cook to bake you a little cake, and then you shall help me to look over your drawers; for I am soon to pack your trunk. Missis intends you to leave Gateshead in a day or two, and you shall choose what toys you like to take with you."

"Bessie, you must promise not to scold me any more till I go."

"Well, I will; but mind you are a very good girl, and don't be afraid of me. Don't start when I chance to speak rather sharply; it's so provoking."

"I don't think I shall ever be afraid of you again, Bessie, because I have got used to you, and I shall soon have another set of people to dread."

"If you dread them they'll dislike you."

"As you do, Bessie?"

"I don't dislike you, Miss; I believe I am fonder of you than of all the others."

"You don't show it."

"You little sharp thing! you've got quite a new way of talking. What makes you so venturesome and hardy?"

"Why, I shall soon be away from you, and besides"—I was going to say something about what had passed between me and Mrs. Reed, but on second thoughts I considered it better to remain silent on that head.

"And so you're glad to leave me?"

"Not at all, Bessie; indeed, just now I'm rather sorry."

"Just now! and rather! How coolly my little lady says it! I dare say now if I were to ask you for a kiss you wouldn't give it me: you'd say you'd RATHER not."

"I'll kiss you and welcome: bend your head down." Bessie stooped; we mutually embraced, and I followed her into the house quite comforted. That afternoon lapsed in peace and harmony; and in the evening Bessie told me some of her most enchaining stories, and sang me some of her sweetest songs. Even for me life had its gleams of sunshine.

Chapter V

Five o'clock had hardly struck on the morning of the 19th of January, when Bessie brought a candle into my closet and found me already up and nearly dressed. I had risen half-an-hour before her entrance, and had washed my face, and put on my clothes by the light of a half-moon just setting, whose rays streamed through the narrow window near my crib. I was to leave Gateshead that day by a coach which passed the lodge gates at six a.m. Bessie was the only person yet risen; she had lit a fire in the nursery, where she now proceeded to make my breakfast. Few children can eat when excited with the thoughts of a journey; nor could I. Bessie, having pressed me in vain to take a few spoonfuls of the boiled milk and bread she had prepared for me, wrapped up some biscuits in a paper and put them into my bag; then she helped me on with my pelisse and bonnet, and wrapping herself in a shawl, she and I left the nursery. As we passed Mrs. Reed's bedroom, she said, "Will you go in and bid Missis good-bye?"

"No, Bessie: she came to my crib last night when you were gone down to supper, and said I need not disturb her in the morning, or my cousins either; and she told me to remember that she had always been my best friend, and to speak of her and be grateful to her accordingly."

"What did you say, Miss?"

"Nothing: I covered my face with the bedclothes, and turned from her to the wall."

"That was wrong, Miss Jane."

"It was quite right, Bessie. Your Missis has not been my friend: she has been my foe."

"O Miss Jane! don't say so!"

"Good-bye to Gateshead!" cried I, as we passed through the hall and went out at the front door.

The moon was set, and it was very dark; Bessie carried a lantern, whose light glanced on wet steps and gravel road sodden by a recent thaw. Raw and chill was the winter morning: my teeth chattered as I hastened down the drive. There was a light in the porter's lodge: when we reached it, we found the porter's wife just kindling her fire: my trunk, which had been carried down the evening before, stood corded at the door. It wanted but a few minutes of six, and shortly after that hour had struck, the distant roll of wheels announced the coming coach; I went to the door and watched its lamps approach rapidly through the gloom.

"Is she going by herself?" asked the porter's wife.

"Yes."

"And how far is it?"

"Fifty miles."

"What a long way! I wonder Mrs. Reed is not afraid to trust her so far alone."

The coach drew up; there it was at the gates with its four horses and its top laden with passengers: the guard and coachman loudly urged haste; my trunk was hoisted up; I was taken from Bessie's neck, to which I clung with kisses.

"Be sure and take good care of her," cried she to the guard, as he lifted me into the inside.

"Ay, ay!" was the answer: the door was slapped to, a voice exclaimed "All right," and on we drove. Thus was I severed from Bessie and Gateshead; thus whirled away to unknown, and, as I then deemed, remote and mysterious regions.

I remember but little of the journey; I only know that the day seemed to me of a preternatural length, and that we appeared to travel over hundreds of miles of road. We passed through several towns, and in one, a very large one, the coach stopped; the horses were taken out, and the passengers alighted to dine. I was carried into an inn, where the guard wanted me to have some dinner; but, as I had no appetite, he left me in an immense room with a fireplace at each end, a chandelier pendent from the ceiling, and a little red gallery high up against the wall filled with musical instruments. Here I walked about for a long time, feeling very strange, and mortally apprehensive of some one coming in and kidnapping me; for I believed in kidnappers, their exploits having frequently figured in Bessie's fireside chronicles. At last the guard returned; once more I was stowed away in the coach, my protector mounted his own seat, sounded his hollow horn, and away we rattled over the "stony street" of L——.

The afternoon came on wet and somewhat misty: as it waned into dusk, I began to feel that we were getting very far indeed from Gateshead: we ceased to pass through towns; the country changed; great grey hills heaved up round the horizon: as twilight deepened, we descended a valley, dark with wood, and long after night had over-clouded the prospect, I heard a wild wind rushing amongst trees.

Lulled by the sound, I at last dropped asleep; I had not long slumbered when the sudden cessation of motion awoke me; the coach-door was open, and a person like a servant was standing at it: I saw her face and dress by the light of the lamps.

"Is there a little girl called Jane Eyre here?" she asked. I answered "Yes," and was then lifted out; my trunk was handed down, and the coach instantly drove away.

I was stiff with long sitting, and bewildered with the noise and motion of the coach: Gathering my faculties, I looked about me. Rain, wind, and darkness filled the air; nevertheless, I dimly discerned a wall before me and a door open in it; through this door I passed with my new guide: she shut and locked it behind her. There was now visible a house or houses—for the building spread far—with many windows, and lights burning in some; we went up a broad pebbly path, splashing wet, and were admitted at a door; then the servant led me through a passage into a room with a fire, where she left me alone.

I stood and warmed my numbed fingers over the blaze, then I looked round; there was no candle, but the uncertain light from the hearth showed, by intervals, papered walls, carpet, curtains, shining mahogany furniture: it was a parlour, not so spacious or splendid as the drawing-room at Gateshead, but comfortable enough. I was puzzling to make out the subject of a picture on the wall, when the door opened, and an individual carrying a light entered; another followed close behind.

The first was a tall lady with dark hair, dark eyes, and a pale and large forehead; her figure was partly enveloped in a shawl, her countenance was grave, her bearing erect.

"The child is very young to be sent alone," said she, putting her candle down on the table. She considered me attentively for a minute or two, then further added—

"She had better be put to bed soon; she looks tired: are you tired?" she asked, placing her hand on my shoulder.

"A little, ma'am."

"And hungry too, no doubt: let her have some supper before she goes to bed, Miss Miller. Is this the first time you have left your parents to come to school, my little girl?"

I explained to her that I had no parents. She inquired how long they had been dead: then how old I was, what was my name, whether I could read, write, and sew a little: then she touched my cheek gently with her forefinger, and saying, "She hoped I should be a good child," dismissed me along with Miss Miller.

The lady I had left might be about twenty-nine; the one who went with me appeared some years younger: the first impressed me by her voice, look, and air. Miss Miller was more ordinary; ruddy in complexion, though of a careworn countenance; hurried in gait and action, like one who had always a multiplicity of tasks on hand: she looked, indeed, what I afterwards found she really was, an under-teacher. Led by her, I passed from compartment to compartment, from passage to passage, of a large and irregular building; till, emerging from the total and somewhat dreary silence pervading that portion of the house we had traversed, we came upon the hum of many voices, and presently entered a wide, long room, with great deal tables, two at each end, on each of which burnt a pair of candles, and seated all round on benches, a congregation of girls of every age, from nine or ten to twenty. Seen by the dim light of the dips, their number to me appeared countless, though not in reality exceeding eighty; they were uniformly dressed in brown stuff frocks of quaint fashion, and long holland pinafores. It was the hour of study; they were engaged in conning over their to-morrow's task, and the hum I had heard was the combined result of their whispered repetitions.

Miss Miller signed to me to sit on a bench near the door, then walking up to the top of the long room she cried out—

"Monitors, collect the lesson-books and put them away! Four tall girls arose from different tables, and going round, gathered the books and removed them. Miss Miller again gave the word of command—

"Monitors, fetch the supper-trays!"

The tall girls went out and returned presently, each bearing a tray, with portions of something, I knew not what, arranged thereon, and a pitcher of water and mug in the middle of each tray. The portions were handed round; those who liked took a draught of the water, the mug being common to all. When it came to my turn, I drank, for I was thirsty, but did not touch the food, excitement and fatigue rendering me incapable of eating: I now saw, however, that it was a thin oaten cake shared into fragments.

The meal over, prayers were read by Miss Miller, and the classes filed off, two and two, upstairs. Overpowered by this time with weariness, I scarcely noticed what sort of a place the bedroom was, except that, like the schoolroom, I saw it was very long. To-night I was to be Miss Miller's bed-fellow; she helped me to undress: when laid down I glanced at the long rows of beds, each of which was quickly filled with two occupants; in ten minutes the single light was extinguished, and amidst silence and complete darkness I fell asleep.

The night passed rapidly. I was too tired even to dream; I only once awoke to hear the wind rave in furious gusts, and the rain fall in torrents, and to be sensible that Miss Miller had taken her place by my side. When I again unclosed my eyes, a loud bell was ringing; the girls were up and dressing; day had not yet begun to dawn, and a rushlight or two burned in the room. I too rose reluctantly; it was bitter cold, and I dressed as well as I could for shivering, and washed when there was a basin at liberty, which did not occur soon, as there was but one basin to six girls, on the stands down the middle of the room. Again the bell rang: all formed in file, two and two, and in that order descended the stairs and entered the cold and dimly lit schoolroom: here prayers were read by Miss Miller; afterwards she called out—

"Form classes!"

A great tumult succeeded for some minutes, during which Miss Miller repeatedly exclaimed, "Silence!" and "Order!" When it subsided, I saw them all drawn up in four semicircles, before four chairs, placed at the four tables; all held books in their hands, and a great book, like a Bible, lay on each table, before the vacant seat. A pause of some seconds succeeded, filled up by the low, vague hum of numbers; Miss Miller walked from class to class, hushing this indefinite sound.

A distant bell tinkled: immediately three ladies entered the room, each walked to a table and took her seat. Miss Miller assumed the fourth vacant chair, which was that nearest the door, and around which the smallest of the children were assembled: to this inferior class I was called, and placed at the bottom of it.

Business now began, the day's Collect was repeated, then certain texts of Scripture were said, and to these succeeded a protracted reading of chapters in the Bible, which lasted an hour. By the time that exercise was terminated, day had fully dawned. The indefatigable bell now sounded for the fourth time: the classes were marshalled and marched into another room to breakfast: how glad I was to behold a prospect of getting something to eat! I was now nearly sick from inanition, having taken so little the day before.

The refectory was a great, low-ceiled, gloomy room; on two long tables smoked basins of something hot, which, however, to my dismay, sent forth an odour far from inviting. I saw a universal manifestation of discontent when the fumes of the repast met the nostrils of those destined to swallow it; from the van of the procession, the tall girls of the first class, rose the whispered words—

"Disgusting! The porridge is burnt again!"

"Silence!" ejaculated a voice; not that of Miss Miller, but one of the upper teachers, a little and dark personage, smartly dressed, but of somewhat morose aspect, who installed herself at the top of one table, while a more buxom lady presided at the other. I looked in vain for her I had first seen the night before; she was not visible: Miss Miller occupied the foot of the table where I sat, and a strange, foreign-looking, elderly lady, the French teacher, as I afterwards found, took the corresponding seat at the other board. A long grace was said and a hymn sung; then a servant brought in some tea for the teachers, and the meal began.

Ravenous, and now very faint, I devoured a spoonful or two of my portion without thinking of its taste; but the first edge of hunger blunted, I perceived I had got in hand a nauseous mess; burnt porridge is almost as bad as rotten potatoes; famine itself soon sickens over it. The spoons were moved slowly: I saw each girl taste her food and try to swallow it; but in most cases the effort was soon relinquished. Breakfast was over, and none had breakfasted. Thanks being returned for what we had not got, and a second hymn chanted, the refectory was evacuated for the schoolroom. I was one of the last to go out, and in passing the tables, I saw one teacher take a basin of the porridge and taste it; she looked at the others; all their countenances expressed displeasure, and one of them, the stout one, whispered—

"Abominable stuff! How shameful!"

A quarter of an hour passed before lessons again began, during which the schoolroom was in a glorious tumult; for that space of time it seemed to be permitted to talk loud and more freely, and they used their privilege. The whole conversation ran on the breakfast, which one and all abused roundly. Poor things! it was the sole consolation they had. Miss Miller was now the only teacher in the room: a group of great girls standing about her spoke with serious and sullen gestures. I heard the name of Mr. Brocklehurst pronounced by some lips; at which Miss Miller shook her head disapprovingly; but she made no great effort to cheek the general wrath; doubtless she shared in it.

A clock in the schoolroom struck nine; Miss Miller left her circle, and standing in the middle of the room, cried—

"Silence! To your seats!"

Discipline prevailed: in five minutes the confused throng was resolved into order, and comparative silence quelled the Babel clamour of tongues. The upper teachers now punctually resumed their posts: but still, all seemed to wait. Ranged on benches down the sides of the room, the eighty girls sat motionless and erect; a quaint assemblage they appeared, all with plain locks combed from their faces, not a curl visible; in brown dresses, made high and surrounded by a narrow tucker about the throat, with little pockets of holland (shaped something like a Highlander's purse) tied in front of their frocks, and destined to serve the purpose of a work-bag: all, too, wearing woollen stockings and country-made shoes, fastened with brass buckles. Above twenty of those clad in this costume were full-grown girls, or rather young women; it suited them ill, and gave an air of oddity even to the prettiest.

I was still looking at them, and also at intervals examining the teachers—none of whom precisely pleased me; for the stout one was a little coarse, the dark one not a little fierce, the foreigner harsh and grotesque, and Miss Miller, poor thing! looked purple, weather-beaten, and over-worked—when, as my eye wandered from face to face, the whole school rose simultaneously, as if moved by a common spring.

What was the matter? I had heard no order given: I was puzzled. Ere I had gathered my wits, the classes were again seated: but as all eyes were now turned to one point, mine followed the general direction, and encountered the personage who had received me last night. She stood at the bottom of the long room, on the hearth; for there was a fire at each end; she surveyed the two rows of girls silently and gravely. Miss Miller approaching, seemed to ask her a question, and having received her answer, went back to her place, and said aloud—

"Monitor of the first class, fetch the globes!"

While the direction was being executed, the lady consulted moved slowly up the room. I suppose I have a considerable organ of veneration, for I retain yet the sense of admiring awe with which my eyes traced her steps. Seen now, in broad daylight, she looked tall, fair, and shapely; brown eyes with a benignant light in their irids, and a fine pencilling of long lashes round, relieved the whiteness of her large front; on each of her temples her hair, of a very dark brown, was clustered in round curls, according to the fashion of those times, when neither smooth bands nor long ringlets were in vogue; her dress, also in the mode of the day, was of purple cloth, relieved by a sort of Spanish trimming of black velvet; a gold watch (watches were not so common then as now) shone at her girdle. Let the reader add, to complete the picture, refined features; a complexion, if pale, clear; and a stately air and carriage, and he will have, at least, as clearly as words can give it, a correct idea of the exterior of Miss Temple—Maria Temple, as I afterwards saw the name written in a prayer-book intrusted to me to carry to church.

The superintendent of Lowood (for such was this lady) having taken her seat before a pair of globes placed on one of the tables, summoned the first class round her, and commenced giving a lesson on geography; the lower classes were called by the teachers: repetitions in history, grammar, &c., went on for an hour; writing and arithmetic succeeded, and music lessons were given by Miss Temple to some of the elder girls. The duration of each lesson was measured by the clock, which at last struck twelve. The superintendent rose—

"I have a word to address to the pupils," said she.

The tumult of cessation from lessons was already breaking forth, but it sank at her voice. She went on—

"You had this morning a breakfast which you could not eat; you must be hungry:—I have ordered that a lunch of bread and cheese shall be served to all."

The teachers looked at her with a sort of surprise.

"It is to be done on my responsibility," she added, in an explanatory tone to them, and immediately afterwards left the room.

The bread and cheese was presently brought in and distributed, to the high delight and refreshment of the whole school. The order was now given "To the garden!" Each put on a coarse straw bonnet, with strings of coloured calico, and a cloak of grey frieze. I was similarly equipped, and, following the stream, I made my way into the open air.

The garden was a wide inclosure, surrounded with walls so high as to exclude every glimpse of prospect; a covered verandah ran down one side, and broad walks bordered a middle space divided into scores of little beds: these beds were assigned as gardens for the pupils to cultivate, and each bed had an owner. When full of flowers they would doubtless look pretty; but now, at the latter end of January, all was wintry blight and brown decay. I shuddered as I stood and looked round me: it was an inclement day for outdoor exercise; not positively rainy, but darkened by a drizzling yellow fog; all under foot was still soaking wet with the floods of yesterday. The stronger among the girls ran about and engaged in active games, but sundry pale and thin ones herded together for shelter and warmth in the verandah; and amongst these, as the dense mist penetrated to their shivering frames, I heard frequently the sound of a hollow cough.

As yet I had spoken to no one, nor did anybody seem to take notice of me; I stood lonely enough: but to that feeling of isolation I was accustomed; it did not oppress me much. I leant against a pillar of the verandah, drew my grey mantle close about me, and, trying to forget the cold which nipped me without, and the unsatisfied hunger which gnawed me within, delivered myself up to the employment of watching and thinking. My reflections were too undefined and fragmentary to merit record: I hardly yet knew where I was; Gateshead and my past life seemed floated away to an immeasurable distance; the present was vague and strange, and of the future I could form no conjecture. I looked round the convent-like garden, and then up at the house—a large building, half of which seemed grey and old, the other half quite new. The new part, containing the schoolroom and dormitory, was lit by mullioned and latticed windows, which gave it a church-like aspect; a stone tablet over the door bore this inscription:-

"Lowood Institution.—This portion was rebuilt A.D.—, by
Naomi Brocklehurst, of Brocklehurst Hall, in this county."
"Let your light so shine before men, that they may see your
good works, and glorify your Father which is in heaven."
—St. Matt. v. 16.

I read these words over and over again: I felt that an explanation belonged to them, and was unable fully to penetrate their import. I was still pondering the signification of "Institution," and endeavouring to make out a connection between the first words and the verse of Scripture, when the sound of a cough close behind me made me turn my head. I saw a girl sitting on a stone bench near; she was bent over a book, on the perusal of which she seemed intent: from where I stood I could see the title—it was "Rasselas;" a name that struck me as strange, and consequently attractive. In turning a leaf she happened to look up, and I said to her directly—

"Is your book interesting?" I had already formed the intention of asking her to lend it to me some day.

"I like it," she answered, after a pause of a second or two, during which she examined me.

"What is it about?" I continued. I hardly know where I found the hardihood thus to open a conversation with a stranger; the step was contrary to my nature and habits: but I think her occupation touched a chord of sympathy somewhere; for I too liked reading, though of a frivolous and childish kind; I could not digest or comprehend the serious or substantial.

"You may look at it," replied the girl, offering me the book.

I did so; a brief examination convinced me that the contents were less taking than the title: "Rasselas" looked dull to my trifling taste; I saw nothing about fairies, nothing about genii; no bright variety seemed spread over the closely-printed pages. I returned it to her; she received it quietly, and without saying anything she was about to relapse into her former studious mood: again I ventured to disturb her—

"Can you tell me what the writing on that stone over the door means? What is Lowood Institution?"

"This house where you are come to live."

"And why do they call it Institution? Is it in any way different from other schools?"

"It is partly a charity-school: you and I, and all the rest of us, are charity-children. I suppose you are an orphan: are not either your father or your mother dead?"

"Both died before I can remember."

"Well, all the girls here have lost either one or both parents, and this is called an institution for educating orphans."

"Do we pay no money? Do they keep us for nothing?"

"We pay, or our friends pay, fifteen pounds a year for each."

"Then why do they call us charity-children?"

"Because fifteen pounds is not enough for board and teaching, and the deficiency is supplied by subscription."

"Who subscribes?"

"Different benevolent-minded ladies and gentlemen in this neighbourhood and in London."

"Who was Naomi Brocklehurst?"

"The lady who built the new part of this house as that tablet records, and whose son overlooks and directs everything here."

"Why?"

"Because he is treasurer and manager of the establishment."

"Then this house does not belong to that tall lady who wears a watch, and who said we were to have some bread and cheese?"

"To Miss Temple? Oh, no! I wish it did: she has to answer to Mr. Brocklehurst for all she does. Mr. Brocklehurst buys all our food and all our clothes."

"Does he live here?"

"No—two miles off, at a large hall."

"Is he a good man?"

"He is a clergyman, and is said to do a great deal of good."

"Did you say that tall lady was called Miss Temple?"

"Yes."

"And what are the other teachers called?"

"The one with red cheeks is called Miss Smith; she attends to the work, and cuts out—for we make our own clothes, our frocks, and pelisses, and everything; the little one with black hair is Miss Scatcherd; she teaches history and grammar, and hears the second class repetitions; and the one who wears a shawl, and has a pocket-handkerchief tied to her side with a yellow ribband, is Madame Pierrot: she comes from Lisle, in France, and teaches French."

"Do you like the teachers?"

"Well enough."

"Do you like the little black one, and the Madame-?—I cannot pronounce her name as you do."

"Miss Scatcherd is hasty—you must take care not to offend her; Madame Pierrot is not a bad sort of person."

"But Miss Temple is the best—isn't she?"

"Miss Temple is very good and very clever; she is above the rest, because she knows far more than they do."

"Have you been long here?"

"Two years."

"Are you an orphan?"

"My mother is dead."

"Are you happy here?"

"You ask rather too many questions. I have given you answers enough for the present: now I want to read."

But at that moment the summons sounded for dinner; all re-entered the house. The odour which now filled the refectory was scarcely more appetising than that which had regaled our nostrils at breakfast: the dinner was served in two huge tin-plated vessels, whence rose a strong steam redolent of rancid fat. I found the mess to consist of indifferent potatoes and strange shreds of rusty meat, mixed and cooked together. Of this preparation a tolerably abundant plateful was apportioned to each pupil. I ate what I could, and wondered within myself whether every day's fare would be like this.

After dinner, we immediately adjourned to the schoolroom: lessons recommenced, and were continued till five o'clock.

The only marked event of the afternoon was, that I saw the girl with whom I had conversed in the verandah dismissed in disgrace by Miss Scatcherd from a history class, and sent to stand in the middle of the large schoolroom. The punishment seemed to me in a high degree ignominious, especially for so great a girl—she looked thirteen or upwards. I expected she would show signs of great distress and shame; but to my surprise she neither wept nor blushed: composed, though grave, she stood, the central mark of all eyes. "How can she bear it so quietly—so firmly?" I asked of myself. "Were I in her place, it seems to me I should wish the earth to open and swallow me up. She looks as if she were thinking of something beyond her punishment—beyond her situation: of something not round her nor before her. I have heard of day-dreams—is she in a day-dream now? Her eyes are fixed on the floor, but I am sure they do not see it—her sight seems turned in, gone down into her heart: she is looking at what she can remember, I believe; not at what is really present. I wonder what sort of a girl she is—whether good or naughty."

Soon after five p.m. we had another meal, consisting of a small mug of coffee, and half-a-slice of brown bread. I devoured my bread and drank my coffee with relish; but I should have been glad of as much more—I was still hungry. Half-an-hour's recreation succeeded, then study; then the glass of water and the piece of oat-cake, prayers, and bed. Such was my first day at Lowood.

Chapter VI

The next day commenced as before, getting up and dressing by rush-light; but this morning we were obliged to dispense with the ceremony of washing; the water in the pitchers was frozen. A change had taken place in the weather the preceding evening, and a keen north-east wind, whistling through the crevices of our bedroom windows all night long, had made us shiver in our beds, and turned the contents of the ewers to ice.

Before the long hour and a half of prayers and Bible-reading was over, I felt ready to perish with cold. Breakfast-time came at last, and this morning the porridge was not burnt; the quality was eatable, the quantity small. How small my portion seemed! I wished it had been doubled.

In the course of the day I was enrolled a member of the fourth class, and regular tasks and occupations were assigned me: hitherto, I had only been a spectator of the proceedings at Lowood; I was now to become an actor therein. At first, being little accustomed to learn by heart, the lessons appeared to me both long and difficult; the frequent change from task to task, too, bewildered me; and I was glad when, about three o'clock in the afternoon, Miss Smith put into my hands a border of muslin two yards long, together with needle, thimble, &c., and sent me to sit in a quiet corner of the schoolroom, with directions to hem the same. At that hour most of the others were sewing likewise; but one class still stood round Miss Scatcherd's chair reading, and as all was quiet, the subject of their lessons could be heard, together with the manner in which each girl acquitted herself, and the animadversions or commendations of Miss Scatcherd on the performance. It was English history: among the readers I observed my acquaintance of the verandah: at the commencement of the lesson, her place had been at the top of the class, but for some error of pronunciation, or some inattention to stops, she was suddenly sent to the very bottom. Even in that obscure position, Miss Scatcherd continued to make her an object of constant notice: she was continually addressing to her such phrases as the following:—

"Burns" (such it seems was her name: the girls here were all called by their surnames, as boys are elsewhere), "Burns, you are standing on the side of your shoe; turn your toes out immediately." "Burns, you poke your chin most unpleasantly; draw it in." "Burns, I insist on your holding your head up; I will not have you before me in that attitude," &c. &c.

A chapter having been read through twice, the books were closed and the girls examined. The lesson had comprised part of the reign of Charles I., and there were sundry questions about tonnage and poundage and ship-money, which most of them appeared unable to answer; still, every little difficulty was solved instantly when it reached Burns: her memory seemed to have retained the substance of the whole lesson, and she was ready with answers on every point. I kept expecting that Miss Scatcherd would praise her attention; but, instead of that, she suddenly cried out—

"You dirty, disagreeable girl! you have never cleaned your nails this morning!"

Burns made no answer: I wondered at her silence. "Why," thought I, "does she not explain that she could neither clean her nails nor wash her face, as the water was frozen?"

My attention was now called off by Miss Smith desiring me to hold a skein of thread: while she was winding it, she talked to me from time to time, asking whether I had ever been at school before, whether I could mark, stitch, knit, &c.; till she dismissed me, I could not pursue my observations on Miss Scatcherd's movements. When I returned to my seat, that lady was just delivering an order of which I did not catch the import; but Burns immediately left the class, and going into the small inner room where the books were kept, returned in half a minute, carrying in her hand a bundle of twigs tied together at one end. This ominous tool she presented to Miss Scatcherd with a respectful curtesy; then she quietly, and without being told, unloosed her pinafore, and the teacher instantly and sharply inflicted on her neck a dozen strokes with the bunch of twigs. Not a tear rose to Burns' eye; and, while I paused from my sewing, because my fingers quivered at this spectacle with a sentiment of unavailing and impotent anger, not a feature of her pensive face altered its ordinary expression.

"Hardened girl!" exclaimed Miss Scatcherd; "nothing can correct you of your slatternly habits: carry the rod away."

Burns obeyed: I looked at her narrowly as she emerged from the book-closet; she was just putting back her handkerchief into her pocket, and the trace of a tear glistened on her thin cheek.

The play-hour in the evening I thought the pleasantest fraction of the day at Lowood: the bit of bread, the draught of coffee swallowed at five o'clock had revived vitality, if it had not satisfied hunger: the long restraint of the day was slackened; the schoolroom felt warmer than in the morning—its fires being allowed to burn a little more brightly, to supply, in some measure, the place of candles, not yet introduced: the ruddy gloaming, the licensed uproar, the confusion of many voices gave one a welcome sense of liberty.

On the evening of the day on which I had seen Miss Scatcherd flog her pupil, Burns, I wandered as usual among the forms and tables and laughing groups without a companion, yet not feeling lonely: when I passed the windows, I now and then lifted a blind, and looked out; it snowed fast, a drift was already forming against the lower panes; putting my ear close to the window, I could distinguish from the gleeful tumult within, the disconsolate moan of the wind outside.

Probably, if I had lately left a good home and kind parents, this would have been the hour when I should most keenly have regretted the separation; that wind would then have saddened my heart; this obscure chaos would have disturbed my peace! as it was, I derived from both a strange excitement, and reckless and feverish, I wished the wind to howl more wildly, the gloom to deepen to darkness, and the confusion to rise to clamour.

Jumping over forms, and creeping under tables, I made my way to one of the fire-places; there, kneeling by the high wire fender, I found Burns, absorbed, silent, abstracted from all round her by the companionship of a book, which she read by the dim glare of the embers.

"Is it still 'Rasselas'?" I asked, coming behind her.

"Yes," she said, "and I have just finished it."

And in five minutes more she shut it up. I was glad of this. "Now," thought I, "I can perhaps get her to talk." I sat down by her on the floor.

"What is your name besides Burns?"

"Helen."

"Do you come a long way from here?"

"I come from a place farther north, quite on the borders of Scotland."

"Will you ever go back?"

"I hope so; but nobody can be sure of the future."

"You must wish to leave Lowood?"

"No! why should I? I was sent to Lowood to get an education; and it would be of no use going away until I have attained that object."

"But that teacher, Miss Scatcherd, is so cruel to you?"

"Cruel? Not at all! She is severe: she dislikes my faults."

"And if I were in your place I should dislike her; I should resist her. If she struck me with that rod, I should get it from her hand; I should break it under her nose."

"Probably you would do nothing of the sort: but if you did, Mr. Brocklehurst would expel you from the school; that would be a great grief to your relations. It is far better to endure patiently a smart which nobody feels but yourself, than to commit a hasty action whose evil consequences will extend to all connected with you; and besides, the Bible bids us return good for evil."

"But then it seems disgraceful to be flogged, and to be sent to stand in the middle of a room full of people; and you are such a great girl: I am far younger than you, and I could not bear it."

"Yet it would be your duty to bear it, if you could not avoid it: it is weak and silly to say you CANNOT BEAR what it is your fate to be required to bear."

I heard her with wonder: I could not comprehend this doctrine of endurance; and still less could I understand or sympathise with the forbearance she expressed for her chastiser. Still I felt that Helen Burns considered things by a light invisible to my eyes. I suspected she might be right and I wrong; but I would not ponder the matter deeply; like Felix, I put it off to a more convenient season.

"You say you have faults, Helen: what are they? To me you seem very good."

"Then learn from me, not to judge by appearances: I am, as Miss Scatcherd said, slatternly; I seldom put, and never keep, things, in order; I am careless; I forget rules; I read when I should learn my lessons; I have no method; and sometimes I say, like you, I cannot BEAR to be subjected to systematic arrangements. This is all very provoking to Miss Scatcherd, who is naturally neat, punctual, and particular."

"And cross and cruel," I added; but Helen Burns would not admit my addition: she kept silence.

"Is Miss Temple as severe to you as Miss Scatcherd?"

At the utterance of Miss Temple's name, a soft smile flitted over her grave face.

"Miss Temple is full of goodness; it pains her to be severe to any one, even the worst in the school: she sees my errors, and tells me of them gently; and, if I do anything worthy of praise, she gives me my meed liberally. One strong proof of my wretchedly defective nature is, that even her expostulations, so mild, so rational, have not influence to cure me of my faults; and even her praise, though I value it most highly, cannot stimulate me to continued care and foresight."

"That is curious," said I, "it is so easy to be careful."

"For YOU I have no doubt it is. I observed you in your class this morning, and saw you were closely attentive: your thoughts never seemed to wander while Miss Miller explained the lesson and questioned you. Now, mine continually rove away; when I should be listening to Miss Scatcherd, and collecting all she says with assiduity, often I lose the very sound of her voice; I fall into a sort of dream. Sometimes I think I am in Northumberland, and that the noises I hear round me are the bubbling of a little brook which runs through Deepden, near our house;—then, when it comes to my turn to reply, I have to be awakened; and having heard nothing of what was read for listening to the visionary brook, I have no answer ready."

"Yet how well you replied this afternoon."

"It was mere chance; the subject on which we had been reading had interested me. This afternoon, instead of dreaming of Deepden, I was wondering how a man who wished to do right could act so unjustly and unwisely as Charles the First sometimes did; and I thought what a pity it was that, with his integrity and conscientiousness, he could see no farther than the prerogatives of the crown. If he had but been able to look to a distance, and see how what they call the spirit of the age was tending! Still, I like Charles—I respect him—I pity him, poor murdered king! Yes, his enemies were the worst: they shed blood they had no right to shed. How dared they kill him!"

Helen was talking to herself now: she had forgotten I could not very well understand her—that I was ignorant, or nearly so, of the subject she discussed. I recalled her to my level.

"And when Miss Temple teaches you, do your thoughts wander then?"

"No, certainly, not often; because Miss Temple has generally something to say which is newer than my own reflections; her language is singularly agreeable to me, and the information she communicates is often just what I wished to gain."

"Well, then, with Miss Temple you are good?"

"Yes, in a passive way: I make no effort; I follow as inclination guides me. There is no merit in such goodness."

"A great deal: you are good to those who are good to you. It is all I ever desire to be. If people were always kind and obedient to those who are cruel and unjust, the wicked people would have it all their own way: they would never feel afraid, and so they would never alter, but would grow worse and worse. When we are struck at without a reason, we should strike back again very hard; I am sure we should—so hard as to teach the person who struck us never to do it again."

"You will change your mind, I hope, when you grow older: as yet you are but a little untaught girl."

"But I feel this, Helen; I must dislike those who, whatever I do to please them, persist in disliking me; I must resist those who punish me unjustly. It is as natural as that I should love those who show me affection, or submit to punishment when I feel it is deserved."

"Heathens and savage tribes hold that doctrine, but Christians and civilised nations disown it."

"How? I don't understand."

"It is not violence that best overcomes hate—nor vengeance that most certainly heals injury."

"What then?"

"Read the New Testament, and observe what Christ says, and how He acts; make His word your rule, and His conduct your example."

"What does He say?"

"Love your enemies; bless them that curse you; do good to them that hate you and despitefully use you."

"Then I should love Mrs. Reed, which I cannot do; I should bless her son John, which is impossible."

In her turn, Helen Burns asked me to explain, and I proceeded forthwith to pour out, in my own way, the tale of my sufferings and resentments. Bitter and truculent when excited, I spoke as I felt, without reserve or softening.

Helen heard me patiently to the end: I expected she would then make a remark, but she said nothing.

"Well," I asked impatiently, "is not Mrs. Reed a hard-hearted, bad woman?"

"She has been unkind to you, no doubt; because you see, she dislikes your cast of character, as Miss Scatcherd does mine; but how minutely you remember all she has done and said to you! What a singularly deep impression her injustice seems to have made on your heart! No ill-usage so brands its record on my feelings. Would you not be happier if you tried to forget her severity, together with the passionate emotions it excited? Life appears to me too short to be spent in nursing animosity or registering wrongs. We are, and must be, one and all, burdened with faults in this world: but the time will soon come when, I trust, we shall put them off in putting off our corruptible bodies; when debasement and sin will fall from us with this cumbrous frame of flesh, and only the spark of the spirit will remain,—the impalpable principle of light and thought, pure as when it left the Creator to inspire the creature: whence it came it will return; perhaps again to be communicated to some being higher than man—perhaps to pass through gradations of glory, from the pale human soul to brighten to the seraph! Surely it will never, on the contrary, be suffered to degenerate from man to fiend? No; I cannot believe that: I hold another creed: which no one ever taught me, and which I seldom mention; but in which I delight, and to which I cling: for it extends hope to all: it makes Eternity a rest—a mighty home, not a terror and an abyss. Besides, with this creed, I can so clearly distinguish between the criminal and his crime; I can so sincerely forgive the first while I abhor the last: with this creed revenge never worries my heart, degradation never too deeply disgusts me, injustice never crushes me too low: I live in calm, looking to the end."

Helen's head, always drooping, sank a little lower as she finished this sentence. I saw by her look she wished no longer to talk to me, but rather to converse with her own thoughts. She was not allowed much time for meditation: a monitor, a great rough girl, presently came up, exclaiming in a strong Cumberland accent—

"Helen Burns, if you don't go and put your drawer in order, and fold up your work this minute, I'll tell Miss Scatcherd to come and look at it!"

Helen sighed as her reverie fled, and getting up, obeyed the monitor without reply as without delay.

Chapter VII

My first quarter at Lowood seemed an age; and not the golden age either; it comprised an irksome struggle with difficulties in habituating myself to new rules and unwonted tasks. The fear of failure in these points harassed me worse than the physical hardships of my lot; though these were no trifles.

During January, February, and part of March, the deep snows, and, after their melting, the almost impassable roads, prevented our stirring beyond the garden walls, except to go to church; but within these limits we had to pass an hour every day in the open air. Our clothing was insufficient to protect us from the severe cold: we had no boots, the snow got into our shoes and melted there: our ungloved hands became numbed and covered with chilblains, as were our feet: I remember well the distracting irritation I endured from this cause every evening, when my feet inflamed; and the torture of thrusting the swelled, raw, and stiff toes into my shoes in the morning. Then the scanty supply of food was distressing: with the keen appetites of growing children, we had scarcely sufficient to keep alive a delicate invalid. From this deficiency of nourishment resulted an abuse, which pressed hardly on the younger pupils: whenever the famished great girls had an opportunity, they would coax or menace the little ones out of their portion. Many a time I have shared between two claimants the precious morsel of brown bread distributed at tea-time; and after relinquishing to a third half the contents of my mug of coffee, I have swallowed the remainder with an accompaniment of secret tears, forced from me by the exigency of hunger.

Sundays were dreary days in that wintry season. We had to walk two miles to Brocklebridge Church, where our patron officiated. We set out cold, we arrived at church colder: during the morning service we became almost paralysed. It was too far to return to dinner, and an allowance of cold meat and bread, in the same penurious proportion observed in our ordinary meals, was served round between the services.

At the close of the afternoon service we returned by an exposed and hilly road, where the bitter winter wind, blowing over a range of snowy summits to the north, almost flayed the skin from our faces.

I can remember Miss Temple walking lightly and rapidly along our drooping line, her plaid cloak, which the frosty wind fluttered, gathered close about her, and encouraging us, by precept and example, to keep up our spirits, and march forward, as she said, "like stalwart soldiers." The other teachers, poor things, were generally themselves too much dejected to attempt the task of cheering others.

How we longed for the light and heat of a blazing fire when we got back! But, to the little ones at least, this was denied: each hearth in the schoolroom was immediately surrounded by a double row of great girls, and behind them the younger children crouched in groups, wrapping their starved arms in their pinafores.

A little solace came at tea-time, in the shape of a double ration of bread—a whole, instead of a half, slice—with the delicious addition of a thin scrape of butter: it was the hebdomadal treat to which we all looked forward from Sabbath to Sabbath. I generally contrived to reserve a moiety of this bounteous repast for myself; but the remainder I was invariably obliged to part with.

The Sunday evening was spent in repeating, by heart, the Church Catechism, and the fifth, sixth, and seventh chapters of St. Matthew; and in listening to a long sermon, read by Miss Miller, whose irrepressible yawns attested her weariness. A frequent interlude of these performances was the enactment of the part of Eutychus by some half-dozen of little girls, who, overpowered with sleep, would fall down, if not out of the third loft, yet off the fourth form, and be taken up half dead. The remedy was, to thrust them forward into the centre of the schoolroom, and oblige them to stand there till the sermon was finished. Sometimes their feet failed them, and they sank together in a heap; they were then propped up with the monitors' high stools.

I have not yet alluded to the visits of Mr. Brocklehurst; and indeed that gentleman was from home during the greater part of the first month after my arrival; perhaps prolonging his stay with his friend the archdeacon: his absence was a relief to me. I need not say that I had my own reasons for dreading his coming: but come he did at last.

One afternoon (I had then been three weeks at Lowood), as I was sitting with a slate in my hand, puzzling over a sum in long division, my eyes, raised in abstraction to the window, caught sight of a figure just passing: I recognised almost instinctively that gaunt outline; and when, two minutes after, all the school, teachers included, rose en masse, it was not necessary for me to look up in order to ascertain whose entrance they thus greeted. A long stride measured the schoolroom, and presently beside Miss Temple, who herself had risen, stood the same black column which had frowned on me so ominously from the hearthrug of Gateshead. I now glanced sideways at this piece of architecture. Yes, I was right: it was Mr. Brocklehurst, buttoned up in a surtout, and looking longer, narrower, and more rigid than ever.

I had my own reasons for being dismayed at this apparition; too well I remembered the perfidious hints given by Mrs. Reed about my disposition, &c.; the promise pledged by Mr. Brocklehurst to apprise Miss Temple and the teachers of my vicious nature. All along I had been dreading the fulfilment of this promise,—I had been looking out daily for the "Coming Man," whose information respecting my past life and conversation was to brand me as a bad child for ever: now there he was.

He stood at Miss Temple's side; he was speaking low in her ear: I did not doubt he was making disclosures of my villainy; and I watched her eye with painful anxiety, expecting every moment to see its dark orb turn on me a glance of repugnance and contempt. I listened too; and as I happened to be seated quite at the top of the room, I caught most of what he said: its import relieved me from immediate apprehension.

"I suppose, Miss Temple, the thread I bought at Lowton will do; it struck me that it would be just of the quality for the calico chemises, and I sorted the needles to match. You may tell Miss Smith that I forgot to make a memorandum of the darning needles, but she shall have some papers sent in next week; and she is not, on any account, to give out more than one at a time to each pupil: if they have more, they are apt to be careless and lose them. And, O ma'am! I wish the woollen stockings were better looked to!—when I was here last, I went into the kitchen-garden and examined the clothes drying on the line; there was a quantity of black hose in a very bad state of repair: from the size of the holes in them I was sure they had not been well mended from time to time."

He paused.

"Your directions shall be attended to, sir," said Miss Temple.

"And, ma'am," he continued, "the laundress tells me some of the girls have two clean tuckers in the week: it is too much; the rules limit them to one."

"I think I can explain that circumstance, sir. Agnes and Catherine Johnstone were invited to take tea with some friends at Lowton last Thursday, and I gave them leave to put on clean tuckers for the occasion."

Mr. Brocklehurst nodded.

"Well, for once it may pass; but please not to let the circumstance occur too often. And there is another thing which surprised me; I find, in settling accounts with the housekeeper, that a lunch, consisting of bread and cheese, has twice been served out to the girls during the past fortnight. How is this? I looked over the regulations, and I find no such meal as lunch mentioned. Who introduced this innovation? and by what authority?"

"I must be responsible for the circumstance, sir," replied Miss Temple: "the breakfast was so ill prepared that the pupils could not possibly eat it; and I dared not allow them to remain fasting till dinner-time."

"Madam, allow me an instant. You are aware that my plan in bringing up these girls is, not to accustom them to habits of luxury and indulgence, but to render them hardy, patient, self-denying. Should any little accidental disappointment of the appetite occur, such as the spoiling of a meal, the under or the over dressing of a dish, the incident ought not to be neutralised by replacing with something more delicate the comfort lost, thus pampering the body and obviating the aim of this institution; it ought to be improved to the spiritual edification of the pupils, by encouraging them to evince fortitude under temporary privation. A brief address on those occasions would not be mistimed, wherein a judicious instructor would take the opportunity of referring to the sufferings of the primitive Christians; to the torments of martyrs; to the exhortations of our blessed Lord Himself, calling upon His disciples to take up their cross and follow Him; to His warnings that man shall not live by bread alone, but by every word that proceedeth out of the mouth of God; to His divine consolations, "If ye suffer hunger or thirst for My sake, happy are ye." Oh, madam, when you put bread and cheese, instead of burnt porridge, into these children's mouths, you may indeed feed their vile bodies, but you little think how you starve their immortal souls!"

Mr. Brocklehurst again paused—perhaps overcome by his feelings. Miss Temple had looked down when he first began to speak to her; but she now gazed straight before her, and her face, naturally pale as marble, appeared to be assuming also the coldness and fixity of that material; especially her mouth, closed as if it would have required a sculptor's chisel to open it, and her brow settled gradually into petrified severity.

Meantime, Mr. Brocklehurst, standing on the hearth with his hands behind his back, majestically surveyed the whole school. Suddenly his eye gave a blink, as if it had met something that either dazzled or shocked its pupil; turning, he said in more rapid accents than he had hitherto used—

"Miss Temple, Miss Temple, what—WHAT is that girl with curled hair? Red hair, ma'am, curled—curled all over?" And extending his cane he pointed to the awful object, his hand shaking as he did so.

"It is Julia Severn," replied Miss Temple, very quietly.

"Julia Severn, ma'am! And why has she, or any other, curled hair? Why, in defiance of every precept and principle of this house, does she conform to the world so openly—here in an evangelical, charitable establishment—as to wear her hair one mass of curls?"

"Julia's hair curls naturally," returned Miss Temple, still more quietly.

"Naturally! Yes, but we are not to conform to nature; I wish these girls to be the children of Grace: and why that abundance? I have again and again intimated that I desire the hair to be arranged closely, modestly, plainly. Miss Temple, that girl's hair must be cut off entirely; I will send a barber to-morrow: and I see others who have far too much of the excrescence—that tall girl, tell her to turn round. Tell all the first form to rise up and direct their faces to the wall."

Miss Temple passed her handkerchief over her lips, as if to smooth away the involuntary smile that curled them; she gave the order, however, and when the first class could take in what was required of them, they obeyed. Leaning a little back on my bench, I could see the looks and grimaces with which they commented on this manoeuvre: it was a pity Mr. Brocklehurst could not see them too; he would perhaps have felt that, whatever he might do with the outside of the cup and platter, the inside was further beyond his interference than he imagined.

He scrutinised the reverse of these living medals some five minutes, then pronounced sentence. These words fell like the knell of doom—

"All those top-knots must be cut off."

Miss Temple seemed to remonstrate.

"Madam," he pursued, "I have a Master to serve whose kingdom is not of this world: my mission is to mortify in these girls the lusts of the flesh; to teach them to clothe themselves with shame-facedness and sobriety, not with braided hair and costly apparel; and each of the young persons before us has a string of hair twisted in plaits which vanity itself might have woven; these, I repeat, must be cut off; think of the time wasted, of—"

Mr. Brocklehurst was here interrupted: three other visitors, ladies, now entered the room. They ought to have come a little sooner to have heard his lecture on dress, for they were splendidly attired in velvet, silk, and furs. The two younger of the trio (fine girls of sixteen and seventeen) had grey beaver hats, then in fashion, shaded with ostrich plumes, and from under the brim of this graceful head-dress fell a profusion of light tresses, elaborately curled; the elder lady was enveloped in a costly velvet shawl, trimmed with ermine, and she wore a false front of French curls.

These ladies were deferentially received by Miss Temple, as Mrs. and the Misses Brocklehurst, and conducted to seats of honour at the top of the room. It seems they had come in the carriage with their reverend relative, and had been conducting a rummaging scrutiny of the room upstairs, while he transacted business with the housekeeper, questioned the laundress, and lectured the superintendent. They now proceeded to address divers remarks and reproofs to Miss Smith, who was charged with the care of the linen and the inspection of the dormitories: but I had no time to listen to what they said; other matters called off and enchanted my attention.

Hitherto, while gathering up the discourse of Mr. Brocklehurst and Miss Temple, I had not, at the same time, neglected precautions to secure my personal safety; which I thought would be effected, if I could only elude observation. To this end, I had sat well back on the form, and while seeming to be busy with my sum, had held my slate in such a manner as to conceal my face: I might have escaped notice, had not my treacherous slate somehow happened to slip from my hand, and falling with an obtrusive crash, directly drawn every eye upon me; I knew it was all over now, and, as I stooped to pick up the two fragments of slate, I rallied my forces for the worst. It came.

"A careless girl!" said Mr. Brocklehurst, and immediately after—"It is the new pupil, I perceive." And before I could draw breath, "I must not forget I have a word to say respecting her." Then aloud: how loud it seemed to me! "Let the child who broke her slate come forward!"

Of my own accord I could not have stirred; I was paralysed: but the two great girls who sit on each side of me, set me on my legs and pushed me towards the dread judge, and then Miss Temple gently assisted me to his very feet, and I caught her whispered counsel—

"Don't be afraid, Jane, I saw it was an accident; you shall not be punished."

The kind whisper went to my heart like a dagger.

"Another minute, and she will despise me for a hypocrite," thought I; and an impulse of fury against Reed, Brocklehurst, and Co. bounded in my pulses at the conviction. I was no Helen Burns.

"Fetch that stool," said Mr. Brocklehurst, pointing to a very high one from which a monitor had just risen: it was brought.

"Place the child upon it."

And I was placed there, by whom I don't know: I was in no condition to note particulars; I was only aware that they had hoisted me up to the height of Mr. Brocklehurst's nose, that he was within a yard of me, and that a spread of shot orange and purple silk pelisses and a cloud of silvery plumage extended and waved below me.

Mr. Brocklehurst hemmed.

"Ladies," said he, turning to his family, "Miss Temple, teachers, and children, you all see this girl?"

Of course they did; for I felt their eyes directed like burning-glasses against my scorched skin.

"You see she is yet young; you observe she possesses the ordinary form of childhood; God has graciously given her the shape that He has given to all of us; no signal deformity points her out as a marked character. Who would think that the Evil One had already found a servant and agent in her? Yet such, I grieve to say, is the case."

A pause—in which I began to steady the palsy of my nerves, and to feel that the Rubicon was passed; and that the trial, no longer to be shirked, must be firmly sustained.

"My dear children," pursued the black marble clergyman, with pathos, "this is a sad, a melancholy occasion; for it becomes my duty to warn you, that this girl, who might be one of God's own lambs, is a little castaway: not a member of the true flock, but evidently an interloper and an alien. You must be on your guard against her; you must shun her example; if necessary, avoid her company, exclude her from your sports, and shut her out from your converse. Teachers, you must watch her: keep your eyes on her movements, weigh well her words, scrutinise her actions, punish her body to save her soul: if, indeed, such salvation be possible, for (my tongue falters while I tell it) this girl, this child, the native of a Christian land, worse than many a little heathen who says its prayers to Brahma and kneels before Juggernaut—this girl is—a liar!"

Now came a pause of ten minutes, during which I, by this time in perfect possession of my wits, observed all the female Brocklehursts produce their pocket-handkerchiefs and apply them to their optics, while the elderly lady swayed herself to and fro, and the two younger ones whispered, "How shocking!" Mr. Brocklehurst resumed.

"This I learned from her benefactress; from the pious and charitable lady who adopted her in her orphan state, reared her as her own daughter, and whose kindness, whose generosity the unhappy girl repaid by an ingratitude so bad, so dreadful, that at last her excellent patroness was obliged to separate her from her own young ones, fearful lest her vicious example should contaminate their purity: she has sent her here to be healed, even as the Jews of old sent their diseased to the troubled pool of Bethesda; and, teachers, superintendent, I beg of you not to allow the waters to stagnate round her."

With this sublime conclusion, Mr. Brocklehurst adjusted the top button of his surtout, muttered something to his family, who rose, bowed to Miss Temple, and then all the great people sailed in state from the room. Turning at the door, my judge said—

"Let her stand half-an-hour longer on that stool, and let no one speak to her during the remainder of the day."

There was I, then, mounted aloft; I, who had said I could not bear the shame of standing on my natural feet in the middle of the room, was now exposed to general view on a pedestal of infamy. What my sensations were no language can describe; but just as they all rose, stifling my breath and constricting my throat, a girl came up and passed me: in passing, she lifted her eyes. What a strange light inspired them! What an extraordinary sensation that ray sent through me! How the new feeling bore me up! It was as if a martyr, a hero, had passed a slave or victim, and imparted strength in the transit. I mastered the rising hysteria, lifted up my head, and took a firm stand on the stool. Helen Burns asked some slight question about her work of Miss Smith, was chidden for the triviality of the inquiry, returned to her place, and smiled at me as she again went by. What a smile! I remember it now, and I know that it was the effluence of fine intellect, of true courage; it lit up her marked lineaments, her thin face, her sunken grey eye, like a reflection from the aspect of an angel. Yet at that moment Helen Burns wore on her arm "the untidy badge;" scarcely an hour ago I had heard her condemned by Miss Scatcherd to a dinner of bread and water on the morrow because she had blotted an exercise in copying it out. Such is the imperfect nature of man! such spots are there on the disc of the clearest planet; and eyes like Miss Scatcherd's can only see those minute defects, and are blind to the full brightness of the orb.

Chapter VIII

Ere the half-hour ended, five o'clock struck; school was dismissed, and all were gone into the refectory to tea. I now ventured to descend: it was deep dusk; I retired into a corner and sat down on the floor. The spell by which I had been so far supported began to dissolve; reaction took place, and soon, so overwhelming was the grief that seized me, I sank prostrate with my face to the ground. Now I wept: Helen Burns was not here; nothing sustained me; left to myself I abandoned myself, and my tears watered the boards. I had meant to be so good, and to do so much at Lowood: to make so many friends, to earn respect and win affection. Already I had made visible progress: that very morning I had reached the head of my class; Miss Miller had praised me warmly; Miss Temple had smiled approbation; she had promised to teach me drawing, and to let me learn French, if I continued to make similar improvement two months longer: and then I was well received by my fellow-pupils; treated as an equal by those of my own age, and not molested by any; now, here I lay again crushed and trodden on; and could I ever rise more?

"Never," I thought; and ardently I wished to die. While sobbing out this wish in broken accents, some one approached: I started up—again Helen Burns was near me; the fading fires just showed her coming up the long, vacant room; she brought my coffee and bread.

"Come, eat something," she said; but I put both away from me, feeling as if a drop or a crumb would have choked me in my present condition. Helen regarded me, probably with surprise: I could not now abate my agitation, though I tried hard; I continued to weep aloud. She sat down on the ground near me, embraced her knees with her arms, and rested her head upon them; in that attitude she remained silent as an Indian. I was the first who spoke—

"Helen, why do you stay with a girl whom everybody believes to be a liar?"

"Everybody, Jane? Why, there are only eighty people who have heard you called so, and the world contains hundreds of millions."

"But what have I to do with millions? The eighty, I know, despise me."

"Jane, you are mistaken: probably not one in the school either despises or dislikes you: many, I am sure, pity you much."

"How can they pity me after what Mr. Brocklehurst has said?"

"Mr. Brocklehurst is not a god: nor is he even a great and admired man: he is little liked here; he never took steps to make himself liked. Had he treated you as an especial favourite, you would have found enemies, declared or covert, all around you; as it is, the greater number would offer you sympathy if they dared. Teachers and pupils may look coldly on you for a day or two, but friendly feelings are concealed in their hearts; and if you persevere in doing well, these feelings will ere long appear so much the more evidently for their temporary suppression. Besides, Jane"—she paused.

"Well, Helen?" said I, putting my hand into hers: she chafed my fingers gently to warm them, and went on—

"If all the world hated you, and believed you wicked, while your own conscience approved you, and absolved you from guilt, you would not be without friends."

"No; I know I should think well of myself; but that is not enough: if others don't love me I would rather die than live—I cannot bear to be solitary and hated, Helen. Look here; to gain some real affection from you, or Miss Temple, or any other whom I truly love, I would willingly submit to have the bone of my arm broken, or to let a bull toss me, or to stand behind a kicking horse, and let it dash its hoof at my chest—"

"Hush, Jane! you think too much of the love of human beings; you are too impulsive, too vehement; the sovereign hand that created your frame, and put life into it, has provided you with other resources than your feeble self, or than creatures feeble as you. Besides this earth, and besides the race of men, there is an invisible world and a kingdom of spirits: that world is round us, for it is everywhere; and those spirits watch us, for they are commissioned to guard us; and if we were dying in pain and shame, if scorn smote us on all sides, and hatred crushed us, angels see our tortures, recognise our innocence (if innocent we be: as I know you are of this charge which Mr. Brocklehurst has weakly and pompously repeated at second-hand from Mrs. Reed; for I read a sincere nature in your ardent eyes and on your clear front), and God waits only the separation of spirit from flesh to crown us with a full reward. Why, then, should we ever sink overwhelmed with distress, when life is so soon over, and death is so certain an entrance to happiness—to glory?"

I was silent; Helen had calmed me; but in the tranquillity she imparted there was an alloy of inexpressible sadness. I felt the impression of woe as she spoke, but I could not tell whence it came; and when, having done speaking, she breathed a little fast and coughed a short cough, I momentarily forgot my own sorrows to yield to a vague concern for her.

Resting my head on Helen's shoulder, I put my arms round her waist; she drew me to her, and we reposed in silence. We had not sat long thus, when another person came in. Some heavy clouds, swept from the sky by a rising wind, had left the moon bare; and her light, streaming in through a window near, shone full both on us and on the approaching figure, which we at once recognised as Miss Temple.

"I came on purpose to find you, Jane Eyre," said she; "I want you in my room; and as Helen Burns is with you, she may come too."

We went; following the superintendent's guidance, we had to thread some intricate passages, and mount a staircase before we reached her apartment; it contained a good fire, and looked cheerful. Miss Temple told Helen Burns to be seated in a low arm-chair on one side of the hearth, and herself taking another, she called me to her side.

"Is it all over?" she asked, looking down at my face. "Have you cried your grief away?"

"I am afraid I never shall do that."

"Why?"

"Because I have been wrongly accused; and you, ma'am, and everybody else, will now think me wicked."

"We shall think you what you prove yourself to be, my child. Continue to act as a good girl, and you will satisfy us."

"Shall I, Miss Temple?"

"You will," said she, passing her arm round me. "And now tell me who is the lady whom Mr. Brocklehurst called your benefactress?"

"Mrs. Reed, my uncle's wife. My uncle is dead, and he left me to her care."

"Did she not, then, adopt you of her own accord?"

"No, ma'am; she was sorry to have to do it: but my uncle, as I have often heard the servants say, got her to promise before he died that she would always keep me."

"Well now, Jane, you know, or at least I will tell you, that when a criminal is accused, he is always allowed to speak in his own defence. You have been charged with falsehood; defend yourself to me as well as you can. Say whatever your memory suggests is true; but add nothing and exaggerate nothing."

I resolved, in the depth of my heart, that I would be most moderate—most correct; and, having reflected a few minutes in order to arrange coherently what I had to say, I told her all the story of my sad childhood. Exhausted by emotion, my language was more subdued than it generally was when it developed that sad theme; and mindful of Helen's warnings against the indulgence of resentment, I infused into the narrative far less of gall and wormwood than ordinary. Thus restrained and simplified, it sounded more credible: I felt as I went on that Miss Temple fully believed me.

In the course of the tale I had mentioned Mr. Lloyd as having come to see me after the fit: for I never forgot the, to me, frightful episode of the red-room: in detailing which, my excitement was sure, in some degree, to break bounds; for nothing could soften in my recollection the spasm of agony which clutched my heart when Mrs. Reed spurned my wild supplication for pardon, and locked me a second time in the dark and haunted chamber.

I had finished: Miss Temple regarded me a few minutes in silence; she then said—

"I know something of Mr. Lloyd; I shall write to him; if his reply agrees with your statement, you shall be publicly cleared from every imputation; to me, Jane, you are clear now."

She kissed me, and still keeping me at her side (where I was well contented to stand, for I derived a child's pleasure from the contemplation of her face, her dress, her one or two ornaments, her white forehead, her clustered and shining curls, and beaming dark eyes), she proceeded to address Helen Burns.

"How are you to-night, Helen? Have you coughed much to-day?"

"Not quite so much, I think, ma'am."

"And the pain in your chest?"

"It is a little better."

Miss Temple got up, took her hand and examined her pulse; then she returned to her own seat: as she resumed it, I heard her sigh low. She was pensive a few minutes, then rousing herself, she said cheerfully—

"But you two are my visitors to-night; I must treat you as such." She rang her bell.

"Barbara," she said to the servant who answered it, "I have not yet had tea; bring the tray and place cups for these two young ladies."

And a tray was soon brought. How pretty, to my eyes, did the china cups and bright teapot look, placed on the little round table near the fire! How fragrant was the steam of the beverage, and the scent of the toast! of which, however, I, to my dismay (for I was beginning to be hungry) discerned only a very small portion: Miss Temple discerned it too.

"Barbara," said she, "can you not bring a little more bread and butter? There is not enough for three."

Barbara went out: she returned soon—

"Madam, Mrs. Harden says she has sent up the usual quantity."

Mrs. Harden, be it observed, was the housekeeper: a woman after Mr. Brocklehurst's own heart, made up of equal parts of whalebone and iron.

"Oh, very well!" returned Miss Temple; "we must make it do, Barbara, I suppose." And as the girl withdrew she added, smiling, "Fortunately, I have it in my power to supply deficiencies for this once."

Having invited Helen and me to approach the table, and placed before each of us a cup of tea with one delicious but thin morsel of toast, she got up, unlocked a drawer, and taking from it a parcel wrapped in paper, disclosed presently to our eyes a good-sized seed-cake.

"I meant to give each of you some of this to take with you," said she, "but as there is so little toast, you must have it now," and she proceeded to cut slices with a generous hand.

We feasted that evening as on nectar and ambrosia; and not the least delight of the entertainment was the smile of gratification with which our hostess regarded us, as we satisfied our famished appetites on the delicate fare she liberally supplied.

Tea over and the tray removed, she again summoned us to the fire; we sat one on each side of her, and now a conversation followed between her and Helen, which it was indeed a privilege to be admitted to hear.

Miss Temple had always something of serenity in her air, of state in her mien, of refined propriety in her language, which precluded deviation into the ardent, the excited, the eager: something which chastened the pleasure of those who looked on her and listened to her, by a controlling sense of awe; and such was my feeling now: but as to Helen Burns, I was struck with wonder.

The refreshing meal, the brilliant fire, the presence and kindness of her beloved instructress, or, perhaps, more than all these, something in her own unique mind, had roused her powers within her. They woke, they kindled: first, they glowed in the bright tint of her cheek, which till this hour I had never seen but pale and bloodless;

then they shone in the liquid lustre of her eyes, which had suddenly acquired a beauty more singular than that of Miss Temple's—a beauty neither of fine colour nor long eyelash, nor pencilled brow, but of meaning, of movement, of radiance. Then her soul sat on her lips, and language flowed, from what source I cannot tell. Has a girl of fourteen a heart large enough, vigorous enough, to hold the swelling spring of pure, full, fervid eloquence? Such was the characteristic of Helen's discourse on that, to me, memorable evening; her spirit seemed hastening to live within a very brief span as much as many live during a protracted existence.

They conversed of things I had never heard of; of nations and times past; of countries far away; of secrets of nature discovered or guessed at: they spoke of books: how many they had read! What stores of knowledge they possessed! Then they seemed so familiar with French names and French authors: but my amazement reached its climax when Miss Temple asked Helen if she sometimes snatched a moment to recall the Latin her father had taught her, and taking a book from a shelf, bade her read and construe a page of Virgil; and Helen obeyed, my organ of veneration expanding at every sounding line. She had scarcely finished ere the bell announced bedtime! no delay could be admitted; Miss Temple embraced us both, saying, as she drew us to her heart—

"God bless you, my children!"

Helen she held a little longer than me: she let her go more reluctantly; it was Helen her eye followed to the door; it was for her she a second time breathed a sad sigh; for her she wiped a tear from her cheek.

On reaching the bedroom, we heard the voice of Miss Scatcherd: she was examining drawers; she had just pulled out Helen Burns's, and when we entered Helen was greeted with a sharp reprimand, and told that to-morrow she should have half-a-dozen of untidily folded articles pinned to her shoulder.

"My things were indeed in shameful disorder," murmured Helen to me, in a low voice: "I intended to have arranged them, but I forgot."

Next morning, Miss Scatcherd wrote in conspicuous characters on a piece of pasteboard the word "Slattern," and bound it like a phylactery round Helen's large, mild, intelligent, and benign-looking forehead. She wore it till evening, patient, unresentful, regarding it as a deserved punishment. The moment Miss Scatcherd withdrew after afternoon school, I ran to Helen, tore it off, and thrust it into the fire: the fury of which she was incapable had been burning in my soul all day, and tears, hot and large, had continually been scalding my cheek; for the spectacle of her sad resignation gave me an intolerable pain at the heart.

About a week subsequently to the incidents above narrated, Miss Temple, who had written to Mr. Lloyd, received his answer: it appeared that what he said went to corroborate my account. Miss Temple, having assembled the whole school, announced that inquiry had been made into the charges alleged against Jane Eyre, and that she was most happy to be able to pronounce her completely cleared from every imputation. The teachers then shook hands with me and kissed me, and a murmur of pleasure ran through the ranks of my companions.

Thus relieved of a grievous load, I from that hour set to work afresh, resolved to pioneer my way through every difficulty: I toiled hard, and my success was proportionate to my efforts; my memory, not naturally tenacious, improved with practice; exercise sharpened my wits; in a few weeks I was promoted to a higher class; in less than two months I was allowed to commence French and drawing. I learned the first two tenses of the verb ETRE, and sketched my first cottage (whose walls, by-the-bye, outrivalled in slope those of the leaning tower of Pisa), on the same day. That night, on going to bed, I forgot to prepare in imagination the Barmecide supper of hot roast potatoes, or white bread and new milk, with which I was wont to amuse my inward cravings: I feasted instead on the spectacle of ideal drawings, which I saw in the dark; all the work of my own hands: freely pencilled houses and trees, picturesque rocks and ruins, Cuyp-like groups of cattle, sweet paintings of butterflies hovering over unblown roses, of birds picking at ripe cherries, of wren's nests enclosing pearl-like eggs, wreathed about with young ivy sprays. I examined, too, in thought, the possibility of my ever being able to translate currently a certain little French story which Madame Pierrot had that day shown me; nor was that problem solved to my satisfaction ere I fell sweetly asleep.

Well has Solomon said—"Better is a dinner of herbs where love is, than a stalled ox and hatred therewith."

I would not now have exchanged Lowood with all its privations for Gateshead and its daily luxuries.

Chapter IX

But the privations, or rather the hardships, of Lowood lessened. Spring drew on: she was indeed already come; the frosts of winter had ceased; its snows were melted, its cutting winds ameliorated. My wretched feet, flayed and swollen to lameness by the sharp air of January, began to heal and subside under the gentler breathings of April; the nights and mornings no longer by their Canadian temperature froze the very blood in our veins; we could now endure the play-hour passed in the garden: sometimes on a sunny day it began even to be pleasant and genial, and a greenness grew over those brown beds, which, freshening daily, suggested the thought that Hope traversed them at night, and left each morning brighter traces of her steps. Flowers peeped out amongst the leaves; snow-drops, crocuses, purple auriculas, and golden-eyed pansies. On Thursday afternoons (half-holidays) we now took walks, and found still sweeter flowers opening by the wayside, under the hedges.

I discovered, too, that a great pleasure, an enjoyment which the horizon only bounded, lay all outside the high and spike-guarded walls of our garden: this pleasure consisted in prospect of noble summits girdling a great hill-hollow, rich in verdure and shadow; in a bright beck, full of dark stones and sparkling eddies. How different had this scene looked when I viewed it laid out beneath the iron sky of winter, stiffened in frost, shrouded with snow!—when mists as chill as death wandered to the impulse of east winds along those purple peaks, and rolled down "ing" and holm till they blended with the frozen fog of the beck! That beck itself was then a torrent, turbid and curbless: it tore asunder the wood, and sent a raving sound through the air, often thickened with wild rain or whirling sleet; and for the forest on its banks, THAT showed only ranks of skeletons.

April advanced to May: a bright serene May it was; days of blue sky, placid sunshine, and soft western or southern gales filled up its duration. And now vegetation matured with vigour; Lowood shook loose its tresses; it became all green, all flowery; its great elm, ash, and oak skeletons were restored to majestic life; woodland plants sprang up profusely in its recesses; unnumbered varieties of moss filled its hollows, and it made a strange ground-sunshine out of the wealth of its wild primrose plants: I have seen their pale gold gleam in overshadowed spots like scatterings of the sweetest lustre. All this I enjoyed often and fully, free, unwatched, and almost alone: for this unwonted liberty and pleasure there was a cause, to which it now becomes my task to advert.

Have I not described a pleasant site for a dwelling, when I speak of it as bosomed in hill and wood, and rising from the verge of a stream? Assuredly, pleasant enough: but whether healthy or not is another question.

That forest-dell, where Lowood lay, was the cradle of fog and fog-bred pestilence; which, quickening with the quickening spring, crept into the Orphan Asylum, breathed typhus through its crowded schoolroom and dormitory, and, ere May arrived, transformed the seminary into an hospital.

Semi-starvation and neglected colds had predisposed most of the pupils to receive infection: forty-five out of the eighty girls lay ill at one time. Classes were broken up, rules relaxed. The few who continued well were allowed almost unlimited license; because the medical attendant insisted on the necessity of frequent exercise to keep them in health: and had it been otherwise, no one had leisure to watch or restrain them. Miss Temple's whole attention was absorbed by the patients: she lived in the sick-room, never quitting it except to snatch a few hours' rest at night. The teachers were fully occupied with packing up and making other necessary preparations for the departure of those girls who were fortunate enough to have friends and relations able and willing to remove them from the seat of contagion. Many, already smitten, went home only to die: some died at the school, and were buried quietly and quickly, the nature of the malady forbidding delay.

While disease had thus become an inhabitant of Lowood, and death its frequent visitor; while there was gloom and fear within its walls; while its rooms and passages steamed with hospital smells, the drug and the pastille striving vainly to overcome the effluvia of mortality, that bright May shone unclouded over the bold hills and beautiful woodland out of doors. Its garden, too, glowed with flowers: hollyhocks had sprung up tall as trees, lilies had opened, tulips and roses were in bloom; the borders of the little beds were gay with pink thrift and crimson double daisies; the sweetbriars gave out, morning and evening, their scent of spice and apples; and these fragrant treasures were all useless for most of the inmates of Lowood, except to furnish now and then a handful of herbs and blossoms to put in a coffin.

But I, and the rest who continued well, enjoyed fully the beauties of the scene and season; they let us ramble in the wood, like gipsies, from morning till night; we did what we liked, went where we liked: we lived better too. Mr. Brocklehurst and his family never came near Lowood now: household matters were not scrutinised into; the cross housekeeper was gone, driven away by the fear of infection; her successor, who had been matron at the Lowton Dispensary, unused to the ways of her new abode, provided with comparative liberality. Besides, there were fewer to feed; the sick could eat little; our breakfast-basins were better filled; when there was no time to prepare a regular dinner, which often happened, she would give us a large piece of cold pie, or a thick slice of bread and cheese, and this we carried away with us to the wood, where we each chose the spot we liked best, and dined sumptuously.

My favourite seat was a smooth and broad stone, rising white and dry from the very middle of the beck, and only to be got at by wading through the water; a feat I accomplished barefoot. The stone was just broad enough to accommodate, comfortably, another girl and me, at that time my chosen comrade—one Mary Ann Wilson; a shrewd, observant personage, whose society I took pleasure in, partly because she was witty and original, and partly because she had a manner which set me at my ease. Some years older than I, she knew more of the world, and could tell me many things I liked to hear: with her my curiosity found gratification: to my faults also she gave ample indulgence, never imposing curb or rein on anything I said. She had a turn for narrative, I for analysis; she liked to inform, I to question; so we got on swimmingly together, deriving much entertainment, if not much improvement, from our mutual intercourse.

And where, meantime, was Helen Burns? Why did I not spend these sweet days of liberty with her? Had I forgotten her? or was I so worthless as to have grown tired of her pare society? Surely the Mary Arm Wilson I have mentioned was inferior to my first acquaintance: she could only tell me amusing stories, and reciprocate any racy and pungent gossip I chose to indulge in; while, if I have spoken truth of Helen, she was qualified to give those who enjoyed the privilege of her converse a taste of far higher things.

True, reader; and I knew and felt this: and though I am a defective being, with many faults and few redeeming points, yet I never tired of Helen Burns; nor ever ceased to cherish for her a sentiment of attachment, as strong, tender, and respectful as any that ever animated my heart. How could it be otherwise, when Helen, at all times and under all circumstances, evinced for me a quiet and faithful friendship, which ill-humour never soured, nor irritation never troubled? But Helen was ill at present: for some weeks she had been removed from my sight to I knew not what room upstairs. She was not, I was told, in the hospital portion of the house with the fever patients; for her complaint was consumption, not typhus: and by consumption I, in my ignorance, understood something mild, which time and care would be sure to alleviate.

I was confirmed in this idea by the fact of her once or twice coming downstairs on very warm sunny afternoons, and being taken by Miss Temple into the garden; but, on these occasions, I was not allowed to go and speak to her; I only saw her from the schoolroom window, and then not distinctly; for she was much wrapped up, and sat at a distance under the verandah.

One evening, in the beginning of June, I had stayed out very late with Mary Ann in the wood; we had, as usual, separated ourselves from the others, and had wandered far; so far that we lost our way, and had to ask it at a lonely cottage, where a man and woman lived, who looked after a herd of half-wild swine that fed on the mast in the wood. When we got back, it was after moonrise: a pony, which we knew to be the surgeon's, was standing at the garden door. Mary Ann remarked that she supposed some one must be very ill, as Mr. Bates had been sent for at that time of the evening. She went into the house; I stayed behind a few minutes to plant in my garden a handful of roots I had dug up in the forest, and which I feared would wither if I left them till the morning. This done, I lingered yet a little longer: the flowers smelt so sweet as the dew fell; it was such a pleasant evening, so serene, so warm; the still glowing west promised so fairly another fine day on the morrow; the moon rose with such majesty in the grave east. I was noting these things and enjoying them as a child might, when it entered my mind as it had never done before:—

"How sad to be lying now on a sick bed, and to be in danger of dying! This world is pleasant—it would be dreary to be called from it, and to have to go who knows where?"

And then my mind made its first earnest effort to comprehend what had been infused into it concerning heaven and hell; and for the first time it recoiled, baffled; and for the first time glancing behind, on each side, and before it, it saw all round an unfathomed gulf: it felt the one point where it stood—the present; all the rest was formless cloud and vacant depth; and it shuddered at the thought of tottering, and plunging amid that chaos. While pondering this new idea, I heard the front door open; Mr. Bates came out, and with him was a nurse. After she had seen him mount his horse and depart, she was about to close the door, but I ran up to her.

"How is Helen Burns?"

"Very poorly," was the answer.

"Is it her Mr. Bates has been to see?"

"Yes."

"And what does he say about her?"

"He says she'll not be here long."

This phrase, uttered in my hearing yesterday, would have only conveyed the notion that she was about to be removed to Northumberland, to her own home. I should not have suspected that it meant she was dying; but I knew instantly now! It opened clear on my comprehension that Helen Burns was numbering her last days in this world, and that she was going to be taken to the region of spirits, if such region there were. I experienced a shock of horror, then a strong thrill of grief, then a desire—a necessity to see her; and I asked in what room she lay.

"She is in Miss Temple's room," said the nurse.

"May I go up and speak to her?"

"Oh no, child! It is not likely; and now it is time for you to come in; you'll catch the fever if you stop out when the dew is falling."

The nurse closed the front door; I went in by the side entrance which led to the schoolroom: I was just in time; it was nine o'clock, and Miss Miller was calling the pupils to go to bed.

It might be two hours later, probably near eleven, when I—not having been able to fall asleep, and deeming, from the perfect silence of the dormitory, that my companions were all wrapt in profound repose—rose softly, put on my frock over my night-dress, and, without shoes, crept from the apartment, and set off in quest of Miss Temple's room. It was quite at the other end of the house; but I knew my way; and the light of the unclouded summer moon, entering here and there at passage windows, enabled me to find it without difficulty. An odour of camphor and burnt vinegar warned me when I came near the fever room: and I passed its door quickly, fearful lest the nurse who sat up all night should hear me. I dreaded being discovered and sent back; for I MUST see Helen,—I must embrace her before she died,—I must give her one last kiss, exchange with her one last word.

Having descended a staircase, traversed a portion of the house below, and succeeded in opening and shutting, without noise, two doors, I reached another flight of steps; these I mounted, and then just opposite to me was Miss Temple's room. A light shone through the keyhole and from under the door; a profound stillness pervaded the vicinity. Coming near, I found the door slightly ajar; probably to admit some fresh air into the close abode of sickness. Indisposed to hesitate, and full of impatient impulses—soul and senses quivering with keen throes—I put it back and looked in. My eye sought Helen, and feared to find death.

Close by Miss Temple's bed, and half covered with its white curtains, there stood a little crib. I saw the outline of a form under the clothes, but the face was hid by the hangings: the nurse I had spoken to in the garden sat in an easy-chair asleep; an unsnuffed candle burnt dimly on the table. Miss Temple was not to be seen: I knew afterwards that she had been called to a delirious patient in the fever-room. I advanced; then paused by the crib side: my hand was on the curtain, but I preferred speaking before I withdrew it. I still recoiled at the dread of seeing a corpse.

"Helen!" I whispered softly, "are you awake?"

She stirred herself, put back the curtain, and I saw her face, pale, wasted, but quite composed: she looked so little changed that my fear was instantly dissipated.

"Can it be you, Jane?" she asked, in her own gentle voice.

"Oh!" I thought, "she is not going to die; they are mistaken: she could not speak and look so calmly if she were."

I got on to her crib and kissed her: her forehead was cold, and her cheek both cold and thin, and so were her hand and wrist; but she smiled as of old.

"Why are you come here, Jane? It is past eleven o'clock: I heard it strike some minutes since."

"I came to see you, Helen: I heard you were very ill, and I could not sleep till I had spoken to you."

"You came to bid me good-bye, then: you are just in time probably."

"Are you going somewhere, Helen? Are you going home?"

"Yes; to my long home—my last home."

"No, no, Helen!" I stopped, distressed. While I tried to devour my tears, a fit of coughing seized Helen; it did not, however, wake the nurse; when it was over, she lay some minutes exhausted; then she whispered—

"Jane, your little feet are bare; lie down and cover yourself with my quilt."

I did so: she put her arm over me, and I nestled close to her. After a long silence, she resumed, still whispering—

"I am very happy, Jane; and when you hear that I am dead, you must be sure and not grieve: there is nothing to grieve about. We all must die one day, and the illness which is removing me is not painful; it is gentle and gradual: my mind is at rest. I leave no one to regret me much: I have only a father; and he is lately married, and will not miss me. By dying young, I shall escape great sufferings. I had not qualities or talents to make my way very well in the world: I should have been continually at fault."

"But where are you going to, Helen? Can you see? Do you know?"

"I believe; I have faith: I am going to God."

"Where is God? What is God?"

"My Maker and yours, who will never destroy what He created. I rely implicitly on His power, and confide wholly in His goodness: I count the hours till that eventful one arrives which shall restore me to Him, reveal Him to me."

"You are sure, then, Helen, that there is such a place as heaven, and that our souls can get to it when we die?"

"I am sure there is a future state; I believe God is good; I can resign my immortal part to Him without any misgiving. God is my father; God is my friend: I love Him; I believe He loves me."

"And shall I see you again, Helen, when I die?"

"You will come to the same region of happiness: be received by the same mighty, universal Parent, no doubt, dear Jane."

Again I questioned, but this time only in thought. "Where is that region? Does it exist?" And I clasped my arms closer round Helen; she seemed dearer to me than ever; I felt as if I could not let her go; I lay with my face hidden on her neck. Presently she said, in the sweetest tone—

"How comfortable I am! That last fit of coughing has tired me a little; I feel as if I could sleep: but don't leave me, Jane; I like to have you near me."

"I'll stay with you, DEAR Helen: no one shall take me way."

"Are you warm, darling?"

"Yes."

"Good-night, Jane."

"Good-night, Helen."

She kissed me, and I her, and we both soon slumbered.

When I awoke it was day: an unusual movement roused me; I looked up; I was in somebody's arms; the nurse held me; she was carrying me through the passage back to the dormitory. I was not reprimanded for leaving my bed; people had something else to think about; no explanation was afforded then to my many questions; but a day or two afterwards I learned that Miss Temple, on returning to her own room at dawn, had found me laid in the little crib; my face against Helen Burns's shoulder, my arms round her neck. I was asleep, and Helen was—dead.

Her grave is in Brocklebridge churchyard: for fifteen years after her death it was only covered by a grassy mound; but now a grey marble tablet marks the spot, inscribed with her name, and the word "Resurgam."

Chapter X

Hitherto I have recorded in detail the events of my insignificant existence: to the first ten years of my life I have given almost as many chapters. But this is not to be a regular autobiography. I am only bound to invoke Memory where I know her responses will possess some degree of interest; therefore I now pass a space of eight years almost in silence: a few lines only are necessary to keep up the links of connection.

When the typhus fever had fulfilled its mission of devastation at Lowood, it gradually disappeared from thence; but not till its virulence and the number of its victims had drawn public attention on the school. Inquiry was made into the origin of the scourge, and by degrees various facts came out which excited public indignation in a high degree. The unhealthy nature of the site; the quantity and quality of the children's food; the brackish, fetid water used in its preparation; the pupils' wretched clothing and accommodations—all these things were discovered, and the discovery produced a result mortifying to Mr. Brocklehurst, but beneficial to the institution.

Several wealthy and benevolent individuals in the county subscribed largely for the erection of a more convenient building in a better situation; new regulations were made; improvements in diet and clothing introduced; the funds of the school were intrusted to the management of a committee. Mr. Brocklehurst, who, from his wealth and family connections, could not be overlooked, still retained the post of treasurer; but he was aided in the discharge of his duties by gentlemen of rather more enlarged and sympathising minds: his office of inspector, too, was shared by those who knew how to combine reason with strictness, comfort with economy, compassion with uprightness. The school, thus improved, became in time a truly useful and noble institution. I remained an inmate of its walls, after its regeneration, for eight years: six as pupil, and two as teacher; and in both capacities I bear my testimony to its value and importance.

During these eight years my life was uniform: but not unhappy, because it was not inactive. I had the means of an excellent education placed within my reach; a fondness for some of my studies, and a desire to excel in all, together with a great delight in pleasing my teachers, especially such as I loved, urged me on: I availed myself fully of the advantages offered me. In time I rose to be the first girl of the first class; then I was invested with the office of teacher; which I discharged with zeal for two years: but at the end of that time I altered.

Miss Temple, through all changes, had thus far continued superintendent of the seminary: to her instruction I owed the best part of my acquirements; her friendship and society had been my continual solace; she had stood me in the stead of mother, governess, and, latterly, companion. At this period she married, removed with her husband (a clergyman, an excellent man, almost worthy of such a wife) to a distant county, and consequently was lost to me.

From the day she left I was no longer the same: with her was gone every settled feeling, every association that had made Lowood in some degree a home to me. I had imbibed from her something of her nature and much of her habits: more harmonious thoughts: what seemed better regulated feelings had become the inmates of my mind. I had given in allegiance to duty and order; I was quiet; I believed I was content: to the eyes of others, usually even to my own, I appeared a disciplined and subdued character.

But destiny, in the shape of the Rev. Mr. Nasmyth, came between me and Miss Temple: I saw her in her travelling dress step into a post-chaise, shortly after the marriage ceremony; I watched the chaise mount the hill and disappear beyond its brow; and then retired to my own room, and there spent in solitude the greatest part of the half-holiday granted in honour of the occasion.

I walked about the chamber most of the time. I imagined myself only to be regretting my loss, and thinking how to repair it; but when my reflections were concluded, and I looked up and found that the afternoon was gone, and evening far advanced, another discovery dawned on me, namely, that in the interval I had undergone a transforming process; that my mind had put off all it had borrowed of Miss Temple—or rather that she had taken with her the serene atmosphere I had been breathing in her vicinity—and that now I was left in my natural element, and beginning to feel the stirring of old emotions. It did not seem as if a prop were withdrawn, but rather as if a motive were gone: it was not the power to be tranquil which had failed me, but the reason for tranquillity was no more. My world had for some years been in Lowood: my experience had been of its rules and systems; now I remembered that the real world was wide, and that a varied field of hopes and fears, of sensations and excitements, awaited those who had courage to go forth into its expanse, to seek real knowledge of life amidst its perils.

I went to my window, opened it, and looked out. There were the two wings of the building; there was the garden; there were the skirts of Lowood; there was the hilly horizon. My eye passed all other objects to rest on those most remote, the blue peaks; it was those I longed to surmount; all within their boundary of rock and heath seemed prison-ground, exile limits. I traced the white road winding round the base of one mountain, and vanishing in a gorge between two; how I longed to follow it farther! I recalled the time when I had travelled that very road in a coach; I remembered descending that hill at twilight; an age seemed to have elapsed since the day which brought me first to Lowood, and I had never quitted it since. My vacations had all been spent at school: Mrs. Reed had never sent for me to Gateshead; neither she nor any of her family had ever been to visit me. I had had no communication by letter or message with the outer world: school-rules, school-duties, school-habits and notions, and voices, and faces, and phrases, and costumes, and preferences, and antipathies—such was what I knew of existence. And now I felt that it was not enough; I tired of the routine of eight years in one afternoon. I desired liberty; for liberty I gasped; for liberty I uttered a prayer; it seemed scattered on the wind then faintly blowing. I abandoned it and framed a humbler supplication; for change, stimulus: that petition, too, seemed swept off into vague space: "Then," I cried, half desperate, "grant me at least a new servitude!"

Here a bell, ringing the hour of supper, called me downstairs.

I was not free to resume the interrupted chain of my reflections till bedtime: even then a teacher who occupied the same room with me kept me from the subject to which I longed to recur, by a prolonged effusion of small talk. How I wished sleep would silence her. It seemed as if, could I but go back to the idea which had last entered my mind as I stood at the window, some inventive suggestion would rise for my relief.

Miss Gryce snored at last; she was a heavy Welshwoman, and till now her habitual nasal strains had never been regarded by me in any other light than as a nuisance; to-night I hailed the first deep notes with satisfaction; I was debarrassed of interruption; my half-effaced thought instantly revived.

"A new servitude! There is something in that," I soliloquised (mentally, be it understood; I did not talk aloud), "I know there is, because it does not sound too sweet; it is not like such words as Liberty, Excitement, Enjoyment: delightful sounds truly; but no more than sounds for me; and so hollow and fleeting that it is mere waste of time to listen to them. But Servitude! That must be matter of fact. Any one may serve: I have served here eight years; now all I want is to serve elsewhere. Can I not get so much of my own will? Is not the thing feasible? Yes—yes—the end is not so difficult; if I had only a brain active enough to ferret out the means of attaining it."

I sat up in bed by way of arousing this said brain: it was a chilly night; I covered my shoulders with a shawl, and then I proceeded TO THINK again with all my might.

"What do I want? A new place, in a new house, amongst new faces, under new circumstances: I want this because it is of no use wanting anything better. How do people do to get a new place? They apply to friends, I suppose: I have no friends. There are many others who have no friends, who must look about for themselves and be their own helpers; and what is their resource?"

I could not tell: nothing answered me; I then ordered my brain to find a response, and quickly. It worked and worked faster: I felt the pulses throb in my head and temples; but for nearly an hour it worked in chaos; and no result came of its efforts. Feverish with vain labour, I got up and took a turn in the room; undrew the curtain, noted a star or two, shivered with cold, and again crept to bed.

A kind fairy, in my absence, had surely dropped the required suggestion on my pillow; for as I lay down, it came quietly and naturally to my mind.—"Those who want situations advertise; you must advertise in the——shire Herald."

"How? I know nothing about advertising."

Replies rose smooth and prompt now:—

"You must enclose the advertisement and the money to pay for it under a cover directed to the editor of the Herald; you must put it, the first opportunity you have, into the post at Lowton; answers must be addressed to J.E., at the post-office there; you can go and inquire in about a week after you send your letter, if any are come, and act accordingly."

This scheme I went over twice, thrice; it was then digested in my mind; I had it in a clear practical form: I felt satisfied, and fell asleep.

With earliest day, I was up: I had my advertisement written, enclosed, and directed before the bell rang to rouse the school; it ran thus:—

"A young lady accustomed to tuition" (had I not been a teacher two years?) "is desirous of meeting with a situation in a private family where the children are under fourteen (I thought that as I was barely eighteen, it would not do to undertake the guidance of pupils nearer my own age). She is qualified to teach the usual branches of a good English education, together with French, Drawing, and Music" (in those days, reader, this now narrow catalogue of accomplishments, would have been held tolerably comprehensive). "Address, J.E., Post-office, Lowton,——shire."

This document remained locked in my drawer all day: after tea, I asked leave of the new superintendent to go to Lowton, in order to perform some small commissions for myself and one or two of my fellow-teachers; permission was readily granted; I went. It was a walk of two miles, and the evening was wet, but the days were still long; I visited a shop or two, slipped the letter into the post-office, and came back through heavy rain, with streaming garments, but with a relieved heart.

The succeeding week seemed long: it came to an end at last, however, like all sublunary things, and once more, towards the close of a pleasant autumn day, I found myself afoot on the road to Lowton. A picturesque track it was, by the way; lying along the side of the beck and through the sweetest curves of the dale: but that day I thought more of the letters, that might or might not be awaiting me at the little burgh whither I was bound, than of the charms of lea and water.

My ostensible errand on this occasion was to get measured for a pair of shoes; so I discharged that business first, and when it was done, I stepped across the clean and quiet little street from the shoemaker's to the post-office: it was kept by an old dame, who wore horn spectacles on her nose, and black mittens on her hands.

"Are there any letters for J.E.?" I asked.

She peered at me over her spectacles, and then she opened a drawer and fumbled among its contents for a long time, so long that my hopes began to falter. At last, having held a document before her glasses for nearly five minutes, she presented it across the counter, accompanying the act by another inquisitive and mistrustful glance—it was for J.E.

"Is there only one?" I demanded.

"There are no more," said she; and I put it in my pocket and turned my face homeward: I could not open it then; rules obliged me to be back by eight, and it was already half-past seven.

Various duties awaited me on my arrival. I had to sit with the girls during their hour of study; then it was my turn to read prayers; to see them to bed: afterwards I supped with the other teachers. Even when we finally retired for the night, the inevitable Miss Gryce was still my companion: we had only a short end of candle in our candlestick, and I dreaded lest she should talk till it was all burnt out; fortunately, however, the heavy supper she had eaten produced a soporific effect: she was already snoring before I had finished undressing. There still remained an inch of candle: I now took out my letter; the seal was an initial F.; I broke it; the contents were brief.

"If J.E., who advertised in the——shire Herald of last Thursday, possesses the acquirements mentioned, and if she is in a position to give satisfactory references as to character and competency, a situation can be offered her where there is but one pupil, a little girl, under ten years of age; and where the salary is thirty pounds per annum. J.E. is requested to send references, name, address, and all particulars to the direction:—

"Mrs. Fairfax, Thornfield, near Millcote,——shire."

I examined the document long: the writing was old-fashioned and rather uncertain, like that of in elderly lady. This circumstance was satisfactory: a private fear had haunted me, that in thus acting for myself, and by my own guidance, I ran the risk of getting into some scrape; and, above all things, I wished the result of my endeavours to be respectable, proper, en regle. I now felt that an elderly lady was no bad ingredient in the business I had on hand. Mrs. Fairfax! I saw her in a black gown and widow's cap; frigid, perhaps, but not uncivil: a model of elderly English respectability. Thornfield! that, doubtless, was the name of her house: a neat orderly spot, I was sure; though I failed in my efforts to conceive a correct plan of the premises. Millcote,——shire; I brushed up my recollections of the map of England, yes, I saw it; both the shire and the town.——shire was seventy miles nearer London than the remote county where I now resided: that was a recommendation to me. I longed to go where there was life and movement: Millcote was a large manufacturing town on the banks of the A——; a busy place enough, doubtless: so much the better; it would be a complete change at least. Not that my fancy was much captivated by the idea of long chimneys and clouds of smoke—"but," I argued, "Thornfield will, probably, be a good way from the town."

Here the socket of the candle dropped, and the wick went out.

Next day new steps were to be taken; my plans could no longer be confined to my own breast; I must impart them in order to achieve their success. Having sought and obtained an audience of the superintendent during the noontide recreation, I told her I had a prospect of getting a new situation where the salary would be double what I now received (for at Lowood I only got 15 pounds per annum); and requested she would break the matter for me to Mr. Brocklehurst, or some of the committee, and ascertain whether they would permit me to mention them as references. She obligingly consented to act as mediatrix in the matter. The next day she laid the affair before Mr. Brocklehurst, who said that Mrs. Reed must be written to, as she was my natural guardian. A note was accordingly addressed to that lady, who returned for answer, that "I might do as I pleased: she had long relinquished all interference in my affairs." This note went the round of the committee, and at last, after what appeared to me most tedious delay, formal leave was given me to better my condition if I could; and an assurance added, that as I had always conducted myself well, both as teacher and pupil, at Lowood, a testimonial of character and capacity, signed by the inspectors of that institution, should forthwith be furnished me.

This testimonial I accordingly received in about a month, forwarded a copy of it to Mrs. Fairfax, and got that lady's reply, stating that she was satisfied, and fixing that day fortnight as the period for my assuming the post of governess in her house.

I now busied myself in preparations: the fortnight passed rapidly. I had not a very large wardrobe, though it was adequate to my wants; and the last day sufficed to pack my trunk,—the same I had brought with me eight years ago from Gateshead.

The box was corded, the card nailed on. In half-an-hour the carrier was to call for it to take it to Lowton, whether I myself was to repair at an early hour the next morning to meet the coach. I had brushed my black stuff travelling-dress, prepared my bonnet, gloves, and muff; sought in all my drawers to see that no article was left behind; and now having nothing more to do, I sat down and tried to rest. I could not; though I had been on foot all day, I could not now repose an instant; I was too much excited. A phase of my life was closing to-night, a new one opening to-morrow: impossible to slumber in the interval; I must watch feverishly while the change was being accomplished.

"Miss," said a servant who met me in the lobby, where I was wandering like a troubled spirit, "a person below wishes to see you."

"The carrier, no doubt," I thought, and ran downstairs without inquiry. I was passing the back-parlour or teachers' sitting-room, the door of which was half open, to go to the kitchen, when some one ran out—

"It's her, I am sure!—I could have told her anywhere!" cried the individual who stopped my progress and took my hand.

I looked: I saw a woman attired like a well-dressed servant, matronly, yet still young; very good-looking, with black hair and eyes, and lively complexion.

"Well, who is it?" she asked, in a voice and with a smile I half recognised; "you've not quite forgotten me, I think, Miss Jane?"

In another second I was embracing and kissing her rapturously: "Bessie! Bessie! Bessie!" that was all I said; whereat she half laughed, half cried, and we both went into the parlour. By the fire stood a little fellow of three years old, in plaid frock and trousers.

"That is my little boy," said Bessie directly.

"Then you are married, Bessie?"

"Yes; nearly five years since to Robert Leaven, the coachman; and I've a little girl besides Bobby there, that I've christened Jane."

"And you don't live at Gateshead?"

"I live at the lodge: the old porter has left."

"Well, and how do they all get on? Tell me everything about them, Bessie: but sit down first; and, Bobby, come and sit on my knee, will you?" but Bobby preferred sidling over to his mother.

"You're not grown so very tall, Miss Jane, nor so very stout," continued Mrs. Leaven. "I dare say they've not kept you too well at school: Miss Reed is the head and shoulders taller than you are; and Miss Georgiana would make two of you in breadth."

"Georgiana is handsome, I suppose, Bessie?"

"Very. She went up to London last winter with her mama, and there everybody admired her, and a young lord fell in love with her: but his relations were against the match; and—what do you think?—he and Miss Georgiana made it up to run away; but they were found out and stopped. It was Miss Reed that found them out: I believe she was envious; and now she and her sister lead a cat and dog life together; they are always quarrelling—"

"Well, and what of John Reed?"

"Oh, he is not doing so well as his mama could wish. He went to college, and he got—plucked, I think they call it: and then his uncles wanted him to be a barrister, and study the law: but he is such a dissipated young man, they will never make much of him, I think."

"What does he look like?"

"He is very tall: some people call him a fine-looking young man; but he has such thick lips."

"And Mrs. Reed?"

"Missis looks stout and well enough in the face, but I think she's not quite easy in her mind: Mr. John's conduct does not please her—he spends a deal of money."

"Did she send you here, Bessie?"

"No, indeed: but I have long wanted to see you, and when I heard that there had been a letter from you, and that you were going to another part of the country, I thought I'd just set of, and get a look at you before you were quite out of my reach."

"I am afraid you are disappointed in me, Bessie." I said this laughing: I perceived that Bessie's glance, though it expressed regard, did in no shape denote admiration.

"No, Miss Jane, not exactly: you are genteel enough; you look like a lady, and it is as much as ever I expected of you: you were no beauty as a child."

I smiled at Bessie's frank answer: I felt that it was correct, but I confess I was not quite indifferent to its import: at eighteen most people wish to please, and the conviction that they have not an exterior likely to second that desire brings anything but gratification.

"I dare say you are clever, though," continued Bessie, by way of solace. "What can you do? Can you play on the piano?"

"A little."

There was one in the room; Bessie went and opened it, and then asked me to sit down and give her a tune: I played a waltz or two, and she was charmed.

"The Miss Reeds could not play as well!" said she exultingly. "I always said you would surpass them in learning: and can you draw?"

"That is one of my paintings over the chimney-piece." It was a landscape in water colours, of which I had made a present to the superintendent, in acknowledgment of her obliging mediation with the committee on my behalf, and which she had framed and glazed.

"Well, that is beautiful, Miss Jane! It is as fine a picture as any Miss Reed's drawing-master could paint, let alone the young ladies themselves, who could not come near it: and have you learnt French?"

"Yes, Bessie, I can both read it and speak it."

"And you can work on muslin and canvas?"

"I can."

"Oh, you are quite a lady, Miss Jane! I knew you would be: you will get on whether your relations notice you or not. There was something I wanted to ask you. Have you ever heard anything from your father's kinsfolk, the Eyres?"

"Never in my life."

"Well, you know Missis always said they were poor and quite despicable: and they may be poor; but I believe they are as much gentry as the Reeds are; for one day, nearly seven years ago, a Mr. Eyre came to Gateshead and wanted to see you; Missis said you were it school fifty miles off; he seemed so much disappointed, for he could not stay: he was going on a voyage to a foreign country, and the ship was to sail from London in a day or two. He looked quite a gentleman, and I believe he was your father's brother."

"What foreign country was he going to, Bessie?"

"An island thousands of miles off, where they make wine—the butler did tell me—"

"Madeira?" I suggested.

"Yes, that is it—that is the very word."

"So he went?"

"Yes; he did not stay many minutes in the house: Missis was very high with him; she called him afterwards a 'sneaking tradesman.' My Robert believes he was a wine-merchant."

"Very likely," I returned; "or perhaps clerk or agent to a wine-merchant."

Bessie and I conversed about old times an hour longer, and then she was obliged to leave me: I saw her again for a few minutes the next morning at Lowton, while I was waiting for the coach. We parted finally at the door of the Brocklehurst Arms there: each went her separate way; she set off for the brow of Lowood Fell to meet the conveyance which was to take her back to Gateshead, I mounted the vehicle which was to bear me to new duties and a new life in the unknown environs of Millcote.

Chapter XI

A new chapter in a novel is something like a new scene in a play; and when I draw up the curtain this time, reader, you must fancy you see a room in the George Inn at Millcote, with such large figured papering on the walls as inn rooms have; such a carpet, such furniture, such ornaments on the mantelpiece, such prints, including a portrait of George the Third, and another of the Prince of Wales, and a representation of the death of Wolfe. All this is visible to you by the light of an oil lamp hanging from the ceiling, and by that of an excellent fire, near which I sit in my cloak and bonnet; my muff and umbrella lie on the table, and I am warming away the numbness and chill contracted by sixteen hours' exposure to the rawness of an October day: I left Lowton at four o'clock a.m., and the Millcote town clock is now just striking eight.

Reader, though I look comfortably accommodated, I am not very tranquil in my mind. I thought when the coach stopped here there would be some one to meet me; I looked anxiously round as I descended the wooden steps the "boots" placed for my convenience, expecting to hear my name pronounced, and to see some description of carriage waiting to convey me to Thornfield. Nothing of the sort was visible; and when I asked a waiter if any one had been to inquire after a Miss Eyre, I was answered in the negative: so I had no resource but to request to be shown into a private room: and here I am waiting, while all sorts of doubts and fears are troubling my thoughts.

It is a very strange sensation to inexperienced youth to feel itself quite alone in the world, cut adrift from every connection, uncertain whether the port to which it is bound can be reached, and prevented by many impediments from returning to that it has quitted. The charm of adventure sweetens that sensation, the glow of pride warms it; but then the throb of fear disturbs it; and fear with me became predominant when half-an-hour elapsed and still I was alone. I bethought myself to ring the bell.

"Is there a place in this neighbourhood called Thornfield?" I asked of the waiter who answered the summons.

"Thornfield? I don't know, ma'am; I'll inquire at the bar." He vanished, but reappeared instantly—

"Is your name Eyre, Miss?"

"Yes."

"Person here waiting for you."

I jumped up, took my muff and umbrella, and hastened into the inn-passage: a man was standing by the open door, and in the lamp-lit street I dimly saw a one-horse conveyance.

"This will be your luggage, I suppose?" said the man rather abruptly when he saw me, pointing to my trunk in the passage.

"Yes." He hoisted it on to the vehicle, which was a sort of car, and then I got in; before he shut me up, I asked him how far it was to Thornfield.

"A matter of six miles."

"How long shall we be before we get there?"

"Happen an hour and a half."

He fastened the car door, climbed to his own seat outside, and we set off. Our progress was leisurely, and gave me ample time to reflect; I was content to be at length so near the end of my journey; and as I leaned back in the comfortable though not elegant conveyance, I meditated much at my ease.

"I suppose," thought I, "judging from the plainness of the servant and carriage, Mrs. Fairfax is not a very dashing person: so much the better; I never lived amongst fine people but once, and I was very miserable with them. I wonder if she lives alone except this little girl; if so, and if she is in any degree amiable, I shall surely be able to get on with her; I will do my best; it is a pity that doing one's best does not always answer. At Lowood, indeed, I took that resolution, kept it, and succeeded in pleasing; but with Mrs. Reed, I remember my best was always spurned with scorn. I pray God Mrs. Fairfax may not turn out a second Mrs. Reed; but if she does, I am not bound to stay with her! let the worst come to the worst, I can advertise again. How far are we on our road now, I wonder?"

I let down the window and looked out; Millcote was behind us; judging by the number of its lights, it seemed a place of considerable magnitude, much larger than Lowton. We were now, as far as I could see, on a sort of common; but there were houses scattered all over the district; I felt we were in a different region to Lowood, more populous, less picturesque; more stirring, less romantic.

The roads were heavy, the night misty; my conductor let his horse walk all the way, and the hour and a half extended, I verify believe, to two hours; at last he turned in his seat and said—

"You're noan so far fro' Thornfield now."

Again I looked out: we were passing a church; I saw its low broad tower against the sky, and its bell was tolling a quarter; I saw a narrow galaxy of lights too, on a hillside, marking a village or hamlet. About ten minutes after, the driver got down and opened a pair of gates: we passed through, and they clashed to behind us. We now slowly ascended a drive, and came upon the long front of a house: candlelight gleamed from one curtained bow-window; all the rest were dark. The car stopped at the front door; it was opened by a maid-servant; I alighted and went in.

"Will you walk this way, ma'am?" said the girl; and I followed her across a square hall with high doors all round: she ushered me into a room whose double illumination of fire and candle at first dazzled me, contrasting as it did with the darkness to which my eyes had been for two hours inured; when I could see, however, a cosy and agreeable picture presented itself to my view.

A snug small room; a round table by a cheerful fire; an arm-chair high-backed and old-fashioned, wherein sat the neatest imaginable little elderly lady, in widow's cap, black silk gown, and snowy muslin apron; exactly like what I had fancied Mrs. Fairfax, only less stately and milder looking. She was occupied in knitting; a large cat sat demurely at her feet; nothing in short was wanting to complete the beau-ideal of domestic comfort. A more reassuring introduction for a new governess could scarcely be conceived; there was no grandeur to overwhelm, no stateliness to embarrass; and then, as I entered, the old lady got up and promptly and kindly came forward to meet me.

"How do you do, my dear? I am afraid you have had a tedious ride; John drives so slowly; you must be cold, come to the fire."

"Mrs. Fairfax, I suppose?" said I.

"Yes, you are right: do sit down."

She conducted me to her own chair, and then began to remove my shawl and untie my bonnet-strings; I begged she would not give herself so much trouble.

"Oh, it is no trouble; I dare say your own hands are almost numbed with cold. Leah, make a little hot negus and cut a sandwich or two: here are the keys of the storeroom."

And she produced from her pocket a most housewifely bunch of keys, and delivered them to the servant.

"Now, then, draw nearer to the fire," she continued. "You've brought your luggage with you, haven't you, my dear?"

"Yes, ma'am."

"I'll see it carried into your room," she said, and bustled out.

"She treats me like a visitor," thought I. "I little expected such a reception; I anticipated only coldness and stiffness: this is not like what I have heard of the treatment of governesses; but I must not exult too soon."

She returned; with her own hands cleared her knitting apparatus and a book or two from the table, to make room for the tray which Leah now brought, and then herself handed me the refreshments. I felt rather confused at being the object of more attention than I had ever before received, and, that too, shown by my employer and superior; but as she did not herself seem to consider she was doing anything out of her place, I thought it better to take her civilities quietly.

"Shall I have the pleasure of seeing Miss Fairfax to-night?" I asked, when I had partaken of what she offered me.

"What did you say, my dear? I am a little deaf," returned the good lady, approaching her ear to my mouth.

I repeated the question more distinctly.

"Miss Fairfax? Oh, you mean Miss Varens! Varens is the name of your future pupil."

"Indeed! Then she is not your daughter?"

"No,—I have no family."

I should have followed up my first inquiry, by asking in what way Miss Varens was connected with her; but I recollected it was not polite to ask too many questions: besides, I was sure to hear in time.

"I am so glad," she continued, as she sat down opposite to me, and took the cat on her knee; "I am so glad you are come; it will be quite pleasant living here now with a companion. To be sure it is pleasant at any time; for Thornfield is a fine old hall, rather neglected of late years perhaps, but still it is a respectable place; yet you know in winter-time one feels dreary quite alone in the best quarters. I say alone—Leah is a nice girl to be sure, and John and his wife are very decent people; but then you see they are only servants, and one can't converse with them on terms of equality: one must keep them at due distance, for fear of losing one's authority. I'm sure last winter (it was a very severe one, if you recollect, and when it did not snow, it rained and blew), not a creature but the butcher and postman came to the house, from November till February; and I really got quite melancholy with sitting night after night alone; I had Leah in to read to me sometimes; but I don't think the poor girl liked the task much: she felt it confining. In spring and summer one got on better: sunshine and long days make such a difference; and then, just at the commencement of this autumn, little Adela Varens came and her nurse: a child makes a house alive all at once; and now you are here I shall be quite gay."

My heart really warmed to the worthy lady as I heard her talk; and I drew my chair a little nearer to her, and expressed my sincere wish that she might find my company as agreeable as she anticipated.

"But I'll not keep you sitting up late to-night," said she; "it is on the stroke of twelve now, and you have been travelling all day: you must feel tired. If you have got your feet well warmed, I'll show you your bedroom. I've had the room next to mine prepared for you; it is only a small apartment, but I thought you would like it better than one of the large front chambers: to be sure they have finer furniture, but they are so dreary and solitary, I never sleep in them myself."

I thanked her for her considerate choice, and as I really felt fatigued with my long journey, expressed my readiness to retire. She took her candle, and I followed her from the room. First she went to see if the hall-door was fastened; having taken the key from the lock, she led the way upstairs. The steps and banisters were of oak; the staircase window was high and latticed; both it and the long gallery into which the bedroom doors opened looked as if they belonged to a church rather than a house. A very chill and vault-like air pervaded the stairs and gallery, suggesting cheerless ideas of space and solitude; and I was glad, when finally ushered into my chamber, to find it of small dimensions, and furnished in ordinary, modern style.

When Mrs. Fairfax had bidden me a kind good-night, and I had fastened my door, gazed leisurely round, and in some measure effaced the eerie impression made by that wide hall, that dark and spacious staircase, and that long, cold gallery, by the livelier aspect of my little room, I remembered that, after a day of bodily fatigue and mental anxiety, I was now at last in safe haven. The impulse of gratitude swelled my heart, and I knelt down at the bedside, and offered up thanks where thanks were due; not forgetting, ere I rose, to implore aid on my further path, and the power of meriting the kindness which seemed so frankly offered me before it was earned. My couch had no thorns in it that night; my solitary room no fears. At once weary and content, I slept soon and soundly: when I awoke it was broad day.

The chamber looked such a bright little place to me as the sun shone in between the gay blue chintz window curtains, showing papered walls and a carpeted floor, so unlike the bare planks and stained plaster of Lowood, that my spirits rose at the view. Externals have a great effect on the young: I thought that a fairer era of life was beginning for me, one that was to have its flowers and pleasures, as well as its thorns and toils. My faculties, roused by the change of scene, the new field offered to hope, seemed all astir. I cannot precisely define what they expected, but it was something pleasant: not perhaps that day or that month, but at an indefinite future period.

I rose; I dressed myself with care: obliged to be plain—for I had no article of attire that was not made with extreme simplicity—I was still by nature solicitous to be neat. It was not my habit to be disregardful of appearance or careless of the impression I made: on the contrary, I ever wished to look as well as I could, and to please as much as my want of beauty would permit. I sometimes regretted that I was not handsomer; I sometimes wished to have rosy cheeks, a straight nose, and small cherry mouth; I desired to be tall, stately, and finely developed in figure; I felt it a misfortune that I was so little, so pale, and had features so irregular and so marked. And why had I these aspirations and these regrets? It would be difficult to say: I could not then distinctly say it to myself; yet I had a reason, and a logical, natural reason too. However, when I had brushed my hair very smooth, and put on my black frock—which, Quakerlike as it was, at least had the merit of fitting to a nicety—and adjusted my clean white tucker, I thought I should do respectably enough to appear before

Mrs. Fairfax, and that my new pupil would not at least recoil from me with antipathy. Having opened my chamber window, and seen that I left all things straight and neat on the toilet table, I ventured forth.

Traversing the long and matted gallery, I descended the slippery steps of oak; then I gained the hall: I halted there a minute; I looked at some pictures on the walls (one, I remember, represented a grim man in a cuirass, and one a lady with powdered hair and a pearl necklace), at a bronze lamp pendent from the ceiling, at a great clock whose case was of oak curiously carved, and ebon black with time and rubbing. Everything appeared very stately and imposing to me; but then I was so little accustomed to grandeur. The hall-door, which was half of glass, stood open; I stepped over the threshold. It was a fine autumn morning; the early sun shone serenely on embrowned groves and still green fields; advancing on to the lawn, I looked up and surveyed the front of the mansion. It was three storeys high, of proportions not vast, though considerable: a gentleman's manor-house, not a nobleman's seat: battlements round the top gave it a picturesque look. Its grey front stood out well from the background of a rookery, whose cawing tenants were now on the wing: they flew over the lawn and grounds to alight in a great meadow, from which these were separated by a sunk fence, and where an array of mighty old thorn trees, strong, knotty, and broad as oaks, at once explained the etymology of the mansion's designation. Farther off were hills: not so lofty as those round Lowood, nor so craggy, nor so like barriers of separation from the living world; but yet quiet and lonely hills enough, and seeming to embrace Thornfield with a seclusion I had not expected to find existent so near the stirring locality of Millcote. A little hamlet, whose roofs were blent with trees, straggled up the side of one of these hills; the church of the district stood nearer Thornfield: its old tower-top looked over a knoll between the house and gates.

I was yet enjoying the calm prospect and pleasant fresh air, yet listening with delight to the cawing of the rooks, yet surveying the wide, hoary front of the hall, and thinking what a great place it was for one lonely little dame like Mrs. Fairfax to inhabit, when that lady appeared at the door.

"What! out already?" said she. "I see you are an early riser." I went up to her, and was received with an affable kiss and shake of the hand.

"How do you like Thornfield?" she asked. I told her I liked it very much.

"Yes," she said, "it is a pretty place; but I fear it will be getting out of order, unless Mr. Rochester should take it into his head to come and reside here permanently; or, at least, visit it rather oftener: great houses and fine grounds require the presence of the proprietor."

"Mr. Rochester!" I exclaimed. "Who is he?"

"The owner of Thornfield," she responded quietly. "Did you not know he was called Rochester?"

Of course I did not—I had never heard of him before; but the old lady seemed to regard his existence as a universally understood fact, with which everybody must be acquainted by instinct.

"I thought," I continued, "Thornfield belonged to you."

"To me? Bless you, child; what an idea! To me! I am only the housekeeper—the manager. To be sure I am distantly related to the Rochesters by the mother's side, or at least my husband was; he was a clergyman, incumbent of Hay—that little village yonder on the hill—and that church near the gates was his. The present Mr. Rochester's mother was a Fairfax, and second cousin to my husband: but I never presume on the connection—in fact, it is nothing to me; I consider myself quite in the light of an ordinary housekeeper: my employer is always civil, and I expect nothing more."

"And the little girl—my pupil!"

"She is Mr. Rochester's ward; he commissioned me to find a governess for her. He intended to have her brought up in-shire, I believe. Here she comes, with her 'bonne,' as she calls her nurse." The enigma then was explained: this affable and kind little widow was no great dame; but a dependant like myself. I did not like her the worse for that; on the contrary, I felt better pleased than ever. The equality between her and me was real; not the mere result of condescension on her part: so much the better—my position was all the freer.

As I was meditating on this discovery, a little girl, followed by her attendant, came running up the lawn. I looked at my pupil, who did not at first appear to notice me: she was quite a child, perhaps seven or eight years old, slightly built, with a pale, small-featured face, and a redundancy of hair falling in curls to her waist.

"Good morning, Miss Adela," said Mrs. Fairfax. "Come and speak to the lady who is to teach you, and to make you a clever woman some day." She approached.

"C'est le ma gouverante!" said she, pointing to me, and addressing her nurse; who answered—

"Mais oui, certainement."

"Are they foreigners?" I inquired, amazed at hearing the French language.

"The nurse is a foreigner, and Adela was born on the Continent; and, I believe, never left it till within six months ago. When she first came here she could speak no English; now she can make shift to talk it a little: I don't understand her, she mixes it so with French; but you will make out her meaning very well, I dare say."

Fortunately I had had the advantage of being taught French by a French lady; and as I had always made a point of conversing with Madame Pierrot as often as I could, and had besides, during the last seven years, learnt a portion of French by heart daily—applying myself to take pains with my accent, and imitating as closely as possible the pronunciation of my teacher, I had acquired a certain degree of readiness and correctness in the language, and was not likely to be much at a loss with Mademoiselle Adela. She came and shook hand with me when she heard that I was her governess; and as I led her in to breakfast, I addressed some phrases to her in her own tongue: she replied briefly at first, but after we were seated at the table, and she had examined me some ten minutes with her large hazel eyes, she suddenly commenced chattering fluently.

"Ah!" cried she, in French, "you speak my language as well as Mr. Rochester does: I can talk to you as I can to him, and so can Sophie. She will be glad: nobody here understands her: Madame Fairfax is all English. Sophie is my nurse; she came with me over the sea in a great ship with a chimney that smoked—how it did smoke!—and I was sick, and so was Sophie, and so was Mr. Rochester. Mr. Rochester lay down on a sofa in a pretty room called the salon, and Sophie and I had little beds in another place. I nearly fell out of mine; it was like a shelf. And Mademoiselle—what is your name?"

"Eyre—Jane Eyre."

"Aire? Bah! I cannot say it. Well, our ship stopped in the morning, before it was quite daylight, at a great city—a huge city, with very dark houses and all smoky; not at all like the pretty clean town I came from; and Mr. Rochester carried me in his arms over a plank to the land, and Sophie came after, and we all got into a coach, which took us to a beautiful large house, larger than this and finer, called an hotel. We stayed there nearly a week: I and Sophie used to walk every day in a great green place full of trees, called the Park; and there were many children there besides me, and a pond with beautiful birds in it, that I fed with crumbs."

"Can you understand her when she runs on so fast?" asked Mrs. Fairfax.

I understood her very well, for I had been accustomed to the fluent tongue of Madame Pierrot.

"I wish," continued the good lady, "you would ask her a question or two about her parents: I wonder if she remembers them?"

"Adele," I inquired, "with whom did you live when you were in that pretty clean town you spoke of?"

"I lived long ago with mama; but she is gone to the Holy Virgin. Mama used to teach me to dance and sing, and to say verses. A great many gentlemen and ladies came to see mama, and I used to dance before them, or to sit on their knees and sing to them: I liked it. Shall I let you hear me sing now?"

She had finished her breakfast, so I permitted her to give a specimen of her accomplishments. Descending from her chair, she came and placed herself on my knee; then, folding her little hands demurely before her, shaking back her curls and lifting her eyes to the ceiling, she commenced singing a song from some opera. It was the strain of a forsaken lady, who, after bewailing the perfidy of her lover, calls pride to her aid; desires her attendant to deck her in her brightest jewels and richest robes, and resolves to meet the false one that night at a ball, and prove to him, by the gaiety of her demeanour, how little his desertion has affected her.

The subject seemed strangely chosen for an infant singer; but I suppose the point of the exhibition lay in hearing the notes of love and jealousy warbled with the lisp of childhood; and in very bad taste that point was: at least I thought so.

Adele sang the canzonette tunefully enough, and with the naivete of her age. This achieved, she jumped from my knee and said, "Now, Mademoiselle, I will repeat you some poetry."

Assuming an attitude, she began, "La Ligue des Rats: fable de La Fontaine." She then declaimed the little piece with an attention to punctuation and emphasis, a flexibility of voice and an appropriateness of gesture, very unusual indeed at her age, and which proved she had been carefully trained.

"Was it your mama who taught you that piece?" I asked.

"Yes, and she just used to say it in this way: 'Qu' avez vous donc? lui dit un de ces rats; parlez!' She made me lift my hand—so—to remind me to raise my voice at the question. Now shall I dance for you?"

"No, that will do: but after your mama went to the Holy Virgin, as you say, with whom did you live then?"

"With Madame Frederic and her husband: she took care of me, but she is nothing related to me. I think she is poor, for she had not so fine a house as mama. I was not long there. Mr. Rochester asked me if I would like to go and live with him in England, and I said yes; for I knew Mr. Rochester before I knew Madame Frederic, and he was always kind to me and gave me pretty dresses and toys: but you see he has not kept his word, for he has brought me to England, and now he is gone back again himself, and I never see him."

After breakfast, Adele and I withdrew to the library, which room, it appears, Mr. Rochester had directed should be used as the schoolroom. Most of the books were locked up behind glass doors; but there was one bookcase left open containing everything that could be needed in the way of elementary works, and several volumes of light literature, poetry, biography, travels, a few romances, &c. I suppose he had considered that these were all the governess would require for her private perusal; and, indeed, they contented me amply for the present; compared with the scanty pickings I had now and then been able to glean at Lowood, they seemed to offer an abundant harvest of entertainment and information. In this room, too, there was a cabinet piano, quite new and of superior tone; also an easel for painting and a pair of globes.

I found my pupil sufficiently docile, though disinclined to apply: she had not been used to regular occupation of any kind. I felt it would be injudicious to confine her too much at first; so, when I had talked to her a great deal, and got her to learn a little, and when the morning had advanced to noon, I allowed her to return to her nurse. I then proposed to occupy myself till dinner-time in drawing some little sketches for her use.

As I was going upstairs to fetch my portfolio and pencils, Mrs. Fairfax called to me: "Your morning school-hours are over now, I suppose," said she. She was in a room the folding-doors of which stood open: I went in when she addressed me. It was a large, stately apartment, with purple chairs and curtains, a Turkey carpet, walnut-panelled walls, one vast window rich in slanted glass, and a lofty ceiling, nobly moulded. Mrs. Fairfax was dusting some vases of fine purple spar, which stood on a sideboard.

"What a beautiful room!" I exclaimed, as I looked round; for I had never before seen any half so imposing.

"Yes; this is the dining-room. I have just opened the window, to let in a little air and sunshine; for everything gets so damp in apartments that are seldom inhabited; the drawing-room yonder feels like a vault."

She pointed to a wide arch corresponding to the window, and hung like it with a Tyrian-dyed curtain, now looped up. Mounting to it by two broad steps, and looking through, I thought I caught a glimpse of a fairy place, so bright to my novice-eyes appeared the view beyond. Yet it was merely a very pretty drawing-room, and within it a boudoir, both spread with white carpets, on which seemed laid brilliant garlands of flowers; both ceiled with snowy mouldings of white grapes and vine-leaves, beneath which glowed in rich contrast crimson couches and ottomans; while the ornaments on the pale Pariain mantelpiece were of sparkling Bohemian glass, ruby red; and between the windows large mirrors repeated the general blending of snow and fire.

"In what order you keep these rooms, Mrs. Fairfax!" said I. "No dust, no canvas coverings: except that the air feels chilly, one would think they were inhabited daily."

"Why, Miss Eyre, though Mr. Rochester's visits here are rare, they are always sudden and unexpected; and as I observed that it put him out to find everything swathed up, and to have a bustle of arrangement on his arrival, I thought it best to keep the rooms in readiness."

"Is Mr. Rochester an exacting, fastidious sort of man?"

"Not particularly so; but he has a gentleman's tastes and habits, and he expects to have things managed in conformity to them."

"Do you like him? Is he generally liked?"

"Oh, yes; the family have always been respected here. Almost all the land in this neighbourhood, as far as you can see, has belonged to the Rochesters time out of mind."

"Well, but, leaving his land out of the question, do you like him? Is he liked for himself?"

"I have no cause to do otherwise than like him; and I believe he is considered a just and liberal landlord by his tenants: but he has never lived much amongst them."

"But has he no peculiarities? What, in short, is his character?"

"Oh! his character is unimpeachable, I suppose. He is rather peculiar, perhaps: he has travelled a great deal, and seen a great deal of the world, I should think. I dare say he is clever, but I never had much conversation with him."

"In what way is he peculiar?"

"I don't know—it is not easy to describe—nothing striking, but you feel it when he speaks to you; you cannot be always sure whether he is in jest or earnest, whether he is pleased or the contrary; you don't thoroughly understand him, in short—at least, I don't: but it is of no consequence, he is a very good master."

This was all the account I got from Mrs. Fairfax of her employer and mine. There are people who seem to have no notion of sketching a character, or observing and describing salient points, either in persons or things: the good lady evidently belonged to this class; my queries puzzled, but did not draw her out. Mr. Rochester was Mr. Rochester in her eyes; a gentleman, a landed proprietor—nothing more: she inquired and searched no further, and evidently wondered at my wish to gain a more definite notion of his identity.

When we left the dining-room, she proposed to show me over the rest of the house; and I followed her upstairs and downstairs, admiring as I went; for all was well arranged and handsome. The large front chambers I thought especially grand: and some of the third-storey rooms, though dark and low, were interesting from their air of antiquity. The furniture once appropriated to the lower apartments had from time to time been removed here, as fashions changed: and the imperfect light entering by their narrow casement showed bedsteads of a hundred years old; chests in oak or walnut, looking, with their strange carvings of palm branches and cherubs' heads, like types of the Hebrew ark; rows of venerable chairs, high-backed and narrow; stools still more antiquated, on whose cushioned tops were yet apparent traces of half-effaced embroideries, wrought by fingers that for two generations had been coffin-dust. All these relics gave to the third storey of Thornfield Hall the aspect of a home of the past: a shrine of memory. I liked the hush, the gloom, the quaintness of these retreats in the day; but I by no means coveted a night's repose on one of those wide and heavy beds: shut in, some of them, with doors of oak; shaded, others, with wrought old English hangings crusted with thick work, portraying effigies of strange flowers, and stranger birds, and strangest human beings,—all which would have looked strange, indeed, by the pallid gleam of moonlight.

"Do the servants sleep in these rooms?" I asked.

"No; they occupy a range of smaller apartments to the back; no one ever sleeps here: one would almost say that, if there were a ghost at Thornfield Hall, this would be its haunt."

"So I think: you have no ghost, then?"

"None that I ever heard of," returned Mrs. Fairfax, smiling.

"Nor any traditions of one? no legends or ghost stories?"

"I believe not. And yet it is said the Rochesters have been rather a violent than a quiet race in their time: perhaps, though, that is the reason they rest tranquilly in their graves now."

"Yes—'after life's fitful fever they sleep well,'" I muttered. "Where are you going now, Mrs. Fairfax?" for she was moving away.

"On to the leads; will you come and see the view from thence?" I followed still, up a very narrow staircase to the attics, and thence by a ladder and through a trap-door to the roof of the hall. I was now on a level with the crow colony, and could see into their nests. Leaning over the battlements and looking far down, I surveyed the grounds laid out like a map: the bright and velvet lawn closely girdling the grey base of the mansion; the field, wide as a park, dotted with its ancient timber; the wood, dun and sere, divided by a path visibly overgrown, greener with moss than the trees were with foliage; the church at the gates, the road, the tranquil hills, all reposing in the autumn day's sun; the horizon bounded by a propitious sky, azure, marbled with pearly white. No feature in the scene was extraordinary, but all was pleasing. When I turned from it and repassed the trap-door, I could scarcely see my way down the ladder; the attic seemed black as a vault compared with that arch of blue air to which I had been looking up, and to that sunlit scene of grove, pasture, and green hill, of which the hall was the centre, and over which I had been gazing with delight.

Mrs. Fairfax stayed behind a moment to fasten the trap-door; I, by drift of groping, found the outlet from the attic, and proceeded to descend the narrow garret staircase. I lingered in the long passage to which this led, separating the front and back rooms of the third storey: narrow, low, and dim, with only one little window at the far end, and looking, with its two rows of small black doors all shut, like a corridor in some Bluebeard's castle.

While I paced softly on, the last sound I expected to hear in so still a region, a laugh, struck my ear. It was a curious laugh; distinct, formal, mirthless. I stopped: the sound ceased, only for an instant; it began again, louder: for at first, though distinct, it was very low. It passed off in a clamorous peal that seemed to wake an echo in every lonely chamber; though it originated but in one, and I could have pointed out the door whence the accents issued.

"Mrs. Fairfax!" I called out: for I now heard her descending the great stairs. "Did you hear that loud laugh? Who is it?"

"Some of the servants, very likely," she answered: "perhaps Grace Poole."

"Did you hear it?" I again inquired.

"Yes, plainly: I often hear her: she sews in one of these rooms. Sometimes Leah is with her; they are frequently noisy together."

The laugh was repeated in its low, syllabic tone, and terminated in an odd murmur.

"Grace!" exclaimed Mrs. Fairfax.

I really did not expect any Grace to answer; for the laugh was as tragic, as preternatural a laugh as any I ever heard; and, but that it was high noon, and that no circumstance of ghostliness accompanied the curious cachinnation; but that neither scene nor season favoured fear, I should have been superstitiously afraid. However, the event showed me I was a fool for entertaining a sense even of surprise.

The door nearest me opened, and a servant came out,—a woman of between thirty and forty; a set, square-made figure, red-haired, and with a hard, plain face: any apparition less romantic or less ghostly could scarcely be conceived.

"Too much noise, Grace," said Mrs. Fairfax. "Remember directions!" Grace curtseyed silently and went in.

"She is a person we have to sew and assist Leah in her house-maid's work," continued the widow; "not altogether unobjectionable in some points, but she does well enough. By-the-bye, how have you got on with your new pupil this morning?"

The conversation, thus turned on Adele, continued till we reached the light and cheerful region below. Adele came running to meet us in the hall, exclaiming—

"Mesdames, vous etes servies!" adding, "J'ai bien faim, moi!"

We found dinner ready, and waiting for us in Mrs. Fairfax's room.

Chapter XII

The promise of a smooth career, which my first calm introduction to Thornfield Hall seemed to pledge, was not belied on a longer acquaintance with the place and its inmates. Mrs. Fairfax turned out to be what she appeared, a placid-tempered, kind-natured woman, of competent education and average intelligence. My pupil was a lively child, who had been spoilt and indulged, and therefore was sometimes wayward; but as she was committed entirely to my care, and no injudicious interference from any quarter ever thwarted my plans for her improvement, she soon forgot her little freaks, and became obedient and teachable. She had no great talents, no marked traits of character, no peculiar development of feeling or taste which raised her one inch above the ordinary level of childhood; but neither had she any deficiency or vice which sunk her below it. She made reasonable progress, entertained for me a vivacious, though perhaps not very profound, affection; and by her simplicity, gay prattle, and efforts to please, inspired me, in return, with a degree of attachment sufficient to make us both content in each other's society.

This, par parenthese, will be thought cool language by persons who entertain solemn doctrines about the angelic nature of children, and the duty of those charged with their education to conceive for them an idolatrous devotion: but I am not writing to flatter parental egotism, to echo cant, or prop up humbug; I am merely telling the truth. I felt a conscientious solicitude for Adele's welfare and progress, and a quiet liking for her little self: just as I cherished towards Mrs. Fairfax a thankfulness for her kindness, and a pleasure in her society proportionate to the tranquil regard she had for me, and the moderation of her mind and character.

Anybody may blame me who likes, when I add further, that, now and then, when I took a walk by myself in the grounds; when I went down to the gates and looked through them along the road; or when, while Adele played with her nurse, and Mrs. Fairfax made jellies in the storeroom, I climbed the three staircases, raised the trap-door of the attic, and having reached the leads, looked out afar over sequestered field and hill, and along dim sky-line—that then I longed for a power of vision which might overpass that limit; which might reach the busy world, towns, regions full of life I had heard of but never seen—that then I desired more of practical experience than I possessed; more of intercourse with my kind, of acquaintance with variety of character, than was here within my reach. I valued what was good in Mrs. Fairfax, and what was good in Adele; but I believed in the existence of other and more vivid kinds of goodness, and what I believed in I wished to behold.

Who blames me? Many, no doubt; and I shall be called discontented. I could not help it: the restlessness was in my nature; it agitated me to pain sometimes. Then my sole relief was to walk along the corridor of the third storey, backwards and forwards, safe in the silence and solitude of the spot, and allow my mind's eye to dwell on whatever bright visions rose before it—and, certainly, they were many and glowing; to let my heart be heaved by the exultant movement, which, while it swelled it in trouble, expanded it with life; and, best of all, to open my inward ear to a tale that was never ended—a tale my imagination created, and narrated continuously; quickened with all of incident, life, fire, feeling, that I desired and had not in my actual existence.

It is in vain to say human beings ought to be satisfied with tranquillity: they must have action; and they will make it if they cannot find it. Millions are condemned to a stiller doom than mine, and millions are in silent revolt against their lot. Nobody knows how many rebellions besides political rebellions ferment in the masses of life which people earth. Women are supposed to be very calm generally: but women feel just as men feel; they need exercise for their faculties, and a field for their efforts, as much as their brothers do; they suffer from too rigid a restraint, too absolute a stagnation, precisely as men would suffer; and it is narrow-minded in their more privileged fellow-creatures to say that they ought to confine themselves to making puddings and knitting stockings, to playing on the piano and embroidering bags. It is thoughtless to condemn them, or laugh at them, if they seek to do more or learn more than custom has pronounced necessary for their sex.

When thus alone, I not unfrequently heard Grace Poole's laugh: the same peal, the same low, slow ha! ha! which, when first heard, had thrilled me: I heard, too, her eccentric murmurs; stranger than her laugh. There were days when she was quite silent; but there were others when I could not account for the sounds she made. Sometimes I saw her: she would come out of her room with a basin, or a plate, or a tray in her hand, go down to the kitchen and shortly return, generally (oh, romantic reader, forgive me for telling the plain truth!) bearing a pot of porter. Her appearance always acted as a damper to the curiosity raised by her oral oddities: hard-featured and staid, she had no point to which interest could attach. I made some attempts to draw her into conversation, but she seemed a person of few words: a monosyllabic reply usually cut short every effort of that sort.

The other members of the household, viz., John and his wife, Leah the housemaid, and Sophie the French nurse, were decent people; but in no respect remarkable; with Sophie I used to talk French, and sometimes I asked her questions about her native country; but she was not of a descriptive or narrative turn, and generally gave such vapid and confused answers as were calculated rather to check than encourage inquiry.

October, November, December passed away. One afternoon in January, Mrs. Fairfax had begged a holiday for Adele, because she had a cold; and, as Adele seconded the request with an ardour that reminded me how precious occasional holidays had been to me in my own childhood, I accorded it, deeming that I did well in showing pliability on the point. It was a fine, calm day, though very cold; I was tired of sitting still in the library through a whole long morning: Mrs. Fairfax had just written a letter which was waiting to be posted, so I put on my bonnet and cloak and volunteered to carry it to Hay; the distance, two miles, would be a pleasant winter afternoon walk. Having seen Adele comfortably seated in her little chair by Mrs. Fairfax's parlour fireside, and given her her best wax doll (which I usually kept enveloped in silver paper in a drawer) to play with, and a story-book for change of amusement; and having replied to her "Revenez bientot, ma bonne amie, ma chere Mdlle. Jeannette," with a kiss I set out.

The ground was hard, the air was still, my road was lonely; I walked fast till I got warm, and then I walked slowly to enjoy and analyse the species of pleasure brooding for me in the hour and situation. It was three o'clock; the church bell tolled as I passed under the belfry: the charm of the hour lay in its approaching dimness, in the low-gliding and pale-beaming sun. I was a mile from Thornfield, in a lane noted for wild roses in summer, for nuts and blackberries in autumn, and even now possessing a few coral treasures in hips and haws, but whose best winter delight lay in its utter solitude and leafless repose. If a breath of air stirred, it made no sound here; for there was not a holly, not an evergreen to rustle, and the stripped hawthorn and hazel bushes were as still as the white, worn stones which causewayed the middle of the path. Far and wide, on each side, there were only fields, where no cattle now browsed; and the little brown birds, which stirred occasionally in the hedge, looked like single russet leaves that had forgotten to drop.

This lane inclined up-hill all the way to Hay; having reached the middle, I sat down on a stile which led thence into a field. Gathering my mantle about me, and sheltering my hands in my muff, I did not feel the cold, though it froze keenly; as was attested by a sheet of ice covering the causeway, where a little brooklet, now congealed, had overflowed after a rapid thaw some days since. From my seat I could look down on Thornfield: the grey and battlemented hall was the principal object in the vale below me; its woods and dark rookery rose against the west. I lingered till the sun went down amongst the trees, and sank crimson and clear behind them. I then turned eastward.

On the hill-top above me sat the rising moon; pale yet as a cloud, but brightening momentarily, she looked over Hay, which, half lost in trees, sent up a blue smoke from its few chimneys: it was yet a mile distant, but in the absolute hush I could hear plainly its thin murmurs of life. My ear, too, felt the flow of currents; in what dales and depths I could not tell: but there were many hills beyond Hay, and doubtless many becks threading their passes. That evening calm betrayed alike the tinkle of the nearest streams, the sough of the most remote.

A rude noise broke on these fine ripplings and whisperings, at once so far away and so clear: a positive tramp, tramp, a metallic clatter, which effaced the soft wave-wanderings; as, in a picture, the solid mass of a crag, or the rough boles of a great oak, drawn in dark and strong on the foreground, efface the aerial distance of azure hill, sunny horizon, and blended clouds where tint melts into tint.

The din was on the causeway: a horse was coming; the windings of the lane yet hid it, but it approached. I was just leaving the stile; yet, as the path was narrow, I sat still to let it go by. In those days I was young, and all sorts of fancies bright and dark tenanted my mind: the memories of nursery stories were there amongst other rubbish; and when they recurred, maturing youth added to them a vigour and vividness beyond what childhood could give. As this horse approached, and as I watched for it to appear through the dusk, I remembered certain of Bessie's tales, wherein figured a North-of-England spirit called a "Gytrash," which, in the form of horse, mule, or large dog, haunted solitary ways, and sometimes came upon belated travellers, as this horse was now coming upon me.

It was very near, but not yet in sight; when, in addition to the tramp, tramp, I heard a rush under the hedge, and close down by the hazel stems glided a great dog, whose black and white colour made him a distinct object against the trees. It was exactly one form of Bessie's Gytrash—a lion-like creature with long hair and a huge head: it passed me, however, quietly enough; not staying to look up, with strange pretercanine eyes, in my face, as I half expected it would. The horse followed,—a tall steed, and on its back a rider. The man, the human being, broke the spell at once. Nothing ever rode the Gytrash: it was always alone; and goblins, to my notions, though they might tenant the dumb carcasses of beasts, could scarce covet shelter in the commonplace human form. No Gytrash was this,—only a traveller taking the short cut to Millcote. He passed, and I went on; a few steps, and I turned: a sliding sound and an exclamation of "What the deuce is to do now?" and a clattering tumble, arrested my attention. Man and horse were down; they had slipped on the sheet of ice which glazed the causeway. The dog came bounding back, and seeing his master in a predicament, and hearing the horse groan, barked till the evening hills echoed the sound, which was deep in proportion to his magnitude. He snuffed round the prostrate group, and then he ran up to me; it was all he could do,—there was no other help at hand to summon. I obeyed him, and walked down to the traveller, by this time struggling himself free of his steed. His efforts were so vigorous, I thought he could not be much hurt; but I asked him the question—

"Are you injured, sir?"

I think he was swearing, but am not certain; however, he was pronouncing some formula which prevented him from replying to me directly.

"Can I do anything?" I asked again.

"You must just stand on one side," he answered as he rose, first to his knees, and then to his feet. I did; whereupon began a heaving, stamping, clattering process, accompanied by a barking and baying which removed me effectually some yards' distance; but I would not be driven quite away till I saw the event. This was finally fortunate; the horse was re-established, and the dog was silenced with a "Down, Pilot!" The traveller now, stooping, felt his foot and leg, as if trying whether they were sound; apparently something ailed them, for he halted to the stile whence I had just risen, and sat down.

I was in the mood for being useful, or at least officious, I think, for I now drew near him again.

"If you are hurt, and want help, sir, I can fetch some one either from Thornfield Hall or from Hay."

"Thank you: I shall do: I have no broken bones,—only a sprain;" and again he stood up and tried his foot, but the result extorted an involuntary "Ugh!"

Something of daylight still lingered, and the moon was waxing bright: I could see him plainly. His figure was enveloped in a riding cloak, fur collared and steel clasped; its details were not apparent, but I traced the general points of middle height and considerable breadth of chest. He had a dark face, with stern features and a heavy brow; his eyes and gathered eyebrows looked ireful and thwarted just now; he was past youth, but had not reached middle-age; perhaps he might be thirty-five. I felt no fear of him, and but little shyness. Had he been a handsome, heroic-looking young gentleman, I should not have dared to stand thus questioning him against his will, and offering my services unasked. I had hardly ever seen a handsome youth; never in my life spoken to one. I had a theoretical reverence and homage for beauty, elegance, gallantry, fascination; but had I met those qualities incarnate in masculine shape, I should have known instinctively that they neither had nor could have sympathy with anything in me, and should have shunned them as one would fire, lightning, or anything else that is bright but antipathetic.

If even this stranger had smiled and been good-humoured to me when I addressed him; if he had put off my offer of assistance gaily and with thanks, I should have gone on my way and not felt any vocation to renew inquiries: but the frown, the roughness of the traveller, set me at my ease: I retained my station when he waved to me to go, and announced—

"I cannot think of leaving you, sir, at so late an hour, in this solitary lane, till I see you are fit to mount your horse."

He looked at me when I said this; he had hardly turned his eyes in my direction before.

"I should think you ought to be at home yourself," said he, "if you have a home in this neighbourhood: where do you come from?"

"From just below; and I am not at all afraid of being out late when it is moonlight: I will run over to Hay for you with pleasure, if you wish it: indeed, I am going there to post a letter."

"You live just below—do you mean at that house with the battlements?" pointing to Thornfield Hall, on which the moon cast a hoary gleam, bringing it out distinct and pale from the woods that, by contrast with the western sky, now seemed one mass of shadow.

"Yes, sir."

"Whose house is it?"

"Mr. Rochester's."

"Do you know Mr. Rochester?"

"No, I have never seen him."

"He is not resident, then?"

"No."

"Can you tell me where he is?"

"I cannot."

"You are not a servant at the hall, of course. You are—" He stopped, ran his eye over my dress, which, as usual, was quite simple: a black merino cloak, a black beaver bonnet; neither of them half fine enough for a lady's-maid. He seemed puzzled to decide what I was; I helped him.

"I am the governess."

"Ah, the governess!" he repeated; "deuce take me, if I had not forgotten! The governess!" and again my raiment underwent scrutiny. In two minutes he rose from the stile: his face expressed pain when he tried to move.

"I cannot commission you to fetch help," he said; "but you may help me a little yourself, if you will be so kind."

"Yes, sir."

"You have not an umbrella that I can use as a stick?"

"No."

"Try to get hold of my horse's bridle and lead him to me: you are not afraid?"

I should have been afraid to touch a horse when alone, but when told to do it, I was disposed to obey. I put down my muff on the stile, and went up to the tall steed; I endeavoured to catch the bridle, but it was a spirited thing, and would not let me come near its head; I made effort on effort, though in vain: meantime, I was mortally afraid of its trampling fore-feet. The traveller waited and watched for some time, and at last he laughed.

"I see," he said, "the mountain will never be brought to Mahomet, so all you can do is to aid Mahomet to go to the mountain; I must beg of you to come here."

I came. "Excuse me," he continued: "necessity compels me to make you useful." He laid a heavy hand on my shoulder, and leaning on me with some stress, limped to his horse. Having once caught the bridle, he mastered it directly and sprang to his saddle; grimacing grimly as he made the effort, for it wrenched his sprain.

"Now," said he, releasing his under lip from a hard bite, "just hand me my whip; it lies there under the hedge."

I sought it and found it.

"Thank you; now make haste with the letter to Hay, and return as fast as you can."

A touch of a spurred heel made his horse first start and rear, and then bound away; the dog rushed in his traces; all three vanished,

"Like heath that, in the wilderness,
The wild wind whirls away."

I took up my muff and walked on. The incident had occurred and was gone for me: it WAS an incident of no moment, no romance, no interest in a sense; yet it marked with change one single hour of a monotonous life. My help had been needed and claimed; I had given it: I was pleased to have done something; trivial, transitory though the deed was, it was yet an active thing, and I was weary of an existence all passive. The new face, too, was like a new picture introduced to the gallery of memory; and it was dissimilar to all the others hanging there: firstly, because it was masculine; and, secondly, because it was dark, strong, and stern. I had it still before me when I entered Hay, and slipped the letter into the post-office; I saw it as I walked fast down-hill all the way home. When I came to the stile, I stopped a minute, looked round and listened, with an idea that a horse's hoofs might ring on the causeway again, and that a rider in a cloak, and a Gytrash-like Newfoundland dog, might be again apparent: I saw only the hedge and a pollard willow before me, rising up still and straight to meet the moonbeams; I heard only the faintest waft of wind roaming fitful among the trees round Thornfield, a mile distant; and when I glanced down in the direction of the murmur, my eye, traversing the hall-front, caught a light kindling in a window: it reminded me that I was late, and I hurried on.

I did not like re-entering Thornfield. To pass its threshold was to return to stagnation; to cross the silent hall, to ascend the darksome staircase, to seek my own lonely little room, and then to meet tranquil Mrs. Fairfax, and spend the long winter evening with her, and her only, was to quell wholly the faint excitement wakened by my walk,—to slip again over my faculties the viewless fetters of an uniform and too still existence; of an existence whose very privileges of security and ease I was becoming incapable of appreciating. What good it would have done me at that time to have been tossed in the storms of an uncertain struggling life, and to have been taught by rough and bitter experience to long for the calm amidst which I now repined! Yes, just as much good as it would do a man tired of sitting still in a "too easy chair" to take a long walk: and just as natural was the wish to stir, under my circumstances, as it would be under his.

I lingered at the gates; I lingered on the lawn; I paced backwards and forwards on the pavement; the shutters of the glass door were closed; I could not see into the interior; and both my eyes and spirit seemed drawn from the gloomy house—from the grey-hollow filled with rayless cells, as it appeared to me—to that sky expanded before me,—a blue sea absolved from taint of cloud; the moon ascending it in solemn march; her orb seeming to look up as she left the hill-tops, from behind which she had come, far and farther below her, and aspired to the zenith, midnight dark in its fathomless depth and measureless distance; and for those trembling stars that followed her course; they made my heart tremble, my veins glow when I viewed them. Little things recall us to earth; the clock struck in the hall; that sufficed; I turned from moon and stars, opened a side-door, and went in.

The hall was not dark, nor yet was it lit, only by the high-hung bronze lamp; a warm glow suffused both it and the lower steps of the oak staircase. This ruddy shine issued from the great dining-room, whose two-leaved door stood open, and showed a genial fire in the grate, glancing on marble hearth and brass fire-irons, and revealing purple draperies and polished furniture, in the most pleasant radiance. It revealed, too, a group near the mantelpiece: I had scarcely caught it, and scarcely become aware of a cheerful mingling of voices, amongst which I seemed to distinguish the tones of Adele, when the door closed.

I hastened to Mrs. Fairfax's room; there was a fire there too, but no candle, and no Mrs. Fairfax. Instead, all alone, sitting upright on the rug, and gazing with gravity at the blaze, I beheld a great black and white long-haired dog, just like the Gytrash of the lane. It was so like it that I went forward and said—"Pilot" and the thing got up and came to me and snuffed me. I caressed him, and he wagged his great tail; but he looked an eerie creature to be alone with, and I could not tell whence he had come. I rang the bell, for I wanted a candle; and I wanted, too, to get an account of this visitant. Leah entered.

"What dog is this?"

"He came with master."

"With whom?"

"With master—Mr. Rochester—he is just arrived."

"Indeed! and is Mrs. Fairfax with him?"

"Yes, and Miss Adele; they are in the dining-room, and John is gone for a surgeon; for master has had an accident; his horse fell and his ankle is sprained."

"Did the horse fall in Hay Lane?"

"Yes, coming down-hill; it slipped on some ice."

"Ah! Bring me a candle will you Leah?"

Leah brought it; she entered, followed by Mrs. Fairfax, who repeated the news; adding that Mr. Carter the surgeon was come, and was now with Mr. Rochester: then she hurried out to give orders about tea, and I went upstairs to take off my things.

Chapter XIII

Mr. Rochester, it seems, by the surgeon's orders, went to bed early that night; nor did he rise soon next morning. When he did come down, it was to attend to business: his agent and some of his tenants were arrived, and waiting to speak with him.

Adele and I had now to vacate the library: it would be in daily requisition as a reception-room for callers. A fire was lit in an apartment upstairs, and there I carried our books, and arranged it for the future schoolroom. I discerned in the course of the morning that Thornfield Hall was a changed place: no longer silent as a church, it echoed every hour or two to a knock at the door, or a clang of the bell; steps, too, often traversed the hall, and new voices spoke in different keys below; a rill from the outer world was flowing through it; it had a master: for my part, I liked it better.

Adele was not easy to teach that day; she could not apply: she kept running to the door and looking over the banisters to see if she could get a glimpse of Mr. Rochester; then she coined pretexts to go downstairs, in order, as I shrewdly suspected, to visit the library, where I knew she was not wanted; then, when I got a little angry, and made her sit still, she continued to talk incessantly of her "ami, Monsieur Edouard Fairfax DE Rochester," as she dubbed him (I had not before heard his prenomens), and to conjecture what presents he had brought her: for it appears he had intimated the night before, that when his luggage came from Millcote, there would be found amongst it a little box in whose contents she had an interest.

"Et cela doit signifier," said she, "qu'il y aura le dedans un cadeau pour moi, et peut-etre pour vous aussi, mademoiselle. Monsieur a parle de vous: il m'a demande le nom de ma gouvernante, et si elle n'etait pas une petite personne, assez mince et un peu pale. J'ai dit qu'oui: car c'est vrai, n'est-ce pas, mademoiselle?"

I and my pupil dined as usual in Mrs. Fairfax's parlour; the afternoon was wild and snowy, and we passed it in the schoolroom. At dark I allowed Adele to put away books and work, and to run downstairs; for, from the comparative silence below, and from the cessation of appeals to the door-bell, I conjectured that Mr. Rochester was now at liberty. Left alone, I walked to the window; but nothing was to be seen thence: twilight and snowflakes together thickened the air, and hid the very shrubs on the lawn. I let down the curtain and went back to the fireside.

In the clear embers I was tracing a view, not unlike a picture I remembered to have seen of the castle of Heidelberg, on the Rhine, when Mrs. Fairfax came in, breaking up by her entrance the fiery mosaic I had been piercing together, and scattering too some heavy unwelcome thoughts that were beginning to throng on my solitude.

"Mr. Rochester would be glad if you and your pupil would take tea with him in the drawing-room this evening," said she: "he has been so much engaged all day that he could not ask to see you before."

"When is his tea-time?" I inquired.

"Oh, at six o'clock: he keeps early hours in the country. You had better change your frock now; I will go with you and fasten it. Here is a candle."

"Is it necessary to change my frock?"

"Yes, you had better: I always dress for the evening when Mr. Rochester is here."

This additional ceremony seemed somewhat stately; however, I repaired to my room, and, with Mrs. Fairfax's aid, replaced my black stuff dress by one of black silk; the best and the only additional one I had, except one of light grey, which, in my Lowood notions of the toilette, I thought too fine to be worn, except on first-rate occasions.

"You want a brooch," said Mrs. Fairfax. I had a single little pearl ornament which Miss Temple gave me as a parting keepsake: I put it on, and then we went downstairs. Unused as I was to strangers, it was rather a trial to appear thus formally summoned in Mr. Rochester's presence. I let Mrs. Fairfax precede me into the dining-room, and kept in her shade as we crossed that apartment; and, passing the arch, whose curtain was now dropped, entered the elegant recess beyond.

Two wax candles stood lighted on the table, and two on the mantelpiece; basking in the light and heat of a superb fire, lay Pilot—Adele knelt near him. Half reclined on a couch appeared Mr. Rochester, his foot supported by the cushion; he was looking at Adele and the dog: the fire shone full on his face. I knew my traveller with his broad and jetty eyebrows; his square forehead, made squarer by the horizontal sweep of his black hair. I recognised his decisive nose, more remarkable for character than beauty; his full nostrils, denoting, I thought, choler; his grim mouth, chin, and jaw—yes, all three were very grim, and no mistake. His shape, now divested of cloak, I perceived harmonised in squareness with his physiognomy: I suppose it was a good figure in the athletic sense of the term—broad chested and thin flanked, though neither tall nor graceful.

Mr. Rochester must have been aware of the entrance of Mrs. Fairfax and myself; but it appeared he was not in the mood to notice us, for he never lifted his head as we approached.

"Here is Miss Eyre, sir," said Mrs. Fairfax, in her quiet way. He bowed, still not taking his eyes from the group of the dog and child.

"Let Miss Eyre be seated," said he: and there was something in the forced stiff bow, in the impatient yet formal tone, which seemed further to express, "What the deuce is it to me whether Miss Eyre be there or not? At this moment I am not disposed to accost her."

I sat down quite disembarrassed. A reception of finished politeness would probably have confused me: I could not have returned or repaid it by answering grace and elegance on my part; but harsh caprice laid me under no obligation; on the contrary, a decent quiescence, under the freak of manner, gave me the advantage. Besides, the eccentricity of the proceeding was piquant: I felt interested to see how he would go on.

He went on as a statue would, that is, he neither spoke nor moved. Mrs. Fairfax seemed to think it necessary that some one should be amiable, and she began to talk. Kindly, as usual—and, as usual, rather trite—she condoled with him on the pressure of business he had had all day; on the annoyance it must have been to him with that painful sprain: then she commended his patience and perseverance in going through with it.

"Madam, I should like some tea," was the sole rejoinder she got. She hastened to ring the bell; and when the tray came, she proceeded to arrange the cups, spoons, &c., with assiduous celerity. I and Adele went to the table; but the master did not leave his couch.

"Will you hand Mr. Rochester's cup?" said Mrs. Fairfax to me; "Adele might perhaps spill it."

I did as requested. As he took the cup from my hand, Adele, thinking the moment propitious for making a request in my favour, cried out—

"N'est-ce pas, monsieur, qu'il y a un cadeau pour Mademoiselle Eyre dans votre petit coffre?"

"Who talks of cadeaux?" said he gruffly. "Did you expect a present, Miss Eyre? Are you fond of presents?" and he searched my face with eyes that I saw were dark, irate, and piercing.

"I hardly know, sir; I have little experience of them: they are generally thought pleasant things."

"Generally thought? But what do YOU think?"

"I should be obliged to take time, sir, before I could give you an answer worthy of your acceptance: a present has many faces to it, has it not? and one should consider all, before pronouncing an opinion as to its nature."

"Miss Eyre, you are not so unsophisticated as Adele: she demands a 'cadeau,' clamorously, the moment she sees me: you beat about the bush."

"Because I have less confidence in my deserts than Adele has: she can prefer the claim of old acquaintance, and the right too of custom; for she says you have always been in the habit of giving her playthings; but if I had to make out a case I should be puzzled, since I am a stranger, and have done nothing to entitle me to an acknowledgment."

"Oh, don't fall back on over-modesty! I have examined Adele, and find you have taken great pains with her: she is not bright, she has no talents; yet in a short time she has made much improvement."

"Sir, you have now given me my 'cadeau;' I am obliged to you: it is the meed teachers most covet—praise of their pupils' progress."

"Humph!" said Mr. Rochester, and he took his tea in silence.

"Come to the fire," said the master, when the tray was taken away, and Mrs. Fairfax had settled into a corner with her knitting; while Adele was leading me by the hand round the room, showing me the beautiful books and ornaments on the consoles and chiffonnieres. We obeyed, as in duty bound; Adele wanted to take a seat on my knee, but she was ordered to amuse herself with Pilot.

"You have been resident in my house three months?"

"Yes, sir."

"And you came from——?"

"From Lowood school, in——shire."

"Ah! a charitable concern. How long were you there?"

"Eight years."

"Eight years! you must be tenacious of life. I thought half the time in such a place would have done up any constitution! No wonder you have rather the look of another world. I marvelled where you had got that sort of face. When you came on me in Hay Lane last night, I thought unaccountably of fairy tales, and had half a mind to demand whether you had bewitched my horse: I am not sure yet. Who are your parents?"

"I have none."

"Nor ever had, I suppose: do you remember them?"

"No."

"I thought not. And so you were waiting for your people when you sat on that stile?"

"For whom, sir?"

"For the men in green: it was a proper moonlight evening for them. Did I break through one of your rings, that you spread that damned ice on the causeway?"

I shook my head. "The men in green all forsook England a hundred years ago," said I, speaking as seriously as he had done. "And not even in Hay Lane, or the fields about it, could you find a trace of them. I don't think either summer or harvest, or winter moon, will ever shine on their revels more."

Mrs. Fairfax had dropped her knitting, and, with raised eyebrows, seemed wondering what sort of talk this was.

"Well," resumed Mr. Rochester, "if you disown parents, you must have some sort of kinsfolk: uncles and aunts?"

"No; none that I ever saw."

"And your home?"

"I have none."

"Where do your brothers and sisters live?"

"I have no brothers or sisters."

"Who recommended you to come here?"

"I advertised, and Mrs. Fairfax answered my advertisement."

"Yes," said the good lady, who now knew what ground we were upon, "and I am daily thankful for the choice Providence led me to make. Miss Eyre has been an invaluable companion to me, and a kind and careful teacher to Adele."

"Don't trouble yourself to give her a character," returned Mr. Rochester: "eulogiums will not bias me; I shall judge for myself. She began by felling my horse."

"Sir?" said Mrs. Fairfax.

"I have to thank her for this sprain."

The widow looked bewildered.

"Miss Eyre, have you ever lived in a town?"

"No, sir."

"Have you seen much society?"

"None but the pupils and teachers of Lowood, and now the inmates of Thornfield."

"Have you read much?"

"Only such books as came in my way; and they have not been numerous or very learned."

"You have lived the life of a nun: no doubt you are well drilled in religious forms;—Brocklehurst, who I understand directs Lowood, is a parson, is he not?"

"Yes, sir."

"And you girls probably worshipped him, as a convent full of religieuses would worship their director."

"Oh, no."

"You are very cool! No! What! a novice not worship her priest! That sounds blasphemous."

"I disliked Mr. Brocklehurst; and I was not alone in the feeling. He is a harsh man; at once pompous and meddling; he cut off our hair; and for economy's sake bought us bad needles and thread, with which we could hardly sew."

"That was very false economy," remarked Mrs. Fairfax, who now again caught the drift of the dialogue.

"And was that the head and front of his offending?" demanded Mr. Rochester.

"He starved us when he had the sole superintendence of the provision department, before the committee was appointed; and he bored us with long lectures once a week, and with evening readings from books of his own inditing, about sudden deaths and judgments, which made us afraid to go to bed."

"What age were you when you went to Lowood?"

"About ten."

"And you stayed there eight years: you are now, then, eighteen?"

I assented.

"Arithmetic, you see, is useful; without its aid, I should hardly have been able to guess your age. It is a point difficult to fix where the features and countenance are so much at variance as in your case. And now what did you learn at Lowood? Can you play?"

"A little."

"Of course: that is the established answer. Go into the library—I mean, if you please.—(Excuse my tone of command; I am used to say, 'Do this,' and it is done: I cannot alter my customary habits for one new inmate.)—Go, then, into the library; take a candle with you; leave the door open; sit down to the piano, and play a tune."

I departed, obeying his directions.

"Enough!" he called out in a few minutes. "You play A LITTLE, I see; like any other English school-girl; perhaps rather better than some, but not well."

I closed the piano and returned. Mr. Rochester continued— "Adele showed me some sketches this morning, which she said were yours. I don't know whether they were entirely of your doing; probably a master aided you?"

"No, indeed!" I interjected.

"Ah! that pricks pride. Well, fetch me your portfolio, if you can vouch for its contents being original; but don't pass your word unless you are certain: I can recognise patchwork."

"Then I will say nothing, and you shall judge for yourself, sir."

I brought the portfolio from the library.

"Approach the table," said he; and I wheeled it to his couch. Adele and Mrs. Fairfax drew near to see the pictures.

"No crowding," said Mr. Rochester: "take the drawings from my hand as I finish with them; but don't push your faces up to mine."

He deliberately scrutinised each sketch and painting. Three he laid aside; the others, when he had examined them, he swept from him.

"Take them off to the other table, Mrs. Fairfax," said he, and look at them with Adele;—you" (glancing at me) "resume your seat, and answer my questions. I perceive those pictures were done by one hand: was that hand yours?"

"Yes."

"And when did you find time to do them? They have taken much time, and some thought."

"I did them in the last two vacations I spent at Lowood, when I had no other occupation."

"Where did you get your copies?"

"Out of my head."

"That head I see now on your shoulders?"

"Yes, sir."

"Has it other furniture of the same kind within?"

"I should think it may have: I should hope—better."

He spread the pictures before him, and again surveyed them alternately.

While he is so occupied, I will tell you, reader, what they are: and first, I must premise that they are nothing wonderful. The subjects had, indeed, risen vividly on my mind. As I saw them with the spiritual eye, before I attempted to embody them, they were striking; but my hand would not second my fancy, and in each case it had wrought out but a pale portrait of the thing I had conceived.

These pictures were in water-colours. The first represented clouds low and livid, rolling over a swollen sea: all the distance was in eclipse; so, too, was the foreground; or rather, the nearest billows, for there was no land. One gleam of light lifted into relief a half-submerged mast, on which sat a cormorant, dark and large, with wings flecked with foam; its beak held a gold bracelet set with gems, that I had touched with as brilliant tints as my palette could yield, and as glittering distinctness as my pencil could impart. Sinking below the bird and mast, a drowned corpse glanced through the green water; a fair arm was the only limb clearly visible, whence the bracelet had been washed or torn.

The second picture contained for foreground only the dim peak of a hill, with grass and some leaves slanting as if by a breeze. Beyond and above spread an expanse of sky, dark blue as at twilight: rising into the sky was a woman's shape to the bust, portrayed in tints as dusk and soft as I could combine. The dim forehead was crowned with a star; the lineaments below were seen as through the suffusion of vapour; the eyes shone dark and wild; the hair streamed shadowy, like a beamless cloud torn by storm or by electric travail. On the neck lay a pale reflection like moonlight; the same faint lustre touched the train of thin clouds from which rose and bowed this vision of the Evening Star.

The third showed the pinnacle of an iceberg piercing a polar winter sky: a muster of northern lights reared their dim lances, close serried, along the horizon. Throwing these into distance, rose, in the foreground, a head,—a colossal head, inclined towards the iceberg, and resting against it. Two thin hands, joined under the forehead, and supporting it, drew up before the lower features a sable veil, a brow quite bloodless, white as bone, and an eye hollow and fixed, blank of meaning but for the glassiness of despair, alone were visible. Above the temples, amidst wreathed turban folds of black drapery, vague in its character and consistency as cloud, gleamed a ring of white flame, gemmed with sparkles of a more lurid tinge. This pale crescent was "the likeness of a kingly crown;" what it diademed was "the shape which shape had none."

"Were you happy when you painted these pictures?" asked Mr. Rochester presently.

"I was absorbed, sir: yes, and I was happy. To paint them, in short, was to enjoy one of the keenest pleasures I have ever known."

"That is not saying much. Your pleasures, by your own account, have been few; but I daresay you did exist in a kind of artist's dream-land while you blent and arranged these strange tints. Did you sit at them long each day?"

"I had nothing else to do, because it was the vacation, and I sat at them from morning till noon, and from noon till night: the length of the midsummer days favoured my inclination to apply."

"And you felt self-satisfied with the result of your ardent labours?"

"Far from it. I was tormented by the contrast between my idea and my handiwork: in each case I had imagined something which I was quite powerless to realise."

"Not quite: you have secured the shadow of your thought; but no more, probably. You had not enough of the artist's skill and science to give it full being: yet the drawings are, for a school-girl, peculiar. As to the thoughts, they are elfish. These eyes in the Evening Star you must have seen in a dream. How could you make them look so clear, and yet not at all brilliant? for the planet above quells their rays. And what meaning is that in their solemn depth? And who taught you to paint wind. There is a high gale in that sky, and on this hill-top. Where did you see Latmos? For that is Latmos. There! put the drawings away!"

I had scarce tied the strings of the portfolio, when, looking at his watch, he said abruptly—

"It is nine o'clock: what are you about, Miss Eyre, to let Adele sit up so long? Take her to bed."

Adele went to kiss him before quitting the room: he endured the caress, but scarcely seemed to relish it more than Pilot would have done, nor so much.

"I wish you all good-night, now," said he, making a movement of the hand towards the door, in token that he was tired of our company, and wished to dismiss us. Mrs. Fairfax folded up her knitting: I took my portfolio: we curtseyed to him, received a frigid bow in return, and so withdrew.

"You said Mr. Rochester was not strikingly peculiar, Mrs. Fairfax," I observed, when I rejoined her in her room, after putting Adele to bed.

"Well, is he?"

"I think so: he is very changeful and abrupt."

"True: no doubt he may appear so to a stranger, but I am so accustomed to his manner, I never think of it; and then, if he has peculiarities of temper, allowance should be made."

"Why?"

"Partly because it is his nature—and we can none of us help our nature; and partly because he has painful thoughts, no doubt, to harass him, and make his spirits unequal."

"What about?"

"Family troubles, for one thing."

"But he has no family."

"Not now, but he has had—or, at least, relatives. He lost his elder brother a few years since."

"His ELDER brother?"

"Yes. The present Mr. Rochester has not been very long in possession of the property; only about nine years."

"Nine years is a tolerable time. Was he so very fond of his brother as to be still inconsolable for his loss?"

"Why, no—perhaps not. I believe there were some misunderstandings between them. Mr. Rowland Rochester was not quite just to Mr. Edward; and perhaps he prejudiced his father against him. The old gentleman was fond of money, and anxious to keep the family estate together. He did not like to diminish the property by division, and yet he was anxious that Mr. Edward should have wealth, too, to keep up the consequence of the name; and, soon after he was of age, some steps were taken that were not quite fair, and made a great deal of mischief. Old Mr. Rochester and Mr. Rowland combined to bring Mr. Edward into what he considered a painful position, for the sake of making his fortune: what the precise nature of that position was I never clearly knew, but his spirit could not brook what he had to suffer in it. He is not very forgiving: he broke with his family, and now for many years he has led an unsettled kind of life. I don't think he has ever been resident at Thornfield for a fortnight together, since the death of his brother without a will left him master of the estate; and, indeed, no wonder he shuns the old place."

"Why should he shun it?"

"Perhaps he thinks it gloomy."

The answer was evasive. I should have liked something clearer; but Mrs. Fairfax either could not, or would not, give me more explicit information of the origin and nature of Mr. Rochester's trials. She averred they were a mystery to herself, and that what she knew was chiefly from conjecture. It was evident, indeed, that she wished me to drop the subject, which I did accordingly.

Chapter XIV

For several subsequent days I saw little of Mr. Rochester. In the mornings he seemed much engaged with business, and, in the afternoon, gentlemen from Millcote or the neighbourhood called, and sometimes stayed to dine with him. When his sprain was well enough to admit of horse exercise, he rode out a good deal; probably to return these visits, as he generally did not come back till late at night.

During this interval, even Adele was seldom sent for to his presence, and all my acquaintance with him was confined to an occasional rencontre in the hall, on the stairs, or in the gallery, when he would sometimes pass me haughtily and coldly, just acknowledging my presence by a distant nod or a cool glance, and sometimes bow and smile with gentlemanlike affability. His changes of mood did not offend me, because I saw that I had nothing to do with their alternation; the ebb and flow depended on causes quite disconnected with me.

One day he had had company to dinner, and had sent for my portfolio; in order, doubtless, to exhibit its contents: the gentlemen went away early, to attend a public meeting at Millcote, as Mrs.

Fairfax informed me; but the night being wet and inclement, Mr. Rochester did not accompany them. Soon after they were gone he rang the bell: a message came that I and Adele were to go downstairs. I brushed Adele's hair and made her neat, and having ascertained that I was myself in my usual Quaker trim, where there was nothing to retouch—all being too close and plain, braided locks included, to admit of disarrangement—we descended, Adele wondering whether the petit coffre was at length come; for, owing to some mistake, its arrival had hitherto been delayed. She was gratified: there it stood, a little carton, on the table when we entered the dining-room. She appeared to know it by instinct.

"Ma boite! ma boite!" exclaimed she, running towards it.

"Yes, there is your 'boite' at last: take it into a corner, you genuine daughter of Paris, and amuse yourself with disembowelling it," said the deep and rather sarcastic voice of Mr. Rochester, proceeding from the depths of an immense easy-chair at the fireside. "And mind," he continued, "don't bother me with any details of the anatomical process, or any notice of the condition of the entrails: let your operation be conducted in silence: tiens-toi tranquille, enfant; comprends-tu?"

Adele seemed scarcely to need the warning—she had already retired to a sofa with her treasure, and was busy untying the cord which secured the lid. Having removed this impediment, and lifted certain silvery envelopes of tissue paper, she merely exclaimed—

"Oh ciel! Que c'est beau!" and then remained absorbed in ecstatic contemplation.

"Is Miss Eyre there?" now demanded the master, half rising from his seat to look round to the door, near which I still stood.

"Ah! well, come forward; be seated here." He drew a chair near his own. "I am not fond of the prattle of children," he continued; "for, old bachelor as I am, I have no pleasant associations connected with their lisp. It would be intolerable to me to pass a whole evening tete-e-tete with a brat. Don't draw that chair farther off, Miss Eyre; sit down exactly where I placed it—if you please, that is. Confound these civilities! I continually forget them. Nor do I particularly affect simple-minded old ladies. By-the-bye, I must have mine in mind; it won't do to neglect her; she is a Fairfax, or wed to one; and blood is said to be thicker than water."

He rang, and despatched an invitation to Mrs. Fairfax, who soon arrived, knitting-basket in hand.

"Good evening, madam; I sent to you for a charitable purpose. I have forbidden Adele to talk to me about her presents, and she is bursting with repletion: have the goodness to serve her as auditress and interlocutrice; it will be one of the most benevolent acts you ever performed."

Adele, indeed, no sooner saw Mrs. Fairfax, than she summoned her to her sofa, and there quickly filled her lap with the porcelain, the ivory, the waxen contents of her "boite;" pouring out, meantime, explanations and raptures in such broken English as she was mistress of.

"Now I have performed the part of a good host," pursued Mr. Rochester, "put my guests into the way of amusing each other, I ought to be at liberty to attend to my own pleasure. Miss Eyre, draw your chair still a little farther forward: you are yet too far back; I cannot see you without disturbing my position in this comfortable chair, which I have no mind to do."

I did as I was bid, though I would much rather have remained somewhat in the shade; but Mr. Rochester had such a direct way of giving orders, it seemed a matter of course to obey him promptly.

We were, as I have said, in the dining-room: the lustre, which had been lit for dinner, filled the room with a festal breadth of light; the large fire was all red and clear; the purple curtains hung rich and ample before the lofty window and loftier arch; everything was still, save the subdued chat of Adele (she dared not speak loud), and, filling up each pause, the beating of winter rain against the panes.

Mr. Rochester, as he sat in his damask-covered chair, looked different to what I had seen him look before; not quite so stern—much less gloomy. There was a smile on his lips, and his eyes sparkled, whether with wine or not, I am not sure; but I think it very probable. He was, in short, in his after-dinner mood; more expanded and genial, and also more self-indulgent than the frigid and rigid temper of the morning; still he looked preciously grim, cushioning his massive head against the swelling back of his chair, and receiving the light of the fire on his granite-hewn features, and in his great, dark eyes; for he had great, dark eyes, and very fine eyes, too—not without a certain change in their depths sometimes, which, if it was not softness, reminded you, at least, of that feeling.

He had been looking two minutes at the fire, and I had been looking the same length of time at him, when, turning suddenly, he caught my gaze fastened on his physiognomy.

"You examine me, Miss Eyre," said he: "do you think me handsome?"

I should, if I had deliberated, have replied to this question by something conventionally vague and polite; but the answer somehow slipped from my tongue before I was aware—"No, sir."

"Ah! By my word! there is something singular about you," said he: "you have the air of a little nonnette; quaint, quiet, grave, and simple, as you sit with your hands before you, and your eyes generally bent on the carpet (except, by-the-bye, when they are directed piercingly to my face; as just now, for instance); and when one asks you a question, or makes a remark to which you are obliged to reply, you rap out a round rejoinder, which, if not blunt, is at least brusque. What do you mean by it?"

"Sir, I was too plain; I beg your pardon. I ought to have replied that it was not easy to give an impromptu answer to a question about appearances; that tastes mostly differ; and that beauty is of little consequence, or something of that sort."

"You ought to have replied no such thing. Beauty of little consequence, indeed! And so, under pretence of softening the previous outrage, of stroking and soothing me into placidity, you stick a sly penknife under my ear! Go on: what fault do you find with me, pray? I suppose I have all my limbs and all my features like any other man?"

"Mr. Rochester, allow me to disown my first answer: I intended no pointed repartee: it was only a blunder."

"Just so: I think so: and you shall be answerable for it. Criticise me: does my forehead not please you?"

He lifted up the sable waves of hair which lay horizontally over his brow, and showed a solid enough mass of intellectual organs, but an abrupt deficiency where the suave sign of benevolence should have risen.

"Now, ma'am, am I a fool?"

"Far from it, sir. You would, perhaps, think me rude if I inquired in return whether you are a philanthropist?"

"There again! Another stick of the penknife, when she pretended to pat my head: and that is because I said I did not like the society of children and old women (low be it spoken!). No, young lady, I am not a general philanthropist; but I bear a conscience;" and he pointed to the prominences which are said to indicate that faculty, and which, fortunately for him, were sufficiently conspicuous; giving, indeed, a marked breadth to the upper part of his head: "and, besides, I once had a kind of rude tenderness of heart. When I was as old as you, I was a feeling fellow enough, partial to the unfledged, unfostered, and unlucky; but Fortune has knocked me about since: she has even kneaded me with her knuckles, and now I flatter myself I am hard and tough as an India-rubber ball; pervious, though, through a chink or two still, and with one sentient point in the middle of the lump. Yes: does that leave hope for me?"

"Hope of what, sir?"

"Of my final re-transformation from India-rubber back to flesh?"

"Decidedly he has had too much wine," I thought; and I did not know what answer to make to his queer question: how could I tell whether he was capable of being re-transformed?

"You looked very much puzzled, Miss Eyre; and though you are not pretty any more than I am handsome, yet a puzzled air becomes you; besides, it is convenient, for it keeps those searching eyes of yours away from my physiognomy, and busies them with the worsted flowers of the rug; so puzzle on. Young lady, I am disposed to be gregarious and communicative to-night."

With this announcement he rose from his chair, and stood, leaning his arm on the marble mantelpiece: in that attitude his shape was seen plainly as well as his face; his unusual breadth of chest, disproportionate almost to his length of limb. I am sure most people would have thought him an ugly man; yet there was so much unconscious pride in his port; so much ease in his demeanour; such a look of complete indifference to his own external appearance; so haughty a reliance on the power of other qualities, intrinsic or adventitious, to atone for the lack of mere personal attractiveness, that, in looking at him, one inevitably shared the indifference, and, even in a blind, imperfect sense, put faith in the confidence.

"I am disposed to be gregarious and communicative to-night," he repeated, "and that is why I sent for you: the fire and the chandelier were not sufficient company for me; nor would Pilot have been, for none of these can talk. Adele is a degree better, but still far below the mark; Mrs. Fairfax ditto; you, I am persuaded, can suit me if you will:

you puzzled me the first evening I invited you down here. I have almost forgotten you since: other ideas have driven yours from my head; but to-night I am resolved to be at ease; to dismiss what importunes, and recall what pleases. It would please me now to draw you out—to learn more of you—therefore speak."

Instead of speaking, I smiled; and not a very complacent or submissive smile either.

"Speak," he urged.

"What about, sir?"

"Whatever you like. I leave both the choice of subject and the manner of treating it entirely to yourself."

Accordingly I sat and said nothing: "If he expects me to talk for the mere sake of talking and showing off, he will find he has addressed himself to the wrong person," I thought.

"You are dumb, Miss Eyre."

I was dumb still. He bent his head a little towards me, and with a single hasty glance seemed to dive into my eyes.

"Stubborn?" he said, "and annoyed. Ah! it is consistent. I put my request in an absurd, almost insolent form. Miss Eyre, I beg your pardon. The fact is, once for all, I don't wish to treat you like an inferior: that is" (correcting himself), "I claim only such superiority as must result from twenty years' difference in age and a century's advance in experience. This is legitimate, et j'y tiens, as Adele would say; and it is by virtue of this superiority, and this alone, that I desire you to have the goodness to talk to me a little now, and divert my thoughts, which are galled with dwelling on one point—cankering as a rusty nail."

He had deigned an explanation, almost an apology, and I did not feel insensible to his condescension, and would not seem so.

"I am willing to amuse you, if I can, sir—quite willing; but I cannot introduce a topic, because how do I know what will interest you? Ask me questions, and I will do my best to answer them."

"Then, in the first place, do you agree with me that I have a right to be a little masterful, abrupt, perhaps exacting, sometimes, on the grounds I stated, namely, that I am old enough to be your father, and that I have battled through a varied experience with many men of many nations, and roamed over half the globe, while you have lived quietly with one set of people in one house?"

"Do as you please, sir."

"That is no answer; or rather it is a very irritating, because a very evasive one. Reply clearly."

"I don't think, sir, you have a right to command me, merely because you are older than I, or because you have seen more of the world than I have; your claim to superiority depends on the use you have made of your time and experience."

"Humph! Promptly spoken. But I won't allow that, seeing that it would never suit my case, as I have made an indifferent, not to say a bad, use of both advantages. Leaving superiority out of the question, then, you must still agree to receive my orders now and then, without being piqued or hurt by the tone of command. Will you?"

I smiled: I thought to myself Mr. Rochester IS peculiar—he seems to forget that he pays me 30 pounds per annum for receiving his orders.

"The smile is very well," said he, catching instantly the passing expression; "but speak too."

"I was thinking, sir, that very few masters would trouble themselves to inquire whether or not their paid subordinates were piqued and hurt by their orders."

"Paid subordinates! What! you are my paid subordinate, are you? Oh yes, I had forgotten the salary! Well then, on that mercenary ground, will you agree to let me hector a little?"

"No, sir, not on that ground; but, on the ground that you did forget it, and that you care whether or not a dependent is comfortable in his dependency, I agree heartily."

"And will you consent to dispense with a great many conventional forms and phrases, without thinking that the omission arises from insolence?"

"I am sure, sir, I should never mistake informality for insolence: one I rather like, the other nothing free-born would submit to, even for a salary."

"Humbug! Most things free-born will submit to anything for a salary; therefore, keep to yourself, and don't venture on generalities of which you are intensely ignorant. However, I mentally shake hands with you for your answer, despite its inaccuracy; and as much for the manner in which it was said, as for the substance of the speech; the manner was frank and sincere; one does not often see such a manner:

no, on the contrary, affectation, or coldness, or stupid, coarse-minded misapprehension of one's meaning are the usual rewards of candour. Not three in three thousand raw school-girl-governesses would have answered me as you have just done. But I don't mean to flatter you: if you are cast in a different mould to the majority, it is no merit of yours: Nature did it. And then, after all, I go too fast in my conclusions: for what I yet know, you may be no better than the rest; you may have intolerable defects to counterbalance your few good points."

"And so may you," I thought. My eye met his as the idea crossed my mind: he seemed to read the glance, answering as if its import had been spoken as well as imagined—

"Yes, yes, you are right," said he; "I have plenty of faults of my own: I know it, and I don't wish to palliate them, I assure you. God wot I need not be too severe about others; I have a past existence, a series of deeds, a colour of life to contemplate within my own breast, which might well call my sneers and censures from my neighbours to myself. I started, or rather (for like other defaulters, I like to lay half the blame on ill fortune and adverse circumstances) was thrust on to a wrong tack at the age of one-and-twenty, and have never recovered the right course since: but I might have been very different; I might have been as good as you—wiser—almost as stainless. I envy you your peace of mind, your clean conscience, your unpolluted memory. Little girl, a memory without blot or contamination must be an exquisite treasure—an inexhaustible source of pure refreshment: is it not?"

"How was your memory when you were eighteen, sir?"

"All right then; limpid, salubrious: no gush of bilge water had turned it to fetid puddle. I was your equal at eighteen—quite your equal. Nature meant me to be, on the whole, a good man, Miss Eyre; one of the better kind, and you see I am not so. You would say you don't see it; at least I flatter myself I read as much in your eye (beware, by-the-bye, what you express with that organ; I am quick at interpreting its language). Then take my word for it,—I am not a villain: you are not to suppose that—not to attribute to me any such bad eminence; but, owing, I verily believe, rather to circumstances than to my natural bent, I am a trite commonplace sinner, hackneyed in all the poor petty dissipations with which the rich and worthless try to put on life. Do you wonder that I avow this to you? Know, that in the course of your future life you will often find yourself elected the involuntary confidant of your acquaintances' secrets: people will instinctively find out, as I have done, that it is not your forte to tell of yourself, but to listen while others talk of themselves; they will feel, too, that you listen with no malevolent scorn of their indiscretion, but with a kind of innate sympathy; not the less comforting and encouraging because it is very unobtrusive in its manifestations."

"How do you know?—how can you guess all this, sir?"

"I know it well; therefore I proceed almost as freely as if I were writing my thoughts in a diary. You would say, I should have been superior to circumstances; so I should—so I should; but you see I was not. When fate wronged me, I had not the wisdom to remain cool: I turned desperate; then I degenerated. Now, when any vicious simpleton excites my disgust by his paltry ribaldry, I cannot flatter myself that I am better than he: I am forced to confess that he and I are on a level. I wish I had stood firm—God knows I do! Dread remorse when you are tempted to err, Miss Eyre; remorse is the poison of life."

"Repentance is said to be its cure, sir."

"It is not its cure. Reformation may be its cure; and I could reform—I have strength yet for that—if—but where is the use of thinking of it, hampered, burdened, cursed as I am? Besides, since happiness is irrevocably denied me, I have a right to get pleasure out of life: and I WILL get it, cost what it may."

"Then you will degenerate still more, sir."

"Possibly: yet why should I, if I can get sweet, fresh pleasure? And I may get it as sweet and fresh as the wild honey the bee gathers on the moor."

"It will sting—it will taste bitter, sir."

"How do you know?—you never tried it. How very serious—how very solemn you look: and you are as ignorant of the matter as this cameo head" (taking one from the mantelpiece). "You have no right to preach to me, you neophyte, that have not passed the porch of life, and are absolutely unacquainted with its mysteries."

"I only remind you of your own words, sir: you said error brought remorse, and you pronounced remorse the poison of existence."

"And who talks of error now? I scarcely think the notion that flittered across my brain was an error. I believe it was an inspiration rather than a temptation: it was very genial, very soothing—I know that. Here it comes again! It is no devil, I assure you; or if it be, it has put on the robes of an angel of light. I think I must admit so fair a guest when it asks entrance to my heart."

"Distrust it, sir; it is not a true angel."

"Once more, how do you know? By what instinct do you pretend to distinguish between a fallen seraph of the abyss and a messenger from the eternal throne—between a guide and a seducer?"

"I judged by your countenance, sir, which was troubled when you said the suggestion had returned upon you. I feel sure it will work you more misery if you listen to it."

"Not at all—it bears the most gracious message in the world: for the rest, you are not my conscience-keeper, so don't make yourself uneasy. Here, come in, bonny wanderer!"

He said this as if he spoke to a vision, viewless to any eye but his own; then, folding his arms, which he had half extended, on his chest, he seemed to enclose in their embrace the invisible being.

"Now," he continued, again addressing me, "I have received the pilgrim—a disguised deity, as I verify believe. Already it has done me good: my heart was a sort of charnel; it will now be a shrine."

"To speak truth, sir, I don't understand you at all: I cannot keep up the conversation, because it has got out of my depth. Only one thing, I know: you said you were not as good as you should like to be, and that you regretted your own imperfection;—one thing I can comprehend: you intimated that to have a sullied memory was a perpetual bane. It seems to me, that if you tried hard, you would in time find it possible to become what you yourself would approve; and that if from this day you began with resolution to correct your thoughts and actions, you would in a few years have laid up a new and stainless store of recollections, to which you might revert with pleasure."

"Justly thought; rightly said, Miss Eyre; and, at this moment, I am paving hell with energy."

"Sir?"

"I am laying down good intentions, which I believe durable as flint. Certainly, my associates and pursuits shall be other than they have been."

"And better?"

"And better—so much better as pure ore is than foul dross. You seem to doubt me; I don't doubt myself: I know what my aim is, what my motives are; and at this moment I pass a law, unalterable as that of the Medes and Persians, that both are right."

"They cannot be, sir, if they require a new statute to legalise them."

"They are, Miss Eyre, though they absolutely require a new statute: unheard-of combinations of circumstances demand unheard-of rules."

"That sounds a dangerous maxim, sir; because one can see at once that it is liable to abuse."

"Sententious sage! so it is: but I swear by my household gods not to abuse it."

"You are human and fallible."

"I am: so are you—what then?"

"The human and fallible should not arrogate a power with which the divine and perfect alone can be safely intrusted."

"What power?"

"That of saying of any strange, unsanctioned line of action,—'Let it be right.'"

"'Let it be right'—the very words: you have pronounced them."

"MAY it be right then," I said, as I rose, deeming it useless to continue a discourse which was all darkness to me; and, besides, sensible that the character of my interlocutor was beyond my penetration; at least, beyond its present reach; and feeling the uncertainty, the vague sense of insecurity, which accompanies a conviction of ignorance.

"Where are you going?"

"To put Adele to bed: it is past her bedtime."

"You are afraid of me, because I talk like a Sphynx."

"Your language is enigmatical, sir: but though I am bewildered, I am certainly not afraid."

"You ARE afraid—your self-love dreads a blunder."

"In that sense I do feel apprehensive—I have no wish to talk nonsense."

"If you did, it would be in such a grave, quiet manner, I should mistake it for sense. Do you never laugh, Miss Eyre? Don't trouble yourself to answer—I see you laugh rarely; but you can laugh very merrily: believe me, you are not naturally austere, any more than I am naturally vicious. The Lowood constraint still clings to you somewhat; controlling your features, muffling your voice, and restricting your limbs; and you fear in the presence of a man and a brother—or father, or master, or what you will—to smile too gaily, speak too freely, or move too quickly: but, in time, I think you will learn to be natural with me, as I find it impossible to be conventional with you; and then your looks and movements will have more vivacity and variety than they dare offer now. I see at intervals the glance of a curious sort of bird through the close-set bars of a cage: a vivid, restless, resolute captive is there; were it but free, it would soar cloud-high. You are still bent on going?"

"It has struck nine, sir."

"Never mind,—wait a minute: Adele is not ready to go to bed yet. My position, Miss Eyre, with my back to the fire, and my face to the room, favours observation. While talking to you, I have also occasionally watched Adele (I have my own reasons for thinking her a curious study,—reasons that I may, nay, that I shall, impart to you some day). She pulled out of her box, about ten minutes ago, a little pink silk frock; rapture lit her face as she unfolded it; coquetry runs in her blood, blends with her brains, and seasons the marrow of her bones. 'Il faut que je l'essaie!' cried she, 'et e l'instant meme!' and she rushed out of the room. She is now with Sophie, undergoing a robing process: in a few minutes she will re-enter; and I know what I shall see,—a miniature of Celine Varens, as she used to appear on the boards at the rising of—But never mind that. However, my tenderest feelings are about to receive a shock: such is my presentiment; stay now, to see whether it will be realised."

Ere long, Adele's little foot was heard tripping across the hall. She entered, transformed as her guardian had predicted. A dress of rose-coloured satin, very short, and as full in the skirt as it could be gathered, replaced the brown frock she had previously worn; a wreath of rosebuds circled her forehead; her feet were dressed in silk stockings and small white satin sandals.

"Est-ce que ma robe va bien?" cried she, bounding forwards; "et mes souliers? et mes bas? Tenez, je crois que je vais danser!"

And spreading out her dress, she chasseed across the room till, having reached Mr. Rochester, she wheeled lightly round before him on tip-toe, then dropped on one knee at his feet, exclaiming—

"Monsieur, je vous remercie mille fois de votre bonte;" then rising, she added, "C'est comme cela que maman faisait, n'est-ce pas, monsieur?"

"Pre-cise-ly!" was the answer; "and, 'comme cela,' she charmed my English gold out of my British breeches' pocket. I have been green, too, Miss Eyre,—ay, grass green: not a more vernal tint freshens you now than once freshened me. My Spring is gone, however, but it has left me that French floweret on my hands, which, in some moods, I would fain be rid of. Not valuing now the root whence it sprang; having found that it was of a sort which nothing but gold dust could manure, I have but half a liking to the blossom, especially when it looks so artificial as just now. I keep it and rear it rather on the Roman Catholic principle of expiating numerous sins, great or small, by one good work. I'll explain all this some day. Good-night."

Chapter XV

Mr. Rochester did, on a future occasion, explain it. It was one afternoon, when he chanced to meet me and Adele in the grounds: and while she played with Pilot and her shuttlecock, he asked me to walk up and down a long beech avenue within sight of her.

He then said that she was the daughter of a French opera-dancer, Celine Varens, towards whom he had once cherished what he called a "grande passion." This passion Celine had professed to return with even superior ardour. He thought himself her idol, ugly as he was: he believed, as he said, that she preferred his "taille d'athlete" to the elegance of the Apollo Belvidere.

"And, Miss Eyre, so much was I flattered by this preference of the Gallic sylph for her British gnome, that I installed her in an hotel; gave her a complete establishment of servants, a carriage, cashmeres, diamonds, dentelles, &c. In short, I began the process of ruining myself in the received style, like any other spoony. I had not, it seems, the originality to chalk out a new road to shame and destruction, but trode the old track with stupid exactness not to deviate an inch from the beaten centre. I had—as I deserved to have—the fate of all other spoonies. Happening to call one evening when Celine did not expect me, I found her out; but it was a warm night, and I was tired with strolling through Paris, so I sat down in her boudoir; happy to breathe the air consecrated so lately by her presence. No,—I exaggerate; I never thought there was any consecrating virtue about her: it was rather a sort of pastille perfume she had left; a scent of musk and amber, than an odour of sanctity. I was just beginning to stifle with the fumes of conservatory flowers and sprinkled essences, when I bethought myself to open the window and step out on to the balcony. It was moonlight and gaslight besides, and very still and serene. The balcony was furnished with a chair or two; I sat down, and took out a cigar,—I will take one now, if you will excuse me."

Here ensued a pause, filled up by the producing and lighting of a cigar; having placed it to his lips and breathed a trail of Havannah incense on the freezing and sunless air, he went on—

"I liked bonbons too in those days, Miss Eyre, and I was croquant—(overlook the barbarism)—croquant chocolate comfits, and smoking alternately, watching meantime the equipages that rolled along the fashionable streets towards the neighbouring opera-house, when in an elegant close carriage drawn by a beautiful pair of English horses, and distinctly seen in the brilliant city-night, I recognised the 'voiture' I had given Celine. She was returning: of course my heart thumped with impatience against the iron rails I leant upon. The carriage stopped, as I had expected, at the hotel door; my flame (that is the very word for an opera inamorata) alighted: though muffed in a cloak—an unnecessary encumbrance, by-the-bye, on so warm a June evening—I knew her instantly by her little foot, seen peeping from the skirt of her dress, as she skipped from the carriage-step. Bending over the balcony, I was about to murmur 'Mon ange'—in a tone, of course, which should be audible to the ear of love alone—when a figure jumped from the carriage after her; cloaked also; but that was a spurred heel which had rung on the pavement, and that was a hatted head which now passed under the arched porte cochere of the hotel.

"You never felt jealousy, did you, Miss Eyre? Of course not: I need not ask you; because you never felt love. You have both sentiments yet to experience: your soul sleeps; the shock is yet to be given which shall waken it. You think all existence lapses in as quiet a flow as that in which your youth has hitherto slid away. Floating on with closed eyes and muffled ears, you neither see the rocks bristling not far off in the bed of the flood, nor hear the breakers boil at their base. But I tell you—and you may mark my words—you will come some day to a craggy pass in the channel, where the whole of life's stream will be broken up into whirl and tumult, foam and noise: either you will be dashed to atoms on crag points, or lifted up and borne on by some master-wave into a calmer current—as I am now.

"I like this day; I like that sky of steel; I like the sternness and stillness of the world under this frost. I like Thornfield, its antiquity, its retirement, its old crow-trees and thorn-trees, its grey facade, and lines of dark windows reflecting that metal welkin: and yet how long have I abhorred the very thought of it, shunned it like a great plague-house? How I do still abhor-"

He ground his teeth and was silent: he arrested his step and struck his boot against the hard ground. Some hated thought seemed to have him in its grip, and to hold him so tightly that he could not advance.

We were ascending the avenue when he thus paused; the hall was before us. Lifting his eye to its battlements, he cast over them a glare such as I never saw before or since. Pain, shame, ire, impatience, disgust, detestation, seemed momentarily to hold a quivering conflict in the large pupil dilating under his ebon eyebrow. Wild was the wrestle which should be paramount; but another feeling rose and triumphed: something hard and cynical: self-willed and resolute: it settled his passion and petrified his countenance: he went on—

"During the moment I was silent, Miss Eyre, I was arranging a point with my destiny. She stood there, by that beech-trunk—a hag like one of those who appeared to Macbeth on the heath of Forres. 'You like Thornfield?' she said, lifting her finger; and then she wrote in the air a memento, which ran in lurid hieroglyphics all along the house-front, between the upper and lower row of windows, 'Like it if you can! Like it if you dare!'

"'I will like it,' said I; 'I dare like it;' and" (he subjoined moodily) "I will keep my word; I will break obstacles to happiness, to goodness—yes, goodness. I wish to be a better man than I have been, than I am; as Job's leviathan broke the spear, the dart, and the habergeon, hindrances which others count as iron and brass, I will esteem but straw and rotten wood."

Adele here ran before him with her shuttlecock. "Away!" he cried harshly; "keep at a distance, child; or go in to Sophie!" Continuing then to pursue his walk in silence, I ventured to recall him to the point whence he had abruptly diverged—

"Did you leave the balcony, sir," I asked, "when Mdlle. Varens entered?"

I almost expected a rebuff for this hardly well-timed question, but, on the contrary, waking out of his scowling abstraction, he turned his eyes towards me, and the shade seemed to clear off his brow. "Oh, I had forgotten Celine! Well, to resume. When I saw my charmer thus come in accompanied by a cavalier, I seemed to hear a hiss, and the green snake of jealousy, rising on undulating coils from the moonlit balcony, glided within my waistcoat, and ate its way in two minutes to my heart's core. Strange!" he exclaimed, suddenly starting again from the point. "Strange that I should choose you for the confidant of all this, young lady; passing strange that you should listen to me quietly, as if it were the most usual thing in the world for a man like me to tell stories of his opera-mistresses to a quaint, inexperienced girl like you! But the last singularity explains the first, as I intimated once before: you, with your gravity, considerateness, and caution were made to be the recipient of secrets. Besides, I know what sort of a mind I have placed in communication with my own: I know it is one not liable to take infection: it is a peculiar mind: it is a unique one. Happily I do not mean to harm it: but, if I did, it would not take harm from me. The more you and I converse, the better; for while I cannot blight you, you may refresh me." After this digression he proceeded—

"I remained in the balcony. 'They will come to her boudoir, no doubt,' thought I: 'let me prepare an ambush.' So putting my hand in through the open window, I drew the curtain over it, leaving only an opening through which I could take observations; then I closed the casement, all but a chink just wide enough to furnish an outlet to lovers' whispered vows: then I stole back to my chair; and as I resumed it the pair came in. My eye was quickly at the aperture. Celine's chamber-maid entered, lit a lamp, left it on the table, and withdrew. The couple were thus revealed to me clearly: both removed their cloaks, and there was 'the Varens,' shining in satin and jewels,—my gifts of course,—and there was her companion in an officer's uniform; and I knew him for a young roue of a vicomte—a brainless and vicious youth whom I had sometimes met in society, and had never thought of hating because I despised him so absolutely. On recognising him, the fang of the snake Jealousy was instantly broken; because at the same moment my love for Celine sank under an extinguisher. A woman who could betray me for such a rival was not worth contending for; she deserved only scorn; less, however, than I, who had been her dupe.

"They began to talk; their conversation eased me completely: frivolous, mercenary, heartless, and senseless, it was rather calculated to weary than enrage a listener. A card of mine lay on the table; this being perceived, brought my name under discussion. Neither of them possessed energy or wit to belabour me soundly, but they insulted me as coarsely as they could in their little way: especially Celine, who even waxed rather brilliant on my personal defects—deformities she termed them. Now it had been her custom to launch out into fervent admiration of what she called my 'beaute male:' wherein she differed diametrically from you, who told me point-blank, at the second interview, that you did not think me handsome. The contrast struck me at the time and——"

Adele here came running up again.

"Monsieur, John has just been to say that your agent has called and wishes to see you."

"Ah! in that case I must abridge. Opening the window, I walked in upon them; liberated Celine from my protection; gave her notice to vacate her hotel; offered her a purse for immediate exigencies; disregarded screams, hysterics, prayers, protestations, convulsions; made an appointment with the vicomte for a meeting at the Bois de Boulogne. Next morning I had the pleasure of encountering him; left a bullet in one of his poor etiolated arms, feeble as the wing of a chicken in the pip, and then thought I had done with the whole crew. But unluckily the Varens, six months before, had given me this filette Adele, who, she affirmed, was my daughter; and perhaps she may be, though I see no proofs of such grim paternity written in her countenance: Pilot is more like me than she. Some years after I had broken with the mother, she abandoned her child, and ran away to Italy with a musician or singer. I acknowledged no natural claim on Adele's part to be supported by me, nor do I now acknowledge any, for I am not her father; but hearing that she was quite destitute, I e'en took the poor thing out of the slime and mud of Paris, and transplanted it here, to grow up clean in the wholesome soil of an English country garden. Mrs. Fairfax found you to train it; but now you know that it is the illegitimate offspring of a French opera-girl, you will perhaps think differently of your post and protegee: you will be coming to me some day with notice that you have found another place—that you beg me to look out for a new governess, &c.—Eh?"

"No: Adele is not answerable for either her mother's faults or yours: I have a regard for her; and now that I know she is, in a sense, parentless—forsaken by her mother and disowned by you, sir—I shall cling closer to her than before. How could I possibly prefer the spoilt pet of a wealthy family, who would hate her governess as a nuisance, to a lonely little orphan, who leans towards her as a friend?"

"Oh, that is the light in which you view it! Well, I must go in now; and you too: it darkens."

But I stayed out a few minutes longer with Adele and Pilot—ran a race with her, and played a game of battledore and shuttlecock. When we went in, and I had removed her bonnet and coat, I took her on my knee; kept her there an hour, allowing her to prattle as she liked: not rebuking even some little freedoms and trivialities into which she was apt to stray when much noticed, and which betrayed in her a superficiality of character, inherited probably from her mother, hardly congenial to an English mind. Still she had her merits; and I was disposed to appreciate all that was good in her to the utmost. I sought in her countenance and features a likeness to Mr. Rochester, but found none: no trait, no turn of expression announced relationship. It was a pity: if she could but have been proved to resemble him, he would have thought more of her.

It was not till after I had withdrawn to my own chamber for the night, that I steadily reviewed the tale Mr. Rochester had told me. As he had said, there was probably nothing at all extraordinary in the substance of the narrative itself: a wealthy Englishman's passion for a French dancer, and her treachery to him, were every-day matters enough, no doubt, in society; but there was something decidedly strange in the paroxysm of emotion which had suddenly seized him when he was in the act of expressing the present contentment of his mood, and his newly revived pleasure in the old hall and its environs. I meditated wonderingly on this incident; but gradually quitting it, as I found it for the present inexplicable, I turned to the consideration of my master's manner to myself. The confidence he had thought fit to repose in me seemed a tribute to my discretion: I regarded and accepted it as such. His deportment had now for some weeks been more uniform towards me than at the first. I never seemed in his way; he did not take fits of chilling hauteur: when he met me unexpectedly, the encounter seemed welcome; he had always a word and sometimes a smile for me: when summoned by formal invitation to his presence, I was honoured by a cordiality of reception that made me feel I really possessed the power to amuse him, and that these evening conferences were sought as much for his pleasure as for my benefit.

I, indeed, talked comparatively little, but I heard him talk with relish. It was his nature to be communicative; he liked to open to a mind unacquainted with the world glimpses of its scenes and ways (I do not mean its corrupt scenes and wicked ways, but such as derived their interest from the great scale on which they were acted, the strange novelty by which they were characterised); and I had a keen delight in receiving the new ideas he offered, in imagining the new pictures he portrayed, and following him in thought through the new regions he disclosed, never startled or troubled by one noxious allusion.

The ease of his manner freed me from painful restraint: the friendly frankness, as correct as cordial, with which he treated me, drew me to him. I felt at times as if he were my relation rather than my master: yet he was imperious sometimes still; but I did not mind that; I saw it was his way. So happy, so gratified did I become with this new interest added to life, that I ceased to pine after kindred: my thin crescent-destiny seemed to enlarge; the blanks of existence were filled up; my bodily health improved; I gathered flesh and strength.

And was Mr. Rochester now ugly in my eyes? No, reader: gratitude, and many associations, all pleasurable and genial, made his face the object I best liked to see; his presence in a room was more cheering than the brightest fire. Yet I had not forgotten his faults; indeed, I could not, for he brought them frequently before me. He was proud, sardonic, harsh to inferiority of every description: in my secret soul I knew that his great kindness to me was balanced by unjust severity to many others. He was moody, too; unaccountably so; I more than once, when sent for to read to him, found him sitting in his library alone, with his head bent on his folded arms; and, when he looked up, a morose, almost a malignant, scowl blackened his features. But I believed that his moodiness, his harshness, and his former faults of morality (I say FORMER, for now he seemed corrected of them) had their source in some cruel cross of fate. I believed he was naturally a man of better tendencies, higher principles, and purer tastes than such as circumstances had developed, education instilled, or destiny encouraged. I thought there were excellent materials in him; though for the present they hung together somewhat spoiled and tangled. I cannot deny that I grieved for his grief, whatever that was, and would have given much to assuage it.

Though I had now extinguished my candle and was laid down in bed, I could not sleep for thinking of his look when he paused in the avenue, and told how his destiny had risen up before him, and dared him to be happy at Thornfield.

"Why not?" I asked myself. "What alienates him from the house? Will he leave it again soon? Mrs. Fairfax said he seldom stayed here longer than a fortnight at a time; and he has now been resident eight weeks. If he does go, the change will be doleful. Suppose he should be absent spring, summer, and autumn: how joyless sunshine and fine days will seem!"

I hardly know whether I had slept or not after this musing; at any rate, I started wide awake on hearing a vague murmur, peculiar and lugubrious, which sounded, I thought, just above me. I wished I had kept my candle burning: the night was drearily dark; my spirits were depressed. I rose and sat up in bed, listening. The sound was hushed.

I tried again to sleep; but my heart beat anxiously: my inward tranquillity was broken. The clock, far down in the hall, struck two. Just then it seemed my chamber-door was touched; as if fingers had swept the panels in groping a way along the dark gallery outside. I said, "Who is there?" Nothing answered. I was chilled with fear.

All at once I remembered that it might be Pilot, who, when the kitchen-door chanced to be left open, not unfrequently found his way up to the threshold of Mr. Rochester's chamber: I had seen him lying there myself in the mornings. The idea calmed me somewhat: I lay down. Silence composes the nerves; and as an unbroken hush now reigned again through the whole house, I began to feel the return of slumber. But it was not fated that I should sleep that night. A dream had scarcely approached my ear, when it fled affrighted, scared by a marrow-freezing incident enough.

This was a demoniac laugh—low, suppressed, and deep—uttered, as it seemed, at the very keyhole of my chamber door. The head of my bed was near the door, and I thought at first the goblin-laugher stood at my bedside—or rather, crouched by my pillow: but I rose, looked round, and could see nothing; while, as I still gazed, the unnatural sound was reiterated: and I knew it came from behind the panels. My first impulse was to rise and fasten the bolt; my next, again to cry out, "Who is there?"

Something gurgled and moaned. Ere long, steps retreated up the gallery towards the third-storey staircase: a door had lately been made to shut in that staircase; I heard it open and close, and all was still.

"Was that Grace Poole? and is she possessed with a devil?" thought I. Impossible now to remain longer by myself: I must go to Mrs. Fairfax. I hurried on my frock and a shawl; I withdrew the bolt and opened the door with a trembling hand. There was a candle burning just outside, and on the matting in the gallery. I was surprised at this circumstance: but still more was I amazed to perceive the air quite dim, as if filled with smoke; and, while looking to the right hand and left, to find whence these blue wreaths issued, I became further aware of a strong smell of burning.

Something creaked: it was a door ajar; and that door was Mr. Rochester's, and the smoke rushed in a cloud from thence. I thought no more of Mrs. Fairfax; I thought no more of Grace Poole, or the laugh: in an instant, I was within the chamber. Tongues of flame darted round the bed: the curtains were on fire. In the midst of blaze and vapour, Mr. Rochester lay stretched motionless, in deep sleep.

"Wake! wake!" I cried. I shook him, but he only murmured and turned: the smoke had stupefied him. Not a moment could be lost: the very sheets were kindling, I rushed to his basin and ewer; fortunately, one was wide and the other deep, and both were filled with water. I heaved them up, deluged the bed and its occupant, flew back to my own room, brought my own water-jug, baptized the couch afresh, and, by God's aid, succeeded in extinguishing the flames which were devouring it.

The hiss of the quenched element, the breakage of a pitcher which I flung from my hand when I had emptied it, and, above all, the splash of the shower-bath I had liberally bestowed, roused Mr. Rochester at last. Though it was now dark, I knew he was awake; because I heard him fulminating strange anathemas at finding himself lying in a pool of water.

"Is there a flood?" he cried.

"No, sir," I answered; "but there has been a fire: get up, do; you are quenched now; I will fetch you a candle."

"In the name of all the elves in Christendom, is that Jane Eyre?" he demanded. "What have you done with me, witch, sorceress? Who is in the room besides you? Have you plotted to drown me?"

"I will fetch you a candle, sir; and, in Heaven's name, get up. Somebody has plotted something: you cannot too soon find out who and what it is."

"There! I am up now; but at your peril you fetch a candle yet: wait two minutes till I get into some dry garments, if any dry there be—yes, here is my dressing-gown. Now run!"

I did run; I brought the candle which still remained in the gallery. He took it from my hand, held it up, and surveyed the bed, all blackened and scorched, the sheets drenched, the carpet round swimming in water.

"What is it? and who did it?" he asked. I briefly related to him what had transpired: the strange laugh I had heard in the gallery: the step ascending to the third storey; the smoke,—the smell of fire which had conducted me to his room; in what state I had found matters there, and how I had deluged him with all the water I could lay hands on.

He listened very gravely; his face, as I went on, expressed more concern than astonishment; he did not immediately speak when I had concluded.

"Shall I call Mrs. Fairfax?" I asked.

"Mrs. Fairfax? No; what the deuce would you call her for? What can she do? Let her sleep unmolested."

"Then I will fetch Leah, and wake John and his wife."

"Not at all: just be still. You have a shawl on. If you are not warm enough, you may take my cloak yonder; wrap it about you, and sit down in the arm-chair: there,—I will put it on. Now place your feet on the stool, to keep them out of the wet. I am going to leave you a few minutes. I shall take the candle. Remain where you are till I return; be as still as a mouse. I must pay a visit to the second storey. Don't move, remember, or call any one."

He went: I watched the light withdraw. He passed up the gallery very softly, unclosed the staircase door with as little noise as possible, shut it after him, and the last ray vanished. I was left in total darkness. I listened for some noise, but heard nothing. A very long time elapsed. I grew weary: it was cold, in spite of the cloak; and then I did not see the use of staying, as I was not to rouse the house. I was on the point of risking Mr. Rochester's displeasure by disobeying his orders, when the light once more gleamed dimly on the gallery wall, and I heard his unshod feet tread the matting. "I hope it is he," thought I, "and not something worse."

He re-entered, pale and very gloomy. "I have found it all out," said he, setting his candle down on the washstand; "it is as I thought."

"How, sir?"

He made no reply, but stood with his arms folded, looking on the ground. At the end of a few minutes he inquired in rather a peculiar tone—

"I forget whether you said you saw anything when you opened your chamber door."

"No, sir, only the candlestick on the ground."

"But you heard an odd laugh? You have heard that laugh before, I should think, or something like it?"

"Yes, sir: there is a woman who sews here, called Grace Poole,—she laughs in that way. She is a singular person."

"Just so. Grace Poole—you have guessed it. She is, as you say, singular—very. Well, I shall reflect on the subject. Meantime, I am glad that you are the only person, besides myself, acquainted with the precise details of to-night's incident. You are no talking fool: say nothing about it. I will account for this state of affairs" (pointing to the bed): "and now return to your own room. I shall do very well on the sofa in the library for the rest of the night. It is near four:-in two hours the servants will be up."

"Good-night, then, sir," said I, departing.

He seemed surprised—very inconsistently so, as he had just told me to go.

"What!" he exclaimed, "are you quitting me already, and in that way?"

"You said I might go, sir."

"But not without taking leave; not without a word or two of acknowledgment and good-will: not, in short, in that brief, dry fashion. Why, you have saved my life!—snatched me from a horrible and excruciating death! and you walk past me as if we were mutual strangers! At least shake hands."

He held out his hand; I gave him mine: he took it first in one, them in both his own.

"You have saved my life: I have a pleasure in owing you so immense a debt. I cannot say more. Nothing else that has being would have been tolerable to me in the character of creditor for such an obligation: but you: it is different;—I feel your benefits no burden, Jane."

He paused; gazed at me: words almost visible trembled on his lips,—but his voice was checked.

"Good-night again, sir. There is no debt, benefit, burden, obligation, in the case."

"I knew," he continued, "you would do me good in some way, at some time;—I saw it in your eyes when I first beheld you: their expression and smile did not"—(again he stopped)—"did not" (he proceeded hastily) "strike delight to my very inmost heart so for nothing. People talk of natural sympathies; I have heard of good genii: there are grains of truth in the wildest fable. My cherished preserver, goodnight!"

Strange energy was in his voice, strange fire in his look.

"I am glad I happened to be awake," I said: and then I was going.

"What! you WILL go?"

"I am cold, sir."

"Cold? Yes,—and standing in a pool! Go, then, Jane; go!" But he still retained my hand, and I could not free it. I bethought myself of an expedient.

"I think I hear Mrs. Fairfax move, sir," said I.

"Well, leave me:" he relaxed his fingers, and I was gone.

I regained my couch, but never thought of sleep. Till morning dawned I was tossed on a buoyant but unquiet sea, where billows of trouble rolled under surges of joy. I thought sometimes I saw beyond its wild waters a shore, sweet as the hills of Beulah; and now and then a freshening gale, wakened by hope, bore my spirit triumphantly towards the bourne: but I could not reach it, even in fancy—a counteracting breeze blew off land, and continually drove me back. Sense would resist delirium: judgment would warn passion. Too feverish to rest, I rose as soon as day dawned.

Chapter XVI

I both wished and feared to see Mr. Rochester on the day which followed this sleepless night: I wanted to hear his voice again, yet feared to meet his eye. During the early part of the morning, I momentarily expected his coming; he was not in the frequent habit of entering the schoolroom, but he did step in for a few minutes sometimes, and I had the impression that he was sure to visit it that day.

But the morning passed just as usual: nothing happened to interrupt the quiet course of Adele's studies; only soon after breakfast, I heard some bustle in the neighbourhood of Mr. Rochester's chamber, Mrs. Fairfax's voice, and Leah's, and the cook's—that is, John's wife—and even John's own gruff tones. There were exclamations of "What a mercy master was not burnt in his bed!" "It is always dangerous to keep a candle lit at night." "How providential that he had presence of mind to think of the water-jug!" "I wonder he waked nobody!" "It is to be hoped he will not take cold with sleeping on the library sofa," &c.

To much confabulation succeeded a sound of scrubbing and setting to rights; and when I passed the room, in going downstairs to dinner, I saw through the open door that all was again restored to complete order; only the bed was stripped of its hangings. Leah stood up in the window-seat, rubbing the panes of glass dimmed with smoke. I was about to address her, for I wished to know what account had been given of the affair: but, on advancing, I saw a second person in the chamber—a woman sitting on a chair by the bedside, and sewing rings to new curtains. That woman was no other than Grace Poole.

There she sat, staid and taciturn-looking, as usual, in her brown stuff gown, her check apron, white handkerchief, and cap. She was intent on her work, in which her whole thoughts seemed absorbed: on her hard forehead, and in her commonplace features, was nothing either of the paleness or desperation one would have expected to see marking the countenance of a woman who had attempted murder, and whose intended victim had followed her last night to her lair, and (as I believed), charged her with the crime she wished to perpetrate. I was amazed—confounded. She looked up, while I still gazed at her: no start, no increase or failure of colour betrayed emotion, consciousness of guilt, or fear of detection. She said "Good morning, Miss," in her usual phlegmatic and brief manner; and taking up another ring and more tape, went on with her sewing.

"I will put her to some test," thought I: "such absolute impenetrability is past comprehension."

"Good morning, Grace," I said. "Has anything happened here? I thought I heard the servants all talking together a while ago."

"Only master had been reading in his bed last night; he fell asleep with his candle lit, and the curtains got on fire; but, fortunately, he awoke before the bed-clothes or the wood-work caught, and contrived to quench the flames with the water in the ewer.

"A strange affair!" I said, in a low voice: then, looking at her fixedly—"Did Mr. Rochester wake nobody? Did no one hear him move?"

She again raised her eyes to me, and this time there was something of consciousness in their expression. She seemed to examine me warily; then she answered—

"The servants sleep so far off, you know, Miss, they would not be likely to hear. Mrs. Fairfax's room and yours are the nearest to master's; but Mrs. Fairfax said she heard nothing: when people get elderly, they often sleep heavy." She paused, and then added, with a sort of assumed indifference, but still in a marked and significant tone—"But you are young, Miss; and I should say a light sleeper: perhaps you may have heard a noise?"

"I did," said I, dropping my voice, so that Leah, who was still polishing the panes, could not hear me, "and at first I thought it was Pilot: but Pilot cannot laugh; and I am certain I heard a laugh, and a strange one."

She took a new needleful of thread, waxed it carefully, threaded her needle with a steady hand, and then observed, with perfect composure—

"It is hardly likely master would laugh, I should think, Miss, when he was in such danger: You must have been dreaming."

"I was not dreaming," I said, with some warmth, for her brazen coolness provoked me. Again she looked at me; and with the same scrutinising and conscious eye.

"Have you told master that you heard a laugh?" she inquired.

"I have not had the opportunity of speaking to him this morning."

"You did not think of opening your door and looking out into the gallery?" she further asked.

She appeared to be cross-questioning me, attempting to draw from me information unawares. The idea struck me that if she discovered I knew or suspected her guilt, she would be playing of some of her malignant pranks on me; I thought it advisable to be on my guard.

"On the contrary," said I, "I bolted my door."

"Then you are not in the habit of bolting your door every night before you get into bed?"

"Fiend! she wants to know my habits, that she may lay her plans accordingly!" Indignation again prevailed over prudence: I replied sharply, "Hitherto I have often omitted to fasten the bolt: I did not think it necessary. I was not aware any danger or annoyance was to be dreaded at Thornfield Hall: but in future" (and I laid marked stress on the words) "I shall take good care to make all secure before I venture to lie down."

"It will be wise so to do," was her answer: "this neighbourhood is as quiet as any I know, and I never heard of the hall being attempted by robbers since it was a house; though there are hundreds of pounds' worth of plate in the plate-closet, as is well known. And you see, for such a large house, there are very few servants, because master has never lived here much; and when he does come, being a bachelor, he needs little waiting on: but I always think it best to err on the safe side; a door is soon fastened, and it is as well to have a drawn bolt between one and any mischief that may be about. A deal of people, Miss, are for trusting all to Providence; but I say Providence will not dispense with the means, though He often blesses them when they are used discreetly." And here she closed her harangue: a long one for her, and uttered with the demureness of a Quakeress.

I still stood absolutely dumfoundered at what appeared to me her miraculous self-possession and most inscrutable hypocrisy, when the cook entered.

"Mrs. Poole," said she, addressing Grace, "the servants' dinner will soon be ready: will you come down?"

"No; just put my pint of porter and bit of pudding on a tray, and I'll carry it upstairs."

"You'll have some meat?"

"Just a morsel, and a taste of cheese, that's all."

"And the sago?"

"Never mind it at present: I shall be coming down before teatime: I'll make it myself."

The cook here turned to me, saying that Mrs. Fairfax was waiting for me: so I departed.

I hardly heard Mrs. Fairfax's account of the curtain conflagration during dinner, so much was I occupied in puzzling my brains over the enigmatical character of Grace Poole, and still more in pondering the problem of her position at Thornfield and questioning why she had not been given into custody that morning, or, at the very least, dismissed from her master's service. He had almost as much as declared his conviction of her criminality last night: what mysterious cause withheld him from accusing her? Why had he enjoined me, too, to secrecy? It was strange: a bold, vindictive, and haughty gentleman seemed somehow in the power of one of the meanest of his dependants; so much in her power, that even when she lifted her hand against his life, he dared not openly charge her with the attempt, much less punish her for it.

Had Grace been young and handsome, I should have been tempted to think that tenderer feelings than prudence or fear influenced Mr. Rochester in her behalf; but, hard-favoured and matronly as she was, the idea could not be admitted. "Yet," I reflected, "she has been young once; her youth would be contemporary with her master's: Mrs. Fairfax told me once, she had lived here many years. I don't think she can ever have been pretty; but, for aught I know, she may possess originality and strength of character to compensate for the want of personal advantages. Mr. Rochester is an amateur of the decided and eccentric: Grace is eccentric at least. What if a former caprice (a freak very possible to a nature so sudden and headstrong as his) has delivered him into her power, and she now exercises over his actions a secret influence, the result of his own indiscretion, which he cannot shake off, and dare not disregard?" But, having reached this point of conjecture, Mrs. Poole's square, flat figure, and uncomely, dry, even coarse face, recurred so distinctly to my mind's eye, that I thought, "No; impossible! my supposition cannot be correct. Yet," suggested the secret voice which talks to us in our own hearts, "you are not beautiful either, and perhaps Mr. Rochester approves you: at any rate, you have often felt as if he did; and last night—remember his words; remember his look; remember his voice!"

I well remembered all; language, glance, and tone seemed at the moment vividly renewed. I was now in the schoolroom; Adele was drawing; I bent over her and directed her pencil. She looked up with a sort of start.

"Qu' avez-vous, mademoiselle?" said she. "Vos doigts tremblent comme la feuille, et vos joues sont rouges: mais, rouges comme des cerises!"

"I am hot, Adele, with stooping!" She went on sketching; I went on thinking.

I hastened to drive from my mind the hateful notion I had been conceiving respecting Grace Poole; it disgusted me. I compared myself with her, and found we were different. Bessie Leaven had said I was quite a lady; and she spoke truth—I was a lady. And now I looked much better than I did when Bessie saw me; I had more colour and more flesh, more life, more vivacity, because I had brighter hopes and keener enjoyments.

"Evening approaches," said I, as I looked towards the window. "I have never heard Mr. Rochester's voice or step in the house to-day; but surely I shall see him before night: I feared the meeting in the morning; now I desire it, because expectation has been so long baffled that it is grown impatient."

When dusk actually closed, and when Adele left me to go and play in the nursery with Sophie, I did most keenly desire it. I listened for the bell to ring below; I listened for Leah coming up with a message; I fancied sometimes I heard Mr. Rochester's own tread, and I turned to the door, expecting it to open and admit him. The door remained shut; darkness only came in through the window. Still it was not late; he often sent for me at seven and eight o'clock, and it was yet but six. Surely I should not be wholly disappointed to-night, when I had so many things to say to him! I wanted again to introduce the subject of Grace Poole, and to hear what he would answer; I wanted to ask him plainly if he really believed it was she who had made last night's hideous attempt; and if so, why he kept her wickedness a secret. It little mattered whether my curiosity irritated him; I knew the pleasure of vexing and soothing him by turns; it was one I chiefly delighted in, and a sure instinct always prevented me from going too far; beyond the verge of provocation I never ventured; on the extreme brink I liked well to try my skill. Retaining every minute form of respect, every propriety of my station, I could still meet him in argument without fear or uneasy restraint; this suited both him and me.

A tread creaked on the stairs at last. Leah made her appearance; but it was only to intimate that tea was ready in Mrs. Fairfax's room. Thither I repaired, glad at least to go downstairs; for that brought me, I imagined, nearer to Mr. Rochester's presence.

"You must want your tea," said the good lady, as I joined her; "you ate so little at dinner. I am afraid," she continued, "you are not well to-day: you look flushed and feverish."

"Oh, quite well! I never felt better."

"Then you must prove it by evincing a good appetite; will you fill the teapot while I knit off this needle?" Having completed her task, she rose to draw down the blind, which she had hitherto kept up, by way, I suppose, of making the most of daylight, though dusk was now fast deepening into total obscurity.

"It is fair to-night," said she, as she looked through the panes, "though not starlight; Mr. Rochester has, on the whole, had a favourable day for his journey."

"Journey!—Is Mr. Rochester gone anywhere? I did not know he was out."

"Oh, he set of the moment he had breakfasted! He is gone to the Leas, Mr. Eshton's place, ten miles on the other side Millcote. I believe there is quite a party assembled there; Lord Ingram, Sir George Lynn, Colonel Dent, and others."

"Do you expect him back to-night?"

"No—nor to-morrow either; I should think he is very likely to stay a week or more: when these fine, fashionable people get together, they are so surrounded by elegance and gaiety, so well provided with all that can please and entertain, they are in no hurry to separate. Gentlemen especially are often in request on such occasions; and Mr. Rochester is so talented and so lively in society, that I believe he is a general favourite: the ladies are very fond of him; though you would not think his appearance calculated to recommend him particularly in their eyes: but I suppose his acquirements and abilities, perhaps his wealth and good blood, make amends for any little fault of look."

"Are there ladies at the Leas?"

"There are Mrs. Eshton and her three daughters—very elegant young ladies indeed; and there are the Honourable Blanche and Mary Ingram, most beautiful women, I suppose: indeed I have seen Blanche, six or seven years since, when she was a girl of eighteen. She came here to a Christmas ball and party Mr. Rochester gave. You should have seen the dining-room that day—how richly it was decorated, how brilliantly lit up! I should think there were fifty ladies and gentlemen present—all of the first county families; and Miss Ingram was considered the belle of the evening."

"You saw her, you say, Mrs. Fairfax: what was she like?"

"Yes, I saw her. The dining-room doors were thrown open; and, as it was Christmas-time, the servants were allowed to assemble in the hall, to hear some of the ladies sing and play. Mr. Rochester would have me to come in, and I sat down in a quiet corner and watched them. I never saw a more splendid scene: the ladies were magnificently dressed; most of them—at least most of the younger ones—looked handsome; but Miss Ingram was certainly the queen."

"And what was she like?"

"Tall, fine bust, sloping shoulders; long, graceful neck: olive complexion, dark and clear; noble features; eyes rather like Mr. Rochester's: large and black, and as brilliant as her jewels. And then she had such a fine head of hair; raven-black and so becomingly arranged: a crown of thick plaits behind, and in front the longest, the glossiest curls I ever saw. She was dressed in pure white; an amber-coloured scarf was passed over her shoulder and across her breast, tied at the side, and descending in long, fringed ends below her knee. She wore an amber-coloured flower, too, in her hair: it contrasted well with the jetty mass of her curls."

"She was greatly admired, of course?"

"Yes, indeed: and not only for her beauty, but for her accomplishments. She was one of the ladies who sang: a gentleman accompanied her on the piano. She and Mr. Rochester sang a duet."

"Mr. Rochester? I was not aware he could sing."

"Oh! he has a fine bass voice, and an excellent taste for music."

"And Miss Ingram: what sort of a voice had she?"

"A very rich and powerful one: she sang delightfully; it was a treat to listen to her;—and she played afterwards. I am no judge of music, but Mr. Rochester is; and I heard him say her execution was remarkably good."

"And this beautiful and accomplished lady, she is not yet married?"

"It appears not: I fancy neither she nor her sister have very large fortunes. Old Lord Ingram's estates were chiefly entailed, and the eldest son came in for everything almost."

"But I wonder no wealthy nobleman or gentleman has taken a fancy to her: Mr. Rochester, for instance. He is rich, is he not?"

"Oh! yes. But you see there is a considerable difference in age: Mr. Rochester is nearly forty; she is but twenty-five."

"What of that? More unequal matches are made every day."

"True: yet I should scarcely fancy Mr. Rochester would entertain an idea of the sort. But you eat nothing: you have scarcely tasted since you began tea."

"No: I am too thirsty to eat. Will you let me have another cup?"

I was about again to revert to the probability of a union between Mr. Rochester and the beautiful Blanche; but Adele came in, and the conversation was turned into another channel.

When once more alone, I reviewed the information I had got; looked into my heart, examined its thoughts and feelings, and endeavoured to bring back with a strict hand such as had been straying through imagination's boundless and trackless waste, into the safe fold of common sense.

Arraigned at my own bar, Memory having given her evidence of the hopes, wishes, sentiments I had been cherishing since last night—of the general state of mind in which I had indulged for nearly a fortnight past; Reason having come forward and told, in her own quiet way a plain, unvarnished tale, showing how I had rejected the real, and rabidly devoured the ideal;—I pronounced judgment to this effect:—

That a greater fool than Jane Eyre had never breathed the breath of life; that a more fantastic idiot had never surfeited herself on sweet lies, and swallowed poison as if it were nectar.

"YOU," I said, "a favourite with Mr. Rochester? YOU gifted with the power of pleasing him? YOU of importance to him in any way? Go! your folly sickens me. And you have derived pleasure from occasional tokens of preference—equivocal tokens shown by a gentleman of family and a man of the world to a dependent and a novice. How dared you? Poor stupid dupe!—Could not even self-interest make you wiser? You repeated to yourself this morning the brief scene of last night?—Cover your face and be ashamed! He said something in praise of your eyes, did he? Blind puppy! Open their bleared lids and look on your own accursed senselessness! It does good to no woman to be flattered by her superior, who cannot possibly intend to marry her; and it is madness in all women to let a secret love kindle within them, which, if unreturned and unknown, must devour the life that feeds it; and, if discovered and responded to, must lead, ignis-fatus-like, into miry wilds whence there is no extrication.

"Listen, then, Jane Eyre, to your sentence: tomorrow, place the glass before you, and draw in chalk your own picture, faithfully, without softening one defect; omit no harsh line, smooth away no displeasing irregularity; write under it, 'Portrait of a Governess, disconnected, poor, and plain.'

"Afterwards, take a piece of smooth ivory—you have one prepared in your drawing-box: take your palette, mix your freshest, finest, clearest tints; choose your most delicate camel-hair pencils; delineate carefully the loveliest face you can imagine; paint it in your softest shades and sweetest lines, according to the description given by Mrs. Fairfax of Blanche Ingram; remember the raven ringlets, the oriental eye;—What! you revert to Mr. Rochester as a model! Order! No snivel!—no sentiment!—no regret! I will endure only sense and resolution. Recall the august yet harmonious lineaments, the Grecian neck and bust; let the round and dazzling arm be visible, and the delicate hand; omit neither diamond ring nor gold bracelet; portray faithfully the attire, aerial lace and glistening satin, graceful scarf and golden rose; call it 'Blanche, an accomplished lady of rank.'

"Whenever, in future, you should chance to fancy Mr. Rochester thinks well of you, take out these two pictures and compare them: say, 'Mr. Rochester might probably win that noble lady's love, if he chose to strive for it; is it likely he would waste a serious thought on this indigent and insignificant plebeian?'"

"I'll do it," I resolved: and having framed this determination, I grew calm, and fell asleep.

I kept my word. An hour or two sufficed to sketch my own portrait in crayons; and in less than a fortnight I had completed an ivory miniature of an imaginary Blanche Ingram. It looked a lovely face enough, and when compared with the real head in chalk, the contrast was as great as self-control could desire. I derived benefit from the task: it had kept my head and hands employed, and had given force and fixedness to the new impressions I wished to stamp indelibly on my heart.

Ere long, I had reason to congratulate myself on the course of wholesome discipline to which I had thus forced my feelings to submit. Thanks to it, I was able to meet subsequent occurrences with a decent calm, which, had they found me unprepared, I should probably have been unequal to maintain, even externally.

Chapter XVII

A week passed, and no news arrived of Mr. Rochester: ten days, and still he did not come. Mrs. Fairfax said she should not be surprised if he were to go straight from the Leas to London, and thence to the Continent, and not show his face again at Thornfield for a year to come; he had not unfrequently quitted it in a manner quite as abrupt and unexpected. When I heard this, I was beginning to feel a strange chill and failing at the heart. I was actually permitting myself to experience a sickening sense of disappointment; but rallying my wits, and recollecting my principles, I at once called my sensations to order; and it was wonderful how I got over the temporary blunder—how I cleared up the mistake of supposing Mr. Rochester's movements a matter in which I had any cause to take a vital interest. Not that I humbled myself by a slavish notion of inferiority: on the contrary, I just said—

"You have nothing to do with the master of Thornfield, further than to receive the salary he gives you for teaching his protegee, and to be grateful for such respectful and kind treatment as, if you do your duty, you have a right to expect at his hands. Be sure that is the only tie he seriously acknowledges between you and him; so don't make him the object of your fine feelings, your raptures, agonies, and so forth. He is not of your order: keep to your caste, and be too self-respecting to lavish the love of the whole heart, soul, and strength, where such a gift is not wanted and would be despised."

I went on with my day's business tranquilly; but ever and anon vague suggestions kept wandering across my brain of reasons why I should quit Thornfield; and I kept involuntarily framing advertisements and pondering conjectures about new situations: these thoughts I did not think check; they might germinate and bear fruit if they could.

Mr. Rochester had been absent upwards of a fortnight, when the post brought Mrs. Fairfax a letter.

"It is from the master," said she, as she looked at the direction. "Now I suppose we shall know whether we are to expect his return or not."

And while she broke the seal and perused the document, I went on taking my coffee (we were at breakfast): it was hot, and I attributed to that circumstance a fiery glow which suddenly rose to my face. Why my hand shook, and why I involuntarily spilt half the contents of my cup into my saucer, I did not choose to consider.

"Well, I sometimes think we are too quiet; but we run a chance of being busy enough now: for a little while at least," said Mrs. Fairfax, still holding the note before her spectacles.

Ere I permitted myself to request an explanation, I tied the string of Adele's pinafore, which happened to be loose: having helped her also to another bun and refilled her mug with milk, I said, nonchalantly—

"Mr. Rochester is not likely to return soon, I suppose?"

"Indeed he is—in three days, he says: that will be next Thursday; and not alone either. I don't know how many of the fine people at the Leas are coming with him: he sends directions for all the best bedrooms to be prepared; and the library and drawing-rooms are to be cleaned out; I am to get more kitchen hands from the George Inn, at Millcote, and from wherever else I can; and the ladies will bring their maids and the gentlemen their valets: so we shall have a full house of it." And Mrs. Fairfax swallowed her breakfast and hastened away to commence operations.

The three days were, as she had foretold, busy enough. I had thought all the rooms at Thornfield beautifully clean and well arranged; but it appears I was mistaken. Three women were got to help; and such scrubbing, such brushing, such washing of paint and beating of carpets, such taking down and putting up of pictures, such polishing of mirrors and lustres, such lighting of fires in bedrooms, such airing of sheets and feather-beds on hearths, I never beheld, either before or since. Adele ran quite wild in the midst of it: the preparations for company and the prospect of their arrival, seemed to throw her into ecstasies. She would have Sophie to look over all her "toilettes," as she called frocks; to furbish up any that were "passees," and to air and arrange the new. For herself, she did nothing but caper about in the front chambers, jump on and off the bedsteads, and lie on the mattresses and piled-up bolsters and pillows before the enormous fires roaring in the chimneys. From school duties she was exonerated: Mrs. Fairfax had pressed me into her service, and I was all day in the storeroom, helping (or hindering) her and the cook; learning to make custards and cheese-cakes and French pastry, to truss game and garnish desert-dishes.

The party were expected to arrive on Thursday afternoon, in time for dinner at six. During the intervening period I had no time to nurse chimeras; and I believe I was as active and gay as anybody—Adele excepted. Still, now and then, I received a damping check to my cheerfulness; and was, in spite of myself, thrown back on the region of doubts and portents, and dark conjectures. This was when I chanced to see the third-storey staircase door (which of late had always been kept locked) open slowly, and give passage to the form of Grace Poole, in prim cap, white apron, and handkerchief; when I watched her glide along the gallery, her quiet tread muffled in a list slipper; when I saw her look into the bustling, topsy-turvy bedrooms,—just say a word, perhaps, to the charwoman about the proper way to polish a grate, or clean a marble mantelpiece, or take stains from papered walls, and then pass on. She would thus descend to the kitchen once a day, eat her dinner, smoke a moderate pipe on the hearth, and go back, carrying her pot of porter with her, for her private solace, in her own gloomy, upper haunt. Only one hour in the twenty-four did she pass with her fellow-servants below; all the rest of her time was spent in some low-ceiled, oaken chamber of the second storey: there she sat and sewed—and probably laughed drearily to herself,—as companionless as a prisoner in his dungeon.

The strangest thing of all was, that not a soul in the house, except me, noticed her habits, or seemed to marvel at them: no one discussed her position or employment; no one pitied her solitude or isolation. I once, indeed, overheard part of a dialogue between Leah and one of the charwomen, of which Grace formed the subject. Leah had been saying something I had not caught, and the charwoman remarked—

"She gets good wages, I guess?"

"Yes," said Leah; "I wish I had as good; not that mine are to complain of,—there's no stinginess at Thornfield; but they're not one fifth of the sum Mrs. Poole receives. And she is laying by: she goes every quarter to the bank at Millcote. I should not wonder but she has saved enough to keep her independent if she liked to leave; but I suppose she's got used to the place; and then she's not forty yet, and strong and able for anything. It is too soon for her to give up business."

"She is a good hand, I daresay," said the charwoman.

"Ah!—she understands what she has to do,—nobody better," rejoined Leah significantly; "and it is not every one could fill her shoes—not for all the money she gets."

"That it is not!" was the reply. "I wonder whether the master—"

The charwoman was going on; but here Leah turned and perceived me, and she instantly gave her companion a nudge.

"Doesn't she know?" I heard the woman whisper.

Leah shook her head, and the conversation was of course dropped. All I had gathered from it amounted to this,—that there was a mystery at Thornfield; and that from participation in that mystery I was purposely excluded.

Thursday came: all work had been completed the previous evening; carpets were laid down, bed-hangings festooned, radiant white counterpanes spread, toilet tables arranged, furniture rubbed, flowers piled in vases: both chambers and saloons looked as fresh and bright as hands could make them. The hall, too, was scoured; and the great carved clock, as well as the steps and banisters of the staircase, were polished to the brightness of glass; in the dining-room, the sideboard flashed resplendent with plate; in the drawing-room and boudoir, vases of exotics bloomed on all sides.

Afternoon arrived: Mrs. Fairfax assumed her best black satin gown, her gloves, and her gold watch; for it was her part to receive the company,—to conduct the ladies to their rooms, &c. Adele, too, would be dressed: though I thought she had little chance of being introduced to the party that day at least. However, to please her, I allowed Sophie to apparel her in one of her short, full muslin frocks. For myself, I had no need to make any change; I should not be called upon to quit my sanctum of the schoolroom; for a sanctum it was now become to me,—"a very pleasant refuge in time of trouble."

It had been a mild, serene spring day—one of those days which, towards the end of March or the beginning of April, rise shining over the earth as heralds of summer. It was drawing to an end now; but the evening was even warm, and I sat at work in the schoolroom with the window open.

"It gets late," said Mrs. Fairfax, entering in rustling state. "I am glad I ordered dinner an hour after the time Mr. Rochester mentioned; for it is past six now. I have sent John down to the gates to see if there is anything on the road: one can see a long way from thence in the direction of Millcote." She went to the window. "Here he is!" said she. "Well, John" (leaning out), "any news?"

"They're coming, ma'am," was the answer. "They'll be here in ten minutes."

Adele flew to the window. I followed, taking care to stand on one side, so that, screened by the curtain, I could see without being seen.

The ten minutes John had given seemed very long, but at last wheels were heard; four equestrians galloped up the drive, and after them came two open carriages. Fluttering veils and waving plumes filled the vehicles; two of the cavaliers were young, dashing-looking gentlemen; the third was Mr. Rochester, on his black horse, Mesrour, Pilot bounding before him; at his side rode a lady, and he and she were the first of the party. Her purple riding-habit almost swept the ground, her veil streamed long on the breeze; mingling with its transparent folds, and gleaming through them, shone rich raven ringlets.

"Miss Ingram!" exclaimed Mrs. Fairfax, and away she hurried to her post below.

The cavalcade, following the sweep of the drive, quickly turned the angle of the house, and I lost sight of it. Adele now petitioned to go down; but I took her on my knee, and gave her to understand that she must not on any account think of venturing in sight of the ladies, either now or at any other time, unless expressly sent for: that Mr. Rochester would be very angry, &c. "Some natural tears she shed" on being told this; but as I began to look very grave, she consented at last to wipe them.

A joyous stir was now audible in the hall: gentlemen's deep tones and ladies' silvery accents blent harmoniously together, and distinguishable above all, though not loud, was the sonorous voice of the master of Thornfield Hall, welcoming his fair and gallant guests under its roof. Then light steps ascended the stairs; and there was a tripping through the gallery, and soft cheerful laughs, and opening and closing doors, and, for a time, a hush.

"Elles changent de toilettes," said Adele; who, listening attentively, had followed every movement; and she sighed.

"Chez maman," said she, "quand il y avait du monde, je le suivais partout, au salon et e leurs chambres; souvent je regardais les femmes de chambre coiffer et habiller les dames, et c'etait si amusant: comme cela on apprend."

"Don't you feel hungry, Adele?"

"Mais oui, mademoiselle: voile cinq ou six heures que nous n'avons pas mange."

"Well now, while the ladies are in their rooms, I will venture down and get you something to eat."

And issuing from my asylum with precaution, I sought a backstairs which conducted directly to the kitchen. All in that region was fire and commotion; the soup and fish were in the last stage of projection, and the cook hung over her crucibles in a frame of mind and body threatening spontaneous combustion. In the servants' hall two coachmen and three gentlemen's gentlemen stood or sat round the fire; the abigails, I suppose, were upstairs with their mistresses; the new servants, that had been hired from Millcote, were bustling about everywhere. Threading this chaos, I at last reached the larder; there I took possession of a cold chicken, a roll of bread, some tarts, a plate or two and a knife and fork: with this booty I made a hasty retreat. I had regained the gallery, and was just shutting the back-door behind me, when an accelerated hum warned me that the ladies were about to issue from their chambers. I could not proceed to the schoolroom without passing some of their doors, and running the risk of being surprised with my cargo of victualage; so I stood still at this end, which, being windowless, was dark: quite dark now, for the sun was set and twilight gathering.

Presently the chambers gave up their fair tenants one after another: each came out gaily and airily, with dress that gleamed lustrous through the dusk. For a moment they stood grouped together at the other extremity of the gallery, conversing in a key of sweet subdued vivacity: they then descended the staircase almost as noiselessly as a bright mist rolls down a hill. Their collective appearance had left on me an impression of high-born elegance, such as I had never before received.

I found Adele peeping through the schoolroom door, which she held ajar. "What beautiful ladies!" cried she in English. "Oh, I wish I might go to them! Do you think Mr. Rochester will send for us by-and-bye, after dinner?"

"No, indeed, I don't; Mr. Rochester has something else to think about. Never mind the ladies to-night; perhaps you will see them to-morrow: here is your dinner."

She was really hungry, so the chicken and tarts served to divert her attention for a time. It was well I secured this forage, or both she, I, and Sophie, to whom I conveyed a share of our repast, would have run a chance of getting no dinner at all: every one downstairs was too much engaged to think of us. The dessert was not carried out till after nine and at ten footmen were still running to and fro with trays and coffee-cups. I allowed Adele to sit up much later than usual; for she declared she could not possibly go to sleep while the doors kept opening and shutting below, and people bustling about. Besides, she added, a message might possibly come from Mr. Rochester when she was undressed; "et alors quel dommage!"

I told her stories as long as she would listen to them; and then for a change I took her out into the gallery. The hall lamp was now lit, and it amused her to look over the balustrade and watch the servants passing backwards and forwards. When the evening was far advanced, a sound of music issued from the drawing-room, whither the piano had been removed; Adele and I sat down on the top step of the stairs to listen. Presently a voice blent with the rich tones of the instrument; it was a lady who sang, and very sweet her notes were. The solo over, a duet followed, and then a glee: a joyous conversational murmur filled up the intervals. I listened long: suddenly I discovered that my ear was wholly intent on analysing the mingled sounds, and trying to discriminate amidst the confusion of accents those of Mr. Rochester; and when it caught them, which it soon did, it found a further task in framing the tones, rendered by distance inarticulate, into words.

The clock struck eleven. I looked at Adele, whose head leant against my shoulder; her eyes were waxing heavy, so I took her up in my arms and carried her off to bed. It was near one before the gentlemen and ladies sought their chambers.

The next day was as fine as its predecessor: it was devoted by the party to an excursion to some site in the neighbourhood. They set out early in the forenoon, some on horseback, the rest in carriages; I witnessed both the departure and the return. Miss Ingram, as before, was the only lady equestrian; and, as before, Mr. Rochester galloped at her side; the two rode a little apart from the rest. I pointed out this circumstance to Mrs. Fairfax, who was standing at the window with me—

"You said it was not likely they should think of being married," said I, "but you see Mr. Rochester evidently prefers her to any of the other ladies."

"Yes, I daresay: no doubt he admires her."

"And she him," I added; "look how she leans her head towards him as if she were conversing confidentially; I wish I could see her face; I have never had a glimpse of it yet."

"You will see her this evening," answered Mrs. Fairfax. "I happened to remark to Mr. Rochester how much Adele wished to be introduced to the ladies, and he said: 'Oh! let her come into the drawing-room after dinner; and request Miss Eyre to accompany her.'"

"Yes; he said that from mere politeness: I need not go, I am sure," I answered.

"Well, I observed to him that as you were unused to company, I did not think you would like appearing before so gay a party—all strangers; and he replied, in his quick way—'Nonsense! If she objects, tell her it is my particular wish; and if she resists, say I shall come and fetch her in case of contumacy.'"

"I will not give him that trouble," I answered. "I will go, if no better may be; but I don't like it. Shall you be there, Mrs. Fairfax?"

"No; I pleaded off, and he admitted my plea. I'll tell you how to manage so as to avoid the embarrassment of making a formal entrance, which is the most disagreeable part of the business. You must go into the drawing-room while it is empty, before the ladies leave the dinner-table; choose your seat in any quiet nook you like; you need not stay long after the gentlemen come in, unless you please: just let Mr. Rochester see you are there and then slip away—nobody will notice you."

"Will these people remain long, do you think?"

"Perhaps two or three weeks, certainly not more. After the Easter recess, Sir George Lynn, who was lately elected member for Millcote, will have to go up to town and take his seat; I daresay Mr. Rochester will accompany him: it surprises me that he has already made so protracted a stay at Thornfield."

It was with some trepidation that I perceived the hour approach when I was to repair with my charge to the drawing-room. Adele had been in a state of ecstasy all day, after hearing she was to be presented to the ladies in the evening; and it was not till Sophie commenced the operation of dressing her that she sobered down. Then the importance of the process quickly steadied her, and by the time she had her curls arranged in well-smoothed, drooping clusters, her pink satin frock put on, her long sash tied, and her lace mittens adjusted, she looked as grave as any judge. No need to warn her not to disarrange her attire: when she was dressed, she sat demurely down in her little chair, taking care previously to lift up the satin skirt for fear she should crease it, and assured me she would not stir thence till I was ready. This I quickly was: my best dress (the silver-grey one, purchased for Miss Temple's wedding, and never worn since) was soon put on; my hair was soon smoothed; my sole ornament, the pearl brooch, soon assumed. We descended.

Fortunately there was another entrance to the drawing-room than that through the saloon where they were all seated at dinner. We found the apartment vacant; a large fire burning silently on the marble hearth, and wax candles shining in bright solitude, amid the exquisite flowers with which the tables were adorned. The crimson curtain hung before the arch: slight as was the separation this drapery formed from the party in the adjoining saloon, they spoke in so low a key that nothing of their conversation could be distinguished beyond a soothing murmur.

Adele, who appeared to be still under the influence of a most solemnising impression, sat down, without a word, on the footstool I pointed out to her. I retired to a window-seat, and taking a book from a table near, endeavoured to read. Adele brought her stool to my feet; ere long she touched my knee.

"What is it, Adele?"

"Est-ce que je ne puis pas prendrie une seule de ces fleurs magnifiques, mademoiselle? Seulement pour completer ma toilette."

"You think too much of your 'toilette,' Adele: but you may have a flower." And I took a rose from a vase and fastened it in her sash. She sighed a sigh of ineffable satisfaction, as if her cup of happiness were now full. I turned my face away to conceal a smile I could not suppress: there was something ludicrous as well as painful in the little Parisienne's earnest and innate devotion to matters of dress.

A soft sound of rising now became audible; the curtain was swept back from the arch; through it appeared the dining-room, with its lit lustre pouring down light on the silver and glass of a magnificent dessert-service covering a long table; a band of ladies stood in the opening; they entered, and the curtain fell behind them.

There were but eight; yet, somehow, as they flocked in, they gave the impression of a much larger number. Some of them were very tall; many were dressed in white; and all had a sweeping amplitude of array that seemed to magnify their persons as a mist magnifies the moon. I rose and curtseyed to them: one or two bent their heads in return, the others only stared at me.

They dispersed about the room, reminding me, by the lightness and buoyancy of their movements, of a flock of white plumy birds. Some of them threw themselves in half-reclining positions on the sofas and ottomans: some bent over the tables and examined the flowers and books: the rest gathered in a group round the fire: all talked in a low but clear tone which seemed habitual to them. I knew their names afterwards, and may as well mention them now.

First, there was Mrs. Eshton and two of her daughters. She had evidently been a handsome woman, and was well preserved still. Of her daughters, the eldest, Amy, was rather little: naive, and child-like in face and manner, and piquant in form; her white muslin dress and blue sash became her well. The second, Louisa, was taller and more elegant in figure; with a very pretty face, of that order the French term minois chiffone: both sisters were fair as lilies.

Lady Lynn was a large and stout personage of about forty, very erect, very haughty-looking, richly dressed in a satin robe of changeful sheen: her dark hair shone glossily under the shade of an azure plume, and within the circlet of a band of gems.

Mrs. Colonel Dent was less showy; but, I thought, more lady-like. She had a slight figure, a pale, gentle face, and fair hair. Her black satin dress, her scarf of rich foreign lace, and her pearl ornaments, pleased me better than the rainbow radiance of the titled dame.

But the three most distinguished—partly, perhaps, because the tallest figures of the band—were the Dowager Lady Ingram and her daughters, Blanche and Mary. They were all three of the loftiest stature of women. The Dowager might be between forty and fifty: her shape was still fine; her hair (by candle-light at least) still black; her teeth, too, were still apparently perfect. Most people would have termed her a splendid woman of her age: and so she was, no doubt, physically speaking; but then there was an expression of almost insupportable haughtiness in her bearing and countenance. She had Roman features and a double chin, disappearing into a throat like a pillar: these features appeared to me not only inflated and darkened, but even furrowed with pride; and the chin was sustained by the same principle, in a position of almost preternatural erectness. She had, likewise, a fierce and a hard eye: it reminded me of Mrs. Reed's; she mouthed her words in speaking; her voice was deep, its inflections very pompous, very dogmatical,—very intolerable, in short. A crimson velvet robe, and a shawl turban of some gold-wrought Indian fabric, invested her (I suppose she thought) with a truly imperial dignity.

Blanche and Mary were of equal stature,—straight and tall as poplars. Mary was too slim for her height, but Blanche was moulded like a Dian. I regarded her, of course, with special interest. First, I wished to see whether her appearance accorded with Mrs. Fairfax's description; secondly, whether it at all resembled the fancy miniature I had painted of her; and thirdly—it will out!—whether it were such as I should fancy likely to suit Mr. Rochester's taste.

As far as person went, she answered point for point, both to my picture and Mrs. Fairfax's description. The noble bust, the sloping shoulders, the graceful neck, the dark eyes and black ringlets were all there;—but her face? Her face was like her mother's; a youthful unfurrowed likeness: the same low brow, the same high features, the same pride. It was not, however, so saturnine a pride! she laughed continually; her laugh was satirical, and so was the habitual expression of her arched and haughty lip.

Genius is said to be self-conscious. I cannot tell whether Miss Ingram was a genius, but she was self-conscious—remarkably self-conscious indeed. She entered into a discourse on botany with the gentle Mrs. Dent. It seemed Mrs. Dent had not studied that science: though, as she said, she liked flowers, "especially wild ones;" Miss Ingram had, and she ran over its vocabulary with an air. I presently perceived she was (what is vernacularly termed) TRAILING Mrs. Dent; that is, playing on her ignorance—her TRAIL might be clever, but it was decidedly not good-natured. She played: her execution was brilliant; she sang: her voice was fine; she talked French apart to her mamma; and she talked it well, with fluency and with a good accent.

Mary had a milder and more open countenance than Blanche; softer features too, and a skin some shades fairer (Miss Ingram was dark as a Spaniard)—but Mary was deficient in life: her face lacked expression, her eye lustre; she had nothing to say, and having once taken her seat, remained fixed like a statue in its niche. The sisters were both attired in spotless white.

And did I now think Miss Ingram such a choice as Mr. Rochester would be likely to make? I could not tell—I did not know his taste in female beauty. If he liked the majestic, she was the very type of majesty: then she was accomplished, sprightly. Most gentlemen would admire her, I thought; and that he DID admire her, I already seemed to have obtained proof: to remove the last shade of doubt, it remained but to see them together.

You are not to suppose, reader, that Adele has all this time been sitting motionless on the stool at my feet: no; when the ladies entered, she rose, advanced to meet them, made a stately reverence, and said with gravity—

"Bon jour, mesdames."

And Miss Ingram had looked down at her with a mocking air, and exclaimed, "Oh, what a little puppet!"

Lady Lynn had remarked, "It is Mr. Rochester's ward, I suppose—the little French girl he was speaking of."

Mrs. Dent had kindly taken her hand, and given her a kiss.

Amy and Louisa Eshton had cried out simultaneously—"What a love of a child!"

And then they had called her to a sofa, where she now sat, ensconced between them, chattering alternately in French and broken English; absorbing not only the young ladies' attention, but that of Mrs. Eshton and Lady Lynn, and getting spoilt to her heart's content.

At last coffee is brought in, and the gentlemen are summoned. I sit in the shade—if any shade there be in this brilliantly-lit apartment; the window-curtain half hides me. Again the arch yawns; they come. The collective appearance of the gentlemen, like that of the ladies, is very imposing: they are all costumed in black; most of them are tall, some young. Henry and Frederick Lynn are very dashing sparks indeed; and Colonel Dent is a fine soldierly man. Mr. Eshton, the magistrate of the district, is gentleman-like: his hair is quite white, his eyebrows and whiskers still dark, which gives him something of the appearance of a "pere noble de theatre." Lord Ingram, like his sisters, is very tall; like them, also, he is handsome; but he shares Mary's apathetic and listless look: he seems to have more length of limb than vivacity of blood or vigour of brain.

And where is Mr. Rochester?

He comes in last: I am not looking at the arch, yet I see him enter. I try to concentrate my attention on those netting-needles, on the meshes of the purse I am forming—I wish to think only of the work I have in my hands, to see only the silver beads and silk threads that lie in my lap; whereas, I distinctly behold his figure, and I inevitably recall the moment when I last saw it; just after I had rendered him, what he deemed, an essential service, and he, holding my hand, and looking down on my face, surveyed me with eyes that revealed a heart full and eager to overflow; in whose emotions I had a part. How near had I approached him at that moment! What had occurred since, calculated to change his and my relative positions? Yet now, how distant, how far estranged we were! So far estranged, that I did not expect him to come and speak to me. I did not wonder, when, without looking at me, he took a seat at the other side of the room, and began conversing with some of the ladies.

No sooner did I see that his attention was riveted on them, and that I might gaze without being observed, than my eyes were drawn involuntarily to his face; I could not keep their lids under control: they would rise, and the irids would fix on him. I looked, and had an acute pleasure in looking,—a precious yet poignant pleasure; pure gold, with a steely point of agony: a pleasure like what the thirst-perishing man might feel who knows the well to which he has crept is poisoned, yet stoops and drinks divine draughts nevertheless.

Most true is it that "beauty is in the eye of the gazer." My master's colourless, olive face, square, massive brow, broad and jetty eyebrows, deep eyes, strong features, firm, grim mouth,—all energy, decision, will,—were not beautiful, according to rule; but they were more than beautiful to me; they were full of an interest, an influence that quite mastered me,—that took my feelings from my own power and fettered them in his. I had not intended to love him; the reader knows I had wrought hard to extirpate from my soul the germs of love there detected; and now, at the first renewed view of him, they spontaneously arrived, green and strong! He made me love him without looking at me.

I compared him with his guests. What was the gallant grace of the Lynns, the languid elegance of Lord Ingram,—even the military distinction of Colonel Dent, contrasted with his look of native pith and genuine power? I had no sympathy in their appearance, their expression: yet I could imagine that most observers would call them attractive, handsome, imposing; while they would pronounce Mr. Rochester at once harsh-featured and melancholy-looking. I saw them smile, laugh—it was nothing; the light of the candles had as much soul in it as their smile; the tinkle of the bell as much significance as their laugh. I saw Mr. Rochester smile:-his stern features softened; his eye grew both brilliant and gentle, its ray both searching and sweet. He was talking, at the moment, to Louisa and Amy Eshton. I wondered to see them receive with calm that look which seemed to me so penetrating: I expected their eyes to fall, their colour to rise under it; yet I was glad when I found they were in no sense moved. "He is not to them what he is to me," I thought: "he is not of their kind. I believe he is of mine;—I am sure he is—I feel akin to him—I understand the language of his countenance and movements: though rank and wealth sever us widely, I have something in my brain and heart, in my blood and nerves, that assimilates me mentally to him. Did I say, a few days since, that I had nothing to do with him but to receive my salary at his hands? Did I forbid myself to think of him in any other light than as a paymaster? Blasphemy against nature! Every good, true, vigorous feeling I have gathers impulsively round him. I know I must conceal my sentiments: I must smother hope; I must remember that he cannot care much for me. For when I say that I am of his kind, I do not mean that I have his force to influence, and his spell to attract; I mean only that I have certain tastes and feelings in common with him. I must, then, repeat continually that we are for ever sundered:-and yet, while I breathe and think, I must love him."

Coffee is handed. The ladies, since the gentlemen entered, have become lively as larks; conversation waxes brisk and merry. Colonel Dent and Mr. Eshton argue on politics; their wives listen. The two proud dowagers, Lady Lynn and Lady Ingram, confabulate together. Sir George—whom, by-the-bye, I have forgotten to describe,—a very big, and very fresh-looking country gentleman, stands before their sofa, coffee-cup in hand, and occasionally puts in a word. Mr. Frederick Lynn has taken a seat beside Mary Ingram, and is showing her the engravings of a splendid volume: she looks, smiles now and then, but apparently says little. The tall and phlegmatic Lord Ingram leans with folded arms on the chair-back of the little and lively Amy Eshton; she glances up at him, and chatters like a wren: she likes him better than she does Mr. Rochester. Henry Lynn has taken possession of an ottoman at the feet of Louisa: Adele shares it with him: he is trying to talk French with her, and Louisa laughs at his blunders. With whom will Blanche Ingram pair? She is standing alone at the table, bending gracefully over an album. She seems waiting to be sought; but she will not wait too long: she herself selects a mate.

Mr. Rochester, having quitted the Eshtons, stands on the hearth as solitary as she stands by the table: she confronts him, taking her station on the opposite side of the mantelpiece.

"Mr. Rochester, I thought you were not fond of children?"

"Nor am I."

"Then, what induced you to take charge of such a little doll as that?" (pointing to Adele). "Where did you pick her up?"

"I did not pick her up; she was left on my hands."

"You should have sent her to school."

"I could not afford it: schools are so dear."

"Why, I suppose you have a governess for her: I saw a person with her just now—is she gone? Oh, no! there she is still, behind the window-curtain. You pay her, of course; I should think it quite as expensive,—more so; for you have them both to keep in addition."

I feared—or should I say, hoped?—the allusion to me would make Mr. Rochester glance my way; and I involuntarily shrank farther into the shade: but he never turned his eyes.

"I have not considered the subject," said he indifferently, looking straight before him.

"No, you men never do consider economy and common sense. You should hear mama on the chapter of governesses: Mary and I have had, I should think, a dozen at least in our day; half of them detestable and the rest ridiculous, and all incubi—were they not, mama?"

"Did you speak, my own?"

The young lady thus claimed as the dowager's special property, reiterated her question with an explanation.

"My dearest, don't mention governesses; the word makes me nervous. I have suffered a martyrdom from their incompetency and caprice. I thank Heaven I have now done with them!"

Mrs. Dent here bent over to the pious lady and whispered something in her ear; I suppose, from the answer elicited, it was a reminder that one of the anathematised race was present.

"Tant pis!" said her Ladyship, "I hope it may do her good!" Then, in a lower tone, but still loud enough for me to hear, "I noticed her; I am a judge of physiognomy, and in hers I see all the faults of her class."

"What are they, madam?" inquired Mr. Rochester aloud.

"I will tell you in your private ear," replied she, wagging her turban three times with portentous significancy.

"But my curiosity will be past its appetite; it craves food now."

"Ask Blanche; she is nearer you than I."

"Oh, don't refer him to me, mama! I have just one word to say of the whole tribe; they are a nuisance. Not that I ever suffered much from them; I took care to turn the tables. What tricks Theodore and I used to play on our Miss Wilsons, and Mrs. Greys, and Madame Jouberts! Mary was always too sleepy to join in a plot with spirit. The best fun was with Madame Joubert: Miss Wilson was a poor sickly thing, lachrymose and low-spirited, not worth the trouble of vanquishing, in short; and Mrs. Grey was coarse and insensible; no blow took effect on her. But poor Madame Joubert! I see her yet in her raging passions, when we had driven her to extremities—spilt our tea, crumbled our bread and butter, tossed our books up to the ceiling, and played a charivari with the ruler and desk, the fender and fire-irons. Theodore, do you remember those merry days?"

"Yaas, to be sure I do," drawled Lord Ingram; "and the poor old stick used to cry out 'Oh you villains childs!'—and then we sermonised her on the presumption of attempting to teach such clever blades as we were, when she was herself so ignorant."

"We did; and, Tedo, you know, I helped you in prosecuting (or persecuting) your tutor, whey-faced Mr. Vining—the parson in the pip, as we used to call him. He and Miss Wilson took the liberty of falling in love with each other—at least Tedo and I thought so; we surprised sundry tender glances and sighs which we interpreted as tokens of 'la belle passion,' and I promise you the public soon had the benefit of our discovery; we employed it as a sort of lever to hoist our dead-weights from the house. Dear mama, there, as soon as she got an inkling of the business, found out that it was of an immoral tendency. Did you not, my lady-mother?"

"Certainly, my best. And I was quite right: depend on that: there are a thousand reasons why liaisons between governesses and tutors should never be tolerated a moment in any well-regulated house; firstly—"

"Oh, gracious, mama! Spare us the enumeration! Au reste, we all know them: danger of bad example to innocence of childhood; distractions and consequent neglect of duty on the part of the attached—mutual alliance and reliance; confidence thence resulting—insolence accompanying—mutiny and general blow-up. Am I right, Baroness Ingram, of Ingram Park?"

"My lily-flower, you are right now, as always."

"Then no more need be said: change the subject."

Amy Eshton, not hearing or not heeding this dictum, joined in with her soft, infantine tone: "Louisa and I used to quiz our governess too; but she was such a good creature, she would bear anything: nothing put her out. She was never cross with us; was she, Louisa?"

"No, never: we might do what we pleased; ransack her desk and her workbox, and turn her drawers inside out; and she was so good-natured, she would give as anything we asked for."

"I suppose, now," said Miss Ingram, curling her lip sarcastically, "we shall have an abstract of the memoirs of all the governesses extant: in order to avert such a visitation, I again move the introduction of a new topic. Mr. Rochester, do you second my motion?"

"Madam, I support you on this point, as on every other."

"Then on me be the onus of bringing it forward. Signior Eduardo, are you in voice to-night?"

"Donna Bianca, if you command it, I will be."

"Then, signior, I lay on you my sovereign behest to furbish up your lungs and other vocal organs, as they will be wanted on my royal service."

"Who would not be the Rizzio of so divine a Mary?"

"A fig for Rizzio!" cried she, tossing her head with all its curls, as she moved to the piano. "It is my opinion the fiddler David must have been an insipid sort of fellow; I like black Bothwell better: to my mind a man is nothing without a spice of the devil in him; and history may say what it will of James Hepburn, but I have a notion, he was just the sort of wild, fierce, bandit hero whom I could have consented to gift with my hand."

"Gentlemen, you hear! Now which of you most resembles Bothwell?" cried Mr. Rochester.

"I should say the preference lies with you," responded Colonel Dent.

"On my honour, I am much obliged to you," was the reply.

Miss Ingram, who had now seated herself with proud grace at the piano, spreading out her snowy robes in queenly amplitude, commenced a brilliant prelude; talking meantime. She appeared to be on her high horse to-night; both her words and her air seemed intended to excite not only the admiration, but the amazement of her auditors: she was evidently bent on striking them as something very dashing and daring indeed.

"Oh, I am so sick of the young men of the present day!" exclaimed she, rattling away at the instrument. "Poor, puny things, not fit to stir a step beyond papa's park gates: nor to go even so far without mama's permission and guardianship! Creatures so absorbed in care about their pretty faces, and their white hands, and their small feet; as if a man had anything to do with beauty! As if loveliness were not the special prerogative of woman—her legitimate appanage and heritage! I grant an ugly WOMAN is a blot on the fair face of creation; but as to the GENTLEMEN, let them be solicitous to possess only strength and valour: let their motto be:-Hunt, shoot, and fight: the rest is not worth a fillip. Such should be my device, were I a man."

"Whenever I marry," she continued after a pause which none interrupted, "I am resolved my husband shall not be a rival, but a foil to me. I will suffer no competitor near the throne; I shall exact an undivided homage: his devotions shall not be shared between me and the shape he sees in his mirror. Mr. Rochester, now sing, and I will play for you."

"I am all obedience," was the response.

"Here then is a Corsair-song. Know that I doat on Corsairs; and for that reason, sing it con spirito."

"Commands from Miss Ingram's lips would put spirit into a mug of milk and water."

"Take care, then: if you don't please me, I will shame you by showing how such things SHOULD be done."

"That is offering a premium on incapacity: I shall now endeavour to fail."

"Gardez-vous en bien! If you err wilfully, I shall devise a proportionate punishment."

"Miss Ingram ought to be clement, for she has it in her power to inflict a chastisement beyond mortal endurance."

"Ha! explain!" commanded the lady.

"Pardon me, madam: no need of explanation; your own fine sense must inform you that one of your frowns would be a sufficient substitute for capital punishment."

"Sing!" said she, and again touching the piano, she commenced an accompaniment in spirited style.

"Now is my time to slip away," thought I: but the tones that then severed the air arrested me. Mrs. Fairfax had said Mr. Rochester possessed a fine voice: he did—a mellow, powerful bass, into which he threw his own feeling, his own force; finding a way through the ear to the heart, and there waking sensation strangely. I waited till the last deep and full vibration had expired—till the tide of talk, checked an instant, had resumed its flow; I then quitted my sheltered corner and made my exit by the side-door, which was fortunately near. Thence a narrow passage led into the hall: in crossing it, I perceived my sandal was loose; I stopped to tie it, kneeling down for that purpose on the mat at the foot of the staircase. I heard the dining-room door unclose; a gentleman came out; rising hastily, I stood face to face with him: it was Mr. Rochester.

"How do you do?" he asked.

"I am very well, sir."

"Why did you not come and speak to me in the room?"

I thought I might have retorted the question on him who put it: but I would not take that freedom. I answered—

"I did not wish to disturb you, as you seemed engaged, sir."

"What have you been doing during my absence?"

"Nothing particular; teaching Adele as usual."

"And getting a good deal paler than you were—as I saw at first sight. What is the matter?"

"Nothing at all, sir."

"Did you take any cold that night you half drowned me?"

"Not she least."

"Return to the drawing-room: you are deserting too early."

"I am tired, sir."

He looked at me for a minute.

"And a little depressed," he said. "What about? Tell me."

"Nothing—nothing, sir. I am not depressed."

"But I affirm that you are: so much depressed that a few more words would bring tears to your eyes—indeed, they are there now, shining and swimming; and a bead has slipped from the lash and fallen on to the flag. If I had time, and was not in mortal dread of some prating prig of a servant passing, I would know what all this means. Well, to-night I excuse you; but understand that so long as my visitors stay, I expect you to appear in the drawing-room every evening; it is my wish; don't neglect it. Now go, and send Sophie for Adele. Good-night, my—" He stopped, bit his lip, and abruptly left me.

Chapter XVIII

Merry days were these at Thornfield Hall; and busy days too: how different from the first three months of stillness, monotony, and solitude I had passed beneath its roof! All sad feelings seemed now driven from the house, all gloomy associations forgotten: there was life everywhere, movement all day long. You could not now traverse the gallery, once so hushed, nor enter the front chambers, once so tenantless, without encountering a smart lady's-maid or a dandy valet.

The kitchen, the butler's pantry, the servants' hall, the entrance hall, were equally alive; and the saloons were only left void and still when the blue sky and halcyon sunshine of the genial spring weather called their occupants out into the grounds. Even when that weather was broken, and continuous rain set in for some days, no damp seemed cast over enjoyment: indoor amusements only became more lively and varied, in consequence of the stop put to outdoor gaiety.

I wondered what they were going to do the first evening a change of entertainment was proposed: they spoke of "playing charades," but in my ignorance I did not understand the term. The servants were called in, the dining-room tables wheeled away, the lights otherwise disposed, the chairs placed in a semicircle opposite the arch. While Mr. Rochester and the other gentlemen directed these alterations, the ladies were running up and down stairs ringing for their maids. Mrs. Fairfax was summoned to give information respecting the resources of the house in shawls, dresses, draperies of any kind; and certain wardrobes of the third storey were ransacked, and their contents, in the shape of brocaded and hooped petticoats, satin sacques, black modes, lace lappets, &c., were brought down in armfuls by the abigails; then a selection was made, and such things as were chosen were carried to the boudoir within the drawing-room.

Meantime, Mr. Rochester had again summoned the ladies round him, and was selecting certain of their number to be of his party. "Miss Ingram is mine, of course," said he: afterwards he named the two Misses Eshton, and Mrs. Dent. He looked at me: I happened to be near him, as I had been fastening the clasp of Mrs. Dent's bracelet, which had got loose.

"Will you play?" he asked. I shook my head. He did not insist, which I rather feared he would have done; he allowed me to return quietly to my usual seat.

He and his aids now withdrew behind the curtain: the other party, which was headed by Colonel Dent, sat down on the crescent of chairs. One of the gentlemen, Mr. Eshton, observing me, seemed to propose that I should be asked to join them; but Lady Ingram instantly negatived the notion.

"No," I heard her say: "she looks too stupid for any game of the sort."

Ere long a bell tinkled, and the curtain drew up. Within the arch, the bulky figure of Sir George Lynn, whom Mr. Rochester had likewise chosen, was seen enveloped in a white sheet: before him, on a table, lay open a large book; and at his side stood Amy Eshton, draped in Mr. Rochester's cloak, and holding a book in her hand. Somebody, unseen, rang the bell merrily; then Adele (who had insisted on being one of her guardian's party), bounded forward, scattering round her the contents of a basket of flowers she carried on her arm. Then appeared the magnificent figure of Miss Ingram, clad in white, a long veil on her head, and a wreath of roses round her brow; by her side walked Mr. Rochester, and together they drew near the table. They knelt; while Mrs. Dent and Louisa Eshton, dressed also in white, took up their stations behind them. A ceremony followed, in dumb show, in which it was easy to recognise the pantomime of a marriage. At its termination, Colonel Dent and his party consulted in whispers for two minutes, then the Colonel called out—

"Bride!" Mr. Rochester bowed, and the curtain fell.

A considerable interval elapsed before it again rose. Its second rising displayed a more elaborately prepared scene than the last. The drawing-room, as I have before observed, was raised two steps above the dining-room, and on the top of the upper step, placed a yard or two back within the room, appeared a large marble basin—which I recognised as an ornament of the conservatory—where it usually stood, surrounded by exotics, and tenanted by gold fish—and whence it must have been transported with some trouble, on account of its size and weight.

Seated on the carpet, by the side of this basin, was seen Mr. Rochester, costumed in shawls, with a turban on his head. His dark eyes and swarthy skin and Paynim features suited the costume exactly: he looked the very model of an Eastern emir, an agent or a victim of the bowstring. Presently advanced into view Miss Ingram. She, too, was attired in oriental fashion: a crimson scarf tied sash-like round the waist: an embroidered handkerchief knotted about her temples; her beautifully-moulded arms bare, one of them upraised in the act of supporting a pitcher, poised gracefully on her head. Both her cast of form and feature, her complexion and her general air, suggested the idea of some Israelitish princess of the patriarchal days; and such was doubtless the character she intended to represent.

She approached the basin, and bent over it as if to fill her pitcher; she again lifted it to her head. The personage on the well-brink now seemed to accost her; to make some request:-"She hasted, let down her pitcher on her hand, and gave him to drink." From the bosom of his robe he then produced a casket, opened it and showed magnificent bracelets and earrings; she acted astonishment and admiration; kneeling, he laid the treasure at her feet; incredulity and delight were expressed by her looks and gestures; the stranger fastened the bracelets on her arms and the rings in her ears. It was Eliezer and Rebecca: the camels only were wanting.

The divining party again laid their heads together: apparently they could not agree about the word or syllable the scene illustrated. Colonel Dent, their spokesman, demanded "the tableau of the whole;" whereupon the curtain again descended.

On its third rising only a portion of the drawing-room was disclosed; the rest being concealed by a screen, hung with some sort of dark and coarse drapery. The marble basin was removed; in its place, stood a deal table and a kitchen chair: these objects were visible by a very dim light proceeding from a horn lantern, the wax candles being all extinguished.

Amidst this sordid scene, sat a man with his clenched hands resting on his knees, and his eyes bent on the ground. I knew Mr. Rochester; though the begrimed face, the disordered dress (his coat hanging loose from one arm, as if it had been almost torn from his back in a scuffle), the desperate and scowling countenance, the rough, bristling hair might well have disguised him. As he moved, a chain clanked; to his wrists were attached fetters.

"Bridewell!" exclaimed Colonel Dent, and the charade was solved.

A sufficient interval having elapsed for the performers to resume their ordinary costume, they re-entered the dining-room. Mr. Rochester led in Miss Ingram; she was complimenting him on his acting.

"Do you know," said she, "that, of the three characters, I liked you in the last best? Oh, had you but lived a few years earlier, what a gallant gentleman-highwayman you would have made!"

"Is all the soot washed from my face?" he asked, turning it towards her.

"Alas! yes: the more's the pity! Nothing could be more becoming to your complexion than that ruffian's rouge."

"You would like a hero of the road then?"

"An English hero of the road would be the next best thing to an Italian bandit; and that could only be surpassed by a Levantine pirate."

"Well, whatever I am, remember you are my wife; we were married an hour since, in the presence of all these witnesses." She giggled, and her colour rose.

"Now, Dent," continued Mr. Rochester, "it is your turn." And as the other party withdrew, he and his band took the vacated seats. Miss Ingram placed herself at her leader's right hand; the other diviners filled the chairs on each side of him and her. I did not now watch the actors; I no longer waited with interest for the curtain to rise; my attention was absorbed by the spectators; my eyes, erewhile fixed on the arch, were now irresistibly attracted to the semicircle of chairs. What charade Colonel Dent and his party played, what word they chose, how they acquitted themselves, I no longer remember; but I still see the consultation which followed each scene: I see Mr. Rochester turn to Miss Ingram, and Miss Ingram to him; I see her incline her head towards him, till the jetty curls almost touch his shoulder and wave against his cheek; I hear their mutual whisperings; I recall their interchanged glances; and something even of the feeling roused by the spectacle returns in memory at this moment.

I have told you, reader, that I had learnt to love Mr. Rochester: I could not unlove him now, merely because I found that he had ceased to notice me—because I might pass hours in his presence, and he would never once turn his eyes in my direction—because I saw all his attentions appropriated by a great lady, who scorned to touch me with the hem of her robes as she passed; who, if ever her dark and imperious eye fell on me by chance, would withdraw it instantly as from an object too mean to merit observation. I could not unlove him, because I felt sure he would soon marry this very lady—because I read daily in her a proud security in his intentions respecting her—because I witnessed hourly in him a style of courtship which, if careless and choosing rather to be sought than to seek, was yet, in its very carelessness, captivating, and in its very pride, irresistible.

There was nothing to cool or banish love in these circumstances, though much to create despair. Much too, you will think, reader, to engender jealousy: if a woman, in my position, could presume to be jealous of a woman in Miss Ingram's. But I was not jealous: or very rarely;—the nature of the pain I suffered could not be explained by that word. Miss Ingram was a mark beneath jealousy: she was too inferior to excite the feeling. Pardon the seeming paradox; I mean what I say. She was very showy, but she was not genuine: she had a fine person, many brilliant attainments; but her mind was poor, her heart barren by nature: nothing bloomed spontaneously on that soil; no unforced natural fruit delighted by its freshness. She was not good; she was not original: she used to repeat sounding phrases from books: she never offered, nor had, an opinion of her own. She advocated a high tone of sentiment; but she did not know the sensations of sympathy and pity; tenderness and truth were not in her. Too often she betrayed this, by the undue vent she gave to a spiteful antipathy she had conceived against little Adele: pushing her away with some contumelious epithet if she happened to approach her; sometimes ordering her from the room, and always treating her with coldness and acrimony. Other eyes besides mine watched these manifestations of character—watched them closely, keenly, shrewdly. Yes; the future bridegroom, Mr. Rochester himself, exercised over his intended a ceaseless surveillance; and it was from this sagacity—this guardedness of his—this perfect, clear consciousness of his fair one's defects—this obvious absence of passion in his sentiments towards her, that my ever-torturing pain arose.

I saw he was going to marry her, for family, perhaps political reasons, because her rank and connections suited him; I felt he had not given her his love, and that her qualifications were ill adapted to win from him that treasure. This was the point—this was where the nerve was touched and teased—this was where the fever was sustained and fed: SHE COULD NOT CHARM HIM.

If she had managed the victory at once, and he had yielded and sincerely laid his heart at her feet, I should have covered my face, turned to the wall, and (figuratively) have died to them. If Miss Ingram had been a good and noble woman, endowed with force, fervour, kindness, sense, I should have had one vital struggle with two tigers—jealousy and despair: then, my heart torn out and devoured, I should have admired her—acknowledged her excellence, and been quiet for the rest of my days: and the more absolute her superiority, the deeper would have been my admiration—the more truly tranquil my quiescence. But as matters really stood, to watch Miss Ingram's efforts at fascinating Mr. Rochester, to witness their repeated failure—herself unconscious that they did fail; vainly fancying that each shaft launched hit the mark, and infatuatedly pluming herself on success, when her pride and self-complacency repelled further and further what she wished to allure—to witness THIS, was to be at once under ceaseless excitation and ruthless restraint.

Because, when she failed, I saw how she might have succeeded. Arrows that continually glanced off from Mr. Rochester's breast and fell harmless at his feet, might, I knew, if shot by a surer hand, have quivered keen in his proud heart—have called love into his stern eye, and softness into his sardonic face; or, better still, without weapons a silent conquest might have been won.

"Why can she not influence him more, when she is privileged to draw so near to him?" I asked myself. "Surely she cannot truly like him, or not like him with true affection! If she did, she need not coin her smiles so lavishly, flash her glances so unremittingly, manufacture airs so elaborate, graces so multitudinous. It seems to me that she might, by merely sitting quietly at his side, saying little and looking less, get nigher his heart. I have seen in his face a far different expression from that which hardens it now while she is so vivaciously accosting him; but then it came of itself: it was not elicited by meretricious arts and calculated manoeuvres; and one had but to accept it—to answer what he asked without pretension, to address him when needful without grimace—and it increased and grew kinder and more genial, and warmed one like a fostering sunbeam. How will she manage to please him when they are married? I do not think she will manage it; and yet it might be managed; and his wife might, I verily believe, be the very happiest woman the sun shines on."

I have not yet said anything condemnatory of Mr. Rochester's project of marrying for interest and connections. It surprised me when I first discovered that such was his intention: I had thought him a man unlikely to be influenced by motives so commonplace in his choice of a wife; but the longer I considered the position, education, &c., of the parties, the less I felt justified in judging and blaming either him or Miss Ingram for acting in conformity to ideas and principles instilled into them, doubtless, from their childhood. All their class held these principles: I supposed, then, they had reasons for holding them such as I could not fathom. It seemed to me that, were I a gentleman like him, I would take to my bosom only such a wife as I could love; but the very obviousness of the advantages to the husband's own happiness offered by this plan convinced me that there must be arguments against its general adoption of which I was quite ignorant: otherwise I felt sure all the world would act as I wished to act.

But in other points, as well as this, I was growing very lenient to my master: I was forgetting all his faults, for which I had once kept a sharp look-out. It had formerly been my endeavour to study all sides of his character: to take the bad with the good; and from the just weighing of both, to form an equitable judgment. Now I saw no bad. The sarcasm that had repelled, the harshness that had startled me once, were only like keen condiments in a choice dish: their presence was pungent, but their absence would be felt as comparatively insipid. And as for the vague something—was it a sinister or a sorrowful, a designing or a desponding expression?—that opened upon a careful observer, now and then, in his eye, and closed again before one could fathom the strange depth partially disclosed; that something which used to make me fear and shrink, as if I had been wandering amongst volcanic-looking hills, and had suddenly felt the ground quiver and seen it gape: that something, I, at intervals, beheld still; and with throbbing heart, but not with palsied nerves. Instead of wishing to shun, I longed only to dare—to divine it; and I thought Miss Ingram happy, because one day she might look into the abyss at her leisure, explore its secrets and analyse their nature.

Meantime, while I thought only of my master and his future bride—saw only them, heard only their discourse, and considered only their movements of importance—the rest of the party were occupied with their own separate interests and pleasures. The Ladies Lynn and Ingram continued to consort in solemn conferences, where they nodded their two turbans at each other, and held up their four hands in confronting gestures of surprise, or mystery, or horror, according to the theme on which their gossip ran, like a pair of magnified puppets. Mild Mrs. Dent talked with good-natured Mrs. Eshton; and the two sometimes bestowed a courteous word or smile on me. Sir George Lynn, Colonel Dent, and Mr. Eshton discussed politics, or county affairs, or justice business. Lord Ingram flirted with Amy Eshton; Louisa played and sang to and with one of the Messrs. Lynn; and Mary Ingram listened languidly to the gallant speeches of the other. Sometimes all, as with one consent, suspended their by-play to observe and listen to the principal actors: for, after all, Mr. Rochester and—because closely connected with him—Miss Ingram were the life and soul of the party. If he was absent from the room an hour, a perceptible dulness seemed to steal over the spirits of his guests; and his re-entrance was sure to give a fresh impulse to the vivacity of conversation.

The want of his animating influence appeared to be peculiarly felt one day that he had been summoned to Millcote on business, and was not likely to return till late. The afternoon was wet: a walk the party had proposed to take to see a gipsy camp, lately pitched on a common beyond Hay, was consequently deferred. Some of the gentlemen were gone to the stables: the younger ones, together with the younger ladies, were playing billiards in the billiard-room. The dowagers Ingram and Lynn sought solace in a quiet game at cards. Blanche Ingram, after having repelled, by supercilious taciturnity, some efforts of Mrs. Dent and Mrs. Eshton to draw her into conversation, had first murmured over some sentimental tunes and airs on the piano, and then, having fetched a novel from the library, had flung herself in haughty listlessness on a sofa, and prepared to beguile, by the spell of fiction, the tedious hours of absence. The room and the house were silent: only now and then the merriment of the billiard-players was heard from above.

It was verging on dusk, and the clock had already given warning of the hour to dress for dinner, when little Adele, who knelt by me in the drawing-room window-seat, suddenly exclaimed—

"Voile, Monsieur Rochester, qui revient!"

I turned, and Miss Ingram darted forwards from her sofa: the others, too, looked up from their several occupations; for at the same time a crunching of wheels and a splashing tramp of horse-hoofs became audible on the wet gravel. A post-chaise was approaching.

"What can possess him to come home in that style?" said Miss Ingram. "He rode Mesrour (the black horse), did he not, when he went out? and Pilot was with him:—what has he done with the animals?"

As she said this, she approached her tall person and ample garments so near the window, that I was obliged to bend back almost to the breaking of my spine: in her eagerness she did not observe me at first, but when she did, she curled her lip and moved to another casement. The post-chaise stopped; the driver rang the door-bell, and a gentleman alighted attired in travelling garb; but it was not Mr. Rochester; it was a tall, fashionable-looking man, a stranger.

"How provoking!" exclaimed Miss Ingram: "you tiresome monkey!" (apostrophising Adele), "who perched you up in the window to give false intelligence?" and she cast on me an angry glance, as if I were in fault.

Some parleying was audible in the hall, and soon the new-comer entered. He bowed to Lady Ingram, as deeming her the eldest lady present.

"It appears I come at an inopportune time, madam," said he, "when my friend, Mr. Rochester, is from home; but I arrive from a very long journey, and I think I may presume so far on old and intimate acquaintance as to instal myself here till he returns."

His manner was polite; his accent, in speaking, struck me as being somewhat unusual,—not precisely foreign, but still not altogether English: his age might be about Mr. Rochester's,—between thirty and forty; his complexion was singularly sallow: otherwise he was a fine-looking man, at first sight especially. On closer examination, you detected something in his face that displeased, or rather that failed to please. His features were regular, but too relaxed: his eye was large and well cut, but the life looking out of it was a tame, vacant life—at least so I thought.

The sound of the dressing-bell dispersed the party. It was not till after dinner that I saw him again: he then seemed quite at his ease. But I liked his physiognomy even less than before: it struck me as being at the same time unsettled and inanimate. His eye wandered, and had no meaning in its wandering: this gave him an odd look, such as I never remembered to have seen. For a handsome and not an unamiable-looking man, he repelled me exceedingly: there was no power in that smooth-skinned face of a full oval shape: no firmness in that aquiline nose and small cherry mouth; there was no thought on the low, even forehead; no command in that blank, brown eye.

As I sat in my usual nook, and looked at him with the light of the girandoles on the mantelpiece beaming full over him—for he occupied an arm-chair drawn close to the fire, and kept shrinking still nearer, as if he were cold, I compared him with Mr. Rochester. I think (with deference be it spoken) the contrast could not be much greater between a sleek gander and a fierce falcon: between a meek sheep and the rough-coated keen-eyed dog, its guardian.

He had spoken of Mr. Rochester as an old friend. A curious friendship theirs must have been: a pointed illustration, indeed, of the old adage that "extremes meet."

Two or three of the gentlemen sat near him, and I caught at times scraps of their conversation across the room. At first I could not make much sense of what I heard; for the discourse of Louisa Eshton and Mary Ingram, who sat nearer to me, confused the fragmentary sentences that reached me at intervals. These last were discussing the stranger; they both called him "a beautiful man." Louisa said he was "a love of a creature," and she "adored him;" and Mary instanced his "pretty little mouth, and nice nose," as her ideal of the charming.

"And what a sweet-tempered forehead he has!" cried Louisa,—"so smooth—none of those frowning irregularities I dislike so much; and such a placid eye and smile!"

And then, to my great relief, Mr. Henry Lynn summoned them to the other side of the room, to settle some point about the deferred excursion to Hay Common.

I was now able to concentrate my attention on the group by the fire, and I presently gathered that the new-comer was called Mr. Mason; then I learned that he was but just arrived in England, and that he came from some hot country: which was the reason, doubtless, his face was so sallow, and that he sat so near the hearth, and wore a surtout in the house. Presently the words Jamaica, Kingston, Spanish Town, indicated the West Indies as his residence; and it was with no little surprise I gathered, ere long, that he had there first seen and become acquainted with Mr. Rochester. He spoke of his friend's dislike of the burning heats, the hurricanes, and rainy seasons of that region. I knew Mr. Rochester had been a traveller: Mrs. Fairfax had said so; but I thought the continent of Europe had bounded his wanderings; till now I had never heard a hint given of visits to more distant shores.

I was pondering these things, when an incident, and a somewhat unexpected one, broke the thread of my musings. Mr. Mason, shivering as some one chanced to open the door, asked for more coal to be put on the fire, which had burnt out its flame, though its mass of cinder still shone hot and red. The footman who brought the coal, in going out, stopped near Mr. Eshton's chair, and said something to him in a low voice, of which I heard only the words, "old woman,"—"quite troublesome."

"Tell her she shall be put in the stocks if she does not take herself off," replied the magistrate.

"No—stop!" interrupted Colonel Dent. "Don't send her away, Eshton; we might turn the thing to account; better consult the ladies." And speaking aloud, he continued—"Ladies, you talked of going to Hay Common to visit the gipsy camp; Sam here says that one of the old Mother Bunches is in the servants' hall at this moment, and insists upon being brought in before 'the quality,' to tell them their fortunes. Would you like to see her?"

"Surely, colonel," cried Lady Ingram, "you would not encourage such a low impostor? Dismiss her, by all means, at once!"

"But I cannot persuade her to go away, my lady," said the footman; "nor can any of the servants: Mrs. Fairfax is with her just now, entreating her to be gone; but she has taken a chair in the chimney-corner, and says nothing shall stir her from it till she gets leave to come in here."

"What does she want?" asked Mrs. Eshton.

"'To tell the gentry their fortunes,' she says, ma'am; and she swears she must and will do it."

"What is she like?" inquired the Misses Eshton, in a breath.

"A shockingly ugly old creature, miss; almost as black as a crock."

"Why, she's a real sorceress!" cried Frederick Lynn. "Let us have her in, of course."

"To be sure," rejoined his brother; "it would be a thousand pities to throw away such a chance of fun."

"My dear boys, what are you thinking about?" exclaimed Mrs. Lynn.

"I cannot possibly countenance any such inconsistent proceeding," chimed in the Dowager Ingram.

"Indeed, mama, but you can—and will," pronounced the haughty voice of Blanche, as she turned round on the piano-stool; where till now she had sat silent, apparently examining sundry sheets of music. "I have a curiosity to hear my fortune told: therefore, Sam, order the beldame forward."

"My darling Blanche! recollect—"

"I do—I recollect all you can suggest; and I must have my will—quick, Sam!"

"Yes—yes—yes!" cried all the juveniles, both ladies and gentlemen. "Let her come—it will be excellent sport!"

The footman still lingered. "She looks such a rough one," said he.

"Go!" ejaculated Miss Ingram, and the man went.

Excitement instantly seized the whole party: a running fire of raillery and jests was proceeding when Sam returned.

"She won't come now," said he. "She says it's not her mission to appear before the 'vulgar herd' (them's her words). I must show her into a room by herself, and then those who wish to consult her must go to her one by one."

"You see now, my queenly Blanche," began Lady Ingram, "she encroaches. Be advised, my angel girl—and—"

"Show her into the library, of course," cut in the "angel girl." "It is not my mission to listen to her before the vulgar herd either: I mean to have her all to myself. Is there a fire in the library?"

"Yes, ma'am—but she looks such a tinkler."

"Cease that chatter, blockhead! and do my bidding."

Again Sam vanished; and mystery, animation, expectation rose to full flow once more.

"She's ready now," said the footman, as he reappeared. "She wishes to know who will be her first visitor."

"I think I had better just look in upon her before any of the ladies go," said Colonel Dent.

"Tell her, Sam, a gentleman is coming."

Sam went and returned.

"She says, sir, that she'll have no gentlemen; they need not trouble themselves to come near her; nor," he added, with difficulty suppressing a titter, "any ladies either, except the young, and single."

"By Jove, she has taste!" exclaimed Henry Lynn.

Miss Ingram rose solemnly: "I go first," she said, in a tone which might have befitted the leader of a forlorn hope, mounting a breach in the van of his men.

"Oh, my best! oh, my dearest! pause—reflect!" was her mama's cry; but she swept past her in stately silence, passed through the door which Colonel Dent held open, and we heard her enter the library.

A comparative silence ensued. Lady Ingram thought it "le cas" to wring her hands: which she did accordingly. Miss Mary declared she felt, for her part, she never dared venture. Amy and Louisa Eshton tittered under their breath, and looked a little frightened.

The minutes passed very slowly: fifteen were counted before the library-door again opened. Miss Ingram returned to us through the arch.

Would she laugh? Would she take it as a joke? All eyes met her with a glance of eager curiosity, and she met all eyes with one of rebuff and coldness; she looked neither flurried nor merry: she walked stiffly to her seat, and took it in silence.

"Well, Blanche?" said Lord Ingram.

"What did she say, sister?" asked Mary.

"What did you think? How do you feel?—Is she a real fortune-teller?" demanded the Misses Eshton.

"Now, now, good people," returned Miss Ingram, "don't press upon me. Really your organs of wonder and credulity are easily excited: you seem, by the importance of you all—my good mama included—ascribe to this matter, absolutely to believe we have a genuine witch in the house, who is in close alliance with the old gentleman. I have seen a gipsy vagabond; she has practised in hackneyed fashion the science of palmistry and told me what such people usually tell. My whim is gratified; and now I think Mr. Eshton will do well to put the hag in the stocks to-morrow morning, as he threatened."

Miss Ingram took a book, leant back in her chair, and so declined further conversation. I watched her for nearly half-an-hour: during all that time she never turned a page, and her face grew momently darker, more dissatisfied, and more sourly expressive of disappointment. She had obviously not heard anything to her advantage: and it seemed to me, from her prolonged fit of gloom and taciturnity, that she herself, notwithstanding her professed indifference, attached undue importance to whatever revelations had been made her.

Meantime, Mary Ingram, Amy and Louisa Eshton, declared they dared not go alone; and yet they all wished to go. A negotiation was opened through the medium of the ambassador, Sam; and after much pacing to and fro, till, I think, the said Sam's calves must have ached with the exercise, permission was at last, with great difficulty, extorted from the rigorous Sibyl, for the three to wait upon her in a body.

Their visit was not so still as Miss Ingram's had been: we heard hysterical giggling and little shrieks proceeding from the library; and at the end of about twenty minutes they burst the door open, and came running across the hall, as if they were half-scared out of their wits.

"I am sure she is something not right!" they cried, one and all. "She told us such things! She knows all about us!" and they sank breathless into the various seats the gentlemen hastened to bring them.

Pressed for further explanation, they declared she had told them of things they had said and done when they were mere children; described books and ornaments they had in their boudoirs at home: keepsakes that different relations had presented to them. They affirmed that she had even divined their thoughts, and had whispered in the ear of each the name of the person she liked best in the world, and informed them of what they most wished for.

Here the gentlemen interposed with earnest petitions to be further enlightened on these two last-named points; but they got only blushes, ejaculations, tremors, and titters, in return for their importunity. The matrons, meantime, offered vinaigrettes and wielded fans; and again and again reiterated the expression of their concern that their warning had not been taken in time; and the elder gentlemen laughed, and the younger urged their services on the agitated fair ones.

In the midst of the tumult, and while my eyes and ears were fully engaged in the scene before me, I heard a hem close at my elbow: I turned, and saw Sam.

"If you please, miss, the gipsy declares that there is another young single lady in the room who has not been to her yet, and she swears she will not go till she has seen all. I thought it must be you: there is no one else for it. What shall I tell her?"

"Oh, I will go by all means," I answered: and I was glad of the unexpected opportunity to gratify my much-excited curiosity. I slipped out of the room, unobserved by any eye—for the company were gathered in one mass about the trembling trio just returned—and I closed the door quietly behind me.

"If you like, miss," said Sam, "I'll wait in the hall for you; and if she frightens you, just call and I'll come in."

"No, Sam, return to the kitchen: I am not in the least afraid." Nor was I; but I was a good deal interested and excited.

Chapter XIX

The library looked tranquil enough as I entered it, and the Sibyl—if Sibyl she were—was seated snugly enough in an easy-chair at the chimney-corner. She had on a red cloak and a black bonnet: or rather, a broad-brimmed gipsy hat, tied down with a striped handkerchief under her chin. An extinguished candle stood on the table; she was bending over the fire, and seemed reading in a little black book, like a prayer-book, by the light of the blaze: she muttered the words to herself, as most old women do, while she read; she did not desist immediately on my entrance: it appeared she wished to finish a paragraph.

I stood on the rug and warmed my hands, which were rather cold with sitting at a distance from the drawing-room fire. I felt now as composed as ever I did in my life: there was nothing indeed in the gipsy's appearance to trouble one's calm. She shut her book and slowly looked up; her hat-brim partially shaded her face, yet I could see, as she raised it, that it was a strange one. It looked all brown and black: elf-locks bristled out from beneath a white band which passed under her chin, and came half over her cheeks, or rather jaws: her eye confronted me at once, with a bold and direct gaze.

"Well, and you want your fortune told?" she said, in a voice as decided as her glance, as harsh as her features.

"I don't care about it, mother; you may please yourself: but I ought to warn you, I have no faith."

"It's like your impudence to say so: I expected it of you; I heard it in your step as you crossed the threshold."

"Did you? You've a quick ear."

"I have; and a quick eye and a quick brain."

"You need them all in your trade."

"I do; especially when I've customers like you to deal with. Why don't you tremble?"

"I'm not cold."

"Why don't you turn pale?"

"I am not sick."

"Why don't you consult my art?"

"I'm not silly."

The old crone "nichered" a laugh under her bonnet and bandage; she then drew out a short black pipe, and lighting it began to smoke. Having indulged a while in this sedative, she raised her bent body, took the pipe from her lips, and while gazing steadily at the fire, said very deliberately—"You are cold; you are sick; and you are silly."

"Prove it," I rejoined.

"I will, in few words. You are cold, because you are alone: no contact strikes the fire from you that is in you. You are sick; because the best of feelings, the highest and the sweetest given to man, keeps far away from you. You are silly, because, suffer as you may, you will not beckon it to approach, nor will you stir one step to meet it where it waits you."

She again put her short black pipe to her lips, and renewed her smoking with vigour.

"You might say all that to almost any one who you knew lived as a solitary dependent in a great house."

"I might say it to almost any one: but would it be true of almost any one?"

"In my circumstances."

"Yes; just so, in YOUR circumstances: but find me another precisely placed as you are."

"It would be easy to find you thousands."

"You could scarcely find me one. If you knew it, you are peculiarly situated: very near happiness; yes, within reach of it. The materials are all prepared; there only wants a movement to combine them. Chance laid them somewhat apart; let them be once approached and bliss results."

"I don't understand enigmas. I never could guess a riddle in my life."

"If you wish me to speak more plainly, show me your palm."

"And I must cross it with silver, I suppose?"

"To be sure."

I gave her a shilling: she put it into an old stocking-foot which she took out of her pocket, and having tied it round and returned it, she told me to hold out my hand. I did. She ached her face to the palm, and pored over it without touching it.

"It is too fine," said she. "I can make nothing of such a hand as that; almost without lines: besides, what is in a palm? Destiny is not written there."

"I believe you," said I.

"No," she continued, "it is in the face: on the forehead, about the eyes, in the lines of the mouth. Kneel, and lift up your head."

"Ah! now you are coming to reality," I said, as I obeyed her. "I shall begin to put some faith in you presently."

I knelt within half a yard of her. She stirred the fire, so that a ripple of light broke from the disturbed coal: the glare, however, as she sat, only threw her face into deeper shadow: mine, it illumined.

"I wonder with what feelings you came to me to-night," she said, when she had examined me a while. "I wonder what thoughts are busy in your heart during all the hours you sit in yonder room with the fine people flitting before you like shapes in a magic-lantern: just as little sympathetic communion passing between you and them as if they were really mere shadows of human forms, and not the actual substance."

"I feel tired often, sleepy sometimes, but seldom sad."

"Then you have some secret hope to buoy you up and please you with whispers of the future?"

"Not I. The utmost I hope is, to save money enough out of my earnings to set up a school some day in a little house rented by myself."

"A mean nutriment for the spirit to exist on: and sitting in that window-seat (you see I know your habits)—"

"You have learned them from the servants."

"Ah! you think yourself sharp. Well, perhaps I have: to speak truth, I have an acquaintance with one of them, Mrs. Poole—"

I started to my feet when I heard the name.

"You have—have you?" thought I; "there is diablerie in the business after all, then!"

"Don't be alarmed," continued the strange being; "she's a safe hand is Mrs. Poole: close and quiet; any one may repose confidence in her. But, as I was saying: sitting in that window-seat, do you think of nothing but your future school? Have you no present interest in any of the company who occupy the sofas and chairs before you? Is there not one face you study? one figure whose movements you follow with at least curiosity?"

"I like to observe all the faces and all the figures."

"But do you never single one from the rest—or it may be, two?"

"I do frequently; when the gestures or looks of a pair seem telling a tale: it amuses me to watch them."

"What tale do you like best to hear?"

"Oh, I have not much choice! They generally run on the same theme—courtship; and promise to end in the same catastrophe—marriage."

"And do you like that monotonous theme?"

"Positively, I don't care about it: it is nothing to me."

"Nothing to you? When a lady, young and full of life and health, charming with beauty and endowed with the gifts of rank and fortune, sits and smiles in the eyes of a gentleman you—"

"I what?"

"You know—and perhaps think well of."

"I don't know the gentlemen here. I have scarcely interchanged a syllable with one of them; and as to thinking well of them, I consider some respectable, and stately, and middle-aged, and others young, dashing, handsome, and lively: but certainly they are all at liberty to be the recipients of whose smiles they please, without my feeling disposed to consider the transaction of any moment to me."

"You don't know the gentlemen here? You have not exchanged a syllable with one of them? Will you say that of the master of the house!"

"He is not at home."

"A profound remark! A most ingenious quibble! He went to Millcote this morning, and will be back here to-night or to-morrow: does that circumstance exclude him from the list of your acquaintance—blot him, as it were, out of existence?"

"No; but I can scarcely see what Mr. Rochester has to do with the theme you had introduced."

"I was talking of ladies smiling in the eyes of gentlemen; and of late so many smiles have been shed into Mr. Rochester's eyes that they overflow like two cups filled above the brim: have you never remarked that?"

"Mr. Rochester has a right to enjoy the society of his guests."

"No question about his right: but have you never observed that, of all the tales told here about matrimony, Mr. Rochester has been favoured with the most lively and the most continuous?"

"The eagerness of a listener quickens the tongue of a narrator." I said this rather to myself than to the gipsy, whose strange talk, voice, manner, had by this time wrapped me in a kind of dream. One unexpected sentence came from her lips after another, till I got involved in a web of mystification; and wondered what unseen spirit had been sitting for weeks by my heart watching its workings and taking record of every pulse.

"Eagerness of a listener!" repeated she: "yes; Mr. Rochester has sat by the hour, his ear inclined to the fascinating lips that took such delight in their task of communicating; and Mr. Rochester was so willing to receive and looked so grateful for the pastime given him; you have noticed this?"

"Grateful! I cannot remember detecting gratitude in his face."

"Detecting! You have analysed, then. And what did you detect, if not gratitude?"

I said nothing.

"You have seen love: have you not?—and, looking forward, you have seen him married, and beheld his bride happy?"

"Humph! Not exactly. Your witch's skill is rather at fault sometimes."

"What the devil have you seen, then?"

"Never mind: I came here to inquire, not to confess. Is it known that Mr. Rochester is to be married?"

"Yes; and to the beautiful Miss Ingram."

"Shortly?"

"Appearances would warrant that conclusion: and, no doubt (though, with an audacity that wants chastising out of you, you seem to question it), they will be a superlatively happy pair. He must love such a handsome, noble, witty, accomplished lady; and probably she loves him, or, if not his person, at least his purse. I know she considers the Rochester estate eligible to the last degree; though (God pardon me!) I told her something on that point about an hour ago which made her look wondrous grave: the corners of her mouth fell half an inch. I would advise her blackaviced suitor to look out: if another comes, with a longer or clearer rent-roll,—he's dished—"

"But, mother, I did not come to hear Mr. Rochester's fortune: I came to hear my own; and you have told me nothing of it."

"Your fortune is yet doubtful: when I examined your face, one trait contradicted another. Chance has meted you a measure of happiness: that I know. I knew it before I came here this evening. She has laid it carefully on one side for you. I saw her do it. It depends on yourself to stretch out your hand, and take it up: but whether you will do so, is the problem I study. Kneel again on the rug."

"Don't keep me long; the fire scorches me."

I knelt. She did not stoop towards me, but only gazed, leaning back in her chair. She began muttering,—

"The flame flickers in the eye; the eye shines like dew; it looks soft and full of feeling; it smiles at my jargon: it is susceptible; impression follows impression through its clear sphere; where it ceases to smile, it is sad; an unconscious lassitude weighs on the lid: that signifies melancholy resulting from loneliness. It turns from me; it will not suffer further scrutiny; it seems to deny, by a mocking glance, the truth of the discoveries I have already made,—to disown the charge both of sensibility and chagrin: its pride and reserve only confirm me in my opinion. The eye is favourable.

"As to the mouth, it delights at times in laughter; it is disposed to impart all that the brain conceives; though I daresay it would be silent on much the heart experiences. Mobile and flexible, it was never intended to be compressed in the eternal silence of solitude: it is a mouth which should speak much and smile often, and have human affection for its interlocutor. That feature too is propitious.

"I see no enemy to a fortunate issue but in the brow; and that brow professes to say,—'I can live alone, if self-respect, and circumstances require me so to do. I need not sell my soul to buy bliss. I have an inward treasure born with me, which can keep me alive if all extraneous delights should be withheld, or offered only at a price I cannot afford to give.' The forehead declares, 'Reason sits firm and holds the reins, and she will not let the feelings burst away and hurry her to wild chasms. The passions may rage furiously, like true heathens, as they are; and the desires may imagine all sorts of vain things: but judgment shall still have the last word in every argument, and the casting vote in every decision. Strong wind, earthquake-shock, and fire may pass by: but I shall follow the guiding of that still small voice which interprets the dictates of conscience.'

"Well said, forehead; your declaration shall be respected. I have formed my plans—right plans I deem them—and in them I have attended to the claims of conscience, the counsels of reason. I know how soon youth would fade and bloom perish, if, in the cup of bliss offered, but one dreg of shame, or one flavour of remorse were detected; and I do not want sacrifice, sorrow, dissolution—such is not my taste. I wish to foster, not to blight—to earn gratitude, not to wring tears of blood—no, nor of brine: my harvest must be in smiles, in endearments, in sweet—That will do. I think I rave in a kind of exquisite delirium. I should wish now to protract this moment ad infinitum; but I dare not. So far I have governed myself thoroughly. I have acted as I inwardly swore I would act; but further might try me beyond my strength. Rise, Miss Eyre: leave me; the play is played out.'"

Where was I? Did I wake or sleep? Had I been dreaming? Did I dream still? The old woman's voice had changed: her accent, her gesture, and all were familiar to me as my own face in a glass—as the speech of my own tongue. I got up, but did not go. I looked; I stirred the fire, and I looked again: but she drew her bonnet and her bandage closer about her face, and again beckoned me to depart. The flame illuminated her hand stretched out: roused now, and on the alert for discoveries, I at once noticed that hand. It was no more the withered limb of eld than my own; it was a rounded supple member, with smooth fingers, symmetrically turned; a broad ring flashed on the little finger, and stooping forward, I looked at it, and saw a gem I had seen a hundred times before. Again I looked at the face; which was no longer turned from me—on the contrary, the bonnet was doffed, the bandage displaced, the head advanced.

"Well, Jane, do you know me?" asked the familiar voice.

"Only take off the red cloak, sir, and then—"

"But the string is in a knot—help me."

"Break it, sir."

"There, then—'Off, ye lendings!'" And Mr. Rochester stepped out of his disguise.

"Now, sir, what a strange idea!"

"But well carried out, eh? Don't you think so?"

"With the ladies you must have managed well."

"But not with you?"

"You did not act the character of a gipsy with me."

"What character did I act? My own?"

"No; some unaccountable one. In short, I believe you have been trying to draw me out—or in; you have been talking nonsense to make me talk nonsense. It is scarcely fair, sir."

"Do you forgive me, Jane?"

"I cannot tell till I have thought it all over. If, on reflection, I find I have fallen into no great absurdity, I shall try to forgive you; but it was not right."

"Oh, you have been very correct—very careful, very sensible."

I reflected, and thought, on the whole, I had. It was a comfort; but, indeed, I had been on my guard almost from the beginning of the interview. Something of masquerade I suspected. I knew gipsies and fortune-tellers did not express themselves as this seeming old woman had expressed herself; besides I had noted her feigned voice, her anxiety to conceal her features. But my mind had been running on Grace Poole—that living enigma, that mystery of mysteries, as I considered her. I had never thought of Mr. Rochester.

"Well," said he, "what are you musing about? What does that grave smile signify?"

"Wonder and self-congratulation, sir. I have your permission to retire now, I suppose?"

"No; stay a moment; and tell me what the people in the drawing-room yonder are doing."

"Discussing the gipsy, I daresay."

"Sit down!—Let me hear what they said about me."

"I had better not stay long, sir; it must be near eleven o'clock. Oh, are you aware, Mr. Rochester, that a stranger has arrived here since you left this morning?"

"A stranger!—no; who can it be? I expected no one; is he gone?"

"No; he said he had known you long, and that he could take the liberty of installing himself here till you returned."

"The devil he did! Did he give his name?"

"His name is Mason, sir; and he comes from the West Indies; from Spanish Town, in Jamaica, I think."

Mr. Rochester was standing near me; he had taken my hand, as if to lead me to a chair. As I spoke he gave my wrist a convulsive grip; the smile on his lips froze: apparently a spasm caught his breath.

"Mason!—the West Indies!" he said, in the tone one might fancy a speaking automaton to enounce its single words; "Mason!—the West Indies!" he reiterated; and he went over the syllables three times, growing, in the intervals of speaking, whiter than ashes: he hardly seemed to know what he was doing.

"Do you feel ill, sir?" I inquired.

"Jane, I've got a blow; I've got a blow, Jane!" He staggered.

"Oh, lean on me, sir."

"Jane, you offered me your shoulder once before; let me have it now."

"Yes, sir, yes; and my arm."

He sat down, and made me sit beside him. Holding my hand in both his own, he chafed it; gazing on me, at the same time, with the most troubled and dreary look.

"My little friend!" said he, "I wish I were in a quiet island with only you; and trouble, and danger, and hideous recollections removed from me."

"Can I help you, sir?—I'd give my life to serve you."

"Jane, if aid is wanted, I'll seek it at your hands; I promise you that."

"Thank you, sir. Tell me what to do,—I'll try, at least, to do it."

"Fetch me now, Jane, a glass of wine from the dining-room: they will be at supper there; and tell me if Mason is with them, and what he is doing."

I went. I found all the party in the dining-room at supper, as Mr. Rochester had said; they were not seated at table,—the supper was arranged on the sideboard; each had taken what he chose, and they stood about here and there in groups, their plates and glasses in their hands. Every one seemed in high glee; laughter and conversation were general and animated. Mr. Mason stood near the fire, talking to Colonel and Mrs. Dent, and appeared as merry as any of them. I filled a wine-glass (I saw Miss Ingram watch me frowningly as I did so: she thought I was taking a liberty, I daresay), and I returned to the library.

Mr. Rochester's extreme pallor had disappeared, and he looked once more firm and stern. He took the glass from my hand.

"Here is to your health, ministrant spirit!" he said. He swallowed the contents and returned it to me. "What are they doing, Jane?"

"Laughing and talking, sir."

"They don't look grave and mysterious, as if they had heard something strange?"

"Not at all: they are full of jests and gaiety."

"And Mason?"

"He was laughing too."

"If all these people came in a body and spat at me, what would you do, Jane?"

"Turn them out of the room, sir, if I could."

He half smiled. "But if I were to go to them, and they only looked at me coldly, and whispered sneeringly amongst each other, and then dropped off and left me one by one, what then? Would you go with them?"

"I rather think not, sir: I should have more pleasure in staying with you."

"To comfort me?"

"Yes, sir, to comfort you, as well as I could."

"And if they laid you under a ban for adhering to me?"

"I, probably, should know nothing about their ban; and if I did, I should care nothing about it."

"Then, you could dare censure for my sake?"

"I could dare it for the sake of any friend who deserved my adherence; as you, I am sure, do."

"Go back now into the room; step quietly up to Mason, and whisper in his ear that Mr. Rochester is come and wishes to see him: show him in here and then leave me."

"Yes, sir."

I did his behest. The company all stared at me as I passed straight among them. I sought Mr. Mason, delivered the message, and preceded him from the room: I ushered him into the library, and then I went upstairs.

At a late hour, after I had been in bed some time, I heard the visitors repair to their chambers: I distinguished Mr. Rochester's voice, and heard him say, "This way, Mason; this is your room."

He spoke cheerfully: the gay tones set my heart at ease. I was soon asleep.

Chapter XX

I had forgotten to draw my curtain, which I usually did, and also to let down my window-blind. The consequence was, that when the moon, which was full and bright (for the night was fine), came in her course to that space in the sky opposite my casement, and looked in at me through the unveiled panes, her glorious gaze roused me. Awaking in the dead of night, I opened my eyes on her disk—silver-white and crystal clear. It was beautiful, but too solemn; I half rose, and stretched my arm to draw the curtain.

Good God! What a cry!

The night—its silence—its rest, was rent in twain by a savage, a sharp, a shrilly sound that ran from end to end of Thornfield Hall.

My pulse stopped: my heart stood still; my stretched arm was paralysed. The cry died, and was not renewed. Indeed, whatever being uttered that fearful shriek could not soon repeat it: not the widest-winged condor on the Andes could, twice in succession, send out such a yell from the cloud shrouding his eyrie. The thing delivering such utterance must rest ere it could repeat the effort.

It came out of the third storey; for it passed overhead. And overhead—yes, in the room just above my chamber-ceiling—I now heard a struggle: a deadly one it seemed from the noise; and a half-smothered voice shouted—

"Help! help! help!" three times rapidly.

"Will no one come?" it cried; and then, while the staggering and stamping went on wildly, I distinguished through plank and plaster:-

"Rochester! Rochester! for God's sake, come!"

A chamber-door opened: some one ran, or rushed, along the gallery. Another step stamped on the flooring above and something fell; and there was silence.

I had put on some clothes, though horror shook all my limbs; I issued from my apartment. The sleepers were all aroused: ejaculations, terrified murmurs sounded in every room; door after door unclosed; one looked out and another looked out; the gallery filled. Gentlemen and ladies alike had quitted their beds; and "Oh! what is it?"—"Who is hurt?"—"What has happened?"—"Fetch a light!"—"Is it fire?"—"Are there robbers?"—"Where shall we run?" was demanded confusedly on all hands. But for the moonlight they would have been in complete darkness. They ran to and fro; they crowded together: some sobbed, some stumbled: the confusion was inextricable.

"Where the devil is Rochester?" cried Colonel Dent. "I cannot find him in his bed."

"Here! here!" was shouted in return. "Be composed, all of you: I'm coming."

And the door at the end of the gallery opened, and Mr. Rochester advanced with a candle: he had just descended from the upper storey. One of the ladies ran to him directly; she seized his arm: it was Miss Ingram.

"What awful event has taken place?" said she. "Speak! let us know the worst at once!"

"But don't pull me down or strangle me," he replied: for the Misses Eshton were clinging about him now; and the two dowagers, in vast white wrappers, were bearing down on him like ships in full sail.

"All's right!—all's right!" he cried. "It's a mere rehearsal of Much Ado about Nothing. Ladies, keep off, or I shall wax dangerous."

And dangerous he looked: his black eyes darted sparks. Calming himself by an effort, he added—

"A servant has had the nightmare; that is all. She's an excitable, nervous person: she construed her dream into an apparition, or something of that sort, no doubt; and has taken a fit with fright. Now, then, I must see you all back into your rooms; for, till the house is settled, she cannot be looked after. Gentlemen, have the goodness to set the ladies the example. Miss Ingram, I am sure you will not fail in evincing superiority to idle terrors. Amy and Louisa, return to your nests like a pair of doves, as you are. Mesdames" (to the dowagers), "you will take cold to a dead certainty, if you stay in this chill gallery any longer."

And so, by dint of alternate coaxing and commanding, he contrived to get them all once more enclosed in their separate dormitories. I did not wait to be ordered back to mine, but retreated unnoticed, as unnoticed I had left it.

Not, however, to go to bed: on the contrary, I began and dressed myself carefully. The sounds I had heard after the scream, and the words that had been uttered, had probably been heard only by me; for they had proceeded from the room above mine: but they assured me that it was not a servant's dream which had thus struck horror through the house; and that the explanation Mr. Rochester had given was merely an invention framed to pacify his guests. I dressed, then, to be ready for emergencies. When dressed, I sat a long time by the window looking out over the silent grounds and silvered fields and waiting for I knew not what. It seemed to me that some event must follow the strange cry, struggle, and call.

No: stillness returned: each murmur and movement ceased gradually, and in about an hour Thornfield Hall was again as hushed as a desert. It seemed that sleep and night had resumed their empire. Meantime the moon declined: she was about to set. Not liking to sit in the cold and darkness, I thought I would lie down on my bed, dressed as I was. I left the window, and moved with little noise across the carpet; as I stooped to take off my shoes, a cautious hand tapped low at the door.

"Am I wanted?" I asked.

"Are you up?" asked the voice I expected to hear, viz., my master's.

"Yes, sir."

"And dressed?"

"Yes."

"Come out, then, quietly."

I obeyed. Mr. Rochester stood in the gallery holding a light.

"I want you," he said: "come this way: take your time, and make no noise."

My slippers were thin: I could walk the matted floor as softly as a cat. He glided up the gallery and up the stairs, and stopped in the dark, low corridor of the fateful third storey: I had followed and stood at his side.

"Have you a sponge in your room?" he asked in a whisper.

"Yes, sir."

"Have you any salts—volatile salts? Yes."

"Go back and fetch both."

I returned, sought the sponge on the washstand, the salts in my drawer, and once more retraced my steps. He still waited; he held a key in his hand: approaching one of the small, black doors, he put it in the lock; he paused, and addressed me again.

"You don't turn sick at the sight of blood?"

"I think I shall not: I have never been tried yet."

I felt a thrill while I answered him; but no coldness, and no faintness.

"Just give me your hand," he said: "it will not do to risk a fainting fit."

I put my fingers into his. "Warm and steady," was his remark: he turned the key and opened the door.

I saw a room I remembered to have seen before, the day Mrs. Fairfax showed me over the house: it was hung with tapestry; but the tapestry was now looped up in one part, and there was a door apparent, which had then been concealed. This door was open; a light shone out of the room within: I heard thence a snarling, snatching sound, almost like a dog quarrelling. Mr. Rochester, putting down his candle, said to me, "Wait a minute," and he went forward to the inner apartment. A shout of laughter greeted his entrance; noisy at first, and terminating in Grace Poole's own goblin ha! ha! SHE then was there. He made some sort of arrangement without speaking, though I heard a low voice address him: he came out and closed the door behind him.

"Here, Jane!" he said; and I walked round to the other side of a large bed, which with its drawn curtains concealed a considerable portion of the chamber. An easy-chair was near the bed-head: a man sat in it, dressed with the exception of his coat; he was still; his head leant back; his eyes were closed. Mr. Rochester held the candle over him; I recognised in his pale and seemingly lifeless face—the stranger, Mason: I saw too that his linen on one side, and one arm, was almost soaked in blood.

"Hold the candle," said Mr. Rochester, and I took it: he fetched a basin of water from the washstand: "Hold that," said he. I obeyed. He took the sponge, dipped it in, and moistened the corpse-like face; he asked for my smelling-bottle, and applied it to the nostrils. Mr. Mason shortly unclosed his eyes; he groaned. Mr. Rochester opened the shirt of the wounded man, whose arm and shoulder were bandaged: he sponged away blood, trickling fast down.

"Is there immediate danger?" murmured Mr. Mason.

"Pooh! No—a mere scratch. Don't be so overcome, man: bear up! I'll fetch a surgeon for you now, myself: you'll be able to be removed by morning, I hope. Jane," he continued.

"Sir?"

"I shall have to leave you in this room with this gentleman, for an hour, or perhaps two hours: you will sponge the blood as I do when it returns: if he feels faint, you will put the glass of water on that stand to his lips, and your salts to his nose. You will not speak to him on any pretext—and—Richard, it will be at the peril of your life if you speak to her: open your lips—agitate yourself—and I'll not answer for the consequences."

Again the poor man groaned; he looked as if he dared not move; fear, either of death or of something else, appeared almost to paralyse him. Mr. Rochester put the now bloody sponge into my hand, and I proceeded to use it as he had done. He watched me a second, then saying, "Remember!—No conversation," he left the room. I experienced a strange feeling as the key grated in the lock, and the sound of his retreating step ceased to be heard.

Here then I was in the third storey, fastened into one of its mystic cells; night around me; a pale and bloody spectacle under my eyes and hands; a murderess hardly separated from me by a single door: yes—that was appalling—the rest I could bear; but I shuddered at the thought of Grace Poole bursting out upon me.

I must keep to my post, however. I must watch this ghastly countenance—these blue, still lips forbidden to unclose—these eyes now shut, now opening, now wandering through the room, now fixing on me, and ever glazed with the dulness of horror. I must dip my hand again and again in the basin of blood and water, and wipe away the trickling gore. I must see the light of the unsnuffed candle wane on my employment; the shadows darken on the wrought, antique tapestry round me, and grow black under the hangings of the vast old bed, and quiver strangely over the doors of a great cabinet opposite—whose front, divided into twelve panels, bore, in grim design, the heads of the twelve apostles, each enclosed in its separate panel as in a frame; while above them at the top rose an ebon crucifix and a dying Christ.

According as the shifting obscurity and flickering gleam hovered here or glanced there, it was now the bearded physician, Luke, that bent his brow; now St. John's long hair that waved; and anon the devilish face of Judas, that grew out of the panel, and seemed gathering life and threatening a revelation of the arch-traitor—of Satan himself—in his subordinate's form.

Amidst all this, I had to listen as well as watch: to listen for the movements of the wild beast or the fiend in yonder side den. But since Mr. Rochester's visit it seemed spellbound: all the night I heard but three sounds at three long intervals,—a step creak, a momentary renewal of the snarling, canine noise, and a deep human groan.

Then my own thoughts worried me. What crime was this that lived incarnate in this sequestered mansion, and could neither be expelled nor subdued by the owner?—what mystery, that broke out now in fire and now in blood, at the deadest hours of night? What creature was it, that, masked in an ordinary woman's face and shape, uttered the voice, now of a mocking demon, and anon of a carrion-seeking bird of prey?

And this man I bent over—this commonplace, quiet stranger—how had he become involved in the web of horror? and why had the Fury flown at him? What made him seek this quarter of the house at an untimely season, when he should have been asleep in bed? I had heard Mr. Rochester assign him an apartment below—what brought him here! And why, now, was he so tame under the violence or treachery done him? Why did he so quietly submit to the concealment Mr. Rochester enforced? Why DID Mr. Rochester enforce this concealment? His guest had been outraged, his own life on a former occasion had been hideously plotted against; and both attempts he smothered in secrecy and sank in oblivion! Lastly, I saw Mr. Mason was submissive to Mr. Rochester; that the impetuous will of the latter held complete sway over the inertness of the former: the few words which had passed between them assured me of this. It was evident that in their former intercourse, the passive disposition of the one had been habitually influenced by the active energy of the other: whence then had arisen Mr. Rochester's dismay when he heard of Mr. Mason's arrival? Why had the mere name of this unresisting individual—whom his word now sufficed to control like a child—fallen on him, a few hours since, as a thunderbolt might fall on an oak?

Oh! I could not forget his look and his paleness when he whispered: "Jane, I have got a blow—I have got a blow, Jane." I could not forget how the arm had trembled which he rested on my shoulder: and it was no light matter which could thus bow the resolute spirit and thrill the vigorous frame of Fairfax Rochester.

"When will he come? When will he come?" I cried inwardly, as the night lingered and lingered—as my bleeding patient drooped, moaned, sickened: and neither day nor aid arrived. I had, again and again, held the water to Mason's white lips; again and again offered him the stimulating salts: my efforts seemed ineffectual: either bodily or mental suffering, or loss of blood, or all three combined, were fast prostrating his strength. He moaned so, and looked so weak, wild, and lost, I feared he was dying; ant I might not even speak to him.

The candle, wasted at last, went out; as it expired, I perceived streaks of grey light edging the window curtains: dawn was then approaching. Presently I heard Pilot bark far below, out of his distant kennel in the courtyard: hope revived. Nor was it unwarranted: in five minutes more the grating key, the yielding lock, warned me my watch was relieved. It could not have lasted more than two hours: many a week has seemed shorter.

Mr. Rochester entered, and with him the surgeon he had been to fetch.

"Now, Carter, be on the alert," he said to this last: "I give you but half-an-hour for dressing the wound, fastening the bandages, getting the patient downstairs and all."

"But is he fit to move, sir?"

"No doubt of it; it is nothing serious; he is nervous, his spirits must be kept up. Come, set to work."

Mr. Rochester drew back the thick curtain, drew up the holland blind, let in all the daylight he could; and I was surprised and cheered to see how far dawn was advanced: what rosy streaks were beginning to brighten the east. Then he approached Mason, whom the surgeon was already handling.

"Now, my good fellow, how are you?" he asked.

"She's done for me, I fear," was the faint reply.

"Not a whit!—courage! This day fortnight you'll hardly be a pin the worse of it: you've lost a little blood; that's all Carter, assure him there's no danger."

"I can do that conscientiously," said Carter, who had now undone the bandages; "only I wish I could have got here sooner: he would not have bled so much—but how is this? The flesh on the shoulder is torn as well as cut. This wound was not done with a knife: there have been teeth here!"

"She bit me," he murmured. "She worried me like a tigress, when Rochester got the knife from her."

"You should not have yielded: you should have grappled with her at once," said Mr. Rochester.

"But under such circumstances, what could one do?" returned Mason. "Oh, it was frightful!" he added, shuddering. "And I did not expect it: she looked so quiet at first."

"I warned you," was his friend's answer; "I said—be on your guard when you go near her. Besides, you might have waited till to-morrow, and had me with you: it was mere folly to attempt the interview to-night, and alone."

"I thought I could have done some good."

"You thought! you thought! Yes, it makes me impatient to hear you: but, however, you have suffered, and are likely to suffer enough for not taking my advice; so I'll say no more. Carter—hurry!—hurry! The sun will soon rise, and I must have him off."

"Directly, sir; the shoulder is just bandaged. I must look to this other wound in the arm: she has had her teeth here too, I think."

"She sucked the blood: she said she'd drain my heart," said Mason.

I saw Mr. Rochester shudder: a singularly marked expression of disgust, horror, hatred, warped his countenance almost to distortion; but he only said—

"Come, be silent, Richard, and never mind her gibberish: don't repeat it."

"I wish I could forget it," was the answer.

"You will when you are out of the country: when you get back to Spanish Town, you may think of her as dead and buried—or rather, you need not think of her at all."

"Impossible to forget this night!"

"It is not impossible: have some energy, man. You thought you were as dead as a herring two hours since, and you are all alive and talking now. There!—Carter has done with you or nearly so; I'll make you decent in a trice. Jane" (he turned to me for the first time since his re-entrance), "take this key: go down into my bedroom, and walk straight forward into my dressing-room: open the top drawer of the wardrobe and take out a clean shirt and neck-handkerchief: bring them here; and be nimble."

I went; sought the repository he had mentioned, found the articles named, and returned with them.

"Now," said he, "go to the other side of the bed while I order his toilet; but don't leave the room: you may be wanted again."

I retired as directed.

"Was anybody stirring below when you went down, Jane?" inquired Mr. Rochester presently.

"No, sir; all was very still."

"We shall get you off cannily, Dick: and it will be better, both for your sake, and for that of the poor creature in yonder. I have striven long to avoid exposure, and I should not like it to come at last. Here, Carter, help him on with his waist-coat. Where did you leave your furred cloak? You can't travel a mile without that, I know, in this damned cold climate. In your room?—Jane, run down to Mr. Mason's room,—the one next mine,—and fetch a cloak you will see there."

Again I ran, and again returned, bearing an immense mantle lined and edged with fur.

"Now, I've another errand for you," said my untiring master; "you must away to my room again. What a mercy you are shod with velvet, Jane!—a clod-hopping messenger would never do at this juncture. You must open the middle drawer of my toilet-table and take out a little phial and a little glass you will find there,—quick!"

I flew thither and back, bringing the desired vessels.

"That's well! Now, doctor, I shall take the liberty of administering a dose myself, on my own responsibility. I got this cordial at Rome, of an Italian charlatan—a fellow you would have kicked, Carter. It is not a thing to be used indiscriminately, but it is good upon occasion: as now, for instance. Jane, a little water."

He held out the tiny glass, and I half filled it from the water-bottle on the washstand.

"That will do;—now wet the lip of the phial."

I did so; he measured twelve drops of a crimson liquid, and presented it to Mason.

"Drink, Richard: it will give you the heart you lack, for an hour or so."

"But will it hurt me?—is it inflammatory?"

"Drink! drink! drink!"

Mr. Mason obeyed, because it was evidently useless to resist. He was dressed now: he still looked pale, but he was no longer gory and sullied. Mr. Rochester let him sit three minutes after he had swallowed the liquid; he then took his arm—

"Now I am sure you can get on your feet," he said—"try."

The patient rose.

"Carter, take him under the other shoulder. Be of good cheer, Richard; step out—that's it!"

"I do feel better," remarked Mr. Mason.

"I am sure you do. Now, Jane, trip on before us away to the backstairs; unbolt the side-passage door, and tell the driver of the post-chaise you will see in the yard—or just outside, for I told him not to drive his rattling wheels over the pavement—to be ready; we are coming: and, Jane, if any one is about, come to the foot of the stairs and hem."

It was by this time half-past five, and the sun was on the point of rising; but I found the kitchen still dark and silent. The side-passage door was fastened; I opened it with as little noise as possible: all the yard was quiet; but the gates stood wide open, and there was a post-chaise, with horses ready harnessed, and driver seated on the box, stationed outside. I approached him, and said the gentlemen were coming; he nodded: then I looked carefully round and listened. The stillness of early morning slumbered everywhere; the curtains were yet drawn over the servants' chamber windows; little birds were just twittering in the blossom-blanched orchard trees, whose boughs drooped like white garlands over the wall enclosing one side of the yard; the carriage horses stamped from time to time in their closed stables: all else was still.

The gentlemen now appeared. Mason, supported by Mr. Rochester and the surgeon, seemed to walk with tolerable ease: they assisted him into the chaise; Carter followed.

"Take care of him," said Mr. Rochester to the latter, "and keep him at your house till he is quite well: I shall ride over in a day or two to see how he gets on. Richard, how is it with you?"

"The fresh air revives me, Fairfax."

"Leave the window open on his side, Carter; there is no wind—good-bye, Dick."

"Fairfax—"

"Well what is it?"

"Let her be taken care of; let her be treated as tenderly as may be: let her——" he stopped and burst into tears.

"I do my best; and have done it, and will do it," was the answer: he shut up the chaise door, and the vehicle drove away.

"Yet would to God there was an end of all this!" added Mr. Rochester, as he closed and barred the heavy yard-gates.

This done, he moved with slow step and abstracted air towards a door in the wall bordering the orchard. I, supposing he had done with me, prepared to return to the house; again, however, I heard him call "Jane!" He had opened feel portal and stood at it, waiting for me.

"Come where there is some freshness, for a few moments," he said; "that house is a mere dungeon: don't you feel it so?"

"It seems to me a splendid mansion, sir."

"The glamour of inexperience is over your eyes," he answered; "and you see it through a charmed medium: you cannot discern that the gilding is slime and the silk draperies cobwebs; that the marble is sordid slate, and the polished woods mere refuse chips and scaly bark. Now HERE" (he pointed to the leafy enclosure we had entered) "all is real, sweet, and pure."

He strayed down a walk edged with box, with apple trees, pear trees, and cherry trees on one side, and a border on the other full of all sorts of old-fashioned flowers, stocks, sweet-williams, primroses, pansies, mingled with southernwood, sweet-briar, and various fragrant herbs. They were fresh now as a succession of April showers and gleams, followed by a lovely spring morning, could make them: the sun was just entering the dappled east, and his light illumined the wreathed and dewy orchard trees and shone down the quiet walks under them.

"Jane, will you have a flower?"

He gathered a half-blown rose, the first on the bush, and offered it to me.

"Thank you, sir."

"Do you like this sunrise, Jane? That sky with its high and light clouds which are sure to melt away as the day waxes warm—this placid and balmly atmosphere?"

"I do, very much."

"You have passed a strange night, Jane."

"Yes, sir."

"And it has made you look pale—were you afraid when I left you alone with Mason?"

"I was afraid of some one coming out of the inner room."

"But I had fastened the door—I had the key in my pocket: I should have been a careless shepherd if I had left a lamb—my pet lamb—so near a wolf's den, unguarded: you were safe."

"Will Grace Poole live here still, sir?"

"Oh yes! don't trouble your head about her—put the thing out of your thoughts."

"Yet it seems to me your life is hardly secure while she stays."

"Never fear—I will take care of myself."

"Is the danger you apprehended last night gone by now, sir?"

"I cannot vouch for that till Mason is out of England: nor even then. To live, for me, Jane, is to stand on a crater-crust which may crack and spue fire any day."

"But Mr. Mason seems a man easily led. Your influence, sir, is evidently potent with him: he will never set you at defiance or wilfully injure you."

"Oh, no! Mason will not defy me; nor, knowing it, will he hurt me—but, unintentionally, he might in a moment, by one careless word, deprive me, if not of life, yet for ever of happiness."

"Tell him to be cautious, sir: let him know what you fear, and show him how to avert the danger."

He laughed sardonically, hastily took my hand, and as hastily threw it from him.

"If I could do that, simpleton, where would the danger be? Annihilated in a moment. Ever since I have known Mason, I have only had to say to him 'Do that,' and the thing has been done. But I cannot give him orders in this case: I cannot say 'Beware of harming me, Richard;' for it is imperative that I should keep him ignorant that harm to me is possible. Now you look puzzled; and I will puzzle you further. You are my little friend, are you not?"

"I like to serve you, sir, and to obey you in all that is right."

"Precisely: I see you do. I see genuine contentment in your gait and mien, your eye and face, when you are helping me and pleasing me—working for me, and with me, in, as you characteristically say, 'ALL THAT IS RIGHT:' for if I bid you do what you thought wrong, there would be no light-footed running, no neat-handed alacrity, no lively glance and animated complexion. My friend would then turn to me, quiet and pale, and would say, 'No, sir; that is impossible: I cannot do it, because it is wrong;' and would become immutable as a fixed star. Well, you too have power over me, and may injure me: yet I dare not show you where I am vulnerable, lest, faithful and friendly as you are, you should transfix me at once."

"If you have no more to fear from Mr. Mason than you have from me, sir, you are very safe."

"God grant it may be so! Here, Jane, is an arbour; sit down."

The arbour was an arch in the wall, lined with ivy; it contained a rustic seat. Mr. Rochester took it, leaving room, however, for me: but I stood before him.

"Sit," he said; "the bench is long enough for two. You don't hesitate to take a place at my side, do you? Is that wrong, Jane?"

I answered him by assuming it: to refuse would, I felt, have been unwise.

"Now, my little friend, while the sun drinks the dew—while all the flowers in this old garden awake and expand, and the birds fetch their young ones' breakfast out of the Thornfield, and the early bees do their first spell of work—I'll put a case to you, which you must endeavour to suppose your own: but first, look at me, and tell me you are at ease, and not fearing that I err in detaining you, or that you err in staying."

"No, sir; I am content."

"Well then, Jane, call to aid your fancy:-suppose you were no longer a girl well reared and disciplined, but a wild boy indulged from childhood upwards; imagine yourself in a remote foreign land; conceive that you there commit a capital error, no matter of what nature or from what motives, but one whose consequences must follow you through life and taint all your existence. Mind, I don't say a CRIME; I am not speaking of shedding of blood or any other guilty act, which might make the perpetrator amenable to the law: my word is ERROR. The results of what you have done become in time to you utterly insupportable; you take measures to obtain relief: unusual measures, but neither unlawful nor culpable. Still you are miserable; for hope has quitted you on the very confines of life: your sun at noon darkens in an eclipse, which you feel will not leave it till the time of setting. Bitter and base associations have become the sole food of your memory: you wander here and there, seeking rest in exile: happiness in pleasure—I mean in heartless, sensual pleasure—such as dulls intellect and blights feeling. Heart-weary and soul-withered, you come home after years of voluntary banishment: you make a new acquaintance—how or where no matter: you find in this stranger much of the good and bright qualities which you have sought for twenty years, and never before encountered; and they are all fresh, healthy, without soil and without taint. Such society revives, regenerates: you feel better days come back—higher wishes, purer feelings; you desire to recommence your life, and to spend what remains to you of days in a way more worthy of an immortal being. To attain this end, are you justified in overleaping an obstacle of custom—a mere conventional impediment which neither your conscience sanctifies nor your judgment approves?"

He paused for an answer: and what was I to say? Oh, for some good spirit to suggest a judicious and satisfactory response! Vain aspiration! The west wind whispered in the ivy round me; but no gentle Ariel borrowed its breath as a medium of speech: the birds sang in the tree-tops; but their song, however sweet, was inarticulate.

Again Mr. Rochester propounded his query:

"Is the wandering and sinful, but now rest-seeking and repentant, man justified in daring the world's opinion, in order to attach to him for ever this gentle, gracious, genial stranger, thereby securing his own peace of mind and regeneration of life?"

"Sir," I answered, "a wanderer's repose or a sinner's reformation should never depend on a fellow-creature. Men and women die; philosophers falter in wisdom, and Christians in goodness: if any one you know has suffered and erred, let him look higher than his equals for strength to amend and solace to heal."

"But the instrument—the instrument! God, who does the work, ordains the instrument. I have myself—I tell it you without parable—been a worldly, dissipated, restless man; and I believe I have found the instrument for my cure in—"

He paused: the birds went on carolling, the leaves lightly rustling. I almost wondered they did not check their songs and whispers to catch the suspended revelation; but they would have had to wait many minutes—so long was the silence protracted. At last I looked up at the tardy speaker: he was looking eagerly at me.

"Little friend," said he, in quite a changed tone—while his face changed too, losing all its softness and gravity, and becoming harsh and sarcastic—"you have noticed my tender penchant for Miss Ingram: don't you think if I married her she would regenerate me with a vengeance?"

He got up instantly, went quite to the other end of the walk, and when he came back he was humming a tune.

"Jane, Jane," said he, stopping before me, "you are quite pale with your vigils: don't you curse me for disturbing your rest?"

"Curse you? No, sir."

"Shake hands in confirmation of the word. What cold fingers! They were warmer last night when I touched them at the door of the mysterious chamber. Jane, when will you watch with me again?"

"Whenever I can be useful, sir."

"For instance, the night before I am married! I am sure I shall not be able to sleep. Will you promise to sit up with me to bear me company? To you I can talk of my lovely one: for now you have seen her and know her."

"Yes, sir."

"She's a rare one, is she not, Jane?"

"Yes, sir."

"A strapper—a real strapper, Jane: big, brown, and buxom; with hair just such as the ladies of Carthage must have had. Bless me! there's Dent and Lynn in the stables! Go in by the shrubbery, through that wicket."

As I went one way, he went another, and I heard him in the yard, saying cheerfully—

"Mason got the start of you all this morning; he was gone before sunrise: I rose at four to see him off."

Chapter XXI

Presentiments are strange things! and so are sympathies; and so are signs; and the three combined make one mystery to which humanity has not yet found the key. I never laughed at presentiments in my life, because I have had strange ones of my own. Sympathies, I believe, exist (for instance, between far-distant, long-absent, wholly estranged relatives asserting, notwithstanding their alienation, the unity of the source to which each traces his origin) whose workings baffle mortal comprehension. And signs, for aught we know, may be but the sympathies of Nature with man.

When I was a little girl, only six years old, I one night heard Bessie Leaven say to Martha Abbot that she had been dreaming about a little child; and that to dream of children was a sure sign of trouble, either to one's self or one's kin. The saying might have worn out of my memory, had not a circumstance immediately followed which served indelibly to fix it there. The next day Bessie was sent for home to the deathbed of her little sister.

Of late I had often recalled this saying and this incident; for during the past week scarcely a night had gone over my couch that had not brought with it a dream of an infant, which I sometimes hushed in my arms, sometimes dandled on my knee, sometimes watched playing with daisies on a lawn, or again, dabbling its hands in running water. It was a wailing child this night, and a laughing one the next: now it nestled close to me, and now it ran from me; but whatever mood the apparition evinced, whatever aspect it wore, it failed not for seven successive nights to meet me the moment I entered the land of slumber.

I did not like this iteration of one idea—this strange recurrence of one image, and I grew nervous as bedtime approached and the hour of the vision drew near. It was from companionship with this baby-phantom I had been roused on that moonlight night when I heard the cry; and it was on the afternoon of the day following I was summoned downstairs by a message that some one wanted me in Mrs. Fairfax's room. On repairing thither, I found a man waiting for me, having the appearance of a gentleman's servant: he was dressed in deep mourning, and the hat he held in his hand was surrounded with a crape band.

"I daresay you hardly remember me, Miss," he said, rising as I entered; "but my name is Leaven: I lived coachman with Mrs. Reed when you were at Gateshead, eight or nine years since, and I live there still."

"Oh, Robert! how do you do? I remember you very well: you used to give me a ride sometimes on Miss Georgiana's bay pony. And how is Bessie? You are married to Bessie?"

"Yes, Miss: my wife is very hearty, thank you; she brought me another little one about two months since—we have three now—and both mother and child are thriving."

"And are the family well at the house, Robert?"

"I am sorry I can't give you better news of them, Miss: they are very badly at present—in great trouble."

"I hope no one is dead," I said, glancing at his black dress. He too looked down at the crape round his hat and replied—

"Mr. John died yesterday was a week, at his chambers in London."

"Mr. John?"

"Yes."

"And how does his mother bear it?"

"Why, you see, Miss Eyre, it is not a common mishap: his life has been very wild: these last three years he gave himself up to strange ways, and his death was shocking."

"I heard from Bessie he was not doing well."

"Doing well! He could not do worse: he ruined his health and his estate amongst the worst men and the worst women. He got into debt and into jail: his mother helped him out twice, but as soon as he was free he returned to his old companions and habits. His head was not strong: the knaves he lived amongst fooled him beyond anything I ever heard. He came down to Gateshead about three weeks ago and wanted missis to give up all to him. Missis refused: her means have long been much reduced by his extravagance; so he went back again, and the next news was that he was dead. How he died, God knows!—they say he killed himself."

I was silent: the things were frightful. Robert Leaven resumed—

"Missis had been out of health herself for some time: she had got very stout, but was not strong with it; and the loss of money and fear of poverty were quite breaking her down. The information about Mr. John's death and the manner of it came too suddenly: it brought on a stroke. She was three days without speaking; but last Tuesday she seemed rather better: she appeared as if she wanted to say something, and kept making signs to my wife and mumbling. It was only yesterday morning, however, that Bessie understood she was pronouncing your name; and at last she made out the words, 'Bring Jane—fetch Jane Eyre: I want to speak to her.' Bessie is not sure whether she is in her right mind, or means anything by the words; but she told Miss Reed and Miss Georgiana, and advised them to send for you. The young ladies put it off at first; but their mother grew so restless, and said, 'Jane, Jane,' so many times, that at last they consented. I left Gateshead yesterday: and if you can get ready, Miss, I should like to take you back with me early to-morrow morning."

"Yes, Robert, I shall be ready: it seems to me that I ought to go."

"I think so too, Miss. Bessie said she was sure you would not refuse: but I suppose you will have to ask leave before you can get off?"

"Yes; and I will do it now;" and having directed him to the servants' hall, and recommended him to the care of John's wife, and the attentions of John himself, I went in search of Mr. Rochester.

He was not in any of the lower rooms; he was not in the yard, the stables, or the grounds. I asked Mrs. Fairfax if she had seen him;—yes: she believed he was playing billiards with Miss Ingram. To the billiard-room I hastened: the click of balls and the hum of voices resounded thence; Mr. Rochester, Miss Ingram, the two Misses Eshton, and their admirers, were all busied in the game. It required some courage to disturb so interesting a party; my errand, however, was one I could not defer, so I approached the master where he stood at Miss Ingram's side. She turned as I drew near, and looked at me haughtily: her eyes seemed to demand, "What can the creeping creature want now?" and when I said, in a low voice, "Mr. Rochester," she made a movement as if tempted to order me away. I remember her appearance at the moment—it was very graceful and very striking: she wore a morning robe of sky-blue crape; a gauzy azure scarf was twisted in her hair. She had been all animation with the game, and irritated pride did not lower the expression of her haughty lineaments.

"Does that person want you?" she inquired of Mr. Rochester; and Mr. Rochester turned to see who the "person" was. He made a curious grimace—one of his strange and equivocal demonstrations—threw down his cue and followed me from the room.

"Well, Jane?" he said, as he rested his back against the schoolroom door, which he had shut.

"If you please, sir, I want leave of absence for a week or two."

"What to do?—where to go?"

"To see a sick lady who has sent for me."

"What sick lady?—where does she live?"

"At Gateshead; in——shire."

"——shire? That is a hundred miles off! Who may she be that sends for people to see her that distance?"

"Her name is Reed, sir—Mrs. Reed."

"Reed of Gateshead? There was a Reed of Gateshead, a magistrate."

"It is his widow, sir."

"And what have you to do with her? How do you know her?"

"Mr. Reed was my uncle—my mother's brother."

"The deuce he was! You never told me that before: you always said you had no relations."

"None that would own me, sir. Mr. Reed is dead, and his wife cast me off."

"Why?"

"Because I was poor, and burdensome, and she disliked me."

"But Reed left children?—you must have cousins? Sir George Lynn was talking of a Reed of Gateshead yesterday, who, he said, was one of the veriest rascals on town; and Ingram was mentioning a Georgiana Reed of the same place, who was much admired for her beauty a season or two ago in London."

"John Reed is dead, too, sir: he ruined himself and half-ruined his family, and is supposed to have committed suicide. The news so shocked his mother that it brought on an apoplectic attack."

"And what good can you do her? Nonsense, Jane! I would never think of running a hundred miles to see an old lady who will, perhaps, be dead before you reach her: besides, you say she cast you off."

"Yes, sir, but that is long ago; and when her circumstances were very different: I could not be easy to neglect her wishes now."

"How long will you stay?"

"As short a time as possible, sir."

"Promise me only to stay a week——"

"I had better not pass my word: I might be obliged to break it."

"At all events you WILL come back: you will not be induced under any pretext to take up a permanent residence with her?"

"Oh, no! I shall certainly return if all be well."

"And who goes with you? You don't travel a hundred miles alone."

"No, sir, she has sent her coachman."

"A person to be trusted?"

"Yes, sir, he has lived ten years in the family."

Mr. Rochester meditated. "When do you wish to go?"

"Early to-morrow morning, sir."

"Well, you must have some money; you can't travel without money, and I daresay you have not much: I have given you no salary yet. How much have you in the world, Jane?" he asked, smiling.

I drew out my purse; a meagre thing it was. "Five shillings, sir." He took the purse, poured the hoard into his palm, and chuckled over it as if its scantiness amused him. Soon he produced his pocket-book: "Here," said he, offering me a note; it was fifty pounds, and he owed me but fifteen. I told him I had no change.

"I don't want change; you know that. Take your wages."

I declined accepting more than was my due. He scowled at first; then, as if recollecting something, he said—

"Right, right! Better not give you all now: you would, perhaps, stay away three months if you had fifty pounds. There are ten; is it not plenty?"

"Yes, sir, but now you owe me five."

"Come back for it, then; I am your banker for forty pounds."

"Mr. Rochester, I may as well mention another matter of business to you while I have the opportunity."

"Matter of business? I am curious to hear it."

"You have as good as informed me, sir, that you are going shortly to be married?"

"Yes; what then?"

"In that case, sir, Adele ought to go to school: I am sure you will perceive the necessity of it."

"To get her out of my bride's way, who might otherwise walk over her rather too emphatically? There's sense in the suggestion; not a doubt of it. Adele, as you say, must go to school; and you, of course, must march straight to—the devil?"

"I hope not, sir; but I must seek another situation somewhere."

"In course!" he exclaimed, with a twang of voice and a distortion of features equally fantastic and ludicrous. He looked at me some minutes.

"And old Madam Reed, or the Misses, her daughters, will be solicited by you to seek a place, I suppose?"

"No, sir; I am not on such terms with my relatives as would justify me in asking favours of them—but I shall advertise."

"You shall walk up the pyramids of Egypt!" he growled. "At your peril you advertise! I wish I had only offered you a sovereign instead of ten pounds. Give me back nine pounds, Jane; I've a use for it."

"And so have I, sir," I returned, putting my hands and my purse behind me. "I could not spare the money on any account."

"Little niggard!" said he, "refusing me a pecuniary request! Give me five pounds, Jane."

"Not five shillings, sir; nor five pence."

"Just let me look at the cash."

"No, sir; you are not to be trusted."

"Jane!"

"Sir?"

"Promise me one thing."

"I'll promise you anything, sir, that I think I am likely to perform."

"Not to advertise: and to trust this quest of a situation to me. I'll find you one in time."

"I shall be glad so to do, sir, if you, in your turn, will promise that I and Adele shall be both safe out of the house before your bride enters it."

"Very well! very well! I'll pledge my word on it. You go to-morrow, then?"

"Yes, sir; early."

"Shall you come down to the drawing-room after dinner?"

"No, sir, I must prepare for the journey."

"Then you and I must bid good-bye for a little while?"

"I suppose so, sir."

"And how do people perform that ceremony of parting, Jane? Teach me; I'm not quite up to it."

"They say, Farewell, or any other form they prefer."

"Then say it."

"Farewell, Mr. Rochester, for the present."

"What must I say?"

"The same, if you like, sir."

"Farewell, Miss Eyre, for the present; is that all?"

"Yes?"

"It seems stingy, to my notions, and dry, and unfriendly. I should like something else: a little addition to the rite. If one shook hands, for instance; but no—that would not content me either. So you'll do no more than say Farewell, Jane?"

"It is enough, sir: as much good-will may be conveyed in one hearty word as in many."

"Very likely; but it is blank and cool—'Farewell.'"

"How long is he going to stand with his back against that door?" I asked myself; "I want to commence my packing." The dinner-bell rang, and suddenly away he bolted, without another syllable: I saw him no more during the day, and was off before he had risen in the morning.

I reached the lodge at Gateshead about five o'clock in the afternoon of the first of May: I stepped in there before going up to the hall. It was very clean and neat: the ornamental windows were hung with little white curtains; the floor was spotless; the grate and fire-irons were burnished bright, and the fire burnt clear. Bessie sat on the hearth, nursing her last-born, and Robert and his sister played quietly in a corner.

"Bless you!—I knew you would come!" exclaimed Mrs. Leaven, as I entered.

"Yes, Bessie," said I, after I had kissed her; "and I trust I am not too late. How is Mrs. Reed?—Alive still, I hope."

"Yes, she is alive; and more sensible and collected than she was. The doctor says she may linger a week or two yet; but he hardly thinks she will finally recover."

"Has she mentioned me lately?"

"She was talking of you only this morning, and wishing you would come, but she is sleeping now, or was ten minutes ago, when I was up at the house. She generally lies in a kind of lethargy all the afternoon, and wakes up about six or seven. Will you rest yourself here an hour, Miss, and then I will go up with you?"

Robert here entered, and Bessie laid her sleeping child in the cradle and went to welcome him: afterwards she insisted on my taking off my bonnet and having some tea; for she said I looked pale and tired. I was glad to accept her hospitality; and I submitted to be relieved of my travelling garb just as passively as I used to let her undress me when a child.

Old times crowded fast back on me as I watched her bustling about—setting out the tea-tray with her best china, cutting bread and butter, toasting a tea-cake, and, between whiles, giving little Robert or Jane an occasional tap or push, just as she used to give me in former days. Bessie had retained her quick temper as well as her light foot and good looks.

Tea ready, I was going to approach the table; but she desired me to sit still, quite in her old peremptory tones. I must be served at the fireside, she said; and she placed before me a little round stand with my cup and a plate of toast, absolutely as she used to accommodate me with some privately purloined dainty on a nursery chair: and I smiled and obeyed her as in bygone days.

She wanted to know if I was happy at Thornfield Hall, and what sort of a person the mistress was; and when I told her there was only a master, whether he was a nice gentleman, and if I liked him. I told her he rather an ugly man, but quite a gentleman; and that he treated me kindly, and I was content. Then I went on to describe to her the gay company that had lately been staying at the house; and to these details Bessie listened with interest: they were precisely of the kind she relished.

In such conversation an hour was soon gone: Bessie restored to me my bonnet, &c., and, accompanied by her, I quitted the lodge for the hall. It was also accompanied by her that I had, nearly nine years ago, walked down the path I was now ascending. On a dark, misty, raw morning in January, I had left a hostile roof with a desperate and embittered heart—a sense of outlawry and almost of reprobation—to seek the chilly harbourage of Lowood: that bourne so far away and unexplored. The same hostile roof now again rose before me: my prospects were doubtful yet; and I had yet an aching heart. I still felt as a wanderer on the face of the earth; but I experienced firmer trust in myself and my own powers, and less withering dread of oppression. The gaping wound of my wrongs, too, was now quite healed; and the flame of resentment extinguished.

"You shall go into the breakfast-room first," said Bessie, as she preceded me through the hall; "the young ladies will be there."

In another moment I was within that apartment. There was every article of furniture looking just as it did on the morning I was first introduced to Mr. Brocklehurst: the very rug he had stood upon still covered the hearth. Glancing at the bookcases, I thought I could distinguish the two volumes of Bewick's British Birds occupying their old place on the third shelf, and Gulliver's Travels and the Arabian Nights ranged just above. The inanimate objects were not changed; but the living things had altered past recognition.

Two young ladies appeared before me; one very tall, almost as tall as Miss Ingram—very thin too, with a sallow face and severe mien. There was something ascetic in her look, which was augmented by the extreme plainness of a straight-skirted, black, stuff dress, a starched linen collar, hair combed away from the temples, and the nun-like ornament of a string of ebony beads and a crucifix. This I felt sure was Eliza, though I could trace little resemblance to her former self in that elongated and colourless visage.

The other was as certainly Georgiana: but not the Georgiana I remembered—the slim and fairy-like girl of eleven. This was a full-blown, very plump damsel, fair as waxwork, with handsome and regular features, languishing blue eyes, and ringleted yellow hair. The hue of her dress was black too; but its fashion was so different from her sister's—so much more flowing and becoming—it looked as stylish as the other's looked puritanical.

In each of the sisters there was one trait of the mother—and only one; the thin and pallid elder daughter had her parent's Cairngorm eye:

the blooming and luxuriant younger girl had her contour of jaw and chin—perhaps a little softened, but still imparting an indescribable hardness to the countenance otherwise so voluptuous and buxom.

Both ladies, as I advanced, rose to welcome me, and both addressed me by the name of "Miss Eyre." Eliza's greeting was delivered in a short, abrupt voice, without a smile; and then she sat down again, fixed her eyes on the fire, and seemed to forget me. Georgiana added to her "How d'ye do?" several commonplaces about my journey, the weather, and so on, uttered in rather a drawling tone: and accompanied by sundry side-glances that measured me from head to foot—now traversing the folds of my drab merino pelisse, and now lingering on the plain trimming of my cottage bonnet. Young ladies have a remarkable way of letting you know that they think you a "quiz" without actually saying the words. A certain superciliousness of look, coolness of manner, nonchalance of tone, express fully their sentiments on the point, without committing them by any positive rudeness in word or deed.

A sneer, however, whether covert or open, had now no longer that power over me it once possessed: as I sat between my cousins, I was surprised to find how easy I felt under the total neglect of the one and the semi-sarcastic attentions of the other—Eliza did not mortify, nor Georgiana ruffle me. The fact was, I had other things to think about; within the last few months feelings had been stirred in me so much more potent than any they could raise—pains and pleasures so much more acute and exquisite had been excited than any it was in their power to inflict or bestow—that their airs gave me no concern either for good or bad.

"How is Mrs. Reed?" I asked soon, looking calmly at Georgiana, who thought fit to bridle at the direct address, as if it were an unexpected liberty.

"Mrs. Reed? Ah! mama, you mean; she is extremely poorly: I doubt if you can see her to-night."

"If," said I, "you would just step upstairs and tell her I am come, I should be much obliged to you."

Georgiana almost started, and she opened her blue eyes wild and wide. "I know she had a particular wish to see me," I added, "and I would not defer attending to her desire longer than is absolutely necessary."

"Mama dislikes being disturbed in an evening," remarked Eliza. I soon rose, quietly took off my bonnet and gloves, uninvited, and said I would just step out to Bessie—who was, I dared say, in the kitchen—and ask her to ascertain whether Mrs. Reed was disposed to receive me or not to-night. I went, and having found Bessie and despatched her on my errand, I proceeded to take further measures. It had heretofore been my habit always to shrink from arrogance: received as I had been to-day, I should, a year ago, have resolved to quit Gateshead the very next morning; now, it was disclosed to me all at once that that would be a foolish plan. I had taken a journey of a hundred miles to see my aunt, and I must stay with her till she was better—or dead: as to her daughters' pride or folly, I must put it on one side, make myself independent of it. So I addressed the housekeeper; asked her to show me a room, told her I should probably be a visitor here for a week or two, had my trunk conveyed to my chamber, and followed it thither myself: I met Bessie on the landing.

"Missis is awake," said she; "I have told her you are here: come and let us see if she will know you."

I did not need to be guided to the well-known room, to which I had so often been summoned for chastisement or reprimand in former days. I hastened before Bessie; I softly opened the door: a shaded light stood on the table, for it was now getting dark. There was the great four-post bed with amber hangings as of old; there the toilet-table, the arm-chair, and the footstool, at which I had a hundred times been sentenced to kneel, to ask pardon for offences by me uncommitted. I looked into a certain corner near, half-expecting to see the slim outline of a once dreaded switch which used to lurk there, waiting to leap out imp-like and lace my quivering palm or shrinking neck. I approached the bed; I opened the curtains and leant over the high-piled pillows.

Well did I remember Mrs. Reed's face, and I eagerly sought the familiar image. It is a happy thing that time quells the longings of vengeance and hushes the promptings of rage and aversion. I had left this woman in bitterness and hate, and I came back to her now with no other emotion than a sort of ruth for her great sufferings, and a strong yearning to forget and forgive all injuries—to be reconciled and clasp hands in amity.

The well-known face was there: stern, relentless as ever—there was that peculiar eye which nothing could melt, and the somewhat raised, imperious, despotic eyebrow. How often had it lowered on me menace and hate! and how the recollection of childhood's terrors and sorrows revived as I traced its harsh line now! And yet I stooped down and kissed her: she looked at me.

"Is this Jane Eyre?" she said.

"Yes, Aunt Reed. How are you, dear aunt?"

I had once vowed that I would never call her aunt again: I thought it no sin to forget and break that vow now. My fingers had fastened on her hand which lay outside the sheet: had she pressed mine kindly, I should at that moment have experienced true pleasure. But unimpressionable natures are not so soon softened, nor are natural antipathies so readily eradicated. Mrs. Reed took her hand away, and, turning her face rather from me, she remarked that the night was warm. Again she regarded me so icily, I felt at once that her opinion of me—her feeling towards me—was unchanged and unchangeable. I knew by her stony eye—opaque to tenderness, indissoluble to tears—that she was resolved to consider me bad to the last; because to believe me good would give her no generous pleasure: only a sense of mortification.

I felt pain, and then I felt ire; and then I felt a determination to subdue her—to be her mistress in spite both of her nature and her will. My tears had risen, just as in childhood: I ordered them back to their source. I brought a chair to the bed-head: I sat down and leaned over the pillow.

"You sent for me," I said, "and I am here; and it is my intention to stay till I see how you get on."

"Oh, of course! You have seen my daughters?"

"Yes."

"Well, you may tell them I wish you to stay till I can talk some things over with you I have on my mind: to-night it is too late, and I have a difficulty in recalling them. But there was something I wished to say—let me see—"

The wandering look and changed utterance told what wreck had taken place in her once vigorous frame. Turning restlessly, she drew the bedclothes round her; my elbow, resting on a corner of the quilt, fixed it down: she was at once irritated.

"Sit up!" said she; "don't annoy me with holding the clothes fast. Are you Jane Eyre?"

"I am Jane Eyre."

"I have had more trouble with that child than any one would believe. Such a burden to be left on my hands—and so much annoyance as she caused me, daily and hourly, with her incomprehensible disposition, and her sudden starts of temper, and her continual, unnatural watchings of one's movements! I declare she talked to me once like something mad, or like a fiend—no child ever spoke or looked as she did; I was glad to get her away from the house. What did they do with her at Lowood? The fever broke out there, and many of the pupils died. She, however, did not die: but I said she did—I wish she had died!"

"A strange wish, Mrs. Reed; why do you hate her so?"

"I had a dislike to her mother always; for she was my husband's only sister, and a great favourite with him: he opposed the family's disowning her when she made her low marriage; and when news came of her death, he wept like a simpleton. He would send for the baby; though I entreated him rather to put it out to nurse and pay for its maintenance. I hated it the first time I set my eyes on it—a sickly, whining, pining thing! It would wail in its cradle all night long—not screaming heartily like any other child, but whimpering and moaning. Reed pitied it; and he used to nurse it and notice it as if it had been his own: more, indeed, than he ever noticed his own at that age. He would try to make my children friendly to the little beggar: the darlings could not bear it, and he was angry with them when they showed their dislike. In his last illness, he had it brought continually to his bedside; and but an hour before he died, he bound me by vow to keep the creature. I would as soon have been charged with a pauper brat out of a workhouse: but he was weak, naturally weak. John does not at all resemble his father, and I am glad of it: John is like me and like my brothers—he is quite a Gibson. Oh, I wish he would cease tormenting me with letters for money? I have no more money to give him: we are getting poor. I must send away half the servants and shut up part of the house; or let it off. I can never submit to do that—yet how are we to get on? Two-thirds of my income goes in paying the interest of mortgages. John gambles dreadfully, and always loses—poor boy! He is beset by sharpers: John is sunk and degraded—his look is frightful—I feel ashamed for him when I see him."

She was getting much excited. "I think I had better leave her now," said I to Bessie, who stood on the other side of the bed.

"Perhaps you had, Miss: but she often talks in this way towards night—in the morning she is calmer."

I rose. "Stop!" exclaimed Mrs. Reed, "there is another thing I wished to say. He threatens me—he continually threatens me with his own death, or mine: and I dream sometimes that I see him laid out with a great wound in his throat, or with a swollen and blackened face. I am come to a strange pass: I have heavy troubles. What is to be done? How is the money to be had?"

Bessie now endeavoured to persuade her to take a sedative draught: she succeeded with difficulty. Soon after, Mrs. Reed grew more composed, and sank into a dozing state. I then left her.

More than ten days elapsed before I had again any conversation with her. She continued either delirious or lethargic; and the doctor forbade everything which could painfully excite her. Meantime, I got on as well as I could with Georgiana and Eliza. They were very cold, indeed, at first. Eliza would sit half the day sewing, reading, or writing, and scarcely utter a word either to me or her sister. Georgiana would chatter nonsense to her canary bird by the hour, and take no notice of me. But I was determined not to seem at a loss for occupation or amusement: I had brought my drawing materials with me, and they served me for both.

Provided with a case of pencils, and some sheets of paper, I used to take a seat apart from them, near the window, and busy myself in sketching fancy vignettes, representing any scene that happened momentarily to shape itself in the ever-shifting kaleidoscope of imagination: a glimpse of sea between two rocks; the rising moon, and a ship crossing its disk; a group of reeds and water-flags, and a naiad's head, crowned with lotus-flowers, rising out of them; an elf sitting in a hedge-sparrow's nest, under a wreath of hawthorn-bloom

One morning I fell to sketching a face: what sort of a face it was to be, I did not care or know. I took a soft black pencil, gave it a broad point, and worked away. Soon I had traced on the paper a broad and prominent forehead and a square lower outline of visage: that contour gave me pleasure; my fingers proceeded actively to fill it with features. Strongly-marked horizontal eyebrows must be traced under that brow; then followed, naturally, a well-defined nose, with a straight ridge and full nostrils; then a flexible-looking mouth, by no means narrow; then a firm chin, with a decided cleft down the middle of it: of course, some black whiskers were wanted, and some jetty hair, tufted on the temples, and waved above the forehead. Now for the eyes: I had left them to the last, because they required the most careful working. I drew them large; I shaped them well: the eyelashes I traced long and sombre; the irids lustrous and large. "Good! but not quite the thing," I thought, as I surveyed the effect: "they want more force and spirit;" and I wrought the shades blacker, that the lights might flash more brilliantly—a happy touch or two secured success. There, I had a friend's face under my gaze; and what did it signify that those young ladies turned their backs on me? I looked at it; I smiled at the speaking likeness: I was absorbed and content.

"Is that a portrait of some one you know?" asked Eliza, who had approached me unnoticed. I responded that it was merely a fancy head, and hurried it beneath the other sheets. Of course, I lied: it was, in fact, a very faithful representation of Mr. Rochester. But what was that to her, or to any one but myself? Georgiana also advanced to look. The other drawings pleased her much, but she called that "an ugly man." They both seemed surprised at my skill. I offered to sketch their portraits; and each, in turn, sat for a pencil outline. Then Georgiana produced her album. I promised to contribute a water-colour drawing: this put her at once into good humour. She proposed a walk in the grounds. Before we had been out two hours, we were deep in a confidential conversation: she had favoured me with a description of the brilliant winter she had spent in London two seasons ago—of the admiration she had there excited—the attention she had received; and I even got hints of the titled conquest she had made. In the course of the afternoon and evening these hints were enlarged on: various soft conversations were reported, and sentimental scenes represented; and, in short, a volume of a novel of fashionable life was that day improvised by her for my benefit. The communications were renewed from day to day: they always ran on the same theme—herself, her loves, and woes. It was strange she never once adverted either to her mother's illness, or her brother's death, or the present gloomy state of the family prospects. Her mind seemed wholly taken up with reminiscences of past gaiety, and aspirations after dissipations to come. She passed about five minutes each day in her mother's sick-room, and no more.

Eliza still spoke little: she had evidently no time to talk. I never saw a busier person than she seemed to be; yet it was difficult to say what she did: or rather, to discover any result of her diligence. She had an alarm to call her up early. I know not how she occupied herself before breakfast, but after that meal she divided her time into regular portions, and each hour had its allotted task. Three times a day she studied a little book, which I found, on inspection, was a Common Prayer Book. I asked her once what was the great attraction of that volume, and she said, "the Rubric." Three hours she gave to stitching, with gold thread, the border of a square crimson cloth, almost large enough for a carpet. In answer to my inquiries after the use of this article, she informed me it was a covering for the altar of a new church lately erected near Gateshead. Two hours she devoted to her diary; two to working by herself in the kitchen-garden; and one to the regulation of her accounts. She seemed to want no company; no conversation. I believe she was happy in her way: this routine sufficed for her; and nothing annoyed her so much as the occurrence of any incident which forced her to vary its clockwork regularity.

She told me one evening, when more disposed to be communicative than usual, that John's conduct, and the threatened ruin of the family, had been a source of profound affliction to her: but she had now, she said, settled her mind, and formed her resolution. Her own fortune she had taken care to secure; and when her mother died—and it was wholly improbable, she tranquilly remarked, that she should either recover or linger long—she would execute a long-cherished project: seek a retirement where punctual habits would be permanently secured from disturbance, and place safe barriers between herself and a frivolous world. I asked if Georgiana would accompany her.

"Of course not. Georgiana and she had nothing in common: they never had had. She would not be burdened with her society for any consideration. Georgiana should take her own course; and she, Eliza, would take hers."

Georgiana, when not unburdening her heart to me, spent most of her time in lying on the sofa, fretting about the dulness of the house, and wishing over and over again that her aunt Gibson would send her an invitation up to town. "It would be so much better," she said, "if she could only get out of the way for a month or two, till all was over." I did not ask what she meant by "all being over," but I suppose she referred to the expected decease of her mother and the gloomy sequel of funeral rites. Eliza generally took no more notice of her sister's indolence and complaints than if no such murmuring, lounging object had been before her. One day, however, as she put away her account-book and unfolded her embroidery, she suddenly took her up thus—

"Georgiana, a more vain and absurd animal than you was certainly never allowed to cumber the earth. You had no right to be born, for you make no use of life. Instead of living for, in, and with yourself, as a reasonable being ought, you seek only to fasten your feebleness on some other person's strength: if no one can be found willing to burden her or himself with such a fat, weak, puffy, useless thing, you cry out that you are ill-treated, neglected, miserable. Then, too, existence for you must be a scene of continual change and excitement, or else the world is a dungeon: you must be admired, you must be courted, you must be flattered—you must have music, dancing, and society—or you languish, you die away. Have you no sense to devise a system which will make you independent of all efforts, and all wills, but your own? Take one day; share it into sections; to each section apportion its task: leave no stray unemployed quarters of an hour, ten minutes, five minutes—include all; do each piece of business in its turn with method, with rigid regularity. The day will close almost before you are aware it has begun; and you are indebted to no one for helping you to get rid of one vacant moment: you have had to seek no one's company, conversation, sympathy, forbearance; you have lived, in short, as an independent being ought to do. Take this advice: the first and last I shall offer you; then you will not want me or any one else, happen what may. Neglect it—go on as heretofore, craving, whining, and idling—and suffer the results of your idiocy, however bad and insuperable they may be. I tell you this plainly; and listen: for though I shall no more repeat what I am now about to say, I shall steadily act on it. After my mother's death, I wash my hands of you: from the day her coffin is carried to the vault in Gateshead Church, you and I will be as separate as if we had never known each other. You need not think that because we chanced to be born of the same parents, I shall suffer you to fasten me down by even the feeblest claim: I can tell you this—if the whole human race, ourselves excepted, were swept away, and we two stood alone on the earth, I would leave you in the old world, and betake myself to the new."

She closed her lips.

"You might have spared yourself the trouble of delivering that tirade," answered Georgiana. "Everybody knows you are the most selfish, heartless creature in existence: and I know your spiteful hatred towards me: I have had a specimen of it before in the trick you played me about Lord Edwin Vere: you could not bear me to be raised above you, to have a title, to be received into circles where you dare not show your face, and so you acted the spy and informer, and ruined my prospects for ever." Georgiana took out her handkerchief and blew her nose for an hour afterwards; Eliza sat cold, impassable, and assiduously industrious.

True, generous feeling is made small account of by some, but here were two natures rendered, the one intolerably acrid, the other despicably savourless for the want of it. Feeling without judgment is a washy draught indeed; but judgment untempered by feeling is too bitter and husky a morsel for human deglutition.

It was a wet and windy afternoon: Georgiana had fallen asleep on the sofa over the perusal of a novel; Eliza was gone to attend a saint's-day service at the new church—for in matters of religion she was a rigid formalist: no weather ever prevented the punctual discharge of what she considered her devotional duties; fair or foul, she went to church thrice every Sunday, and as often on week-days as there were prayers.

I bethought myself to go upstairs and see how the dying woman sped, who lay there almost unheeded: the very servants paid her but a remittent attention: the hired nurse, being little looked after, would slip out of the room whenever she could. Bessie was faithful; but she had her own family to mind, and could only come occasionally to the hall. I found the sick-room unwatched, as I had expected: no nurse was there; the patient lay still, and seemingly lethargic; her livid face sunk in the pillows: the fire was dying in the grate. I renewed the fuel, re-arranged the bedclothes, gazed awhile on her who could not now gaze on me, and then I moved away to the window.

The rain beat strongly against the panes, the wind blew tempestuously: "One lies there," I thought, "who will soon be beyond the war of earthly elements. Whither will that spirit—now struggling to quit its material tenement—flit when at length released?"

In pondering the great mystery, I thought of Helen Burns, recalled her dying words—her faith—her doctrine of the equality of disembodied souls. I was still listening in thought to her well-remembered tones—still picturing her pale and spiritual aspect, her wasted face and sublime gaze, as she lay on her placid deathbed, and whispered her longing to be restored to her divine Father's bosom—when a feeble voice murmured from the couch behind: "Who is that?"

I knew Mrs. Reed had not spoken for days: was she reviving? I went up to her.

"It is I, Aunt Reed."

"Who—I?" was her answer. "Who are you?" looking at me with surprise and a sort of alarm, but still not wildly. "You are quite a stranger to me—where is Bessie?"

"She is at the lodge, aunt."

"Aunt," she repeated. "Who calls me aunt? You are not one of the Gibsons; and yet I know you—that face, and the eyes and forehead, are quiet familiar to me: you are like—why, you are like Jane Eyre!"

I said nothing: I was afraid of occasioning some shock by declaring my identity.

"Yet," said she, "I am afraid it is a mistake: my thoughts deceive me. I wished to see Jane Eyre, and I fancy a likeness where none exists: besides, in eight years she must be so changed." I now gently assured her that I was the person she supposed and desired me to be: and seeing that I was understood, and that her senses were quite collected, I explained how Bessie had sent her husband to fetch me from Thornfield.

"I am very ill, I know," she said ere long. "I was trying to turn myself a few minutes since, and find I cannot move a limb. It is as well I should ease my mind before I die: what we think little of in health, burdens us at such an hour as the present is to me. Is the nurse here? or is there no one in the room but you?"

I assured her we were alone.

"Well, I have twice done you a wrong which I regret now. One was in breaking the promise which I gave my husband to bring you up as my own child; the other—" she stopped. "After all, it is of no great importance, perhaps," she murmured to herself: "and then I may get better; and to humble myself so to her is painful."

She made an effort to alter her position, but failed: her face changed; she seemed to experience some inward sensation—the precursor, perhaps, of the last pang.

"Well, I must get it over. Eternity is before me: I had better tell her.—Go to my dressing-case, open it, and take out a letter you will see there."

I obeyed her directions. "Read the letter," she said.

It was short, and thus conceived:—

"Madam,—

Will you have the goodness to send me the address of my niece, Jane Eyre, and to tell me how she is? It is my intention to write shortly and desire her to come to me at Madeira. Providence has blessed my endeavours to secure a competency; and as I am unmarried and childless, I wish to adopt her during my life, and bequeath her at my death whatever I may have to leave.—I am, Madam, &c., &c.,

"JOHN EYRE, Madeira."

It was dated three years back.

"Why did I never hear of this?" I asked.

"Because I disliked you too fixedly and thoroughly ever to lend a hand in lifting you to prosperity. I could not forget your conduct to me, Jane—the fury with which you once turned on me; the tone in which you declared you abhorred me the worst of anybody in the world; the unchildlike look and voice with which you affirmed that the very thought of me made you sick, and asserted that I had treated you with miserable cruelty. I could not forget my own sensations when you thus started up and poured out the venom of your mind: I felt fear as if an animal that I had struck or pushed had looked up at me with human eyes and cursed me in a man's voice.—Bring me some water! Oh, make haste!"

"Dear Mrs. Reed," said I, as I offered her the draught she required, "think no more of all this, let it pass away from your mind. Forgive me for my passionate language: I was a child then; eight, nine years have passed since that day."

She heeded nothing of what I said; but when she had tasted the water and drawn breath, she went on thus—

"I tell you I could not forget it; and I took my revenge: for you to be adopted by your uncle, and placed in a state of ease and comfort, was what I could not endure. I wrote to him; I said I was sorry for his disappointment, but Jane Eyre was dead: she had died of typhus fever at Lowood. Now act as you please: write and contradict my assertion—expose my falsehood as soon as you like. You were born, I think, to be my torment: my last hour is racked by the recollection of a deed which, but for you, I should never have been tempted to commit."

"If you could but be persuaded to think no more of it, aunt, and to regard me with kindness and forgiveness"

"You have a very bad disposition," said she, "and one to this day I feel it impossible to understand: how for nine years you could be patient and quiescent under any treatment, and in the tenth break out all fire and violence, I can never comprehend."

"My disposition is not so bad as you think: I am passionate, but not vindictive. Many a time, as a little child, I should have been glad to love you if you would have let me; and I long earnestly to be reconciled to you now: kiss me, aunt."

I approached my cheek to her lips: she would not touch it. She said I oppressed her by leaning over the bed, and again demanded water. As I laid her down—for I raised her and supported her on my arm while she drank—I covered her ice-cold and clammy hand with mine: the feeble fingers shrank from my touch—the glazing eyes shunned my gaze.

"Love me, then, or hate me, as you will," I said at last, "you have my full and free forgiveness: ask now for God's, and be at peace."

Poor, suffering woman! it was too late for her to make now the effort to change her habitual frame of mind: living, she had ever hated me—dying, she must hate me still.

The nurse now entered, and Bessie followed. I yet lingered half-an-hour longer, hoping to see some sign of amity: but she gave none. She was fast relapsing into stupor; nor did her mind again rally: at twelve o'clock that night she died. I was not present to close her eyes, nor were either of her daughters. They came to tell us the next morning that all was over. She was by that time laid out. Eliza and I went to look at her: Georgiana, who had burst out into loud weeping, said she dared not go. There was stretched Sarah Reed's once robust and active frame, rigid and still: her eye of flint was covered with its cold lid; her brow and strong traits wore yet the impress of her inexorable soul. A strange and solemn object was that corpse to me. I gazed on it with gloom and pain: nothing soft, nothing sweet, nothing pitying, or hopeful, or subduing did it inspire; only a grating anguish for HER woes—not MY loss—and a sombre tearless dismay at the fearfulness of death in such a form.

Eliza surveyed her parent calmly. After a silence of some minutes she observed—

"With her constitution she should have lived to a good old age: her life was shortened by trouble." And then a spasm constricted her mouth for an instant: as it passed away she turned and left the room, and so did I. Neither of us had dropt a tear.

Chapter XXII

Mr. Rochester had given me but one week's leave of absence: yet a month elapsed before I quitted Gateshead. I wished to leave immediately after the funeral, but Georgiana entreated me to stay till she could get off to London, whither she was now at last invited by her uncle, Mr. Gibson, who had come down to direct his sister's interment and settle the family affairs. Georgiana said she dreaded being left alone with Eliza; from her she got neither sympathy in her dejection, support in her fears, nor aid in her preparations; so I bore with her feeble-minded wailings and selfish lamentations as well as I could, and did my best in sewing for her and packing her dresses. It is true, that while I worked, she would idle; and I thought to myself, "If you and I were destined to live always together, cousin, we would commence matters on a different footing. I should not settle tamely down into being the forbearing party; I should assign you your share of labour, and compel you to accomplish it, or else it should be left undone: I should insist, also, on your keeping some of those drawling, half-insincere complaints hushed in your own breast. It is only because our connection happens to be very transitory, and comes at a peculiarly mournful season, that I consent thus to render it so patient and compliant on my part."

At last I saw Georgiana off; but now it was Eliza's turn to request me to stay another week. Her plans required all her time and attention, she said; she was about to depart for some unknown bourne; and all day long she stayed in her own room, her door bolted within, filling trunks, emptying drawers, burning papers, and holding no communication with any one. She wished me to look after the house, to see callers, and answer notes of condolence.

One morning she told me I was at liberty. "And," she added, "I am obliged to you for your valuable services and discreet conduct! There is some difference between living with such an one as you and with Georgiana: you perform your own part in life and burden no one. To-morrow," she continued, "I set out for the Continent. I shall take up my abode in a religious house near Lisle—a nunnery you would call it; there I shall be quiet and unmolested. I shall devote myself for a time to the examination of the Roman Catholic dogmas, and to a careful study of the workings of their system: if I find it to be, as I half suspect it is, the one best calculated to ensure the doing of all things decently and in order, I shall embrace the tenets of Rome and probably take the veil."

I neither expressed surprise at this resolution nor attempted to dissuade her from it. "The vocation will fit you to a hair," I thought: "much good may it do you!"

When we parted, she said: "Good-bye, cousin Jane Eyre; I wish you well: you have some sense."

I then returned: "You are not without sense, cousin Eliza; but what you have, I suppose, in another year will be walled up alive in a French convent. However, it is not my business, and so it suits you, I don't much care."

"You are in the right," said she; and with these words we each went our separate way. As I shall not have occasion to refer either to her or her sister again, I may as well mention here, that Georgiana made an advantageous match with a wealthy worn-out man of fashion, and that Eliza actually took the veil, and is at this day superior of the convent where she passed the period of her novitiate, and which she endowed with her fortune.

How people feel when they are returning home from an absence, long or short, I did not know: I had never experienced the sensation. I had known what it was to come back to Gateshead when a child after a long walk, to be scolded for looking cold or gloomy; and later, what it was to come back from church to Lowood, to long for a plenteous meal and a good fire, and to be unable to get either. Neither of these returnings was very pleasant or desirable: no magnet drew me to a given point, increasing in its strength of attraction the nearer I came. The return to Thornfield was yet to be tried.

My journey seemed tedious—very tedious: fifty miles one day, a night spent at an inn; fifty miles the next day. During the first twelve hours I thought of Mrs. Reed in her last moments; I saw her disfigured and discoloured face, and heard her strangely altered voice. I mused on the funeral day, the coffin, the hearse, the black train of tenants and servants—few was the number of relatives—the gaping vault, the silent church, the solemn service. Then I thought of Eliza and Georgiana; I beheld one the cynosure of a ball-room, the other the inmate of a convent cell; and I dwelt on and analysed their separate peculiarities of person and character. The evening arrival at the great town of—scattered these thoughts; night gave them quite another turn: laid down on my traveller's bed, I left reminiscence for anticipation.

I was going back to Thornfield: but how long was I to stay there? Not long; of that I was sure. I had heard from Mrs. Fairfax in the interim of my absence: the party at the hall was dispersed; Mr. Rochester had left for London three weeks ago, but he was then expected to return in a fortnight. Mrs. Fairfax surmised that he was gone to make arrangements for his wedding, as he had talked of purchasing a new carriage: she said the idea of his marrying Miss Ingram still seemed strange to her; but from what everybody said, and from what she had herself seen, she could no longer doubt that the event would shortly take place. "You would be strangely incredulous if you did doubt it," was my mental comment. "I don't doubt it."

The question followed, "Where was I to go?" I dreamt of Miss Ingram all the night: in a vivid morning dream I saw her closing the gates of Thornfield against me and pointing me out another road; and Mr. Rochester looked on with his arms folded—smiling sardonically, as it seemed, at both her and me.

I had not notified to Mrs. Fairfax the exact day of my return; for I did not wish either car or carriage to meet me at Millcote. I proposed to walk the distance quietly by myself; and very quietly, after leaving my box in the ostler's care, did I slip away from the George Inn, about six o'clock of a June evening, and take the old road to Thornfield: a road which lay chiefly through fields, and was now little frequented.

It was not a bright or splendid summer evening, though fair and soft: the haymakers were at work all along the road; and the sky, though far from cloudless, was such as promised well for the future: its blue—where blue was visible—was mild and settled, and its cloud strata high and thin. The west, too, was warm: no watery gleam chilled it—it seemed as if there was a fire lit, an altar burning behind its screen of marbled vapour, and out of apertures shone a golden redness.

I felt glad as the road shortened before me: so glad that I stopped once to ask myself what that joy meant: and to remind reason that it was not to my home I was going, or to a permanent resting-place, or to a place where fond friends looked out for me and waited my arrival. "Mrs. Fairfax will smile you a calm welcome, to be sure," said I; "and little Adele will clap her hands and jump to see you: but you know very well you are thinking of another than they, and that he is not thinking of you."

But what is so headstrong as youth? What so blind as inexperience? These affirmed that it was pleasure enough to have the privilege of again looking on Mr. Rochester, whether he looked on me or not; and they added—"Hasten! hasten! be with him while you may: but a few more days or weeks, at most, and you are parted from him for ever!" And then I strangled a new-born agony—a deformed thing which I could not persuade myself to own and rear—and ran on.

They are making hay, too, in Thornfield meadows: or rather, the labourers are just quitting their work, and returning home with their rakes on their shoulders, now, at the hour I arrive. I have but a field or two to traverse, and then I shall cross the road and reach the gates. How full the hedges are of roses! But I have no time to gather any; I want to be at the house. I passed a tall briar, shooting leafy and flowery branches across the path; I see the narrow stile with stone steps; and I see—Mr. Rochester sitting there, a book and a pencil in his hand; he is writing.

Well, he is not a ghost; yet every nerve I have is unstrung: for a moment I am beyond my own mastery. What does it mean? I did not think I should tremble in this way when I saw him, or lose my voice or the power of motion in his presence. I will go back as soon as I can stir:

I need not make an absolute fool of myself. I know another way to the house. It does not signify if I knew twenty ways; for he has seen me.

"Hillo!" he cries; and he puts up his book and his pencil. "There you are! Come on, if you please."

I suppose I do come on; though in what fashion I know not; being scarcely cognisant of my movements, and solicitous only to appear calm; and, above all, to control the working muscles of my face—which I feel rebel insolently against my will, and struggle to express what I had resolved to conceal. But I have a veil—it is down: I may make shift yet to behave with decent composure.

"And this is Jane Eyre? Are you coming from Millcote, and on foot? Yes—just one of your tricks: not to send for a carriage, and come clattering over street and road like a common mortal, but to steal into the vicinage of your home along with twilight, just as if you were a dream or a shade. What the deuce have you done with yourself this last month?"

"I have been with my aunt, sir, who is dead."

"A true Janian reply! Good angels be my guard! She comes from the other world—from the abode of people who are dead; and tells me so when she meets me alone here in the gloaming! If I dared, I'd touch you, to see if you are substance or shadow, you elf!—but I'd as soon offer to take hold of a blue ignis fatuus light in a marsh. Truant! truant!" he added, when he had paused an instant. "Absent from me a whole month, and forgetting me quite, I'll be sworn!"

I knew there would be pleasure in meeting my master again, even though broken by the fear that he was so soon to cease to be my master, and by the knowledge that I was nothing to him: but there was ever in Mr. Rochester (so at least I thought) such a wealth of the power of communicating happiness, that to taste but of the crumbs he scattered to stray and stranger birds like me, was to feast genially. His last words were balm: they seemed to imply that it imported something to him whether I forgot him or not. And he had spoken of Thornfield as my home—would that it were my home!

He did not leave the stile, and I hardly liked to ask to go by. I inquired soon if he had not been to London.

"Yes; I suppose you found that out by second-sight."

"Mrs. Fairfax told me in a letter."

"And did she inform you what I went to do?"

"Oh, yes, sir! Everybody knew your errand."

"You must see the carriage, Jane, and tell me if you don't think it will suit Mrs. Rochester exactly; and whether she won't look like Queen Boadicea, leaning back against those purple cushions. I wish, Jane, I were a trifle better adapted to match with her externally. Tell me now, fairy as you are—can't you give me a charm, or a philter, or something of that sort, to make me a handsome man?"

"It would be past the power of magic, sir;" and, in thought, I added, "A loving eye is all the charm needed: to such you are handsome enough; or rather your sternness has a power beyond beauty."

Mr. Rochester had sometimes read my unspoken thoughts with an acumen to me incomprehensible: in the present instance he took no notice of my abrupt vocal response; but he smiled at me with a certain smile he had of his own, and which he used but on rare occasions. He seemed to think it too good for common purposes: it was the real sunshine of feeling—he shed it over me now.

"Pass, Janet," said he, making room for me to cross the stile: "go up home, and stay your weary little wandering feet at a friend's threshold."

All I had now to do was to obey him in silence: no need for me to colloquise further. I got over the stile without a word, and meant to leave him calmly. An impulse held me fast—a force turned me round. I said—or something in me said for me, and in spite of me—

"Thank you, Mr. Rochester, for your great kindness. I am strangely glad to get back again to you: and wherever you are is my home—my only home."

I walked on so fast that even he could hardly have overtaken me had he tried. Little Adele was half wild with delight when she saw me. Mrs. Fairfax received me with her usual plain friendliness. Leah smiled, and even Sophie bid me "bon soir" with glee. This was very pleasant; there is no happiness like that of being loved by your fellow-creatures, and feeling that your presence is an addition to their comfort.

I that evening shut my eyes resolutely against the future: I stopped my cars against the voice that kept warning me of near separation and coming grief. When tea was over and Mrs. Fairfax had taken her knitting, and I had assumed a low seat near her, and Adele, kneeling on the carpet, had nestled close up to me, and a sense of mutual affection seemed to surround us with a ring of golden peace, I uttered a silent prayer that we might not be parted far or soon; but when, as we thus sat, Mr. Rochester entered, unannounced, and looking at us, seemed to take pleasure in the spectacle of a group so amicable—when he said he supposed the old lady was all right now that she had got her adopted daughter back again, and added that he saw Adele was "prete e croquer sa petite maman Anglaise"—I half ventured to hope that he would, even after his marriage, keep us together somewhere under the shelter of his protection, and not quite exiled from the sunshine of his presence.

A fortnight of dubious calm succeeded my return to Thornfield Hall. Nothing was said of the master's marriage, and I saw no preparation going on for such an event. Almost every day I asked Mrs. Fairfax if she had yet heard anything decided: her answer was always in the negative. Once she said she had actually put the question to Mr. Rochester as to when he was going to bring his bride home; but he had answered her only by a joke and one of his queer looks, and she could not tell what to make of him.

One thing specially surprised me, and that was, there were no journeyings backward and forward, no visits to Ingram Park: to be sure it was twenty miles off, on the borders of another county; but what was that distance to an ardent lover? To so practised and indefatigable a horseman as Mr. Rochester, it would be but a morning's ride. I began to cherish hopes I had no right to conceive: that the match was broken off; that rumour had been mistaken; that one or both parties had changed their minds. I used to look at my master's face to see if it were sad or fierce; but I could not remember the time when it had been so uniformly clear of clouds or evil feelings. If, in the moments I and my pupil spent with him, I lacked spirits and sank into inevitable dejection, he became even gay. Never had he called me more frequently to his presence; never been kinder to me when there—and, alas! never had I loved him so well.

Chapter XXIII

A splendid Midsummer shone over England: skies so pure, suns so radiant as were then seen in long succession, seldom favour even singly, our wave-girt land. It was as if a band of Italian days had come from the South, like a flock of glorious passenger birds, and lighted to rest them on the cliffs of Albion. The hay was all got in; the fields round Thornfield were green and shorn; the roads white and baked; the trees were in their dark prime; hedge and wood, full-leaved and deeply tinted, contrasted well with the sunny hue of the cleared meadows between.

On Midsummer-eve, Adele, weary with gathering wild strawberries in Hay Lane half the day, had gone to bed with the sun. I watched her drop asleep, and when I left her, I sought the garden.

It was now the sweetest hour of the twenty-four:-"Day its fervid fires had wasted," and dew fell cool on panting plain and scorched summit. Where the sun had gone down in simple state—pure of the pomp of clouds—spread a solemn purple, burning with the light of red jewel and furnace flame at one point, on one hill-peak, and extending high and wide, soft and still softer, over half heaven. The east had its own charm or fine deep blue, and its own modest gem, a casino and solitary star: soon it would boast the moon; but she was yet beneath the horizon.

I walked a while on the pavement; but a subtle, well-known scent—that of a cigar—stole from some window; I saw the library casement open a handbreadth; I knew I might be watched thence; so I went apart into the orchard. No nook in the grounds more sheltered and more Eden-like; it was full of trees, it bloomed with flowers: a very high wall shut it out from the court, on one side; on the other, a beech avenue screened it from the lawn. At the bottom was a sunk fence; its sole separation from lonely fields: a winding walk, bordered with laurels and terminating in a giant horse-chestnut, circled at the base by a seat, led down to the fence. Here one could wander unseen. While such honey-dew fell, such silence reigned, such gloaming gathered, I felt as if I could haunt such shade for ever; but in threading the flower and fruit parterres at the upper part of the enclosure, enticed there by the light the now rising moon cast on this more open quarter, my step is stayed—not by sound, not by sight, but once more by a warning fragrance.

Sweet-briar and southernwood, jasmine, pink, and rose have long been yielding their evening sacrifice of incense: this new scent is neither of shrub nor flower; it is—I know it well—it is Mr. Rochester's cigar. I look round and I listen. I see trees laden with ripening fruit. I hear a nightingale warbling in a wood half a mile off; no moving form is visible, no coming step audible; but that perfume increases: I must flee. I make for the wicket leading to the shrubbery, and I see Mr. Rochester entering. I step aside into the ivy recess; he will not stay long: he will soon return whence he came, and if I sit still he will never see me.

But no—eventide is as pleasant to him as to me, and this antique garden as attractive; and he strolls on, now lifting the gooseberry-tree branches to look at the fruit, large as plums, with which they are laden; now taking a ripe cherry from the wall; now stooping towards a knot of flowers, either to inhale their fragrance or to admire the dew-beads on their petals. A great moth goes humming by me; it alights on a plant at Mr. Rochester's foot: he sees it, and bends to examine it.

"Now, he has his back towards me," thought I, "and he is occupied too; perhaps, if I walk softly, I can slip away unnoticed."

I trode on an edging of turf that the crackle of the pebbly gravel might not betray me: he was standing among the beds at a yard or two distant from where I had to pass; the moth apparently engaged him. "I shall get by very well," I meditated. As I crossed his shadow, thrown long over the garden by the moon, not yet risen high, he said quietly, without turning—

"Jane, come and look at this fellow."

I had made no noise: he had not eyes behind—could his shadow feel? I started at first, and then I approached him.

"Look at his wings," said he, "he reminds me rather of a West Indian insect; one does not often see so large and gay a night-rover in England; there! he is flown."

The moth roamed away. I was sheepishly retreating also; but Mr. Rochester followed me, and when we reached the wicket, he said—

"Turn back: on so lovely a night it is a shame to sit in the house; and surely no one can wish to go to bed while sunset is thus at meeting with moonrise."

It is one of my faults, that though my tongue is sometimes prompt enough at an answer, there are times when it sadly fails me in framing an excuse; and always the lapse occurs at some crisis, when a facile word or plausible pretext is specially wanted to get me out of painful embarrassment. I did not like to walk at this hour alone with Mr. Rochester in the shadowy orchard; but I could not find a reason to allege for leaving him. I followed with lagging step, and thoughts busily bent on discovering a means of extrication; but he himself looked so composed and so grave also, I became ashamed of feeling any confusion: the evil—if evil existent or prospective there was—seemed to lie with me only; his mind was unconscious and quiet.

"Jane," he recommenced, as we entered the laurel walk, and slowly strayed down in the direction of the sunk fence and the horse-chestnut, "Thornfield is a pleasant place in summer, is it not?"

"Yes, sir."

"You must have become in some degree attached to the house,—you, who have an eye for natural beauties, and a good deal of the organ of Adhesiveness?"

"I am attached to it, indeed."

"And though I don't comprehend how it is, I perceive you have acquired a degree of regard for that foolish little child Adele, too; and even for simple dame Fairfax?"

"Yes, sir; in different ways, I have an affection for both."

"And would be sorry to part with them?"

"Yes."

"Pity!" he said, and sighed and paused. "It is always the way of events in this life," he continued presently: "no sooner have you got settled in a pleasant resting-place, than a voice calls out to you to rise and move on, for the hour of repose is expired."

"Must I move on, sir?" I asked. "Must I leave Thornfield?"

"I believe you must, Jane. I am sorry, Janet, but I believe indeed you must."

This was a blow: but I did not let it prostrate me.

"Well, sir, I shall be ready when the order to march comes."

"It is come now—I must give it to-night."

"Then you ARE going to be married, sir?"

"Ex-act-ly—pre-cise-ly: with your usual acuteness, you have hit the nail straight on the head."

"Soon, sir?"

"Very soon, my—that is, Miss Eyre: and you'll remember, Jane, the first time I, or Rumour, plainly intimated to you that it was my intention to put my old bachelor's neck into the sacred noose, to enter into the holy estate of matrimony—to take Miss Ingram to my bosom, in short (she's an extensive armful: but that's not to the point—one can't have too much of such a very excellent thing as my beautiful Blanche): well, as I was saying—listen to me, Jane! You're not turning your head to look after more moths, are you? That was only a lady-clock, child, 'flying away home.' I wish to remind you that it was you who first said to me, with that discretion I respect in you—with that foresight, prudence, and humility which befit your responsible and dependent position—that in case I married Miss Ingram, both you and little Adele had better trot forthwith. I pass over the sort of slur conveyed in this suggestion on the character of my beloved; indeed, when you are far away, Janet, I'll try to forget it: I shall notice only its wisdom; which is such that I have made it my law of action. Adele must go to school; and you, Miss Eyre, must get a new situation."

"Yes, sir, I will advertise immediately: and meantime, I suppose—" I was going to say, "I suppose I may stay here, till I find another shelter to betake myself to:" but I stopped, feeling it would not do to risk a long sentence, for my voice was not quite under command.

"In about a month I hope to be a bridegroom," continued Mr. Rochester; "and in the interim, I shall myself look out for employment and an asylum for you."

"Thank you, sir; I am sorry to give——"

"Oh, no need to apologise! I consider that when a dependent does her duty as well as you have done yours, she has a sort of claim upon her employer for any little assistance he can conveniently render her; indeed I have already, through my future mother-in-law, heard of a place that I think will suit: it is to undertake the education of the five daughters of Mrs. Dionysius O'Gall of Bitternutt Lodge, Connaught, Ireland. You'll like Ireland, I think: they're such warm-hearted people there, they say."

"It is a long way off, sir."

"No matter—a girl of your sense will not object to the voyage or the distance."

"Not the voyage, but the distance: and then the sea is a barrier——"

"From what, Jane?"

"From England and from Thornfield: and——"

"Well?"

"From YOU, sir."

I said this almost involuntarily, and, with as little sanction of free will, my tears gushed out. I did not cry so as to be heard, however; I avoided sobbing. The thought of Mrs. O'Gall and Bitternutt Lodge struck cold to my heart; and colder the thought of all the brine and foam, destined, as it seemed, to rush between me and the master at whose side I now walked, and coldest the remembrance of the wider ocean—wealth, caste, custom intervened between me and what I naturally and inevitably loved.

"It is a long way," I again said.

"It is, to be sure; and when you get to Bitternutt Lodge, Connaught, Ireland, I shall never see you again, Jane: that's morally certain. I never go over to Ireland, not having myself much of a fancy for the country. We have been good friends, Jane; have we not?"

"Yes, sir."

"And when friends are on the eve of separation, they like to spend the little time that remains to them close to each other. Come! we'll talk over the voyage and the parting quietly half-an-hour or so, while the stars enter into their shining life up in heaven yonder: here is the chestnut tree: here is the bench at its old roots. Come, we will sit there in peace to-night, though we should never more be destined to sit there together." He seated me and himself.

"It is a long way to Ireland, Janet, and I am sorry to send my little friend on such weary travels: but if I can't do better, how is it to be helped? Are you anything akin to me, do you think, Jane?"

I could risk no sort of answer by this time: my heart was still.

"Because," he said, "I sometimes have a queer feeling with regard to you—especially when you are near me, as now: it is as if I had a string somewhere under my left ribs, tightly and inextricably knotted to a similar string situated in the corresponding quarter of your little frame. And if that boisterous Channel, and two hundred miles or so of land come broad between us, I am afraid that cord of communion will be snapt; and then I've a nervous notion I should take to bleeding inwardly. As for you,—you'd forget me."

"That I NEVER should, sir: you know—" Impossible to proceed.

"Jane, do you hear that nightingale singing in the wood? Listen!"

In listening, I sobbed convulsively; for I could repress what I endured no longer; I was obliged to yield, and I was shaken from head to foot with acute distress. When I did speak, it was only to express an impetuous wish that I had never been born, or never come to Thornfield.

"Because you are sorry to leave it?"

The vehemence of emotion, stirred by grief and love within me, was claiming mastery, and struggling for full sway, and asserting a right to predominate, to overcome, to live, rise, and reign at last: yes,—and to speak.

"I grieve to leave Thornfield: I love Thornfield:-I love it, because I have lived in it a full and delightful life,—momentarily at least. I have not been trampled on. I have not been petrified. I have not been buried with inferior minds, and excluded from every glimpse of communion with what is bright and energetic and high. I have talked, face to face, with what I reverence, with what I delight in,—with an original, a vigorous, an expanded mind. I have known you, Mr. Rochester; and it strikes me with terror and anguish to feel I absolutely must be torn from you for ever. I see the necessity of departure; and it is like looking on the necessity of death."

"Where do you see the necessity?" he asked suddenly.

"Where? You, sir, have placed it before me."

"In what shape?"

"In the shape of Miss Ingram; a noble and beautiful woman,—your bride."

"My bride! What bride? I have no bride!"

"But you will have."

"Yes;—I will!—I will!" He set his teeth.

"Then I must go:-you have said it yourself."

"No: you must stay! I swear it—and the oath shall be kept."

"I tell you I must go!" I retorted, roused to something like passion. "Do you think I can stay to become nothing to you? Do you think I am an automaton?—a machine without feelings? and can bear to have my morsel of bread snatched from my lips, and my drop of living water dashed from my cup? Do you think, because I am poor, obscure, plain, and little, I am soulless and heartless? You think wrong!—I have as much soul as you,—and full as much heart! And if God had gifted me with some beauty and much wealth, I should have made it as hard for you to leave me, as it is now for me to leave you. I am not talking to you now through the medium of custom, conventionalities, nor even of mortal flesh;—it is my spirit that addresses your spirit; just as if both had passed through the grave, and we stood at God's feet, equal,—as we are!"

"As we are!" repeated Mr. Rochester—"so," he added, enclosing me in his arms. Gathering me to his breast, pressing his lips on my lips: "so, Jane!"

"Yes, so, sir," I rejoined: "and yet not so; for you are a married man—or as good as a married man, and wed to one inferior to you—to one with whom you have no sympathy—whom I do not believe you truly love; for I have seen and heard you sneer at her. I would scorn such a union: therefore I am better than you—let me go!"

"Where, Jane? To Ireland?"

"Yes—to Ireland. I have spoken my mind, and can go anywhere now."

"Jane, be still; don't struggle so, like a wild frantic bird that is rending its own plumage in its desperation."

"I am no bird; and no net ensnares me; I am a free human being with an independent will, which I now exert to leave you."

Another effort set me at liberty, and I stood erect before him.

"And your will shall decide your destiny," he said: "I offer you my hand, my heart, and a share of all my possessions."

"You play a farce, which I merely laugh at."

"I ask you to pass through life at my side—to be my second self, and best earthly companion."

"For that fate you have already made your choice, and must abide by it."

"Jane, be still a few moments: you are over-excited: I will be still too."

A waft of wind came sweeping down the laurel-walk, and trembled through the boughs of the chestnut: it wandered away—away—to an indefinite distance—it died. The nightingale's song was then the only voice of the hour: in listening to it, I again wept. Mr. Rochester sat quiet, looking at me gently and seriously. Some time passed before he spoke; he at last said—

"Come to my side, Jane, and let us explain and understand one another."

"I will never again come to your side: I am torn away now, and cannot return."

"But, Jane, I summon you as my wife: it is you only I intend to marry."

I was silent: I thought he mocked me.

"Come, Jane—come hither."

"Your bride stands between us."

He rose, and with a stride reached me.

"My bride is here," he said, again drawing me to him, "because my equal is here, and my likeness. Jane, will you marry me?"

Still I did not answer, and still I writhed myself from his grasp: for I was still incredulous.

"Do you doubt me, Jane?"

"Entirely."

"You have no faith in me?"

"Not a whit."

"Am I a liar in your eyes?" he asked passionately. "Little sceptic, you SHALL be convinced. What love have I for Miss Ingram? None: and that you know. What love has she for me? None: as I have taken pains to prove: I caused a rumour to reach her that my fortune was not a third of what was supposed, and after that I presented myself to see the result; it was coldness both from her and her mother. I would not—I could not—marry Miss Ingram. You—you strange, you almost unearthly thing!—I love as my own flesh. You—poor and obscure, and small and plain as you are—I entreat to accept me as a husband."

"What, me!" I ejaculated, beginning in his earnestness—and especially in his incivility—to credit his sincerity: "me who have not a friend in the world but you-if you are my friend: not a shilling but what you have given me?"

"You, Jane, I must have you for my own—entirely my own. Will you be mine? Say yes, quickly."

"Mr. Rochester, let me look at your face: turn to the moonlight."

"Why?"

"Because I want to read your countenance—turn!"

"There! you will find it scarcely more legible than a crumpled, scratched page. Read on: only make haste, for I suffer."

His face was very much agitated and very much flushed, and there were strong workings in the features, and strange gleams in the eyes

"Oh, Jane, you torture me!" he exclaimed. "With that searching and yet faithful and generous look, you torture me!"

"How can I do that? If you are true, and your offer real, my only feelings to you must be gratitude and devotion—they cannot torture."

"Gratitude!" he ejaculated; and added wildly—"Jane accept me quickly. Say, Edward—give me my name—Edward—I will marry you."

"Are you in earnest? Do you truly love me? Do you sincerely wish me to be your wife?"

"I do; and if an oath is necessary to satisfy you, I swear it."

"Then, sir, I will marry you."

"Edward—my little wife!"

"Dear Edward!"

"Come to me—come to me entirely now," said he; and added, in his deepest tone, speaking in my ear as his cheek was laid on mine, "Make my happiness—I will make yours."

"God pardon me!" he subjoined ere long; "and man meddle not with me: I have her, and will hold her."

"There is no one to meddle, sir. I have no kindred to interfere."

"No—that is the best of it," he said. And if I had loved him less I should have thought his accent and look of exultation savage; but, sitting by him, roused from the nightmare of parting—called to the paradise of union—I thought only of the bliss given me to drink in so abundant a flow. Again and again he said, "Are you happy, Jane?" And again and again I answered, "Yes." After which he murmured, "It will atone—it will atone. Have I not found her friendless, and cold, and comfortless? Will I not guard, and cherish, and solace her? Is there not love in my heart, and constancy in my resolves? It will expiate at God's tribunal. I know my Maker sanctions what I do. For the world's judgment—I wash my hands thereof. For man's opinion—I defy it."

But what had befallen the night? The moon was not yet set, and we were all in shadow: I could scarcely see my master's face, near as I was. And what ailed the chestnut tree? it writhed and groaned; while wind roared in the laurel walk, and came sweeping over us.

"We must go in," said Mr. Rochester: "the weather changes. I could have sat with thee till morning, Jane."

"And so," thought I, "could I with you." I should have said so, perhaps, but a livid, vivid spark leapt out of a cloud at which I was looking, and there was a crack, a crash, and a close rattling peal; and I thought only of hiding my dazzled eyes against Mr. Rochester's shoulder.

The rain rushed down. He hurried me up the walk, through the grounds, and into the house; but we were quite wet before we could pass the threshold. He was taking off my shawl in the hall, and shaking the water out of my loosened hair, when Mrs. Fairfax emerged from her room. I did not observe her at first, nor did Mr. Rochester. The lamp was lit. The clock was on the stroke of twelve.

"Hasten to take off your wet things," said he; "and before you go, good-night—good-night, my darling!"

He kissed me repeatedly. When I looked up, on leaving his arms, there stood the widow, pale, grave, and amazed. I only smiled at her, and ran upstairs. "Explanation will do for another time," thought I. Still, when I reached my chamber, I felt a pang at the idea she should even temporarily misconstrue what she had seen. But joy soon effaced every other feeling; and loud as the wind blew, near and deep as the thunder crashed, fierce and frequent as the lightning gleamed, cataract-like as the rain fell during a storm of two hours' duration, I experienced no fear and little awe. Mr. Rochester came thrice to my door in the course of it, to ask if I was safe and tranquil: and that was comfort, that was strength for anything.

Before I left my bed in the morning, little Adele came running in to tell me that the great horse-chestnut at the bottom of the orchard had been struck by lightning in the night, and half of it split away.

Chapter XXIV

As I rose and dressed, I thought over what had happened, and wondered if it were a dream. I could not be certain of the reality till I had seen Mr. Rochester again, and heard him renew his words of love and promise.

While arranging my hair, I looked at my face in the glass, and felt it was no longer plain: there was hope in its aspect and life in its colour; and my eyes seemed as if they had beheld the fount of fruition, and borrowed beams from the lustrous ripple. I had often been unwilling to look at my master, because I feared he could not be pleased at my look; but I was sure I might lift my face to his now, and not cool his affection by its expression. I took a plain but clean and light summer dress from my drawer and put it on: it seemed no attire had ever so well become me, because none had I ever worn in so blissful a mood.

I was not surprised, when I ran down into the hall, to see that a brilliant June morning had succeeded to the tempest of the night; and to feel, through the open glass door, the breathing of a fresh and fragrant breeze. Nature must be gladsome when I was so happy. A beggar-woman and her little boy—pale, ragged objects both—were coming up the walk, and I ran down and gave them all the money I happened to have in my purse—some three or four shillings: good or bad, they must partake of my jubilee. The rooks cawed, and blither birds sang; but nothing was so merry or so musical as my own rejoicing heart.

Mrs. Fairfax surprised me by looking out of the window with a sad countenance, and saying gravely—"Miss Eyre, will you come to breakfast?" During the meal she was quiet and cool: but I could not undeceive her then. I must wait for my master to give explanations; and so must she. I ate what I could, and then I hastened upstairs. I met Adele leaving the schoolroom.

"Where are you going? It is time for lessons."

"Mr. Rochester has sent me away to the nursery."

"Where is he?"

"In there," pointing to the apartment she had left; and I went in, and there he stood.

"Come and bid me good-morning," said he. I gladly advanced; and it was not merely a cold word now, or even a shake of the hand that I received, but an embrace and a kiss. It seemed natural: it seemed genial to be so well loved, so caressed by him.

"Jane, you look blooming, and smiling, and pretty," said he: "truly pretty this morning. Is this my pale, little elf? Is this my mustard-seed? This little sunny-faced girl with the dimpled cheek and rosy lips; the satin-smooth hazel hair, and the radiant hazel eyes?" (I had green eyes, reader; but you must excuse the mistake: for him they were new-dyed, I suppose.)

"It is Jane Eyre, sir."

"Soon to be Jane Rochester," he added: "in four weeks, Janet; not a day more. Do you hear that?"

I did, and I could not quite comprehend it: it made me giddy. The feeling, the announcement sent through me, was something stronger than was consistent with joy—something that smote and stunned. It was, I think almost fear.

"You blushed, and now you are white, Jane: what is that for?"

"Because you gave me a new name—Jane Rochester; and it seems so strange."

"Yes, Mrs. Rochester," said he; "young Mrs. Rochester—Fairfax Rochester's girl-bride."

"It can never be, sir; it does not sound likely. Human beings never enjoy complete happiness in this world. I was not born for a different destiny to the rest of my species: to imagine such a lot befalling me is a fairy tale—a day-dream."

"Which I can and will realise. I shall begin to-day. This morning I wrote to my banker in London to send me certain jewels he has in his keeping,—heirlooms for the ladies of Thornfield. In a day or two I hope to pour them into your lap: for every privilege, every attention shall be yours that I would accord a peer's daughter, if about to marry her."

"Oh, sir!—never rain jewels! I don't like to hear them spoken of. Jewels for Jane Eyre sounds unnatural and strange: I would rather not have them."

"I will myself put the diamond chain round your neck, and the circlet on your forehead,—which it will become: for nature, at least, has stamped her patent of nobility on this brow, Jane; and I will clasp the bracelets on these fine wrists, and load these fairy-like fingers with rings."

"No, no, sir! think of other subjects, and speak of other things, and in another strain. Don't address me as if I were a beauty; I am your plain, Quakerish governess."

"You are a beauty in my eyes, and a beauty just after the desire of my heart,—delicate and aerial."

"Puny and insignificant, you mean. You are dreaming, sir,—or you are sneering. For God's sake don't be ironical!"

"I will make the world acknowledge you a beauty, too," he went on, while I really became uneasy at the strain he had adopted, because I felt he was either deluding himself or trying to delude me. "I will attire my Jane in satin and lace, and she shall have roses in her hair; and I will cover the head I love best with a priceless veil."

"And then you won't know me, sir; and I shall not be your Jane Eyre any longer, but an ape in a harlequin's jacket—a jay in borrowed plumes. I would as soon see you, Mr. Rochester, tricked out in stage-trappings, as myself clad in a court-lady's robe; and I don't call you handsome, sir, though I love you most dearly: far too dearly to flatter you. Don't flatter me."

He pursued his theme, however, without noticing my deprecation. "This very day I shall take you in the carriage to Millcote, and you must choose some dresses for yourself. I told you we shall be married in four weeks. The wedding is to take place quietly, in the church down below yonder; and then I shall waft you away at once to town. After a brief stay there, I shall bear my treasure to regions nearer the sun: to French vineyards and Italian plains; and she shall see whatever is famous in old story and in modern record: she shall taste, too, of the life of cities; and she shall learn to value herself by just comparison with others."

"Shall I travel?—and with you, sir?"

"You shall sojourn at Paris, Rome, and Naples: at Florence, Venice, and Vienna: all the ground I have wandered over shall be retrodden by you: wherever I stamped my hoof, your sylph's foot shall step also. Ten years since, I flew through Europe half mad; with disgust, hate, and rage as my companions: now I shall revisit it healed and cleansed, with a very angel as my comforter."

I laughed at him as he said this. "I am not an angel," I asserted; "and I will not be one till I die: I will be myself. Mr. Rochester, you must neither expect nor exact anything celestial of me—for you will not get it, any more than I shall get it of you: which I do not at all anticipate."

"What do you anticipate of me?"

"For a little while you will perhaps be as you are now,—a very little while; and then you will turn cool; and then you will be capricious; and then you will be stern, and I shall have much ado to please you: but when you get well used to me, you will perhaps like me again,—LIKE me, I say, not LOVE me. I suppose your love will effervesce in six months, or less. I have observed in books written by men, that period assigned as the farthest to which a husband's ardour extends. Yet, after all, as a friend and companion, I hope never to become quite distasteful to my dear master."

"Distasteful! and like you again! I think I shall like you again, and yet again: and I will make you confess I do not only LIKE, but LOVE you—with truth, fervour, constancy."

"Yet are you not capricious, sir?"

"To women who please me only by their faces, I am the very devil when I find out they have neither souls nor hearts—when they open to me a perspective of flatness, triviality, and perhaps imbecility, coarseness, and ill-temper: but to the clear eye and eloquent tongue, to the soul made of fire, and the character that bends but does not break—at once supple and stable, tractable and consistent—I am ever tender and true."

"Had you ever experience of such a character, sir? Did you ever love such an one?"

"I love it now."

"But before me: if I, indeed, in any respect come up to your difficult standard?"

"I never met your likeness. Jane, you please me, and you master me—you seem to submit, and I like the sense of pliancy you impart; and while I am twining the soft, silken skein round my finger, it sends a thrill up my arm to my heart. I am influenced—conquered; and the influence is sweeter than I can express; and the conquest I undergo has a witchery beyond any triumph I can win. Why do you smile, Jane? What does that inexplicable, that uncanny turn of countenance mean?"

"I was thinking, sir (you will excuse the idea; it was involuntary), I was thinking of Hercules and Samson with their charmers—"

"You were, you little elfish—"

"Hush, sir! You don't talk very wisely just now; any more than those gentlemen acted very wisely. However, had they been married, they would no doubt by their severity as husbands have made up for their softness as suitors; and so will you, I fear. I wonder how you will answer me a year hence, should I ask a favour it does not suit your convenience or pleasure to grant."

"Ask me something now, Jane,—the least thing: I desire to be entreated—"

"Indeed I will, sir; I have my petition all ready."

"Speak! But if you look up and smile with that countenance, I shall swear concession before I know to what, and that will make a fool of me."

"Not at all, sir; I ask only this: don't send for the jewels, and don't crown me with roses: you might as well put a border of gold lace round that plain pocket handkerchief you have there."

"I might as well 'gild refined gold.' I know it: you request is granted then—for the time. I will remand the order I despatched to my banker. But you have not yet asked for anything; you have prayed a gift to be withdrawn: try again."

"Well then, sir, have the goodness to gratify my curiosity, which is much piqued on one point."

He looked disturbed. "What? what?" he said hastily. "Curiosity is a dangerous petition: it is well I have not taken a vow to accord every request—"

"But there can be no danger in complying with this, sir."

"Utter it, Jane: but I wish that instead of a mere inquiry into, perhaps, a secret, it was a wish for half my estate."

"Now, King Ahasuerus! What do I want with half your estate? Do you think I am a Jew-usurer, seeking good investment in land? I would much rather have all your confidence. You will not exclude me from your confidence if you admit me to your heart?"

"You are welcome to all my confidence that is worth having, Jane; but for God's sake, don't desire a useless burden! Don't long for poison—don't turn out a downright Eve on my hands!"

"Why not, sir? You have just been telling me how much you liked to be conquered, and how pleasant over-persuasion is to you. Don't you think I had better take advantage of the confession, and begin and coax and entreat—even cry and be sulky if necessary—for the sake of a mere essay of my power?"

"I dare you to any such experiment. Encroach, presume, and the game is up."

"Is it, sir? You soon give in. How stern you look now! Your eyebrows have become as thick as my finger, and your forehead resembles what, in some very astonishing poetry, I once saw styled, 'a blue-piled thunderloft.' That will be your married look, sir, I suppose?"

"If that will be YOUR married look, I, as a Christian, will soon give up the notion of consorting with a mere sprite or salamander. But what had you to ask, thing,—out with it?"

"There, you are less than civil now; and I like rudeness a great deal better than flattery. I had rather be a THING than an angel. This is what I have to ask,—Why did you take such pains to make me believe you wished to marry Miss Ingram?"

"Is that all? Thank God it is no worse!" And now he unknit his black brows; looked down, smiling at me, and stroked my hair, as if well pleased at seeing a danger averted. "I think I may confess," he continued, "even although I should make you a little indignant, Jane—and I have seen what a fire-spirit you can be when you are indignant. You glowed in the cool moonlight last night, when you mutinied against fate, and claimed your rank as my equal. Janet, by-the-bye, it was you who made me the offer."

"Of course I did. But to the point if you please, sir—Miss Ingram?"

"Well, I feigned courtship of Miss Ingram, because I wished to render you as madly in love with me as I was with you; and I knew jealousy would be the best ally I could call in for the furtherance of that end."

"Excellent! Now you are small—not one whit bigger than the end of my little finger. It was a burning shame and a scandalous disgrace to act in that way. Did you think nothing of Miss Ingram's feelings, sir?"

"Her feelings are concentrated in one—pride; and that needs humbling. Were you jealous, Jane?"

"Never mind, Mr. Rochester: it is in no way interesting to you to know that. Answer me truly once more. Do you think Miss Ingram will not suffer from your dishonest coquetry? Won't she feel forsaken and deserted?"

"Impossible!—when I told you how she, on the contrary, deserted me: the idea of my insolvency cooled, or rather extinguished, her flame in a moment."

"You have a curious, designing mind, Mr. Rochester. I am afraid your principles on some points are eccentric."

"My principles were never trained, Jane: they may have grown a little awry for want of attention."

"Once again, seriously; may I enjoy the great good that has been vouchsafed to me, without fearing that any one else is suffering the bitter pain I myself felt a while ago?"

"That you may, my good little girl: there is not another being in the world has the same pure love for me as yourself—for I lay that pleasant unction to my soul, Jane, a belief in your affection."

I turned my lips to the hand that lay on my shoulder. I loved him very much—more than I could trust myself to say—more than words had power to express.

"Ask something more," he said presently; "it is my delight to be entreated, and to yield."

I was again ready with my request. "Communicate your intentions to Mrs. Fairfax, sir: she saw me with you last night in the hall, and she was shocked. Give her some explanation before I see her again. It pains me to be misjudged by so good a woman."

"Go to your room, and put on your bonnet," he replied. "I mean you to accompany me to Millcote this morning; and while you prepare for the drive, I will enlighten the old lady's understanding. Did she think, Janet, you had given the world for love, and considered it well lost?"

"I believe she thought I had forgotten my station, and yours, sir."

"Station! station!—your station is in my heart, and on the necks of those who would insult you, now or hereafter.—Go."

I was soon dressed; and when I heard Mr. Rochester quit Mrs. Fairfax's parlour, I hurried down to it. The old lady, had been reading her morning portion of Scripture—the Lesson for the day; her Bible lay open before her, and her spectacles were upon it. Her occupation, suspended by Mr. Rochester's announcement, seemed now forgotten: her eyes, fixed on the blank wall opposite, expressed the surprise of a quiet mind stirred by unwonted tidings. Seeing me, she roused herself: she made a sort of effort to smile, and framed a few words of congratulation; but the smile expired, and the sentence was abandoned unfinished. She put up her spectacles, shut the Bible, and pushed her chair back from the table.

"I feel so astonished," she began, "I hardly know what to say to you, Miss Eyre. I have surely not been dreaming, have I? Sometimes I half fall asleep when I am sitting alone and fancy things that have never happened. It has seemed to me more than once when I have been in a doze, that my dear husband, who died fifteen years since, has come in and sat down beside me; and that I have even heard him call me by my name, Alice, as he used to do. Now, can you tell me whether it is actually true that Mr. Rochester has asked you to marry him? Don't laugh at me. But I really thought he came in here five minutes ago, and said that in a month you would be his wife."

"He has said the same thing to me," I replied.

"He has! Do you believe him? Have you accepted him?"

"Yes."

She looked at me bewildered. "I could never have thought it. He is a proud man: all the Rochesters were proud: and his father, at least, liked money. He, too, has always been called careful. He means to marry you?"

"He tells me so."

She surveyed my whole person: in her eyes I read that they had there found no charm powerful enough to solve the enigma.

"It passes me!" she continued; "but no doubt, it is true since you say so. How it will answer, I cannot tell: I really don't know. Equality of position and fortune is often advisable in such cases; and there are twenty years of difference in your ages. He might almost be your father."

"No, indeed, Mrs. Fairfax!" exclaimed I, nettled; "he is nothing like my father! No one, who saw us together, would suppose it for an instant. Mr. Rochester looks as young, and is as young, as some men at five-and-twenty."

"Is it really for love he is going to marry you?" she asked.

I was so hurt by her coldness and scepticism, that the tears rose to my eyes.

"I am sorry to grieve you," pursued the widow; "but you are so young, and so little acquainted with men, I wished to put you on your guard. It is an old saying that 'all is not gold that glitters;' and in this case I do fear there will be something found to be different to what either you or I expect."

"Why?—am I a monster?" I said: "is it impossible that Mr. Rochester should have a sincere affection for me?"

"No: you are very well; and much improved of late; and Mr. Rochester, I daresay, is fond of you. I have always noticed that you were a sort of pet of his. There are times when, for your sake, I have been a little uneasy at his marked preference, and have wished to put you on your guard: but I did not like to suggest even the possibility of wrong. I knew such an idea would shock, perhaps offend you; and you were so discreet, and so thoroughly modest and sensible, I hoped you might be trusted to protect yourself. Last night I cannot tell you what I suffered when I sought all over the house, and could find you nowhere, nor the master either; and then, at twelve o'clock, saw you come in with him."

"Well, never mind that now," I interrupted impatiently; "it is enough that all was right."

"I hope all will be right in the end," she said: "but believe me, you cannot be too careful. Try and keep Mr. Rochester at a distance: distrust yourself as well as him. Gentlemen in his station are not accustomed to marry their governesses."

I was growing truly irritated: happily, Adele ran in.

"Let me go,—let me go to Millcote too!" she cried. "Mr. Rochester won't: though there is so much room in the new carriage. Beg him to let me go mademoiselle."

"That I will, Adele;" and I hastened away with her, glad to quit my gloomy monitress. The carriage was ready: they were bringing it round to the front, and my master was the pavement, Pilot following him backwards and forwards.

"Adele may accompany us, may she not, sir?"

"I told her no. I'll have no brats!—I'll have only you."

"Do let her go, Mr. Rochester, if you please: it would be better."

"Not it: she will be a restraint."

He was quite peremptory, both in look and voice. The chill of Mrs. Fairfax's warnings, and the damp of her doubts were upon me: something of unsubstantiality and uncertainty had beset my hopes. I half lost the sense of power over him. I was about mechanically to obey him, without further remonstrance; but as he helped me into the carriage, he looked at my face.

"What is the matter?" he asked; "all the sunshine is gone. Do you really wish the bairn to go? Will it annoy you if she is left behind?"

"I would far rather she went, sir."

"Then off for your bonnet, and back like a flash of lightning!" cried he to Adele.

She obeyed him with what speed she might.

"After all, a single morning's interruption will not matter much," said he, "when I mean shortly to claim you—your thoughts, conversation, and company—for life."

Adele, when lifted in, commenced kissing me, by way of expressing her gratitude for my intercession: she was instantly stowed away into a corner on the other side of him. She then peeped round to where I sat; so stern a neighbour was too restrictive to him, in his present fractious mood, she dared whisper no observations, nor ask of him any information.

"Let her come to me," I entreated: "she will, perhaps, trouble you, sir: there is plenty of room on this side."

He handed her over as if she had been a lapdog. "I'll send her to school yet," he said, but now he was smiling.

Adele heard him, and asked if she was to go to school "sans mademoiselle?"

"Yes," he replied, "absolutely sans mademoiselle; for I am to take mademoiselle to the moon, and there I shall seek a cave in one of the white valleys among the volcano-tops, and mademoiselle shall live with me there, and only me."

"She will have nothing to eat: you will starve her," observed Adele.

"I shall gather manna for her morning and night: the plains and hillsides in the moon are bleached with manna, Adele."

"She will want to warm herself: what will she do for a fire?"

"Fire rises out of the lunar mountains: when she is cold, I'll carry her up to a peak, and lay her down on the edge of a crater."

"Oh, qu' elle y sera mal—peu comfortable! And her clothes, they will wear out: how can she get new ones?"

Mr. Rochester professed to be puzzled. "Hem!" said he. "What would you do, Adele? Cudgel your brains for an expedient. How would a white or a pink cloud answer for a gown, do you think? And one could cut a pretty enough scarf out of a rainbow."

"She is far better as she is," concluded Adele, after musing some time: "besides, she would get tired of living with only you in the moon. If I were mademoiselle, I would never consent to go with you."

"She has consented: she has pledged her word."

"But you can't get her there; there is no road to the moon: it is all air; and neither you nor she can fly."

"Adele, look at that field." We were now outside Thornfield gates, and bowling lightly along the smooth road to Millcote, where the dust was well laid by the thunderstorm, and, where the low hedges and lofty timber trees on each side glistened green and rain-refreshed.

"In that field, Adele, I was walking late one evening about a fortnight since—the evening of the day you helped me to make hay in the orchard meadows; and, as I was tired with raking swaths, I sat down to rest me on a stile; and there I took out a little book and a pencil, and began to write about a misfortune that befell me long ago, and a wish I had for happy days to come: I was writing away very fast, though daylight was fading from the leaf, when something came up the path and stopped two yards off me. I looked at it. It was a little thing with a veil of gossamer on its head. I beckoned it to come near me; it stood soon at my knee. I never spoke to it, and it never spoke to me, in words; but I read its eyes, and it read mine; and our speechless colloquy was to this effect—

"It was a fairy, and come from Elf-land, it said; and its errand was to make me happy: I must go with it out of the common world to a lonely place—such as the moon, for instance—and it nodded its head towards her horn, rising over Hay-hill: it told me of the alabaster cave and silver vale where we might live. I said I should like to go; but reminded it, as you did me, that I had no wings to fly.

"'Oh,' returned the fairy, 'that does not signify! Here is a talisman will remove all difficulties;' and she held out a pretty gold ring. 'Put it,' she said, 'on the fourth finger of my left hand, and I am yours, and you are mine; and we shall leave earth, and make our own heaven yonder.' She nodded again at the moon. The ring, Adele, is in my breeches-pocket, under the disguise of a sovereign: but I mean soon to change it to a ring again."

"But what has mademoiselle to do with it? I don't care for the fairy: you said it was mademoiselle you would take to the moon?"

"Mademoiselle is a fairy," he said, whispering mysteriously. Whereupon I told her not to mind his badinage; and she, on her part, evinced a fund of genuine French scepticism: denominating Mr. Rochester "un vrai menteur," and assuring him that she made no account whatever of his "contes de fee," and that "du reste, il n'y avait pas de fees, et quand meme il y en avait:" she was sure they would never appear to him, nor ever give him rings, or offer to live with him in the moon.

The hour spent at Millcote was a somewhat harassing one to me. Mr. Rochester obliged me to go to a certain silk warehouse: there I was ordered to choose half-a-dozen dresses. I hated the business, I begged leave to defer it: no—it should be gone through with now. By dint of entreaties expressed in energetic whispers, I reduced the half-dozen to two: these however, he vowed he would select himself. With anxiety I watched his eye rove over the gay stores: he fixed on a rich silk of the most brilliant amethyst dye, and a superb pink satin. I told him in a new series of whispers, that he might as well buy me a gold gown and a silver bonnet at once: I should certainly never venture to wear his choice. With infinite difficulty, for he was stubborn as a stone, I persuaded him to make an exchange in favour of a sober black satin and pearl-grey silk. "It might pass for the present," he said; "but he would yet see me glittering like a parterre."

Glad was I to get him out of the silk warehouse, and then out of a jewellers shop: the more he bought me, the more my cheek burned with a sense of annoyance and degradation. As we re-entered the carriage, and I sat back feverish and fagged, I remembered what, in the hurry of events, dark and bright, I had wholly forgotten—the letter of my uncle, John Eyre, to Mrs. Reed: his intention to adopt me and make me his legatee. "It would, indeed, be a relief," I thought, "if I had ever so small an independency; I never can bear being dressed like a doll by Mr. Rochester, or sitting like a second Danae with the golden shower falling daily round me. I will write to Madeira the moment I get home, and tell my uncle John I am going to be married, and to whom: if I had but a prospect of one day bringing Mr. Rochester an accession of fortune, I could better endure to be kept by him now." And somewhat relieved by this idea (which I failed not to execute that day), I ventured once more to meet my master's and lover's eye, which most pertinaciously sought mine, though I averted both face and gaze. He smiled; and I thought his smile was such as a sultan might, in a blissful and fond moment, bestow on a slave his gold and gems had enriched: I crushed his hand, which was ever hunting mine, vigorously, and thrust it back to him red with the passionate pressure.

"You need not look in that way," I said; "if you do, I'll wear nothing but my old Lowood frocks to the end of the chapter. I'll be married in this lilac gingham: you may make a dressing-gown for yourself out of the pearl-grey silk, and an infinite series of waistcoats out of the black satin."

He chuckled; he rubbed his hands. "Oh, it is rich to see and hear her?" he exclaimed. "Is she original? Is she piquant? I would not exchange this one little English girl for the Grand Turk's whole seraglio, gazelle-eyes, houri forms, and all!"

The Eastern allusion bit me again. "I'll not stand you an inch in the stead of a seraglio," I said; "so don't consider me an equivalent for one. If you have a fancy for anything in that line, away with you, sir, to the bazaars of Stamboul without delay, and lay out in extensive slave-purchases some of that spare cash you seem at a loss to spend satisfactorily here."

"And what will you do, Janet, while I am bargaining for so many tons of flesh and such an assortment of black eyes?"

"I'll be preparing myself to go out as a missionary to preach liberty to them that are enslaved—your harem inmates amongst the rest. I'll get admitted there, and I'll stir up mutiny; and you, three-tailed bashaw as you are, sir, shall in a trice find yourself fettered amongst our hands: nor will I, for one, consent to cut your bonds till you have signed a charter, the most liberal that despot ever yet conferred."

"I would consent to be at your mercy, Jane."

"I would have no mercy, Mr. Rochester, if you supplicated for it with an eye like that. While you looked so, I should be certain that whatever charter you might grant under coercion, your first act, when released, would be to violate its conditions."

"Why, Jane, what would you have? I fear you will compel me to go through a private marriage ceremony, besides that performed at the altar. You will stipulate, I see, for peculiar terms—what will they be?"

"I only want an easy mind, sir; not crushed by crowded obligations. Do you remember what you said of Celine Varens?—of the diamonds, the cashmeres you gave her? I will not be your English Celine Varens. I shall continue to act as Adele's governess; by that I shall earn my board and lodging, and thirty pounds a year besides. I'll furnish my own wardrobe out of that money, and you shall give me nothing but—"

"Well, but what?"

"Your regard; and if I give you mine in return, that debt will be quit."

"Well, for cool native impudence and pure innate pride, you haven't your equal," said he. We were now approaching Thornfield. "Will it please you to dine with me to-day?" he asked, as we re-entered the gates.

"No, thank you, sir."

"And what for, 'no, thank you?' if one may inquire."

"I never have dined with you, sir: and I see no reason why I should now: till—"

"Till what? You delight in half-phrases."

"Till I can't help it."

"Do you suppose I eat like an ogre or a ghoul, that you dread being the companion of my repast?"

"I have formed no supposition on the subject, sir; but I want to go on as usual for another month."

"You will give up your governessing slavery at once."

"Indeed, begging your pardon, sir, I shall not. I shall just go on with it as usual. I shall keep out of your way all day, as I have been accustomed to do: you may send for me in the evening, when you feel disposed to see me, and I'll come then; but at no other time."

"I want a smoke, Jane, or a pinch of snuff, to comfort me under all this, 'pour me donner une contenance,' as Adele would say; and unfortunately I have neither my cigar-case, nor my snuff-box. But listen—whisper. It is your time now, little tyrant, but it will be mine presently; and when once I have fairly seized you, to have and to hold, I'll just—figuratively speaking—attach you to a chain like this" (touching his watch-guard). "Yes, bonny wee thing, I'll wear you in my bosom, lest my jewel I should tyne."

He said this as he helped me to alight from the carriage, and while he afterwards lifted out Adele, I entered the house, and made good my retreat upstairs.

He duly summoned me to his presence in the evening. I had prepared an occupation for him; for I was determined not to spend the whole time in a tete-e-tete conversation. I remembered his fine voice; I knew he liked to sing—good singers generally do. I was no vocalist myself, and, in his fastidious judgment, no musician, either; but I delighted in listening when the performance was good. No sooner had twilight, that hour of romance, began to lower her blue and starry banner over the lattice, than I rose, opened the piano, and entreated him, for the love of heaven, to give me a song. He said I was a capricious witch, and that he would rather sing another time; but I averred that no time was like the present.

"Did I like his voice?" he asked.

"Very much." I was not fond of pampering that susceptible vanity of his; but for once, and from motives of expediency, I would e'en soothe and stimulate it.

"Then, Jane, you must play the accompaniment."

"Very well, sir, I will try."

I did try, but was presently swept off the stool and denominated "a little bungler." Being pushed unceremoniously to one side—which was precisely what I wished—he usurped my place, and proceeded to accompany himself: for he could play as well as sing. I hied me to the window-recess. And while I sat there and looked out on the still trees and dim lawn, to a sweet air was sung in mellow tones the following strain:-

"The truest love that ever heart
    Felt at its kindled core,
Did through each vein, in quickened start,
    The tide of being pour.

Her coming was my hope each day,
    Her parting was my pain;
The chance that did her steps delay
    Was ice in every vein.

I dreamed it would be nameless bliss,
    As I loved, loved to be;
And to this object did I press
    As blind as eagerly.

But wide as pathless was the space
    That lay our lives between,
And dangerous as the foamy race
    Of ocean-surges green.

And haunted as a robber-path
    Through wilderness or wood;
For Might and Right, and Woe and Wrath,
    Between our spirits stood.

I dangers dared; I hindrance scorned;
    I omens did defy:
Whatever menaced, harassed, warned,
    I passed impetuous by.

On sped my rainbow, fast as light;
    I flew as in a dream;
For glorious rose upon my sight
    That child of Shower and Gleam.

Still bright on clouds of suffering dim
    Shines that soft, solemn joy;
Nor care I now, how dense and grim
    Disasters gather nigh.

I care not in this moment sweet,
    Though all I have rushed o'er
Should come on pinion, strong and fleet,
    Proclaiming vengeance sore:

Though haughty Hate should strike me down,
    Right, bar approach to me,
And grinding Might, with furious frown,
    Swear endless enmity.

My love has placed her little hand
    With noble faith in mine,
And vowed that wedlock's sacred band
    Our nature shall entwine.

My love has sworn, with sealing kiss,
    With me to live—to die;
I have at last my nameless bliss.
    As I love—loved am I!"

He rose and came towards me, and I saw his face all kindled, and his full falcon-eye flashing, and tenderness and passion in every lineament. I quailed momentarily—then I rallied. Soft scene, daring demonstration, I would not have; and I stood in peril of both: a weapon of defence must be prepared—I whetted my tongue: as he reached me, I asked with asperity, "whom he was going to marry now?"

"That was a strange question to be put by his darling Jane."

"Indeed! I considered it a very natural and necessary one: he had talked of his future wife dying with him. What did he mean by such a pagan idea? I had no intention of dying with him—he might depend on that."

"Oh, all he longed, all he prayed for, was that I might live with him! Death was not for such as I."

"Indeed it was: I had as good a right to die when my time came as he had: but I should bide that time, and not be hurried away in a suttee."

"Would I forgive him for the selfish idea, and prove my pardon by a reconciling kiss?"

"No: I would rather be excused."

Here I heard myself apostrophised as a "hard little thing;" and it was added, "any other woman would have been melted to marrow at hearing such stanzas crooned in her praise."

I assured him I was naturally hard—very flinty, and that he would often find me so; and that, moreover, I was determined to show him divers rugged points in my character before the ensuing four weeks elapsed: he should know fully what sort of a bargain he had made, while there was yet time to rescind it.

"Would I be quiet and talk rationally?"

"I would be quiet if he liked, and as to talking rationally, I flattered myself I was doing that now."

He fretted, pished, and pshawed. "Very good," I thought; "you may fume and fidget as you please: but this is the best plan to pursue with you, I am certain. I like you more than I can say; but I'll not sink into a bathos of sentiment: and with this needle of repartee I'll keep you from the edge of the gulf too; and, moreover, maintain by its pungent aid that distance between you and myself most conducive to our real mutual advantage."

From less to more, I worked him up to considerable irritation; then, after he had retired, in dudgeon, quite to the other end of the room, I got up, and saying, "I wish you good-night, sir," in my natural and wonted respectful manner, I slipped out by the side-door and got away.

The system thus entered on, I pursued during the whole season of probation; and with the best success. He was kept, to be sure, rather cross and crusty; but on the whole I could see he was excellently entertained, and that a lamb-like submission and turtle-dove sensibility, while fostering his despotism more, would have pleased his judgment, satisfied his common-sense, and even suited his taste less.

In other people's presence I was, as formerly, deferential and quiet; any other line of conduct being uncalled for: it was only in the evening conferences I thus thwarted and afflicted him. He continued to send for me punctually the moment the clock struck seven; though when I appeared before him now, he had no such honeyed terms as "love" and "darling" on his lips: the best words at my service were "provoking puppet," "malicious elf," "sprite," "changeling," &c. For caresses, too, I now got grimaces; for a pressure of the hand, a pinch on the arm; for a kiss on the cheek, a severe tweak of the ear. It was all right: at present I decidedly preferred these fierce favours to anything more tender. Mrs. Fairfax, I saw, approved me: her anxiety on my account vanished; therefore I was certain I did well. Meantime, Mr. Rochester affirmed I was wearing him to skin and bone, and threatened awful vengeance for my present conduct at some period fast coming. I laughed in my sleeve at his menaces. "I can keep you in reasonable check now," I reflected; "and I don't doubt to be able to do it hereafter: if one expedient loses its virtue, another must be devised."

Yet after all my task was not an easy one; often I would rather have pleased than teased him. My future husband was becoming to me my whole world; and more than the world: almost my hope of heaven. He stood between me and every thought of religion, as an eclipse intervenes between man and the broad sun. I could not, in those days, see God for His creature: of whom I had made an idol.

Chapter XXV

The month of courtship had wasted: its very last hours were being numbered. There was no putting off the day that advanced—the bridal day; and all preparations for its arrival were complete. I, at least, had nothing more to do: there were my trunks, packed, locked, corded, ranged in a row along the wall of my little chamber; to-morrow, at this time, they would be far on their road to London: and so should I (D.V.),—or rather, not I, but one Jane Rochester, a person whom as yet I knew not. The cards of address alone remained to nail on: they lay, four little squares, in the drawer. Mr. Rochester had himself written the direction, "Mrs. Rochester,—Hotel, London," on each: I could not persuade myself to affix them, or to have them affixed. Mrs. Rochester! She did not exist: she would not be born till to-morrow, some time after eight o'clock a.m.; and I would wait to be assured she had come into the world alive before I assigned to her all that property. It was enough that in yonder closet, opposite my dressing-table, garments said to be hers had already displaced my black stuff Lowood frock and straw bonnet: for not to me appertained that suit of wedding raiment;

the pearl-coloured robe, the vapoury veil pendent from the usurped portmanteau. I shut the closet to conceal the strange, wraith-like apparel it contained; which, at this evening hour—nine o'clock—gave out certainly a most ghostly shimmer through the shadow of my apartment. "I will leave you by yourself, white dream," I said. "I am feverish: I hear the wind blowing: I will go out of doors and feel it."

It was not only the hurry of preparation that made me feverish; not only the anticipation of the great change—the new life which was to commence to-morrow: both these circumstances had their share, doubtless, in producing that restless, excited mood which hurried me forth at this late hour into the darkening grounds: but a third cause influenced my mind more than they.

I had at heart a strange and anxious thought. Something had happened which I could not comprehend; no one knew of or had seen the event but myself: it had taken place the preceding night. Mr. Rochester that night was absent from home; nor was he yet returned: business had called him to a small estate of two or three farms he possessed thirty miles off—business it was requisite he should settle in person, previous to his meditated departure from England. I waited now his return; eager to disburthen my mind, and to seek of him the solution of the enigma that perplexed me. Stay till he comes, reader; and, when I disclose my secret to him, you shall share the confidence.

I sought the orchard, driven to its shelter by the wind, which all day had blown strong and full from the south, without, however, bringing a speck of rain. Instead of subsiding as night drew on, it seemed to augment its rush and deepen its roar: the trees blew steadfastly one way, never writhing round, and scarcely tossing back their boughs once in an hour; so continuous was the strain bending their branchy heads northward—the clouds drifted from pole to pole, fast following, mass on mass: no glimpse of blue sky had been visible that July day.

It was not without a certain wild pleasure I ran before the wind, delivering my trouble of mind to the measureless air-torrent thundering through space. Descending the laurel walk, I faced the wreck of the chestnut-tree; it stood up black and riven: the trunk, split down the centre, gasped ghastly. The cloven halves were not broken from each other, for the firm base and strong roots kept them unsundered below; though community of vitality was destroyed—the sap could flow no more: their great boughs on each side were dead, and next winter's tempests would be sure to fell one or both to earth: as yet, however, they might be said to form one tree—a ruin, but an entire ruin.

"You did right to hold fast to each other," I said: as if the monster-splinters were living things, and could hear me. "I think, scathed as you look, and charred and scorched, there must be a little sense of life in you yet, rising out of that adhesion at the faithful, honest roots: you will never have green leaves more—never more see birds making nests and singing idyls in your boughs; the time of pleasure and love is over with you: but you are not desolate: each of you has a comrade to sympathise with him in his decay." As I looked up at them, the moon appeared momentarily in that part of the sky which filled their fissure; her disk was blood-red and half overcast; she seemed to throw on me one bewildered, dreary glance, and buried herself again instantly in the deep drift of cloud. The wind fell, for a second, round Thornfield; but far away over wood and water, poured a wild, melancholy wail: it was sad to listen to, and I ran off again.

Here and there I strayed through the orchard, gathered up the apples with which the grass round the tree roots was thickly strewn; then I employed myself in dividing the ripe from the unripe; I carried them into the house and put them away in the store-room. Then I repaired to the library to ascertain whether the fire was lit, for, though summer, I knew on such a gloomy evening Mr. Rochester would like to see a cheerful hearth when he came in: yes, the fire had been kindled some time, and burnt well. I placed his arm-chair by the chimney-corner: I wheeled the table near it: I let down the curtain, and had the candles brought in ready for lighting. More restless than ever, when I had completed these arrangements I could not sit still, nor even remain in the house: a little time-piece in the room and the old clock in the hall simultaneously struck ten.

"How late it grows!" I said. "I will run down to the gates: it is moonlight at intervals; I can see a good way on the road. He may be coming now, and to meet him will save some minutes of suspense."

The wind roared high in the great trees which embowered the gates; but the road as far as I could see, to the right hand and the left, was all still and solitary: save for the shadows of clouds crossing it at intervals as the moon looked out, it was but a long pale line, unvaried by one moving speck.

A puerile tear dimmed my eye while I looked—a tear of disappointment and impatience; ashamed of it, I wiped it away. I lingered; the moon shut herself wholly within her chamber, and drew close her curtain of dense cloud: the night grew dark; rain came driving fast on the gale.

"I wish he would come! I wish he would come!" I exclaimed, seized with hypochondriac foreboding. I had expected his arrival before tea; now it was dark: what could keep him? Had an accident happened? The event of last night again recurred to me. I interpreted it as a warning of disaster. I feared my hopes were too bright to be realised; and I had enjoyed so much bliss lately that I imagined my fortune had passed its meridian, and must now decline.

"Well, I cannot return to the house," I thought; "I cannot sit by the fireside, while he is abroad in inclement weather: better tire my limbs than strain my heart; I will go forward and meet him."

I set out; I walked fast, but not far: ere I had measured a quarter of a mile, I heard the tramp of hoofs; a horseman came on, full gallop; a dog ran by his side. Away with evil presentiment! It was he: here he was, mounted on Mesrour, followed by Pilot. He saw me; for the moon had opened a blue field in the sky, and rode in it watery bright: he took his hat off, and waved it round his head. I now ran to meet him.

"There!" he exclaimed, as he stretched out his hand and bent from the saddle: "You can't do without me, that is evident. Step on my boot-toe; give me both hands: mount!"

I obeyed: joy made me agile: I sprang up before him. A hearty kissing I got for a welcome, and some boastful triumph, which I swallowed as well as I could. He checked himself in his exultation to demand, "But is there anything the matter, Janet, that you come to meet me at such an hour? Is there anything wrong?"

"No, but I thought you would never come. I could not bear to wait in the house for you, especially with this rain and wind."

"Rain and wind, indeed! Yes, you are dripping like a mermaid; pull my cloak round you: but I think you are feverish, Jane: both your cheek and hand are burning hot. I ask again, is there anything the matter?

"Nothing now; I am neither afraid nor unhappy."

"Then you have been both?"

"Rather: but I'll tell you all about it by-and-bye, sir; and I daresay you will only laugh at me for my pains."

"I'll laugh at you heartily when to-morrow is past; till then I dare not: my prize is not certain. This is you, who have been as slippery as an eel this last month, and as thorny as a briar-rose? I could not lay a finger anywhere but I was pricked; and now I seem to have gathered up a stray lamb in my arms. You wandered out of the fold to seek your shepherd, did you, Jane?"

"I wanted you: but don't boast. Here we are at Thornfield: now let me get down."

He landed me on the pavement. As John took his horse, and he followed me into the hall, he told me to make haste and put something dry on, and then return to him in the library; and he stopped me, as I made for the staircase, to extort a promise that I would not be long: nor was I long; in five minutes I rejoined him. I found him at supper.

"Take a seat and bear me company, Jane: please God, it is the last meal but one you will eat at Thornfield Hall for a long time."

I sat down near him, but told him I could not eat. "Is it because you have the prospect of a journey before you, Jane? Is it the thoughts of going to London that takes away your appetite?"

"I cannot see my prospects clearly to-night, sir; and I hardly know what thoughts I have in my head. Everything in life seems unreal."

"Except me: I am substantial enough—touch me."

"You, sir, are the most phantom-like of all: you are a mere dream."

He held out his hand, laughing. "Is that a dream?" said he, placing it close to my eyes. He had a rounded, muscular, and vigorous hand, as well as a long, strong arm.

"Yes; though I touch it, it is a dream," said I, as I put it down from before my face. "Sir, have you finished supper?"

"Yes, Jane."

I rang the bell and ordered away the tray. When we were again alone, I stirred the fire, and then took a low seat at my master's knee.

"It is near midnight," I said.

"Yes: but remember, Jane, you promised to wake with me the night before my wedding."

"I did; and I will keep my promise, for an hour or two at least: I have no wish to go to bed."

"Are all your arrangements complete?"

"All, sir."

"And on my part likewise," he returned, "I have settled everything; and we shall leave Thornfield to-morrow, within half-an-hour after our return from church."

"Very well, sir."

"With what an extraordinary smile you uttered that word—'very well,' Jane! What a bright spot of colour you have on each cheek! and how strangely your eyes glitter! Are you well?"

"I believe I am."

"Believe! What is the matter? Tell me what you feel."

"I could not, sir: no words could tell you what I feel. I wish this present hour would never end: who knows with what fate the next may come charged?"

"This is hypochondria, Jane. You have been over-excited, or over-fatigued."

"Do you, sir, feel calm and happy?"

"Calm?—no: but happy—to the heart's core."

I looked up at him to read the signs of bliss in his face: it was ardent and flushed.

"Give me your confidence, Jane," he said: "relieve your mind of any weight that oppresses it, by imparting it to me. What do you fear?—that I shall not prove a good husband?"

"It is the idea farthest from my thoughts."

"Are you apprehensive of the new sphere you are about to enter?—of the new life into which you are passing?"

"No."

"You puzzle me, Jane: your look and tone of sorrowful audacity perplex and pain me. I want an explanation."

"Then, sir, listen. You were from home last night?"

"I was: I know that; and you hinted a while ago at something which had happened in my absence:-nothing, probably, of consequence; but, in short, it has disturbed you. Let me hear it. Mrs. Fairfax has said something, perhaps? or you have overheard the servants talk?—your sensitive self-respect has been wounded?"

"No, sir." It struck twelve—I waited till the time-piece had concluded its silver chime, and the clock its hoarse, vibritting stroke, and then I proceeded.

"All day yesterday I was very busy, and very happy in my ceaseless bustle; for I am not, as you seem to think, troubled by any haunting fears about the new sphere, et cetera: I think it a glorious thing to have the hope of living with you, because I love you. No, sir, don't caress me now—let me talk undisturbed. Yesterday I trusted well in Providence, and believed that events were working together for your good and mine: it was a fine day, if you recollect—the calmness of the air and sky forbade apprehensions respecting your safety or comfort on your journey. I walked a little while on the pavement after tea, thinking of you; and I beheld you in imagination so near me, I scarcely missed your actual presence. I thought of the life that lay before me—YOUR life, sir—an existence more expansive and stirring than my own: as much more so as the depths of the sea to which the brook runs are than the shallows of its own strait channel. I wondered why moralists call this world a dreary wilderness: for me it blossomed like a rose. Just at sunset, the air turned cold and the sky cloudy: I went in, Sophie called me upstairs to look at my wedding-dress, which they had just brought; and under it in the box I found your present—the veil which, in your princely extravagance, you sent for from London: resolved, I suppose, since I would not have jewels, to cheat me into accepting something as costly. I smiled as I unfolded it, and devised how I would tease you about your aristocratic tastes, and your efforts to masque your plebeian bride in the attributes of a peeress. I though how I would carry down to you the square of unembroidered blond I had myself prepared as a covering for my low-born head, and ask if that was not good enough for a woman who could bring her husband neither fortune, beauty, nor connections. I saw plainly how you would look; and heard your impetuous republican answers, and your haughty disavowal of any necessity on your part to augment your wealth, or elevate your standing, by marrying either a purse or a coronet."

"How well you read me, you witch!" interposed Mr. Rochester: "but what did you find in the veil besides its embroidery? Did you find poison, or a dagger, that you look so mournful now?"

"No, no, sir; besides the delicacy and richness of the fabric, I found nothing save Fairfax Rochester's pride; and that did not scare me, because I am used to the sight of the demon. But, sir, as it grew dark, the wind rose: it blew yesterday evening, not as it blows now—wild and high—but 'with a sullen, moaning sound' far more eerie. I wished you were at home. I came into this room, and the sight of the empty chair and fireless hearth chilled me. For some time after I went to bed, I could not sleep—a sense of anxious excitement distressed me. The gale still rising, seemed to my ear to muffle a mournful under-sound; whether in the house or abroad I could not at first tell, but it recurred, doubtful yet doleful at every lull; at last I made out it must be some dog howling at a distance. I was glad when it ceased. On sleeping, I continued in dreams the idea of a dark and gusty night. I continued also the wish to be with you, and experienced a strange, regretful consciousness of some barrier dividing us. During all my first sleep, I was following the windings of an unknown road; total obscurity environed me; rain pelted me; I was burdened with the charge of a little child: a very small creature, too young and feeble to walk, and which shivered in my cold arms, and wailed piteously in my ear. I thought, sir, that you were on the road a long way before me; and I strained every nerve to overtake you, and made effort on effort to utter your name and entreat you to stop—but my movements were fettered, and my voice still died away inarticulate; while you, I felt, withdrew farther and farther every moment."

"And these dreams weigh on your spirits now, Jane, when I am close to you? Little nervous subject! Forget visionary woe, and think only of real happiness! You say you love me, Janet: yes—I will not forget that; and you cannot deny it. THOSE words did not die inarticulate on your lips. I heard them clear and soft: a thought too solemn perhaps, but sweet as music—'I think it is a glorious thing to have the hope of living with you, Edward, because I love you.' Do you love me, Jane?—repeat it."

"I do, sir—I do, with my whole heart."

"Well," he said, after some minutes' silence, "it is strange; but that sentence has penetrated by breast painfully. Why? I think because you said it with such an earnest, religious energy, and because your upward gaze at me now is the very sublime of faith, truth, and devotion: it is too much as if some spirit were near me. Look wicked, Jane: as you know well how to look: coin one of your wild, shy, provoking smiles; tell me you hate me—tease me, vex me; do anything but move me: I would rather be incensed than saddened."

"I will tease you and vex you to your heart's content, when I have finished my tale: but hear me to the end."

"I thought, Jane, you had told me all. I thought I had found the source of your melancholy in a dream."

I shook my head. "What! is there more? But I will not believe it to be anything important. I warn you of incredulity beforehand. Go on."

The disquietude of his air, the somewhat apprehensive impatience of his manner, surprised me: but I proceeded.

"I dreamt another dream, sir: that Thornfield Hall was a dreary ruin, the retreat of bats and owls. I thought that of all the stately front nothing remained but a shell-like wall, very high and very fragile-looking. I wandered, on a moonlight night, through the grass-grown enclosure within: here I stumbled over a marble hearth, and there over a fallen fragment of cornice. Wrapped up in a shawl, I still carried the unknown little child: I might not lay it down anywhere, however tired were my arms—however much its weight impeded my progress, I must retain it. I heard the gallop of a horse at a distance on the road; I was sure it was you; and you were departing for many years and for a distant country. I climbed the thin wall with frantic perilous haste, eager to catch one glimpse of you from the top: the stones rolled from under my feet, the ivy branches I grasped gave way, the child clung round my neck in terror, and almost strangled me; at last I gained the summit. I saw you like a speck on a white track, lessening every moment. The blast blew so strong I could not stand. I sat down on the narrow ledge; I hushed the scared infant in my lap: you turned an angle of the road: I bent forward to take a last look; the wall crumbled; I was shaken; the child rolled from my knee, I lost my balance, fell, and woke."

"Now, Jane, that is all."

"All the preface, sir; the tale is yet to come. On waking, a gleam dazzled my eyes; I thought—Oh, it is daylight! But I was mistaken; it was only candlelight. Sophie, I supposed, had come in. There was a light in the dressing-table, and the door of the closet, where, before going to bed, I had hung my wedding-dress and veil, stood open; I heard a rustling there. I asked, 'Sophie, what are you doing?' No one answered; but a form emerged from the closet; it took the light, held it aloft, and surveyed the garments pendent from the portmanteau. 'Sophie! Sophie!' I again cried: and still it was silent. I had risen up in bed, I bent forward: first surprise, then bewilderment, came over me; and then my blood crept cold through my veins. Mr. Rochester, this was not Sophie, it was not Leah, it was not Mrs. Fairfax: it was not—no, I was sure of it, and am still—it was not even that strange woman, Grace Poole."

"It must have been one of them," interrupted my master.

"No, sir, I solemnly assure you to the contrary. The shape standing before me had never crossed my eyes within the precincts of Thornfield Hall before; the height, the contour were new to me."

"Describe it, Jane."

"It seemed, sir, a woman, tall and large, with thick and dark hair hanging long down her back. I know not what dress she had on: it was white and straight; but whether gown, sheet, or shroud, I cannot tell."

"Did you see her face?"

"Not at first. But presently she took my veil from its place; she held it up, gazed at it long, and then she threw it over her own head, and turned to the mirror. At that moment I saw the reflection of the visage and features quite distinctly in the dark oblong glass."

"And how were they?"

"Fearful and ghastly to me—oh, sir, I never saw a face like it! It was a discoloured face—it was a savage face. I wish I could forget the roll of the red eyes and the fearful blackened inflation of the lineaments!"

"Ghosts are usually pale, Jane."

"This, sir, was purple: the lips were swelled and dark; the brow furrowed: the black eyebrows widely raised over the bloodshot eyes. Shall I tell you of what it reminded me?"

"You may."

"Of the foul German spectre—the Vampyre."

"Ah!—what did it do?"

"Sir, it removed my veil from its gaunt head, rent it in two parts, and flinging both on the floor, trampled on them."

"Afterwards?"

"It drew aside the window-curtain and looked out; perhaps it saw dawn approaching, for, taking the candle, it retreated to the door. Just at my bedside, the figure stopped: the fiery eyes glared upon me—she thrust up her candle close to my face, and extinguished it under my eyes. I was aware her lurid visage flamed over mine, and I lost consciousness: for the second time in my life—only the second time—I became insensible from terror."

"Who was with you when you revived?"

"No one, sir, but the broad day. I rose, bathed my head and face in water, drank a long draught; felt that though enfeebled I was not ill, and determined that to none but you would I impart this vision. Now, sir, tell me who and what that woman was?"

"The creature of an over-stimulated brain; that is certain. I must be careful of you, my treasure: nerves like yours were not made for rough handling."

"Sir, depend on it, my nerves were not in fault; the thing was real: the transaction actually took place."

"And your previous dreams, were they real too? Is Thornfield Hall a ruin? Am I severed from you by insuperable obstacles? Am I leaving you without a tear—without a kiss—without a word?"

"Not yet."

"Am I about to do it? Why, the day is already commenced which is to bind us indissolubly; and when we are once united, there shall be no recurrence of these mental terrors: I guarantee that."

"Mental terrors, sir! I wish I could believe them to be only such: I wish it more now than ever; since even you cannot explain to me the mystery of that awful visitant."

"And since I cannot do it, Jane, it must have been unreal."

"But, sir, when I said so to myself on rising this morning, and when I looked round the room to gather courage and comfort from the cheerful aspect of each familiar object in full daylight, there—on the carpet—I saw what gave the distinct lie to my hypothesis,—the veil, torn from top to bottom in two halves!"

I felt Mr. Rochester start and shudder; he hastily flung his arms round me. "Thank God!" he exclaimed, "that if anything malignant did come near you last night, it was only the veil that was harmed. Oh, to think what might have happened!"

He drew his breath short, and strained me so close to him, I could scarcely pant. After some minutes' silence, he continued, cheerily—

"Now, Janet, I'll explain to you all about it. It was half dream, half reality. A woman did, I doubt not, enter your room: and that woman was—must have been—Grace Poole. You call her a strange being yourself: from all you know, you have reason so to call her—what did she do to me? what to Mason? In a state between sleeping and waking, you noticed her entrance and her actions; but feverish, almost delirious as you were, you ascribed to her a goblin appearance different from her own: the long dishevelled hair, the swelled black face, the exaggerated stature, were figments of imagination; results of nightmare: the spiteful tearing of the veil was real: and it is like her. I see you would ask why I keep such a woman in my house: when we have been married a year and a day, I will tell you; but not now. Are you satisfied, Jane? Do you accept my solution of the mystery?"

I reflected, and in truth it appeared to me the only possible one: satisfied I was not, but to please him I endeavoured to appear so—relieved, I certainly did feel; so I answered him with a contented smile. And now, as it was long past one, I prepared to leave him.

"Does not Sophie sleep with Adele in the nursery?" he asked, as I lit my candle.

"Yes, sir."

"And there is room enough in Adele's little bed for you. You must share it with her to-night, Jane: it is no wonder that the incident you have related should make you nervous, and I would rather you did not sleep alone: promise me to go to the nursery."

"I shall be very glad to do so, sir."

"And fasten the door securely on the inside. Wake Sophie when you go upstairs, under pretence of requesting her to rouse you in good time to-morrow; for you must be dressed and have finished breakfast before eight. And now, no more sombre thoughts: chase dull care away, Janet. Don't you hear to what soft whispers the wind has fallen? and there is no more beating of rain against the window-panes: look here" (he lifted up the curtain)—"it is a lovely night!"

It was. Half heaven was pure and stainless: the clouds, now trooping before the wind, which had shifted to the west, were filing off eastward in long, silvered columns. The moon shone peacefully.

"Well," said Mr. Rochester, gazing inquiringly into my eyes, "how is my Janet now?"

"The night is serene, sir; and so am I."

"And you will not dream of separation and sorrow to-night; but of happy love and blissful union."

This prediction was but half fulfilled: I did not indeed dream of sorrow, but as little did I dream of joy; for I never slept at all. With little Adele in my arms, I watched the slumber of childhood—so tranquil, so passionless, so innocent—and waited for the coming day: all my life was awake and astir in my frame: and as soon as the sun rose I rose too. I remember Adele clung to me as I left her: I remember I kissed her as I loosened her little hands from my neck; and I cried over her with strange emotion, and quitted her because I feared my sobs would break her still sound repose. She seemed the emblem of my past life; and he I was now to array myself to meet, the dread, but adored, type of my unknown future day.

Chapter XXVI

Sophie came at seven to dress me: she was very long indeed in accomplishing her task; so long that Mr. Rochester, grown, I suppose, impatient of my delay, sent up to ask why I did not come. She was just fastening my veil (the plain square of blond after all) to my hair with a brooch; I hurried from under her hands as soon as I could.

"Stop!" she cried in French. "Look at yourself in the mirror: you have not taken one peep."

So I turned at the door: I saw a robed and veiled figure, so unlike my usual self that it seemed almost the image of a stranger. "Jane!" called a voice, and I hastened down. I was received at the foot of the stairs by Mr. Rochester.

"Lingerer!" he said, "my brain is on fire with impatience, and you tarry so long!"

He took me into the dining-room, surveyed me keenly all over, pronounced me "fair as a lily, and not only the pride of his life, but the desire of his eyes," and then telling me he would give me but ten minutes to eat some breakfast, he rang the bell. One of his lately hired servants, a footman, answered it.

"Is John getting the carriage ready?"

"Yes, sir."

"Is the luggage brought down?"

"They are bringing it down, sir."

"Go you to the church: see if Mr. Wood (the clergyman) and the clerk are there: return and tell me."

The church, as the reader knows, was but just beyond the gates; the footman soon returned.

"Mr. Wood is in the vestry, sir, putting on his surplice."

"And the carriage?"

"The horses are harnessing."

"We shall not want it to go to church; but it must be ready the moment we return: all the boxes and luggage arranged and strapped on, and the coachman in his seat."

"Yes, sir."

"Jane, are you ready?"

I rose. There were no groomsmen, no bridesmaids, no relatives to wait for or marshal: none but Mr. Rochester and I. Mrs. Fairfax stood in the hall as we passed. I would fain have spoken to her, but my hand was held by a grasp of iron: I was hurried along by a stride I could hardly follow; and to look at Mr. Rochester's face was to feel that not a second of delay would be tolerated for any purpose. I wonder what other bridegroom ever looked as he did—so bent up to a purpose, so grimly resolute: or who, under such steadfast brows, ever revealed such flaming and flashing eyes.

I know not whether the day was fair or foul; in descending the drive, I gazed neither on sky nor earth: my heart was with my eyes; and both seemed migrated into Mr. Rochester's frame. I wanted to see the invisible thing on which, as we went along, he appeared to fasten a glance fierce and fell. I wanted to feel the thoughts whose force he seemed breasting and resisting.

At the churchyard wicket he stopped: he discovered I was quite out of breath. "Am I cruel in my love?" he said. "Delay an instant: lean on me, Jane."

And now I can recall the picture of the grey old house of God rising calm before me, of a rook wheeling round the steeple, of a ruddy morning sky beyond. I remember something, too, of the green grave-mounds; and I have not forgotten, either, two figures of strangers straying amongst the low hillocks and reading the mementoes graven on the few mossy head-stones. I noticed them, because, as they saw us, they passed round to the back of the church; and I doubted not they were going to enter by the side-aisle door and witness the ceremony. By Mr. Rochester they were not observed; he was earnestly looking at my face from which the blood had, I daresay, momentarily fled: for I felt my forehead dewy, and my cheeks and lips cold. When I rallied, which I soon did, he walked gently with me up the path to the porch.

We entered the quiet and humble temple; the priest waited in his white surplice at the lowly altar, the clerk beside him. All was still: two shadows only moved in a remote corner. My conjecture had been correct: the strangers had slipped in before us, and they now stood by the vault of the Rochesters, their backs towards us, viewing through the rails the old time-stained marble tomb, where a kneeling angel guarded the remains of Damer de Rochester, slain at Marston Moor in the time of the civil wars, and of Elizabeth, his wife.

Our place was taken at the communion rails. Hearing a cautious step behind me, I glanced over my shoulder: one of the strangers—a gentleman, evidently—was advancing up the chancel. The service began. The explanation of the intent of matrimony was gone through; and then the clergyman came a step further forward, and, bending slightly towards Mr. Rochester, went on.

"I require and charge you both (as ye will answer at the dreadful day of judgment, when the secrets of all hearts shall be disclosed), that if either of you know any impediment why ye may not lawfully be joined together in matrimony, ye do now confess it; for be ye well assured that so many as are coupled together otherwise than God's Word doth allow, are not joined together by God, neither is their matrimony lawful."

He paused, as the custom is. When is the pause after that sentence ever broken by reply? Not, perhaps, once in a hundred years. And the clergyman, who had not lifted his eyes from his book, and had held his breath but for a moment, was proceeding: his hand was already stretched towards Mr. Rochester, as his lips unclosed to ask, "Wilt thou have this woman for thy wedded wife?"—when a distinct and near voice said—

"The marriage cannot go on: I declare the existence of an impediment."

The clergyman looked up at the speaker and stood mute; the clerk did the same; Mr. Rochester moved slightly, as if an earthquake had rolled under his feet: taking a firmer footing, and not turning his head or eyes, he said, "Proceed."

Profound silence fell when he had uttered that word, with deep but low intonation. Presently Mr. Wood said—

"I cannot proceed without some investigation into what has been asserted, and evidence of its truth or falsehood."

"The ceremony is quite broken off," subjoined the voice behind us. "I am in a condition to prove my allegation: an insuperable impediment to this marriage exists."

Mr. Rochester heard, but heeded not: he stood stubborn and rigid, making no movement but to possess himself of my hand. What a hot and strong grasp he had! and how like quarried marble was his pale, firm, massive front at this moment! How his eye shone, still watchful, and yet wild beneath!

Mr. Wood seemed at a loss. "What is the nature of the impediment?" he asked. "Perhaps it may be got over—explained away?"

"Hardly," was the answer. "I have called it insuperable, and I speak advisedly."

The speaker came forward and leaned on the rails. He continued, uttering each word distinctly, calmly, steadily, but not loudly—

"It simply consists in the existence of a previous marriage. Mr. Rochester has a wife now living."

My nerves vibrated to those low-spoken words as they had never vibrated to thunder—my blood felt their subtle violence as it had never felt frost or fire; but I was collected, and in no danger of swooning. I looked at Mr. Rochester: I made him look at me. His whole face was colourless rock: his eye was both spark and flint. He disavowed nothing: he seemed as if he would defy all things. Without speaking, without smiling, without seeming to recognise in me a human being, he only twined my waist with his arm and riveted me to his side.

"Who are you?" he asked of the intruder.

"My name is Briggs, a solicitor of——Street, London."

"And you would thrust on me a wife?"

"I would remind you of your lady's existence, sir, which the law recognises, if you do not."

"Favour me with an account of her—with her name, her parentage, her place of abode."

"Certainly." Mr. Briggs calmly took a paper from his pocket, and read out in a sort of official, nasal voice:-

"'I affirm and can prove that on the 20th of October A.D.——(a date of fifteen years back), Edward Fairfax Rochester, of Thornfield Hall, in the county of——, and of Ferndean Manor, in——shire, England, was married to my sister, Bertha Antoinetta Mason, daughter of Jonas Mason, merchant, and of Antoinetta his wife, a Creole, at——church, Spanish Town, Jamaica. The record of the marriage will be found in the register of that church—a copy of it is now in my possession. Signed, Richard Mason.'"

"That—if a genuine document—may prove I have been married, but it does not prove that the woman mentioned therein as my wife is still living."

"She was living three months ago," returned the lawyer.

"How do you know?"

"I have a witness to the fact, whose testimony even you, sir, will scarcely controvert."

"Produce him—or go to hell."

"I will produce him first—he is on the spot. Mr. Mason, have the goodness to step forward."

Mr. Rochester, on hearing the name, set his teeth; he experienced, too, a sort of strong convulsive quiver; near to him as I was, I felt the spasmodic movement of fury or despair run through his frame. The second stranger, who had hitherto lingered in the background, now drew near; a pale face looked over the solicitor's shoulder—yes, it was Mason himself. Mr. Rochester turned and glared at him. His eye, as I have often said, was a black eye: it had now a tawny, nay, a bloody light in its gloom; and his face flushed—olive cheek and hueless forehead received a glow as from spreading, ascending heart-fire: and he stirred, lifted his strong arm—he could have struck Mason, dashed him on the church-floor, shocked by ruthless blow the breath from his body—but Mason shrank away, and cried faintly, "Good God!" Contempt fell cool on Mr. Rochester—his passion died as if a blight had shrivelled it up: he only asked—"What have YOU to say?"

An inaudible reply escaped Mason's white lips.

"The devil is in it if you cannot answer distinctly. I again demand, what have you to say?"

"Sir—sir," interrupted the clergyman, "do not forget you are in a sacred place." Then addressing Mason, he inquired gently, "Are you aware, sir, whether or not this gentleman's wife is still living?"

"Courage," urged the lawyer,—"speak out."

"She is now living at Thornfield Hall," said Mason, in more articulate tones: "I saw her there last April. I am her brother."

"At Thornfield Hall!" ejaculated the clergyman. "Impossible! I am an old resident in this neighbourhood, sir, and I never heard of a Mrs. Rochester at Thornfield Hall."

I saw a grim smile contort Mr. Rochester's lips, and he muttered—

"No, by God! I took care that none should hear of it—or of her under that name." He mused—for ten minutes he held counsel with himself: he formed his resolve, and announced it—

"Enough! all shall bolt out at once, like the bullet from the barrel. Wood, close your book and take off your surplice; John Green (to the clerk), leave the church: there will be no wedding to-day." The man obeyed.

Mr. Rochester continued, hardily and recklessly: "Bigamy is an ugly word!—I meant, however, to be a bigamist; but fate has out-manoeuvred me, or Providence has checked me,—perhaps the last. I am little better than a devil at this moment; and, as my pastor there would tell me, deserve no doubt the sternest judgments of God, even to the quenchless fire and deathless worm. Gentlemen, my plan is broken up:-what this lawyer and his client say is true: I have been married, and the woman to whom I was married lives! You say you never heard of a Mrs. Rochester at the house up yonder, Wood; but I daresay you have many a time inclined your ear to gossip about the mysterious lunatic kept there under watch and ward. Some have whispered to you that she is my bastard half-sister: some, my cast-off mistress. I now inform you that she is my wife, whom I married fifteen years ago,—Bertha Mason by name; sister of this resolute personage, who is now, with his quivering limbs and white cheeks, showing you what a stout heart men may bear. Cheer up, Dick!—never fear me!—I'd almost as soon strike a woman as you. Bertha Mason is mad; and she came of a mad family; idiots and maniacs through three generations? Her mother, the Creole, was both a madwoman and a drunkard!—as I found out after I had wed the daughter: for they were silent on family secrets before. Bertha, like a dutiful child, copied her parent in both points. I had a charming partner—pure, wise, modest: you can fancy I was a happy man. I went through rich scenes! Oh! my experience has been heavenly, if you only knew it! But I owe you no further explanation. Briggs, Wood, Mason, I invite you all to come up to the house and visit Mrs. Poole's patient, and MY WIFE! You shall see what sort of a being I was cheated into espousing, and judge whether or not I had a right to break the compact, and seek sympathy with something at least human. This girl," he continued, looking at me, "knew no more than you, Wood, of the disgusting secret: she thought all was fair and legal and never dreamt she was going to be entrapped into a feigned union with a defrauded wretch, already bound to a bad, mad, and embruted partner! Come all of you—follow!"

Still holding me fast, he left the church: the three gentlemen came after. At the front door of the hall we found the carriage.

"Take it back to the coach-house, John," said Mr. Rochester coolly; "it will not be wanted to-day."

At our entrance, Mrs. Fairfax, Adele, Sophie, Leah, advanced to meet and greet us.

"To the right-about—every soul!" cried the master; "away with your congratulations! Who wants them? Not I!—they are fifteen years too late!"

He passed on and ascended the stairs, still holding my hand, and still beckoning the gentlemen to follow him, which they did. We mounted the first staircase, passed up the gallery, proceeded to the third storey: the low, black door, opened by Mr. Rochester's master-key, admitted us to the tapestried room, with its great bed and its pictorial cabinet.

"You know this place, Mason," said our guide; "she bit and stabbed you here."

He lifted the hangings from the wall, uncovering the second door: this, too, he opened. In a room without a window, there burnt a fire guarded by a high and strong fender, and a lamp suspended from the ceiling by a chain. Grace Poole bent over the fire, apparently cooking something in a saucepan. In the deep shade, at the farther end of the room, a figure ran backwards and forwards. What it was, whether beast or human being, one could not, at first sight, tell: it grovelled, seemingly, on all fours; it snatched and growled like some strange wild animal: but it was covered with clothing, and a quantity of dark, grizzled hair, wild as a mane, hid its head and face.

"Good-morrow, Mrs. Poole!" said Mr. Rochester. "How are you? and how is your charge to-day?"

"We're tolerable, sir, I thank you," replied Grace, lifting the boiling mess carefully on to the hob: "rather snappish, but not 'rageous."

A fierce cry seemed to give the lie to her favourable report: the clothed hyena rose up, and stood tall on its hind-feet.

"Ah! sir, she sees you!" exclaimed Grace: "you'd better not stay."

"Only a few moments, Grace: you must allow me a few moments."

"Take care then, sir!—for God's sake, take care!"

The maniac bellowed: she parted her shaggy locks from her visage, and gazed wildly at her visitors. I recognised well that purple face,—those bloated features. Mrs. Poole advanced.

"Keep out of the way," said Mr. Rochester, thrusting her aside: "she has no knife now, I suppose, and I'm on my guard."

"One never knows what she has, sir: she is so cunning: it is not in mortal discretion to fathom her craft."

"We had better leave her," whispered Mason.

"Go to the devil!" was his brother-in-law's recommendation.

"'Ware!" cried Grace. The three gentlemen retreated simultaneously. Mr. Rochester flung me behind him: the lunatic sprang and grappled his throat viciously, and laid her teeth to his cheek: they struggled. She was a big woman, in stature almost equalling her husband, and corpulent besides: she showed virile force in the contest—more than once she almost throttled him, athletic as he was. He could have settled her with a well-planted blow; but he would not strike: he would only wrestle. At last he mastered her arms; Grace Poole gave him a cord, and he pinioned them behind her: with more rope, which was at hand, he bound her to a chair. The operation was performed amidst the fiercest yells and the most convulsive plunges. Mr. Rochester then turned to the spectators: he looked at them with a smile both acrid and desolate.

"That is MY WIFE," said he. "Such is the sole conjugal embrace I am ever to know—such are the endearments which are to solace my leisure hours! And THIS is what I wished to have" (laying his hand on my shoulder): "this young girl, who stands so grave and quiet at the mouth of hell, looking collectedly at the gambols of a demon, I wanted her just as a change after that fierce ragout. Wood and Briggs, look at the difference! Compare these clear eyes with the red balls yonder—this face with that mask—this form with that bulk; then judge me, priest of the gospel and man of the law, and remember with what judgment ye judge ye shall be judged! Off with you now. I must shut up my prize."

We all withdrew. Mr. Rochester stayed a moment behind us, to give some further order to Grace Poole. The solicitor addressed me as he descended the stair.

"You, madam," said he, "are cleared from all blame: your uncle will be glad to hear it—if, indeed, he should be still living—when Mr. Mason returns to Madeira."

"My uncle! What of him? Do you know him?"

"Mr. Mason does. Mr. Eyre has been the Funchal correspondent of his house for some years. When your uncle received your letter intimating the contemplated union between yourself and Mr. Rochester, Mr. Mason, who was staying at Madeira to recruit his health, on his way back to Jamaica, happened to be with him. Mr. Eyre mentioned the intelligence; for he knew that my client here was acquainted with a gentleman of the name of Rochester. Mr. Mason, astonished and distressed as you may suppose, revealed the real state of matters. Your uncle, I am sorry to say, is now on a sick bed; from which, considering the nature of his disease—decline—and the stage it has reached, it is unlikely he will ever rise. He could not then hasten to England himself, to extricate you from the snare into which you had fallen, but he implored Mr. Mason to lose no time in taking steps to prevent the false marriage. He referred him to me for assistance. I used all despatch, and am thankful I was not too late: as you, doubtless, must be also. Were I not morally certain that your uncle will be dead ere you reach Madeira, I would advise you to accompany Mr. Mason back; but as it is, I think you had better remain in England till you can hear further, either from or of Mr. Eyre. Have we anything else to stay for?" he inquired of Mr. Mason.

"No, no—let us be gone," was the anxious reply; and without waiting to take leave of Mr. Rochester, they made their exit at the hall door. The clergyman stayed to exchange a few sentences, either of admonition or reproof, with his haughty parishioner; this duty done, he too departed.

I heard him go as I stood at the half-open door of my own room, to which I had now withdrawn. The house cleared, I shut myself in, fastened the bolt that none might intrude, and proceeded—not to weep, not to mourn, I was yet too calm for that, but—mechanically to take off the wedding dress, and replace it by the stuff gown I had worn yesterday, as I thought, for the last time. I then sat down: I felt weak and tired. I leaned my arms on a table, and my head dropped on them. And now I thought: till now I had only heard, seen, moved—followed up and down where I was led or dragged—watched event rush on event, disclosure open beyond disclosure: but NOW, I THOUGHT.

The morning had been a quiet morning enough—all except the brief scene with the lunatic: the transaction in the church had not been noisy; there was no explosion of passion, no loud altercation, no dispute, no defiance or challenge, no tears, no sobs: a few words had been spoken, a calmly pronounced objection to the marriage made; some stern, short questions put by Mr. Rochester; answers, explanations given, evidence adduced; an open admission of the truth had been uttered by my master; then the living proof had been seen; the intruders were gone, and all was over.

I was in my own room as usual—just myself, without obvious change: nothing had smitten me, or scathed me, or maimed me. And yet where was the Jane Eyre of yesterday?—where was her life?—where were her prospects?

Jane Eyre, who had been an ardent, expectant woman—almost a bride, was a cold, solitary girl again: her life was pale; her prospects were desolate. A Christmas frost had come at midsummer; a white December storm had whirled over June; ice glazed the ripe apples, drifts crushed the blowing roses; on hayfield and cornfield lay a frozen shroud: lanes which last night blushed full of flowers, to-day were pathless with untrodden snow; and the woods, which twelve hours since waved leafy and flagrant as groves between the tropics, now spread, waste, wild, and white as pine-forests in wintry Norway. My hopes were all dead—struck with a subtle doom, such as, in one night, fell on all the first-born in the land of Egypt. I looked on my cherished wishes, yesterday so blooming and glowing; they lay stark, chill, livid corpses that could never revive. I looked at my love: that feeling which was my master's—which he had created; it shivered in my heart, like a suffering child in a cold cradle; sickness and anguish had seized it; it could not seek Mr. Rochester's arms—it could not derive warmth from his breast. Oh, never more could it turn to him; for faith was blighted—confidence destroyed! Mr. Rochester was not to me what he had been; for he was not what I had thought him. I would not ascribe vice to him; I would not say he had betrayed me; but the attribute of stainless truth was gone from his idea, and from his presence I must go: THAT I perceived well. When—how—whither, I could not yet discern; but he himself, I doubted not, would hurry me from Thornfield. Real affection, it seemed, he could not have for me; it had been only fitful passion: that was balked; he would want me no more. I should fear even to cross his path now: my view must be hateful to him. Oh, how blind had been my eyes! How weak my conduct!

My eyes were covered and closed: eddying darkness seemed to swim round me, and reflection came in as black and confused a flow. Self-abandoned, relaxed, and effortless, I seemed to have laid me down in the dried-up bed of a great river; I heard a flood loosened in remote mountains, and felt the torrent come: to rise I had no will, to flee I had no strength. I lay faint, longing to be dead. One idea only still throbbed life-like within me—a remembrance of God: it begot an unuttered prayer: these words went wandering up and down in my rayless mind, as something that should be whispered, but no energy was found to express them—

"Be not far from me, for trouble is near: there is none to help."

It was near: and as I had lifted no petition to Heaven to avert it—as I had neither joined my hands, nor bent my knees, nor moved my lips—it came: in full heavy swing the torrent poured over me. The whole consciousness of my life lorn, my love lost, my hope quenched, my faith death-struck, swayed full and mighty above me in one sullen mass. That bitter hour cannot be described: in truth, "the waters came into my soul; I sank in deep mire: I felt no standing; I came into deep waters; the floods overflowed me."

Chapter XXVII

Some time in the afternoon I raised my head, and looking round and seeing the western sun gilding the sign of its decline on the wall, I asked, "What am I to do?"

But the answer my mind gave—"Leave Thornfield at once"—was so prompt, so dread, that I stopped my ears. I said I could not bear such words now. "That I am not Edward Rochester's bride is the least part of my woe," I alleged: "that I have wakened out of most glorious dreams, and found them all void and vain, is a horror I could bear and master; but that I must leave him decidedly, instantly, entirely, is intolerable. I cannot do it."

But, then, a voice within me averred that I could do it and foretold that I should do it. I wrestled with my own resolution: I wanted to be weak that I might avoid the awful passage of further suffering I saw laid out for me; and Conscience, turned tyrant, held Passion by the throat, told her tauntingly, she had yet but dipped her dainty foot in the slough, and swore that with that arm of iron he would thrust her down to unsounded depths of agony.

"Let me be torn away," then I cried. "Let another help me!"

"No; you shall tear yourself away, none shall help you: you shall yourself pluck out your right eye; yourself cut off your right hand: your heart shall be the victim, and you the priest to transfix it."

I rose up suddenly, terror-struck at the solitude which so ruthless a judge haunted,—at the silence which so awful a voice filled. My head swam as I stood erect. I perceived that I was sickening from excitement and inanition; neither meat nor drink had passed my lips that day, for I had taken no breakfast. And, with a strange pang, I now reflected that, long as I had been shut up here, no message had been sent to ask how I was, or to invite me to come down: not even little Adele had tapped at the door; not even Mrs. Fairfax had sought me. "Friends always forget those whom fortune forsakes," I murmured, as I undrew the bolt and passed out. I stumbled over an obstacle: my head was still dizzy, my sight was dim, and my limbs were feeble. I could not soon recover myself. I fell, but not on to the ground: an outstretched arm caught me. I looked up—I was supported by Mr. Rochester, who sat in a chair across my chamber threshold.

"You come out at last," he said. "Well, I have been waiting for you long, and listening: yet not one movement have I heard, nor one sob: five minutes more of that death-like hush, and I should have forced the lock like a burglar. So you shun me?—you shut yourself up and grieve alone! I would rather you had come and upbraided me with vehemence. You are passionate. I expected a scene of some kind. I was prepared for the hot rain of tears; only I wanted them to be shed on my breast: now a senseless floor has received them, or your drenched handkerchief. But I err: you have not wept at all! I see a white cheek and a faded eye, but no trace of tears. I suppose, then, your heart has been weeping blood?"

"Well, Jane! not a word of reproach? Nothing bitter—nothing poignant? Nothing to cut a feeling or sting a passion? You sit quietly where I have placed you, and regard me with a weary, passive look."

"Jane, I never meant to wound you thus. If the man who had but one little ewe lamb that was dear to him as a daughter, that ate of his bread and drank of his cup, and lay in his bosom, had by some mistake slaughtered it at the shambles, he would not have rued his bloody blunder more than I now rue mine. Will you ever forgive me?"

Reader, I forgave him at the moment and on the spot. There was such deep remorse in his eye, such true pity in his tone, such manly energy in his manner; and besides, there was such unchanged love in his whole look and mien—I forgave him all: yet not in words, not outwardly; only at my heart's core.

"You know I am a scoundrel, Jane?" ere long he inquired wistfully—wondering, I suppose, at my continued silence and tameness, the result rather of weakness than of will.

"Yes, sir."

"Then tell me so roundly and sharply—don't spare me."

"I cannot: I am tired and sick. I want some water." He heaved a sort of shuddering sigh, and taking me in his arms, carried me downstairs. At first I did not know to what room he had borne me; all was cloudy to my glazed sight: presently I felt the reviving warmth of a fire; for, summer as it was, I had become icy cold in my chamber. He put wine to my lips; I tasted it and revived; then I ate something he offered me, and was soon myself. I was in the library—sitting in his chair—he was quite near. "If I could go out of life now, without too sharp a pang, it would be well for me," I thought; "then I should not have to make the effort of cracking my heart-strings in rending them from among Mr. Rochester's. I must leave him, it appears. I do not want to leave him—I cannot leave him."

"How are you now, Jane?"

"Much better, sir; I shall be well soon."

"Taste the wine again, Jane."

I obeyed him; then he put the glass on the table, stood before me, and looked at me attentively. Suddenly he turned away, with an inarticulate exclamation, full of passionate emotion of some kind; he walked fast through the room and came back; he stooped towards me as if to kiss me; but I remembered caresses were now forbidden. I turned my face away and put his aside.

"What!—How is this?" he exclaimed hastily. "Oh, I know! you won't kiss the husband of Bertha Mason? You consider my arms filled and my embraces appropriated?"

"At any rate, there is neither room nor claim for me, sir."

"Why, Jane? I will spare you the trouble of much talking; I will answer for you—Because I have a wife already, you would reply.—I guess rightly?"

"Yes."

"If you think so, you must have a strange opinion of me; you must regard me as a plotting profligate—a base and low rake who has been simulating disinterested love in order to draw you into a snare deliberately laid, and strip you of honour and rob you of self-respect. What do you say to that? I see you can say nothing in the first place, you are faint still, and have enough to do to draw your breath; in the second place, you cannot yet accustom yourself to accuse and revile me, and besides, the flood-gates of tears are opened, and they would rush out if you spoke much; and you have no desire to expostulate, to upbraid, to make a scene: you are thinking how TO ACT—TALKING you consider is of no use. I know you—I am on my guard."

"Sir, I do not wish to act against you," I said; and my unsteady voice warned me to curtail my sentence.

"Not in your sense of the word, but in mine you are scheming to destroy me. You have as good as said that I am a married man—as a married man you will shun me, keep out of my way: just now you have refused to kiss me. You intend to make yourself a complete stranger to me: to live under this roof only as Adele's governess; if ever I say a friendly word to you, if ever a friendly feeling inclines you again to me, you will say,—'That man had nearly made me his mistress: I must be ice and rock to him;' and ice and rock you will accordingly become."

I cleared and steadied my voice to reply: "All is changed about me, sir; I must change too—there is no doubt of that; and to avoid fluctuations of feeling, and continual combats with recollections and associations, there is only one way—Adele must have a new governess, sir."

"Oh, Adele will go to school—I have settled that already; nor do I mean to torment you with the hideous associations and recollections of Thornfield Hall—this accursed place—this tent of Achan—this insolent vault, offering the ghastliness of living death to the light of the open sky—this narrow stone hell, with its one real fiend, worse than a legion of such as we imagine. Jane, you shall not stay here, nor will I. I was wrong ever to bring you to Thornfield Hall, knowing as I did how it was haunted. I charged them to conceal from you, before I ever saw you, all knowledge of the curse of the place; merely because I feared Adele never would have a governess to stay if she knew with what inmate she was housed, and my plans would not permit me to remove the maniac elsewhere—though I possess an old house, Ferndean Manor, even more retired and hidden than this, where I could have lodged her safely enough, had not a scruple about the unhealthiness of the situation, in the heart of a wood, made my conscience recoil from the arrangement. Probably those damp walls would soon have eased me of her charge: but to each villain his own vice; and mine is not a tendency to indirect assassination, even of what I most hate.

"Concealing the mad-woman's neighbourhood from you, however, was something like covering a child with a cloak and laying it down near a upas-tree: that demon's vicinage is poisoned, and always was. But I'll shut up Thornfield Hall: I'll nail up the front door and board the lower windows: I'll give Mrs. Poole two hundred a year to live here with MY WIFE, as you term that fearful hag: Grace will do much for money, and she shall have her son, the keeper at Grimsby Retreat, to bear her company and be at hand to give her aid in the paroxysms, when MY WIFE is prompted by her familiar to burn people in their beds at night, to stab them, to bite their flesh from their bones, and so on—"

"Sir," I interrupted him, "you are inexorable for that unfortunate lady: you speak of her with hate—with vindictive antipathy. It is cruel—she cannot help being mad."

"Jane, my little darling (so I will call you, for so you are), you don't know what you are talking about; you misjudge me again: it is not because she is mad I hate her. If you were mad, do you think I should hate you?"

"I do indeed, sir."

"Then you are mistaken, and you know nothing about me, and nothing about the sort of love of which I am capable. Every atom of your flesh is as dear to me as my own: in pain and sickness it would still be dear. Your mind is my treasure, and if it were broken, it would be my treasure still: if you raved, my arms should confine you, and not a strait waistcoat—your grasp, even in fury, would have a charm for me: if you flew at me as wildly as that woman did this morning, I should receive you in an embrace, at least as fond as it would be restrictive. I should not shrink from you with disgust as I did from her: in your quiet moments you should have no watcher and no nurse but me; and I could hang over you with untiring tenderness, though you gave me no smile in return; and never weary of gazing into your eyes, though they had no longer a ray of recognition for me.—But why do I follow that train of ideas? I was talking of removing you from Thornfield. All, you know, is prepared for prompt departure: to-morrow you shall go. I only ask you to endure one more night under this roof, Jane; and then, farewell to its miseries and terrors for ever! I have a place to repair to, which will be a secure sanctuary from hateful reminiscences, from unwelcome intrusion—even from falsehood and slander."

"And take Adele with you, sir," I interrupted; "she will be a companion for you."

"What do you mean, Jane? I told you I would send Adele to school; and what do I want with a child for a companion, and not my own child,—a French dancer's bastard? Why do you importune me about her! I say, why do you assign Adele to me for a companion?"

"You spoke of a retirement, sir; and retirement and solitude are dull: too dull for you."

"Solitude! solitude!" he reiterated with irritation. "I see I must come to an explanation. I don't know what sphynx-like expression is forming in your countenance. You are to share my solitude. Do you understand?"

I shook my head: it required a degree of courage, excited as he was becoming, even to risk that mute sign of dissent. He had been walking fast about the room, and he stopped, as if suddenly rooted to one spot. He looked at me long and hard: I turned my eyes from him, fixed them on the fire, and tried to assume and maintain a quiet, collected aspect.

"Now for the hitch in Jane's character," he said at last, speaking more calmly than from his look I had expected him to speak. "The reel of silk has run smoothly enough so far; but I always knew there would come a knot and a puzzle: here it is. Now for vexation, and exasperation, and endless trouble! By God! I long to exert a fraction of Samson's strength, and break the entanglement like tow!"

He recommenced his walk, but soon again stopped, and this time just before me.

"Jane! will you hear reason?" (he stooped and approached his lips to my ear); "because, if you won't, I'll try violence." His voice was hoarse; his look that of a man who is just about to burst an insufferable bond and plunge headlong into wild license. I saw that in another moment, and with one impetus of frenzy more, I should be able to do nothing with him. The present—the passing second of time—was all I had in which to control and restrain him—a movement of repulsion, flight, fear would have sealed my doom,—and his. But I was not afraid: not in the least. I felt an inward power; a sense of influence, which supported me. The crisis was perilous; but not without its charm: such as the Indian, perhaps, feels when he slips over the rapid in his canoe. I took hold of his clenched hand, loosened the contorted fingers, and said to him, soothingly—

"Sit down; I'll talk to you as long as you like, and hear all you have to say, whether reasonable or unreasonable."

He sat down: but he did not get leave to speak directly. I had been struggling with tears for some time: I had taken great pains to repress them, because I knew he would not like to see me weep. Now, however, I considered it well to let them flow as freely and as long as they liked. If the flood annoyed him, so much the better. So I gave way and cried heartily.

Soon I heard him earnestly entreating me to be composed. I said I could not while he was in such a passion.

"But I am not angry, Jane: I only love you too well; and you had steeled your little pale face with such a resolute, frozen look, I could not endure it. Hush, now, and wipe your eyes."

His softened voice announced that he was subdued; so I, in my turn, became calm. Now he made an effort to rest his head on my shoulder, but I would not permit it. Then he would draw me to him: no.

"Jane! Jane!" he said, in such an accent of bitter sadness it thrilled along every nerve I had; "you don't love me, then? It was only my station, and the rank of my wife, that you valued? Now that you think me disqualified to become your husband, you recoil from my touch as if I were some toad or ape."

These words cut me: yet what could I do or I say? I ought probably to have done or said nothing; but I was so tortured by a sense of remorse at thus hurting his feelings, I could not control the wish to drop balm where I had wounded.

"I DO love you," I said, "more than ever: but I must not show or indulge the feeling: and this is the last time I must express it."

"The last time, Jane! What! do you think you can live with me, and see me daily, and yet, if you still love me, be always cold and distant?"

"No, sir; that I am certain I could not; and therefore I see there is but one way: but you will be furious if I mention it."

"Oh, mention it! If I storm, you have the art of weeping."

"Mr. Rochester, I must leave you."

"For how long, Jane? For a few minutes, while you smooth your hair—which is somewhat dishevelled; and bathe your face—which looks feverish?"

"I must leave Adele and Thornfield. I must part with you for my whole life: I must begin a new existence among strange faces and strange scenes."

"Of course: I told you you should. I pass over the madness about parting from me. You mean you must become a part of me. As to the new existence, it is all right: you shall yet be my wife: I am not married. You shall be Mrs. Rochester—both virtually and nominally. I shall keep only to you so long as you and I live. You shall go to a place I have in the south of France: a whitewashed villa on the shores of the Mediterranean. There you shall live a happy, and guarded, and most innocent life. Never fear that I wish to lure you into error—to make you my mistress. Why did you shake your head? Jane, you must be reasonable, or in truth I shall again become frantic."

His voice and hand quivered: his large nostrils dilated; his eye blazed: still I dared to speak.

"Sir, your wife is living: that is a fact acknowledged this morning by yourself. If I lived with you as you desire, I should then be your mistress: to say otherwise is sophistical—is false."

"Jane, I am not a gentle-tempered man—you forget that: I am not long-enduring; I am not cool and dispassionate. Out of pity to me and yourself, put your finger on my pulse, feel how it throbs, and—beware!"

He bared his wrist, and offered it to me: the blood was forsaking his cheek and lips, they were growing livid; I was distressed on all hands. To agitate him thus deeply, by a resistance he so abhorred, was cruel: to yield was out of the question. I did what human beings do instinctively when they are driven to utter extremity—looked for aid to one higher than man: the words "God help me!" burst involuntarily from my lips.

"I am a fool!" cried Mr. Rochester suddenly. "I keep telling her I am not married, and do not explain to her why. I forget she knows nothing of the character of that woman, or of the circumstances attending my infernal union with her. Oh, I am certain Jane will agree with me in opinion, when she knows all that I know! Just put your hand in mine, Janet—that I may have the evidence of touch as well as sight, to prove you are near me—and I will in a few words show you the real state of the case. Can you listen to me

"Yes, sir; for hours if you will."

"I ask only minutes. Jane, did you ever hear or know at I was not the eldest son of my house: that I had once a brother older than I?"

"I remember Mrs. Fairfax told me so once."

"And did you ever hear that my father was an avaricious, grasping man?"

"I have understood something to that effect."

"Well, Jane, being so, it was his resolution to keep the property together; he could not bear the idea of dividing his estate and leaving me a fair portion: all, he resolved, should go to my brother, Rowland. Yet as little could he endure that a son of his should be a poor man. I must be provided for by a wealthy marriage. He sought me a partner betimes. Mr. Mason, a West India planter and merchant, was his old acquaintance. He was certain his possessions were real and vast: he made inquiries. Mr. Mason, he found, had a son and daughter; and he learned from him that he could and would give the latter a fortune of thirty thousand pounds: that sufficed. When I left college, I was sent out to Jamaica, to espouse a bride already courted for me. My father said nothing about her money; but he told me Miss Mason was the boast of Spanish Town for her beauty: and this was no lie. I found her a fine woman, in the style of Blanche Ingram: tall, dark, and majestic. Her family wished to secure me because I was of a good race; and so did she. They showed her to me in parties, splendidly dressed. I seldom saw her alone, and had very little private conversation with her. She flattered me, and lavishly displayed for my pleasure her charms and accomplishments. All the men in her circle seemed to admire her and envy me. I was dazzled, stimulated: my senses were excited; and being ignorant, raw, and inexperienced, I thought I loved her. There is no folly so besotted that the idiotic rivalries of society, the prurience, the rashness, the blindness of youth, will not hurry a man to its commission. Her relatives encouraged me; competitors piqued me; she allured me: a marriage was achieved almost before I knew where I was. Oh, I have no respect for myself when I think of that act!—an agony of inward contempt masters me. I never loved, I never esteemed, I did not even know her. I was not sure of the existence of one virtue in her nature: I had marked neither modesty, nor benevolence, nor candour, nor refinement in her mind or manners—and, I married her:-gross, grovelling, mole-eyed blockhead that I was! With less sin I might have—But let me remember to whom I am speaking."

"My bride's mother I had never seen: I understood she was dead. The honeymoon over, I learned my mistake; she was only mad, and shut up in a lunatic asylum. There was a younger brother, too—a complete dumb idiot. The elder one, whom you have seen (and whom I cannot hate, whilst I abhor all his kindred, because he has some grains of affection in his feeble mind, shown in the continued interest he takes in his wretched sister, and also in a dog-like attachment he once bore me), will probably be in the same state one day. My father and my brother Rowland knew all this; but they thought only of the thirty thousand pounds, and joined in the plot against me."

"These were vile discoveries; but except for the treachery of concealment, I should have made them no subject of reproach to my wife, even when I found her nature wholly alien to mine, her tastes obnoxious to me, her cast of mind common, low, narrow, and singularly incapable of being led to anything higher, expanded to anything larger—when I found that I could not pass a single evening, nor even a single hour of the day with her in comfort; that kindly conversation could not be sustained between us, because whatever topic I started, immediately received from her a turn at once coarse and trite, perverse and imbecile—when I perceived that I should never have a quiet or settled household, because no servant would bear the continued outbreaks of her violent and unreasonable temper, or the vexations of her absurd, contradictory, exacting orders—even then I restrained myself: I eschewed upbraiding, I curtailed remonstrance; I tried to devour my repentance and disgust in secret; I repressed the deep antipathy I felt.

"Jane, I will not trouble you with abominable details: some strong words shall express what I have to say. I lived with that woman upstairs four years, and before that time she had tried me indeed: her character ripened and developed with frightful rapidity; her vices sprang up fast and rank: they were so strong, only cruelty could check them, and I would not use cruelty. What a pigmy intellect she had, and what giant propensities! How fearful were the curses those propensities entailed on me! Bertha Mason, the true daughter of an infamous mother, dragged me through all the hideous and degrading agonies which must attend a man bound to a wife at once intemperate and unchaste.

"My brother in the interval was dead, and at the end of the four years my father died too. I was rich enough now—yet poor to hideous indigence: a nature the most gross, impure, depraved I ever saw, was associated with mine, and called by the law and by society a part of me. And I could not rid myself of it by any legal proceedings: for the doctors now discovered that MY WIFE was mad—her excesses had prematurely developed the germs of insanity. Jane, you don't like my narrative; you look almost sick—shall I defer the rest to another day?"

"No, sir, finish it now; I pity you—I do earnestly pity you."

"Pity, Jane, from some people is a noxious and insulting sort of tribute, which one is justified in hurling back in the teeth of those who offer it; but that is the sort of pity native to callous, selfish hearts; it is a hybrid, egotistical pain at hearing of woes, crossed with ignorant contempt for those who have endured them. But that is not your pity, Jane; it is not the feeling of which your whole face is full at this moment—with which your eyes are now almost overflowing—with which your heart is heaving—with which your hand is trembling in mine. Your pity, my darling, is the suffering mother of love: its anguish is the very natal pang of the divine passion. I accept it, Jane; let the daughter have free advent—my arms wait to receive her."

"Now, sir, proceed; what did you do when you found she was mad?"

"Jane, I approached the verge of despair; a remnant of self-respect was all that intervened between me and the gulf. In the eyes of the world, I was doubtless covered with grimy dishonour; but I resolved to be clean in my own sight—and to the last I repudiated the contamination of her crimes, and wrenched myself from connection with her mental defects. Still, society associated my name and person with hers; I yet saw her and heard her daily: something of her breath (faugh!) mixed with the air I breathed; and besides, I remembered I had once been her husband—that recollection was then, and is now, inexpressibly odious to me; moreover, I knew that while she lived I could never be the husband of another and better wife; and, though five years my senior (her family and her father had lied to me even in the particular of her age), she was likely to live as long as I, being as robust in frame as she was infirm in mind. Thus, at the age of twenty-six, I was hopeless.

"One night I had been awakened by her yells—(since the medical men had pronounced her mad, she had, of course, been shut up)—it was a fiery West Indian night; one of the description that frequently precede the hurricanes of those climates. Being unable to sleep in bed, I got up and opened the window. The air was like sulphur-steams—I could find no refreshment anywhere. Mosquitoes came buzzing in and hummed sullenly round the room; the sea, which I could hear from thence, rumbled dull like an earthquake—black clouds were casting up over it; the moon was setting in the waves, broad and red, like a hot cannon-ball—she threw her last bloody glance over a world quivering with the ferment of tempest. I was physically influenced by the atmosphere and scene, and my ears were filled with the curses the maniac still shrieked out; wherein she momentarily mingled my name with such a tone of demon-hate, with such language!—no professed harlot ever had a fouler vocabulary than she: though two rooms off, I heard every word—the thin partitions of the West India house opposing but slight obstruction to her wolfish cries.

"'This life,' said I at last, 'is hell: this is the air—those are the sounds of the bottomless pit! I have a right to deliver myself from it if I can. The sufferings of this mortal state will leave me with the heavy flesh that now cumbers my soul. Of the fanatic's burning eternity I have no fear: there is not a future state worse than this present one—let me break away, and go home to God!'

"I said this whilst I knelt down at, and unlocked a trunk which contained a brace of loaded pistols: I mean to shoot myself. I only entertained the intention for a moment; for, not being insane, the crisis of exquisite and unalloyed despair, which had originated the wish and design of self-destruction, was past in a second.

"A wind fresh from Europe blew over the ocean and rushed through the open casement: the storm broke, streamed, thundered, blazed, and the air grew pure. I then framed and fixed a resolution. While I walked under the dripping orange-trees of my wet garden, and amongst its drenched pomegranates and pine-apples, and while the refulgent dawn of the tropics kindled round me—I reasoned thus, Jane—and now listen; for it was true Wisdom that consoled me in that hour, and showed me the right path to follow.

"The sweet wind from Europe was still whispering in the refreshed leaves, and the Atlantic was thundering in glorious liberty; my heart, dried up and scorched for a long time, swelled to the tone, and filled with living blood—my being longed for renewal—my soul thirsted for a pure draught. I saw hope revive—and felt regeneration possible. From a flowery arch at the bottom of my garden I gazed over the sea—bluer than the sky: the old world was beyond; clear prospects opened thus:-

"'Go,' said Hope, 'and live again in Europe: there it is not known what a sullied name you bear, nor what a filthy burden is bound to you. You may take the maniac with you to England; confine her with due attendance and precautions at Thornfield: then travel yourself to what clime you will, and form what new tie you like. That woman, who has so abused your long-suffering, so sullied your name, so outraged your honour, so blighted your youth, is not your wife, nor are you her husband. See that she is cared for as her condition demands, and you have done all that God and humanity require of you. Let her identity, her connection with yourself, be buried in oblivion: you are bound to impart them to no living being. Place her in safety and comfort: shelter her degradation with secrecy, and leave her.'

"I acted precisely on this suggestion. My father and brother had not made my marriage known to their acquaintance; because, in the very first letter I wrote to apprise them of the union—having already begun to experience extreme disgust of its consequences, and, from the family character and constitution, seeing a hideous future opening to me—I added an urgent charge to keep it secret: and very soon the infamous conduct of the wife my father had selected for me was such as to make him blush to own her as his daughter-in-law. Far from desiring to publish the connection, he became as anxious to conceal it as myself.

"To England, then, I conveyed her; a fearful voyage I had with such a monster in the vessel. Glad was I when I at last got her to Thornfield, and saw her safely lodged in that third-storey room, of whose secret inner cabinet she has now for ten years made a wild beast's den—a goblin's cell. I had some trouble in finding an attendant for her, as it was necessary to select one on whose fidelity dependence could be placed; for her ravings would inevitably betray my secret: besides, she had lucid intervals of days—sometimes weeks—which she filled up with abuse of me. At last I hired Grace Poole from the

Grimbsy Retreat. She and the surgeon, Carter (who dressed Mason's wounds that night he was stabbed and worried), are the only two I have ever admitted to my confidence. Mrs. Fairfax may indeed have suspected something, but she could have gained no precise knowledge as to facts. Grace has, on the whole, proved a good keeper; though, owing partly to a fault of her own, of which it appears nothing can cure her, and which is incident to her harassing profession, her vigilance has been more than once lulled and baffled. The lunatic is both cunning and malignant; she has never failed to take advantage of her guardian's temporary lapses; once to secrete the knife with which she stabbed her brother, and twice to possess herself of the key of her cell, and issue therefrom in the night-time. On the first of these occasions, she perpetrated the attempt to burn me in my bed; on the second, she paid that ghastly visit to you. I thank Providence, who watched over you, that she then spent her fury on your wedding apparel, which perhaps brought back vague reminiscences of her own bridal days: but on what might have happened, I cannot endure to reflect. When I think of the thing which flew at my throat this morning, hanging its black and scarlet visage over the nest of my dove, my blood curdles

"And what, sir," I asked, while he paused, "did you do when you had settled her here? Where did you go?"

"What did I do, Jane? I transformed myself into a will-o'-the-wisp. Where did I go? I pursued wanderings as wild as those of the March-spirit. I sought the Continent, and went devious through all its lands. My fixed desire was to seek and find a good and intelligent woman, whom I could love: a contrast to the fury I left at Thornfield—"

"But you could not marry, sir."

"I had determined and was convinced that I could and ought. It was not my original intention to deceive, as I have deceived you. I meant to tell my tale plainly, and make my proposals openly: and it appeared to me so absolutely rational that I should be considered free to love and be loved, I never doubted some woman might be found willing and able to understand my case and accept me, in spite of the curse with which I was burdened."

"Well, sir?"

"When you are inquisitive, Jane, you always make me smile. You open your eyes like an eager bird, and make every now and then a restless movement, as if answers in speech did not flow fast enough for you, and you wanted to read the tablet of one's heart. But before I go on, tell me what you mean by your 'Well, sir?' It is a small phrase very frequent with you; and which many a time has drawn me on and on through interminable talk: I don't very well know why."

"I mean,—What next? How did you proceed? What came of such an event?"

"Precisely! and what do you wish to know now?"

"Whether you found any one you liked: whether you asked her to marry you; and what she said."

"I can tell you whether I found any one I liked, and whether I asked her to marry me: but what she said is yet to be recorded in the book of Fate. For ten long years I roved about, living first in one capital, then another: sometimes in St. Petersburg; oftener in Paris; occasionally in Rome, Naples, and Florence. Provided with plenty of money and the passport of an old name, I could choose my own society: no circles were closed against me. I sought my ideal of a woman amongst English ladies, French countesses, Italian signoras, and German grafinnen. I could not find her. Sometimes, for a fleeting moment, I thought I caught a glance, heard a tone, beheld a form, which announced the realisation of my dream: but I was presently undeserved. You are not to suppose that I desired perfection, either of mind or person. I longed only for what suited me—for the antipodes of the Creole: and I longed vainly. Amongst them all I found not one whom, had I been ever so free, I—warned as I was of the risks, the horrors, the loathings of incongruous unions—would have asked to marry me. Disappointment made me reckless. I tried dissipation—never debauchery: that I hated, and hate. That was my Indian Messalina's attribute: rooted disgust at it and her restrained me much, even in pleasure. Any enjoyment that bordered on riot seemed to approach me to her and her vices, and I eschewed it.

"Yet I could not live alone; so I tried the companionship of mistresses. The first I chose was Celine Varens—another of those steps which make a man spurn himself when he recalls them. You already know what she was, and how my liaison with her terminated. She had two successors: an Italian, Giacinta, and a German, Clara; both considered singularly handsome. What was their beauty to me in a few weeks? Giacinta was unprincipled and violent: I tired of her in three months. Clara was honest and quiet; but heavy, mindless, and unimpressible: not one whit to my taste. I was glad to give her a sufficient sum to set her up in a good line of business, and so get decently rid of her. But, Jane, I see by your face you are not forming a very favourable opinion of me just now. You think me an unfeeling, loose-principled rake: don't you?"

"I don't like you so well as I have done sometimes, indeed, sir. Did it not seem to you in the least wrong to live in that way, first with one mistress and then another? You talk of it as a mere matter of course."

"It was with me; and I did not like it. It was a grovelling fashion of existence: I should never like to return to it. Hiring a mistress is the next worse thing to buying a slave: both are often by nature, and always by position, inferior: and to live familiarly with inferiors is degrading. I now hate the recollection of the time I passed with Celine, Giacinta, and Clara."

I felt the truth of these words; and I drew from them the certain inference, that if I were so far to forget myself and all the teaching that had ever been instilled into me, as—under any pretext—with any justification—through any temptation—to become the successor of these poor girls, he would one day regard me with the same feeling which now in his mind desecrated their memory. I did not give utterance to this conviction: it was enough to feel it. I impressed it on my heart, that it might remain there to serve me as aid in the time of trial.

"Now, Jane, why don't you say 'Well, sir?' I have not done. You are looking grave. You disapprove of me still, I see. But let me come to the point. Last January, rid of all mistresses—in a harsh, bitter frame of mind, the result of a useless, roving, lonely life—corroded with disappointment, sourly disposed against all men, and especially against all womankind (for I began to regard the notion of an intellectual, faithful, loving woman as a mere dream), recalled by business, I came back to England.

"On a frosty winter afternoon, I rode in sight of Thornfield Hall. Abhorred spot! I expected no peace—no pleasure there. On a stile in Hay Lane I saw a quiet little figure sitting by itself. I passed it as negligently as I did the pollard willow opposite to it: I had no presentiment of what it would be to me; no inward warning that the arbitress of my life—my genius for good or evil—waited there in humble guise. I did not know it, even when, on the occasion of Mesrour's accident, it came up and gravely offered me help. Childish and slender creature! It seemed as if a linnet had hopped to my foot and proposed to bear me on its tiny wing. I was surly; but the thing would not go: it stood by me with strange perseverance, and looked and spoke with a sort of authority. I must be aided, and by that hand: and aided I was.

"When once I had pressed the frail shoulder, something new—a fresh sap and sense—stole into my frame. It was well I had learnt that this elf must return to me—that it belonged to my house down below—or I could not have felt it pass away from under my hand, and seen it vanish behind the dim hedge, without singular regret. I heard you come home that night, Jane, though probably you were not aware that I thought of you or watched for you. The next day I observed you—myself unseen—for half-an-hour, while you played with Adele in the gallery. It was a snowy day, I recollect, and you could not go out of doors. I was in my room; the door was ajar: I could both listen and watch. Adele claimed your outward attention for a while; yet I fancied your thoughts were elsewhere: but you were very patient with her, my little Jane; you talked to her and amused her a long time. When at last she left you, you lapsed at once into deep reverie: you betook yourself slowly to pace the gallery. Now and then, in passing a casement, you glanced out at the thick-falling snow; you listened to the sobbing wind, and again you paced gently on and dreamed. I think those day visions were not dark: there was a pleasurable illumination in your eye occasionally, a soft excitement in your aspect, which told of no bitter, bilious, hypochondriac brooding: your look revealed rather the sweet musings of youth when its spirit follows on willing wings the flight of Hope up and on to an ideal heaven. The voice of Mrs. Fairfax, speaking to a servant in the hall, wakened you: and how curiously you smiled to and at yourself, Janet! There was much sense in your smile: it was very shrewd, and seemed to make light of your own abstraction. It seemed to say—'My fine visions are all very well, but I must not forget they are absolutely unreal. I have a rosy sky and a green flowery Eden in my brain; but without, I am perfectly aware, lies at my feet a rough tract to travel, and around me gather black tempests to encounter.' You ran downstairs and demanded of Mrs. Fairfax some occupation: the weekly house accounts to make up, or something of that sort, I think it was. I was vexed with you for getting out of my sight.

"Impatiently I waited for evening, when I might summon you to my presence. An unusual—to me—a perfectly new character I suspected was yours: I desired to search it deeper and know it better. You entered the room with a look and air at once shy and independent: you were quaintly dressed—much as you are now. I made you talk: ere long I found you full of strange contrasts. Your garb and manner were restricted by rule; your air was often diffident, and altogether that of one refined by nature, but absolutely unused to society, and a good deal afraid of making herself disadvantageously conspicuous by some solecism or blunder; yet when addressed, you lifted a keen, a daring, and a glowing eye to your interlocutor's face: there was penetration and power in each glance you gave; when plied by close questions, you found ready and round answers. Very soon you seemed to get used to me: I believe you felt the existence of sympathy between you and your grim and cross master, Jane; for it was astonishing to see how quickly a certain pleasant ease tranquillised your manner: snarl as I would, you showed no surprise, fear, annoyance, or displeasure at my moroseness; you watched me, and now and then smiled at me with a simple yet sagacious grace I cannot describe. I was at once content and stimulated with what I saw: I liked what I had seen, and wished to see more. Yet, for a long time, I treated you distantly, and sought your company rarely. I was an intellectual epicure, and wished to prolong the gratification of making this novel and piquant acquaintance: besides, I was for a while troubled with a haunting fear that if I handled the flower freely its bloom would fade—the sweet charm of freshness would leave it. I did not then know that it was no transitory blossom, but rather the radiant resemblance of one, cut in an indestructible gem. Moreover, I wished to see whether you would seek me if I shunned you—but you did not; you kept in the schoolroom as still as your own desk and easel; if by chance I met you, you passed me as soon, and with as little token of recognition, as was consistent with respect. Your habitual expression in those days, Jane, was a thoughtful look; not despondent, for you were not sickly; but not buoyant, for you had little hope, and no actual pleasure. I wondered what you thought of me, or if you ever thought of me, and resolved to find this out.

"I resumed my notice of you. There was something glad in your glance, and genial in your manner, when you conversed: I saw you had a social heart; it was the silent schoolroom—it was the tedium of your life—that made you mournful. I permitted myself the delight of being kind to you; kindness stirred emotion soon: your face became soft in expression, your tones gentle; I liked my name pronounced by your lips in a grateful happy accent. I used to enjoy a chance meeting with you, Jane, at this time: there was a curious hesitation in your manner: you glanced at me with a slight trouble—a hovering doubt: you did not know what my caprice might be—whether I was going to play the master and be stern, or the friend and be benignant. I was now too fond of you often to simulate the first whim; and, when I stretched my hand out cordially, such bloom and light and bliss rose to your young, wistful features, I had much ado often to avoid straining you then and there to my heart."

"Don't talk any more of those days, sir," I interrupted, furtively dashing away some tears from my eyes; his language was torture to me; for I knew what I must do—and do soon—and all these reminiscences, and these revelations of his feelings only made my work more difficult.

"No, Jane," he returned: "what necessity is there to dwell on the Past, when the Present is so much surer—the Future so much brighter?"

I shuddered to hear the infatuated assertion.

"You see now how the case stands—do you not?" he continued. "After a youth and manhood passed half in unutterable misery and half in dreary solitude, I have for the first time found what I can truly love—I have found you. You are my sympathy—my better self—my good angel. I am bound to you with a strong attachment. I think you good, gifted, lovely: a fervent, a solemn passion is conceived in my heart; it leans to you, draws you to my centre and spring of life, wraps my existence about you, and, kindling in pure, powerful flame, fuses you and me in one.

"It was because I felt and knew this, that I resolved to marry you. To tell me that I had already a wife is empty mockery: you know now that I had but a hideous demon. I was wrong to attempt to deceive you; but I feared a stubbornness that exists in your character. I feared early instilled prejudice: I wanted to have you safe before hazarding confidences. This was cowardly: I should have appealed to your nobleness and magnanimity at first, as I do now—opened to you plainly my life of agony—described to you my hunger and thirst after a higher and worthier existence—shown to you, not my RESOLUTION (that word is weak), but my resistless BENT to love faithfully and well, where I am faithfully and well loved in return. Then I should have asked you to accept my pledge of fidelity and to give me yours. Jane—give it me now."

A pause.

"Why are you silent, Jane?"

I was experiencing an ordeal: a hand of fiery iron grasped my vitals. Terrible moment: full of struggle, blackness, burning! Not a human being that ever lived could wish to be loved better than I was loved; and him who thus loved me I absolutely worshipped: and I must renounce love and idol. One drear word comprised my intolerable duty—"Depart!"

"Jane, you understand what I want of you? Just this promise—'I will be yours, Mr. Rochester.'"

"Mr. Rochester, I will NOT be yours."

Another long silence.

"Jane!" recommenced he, with a gentleness that broke me down with grief, and turned me stone-cold with ominous terror—for this still voice was the pant of a lion rising—"Jane, do you mean to go one way in the world, and to let me go another?"

"I do."

"Jane" (bending towards and embracing me), "do you mean it now?"

"I do."

"And now?" softly kissing my forehead and cheek.

"I do," extricating myself from restraint rapidly and completely.

"Oh, Jane, this is bitter! This—this is wicked. It would not be wicked to love me."

"It would to obey you."

A wild look raised his brows—crossed his features: he rose; but he forebore yet. I laid my hand on the back of a chair for support: I shook, I feared—but I resolved.

"One instant, Jane. Give one glance to my horrible life when you are gone. All happiness will be torn away with you. What then is left? For a wife I have but the maniac upstairs: as well might you refer me to some corpse in yonder churchyard. What shall I do, Jane? Where turn for a companion and for some hope?"

"Do as I do: trust in God and yourself. Believe in heaven. Hope to meet again there."

"Then you will not yield?"

"No."

"Then you condemn me to live wretched and to die accursed?" His voice rose.

"I advise you to live sinless, and I wish you to die tranquil."

"Then you snatch love and innocence from me? You fling me back on lust for a passion—vice for an occupation?"

"Mr. Rochester, I no more assign this fate to you than I grasp at it for myself. We were born to strive and endure—you as well as I: do so. You will forget me before I forget you."

"You make me a liar by such language: you sully my honour. I declared I could not change: you tell me to my face I shall change soon. And what a distortion in your judgment, what a perversity in your ideas, is proved by your conduct! Is it better to drive a fellow-creature to despair than to transgress a mere human law, no man being injured by the breach? for you have neither relatives nor acquaintances whom you need fear to offend by living with me?"

This was true: and while he spoke my very conscience and reason turned traitors against me, and charged me with crime in resisting him. They spoke almost as loud as Feeling: and that clamoured wildly. "Oh, comply!" it said. "Think of his misery; think of his danger—look at his state when left alone; remember his headlong nature; consider the recklessness following on despair—soothe him; save him; love him; tell him you love him and will be his. Who in the world cares for YOU? or who will be injured by what you do?"

Still indomitable was the reply—"I care for myself. The more solitary, the more friendless, the more unsustained I am, the more I will respect myself. I will keep the law given by God; sanctioned by man. I will hold to the principles received by me when I was sane, and not mad—as I am now. Laws and principles are not for the times when there is no temptation: they are for such moments as this, when body and soul rise in mutiny against their rigour; stringent are they; inviolate they shall be. If at my individual convenience I might break them, what would be their worth? They have a worth—so I have always believed; and if I cannot believe it now, it is because I am insane—quite insane: with my veins running fire, and my heart beating faster than I can count its throbs. Preconceived opinions, foregone determinations, are all I have at this hour to stand by: there I plant my foot."

I did. Mr. Rochester, reading my countenance, saw I had done so. His fury was wrought to the highest: he must yield to it for a moment, whatever followed; he crossed the floor and seized my arm and grasped my waist. He seemed to devour me with his flaming glance: physically, I felt, at the moment, powerless as stubble exposed to the draught and glow of a furnace: mentally, I still possessed my soul, and with it the certainty of ultimate safety. The soul, fortunately, has an interpreter—often an unconscious, but still a truthful interpreter—in the eye. My eye rose to his; and while I looked in his fierce face I gave an involuntary sigh; his gripe was painful, and my over-taxed strength almost exhausted.

"Never," said he, as he ground his teeth, "never was anything at once so frail and so indomitable. A mere reed she feels in my hand!" (And he shook me with the force of his hold.) "I could bend her with my finger and thumb: and what good would it do if I bent, if I uptore, if I crushed her? Consider that eye: consider the resolute, wild, free thing looking out of it, defying me, with more than courage—with a stern triumph. Whatever I do with its cage, I cannot get at it—the savage, beautiful creature! If I tear, if I rend the slight prison, my outrage will only let the captive loose. Conqueror I might be of the house; but the inmate would escape to heaven before I could call myself possessor of its clay dwelling-place. And it is you, spirit—with will and energy, and virtue and purity—that I want: not alone your brittle frame. Of yourself you could come with soft flight and nestle against my heart, if you would: seized against your will, you will elude the grasp like an essence—you will vanish ere I inhale your fragrance. Oh! come, Jane, come!"

As he said this, he released me from his clutch, and only looked at me. The look was far worse to resist than the frantic strain: only an idiot, however, would have succumbed now. I had dared and baffled his fury; I must elude his sorrow: I retired to the door.

"You are going, Jane?"

"I am going, sir."

"You are leaving me?"

"Yes."

"You will not come? You will not be my comforter, my rescuer? My deep love, my wild woe, my frantic prayer, are all nothing to you?"

What unutterable pathos was in his voice! How hard it was to reiterate firmly, "I am going."

"Jane!"

"Mr. Rochester!"

"Withdraw, then,—I consent; but remember, you leave me here in anguish. Go up to your own room; think over all I have said, and, Jane, cast a glance on my sufferings—think of me."

He turned away; he threw himself on his face on the sofa. "Oh, Jane! my hope—my love—my life!" broke in anguish from his lips. Then came a deep, strong sob.

I had already gained the door; but, reader, I walked back—walked back as determinedly as I had retreated. I knelt down by him; I turned his face from the cushion to me; I kissed his cheek; I smoothed his hair with my hand.

"God bless you, my dear master!" I said. "God keep you from harm and wrong—direct you, solace you—reward you well for your past kindness to me."

"Little Jane's love would have been my best reward," he answered; "without it, my heart is broken. But Jane will give me her love: yes—nobly, generously."

Up the blood rushed to his face; forth flashed the fire from his eyes; erect he sprang; he held his arms out; but I evaded the embrace, and at once quitted the room.

"Farewell!" was the cry of my heart as I left him. Despair added, "Farewell for ever!"

That night I never thought to sleep; but a slumber fell on me as soon as I lay down in bed. I was transported in thought to the scenes of childhood: I dreamt I lay in the red-room at Gateshead; that the night was dark, and my mind impressed with strange fears. The light that long ago had struck me into syncope, recalled in this vision, seemed glidingly to mount the wall, and tremblingly to pause in the centre of the obscured ceiling. I lifted up my head to look: the roof resolved to clouds, high and dim; the gleam was such as the moon imparts to vapours she is about to sever. I watched her come—watched with the strangest anticipation; as though some word of doom were to be written on her disk. She broke forth as never moon yet burst from cloud: a hand first penetrated the sable folds and waved them away; then, not a moon, but a white human form shone in the azure, inclining a glorious brow earthward. It gazed and gazed on me. It spoke to my spirit: immeasurably distant was the tone, yet so near, it whispered in my heart—

"My daughter, flee temptation."

"Mother, I will."

So I answered after I had waked from the trance-like dream. It was yet night, but July nights are short: soon after midnight, dawn comes. "It cannot be too early to commence the task I have to fulfil," thought I. I rose: I was dressed; for I had taken off nothing but my shoes. I knew where to find in my drawers some linen, a locket, a ring. In seeking these articles, I encountered the beads of a pearl necklace Mr. Rochester had forced me to accept a few days ago. I left that; it was not mine: it was the visionary bride's who had melted in air. The other articles I made up in a parcel; my purse, containing twenty shillings (it was all I had), I put in my pocket: I tied on my straw bonnet, pinned my shawl, took the parcel and my slippers, which I would not put on yet, and stole from my room.

"Farewell, kind Mrs. Fairfax!" I whispered, as I glided past her door. "Farewell, my darling Adele!" I said, as I glanced towards the nursery. No thought could be admitted of entering to embrace her. I had to deceive a fine ear: for aught I knew it might now be listening.

I would have got past Mr. Rochester's chamber without a pause; but my heart momentarily stopping its beat at that threshold, my foot was forced to stop also. No sleep was there: the inmate was walking restlessly from wall to wall; and again and again he sighed while I listened. There was a heaven—a temporary heaven—in this room for me, if I chose: I had but to go in and to say—

"Mr. Rochester, I will love you and live with you through life till death," and a fount of rapture would spring to my lips. I thought of this.

That kind master, who could not sleep now, was waiting with impatience for day. He would send for me in the morning; I should be gone. He would have me sought for: vainly. He would feel himself forsaken; his love rejected: he would suffer; perhaps grow desperate. I thought of this too. My hand moved towards the lock: I caught it back, and glided on.

Drearily I wound my way downstairs: I knew what I had to do, and I did it mechanically. I sought the key of the side-door in the kitchen; I sought, too, a phial of oil and a feather; I oiled the key and the lock. I got some water, I got some bread: for perhaps I should have to walk far; and my strength, sorely shaken of late, must not break down. All this I did without one sound. I opened the door, passed out, shut it softly. Dim dawn glimmered in the yard. The great gates were closed and locked; but a wicket in one of them was only latched. Through that I departed: it, too, I shut; and now I was out of Thornfield.

A mile off, beyond the fields, lay a road which stretched in the contrary direction to Millcote; a road I had never travelled, but often noticed, and wondered where it led: thither I bent my steps. No reflection was to be allowed now: not one glance was to be cast back; not even one forward. Not one thought was to be given either to the past or the future. The first was a page so heavenly sweet—so deadly sad—that to read one line of it would dissolve my courage and break down my energy. The last was an awful blank: something like the world when the deluge was gone by.

I skirted fields, and hedges, and lanes till after sunrise. I believe it was a lovely summer morning: I know my shoes, which I had put on when I left the house, were soon wet with dew. But I looked neither to rising sun, nor smiling sky, nor wakening nature. He who is taken out to pass through a fair scene to the scaffold, thinks not of the flowers that smile on his road, but of the block and axe-edge; of the disseverment of bone and vein; of the grave gaping at the end: and I thought of drear flight and homeless wandering—and oh! with agony I thought of what I left. I could not help it. I thought of him now—in his room—watching the sunrise; hoping I should soon come to say I would stay with him and be his. I longed to be his; I panted to return: it was not too late; I could yet spare him the bitter pang of bereavement. As yet my flight, I was sure, was undiscovered. I could go back and be his comforter—his pride; his redeemer from misery, perhaps from ruin. Oh, that fear of his self-abandonment—far worse than my abandonment—how it goaded me! It was a barbed arrow-head in my breast; it tore me when I tried to extract it; it sickened me when remembrance thrust it farther in. Birds began singing in brake and copse: birds were faithful to their mates; birds were emblems of love. What was I? In the midst of my pain of heart and frantic effort of principle, I abhorred myself. I had no solace from self-approbation: none even from self-respect. I had injured—wounded—left my master. I was hateful in my own eyes. Still I could not turn, nor retrace one step. God must have led me on. As to my own will or conscience, impassioned grief had trampled one and stifled the other. I was weeping wildly as I walked along my solitary way: fast, fast I went like one delirious. A weakness, beginning inwardly, extending to the limbs, seized me, and I fell: I lay on the ground some minutes, pressing my face to the wet turf. I had some fear—or hope—that here I should die: but I was soon up; crawling forwards on my hands and knees, and then again raised to my feet—as eager and as determined as ever to reach the road.

When I got there, I was forced to sit to rest me under the hedge; and while I sat, I heard wheels, and saw a coach come on. I stood up and lifted my hand; it stopped. I asked where it was going: the driver named a place a long way off, and where I was sure Mr. Rochester had no connections. I asked for what sum he would take me there; he said thirty shillings; I answered I had but twenty; well, he would try to make it do. He further gave me leave to get into the inside, as the vehicle was empty: I entered, was shut in, and it rolled on its way.

Gentle reader, may you never feel what I then felt! May your eyes never shed such stormy, scalding, heart-wrung tears as poured from mine. May you never appeal to Heaven in prayers so hopeless and so agonised as in that hour left my lips; for never may you, like me, dread to be the instrument of evil to what you wholly love.

Chapter XXVIII

Two days are passed. It is a summer evening; the coachman has set me down at a place called Whitcross; he could take me no farther for the sum I had given, and I was not possessed of another shilling in the world. The coach is a mile off by this time; I am alone. At this moment I discover that I forgot to take my parcel out of the pocket of the coach, where I had placed it for safety; there it remains, there it must remain; and now, I am absolutely destitute.

Whitcross is no town, nor even a hamlet; it is but a stone pillar set up where four roads meet: whitewashed, I suppose, to be more obvious at a distance and in darkness. Four arms spring from its summit: the nearest town to which these point is, according to the inscription, distant ten miles; the farthest, above twenty. From the well-known names of these towns I learn in what county I have lighted; a north-midland shire, dusk with moorland, ridged with mountain: this I see. There are great moors behind and on each hand of me; there are waves of mountains far beyond that deep valley at my feet. The population here must be thin, and I see no passengers on these roads: they stretch out east, west, north, and south—white, broad, lonely; they are all cut in the moor, and the heather grows deep and wild to their very verge. Yet a chance traveller might pass by; and I wish no eye to see me now: strangers would wonder what I am doing, lingering here at the sign-post, evidently objectless and lost. I might be questioned: I could give no answer but what would sound incredible and excite suspicion. Not a tie holds me to human society at this moment—not a charm or hope calls me where my fellow-creatures are—none that saw me would have a kind thought or a good wish for me. I have no relative but the universal mother, Nature: I will seek her breast and ask repose.

I struck straight into the heath; I held on to a hollow I saw deeply furrowing the brown moorside; I waded knee-deep in its dark growth; I turned with its turnings, and finding a moss-blackened granite crag in a hidden angle, I sat down under it. High banks of moor were about me; the crag protected my head: the sky was over that.

Some time passed before I felt tranquil even here: I had a vague dread that wild cattle might be near, or that some sportsman or poacher might discover me. If a gust of wind swept the waste, I looked up, fearing it was the rush of a bull; if a plover whistled, I imagined it a man. Finding my apprehensions unfounded, however, and calmed by the deep silence that reigned as evening declined at nightfall, I took confidence. As yet I had not thought; I had only listened, watched, dreaded; now I regained the faculty of reflection.

What was I to do? Where to go? Oh, intolerable questions, when I could do nothing and go nowhere!—when a long way must yet be measured by my weary, trembling limbs before I could reach human habitation—when cold charity must be entreated before I could get a lodging: reluctant sympathy importuned, almost certain repulse incurred, before my tale could be listened to, or one of my wants relieved!

I touched the heath, it was dry, and yet warm with the beat of the summer day. I looked at the sky; it was pure: a kindly star twinkled just above the chasm ridge. The dew fell, but with propitious softness; no breeze whispered. Nature seemed to me benign and good; I thought she loved me, outcast as I was; and I, who from man could anticipate only mistrust, rejection, insult, clung to her with filial fondness. To-night, at least, I would be her guest, as I was her child: my mother would lodge me without money and without price. I had one morsel of bread yet: the remnant of a roll I had bought in a town we passed through at noon with a stray penny—my last coin. I saw ripe bilberries gleaming here and there, like jet beads in the heath: I gathered a handful and ate them with the bread. My hunger, sharp before, was, if not satisfied, appeased by this hermit's meal. I said my evening prayers at its conclusion, and then chose my couch.

Beside the crag the heath was very deep: when I lay down my feet were buried in it; rising high on each side, it left only a narrow space for the night-air to invade. I folded my shawl double, and spread it over me for a coverlet; a low, mossy swell was my pillow. Thus lodged, I was not, at least—at the commencement of the night, cold.

My rest might have been blissful enough, only a sad heart broke it. It plained of its gaping wounds, its inward bleeding, its riven chords. It trembled for Mr. Rochester and his doom; it bemoaned him with bitter pity; it demanded him with ceaseless longing; and, impotent as a bird with both wings broken, it still quivered its shattered pinions in vain attempts to seek him.

Worn out with this torture of thought, I rose to my knees. Night was come, and her planets were risen: a safe, still night: too serene for the companionship of fear. We know that God is everywhere; but certainly we feel His presence most when His works are on the grandest scale spread before us; and it is in the unclouded night-sky, where His worlds wheel their silent course, that we read clearest His infinitude, His omnipotence, His omnipresence. I had risen to my knees to pray for Mr. Rochester. Looking up, I, with tear-dimmed eyes, saw the mighty Milky-way. Remembering what it was—what countless systems there swept space like a soft trace of light—I felt the might and strength of God. Sure was I of His efficiency to save what He had made: convinced I grew that neither earth should perish, nor one of the souls it treasured. I turned my prayer to thanksgiving: the Source of Life was also the Saviour of spirits. Mr. Rochester was safe; he was God's, and by God would he be guarded. I again nestled to the breast of the hill; and ere long in sleep forgot sorrow.

But next day, Want came to me pale and bare. Long after the little birds had left their nests; long after bees had come in the sweet prime of day to gather the heath honey before the dew was dried—when the long morning shadows were curtailed, and the sun filled earth and sky—I got up, and I looked round me.

What a still, hot, perfect day! What a golden desert this spreading moor! Everywhere sunshine. I wished I could live in it and on it. I saw a lizard run over the crag; I saw a bee busy among the sweet bilberries. I would fain at the moment have become bee or lizard, that I might have found fitting nutriment, permanent shelter here. But I was a human being, and had a human being's wants: I must not linger where there was nothing to supply them. I rose; I looked back at the bed I had left. Hopeless of the future, I wished but this—that my Maker had that night thought good to require my soul of me while I slept; and that this weary frame, absolved by death from further conflict with fate, had now but to decay quietly, and mingle in peace with the soil of this wilderness. Life, however, was yet in my possession, with all its requirements, and pains, and responsibilities. The burden must be carried; the want provided for; the suffering endured; the responsibility fulfilled. I set out.

Whitcross regained, I followed a road which led from the sun, now fervent and high. By no other circumstance had I will to decide my choice. I walked a long time, and when I thought I had nearly done enough, and might conscientiously yield to the fatigue that almost overpowered me—might relax this forced action, and, sitting down on a stone I saw near, submit resistlessly to the apathy that clogged heart and limb—I heard a bell chime—a church bell.

I turned in the direction of the sound, and there, amongst the romantic hills, whose changes and aspect I had ceased to note an hour ago, I saw a hamlet and a spire. All the valley at my right hand was full of pasture-fields, and cornfields, and wood; and a glittering stream ran zig-zag through the varied shades of green, the mellowing grain, the sombre woodland, the clear and sunny lea. Recalled by the rumbling of wheels to the road before me, I saw a heavily-laden waggon labouring up the hill, and not far beyond were two cows and their drover. Human life and human labour were near. I must struggle on: strive to live and bend to toil like the rest.

About two o'clock p.m. I entered the village. At the bottom of its one street there was a little shop with some cakes of bread in the window. I coveted a cake of bread. With that refreshment I could perhaps regain a degree of energy: without it, it would be difficult to proceed. The wish to have some strength and some vigour returned to me as soon as I was amongst my fellow-beings. I felt it would be degrading to faint with hunger on the causeway of a hamlet. Had I nothing about me I could offer in exchange for one of these rolls? I considered. I had a small silk handkerchief tied round my throat; I had my gloves. I could hardly tell how men and women in extremities of destitution proceeded. I did not know whether either of these articles would be accepted: probably they would not; but I must try.

I entered the shop: a woman was there. Seeing a respectably-dressed person, a lady as she supposed, she came forward with civility.

How could she serve me? I was seized with shame: my tongue would not utter the request I had prepared. I dared not offer her the half-worn gloves, the creased handkerchief: besides, I felt it would be absurd. I only begged permission to sit down a moment, as I was tired. Disappointed in the expectation of a customer, she coolly acceded to my request. She pointed to a seat; I sank into it. I felt sorely urged to weep; but conscious how unseasonable such a manifestation would be, I restrained it. Soon I asked her "if there were any dress-maker or plain-workwoman in the village?"

"Yes; two or three. Quite as many as there was employment for."

I reflected. I was driven to the point now. I was brought face to face with Necessity. I stood in the position of one without a resource, without a friend, without a coin. I must do something. What? I must apply somewhere. Where?

"Did she know of any place in the neighbourhood where a servant was wanted?"

"Nay; she couldn't say."

"What was the chief trade in this place? What did most of the people do?"

"Some were farm labourers; a good deal worked at Mr. Oliver's needle-factory, and at the foundry."

"Did Mr. Oliver employ women?"

"Nay; it was men's work."

"And what do the women do?"

"I knawn't," was the answer. "Some does one thing, and some another. Poor folk mun get on as they can."

She seemed to be tired of my questions: and, indeed, what claim had I to importune her? A neighbour or two came in; my chair was evidently wanted. I took leave.

I passed up the street, looking as I went at all the houses to the right hand and to the left; but I could discover no pretext, nor see an inducement to enter any. I rambled round the hamlet, going sometimes to a little distance and returning again, for an hour or more. Much exhausted, and suffering greatly now for want of food, I turned aside into a lane and sat down under the hedge. Ere many minutes had elapsed, I was again on my feet, however, and again searching something—a resource, or at least an informant. A pretty little house stood at the top of the lane, with a garden before it, exquisitely neat and brilliantly blooming. I stopped at it. What business had I to approach the white door or touch the glittering knocker? In what way could it possibly be the interest of the inhabitants of that dwelling to serve me? Yet I drew near and knocked. A mild-looking, cleanly-attired young woman opened the door. In such a voice as might be expected from a hopeless heart and fainting frame—a voice wretchedly low and faltering—I asked if a servant was wanted here?

"No," said she; "we do not keep a servant."

"Can you tell me where I could get employment of any kind?" I continued. "I am a stranger, without acquaintance in this place. I want some work: no matter what."

But it was not her business to think for me, or to seek a place for me: besides, in her eyes, how doubtful must have appeared my character, position, tale. She shook her head, she "was sorry she could give me no information," and the white door closed, quite gently and civilly: but it shut me out. If she had held it open a little longer, I believe I should have begged a piece of bread; for I was now brought low.

I could not bear to return to the sordid village, where, besides, no prospect of aid was visible. I should have longed rather to deviate to a wood I saw not far off, which appeared in its thick shade to offer inviting shelter; but I was so sick, so weak, so gnawed with nature's cravings, instinct kept me roaming round abodes where there was a chance of food. Solitude would be no solitude—rest no rest—while the vulture, hunger, thus sank beak and talons in my side.

I drew near houses; I left them, and came back again, and again I wandered away: always repelled by the consciousness of having no claim to ask—no right to expect interest in my isolated lot. Meantime, the afternoon advanced, while I thus wandered about like a lost and starving dog. In crossing a field, I saw the church spire before me: I hastened towards it. Near the churchyard, and in the middle of a garden, stood a well-built though small house, which I had no doubt was the parsonage. I remembered that strangers who arrive at a place where they have no friends, and who want employment, sometimes apply to the clergyman for introduction and aid. It is the clergyman's function to help—at least with advice—those who wished to help themselves. I seemed to have something like a right to seek counsel here. Renewing then my courage, and gathering my feeble remains of strength, I pushed on. I reached the house, and knocked at the kitchen-door. An old woman opened: I asked was this the parsonage?

"Yes."

"Was the clergyman in?"

"No."

"Would he be in soon?"

"No, he was gone from home."

"To a distance?"

"Not so far—happen three mile. He had been called away by the sudden death of his father: he was at Marsh End now, and would very likely stay there a fortnight longer."

"Was there any lady of the house?"

"Nay, there was naught but her, and she was housekeeper;" and of her, reader, I could not bear to ask the relief for want of which I was sinking; I could not yet beg; and again I crawled away.

Once more I took off my handkerchief—once more I thought of the cakes of bread in the little shop. Oh, for but a crust! for but one mouthful to allay the pang of famine! Instinctively I turned my face again to the village; I found the shop again, and I went in; and though others were there besides the woman I ventured the request—"Would she give me a roll for this handkerchief?"

She looked at me with evident suspicion: "Nay, she never sold stuff i' that way."

Almost desperate, I asked for half a cake; she again refused. "How could she tell where I had got the handkerchief?" she said.

"Would she take my gloves?"

"No! what could she do with them?"

Reader, it is not pleasant to dwell on these details. Some say there is enjoyment in looking back to painful experience past; but at this day I can scarcely bear to review the times to which I allude: the moral degradation, blent with the physical suffering, form too distressing a recollection ever to be willingly dwelt on. I blamed none of those who repulsed me. I felt it was what was to be expected, and what could not be helped: an ordinary beggar is frequently an object of suspicion; a well-dressed beggar inevitably so. To be sure, what I begged was employment; but whose business was it to provide me with employment? Not, certainly, that of persons who saw me then for the first time, and who knew nothing about my character. And as to the woman who would not take my handkerchief in exchange for her bread, why, she was right, if the offer appeared to her sinister or the exchange unprofitable. Let me condense now. I am sick of the subject.

A little before dark I passed a farm-house, at the open door of which the farmer was sitting, eating his supper of bread and cheese. I stopped and said—

"Will you give me a piece of bread? for I am very hungry." He cast on me a glance of surprise; but without answering, he cut a thick slice from his loaf, and gave it to me. I imagine he did not think I was a beggar, but only an eccentric sort of lady, who had taken a fancy to his brown loaf. As soon as I was out of sight of his house, I sat down and ate it.

I could not hope to get a lodging under a roof, and sought it in the wood I have before alluded to. But my night was wretched, my rest broken: the ground was damp, the air cold: besides, intruders passed near me more than once, and I had again and again to change my quarters; no sense of safety or tranquillity befriended me. Towards morning it rained; the whole of the following day was wet. Do not ask me, reader, to give a minute account of that day; as before, I sought work; as before, I was repulsed; as before, I starved; but once did food pass my lips. At the door of a cottage I saw a little girl about to throw a mess of cold porridge into a pig trough. "Will you give me that?" I asked.

She stared at me. "Mother!" she exclaimed, "there is a woman wants me to give her these porridge."

"Well lass," replied a voice within, "give it her if she's a beggar. T pig doesn't want it."

The girl emptied the stiffened mould into my hand, and I devoured it ravenously.

As the wet twilight deepened, I stopped in a solitary bridle-path, which I had been pursuing an hour or more.

"My strength is quite failing me," I said in a soliloquy. "I feel I cannot go much farther. Shall I be an outcast again this night? While the rain descends so, must I lay my head on the cold, drenched ground? I fear I cannot do otherwise: for who will receive me? But it will be very dreadful, with this feeling of hunger, faintness, chill, and this sense of desolation—this total prostration of hope. In all likelihood, though, I should die before morning. And why cannot I reconcile myself to the prospect of death? Why do I struggle to retain a valueless life? Because I know, or believe, Mr. Rochester is living: and then, to die of want and cold is a fate to which nature cannot submit passively. Oh, Providence! sustain me a little longer! Aid!—direct me!"

My glazed eye wandered over the dim and misty landscape. I saw I had strayed far from the village: it was quite out of sight. The very cultivation surrounding it had disappeared. I had, by cross-ways and by-paths, once more drawn near the tract of moorland; and now, only a few fields, almost as wild and unproductive as the heath from which they were scarcely reclaimed, lay between me and the dusky hill.

"Well, I would rather die yonder than in a street or on a frequented road," I reflected. "And far better that crows and ravens—if any ravens there be in these regions—should pick my flesh from my bones, than that they should be prisoned in a workhouse coffin and moulder in a pauper's grave."

To the hill, then, I turned. I reached it. It remained now only to find a hollow where I could lie down, and feel at least hidden, if not secure. But all the surface of the waste looked level. It showed no variation but of tint: green, where rush and moss overgrew the marshes; black, where the dry soil bore only heath. Dark as it was getting, I could still see these changes, though but as mere alternations of light and shade; for colour had faded with the daylight.

My eye still roved over the sullen swell and along the moor-edge, vanishing amidst the wildest scenery, when at one dim point, far in among the marshes and the ridges, a light sprang up. "That is an ignis fatuus," was my first thought; and I expected it would soon vanish. It burnt on, however, quite steadily, neither receding nor advancing. "Is it, then, a bonfire just kindled?" I questioned. I watched to see whether it would spread: but no; as it did not diminish, so it did not enlarge. "It may be a candle in a house," I then conjectured; "but if so, I can never reach it. It is much too far away: and were it within a yard of me, what would it avail? I should but knock at the door to have it shut in my face."

And I sank down where I stood, and hid my face against the ground. I lay still a while: the night-wind swept over the hill and over me, and died moaning in the distance; the rain fell fast, wetting me afresh to the skin. Could I but have stiffened to the still frost—the friendly numbness of death—it might have pelted on; I should not have felt it; but my yet living flesh shuddered at its chilling influence. I rose ere long.

The light was yet there, shining dim but constant through the rain. I tried to walk again: I dragged my exhausted limbs slowly towards it. It led me aslant over the hill, through a wide bog, which would have been impassable in winter, and was splashy and shaking even now, in the height of summer. Here I fell twice; but as often I rose and rallied my faculties. This light was my forlorn hope: I must gain it.

Having crossed the marsh, I saw a trace of white over the moor. I approached it; it was a road or a track: it led straight up to the light, which now beamed from a sort of knoll, amidst a clump of trees—firs, apparently, from what I could distinguish of the character of their forms and foliage through the gloom. My star vanished as I drew near: some obstacle had intervened between me and it. I put out my hand to feel the dark mass before me: I discriminated the rough stones of a low wall—above it, something like palisades, and within, a high and prickly hedge. I groped on. Again a whitish object gleamed before me: it was a gate—a wicket; it moved on its hinges as I touched it. On each side stood a sable bush-holly or yew.

Entering the gate and passing the shrubs, the silhouette of a house rose to view, black, low, and rather long; but the guiding light shone nowhere. All was obscurity. Were the inmates retired to rest? I feared it must be so. In seeking the door, I turned an angle: there shot out the friendly gleam again, from the lozenged panes of a very small latticed window, within a foot of the ground, made still smaller by the growth of ivy or some other creeping plant, whose leaves clustered thick over the portion of the house wall in which it was set. The aperture was so screened and narrow, that curtain or shutter had been deemed unnecessary; and when I stooped down and put aside the spray of foliage shooting over it, I could see all within. I could see clearly a room with a sanded floor, clean scoured; a dresser of walnut, with pewter plates ranged in rows, reflecting the redness and radiance of a glowing peat-fire. I could see a clock, a white deal table, some chairs. The candle, whose ray had been my beacon, burnt on the table; and by its light an elderly woman, somewhat rough-looking, but scrupulously clean, like all about her, was knitting a stocking.

I noticed these objects cursorily only—in them there was nothing extraordinary. A group of more interest appeared near the hearth, sitting still amidst the rosy peace and warmth suffusing it. Two young, graceful women—ladies in every point—sat, one in a low rocking-chair, the other on a lower stool; both wore deep mourning of crape and bombazeen, which sombre garb singularly set off very fair necks and faces: a large old pointer dog rested its massive head on the knee of one girl—in the lap of the other was cushioned a black cat.

A strange place was this humble kitchen for such occupants! Who were they? They could not be the daughters of the elderly person at the table; for she looked like a rustic, and they were all delicacy and cultivation. I had nowhere seen such faces as theirs: and yet, as I gazed on them, I seemed intimate with every lineament. I cannot call them handsome—they were too pale and grave for the word: as they each bent over a book, they looked thoughtful almost to severity. A stand between them supported a second candle and two great volumes, to which they frequently referred, comparing them, seemingly, with the smaller books they held in their hands, like people consulting a dictionary to aid them in the task of translation. This scene was as silent as if all the figures had been shadows and the firelit apartment a picture: so hushed was it, I could hear the cinders fall from the grate, the clock tick in its obscure corner; and I even fancied I could distinguish the click-click of the woman's knitting-needles. When, therefore, a voice broke the strange stillness at last, it was audible enough to me.

"Listen, Diana," said one of the absorbed students; "Franz and old Daniel are together in the night-time, and Franz is telling a dream from which he has awakened in terror—listen!" And in a low voice she read something, of which not one word was intelligible to me; for it was in an unknown tongue—neither French nor Latin. Whether it were Greek or German I could not tell.

"That is strong," she said, when she had finished: "I relish it." The other girl, who had lifted her head to listen to her sister, repeated, while she gazed at the fire, a line of what had been read. At a later day, I knew the language and the book; therefore, I will here quote the line: though, when I first heard it, it was only like a stroke on sounding brass to me—conveying no meaning:-

"'Da trat hervor Einer, anzusehen wie die Sternen Nacht.' Good! good!" she exclaimed, while her dark and deep eye sparkled. "There you have a dim and mighty archangel fitly set before you! The line is worth a hundred pages of fustian. 'Ich wage die Gedanken in der Schale meines Zornes und die Werke mit dem Gewichte meines Grimms.' I like it!"

Both were again silent.

"Is there ony country where they talk i' that way?" asked the old woman, looking up from her knitting.

"Yes, Hannah—a far larger country than England, where they talk in no other way."

"Well, for sure case, I knawn't how they can understand t' one t'other: and if either o' ye went there, ye could tell what they said, I guess?"

"We could probably tell something of what they said, but not all—for we are not as clever as you think us, Hannah. We don't speak German, and we cannot read it without a dictionary to help us."

"And what good does it do you?"

"We mean to teach it some time—or at least the elements, as they say; and then we shall get more money than we do now."

"Varry like: but give ower studying; ye've done enough for to-night."

"I think we have: at least I'm tired. Mary, are you?"

"Mortally: after all, it's tough work fagging away at a language with no master but a lexicon."

"It is, especially such a language as this crabbed but glorious Deutsch. I wonder when St. John will come home."

"Surely he will not be long now: it is just ten (looking at a little gold watch she drew from her girdle). It rains fast, Hannah: will you have the goodness to look at the fire in the parlour?"

The woman rose: she opened a door, through which I dimly saw a passage: soon I heard her stir a fire in an inner room; she presently came back.

"Ah, childer!" said she, "it fair troubles me to go into yond' room now: it looks so lonesome wi' the chair empty and set back in a corner."

She wiped her eyes with her apron: the two girls, grave before, looked sad now.

"But he is in a better place," continued Hannah: "we shouldn't wish him here again. And then, nobody need to have a quieter death nor he had."

"You say he never mentioned us?" inquired one of the ladies.

"He hadn't time, bairn: he was gone in a minute, was your father. He had been a bit ailing like the day before, but naught to signify; and when Mr. St. John asked if he would like either o' ye to be sent for, he fair laughed at him. He began again with a bit of a heaviness in his head the next day—that is, a fortnight sin'—and he went to sleep and niver wakened: he wor a'most stark when your brother went into t' chamber and fand him. Ah, childer! that's t' last o' t' old stock—for ye and Mr. St. John is like of different soart to them 'at's gone; for all your mother wor mich i' your way, and a'most as book-learned. She wor the pictur' o' ye, Mary: Diana is more like your father."

I thought them so similar I could not tell where the old servant (for such I now concluded her to be) saw the difference. Both were fair complexioned and slenderly made; both possessed faces full of distinction and intelligence. One, to be sure, had hair a shade darker than the other, and there was a difference in their style of wearing it; Mary's pale brown locks were parted and braided smooth: Diana's duskier tresses covered her neck with thick curls. The clock struck ten.

"Ye'll want your supper, I am sure," observed Hannah; "and so will Mr. St. John when he comes in."

And she proceeded to prepare the meal. The ladies rose; they seemed about to withdraw to the parlour. Till this moment, I had been so intent on watching them, their appearance and conversation had excited in me so keen an interest, I had half-forgotten my own wretched position: now it recurred to me. More desolate, more desperate than ever, it seemed from contrast. And how impossible did it appear to touch the inmates of this house with concern on my behalf; to make them believe in the truth of my wants and woes—to induce them to vouchsafe a rest for my wanderings! As I groped out the door, and knocked at it hesitatingly, I felt that last idea to be a mere chimera. Hannah opened.

"What do you want?" she inquired, in a voice of surprise, as she surveyed me by the light of the candle she held.

"May I speak to your mistresses?" I said.

"You had better tell me what you have to say to them. Where do you come from?"

"I am a stranger."

"What is your business here at this hour?"

"I want a night's shelter in an out-house or anywhere, and a morsel of bread to eat."

Distrust, the very feeling I dreaded, appeared in Hannah's face. "I'll give you a piece of bread," she said, after a pause; "but we can't take in a vagrant to lodge. It isn't likely."

"Do let me speak to your mistresses."

"No, not I. What can they do for you? You should not be roving about now; it looks very ill."

"But where shall I go if you drive me away? What shall I do?"

"Oh, I'll warrant you know where to go and what to do. Mind you don't do wrong, that's all. Here is a penny; now go—"

"A penny cannot feed me, and I have no strength to go farther. Don't shut the door:-oh, don't, for God's sake!"

"I must; the rain is driving in—"

"Tell the young ladies. Let me see them-"

"Indeed, I will not. You are not what you ought to be, or you wouldn't make such a noise. Move off."

"But I must die if I am turned away."

"Not you. I'm fear'd you have some ill plans agate, that bring you about folk's houses at this time o' night. If you've any followers—housebreakers or such like—anywhere near, you may tell them we are not by ourselves in the house; we have a gentleman, and dogs, and guns." Here the honest but inflexible servant clapped the door to and bolted it within.

This was the climax. A pang of exquisite suffering—a throe of true despair—rent and heaved my heart. Worn out, indeed, I was; not another step could I stir. I sank on the wet doorstep: I groaned—I wrung my hands—I wept in utter anguish. Oh, this spectre of death! Oh, this last hour, approaching in such horror! Alas, this isolation—this banishment from my kind! Not only the anchor of hope, but the footing of fortitude was gone—at least for a moment; but the last I soon endeavoured to regain.

"I can but die," I said, "and I believe in God. Let me try to wait His will in silence."

These words I not only thought, but uttered; and thrusting back all my misery into my heart, I made an effort to compel it to remain there—dumb and still.

"All men must die," said a voice quite close at hand; "but all are not condemned to meet a lingering and premature doom, such as yours would be if you perished here of want."

"Who or what speaks?" I asked, terrified at the unexpected sound, and incapable now of deriving from any occurrence a hope of aid. A form was near—what form, the pitch-dark night and my enfeebled vision prevented me from distinguishing. With a loud long knock, the new-comer appealed to the door.

"Is it you, Mr. St. John?" cried Hannah.

"Yes—yes; open quickly."

"Well, how wet and cold you must be, such a wild night as it is! Come in—your sisters are quite uneasy about you, and I believe there are bad folks about. There has been a beggar-woman—I declare she is not gone yet!—laid down there. Get up! forx shame! Move off, I say!"

"Hush, Hannah! I have a word to say to the woman. You have done your duty in excluding, now let me do mine in admitting her. I was near, and listened to both you and her. I think this is a peculiar case—I must at least examine into it. Young woman, rise, and pass before me into the house."

With difficulty I obeyed him. Presently I stood within that clean, bright kitchen—on the very hearth—trembling, sickening; conscious of an aspect in the last degree ghastly, wild, and weather-beaten. The two ladies, their brother, Mr. St. John, the old servant, were all gazing at me.

"St. John, who is it?" I heard one ask.

"I cannot tell: I found her at the door," was the reply.

"She does look white," said Hannah.

"As white as clay or death," was responded. "She will fall: let her sit."

And indeed my head swam: I dropped, but a chair received me. I still possessed my senses, though just now I could not speak.

"Perhaps a little water would restore her. Hannah, fetch some. But she is worn to nothing. How very thin, and how very bloodless!"

"A mere spectre!"

"Is she ill, or only famished?"

"Famished, I think. Hannah, is that milk? Give it me, and a piece of bread."

Diana (I knew her by the long curls which I saw drooping between me and the fire as she bent over me) broke some bread, dipped it in milk, and put it to my lips. Her face was near mine: I saw there was pity in it, and I felt sympathy in her hurried breathing. In her simple words, too, the same balm-like emotion spoke: "Try to eat."

"Yes—try," repeated Mary gently; and Mary's hand removed my sodden bonnet and lifted my head. I tasted what they offered me: feebly at first, eagerly soon.

"Not too much at first—restrain her," said the brother; "she has had enough." And he withdrew the cup of milk and the plate of bread.

"A little more, St. John—look at the avidity in her eyes."

"No more at present, sister. Try if she can speak now—ask her her name."

I felt I could speak, and I answered—"My name is Jane Elliott." Anxious as ever to avoid discovery, I had before resolved to assume an ALIAS.

"And where do you live? Where are your friends?"

I was silent.

"Can we send for any one you know?"

I shook my head.

"What account can you give of yourself?"

Somehow, now that I had once crossed the threshold of this house, and once was brought face to face with its owners, I felt no longer outcast, vagrant, and disowned by the wide world. I dared to put off the mendicant—to resume my natural manner and character. I began once more to know myself; and when Mr. St. John demanded an account—which at present I was far too weak to render—I said after a brief pause—

"Sir, I can give you no details to-night."

"But what, then," said he, "do you expect me to do for you?"

"Nothing," I replied. My strength sufficed for but short answers. Diana took the word—

"Do you mean," she asked, "that we have now given you what aid you require? and that we may dismiss you to the moor and the rainy night?"

I looked at her. She had, I thought, a remarkable countenance, instinct both with power and goodness. I took sudden courage. Answering her compassionate gate with a smile, I said—"I will trust you. If I were a masterless and stray dog, I know that you would not turn me from your hearth to-night: as it is, I really have no fear. Do with me and for me as you like; but excuse me from much discourse—my breath is short—I feel a spasm when I speak." All three surveyed me, and all three were silent.

"Hannah," said Mr. St. John, at last, "let her sit there at present, and ask her no questions; in ten minutes more, give her the remainder of that milk and bread. Mary and Diana, let us go into the parlour and talk the matter over."

They withdrew. Very soon one of the ladies returned—I could not tell which. A kind of pleasant stupor was stealing over me as I sat by the genial fire. In an undertone she gave some directions to Hannah. Ere long, with the servant's aid, I contrived to mount a staircase; my dripping clothes were removed; soon a warm, dry bed received me. I thanked God—experienced amidst unutterable exhaustion a glow of grateful joy—and slept.

Chapter XXIX

The recollection of about three days and nights succeeding this is very dim in my mind. I can recall some sensations felt in that interval; but few thoughts framed, and no actions performed. I knew I was in a small room and in a narrow bed. To that bed I seemed to have grown; I lay on it motionless as a stone; and to have torn me from it would have been almost to kill me. I took no note of the lapse of time—of the change from morning to noon, from noon to evening. I observed when any one entered or left the apartment: I could even tell who they were; I could understand what was said when the speaker stood near to me; but I could not answer; to open my lips or move my limbs was equally impossible. Hannah, the servant, was my most frequent visitor. Her coming disturbed me. I had a feeling that she wished me away: that she did not understand me or my circumstances; that she was prejudiced against me. Diana and Mary appeared in the chamber once or twice a day. They would whisper sentences of this sort at my bedside—

"It is very well we took her in."

"Yes; she would certainly have been found dead at the door in the morning had she been left out all night. I wonder what she has gone through?"

"Strange hardships, I imagine—poor, emaciated, pallid wanderer?"

"She is not an uneducated person, I should think, by her manner of speaking; her accent was quite pure; and the clothes she took off, though splashed and wet, were little worn and fine."

"She has a peculiar face; fleshless and haggard as it is, I rather like it; and when in good health and animated, I can fancy her physiognomy would be agreeable."

Never once in their dialogues did I hear a syllable of regret at the hospitality they had extended to me, or of suspicion of, or aversion to, myself. I was comforted.

Mr. St. John came but once: he looked at me, and said my state of lethargy was the result of reaction from excessive and protracted fatigue. He pronounced it needless to send for a doctor: nature, he was sure, would manage best, left to herself. He said every nerve had been overstrained in some way, and the whole system must sleep torpid a while. There was no disease. He imagined my recovery would be rapid enough when once commenced. These opinions he delivered in a few words, in a quiet, low voice; and added, after a pause, in the tone of a man little accustomed to expansive comment, "Rather an unusual physiognomy; certainly, not indicative of vulgarity or degradation."

"Far otherwise," responded Diana. "To speak truth, St. John, my heart rather warms to the poor little soul. I wish we may be able to benefit her permanently."

"That is hardly likely," was the reply. "You will find she is some young lady who has had a misunderstanding with her friends, and has probably injudiciously left them. We may, perhaps, succeed in restoring her to them, if she is not obstinate: but I trace lines of force in her face which make me sceptical of her tractability." He stood considering me some minutes; then added, "She looks sensible, but not at all handsome."

"She is so ill, St. John."

"Ill or well, she would always be plain. The grace and harmony of beauty are quite wanting in those features."

On the third day I was better; on the fourth, I could speak, move, rise in bed, and turn. Hannah had brought me some gruel and dry toast, about, as I supposed, the dinner-hour. I had eaten with relish: the food was good—void of the feverish flavour which had hitherto poisoned what I had swallowed. When she left me, I felt comparatively strong and revived: ere long satiety of repose and desire for action stirred me. I wished to rise; but what could I put on? Only my damp and bemired apparel; in which I had slept on the ground and fallen in the marsh. I felt ashamed to appear before my benefactors so clad. I was spared the humiliation.

On a chair by the bedside were all my own things, clean and dry. My black silk frock hung against the wall. The traces of the bog were removed from it; the creases left by the wet smoothed out: it was quite decent. My very shoes and stockings were purified and rendered presentable. There were the means of washing in the room, and a comb and brush to smooth my hair. After a weary process, and resting every five minutes, I succeeded in dressing myself. My clothes hung loose on me; for I was much wasted, but I covered deficiencies with a shawl, and once more, clean and respectable looking—no speck of the dirt, no trace of the disorder I so hated, and which seemed so to degrade me, left—I crept down a stone staircase with the aid of the banisters, to a narrow low passage, and found my way presently to the kitchen.

It was full of the fragrance of new bread and the warmth of a generous fire. Hannah was baking. Prejudices, it is well known, are most difficult to eradicate from the heart whose soil has never been loosened or fertilised by education: they grow there, firm as weeds among stones. Hannah had been cold and stiff, indeed, at the first: latterly she had begun to relent a little; and when she saw me come in tidy and well-dressed, she even smiled.

"What, you have got up!" she said. "You are better, then. You may sit you down in my chair on the hearthstone, if you will."

She pointed to the rocking-chair: I took it. She bustled about, examining me every now and then with the corner of her eye. Turning to me, as she took some loaves from the oven, she asked bluntly—

"Did you ever go a-begging afore you came here?"

I was indignant for a moment; but remembering that anger was out of the question, and that I had indeed appeared as a beggar to her, I answered quietly, but still not without a certain marked firmness—

"You are mistaken in supposing me a beggar. I am no beggar; any more than yourself or your young ladies."

After a pause she said, "I dunnut understand that: you've like no house, nor no brass, I guess?"

"The want of house or brass (by which I suppose you mean money) does not make a beggar in your sense of the word."

"Are you book-learned?" she inquired presently.

"Yes, very."

"But you've never been to a boarding-school?"

"I was at a boarding-school eight years."

She opened her eyes wide. "Whatever cannot ye keep yourself for, then?"

"I have kept myself; and, I trust, shall keep myself again. What are you going to do with these gooseberries?" I inquired, as she brought out a basket of the fruit.

"Mak' 'em into pies."

"Give them to me and I'll pick them."

"Nay; I dunnut want ye to do nought."

"But I must do something. Let me have them."

She consented; and she even brought me a clean towel to spread over my dress, "lest," as she said, "I should mucky it."

"Ye've not been used to sarvant's wark, I see by your hands," she remarked. "Happen ye've been a dressmaker?"

"No, you are wrong. And now, never mind what I have been: don't trouble your head further about me; but tell me the name of the house where we are."

"Some calls it Marsh End, and some calls it Moor House."

"And the gentleman who lives here is called Mr. St. John?"

"Nay; he doesn't live here: he is only staying a while. When he is at home, he is in his own parish at Morton."

"That village a few miles off?

"Aye."

"And what is he?"

"He is a parson."

I remembered the answer of the old housekeeper at the parsonage, when I had asked to see the clergyman. "This, then, was his father's residence?"

"Aye; old Mr. Rivers lived here, and his father, and grandfather, and gurt (great) grandfather afore him."

"The name, then, of that gentleman, is Mr. St. John Rivers?"

"Aye; St. John is like his kirstened name."

"And his sisters are called Diana and Mary Rivers?"

"Yes."

"Their father is dead?"

"Dead three weeks sin' of a stroke."

"They have no mother?"

"The mistress has been dead this mony a year."

"Have you lived with the family long?"

"I've lived here thirty year. I nursed them all three."

"That proves you must have been an honest and faithful servant. I will say so much for you, though you have had the incivility to call me a beggar."

She again regarded me with a surprised stare. "I believe," she said, "I was quite mista'en in my thoughts of you: but there is so mony cheats goes about, you mun forgie me."

"And though," I continued, rather severely, "you wished to turn me from the door, on a night when you should not have shut out a dog."

"Well, it was hard: but what can a body do? I thought more o' th' childer nor of mysel: poor things! They've like nobody to tak' care on 'em but me. I'm like to look sharpish."

I maintained a grave silence for some minutes.

"You munnut think too hardly of me," she again remarked.

"But I do think hardly of you," I said; "and I'll tell you why—not so much because you refused to give me shelter, or regarded me as an impostor, as because you just now made it a species of reproach that I had no 'brass' and no house. Some of the best people that ever lived have been as destitute as I am; and if you are a Christian, you ought not to consider poverty a crime."

"No more I ought," said she: "Mr. St. John tells me so too; and I see I wor wrang—but I've clear a different notion on you now to what I had. You look a raight down dacent little crater."

"That will do—I forgive you now. Shake hands."

She put her floury and horny hand into mine; another and heartier smile illumined her rough face, and from that moment we were friends.

Hannah was evidently fond of talking. While I picked the fruit, and she made the paste for the pies, she proceeded to give me sundry details about her deceased master and mistress, and "the childer," as she called the young people.

Old Mr. Rivers, she said, was a plain man enough, but a gentleman, and of as ancient a family as could be found. Marsh End had belonged to the Rivers ever since it was a house: and it was, she affirmed, "aboon two hundred year old—for all it looked but a small, humble place, naught to compare wi' Mr. Oliver's grand hall down i' Morton Vale. But she could remember Bill Oliver's father a journeyman needlemaker; and th' Rivers wor gentry i' th' owd days o' th' Henrys, as onybody might see by looking into th' registers i' Morton Church vestry." Still, she allowed, "the owd maister was like other folk—naught mich out o' t' common way: stark mad o' shooting, and farming, and sich like." The mistress was different. She was a great reader, and studied a deal; and the "bairns" had taken after her. There was nothing like them in these parts, nor ever had been; they had liked learning, all three, almost from the time they could speak; and they had always been "of a mak' of their own." Mr. St. John, when he grew up, would go to college and be a parson; and the girls, as soon as they left school, would seek places as governesses: for they had told her their father had some years ago lost a great deal of money by a man he had trusted turning bankrupt; and as he was now not rich enough to give them fortunes, they must provide for themselves. They had lived very little at home for a long while, and were only come now to stay a few weeks on account of their father's death; but they did so like Marsh End and Morton, and all these moors and hills about. They had been in London, and many other grand towns; but they always said there was no place like home; and then they were so agreeable with each other—never fell out nor "threaped." She did not know where there was such a family for being united.

Having finished my task of gooseberry picking, I asked where the two ladies and their brother were now.

"Gone over to Morton for a walk; but they would be back in half-an-hour to tea."

They returned within the time Hannah had allotted them: they entered by the kitchen door. Mr. St. John, when he saw me, merely bowed and passed through; the two ladies stopped: Mary, in a few words, kindly and calmly expressed the pleasure she felt in seeing me well enough to be able to come down; Diana took my hand: she shook her head at me.

"You should have waited for my leave to descend," she said. "You still look very pale—and so thin! Poor child!—poor girl!"

Diana had a voice toned, to my ear, like the cooing of a dove. She possessed eyes whose gaze I delighted to encounter. Her whole face seemed to me fill of charm. Mary's countenance was equally intelligent—her features equally pretty; but her expression was more reserved, and her manners, though gentle, more distant. Diana looked and spoke with a certain authority: she had a will, evidently. It was my nature to feel pleasure in yielding to an authority supported like hers, and to bend, where my conscience and self-respect permitted, to an active will.

"And what business have you here?" she continued. "It is not your place. Mary and I sit in the kitchen sometimes, because at home we like to be free, even to license—but you are a visitor, and must go into the parlour."

"I am very well here."

"Not at all, with Hannah bustling about and covering you with flour."

"Besides, the fire is too hot for you," interposed Mary.

"To be sure," added her sister. "Come, you must be obedient." And still holding my hand she made me rise, and led me into the inner room.

"Sit there," she said, placing me on the sofa, "while we take our things off and get the tea ready; it is another privilege we exercise in our little moorland home—to prepare our own meals when we are so inclined, or when Hannah is baking, brewing, washing, or ironing."

She closed the door, leaving me solus with Mr. St. John, who sat opposite, a book or newspaper in his hand. I examined first, the parlour, and then its occupant.

The parlour was rather a small room, very plainly furnished, yet comfortable, because clean and neat. The old-fashioned chairs were very bright, and the walnut-wood table was like a looking-glass. A few strange, antique portraits of the men and women of other days decorated the stained walls; a cupboard with glass doors contained some books and an ancient set of china. There was no superfluous ornament in the room—not one modern piece of furniture, save a brace of workboxes and a lady's desk in rosewood, which stood on a side-table: everything—including the carpet and curtains—looked at once well worn and well saved.

Mr. St. John—sitting as still as one of the dusty pictures on the walls, keeping his eyes fixed on the page he perused, and his lips mutely sealed—was easy enough to examine. Had he been a statue instead of a man, he could not have been easier. He was young—perhaps from twenty-eight to thirty—tall, slender; his face riveted the eye; it was like a Greek face, very pure in outline: quite a straight, classic nose; quite an Athenian mouth and chin. It is seldom, indeed, an English face comes so near the antique models as did his. He might well be a little shocked at the irregularity of my lineaments, his own being so harmonious. His eyes were large and blue, with brown lashes; his high forehead, colourless as ivory, was partially streaked over by careless locks of fair hair.

This is a gentle delineation, is it not, reader? Yet he whom it describes scarcely impressed one with the idea of a gentle, a yielding, an impressible, or even of a placid nature. Quiescent as he now sat, there was something about his nostril, his mouth, his brow, which, to my perceptions, indicated elements within either restless, or hard, or eager. He did not speak to me one word, nor even direct to me one glance, till his sisters returned. Diana, as she passed in and out, in the course of preparing tea, brought me a little cake, baked on the top of the oven.

"Eat that now," she said: "you must be hungry. Hannah says you have had nothing but some gruel since breakfast."

I did not refuse it, for my appetite was awakened and keen. Mr. Rivers now closed his book, approached the table, and, as he took a seat, fixed his blue pictorial-looking eyes full on me. There was an unceremonious directness, a searching, decided steadfastness in his gaze now, which told that intention, and not diffidence, had hitherto kept it averted from the stranger.

"You are very hungry," he said.

"I am, sir." It is my way—it always was my way, by instinct—ever to meet the brief with brevity, the direct with plainness.

"It is well for you that a low fever has forced you to abstain for the last three days: there would have been danger in yielding to the cravings of your appetite at first. Now you may eat, though still not immoderately."

"I trust I shall not eat long at your expense, sir," was my very clumsily-contrived, unpolished answer.

"No," he said coolly: "when you have indicated to us the residence of your friends, we can write to them, and you may be restored to home."

"That, I must plainly tell you, is out of my power to do; being absolutely without home and friends."

The three looked at me, but not distrustfully; I felt there was no suspicion in their glances: there was more of curiosity. I speak particularly of the young ladies. St. John's eyes, though clear enough in a literal sense, in a figurative one were difficult to fathom. He seemed to use them rather as instruments to search other people's thoughts, than as agents to reveal his own: the which combination of keenness and reserve was considerably more calculated to embarrass than to encourage.

"Do you mean to say," he asked, "that you are completely isolated from every connection?"

"I do. Not a tie links me to any living thing: not a claim do I possess to admittance under any roof in England."

"A most singular position at your age!"

Here I saw his glance directed to my hands, which were folded on the table before me. I wondered what he sought there: his words soon explained the quest.

"You have never been married? You are a spinster?"

Diana laughed. "Why, she can't he above seventeen or eighteen years old, St. John," said she.

"I am near nineteen: but I am not married. No."

I felt a burning glow mount to my face; for bitter and agitating recollections were awakened by the allusion to marriage. They all saw the embarrassment and the emotion. Diana and Mary relieved me by turning their eyes elsewhere than to my crimsoned visage; but the colder and sterner brother continued to gaze, till the trouble he had excited forced out tears as well as colour.

"Where did you last reside?" he now asked.

"You are too inquisitive, St. John," murmured Mary in a low voice; but he leaned over the table and required an answer by a second firm and piercing look.

"The name of the place where, and of the person with whom I lived, is my secret," I replied concisely.

"Which, if you like, you have, in my opinion, a right to keep, both from St. John and every other questioner," remarked Diana.

"Yet if I know nothing about you or your history, I cannot help you," he said. "And you need help, do you not?"

"I need it, and I seek it so far, sir, that some true philanthropist will put me in the way of getting work which I can do, and the remuneration for which will keep me, if but in the barest necessaries of life."

"I know not whether I am a true philanthropist; yet I am willing to aid you to the utmost of my power in a purpose so honest. First, then, tell me what you have been accustomed to do, and what you CAN do."

I had now swallowed my tea. I was mightily refreshed by the beverage; as much so as a giant with wine: it gave new tone to my unstrung nerves, and enabled me to address this penetrating young judge steadily.

"Mr. Rivers," I said, turning to him, and looking at him, as he looked at me, openly and without diffidence, "you and your sisters have done me a great service—the greatest man can do his fellow-being; you have rescued me, by your noble hospitality, from death. This benefit conferred gives you an unlimited claim on my gratitude, and a claim, to a certain extent, on my confidence. I will tell you as much of the history of the wanderer you have harboured, as I can tell without compromising my own peace of mind—my own security, moral and physical, and that of others.

"I am an orphan, the daughter of a clergyman. My parents died before I could know them. I was brought up a dependant; educated in a charitable institution. I will even tell you the name of the establishment, where I passed six years as a pupil, and two as a teacher—Lowood Orphan Asylum,——shire: you will have heard of it, Mr. Rivers?—the Rev. Robert Brocklehurst is the treasurer."

"I have heard of Mr. Brocklehurst, and I have seen the school."

"I left Lowood nearly a year since to become a private governess. I obtained a good situation, and was happy. This place I was obliged to leave four days before I came here. The reason of my departure I cannot and ought not to explain: it would be useless, dangerous, and would sound incredible. No blame attached to me: I am as free from culpability as any one of you three. Miserable I am, and must be for a time; for the catastrophe which drove me from a house I had found a paradise was of a strange and direful nature. I observed but two points in planning my departure—speed, secrecy: to secure these, I had to leave behind me everything I possessed except a small parcel; which, in my hurry and trouble of mind, I forgot to take out of the coach that brought me to Whitcross. To this neighbourhood, then, I came, quite destitute. I slept two nights in the open air, and wandered about two days without crossing a threshold: but twice in that space of time did I taste food; and it was when brought by hunger, exhaustion, and despair almost to the last gasp, that you, Mr. Rivers, forbade me to perish of want at your door, and took me under the shelter of your roof. I know all your sisters have done for me since—for I have not been insensible during my seeming torpor—and I owe to their spontaneous, genuine, genial compassion as large a debt as to your evangelical charity."

"Don't make her talk any more now, St. John," said Diana, as I paused; "she is evidently not yet fit for excitement. Come to the sofa and sit down now, Miss Elliott."

I gave an involuntary half start at hearing the alias: I had forgotten my new name. Mr. Rivers, whom nothing seemed to escape, noticed it at once.

"You said your name was Jane Elliott?" he observed.

"I did say so; and it is the name by which I think it expedient to be called at present, but it is not my real name, and when I hear it, it sounds strange to me."

"Your real name you will not give?"

"No: I fear discovery above all things; and whatever disclosure would lead to it, I avoid."

"You are quite right, I am sure," said Diana. "Now do, brother, let her be at peace a while."

But when St. John had mused a few moments he recommenced as imperturbably and with as much acumen as ever.

"You would not like to be long dependent on our hospitality—you would wish, I see, to dispense as soon as may be with my sisters' compassion, and, above all, with my CHARITY (I am quite sensible of the distinction drawn, nor do I resent it—it is just): you desire to be independent of us?"

"I do: I have already said so. Show me how to work, or how to seek work: that is all I now ask; then let me go, if it be but to the meanest cottage; but till then, allow me to stay here: I dread another essay of the horrors of homeless destitution."

"Indeed you SHALL stay here," said Diana, putting her white hand on my head. "You SHALL," repeated Mary, in the tone of undemonstrative sincerity which seemed natural to her.

"My sisters, you see, have a pleasure in keeping you," said Mr. St. John, "as they would have a pleasure in keeping and cherishing a half-frozen bird, some wintry wind might have driven through their casement. I feel more inclination to put you in the way of keeping yourself, and shall endeavour to do so; but observe, my sphere is narrow. I am but the incumbent of a poor country parish: my aid must be of the humblest sort. And if you are inclined to despise the day of small things, seek some more efficient succour than such as I can offer."

"She has already said that she is willing to do anything honest she can do," answered Diana for me; "and you know, St. John, she has no choice of helpers: she is forced to put up with such crusty people as you."

"I will be a dressmaker; I will be a plain-workwoman; I will be a servant, a nurse-girl, if I can be no better," I answered.

"Right," said Mr. St. John, quite coolly. "If such is your spirit, I promise to aid you, in my own time and way."

He now resumed the book with which he had been occupied before tea. I soon withdrew, for I had talked as much, and sat up as long, as my present strength would permit.

Chapter XXX

The more I knew of the inmates of Moor House, the better I liked them. In a few days I had so far recovered my health that I could sit up all day, and walk out sometimes. I could join with Diana and Mary in all their occupations; converse with them as much as they wished, and aid them when and where they would allow me. There was a reviving pleasure in this intercourse, of a kind now tasted by me for the first time-the pleasure arising from perfect congeniality of tastes, sentiments, and principles.

I liked to read what they liked to read: what they enjoyed, delighted me; what they approved, I reverenced. They loved their sequestered home. I, too, in the grey, small, antique structure, with its low roof, its latticed casements, its mouldering walls, its avenue of aged firs—all grown aslant under the stress of mountain winds; its garden, dark with yew and holly—and where no flowers but of the hardiest species would bloom—found a charm both potent and permanent. They clung to the purple moors behind and around their dwelling—to the hollow vale into which the pebbly bridle-path leading from their gate descended, and which wound between fern-banks first, and then amongst a few of the wildest little pasture-fields that ever bordered a wilderness of heath, or gave sustenance to a flock of grey moorland sheep, with their little mossy-faced lambs:-they clung to this scene, I say, with a perfect enthusiasm of attachment. I could comprehend the feeling, and share both its strength and truth. I saw the fascination of the locality. I felt the consecration of its loneliness: my eye feasted on the outline of swell and sweep—on the wild colouring communicated to ridge and dell by moss, by heath-bell, by flower-sprinkled turf, by brilliant bracken, and mellow granite crag. These details were just to me what they were to them—so many pure and sweet sources of pleasure. The strong blast and the soft breeze; the rough and the halcyon day; the hours of sunrise and sunset; the moonlight and the clouded night, developed for me, in these regions, the same attraction as for them—wound round my faculties the same spell that entranced theirs.

Indoors we agreed equally well. They were both more accomplished and better read than I was; but with eagerness I followed in the path of knowledge they had trodden before me. I devoured the books they lent me: then it was full satisfaction to discuss with them in the evening what I had perused during the day. Thought fitted thought; opinion met opinion: we coincided, in short, perfectly.

If in our trio there was a superior and a leader, it was Diana. Physically, she far excelled me: she was handsome; she was vigorous. In her animal spirits there was an affluence of life and certainty of flow, such as excited my wonder, while it baffled my comprehension. I could talk a while when the evening commenced, but the first gush of vivacity and fluency gone, I was fain to sit on a stool at Diana's feet, to rest my head on her knee, and listen alternately to her and Mary, while they sounded thoroughly the topic on which I had but touched. Diana offered to teach me German. I liked to learn of her: I saw the part of instructress pleased and suited her; that of scholar pleased and suited me no less. Our natures dovetailed: mutual affection—of the strongest kind—was the result. They discovered I could draw: their pencils and colour-boxes were immediately at my service. My skill, greater in this one point than theirs, surprised and charmed them. Mary would sit and watch me by the hour together: then she would take lessons; and a docile, intelligent, assiduous pupil she made. Thus occupied, and mutually entertained, days passed like hours, and weeks like days.

As to Mr. St John, the intimacy which had arisen so naturally and rapidly between me and his sisters did not extend to him. One reason of the distance yet observed between us was, that he was comparatively seldom at home: a large proportion of his time appeared devoted to visiting the sick and poor among the scattered population of his parish.

No weather seemed to hinder him in these pastoral excursions: rain or fair, he would, when his hours of morning study were over, take his hat, and, followed by his father's old pointer, Carlo, go out on his mission of love or duty—I scarcely know in which light he regarded it. Sometimes, when the day was very unfavourable, his sisters would expostulate. He would then say, with a peculiar smile, more solemn than cheerful—

"And if I let a gust of wind or a sprinkling of rain turn me aside from these easy tasks, what preparation would such sloth be for the future I propose to myself?"

Diana and Mary's general answer to this question was a sigh, and some minutes of apparently mournful meditation.

But besides his frequent absences, there was another barrier to friendship with him: he seemed of a reserved, an abstracted, and even of a brooding nature. Zealous in his ministerial labours, blameless in his life and habits, he yet did not appear to enjoy that mental serenity, that inward content, which should bet he reward of every sincere Christian and practical philanthropist. Often, of an evening, when he sat at the window, his desk and papers before him, he would cease reading or writing, rest his chin on his hand, and deliver himself up to I know not what course of thought; but that it was perturbed and exciting might be seen in the frequent flash and changeful dilation of his eye.

I think, moreover, that Nature was not to him that treasury of delight it was to his sisters. He expressed once, and but once in my hearing, a strong sense of the rugged charm of the hills, and an inborn affection for the dark roof and hoary walls he called his home; but there was more of gloom than pleasure in the tone and words in which the sentiment was manifested; and never did he seem to roam the moors for the sake of their soothing silence—never seek out or dwell upon the thousand peaceful delights they could yield.

Incommunicative as he was, some time elapsed before I had an opportunity of gauging his mind. I first got an idea of its calibre when I heard him preach in his own church at Morton. I wish I could describe that sermon: but it is past my power. I cannot even render faithfully the effect it produced on me.

It began calm—and indeed, as far as delivery and pitch of voice went, it was calm to the end: an earnestly felt, yet strictly restrained zeal breathed soon in the distinct accents, and prompted the nervous language. This grew to force—compressed, condensed, controlled. The heart was thrilled, the mind astonished, by the power of the preacher: neither were softened. Throughout there was a strange bitterness; an absence of consolatory gentleness; stern allusions to Calvinistic doctrines—election, predestination, reprobation—were frequent; and each reference to these points sounded like a sentence pronounced for doom. When he had done, instead of feeling better, calmer, more enlightened by his discourse, I experienced an inexpressible sadness; for it seemed to me—I know not whether equally so to others—that the eloquence to which I had been listening had sprung from a depth where lay turbid dregs of disappointment—where moved troubling impulses of insatiate yearnings and disquieting aspirations. I was sure St. John Rivers—pure-lived, conscientious, zealous as he was—had not yet found that peace of God which passeth all understanding: he had no more found it, I thought, than had I with my concealed and racking regrets for my broken idol and lost elysium—regrets to which I have latterly avoided referring, but which possessed me and tyrannised over me ruthlessly.

Meantime a month was gone. Diana and Mary were soon to leave Moor House, and return to the far different life and scene which awaited them, as governesses in a large, fashionable, south-of-England city, where each held a situation in families by whose wealthy and haughty members they were regarded only as humble dependants, and who neither knew nor sought out their innate excellences, and appreciated only their acquired accomplishments as they appreciated the skill of their cook or the taste of their waiting-woman. Mr. St. John had said nothing to me yet about the employment he had promised to obtain for me; yet it became urgent that I should have a vocation of some kind. One morning, being left alone with him a few minutes in the parlour, I ventured to approach the window-recess—which his table, chair, and desk consecrated as a kind of study—and I was going to speak, though not very well knowing in what words to frame my inquiry—for it is at all times difficult to break the ice of reserve glassing over such natures as his—when he saved me the trouble by being the first to commence a dialogue.

Looking up as I drew near—"You have a question to ask of me?" he said.

"Yes; I wish to know whether you have heard of any service I can offer myself to undertake?"

"I found or devised something for you three weeks ago; but as you seemed both useful and happy here—as my sisters had evidently become attached to you, and your society gave them unusual pleasure—I deemed it inexpedient to break in on your mutual comfort till their approaching departure from Marsh End should render yours necessary."

"And they will go in three days now?" I said.

"Yes; and when they go, I shall return to the parsonage at Morton: Hannah will accompany me; and this old house will be shut up."

I waited a few moments, expecting he would go on with the subject first broached: but he seemed to have entered another train of reflection: his look denoted abstraction from me and my business. I was obliged to recall him to a theme which was of necessity one of close and anxious interest to me.

"What is the employment you had in view, Mr. Rivers? I hope this delay will not have increased the difficulty of securing it."

"Oh, no; since it is in employment which depends only on me to give, and you to accept."

He again paused: there seemed a reluctance to continue. I grew impatient: a restless movement or two, and an eager and exacting glance fastened on his face, conveyed the feeling to him as effectually as words could have done, and with less trouble.

"You need be in no hurry to hear," he said: "let me frankly tell you, I have nothing eligible or profitable to suggest. Before I explain, recall, if you please, my notice, clearly given, that if I helped you, it must be as the blind man would help the lame. I am poor; for I find that, when I have paid my father's debts, all the patrimony remaining to me will be this crumbling grange, the row of scathed firs behind, and the patch of moorish soil, with the yew-trees and holly-bushes in front. I am obscure: Rivers is an old name; but of the three sole descendants of the race, two earn the dependant's crust among strangers, and the third considers himself an alien from his native country—not only for life, but in death. Yes, and deems, and is bound to deem, himself honoured by the lot, and aspires but after the day when the cross of separation from fleshly ties shall be laid on his shoulders, and when the Head of that church-militant of whose humblest members he is one, shall give the word, 'Rise, follow Me!'"

St. John said these words as he pronounced his sermons, with a quiet, deep voice; with an unflushed cheek, and a coruscating radiance of glance. He resumed—

"And since I am myself poor and obscure, I can offer you but a service of poverty and obscurity. YOU may even think it degrading—for I see now your habits have been what the world calls refined: your tastes lean to the ideal, and your society has at least been amongst the educated; but I consider that no service degrades which can better our race. I hold that the more arid and unreclaimed the soil where the Christian labourer's task of tillage is appointed him—the scantier the meed his toil brings—the higher the honour. His, under such circumstances, is the destiny of the pioneer; and the first pioneers of the Gospel were the Apostles—their captain was Jesus, the Redeemer, Himself."

"Well?" I said, as he again paused—"proceed."

He looked at me before he proceeded: indeed, he seemed leisurely to read my face, as if its features and lines were characters on a page. The conclusions drawn from this scrutiny he partially expressed in his succeeding observations.

"I believe you will accept the post I offer you," said he, "and hold it for a while: not permanently, though: any more than I could permanently keep the narrow and narrowing—the tranquil, hidden office of English country incumbent; for in your nature is an alloy as detrimental to repose as that in mine, though of a different kind."

"Do explain," I urged, when he halted once more.

"I will; and you shall hear how poor the proposal is,—how trivial—how cramping. I shall not stay long at Morton, now that my father is dead, and that I am my own master. I shall leave the place probably in the course of a twelve-month; but while I do stay, I will exert myself to the utmost for its improvement. Morton, when I came to it two years ago, had no school: the children of the poor were excluded from every hope of progress. I established one for boys: I mean now to open a second school for girls. I have hired a building for the purpose, with a cottage of two rooms attached to it for the mistress's house. Her salary will be thirty pounds a year: her house is already furnished, very simply, but sufficiently, by the kindness of a lady, Miss Oliver; the only daughter of the sole rich man in my parish—Mr. Oliver, the proprietor of a needle-factory and iron-foundry in the valley. The same lady pays for the education and clothing of an orphan from the workhouse, on condition that she shall aid the mistress in such menial offices connected with her own house and the school as her occupation of teaching will prevent her having time to discharge in person. Will you be this mistress?"

He put the question rather hurriedly; he seemed half to expect an indignant, or at least a disdainful rejection of the offer: not knowing all my thoughts and feelings, though guessing some, he could not tell in what light the lot would appear to me. In truth it was humble—but then it was sheltered, and I wanted a safe asylum: it was plodding—but then, compared with that of a governess in a rich house, it was independent; and the fear of servitude with strangers entered my soul like iron: it was not ignoble—not unworthy—not mentally degrading, I made my decision.

"I thank you for the proposal, Mr. Rivers, and I accept it with all my heart."

"But you comprehend me?" he said. "It is a village school: your scholars will be only poor girls—cottagers' children—at the best, farmers' daughters. Knitting, sewing, reading, writing, ciphering, will be all you will have to teach. What will you do with your accomplishments? What, with the largest portion of your mind—sentiments—tastes?"

"Save them till they are wanted. They will keep."

"You know what you undertake, then?"

"I do."

He now smiled: and not a bitter or a sad smile, but one well pleased and deeply gratified.

"And when will you commence the exercise of your function?"

"I will go to my house to-morrow, and open the school, if you like, next week."

"Very well: so be it."

He rose and walked through the room. Standing still, he again looked at me. He shook his head.

"What do you disapprove of, Mr. Rivers?" I asked.

"You will not stay at Morton long: no, no!"

"Why? What is your reason for saying so?"

"I read it in your eye; it is not of that description which promises the maintenance of an even tenor in life."

"I am not ambitious."

He started at the word "ambitious." He repeated, "No. What made you think of ambition? Who is ambitious? I know I am: but how did you find it out?"

"I was speaking of myself."

"Well, if you are not ambitious, you are—" He paused.

"What?"

"I was going to say, impassioned: but perhaps you would have misunderstood the word, and been displeased. I mean, that human affections and sympathies have a most powerful hold on you. I am sure you cannot long be content to pass your leisure in solitude, and to devote your working hours to a monotonous labour wholly void of stimulus: any more than I can be content," he added, with emphasis, "to live here buried in morass, pent in with mountains—my nature, that God gave me, contravened; my faculties, heaven-bestowed, paralysed—made useless. You hear now how I contradict myself. I, who preached contentment with a humble lot, and justified the vocation even of hewers of wood and drawers of water in God's service—I, His ordained minister, almost rave in my restlessness. Well, propensities and principles must be reconciled by some means."

He left the room. In this brief hour I had learnt more of him than in the whole previous month: yet still he puzzled me.

Diana and Mary Rivers became more sad and silent as the day approached for leaving their brother and their home. They both tried to appear as usual; bat the sorrow they had to struggle against was one that could not be entirely conquered or concealed. Diana intimated that this would be a different parting from any they had ever yet known. It would probably, as far as St. John was concerned, be a parting for years: it might be a parting for life.

"He will sacrifice all to his long-framed resolves," she said: "natural affection and feelings more potent still. St. John looks quiet, Jane; but he hides a fever in his vitals. You would think him gentle, yet in some things he is inexorable as death; and the worst of it is, my conscience will hardly permit me to dissuade him from his severe decision: certainly, I cannot for a moment blame him for it. It is right, noble, Christian: yet it breaks my heart!" And the tears gushed to her fine eyes. Mary bent her head low over her work.

"We are now without father: we shall soon be without home and brother," she murmured,

At that moment a little accident supervened, which seemed decreed by fate purposely to prove the truth of the adage, that "misfortunes never come singly," and to add to their distresses the vexing one of the slip between the cup and the lip. St. John passed the window reading a letter. He entered.

"Our uncle John is dead," said he.

Both the sisters seemed struck: not shocked or appalled; the tidings appeared in their eyes rather momentous than afflicting.

"Dead?" repeated Diana.

"Yes."

She riveted a searching gaze on her brother's face. "And what then?" she demanded, in a low voice.

"What then, Die?" he replied, maintaining a marble immobility of feature. "What then? Why—nothing. Read."

He threw the letter into her lap. She glanced over it, and handed it to Mary. Mary perused it in silence, and returned it to her brother. All three looked at each other, and all three smiled—a dreary, pensive smile enough.

"Amen! We can yet live," said Diana at last.

"At any rate, it makes us no worse off than we were before," remarked Mary.

"Only it forces rather strongly on the mind the picture of what MIGHT HAVE BEEN," said Mr. Rivers, "and contrasts it somewhat too vividly with what IS."

He folded the letter, locked it in his desk, and again went out.

For some minutes no one spoke. Diana then turned to me.

"Jane, you will wonder at us and our mysteries," she said, "and think us hard-hearted beings not to be more moved at the death of so near a relation as an uncle; but we have never seen him or known him. He was my mother's brother. My father and he quarrelled long ago. It was by his advice that my father risked most of his property in the speculation that ruined him. Mutual recrimination passed between them: they parted in anger, and were never reconciled. My uncle engaged afterwards in more prosperous undertakings: it appears he realised a fortune of twenty thousand pounds. He was never married, and had no near kindred but ourselves and one other person, not more closely related than we. My father always cherished the idea that he would atone for his error by leaving his possessions to us; that letter informs us that he has bequeathed every penny to the other relation, with the exception of thirty guineas, to be divided between St. John, Diana, and Mary Rivers, for the purchase of three mourning rings. He had a right, of course, to do as he pleased: and yet a momentary damp is cast on the spirits by the receipt of such news. Mary and I would have esteemed ourselves rich with a thousand pounds each; and to St. John such a sum would have been valuable, for the good it would have enabled him to do."

This explanation given, the subject was dropped, and no further reference made to it by either Mr. Rivers or his sisters. The next day I left Marsh End for Morton. The day after, Diana and Mary quitted it for distant B-. In a week, Mr. Rivers and Hannah repaired to the parsonage: and so the old grange was abandoned.

Chapter XXXI

My home, then, when I at last find a home,—is a cottage; a little room with whitewashed walls and a sanded floor, containing four painted chairs and a table, a clock, a cupboard, with two or three plates and dishes, and a set of tea-things in delf. Above, a chamber of the same dimensions as the kitchen, with a deal bedstead and chest of drawers; small, yet too large to be filled with my scanty wardrobe: though the kindness of my gentle and generous friends has increased that, by a modest stock of such things as are necessary.

It is evening. I have dismissed, with the fee of an orange, the little orphan who serves me as a handmaid. I am sitting alone on the hearth. This morning, the village school opened. I had twenty scholars. But three of the number can read: none write or cipher. Several knit, and a few sew a little. They speak with the broadest accent of the district. At present, they and I have a difficulty in understanding each other's language. Some of them are unmannered, rough, intractable, as well as ignorant; but others are docile, have a wish to learn, and evince a disposition that pleases me. I must not forget that these coarsely-clad little peasants are of flesh and blood as good as the scions of gentlest genealogy; and that the germs of native excellence, refinement, intelligence, kind feeling, are as likely to exist in their hearts as in those of the best-born. My duty will be to develop these germs: surely I shall find some happiness in discharging that office. Much enjoyment I do not expect in the life opening before me: yet it will, doubtless, if I regulate my mind, and exert my powers as I ought, yield me enough to live on from day to day.

Was I very gleeful, settled, content, during the hours I passed in yonder bare, humble schoolroom this morning and afternoon? Not to deceive myself, I must reply—No: I felt desolate to a degree. I felt—yes, idiot that I am—I felt degraded. I doubted I had taken a step which sank instead of raising me in the scale of social existence. I was weakly dismayed at the ignorance, the poverty, the coarseness of all I heard and saw round me. But let me not hate and despise myself too much for these feelings; I know them to be wrong—that is a great step gained; I shall strive to overcome them. To-morrow, I trust, I shall get the better of them partially; and in a few weeks, perhaps, they will be quite subdued. In a few months, it is possible, the happiness of seeing progress, and a change for the better in my scholars may substitute gratification for disgust.

Meantime, let me ask myself one question—Which is better?—To have surrendered to temptation; listened to passion; made no painful effort—no struggle;—but to have sunk down in the silken snare; fallen asleep on the flowers covering it; wakened in a southern clime, amongst the luxuries of a pleasure villa: to have been now living in France, Mr. Rochester's mistress; delirious with his love half my time—for he would—oh, yes, he would have loved me well for a while. He DID love me—no one will ever love me so again. I shall never more know the sweet homage given to beauty, youth, and grace—for never to any one else shall I seem to possess these charms. He was fond and proud of me—it is what no man besides will ever be.—But where am I wandering, and what am I saying, and above all, feeling? Whether is it better, I ask, to be a slave in a fool's paradise at Marseilles—fevered with delusive bliss one hour—suffocating with the bitterest tears of remorse and shame the next—or to be a village-schoolmistress, free and honest, in a breezy mountain nook in the healthy heart of England?

Yes; I feel now that I was right when I adhered to principle and law, and scorned and crushed the insane promptings of a frenzied moment. God directed me to a correct choice: I thank His providence for the guidance!

Having brought my eventide musings to this point, I rose, went to my door, and looked at the sunset of the harvest-day, and at the quiet fields before my cottage, which, with the school, was distant half a mile from the village. The birds were singing their last strains—

"The air was mild, the dew was balm."

While I looked, I thought myself happy, and was surprised to find myself ere long weeping—and why? For the doom which had reft me from adhesion to my master: for him I was no more to see; for the desperate grief and fatal fury—consequences of my departure—which might now, perhaps, be dragging him from the path of right, too far to leave hope of ultimate restoration thither. At this thought, I turned my face aside from the lovely sky of eve and lonely vale of Morton—I say LONELY, for in that bend of it visible to me there was no building apparent save the church and the parsonage, half-hid in trees, and, quite at the extremity, the roof of Vale Hall, where the rich Mr. Oliver and his daughter lived. I hid my eyes, and leant my head against the stone frame of my door; but soon a slight noise near the wicket which shut in my tiny garden from the meadow beyond it made me look up. A dog—old Carlo, Mr. Rivers' pointer, as I saw in a moment—was pushing the gate with his nose, and St. John himself leant upon it with folded arms; his brow knit, his gaze, grave almost to displeasure, fixed on me. I asked him to come in.

"No, I cannot stay; I have only brought you a little parcel my sisters left for you. I think it contains a colour-box, pencils, and paper."

I approached to take it: a welcome gift it was. He examined my face, I thought, with austerity, as I came near: the traces of tears were doubtless very visible upon it.

"Have you found your first day's work harder than you expected?" he asked.

"Oh, no! On the contrary, I think in time I shall get on with my scholars very well."

"But perhaps your accommodations—your cottage—your furniture—have disappointed your expectations? They are, in truth, scanty enough; but——" I interrupted—

"My cottage is clean and weather-proof; my furniture sufficient and commodious. All I see has made me thankful, not despondent. I am not absolutely such a fool and sensualist as to regret the absence of a carpet, a sofa, and silver plate; besides, five weeks ago I had nothing—I was an outcast, a beggar, a vagrant; now I have acquaintance, a home, a business. I wonder at the goodness of God; the generosity of my friends; the bounty of my lot. I do not repine."

"But you feel solitude an oppression? The little house there behind you is dark and empty."

"I have hardly had time yet to enjoy a sense of tranquillity, much less to grow impatient under one of loneliness."

"Very well; I hope you feel the content you express: at any rate, your good sense will tell you that it is too soon yet to yield to the vacillating fears of Lot's wife. What you had left before I saw you, of course I do not know; but I counsel you to resist firmly every temptation which would incline you to look back: pursue your present career steadily, for some months at least."

"It is what I mean to do," I answered. St. John continued—

"It is hard work to control the workings of inclination and turn the bent of nature; but that it may be done, I know from experience. God has given us, in a measure, the power to make our own fate; and when our energies seem to demand a sustenance they cannot get—when our will strains after a path we may not follow—we need neither starve from inanition, nor stand still in despair: we have but to seek another nourishment for the mind, as strong as the forbidden food it longed to taste—and perhaps purer; and to hew out for the adventurous foot a road as direct and broad as the one Fortune has blocked up against us, if rougher than it.

"A year ago I was myself intensely miserable, because I thought I had made a mistake in entering the ministry: its uniform duties wearied me to death. I burnt for the more active life of the world—for the more exciting toils of a literary career—for the destiny of an artist, author, orator; anything rather than that of a priest: yes, the heart of a politician, of a soldier, of a votary of glory, a lover of renown, a luster after power, beat under my curate's surplice. I considered; my life was so wretched, it must be changed, or I must die. After a season of darkness and struggling, light broke and relief fell: my cramped existence all at once spread out to a plain without bounds—my powers heard a call from heaven to rise, gather their full strength, spread their wings, and mount beyond ken. God had an errand for me; to bear which afar, to deliver it well, skill and strength, courage and eloquence, the best qualifications of soldier, statesman, and orator, were all needed: for these all centre in the good missionary.

"A missionary I resolved to be. From that moment my state of mind changed; the fetters dissolved and dropped from every faculty, leaving nothing of bondage but its galling soreness—which time only can heal. My father, indeed, imposed the determination, but since his death, I have not a legitimate obstacle to contend with; some affairs settled, a successor for Morton provided, an entanglement or two of the feelings broken through or cut asunder—a last conflict with human weakness, in which I know I shall overcome, because I have vowed that I WILL overcome—and I leave Europe for the East."

He said this, in his peculiar, subdued, yet emphatic voice; looking, when he had ceased speaking, not at me, but at the setting sun, at which I looked too. Both he and I had our backs towards the path leading up the field to the wicket. We had heard no step on that grass-grown track; the water running in the vale was the one lulling sound of the hour and scene; we might well then start when a gay voice, sweet as a silver bell, exclaimed—

"Good evening, Mr. Rivers. And good evening, old Carlo. Your dog is quicker to recognise his friends than you are, sir; he pricked his ears and wagged his tail when I was at the bottom of the field, and you have your back towards me now."

It was true. Though Mr. Rivers had started at the first of those musical accents, as if a thunderbolt had split a cloud over his head, he stood yet, at the close of the sentence, in the same attitude in which the speaker had surprised him—his arm resting on the gate, his face directed towards the west. He turned at last, with measured deliberation. A vision, as it seemed to me, had risen at his side. There appeared, within three feet of him, a form clad in pure white—a youthful, graceful form: full, yet fine in contour; and when, after bending to caress Carlo, it lifted up its head, and threw back a long veil, there bloomed under his glance a face of perfect beauty. Perfect beauty is a strong expression; but I do not retrace or qualify it: as sweet features as ever the temperate clime of Albion moulded; as pure hues of rose and lily as ever her humid gales and vapoury skies generated and screened, justified, in this instance, the term. No charm was wanting, no defect was perceptible; the young girl had regular and delicate lineaments; eyes shaped and coloured as we see them in lovely pictures, large, and dark, and full; the long and shadowy eyelash which encircles a fine eye with so soft a fascination; the pencilled brow which gives such clearness; the white smooth forehead, which adds such repose to the livelier beauties of tint and ray; the cheek oval, fresh, and smooth; the lips, fresh too, ruddy, healthy, sweetly formed; the even and gleaming teeth without flaw; the small dimpled chin; the ornament of rich, plenteous tresses—all advantages, in short, which, combined, realise the ideal of beauty, were fully hers. I wondered, as I looked at this fair creature: I admired her with my whole heart. Nature had surely formed her in a partial mood; and, forgetting her usual stinted step-mother dole of gifts, had endowed this, her darling, with a grand-dame's bounty.

What did St. John Rivers think of this earthly angel? I naturally asked myself that question as I saw him turn to her and look at her; and, as naturally, I sought the answer to the inquiry in his countenance. He had already withdrawn his eye from the Peri, and was looking at a humble tuft of daisies which grew by the wicket.

"A lovely evening, but late for you to be out alone," he said, as he crushed the snowy heads of the closed flowers with his foot.

"Oh, I only came home from S——" (she mentioned the name of a large town some twenty miles distant) "this afternoon. Papa told me you had opened your school, and that the new mistress was come; and so I put on my bonnet after tea, and ran up the valley to see her: this is she?" pointing to me.

"It is," said St. John.

"Do you think you shall like Morton?" she asked of me, with a direct and naive simplicity of tone and manner, pleasing, if child-like.

"I hope I shall. I have many inducements to do so."

"Did you find your scholars as attentive as you expected?"

"Quite."

"Do you like your house?"

"Very much."

"Have I furnished it nicely?"

"Very nicely, indeed."

"And made a good choice of an attendant for you in Alice Wood?"

"You have indeed. She is teachable and handy." (This then, I thought, is Miss Oliver, the heiress; favoured, it seems, in the gifts of fortune, as well as in those of nature! What happy combination of the planets presided over her birth, I wonder?)

"I shall come up and help you to teach sometimes," she added. "It will be a change for me to visit you now and then; and I like a change. Mr. Rivers, I have been SO gay during my stay at S——. Last night, or rather this morning, I was dancing till two o'clock. The-th regiment are stationed there since the riots; and the officers are the most agreeable men in the world: they put all our young knife-grinders and scissor merchants to shame."

It seemed to me that Mr. St. John's under lip protruded, and his upper lip curled a moment. His mouth certainly looked a good deal compressed, and the lower part of his face unusually stern and square, as the laughing girl gave him this information. He lifted his gaze, too, from the daisies, and turned it on her. An unsmiling, a searching, a meaning gaze it was. She answered it with a second laugh, and laughter well became her youth, her roses, her dimples, her bright eyes.

As he stood, mute and grave, she again fell to caressing Carlo. "Poor Carlo loves me," said she. "HE is not stern and distant to his friends; and if he could speak, he would not be silent."

As she patted the dog's head, bending with native grace before his young and austere master, I saw a glow rise to that master's face. I saw his solemn eye melt with sudden fire, and flicker with resistless emotion. Flushed and kindled thus, he looked nearly as beautiful for a man as she for a woman. His chest heaved once, as if his large heart, weary of despotic constriction, had expanded, despite the will, and made a vigorous bound for the attainment of liberty. But he curbed it, I think, as a resolute rider would curb a rearing steed. He responded neither by word nor movement to the gentle advances made him.

"Papa says you never come to see us now," continued Miss Oliver, looking up. "You are quite a stranger at Vale Hall. He is alone this evening, and not very well: will you return with me and visit him?"

"It is not a seasonable hour to intrude on Mr. Oliver," answered St. John.

"Not a seasonable hour! But I declare it is. It is just the hour when papa most wants company: when the works are closed and he has no business to occupy him. Now, Mr. Rivers, DO come. Why are you so very shy, and so very sombre?" She filled up the hiatus his silence left by a reply of her own.

"I forgot!" she exclaimed, shaking her beautiful curled head, as if shocked at herself. "I am so giddy and thoughtless! DO excuse me. It had slipped my memory that you have good reasons to be indisposed for joining in my chatter. Diana and Mary have left you, and Moor House is shut up, and you are so lonely. I am sure I pity you. Do come and see papa."

"Not to-night, Miss Rosamond, not to-night."

Mr. St. John spoke almost like an automaton: himself only knew the effort it cost him thus to refuse.

"Well, if you are so obstinate, I will leave you; for I dare not stay any longer: the dew begins to fall. Good evening!"

She held out her hand. He just touched it. "Good evening!" he repeated, in a voice low and hollow as an echo. She turned, but in a moment returned.

"Are you well?" she asked. Well might she put the question: his face was blanched as her gown.

"Quite well," he enunciated; and, with a bow, he left the gate. She went one way; he another. She turned twice to gaze after him as she tripped fairy-like down the field; he, as he strode firmly across, never turned at all.

This spectacle of another's suffering and sacrifice rapt my thoughts from exclusive meditation on my own. Diana Rivers had designated her brother "inexorable as death." She had not exaggerated.

Chapter XXXII

I continued the labours of the village-school as actively and faithfully as I could. It was truly hard work at first. Some time elapsed before, with all my efforts, I could comprehend my scholars and their nature. Wholly untaught, with faculties quite torpid, they seemed to me hopelessly dull; and, at first sight, all dull alike: but I soon found I was mistaken. There was a difference amongst them as amongst the educated; and when I got to know them, and they me, this difference rapidly developed itself. Their amazement at me, my language, my rules, and ways, once subsided, I found some of these heavy-looking, gaping rustics wake up into sharp-witted girls enough. Many showed themselves obliging, and amiable too; and I discovered amongst them not a few examples of natural politeness, and innate self-respect, as well as of excellent capacity, that won both my goodwill and my admiration. These soon took a pleasure in doing their work well, in keeping their persons neat, in learning their tasks regularly, in acquiring quiet and orderly manners. The rapidity of their progress, in some instances, was even surprising; and an honest and happy pride I took in it: besides, I began personally to like some of the best girls; and they liked me. I had amongst my scholars several farmers' daughters: young women grown, almost. These could already read, write, and sew; and to them I taught the elements of grammar, geography, history, and the finer kinds of needlework. I found estimable characters amongst them—characters desirous of information and disposed for improvement—with whom I passed many a pleasant evening hour in their own homes. Their parents then (the farmer and his wife) loaded me with attentions. There was an enjoyment in accepting their simple kindness, and in repaying it by a consideration—a scrupulous regard to their feelings—to which they were not, perhaps, at all times accustomed, and which both charmed and benefited them; because, while it elevated them in their own eyes, it made them emulous to merit the deferential treatment they received.

I felt I became a favourite in the neighbourhood. Whenever I went out, I heard on all sides cordial salutations, and was welcomed with friendly smiles. To live amidst general regard, though it be but the regard of working people, is like "sitting in sunshine, calm and sweet;" serene inward feelings bud and bloom under the ray. At this period of my life, my heart far oftener swelled with thankfulness than sank with dejection: and yet, reader, to tell you all, in the midst of this calm, this useful existence—after a day passed in honourable exertion amongst my scholars, an evening spent in drawing or reading contentedly alone—I used to rush into strange dreams at night: dreams many-coloured, agitated, full of the ideal, the stirring, the stormy—dreams where, amidst unusual scenes, charged with adventure, with agitating risk and romantic chance, I still again and again met Mr. Rochester, always at some exciting crisis; and then the sense of being in his arms, hearing his voice, meeting his eye, touching his hand and cheek, loving him, being loved by him—the hope of passing a lifetime at his side, would be renewed, with all its first force and fire. Then I awoke. Then I recalled where I was, and how situated. Then I rose up on my curtainless bed, trembling and quivering; and then the still, dark night witnessed the convulsion of despair, and heard the burst of passion. By nine o'clock the next morning I was punctually opening the school; tranquil, settled, prepared for the steady duties of the day.

Rosamond Oliver kept her word in coming to visit me. Her call at the school was generally made in the course of her morning ride. She would canter up to the door on her pony, followed by a mounted livery servant. Anything more exquisite than her appearance, in her purple habit, with her Amazon's cap of black velvet placed gracefully above the long curls that kissed her cheek and floated to her shoulders, can scarcely be imagined: and it was thus she would enter the rustic building, and glide through the dazzled ranks of the village children. She generally came at the hour when Mr. Rivers was engaged in giving his daily catechising lesson. Keenly, I fear, did the eye of the visitress pierce the young pastor's heart. A sort of instinct seemed to warn him of her entrance, even when he did not see it; and when he was looking quite away from the door, if she appeared at it, his cheek would glow, and his marble-seeming features, though they refused to relax, changed indescribably, and in their very quiescence became expressive of a repressed fervour, stronger than working muscle or darting glance could indicate.

Of course, she knew her power: indeed, he did not, because he could not, conceal it from her. In spite of his Christian stoicism, when she went up and addressed him, and smiled gaily, encouragingly, even fondly in his face, his hand would tremble and his eye burn. He seemed to say, with his sad and resolute look, if he did not say it with his lips, "I love you, and I know you prefer me. It is not despair of success that keeps me dumb. If I offered my heart, I believe you would accept it. But that heart is already laid on a sacred altar: the fire is arranged round it. It will soon be no more than a sacrifice consumed."

And then she would pout like a disappointed child; a pensive cloud would soften her radiant vivacity; she would withdraw her hand hastily from his, and turn in transient petulance from his aspect, at once so heroic and so martyr-like. St. John, no doubt, would have given the world to follow, recall, retain her, when she thus left him; but he would not give one chance of heaven, nor relinquish, for the elysium of her love, one hope of the true, eternal Paradise. Besides, he could not bind all that he had in his nature—the rover, the aspirant, the poet, the priest—in the limits of a single passion. He could not—he would not—renounce his wild field of mission warfare for the parlours and the peace of Vale Hall. I learnt so much from himself in an inroad I once, despite his reserve, had the daring to make on his confidence.

Miss Oliver already honoured me with frequent visits to my cottage. I had learnt her whole character, which was without mystery or disguise: she was coquettish but not heartless; exacting, but not worthlessly selfish. She had been indulged from her birth, but was not absolutely spoilt. She was hasty, but good-humoured; vain (she could not help it, when every glance in the glass showed her such a flush of loveliness), but not affected; liberal-handed; innocent of the pride of wealth; ingenuous; sufficiently intelligent; gay, lively, and unthinking: she was very charming, in short, even to a cool observer of her own sex like me; but she was not profoundly interesting or thoroughly impressive. A very different sort of mind was hers from that, for instance, of the sisters of St. John. Still, I liked her almost as I liked my pupil Adele; except that, for a child whom we have watched over and taught, a closer affection is engendered than we can give an equally attractive adult acquaintance.

She had taken an amiable caprice to me. She said I was like Mr. Rivers, only, certainly, she allowed, "not one-tenth so handsome, though I was a nice neat little soul enough, but he was an angel." I was, however, good, clever, composed, and firm, like him. I was a lusus naturae, she affirmed, as a village schoolmistress: she was sure my previous history, if known, would make a delightful romance.

One evening, while, with her usual child-like activity, and thoughtless yet not offensive inquisitiveness, she was rummaging the cupboard and the table-drawer of my little kitchen, she discovered first two French books, a volume of Schiller, a German grammar and dictionary, and then my drawing-materials and some sketches, including a pencil-head of a pretty little cherub-like girl, one of my scholars, and sundry views from nature, taken in the Vale of Morton and on the surrounding moors. She was first transfixed with surprise, and then electrified with delight.

"Had I done these pictures? Did I know French and German? What a love—what a miracle I was! I drew better than her master in the first school in S——. Would I sketch a portrait of her, to show to papa?"

"With pleasure," I replied; and I felt a thrill of artist—delight at the idea of copying from so perfect and radiant a model. She had then on a dark-blue silk dress; her arms and her neck were bare; her only ornament was her chestnut tresses, which waved over her shoulders with all the wild grace of natural curls. I took a sheet of fine card-board, and drew a careful outline. I promised myself the pleasure of colouring it; and, as it was getting late then, I told her she must come and sit another day.

She made such a report of me to her father, that Mr. Oliver himself accompanied her next evening—a tall, massive-featured, middle-aged, and grey-headed man, at whose side his lovely daughter looked like a bright flower near a hoary turret. He appeared a taciturn, and perhaps a proud personage; but he was very kind to me. The sketch of Rosamond's portrait pleased him highly: he said I must make a finished picture of it. He insisted, too, on my coming the next day to spend the evening at Vale Hall.

I went. I found it a large, handsome residence, showing abundant evidences of wealth in the proprietor. Rosamond was full of glee and pleasure all the time I stayed. Her father was affable; and when he entered into conversation with me after tea, he expressed in strong terms his approbation of what I had done in Morton school, and said he only feared, from what he saw and heard, I was too good for the place, and would soon quit it for one more suitable.

"Indeed," cried Rosamond, "she is clever enough to be a governess in a high family, papa."

I thought I would far rather be where I am than in any high family in the land. Mr. Oliver spoke of Mr. Rivers—of the Rivers family—with great respect. He said it was a very old name in that neighbourhood; that the ancestors of the house were wealthy; that all Morton had once belonged to them; that even now he considered the representative of that house might, if he liked, make an alliance with the best. He accounted it a pity that so fine and talented a young man should have formed the design of going out as a missionary; it was quite throwing a valuable life away. It appeared, then, that her father would throw no obstacle in the way of Rosamond's union with St. John. Mr. Oliver evidently regarded the young clergyman's good birth, old name, and sacred profession as sufficient compensation for the want of fortune.

It was the 5th of November, and a holiday. My little servant, after helping me to clean my house, was gone, well satisfied with the fee of a penny for her aid. All about me was spotless and bright—scoured floor, polished grate, and well-rubbed chairs. I had also made myself neat, and had now the afternoon before me to spend as I would.

The translation of a few pages of German occupied an hour; then I got my palette and pencils, and fell to the more soothing, because easier occupation, of completing Rosamond Oliver's miniature. The head was finished already: there was but the background to tint and the drapery to shade off; a touch of carmine, too, to add to the ripe lips—a soft curl here and there to the tresses—a deeper tinge to the shadow of the lash under the azured eyelid. I was absorbed in the execution of these nice details, when, after one rapid tap, my door unclosed, admitting St. John Rivers.

"I am come to see how you are spending your holiday," he said. "Not, I hope, in thought? No, that is well: while you draw you will not feel lonely. You see, I mistrust you still, though you have borne up wonderfully so far. I have brought you a book for evening solace," and he laid on the table a new publication—a poem: one of those genuine productions so often vouchsafed to the fortunate public of those days—the golden age of modern literature. Alas! the readers of our era are less favoured. But courage! I will not pause either to accuse or repine. I know poetry is not dead, nor genius lost; nor has Mammon gained power over either, to bind or slay: they will both assert their existence, their presence, their liberty and strength again one day. Powerful angels, safe in heaven! they smile when sordid souls triumph, and feeble ones weep over their destruction. Poetry destroyed? Genius banished? No! Mediocrity, no: do not let envy prompt you to the thought. No; they not only live, but reign and redeem: and without their divine influence spread everywhere, you would be in hell—the hell of your own meanness.

While I was eagerly glancing at the bright pages of "Marmion" (for "Marmion" it was), St. John stooped to examine my drawing. His tall figure sprang erect again with a start: he said nothing. I looked up at him: he shunned my eye. I knew his thoughts well, and could read his heart plainly; at the moment I felt calmer and cooler than he: I had then temporarily the advantage of him, and I conceived an inclination to do him some good, if I could.

"With all his firmness and self-control," thought I, "he tasks himself too far: locks every feeling and pang within—expresses, confesses, imparts nothing. I am sure it would benefit him to talk a little about this sweet Rosamond, whom he thinks he ought not to marry: I will make him talk."

I said first, "Take a chair, Mr. Rivers." But he answered, as he always did, that he could not stay. "Very well," I responded, mentally, "stand if you like; but you shall not go just yet, I am determined: solitude is at least as bad for you as it is for me. I'll try if I cannot discover the secret spring of your confidence, and find an aperture in that marble breast through which I can shed one drop of the balm of sympathy."

"Is this portrait like?" I asked bluntly.

"Like! Like whom? I did not observe it closely."

"You did, Mr. Rivers."

He almost started at my sudden and strange abruptness: he looked at me astonished. "Oh, that is nothing yet," I muttered within. "I don't mean to be baffled by a little stiffness on your part; I'm prepared to go to considerable lengths." I continued, "You observed it closely and distinctly; but I have no objection to your looking at it again," and I rose and placed it in his hand.

"A well-executed picture," he said; "very soft, clear colouring; very graceful and correct drawing."

"Yes, yes; I know all that. But what of the resemblance? Who is it like?"

Mastering some hesitation, he answered, "Miss Oliver, I presume."

"Of course. And now, sir, to reward you for the accurate guess, I will promise to paint you a careful and faithful duplicate of this very picture, provided you admit that the gift would be acceptable to you. I don't wish to throw away my time and trouble on an offering you would deem worthless."

He continued to gaze at the picture: the longer he looked, the firmer he held it, the more he seemed to covet it. "It is like!" he murmured; "the eye is well managed: the colour, light, expression, are perfect. It smiles!"

"Would it comfort, or would it wound you to have a similar painting? Tell me that. When you are at Madagascar, or at the Cape, or in India, would it be a consolation to have that memento in your possession? or would the sight of it bring recollections calculated to enervate and distress?"

He now furtively raised his eyes: he glanced at me, irresolute, disturbed: he again surveyed the picture.

"That I should like to have it is certain: whether it would be judicious or wise is another question."

Since I had ascertained that Rosamond really preferred him, and that her father was not likely to oppose the match, I—less exalted in my views than St. John—had been strongly disposed in my own heart to advocate their union. It seemed to me that, should he become the possessor of Mr. Oliver's large fortune, he might do as much good with it as if he went and laid his genius out to wither, and his strength to waste, under a tropical sun. With this persuasion I now answered—

"As far as I can see, it would be wiser and more judicious if you were to take to yourself the original at once."

By this time he had sat down: he had laid the picture on the table before him, and with his brow supported on both hands, hung fondly over it. I discerned he was now neither angry nor shocked at my audacity. I saw even that to be thus frankly addressed on a subject he had deemed unapproachable—to hear it thus freely handled—was beginning to be felt by him as a new pleasure—an unhoped-for relief. Reserved people often really need the frank discussion of their sentiments and griefs more than the expansive. The sternest-seeming stoic is human after all; and to "burst" with boldness and good-will into "the silent sea" of their souls is often to confer on them the first of obligations.

"She likes you, I am sure," said I, as I stood behind his chair, "and her father respects you. Moreover, she is a sweet girl—rather thoughtless; but you would have sufficient thought for both yourself and her. You ought to marry her."

"DOES she like me?" he asked.

"Certainly; better than she likes any one else. She talks of you continually: there is no subject she enjoys so much or touches upon so often."

"It is very pleasant to hear this," he said—"very: go on for another quarter of an hour." And he actually took out his watch and laid it upon the table to measure the time.

"But where is the use of going on," I asked, "when you are probably preparing some iron blow of contradiction, or forging a fresh chain to fetter your heart?"

"Don't imagine such hard things. Fancy me yielding and melting, as I am doing: human love rising like a freshly opened fountain in my mind and overflowing with sweet inundation all the field I have so carefully and with such labour prepared—so assiduously sown with the seeds of good intentions, of self-denying plans. And now it is deluged with a nectarous flood—the young germs swamped—delicious poison cankering them: now I see myself stretched on an ottoman in the drawing-room at Vale Hall at my bride Rosamond Oliver's feet: she is talking to me with her sweet voice—gazing down on me with those eyes your skilful hand has copied so well—smiling at me with these coral lips. She is mine—I am hers—this present life and passing world suffice to me. Hush! say nothing—my heart is full of delight—my senses are entranced—let the time I marked pass in peace."

I humoured him: the watch ticked on: he breathed fast and low: I stood silent. Amidst this hush the quartet sped; he replaced the watch, laid the picture down, rose, and stood on the hearth.

"Now," said he, "that little space was given to delirium and delusion. I rested my temples on the breast of temptation, and put my neck voluntarily under her yoke of flowers. I tasted her cup. The pillow was burning: there is an asp in the garland: the wine has a bitter taste: her promises are hollow—her offers false: I see and know all this."

I gazed at him in wonder.

"It is strange," pursued he, "that while I love Rosamond Oliver so wildly—with all the intensity, indeed, of a first passion, the object of which is exquisitely beautiful, graceful, fascinating—I experience at the same time a calm, unwarped consciousness that she would not make me a good wife; that she is not the partner suited to me; that I should discover this within a year after marriage; and that to twelve months' rapture would succeed a lifetime of regret. This I know."

"Strange indeed!" I could not help ejaculating.

"While something in me," he went on, "is acutely sensible to her charms, something else is as deeply impressed with her defects: they are such that she could sympathise in nothing I aspired to—co-operate in nothing I undertook. Rosamond a sufferer, a labourer, a female apostle? Rosamond a missionary's wife? No!"

"But you need not be a missionary. You might relinquish that scheme."

"Relinquish! What! my vocation? My great work? My foundation laid on earth for a mansion in heaven? My hopes of being numbered in the band who have merged all ambitions in the glorious one of bettering their race—of carrying knowledge into the realms of ignorance—of substituting peace for war—freedom for bondage—religion for superstition—the hope of heaven for the fear of hell? Must I relinquish that? It is dearer than the blood in my veins. It is what I have to look forward to, and to live for."

After a considerable pause, I said—"And Miss Oliver? Are her disappointment and sorrow of no interest to you?"

"Miss Oliver is ever surrounded by suitors and flatterers: in less than a month, my image will be effaced from her heart. She will forget me; and will marry, probably, some one who will make her far happier than I should do."

"You speak coolly enough; but you suffer in the conflict. You are wasting away."

"No. If I get a little thin, it is with anxiety about my prospects, yet unsettled—my departure, continually procrastinated. Only this morning, I received intelligence that the successor, whose arrival I have been so long expecting, cannot be ready to replace me for three months to come yet; and perhaps the three months may extend to six."

"You tremble and become flushed whenever Miss Oliver enters the schoolroom."

Again the surprised expression crossed his face. He had not imagined that a woman would dare to speak so to a man. For me, I felt at home in this sort of discourse. I could never rest in communication with strong, discreet, and refined minds, whether male or female, till I had passed the outworks of conventional reserve, and crossed the threshold of confidence, and won a place by their heart's very hearthstone.

"You are original," said he, "and not timid. There is something brave in your spirit, as well as penetrating in your eye; but allow me to assure you that you partially misinterpret my emotions. You think them more profound and potent than they are. You give me a larger allowance of sympathy than I have a just claim to. When I colour, and when I shade before Miss Oliver, I do not pity myself. I scorn the weakness. I know it is ignoble: a mere fever of the flesh: not, I declare, the convulsion of the soul. THAT is just as fixed as a rock, firm set in the depths of a restless sea. Know me to be what I am—a cold hard man."

I smiled incredulously.

"You have taken my confidence by storm," he continued, "and now it is much at your service. I am simply, in my original state—stripped of that blood-bleached robe with which Christianity covers human deformity—a cold, hard, ambitious man. Natural affection only, of all the sentiments, has permanent power over me. Reason, and not feeling, is my guide; my ambition is unlimited: my desire to rise higher, to do more than others, insatiable. I honour endurance, perseverance, industry, talent; because these are the means by which men achieve great ends and mount to lofty eminence. I watch your career with interest, because I consider you a specimen of a diligent, orderly, energetic woman: not because I deeply compassionate what you have gone through, or what you still suffer."

"You would describe yourself as a mere pagan philosopher," I said.

"No. There is this difference between me and deistic philosophers: I believe; and I believe the Gospel. You missed your epithet. I am not a pagan, but a Christian philosopher—a follower of the sect of Jesus. As His disciple I adopt His pure, His merciful, His benignant doctrines. I advocate them: I am sworn to spread them. Won in youth to religion, she has cultivated my original qualities thus:-From the minute germ, natural affection, she has developed the overshadowing tree, philanthropy. From the wild stringy root of human uprightness, she has reared a due sense of the Divine justice. Of the ambition to win power and renown for my wretched self, she has formed the ambition to spread my Master's kingdom; to achieve victories for the standard of the cross. So much has religion done for me; turning the original materials to the best account; pruning and training nature.

But she could not eradicate nature: nor will it be eradicated 'till this mortal shall put on immortality.'"

Having said this, he took his hat, which lay on the table beside my palette. Once more he looked at the portrait.

"She IS lovely," he murmured. "She is well named the Rose of the World, indeed!"

"And may I not paint one like it for you?"

"CUI BONO? No."

He drew over the picture the sheet of thin paper on which I was accustomed to rest my hand in painting, to prevent the cardboard from being sullied. What he suddenly saw on this blank paper, it was impossible for me to tell; but something had caught his eye. He took it up with a snatch; he looked at the edge; then shot a glance at me, inexpressibly peculiar, and quite incomprehensible: a glance that seemed to take and make note of every point in my shape, face, and dress; for it traversed all, quick, keen as lightning. His lips parted, as if to speak: but he checked the coming sentence, whatever it was.

"What is the matter?" I asked.

"Nothing in the world," was the reply; and, replacing the paper, I saw him dexterously tear a narrow slip from the margin. It disappeared in his glove; and, with one hasty nod and "good-afternoon," he vanished.

"Well!" I exclaimed, using an expression of the district, "that caps the globe, however!"

I, in my turn, scrutinised the paper; but saw nothing on it save a few dingy stains of paint where I had tried the tint in my pencil. I pondered the mystery a minute or two; but finding it insolvable, and being certain it could not be of much moment, I dismissed, and soon forgot it.

Chapter XXXIII

When Mr. St. John went, it was beginning to snow; the whirling storm continued all night. The next day a keen wind brought fresh and blinding falls; by twilight the valley was drifted up and almost impassable. I had closed my shutter, laid a mat to the door to prevent the snow from blowing in under it, trimmed my fire, and after sitting nearly an hour on the hearth listening to the muffled fury of the tempest, I lit a candle, took down "Marmion," and beginning—

"Day set on Norham's castled steep,
And Tweed's fair river broad and deep,
    And Cheviot's mountains lone;
The massive towers, the donjon keep,
The flanking walls that round them sweep,
    In yellow lustre shone"—

I soon forgot storm in music.

I heard a noise: the wind, I thought, shook the door. No; it was St. John Rivers, who, lifting the latch, came in out of the frozen hurricane—the howling darkness—and stood before me: the cloak that covered his tall figure all white as a glacier. I was almost in consternation, so little had I expected any guest from the blocked-up vale that night.

"Any ill news?" I demanded. "Has anything happened?"

"No. How very easily alarmed you are?" he answered, removing his cloak and hanging it up against the door, towards which he again coolly pushed the mat which his entrance had deranged. He stamped the snow from his boots.

"I shall sully the purity of your floor," said he, "but you must excuse me for once." Then he approached the fire. "I have had hard work to get here, I assure you," he observed, as he warmed his hands over the flame. "One drift took me up to the waist; happily the snow is quite soft yet."

"But why are you come?" I could not forbear saying.

"Rather an inhospitable question to put to a visitor; but since you ask it, I answer simply to have a little talk with you; I got tired of my mute books and empty rooms. Besides, since yesterday I have experienced the excitement of a person to whom a tale has been half-told, and who is impatient to hear the sequel."

He sat down. I recalled his singular conduct of yesterday, and really I began to fear his wits were touched. If he were insane, however, his was a very cool and collected insanity: I had never seen that handsome-featured face of his look more like chiselled marble than it did just now, as he put aside his snow-wet hair from his forehead and let the firelight shine free on his pale brow and cheek as pale, where it grieved me to discover the hollow trace of care or sorrow now so plainly graved. I waited, expecting he would say something I could at least comprehend; but his hand was now at his chin, his finger on his lip: he was thinking. It struck me that his hand looked wasted like his face. A perhaps uncalled-for gush of pity came over my heart: I was moved to say—

"I wish Diana or Mary would come and live with you: it is too bad that you should be quite alone; and you are recklessly rash about your own health."

"Not at all," said he: "I care for myself when necessary. I am well now. What do you see amiss in me?"

This was said with a careless, abstracted indifference, which showed that my solicitude was, at least in his opinion, wholly superfluous. I was silenced.

He still slowly moved his finger over his upper lip, and still his eye dwelt dreamily on the glowing grate; thinking it urgent to say something, I asked him presently if he felt any cold draught from the door, which was behind him.

"No, no!" he responded shortly and somewhat testily.

"Well," I reflected, "if you won't talk, you may be still; I'll let you alone now, and return to my book."

So I snuffed the candle and resumed the perusal of "Marmion." He soon stirred; my eye was instantly drawn to his movements; he only took out a morocco pocket-book, thence produced a letter, which he read in silence, folded it, put it back, relapsed into meditation. It was vain to try to read with such an inscrutable fixture before me; nor could I, in impatience, consent to be dumb; he might rebuff me if my he liked, but talk I would.

"Have you heard from Diana and Mary lately?"

"Not since the letter I showed you a week ago."

"There has not been any change made about your own arrangements? You will not be summoned to leave England sooner than you expected?"

"I fear not, indeed: such chance is too good to befall me." Baffled so far, I changed my ground. I bethought myself to talk about the school and my scholars.

"Mary Garrett's mother is better, and Mary came back to the school this morning, and I shall have four new girls next week from the Foundry Close—they would have come to-day but for the snow."

"Indeed!"

"Mr. Oliver pays for two."

"Does he?"

"He means to give the whole school a treat at Christmas."

"I know."

"Was it your suggestion?"

"No."

"Whose, then?"

"His daughter's, I think."

"It is like her: she is so good-natured."

"Yes."

Again came the blank of a pause: the clock struck eight strokes. It aroused him; he uncrossed his legs, sat erect, turned to me.

"Leave your book a moment, and come a little nearer the fire," he said.

Wondering, and of my wonder finding no end, I complied.

"Half-an-hour ago," he pursued, "I spoke of my impatience to hear the sequel of a tale: on reflection, I find the matter will be better managed by my assuming the narrator's part, and converting you into a listener. Before commencing, it is but fair to warn you that the story will sound somewhat hackneyed in your ears; but stale details often regain a degree of freshness when they pass through new lips. For the rest, whether trite or novel, it is short.

"Twenty years ago, a poor curate—never mind his name at this moment—fell in love with a rich man's daughter; she fell in love with him, and married him, against the advice of all her friends, who consequently disowned her immediately after the wedding. Before two years passed, the rash pair were both dead, and laid quietly side by side under one slab. (I have seen their grave; it formed part of the pavement of a huge churchyard surrounding the grim, soot-black old cathedral of an overgrown manufacturing town in-shire.) They left a daughter, which, at its very birth, Charity received in her lap—cold as that of the snow-drift I almost stuck fast in to-night. Charity carried the friendless thing to the house of its rich maternal relations; it was reared by an aunt-in-law, called (I come to names now) Mrs. Reed of Gateshead. You start—did you hear a noise? I daresay it is only a rat scrambling along the rafters of the adjoining schoolroom: it was a barn before I had it repaired and altered, and barns are generally haunted by rats.—To proceed. Mrs. Reed kept the orphan ten years: whether it was happy or not with her, I cannot say, never having been told; but at the end of that time she transferred it to a place you know—being no other than Lowood School, where you so long resided yourself. It seems her career there was very honourable: from a pupil, she became a teacher, like yourself—really it strikes me there are parallel points in her history and yours—she left it to be a governess: there, again, your fates were analogous; she undertook the education of the ward of a certain Mr. Rochester."

"Mr. Rivers!" I interrupted.

"I can guess your feelings," he said, "but restrain them for a while: I have nearly finished; hear me to the end. Of Mr. Rochester's character I know nothing, but the one fact that he professed to offer honourable marriage to this young girl, and that at the very altar she discovered he had a wife yet alive, though a lunatic. What his subsequent conduct and proposals were is a matter of pure conjecture; but when an event transpired which rendered inquiry after the governess necessary, it was discovered she was gone—no one could tell when, where, or how. She had left Thornfield Hall in the night; every research after her course had been vain: the country had been scoured far and wide; no vestige of information could be gathered respecting her. Yet that she should be found is become a matter of serious urgency: advertisements have been put in all the papers; I myself have received a letter from one Mr. Briggs, a solicitor, communicating the details I have just imparted. Is it not an odd tale?"

"Just tell me this," said I, "and since you know so much, you surely can tell it me—what of Mr. Rochester? How and where is he? What is he doing? Is he well?"

"I am ignorant of all concerning Mr. Rochester: the letter never mentions him but to narrate the fraudulent and illegal attempt I have adverted to. You should rather ask the name of the governess—the nature of the event which requires her appearance."

"Did no one go to Thornfield Hall, then? Did no one see Mr. Rochester?"

"I suppose not."

"But they wrote to him?"

"Of course."

"And what did he say? Who has his letters?"

"Mr. Briggs intimates that the answer to his application was not from Mr. Rochester, but from a lady: it is signed 'Alice Fairfax.'"

I felt cold and dismayed: my worst fears then were probably true: he had in all probability left England and rushed in reckless desperation to some former haunt on the Continent. And what opiate for his severe sufferings—what object for his strong passions—had he sought there? I dared not answer the question. Oh, my poor master—once almost my husband—whom I had often called "my dear Edward!"

"He must have been a bad man," observed Mr. Rivers.

"You don't know him—don't pronounce an opinion upon him," I said, with warmth.

"Very well," he answered quietly: "and indeed my head is otherwise occupied than with him: I have my tale to finish. Since you won't ask the governess's name, I must tell it of my own accord. Stay! I have it here—it is always more satisfactory to see important points written down, fairly committed to black and white."

And the pocket-book was again deliberately produced, opened, sought through; from one of its compartments was extracted a shabby slip of paper, hastily torn off: I recognised in its texture and its stains of ultra-marine, and lake, and vermillion, the ravished margin of the portrait-cover. He got up, held it close to my eyes: and I read, traced in Indian ink, in my own handwriting, the words "JANE EYRE"—the work doubtless of some moment of abstraction.

"Briggs wrote to me of a Jane Eyre:" he said, "the advertisements demanded a Jane Eyre: I knew a Jane Elliott.—I confess I had my suspicions, but it was only yesterday afternoon they were at once resolved into certainty. You own the name and renounce the alias?"

"Yes—yes; but where is Mr. Briggs? He perhaps knows more of Mr. Rochester than you do."

"Briggs is in London. I should doubt his knowing anything at all about Mr. Rochester; it is not in Mr. Rochester he is interested. Meantime, you forget essential points in pursuing trifles: you do not inquire why Mr. Briggs sought after you—what he wanted with you."

"Well, what did he want?"

"Merely to tell you that your uncle, Mr. Eyre of Madeira, is dead; that he has left you all his property, and that you are now rich—merely that—nothing more."

"I!—rich?"

"Yes, you, rich—quite an heiress."

Silence succeeded.

"You must prove your identity of course," resumed St. John presently: "a step which will offer no difficulties; you can then enter on immediate possession. Your fortune is vested in the English funds; Briggs has the will and the necessary documents."

Here was a new card turned up! It is a fine thing, reader, to be lifted in a moment from indigence to wealth—a very fine thing; but not a matter one can comprehend, or consequently enjoy, all at once. And then there are other chances in life far more thrilling and rapture-giving: THIS is solid, an affair of the actual world, nothing ideal about it: all its associations are solid and sober, and its manifestations are the same. One does not jump, and spring, and shout hurrah! at hearing one has got a fortune; one begins to consider responsibilities, and to ponder business; on a base of steady satisfaction rise certain grave cares, and we contain ourselves, and blood over our bliss with a solemn brow.

Besides, the words Legacy, Bequest, go side by side with the words, Death, Funeral. My uncle I had heard was dead—my only relative; ever since being made aware of his existence, I had cherished the hope of one day seeing him: now, I never should. And then this money came only to me: not to me and a rejoicing family, but to my isolated self. It was a grand boon doubtless; and independence would be glorious—yes, I felt that—that thought swelled my heart.

"You unbend your forehead at last," said Mr. Rivers. "I thought Medusa had looked at you, and that you were turning to stone. Perhaps now you will ask how much you are worth?"

"How much am I worth?"

"Oh, a trifle! Nothing of course to speak of—twenty thousand pounds, I think they say—but what is that?"

"Twenty thousand pounds?"

Here was a new stunner—I had been calculating on four or five thousand. This news actually took my breath for a moment: Mr. St. John, whom I had never heard laugh before, laughed now.

"Well," said he, "if you had committed a murder, and I had told you your crime was discovered, you could scarcely look more aghast."

"It is a large sum—don't you think there is a mistake?"

"No mistake at all."

"Perhaps you have read the figures wrong—it may be two thousand!"

"It is written in letters, not figures,—twenty thousand."

I again felt rather like an individual of but average gastronomical powers sitting down to feast alone at a table spread with provisions for a hundred. Mr. Rivers rose now and put his cloak on.

"If it were not such a very wild night," he said, "I would send Hannah down to keep you company: you look too desperately miserable to be left alone. But Hannah, poor woman! could not stride the drifts so well as I: her legs are not quite so long: so I must e'en leave you to your sorrows. Good-night."

He was lifting the latch: a sudden thought occurred to me. "Stop one minute!" I cried.

"Well?"

"It puzzles me to know why Mr. Briggs wrote to you about me; or how he knew you, or could fancy that you, living in such an out-of-the-way place, had the power to aid in my discovery."

"Oh! I am a clergyman," he said; "and the clergy are often appealed to about odd matters." Again the latch rattled.

"No; that does not satisfy me!" I exclaimed: and indeed there was something in the hasty and unexplanatory reply which, instead of allaying, piqued my curiosity more than ever.

"It is a very strange piece of business," I added; "I must know more about it."

"Another time."

"No; to-night!—to-night!" and as he turned from the door, I placed myself between it and him. He looked rather embarrassed.

"You certainly shall not go till you have told me all," I said.

"I would rather not just now."

"You shall!—you must!"

"I would rather Diana or Mary informed you."

Of course these objections wrought my eagerness to a climax: gratified it must be, and that without delay; and I told him so.

"But I apprised you that I was a hard man," said he, "difficult to persuade."

"And I am a hard woman,—impossible to put off."

"And then," he pursued, "I am cold: no fervour infects me."

"Whereas I am hot, and fire dissolves ice. The blaze there has thawed all the snow from your cloak; by the same token, it has streamed on to my floor, and made it like a trampled street. As you hope ever to be forgiven, Mr. Rivers, the high crime and misdemeanour of spoiling a sanded kitchen, tell me what I wish to know."

"Well, then," he said, "I yield; if not to your earnestness, to your perseverance: as stone is worn by continual dropping. Besides, you must know some day,—as well now as later. Your name is Jane Eyre?"

"Of course: that was all settled before."

"You are not, perhaps, aware that I am your namesake?—that I was christened St. John Eyre Rivers?"

"No, indeed! I remember now seeing the letter E. comprised in your initials written in books you have at different times lent me; but I never asked for what name it stood. But what then? Surely——"

I stopped: I could not trust myself to entertain, much less to express, the thought that rushed upon me—that embodied itself,—that, in a second, stood out a strong, solid probability. Circumstances knit themselves, fitted themselves, shot into order: the chain that had been lying hitherto a formless lump of links was drawn out straight,—every ring was perfect, the connection complete. I knew, by instinct, how the matter stood, before St. John had said another word; but I cannot expect the reader to have the same intuitive perception, so I must repeat his explanation.

"My mother's name was Eyre; she had two brothers; one a clergyman, who married Miss Jane Reed, of Gateshead; the other, John Eyre, Esq., merchant, late of Funchal, Madeira. Mr. Briggs, being Mr. Eyre's solicitor, wrote to us last August to inform us of our uncle's death, and to say that he had left his property to his brother the clergyman's orphan daughter, overlooking us, in consequence of a quarrel, never forgiven, between him and my father. He wrote again a few weeks since, to intimate that the heiress was lost, and asking if we knew anything of her. A name casually written on a slip of paper has enabled me to find her out. You know the rest." Again he was going, but I set my back against the door.

"Do let me speak," I said; "let me have one moment to draw breath and reflect." I paused—he stood before me, hat in hand, looking composed enough. I resumed—

"Your mother was my father's sister?"

"Yes."

"My aunt, consequently?"

He bowed.

"My uncle John was your uncle John? You, Diana, and Mary are his sister's children, as I am his brother's child?"

"Undeniably."

"You three, then, are my cousins; half our blood on each side flows from the same source?"

"We are cousins; yes."

I surveyed him. It seemed I had found a brother: one I could be proud of,—one I could love; and two sisters, whose qualities were such, that, when I knew them but as mere strangers, they had inspired me with genuine affection and admiration. The two girls, on whom, kneeling down on the wet ground, and looking through the low, latticed window of Moor House kitchen, I had gazed with so bitter a mixture of interest and despair, were my near kinswomen; and the young and stately gentleman who had found me almost dying at his threshold was my blood relation. Glorious discovery to a lonely wretch! This was wealth indeed!—wealth to the heart!—a mine of pure, genial affections. This was a blessing, bright, vivid, and exhilarating;—not like the ponderous gift of gold: rich and welcome enough in its way, but sobering from its weight. I now clapped my hands in sudden joy—my pulse bounded, my veins thrilled.

"Oh, I am glad!—I am glad!" I exclaimed.

St. John smiled. "Did I not say you neglected essential points to pursue trifles?" he asked. "You were serious when I told you you had got a fortune; and now, for a matter of no moment, you are excited."

"What can you mean? It may be of no moment to you; you have sisters and don't care for a cousin; but I had nobody; and now three relations,—or two, if you don't choose to be counted,—are born into my world full-grown. I say again, I am glad!"

I walked fast through the room: I stopped, half suffocated with the thoughts that rose faster than I could receive, comprehend, settle them:-thoughts of what might, could, would, and should be, and that ere long. I looked at the blank wall: it seemed a sky thick with ascending stars,—every one lit me to a purpose or delight. Those who had saved my life, whom, till this hour, I had loved barrenly, I could now benefit. They were under a yoke,—I could free them: they were scattered,—I could reunite them: the independence, the affluence which was mine, might be theirs too. Were we not four? Twenty thousand pounds shared equally would be five thousand each, justice—enough and to spare: justice would be done,—mutual happiness secured. Now the wealth did not weigh on me: now it was not a mere bequest of coin,—it was a legacy of life, hope, enjoyment.

How I looked while these ideas were taking my spirit by storm, I cannot tell; but I perceived soon that Mr. Rivers had placed a chair behind me, and was gently attempting to make me sit down on it. He also advised me to be composed; I scorned the insinuation of helplessness and distraction, shook off his hand, and began to walk about again.

"Write to Diana and Mary to-morrow," I said, "and tell them to come home directly. Diana said they would both consider themselves rich with a thousand pounds, so with five thousand they will do very well."

"Tell me where I can get you a glass of water," said St. John; "you must really make an effort to tranquillise your feelings."

"Nonsense! and what sort of an effect will the bequest have on you? Will it keep you in England, induce you to marry Miss Oliver, and settle down like an ordinary mortal?"

"You wander: your head becomes confused. I have been too abrupt in communicating the news; it has excited you beyond your strength."

"Mr. Rivers! you quite put me out of patience: I am rational enough; it is you who misunderstand, or rather who affect to misunderstand."

"Perhaps, if you explained yourself a little more fully, I should comprehend better."

"Explain! What is there to explain? You cannot fail to see that twenty thousand pounds, the sum in question, divided equally between the nephew and three nieces of our uncle, will give five thousand to each? What I want is, that you should write to your sisters and tell them of the fortune that has accrued to them."

"To you, you mean."

"I have intimated my view of the case: I am incapable of taking any other. I am not brutally selfish, blindly unjust, or fiendishly ungrateful. Besides, I am resolved I will have a home and connections. I like Moor House, and I will live at Moor House; I like Diana and Mary, and I will attach myself for life to Diana and Mary. It would please and benefit me to have five thousand pounds; it would torment and oppress me to have twenty thousand; which, moreover, could never be mine in justice, though it might in law. I abandon to you, then, what is absolutely superfluous to me. Let there be no opposition, and no discussion about it; let us agree amongst each other, and decide the point at once."

"This is acting on first impulses; you must take days to consider such a matter, ere your word can be regarded as valid."

"Oh! if all you doubt is my sincerity, I am easy: you see the justice of the case?"

"I DO see a certain justice; but it is contrary to all custom. Besides, the entire fortune is your right: my uncle gained it by his own efforts; he was free to leave it to whom he would: he left it to you. After all, justice permits you to keep it: you may, with a clear conscience, consider it absolutely your own."

"With me," said I, "it is fully as much a matter of feeling as of conscience: I must indulge my feelings; I so seldom have had an opportunity of doing so. Were you to argue, object, and annoy me for a year, I could not forego the delicious pleasure of which I have caught a glimpse—that of repaying, in part, a mighty obligation, and winning to myself lifelong friends."

"You think so now," rejoined St. John, "because you do not know what it is to possess, nor consequently to enjoy wealth: you cannot form a notion of the importance twenty thousand pounds would give you; of the place it would enable you to take in society; of the prospects it would open to you: you cannot——"

"And you," I interrupted, "cannot at all imagine the craving I have for fraternal and sisterly love. I never had a home, I never had brothers or sisters; I must and will have them now: you are not reluctant to admit me and own me, are you?"

"Jane, I will be your brother—my sisters will be your sisters—without stipulating for this sacrifice of your just rights."

"Brother? Yes; at the distance of a thousand leagues! Sisters? Yes; slaving amongst strangers! I, wealthy—gorged with gold I never earned and do not merit! You, penniless! Famous equality and fraternisation! Close union! Intimate attachment!"

"But, Jane, your aspirations after family ties and domestic happiness may be realised otherwise than by the means you contemplate: you may marry."

"Nonsense, again! Marry! I don't want to marry, and never shall marry."

"That is saying too much: such hazardous affirmations are a proof of the excitement under which you labour."

"It is not saying too much: I know what I feel, and how averse are my inclinations to the bare thought of marriage. No one would take me for love; and I will not be regarded in the light of a mere money speculation. And I do not want a stranger—unsympathising, alien, different from me; I want my kindred: those with whom I have full fellow-feeling. Say again you will be my brother: when you uttered the words I was satisfied, happy; repeat them, if you can, repeat them sincerely."

"I think I can. I know I have always loved my own sisters; and I know on what my affection for them is grounded,—respect for their worth and admiration of their talents. You too have principle and mind: your tastes and habits resemble Diana's and Mary's; your presence is always agreeable to me; in your conversation I have already for some time found a salutary solace. I feel I can easily and naturally make room in my heart for you, as my third and youngest sister."

"Thank you: that contents me for to-night. Now you had better go; for if you stay longer, you will perhaps irritate me afresh by some mistrustful scruple."

"And the school, Miss Eyre? It must now be shut up, I suppose?"

"No. I will retain my post of mistress till you get a substitute."

He smiled approbation: we shook hands, and he took leave.

I need not narrate in detail the further struggles I had, and arguments I used, to get matters regarding the legacy settled as I wished. My task was a very hard one; but, as I was absolutely resolved—as my cousins saw at length that my mind was really and immutably fixed on making a just division of the property—as they must in their own hearts have felt the equity of the intention; and must, besides, have been innately conscious that in my place they would have done precisely what I wished to do—they yielded at length so far as to consent to put the affair to arbitration. The judges chosen were Mr. Oliver and an able lawyer: both coincided in my opinion: I carried my point. The instruments of transfer were drawn out: St. John, Diana, Mary, and I, each became possessed of a competency.

Chapter XXXIV

It was near Christmas by the time all was settled: the season of general holiday approached. I now closed Morton school, taking care that the parting should not be barren on my side. Good fortune opens the hand as well as the heart wonderfully; and to give somewhat when we have largely received, is but to afford a vent to the unusual ebullition of the sensations. I had long felt with pleasure that many of my rustic scholars liked me, and when we parted, that consciousness was confirmed: they manifested their affection plainly and strongly. Deep was my gratification to find I had really a place in their unsophisticated hearts: I promised them that never a week should pass in future that I did not visit them, and give them an hour's teaching in their school.

Mr. Rivers came up as, having seen the classes, now numbering sixty girls, file out before me, and locked the door, I stood with the key in my hand, exchanging a few words of special farewell with some half-dozen of my best scholars: as decent, respectable, modest, and well-informed young women as could be found in the ranks of the British peasantry. And that is saying a great deal; for after all, the British peasantry are the best taught, best mannered, most self-respecting of any in Europe: since those days I have seen paysannes and Bauerinnen; and the best of them seemed to me ignorant, coarse, and besotted, compared with my Morton girls.

"Do you consider you have got your reward for a season of exertion?" asked Mr. Rivers, when they were gone. "Does not the consciousness of having done some real good in your day and generation give pleasure?"

"Doubtless."

"And you have only toiled a few months! Would not a life devoted to the task of regenerating your race be well spent?"

"Yes," I said; "but I could not go on for ever so: I want to enjoy my own faculties as well as to cultivate those of other people. I must enjoy them now; don't recall either my mind or body to the school; I am out of it and disposed for full holiday."

He looked grave. "What now? What sudden eagerness is this you evince? What are you going to do?"

"To be active: as active as I can. And first I must beg you to set Hannah at liberty, and get somebody else to wait on you."

"Do you want her?"

"Yes, to go with me to Moor House. Diana and Mary will be at home in a week, and I want to have everything in order against their arrival."

"I understand. I thought you were for flying off on some excursion. It is better so: Hannah shall go with you."

"Tell her to be ready by to-morrow then; and here is the schoolroom key: I will give you the key of my cottage in the morning."

He took it. "You give it up very gleefully," said he; "I don't quite understand your light-heartedness, because I cannot tell what employment you propose to yourself as a substitute for the one you are relinquishing. What aim, what purpose, what ambition in life have you now?"

"My first aim will be to CLEAN DOWN (do you comprehend the full force of the expression?)—to CLEAN DOWN Moor House from chamber to cellar; my next to rub it up with bees-wax, oil, and an indefinite number of cloths, till it glitters again; my third, to arrange every chair, table, bed, carpet, with mathematical precision; afterwards I shall go near to ruin you in coals and peat to keep up good fires in every room; and lastly, the two days preceding that on which your sisters are expected will be devoted by Hannah and me to such a beating of eggs, sorting of currants, grating of spices, compounding of Christmas cakes, chopping up of materials for mince-pies, and solemnising of other culinary rites, as words can convey but an inadequate notion of to the uninitiated like you. My purpose, in short, is to have all things in an absolutely perfect state of readiness for Diana and Mary before next Thursday; and my ambition is to give them a beau-ideal of a welcome when they come."

St. John smiled slightly: still he was dissatisfied.

"It is all very well for the present," said he; "but seriously, I trust that when the first flush of vivacity is over, you will look a little higher than domestic endearments and household joys."

"The best things the world has!" I interrupted.

"No, Jane, no: this world is not the scene of fruition; do not attempt to make it so: nor of rest; do not turn slothful."

"I mean, on the contrary, to be busy."

"Jane, I excuse you for the present: two months' grace I allow you for the full enjoyment of your new position, and for pleasing yourself with this late-found charm of relationship; but THEN, I hope you will begin to look beyond Moor House and Morton, and sisterly society, and the selfish calm and sensual comfort of civilised affluence. I hope your energies will then once more trouble you with their strength."

I looked at him with surprise. "St. John," I said, "I think you are almost wicked to talk so. I am disposed to be as content as a queen, and you try to stir me up to restlessness! To what end?"

"To the end of turning to profit the talents which God has committed to your keeping; and of which He will surely one day demand a strict account. Jane, I shall watch you closely and anxiously—I warn you of that. And try to restrain the disproportionate fervour with which you throw yourself into commonplace home pleasures. Don't cling so tenaciously to ties of the flesh; save your constancy and ardour for an adequate cause; forbear to waste them on trite transient objects. Do you hear, Jane?"

"Yes; just as if you were speaking Greek. I feel I have adequate cause to be happy, and I WILL be happy. Goodbye!"

Happy at Moor House I was, and hard I worked; and so did Hannah: she was charmed to see how jovial I could be amidst the bustle of a house turned topsy-turvy—how I could brush, and dust, and clean, and cook. And really, after a day or two of confusion worse confounded, it was delightful by degrees to invoke order from the chaos ourselves had made. I had previously taken a journey to S-to purchase some new furniture: my cousins having given me CARTE BLANCHE TO effect what alterations I pleased, and a sum having been set aside for that purpose. The ordinary sitting-room and bedrooms I left much as they were: for I knew Diana and Mary would derive more pleasure from seeing again the old homely tables, and chairs, and beds, than from the spectacle of the smartest innovations. Still some novelty was necessary, to give to their return the piquancy with which I wished it to be invested. Dark handsome new carpets and curtains, an arrangement of some carefully selected antique ornaments in porcelain and bronze, new coverings, and mirrors, and dressing-cases, for the toilet tables, answered the end: they looked fresh without being glaring. A spare parlour and bedroom I refurnished entirely, with old mahogany and crimson upholstery: I laid canvas on the passage, and carpets on the stairs. When all was finished, I thought Moor House as complete a model of bright modest snugness within, as it was, at this season, a specimen of wintry waste and desert dreariness without.

The eventful Thursday at length came. They were expected about dark, and ere dusk fires were lit upstairs and below; the kitchen was in perfect trim; Hannah and I were dressed, and all was in readiness.

St. John arrived first. I had entreated him to keep quite clear of the house till everything was arranged: and, indeed, the bare idea of the commotion, at once sordid and trivial, going on within its walls sufficed to scare him to estrangement. He found me in the kitchen, watching the progress of certain cakes for tea, then baking. Approaching the hearth, he asked, "If I was at last satisfied with housemaid's work?" I answered by inviting him to accompany me on a general inspection of the result of my labours. With some difficulty, I got him to make the tour of the house. He just looked in at the doors I opened; and when he had wandered upstairs and downstairs, he said I must have gone through a great deal of fatigue and trouble to have effected such considerable changes in so short a time: but not a syllable did he utter indicating pleasure in the improved aspect of his abode.

This silence damped me. I thought perhaps the alterations had disturbed some old associations he valued. I inquired whether this was the case: no doubt in a somewhat crest-fallen tone.

"Not at all; he had, on the contrary, remarked that I had scrupulously respected every association: he feared, indeed, I must have bestowed more thought on the matter than it was worth. How many minutes, for instance, had I devoted to studying the arrangement of this very room?—By-the-bye, could I tell him where such a book was?"

I showed him the volume on the shelf: he took it down, and withdrawing to his accustomed window recess, he began to read it.

Now, I did not like this, reader. St. John was a good man; but I began to feel he had spoken truth of himself when he said he was hard and cold. The humanities and amenities of life had no attraction for him—its peaceful enjoyments no charm. Literally, he lived only to aspire—after what was good and great, certainly; but still he would never rest, nor approve of others resting round him. As I looked at his lofty forehead, still and pale as a white stone—at his fine lineaments fixed in study—I comprehended all at once that he would hardly make a good husband: that it would be a trying thing to be his wife. I understood, as by inspiration, the nature of his love for Miss Oliver; I agreed with him that it was but a love of the senses. I comprehended how he should despise himself for the feverish influence it exercised over him; how he should wish to stifle and destroy it; how he should mistrust its ever conducting permanently to his happiness or hers. I saw he was of the material from which nature hews her heroes—Christian and Pagan—her lawgivers, her statesmen, her conquerors: a steadfast bulwark for great interests to rest upon; but, at the fireside, too often a cold cumbrous column, gloomy and out of place.

"This parlour is not his sphere," I reflected: "the Himalayan ridge or Caffre bush, even the plague-cursed Guinea Coast swamp would suit him better. Well may he eschew the calm of domestic life; it is not his element: there his faculties stagnate—they cannot develop or appear to advantage. It is in scenes of strife and danger—where courage is proved, and energy exercised, and fortitude tasked—that he will speak and move, the leader and superior. A merry child would have the advantage of him on this hearth. He is right to choose a missionary's career—I see it now."

"They are coming! they are coming!" cried Hannah, throwing open the parlour door. At the same moment old Carlo barked joyfully. Out I ran. It was now dark; but a rumbling of wheels was audible. Hannah soon had a lantern lit. The vehicle had stopped at the wicket; the driver opened the door: first one well-known form, then another, stepped out. In a minute I had my face under their bonnets, in contact first with Mary's soft cheek, then with Diana's flowing curls. They laughed—kissed me—then Hannah: patted Carlo, who was half wild with delight; asked eagerly if all was well; and being assured in the affirmative, hastened into the house.

They were stiff with their long and jolting drive from Whitcross, and chilled with the frosty night air; but their pleasant countenances expanded to the cheerful firelight. While the driver and Hannah brought in the boxes, they demanded St. John. At this moment he advanced from the parlour. They both threw their arms round his neck at once. He gave each one quiet kiss, said in a low tone a few words of welcome, stood a while to be talked to, and then, intimating that he supposed they would soon rejoin him in the parlour, withdrew there as to a place of refuge.

I had lit their candles to go upstairs, but Diana had first to give hospitable orders respecting the driver; this done, both followed me. They were delighted with the renovation and decorations of their rooms; with the new drapery, and fresh carpets, and rich tinted china vases: they expressed their gratification ungrudgingly. I had the pleasure of feeling that my arrangements met their wishes exactly, and that what I had done added a vivid charm to their joyous return home.

Sweet was that evening. My cousins, full of exhilaration, were so eloquent in narrative and comment, that their fluency covered St. John's taciturnity: he was sincerely glad to see his sisters; but in their glow of fervour and flow of joy he could not sympathise. The event of the day—that is, the return of Diana and Mary—pleased him; but the accompaniments of that event, the glad tumult, the garrulous glee of reception irked him: I saw he wished the calmer morrow was come. In the very meridian of the night's enjoyment, about an hour after tea, a rap was heard at the door. Hannah entered with the intimation that "a poor lad was come, at that unlikely time, to fetch Mr. Rivers to see his mother, who was drawing away."

"Where does she live, Hannah?"

"Clear up at Whitcross Brow, almost four miles off, and moor and moss all the way."

"Tell him I will go."

"I'm sure, sir, you had better not. It's the worst road to travel after dark that can be: there's no track at all over the bog. And then it is such a bitter night—the keenest wind you ever felt. You had better send word, sir, that you will be there in the morning."

But he was already in the passage, putting on his cloak; and without one objection, one murmur, he departed. It was then nine o'clock: he did not return till midnight. Starved and tired enough he was: but he looked happier than when he set out. He had performed an act of duty; made an exertion; felt his own strength to do and deny, and was on better terms with himself.

I am afraid the whole of the ensuing week tried his patience. It was Christmas week: we took to no settled employment, but spent it in a sort of merry domestic dissipation. The air of the moors, the freedom of home, the dawn of prosperity, acted on Diana and Mary's spirits like some life-giving elixir: they were gay from morning till noon, and from noon till night. They could always talk; and their discourse, witty, pithy, original, had such charms for me, that I preferred listening to, and sharing in it, to doing anything else. St. John did not rebuke our vivacity; but he escaped from it: he was seldom in the house; his parish was large, the population scattered, and he found daily business in visiting the sick and poor in its different districts.

One morning at breakfast, Diana, after looking a little pensive for some minutes, asked him, "If his plans were yet unchanged."

"Unchanged and unchangeable," was the reply. And he proceeded to inform us that his departure from England was now definitively fixed for the ensuing year.

"And Rosamond Oliver?" suggested Mary, the words seeming to escape her lips involuntarily: for no sooner had she uttered them, than she made a gesture as if wishing to recall them. St. John had a book in his hand—it was his unsocial custom to read at meals—he closed it, and looked up,

"Rosamond Oliver," said he, "is about to be married to Mr. Granby, one of the best connected and most estimable residents in S——, grandson and heir to Sir Frederic Granby: I had the intelligence from her father yesterday."

His sisters looked at each other and at me; we all three looked at him: he was serene as glass.

"The match must have been got up hastily," said Diana: "they cannot have known each other long."

"But two months: they met in October at the county ball at S——. But where there are no obstacles to a union, as in the present case, where the connection is in every point desirable, delays are unnecessary: they will be married as soon as S-Place, which Sir Frederic gives up to them, can he refitted for their reception."

The first time I found St. John alone after this communication, I felt tempted to inquire if the event distressed him: but he seemed so little to need sympathy, that, so far from venturing to offer him more, I experienced some shame at the recollection of what I had already hazarded. Besides, I was out of practice in talking to him: his reserve was again frozen over, and my frankness was congealed beneath it. He had not kept his promise of treating me like his sisters; he continually made little chilling differences between us, which did not at all tend to the development of cordiality: in short, now that I was acknowledged his kinswoman, and lived under the same roof with him, I felt the distance between us to be far greater than when he had known me only as the village schoolmistress. When I remembered how far I had once been admitted to his confidence, I could hardly comprehend his present frigidity.

Such being the case, I felt not a little surprised when he raised his head suddenly from the desk over which he was stooping, and said—

"You see, Jane, the battle is fought and the victory won."

Startled at being thus addressed, I did not immediately reply: after a moment's hesitation I answered—

"But are you sure you are not in the position of those conquerors whose triumphs have cost them too dear? Would not such another ruin you?"

"I think not; and if I were, it does not much signify; I shall never be called upon to contend for such another. The event of the conflict is decisive: my way is now clear; I thank God for it!" So saying, he returned to his papers and his silence.

As our mutual happiness (i.e., Diana's, Mary's, and mine) settled into a quieter character, and we resumed our usual habits and regular studies, St. John stayed more at home: he sat with us in the same room, sometimes for hours together. While Mary drew, Diana pursued a course of encyclopaedic reading she had (to my awe and amazement) undertaken, and I fagged away at German, he pondered a mystic lore of his own: that of some Eastern tongue, the acquisition of which he thought necessary to his plans.

Thus engaged, he appeared, sitting in his own recess, quiet and absorbed enough; but that blue eye of his had a habit of leaving the outlandish-looking grammar, and wandering over, and sometimes fixing upon us, his fellow-students, with a curious intensity of observation: if caught, it would be instantly withdrawn; yet ever and anon, it returned searchingly to our table. I wondered what it meant: I wondered, too, at the punctual satisfaction he never failed to exhibit on an occasion that seemed to me of small moment, namely, my weekly visit to Morton school; and still more was I puzzled when, if the day was unfavourable, if there was snow, or rain, or high wind, and his sisters urged me not to go, he would invariably make light of their solicitude, and encourage me to accomplish the task without regard to the elements.

"Jane is not such a weakling as you would make her," he would say: "she can bear a mountain blast, or a shower, or a few flakes of snow, as well as any of us. Her constitution is both sound and elastic;—better calculated to endure variations of climate than many more robust."

And when I returned, sometimes a good deal tired, and not a little weather-beaten, I never dared complain, because I saw that to murmur would be to vex him: on all occasions fortitude pleased him; the reverse was a special annoyance.

One afternoon, however, I got leave to stay at home, because I really had a cold. His sisters were gone to Morton in my stead: I sat reading Schiller; he, deciphering his crabbed Oriental scrolls. As I exchanged a translation for an exercise, I happened to look his way: there I found myself under the influence of the ever-watchful blue eye. How long it had been searching me through and through, and over and over, I cannot tell: so keen was it, and yet so cold, I felt for the moment superstitious—as if I were sitting in the room with something uncanny.

"Jane, what are you doing?"

"Learning German."

"I want you to give up German and learn Hindostanee."

"You are not in earnest?"

"In such earnest that I must have it so: and I will tell you why."

He then went on to explain that Hindostanee was the language he was himself at present studying; that, as he advanced, he was apt to forget the commencement; that it would assist him greatly to have a pupil with whom he might again and again go over the elements, and so fix them thoroughly in his mind; that his choice had hovered for some time between me and his sisters; but that he had fixed on me because he saw I could sit at a task the longest of the three. Would I do him this favour? I should not, perhaps, have to make the sacrifice long, as it wanted now barely three months to his departure.

St. John was not a man to be lightly refused: you felt that every impression made on him, either for pain or pleasure, was deep-graved and permanent. I consented. When Diana and Mary returned, the former found her scholar transferred from her to her brother: she laughed, and both she and Mary agreed that St. John should never have persuaded them to such a step. He answered quietly—

"I know it."

I found him a very patient, very forbearing, and yet an exacting master: he expected me to do a great deal; and when I fulfilled his expectations, he, in his own way, fully testified his approbation. By degrees, he acquired a certain influence over me that took away my liberty of mind: his praise and notice were more restraining than his indifference. I could no longer talk or laugh freely when he was by, because a tiresomely importunate instinct reminded me that vivacity (at least in me) was distasteful to him. I was so fully aware that only serious moods and occupations were acceptable, that in his presence every effort to sustain or follow any other became vain: I fell under a freezing spell. When he said "go," I went; "come," I came; "do this," I did it. But I did not love my servitude: I wished, many a time, he had continued to neglect me.

One evening when, at bedtime, his sisters and I stood round him, bidding him good-night, he kissed each of them, as was his custom; and, as was equally his custom, he gave me his hand. Diana, who chanced to be in a frolicsome humour (SHE was not painfully controlled by his will; for hers, in another way, was as strong), exclaimed—

"St. John! you used to call Jane your third sister, but you don't treat her as such: you should kiss her too."

She pushed me towards him. I thought Diana very provoking, and felt uncomfortably confused; and while I was thus thinking and feeling, St. John bent his head; his Greek face was brought to a level with mine, his eyes questioned my eyes piercingly—he kissed me. There are no such things as marble kisses or ice kisses, or I should say my ecclesiastical cousin's salute belonged to one of these classes; but there may be experiment kisses, and his was an experiment kiss. When given, he viewed me to learn the result; it was not striking: I am sure I did not blush; perhaps I might have turned a little pale, for I felt as if this kiss were a seal affixed to my fetters. He never omitted the ceremony afterwards, and the gravity and quiescence with which I underwent it, seemed to invest it for him with a certain charm.

As for me, I daily wished more to please him; but to do so, I felt daily more and more that I must disown half my nature, stifle half my faculties, wrest my tastes from their original bent, force myself to the adoption of pursuits for which I had no natural vocation. He wanted to train me to an elevation I could never reach; it racked me hourly to aspire to the standard he uplifted. The thing was as impossible as to mould my irregular features to his correct and classic pattern, to give to my changeable green eyes the sea-blue tint and solemn lustre of his own.

Not his ascendancy alone, however, held me in thrall at present. Of late it had been easy enough for me to look sad: a cankering evil sat at my heart and drained my happiness at its source—the evil of suspense.

Perhaps you think I had forgotten Mr. Rochester, reader, amidst these changes of place and fortune. Not for a moment. His idea was still with me, because it was not a vapour sunshine could disperse, nor a sand-traced effigy storms could wash away; it was a name graven on a tablet, fated to last as long as the marble it inscribed. The craving to know what had become of him followed me everywhere; when I was at Morton, I re-entered my cottage every evening to think of that; and now at Moor House, I sought my bedroom each night to brood over it.

In the course of my necessary correspondence with Mr. Briggs about the will, I had inquired if he knew anything of Mr. Rochester's present residence and state of health; but, as St. John had conjectured, he was quite ignorant of all concerning him. I then wrote to Mrs. Fairfax, entreating information on the subject. I had calculated with certainty on this step answering my end: I felt sure it would elicit an early answer. I was astonished when a fortnight passed without reply; but when two months wore away, and day after day the post arrived and brought nothing for me, I fell a prey to the keenest anxiety.

I wrote again: there was a chance of my first letter having missed. Renewed hope followed renewed effort: it shone like the former for some weeks, then, like it, it faded, flickered: not a line, not a word reached me. When half a year wasted in vain expectancy, my hope died out, and then I felt dark indeed.

A fine spring shone round me, which I could not enjoy. Summer approached; Diana tried to cheer me: she said I looked ill, and wished to accompany me to the sea-side. This St. John opposed; he said I did not want dissipation, I wanted employment; my present life was too purposeless, I required an aim; and, I suppose, by way of supplying deficiencies, he prolonged still further my lessons in Hindostanee, and grew more urgent in requiring their accomplishment: and I, like a fool, never thought of resisting him—I could not resist him.

One day I had come to my studies in lower spirits than usual; the ebb was occasioned by a poignantly felt disappointment. Hannah had told me in the morning there was a letter for me, and when I went down to take it, almost certain that the long-looked for tidings were vouchsafed me at last, I found only an unimportant note from Mr. Briggs on business. The bitter check had wrung from me some tears; and now, as I sat poring over the crabbed characters and flourishing tropes of an Indian scribe, my eyes filled again.

St. John called me to his side to read; in attempting to do this my voice failed me: words were lost in sobs. He and I were the only occupants of the parlour: Diana was practising her music in the drawing-room, Mary was gardening—it was a very fine May day, clear, sunny, and breezy. My companion expressed no surprise at this emotion, nor did he question me as to its cause; he only said—

"We will wait a few minutes, Jane, till you are more composed." And while I smothered the paroxysm with all haste, he sat calm and patient, leaning on his desk, and looking like a physician watching with the eye of science an expected and fully understood crisis in a patient's malady. Having stifled my sobs, wiped my eyes, and muttered something about not being very well that morning, I resumed my task, and succeeded in completing it. St. John put away my books and his, locked his desk, and said—

"Now, Jane, you shall take a walk; and with me."

"I will call Diana and Mary."

"No; I want only one companion this morning, and that must be you. Put on your things; go out by the kitchen-door: take the road towards the head of Marsh Glen: I will join you in a moment."

I know no medium: I never in my life have known any medium in my dealings with positive, hard characters, antagonistic to my own, between absolute submission and determined revolt. I have always faithfully observed the one, up to the very moment of bursting, sometimes with volcanic vehemence, into the other; and as neither present circumstances warranted, nor my present mood inclined me to mutiny, I observed careful obedience to St. John's directions; and in ten minutes I was treading the wild track of the glen, side by side with him.

The breeze was from the west: it came over the hills, sweet with scents of heath and rush; the sky was of stainless blue; the stream descending the ravine, swelled with past spring rains, poured along plentiful and clear, catching golden gleams from the sun, and sapphire tints from the firmament. As we advanced and left the track, we trod a soft turf, mossy fine and emerald green, minutely enamelled with a tiny white flower, and spangled with a star-like yellow blossom: the hills, meantime, shut us quite in; for the glen, towards its head, wound to their very core.

"Let us rest here," said St. John, as we reached the first stragglers of a battalion of rocks, guarding a sort of pass, beyond which the beck rushed down a waterfall; and where, still a little farther, the mountain shook off turf and flower, had only heath for raiment and crag for gem—where it exaggerated the wild to the savage, and exchanged the fresh for the frowning—where it guarded the forlorn hope of solitude, and a last refuge for silence.

I took a seat: St. John stood near me. He looked up the pass and down the hollow; his glance wandered away with the stream, and returned to traverse the unclouded heaven which coloured it: he removed his hat, let the breeze stir his hair and kiss his brow. He seemed in communion with the genius of the haunt: with his eye he bade farewell to something.

"And I shall see it again," he said aloud, "in dreams when I sleep by the Ganges: and again in a more remote hour—when another slumber overcomes me—on the shore of a darker stream!"

Strange words of a strange love! An austere patriot's passion for his fatherland! He sat down; for half-an-hour we never spoke; neither he to me nor I to him: that interval past, he recommenced—

"Jane, I go in six weeks; I have taken my berth in an East Indiaman which sails on the 20th of June."

"God will protect you; for you have undertaken His work," I answered.

"Yes," said he, "there is my glory and joy. I am the servant of an infallible Master. I am not going out under human guidance, subject to the defective laws and erring control of my feeble fellow-worms: my king, my lawgiver, my captain, is the All-perfect. It seems strange to me that all round me do not burn to enlist under the same banner,—to join in the same enterprise."

"All have not your powers, and it would be folly for the feeble to wish to march with the strong."

"I do not speak to the feeble, or think of them: I address only such as are worthy of the work, and competent to accomplish it."

"Those are few in number, and difficult to discover."

"You say truly; but when found, it is right to stir them up—to urge and exhort them to the effort—to show them what their gifts are, and why they were given—to speak Heaven's message in their ear,—to offer them, direct from God, a place in the ranks of His chosen."

"If they are really qualified for the task, will not their own hearts be the first to inform them of it?"

I felt as if an awful charm was framing round and gathering over me: I trembled to hear some fatal word spoken which would at once declare and rivet the spell.

"And what does YOUR heart say?" demanded St. John.

"My heart is mute,—my heart is mute," I answered, struck and thrilled.

"Then I must speak for it," continued the deep, relentless voice. "Jane, come with me to India: come as my helpmeet and fellow-labourer."

The glen and sky spun round: the hills heaved! It was as if I had heard a summons from Heaven—as if a visionary messenger, like him of Macedonia, had enounced, "Come over and help us!" But I was no apostle,—I could not behold the herald,—I could not receive his call.

"Oh, St. John!" I cried, "have some mercy!"

I appealed to one who, in the discharge of what he believed his duty, knew neither mercy nor remorse. He continued—

"God and nature intended you for a missionary's wife. It is not personal, but mental endowments they have given you: you are formed for labour, not for love. A missionary's wife you must—shall be. You shall be mine: I claim you—not for my pleasure, but for my Sovereign's service."

"I am not fit for it: I have no vocation," I said.

He had calculated on these first objections: he was not irritated by them. Indeed, as he leaned back against the crag behind him, folded his arms on his chest, and fixed his countenance, I saw he was prepared for a long and trying opposition, and had taken in a stock of patience to last him to its close—resolved, however, that that close should be conquest for him.

"Humility, Jane," said he, "is the groundwork of Christian virtues: you say right that you are not fit for the work. Who is fit for it? Or who, that ever was truly called, believed himself worthy of the summons? I, for instance, am but dust and ashes. With St. Paul, I acknowledge myself the chiefest of sinners; but I do not suffer this sense of my personal vileness to daunt me. I know my Leader: that He is just as well as mighty; and while He has chosen a feeble instrument to perform a great task, He will, from the boundless stores of His providence, supply the inadequacy of the means to the end. Think like me, Jane—trust like me. It is the Rock of Ages I ask you to lean on: do not doubt but it will bear the weight of your human weakness."

"I do not understand a missionary life: I have never studied missionary labours."

"There I, humble as I am, can give you the aid you want: I can set you your task from hour to hour; stand by you always; help you from moment to moment. This I could do in the beginning: soon (for I know your powers) you would be as strong and apt as myself, and would not require my help."

"But my powers—where are they for this undertaking? I do not feel them. Nothing speaks or stirs in me while you talk. I am sensible of no light kindling—no life quickening—no voice counselling or cheering. Oh, I wish I could make you see how much my mind is at this moment like a rayless dungeon, with one shrinking fear fettered in its depths—the fear of being persuaded by you to attempt what I cannot accomplish!"

"I have an answer for you—hear it. I have watched you ever since we first met: I have made you my study for ten months. I have proved you in that time by sundry tests: and what have I seen and elicited? In the village school I found you could perform well, punctually, uprightly, labour uncongenial to your habits and inclinations; I saw you could perform it with capacity and tact: you could win while you controlled. In the calm with which you learnt you had become suddenly rich, I read a mind clear of the vice of Demas:-lucre had no undue power over you. In the resolute readiness with which you cut your wealth into four shares, keeping but one to yourself, and relinquishing the three others to the claim of abstract justice, I recognised a soul that revelled in the flame and excitement of sacrifice. In the tractability with which, at my wish, you forsook a study in which you were interested, and adopted another because it interested me; in the untiring assiduity with which you have since persevered in it—in the unflagging energy and unshaken temper with which you have met its difficulties—I acknowledge the complement of the qualities I seek. Jane, you are docile, diligent, disinterested, faithful, constant, and courageous; very gentle, and very heroic: cease to mistrust yourself—I can trust you unreservedly. As a conductress of Indian schools, and a helper amongst Indian women, your assistance will be to me invaluable."

My iron shroud contracted round me; persuasion advanced with slow sure step. Shut my eyes as I would, these last words of his succeeded in making the way, which had seemed blocked up, comparatively clear. My work, which had appeared so vague, so hopelessly diffuse, condensed itself as he proceeded, and assumed a definite form under his shaping hand. He waited for an answer. I demanded a quarter of an hour to think, before I again hazarded a reply.

"Very willingly," he rejoined; and rising, he strode a little distance up the pass, threw himself down on a swell of heath, and there lay still.

"I CAN do what he wants me to do: I am forced to see and acknowledge that," I meditated,—"that is, if life be spared me. But I feel mine is not the existence to be long protracted under an Indian sun. What then? He does not care for that: when my time came to die, he would resign me, in all serenity and sanctity, to the God who gave me. The case is very plain before me. In leaving England, I should leave a loved but empty land—Mr. Rochester is not there; and if he were, what is, what can that ever be to me? My business is to live without him now: nothing so absurd, so weak as to drag on from day to day, as if I were waiting some impossible change in circumstances, which might reunite me to him. Of course (as St. John once said) I must seek another interest in life to replace the one lost: is not the occupation he now offers me truly the most glorious man can adopt or God assign? Is it not, by its noble cares and sublime results, the one best calculated to fill the void left by uptorn affections and demolished hopes? I believe I must say, Yes—and yet I shudder. Alas! If I join St. John, I abandon half myself: if I go to India, I go to premature death. And how will the interval between leaving England for India, and India for the grave, be filled? Oh, I know well! That, too, is very clear to my vision. By straining to satisfy St. John till my sinews ache, I SHALL satisfy him—to the finest central point and farthest outward circle of his expectations. If I DO go with him—if I DO make the sacrifice he urges, I will make it absolutely: I will throw all on the altar—heart, vitals, the entire victim. He will never love me; but he shall approve me; I will show him energies he has not yet seen, resources he has never suspected. Yes, I can work as hard as he can, and with as little grudging.

"Consent, then, to his demand is possible: but for one item—one dreadful item. It is—that he asks me to be his wife, and has no more of a husband's heart for me than that frowning giant of a rock, down which the stream is foaming in yonder gorge. He prizes me as a soldier would a good weapon; and that is all. Unmarried to him, this would never grieve me; but can I let him complete his calculations—coolly put into practice his plans—go through the wedding ceremony? Can I receive from him the bridal ring, endure all the forms of love (which I doubt not he would scrupulously observe) and know that the spirit was quite absent? Can I bear the consciousness that every endearment he bestows is a sacrifice made on principle? No: such a martyrdom would be monstrous. I will never undergo it. As his sister, I might accompany him—not as his wife: I will tell him so."

I looked towards the knoll: there he lay, still as a prostrate column; his face turned to me: his eye beaming watchful and keen. He started to his feet and approached me.

"I am ready to go to India, if I may go free."

"Your answer requires a commentary," he said; "it is not clear."

"You have hitherto been my adopted brother—I, your adopted sister: let us continue as such: you and I had better not marry."

He shook his head. "Adopted fraternity will not do in this case. If you were my real sister it would be different: I should take you, and seek no wife. But as it is, either our union must be consecrated and sealed by marriage, or it cannot exist: practical obstacles oppose themselves to any other plan. Do you not see it, Jane? Consider a moment—your strong sense will guide you."

I did consider; and still my sense, such as it was, directed me only to the fact that we did not love each other as man and wife should: and therefore it inferred we ought not to marry. I said so. "St. John," I returned, "I regard you as a brother—you, me as a sister: so let us continue."

"We cannot—we cannot," he answered, with short, sharp determination: "it would not do. You have said you will go with me to India: remember—you have said that."

"Conditionally."

"Well—well. To the main point—the departure with me from England, the co-operation with me in my future labours—you do not object. You have already as good as put your hand to the plough: you are too consistent to withdraw it. You have but one end to keep in view—how the work you have undertaken can best be done. Simplify your complicated interests, feelings, thoughts, wishes, aims; merge all considerations in one purpose: that of fulfilling with effect—with power—the mission of your great Master. To do so, you must have a coadjutor: not a brother—that is a loose tie—but a husband. I, too, do not want a sister: a sister might any day be taken from me. I want a wife: the sole helpmeet I can influence efficiently in life, and retain absolutely till death."

I shuddered as he spoke: I felt his influence in my marrow—his hold on my limbs.

"Seek one elsewhere than in me, St. John: seek one fitted to you."

"One fitted to my purpose, you mean—fitted to my vocation. Again I tell you it is not the insignificant private individual—the mere man, with the man's selfish senses—I wish to mate: it is the missionary."

"And I will give the missionary my energies—it is all he wants—but not myself: that would be only adding the husk and shell to the kernel. For them he has no use: I retain them."

"You cannot—you ought not. Do you think God will be satisfied with half an oblation? Will He accept a mutilated sacrifice? It is the cause of God I advocate: it is under His standard I enlist you. I cannot accept on His behalf a divided allegiance: it must be entire."

"Oh! I will give my heart to God," I said. "YOU do not want it."

I will not swear, reader, that there was not something of repressed sarcasm both in the tone in which I uttered this sentence, and in the feeling that accompanied it. I had silently feared St. John till now, because I had not understood him. He had held me in awe, because he had held me in doubt. How much of him was saint, how much mortal, I could not heretofore tell: but revelations were being made in this conference: the analysis of his nature was proceeding before my eyes. I saw his fallibilities: I comprehended them. I understood that, sitting there where I did, on the bank of heath, and with that handsome form before me, I sat at the feet of a man, caring as I. The veil fell from his hardness and despotism. Having felt in him the presence of these qualities, I felt his imperfection and took courage. I was with an equal—one with whom I might argue—one whom, if I saw good, I might resist.

He was silent after I had uttered the last sentence, and I presently risked an upward glance at his countenance.

His eye, bent on me, expressed at once stern surprise and keen inquiry. "Is she sarcastic, and sarcastic to ME!" it seemed to say. "What does this signify?"

"Do not let us forget that this is a solemn matter," he said ere long; "one of which we may neither think nor talk lightly without sin. I trust, Jane, you are in earnest when you say you will serve your heart to God: it is all I want. Once wrench your heart from man, and fix it on your Maker, the advancement of that Maker's spiritual kingdom on earth will be your chief delight and endeavour; you will be ready to do at once whatever furthers that end. You will see what impetus would be given to your efforts and mine by our physical and mental union in marriage: the only union that gives a character of permanent conformity to the destinies and designs of human beings; and, passing over all minor caprices—all trivial difficulties and delicacies of feeling—all scruple about the degree, kind, strength or tenderness of mere personal inclination—you will hasten to enter into that union at once."

"Shall I?" I said briefly; and I looked at his features, beautiful in their harmony, but strangely formidable in their still severity; at his brow, commanding but not open; at his eyes, bright and deep and searching, but never soft; at his tall imposing figure; and fancied myself in idea HIS WIFE. Oh! it would never do! As his curate, his comrade, all would be right: I would cross oceans with him in that capacity; toil under Eastern suns, in Asian deserts with him in that office; admire and emulate his courage and devotion and vigour; accommodate quietly to his masterhood; smile undisturbed at his ineradicable ambition; discriminate the Christian from the man: profoundly esteem the one, and freely forgive the other. I should suffer often, no doubt, attached to him only in this capacity: my body would be under rather a stringent yoke, but my heart and mind would be free. I should still have my unblighted self to turn to: my natural unenslaved feelings with which to communicate in moments of loneliness. There would be recesses in my mind which would be only mine, to which he never came, and sentiments growing there fresh and sheltered which his austerity could never blight, nor his measured warrior-march trample down: but as his wife—at his side always, and always restrained, and always checked—forced to keep the fire of my nature continually low, to compel it to burn inwardly and never utter a cry, though the imprisoned flame consumed vital after vital—THIS would be unendurable.

"St. John!" I exclaimed, when I had got so far in my meditation.

"Well?" he answered icily.

"I repeat I freely consent to go with you as your fellow-missionary, but not as your wife; I cannot marry you and become part of you."

"A part of me you must become," he answered steadily; "otherwise the whole bargain is void. How can I, a man not yet thirty, take out with me to India a girl of nineteen, unless she be married to me? How can we be for ever together—sometimes in solitudes, sometimes amidst savage tribes—and unwed?"

"Very well," I said shortly; "under the circumstances, quite as well as if I were either your real sister, or a man and a clergyman like yourself."

"It is known that you are not my sister; I cannot introduce you as such: to attempt it would be to fasten injurious suspicions on us both.

And for the rest, though you have a man's vigorous brain, you have a woman's heart and—it would not do."

"It would do," I affirmed with some disdain, "perfectly well. I have a woman's heart, but not where you are concerned; for you I have only a comrade's constancy; a fellow-soldier's frankness, fidelity, fraternity, if you like; a neophyte's respect and submission to his hierophant: nothing more—don't fear."

"It is what I want," he said, speaking to himself; "it is just what I want. And there are obstacles in the way: they must be hewn down. Jane, you would not repent marrying me—be certain of that; we MUST be married. I repeat it: there is no other way; and undoubtedly enough of love would follow upon marriage to render the union right even in your eyes."

"I scorn your idea of love," I could not help saying, as I rose up and stood before him, leaning my back against the rock. "I scorn the counterfeit sentiment you offer: yes, St. John, and I scorn you when you offer it."

He looked at me fixedly, compressing his well-cut lips while he did so. Whether he was incensed or surprised, or what, it was not easy to tell: he could command his countenance thoroughly.

"I scarcely expected to hear that expression from you," he said: "I think I have done and uttered nothing to deserve scorn."

I was touched by his gentle tone, and overawed by his high, calm mien.

"Forgive me the words, St. John; but it is your own fault that I have been roused to speak so unguardedly. You have introduced a topic on which our natures are at variance—a topic we should never discuss: the very name of love is an apple of discord between us. If the reality were required, what should we do? How should we feel? My dear cousin, abandon your scheme of marriage—forget it."

"No," said he; "it is a long-cherished scheme, and the only one which can secure my great end: but I shall urge you no further at present. To-morrow, I leave home for Cambridge: I have many friends there to whom I should wish to say farewell. I shall be absent a fortnight—take that space of time to consider my offer: and do not forget that if you reject it, it is not me you deny, but God. Through my means, He opens to you a noble career; as my wife only can you enter upon it. Refuse to be my wife, and you limit yourself for ever to a track of selfish ease and barren obscurity. Tremble lest in that case you should be numbered with those who have denied the faith, and are worse than infidels!"

He had done. Turning from me, he once more

"Looked to river, looked to hill."

But this time his feelings were all pent in his heart: I was not worthy to hear them uttered. As I walked by his side homeward, I read well in his iron silence all he felt towards me: the disappointment of an austere and despotic nature, which has met resistance where it expected submission—the disapprobation of a cool, inflexible judgment, which has detected in another feelings and views in which it has no power to sympathise: in short, as a man, he would have wished to coerce me into obedience: it was only as a sincere Christian he bore so patiently with my perversity, and allowed so long a space for reflection and repentance.

That night, after he had kissed his sisters, he thought proper to forget even to shake hands with me, but left the room in silence. I—who, though I had no love, had much friendship for him—was hurt by the marked omission: so much hurt that tears started to my eyes.

"I see you and St. John have been quarrelling, Jane," said Diana, "during your walk on the moor. But go after him; he is now lingering in the passage expecting you—he will make it up."

I have not much pride under such circumstances: I would always rather be happy than dignified; and I ran after him—he stood at the foot of the stairs.

"Good-night, St. John," said I.

"Good-night, Jane," he replied calmly.

"Then shake hands," I added.

What a cold, loose touch, he impressed on my fingers! He was deeply displeased by what had occurred that day; cordiality would not warm, nor tears move him. No happy reconciliation was to be had with him—no cheering smile or generous word: but still the Christian was patient and placid; and when I asked him if he forgave me, he answered that he was not in the habit of cherishing the remembrance of vexation; that he had nothing to forgive, not having been offended.

And with that answer he left me. I would much rather he had knocked me down.

Chapter XXXV

He did not leave for Cambridge the next day, as he had said he would. He deferred his departure a whole week, and during that time he made me feel what severe punishment a good yet stern, a conscientious yet implacable man can inflict on one who has offended him. Without one overt act of hostility, one upbraiding word, he contrived to impress me momently with the conviction that I was put beyond the pale of his favour.

Not that St. John harboured a spirit of unchristian vindictiveness—not that he would have injured a hair of my head, if it had been fully in his power to do so. Both by nature and principle, he was superior to the mean gratification of vengeance: he had forgiven me for saying I scorned him and his love, but he had not forgotten the words; and as long as he and I lived he never would forget them. I saw by his look, when he turned to me, that they were always written on the air between me and him; whenever I spoke, they sounded in my voice to his ear, and their echo toned every answer he gave me.

He did not abstain from conversing with me: he even called me as usual each morning to join him at his desk; and I fear the corrupt man within him had a pleasure unimparted to, and unshared by, the pure Christian, in evincing with what skill he could, while acting and speaking apparently just as usual, extract from every deed and every phrase the spirit of interest and approval which had formerly communicated a certain austere charm to his language and manner. To me, he was in reality become no longer flesh, but marble; his eye was a cold, bright, blue gem; his tongue a speaking instrument—nothing more.

All this was torture to me—refined, lingering torture. It kept up a slow fire of indignation and a trembling trouble of grief, which harassed and crushed me altogether. I felt how—if I were his wife, this good man, pure as the deep sunless source, could soon kill me, without drawing from my veins a single drop of blood, or receiving on his own crystal conscience the faintest stain of crime. Especially I felt this when I made any attempt to propitiate him. No ruth met my ruth. HE experienced no suffering from estrangement—no yearning after reconciliation; and though, more than once, my fast falling tears blistered the page over which we both bent, they produced no more effect on him than if his heart had been really a matter of stone or metal. To his sisters, meantime, he was somewhat kinder than usual: as if afraid that mere coldness would not sufficiently convince me how completely I was banished and banned, he added the force of contrast; and this I am sure he did not by force, but on principle.

The night before he left home, happening to see him walking in the garden about sunset, and remembering, as I looked at him, that this man, alienated as he now was, had once saved my life, and that we were near relations, I was moved to make a last attempt to regain his friendship. I went out and approached him as he stood leaning over the little gate; I spoke to the point at once.

"St. John, I am unhappy because you are still angry with me. Let us be friends."

"I hope we are friends," was the unmoved reply; while he still watched the rising of the moon, which he had been contemplating as I approached.

"No, St. John, we are not friends as we were. You know that."

"Are we not? That is wrong. For my part, I wish you no ill and all good."

"I believe you, St. John; for I am sure you are incapable of wishing any one ill; but, as I am your kinswoman, I should desire somewhat more of affection than that sort of general philanthropy you extend to mere strangers."

"Of course," he said. "Your wish is reasonable, and I am far from regarding you as a stranger."

This, spoken in a cool, tranquil tone, was mortifying and baffling enough. Had I attended to the suggestions of pride and ire, I should immediately have left him; but something worked within me more strongly than those feelings could. I deeply venerated my cousin's talent and principle. His friendship was of value to me: to lose it tried me severely. I would not so soon relinquish the attempt to reconquer it.

"Must we part in this way, St. John? And when you go to India, will you leave me so, without a kinder word than you have yet spoken?"

He now turned quite from the moon and faced me.

"When I go to India, Jane, will I leave you! What! do you not go to India?"

"You said I could not unless I married you."

"And you will not marry me! You adhere to that resolution?"

Reader, do you know, as I do, what terror those cold people can put into the ice of their questions? How much of the fall of the avalanche is in their anger? of the breaking up of the frozen sea in their displeasure?

"No. St. John, I will not marry you. I adhere to my resolution."

The avalanche had shaken and slid a little forward, but it did not yet crash down.

"Once more, why this refusal?" he asked.

"Formerly," I answered, "because you did not love me; now, I reply, because you almost hate me. If I were to marry you, you would kill me. You are killing me now."

His lips and cheeks turned white—quite white.

"I SHOULD KILL YOU—I AM KILLING YOU? Your words are such as ought not to be used: violent, unfeminine, and untrue. They betray an unfortunate state of mind: they merit severe reproof: they would seem inexcusable, but that it is the duty of man to forgive his fellow even until seventy-and-seven times."

I had finished the business now. While earnestly wishing to erase from his mind the trace of my former offence, I had stamped on that tenacious surface another and far deeper impression, I had burnt it in.

"Now you will indeed hate me," I said. "It is useless to attempt to conciliate you: I see I have made an eternal enemy of you."

A fresh wrong did these words inflict: the worse, because they touched on the truth. That bloodless lip quivered to a temporary spasm. I knew the steely ire I had whetted. I was heart-wrung.

"You utterly misinterpret my words," I said, at once seizing his hand: "I have no intention to grieve or pain you—indeed, I have not."

Most bitterly he smiled—most decidedly he withdrew his hand from mine. "And now you recall your promise, and will not go to India at all, I presume?" said he, after a considerable pause.

"Yes, I will, as your assistant," I answered.

A very long silence succeeded. What struggle there was in him between Nature and Grace in this interval, I cannot tell: only singular gleams scintillated in his eyes, and strange shadows passed over his face. He spoke at last.

"I before proved to you the absurdity of a single woman of your age proposing to accompany abroad a single man of mine. I proved it to you in such terms as, I should have thought, would have prevented your ever again alluding to the plan. That you have done so, I regret—for your sake."

I interrupted him. Anything like a tangible reproach gave me courage at once. "Keep to common sense, St. John: you are verging on nonsense. You pretend to be shocked by what I have said. You are not really shocked: for, with your superior mind, you cannot be either so dull or so conceited as to misunderstand my meaning. I say again, I will be your curate, if you like, but never your wife."

Again he turned lividly pale; but, as before, controlled his passion perfectly. He answered emphatically but calmly—

"A female curate, who is not my wife, would never suit me. With me, then, it seems, you cannot go: but if you are sincere in your offer, I will, while in town, speak to a married missionary, whose wife needs a coadjutor. Your own fortune will make you independent of the Society's aid; and thus you may still be spared the dishonour of breaking your promise and deserting the band you engaged to join."

Now I never had, as the reader knows, either given any formal promise or entered into any engagement; and this language was all much too hard and much too despotic for the occasion. I replied—

"There is no dishonour, no breach of promise, no desertion in the case. I am not under the slightest obligation to go to India, especially with strangers. With you I would have ventured much, because I admire, confide in, and, as a sister, I love you; but I am convinced that, go when and with whom I would, I should not live long in that climate."

"Ah! you are afraid of yourself," he said, curling his lip.

"I am. God did not give me my life to throw away; and to do as you wish me would, I begin to think, be almost equivalent to committing suicide. Moreover, before I definitively resolve on quitting England, I will know for certain whether I cannot be of greater use by remaining in it than by leaving it."

"What do you mean?"

"It would be fruitless to attempt to explain; but there is a point on which I have long endured painful doubt, and I can go nowhere till by some means that doubt is removed."

"I know where your heart turns and to what it clings. The interest you cherish is lawless and unconsecrated. Long since you ought to have crushed it: now you should blush to allude to it. You think of Mr. Rochester?"

It was true. I confessed it by silence.

"Are you going to seek Mr. Rochester?"

"I must find out what is become of him."

"It remains for me, then," he said, "to remember you in my prayers, and to entreat God for you, in all earnestness, that you may not indeed become a castaway. I had thought I recognised in you one of the chosen. But God sees not as man sees: HIS will be done—"

He opened the gate, passed through it, and strayed away down the glen. He was soon out of sight.

On re-entering the parlour, I found Diana standing at the window, looking very thoughtful. Diana was a great deal taller than I: she put her hand on my shoulder, and, stooping, examined my face.

"Jane," she said, "you are always agitated and pale now. I am sure there is something the matter. Tell me what business St. John and you have on hands. I have watched you this half hour from the window; you must forgive my being such a spy, but for a long time I have fancied I hardly know what. St. John is a strange being——"

She paused—I did not speak: soon she resumed—

"That brother of mine cherishes peculiar views of some sort respecting you, I am sure: he has long distinguished you by a notice and interest he never showed to any one else—to what end? I wish he loved you—does he, Jane?"

I put her cool hand to my hot forehead; "No, Die, not one whit."

"Then why does he follow you so with his eyes, and get you so frequently alone with him, and keep you so continually at his side? Mary and I had both concluded he wished you to marry him."

"He does—he has asked me to be his wife."

Diana clapped her hands. "That is just what we hoped and thought! And you will marry him, Jane, won't you? And then he will stay in England."

"Far from that, Diana; his sole idea in proposing to me is to procure a fitting fellow-labourer in his Indian toils."

"What! He wishes you to go to India?"

"Yes."

"Madness!" she exclaimed. "You would not live three months there, I am certain. You never shall go: you have not consented, have you, Jane?"

"I have refused to marry him——"

"And have consequently displeased him?" she suggested.

"Deeply: he will never forgive me, I fear: yet I offered to accompany him as his sister."

"It was frantic folly to do so, Jane. Think of the task you undertook—one of incessant fatigue, where fatigue kills even the strong, and you are weak. St. John—you know him—would urge you to impossibilities: with him there would be no permission to rest during the hot hours; and unfortunately, I have noticed, whatever he exacts, you force yourself to perform. I am astonished you found courage to refuse his hand. You do not love him then, Jane?"

"Not as a husband."

"Yet he is a handsome fellow."

"And I am so plain, you see, Die. We should never suit."

"Plain! You? Not at all. You are much too pretty, as well as too good, to be grilled alive in Calcutta." And again she earnestly conjured me to give up all thoughts of going out with her brother.

"I must indeed," I said; "for when just now I repeated the offer of serving him for a deacon, he expressed himself shocked at my want of decency. He seemed to think I had committed an impropriety in proposing to accompany him unmarried: as if I had not from the first hoped to find in him a brother, and habitually regarded him as such."

"What makes you say he does not love you, Jane?"

"You should hear himself on the subject. He has again and again explained that it is not himself, but his office he wishes to mate. He has told me I am formed for labour—not for love: which is true, no doubt. But, in my opinion, if I am not formed for love, it follows that I am not formed for marriage. Would it not be strange, Die, to be chained for life to a man who regarded one but as a useful tool?"

"Insupportable—unnatural—out of the question!"

"And then," I continued, "though I have only sisterly affection for him now, yet, if forced to be his wife, I can imagine the possibility of conceiving an inevitable, strange, torturing kind of love for him, because he is so talented; and there is often a certain heroic grandeur in his look, manner, and conversation. In that case, my lot would become unspeakably wretched. He would not want me to love him; and if I showed the feeling, he would make me sensible that it was a superfluity, unrequired by him, unbecoming in me. I know he would."

"And yet St. John is a good man," said Diana.

"He is a good and a great man; but he forgets, pitilessly, the feelings and claims of little people, in pursuing his own large views. It is better, therefore, for the insignificant to keep out of his way, lest, in his progress, he should trample them down. Here he comes! I will leave you, Diana." And I hastened upstairs as I saw him entering the garden.

But I was forced to meet him again at supper. During that meal he appeared just as composed as usual. I had thought he would hardly speak to me, and I was certain he had given up the pursuit of his matrimonial scheme: the sequel showed I was mistaken on both points. He addressed me precisely in his ordinary manner, or what had, of late, been his ordinary manner—one scrupulously polite. No doubt he had invoked the help of the Holy Spirit to subdue the anger I had roused in him, and now believed he had forgiven me once more.

For the evening reading before prayers, he selected the twenty-first chapter of Revelation. It was at all times pleasant to listen while from his lips fell the words of the Bible: never did his fine voice sound at once so sweet and full—never did his manner become so impressive in its noble simplicity, as when he delivered the oracles of God: and to-night that voice took a more solemn tone—that manner a more thrilling meaning—as he sat in the midst of his household circle (the May moon shining in through the uncurtained window, and rendering almost unnecessary the light of the candle on the table): as he sat there, bending over the great old Bible, and described from its page the vision of the new heaven and the new earth—told how God would come to dwell with men, how He would wipe away all tears from their eyes, and promised that there should be no more death, neither sorrow nor crying, nor any more pain, because the former things were passed away.

The succeeding words thrilled me strangely as he spoke them: especially as I felt, by the slight, indescribable alteration in sound, that in uttering them, his eye had turned on me.

"He that overcometh shall inherit all things; and I will be his God, and he shall be my son. But," was slowly, distinctly read, "the fearful, the unbelieving, &c., shall have their part in the lake which burneth with fire and brimstone, which is the second death."

Henceforward, I knew what fate St. John feared for me.

A calm, subdued triumph, blent with a longing earnestness, marked his enunciation of the last glorious verses of that chapter. The reader believed his name was already written in the Lamb's book of life, and he yearned after the hour which should admit him to the city to which the kings of the earth bring their glory and honour; which has no need of sun or moon to shine in it, because the glory of God lightens it, and the Lamb is the light thereof.

In the prayer following the chapter, all his energy gathered—all his stern zeal woke: he was in deep earnest, wrestling with God, and resolved on a conquest. He supplicated strength for the weak-hearted; guidance for wanderers from the fold: a return, even at the eleventh hour, for those whom the temptations of the world and the flesh were luring from the narrow path. He asked, he urged, he claimed the boon of a brand snatched from the burning. Earnestness is ever deeply solemn: first, as I listened to that prayer, I wondered at his; then, when it continued and rose, I was touched by it, and at last awed. He felt the greatness and goodness of his purpose so sincerely: others who heard him plead for it, could not but feel it too.

The prayer over, we took leave of him: he was to go at a very early hour in the morning. Diana and Mary having kissed him, left the room—in compliance, I think, with a whispered hint from him: I tendered my hand, and wished him a pleasant journey.

"Thank you, Jane. As I said, I shall return from Cambridge in a fortnight: that space, then, is yet left you for reflection. If I listened to human pride, I should say no more to you of marriage with me; but I listen to my duty, and keep steadily in view my first aim—to do all things to the glory of God. My Master was long-suffering: so will I be. I cannot give you up to perdition as a vessel of wrath: repent—resolve, while there is yet time. Remember, we are bid to work while it is day—warned that 'the night cometh when no man shall work.' Remember the fate of Dives, who had his good things in this life. God give you strength to choose that better part which shall not be taken from you!"

He laid his hand on my head as he uttered the last words. He had spoken earnestly, mildly: his look was not, indeed, that of a lover beholding his mistress, but it was that of a pastor recalling his wandering sheep—or better, of a guardian angel watching the soul for which he is responsible. All men of talent, whether they be men of feeling or not; whether they be zealots, or aspirants, or despots—provided only they be sincere—have their sublime moments, when they subdue and rule. I felt veneration for St. John—veneration so strong that its impetus thrust me at once to the point I had so long shunned. I was tempted to cease struggling with him—to rush down the torrent of his will into the gulf of his existence, and there lose my own. I was almost as hard beset by him now as I had been once before, in a different way, by another. I was a fool both times. To have yielded then would have been an error of principle; to have yielded now would have been an error of judgment. So I think at this hour, when I look back to the crisis through the quiet medium of time: I was unconscious of folly at the instant.

I stood motionless under my hierophant's touch. My refusals were forgotten—my fears overcome—my wrestlings paralysed. The Impossible—I.E., my marriage with St. John—was fast becoming the Possible. All was changing utterly with a sudden sweep. Religion called—Angels beckoned—God commanded—life rolled together like a scroll—death's gates opening, showed eternity beyond: it seemed, that for safety and bliss there, all here might be sacrificed in a second. The dim room was full of visions.

"Could you decide now?" asked the missionary. The inquiry was put in gentle tones: he drew me to him as gently. Oh, that gentleness! how far more potent is it than force! I could resist St. John's wrath: I grew pliant as a reed under his kindness. Yet I knew all the time, if I yielded now, I should not the less be made to repent, some day, of my former rebellion. His nature was not changed by one hour of solemn prayer: it was only elevated.

"I could decide if I were but certain," I answered: "were I but convinced that it is God's will I should marry you, I could vow to marry you here and now—come afterwards what would!"

"My I prayers are heard!" ejaculated St. John. He pressed his hand firmer on my head, as if he claimed me: he surrounded me with his arm, ALMOST as if he loved me (I say ALMOST—I knew the difference—for I had felt what it was to be loved; but, like him, I had now put love out of the question, and thought only of duty). I contended with my inward dimness of vision, before which clouds yet rolled. I sincerely, deeply, fervently longed to do what was right; and only that. "Show me, show me the path!" I entreated of Heaven. I was excited more than I had ever been; and whether what followed was the effect of excitement the reader shall judge.

All the house was still; for I believe all, except St. John and myself, were now retired to rest. The one candle was dying out: the room was full of moonlight. My heart beat fast and thick: I heard its throb. Suddenly it stood still to an inexpressible feeling that thrilled it through, and passed at once to my head and extremities. The feeling was not like an electric shock, but it was quite as sharp, as strange, as startling: it acted on my senses as if their utmost activity hitherto had been but torpor, from which they were now summoned and forced to wake. They rose expectant: eye and ear waited while the flesh quivered on my bones.

"What have you heard? What do you see?" asked St. John. I saw nothing, but I heard a voice somewhere cry—

"Jane! Jane! Jane!"—nothing more.

"O God! what is it?" I gasped.

I might have said, "Where is it?" for it did not seem in the room—nor in the house—nor in the garden; it did not come out of the air—nor from under the earth—nor from overhead. I had heard it—where, or whence, for ever impossible to know! And it was the voice of a human being—a known, loved, well-remembered voice—that of Edward Fairfax Rochester; and it spoke in pain and woe, wildly, eerily, urgently.

"I am coming!" I cried. "Wait for me! Oh, I will come!" I flew to the door and looked into the passage: it was dark. I ran out into the garden: it was void.

"Where are you?" I exclaimed.

The hills beyond Marsh Glen sent the answer faintly back—"Where are you?" I listened. The wind sighed low in the firs: all was moorland loneliness and midnight hush.

"Down superstition!" I commented, as that spectre rose up black by the black yew at the gate. "This is not thy deception, nor thy witchcraft: it is the work of nature. She was roused, and did—no miracle—but her best."

I broke from St. John, who had followed, and would have detained me. It was MY time to assume ascendency. MY powers were in play and in force. I told him to forbear question or remark; I desired him to leave me: I must and would be alone. He obeyed at once. Where there is energy to command well enough, obedience never fails. I mounted to my chamber; locked myself in; fell on my knees; and prayed in my way—a different way to St. John's, but effective in its own fashion. I seemed to penetrate very near a Mighty Spirit; and my soul rushed out in gratitude at His feet. I rose from the thanksgiving—took a resolve—and lay down, unscared, enlightened—eager but for the daylight.

Chapter XXXVI

The daylight came. I rose at dawn. I busied myself for an hour or two with arranging my things in my chamber, drawers, and wardrobe, in the order wherein I should wish to leave them during a brief absence. Meantime, I heard St. John quit his room. He stopped at my door: I feared he would knock—no, but a slip of paper was passed under the door. I took it up. It bore these words—

"You left me too suddenly last night. Had you stayed but a little longer, you would have laid your hand on the Christian's cross and the angel's crown. I shall expect your clear decision when I return this day fortnight. Meantime, watch and pray that you enter not into temptation: the spirit, I trust, is willing, but the flesh, I see, is weak. I shall pray for you hourly.—Yours, ST. JOHN."

"My spirit," I answered mentally, "is willing to do what is right; and my flesh, I hope, is strong enough to accomplish the will of Heaven, when once that will is distinctly known to me. At any rate, it shall be strong enough to search—inquire—to grope an outlet from this cloud of doubt, and find the open day of certainty."

It was the first of June; yet the morning was overcast and chilly: rain beat fast on my casement. I heard the front-door open, and St. John pass out. Looking through the window, I saw him traverse the garden. He took the way over the misty moors in the direction of Whitcross—there he would meet the coach.

"In a few more hours I shall succeed you in that track, cousin," thought I: "I too have a coach to meet at Whitcross. I too have some to see and ask after in England, before I depart for ever."

It wanted yet two hours of breakfast-time. I filled the interval in walking softly about my room, and pondering the visitation which had given my plans their present bent. I recalled that inward sensation I had experienced: for I could recall it, with all its unspeakable strangeness. I recalled the voice I had heard; again I questioned whence it came, as vainly as before: it seemed in ME—not in the external world. I asked was it a mere nervous impression—a delusion? I could not conceive or believe: it was more like an inspiration. The wondrous shock of feeling had come like the earthquake which shook the foundations of Paul and Silas's prison; it had opened the doors of the soul's cell and loosed its bands—it had wakened it out of its sleep, whence it sprang trembling, listening, aghast; then vibrated thrice a cry on my startled ear, and in my quaking heart and through my spirit, which neither feared nor shook, but exulted as if in joy over the success of one effort it had been privileged to make, independent of the cumbrous body.

"Ere many days," I said, as I terminated my musings, "I will know something of him whose voice seemed last night to summon me. Letters have proved of no avail—personal inquiry shall replace them."

At breakfast I announced to Diana and Mary that I was going a journey, and should be absent at least four days.

"Alone, Jane?" they asked.

"Yes; it was to see or hear news of a friend about whom I had for some time been uneasy."

They might have said, as I have no doubt they thought, that they had believed me to be without any friends save them: for, indeed, I had often said so; but, with their true natural delicacy, they abstained from comment, except that Diana asked me if I was sure I was well enough to travel. I looked very pale, she observed. I replied, that nothing ailed me save anxiety of mind, which I hoped soon to alleviate.

It was easy to make my further arrangements; for I was troubled with no inquiries—no surmises. Having once explained to them that I could not now be explicit about my plans, they kindly and wisely acquiesced in the silence with which I pursued them, according to me the privilege of free action I should under similar circumstances have accorded them.

I left Moor House at three o'clock p.m., and soon after four I stood at the foot of the sign-post of Whitcross, waiting the arrival of the coach which was to take me to distant Thornfield. Amidst the silence of those solitary roads and desert hills, I heard it approach from a great distance. It was the same vehicle whence, a year ago, I had alighted one summer evening on this very spot—how desolate, and hopeless, and objectless! It stopped as I beckoned. I entered—not now obliged to part with my whole fortune as the price of its accommodation. Once more on the road to Thornfield, I felt like the messenger-pigeon flying home.

It was a journey of six-and-thirty hours. I had set out from Whitcross on a Tuesday afternoon, and early on the succeeding Thursday morning the coach stopped to water the horses at a wayside inn, situated in the midst of scenery whose green hedges and large fields and low pastoral hills (how mild of feature and verdant of hue compared with the stern North-Midland moors of Morton!) met my eye like the lineaments of a once familiar face. Yes, I knew the character of this landscape: I was sure we were near my bourne.

"How far is Thornfield Hall from here?" I asked of the ostler.

"Just two miles, ma'am, across the fields."

"My journey is closed," I thought to myself. I got out of the coach, gave a box I had into the ostler's charge, to be kept till I called for it; paid my fare; satisfied the coachman, and was going: the brightening day gleamed on the sign of the inn, and I read in gilt letters, "The Rochester Arms." My heart leapt up: I was already on my master's very lands. It fell again: the thought struck it:-

"Your master himself may be beyond the British Channel, for aught you know: and then, if he is at Thornfield Hall, towards which you hasten, who besides him is there? His lunatic wife: and you have nothing to do with him: you dare not speak to him or seek his presence. You have lost your labour—you had better go no farther," urged the monitor. "Ask information of the people at the inn; they can give you all you seek: they can solve your doubts at once. Go up to that man, and inquire if Mr. Rochester be at home."

The suggestion was sensible, and yet I could not force myself to act on it. I so dreaded a reply that would crush me with despair. To prolong doubt was to prolong hope. I might yet once more see the Hall under the ray of her star. There was the stile before me—the very fields through which I had hurried, blind, deaf, distracted with a revengeful fury tracking and scourging me, on the morning I fled from Thornfield: ere I well knew what course I had resolved to take, I was in the midst of them. How fast I walked! How I ran sometimes! How I looked forward to catch the first view of the well-known woods! With what feelings I welcomed single trees I knew, and familiar glimpses of meadow and hill between them!

At last the woods rose; the rookery clustered dark; a loud cawing broke the morning stillness. Strange delight inspired me: on I hastened. Another field crossed—a lane threaded—and there were the courtyard walls—the back offices: the house itself, the rookery still hid. "My first view of it shall be in front," I determined, "where its bold battlements will strike the eye nobly at once, and where I can single out my master's very window: perhaps he will be standing at it—he rises early: perhaps he is now walking in the orchard, or on the pavement in front. Could I but see him!—but a moment! Surely, in that case, I should not be so mad as to run to him? I cannot tell—I am not certain. And if I did—what then? God bless him! What then? Who would be hurt by my once more tasting the life his glance can give me? I rave: perhaps at this moment he is watching the sun rise over the Pyrenees, or on the tideless sea of the south."

I had coasted along the lower wall of the orchard—turned its angle: there was a gate just there, opening into the meadow, between two stone pillars crowned by stone balls. From behind one pillar I could peep round quietly at the full front of the mansion. I advanced my head with precaution, desirous to ascertain if any bedroom window-blinds were yet drawn up: battlements, windows, long front—all from this sheltered station were at my command.

The crows sailing overhead perhaps watched me while I took this survey. I wonder what they thought. They must have considered I was very careful and timid at first, and that gradually I grew very bold and reckless. A peep, and then a long stare; and then a departure from my niche and a straying out into the meadow; and a sudden stop full in front of the great mansion, and a protracted, hardy gaze towards it. "What affectation of diffidence was this at first?" they might have demanded; "what stupid regardlessness now?"

Hear an illustration, reader.

A lover finds his mistress asleep on a mossy bank; he wishes to catch a glimpse of her fair face without waking her. He steals softly over the grass, careful to make no sound; he pauses—fancying she has stirred: he withdraws: not for worlds would he be seen. All is still: he again advances: he bends above her; a light veil rests on her features: he lifts it, bends lower; now his eyes anticipate the vision of beauty—warm, and blooming, and lovely, in rest. How hurried was their first glance! But how they fix! How he starts! How he suddenly and vehemently clasps in both arms the form he dared not, a moment since, touch with his finger! How he calls aloud a name, and drops his burden, and gazes on it wildly! He thus grasps and cries, and gazes, because he no longer fears to waken by any sound he can utter—by any movement he can make. He thought his love slept sweetly: he finds she is stone dead.

I looked with timorous joy towards a stately house: I saw a blackened ruin.

No need to cower behind a gate-post, indeed!—to peep up at chamber lattices, fearing life was astir behind them! No need to listen for doors opening—to fancy steps on the pavement or the gravel-walk! The lawn, the grounds were trodden and waste: the portal yawned void.

The front was, as I had once seen it in a dream, but a well-like wall, very high and very fragile-looking, perforated with paneless windows: no roof, no battlements, no chimneys—all had crashed in.

And there was the silence of death about it: the solitude of a lonesome wild. No wonder that letters addressed to people here had never received an answer: as well despatch epistles to a vault in a church aisle. The grim blackness of the stones told by what fate the Hall had fallen—by conflagration: but how kindled? What story belonged to this disaster? What loss, besides mortar and marble and wood-work had followed upon it? Had life been wrecked as well as property? If so, whose? Dreadful question: there was no one here to answer it—not even dumb sign, mute token.

In wandering round the shattered walls and through the devastated interior, I gathered evidence that the calamity was not of late occurrence. Winter snows, I thought, had drifted through that void arch, winter rains beaten in at those hollow casements; for, amidst the drenched piles of rubbish, spring had cherished vegetation: grass and weed grew here and there between the stones and fallen rafters. And oh! where meantime was the hapless owner of this wreck? In what land? Under what auspices? My eye involuntarily wandered to the grey church tower near the gates, and I asked, "Is he with Damer de Rochester, sharing the shelter of his narrow marble house?"

Some answer must be had to these questions. I could find it nowhere but at the inn, and thither, ere long, I returned. The host himself brought my breakfast into the parlour. I requested him to shut the door and sit down: I had some questions to ask him. But when he complied, I scarcely knew how to begin; such horror had I of the possible answers. And yet the spectacle of desolation I had just left prepared me in a measure for a tale of misery. The host was a respectable-looking, middle-aged man.

"You know Thornfield Hall, of course?" I managed to say at last.

"Yes, ma'am; I lived there once."

"Did you?" Not in my time, I thought: you are a stranger to me.

"I was the late Mr. Rochester's butler," he added.

The late! I seem to have received, with full force, the blow I had been trying to evade.

"The late!" gasped. "Is he dead?"

"I mean the present gentleman, Mr. Edward's father," he explained. I breathed again: my blood resumed its flow. Fully assured by these words that Mr. Edward—MY Mr. Rochester (God bless him, wherever he was!)—was at least alive: was, in short, "the present gentleman." Gladdening words! It seemed I could hear all that was to come—whatever the disclosures might be—with comparative tranquillity. Since he was not in the grave, I could bear, I thought, to learn that he was at the Antipodes.

"Is Mr. Rochester living at Thornfield Hall now?" I asked, knowing, of course, what the answer would be, but yet desirous of deferring the direct question as to where he really was.

"No, ma'am—oh, no! No one is living there. I suppose you are a stranger in these parts, or you would have heard what happened last autumn,—Thornfield Hall is quite a ruin: it was burnt down just about harvest-time. A dreadful calamity! such an immense quantity of valuable property destroyed: hardly any of the furniture could be saved. The fire broke out at dead of night, and before the engines arrived from Millcote, the building was one mass of flame. It was a terrible spectacle: I witnessed it myself."

"At dead of night!" I muttered. Yes, that was ever the hour of fatality at Thornfield. "Was it known how it originated?" I demanded.

"They guessed, ma'am: they guessed. Indeed, I should say it was ascertained beyond a doubt. You are not perhaps aware," he continued, edging his chair a little nearer the table, and speaking low, "that there was a lady—a—a lunatic, kept in the house?"

"I have heard something of it."

"She was kept in very close confinement, ma'am: people even for some years was not absolutely certain of her existence. No one saw her: they only knew by rumour that such a person was at the Hall; and who or what she was it was difficult to conjecture. They said Mr. Edward had brought her from abroad, and some believed she had been his mistress. But a queer thing happened a year since—a very queer thing."

I feared now to hear my own story. I endeavoured to recall him to the main fact.

"And this lady?"

"This lady, ma'am," he answered, "turned out to be Mr. Rochester's wife! The discovery was brought about in the strangest way. There was a young lady, a governess at the Hall, that Mr. Rochester fell in—"

"But the fire," I suggested.

"I'm coming to that, ma'am—that Mr. Edward fell in love with. The servants say they never saw anybody so much in love as he was: he was after her continually. They used to watch him—servants will, you know, ma'am—and he set store on her past everything: for all, nobody but him thought her so very handsome. She was a little small thing, they say, almost like a child. I never saw her myself; but I've heard Leah, the house-maid, tell of her. Leah liked her well enough. Mr. Rochester was about forty, and this governess not twenty; and you see, when gentlemen of his age fall in love with girls, they are often like as if they were bewitched. Well, he would marry her."

"You shall tell me this part of the story another time," I said; "but now I have a particular reason for wishing to hear all about the fire. Was it suspected that this lunatic, Mrs. Rochester, had any hand in it?"

"You've hit it, ma'am: it's quite certain that it was her, and nobody but her, that set it going. She had a woman to take care of her called Mrs. Poole—an able woman in her line, and very trustworthy, but for one fault—a fault common to a deal of them nurses and matrons—she KEPT A PRIVATE BOTTLE OF GIN BY HER, and now and then took a drop over-much. It is excusable, for she had a hard life of it: but still it was dangerous; for when Mrs. Poole was fast asleep after the gin and water, the mad lady, who was as cunning as a witch, would take the keys out of her pocket, let herself out of her chamber, and go roaming about the house, doing any wild mischief that came into her head. They say she had nearly burnt her husband in his bed once: but I don't know about that. However, on this night, she set fire first to the hangings of the room next her own, and then she got down to a lower storey, and made her way to the chamber that had been the governess's—(she was like as if she knew somehow how matters had gone on, and had a spite at her)—and she kindled the bed there; but there was nobody sleeping in it, fortunately. The governess had run away two months before; and for all Mr. Rochester sought her as if she had been the most precious thing he had in the world, he never could hear a word of her; and he grew savage—quite savage on his disappointment: he never was a wild man, but he got dangerous after he lost her. He would be alone, too. He sent Mrs. Fairfax, the housekeeper, away to her friends at a distance; but he did it handsomely, for he settled an annuity on her for life: and she deserved it—she was a very good woman. Miss Adele, a ward he had, was put to school. He broke off acquaintance with all the gentry, and shut himself up like a hermit at the Hall."

"What! did he not leave England?"

"Leave England? Bless you, no! He would not cross the door-stones of the house, except at night, when he walked just like a ghost about the grounds and in the orchard as if he had lost his senses—which it is my opinion he had; for a more spirited, bolder, keener gentleman than he was before that midge of a governess crossed him, you never saw, ma'am. He was not a man given to wine, or cards, or racing, as some are, and he was not so very handsome; but he had a courage and a will of his own, if ever man had. I knew him from a boy, you see: and for my part, I have often wished that Miss Eyre had been sunk in the sea before she came to Thornfield Hall."

"Then Mr. Rochester was at home when the fire broke out?"

"Yes, indeed was he; and he went up to the attics when all was burning above and below, and got the servants out of their beds and helped them down himself, and went back to get his mad wife out of her cell. And then they called out to him that she was on the roof, where she was standing, waving her arms, above the battlements, and shouting out till they could hear her a mile off: I saw her and heard her with my own eyes. She was a big woman, and had long black hair: we could see it streaming against the flames as she stood. I witnessed, and several more witnessed, Mr. Rochester ascend through the skylight on to the roof; we heard him call 'Bertha!' We saw him approach her; and then, ma'am, she yelled and gave a spring, and the next minute she lay smashed on the pavement."

"Dead?"

"Dead! Ay, dead as the stones on which her brains and blood were scattered."

"Good God!"

"You may well say so, ma'am: it was frightful!"

He shuddered.

"And afterwards?" I urged.

"Well, ma'am, afterwards the house was burnt to the ground: there are only some bits of walls standing now."

"Were any other lives lost?"

"No—perhaps it would have been better if there had."

"What do you mean?"

"Poor Mr. Edward!" he ejaculated, "I little thought ever to have seen it! Some say it was a just judgment on him for keeping his first marriage secret, and wanting to take another wife while he had one living: but I pity him, for my part."

"You said he was alive?" I exclaimed.

"Yes, yes: he is alive; but many think he had better he dead."

"Why? How?" My blood was again running cold. "Where is he?" I demanded. "Is he in England?"

"Ay—ay—he's in England; he can't get out of England, I fancy—he's a fixture now."

What agony was this! And the man seemed resolved to protract it.

"He is stone-blind," he said at last. "Yes, he is stone-blind, is Mr. Edward."

I had dreaded worse. I had dreaded he was mad. I summoned strength to ask what had caused this calamity.

"It was all his own courage, and a body may say, his kindness, in a way, ma'am: he wouldn't leave the house till every one else was out before him. As he came down the great staircase at last, after Mrs. Rochester had flung herself from the battlements, there was a great crash—all fell. He was taken out from under the ruins, alive, but sadly hurt: a beam had fallen in such a way as to protect him partly; but one eye was knocked out, and one hand so crushed that Mr. Carter, the surgeon, had to amputate it directly. The other eye inflamed: he lost the sight of that also. He is now helpless, indeed—blind and a cripple."

"Where is he? Where does he now live?"

"At Ferndean, a manor-house on a farm he has, about thirty miles off: quite a desolate spot."

"Who is with him?"

"Old John and his wife: he would have none else. He is quite broken down, they say."

"Have you any sort of conveyance?"

"We have a chaise, ma'am, a very handsome chaise."

"Let it be got ready instantly; and if your post-boy can drive me to Ferndean before dark this day, I'll pay both you and him twice the hire you usually demand."

Chapter XXXVII

The manor-house of Ferndean was a building of considerable antiquity, moderate size, and no architectural pretensions, deep buried in a wood. I had heard of it before. Mr. Rochester often spoke of it, and sometimes went there. His father had purchased the estate for the sake of the game covers. He would have let the house, but could find no tenant, in consequence of its ineligible and insalubrious site. Ferndean then remained uninhabited and unfurnished, with the exception of some two or three rooms fitted up for the accommodation of the squire when he went there in the season to shoot.

To this house I came just ere dark on an evening marked by the characteristics of sad sky, cold gale, and continued small penetrating rain. The last mile I performed on foot, having dismissed the chaise and driver with the double remuneration I had promised. Even when within a very short distance of the manor-house, you could see nothing of it, so thick and dark grew the timber of the gloomy wood about it. Iron gates between granite pillars showed me where to enter, and passing through them, I found myself at once in the twilight of close-ranked trees. There was a grass-grown track descending the forest aisle between hoar and knotty shafts and under branched arches. I followed it, expecting soon to reach the dwelling; but it stretched on and on, it would far and farther: no sign of habitation or grounds was visible.

I thought I had taken a wrong direction and lost my way. The darkness of natural as well as of sylvan dusk gathered over me. I looked round in search of another road. There was none: all was interwoven stem, columnar trunk, dense summer foliage—no opening anywhere.

I proceeded: at last my way opened, the trees thinned a little; presently I beheld a railing, then the house—scarce, by this dim light, distinguishable from the trees; so dank and green were its decaying walls. Entering a portal, fastened only by a latch, I stood amidst a space of enclosed ground, from which the wood swept away in a semicircle. There were no flowers, no garden-beds; only a broad gravel-walk girdling a grass-plat, and this set in the heavy frame of the forest. The house presented two pointed gables in its front; the windows were latticed and narrow: the front door was narrow too, one step led up to it. The whole looked, as the host of the Rochester Arms had said, "quite a desolate spot." It was as still as a church on a week-day: the pattering rain on the forest leaves was the only sound audible in its vicinage.

"Can there be life here?" I asked.

Yes, life of some kind there was; for I heard a movement—that narrow front-door was unclosing, and some shape was about to issue from the grange.

It opened slowly: a figure came out into the twilight and stood on the step; a man without a hat: he stretched forth his hand as if to feel whether it rained. Dusk as it was, I had recognised him—it was my master, Edward Fairfax Rochester, and no other.

I stayed my step, almost my breath, and stood to watch him—to examine him, myself unseen, and alas! to him invisible. It was a sudden meeting, and one in which rapture was kept well in check by pain. I had no difficulty in restraining my voice from exclamation, my step from hasty advance.

His form was of the same strong and stalwart contour as ever: his port was still erect, his heir was still raven black; nor were his features altered or sunk: not in one year's space, by any sorrow, could his athletic strength be quelled or his vigorous prime blighted. But in his countenance I saw a change: that looked desperate and brooding—that reminded me of some wronged and fettered wild beast or bird, dangerous to approach in his sullen woe. The caged eagle, whose gold-ringed eyes cruelty has extinguished, might look as looked that sightless Samson.

And, reader, do you think I feared him in his blind ferocity?—if you do, you little know me. A soft hope blest with my sorrow that soon I should dare to drop a kiss on that brow of rock, and on those lips so sternly sealed beneath it: but not yet. I would not accost him yet.

He descended the one step, and advanced slowly and gropingly towards the grass-plat. Where was his daring stride now? Then he paused, as if he knew not which way to turn. He lifted his hand and opened his eyelids; gazed blank, and with a straining effort, on the sky, and toward the amphitheatre of trees: one saw that all to him was void darkness. He stretched his right hand (the left arm, the mutilated one, he kept hidden in his bosom); he seemed to wish by touch to gain an idea of what lay around him: he met but vacancy still; for the trees were some yards off where he stood. He relinquished the endeavour, folded his arms, and stood quiet and mute in the rain, now falling fast on his uncovered head. At this moment John approached him from some quarter.

"Will you take my arm, sir?" he said; "there is a heavy shower coming on: had you not better go in?"

"Let me alone," was the answer.

John withdrew without having observed me. Mr. Rochester now tried to walk about: vainly,—all was too uncertain. He groped his way back to the house, and, re-entering it, closed the door.

I now drew near and knocked: John's wife opened for me. "Mary," I said, "how are you?"

She started as if she had seen a ghost: I calmed her. To her hurried "Is it really you, miss, come at this late hour to this lonely place?" I answered by taking her hand; and then I followed her into the kitchen, where John now sat by a good fire. I explained to them, in few words, that I had heard all which had happened since I left Thornfield, and that I was come to see Mr. Rochester. I asked John to go down to the turn-pike-house, where I had dismissed the chaise, and bring my trunk, which I had left there: and then, while I removed my bonnet and shawl, I questioned Mary as to whether I could be accommodated at the Manor House for the night; and finding that arrangements to that effect, though difficult, would not be impossible, I informed her I should stay. Just at this moment the parlour-bell rang.

"When you go in," said I, "tell your master that a person wishes to speak to him, but do not give my name."

"I don't think he will see you," she answered; "he refuses everybody."

When she returned, I inquired what he had said. "You are to send in your name and your business," she replied. She then proceeded to fill a glass with water, and place it on a tray, together with candles.

"Is that what he rang for?" I asked.

"Yes: he always has candles brought in at dark, though he is blind."

"Give the tray to me; I will carry it in."

I took it from her hand: she pointed me out the parlour door. The tray shook as I held it; the water spilt from the glass; my heart struck my ribs loud and fast. Mary opened the door for me, and shut it behind me.

This parlour looked gloomy: a neglected handful of fire burnt low in the grate; and, leaning over it, with his head supported against the high, old-fashioned mantelpiece, appeared the blind tenant of the room. His old dog, Pilot, lay on one side, removed out of the way, and coiled up as if afraid of being inadvertently trodden upon. Pilot pricked up his ears when I came in: then he jumped up with a yelp and a whine, and bounded towards me: he almost knocked the tray from my hands. I set it on the table; then patted him, and said softly, "Lie down!" Mr. Rochester turned mechanically to SEE what the commotion was: but as he SAW nothing, he returned and sighed.

"Give me the water, Mary," he said.

I approached him with the now only half-filled glass; Pilot followed me, still excited.

"What is the matter?" he inquired.

"Down, Pilot!" I again said. He checked the water on its way to his lips, and seemed to listen: he drank, and put the glass down. "This is you, Mary, is it not?"

"Mary is in the kitchen," I answered.

He put out his hand with a quick gesture, but not seeing where I stood, he did not touch me. "Who is this? Who is this?" he demanded, trying, as it seemed, to SEE with those sightless eyes—unavailing and distressing attempt! "Answer me—speak again!" he ordered, imperiously and aloud.

"Will you have a little more water, sir? I spilt half of what was in the glass," I said.

"WHO is it? WHAT is it? Who speaks?"

"Pilot knows me, and John and Mary know I am here. I came only this evening," I answered.

"Great God!—what delusion has come over me? What sweet madness has seized me?"

"No delusion—no madness: your mind, sir, is too strong for delusion, your health too sound for frenzy."

"And where is the speaker? Is it only a voice? Oh! I CANNOT see, but I must feel, or my heart will stop and my brain burst. Whatever—whoever you are—be perceptible to the touch or I cannot live!"

He groped; I arrested his wandering hand, and prisoned it in both mine.

"Her very fingers!" he cried; "her small, slight fingers! If so there must be more of her."

The muscular hand broke from my custody; my arm was seized, my shoulder—neck—waist—I was entwined and gathered to him.

"Is it Jane? WHAT is it? This is her shape—this is her size——"

"And this her voice," I added. "She is all here: her heart, too. God bless you, sir! I am glad to be so near you again."

"Jane Eyre!—Jane Eyre," was all he said.

"My dear master," I answered, "I am Jane Eyre: I have found you out—I am come back to you."

"In truth?—in the flesh? My living Jane?"

"You touch me, sir,—you hold me, and fast enough: I am not cold like a corpse, nor vacant like air, am I?"

"My living darling! These are certainly her limbs, and these her features; but I cannot be so blest, after all my misery. It is a dream; such dreams as I have had at night when I have clasped her once more to my heart, as I do now; and kissed her, as thus—and felt that she loved me, and trusted that she would not leave me."

"Which I never will, sir, from this day."

"Never will, says the vision? But I always woke and found it an empty mockery; and I was desolate and abandoned—my life dark, lonely, hopeless—my soul athirst and forbidden to drink—my heart famished and never to be fed. Gentle, soft dream, nestling in my arms now, you will fly, too, as your sisters have all fled before you: but kiss me before you go—embrace me, Jane."

"There, sir—and there!"'

I pressed my lips to his once brilliant and now rayless eyes—I swept his hair from his brow, and kissed that too. He suddenly seemed to arouse himself: the conviction of the reality of all this seized him.

"It is you—is it, Jane? You are come back to me then?"

"I am."

"And you do not lie dead in some ditch under some stream? And you are not a pining outcast amongst strangers?"

"No, sir! I am an independent woman now."

"Independent! What do you mean, Jane?"

"My uncle in Madeira is dead, and he left me five thousand pounds."

"Ah! this is practical—this is real!" he cried: "I should never dream that. Besides, there is that peculiar voice of hers, so animating and piquant, as well as soft: it cheers my withered heart; it puts life into it.—What, Janet! Are you an independent woman? A rich woman?"

"If you won't let me live with you, I can build a house of my own close up to your door, and you may come and sit in my parlour when you want company of an evening."

"But as you are rich, Jane, you have now, no doubt, friends who will look after you, and not suffer you to devote yourself to a blind lameter like me?"

"I told you I am independent, sir, as well as rich: I am my own mistress."

"And you will stay with me?"

"Certainly—unless you object. I will be your neighbour, your nurse, your housekeeper. I find you lonely: I will be your companion—to read to you, to walk with you, to sit with you, to wait on you, to be eyes and hands to you. Cease to look so melancholy, my dear master; you shall not be left desolate, so long as I live."

He replied not: he seemed serious—abstracted; he sighed; he half-opened his lips as if to speak: he closed them again. I felt a little embarrassed. Perhaps I had too rashly over-leaped conventionalities; and he, like St. John, saw impropriety in my inconsiderateness. I had indeed made my proposal from the idea that he wished and would ask me to be his wife: an expectation, not the less certain because unexpressed, had buoyed me up, that he would claim me at once as his own. But no hint to that effect escaping him and his countenance becoming more overcast, I suddenly remembered that I might have been all wrong, and was perhaps playing the fool unwittingly; and I began gently to withdraw myself from his arms—but he eagerly snatched me closer.

"No—no—Jane; you must not go. No—I have touched you, heard you, felt the comfort of your presence—the sweetness of your consolation: I cannot give up these joys. I have little left in myself—I must have you. The world may laugh—may call me absurd, selfish—but it does not signify. My very soul demands you: it will be satisfied, or it will take deadly vengeance on its frame."

"Well, sir, I will stay with you: I have said so."

"Yes—but you understand one thing by staying with me; and I understand another. You, perhaps, could make up your mind to be about my hand and chair—to wait on me as a kind little nurse (for you have an affectionate heart and a generous spirit, which prompt you to make sacrifices for those you pity), and that ought to suffice for me no doubt. I suppose I should now entertain none but fatherly feelings for you: do you think so? Come—tell me."

"I will think what you like, sir: I am content to be only your nurse, if you think it better."

"But you cannot always be my nurse, Janet: you are young—you must marry one day."

"I don't care about being married."

"You should care, Janet: if I were what I once was, I would try to make you care—but—a sightless block!"

He relapsed again into gloom. I, on the contrary, became more cheerful, and took fresh courage: these last words gave me an insight as to where the difficulty lay; and as it was no difficulty with me, I felt quite relieved from my previous embarrassment. I resumed a livelier vein of conversation.

"It is time some one undertook to rehumanise you," said I, parting his thick and long uncut locks; "for I see you are being metamorphosed into a lion, or something of that sort. You have a 'faux air' of Nebuchadnezzar in the fields about you, that is certain: your hair reminds me of eagles' feathers; whether your nails are grown like birds' claws or not, I have not yet noticed."

"On this arm, I have neither hand nor nails," he said, drawing the mutilated limb from his breast, and showing it to me. "It is a mere stump—a ghastly sight! Don't you think so, Jane?"

"It is a pity to see it; and a pity to see your eyes—and the scar of fire on your forehead: and the worst of it is, one is in danger of loving you too well for all this; and making too much of you."

"I thought you would be revolted, Jane, when you saw my arm, and my cicatrised visage."

"Did you? Don't tell me so—lest I should say something disparaging to your judgment. Now, let me leave you an instant, to make a better fire, and have the hearth swept up. Can you tell when there is a good fire?"

"Yes; with the right eye I see a glow—a ruddy haze."

"And you see the candles?"

"Very dimly—each is a luminous cloud."

"Can you see me?"

"No, my fairy: but I am only too thankful to hear and feel you."

"When do you take supper?"

"I never take supper."

"But you shall have some to-night. I am hungry: so are you, I daresay, only you forget."

Summoning Mary, I soon had the room in more cheerful order: I prepared him, likewise, a comfortable repast. My spirits were excited, and with pleasure and ease I talked to him during supper, and for a long time after. There was no harassing restraint, no repressing of glee and vivacity with him; for with him I was at perfect ease, because I knew I suited him; all I said or did seemed either to console or revive him. Delightful consciousness! It brought to life and light my whole nature: in his presence I thoroughly lived; and he lived in mine. Blind as he was, smiles played over his face, joy dawned on his forehead: his lineaments softened and warmed.

After supper, he began to ask me many questions, of where I had been, what I had been doing, how I had found him out; but I gave him only very partial replies: it was too late to enter into particulars that night. Besides, I wished to touch no deep-thrilling chord—to open no fresh well of emotion in his heart: my sole present aim was to cheer him. Cheered, as I have said, he was: and yet but by fits. If a moment's silence broke the conversation, he would turn restless, touch me, then say, "Jane."

"You are altogether a human being, Jane? You are certain of that?"

"I conscientiously believe so, Mr. Rochester."

"Yet how, on this dark and doleful evening, could you so suddenly rise on my lone hearth? I stretched my hand to take a glass of water from a hireling, and it was given me by you: I asked a question, expecting John's wife to answer me, and your voice spoke at my ear."

"Because I had come in, in Mary's stead, with the tray."

"And there is enchantment in the very hour I am now spending with you. Who can tell what a dark, dreary, hopeless life I have dragged on for months past? Doing nothing, expecting nothing; merging night in day; feeling but the sensation of cold when I let the fire go out, of hunger when I forgot to eat: and then a ceaseless sorrow, and, at times, a very delirium of desire to behold my Jane again. Yes: for her restoration I longed, far more than for that of my lost sight. How can it be that Jane is with me, and says she loves me? Will she not depart as suddenly as she came? To-morrow, I fear I shall find her no more."

A commonplace, practical reply, out of the train of his own disturbed ideas, was, I was sure, the best and most reassuring for him in this frame of mind. I passed my finger over his eyebrows, and remarked that they were scorched, and that I would apply something which would make them grow as broad and black as ever.

"Where is the use of doing me good in any way, beneficent spirit, when, at some fatal moment, you will again desert me—passing like a shadow, whither and how to me unknown, and for me remaining afterwards undiscoverable?

"Have you a pocket-comb about you, sir?"

"What for, Jane?"

"Just to comb out this shaggy black mane. I find you rather alarming, when I examine you close at hand: you talk of my being a fairy, but I am sure, you are more like a brownie."

"Am I hideous, Jane?"

"Very, sir: you always were, you know."

"Humph! The wickedness has not been taken out of you, wherever you have sojourned."

"Yet I have been with good people; far better than you: a hundred times better people; possessed of ideas and views you never entertained in your life: quite more refined and exalted."

"Who the deuce have you been with?"

"If you twist in that way you will make me pull the hair out of your head; and then I think you will cease to entertain doubts of my substantiality."

"Who have you been with, Jane?"

"You shall not get it out of me to-night, sir; you must wait till to-morrow; to leave my tale half told, will, you know, be a sort of security that I shall appear at your breakfast table to finish it. By the bye, I must mind not to rise on your hearth with only a glass of water then: I must bring an egg at the least, to say nothing of fried ham."

"You mocking changeling—fairy-born and human-bred! You make me feel as I have not felt these twelve months. If Saul could have had you for his David, the evil spirit would have been exorcised without the aid of the harp."

"There, sir, you are redd up and made decent. Now I'll leave you: I have been travelling these last three days, and I believe I am tired. Good night."

"Just one word, Jane: were there only ladies in the house where you have been?"

I laughed and made my escape, still laughing as I ran upstairs. "A good idea!" I thought with glee. "I see I have the means of fretting him out of his melancholy for some time to come."

Very early the next morning I heard him up and astir, wandering from one room to another. As soon as Mary came down I heard the question: "Is Miss Eyre here?" Then: "Which room did you put her into? Was it dry? Is she up? Go and ask if she wants anything; and when she will come down."

I came down as soon as I thought there was a prospect of breakfast. Entering the room very softly, I had a view of him before he discovered my presence. It was mournful, indeed, to witness the subjugation of that vigorous spirit to a corporeal infirmity. He sat in his chair—still, but not at rest: expectant evidently; the lines of now habitual sadness marking his strong features. His countenance reminded one of a lamp quenched, waiting to be re-lit—and alas! it was not himself that could now kindle the lustre of animated expression: he was dependent on another for that office! I had meant to be gay and careless, but the powerlessness of the strong man touched my heart to the quick: still I accosted him with what vivacity I could.

"It is a bright, sunny morning, sir," I said. "The rain is over and gone, and there is a tender shining after it: you shall have a walk soon."

I had wakened the glow: his features beamed.

"Oh, you are indeed there, my skylark! Come to me. You are not gone: not vanished? I heard one of your kind an hour ago, singing high over the wood: but its song had no music for me, any more than the rising sun had rays. All the melody on earth is concentrated in my Jane's tongue to my ear (I am glad it is not naturally a silent one): all the sunshine I can feel is in her presence."

The water stood in my eyes to hear this avowal of his dependence; just as if a royal eagle, chained to a perch, should be forced to entreat a sparrow to become its purveyor. But I would not be lachrymose: I dashed off the salt drops, and busied myself with preparing breakfast.

Most of the morning was spent in the open air. I led him out of the wet and wild wood into some cheerful fields: I described to him how brilliantly green they were; how the flowers and hedges looked refreshed; how sparklingly blue was the sky. I sought a seat for him in a hidden and lovely spot, a dry stump of a tree; nor did I refuse to let him, when seated, place me on his knee. Why should I, when both he and I were happier near than apart? Pilot lay beside us: all was quiet. He broke out suddenly while clasping me in his arms—

"Cruel, cruel deserter! Oh, Jane, what did I feel when I discovered you had fled from Thornfield, and when I could nowhere find you; and, after examining your apartment, ascertained that you had taken no money, nor anything which could serve as an equivalent! A pearl necklace I had given you lay untouched in its little casket; your trunks were left corded and locked as they had been prepared for the bridal tour. What could my darling do, I asked, left destitute and penniless? And what did she do? Let me hear now."

Thus urged, I began the narrative of my experience for the last year. I softened considerably what related to the three days of wandering and starvation, because to have told him all would have been to inflict unnecessary pain: the little I did say lacerated his faithful heart deeper than I wished.

I should not have left him thus, he said, without any means of making my way: I should have told him my intention. I should have confided in him: he would never have forced me to be his mistress. Violent as he had seemed in his despair, he, in truth, loved me far too well and too tenderly to constitute himself my tyrant: he would have given me half his fortune, without demanding so much as a kiss in return, rather than I should have flung myself friendless on the wide world. I had endured, he was certain, more than I had confessed to him.

"Well, whatever my sufferings had been, they were very short," I answered: and then I proceeded to tell him how I had been received at Moor House; how I had obtained the office of schoolmistress, &c. The accession of fortune, the discovery of my relations, followed in due order. Of course, St. John Rivers' name came in frequently in the progress of my tale. When I had done, that name was immediately taken up.

"This St. John, then, is your cousin?"

"Yes."

"You have spoken of him often: do you like him?"

"He was a very good man, sir; I could not help liking him."

"A good man. Does that mean a respectable well-conducted man of fifty? Or what does it mean?"

"St John was only twenty-nine, sir."

"'Jeune encore,' as the French say. Is he a person of low stature, phlegmatic, and plain. A person whose goodness consists rather in his guiltlessness of vice, than in his prowess in virtue."

"He is untiringly active. Great and exalted deeds are what he lives to perform."

"But his brain? That is probably rather soft? He means well: but you shrug your shoulders to hear him talk?"

"He talks little, sir: what he does say is ever to the point. His brain is first-rate, I should think not impressible, but vigorous."

"Is he an able man, then?"

"Truly able."

"A thoroughly educated man?"

"St. John is an accomplished and profound scholar."

"His manners, I think, you said are not to your taste?—priggish and parsonic?"

"I never mentioned his manners; but, unless I had a very bad taste, they must suit it; they are polished, calm, and gentlemanlike."

"His appearance,—I forget what description you gave of his appearance;—a sort of raw curate, half strangled with his white neck-cloth, and stilted up on his thick-soled high-lows, eh?"

"St. John dresses well. He is a handsome man: tall, fair, with blue eyes, and a Grecian profile."

(Aside.) "Damn him!"—(To me.) "Did you like him, Jane?"

"Yes, Mr. Rochester, I liked him: but you asked me that before."

I perceived, of course, the drift of my interlocutor. Jealousy had got hold of him: she stung him; but the sting was salutary: it gave him respite from the gnawing fang of melancholy. I would not, therefore, immediately charm the snake.

"Perhaps you would rather not sit any longer on my knee, Miss Eyre?" was the next somewhat unexpected observation.

"Why not, Mr. Rochester?"

"The picture you have just drawn is suggestive of a rather too overwhelming contrast. Your words have delineated very prettily a graceful Apollo: he is present to your imagination,—tall, fair, blue-eyed, and with a Grecian profile. Your eyes dwell on a Vulcan,—a real blacksmith, brown, broad-shouldered: and blind and lame into the bargain."

"I never thought of it, before; but you certainly are rather like Vulcan, sir."

"Well, you can leave me, ma'am: but before you go" (and he retained me by a firmer grasp than ever), "you will be pleased just to answer me a question or two." He paused.

"What questions, Mr. Rochester?"

Then followed this cross-examination.

"St. John made you schoolmistress of Morton before he knew you were his cousin?"

"Yes."

"You would often see him? He would visit the school sometimes?"

"Daily."

"He would approve of your plans, Jane? I know they would be clever, for you are a talented creature!"

"He approved of them—yes."

"He would discover many things in you he could not have expected to find? Some of your accomplishments are not ordinary."

"I don't know about that."

"You had a little cottage near the school, you say: did he ever come there to see you?"

"Now and then?"

"Of an evening?"

"Once or twice."

A pause.

"How long did you reside with him and his sisters after the cousinship was discovered?"

"Five months."

"Did Rivers spend much time with the ladies of his family?"

"Yes; the back parlour was both his study and ours: he sat near the window, and we by the table."

"Did he study much?"

"A good deal."

"What?"

"Hindostanee."

"And what did you do meantime?"

"I learnt German, at first."

"Did he teach you?"

"He did not understand German."

"Did he teach you nothing?"

"A little Hindostanee."

"Rivers taught you Hindostanee?"

"Yes, sir."

"And his sisters also?"

"No."

"Only you?"

"Only me."

"Did you ask to learn?"

"No."

"He wished to teach you?"

"Yes."

A second pause.

"Why did he wish it? Of what use could Hindostanee be to you?"

"He intended me to go with him to India."

"Ah! here I reach the root of the matter. He wanted you to marry him?"

"He asked me to marry him."

"That is a fiction—an impudent invention to vex me."

"I beg your pardon, it is the literal truth: he asked me more than once, and was as stiff about urging his point as ever you could be."

"Miss Eyre, I repeat it, you can leave me. How often am I to say the same thing? Why do you remain pertinaciously perched on my knee, when I have given you notice to quit?"

"Because I am comfortable there."

"No, Jane, you are not comfortable there, because your heart is not with me: it is with this cousin—this St. John. Oh, till this moment, I thought my little Jane was all mine! I had a belief she loved me even when she left me: that was an atom of sweet in much bitter. Long as we have been parted, hot tears as I have wept over our separation, I never thought that while I was mourning her, she was loving another! But it is useless grieving. Jane, leave me: go and marry Rivers."

"Shake me off, then, sir,—push me away, for I'll not leave you of my own accord."

"Jane, I ever like your tone of voice: it still renews hope, it sounds so truthful. When I hear it, it carries me back a year. I forget that you have formed a new tie. But I am not a fool—go—"

"Where must I go, sir?"

"Your own way—with the husband you have chosen."

"Who is that?"

"You know—this St. John Rivers."

"He is not my husband, nor ever will be. He does not love me: I do not love him. He loves (as he CAN love, and that is not as you love) a beautiful young lady called Rosamond. He wanted to marry me only because he thought I should make a suitable missionary's wife, which she would not have done. He is good and great, but severe; and, for me, cold as an iceberg. He is not like you, sir: I am not happy at his side, nor near him, nor with him. He has no indulgence for me—no fondness. He sees nothing attractive in me; not even youth—only a few useful mental points.—Then I must leave you, sir, to go to him?"

I shuddered involuntarily, and clung instinctively closer to my blind but beloved master. He smiled.

"What, Jane! Is this true? Is such really the state of matters between you and Rivers?"

"Absolutely, sir! Oh, you need not be jealous! I wanted to tease you a little to make you less sad: I thought anger would be better than grief. But if you wish me to love you, could you but see how much I DO love you, you would be proud and content. All my heart is yours, sir: it belongs to you; and with you it would remain, were fate to exile the rest of me from your presence for ever."

Again, as he kissed me, painful thoughts darkened his aspect. "My scared vision! My crippled strength!" he murmured regretfully.

I caressed, in order to soothe him. I knew of what he was thinking, and wanted to speak for him, but dared not. As he turned aside his face a minute, I saw a tear slide from under the sealed eyelid, and trickle down the manly cheek. My heart swelled.

"I am no better than the old lightning-struck chestnut-tree in Thornfield orchard," he remarked ere long. "And what right would that ruin have to bid a budding woodbine cover its decay with freshness?"

"You are no ruin, sir—no lightning-struck tree: you are green and vigorous. Plants will grow about your roots, whether you ask them or not, because they take delight in your bountiful shadow; and as they grow they will lean towards you, and wind round you, because your strength offers them so safe a prop."

Again he smiled: I gave him comfort.

"You speak of friends, Jane?" he asked.

"Yes, of friends," I answered rather hesitatingly: for I knew I meant more than friends, but could not tell what other word to employ. He helped me.

"Ah! Jane. But I want a wife."

"Do you, sir?"

"Yes: is it news to you?"

"Of course: you said nothing about it before."

"Is it unwelcome news?"

"That depends on circumstances, sir—on your choice."

"Which you shall make for me, Jane. I will abide by your decision."

"Choose then, sir—HER WHO LOVES YOU BEST."

"I will at least choose—HER I LOVE BEST. Jane, will you marry me?"

"Yes, sir."

"A poor blind man, whom you will have to lead about by the hand?"

"Yes, sir."

"A crippled man, twenty years older than you, whom you will have to wait on?"

"Yes, sir."

"Truly, Jane?"

"Most truly, sir."

"Oh! my darling! God bless you and reward you!"

"Mr. Rochester, if ever I did a good deed in my life—if ever I thought a good thought—if ever I prayed a sincere and blameless prayer—if ever I wished a righteous wish,—I am rewarded now. To be your wife is, for me, to be as happy as I can be on earth."

"Because you delight in sacrifice."

"Sacrifice! What do I sacrifice? Famine for food, expectation for content. To be privileged to put my arms round what I value—to press my lips to what I love—to repose on what I trust: is that to make a sacrifice? If so, then certainly I delight in sacrifice."

"And to bear with my infirmities, Jane: to overlook my deficiencies."

"Which are none, sir, to me. I love you better now, when I can really be useful to you, than I did in your state of proud independence, when you disdained every part but that of the giver and protector."

"Hitherto I have hated to be helped—to be led: henceforth, I feel I shall hate it no more. I did not like to put my hand into a hireling's, but it is pleasant to feel it circled by Jane's little fingers. I preferred utter loneliness to the constant attendance of servants; but Jane's soft ministry will be a perpetual joy. Jane suits me: do I suit her?"

"To the finest fibre of my nature, sir."

"The case being so, we have nothing in the world to wait for: we must be married instantly."

He looked and spoke with eagerness: his old impetuosity was rising.

"We must become one flesh without any delay, Jane: there is but the licence to get—then we marry."

"Mr. Rochester, I have just discovered the sun is far declined from its meridian, and Pilot is actually gone home to his dinner. Let me look at your watch."

"Fasten it into your girdle, Janet, and keep it henceforward: I have no use for it."

"It is nearly four o'clock in the afternoon, sir. Don't you feel hungry?"

"The third day from this must be our wedding-day, Jane. Never mind fine clothes and jewels, now: all that is not worth a fillip."

"The sun has dried up all the rain-drops, sir. The breeze is still: it is quite hot."

"Do you know, Jane, I have your little pearl necklace at this moment fastened round my bronze scrag under my cravat? I have worn it since the day I lost my only treasure, as a memento of her."

"We will go home through the wood: that will be the shadiest way."

He pursued his own thoughts without heeding me.

"Jane! you think me, I daresay, an irreligious dog: but my heart swells with gratitude to the beneficent God of this earth just now. He sees not as man sees, but far clearer: judges not as man judges, but far more wisely. I did wrong: I would have sullied my innocent flower—breathed guilt on its purity: the Omnipotent snatched it from me. I, in my stiff-necked rebellion, almost cursed the dispensation: instead of bending to the decree, I defied it. Divine justice pursued its course; disasters came thick on me: I was forced to pass through the valley of the shadow of death. HIS chastisements are mighty; and one smote me which has humbled me for ever. You know I was proud of my strength: but what is it now, when I must give it over to foreign guidance, as a child does its weakness? Of late, Jane—only—only of late—I began to see and acknowledge the hand of God in my doom. I began to experience remorse, repentance; the wish for reconcilement to my Maker. I began sometimes to pray: very brief prayers they were, but very sincere.

"Some days since: nay, I can number them—four; it was last Monday night, a singular mood came over me: one in which grief replaced frenzy—sorrow, sullenness. I had long had the impression that since I could nowhere find you, you must be dead. Late that night—perhaps it might be between eleven and twelve o'clock—ere I retired to my dreary rest, I supplicated God, that, if it seemed good to Him, I might soon be taken from this life, and admitted to that world to come, where there was still hope of rejoining Jane.

"I was in my own room, and sitting by the window, which was open: it soothed me to feel the balmy night-air; though I could see no stars and only by a vague, luminous haze, knew the presence of a moon. I longed for thee, Janet! Oh, I longed for thee both with soul and flesh! I asked of God, at once in anguish and humility, if I had not been long enough desolate, afflicted, tormented; and might not soon taste bliss and peace once more. That I merited all I endured, I acknowledged—that I could scarcely endure more, I pleaded; and the alpha and omega of my heart's wishes broke involuntarily from my lips in the words—'Jane! Jane! Jane!'"

"Did you speak these words aloud?"

"I did, Jane. If any listener had heard me, he would have thought me mad: I pronounced them with such frantic energy."

"And it was last Monday night, somewhere near midnight?"

"Yes; but the time is of no consequence: what followed is the strange point. You will think me superstitious,—some superstition I have in my blood, and always had: nevertheless, this is true—true at least it is that I heard what I now relate.

"As I exclaimed 'Jane! Jane! Jane!' a voice—I cannot tell whence the voice came, but I know whose voice it was—replied, 'I am coming: wait for me;' and a moment after, went whispering on the wind the words—'Where are you?'

"I'll tell you, if I can, the idea, the picture these words opened to my mind: yet it is difficult to express what I want to express. Ferndean is buried, as you see, in a heavy wood, where sound falls dull, and dies unreverberating. 'Where are you?' seemed spoken amongst mountains; for I heard a hill-sent echo repeat the words. Cooler and fresher at the moment the gale seemed to visit my brow: I could have deemed that in some wild, lone scene, I and Jane were meeting. In spirit, I believe we must have met. You no doubt were, at that hour, in unconscious sleep, Jane: perhaps your soul wandered from its cell to comfort mine; for those were your accents—as certain as I live—they were yours!"

Reader, it was on Monday night—near midnight—that I too had received the mysterious summons: those were the very words by which I replied to it. I listened to Mr. Rochester's narrative, but made no disclosure in return. The coincidence struck me as too awful and inexplicable to be communicated or discussed. If I told anything, my tale would be such as must necessarily make a profound impression on the mind of my hearer: and that mind, yet from its sufferings too prone to gloom, needed not the deeper shade of the supernatural. I kept these things then, and pondered them in my heart.

"You cannot now wonder," continued my master, "that when you rose upon me so unexpectedly last night, I had difficulty in believing you any other than a mere voice and vision, something that would melt to silence and annihilation, as the midnight whisper and mountain echo had melted before. Now, I thank God! I know it to be otherwise. Yes, I thank God!"

He put me off his knee, rose, and reverently lifting his hat from his brow, and bending his sightless eyes to the earth, he stood in mute devotion. Only the last words of the worship were audible.

"I thank my Maker, that, in the midst of judgment, he has remembered mercy. I humbly entreat my Redeemer to give me strength to lead henceforth a purer life than I have done hitherto!"

Then he stretched his hand out to be led. I took that dear hand, held it a moment to my lips, then let it pass round my shoulder: being so much lower of stature than he, I served both for his prop and guide. We entered the wood, and wended homeward.

Chapter XXXVIII—CONCLUSION

Reader, I married him. A quiet wedding we had: he and I, the parson and clerk, were alone present. When we got back from church, I went into the kitchen of the manor-house, where Mary was cooking the dinner and John cleaning the knives, and I said—

"Mary, I have been married to Mr. Rochester this morning." The housekeeper and her husband were both of that decent phlegmatic order of people, to whom one may at any time safely communicate a remarkable piece of news without incurring the danger of having one's ears pierced by some shrill ejaculation, and subsequently stunned by a torrent of wordy wonderment. Mary did look up, and she did stare at me: the ladle with which she was basting a pair of chickens roasting at the fire, did for some three minutes hang suspended in air; and for the same space of time John's knives also had rest from the polishing process: but Mary, bending again over the roast, said only—

"Have you, Miss? Well, for sure!"

A short time after she pursued—"I seed you go out with the master, but I didn't know you were gone to church to be wed;" and she basted away. John, when I turned to him, was grinning from ear to ear.

"I telled Mary how it would be," he said: "I knew what Mr. Edward" (John was an old servant, and had known his master when he was the cadet of the house, therefore, he often gave him his Christian name)—"I knew what Mr. Edward would do; and I was certain he would not wait long neither: and he's done right, for aught I know. I wish you joy, Miss!" and he politely pulled his forelock.

"Thank you, John. Mr. Rochester told me to give you and Mary this." I put into his hand a five-pound note. Without waiting to hear more, I left the kitchen. In passing the door of that sanctum some time after, I caught the words—

"She'll happen do better for him nor ony o't' grand ladies." And again, "If she ben't one o' th' handsomest, she's noan faal and varry good-natured; and i' his een she's fair beautiful, onybody may see that."

I wrote to Moor House and to Cambridge immediately, to say what I had done: fully explaining also why I had thus acted. Diana and Mary approved the step unreservedly. Diana announced that she would just give me time to get over the honeymoon, and then she would come and see me.

"She had better not wait till then, Jane," said Mr. Rochester, when I read her letter to him; "if she does, she will be too late, for our honeymoon will shine our life long: its beams will only fade over your grave or mine."

How St. John received the news, I don't know: he never answered the letter in which I communicated it: yet six months after he wrote to me, without, however, mentioning Mr. Rochester's name or alluding to my marriage. His letter was then calm, and, though very serious, kind. He has maintained a regular, though not frequent, correspondence ever since: he hopes I am happy, and trusts I am not of those who live without God in the world, and only mind earthly things.

You have not quite forgotten little Adele, have you, reader? I had not; I soon asked and obtained leave of Mr. Rochester, to go and see her at the school where he had placed her. Her frantic joy at beholding me again moved me much. She looked pale and thin: she said she was not happy. I found the rules of the establishment were too strict, its course of study too severe for a child of her age: I took her home with me. I meant to become her governess once more, but I soon found this impracticable; my time and cares were now required by another—my husband needed them all. So I sought out a school conducted on a more indulgent system, and near enough to permit of my visiting her often, and bringing her home sometimes. I took care she should never want for anything that could contribute to her comfort: she soon settled in her new abode, became very happy there, and made fair progress in her studies. As she grew up, a sound English education corrected in a great measure her French defects; and when she left school, I found in her a pleasing and obliging companion: docile, good-tempered, and well-principled. By her grateful attention to me and mine, she has long since well repaid any little kindness I ever had it in my power to offer her.

My tale draws to its close: one word respecting my experience of married life, and one brief glance at the fortunes of those whose names have most frequently recurred in this narrative, and I have done.

I have now been married ten years. I know what it is to live entirely for and with what I love best on earth. I hold myself supremely blest—blest beyond what language can express; because I am my husband's life as fully is he is mine. No woman was ever nearer to her mate than I am: ever more absolutely bone of his bone and flesh of his flesh. I know no weariness of my Edward's society: he knows none of mine, any more than we each do of the pulsation of the heart that beats in our separate bosoms; consequently, we are ever together. To be together is for us to be at once as free as in solitude, as gay as in company. We talk, I believe, all day long: to talk to each other is but a more animated and an audible thinking. All my confidence is bestowed on him, all his confidence is devoted to me; we are precisely suited in character—perfect concord is the result.

Mr. Rochester continued blind the first two years of our union; perhaps it was that circumstance that drew us so very near—that knit us so very close: for I was then his vision, as I am still his right hand. Literally, I was (what he often called me) the apple of his eye. He saw nature—he saw books through me; and never did I weary of gazing for his behalf, and of putting into words the effect of field, tree, town, river, cloud, sunbeam—of the landscape before us; of the weather round us—and impressing by sound on his ear what light could no longer stamp on his eye. Never did I weary of reading to him; never did I weary of conducting him where he wished to go: of doing for him what he wished to be done. And there was a pleasure in my services, most full, most exquisite, even though sad—because he claimed these services without painful shame or damping humiliation. He loved me so truly, that he knew no reluctance in profiting by my attendance: he felt I loved him so fondly, that to yield that attendance was to indulge my sweetest wishes.

One morning at the end of the two years, as I was writing a letter to his dictation, he came and bent over me, and said—"Jane, have you a glittering ornament round your neck?"

I had a gold watch-chain: I answered "Yes."

"And have you a pale blue dress on?"

I had. He informed me then, that for some time he had fancied the obscurity clouding one eye was becoming less dense; and that now he was sure of it.

He and I went up to London. He had the advice of an eminent oculist; and he eventually recovered the sight of that one eye. He cannot now see very distinctly: he cannot read or write much; but he can find his way without being led by the hand: the sky is no longer a blank to him—the earth no longer a void. When his first-born was put into his arms, he could see that the boy had inherited his own eyes, as they once were—large, brilliant, and black. On that occasion, he again, with a full heart, acknowledged that God had tempered judgment with mercy.

My Edward and I, then, are happy: and the more so, because those we most love are happy likewise. Diana and Mary Rivers are both married: alternately, once every year, they come to see us, and we go to see them. Diana's husband is a captain in the navy, a gallant officer and a good man. Mary's is a clergyman, a college friend of her brother's, and, from his attainments and principles, worthy of the connection. Both Captain Fitzjames and Mr. Wharton love their wives, and are loved by them.

As to St. John Rivers, he left England: he went to India. He entered on the path he had marked for himself; he pursues it still. A more resolute, indefatigable pioneer never wrought amidst rocks and dangers. Firm, faithful, and devoted, full of energy, and zeal, and truth, he labours for his race; he clears their painful way to improvement; he hews down like a giant the prejudices of creed and caste that encumber it. He may be stern; he may be exacting; he may be ambitious yet; but his is the sternness of the warrior Greatheart, who guards his pilgrim convoy from the onslaught of Apollyon. His is the exaction of the apostle, who speaks but for Christ, when he says—"Whosoever will come after me, let him deny himself, and take up his cross and follow me." His is the ambition of the high master-spirit, which aims to fill a place in the first rank of those who are redeemed from the earth—who stand without fault before the throne of God, who share the last mighty victories of the Lamb, who are called, and chosen, and faithful.

St. John is unmarried: he never will marry now. Himself has hitherto sufficed to the toil, and the toil draws near its close: his glorious sun hastens to its setting. The last letter I received from him drew from my eves human tears, and yet filled my heart with divine joy: he anticipated his sure reward, his incorruptible crown. I know that a stranger's hand will write to me next, to say that the good and faithful servant has been called at length into the joy of his Lord. And why weep for this? No fear of death will darken St. John's last hour: his mind will be unclouded, his heart will be undaunted, his hope will be sure, his faith steadfast. His own words are a pledge of this—

"My Master," he says, "has forewarned me. Daily He announces more distinctly,—'Surely I come quickly!' and hourly I more eagerly respond,—'Amen; even so come, Lord Jesus!'"